RISK

Dick Francis has written thirty-nine international worldwide bestsellers and is widely acclaimed as one of the world's finest thriller writers. His awards include the Crime Writers' Association's Cartier Diamond Dagger for his outstanding contribution to the crime genre, and an honorary Doctorate of Humane Letters from Tufts University of Boston. In 1996 Dick Francis was made a Mystery Writers of America Grand Master for a lifetime's achievement.

Also by Dick Francis in Pan Books

THE SPORT OF QUEENS
(autobiography)

LESTER: The Official
Biography

DEAD CERT
NERVE
FOR KICKS
ODDS AGAINST
FLYING FINISH
BLOOD SPORT
FORFEIT
ENQUIRY
RAT RACE
BONECRACK
SMOKESCREEN
SLAY-RIDE
KNOCK DOWN
HIGH STAKES
IN THE FRAME
TRIAL RUN
WHIP HAND
REFLEX
TWICE SHY
BANKER
THE DANGER
PROOF
BREAK IN
BOLT
HOT MONEY
THE EDGE
STRAIGHT
LONGSHOT
COMEBACK
DRIVING FORCE
DECIDER
WILD HORSES
COME TO GRIEF
TO THE HILT
10lb PENALTY
FIELD OF THIRTEEN
SECOND WIND
SHATTERED

Dick Francis

RISK

PAN BOOKS

First published 1977 by Michael Joseph Ltd

This edition first published 1979 by Pan Books
an imprint of Pan Macmillan Ltd
Pan Macmillan, 20 New Wharf Road, London N1 9RR
Basingstoke and Oxford
Associated companies throughout the world
www.panmacmillan.com

ISBN 0 330 25712 9

37 39 38 36

A CIP catalogue record for this book is available from the British Library.

Printed and bound in Great Britain by
Mackays of Chatham plc, Chatham, Kent

To the memory of
Lionel Vick,
first a professional steeplechase jockey,
then a certified accountant;
always a brave man.
And my thanks to his associate,
Michael Footé.

CHAPTER ONE

Thursday, March 17th, I spent the morning in anxiety, the afternoon in ecstasy, and the evening unconscious.

Thursday night, somewhere between dark and dawn, I slowly surfaced into a nightmare which would have been all right if I'd been asleep.

It took me a good long time to realize I was actually awake. Half awake, anyway.

There was no light. I thought my eyes were open, but the blackness was absolute.

There was a lot of noise. Different noises, loud and confusing. A heavy engine. Rattling noises. Creaks. Rushing noises. I lay in a muzzy state and felt battered by too much sound.

Lay . . . I was lying on some sort of mattress. On my back. Cold, sick and stiff. Aching. Shivering. Physically wretched and mentally bewildered.

I tried to move. Couldn't for some reason lift either hand to my face. They seemed to be stuck to my legs. Very odd.

An interminable time passed. I grew colder, sicker, stiffer, and wide awake.

Tried to sit up. Banged my head on something close above. Lay down again, fought a sudden spurt of panic, and made myself take it step by step.

Hands. Why couldn't I move my hands? Because my wrists seemed to be fastened to my trousers. It didn't make sense, but that was what it felt like.

Space. What of space? I stiffly moved my freezing feet, exploring. Found I had no shoes on. Only socks. On the immediate left, a wall. Close above, a ceiling. On the immediate right, a softer barrier. Possibly cloth.

I shifted my whole body a fraction to the right, and felt with my fingers. Not cloth, but netting. Like a tennis net. Pulled tight. Keeping me in. I pushed my fingers through the mesh, but could feel nothing at all on the far side.

Eyes. If I hadn't gone suddenly blind (and it didn't feel like it), I was lying somewhere where no light penetrated. Brilliant deduction. Most constructive. Ha bloody ha.

Ears. Almost the worst problem. Constant din assaulted them, shutting me close in the narrow black box, preventing me hearing any further than the powerful, nearby, racketing engine. I had a frightening feeling that even if I screamed no one would hear me. I had a sudden even more frightening feeling of *wanting* to scream. To make someone come. To make someone tell me where I was, and why I was there, and what on earth was happening.

I opened my mouth and yelled.

I yelled 'Hey' and 'Come here' and 'Bloody bastard, come and let me out', and thrashed about in useless rage, and all that happened was that my voice and fear bounded back in the confined space and made things worse. Chain reaction. One-way trip to exhaustion.

In the end I stopped shouting and lay still. Swallowed. Ground my teeth. Tried to force my mind into holding on to sense. Disorientation was the road to gibbering.

Concentrate, I told myself. *Think*.

That engine . . .

A big one. Doing a job of work. Situated somewhere close, but not where I was. The other side of a wall. Perhaps behind my head.

If it would only stop, I thought numbly, I would feel less sick, less pulverized, less panicky, less threatened.

The engine went right on hammering, its vibration reaching me through the walls. Not a turbine engine: not smooth enough, and no whine. A piston engine. Heavy duty, like a tractor . . . or a lorry. But I wasn't in a lorry. There was no feeling of movement; and the engine never altered its rate. No slowing or accelerating. No changes of gear. Not a lorry.

A generator. It's a generator, I thought. Making electricity.

I was lying tied up in the dark and on a sort of shelf near an electric generator. Cold, sick and frightened. And where?

As to how I'd got there . . . well, I knew that, up to a

point. I remembered the beginning, well enough. I would never forget Thursday, March 17th.

The most shattering questions were those to which I could think of no answer at all.

Why? What for? And *what next?*

CHAPTER TWO

That Thursday morning a client with his life in ruins kept me in the office in Newbury long after I should have left for Cheltenham races, and it seemed churlish to say, 'Yes, Mr Wells, terribly sorry about your agony, but I can't stop to help you now because I want to nip off and enjoy myself.' Mr Wells, staring-eyed and suicidal, simply had to be hauled in from his quicksand.

It took three and a half hours of analysis, sympathy, brandy, discussion of ways and means, and general pep-talk, to restore the slightest hope to his horizon, and I wasn't his doctor, priest, solicitor or other assorted hand-holder, but only the accountant he'd engaged in a frenzy the night before.

Mr Wells had bitten the dust in the hands of a crooked financial adviser. Mr Wells, frantic, desperate, had heard that Roland Britten, although young, had done other salvage jobs. Mr Wells on the telephone had offered double fees, tears, and lifelong gratitude as inducements: and Mr Wells was a confounded nuisance.

For the first and probably the only time in my life I

was that day going to ride in the Cheltenham Gold Cup, the race which ranked next to the Grand National in the lives of British steeplechase riders. No matter that the tipsters gave my mount little chance or the bookies were offering ante-post odds of forty-to-one, the fact remained that for a part-time amateur like myself the offer of a ride in the Gold Cup was as high as one could go.

Thanks to Mr Wells I did not leave the office calmly and early after a quick shuffle through the day's mail. Not until a quarter to one did I begin to unstick his leech-like dependence and get him moving, and only then by promising another long session on the following Monday. Halfway through the door, he froze yet again. Was I sure we had covered every angle? Couldn't I give him the afternoon? Monday, I said firmly. Wasn't there anyone else he could see, then?

'Sorry,' I said. 'My senior partner is away on holiday.'

'Mr King?' he asked, pointing to the neat notice 'King and Britten' painted on the open door.

I nodded, reflecting gloomily that my senior partner, if he hadn't been touring somewhere in Spain, would have been most insistent that I got off to Cheltenham in good time. Trevor King, big, silver-haired, authoritative and worldly, had my priorities right.

We had worked together for six years, ever since he'd enticed me, from the city office where I'd been trained, with the one inducement I couldn't refuse: flexible working hours which allowed time to go racing. He already had five or six clients from the racing world,

Newbury being central for many of the racing stables strung out along the Berkshire Downs, and, needing a replacement for a departing assistant, he'd reckoned that if he engaged me he might acquire a good deal more business in that direction. Not that he'd ever actually said so, because he was not a man to use two words where one would do; but his open satisfaction as his plan had gradually worked made it obvious.

All he had apparently done towards checking my ability as an accountant, as opposed to amateur jockey, was to ask my former employers if they would offer me a substantial raise in salary in order to keep me. They said yes, and did so. Trevor, it seemed, had smiled like a gentle shark, and gone away. His subsequent offer to me had been for a full partnership and lots of racing time; the partnership would cost me ten thousand pounds and I could pay it to him over several years out of my earnings. What did I think?

I'd thought it might turn out just fine; and it had.

In some ways I knew Trevor no better than on that first day. Our real relationship began and ended at the office door, social contact outside being confined to one formal dinner party each year, to which I was invited by letter by his wife. His house was opulent: building and contents circa nineteen twenties, with heavy plate glass cut to fit the top surfaces of polished furniture, and an elaborate bar built into the room he called his 'snug'. Friends tended to be top management types or county councillors, worthy substantial citizens like Trevor himself.

On the professional level, I knew him well. Orthodox establishment outlook, sober and traditional. Patriarchal, but not pompous. Giving the sort of gilt-edged advice that still appeared sound even if in hindsight it turned out not to be.

Something punitive about him, perhaps. He seemed to me sometimes to get a positive pleasure from detailing the extent of a client's tax liabilities, and watching the client droop.

Precise in mind and method, discreetly ambitious, pleased to be a noted local personage, and at his charming best with rich old ladies. His favourite clients were prosperous companies; his least favourite, incompetent individuals with their affairs in a mess.

I finally got rid of the incompetent Mr Wells and took my tensions down to the office car park. It was sixty miles from Newbury to Cheltenham and on the way I chewed my fingernails through two lots of roadworks and an army convoy, knowing also that near the course the crawling racegoing jams would mean half an hour for the last mile. There had been enough said already about the risks of putting up an amateur ('however good' some kind columnist had written) against the top brass of the professionals on the country's best horses in the most important race of the season's most prestigious meeting. 'The best thing Roland Britten can do is to keep Tapestry out of everyone else's way' was the offering of a less kind writer, and although I more or less agreed with him I hadn't meant to do it by not arriving in time. Of all possible unprofessional behaviour, that would be the worst.

Lateness was the last and currently the most acute of a whole list of pressures. I had been riding as an amateur in jump races since my sixteenth birthday, but was now, with thirty-two in sight, finding it increasingly difficult to keep fit. Age and desk work were nibbling away at a stamina I'd always taken for granted: it now needed a lot of effort to do what I'd once done without thought. The hour and a half I spent early every morning riding exercise for a local trainer were no longer enough. Recently, in a couple of tight finishes, I'd felt the strength draining like bathwater from my creaking muscles, and had lost at least one race because of it. I couldn't swear to myself that I was tuned up tight for the Gold Cup.

Work in the office had multiplied to the point where doing it properly was a problem in itself. Half-days off for racing had begun to feel like treachery. Saturdays were fine, but impatient clients viewed Wednesdays at Ascot or Thursdays at Stratford-upon-Avon with irritation. That I worked at home in the evenings to make up for it satisfied Trevor, but no one else. And my case load, as jargon would put it, was swamping me.

Apart from Mr Wells, there had been other jobs I should have done that morning. I should have sent an appeal against a top jockey's tax assessment; I should have signed a certificate for a solicitor; and there had been two summonses for clients to appear before the Tax Commissioners, which needed instant action, even if only evasive.

'I'll apply for postponements,' I told Peter, one of our two assistants. 'Ring both of those clients, and tell them not to worry, I'll start on their cases at once. And check that we've all the papers we need. Ask them to send any that are missing.'

Peter nodded sullenly, unwillingly, implying that I was always giving him too much work. And maybe I was.

Trevor's plans to take on another assistant had been so far halted by an offer which was currently giving both of us headaches. A big London firm wanted to move in on us, merge, amalgamate, and establish a large branch of itself on our patch, with us inside. Materially, we would benefit, as at present the steeply rising cost of overheads like office rent, electricity and secretarial wages was coming straight out of our pockets. We would also be under less stress, as at present when one of us was ill or on holiday, the burden on the other was heavy. But Trevor agonized over the prospect of demotion from absolute boss, and I over the threat of loss of liberty. We had postponed a decision until Trevor's return from Spain in two weeks' time, but at that point bleak realities would have to be faced.

I drummed my fingers on the steering wheel of my Dolomite and waited impatiently for the roadworks' traffic lights to turn green. Looked at my watch for the hundredth time. 'Come on,' I said aloud. 'Come *on*.' Binny Tomkins would be absolutely furious.

Binny, Tapestry's trainer, didn't want me on the horse. 'Not in the Gold Cup,' he'd said positively, when the owner had proposed it. They'd faced each other belligerently outside the weighing room of Newbury racecourse, where Tapestry had just obliged in the three mile 'chase: Mrs Moira Longerman, small, blonde and bird-like, versus sixteen stone of frustrated male.

'. . . just because he's your *accountant*,' Binny was saying in exasperation when I rejoined them after weighing-in. 'It's bloody ridiculous.'

'Well, he won today, didn't he?' she said.

Binny threw his arms wide, breathing heavily. Mrs Longerman had offered me the Newbury ride on the spur of the moment when the stable jockey had broken his ankle in a fall in the previous race. Binny had accepted me as a temporary arrangement with fair grace, but Tapestry was the best horse in his yard, and for a middle-ranker like him a runner in the Gold Cup was an event. He wanted the best professional jockey he could get. He did not want Mrs Longerman's accountant who rode in thirty races in a year, if he was lucky. Mrs Longerman, however, had murmured something about removing Tapestry to a more accommodating trainer, and I had not been unselfish enough to decline the offer, and Binny had fumed in vain.

Mrs Longerman's previous accountant had for years let her pay to the Inland Revenue a lot more tax than she'd needed, and I'd got her a refund of thousands. It wasn't the best grounds for choosing a jockey to ride for you in the Gold Cup, but I understood she was thanking me by giving me something beyond price. I quite passionately did not want to let her down; and that, too, was a pressure.

I was worried about making a reasonable show, but not about falling. When one worried about falling, it was time to stop racing: it would happen to me one day, I supposed, but it hadn't yet. I worried about being unfit, unwanted, and late. Enough to be going on with.

Binny was spluttering like a lit fuse when I finally arrived, panting, in the weighing room.

'Where the hell have you been?' he demanded. 'Do you realize the first race is over already and in another five minutes you'd be fined for not turning up?'

'Sorry.'

I carried my saddle, helmet, and bag of gear through into the changing room, sat down thankfully on the bench, and tried to stop sweating. The usual bustle went on around me; jockeys dressing, undressing, swearing, laughing, accepting me from long acquaintance as a part of the scenery. I did the accounts for thirty-two jockeys and had unofficially filled in tax assessment forms for a dozen more. I was also to date employed as accountant by thirty-one trainers, fifteen stud farms, two Stewards of the Jockey Club, one racecourse, thirteen bookmakers, two horse-transport firms, one blacksmith, five forage merchants, and upwards of forty people who owned racehorses. I probably knew more about the private financial affairs of the racing world than any other single person on the racecourse.

In the parade ring Moira Longerman twittered with happy nerves, her button nose showing kittenishly just above a fluffy upstanding sable collar. Below the collar she snuggled into a coat to match, and on the blonde curls floated a fluffy sable hat. Her middle-aged blue eyes brimmed with excitement, and in the straightforward gaiety of her manner one could see why it was that so many thousands of people spent their hobby money on owning racehorses. Not just for the gambling, nor the display: more likely for the kick from extra adrenalin, and the feeling of being involved. She knew well enough that the fun could turn to disappointment, to tears. The lurking valleys made the mountaintops more precious.

'Doesn't Tapestry look *marvellous*?' she said, her small gloved hands fluttering in the horse's direction as he plodded round the ring under the gaze of the ten-deep banks of intent spectators.

'Great,' I said truthfully.

Binny scowled at the cold sunny sky. He had produced the horse with a gloss seldom achieved by his other runners: impeccably plaited mane and tail, oiled hooves, a new rug, gleamingly polished leather tack, and an intricate geometric pattern brushed into the well-groomed hairs of the hindquarters. Binny was busy telling the world that if his horse failed it would not be from lack of preparation. Binny was going to use me for evermore as his reason for not having won the Gold Cup.

I can't say that it disturbed me very much. Like Moira Longerman, I was feeling the throat-catching once-in-a-lifetime thrill of a profound experience waiting just ahead. Disaster might follow, but whatever happened I would have had my ride in the Gold Cup.

There were eight runners, including Tapestry. We mounted, walked out on to the course, paraded in front of the packed and noisy stands, cantered down to the start. I could feel myself trembling, and knew it was stupid. Only a cool head could produce a worthy result. Tell that to the adrenal glands.

I could pretend, anyway. Stifle the butterfly nerves and act as if races of this calibre came my way six times a season. None of the other seven riders looked anxious or strung up, yet I guessed that some of them must be. Even for the top pros, this was an occasion. I reckoned that their placid expressions were nearly as phoney as mine, and felt better.

We advanced to the tapes in a bouncing line, restraining the eager heads on short reins, and keeping the weight still back in the saddle. Then the starter pressed his lever and let the tapes fly up, and Tapestry took a great bite of air and practically yanked my arms out of their sockets.

Most three and a quarter mile 'chases started moderately, speeded up a mile from home, and maybe finished in a decelerating procession. The Gold Cup field that day set off as if to cover the whole distance in record Derby time, and Moira Longerman told me later that Binny used words she'd never heard before when I failed to keep Tapestry close in touch.

By the time we'd swept over the first two fences, by the stands, I was last by a good six lengths, a gap not much in itself but still an I-told-you-so sort of distance so early in the proceedings. I couldn't in fact make up my mind. Should I go faster? Stick closer to the tails in front? Tapestry had set off at a greater speed already than when he'd won with me at Newbury. If I let him zip along with the others he could be exhausted and tailed off at half-way. If I held him up, we might at least finish the race.

Over the third fence and over the water I saw the gap lengthening and still dithered about tactics. I hadn't expected the others to go off so fast. I didn't know if they hoped to maintain that speed throughout, or whether they would slow and come back to me later. I couldn't decide which was more likely.

But what would Binny say if I guessed wrong and was last the whole way? What wouldn't he say?

What was I doing in this race, out of my class?

Making an utter fool of myself.

Oh God, I thought, why did I try it?

Accountants are held to be cautious by nature but at that point I threw caution to the winds. Almost anything would be better than starting last and staying last.

Prudence would get me nowhere. I gave Tapestry a kick which he didn't expect and he shot forward like an arrow.

'Steady,' I gasped. 'Steady, dammit.'

Shorten the gap, I thought, but not too fast. Spurt too fast and I'd use the reserves we'd need for the last stretch uphill. If we ever got there. If I didn't fall off. If I didn't let Tapestry meet a fence wrong, or run out, or refuse to jump at all.

Only a mile done, and I'd lived a couple of lifetimes.

I was still last by the end of the first circuit, but no longer a disgrace. Once more round . . . and maybe we'd pass one or two before we'd done. I began at that point to enjoy myself, a background feeling mostly smothered by anxious concentration, but there all the same, and I knew from other days that it would be the enjoyment I remembered most afterwards, not the doubts.

Over the water-jump, still last, the others all in a group just ahead. Open ditch next; Tapestry met it just right and we pegged it back a length in mid-air. Landed nose to tail with the horse in front. Stayed there to the next fence, and again won ground in flight, setting off that time beside the next horse, not behind.

Great. I was no longer last. Just joint last. Whatever I might fear about Tapestry staying to the end, he was surging over the jumps meanwhile with zest and courage.

It was at the next fence, on the far side of the course, that the race came apart. The favourite fell, and the second favourite tripped over him. Tapestry swerved violently as he landed among the rolling bodies and crashed into the horse alongside. The rider of that horse fell off.

It happened so fast. One second, an orderly Gold Cup. Next second, a shambles. Three down, the high hopes of owners, trainers, lads and punters blown to the wind. Tapestry forged his way out like a bull, but when we tackled the hill ahead, we again lay last.

Never try to accelerate uphill, they say, because the horses you pass will pass you again on the way down. Save your strength, don't waste it. I saved Tapestry's strength in last place up the hill and it seemed to me that at the crest the others suddenly swooped away from me, piling on every ounce of everything they had, shooting off while I was still freewheeling.

Come on, I thought urgently, come on, it's now or never. Now, or absolutely never. Get on, Tapestry. Get going. I went down the hill faster than I'd ever ridden in my life.

A fence half-way down. A fractional change of stride. A leap to shame the chamoix.

Another jockey lay on the ground there, curled in a ball to avoid being kicked. Hard luck . . . Too bad . . .

Three horses in front. Two fences to go. I realized abruptly that the three horses in front were all there were. Not far in front, either. My God, I thought, almost laughing, just supposing I can pass one, I'll finish third. Third in the Gold Cup. A dream to last till death.

I urged Tapestry ever faster, and amazingly, he responded. This was the horse whose finishing speed was doubtful, who had to be nursed. This horse, thundering along like a sprinter.

Round the bend . . . only one fence to go . . . I was approaching it faster than the others . . . took off alongside the third horse, landed in front . . . with only the last taxing uphill stretch to the post. I'm third, I thought exultantly. I'm *bloody* third.

Some horses find the Cheltenham finish a painful struggle. Some wander sideways from tiredness, swish their tails and falter when in front, slow to a leaden all-spent pace that barely takes them to the post.

Nothing like that happened to Tapestry, but it did to both of the horses in front. One of them wavered up the straight at a widening angle. The other seemed to be stopping second by second. To my own and everyone else's disbelief, Tapestry scorched past both of them at a flat gallop and won the Gold Cup.

I didn't give a damn that everyone would say (and did say) that if the favourite and second favourite hadn't fallen, I wouldn't have had a chance. I didn't care a fig that it would go down in history as a 'bad' Gold Cup. I lived through such a peak of ecstasy on the lengthy walk round from the winning post to the unsaddling enclosure that nothing after, I thought, could ever match it.

It was impossible . . . and it had happened. Mrs Longerman's accountant had brought her a tax-free capital gain.

A misty hour later, changed into street clothes, with champagne flowing in the weighing room and all the hands I'd ever want slapping me on the shoulder, I was still so wildly happy that I wanted to run up the walls and laugh aloud and turn hand-springs. Speeches, presentations, Moira Longerman's excited tears, Binny's incredulous embarrassment, all had passed in a jumble which I would sort out later. I was high on the sort of glory wave which would put poppies out of business.

Into this ball of a day came a man in a St John's Ambulance uniform, asking for me.

'You Roland Britten?' he said.

I nodded over a glass of bubbles.

'There's a jockey wanting you. In the ambulance. Says he won't go off to hospital before he's talked to you. Proper fussed, he is. So would you come?'

'Who is it?' I asked, putting my drink down.

'Budley. Fell in the last race.'

'Is he badly hurt?'

We walked out of the weighing room and across the crowded stretch of tarmac towards the ambulance which stood waiting just outside the gates. It was five minutes before the time for the last race of the day, and thousands were scurrying about, making for the stands, hurrying to put on the last bet of the meeting. The ambulance man and I walked in the counter-current of those making for the car park before the greater rush began.

'Broken leg,' said the ambulance man.

'What rotten luck.'

I couldn't imagine what Bobby Budley wanted me for. There had been nothing wrong with his last annual accounts and we'd had them agreed by the Inspector of Taxes. He shouldn't have had any urgent problems.

We reached the back doors of the white ambulance, and the St John's man opened them.

'He's inside,' he said.

Not one of the big ambulances, I thought, stepping up. More like a white van, with not quite enough headroom to stand upright. They were short of regular ambulances, I supposed, on race days.

Inside there was a stretcher, with a figure on it under a blanket. I went a step towards it, head bent under the low roof.

'Bobby?' I said.

It wasn't Bobby. It was someone I'd never seen before. Young, agile, and in no way hurt. He sprang upwards off the stretcher shedding dark grey blanket like a cloud.

I turned to retreat. Found the ambulance man up beside me, inside the van. Behind him the doors were already shut. His expression was far from gentle and when I tried to push him out of the way he kicked my shin.

I turned again. The stretcher case was ripping open a plastic bag which seemed to contain a hand-sized wad of damp cotton wool. The ambulance man caught hold of one of my arms and the stretcher case the other, and despite fairly desperate heavings and struggles on my part they managed between them to hold the damp cotton wool over my nose and mouth.

It's difficult to fight effectively when you can't stand up straight and every breath you draw is pure ether. The last thing I saw in a greying world was the ambulance man's peaked cap falling off. His light brown hair tumbled out loose into a shaggy mop and turned him from an angel of mercy into a straightforward villain.

I had left racecourses once or twice before on a stretcher, but never fast asleep.

Awake in the noisy dark I could make no sense of it.

Why should they take me? Did it have anything to do with winning the Gold Cup? And if so, what?

It seemed to me that I had grown colder, and still sicker, and that the peripheral noises of creaks and rushing sounds had grown louder. There was also now an uncoordinated feeling of movement: yet I was not in a lorry.

Where, then? In an aeroplane?

The sickness suddenly identified itself into being not the aftermath of ether, as I'd vaguely thought, but a familiar malaise I'd suffered on and off from childhood.

I was seasick.

On a boat.

CHAPTER THREE

I was lying, I realized, on a bunk. The tight net across the open side on my right was to prevent me from falling off. The rushing noises were from the waves washing against the hull. The creaks and rattles were the result of a solid body being pushed by an engine through the resistance of water.

To have made at least some sense of my surroundings was an enormous relief. I could relate myself to space again, and visualize my condition. On the other hand, sorting out the most disorientating part of the mystery left me feeling more acutely the physical discomforts. Cold. Hands tied to legs. Muscles stiff from immobility: and knowing I was on a boat, and knowing boats always made me sick, was definitely making me feel a lot sicker.

Ignorance was a great tranquillizer, I thought. The intensity of a pain depended on the amount of attention one gave it, and one never felt half as bad talking to people in daylight as alone in the dark. If someone would come and talk to me I might feel less cold and less miserable and less quite horribly sick.

No one came for a century or so.

The motion of the boat increased, and my queasiness with it. I could feel my weight rolling slightly from side to side, and had an all too distinct impression that I was also pitching lengthwise, first toe down, then head down, as the bows lifted and fell with the waves.

Out at sea, I thought helplessly. It wouldn't be so rough on a river.

I tried for a while with witticisms like 'Press-ganged, by God', and 'Shanghaied!' and 'Jim lad, Long John Silver's got you', to put a twist of lightness into the situation. Not a deafening success.

In time also I gave up trying to work out why I was there. I gave up feeling apprehensive. I gave up feeling cold and uncomfortable. Finally I was concentrating only on not actually vomiting, and the fact that I'd eaten nothing since breakfast was all that helped.

Breakfast . . .? I had lost all idea of time. I didn't know how long I'd been unconscious, or even how long I'd lain awake in the dark. Unconscious long enough to be shipped from Cheltenham to the coast, and to be carried on board. Awake long enough to long for sleep.

The engine stopped.

The sudden quiet was so marvellous that I only fully realized then how exhausting had been the assault of noise. I actively feared that it would start again. And was this, I wondered, the basis of brainwashing?

There was a new noise, suddenly, from overhead. Dragging sounds, and then metallic sounds, and then, devastatingly, a shaft of daylight.

I shut my dark-adjusted eyes, wincing, and opened them again slowly. Above my head, the shaft had grown to a square. Someone had opened a hatch.

Fresh air blew in like a shower, cold and damp. Without much enthusiasm I glanced around, seeing a small world through a wide-meshed white net.

I was in what one might call the sharp end. In the bows. The bunk where I lay grew narrower at my feet, the side walls of the cabin angling to meet in the centre, like an arrowhead.

The bunk was about two feet wide, and had another bunk above it. I was lying on a cloth-covered mattress; navy blue.

Most of the rest of the cabin was taken up by two large, open-topped, built-in, varnished wooden bins. For stowing sails, I thought. I was in the sail locker of a sailing boat.

Behind my right shoulder a door, now firmly shut, presumably led back to warmth, life, the galley and the saloon.

The matter of my wrists, too, became clear. They were indeed tied to my trousers, one on each side. From what I could see, someone had punched a couple of holes through the material in the region of each side pocket, threaded something which looked like bandage through the holes, and effectively tied each of my wrists to a bunch of cloth.

A good pair of trousers ruined: but then all disasters were relative.

A head appeared above me, framed by the hatch. Indistinctly, seeing him through the net and silhouetted against the grey sky, I got the impression he was fairly young and uncompromisingly tough.

'Are you awake?' he said, peering down.

'Yes,' I said.

'Right.'

He went away, but presently returned, leaning head and shoulders into the hatch.

'If you act sensible, I'll untie you,' he said.

His voice had the bossy strength of one accustomed to dictate, not cajole. A voice which had come up the hard way, gathering aggression on the journey.

'Have you got any dramamine?' I asked.

'No,' he said. 'There's a toilet in the cabin. You can throw up into that. You're going to have to agree you'll act quiet if I come down and untie you. Otherwise I won't. Right?'

'I agree,' I said.

'Right.'

Without more ado he lowered himself easily through the hatch and stood six feet three in his canvas shoes, practically filling all available space. His body moved in effortless balance in the boat's tossing.

'Here,' he said, lifting the lid of what had looked like a

built-in varnished box. 'Here's the head. You open the stop-cock and pump sea water through with that lever. Turn the water off when you've done, or you'll have a flood.' He shut the lid and opened a locker door on the wall above. 'In here there's a bottle of drinking water and some paper cups. You'll get your meals when we get ours.' He fished deep into one of the sail bins, which otherwise seemed empty. 'Here's a blanket. And a pillow.' He lifted them out, showed them to me, both dark blue, dropped them back.

He looked upwards to the generous square of open sky above him.

'I'll fix you the hatch so you'll have air and light. You won't be able to get out. And there's nothing to get out for. We're out of sight of land.'

He stood for a moment, considering, then began to unfasten the net, which was held simply by chrome hooks slotted into eyelets on the bunk above.

'You can hook the net up if it gets rough,' he said.

Seen without intervening white meshes, he was not reassuring. A strong face with vigorous bones. Smallish eyes, narrow-lipped mouth, open air skin and straight brown floppy hair. My own sort of age: no natural kinship, though. He looked down at me without any hint of sadistic enjoyment, for which I was grateful, but also without apology or compassion.

'Where am I?' I said. 'Why am I here? Where are we going? And who are you?'

He said, 'If I untie your hands and you try anything, I'll bash you.'

You must be joking, I thought. Six foot three of healthy muscle against a cold, stiff, seasick five foot ten. No thank you very much.

'What *is* this all about?' I said. Even to my ears, it sounded pretty weak. But then, pretty weak was exactly how I felt.

He didn't answer. He merely bent down, leaned in and over me, and unknotted the bandage from my left wrist. Extracting himself from the small space between the bunks, he repeated the process on the right.

'Stay lying down until I'm out of here,' he said.

'Tell me what's going on.'

He put a foot on the edge of the sail bins, and his hands on the sides of the hatch, and pulled himself halfway up into the outside world.

'I'll tell you,' he said unemotionally, looking down, 'that you're a bloody nuisance to me. I'm having to stow all the sails on deck.'

He gave a heave, a wriggle, and a kick, and hauled himself out.

'Tell me,' I shouted urgently. 'Why am I here?'

He didn't answer. He was fiddling with the hatch. I swung my feet over the side of the bunk and rolled in an exceedingly wobbly fashion to my feet. The pitching of the boat promptly threw me off balance and I ended in a heap on the floor.

'Tell me,' I shouted, pulling myself up again and holding on to things. 'Tell me, God dammit.'

The hatch cover slid over and shut out most of the sky. This time, though, it was not clamped down tight, but rested on metal stays, which left a three-inch gap all round: like a lid held three inches above a box.

I put a hand up through the gap and yelled again 'Tell me.'

The only reply I got was the sound of the hatch being made secure against any attempt of mine to dislodge it. Then even those sounds ceased, and I knew he'd gone away; and a minute or two later the engine started again.

The boat rolled and tossed wildly, and the sickness won with a rush. I knelt on the floor with my head over the lavatory bowl and heaved and retched as if trying to rid myself of my stomach itself. I hadn't eaten for so long that all that actually came up was bright yellow bile, but that made nothing any better. The misery of seasickness was that one's body never seemed to realize that there was nothing left to vomit.

I dragged myself onto the bunk and lay there both sweating and shivering, wanting to die.

Blanket and pillow, I thought. In the sail bin.

A terrible effort to get up and get them. I leaned down to pick them up, and my head whirled alarmingly.

Another frightful session over the bowl. Curse the blanket and pillow. But I was so cold.

I got them at the second attempt. Wrapped myself closely in the thick navy wool and put my head thankfully on the navy pillow. There was mercy somewhere, it seemed. I had a bed and a blanket and light and air and a water closet, and a lot of shipboard prisoners before me would have given their souls for all that. It seemed unreasonable to want an explanation as well.

The day passed with increasing awfulness. Anyone who has been comprehensively seasick won't need telling. Head ached and swam, skin sweated, stomach heaved, entire system felt unbelievably ill. If I opened my eyes it was worse.

How long, I thought, will this be going on? Were we crossing the Channel? Surely this relentless churning would soon end. Wherever we were going, it couldn't be far.

At some point he came back and undid the hatch.

'Food,' he said, shouting to be heard against the engine's din.

I didn't answer; couldn't be bothered.

'Food,' he shouted again.

I flapped a weak hand in the air, making go away signals.

I could swear he laughed. Extraordinary how funny seasickness is to those who don't have it. He pushed the hatch into place again and left me to it.

The light faded to dark. I slid in and out of dreams which were a good deal more comforting than reality; and during one of those brief sleeps someone came and fastened the hatch. I didn't care very much. If the boat had sunk, I would have looked upon drowning as a blessed release.

The next time the engine stopped it was only a minor relief compared with the general level of misery. I had supposed it was only in my imagination that the boat was tossing in a storm, but when the engine stopped I rolled clean off the bunk.

Climbing clumsily to my feet, holding on with one hand to the upper bunk, I felt for the door and the light switch beside it. Found the switch, and pressed it. No light. No damned light. Bloody stinking sods, giving me no light.

I fumbled my way back to the lower bunk in the blackness. Tripped over the blanket. Rolled it around me and lay down, feeling most insecure. Felt around for the net: fastened a couple of the hooks, groaning and grunting; not tidily, but enough to do the job.

From the next lot of noises from the outside world, I gathered that someone was putting up sails. On a sailing boat that merely made sense. There were rattlings and flappings and indistinct shouts, about none of which I cared a drip. It seemed vaguely strange someone should be sluicing the decks with buckets of water at such a time, until it dawned on me that the heavy intermittent splashes were made by waves breaking over the bows. The tight-closed hatch made sense. I had never wished for anything more passionately than to get my feet on warm, steady, dry land.

I entirely lost touch of time. Life became merely a matter of total wretchedness, seemingly without end. I would quite have liked a drink of water, but partly couldn't raise the energy to search for it, and partly feared to spill it in the dark, but mostly I didn't bother because every time I lifted my head the whirling bouts of sickness sent me retching to my knees. Water would be no sooner down than up.

He came and undid the hatch: not wide, but enough to let in grey daylight and a flood of fresh air. He did not, it seemed, intend me to die of suffocation.

It was raining hard outside: or maybe it was spray. I saw the bright shine of his yellow oilskins as a shower of heavy drops spattered in through the narrow gap.

His voice came to me, shouting. 'Do you want food?'

I lay apathetically, not answering.

He shouted again. 'Wave your hand if you are all right.'

I reckoned all right was a relative term, but raised a faint flap.

He said something which sounded like 'Gale', and shut the hatch again.

Bloody hell, I thought bitterly. Where were we going that we should run into gales? Out into the Atlantic? And *what for*?

The old jingle about seasickness ran through my head: 'One minute you're afraid you're dying, next minute you're afraid you're not.' For hours through the storm I groaned miserably into the pillow, incredibly ill from nothing but motion.

*

I woke from a sunny dream, the umpteenth awakening into total darkness.

Something different, I thought hazily. Same wild weather outside, the bows crashing against the seas and shipping heavy waves over the deck. Same creaking and slapping of wind-strained rigging. But inside, in me, something quite different.

I breathed deeply from relief. The sickness was going, subsiding slowly like an ebb tide, leaving me acclimatized to an alien environment. I lay for a while in simple contentment, while normality crept back like a forgotten luxury: but then, insistently, other troubles began to surface instead. Thirst, hunger, exhaustion, and an oppressive headache which I eventually put down to dehydration and a dearth of fresh air. A sour taste. An itching stubble of beard. A sweaty feeling of having worn the same clothes for a month. But worse than physical pinpricks, the mental rocks.

Confusion had had its points. Clarity brought no comfort at all. The more I was able to think straight, the less I liked the prospects.

There had to be a reason for any abduction, but the most usual reason made least sense. Ransom . . . it couldn't be. There was no one to pay a million for my release: no parents, rich or poor. Hostage . . . but hostages were mostly taken at random, not elaborately, from a public place. I had no political significance and no special knowledge: I couldn't be bartered, didn't know any secrets, had no access to Government papers or defence plans or scientific discoveries. No one would care more than a passing pang whether I lived or died, except perhaps Trevor, who would count it a nuisance to have to find a replacement.

I considered as dispassionately as possible the thought of death, but eventually discarded it. If I was there to be murdered, it would already have been done. The cabin had been made ready for a living prisoner, not a prospective corpse. Once out at sea, a weighted heave-ho would have done the trick. So, with luck, I was going to live.

However unrealistic it seemed to me, the only reason I could raise which made any sense at all was that I was there for revenge.

Although the majority of mankind think of auditing accountants as dry-as-dust creatures burrowing dimly into columns of boring figures, the dishonest regard them as deadly enemies.

I had had my share of uncovering frauds. I'd lost a dozen people their jobs and set the Revenue onto others, and seen five embezzlers go to prison, and the spite in some of those eyes had been like acid.

If Connaught Powys, for instance, had arranged this trip, my troubles had hardly started. Four years ago, when I'd last seen him, in court and newly convicted, he'd sworn to get even. He would be out of Leyhill about now. If by getting even he meant the full four years in a sail locker . . . well, it couldn't be that. It couldn't. I swallowed, convincing myself that from the solely practical viewpoint, it was impossible.

My throat was dry. From thirst, I told myself firmly: not from fear. Fear would get me nowhere.

I eased myself out of the bunk and onto the small patch of floor, holding on tight to the upper bunk. The black world went on corkscrewing around, but the vertigo had really gone. The fluid in my ears' semicircular canals had finally got used to sloshing about chaotically: a pity it hadn't done it with less fuss.

I found the catch of the wall locker, opened it, and felt around inside. Paper cups, as promised. Bottle of water, ditto. Big plastic bottle with a screw cap. It was hopeless in the dark to use one of the cups: I wedged myself on the only available seat, which was the lowered lid of the loo, and drank straight from the bottle. Even then, with the violent rolling and pitching, a good deal of it ran down my neck.

I screwed the cap on again carefully and groped my way back to the bunk, taking the bottle with me. Hooked up the net again. Lay on my back with my head propped up on the pillow, holding the water on my chest and whistling 'Oh Susanna' to prove I was alive.

A long time passed during which I drank a good deal and whistled every tune I could think of.

After that I stood up and banged on the cabin door with my fists and the bottle, and shouted at the top of my voice that I was awake and hungry and furious at the whole bloody charade. I used a good deal of energy and the results were an absolute zero.

Back in the bunk I took to swearing instead of whistling. It made a change.

The elements went on giving the boat a bad time. I speculated fruitlessly about where we were, and how big the boat was, and how many people were sailing it, and whether they were any good. I thought about hot sausages and crusty bread and red wine, and for a fairly cheerful hour I thought about winning the Gold Cup.

At about the time that I began to wonder seriously if everyone except me had been washed overboard, the hatch-opening noises returned. He was there, still in his oilskins. I gulped in the refreshing blast of cold air and wondered just how much of a stinking fug was rushing out to meet him.

I unhooked the net and stood up, holding on and swaying. The wind outside shrieked like starlings.

He shouted, 'Do you want food?'

'Yes,' I yelled. 'And more water.' I held the nearly empty bottle up to him, and he reached down for it.

'Right.'

He shut the hatch and went away, but not before I had a terrifying glimpse of the outside world. The boat rolled heavily as usual to one side, to the left, and before it rolled back to the right I saw the sea. A huge uneven wave, towering to obliterate the sky, charcoal grey, shining, swept with gusts of spray. The next heavy crash of water over the hatch made me think happier thoughts of my dry cabin.

He came back, opened the hatch a few inches, and

lowered in a plastic carrier bag on a loop of rope. He shouted down at me.

'Next time I bring you food, you give me back this carrier. Understand?'

'Yes,' I shouted back, untying the rope. 'What time is it?'

'Five o'clock. Afternoon.'

'What day?'

'Sunday.' He pulled the rope up and began to shut the hatch.

'Give me some light,' I yelled.

He shouted something which sounded like 'Batteries' and put me back among the blind. Yes, well . . . one could live perfectly well without sight. I slid back onto the bunk, fastened the net, and investigated the carrier bag.

The water bottle, full; an apple; and a packet of two thick sandwiches, faintly warm. They turned out to be hamburgers in bread, not buns; and very good too. I ate the lot.

Five o'clock on Sunday. Three whole damned days since I'd stepped into the white van.

I wondered if anyone had missed me seriously enough to go to the police. I had disappeared abruptly from the weighing room, but no one would think it sinister. The changing room valet might be surprised that I hadn't collected from him my wallet and keys and watch, which he'd been holding as usual in safe keeping while I raced, and that I hadn't in fact paid him, either; but he would have put my absent-mindedness down to excitement. My car would still, I supposed, be standing in the jockeys' car park, but no one yet would have begun to worry about it.

I lived alone in a cottage three miles outside Newbury: my next-door neighbour would merely think I was away celebrating for the weekend. Our two office assistants, one boy, one girl, would have made indulgent allowances, or caustic allowances perhaps, when I hadn't turned up for work on Friday. The clients I had been supposed to see would have been irritated, but no more.

Trevor was away on his holidays. So no one, I concluded, would be looking for me.

On Monday morning, the bankrupt Mr Wells might make a fuss. But even if people began to realize I had vanished, how would they ever find me? The fact had to be faced that they wouldn't. Rescue was unlikely. Unless I escaped, I would be staying in the sail locker until someone chose to let me out.

Sunday to Monday was a long, cold, wild, depressing night.

CHAPTER FOUR

On Monday, March 21st the hatch opened twice to let in air, food, sprays of water, and brief views of constantly grey skies. On each occasion I demanded information, and got none. The oilskins gave merely an impression that the crew had more than enough to do with sailing the boat in those conditions, and had no time to answer damn fool questions.

I was used to being alone. I lived alone and to a great extent worked alone; solitary by nature, and seldom lonely. An only child, long accustomed to my own company, I tended often to feel oppressed by the constant companionship of a large number of people, and to seek escape as soon as possible. All the same, as the hours dragged on, I found life alone in the sail locker increasingly wearing.

Limbo existence, I thought. Lying in a black capsule, endlessly tossing. How long did it take for the human mind to disintegrate, left alone in uncertainty in the rattling, corkscrewing dark?

A bloody long time, I answered myself rebelliously. If

the purpose of all this incarceration was to reduce me to a crying wreck, then it wasn't going to succeed. Tough thoughts, tough words . . . I reckoned more realistically that it depended on the true facts. I could survive another week of it passably, and two weeks with difficulty. After that . . . unknown territory.

Where could we be going? Across the Atlantic? Or, if the idea really was to break me up, maybe just up and down the Irish Sea? They might reckon that any suitable stretch of rough water would do the trick.

And who were 'they'?

Not him in the oilskins. He looked upon me as a nuisance, not a target for malice. He probably had instructions regarding me, and was carrying them out. How unfunny if his instructions were to take me home once I'd gone mad.

Dammit, I thought. Dammit to bloody hell. He'd have a bloody long job. Bugger him. Bugger and sod him.

There was a great sane comfort to be found in swearing.

At some long time after my second Monday glimpse of the outside, it seemed that the demented motion of the boat was slowly steadying. Standing up out of the bunk was no longer quite such a throw-around affair. Holding on was still necessary, but not holding on for dear life. The bows crashed more gently against the waves. The thuds of water over the hatch diminished in number and weight. There were shouts on deck and a good deal of pulley noise, and I guessed they were resetting the sails.

I found also that for the first time since my first awakening, I was no longer cold.

I was still wearing the clothes I had put on in the far off world of sanity: charcoal business suit, sleeveless waistcoat-shaped pullover underneath, pale blue shirt, underpants, and socks. Somewhere on the floor in the dark was my favourite Italian silk tie, worn to celebrate the Gold Cup. Shoes had vanished altogether. From being inadequate even when reinforced by a blanket, the long-suffering ensemble was suddenly too much.

I took off my jacket and rolled it into a tidy ball. As gent's natty suiting it was already a past number: as an extra pillow it added considerably to life's luxuries. Amazing how deprivation made the smallest extras marvellous.

Time had become a lost faculty. Drifting in and out of sleep with no external references was a queer business. I mostly couldn't tell whether I'd been asleep for minutes or hours. Dreams occurred in a semi-waking state, sometimes in such short snatches that I could have counted them in seconds. Other dreams were deeper and longer, and I knew that they were the product of sounder sleep. None of them seemed to have anything to do with my present predicament, and not one came up with any useful subconscious information as to why I should be there. In my innermost soul, it seemed, I didn't know.

Tuesday morning – it must have been Tuesday

morning – he came without the oilskins. The air which flowed in through the open hatch was as always fresh and clean, but now dry and faintly warm. The sky was pale blue. I could see a patch of white sail and hear the hissing of the hull as it cut through the water.

'Food,' he said, lowering one of the by now familiar plastic carriers.

'Tell me why I'm here,' I said, untying the knot.

He didn't answer. I took the carrier off, and tied on the empty one, and held on to the rope.

'Who are you? What is this boat? Why am I here?' I said.

His face showed no response except faint irritation.

'I'm not here to answer your questions.'

'Then what *are* you here for?' I said.

'None of your business. Let go of the rope.'

I held on to it. 'Please tell me why I'm here,' I said.

He stared down, unmoved. 'If you ask any more questions, and you don't leave go of the rope, you'll get no supper.'

The simplicity of the threat, and the simplicity of the mind that made it, was a bit of a stunner. I let go of the rope, but I made one more try.

'Then please just tell me how long you're going to keep me here.'

He gave me a stubborn scowl as he pulled up the carrier.

'You'll get no supper,' he said, withdrawing his head out of sight, and beginning to shut the hatch.

'Leave the hatch open,' I shouted.

I got no joy from that either. He firmly fastened me back in the dark. I stood swaying with the boat, holding onto the upper bunk, and trying to fight down a sudden overwhelming tide of furious anger. How *dared* they abduct me and imprison me in this tiny place and treat me like a naughty child. How dared they give me no reasons and no horizons. How dared they thrust me into the squalor of my own unwashed, unbrushed, unshaven state. There was a great deal of insulted pride and soaring temper in the fiery outrage with which I literally shook.

I could go berserk and smash up the place, I thought, or calm down again and eat whatever he'd brought in the carrier: and the fact that I'd recognized the choice made it certain I'd choose the latter. The bitter, frustrated fury didn't exactly go away, but at least with a sigh I had it back under control.

The intensity of what I'd felt, and its violent, unexpected onset, both alarmed me. I would have to be careful, I thought. There were so many roads to destruction, and rage, it seemed, was one of them.

If a psychiatrist had been shut up like this, I wondered, would he have had any safety nets that I hadn't? Would his knowledge of what might happen to the mind of someone in this position help him to withstand the symptoms when they occurred? Probably I should have studied psychology, not accountancy. More useful if one were kidnapped. Stood to reason.

The carrier contained two shelled hard-boiled eggs, an apple, and three small foil-wrapped triangles of processed cheese. I saved one of the eggs and two pieces of cheese for later, in case he meant it about no supper.

He did mean it. Uncountable hours passed. I ate the second egg and the rest of the cheese. Drank some water. As the day's total entertainment, hardly a riot.

When the hatch was next opened, it was dark outside, though dark with a luminous greyness quite unlike the black inside the cabin. No carrier of food materialized, and I gathered that the respite was only so that I shouldn't asphyxiate. He had opened the hatch and gone before I got round to risking any more questions.

Gone.

The hatch was wide open. Out on the deck there were voices and a good deal of activity with ropes and sails.

'Let go.'

'You're letting the effing thing fall into the sea . . .'

'Catch that effing sheet . . . Move, can't you . . .'

'You'll have to stow the gennie along the rail . . .'

Mostly his voice, from close by, directing things.

I put one foot on the thigh-high rim of the sail bin, as he had done, and hooked my hands over the side of the hatch, and heaved. My head popped out into the free world and it was about two whole seconds before he noticed.

'Get back,' he said brusquely, punctuating his remark by stamping on my fingers. 'Get down and stay down.' He kicked at my other hand. 'Do you want a bash on the head?' He was holding a heavy chromium winch handle, and he swung it in an unmistakable gesture.

'There's no land in sight,' he said, kicking again. 'So get down.'

I dropped back to the floor, and he shut the hatch. I hugged my stinging fingers and counted it fortunate that no one went sailing in hob-nailed boots.

Two seconds' uninterrupted view of the boat had been worth it, though. I sat on the lid of the loo with my feet on the side of the lower bunk opposite, and thought about the pictures still alive on my retinas. Even in night light, with eyes adjusted to a deeper darkness, I'd been able to see a good deal.

For a start, I'd seen three men.

The one I knew, who seemed to be not only in charge of me but of the whole boat. Two others, both young, hauling in a voluminous sail which hung half over the side, pulling it in with outstretched arms and trying to stop it billowing again once they'd got it on deck.

There might be a fourth one steering: I hadn't been able to see. About ten feet directly aft of the hatch the single mast rose majestically skywards, and with all the cleats and pulleys and ropes clustered around its base it had formed a block to any straight view towards the stern. There might have been a helmsman and three or four crewmen resting below. Or there might have been automatic steering and all hands visible on deck. It seemed a huge boat, though, to be managed by three.

From the roughest of guesses and distant gleams from

chromium winches I would have put it at about a cricket pitch long. Say sixty-five feet. Or say, if you preferred it, nineteen point eight one metres. Give or take an octave.

Not exactly a nippy little dinghy for Sunday afternoons on the Thames. An ocean racer, more like.

I had had a client once who had bought himself a second-hand ocean racer. He'd paid twenty-five thousand for thirty feet of adventure, and beamed every time he thought of it. His voice came back over the years: 'The people who race seriously have to buy new boats every year. There's always something new. If they don't get a better boat they can't possibly win, and the possibility of winning is what it's all about. Now me, all I want is to be able to sail round Britain comfortably at weekends in the summer. So I buy one of the big boys' cast-offs, because they're well-built boats, and just the job.' He had once invited me to Sunday lunch on board. I had enjoyed looking over his pride and joy, but privately had been most relieved when a sudden gale had prevented us leaving the moorings at his yacht club for the promised afternoon's sail.

Highly probable, I thought, that I was now being entertained on some other big boy's cast-off. The great question was, at whose expense?

The improvement in the weather was a mixed blessing, because the engine started again. The din seemed an even worse assault on my nerves than it had at the beginning. I lay on the bunk and tried to shut my ears with the pillow and my fingers, but the roaring vibration easily by-passed such frivolous barriers. I'd either got to get used to it and ignore it, I thought, or go raving, screaming bonkers.

I got used to it.

Wednesday. Was it Wednesday? I got food and air twice. I said nothing to him, and he said nothing to me. The constant noise of the engine made talking difficult. Wednesday was a black desert.

Thursday. I'd been there a week.

When he opened the hatch, I shouted, 'Is it Thursday?'

He looked surprised. Hesitated, then shouted back, 'Yes.' He looked at his watch. 'Quarter to eleven.'

He was wearing a blue cotton tee shirt, and the day outside seemed fine. The light tended to hurt my eyes.

I untied the carrier and fastened on the previous one, which as usual contained an empty water bottle. I looked up at him as he pulled it out, and he stared down at my face. He looked his normal unsmiling self: a hard young man, unfeeling rather than positively brutal.

I didn't consciously ask him, but after a pause, during which he seemed to be inspecting the horizon, he began to fix the hatch as he had done on the first day, so that it was a uniform three inches above the deck, letting in continuous air and light.

The relief at not being locked back in the dark was absolutely shattering. I found I was trembling from head to foot. I swallowed, trying to guard against the possibility that he would change his mind. Trying to tell myself that even if it proved to be only for five minutes, I should be grateful for that.

He finished securing the hatch and went away. I took some shaky deep breaths and gave myself an ineffective lecture about stoical responses, come dark, come shine.

After a while I sat on the lid of the loo and ate the first shipboard meal that I could actually see. Two hard-boiled eggs, some crispbread, three triangles of cheese and an apple. Never much variety in the diet, but at least no one intended me to starve.

He came back about half an hour after he'd gone away.

Hell, I thought. Half an hour. Be grateful for that. I had at least talked myself into facing another dose of darkness without collapsing into rubble.

He didn't, however, shut the hatch. Without altering the way it was fixed, he slid another plastic carrier through the gap. It was not this time tied to a rope, because when he let go of it, it fell to the floor; and before I could raise any remark, he had gone again.

I picked up the carrier, which seemed light and almost empty, and looked inside.

For God's sake, I thought. Laugh. Laugh, but don't bloody snivel. An ounce of kindness was more devastating than a week of misery.

He'd given me a pair of clean socks and a paperback novel.

I spent a good deal of the day trying to look out of the gap. With one foot on the rim of the sail bins, and my hands grasping the hatch opening, I could get my head up to the top well enough, but the view would have been more comprehensive if either the gap had been a couple of inches deeper or my eyes had been located halfway up my forehead. What I did see, mostly by tilting my head and applying one eye at a time, was a lot of ropes, pulleys, and rolled up sails, a lot of green sea, and a dark line of land on the horizon ahead.

None of these things changed all day except that the smudge of land grew slowly thicker, but I never tired of looking.

At closer quarters I also looked at the fittings of the hatch itself, which, I realized after a time, had been modified slightly for my visit. The metal props which held it open were hinged, and folded down inside the cabin when the hatch was closed. Out on deck the hatch cover was mounted on two heavier extending hinges, which allowed it to open outwards completely and lie flat on its back.

Inside the cabin there were two sturdy clips for securing the hatch shut from below, and outside there were two others, for securing the hatch from above.

So far, all as planned by the ship builders. What had been added, though, was extra provision to prevent someone inside the cabin from pushing the hatch wide open after releasing it from the hinged props. Normally, one could have done this. Sail locker hatches were supposed to open easily and wide, so that the sails could be pulled in and out. There was no point in ordinary circumstances in making things difficult. But now, outside, crossing from fore to aft and from port to starboard over the top of the hatch cover, were two lengths of chain, each secured at both ends to cleats which to my eyes looked newly screwed to the deck. The chains held the hatch cover down on the props like guy ropes, taut and forceful. If I could dislodge those chains, I thought, I could get out. If I had anything to dislodge them with. A couple of Everest-sized ifs. I could get my hands out through the three inch gap, but not much arm. Not enough to reach the cleats, let alone undo the chains. As for levers, screwdrivers, hammers and files, all I had were paper cups, a flimsy carrier and a plastic water bottle. Tantalizing, all those hours looking out at unreachable freedom.

In between the long bouts of balancing up by the ceiling I sat on the loo lid and read the book, which was an American private-eye thriller with a karate-trained hero who would have chopped his way out of a sail locker in five minutes.

Inspired by him, I had another go at the cabin door. It withstood my efforts like a stolid wall. Obviously I should have studied karate as well as psychiatry. Better luck next time.

The day whizzed past. The light began to fade. Outside the smudge of land had grown into an approaching certainty, and I had no idea what land it was.

He came back, lowered the carrier, and waited while I tied on the empty ones.

'Thank you,' I shouted, as he pulled them up, 'for the book and socks.'

He nodded, and began to close the hatch.

'Please don't,' I shouted.

He paused and looked down. It seemed to be still be-kind-to-prisoners day, because he provided his first explanation.

'We are going into port. Don't waste your breath making a noise when we stop. We'll be anchored. No one will hear you.'

He shut the hatch. I ate sliced tinned ham and a hot baked potato in the noisy stupefying dark, and to cheer myself up thought that now that the journey was ending they surely wouldn't keep me there much longer. Tomorrow, perhaps, I would be out. And after that I might get some answers.

I stifled the gloomy doubts.

*

The engine slowed, the first time it had changed its note. There were footsteps on deck, and shouts, and the anchor went over with a splash. The anchor chain rattled out, sounding as if it were passing practically through the sail locker; behind the panelling, no doubt.

The engine was switched off. There was no sound from anywhere. The creakings and rushing noises had stopped. No perceptible motion any more. I had expected the peace to be a relief, but as time passed it was the opposite. Even aggravating stimuli, it seemed, were better than none at all. I slept in disjointed snatches and lay emptily awake for hours and hours wondering if one really could go mad from too much nothing.

When he next opened the hatch it was full daylight outside. Friday; mid-morning. He lowered the carrier, waited for the exchange, raised the rope, and began to close the hatch.

I made involuntarily a vague imploring gesture with my hands. He paused, looking down.

'I can't let you see where we are,' he said.

It was the nearest he had come to an apology, the nearest to admitting that he might have treated me better, if he didn't have his orders.

'Wait,' I yelled, as he pulled the hatch over.

He paused again: prepared at least to listen.

'Can't you put screens round if you don't want me to see the land?' I said. 'Leave the hatch open . . .'

He considered it. 'I'll see,' he said, 'later.'

It seemed an awfully long time later, but he did come

back, and he did open the hatch. While he was fastening it, I said, 'When are you going to let me out?'

'Don't ask questions.'

'I *must*,' I said explosively. 'I have to know.'

'Do you want me to shut the hatch?'

'No.'

'Then don't ask questions.'

It may have been spineless of me, but I didn't ask any more. He hadn't given me one useful answer in eight days, and if I persevered, all I would get would be no light and no supper and an end to the new era of partial humanity.

When he'd gone I climbed up for a look, and found he had surrounded the hatch area with bulging bolsters of rolled sails. My field of vision had come down to about eighteen inches.

I lay on the top bunk for a change, and tried to imagine what it was about the port, so hopelessly near, that I might recognize. The sky was pale blue, with sun shining through high, hazy cloud. It was warm, like a fine spring day. There were even seagulls.

It evoked in me such a strong picture that I became convinced that if I could only see over the sail bolsters, I would be looking at the harbour and beaches where I'd played as a child. Maybe all that frantic sailing had been nowhere but up and down the English Channel, and we were now safe back home in Ryde, Isle of Wight.

I shook the comforting dream away. All one could

actually tell for sure was that it was not in the Arctic Circle.

There were occasional sounds from outside, but all distant, and nothing of any use. I read the American thriller again, and thought a good deal about escape.

When the day was fading he came back with supper, but this time, after I'd swopped the carriers, he didn't shut the hatch. That evening I watched the light die to dusk and night, and breathed sweet air. Small mercies could be huge mercies, I thought.

Saturday, March 26th. The morning carrier contained fresh bread, fresh cheese, fresh tomatoes: someone had been shopping ashore. It also contained an extra bottle of water and a well-worn piece of soap. I looked at the soap and wondered if it was there from kindness or because I stank; and then with wildly leaping hope wondered if it was there so that I should at least be clean when they turned me loose.

I took off all my clothes and washed from head to foot, using a sock as a sponge. After the week's desultory efforts with salt water from the loo, the lather was a fantastic physical delight. I washed my face and ears and neck and wondered what I looked like with a beard.

After that, dressed in shirt and underpants which were both long overdue for the same treatment, I ate the morning meal.

After that, I tidied the cabin, folding the blanket and my extra clothes and stacking everything neatly.

After that, I still couldn't face for a long time that my soaring hope was unfounded. No one came to let me out.

It was odd how soon the most longed-for luxury became commonplace and not enough. In the dark, I had ached for light. Now that I had light, I took it for granted and ached for room to move.

The cabin was triangular, its three sides each about six feet long. The bunks on the port side, and the loo and sail bins on the starboard side, took up most of the space. The floor area in the centre was roughly two feet wide by the cabin door, but narrowed to a point about four feet in, where the bunks and the forward sail bin met. There was room to take two small paces, or one large. Any attempt at knees-bend-arms-stretch involved unplanned contact with the surrounding woodwork. There was more or less enough space to stand on one's head by the cabin door. I did that a couple of times. It just shows how potty one can get. The second time I bashed my ankle on the edge of the sail bin coming down, and decided to give Yoga a miss. If I'd tried the Lotus position, I'd have been wedged for life.

I felt a continuous urge to scream and shout. I knew that no one would hear me, but the impulse had nothing to do with reason. It stemmed from frustration, fury and induced claustrophobia. I knew that if I gave way to it, and yelled and yelled, I would probably end up sobbing.

The thought that maybe that was precisely what someone wanted to happen to me was an enormous support. I couldn't stop the screaming and shouting from going on inside my head, but at least it didn't get out.

After I'd finally come to terms with the thought that it wasn't Exodus day, I spent a good deal of time contemplating the loo. Not metaphysically: mechanically.

Everything in the cabin was either built-in, or soft. From the beginning I'd been given no possible weapons, no possible implements. All the food had been for eating with my fingers, and came wrapped only in paper or plastic, if at all. No plates. Nothing made of metal, china or glass. The light bulb had not only been unscrewed from its socket, but the glass cover for it, which I guessed should be there, was not.

The pockets of my suit had been emptied. The nail file I usually carried in my breast pocket was no longer there: nor were my pens clipped inside: and my penknife had gone from my trousers.

I sat on the floor, lifted the lid, and at close quarters glared at the loo's mechanics.

Bowl, flushing lever, pump. A good deal of tubing. The stopcock for turning the sea water on and off. Everything made with the strength and durability demanded by the wild motions of the sea, which shook flimsy contraptions to pieces.

The lever was fastened at the back, hinged to the built-in casing of the fitment. At the front, it ended in a wooden handle. Attached at about a third of the way back was the rod which led directly down into the pump, to pull the piston there up and down. The whole lever, from handle to hinge, measured about eighteen inches.

I lusted for that lever like a rapist, but I could see no way, without tools, of getting it off. The hinge and the piston linkage were each fastened with a nut and bolt, and appeared to have been tightened by Atlas. Nut versus thumb and finger was no contest. I had tried on and off for two days.

A spanner. My kingdom for a spanner, I thought.

Failing a spanner, what else?

I tried with my shirt. The cloth saved the pressure on skin and bones, but gave no extra purchase. The nuts sat there like rocks. It was like trying to change a wheel with only fingers and a handkerchief.

Trousers? The cloth itself tended to slip more easily than my shirt. I tried the waistband, and found it a great deal better. Around the inside of the waist was a strip with two narrow rows of rough-surfaced rubber let into it. The real purpose of the strip was to help belt-less trousers stay up by providing a friction grip against a tucked-in shirt. Applying trouser-band to nut gave a good grip and slightly more hope, but despite a lot of heavy effort, no results.

The day ground on. I went on sitting on the floor futilely trying to unscrew nuts which wouldn't unscrew, simply because there was nothing else to do.

*

Tinned ham again for supper. I carefully peeled off all the fat, and ate the lean.

The hatch stayed open.

I said thanks for the soap, and asked no questions.

Sunday. Another Sunday. How *could* anyone keep me locked up so long without explanation? The whole modern world was churning along outside, and there I was cooped up like the man in the iron mask, or as near as dammit.

I applied the strips of ham fat to the nuts, to see if grease would have any effect. I spent most of the day warming the piston-rod nut in my fingers, rubbing fat round its edges, and hauling at it with my trousers.

Nothing happened.

Now and again I stood up and stretched, and climbed up to see if the sail bolsters were still obstructing the view, which they always were. I read bits of the thriller again. I closed the loo lid and sat on it, and looked at the walls. I listened to the seagulls.

My ordinary life seemed far removed. Reality was inside the sail locker. Reality was a mystery. Reality was mind-cracking acres of empty time.

Sunday night drifted in and darkened and slowly became Monday. He came much earlier than usual with my breakfast, and when he had lifted out the exchange carrier, he began to close the hatch.

'Don't,' I yelled.

He paused only briefly, staring down unmoved.

'Necessary,' he said.

I went on yelling for him to open it for a long time after he'd gone away and left me in the dark. Once I'd started making a noise, I found it difficult to stop: all the stifled screams and shouts were trying to burst out through the hole in the dam. If the dam broke up, so would I. I stuffed the pillow into my mouth to make myself shut up, and resisted a desire to bang my head against the door instead.

The engine started. Din and vibration and darkness, all as before. It's too much, I thought. Too much. But there were only two basic alternatives. Stay sane or go crazy. Sanity was definitely getting harder.

Think rational thoughts, I told myself. Repeat verses, do mental arithmetic, remember all the tricks that other solitary prisoners have used to see them through weeks and months and years.

I tore my mind away from such impossible periods and directed it to the present.

The engine ran on fuel. It had used a good deal of fuel on the journey. Therefore if the boat was going far, it would need more.

Engines were always switched off during refuelling. If I made the most colossal racket when we refuelled, just possibly someone might hear. I didn't honestly see how any noise I could make would attract enough attention, but I could try.

The chain rattled back through its hidden chute as the anchor came up, and I presumed the boat was moving, although there was no feeling of motion.

Then someone came and put a radio on top of the hatch, and turned the volume up loud. The music fought a losing battle against the engine for a while, but shortly I felt the boat bump, and almost at once the engine switched off.

I knew we were refuelling. I could hear only loud pop music. And no one on the quayside, whatever I did, could possibly have heard *me*.

After a fairly short while the engine started again. There were a few small thuds outside, felt through the hull, and then nothing. Someone came and collected the radio: I yelled for the hatch to be opened, but might as well not have bothered.

Motion slowly returned to the boat, bringing hopeless recognition with it.

Going out to sea again.

Out to sea, in the noise and the dark. Still not knowing why I was there, or for how long. Growing less fit from lack of exercise and less able to deal with mental pressure. Starting last week's torments all over again.

I sat on the floor with my back against the cabin door, and folded my arms over my knees, and put my head on my arms, and wondered how I could possibly endure it.

Monday I spent in full-blown despair.

On Tuesday, I got out.

CHAPTER FIVE

Monday night the boat was anchored somewhere, but it stopped after I got my supper and started again before Tuesday mid-morning. It rained most of the time, drumming on the hatch. I was glad of the respite from the engine but in general the misery level was a pain.

When he brought the morning food he fixed the hatch open. The extent of my relief was pathetic.

Shortly after, they stopped the engine and put up the sails, and the grey sky outside slowly cleared to blue.

I ate the hard boiled eggs and the apple and thought about the thick slice of bread, upon which, for the first time, he had given me butter. Then I pulled a button off my shirt to use as a scraper, and transferred as much of the butter as I could to the stubborn nuts and bolts on the flushing lever. Then I ate the bread. Then I sat on the floor and one after the other warmed the nuts with my hand in the hope that the butter and ham fat would melt into the screw threads.

After that I ripped a length of the rubberized waistband from my trousers, and fished out of the bottom of one of the sail bins the white net which I had stored there after the storms.

It was activity for activity's sake, more than any real hope. I wound the waistband twice round the piston-rod nut, because it was the nearest, and fitted over that the chromium hook which had attached the net to the upper berth. Then I tugged the net.

After a second of gripping, the hook slid round on the cloth and fell off. I tried again, folding the waistband so that it had an elasticated side against the hook as well as against the nut. That time the hook stayed in place; but so did the nut.

I tugged several times. If I tugged very hard, hook, waistband and all came off. Nothing else happened. I slung the net back into the sail bin in depression.

After that I sat for ages with my hand on the piston-rod nut, until it was as warm as a handful of pennies clutched by a child. Then I wound the strip of waistband round quickly three times, to make the nut larger to grip, and then I tried it with all my remaining muscle power.

The waistband turned in my hand.

Damn it to hell, I thought hopelessly. I pulled it off and wound it on again, trying to grip it more tightly.

It turned again.

It may seem ridiculous, but it was not until it turned more easily the third time that I realized I was turning the nut on the bolt, not the waistband on the nut.

Unbelievable. I sat there looking idiotic, with my

mouth open. Excitement fluttered in my throat like a stifled laugh. If I could get one off, what about the other?

Time hadn't mattered for the first one. I'd had nothing else to do. For the second one, the hinge, I was feverishly impatient.

I warmed the nut, and wound on the waistband, and heaved; and nothing happened.

Heaved again.

A blob.

It had to move, I thought furiously. It simply had to. After several more useless attempts, I went back to basics.

Perhaps after all the tugging session with the hook had had some effect. I scooped out the net and applied it to the hinge nut, and tugged away with enthusiasm, replacing the hook every time it fell off. Then I made myself warm the nut as thoroughly as I had the other one, so that the heat from my hand was conducted right to the inside, where the melted grease and the minute heat-expansion of the metal could do their work. Then I wound on the waistband again and practically tore all the ligaments in my arm and back with a long and mighty heave.

And that time, the waistband turned. That time again I couldn't be sure until the third turn, when the nut started moving more freely, that I'd really done it.

I climbed up on the sail bin and squinted out at the free world. To the left all I could see was sky and a sparkle of sun on the water. I turned my head to the right and nearly fell off my perch. To the right there was a sail, and shining below it, green and rocky and moderately close, there was land.

I thought that if he came along at that moment to shut the hatch I would perversely be grateful.

Only desperation made me do what I did next, because I was sure that if he caught me in mid-escape he'd tie my hands and leave me in the dark on starvation rations.

The risk that I wouldn't get out unseen was appalling. My present conditions were just about bearable; my future afterwards wouldn't be.

Yet if I hadn't meant to risk it, why had I laboured so long on the nuts?

I went back to the loo and unscrewed the nuts completely. I knocked the bolts out, and pulled the whole lever free.

Without it, no one could flush the loo. I thought grimly that it would be an added complication if I found myself back in the cabin with it gone.

There was no sign of anyone on deck, and as usual I couldn't see if the boat was on automatic steering or whether there was anyone at the helm.

Hesitation was only in my mind. Looking back, it seemed as if I did everything very fast.

I pulled the hinged props of the hatch down inside the cabin, which one would do in the normal way if one wanted to shut the hatch oneself from the inside. This had the effect of slackening the guy-rope action of the chains crossed over the top.

Through the much reduced gap, little more than a slit, I poked the lever, aiming at where a link of chain was hooked over the top.

Long hours of inspection had given me the impression that those chains had no other fastening. Putting a link over the hook of the cleat must have seemed safe enough, because they were certain I had no means of dislodging them. I stuck the lever into the chain on the right, wedged it securely, and pushed. With almost miraculous elegance the whole chain slid loosely outwards, and the link fell off the cleat.

Without pausing for anything but mental hip-hoorays I applied the lever again, this time to where the fore and aft chain was fastened on the bow side. Again, with no more fuss, the link slid off.

I was committed. I couldn't get the chains back on again. I had to open the hatch now, and climb out. There was no retreat.

I took the lever with me as a last resort against recapture, putting it out first onto the deck. Then with both hands I released the hatch from the hinged props and pushed it wide. Eased it down gently until it lay flat, fearing to let it crash open and bring them running.

I snaked out onto the deck on my stomach. Rolled to the right, under the jib sail. Reached the railing, grabbed it with both hands, and bunny-hopped fast over the side, going down into the sea straight and feet first, like a pillar.

It wasn't the safest way of disembarking, but I survived it, staying down under the surface until my lungs protested. Surfacing was one of the most anxious moments of my life, but when I cautiously lifted mouth, nose and eyes above the water, there was the boat a hundred yards away, steadily sailing on.

With a great intake of air I sank down again and began to swim underwater towards the shore; gently, so as to make no notice-attracting splash.

The water was chilly, but not as cold as I'd expected. The shore, when I came up again, looked about a mile away, though distances at sea were deceptive.

The boat sailed on peacefully. It must have had a name on it, I supposed, though in the flurry I hadn't seen one. I wondered how long it would be before they found I had gone. Supper time, with luck.

The land ahead looked a most promising haven. To the left it was rocky, with grassy cliffs, but straight ahead lay a much greener part, with houses and hotels, and a strip of sand. Civilization, hot baths, freedom and a razor. I swam towards them steadily, taking rests. A mile was a long way for a moderate swimmer, and I was nothing like as strong as I had been twelve days earlier.

I looked back at the boat. It had gone a good way along the coast: growing smaller.

The big mainsail was sagging down the mast.

God, I thought, my heart lurching, if they're taking down the sails they'll see the open hatch.

Time had run out. They knew I had gone.

I ploughed for the shore until I felt dizzy with the effort. Swam until I had grey dots before the eyes and even greyer dots in the mind.

I wasn't going back into that dark hole. I absolutely couldn't.

When I next looked back all the sails were down and the boat was turning.

The hotels ahead were in a sandy bay. Two big hotels, white, with rows of balconies, and a lot of smaller buildings all around. There were some people on the beach, and four or five standing in the water.

Five hundred yards, perhaps.

It would take me years to swim five hundred yards.

I pushed my absolutely useless muscles into frantic efforts. If I could only reach the other bathers, I would be just one more head.

The boat had not been travelling very fast under sail. They would motor back faster. I feared to look around; to see them close. My imagination heard him shouting and pointing, and steering the boat to intercept me, felt them grabbing me with boathooks and pulling me in. When in the end I did nerve myself for a look, it was bad enough, but still too far to distinguish anyone clearly.

Next time I looked, it was alarming. They were catching up like hares. The nearest point of land was still about three hundred yards away, and it was uneven rock, not easy shelving beach. The sand lay in the centre of the bay: the curving arms were shallow cliffs. I would never reach the sand, I thought.

And yet . . . sailing boats had deep keels. They wouldn't be able to motor right up to the beach. Perhaps, after all, I could get there.

I had never felt so tired, so leaden. The hardest steeplechase had never demolished me so completely, even those I'd lost from being unfit. My progress through the water grew slower and slower, when speed was all that mattered. In the end it took me all my time to stay afloat.

There was a current, which I hadn't noticed at first, carrying me to the left, drifting me off my line to the beach. Nothing fierce; but simply sapping. I hadn't enough kick left to overcome it.

Another look back.

Literally terrifying. I could see him on deck, standing in the bows, shading his eyes with his hand. He had come back on a course closer to the shore than when I'd jumped, and it was the shoreline he seemed to be scouring most closely.

I swam on with feeble, futile strokes. I could see that I was not going to reach the sand. The current was taking me inexorably towards the higher, left hand side of the bay, where there were trees to within ten feet of the waterline, and rocks below the trees.

When I'd got to the numb stage of thinking drowning would be preferable to recapture, and doubting if one *could* drown oneself in cold blood, I found suddenly that I could no longer see for miles along the coast. I had at last got within the embracing arms of the bay. When I looked back, I couldn't see the boat.

It didn't stay out of sight long. It crept along in a straight line until it reached the centre of the bay, and there dropped anchor. I watched it in sick glimpses over my shoulder. Saw them unbuckle a black rubber dinghy and lower it over the side. Caught an impression of them lowering an outboard engine, and oars, and of two of them climbing down into the boat.

I heard the outboard splutter into life. Only about thirty feet to go to touch the land. It seemed like thirty miles.

There was a man-made strip of concrete set into the rocks ahead of me at the water's edge. I glanced along the shore towards the beach, and saw that there were others. Aids to bathers. The most heartening aid in the world to the bather approaching at snail's pace with the hounds of hell at his back.

The dinghy pulled away from the anchored boat and pointed its bulky black shape towards the shore.

I reached the strip of concrete. It was a flat step, set only inches above the water.

No grips for hauling oneself out. Just a step. I put one hand flat on it and raised a foot to it, and used jelly muscles to flounder up onto my stomach.

Not enough. Not enough. The dinghy would come while I was lying there.

My heart was pounding. Effort and fear in equal measures. Utter desperation took me to hands and knees and set me crawling up the rocks to find shelter.

Ordinarily it would have been easy. It was a gentle shore, undemanding. A child could have jumped where I laboured. I climbed up about six feet of tumbled rocks and found a shallow gully, half full of water. I rolled into the hollow and lay there panting, hopelessly exhausted, listening to the outboard engine grow steadily louder.

They must have seen me, I thought despairingly. Seen me climbing up out of the sea. Yet if I'd stayed at the water's edge they would have found me just as surely. I lay in defeated misery and wondered how on earth I could live through whatever was coming.

The dinghy approached. I kept my head down. They were going to have to come and find me and carry me, and if I could raise enough breath I'd yell until some of the people on the beach took notice, except that they were far enough away to think it was all a game.

The engine died and I heard his voice, raised but not exactly shouting.

He said, 'Excuse me, but have you seen a friend of ours swim in from the sea? We think he fell overboard.'

A woman's voice answered him, from so close to me that I almost fainted.

'No, I haven't seen anybody.'

He said, 'He takes drugs. He might have been acting funny.'

'Serves him right, then,' she said, sanctimoniously.

'I've been reading. I haven't seen him. Have you come from that boat?'

'That's right. We think he fell overboard about here. We heard a splash, but we thought it was just a fish. Till after.'

'Sorry,' she said. 'Why don't you ask along the beach?'

'Just starting this side,' he said. 'We'll work round.'

There was a noise of oars being fitted into rowlocks, and the splash and squeak as they pulled away. I stayed where I was without moving, hoping she wouldn't have hysterics when she saw me, dreading that she would call them back.

I could hear him, away along the shore, loudly asking the same question of someone else.

Her voice said, 'Don't be frightened. I know you're there.'

I didn't answer her. She'd taken away what was left of my breath.

After a pause she said, 'Do you take drugs?'

'No,' I said. It was little more than a whisper.

'What did you say?'

'No.'

'Hm. Well, you'd better not move. They're methodical. I think I'll go on reading.'

Incredulously, I took her advice, lying half in and half out of the water, feeling heart and lungs subside slowly to a more manageable rhythm.

'They've landed on the beach,' she said.

My heart stirred up again. 'Are they searching?' I said anxiously.

'No. Asking questions, I should think.' She paused. 'Are they criminals?'

'I don't know.'

'But . . . would they take you from here by force? With people watching?'

'Yes. You heard them. If I shouted for help, they'd say I was crazy with drugs. No one would stop them.'

'They're walking round the far side of the bay,' she said. 'Asking people.'

'My name is Roland Britten,' I said. 'I live in Newbury, and I'm an accountant. I was kidnapped twelve days ago, and they've kept me on that boat ever since, and I don't know why. So please, whoever you are, if they do manage to get me back there, will you tell the police? I really do most desperately need help.'

There was a short silence. I thought that I must have overdone it; that she didn't believe me. Yet I'd had to tell her, as a precaution.

She apparently made up her mind. 'Well then,' she said briskly, 'time for you to vanish.'

'Where to?'

'My bedroom,' she said.

She was a great one for punches in the mental solar plexus. In spite of the grimness of things in general, I almost laughed.

'Can you see me?' I said.

'I can see your feet. I saw all of you when you climbed out of the sea and scrambled up here.'

'And how do I get to your bedroom dressed in a wet shirt and underpants and nothing else?'

'Do you want to avoid those men, or don't you?'

There was no answer to that.

'Stay still,' she said sharply, though I had not in fact moved. 'They're looking this way. Someone over there seems to be pointing in this direction.'

'Oh God.'

'Stay still.' There was a longish pause, then she said, 'They are walking back along the beach, towards their boat. If they don't stop there, but come on this way, we will go.'

I waited dumbly, and more or less prayed.

'There's a path above us,' she said. 'I will hand you a towel. Wrap it round you, and climb up to the path.'

'Are they coming?'

'Yes.'

A triangle of brightly striped bathing towel appeared over the rock by my head. There was little I'd ever wanted to do less than stand up out of my secure hiding place. My nerves were all against it.

'Hurry up,' she said. 'Don't look back.'

I stood up, dripping, with my back to the sea. Pulled the towel towards me, wrapped it round like a sarong, and tackled the rocky upgrade to the path. The respite in the gully had given me back a surprising amount of energy: or perhaps it was plain fear. In any case I climbed the second stage a great deal more nimbly than the first.

'I'm behind you,' her voice said. 'Don't look back. Turn right when you reach the path. And don't run.'

'Yes ma'am,' I said under my breath. Never argue with a guardian angel.

The path was fringed on both sides with trees, with a mixture of sand and bare rock underfoot. The sunshine dappled through the branches and at any other time would have looked pretty.

When the path widened she fell into step beside me, between me and the sea.

'Take the branch path to the left,' she said, drawing level. 'And don't walk too fast.'

I glanced at her, curious to see what she looked like. She matched her voice: a no-nonsense middle-aged lady with spectacles and a practical air. Self-confident. Tall: almost six feet. Thin, and far from a beauty.

She was wearing a pale-pink blouse, fawn cotton trousers, and sandshoes, and she carried a capacious canvas beach bag.

Beach. Swimming. In March.

'Where is this place?' I said.

'Cala St Galdana.'

'Where's that?'

'Minorca, of course.'

'*Where*?'

'Don't stop walking. Minorca.'

'Island next to Majorca?'

'Of course.' She paused. 'Didn't you know?'

I shook my head. The branch path reached the top of a shallow gradient and began to descend through more trees on the far side.

She peered to the right as we went over the brow.

'Those men are just coming along the lower path, heading towards where I was sitting. I think it would be a good idea to hurry a little now, don't you?'

'Understatement,' I said.

Hurrying meant stubbing my bare toes on various half-buried stones and feeling the dismal weakness again make rubber of my legs.

'While they are looking for you on the rocks, we will reach my hotel,' she said.

I shuffled along and saved my breath. Glanced over my shoulder. Only empty path. No pursuing furies. So why did I feel that they could see through earth and trees and know exactly where to find me?

'Over that little bridge, and across the road. Over there.' She pointed. 'That's the hotel.'

It was one of the two big white ones. We reached the wide glass doors and went inside. Made it unchallenged across the hall and into the lift. Rose to the fifth floor. She scooped some keys out of her beach bag, and let us into 507.

We had seen almost nobody on the way. Still enough warm sun for holidaymakers to be out on the beach and for the staff to be sleeping.

507 had a sea-view balcony, twin beds, two armchairs,

a yellow carpet, and orange and brown curtains. Regulation hotel room, with almost none of my saviour's belongings in sight.

She walked over to the glass door, which was wide open, and half stepped onto the balcony.

'Do you want to watch?' she said.

I looked cautiously over her shoulder. From that height one could see the whole panorama of the bay. There was the boat, anchored in the centre. There was the dinghy on the sand. The headland where I'd crawled out of the sea was to the right, the path leading to it from the beach showing clearly through the trees like a dappled yellow snake.

Along the path came the two men, my familiar warder in front, making for the sand. They trudged slowly across to the dinghy, still looking continually around, and pushed it into the sea.

They both climbed in. They started the outboard. They steered away from the beach.

I felt utterly drained.

'Do you mind if I sit down?' I said.

CHAPTER SIX

Thanks to telephones, consul, bank, and friends, I flew back to England the following evening, but not before I had collected further unforgettable memories of Miss Hilary Margaret Pinlock.

She asked me my measurements, descended to the local boutiques, and returned with new clothes.

She lent me her bathroom, inspected me cleaned and dressed, and decided to go shopping for a razor. I protested. She went. It was as easy to stop Miss Pinlock as an avalanche.

With some relief I scratched the twelve days' scruffy dark stubble off my face, one glance in the looking glass having persuaded me that I was not going to look better in a beard. The twelve days of indoor life had left me thin and pale, with grey hollows in cheeks and eye sockets which I didn't remember having before. Nothing that a little freedom wouldn't fix.

On her second expedition she had also bought bread, cheese and fruit, explaining that she was there on a package holiday, and that the hotel didn't cater for random visitors.

'I'll go down to dinner at seven as usual,' she said. 'You can eat here.'

Throughout all her remarks and actions ran the positive decision-making of one accustomed to command.

'Are you a children's nurse?' I asked curiously.

'No,' she said, unsmiling. 'A headmistress.'

'Oh.'

The smile came, briefly. 'Of a girls-only comprehensive, in Surrey.'

With a touch of sardonic humour she watched me reassess her in the light of that revelation. Not a do-gooding bossy spinster, but a fulfilled career woman of undoubted power.

'Yes. Well . . .' she shrugged. 'If you give me the numbers, I'll ask the switchboard for your calls.'

'And I need a bedroom,' I said.

'Your friends might return and ask about strangers needing bedrooms,' she said.

It had occurred to me too. 'Yes, but . . .' I said.

She pointed to one of the twin beds. 'You can sleep there. I am here alone. The friend who was coming with me had to cry off at the last minute.'

'But . . .' I stopped.

She waited calmly.

'All right,' I said. 'Thank you.'

When she returned from dinner she brought with her a piece of news and a bottle of wine.

'Your friend from the boat was downstairs in the lobby, asking everyone who speaks English if they saw a crazy young man come ashore today. Everyone said no. He looks extremely worried.'

'Probably thinks I drowned.'

The boat had gone from the bay. He must have reached another mooring and returned to Cala St Galdana by road. I wondered how long and how thoroughly he would persevere in his search: the more he feared whoever he was working for, the less he would give up.

The evening air was chilly. Miss Pinlock shut the glass door against the night sky and expertly opened her bottle of Marqués de Riscal.

'Tell me about your journey,' she said, handing me a glass.

I told her the beginning and the end, and not much of the middle.

'Extraordinary,' she said.

'When I get home I'll have a go at finding out what it was all about . . .'

She looked at me gravely. 'It may not be over.'

She had an uncomfortable habit of putting my worst fears into speech.

We drank the excellent wine and she told me a little of her busy life.

'I enjoy it,' she said positively.

'Yes, I see that.'

There was a pause. She looked carefully at the wine in her glass.

She said, 'Will you go to bed with me?'

I suppose I sat in an ungentlemanly heap with my mouth open. I closed it, conscious of the insult it conveyed.

When I'd got over the first shock, she looked up. Her face was calm and businesslike as before, but also suddenly there was vulnerability and self-consciousness. A blush started on her neck, and spread painfully upwards.

She was between forty-two and forty-six, I guessed. She had dark brown wavy hair, going grey, cut with shape but not much style. A broad, lined forehead, large nose, mouth turning down naturally at the corners, and small chin. Behind her glasses her eyes were brown and looked small, probably the effect of the lenses. Wrinkles grew where wrinkles grow; and there was no glow to her skin. A face of character, but not sexually attractive, at least not to me.

'Why?' I said, which was a pretty stupid question.

She blushed a little deeper and shook her head.

'Look,' I said, 'it isn't as simple as that. I can't . . . I mean, one can't just sort of switch that sort of thing on and off, like a tap.'

We sat in awkward silence. She put down her glass, and said, 'I'm sorry. It was a ridiculous thing to say. Please try and forget it.'

'You said it because it was in your mind. So . . . well . . . you must have meant it.'

She half smiled, ruefully. 'It's been in my mind, now and again, for a long time. You will find it extraordinary, but I have never . . . so to speak, slept with a man.'

'In this permissive age?' I said.

'There you are, you see. You find it hard to believe. But I've never been pretty, even as a child. And also I've always been, well . . . able to do things. Learn. Teach. Organize. Administrate. All the unfeminine things. All my life people have relied on me, because I was capable. I've always had health and energy, and I've enjoyed getting on, being given senior posts, and five years ago, being offered a headship. In most ways my life has been absorbing and gratifyingly successful.'

'But?' I suggested.

She nodded. 'But. I was never interested in boys when I was in my teens, and then I thought them callow, and at university I worked all hours to get a First, and after that I've always taught in girls' schools because frankly it is usually a man who's given the headship in a mixed school, and I've never fancied the role of male-ego-massager in second place. Nothing I've ever been or done has been geared to romance.'

'So why *now*?'

'I hope you won't be angry, but it is mostly curiosity, and the pursuit of knowledge.'

I wasn't angry. Just astounded.

Her blush had subsided as fast as it had risen. She was back on surer ground.

'For some time I've thought I ought to have had the

experience. Of sexual intercourse, that is. It didn't come my way when I was young, but I didn't expect it, you see. I think now that I should have tried to find a man, but then, when I was at college, I was half scared of it, and I didn't have any great urge, and I was engrossed in my work. Afterwards for years it didn't bother me, until I was thirty or so, and of course by that time all the men one meets are married, and in any case, teaching among women, one rarely meets any men, except officials, and so on. I go to many official functions, of course, but people tend not to ask unmarried women to private social occasions.'

'What changed your mind?' I asked, fascinated.

'Oh, having to cope with highly-sexed young girls. The modern lot are so clued up. So brash and outspoken. I like them. But I have to arrange their sex-education lessons, and in my time I've even taught them, from text books. I feel it would be a great deal better if I knew . . . what the sex act felt like. I feel at a disadvantage with many of the older girls, particularly as this last term I had to advise a pregnant fourteen-year-old. Fourteen! She knows more than I do. How can I advise her?'

'Catholic priests don't have this problem,' I commented.

'Catholic priests may be respected for virginity, but school-mistresses are not.' She paused, hesitating, and went on. 'To be honest, I also find myself at a disadvantage with the married members of my staff. Some of them have a tendency to patronize me, even unconsciously. I don't like it. I would be able to cope with it perfectly, though, if I actually knew what they know.'

'Am I,' I said slowly, 'the first man you have asked?'

'Oh yes.' She smiled slightly and drank some wine. 'There are practically no men one *can* ask. Especially if one is a headmistress, and widely known. I certainly wouldn't jeopardize my job.'

'I can see that it would be difficult,' I said, thinking about it.

'So of course holidays are the only possibility,' she said. 'I've been on archaeological cruises to Greece, and all that sort of thing, and I've seen other couples join up, but it never happened to me. And then I've heard that some lonely women throw themselves at ski-instructors and waiters and men who perform for money, but somehow that isn't what I want. I mean, I don't want to despise myself. I want knowledge without guilt or shame.'

'The dream of Eden,' I said.

'What? Oh, yes.'

'What about your friend?' I said, pointing to the second bed.

She smiled twistedly. 'No friend, just an excuse for having come alone.'

'Friends being death to the pursuit of knowledge?'

'Exactly.'

We drank some more wine.

'I've been here since last Saturday,' she said. 'I always

take a complete break straight after the end of term, and then go back refreshed for the new work.'

'A perfect system,' I said absently. 'Why didn't you . . . er . . . throw me back, when the men in the dinghy came after me?'

'If you mean, did I immediately see you as a . . . *possible* . . . then no, of course not. I was fascinated, in a way. I'd never seen anyone in such terror before. I watched you from quite a long way out. Swimming, and looking back. It wasn't until you reached the concrete step, though, and I saw your face clearly, that I realized that you were being *hunted*. It would take a certain mentality to point the hounds at an exhausted quarry gone to ground, and I don't have it.'

'And thank God for that,' I said.

I stood up, and opened the glass door, and went out onto the balcony. The cool night was clear, with bright stars over the ageless Mediterranean. Waves rippled softly round the edges of the bay, and the gentle moonlight shone on the wide, empty expanse where the boat had been anchored.

It was the weirdest of debts. She had saved me from recapture. I certainly owed her my wholeness of mind, if not life itself. If the only payment she wanted was something I didn't much want to give, then that was simply too bad. One extreme favour, I thought sardonically, deserved another.

I went in, and sat down. Drank some wine with a dry mouth.

'We'll try, if you like,' I said.

She sat very still. I had a swift impression that now I'd agreed she was hastily retreating: that the half-fear of her student days was definitely still there.

'You don't have to,' she said.

'No. I want to.' Heaven forgive all liars.

She said, as if speaking to herself, and not to me: 'I'll never have another chance.'

The voice of longing teetering on the brink of the leap in the dark. Her strength of mind, I saw, would carry her through. I admired her. I determined to make Hilary Pinlock's leap something that at least she wouldn't regret: if I could.

'First of all,' I said, 'we'll switch off the lights and sit by the window for a while, and talk about it.'

We sat facing each other in dim reflected moonlight, and I asked her some fairly medical questions, to which she gave straightforward replies.

'What if you get pregnant?' I said.

'I'd solve that later.'

'You want to go ahead?'

She took a deep breath. 'If you do.'

If I *can*, I thought.

'Then I think the best thing to do first would be to get undressed,' I said. 'Do you have a nightdress? And could you lend me a dressing gown?'

I reflected, as I put on her blue candlewick in the privacy of the bathroom, that deep physical tiredness was a rotten basis for the matter in hand. I yawned. I wanted above all to go to sleep.

When I went out she was sitting by the window in a long cotton nightgown which had a frill round the neckline, but was not, of course, transparent.

'Come on,' I said. 'We'll sit on the bed.'

She stood up. The nightgown accentuated her height and thinness, and revealed long narrow feet. I pulled back the bed-clothes, sat on the white sheet, and held my hand out towards her. She came, gripped my hand, and sat beside me.

'Right,' I said. 'Now, if at any point you want to stop, you've only got to say so.'

She nodded.

'Lie down, then,' I said, 'and imagine you are twenty.'

'Why?'

'Because this is not a brain matter. It's about the stimulation of nerve endings. About feeling, not thinking. If you think all the time of who you are, you may find it inhibiting. Age doesn't exist in the dark. If you imagine you are twenty, you will be twenty, and you'll find it liberating.'

'You're a most unusual man.'

'Oh sure,' I said. 'And you're a most unusual woman. So lie down.'

She gave a small unexpected chuckle, and did as I said.

'Take off your glasses,' I said, and she put them without comment on the bedside table. In the dim light her eyes looked larger, as I'd guessed, and her big nose smaller, and her determined mouth softer. I leaned over and kissed her lips, and if it was basically a nephew-to-aunt gesture it brought a smile to her face and a grin to my own.

It was the strangest lovemaking, but it did work. I looked back afterwards to the moment when she first took pleasure in the sensation of my stroking her skin; the ripple of surprise when she felt with her hands the size of an erect man; the passion with which she finally responded; and the stunning release into gasping incredulity.

'Is that,' she said, out of breath, 'is that what every woman feels?'

I knew she had reached a most satisfactory climax. 'I guess so,' I said. 'On good days.'

'Oh my goodness,' she said in a sort of exultation. 'So now I *know*.'

CHAPTER SEVEN

Thursday morning I went back to the office and tried to take up my life where it had left off.

The same smell of typewriters, filing cabinets, reams of paper. Same bustle, adding machines, telephones. Same heaps of too much work. All familiar, all unreal.

Our two assistants, Debbie and Peter, had had a rough time, they said aggrievedly, trying to account to everyone for my unaccountable absence. They had reported my disappearance to the police, who had said I was over twenty-one and had the right to duck out if I wanted to, and that they would look for me only if I'd committed a crime, or was clearly a missing victim. They had thought I had merely gone off on a celebratory binge after winning the Gold Cup.

'We told them you wouldn't have gone away for so long,' Peter said. 'But they didn't show much interest.'

'We wanted them to get in touch with Mr King, through Interpol,' Debbie complained. 'And they laughed at the idea.'

'I expect they would,' I said. 'So Trevor is still on his holiday?'

'He's not due back until Monday,' Peter said, surprised that I should have forgotten something I knew so well.

'Oh yes . . .'

I spent the morning re-organizing the timetable and getting Peter to make new appointments to replace those I'd missed, and the afternoon discovering that as far as the police were concerned, my troubles were still of little interest. I was back home, wasn't I? Unharmed. Without having to pay a ransom? Was there any form of extortion? No. Was I starved? No. Beaten? No. Tied with ropes, straps, shackles? No. Was I sure it wasn't a practical joke? They would look into it, they said: but one of them remarked that *he* wouldn't mind a free fortnight's trip to the Mediterranean, and his colleague laughed. I gathered that if I seriously wanted to get to know, I would have to do the investigating myself.

I did want to know. Not knowing felt dangerously unsafe, like standing behind a bad-tempered horse. If I didn't know why I'd been taken the first time, how was I to stop it happening again?

Thursday evening I collected my Dolomite, which had been moved to the Cheltenham racecourse manager's front drive. ('Where on earth have you been? We traced that it was your car through the police.') Next I drove to the house of the racecourse valet to pick up my wallet and keys and racing saddle. ('Where on earth have you been? I gave the racecourse manager your car keys, I hope that's all right.') Then I drove back to my cottage (having spent the previous night in an airport hotel), and with faint-hearted caution let myself in.

No one was waiting there in the dark, with coshes or ether or one-way tickets to sail lockers. I switched on all the lights and poured myself a stiff Scotch and told myself to calm down and take a better grip.

I telephoned the trainer I regularly rode early morning exercise for ('Where on earth have you been?') and arranged to start again on Monday: and I rang a man who had asked me to ride in a hunter 'chase, to apologize for not turning up. I saw no reason not to answer the questions about where I'd been, so I told them all: abducted and taken on a boat to Minorca, and I didn't know why. I thought at least that someone might come up with a possible explanation, but everyone I told sounded as flummoxed as I felt.

There wasn't much food in the cottage, and the steak in the fridge had grown whiskers. I decided on spaghetti, with chopped up cheese melting on it, but before starting to cook I went upstairs to change new jacket for old sweater, and to make a detour to the bathroom.

I glanced casually out of the bathroom window and spent a frozen instant in pure panic.

There was a man in the garden, looking towards the downstairs rooms of the cottage. The light from the sitting-room window fell brightly on his face.

I hadn't consciously remembered him, but I knew him

at once, in one heart-stopping flash of the inner eye. He was the fake St John's Ambulance man from Cheltenham races.

Behind him, in the road, stood a car, with gleams of light edging its roof and windows. A second man was levering himself out of the passenger's seat, carrying what looked like a plastic bag containing cotton wool. A third figure, dimly seen, was heading through the garden to the back of the house.

They couldn't, I thought: surely they couldn't think they would trick me again. But with three of them, they hardly needed tricks.

The St John's man waved his arm to the man by the car, and pointed, and the two of them took up positions, one on each side of my front door, out of sight of anyone opening it from the inside. The St John's man stretched out an arm and rang my bell.

I unfroze.

Wonderful how terror sharpened the wits. There was only one place I could hide, and that was in my bedroom. The speed with which I'd gone over the side of the boat was nothing compared with my disappearance inside the cottage.

Downstairs in the sitting-room the huge old fireplace had at one side incorporated a bread oven, which the people living there before me had removed, constructing instead a head-high alcove with display shelves. Wanting a safe place in which to keep valuables, they had opened the upper part of the bread oven space into the bedroom above, where it formed a sort of box below the floor of the built-in wardrobe. Not having much in the way of valuables, I stored my two suitcases in there instead.

I opened the wardrobe door, and pulled up the hinged flap of flooring, and hauled out the cases.

The door bell rang again, insistently.

Lowering myself into the space took seconds, and I had the wardrobe door shut and the flap of floor almost in place when they burst in through the front door.

They rampaged through the place, opening and slamming doors, and shouting, and finally gathering all together downstairs.

'He must be bloody here.'

'Britten! Britten, come out, we know you're here.'

'The effing bastard's scarpered.'

I could hear every loud word through the chipboard partition between my hiding place and the sitting-room. I felt horribly vulnerable sitting there, level with the picture over the mantelshelf, practically in the room with them, hidden only by a thin piece of wall.

'He couldn't have seen us coming.'

'He never got out of the back, I'll tell you that for sure.'

'Then where the bleeding hell is he?'

'How about those suitcases of his upstairs?'

'No. He ain't in them. They're too small. And I looked.'

'He must be meaning to bleeding scarper.'

'Yeah.'

'Take another butcher's upstairs. He must be here somewhere.'

They searched the whole house again, crashing about with heavy boots.

One of them opened the wardrobe above me for the second time, and saw nothing but clothes, as before. I sat under their feet and sweated, and felt my pulse shoot up to the hundreds.

'Look under the bed,' he said.

'Can't. The bed's right on the floor.'

'How about the other bedroom, then?'

'I looked. He ain't there.'

'Well, bleeding well look again.'

The wardrobe door closed above me. I wiped the sweat out of my eyes and tried to ease my legs without scraping my shoes on the wall and making a noise. I was half sitting, half lying, in a recess about three feet long by two feet deep, and just wide enough for my shoulders. My knees were bent acutely, with my heels against the backs of my thighs. It was a bad position for every muscle I could think of.

Two of them came into the sitting-room, one after the other.

'What you got there? Here, let me see.'

'None of your bleeding business.'

'It's his wallet. You've got his wallet.'

'Yeah. Well, it was in his bedroom.'

'Well, bleeding well put it back.'

'Not likely, he's got thirty quid in it.'

'You'll effing well do as I say. You know the orders, same as I do. Don't steal nothink, don't break nothink. I told you.'

'You can have half, then.'

'Give it to me. I'll put it back. I don't trust you.' It was the St John's man talking, I thought.

'It's bloody stupid, not nicking what we can get.'

'You want the fuzz on our necks? They didn't bloody look for him last time, and they won't bloody look for him this time, either, but they will if they find his place has been turned over. Use your bloody loaf.'

'We ain't got him yet.'

'Matter of time. He's round here some place. Bound to be.'

'He won't come back if he sees us in here.'

'No, you got a point there. Tell you what, we'll turn the lights off and wait for him, and jump him, like.'

'He left all the lights on, himself. He won't come in if they're off.'

'Best if one of us waits in the kitchen, like, and the other two in the garden. Then when he gets here we can jump him from both sides, right, just as he's coming back through the door.'

'Yeah.'

Into these plans there suddenly came a fresh voice, female and enquiring.

'Mr Britten? Mr Britten, are you there?'

I heard her push the front door open and take the step into the sitting-room.

The voice of my next-door neighbour.

Yes, Mrs Morris, I'm here, I thought. And it would take more than me and a small plump senior citizen to fight off my unwanted guests.

'Who are you?' she said.

'Friends of his. Calling on him, like.'

'He's away,' she said sharply.

'No he's not. He's back. His car's round the side. And he's having a drink, see? Whisky.'

'Then where is he? Mr Britten?' she called.

'Ain't no use, lady. He's out. We're waiting for him, like.'

'I don't think you should be in here.' A brave lady, old Mrs Morris.

'We're friends of his, see.'

'You don't look like his friends,' she said.

'Know his friends, then, do yer?'

A certain nervousness crept into her voice, but the resolution was still there.

'I think you'd better wait outside.'

There was a pause, then the St John's man said, 'Where do you think he could be? We've searched all over for him.'

Let her not know about this hiding place, I prayed. Let her not think of it.

'He might've gone to the pub,' she said. 'Why don't you go down there? To the Fox.'

'Yeah, maybe.'

'Anyway, I think I'll just see you out.'

Intrepid little Mrs Morris. I heard them all go out, and shut the front door behind them. The lock clicked decisively. The cottage was suddenly still.

I lay quiet, listening for their car to start.

Nothing happened.

They were still there, I thought. Outside. Round my house. Waiting.

On the mantelshelf, the clock ticked.

I cautiously pushed up the flap over my head, and sat up, straightening knees, back and neck, with relief.

The light in my bedroom was still on, shining in a crack under the wardrobe door. I left the door shut. If they saw so much as a shadow move they would know for sure I was inside the house.

I reflected that I had had a good deal too much practice at passing uncertain hours in small dark places.

The lock clicked on my front door.

One gets to know the noises of one's own house so well that sight is unnecessary for interpretation. I heard the unmistakable sound of the hinges, and the gritty sound of a shoe on the bare flagstones of the entrance hall. Then there were quiet noises in the sitting-room itself, and low voices, and the squeak of the door to the kitchen. They had come back in a way that would not bring Mrs Morris.

I sat rigidly, wondering whether to slide down into the smaller space and risk them hearing my movements, or stay with head and shoulders above floor level and risk them searching my clothes cupboard yet again. If I coughed or sneezed, or as much as knocked the chipboard with my elbow as I slid down into the safer hiding place, they would hear me. I sat immobile, stretching my own ears and wondering despairingly how long they would stay.

Breathing evenly was difficult, controlling my heartbeat was impossible. Acute anxiety over a period of hours was highly shattering to the nerves.

From time to time I could hear them moving and murmuring, but could no longer distinctly hear their words. I supposed that they too were hiding, waiting out of sight for me to come home. It was almost funny when one thought of it: them hiding behind the furniture and me within the walls.

Unfunny if they found me. More like unfaceable.

I took a deep, shaky breath, one of many.

Someone began to come quietly upstairs. The familiar creaks of the old treads fizzed through my body like electric shocks. The risk of moving had to be taken. I tucked my elbows in and bent my knees, and eased myself back under the floor. The flap came down hard on my hair and I thought wildly that they must have heard it: but no one arrived with triumphant shouts, and the awful suspense just went on and on.

I got pains from being bent up, and I got cramps, but there was nothing I could do about that except surrender.

One of them spent a good time in my bedroom. I could hear his footfall through the floorboards, and the small thuds of drawers shutting. Guessed he was no longer looking for me, but at what I owned. It didn't make his nearness to me any safer.

The fear seemed endless; but everything ends. I heard them murmuring again in the sitting-room, and shutting the kitchen door. The man upstairs went down again. More murmurings: a chorus. Then silence for a while. Then a step or two in the hall, and the click of the front door closing.

I waited, thinking that only one of them had gone out.

Their car started. Shifted quietly into gear. Drove off.

I still lay without moving, not trusting that it was over, that it wasn't a trick: but the absolute quietness persisted, and in the end I pushed up the flap of the floor and levered myself with much wincing and pins and needles onto my bedroom carpet.

The lights were still on, but the black square of window was grey. The whole night had passed. It was dawn.

I threw a few things into one of the suitcases and left the cottage ten minutes later.

The Yale lock on the front door showed no signs of forcing, and I guessed they must have opened it with a credit card, as I myself had done once when I'd locked myself out. My car stood untouched where I'd left it, and even my half-drunk glass of Scotch was still on the sitting-room table.

Feeling distinctly unsettled I had a wash, shave and breakfast at the Chequers Hotel, and then went to the police.

'Back again?' they said.

They listened, made notes, asked questions.

'Do you know who they were?'

'No.'

'Any evidence of a forced entry?'

'No.'

'Anything stolen?'

'No.'

'Nothing we can do, sir.'

'Look,' I said, 'these people are trying to abduct me. They've succeeded once, and they're trying again. Can't you do a damn thing to help?'

They seemed fairly sympathetic, but the answer was no. They hadn't enough men or money to mount a round-the-clock guard on anyone for an indefinite period without a very good reason.

'Isn't the threat of abduction a very good reason?'

'No. If you believe the threat, you could hire yourself a private bodyguard.'

'Thanks very much,' I said. 'But if anyone reports me missing again, I won't have gone by choice, and you might do me a favour and start looking.'

'If they do, sir, we will.'

*

I went to the office and sat at my desk and watched my hands shake. Whatever I normally had in the way of mental and physical stamina was at a very low ebb.

Peter came in with a cable and his usual expression of not quite grasping the point, and handed me the bad news. CAR BROKEN DOWN RETURNING WEDNESDAY APOLOGIES TREVOR.

'You read this?' I asked Peter.

'Yes.'

'Well, you'd better fetch Mr King's list, for next week, and his appointment book.'

He went on the errand and I sat and looked blankly at the cable. Trevor had sent it from some town I'd never heard of in France, and had given no return address. He wouldn't be worried, wherever he was. He would be sure I could take his extra few days in my stride.

Peter came back with the list and I laced my fingers together to keep them still. What did people take for tranquillizers?

'Get me some coffee,' I said to Peter. His eyebrows rose. 'I know it's only a quarter past nine,' I said, 'but get me some coffee . . . please.'

When he brought the coffee I sent him to fetch Debbie, so that I could share between them the most urgent jobs. Neither of them had a good brain, but they were both persistent, meticulous plodders, invaluable qualities in accountants' assistants. In many offices the assistants were bright and actively studying to become accountants themselves, but Trevor for some reason seemed always to prefer working with the unambitious sort. Peter was twenty-two, Debbie twenty-four. Peter, I thought, was a latent homosexual who hadn't quite realized it. Debbie, mousy-haired, big-busted, and pious, had a boyfriend working in a hardware shop. Peter occasionally made jokes about screws, which shocked her.

They sat opposite my desk with notebooks poised, both of them looking at me with misgiving.

'You really look awfully ill,' Debbie said. 'Worse even than yesterday. Grey, sort of.' There seemed to be more ghoulish relish in her voice than concern.

'Yes, well, never mind that,' I said. 'I've looked at Mr King's list, and there are a few accounts that won't wait until he gets back.' There were two he should have seen to before he went, but no one was perfect. 'Certificate for the solicitors, Mr Crest, and Mr Grant. I'm afraid they are already overdue. Could you bring all the papers for those two in here, Debbie? Later, I mean. Not this instant. Then there are the two summonses to appear before the Commissioners next Thursday. I'll apply for postponements for those, but you'd better bring all the books in here, Debbie, anyway, and I'll try and make a start on them.'

'That's the Axwood stables, is it? And Millrace Stud?'

'Not the stud; that's the week after. Mr King can deal with that. The Axwood stables, yes, and those corn merchants, Coley Young.'

'The Coley Young books aren't here yet,' Peter said.

'Well, for crying out loud, didn't you do what I said two weeks ago, and tell them to send them?' I could hear the scratch in my voice and did my best to stop it. 'OK,' I said slowly. 'Did you ask them to send them?'

'Yes, I did.' Peter tended to look sulky. 'But they haven't come.'

'Ring them again, would you? And what about the Axwood stables?'

'You checked those yourself, if you remember.'

'Did I?' I looked back as if to a previous existence. The two summonses to appear before the Commissioners were not particularly serious. We seldom actually went. The summonses were issued when the Inland Revenue thought a particular set of accounts were long overdue: a sort of goad to action. It meant that Trevor or I asked for a postponement, did the accounts, and sent them in before the revised date. End of drama. The two summonses in question had arrived after Trevor had left for his holidays, which was why he hadn't dealt with them himself.

'You said the petty cash book hadn't arrived,' Peter said.

'Did I? Did you ask them to send it?'

'Yes, I did, but it hasn't come.'

I sighed. 'Ring them again.'

A great many clients saw no urgency at all in getting their accounts done, and requests from us for further information or relevant papers were apt to be ignored for weeks.

'Tell them both they really will have to go before the Commissioners if they don't send those books.'

'But they won't really, will they?' Peter said. Not the brightest of boys, I thought.

'I'll get adjournments anyway,' I said patiently, 'but Trevor will need those books to hand the second he gets back.'

Debbie said, 'Mr Wells rang three times yesterday afternoon.'

'Who is Mr Wells? Oh yes. Mr Wells.'

'He says one of his creditors is applying to have him made bankrupt and he wants to know what you're going to do about it.'

I'd forgotten all the details of Mr Wells' troubles. 'Where are his books?' I asked.

'In one of those boxes,' Debbie said, pointing. A three-high row of large cardboard boxes ran along the wall under the window. Each box had the name of the client on it, in large black letters, and each contained the cash books, invoices, receipts, ledgers, paying-in books, bank statements, petty cash records, stocktakings and general paraphernalia needed for the assessment of taxes. Each of the boxes represented a task I had yet to do.

It took me an average of two working days to draw up the annual accounts for each client. Some audits took longer. I had roughly two hundred clients. The thing was impossible.

Trevor had collared the bigger firms and liked to

spend nearly a week on each. He dealt with seven clients. No wonder Commissioners' summonses fell on us like snow.

Peter and Debbie did most of the routine work, checking bank statements against cheque numbers, and against invoices paid. Someone extra to share that work would only help Trevor and me to a certain extent. Taking a third, fully equal partner would certainly reduce the pressure, but it would also entail dividing the firm's profits into three instead of two, which would mean a noticeable drop in income. Trevor was totally opposed. Amalgamation with the London firm meant Trevor not being boss and me not going racing . . . a fair sized impasse, all in all.

'Debbie and I didn't get our pay cheques last week,' Peter said. 'Nor did Bess.' Bess was the typist.

'And the water heater in the washroom is running cold,' Debbie added. 'And you did say I could go to the dentist this afternoon at three-thirty.'

'Sorry about all the extra work,' Peter said, not sounding it, 'but I'm afraid it's my Friday for the Institute of Accounting Staff class.'

'Mm,' I said. 'Peter, telephone to Leyhill Prison and ask if Connaught Powys is still there.'

'What?'

'Leyhill Prison. Somewhere in Gloucestershire. Get the number from directory enquiries.'

'But . . .'

'Just go and do it,' I said. 'Connaught Powys. Is he still there.'

He went out looking mystified, but then he, like Debbie, dated from after the searchingly difficult court case. Debbie went to fetch the first batch of the papers I needed, and I began on the solicitors' certificates.

Since embezzlement of clients' trust monies had become a flourishing industry, laws had been passed to ensure that auditors checked every six months to see that the cash and securities which were supposed to be in a solicitor's care actually were there. If they weren't, Nemesis swiftly struck the solicitor off the Roll. If they were, the auditor signed the certificate and pocketed his fee.

Peter returned as if he'd come from a dangerous mission, looking noble.

'The prison said he was released six weeks ago, on February 16th.'

'Thanks.'

'I had a good deal of trouble in getting through.'

'Er . . . well done,' I said. He still looked as if he thought more praise was due, but he didn't get it.

If Connaught Powys had been out for six weeks, he would have had a whole month to fix me up with a voyage. I tried hard to concentrate on the checking for the certificates but the sail locker kept getting in the way.

Solicitor Grant's affair tallied at about the third shot, but I kept making errors with Denby Crest's. I realized I'd always taken clarity of mind for granted, like walking:

one of those things you don't consciously value until you've lost it. Numbers, from my infancy, had been like a second language, understood without effort. I checked Denby Crest's figures five times and kept getting a fifty thousand pounds' discrepancy, and knowing him, as he occasionally did work for us, it was ridiculous. Denby Crest was no crook, I thought in exasperation. It's my useless muddle-headed thought processes. Somewhere I was transposing a decimal point, making a mountain out of a molehill discrepancy of probably five pounds or fifty pence.

In the end I telephoned his office and asked to speak to him.

'Look, Denby,' I said, 'I'm most awfully sorry, but are you sure we've got all the relevant papers?'

'I expect so,' he said, sounding impatient. 'Why don't you leave it for Trevor? He gets back to England tomorrow, doesn't he?'

I explained about the broken-down car. 'He won't be back in the office until Wednesday or Thursday.'

'Oh.' He sounded disconcerted and there was a perceptible pause. 'All the same,' he said, 'Trevor is used to our ways. Please leave our certificate until he gets back.'

'But it's overdue,' I said.

'Tell Trevor to call me,' he said. 'And now, I'm sorry, but I have a client with me. So if you'll excuse me . . .'

He disconnected. I shuffled his papers together thankfully and thought that if he wanted to risk waiting for Trevor it was certainly all right by me.

At twelve-thirty Peter and Debbie went out to lunch, but I didn't feel hungry. I sat in shirtsleeves before the newly tackled sea of Mr Wells' depressing papers: put my elbows on the desk, and propped my forehead on the knuckles of my right hand, and shut my eyes. Thought a lot of rotten thoughts and wondered about buying myself a one-way ticket to Antarctica.

A voice said, 'Are you ill, asleep or posing for Rodin?'

I looked up, startled.

She was standing in the doorway. Young, fair, slender pretty.

'I'm looking for Trevor,' she said.

One couldn't have everything, I supposed.

CHAPTER EIGHT

'Don't I know you?' I said, puzzled, standing up.

'Sure.' She looked resigned, as if this sort of thing happened often. 'Cast your mind back to long hair, no lipstick, dirty jeans and ponies.'

I looked at the short bouncy bob, the fashionable make-up, the swirling brown skirt topped by a neat waist-length fur-fabric jacket. Someone's daughter, I thought; recently and satisfactorily grown up.

'Whose daughter?' I said.

'My own woman.'

'Reasonable.'

She was enjoying herself, pleased with her impact on men.

'Jossie Finch, actually.'

'Wow,' I said.

'Every grub spreads its wings.'

'To where will you fly?'

'Yes,' she said, 'I've heard you were smooth.'

'Trevor isn't here, I'm afraid.'

'Mm. Still on his hols?'

I nodded.

'Then I was to deliver the same message to you, if you were here instead.'

'Sit down?' I suggested, gesturing to a chair.

'Can't stop. Sorry. Message from Dad. What are you doing about the Commissioners? He said he was absolutely not going before any so-and-so Commissioners next Thursday, or lurid words to that effect.'

'No, he won't have to.'

'He also says he would have sent the petty cash book, or whatever, in with me this morning, but his secretary is sick, and if you ask me she's the sickest thing that ever broke fingernails on a typewriter, and she has not done something or other with petty cash receipts or vouchers, or whatever it is you need. However . . .' she paused, drawing an exaggerated breath. 'Dad says, if you would like to drop in this evening you could go round the yard with him at evening stables, and have a noggin afterwards, and he will personally press into your hot little palms the book your assistant has been driving him mad about.'

'I'd like that,' I said.

'Good. I'll tell him.'

'And will you be there?'

'Ah,' she said, her eyes laughing, 'a little uncertainty is the HP sauce on the chips.'

'And the spice of life to you, too.'

She gave me an excellent smile, spun on her heel so

that the skirt swirled and the hair bounced, and walked out of the office.

Jossie Finch, daughter of William Finch, master of Axwood Stables. I knew her father in the way all long-time amateur riders knew all top trainers; enough to greet and chat to at the races. Since his was one of the racing accounts which pre-dated my arrival in the firm, and which Trevor liked to do himself, I had never before actually visited his yard.

I was interested enough to want to go, in spite of all my troubles. He had approximately ninety horses in his care, both jumpers and flat racers, and winners were taken for granted. Apart from Tapestry, most of the horses I usually rode were of moderate class, owned with more hope than expectation. To see a big stableful of top performers was always a feast. I would be safe from abduction there. And Jossie looked a cherry on the top.

When Peter and Debbie came back I laid into them for going out and leaving the outer door unlocked, and they adopted put-upon expressions and said they thought it was all right, as I was there, which would stop people sneaking in to steal things.

My fault, I thought more reasonably. I should have locked it after them myself. I would have to reshape a lot of habits. It could easily have been the enemy who walked in, not Jossie Finch.

I spent part of the afternoon on Mr Wells, but more of it trying to trace Connaught Powys.

We had his original address on file, left over from the

days when he had rigged the computer and milked his firm of a quarter of a million pounds in five years. The firm's audit was normally Trevor's affair, but one year, when Trevor was away a great deal with an ulcer, I had done it instead, and by some fluke had discovered the fraud. It had been one of those things you don't believe even when it is in front of your eyes. Connaught Powys had been an active director, and had paid his taxes on a comfortable income. The solid, untaxed lolly had disappeared without trace, but Connaught himself hadn't been quick enough.

I tried his old address. A sharp voice on the telephone told me the new occupants knew nothing of the Powys' whereabouts, and wished people would stop bothering them, and regretted the day they'd ever moved into a crook's house.

I tried his solicitors, who froze when they heard who was trying to find him. They could not, they said, divulge his present address without his express permission: which, their tone added, he was as likely to give as Shylock to a church bazaar.

I tried Leyhill Prison. No good.

I tried finally a racing acquaintance called Vivian Iverson who ran a gambling club in London and always seemed to know of corruption scandals before the stories publicly broke.

'My dear Ro,' he said, 'you're fairly non gratis in that quarter, don't you know.'

'I could guess.'

'You put the shivers up embezzlers, my friend. They're leaving the Newbury area in droves.'

'Oh sure. And I pick the Derby winner every year.'

'You may well jest, my dear chap, but the whisper has gone round.' He hesitated. 'Those two little dazzlers, Glitberg and Ownslow, have been seen talking to Powys, who has got rid of his indoor pallor under a sun lamp. The gist, so I'm fairly reliably told, was a hate-Britten chorus.'

'With vengeance intended?'

'No information, my dear chap.'

'Could you find out?'

'I only *listen*, my dear Ro,' he said. 'If I hear the knives are out, I'll tell you.'

'You're a pet,' I said dryly.

He laughed. 'Connaught Powys comes here to play, most Fridays.'

'What time?'

'You do ask a lot, my dear chap. After dinner to dawn.'

'How about making me an instant member?'

He sighed heavily. 'If you are bent on suicide, I'll tell the desk to let you in.'

'See you,' I said. 'And thanks.'

I put down the receiver and stared gloomily into space. Glitberg and Ownslow. Six years apiece, reduced for good behaviour . . . They could have met Connaught Powys in Leyhill, and it would have been no joy to any of them that I had put them all there.

Glitberg and Ownslow had served on a local council and robbed the ratepayers blind, and I'd turned them up through some dealings they'd done with one of my clients. My client had escaped with a fine, and had removed his custom from me with violent curses.

I wondered how much time all the embezzlers and bent solicitors and corrupted politicians in Leyhill Prison spent in thinking up new schemes for when they got out. Glitberg and Ownslow must already have been out for about six months.

Debbie had gone to the dentist and Peter to his Institute of Accounting Staff class, and this time I did lock the door behind them.

I felt too wretchedly tired to bother any further with Mr Wells. The shakes of the morning had gone, but even the swift tonic of Jossie Finch couldn't lift the persistent feeling of threat. I spent an hour dozing in the armchair we kept for favoured clients and when it was time, locked the filing cabinets and my desk and every door in the office, and went down to my car.

There was no one hiding behind the front seats. No one lurking round the edges of the car park. Nothing in the boot except the suitcase I'd stowed there that morning. I started up and drove out into the road, assaulted by nothing but my own nerves.

William Finch's yard lay south-west of Newbury: a huge spread of buildings sheltering in a hollow, with a creeper-covered Victorian mansion rising on the hillside above. I arrived at the house just as Finch was coming out of it, and we walked down together to the first cluster of boxes.

'Glad you could come,' he said.

'It's a treat.'

He smiled with easy charm. A tall man, going grey at about fifty, very much in command of himself and everything else. He had a broad face, fine well-shaped mouth, and the eyes of experience. Horses and owners thrived in his care, and years of success had given him a stature he plainly enjoyed.

We went from box to box, spending a couple of minutes in each. Finch told me which horse we were looking at, with some of its breeding and form. He held brief reassurance conversations in each case with the lad holding the horse's head, and with his head lad, who walked round with us. If all was well, he patted the horse's neck and fed him a carrot from a bag which his head lad carried. A practised important routine evening inspection, as carried out by every trainer in the country.

We came to an empty box in a full row. Finch gestured to it with a smile.

'Ivansky. My National runner. He's gone up to Liverpool.'

I almost gaped like an idiot. I'd been out of touch with the normal world so much that I had completely forgotten that the Grand National was due that Saturday.

I cleared my throat. 'He should . . . er . . . have a fair chance at the weights.' It seemed a fairly safe comment, but he disagreed.

'Ten twelve is far too much on his Haydock form. He's badly in with Wasserman, don't you think?'

I raked back for all the opinions I'd held in the safe and distant life of three weeks ago. Nothing much surfaced.

'I'm sure he'll do well,' I said.

He nodded as if he hadn't noticed the feebleness of the remark, and we went on. The horses were truly an impressive bunch, glowing with good feeding, thorough grooming and well-judged exercise. I ran out of compliments long before he ran out of horses.

'Drink?' he said, as the head lad shut the last door.

'Great.'

We walked up to the house, and he led the way into a sitting-room-cum-office. Chintz-covered sofa and chairs, big desk, table with drinks and glasses, walls covered with framed racing photographs. Normal affluent trainer ambience.

'Gin?' he said.

'Scotch, if you have it.'

He gave me a stiff one and poured gin like water for himself.

'Your health,' he said.

'And yours.'

We drank the ritual first sip, and he gestured to me to sit down.

'I've found that damned cash book for you,' he said, opening a drawer in the desk. 'There you are. Book, and file of petty cash receipts.'

'That's fine.'

'And what about these Commissioners?'

'Don't worry, I've applied for a postponement.'

'But will they grant it?'

'Never refused us yet,' I said. 'They'll set a new date about a month ahead, and we'll do your accounts and audit before then.'

He relaxed contentedly over his draught of gin. 'We can expect Trevor here next week, then? Counting hay bales and saddles?' There was humour in his voice at the thoroughness ahead.

'Well,' I said, 'maybe at the end of the week, or the one after. He won't be back until Wednesday or Thursday.' Did 'Returning Wednesday', I wondered, mean *travelling* Wednesday, or turning up for work? 'I'll do a lot of the preliminary paperwork for him, to save time.'

Finch turned to the drinks table and unscrewed the gin. 'I thought he was due back on Monday.'

'His car's broken down somewhere in France.'

'That'll please him.' He drank deeply. 'Still, if you make a start on things, the audit should get done in time.'

'Don't worry about the Commissioners,' I said; but everyone did worry when the peremptory summons dropped through their door. If one neither asked for a postponement nor attended at the due hour, the Commissioners would fix one's year's tax at whatever figure they cared to, and to that assessment there was no appeal. As such assessments were customarily far higher than the amount of tax actually due, one avoided them like black ice.

To my pleasure, the swirly brown skirt and bouncy fair hair made a swooping entrance. She was holding a marmalade cat which was trying to jump out of her arms.

'Damn thing,' she said, 'why won't he be *stroked*.'

'It's a mouser,' said her father, unemotionally.

'You'd think it would be glad of a cuddle.'

The cat freed itself and bolted. Jossie shrugged. 'Hello,' she said to me. 'So you got here.'

'Mm.'

'Well,' she said to her father, 'what did he say?'

'Eh? Oh . . . I haven't asked him yet.'

She gave him a fond exasperated smile and said to me, 'He wants to ask you to ride a horse for him.'

Finch shook his head at her, and I said, 'When?'

'Tomorrow,' Jossie said. 'At Towcester.'

'Er,' I said, 'I'm not really ultra fit.'

'Nonsense. You won the Gold Cup a fortnight ago. You must be.'

'Josephine,' her father said. 'Clam up.' He turned to me. 'I'm flying up to Liverpool in the morning, but I have this horse in at Towcester, and to be blunt he's still entered there only because someone forgot to scratch him by the eleven o'clock deadline this morning . . .'

'The chronically sick secretary,' muttered Jossie.

'So we've either got to run him after all or pay a fine, and I was toying with the idea of sending him up there, if I could get a suitable jockey.'

'Most of them having gone to the National,' Jossie added.

'Which horse?' I said.

'Notebook. Novice hurdler. Four-year-old chestnut gelding, in the top yard.'

'The one with the flaxen mane and tail?'

'That's right. He's run a couple of times so far. Shows promise, but still green.'

'Last of twenty-six at Newbury,' Jossie said cheerfully. 'It won't matter a curse if you're not fit.' She paused. 'I've been delegated to saddle it up, so you might do us a favour and come and ride it.'

'Up to you,' Finch said.

The delegated saddler was a powerful attraction, even if Notebook himself was nothing much.

'Yes,' I said weakly. 'OK.'

'Good.' Jossie gave me a flashing smile. 'I'll drive you up there, if you like.'

'I would like,' I said regretfully, 'but I'll be in London tonight. I'll go straight to Towcester from there.'

'I'll meet you outside the weighing room, then. He's in the last race, by the way. He would be.'

Novice hurdles were customarily first or last (or both), on a day's programme: the races a lot of racegoers chose to miss through lunch or leaving early to avoid the crush. The poor-relation races for the mediocre majority, where every so often a new blazing star scorched out of the ruck on its way to fame.

Running horses in novice hurdles meant starting from

home early or getting back late; but there were far more runners in novice hurdles than in any other type of race.

When I left it was Jossie who came back with me through the entrance hall to see me off. As we crossed a vast decrepit Persian rug I glanced at the large dark portraits occupying acres of wall space.

'Those are Nantuckets, of course,' she said, following my gaze. 'They came with the house.'

'Po-faced lot,' I said.

'You did know that Dad doesn't actually own all this?'

'Yes, I actually did know.' I smiled to myself, but she saw it.

She said defensively, 'All right, but you'd be surprised how many people make up to me, thinking that they'll marry the trainer's daughter and step into all this when he retires.'

'So you like to establish the ground rules first?'

'OK, greyhound-brain, I'd forgotten you'd know from Trevor.'

I knew in general that Axwood Stables Ltd belonged to an American family, the Nantuckets, who rarely took much personal interest in the place except as a business asset. It had been bought and brought to greatness in the fifties by a rumbustious tycoon thrown up atypically from prudent banking stock. Old Naylor Nantucket had brought his energies and enterprise to England, had fallen in love with English racing, had built a splendid modern stable yard and filled it with splendid horses. He had engaged the young William Finch to train them for him, and the middle-aged William Finch was still doing it for his heirs, except that nowadays nine tenths of the horses belonged to other owners, and the young Nantuckets, faintly ashamed of Uncle Naylor, never crossed the Atlantic to see their own horses perform.

'Doesn't your father ever get tired of training for absent owners?' I said.

'No. They don't argue. They don't ring him up in the middle of the night. And when they lose, they don't complain. He says training would be a lot easier if *all* owners lived in New York.'

She stood on the doorstep to wave me goodbye, assured and half-mocking, a girl with bright brown eyes, graceful neck, and neat nose and mouth in between.

I booked into the Gloucester Hotel, where I'd never stayed before, and ate a leisurely and much needed dinner in a nearby restaurant. I shouldn't have accepted the ride on Notebook, I thought ruefully; I'd hardly enough strength to cut up a steak.

A strong feeling of walking blindfold towards a precipice dragged at my feet all the way to Vivian Iverson's gambling club. I didn't know which way the precipice lay: ahead, behind, or all round. I only suspected that it was still there, and if I did nothing about finding it, I could walk straight over.

The Vivat Club proved as suave and well-manicured as its owner, and was a matter of interconnecting small rooms, not open expanses like casinos. There were no croupiers in eye-shades with bright dramatic spotlights over the tables, and no ladies tinkling with diamonds in half shadow. There were however two or three discreet chandeliers, a good deal of cigar smoke, and a sort of reverent hush.

Vivian, good as his word, had left a note for me to be let in, and as an extra, treated as a guest. I walked slowly from room to room, balloon glass of brandy in hand, looking for his elegant shape, and not finding it.

There were a good many businessmen in lounge suits earnestly playing chemin-de-fer, and women among them with eyes that flicked concentratedly from side to side with every delivered card. I'd never had an urge towards betting for hours on the turn of a card, but everyone to his own poison.

'Ro, my dear fellow,' Vivian said behind me. 'Come to play?'

'On an accountant's earnings?' I said, turning to him and smiling. 'What are the stakes?'

'Whatever you can afford to lose, my dear fellow.'

'Life, liberty, and a ticket to the Cup Final.'

His eyes didn't smile as thoroughly as his mouth. 'Some people lose honour, fortunes, reputation, and their heads.'

'Does it disturb you?' I asked.

He made a small waving gesture towards the chemin-de-fer. 'I provide a pastime to cater for an impulse. Like bingo.'

He put his hand on my shoulder as if we were long-lost friends and steered me towards a further room. There were heavy gold links in his cuffs, and a silk cord edging to his blue velvet jacket. Dark glossy hair on a well-shaped head, flat stomach, faint smell of fresh talc. About thirty-five, and shrewdly succeeding where others had fallen to bailiffs.

There was a green baize raised-edge gaming table in the further room, but no one was playing cards.

Behind the table, in the club's ubiquitous wooden-armed, studded-leather armchairs, sat three men.

They were all large, smoothly dressed, and unfriendly. I knew them, from way back.

Connaught Powys. Glitberg. Ownslow.

'We hear you're looking for us,' Connaught Powys said.

CHAPTER NINE

I stood still. Vivian closed the door behind me and sat in another armchair on the edge of my left-hand vision. He crossed one leg elegantly over the other and eased the cloth over the knee with a languid hand.

Ownslow watched with disfavour.

'Piss off,' he said.

Vivian's answer was an extra-sophisticated drawl. 'My dear fellow, I may have set him up, but you've no licence to knock him down.'

There were several other empty chairs, pulled back haphazardly from the centre table. I sat unhurriedly in one of them and did my best with Vivian's leg-crossing ritual, hoping that casualness would reduce the atmosphere from bash-up to boardroom. Ownslow's malevolent stare hardly persuaded me that I'd succeeded.

Ownslow and Glitberg had run a flourishing construction racket for years, robbing the ratepayers of literally millions. Like all huge frauds, theirs had been done on paper, with Glitberg in the council's Planning Office, and

Ownslow in the Works and Maintenance. They had simply invented a large number of buildings: offices, flats and housing estates. The whole council having approved the buildings in principle, Glitberg, in his official capacity, advertised for tenders from developers. The lowest good-looking tender often came from a firm called National Construction (Wessex) Ltd and the council confidently entrusted the building to them.

National Construction (Wessex) Ltd did not exist except as expensively produced lettterheads. The sanctioned buildings were never built. Huge sums of money were authorized and paid to National Construction (Wessex) Ltd, and regular reports of the buildings' progress came back as Glitberg, from Planning, made regular inspections. After the point when the buildings were passed as ready for occupation the Maintenance department took over. Ownslow's men maintained bona-fide buildings, and Ownslow also requisitioned huge sums for the maintenance of the well-documented imaginary lot.

All the paperwork had been punctiliously, even brilliantly, completed. There were full records of rents received from the imaginary buildings, and rates paid by the imaginary tenants; but as all councils took it for granted that council buildings had to be heavily subsidized, the permanent gap between revenue and expenditure was accepted as normal.

Like many big frauds it had been uncovered by accident, and the accident had been my digging a little too deeply into the affairs of one of the smaller operators sharing in the crumbs of the greater rip-off.

The council, when I'd informed them, had refused to believe me. Not, that was, until they toured their area in detail, and found weedy grass where they had paid for, among other things, six storeys of flats for low-income families, a cul-de-sac of maisonettes for single pensioners, and two roadfuls of semi-detached bungalows for the retired and handicapped.

Blind-eye money had obviously been passed to various council members, but bribery in cash was hard to prove. The council had been publicly embarrassed and had not forgiven me. Glitberg and Ownslow, who had seen that the caper could not continue for ever, had been already preparing a quiet departure when the police descended on them in force on a Sunday afternoon. They had not exactly forgiven me either.

In line with all their other attention to detail, neither of them had made the mistake of living above his legal income. The huge sums they had creamed off had been withdrawn from the National Construction (Wessex) Ltd bank account over the years as a stream of cheques and cash which had aroused no suspicion at the bank, and had then apparently vanished into thin air. Of the million-plus which they had each stolen, not a pound had been recovered.

'Whatever you want from us,' Glitberg said, 'you're not going to get.'

'You're a danger to us,' Connaught Powys said.

'And like a wasp, you'll get swatted,' said Ownslow.

I looked at their faces. All three showed the pudgy roundness of self-indulgence, and all three had the sharp, wary eyes of guilt. Separately, Connaught Powys, with his sun-lamp tan and smoothly brushed hair, looked a high-up City gent. Heavy of body, in navy blue pin-stripes. Pale grey silk tie. Overall air of power and opulence, and not a whisper of cell-fug and slopping-out in the mornings.

Ownslow in jail was an easier picture. Fairish hair straggled to his collar from a fringe round a bald dome. Thick neck, bull shoulders, hands like baseball gloves. A hard, tough man whose accent came from worlds away from Connaught Powys.

Glitberg, in glasses, had short bushy grey hair and a fanned-out spread of white side-whiskers, which made him look like a species of ape. If Connaught Powys was power, and Ownslow was muscle, Glitberg was venom.

'Have you already tried?' I said.

'Tried what?' Ownslow said.

'Swatting.'

They stared, all three of them, without expression, at some point in the air between myself and Vivian.

'Someone has,' I said.

Connaught Powys smiled very slightly. 'Whatever we have done, or intend to do, about you,' he said, 'we are not going to be so insane as to admit it in front of a witness.'

'You'll be looking over your shoulder for the rest of your life,' Glitberg said, with satisfaction.

'Don't go near building sites on a dark night,' Ownslow said. 'There's a bit of advice, free, gratis and for nothing.'

'How about a sailing boat on a dark night?' I said. 'An ocean-going sailing boat.'

I wished at once that I hadn't said it. The unfriendliness on all three faces hardened to menace, and the whole room became very still.

Into the silence came Vivian's voice, relaxed and drawling. 'Ro . . . time you and I had a drink together, don't you think?'

He unfolded himself from his chair, and I, feeling fairly weak at the knees, stood up from mine.

Connaught Powys, Glitberg, and Ownslow delivered a collective look of such hatred that even Vivian began to look nervous. His hand fumbled with the door knob, and as he left the room, behind me, he almost tripped over his own feet.

'Whew,' he said in my ear. 'You do play with big rough boys, my dear fellow.' He steered me this time into a luxurious little office; three armchairs, all safely unoccupied. He waved me to one of them and poured brandy into two balloons.

'It's not what they say,' he said, 'as how they say it.'

'And what they don't say.'

He looked at me speculatively over his glass.

'Did you get what you wanted? I mean, was it worth your while, running under their guns?'

I smiled twistedly. 'I think I got an answer.'

'Well then.'

'Yes. But it was to a question I didn't ask.'

'I don't follow you.'

'I'm afraid,' I said slowly, 'that I've made everything a great deal worse.'

I slept soundly at the Gloucester, but more from exhaustion than an easy mind.

From the racing page of the newspaper delivered under my door in the morning I saw that my name was down in the list of runners as the rider of Notebook in the last race at Towcester. I sucked my teeth. I hadn't thought of asking William Finch not to include me in his list for the press, and now the whole world would learn where I would be that afternoon at four-thirty. If, that was, they bothered to turn to an insignificant race at a minor meeting on Grand National day.

'You'll be looking over your shoulder for the rest of your life,' Glitberg had said.

I didn't intend to. Life would be impossible if I feared for demons in every shadow. I wouldn't climb trustingly into any ambulances at Towcester, but I would go and ride there. There was an awfully thin line, it seemed to me, between cowardice and caution.

Jossie, waiting outside the weighing room, sent the heeby-jeebies flying.

'Hello,' she said. 'Notebook is here, looking his usual noble self and about to turn in his standard useless performance.'

'Charming.'

'The trainer's orders to the jockey,' she said, 'are succinct. Stay on, and stay out of trouble. He doesn't want you getting hurt.'

'Nor do I,' I said with feeling.

'He doesn't want anything to spoil the day if Ivansky wins the National.'

'Ah,' I said. 'Does he think he will?'

'He flew off in the air-taxi this morning in the usual agonized euphoria,' she said, with affection. 'Hope zigzagging from conviction to doubt.'

Finch had sent two horses to Towcester, the second of them, Stoolery, being the real reason for Jossie's journey. I helped her saddle it for the two mile handicap 'chase, and cheered with her on the stands when it won. The Grand National itself was transmitted on television all over the racecourse straight afterwards, so that Jossie was already consoled when Ivansky finished fifth.

'Oh well.' She shrugged. 'That's that. Dad will feel flat, the owners will feel flat, the lads will get gloomily drunk, and then they'll all start talking about next year.'

We strolled along without much purpose and arrived at the door to the bar.

'Like a drink?' I asked.

'Might pass the time.'

The bar was crowded with people dissecting the National result, and the elbowing customers jockeying for service were four deep.

'Don't let's bother,' Jossie said.

I agreed. We turned to leave, and a thin hand stretched out from the tight pressed ranks and gripped my wrist hard.

'What do you want?' a voice shouted over the din. 'I've just got served. What do you want? Quick!'

The hand, I saw, belonged to Moira Longerman, and beyond her, scowling as usual, stood Binny Tomkins.

'Jossie?' I said.

'Fruit juice. Grapefruit if poss.'

'Two grapefruit juice,' I said.

The hand let go and disappeared, shortly to reappear with a glass in it. I took it, and also the next issue, and finally Moira Longerman herself, followed by Binny, fought her way out of the throng, holding two glasses high to avoid having the expensive thimblefuls knocked flying.

'How super!' she said. 'I saw you in the distance just now. I've been trying to telephone you for weeks and now I hear some extraordinary story about you being kidnapped.'

I introduced Jossie who was looking disbelievingly at what Moira had said.

'Kidnapped?' Her eyebrows rose comically. 'You?'

'You may well laugh,' I said ruefully.

Moira handed a glass to Binny, who nodded a scant thanks. Graceless man, I thought. Extraordinary to leave any woman to fight her way to get him a drink, let alone the owner of the most important horse in his yard. She was paying, of course.

'My *dear*,' Moira Longerman said to Jossie. 'Right after Ro won the Gold Cup on my darling Tapestry, someone kidnapped him from the racecourse. Isn't that right?' She beamed quizzically up at my face, her blue eyes alight with friendly interest.

'Sure is,' I agreed.

Binny scowled some more.

'How's the horse?' I said.

Binny gave me a hard stare and didn't answer, but Moira Longerman was overflowing with news and enthusiasm.

'I do so want you to ride Tapestry in all his races from now on, Ro, so I hope you will. He's ready for Ascot next Wednesday, Binny says, and I've been trying and trying to get hold of you to see if you'll ride him.'

Binny said sourly, 'I've already engaged another jockey.'

'Then disengage him, Binny dear.' Underneath the friendly birdlike brightness there was the same touch of steel which had got me the Gold Cup ride in the first place. Moira might be half Binny's physical weight but she had twice the mental muscle.

'It might be better to let this other chap ride . . .' I began.

'No, no,' she interrupted. 'It's you I want, Ro. I won't have anyone else. I told Binny that, quite definitely, the very moment after you'd won the Cup. Now you're back and safe again it will either be you on my horse or I won't run him.' She glanced defiantly at Binny, impishly at Jossie, and with a determined nod of her blonde curly head, expectantly turned to me. 'Well? What do you say?'

'Er,' I said, which was hardly helpful.

'Oh go on,' Jossie said. 'You'll have to.'

Binny's scowl switched targets. Jossie caught the full blast and showed no discomfiture at all.

'He did win the Gold Cup,' she said. 'You can't say he isn't capable.'

'He does say that, my dear,' beamed Moira Longerman happily. 'Isn't it odd?'

Binny muttered something blackly of which the only audible word was 'amateurs'.

'I think that what Binny really means,' said Moira sweetly and distinctly. 'is that Ro, like most amateurs, always tries very hard to win, and won't listen to propositions to the contrary.'

Binny's face turned a dark red. Jossie practically giggled. Moira looked at me with limpid blue eyes as if not quite aware of what she'd said, and I chewed around helplessly for a sensible answer.

'Like most *jockeys*,' I said finally.

'You're so nice, Ro,' she said. 'You think everyone's honest.'

I tended, like most accountants, to think exactly the opposite, but as it happened I had never much wondered about Binny. To train a horse like Tapestry should have been enough, without trying to rig his results.

Binny himself had decided to misunderstand what Moira had said, and was pretending that he hadn't seen the chasm that was opening at his feet. Moira gave him a mischievous glance and allowed him no illusions about her power to push him in.

'Binny dear,' she said, 'I'll never desert the man who trained a Gold Cup winner for me. Not as long as he keeps turning out my horses beautifully fit, and I choose who rides them.'

Jossie cleared her throat in the following silence and said encouragingly to Binny, 'I expect you had a good bet in the Gold Cup? My father always puts a bit on in the Cup and the National. Too awful if you win, and you haven't. Makes you look such an ass, he says.'

If she had tried to rub salt into his raw wounds, it appeared she couldn't have done a better job. Moira Longerman gave a delighted laugh.

'You naughty girl,' she said, patting Jossie's arm. 'Poor Binny had so little faith, you see, that not only did he not back Tapestry to win, but I've heard he unfortunately laid it to lose. Such a pity. Poor Binny, winning the Gold Cup and ending up out of pocket.'

Binny looked so appalled that I gathered the extent of her information was a nasty shock to him.

'Never mind,' Moira said kindly. 'What's past is past.

And if Ro rides Tapestry next Wednesday, all will be well.'

Binny looked as if everything would be very far from well. I wondered idly if he could possibly have already arranged that Tapestry should lose on Wednesday. On his first outing after a Gold Cup win, any horse would start at short odds. Many a bookmaker would be grateful to know for certain that he wouldn't have to pay out. Binny could already have sold that welcome information, thinking that I wasn't around to upset things. Binny was having a thoroughly bad time.

I reflected that I simply couldn't afford to take Wednesday off. The mountains of undone work made me feel faintly sick.

'Ro?' Moira said persuasively.

'Yes,' I said. 'Nothing I'd like better in the world.'

'Oh goody!' Her eyes sparkled with pleasure. 'I'll see you at Ascot, then. Binny will ring you, of course, if there's a change of plan.'

Binny scowled.

'Tell me all,' Jossie demanded as we walked across to the trainers' stand to watch the next race. 'All this drama about you being kidnapped.'

I told her briefly, without much detail.

'Do you mean they just popped you on a boat and sailed off with you to the Med?'

'That's right.'

'What a lark.'

'It was inconvenient,' I said mildly.

'I'll bet.' She paused. 'You said you escaped. How did you do that?'

'Jumped overboard.'

Her mouth twisted with sympathy. I reflected that it was only four days since that frantic swim. It seemed another world.

Jossie was of the real, sensible world, where things were understandable, if not always pleasant. Being with her made me feel a great deal more settled, more normal, and safer.

'How about dinner,' I said, 'on the way home?'

'We've got two cars,' she said.

'Nothing to prevent them both stopping at the same place.'

'How true.'

She was again wearing swirly clothes: a soft rusty red, this time. There was nothing tailored about her, and nothing untidy. An organized girl, amusing and amused.

'There's a fair pub near Oxford,' I said.

'I'll follow you, then.'

I changed in due course for Notebook's race, and weighed out, and gave my lightest saddle to the Axwood travelling head lad, who was waiting for it by the door.

'Carrying overweight, are you?' he said sardonically.

'Four pounds.'

He made an eyes-to-heaven gesture, saying louder than words that trainers should put up professionals in novice hurdle races, not amateurs who couldn't do ten stone six. I didn't mention that on Gold Cup day I'd weighed eight pounds more.

When I went out to the parade ring, he and Jossie were waiting, while a lad led the noble Notebook round and round, now wearing my saddle over a number cloth. Number thirteen. So who was superstitious?

'He bucks a bit,' said the travelling head lad, with satisfaction.

'When you get home,' Jossie said to him, 'please tell my father I'm stopping on the way back for dinner with Roland. So that he doesn't worry about car crashes.'

'Right.'

'Dad fusses,' Jossie said.

The travelling head lad gave me another look which needed no words, and which speculated on whether I would get her into bed. I wasn't so sure that I cared all that much for the travelling head lad.

A good many people had already gone home, and from the parade ring one could see a steady drift to the gate. There were few things as disheartening, I thought, as playing to a vanishing audience. On the other hand, if one made a frightful mess, the fewer who saw it, the better.

'They said "jockeys get mounted" half an hour ago,' Jossie said.

'Two seconds,' I said. 'I was listening.'

The travelling head lad gave me a leg up. Notebook gave a trial buck.

'Stay out of trouble,' Jossie said.

'It's underneath me,' I said, feeling the noble animal again try to shoot me off.

She grinned unfeelingly. Notebook bounced away, hiccupped sideways down to the start, and then kept everyone waiting while he did a circus act on his hind legs. 'Bucks a bit', I thought bitterly. I'd fall off before the tapes went up, if I wasn't careful.

The race started, and Notebook magnanimously decided to take part, setting off at an uncoordinated gallop which involved a good deal of head-shaking and yawing from side to side. His approach to the first hurdle induced severe loss of confidence in his rider, as he seemed to be trying to jump it sideways, like a crab.

As I hadn't taken the precaution of dropping him out firmly at the back, always supposing I could actually have managed it, as he was as strong as he was wilful, his diagonal crossing of the flight of hurdles harvested a barrage of curses from the other jockeys. 'Sorry' was a useless word in a hurdle race, particularly from an unfit amateur who should have known better than to be led astray by a pretty girl. I yanked Notebook's head straight at the next hurdle with a force which would have had the Cruelty to Animals people swooning. He retaliated by screwing his hindquarters sideways in mid-air and landing on all four feet at once, pointing east-north-east to the rails.

This manoeuvre at least dropped him out into last place, which he tried to put right by running away with me up the stretch in front of the stands. As we fought each other on the way outwards round the mile-and-a-half circuit I understood the full meaning of the trainer's orders to his jockey. 'Stay on, and stay out of trouble.' My God.

I was not in the least surprised that Notebook had finished last of twenty-six at Newbury. He would have been last of a hundred and twenty-six, if his jockey had had any sense. Last place on Notebook was not exactly safe, but if one had to be anywhere on him, last place was wisest. No one, however, had got the message through to the horse.

The circuit at Towcester went out downhill from the stands, flattened into a straight stretch on the far side, and ended with a stamina-sapping uphill pull to the finishing straight and the winning post. Some of the world's slowest finishes had been slogged out there on muddy days at the end of three-mile 'chases. Notebook however set off downhill on firm going at a graceless rush, roller-coastered over the most distant hurdles, and only began to lose interest when he hit the sharply rising ground on the way back.

By that time the nineteen other runners were ahead as of right, as Notebook's stop-go and sideways type of jumping lost at every flight the lengths he made up on the flat.

I suppose I relaxed a little. He met the next hurdle all wrong, ignored my bid to help him, screwed wildly in mid-air, and landed with his nose on the turf and all four feet close together behind it. Not radically different from six other landings, just more extreme.

Being catapulted off at approximately thirty miles an hour is a kaleidoscopic business. Sky, trees, rails and grass somersaulted around my vision in a disjointed jumble, and if I tucked my head in it was from instinct, not thought. The turf smacked me sharply in several places, and Notebook delivered a parting kick on the thigh. The world stopped rolling, and half a ton of horse had not come crashing down on top of me. Life would go on.

I sat up slowly, all breath knocked out, and watched the noble hindquarters charge heedlessly away.

An ambulance man ran towards me, in the familiar black St John's uniform. I felt a flood of panic. A conditioned reflex. He had a kind face: a total stranger.

'All right, mate?' he said.

I nodded weakly.

'You came a proper purler.'

'Mm.' I unclipped my helmet, and pulled it off. Speech was impossible. My chest heaved from lack of air. He put a hand under one of my armpits and helped me as far as my knees, and from there, once I could breathe properly, to my feet.

'Bones OK?'

I nodded.

'Just winded,' he said cheerfully.

'Mm.'

A Land Rover arrived beside us with a jerk, and the vet inside it said that as there were no injured horses needing his attention, he could offer me a lift back to the stands.

'You fell off,' Jossie observed, as I emerged with normal breath and clean bill of health from the doctor in the First Aid room.

I smiled, 'Granted.'

She gave me a sideways glance from the huge eyes.

'I thought all jockeys were frightfully touchy about being told they fell off,' she said. 'All that guff about it's the horse that falls, and the jockey just goes down with the ship.'

'Quite right,' I said.

'But Notebook didn't actually fall, so you fell off.' Her voice was lofty, teasing.

'I don't dispute it.'

'No, aren't you boring.' She smiled. 'They caught Notebook in the next parish, so while you change I'll go along to the stables and see he's OK, and I'll meet you in the car park.'

'Fine.'

I changed into street clothes, fixed with the valet to take my saddles, helmet, and other gear to Ascot for the following Wednesday, and walked the short distance to the car park.

The crowds had gone, and only the stragglers like me were leaving now in twos and threes. The cars still remaining stood singly, haphazardly scattered instead of in orderly rows.

I looked into the back of mine, behind the front seats.

No one there.

I wondered with a shiver what I would have done if there had been. Run a mile, no doubt. I stood leaning on my car waiting for Jossie, and no one looked in the least like trying to carry me off. A quiet spring-like Saturday evening in the Northamptonshire countryside, as friendly as beer.

CHAPTER TEN

She followed me in her pale blue Midget to the pub on the south side of Oxford, and chose a long cold drink with fruit on the top and a kick in the tail.

'Dad has schooled Notebook until he's blue in the face,' she said, pursing her lips to the straw which stuck up like a mast from the log-jam of fruit.

'Some of them never learn,' I said.

She nodded. Polite transaction achieved, I thought: she had obliquely apologized for the horse's frightful behaviour, and I had accepted that her father had done his best to teach him to jump. Some trainers, but not those of William Finch's standing, seemed to think that the best place for a green novice to learn to jump was actually in a race: rather like urging a child up the Eiger without showing him how to climb.

'What made you become an accountant?' she said. 'It's such a dull sort of job.'

'Do you think so?'

She gave me the full benefit of the big eyes. 'You obviously don't,' she said. She tilted her head a little, considering. 'You don't *look* boring and stuffy, and you don't *act* boring and stuffy, so give.'

'Judges are sober, nurses are dedicated, miners are heroes, writers drink.'

'Or in other words, don't expect people to fit the image?'

'As you say,' I said.

She smiled. 'I've known Trevor since I was six.'

A nasty one. Trevor, without any stretch of imagination, could fairly be classed as stuffy and boring.

'Carry on,' she said. 'Why?'

'Security. Steady employment. Good pay. The usual inducements.'

She looked at me levelly. 'You're lying.'

'What makes you think so?'

'People who risk their necks for nothing in jump races are not hell-bent on security, steady employment, and money.'

'Because of me Mum, then,' I said flippantly.

'She bossed you into it?'

'No.' I hesitated, because in fact I never had told anyone why I'd grown up with a fiery zeal as powerful as a vocation. Jossie waited with quizzical expectation.

'She had a rotten accountant,' I said. 'I promised her that when I grew up I would take over. As corny as that.'

'And did you?'

'No. She died.'

'Sob story.'

'Yes, I told you. Pure corn.'

She stirred the fruit with her straw, looking less mocking. 'You're afraid I'll laugh at you.'

'Sure of it,' I said.

'Try me, then.'

'Well . . . she was a rotten businesswoman, my Mum. My father got killed in a pointless sort of accident, and she was left having to bring me up alone. She was about thirty. I was nine.' I paused. Jossie was not actually laughing, so I struggled on. 'She rented a house just off the sea-front at Ryde and ran it as a holiday hotel, half a step up from a boarding house. Comfortable, but no drinks licence; that sort of thing. So she could be there when I got home from school, and in the holidays.'

'Brave of her,' Jossie said. 'Go on.'

'You can guess.'

She sucked down to the dregs of her glass and made a bubbling noise through the straw. 'Sure,' she said. 'She was good at cooking and welcoming people and lousy at working out how much to charge.'

'She was also paying tax on money she should have claimed as expenses.'

'And that's bad?'

'Crazy.'

'Well, go on,' she said encouragingly. 'Digging a story out of you is worse than looking for mushrooms.'

'I found her crying sometimes, mostly in the winter when there weren't any guests. It's pretty upsetting for a kid of ten or so to find his mother crying, so you can say I was upset. Protective also, probably. Anyway, at first

I thought it was still because of losing Dad. Then I realized she always cried when she'd been seeing Mr Jones, who was her accountant. I tried to get her to open up on her troubles, but she said I was too young.'

I stopped again. Jossie sighed with exasperation and said, 'Do get *on* with it.'

'I told her to ditch Mr Jones and get someone else. She said I didn't understand, I was too young. I promised her that when I got older I would be an accountant, and I'd put her affairs to rights.' I smiled lopsidedly. 'When I was thirteen she went down to Boots one morning and bought two hundred aspirins. She stirred them into a glass of water, and drank them. I found her lying on her bed when I came home from school. She left me a note.'

'What did it say?'

'It said "Dear Ro, Sorry, Love, Mum." '

'Poor girl.' Jossie blinked. Not laughing.

'She'd made a will,' I said. 'One of those simple things on a form from the stationers. She left me everything, which was actually nothing much except her own personal things. I kept all the account books and bank statements. I got shuttled around uncles and aunts for a few years, but I kept those account books safe, and then I got another accountant to look at them. He told me Mr Jones seemed to have thought he was working for the Inland Revenue, not his client. I told him I wanted to be an accountant, and I got him to show me exactly what Mr Jones had done wrong. So there you are. That's all.'

'Are you still killing Mr Jones to dry your mother's tears?' The teasing note was back, but gentler.

I smiled, 'I enjoy accountancy. I might never have thought of it if it hadn't been for Mr Jones.'

'So God bless villains.'

'He was ultra-righteous. A smug pompous ass. There are still a lot of Mr Joneses around, not pointing out to their clients all the legitimate ways of avoiding tax.'

'Huh?'

'It's silly to pay tax when you don't have to.'

'That's obvious.'

'A lot of people do, though, from ignorance or bad advice.'

I ordered refill drinks and told Jossie it was her turn to unbutton with the family skeletons.

'My Ma?' she said in surprise. 'I thought the whole world knew about my Ma. She canoes up and down the Amazon like a yo-yo, digging up ancient tribes. Sends back dispatches in the shape of earnest papers to obscure magazines. Dad and I haven't seen her for years. We get telegrams in January saying Happy Christmas.'

Revelation dawned. 'Christabel Saffray Finch! Intrepid female explorer, storming about in rain forests?'

'Ma,' Jossie nodded.

'Good heavens.'

'Good grief, more like.'

'Trevor never told me,' I said. 'But then he wouldn't, I suppose.'

Jossie grinned. 'Trevor disapproves. Trevor also

always disapproves of Dad's little consolations. Aunts, I used to call them. Now I call them Lida and Sandy.'

'He's very discreet.' Even on the racecourse, where gossip was a second occupation, I hadn't heard of Lida and Sandy. Or that Christabel Saffray Finch, darling of anthropological documentaries, was William's wife.

'Sandy is his ever-sick secretary,' Jossie said, 'perpetually shuttling between bronchitis, backache and abortion.'

I laughed. 'And Lida?'

Jossie made a face, suddenly vulnerable under all the bright froth.

'Lida's got her hooks into him like a tapeworm. I can't stand her. Let's talk about food; I'm starving.'

We read the menu and ordered, and finished our drinks, and went in to dinner in the centuries-old dining-room: stone walls, uncovered oak beams, red velvet and soft lights.

Jossie ate as if waistlines never expanded, which was refreshing after the finicky picker I'd taken out last.

'Luck of the draw,' she said complacently, smothering a baked-in-the-skin potato with a butter mountain. I reflected that she'd drawn lucky in more ways than metabolism. A quick mind, fascinating face, tall, slender body: there was nothing egalitarian about nature.

Most of the tables around us were filled with softly chattering groups of twos and fours, but over by a far wall a larger party were making the lion's share of the noise.

'They keep looking over here,' Jossie said. 'Do you know them?'

'It looks like Sticks Elroy with his back to us.'

'Is it? Celebrating his winner?'

Sticks Elroy, named for the extreme thinness of his legs, had studiously avoided me in the Towcester changing room, and must have been thoroughly disconcerted to find me having dinner in his local pub. He was one of my jockey clients, but for how much longer was problematical. I was not currently his favourite person.

The noise, however, was coming not from him but from the host of the party, a stubborn-looking man with a naturally loud voice.

'Avert your gaze,' I said to Jossie.

The large eyes regarded me over salad and steak.

'An ostrich act?' she said.

I nodded. 'If we bury our heads, maybe the storm won't notice us.'

The storm, however, seemed to be gathering force. Words like 'bastard' rose easily above the prevailing clatter and the uninvolved majority began to look interested.

'Trouble,' Josie said without visible regret, 'is on its feet and heading this way.'

'Damn.'

She grinned. 'Faint heart.'

Trouble arrived with the deliberate movements of the slightly drunk. Late forties, I judged. About five feet eight, short dark hair, flushed cheeks and aggressive eyes. He stood four-square and ignored Jossie altogether.

'My son tells me you're that bastard Roland Britten.' His voice, apart from fortissimo, was faintly slurred.

To ignore him was to invite a punch-up. I laid down my knife and fork. Leaned back in my chair. Behaved as if the enquiry was polite.

'Is Sticks Elroy your son?'

'Too right, he bloody is,' he said.

'He had a nice winner today,' I said. 'Well done.'

It stopped him for barely two seconds.

'He doesn't need your bloody "well done".'

I waited mildly, without answering. Elroy senior bent down, breathed alcohol heavily, and pointed an accusing finger under my nose.

'You leave my son alone, see? He isn't doing anyone any harm. He doesn't want any bastard like you snitching on him to the bloody tax man. Judas, that's what you are. Going behind his back. Bloody informer, that's what you are.'

'I haven't informed on him.'

'What's that?' He wagged the finger to and fro, belligerently. 'Costing him hundreds, aren't you, with the bloody tax man. Bastard like you ought to be locked up. Serve you bloody well right.'

The head waiter arrived smoothly at Elroy's shoulder.

'Excuse me, sir,' he began.

Elroy turned on him like a bull. 'You trot off. You majordomo, or whatever you are. You trot off. I'll have my say, and when I've had my say I'll sit down, see? Not before.'

The head waiter cravenly retired, and Elroy returned to his prime target. Jossie's eyes stared at him with disfavour, which deflected him not at all.

'I hear someone locked you up for ten days or so just now, and you got out. Bloody shame. You deserve to be locked up, you do. Bastard like you. Whoever it was locked you up had the right idea.'

I said nothing. Elroy half turned away, but he had by no means finished. Merely addressing a wider audience.

'You know what this bastard did to my son?' The audience removed its eyes in thoroughly British embarrassment, but they got told the answer whether they liked it or not.

'This boot-licking, creeping bastard went crawling to the tax man and told him my son had some cash he hadn't paid taxes on.'

'I didn't,' I said to Jossie.

He swung round to me again and poked the finger rigidly under my nose. 'Bloody liar. Locking up's too bloody good for bastards like you.'

The manager arrived, with the head waiter hovering behind.

'Mr Elroy,' the manager said courteously. 'A bottle of wine for your party, compliments of the management.' He beckoned a finger to the head waiter, who deftly proffered a bottle of claret.

The manager was young and well-dressed, and

reminded me of Vivian Iverson. His unexpected oil worked marvels on the storm, which abated amid a few extra 'bastards' and went back to its table muttering under its breath.

The people at the other tables watched from the cover of animated conversation, while the head waiter drew the cork for Elroy and poured the free wine. The manager drifted casually back to Jossie and me.

'There will be no charge for your dinner, sir.' He paused delicately. 'Mr Elroy is a valued customer.' He bowed very slightly and drifted on without waiting for an answer.

'How cool of him,' Josie said, near explosion.

'How professional.'

She stared at me. 'Do you often sit still and let people call you a bastard?'

'Once a week and twice on Sundays.'

'Spineless.'

'If I'd stood up and slogged him, our steaks would have gone cold.'

'Mine has, anyway.'

'Have another,' I said. I started to eat again where I had left off, and so, after a moment or two, did Jossie.

'Go on,' she said. 'I'm all agog. Just what was that all about?' She looked round the restaurant. 'You are now the target of whispers, and the consensus looks unfavourable.'

'In general,' I said, spearing lettuce, 'people shouldn't expect their accountants to help them break the law.'

'Sticks?'

'And accountants unfortunately cannot discuss their clients.'

'Are you being serious?'

I sighed. 'A client who wants his accountant to connive at a massive piece of tax-dodging is not going to be madly pleased when the accountant refuses to do it.'

'Mm.' She chewed cheerfully. 'I do see that.'

'And,' I went on, 'an accountant who advises such a client to declare the loot and pay the tax, because otherwise the nasty Revenue men will undoubtedly find out, and the client will have to pay fines on top of tax and will end up very poorly all round, because not only will he get it in the neck for that one offence, but every tax return he makes in the future will be inspected with magnifying glasses and he'll be hounded for evermore over every penny and have inspectors ransacking every cranny of his house at two in the morning . . .' I took a breath ' . . . such an accountant may be unpopular.'

'Unreasonable.'

'And an accountant who refuses to break the law, and says that if his client insists on doing so he will have to take his custom somewhere else, such an accountant may possibly be called a bastard.'

She finished her steak and laid down her knife and fork. 'Does this hypothetical accountant snitch to the tax man?'

I smiled. 'If the client is no longer his client, he doesn't know whether his ex-client is tax-dodging or not. So no, he doesn't snitch.'

'Elroy had it all wrong, then.'

'Er,' I said, 'it was he who set up the scheme from which Sticks drew the cash. That's why he is so furious. And I shouldn't be telling you that.'

'You'll be struck off, or strung up, or whatever.'

'Sky high.' I drank some wine. 'It's quite extraordinary how many people try to get their accountants to help them with tax fiddles. I reckon if someone wants to fiddle, the last person he should tell should be his accountant.'

'Just get on with it, and keep quiet?'

'If they want to take the risk.'

She half laughed. 'What risk? Tax-dodging is a national sport.'

People never understood about taxation, I thought. The ruthlessness with which tax could be collected put Victorian landlords in the shade, and the Revenue people now had frightening extra powers of entry and search.

'It's much safer to steal from your employer than the tax man,' I said.

'You must be joking.'

'Have some profiteroles,' I said.

Jossie eyed the approaching trolley of super-puds and agreed on four small cream-filled buns smothered in chocolate sauce.

'Aren't you having any?' she demanded.

'Think of Tapestry on Wednesday.'

'No wonder jockeys get fat when they finally let themselves eat.' She spooned up the dark brown goo with satisfaction. 'Why is it safer to steal from your employer?'

'He can't sell your belongings to get his money back.'

The big eyes widened.

'Golly!' she said.

'If you run up debts, the courts can send bailiffs to take your furniture. If you steal instead, they can't.'

She paused blankly in mid-mouthful, then went on chewing, and swallowed. 'Carry right on,' she said. 'I'm riveted.'

'Well . . . it's theft which is the national sport, not tax-dodging. Petty theft. Knocking off. Nicking. Most shop-lifting is done by the staff, not the customers. No one really blames a girl who sells tights all day if she tucks a pair into her handbag when she goes home. Pinching from employers is almost regarded as a rightful perk, and if ever a manufacturing firm puts an efficient checker on the staff exits there's practically a riot until he's removed.'

'Because he stops the outward march of spanners and fork-lift trucks?'

I grinned. 'You could feed an army on what disappears from the fridges of hotels.'

'Accountants,' she said, 'shouldn't find it amusing.'

'Especially as they spend their lives looking for fraud.'

'Do you?' she said, surprised. 'Do you really? I thought accountants just did sums.'

'The main purpose of an audit is to turn up fiddles.'

'I thought it was . . . well . . . to add up the profit or loss.'

'Not really.'

She thought. 'But when Trevor comes to count the hay and saddles and stuff, that's stocktaking.'

I shook my head. 'More like checking on behalf of your father that he hasn't got a stable lad selling the odd bale or bridle on the quiet.'

'Good heavens.' She was truly astounded. 'I'll have to stop thinking of auditors as fuddy-duddies. Change their image to fraud squad policemen.'

'Not that, either.'

'Why not?'

'If an auditor finds that a firm is being swindled by its cashier, for instance, he simply tells the firm. He doesn't arrest the cashier. He leaves it to the firm to decide whether to call in the handcuffs.'

'But surely they always do.'

'Absolutely not. Firms get red faces and tend to lose business if everyone knows their cashier took them for a ride. They sack the cashier and keep quiet, mostly.'

'Are you bored with telling me all this?'

'No,' I said truthfully.

'Then tell me a good fraud.'

I laughed. 'Heard any good frauds lately?'

'Get on with it.'

'Um . . .' I thought. 'A lot of the best frauds are complicated juggling with figures. It's the paperwork which deceives the eye, like a three card trick. I paused, then smiled. 'I know a good one, though they weren't my clients, thank God. There was a manager of a broiler-chicken factory farm which sold thousands of chickens every week to a freezing firm. The manager was also quietly selling a hundred a week to a butcher who didn't know the chickens had fallen off the back of a lorry, so to speak. No one could ever tell how many chickens there actually were on the farm, because the turnover was so huge and fast, and baby chicks tend to die. The manager pocketed a neat little untaxed regular income, and like most good frauds it was discovered by accident.'

'What accident?'

'The butcher used to pay the manager by cheque, made out in the manager's name. One day he happened to meet one of the directors of the firm which owned the chicken farm, and to save postage he got out his chequebook, wrote a cheque in the manager's name, and asked the director to give it to him, to pay for that month's delivery of chickens.'

'And the lid blew off.'

'With a bang. They sacked the manager.'

'No prosecution?'

'No. The last I heard, he was selling rose bushes by mail order.'

'And you wondered for whose nursery he was working?'

I grinned and nodded. She was quick and funny, and it seemed incredible that I'd met her only the day before.

We drank coffee and talked about horses. She said she had been trying her hand at three-day-eventing, but would be giving it up soon.

'Why?' I asked.

'Lack of talent.'

'What will you do instead?'

'Marry.'

'Oh.' I felt obscurely disappointed. 'Who?'

'I've no idea. Someone will turn up.'

'Just like that?'

'Of course just like that. One finds husbands in the oddest places.'

'What are you doing tomorrow?' I said.

Her eyes gleamed with light and life. 'Visiting a girl friend. What will you do instead?'

'Sums, I expect.'

'But tomorrow's Sunday.'

'And I can have the office to myself all day, without any interruption. I often work on Sundays. Nearly always.'

'Good grief.'

We went out to where the Midget and the Dolomite stood side by side in the car park.

'Thanks for the grub,' Jossie said.

'And for your company.'

'Do you feel all right?'

'Yes,' I said, surprised. 'Why?'

'Just checking,' she said. 'Dad'll ask. It looked such a crunching fall.'

I shook my head. 'A bruise or two.'

'Good. Well, goodnight.'

'Goodnight.' I kissed her cheek.

Her eyes glinted in the dim light from the pub's windows. I kissed her mouth, rather briefly, with closed lips. She gave me the same sort of kiss in return.

'Hm,' she said, standing back. 'That wasn't bad. I do hate wet slobbers.'

She slid expertly into the Midget and started the engine.

'See you in the hay,' she said. 'Counting it.'

She was smiling as she drove away, probably with a mirror expression of my own. I unlocked my car door, and, feeling slightly silly, I looked into the dark area behind the front seats.

No one there.

I sat in the car and started it, debating whether or not to risk going home to the cottage. Friday and Saturday had passed safely enough; but maybe the cats were still watching the mousehole. I decided that another night away would be prudent, and from the pub drove northwards around Oxford again, to the anonymity of the large motel and service station built beside a busy route-connecting roundabout.

The place as usual was bright with lights and bustle: flags flying on tall poles and petrol pumps rattling. I booked in at the reception office, took the key, and drove round to the slightly quieter wing of bedrooms at the rear.

Sleep would be no problem, I thought. The constant rumble of traffic would be soporific. A lullaby.

I yawned, took out my suitcase, locked the car, and fitted the key into the bedroom door.

Something hit me very hard between the shoulders. I fell against the still closed door, and something immediately hit me very hard on the head.

This time, it was brutal. This time, no ether.

I slid in a daze down the door and saw only dark unrecognizable figures bending over to punch and kick. The thuds shuddered through my bones, and another bang on the head slid me deep into peaceful release.

CHAPTER ELEVEN

I awoke in the dark. Black, total darkness.

I couldn't make out why I should be lying on a hard surface in total darkness, aching all over.

A fall, I thought. I had a fall at Towcester. Why couldn't I remember?

I felt cold. Chilled through and through. When I moved, the aches were worse.

I suddenly remembered having dinner with Jossie. Remembered it all clearly, down to kissing her goodnight in the car park.

So then what?

I tried to sit up, but raising my head was as far as I got. The result was whirling nausea and a pile-driving headache. I inched my fingers tentatively through my hair and found a wince-making area of swelling. I let my head down again, gingerly.

There was no sound except the rustle of my clothes. No engine. No creakings or rushings or water noises. I was not lying on a bunk, but on a larger surface, hard and flat.

I might not be in a sail locker, but I was certainly still in the dark. In the dark in every sense. Weak frustrated anger mocked me that in four days of freedom I hadn't found out enough to save me from the gloomy present.

Every movement told me what I still couldn't remember. I knew only that the fall off Notebook could not be the source of the soreness all over my body. There would have been a few bruises which would have stiffened up overnight, but nothing like the overall feeling of having been kneaded like dough. I rolled with a grunt on to my stomach and put my head on my folded arms. The only good thing that I could think of was that they hadn't tied my hands.

They. Who were *they?*

When my head stopped hammering, I thought, I would have enough energy to find out where I was and try to get out. Meanwhile it was enough just to lie still and wait for things to get better.

Another thing to be grateful for, I thought. The hard flat surface I was lying on was not swaying about. With luck, I was not on a boat. I wasn't going to be sick. A bruised body was absolutely nothing compared with the agonies of seasickness.

I had no shoes on, just socks. When I squinted at my wrist there was no luminous dial there: no watch. I couldn't be bothered to check all my pockets. I was certain they'd be empty.

After a while I remembered deciding to go to the

motel, and after that, bit by bit, I remembered booking in, and the affray on the doorstep.

They must have followed me all the way from Towcester, I thought. Waited through dinner with Jossie. Followed me to the motel. I hadn't spotted them once. I hadn't even heard their footsteps behind me, against the constant noise of traffic.

My instinctive feeling of being safe with Jossie had been dead right.

Ages passed.

The racket inside my skull gradually subsided. Nothing else happened.

I had a feeling that it was nearly dawn, and time to wake up. It had been ten-thirty when I'd been knocked out. There was no telling how long I'd been unconscious, or lain feebly in my present state, but the body had its own clock, and mine was saying six in the morning.

The dawn feeling stirred me to some sort of action, though if there was dawn outside it was not making its way through to me. Perhaps, I thought uneasily, I was wrong about the time. It was still night outside. I prayed for it to be still night outside.

I had another go at sitting up. One couldn't say that I felt superbly healthy. Concussion took a while to go away, and cold was notoriously bad for bruised muscles. The combination made every movement a nuisance. A familiar sort of pain, because of racing falls in the past. Just worse.

The surface beneath me was dirty: I could feel the gritty dust. It smelled faintly of oil. It was flat and smooth and not wood.

I felt around me in all directions, and on my left connected with a wall. Slithering on one hip, I inched that way and cautiously explored with my fingers.

Another smooth flat surface, at right angles to the floor. I banged it gently with my fist, and got back the noise and vibration of metal.

I thought that if I sat for a while with my back against the wall it would soon get light, and it would be easy then to see where I was. It had to get light, I thought forlornly. It simply had to.

It didn't, of course.

When they'd given me light on the boat, I'd escaped. A mistake to be avoided.

It had to be faced. The darkness was deliberate, and would go on. It was no good, I told myself severely, sitting in a miserable huddle feeling sorry for myself.

I made a further exploration into unmapped territory, and found that my world was a good deal smaller than Columbus's. It seemed prudent to move while still sitting down, on the flat-earth theory that one might fall over the edge; but two feet of shuffling to the right brought me to a corner.

The adjacent wall was also flat, smooth, and metal. I

shifted my spine round on to it, and set off again to the right.

The traverse was short. I came almost at once to another corner. I found that if I sat in the centre of the wall I could reach both side walls at once quite easily with my fingertips. Five feet, approximately, from side to side.

I shuffled round the second corner and pressed on. Three feet down that side, I knew where I was. The flatness of the metal wall was broken there by a big rounded bulge, whose meaning was as clear to my touch as if I'd been seeing it.

It was the semi-circular casing over a wheel; and I was inside a van.

I had a powerful, immediate picture of the fake ambulance I'd climbed into at Cheltenham. A white van, of a standard pattern, with the doors opening outwards at the rear. If I continued past the wheel, I would come to the rear doors.

And I would feel a proper fool, I thought, if all I had to do was open the doors and step out.

I wouldn't have minded feeling a proper fool. The doors were firmly shut, and likely to remain so. There was no handle on the inside.

In the fourth corner I came across what I had this time been given in the way of life support systems, and if my spirits had already been at zero, at that point they went way below.

There was a five-gallon plastic jerrycan full of liquid, and a large carrier bag.

I unscrewed the cap of the jerrycan and sniffed at the contents. No smell. Sloshed some of the liquid out on to my hand, and tasted it.

Water.

I screwed the cap on again, fumbling in the dark.

Five gallons of water.

Oh no, I thought numbly. Oh dear God.

The carrier was packed to the top with flat plastic packets, each about four inches square. There was again no smell. I pulled one of the packets open, and found the contents were thin four-inch squares of sliced processed cheese.

I counted the packets with a sinking heart, taking them one by one from the carrier and stacking them on the floor. There were sixty of them. All, as far as I could tell, exactly the same.

Wretchedly I counted them from the floor back into the carrier, one by one, and there were still sixty. They had given me enough food and water to last for at least four weeks. There were going to be no twice a day visits: no one to talk to at all.

Sod them, I thought violently. If this was revenge, it was worse than anything I'd ever brought on any crook.

Spurred by anger, I stood without caution to explore the top part of the van, and banged my sore head on the roof. It was very nearly altogether too much. I found myself back on my knees, cursing and holding my head, and trying not to weep. A battered feeble figure, sniffing in the dark.

It wouldn't do, I thought. It was necessary to be sternly unemotional. To ignore the aches and pains. To take a good cold grip of things, and make a plan and routine for survival.

When the fresh waves of headache passed, I got on with it.

The presence of food and drink meant, I thought, that survival was expected. That one day, if I didn't manage a second escape, I would be released. Death, again, was not apparently on the agenda. Well, then, why was I getting into such a fuss?

I had read once of a man who had spent weeks down a pothole in silence and darkness to see how a total lack of external reference would affect the human body. He had survived with his mind intact and his body none the worse for wear, and his sense of time had gone remarkably little astray. What he could do, so could I. It was irrelevant, I thought sternly, that the scientist had volunteered for his incarceration, and had had his heartbeat and other vital signs monitored on the surface, and could have got out again any time he felt he'd had enough.

Feeling a good deal steadier for the one-man pep-talk, I got more slowly to my feet, sliding my spine up the side wall, and feeling for the roof with my hands. It was too low for me to stand upright, by four or six inches. With head and knees bent, I felt my way again right round the van.

Both sides were completely blank. The front wall was broken by the shape of a small panel which must have opened through to the driving cab. It seemed to be intended to slide, but was fastened shut as firmly as if it had been welded. There was no handle or bolt on the inside; only smoothed metal.

The rear doors at first seemed to be promising, as I discovered they were not entirely solid, but had windows. One each side, about twelve inches across, the distance from my wrist to my elbow, and half as high.

There was no glass in the windows. I stretched my hand cautiously through the one on the right, and immediately came to a halt. Something hard was jammed against the doors on the outside, holding them shut.

I was concentrating so much on the message from my fingers that I realized that I was crouching there with my eyes shut. Funny, really. I opened them. No light. What good were eyes without light?

Outside each window there was an area of coarse cloth, which felt like heavy canvas. At the outer sides of the window it was possible to push the canvas, to move it three or four inches away from the van. On the inner halves it was held tight against the van by whatever was jamming the doors shut.

I put an arm out of each outer section of window in turn, and felt as much of the outside of the van as I could reach. It was very little, and of no use. The whole of the back of the van was sheeted in canvas.

I slid down again to the floor and tried to visualize

what I'd felt. A van covered in canvas with its rear doors jammed shut. Where could one park such a thing so that it wouldn't be immediately discovered? In a garage? A barn? If I banged on the sides, would anyone hear me?

I banged on the sides of the van, but my fists made little noise, and there was nothing else to bang with. I shouted 'Help' a good many times through the windows, but no one came.

There was air perceptibly leaking in through the missing windows: I could feel it when I pushed the canvas outwards. No fear of asphyxiation.

It irritated me that I could do nothing useful with those windows. They were too small to crawl through, even without the canvas and whatever was holding it against the van. I couldn't get my head through the spaces, let alone my shoulders.

I decided to eat some cheese and think things over. The cheese wasn't bad. The thoughts produced the unwelcome reflection that this time I had no mattress, no blanket, no pillow, and no loo. Also no paperback novel, spare socks, or soap. The sail locker had been a Hilton compared with the van.

On the other hand, in an odd sort of way the time in the sail locker had prepared me better for this dourer cell. Instead of feeling more frightened, more hysterical, more despairing, I felt less. I had already been through all the horrors. Also, during the four days of freedom, I had not gone to the South Pole to avoid capture. I'd feared it and done my best to dodge it, but in returning to my usual life, I'd known it might come.

The reason for the first abduction presumably still existed. I had escaped before the intended time, and in someone's eyes this had been a very bad thing. Bad enough to send the squad to retake me, from the cottage, within a day of my return to England. Bad enough to risk carting me off again when this time there would, I hoped, be a police search.

I was pretty sure I must still be in England. I certainly had no memory of being transported from the motel to wherever I was now, but the impression that I'd been unconscious for only an hour or two was convincingly strong.

Sunday morning. No one would miss me. It would be Monday before Debbie and Peter began to wonder. Tuesday, perhaps, before the police took it seriously, if indeed they did, in spite of their assurance. A day or two more before anyone really started looking: and I had no wife or parents to keep the search alive, if I wasn't to be found soon after that.

Jossie might have done, I thought regretfully, if I'd known her for longer. Jossie with her bright eyes and forthright tongue.

At the very least, at the most hopeful assessment, the future still looked a long, hard, weary grind.

Shortening the perspective dramatically, it was becoming imperative to solve immediately the question of liquid waste disposal. I might be having to live in a tin box, but not, if I could help it, in a filthy stinking tin box.

Necessity concentrated the mind wonderfully, as others before me had observed. I took the cheese slices out of one of the thick plastic packets, and used that, and emptied it in relays out of the rear window, pushing the canvas away from the van as far as I could. Not the most sanitary of arrangements, but better than nothing.

After that little excitement, I sat down again. I was still cold, though not now with the through-and-through chill of injury-shock. I could perhaps have done some warming-up arm-swinging exercises, if it hadn't been for protesting bruises. As things were, with every muscle movement a reminder, I simply sat.

Exploration had kept me busy up to that point, but the next few hours revealed the true extent of my isolation.

There was absolutely no external sound. If I suppressed the faint noise of my own breathing, I could hear literally nothing. No traffic, no hum of aircraft, no wind, no creak, no rustle. Nothing.

There was absolutely no light. Air came steadily in from between the outside of the van and its canvas shroud, but no light came with it. Eyes wide open, or firmly shut, it was all the same.

There was no perceptible change in temperature. It remained just too low for comfort, defying my body's efforts to acclimatize. I had been left trousers, underpants, shirt, sports jacket and socks, though no tie, no belt, no loose belongings of any sort. It was Sunday, April 3rd. It might have been a sunny spring day outside, but wherever I was, it was simply too cold.

People would be reading about the Grand National in their Sunday newspapers, I thought. Lying in bed, warm and comfortable. Getting up and strolling to the pub. Eating hot meals, playing with the kids, deciding not to mow the lawn for another week. Millions of people, living their Sunday.

I served myself a Sunday lunch of cheese slices, and with great care drank some water from the can. It was heavy, being full, and I couldn't afford to tip it over. Enough water went down my neck to make me think of the uses of cheese packets as drinking cups.

After lunch, a snooze, I thought. I made a fairly reasonable pillow by rearranging the cheese packets inside the carrier, and resolutely tried to sleep, but the sum of discomfort kept me awake.

Well, then, I thought, lying on my back and staring at the invisible ceiling, I could sort out what I'd learned during my four free days.

The first of them could be discounted, as I'd spent it in Minorca, organizing my return home. That left two days in the office and one at the races. One night hiding in the cottage, one sleeping soundly in the Gloucester hotel. For all of that period I'd been looking for reasons, which made this present dose of imprisonment a great deal different from the first. Then, I'd been completely bewildered. This time I had at least one or two ideas.

Hours passed.

Nothing got any better.

I sat up for a while, and lay down again, and everything hurt, just the same. I cheered myself up with the thought that the stiff ache of bruises always finally got better, never worse. Suppose, for instance, it had been appendicitis. I'd heard that people going off to Everest or other Backs of Beyond had their perfectly healthy appendix removed, just in case. I wished on the whole that I hadn't thought of appendicitis.

Or toothache.

I had a feeling that it was evening, and then that it was night.

There was no change, except in me. I grew slowly even colder, but as if from the inside out. My eyelids stayed heavily shut. I drifted gradually in and out of sleep, a long drowsy twilight punctuated by short groaning awakenings every time I moved. When I woke with a clear mind, it felt like dawn.

If the cycle held, I thought, I could keep a calendar. One empty cheese packet for every day, stacked in the right-hand front corner of the van. If I put one there at every dawn, I would know the days. One for Sunday: a second for Monday. I extracted two wads of cheese slices and shuffled carefully a couple of feet forward to leave the empties.

I ate and drank what I thought of as breakfast: and I had become, I realized, much more at home in the dark. Physically, I was less clumsy. I found it easier to manage the water can, for instance, and no longer tended to put the cap on the floor and feel frustrated when I couldn't at once find it after I'd drunk. I now put my hand back automatically to where I'd parked the cap in the first place.

Mentally, too, it was less of a burden. On the boat I'd loathed it, and of all the rotten prospects of a second term of imprisonment, it had been being thrown back into the dark which I had shrunk from most. I still hated it, but its former heavy oppression was passing. I found that I no longer feared that the darkness on its own would set me climbing the walls.

I spent the morning thinking about reasons for abduction, and in the afternoon made an abacus out of pieces of cheese arranged in rows, and did a string of mathematical computations. I knew that other solitary captives had kept their minds occupied by repeating verses, but I'd always found it easier to think in numbers and symbols, and I'd not learned enough words by heart for them to be of any present use. Goosey goosey gander had its limitations.

*

Monday night came and went. When I woke I planted another cheese packet in the front right-hand corner, and flexed arms and legs which were no longer too sore to be worth it.

Tuesday morning I spent doing exercises and thinking about reasons for abduction, and Tuesday afternoon I felt my way delicately round the abacus, enlarging its scope as a calculator. Tuesday evening I sat and hugged my knees, and thought disconsolately that it was all very well telling myself to be staunch and resolute, but that staunch and resolute was not really how I felt.

Three days since I'd had dinner with Jossie. Well . . . at least I had her to think about, which I hadn't had on the boat.

The dozing period came round again. I lay down and let it wash over me for hours, and counted it Tuesday night.

Wednesday, for the twentieth time, I felt round the van inch by inch, looking for a possible way out. For the twentieth time, I didn't find one.

There were no bolts to undo. No levers. There was nothing. No way out. I knew it, but I couldn't stop searching.

Wednesday was the day I was supposed to be riding Tapestry at Ascot. Whether because of that, or simply because my body was back approximately to normal, the time passed more slowly than ever.

I whistled and sang, and felt restless, and wished passionately that there was room to stand up straight. The only way to straighten my spine was to lie down flat. I could feel my hard-won calm slipping away round the edges, and it was a considerable effort to give myself something to do with the pieces-of-cheese slide rule.

Wednesday I lost track of whether it was noon or evening, and the idea of days and days more of that existence was demoralizing. Dammit, I thought mordantly. Shut up, shut up with the gloomsville. One day at a time. One day, one hour, one minute at a time.

I ate some cheese and felt sleepy, and that at long last was Wednesday done.

Thursday midday, I heard a noise.

I couldn't believe it.

Some distant clicks, and a grinding noise. I was lying on my back doing bicycling exercises with my legs in the air, and I practically disconnected myself getting to my knees and scrambling over to the rear doors.

I pushed the canvas away from one of the windows, and shouted at the top of my lungs.

'Hey . . . hey . . . Come here.'

There were footsteps; more than one set. Soft footsteps, but in that huge dead silence, quite clear.

I swallowed. Whoever it was, there was no point in keeping quiet.

'Hey,' I shouted again. 'Come here.'

The footsteps stopped.

A man's voice, close to the van, spoke very loudly.

'Are you Roland Britten?'

I said weakly, 'Yes . . . who are you?'

'Police, sir,' he said.

CHAPTER TWELVE

They took a good long while getting me out, because, as the disembodied voice explained, they would have to take photographs and notes for use in any future prosecution. Also there was the matter of fingerprints, which would mean further delay.

'And we can't get you out without moving the van, you see, sir,' said the voice. 'On account of it's backed hard up against a brick pillar, and we can't open the rear doors. On top of that the driving cab doors are both locked, and the brake's hard on, and there's no key in the ignition. So if you'll be patient, sir, we'll have you out as soon as we can.'

He sounded as if he were reassuring a small child who might scream the place down at any minute, but I found it easy to be patient, if only he knew.

There were several voices outside after a while, and from time to time they asked me if I was all right, and I said yes; and in the end they started the van's engine and drove it forward a few feet, and pulled off the canvas cover.

The return of sight was extraordinary. The two small windows appeared as oblongs of grey, and I had difficulty in focusing. A face looked in, roundly healthy, enquiring and concerned, topped by a uniform cap.

'Have you out in a jiffy now, sir,' he said. 'We're having a bit of difficulty with these doors, see, as the handle's been sabotaged.'

'Fine,' I said vaguely. The light was still pretty dim, but to me a luxury like no other on earth. A half-forgotten joy, newly discovered. Like meeting a dead friend. Familiar, lost, precious, and restored.

I sat on the floor and looked around my prison. It was smaller than I'd imagined: cramped and claustrophobic, now that I could see the grey enclosing walls.

The jerrycan of water was of white plastic, with a red cap. The carrier was brown, as I'd imagined it. The little calendar stack of five empty packets lay in its corner, and the hardening pieces of cheese from my counting machine, in another. There was nothing else, except me and dust.

They opened the doors eventually and helped me out, and then took notes and photographs of where I'd been. I stood a pace or two away and looked curiously at my surroundings.

The van was indeed the white one from Cheltenham, or one exactly like it. An old Ford. No tax disc, and no number-plates. The canvas which had covered it was a huge, dirty dark grey tarpaulin, the sort used for sheeting loads on lorries. The van had been wrapped in it like a parcel, and tied with ropes threaded through eyelets in the tarpaulin's edges.

The van, the police and I were all inside a building of about a hundred feet square. All round the walls rose huge lumpy heaps of dust-covered unidentifiable bundles, grey shapes of boxes and things that looked like sandbags. Some of the piles reached the low flat ceiling, which was supported at strategic points by four sturdy brick pillars.

It was against one of these, in the small clear area in the centre, that the van had been jammed.

'What is this place?' I said to the policeman beside me.

'Are you all right, sir?' he said. He shivered slightly. 'It's cold in here.'

'Yes,' I said. 'Where exactly are we?'

'It used to be one of those army surplus stores, selling stuff to the public. Went bust a while back, though, and no one's ever shifted all the muck.'

'Oh. Well . . . whereabouts is it?'

'Down one of those tracks that used to be the railway branch line, before they closed it.'

'Yes,' I said apologetically. 'But what town?'

'Eh?' He looked at me in surprise. 'Newbury, of course, sir.'

The town clocks pointed to five o'clock when the police drove me down to the station. My body's own time had proved remarkably constant, I thought. Much better than on the boat, where noise and tossing and sickness had upset things.

I was given a chair in the office of one of the same policemen as before, who showed no regrets at having earlier thought I was exaggerating.

'How did you find me?' I said.

He tapped his teeth with a pencil, a hard-working Detective Inspector with an air of suspecting the innocent until they were found guilty.

'Scotland Yard had a call,' he said grudgingly. 'We'll want a statement from you, sir, if you don't mind.'

'A cup of tea first,' I suggested.

His gaze wandered over my face and clothes. I must have looked a wreck. He came somewhere near a smile, and sent a young constable on the errand.

The tea tasted marvellous, though I daresay it wasn't. I drank it slowly and told him fairly briefly what had happened.

'So you didn't see their faces at all, this time?'

'No,' I said.

'Pity.'

'Do you think,' I said tentatively, 'that some one could drive me back to the motel, so I can collect my car?'

'No need, sir,' he said. 'It's parked beside your cottage.'

'What?'

He nodded. 'With a lot of your possessions in it. Suitcase. Wallet. Shoes. Keys. All in the boot. Your assistants notified us on Monday that you were missing again. We sent a man along to your cottage. He reported your car was there, but you weren't. We did what you asked, sir. We did look for you. The whole country's been looking for you, come to that. The motel rang us yesterday to say you'd booked in there last Saturday but hadn't used the room, but apart from that there was nothing to go on. No trace at all. We thought you might have been taken off on another boat, to be frank.'

I finished the tea, and thanked him for it.

'Will you run me back to the cottage, then?'

He thought it could be arranged. He came with me out to the entrance hall, to fix it.

A large man with an over-anxious expression came bustling in from the street, swinging the door wide and assessing rapidly the direction from which he would get most satisfaction. My partner at his most bombastic, his deep voice echoing round the hall as he demanded information.

'Hello, Trevor,' I said. 'Take it easy.'

He stopped in mid-commotion, and stared at me as if I were an intrusive stranger. Then he recognized me, and took in my general appearance, and his face went stiff with shock.

'Ro!' He seemed to have trouble with his voice. 'Ro, my dear fellow. My dear fellow. I've just heard . . . My God, Ro . . .'

I sighed. 'Calm down, Trevor. All I need is a razor.'

'But you're so *thin*.' His eyes were appalled. I reflected

that I was probably a good deal thinner than when he'd seen me last, some time in the dim, distant, and safe past.

'Mr King has been bombarding us all day,' said the Detective Inspector with a touch of impatience.

'My dear Ro, you must come back with me. We'll look after you. My *God*, Ro . . .'

I shook my head. 'I'm fine, Trevor. I'm grateful to you, but I'd really rather go home.'

'Alone?' he said anxiously. 'Suppose . . . I mean . . . do you think it's safe?'

'Oh yes,' I nodded. 'Whoever put me in, let me out. It's all over, I think.'

'What's all over?'

'That,' I said soberly, 'is a whole new ball game.'

The cottage embraced me like a balm.

I had a bath, and shaved, and a grey face of gaunt shadows looked at me out of the mirror. No wonder Trevor had been shocked. Just as well, I thought, that he hadn't seen the black and yellow blotches of fading bruises which covered me from head to foot.

I shrugged, and thought the same as before: nothing that a few days' freedom wouldn't fix. I put on jeans and a jersey and went downstairs in search of a large Scotch, and that was the last peaceful moment of the evening.

The telephone rang non-stop. Reporters, to my amazement, arrived at the doorstep. A television camera appeared. When they saw I was astounded, they said hadn't I read the papers.

'What papers?'

They produced them, and spread them out.

The Sporting Life: headline on Tuesday: 'Where is Roland Britten?' followed by an article about my sea trip, as told by me to friends. I had not been seen since Towcester. Friends were worried.

On Wednesday, paragraphs in all the dailies: 'Tapestry's rider again missing' in one of the staider, and 'Fun Jock Twice Removed?' from a tits-and-bums.

Thursday – that day – many front pages carried a broadly smiling picture of me, taken five minutes after the Gold Cup. 'Find Roland Britten' ordered one, and 'Fears for Jockey's Life' gloomed another. I glanced over them in amazement, remembering ironically that I'd been afraid no one would really look for me at all.

The telephone rang beside my hand. I picked up the receiver and said hello.

'Ro? Is that you?' The voice was fresh and unmistakable.

'Jossie!'

'Where the hell have you been?'

'Have dinner with me tomorrow, and I'll tell you.'

'Pick me up at eight,' she said. 'What's all that noise?'

'I'm pressed by Press,' I said. 'Journalists.'

'Good grief.' She laughed. 'Are you all right?'

'Yes, fine.'

'It was on the news, that you'd been found.'

'I don't believe it.'

'Big stuff, buddy boy.' The mockery was loud and clear.

'Did you start it . . . all this publicity?' I said.

'Not me, no. Moira Longerman. Mrs Tapestry. She tried to get you Sunday, and she tried your office on Monday, and they told her you were missing, and they thought you might have been kidnapped again, so she rang up the editor of *The Sporting Life*, who's a friend of hers, to ask him to help.'

'A determined lady,' I said gratefully.

'She didn't run Tapestry yesterday, you know. There's a sob-stuff bit in *The Sporting Life*. "How can I run my horse while Roland is missing" and all that guff. Fair turns your stomach.'

'Fair turned Binny Tomkins's, I'll bet.'

She laughed. 'I can hear the wolves howling for you. See you tomorrow. Don't vanish before eight.'

I put the telephone down, but the wolves had to wait a little longer, as the bell immediately rang again.

Moira Longerman, excited and twittering, coming down the wire like an electric current.

'Thank heavens you're free. Isn't it marvellous? Are you all right? Can you ride Tapestry on Saturday? Do tell me all about the horrible place where they found you . . . and Roland, dear, I don't want you listening to a word Binny Tomkins says about you not being fit to ride after all you've been through.'

'Moira,' I said, vainly trying to stop the flow. 'Thank you very much.'

'My dear,' she said, 'it was rather *fun*, getting everyone mobilized. Of course I was truly dreadfully worried that something awful had happened to you, and it was quite clear that somebody had to do *something*, otherwise you might stay kidnapped for *weeks*, and it seemed to me that a jolly good fuss was what was wanted. I thought that if the whole country was looking for you, whoever had taken you might get cold feet and turn you loose, and that's precisely what happened, so I was right and the silly police were all wrong.'

'What silly police?' I said.

'Telling me I might have put you in danger by getting *The Sporting Life* to say you'd vanished again. I ask you! They said if kidnappers get panicky they could kill their victim. Anyway, they were wrong, weren't they?'

'Fortunately,' I agreed.

'So do tell me all about it,' she said. 'Is it true you were shut up in a van? What was it like?'

'Boring,' I said.

'Roland, *really*. Is that all you've got to say?'

'I thought about you all day on Wednesday, imagining you'd be furious when I didn't turn up at Ascot.'

'That's better.' She laughed her tinkly laugh. 'You can make up for it on Saturday. Tapestry's in the Oasthouse Cup at Kempton, though of course he's got top weight there, which was why we wanted to run at Ascot instead. But now we're going to Kempton.'

'I'm afraid . . .' I said, 'that Binny's right. This time, I'm really not fit enough. I'd love to ride him, but . . . well . . . at the moment I couldn't go two rounds with a kitten.'

There was a short silence at the other end.

'Do you mean it?' she demanded doubtfully.

'I hate to say so, but I do.'

The doubt in her voice subsided. 'I'm sure you'll be a hundred per cent after a good night's sleep. After all, you'll have nearly two days to recover, and even Binny admits you're pretty tough as amateurs go . . . so *please*, Roland, *please* ride on Saturday, because the horse is jumping out of his skin, and the opposition is not so strong as it will be in the Whitbread Gold Cup in two weeks' time, and I feel in my bones that he'll win this race but not the other. And I don't want Binny putting up any other jockey, as to be frank I only trust you, which you know. So *please* say you will. I was so *thrilled* when I heard you were free, so that you could ride on Saturday.'

I rubbed my hand across my eyes. I knew I shouldn't agree, and that I was highly unlikely to be fit enough even to walk the course on my feet, let alone control half a ton of thoroughbred muscle on the rampage. Yet to her, if I refused, it would seem like gross ingratitude after her lively campaign to free me, and I too suspected that if Tapestry started favourite with a different jockey of Binny's choice, he wouldn't win. There was also the insidious old desire to race which raised its head in defiance of common sense. Reason told me I'd fall off from weakness at the first fence, and the irresistible temptation of a go at another of the season's top 'chases kidded me not to believe it.

'Well . . .' I said, hesitating.

'Oh, you *will*,' she said delightedly. 'Oh Roland, I'm so *glad*.'

'I shouldn't.'

'If you don't win,' she said gaily, 'I promise I won't blame you.'

I'd blame myself, I thought, and I'd deserve it.

I went to the office at nine the next morning, and Trevor fussed about a great deal too much.

'You need rest, Ro. You should be in bed.'

'I need people and life and things to do.'

He sat in the clients' armchair in my office and looked worried. The sun-tan of his holiday suited him, increasing his air of distinction. His silvery hair was fluffier than usual, and his comfortable stomach looked rounder.

'Did you have a good time,' I said, 'in Spain?'

'What? Oh yes, splendid. Splendid. Until the car broke down, of course. And all the time, while we were enjoying ourselves, you . . .' He stopped and shook his head.

'I'm afraid,' I said wryly, 'that I'm dreadfully behind with the work.'

'For heaven's sake . . .'

'I'll try to catch up,' I said.

'I wish you'd take it easy for a few days.' He looked as

if he meant it, his eyes full of troubled concern. 'It won't do either of us any good if you crack up.'

My lips twitched. That was more like the authentic Trevor.

'I'm made of plasticine,' I said; and despite his protests I stayed where I was and once again tried to sort out the trail of broken appointments.

Mr Wells was in a worse mess than ever, having sent a cheque which had promptly bounced. A prosecution for that was in the offing.

'But you knew the bank wouldn't pay it,' I protested when he telephoned with this latest trouble.

'Yes . . . but I thought they *might*.'

His naïvety was frightening: the same stupid hopefulness which had got him enmeshed in the first place. He blanked out reality and believed in fantasies. I'd known others like him, and I'd never known them change.

'Come on Monday afternoon,' I said resignedly.

'Supposing someone kidnaps you again.'

'They won't,' I said. 'Two-thirty, Monday.'

I went through the week's letters with Debbie and sorted out the most urgent. Their complexity made me wilt.

'We'll answer them on Monday morning,' I said.

Debbie fetched some coffee and said at her most pious that I wasn't fit to be at work.

'Did we get those postponements from the Commissioners for Axwood Stables and Coley Young?' I said.

'Yes, they came on Wednesday.'

'And what about Denby Crest's certificate?'

'Mr King said he'd see about that this morning.'

I rubbed a hand over my face. No use kidding myself. However much I disliked it, I did feel pathetically weak. Agreeing to ride Tapestry had been a selfish folly. The only sensible course was to ring Moira Longerman at once, and cry off: but when it came to race-riding, I'd never been sensible.

'Debbie,' I said, 'please would you go down to the store in the basement, and bring up all the old files on Connaught Powys, and on Glitberg and Ownslow.'

'Who?'

I wrote the names down for her. She glanced at them, nodded, and went away.

Sticks Elroy telephoned, words tumbling out in a rush, incoherent and thick with Oxfordshire accent. A lot more talkative than he'd been at dinner in the pub, when overshadowed by his bull-like dad.

'Stop,' I said. 'I didn't hear a word. Say it slowly.'

'I said I was ever so sorry you got shut up in that van.'

'Well . . . thanks.'

'My old man couldn't have done it, you know.' He sounded anxious, more seeking to convince than convinced.

'Don't you think so?'

'I know he said . . . Look, well, he went on cursing all evening, and I know he's got a van, and all, which is off somewhere getting the gearbox fixed, or something, and I know he was that furious, and he said you should be locked up, but I don't reckon he could have done it, not for real.'

'Did you ask him?' I said curiously.

'Yeah.' He hesitated. 'See . . . we had a bloody big row, him and me.' Another pause. 'He always knocked us about when we were kids. Straps, boots, anything.' A pause. 'I asked him about you . . . he punched me in the face.'

'Mm,' I said. 'What did you decide to do about that cash?'

'Yeah, well, that's what the row was about, see. I reckoned you were right and I didn't want any trouble with the law, and Dad blew his top and said I'd never been grateful for everything he'd done for me. He says if I declare that cash and pay tax on it he'll be in trouble himself, see, and I reckon he was mad enough to do anything.'

I reflected a bit. 'What colour is his van?'

'White, sort of. An old Ford.'

'Um. When did you decide to go to that pub for dinner?'

'Dad drove there straight from the races, for a drink, like, and then he phoned and said they could fit us all in for dinner, and we might as well celebrate my win.'

'Would he be likely,' I said, 'to be able to lay his hands on sixty packets of cheese slices?'

'Whatever are you on about?'

I sighed. 'They were in the van with me.'

'Well, I don't know, do I? I don't live with him any

more. I wouldn't reckon on him going to a supermarket, though. Women's work, see?'

'Yes. If you've decided to declare that cash, there are some legitimate expenses to set off against the profit.'

'Bloody tax,' he said. 'Sucks you dry. I'm not going to bother sweating my guts out on any more schemes. Not bloody worth it.'

He made an appointment for the following week and grumbled his way off the phone.

I sat and stared into space, thinking of Sticks Elroy and his violent father. Heavy taxation was always self-defeating, with the country losing progressively more for every tightening of the screw. Overtime and enterprise weren't worth it. Emigration was. The higher the tax rates, the less there was to tax. It was crazy. If I'd been Chancellor, I'd have made Britain a tax haven, and welcomed back all the rich who had taken their money and left. A fifty per cent tax on millions would be better for the country than a ninety-eight per cent on nothing. As it was, I had to interpret and advise in accordance with what I thought of as bad economics; uphold laws which I thought irrational. If the fury the Elroys felt against the system took the form of abuse of the accountant who forced them to face nasty facts, it wasn't unduly surprising. I did doubt though that even Elroy senior would make his abuse physical. Calling me a bastard was a long way from imprisonment.

Debbie came in with her arms full of files and her face full of fluster.

'There's a lady outside who insists on seeing you. She hasn't got an appointment and Mr King said you were definitely not to be worried today, but she won't go away. Oh!'

The lady in question was walking into the office in Debbie's wake. Tall, thin, assured, and middle-aged.

I stood up, smiling, and shook hands with Hilary Margaret Pinlock.

'It's all right, Debbie,' I said.

'Oh, very well.' She shrugged, put down the files, and went out.

'How are you?' I said. 'Sit down.'

Hilary Margaret Pinlock sat in the clients' chair and crossed her thin legs.

'You,' she said, 'look half-dead.'

'A half-empty bottle is also half-full.'

'And you're an optimist?'

'Usually,' I said.

She was wearing a brownish-grey flecked tweed coat, to which the sunless April day added nothing in the way of life. Behind the spectacles the eyes looked small and bright, and coral-pink lipstick lent warmth to her mouth.

'I've come to tell you something,' she said. 'Quite a lot of things, I suppose.'

'Good or bad?'

'Facts.'

'You're not pregnant?'

She was amused. 'I don't know yet.'

'Would you like some sherry?'

'Yes, please.'

I stood up and produced a bottle and two glasses from a filing cupboard. Poured. Handed her a generous slug of Harvey's Luncheon Dry.

'I came home yesterday,' she said. 'I read about you being kidnapped again, on the aeroplane coming back. They had newspapers. Then I heard on the news that you were found, and safe. I thought I would come and see you myself, instead of taking my information to the police.'

'What information?' I said. 'And I thought you were due back home last Saturday.'

She sipped her sherry sedately.

'Yes, I was. I stayed on, though. Because of you. It cost me a fortune.' She looked at me over her glass. 'I was sorry to read you had been recaptured after all. I had seen . . . your fear of it.'

'Mm,' I said ruefully.

'I found out about that boat for you,' she said.

I almost spilled the sherry.

She smiled. 'About the man, to be more exact. The man in the dinghy, who was chasing you.'

'How?' I said.

'After you'd gone, I hired a car and drove to all the places on Minorca where they said yachts could be moored. The nearest good harbour to Cala St Galdana was Ciudadela, and I should think that's where the boat went after they lost you, but it had gone by the time I started looking.' She drank some sherry. 'I asked some

English people on a yacht there, and they said there had been an English crew on a sixty-footer there the night before, and they'd overheard them talking about wind for a passage to Palma. I asked them to describe the captain, and they said there didn't seem to be a proper captain, only a tall young man who looked furious.' She stopped and considered, and explained further. 'All the yachts at Ciudadela were moored at right angles to the quayside, you see. Stern on. So that they were all close together, side by side, and you walked straight off the back of them on to dry land.'

'Yes,' I said. 'I see.'

'So I just walked along the whole row, asking. There were Spaniards, Germans, French, Swedes . . . all sorts. The English people had noticed the other English crew just because they *were* English, if you see what I mean.'

'I do,' I said.

'And also because it had been the biggest yacht that night in the harbour.' She paused. 'So instead of flying home on Saturday, I went to Palma.'

'It's a big place,' I said.

She nodded. 'It took me three days. But I found out that young man's name, and quite a lot about him.'

'Would you like some lunch?' I said.

CHAPTER THIRTEEN

We walked along to La Riviera at the end of the High Street and ordered moussaka. The place was full as usual, and Hilary leaned forward across the table to make herself privately heard. Her strong plain face was full of the interest and vigour she had put into her search on my behalf, and it was typical of her self-confidence that she was concentrating only on the subject in hand and not the impression she was making as a woman. A headmistress, I thought: not a lover.

'His name,' she said, 'is Alastair Yardley. He is one of a whole host of young men who seem to wander around the Mediterranean looking after boats while the owners are home in England, Italy, France, and wherever. They live in the sun, on the water's edge, picking up jobs where they can, and leading an odd sort of drop-out existence which supplies a useful service to boat owners.'

'Sounds attractive.'

'It's bumming around,' she said succinctly.

'I wouldn't mind dropping out, right now,' I said.

'You're made of sterner stuff.'

Plasticine, I thought.

'Go on about Alastair Yardley,' I said.

'I asked around for two days without any success. My description of him seemed to fit half the population, and although I'd seen the boat, of course, I wasn't sure I would know it again, as I haven't an educated eye for that sort of thing. There are two big marinas at Palma, both of them packed with boats. Some boats are moored stern-on, like at Ciudadela, but dozens more were anchored away from the quays. I hired a boatman to take me round the whole harbour in his motorboat, but with no results. I'm sure he thought I was potty. I was pretty discouraged, actually, and was admitting defeat, when he – the boatman, that is – said there was another small harbour less than a day's sail away, and why didn't I look there. So on Wednesday I took a taxi to the port of Andraitx.'

She stopped to eat some moussaka, which had arrived and smelled magnificent.

'Eat,' she said, scooping up a third generous forkful and waving at my still full plate.

'Yes,' I said. It was the first proper meal I'd approached since the dinner with Jossie, and I should have been ravenous. Instead, the diet of processed cheese seemed to have played havoc with my appetite, and I found difficulty in eating much at all. I hadn't been able to face any supper, the evening before, when the journalists had finally gone, and not much breakfast either.

'Tell me about Andraitx,' I said.

'In a minute,' she said. 'I'm not letting this delicious food get cold.' She ate with enjoyment and disapproved of my unsuccessful efforts to do the same. I had to wait for the next instalment until she had finished the last morsel and lain down her fork.

'That was *good*,' she said. 'A great treat.'

'Andraitx,' I said.

She half laughed. 'All right, then. Andraitx. Small by Palma's standards, but bigger than Ciudadela. The small ports and harbours are the old parts of the islands. The buildings are old . . . there are no new ritzy hotels there, because there are no beaches. Deep water, rocky cliffs, and so on. I found out so much more about the islands this week than if I'd stopped in Cala St Galdana for my week and come home last Saturday. They have such a bloody history of battles and sieges and invasions. A horrible violent history. One may sneer now at the way they've been turned into a tourist paradise, but the brassy modern civilization must be better than the murderous past.'

'Dearest Hilary,' I said. 'Cut the lecture and come to the grit.'

'It was the biggest yacht in Andraitx,' she said. 'I was sure almost at once, and then I saw the young man on the quayside, not far from where I paid off the taxi. He came out of a shop and walked across the big open space that there is there, between the buildings and the water. He was carrying a heavy box of provisions. He dumped it on the edge of the quay, beside that black rubber dinghy which he brought ashore at Cala St Galdana. Then he went off again, up a street leading away from the quay. I didn't exactly follow him, I just watched. He went into a doorway a little way up the street, and soon came out again carrying a bundle wrapped in plastic. He went back to the dinghy, and loaded the box and the bundle and himself, and motored out to the yacht.'

The waiter came to take our plates and ask about puddings and coffee.

'Cheese,' Hilary decided.

'Just coffee,' I said. 'And do go on.'

'Well . . . I went into the shop he'd come out of, and asked about him, but they spoke only Spanish, and I don't. So then I walked up the street to the doorway I'd seen him go into, and that was where I hit the jackpot.'

She stopped to cut cheese from a selection on a board. I wondered how long it would be before I liked the stuff again.

'It was a laundry,' she said. 'All white and airy. And run by an English couple who'd gone to Majorca originally for a holiday and fallen in love with the place. A nice couple. Friendly, happy, busy, and very, very helpful. They knew the young man fairly well, they said, because he always took his washing in when he was in Andraitx. They do the boat people's laundry all the time. They reckon to have a bag of dirty clothes washed and ironed in half a day.'

She ate a biscuit and some cheese, and I waited.

'Alastair Yardley,' she said. 'The laundry people said he is a good sailor. Better than most of his kind. He often takes yachts from one place to another, so that they'll be wherever the owner wants. He can handle big boats, and is known for it. He sails into Andraitx four or five times a year, but three years ago he had a flat there, and used it as his base. The laundry people said they don't really know much about him, except that his father worked in a boat-building yard. He told them once that he'd learned to sail as soon as walk, and his first job was as a paid deck-hand in sea-trials for ocean-racing yachts. Apart from that, he hasn't said much about himself or who he's working for now, and the laundry people don't know because they aren't the prying sort, just chatty.'

'You're marvellous,' I said.

'Hm. I took some photographs of the boat, and I've had them processed at an overnight developers.' She opened her handbag, and drew out a yellow packet, which contained, among holiday scenes, three clear colour photographs of my first prison. Three different views, taken as the boat swung round with the tide.

'You can have them, if you like,' she said.

'I could kiss you.'

Her face lit with amusement. 'If you shuffle through that pack, you'll find a rather bad picture of Alastair Yardley. I didn't get the focus right. I was in a bit of a hurry, and he was walking towards me with his laundry, and I didn't want him to think I was taking a picture of him personally. I had to pretend to be taking a general view of the port, you see, and so I'm afraid it isn't very good.'

She had caught him from the waist up, and, as she said, slightly out of focus, but still recognizable to anyone who knew him. Looking ahead, not at the camera, with a white-wrapped bundle under his arm. Even in fuzzy outline, the uncompromising bones gave his face a powerful toughness, a look of aggressive determination. I thought that I might have liked him, if we'd met another way.

'Will you take the photos to the police?' Hilary asked.

'I don't know.' I considered it. 'Could you lend me the negatives, to have more prints made?'

'Sort them out and take them,' she said.

I did that, and we lingered over our coffee.

'I suppose,' she said, 'that you have thought once or twice about . . . the time we spent together?'

'Yes.'

She looked at me with a smile in the spectacled eyes. 'Do you regret it?'

'Of course not. Do you?'

She shook her head. 'It may be too soon to say, but I think it will have changed my entire life.'

'How could it?' I said.

'I think you have released in me an enormous amount of mental energy. I was being held back by feelings of ignorance and even inferiority. These feelings have entirely gone. I feel full of rocket fuel, ready for blast off.'

'Where to?' I said. 'What's higher than a headmistress?'

'Nothing measurable. But my school will be better, and there are such things as power and influence, and the ear of policy makers.'

'Miss Pinlock will be a force in the land?'

'We'll have to see,' she said.

I thought back to the time I'd first slept with a girl, when I was eighteen. It had been a relief to find out what everyone had been going on about, but I couldn't remember any accompanying upsurge of power. Perhaps, for me, the knowledge had come too easily, and too young. More likely that I'd never had the Pinlock potential in the first place.

I paid the bill and went out into the street. The April air was cold, as it had been for the past entire week, and Hilary shivered slightly inside her coat.

'The trouble with warm rooms . . . life blasts you when you leave.'

'Speaking allegorically?' I said.

'Of course.'

We began to walk back towards the office, up the High Street, beside the shops. People scurried in and out of the doorways like bees at a hive mouth. The familiar street scene, after the last three weeks, seemed superficial and unreal.

We drew level with a bank: not, as it happened, the one where I kept my own money, nor that which we used as a firm, but one which dealt with the affairs of many of our clients.

'Would you wait a sec?' I said. 'I've had a thought or two this week . . . just want to check something.'

Hilary smiled and nodded cheerfully, and waited without comment while I went on my short errand.

'OK?' I said, rejoining her.

'Fine,' she said. 'Where did they keep you, in that van?'

'In a warehouse.' I looked at my watch. 'Do you want to see it? I want to go back for another look.'

'All right.'

'My car's behind the office.'

We walked on, past a small, pleasant-looking dress shop. I glanced idly into the window, and walked two strides past, and then stopped.

'Hilary . . .'

'Yes?'

'I want to give you a present.'

'Don't be ridiculous,' she said.

She protested her way into the shop and was reduced to silence only by the sight of what I wanted her to wear: the garment I'd seen in the window; a long bold scarlet cloak.

'Try it,' I said.

Shaking her head, she removed the dull tweed coat and let the girl assistant lower the bright swirling cape on to her shoulders. She stood immobile while the girl fastened the buttons and arranged the neat collar. Looked at herself in the glass.

Duck into swan, I thought. She looked imposing and magnificent, a plain woman transfigured, her height making dramatic folds in the drop of clear red wool.

'Rockets,' I said, 'are powered by flame.'

'You can't buy me this.'

'Why not?'

I wrote the girl a cheque, and Hilary for once seemed to be speechless.

'Keep it on,' I said. 'It looks marvellous.'

The girl packed the old coat into a carrier, and we continued our walk to the office. People looked at Miss Pinlock as they passed, as they had not done before.

'It takes courage,' she said, raising her chin.

'First flights always do.'

She thought instantly of the night in Cala St Galdana: I saw it in the movement of her eyes. She smiled to herself, and straightened a fraction to her full height. Nothing wrong with the Pinlock nerve, then or ever.

From the front the warehouse looked small and dilapidated, its paint peeling off like white scabs to leave uneven grey scars underneath. A weatherboard screwed to the wall offered 10,500 square feet to let, but judging from the aged dimness of the sign, the customers had hardly queued.

The building stood on its own at the end of a side road

which now had no destination, owing to the close-down of the branch railway and the subsequent massive re-organization of the landscape into motorways and roundabouts.

There was a small door let into a large one on rollers at the entrance, neither of them locked. The locks, in fact, appeared to have been smashed, but in time gone by. The splintered wood around them had weathered grey with age.

I pushed open the small door for Hilary, and we stepped in. The gloom as the door swung behind us was as blinding as too much light; I propped the door open with a stone, but even then there were enfolding shadows at every turn. It was clear why vandals had stopped at breaking down the doors. Everything inside was so thick with dust that to kick anything was to start a choking cloud.

Sounds were immediately deadened, as if the high, mouldering piles of junk were soaking up every echo before it could go a yard.

I shouted 'Hey' into the small central space, and it seemed to reach no further than my own throat.

'It's cold in here,' Hilary said. 'Colder than outside.'

'Something to do with ventilation bricks, I expect,' I said. 'A draught, bringing in dust and lowering the temperature.'

Our voices had no resonance. We walked the short distance to where the white van stood, with the dark tarpaulin sprawling in a huge heap beside it.

With eyes adjusting to the dim light, we looked inside. The police had taken the water carrier and the bag of cheese, and the van was empty.

It was a small space. Dirty, and hard.

'You spent nearly a week in there,' Hilary said, disbelievingly.

'Five nights and four and a half days,' I said. 'Let's not exaggerate.'

'Let's not,' she said dryly.

We stood looking at the van for a minute or two, and the deadness and chill of the place began to soak into our brains. I shuddered slightly and walked away, out through the door into the living air.

Hilary followed me, and kicked away the door-stop. The peeling door swung shut.

'Did you sleep well, last night?' she said bleakly.

'No.'

'Nightmares?'

I looked up to the grey sky, and breathed deep luxurious breaths.

'Well . . . dreams,' I said.

She swallowed. 'Why did you want to come back here?'

'To see the name of the estate agent who has this place on his books. It's on the board, on the wall. I wasn't noticing things much when the police took me out of here yesterday.'

She gave a small explosive laugh of escaping tension. 'So practical!'

'Whoever put the van in there knew the place existed,' I said. 'I didn't, and I've lived in Newbury for six years.'

'Leave it to the police,' she said seriously. 'After all, they did find you.'

I shook my head. 'Someone rang Scotland Yard to tell them where I was.'

'Leave it to them,' she urged. 'You're out of it now.'

'I don't know. To coin a cliché, there's a great big iceberg blundering around here, and that van's only the tip.'

We got into my car, and I drove her back to the park in town where she'd left her own. She stood beside it, tall in her scarlet cloak, and fished in her handbag for a pen and notebook.

'Here,' she said, writing. 'This is my address and telephone number. You can come at any time. You might need . . .' She paused an instant, ' . . . a safe place.'

'Can I come for advice?' I said.

'For anything.'

I smiled.

'No,' she said. 'Not for that. I want a memory, not a habit.'

'Take your glasses off,' I said.

'To see you better?' She took them off, humouring me quizzically.

'Why don't you wear contact lenses?' I said. 'Without glasses, your eyes are great.'

*

On the way back to the office I stopped to buy food, on the premise that if I didn't stock up with things I liked, I wouldn't get back to normal eating. I also left Hilary's negatives for a rush reprint, so that it was nearly five before I went through the door.

Debbie and Peter had both done their usual Friday afternoon bolt, for which dentists and classes were only sample reasons. The variety they had come up with over the years would have been valuable if applied to their work: but I knew from experience that if I forced them both to stay until five I got nothing productive done after a quarter past four. Bess, infected by them, had already covered her typewriter, and was busy applying thick new make-up on top of the old. Bess, eighteen and curvy, thought of work as a boring interruption of her sex life. She gave me a bright smile, ran her tongue round the fresh glistening lipstick, and swung her hips provocatively on her way to the weekend's sport.

There were voices in Trevor's room. Trevor's loud voice in short sentences, and a client's softer tones in long paragraphs.

I tidied my own desk, and carried the Glitberg, Ownslow and Connaught Powys files into the outer office on my way to the car.

The door to Trevor's room opened suddenly, and Trevor and his client were revealed there, warmly shaking hands.

The client was Denby Crest, solicitor, a short plump man with a stiff moustache and a mouth permanently twisted in irritation. Even when he smiled at you personally, he gave an impression of annoyance at the state of things in general. Many of his own clients saw that as sympathy for their troubles, which was their mistake.

'I'll make it worth your while, Trevor,' he was saying. 'I'm eternally grateful.'

Trevor suddenly saw me standing there and stared at me blankly.

'I thought you'd gone, Ro,' he said.

'Came back for some files,' I said, glancing down at them in my arms. 'Good afternoon, Denby.'

'Good afternoon, Roland.'

He gave me a brief nod and made a brisk dive for the outer door; a brusque departure, even by his standards. I watched his fast disappearing back and said to Trevor, 'Did you sign his certificate? He said he would wait until you got back.'

'Yes, I did,' Trevor said. He too showed no inclination for leisurely chat, and turned away from me towards his own desk.

'What was I doing wrong?' I said. 'I kept making him fifty thousand pounds short.'

'Decimal point in the wrong place,' he said shortly.

'Show me,' I said.

'Not now, Ro. It's time to go home.'

I put the files down on Bess's desk and walked into Trevor's office. It was larger than mine, and much tidier, with no wall of waiting cardboard boxes. There were three armchairs for clients, some Stubbs prints on the walls, and a bowl of flowering daffodils on his desk.

'Trevor . . .'

He was busy putting together what I recognized as Denby Crest's papers, and didn't look up. I stood in his room, waiting, until in the end he had to take notice. His face was bland, calm, uninformative, and if there had been any tension there a minute ago, it had now evaporated.

'Trevor,' I said. 'Please show me where I went wrong.'

'Leave it, Ro,' he said pleasantly. 'There's a good chap.'

'If you did sign his certificate, and he really is fifty thousand pounds short, then it concerns me too.'

'You're dead tired, Ro, and you look ill, and this is not a good time to discuss it.' He came round his desk and put his hand gently on my arm. 'My dear chap, you know how horrified and worried I am about what has been happening to you. I am most concerned that you should take things easy and recover your strength.'

It was a long speech for him, and confusing. When he saw me hesitate, he added. 'There's nothing wrong with Denby's affairs. We'll go through them, if you like, on Monday.'

'It had better be now,' I said.

'No.' He was stubbornly positive. 'We have friends coming for the evening, and I promised to be home early. Monday, Ro. It will keep perfectly well until Monday.'

I gave in, partly because I simply didn't want to face

what I guessed to be true, that Trevor had signed the certificate knowing the figures were false. I'd done the sums over and over on my cheese abacus, and the answer came monotonously the same, whichever method I used to work them out.

He shepherded me like an uncle to his door, and watched while I picked up the heap of files from Bess's desk.

'What are those?' he said. 'You really mustn't work this weekend.'

'They're not exactly work. They're back files. I just thought I'd take a look.'

He walked over and peered down at the labels, moving the top file to see what was underneath.

'Why these, for heaven's sake?' he said, frowning, coming across Connaught Powys.

'I don't know . . .' I sighed. 'I just thought they might possibly have some connection with my being abducted.'

He looked at me with compassion. 'My dear Ro, why don't you leave it all to the police?'

'I'm not hindering them.' I picked up the armful of files and smiled. 'I don't think I'm high on their urgency list, though. I wasn't robbed, ransomed, or held hostage, and a spot of unlawful imprisonment on its own probably ranks lower than parking on double yellow lines.'

'But,' he said doubtfully, 'don't you think they will ever discover who, or why?'

'It depends on where they look, I should think.' I shrugged a shoulder, walked to the door, and stopped to look back. He was standing by Bess's desk, clearly troubled. 'Trevor,' I said, 'I don't mind one way or the other whether the police come up with answers. I don't madly want public revenge, and I've had my fill of court-case publicity, as a witness. I certainly don't relish it as a victim. But for my own peace of mind, I would like to know. If I find out, I won't necessarily act on the knowledge. The police would have to. So there's the difference. It might be better – you never know – if it's I who did the digging, not the police.'

He shook his head, perturbed and unconvinced.

'See you Monday,' I said.

CHAPTER FOURTEEN

Jossie met me on the doorstep, fizzing with life.

'Dad says please come in for a drink.' She held the door open for me and looked uncertainly at my face. 'Are you all right? I mean . . . I suppose I didn't realize . . .'

I kissed her mouth. Soft and sweet. It made me hungry.

'A drink would be fine,' I said.

William Finch was already pouring Scotch as we walked into his office-sitting-room. He greeted me with a smile and held out the glass.

'You look as if you could do with it,' he said. 'You've been having a rough time, by all accounts.'

'I've a fellow feeling for footballs.' I took the glass, lifted it in a token toast, and sipped the pale fine spirit.

Jossie said, 'Kicked around?'

I nodded, smiling. 'Somebody,' I said, 'is playing a strategic game.'

Finch looked at me curiously. 'Do you know who?'

'Not exactly. Not yet.'

Jossie stood beside her father, pouring grapefruit juice

out of a small bottle. One could see heredity clearly at work: they both had the same tall, well-proportioned frame, the same high carriage of head on long neck, the same air of bending the world to their ways, instead of being themselves bent. He looked at her fondly, a hint of civilized amusement in his fatherly pride. Even her habitual mockery, it seemed, stemmed from him.

He turned his greying head to me again, and said he expected the police would sort out all the troubles, in time.

'I expect so,' I said neutrally.

'And I hope the villains get shut up in small spaces for years and years,' Jossie said.

'Well,' I said, 'they may.'

Finch buried his nose in a large gin and tonic and surfaced with a return to the subject which interested him most. Kidnappings came a poor second to racing.

'My next ride?' I echoed. 'Tomorrow, as a matter of fact. Tapestry runs in the Oasthouse Cup.'

His astonishment scarcely boosted my non-existent confidence. 'Good heavens,' he said. 'I mean, to be frank, Ro, is it wise?'

'Totally not.'

'Then why?'

'I have awful difficulty in saying no.'

Jossie laughed. 'Spineless,' she said.

The door opened and a dark-haired woman came in, walking beautifully in a long black dress. She seemed to move in a glow of her own; and the joy died out of Jossie like an extinguished fire.

Finch went towards the newcomer with a welcoming smile, took her elbow proprietorially, and steered her in my direction. 'Lida, my dear, this is Roland Britten. Ro, Lida Swann.'

A tapeworm with hooks, Jossie had said. The tapeworm had a broad expanse of unlined forehead, dark blue eyes, and raven hair combed smoothly back. As we shook hands, she pressed my fingers warmly. Her heavy, sweet scent broadcast the same message as full breasts, tiny waist, narrow hips, and challenging smile: the sexual woman in full bloom. Diametrically opposite, I reflected, to my own preference for astringency and humour. Jossie watched our polite social exchanges with a scowl, and I wanted to walk over and hug her.

Why not, I thought. I disengaged myself from the sultry aura of Lida, took the necessary steps, and slid my arm firmly round Jossie's waist.

'We'll be off, then,' I said. 'To feed the starving.'

Jossie's scowl persisted across the hall, into the car, and five miles down the road.

'I hate her,' she said. 'That sexy throaty voice . . . it's all put on.'

'It's gin,' I said.

'What?'

'Too much gin alters the vocal chords.'

'You're having me on.'

'I think I love you,' I said.

'That's a damn silly thing to say.'

'Why?'

'You can't love someone just because she hates her father's girlfriend.'

'A better reason than many.'

She turned her big eyes searchingly my way. I kept my own looking straight ahead, dealing with night on the country road.

'Strong men fall for her like ninepins,' she said.

'But I'm weak.'

'Spineless.' She cheered up a good deal, and finally managed a smile. 'Do you want me to come to Kempton tomorrow and cheer you on?'

'Come and give Moira Longerman a double brandy when I fall off.'

Over dinner she said with some seriousness, 'I suppose it's occurred to you that the last twice you've raced, you've been whipped off into black holes straight after?'

'It has,' I said.

'So are you – uh – at all scared, about tomorrow?'

'I'd be surprised if it happened again.'

'Surprise wouldn't help you much.'

'True.'

'You're absolutely infuriating,' she said explosively. 'If you know why you were abducted, why not tell me?'

'I might be wrong, and I want to ask some questions first.'

'What questions?'

'What are you doing on Sunday?'

'That's not a question.'

'Yes, it is,' I said. 'Would you care for a day on the Isle of Wight?'

With guilty misgivings about riding Tapestry I did my best to eat, and later, after leaving Jossie on her doorstep, to go home and sleep. As my system seemed to be stubbornly resisting my intention that it should return to normal, both enterprises met with only partial success. The Saturday morning face in the shaving mirror would have inspired faith in no one, not even Moira herself.

'You're a bloody fool,' I said aloud, and my reflection agreed.

Coffee, boiled egg and toast to the good, I went down into the town to seek out owners of destitute warehouses. The estate agents, busy with hand-holding couples, told me impatiently that they had already given the information to the police.

'Give it to me, too, then,' I said. 'It's hardly a secret, is it?'

The bearded pale-faced man I'd asked looked harried and went off to consult. He came back with a slip of paper which he handed over as if contact with it had sullied his soul.

'We have ceased to act for these people,' he said earnestly. 'Our board should no longer be affixed to the wall.'

I'd never known anyone actually say the word 'affixed'

before. It wasn't all he could say, either. 'We wish to be considered as disassociated from the whole situation.'

I read the words written on the paper. 'I'm sure you do,' I said. 'Could you tell me when you last heard from these people? And has anyone been enquiring recently about hiring or using the warehouse?'

'Those people,' he said disapprovingly, 'appear to have let the warehouse several years ago to some army surplus suppliers, without informing us or paying fees due to us. We have received no instructions from them, then or since, regarding any further letting or sub-letting.'

'Ta ever so,' I said, and went grinning out to the street.

The words on the paper, which had so fussed the agents in retrospect, were 'National Construction (Wessex) Ltd', or in other words the mythical builders invented by Ownslow and Glitberg.

I picked up the rush reprint enlargements of Hilary's photographs, and walked along to the office. All quiet there, as usual on Saturdays, with undone work still sitting reproachfully in heaps.

Averting my eyes, I telephoned the police.

'Any news?' I said; and they said no there wasn't.

'Did you trace the owner of the van?' I asked. No, they hadn't.

'Did it have an engine number?' I said. Yes, they said, but it was not the original number for that particular vehicle, said vehicle having probably passed through many hands and rebuilding processes on its way to the warehouse.

'And have you asked Mr Glitberg and Mr Ownslow what I was doing in a van inside their warehouse?'

There was silence at the other end.

'Have you?' I repeated.

They wanted to know why I should ask.

'Oh come off it,' I said. 'I've been to the estate agents, same as you.'

Mr Glitberg and Mr Ownslow, it appeared, had been totally mystified as to why their warehouse should have been used in such a way. As far as they were concerned, it was let to an army surplus supply company, and the police should direct their enquiries to them.

'Can you find these army surplus people?' I asked. Not so far, they said. They cleared the police throat and cautiously added that Mr Glitberg and Mr Ownslow had categorically denied that they had imprisoned Mr Britten in a van in their warehouse, or anywhere else, for that matter, as revenge for the said Mr Britten having been instrumental in their custodial sentences for fraud.

'Their actual words?' I asked with interest. Not exactly. I had been given the gist.

I thanked them for the information, and disconnected. I thought they had probably not passed on everything they knew, but then neither had I, which made us quits.

The door of Trevor's private office was locked, as mine had been, but we both had keys for each other's rooms. I knew all the same that he wouldn't have been pleased to see me searching uninvited through the papers in his filing cupboard, but I reckoned that as I'd had access to them anyway while he was on holiday, another peep would be no real invasion. I spent a concentrated hour reading cash books and ledgers; and then with a mind functioning more or less as normal I checked through the Denby Crest figures yet again. I had made no mistake with them, even in a daze. Fifty thousand pounds of clients' trust funds were missing. I stared unseeingly at 'Lady and Gentleman in a Carriage' and thought bleakly about consequences.

There was a photocopier in the outer office, busily operated every weekday by Debbie and Peter. I spent another hour of that quiet Saturday morning methodically printing private copies for my own use. Then I put all the books and papers back where I'd found them, locked Trevor's office, and went down to the store in the basement.

The files I was looking for there were easy to find but were slim and uninformative, containing only copies of audits and not all the invoices, cash books and paying-in books from which the accounts had been drawn.

There was nothing odd in that. Under the Companies Act 1976, and also under the value added tax system, all such papers had to be kept available for three years and could legally be thrown away only after that, but most accountants returned the books to their clients for keeping, as like us they simply didn't have enough storage space for everyone.

I left the files where they were, locked all the office doors, sealed my folder of photocopies into a large envelope, and took it with me in some depression to Kempton Park.

The sight of Jossie in her swirly brown skirt brought the sun out considerably, and we despatched grapefruit juice in amicable understanding.

'Dad's brought the detestable Lida,' she said, 'so I came on my own.'

'Does she live with you?' I asked.

'No, thank God.' The idea alarmed her. 'Five miles away, and that's five thousand miles too close.'

'What does the ever-sick secretary have to say about her?'

'Sandy? It makes her even sicker.' She drank the remains of her juice, smiling over the glass. 'Actually Sandy wouldn't be so bad, if she weren't so wet. And you can cast out any slick theories about daughters being possessive of their footloose fathers, because actually I would have liked it rather a lot if he'd fallen for a peach.'

'Does he know you don't like Lida?'

'Oh sure,' she sighed. 'I told him she was a flesh-eating orchid and he said I didn't understand. End of conversation. The funny thing is,' she added, 'that it's only when I'm with you that I can think of her without spitting.'

'Appendicitis diverts the mind from toothache,' I said.

'What?'

'Thoughts from inside little white vans.'

'Half the time,' she said, 'I think you're crazy.'

She met some friends and went off with them, and I repaired to the weighing room to change into breeches, boots, and Moira Longerman's red and white colours. When I came out, with my jacket on over the bright shirt, Binny Tomkins was waiting. On his countenance, the reverse of warmth and light.

'I want to talk to you,' he said.

'Fine. Why not?'

He scowled. 'Not here. Too many people. Walk down this way.' He pointed to the path taken by the horses on their way from parade ring to track: a broad stretch of grass mostly unpopulated by racegoing crowds.

'What is it?' I said, as we emerged from the throng round the weighing room door, and started in the direction he wanted. 'Is there something wrong with Tapestry?'

He shook his head impatiently, as if the idea were silly.

'I want you to give the horse an easy race.'

I stopped walking. An easy race, in those terms, meant trying not to win.

'No,' I said.

'Come on, there's more . . .' He went on a pace or two, looking back and waiting for me to follow. 'I must talk to you. You must listen.'

There was more than usual scowling bad temper in his manner. Something like plain fear. Shaking my head, I went on with him, across the grass.

'How much would you want?' he said.

I stopped again. 'I'm not doing it,' I said.

'I know, but . . . How about two hundred, tax free?'

'You're stupid, Binny.'

'It's all right for you,' he said furiously. 'But if Tapestry wins today I'll lose everything. My yard, my livelihood – everything.'

'Why?'

He was trembling with tension. 'I owe a lot of money.'

'To bookmakers?' I said.

'Of course to bookmakers.'

'You're a fool,' I said flatly.

'Smug bastard,' he said furiously. 'I'd give anything to have you back inside that van, and not here today.'

I looked at him thoughtfully. 'Tapestry may not win anyway,' I said. 'Nothing's a certainty.'

'I've got to know in advance,' he said incautiously.

'And if you assure your bookmaker Tapestry won't win, he'll let you off the hook?'

'He'll let me off a bit,' he said. 'He won't press for the rest.'

'Until next time,' I said. 'Until you're in deeper still.'

Binny's eyes stared inwards to the hopeless future, and I guessed he would never take the first step back to firm ground, which was in his case to stop gambling altogether.

'There are easier ways for trainers to lose races,' I pointed out, 'than trying to bribe the jockey.'

His scowl reached Neanderthal proportions. 'She pays the lad who does her horse to watch him like a hawk and give her a report on everything that happens. I can't sack him or change him to another horse, because she says if I do she'll send Tapestry to another trainer.'

'I'm amazed she hasn't already,' I said: and she would have done, I thought, if she'd been able to hear that conversation.

'You've only got to ride a bad race,' he said. 'Get boxed in down the far side and swing wide coming into the straight.'

'No,' I said. 'Not on purpose.'

I seemed to be remarkably good at inspiring fury. Binny would happily have seen me fall dead at his feet.

'Look,' I said, 'I'm sorry about the fix you're in. I really am, whether you believe it or not. But I'm not going to try to get you out of it by cheating Moira or the horse or the punters or myself, and that's that.'

'You *bastard*,' he said.

Five minutes later, when I was back in the hub of the racecourse outside the weighing room, a hand touched me on the arm and a drawly voice spoke behind my ear.

'My dear Ro, what are your chances?'

I turned, smiling, to the intelligent face of Vivian Iverson. In the daylight on a racecourse, where I'd first met him, he wore his clothes with the same elegance and flair that he had extended to his Vivat Club. Dark green blazer over grey checked trousers; hair shining black in the April sun. Quiet amusement in the observant eyes.

'In love, war, or the three-thirty?' I said.

'Of remaining at liberty, my dear chap.'

I blinked. 'Um,' I said. 'What would you offer?'

'Five to four against?'

'I hope you're wrong,' I said.

Underneath the banter, he was detectably serious. 'It just so happens that last night in the club I heard our friend Connaught Powys talking on the telephone. To be frank, my dear Ro, after I'd heard your name mentioned, I more or less deliberately *listened*.'

'On an extension?'

'Tut tut,' he said reprovingly. 'Unfortunately not. I don't know who he was talking to. But he said – his exact words – "As far as Britten is concerned you must agree that precaution is better than cure," and a bit later he said "If dogs start sniffing around, the best thing to do is chain them up." '

'Charming,' I said blankly.

'Do you need a bodyguard?'

'Are you offering yourself?'

He shook his head, smiling. 'I could hire you one. Karate. Bulletproof glass. All the mod cons.'

'I think,' I said thoughtfully, 'that I'll just increase the insurance policies.'

'Against kidnapping? No one will take you on.'

'Checks and balances,' I said. 'No one'll push me off a spring-board if it means a rock falling on their own head.'

'Be sure to let them know the rock exists.'

'Your advice,' I said, smiling, 'is worth its weight in ocean-going sailing boats.'

*

Moira Longerman twinkled with her bright bird-eyes in the parade ring before Tapestry's race and stroked my arm repeatedly, her small thin hand sliding delicately over the shiny scarlet sleeve.

'Now, Roland, you'll do your best, I know you'll do your best.'

'Yes,' I said guiltily, flexing several flabby muscles and watching Tapestry's highly tuned ones ripple under his coat as he walked round the ring with his lad.

'I saw you talking to Binny just now, Roland.'

'Did you, Moira?' I switched my gaze to her face.

'Yes, I did.' She nodded brightly. 'I was up in the stands, up there in the bar, looking down to the paddock. I saw Binny take you away for a talk.'

She looked at me steadily, shrewdly, asking the vital question in total silence. Her hand went on stroking. She waited intently, expecting an answer.

'I promise you,' I said plainly, 'that if I make a hash of it, it'll be against my will.'

She stopped stroking, patted my arm instead, and smiled. 'That will do nicely, Roland.'

Binny stood ten feet away, unable to make even a show of the civility due from trainer to owner. His face was rigid, his eyes expressionless, and even the usual scowl had frozen into a more general and powerful gloom. I thought I had probably been wrong to think of Binny as a stupid fool. There was something about him at that moment which raised prickles on the skin and images of murder.

The bell rang for jockeys to mount, and it was the lad, not Binny, who gave me a leg-up into the saddle.

'I'm not going to take much more of this,' Moira said pleasantly to the world in general.

Binny ignored her as if he hadn't heard; and maybe he hadn't. He'd also given me no riding instructions, which I didn't mind in the least. He seemed wholly withdrawn and unresponsive, and when Moira waved briefly as I walked away on Tapestry, he did not accompany her across to the stands. Even for him, his behaviour was incredible.

Tapestry himself was in a great mood, tossing his head with excitement and bouncing along in tiny cantering strides as if he had April spring fever in all his veins. I remembered his plunging start in the Gold Cup and realized that this time I'd be lucky if he didn't bolt with me from the post. Far from being last from indecision, this time, in my weakened state, I could be forty lengths in front by the second fence, throwing away all chance of staying power at the end.

Tapestry bounced gently on his toes in the parade past the stands, while the other runners walked. Bounced playfully back at a canter to the start, which in three mile 'chases at Kempton Park was to the left of the stands and in full view of most of the crowd.

There were eleven other jockeys walking around there, making final adjustments to girths and goggles and answering to the starter's roll call. The starter's assistant, tightening the girths of the horse beside me, looked over his shoulder and asked me if mine were all right, or should he tighten those too.

If I hadn't recently been through so many wringers, I would simply have said yes, and he would have pulled the buckles up a notch or two, and I wouldn't have given it another thought. As it was, in my over-cautious state, I had a sudden sharp vision of Binny's dangerous detachment, and remembered the desperation behind his appeal to me to lose. The prickles returned in force.

I slid off Tapestry's back and looped his reins over my arm.

'Just want to check . . .' I said vaguely to the starter's assistant.

He nodded briefly, glancing at his watch. One minute to racetime, his face said, so hurry up.

It was my own saddle. I intimately knew its every flap, buckle, scratch and stain. I checked it thoroughly inch by inch with fingers and eyes, and could see nothing wrong. Girths, stirrups, leathers, buckles; everything as it should be. I pulled the girths tighter myself, and the starter told me to get mounted.

Looking over my shoulder, I thought, for the rest of my life. Seeing demons in shadows. But the feeling of danger wouldn't go away.

'Hurry up, Britten.'

'Yes, sir.'

I stood on the ground, looking at Tapestry tossing his head.

'*Britten!*'

Reins, I thought. Bridle. Bit Reins. If the bridle broke, I couldn't control the horse and he wouldn't win the race. Many races had been lost, from broken bridles.

It was not too difficult to see, if one looked really closely. The leather reins were stitched on to the rings at each side of the bit, and the stitches on the off-side rein had nearly all been severed.

Three miles and twenty fences at bucketing speed with just two strands of thread holding my right-hand rein.

'*Britten!*'

I gave a jerking tug, and the remaining stitches came apart in my hand. I pulled the rein off the ring and waved the free end in the air.

'Sorry, sir,' I said. 'I need another bridle.'

'What? Oh very well . . .' He used his telephone to call the weighing room to send a replacement out quickly. Tapestry's lad appeared, looking worried, to help change the headpiece, and I pointed out to him, as I gave him Binny's bridle, the parted stitching.

'I don't know how it could have got like that,' he said anxiously. 'I didn't know it was like that, honest. I cleaned it yesterday, and all.'

'Don't worry,' I said. 'It's not your fault.'

'Yes, but . . .'

'Give me a leg-up,' I said, 'and don't worry.'

He continued all the same to look upset. Good lads took it grievously to heart if anything was proved lacking in the way they turned out their horses, and Tapestry's lad was as good as the horse deserved. Binny, I thought not for the first time, was an all-out, one-man disaster area, a blight to himself and everyone around.

'Line up,' shouted the starter, with his hand on the lever. 'We're five minutes late.'

Tapestry did his best to put that right two seconds later with another arm-wrenching departure, but owing to one or two equally impetuous opponents I thankfully got him anchored in mid-field; and there we stayed for all of the first circuit. The pace, once we'd settled down, was nothing like as fast as the Gold Cup, and I had time to worry about the more usual things, like meeting the fences right, and not running out altogether, which was an added hazard at Kempton where the wings leading to the fences were smaller and lower than on other courses, and tended to give tricky horses bad ideas.

During the second circuit my state of unfitness raised its ugly head in no uncertain way, and it would be fair to say that for the last mile Tapestry's jockey did little except cling on. Tapestry truly was, however, a great performer, and in consequence of the cheers and acclaim in the unsaddling enclosure after the Gold Cup, he seemed, like many much-fêted horses, to have become conscious of his own star status. It was the extra dimension of his new pride which took us in a straight faultless run over the last three fences in the straight, and his own will to win which extended his neck and his stride on the run-in. Tapestry won the Oasthouse Cup by four lengths, and it was all the horse's doing, not mine.

Moira kissed her horse with tears running down her

cheeks, and kissed me as well, and everyone else within mouth-shot, indiscriminately. There was nothing uptight or inhibited about the Longerman joy, and the most notable person not there to share it was the horse's trainer. Binny Tomkins was nowhere to be seen.

'Drink,' Moira shrieked at me. 'Owners and trainers bar.'

I nodded, speechless from exertion and back-slapping, and struggled through the throng with my saddle to be weighed in. It was fabulous, I thought dazedly; fantastic, winning another big race. More than I'd ever reckoned possible. A bursting delight like no other on earth. Even knowing how little I'd contributed couldn't dampen the wild inner rejoicing. I'd never be able to give it up, I thought. I'd still be struggling round in the mud and the rain at fifty, chasing the marvellous dream. Addiction wasn't only a matter of needles in the arm.

Moira in the bar was dispensing champagne and bright laughs in copious quantities, and had taken Jossie closely in tow.

'Ro, darling Ro,' Moira said, 'have you seen Binny anywhere?'

'No, I haven't.'

'Wasn't it odd, the bridle breaking like that?' Her innocent-seeming eyes stared up into my own. 'I talked to the lad, you see.'

'These things do happen,' I said.

'You mean, no one can prove anything?'

'Roughly that.'

'But aren't you the teeniest bit angry?'

I smiled from the glowing inner pleasure. 'We won the race. What else matters?'

She shook her head. 'It was a wicked thing to do.'

Desperation, I thought, could spawn deeds the doers wouldn't sanely contemplate. Like cutting loose a rein. Like kidnapping the enemy. Like whatever else lay ahead before we were done. I shut out the shadowy devils and drank to life and the Oasthouse Cup.

Jossie, too, had a go at me when we wandered later out to the car park.

'Is Moira right?' she demanded. 'Did Binny rig it for you to come to grief?'

'I should think so.'

'She says you ought to report it.'

'There's no need.'

'Why not?'

'He's programmed to self-destruct before the end of the season.'

'Do you mean *suicide*?' she said.

'You're too literal. I mean he'll go bust to the bookies with a reverberating bang.'

'You're drunk.'

I shook my head, grinning. 'High. Quite different. Care to join me on my cloud?'

'A puff of wind,' she said, 'and you'd evaporate.'

CHAPTER FIFTEEN

Jossie drove off to some party or other in London, and I, mindful of earlier unscheduled destinations after racing, took myself circumspectly down the road to the nearest public telephone box. No one followed, that I could see.

Hilary Margaret Pinlock answered at the twentieth ring, when I had all but given up, and said breathlessly that she had only that second reached home; she'd been out playing tennis.

'Are you busy this evening?' I said.

'Nothing special.'

'Can I come and see you?'

'Yes.' She hesitated a fraction. 'What do you want? Food? A bed?'

'An ear,' I said. 'And baked beans, perhaps. But no bed.'

'Right,' she said calmly. 'Where are you? Do you need directions?'

She told me clearly how to find her, and I drew up forty minutes later outside a large Edwardian house in a leafy road on the outskirts of a sprawling Surrey town.

Hilary, it transpired, owned the ground floor, a matter of two large, high-ceilinged rooms, modern kitchen, functional bathroom, and a pleasant old-fashioned conservatory with plants, cane armchairs, and steps down to an unkempt garden.

Inside, everything was orderly and organized, and comfortable in an uninspired sort of way. Well-built easy chairs in dim covers, heavy curtains in good velvet but of a deadening colour somewhere between brown and green, patterned carpet in olive and fawn. The home of a vigorous academic mind with no inborn response to refracted light. I wondered just how much she would wear the alien scarlet cloak.

The evening sun still shone into the conservatory, and there we sat, in the cane armchairs, drinking sherry, greenly surrounded by palms and rubber plants and *Monstera deliciosa*.

'I don't mind *watering*,' Hilary said. 'But I detest *gardening*. The people upstairs are supposed to do the garden, but they don't.' She waved disgustedly towards the view of straggly bushes, unpruned roses, weedy paths, and dried coffee-coloured stalks of last year's unmown grass.

'It's better than concrete,' I said.

'I'll use you as a parable for the children,' she said, smiling.

'Hm?'

'When things are bad, you endure what you must, and thank God it's not worse.'

I made a protesting sound in my throat, much taken aback. 'Well,' I said helplessly, 'what else is there to do?'

'Go screaming off to the Social Services.'

'For a gardener?'

'You know darned well what I mean.'

'Endurance is like tax,' I said. 'You're silly to pay more than you have to, but you can't always escape it.'

'And you can whine,' she said, nodding, 'or suffer with good grace.'

She drank her sherry collectedly and invited me to say why I'd come.

'To ask you to keep a parcel safe for me,' I said.

'But of course.'

'And to listen to a fairly long tale, so that . . .' I paused. 'I mean, I want someone to know . . .' I stopped once more.

'In case you disappear again?' she said matter-of-factly.

I was grateful for her calmness.

'Yes,' I said. I told her about meeting Vivian Iverson at the races, and our thoughts on insurance, springboards, and rocks. 'So you see,' I ended, 'you'll be the rock, if you will.'

'You can expect,' she said, 'rock-like behaviour.'

'Well,' I said, 'I've brought a sealed package of photocopied documents. It's in the car.'

'Fetch it,' she said.

I went out to the street and collected the thick envelope from the boot. Habit induced me to look into the back seat floor space, and to scan the harmless street. No one hiding, no one watching, that I could see. No one had followed me from the racecourse, I was sure.

Looking over my shoulder for the rest of my life.

I took the parcel indoors and gave it to Hilary, and also the negatives of her photographs, explaining that I already had the extra prints. She put everything on the table beside her and told me to sit down and get on with the tale.

'I'll tell you a bit about my job,' I said. 'And then you'll understand better.' I stretched out with luxurious weariness in the cane chair and looked at the intent interest on her strong plain face. A pity, I thought, about the glasses.

'An accountant working for a long time in one area, particularly in an area like a country town, tends to get an overall picture of the local life.'

'I follow you,' she said. 'Go on.'

'The transactions of one client tend to turn up in the accounts of others. For instance, a racehorse trainer buys horse food from the forage merchants. I check the invoice through the trainer's accounts, and then, because the forage merchant is also my client, I later check it again through his. I see that the forage merchant has paid a builder for an extension to his house, and later, in the builder's accounts, I see what *he* paid for the bricks and cement. I see that a jockey had paid *x* pounds on an air-taxi, and later, because the air-taxi firm is also my client, I see the receipt of *x* pounds from the jockey. I see the movement of money around the neighbourhood . . . the interlocking of interests . . . the pattern of commerce. I learn the names of suppliers, the size of businesses, and the kinds of services people use. My knowledge increases until I have a sort of mental map like a wide landscape, in which all the names are familiar and occur in the proper places.'

'Fascinating,' Hilary said.

'Well,' I said, 'if a totally strange name crops up, and you can't cross-reference it with anything else, you begin to ask questions. At first of yourself, and then of others. Discreetly. And that was how I ran into trouble in the shape of two master criminals called Glitberg and Ownslow.'

'They sound like a music-hall turn.'

'They're as funny as the Black Death.' I drank some sherry ruefully. 'They worked for the council, and the council's accounts and audits were done by a large firm in London, who naturally didn't have any intimate local knowledge. Ownslow and Glitberg had invented a construction firm called National Construction (Wessex) Limited, through which they had syphoned off more than a million pounds each of taxpayers' money. And I had a client, a builders' merchant, who had received several cheques from National Construction (Wessex). I'd never heard of National Construction (Wessex) in any other context, and I asked my client some searching questions, to which his reply was unmistakable panic. Glitberg and

Ownslow were prosecuted and went to jail swearing to be revenged.'

'On you?'

'On me.'

'Nasty.'

'A few weeks later,' I said, 'much the same thing happened. I turned up some odd payments made by a director of an electronics firm through the company's computer. His name was Connaught Powys. He'd taken his firm for over a quarter of a million, and he too went to jail swearing to get even. He's out again now, and so are Glitberg and Ownslow. Since then I've been the basic cause of the downfall of two more big-time embezzlers, both of whom descended to the cells swearing severally to tear my guts out and cut my throat.' I sighed. 'Luckily, they're both still inside.'

'And I thought accountants led dull lives!'

'Maybe some do.' I drained my sherry. 'There's another thing that those five embezzlers have in common besides me, and that is that not a penny of what they stole has been recovered.'

'Really?' She seemed not to find it greatly significant. 'I expect it's all sitting around in bank deposits, under different names.'

I shook my head. 'Not unless it is in literally thousands of tiny weeny deposits, which doesn't seem likely.'

'Why thousands?'

'Banks nowadays have to inform the Tax Inspectors of the existence of any deposit account for which the annual interest is £15 or more. That means the Inspectors know of all deposits of over three or four hundred quid.'

'I had no idea,' she said blankly.

'Anyway,' I said, 'I wanted to know if it could be Powys or Glitberg or Ownslow who had kidnapped me for revenge, so I asked them.'

'Good heavens.'

'Yeah. It wasn't a good idea. They wouldn't say yes or no.' I looked back to the night at the Vivat Club. 'They did tell me something else, though . . .' I said, and told Hilary what it was. Her eyes widened behind the glasses and she nodded once or twice.

'I see. Yes,' she said.

'So now,' I said. 'Here we are a few years later, and now I have not only my local area mental map but a broad view of most of the racing world, with uncountable interconnections. I do the accounts for so many racing people, their lives spread out like a carpet, touching, overlapping, each small transaction adding to my understanding of the whole. I'm part of it myself, as a jockey. I feel the fabric around me. I know how much saddles cost, and which saddler does most business, and which owners don't pay their bills, and who bets and who drinks, who saves, who gives to charity, who keeps a mistress. I know how much the woman whose horse I rode today paid to have him photographed for the Christmas cards she sent last year, and how much a bookmaker gave for his Rolls, and thousands and thousands of similar facts. All fitting, all harmless. It's when they don't fit . . . like a jockey suddenly spending more than he's earned, and I find he's running a whole new business and not declaring a penny of it . . . it's when the bits don't fit that I see the monster in the waves. Glimpsed, hidden . . . But definitely there.'

'Like now?' she said, frowning. 'Your iceberg?'

'Mm.' I hesitated. 'Another embezzler.'

'And this one – will he too go to jail swearing to cut your throat?'

I didn't answer at once, and she added dryly, 'Or is he likely to cut your throat before you get him there?'

I gave her half a grin. 'Not with a rock like you, he won't.'

'You be careful, Roland,' she said seriously. 'This doesn't feel to me like a joke.'

She stood up restlessly, towering among the palm fronds, as thin in her way as their stems.

'Come into the kitchen. What do you want to eat? I can do a Spanish omelette, if you like.'

I sat with my elbows on the kitchen table, and while she chopped onions and potatoes and green peppers I told her a good deal more, most of it highly unethical, as an accountant should never disclose the affairs of a client. She listened with increasing dismay, her cooking actions growing slower. Finally she laid down the knife and simply stood.

'Your partner,' she said.

'I don't know how much he's condoned,' I said, 'but on Monday . . . I have to find out.'

'Tell the police,' she said. 'Let them find out.'

'No. I've worked with Trevor for six years. We've always got on well together, and he seems fond of me, in his distant way. I can't shop him, just like that.'

'You'll warn him.'

'Yes,' I said. 'And I'll tell him of the existence of . . . the rock.'

She started cooking again, automatically, her thoughts busy behind her eyes.

'Do you think,' she said, 'that your partner knew about the other embezzlers, and tried to hush them up?'

I shook my head. 'Not Glitberg and Ownslow. Positively not. Not the last two, either. The firms they worked for were both my clients, and Trevor had no contact with them. But Connaught Powys . . .' I sighed. 'I really don't know. Trevor always used to spend about a week at that firm, doing the audit on the spot, as one nearly always does for big concerns, and I went one year only because he had an ulcer. It was Connaught Powys's bad luck that I cottoned on to what he was doing. Trevor might genuinely have missed the warning signs, because he doesn't always work the way I do.'

'How do you mean?'

'Well, a lot of an accountant's work is fairly mechanical. Vouching, for instance. That's checking that cheques written down in the cash book really were issued for the amount stated or, in other words, if the cashier writes down that cheque number 1234 was issued to Joe Bloggs in the sum of eighty pounds to pay for a load of sand, the auditor checks that the bank actually paid eighty pounds to Joe Bloggs on cheque no. 1234. It's routine work and takes a fairly long time on a big account, and it's often, or even usually, done, not by the accountant or auditor himself, but by an assistant. Assistants in our firm tend to come and go, and don't necessarily develop a sense of probability. The present ones wouldn't be likely to query, for instance, whether Joe Bloggs really existed, or sold sand, or sold eighty quid's worth, or delivered only fifty quid's worth, with Joe Bloggs and the cashier conspiring to pocket the thirty pounds profit.'

'Roland!'

I grinned. 'Small fiddles abound. It's the first violins that threaten to cut your throat.'

She broke four eggs into a bowl. 'Do you do all your own . . . er . . . vouching, then?'

'No, not all. It would take too long. But I do all of it for some accounts, and some of it for all accounts. To get the feel of things. To know where I am.'

'To fit into the landscape,' she said.

'Yes.'

'And Trevor doesn't?'

'He does a few himself, but on the whole not. Don't get me wrong. More accountants do as Trevor does, it's absolutely normal practice.'

'You want my advice?' she said.

'Yes, please.'

'Go straight to the police.'

'Thank you. Get on with the omelette.'

She sizzled it in the pan and divided it, succulent and

soft in the centre, onto the plates. It tasted like a testimonial to her own efficiency, the best I'd ever had. Over coffee, afterwards, I told her a great deal about Jossie.

She looked into her cup. 'Do you love her?' she said.

'I don't know. It's too soon to say.'

'You sound,' she said dryly, 'bewitched.'

'There have been other girls. But not the same.' I looked at her downturned face. My mouth twitched. 'In case you're wondering about Jossie,' I said, 'no, I haven't.'

She looked up, the spectacles flashing, her eyes suddenly laughing, and a blush starting on her neck. She uttered an unheadmistressly opinion.

'You're a sod,' she said.

It was an hour's drive home from Hilary's house. No one followed me, or took the slightest interest, that I could see.

I rolled quietly down the lane towards the cottage with the car lights switched off, and made a silent reconnoitre on foot for the last hundred yards.

Everything about my home was dark and peaceful. The lights of Mrs Morris's sitting-room, next door, shone dimly through the pattern of her curtains. The night sky was powdered with stars, and the air was cool.

I waited for a while, listening, and was slowly reassured. No horrors in the shadows. No shattering black prisons yawning like mantraps before my feet. No cut-throats with ready steel.

To be afraid, I thought, was no way to live; yet I couldn't help it.

I unlocked the cottage and switched on all the lights; and it was empty, welcoming and sane. I fetched the car from the lane, locked myself into the cottage, pulled shut the curtains, switched on the heaters, and hugged round myself the comforting illusion of being safe in the burrow.

After that I made a pot of coffee, fished out some brandy, and sprawled into an armchair with the ancient records of the misdeeds of Powys, Glitberg and Ownslow.

At one time I'd known every detail in those files with blinding clarity, but the years had blurred my memory. I found notes in my own handwriting about inferences I couldn't remember drawing, and conclusions as startling as acid. I was amazed, actually, at the quality of work I'd done, and it was weird to see it from an objective distance, as with a totally fresh eye. I supposed I could understand the comment there had been then, though at the time what I was doing had seemed a perfectly natural piece of work, done merely as best I could. I smiled to myself in pleased surprise. In that far-off time, I must have been hell to embezzlers. Not like nowadays, when it took me six shots to see Denby Crest.

I came across pages of notes about the workings of computers, details of which I had forgotten as fast as I'd learned them on a crash course in an electronics firm much like Powys's. It had pleased me at the time to be able to dissect and explain just what he'd done, and nothing had made him more furious. It had been vanity on my part, I thought: and I was still vain. Admiring your own work was one of the deadlier intellectual sins.

I sighed. I was never going to be perfect, so why worry.

There was no record anywhere in the Glitberg/Ownslow file of the buying of the warehouse, but it did seem possible, as I dug deeper in the search for clues, that it actually had been built by Glitberg and Ownslow, and was the sole concrete fabrication of National Construction (Wessex). Anyone who could invent whole streets of dwellings could put up a real warehouse without much trouble.

I wondered why they'd needed it, when everything else had been achieved on paper.

A tangible asset, uncashed, gone to seed, in which I had been dumped. The police had been told I was there, and the estate agent trail had led without difficulty straight to Ownslow and Glitberg.

Why?

I sat and thought about it for a good long time, and then I finished the coffee and brandy and went to bed.

I picked Jossie up at ten in the grey morning, and drove to Portsmouth for the hovercraft ferry to the Isle of Wight.

'The nostalgia kick?' Jossie said. 'Back to the boarding house?'

I nodded. 'The sunny isle of childhood.'

'Oh yeah?' She took me literally and looked up meaningfully at the cloudy sky.

'It heads the British sunshine league,' I said.

'Tell that to Torquay.'

A ten-minute zip in the hovercraft took us across the sea at Spithead, and when we stepped ashore at Ryde, the clouds were behind us, hovering like a grey sheet over the mainland.

'It's unfair,' Jossie said, smiling.

'It's often like that.'

The town was bright with new spring paint, the Regency buildings clean and graceful in the sun. Every year, before the holiday-makers came, there was the big brush-up and every winter, when they'd gone, the comfortable relapse into carpet slippers and salt-caked windows.

'Ryde pier,' I said, 'is two thousand, three hundred and five feet long, and was opened in 1814.'

'I don't want to know that.'

'There are approximately six hundred hotels, motels and boarding houses on this sunny island.'

'Nor that.'

'Nine towns, two castles, a lot of flamingoes and Parkhurst Prison.'

'Nor that, for God's sake.'

'My Uncle Rufus,' I said, 'was chief mucker-out at the local riding school.'

'Good grief.'

'As his assistant mucker-out,' I said, 'I scrambled under horses' bellies from the age of six.'

'That figures.'

'I used to exercise the horses and ponies all winter when the holiday people had gone home. And break in new ones. I can't really remember not being able to ride, but there's no racing here, of course. The first race I ever rode in was the Isle of Wight Foxhounds point-to-point over on the mainland, and I fell off.'

We walked along the Esplanade with the breeze blowing Jossie's long green scarf out like streamers. She waved an arm at the sparkling water and said, 'Why horses? Why not boats, for heaven's sake, when you had them on your doorstep.'

'They made me seasick.'

She laughed. 'Like going to heaven and being allergic to harps.'

I took her to a hotel I knew, where there was a sunny terrace sheltered from the breeze, with a stunning view of the Solent and the shipping tramping by to Southampton. We drank hot chocolate and read the lunch menu, and talked of this and that and nothing much, and the time slid away like a mill-stream.

After roast beef for both of us, and apple pie, ice-cream and cheese for Jossie, we whistled up a taxi. There weren't many operating on a Sunday afternoon in April, but there was no point in being a native if one didn't know where to find the pearls.

The driver knew me, and didn't approve of my having deserted to become a 'mainlander', but as he also knew I knew the roads backwards, we got a straight run over Blackgang Chine to the wild cliffs on the south-west coast, and no roundabout guff to add mileage. We dawdled along there for about an hour, stopping often to stand out of the car, on the windswept grass. Jossie took in great lungfuls of the soul-filling landscape and said whyever did I live in Newbury.

'Racing,' I said.

'So simple.'

'Do you mind if we call on a friend on the way back?' I said. 'Ten minutes or so?'

'Of course not.'

'Wootton Bridge, then,' I said to the driver. 'Frederick's boatyard.'

'They'll be shut. It's Sunday.'

'We'll try, anyway.'

He shrugged heavily, leaving me to the consequences of my own stupidity, and drove back across the island, through Newport and out on the Ryde road to the deep inlet which formed a natural harbour for hundreds of small yachts.

The white-painted façade of the boatyard showed closed doors and no sign of life.

'There you are,' said the driver. 'I told you so.'

I got out of the car and walked over to the door

marked 'Office', and knocked on it. Within a few moments it opened, and I grinned back to Jossie and jerked my head for her to join me.

'I got your message,' Johnny Frederick said. 'And Sunday afternoon, I sleep.'

'At your age?'

His age was the same as mine, almost to the day: we'd shared a desk at school and many a snigger in the lavatories. The round-faced, impish boy had grown into a muscular, salt-tanned man with craftsman's hands and a respectable hatred of paperwork. He occasionally telephoned me to find out if his own local accountant was doing things right, and bombarded the poor man with my advice.

'How's your father?' I said.

'Much the same.'

A balk of timber had fallen on Johnny's father's head in days gone by. There had been a lot of unkind jokes about thick as two planks before, three planks after, but the net result had been that an ailing family business had woken up in the hands of a bright new mind. With Johnny's designs and feeling for materials, Frederick Boats were a growing name.

I introduced Jossie, who got a shrewd once-over for aerodynamic lines and a shake from a hand like a piece of calloused teak.

'Pleased to meet you,' he said, which was about the nearest he ever got to social small-talk. He switched his gaze to me. 'You've been in the wars a bit, according to the papers.'

'You might say so.' I grinned. 'What are you building, these days?'

'Come and see.'

He walked across the functional little office and opened the far door, which led straight into the boatyard itself. We went through, and Jossie exclaimed aloud at the unexpected size of the huge shed which sloped away down to the water.

There were several smallish fibreglass hulls supported in building frames, and two large ones, side by side in the centre, with five-foot keels.

'What size are those?' Jossie said.

'Thirty-seven feet overall.'

'They look bigger.'

'They won't on the water. It's the largest size we do, at present.' Johnny walked us round one of them, pointing out subtleties of hull design with pride. 'It handles well in heavy seas. It's stable, and not too difficult to sail, which is what most people want.'

'Not a racer?' I said.

He shook his head. 'Those dinghies are. But the big ocean-racers are specialist jobs. This yard isn't large enough; not geared to that class. And anyway, I like cruisers. A bit of carpet in the saloon and lockers that slide like silk.'

Jossie wandered off down the concrete slope, peering into the half-fitted dinghies and looking contentedly interested. I pulled the envelope of enlarged photographs from my inner pocket and showed them to Johnny. Three views of a sailing boat, one of an out-of-focus man.

'That's the boat I was abducted on. Can you tell anything about it from these photos?'

He peered at them, his head on one side. 'If you leave them with me, maybe. I'll look through the catalogues, and ask the boys over at Cowes. Was there anything special about it, that you remember?'

I explained that I hadn't seen much except the sail locker. 'The boat was pretty new, I think. Or at any rate well maintained. And it sailed from England on Thursday, March 17th, some time in the evening.'

He shuffled the prints to look at the man.

'His name is Alastair Yardley,' I said. 'I've written it on the back. He came from Bristol, and worked from there as a deck-hand on sea-trials for ocean-going yachts. He skippered the boat. He's about our age.'

'Are you in a hurry for all this info?'

'Quicker the better.'

'OK. I'll ring a few guys. Let you know tomorrow, if I come up with anything.'

'That's great.'

He tucked the prints into their envelope and let his gaze wander to Jossie.

'A racing filly,' he said. 'Good lines.'

'Eyes off.'

'I like earthier ones, mate. Big boobs and not too bright.'

'Boring.'

'When I get home, I want a hot tea, and a cuddle when I feel like it, and no backchat about women's lib.'

When I got home, I thought, I wouldn't mind Jossie.

She walked up the concrete with big strides of her long legs, and came to a stop at our side. 'I had a friend whose boyfriend insisted on taking her sailing,' she said. 'She said she didn't terribly mind being wet, or cold, or hungry, or seasick, or frightened. She just didn't like them all at once.'

Johnny's eyes slid my way. 'With this boyfriend she'd be all right. He gets sick in harbour.'

Jossie nodded. 'Feeble.'

'Thanks,' I said.

'Be my guest.'

We went back through the office and into the taxi, and Johnny waved us goodbye.

'Any more chums?' Jossie said.

'Not this trip. If I start on the aunts, we'll be here for ever. Visit one, visit all, or there's a dust-up.'

We drove, however, at Jossie's request, past the guest house where I'd lived with my mother. There was a new glass sun lounge across the whole of the front, and a car park where there had been garden. Tubs of flowers, bright sun-awnings, and a swinging sign saying 'Vacancies'.

'Brave,' Jossie said, clearly moved. 'Don't you think?'

I paid off the taxi there and we walked down to the sea, with seagulls squawking overhead and the white little town sleeping to tea-time on its sunny hillside.

'It's pretty,' Jossie said. 'And I see why you left.'

She seemed as content as I to dawdle away the rest of the day. We crossed again in the hovercraft, and made our way slowly northwards, stopping at a pub at dusk for a drink and rubbery pork pie, and arriving finally outside the sprawling pile of Axwood House more than twelve hours after we'd left.

'That car,' Jossie said, pointing with disfavour at an inoffensive Volvo parked ahead, 'belongs to the detestable Lida.'

The light over the front door shone on her disgruntled face. I smiled, and she transferred the disfavour to me.

'It's all right for you. You aren't threatened with her moving into your home.'

'You could move out,' I said mildly.

'Just like that?'

'To my cottage, perhaps.'

'Good grief!'

'You could inspect it,' I said, 'for cleanliness, dry rot and spiders.'

She gave me her most intolerant stare. 'Butler, cook, and housemaids?'

'Six footmen and a lady's maid.'

'I'll come to tea and cucumber sandwiches. I suppose you do have cucumber sandwiches?'

'Of course.'

'Thin, and without crusts?'

'Naturally.'

I had really surprised her, I saw. She didn't know what to answer. It was quite clear, though, that she was not going to fall swooning into my arms. There was a good deal I would have liked to say, but I didn't know how to. Things about caring, and reassurance, and looking ahead.

'Next Sunday,' she said. 'At half past three. For tea.'

'I'll line up the staff.'

She decided to get out of the car, and I went round to open the door for her. Her eyes looked huge.

'Are you serious?' she said.

'Oh yes. It'll be up to you . . . to decide.'

'After tea?'

I shook my head. 'At any time.'

Her expression slowly softened to unaccustomed gentleness. I kissed her, and then kissed her again with conviction.

'I think I'll go in,' she said waveringly, turning away.

'Jossie . . .'

'What?'

I swallowed. Shook my head. 'Come to tea,' I said helplessly. 'Come to tea.'

CHAPTER SIXTEEN

Monday morning, after another night free of alarms and excursions, I went back to the office with good intentions of actually doing some work. Peter was sulking with Monday morning glooms, Bess had menstrual pains, and Debbie was tearful from a row with the screw-selling fiancé: par for office life as I knew it.

Trevor came into my room looking fatherly and anxious, and seemed reassured to find my appearance less deathly than on Friday.

'You did rest, then, Ro,' he said relievedly.

'I rode in a race and took a girl to the seaside.'

'Good heavens. At any rate, it seems to have done you good. Better than spending your time working.'

'Yes . . .' I said. 'Trevor, I did come into the office on Saturday morning, for a couple of hours.'

His air of worry crept subtly back. He waited for me to go on with the manner of a patient expecting bad news from his doctor: and I felt the most tremendous regret in having to give it to him.

'Denby Crest,' I said.

'Ro . . .' He spread out his hands, palms downwards, in a gesture that spoke of paternal distress at a rebellious son who wouldn't take his senior's word for things.

'I can't help it,' I said. 'I know he's a client, and a friend of yours, but if he's misappropriated fifty thousand pounds and you've condoned it, it concerns us both. It concerns this office, this partnership, and our future. You must see that. We can't just ignore the whole thing and pretend it hasn't happened.'

'Ro, believe me, everything will be all right.'

I shook my head. 'Trevor, you telephone Denby Crest and tell him to come over here today, to discuss what we're going to do.'

'No.'

'Yes,' I said positively. 'I'm not having it, Trevor. I'm half of this firm, and it's not going to do anything illegal.'

'You're uncompromising.' The mixture of sorrow and irritation had intensified. The two emotions, I thought fleetingly, that gave you regrets while you shot the rabbit.

'Get him here at four o'clock,' I said.

'You can't bully him like that.'

'There are worse consequences,' I said. I spoke without emphasis, but he knew quite well that it was a threat.

Irritation won hands down over sorrow. 'Very well, Ro,' he said sourly. 'Very well.'

He went out of my room with none of the sympathetic concern for me with which he had come in, and I felt a lonely sense of loss. I could forgive him anything myself,

I thought in depression, but the law wouldn't. I lived by the law, both by inclination and choice. If my friend broke the law, should I abandon it for his sake: or should I abandon my friend for the sake of the law? In the abstract, there was no difficulty in my mind. In the flesh, I shrank. There was nothing frightfully jolly in being the instrument of distress, ruin, and prosecution. How much easier if the miscreant would confess of his own free will, instead of compelling his friend to denounce him: a sentimental solution, I thought sardonically, which happened only in weepy films. I was afraid that for myself there would be no such easy way out.

Those pessimistic musings were interrupted by a telephone call from Hilary, whose voice, when I answered, sounded full of relief.

'What's the matter?' I said.

'Nothing. I just . . .' She stopped.

'Just what?'

'Just wanted to know you were there, as a matter of fact.'

'Hilary!'

'Sounds stupid, I suppose, now that we both know you *are* there. But I just wanted to be sure. After all, you wouldn't have cast me in the role of rock if you thought you were in no danger at all.'

'Um,' I said, smiling down the telephone. 'Sermons in stones.'

She laughed. 'You just take care of yourself, Ro.'

'Yes, ma'am.'

I put down the receiver, marvelling at her kindness; and almost immediately the bell rang again.

'Roland?'

'Yes, Moira?'

Her sigh came audibly down the wire. 'Thank goodness! I tried all day yesterday to reach you, and there was no reply.'

'I was out all day.'

'Yes, but I didn't know that. I mean, I was imagining all sorts of things, like you being kidnapped again, and all because of me.'

'I'm so sorry.'

'Oh, I don't mind, now that I know you're safe. I've had this terrible picture of you shut up again, and needing someone to rescue you. I've been so worried, because of Binny.'

'What about Binny?'

'I think he's gone really *mad*,' she said. 'Insane. I went over to his stables yesterday morning to see if Tapestry was all right after his race, and he wouldn't let me into the yard. Binny, I mean. All the gates were shut and locked with padlocks and chains. It's insane. He came and stood on the inside of the gate to the yard where Tapestry is, and waved his arms about, and told me to go away. I mean, it's *insane*.'

'It certainly is.'

'I told him he could have caused a terrible accident, tampering with that rein, and he screamed that he hadn't done it, and I couldn't prove it, and anything that happened to you was my fault for insisting that you rode the horse.' She paused for breath. 'He looked so . . . well, so *dangerous.* And I'd never thought of him being dangerous, but just a fool. You'll think I'm silly, but I was quite frightened.'

'I don't think you were silly,' I said truthfully.

'And then it came to me, like a revelation,' she said, 'that it had been Binny who had kidnapped you before, both times, and that he'd done it again, or something even worse . . .'

'Moira . . .'

'Yes, but you didn't *see* him. And then there was no answer to your telephone. I know you'll think I'm silly, but I was so worried.'

'I'm very grateful . . .' I started to say.

'You see, Binny never thought you'd win the Gold Cup,' she said, rushing on. 'And the very second you had, I told him you'd ride Tapestry always from then on, and he was *furious*, absolutely furious. You wouldn't believe. So of course he had you kidnapped at once, so that you'd be out of the way, and I'd *have* to have someone else, and then you escaped, and you were going to ride at Ascot, so he kidnapped you *again*, and he went absolutely berserk when I wouldn't let Tapestry go at Ascot with another jockey. And I made such a fuss in the press that he had to let you out, and so he had to try something else, like cutting the rein, and now I think he's so insane that he doesn't really know what he's doing. I mean, I think he thinks that if he kidnaps you, or kills you even, that I'll *have* to get another jockey for the Whitbread Gold Cup a week next Saturday, and honestly I think he's out of his *senses*, and really awfully dangerous because of that *obsession*, and so you see I really was terribly worried.'

'I do see,' I said. 'And I'm incredibly grateful for your concern.'

'But what are you going to *do*?' she wailed.

'About Binny? Listen, Moira, please listen.'

'Yes,' she said, her voice calming down. 'I'm listening.'

'Do absolutely nothing.'

'But *Roland*,' she protested.

'Listen. I'm sure you are quite right that Binny is in a dangerous mental state, but anything you or I could do would make him worse. Let him cool down. Give him several days. Then send a horsebox with if possible a police escort – and you can get policemen for private jobs like that, you just apply to the local nick, and offer to pay for their time – collect Tapestry, and send him to another trainer.'

'Roland!'

'You can carry loyalty too far,' I said. 'Binny's done marvels with training the horse, I agree, but you owe him nothing. If it weren't for your own strength of mind he'd have manipulated the horse to make money only for himself, as well you know, and your enjoyment would have come nowhere.'

'But about kidnapping you . . .' she began.

'No, Moira,' I said. 'He didn't; it wasn't Binny. I don't doubt he was delighted it was done, but he didn't do it.'

She was astonished. 'He must have.'

'No.'

'But why not?'

'Lots of complicated reasons. But for one thing, he wouldn't have kidnapped me straight after the Gold Cup. He wouldn't have had any need to. If he'd wanted to abduct me to stop me riding Tapestry, he wouldn't have done it until just before the horse's next race, nearly three weeks later.'

'Oh,' she said doubtfully.

'The first abduction was quite elaborate,' I said. 'Binny couldn't possibly have had time to organize it between the Gold Cup and the time I was taken, which was only an hour or so later.'

'Are you sure?'

'Yes, Moira, quite sure. And when he really did try to stop me winning, he did very direct and simple things, not difficult like kidnapping. He offered me a bribe, and cut the rein. Much more in character. He always was a fool, and now he's a dangerous fool, but he isn't a kidnapper.'

'Oh dear,' she said, sounding disappointed. 'And I was so *sure*.'

She cheered up a bit and asked me to ride Tapestry in the Whitbread. I said I'd be delighted, and she deflated my ego by passing on the opinion of a press friend of hers to the effect that Tapestry was one of those horses who liked to be in charge, and an amateur who just sat there doing nothing very much was exactly what suited him best.

Grinning to myself I put down the receiver. The press friend was right; but who cared.

For the rest of the morning I tried to make inroads into the backlog of correspondence, but found it impossible to concentrate. The final fruit of two hours of reading letters and shuffling them around was three heaps marked 'overdue', 'urgent', and 'if you don't get these off today there will be trouble'.

Debbie looked down her pious nose at my inability to apply myself, and primly remarked that I was under-utilizing her capability. Under-utilizing ... Ye Gods! Where did the gobbledegook jargon come from?

'You mean I'm not giving you enough to do.'

'That's what I said.'

At luncheon I stayed alone in the office and stared into space: and my telephone rang again.

Johnny Frederick, full of news.

'Do you mind if I send you a bill for 'phone calls?' he said. 'I must have spent thirty quid. I've been talking all morning.'

'I'll send you a cheque.'

'OK. Well, mate, pin back your lugholes. That boat you were on was built at Lymington, and she sailed from there after dark on March 17th. She was brand spanking new, and she hadn't completed her trials, and she wasn't registered or named. She was built by a top-notch shipyard called Goldenwave Marine, for a client called Arthur Robinson.'

'Who?'

'Arthur Robinson. That's what he said his name was, anyway. And there was only one slightly unusual thing about Mr Robinson, and that was that he paid for the boat in cash.'

He waited expectantly.

'How much cash?' I said.

'Two hundred thousand pounds.'

'Crikey.'

'Mind you,' Johnny said, 'that's bargain basement stuff for Goldenwave. They do a nice job in mini-liners at upwards of a million, with gold taps, for Arabs.'

'In cash?'

'Near enough, I dare say. Anyway, Arthur Robinson always paid on the nail, in instalments as they came due during the boat-building, but always in your actual folding. Goldenwave Marine wouldn't be interested in knowing whether the cash had had tax paid on it. None of their business.'

'Quite,' I said. 'Go on.'

'That Thursday – March 17th – in the morning, some time, Arthur Robinson rang Goldenwave and said he wanted to take some friends aboard for a party that evening, and would they please see that the water and fuel tanks were topped up, and everything shipshape. Which Goldenwave did.'

'Without question.'

'Of course. You don't argue with two hundred thousand quid. Anyway, the boat was out on a mooring in the deep water passage, so they left her fit for the owner's visit and brought her tender ashore, for him to use when he got there.'

'A black rubber dinghy?'

'I didn't ask. The nightwatchman had been told to expect the party, so he let them in, and helped generally, and saw them off. I got him out of bed this morning to talk to him, and he was none too pleased, but he remembers the evening quite well, because of course the boat sailed off that night and never came back.'

'What did he say?'

'There were two lots of people, he said. One lot came in an old white van, which he didn't think much of for an owner of such a boat. You'd expect a Rolls, he said.' Johnny chuckled. 'The first arrivals, three people, were the crew. They unloaded stores from an estate car and made two trips out to the boat. Then the white van arrived with several more men, and one of those was lying down. They told the nightwatchman he was dead drunk, and that was you, I reckon. Then the first three men and the drunk man went out to the boat, and the other men drove away in the old van and the estate car, and that was that. The nightwatchman thought it a very boring sort of party, and noted the embarkation in his log, and paid no more attention. Next morning, no boat.'

'And no report to the police?'

'The owner had taken his own property, which he'd fully paid for. Goldenwave had expected him to take command of her a week later, anyway, so they made no fuss.'

'You've done absolute marvels,' I said.

'Do you want to hear about Alastair Yardley?'

'There's more?'

'There sure is. He seems to be quite well-known. Several of the bigger shipyards have recommended him to people who want their boats sailed from England, say, to Bermuda, or the Caribbean, and so on, and don't have a regular crew, and also don't want to cross oceans themselves. He signs on his own crew, and pays them himself. He's no crook. Got a good reputation. Tough, though. And he's not cheap. If he agreed to help shanghai you, you can bet Mr Arthur Robinson paid through the nose for the service. But you can ask him yourself, if you like.'

'What do you mean?'

Johnny was justifiably triumphant. 'I struck dead lucky, mate. Mind you, I chased him round six shipyards, but he's in England now to fetch another yacht, and he'll talk to you if you ring him more or less at once.'

'I don't believe it!'

'Here's the number.' He read out the numbers, and I wrote them down. 'Ring him before two o'clock. You can also talk to the chap in charge of Goldenwave, if you like. This is his number. He said he'd help in any way he could.'

'You're fantastic,' I said, stunned to breathlessness by his success.

'We got a real lucky break, mate, because when I took those photographs to Cowes first thing this morning, I asked around everybody, and there was a feller in the third yard I tried who'd worked at Goldenwave last year, and he said it looked like their Golden Sixty Five, so I rang them, and it was the departure date that clinched it.'

'I can't begin to thank you.'

'To tell you the truth, mate, it's been a bit of excitement, and there isn't all that much about, these days. I've enjoyed this morning, and that's a fact.'

'I'll give you a ring. Tell you how things turn out.'

'Great. Can't wait. And see you.'

He disconnected, and with an odd sinking feeling in my stomach I rang the first of the numbers he'd given me. A shipyard. Could I speak to Alastair Yardley? Hang on, said the switchboard. I hung.

'Hullo?'

The familiar voice. Bold, self-assertive, challenging the world.

'It's Roland Britten,' I said.

There was a silence, then he said, 'Yeah,' slowly.

'You said you'd talk to me.'

'Yeah.' He paused. 'Your friend this morning, John Frederick, the boat-builder, he tells me I was sold a pup about you.'

'How do you mean?'

'I was told you were a blackmailer.'

'A *what*?'

'Yeah.' He sighed. 'Well, this guy Arthur Robinson, he said you'd set up his wife in some compromising photographs and were trying to blackmail her, and he wanted you taught a lesson.'

'Oh,' I said blankly. It explained a great deal, I thought.

'Your friend Frederick told me that was all crap. He said I'd been conned. I reckon I was. All the other guys in the yard here know all about you winning that race and going missing. They just told me. Seems it was in all the papers. But I didn't see them, of course.'

'How long,' I said, 'were you supposed to keep me on board?'

'He said to ring him Monday evening, April 4th, and he'd tell me when and where and how to set you loose. But of course, you jumped ship the Tuesday before, and how you got that lever off is a bloody mystery . . . I rang him that night, and he was so bloody angry he couldn't get the words out. So then he said he wouldn't pay me for the job on you, and I said if he didn't he could whistle for his boat, I'd just sail it into some port somewhere and walk away, and he'd have God's own job finding it. So I said he could send me the money to Palma, where I bank, and when I got it I'd do what he wanted, which was to take his boat to Antibes and deliver it to the ship brokers there.'

'Brokers?'

'Yeah. Funny, that. He'd only just bought it. What did he want to sell it for?'

'Well . . .' I said. 'Do you remember his telephone number?'

'No. Threw it away, didn't I, as soon as I was shot of his boat.'

'At Antibes?'

'That's right.'

'Did you meet him?' I asked.

'Yeah. That night at Lymington. He told me not to talk to you, and not to listen, because you'd tell me lies, and not to let you know where we were, and not to leave a mark on you, and to watch out because you were as slippery as an eel.' He paused a second. 'He was right about that, come to think.'

'Do you remember what he looked like?'

'Yeah,' he said, 'what I saw of him; but it was mostly in the dark, out on the quay.' He described Arthur Robinson as I'd expected, and well enough to be conclusive.

'I wasn't intending to go for another week,' he said. 'The weather forecasts were all bad for Biscay, and I'd only been out in her once, in light air, not enough to know how she'd handle in a gale, but he rang Goldenwave that morning and spoke to me, and told me about you, and said gale or no gale he'd make it worth my while if I'd go that evening and take you with me.'

'I hope it was worth it,' I said.

'Yeah,' he said frankly. 'I got paid double.'

I laughed in my throat. 'Er . . .' I said, 'is it possible for a boat just to sail off from England and wander round Mediterranean ports, when it hasn't even got a name? I mean, do you have to pass Customs, and things like that?'

'You can pass Customs if you want to waste a bloody lot of time. Otherwise, unless you tell them, a port doesn't know whether you've come from two miles down the coast, or two thousand. The big ports collect mooring fees, that's all they're interested in. If you drop anchor at somewhere like Formentor, which we did one night with you, no one takes a blind bit of notice. Easy come, easy go, that's what it's like on the sea. Best way to live, I reckon.'

'It sounds marvellous,' I sighed enviously.

'Yeah. Look . . .' he paused a second, 'are you going to set the police on me, or anything? Because I'm off today, on the afternoon tide, and I'm not telling where.'

'No,' I said. 'No police.'

He let his breath out audibly in relief. 'I reckon . . .' He paused. 'Thanks, then. And well, sorry, like.'

I remembered the paperback, and the socks, and the soap and I had no quarrel with him.

From Goldenwave Marine, ten minutes later, I learned a good many background facts about big boats in general and Arthur Robinson in particular.

Goldenwave had four more Golden Sixty Fives on the stocks at the moment, all commissioned by private customers, and Arthur Robinson had been one of a stream. Their Golden Sixty Five had been a successful design, they were pleased and proud to say, and their standard of ship-building was respected the world over.

End of commercial.

I replaced the receiver gratefully. Sat, thinking, chewing bits off my fingernails. Decided, without joy, to take a slightly imprudent course.

Debbie, Peter, Bess and Trevor came back, and the place filled up with tap-tap and bustle. Mr Wells arrived for his appointment twenty minutes before the due time, reminding me of the psychiatrists'-eye-view of patients: if they're early, they're anxious, if they're late, they're aggressive, and if they're on time, they're pathological. I often thought the psychiatrists didn't understand about trains, buses and traffic flow, but in this case there wasn't much doubt about the anxiety. Mr Wells' hair, manner and eyes were all out of control.

'I rang the people you sent the rubber cheque to,' I said. 'They were a bit sticky, but they've agreed not to prosecute if you take care of them after the inevitable Receiving Order.'

'I what?'

'Pay them later,' I said. Jargon . . . I did it myself.

'Oh.'

'The order of paying,' I said, 'will be first the Inland Revenue, who will collect tax in full, and will also charge interest for every day overdue.'

'But I haven't anything to pay them with.'

'Did you sell your car, as we agreed you should?'

He nodded, but wouldn't meet my eyes.

'What have you done with the money?' I said.

'Nothing.'

'Pay it to the Revenue, then, on account.'

He looked away evasively, and I sighed at his folly. 'What have you done with the money?' I repeated.

He wouldn't tell me, and I concluded that he had been following the illegal path of many an imminent bankrupt, selling off his goods and banking the proceeds distantly under a false name, so that when the bailiffs came there wouldn't be much left. I gave him some good advice which I knew he wouldn't take. The suicidal hysterics of his earlier visit had settled into resentment against everyone pressing him, including me. He listened with a mulish stubbornness which I'd seen often enough before, and all he would positively agree to was not to write any more cheques.

By three-thirty I'd had enough of Mr Wells, and he of me.

'You need a good solicitor,' I said. 'He'll tell you the same as me, but maybe you'll listen.'

'It was a solicitor who gave me your name,' he said glumly.

'Who's your solicitor?'

'Fellow called Denby Crest.'

It was a small community, I thought. Touching, overlapping, a patchwork fabric. When the familiar names kept turning up, things were normal.

As it happened, Trevor was in the outer office when I showed Mr Wells to the door. I introduced them, explaining that Denby had sent him to see us. Trevor cast a benign eye, which would have been jaundiced had he known the Wells state of dickiness, and made affable small talk. Mr Wells took in Trevor's substantial air, seniority, and general impression of worldliness, and I practically saw the thought cross his mind that perhaps he had consulted the wrong partner.

And perhaps, I thought cynically, he had.

When he'd gone, Trevor looked at me sombrely.

'Come into my office,' he sighed.

CHAPTER SEVENTEEN

I sat in one of the clients' chairs, with Trevor magisterially behind his desk. His manner was somewhere between unease and cajoling, as if he were not quite sure of his ground.

'Denby said he'd be here by four.'

'Good.'

'But Ro . . . he'll explain. He'll satisfy you, I'm sure. I think I'll leave it to him to explain, and then you'll see . . . that there's nothing for us to worry about.'

He raised an unconvincing smile and rippled his fingertips on his blotter. I looked at the familiar, friendly figure, and wished with all my heart that things were not as they were.

Denby came ten minutes early, which would have gratified the psychiatrists, and he was wound up like a tight spring, as well he might be. His backbone was ramrod stiff inside the short plump frame, the moustache bristling on the forward jutting mouth, the irritated air plainer than ever.

He didn't shake hands with me: merely nodded.

Trevor came round his desk to offer a chair, a politeness I thought excessive.

'Well, Ro,' Denby said crossly. 'I hear you have reservations about my certificate.'

'That's so.'

'What, exactly?'

'Well,' I said. 'To be exact . . . fifty thousand pounds missing from the clients' deposit account.'

'Rubbish.'

I sighed. 'You transferred money belonging to three separate clients from the clients' deposit to the clients' current account,' I said. 'You then drew five cheques from the current account, made out to yourself, in varying sums, over a period of six weeks, three to four months ago. Those cheques add up to fifty thousand pounds exactly.'

'But I've repaid the money. If you'd've looked more carefully you'd have seen the counter credits on the bank statement.' He was irritated. Impatient.

'I couldn't make out where those credits had come from,' I said, 'so I asked the bank to send a duplicate statement. It came this morning.'

Denby sat as if turned to stone.

'The duplicate statement,' I said regretfully, 'shows no record of the money having been repaid. The bank statement you gave us was . . . well . . . a forgery.'

Time ticked by.

Trevor looked unhappy. Denby revised his position.

'I've only *borrowed* the money,' he said. There was

still no regret, and no real fear. 'It's perfectly safe. It will be repaid very shortly. You have my word for it.'

'Um . . .' I said. 'Your word isn't enough.'

'Really, Ro, this is ridiculous. If I say it will be repaid, it will be repaid. Surely you know me well enough for that?'

'If you mean,' I said, 'would I have thought you a thief, then no, I wouldn't.'

'I'm not a thief,' he said angrily. 'I told you, I borrowed the money. A temporary expediency. It's unfortunate that . . . as things turned out . . . I was not able to repay it before the certificate became due. But as I explained to Trevor, it is only a matter of a few weeks, at the most.'

'The clients' money,' I said reasonably, 'is not entrusted to you so that you can use it for a private loan to yourself.'

'We all know that,' Denby said snappily, in a teaching-grandmother-to-suck-eggs manner. My grandmother, I reflected fleetingly, had never sucked an egg in her life.

'You're fifty thousand short,' I said, 'and Trevor's condoned it, and neither of you seems to realize you'll be out of business if it comes to light.'

They both looked at me as if I were a child.

'But there's no need for it to come to light, Ro,' Trevor said. 'Denby will repay the money soon, and all will be well. Like I told you.'

'It isn't ethical,' I said.

'Don't be so pompous, Ro,' Trevor said, at his most fatherly, shaking his head with sorrow.

'Why did you take the money?' I asked Denby. 'What for?'

Denby looked across enquiringly at Trevor, who nodded.

'You'll have to tell him everything, Denby. He's very persistent. Better tell him, then he'll understand, and we can clear the whole thing up.'

Denby complied with bad grace. 'I had a chance,' he said, 'of buying a small block of flats. Brand new. Not finished. Builder in difficulties, wanted a quick sale, that sort of thing. Flats were going cheap, of course. So I bought them. Too good to miss. Done that sort of deal before, of course. Not a fool, you know. Knew what I was doing, and all that.'

'Your own conveyancer?' I said.

'What? Oh yes.' He nodded. 'Well, then, I needed a bit more extra capital to finance the deal. Perfectly safe. Good flats. Nothing wrong with them.'

'But they haven't sold?' I said.

'Takes time. Market's sluggish in the winter. But they're all sold now, subject to contracts. Formalities, mortgages, all that. Takes time.'

'Mm.' I said. 'How many flats in the block, and where is it?'

'Eight flats, small, of course. At Newquay, Cornwall.'

'Have you seen them?' I said.

'Of course.'

'Do you mind if I do?' I said. 'And will you give me the

addresses of all the people who are buying the flats, and tell me how much each is paying?'

Denby bristled. 'Are you saying you don't believe me?'

'I'm an auditor,' I said. 'I don't believe. I check.'

'You can take my word for it.'

I shook my head. 'You sent us a forged bank statement. I can't take your word for anything.'

There was a silence.

'If those flats exist, and if you repay that money this week, I'll keep quiet,' I said. 'I'll want confirmation by letter from the bank. The money must be there by Friday, and the letter here by Saturday. Otherwise, no deal.'

'I can't get the money this week,' Denby said peevishly.

'Borrow it from a loan shark.'

'But that's ridiculous. The interest I would have to pay would wipe out all my profit.'

Serve you right, I thought unfeelingly. I said, 'Unless the clients' money is back in the bank by Friday, the Law Society will have to be told.'

'Ro!' Trevor protested.

'However much you try to wrap it up as "unfortunate" and "expedient",' I said, 'the fact remains that all three of us know that what Denby has done is a criminal offence. I'm not putting my name to it as a partner of this firm. If the money is not repaid by Friday, I'll write a letter explaining that in the light of fresh knowledge we wish to cancel the certificate just issued.'

'But Denby would be struck off!' Trevor said.

They both looked as if the stark realities of life were something that only happened to other people.

'Unfriendly,' Denby said angrily. 'Unnecessarily aggressive, that's what you are, Ro. Righteous. Unbending.'

'All those, I dare say,' I said.

'It's no good, I suppose, suggesting I . . . er . . . cut you in?'

Trevor made a quick horrified gesture, trying to stop him.

'Denby, Denby,' he said, distressed. 'You'll never bribe him. For God's sake have some sense. If you really want to antagonize Ro, you offer him a bribe.'

Denby scowled at me and got explosively to his feet.

'All right,' he said bitterly. 'I'll get the money by Friday. And don't ever expect any favours from me for the rest of your life.'

He strode furiously out of the office leaving eddies of disturbed air and longer trails of disturbed friendship. Turbulent wake, I thought. Churning and destructive, overturning everything it touched.

'Are you satisfied, Ro?' Trevor said gently, in sorrow.

I sat without answering.

I felt like a man on a high diving board, awaiting the moment of strength. Ahead, the plunge. Behind, the quiet way down. The choice, within me.

I could walk away, I thought. Pretend I didn't know what I knew. Settle for silence, friendship and peace.

Refrain from bringing distress and disgrace and dreary unhappiness.

My friend or the law. To which did I belong? To the law or my own pleasure . . .

O great God almighty.

I swallowed with a dry mouth.

'Trevor,' I said, 'do you know Arthur Robinson?'

There was no fun, no fun at all, in looking into the face of ultimate disaster.

The blood slowly drained from Trevor's skin, leaving his eyes like great dark smudges.

'I'll get you some brandy,' I said.

'Ro . . .'

'Wait.'

I fetched him a tumbler, from his entertaining cupboard, heavy with alcohol, light on soda.

'Drink it,' I said with compassion. 'I'm afraid I've given you a shock.'

'How . . .' His mouth quivered suddenly, and he put the glass to his lips to hide it. He drank slowly, and took the glass a few inches away: a present help in trouble. 'How much . . . do you know?' he said.

'Why I was abducted. Who did it. Who owns the boat. Who sailed her. Where she is now. How much she cost. And where the money comes from.'

'My God . . . My God . . .' His hands shook.

'I want to talk to him,' I said. 'To Arthur Robinson.'

A faint flash of something like hope shone in his eyes.

'Do you know . . . his other name?'

I told him what it was. The spark of light died to a pebble-like dullness. He clattered the glass against his teeth.

'I want you to telephone,' I said. 'Tell him I know. Tell him I want to talk. Tell him, if he has any ideas of doing anything but what I ask, I'll go straight from this office to the police. I want to talk to him tonight.'

'But Ro, knowing you . . .' He sounded despairing. 'You'll go to the police anyway.'

'Tomorrow morning,' I said.

He stared at me for a long, long time. Then with a heavy half-groaning sigh, he stretched out his hand to the telephone.

We went to Trevor's house. Better for talking, he suggested, than the office.

'Your wife?' I said.

'She's staying with her sister, tonight. She often does.'

We drove in two cars, and judging by the daze of his expression Trevor saw nothing consciously of the road for the whole four miles.

His big house sat opulently in the late afternoon sunshine, nineteen-twenties respectability in every brick. Acres of diamond-shaped leaded window panes, black paint, a wide portico with corkscrew pillars, wisteria creeping here and there, lots of gables with beams stuck on for effect.

Trevor unlocked the front door and led the way into dead inside air which smelled of old coffee and furniture polish. Parquet flooring in the roomy hall, and rugs.

'Come into the snug,' he said, walking ahead.

The snug was a longish room which lay between the more formal sitting and dining rooms, looking outwards to the pillared loggia, with the lawn beyond it. To Trevor the snug was psychologically as well as geographically the heart of the house, the place where he most felt a host to his businessmen friends.

There was the bar, built in, where he liked to stand, genially pouring drinks. Several dark red leather armchairs. A small, sturdy dining table, with four leather-seated dining chairs. A large television. Bookshelves. An open brick fireplace, with a leather screen. A palm in a brass pot. More Stubbs prints. Several small chair-side tables. A leaf-patterned carpet. Heavy red velvet curtains. Red lampshades. On winter evenings, with the fire lit, curtains drawn, and lights glowing warmly, snug, in spite of its size, described it.

Trevor switched on the lights, and although it was full daylight, drew the curtains. Then he made straight for the bar.

'Do you want a drink?' he said.

I shook my head. He fixed himself a brandy of twice the size I'd given him in the office.

'I can't believe any of this is happening,' he said.

He took his filled glass and slumped down in one of the red leather armchairs, staring into space. I hitched a hip on to the table, which like so much in that house was protected by a sheet of plate glass. We both waited, neither of us enjoying our thoughts. We waited nearly an hour.

Nothing violent, I told myself numbly, would happen in that genteel house. Violence occurred in back alleys and dark corners. Not in a well-to-do sitting-room on a Monday evening. I felt the flutter of apprehension in every nerve and thought about eyes black with the lust for revenge.

A car drew up outside. A door slammed. There were footsteps outside on the gravel. Footsteps crossing the threshold, coming through the open front door, treading across the parquet, coming to the door of the snug. Stopping there.

'Trevor?' he said.

Trevor looked up dully. He waved a hand towards me, where I sat to one side, masked by the open door.

He pushed the door wider. Stepped into the room.

He held a shotgun; balanced over his forearm, butt under the armpit, twin barrels pointing to the floor.

I took a deep steadying breath, and looked into his firm, familiar face.

Jossie's father. William Finch.

*

'Shooting me,' I said, 'won't solve anything. I've left photostats and all facts with a friend.'

'If I shoot your foot off, you'll ride no more races.'

His voice already vibrated with the smashing hate: and this time I saw it not from across a courtroom thick with policemen, but from ten feet at the wrong end of a gun.

Trevor made jerky calming gestures with his hands.

'William . . . surely you see. Shooting Ro would be disastrous. Irretrievably disastrous.'

'The situation is already irretrievable.' His voice was thick, roughened and deepened by the tension in throat and neck. 'This little creep has seen to that.'

'Well,' I said, and heard the tension in my own voice, 'I didn't make you steal.'

It wasn't the best of remarks. Did nothing to reduce the critical mass: and William Finch was like a nuclear reactor with the rods too far out already. The barrels of the gun swung up into his hands and pointed at my loins.

'William, for God's sake,' Trevor said urgently, climbing ponderously out of his armchair. 'Use your reason. If he says killing him would do no good, you must believe him. He'd never have risked coming here if it wasn't true.'

Finch vibrated with fury through all his elegant height. The conflict between hatred and common sense was plain in the bunching muscles along his jaw and the claw-like curve of his fingers. There was a fearful moment when I was certain that the blood-lust urge to avenge himself would blot out all fear of consequences, and I thought disconnectedly that I wouldn't feel it . . . you never felt the worst of wounds in the first few seconds. It was only after, if you lived, that the tide came in. I wouldn't know . . . I wouldn't feel it, and I might not even know . . .

He swung violently away from me and thrust the shotgun into Trevor's arms.

'Take it. Take it,' he said through his teeth. 'I don't trust myself.'

I could feel the tremors down my legs, and the prickling of sweat over half my body. He hadn't killed me at the very start, when it would have been effective, and it was all very well risking he wouldn't do it now when he'd nothing to gain. It had come a good deal too close.

I leaned my behind weakly against the table, and worked some saliva into my mouth. Tried to set things out in a dry-as-dust manner, as if we were discussing a small point of policy.

'Look . . .' It came out half-strangled. I cleared my throat and tried again. 'Tomorrow I will have to telephone to New York, to talk to the Nantucket family. Specifically, to talk to one of the directors on the board of their family empire; the director to whom Trevor sends the annual Axwood audited accounts.'

Trevor took the shotgun and stowed it away out of sight behind the ornate bar. William Finch stood in the centre of the room with unreleased energy quivering through all his frame. I watched his hands clench and unclench, and his legs move inside his trousers, as if wanting to stride about.

'What will you tell them, then?' he said fiercely. 'What?'

'That you've been . . . er . . . defrauding the Nantucket family business during the past financial year.'

For the first time some of the heat went out of him.

'During the past . . .' He stopped.

'I can't tell,' I said, 'about earlier years. I didn't do the audits. I've never seen the books, and they are not in our office. They have to be kept for three years, of course, so I expect you have them.'

There was a lengthy silence.

'I'm afraid,' I said, 'that the Nantucket director will tell me to go at once to the police. If it was old Naylor Nantucket who was involved, it might be different. He might just have hushed everything up, for your sake. But this new generation, they don't know you. They're hard-nosed businessmen who disapprove of the stable anyway. They never come near the place. They do look upon it as a business proposition, though, and they pay you a good salary to manage it, and they undoubtedly regard any profits as being theirs. However mildly I put it, and I'm not looking forward to it at all, they are going to have to know that for this financial year their profits have gone to you.'

My deadpan approach began to have its results. Trevor poured two drinks and thrust one into William

Finch's hand. He looked at it unseeingly and after a few moments put it down on the bar.

'And Trevor?' he said.

'I'll have to tell the Nantucket director,' I said regretfully, 'that the auditor they appointed has helped to rip them off.'

'Ro,' Trevor said, protesting, I gathered, at the slang expression more than the truth of it.

'Those Axwood books are a work of fiction,' I said to him. 'Cash books, ledgers, invoices . . . all ingenious lies. William would never have got away with such a wholesale fraud without your help. Without, anyway . . .' I said, modifying it slightly, 'without you knowing, and turning a blind eye.'

'And raking off a bloody big cut,' Finch said violently, making sure he took his friend down with him.

Trevor made a gesture of distaste, but it had to be right. Trevor had a hearty appetite for money, and would never have taken such a risk without the gain.

'These books look all right at first sight,' I said. 'They would have satisfied an outside auditor, if the Nantuckets had wanted a check from a London firm, or one in New York. But as for Trevor, and as for me, living here . . .' I shook my head. 'Axwood Stables have paid thousands to forage merchants who didn't receive the money, to saddlers who don't exist, to maintenance men, electricians and plumbers who did no work. The invoices are there, all nicely printed, but the transactions they refer to are thin air. The cash went straight to William Finch.'

Some of the slowly evaporating heat returned fast to Finch's manner, and I thought it wiser not to catalogue aloud all the rest of the list of frauds.

He'd charged the Nantuckets wages for several more lads than he'd employed: a dodge hard to pin down, as the stable-lad population floated from yard to yard.

He'd charged the Nantucket company more than nine thousand pounds for the rent of extra loose boxes and keep for horses by a local farmer, when I knew he had paid only a fraction of that, as the farmer was one of my clients.

He'd charged much more for shares in jockeys' retainers than the jockeys had received; and had invented travelling expenses to the races for horses which according to the form books had never left the yard.

He had pocketed staggering sums from a bloodstock agent in the form of commission on the sales of Nantucket horses to outside owners: fifty thousand or so in the past year, the agent had confirmed casually on the telephone, not knowing that Finch had no right to it.

I imagined Finch had also been sending enlarged bills to all the non-Nantucket owners, getting them to make out their cheques to him personally rather than to the company, and then diverting a slice to himself before paying a reasonable sum into the business.

The Nantuckets were far away, and uninterested. All I guessed they'd wanted had been a profit on the bottom line, and he'd given them just enough to keep them quiet.

As a final irony, he'd charged the Nantuckets six thousand pounds for auditors' fees, and nowhere in our books was there a trace of six thousand pounds from Axwood Stables. Trevor might have had his half, though, on the quiet: it was enough to make you laugh.

A long list of varied frauds. Much harder to detect than one large one. Adding up, though, to an average rake-off for Finch of over two thousand pounds a week. Untaxed.

Year in, year out.

Assisted by his auditor.

Assisted also, it was certain, by the ever-sick secretary, Sandy, though with or without her knowledge I didn't know. If she was ill as often as all that, and away from her post, maybe she didn't know. Or maybe the knowledge made her ill. But as in most big frauds, the paperwork had to be done well, and in the Axwood Stables case, there had been a great deal of it done well.

Ninety to a hundred horses. Well trained, well raced. A big stable with a huge weekly turnover. A top trainer. A trainer, I thought, who didn't own his own stable, who was paid only a salary, and a highly taxed one at that, and who faced having no capital to live on in old age, in a time of inflation. A man in his fifties, an employee, seeing into a future without enough money. An enforced retirement. No house of his own. No power. A man with money at present passing daily through his hands like a river in flood.

All racehorse trainers were entrepreneurs, with

organizing minds. Most were in business on their own account, and had no absent company to defraud. If William Finch had been his own master, I doubted that he would ever have thought of embezzlement. With his abilities, in the normal course of things, he would have had no need.

Need. Ability. Opportunity. I wondered how big a step it had been to dishonesty. To crime.

Probably not very big. A pay-packet for a non-existent stable lad, for a little extra regular cash. The cost of an unordered ton of hay.

Small steps, ingenious swindles, multiplying and swelling, leading to a huge swathing highway.

'Trevor,' I said mildly, 'how long ago did you spot William's . . . irregularities?'

Trevor looked at me sorrowfully, and I half-smiled.

'You saw them . . . some of the first ones . . . in the books,' I said, 'and you told him it wouldn't do.'

'Of course.'

'You suggested,' I said, 'that if he really put his mind to it you would both be a great deal better off.'

Finch reacted strongly with a violent gesture of his whole arm, but Trevor's air of sorrow merely intensified.

'Just like Connaught Powys,' I said. 'I tried hard to believe that you genuinely hadn't seen how he was rigging that computer, but I reckon . . . I have to face it that you were doing it together.'

'Ro . . .' he said sadly.

'Anyway,' I said to Finch, 'you sent the books in for

the annual audit, and after all this time neither you nor Trevor are particularly nervous. Trevor and I have been chronically behind with our work for ages, so I guess he just locked them in his cupboard, to see to as soon as he could. He would know I wouldn't look at your books. I never had, in six years; and I had too many clients of my own. And then, when Trevor was away on his holidays, the unforeseen happened. On Gold Cup day, through your letterbox, and mine, came the summons for you to appear before the Tax Commissioners a fortnight later.'

He stared at me with furious dark eyes, his strong, elegant figure tall and straight like a great stag at bay against an impudent hound. Round the edges of the curtains the daylight was fading to dark. Inside, electric lights shone smoothly on civilized man.

I smiled twistedly. 'I sent you a message. Don't worry, I said, Trevor's on holiday, but I'll apply for a postponement, and make a start on the books myself. I went straight off to ride in the Gold Cup and never gave it another thought. But you, to you, that message meant ruin. Degradation, prosecution, probably prison.'

A quiver ran through him. Muscles moved along his jaw.

'I imagine,' I said, 'that you thought the simplest thing would be to get the books back; but they were locked in Trevor's cupboard, and only he and I have keys. And in any case I would have thought it very suspicious, if, with the Commissioners breathing down our necks, you refused to let me see the books. Especially suspicious if the office had been broken into and those papers stolen. Anything along those lines would have led to investigation, and disaster. So as you couldn't keep the books from *me*, you decided to keep *me* from the books. You had the means to hand. A new boat, nearly ready to sail. You simply arranged for it to go early, and take me with it. If you could keep me away from the office until Trevor returned, all would be well.'

'This is all nonsense,' he said stiffly.

'Don't be silly. It's past denying. Trevor was due back in the office on Monday, April 4th, which would give him three days to apply for a postponement to the Commissioners. A perfectly safe margin. Trevor would then do the Axwood books as usual, and I would be set free, never knowing why I'd been abducted.'

Trevor buried his face in his brandy, which made me thirsty.

'If you've any mineral water, or tonic, Trevor, I'd like some,' I said.

'Give him nothing,' Finch said, the pent-up violence still thick in his voice.

Trevor made fluttery motions with his hands, but after a moment, with apologetic glances at Finch's tightened mouth, he fetched a tumbler and poured into it a bottle of tonic water.

'Ro . . .' he said, giving me the glass. 'My dear chap . . .'

'My dear *shit*,' Finch said.

I drank the fizzy quinine water gratefully.

'I bust things up by getting home a few days early,' I

said. 'I suppose you were frantic. Enough, anyway, to send the kidnapping squads to my cottage to pick me up again. And when they didn't manage it, you sent someone else.' I drank bubbles and tasted gall. 'Next day, you sent your daughter Jossie.'

'She knows nothing, Ro,' Trevor said.

'Shut up,' Finch said. 'She strung him along by the nose.'

'Maybe she did,' I said. 'It was supposed to be only for a day or two. Trevor was due back that Sunday. But I told you, while you were busy filling my time by showing me round your yard, that Trevor's car had broken down in France, and he wouldn't be back until Wednesday or Thursday. And I assured you again that you didn't have to worry, I had already applied for the postponement, and I would start the audit myself. The whole situation was back to square one, and the outlook was as deadly as ever.'

Finch glared, denying nothing.

'You offered me a day at the races with Jossie,' I said. 'And a ride in the novice hurdle. I'm a fool about accepting rides. Never know when to say no. You must have known that Notebook was unable to jump properly. You must have hoped when you flew off to the Grand National, that I'd fall with him and break a leg.'

'Your neck,' he said vindictively, with no vestige of a joke.

Trevor glanced at his face and away again, as if embarrassed by so much raw emotion.

'Your men must have been standing by in case I survived undamaged, which of course I did,' I said. 'They followed us to the pub where I had dinner with Jossie, and then to the motel where I planned to stay. Your second attempt at abduction was more successful, in that I couldn't get out. And when Trevor was safely back, you rang Scotland Yard, and the police set me free. From one point of view all your efforts had produced precisely the desired result, because I had not in fact by then seen one page or one entry of the Axwood books.'

I thought back, and amended that statement. 'I hadn't seen any except the petty cash book, which you gave me yourself. And that, I imagine, was your own private accurate record, and not the one re-written and padded for the sake of the audit. It was left in my car with all my other belongings, and I took it to the office when I went back last Friday. It was still there on Saturday. It was Saturday morning that I got out the Axwood books and studied them, and made the photocopies.'

'But why, Ro?' Trevor asked frustratedly. 'What made you think . . . Why did you think of William?'

'The urgency,' I said. 'The ruthless haste, and the time factors. I believed, you see, when I was on the boat, that I'd been kidnapped for revenge. Any auditor who's been the downfall of embezzlers would think that, if he'd found himself in such a position. Especially if he's been directly threatened, face to face, as I had, by Connaught Powys, and earlier by Ownslow and Glitberg, and later also by others. But when I escaped and came home, there was hardly any interval before I was in danger again. Hunted, really. And caught. So the second time, last week, in the van, I began to think . . . that perhaps it wasn't revenge, but *prevention*, and after that, it was a matter of deduction, elimination, boring things, on the whole. But I had hours . . .' I swallowed involuntarily, remembering. 'I had hours in which to think of all the possible people, and work it out. So then, on Saturday morning, I went to the office, when I had the place to myself, and checked.'

Finch turned on Trevor, looking for a whipping boy. 'Why the hell did you keep those books where he could see them? Why didn't you lock them in the bloody safe?'

'I've a key to the safe,' I said dryly.

'Christ!' He raised his hands in a violent, exploding, useless gesture. 'Why didn't you take them home?'

'I never take books home,' Trevor said. 'And you told me that Ro was going to the races Saturday, and out with Jossie Sunday, so we'd nothing to worry about. And anyway, neither of us dreamt that he knew . . . or guessed.'

Finch swung his desperate face in my direction.

'What's your price?' he said. 'How much?'

I didn't answer. Trevor said protestingly, 'William . . .'

'He must want something,' Finch said. 'Why is he telling us all this instead of going straight to the police? Because he wants a deal, that's why.'

'Not money,' I said.

Finch continued to look like a bolt of lightning

trapped in bones and flesh, but he didn't pursue the subject. He knew, as he'd always known, that it wasn't a question of money.

'Where did you get the men who abducted me?' I said.

'You know so much. You can bloody well find out.'

Rent-a-thug, I thought cynically. Someone, somewhere, knew how to hire some bully boys. The police could find out, I thought, if they wanted to. I wouldn't bother.

'The second time,' I said. 'Did you tell them not to leave a mark on me?'

'So what?'

'Did you?' I said.

'I didn't want the police taking any serious interest,' he said. 'No marks. No stealing. Made you a minor case.'

So the fists and boots, I thought, had been a spot of private enterprise. Payment for the general run-around I'd given the troops. Not orders from above. I supposed I was glad, in a sour sort of way.

He'd chosen the warehouse, I guessed, because it couldn't have been easy to find a safer place in a hurry: and because he thought it would divert my attention even more strongly towards Ownslow and Glitberg, and away from any thought of himself.

Trevor said, 'Well . . . What . . . what are we going to do now?' but no one answered, because there were wheels outside on the gravel. Car doors slammed.

'Did you leave the front door open?' Trevor said.

Finch didn't need to answer. He had. Several feet

tramped straight in, crossed the hall, and made unerringly for the snug.

'Here we are then,' said a powerful voice. 'Let's get on with it.'

The light of triumph shone in Finch's face, and he smiled with grateful welcome at the newcomers crowding into the room.

Glitberg. Ownslow. Connaught Powys.

'Got the rat cornered, then?' Powys said.

CHAPTER EIGHTEEN

I had an everlasting picture of the five of them, in that freezing moment. I straightened to my feet, and my heart thumped, and I looked at them one by one.

Connaught Powys in his city suit, as Establishment as a pillar of the government. Coffee-coloured tan on his fleshy face. Smooth hair; pale hands. A large man aiming to throw his weight about, and enjoying it.

Glitberg with his mean eyes and the repulsive four-inch frill of white whiskers, which stood out sideways from his cheeks like a ruff. Little pink lips, and a smirk.

Ownslow the bull, with his bald crown and long straggling blond hair. He'd shut the door of the snug and leaned against it, and folded his arms with massive satisfaction.

William Finch, tall and distinguished, vibrating in the centre of the room in a tangle of fear, and anger, and unpleasant pleasure.

Trevor, silver-haired, worldly, come to dust. Sitting apprehensively in his armchair, facing his future with more sorrow than horror. The only one of them who showed the slightest sign of realizing that it was they who had got themselves into trouble, not I.

Embezzlers were not normally men of violence. They robbed on paper, not with their fists. They might hate and threaten, but actual physical assault wasn't natural to them. I looked bleakly at the five faces and thought again of the nuclear effect of critical mass. Small separate amounts of radio-active matter could release harnessable energy. If small amounts got together into a larger mass, they exploded.

'Why did you come?' Trevor said.

'Finchy rang and told us he'd be here,' Powys said, jerking his head in my direction. 'Never get another opportunity like it, will we? Seeing as you and Finchy will be out of circulation, for a bit.'

Finch shook his head fiercely: but I reckoned there were different sorts of circulation, and it would be a very long time before he was back on a racetrack. I wouldn't have wanted to face the ruin before him: the crash from such a height.

Glitberg said, 'Four years locked in a cell. Four sodding years, because of him.'

'Don't bellyache,' I said. 'Four years in jail for a million pounds is a damned good bargain. You offer it around, you'd get a lot of takers.'

'Prison is dehumanizing,' Powys said. 'They treat you worse than animals.'

'Don't make me cry,' I said. 'You chose the way that led there. And all of you have got what you wanted.

Money, money, money. So run away and play with it.' Maybe I spoke with too much heat, but nothing was going to defuse the developing bomb.

Anger that I'd let myself in for such a mess was a stab in the mind. I simply hadn't thought of Finch summoning reinforcements. He'd had no need of it: it had been merely spite. I'd believed I could manage Finch and Trevor with reasonable safety, and here all of a sudden was a whole new battle.

'Trevor,' I said, flatly, 'don't forget the photostats I left with a friend.'

'What friend?' Finch said, gaining belligerence from his supporters.

'Barclays Bank,' I said.

Finch was furious, but he couldn't prove it wasn't true, and even he must have seen that any serious attempt at wringing out a different answer might cost them more time in the clink.

I had hoped originally to make a bargain with Finch, but it was no longer possible. I thought merely, at that point, of getting through whatever was going to happen with some semblance of grace. A doubtful proposition, it seemed to me.

'How much does he know?' Ownslow demanded of Trevor.

'Enough . . .' Trevor said. 'Everything.'

'Bloody hell.'

'How did he find out?' Glitberg demanded.

'Because William took him on his boat,' Trevor said.

'A mistake,' Powys said. 'That was a mistake, Finchy. He came sniffing round us in London, asking about boats. Like I told you.'

'You chain dogs up,' Finch said.

'But not in a floating kennel, Finchy. Not this bastard here with his bloody quick eyes. You should have kept him away from your boat.'

'I don't see that it matters,' Trevor said. 'Like he said, we've all got our money.'

'And what if he tells?' Ownslow demanded.

'Oh, he'll tell,' Trevor said with certainty. 'And of course there will be trouble. Questions and enquiries and a lot of fuss. But in the end, if we're careful, we should keep the cash.'

'Should isn't enough,' Powys said fiercely.

'Nothing's certain,' Trevor said.

'One thing's certain,' Ownslow said. 'This creep's going to get his come-uppance.'

All five of the faces turned my way together, and in each one, even in Trevor's, I read the same intent.

'That's what we came for,' Powys said.

'Four bloody years,' Ownslow said. 'And the sneers my kids suffered.' He pushed off the door and uncrossed his arms.

Glitberg said, 'Judges looking down their bloody noses.'

They all, quite slowly, came nearer.

It was uncanny, and frightening. The forming of a pack.

Behind me there was the table, and behind that, solid wall. They were between me and the windows, and between me and the door.

'Don't leave any marks,' Powys said. 'If he goes to the police it'll be his word against ours, and if he's nothing to show that can't do much.' To me, directly, he said, 'We'll have a bloody good alibi, I'll tell you that.'

The odds looked appalling. I made a sudden thrusting jump to one side, to dodge the menacing advance, outflank the cohorts, scramble for the door.

I got precisely nowhere. Two strides, no more. Their hands clutched me from every direction, dragging me back, their bodies pushing against me with their collective weight. It was as if my attempt to escape had triggered them off. They were determined, heavy, and grunting. I struggled with flooding fury to disentangle myself, and I might as well have wrestled with an octopus.

They lifted me up bodily and sat me on the end of the table. Three of them held me there with hands like clamps.

Finch pulled open a drawer in the side of the table, and threw out a checked red and white table cloth, which floated across the room and fell on a chair. Under the cloth, several big square napkins. Red and white checks. Tapestry's racing colours. Ridiculous thought at such a moment.

Finch and Connaught Powys each rolled a napkin into a shape like a bandage and knotted it round one of my ankles. They tied my ankles to the legs of the table. They pulled my jacket off. They rolled and tied a red and white napkin round each of my wrists, pulling the knots tight and leaving cheerful bright loose ends like streamers.

They did it fast.

All of the faces were flushed, and the eyes fuzzy, in the fulfilment of lust. Glitberg and Ownslow, one on each side, pushed me down flat on my back. Finch and Connaught Powys pulled my arms over my head and tied the napkins on my wrists to the other two legs of the table. My resistance made them rougher.

The table was, I supposed, about two feet by four. Long enough to reach from my knees to the top of my head. Hard, covered with glass, uncomfortable.

They stood back to admire their handiwork. All breathing heavily from my useless fight. All overweight, out of condition, ripe to drop dead from coronaries at any moment. They went on living.

'Now what?' said Ownslow, considering. He went down on his knees and took off my shoes.

'Nothing,' Trevor said. 'That's enough.'

The pack instinct had died out of him fastest. He turned away, refusing to meet my eyes.

'Enough!' Glitberg said. 'We've done nothing yet.'

Powys eyed me assessingly from head to foot, and maybe he saw just what they had done.

'Yes,' he said slowly. 'That's enough.'

Ownslow said 'Here!' furiously, and Glitberg said,

'Not on your life.' Powys ignored them and turned to Finch.

'He's yours,' he said. 'But if I were you I'd just leave him here.'

'*Leave* him?'

'You've got better things to do than fool around with him. You don't want to leave marks on him, and I'm telling you, the way we've tied him will be enough.'

William Finch thought about it, and nodded, and came half way back to cold sense. He stepped closer until he stood near my ribs. He stared down, eyes full of the familiar hate.

'I hope you're satisfied,' he said.

He spat in my face.

Powys, Glitberg and Ownslow thought it a marvellous idea. They did it in turn, as disgustingly as they could.

Not Trevor. He looked on uncomfortably and made small useless gestures of protest with his hands.

I could hardly see for slime. It felt horrible, and I couldn't get it off.

'All right,' Powys said. 'That's it, then. You push off now, Finchy, and you get packed, Trevor, and then we'll all leave.'

'Here!' Ownslow said again, protestingly.

'Do you want an alibi, or don't you?' Powys said. 'You got to make some effort. Be seen by a few squares. Help the lies along.'

Ownslow gave in with a bad grace, and contented

himself with making sure that none of the table napkins had worked loose. Which they hadn't.

Finch had gone from my diminished sight and also, it appeared, from my life. A car started in the drive, crunched on the gravel, and faded away.

Trevor went out of the room and presently returned carrying a suitcase. In the interval Ownslow sniggered, Glitberg jeered, and Powys tested the amount that I could move my arms. Half an inch, at the most.

'You won't get out of that,' he said. He shook my elbow and watched the results. 'I reckon this'll make us even.' He turned as Trevor came back. 'Are all doors locked?'

'All except the front one,' Trevor said.

'Right. Then let's be off.'

'But what about *him?*' Trevor said. 'We can't just leave him like that.'

'Can't we? Why not?'

'But . . .' Trevor said: and fell silent.

'Someone will find him tomorrow,' Powys said. 'A cleaner, or something. Do you have a cleaner?'

'Yes,' Trevor said doubtfully. 'But she doesn't come in on Tuesdays. My wife will be back though.'

'There you are, then.'

'All right.' He hesitated. 'My wife keeps some money in the kitchen. I'll just fetch it.'

'Right.'

Trevor went on his errand and came back. He stood near me, looking worried.

'Ro . . .'

'Come on,' said Powys impatiently. 'He's ruined you, like he ruined us. You owe him bloody nothing.'

He shepherded them out of the door; Trevor unhappy, Glitberg sneering, Ownslow unassuaged. Powys looked back from the doorway, his own face, what I could see of it, full of smug satisfaction.

'I'll think of you,' he said. 'All night.'

He pulled the door towards him, to shut it, and switched off the light.

Human bodies were not designed to remain for hours in one position. Even in sleep, they regularly shifted. Joints bent and unbent, muscles contracted and relaxed.

No human body was designed to lie as I was lying, with constant strain already running up through legs, stomach, chest, shoulders and arms. Within five minutes, while they were still there, it had become in any normal way intolerable. One would not have stayed in that attitude from choice.

When they had gone, I simply could not visualize the time ahead. My imagination short-circuited. Blanked out. What did one do if one couldn't bear something, and had to?

The worst of the spit slid slowly off my face, but the rest remained, sticky and itching. I blinked my eyes wide open in the dark and thought of being at home in my own quiet bed, as I'd hoped to be that night.

I realized that I was having a surprising amount of difficulty in breathing. One took breathing so much for granted; but the mechanics weren't all that simple. The muscles between the ribs pulled the ribcage out and upwards, allowing air to rush down to the lungs. It wasn't, so to speak, the air going in which expanded the chest, but the expansion of the chest which drew in the air. With the ribcage pulled continuously up, the normal amount of muscle movement was much curtailed.

I still wore a collar and tie. I would choke, I thought.

The other bit that breathed for you was the diaphragm, a nice hefty floor of muscle between the heart-lung cavity and the lower lot of guts. Thank God for diaphragms, I thought. Long may they reign. Mine chugged away, doing its best.

If I passed the night in delirium, I thought, it would be a good idea. If I'd studied Yoga . . . mind out of body. Too late for that. I was always too late. Never prepared.

Stabs of strain afflicted both my shoulders. Needles. Swords.

Think of something else.

Boats. Think of boats. Big expensive boats, built to high standards in top British boat yards, sailing away out of Britain to ship-brokers in Antibes and Antigua.

Huge floating assets in negotiable form. None of the usual bureaucratic trouble about transferring money abroad in huge amounts. No dollar premiums to worry about, or other such hurdles set up by grasping governments. Just put your money in fibreglass and ropes and sails, and float away on it on the tide.

The man at Goldenwave had told me they never lacked for orders. Boats, he said, didn't deteriorate like aeroplanes or cars. Put a quarter of a million into a boat, and it would most likely increase in value, as years went by. Sell the boat, bank the money, and hey presto, all nicely, tidily, and legally done.

There were frightful protests from my arms and legs. I couldn't move them in any way more than an inch: could give them no respite. It really was, I thought, an absolutely bloody revenge.

No use reflecting that it was I who had stirred up Powys and Ownslow and Glitberg. Poke a rattlesnake with a stick, don't be surprised if he bites you. I'd gone to find out if it was they who'd abducted me, and found out instead what they'd done with all the missing money.

Paid for boats. The mention of boats had produced the menace, not the mention of abduction. Boats paid for by the taxpayers, the electronics firm, and the Nantuckets of New York. Gone with the four winds. Exchanged for a pile of nice strong currency, lying somewhere in a foreign bank, waiting for the owners to stroll along and collect.

Trevor linked them all. Maybe the boats had originally been his idea. I hadn't thought of William Finch knowing Connaught Powys: certainly not as well as he clearly did. But through Trevor, along the track from embezzlement to ship building . . . along the way, they had met.

The pains in my arms and legs intensified, and there was a great shaft of soreness up my chest.

I thought: I don't know how to face this. I don't know how. It isn't possible.

Trevor, I thought. Surely Trevor wouldn't have left me like this . . . not like this . . . if he had realized. Trevor, who had been so distressed at my dishevelled appearance in the police station, who as far as I could see had really cared about my health.

Ye Gods, I thought, I'd go gladly back to the sail locker . . . to the van . . . to almost anywhere one could think of.

Some of my muscles were trembling. Would the fibres simply collapse? I wondered. Would the muscles just tear apart; the ligaments disconnect from the bones? Oh for God's sake, I told myself, you've got enough to worry about, without that. Think of something cheerful.

I couldn't, off-hand. Even cheerful subjects like Tapestry were no good. I couldn't see me being able to ride in the Whitbread Gold Cup.

Minutes dragged and telescoped, stretching to hours. The various separate pains gradually coalesced into an all pervading fire. Thought became fragmentary, and then, I reckon, more or less stopped.

The unbearable was there, inside, savage and consuming. Unbearable . . . there was no such word.

By morning I'd gone a long way into an extreme land I hadn't known existed. A different dimension, where the memory of ordinary pain was a laugh.

An internal place; a heavy core. The external world had retreated. I no longer felt as if I were any particular shape: had no picture of hands or feet, or where they were. Everything was crimson and dark.

I existed as a mass. Unified. A single lump of matter, of a weight and fire like the centre of the earth.

There was nothing else. No thought. Just feeling, and eternity.

A noise dragged me back.

People talking. Voices in the house.

I saw that daylight had returned and was trickling in round the edge of the curtains. I tried to call out, and could not.

Footsteps crossed and recrossed the hall, and at last, at last, someone opened the door, and switched on the light.

Two women came in. I stared at them, and they stared at me: on both sides with disbelief.

They were Hilary Pinlock, and Jossie.

Hilary cut through the red checked table napkins with a small pair of scissors from her handbag.

I tried to sit up and behave with sangfroid, but my stretched muscles wouldn't respond to directions. I ended somehow with my face against her chest and my throat heaving with unstoppable half-stifled groans.

'It's all right, Ro. It's all right, my dear, my dear.'

Her thin arms held me close and tight, rocking me

gently, taking into herself the impossible pain, suffering for me like a mother. Mother, sister, lover, child . . . a woman who crossed the categories and left them blurred.

I had a mouthful of blouse button and was comforted to my soul.

She put an arm round my waist and more or less carried me to the nearest chair. Jossie stood looking on, her face filled with a greater shock than finding me there.

'Do you realize,' she said, 'that Dad's gone?'

I didn't feel like saying much.

'Did you hear?' Jossie said. Her voice was tight, unfriendly. 'Dad's gone. Walked out. Left all the horses. Do you hear? He's cleared half the papers out of the office and burned them in the incinerator, and this lady says it is because my father is an embezzler, and you . . . you are going to give him away to the Nantuckets, and the police.'

The big eyes were hard. 'And Trevor, too. Trevor. I've known him all my life. How could you? And you *knew* . . . you knew on Sunday . . . all day . . . what you were going to do. You took me out, and you knew you were going to ruin all our lives. I think you're hateful.'

Hilary took two strides, gripped her by the shoulders, and positively shook her.

'Stop it, you silly girl. Open your silly eyes. He did all this for you.'

Jossie tore herself free. 'What do you mean?' she demanded.

'He didn't want your father to go to prison. Because he's your father. He's sent others there, but he didn't want it to happen to your father, or to Trevor King. So he warned them, and gave them time to destroy things. Evidence. Paper and records.' She glanced back at me. 'He told me on Saturday what he planned . . . to tell your father how much he knew, and to offer him a bargain. Time, enough time, if he would destroy his tracks and go, in a way which would cause you least pain. Time to go before the police arrived to confiscate his passport. Time to arrange his life as best he could. And they made him pay for the time he gave them. He paid for every second of it . . .' She gestured in frustrated disgust towards the table and the cut pieces of cloth, ' . . . in *agony.*'

'Hilary,' I protested.

There never had been any stopping Hilary Pinlock in full flight. She said fiercely to Jossie, 'He can put up with a lot, but I reckon it's too much to have you reviling him for what he's suffered for your sake. So you just get some sense into your little bird-brain, and beg his pardon.'

I helplessly shook my head. Jossie stood with her mouth open in shattered shock, and then she looked at the table, and discarded the thought.

'Dad would never have done that,' she said.

'There were five of them,' I said wearily. 'People do

things in gangs which they would never have done on their own.'

She looked at me with shadowed eyes. Then she turned abruptly on her heel and walked out of the room.

'She's terribly upset,' Hilary said, making allowances.

'Yes.'

'Are you all right?'

'No.'

She made a face. 'I'll get you something. They must at least have aspirins in this house.'

'Tell me first,' I said, 'how you got here.'

'Oh. I was worried. I rang your cottage all evening. Late into the night. And again this morning, early. I had a feeling . . . I didn't think it would hurt if I came over to check, so I drove to your cottage . . . but of course you weren't there. I saw your neighbour, Mrs Morris, and she said you hadn't been home all night. So then I went to your office. They were in a tizzy because some time between last night and this morning your partner had taken away a great many papers, and neither of you had turned up for work.'

'What time . . .' I said.

'About half past nine, when I went to the office.' She looked at her watch. 'It's a quarter to eleven, now.'

Fourteen hours, I thought numbly. It must have been at least fourteen hours, that I'd been lying there.

'Well, I drove to Finch's house,' she said. 'I had a bit of

trouble finding the way, and when I got there, everything was in a shambles. There was a girl secretary weeping all over the place. People asking what was going on . . . and your girl Jossie in a dumbstruck state. I asked her if she'd seen you. I said I thought you could be in real trouble. I asked her where Trevor King lived. I made her come with me, to show me the way. I tried to tell her what her father had been doing, and how he'd abducted you, but she didn't want to believe it.'

'No.'

'So then we arrived here, and found you.'

'How did you get in?'

'The back door was wide open.'

'Wide . . .?'

I had a sudden picture of Trevor going out to the kitchen, saying it was to fetch some money. To open the door. To give me a tiny chance. Poor Trevor.

'That package I gave you,' I said. 'With all the photostats. When you get home, will you burn it?'

'If that's what you want.'

'Mm.'

Jossie came back and sprawled in a red armchair, all angular legs.

'Sorry,' she said abruptly.

'So am I.'

'You did help him,' she said.

Hilary said, 'Do good to those who despitefully use you.'

I slid my eyes her way. 'That's enough of that.'

'What are you talking about?' Jossie demanded.

Hilary shook her head with a smile and went on an aspirin hunt. Butazolidin, I imagined, would do more good. Things were better now I was sitting in a chair, but a long old way from right.

'He left me a letter,' Jossie said. 'More or less the same as yours.'

'How do you mean?'

'Dear Jossie, Sorry, Love, Dad.'

'Oh.'

'He said he was going to France . . .' She broke off, and stared ahead of her, her face full of misery. 'Life's going to be unutterably bloody, isn't it,' she said, 'for a long time to come?'

'Mm.'

'What am I going to do?' The question was a rhetorical wail, but I answered it.

'I did want to warn you,' I said. 'But I couldn't . . . before I'd talked to your father. I meant it, though, about you coming to live in the cottage. If you thought . . . that you could.'

'Ro . . .' Her voice was little more than a breath.

I sat and ached, and thought in depression about telephoning the Nantuckets, and the chaos I'd have to deal with in the office.

Jossie turned her head towards me and gave me a long inspection.

'You look spineless,' she said. Her voice was halfway back in spirit to the old healthy mockery; shaky, but doing its best. 'And I'll tell you something else.' She paused and swallowed.

'When Dad went, he left *me* behind, but he took the detestable Lida with him.'

There was enough, in that, for the future.

10lb PENALTY

Dick Francis has written thirty-nine international bestsellers and is widely acclaimed as one of the world's finest thriller writers. His awards include the Crime Writers' Association's Cartier Diamond Dagger for his outstanding contribution to the crime genre, and an honorary Doctorate of Humane Letters from Tufts University of Boston. In 1996 Dick Francis was made a Mystery Writers of America Grand Master for a lifetime's achievement.

Also by Dick Francis in Pan Books

DEAD CERT
NERVE
FOR KICKS
ODDS AGAINST
FLYING FINISH
BLOOD SPORT
FORFEIT
ENQUIRY
RAT RACE
BONECRACK
SMOKESCREEN
SLAY-RIDE
KNOCK DOWN
HIGH STAKES
IN THE FRAME
RISK
TRIAL RUN
WHIP HAND
REFLEX
TWICE SHY
BANKER
THE DANGER
PROOF
BREAK IN
BOLT
HOT MONEY
THE EDGE
STRAIGHT
LONGSHOT
COMEBACK
DRIVING FORCE
DECIDER
WILD HORSES
COME TO GRIEF
TO THE HILT
FIELD OF THIRTEEN
SECOND WIND
SHATTERED

THE SPORT OF QUEENS
(autobiography)

LESTER: The Official
Biography

DICK FRANCIS
OMNIBUS ONE:
Long Shot, Straight, High
Stakes

DICK FRANCIS
OMNIBUS TWO:
Forfeit, Risk,
Reflex

Dick Francis

10lb PENALTY

PAN BOOKS

First published 1997 by Michael Joseph Ltd

This edition published 1998 by Pan Books
an imprint of Pan Macmillan Ltd
Pan Macmillan, 20 New Wharf Road, London N1 9RR
Basingstoke and Oxford
Associated companies throughout the world
www.panmacmillan.com

ISBN 0 330 37001 4

11 13 15 17 19 18 16 14 12 10

A CIP catalogue record for this book is available from
the British Library.

Phototypeset by Intype London Ltd
Printed by Mackays of Chatham plc, Chatham, Kent

With thanks to my grandson
MATTHEW FRANCIS
aged eighteen

and to

Weatherbys
and
No. 10 Downing Street

CHAPTER ONE

Glue-sniffing jockeys don't win the Derby.

I'd never sniffed glue in my life.

All the same, I stood before the man whose horses I rode and listened to him telling me he had no further use for my services. He sat behind his large antique paper-covered desk fidgeting with his clean fingernails. His hands were a yellowish white, very smooth.

'I have it on good authority,' he said.

'But I don't!' I protested in bewilderment. 'I've never sniffed glue or anything else. Certainly not cocaine. I've never even smoked pot. It's not true.'

He looked at me coldly with the knowing eyes of a rich, powerful, assured and physically bulky man who had inherited a good brain and a chunk of merchant bank, and trained racehorses prestigiously out of obsession.

I was not yet eighteen at that point and, I now know, immature for my age, though of course I wasn't aware of it at the time. I felt helpless, though, in the face of his inaccurate certainty, and had no idea how to deal with it.

'Sir Vivian ...' I began with desperation, but he effortlessly cut me off with his heavier authoritative voice.

'You can clear off at once, Benedict,' he said. 'I'll not have my stable contaminated by rumours of a drug-taking jockey, even if he is an amateur and not much good.' He saw me flinch but went on relentlessly. 'You'll never be a top race rider. You're too big, for one thing, or at least you will be in a year or two and, frankly, you look clumsy on a horse. All arms and legs. In your hands, the most collected jumper turns in a sprawling performance. With that and an unsatisfactory reputation ... well, I no longer want you associated with my stable.'

I stared at him numbly, hurt more deeply by his fairly brutal assessment of my lack of riding ability, which could perhaps be substantiated, rather than by the accusations of drug-taking, which couldn't.

Around me the familiar walls of his stable office seemed to recede, leaving me isolated with a thumping heart and no feeling below the ankles. All the framed photographs of past winners, all the bookshelves and the olive-green wallpaper faded away. I saw only the stony faces spelling out the effective end of my long-held dream of winning all races from the Grand National down.

I expect seventeen is a better age than most to be

chopped off at the ambitious knees. It just didn't feel like it at that moment of the slice of the axe.

'Outside that window,' said Sir Vivian Durridge, pointing, 'a car is waiting for you. The driver says he has a message for you. He's been waiting a good hour or more, while you've been out at riding exercise.'

I followed the direction of his finger, and saw, some way across the raked gravel of the imposing entrance driveway to his porticoed domain, a large black car inhabited solely by a chauffeur in a peaked cap.

'Who is it?' I asked blankly.

Vivian Durridge either didn't know or wasn't telling. He said merely, 'On your way out, you can ask him.'

'But, sir . . .' I began again, and dried to fresh silence in the continuing negation of his distrust.

'I advise you to clean up your act,' he said, making a gesture that directed me to leave. 'And now, I have work to do.'

He looked steadfastly down at his desk and ignored me, and after a few seconds I walked unsteadily over to the high polished door with its gilded knob and let myself out.

It was unfair. I had not cried much in my life but I felt weak then and near to weeping. No one before had pitilessly accused me of something I hadn't done. No one had so ruthlessly despised my riding. I still had a thin skin.

No other good trainer would let me into his stable if Vivian Durridge had kicked me out of his.

In a mist of bewildered misery I crossed the wide Durridge entrance hall, made my way through the heavy front door and crunched across the gravel to where the car and chauffeur waited.

I knew neither of them. The August morning sun gleamed on black spotless bodywork, and the chauffeur with the shiny black peak to his cap let down the window beside him and stretched out a black uniformed arm, silently offering me a white unaddressed envelope.

I took it. The flap was only lightly glued. I peeled it open, drew out a single white card from inside, and read the brief message.

'*Get in the car.*'

Underneath an afterthought had been added.

'*Please.*'

I looked back towards the big house from which I'd been so roughly banned and saw Vivian Durridge standing by his window, watching me. He made no movement: no reconsidering action, no farewell.

I understood none of it.

The handwriting on the card was my father's.

I sat on the back seat of the car for almost an hour while the chauffeur drove at a slow pace through

Sussex, south of London, approaching finally the seaside spread of Brighton.

He would answer none of my questions except to say that he was following instructions, and after a while I stopped asking. Short of jumping out and running free at any of the few traffic-light stops, it seemed I was going to go wherever my father had ordained, and as I had no fear of him I would, from long conditioned habit, do what he asked.

I thought chiefly – and in a mixture of rage and unhappiness – of the scene in Durridge's study, his words circling endlessly in memory and not getting more bearable as time went by.

The black car drifted past Regency town houses and open-fronted souvenir shops, past old grandeur and new-world commercialism, and sighed to a stop on the sea front outside the main door of a large hotel of ancient French architectural pedigree with bright beach towels drying on its decorative wrought-iron balconies.

Porters appeared solicitously. The chauffeur climbed out of his seat and ceremoniously opened the door beside me and, thus prompted, I stood up into the sea air, hearing gulls crying and voices in the distance calling on the wet ebb-tide strand, smelling the salt on the wind and unexpectedly feeling the lift of spirits of the sandcastle holidays of childhood.

The chauffeur made me a small sketch of a bow and pointed at the hotel's main door, and then, still without explaining, he returned to his driving seat and at a convenient moment inserted himself into the flow of traffic and smoothly slid away.

'Luggage, sir?' one of the porters suggested. He was barely older than myself.

I shook my head. For luggage I wore the clothes suitable for first-lot August morning exercise with the Durridge string: jodhpurs, jodhpur boots, short-sleeved sports shirt and harlequin-printed lightweight zipped jacket (unzipped). I carried by its chin-strap my shiny blue helmet. With a conscious effort I walked these inappropriate garments into the grand hotel, but I needn't have worried: the once-formal lobby buzzed like a beehive with people looking normal in cut-off shorts, flip-flop sandals and message-laden T-shirts. The composed woman at the reception desk gave my riding clothes an incurious but definite assessment like a click on an identification parade and answered my slightly hoarse enquiry.

'Mr George Juliard?' she repeated. 'Who shall I say is asking for him?'

'His son.'

She picked up a telephone receiver, pressed buttons, spoke, listened, gave me the news.

'Please go up. Room four-twelve. The lift is to your left.'

My father was standing in an open doorway as I walked down a passage to locate four-twelve. I stopped as I approached him and watched him inspect me, as he customarily did, from my dark curly hair (impervious to straightening by water), to my brown eyes, thin face, lean frame, five foot eleven (or thereabouts) of long legs to unpolished boots: not in any way an impressive experience for an ambitious parent.

'Ben,' he said. He breathed down his nose as if accepting a burden. 'Come in.'

He tried hard always to be a good father, but gave no weight to my infrequent assurances that he succeeded. I was a child he hadn't wanted, the accidental consequence of his teenage infatuation with a woman biologically just old enough to be his own mother. On the day I went to Brighton I was almost as old as he had been when he fathered me.

Over the years I'd gleaned the details. There had been a hullabaloo in both extended families when they were told of the pregnancy, an even worse fuss (product of the times) when my mother refused an abortion, and a frosty turning of backs at the hasty (and happy) wedding.

The marriage-day photograph was the only record I had of my mother, who ironically died of pre-eclampsia at my birth, leaving her very young husband literally holding the baby with his envisaged bright future in ruins, so it was said.

George Juliard, however, who wasn't considered bright for nothing, promptly rearranged his whole life, jettisoning the intended Oxford degree and career in law, persuading his dead wife's sister to add me to her already large family of four sons, and setting forth into the City to learn how to make money. He had paid from the beginning for my keep and later for my education and had further fulfilled his duties by turning up at parent–teacher meetings and punctiliously sending me cards and gifts at Christmas and birthdays. A year ago for my birthday he'd given me an air ticket to America so that I could spend the summer holidays on a horse farm in Virginia owned by the family of a school friend. Many fathers had done less.

I followed him into four-twelve and found without surprise that I was in the sitting-room of a suite directly facing the sea, the English Channel stretching blue-grey to the horizon. When George Juliard had set out with the goal of making money, he had spectacularly hit his target.

'Have you had breakfast?' he asked.

'I'm not hungry.'

He ignored the untruth. 'What did Vivian Durridge say to you?'

'He sacked me.'

'Yes, but what did he *say*?'

'He said I couldn't ride and that I sniffed glue and also cocaine.'

My father stared. 'He said *what*?'

'He said what you asked him to, didn't he? He said he had it on good authority that I took drugs.'

'Did you ask him who his "good authority" was?'

'No.' I hadn't thought of it until too late, in the car.

'You've a lot to learn,' my father said.

'It was no coincidence that you sent a car to wait for me.'

He smiled marginally, light gleaming in his eyes. He was taller than I, with wider shoulders, and in many ways inhabited an intenser, more powerful version of the body I had been growing into during the past five years. His hair was darker than mine, and curlier, a close rug on his Grecian-like head. The firmness in his face, now that he was approaching his late thirties, had already been apparent in his wedding photograph, when the gap in age had showed not at all, where the bridegroom had looked the dominant partner and the bride, smiling in her blue silk dress outside the registry office, had shone with youthful beauty.

'Why did you do it?' I asked, trying to sound more adult than bitter, and not managing it.

'Do what?'

'Get me kicked out.'

'Ah.'

He walked over to a pair of glass doors leading to a balcony and opened them, letting in the vivid coastal air and the high voices from the beach. He stood there silently for a while, breathing deeply, and then, as if making up his mind, he closed the windows purposefully and turned towards me.

'I have a proposition for you,' he said.

'What proposition?'

'It will take a good while to explain.' He lifted a telephone receiver and told the room service that whether or not breakfast had been officially over an hour ago, they were to send up immediately a tray of cereal, milk, hot toast, grilled bacon with tomatoes and mushrooms, an apple, a banana and a pot of tea. 'And don't argue,' he said to me, disconnecting, 'you look as if you haven't eaten for a week.'

I said, 'Did *you* tell Sir Vivian that I take drugs?'

'No, I didn't. Do you?'

'No.'

We looked at each other, virtual strangers though as closely tied as genetically possible. I had lived according to his edicts, had been to his choice of schools, had learned to ride, to ski and to shoot because he had distantly funded my preference for those pursuits, and I had not received tickets for Beyreuth, Covent Garden or La Scala because he didn't enthuse over time spent that way.

I was his product, as most teenage sons were of their fathers. I was also aware of his strict sense of honour, his clear vision of right and wrong and his insistence that shameful acts be acknowledged and paid for, not lied about and covered up. He was, as my four older cousins/brothers told me pityingly, a hard act to follow.

'Sit down,' he said.

The room was warm. I took off my jazzy zipped

jacket and laid it on the floor with my helmet and sat in a light armchair, where he pointed.

'I have been selected,' he said, 'as a candidate in the Hoopwestern by-election, in place of the sitting MP who has died.'

'Er . . .' I blinked, not quickly taking it in.

'Did you hear what I said?'

'Do you mean . . . you are running for office?'

'Your American friend Chuck would say I'm running for office, but as this is England, I am standing for Parliament.'

I didn't know what I should say. *Great? How awful? Why?* I said blunderingly, 'Will you get in?'

'It's a marginal seat. A toss up.'

I looked vaguely round the impersonal room. He waited with a shade of impatience.

'What is the proposition?' I asked.

'Well, now . . .' Somewhere within him he relaxed. 'Vivian Durridge treated you harshly.'

'Yes, he did.'

'Accusing you of taking drugs . . . That was his own invention.'

'But what *for*?' I asked, bewildered. 'If he didn't want me around, why didn't he just say so?'

'He told me you would never be more than an average-standard amateur. Never a top professional jockey. What you were doing was a waste of time.'

I didn't want to believe it. I couldn't face believing it. I protested vehemently, 'But I enjoy it.'

'Yes, and if you look honestly inside yourself, you'll admit that a pleasant waste of time isn't enough for you at this stage.'

'I'm not you,' I said. 'I don't have your . . . your . . .'

'Drive?' he suggested.

I thought it over weakly, and nodded.

'I am satisfied, though,' he said, 'that you have sufficient intelligence and . . . well . . . *courage* . . . for what I have in mind.'

If he intended to flatter me, of course he succeeded. Few young boys could throw overboard such an assessment.

'Father – ' I began.

'I thought we agreed you should call me Dad.'

He had insisted at parent-teacher-schoolboy meetings I should refer to him as 'Dad', and I had done so, but in my mind he was always Father, my formal and controlling authority.

'What do you want me to do?' I said.

He still wouldn't answer straightaway. He looked absent-mindedly out of the window and at my jacket on the floor. He fiddled with his fingers in a way that reminded me of Sir Vivian, and finally he said, 'I want you to take up the place you've been offered at Exeter University.'

'Oh.' I tried not to appear either astonished or annoyed, though I felt both. He went on, however, as if I'd launched into a long audible harangue.

'You've promised yourself a gap year, is that it?'

A gap year, so-called, was the currently fashionable pause between school and university, much praised and prized in terms of growing up in worldly experience before graduating academically. A lot to be said for it . . . little against.

'You agreed I should have a gap year,' I protested.

'I didn't prohibit it. That's different.'

'But . . . *can* you prohibit it? And why do you want to?'

'Until you are eighteen I can legally do almost anything that's for your own good or, rather, that I consider is for your own good. You're no fool, Ben. You know that's a fact. For the next three weeks, until your birthday on August thirty-first, I am still in charge of your life.'

I did know it. I also knew that though by right I would receive basic university tuition fees from the state, I would not qualify for living expenses or other grants because of my father's wealth. Working one's way through college, although just possible in some countries, was hardly an option in Britain. Realistically, if my father wouldn't pay for my keep, I wouldn't be going to university, whether Exeter or anywhere else.

I said neutrally, 'When I asked you, ages ago, you said you thought a gap year was a good idea.'

'I didn't know that you intended your gap year to be spent on a racecourse.'

'It's a growing-up experience!'

'It's a minefield of moral traps.'

'You don't trust me!' Even I could hear the outraged self-regard in my voice. Too near a whine. I said more frostily, 'Because of your example, I would keep out of trouble.'

'No bribes, do you mean?' He was unimpressed by my own shot at flattery. 'You'd throw no races? Everyone would believe in your incorruptibility? Is that it? What about a rumour that you take drugs? Rumours destroy reputations quicker than truth.'

I was silenced. An unproven accusation had that morning rent apart my comfortable illusion that innocence could shield one from defamation. My father would no doubt categorise the revelation as 'growing up'.

A knock on the door punctuated my bitter thoughts with the arrival of a breakfast designed to give me a practically guilt-free release from chronic hunger. The necessity of keeping down to a low racing weight had occasionally made me giddy from deprivation. Even as I fell on the food ravenously I marvelled at my father's understanding of what I would actually eat and what I would reject.

'While you eat, you can listen,' he said. 'If you were going to be the world's greatest steeplechase jockey, I wouldn't ask . . . what I'm going to ask of you. If you were going to be, say, Isaac Newton, or Mozart, or some other genius, it would be pointless to ask that you should give it up. And I'm not asking you to give up riding altogether, just to give up trying to make it your life.'

Cornflakes and milk were wonderful.

'I have a suspicion,' he said, 'that you intended your gap year to go on for ever.'

I paused in mid munch. Couldn't deny he was right.

'So go to Exeter, Ben. Do your growing up *there.* I don't expect you to get a First. A Second would be fine; a Third is OK, though I guess you'll manage good results, as you always have done, in spite of the disadvantage of your birth date.'

I zoomed through the bacon, tomatoes and mushrooms and accompanied them with toast. Because of the rigid education system that graded schoolchildren by age and not ability, and because I'd been born on the last day of the age-grading year (September 1st would have given me an extra twelve months), I had always been the youngest in the class, always faced with the task of keeping up. A gap year would have levelled things nicely. And he was telling me, of course, that he understood all that, and was forgiving a poor outcome in the degree stakes before I'd even started.

'Before Exeter,' he said, 'I'd like you to work for *me.* I'd like you to come with me to Hoopwestern and help me get elected.'

I stared at him, chewing slowly but no longer tasting the mouthful.

'But,' I said, swallowing, 'I don't know anything about politics.'

'You don't have to. I don't want you to make speeches or any policy statements. I just want you to be with me, to be part of my scene.'

'I don't . . . I mean,' I more or less stuttered, 'I don't understand what I could do.'

'Eat your apple,' he said calmly, 'and I'll explain.'

He sat in one of the armchairs and crossed his legs with deliberation, as if he had rehearsed the next bit, and I thought that probably he had indeed gone over it repeatedly in his mind.

'The selection committee who chose me as their candidate,' he said, 'would frankly have preferred me to be married. They said so. They saw my bachelor state as a drawback. I told them therefore that I *had* been married, that my wife had died, and that I had a son. That cheered them up no end. What I'm asking you to do is to be a sort of substitute wife. To come with me in public. To be terribly *nice* to people.'

I said absentmindedly, 'To kiss babies?'

'*I'll* kiss the babies.' He was amused. '*You* can chat up the old ladies, and talk football, cricket and racing to the men.'

I thought of the wild thrill of riding in races. I thought of the intoxication of risking my neck, of pitting such skill as I had against fate and disaster, of completing the bucketing journeys without disgrace. A far cry from chatting up babies.

I yearned for the simple life of carefree reckless speed; the gift given by horses, the gift of skis; and I was beginning to learn, as everyone has to in the end, that all of life's pleasures have strings attached.

I said, 'How could anyone think I would bother with drugs when race-riding itself gives you the biggest high on earth?'

My father said, 'If Vivian said he would take you back, would you go?'

'No.' My answer came instinctively, without thought. Things couldn't be the same. I had gone a long way down reality's road in those few hours of an August Wednesday. I could acknowledge grimly that I would never be my dream jockey. I would never win my Grand National. But patting babies instead? Good grief!

'Polling day,' he said, 'is more than three weeks before term starts at Exeter. You will be eighteen by then . . .'

'And,' I said, without either joy or regret, 'I wrote to Exeter to say I wouldn't be taking up the place they'd offered me. Even if you instruct me to go, I can't.'

'I overruled your decision,' he told me flatly. 'I thought you might do that. I've observed you, you know, throughout your young life, even if we've never been particularly close. I got in touch with Exeter and reversed your cancellation. They are now expecting your registration. They have arranged lodging for you on campus. Unless you totally rebel and run away, you'll go ahead with your degree.'

I felt a lurching and familiar recognition of this man's power as a force that far outweighed any ordinary family relationship. Even Exeter University had done his bidding.

'But, Father . . .' I said feebly.

'Dad.'

'Dad . . .' The word was wholly inappropriate both for the image of him as the conventionally supportive parent of a schoolboy and for my perception of him as something far different from an average man in a business suit.

The Grand National, for him, I saw, was the road to Downing Street. Winning the race was the Prime Ministership in Number Ten. He was asking me to abandon my own unobtainable dream to help him have a chance of achieving his own.

I looked at the untouched apple and banana and had no more appetite.

I said, 'You don't need me.'

'I need to win votes. You can help with that. If I weren't totally convinced of your value as a constituent-pleaser you wouldn't be sitting here now.'

'Well . . .' I hesitated, 'to be honest, I wish I wasn't.'

I would have been pottering about happily in Vivian Durridge's stable yard, untroubled in my illusions. And I would have been drifting towards a less abrupt, less brutal awakening. I would also, I supposed, have been going to be cumulatively depressed. The alternative future thrust at me now was at least challenging, not a slow slide to nowhere.

'Ben,' he said briskly, almost as if he could read my thoughts, 'give it a try. Enjoy it.'

He gave me an envelope full of money and told me to go out and buy clothes. 'Get anything you need. We're going to Hoopwestern from here.'

'But my stuff – ' I began.

'Your stuff, as you call it, is being packed into a box by Mrs Wells.' Mrs Wells had rented me a room in her house along the road from the Durridge stable. 'I'm paying her until the end of the month,' my father said. 'She's quite pleased about that, though she said, you'd like to know, that you were a nice quiet boy, a pleasure to have around.' He smiled. 'I've arranged for your things to be collected. You'll be reunited with them soon, perhaps tomorrow.'

It was a bit, I thought, like being hit by a tidal wave, and it wasn't the first time he had yanked me out of one easy way of life and set me down on a different path. My dead mother's sister, Aunt Susan (and her husband Harry) who had reluctantly agreed to bring me up, had felt affronted, and said so bitterly and often, when my father plucked me out of the comprehensive school that had been 'good enough' for her four sons, and insisted that I take diction lessons and extra tuition in maths, my best subject, and had by one way or another seen to it that I spent five years of intensive learning in a top fee-paying school, Malvern College.

My cousins/brothers had both envied and sneered, so that effectively I had become the 'only' child that I actually was, not the petted last addition to a big family.

The father who had planned my life to the point of my unsought arrival in Brighton took it for granted that in the last three weeks of his legal guardianship I would still act as he directed.

I suppose, looking back, that many boys of seventeen would have complained and rebelled. All I can say is that they weren't dealing with a trusted and proven benevolent tyranny: and since I knew he meant me the opposite of harm, I took the envelope of money and spent it in the Brighton shops on clothes I thought his constituents would have voted for if they'd been judging a candidate by his teenage son's appearance.

We left Brighton soon after three in the afternoon, and not in the morning's overpowering black car with the unnervingly silent chauffeur (obeying my father's 'no explanation' instructions, it seemed) but in a cheerful metallic coffee-coloured Range Rover with silver and gold garlands of daisy-like flowers in metal paint shining along the sides.

'I'm new in the constituency,' my father said, grinning. 'I need to get myself noticed and recognised.'

He could hardly be missed, I thought. Heads turned

to watch us all along the south coast. Even so, I was unprepared for Hoopwestern (in Dorset), where it seemed that every suitable pole and tree bore a placard saying simply 'VOTE JULIARD'. No one in the town could avoid the message.

He had driven the advertisement-on-wheels from Brighton, with me sitting beside him on the front seat, and on the way he gave me non-stop instruction on what I should say and not say, do and not do, in my new role.

'Politicians,' he said, 'should seldom tell the whole truth.'

'But – '

'And politicians,' he went on, 'should *never* lie.'

'But you told me always to tell the truth.'

He smiled sideways at my simplicity. 'You better damn well tell *me* the truth. But people as a rule believe only what they *want* to believe, and if you tell them anything else they'll call you a trouble-maker and get rid of you and never give you your job back, even if what you said is proved spot on right by time.'

I said slowly, 'I suppose I do know that.'

'On the other hand, to be caught out in a lie is political death, so I don't do it.'

'But what do you say if you're asked a direct question and you can't tell the truth and you can't tell a lie?'

'You say "how very interesting" and change the subject.'

He drove the Range Rover with both speed and caution, the way he lived his whole life.

'During the next weeks,' he said, 'people will ask you what I think about this and that. Always say you don't know, they'd better ask me themselves. *Never* repeat to anyone anything I've said, even if I've said it in public. OK?'

'If you say so.'

'Remember this election is a contest. I have political enemies. Not every smiling face is a friend.'

'Do you mean . . . don't trust anyone?'

'That's exactly what I mean. People always kill Caesar. Don't trust *anyone*.'

'But that's cynical!'

'It's the first law of self-preservation.'

I said, 'I'd rather be a jockey.'

He shook his head in sorrow. 'I'm afraid you'll find that every world has its share of villains and cheats, jockeys not excepted.'

He drove into the centre of Hoopwestern, which proved to be one of those old indigenous market towns whose ancient heart had been petrified into a quaint cobbled pedestrian precinct, with the raw pulse of modern commerce springing up in huge office buildings and shopping malls on three sides around a ring road.

'This used to be a farming community,' my father said neutrally. 'Farming is now an industry like the factory here that makes light bulbs and employs more people. I need the light-bulb votes.'

His campaign headquarters, I found, were in a remarkable back-to-back hybrid house with an old bay-windowed frontage facing the cobbled square and a box-like featureless shop behind, one of a row looking out over a half-acre of car park. The house, with basic living accommodation for him (and me) upstairs, had once been a shoe store (now bankrupt because of an aggressive local mall) and was the twin of the place next door to it, a charity gift shop.

The political headquarters bustled with earnest endeavour, brightly coloured telephones, a click-clacking floor-standing photocopier, constant cups of tea, desks, computers, maps on the walls with coloured pins in, directories in heaps, envelopes by the carton-load and three middle-aged women enjoying the fuss.

We had parked in the car park and walked to the unmistakable glass-fronted premises where it not only said VOTE JULIARD in huge letters but displayed three large pictures of my father, all of them projecting a good-natured, intelligent, forward-looking person who would do an excellent job at Westminster.

The three women greeted him with merry cries of pleasure and a stack of problems.

'This is my son,' he said.

The merry smiles were bent my way. They looked me up and down. Three witches, I thought.

'Come in, dear,' one of them said. 'Cup of tea?'

CHAPTER TWO

The double shop, I found, was the regular constituency office of the party to which my father belonged. It was where Dennis Nagle, the previous Member, had lately held his Saturday 'surgeries', being present himself to listen to local problems and do his best to sort them out. Still in his fifties, he had died, poor fellow, of pancreatic cancer. His ambitious wife, Orinda, was reportedly steaming with vitriolic anger since the selection committee had passed her over in favour of my parent to fight to retain the vacant seat at the behest of the central party.

I learned about Orinda by sitting on an inconspicuous stool in a corner and listening to the three helpers describe to my father a visit the dispossessed lady had paid that day to the office.

The thinnest, least motherly help, who was also the most malicious, said with lip-curling glee, 'You'd think she'd be grieving for Dennis, but she just seems furious with him for dying. She talks about "*our* constituents", like she always did. She says she wrote his speeches and formed his opinions. She said it was understood from when Dennis was first ill that she would take his place. She says we three are traitors to be working for you, George. She was absolutely stuttering with rage. She says if you think she'll meekly go away, you have another think coming. And she says she is going to tonight's dinner!'

My father grimaced.

I thought that the selection committee had probably acted with good sense.

From my stool I also learned that the main opposition party was fielding 'a fat slob with zero sex appeal' against my father. His – Paul Bethune's – party had recently picked up a couple of marginal seats in by-elections and were confident of taking Hoopwestern since 'the need for change' was in the air.

In the days that followed I saw his picture everywhere: a grin above the slogan '*Bethune is better. Give him your X.*'

It made me laugh. Was he collecting divorcées?

On that first evening, though, all I learned of him was that he was a local councillor and losing his hair. Incipient baldness might in fact lose him the election, it seemed (never mind his mental suitability). America hadn't elected a bald president since the soldier-hero Eisenhower, and few people nowadays named their babies Dwight.

I learned that votes were won by laughter and lost by dogma. I learned that the virility of George Juliard acted like a friction rub on the pink faces of his helpers.

'My son will come with me to the dinner tonight,' he said. 'He can have Mervyn's place.' Mervyn Teck, he explained was the agent, his chief of staff, who was unavoidably detained in the Midlands.

The three aroused ladies looked me over again, nodding.

'The dinner,' he explained to me briefly, 'is being held at the Sleeping Dragon, the hotel straight across the square from here.' He pointed through the bow-fronted windows, showing me a multi-gabled façade, adorned with endless geraniums in hanging baskets, barely a hundred yards away. 'We'll walk over there at seven-thirty. Short reception. Dinner. Public meeting in the hall to the rear of the hotel. If we get some good hecklers, it may last until midnight.'

'You *want* hecklers?' I said, surprised.

'Of course. They set fire to things. Very dull otherwise.'

I asked weakly, 'What do I wear?'

'Just look tidy. There's a Front Bench bigwig coming. They wheel out the big guns to support a by-election as marginal as this. I'll wear a dinner jacket to start with, but I'll strip off my black tie later. Maybe unbutton my shirt a bit. See how it goes.' He smiled almost calmly, but I could sense excitement running in him deeply. He's a *fighter*, I thought. He's my father, this extraordinary man. He's kicked my dreams away and shown me a different world that I don't like very much, but I'll go with him, as he wants, for a month, and I'll do my best for him, and then we'll see. See how it goes . . . as he'd said.

We walked across the square at seven-thirty, I in grey trousers and navy blazer (new from the Brighton shops), he in black tailoring that was in itself a step forward in my education.

He was received with acclaim and clapping. I smiled and smiled at his shoulder and was terribly *nice* to everyone, and shook hand after hand as required. No babies in sight.

'My son,' he gestured. 'This is my son.'

Some of the perhaps eighty people at the reception and dinner were dressed formally like my father, others made political-equality statements like open-necked shirts and gingham with studs.

The Front Bench bigwig came with black bow sharply tied, his wife discreetly diamonded. I watched her being unpretentiously and endlessly charming to strangers, and when I in my turn was introduced to her she clasped my hand warmly and grinned into my eyes as if meeting me was a highlight of her evening. I had a long way to go, I thought, before I could put that amount of genuine and spontaneous friendliness into every greeting. I saw also that Mrs Bigwig's smile was worth a ballot-box full of Xs.

I realised slowly, as the room filled up, that the dinner was a ticket affair; that, except for the Bigwigs and my father, everyone had paid for their presence. My father, it appeared, had paid for me. One of the evening's organising committee was telling him he didn't have to.

'Never accept gifts,' he had warned me on the drive from Brighton. 'Gifts may look harmless, but they can come back to haunt you. Say no. Pay for yourself, understand?'

'Yes, I think so.'

'Never put yourself into the position of having to return a heavy favour when you know what you're being asked to do is wrong.'

'Don't take sweets from strangers?'

'Exactly so.'

The organising lady informed my father that if he had had a wife, her ticket would have been free.

He said with gentle, smiling finality, 'I will pay for my son. Dearest Polly, don't argue.'

Dearest Polly turned to me with mock exasperation. 'Your father. What a man!' Her gaze slid past me and her face and voice changed from blue skies to storm. '*Bugger*,' she said.

I looked, of course, to see the cause of the almost comic disapproval and found it was an earnest-eyed thin woman of forty or so sun-baked summers, whose tan glowed spectacularly against a sleeveless white dress. Blonde streaked hair. Vitality plus.

Dearest Polly said, 'Orinda!' under her breath.

Orinda, the passed-over candidate, was doing her

best to eclipse the chosen rival by wafting round the room embracing everyone extravagantly while saying loudly, 'Daaarling, we must all do our best for the party even if the selectors have made this *ghastly* mistake . . .'

'Damn her,' said Dearest Polly who had been, she told me, a selector herself.

Everyone knew Orinda, of course. She managed to get the cameraman from the local television company to follow her around, so that her white slenderness would hog whatever footage reached the screen.

Dearest Polly quietly fumed, throwing out sizzling news snippets my way as if she would explode if she kept them in.

'Dennis was a cuddly precious, you know. Can't think why he married that *harpy*.'

Dearest Polly, herself on the angular side of cuddly, had one of those long-jawed faces from which condensed kindness and goodwill flowed forth unmistakably. She wore dark red lipstick as if she didn't usually: it was the wrong colour for her yellowish skin.

'Dennis told us he wanted us to select Orinda. She *made* him say it. He knew he was dying.'

Orinda flashed her white teeth at a second cameraman.

'That man's from the *Hoopwestern Gazette*,' Dearest Polly said disgustedly. 'She'll make the front page.'

'But she won't get to Parliament,' I said.

Polly's eyes focused on me with awakening

amusement. 'Your father's son, aren't you, then! It was George's ability to identify the essential points that swayed us in his favour. There were seventeen of us on the selection panel, and to begin with most people thought Orinda the obvious choice. I know she took it for granted . . .'

And she'd reckoned without Dearest Polly, I thought. Polly and others of like mind.

Polly said, 'I don't know how she has the nerve to bring her lover!'

'Er . . .' I said. 'What?'

'That man just behind her. He was Dennis's best friend.'

I didn't see how being Dennis's best friend made anyone automatically Orinda's lover, but before I could ask, Polly was claimed away. Dennis's best friend, a person who managed to look unremarkable even in a dinner jacket, seemed abstracted more than attentive, but he did stick faithfully to Orinda's back: rather like a bodyguard, I thought.

I realised in consequence that Mr Bigwig himself had a genuinely serious bodyguard, a young muscular-looking shadow whose attention was directed to the crowd, not his master.

I wondered if my father accepted that bodyguards would be the price of success as he went up his chosen ladder.

He began circling the room and gestured for me to

join him, and I practised being Mrs Bigwig but fell far short of her standard. I could act, but she was real.

There was a general movement into the dining-room next door, where too many tables laid for ten people each were crowded into too small a space. Places were allocated to everyone by name and, my father and I entering almost last, I found that not only were we not expected at the same table – he was put naturally with the Bigwigs and the Constituency Association's chairman – but I was squeezed against a distant wall between a Mrs Leonard Kitchens and Orinda herself.

When she discovered her ignominious location Orinda flamed with fury like a white-hot torch. She stood and quivered and tried to get general attention by tapping a glass with a knife, but the noise was lost in the general bustle of eighty people chattering and clattering into their places. Orinda's angry outburst barely reached further than her knives and forks.

'This is an insult! I always sit at the top table! I *demand* . . .'

No one listened.

Through the throng I saw Dearest Polly busily settling my father into a place of honour and guessed with irony that Orinda's quandary was Polly's mischief.

Orinda glared at me as I hovered politely waiting for her to sit. She had green eyes, black lashed. Stage grease-paint skin.

'And who are *you*?' she demanded; then bent down

and snatched up the name card in front of my place. My identity left her speechless with her red mouth open.

'I'm his son,' I said lamely. 'Can I help you with your chair?'

She turned her back on me and spoke to her bodyguard (lover?) best friend of her dead husband, a characterless-seeming entity with a passive face.

'Do something!' Orinda instructed him.

He glanced past her in my direction and with flat expressionless eyes dismissed me as of no consequence. He silently held Orinda's chair for her to sit down and to my surprise she folded away most of her aggression and sat stonily and with a stiff back, enduring what she couldn't get changed.

At school one learned a good deal about power: who had it and who didn't. (I didn't.) Orinda's understated companion had power that easily eclipsed her own, all the more effective for being quiet.

Mrs Leonard Kitchens, on my right, patted my chair with invitation and told me to occupy it. Mrs Leonard Kitchens, large, comfortable in a loose floral dress and with the lilt of a Dorset accent on her tongue, told me that my father looked too young to have a son my size.

'Yes, doesn't he,' I said.

Leonard himself, on her other side, bristled with a bad-tempered moustache and tried unsuccessfully to talk to Orinda across his wife and me. I offered to change places with him: his wife said sharply, 'No.'

Mrs Leonard Kitchens' gift for small talk took us cosily through dinner (egg salad, chicken, strawberries), and I learned that 'my Leonard', her husband, was a nurseryman by trade with fanatical political beliefs and a loathing for Manchester United.

With the chicken Mrs Kitchens, to my surprise, mentioned that Dennis Nagle had been an Under-Secretary of State in the Department of Trade and Industry, not a simple backbencher, as I had somehow surmised. If my father won the seat, he would be a long way behind Dennis in career terms.

Mrs Leonard Kitchens spoke conspiratorily into my right ear. 'Perhaps I shouldn't tell you, dear, but Polly very naughtily changed the name cards over, so as to put Orinda next to you. I saw her. She just laughed. She's never *liked* Orinda.' The semi-whispering voice grew even quieter, so as not to reach the ears on my left. 'Orinda made a great constituency wife, very good at opening fêtes and that sort of thing, but one has to admit she did tend to boss Dennis sometimes. My Leonard was on the selection panel and he voted for her, of course. Men always fall for her, you know.' She drew back and looked at me with her big head on one side. 'You're too young, of course.'

To my dismay I could feel myself going red. Mrs Kitchens laughed her worldly laugh and shovelled her strawberries. Orinda Nagle ignored me throughout, while pouring out non-stop complaints to her companion, who mostly replied with grunts. I thought I would rather be almost anywhere else.

Dinner finally over, the talkative throng rose to its collective feet and transferred down a passage into the large room lit by chandeliers which made the Sleeping Dragon the area's popular magnet for dances, weddings and – as now – political free-for-alls.

Orinda's companion left his name card on the table, and out of not-very-strong curiosity I picked it up.

Mr A.L. Wyvern, it said.

I let 'Mr A.L. Wyvern' fall back among the debris of napkins and coffee cups and, without enthusiasm, drifted along with everyone else to the rows of folding chairs set up for the meeting. I'd read somewhere that affairs like this could draw tiny crowds unworthy of the name, but perhaps because my father was new to the district, almost double the number of the diners had turned up, and the whole place buzzed with the expectation of enjoyment.

It was the first political meeting I'd attended and at that point I would have been happy if it had been my last.

There were speeches from the small row of people up on a platform. The chairman of the Constituency Association rambled on a bit. Mr Bigwig was on his feet for twenty minutes. Mrs Bigwig smiled approvingly throughout.

My father stood up and lightened the proceedings

by making everyone laugh. I could feel my face arranging itself into Mrs Bigwig-type soppiness and knew that in my case anyway it had a lot to do with relief. I had been anxious that he wouldn't grab his audience, that he would embarrass me into squirming agony by being boring.

I suppose I should have known better. He told them what was right with the country, and why. He told them what was wrong with the country, and how to fix it. He gave them a palatable recipe. He told them what they wanted to believe, and he had them stamping their feet and roaring their applause.

The local TV station cameraman filmed the cheers.

Predictably, Orinda hated it. She sat rigidly, her neck as stiff as if she had an unbending rod there instead of vertebrae. I could see the sharp line of her jaw and the grim tight muscles round her mouth. She shouldn't have come, I thought: but perhaps she truly had believed that the selectors had made a ghastly mistake.

Dearest Polly, chief de-selector of Dennis's widow, regarded my father euphorically, as if she had invented him herself; and, indeed, without her he might not have been there to seize the first rung of his destiny.

Eyes alight with the triumph of his reception he asked for questions and, true to his intention, he stripped off his tie. He flung it on the table in front of him, and then he rounded the table so that there was nothing between him on the platform and the crowd below. He opened his arms wide, embracing them. He invited them to join him in a political adventure, to build for a better world and in particular for a better world for the constituents of Hoopwestern.

He held them in his hands. He had them laughing. His timing could have been learned from stand-up comics. He generated excitement, belief, purpose; and I, in my inconspicuous end-of-row seat, I swelled with a mixture of amazement, understanding and finally pride that my parent was publicly delivering the goods.

'I'm here for you,' he said. 'Come to my office across the square. Tell me your concerns, tell me what's troubling you here in Hoopwestern. Tell me who to see, who to listen to. Tell me your history . . . and I'll tell you your future. If you elect me I'll work for you, I'll take your wishes to Westminster, I'll be your voice where it matters. I'll light a bulb or two in the House of Commons . . .'

Laughter drowned him. The light-bulb factory fuelled the town's economy, and he wanted the light-bulb votes.

To do good one needed power, he said. Light bulbs were so much wire and glass without power. In humans, power came from inside, not delivered and metered. Power gave light and warmth. 'If you give me power, I'll light your lamps.'

My father's own electricity galvanised the crowd. They shouted questions, he shouted answers. He was serious where it mattered and funny everywhere else.

He had horror for genocide and sympathy for cats. He dodged cornering demands and promised never to put his name to anything whose consequences he didn't understand.

'Legislation,' he said jokingly, 'often achieves exactly what it is designed to avoid. We all know it. We moan about the results. I promise not to jump into emotional deep ends on your behalf. I beg the brains and common sense of Hoopwesterners to foresee disaster and warn me. I'll raise your voices in whispers, not shouts, because shouts annoy but whispers go round persuasively and travel sweetly to the heart of things, and lead to sensible action.'

Whether they understood him or not, they loved him.

The most dedicated hecklers of the evening proved not to be the Paul Bethune opposition supporters, several of whom had bought tickets to the dinner and who had afterwards formed an aggressive bunch on the flip-up chairs, but my father's presumed political allies (but in fact personal enemies), Orinda Nagle and Leonard Kitchens.

Both of them demanded firm commitments to policies they both approved. Both shouted and pointed fingers. My father answered with unfailing good humour and stuck to the party's overall stated position: he needed also to keep the die-hard backbone votes safely in his bag.

Orinda was professional enough to see she was

outgunned, but she didn't give up trying. Mr A.L. Wyvern narrowed his eyes and sank his ears down into his collar. Mr A.L. Wyvern's influence over Dennis and Orinda waned before my eyes.

My father paid tribute to Dennis Nagle. Orinda, far from placated, said that no way could an inexperienced novice like George Juliard replace her husband, however Hollywood-handsome he might be, however manly his hairy chest, however witty, quick-tongued, charismatic. None of that made up for political know-how.

Someone at the back of the hall booed. There was general laughter, a nervous release of the tension Orinda had begun to build up. The impetus swung back to my father, who sincerely thanked Orinda for her years of service to the party cause and deftly led an appreciation to her by clapping in her direction and encouraging everyone else to copy him. The clapping grew. The crowd gave generous but unaffectionate acclaim.

Orinda, to her impotent fury, was silenced and defeated by this vote of thanks. Leonard Kitchens bounced to his feet to defend her, but was shouted down. Leonard's moustache quivered with frustration, his thick glasses flashing in the light as he swung from side to side like a wounded bull. His cosy wife looked as if she would deliver the *coup de grâce* when she got him home.

My father courteously admired Leonard for his

faithfulness and told him and everyone that if elected he would aim always for Dennis Nagle's high and honest standard. Nothing less was worthy of the people of Hoopwestern.

He had them cheering. He exhorted them again to talk to him personally and the crowd stood and surged forward round the seats to take him at his word.

Dearest Polly chatted happily with the Bigwigs and beckoned me up onto the platform, and Mr Bigwig, regarding the clamorous excited throng, told me that my father already had all the skills that would propel him into high office. 'All he needs is luck – and to keep out of trouble,' he said.

'Trouble like Paul Bethune,' Polly said, nodding.

'What trouble?' asked Bigwig.

'Oh dear!' Polly looked flustered. 'George forbids us to attack Paul Bethune's character. George says negative campaigning can rebound on you. Paul Bethune has a mistress with an illegitimate daughter by him which he's tried hard to hush up and George won't attack him for it.'

Mrs Bigwig looked at me assessingly. 'I suppose there's no shadow over *your* birth, is there, young Ben?'

Polly assured her vehemently. 'No, of course not,' and I wondered if my father, all those years ago, could possibly have reckoned that my legitimacy would one day be important to him. After what I'd learned of him that day I saw that anything was possible, but in fact I stayed as convinced as I'd always been that his marriage to my mother had been an act of natural characteristic honour. I still believed, as I always had, that he would never shirk responsibility for his actions. I knew my birth had been a mistake and, as I'd often said, I had no quarrel at all with the quality of life he'd given me since.

It was indeed midnight by the time most of the crowd left to go home. Mr and Mrs Bigwig had long gone, with chauffeur and bodyguard in attendance. Polly yawned with well-earned fatigue. Orinda and Mr A.L. Wyvern were nowhere to be seen and Mrs Leonard Kitchens had hauled her Leonard away with the rough edge of her energetic tongue.

I waited for my father to the end, not only because I had no key to get into my bedroom above the campaign headquarters but also because he would need someone to unwind on after the cheers had died away. Even at not quite eighteen I knew that triumph needed human company afterwards. I'd gone back to an empty room in Mrs Wells's house after three (infrequent) wins in steeplechases and had had no one to bounce round the place with, no one to hug and yell with, no one to share the uncontainable joy. That night my father needed me. A wife would have been better; but he certainly would need *someone.* So I stayed.

He put his arm round my shoulders.

'*God,*' he said.

'You'll be Prime Minister,' I told him. 'Mr Bigwig fears it.'

He looked at me vaguely, his eyes shining. 'Why should he or anyone fear it?'

'They always kill Caesar. You said so.'

'What?'

'You were brilliant.'

'I can do without your sarcasm, Ben.'

'No, seriously, Father . . .'

'Dad.'

'Dad . . .' I was tongue-tied. I couldn't talk to him as Dad. Dads were people who drove you to school and threw snowballs and ticked you off for coming home late. Dads didn't send you a ticket to ski school in a Christmas card. Dads didn't send an impersonal fax to a hotel saying 'well done' when one won a teenage downhill ski race. Dads were there to watch. Fathers weren't.

Remnants of the meeting came up with shining faces to add congratulations. He took his arm off my shoulder and shook their hands, friendly and positive to all; and I had a vision of them going around for the next four weeks saying, 'Juliard, a very good man, just what we need . . . Vote Juliard, couldn't do better.' The ripple from that night would reach the Hoopwestern boundaries and eddy along its roads.

My father slowly came down a little from his high and decided he'd done enough for one day. We left the hall, returned to the hotel and eventually through a harmony of 'Good Nights' made our way out into the warm August night to walk across to the dimly lit bow-front opposite.

There were street lights round the square and the hotel lights at our back, but underfoot the decorative cobbles were dark and lumpy. In icy winters, I learned later, elderly people tended to skid on them and fall and crunch their bones; and on that euphoric night my father tripped on the uneven surface and went down forward on one knee, trying not to topple entirely and not managing it.

At exactly the same moment there was a loud bang and a sharp zzing and a scrunch of glass breaking.

I bent down over my father and saw in the light that his eyes were stretched wide with anxiety and his mouth grim and urgent with pain.

'Run,' he said. 'Run for cover. God dammit, *run*.'

I stayed where I was, however.

'Ben,' he said, 'for God's sake. That was a gunshot.'

'Yes, I know.'

We were halfway across the square, easy immobile targets. He struggled to get to his feet and told me again to run: and for once in my life I made a judgement and disobeyed him.

He couldn't put his weight on his left ankle. He half rose and fell down again and beseeched me to run.

'Stay down,' I told him.

'You don't understand . . .' His voice was anguished.

'Are you bleeding?'

'What? I don't think so. I twisted my ankle.'

People ran out of the hotel, drawn by the bang that had re-echoed round the buildings fringing the square. People came over to my father and me and stood around us, curious and unsettled, noncomprehension wrinkling their foreheads.

There was confusion and people saying, 'What happened, what happened?' and hands stretching down to my father to help him up, cushioning him with a lot of well-meaning concern and kindness.

When he was well surrounded he did finally take my arm and lean on other people and pull himself to his feet: or rather, to his right foot, because putting his left foot down caused him to exclaim with strong discomfort. He began to be embarrassed rather than frightened and told the crowding well-wishers that he felt stupid, losing his footing so carelessly. He apologised. He said he was fine. He smiled to prove it. He cursed mildly, to crowd approval.

'But that *noise*,' a woman said.

Heads nodded. 'It sounded like . . .'

'Not here in Hoopwestern . . .'

'Was it . . . a *gun*?'

An important-looking man said impatiently, 'A rifle shot. I'd know it anywhere. Some madman . . .'

'But where? There's no one here with a gun.'

Everyone looked round, but it was far too late to see the rifle, let alone the person taking pot-shots.

My father put his arm round my shoulders again,

but this time for a different, more practical sort of support, and cheerfully indicated to everyone that we should set off again to finish the crossing of the square.

The important-looking man literally shoved me out of the way, taking my place as crutch and saying in his loud authoritative way, 'Let me do this. I'm stronger than the lad. I'll have you over to your office in a jiffy, Mr Juliard. You just lean on *me*.'

My father looked over his shoulder to where I now stood behind him and would have protested on my behalf, I could see, but the change suited me fine and I simply waved for him to go on. The important-looking man efficiently half-carried my hopping father over the remaining stretch of square, the bunch of onlookers crowding round with murmurs of sympathy and helpful suggestions.

I walked behind my father. It came naturally, to do that. There was a high voice calling then, and I turned to find Polly running towards us, stumbling on the cobbles in strappy sandals and sounding very distressed.

'Ben . . . Ben . . . has George been shot?'

'No, Polly.' I tried to reassure her. 'No.'

'Someone said George had been shot.' She was out of breath and full of disbelief.

'Look, there he is.' I took her arm and pointed. 'There. Hopping. And hopping mad with himself for twisting his ankle and needing someone to help him along.'

Polly's arm was vibrating with the inner shakes, which only slowly abated when she could see that indeed George was alive and healthily swearing.

'But . . . the shot . . .'

I said, 'It seems someone did fire a gun at the same moment that he tripped on the cobbles, but I promise you he wasn't hit. No blood.'

'But you're so young, Ben.' Her doubts still showed.

'Even a tiny kid could tell you there's no blood.' I said it teasingly, but I guess it was my own relief that finally convinced her. She walked beside me and followed the pied-piper-like procession to the head-quarters' door, where my father produced a key and let everyone in.

He hopped across to his swivel chair behind his accustomed desk and, consulting a list, telephoned the local police.

'They've had several complaints already,' he told everyone, putting down the receiver. 'They're on their way here. Letting off a firearm . . . disturbing the peace . . . that sort of thing.'

Someone said, 'What you need is a doctor . . .' and someone else arranged for one to come.

'So kind. You're all so bloody kind,' my father said.

I left the hubbub and went to the open door, looking across the square to the Sleeping Dragon, who perversely had every eye wide open, with people leaning out of upstairs windows and people standing in brightly lit doorways below.

I remembered the '*zzing*' of the passing bullet and thought of ricochets. My father and I had been steering a straight line from hotel to headquarters; and *if* the bullet had been aimed at *him*, and *if* he'd stumbled at the exact second that the trigger was squeezed, and *if* the bullet's trajectory had been from upstairs somewhere in the Sleeping Dragon (and not from downstairs because there were still too many people about), and *if* the bullet had smashed some glass so that I heard the tinkle, then why was every pane of the window in the bow-fronted headquarters intact?

Because, I told myself, the whole thing had been a coincidence. The bullet had not been intended to stop George Juliard's political career before it started. Of course not. Dramatics were childish.

I turned to go back inside, and saw for an instant a flash of light on broken glass down on the ground.

It was a window of the charity shop next door that had been hit.

Zzing. Ricochet. Smash. The straight trajectory could have been deflected by the curve of a cobble. A rifle bullet travelling straight and true would very likely have gone right through glass without breaking it, but a wobbling bullet . . . that might set up glass-smashing vibrations.

The police arrived at the car-park side of the headquarters, and the doctor also. Everyone talked at once.

The doctor, bandaging, said he thought the injury a strain, not a break. Ice and elevation, he prescribed.

The police listened to the self-important man's view on gunshots.

I stood to one side and at one point found my father looking at me through the throng, his expression both surprised and questioning. I smiled at him a bit, and the window of line of sight closed again as people moved.

I did tell a junior-looking uniformed policeman that the glass of the charity shop's bow-front was broken, and he did come outside to look. But when I tentatively mentioned ricochets he looked quizzical and asked how old I was. I had done a bit of rifle shooting at school, I said. He nodded, unimpressed, and made a note. I followed when he returned to join his colleagues.

Dearest Polly stood at my father's side and listened to everything worriedly. A man with a camera flashed several pictures. Considering that no one had actually been shot the fuss went on for a long time and it was nearly two o'clock when I finally closed and bolted the doors, front and back, and switched off a few of the lights.

My father decided to go upstairs backwards, sitting down. He would accept only minimal help and winced himself in and out of the bathroom and into one of the single beds in the bedroom. I was to sleep on the pull-out sofa-bed in the small sitting-room, but I ended up lying on the second single bed, next to my father, half dressed and not at all sleepy.

I had in the past twenty hours hummed along from Mrs Wells's house on my bicycle and ridden a canter on grassy sunlit Downs. I'd had my life torn apart and entered a new world, and for long minutes I'd wondered if I would collect a bullet in the back. How could I sleep?

I switched off the bedside light.

In the dark, my father said, 'Ben, why didn't you run?'

After a pause I answered. 'Why did you tell me to?'

'I didn't want you to get shot.'

'Mm. Well, that's why I didn't run. I didn't want you to get shot.'

'So you stood in the way . . .?'

'More fun than patting babies.'

'*Ben!*'

After a while, I said, 'I'd say it was a .22 rifle, the sort used for target shooting. I'd say it was a high-velocity bullet. I know that noise well. If a .22 bullet hits you in the body, it quite likely won't kill you. You need to hit the head or the neck to be most probably lethal. All I did was shield your head.'

There was a silence from the other bed. Then he said, 'I'd forgotten you could shoot.'

'I was in the school team. We were taught by one of the country's best marksmen.' I smiled in the dark. 'You paid for it, you know.'

CHAPTER THREE

Before nine the next morning I went downstairs and unbolted the door to the car park at the shrill summons of a man who was standing there with his finger on the bell button. He was short, black-haired, softly plump, held a bunch of keys in his hand and was very annoyed.

'Who are *you*?' he demanded. 'What are you doing in here? Why is the door bolted?'

'Benedict – ' I began.

'What?'

'Juliard.'

He stared at me for a moment, then brushed past and began bad-temperedly setting to rights the untidiness left all over both front and back offices by the events of the night.

'You're the son, I suppose,' he said, picking up scattered envelopes. 'George wasted all of yesterday going to collect you. As you're here, do something useful.' He gestured to the mess. 'Where is George, anyway? The radio is red hot. What did happen last night?'

'Upstairs. He sprained his ankle. And . . . er . . . who are *you*?'

'Mervyn Teck, of course.' He looked impatiently at my blank face. 'I'm the agent. Don't you know *anything*?'

'Not much.'

'I'm running this election. I'm here to get George Juliard into Parliament. The radio says someone shot at him. Is that true?' He seemed unconcerned and went on straightening papers.

'Possibly,' I said.

'Good.'

I said, 'Er . . .?'

'Free publicity. We can't afford to buy air time.'

'Oh.'

'It will get rid of Titmuss and Whistle.'

'Who are they?' I asked.

'Fringe candidates. We don't need to worry about them.'

My father hobbled downstairs saying, 'Morning, Mervyn. I see you've met my son.'

Mervyn gave me an unenthusiastic glance.

'Lucky he's here,' my father said. 'He can drive me around.'

I'd told him on the way from Brighton that I'd done errands to earn money for driving lessons and had held a full licence by then for nearly five weeks.

'Good,' he'd said.

'But I haven't driven since the test.'

'All in good time.' His bland expression now forbade me to reveal my inexperience. There was tolerance between the candidate and the agent, I saw, but no warmth.

A sharp-boned young woman arrived with disciplined hair and a power-dressing grey suit with a bright 'Juliard' rosette pinned to one shoulder. She was introduced as Crystal Harley, Mervyn Teck's secretary, and, as I learned during the morning, she was the only person, besides Mervyn himself, who received pay for running the by-election. Everyone else was a volunteer.

The three volunteer witches from the day before arrived one by one and smothered my father with cooing solicitude and endless coffee.

I had forgotten their names: Faith, Marge and Lavender, Faith chided me gently.

'Sorry.'

'A good politician remembers names,' Lavender told me severely. 'You won't be much use to your father if you forget who people are.' The thin lady with the sweet-smelling name was the one who had disapproved of Orinda Nagle. Difficult to please her, I thought.

Mervyn Teck and my father discussed streets and leaflet distributions. Crystal Harley entered endless details into a computer. Motherly Faith went round with a duster and Marge set the photocopier humming.

I sat on my stool and simply listened, and learned many surprising (to me) facts of electoral life, chief among which was the tiny amount of money allowed to be spent. No one could buy themselves into Parliament: every candidate had to rely on an army of unpaid helpers for door-to-door persuasions and the nailing of 'Vote for Me' posters to suitable trees.

There were Representation of the People Acts, Crystal told me crisply, her fingers busy on the keyboard, her eyes unwaveringly turned to the screen. The Acts severely limited what one could spend.

'There are about seventy thousand voters in this constituency,' she said. 'You couldn't buy seventy thousand half-pints of beer with what we're allowed to spend. It's impossible to *bribe* the British voters. You have to *persuade* them. That's your father's job.'

'Don't buy a stamp, dear, for a local letter,' Faith said, smiling. 'Get on a bicycle and deliver it by hand.'

'Do you mean you can't buy *stamps*?'

'You have to write down every cent you spend,' Crystal nodded. 'You have to make an itemised return after the election to show where the money went, and you can bet your sweet life Paul Bethune's people will be hoping like hell they'll find we've gone over the limit, just like we'll be scrutinising his return with a magnifying glass looking for any twopenny wickedness.'

'Then last night's dinner . . .' I began.

'Last night's dinner was paid for by the people who ate it, and cost the local Constituency Association nothing,' Crystal said. She paused, then went on with my education. 'Mervyn and I are employed by the local Constituency Association of this party, not directly by Westminster. The local association pays for these offices here, and the whole caboodle relies on gifts and fundraising.'

She approved of the way things were set up, and I wondered vaguely why, with everything carefully regulated to ensure the election of the fittest, there were still so many nutcases in the House.

The relative peace of just seven bodies in the offices lasted only until an influx of the previous night's social mix trooped in through both doors and asked endless questions to which there seemed no answers.

Mervyn Teck loved it. The police, the media people, the party enthusiasts and the merely curious, he expansively welcomed them all. His candidate was not only alive but being perfectly charming to every enquirer. The TV cameraman shone his bright spotlight on my father's face and taped the sincerity of his smile. Local newspapermen had been augmented by several from the major dailies. Cameras flashed. Microphones were offered to catch anything worth saying, and I, doing my bit, simply smiled and smiled and was terribly nice to everyone and referred every question to my parent.

Crystal, trying to continue working but having to cling physically to her desk to avoid being swept round the place like flotsam, remarked to me tartly that there would hardly have been more fuss if George Juliard had been killed.

'Lucky he wasn't,' I said, wedging my stool next to her to keep us both anchored.

'Did the noise of the gunshot make him trip?' she asked.

'No. He tripped first.'

'Why are you so sure?'

'Because the bang of a high-velocity bullet reaches you after the bullet itself.'

She looked disbelieving.

'I learned it in physics lessons,' I said.

She glanced at my beardless face. 'How old are you?' she asked.

'Seventeen.'

'You can't even vote!'

'I don't actually want to.'

She looked across to where my father was winning media allies with modesty and grace.

'I've met a fair number of politicians,' she said. 'Your father's different.'

'In what way?'

'Can't you feel his power? Perhaps you can't, as you're his son. You're too close to him.'

'I do sometimes feel it.' It stunned me, I should have said.

'Look at last night,' Crystal went on without pausing. 'I was there in the hall, sitting at the back. He set that place alight. He's a natural speaker. I mean, I *work* here, and he had my pulse racing. Poor old Dennis Nagle, he was a nice worthy man, pretty capable in a quiet way, but he could never have got a crowd cheering and stamping their feet like last night.'

'Could Orinda?' I asked.

Crystal was startled. 'No, she can't make people laugh. But don't judge her by last night. She's done devoted work in the constituency. She was always at Dennis's side. She's feeling very hurt that she wasn't selected to follow Dennis, because until your father galvanised the selection panel she was unopposed.'

'In fact,' I said, 'if *anyone* had a motive for bumping off my father, it would be her.'

'Oh, but she wouldn't!' Crystal was honestly dismayed. 'She can sometimes be a darling, you know. Mervyn *loves* her. He's quite put out that he's not working to get *her* elected. He was looking forward to it.'

My first impression of Crystal's sharp spikiness had been right only as regarded her outward appearance. She was kinder and more patient than she looked. I wondered if at one time she had been anorexic: I had known anorexic girls at school. The teeth of one of them had fallen out.

Crystal's teeth were straight and white, though seldom visible, owing to an overall serious view of life. I thought she was probably twenty-five or -six and hadn't had enough in life to smile about.

Mervyn Teck zig-zagged to my elbow through the busy crowd and said it was time to think about driving my father to his day's engagements in the outlying town of Quindle. The constituency was large in area with separate pockets of concentrated inhabitation: Mervyn gave me a map with roads and destinations marked, but looked at me doubtfully.

'Are you sure you're competent enough?'

I said, 'Yes,' with more confidence than I felt.

'One incident like last night's is a godsend,' he said. 'A car crash on top would be too much. We don't want any whiff of accident-prone.'

'No,' I said.

Across the room my father was dangling the Range Rover's keys in my direction. I went over to him and took them and he, with the help of a walking stick, detached himself from the chattering well-wishers (the police and media had long gone) and limped through the office and out to the car park.

Crowds beget crowds. There was a bunch of people outside the rear door who clapped and smiled at my father and gave him thumbs-up signs. I looked across the car park to where we had left the Range Rover on our arrival from Brighton the previous afternoon and my father asked me to fetch it over so that he wouldn't need to hobble that far.

I walked across to the conspicuous vehicle and stopped beside it, the keys in my hand. The sun shone again that day, gleaming on the gold-and-silver-painted garlands; and after a moment I turned away and went back to my father.

'What's the matter?' he said, half annoyed. 'Can't you drive it?'

'Is it insured for someone my age?'

'Yes, of course. I wouldn't suggest it otherwise. Go and fetch it, Ben.'

I frowned and went back into the offices, ignoring his displeasure.

'It's time you went,' Mervyn said, equally impatient. 'You said you could drive George's car.'

I nodded. 'But I'd be better in a smaller car. Like you said, we don't want an accident. Do you have a smaller one? Could I borrow yours?'

Mervyn said with obvious aggravation, 'My car isn't insured for drivers under twenty-one.'

'Mine is, though,' Crystal said. 'My nineteen-year-old brother drives it. But it's not very glamorous. Not like the Range Rover.'

She dug the keys out of her handbag and said that Mervyn (to his impatience) would give her a lift home if we were not back by five-thirty, and would pick her up again in the morning. I thanked her with an awkward kiss on the cheek, and with Mervyn Teck repeating his disapproval, went out to rejoin my father.

'I'm disappointed in you, Ben,' he said, when Mervyn Teck explained. 'You'd better practise in the Range Rover tomorrow.'

'OK. But today, now, before we go, would you arrange for some mechanics to come here and make sure there's nothing wrong with it?'

'Of course there's nothing wrong with it. I drove it to Brighton and back yesterday and it was running perfectly.'

'Yes, but it's been standing out in the car park all night. Last night it's possible someone tried to shoot you. Suppose someone's hammered a nail or two into the Range Rover's tyres? Or anything.' I finished self-deprecatingly, as if I thought sabotage a childish fantasy; but after a brief thoughtful silence my father said to Mervyn, 'I'll go in Crystal's car. Ben can practise on the Range Rover tomorrow. Meanwhile, Mervyn, get the Range Rover overhauled, would you?'

Mervyn gave me a sour look, but it was he, after all, who had most wanted to avoid the accident-prone label: or so he'd said.

In Crystal's small work-a-day box on wheels I therefore drove the candidate safely to his far-flung appointments, and again I saw and heard him shake awake the apathetic voting public, progressively attracting more and more people as his voice raised laughter and applause. His audience approved with their eyes and shouted questions, some friendly, some hostile, all of them getting thoughtful answers, lightly phrased.

I didn't know how much of the day's flashing enthusiasm would actually carry the feet to the polling booths, but it was enough, my father assured me, if they didn't walk into the opposition camp and write their X for Bethune.

We had squeezed into Crystal's car an invention of my father's that was basically two wooden boxes, each a foot high, one larger than the other, that would bolt together, one on top of the other, to form an impromptu stepped platform to raise a speaker above his listeners: just enough for him to be comfortably heard, not high enough to be psychologically threatening. 'My soapbox' my father called it, though it was many years since such crowd-pulling structures had contained soap.

I assembled the 'soapbox' in three places in the town's scattered focal points, and at each place a crowd gathered, curious, or anti, or uncommitted, and at each place, as I unbolted, or assembled or packed away the stepped platform, people would crowd round me with (mostly) friendly enquiries.

'Are you his chauffeur?'

'Yes.'

'Is he as knowledgeable as he seems?'

'More so.'

'What does he think about education?'

I smiled. 'He's in favour of it.'

'Yes, but – '

'I can't answer for him. Please ask him yourself.'

They turned away and asked him, and got politically correct and truthful answers that would never be implemented without a huge increase in taxes: I was learning the economic facts as rapidly as I'd ever assimilated quadratic equations.

My father's appearance in Quindle had been well publicised in advance by posters all over the town. Volunteers had distributed them and volunteers met and escorted us everywhere, their faces shining with commitment. My own commitment, I had already found, was to my father himself, not to his party nor his beliefs. My private views, if I had any, were that good ideas were scattered around, not solely the property of any shade of rosette: and of course what were to me good ideas were hateful errors to others. I didn't embrace any single whole agenda package, and it was always those who didn't care passionately, those who changed their minds and swung with the wind, those who felt vaguely dissatisfied, they it was who swayed one side in or another side out. The 'floating voters', who washed back and forth with the tide, those were my father's target.

Quindle, like Hoopwestern, had grown in response to industries planted in the surrounding fields; not light bulbs this time, but furniture and paint. There had then been a long policy of 'infilling' – the building of large numbers of small houses on every patch of vacant grass. The resulting town strained against its green belt and suffered from interior traffic snarl-ups on a standstill scale. It worked well for soapbox orators: in the summer heat cars crept past with their windows down, getting the message.

Among the blizzard of VOTE JULIARD posters there were some for TITMUSS and WHISTLE and, of course, many for BETHUNE IS BETTER. GIVE HIM YOUR X. Bethune's notices on the whole looked tattered, and I found it wasn't merely because it was three days since he'd stomped inner Quindle on his own soapbox tour, but because the local weekly paper, the *Quindle Diary*, had hit the newsagents with 'Bethune for Sleaze' as its headline.

One of the volunteers having tucked the *Quindle Diary* under my elbow, I read the front page, as who wouldn't.

'As our representative in Westminster, do we want an adulterer who says he upholds the family values to which this newspaper in this young town is dedicated? Do we believe the promises of one who can't keep a solemn vow?'

I read to the end and thought the whole tone insufferably pompous, but I didn't suppose it would do the Bethune camp much good.

At each of his three ascents of the soapbox, my father was bombarded with demands that he should at least deplore the Bethune hypocrisy, and at each place, carefully side-stepping the loaded come-ons, he attacked Bethune and his party only for their political aims and methods.

His restraint didn't altogether please his own army of volunteers.

'George could *demolish* Bethune if he would only take a hatchet to his character,' one of them complained. 'Why won't he do it?'

'He doesn't believe in it,' I said.

'You have to play the aces you're given.'

'Not five aces,' I said.

'What?'

'He would think it cheating.'

The volunteer raised his eyes to heaven but changed his approach. 'You see that thin man standing near your father, writing in a notebook?'

'Do you mean the one in a pink jogging suit and a baseball hat on backwards?'

'I do indeed. He's called Usher Rudd. He writes for the *Hoopwestern Gazette* and his column is also syndicated to the *Quindle Diary.* It's he who wrote the personal attacks on Paul Bethune. He's been following Bethune around ever since his party chose him as their candidate. Rudd's a highly professional siever of mud. Never, *never* trust him.'

I said in apprehension, 'Does my father know who he is?'

'I told George that Usher Rudd would be bound to turn up again, but he doesn't always look the same. The pink overalls and baseball cap are new.'

'Usher Rudd's an unusual name.'

The volunteer laughed. 'He's really young Bobby Rudd, always a menace. His mother was Gracie Usher before she married a Rudd. The Rudd family have a string of repair garages, for anything from bicycles to combine harvesters, but fixing cars isn't to young

Bobby's taste. He calls himself an investigative journalist. More like a muck-raker, I'd say.'

I said tentatively, 'Was he at the dinner last night?'

'That big do at the Sleeping Dragon? He would have been for a certainty. He'll be furious that the gunshot and all that happened was too late for today's *Gazette.* The *Gazette* is only twenty-four pages long, mostly advertisements, sports results, local news and re-hashed world events. Everyone buys it for the dirt Rudd digs up. He was a rotten peeping tom as a little boy, always had his snotty nose glued to people's windows, and he hasn't got better with time. If you want to have sex with the vicar, don't do it in Quindle.'

I said dryly, 'Thanks for the advice.'

He laughed. 'Beware of Bobby Rudd, that's all.'

With the present crowd listening to my galvanic father with devouring eyes as much as persuadable ears, I slowly strolled round to guard his back; I was some poor sort of guardian to my parent, I thought with self-condemnation, if I left him wide open to repeat bullets or other jokers.

I did my best to look purposeless, but clearly failed with that message as Usher Rudd, also as if guileless, came to stand casually beside me. His baseball cap advertised vigorous sports goods, as did his footwear, and he wore between, from neck to ankle, a soft rose-pink loose exercise suit of nylon-like fabric which, instead of hiding the thinness of his body inside, gave an impression that the arms and legs functioned on a system of articulated rods. I, in my jeans and T-shirt, looked almost invisibly ordinary.

'Hello,' he said. 'Where is the Juliard battle-wagon?'

Puzzled, I answered, 'We came in a different car.'

'I'm Usher Rudd.'

His accent was unreconstructed Dorset, his manner confident to arrogant. He had unexcited blue eyes, sandy lashes and dry freckled skin: the small-boy menace who had peeped through windows still lived close to the surface and made me for once feel older than my years.

'What's your name?' he demanded, as I made no response.

'Benedict,' I said.

'Ben,' he asserted, nodding his recognition, 'Ben Juliard.'

'That's right.'

'How old are you?' He was abrupt, as if he had a right to the information.

'Seventeen,' I said without offence. 'How old are *you*?'

'That's none of your business.'

I gazed at him with a perplexity that was at least half genuine. Why should he think he could ask questions that he himself would not answer? I had a lot to learn, as my father had said; but I instinctively didn't like him.

Close behind my back my father was answering the sort of questions it was proper he should be asked:

where did he stand on education, foreign policy, taxes, the dis-united kingdom and the inability of bishops to uphold the ten commandments? 'Shouldn't sins be modernised?' someone shouted. Moses was out of date.

My father, who certainly lived by 'thou shalt not' rather than by 'what can I get away with?' replied with humour, 'By all means pension off Moses if you would like your neighbour to covet your ox and your ass and carry off your wife and your lawn mower . . .'

The end of his sentence drowned in laughter and cheers, and for fifteen more minutes he had them spellbound, feeding them political nuggets in nourishing soup, producing a performance without microphone or footlights that they would never forget. All my life people would say to me, 'I heard your father speak in Quindle,' as if it had been a revelation in their existence: and it wasn't altogether *what* he said that mattered, I reckoned, but his whole, honest, joyous, vigorous presentation.

Against the final applause, Usher Rudd said to me, 'Birthday?'

'What?'

'Your birthday?'

'Yes,' I said.

'Yes, what?'

'Yes, I do have a birthday.'

He thought me dim. 'What's your mother's name?' he said.

'Sarah.'

'Her last name?'

'Yes. She's dead.'

His expression changed. His gaze grew thoughtful and flicked downward to the *Quindle Diary* that I held rolled in my hand. I saw him understand the obtuseness of my answers.

'Bethune deserves it,' he said sharply.

'I don't know anything about him,' I said.

'Then read my column.'

'Even then . . .'

'Everyone has secrets,' he declared with relish. 'I just find them out. I enjoy doing it. They deserve it.'

'The public has a right to know?' I asked.

'Of course they do. If someone is setting themselves up to make our laws and rule our lives they shouldn't sleaze it off with dirty sex on the side, should they?'

'I haven't thought about it.'

'If old George is hiding dirty secrets, I'll find them out. What's your mother's name?'

'Sarah. She's dead.'

He gave me a bitter antagonistic glare.

'I'm sure you do a good detective job,' I said mildly. 'My mother's name was Sarah Juliard. Married. Dead. Sorry about that.'

'I'll find out,' he threatened.

'Be my guest.'

My father disengaged himself from eager clutching

voters and turned to say he was ready for his lunch engagement: a volunteers' gathering in a pub.

'This,' I said, indicating the inhabitant of the pink tracksuit and the energetic shoes and baseball hat, 'is Usher Rudd.'

'Nice to know you,' my father said, automatically ready to shake hands. 'Do you work for the party, er . . . Usher?'

'He writes for newspapers,' I said. I unrolled the *Quindle Diary* so he could see the front page. 'He wrote this. He wants me to tell him my mother's name.'

I was getting to know my father. Twenty-four hours earlier I wouldn't have been aware that a tiny tensing of muscles and a beat of silence meant a fizzingly fast assessment of unwelcome facts. Not only powerful but dauntingly rapid: not only analytical but an instant calculator of down-the-line consequences. Some brain.

He smiled politely at Usher Rudd. 'My wife's name was Sarah. Unfortunately she died.'

'What of?' Usher Rudd, disconcerted by my father's pleasant frankness, sounded aggressively rude.

'It was a long time ago.' My father remained civil. 'Come on, Ben, or we'll be late.'

We turned away and walked three paces; and Bobby Usher Rudd, darting round and wheeling in the running shoes, came to a halt facing us, standing in our way.

His voice was thin, malicious and triumphant. 'I'll get you de-selected. Orinda Nagle will have her rights.'

'Ah.' My father packed all the understanding in the world into one syllable. 'So you rubbished Paul Bethune to give her a clear run, is that it?'

Usher Rudd was furious. 'She's worth ten of you.'

'She's a lucky woman to have so many fans.'

'You'll lose.' Usher Rudd almost danced with rage. 'She would have won.'

'Well . . .' My father detoured past him with me at his heels, and Usher Rudd behind us yelled the question I would never have asked but wanted like crazy to know the answer to. 'If your wife died long ago, what do you do for sex?'

My father certainly heard but there wasn't a falter in his step. I risked a flick of a glance at his face but learned nothing: he showed no embarrassment or anxiety, only, if anything, *amusement*.

The lunch in the pub was up-beat, the volunteers all intoxicated with the speech stops of the morning. In the afternoon we toured a furniture factory and then a paint factory, where the candidate (leaning on his walking stick) listened intently to local problems and promised remedies if he were elected. He shook countless hands and signed countless autographs, and left behind an atmosphere of hope.

When Mervyn Teck had made his plans he had expected it to be Orinda who charmed the woodworkers and the colour mixers, and there had been resistance in parts of the factories to the one seen as a usurper. My father defused criticism by praising

Orinda steadfastly without apologising for having been chosen to take her place.

'A natural-born politician,' one of the lady volunteers said in my ear. 'The way the country's leaning, we'd lose this marginal seat with Orinda, though she doesn't believe that, of course. With your father we've a better chance, but voters are unpredictable and can often be downright vindictive, and they mostly vote for party, not for individuals, and the sleaze accusations won't hurt Paul Bethune much, especially with male voters who privately don't think a spot of adultery too much of a big deal, and will think "good luck to him". And you'd fancy women wouldn't vote for adulterers, but they do.'

'Doesn't Usher Rudd shift the Xs from one slot to another?'

'Not as much as he believes, the little weasel. It's not the locals that pay attention to him as much as the big noises in Westminster. They're all shit-scared of him digging into their pasts, and the higher they climb the more they hate him. Haven't you noticed that when an MP screws up his or her reputation, it's their own party that dumps them quickest?'

The correct answer was no, I hadn't noticed, because I hadn't been looking.

On our way back to Hoopwestern I asked my father what he thought of Usher Rudd but he yawned, said he was flaked out and his ankle hurt, and promptly went to sleep. I drove carefully, still not instinctive in traffic, and woke the candidate by a jerking halt at a red light at a crossroads.

'Usher Rudd,' he said without preamble, as if twenty minutes hadn't passed between question and answer, 'will burn his fingers on privacy laws.'

I said, 'I didn't know there were any privacy laws.'

'There will be.'

'Oh.'

'Usher Rudd has red hair under that baseball cap.'

'How do you know?'

'He came to the meeting after last night's dinner. Polly pointed him out to me. He wore a black tracksuit and black trainers. Didn't you see him?'

'I don't remember him.'

'Find out if he can shoot.'

I opened my mouth to say 'Wow' or 'How?' and thought better of both. My father glanced at me sideways, and I felt him smile.

'I don't think it was him,' I said.

'Why not?'

'His bullets of choice are acid ink.'

'Are you sure you want to be a mathematician? Why don't you try writing?'

'I want to be a jockey.' Might as well walk on the moon.

'Exeter University required to know where you would spend your gap year before they offered you a deferred entry: that is to say, you're going there not this October, but next year. They weren't enthusiastic about racecourses.'

'There's an Exeter racecourse.'

'You know damned well what they mean.'

'I don't like politics.' Change the subject.

'Politics are the oil of the world.'

'You mean . . . the world doesn't run without oil?'

He nodded. 'When politics jam solid, you get wars.'

'Father – ' I said.

'Dad.'

'No. Father. Why do you want to be a politician?'

After a pause he said, 'I am one. I can't help it.'

'But you've never . . . I mean . . .'

'I've never made a move before? Don't think I haven't considered it. I've known since I was your age or younger that one day I would try for Parliament. But I needed a solid base. I needed to prove to myself that I could make money. I needed to understand economics. And then there came a time not long ago when I said to myself "now or never". So it's now.'

It was the longest statement about himself that he'd ever made in my hearing; and he had simplified for my sake, I thought, an urge that had taken time to ripen and had burst out fully grown at the Sleeping Dragon. The Juliard dragon was awake now and roaring and prowling up broad Whitehall towards Number 10.

Thinking about him, I lost the way home. He made no sarcastic comment when I stopped, consulted the map, worked out where I'd gone wrong and finally arrived in the car park from an unexpected direction; and for that forbearance alone I would have served him as an esquire to a knight. How old-fashioned could one get?

It was well after six o'clock when we reached the car park which, in consequence, was almost empty. All the bordering shops had closed for the day. The late afternoon sunshine weakened to soft gold as I pulled up and applied Crystal's brakes.

There were dim lights in the office, but no people. I unlocked the door and we found a large note laid out prominently on Mervyn Teck's desk.

'The Range Rover is in Rudd's Repair Garage. They thoroughly overhauled it, and found nothing wrong.'

CHAPTER FOUR

I would have expected the nervous energy of the day-long performance in Quindle to have earned my father an evening's rest, but I had barely begun to wake up to the stamina demanded of would-be public servants. It seemed that far from a quiet top-up of batteries, he was committed to another marathon shake-hands-and-smile, not this time in the chandeliered magnificence of the Sleeping Dragon's all-purpose hall, but in much more basic space normally used as a schooling ground for five-year-olds in Hoopwestern's outer regions.

There were kids' attempts at pictures pinned to cork boards all round the walls, mostly thin figures with big heads and spiky hair sticking straight out like Medusa's snakes. There were simple notices – 'do not run' and 'raise your hand' – all written in self-conscious lower case letters.

Primary colours everywhere bombarded the eyesight to saturation point, and I couldn't believe that this sort of thing had been my own educational springboard; but it had. Another world, long left behind.

There were several rows of the temporary flip-up seats that grew more and more familiar to me as the days passed, and a makeshift speaker's platform, this time with a microphone that squeaked whenever tested, and on several other occasions when switched on or off.

The lighting was of unflattering greenish-white fluorescent strips, and there weren't enough of them to raise spirits above depression. Limbo must look like this, I thought: and the unenticing room had in fact drawn the sort of audience you could count on fingers and toes and still have enough left over for an abacus.

Mervyn Teck met us on the doorstep looking at his watch and checking, but by good luck and asking the way (less pride on my part than shame of arriving late) we had turned up at the exact minute advertised by a scatter of leaflets.

On the table on the platform, beside the temperamental microphone, there was a gavel for calling the meeting to order and two large plates of sandwiches secured by cling film.

Two or three earnest lady volunteers crowded round the candidate with goodwill, but it was plain, ten minutes after start time, that apathy, and not enthusiasm, had won the evening.

I expected my father to be embarrassed by the small turn-out and to hurry through the unsatisfactory proceedings, but he made a joke of it, abandoning the microphone and sitting on the edge of the platform, beckoning the sparse and scattered congregation to come forward into the first few rows, to make the meeting more coherent.

His magic worked. Everyone moved forward. He spoke to them familiarly, as if addressing a roomful of friends, and I watched him turn a disaster into a useful exercise in public relations. By the time the sandwiches had been liberated from the cling film even the few who had come to heckle had been tamed to silence.

Mervyn Teck looked both thoughtful and displeased.

'Something the matter?' I asked.

He said sourly, 'Orinda would have drawn a much better house. She'd have packed the hall. They love her here: she presents prizes to the children here every term. She buys them herself.'

'I'm sure she'll go on doing it.'

I meant it without irony, but Mervyn Teck gave me a glance of dislike and moved away. One of the lady volunteers sweetly told me that the time of the meeting had clashed with the current rave series on the television, and that even the pubs were suffering from it on Thursday nights. Tomorrow would be different, she said. Tomorrow the Town Hall would be packed.

'Er . . .' I said, 'what's happening in the Town Hall?'

'But you're his son, aren't you?'

'Yes, but . . .'

'But you don't know that tomorrow night your

father goes face to face in a debate with Paul Bethune?'

I shook my head.

'Fireworks,' she said happily. 'I wouldn't miss it for the world.'

My father, when I asked him about it on the short drive back to the centre of Hoopwestern, seemed full of equal relish.

'I suppose,' I said, 'there'll be more point to it than the sort of fiasco tonight could have been.'

'Every vote counts,' he corrected me. 'If I won only a few tonight, that's fine. You have to win the floaters over to your side, and they have to be persuaded one by one.'

'I'm hungry,' I said as we passed a brightly lit take-away, so we backtracked and bought chicken wings with banana and bacon, and even there my father, recognised, fell into political chat with the man deep-frying chips.

In the morning early I went out and bought a copy of the *Gazette*. Sleaze and Paul Bethune filled pages four and five (with photographs) but the front-page topic of concern was headlined 'JULIARD SHOT?'

Columns underneath said Yes (eyewitnesses) and No (he wasn't hurt). Statements from the police said nothing much (they couldn't find a gun). Statements from onlookers, like the self-important gunshot expert, said Juliard had definitely been the object of an assassination attempt. He thought so and he was always right.

The consensus theory of the reporters (including Usher Rudd) was that resentment against Juliard was running high in the Orinda Nagle camp. The editor's leader column didn't believe that political assassination ever took place at so low a level. World leaders, perhaps. Unelected local candidates, never.

I walked through the town to the ring road looking for Rudd's Repair Garage and found the staff unlocking their premises for the day. They had a large covered workshop and an even larger wire-fenced compound where jobs done or waiting stood in haphazard rows. The Range Rover was parked in that compound, sunlight already gleaming on its metallic paint.

I asked for, and reached, the manager, whose name was Basil Rudd. Thin, red-haired, freckled and energetic, his likeness to Usher Rudd made twins a possibility.

'Don't ask,' he said, eyeing my newspaper. 'He's my cousin. I disown him, and if you're out to be busy with your fists, you've reached the wrong man.'

'Well, I really came to collect that Range Rover. It's my father's.'

'Oh?' He blinked. 'I'll need proof of identity.'

I showed him a letter of authorisation signed by my parent and also my driving licence.

'Fair enough.' He opened a drawer, picked out a labelled ring bearing two keys and held them out for me to take. 'Don't forget to switch off the alarms. I'll send the bill to Mr Juliard's party headquarters. OK?'

'Yes. Thank you. Was there anything wrong?'

He shrugged. 'If there was, there isn't now.' He consulted a spiked worksheet. 'Oil change. General check. That's all.'

'Do you think I could talk to whoever did the job?'

'Whatever for?'

'Er . . . I've got to drive my father round in that vehicle and I've never driven it before . . . and I thought I might get some tips about engine management . . . so I don't overheat it by crawling along the roads canvassing door to door.'

Basil Rudd shrugged. 'Ask for Terry. He did the work.'

I thanked him and sought out Terry who gave three instant physical impressions: big; bald; belly. Brown overalls, grease-stained from his job.

He too eyed my newspaper. He spoke with venom in a powerful Dorset voice.

'Don't mention Bobby bloody Rudd round here.'

I hadn't been going to, but I said, 'Why not?'

'He'll listen to you and your missus in bed with one of them window-vibrating bugging contraptions and before you know it, never mind the sex, he'll be printing what you said about the boss having his hand up a customer's skirt when she brings her car in for the twentieth time to be overhauled, though there's bugger all wrong with it in the first place. Got me sacked, Bobby did.'

'But,' I suggested, 'you're still here.'

'Yeah, see, Basil took me on because he loathes Bobby, who's his cousin, see. It was over in Quindle I got sacked by Bobby's dad, that's Basil's uncle, drunk half the time . . .' He broke off. 'If it's not to complain about Bobby Usher bleeding Rudd, what is it you want, lad?'

'I . . . er . . . you serviced my father's Range Rover. What was wrong with it?'

'Apart from the fancy paintwork?' He scratched his shiny head. 'Foreign body in the oil sump. I suppose you might say that. Nothing else. I gave it a good clean-out.'

'What sort of foreign body?'

He looked at me dubiously. 'I don't rightly know.'

'Well, um . . . how do you know it was there?'

He took his time in answering by starting at the beginning of his involvement. 'A man in your party's headquarters – said his name was Teck or some such – he phones Basil saying there might be something dicey about a fancy Range Rover they'd got there and to send someone over pronto to take a decko, so I went over there and this Mr Teck gave me the keys and the Range Rover started at first touch, sweet as anything.'

I looked at him without comment.

'Yeah, well,' he said, scratching his bald head again. 'This Teck guy said something about maybe someone took a pot shot at your old man and to check that the Range Rover's brakes hadn't been mucked about with or anything, so I looked it all over and could see nothing wrong. No bombs, nothing like that, but anyway this Teck guy said to bring it here and do a thorough service, so I did.'

He stopped for effect. I said obligingly, 'What did you find?'

'See, it was what I *didn't* find.'

'I wish you'd explain.'

'No plug on the sump.'

'What?'

'Oil change. Routine service. I run the Range Rover over the inspection pit and I take a spanner to unscrew the sump-plug to drain out the old oil, and there you are, no plug. *No plug*, I ask you. But there's oil there, according to the dipstick. Normal. Full. So I run the engine a bit and the oil pressure gauge reads normal, like it did on my way round here, so there has to be oil circulating round the engine, see, so why, if the sump-plug is missing, why hasn't the oil all emptied out?'

'Well, why?'

'Because there's something else plugging up the hole, that's why.'

'A rag?' I suggested. 'A wad of tissues?'

'Nothing like that, I don't think. Something harder.

Anyway, I poked a bit of wire into the hole and freed whatever was there and the oil poured out like it always does. Not filthy oil, mind you. It hadn't been long since the last oil change.'

'So the plug, whatever it is, is still in the sump?'

He shrugged. 'I dare say so. It won't do much harm there. The sump drain-hole's not much bigger than a little finger.' He held up his own grimy hand. 'It wasn't a *big* plug, see.'

'Mm.' I hesitated. 'Did you tell Basil Rudd about it?'

He shook his big head. 'He'd gone home for the day when I put the work-done sheets in his office, and I didn't think much of it. I found a new plug that fits the Range Rover and screwed it up tight. Then I filled up with clean oil, same as usual, and put the Range Rover out in the yard, where it is now. It's all hunky-dory. You'll have no trouble with it.'

'I'll take it in a minute,' I said. 'I'll just go back into the office to see about settling up.'

I went into the office and asked Basil Rudd if I could telephone my father in the party headquarters and he obligingly held out the receiver to me with a be-my-guest invitation.

I said to my father, 'Please could you ask whoever it was who worked on your Range Rover last if there was a normal plug on the oil-sump drain.' I relayed Terry's finding and his solution to the problem.

Basil Rudd looked up sharply from a sheet of paper

he was writing on and began to protest, but I smiled, said it was an unimportant enquiry, and waited for my father's answer. He told me to stay right where I was and five minutes later was back on the line.

'My mechanic is very annoyed at any suggestion that there was any irregularity at all with any part of the Range Rover. He did a complete overhaul on Monday. So what is going on?'

'I don't exactly know. It's probably nothing.'

'Bring the Range Rover back. We need it today.'

'Yes,' I said.

I gave the receiver back to Basil Rudd and thanked him for the call.

'Just what is this all about?' he said.

'I don't know enough,' I replied. 'I haven't been driving long. But I am concerned with keeping my father safe since the episode with the gun . . .' I waved the newspaper, 'so I'm probably being fussy over nothing. But on its last overhaul there was an ordinary plug screwed into the sump drain, and yesterday there wasn't.'

Basil Rudd showed first of all impatience and then anxiety, and finally stood up and came with me back to talk to Terry.

Terry, for a change, was scratching his brown-overalled belly.

I said, 'I'm not complaining about anything here, and please don't think I am. I do want to know what was plugging the sump, though, because I'm frankly scared of mysteries concerning anything to do with my father. So, please, how would you put a substitute plug in the drain-hole, and most of all, why?'

The two motor men stood in silence, not knowing the answers.

'The oil was quite clean,' Terry said.

Another silence.

Basil Rudd said, 'If you drain the new oil out again, and take the engine apart, you'll find whatever the stopper was that Terry pushed through the sump, but that's a very expensive procedure and not justified, I don't think.'

Another silence.

'I'll ask my father,' I said.

We trooped back to the office and I reported the last-resort expensive solution of dismantling the engine.

'Do nothing. Stay where you are,' my father commanded. 'Just do nothing, and wait. Let me speak to Basil Rudd.'

The chit-chat went on for several minutes. Basil Rudd said he thought the boy – meaning me – was making a hullabaloo over nothing much, but in the end he shrugged and said, 'Yes, yes, all right.' He put down the receiver and said to me, 'Your father is sending someone for the Range Rover. He wants you to stay here for now.'

Terry muttered that he had done a proper service on the Range Rover and no one could tell him different. Basil Rudd gave me a look of disfavour and said he couldn't waste any more time, he had mountains of paperwork to see to. I didn't exactly apologise, but I said I would wait outside in the Range Rover and walked peacefully across to where it stood in the wire-fenced compound. I disarmed the alarms, opened the door and sat behind the driving wheel, going through the systems and reading the instruction book.

I waited for over an hour until Basil Rudd appeared at the window beside me. I opened the door, stepped down to the ground and met the man accompanying the garage owner, who announced with a glint of irony that he had come to solve the mystery of the missing sump-plug. His name, he said, was Foster Fordham. He looked more like a lawyer than a mechanic: no blue collar to his grey and white pinstriped shirt or his neat dark suit. He had straight, dark, well-brushed hair, light-framed glasses and polished black shoes.

Basil Rudd, turning away, asked Foster Fordham to report to him in the office before leaving and, watching Rudd's departing back, Fordham, apparently bored to inertia, informed me that he was here to do my father a big favour, as normally he was a consultant engineer, not a hands-on minion.

I began to explain about the gunshot, but he interrupted that he knew all about it, and all about the missing plug.

'I work in car-racing circles,' he said. 'My field is sabotage.'

I no doubt looked as inadequate as I felt in the face of his quiet assurance.

He said, 'I understand that yesterday you were going to drive this vehicle from here to Quindle. How far is that?'

'About twelve miles.'

'Dual carriageway? Flat straight roads?'

'Mostly single lane, a lot of sharp corners, and some of it uphill.'

He nodded. He said we would now take the road to Quindle and he would drive.

Perplexed but trusting I climbed into the passenger seat beside him and listened to the healthy purr of the engine as he started up and drove off out of the garage compound onto the ring road round Hoopwestern, bound for Quindle. He drove fast in silence, watching the instrument panel as intently as the road, and said nothing until we had reached the top of the long steep incline halfway to what I thought was our destination. He stopped up there, however, and, still without explaining, did a U-turn and drove straight back to Rudd's garage.

Cars flashed past, appearing fast towards us from blind corners, as they had the day before. Fordham drove faster than I'd felt safe doing in Crystal's car, but if his field was racing, that was hardly surprising.

At the garage he told Terry to drain the engine oil into a clean container. Terry said the oil was too hot to handle. Fordham agreed to wait a little, but insisted that the oil should still be hot when it was drained.

'Why?' Terry asked. 'It's clean. I did the oil change yesterday.'

Fordham didn't answer. Eventually, wearing heavy gloves, Terry unscrewed the sump-plug and let the hot oil drain out as requested into a clean plastic five-gallon container. Fordham had him put the container into the luggage space at the back of the Range Rover and then suggested he should screw the sump-plug back into place and refill the engine with fresh cool oil.

Terry signalled exasperation with his eyebrows but did as he was asked. Mr Fordham, calm throughout, then told me that he had finished his investigation and suggested we say farewell to Basil Rudd and return in the Range Rover to my father's headquarters. Basil Rudd, of course, wanted to know reasons. Fordham told him with great politeness that he would receive a written report, and meanwhile not to worry, all was well.

Fordham drove composedly to the car park outside my father's headquarters and, with me faithfully following, walked into the offices where my father was sitting with Mervyn Teck discussing tactics.

My father stood at the sight of us and limped outside with Fordham to the Range Rover. Through the window I watched them talking earnestly, then Fordham took the plastic container of oil out of the

Range Rover, put it into the boot of a Mercedes standing nearby, climbed into the driver's seat, and neatly departed.

My father, returning, told Mervyn cheerfully that there was now nothing wrong with the Range Rover and it could safely be driven all round the town.

We finally set off. I drove, feeling my way cautiously through the gears, learning the positive message of the four-wheel drive. My father sat beside me, accompanied by his walking stick. Mervyn Teck, carrying a megaphone, sat in the rear seat, squeezing his lumpy knees together to allow more space for two volunteer helpers, thin bittersweet Lavender and motherly Faith.

The rear-seaters knew their drill from much past practice, and I with eye-opening wonderment became acquainted with the hardest graft in politics, the door-to-door begging for a 'yes' vote.

The first chosen residential street consisted of identical semi-detached houses with clipped garden-defining hedges and short concrete drives up to firmly closed garage doors. Some of the front windows were adorned with stickers simply announcing 'BETHUNE': he had worked this land before us.

'This road is awash with floaters,' Mervyn said with rare amusement. 'Let's see what we can do about turning the tide our way.'

Directing me to stop the vehicle, he untucked himself from his seatbelt and, standing in the open air, began to exhort the invisible residents through the reverberating megaphone, to vote JULIARD, JULIARD, JULIARD.

I found it odd to have my name bouncing off the house fronts, but the candidate himself nodded with smiling approval.

Lavender and Faith followed Mervyn out of the car, each of them carrying a bundle of stickers printed JULIARD in slightly larger letters than BETHUNE. Taking one side of the road each they began ringing front door bells and knocking knockers and, where they got no response, tucking a sticker through the letter-box.

If a door was opened to them they smiled and pointed to the Range Rover from where my father would limp bravely up the garden path to put on his act, at which he was clearly terrific. I crawled up the road in low gear, my father limped uncomplainingly, Mervyn activated his megaphone and Lavender and Faith wasted not a leaflet. In our slow wake we left friendly waves and a few JULIARDs in windows. By the end of the street I was bored to death, but it seemed Lavender and Faith both revelled in persuasion tactics and were counting the road a victory for their side.

After two more long sweeps through suburbia (in which at least one baby got kissed) we respited for a late sandwich lunch in a pub.

'If ever you get invited into someone's home,' my father said (as he had been invited five or six times that morning), 'you go into the sitting-room and you say, "Oh, what an attractive room!" even if you think it's hideous.'

Lavender, Faith and Mervyn all nodded, and I said, 'That's cynical.'

'You've a lot to learn.'

We were sitting by a window. I looked through it to the Range Rover parked outside in plain view and reckoned that one way or another I actually had learned a lot that morning, and that what I'd learned had probably saved a good many votes.

My father, as if following my thoughts, said lightly, 'We'll talk about it later,' but it wasn't until we were changing before going to the Town Hall debate that he would discuss Foster Fordham.

By then I'd persuaded Mervyn to arrange a securely locked overnight garage for the Range Rover, backed by my casual parent who said mildly, 'The boy's got a point, Mervyn. It might be more satisfactory for us all. No harm, anyway, in keeping it safe from thieves,' and as the car belonged to my father himself and not to the party, he had his way.

'Foster Fordham wasn't sure how much you understood,' he said, combing through his tightly curled dark hair and leaving it much as it had been before. 'He was surprised you didn't ask him questions.'

'Terry – the mechanic – did ask. Fordham wouldn't answer.'

'So what do you conclude it was all about?'

'Well . . . if you or I or anyone else had driven the

Range Rover yesterday towards Quindle, it would quite likely have crashed. Or, at least, I think so.'

My father put down his comb and with stillness said, 'Go on.'

I said, 'I do think the bullet that came so near us was deliberately aimed at you, and even if it hadn't killed you, it would have stopped your campaign if you'd been badly injured. But all the town could see that all you'd done was twist your ankle. So if anyone was looking around for another way to put a stopper on you, there was the Range Rover, just standing there unguarded all night in the car park, conspicuously yours and painted with silver and gold to attract attention.'

'Yes.'

'When I was taking driving lessons, which was mostly in the Easter holidays, I read a lot of motoring magazines – '

'I thought you were supposed to be revising for your A levels, your university entrance exams.'

'Um . . . I was riding for Sir Vivian, too. I mean, I can *think* in algebra. I just had to make sure I understood all the exam questions that have been set before, set in the past. I don't mean to sound big-headed, really I don't, but I had sort of a lot of spare mental time, so I read the motor magazines. I didn't know you had a Range Rover – but I read about them. I read about their anti-thief devices. So when your Range Rover had stood quiet in the car park all night, and you had the only keys to disarm the screech alarms, then if anyone had done any harm it had to have been from outside . . . or underneath . . .' I tapered off, feeling silly, but he waved for me to go on.

'I thought the brake fluid might have been drained so that the brakes wouldn't work,' I said. 'I thought the tyres might have been slashed so that you'd have a blow-out when you were going fast. Things come whizzing round corners on that road to Quindle . . . you wouldn't have much chance in a car out of control, but a Range Rover is pretty well built like a tank – so *you* might be unhurt in a crash, but you might kill the people you crashed *into* . . . or at least injure them badly . . . and that would stop you being elected, wouldn't it?'

My father took his time in moving, and in answering. 'It wasn't the brakes or the tyres,' he said.

'It was the engine oil.'

He nodded. 'Tell me what you think.'

I said, 'I think Fordham knew what was wrong before he came. He said he was an expert in sabotage in motor racing, and nothing about the Range Rover surprised him. It must have seemed pretty elementary to him.'

My father, smiling, said, 'I've known him a long time. So, what did he tell me?'

This is some sort of test, I thought. I could only guess at answers; but anyhow, I guessed. 'Someone unscrewed the sump-plug and removed it, and stuffed up the hole so that the oil couldn't all run out.'

'Go on.'

'The stopper was something that would fall out later, so the oil would all drain out of the engine when it was going along, and the engine would seize up solid, and as it's a four-wheel drive you wouldn't be able to steer and you would be like a block of stone in the middle of the road.'

'Not bad.'

'But Terry – the mechanic – pushed the substitute plug right through into the sump like a cork in a bottle, which I honestly don't think he should have done, and screwed in a new plug before he refilled with clean oil . . . like I told you on the phone.'

'Mm. So what was the substitute plug made of?'

I'd been thinking about it while we drove round the suburbs. I said hesitantly, 'To begin with I thought it would be something chemical that could react with the oil and make it like jelly, or something, so that it couldn't be pumped round the pistons and they would seize up in the cylinders, but that can't have been right as the plug was in the sump when Foster Fordham drove fast towards Quindle and deliberately made the engine very hot, and he insisted on Terry draining out the clean oil again when it was still hot, so I thought that perhaps the temporary stopper had *melted*, and Fordham has taken the oil away to see what was in it.'

'Yes,' my father said.

'Because if it had melted away in the sump drain-hole when we were on our way to Quindle yesterday, it would have taken only about a minute for all the oil to drain out and ruin the engine. When the oil was hot this morning, when Terry drained it, it ran out as thin as water.'

'Fordham says it's an old trick. So old, it's never attempted now in motor racing.'

'Well . . . what was the plug made of?'

'What would you think?'

I hesitated. 'It had to be pretty simple. I mean, almost spur-of-the-moment, after the bullet had missed.'

'So?'

'So how about shoving a candle up the spout, and cutting it off? How about *wax*?'

My father peacefully tied his unexuberantly striped tie. 'Foster Fordham,' he said, 'will let us know.'

It was extraordinary, I thought, as we entered the Town Hall for the Bethune face-to-face confrontation, how many people I'd come to recognise in only two days.

Orinda was there, torturing herself, wearing a very short gold dress with a black feather boa that twisted round her neck and arms like the snake it was named for, and demanded admiring attention. Her green eyes flashed. An emerald and diamond bracelet sparkled on her wrist. No one could be unaware of her vibrant attendance.

A pace behind her, as ever, stood her shadow, whose name I remembered with an effort was A.L. Wyvern. 'A.L.', I thought, 'Anonymous Lover' Wyvern. He had looked uninteresting in a dinner jacket at the Sleeping Dragon dinner: in the Town Hall, in a grey suit and a blue shirt, he filled space without making an impression.

Large Mrs Kitchens, eagle-eyed, in navy blue with purple frills, held tight to 'my Leonard's' arm and succeeded in preventing him from beaming his sickly moustache into Orinda's airspace. Mrs Kitchens gave me a cheery wave and a leer – and I would *not* let her embarrass me.

Mervyn, of course, had arrived with Crystal at his side to take notes. The three witches were helping to seat people, and Dearest Polly, at the sight of us, made an enthusiastic little run in our direction, and bore off my father like a trophy to show him the lectern behind which he was to stand on the platform. Dearest Polly, it seemed, was stage-managing the evening.

As if with a flourish of trumpets the Bethune camp arrived. There was a stir and a rustle in the hall and a sprinkle of clapping. Hooray for adultery, I thought.

Paul Bethune, seen for the first time, was a portly and portentous-looking fifty or so with a double chin and the thinning hair that might in the end confound his chances more thoroughly than a love-child. He was accompanied by a busy Mervyn Teck lookalike, who was indeed his agent, and by a nervous woman who looked at the world in general in upward glances from under her eyebrows. She was shown to a seat in the front row of spectators and Dearest Polly, beckoning to me strongly, introduced me to Paul Bethune's wife, Isobel.

Isobel emitted severe discomfort at having me to sit beside her, but I gave her my best harmless grin and told her she couldn't want to avoid being there more than I did myself.

'I've only just left school,' I said. 'I don't know anything about politics. I understand this is the third campaign for you and Mr Bethune, so you probably don't find it as confusing as I do.'

'Oh dear,' she said. 'You're such a child, you can't possibly know . . .'

'I'm nearly eighteen.'

She smiled weakly, then suddenly stiffened to immobility, her face pale with a worse disaster than my proximity.

I said, 'What's the matter, Mrs Bethune?'

'That man,' she murmured. 'Oh God.'

I looked where she was looking, and saw Basil Rudd.

'That's not Usher Rudd, the newspaperman,' I said, understanding. 'That's his cousin. That's Basil Rudd. He mends cars.'

'It's *him*. That beastly writer.'

'No, Mrs Bethune. It's his cousin. They look alike, but that's Basil.'

To my absolute horror, she began to cry. I looked around urgently for help but Polly was elbow-deep in wires to microphones and television cameras, and Paul Bethune, eyeing his wife's distress, turned away deliberately with a sharply displeased grimace.

Unkind bastard, I thought. Stupid, too. A show of fondness might have earned him votes.

Isobel Bethune stumbled to her feet, searching unsuccessfully in her well-worn black handbag for something to mop up tears, and I, clumsily but with pity, offered her an arm to hold on to while I cleared a path towards the door.

She talked all the way in broken half-intelligible explanations. 'Paul insisted I came . . . I didn't want to, but he said I might as well stab him in the back if I didn't . . . and now he'll be so *furious*, but what does he expect me to do after all those pictures in the paper of him and that girl . . . and she had nothing on, well, next to nothing. He wants me to smile and pretend I don't mind, but he makes me look a fool and I suppose I am, but I didn't know about that girl until it was in the paper, and he doesn't deny it. He says what did I expect . . .'

We went through the entrance hall and out into the fresh air with everyone arriving and staring at Isobel's tears with hungry curiosity. At seven-thirty in the evening merciful dusk was still some time ahead, so I veered away from the entrance and she, wholly without resistance, came with me round the nearest corner.

The Town Hall formed one of the sides of the cobbled square. The Sleeping Dragon took up an adjoining side, with shops (and party headquarters) along the other two. Wide alleyways, that once had been open roads, led away from every corner, and on one of them lay the main Town Hall entrance doors. Along the side of the Town Hall that faced onto the square, there was a sort of cloister – a covered walkway with pillars and benches giving shelter and rest. Isobel Bethune crumpled onto one of the benches and, after a craven moment of wanting to ditch her, I sat beside her and wondered what to say.

I needn't have worried. She compulsively went on sobbing and pouring out her unhappiness and resentment at the unfairness of things. I half listened, watching the wretchedness that twisted her lipsticked mouth, and seeing in her swelling eyes and grey-flecked hair that not long ago she'd been quite pretty, before Usher Rudd had taken a photographic sledgehammer to her complacent world.

Her sons were just as bad, she sobbed. Fifteen, seventeen, they sulked and argued with everything she said and complained non-stop. If Paul got elected it would at least take him away from home more, and, oh dear, she didn't mean to say that, but it was either him or her – and where would she go? She was at her wit's end, she said.

She was on the point of a full breakdown, I thought. I had been only about twelve when my Aunt Susan had screamed and yelled and slammed doors, had driven the family car across the lawn into a hedge and been taken to hospital, and had then got worse when her second son left to join a rap group and grew a beard and got AIDS. My Uncle Harry had gone to my father for help, and somehow or other my parent had restored general order and put some balance back in Susan; and if it was never a rapturously happy household after that, there was no actual abuse.

I asked Isobel Bethune, 'Do your sons want Mr Bethune to be elected?'

'They just grunt. You can't get a word out of them.' She sniffed, wiping her eyes with her fingers. 'Paul thinks he would have beaten Orinda easily, but he says George Juliard is different. Oh! I'd forgotten, you're his son! I shouldn't talk to you like this. Paul will be so cross.'

'Don't tell him.'

'No . . . would you like a drink?' She looked across at the Sleeping Dragon. 'Brandy?'

I shook my head but she said she badly needed a nerve-steadier and she wouldn't drink alone, so I went across the square with her and drank Coke while she dealt with a double Rémy Martin on ice. We sat at a small table in the bar, which was Friday-night busy with couples.

Both of Isobel's hands were shaking.

She left me to go and 'tidy up', returning with combed hair, freshened lipstick and powdered eyelids, still clutching a tissue but much more in control.

She ordered more brandy. I said no to Coke.

'I'm not going back to the Town Hall,' she said. 'I'll walk home from here. It's not all that far.'

When she picked up her refilled glass, the ice still clattered and shook in her grasp.

'Could I get you a taxi?' I asked.

She leaned across the table and put her hand on mine. 'You're a nice boy,' she said, 'whoever your father is.'

There was a familiar bright flash and the whine of a film winding on and there, a few feet away, stood the other Rudd, Bobby Usher himself, grinning triumphantly and radiating ill nature in megawatts.

Isobel Bethune lunged furiously to her feet but Usher Rudd, quick at getaways, was out of the door before she could draw breath to shout. 'I *hate* him,' she said, again near to tears. 'I'll kill him.'

I asked the barman to phone for a taxi.

'Mrs Bethune still owes for the drinks.'

'Oh.'

'I haven't any money,' she said. 'Pay for me, there's a dear.'

I salvaged from my pockets the remains of the

money my father had given me in Brighton and handed her all of it.

'You pay the man for the drinks. I'm not old enough yet to buy alcohol and I'm not getting into that sort of trouble.'

Both the barman and Isobel, open-mouthed, completed the sale.

CHAPTER FIVE

Back at the Town Hall the debate had passed through lukewarm and was heating towards chopping motions with the hands of the two protagonists.

A local chess champion, brought in as referee, had come to the fray with a pinging time clock and, making his own set of rules, he had decreed that each candidate would in turn answer specific questions, the answers to last a maximum of five minutes before being silenced by the time clock's arbitration.

The format seemed to be working quite well, chiefly because both candidates knew how to speak. I was no longer surprised by my father's ability to rouse, amuse and convince, but somehow I'd expected Paul Bethune to be as bombastic and unkind as he'd seemed to his wife. Instead he delivered dryly witty and well-prepared responses to the questions and it was only afterwards that I wondered if he'd learned his best phrases by heart and had used them before.

The Town Hall was full. The seats given by Polly to me and Isobel Bethune now held the Mayor and his missus and, glad to be less exposed, I stood by the door and watched the waves of animation and agreement and fury roll in turn across the faces of the audience, and thought that at least they were *listening*, and obviously cared.

There could be no winner that night. They both won. Everyone applauded and went away talking.

Orinda had several times clapped Bethune. Leonard Kitchens kept his hands for ever in his pockets. Dearest Polly's long face glowed with goodness and pleasure, and freckly Basil Rudd looked even more like his obnoxious cousin when he smiled.

No one produced a gun.

My father and Paul Bethune shook hands.

Like star actors they left the stage last, each surrounded at once by chattering satellites, all with something to say, questions to ask, points to make. My father genuinely enjoyed it, and again his spirits were helium-ballooning as we headed back to our base.

'It's quicker if we walk straight across the square,' my parent objected as I tried to persuade him to take to the cloister. 'Why do you want to walk two sides of a triangle, not one, and you a mathematician?'

'Bullets,' I said.

'My God.' He stopped dead. 'But no one would try again!'

'You'd have said no one would try the first time, but they did.'

'We don't know for sure.'

'And the sump-plug?'

He shook his head as if in general disbelief, but he made no further objection to the cloister route, and seemed not to notice that I walked between him and the well-lit open square.

He wanted to talk about the debate. He also wanted to know why I'd missed half of it and where I'd been. I told him all of Isobel's troubles but I could feel he was barely attending: his mind and his tongue were still busy with points made and lost against the lady's unfaithful man.

'He's dedicated, you know. I can't stand his politics.'

I said, 'I hate what you say, but I'll defend to the death your right to say it.'

'Bull's eye. Don't tell me all those school fees weren't wasted.'

'Come down,' I begged. 'You're too high in the sky.'

Again he stopped walking. We had by then left the cloister and were passing dimly lit shop fronts on the way to the bay windows of first the charity gift shop and, next door, the party headquarters.

'You have no idea what it's like to hold an audience in your hand.'

'No.' Winners at long odds got little praise, and I'd never won on a favourite.

We walked on to the doorway.

Dearest Polly waited there, puzzled. 'Where have you been? You left ahead of me.'

'The boy,' my father said, pointing at me though

there were precious few other boys in sight. 'Benedict, my son, has this fixed idea that someone is violently seeking to put paid to my campaign, if not to my life. Dearest Polly, tell him I'll take my chances and I don't want him ever again to risk his own neck to preserve mine.'

'Dearest Polly,' I said – and she smiled vividly with sweetness – 'this is the only father I'm ever likely to have. Persuade him to give me a real job in this election. Persuade him he needs a full-time bodyguard. Persuade him to let me try to keep him safe.'

'I don't need a bodyguard,' he insisted. 'I need you to be a social asset. Isobel Bethune is useless to Paul, but you have this extraordinary gift – which I admit I didn't expect – of getting people to talk to you. Look at Isobel Bethune! Look at Crystal Harley! I haven't got a word out of her and she chatters away to you. Look at Mrs Kitchens, pouring information into your ears.'

Polly nodded, smiling. 'You're so young, you're no threat to anyone. They all need to talk, and you're safe.'

I said pensively, 'How about Orinda? She turned her back on me at the dinner and wouldn't say a word.'

Polly clapped her hands together with laughter. 'I'll give you Orinda. I'll manage it again.'

'But alone,' I said. 'I could talk to her if she was

alone, but the Anonymous Lover never leaves her side.'

'Who?'

'A.L. Wyvern.'

'Anonymous Lover!' Polly exclaimed. 'Enchanting. His name's really Alderney, I think. He plays golf. He used to play golf with Dennis.'

She moved around smoothly, at home in the office, sorting out mugs and making coffee. I couldn't guess her age nearer than ten years: somewhere between forty or fifty, I thought, but knew I could be wrong. She was again wearing the inappropriate crimson lipstick, this time with a green jacket over a long skirt of brownish tweed: heavy for August. Somehow, with the opaque stockings and 'sensible' shoes, one would have expected her to be clumsy, but she was paradoxically graceful, as if she had once been a dancer. She had no rings on her long capable fingers and for jewellery relied on a single strand of maidenly pearls.

One could have felt sorry for Polly at first sight, I thought, but that would have been a great mistake. She had an inner certainty to go with the goodness. She carried the fuddy-duddy clothes without self-consciousness. She was – I fished for the word – serene.

She said, pouring hot water onto instant coffee granules, 'I don't see any harm in Benedict appointing himself officially to look after you. After all, he hasn't done a bad job so far. Mervyn grumbled all over the Town Hall tonight about having to find a lock-up garage because Benedict wanted one. He says he doesn't like Benedict giving him orders.'

'It was a suggestion, not an order,' my father said.

'It felt like an order to Mervyn, therefore to him it *was* an order. Mervyn resents Benedict's influence over you. Mervyn likes to be in charge.'

'Ben's only been here two days,' my father protested.

Polly smiled. 'Ten minutes was probably enough. You're a brilliant politician on a grand scale, George, but it's your son who sees into individual minds.'

My father looked at me thoughtfully.

'He's good at it now,' Polly said, 'and he's not yet eighteen. Just wait ten years or so. You brought him here to give yourself social credibility, proving you had a son, you weren't a bachelor, confirmed or otherwise, and you've found an asset you didn't expect, so use him, George.'

She stirred the mugs of coffee and distributed it black. My father absentmindedly fished a small container out of a pocket and tapped a sweetener into his drink.

'George?' Polly prompted.

He opened his mouth to answer but before he could speak the telephone rang, and as I was nearest I picked up the receiver.

'Juliard?' a voice said.

'Benedict. Do you want my father? He's here.'

'No. You'll do. Do you know who you're talking to?'

'Foster Fordham,' I said.

'Right. And have you worked out what was plugging your sump?'

'Something that would melt when the oil got really hot.'

He laughed. 'I refrigerated the oil and filtered it. There were enough wax globules to make a good thick plug. There are also cotton fibres which may have been from the wick of a candle. Now let me talk to your father.'

I handed over the receiver and listened to half of a long discussion that was apparently about whether or not to report the sabotage to the police. There had been no further action that my father knew of over the rifle shot but, he thought, and his opinion persuaded, that his friend Foster should write an account of what he'd done and what he'd found, and that my father should give a copy of it to the boys in blue as a precaution.

Polly and I listened to snatches. 'They don't have the manpower for surveillance . . . they won't do it . . . you can't guard against a determined assassin . . . yes . . .' my father's gaze slid my way, ' . . . but he's too young . . . all right, then . . . we're agreed.' He put down the receiver carefully and with deliberation and a sigh said, 'Foster Fordham will write a report for the police. Ben will nanny me to the best of his ability and Mervyn will have to put up with it. And now, dearest Polly, I'm going to abandon tomorrow's canvassing and go where I'm not expected.'

Hanging from a hook on one wall was a large appointments calendar with an extensive square allocated to each day. Crystal had entered the basics of my father's advance plans in the squares so that one could see at a glance what he would be doing on each day.

The programme had started the previous Tuesday with 'Candidate arrives. Office familiarisation.' Wednesday's schedule of 'Drive round constituency' had been crossed off, and 'Fetch son from Brighton' inserted instead and, underneath that, 'Dinner at Sleeping Dragon'. Nothing about being shot at on the way home.

The Quindle engagements and the infant school evening were listed for Thursday, and door-to-door canvassing and the Town Hall debate for Friday.

More of the same stretched ahead. If I hadn't had the interest of attempting to foil seriously dangerous attacks on said candidate I would have suffered severe strain of the smiling muscles long before polling day.

How could he face it? I wondered. How could he *enjoy* it, as he clearly did?

'Tomorrow,' he said, pleased with his inspiration, 'tomorrow we'll go to Dorset County racecourse. Tomorrow will be for Ben. We'll go to the races.'

My first reaction was joy, which he noted. Fast on

joy's heels came a sort of devastation that I couldn't hope to be riding there, that I would spend the afternoon as an exile, envying my neighbour his ox and his ass and his saddle in the amateurs' steeplechase; but I let only the joy show, I think.

'We'll go in the Range Rover,' my father said decisively, pleased with his plan. 'And Polly will come with us, won't you, Poll?'

Polly said she would love to.

Did Polly ever lie?

We drank the coffee without stress, my father finally as calm as he'd achieved during this whole strange week. Polly went out through the back office to retrieve her car and drive home, which I understood was a house in a wood outside the town, and my father and I, bolting everything securely, climbed the steep little staircase and slept undisturbed until Saturday morning.

Mervyn leaned in heavy annoyance on the bell at breakfast time and of course frowned heavily over the change of destination. How did George ever hope to be successful in a marginal seat if he neglected the door-to-door persuasion routine, which was of *paramount* importance? The Dorset County racecourse, sin of sins, was outside the Hoopwestern catchment area.

Never mind, my father soothed him, the many

Hoopwestern voters who went to the races might approve.

Mervyn, unconvinced, shut his mouth grimly for half an hour, but as the day expanded decided to salvage at least crumbs from what he considered the ruins of canvassing's best weekend opportunity and got busy on the telephone, with the result that we were invited to lunch with the racecourse Stewards and were otherwise showered with useful tickets. Mervyn, from long experience, knew everyone of influence in the county.

He blamed me, of course, for the switch, and perhaps with reason. If he'd had his way he would have been dancing happy attendance on Orinda, walking backwards in her presence. What he would have done with A.L. Wyvern I couldn't guess, but presumably he was used to the enigmatic shadow, as the Anonymous Lover had been deceased Dennis Nagle's best friend also. They played golf.

Mervyn's disappointments, I thought, shrugging off his ill will, were just too bad. In his life's terms, success lay in getting his candidate elected, or, if not elected, a close runner-up. Mervyn was not about to ruin his own reputation as agent out of tetchiness with Juliards, father or son.

The chilly atmosphere in the offices was lightened by an unexpected visit from the woman who ran the charity shop next door. She and Mervyn knew each other well, but she was fascinated to meet the new candidate, she said; she had seen us come and go, she wanted to shake hands with George, she'd heard his son was a doll, she wondered if we would like a home-made apple pie.

She put her offering on my father's desk.

'Kind of you, Amy,' Mervyn said, and in his manner I read that not only had he known his neighbour a long time but he'd undervalued her for probably the whole period.

Amy was one of those people easy to undervalue; an apologetic unassuming middle-aged widow (Polly said) who received gifts of unwanted junk, spruced them up a bit to sell, and would never have dipped into the till before passing on the proceeds to the charity that maintained her. Amy was fluffy, honest and halfway to stupid: also kind and talkative. One day of unadulterated Amy, I thought, would last a lifetime.

It was easy not to listen to every word in the flow, but she did grab our attention at one point.

'Someone broke a pane of glass in our window on Wednesday night and I've had a terrible job getting it mended.' She told us at far too much length how she'd managed it. 'A policeman called, you know, and asked if the window had been broken by a rifle bullet but I said, of course not, I clean the floor first thing when I arrive every morning because, of course, I don't live upstairs like you can here. There's only a bath-room and one small room I use for storage, though sometimes I do let a homeless person sleep there in an emergency. Anyway, of course I didn't find a bullet. I told the policeman, Joe it was, whose mother drives a school bus, and he came in for a look round and made a note or two. I saw it in the paper about the gun going off and maybe someone was shooting at Mr Juliard, you never feel safe these days, do you? And then, just now when I was dusting an old what-not that I can't seem to sell to anybody, I came to this *bump*, and I pulled it out, and I wonder if this was what Joe was looking for, so do you think I should tell him?'

She plunged a hand into a pocket in her drab droopy cardigan and put down on the desk, beside the apple pie, a squashed-looking piece of metal that had certainly flown at high speed from a .22 rifle.

'I do think,' my father said carefully, 'that you should tell your friend Joe, whose mother drives a school bus, that you've found the little lump of metal stuck in a what-not.'

'Do you really?'

'Yes, I do.'

Amy picked up the bullet, squinted at it, and polished it a bit on her cardigan. So much for residual fingerprints, I thought.

'All right, then,' Amy said cheerfully, putting the prize back in her pocket. 'I was sure you would know what I should do.'

She invited him to look around her shop, but he

cravenly sent me instead, and so I found myself staring at an ugly six-foot-high cane and wicker what-not that had stood near the window and had stopped the slug.

'I call it an *étagère* these days,' Amy said sadly. 'But still nobody wants it. I don't suppose *you* . . .?'

'No,' I said. And nor did I want any of the silver spoons or children's toys or second-hand clothes neatly and cleanly arranged to do good.

I retrieved the Range Rover from its safe haven, picked up my father and (following Mervyn's ungracious directions) found Polly's unexpectedly grand house in the woods. She sat on the rear seat for our journey to the races and, with a touch of glee, detailed a few telephone calls she had made; a touch of persuasion here, a dangle of carrot there.

'Mr Anonymous Lover Wyvern,' she said, 'received a lovely last-minute invitation to play golf in the county's top pro-am event of the year, an offer he'd have to have been ice to refuse. So off he was due to go with his precious clubs, and that was *him* out of the way.'

'How did you manage it?' my father asked admiringly.

'Inducements,' she said darkly. 'And, shortly afterwards, Orinda got invited to the Stewards' box at the races . . .'

'That's where we're going to!' exclaimed my father.

'You don't say!' Polly teased him. 'Benedict,' she

admonished me, 'I'm giving you Orinda without the lover, so don't waste the day.'

'But what can he do?' my father protested.

'He knows,' Polly said. 'How he'll do it, I can't tell, but trust your son.' She switched her attention back to me. 'Orinda knows bugger all about racing. She's going today for the snob value of a Duke, who's one of the Stewards. You'll have to contend with that. Think you can do it?'

I said a bit helplessly, 'I don't know.' Polly's forthright language always disconcerted me, although everyday lurid stable-talk passed my ears unnoticed.

'Go for shit,' she said.

Orinda was already into lobster mousse with diced cucumber when we reached the Stewards' luncheon room and although she looked outraged at our arrival she could do little but choke and recover with sips of wine, patted delicately on the back by the Duke at her side.

The Duke rose and gave Polly a conspiratorial kiss on the cheek, and I saw how Orinda had been hooked and reeled in.

Orinda wore a white linen suit with a green silk scarf tied and floating from a black lizard handbag that swung from the back of her chair. Sleek, matt-skinned, her presence easily eclipsed every other woman in the room, especially Polly who had dressed as usual as if not sure of the event or the season.

My father shook hands all round, his innate unmistakable power turning every head his way even in a roomful of powerful men. Orinda hated him.

'My son Benedict,' he said, introducing me: but it was he who claimed their eyes.

The Duke, hesitantly, said to me, 'Haven't I met you before? Haven't you ridden against my son Edward?'

'Yes, sir. At Towcester last Easter. He won.'

The Duke had a remembering smile. 'You finished third! It was Eddie's birthday. We had an impromptu party to celebrate. You were there.'

'Yes, sir.'

'Nothing like racing, is there? Best thing on earth, Eddie says.'

My father looked sharply at my face.

'Best thing,' I said.

'Mind you,' the Duke said to my father, 'for all these young men, it's only a hobby. Amateurs can't make a living at it. The best amateurs used to be able to turn pro but for some reason it's hardly ever done these days. Eddie needs a job. Amateurs can't ride for ever. I expect your Benedict knows all that. A good fellow, your Benedict, Eddie says. Sit down, Mr Juliard. It's an excellent lunch.'

He seated my father on the other side of him from Orinda, whose enjoyment of the day had waned to twilight even though the sun outside shone brightly.

She pushed away her unfinished mousse as if she could no longer taste it and had difficulty, with rigid facial muscles, in smiling at her host.

A stocky man of perhaps sixty, the Duke looked less patrician than industrious, a worldly-wise businessman, a managing director more than a figurehead chairman. His son, Eddie, a good fellow himself, had once said he envied the time I could give to racing: his own father insisted he work for his living. Well, I thought ruefully, Vivian Durridge and my own father had more than evened us up. Eddie's father owned horses which the son could ride in races, and mine didn't.

Polly and I were seated several places down the lengthy white-clothed dining table on the other side from the uncomfortable Orinda, and placidly ate our mousse and cucumber which was, as the Duke said, excellent, even though, now I'd been let off near-starvation, I would have preferred a large salami pizza.

There was some sort of curried chicken next. As time ran out towards the first race, the Duke, looking at his watch, told my father that as Chief Steward for the day he (the Duke) would have to leave the party now in order to carry out his duties. As if by accident he saw the near panic on Orinda's face at being left without a buffer zone between herself and her beastly usurper, and found an irresistible and apparently spur-of-the-moment solution.

With a flick of a glance at Polly, who was looking

particularly bland, the Duke said to Orinda kindly, 'Now, Mrs Nagle, I am truly concerned that you should enjoy and understand our splendid sport of steeple-chasing, and as I'll be busily occupied I can think of no one better to entrust you to than young Benedict there. He knows all about racing, in spite of his age, and he will take you round and show you everything, and we will all meet up here again after, say, the second race. So, Benedict,' he spoke to me loudly down the table, 'be a good fellow and take Mrs Nagle down to see the horses walk round the parade ring. Watch the race with her. Answer her questions, right?'

I said, 'Yes, sir,' faintly, and the Duke, nodding benignly, more or less pushed Orinda into my arms. I sensed her begin to stiffen and refuse but the Duke made urging motions towards the door as if there were no possibility of a change of his plans, and over my shoulder, as I followed the white linen suit into the passage outside, I caught glimpses of astonishment on my father's face and a wide grin on Polly's.

Orinda marched along the passage and down the stairs at the end into the open air; and there she stopped dead and said, 'This is ridiculous.'

'Yes,' I said.

'What do you mean, yes?'

'I mean, you're not going to listen to me because you hate my father, which is pretty unreasonable when you look at it, but I'd probably feel the same way, so if you like I'll just leave you here and go and look at the horses which is actually what I want to do anyhow.'

She said irritably, inconsequentially, 'I'm old enough to be your mother.'

'Easily,' I said. Hardly tactful.

In spite of her fury she almost laughed. 'You're supposed to say I couldn't be.'

'Sorry.'

'Mervyn says you're only seventeen.'

'I'll be eighteen in two weeks.'

'What will I do, if you just dump me here?'

'Well,' I said, 'I won't dump you. But if you want me to vanish, well, round that corner you'll find the parade ring where the horses walk round before the race so that everyone can see what they're putting their money on.'

'What if I want to bet?'

'Bookmakers or the Tote?'

'What's going to win?'

I smiled at her with real goodwill. 'If I knew, if anyone knew, I'd be rich.'

'And if you were rich?'

'I'd buy a string of racehorses, and ride them.'

I hadn't expected the question, and the answer I'd given her came straight from the honesty of childhood. I wasn't yet used to being adult. My mind, and also my voice and physical co-ordination, could switch disconcertingly sometimes back to fifteen, even in dreams to thirteen. Some days I could ski downhill with sharp turning certainty: other days I'd crash out on the first bend. Some days I'd move in total harmony with a horse's gallop: other days I'd have gawky arms and legs. Always, so far always, I could shoot and hit the inner or the bull, a two-inch spot at a hundred yards.

Orinda said formally, 'I'd be grateful if you'd accompany me to the parade ring.'

I nodded as if she were conceding nothing, and with minute body signs steered her to where the horses plodded round the ring, the sun shining on their coats, the smell and sound of them piercing my senses, the last four days setting up in me such an acute sense of loss that I wished myself anywhere on earth but on a racecourse.

'What's the matter?' Orinda said.

'Nothing.'

'That's not true.'

'It doesn't matter.'

She had given me a perfect opening for what I wanted to say to her, but I miserably shrank from it. I hadn't expected to feel so grindingly forlorn: an exile looking through a glass barrier at a life denied him.

I found a place for us to stand against the rails of the parade ring, and I gave her my racecard, as she had left her own upstairs. She needed spectacles from her handbag to see small print with, and help in identifying the runners from their number cloths.

'What do all these figures mean?' she asked, scratchily pointing to the card. 'It's double Dutch to me.'

'They tell you the horse's age and how much weight he's carrying in the race. Those very small figures tell you his results in the last races he's run in.' I pointed. 'F means fell, and P means he pulled up and didn't finish.'

'Oh.' She studied the card and read aloud the conditions of entry to the first race, a two-and-a-half-mile hurdle race for novices.

'A race for four-year-olds and upwards, which at the start of the season have not won a hurdle race . . . but if they *have* won a hurdle race since the start of the season, they are to carry a 7-lb penalty.' She looked up, disliking me. 'What's a 7-lb penalty?'

'Extra weight. Most often flat thin sheets of lead carried in pockets in the weight cloth which lies over the horse's back under the number cloth and saddle.' I explained that a jockey had to carry the weight allotted to his horse. 'You get weighed before and after a race . . .'

'Yes, yes, I'm not totally ignorant.'

'Sorry.'

She studied the racecard. 'There's only one horse in this race carrying a 7-lb penalty,' she announced. 'Will he win?'

'He might if he's very good.'

She turned the pages of the card, looking forward.

'In almost every race a horse carries a penalty if it's won recently.'

'Mm.'

'What's the heaviest penalty you can get?'

I said, 'I don't think there's any set limit, but in practice a 10-lb penalty is the most a horse will be faced with. If he had to carry more than ten pounds extra in a handicap he almost certainly wouldn't win, so the trainer wouldn't run him.'

'But you *could* win with a 10-lb penalty?'

'Yes, just about.'

'A lot to ask?'

'It depends how strong the horse is.'

She put her glasses away and wanted me to go with her to the Tote, where she backed the horse that had won on the first day of the season and earned himself an extra seven pounds of lead. 'He must be the best,' she said.

Almost as tall as I was, Orinda walked always a pace ahead of me as if it were natural to her to have her escort to her rear. She was used to being looked at, and I did see that her clothes drew admiration, even if more geared to Ascot than a country meeting in the boondocks of rural far-from-all-crowds Dorset.

We stood on the steps of the grandstand to watch the race. Orinda's choice finished fourth.

'Now what?' she said.

'Same thing all over again.'

'Don't you get bored with it?'

'No.'

She tore her Tote ticket across and let the pieces flutter to the ground like a seasoned loser.

'I don't see much fun in this.' She looked around at a host of people studying racecards. 'What do you do if it rains?'

The simple answer was 'get wet', but it would hardly have pleased her.

'People come to see the horses as much as to gamble,' I said. 'I mean, horses are marvellous.'

She gave me a pitying stare and said that after the following races she would return to the Stewards' room to thank the Duke for his hospitality, and then she would leave. She couldn't see the fascination that jump racing held for everyone.

I said, 'I can't see what fascination politics has for my father, but for him now it's his whole life.'

We were walking back towards the parade ring where the horses were beginning to appear for the second race. She stopped abruptly from one stride to the next and faced me with frank hostility.

'Your father,' she said acidly, biting off each word as if she could crunch them to splinters of glass, 'has stolen my purpose in life. It is *I* who should represent Hoopwestern in Parliament. It was *I* who was supposed to be fighting this election, and I'd have won it too, which is more than your precious father will do for all his machismo.'

'He didn't know you existed,' I said. 'He was sent by the central party in Westminster to fight the by-election, if he could get selected. He didn't set out to replace you personally.'

She demanded, 'How do you know?'

'He told me. He's been giving me a condensed course in politics since last Wednesday, when he brought me here as window dressing. He respects the way you feel. And actually, if he had you on his side, and if because of that he did get elected, then maybe you could be as good a team with him as you were with Mr Nagle.'

'You're a *child*,' she said.

'Yes . . . sorry. But everyone here says how outstanding you are at work in the constituency.'

She made no comment, angry or otherwise, but began as before to study her racecard, leaning on the parade ring rails as if at home.

After a bit she said, 'What your father wants is power.'

'Yes.' I paused. 'Do you?'

'Of course.'

Power stalked past us in the muscular rumps of fully grown steeplechasers, animals capable of covering ground at thirty miles an hour or more for distances of from four and a half miles: the length and speed of the Grand National. No animal on earth could better a racehorse for stamina and speed. That power . . . *that* was power for me. To share it, guide it, jump with it. Oh, dear God, give me that power.

'Usher Rudd,' Orinda said, 'do you know who I mean?'

'Yes.'

'Usher Rudd told my friend Alderney Wyvern – um, do you know who I mean by Alderney Wyvern?'

'Yes again.'

'Usher Rudd says George Juliard is not only lying about you being his legitimate son but maintains you are his catamite.'

'His what?' If I sounded bewildered, it was because I was. 'What's a . . . a cat of mice?'

'You don't know what he means?'

'No.'

'A catamite is a boy . . . a prostitute boy lover.'

I wasn't so much outraged as astonished. In fact, I laughed.

'Usher Rudd,' Orinda said warningly, 'is a tireless researcher. Don't take him lightly.'

'But I thought Paul Bethune was his sleaze target.'

'Anyone is,' Orinda said. 'He makes up lies. He likes to destroy people. He'll do it for money if he can, but if there's no money in it he'll do it for pleasure. He's a butterfly-wing puller. Are you George Juliard's legitimate son?'

'I look like him, a bit.'

She nodded.

'And he did marry my mother – in front of a lot

of witnesses.' (Disapproving witnesses, but never mind.)

The news seemed not to please her.

'I suppose,' I said, 'that you would prefer Usher Rudd to be right? Then you could have got rid of my father?'

'Alderney Wyvern says it will take more than an Usher Rudd fabrication. It's a matter of finding a strong lever.'

She sounded fiercely bitter. Whatever Polly thought of my ability to understand unhappiness and release it, I felt lost in the maze of Orinda's implacable grievances against my father.

'Someone took a shot at him,' I said.

Orinda shook her head. 'Another lie.'

'I was there,' I protested.

'So was Alderney,' she said. 'He saw what happened. George Juliard tripped on the cobbles and someone loosed a single shot out of high spirits and Juliard claimed it had been aimed at him! Utter *rubbish*. He'll do anything for publicity.'

I thought: Orinda herself would never get under a car and unscrew a sump-plug. However careful one might be, oil would run out before one could thrust a candle into the drain. Even if she knew how and where to unscrew the plug, engine oil and Orinda's clothes couldn't be thought of together in a month of canvassing.

Orinda needed glasses to read a racecard: I couldn't envisage her aiming and firing a target rifle.

Orinda might wish my father dead, but couldn't kill him herself, and didn't believe that anyone else had tried.

Orinda, I thought, hadn't asked or paid anyone to get rid of her rival physically. There were limits to her hate.

I took her across the course to watch the second race from near one of the fences, to give her at least some sensation of the speed involved. Her narrow high heels tended to dig into the turf and stick, making walking difficult, which didn't please her. I was not, I acknowledged to myself in depression, making a great success of the afternoon.

She was, though, impressed by the noise and energy of the half-ton horses soaring or crashing through the tops of the big black birch fence, and she could hear the jockeys shouting to each other and to their mounts; could see the straining legs in white breeches and the brilliant colours of the silks in the August sun. And whether she wanted me to know it or not, she did quite suddenly understand why this sort of racing fascinated the Duke and everyone else who had made the effort and the journey to the racecourse.

When the horses had surged past us again and were striving their way to the winning post, while the very air still vibrated with their passage, I said, 'I do understand what you feel about having been passed over by the selectors.'

Orinda said unkindly, 'You can't possibly. You're far too young.'

Almost in desperation I said, 'You've lost what you most wanted, and it's near to unbearable. You were looking forward to a sort of life that would be a joy every day, that would fulfil you and give you inner power to achieve your best dreams, and it's been snatched away. You've been told you can't have it. The pain of it's brutal. Believe me, I do know.'

She stared, the green eyes wide.

'You don't have to be old,' I said. 'You can feel it if you're only six and you passionately want a pony and you've nowhere to keep it and it's not sensible to start with. And I . . .' I swallowed. I wanted to stop again, but this time found the grit for the words. 'I wanted *this*.' I swept an arm to the black fence, to the whole wide racecourse. 'I wanted all of *this*. I've wanted to be a jockey for as long as I can remember. I've grown up in the belief that this would be my life. I've grown up feeling warm and certain of my future, and . . . well . . . this week it's been snatched away from me. This week I've been told I can't live this life, I'm not a good enough rider, I haven't the spark to be the jockey I want to be. The trainer I was riding for told me to leave. My father says he'll pay for me to go to university, but not for me to waste my time riding in races when I'm not going to be brilliant.

It didn't really sink in . . . I didn't know how absolutely *awful* it would be until I came here today . . . but I'd like to scream, actually, and roll on the ground, and if you think you have to be old enough to be my mother to feel as you do, well, you're wrong.'

CHAPTER SIX

At the end of the afternoon I glumly drove the Range Rover back to Polly's house in the woods, feeling that I'd wasted all her planning and not only failed to profit from an unrepeatable opportunity but had positively made things worse.

By the time Orinda and I had recrossed the course (her heels were sticking worse than ever) and regained the Stewards' room, the Duke had disappeared again towards his duties. Orinda watched the third race from the viewing balcony leading out of the luncheon room, her back relentlessly turned towards me, her manner forbidding conversation.

A horse carrying a 7-lb penalty won the race. Orinda hadn't backed it.

When the Duke returned, all smiles at the sight of her, she thanked him charmingly for his hospitality and left. She said nothing to my father or to Polly or to myself, ignoring our existence, and I survived the last three races wishing I were smaller, richer, and at the very least a genius. Settling for the obvious privileges I had seemed dreary compared with the fairy-tale lost.

When Polly invited us into her house my father accepted at once.

'Cheer up,' he commanded to my silent reluctance. 'No one wins all the time. Say something. You haven't said anything for hours.'

'All right . . . Orinda said Usher Rudd wants to know if I'm your catamite.'

My father spluttered into the gin that Polly had poured him.

Polly said, 'What's a catamite?', but my father knew.

I said, 'Usher Rudd's trying to prove I'm not your son. If you have a marriage certificate, put it in a bank vault.'

'And your birth certificate, where's that?'

'With my stuff at Mrs Wells.'

He frowned. My things hadn't followed me so far. He borrowed Polly's phone and called my ex-landlady forthwith. 'She's packed everything,' he reported, 'but the carriers I ordered haven't turned up. I'll see to it again on Monday.'

'My bicycle is at the stables.'

He caught some sense of the wreck he'd made of my aspirations, but I also saw quite clearly that he still expected me to face reality thoroughly and grow up.

'Tough it out,' he said.

'Yes.'

Polly looked from one of us to the other and said, 'The boy's doing his best for you, George.'

Leaving her in her house I drove the Range Rover back to Hoopwestern, familiar at last with the four-wheel drive and the weight and size. I disembarked my parent at a church hall (directions from Mervyn) where he was due to meet and thank the small army of volunteers working for him and the party's sake throughout the whole scattered area of the constituency. The volunteers had brought their families and their neighbours, and also tea, beer, wine and cake to sustain them and my father's inexhaustible enthusiasm to energise them for the next three weeks.

'My son . . . this is my son.' He presented me over and over again, and I shook hands and smiled and smiled and chatted up old ladies and talked football with shaky knowledge and racing with piercing regret.

Mervyn moved from group to group with plans and lists. This ward would be canvassed tomorrow, that ward on Monday: leaflets . . . posters . . . visits . . . leave not one of seventy thousand voters unaware of JULIARD.

Three more weeks of it . . . Even with the spice of looking out for stray attacks, the campaign at that point seemed more like purgatory than appealing.

But I'd said I would do it . . . and I would.

I ate chocolate cake. Still no pizza.

At goodbye time I collected the Range Rover from where I'd parked it in a nearby road and was as sure as possible that no one had tampered with it that evening.

Foster Fordham had given me simple instructions on the telephone. 'Always take with you a carton of dishwasher powder in a box with a spout. When you park the vehicle, sprinkle a thin line of powder on the ground from behind each front wheel back to the rear wheel on the same side. If anyone has moved the vehicle or wriggled under it in your absence, the powder will tell you. Understand?'

'Yes. Thank you.'

'Always set the alarms carefully, and disable them and start the vehicle from a distance, however short a time you've been away.'

I'd followed his instructions faithfully, but our sump-plug merchant had tried no other tricks. I ferried my father safely from the church hall back to the bow-fronted head-quarters and left him there with Mervyn, the two of them endlessly discussing tactics, while I housed the Range Rover in its lock-up and finally ran a pizza to earth in the local take-away.

Mervyn and my father absentmindedly ate half of it. Mervyn laid out dozens of stickers and leaflets in piles, ready for distribution. Yes, he said when I asked him, *of course* by-elections were wildly exciting, they were the peaks of an agent's busy life. And there were the final touches to be arranged for the fund-raising fête organised for next week – such a pity Orinda wasn't in charge of it this time . . .

I yawned and climbed the narrow stairs, leaving my two elders to lock up: and I woke in the night to a strong smell of smoke.

Smoke.

I sat bolt upright in bed.

Without much more than instinct I disentangled my legs from the sheets and violently shook the unconscious lump on the neighbouring mattress, yelling at him, 'We're on fire!' as I leapt to the half-open door to see if what I said was actually, devastatingly true.

It was.

Down the stairs there were fierce yellow leaping flames, devouring and roaring. Smoke funnelled up in growing billows. Ahead of me the sitting-room blazed yellow with flames from the rear-office underneath.

Gasping at once for breath in the smoke, I swivelled fast on one foot and jumped into the bathroom. If I switched on the taps, I thought, the bath and the washbasin would overflow and help to drown the flames: I pushed the stoppers into the plug-holes and opened all the taps to maximum: and I swept a large bath towel into the toilet bowl and pulled the flush. Whisking the sopping towel into the bedroom, I closed the door against the smoke and laid the wet towel along the bottom of the door with a sort of speed near to frenzy.

'The window,' I yelled. 'The bloody window's stuck.'

The window was stuck shut with layers of paint and had been annoying my father for days. We were both wearing only underpants, and the air was growing hot. 'We can't go down the stairs.' Doesn't he understand? I thought. He smoothly picked up the single bedroom chair and smashed it against the window. Glass broke, but the panes were small and the wooden frames barely cracked. We were above the bow windows facing the square. A second smash with the chair burst through the sticky layers of old paint and swung open both sides of the window – but underneath the fire had already eaten through the bay window's roof and was shooting up the wall.

The bay window of the charity shop next door blazed also with manic energy. If anything the fire next door was hotter and older and had reached the roof, with scarlet and gold sparks shooting into the sky above our heads.

I scrambled over to the door, thinking the stairs the only way out after all, but even if the wet towel was still holding back the worst of the smoke it was useless against flame. The door knob was now too hot to touch. The whole door had fire on the far side.

I shouted with fierceness, 'We're burning. The door's on fire.'

My father stared at me briefly across the room.

'We'll have to take our chances and jump. You first.'

He put the damaged chair against the window wall

and motioned me to climb up and leap out as far as I could.

'You go,' I said.

There were people now in the square and voices yelling, and the raucous siren of the fire engine coming nearer.

'Hurry,' my father said. 'Don't bloody argue. Jump.'

I stood on the chair and held onto the window frame. The paint on it scorched my hands.

'*Jump*!'

I couldn't believe it – he was struggling into shirt and trousers and zipping up his fly.

'Go on. *Jump*!'

I put a bare foot on the frame, pulled myself up and leapt out with every scrap of muscle power .... with strong legs and desperation: and I sailed through the flames from the bay window and missed the front burning edge of it by terrifying inches and crashed down onto the dark cobbled ground with a head-stunning disorientating impact. I heard people yelling and felt hands grabbing me to pull me away from the fire and I was choking with smoke and winded by hitting the unyielding ground and rolling, and also fighting to free myself from the firmly clutching hands to help to cushion my father's fall when he jumped down after me. I had no strength. Sat on the ground. Couldn't even speak.

Incredibly there were camera flashes. People were *recording* our extreme danger, our closeness to dying.

I felt helplessly angry. Outraged. Near to sobbing. Illogical, I dare say.

Voices were screaming to my father to jump and voices were screaming to my father *not* to jump, to wait for the bellowing fire engine now charging across the square, scattering onlookers and spilling people in yellow helmets.

'Wait, wait,' people screamed as firemen released their swivelling ladder to extend it to my father, but he was standing up silhouetted in the window with a reddish glow behind him. He was standing on the chair – and the door behind him was burning.

Before the ladder reached him there was an outburst of bright sunlike flame in the room at his back and he stood on the window frame and threw himself out as I had done, flung himself through the climbing fire of the bow windows below into the darkness beyond, knowing he might break his neck and smash his skull, knowing the ground was there but unable to judge how far away: but too near. Break-your-bones near.

A camera flashed.

Two men in yellow suits like moonsuits were sprinting, heavy-gloved hands outstretched, dragging as they went a circular trampoline thing for catching jumpers. No time to position it. They simply ran, and my father crashed down into them, all the figures sprawling, arms and legs flying. People crowded to help them and hid the tangle from my sight but my father's legs had been moving with life, and he had *shoes* on, which he hadn't had upstairs.

I was covered in smoky dirt and bleeding from a few cobble-induced scrapes and grazes, and I had tears running down my face, although I didn't know I was crying: and I was dazed still and was coughing and had blisters forming on my fingers and feet, but none of it mattered. Noise and confusion filled my head. I'd aimed to keep my father safe from danger and I hadn't even *contemplated* a smoke alarm.

His voice said, 'Ben?'

I looked up woozily. He was standing above me; he was *smiling*. How could he?

Men in yellow suits unrolled hoses and poured gallons from the tanker onto the killing bow-fronts. There was steam and smoke and unquenched flame: and there were people putting a red blanket round my bare shoulders and telling me not to worry. I wasn't sure where they had come from, or what I didn't have to worry about.

I wasn't actually *sure* of anything.

'Ben,' my father said in my ear, 'you're concussed.'

'Mm?'

'They say your head hit the ground. Can you hear me?'

'No smoke alarm. My fault . . .'

Ben!' He shook me. People told him not to.

'I'll get you elected,' I said.

'Christ.'

People's familiar faces loomed into my orbit and went away again. I thought it extraordinary that they were walking around fully dressed in the middle of the night but at one point learned that it was barely twenty minutes past eleven, not five to four. I'd gone early to bed and jumped out of the window wearing only my watch and my underpants and got the time wrong.

Amy was there, wringing her hands and weeping. Amy crying for the charity gifts lost to ashes, the ugly what-not gone for ever, still unsold. What's a what-not, Amy? An *étagère*, you know, an upright set of little shelves for filling an odd corner, bearing plates and photographs and what not.

And bullets?

'Oh dear,' she said. 'I left the bullet in my awful cardigan in the shop, and now I've lost it, but never mind, it was only a lump of old lead.'

Mrs Leonard Kitchens patted my shoulder reassuringly. 'Don't you worry, boy, there was nothing in those old shops but junk and paper. Leaflets. Nothing! My Leonard's here somewhere. Have you seen him? Likes a good fire, does my Leonard, but the fun's all over now. I want to go home.'

Usher Rudd stalked his prey backwards, framing his picture, stepping back and clicking. He grinned over my blanket, took time to focus, aimed his lens.

Flash.

The cameraman from the local TV station arrived with his brighter light that was still out-watted by fire.

Mervyn wrung his hands over the lost heaps of JULIARDS. He'd barely been home half an hour before someone had phoned to warn him the charity shop was on fire.

Crystal Harley knelt beside me, dabbing bloody trickles with tissues and said worriedly, 'Do you think I'd better come into work tomorrow?'

Paul and Isobel Bethune illicitly drove into the pedestrian-only precinct. Emergencies made new rules, the local councillor said, bustling towards my father, presenting a surface of urgent concern, all camaraderie for him and with hail-fellow greetings individually for the firemen.

Isobel asked me weakly if I were all right.

'Of course he's not,' Crystal snapped. 'He jumped through fire and hit the ground. What do you expect?'

'And . . . er . . . his father?'

'His father will win the seat,' Crystal said.

God bless politics, I thought.

'Paul was out at a meeting,' Isobel said. 'He came home to collect me when he heard about the fire, to see if there was anything I could do to help. It always looks better if I'm with him, he says.'

Water plumed out of the huge appliance and sizzled on the flames and ran out of the building again, soaking the cobbles. I and my red blanket dripped and chilled.

Another vast tanker in the car park at the rear raised soaring fountains above the roof so that the two arcs of glittering Niagara met and married and fell together as monstrous rain. Leaflets and junk a fiery furnace; two vulnerable organisms shivering outside.

The yellow-helmets prodigally aimed their hoses at the still dark buildings next to the blazing shops and, in time, inevitably, the ravaging tongues of fire ran out of fuel and began to diminish, to whisper instead of roar, to give up the struggle and leave the battlefield so that what fell from the sky into the square was no longer sparks but hot clinging ash, and what assaulted the senses wasn't heat but the acrid after-smell of burning.

Someone fetched the doctor who had seen to my father's ankle three days earlier; he peered into my eyes with bright lights and into my ears and felt the bump on my head and bound up blisters in huge padded dressings so that they wouldn't burst and get infected, and he agreed with my father that all a healthy boy needed was to see him in the morning.

My father solved the interim by enlisting the sympathy of the manager of the Sleeping Dragon, who gave us a bedroom and whose wife found me some clothes.

'You poor dears . . . you poor dears . . .' She mothered us, kind, but enjoying it, and both she and her husband happily welcomed the reporters from the

London dailies who thronged through the doors the next day.

Usher Rudd's admittedly brilliant photograph of my father in mid-leap with the flaming window behind him made the front pages, not only of the *Hoopwestern Gazette* and the next edition of the *Quindle Diary* (JULIARD JINX) but of every major paper in the land (JULIARD JUMPS) and hot on the heels of the factual news came endless comment and criticism and picking-to-pieces.

People will always tell you what you should have done. People will tell you what *they* would have done if they had woken in the night with fire underneath them. People will say that absolutely the first thing to do was call the fire brigade, and no one could be bothered to say how do I call the brigade when the only telephone is downstairs surrounded by flames? How do you call a fire brigade when the telephone line has melted?

Everyone can think logically afterwards, but in the heat and the smell and the noise and the danger, analytical reasoning is more or less out of the question.

People tend to think that wildly unreasonable behaviour in terrifying circumstances can be called 'panic', and forgiven, but it's not so much panic, a form of ultimate illogical fear, but a lack of time to think things through.

Perhaps my father and I would have done differently if we had been presented with the situation as a theoretical exercise with a correct and an incorrect solution.

Perhaps we should have thrown the mattresses out of the window as a possible way of breaking our fall. Perhaps, if we could have got them through the window. As it was, we both nearly died and, as it was, we both lived, but more by luck than reason.

Don't waste time with clothes, they'll tell you. Better go naked into this world than clothed into the next. But they – 'they', whoever they are – haven't jumped in front of the media's sharpened lenses.

I thought afterwards that I should at least have dashed into the burning sitting-room for my jacket and jockey's helmet, instead of bothering with the taps. Also I should have wrapped towels round my hands and feet before grasping the window frame.

But I don't think my father ever regretted the near-to-lethal seconds he spent in putting on his shirt and trousers. He knew in some way, even in that life-or-death split second, that a photograph of him jumping half naked from the flames would haunt his whole career. He knew, even in that fraught moment, that an orderly presentation was everything. Not even the worst that Usher Rudd could dredge up in the future ever showed George Juliard as anything but a fast-thinking headliner who was at his very best – *who put his shoes on* – in a crisis.

*

The police investigation sauntered upwards from Joe, whose mother drove a school bus, to higher ranks at county level, but the firefighters couldn't swear the two bow-fronts had been torched and no one found a .22 rifle to match the lost-again bullet, and Foster Fordham's report on wax in the Range Rover's sump was judged inconclusive.

George Juliard *might* have been the target of three attempts on his candidature, if not on his life, but again he might not. There were no obvious suspects.

In the August doldrums for news, London editors gave the puzzle two full days of wide coverage. George Juliard shone on television nationwide. Every single voter in the Hoopwestern constituency knew who JULIARD was.

While my father dealt with publicity people and Mervyn Teck drove around like an agitated bluebottle searching for inexpensive substitute headquarters, I spent most of the Sunday sitting in an armchair by the window of our Sleeping Dragon room, letting bruises and grazes heal themselves, and looking across the square at the burnt-out building opposite.

From somewhere up here, I thought, from somewhere here among the many hanging baskets of geraniums (her Leonard, the nurseryman, had designed them, Mrs Kitchens had told me with pride), from among all these big clusters of scarlet pompoms and little blue flowers whose name I didn't know, and from among the fluffy white flowers that filled and rounded the bright living displays decorating the whole long frontage of the Sleeping Dragon, from somewhere up here someone had aimed a .22 rifle at my father.

The marksman probably hadn't been in this room given to us in the night, which was much further along towards the Town Hall than the main door of the hotel from which we'd walked. A shot from where I sat would have had to take into account that the target wasn't walking straight ahead but moving sideways. A stalker's shot; but not a stalker's gun.

A ricochet could, of course, take a bullet anywhere, but I thought it unlikely that a ricochet from where I sat would have turned and hit the charity shop.

At one point, shuffling on the padded blisters, I explored the length of the hotel's first floor, glimpsing the square through an open doorway or two and coming to a little lounge area furnished with armchairs and small tables that I reckoned lay directly above the front hall and main door, accessible to the world. Straight ahead through the window from there was the unmarked path I'd taken with my father across the cobbles.

Anyone . . . *anyone* . . . if they had the nerve, could have stood among the floor-length curtains, opened the window, rested the barrel of a .22 on the windowsill and shot through the geraniums and the warm night.

My father, interested, asked the manager for the names of the people sleeping in the bedrooms on

Wednesday night, but although the register was freely opened, no one familiar appeared.

'Nice try, Ben,' my father sighed; and the police had the same nice try in due course, with similar results.

By Monday morning Mervyn had rented an empty shop in a side street and borrowed a desk for Crystal and some flip-up chairs. The campaign hiccupped for two days while he cajoled his friendly neighbourhood printer into replacement leaflet and poster production at grand-prix speed and near-to-cost prices, but by late Tuesday afternoon the indefatigable witches, Faith, Marge and Lavender, had turned the empty shop into a fully working office complete with teapot and mobile phone.

On Monday and Tuesday George Juliard filled the newspapers, and enlivened some chat shows, and on Wednesday morning a miracle happened.

Mervyn had sticky-taped a new large-scale map onto the wall and was pointing out to me the roads I should drive along (feet OK by now) for Faith and Lavender to ring as yet untroubled door-bells. In the absence of a megaphone (burned) I would please occasionally toot the horn, just enough to announce our presence but *not enough*, he lectured me, to anger anyone trying to get a baby to sleep. The mothers of babies (he wagged a finger at me) swayed Xs in the polls like pendulums. Kiss a baby: win a vote. A hundred thousand politicians couldn't all be historically wrong.

'I'll kiss every baby in sight,' I promised recklessly.

He frowned at me, never one to take a joke. I was reminded of my father's most recent lesson: '*Never ever* make a joke to the police, they have *no* sense of humour. *Never* make a political joke, it will always be considered an insult. Always remember that umbrage can be taken by the lift of an eyebrow. Remember that if offence can possibly be taken, it will be.'

I'd gazed at my father. 'Are people that silly?'

'Silly,' he said with mock severity, 'isn't a word you should ever apply to people. They may be totally stupid, in fact, but if you call them silly you've lost their vote.'

'And you want silly people to vote for you?'

He laughed. 'Don't make jokes.'

He had gone to London on Wednesday morning when the miracle happened. There were just Mervyn, Crystal, Faith, Marge, Lavender and me in the makeshift office, just the bunch of us putting the best face possible on the lack of computer (for the totals spent on tea-bags), copier (schedules for volunteers) and fax (reports from distant galaxies like Quindle).

Orinda walked in.

All business stopped.

She wore pale citrus green: trousers, jacket and headband. Gold chains. She carried, beside the black lizard handbag, a substantial roll of papers.

She looked around the bare room, smiled faintly at Marge and fixed her gaze on me.

'I want to talk to you,' she said calmly. 'Outside.'

I followed where she led. We stood on the pavement in the sun, with shoppers passing by.

'Since Saturday,' she announced, 'I have been considering things. On Sunday morning, at half past eight or so, a newspaperman appeared at my house in an invasive procedure I believe is called "door stepping".'

She paused. I nodded faintly.

'He asked if I was glad or sorry that you hadn't been burned to death. You and your father, that is.'

'Oh.'

'It was the first I'd heard about the fire.'

'I'm surprised no one had phoned you.'

'I unplug the telephone when I sleep. I find it hard to sleep in any case.'

I said, 'Oh,' again, vaguely.

'The journalist wanted to know my opinion of the information he'd been given that close-to-death attacks had been made on George Juliard so that he would have to retire from the candidacy, clearing the way for my return.'

She paused, studying my face, and continued: 'I see that that thought isn't new to you.'

'No, but I don't think you did it.'

'Why not?'

'You're hurt. You're furious. But you wouldn't murder.'

'When will you be eighteen?'

'In ten days.'

'Then consider this a coming-of-age present.' She thrust the roll of papers into my hands. 'This is for you. It is because of you . . .' She stopped abruptly, swallowing. 'Use it in any way you like.'

With curiosity I unrolled the stiff sheets, having to hold them wide to prevent them rolling up again. The top one, in very large capital letters, read:

ORINDA NAGLE SAYS VOTE FOR JULIARD

My mouth, I know, fell open.

'There are ten of them,' she said simply. 'They're all the same. I had them printed this morning. They'll print dozens, if you like.'

'Orinda . . .' I was all but speechless.

'You showed me . . . at the races . . .' she began, and stopped again. 'You're so very *young*, but you showed me it's possible to bear an unbearable disappointment. You made me look into myself. Anyway, I will *not* have people thinking I would set fire to our old headquarters in order to get rid of your father, so I'll *join* him. I'll support him from now on in every way. I should never have listened to all those people who told me he had robbed me. I don't know, to be really truthful, and the truth is awful . . . I don't know that I wasn't *relieved* not to be forced to go to Westminster, but I do like working in the constituency and that's what hurts most . . . that the people I've worked so hard for passed me over for some stranger from outside.'

She stopped talking and looked at me in a sort of desperation to see if I could possibly understand, and I understood so well that I leaned forward impulsively and kissed her on the cheek.

A camera flashed.

'I can't *believe* it,' Orinda screeched. 'He follows me round.'

Usher Rudd, with the advantage of surprise, was already scuttling away down the street to get lost in bunches of shoppers.

'He follows me, too,' I said, putting a hand on Orinda's arm, to deter her trying to catch him. 'You warned me and I told my father . . . but unless Usher Rudd breaks the law it seems he can't be stopped, and the law is still on the side of copy-cat Rudds.'

'But my private life is my own affair!' She glanced at me as if it were my fault that it wasn't.

I said, 'Drug dealers would be out of business if people didn't want drugs.'

'What?'

'The so-called war on drugs is fought against the wrong people. Lock up the users. Lock up the demand. Lock up human nature.'

She looked bewildered. 'What have drugs to do with Usher Rudd?'

'If people didn't flock to buy his sleaze, he wouldn't push it.'

'And you mean . . . they always will?'

She needed no answer. She followed me into the shop/office and, after delivering her news, enjoyed a hugging session with Mervyn (no photo) and an ambiguous welcome from the three witches, who had with pink arousal transferred their effective allegiance to the new order.

'Where are you canvassing today, Mervyn?' Orinda asked, and he showed her on the map, with the unexpected result that when I drove the Range Rover round Hoopwestern that morning I had on board Mervyn, Orinda, Faith and Lavender, and all of Orinda's roll of commitment flattened out as placards.

As Mervyn had telephoned the editor of the *Gazette* – gasps of shock at having to U-turn his anti-all-politicians spin – we were greeted in the car park behind the burned shop by a hastily assembled crowd, by the leader-writer of the *Gazette* (the paper was short of news) and by the cameraman who had besottedly followed Orinda with his loving lens round the reception before the dinner a week earlier at the Sleeping Dragon.

Orinda flirted again with his lens (or with him – much the same thing) and told everyone prettily through a non-squeaking microphone that George Juliard, undoubtedly on the brink of becoming a nationally acclaimed politician, was the best possible substitute for her beloved husband Dennis, who had dedicated his life to the good citizens of this glorious part of Dorset.

Applause, applause. She appeared in the sitting-rooms of Hoopwestern on the lunchtime television news against the only slightly orchestrated cheers.

By the time my father returned on the train from London he'd heard of Orinda's media conference with mixed feelings – she might be stealing his limelight or she might just be saving his life – but at another church hall meeting of the faithful that evening he embraced her in a warm hug (reciprocated) that would have been unthinkable a day earlier.

Not everyone was pleased.

Orinda's shadow, Anonymous Lover Wyvern, followed her around like thunder. She, dressed in blackberry-coloured satin and glowing with a sense of generosity and virtue, kept giving him enquiring looks as if unsure of the source of his dudgeon. In her inner release she didn't seem to realise, as I did, albeit only slowly through the evening, that in dumping her anger at not being selected she had in some way lessened his status. He had been Dennis Nagle's best friend, but Orinda was leaving her Dennis behind.

Dearest Polly, to my surprise, positively scowled, even though she had herself delivered Orinda to her change of heart.

'I didn't count on such a radical about-face,' Polly complained. 'She's cast herself in the ongoing role of constituency wife! There's no doubt she was good at it, but she *isn't* George's wife and she can't surely imagine she can go on opening fêtes and things, and I bet that's what she's got in mind. Whatever did you say to her at the races?'

I said, 'I thought you wanted her on my father's side.'

'Well, yes, I do. But I don't want her going around saying all the time that *she* was the one we should have picked.'

'Get him into Parliament, Polly,' I said. 'Put him on the escalator, then he'll deal with Orinda and everything else.'

'*How* old did you say you are?'

'Eighteen at the end of next week. And it was you, dearest Polly, who said I look into people's minds.'

She asked in some alarm, 'Do you see into mine?'

'Sort of.'

She laughed uneasily; but I saw nothing but good.

One could say the opposite about Leonard Kitchens. I had come to notice that the tilt of his prominent moustache acted like a weather-vane, signalling the direction of his feelings. The upward thrust that evening was combative and self-important, a combination looking for a fight. Bulky Mrs Kitchens (in large pink flowers printed on dark blue) followed her Leonard's progress round the meeting with anxiety for a while and then made a straight line to my side.

'Do something,' she hissed into my ear. 'Tell Orinda to leave my Leonard alone.'

It seemed to me that it was the other way round, as Leonard's moustache vibrated by Orinda's neck, but at Mrs Kitchens' urgent and continuous prompting I went over to hear Leonard's agitated and whining drift.

'I would do *anything* for you, Orinda, you know I would, but you're joining the *enemy* and I can't bear to see him slobbering all over you, it's disgusting . . .'

'Wake up, Leonard,' Orinda said lightly, not seeing the seething lava below the faintly ridiculous exterior, 'it's a new world.'

The undercurrents might tug and eddy, but Orinda had definitely unified the party behind JULIARD; yet in our room that night my father would literally not hear a word said about her. In fact, he put a finger decisively against his lips and drew me out into the passage, closing our door behind us.

'What's up?' I asked, mystified.

'Tonight the editor of the *Gazette* asked me if I thought people who voted for me were silly.'

'But that's nonsense. That's – ' I stopped.

'Yes. Think back. When we joked about silly voters we were alone in this bedroom here. Did you repeat what we said?'

'Of course not.'

'Then how did the *Gazette* know?'

I stared at him, and said slowly, 'Usher Rudd.'

He nodded. 'Didn't you tell me that that mechanic – Terry, isn't that what his name is? – got sacked because Usher Rudd had listened to his pillow talk using one of those gadgets that pick up voice waves from the faint vibrations in the windows?'

'Usher Rudd,' I said furiously, 'is trying to prove I'm not your son.'

'Never mind, he's on a loser.'

'He's following Orinda too, not to mention the Bethunes.'

'He thinks if he flings enough mud, some will stick. Don't give him any target.'

As the days went by one could see that Orinda's flip-flop had most impact in Hoopwestern itself, less in Quindle, and not very much in the villages dotting the maps with a church spire, a couple of pubs and a telephone box. Cheers and clapping greeted her near home but news of her arrival to canvass in, say, Middle Lampfield (pop. 637) was more likely to be greeted with a polite 'Oo? Aah' and a swift return to 'Zoo-merzet' cider.

More local draught cider flowed down the constituency throats than babies' formula, and my father's head for the frothy fruit of the apple earned him approval. We rolled every day at lunchtime from pub to pub to pub (I drove) and I got used to hearing the verdict. 'A good chap, your father, he understands what we need in the countryside. Reckon I'll vote for him. That Bethune, that they say is a certainty, he's a *town* councillor, and you know what we think of them lot, thumbs down.'

My father made them laugh. He knew the price of hay. They would have followed him to the South Pole.

Orinda thought the villages a waste of time, and so did Mervyn.

'The bulk of the votes is in the towns,' they lectured. Dennis Nagle had been the star of the businessman circle.

'You vote for a man you play darts with,' my father said, missing double top. 'I buy my own drinks, they buy theirs. Neither of us is beholden.'

Orinda didn't like cider, and she didn't like pubs. Lavender, surprisingly, liked both: my father, Lavender and I therefore spent several days soap-boxing the outskirts in the silver and gold Range Rover, seeing to it (as my father said) that not a voter was left unturned.

The following week it was Orinda who nearly died.

CHAPTER SEVEN

On the Tuesday of the last full week of canvassing, my box of possessions, and my bicycle, finally arrived by carrier from Mrs Wells.

Up in our room, my father picked with interest and curiosity through the meagre debris of my life: two trophies for winning amateur 'chases the previous Easter, several photographs of me on horses and skis, and other photos from school with me sitting in one of those frozen team line-ups (this one for target shooting), with the captain hugging a cup. There were books on mathematics, and racing biographies. Also clothes, but not many as, to my dismay, I was still growing.

My father extracted my passport, my birth certificate and the framed photograph of his wedding to my mother. He took the picture out of its frame and after looking at it for several long minutes he ran his finger over her face and sighed deeply, and it was the only time I'd known him show any emotion at all about his loss.

I said incautiously, 'Do you remember her? If she walked into the room now, would you know her?'

He gave me a look of such bleakness that I realised I'd asked a question of unforgivable intrusion, but after a pause all he said was, 'You never forget your first.'

I swallowed.

He said, 'Have you had your first?'

I felt numb, embarrassed almost beyond speech, but in the end I said truthfully, 'No.'

He nodded. It was a moment of almost unbearable intimacy, the first ever between us, but he remained totally calm and matter-of-fact, and let me recover.

He sorted through some papers he had brought in a briefcase from a recent trip to London, put my own identifications in the case, snapped shut the locks and announced that we were going to call on the *Hoopwestern Gazette.*

We called, in fact, on the editor, who was also the publisher and proprietor of the only local daily. He was a man in shirt-sleeves, harassed, middle-aged, and from the tone of his front pages, censorious. He stood up from his desk as we approached.

'Mr Samson Frazer,' my father said, calling him by name, 'when we met the other evening, you asked if I thought people who vote for me are silly.'

Samson Frazer, for all his importance in Hoopwestern, was no match in power against my parent. Interesting, I thought.

'Er . . .' he said.

'We'll return to that in a minute,' my father told him. 'First, I have some things for you to see.'

He unclipped the briefcase and opened it.

'I have brought the following items,' he said, taking out each paper and putting it down in front of the editor. 'My marriage certificate. My son's birth certificate. Both of our passports. This photograph of my wife and myself taken outside the registry office after our wedding. On the back – ' he turned the picture over, 'you will see the professional photographer's name and copyright, and the date. Here also is my wife's death certificate. She died of complications after the birth of our son. This son, Benedict, my only child, who has been at my side during this by-election.'

The editor gave me a swift glance as if he hadn't until that point taken note of my existence.

'You employ a person called Usher Rudd,' my father said. 'I think you should be careful. He seems to be trying to cast doubt on my son's identity and legitimacy. I'm told he has made scurrilous insinuations.'

He asked the editor just how he'd come to hear of 'silly' votes when he, my father, had only used the word – and in a joke – in the privacy of his own room.

Samson Frazer froze like a dazzled rabbit.

'If I have to,' my father said, 'I will send hair samples for DNA testing. My own hair, my son's hair, and some hair from my wife that she gave me in a locket. I hope you will carefully consider what I've said and what I've shown you.' He began methodically replacing the certificates in the briefcase. 'Because, I assure you,' he went on pleasantly, 'if the *Hoopwestern Gazette* should be so unwise as to cast doubt on my son's origins, I will sue the paper and you personally for defamation and libel, and you might quite likely wish you hadn't done it.' He snapped the locks shut so vigorously that they sounded in themselves like a threat.

'You understand?' he asked.

The editor plainly did.

'Good,' my father said. 'If you catch me in sleaze, that will be fair enough. If you try to manufacture it, I'll hang you out by the toes.'

Samson Frazer found nothing to say.

'Good day to you, sir,' my father said.

He was in high good humour all the way back to the hotel and went upstairs humming.

'What would you say,' he suggested, 'to a pact between us?'

'What sort of pact?'

He put the briefcase down on the table and drew out two sheets of plain paper.

'I've been thinking,' he said, 'of making you a promise, and I want you to make the same promise in return. We both know how vulnerable one is to people like Usher Rudd.'

'And it's not impossible,' I interrupted, 'that he's

listening to us at this moment, particularly if he knows where we've just been.'

My father looked briefly startled, but then grinned. 'The red-haired dung-beetle can listen all he likes. The promise I'll make to you is not to give him, or anyone like him, any grounds ever for messy publicity. I'll be dead boring. There will be no kiss-and-tell bimbos and no illicit payment for favours and no cheating on tax and no nasty pastimes like drugs or kinky sex . . .'

I smiled easily, amused.

'Yes,' he said, 'but I want *you* to make the same promise to *me*. I want you to promise me that if I get elected you'll do nothing throughout my political career that can get me discredited or sacked or disgraced in any way.'

'But I wouldn't,' I protested.

'It's easy for you to say that now while you're young, but you'll find life's full of terrible temptations.'

'I promise,' I said.

He shook his head. 'That's not enough. I want us both to write it down. I want you to be able to see and remember what you promised. Of course, it's in no way a legal document or anything pretentious like that, it's just an affirmation of intent.' He paused, clicking a ball-point pen while he thought, then he wrote very quickly and simply on one sheet of paper, and signed his name, and pushed the paper over for me to read.

It said: 'I will cause no scandal, nor will I perform any shameful or illegal act.'

Wow, I thought. I said, not wanting this to get too serious, 'It's a bit comprehensive, isn't it?'

'It's not worth doing otherwise. But you can write your own version. Write what you're comfortable with.'

I had no sense of binding myself irrevocably to sainthood.

I wrote: 'I'll do nothing that could embarrass my father's political career or drag his name in the dust. I'll do my best to keep him safe from any sort of attack.'

I signed my name lightheartedly and gave him the page. 'Will that do?'

He read it, smiling. 'It'll do.'

He folded both pages together, then picked up the wedding photograph and positioned it face down on the glass in its frame. He then put both of the signed pacts on the photo and replaced the back part of the frame, fastening it with its clips.

'There you are,' he said, turning the frame face up. 'Every time you look at your mother and me, you'll remember the promises behind the photo, inside the frame. Couldn't be simpler.'

He stood the picture on the table and without fuss gave me back my birth certificate and passport.

'Keep them safe.'

'Yes.'

'Right. Then let's get on with this election.'

Stopping only briefly to leave my identity in an envelope in the manager's safe, we went to the new headquarters to collect Mervyn, pamphlets, Faith and Lavender, and start a door-to-door morning round three Hoopwestern housing estates. Light-bulb workers, they said.

Mervyn, proud of himself, had found a replacement megaphone. His friendly printer continued to furnish a torrent of JULIARDS. Mervyn for once seemed content in his world, but his day shone even brighter when Orinda arrived, declaring her readiness for the fray.

With Faith and Lavender cool and Mervyn hot, therefore, six of us squeezed into the Range Rover, leaving behind Crystal (chronically anxious) and Marge (dusting and sweeping).

Only eight days after this one, I thought, and it will be over. And what will I do, I wondered, after that? There would be three or four weeks to fill before the Exeter term started. I mentally shrugged. I would be eighteen. I had a bicycle . . . might get to France . . .

I drove mechanically, stopping wherever Mervyn dictated.

Orinda had come in neat trousers and jacket, light orange-scarlet in colour. As usual, gold chains. Smooth, perfect make-up.

Babies got kissed. My father came across a clutch of child-minding house-husbands, factory shift workers, and learned about tungsten filaments. I chatted up a coffee-morning of old ladies who weren't satisfied until my parent shook their hands. (Pink smiles. A blossoming of votes.) Orinda met old friends. Mervyn alerted the streets to our presence like a musically tinkling fish-and-chip van, and Faith and Lavender left no door-bell un-rung.

When we drove out of the last of the estates we'd seen one or two TITMUSSES, no WHISTLE, not a BETHUNE to speak of, but many a window now proclaimed JULIARD. One could not but hope.

Mervyn and my father decided on one more long street, this time of varied and slightly more prosperous-looking houses. I, by this time, had had enough of door-to-dooring to last me several lifetimes, but as always the others seemed to have an indefatigable appetite. My father's eyes still shone with enthusiasm and people who disagreed with his political theories left him not downcast but stimulated. He never tired, it seemed to me, of trying to convert the heathen.

Without much hope I asked Faith and Lavender if they wouldn't prefer to say they'd done enough; how about lunch? 'No, no,' they insisted with fervour, 'every vote counts.'

Orinda alone seemed uneasy and withdrawn and not her usual positive and extravagant self, and in the end, while she and I waited together on the pavement beside the Range Rover for the others to finish galvanising an old people's home, I asked her what was the matter.

'Nothing,' she said, and I didn't press it, but after a moment or two she said, 'Do you see that white BMW there, along the road?'

'Yes.' I frowned. 'I saw it earlier, in one of the housing estates.'

'He's following us.'

'Who's following us? Is it Usher Rudd?'

'Oh, no.' She found the idea a surprise, which in itself surprised me. 'No, not Usher Rudd. It's Alderney Wyvern.'

It was I, then, who was surprised, and I asked, sounding astonished, 'Why on earth should he follow us?'

Orinda frowned. 'He's still furious with me for supporting your father.'

'Well . . . I'd noticed. But why, exactly?'

'You're too young to understand.'

'I could try.'

'Dennis used to do everything Alderney said. I mean, Alderney actually was how Dennis got advancement. Alderney would tell him what to say. Alderney is very clever, politically.'

'Why doesn't he find a parliamentary seat for himself?'

'He says he doesn't want to.' She paused. 'To be frank, he isn't easy to understand. But I know he expected me to be selected and to retain the seat as

Dennis' widow, and he worked on people like that creepy Leonard Kitchens, with that shudder-making moustache, to make sure I was selected. And then out of the blue the central party in Westminster decided they wanted George Juliard in Parliament, so he came and dazzled the selectors, who always listen to Polly, as a matter of course, and she fell for him like a ton of bricks . . . Anyway, Alderney got nowhere with your father. I sometimes think that that's the sort of power Alderney really wants, to be able to pull the levers behind the scenes.'

It seemed to me at that moment a wacky notion. (I still had a lot to learn.)

'So now that I've joined your father,' Orinda said, 'I'm not listening to Alderney as much. I used to do everything he suggested. We always did, Dennis and I, because Alderney would tell us such and such a thing would happen on the political scene and mostly he was right, and now I'm out with you and your father so much of the time . . . You'll laugh, but I almost think he's *jealous*!'

I didn't laugh. I'd seen my father's powerful effect on every female in Hoopwestern, from acid-tongued Lavender onwards. It wouldn't have surprised me if he'd left a comet-tail of jealousy through the constituency, except that he needed the men to vote for him as well as the women, and I'd watched him keep a tactical distance from their wives.

Alderney Wyvern, along the road, got out of his

car and stood aggressively on the pavement, hands on hips, staring at Orinda.

'I'd better go and talk to him,' Orinda said.

I said instinctively, 'No, don't.'

She caught the alarm in my voice and smiled. 'I've known him for years.'

I hadn't yet come across the adult grossly matured variety of jealousy, only the impotent rage of adolescence, but I felt intuitively that a great – and disturbing – change had taken place in A.L. Wyvern.

He had been by his own choice self-effacing on every occasion I'd seen him: quiet in manner, self-contained, behaving as if he didn't want to be noticed. All that had now gone. The stocky figure seemed heavier, the shoulders hunched, the face, even from a distance, visibly tense with menace. He had the out-of-control anger of a rioter, or of a militant striker.

I said to Orinda, 'Stay here.'

'Don't be silly.'

She walked confidently towards him in her brave orange-red clothes.

I could hear his voice, low and growling, but not what he said. Her reply was light and teasing. She put out a hand as if to stroke his arm affectionately, and he hit her very hard in the face.

She cried out with shock as much as pain. I ran towards her, and although Wyvern saw me coming he hit her again, back-handed, across her nose and mouth.

She squealed, raising her hands to shield her face,

trying at the same time to escape from him, but he clutched the shoulder of her jacket to prevent her running, and drew back his fist for a third blow.

She wrenched herself free. She half-overbalanced. She stumbled off the pavement into the roadway.

The prosperous residential street that had been so peaceful and empty suddenly seemed filled with a heavy lorry that bore down towards Orinda, brakes shrieking, horn blowing in banshee bursts.

Orinda tottered blindly as if disoriented, and I sprinted towards her without calculating speed or distance but simply impelled by the need of the moment.

The lorry driver was swerving about, trying to miss her and actually making things worse because his direction was unpredictable. I might easily have shoved her into his path rather than out of it, but I threw myself at Orinda in a sort of twisting rugby-football tackle so that she fell half under me onto the hard surface and rolled, and the screaming black tyres made skid marks an inch from our feet.

Orinda's nose was bleeding and her eyes were overflowing with pain-induced tears, and beyond that she was dazed and bewildered. I knelt beside her, winded myself and fearful that I'd hurt her unnecessarily when the lorry driver might have avoided her anyway.

The lorry had stopped not far beyond us and the driver, jumping down from his cab and running towards us, was already rehearsing aggrieved innocence.

'She ran out straight in front of me, I didn't have a chance. It isn't my fault . . . I couldn't help it . . . it isn't my fault she's bleeding all down her front.'

Neither Orinda nor I made any reply. It was irrelevant. It hadn't been his fault, and no one would say it had been. The person at fault stood in shocked rage on the pavement directly across the road from us, glaring and rigid and not coming to our aid.

With breath returning I asked Orinda if she was all right. Silly question, really, when her nose was bleeding and there were other marks of Wyvern's dangerous hands on her face. Her jacket was torn. One black shoe was off. The careful make-up was smeared and there was a slack weakness through all her body. The Orinda lying in the road looked far from the assured sophisticated flirter with cameras that I was used to; she looked a shattered, ordinary, middle-aged and rather nice woman trying to gather her wits and understand what had happened.

I leaned forward and slid an arm under her neck to see if she could sit up, and to my relief she let me help her to do that, until she was sitting in the road with her knees bent and her head and her hands on her knees.

She'd broken no bones, I thought gratefully. The fractures were internal and mental and couldn't be mended.

She said tearfully, trying to wipe blood with her fingers, 'Have you got a tissue?'

I hadn't.

'There's one in my bag.'

Her handbag, I knew, was in the Range Rover.

'I'll get it,' I said.

'No . . . Benedict . . . don't leave me!'

'Call an ambulance,' the lorry driver advised bullishly. 'I missed her, I know I did. It's not my fault she's bleeding.'

'No, it's not,' I agreed, standing up. 'But you're a big strong guy and you can help by picking up the lady and carrying her to that goldish Range Rover over there.'

'No fear,' he interrupted. 'I'm not getting her blood on me, it's not my sodding fault, she ran straight out in front of me.'

'Yes. OK,' I said. 'It wasn't your fault. But you did at least stop, so if you'd help and take her along to that vehicle, and if I just jot down your name and the firm you work for, that owns the lorry, then I'm sure you can carry on with whatever you were doing.'

'No police,' he said.

'You don't have to call the police to an accident unless someone's been injured, and you didn't injure this lady, as you said.'

'Straight up? How do you know that? You're only a boy.'

I'd learned it in the course of reading for my driving licence, but I couldn't be bothered to explain. I bent down and tried to get Orinda to her feet, and she stood up shakily, clutching me to stop herself from falling.

I put my arms round her awkwardly. She was trembling all over. My father would simply have scooped her up and carried her to the Range Rover, but apart from my doubt of having adequate strength, I was embarrassed by the difference in our ages. Ridiculous, really. I felt protective, but unsure.

A couple of cars went by, the passengers craning their necks with curiosity.

'Oh, come on, missus,' the driver said suddenly, picking up her scattered shoe and putting it on for her, 'hold onto my arm.'

He offered her a rock-like support, and between the two of us Orinda walked unsteadily, setting her feet down gingerly as if not sure where the ground lay. In that fashion we reached the Range Rover and installed Orinda in the front passenger seat, where she relaxed weakly and thanked the driver.

'Hey!' he said suddenly, surveying the highly noticeable vehicle. 'Doesn't this motor belong to that politician? Some funny name?'

'Juliard.'

'Yeah.'

'I'm his son,' I said. 'This lady, that you cleverly missed hitting, and that you've helped just now, is a Mrs Orinda Nagle, whose husband was the MP here before he died.'

'Cor!' Surprise at least stopped the whine of self-justification. I reckoned he was already rehearsing a revised tale to his masters. 'I live in Quindle,' he said. 'They say your father's got no chance, the way things are, but maybe I'll vote for him now anyway. Can't say fairer than that!'

I wrote down his name, which he gave willingly, and the name of the furniture firm he worked for, and the telephone number, and he positively beamed at Orinda and told her not to worry, and drove off in his lorry giving us a smile – a *smile* – and a wave.

Alderney Wyvern, all this time, had remained as if the soles of his shoes were glued to the ground.

A few people had come out of the houses because of the noise of horn and brakes, but as there'd been no actual crash, and as Orinda had stood up and walked away, their curiosity had died quickly.

For once, with a real story to record, Usher Rudd and his lens had been missing.

My father, Mervyn, Faith and Lavender came out from a triumphant conversion of the old people's home and exclaimed in horror at Orinda's blood and distress. The tissue from her handbag had proved inadequate. Her tears by now were of uncomplicated misery, rolling half-mopped down her cheeks.

'What happened?' my father demanded of me fiercely. 'What have you done?'

'Nothing!' I said. 'I mean . . . nothing.'

Orinda came to my defence. 'George, Benedict

helped me . . . I can't believe it . . .' Her voice wailed. 'Alderney . . . *Alderney* . . . h-h-hit me.'

'He *what*?'

We all looked along the road to where Wyvern still pugnaciously stood his ground, and if I had needed an explanation of the emotions involved, my father didn't. He strode off with purposeful anger towards the visibly unrepentant ex-best friend and challenged him loudly, though we couldn't hear the actual words. Wyvern answered with equal vigour, arms waving.

'Benedict . . .' Orinda begged me, increasingly upset, 'go and stop them.'

It was easy enough for her to say it, but they were both grown men whereas I . . . Well, I went along there fast and caught my father's arm as he drew back his fist for an infuriated swipe at Wyvern who was, incredibly, sneering.

My father swung round and shouted at me, raging, 'Get out of my bloody way.'

'The pact,' I yelled at him. 'Remember the pact.'

'*What*?'

'The *pact*,' I insisted. 'Don't hit him. Father . . . Dad . . . don't hit him.'

The scorching fury went out of his eyes as suddenly as if he were waking up.

'He *wants* you to hit him,' I said. I didn't know how I knew or why I was so certain. It had something to do with the fact that Wyvern had remained on the spot instead of driving off, but it was mostly intuition derived from his body language. He was looking for trouble. He meant all sorts of harm to my father, not least adverse publicity before polling day.

My father gave me a blank look, then walked past me to go back to the Range Rover. I half turned to follow him but was grabbed and spun round by Wyvern, whose always unsmiling face was now set fast with brutal malice. If he couldn't get what he wanted from the father, he would take it out on the son.

I hadn't learned boxing or karate, but I did have naturally fast reflexes and, thanks to riding and ski-ing, an instinctive command of balance. Wyvern might have had weight in his fists, but I ducked and dodged two sizzling punches to the face that would have laid me out flat if they'd connected, and concentrated solely on staying on my feet.

He drove me back against the shoulder-height rough stone wall that divided a garden from the pave-ment, but I squirmed out of his grasp and simply ran, intent on escape and containment, not on winning any battles.

I could hear Wyvern coming after me, and saw my father with renewed fury turning back to my aid.

I yelled at him in frenzy, 'Get in the Range Rover. *Get in the vehicle*,' and he wavered and turned again and marvellously did as I said.

Three steps from the Range Rover I stopped running and swung round fast to face Wyvern, in whom calculation had never been wholly overwhelmed by emotion: he sized up the gallery he was playing to – Orinda, my father, Mervyn, Faith and Lavender – and under the glare of all those sets of eyes he abruptly conceded that further attack would have legal consequences he wouldn't relish and stopped a bare six paces from where I stood.

The venom in his expression shrivelled the saliva in my mouth.

'One day,' he said, 'I'll get you one day.'

But not today, I thought; and today was all that mattered.

He took a few steps backwards, his face smoothing out to its customary flatness, then he turned and walked towards his car as if nothing had happened. Easing into the driver's seat he started the engine and drove collectedly away with no burning of tyres or other histrionics.

He left a lot of speechlessness in and around the Range Rover.

In the end Mervyn, clearing his throat, said, 'Orinda needs a doctor.'

Orinda disagreed. 'I need a tissue.'

Faith and Lavender between them produced some crumpled white squares. Orinda wiped her face, looked in a small mirror and moaned at the wreck it revealed. 'I'm not going anywhere like this.'

'The police . . .?' suggested Faith.

'*No*,' Orinda said, and no one argued.

With everyone subdued I drove the Range Rover

back to the headquarters where my father transferred himself and Orinda into her nearby parked car and set off to her home, with me following to bring him back.

He was silent for the whole of the return journey, but as I braked to a halt at the end of it he said, finally, 'Orinda thinks you saved her from being run over by the lorry.'

'Oh.'

'Did you?'

'The lorry driver missed us.'

He insisted I tell him what had happened.

'Her eyes were watering,' I explained. 'She couldn't see where she was going.'

I made as if to get out of the vehicle, but he stopped me.

'Wait.' He seemed to be searching for words and not finding them.

I waited.

He said in the end, 'I'm afraid I've let you in for more than I expected.'

I half laughed. 'It hasn't been boring.'

He went to Quindle with Mervyn early on the following Saturday to undertake an all-embracing round of the town's suburbs and, because of a dinner that evening and yet more commitments on the Sunday morning, he stayed in Quindle overnight.

That Sunday was my eighteenth birthday. My father had told me he would leave me a birthday card with Crystal, and I was to go along at nine in the morning to collect it. He would return that afternoon, he said, and we would dine together that evening to celebrate. No more political meetings, he said. Just the two of us, with champagne.

When I arrived at the party office at nine the door was locked and fifteen minutes passed before Crystal arrived and made her way inside. Yes, she agreed, my father had left me a card: and many happy returns and all that.

She took an envelope out of the desk and gave it to me, and inside I found a card with a joke on it about growing old, and nothing else. 'Yours, Dad,' he'd written.

'George said,' Crystal told me, 'that you are to go out into the street and find a black car with a chauffeur in it. And don't ask me what it's about, George wouldn't tell me, but he was smiling fit to crack his cheeks. So off you go, then, and find the car.'

'Thanks, Crystal.'

She nodded and waved me off, and I went outside and found the black car and the chauffeur a hundred yards away, patiently parked.

The chauffeur without speaking handed me a white envelope, unaddressed.

The card inside read '*Get in the car.*'

And underneath, '*Please.*'

With a gleam and a breath of good spirits I obeyed the instructions.

It wasn't much of a surprise when the chauffeur (not the same man as before, nor the same car) refused to tell me where we were going. It was, however, clear shortly that the direction was westwards and that many signposts distantly promised Exeter.

The chauffeur aimed at the heart of that city and pulled up outside the main doors of its grandest hotel. As before, the car's rear door was ceremoniously opened for me to step out and again, smiling broadly (not in the script), he pointed silently towards the interior and left me to the uniformed porters enquiring sniffily about my luggage.

My luggage this time again consisted of what I wore: a white long-sleeved sweatshirt, new blue jeans, and well-tried running shoes. With undoubtedly more self-confidence than at Brighton I walked into the grand lobby and asked at the reception desk for George Juliard.

The receptionist pressed buttons on a computer.

'Sorry, no one called Juliard staying at the hotel.'

'Please check again.'

She checked. Gave me a professional smile. Still no one called Juliard, past, present or future.

I was definitely not this time in sawn-off shorts and message-laden T-shirt land. Even on the last summer Sunday of August, business suits here prevailed. Ladies were fifty. In a cathedral city, people had been to church. The chauffeur, I gloomily concluded, had taken me to the wrong place.

The hotel's entrance lobby bulged at one side into a glass-roofed conservatory section with armchairs and green plants, and I sat there for a while considering what I should do next. Had my father intended me to get to know Exeter before I went to its university?

Or what?

After about half an hour a man dressed much as I was myself, though a good ten years older, appeared in the lobby. He looked around and drifted unhurriedly in my direction.

'Juliard?' he said. 'Benedict?'

'Yes.' I stood up, taller than he by an inch or two, which seemed to surprise him. He had yellow-blond hair, white eyelashes and outdoor skin. A man of strong muscles, self-confident, at home in his world.

'I'm Jim,' he said. 'I've come to collect you.'

'Who are you?' I asked. 'Where are we going?'

He smiled and said merely, 'Come on.'

He led the way out of the hotel and round a few corners, fetching up beside a dusty dented red car that contained torn magazines, screwed-up sandwich papers, coffee-stained polystyrene cups and a mixed-parentage dog introduced as Bert.

'Disregard the mess,' Jim said cheerfully, sweeping crumpled newspapers off the front passenger seat onto the floor. 'Happy birthday, by the way.'

'Uh . . . thanks.'

He drove the way I'd been taught not to; jerking acceleration and sudden brakes. Start and stop. Impulse and caution. I would have gone a long way with Jim.

It turned out to be only eight miles westward, as far as I could judge. Out of the city, past a signpost to Exeter University's Streatham Campus (home among much else of the department of mathematics), deep into rural Devon, with heavy thatched roofs frowning over tiny-windowed cottages.

Jim jerked to a halt in front of a larger example of the basic pattern and pointed to a heavy wooden front door.

'Go in there,' he instructed. 'Down the passage, last room on the left.' He grinned. 'And good luck.'

I was quite glad to be getting out of his car, even if only to stop the polymorphous Bert from licking my neck.

'Who lives here?' I asked.

'You'll find out.'

He left me with a simple choice: to do as I'd been told or find a way of returning to Exeter. Alice down the bleeding rabbit hole, I thought.

I opened the heavy door and went along the passage to the last room on the left.

CHAPTER EIGHT

In the last room on the left a man sat behind a large desk, and at first I thought with an unwelcome skipped heart-beat that he was Vivian Durridge, intent on sacking me all over again.

He looked up from his paperwork as I went in and I saw that though he wasn't Vivian Durridge himself he was of the same generation and of the same severe cast of mind.

He gave me no warm greeting, but looked me slowly up and down.

'Your father has gone to a great deal of trouble for you,' he said. 'I hope you're worth it.'

No reply seemed suitable, so I didn't make one.

'Do you know who I am?' he demanded.

'I'm afraid not . . . sir.'

'Stallworthy.'

He waited for the name to trickle through my brain, which it did pretty fast. It was the implication of his name that slowed my reply. Too much hope was bad for the pulse.

'Er . . . do you mean Spencer Stallworthy, the racehorse trainer?'

'I do.' He paused. 'Your father telephoned me. He wants to buy a horse and put it in training here with me, so that you can bicycle over from the university to ride it out at exercise. He asked me to enter it in amateur events so that you can ride it in races.'

He studied my face. I must have looked pretty ecstatic because a slow wintry smile lightened his heavy expression.

'I just hope,' he said, 'that you can ride well enough not to disgrace my stable.'

I just hoped he hadn't been talking to Vivian Durridge.

'Your father asked me to find a suitable horse. We discussed price, of course. I told him I train forty or so horses and one or two of them are always for sale. I have two here at present which might fit the bill. Your father and I agreed that you should come here today and have a ride on both. You are to choose which of them you prefer. He wanted it to be a surprise for your birthday – and I see it is.'

I breathlessly nodded.

'Right. Then go out of the back door. My assistant, Jim – he was the one who brought you here – he'll drive you along to the stables where the horses are ready for you. So off you go, then.'

'Er . . .' I said. 'Thank you . . . very much.'

He nodded and bent his head to his paperwork;

and Jim, grinning widely, drove half a mile to the stable yard that was old, needed paint and had sent out winners by the dozen over the years to small races on West Country courses. Stallworthy didn't aim for Cheltenham, Sandown or Aintree. He trained for local farmers and businessmen and ran their horses near home.

Jim stood in the yard and laconically pointed. 'Tack-room there.' He half turned. 'Horse in number twenty-seven. OK?'

'OK.'

I took a look at the occupant of box 27 and found a heavily muscled chestnut gelding standing there, anxious, it seemed, to be out on the gallops. He had nice short legs, with hocks not too angular, and a broad chest capable of pushing his way over or through any obstacle which came his way. More the type of a tough hardy steeplechaser than an ex-flat racer graduating to jumps.

I guessed at stamina and an unexcitability that might take a tiring amateur steadfastly towards the finish line, and if there were anything against him at first sight it was, perhaps, that he was a bit short in the neck.

Jim whistled up a lad to saddle and bridle the chestnut, though I had the impression that he had at first intended that I should do it myself.

Jim had considered me a sort of a joke. Perhaps my actual presence in the yard had converted me from joke to customer. In any case, neither Jim nor the lad saw anything but ordinary sense when I asked if I could see the chestnut being led round the yard at a walk. Somewhere along the way in my scrappy racing education I'd been told and shown by an avuncular old pro jockey that a horse that walked well galloped well. A long slow stride boded well for long-distance 'chases. A tittupping scratchy little walker meant a nervous scratchy little galloper.

The stride of the chestnut's walk was long enough and slow enough to suggest a temperament that would plod for ever. When he and his lad had completed two circuits of the yard I stopped him and felt his legs (no bumps from past tendon trouble) and looked in his mouth (which perhaps one shouldn't do to a gift horse) and estimated him to be about seven years old, a good solid age for a steeplechaser.

'Where do I ride him?' I asked Jim, and he pointed to a way out of the yard which led to a gate into a vast field that proved to be the chief training ground for the whole stable. There were no wide open down-land gallops, it seemed, in that cosy part of Devon.

'You can trot or canter down to the far end,' Jim said, 'and come back at a half-speed gallop. He . . . the chestnut . . . knows the way.'

I swung onto the chestnut's back and put the toes of my unsuitable running shoes into the stirrups, lengthening the leathers while getting to know the 'feel' of the big creature who would give me half speed and at least an illusion of being where I belonged.

I might never be a great jockey, and I might at times be clumsy and uncoordinated owing to growing in spurts and changing shape myself, but I'd ridden a great many different horses in my school holidays by working for people who wanted a few horses cared for while they went away on trips. I'd begged racehorse experience from trainers, and for the past two years had ridden in any race offered: I had had twenty-six outings to date, with three wins, two thirds and three falls.

The Stallworthy chestnut was in a good mood and let me know it by standing still patiently through the stirrup-leather lengthening and the pause while Jim sorted out a helmet in the tack-room, insisting that I wear it even though it was a size too small.

The chestnut's back was broad with muscles and I hadn't sat on a horse for three and a half weeks; and if he'd been mean-spirited that morning he could have run away with me and made a fool of my deficient strength, but in fact he went out onto the exercise ground as quietly as an old hack.

I didn't enjoy his trot, which was lumpy and threw me about, but his canter was like an armchair. We went in harmony down to the far end of the exercise field where the land dropped away a bit, so that the first part of the gallop home was uphill, good for strengthening legs.

At a half-speed gallop, riding the chestnut was a bit like sitting astride a launched rocket: powerful, purposeful, difficult to deflect. I reined to a slightly breathless walk and went over to where Jim waited beside the gate. 'Right,' he said noncommittally, 'now try the other one.'

The other horse – a bay gelding with a black mane – was of a leaner type and struck me as being more of a speed merchant than the one I'd just ridden. He carried his head higher and was more frisky and eager to set off and get into his stride. Whether that stride would last out over a distance of ground was, perhaps, doubtful.

I stood with my toes in the irons all the way down the field, letting the trot and canter flow beneath me. This was not a horse schooled to give his rider a peaceful look at the countryside; this was a fellow bred to race, for whom nothing else was of interest. At the far end of the field, instead of turning quietly, he did one of those swerving pirouettes with a dropped shoulder, a manoeuvre guaranteed to fling an unwary jockey off sideways. I'd seen many horses do that. I'd been flung off myself. But I was ready for Stallworthy's bay to try it; on his part more from eagerness to gallop than from spite.

His half-speed gallop home was a battle against my arms all the way: he wanted to go much faster. Thoughtfully I slid off his back and led him to Jim at the gate.

'Right,' Jim said. 'Which do you want?'

'Er . . .' I patted the bay's neck. He shook his handsome head vigorously, not in disapproval, I gathered, but in satisfaction.

'How about,' I suggested, 'a look at the form books and the breeding over a sandwich in a pub?'

I was quite good at pub life after three and a half weeks with my father.

Jim briefly laughed. 'I was told I was to fetch a school kid. You're some school kid.'

'I left school last month.'

'Yeah. Makes a difference!'

With good-natured irony he collected the necessary records from inside Stallworthy's house and drove us to a local pub where he was greeted as a friendly regular. We sat on a high-backed wooden settle and he put the form books on the table beside the beer (him) and the diet Coke (me).

In steeplechase breeding it's the dams that matter. A dam who breeds one winner will most likely breed others. The chestnut's dam had never herself won, though two of her progeny had. The chestnut so far hadn't finished nearer than second.

The bay's dam had never even raced, but all of her progeny, except the first foal, had won. The bay had won twice.

Both horses were eight.

'Tell me about them,' I said to Jim. 'What ought I to know?'

There was no way he was going to tell me the absolute truth if he had any commission coming from the sale. Horse traders were as notorious as car salesmen for filling the gear box with chaff.

'Why are they for sale?' I asked.

'Their owners are short of money.'

'My father would need a vet's certificate.'

'I'll see to it. Which horse do you want?'

'I'll talk to my father and let you know.'

Jim gave me a twisted smile. He had white eyebrows as well as white lashes. I needed to make a friend of him if I were to come often to ride exercise, so regrettably, with all my father's wily political sense, I deliberately set about canvassing Jim's pro-Ben vote, and thought that maybe I'd learned a few reprehensible techniques, while being willing to listen to people's troubles and desires.

Jim told me, laughing, that he'd hitched himself to Stallworthy because he hadn't been able to find a comparable trainer with a marriageable daughter. A good job I wasn't Usher Rudd, I thought.

Spencer Stallworthy apparently slept on Sunday afternoons, so I didn't see him again that day. Jim (and Bert) drove me back to Exeter by three o'clock and with a grin and a warm slap on the back he handed me over to the black car with the silent chauffeur.

'See you, then,' Jim said.

'I can hardly wait.'

The future had spectacularly clarified. My father,

instead of giving me a monthly allowance, had through my teens sent me one lump sum at Christmas to last me for the year: consequently I had enough saved away both to find myself a temporary lodging within cycling distance of Spencer Stallworthy and to immerse my brain in the racing press.

The chauffeur took me not to the headquarters from where he'd collected me, but to a playing field on the edge of Hoopwestern where, it appeared, an afternoon amalgam of fête and political rally was drawing to a close. Balloons, bouncy castle, bright plastic chutes and roundabouts had drawn children (and therefore voting parents) and car-boot-type stalls seemed to have sold out of all but hideous vases.

Painted banners promised 'GRAND OPENING BY MRS ORINDA NAGLE AT 3.00' and 'GEORGE JULIARD, 3.15.' Both of them were still present at 5.30, shaking hands all round.

Dearest Polly saw the black car stop at the gate and hurried across dry dusty grass to greet me.

'Happy birthday, Benedict. Did you choose a horse?'

'So he told you?' I looked across the field to where he stood on the soapbox surrounded by autograph books.

'He's been high as a kite all day.' Polly's own smile stretched inches. 'He told me he'd brought you here to Hoopwestern originally as window-dressing for the campaign, and he'd got to know you for the first time ever, and he'd wanted to give you something you would like, to thank you for all you've done here . . .'

'Polly!'

'He told me he hadn't realised how much he'd asked you to give up, with going to university instead of racing, and that you hadn't rebelled or walked out or cursed him. He wanted to give you the best he could.'

I swallowed.

He saw me from across the field and waved, and Polly and I walked over and stopped just outside the hedge of autograph seekers.

'Well?' he said over their heads. 'Did you like one?'

I couldn't think of adequate words. He looked, however, at my face, and smiled at what he saw there, and seemed content with my speechlessness. He stepped off the soapbox and made his way through the offered books, signing left and right, until he was within touching distance, and there he stopped.

We looked at each other in great accord.

'Well, go on,' Polly said to me impatiently, 'hug him.'

But my father shook his head and I didn't touch him, and I realised we had no tradition between us of how to express greeting or emotion, and that until that moment there had never been much intense mutual emotion to express. Far from hugging, we had never shaken hands.

'Thanks,' I said to him.

It sounded inadequate, but he nodded: it was enough.

'I want to tell you about it,' I said.

'Did you choose one?'

'More or less, but I want to talk to you first.'

'At dinner, then.'

'Perfect.'

Orinda was smiling warmly at me, fully recovered, make-up hiding any residual marks, all traces of the shaking, frightened woman in blood-spattered clothes overlaid by Constituency Wife, Mark I, the opener of fêtes and natural hogger of cameras.

'Benedict, daaahling!' She at least had no inhibitions about hugging, and embraced me soundly for public consumption. She smelled sweetly of scent. She wore a copper-coloured dress with green embroidery to match her eyes, and Polly beside me stiffened with the prehistoric reaction of Martha to butterfly.

Dearest Polly. *Dearest* Polly. I was far too young externally to show I understood her, let alone insult her by offering comforts. Dearest Polly wore remnants of the awful lipstick, a chunky necklace of amber beads and heavily strapped sandals below a muddy-green dress. I liked both women, but on the evidence of their clothes, they would never equally like each other.

Instinctively I looked over Orinda's shoulder, expecting the everlasting Anonymous Lover to be back at his post, but Wyvern had once and for all abandoned Hoopwestern as his path to influence. In his place behind Orinda loomed Leonard Kitchens with a soppy grin below his out-of-control moustache. Close on his heels came Mrs Kitchens, looking grim.

Usher Rudd was wandering about with his intrusive malice trying to catch people photographically at a disadvantage but, interestingly, when he caught my eye he pretended he hadn't, and veered away. I had no illusions that he wished me well.

Mervyn Teck and a retinue of dedicated volunteers, stoutly declaring the afternoon a success, drove my father and me back to the Sleeping Dragon. Four days to polling day, I thought; eternity.

Over a good dinner in the hotel dining-room I told my father about the two Stallworthy horses. A phlegmatic chestnut stayer and a sprinting excitable bay with a black mane.

'Well . . .' he said, frowning, 'you love speed. You'll take the bay. What makes you hesitate?'

'The horse I want has a name that might disturb you. I can't change his name: one isn't allowed to, after a thorough-bred has raced. I won't have that horse unless it's OK with you.'

He stared. 'What name could possibly disturb me so much?'

After a pause I said flatly, 'Sarah's Future.'

'Ben!'

'His dam was Sarah Jones; his sire, Bright Future. It's good breeding for a jumper.'

'The bay – ?'

'No,' I said. 'The chestnut. He's the one I want. He's never won yet, though he's been second. A novice has a wider – a better – choice of a race. Apart from that, he felt right. He'd look after me.'

My father absentmindedly crumbled a bread roll to pieces.

'*You*,' he said eventually, '*you* are literally Sarah's future. Let's say she would be pleased. I'll phone Stallworthy in the morning.'

Far from slackening off during the run-up to polling day, the Juliard camp spent the last three days in a non-stop whirl.

I drove the Range Rover from breakfast to bedtime. I drove to Quindle three times, and all around the villages. I screwed together and unclipped the soapbox until I could do it in my sleep. I loaded and unloaded boxes of leaflets. I made cooing noises at babies and played ball games with kids and shook uncountable hands and smiled and smiled and smiled.

I thought of Sarah's Future, and was content.

On the last evening, Wednesday, my father invited all his helpers and volunteers to the Sleeping Dragon for a thank-you supper. Along in a room off the Town Hall, Paul Bethune was doing the same.

The Bethune cavalcade had several times crossed our path, their megaphone louder, their travelling circus larger, their campaign vehicle not a painted

Range Rover but a roofless double-decker bus borrowed from his party headquarters. Bethune's message followed him everywhere: 'Dennis Nagle was out of touch, old-fashioned. Elect Bethune, a local man, who knows the score.'

A recent opinion poll in the constituency had put Bethune a few points ahead. Titmuss and Whistle were nowhere.

The *Gazette* had trumpeted merely 'An End to Sleaze' and waffled on about 'the new morality' without defining it. Though by instinct a Bethune man, the editor had let Usher Rudd loose and thereby both increased his sales and scored an own-goal. The editor, I thought in amusement, had dug his own dilemma.

My father thanked his faithful workers.

'Whatever happens tomorrow,' he said, 'I want you to know how much I appreciate all you've done . . . all the time you've given . . . your tireless energy . . . your friendly good nature. I thank our agent, Mervyn, for his excellent planning. We've all done our best to get the party's message across. Now it's up to the voters to decide.'

He thanked Orinda for rallying to his side. ' . . . All the difference in the world to have her support . . . immensely generous . . . reassuring to the faithful . . .'

Orinda, splendid in gold chains and emerald green, looked modest and loved it.

Polly, beside me, made a noise near to a retch.

I stifled a quivering giggle.

'Don't think I've forgotten,' she said to me severely, 'that it was you who changed Orinda from foe to angel. I bear it only because the central party wants to use your father's talents. Get him *in*, they said. Just like you, they more or less told me to put his feet on the escalator, and he would rise all the way.'

But someone, I thought, had tried to prevent that first step onto the escalator. Had *perhaps* tried. A bullet, a wax plug, an unexplained fire. If someone had tried to halt him by those means and hadn't left it to the ballot-box . . . then *who*? No one had seriously tried to find out.

The speeches done, my father came over to Polly and me, his eyes gleaming with excitement, his whole body alive with purpose. His strong facial bones shouted intelligence. His dark hair curled with healthy animal vigour.

'I'm going to win this by-election,' he said, broadly smiling. 'I'm going to win. I can feel it.'

His euphoria fired everyone in the place to believe him, and lasted in himself through breakfast the next morning. The glooms crowded in with his second cup of coffee and he wasted an hour in doubt and tension, worrying that he hadn't worked hard enough, that there was more he could have done.

'You'll win,' I said.

'But the opinion polls . . .'

'The people who compile the opinion polls don't go round the village pubs at lunchtime.'

'The tide is flowing the wrong way . . .'

'Then go back to the City and make another fortune.'

He stared and then laughed, and we set out on a tour of the polling stations, where the volunteers taking exit polls told him they were pretty even, but not to lose hope.

Here and there we came across Paul Bethune on a similar mission with similar doubts. He and my father were unfailingly polite to each other.

The anxiety went on all day and all evening. After weeks of fine weather it rained hard that afternoon. Both sides thought it might be a disaster. Both sides thought it might be to their advantage. The rain stopped when the light-bulb workers poured out of the day shift and detoured to the polling booths on their way home.

The polls closed at ten o'clock and the counting began.

My father stood at our bedroom window staring out across the cobbled square to the burned-out shell of the bow-fronted shops.

'Stop worrying,' I said. As if he could.

'I was head-hunted, you know,' he said. 'The party leaders came to me and said they wanted to harness my economic skills for the good of the country. What if I've let them down?'

'You won't have,' I assured him.

He smiled twistedly. 'They offered me a marginal

seat to see what I was made of. I was *flattered*. Serves me right.'

'Father . . .'

'Dad.'

'OK, Dad. Good men do lose.'

'Thanks a lot.'

We went in time along the square to the Town Hall where, far from offering peace, the atmosphere was electric with hope and despair. Paul Bethune, surrounded by hugely rosetted supporters, was trying hard to smile. Isobel Bethune, in dark brown, tried to merge into the woodwork.

Mervyn talked to Paul Bethune's agent absent-mindedly and I would have bet neither of them heard what the other was saying.

Usher Rudd took merciless photographs.

There was a smattering of applause at my father's entrance and both Polly (in pinkish grey) and Orinda (in dramatic glittering white) sailed across the floor to greet him personally.

'George, daaahling,' Orinda crowed, offering her smooth cheek for a kiss. 'Dennis is with us, you know.'

George daaahling looked embarrassed.

'It's going quite well, George,' Polly said, giving succour. 'First reports say the town votes are fairly even.'

The counting was going on under all sorts of rigorous supervision. Even those counting the Xs weren't sure who had won.

My father and Paul Bethune looked as calm as neither was feeling.

The hall gradually filled with supporters of both sides. After midnight, getting on for one o'clock, the four candidates and their close supporters appeared on the platform, shuffling about with false smiles. Paul Bethune looked around irritably for his wife, but she'd hidden herself successfully in the crowd. Orinda stood on the platform close beside my father as of right and no one questioned it, though Polly, beside me on the floor, fumed that it should be me up there, not that . . . that . . .

Words failed her.

My father told me afterwards that the result had been whispered to the candidates before they faced the world, presumably so no one would burst into tears, but one couldn't have guessed it from their faces.

Finally the returning officer (whose function was to announce the result) fussed his way onto the centre stage, tapped the microphone to make sure it was working (it was), grinned at the television cameras, and rather unnecessarily asked for silence.

He strung out his moment of importance by looking around as if to make sure everyone was there on the platform who should be and, finally, slowly, in a silence broken only by a throng of heartbeats, read the result.

Alphabetically.

Bethune . . . thousands.

Juliard . . . thousands.

Titmuss . . . hundreds.

Whistle . . . 69.

It took a moment to sink in. Staring down a preliminary cheer from the floor, the returning officer completed his task.

George Juliard is therefore elected . . .

The rest was drowned in cheers.

Polly worked it out. 'He won by just under two thousand. Bloody well done.'

Polly kissed me.

Up on the stage Orinda was loudly kissing the new MP.

It was too much for Dearest Polly, who left my side to go to his.

I found poor sad Isobel Bethune at my elbow instead.

'Look at that *harridan* with your father, pretending it was *she* who won the votes.'

'She did help, to be fair.'

'She would never have won on her own. It was your *father* who won the election. And my Paul lost. He positively *lost*. Your father never mentioned that bimbo of his, not once, though he could have done, but the public never forget those things. Sleaze sticks, you know.'

'Mrs Bethune . . .'

'This is the third time Paul's contested the seat,' she told me hopelessly. 'We knew he would lose to Dennis Nagle the last two times, but this time the party said he was bound to win, with the way the recent by-elections have been swinging in our favour, and with the other party ignoring Orinda and bringing in a stranger, and they'll never let Paul stand again. He's lost worse than ever this time with everything on his side, and it's that *horrid* Usher Rudd's fault and I could *kill* him . . .' She smothered her face in a handkerchief as if to shut out the world and, stroking my arm, mumbled, 'I'll never forget your kindness.'

Up on the stage her stupid husband still looked self-satisfied.

A month ago, I thought, I hadn't known the Bethunes existed.

Dearest Polly had bloomed unseen.

I hadn't heard of Orinda, or of Alderney Wyvern.

I hadn't met Mrs Kitchens nor her fanatical unlovable Leonard, and I hadn't known plump efficient Mervyn or worried Crystal. I never did know the last names of Faith or Marge or Lavender, but I was certain even then that I would never forget the mean-spirited red-haired terror whose delight in life was to find out people's hidden pleasures in order to destroy them. Bobby Usher bleeding Rudd.

CHAPTER NINE

So my father went to Westminster and I to Exeter, and the intense month we had spent in getting to know each other receded from a vivid present experience into a calmer, picture-filled memory.

I might not see him for weeks at a time but we talked now often on the telephone. Parliament was still in its summer recess. He would go back as a new boy, as I would, when my first term began.

Meantime, I rode Sarah's Future every morning under Stallworthy's critical eye and can't have done as badly as for Vivian Durridge because when I asked if he would enter the chestnut in a race for me – any race would do – he chose a novice 'chase at Wincanton on an inconspicuous Thursday and told me he hoped I'd be worth it as it was costing my father extras in the way of horse transport and shoeing with racing plates, not to mention the entry fee.

Laden thus half with glee and half with guilt I went with Jim in his car to Wincanton, where Jim declared and saddled the horse and then watched him win with as much disbelief as I felt when I sailed past the post first.

'He *flew*!' I said, thrilled and astonished, as I unbuckled the saddle in the winner's enclosure. 'He was brilliant.'

'So I saw.'

Jim's lack of much enthusiasm, I discovered, was rooted in his not having had the faith for a bet. Neither was Stallworthy overjoyed. All he said the next morning was, 'You wasted the horse's best win. You haven't any sense. If I'd thought for a moment you would go to the front when the favourite fell, I'd have told you to keep the chestnut on a tight rein so we could have put the stable money on him next time out. What your father will say, I can't imagine.'

What my father said was, 'Very well done.'

'But nobody backed it . . .'

'Don't you listen to Stallworthy. You listen to *me*. That horse is for you to do your best on. To win whenever you can. And don't think I didn't back it. I have an arrangement with a bookmaker that wherever – *whenever* – you ride in a race, I am betting on you at starting price. I won on you at twenties yesterday . . . I'm even learning racing jargon! *Always* try to win. Understand?'

I said, 'Yes,' weakly.

'And I don't care if you lose because some other horse is faster. Just keep to the rules and don't break your neck.'

'OK.'

'Is there anything else you want?'

'Er . . .'

'You'll get nowhere if you're afraid to tell me.'

'I'm not exactly afraid,' I said.

'Well, then?'

'Well . . . will you telephone Stallworthy? Will you ask him to run your horse in the novice 'chase at Newton Abbot a week tomorrow? He's entered him but now he won't want to run him. He'll say it's too soon. He'll say the horse will have to carry a 5-lb penalty because I won on him yesterday.'

'And will he?'

'Yes, but there aren't many more races – suitable races, that is – that I can ride him in before term starts. Stallworthy wants to win but I just want to *race*.'

'Yes, I know.' He paused. 'I'll fix it for Newton Abbot. Anything else?'

'Only . . . thanks.'

His laugh came down the wire. 'Give my regards to Sarah's Future.'

Feeling a bit foolish I passed on the message to the chestnut, though in fact I had fallen into a habit of talking to him, sometimes aloud if we were alone, and sometimes in my mind. Although I had ridden a good many horses, he was the first I had known consistently from day to day. He fitted my body-size and my level of skill. He undoubtedly recognised me and seemed almost to breathe a sigh of relief when I appeared every morning for exercise. We had won the race at Wincanton because we knew and trusted each other, and when I'd asked him for maximum speed at the end he'd understood from past experience what was needed, and had seemed positively to exult in having at last finished first.

Jim forgave the success and grew interested. Jim was by nature in tune with horses and, as I gradually realised, did most of the actual training. Stallworthy, although he watched the gallops most mornings, won his races with pen and entry forms, totting up times and weights and statistical probabilities.

Up the centre of the long exercise field there were two rows of schooling fences, one of three flights of hurdles, and one of birch fences. Jim patiently spent some mornings teaching both me and the chestnut to go up over the birch with increasing precision, measuring our stride for take-off from further and further back before the actual jump.

The riding I'd learned to that date had been from watching other people. Jim taught me, as it were, from inside, so that in that first month with Sarah's Future I began to develop from an uncoordinated windmill with a head full of unrealistic dreams into a reasonably competent amateur rider.

Grumbling at great length about owners who knew nothing at all about racing and should leave all decisions to their trainer, Stallworthy complainingly sent the chestnut to carry his 5-lb penalty at Newton Abbot.

I'd never before ridden on the course and at first sight of it felt foolish not to have listened to Stallworthy's judgment. The steeplechase track was an almost one-and-a-half-mile flat circuit with sharpish turns, and the short grass gave little purchase on rock-hard ground, baked by the sun of August.

Stallworthy, with several other runners from his yard, had brought his critical eye to the course. Jim, saddling Sarah's Future, told me the chestnut knew the course better than I did (I'd walked round it a couple of hours earlier to see the jumps, and the approaches to them, at close quarters) and to remember what I'd learned from him at home, and not to expect too much because of the weight disadvantage and because the other jockeys were all professionals, and this was not an amateur race.

As usual, it was the speed that seduced me and fulfilled, and the fact that we finished third was enough to make my day worthwhile, though Stallworthy, who had incidentally also trained the winner, announced to me several times, 'I told you so. I told your father it was too much to expect. Perhaps you'll listen to me next time.'

'Never mind,' Jim consoled. 'If you'd won today you'd have to have carried a 10-lb penalty at Exeter races next Saturday, always supposing you can persuade the old man to let him run there after this. He'll say it's too soon, which it probably *is*.'

The old man (Stallworthy) conducted a running battle over the telephone with my father.

My father won.

So, blisteringly, by six lengths, did Sarah's Future, because the much longer galloping track, up on Haldon Moor above Exeter, suited him better. He carried a 5-lb penalty, not 10, and made light of it. The starting price, my father assured me later, would pay the training fees until Christmas.

Two days after that, in cooler blood, I went to learn mathematics.

My father learned back-bench tactics, but that wasn't what the party had sent him to Hoopwestern for. He tried to explain to me that the path upward led through the Whips' office, which sounded nastily about flagellation to me, though he laughed.

'The Whips' office is what gives you the thumbs up for advancement towards the ministerial level.'

'And their thumbs are up for you?'

'Well . . . so far . . . yes.'

'Minister of what?' I asked, disbelievingly. 'Surely you're too young?'

'The really forward boys are on their way by twenty-two. At thirty-eight, I'm old.'

'I don't like politics.'

'I can't ride races,' he said.

To have the Whip withdrawn, he explained, meant the virtual end to a political career. If getting elected was the first giant step, then winning the Whips' approval was the second. When the newly elected member for Hoopwestern was shortly appointed as Under-Secretary of State in the Department of Trade and Industry, it was apparently a signal to the whole fabric of government that a bright fast-moving comet had risen over the horizon.

I went to listen to his maiden speech, sitting inconspicuously in the gallery. He spoke about light bulbs and had the whole House laughing; and Hoopwestern's share of the illumination market soared.

I met him for dinner after his speech, when he was again in the high exaltation of post-performance spirits.

'I suppose you haven't been back to Hoopwestern?' he said.

'Well, no.'

'I have, of course. Leonard Kitchens is in trouble.'

'Who?'

'Leonard . . .'

'Oh, yes. Yes, the unbalanced moustache. What sort of trouble?'

'The police now have a rifle which may be the one fired at us that evening.'

'By the police,' I asked as he paused, 'do you mean Joe the policeman whose mother drives a school bus?'

'Joe whose mother drives a school bus is actually Detective Sergeant Joe Duke, and, yes, he's now received from the Sleeping Dragon a very badly rusted .22 rifle. It seems that after the trees shed their leaves the guttering round the roof of the hotel got choked with them, as happens most years, and rainwater overflowed instead of draining down the pipes as it should, so they sent a man up a ladder to clear out the leaves, and they found it wasn't just leaves clogging the guttering, it was the .22 rifle.'

'But what's that got to do with Leonard Kitchens?'

My father ate peppered steak, rare, with spinach.

'Leonard Kitchens is the nurseryman who festoons the Sleeping Dragon with all those baskets of geraniums.'

'But – ' I objected.

'Apparently in a broom cupboard on that bedroom level he keeps a sort of trolley with things for looking after the baskets. Clippers, a long-spouted watering can, fertiliser. They think he could have hidden the gun in the trolley. If you stand on a chair by the window you can reach up far enough outside to put a rifle up in the gutter. And someone *did* put a gun up there.'

I frowned over my food.

'You know what people are like,' my father said. 'Someone says, "I *suppose* Leonard Kitchens could have put the rifle in the gutter, he's always in and out of the hotel," and the next person drops the "I suppose" and repeats the rest as a fact.'

'What does Leonard Kitchens himself say?'

'Of course, he says it wasn't his gun and he didn't put it in the gutter, and he says no one can prove he did.'

'That's what guilty people always say,' I observed.

'Yes, but it's true, no one can prove he ever had the gun. No one has come forward to connect him to rifles in any way.'

'What does Mrs Kitchens say?'

'Leonard's wife is doing him no good at all. She goes around saying her husband was so besotted with Orinda Nagle that he would do anything, including shooting me in the back, to get me out of Orinda's way. Joe Duke asked her if she had ever seen a rifle in her husband's possession, and instead of saying no, as any sensible woman would, she said he had a garden shed full of junk, and it was possible he had *anything* lying around in there.'

'Did Joe by any chance search the shed? I mean, did he have a look round to see if Leonard had any bullets?'

'Joe couldn't get a warrant to search, as there were no real grounds for suspicion. Also, as I suppose you know, it's quite easy to buy high-velocity bullets, and even easier to throw them away. There's no chance of telling that it was indeed that rifle that was used because, even if you could remove all the rust, there is no bullet to match it to, as the one from the what-not finally got lost altogether in the fire. No one ever found any cartridge cases in the hotel either.'

My father continued with his steak. Putting down his knife and fork he said, 'I took the Range Rover to Basil Rudd's garage and had him dismantle the engine for a thorough check of the oil system. There was nothing in the sump except oil. It was actually extremely unprofessional for that mechanic – Terry, I think he is – to push the substitute plug up into the sump, but Basil Rudd won't hear a word against him, and I suppose there was no harm done.'

'There might have been,' I said. I thought for a moment and asked, 'I suppose Leonard Kitchens isn't accused of being in possession of candles?'

'You may laugh,' my father said, 'but in the shop at his garden centre, where they sell plastic gnomes and things, they do have table centre-pieces with candles and ribboned bows and stuff.'

'You can buy candles anywhere,' I said. 'And what about the fire? Was that Leonard Kitchens, too?'

'He was there,' my father reminded me, and I remembered Mrs Kitchens saying her Leonard liked a good fire.

'Did the firemen ever find out how that fire started?'

My father shook his head. 'They didn't at the time. Some of them are now saying unofficially that it could have been started with candles. Leonard Kitchens fiercely denies he had anything to do with it.'

'What do you think, yourself?'

My father drank some wine. He was trying to indoctrinate me into liking burgundy but, to his disgust, I still liked diet Coke better.

He said, 'I think Leonard Kitchens is fanatical enough to do almost anything. It's easy enough to think of him as a bit of a silly ass, with that out-of-proportion moustache, but it's people with obsessions who do the real harm in the world, and if he still has a grudge against me, I want him where I can see him.'

I did my best with the wine, but I didn't really like it.

'There's no point in his arranging accidents for you any more, now that you're elected.'

My father sighed. 'With people like Kitchens you can't be sure that good sense will be in control.'

I stayed with him that night in his Canary Wharf apartment by the Thames. His big windows looked down the wide river where once a flourish of cranes had been busy with shipping, though he himself couldn't remember 'the Docks' except as a long-ago political lever. His old office (he ran his investment-consultant business from home) gave him a two-mile walk along the Embankment to his new office in Whitehall, a leg-stretching that was clearly keeping him muscularly fit. He blazed with vigour and excitement. Even though he was my father I felt both energised and overwhelmed by his vitality.

In a way, I deeply loved him.

In a way I felt wholly incapable of ever equalling

his mental force or his determination. It took me years to realise that I didn't have to.

On the morning after his maiden speech I caught the early train from Paddington to Exeter, clicketing along the rails from reflected fame to anonymity.

In Exeter, one of eight thousand residential students, I coasted through university life without attracting much attention, and absorbed reams of calculus, linear algebra, actuarial science and distribution theory towards a Bachelor of Science degree in Mathematics with Accounting: and as a short language course came with the package I also learned French, increasing my vocabulary from *piste* and *écurie* (track and stable) to law and order.

As often as possible I cycled to Stallworthy's stable to ride Sarah's Future, and on several Saturdays set off from starting gates. After the first flourish as a novice, finding winning races for a steady but unspectacular jumper proved difficult, but also-ran was fine by me: fourth, fifth, sixth, one easy fall and no tailed-offs.

On one very cold December Saturday towards the end of my first term I was standing on the stands at Taunton watching one of Stallworthy's string scud first towards the last flight of hurdles when it crashed and fell in a cascading cartwheel of legs, and snapped its neck.

They put screens round the disaster and winched the body away, and within ten minutes I came across Stallworthy trying to comfort the female owner. Crying ladies were not Stallworthy's speciality. He first asked me to find Jim and then cancelled that instruction and simply passed the weeping woman into my arms, and told me to take her for a drink.

Many trainers went white and shook with emotion when their horses died. Stallworthy shrugged and drew a line across a page.

Mrs Courtney Young, the bereaved owner, wiped away her tears and tried to apologise, while a large bracer of gin took its effect.

'It's all right,' I assured her. 'If my horse died, I'd be devastated.'

'But you're so young. You'd get over it.'

'I'm sure you will too, in time.'

'You don't understand.' Fresh tears rolled. 'I let the horse's insurance lapse because I couldn't afford the premium, and I owe Mr Stallworthy a lot of training fees, and I was sure my horse would win today so I could pay off my debts, and I backed it with a bookie I have an account with, and I haven't any money to pay him. I was going to have to sell my horse anyway if he didn't win, but now I can't do even that . . .'

Poor Mrs Courtney Young.

'She's mad,' Jim told me later, saddling Sarah's Future. 'She bets too much.'

'What will she do?'

'Do?' he exclaimed. 'She'll sell a few more heir-looms. She'll buy another horse. One day she'll lose the lot.'

I grieved very briefly for Mrs Courtney Young, but that evening I telephoned my father and suggested he insure Sarah's Future.

'How did you get on today?' he asked. 'I heard the results and you weren't in the first three.'

'Fourth. What about insurance?'

'Who arranges horse insurance?'

'Weatherbys.'

'Do you want to?'

'For your sake,' I said.

'Then send me the paperwork.'

Weatherbys, the firm that arranged insurance for horses, were the administrators for the whole of racing. It was Weatherbys who kept the records, who registered horses' names and ownership details including colours; Weatherbys to whom trainers sent entries for races; Weatherbys who confirmed a horse was running and sent details of racing programmes to the press; Weatherbys who printed racecards in colour by night and despatched them to racecourses by morning.

Weatherbys published the fixture list, kept the thorough-bred Stud Book and acted as a bank for the transfer of fees to jockeys, prize money to owners, anything to anyone. Weatherbys ran a safe computer database.

There wasn't much in racing, in fact, that Weatherbys didn't do.

It was because of mad, tearful, silly Mrs Courtney Young that I began to think that one distant day I might apply to Weatherbys for a job.

In the spring of my third year of study my father came to Exeter to see me (he had been a couple of times before) and to my surprise brought with him Dearest Polly.

I had spent a week of each Christmas holidays skiing (practising my French!) and I'd been riding and racing in every spare minute, but I also played fair and passed all my exams and assessments with reasonable grades if not with distinction, so when I saw him arrive a quick canter round the guilt reflexes raised no wincing spectres, and I shook his hand (we had at least advanced that far) with uncomplicated pleasure.

'I don't know if you realise,' my father said, 'that we are fast approaching a General Election.'

My immediate reaction was 'Oh, God. No.' I managed not to say it aloud, but it must have been plain on my face.

Dearest Polly laughed and my father said, 'This time I'm not asking you to canvass door to door.'

'But you need a bodyguard . . .'

'I've engaged a professional.'

I felt instantly jealous: ridiculous. It took me a good

ten seconds to say sincerely, 'I hope he'll mind your back.'

'He's a she. All sorts of belts in martial arts.'

'Oh.' I glanced at Polly, who looked merely benign.

'Polly and I,' my father said, 'propose to marry. We came to hear if you had any objections.'

'Polly!'

'Dear Benedict. Your father is so abrupt. I would have asked you more gently.'

'I've no objections,' I said. 'Very much the opposite.'

I kissed her cheek.

'Goodness!' she exclaimed. 'You've grown.'

'Have you?' my father enquired with interest. 'I hadn't noticed.'

'I've stopped at last,' I sighed. 'I'm over an inch taller and fifteen pounds heavier than I was at Hoopwestern.' Too big, I might have added, for much scope as a professional jockey, but an excellent size for an amateur.

Polly herself hadn't changed, except that I saw with interest that the hard crimson lipstick had been jettisoned for an equally inappropriate scarlet. Her clothes still looked unfashionable even by charity shop standards, and no one had taken recent scissors to her hair. With her long face and thin stringy body, she looked a total physical mismatch for my increasingly powerful father, but positive goodness shone out of her as always, and her sincerity, it seemed to me, was now tinged with amusement. There had never been anything gauche or self-conscious in her manner, but only the strength to be her own intelligent, uncompromising self.

More than a marriage of true minds, I thought. A marriage of true morality.

I said sincerely to my father, 'Congratulations,' and he looked pleased.

'What are you doing next Saturday?' he asked.

'Racing at Chepstow.'

He was shaking his head. 'I want you to stand beside me.'

'Do you mean . . .' I hesitated, 'that you are marrying . . . next Saturday?'

'That's right,' he agreed. 'Now that we've decided, and since you seem quite pleased, there's no point in delaying. I'm going to live with Polly in her house in the woods, and I'll also find a larger flat in London.'

Polly, I learned by instalments through that afternoon, had inherited the house in the woods from her parents, along with a fortune that set her financially free to work unpaid wherever she saw the need.

She was two years older than my father. She had never been married: a mischievous glint in her eye both forbade and answered the more intimate question.

She didn't intend, she said, to make a wasteland of Orinda Nagle's life. Orinda and Mervyn Teck had been running the constituency day to day and making a success of it. Polly didn't hunger to open fêtes or flirt with cameras. She would organise, as always, from behind the scenes. And she would be listened to, I thought, where influence mattered.

Six days later she and my father married in the ultimate of quiet weddings. I stood by my father and Polly was supported by the Duke who'd lured Orinda to the races, and all of us signed the certificates.

The bride wore brown with a gold and amber necklet given by my father, and looked distinguished. A photographer, at my request, recorded the event. A discreet paragraph appeared in *The Times*. The *Hoopwestern Gazette* caught up with the story later. Mr and Mrs George Juliard, after a week in Paris, returned to Hoopwestern to keep the light-bulb workers faithful.

I still disliked politics and I was extremely grateful that the approach of my final exams made it impossible for me to repeat my by-election stint.

There were many politically active students at Exeter, but I kept my head down with them too and led a double life only on Stallworthy's gallops and various racetracks. I won no races that spring, but the sensation of speed was all that mattered: and, in an oddity of brain activity, the oftener I raced the more clearly I understood second-order differential equations.

The General Election swelled and broke under me like a Pacific surf, and my father, along with his party, were returned to power. A small majority, but enough.

No one shot at him, no one plugged his sump-drain

with wax, no one set fire to Polly's house, and no one let the martial arts expert earn her fee.

Suspicion of shooting and arson still lay heavily on Leonard Kitchens, but no one could accuse him of anything this time as his formidable and unforgiving wife insisted on his taking her on a double Mediterranean cruise. They were in Athens on polling day.

Poor Isobel Bethune had been right: Paul Bethune's party dumped him as a candidate in favour of a worthy woman magistrate. Though it was no longer hotly scandalous news, Paul Bethune's roving eye had settled again outside his home, and Isobel, at last fed up with it, had shed her marriage and her sullen sons and gone to live with her sister in Wales.

Polly kept me informed, her humour dry. My father couldn't have married anyone better.

I told him to beware of bikini-clad bimbos falling artistically into his lap with Usher Rudd in attendance for accusations of sleaze. Hadn't I heard, he asked, that Usher Rudd had been sacked by the *Gazette* for manufacturing sleaze where it didn't exist? Usher Rudd, my father cheerfully said, was now telephoto-lens-stalking a promiscuous front-bencher of the Opposition.

When the party in power reassembled after the whole country had voted, there was a major reshuffle of jobs. To no one's surprise at Westminster, my father's career skipped upwards like helium and he became a Minister of State in the Ministry of Transport, one step down from a seat in the Cabinet.

I had the best photograph of his wedding to Polly framed and stood it beside the one of him and my mother. I took the pacts we'd signed out of my mother's frame and read them thoughtfully, and put them back. They seemed to belong to a different life. I had indeed grown up at Exeter, and I'd had 'the first' that I would never forget: but the basic promises of those pacts had so far been kept, and although now it might seem a melodramatic statement, I knew that if it ever became necessary, I would indeed defend my father against any form of attack.

I took my final exams and, seeing that I'd probably done enough to gain a Bachelor of Science degree of a reasonable standard, I wrote to Weatherbys and asked for a job.

They replied, what job?

Any, I wrote. I could add, subtract and work computers, and I had ridden in races.

Ah, *that* Juliard. Come for an interview, they said.

Weatherbys, a family business started in 1770 and currently servicing racing in increasingly inventive and efficient ways, stood quietly in red brick surrounded by fields, trees and peaceful countryside near the small ancient town of Wellingborough, some sixty miles north-west of London in Northamptonshire.

Inside, the atmosphere of the furiously busy secretariat was notably calm and quiet also. Knowing the vast scope and daily pressure of the work being done there, I suppose I'd expected something like the clattering frenzy of an old-fashioned newspaper office, but what I walked into was near to silence, with rows of heads bent over computer monitors and people walking among them with thoughtfulness, not scurrying, carrying papers and boxes of disks.

I was handed from department to department and shown around, and in an undemanding interview at the end was asked for my age and references. I went away in disappointment: they had been polite and kind but had asked none of the piercing questions I would have expected if they'd had a job to offer.

Back at Exeter, living in rooms halfway between the university and Stallworthy's yard, I began dispiritedly to send job applications to a list of industries. Weatherbys had seemed my natural home: too bad they didn't see me as their child.

They did, however, follow up on the references I'd given them: my tutor at the university and Stallworthy himself.

The gruff old trainer told me he'd said my character and behaviour were satisfactory. Thanks a lot, I thought. Jim laughed. 'He doesn't want you to leave and take Sarah's Future with you. It's a wonder he didn't call you a loud-mouthed trouble-maker!'

There was a letter from my tutor:

Dear Benedict,

I enclose a photocopy of a reference I have sent to an institution called Weatherbys, that has something to do with horse racing, I believe.

His testimonial in full read:

'Benedict Juliard is likely to have gained a creditable degree in Mathematics with Accounting, though not a brilliant one. He took very little part in student activities during his three years at University, as it seems he was exclusively interested in horses. There are no adverse reports of his character and behaviour.'

Shit, I thought. Oh, well.

Much to my astonishment, I also received a letter from Sir Vivian Durridge:

My dear Benedict,

I am delighted to have seen over the past three years that you have had the opportunity to ride successfully as an amateur on your father's horse, Sarah's Future. I am sure that he has told you he enlisted my help in making you face the fact that you were not cut out for rising to the top three in the steeplechase jockeys' list. Looking back, I see that I was unnecessarily brutal in accusing you of drug-taking, as I knew perfectly well at the time that with your sort of character you did not, but on that particular morning it seemed to me – and I regret it – that it was the only thing that would disturb you so badly that you would do as your father wanted, which was to go to university.

I have now heard from a friend of mine at Weatherbys that you have applied to them for a job. I enclose a photocopy of a letter I have written to them, and I hope that some way this may straighten things between us.

Yours sincerely,
Vivian Durridge

His enclosure read:

To whom it may concern:
Benedict Juliard rode my horses as a sixteen- and seventeen-year-old amateur jockey. I found him completely trustworthy in every respect and would give him my unqualified endorsement in any position he applied for.

I sat down, the pages shaking in my hands. Vivian Durridge was about the last person I would ever have applied to for a thumbs up.

I had vaguely been looking for a safe place to keep my birth certificate, so as not to lose it while I moved from lodgings to lodgings. I knew I wouldn't lose the marriage photographs so I decided to put my birth certificate behind my father and Polly, and as I'd been doing that when Vivian Durridge's remarkable letter arrived, I folded his pages into the frame too.

Three days later the mail brought an envelope bearing the Weatherbys logo, a miniature representation of a stallion standing under an oak tree, from a painting by George Stubbs.

I was cravenly afraid of opening it. It would begin '*We regret . . .*'

Well, it had to be faced.

I opened the envelope, and the letter began '*We are pleased . . .*'

Pleased.

That evening my father telephoned. 'Is it true you've got yourself a job at Weatherbys?'

'Yes. How do you know?'

'Why didn't you ask for my help?'

'I didn't think of it.'

'I despair of you, Ben.' He didn't, though, sound particularly annoyed.

He had been talking to one of the Weatherby cousins at a dinner in the City, he said. The web of insider chat in the City far outdid the Internet.

I asked if I could move Sarah's Future from Devon.

'Find a trainer.'

'Thanks.'

Spencer Stallworthy grumbled. Jim shrugged: life always moved on. I parted from them with gratitude and boxed my chestnut pal to a new home.

Weatherbys took me into their Racing Operations department which handled entries, runners, weights, riders, the draw: all the details of every race run in Britain, amounting to about a thousand transactions most days and up to three thousand at busy times.

All this computer speed took place in airy light expanses of desks and floor space, and in the calm quietness so impressive on my first visit. I'd thought that at a couple of days over twenty-one I might be at a disadvantage from youth, but I found at once that the whole staff were young, and enjoyed what they were doing. Within a month I couldn't imagine working anywhere else.

Every so often my own name cropped up, both whenever I was actually racing, but also in the next door department of Racing Administration that dealt with records of owners. It became a sort of running joke – 'Hey, Juliard, if you race that nag again at Fontwell, he'll suffer a 7-lb penalty,' or 'Hey, Juliard, you carried overweight at Ludlow. Cut down on the plum duff!'

Sarah's Future, as far as I could tell, enjoyed the exchange of the soft air of Devon for the brisker winds of further north. He still acknowledged my morning arrivals with much head-nodding and blow-breathing down his wide black nostrils, and he seemed to think it normal that I should embrace his neck and tell him he was a great fella, and mean it.

Anyone who says there can be true fusing of animal/

human consciousness is probably deluding themselves, but after several intimate years of speed together, that chestnut and I were probably as near to brothers as interspecies relationships could get.

One Saturday, about a year after I'd started at Weatherbys, the horse and I lined up at Towcester for an uneventful three mile 'chase, my father's inconspicuous colours of gold and grey made even less discernible by a persistent drizzle.

No one on the stands seemed afterwards to be sharply clear what happened. From my point of view we were rising cleanly in a well-judged take-off to a big black open ditch fence coming up the hill towards the straight. Another horse tripped and crashed into us, knocking Sarah's Future completely off balance. He had jumped that fence expertly several times over the past years: neither he nor I was expecting disaster. His feet were knocked sideways. He landed in a heap, throwing me off forwards. I connected with the ground in one of those crunching collisions that tells you at once that you've broken a bone without being sure *which* bone. I heard it snap. I rolled, tucking my head in to save it from the hooves of the runners behind me. The remainder of the field of half-ton horses clattered over my head as I lay winded and anxious on the slippery grass with blades of it in my mouth and up my nose, and dislodging my goggles after an uncontrollable slide.

The clamour of the contest faded away towards the

next fence. Two horses and two jockeys weren't going to be worrying about that. The horse that had crashed into Sarah's Future scrambled to its unsteady feet and trotted off as if dazed, and his unseated rider bent over me with 'Are you all right, mate?' as his best effort at an apology.

I gripped his hand to haul myself to my feet and found that the bone I'd broken was somewhere in my left shoulder.

Sarah's Future, also on his feet, was trying to walk but succeeding only in hobbling around in a circle. He couldn't put any weight on one of his forelegs. A groundsman caught him by the bridle and held him.

In hopeless love for the horse I walked over to him and tried to will it not to be true, not to be possible that after so long this closest of companionships should have so suddenly come to the edge of a precipice.

I knew, as every rider of any experience knew, that there was nothing to be done. Sarah's Future, like Sarah herself, was going to eternity in my hands.

I wept. I couldn't help it. It looked like the rain. The horse had broken his near foreleg. His jockey, his left collar-bone.

The horse died.

The jockey lived.

CHAPTER TEN

My father discontinued the insurance of Sarah's Future when I went to work for Weatherbys; partly, he'd said, because the horse was getting old and lessening in value and partly, punctiliously, so that if the horse were killed, Weatherbys would not have to pay up.

He would hear no apologies when I telephoned him. He briefly said, 'Bad luck.'

When I went back to work two days after Towcester, the man who had originally interviewed me drew up a chair at my desk and said, 'We used to insure that horse of yours, of course.'

I explained why my father had let the insurance lapse.

'I didn't come to talk to you about your loss,' the Weatherbys man said, 'though you do have all my sympathy. And is your arm all right? I came to ask you whether you would be interested in transferring yourself from here into our Insurance Services department, to work there from now on.'

The insurance department, mainly one long room

walled by books, more books and files and more files, was inhabited also by two men in their twenties. One was leaving the firm. Would I like his place?

Yes, I would.

Promotion struck the Juliards twice in one week. Another internal upheaval shuffled the cards in the government, and when the hurt feelings settled my father had moved upwards to the Cabinet as Minister of Agriculture, Fisheries and Food.

I congratulated him.

'I would have preferred Secretary of State for Defence.'

'Better luck next time,' I said flippantly.

My father's resigned sigh came down the wire. 'I suppose you've never heard of Hudson Hurst?'

'No.'

'If you think I'm going up fast, he's going up faster. He beat me to Defence. He's currently the can-do-nothing-wrong flavour-of-the-year with the Prime Minister.'

'How's Polly?' I asked.

'You're incorrigible.'

'I'm sure the jellied eels and the brontosaurus-burgers will be safe in your hands.'

There were for once no agricultural crises looming, and both he and I spent the autumn of that year rooting ourselves comfortably in new realms.

Not a great deal to my surprise, I took to insurance with energy: it not only satisfied my inclination to numbers and probabilities, but I got sent out fairly often on verification trips, to see, for instance, if the polo ponies I was asked to set a premium for actually existed.

As Evan, my co-worker and boss in the insurance department, preferred office work and computers, I did more and more of the leg work, and it seemed to be a useful arrangement all round, as I knew what good stables looked like and fast developed a nose and an instinct for the preparatory arrangements for a rip-off. Preventing insurance fraud at the planning stage became a game like chess: you could see the moves ahead and could put the knights where they would zig-zag sideways for the chop.

A great advantage, it transpired, was my youth. I might not look seventeen any more, but often at twenty-two I wasn't taken seriously enough. A mistake.

In the normal everyday honestly intentioned work of the department, Evan (twenty-nine) and I handled bona fide policies on every sort of horse and need, from the chance of infertility in a stallion to barrenness in a mare.

We also arranged cover for stable yards, all buildings, personal accident, public liability, fire, theft and measles. Anything for everyone. As agents, we kept underwriters busy.

I did abominably miss my early mornings on Sarah's Future, but as dawn grew later and colder towards winter, I would have found, as I had the previous year, that only weekends gave me much scope.

As for riding in races, I was lucky in that: the Northamptonshire trainer who'd taken the chestnut phoned me one day to say an owner of his, a farmer, wanted a free jockey – in other words, an amateur – for a runner he thought had no chance.

Why run it? I thought. I happily took the ride and plugged away, and the horse finished third. Delighted, the farmer put me up again, and although I never actually won for him, I got handed around to his friends like a box of chocolates, and cantered down to a start somewhere most Saturdays.

It wasn't the same without Sarah's Future, but I wasn't ready to try to replace him, even if I could have afforded it. One day, I thought. Perhaps. When I'd paid off the instalments on a car.

I had rationalised my liking for speed. Taking intoxicating risks was normal in growing up. Warrior genes were in-bred: it was necessary to fight the birch fences and the ski slopes, perhaps, in lieu of war.

Nearing Christmas my father said we'd been invited to a reception at No. 10 Downing Street – himself, Polly and I – for the customary jolly given by the current Prime Minister to the members of his Cabinet and their families.

Polly wore a reasonable dress and my father hired a chauffeur, and the Juliards in good formation walked through the famous front door. Staff greeted my father as one who belonged there. Polly had been through the portals before, but I couldn't help but feel awed as I trod through the crimson-walled entrance hall over the black-and-white squared floor and through into the inner hall and up the historic staircase in a river of other guests. The brilliant yellow staircase wall, going up round a central wall, was hung with portraits of all the past Prime Ministers; and I knew from the friendly way he looked at them that my father would try his best to join them, one of these days.

Never mind that there were about twenty other Cabinet ministers with the same dream, let alone all the 'shadow' ministers in the Opposition: one never got to hang on that wall without ambition.

The reception was chattering away in the large formal area upstairs known as the pillared drawing-room. (It had pillars. Two.)

We were greeted sweetly by Mrs Prime Minister – her husband was *bound* to arrive shortly – and were wafted onwards to trays of filled glasses and tiny Christmassy mince pies surrounded with holly.

I no longer asked annoyingly for diet Coke. I drank the Prime Ministerial champagne and liked it.

I knew almost no one, of course, even by sight. Polly kept me in tow for a while, though her husband had drifted away as if on wheels, greeting and laughing and making no enemies. Polly could identify all the Cabinet after eighteen months with my father, but knew none of them – as Orinda would have done – as ‘daaahling’.

The Prime Minister did arrive (he was *bound* to, after all) and my father saw to it that the great man shook Polly’s hand with warm recognition and mine with at least a show of interest.

‘You win races, don’t you?’ he asked, brow furrowed.

‘Er . . . sometimes,’ I said weakly.

He nodded. ‘Your father’s proud of you.’

I did, I suppose, look astounded. The Prime Minister, a gently rounded man with a steel handshake, gave me an ironic smile as he passed to the next group, and my father didn’t know whether or not to call him a liar.

Dearest Polly squeezed my arm. ‘George doesn’t *say* he’s proud of you. He just certainly sounds it.’

‘That makes us equal.’

‘You really are a dear boy, Benedict.’

‘And I love you too,’ I said.

My father’s attention had purposefully wandered. ‘You see that man over there?’

There were about twenty men ‘over there’.

Polly said, ‘Do you mean that one with flat white hair and circular eyes? The Home Secretary?’

‘Yes, dearest. But I meant the one he’s talking to. The one who’s looking presidential and suitable for high office. He’s Hudson Hurst.’

Polly shook her head. ‘Surely not. Hudson Hurst has

an oiled black pony-tail and one of those silly little black moustache and beard combinations that frame a man's mouth and distract you from what he's saying.'

'Not any more.' My father smiled, but not with joy. 'Someone must have persuaded Hudson Hurst that the topiary work was a political no-no. He's cut off the hair and shaved off the beard. What you see now are the unadorned petulant lips of the Defence Secretary, God help us all.'

Five minutes later my father was putting a seemingly affectionate hand on the Defence Secretary's shoulder and saying, 'My dear Hud, have you met my wife and my son?'

Love thine enemies . . .

I hated politics.

Hud had a damp cold handclasp that I supposed he couldn't help, and if he had lately had an oiled black pony-tail and a black moustache-beard mouth-circling combination, they had very likely been dyed. His present hair colour was the dark-lightly-flecked-with-grey that a passing girl-friend had told me couldn't be faked, and he'd had a cut in a swept-back and duck-tailed style straight from the films of James Bond. Distinguished. Impressive, one had to admit. It inspired trust.

My father's own mat of natural dark close curls was cut to display to advantage the handsome outline of his skull. Expert stuff. Ah, well.

Hudson Hurst was overpoweringly pleasant to Polly.

Smile and smile, I thought, remembering Hoopwestern: smile and smile and shake the hands and win the votes. He flicked me a glance, but I wasn't important.

Sweet Mrs Prime Minister appeared at my elbow and asked if I was having a good time.

'Oh, yes. Splendid, thank you.'

'You look a bit lost. Come with me.' She led me across to the far side of the big room and stopped beside a sharply dressed woman who reminded me strongly of Orinda. 'Jill, dear, this is George Juliard's son. Do look after him.'

Jill gave me a comprehensive head-to-toe and stared at Mrs Prime Minister's retreating back without enthusiasm.

'I'm really sorry,' I said, 'I don't know your name.'

'Vinicheck. Education.'

'Minister of?'

Her grim lips twitched. 'Certainly.'

She was joined by another woman in the simplest and best of current fashion: another Orinda-clone. Secretary of State for Social Security.

She said bluntly, 'Where does your mother get her clothes?'

I followed her gaze across the room and saw Polly talking unself-consciously to the man with flat white hair and circular eyes: the Home Secretary. Polly's clothes, as always, had nothing to do with popular opinion but very clearly revealed her individual character.

Jill Vinicheck (Education) kindly said, 'Your father may have a bright career in front of him, but your mother will have to change the way she dresses or she'll be clawed to bits by those bitches who write about fashion in the newspapers.'

The Secretary of State for Social Security agreed. 'Every woman in politics gets the hate treatment. Haven't you noticed?'

'Oh, not really, no.'

'Your mother's skirt is the wrong length. You don't mind me telling you? I'm only being helpful. Frankly, it would be the wrong length whatever length it was, according to the fashion bitches. But you can pass on some tips to her from us, if you like.'

'Er . . .'

'Tell her,' Jill Vinicheck said, enjoying herself, 'never to buy clothes in shops.'

Social Security nodded. 'She must have them made.'

Jill Vinicheck: 'Always wool or silk or cotton. Never polyester, or tight.'

'There's a marvellous man who could make your mother really elegant, with her long thin figure. He totally changed the way the papers write about us now. They discuss our policies, not our clothes. And he doesn't do it only for women. Look at the change in Hudson Hurst! Hud frankly looked a bit of a gangster, but now he's a statesman.'

'No time like the present,' Jill Vinicheck said with the briskness that had no doubt propelled her up the ladder. 'Our wand-waving friend is here somewhere. Why don't we introduce him to your mother straight away?'

'Er . . .' I said. 'I don't think she – '

'Oh, *there* he is,' said Social Security, stepping sideways and pouncing. 'Let me introduce you . . .'

She had her hand on his arm and he turned towards her, and I came face to face with A.L. Wyvern.

Alderney Anonymous Lover Wyvern.

No wonder Education and Social Security had reminded me of Orinda. All those years ago his ideas had dressed her, too.

I knew him instantly, but it took him several seconds to add four years to my earlier appearance. Then his face hardened to ill-will and he looked disconcerted, even though with my father in the Cabinet he might have considered that he and I might both be asked to the families' Christmas reception. Maybe he hadn't given it a thought. In any case, my presence there was to him an unwelcome surprise.

So was his to me.

Education and Social Security were looking puzzled.

'Do you two know each other?' one of them asked.

'We've met,' Wyvern said shortly.

His own appearance, too, had changed. At Hoopwestern he had made a point of looking inconspicuous, of being easily forgettable. Four years later he wasn't finding it so simple to fade into the wallpaper.

I had thought him then to be less than forty, but I now saw that to have been probably an underestimate. His skin had begun to show a few wrinkles and his hair to recede, and he was now wearing glasses with narrow dark frames. There was still about him, though, the strong secretive aura of introverted clout.

At the Downing Street Christmas party there was no overt sign of the sleeping anger that had blazed across Orinda's face and nearly killed her. He was not this time saying to me aloud in fury, 'One day I'll get you,' but I could see the intent rise again in his narrowed eyes as if no interval for second thoughts had existed.

The extraordinary response I felt was not fear but excitement. The adrenalin rush in my blood was for fight, not flight. And whether or not he saw my reaction to him as vividly as I felt it, he pulled down the shutters on the malice visible behind the dark-framed lenses and excused himself with the briefest of courtesies to Education and Social Security: when he moved slowly away it was as if every step were consciously controlled.

'Well!' exclaimed Jill Vinicheck. 'I know he's never talkative, but I'm afraid he was . . . impolite.'

Not impolite, I thought.

Murderous.

*

After the reception Polly, my father and I all ate in one of the few good restaurants in London that had taken the din out of dinner. One could mostly hear oneself speak.

My father had enjoyed a buddy-buddy session with the Prime Minister and Polly said she thought the circular eyes of the Home Secretary were not after all an indication of mania.

Didn't the Home Secretary, I asked, keep prisoners *in* and chuck illegal immigrants *out*?

More or less, my father agreed.

I said, 'Did you know there was a list on a sort of easel there detailing all the jobs in government?'

My father, ministerially busy with broccoli that he didn't actually like, nodded, but Polly said she hadn't seen it.

'There are weird jobs,' I said, 'like Minister for Former Countries and Under Secretary for Buses.' Polly looked mystified but my father nodded. 'Every Prime Minister invents titles to describe what he wants done.'

'So,' I said, 'theoretically you could have a minister in charge of banning yellow plastic ducks.'

'You do talk nonsense, Benedict dear,' Polly said.

'What he means,' my father said, 'is that the quickest way to make people want something is to ban it. People always fight to get what they are told they cannot have.'

'All the same,' I said mildly, 'I think the Prime

Minister should introduce a law banning Alderney Wyvern from drinking champagne at No. 10 Downing Street.'

Polly and my father sat with their mouths open.

'He was there,' I said. 'Didn't you see him?'

They shook their heads.

'He kept over the far side of the room, out of your way. He looks a bit different. He's older, balder. He wears spectacles. But he is revered by the Minister of Education, the Secretary of State for Social Security and the Secretary of State for Defence, to name those I am sure of. Orinda and Dennis Nagle were kindergarten stuff. Alderney Wyvern now has his hands on levers he can pull to affect whole sections of the nation.'

'I don't believe it,' my father said.

'The dear ladies of Education and Social Security told me they had a friend who would do wonders for my . . . er, mother's wardrobe. He had already, they said, turned Hudson Hurst from a quasi mobster into a polished gent. What do you think they give Alderney in return?'

'No,' my father said. 'Not classified information. They couldn't!'

He was scandalised. I shook my head.

'What then?' Polly asked. 'What do they give him?'

'I'd guess,' I said, 'that they give him attention. I'd guess they listen to him and act on his advice. Orinda said years ago that he had a terrific understanding of what would happen in politics. He would predict things and tell Dennis Nagle what to do about them and Orinda said he was nearly always right. Dennis Nagle had his feet on the upward path, and if he hadn't died I'd think he'd be in the Cabinet by now with Wyvern at his shoulder.'

My father pushed his broccoli aside. A good thing his broccoli farmers weren't watching. They were agitating for a broccoli awareness week to make the British eat their greens. A law to ban excess broccoli would have had healthier results.

'If he's so clever,' Polly asked, 'why isn't he in the Cabinet himself?'

'Orinda told me the sort of power Alderney really wants is to be able to pull the levers behind the scenes. I thought it a crazy idea. I've grown up since then.'

'Power without responsibility,' my father murmured.

'Allied,' I said ruefully, 'to a frighteningly violent temper which explodes when he's crossed.'

My father hadn't actually seen Wyvern hit Orinda. He hadn't seen the speed and the force and the heartlessness; but he had seen the blood and tears and they alone had driven him to try to retaliate. Wyvern had wanted to damage my father's reputation by provoking my father to hit him. I dimly understood, but still hadn't properly worked it out, that attacking Wyvern would, in the end, destroy the attacker.

My boss Evan agreeing, I'd tied in the No. 10 Thursday evening reception with a Friday morning trip to meet a claims inspector to see if a haybarn had burned by accident or design (accident) and was due to stay again on Friday night in London with Polly and my father, before going to ride at Stratford-upon-Avon on Saturday, but en route I got a message to return to meet my father in Downing Street by two that Friday afternoon.

'I thought you might like to see more of the house,' he said cheerfully. 'You can't see a thing at those receptions.'

He had arranged for one of the household staff – called a messenger – to accompany us and show us round officially, so we went up the yellow staircase again, spending longer over the pictures, and wandered round the three large drawing-rooms leading off the ante-room at the top of the stairs: the white drawing-room, the green drawing-room and the pillared drawing-room where they'd held the reception.

The messenger was proud of the house which he said looked better and was better looked after than at any time in its rickety history. It had once been two houses back to back (rather like the burnt shops of Hoopwestern): the small Downing Street house facing one way, and a mansion to the rear of it facing the other. The interior layout over two and a half centuries had been constantly redesigned, and a modern refurbishment had bestowed overall an eighteenth-century ambience that hadn't been there before.

'The green drawing-room used to be the blue

drawing-room,' the messenger said happily. 'All the beautiful plaster work on nearly all the ceilings is relatively new. So are the classical mantels over the doorways. It all looks now like it always should have done, and never did.'

We admired it all copiously, to his satisfaction.

'Through here,' he said, marching off into one corner of the pillared drawing-room, 'is the small dining-room.' (It seated twelve in comfort.) 'Beyond that is the State Dining-Room.' (Dark panelled walls, seats for twenty-four.)

He told us about all the paintings in every room. I thought of all the past prime ministers for whom this graceful splendour had not existed, who had used this building as an office. It seemed a shame and a waste, somehow.

Back in the ante-room to the drawing-rooms our guide told us, pointing, 'Up those stairs is the Prime Minister's private apartment, and behind that locked door is his own personal room where no one goes unless he invites them. And downstairs . . .' he led the way expertly, via a lift to the ground floor ' . . . along this passage, as of course you know well, sir, is the ante-room to the Cabinet Room itself, sir, and I'll leave you to show those yourself to your son, sir, and I'll see you again just on your way out.'

My father thanked him sincerely for his trouble, and I reflected, slightly overwhelmed, that I'd never before given much of a thought to the living legacy of history my father hoped to inhabit.

The ante-room was any ante-room: just a gathering place, but with brilliant red walls.

The Cabinet Room, at the rear of the old mansion section, was long, with tall windows down one side and across one end, facing out into a peaceful-looking walled garden.

Irish terrorists had lobbed a bomb into that garden while all the Cabinet ministers were in the building. The bomb had done little damage. The grass now looked undisturbed. Peace was relative. Guy Fawkes could rise again.

Extraordinarily, Sir Thomas Knyvet, the magistrate who arrested Guy Fawkes red-handed with his barrels of gun-powder, lived in a house on the exact spot where the developer George Downing later built No. 10.

'This is where I usually sit,' my father said, walking down the room and coming to rest behind one of the two dozen chairs. 'That chair with arms, halfway along the table, that is the Prime Minister's chair. It's the only one with arms.'

The long table down the centre of the room wasn't rectangular but a much elongated oval, in order, my father explained, for the Prime Minister to be able to see the various members more easily.

'Go on, then,' I teased him. 'Take the arms.'

He was half embarrassed, half shy, but he couldn't

resist it. There was only his son to see. He crabbed sideways round the table and sat in the chair with arms; he nestled into it, resting his wrists, living the dream.

Above and behind him on the wall hung the only picture in that room, a portrait of Sir Robert Walpole, the first to be given the title Prime Minister.

'It all suits you,' I said.

He stood up self-consciously and said, as if to take the emotion out of the moment, 'The chair opposite the Prime Minister is normally where the Chancellor of the Exchequer sits.'

'And how many of you put your feet up on the table?'

He gave me a disgusted look. 'You're not fit to be taken anywhere.'

We returned to the front hall, my father looking at his watch. The messenger appeared as if on cue to see us off the premises, and I wondered vaguely if there were interior monitoring video cameras – which would be merely normally prudent – to trace the comings and goings of visitors.

While we said lengthy farewells the front door opened and in walked the Prime Minister, followed by two alert young men: bodyguards.

The Prime Minister said, 'Hello, George,' without surprise and glanced at his own watch revealingly. 'Come this way. And you . . . er . . .'

My father said, 'Ben.'

'Ben, yes. The racerider. You come too.'

He led the way through the front hall and past the staircase into a crowded and busy office crammed with desks, office paraphernalia and people, who all stood up at his approach.

'Now, Ben, you stay here with these good people while I talk to your father.'

He went through the office, opened a door and gestured to my father to follow. The office staff gave me a chair and a friendly welcome and told me that I was in the room where all the real work got done; the running of the Prime Minister's life as opposed to his politics.

They told me that quiet though the house might seem on a Friday afternoon, almost two hundred people worked there in the buildings in connected offices and that someone had once counted how many times the front door of No. 10 had been opened and closed in twenty-four hours, and it was more than nine hundred.

At length, in response to one of the constant telephone calls, I was invited through the office and into the next room in the wake of my father, and found myself in a large quiet tidy place that was part office, part sitting-room.

My father and the Prime Minister sat in the two fattest armchairs, looking relaxed, and I was waved to join them.

'Your father and I,' the Prime Minister said, 'have

been discussing Alderney Wyvern. I've met him once or twice, but I've seen no harm in him. I know that Jill Vinicheck and other women in the Cabinet say they owe him a great deal, and Hudson Hurst, above all, has benefited from a change of presentation. I've seen nothing sinister or unacceptable in any of this. The man is quiet, tactful, and as far as I can see, he hasn't put a foot wrong politically. Jill Vinicheck, in particular, has once or twice found his considered advice helpful, and certainly the Press have stopped making frivolous comments on her clothes, and take her as the serious politician that she is.'

'Er . . .' I said. 'Yes, sir.'

'Your father says that he and you have seen a different side of Alderney Wyvern. A violent side. He says you believe this capacity for violence still exists. I have to tell you that I find this hard to believe, and until I see something of it myself I have to give Wyvern the benefit of the doubt. I am sure you have both acted with the best of intentions in drawing my attention to the influence Wyvern may have with my ministers but, George, if you'll excuse my saying so, your son is a very young man without much experience of the world, and he may be exaggerating trouble where little exists.'

My father looked non-committal. I wondered what the Prime Minister would have thought if he himself had seen Wyvern hit Orinda. Nothing less, it seemed, was going to convince him that the outer shell of the man he'd met hid a totally different creature inside, rather like a beautiful spiky and shiny conch-shell hiding the slippery slug-like mollusc inside, a gastropod inching along on its stomach.

The Prime Minister said, 'I will take note and remember what you have both said, but at the moment I don't see any real grounds for action.'

He stood up, indicating that the meeting was over, and shook hands with my father with unabated good nature; and I remembered my father's teaching on the very first day when I'd driven with him from Brighton to Hoopwestern, that people only believe what they want to believe. It applied, it seemed, even to prime ministers.

After we'd left No. 10 I said glumly to my father, 'I did you no good.'

'He had to be told. He had to be warned. Even if it does my career no good, it was the right thing to do.'

My father's strict sense of right and wrong might destroy him yet, I thought.

CHAPTER ELEVEN

After Christmas that year several things happened that changed a lot of lives.

First of all, on New Year's Eve, a wide tongue of freezing air licked down from the Arctic Circle and froze solid all of Canada, all of northern Europe, and all of the British Isles. Weathermen stopped agitating about global warming and with equally long faces discussed permafrost. No one seemed to mention that when Stonehenge was built in around 3000 B.C. the prevailing climate was warm, and no one remembered that, in the nineteenth century, Britain was so cold in the winters that on the Thames in London, they skated, held fairs and roasted oxen.

In the houses of that time people huddled in wing chairs with their feet on footstools to avoid draughts, and women wore a dozen layers of petticoats.

In the winter when I was twenty-two it rained ice on top of snow. People skated on their lawns and built igloos for their children. Diesel oil congealed to jelly. All racing came to a halt, except on a few specially built all-weather tracks, but even they had to be swept clear of snow. Owners cursed as their training bills kept rolling in, professional jockeys bit their fingernails and amateurs were grounded.

Claims for frost damage avalanched into Weatherbys, and in the middle of all this Evan, my boss, announced that he was leaving the firm to join a growing insurance company as managing director. I expected Weatherbys to replace him, over my head, but instead they told him to spend his three months' notice teaching me his job. I thought I was too young, even by Weatherbys' standards, but they seemed oblivious to my date of birth and merely told me that in following Evan I had a great deal to live up to.

Evan, tall, thin and with a bird-like head on a long neck, had taken over a department that had formerly acted mainly as a convenience for racing's owners and trainers, and in five years had fertilised it with imagination and invention into an agency major by any standard.

In his last three months, in addition to our ordinary busy work, he took me to meet personally all the underwriters he fixed deals with on the telephone, so that in the end I could wander round the 'boxes' at Lloyds knowing and being known in the syndicates and speaking their language.

He taught me scams. 'Beware the friendship scam,' he said.

'What's that?'

'Two friends conspire,' he told me, amused. 'One friend has a horse with something fatally wrong, a kidney ailment, say. OK? Instead of calling in a vet, Friend A sends his sick fellow to the sales. Friend B buys the sick animal at auction, insuring his purchase onwards from the fall of the hammer. Fall-of-the-hammer insurance was introduced to cover accidents like a million-pound colt stumbling on its way out of the sale ring and breaking a leg. Fall-of-the-hammer insurance comes into effect *before* a vet's inspection, see? So Friend B buys and insures a dud horse from the fall-of-the-hammer. Friend A acts all innocent . . . "would never have sold such a horse if I'd known . . ." Friend B humanely kills his dud and collects the insurance. Friends A and B split the proceeds.' He laughed. 'You've a nose for crooks, Ben. You'll do all right.'

During that same three months my father became the front man in an ongoing fish war, discussing at international high level who could take how many fish of such and such a species of such and such a size out of any particular area of the world's oceans. With wit and understanding, and by going to sea himself in freezing salt-crusted net-festooned seasickness factories, he learned the gripes and the legitimate arguments of men who lived close to Davy Jones and his ever-ready locker.

The Press took notice. Headlines appeared: 'JULIARD HOOKS AGREEMENT' and 'JULIARD IN JAPAN'.

People in insurance began to say, 'This Juliard person – no relation of yours, I suppose?'

'My father.'

'Seems to be doing a good job for my fish and chips.'

Fish and chips – the potatoes in agriculture – put my father on the map.

A television station sent a cameraman to sea with him: the cameraman, though sick the whole time, shot fearsomely memorable footage of my father hanging half-overboard in oilskins above the breaking waves and *grinning.*

Schoolchildren recognised pictures of 'the Fish Minister' instantly: his Cabinet colleagues didn't like it.

One of the top tabloids dug up the five-year-old stunning photograph of my father in mid-jump from the burning constituency office and printed it big in a centre-page spread extolling virility and presence of mind and the 'hands-on' policy out on the deep blue sea.

Even the Prime Minister didn't much like *that.* George Juliard as a relative newcomer with a normally quiet department in his charge was fine. George Juliard on the fast track upwards in public acclaim was a threat.

'One mustn't make a Minister a *cult,*' the Prime Minister said in a television interview: but others talked of 'leadership qualities' and 'getting things done', and Polly advised Dearest George to damp it down a bit and not let his success antagonise his colleagues.

My father therefore paid lavish tribute to the army of civil servants behind his fish-war solutions. 'Without their help . . .' and so on and so on. He did a lot of modest grovelling in Cabinet.

Towards the end of the long winter freeze the racing papers – frantic for something to fill their pages after weeks of near stagnation – gave a lot of space to the news that Sir Vivian Durridge, at seventy-four, had decided to retire from training.

The article, full of sonorous clichés like 'long and distinguished career', detailed his winners of the Derby (four) and other great races ('too numerous to mention') and listed both the chief owners he'd trained for ('royalty downwards') and the chief jockeys he'd employed ('champions all').

Tucked away near the end came the riveting information that, according to the form book, 'Benedict Juliard had, for two years, ridden the Durridge horses as an amateur.'

'*Benedict Juliard, as everyone in racing knows, is the son of George Juliard, charismatic Minister of Agriculture, Fisheries and Food. Ben Juliard won three races on horses trained by Sir Vivian, and then left.*'

End of Vivian Durridge. *A happy retirement, Sir Vivian.*

It seemed the freezing temperatures had put a brake even on adultery. Usher Rudd, still active with his telephoto-lens and his mean spirit, had hit a dry patch in his relentless pursuit of the unfortunate Opposition front-bencher, whose progress from bimbo to spanked bimbo (with the odd choir-boy for variety) had either temporarily ceased or he had gone into hiding.

Usher Rudd, sacked by the *Hoopwestern Gazette* as a sleaze generator and definitely now *non grata* under many flags, had all the same as a freelance found a market in weekly sex magazines on the edge of perversion.

The motto he everlastingly lived by: SLEAZE SELLS.

And where it doesn't exist, invent it.

The Opposition front-bencher killed himself.

Shock reverberated through Parliament, and shivered in many a conscience.

He had been the Shadow Chancellor, the one who would have written the country's budget if his party had been in power. Rudd, for all his digging, had found no cent out of place.

Leader writers, hands raised in semi-mock horror, pointed out that though adultery (like suicide) might be a sin, it was not, under British law, a crime. Hounding a man to despair – was that a sin? Was that a crime?

Usher Rudd, smirking and unrepentant, repeated his credo again and again: if people in the public eye chose to behave disgustingly in private, the public had a right to know.

Did they? What was disgusting? Who should judge? Chat shows discussed it endlessly.

Usher Rudd was either 'the watchdog of the people', or a dangerous voyeur.

My father, walking with me in the woods round Polly's house, believed Usher Rudd would now be looking for another target.

'Until he's safely locked on to some other poor bastard,' he said. 'Just you remember how he listened to us in the Sleeping Dragon, so be very careful. He had a go at us then, and we got him sacked.'

'Yes, but,' I said, 'I'm certain you've stuck to what you wrote that day in those pacts: "That you would do nothing shameful or unlawful and would cause no scandal." Usher Rudd can't therefore touch you.'

He smiled. 'Those pacts! Yes, I've kept my bargain. But a small thing like innocence wouldn't stop that red-haired shit. Have you found your side of the promise difficult to keep?'

I shook my head. 'I've kept it.'

It was undoubtedly true, though, that the pact I'd written myself had shaped and inhibited what one might call my sex life. More accurately, my lack of sex life. I'd had two brief but pretty satisfactory interludes, one at university, one in racing, but both times I'd drawn back from any deep involvement. As for promiscuity – Usher Rudd had proved a bigger threat than AIDS.

When the sun at last shone warmingly on the house

in outer Wellingborough where I lived in a 'granny flat' built for a dear-departed granny, the ceilings first drizzled rain from burst pipes in the attic and then fell down completely. As major replastering was obviously required, I packed my stuff again in nomadic boxes and drove them to the office, storing them in the leg-room under my desk.

Evan was stripping the office of the clutter of his five-year tenure. Pin-ups, long lusted over, disappeared. He arranged a thousand files in easy order and gave me an index. He bequeathed me three straggly green plants suffering from sunlight deficiency.

'I can't manage without you,' I said.

'You can always phone me.' His bird-like head inspected his non-personalised end of the room. 'You won't, though. You'll make your own decisions. If anyone thought you couldn't, you wouldn't be taking my place.'

He left in a flurry of farewell beers, and I spent the whole summer at first tiptoeing and then striding into new responsibilities, and in six swift months shed the last remnants of boy and grew in confidence and perhaps in ability until I had settled into the person I would be for the rest of my life.

When I mentioned how I felt to Polly, she said the change was obvious and that I was lucky: some people weren't sure who they were till the far side of thirty.

My father, who'd known who he was at nineteen, had during the early summer consolidated himself in the Cabinet, and by conscientious work had converted his colleagues' jealousy into acceptance, if not admiration. George Juliard had arrived as a political fact.

I asked him about Alderney Wyvern.

My father frowned. 'I haven't seen Wyvern anywhere since Christmas, but he's somewhere about – though the Prime Minister still won't hear a word against him. I'd say both Hudson Hurst and Jill Vinicheck are voting to his tune. They're both apt to say on one day that they haven't made up their minds on a point of discussion, but a couple of days later their minds and opinions are firm, and they always agree with each other . . . and I think those opinions are Wyvern's, though I've no way of proving it.'

'And are they good opinions?'

'Sometimes *very* good, but that's not the point.'

Parliament went into summer recess. Polly and the member for Hoopwestern spent the first part of the break in the constituency, living in Polly's house and working with Mervyn and Orinda. The four of them had settled into an energetic and harmonious team to the great benefit of all the voters, floating or not.

My father then took Polly round the world with stopovers in capital cities to learn about famine and fertilisers and freaks of climate, and came back with a fair understanding of how a billion people fed themselves on the blue planet.

I, in my little world at Wellingborough, computed numbers and risks and moved back into my granny flat when the new ceilings were dry.

Usher Rudd began stalking a bishop. Everyone except His Reverence sighed with relief.

I rode a winner in August and another in September.

Beneath this surface, although none of us knew it, little upheavals were growing and coalescing like cumulonimbus. My father had once said that they always killed Caesar, and when Parliament reconvened the knives were ready to drive into the toga.

My father, worried, told Polly and me that Hudson Hurst intended to challenge the Prime Minister for the leadership of the party. Hudson Hurst was cosying up to each Cabinet member in turn to ask for support. With his now polished manner he was smoothly saying that the party needed a tougher, younger leader who would galvanise the nation to prepare for the big build-up towards the next General Election, three years ahead.

'Alderney Wyvern,' I said, 'is writing the script.'

Polly said, horrified, 'He couldn't.'

My father said, 'It's been Wyvern's aim all along to rule by stealth.'

'Then stop him!' Polly exclaimed.

But Hudson Hurst resigned from the Cabinet and announced to the world that a majority of the party in power was dissatisfied with the decisions being made in its name and that he could do better.

'Stop him,' Polly said again. 'Oppose him.'

The three of us, sitting round the kitchen table in Polly's house, were silenced by the suddenness and size of the task. Sure, my father had aimed if possible one day to be Prime Minister, but had thought of acceding peacefully after a resignation, not of being a contender for the Ides of March.

My father, considering loyalty to be a paramount virtue, went to Downing Street and declared himself the Prime Minister's man. The Prime Minister, however, seeing that the party wanted a change, decided it was time to go just as soon as a new leader was elected. The way was now clear for my father to declare himself as a candidate for the ultimate job. The battle was now joined.

On a harmless-looking Tuesday morning in October I went into Weatherbys as usual and found that no one would look at me. Puzzled but unalarmed I made my way into my office and found that someone had kindly – or unkindly – left on my desk a copy of *SHOUT!* open at the centre pages.

SHOUT! was the weekly magazine that regularly printed Usher Rudd's most virulent outbursts.

There was a photograph, not of my father, but of myself, dressed as a jockey.

The headline in huge letters read, 'DOPE!'

Underneath it said: '*Jockey son of George Juliard, self-aggrandising Minister of Agriculture, Fisheries and Food, was fired for snorting cocaine, says trainer.*'

In disbelief I read the trailing paragraphs.

'*I had to get rid of him,' says Sir Vivian Durridge. 'I could not have a glue-sniffing, drug-taking bad apple, infecting my good stable's reputation. The boy is no good. I am sorry for his father.*'

His father, the magazine pointed out, had entered the ring in the power struggle currently rending apart the Party. How could George Juliard proclaim himself a paragon of all the virtues (including family values) when he had failed as a parent himself, as his only child was a drug addict?

I felt as I had in Vivian Durridge's study on that morning five years earlier; numb from the ankles down. It hadn't been true that I had ever sniffed glue or cocaine or anything else, and it still wasn't true, but I wasn't fool enough now to think that everyone would believe me.

I picked up the magazine and, with eyes speculatively following every step I took, went to see the chairman, the working boss of Weatherbys, in his office. He sat at his desk. I stood before him.

I needn't have taken the magazine with me. He had a copy of it already on his desk.

'It's not true,' I said flatly.

'If it's not true,' the chairman asked, 'why on earth

would Vivian Durridge say it is? Vivian Durridge is one of the most highly respected men in racing.'

'If you'll give me the day off, I'll go and ask him.'

He stared up at me, considering.

'I think,' I said, 'that this is an attack on my father more than on myself. This article was written by a journalist called Usher Rudd who tried to discredit my father once before, in fact five years ago, when he first stood for Parliament in a by-election. My father complained to the editor of the newspaper and Usher Rudd was sacked. This looks like revenge. You'll see that this article says my father is involved in a power struggle in the party and, well, he is. Whoever wins the struggle will be the next Prime Minister. Usher Rudd is determined it won't be George Juliard.'

The chairman still said nothing.

'When I applied here for a job,' I said, 'Sir Vivian sent you a reference about me, and, oh' – I remembered in a blinding flash of joy – 'he sent me a letter, which I'll show you . . .' I turned towards the door. 'It is actually here in this building, in the insurance office.'

I didn't wait for him to comment but hurried back to the long insurance office and retrieved the cardboard box full of my stuff from under my desk. I simply hadn't bothered to take it back to my reconstructed room and clutter the place up again with bits and pieces. Somewhere in that box were my father's wedding photos with wives one and two.

In the frame behind the picture of himself and Polly

the letter from Vivian Durridge was as clean and fresh as the day I received it.

As a precaution, I made several copies of the letter and put them in one file among hundreds, and took the original to the chairman.

He had already, fair man that he was, retrieved from his records the short 'To whom it may concern' reference that Sir Vivian had spontaneously sent. It was lying on his desk on top of the magazine.

I handed him the letter, which he read twice.

'Sit down,' he said, pointing to the chair opposite his desk. 'Tell me what happened the day Sir Vivian Durridge accused you of taking drugs.'

'Five years ago' – it seemed a lifetime – 'like it says in the letter, my father wanted to make me face the reality that I would never be a top jockey.'

I told the chairman about the car and the chauffeur, and the hotel in Brighton facing the sea. I told him that my father had asked me to give him family background to help with his by-election campaign.

The chairman listened and at the end asked, 'Who, besides you and your father, knew that Vivian Durridge had accused you of drug taking?'

'That's just it,' I said slowly. 'I certainly told no one, and I don't think my father did either. Will you let me go and find out?'

He looked at the letter again, and at the reference and at the magazine article with its malice and lies, and made up his mind.

'I'll give you a week,' he said. 'Ten days. Whatever it takes. Before you came, Evan was second in command to an insurance specialist who is now on our board of directors. He will do your job until you come back.'

I was grateful and speechless in the face of his generosity. He merely waved me away with a gesture towards the door and, looking back as I left, I saw him slide the magazine, the letter and the reference into a drawer in his desk and lock it.

Back in my own office the telephone was ringing. My father's voice said, 'What the hell's going on? What does Vivian Durridge think he's doing? I can't get any answer from his telephone.'

The reason he couldn't get any answer from Vivian Durridge's telephone, I discovered three hours later, was because he was not in his own home.

The gravel in the drive was tidily raked. The porticoed front of the near-mansion spoke as usual of effortless wealth, but no one answered the doorbell.

Along in his stable yard there were no horses, but the head lad, who lived in an adjoining cottage, was pottering aimlessly about.

He recognised me without hesitation, though it was over five years since I'd left.

'Well, Ben,' he said, scratching his head, 'I never knew you took drugs.'

He was old and small and bandy-legged and had loved and been loved by the great beasts in his care.

The life he'd lived in their service had pathetically gone, leaving him without anchor, without purpose, with only a fading mental scrap-book of victories past.

'I never did take drugs,' I said.

'No, I wouldn't have thought so, but if Sir Vivian says . . .'

'Where is he?' I asked. 'Do you know?'

'He's ill, of course.'

'Ill?'

'He's gone in the wits, poor old man. He was walking round the yard with me one day at evening stables, same as usual, when all of a sudden he clapped a hand to his head and fell down, and I got the vet to him – '

'The *vet*?'

'There's a telephone in the tack-room and I knew the vet's number.' The head lad shook his own old head. 'So, anyway, the vet came and he brought with him the doctor and they thought Sir Vivian had had a stroke or some such. So an ambulance came for him, and his family, they didn't want us to say he was ga-ga, but he couldn't go on training, poor old man, so they just told everybody he'd retired.'

I wandered round the yard with the once supreme head lad, stopping at each empty box for him to tell me what splendid winners had once stood in each.

All the owners, he said, had been asked to take their horses away and send them somewhere else temporarily, but the weeks had passed and the old man wasn't coming back; one could see that now, and nothing was ever going to be the same again.

'But where,' I asked gently, 'is Sir Vivian at this moment?'

'In the nursing home,' he simply said.

I found the nursing home. A board outside announced 'Haven House'. Sir Vivian sat in a wheelchair, smooth of skin, empty of eye, warmed by a rug over his knees.

'He's confused. He doesn't know anyone,' the nurses warned me; but even if he didn't recognise me, he garrulously talked.

'Oh dear, yes,' he said in a high voice, not like his own gruff tones. 'Of course, I remember Benedict Juliard. He wanted to be a jockey, but I couldn't have him, you know! I couldn't have anyone who sniffed glue.'

Sir Vivian's eyes were wide and guileless. I saw that he now did believe in the fiction he had invented for my father's sake. I understood that from now on he would repeat that version of my leaving him because he truly believed it.

I asked him, 'Did you yourself ever actually see Benedict Juliard sniffing glue, or cocaine, or anything else?'

'Had it on good authority,' he said.

Five years too late I asked him, 'Whose authority?'

'Eh? What? Whose authority? Mine, of course.'

I tried again. 'Did anyone tell you that Benedict

Juliard was addicted to drugs? If anyone told you, who was it?'

The intelligence that had once inhabited the Durridge brain, the worldly experience that had illuminated for so long the racing scene, the grandeur of thought and judgment, all had been wiped out by a devastating haemorrhage in some tiny recess of that splendid personality. Sir Vivian Durridge no longer existed. I spoke to the shell, the chaos. There was no hope that he would ever again remember anything in detail, but he would be for ever open to suggestion.

I sat with him for a while, as it seemed he liked company and, even if he didn't know who I was, he didn't want me to go.

The nurses said, 'It settles him to have people near him. He was a great man once, you know. And you're the second person, outside his family, who has been to see him recently. He is so pleased to have visitors.'

'Who else came?' I asked.

'Such a nice young man. Red hair. Freckles. So friendly, just like you. A journalist, he said. He was asking Sir Vivian about someone called Benedict Juliard, who had ridden his horses for him once. Oh, my goodness – ' the nurses said, clapping hands to surprised mouths. 'Benedict Juliard . . . isn't that who you said you were?'

'That's right. What would Sir Vivian like that he hasn't got?'

The nurses giggled and said, 'Chocolate biscuits and gin, but he isn't supposed to have either.'

'Give him both.'

I handed them money. Vivian Durridge sat in his wheelchair and understood nothing.

I telephoned my father.

'People believe what they want to believe,' I said. 'Hudson Hurst will want to believe your son is a drug addict and he'll go around asserting to your colleagues that that makes you unfit to be Prime Minister. Well, you remember what I wrote that day when we made the pacts . . . that I would do my best to keep you safe from attack?'

'Of course I remember.'

'It's time to do it.'

'But Ben . . . how?'

'I'm going to sue him for libel.'

'Who? Hurst? Usher Rudd? Vivian Durridge?'

'No. The Editor of *SHOUT!*'

After a pause my father said, 'You need a lawyer.'

'Lawyers are expensive. I'll see what I can do myself.'

'Ben, I don't like it.'

'Nor do I. But if I can make a charge of libel stick to *SHOUT!*, Hudson Hurst will have to shut up. And there's no time to lose, is there, as didn't you say the first round of voting for the new leader is next week?'

'It is, yes. Monday.'

'Then you go back to your fish and chips, and I'll take a sword to Usher bleeding Rudd.'

From Durridge's place in Kent I drove across much of southern England to Exeter and round to the training stables that to me seemed like home, the domain of Spencer Stallworthy.

I arrived at about six-thirty, when he was just finishing his round of evening stables.

'Hello,' he said, surprised. 'I didn't know you were coming.'

'No . . .' I watched him feed carrots to the last couple of horses and wandered over to look into the box that had held Sarah's Future for three splendid years. It was inhabited now by a long-necked grey, and I grieved for the simple happiness of days gone.

Jim was still there, closing the boxes for the night, checking that the lads had filled the hay nets and positioned the water buckets: all so familiar, so much missed.

The evening routine finished, I asked if I could talk to them both for a while, which meant a short drive to Stallworthy's house and an issue of well-remembered sherry.

They knew my father was in the Cabinet and I explained about the power struggle. I showed them the centre pages of *SHOUT!*, which shocked them back to the bottle.

Jim blinked his white eyelashes rapidly, always a sign of disturbance, and Stallworthy said, 'But it's not true, is it? You never took drugs. I'd have known it.'

'That's right,' I said gratefully, 'and that's what I'd like you to write for me. A statement that I rode from your stables for three years and won races and showed no sign of ever being interested in drugs. I want as many affidavits as I can get to say that I am not a drug addict and never was as far as you can possibly tell. I'm going to sue this magazine for libel.'

Both Stallworthy and Jim were outraged on my behalf and wrote more fiercely in my defence than I could have asked for.

Stallworthy gave me a bed for the night and a horse to ride in the early morning, and I left after breakfast and drove along the familiar country roads back to the university.

The two years since I'd graduated seemed to vanish. I parked the car in the road outside the Streatham Campus and walked up the steep path to the Laver Building, home of the mathematics department. There, after a good deal of casting about, I found my tutor – the one who had written for me the reference sought by Weatherbys – and explained to him, as to Stallworthy and Jim, what I was asking of him.

'*Drugs*? Of course, a lot of the students experiment and, as you know, we try to get rid of the hard core, but you were about the last student I would have suspected of getting hooked. For a start, drugs and mathematics don't mix, and your work was particularly clear-headed. This magazine article is all rubbish.'

I beseeched him to put those views in writing, which he did with emphasis.

'Good luck,' he said when I left. 'These journalists get away with murder.'

I hiked back to my car and drove across country to my old school at Malvern.

There on its hillside campus, steep like Exeter University, though not so big, I sought out the man who had taught me mathematics. He passed the buck to my one-time house-master, who listened and sent me to the Head.

The Headmaster walked with me down the broad familiar stone-floored passage in the Main Building and up the stone stairs to his study, where I showed him a copy of *SHOUT!* and also a copy of Vivian Durridge's letter.

'Of course I'll support you,' he said without hesitation and wrote, and handed me the handwritten page to read.

It said:

Benedict Juliard attended Malvern College for five years. During the last two, while he was successfully working towards his A levels and university entrance, he spent all breaks either riding racehorses

– he won three steeplechases – or skiing, in which sport he won a European under-18 downhill race.

In addition to those skills he was a considerable marksman with a rifle: he shot in the school team that won the prestigious Ashburton Shield.

In all these activities he showed clear-headedness, natural courage and a high degree of concentration. It is ludicrous to suggest that he was ever under the influence of hallucinatory drugs.

I looked up, not knowing quite what to say.

'I admire your father,' the Headmaster said. 'I'm not saying I agree with him all the time politically, but the country could certainly do worse.'

I said, 'Thank you,' rather feebly, and he shook hands with me on a smile.

Onwards I went to Wellingborough where I briefly called in to see the chairman to tell him what I'd been doing and what I proposed to do. Then, taking a couple of the photocopies of Vivian Durridge's letter and his reference from their folder, and making copies of all the letters I'd collected, I drove to Wellingborough station and, tired of the roads, I caught the train to London.

SHOUT! emanated, it transpired, from a small and grubby-looking building south of the Thames. The editor wouldn't in the least want to see me but, late in the afternoon, I marched straight into his office shedding secretaries like bow-waves. He was sitting in a sweatshirt behind a cluttered desk typing on the keyboard of a computer.

He didn't recognise me, of course. When I told him who I was he invited me to leave.

'I am going to sue you for libel,' I said, opening the copy of *SHOUT!* at the centre pages. 'I see from the small print at the beginning of this magazine that the name of the editor is Rufus Crossmead. If that's who you are, I'll be suing Rufus Crossmead personally.'

He was a small pugnacious man, sticking his chest out and tucking his chin in like a pugilist. I supposed briefly that dealing with wronged and furious victims of his destructive ethos was a regular part of his life.

I remembered how, five years earlier, my father had pulverised the editor of the *Hoopwestern Gazette*, but I couldn't reproduce exactly that quiet degree of menace. I didn't have the commanding strength of his vibrant physical presence. I left Rufus Crossmead, however, in no doubt as to my intentions.

I laid down in front of him copies of the strong letters from Spencer Stallworthy, Jim, my Exeter tutor and the Headmaster of Malvern College, and I gave him finally a copy of the letter Vivian Durridge had sent.

'The only good defence in a libel suit,' I said, 'is to prove that the allegations are true. You can't use that defence, because you've printed lies. It will be easy for me to establish that Sir Vivian Durridge is now hopelessly confused after a stroke and doesn't know what he's saying. Usher Rudd must have been aware of it. He was trying to revenge himself for my father having got him sacked from the *Hoopwestern Gazette*. No reputable paper has employed him since. He suits your style, but he's dropped even you in the shit.'

Rufus Crossmead gloomily read the various papers.

'We'll settle out of court,' he said.

It sounded to me as if he'd said it often before, and it wasn't at all what I'd expected. I wasn't sure it was even what I wanted.

I said slowly, 'I'll tell you what I'll settle for . . .'

'It's up to the proprietors,' Crossmead interrupted. 'They'll make you an offer.'

'They always do?' I asked.

He didn't exactly nod, but it was in the air.

'Then you tell the proprietors,' I said, 'that I'll settle for a retraction and a statement of sincere regret from you that your magazine's accusations were based on incorrect information. Tell your proprietors that I'll settle for a statement appearing very visibly in next Tuesday's issue of *SHOUT*! In addition, you will send immediately – by registered post – a personally signed copy of that retraction and statement of regret to each of the 650 or so Members of Parliament.'

CHAPTER TWELVE

It wasn't enough, I thought, to defend.

I should have written in that pact, 'I will attack my father's attackers.' I should have written that I'd go to war for him if I saw the need.

At almost eighteen, I'd written from easy sentiment. At twenty-three, I saw that, if the pact meant anything at all, it pledged an allegiance that could lead to death. And if that were so, I thought, it would be feeble just to sit around waiting for the axe.

It had been Tuesday when *SHOUT*! had hit the newsagents, and late afternoon on Wednesday when I'd crashed into Rufus Crossmead's editorial office. On Friday I drove from Wellingborough to Hoopwestern, and spent the journey looking back to the end of that confrontation and the answers I'd been given.

I'd asked *SHOUT*!'s editor why he had sent Usher Rudd to see Vivian Durridge, and he'd said he hadn't, it had been Usher Rudd's own idea.

'Usher – well, his name is Bobby – said he'd been asked to dig into everything you'd ever done, and come up with some dirt. He was getting ultra frustrated because he couldn't find any sludge. He went blasting on a bit that no one could be as careful to stay out of trouble as you had been, and then there was this announcement of Sir Vivian Durridge's retirement, which said you had ridden for his stable, so Bobby went off on the off-chance, and he came back laughing. Crowing. He said he'd got you at last. So he wrote the story and I printed it.'

'And you didn't check.'

'If I had to check every word I print,' the editor had said with world-weariness, 'our sales would plummet.'

On Wednesday, early evening, I'd phoned Samson Frazer, the editor of the *Hoopwestern Gazette.*

'If you're thinking of reprinting a story about me from *SHOUT!*,' I'd said, 'don't do it. Usher Rudd wrote it. It's not true and it'll get you into court for libel.'

Gloomy silence.

Then, 'I'll re-set the front page,' he'd said.

On Thursday, with prudent speed, *SHOUT!*'s proprietors had acted to avoid the heavy expenses of a libel action and had written and posted the retractions I'd asked for to the Members of Parliament.

My father, attending the House of Commons on Friday morning, found that several registered letters had already reached their targets. In addition, he gave everyone – from the Prime Minister downwards – a copy of Vivian Durridge's letter to me, along with a brief confirmation from himself that he'd asked Durridge to think of a way of persuading me to leave. Apparently the general reaction had been relief and relaxation, though Hudson Hurst had insisted there had to be some truth in the dope story somewhere.

'Why do you think so?' my father related that he'd asked, and the only reply had been stutter and dismay.

My father said, 'I asked Hudson Hurst if he himself had sent Usher Rudd to Vivian Durridge. He denied it. He looked bewildered. I don't think he did it.'

'No, I agree.'

I now negotiated a roundabout. Fourteen more miles to Hoopwestern.

I thought about Hudson Hurst, the ugly duckling converted to swan by scissors and razor. On television he was smooth, convincing and read his speeches from an auto-cue. No inner fire. A puppet.

Alderney Wyvern pulled his strings.

How to prove it? How to stop him?

Attacking Alderney Wyvern could destroy the attacker. I sensed it strongly. History was littered with the laments of failed invasions.

I arrived at Hoopwestern at noon and parked in the car park behind the old party headquarters. Polly had told me that the charity that had owned the whole of the burned double bow-fronted building had chosen to rebuild it much as before, with new bow windows fronting onto the cobbled square and new shops matching the row at the rear. When I walked in from the car park all that seemed different were heavy fire doors and a rash of big scarlet extinguishers.

Mervyn Teck was there, and greeted me with ambivalent open arms and wary eyes.

'Benedict!' He was plumper than ever. Rotund, nowadays.

'Hi, Mervyn.'

He shook hands awkwardly, and glanced past me to where, on his desk, lay two newspapers, both *SHOUT!* and the *Hoopwestern Gazette.*

'I didn't expect you,' Mervyn said.

'No, well, I'm sorry. I expect my father telephoned to say he couldn't get down this weekend for the surgery?' Most Saturday mornings the public came to headquarters with their complaints. 'I expect you'll do fine without him.'

My father, in fact, was busy in London with secretive little lunches and private dinners, with hurried hidden meetings and promises and bargains, all the undercover manoeuvring of shifts of power. I hoped and trusted that A.L. Wyvern was fully occupied in doing the same.

A young woman sitting behind a computer stood up with unaffected welcome.

'Benedict!'

I said, 'Crystal?' tentatively.

'I'm so glad to see you,' she said edging round her desk to give me a kiss. 'It's such ages since you were here.'

A great change here too had taken place. She was no longer thin and anxious, but rounded and secure; and she wore a wedding ring, I saw.

They gave me coffee and local news, and I read with interest what the *Gazette* had made of *SHOUT!*. 'An unfair attack on our MP through his son. No truth in this allegation . . . shocking . . . libellous . . . retractions and regrets are in the pipeline.'

'The by-line in *SHOUT!* says Usher Rudd.' Mervyn pointed. 'Vicious little nerd.'

'Actually,' I said as their indignation boiled on, 'I came hoping to see Orinda, but she doesn't answer her phone.'

'Oh dear,' Crystal said, 'she isn't here. She went away for the weekend. She won't be back till Monday.'

They didn't know where she'd gone.

I'd made a short list of people I aimed to see. Mervyn, helpful with addresses, knew where to find Isobel Bethune at her sister's house in Wales, and as she – telephoned – was not only at home but would be glad to see me, I drove to Cardiff that afternoon and discovered Paul Bethune's rejuvenated wife in a pretty terraced house in the suburbs.

I'd never before seen her happy. She too was a different woman: the grey lines of worry had smoothed into peaches and cream.

It was she, however, who exclaimed, 'How you've changed. You've grown older.'

'It happens.'

Her sister had gone shopping. I sat with Isobel and listened to her remembering for my benefit how Usher Rudd had uncovered her husband's bimbo affair.

'Usher Rudd just dug away and wrote it up sensationally, but it was all Paul's fault. Men are such bloody fools. He confessed to me in snivelling tears in the end that he'd boasted – *boasted*, I ask you – to some stranger that he was playing golf with that he was having an affair his wife didn't know about. Snigger, snigger. Can you believe it? And that stranger turned out to be that weird nobody that was always hanging about round the Nagles. He used to play golf with Dennis.'

'His name's Wyvern.'

'Yes, I know that now. When Dennis died, that Wyvern person wanted to make sure Orinda got elected, so he arranged to play golf with Paul, to see where Paul was weakest . . . I hated Usher Rudd, but it wasn't until after your father got elected that Paul broke down and told me what had happened.' She sighed. 'I was shattered then, but I don't care now, isn't that odd?'

'How are your sons?'

She laughed. 'They've joined the army. Best place for them. They sometimes send postcards. You're the only one that was kind to me in those days.'

I left her with a kiss on the peaches-and-cream cheek and drove tiredly back to Hoopwestern for the night, staying in Polly's house in the woods and eating potted shrimps from her freezer.

On Saturday morning I went to the police station and asked to see Detective Sergeant Joe Duke, whose mother drove a school bus.

Joe Duke appeared questioningly.

'George Juliard's son? You look older.'

Joe Duke was still a detective sergeant, but his mother no longer drove a bus. 'She's into rabbits,' he said. He took me into a bare little interview room, explaining he was the senior officer on duty and couldn't leave the station.

He thoughtfully repeated my question. 'Do I know if that fire you could have died in was arson? It's all of five years ago.'

'A bit more. But you must have files,' I said.

'I don't need files. Mostly fires in the night are from cigarettes or electrical shorts, but none of you smoked and the place had been re-wired. Is this off the record?'

'On the moon.'

A dedicated policeman in his thirties, Joe had a broad face, a Dorset accent and a realistic attitude to human failings. 'Amy used to let tramps sleep above the charity shop sometimes, but not that night, she says, though that's the official and easy theory of the cause of fire. They say a vagrant was lighting candles downstairs and knocked them over, and then ran away. Nonsense, really. But the fire did start, the fire-fighters reckoned, in the charity shop, and the back door there wasn't bolted, and both shops of the old place were lined and partitioned with dry old wood, though they've rebuilt it with brick and concrete now, and it's awash with smoke alarms. Anyway, I suppose you heard the theory that crazy Leonard Kitchens set light to the place to frighten your father off so that Orinda Nagle could be our MP?'

'I've heard. What do you think?'

'It doesn't much matter now, does it?'

'But still . . .'

'I think he did it. I questioned him, see? But we hadn't a flicker of evidence.'

'And what about the gun in the Sleeping Dragon's gutter?'

'No one knows who put it there.'

'Leonard Kitchens?'

'He swears he didn't. And he's heavy and slow. It needed someone pretty agile to put that gun up high.'

'Did you ever find out where the rifle came from?'

'No, we didn't,' he said. 'They're so common. They've been used in the Olympics for donkey's years. They're licensed and locked away and accounted for these days, but in the past . . . and theft . . .' He shrugged. 'It isn't as if it had killed anyone.'

I said, 'What's the penalty for attempted murder?'

'Do you mean a deliberate attempt that didn't come off?'

'Mm.'

'Same as murder.'

'A 10-lb penalty?'

'Ten years,' he said.

From the police station I drove out to the ring road and stopped in the forecourt of Basil Rudd's car-repair outfit. I walked up the stairs into his glass-walled office that gave him a comprehensive view over his wide workshop below, only half busy on Saturday morning.

'Sorry,' he said, without looking up. 'We close at noon on Saturdays. Can't do anything for you till Monday.'

He was still disconcertingly like his cousin; red hair and freckles and a combative manner.

'I don't want my car fixed,' I said. 'I want to find Usher Rudd.'

It was as though I had jabbed him with a needle. He looked up, and said, 'Who are you? Why do you want him?'

I told him who and why. I asked him if he remembered the Range Rover's questionable sump-plug, but his recollection was hazy. He was quite sharply aware, though, of the political damage that could be done to a father by a son's disgrace. He had a copy of *SHOUT!* on his desk, inevitably open at the centre pages.

'That's me,' I said, pointing at the photograph of the jockey. 'Your cousin is lying. The *Gazette* sacked him for lying once before, and I'm doing my best to get him finally discredited – struck off, or whatever it's called in newspaper-speak – for what is called dishonourable conduct. So where is he?'

Basil Rudd looked helpless. 'How should I know?'

'Find out,' I said forcefully. 'You're a Rudd. Someone in the Rudd clan must know where to find its most notorious son.'

'He's brought us nothing but trouble . . .'

'Find him,' I said, 'and your troubles may end.'

He stretched out a hand to the telephone, saying, 'It may take ages. And it'll cost you.'

'I'll pay your phone bills,' I said. 'When you find him, leave a message on the answer-phone at my father's headquarters. Here's the number.' I gave him a card. 'Don't waste time. It's urgent.'

I went next to the Sleeping Dragon to see the manager. He had been newly installed there at the time of the by-election, but perhaps because of that he had a satisfactorily clear recollection of the night someone had fired a gun into the cobbled square. He was much honoured, he said, to be on first-name terms with my father.

'There were so many people coming and going on that night, and I was only beginning to know who was who. Someone left a set of golf clubs in my office and said they were Dennis Nagle's but, of course, the poor man was dead and I didn't know what to do with them, but I offered them to Mrs Nagle and she said she thought they belonged to her husband's friend, Mr

Wyvern, so I gave them to him.' He frowned. 'It was so long ago. I'm afraid I'm not being much help.'

I left him and walked upstairs and from the little lounge over the main lobby looked down again onto the cobbled square where, on that first night, my father and I had by good luck not been shot.

Golf clubs . . .

Mervyn Teck, at the end of a busy morning surgery, told me where to find Leonard and Mrs Kitchens, and on Saturday afternoon, without enthusiasm, I found their substantial semi-detached house on the outskirts of the town.

The house, its lack of imagination, and the disciplined front garden were all somehow typical of a heavy worthiness: no manic sign of an arsonist.

Mrs Kitchens opened the front door at my ring and, after a moment's hesitation for recognition, said, 'My Leonard isn't in, I'm afraid.'

She took me into a front sitting-room where the air smelled as if it had been undisturbed for weeks, and talked with bitterness and freedom about 'her Leonard's' infatuation for Orinda.

'My Leonard would have done *anything* for that woman. He still would.'

'Er . . .' I said, 'looking back to that fire at the party headquarters – '

'Leonard said,' Mrs Kitchens interrupted, 'that he didn't do it.'

'But *you* think – ?'

'The silly old fool did it,' she said. 'I know he did. But I'm not going to say it to anyone except you. It was that Wyvern who put him up to it, you know. And it was all pointless, as your father is much better for the country than Orinda would have been. Everyone knows that now.'

'People say,' I said gently, 'that Leonard shot a rifle at my father and then put the gun up into the gutter of the Sleeping Dragon.'

Clumsy, large, unhappy Mrs Kitchens wouldn't hear of it. 'My Leonard doesn't know one end of a gun from the other!'

'And does your Leonard change the oil in his own car?'

She looked utterly bewildered. 'He can make plants grow, but he's hopeless at anything else.'

I left poor Mrs Kitchens to her unsatisfactory marriage, and slept again in Polly's house.

For most of Sunday I sat alone in the party's headquarters, wishing and waiting for Basil Rudd to dislike his cousin enough to help me, but it wasn't until nearly six in the evening that the telephone rang.

I picked up the receiver. A voice that was not Basil Rudd's said, 'Is it you that wants to know where to find Bobby Usher Rudd?'

'Yes, it is,' I said. 'Who are you?'

'It doesn't matter a damn who I am. Because of his snooping, my wife left me and I lost my kids. If you want to fix that bastard Usher Rudd, at this very moment he is in the offices of the *Hoopwestern Gazette*.'

The informant at the other end disconnected abruptly.

Usher Rudd was on my doorstep.

I'd expected a longer chase, but the *Hoopwestern Gazette's* offices and printing presses were simply down the road. I locked the party headquarters, jumped in my car, and sped through the Sunday traffic with the devil on my tail, anxious not to lose Usher Rudd now that I'd found him.

He was still at the *Gazette*, though, in mid-furious row with Samson Frazer. When I walked into the editor's office it silenced them both with their hot words half spoken.

They both knew who I was.

Bobby Usher Rudd looked literally struck dumb. Samson Frazer's expression mingled pleasure, apprehension and relief.

He said, 'Bobby swears the dope story's true.'

'Bobby would swear his mother's a chimpanzee.'

Usher Rudd's quivering finger pointed at a copy of Thursday's *Gazette* that lay on Samson's desk, and he found his voice, hoarse with rage.

'You know what you've done?' He was asking me, not Samson Frazer. 'You've got me sacked from *SHOUT!*. You frightened Rufus Crossmead and the proprietors so badly that they won't risk my stuff any more, and I've increased their bloody sales for them over the years . . . it's bloody *unfair*. So now they say they're the laughing stock of the whole industry, printing a false story about someone whose father might be the next Prime Minister. They say the story has backfired. They said it will *help* George Juliard, not finish him. And how was I to know? It's effing unfair.'

I said bitterly. 'You could have seen Vivian Durridge didn't know what he was saying.'

'People who don't know what they're saying are the ones you listen to.'

That confident statement, spoken in rage, popped a light bulb in my understanding of Usher Rudd's success.

I said, 'That day in Quindle, when I first met you, you were already trying to dig up scandal about my father.'

'Natch.'

'He tries to dig up dirt about anyone,' Samson put in.

I shook my head. 'Who,' I asked Usher Rudd, 'told you to attack my father?'

'I don't need to be told.'

Though I wasn't exactly shouting, my voice was loud and my accusation plain. 'As you've known all about cars for the whole of your life, did you stuff up my father's Range Rover's sump-plug drain with a candle?'

'*What?*'

'Did you? Who suggested you do it?'

'I'm not answering your bloody questions.'

The telephone rang on Samson Frazer's desk.

He picked up the receiver, listened briefly, said, 'OK,' and disconnected.

Usher Rudd, not a newspaperman for nothing, said suspiciously, 'Did you give them the OK to roll the presses?'

'Yes.'

Usher Rudd's rage increased to the point where his whole body shook. He shouted, 'You're printing without the change. I insist . . . I'll kill you . . . *stop the presses* . . . if you don't print what I told you to, I'll kill you.'

Samson Frazer didn't believe him, and nor, for all Rudd's passion, did I. Kill was a word used easily, but seldom meant.

'What change?' I demanded.

Samson's voice was high beyond normal. 'He wants me to print that you faked Sir Vivian's letter and forged his signature and that the story about sniffing glue is a hundred per cent sterling, a hundred per cent kosher, and you'll do *anything* . . . *anything* to deny it.'

He picked a typewritten page off his desk and waved it.

'It's Sunday, anyway,' he said. 'There's no one here but me and the print technicians. Tomorrow's paper is locked onto the presses, ready to roll.'

'You can do the changes yourself.' Usher Rudd fairly danced with fury.

'I'm not going to,' Samson said.

'Then don't print the paper.'

'Don't be ridiculous.'

Samson put the typewritten page into my hands.

I glanced down to read it and, as if all he'd been waiting for had been a flicker of inattention on my part, Bobby Rudd did one of his quickest getaways and was out through a door in a flash – not the door to the outside world, but the swinging door into the passage leading deeper into the building; the passage, it transpired, down to the presses.

'Stop him!' yelled Samson, aghast.

'It's only paper,' I said, though making for the door.

'No . . . sabotage . . . he can destroy . . . catch him.'

His agitation convinced me. I sprinted after Usher Rudd and ran down a passage with small empty individual offices to both sides and out through another door at the end and across an expanse inhabited only by huge white rolls of paper – newsprint, the raw material of newspapers – and through a small printroom beyond that with two or three men tending clattering machines turning out coloured pages, and finally through a last swinging door into the long high room containing the heart and muscle of the *Hoopwestern Gazette*, the monster printing presses that every day turned out twenty thousand twenty-four-page community enlightenments to most of Dorset.

The presses were humming quietly when I reached them. There were eight in a row with a tower in the centre. From each end of four, the presses put first a banner in colour – red, green, blue – on the sheets that would be the front and back pages, and then came the closely edited black and white pages set onto rollers in an age-old, but still perfectly functional, offset litho process.

I learned afterwards how the machines technically worked. On that fraught Sunday I saw only wide white paper looping from press to press and in and out of inked rollers as it collected the news page by page on its journey to the central tower, from where it went up in single sheets and came down folded into a publishable newspaper, cut and counted into bundles of fifty.

There were two men tending the presses, adjusting the ink flow and slowly increasing the speed of the paper over the rollers and through the mechanism. Warning bells were ringing. Noise was building.

When I ran into the long thundering area, Usher Rudd was shouting at one of the men to turn everything off. The technician blinked at him and paid no attention.

His colleague activated another alarm bell and switched the presses to a full floor-trembling roar. Monday's edition of the *Hoopwestern Gazette*, twenty thousand copies of it, flowed from press to press and up the tower and down at a speed that reduced each separate page to a blur.

Samson Frazer, catching up with me as I watched with awe, shouted in my ear, 'Don't go near the presses while they're running. If you get your little finger caught in any of the rollers it would pull your whole arm in – it would wrench your arm right out of your body. We can't stop the presses fast enough to save an arm. Do you understand?'

'Yes,' I yelled.

Usher Rudd was screaming at the technician.

Samson Frazer's warning was essential.

There was a space of three or four feet between each machine where one was wholly exposed to the revolving accelerating rollers. When the presses were at rest, the printers – the technicians – walked with safety into these spaces to fit the master sheets onto the cylinders and to check the state of the inking rollers. When the presses, switched on, ran even at minimum inch-by-inch speed, the danger began. An arm could be torn out, not in one jerking terror but worse, in inch by excruciating inevitable inch.

I asked later why no guarding gates kept people away. The machines were old, built before safety standards sky-rocketed, Samson Frazer said, but they did indeed now have gates. It was illegal in Britain to operate without them. These gates pulled across like trellises and locked into place, but they were fiddly, and an extra job. People who worked round these presses knew and respected the danger, and sometimes didn't bother with the gates. He didn't approve, but he'd had no tragedies. There were computerised programs and printers to be had, but the old technology worked perfectly, as it had for a hundred years, and he couldn't afford to scrap the old and to install the new, which often went wrong anyway, and one couldn't guard against maniacs like Usher Rudd. No one had to insure against lunatics.

I could have sold him a policy about that: but on that particular Sunday evening, what we needed for Usher Rudd was a straitjacket, not a premium.

He was still swearing at the technician who looked over the Rudd shoulder and saw Samson Frazer's arrival as deliverance.

Stopping the presses, I learned later, meant hitting one particular button on one of the control panels to be found on the end of each press that regulated the overall speed of the printing. The buttons weren't things the size of door-bells, but scarlet three-inch-diameter flat knobs on springs. Neither the technician nor Samson Frazer pushed the overall stop control, and neither Rudd himself nor I knew which of several scarlet buttons ruled the roost. The presses went on roaring and Bobby Usher Rudd completely lost control.

He knew the terrible danger of the presses. He'd worked for the *Hoopwestern Gazette*. He'd been in and out of newspapers all his adult life.

He grabbed the technician by his overalls and swung him towards unimaginable agony.

The technician, half in and half out of one of the lethal spaces, screamed.

Samson Frazer screamed at Usher Rudd.

The second technician sprinted for refuge in the smaller print-room next door.

I, from instinct, leapt at Usher Rudd and yanked him backwards. He too started screaming. Still clutched by the overalls, the technician stumbled out of the fearsome gap, ingrained awareness keeping his hands close to his body: better to fall on the floor than try to keep his balance by touching the death-dealing machinery.

Usher Rudd let go of the overalls and re-routed his uncontrolled frenzy onto me. He was no longer primarily trying to stop the print-run, but to avenge himself for the cataclysms he had brought on himself.

The glare in his eyes was madness. I saw the intention there of pushing me instead of the technician onto the rollers and had we been alone he might have managed it. But Samson Frazer jumped to grab him while the technician, saved from mutilation, gave a horror-struck final shout as he made his terrified stumbling run for the door, and by unplanned chance barged into Usher Rudd on the way, unbalancing him.

Rudd threw Samson off him like an irrelevance, but it gave me time to put space between me and the nearest press, and although Rudd grasped and lurched in an effort to get me back again into the danger zone, I was fighting more or less for my life and it was amazing how much strength ultimate fear generated.

Samson Frazer, to his supreme credit – and maybe calculating that any death on his premises would ruin him – helped me struggle with the demented kicking and punching and clutching red-haired tornado: and it was Samson who delivered a blow to Rudd's head with a bunched fist that half-dazed his target and knocked him to the ground face downwards. I sat on his squirming back while Samson found some of the wide brown sticky tape used for parcels and with my active help, circled one of Usher Rudd's wrists, and then the other, and fastened his arms behind his back in makeshift handcuffs. Samson tethered the wildly kicking legs in the same way and we rolled Rudd onto his back and stood over him panting.

Then with each of us looping an arm under Rudd's armpits we dragged him into the comparative quiet of the secondary print-room next door and propped him in a chair.

All of the technicians were in that room, wide-eyed and upset. Samson told them unemotionally to go back to work, there was a paper to be got out; and slowly, hesitantly, they obeyed him.

In his chair, Rudd began shouting, 'It's all his fault. Wyvern did it. Wyvern's the one you want, not me.'

'I don't believe it,' I contradicted, though I did.

Usher Rudd tried to convince me. 'Wyvern wanted your father out of the way. He wanted Orinda in Parliament. He wanted to get her promoted, like Dennis. He would have done anything to stop your father being elected.'

'Like sabotaging his car?'

'I didn't want to do it. I would write what he wanted. I trailed Paul Bethune for weeks to find his bimbo, to please Wyvern, so that people would vote for Orinda, but messing up a Range Rover, cutting the brake-lines like Wyvern wanted, that was too much. I didn't do it.'

'Yes, you did,' I told him conclusively.

'No, I didn't.'

'What did you do then?'

'I didn't do anything.'

'Your cousin, Basil, knows what you did.'

Usher Rudd cursed Basil with words I'd hardly ever heard even on a racecourse, and somewhere in the tirade came a description of how he'd wriggled under the Range Rover in the black tracksuit he'd worn to the meeting after the dinner in the Sleeping Dragon. The brilliant performance my father had given that evening had convinced Wyvern that he wouldn't get rid of my father without at least injuring him badly. Wyvern had been furious with Usher Rudd that his sabotage had been so useless.

Usher Rudd's rage slowly ran down and he began

first to whine and then deny that he had ever said what Samson and I had both just heard.

Samson phoned the police. Joe Duke was not on duty, but Samson knew all the force individually and put down the receiver, reporting a promise of immediate action.

Usher Rudd shouted, 'I want a lawyer.'

He got his lawyer, passed a night in the cells and on Monday morning collected a slap on the wrist from busy magistrates (for causing a disturbance indoors at the *Hoopwestern Gazette*) who had no real conception of the speed and noise and danger involved.

No actual damage had been done. The newspaper had appeared as usual. Usher Rudd, meek and respectful, walked out free.

I talked to Joe Duke.

I said, 'It was Usher Rudd who stuffed wax in the sump-drain of the Range Rover, and Leonard Kitchens who started the fire. Both of them were put up to it by Alderney Wyvern.'

Joe Duke slowly nodded. 'But they didn't stop your father, did they? And as for you' – he gave a half smile – 'I'll never forget you that night of the fire, sitting there half-naked on the cobbles with that red blanket over your shoulders and no sign of pain, though you'd burns on your hands and feet and you'd smashed down into the square. Don't you ever feel pain?'

'Of course, but there was so much happening – '

'And you're used to falling off horses?'

'Horses fall . . . Anyway, I suppose so. I've hit the ground quite a lot.'

The smile broadened. 'Then why do it?'

'Speed,' I told him. 'Nothing like it.' I paused. 'If you want something badly enough, you can risk your life for it and consider it normal behaviour.'

He pondered. 'If you want Orinda Nagle to be an MP enough, you'll risk . . .'

'Almost anything. I think it was Wyvern who shot at my father.'

'I'm not saying you're wrong. He could have carried a rifle in his golf bag, with one of those covers on it that they use for clubs.'

'Yes.'

'And he'd had to have had murder in his mind to do that.'

'Uh-huh. And when he heard and saw my father's success at that meeting, he judged he needed to get rid of him at once.'

'He was crazy.'

'He still is.'

Joe Duke knew my father was engaged in a power struggle but was dismayed when I explained about Hudson Hurst.

'You don't think,' Joe said, horrified, 'that Wyvern would try *again* to kill your father?'

'Wyvern's stakes are higher now, and my father still stands in his way. If my father is chosen to lead his party, I'm sure he'll be in appalling danger. It frightens me badly, to be honest.'

Joe said thoughtfully, 'You know what . . .?'

'What?'

'Just in case we're doing Wyvern a great injustice, thinking it was he that shot at you . . . I mean, so far we've only got theory to go on, really. Why don't you and I do an unofficial walk-through . . . a reconstruction? I'll use a walking stick for a gun. I'll transport it in a golf bag. And I'll carry it up into the little lounge, and aim it at you while you're crossing the square, like you did that night, and I'll see how difficult it will be to put the walking stick up in the gutter. What do you think?'

'Can't do any harm.'

'We might come across something we haven't thought of. It often works that way with reconstructions.'

'OK.'

'We'll have to do it at night,' Joe said.

'It was after midnight.'

'After midnight, then. I'll be off duty. It will just be the two of us.'

I agreed that we would meet that evening in the

Sleeping Dragon, and that Joe would tell the manager what we were doing.

I went to see Orinda who had finally returned from her weekend and answered the telephone.

Five years had been kind to her. She looked as striking as ever, the green eyes black-lashed, the greasepaint make-up smooth and blended. She was less brittle, less stressed, more fulfilled.

She called me darling with only two or three 'a's. 'Daaarling.'

'Orinda.' I hugged her.

'How you've grown,' she exclaimed. 'I mean, not just upwards, but older.'

She had made us a salad lunch with diet Coke and coffee after.

She knew about the power struggle going on in the party and mentioned that every time there was this sort of leadership contest, the politicians changed the rules.

'They invent whatever procedure they think will give a result that everyone thinks is fair, even if not everyone is happy with the eventual winner. It's now all up to the party's MPs.'

I had forgotten how much Orinda knew about government.

'I suppose Dennis told you how it all works.'

'No, it was Alderney Wyvern.' She frowned. 'I never want to see that man again.'

I said neutrally, 'Did you know that Wyvern now controls Hudson Hurst, like he used to control you and Dennis? Do you realise that if Hurst wins the ballot and becomes Prime Minister, it will be Alderney Wyvern who effectively governs this country?'

Orinda looked horrified but shook her head. 'Your father's more popular in the country.'

'Don't forget *Schadenfreude*.'

Orinda laughed. 'You mean the malicious enjoyment of someone else's misfortune?'

I nodded. 'Half the Cabinet would like to see my father come a cropper after his spectacular way of fighting the fish war.'

'It will be marvellous for this constituency if he wins.' She smiled widely. 'I never thought I would say that, but it's true.'

I told Orinda about the reconstruction that Joe Duke and I had planned.

I asked, 'Do you remember much about that evening?'

'Of course I do. I was *furious* at not being chosen as candidate.'

'How much were you with Alderney Wyvern after the political meeting?'

'I wasn't. I was angry and miserable and drove straight home.'

'Do you know if Alderney Wyvern had his golf clubs with him at the meeting in the hall?'

'What an extraordinary question! He always used to have them in the back of the car.'

Orinda might have hated my father that night, but not enough to do him harm. She had no wickedness in her nature.

I spent a comfortable hour or two longer with her and then drove to Polly's house to wait for my father to telephone from London with the result of the ballot.

He gave me news from his car. 'It was all indecisive,' he reported. 'It was basically a three-way split. All that's certain is that we have to vote again tomorrow.'

'Do explain,' I begged him.

He described a day that had been full of doubt and manoeuvring, but it seemed that what had finally happened was that neither my father nor Hudson Hurst had received enough votes in the first round to secure victory outright. Jill Vinicheck (Education), the third candidate, had received fewest votes and had been eliminated. The next ballot would be a straight fight between Hurst and Juliard, and no one was predicting who would win.

My father sounded tired. He said he and Polly were on their way to join me at the house for a quiet night. He had done all he could behind the scenes to sway the vote his way: now it was up to his colleagues to choose whom they wanted.

I explained about Joe Duke and the reconstruction and, after a brief discussion with Polly by his side, he said they would meet me in the Sleeping Dragon and we would eat together.

Any thought that we might have had about a peaceful evening disappeared between the soup and the apple pie.

While neither Joe Duke nor I had made any particular secret about our plan for the reconstruction, we had not expected the manager of the hotel to broadcast the scenario. He appeared to have told the whole town. The hotel was buzzing, as it had on the night of the dinner, and people came up to my father in droves to shake his hand and wish him well.

Samson Frazer came from the *Hoopwestern Gazette* with his cameraman and gave my horrified father extra details of how Usher Rudd had spent his Sunday.

Usher Rudd himself came – free, unrepentant, bitter-eyed and steaming with malice, glaring at my father and talking into a mobile phone.

When Joe Duke came, he looked at first aghast at the bustle and movement, but my father resignedly told him, as he joined us for coffee, that the hotel had been packed on the night we were reproducing, and the present crowd would make everything seem more real.

Moreover, my father said he would walk with me across the square as he had done before, and although I didn't like the idea, Joe Duke nodded enthusiastically.

Why wait for midnight? people asked. Everyone was ready *now*, and now was eleven-thirty.

Because Joe explained, half of the lights in the square switched off automatically at twelve o'clock, and if the reconstruction was to mean anything, the conditions had to be as near as possible what they had been before.

Joe Duke brought in a bag of golf clubs from his car and showed everyone the long walking stick with the tartan cover that disguised it.

The manager frowned in puzzlement, and I wanted to ask him if he had remembered something significant, but Joe and the crowd swept all before them, anxious to get started. I would ask him later, I thought.

Midnight came. Half the lights in the square faded to darkness. All that were left glowing threw shadows on the cobbles. Over the far side of the square a few lights showed dimly in the party headquarters and the charity shop.

When my father and I walked out into the square, the only lights blazing brightly were those of the Sleeping Dragon at our back.

It was planned that my father and I would walk halfway across the square and wait while Joe aimed his walking stick out of the window and BANG, and then reached or climbed up to put the stick in the gutter. People would hurry from the Sleeping Dragon towards my father, as they had done before.

It all felt alarmingly real to me, but everyone was smiling.

Joe, surrounded by encouraging crowds, turned to go towards the staircase while I and my father walked out across the cobbles. I stopped after a while to look back at the hotel but my father walked on, calling over his shoulder, 'Come on, Ben, we haven't reached the spot yet.'

I looked up at the hotel. Joe's walking stick was pointing out of one of the windows, half hidden by the seemingly perpetual geraniums.

Three thoughts jammed into my consciousness simultaneously.

First, Joe hadn't had time to get up the stairs and walk along to the lounge and hide behind the curtain.

Second, the stick was pointing out of the wrong window.

Third, there was a gleam on the stick and a hole, a black round hole, in the end of it.

It wasn't a stick. It was a gun.

My father was ten yards ahead of me across the square. I sprinted as I had for Orinda and for the technician in the presses, without pause, without thought, with raw intuition, and I jumped in a flying rugger tackle to knock my father down.

The bang was real enough. The bullet was real enough, but the happy crowd which poured out of the hotel still thought it was a game.

The bullet hit me while I was still in the air, jumping

and colliding with my father, and it would have gone into his back if I hadn't been there.

It entered high on my right thigh and travelled down inside my leg to the knee, the kinetic energy bursting apart all muscles and soft tissue in its path.

The force of it whirled me round so that when I crashed to the cobbles I was facing the Sleeping Dragon; half lying, propped on my left elbow, shuddering throughout all my body with my brain disoriented and protesting with universal outrage.

There was enough pain everywhere to satisfy Joe Duke. My eyes watered with it and my skin sweated. I'd been injured now and then in racing falls, and I'd felt shivery and sore the night of the fire, but nothing had even begun to warn me that there was an unimaginable dimension far beyond cuts and breaks.

It didn't really help that I knew the physics of high-velocity bullets and the damage they could do. I'd fired hundreds of them at targets. I shot in a world where all one hit was paper. I didn't know that I'd ever be able to fire a rifle again.

My father was on his knees beside me, his face screwed up with anxiety. My right trouser leg was dark and saturated with blood. The crowd from the Sleeping Dragon were running now, with Polly at their head. I could hear her agonised voice, 'George . . . oh, George.'

It was all right, I thought. It wasn't George.

My father held my hand.

Besides the encompassing pain I felt remarkably ill. I wanted to lie down, to stand up, to move somehow, and I couldn't. I wanted someone to come along and shoot me again, but in the head; to give me oblivion, like they did with horses.

Time passed. Nothing got better.

Although ordinary traffic was banned from the square, police cars, ambulances and fire engines weren't. Two police cars and one ambulance arrived, roof lights flashing. People from the police cars went into the hotel. Someone from the ambulance came and, with large scissors, cut open my right trouser leg.

I went on wishing for oblivion.

My leg, exposed to the dim light in the square, looked literally a bloody mess. I gathered that the bullet hadn't severed the femoral artery, because if it had I would have already bled to death. There was, however, somewhere in my mangled muscles, a hard white finger-shaped length of what I understood with shock to be bone. Femur. Uncovered, but also unbroken.

The man from the ambulance hid the devastation with a large padded dressing and went back to the ambulance. He'd gone to summon a doctor, my father said: there were all sorts of rules and regulations about gun-shot wounds.

It didn't cross my mind that I might lose my leg and, in fact, I didn't. What I lost, once everything was stitched and repaired, was the strength to ride half-ton steeplechasers over the black birch. What I lost was speed.

People came out of the hotel and got into the police cars. One of them was Alderney Wyvern, in handcuffs.

When the cars had driven away, Joe Duke walked across the square and sat on his heels to talk to my father and me.

He said to me, 'Can you take in what I'm saying?'

'Yes.'

Joe said, 'When I went up the stairs to position the walking stick, the hotel manager hurried up after me and caught me before I reached the little lounge. He said he didn't know if it was just a coincidence, but not long before, in fact at about eleven o'clock, a man had booked in as a guest at the hotel and he too was carrying a bag of golf clubs. And what was slightly odd about him, the manager said, was that he was wearing *gloves*.'

Joe stood up to stretch his legs for a moment, and then sat back on his heels. 'Are you taking in what I'm saying?' he said.

'Yes,' I groggily replied.

'We heard that cracking bang of the gun going off and the manager used his pass-key to open a bedroom door, and inside we found Alderney Wyvern coming towards the door carrying his bag of golf clubs, but when the manager snatched it from him and emptied them out onto the floor, all that was in it was golf clubs.'

Joe went on, 'He hadn't time to put the rifle up in the gutter, but it was there with him all right. He'd put the gun-butt in the hanging basket with the geraniums, with the barrel pointing skywards, among the chains hanging the basket. I then used the room telephone to bring my colleagues from the police station. While we waited for them to arrive I asked, out of curiosity, how Wyvern had known about the reconstruction. How had he known that he would have a chance to shoot George Juliard?'

Joe smiled lopsidedly. 'Wyvern said Usher Rudd had phoned him and told him.' He stood up again.

My father said, 'How did Wyvern think he would get away with it?'

Joe shrugged. 'He did last time. In the commotion, he simply walked away. If it hadn't been for the hotel manager, he quite likely would have done it again. But it was odd. He seemed just plain tired. There was no fight left in him. He could see he hadn't managed to finish either of you, and he simply gave up. We had no trouble arresting him.'

'And what are you charging him with?' my father asked.

'Attempted murder,' Joe said.

I faintly smiled. 'A 10-lb penalty.'

'Ten years,' Joe said.

*

The next Prime Minister held my hand.

I gripped his tight, as if he would give me comfort and security when I needed them badly.

I gripped his hand as if I'd been a little boy.

DICK FRANCIS

Wild Horses

£5.99

'A marvellous storyteller and an immaculate craftsman'
Daily Mail

Movie director Thomas Lyon came to Newmarket to rake the ashes of an old Jockey Club scandal for a new Hollywood film. Too late, he found himself listening to a blacksmith's dying confession. Found himself watching as the past came violently back to life.

Capturing the shockwaves over one woman's macabre death nearly thirty years before is drama. But a frenzied knife attack on the set of *Unstable Times* is definitely attempted murder. Who stood to gain from the threats? Between truth and shadowy fiction, Thomas Lyon already knew too much.

Following the real story could mean the difference between life and death. His own . . .

'Still the best bet for a winning read'
Mail on Sunday

DICK FRANCIS

For Kicks

£5.99

'Absolutely first class . . . warmly recommended'
Sunday Times

Proprietor of a stud farm in the breathtaking region of Australia's Snowy Mountains? Or muck-raking stable boy in Yorkshire?

The Earl of October persuades young Australian Danny Roke to accept the English alternative. It's the change of scene and the challenge that pushes Danny undercover, on the scent of a suspect racehorse dope scandal.

But the pain involved, dealing with vicious swindlers and the Earl's two attractive daughters, could overturn all his pleasure in the chase . . .

'Very lively, hard-bitten account . . . some jolting action scenes'
Financial Times

RAT RACE

Dick Francis has written forty-one international bestsellers and is widely acclaimed as one of the world's finest thriller writers. His awards include the Crime Writers' Association's Cartier Diamond Dagger for his outstanding contribution to the crime genre, and an honorary Doctorate of Humane Letters from Tufts University of Boston. In 1996 Dick Francis was made a Mystery Writers of America Grand Master for a lifetime's achievement and in 2000 he received a CBE in the Queen's Birthday Honours List.

Also by Dick Francis in Pan Books

THE SPORT OF QUEENS
(autobiography)

LESTER: The Official
Biography

DEAD CERT
NERVE
FOR KICKS
ODDS AGAINST
FLYING FINISH
BLOOD SPORT
FORFEIT
ENQUIRY
BONECRACK
SMOKESCREEN
SLAY-RIDE
KNOCK DOWN
HIGH STAKES
IN THE FRAME
RISK
TRIAL RUN
WHIP HAND
REFLEX
TWICE SHY
BANKER
THE DANGER
PROOF
BREAK IN
BOLT
HOT MONEY
THE EDGE
STRAIGHT
LONGSHOT
COMEBACK
DRIVING FORCE
DECIDER
WILD HORSES
COME TO GRIEF
TO THE HILT
10lb PENALTY
FIELD OF THIRTEEN
SECOND WIND
SHATTERED

Dick Francis

RAT RACE

PAN BOOKS

First published in Great Britain 1970 by Michael Joseph Ltd

This edition first published 1972 by Pan Books
an imprint of Macmillan Publishers Ltd
Pan Macmillan, 20 New Wharf Road, London N1 9RR
Basingstoke and Oxford
Associated companies throughout the world
www.panmacmillan.com

ISBN 0 330 02966 5

53 55 57 59 58 56 54 52

A CIP catalogue record for this book is available from the British Library.

Phototypeset by Intype London Ltd
Printed and bound in Great Britain by
Mackays of Chatham plc, Chatham, Kent

INTRODUCTION

I learned to fly in the Royal Air Force during the Second World War, and in the course of the 1940s flew Spitfire fighters and later Wellington and Lancaster bombers, amassing hundreds of hours in the air. On the thrifty novelist's premiss of not wasting any of life's experiences I decided to base one of my stories on flying (but not in wartime), the result being a book called *Flying Finish*.

My wife, Mary, helping me with earlier research for that book, undertook to go up for three flights in a light aircraft to find out about up-to-date civilian air regulations, which of course hadn't been in existence during the War. To our mutual surprise, Mary at once developed an enormous enthusiasm and aptitude at the controls, and in time became a qualified pilot herself.

From this almost accidental beginning she went on to take an Instrument Rating – approximately a master's degree in flying – and was commissioned to write a flying teaching book for absolute beginners which became recommended reading in British Airways pilot training schools.

We bought three light aircraft, two of them to lease to a flying training school and one, a fast little sports-car equivalent, for Mary to fly personally. People like jockeys, trainers and owners began asking her to fly them to the races, and eventually as a result we set up a small professional air-taxi and charter operation, employing six experienced British Airways pilots in their spare time – not Mary herself – to fly our paying passengers round the British Isles and Europe. Mary arranged the flights, smoothed their way and ran the records and business side.

Rat Race is about taxi flying. (Never waste experiences!) While I wrote the book, our own taxi business filled our days so that I was constantly surrounded by the raw materials of the story. Aircraft became the book's central characters, air procedures its structural bones. One might even say that page by page and hour by hour I lived and breathed the same basic concerns as my chief character, pilot Matt Shore.

As *Rat Race* is fiction, Matt Shore's more dangerous problems did *not* arise, I'm glad to say, in the seven years of our own air-taxi firm's life. We sold the successful little business finally to one of our chief customers and it is operating still, though changed and expanded, concentrating more on Euro-businessmen as passengers and less on the racing scene.

CHAPTER ONE

I picked four of them up at White Waltham in the new Cherokee Six 300 that never got a chance to grow old. The pale-blue upholstery still had a new leather smell and there wasn't a scratch on the glossy white fuselage. A nice little aeroplane, while it lasted.

They had ordered me for noon but they were already in the bar when I landed at eleven-forty. Three double whiskies and a lemonade.

Identification was easy: several chairs round a small table were draped with four lightweight raincoats, three binocular cases, two copies of the *Sporting Life* and one very small racing saddle. The four passengers were standing nearby in the sort of spread-about group indicative of people thrown together by business rather than natural friendship. They were not talking to each other, though it looked as though they had been. One, a large man, had a face full of anger. The smallest, evidently a jockey, was flushed and rigid. The two others, an elderly man and a middle-aged woman, were steadfastly staring at nothing in particular in the way that meant a lot of furious activity was going on inside their heads.

I walked towards the four of them across the large lounge reception room and spoke to an indeterminate spot in mid-air.

'Major Tyderman?'

The elderly man, who said 'Yes?', had been made a major a good long time ago. Nearer seventy than sixty; but still with a tough little body, wiry little moustache, sharp little eyes. He had thin salt-and-pepper hair brushed sideways across a balding crown and he carried his head stiffly, with his chin tucked back into his neck. Tense: very tense. And wary, looking at the world with suspicion.

He wore a lightweight speckled fawn suit vaguely reminiscent in cut of his military origins, and unlike the others had not parked his binoculars but wore them with the strap diagonally across his chest and the case facing forwards on his stomach, like a sporran. Club badges of metal and coloured cardboard hung in thick clusters at each side.

'Your aeroplane is here, Major,' I said. 'I'm Matt Shore . . . I'm flying you.'

He glanced over my shoulder, looking for someone else.

'Where's Larry?' he asked abruptly.

'He left,' I said. 'He got a job in Turkey.'

The Major's gaze came back from the search with a click. 'You're new,' he said accusingly.

'Yes,' I agreed.

'I hope you know the way.'

He meant it seriously. I said politely, 'I'll do my best.'

The second of the passengers, the woman on the Major's left, said flatly, 'The last time I flew to the races, the pilot got lost.'

I looked at her, giving her my best approximation to a confidence-boosting smile. 'The weather's good enough today not to have any fear of it.'

It wasn't true. There were cu-nims forecast for the June afternoon. And anyone can get lost any time if enough goes wrong. The woman gave me a disillusioned stare and I stopped wasting my confidence builder. She didn't need it. She had all the confidence in the world. She was fifty and fragile looking, with greying hair cut in a straight-across fringe and a jaw-length bob. There were two mild brown eyes under heavy dark eyebrows and a mouth that looked gentle; yet she held herself and behaved with the easy authority of a much higher command than the Major's. She was the only one of the group not outwardly ruffled.

The Major had been looking at his watch. 'You're early,' he said. 'We've got time for the other half.' He turned to the barman and ordered refills, and as an afterthought said to me, 'Something for you?'

I shook my head. 'No, thank you.'

The woman said indifferently, 'No alcohol for eight hours before a flight. Isn't that the rule?'

'More or less,' I agreed.

The third passenger, the large angry looking man, morosely watched the barman push the measure up twice on the Johnnie Walker. 'Eight hours. Good God,' he said. He looked as if eight hours seldom passed for him without topping up. The bulbous nose, the purple thread veins on his cheeks, the swelling paunch, they had all cost a lot in Excise duty.

The atmosphere I had walked into slowly subsided. The jockey sipped his low calorie lemonade, and the bright pink flush faded from his cheek bones and came out in fainter mottles on his neck. He seemed about twenty-one or two, reddish haired, with a naturally small frame and a moist looking skin. Few weight problems, I thought. No dehydration. Fortunate for him.

The Major and his large friend drank rapidly, muttered unintelligibly, and removed themselves to the Gents. The woman eyed the jockey and said in a voice which sounded more friendly than her comment, 'Are you out of your mind, Kenny Bayst? If you go on antagonizing Major Tyderman you'll be looking for another job.'

Kenny Bayst flicked his eyes to me and away again, compressing his rosebud mouth. He put the half-finished lemonade on the table and picked up one of the raincoats and the racing saddle.

'Which plane?' he said to me. 'I'll stow my gear.'

He had a strong Australian accent with a resentful bite to it. The woman watched him with what would have passed for a smile but for the frost in her eyes.

'The baggage door is locked,' I said. 'I'll come over with you.' To the woman I said, 'Can I carry your coat?'

'Thank you.' She indicated the coat which was obviously hers, a shiny rust-coloured affair with copper buttons. I picked it up, and also the businesslike binoculars lying on top, and followed Kenny Bayst out of the door.

After ten fuming paces he said explosively, 'It's too damn easy to blame the man on top.'

'They always blame the pilot,' I said mildly. 'Fact of life.'

'Huh?' he said. 'Oh yeah. Too right. They do.'

We reached the end of the path and started across the grass. He was still oozing grudge. I wasn't much interested.

'For the record,' I said, 'What are the names of my other passengers? Besides the Major, that is.'

He turned his head in surprise. 'Don't you know her? Our Annie Villars? Looks like someone's cosy old granny and has a tongue that would flay a kangaroo. Everyone knows our little Annie.' His tone was sour and disillusioned.

'I don't know much about racing,' I said.

'Oh? Well, she's a trainer, then. A damned good trainer, I'll say that for her, I wouldn't stay with her else. Not with that tongue of hers. I'll tell you, sport, she can roust her stable lads out of the gallops in words a sergeant-major never thought of. But sweet as milk with the owners. Has them eating out of her little hand.'

'The horses, too?'

'Uh? Oh, yeah. The horses love her. She can ride like a jock, too, when she's a mind to. Not that she does it much now. She must be getting on a bit. Still, she knows what she's at, true enough. She knows what a horse can do and what it can't, and that's most of the battle in this game.'

His voice held resentment and admiration in roughly equal amounts.

I said, 'What is the name of the other man? The big one.'

This time it was pure resentment: no admiration. He spat the name out syllable by deliberate syllable, curling his lips away from his teeth.

'Mister Eric Goldenberg.'

Having got rid of the name he shut his mouth tight and was clearly taking his employer's remarks to heart. We reached the aircraft and stowed the coats and his saddle in the baggage space behind the rear seats.

'We're going to Newbury first, aren't we?' he asked. 'To pick up Colin Ross?'

'Yes.'

He gave me a sardonic look. 'Well, you *must* have heard of Colin Ross.'

'I guess,' I agreed, 'that I have.'

It would have been difficult not to, since the champion jockey was twice as popular as the Prime Minister and earned six times as much. His face appeared on half the billboards in Britain encouraging the populace to drink more milk and there was even a picture strip about him in a children's comic. Everyone, but everyone, had heard of Colin Ross.

Kenny Bayst climbed in through the rear end door and sat in one of the two rear seats. I took a quick look round the outside of the aircraft, even though I'd done a thorough preflight check on it not an hour ago, before I left base. It was my first week, my fourth day, my third flight for Derrydown Sky Taxis, and after the way Fate had clobbered me in the past, I was taking no chances.

There were no nuts loose, no rivets missing on the sharp-nosed little six-seater. There were eight quarts of oil where there should have been eight quarts of oil, there were no dead birds clogging up the air intakes to the engine, there were no punctures in the tyres, no cracks in the green or red glass over the navigation lights, no chips in the propeller blades, no loose radio aerials. The pale-blue cowling over the engine was securely clipped down, and the matching pale-blue cowlings over the struts and wheels of the fixed undercarriage were as solid as rocks.

By the time I'd finished the other three passengers were coming across the grass. Goldenberg was doing the talking with steam still coming out of his ears, while the Major nodded agreement in unhappy little jerks and Annie Villars looked as if she wasn't listening. When they arrived within earshot Goldenberg was saying '. . . can't lay the horse unless we're sure he'll pull it . . .' But he stopped with a snap when the Major gestured sharply in my direction. He need hardly have bothered. I had no curiosity about their affairs.

On the principle that in a light aircraft it is better to have the centre of gravity as far forward as possible, I asked Goldenberg to sit in front in the right-hand seat beside me, and put the Major and Annie Villars in the centre two seats, and left Kenny in the last two, with the empty one ready for Colin Ross. The four rear seats were reached by the port side door, but Goldenberg had to climb in by stepping up on the low wing on the starboard side and lowering into his seat through the forward door. He waited while I got in before him and moved over to my side, then squeezed his bulk in through the door and settled heavily into his seat.

They were all old hands at air taxis: they had their safety belts fastened before I did mine, and when I looked round to check that they were ready to go, the Major was already deep in the *Sporting Life*. Kenny Bayst was cleaning his nails with fierce little jabs, relieving his frustration by hurting himself.

I got clearance from the tower and lifted the little aeroplane away for the twenty-mile hop across Berkshire. Taxi flying was a lot different from the airlines, and finding racecourses looked more difficult to me than being radar vectored into Heathrow. I'd never before flown a racecourse trip, and I'd asked my predecessor Larry about it that morning when he'd come into the office to collect his cards.

'Newbury's a cinch,' he said offhandedly. 'Just point

its nose at that vast runway the Yanks built at Greenham Common. You can practically see it from Scotland. The racecourse is just north of it, and the landing strip is parallel with the white rails of the finishing straight. You can't miss it. Good long strip. No problems. As for Haydock, it's just where the M6 motorway crosses the East Lancs road. Piece of cake.'

He took himself off to Turkey, stopping on one foot at the doorway for some parting advice. 'You'll have to practise short landings before you go to Bath; and avoid Yarmouth in a heatwave. It's all yours now, mate, and the best of British luck.'

It was true that you could see Greenham Common from a long way off, but on a fine day it would anyway have been difficult to lose the way from White Waltham to Newbury; the main railway line to Exeter ran more or less straight from one to the other. My passengers had flown into Newbury before, and the Major helpfully told me to look out for the electric cables strung across the approach. We landed respectably on the newly mown grass and taxied along the strip towards the grandstand end, braking to a stop just before the boundary fence.

Colin Ross wasn't there.

I shut down the engine, and in the sudden silence Annie Villars remarked, 'He's bound to be late. He said he was riding work for Bob Smith, and Bob's never on time getting his horses out.'

The other three nodded vaguely but they were still

not on ordinarily chatty terms with each other, and after about five minutes of heavy silence I asked Goldenberg to let me out to stretch my legs. He grunted and mumbled at having to climb out on to the wing to let me past him and I gathered I was breaking Derrydown's number one rule: never annoy the customers, you're going to need them again.

Once I was out of their company, however, they did start talking. I walked round to the front of the aircraft and leant against the leading edge of the wing; and looked up at the scattered clouds in the blue-grey sky and thought unprofitably about this and that. Behind me their voices rose acrimoniously, and when they opened the door wide to get some air, scraps of what they were saying floated across.

'... simply asking for a dope test.' Annie Villars.

'... if you can't ride a losing race better than last time ... find someone else.' Goldenberg.

'... very difficult position ...' Major Tyderman.

A short sharp snap from Kenny, and Annie Villars' exasperated exclamation. 'Bayst!'

'... not paying you more than last time.' The Major, very emphatically.

Indistinct protest from Kenny, and a violently clear reaction from Goldenberg: 'Bugger your licence.'

Kenny my lad, I thought remotely, if you don't watch out you'll end up like me, still with a licence but with not much else.

A Ford-of-all-work rolled down the road past the

grandstands, came through the gate in the boundary fence, and bounced over the turf towards the aircraft. It stopped about twenty feet away, and two men climbed out. The larger, who had been driving, went round to the back and pulled out a brown canvas and leather overnight grip. The smaller one walked on over the grass. I took my weight off the wing and stood up. He stopped a few paces away, waiting for the larger man to catch up. He was dressed in faded blue jeans and a whitish cotton sweater with navy-blue edgings. Black canvas shoes on his narrow feet. He had nondescript brownish hair over an exceptionally broad forehead, a short straight nose, and a delicate feminine looking chin. All his bones were fine and his waist and hips would have been the despair of Victorian maidens. Yet there was something unmistakably masculine about him: and more than that, he was mature. He looked at me with the small still smile behind the eyes which is the hallmark of those who know what life is really about. His soul was old. He was twenty-six.

'Good morning,' I said.

He held out his hand, and I shook it. His clasp was cool, firm, and brief.

'No Larry?' he inquired.

'He's left. I'm Matt Shore.'

'Fine,' he said noncommittally. He didn't introduce himself. He knew there was no need. I wondered what it was like to be in that position. It hadn't affected Colin Ross. He had none of the 'I am' aura which often clings around the notably successful, and from the extreme understatement of his clothes I gathered that he avoided it consciously.

'We're late, I'm afraid,' he said. 'Have to bend the throttle.'

'Do my best . . .'

The larger man arrived with the grip, and I stowed it in the forward luggage locker between the engine wall and the forward bulkhead of the cabin. By the time the baggage door was securely fastened Colin Ross had found his empty seat and strapped himself into it. Goldenberg with heavy grunts moved out again so that I could get back to my left-hand place. The larger man, who was apparently the dilatory trainer Bob Smith, said his hellos and goodbyes to the passengers, and stood watching afterwards while I started the engine and taxied back to the other end of the strip to turn into wind for take-off.

The flight north was uneventful: I went up the easy way under the Amber One airway, navigating on the radio beacons at Daventry, Lichfield and Oldham. Manchester control routed us right round the north of their zone so that I had to drop down southwards towards Haydock racecourse, and there it was, just as Larry had said, near the interchange of the two giant roads. We touched down on the grass strip indicated in the centre of the course, and I taxied on and parked where the Major told me to, near the rails of the track itself, a mere hundred yards from the grandstand.

The passengers disembarked themselves and their belongings and Colin Ross looked at his watch. A faint smile hovered and was gone. He made no comment. He said merely, 'Are you coming in to the races?'

I shook my head. 'Think I'll stay over here.'

'I'll arrange with the man on the gate to let you into the paddock, if you change your mind.'

'Thanks,' I said in surprise. 'Thanks very much.'

He nodded briefly and set off without waiting for the others, ducking under the white-painted rails and trudging across the track.

'Pilots' perks,' Kenny said, taking his raincoat from my hand and putting his arm forward for the saddle. 'You want to take advantage.'

'Maybe I will,' I said, but I didn't mean to. Horse racing began and ended with the Derby as far as I was concerned, and also I was a non-gambler by nature.

Annie Villars said in her deceptively gentle voice, 'You do understand that we're all going on to Newmarket after the races, and not back to Newbury?'

'Yes,' I assured her. 'That's what I was told.'

'Good.'

'If we don't go to jail,' Kenny said under his breath. Goldenberg looked at me sharply to see if I'd heard that, and I gave no sign of it. Whatever they were about, it was as little my concern as who killed Cock Robin.

Major Tyderman pushed at his moustache with a hand rigid with nervous energy and said, 'Last race at four-thirty. Need a drink after that. Ready to start back at, say, five-fifteen. That all right with you?'

'Perfectly, Major,' I nodded.

'Right,' he said. 'Good.' His gaze was flicking from one to another of his travelling companions, assessing and suspicious. His eyes narrowed fiercely at Kenny Bayst, opened and narrowed again rapidly on Goldenberg, relaxed on Annie Villars and went cold on the vanishing back of Colin Ross. The thoughts behind the outward physical reactions were unguessable, and when he finally looked back at me he didn't really see me, he was busy with the activity inside his head.

'Five-fifteen,' he repeated vaguely. 'Good.'

Kenny said to me, 'Don't waste your money in the three-thirty, sport'; and Goldenberg raised his fist with a face going purple with anger and nearly hit him.

Annie Villars' voice rapped into him, the steel sticking through the cream with a vengeance, the top-brass quality transcendent and withering.

'Control your temper, you stupid man.'

Goldenberg's mouth literally dropped open, to reveal a bottom row of unappetising brown stained teeth. His raised fist lowered slowly, and he looked altogether foolish.

'As for you,' she said to Kenny, 'I told you to keep your tongue still, and that was your last chance.'

'Are you sacking me?' he asked.

'I'll decide that at the end of the afternoon.'

Kenny showed no anxiety about keeping his job, and

I realized that in fact what he had been doing was trying to provoke them into getting rid of him. He'd got himself into nutcrackers and while they squeezed he couldn't get out.

I became mildly curious to see what would happen in the three-thirty. It would help to pass the afternoon.

They straggled off towards the stands, Kenny in front, the Major and Goldenberg together, with Annie Villars several paces behind. The Major kept stopping and looking back and waiting for her, but every time just as she reached him he turned and went off again in front, so that as a piece of courtesy, the whole thing was wasted. He reminded me vividly of an aunt who had taken me for childhood walks in just that way. I remembered quite clearly that it had been infuriating.

I sighed, shut the baggage doors and tidied up the aeroplane. Annie Villars had been smoking thin brown cigars. Goldenberg had been eating indigestion tablets, each from a square wrapper. The Major had left his *Sporting Life* in a tumbled heap on the floor.

While I was fiddling around with the debris, two more aeroplanes flew in, a four-seat high-winged Cessna and a six-seat twin-engined Aztec.

I watched their touchdowns with an uncritical eye, though I wouldn't have given the Aztec pilot a gold medal for his double bounce. Several small men disgorged themselves and made a dart like a flock of starlings across the track towards the paddock. They were followed by three or four larger and slower-moving people slung around with binoculars and what I later learned to be bags for carrying sets of racing colours. Finally out of each aircraft popped the most leisurely of all the inmates, a man dressed very much as I was, in dark trousers, white shirt, neat dark tie.

They strolled towards each other and lit cigarettes. After a while, not wanting to seem unsociable, I wandered across to join them. They turned and watched me come, but with no welcome in unsmiling faces.

'Hello,' I said moderately. 'Nice day.'

'Perhaps,' said one.

'You think so?' said the other.

They offered me fish-eyed stares but no cigarette. I had grown hardened to that sort of thing. I turned half away from them and read the names of the firms they flew for, which were painted on the tails of their aircraft. It was the same name on both. Polyplane Services.

How dreary of them, I thought, to be so antagonistic. I gave them the benefit of a very small doubt and made one more approach.

'Have you come far?'

They didn't answer. Just gave me the stares, like two cod.

I laughed at them as if I thought their behaviour pathetic, which in fact I did, and turned on my heel to go back to my own territory. When I'd gone ten steps one of them called after me, 'Where's Larry Gedge?' He didn't sound as if he liked Larry any better than me.

I decided not to hear: if they really wanted to know,

they could come and ask nicely. It was their turn to cross the grass.

They didn't bother. I wasn't particularly sorry. I had long ago learned that pilots were not all one great happy brotherhood. Pilots could be as bloodyminded to each other as any group on earth.

I climbed back into my seat in the Cherokee and sorted out my maps and flight plans for the return journey. I had four hours to do it in and it took me ten minutes. After that I debated whether to go over to the stands and find some lunch, and decided I wasn't hungry. After that I yawned. It was a habit.

I had been depressed for so long that it had become a permanent state of mind. Expectations might lift the edge of the cloud every time one took a new job, but life never turned out to be as good as the hopes. This was my sixth job since I'd gone to learn flying with stars in my eyes, my fourth since the stars had faded for good. I had thought that taxi flying might be interesting, and after crop spraying, which I'd been doing last, anything would be; and perhaps it would indeed be interesting, but if I'd thought it might be free of gripe and bad temper I'd been kidding myself. For here it all was, as usual. Squabbling passengers and belligerent competitors and no discernible joy anywhere.

There was a small buffet on the side of the fuselage and the jar and sound of someone stepping up on to the wing. The slightly open door was pushed wide with a crash, and into its space appeared a girl, bending at the waist and knees and neck so that she could look inside and across at me.

She was slim and dark haired and she was wearing large square sunglasses. Also she had a blue linen dress and long white boots. She looked great. The afternoon instantly improved.

'You lousy bloody skunk,' she said.

It really was one of those days.

CHAPTER TWO

'Wow,' she said. 'Wrong man.' She took off the sunglasses and folded them away in the white handbag which hung from her shoulder by a thick red, white and blue cord.

'Think nothing of it.'

'Where's Larry?'

'Gone to Turkey.'

'Gone?' she said blankly. 'Do you mean literally gone already, or planning to go, or what?'

I looked at my watch. 'Took off from Heathrow twenty minutes ago, I believe.'

'Damn,' she said forcibly. 'Bloody damn.'

She straightened up so that all I could see of her was from the waist down. A pleasant enough view for any poor aviator. The legs looked about twenty-three years old and there was nothing wrong with them.

She bent down again. Nothing wrong with the rest of her, either.

'When will he be back?'

'He had a three-year contract.'

'Oh, *hell.*' She stared at me in dismay for a few seconds, then said, 'Can I come in there and talk to you for a minute?'

'Sure,' I agreed, and moved my maps and stuff off Goldenberg's seat. She stepped down into the cockpit and slid expertly into place. By no means her first entrance into a light aircraft. I wondered about Larry. Lucky Larry.

'I suppose he didn't give you . . . a parcel . . . or anything . . . to give me, did he?' she said gloomily.

'Nothing, I'm afraid.'

'He's an absolute beast then . . . er, is he a friend of yours?'

'I've met him twice, that's all.'

'He's pinched my hundred quid,' she said bitterly.

'He pinched? . . .'

'He bloody has. Not to mention my handbag and keys and everything.' She stopped and compressed her mouth in anger. Then she added, 'I left my handbag in this aeroplane three weeks ago, when we flew to Doncaster. And Larry has been saying ever since that he'll bring it on the next trip to the races and give it to Colin to give to me, and for three solid weeks he's kept on forgetting it. I suppose he knew he was going to Turkey and he thought if he could put it off long enough he would never have to give my bag back.'

'Colin . . . Colin Ross?' I asked. She nodded abstractedly.

'Is he your husband?'

She looked startled, then laughed. 'Good Lord, no. He's my brother. I saw him just now in the paddock and I said, "Has he brought my handbag?" and he shook his head and started to say something, but I belted off over here in a fury without stopping to listen, and I suppose he was going to tell me it wasn't Larry who had come in the plane . . . Oh damn it, I *hate* being robbed. Colin would have lent him a hundred quid if he was that desperate. He didn't have to pinch it.'

'It was a lot of money to have in a handbag,' I suggested.

'Colin had just given it to me, you see. In the plane. Some owner had handed him a terrific present in readies, and he gave me a hundred of it to pay a bill with, which was really sweet of him, and I can hardly expect him to give me another hundred just because I was silly enough to leave the first one lying about . . .' Her voice tailed off in depression.

'The bill,' she added wryly, 'is for flying lessons.'

I looked at her with interest. 'How far have you got?'

'Oh, I've got my licence,' she said. 'These were instrument flying lessons. And radio navigation, and all that jazz. I've done about ninety-five hours, altogether. Spread over about four years, though, sad to say.'

That put her in the experienced-beginner class and the dangerous time bracket. After eighty hours flying, pilots are inclined to think they know enough. After a hundred hours, they are sure they don't. Between the two, the accident rate is at its peak.

She asked me several questions about the aeroplane, and I answered them. Then she said, 'Well, there's no point in sitting here all afternoon,' and began to lever herself out on to the wing. 'Aren't you coming over to the races?'

'No,' I shook my head.

'Oh come on,' she said. 'Do.'

The sun was shining and she was very pretty. I smiled and said 'OK,' and followed her out on to the grass. It is profitless now to speculate on the different course things would have taken if I'd stayed where I was.

I collected my jacket from the rear baggage compartment and locked all the doors and set off with her across the track. The man on the gate duly let me into the paddock and Colin Ross' sister showed no sign of abandoning me once we were inside. Instead she diagnosed my almost total ignorance and seemed pleased to be able to start dispelling it.

'You see that brown horse over there,' she said, steering me towards the parade ring rails, 'That one walking round the far end, number sixteen, that's Colin's mount in this race. It's come out a bit light but it looks well in its coat.'

'It does?'

She looked at me in amusement. 'Definitely.'

'Shall I back it, then?'

'It's all a joke to you.'

'No,' I protested.

'Oh yes indeed,' she nodded. 'You're looking at this

race meeting in the way I'd look at a lot of spiritualists. Disbelieving and a bit superior.'

'Ouch.'

'But what you're actually seeing is a large export industry in the process of marketing its wares.'

'I'll remember that.'

'And if the industry takes place out of doors on a nice fine sunny day with everyone enjoying themselves, well, so much the better.'

'Put that way,' I agreed, 'it's a lot more jolly than a car factory.'

'You will get involved,' she said with certainty.

'No.' I was equally definite.

She shook her head. 'You will, you know, if you do much racecourse taxi work. It'll bust through that cool shell of yours and make you feel something, for a change.'

I blinked. 'Do you always talk like that to total strangers?'

'No,' she said slowly. 'I don't.'

The bright little jockeys flooded into the parade ring and scattered to small earnest owner-trainer groups where there were a lot of serious conversations and much nodding of heads. On the instructions of Colin Ross' sister I tried moderately hard to take it all seriously. Not with much success.

Colin Ross' sister . . .

'Do you have a name?' I asked.

'Often.'

'Thanks.'

She laughed. 'It's Nancy. What's yours?'

'Matt Shore.'

'Hm. A flat matt name. Very suitable.'

The jockeys were thrown up like confetti and landed in their saddles, and their spindly shining long-legged transportation skittered its way out on to the track. Two-year-olds, Nancy said.

She walked me back towards the stands and proposed to smuggle me into the 'Owners and Trainers'. The large official at the bottom of the flight of steps beamed at her until his eyes disappeared and he failed to inspect me for the right bit of cardboard.

It seemed that nearly everyone on the small rooftop stand knew Nancy, and obvious that they agreed with the beaming official's assessment. She introduced me to several people whose interest collapsed like a soufflé in a draught when they found I didn't understand their opening bids.

'He's a pilot,' Nancy explained apologetically. 'He flew Colin here today.'

'Ah,' they said. 'Ah.'

Two of my other passengers were there. Annie Villars was watching the horses canter past with an intent eye and a pursed mouth: the field-marshal element was showing strongly, the feminine camouflage in abeyance. Major Tyderman, planted firmly with his legs apart and his chin tucked well back into his neck, was scribbling notes into his racecard. When he looked up he saw us, and made his way purposefully across.

'I say,' he said to me, having forgotten my name. 'Did I leave my *Sporting Life* over in the plane, do you know?'

'Yes, you did, Major.'

'Blast,' he said. 'I made some notes on it . . . Must get it, you know. Have to go across after this race.'

'Would you like me to fetch it?' I asked.

'Well, that's very good of you, my dear chap. But . . . no . . . couldn't ask it. Walk will do me good.'

'The aircraft's locked, Major,' I said. 'You'll need the keys.' I took them out of my pocket and gave them to him.

'Right.' He nodded stiffly. 'Good.'

The race started away off down the track and was all over long before I sorted out the colours of Colin Ross. In the event, it wasn't difficult. He had won.

'How's Midge?' Annie Villars said to Nancy, restoring her giant raceglasses to their case.

'Oh, much better, thank you. Getting on splendidly.'

'I'm so glad. She's had a bad time, poor girl.'

Nancy nodded and smiled, and everyone trooped down the stairs to the ground.

'Well now,' Nancy said. 'How about some coffee? And something to munch, perhaps?'

'You must have others you'd prefer to be with . . . I won't get into trouble, you know, on my own.'

Her lips twitched. 'Today I need a bodyguard. I

elected you for the job. Desert me if you like, but if you want to please, stick.'

'Not difficult,' I said.

'Great. Coffee, then.'

It was iced coffee, rather good. Halfway through the turkey sandwiches the reason why Nancy wanted me with her drifted up to the small table where we sat and slobbered all over her. She fended off what looked to me like a random assembly of long hair, beard, beads, fringes and a garment like a tablecloth with a hole in it, and yelled to me through the undergrowth, 'Buddy, your job starts right now.'

I stood up, reached out two hands, caught hold of an assortment of wool and hair, and pulled firmly backwards. The result resolved itself into a youngish man sitting down with surprise much more suddenly than he'd intended.

'Nancy,' he said in an aggrieved voice.

'This is Chanter,' she said to me. 'He's never grown out of the hippie thing, as you can see.'

'I'm an artist,' he said. He had an embroidered band across his forehead and round his head: like the horses' bridles, I thought fleetingly. All the hair was clean and there were shaven parts on his jaw just to prove that it wasn't from pure laziness that he let everything grow. On closer inspection I was sure that it was indeed a dark-green chenille tablecloth, with a central hole for his head. Underneath that he wore low-slung buckskin trousers fringed from hip to ankle, and a creepy crêpy dim mauve shirt curved to fit his concave stomach. Various necklaces and pendants on silver chains hung round his neck. Under all the splendour he had dirty bare feet.

'I went to art school with him,' Nancy said resignedly. 'That was in London. Now he's at Liverpool, just down the road. Any time I come racing up here, he turns up too.'

'Uh,' Chanter said profoundly.

'Do you get grants for ever?' I asked: not sneeringly; I simply wanted to know.

He was not offended. 'Look, man, like, up here I'm the fuzz.'

I nearly laughed. Nancy said, 'You know what he means, then?'

'He teaches,' I said.

'Yeah, man, that's what I said.' He took one of the turkey sandwiches. His fingers were greenish with black streaks. Paint.

'You keep your impure thoughts off this little bird,' he said to me, spitting out bits of bread. 'She's strictly my territory. But strictly, man.'

'Zat so?'

'Zat definitely, but definitely . . . is . . . so, man.'

'How come?'

He gave me a look which was as off beat as his appearance.

'I've still got the salt to put on this little bird's tail,' he said. 'Shan't be satisfied till it's there . . .'

Nancy was looking at him with an expression which

meant that she didn't know whether to laugh at him or be afraid of him. She couldn't decide whether he was Chanter the amorous buffoon or Chanter the frustrated sex maniac. Nor could I. I understood her needing help when he was around.

'He only wants me because I won't,' she said.

'The challenge bit,' I nodded. 'Affront to male pride, and all that.'

'Practically every other girl has,' she said.

'That makes it worse.'

Chanter looked at me broodingly. 'You're a drag, man. I mean, cubic.'

'To each his scene,' I said ironically.

He took the last of the sandwiches, turned his back studiously towards me and said to Nancy, 'Let's you and me lose this dross, huh?'

'Let's you and me do nothing of the sort, Chanter. If you want to tag along, Matt comes in the deal.'

He scowled at the floor and then suddenly stood up so that all the fringes and beads danced and jingled.

'Come on, then. Let's get a look at the horses. Life's a-wasting.'

'He really can draw,' Nancy said as we followed the tablecloth out into the sunshine.

'I wouldn't doubt it. I'll bet half of what he does is caricature, though, with a strong element of cruelty.'

'How d'you know?' she said, startled.

'He just seems like that.'

He padded along beside us in his bare feet and was a

sufficiently unusual sight on a racecourse to attract a barrage of stares ranging from amusement to apoplexy. He didn't seem to notice. Nancy looked as if she were long used to it.

We came to a halt against the parade ring rails where Chanter rested his elbows and exercised his voice.

'Horses,' he said. 'I'm not for the Stubbs and Munnings thing. When I see a racehorse I see a machine, and that's what I paint, a horse-shaped machine with pistons thumping away and muscle fibres like connecting rods and a crack in the crank case with the oil dripping away drop by drop into the body cavity . . .' He broke off abruptly but with the same breath finished. 'How's your sister?'

'She's much better,' Nancy said, not seeming to see any great change of subject. 'She's really quite well now.'

'Good,' he said, and went straight on with his lecture. 'And then I draw some distant bulging stands with hats flying off and everyone cheering and all the time the machine is bursting its gut . . . I see components, I see what's happening to the bits . . . the stresses . . . I see colours in components too . . . nothing on earth is a whole . . . nothing is ever what it seems . . . everything is components.' He stopped abruptly, thinking about what he'd said.

After a suitably appreciative pause, I asked, 'Do you ever sell your paintings?'

'Sell them?' He gave me a scornful, superior stare. 'No, I don't. Money is disgusting.'

'It's more disgusting when you haven't got it,' Nancy said.

'You're a renegade, girl,' he said fiercely.

'Love on a crust,' she said, 'is fine when you're twenty, but pretty squalid when you're sixty.'

'I don't intend to be sixty. Sixty is strictly for grandfathers. Not my scene at all.'

We turned away from the rails and came face to face with Major Tyderman, who was carrying his *Sporting Life* and holding out the aircraft's keys. His gaze swept over Chanter and he controlled himself admirably. Not a twitch.

'I locked up again,' he said, handing me the bunch.

'Thanks, Major.'

He nodded, glanced once more at Chanter, and retreated in good order.

Even for Nancy's sake the official wouldn't let Chanter up the steps to the Owners and Trainers. We watched at grass level with Chanter muttering 'stinking bourgeois' at regular intervals.

Colin Ross finished second. The crowd booed and tore up a lot of tickets. Nancy looked as though she were long used to that, too.

Between the next two races we sat on the grass while Chanter gave us the uninterrupted benefit of his views on the evils of money, racialism, war, religion and marriage. It was regulation stuff, nothing new. I didn't say I thought so. During the discourse he twice without warning stretched over and put his hand on Nancy's breast. Each time without surprise she picked it off again by the wrist and threw it back at him. Neither of them seemed to think it needed comment.

After the next race (Colin was third) Chanter remarked that his throat was dry, and Nancy and I obediently followed him off to the Tattersalls bar for lubrication. Coca-Colas for three, splashed out of the bottles by an overworked barmaid. Chanter busily juggled the three glasses so that it was I who paid, which figured.

The bar was only half full but a great deal of space and attention was being taken up by one man, a large tough-looking individual with a penetrating Australian accent. He had an obviously new white plaster cast on his leg and a pair of crutches which he hadn't mastered. His loud laugh rose above the general buzz as he constantly apologised for knocking into people.

'Haven't got the hang of these props yet . . .'

Chanter regarded him, as he did most things, with some disfavour.

The large Australian went on explaining his state to two receptive acquaintances.

'Mind you, can't say I'm sorry I broke my ankle. Best investment I ever made.' The laugh rang out infectiously and most people in the bar began to grin. Not Chanter, of course.

'See, I only paid my premium the week before, and

then I fell down these steps and I got a thousand quid for it. Now that ain't whistling, that ain't, eh? A thousand bleeding quid for falling down a flight of steps.' He laughed again hugely, enjoying the joke. 'Come on mates,' he said, 'Drink up, and let's go and invest some of this manna from Heaven on my good friend Kenny Bayst.'

I jumped a fraction and looked at my watch. Coming up to three-thirty. Kenny Bayst clearly hadn't told his good friend not to speculate. Absolutely none of my business. Telling him myself would be the worst favour I could do for Kenny Bayst.

The large Australian swung himself out of the bar, followed by the two mates. Chanter's curiosity overcame his disinclination to show himself at a loss.

'Who,' he said crossly, 'is going to give that schmo a thousand quid for breaking his ankle?'

Nancy smiled. 'It's a new insurance fund, specially for people who go racing. Accident insurance. I don't really know. I've heard one or two people mention it lately.'

'Insurance is immoral,' Chanter said dogmatically, sliding round behind her and laying his hand flat on her stomach. Nancy picked it off and stepped away. As a bodyguard, I didn't seem to be doing much good.

Nancy said she particularly wanted to see this race properly, and left Chanter looking moody at the bottom of the staircase. Without asking her I followed her up the steps: a period alone with Chanter held no attractions.

Kenny Bayst, according to my slantways look at Nancy's racecard, was riding a horse called Rudiments: number seven, owned by the Duke of Wessex, trained by Miss Villars, carrying olive green with silver crossbelts and cap. I watched the horse canter down past the stands on the olive-green grass and reflected that the Duke of Wessex had chosen colours which were as easy to distinguish as coal on a black night.

I said to Nancy, 'What did Rudiments do in his last race?'

'Hm?' she said absentmindedly, all her attention on the rose-pink and white shape of her brother. 'Did you say Rudiments?'

'That's right. I brought Kenny Bayst and Annie Villars here, as well.'

'Oh. I see.' She looked down at her racecard. 'Last time out . . . it won. Time before that, it won. Time before that, it came fourth.'

'It's good, then?'

'Fairly, I suppose.' She wrinkled her nose at me. 'I told you you'd get involved.'

I shook my head. 'Just curious.'

'Same thing.'

'Is it favourite?'

'No, Colin is. But . . . you can see over there, on that big board . . . see? . . . Rudiments is second favourite on the Tote at about three to one.'

'Well . . .' I said. 'What does it mean, to lay a horse?'

'It means to stand a bet. It's what bookmakers do. What the Tote does, really, come to that.'

'Can people do it who aren't bookmakers?'

'Oh sure. They do. Say the bookmakers are offering three to one, and you yourself don't think the horse will win, you could say to your friends, I'll lay you four to one; so they'd bet with you because you were offering more. Also, no betting tax. Private wager, you see.'

'And if the horse wins, you pay out?'

'You sure do.'

'I see,' I said. And I did. Eric Goldenberg had laid Rudiments the last time it had run because Kenny Bayst had agreed to lose, and then he'd gone and won. Their tempers were still on the dicky side as a result: and they had been arguing today about whether or not to try again.

'Colin thinks he'll win this,' Nancy said. 'I do hope so.'

Bonanza for Bayst, I thought.

It was a seven furlong race, it seemed. The horses accelerated from standing to 30 mph in times which would have left a Porsche gasping. When they swung away round the far bend Rudiments was as far as I was concerned invisible, and until the last hundred yards I didn't see him once. Then all of a sudden there he was, boxed in in a bunch on the rails and unable to get past Colin Ross directly in front.

Kenny didn't find his opening. He finished the race in

third place, still pinned in by Colin in front and a dappled grey alongside. I couldn't begin to tell whether or not he had done it on purpose.

'Wasn't that *great*?' Nancy exclaimed to the world in general, and a woman on the far side of her agreed that it was, and asked after the health of her sister Midge.

'Oh, she's fine, thanks,' Nancy said. She turned to me and there was less joy in her eyes than in her voice. 'Come over here,' she said. 'You can see them unsaddling the winner.'

The Owners and Trainers turned out to be on the roof of the weighing room. We leaned over the rails at the front and watched Colin and Kenny unbuckle the saddle girths, loop the saddles over their arms, pat their steaming horses, and disappear into the weighing room. The group in the winner's enclosure were busy slapping backs and unburdening to the Press. The group in the third enclosure wore small tight smiles and faraway eyes. I still couldn't tell if they were ecstatic and hiding it, or livid and ditto.

The horses were led away and the groups dispersed. In their place appeared Chanter, staring up and waving his arm.

'Come on down,' he shouted.

'No inhibitions, that's his trouble,' Nancy said. 'If we don't go down, he'll just go on shouting.'

He did. An official strode up manfully to ask him to belt up and buzz off, but it was like ripples trying to push over Bass Rock.

'Come on down, Nancy.' Fortissimo.

She pushed herself away from the rails and took enough steps to be out of his sight.

'Stay with me,' she said. It was more than half a question.

'If you want it.'

'You've seen what he's like. And he's been mild, today. Mild. Thanks to you.'

'I've done absolutely nothing.'

'You're here.'

'Why do you come to Haydock, if he always bothers you too much?'

'Because I'm bloody well not letting him frighten me away.'

'He loves you,' I said.

'No. Can't you tell the difference, for God's sake?'

'Yes,' I said.

She looked startled, then shook her head. 'He loves Chanter, full stop.'

She took three more steps towards the stairs, then stopped again.

'Why is it that I talk to you as if I'd known you for years?'

To a certain extent I knew, but I smiled and shook my head. No one cares to say straight out that it's because one is as negative as wallpaper.

Chanter's plaintive voice floated up the steps. 'Nancy, come on down . . .'

She took another step, and then stopped again. 'Will

you do me another favour? I'm staying up here a few more days with an aunt, but I bought a present for Midge this morning and I've given it to Colin to take home. But he's got a memory like a string vest for everything except horses, so would you check with him that he hasn't left it in the changing room, before you take off?'

'Sure,' I said. 'Your sister . . . I gather she's been ill.'

She looked away up at the sun-filled sky and down again and straight at me, and in a shattering moment of awareness I saw the pain and the cracks behind the bright public façade.

'Has been. Will be,' she said. 'She's got leukaemia.'

After a pause she swallowed and added the unbearable bit.

'She's my identical twin.'

CHAPTER THREE

After the fifth race Chanter gloomily announced that about fifty plastic students were waiting for him to pat their egos and that although he despised the system he was likely to find eating a problem if he actually got the sack. His farewell to Nancy consisted in wiping his hands all over her, front and back, and giving her an open-mouthed kiss which owing to her split-second evasive action landed on her ear.

He glared at me as if it were my fault. Nancy not relenting, he scowled at her and muttered something about salt, and then twirled around on his bare heel so that the tablecloth and all the hair and fringes and beads swung out with centrifugal force, and strode away at high speed towards the exit.

'The soles of his feet are like leather,' she said. 'Disgusting.' But from the hint of indulgence in her face I gathered that Chanter's cause wasn't entirely lost.

She said she was thirsty again and could do with a Coke, and since she seemed to want me still to tag along, I tagged. This time, without Chanter, we went to the members' bar in the Club enclosure, the small downstairs one that was open to the main entrance hall.

The man in the plaster cast was there again. Different audience. Same story. His big cheerful booming voice filled the little bar and echoed round the whole hall outside.

'You can't hear yourself think,' Nancy said.

In a huddle in a far corner were Major Tyderman and Eric Goldenberg, sitting at a small table with what looked like treble whiskies in front of them. Their heads were bent towards each other, close, almost touching, so that they could each hear what the other was saying amid the din, yet not be overheard. Relations between them didn't seem to be at their most cordial. There was a great deal of rigidity in their down-bent faces, and no friendliness in the small flicking glances they occasionally gave each other.

'The *Sporting Life* man,' Nancy said, following my gaze.

'Yes. The big one is a passenger too.'

'They don't look madly happy.'

'They weren't madly happy coming up here, either.'

'Owners of chronic losers?'

'No – well, I don't think so. They came up because of that horse Rudiments which Kenny Bayst rode for Annie Villars, but they aren't down in the racecard as its owners.'

She flicked back through her card. 'Rudiments. Duke

of Wessex. Well, neither of those two is him, poor old booby.'

'Who, the Duke?'

'Yes,' she said, 'Actually I suppose he isn't all that old, but he's dreadfully dim. Big important looking man with a big important looking rank, and as sweet as they come, really, but there's nothing but cotton wool upstairs.'

'You know him well?'

'I've met him often.'

'Subtle difference.'

'Yes.'

The two men scraped back their chairs and began to make their way out of the bar. The man in the plaster cast caught sight of them and his big smile grew even bigger.

'Say, if it isn't Eric Goldenberg, of all people. Come over here, me old sport, come and have a drink.'

Goldenberg looked less than enthusiastic at the invitation and the Major sidled away quickly to avoid being included, giving the Australian a glance full of the dislike of the military for the flamboyant.

The man in the cast put one arm clumsily round Goldenberg's shoulder, the crutch swinging out widely and knocking against Nancy.

'Say,' he said. 'Sorry, lady. I haven't got the hang of these things yet.'

'That's all right,' she said, and Goldenberg said something to him that I couldn't hear, and before we knew where we were we had been encompassed into the Australian's circle and he was busy ordering drinks all round.

Close to, he was a strange-looking man because his face and hair were almost colourless. The skin was whitish, the scalp, half bald, was fringed by silky hair that had been fair and was turning white, the eyelashes and eyebrows made no contrast, and the lips of the smiling mouth were creamy pale. He looked like a man made up to take the part of a large cheerful ghost. His name, it appeared, was Acey Jones.

'Aw, come on,' he said to me in disgust. 'Coke is for milksops, not men.' Even his eyes were pale: a light indeterminate bluey grey.

'Just lay off him, Ace,' Goldenberg said. 'He's flying me home. A drunken pilot I can do without.'

'A pilot, eh?' The big voice broadcast the information to about fifty people who weren't in the least interested. 'One of the fly boys? Most pilots I know are a bunch of proper tearaways. Live hard, love hard, drink hard. Real characters, those guys.' He said it with an expansive smile which hid the implied slight. 'C'mon now, sport, live dangerously. Don't disillusion all these people.'

'Beer, then, please,' I said.

Nancy was equally scornful, but for opposite reasons. 'Why did you climb down?'

'Antagonizing people when you don't have to is like

casting your garbage on the waters. One day it may come floating back, smelling worse.'

She laughed. 'Chanter would say that was immoral. Stands must be made on principles.'

'I won't drink more than half of the beer. Will that do?'

'You're impossible.'

Acey Jones handed me the glass and watched me take a mouthful and went on a bit about hell-raising and beating up the skies and generally living the life of a high-powered gypsy. He made it sound very attractive and his audience smiled and nodded their heads and none of them seemed to know that the picture was fifty years out of date, and that the best thing a pilot can be is careful: sober, meticulous, receptive, and careful. There are old pilots and foolish pilots, but no old foolish pilots. Me, I was old, young, wise, foolish, thirty-four. Also depressed, divorced and broke.

After aviation, Acey Jones switched back to insurance and told Goldenberg and Nancy and me and the fifty other people about getting a thousand pounds for breaking his ankle, and we had to listen to it all again, reacting with the best we could do in surprised appreciation.

'No, look, no kidding, sport,' he said to Goldenberg with his first sign of seriousness. 'You want to get yourself signed up with this outfit. Best fiver I've ever spent . . .'

Several of the fifty onlookers edged nearer to listen,

and Nancy and I filtered towards the outside of the group. I put down the tasted beer on an inconspicuous table out in the hall while Nancy dispatched the bottom half of her Coke, and from there we drifted out into the air.

The sun was still shining, but the small round white clouds were expanding into bigger round clouds with dark-grey centres. I looked at my watch. Four-twenty. Still nearly an hour until the time the Major wanted to leave. The longer we stayed the bumpier the ride was likely to be, because the afternoon forecast for scattered thunderstorms looked accurate.

'Cu-nims forming,' Nancy said, watching them. 'Nasty.'

We went and watched her brother get up on his mount for the last race and then we went up on the Owners and Trainers and watched him win it, and that was about that. She said goodbye to me near the bottom of the steps, outside the weighing room.

'Thanks for the escort duty . . .'

'Enjoyed it . . .'

She had smooth gilded skin and greyish-brown eyes. Straight dark eyebrows. Not much lipstick. No scent. Very much the opposite of my blonde, painted, and departed wife.

'I expect,' she said, 'that we'll meet again, because I sometimes fly with Colin, if there's a spare seat.'

'Do you ever take him yourself?'

'Good Lord no.' She laughed. 'He wouldn't trust me

to get him there on time. And anyway, there are too many days when the weather is beyond what I can do. Maybe one day, though . . .'

She held out her hand and I shook it. A grip very like her brother's, and just as brief.

'See you, then,' she said.

'I hope so.'

She nodded with a faint smile and went away. I watched her neat blue and white back view and stifled a sudden unexpected inclination to run after her and give her a Chanter type farewell.

When I walked across the track towards the aeroplane I met Kenny Bayst coming back from it with his raincoat over his arm. His skin was blotched pink again with fury, clashing with his carroty hair.

'I'm not coming back with you,' he said tightly. 'You tell Miss Annie effing Villars that I'm not coming back with you. There's no bloody pleasing her. Last time I nearly got the push for winning and this time I nearly got the push for not winning. You'd think that both times I'd had the slightest choice in the matter. I'll tell you straight, sport, I'm not coming back in your bloody little aeroplane having them gripe gripe gripe at me all the way back.'

'All right,' I said. I didn't blame him.

'I've just been over to fetch my raincoat. I'll go home by train . . . or get a lift.'

'Raincoat . . . but the aircraft is locked.'

'No it isn't. I just got my raincoat out of the back. Now you tell them I've had enough, right?' I nodded, and while he hurried off I walked on towards the aeroplane puzzled and a bit annoyed. Major Tyderman had said he had locked up again after he had fetched his *Sporting Life*, but apparently he hadn't.

He hadn't. Both the doors on the port side were unlocked, the passenger door and the baggage locker. I wasn't too pleased because Derrydowns had told me explicitly never to leave the aircraft open as they'd had damage done by small boys on several occasions: but all looked well and there were no signs of sticky fingers.

I did all the external checks again and glanced over the flight plan for the return. If we had to avoid too many thunderclouds it might take a little longer to reach Newmarket, but unless there was one settled and active over the landing field there should be no problem.

The passengers of the two Polyplane aircraft assembled by ones and twos, shovelled themselves inside, shut the doors, and were trundled down to the far end of the course. One after the other the two aeroplanes raced back over the grass and lifted away, wheeling like black darts against the blue, grey and white patchwork of the sky.

Annie Villars came first of my lot. Alone, composed, polite; giving nothing away. She handed me her coat and binoculars and I stored them for her. She thanked me. The deceptive mild brown eyes held a certain blankness and every few seconds a spasmodic tightening belied the gentle set of her mouth. A formidable lady, I thought. What was more, she herself knew it. She was so conscious of the strength and range of her power that she deliberately manufactured the disarming exterior in order not exactly to hide it, but to make it palatable. Made a nice change, I thought ironically, from all those who put up a big tough front to disguise their inner lack.

'Kenny Bayst asked me to tell you that he has got a lift home to Newmarket and won't be coming back by air,' I said.

A tiny flash of fire in the brown eyes. The gentle voice, completely controlled, said 'I'm not surprised.' She climbed into the aeroplane and strapped herself into her seat and sat there in silence, looking out over the emptying racecourse with eyes that weren't concentrating on the grass and the trees.

Tyderman and Goldenberg returned together, still deep in discussion. The Major's side mostly consisted of decisive nods, but it was pouring out of Goldenberg. Also he was past worrying about what I overheard.

'I would be surprised if the little shit hasn't been double crossing us all the time and collecting from some bookmaker or other even more than he got from us. Making fools of us, that's what he's been doing. I'll murder the little sod. I told him so, too.'

'What did he say?' the Major asked.

'Said I wouldn't get the chance. Cocky little bastard.'

They thrust their gear angrily into the baggage compartment and stood talking by the rear door in voices rumbling like the distant thunder.

Colin Ross came last, slight and inconspicuous, still wearing the faded jeans and the now crumpled sweat shirt.

I went a few steps to meet him. 'Your sister Nancy asked me to check with you whether you had remembered to bring the present for Midge.'

'Oh damn . . .' More than irritation in his voice there was weariness. He had ridden six hard races, won three of them. He looked as if a toddler could knock him down.

'I'll get it for you, if you like.'

'Would you?' He hesitated, then with a tired flap of his wrist said, 'Well, I'd be grateful. Go into the weighing room and ask for my valet, Ginger Mundy. The parcel's on the shelf over my peg. He'll get it for you.'

I nodded and went back across the track. The parcel, easily found, proved to be a little smaller than a shoe box and was wrapped in pink and gold paper with a pink bow. I took it over to the aeroplane and Colin put it on Kenny Bayst's empty seat.

The Major had already strapped himself in and was drumming with his fingers on his binocular case, which was as usual slung around him. His body was still stiff with tension. I wondered if he ever relaxed.

Goldenberg waited without a smile while I clambered across into my seat, and followed me in and clipped shut the door in gloomy silence. I sighed, started the engine, and taxied down to the far end of the course. Ready for take-off I turned round to my passengers and tried a bright smile.

'All set?'

I got three grudging nods for my pains. Colin Ross was asleep. I took the hilarious party off the ground without enthusiasm, skirted the Manchester zone, and pointed the nose in the general direction of Newmarket. Once up in the sky it was all too clear that the air had become highly unstable. At lower levels, rising pockets of heat from the built-up areas bumped the aeroplane about like a puppet, and to enormous heights great heaps of cumulo-nimbus cloud were boiling up all round the horizon.

Airsick-making weather. I looked round to see if an issue of waterproof bags was going to be required. Needn't have bothered. Colin was still asleep and the other three had too much on their minds to worry about a few lurches. I told Annie Villars where the bags were to be found if wanted, and she seemed to think I had insulted her.

Although by four thousand feet the worst of the bumps were below us, the flight was a bit like a bending race as I tracked left and right to avoid the dark towering cloud masses. Mostly we stayed in the sunshine: occasionally raced through the small veiling clouds which were dotted among the big ones. I wanted to avoid even the medium-sized harmless ones, as these sometimes hid a dangerous whopper just behind, and at a hundred and fifty miles an hour there was little chance to dodge. Inside every well grown cumulo-nimbus there were vertical rushing air currents which could lift and drop even an airliner like a yoyo. Also one could meet hailstones and freezing rain. Nobody's idea of a jolly playground. So it was a good idea to avoid the black churning brutes, but it was a rougher ride than one should aim for with passengers.

Everyone knows the horrible skin-prickling heart-thudding feeling when the normal suddenly goes wrong. Fear, it's called. The best place to feel it is not with a jerk at four thousand feet in a battlefield of cu-nims.

I was used to far worse weather; to bad, beastly, even lethal weather. It wasn't the state of the sky which distracted me, which set the fierce little adrenalin-packed alarm bell ringing like crazy.

There was something wrong with the aeroplane.

Nothing much. I couldn't even tell what it was. But something. Something . . .

My instinct for safety was highly developed. Over-developed, many had said, when it had got me into trouble. Bloody coward, was how they'd put it.

You couldn't ignore it, though. When the instinct switched to danger you couldn't risk ignoring it, not with passengers on board. What you could do when you were alone was a different matter, but civil commercial pilots seldom got a chance to fly alone.

Nothing wrong with the instruments. Nothing wrong with the engine.

Something wrong with the flying controls.

When I swerved gently to avoid yet another lurking cu-nim the nose of the aircraft dropped and I had a shade of difficulty pulling it up again. Once level nothing seemed wrong. All the gauges seemed right. Only the instinct remained. Instinct and the memory of a slightly sluggish response.

The next time I made a turn, the same thing happened. The nose wanted to drop, and it needed more pressure than it should have done to hold it level. At the third turn, it was worse.

I looked down at the map on my knees. We were twenty minutes out of Haydock . . . south of Matlock . . . approaching Nottingham. Another eighty nautical miles to Newmarket.

It was the hinged part of the tailplane which raised or lowered the aircraft's nose. The elevators, they were called. They were linked by wires to the control column in such a way that when you pushed the control column forward the tail went up and tipped the nose down. And vice versa.

The wires ran through rings and over pulleys, between the cabin floor and the outer skin of the fuselage. There wasn't supposed to be any friction.

Friction was what I could feel.

I thought perhaps one of the wires had somehow come off one of the pulleys during the bumpy ride. I'd never heard of it happening before, but that didn't mean it couldn't. Or perhaps a whole pulley had come adrift, or had broken in half . . . If something was rolling around loose it could affect the controls fairly seriously.

I turned to the cheerful company.

'I'm very sorry, but there will be a short delay on the journey. We're going to land for a while at the East Midlands Airport, near Nottingham, while I get a quick precautionary check done to the aircraft.'

I met opposition.

Goldenberg said belligerently, 'I can't see anything wrong.' His eyes swept over the gauges, noticing all the needles pointing to the green safety segments on all the engine instruments. 'It all looks the same as it always does.'

'Are you sure it's necessary?' Annie Villars said. 'I particularly want to get back to see my horses at evening stables.'

The Major said 'Damn it all!' fiercely and frowned heavily and looked more tense than ever.

They woke up Colin Ross.

'The pilot wants to land here and make what he calls a precautionary check. We want to go straight on. We don't want to waste time. There isn't anything wrong with the plane, as far as we can see . . .'

Colin Ross' voice came across, clear and decisive. 'If he says we're going down, we're going down. He's the boss.'

I looked round at them. Except for Colin they were

all more moody and gloomy than ever. Colin unexpectedly gave me a flicker of a wink. I grinned as much to myself as to him, called up East Midlands on the radio, announced our intention to land, and asked them to arrange for a mechanic to be available for a check.

On the way down I regretted it. The friction seemed no worse: if anything it was better. Even in the turbulent air near the ground I had no great trouble in moving the elevators. I'd made a fool of myself and the passengers would be furious and Derrydowns would be scathing about the unnecessary expense, and at any time at all I would be looking for my seventh job.

It was a normal landing. I parked where directed on the apron and suggested everyone got out and went into the airport for a drink, as the check would take half an hour, and maybe more.

They were by then increasingly annoyed. Up in the air they must have had a lingering doubt that I was right about landing. Safe on the ground, they were becoming sure it was unnecessary.

I walked some of the way across the tarmac with them towards the airport passengers' doors, then peeled off to go to the control office for the routine report after landing, and to ask for the mechanic to come for a look-see as soon as possible. I would fetch them from the bar, I said, once the check was done.

'Hurry it up,' Goldenberg said rudely.

'Most annoying. Most annoying indeed.' The Major.

'I was away last night . . . particularly wanted to get

back this evening. Might as well go by road, no point in paying for speed if you don't get it . . .' Annie Villars' irritation overcoming the velvet glove.

Colin Ross said, 'If your horse coughs, don't race it.'

The others looked at him sharply. I said, 'Thanks' gratefully, and bore off at a tangent to the left. I saw them out of the side of my vision, looking briefly back towards the aircraft and then walking unenthusiastically towards the big glass doors.

There was a crack behind me like a snapping branch, and a monstrous boom, and a roaring gust of air.

I'd heard that sequence before. I spun round, appalled.

Where there had stood a smart little blue and white Cherokee there was an exploding ball of fire.

CHAPTER FOUR

The bomb had taken a fraction of a second to detonate. The public impact lasted three days. The investigations dragged on for weeks.

Predictably, the dailies went to town on 'Colin Ross Escapes Death by One Minute' and 'Champion Jockey wins Race against Time'. Annie Villars, looking particularly sweet and frail, said in a television news interview that we had all been fantastically lucky. Major Tyderman was quoted as saying, 'Fortunately there was something wrong with the plane, and we landed for a check. Otherwise . . .' And Colin Ross had apparently finished his sentence for him; 'Otherwise we would all have been raining down on Nottingham in little bits.'

That was after they had recovered, of course. When I reached them at a run near the airport doors their eyes were stretched wide and their faces were stiff with shock. Annie Villars' mouth had dropped open and she was shaking from head to foot. I put my hand on her arm. She looked at me blankly and then made a small mewing sound and crumpled against me in a thoroughly un-

Napoleonic faint. I caught her on the way down and lifted her up in my arms to save her falling on the shower-soaked tarmac. She weighed even less than she looked.

'God,' said Goldenberg automatically. 'God.' His mind and tongue seemed to be stuck on the single word.

The Major's mouth was trembling and he was losing the battle to keep it still with his teeth. Sweat stood out in fine drops on his forehead and he was breathing in short shocked gasps.

Holding Annie Villars I stood beside them and watched the death throes of the aeroplane. The first explosion had blown it apart and almost immediately the fuel tanks had ignited and finished the job. The wreckage lay strewn in burning twisted pieces over a radius of wet tarmac, the parts looking too small ever to have formed the whole. Rivers of burning petrol ran among them, and great curling orange and yellow flames roared round the largest piece, which looked like the front part of the cabin.

My seat. My hot, hot seat.

Trouble followed me around like the rats of Hamelin.

Colin Ross looked as shocked as the others but his nerves were of sterner stuff. 'Was that . . . a bomb?'

'Nothing but,' I said flippantly.

He looked at me sharply. 'It's not funny.'

'It's not tragic, either,' I said. 'We're still here.'

A lot of the stiffness left his face and body. The beginnings of a smile appeared. 'So we are,' he said.

Someone in the control tower had pressed the panic

button. Fire engines screamed up and foam poured out of the giant hoses on to the pathetic scraps. The equipment was designed to deal with jumbos. It took about ten seconds to reduce the Cherokee sized flames to black memories.

Three or four airport cars buzzed around like gnats and one filled with agitated officials dashed in our direction.

'Are you the people who came in that aircraft?'

The first of the questions. By no means the last. I knew what I was in for. I had been taken apart before.

'Which is the pilot? Will you come with us, then, and your passengers can go to the manager's office . . . Is the lady injured?'

'Fainted,' I said.

'Oh . . .' he hesitated. 'Can someone else take her?' He looked at the others. Goldenberg, large and flabby; the Major, elderly; Colin, frail. His eyes passed over Colin and then went back, widening, the incredulity fighting against recognition.

'Excuse me . . . are you? . . .'

'Ross,' said Colin flatly. 'Yes.'

They rolled out the red carpet, after that. They produced smelling salts and a ground hostess for Annie Villars, stiff brandies for the Major and Goldenberg, autograph books for Colin Ross. The manager himself took charge of them. And someone excitedly rang up the national press.

*

The Board of Trade investigators were friendly and polite. As usual. And persistent, scrupulous, and ruthless. As usual.

'Why did you land at East Midlands?'

Friction.

'Had you any idea there was a bomb on board?'

No.

'Had you made a thorough pre-flight investigation?'

Yes.

'And no bomb?'

No.

Did I know that I was nevertheless responsible for the safety of the aircraft and could technically be held responsible for having initiated a flight with a bomb on board?

Yes.

We looked at each other. It was an odd rule. Very few people who took off with a bomb on board lived to be held responsible. The Board of Trade smiled, to show they knew it was silly to think anyone would take off with a bomb, knowing it was there.

'Did you lock the aircraft whenever you left it?'

I did.

'And did it remain locked?'

The knife was in. I told them about the Major. They already knew.

'He says he is sure that he relocked the doors,' they said. 'But even so wasn't it your responsibility to look after the safety of the aircraft, not his?'

Quite so.

'Wouldn't it have been prudent of you to accompany him to fetch the paper?'

No comment.

'The safety of the aircraft is the responsibility of the captain.'

Whichever way you turned, it came back to that.

This was my second interview with the Board of Trade. The first, the day after the explosion, had been friendly and sympathetic, a fact-finding mission during which the word responsibility had not cropped up once. It had hovered delicately in the wings. Inevitably it would be brought on later and pinned to someone's chest.

'During the past three days we have interviewed all your passengers, and none of them has any idea who would have wanted to kill them, or why. We now feel we must go more carefully into the matter of opportunity, so we do hope you don't mind answering what may be a lot of questions. Then we can piece together a statement for you, and we would be glad if you would sign it . . .'

'Do all I can,' I said. Dig my own grave. Again.

'They all agreed that the bomb must have been in the gift wrapped parcel which you yourself carried on board.'

Nice.

'And that the intended victim was Colin Ross.'

I sucked my teeth.

'You don't think so?'

'I honestly have no idea who it was intended for,' I said. 'But I don't think the bomb was in the parcel.'

'Why not?'

'His sister bought it, that morning.'

'We know.' He was a tall man, with inward looking eyes as if they were consulting a computer in his head, feeding in every answer he was given and waiting for the circuits to click out a conclusion. There was no aggression anywhere in his manner, no vengeance in his motivation. A fact-finder, a cause-seeker: like a truffle hound. He knew the scent of truth. Nothing would entice him away.

'And it sat on a shelf in the changing room all afternoon,' I said. 'And no one is allowed into the changing room except jockeys and valets.'

'We understand that that is so,' He smiled. 'Could the parcel have been the bomb? Weightwise?'

'I suppose so.'

'Miss Nancy Ross says it contained a large fancy bottle of bath oil.'

'No pieces in the wreckage?' I asked.

'Not a thing.' The tall man's nose wrinkled. 'I've seldom seen a more thorough disintegration.'

We were sitting in what was called the crew room in the Derrydowns office on the old RAF airfield near Buckingham. Such money as Derrydowns spent on appearances began in the manager's office and ended in the passengers' waiting lounge across the hall. The crew room looked as if the paint and the walls were coming up to their silver wedding. The linoleum had long passed the age of consent. Three of the four cheap armchairs looked as if they had still to reach puberty but the springs in the fourth were so badly broken that it was more comfortable to sit on the floor.

Much of the wall space was taken up by maps and weather charts and various Notices to Airmen, several of them out of date. There was a duty roster upon which my name appeared with the utmost regularity and a notice typed in red capitals to the effect that anyone who failed to take the aircraft's documents with him on a charter flight would get the sack. I had duly taken all the Cherokee's records and maintenance certificates with me, as the Air Navigation Order insisted. Now they were burned to a crisp. I hoped someone somewhere saw some sense in it.

The tall man looked carefully round the dingy room. The other, shorter, broader, silent, sat with his green bitten HB poised over his spiral bound notebook.

'Mr Shore, I understand you hold an Airline Transport Pilot's Licence. And a Flight Navigator's certificate.'

He had been looking me up. I knew he would have.

I said flatly, 'Yes.'

'This taxi work is hardly . . . well . . . what you were intended for.'

I shrugged.

'The highest possible qualifications . . .' He shook his head. 'You were trained by BOAC and flew for them for nine years. First Officer. In line for Captain. And then you left.'

'Yes.' And they never took you back. Policy decision. Never.

He delicately consulted his notes. 'And then you flew as Captain for a private British airline until it went into liquidation? And after that for a South American airline, who, I believe, dismissed you. And then all last year a spot of gun running, and this spring some crop spraying. And now this.'

They never let go. I wondered who had compiled the list.

'It wasn't guns. Food and medical supplies in, refugees and wounded out.'

He smiled faintly. 'To some remote African airstrip on dark nights? Being shot at?'

I looked at him.

He spread out his hands, 'Yes, I know. All legal and respectable, and not our business, of course.' He cleared his throat . . . 'Weren't you the . . . er . . . the subject . . . of an investigation about four years ago? While you were flying for British Interport?'

I took in a slow breath. 'Yes.'

'Mm.' He looked up, down, and sideways. 'I've read an outline of that case. They didn't suspend your licence.'

'No.'

'Though on the face of it one might have expected them to.'

I didn't answer.

'Did Interport pay the fine for you?'

'No.'

'But they kept you on as Captain. You were convicted of gross negligence, but they kept you on.' It was halfway between a statement and a question.

'That's right,' I said.

If he wanted all the details, he could read the full report. He knew it and I knew it. He wasn't going to get me to tell him.

He said, 'Yes . . . well. Who put this bomb in the Cherokee? When and how?'

'I wish I knew.'

His manner hadn't changed. His voice was still friendly. We both ignored his tentative shot at piling on the pressure.

'You stopped at White Waltham and Newbury . . .'

'I didn't lock up at White Waltham. I parked on the grass outside the reception lounge. I could see the aeroplane most of the time, and it was only on the ground for half an hour. I got there early . . . I can't see that anyone had a chance, or could rely on having a chance, to put a bomb on board at White Waltham.'

'Newbury?'

'They all stayed in their seats except me. Colin Ross came . . . We put his overnight bag in the front baggage locker . . .'

The tall man shook his head. 'The explosion was further back. Behind the captain's seat, at the very least.

The blast evidence makes it certain. Some of the metal parts of the captain's seat were embedded in the instrument panel.'

'One minute,' I said reflectively. 'Very nasty.'

'Yes . . . Who had an opportunity at Haydock?'

I sighed inwardly. 'I suppose anyone, from the time I gave the keys to Major Tyderman until I went back to the aircraft.'

'How long was that?'

I'd worked it out. 'Getting on for three hours. But . . .'

'But what?'

'No one could have counted on the aircraft being left unlocked.'

'Trying to wriggle out?'

'Do you think so?'

He dodged an answer: said: 'I'll give it to you that no one could have known whether it would be locked or unlocked. You just made it easy.'

'All right,' I said. 'If you'll also bear in mind that pickers and stealers unlock cars every day of the week, and that aircraft keys are the same type. Anyone who could manufacture and plant a bomb could open a little old lock.'

'Possibly,' he said, and repeated, 'But you made it easy.'

Damn Major Tyderman, I thought bleakly. Stupid, careless old fool. I stifled the thought that I probably would have gone across with him, or insisted on fetching his newspaper for him, if I hadn't been unwilling to walk away and leave Nancy.

'Who could have had access . . . leaving the matter of locks?'

I shrugged one shoulder. 'All the world. They had only to walk across the track.'

'The aircraft was parked opposite the stands, I believe, in full view of the crowds.'

'Yes. About a hundred yards, in fact, from the stands. Not close enough for anyone to see exactly what someone was doing, if he seemed to be walking round peering in through the windows. People do that, you know, pretty often.'

'You didn't notice anyone, yourself?'

I shook my head. 'I looked across several times during the afternoon. Just a casual glance, though. I wasn't thinking about trouble.'

'Hm.' He reflected for a few seconds. Then he said, 'Two of the Polyplanes were there as well, I believe.'

'Yes.'

'I think I'd better talk to the pilots, to see if they noticed anything.'

I didn't comment. His eyes suddenly focused on mine, sharp and black.

'Were they friendly?'

'The pilots? Not particularly.'

'How's the feud?'

'What feud?'

He stared at me assessingly. 'You're not that dumb.

No one could work for Derrydown and not know that they and Polyplanes are permanently engaged in scratching each others' eyes out.'

I sighed. 'I don't give a damn.'

'You will, when they start reporting you.'

'Reporting me? For what? What do you mean?'

He smiled thinly. 'If you infringe the rules by as much as one foot, Polyplanes will be on to us before your wheels have stopped rolling. They're doing their best to put Derrydowns out of business. Most of it we shrug off as simply spite. But if they catch you breaking the regulations, and can produce witnesses, we'd have to take action.'

'Charming.'

He nodded. 'Aviation will never need a special police force to detect crime. Everyone is so busy informing on everyone else. Makes us laugh, sometimes.'

'Or cry,' I said.

'That too.' He nodded wryly. 'There are no permanent friendships in aviation. The people you think are your friends are the first to deny they associate with you at the faintest hint of trouble. The cock crows until it's hoarse, in aviation.' The bitterness in his voice was unmistakable. But impersonal, also.

'You don't approve.'

'No. It makes our job easier, of course. But I like less and less the sight of people scrambling to save themselves at any cost to others. It diminishes them. They are small.'

'You can't always blame them for not always wanting to be involved. Aviation law cases are so fierce, so unforgiving . . .'

'Did your friends at Interport rally round and cheer you up?'

I thought back to those weeks of loneliness. 'They waited to see.'

He nodded. 'Didn't want to be contaminated.'

'It's a long time ago,' I said.

'You never forget rejection,' he said. 'It's a trauma.'

'Interport didn't reject me. They kept me on for another year, until they went bust. And,' I added, 'I didn't have anything to do with *that*.'

He gently laughed. 'Oh I know. My masters in that Government put on one of its great big squeezes and by one means or another forced them out of business.'

I didn't pursue it. The history of aviation was littered with the bodies of murdered air firms. Insolvency sat like a vulture in every boardroom in the industry and constantly pecked away at the bodies before they were dead. British Eagle, Handley Page, Beagle, the list of corpses was endless. Interport had been one of the largest, and Derrydowns, still struggling, one of the smallest, but their problems were identical. Huge inexorable costs. Fickle variable income. Write the sum in red.

I said, 'There is one other place, of course, where the bomb could have been put on board.' I stopped.

'Spell it out, then.'

'Here.'

The tall investigator and his silent friend with the pencil went down to the hangar to interview old Joe.

Harley called me into his office.

'Have they finished?'

'They've gone to ask Joe if he put the bomb in the Cherokee.'

Harley was irritated, which was with him a common state of mind. 'Ridiculous.'

'Or if Larry did.'

'*Larry . . .*'

'He left for Turkey that afternoon,' I pointed out. 'Would he have planted a legacy?'

'No.' Short, snappy and vehement.

'Why did he leave?'

'He wanted to.' He gave me a sharp glance bordering on dislike. 'You sound like the Board of Trade.'

'Sorry,' I said in conciliation. 'Must be catching.'

Harley's office dated back to a more prosperous past. There was a carpet of sorts on the floor and the walls had been painted within living memory, and his good-quality desk had mellowed instead of chipping. Limp blue curtains framed the big window looking out over the airfield and several good photographs of aeroplanes had been framed and hung. Customers, when they visited him, were allowed the nearly new lightweight armchair. Crew sat on the wooden upright.

Harley himself was proprietor, manager, chief flying instructor, booking clerk and window cleaner. His staff consisted of one qualified mechanic past retiring age, one part-time boy helper, one full-time taxi pilot (me) and one part-time pilot who switched from taxiing to teaching, whichever was required, and on alternate days taught in a flying club twenty miles to the north.

Derrydown's other assets had been, before the Cherokee blew up, three useful aircraft and one bright girl.

The remaining two aircraft were a small single engined trainer, and a twin-engined eight-year-old Aztec equipped with every possible flying aid, for which Harley was paying through the nose on a five year lease.

The girl, Honey, his brother's daughter, worked for love and peanuts and was the keystone which held up the arch. I knew her voice better than her face, as she sat up in the control tower all day directing such air traffic as came along. Between times she typed all the letters, kept the records, did the accounts, answered the telephone if her uncle didn't and collected landing fees from visiting pilots. She was reputed to be suffering from a broken heart about Larry and consequently came down from her crow's nest as seldom as possible.

'She's made puff balls out of her eyes, crying for that louse,' was how my part-time colleague put it. 'But you wait just a week or two. She'll lie down for you instead. Never refused a good pilot yet, our Honey hasn't.'

'How about you?' I asked, amused.

'Me? She'd squeezed me like a lemon long before that goddamned Larry ever turned up.'

Harley said crossly, 'We've lost two charters since the bomb. They say the Aztec's too expensive, they would rather go by road.' He ran his hand over his head. 'There's another Cherokee Six up at Liverpool that's available to lease. I've just been talking to them on the phone. It sounds all right. They're bringing it across here tomorrow afternoon, so you can take it up when you get back from Newmarket and see what you think.'

'How about the insurance on the old one?' I asked idly. 'It would be cheaper in the long run to buy rather than lease.'

'It was on hire purchase,' he said gloomily. 'We'll be lucky if we get a penny. And it's not really your business.'

Harley was slightly plump and slightly bald and just not quite forceful enough to lift Derrydowns up by its bootstraps. His manner to me was more bossy than friendly, a reaction I understood well enough.

'The last person on earth to put a bomb on any aircraft would be Joe,' he said explosively. 'He looks after them like a mother. He *polishes* them.'

It was true. The Derrydowns aircraft sparkled outside and were shampooed inside. The engines ran like silk. The general, slightly misleading, air of prosperity which clung around the public face of the firm was mostly Joe's work.

The Board of Trade came back from the hangar looking vaguely sheepish. The rough side of Joe's tongue, I guessed. At sixty-nine and with savings in the bank, he was apt to lay down his own laws. He had taken exception to my theory that a pulley on the elevator wires had come adrift. No such thing was possible in one of his aircraft, he had told me stiffly, and I could take my four gold rings away and I knew what I could do with them. As I hadn't worn my captain's jacket for nearly two years I told him the moths had beaten me to it, and although it was a feeble joke he gave me a less sour look and told me that it couldn't have been a broken pulley, he was sure it couldn't, and if it was, it was the manufacturer's fault, not his.

'It saved Colin Ross' life,' I pointed out. 'You should claim a medal for it.' Which opened his mouth and shut him up.

The Board of Trade trooped into Harley's office. The tall man sat in the armchair and Green Pencil on the hard one. Harley behind his desk. I leant against the wall, on my feet.

'Well now,' said the tall man. 'It seems as if everyone on this airfield had a chance to tamper with the Cherokee. Everyone in the company, and any customers who happened to be here that morning, and any member of the public wandering around for a look-see. We've assumed the bomb was aimed at Colin Ross, but we don't really know that. If it was, someone had a pretty accurate idea of when he would be in the aircraft.'

'Last race four-thirty. He was riding in it,' Harley said. 'Doesn't take too much figuring to assume that at five-forty he'd be in the air.'

'Five forty-seven,' said the tall man. 'Actually.'

'Any time about then,' said Harley irritably.

'I wonder what the bomb was in,' said the tall man reflectively. 'Did you look inside the first-aid tin?'

'No,' I said, startled. 'I just checked that it was there. I've never looked inside it. Or inside the fire extinguishers, or under the seats or inside the life jacket covers . . .'

The tall man nodded. 'It could have been in any of those places. Or it could after all have been in that fancy parcel.'

'Ticking away,' said Harley.

I peeled myself slowly off the wall. 'Suppose,' I said hesitantly, 'suppose it wasn't in any of those places. Suppose it was deeper, out of sight. Somewhere between the cabin wall and the outer skin . . . like a limpet mine, for instance. Suppose that that bumpy ride . . . and all those turns I did to avoid the cu-nims . . . dislodged it, so that it was getting jammed in the elevator wires . . . Suppose that was what I could feel . . . and why I decided to land . . . and that what saved us . . . was the bomb itself.'

CHAPTER FIVE

The next day I took five jockeys and trainers from Newmarket to Newcastle races and back in the Aztec and listened to them grousing over the extra expense, and in the evening I tried out the replacement Cherokee, which flew permanently left wing down on the auto pilot, had an unserviceable fuel flow meter, and an overload somewhere on the electrical circuit.

'It isn't very good,' I told Harley. 'It's old and noisy and it probably drinks fuel and I shouldn't think the battery's charging properly.'

He interrupted me. 'It flies. And it's cheap. And Joe will fix it. I'm taking it.'

'Also it's orange and white, just like the Polyplanes.'

He gave me an irritable glare. 'I'm not blind. I know it is. And it's not surprising, considering it used to belong to them.'

He waited for me to protest so that he could slap me down, so I didn't. I shrugged instead. If he wanted to admit to his bitterest rivals that his standards were down to one of their third hand clapped out old buggies, that was his business.

He signed the lease on the spot and gave it to the pilot who had brought the aeroplane to take back with him on the train, and the pilot smiled a pitying smile and went off shaking his head.

The orange and white Cherokee went down to the hangar for Joe to wave his wand over, and I walked round the perimeter track to home sweet home.

One caravan, pilots' for the use of. Larry had lived in it before me, and others before him: Harley's taxi pilots stayed, on average, eight months, and most of them settled for the caravan because it was easiest. It stood on a dusty square of concrete which had once been the floor of a RAF hut, and it was connected to the mains electricity, water and drainage which had served the long departed airmen.

As caravans go it must once have held up its head, but generations of beer drinking bachelors had left tiny teeth marks of bottle-caps along the edges of all the fitments, and circular greasy head marks on the wall above every seat. Airport dirt had clogged the brown haircord into a greyish cake, relieved here and there by darker irregular stains. Shabby pin-ups of superhuman mammalian development were stuck to the walls with Sellotape, and a scatter of torn-off patches of paint showed where dozens of others had been stuck before. Tired green curtains had opened and shut on a thousand hangovers. The fly-blown mirror had stared back at a lot of disillusion, and the bed springs sagged from the weight of a bored succession of pilots with nothing to do except Honey.

I had forgotten to get anything to eat. There was half a packet of cornflakes in the kitchen and a jar of instant coffee. Neither was much use, as yesterday's half pint of milk had gone sour in the heat. I damned it all and slouched on the two seat approximation to a sofa, and resignedly dragged out of my pocket the two letters which had lain unopened there since this morning.

One was from a television rental firm who said they confirmed that they were transferring the rental from Larry's name to mine, as requested, and could I now be so good as to pay immediately the six weeks for which he was in arrears. The other, from Susan, said briefly that I was late with the alimony yet again.

I put down both the letters and stared unseeingly through the opposite window towards the darkening summer sky. All the empty airfield stretched away into the dusk, calm, quiet, undemanding and shadowy, everything I needed for a few repairs to the spirit. The only trouble was, the process was taking longer than I'd expected. I wondered sometimes whether I'd ever get back to where I'd once been. Maybe if you'd hashed up your life as thoroughly as I had, there was never any going back. Maybe one day soon I'd stop wanting to. Maybe one day I would accept the unsatisfactory present not as a healing period but as all there ever was going to be. That would be a pity, I thought. A pity to let the void take over for always.

I had three pounds in my pocket and sixteen in the bank, but I had finally paid all my debts. The crippling fine, the divorce, and the mountainous bills Susan had run up everywhere in a cold orgy of hatred towards me in the last weeks we were together: everything had been settled. The house had always been in her name because of the nature of my job, and she had clung on to that like a leech. She was still living in it, triumphant, collecting a quarter of everything I earned and writing sharp little letters if I didn't pay on the nail.

I didn't understand how love could curdle so abysmally: looking back, I still couldn't understand. We had screamed at each other: hit each other, intending to hurt. Yet when we married at nineteen we'd been entwined in tenderness, inseparable and sunny. When it started to go wrong she said it was because I was away so much, long ten-day tours to the West Indies all the time, and all she had was her job as a doctor's secretary and the dull endless housework. In an uprush of affection and concern for her I resigned from BOAC and joined Interport instead, where I flew short-haul trips, and spent most of my nights at home. The pay was a shade less good, the prospects a lot less good, but for three months we were happier. After that there was a long period in which we both tried to make the best of it, and a last six months in which we had torn each other's nerves and emotions to shreds.

Since then I had tried more or less deliberately not to feel anything for anybody. Not to get involved. To be private, and apart, and cold. An ice-pack after the tempest.

I hadn't done anything to improve the caravan, to stamp anything of myself upon it. I didn't suppose I would, because I didn't feel the need. I didn't want to get involved, not even with a caravan.

And certainly not with Tyderman, Goldenberg, Annie Villars and Colin Ross.

All of them except Goldenberg were on my next racing trip.

I had spent two more days in the Aztec, chauffeuring some business executives on their regular monthly visit to subsidiary factories in Germany and Luxembourg, but by Saturday Joe had tarted up the replacement Cherokee so I set off in that. The fuel meter still resolutely pointed to nought, which was slightly optimistic, but the electrical fault had been cured: no overload now on the generator. And if it still flew one wing low, at least the wing in question sparkled with a new shine. The cabin smelt of soap and air freshener, and all the ash trays were empty.

The passengers were to be collected that day at Cambridge, and although I flew into the aerodrome half an hour early, the Major was already there, waiting on a seat in a corner of the entrance hall.

I saw him before he saw me, and as I walked towards him he took the binoculars out of their case and put them on the low table beside him. The binoculars were smaller than the case suggested. In went his hand again and out came a silver and pigskin flask. The Major took a six-second swig and with a visible sigh screwed the cap back into place.

I slowed down and let him get the binoculars back on top of his courage before I came to a halt beside him and said good morning.

'Oh . . . Good morning,' he said stiffly. He stood up, fastening the buckle of the case and giving it a pat as it swung into its usual facing forwards position on his stomach. 'All set?'

'The others are not here yet. It's still early.'

'Ah. No. Of course.' He wiped his moustache carefully with his hand and tucked his chin back into his neck. 'No bombs today, I hope?'

He wasn't altogether meaning to joke.

'No bombs,' I assured him.

He nodded, not meeting my eyes. 'Very upsetting, last Friday. Very upsetting, you know.' He paused. 'Nearly didn't come, today, when I heard that Colin . . . er . . .' He stopped.

'I'll stay in the aeroplane all afternoon,' I promised him.

The Major nodded again, sharply. 'Had a Board of Trade fellow come to see me. Did you know that?'

'They told me so.'

'Been to see you too, I suppose.'

'Yes.'

'They get about a bit.'

'They're very thorough. They'll go a hundred miles to get a single answer to a simple question.'

He looked at me sharply. 'Speaking from bitter experience?'

I hadn't known there was any feeling in my voice. I said, 'I've been told they do.'

He grunted. 'Can't think why they don't leave it to the police.'

No such luck, I thought. There was no police force in the world as tenacious as the British Board of Trade.

Annie Villars and Colin Ross arrived together, deep in a persuasive argument that was getting nowhere.

'Just say you'll ride my horses whenever you can.'

'. . . too many commitments.'

'I'm not asking a great deal.'

'There are reasons, Annie. Sorry, but no.' He said it with an air of finality, and she looked startled and upset.

'Good morning,' she said to me abstractedly. 'Morning, Rupert.'

'Morning, Annie,' said the Major.

Colin Ross had achieved narrow pale-grey trousers and a blue open-necked shirt.

'Morning, Matt,' he said.

The Major took a step forward, bristling like a terrier. 'Did I hear you turning down Annie's proposition?'

'Yes, Major.'

'Why?' he asked in an aggrieved tone. 'Our money is as good as anyone else's, and her horses are always fit.'

'I'm sorry, Major, but no. Just let's leave it at that.'

The Major looked affronted and took Annie Villars off to see if the bar was open. Colin sighed and sprawled in a wooden armchair.

'God save me,' he said, 'from crooks.'

I sat down too. 'She doesn't seem crooked to me.'

'Who, Annie? She isn't really. Just not one hundred per cent permanently scrupulous. No, it's that crummy slob Goldenberg that I don't like. She does what he says, a lot too much. I'm not taking indirect riding orders from him.'

'Like Kenny Bayst?' I suggested.

He looked at me sideways. 'The word gets around, I see. Kenny reckons he's well out of it. Well I'm not stepping in.' He paused reflectively. 'The Board of Trade investigator who came to see me asked if I thought there was any significance in Bayst having cried off the return trip the other day.'

'What did you say?'

'I said I didn't. Did you?'

'I confess I wondered, because he did go across to the aeroplane after the races, and he certainly felt murderous, but . . .'

'But,' he agreed, 'would Kenny Bayst be cold blooded enough to kill you and me as well?' He shook his head. 'Not Kenny, I wouldn't have thought.'

'And besides that,' I nodded, 'he only came to the steaming boil after he lost the three-thirty, and just how would he rustle up a bomb at Haydock in a little over one hour?'

'He would have to have arranged it in advance.'

'That would mean that he knew he would lose the race . . .'

'It's been done,' said Colin dryly.

There was a pause. Then I said, 'Anyway, I think we had it with us all the time. Right from before I left base.'

He swivelled his head and considered it. 'In that case . . . Larry?'

'Would he?'

'God knows. Sneaky fellow. Pinched Nancy's hundred quid. But a bomb . . . and what was the point?'

I shook my head.

Colin said, 'Bombs are usually either political or someone's next of kin wanting to collect the insurance.'

'Fanatics or family . . .' I stifled the beginnings of a yawn.

'You don't really care, do you?' he said.

'Not that much.'

'It doesn't disturb you enough to wonder whether the bomb merchant will try again?'

'About as much as it's disturbing you.'

He grinned. 'Yes . . . well. It would be handy to know for sure whose name was on that one. One would look so damn silly taking fiddly precautions if it was the Major who finally got clobbered. Or you.'

'Me?' I said in astonishment.

'Why not?'

I shook my head. 'I don't stand in anyone's way to anything.'

'Someone may think you do.'

'Then they're nuts.'

'It takes a nut . . . a regular psycho . . . to put a bomb in an aeroplane . . .'

Tyderman and Annie Villars came back from the direction of the bar with two more people, a man and a woman.

'Oh Christ,' Colin said under his breath. 'Here comes my own personal Chanter.' He looked at me accusingly. 'You didn't tell me who the other passengers were.'

'I don't know them. Who are they? I don't do the bookings.'

We stood up. The woman, who was in her thirties but dressed like a teenager, made a straight line for Colin and kissed him exuberantly on the cheek.

'Colin, darling, there was a spare seat and Annie said I could come. Wasn't that absolutely super of her?'

Colin glared at Annie who pretended not to notice.

The girl-woman had a strong upper-class accent, white knee socks, a camel-coloured high-waisted dress, several jingling gold bracelets, streaky fair brown long hair, a knock-you-down exotic scent and an air of expecting everyone to curl up and die for her.

She latched her arm through Colin's so that he couldn't disentangle without giving offence, and said with a somehow unattractive gaiety, 'Come along everyone, let's take the plunge. Isn't it all just too unnerving, flying around with Colin these days.'

'You don't actually have to come,' Colin said without quite disguising his wishes.

She seemed oblivious. 'Darling,' she said. 'Too riveting. Nothing would stop me.'

She moved off towards the door, followed by the Major and Annie and the new man together, and finally by me. The new man was large and had the same air as the woman of expecting people to jump to it and smooth his path. The Major and Annie Villars were busy smoothing it, their ears bent deferentially to catch any falling crumbs of wisdom, their heads nodding in agreement over every opinion.

The two just-teenage girls I had stationed beside the locked aircraft were still on duty, retained more by the promise of Colin's autograph than by my money. They got both, and were delighted. No one, they anxiously insisted, had even come close enough to ask what they were doing. No one could possibly have put a piece of chewing gum on to the aeroplane, let alone a bomb.

Colin, signing away, gave me a sidelong look of amusement and appreciation and said safety came cheap at the price. He was less amused to find that the affectionate lady had stationed herself in one of the rear seats and was beckoning him to come and sit beside her.

'Who is she?' I asked.

'Fenella Payne-Percival. Fenella pain in the neck.'

I laughed. 'And the man?'

'Duke of Wessex. Annie's got a horse running for him today.'

'Not Rudiments again?'

He looked up in surprise from the second autograph book.

'Yes. That's right. Bit soon, I would have thought.' He finished the book and gave it back. 'Kenny Bayst isn't riding it.' His voice was dry.

'You don't say.'

The passengers had sorted themselves out so that Annie and the Duke sat in the centre seats, with the Major waiting for me to get in before him into the first two. He nodded his stiff little nod as I stepped up on to the wing, and pushed at his moustache. Less tense, slightly less rigid, than last time. The owner was along instead of Goldenberg and Kenny wasn't there to stir things up. No coup today, I thought. No coup to go wrong.

The flight up was easy and uneventful, homing to the radio beacon on the coast at Ottringham and tracking away from it on a radial to Redcar. We landed without fuss on the racecourse and the passengers yawned and unbuckled themselves.

'I wish every racecourse had a landing strip,' Colin sighed. 'It makes the whole day so much easier. I hate all those dashes from airport to course by taxi.'

The racecourses which catered for aeroplanes were in a minority, which seemed a shame considering there was room enough on most, if anyone cared enough. Harley constantly raved in frustration at having to land ten or fifteen miles away and fix up transportation for the passengers. All the conveniently placed RAF airfields with superb runways who either refused to let private aircraft land at all, or shut their doors firmly at 5 pm weekdays and all day on Saturdays had him on the verge of tears. As also did all the airfields whose owners said they wouldn't take the responsibility of having an aircraft land there or take off if they didn't have a fire engine standing by, even though Harley's own insurance didn't require it.

'The English are as air-minded as earth worms,' Harley said.

On the other hand Honey had tacked a list to the office wall which started in big red letters 'God Bless . . .' and continued with all the friendly and accommodating places like Kempton Park, which let you land up the five furlong straight (except during five furlong races) and RAF stations like Wroughton and Leeming and Old Sarum, who really tried for you, and the airfields who could let you land when they were officially shut, and all the privately owned strips whose owners generously agreed to you using them any time you liked.

Harley's view of Heaven was an open public landing field outside every town and a windsock and a flat four furlongs on every racecourse. It wasn't much to ask, he said plaintively. Not in view of the dozens of enormous airfields which had been built during World War Two and were now disused and wasted.

He could dream, I thought. There was never any money for such schemes, except in wars.

The passengers stretched themselves on to the grass. Fenella Payne-Percival made little up and down jumps of excitement like a small girl, the Major patted his binocular case reassuringly, Annie Villars efficiently picked up her own belongings and directed a look of melting feminine helplessness towards the Duke, Colin looked at his watch and smiled, and the Duke himself glanced interestedly around and said, 'Nice day, what?'

A big man, he had a fine looking head with thick greying hair, eyebrows beginning to sprout, and a strong square jaw, but there wasn't enough living stamped on his face for a man in his fifties, and I remembered what Nancy had said of him: sweet as they come, but nothing but cottonwool upstairs.

Colin said to me, 'Are you coming into the paddock?'

I shook my head. 'Better stay with the aeroplane, this time.'

The Duke said, 'Won't you need some lunch, my dear chap?'

'It's kind of you, sir, but I often don't have any.'

'Really?' He smiled. 'Must have my lunch.'

Annie Villars said, 'We'll leave soon after the last. About a quarter to five.'

'Right,' I agreed.

'Doesn't give us time for a drink, Annie,' complained the Duke.

She swallowed her irritation. 'Any time after that, then.'

'I'll be here,' I said.

'Oh do come on,' said Fenella impatiently. 'The pilot can look after himself, can't he? Let's get going, do. Come on, Colin darling.' She twined her arm in his again and he all but squirmed. They moved away towards the paddock obediently, with only Colin looking back. I laughed at the desperation on his face and he stuck out his tongue.

There were three other aircraft parked in a row. One private, one from a Scottish taxi firm, and one Polyplane. All the pilots seemed to have gone in to the races, but when I climbed out half way through the afternoon to stretch my legs, I found the Polyplane pilot standing ten yards away, staring at the Cherokee with narrowed eyes and smoking a cigarette.

He was one of the two who had been at Haydock. He seemed surprised that I was there.

'Hello,' I said equably. Always a sucker.

He gave me the old hard stare. 'Taking no chances today, I see.'

I ignored the sneer in his voice. 'That's right.'

'We got rid of that aircraft,' he said sarcastically nodding towards it, 'because we'd flown the guts out of it. It's only suitable now for minor operators like you.'

'It shows signs of the way you flew it,' I agreed

politely: and that deadly insult did nothing towards cooling the feud.

He compressed his lips and flicked the end of his cigarette away into the grass. A thin trickle of blue smoke arose from among the tangled green blades. I watched it without comment. He knew as well as I did that smoking near parked aircraft was incredibly foolish, and on all airfields, forbidden.

He said, 'I'm surprised you take the risk of flying Colin Ross. If your firm are proved to be responsible for his death you'll be out of business.'

'He's not dead yet.'

'If I were him I wouldn't risk flying any more with Derrydowns.'

'Did he, by any chance,' I asked, 'once fly with Polyplanes? Is all this sourness due to his having transferred to Derrydowns instead?'

He gave me a bitter stare. 'No,' he said.

I didn't believe him. He saw that I didn't. He turned on his heel and walked away.

Rudiments won the big race. The dim green colours streaked up the centre of the track at the last possible moment and pushed Colin on the favourite into second place. I could hear the boos all the way from the stands.

An hour until the end of racing. I yawned, leaned back in my seat, and went to sleep.

A young voice saying 'Excuse me,' several times,

woke me up. I opened my eyes. He was about ten, slightly shy, ultra well bred. Squatting down on the wing, he spoke through the open door.

'I say, I'm sorry to wake you, but my uncle wanted me to come over and fetch you. He said you hadn't had anything to eat all day. He thinks you ought to. And besides, he's had a winner and he wants you to drink his health.'

'Your uncle is remarkably kind,' I said, 'but I can't leave the aeroplane.'

'Well, actually, he thought of that. I've brought my father's chauffeur over with me, and he is going to sit here for you until you come back.' He smiled with genuine satisfaction at these arrangements.

I looked past him out of the door, and there, sure enough, was the chauffeur, all togged up in dark green with a shining peak to his cap.

'OK,' I said. 'I'll get my jacket.'

He walked with me along the paddock, through the gate, and across to the members' bar.

'Awfully nice chap, my uncle,' he said.

'Unusually thoughtful,' I agreed.

'Soft, my mother says,' he said dispassionately. 'He's her brother. They don't get along very well.'

'What a pity.'

'Oh, I don't know. If they were frightfully chummy she would always be wanting to come with me when I go to stay with him. As it is, I go on my own, and we have some fantastic times, him and me. That's how I know how super he is.' He paused. 'Lots of people think he's terribly thick, I don't know why.' There was a shade of anxiety in his young voice. 'He's really awfully kind.'

I reassured him. 'I only met him this morning, but I think he's very nice.'

His brow cleared. 'You do? Oh, good.'

The Duke was knee deep in cronies all armed with glasses of champagne. His nephew disappeared from my side, dived through the throng, and reappeared tugging at his uncle's arm.

'What?' The kind brown eyes looked round; saw me. 'Oh yes.' He bent down to talk, and presently the boy came back.

'Champagne or coffee?'

'Coffee, please.'

'I'll get it for you.'

'I'll get it,' I suggested.

'No. Let me. Do let me. Uncle gave me the money.' He marched off to the far end of the counter and ordered a cup of coffee and two rounds of smoked salmon sandwiches, and paid for them with a well crushed pound note.

'There,' he said triumphantly. 'How's that?'

'Fine,' I said. 'Terrific. Have a sandwich.'

'All right.'

We munched companionably.

'I say,' he said, 'look at that man over there, he looks like a ghost.'

I turned my head. Big blond man with very pale skin. Pair of clumsy crutches. Large plaster cast. Acey Jones.

Not so noisy today. Drinking beer very quietly in a far corner with a nondescript friend.

'He fell down some steps and broke his ankle and collected a thousand pounds from an insurance policy,' I said.

'Golly,' said the boy. 'Almost worth it.'

'He thinks so, too.'

'Uncle has something to do with insurance. Don't know what, though.'

'An underwriter?' I suggested.

'What's that?'

'Someone who invests money in insurance companies, in a special sort of way.'

'He talks about Lloyd's, sometimes. Is it something to do with Lloyd's?'

'That's right.'

He nodded and looked wistfully at the sandwiches.

'Have another,' I suggested.

'They're yours, really.'

'Go on. I'd like you to.'

He gave me a quick bright glance and bit into number two.

'My name's Matthew,' he said.

I laughed. 'So is mine.'

'Is it really? Do you really mean it?'

'Yes.'

'Wow.'

There was a step behind me and the deep Eton-sounding voice said, 'Is Matthew looking after you all right?'

'Great sir, thank you,' I said.

'His name is Matthew too,' said the boy.

The Duke looked from one of us to the other. 'A couple of Matts, eh? Don't let too many people wipe their feet on you.'

Matthew thought it a great joke but the touch of sadness in the voice was revealing. He was dimly aware that despite his ancestry and position, one or two sharper minds had wiped their feet on *him*.

I began to like the Duke.

'Well done with Rudiments, sir,' I said.

His face lit up. 'Splendid, wasn't it? Absolutely splendid. Nothing on earth gives me more pleasure than seeing my horses win.'

I went back to the Cherokee just before the last race and found the chauffeur safe and sound and reading *Doctor Zhivago*. He stretched, reported nothing doing, and ambled off.

All the same I checked the aircraft inch by inch inside and even unscrewed the panel to the aft baggage compartment so that I could see into the rear part of the fuselage, right back to the tail. Nothing there that shouldn't be. I screwed the panel on again.

Outside the aircraft, I started in the same way.

Started only: because when I was examining every hinge in the tail plane I heard a shout from the next aircraft.

I looked round curiously but without much haste.

Against that side of the Polyplane which faced away from the stands, two large men were laying into Kenny Bayst.

CHAPTER SIX

The pilot of the Polyplane was standing aside and watching. I reached him in six strides.

'For God's sake,' I said. 'Come and help him.'

He gave me a cold stolid stare. 'I've got my medical tomorrow. Do it yourself.'

In three more steps I caught one of the men by the fist as he lifted it high to smash into the crumpling Kenny, bent his arm savagely backwards and kicked him hard in the left hamstring. He fell over on his back with a shout of mixed anger, surprise, and pain, closely echoed in both emotion and volume by his colleague, who received the toe of my shoe very solidly at the base of his spine.

Bashing people was their sort of business, not mine, and Kenny hadn't enough strength left to stand up, let alone fight back, so that I got knocked about a bit here and there. But I imagined that they hadn't expected any serious opposition, and it must have been clear to them from the beginning that I didn't play their rules.

They had big fists all threateningly bunched and the

hard round sort of toecaps which cowards hide behind. I kicked their knees with vigour, stuck my fingers out straight and hard towards their eyes, and chopped the sides of my palms at their throats.

I'd had enough of it before they had. Still, I outlasted them for determination, because I really did not want to fall down and have their boots bust my kidneys. They got tired in the end and limped away quite suddenly, as if called off by a whistle. They took with them some damaged knee cartilage, aching larynxes, and one badly scratched eye; and they left behind a ringing head and a set of sore ribs.

I leaned against the aeroplane getting my breath back and looking down at Kenny where he sat on the grass. There was a good deal of blood on his face. His nose was bleeding, and he had tried to wipe it with the back of his hand.

I bent down presently and helped him up. He came to his feet without any of the terrible slowness of the severely injured and there was nothing wrong with his voice.

'Thanks, sport.' He squinted at me. 'Those sods said they were going to fix me so my riding days were over . . . God . . . I feel crook . . . here, have you got any whisky . . . aah . . . Jesus . . .' He bent double and vomited rakingly on to the turf.

Straightening up afterwards he dragged a large handkerchief out of his pocket and wiped his mouth, looking in dismay at the resulting red stains.

'I'm bleeding . . .'

'It's your nose, that's all.'

'Oh . . .' He coughed weakly. 'Look, sport, thanks. I guess thanks isn't enough . . .' His gaze sharpened on the Polyplane pilot still standing aloof a little way off. 'That bastard didn't lift a finger . . . they'd have crippled me and he wouldn't come . . . I shouted.'

'He's got his medical tomorrow,' I said.

'Sod his bloody medical . . .'

'If you don't pass your medical every six months, you get grounded. If you get grounded for long in the taxi business you lose either your whole job or at least half your income . . .'

'Yeah,' he said. 'And your own medical, when does that come up?'

'Not for two months.'

He laughed a hollow, sick sounding laugh. Swallowed. Swayed. Looked suddenly very small and vulnerable.

'You'd better go over and see the doctor,' I suggested.

'Maybe . . . but I've got the ride on Volume Ten on Monday . . . big race . . . opportunity if I do well of a better job than I've had with Annie Villars . . . don't want to miss it . . .' He smiled twistedly. 'Doesn't do jockeys any good to be grounded either, sport.'

'You're not in very good shape.'

'I'll be all right. Nothing broken . . . except maybe my nose. That won't matter; done it before.' He coughed again. 'Hot bath. Spell in the sauna. Good as new by Monday. Thanks to you.'

'How about telling the police?'

'Yeah. Great idea.' He was sarcastic. 'Just imagine their sort of questions. "Why was anyone trying to cripple you, Mr Bayst?" "Well, officer, I'd promised to fiddle their races see, and this sod Goldenberg, I beg his pardon, gentlemen, Mr Eric Goldenberg, sticks these two heavies on to me to get his own back for all the lolly he had to cough up when I won . . ." "And why did you promise to fiddle the race, Mr Bayst?" "Well, officer, I done it before you see and made a handy bit on the side . . ." ' He gave me a flickering glance and decided he'd said enough. 'Guess I'll see how it looks tomorrow. If I'm in shape to ride Monday I'll just forget it happened.'

'Suppose they try again?'

'No.' He shook his head a fraction. 'They don't do it twice.'

He picked himself off the side of the fuselage and looked at his reflection in the Polyplane's window, licked his handkerchief and wiped most of the blood off his face.

The nose had stopped bleeding. He felt it gingerly between thumb and forefinger.

'It isn't moving. Can't feel it grate. It did, when I broke it.'

Without the blood he looked pale under the red hair

but not leaden. 'Guess I'll be all right. Think I'll get into the plane and sit down, though . . . Came in it, see . . .'

I helped him in. He sagged down weakly in his seat and didn't look like someone who would be fit to ride a racehorse in forty-six hours.

'Hey,' he said, 'I never asked you . . . are you OK yourself?'

'Yes . . . Look, I'll get your pilot to fetch you some whisky.'

His reaction showed how unsettled he still felt. 'That would be . . . fair dinkum. He won't go though.'

'He will,' I said.

He did. British aviation was a small world. Everyone knew someone who knew someone else. News of certain sorts travelled slowly but surely outwards and tended to follow one around. He got the message. He also agreed to buy the whisky himself.

By the time he came back, bearing a full quarter bottle and a scowl, the last race was over and the passengers for all the aeroplanes were turning up in little groups. Kenny began to look less shaky, and when two other jockeys arrived with exclamations and consolations, I went back to the Cherokee.

Annie Villars was waiting, not noticeably elated by her win with Rudiments.

'I thought you said you were going to stay with the plane,' she said. Ice cracked in her voice.

'Didn't take my eyes off it.'

She snorted. I did a quick double check inside, just to

be sure, but no one had stored anything aboard since my last search. The external check I did more slowly and more thoroughly. Still nothing.

The thumping I'd collected started to catch up. The ringing noise in my head was settling into a heavy ache. Various soggy areas on my upper arms were beginning to stiffen. My solar plexus and adjacent areas felt like Henry Cooper's opponents on the morning after.

'Did you know,' I said to Annie Villars conversationally, 'that two men just had a go at beating up Kenny Bayst?'

If she felt any compassion she controlled it admirably. 'Is he badly hurt?'

'An uncomfortable night should see him through.'

'Well then . . . I dare say he deserved it.'

'What for?'

She gave me a direct stare. 'You aren't deaf.'

I shrugged: 'Kenny thinks Mr Goldenberg arranged it.'

She hadn't known it was going to happen. Didn't know whether Goldenberg was responsible or not. I saw her hesitating, summing the information up.

In the end she said vaguely, 'Kenny never could keep his tongue still,' and a minute later, under her breath, 'Stupid thing to do. Stupid man.'

Major Tyderman, the Duke of Wessex and Fenella Payne-in-the-neck arrived together, the Duke still talking happily about his winner.

'Where's Colin?' asked Fenella. 'Isn't he here after

all? What a frantic nuisance. I asked for him at the weighing room and that man, who did he say he was? His valet, oh yes, of course . . . his valet, said that he had already gone to the plane.' She pouted, thrusting out her lower lip. There was champagne in her eyes and petulance in her voice. The gold bracelets jingled. The heavy scent didn't seem to have abated during the afternoon. I thought Colin had dodged very neatly. The Major also had been included in the celebrations. He looked slightly fuzzy round the eyes and a lot less rigid everywhere else. The hand that pushed at the wiry moustache looked almost gentle. The chin was still tucked well back into the neck, but there was nothing aggressive any more: it seemed suddenly only the mannerism of one who used suspiciousness instead of understanding to give himself a reputation for shrewdness.

The Duke asked the Major if he minded changing places on the way home so that he, the Duke, could sit in front. 'I like to see the dials go round,' he explained.

The Major, full of ducal champagne, gracefully agreed. He and Fenella climbed aboard and I waited outside with the Duke.

'Is there anything the matter, my dear chap?' he said.

'No, sir.'

He studied me slowly. 'There is, you know.'

I put my fingers on my forehead and felt the sweat. 'It's a hot day,' I said.

Colin came eventually. He too was sweating: his now

crumpled open shirt had great dark patches under the arms. He had ridden five races. He looked thin and exhausted.

'Are you all right?' he said abruptly.

'I *knew*,' said the Duke.

'Yes, thank you.'

Colin looked back to where the Polyplane still waited on the ground.

'Is Kenny bad?'

'A bit sore. He didn't want anyone to know.'

'One of the jockeys with him on the trip came back over and told us. Kenny said you saved him from a fate worse than death, or words to that effect.'

'What?' said the Duke.

Colin explained. They looked at me suspiciously.

'I'm fit to fly, if that's what's worrying you.'

Colin made a face. 'Yeah, boy, it sure is.' He grinned, took a deep breath, and dived into the back with the tentacly Fenella. The Duke folded himself after me into the front seats and we set off.

There was thick cloud over the Humber at Ottringham and all the way south to Cambridge. As he could see just about as far forward as the propeller, the Duke asked me what guarantee there was that we wouldn't collide with another aircraft.

There wasn't any guarantee. Just probability.

'The sky is huge,' I said. 'And there are strict rules for flying in clouds. Collisions practically never happen.'

His hands visibly relaxed. He shifted into a more

comfortable position. 'How do you know where we are?' he asked.

'Radio,' I said. 'Radio beams from transmitters on the ground. As long as that needle on the dial points centrally downwards, we are going straight to Ottringham, where the signal is coming from.'

'Fascinating,' he said.

The replacement Cherokee had none of the sophistication of the one which had been blown up. That had had an instrument which locked the steering on to the radio beam and took the aircraft automatically to the transmitter. After the attentions of Kenny Bayst's assailants I regretted not having it around.

'How will we know when we get to Cambridge?' asked the Duke.

'The needle on that other dial down there will swing from pointing straight up and point straight down. That will mean we have passed over the top of the transmitter at Cambridge.'

'Wonderful what they think of,' said the Duke.

The needles came up trumps. We let down through the cloud over Cambridge into an overcast, angry looking afternoon and landed on the shower soaked tarmac. I taxied them over close to the buildings, shut down the engine, and took off my head set, which felt a ton heavier than usual.

'Wouldn't have missed it,' said the Duke. 'Always motored everywhere before, you know.' He unfastened his safety belt. 'Annie persuaded me to try flying. Just once, she said. But I'll be coming with you again, my dear chap.'

'That's great, sir.'

He looked at me closely, kindly. 'You want to go straight to bed when you get home, Matthew. Get your wife to tuck you up nice and warm, eh?'

'Yes,' I said.

'Good, good.' He nodded his fine head and began to heave himself cumbersomely out of the door and on to the wing. 'You made a great hit with my nephew, my dear chap. And I respect Matt's opinion. He can spot good 'uns and bad 'uns a mile off.'

'He's a nice boy,' I said.

The Duke smiled happily. 'He's my heir.'

He stepped down from the wing and went round to help Annie Villars put on her coat. No doubt I should have been doing it. I sat with my belt still fastened, feeling too rough to be bothered to move. I didn't relish the thought of the final hop back to Buckingham, up into the clouds again and with no easy well-placed transmitter to help me down at the other end. I'd have to go round the Luton complex . . . could probably get a steer home from there, from the twenty-four hour radar . . .

I ached. I thought of the caravan. Cold little harbour.

The passengers collected their gear, shut the rear door, waved, and walked off towards the buildings. I looked at the map, picked out a heading, planned the return journey in terms of time and the cross references

I'd need to tell me when I'd got to Buckingham, if the radar should be out of service. After that I sat and stared at the flight plan and told myself to get on with it. After that I rested my head on my hand and shut my eyes.

Ridiculous wasting time, I thought. Cambridge airport charged extra for every minute they stayed open after six o'clock, and the passengers were already committed to paying for more than an hour. Every moment I lingered cost them more still.

There was a tap on the window beside me. I raised my head more quickly than proved wise. Colin Ross was standing there, watching me with a gleam of humour. I twisted the catch and opened the window flap on its hinge.

'Fit to fly, didn't you say?' he said.

'That was two hours ago.'

'Ah yes. Makes a difference.' He smiled faintly. 'I just wondered, if you don't feel like going on, whether you'd care to let me take you home for the night? Then, you can finish the trip tomorrow. It might be a fine day, tomorrow.'

He had flown a great deal and understood the difficulties. All the same, I was surprised he had troubled to come back.

'It might,' I agreed. 'But I could stay in Cambridge . . .'

'Get out of there and fix the hangarage,' he said calmly.

'I'll have to check with Derrydowns . . .'

'Check, then.'

I climbed too slowly out of the aeroplane and struggled into my jacket. We walked together across into the building.

'Call your wife, too,' he said.

'Haven't got one.'

'Oh.' He looked at me with speculative curiosity.

'No,' I said. 'Not that. Married twelve years, divorced three.'

Humour crinkled the skin round his eyes. 'Better than me,' he said. 'Married two years, divorced four.'

Harley answered at the first ring.

'Where are you? Cambridge? . . . No, come back now, if you stay at Cambridge we'll have to pay the hangarage.' I hadn't told him about the fight, about the way I felt.

'I'll pay it,' I said. 'You can deduct it from my salary. Colin Ross has asked me to stay with him.' That would clinch it. Harley saw the importance of pleasing, and Colin Ross was his best customer.

'Oh . . . that's different. All right then. Come back in the morning.'

I went into the Control office and arranged for the aircraft to be stowed under cover for the night, one last overtime job for the staff before they all went home. After that I sank into the Ross Aston Martin and let the world take care of itself.

*

He lived in an ordinary looking brick built bungalow on the outskirts of Newmarket. Inside, it was colourful and warm, with a large sitting-room stocked with deep luxurious velvet upholstered armchairs.

'Sit down,' he said.

I did. Put my head back. Shut my eyes.

'Whisky or brandy?' he asked.

'Whichever you like.'

I heard him pouring. It sounded like a tumblerful.

'Here,' he said.

I opened my eyes and gratefully took the glass. It was brandy and water. It did a grand job.

There were sounds of pans from the kitchen and a warm smell of roasting chicken. Colin's nose twitched.

'Dinner will be ready soon . . . I'll go and tell the cooks there will be one extra.'

He went out of the room and came back almost immediately with his two cooks.

I stood up slowly. I hadn't given it a thought; was quite unprepared.

They looked at first sight like two halves of one whole. Nancy and Midge. Same dark hair, tied high on the crown with black velvet bows. Same dark eyes, straight eyebrows, spontaneous smiles.

'The bird man himself,' Nancy said. 'Colin, how did you snare him?'

'Potted a sitting duck . . .'

'This is Midge,' she said. 'Midge . . . Matt.'

'Hi,' she said. 'The bomb man, aren't you?'

When you looked closer, you could see. She was thinner than Nancy, and much paler, and she seemed fragile where Nancy was strong: but without the mirror comparison with her sister there was no impression of her being ill.

'First and last bomb, I hope,' I said.

She shivered. 'A lot too ruddy close.'

Colin poured each of them a Dubonnet and took whisky for himself. 'Bombs, battles . . . some introduction you've had to racing.'

'An eventful change from crop spraying,' I agreed.

'Is that a dull job?' Midge asked, surprised.

'Dull and dangerous. You get bored to death trudging up and down some vast field for six hours a day . . . It's all low flying, you see, so you have to be wide awake, and after a while you start yawning. One day maybe you get careless and touch the ground with your wing in a turn, and you write off an expensive machine, which is apt to be unpopular with the boss.'

Nancy laughed. 'Is that what you did?'

'No . . . I went to sleep for a second in the air one day and woke up twenty feet from a pylon. Missed it by millimetres. So I quit while everything was still in one piece.'

'Never mind,' Midge said. 'The next plane you touched disintegrated beautifully.'

They laughed together, a united family, close.

Colin told them about Kenny Bayst's fracas and they exclaimed sympathetically, which made me feel a humbug: Colin habitually drove himself to exhaustion and Midge was irretrievably afflicted, and all I had were a few minor bruises.

Dinner consisted simply of the hot roast chicken and a tossed green salad, with thick wedges of cheese afterwards. We ate in the kitchen with our elbows on the scarlet table, and chewed the bones. I hadn't passed a more basically satisfying evening for many a long weary year.

'What are you thinking?' Nancy demanded. 'At this moment?'

'Making a note to fall frequently sick at Cambridge.'

'Well,' said Midge. 'Don't bother. Just come any time.' She looked inquiringly at her sister and brother and they nodded. 'Just come,' she repeated. 'Whenever it's handy.'

The old inner warning raised its urgent head: don't get involved, don't feel anything, don't risk it.

Don't get involved.

I said, 'Nothing I'd like better,' and didn't know whether I meant it or not.

The two girls stacked the plates in a dishwasher and made coffee. Nancy poured cream carefully across the top of her cup.

'Do you think that bomb was really intended for Colin?' she asked suddenly.

I shrugged. 'I don't know. It could just as well have been intended for Major Tyderman or Annie Villars or Goldenberg, or even Kenny Bayst, really, because it must have been on board before he decided not to come. Or it might have been intended for putting the firm out of action . . . for Derrydowns, itself, if you see what I mean, because if Colin had been killed, Derrydowns would probably have gone bust.'

'I can't see why anyone would want to kill Colin,' Midge said. 'Sure, people are jealous of him, but jealousy is one thing and killing five people is another . . .'

'Everyone seems to be taking it so calmly,' Nancy suddenly exploded. 'Here is this bloody bomb merchant running around loose with no one knowing just what he'll do next, and no one seems to be trying to find him and lock him up.'

'I don't see how they can find him,' Colin said. 'And anyway, I don't suppose he will risk trying it again.'

'Oh you . . . you . . . *ostrich*,' she said bitterly. 'Doesn't it occur to you that you don't just lightly put a bomb in an aeroplane? Whoever did it must have had an overwhelming reason, however mad it was, and since the whole thing went wrong they still have the same motive rotting away inside them, and what do you think Midge and I will do if next time you get blown to bits?'

I saw Midge looking at her with compassion and understood the extent of Nancy's fear. One day she was certainly going to lose her sister. She couldn't face losing her brother as well.

'It won't happen,' he said calmly.

They looked at him, and at me. There was a long, long pause. Then Midge picked up the wishbone of the chicken and held it out for me to pull. It snapped with the biggest side in her fist.

'I wish,' she said seriously, 'that Colin would stop cutting his toenails in the bath.'

CHAPTER SEVEN

I slept on a divan bed in Colin's study, a small room crammed with racing trophies, filing cabinets and form books. Every wall was lined by rows of framed photographs of horses passing winning posts and owners proudly leading them in. Their hooves thudded through my head most of the night, but all was peace by morning.

Colin brought me a cup of tea, yawning in his dark woolly bathrobe. He put the cup down on the small table beside the divan and pulled back the curtains.

'It's drizzling cats and dogs,' he announced. 'There's no chance of you flying this morning so you may as well relax and go back to sleep.'

I looked out at the misty rain. Didn't mind a bit.

'It's my day off,' I said.

'Couldn't be better.'

He perched his bottom on the edge of the desk.

'Are you OK this morning?'

'Fine,' I said. 'That hot bath loosened things a lot.'

'Every time you moved yesterday evening you could see it hurt.'

I made a face. 'Sorry.'

'Don't be. In this house you say ouch.'

'So I've noticed,' I said dryly.

He grinned. 'Everyone lives on a precipice. All the time. And Midge keeps telling me and Nancy that if we're not careful she'll outlive us both.'

'She's marvellous.'

'Yes, she is.' He looked out of the window. 'It was a terrible shock at first. Terrible. But now . . . I don't know . . . we seem to have accepted it. All of us. Even her.'

I said hesitantly, 'How long? . . .'

'How long will she live? No one knows. It varies so much, apparently. She's had it, they think, for about three years now. It seems a lot of people have it for about a year before it becomes noticeable enough to be diagnosed, so no one knows when it started with Midge. Some people die within days of getting it. Some have lived for twenty years. Nowadays, with all the modern treatments, they say the average after diagnosis is from two to six years, but it will possibly be ten. We've had two . . . We just believe it will be ten . . . and that makes it much easier . . .'

'She doesn't look especially ill.'

'Not at the moment. She had pneumonia a short while ago and the odd thing about that is that it reverses leukaemia for a while. Any fever does it, apparently. Actually makes her better. So do doses of radiation on her arms and legs, and other bones and organs. She's had several relapses and several good long spells of being well. It just goes on like that . . . but her blood is different, and her bones are changing inside all the time . . . I've seen pictures of what is happening . . . and one day . . . well, one day she'll have a sort of extreme relapse, and she won't recover.'

'Poor Midge . . .'

'Poor all of us.'

'What about . . . Nancy? Being her twin . . .'

'Do identical bodies get identical blood diseases, do you mean?' He looked at me across the room, his eyes in shadow. 'There's that too. They say the chances are infinitesimal. They say there are only eighteen known cases of leukaemia occurring twice in the same family unit. You can't catch it, and you can't inherit it. A girl with leukaemia can have a baby, and the baby won't have leukaemia. You can transfuse blood from someone with leukaemia into someone without it, and he won't catch it. They say there's no reason why Nancy should develop it any more than me or you or the postman. But they don't *know*. The books don't record any cases of an identical twin having it, or what became of the other one.' He paused. Swallowed, 'I think we are all more afraid of Nancy getting it too than of anything on earth.'

I stayed until the sky cleared up at five o'clock. Colin spent most of the day working out which races he wanted to ride in during the coming week and answering telephone calls from owners and trainers anxious to engage him. Principally he rode for a stable half a mile down the road, he said, but the terms of his retainer there gave him a good deal of choice.

He worked at a large chart with seven columns, one for each day of the week. Under each day he listed the various meetings, and under each meeting he listed the names, prizes and distances of the races. Towards the end of the afternoon there was a horse's name against a fair proportion of races, especially, I noticed, those with the highest rewards.

He grinned at my interest. 'A business is a business,' he said.

'So I see. A study in time and motion.'

On three of the days he proposed to ride at two meetings.

'Can you get me from Brighton to Windsor fast enough for two races an hour and a half apart? Three o'clock race at Brighton. Four-thirty, Windsor. And on Saturday, three o'clock race at Bath, four-thirty at Brighton?'

'With fast cars both ends, don't see why not.'

'Good.' He crossed out a couple of question marks and wrote ticks instead. 'And next Sunday, can you take me to France?'

'If Harley says so.'

'Harley will say so,' he said with certainty.

'Don't you ever take a day off?'

He raised his eyebrows in surprise. 'Today,' he said, 'is off. Hadn't you noticed?'

'Er . . . yes.'

'The horse I was going over to ride today went lame on Thursday. Otherwise I was going to Paris. BEA, though, for once.'

Nancy said with mock resignation, 'The dynamo whirs non-stop from March to November in England and Europe and then goes whizzing off to Japan and so on, and around about February there might be a day or two when we can all flop back in armchairs and put our feet up.'

Midge said, 'We put them up in the Bahamas last time. It was gorgeous. All that hot sun . . .'

The others laughed. 'It rained the whole of the first week.'

The girls cooked steaks for lunch. 'In your honour,' Midge said to me. 'You're too thin.'

I was fatter than any of them; which wasn't saying much.

Midge cleared the things away afterwards and Nancy covered the kitchen table with maps and charts.

'I really am flying Colin to the races one day soon, and I wondered if you'd help . . .'

'Of course.'

She bent over the table, the long dark hair swinging down over her neck. Don't get involved, I said to myself. Just don't.

'Next week, to Haydock. If the weather's good enough.'

'She's doing you out of a job,' Midge observed, wiping glasses.

'Wait till it thunders.'

'Beast,' Nancy said.

She had drawn a line on the map. She wanted me to tell her how to proceed in the Manchester control zone, and what to do if they gave her instructions she didn't understand.

'Ask them to repeat them. If you still don't understand, ask them to clarify.'

'They'll think I'm stupid,' she protested.

'Better that than barging on regardless and crashing into an airliner.'

'OK,' she sighed. 'Point taken.'

'Colin deserves a medal,' Midge said.

'Just shut up,' Nancy said. 'You're all bloody rude.'

When the drizzle stopped they all three took me back to Cambridge, squashing into the Aston Martin. Midge drove, obviously enjoying it. Nancy sat half on Colin and half on me, and I sat half on the door handle.

They stood in a row, and waved when I took off. I rolled the wings in salute and set course for Buckingham, and tried to ignore the regret I felt to be leaving.

Honey was up in the control tower at Derrydowns, Sunday or no Sunday, and Harley was aloft in the trainer giving someone a lesson. When he heard me on the radio he said snappily 'And about time too,' and I remembered the dimensions of my bank balance and didn't snap back. Chanter, I thought wryly, would have plain despised me.

I left the Cherokee Six in the hangar and walked round to the caravan. It seemed emptier, more sordid, more dilapidated than before. The windows all needed cleaning. The bed wasn't made. Yesterday's milk had gone sour again, and there was still no food.

I sat for a while watching the evening sun struggle through the breaking clouds, watching Harley's pupil stagger through some ropy landings, wondering how long it would be before Derrydowns went broke, and wondering if I could save enough before that happened to buy a car. Harley was paying me forty-five pounds a week, which was more than he could afford and less than I was worth. Of that, Susan, taxes and insurance would be taking exactly half, and with Harley deducting four more for my rent it wasn't going to be easy.

Impatiently I got up and cleaned all the windows, which improved my view of the airfield but not of the future.

When the light began to fade I had a visitor. A ripe shapely girl in the minimum of green cotton dress. Long fair hair. Long legs. Large mouth. Slightly protruding teeth. She walked with a man-eating sway and spoke with the faintest of lisps.

Honey Harley, come down from her tower.

She knocked on her way in. All the same if I'd been naked. As it was, I had my shirt off from the window cleaning and for Honey, it seemed, that was invitation enough. She came over holding out a paper in one hand and putting the other lightly on my shoulder. She let it slide down against my skin to halfway down my back and then brought it up again to the top.

'Uncle and I were making out the list for the next week. We wondered if you fixed anything up with Colin Ross.'

I moved gently away, picked up a nylon sweater, and put it on.

'Yes . . . he wants us Tuesday, Friday, Saturday and Sunday.'

'Great.'

She followed me across the small space. One step farther backwards and I'd be in my bedroom. Internally I tried to stifle a laugh. I stepped casually round her, back towards the door. Her face showed nothing but businesslike calm.

'Look,' she said, 'Monday, that's tomorrow, then, you collect a businessman at Coventry, take him to Rotterdam, wait for him, and bring him back. That's in the Aztec. Tuesday, Colin Ross. Wednesday, nothing yet. Thursday, probably a trainer in Lambourn wanting to look at a horse for sale in Yorkshire, he'll let us know, and then Colin Ross again all the end of the week.'

'OK.'

'And the Board of Trade want to come out and see you again. I told them early Tuesday or Wednesday.'

'All right.' As usual, the automatic sinking of the heart even at the words Board of Trade: though this time, surely, surely, my responsibility was a technicality. This time, surely, I couldn't get ground to bits.

Honey sat down on the two-seat sofa and crossed her legs. She smiled.

'We haven't seen much of each other yet, have we?'

'No,' I said.

'Can I have a cigarette?'

'I'm sorry . . . I don't smoke . . . I haven't any.'

'Oh. Well, give me a drink, then.'

'Look, I really am sorry . . . all I can offer you is black coffee . . . or water.'

'Surely you've got some beer?'

'Afraid not.'

She stared at me. Then she stood up, went into the tiny kitchen, and opened all the cupboards. I thought it was because she thought I was lying, but I'd done her an injustice. Sex minded she might be, but no fool.

'You've no car, have you? And the shops and the pub are nearly two miles away.' She came back frowning, and sat down again. 'Why didn't you ask someone to give you a lift?'

'Didn't want to be a bother.'

She considered it. 'You've been here three weeks and you don't get paid until the end of the month. So . . . have you any money?'

'Enough not to starve,' I said. 'But thanks all the same.'

I'd sent ten pounds to Susan and told her she'd have to wait for the rest until I got my pay cheque. She'd written back short and to the point. Two months, by then, don't forget. As if I could. I had under four pounds left in the world and too much pride.

'Uncle would give you an advance.'

'I wouldn't like to ask him.'

A small smile lifted the corners of her mouth. 'No, I can see that, as he's so intent on slapping you down.'

'Is he?'

'Don't pretend to be surprised. You know he is. You give him a frightful inferiority complex and he's getting back at you for it.'

'It's silly.'

'Oh sure. But you are the two things he longs to be and isn't, a top class pilot and an attractive man. He needs you badly for the business, but he doesn't have to like it. And don't tell me you didn't know all that, because it's been obvious all along that you understand, otherwise you would have lost your temper with him every day at the treatment he's been handing out.'

'You see a lot from your tower,' I said smiling.

'Sure. And I'm very fond of my uncle. And I love this little business, and I'd do anything to keep us afloat.'

She said it with intense feeling. I wondered whether 'anything' meant sleeping with the pilots, or whether that came under the heading of pleasure, not profit. I didn't intend to find out. Not getting involved included Honey, in the biggest possible way.

I said, 'It must have been a blow to the business, losing that new Cherokee.'

She pursed her mouth and put her head on one side. 'Not altogether. In fact, absolutely the reverse. We had too much capital tied up in it. We had to put down a lump sum to start with, and the HP instalments were pretty steep . . . I should think when everything's settled, and we get the insurance, we will have about five thousand pounds back, and with that much to shore us up we can keep going until times get better.'

'If the aircraft hadn't blown up, would you have been able to keep up with the HP?'

She stood up abruptly, seeming to think that she had already said too much. 'Let's just leave it that things are all right as they are.'

The daylight was fading fast. She came and stood close beside me, not quite touching.

'You don't smoke, you don't eat, you don't drink,' she said softly. 'What else don't you do?'

'That too.'

'Not ever?'

'Not now. Not here.'

'I'd give you a good time.'

'Honey . . . I just . . . don't want to.'

She wasn't angry. Not even hurt. 'You're cold,' she said judiciously. 'An iceberg.'

'Perhaps.'

'You'll thaw,' she said. 'One of these days.'

The Board of Trade had sent the same two men, the tall one and the silent one, complete with notebook and bitten green pencil. As before, I sat with them in the crew room and offered them coffee from the slot machine in the passengers' lounge. They accepted, and I went and fetched three plastic cupfuls. The staff as well as the customers had to buy their coffee or whatever from the machine. Honey kept it well stocked. It made a profit.

Outside on the airfield my part-time colleague, Ron, was showing a new pupil how to do the external checks. They crept round the trainer inch by inch. Ron talked briskly. The pupil, a middle-aged man, nodded as if he understood.

The tall man was saying in effect that they had got nowhere with the bomb.

'The police have been happy to leave the investigations with us, but frankly in these cases it is almost impossible to find the identity of the perpetrator. Of course if someone on board is a major political figure, or a controversial agitator . . . Or if there is a great sum of personal insurance involved . . . But in this case there is nothing like that.'

'Isn't Colin Ross insured?' I asked.

'Yes, but he has no new policy, or anything exceptional. And the beneficiaries are his twin sisters. I cannot believe . . .'

'Impossible,' I said with conviction.

'Quite so.'

'How about the others?'

He shook his head. 'They all said, in fact, that they ought to be better insured than they were.' He coughed discreetly. 'There is, of course, the matter of yourself.'

'What do you mean?'

His sharp eyes stared at me unblinkingly.

'Several years ago you took out a policy for the absolute benefit of your wife. Although she is now your ex-wife, she would still be the beneficiary. You can't change that sort of policy.'

'Who told you all this?'

'She did,' he said. 'We went to see her in the course of our inquiries.' He paused. 'She didn't speak kindly of you.'

I compressed my mouth. 'No. I can imagine. Still, I'm worth more to her alive than dead. She'll want me to live as long as possible.'

'And if she wanted to get married again? Your alimony payments would stop then, and a lump sum from insurance might be welcome.'

I shook my head. 'She might have killed me in a fury three years ago, but not now, cold bloodedly, with other people involved. It isn't in her nature. And besides, she doesn't know anything about bombs and she had no opportunity . . . You'll have to cross out that theory too.'

'She has been going out occasionally with an executive from a firm specializing in demolitions.'

He kept his voice dead even, but he had clearly expected more reaction than he got. I wasn't horrified or even much taken aback.

'She wouldn't do it. Or put anyone else up to doing it. Ordinarily, she was too . . . too kind hearted. Too sensible, anyway. She used to be so angry whenever innocent passengers were blown up . . . she would never do it herself. Never.'

He watched me for a while in the special Board of Trade brand of unnerving silence. I didn't see what I could add. Didn't know what he was after.

Outside on the airfield the trainer started up and taxied away. The engine noise faded. It was very quiet. I sat. I waited.

Finally he stirred. 'All in all, for all our trouble, we have come up with only one probability. And even that gets us no nearer knowing who the bomb was intended for, or who put it on board.'

He put his hand in his inner pocket and brought out a stiff brown envelope. Out of that he shook on to the crew room table a twisted piece of metal. I picked it up and looked at it. Beyond the impression that it had once been round and flat, like a button, it meant nothing.

'What is it?'

'The remains,' he said, 'of an amplifier.'

I looked up, puzzled. 'Out of the radio?'

'We don't think so.' He chewed his lip. 'We think it was in the bomb. We found it embedded in what had been the tail plane.'

'Do you mean . . . it wasn't a time bomb after all?'

'Well . . . probably not. It looks as if it was exploded by a radio transmission. Which puts, do you see, a different slant on things.'

'What difference? I don't know much about bombs. How does a radio bomb differ from a time bomb?'

'They can differ a lot, though in many the actual explosive is the same. In those cases it's just the trigger mechanism that's different.' He paused. 'Well, say you have a quantity of plastic explosive. Unfortunately that's all too easy to get hold of, nowadays. In fact, if you happen to be in Greece, you can go into any hardware shop and buy it over the counter. On its own, it won't explode. It needs a detonator. Gunpowder, old-fashioned gunpowder, is the best. You also need something to ignite the gunpowder before it will detonate the plastic. Are you with me?'

'Faint but pursuing,' I said.

'Right. The easiest way to ignite gunpowder, from a distance, that is, is to pack it round a thin filament of fuse wire. Then you pass an electric current through the filament. It becomes red hot, ignites the gunpowder . . .'

'And boom, you have no Cherokee Six.'

'Er, yes. Now, in this type of bomb you have a battery, a high voltage battery about the size of a sixpence, to provide the electric current. The filament will heat up if you bend it round and fasten one end to one terminal of the battery, and the other to the other.'

'Clear,' I said. 'And the bomb goes off immediately.'

He raised his eyes to Heaven. 'Why did I ever start this? Yes, it would go off immediately. So it is necessary to have a mechanism that will complete the circuit after the manufacturer is safely out of the way.'

'By a spring?' I suggested.

'Yes. You hold the circuit open by a hair spring on a catch. When the catch is removed, the spring snaps the circuit shut, and that's that. Right? Now, the catch can be released by a time mechanism like an ordinary alarm clock. Or it can be released by a radio signal from a distance, via a receiver, an amplifier and a solenoid, like mechanisms in a space craft.'

'What is a solenoid, exactly?'

'A sort of electric magnet, a coil with a rod in the centre. The rod moves up and down inside the coil, when a pulse is passed through the coil. Say the top of the rod is sticking up out of the coil to form the catch on the spring, when the rod moves down into the coil the spring is released.'

I considered it. 'What is there to stop someone detonating the bomb by accident, by unknowingly transmitting on the right frequency? The air is packed with radio waves . . . surely radio bombs are impossibly risky?'

He cleared his throat. 'It is possible to make a

combination type release mechanism. One could make a bomb in which, say, three radio signals had to be received in the correct order before the circuit could be completed. For such a release mechanism, you would need three separate sets of receivers, amplifiers and solenoids to complete the circuit . . . We were exceptionally fortunate to find this amplifier. We doubt if it was the only one . . .'

'It sounds much more complicated than the alarm clock.'

'Oh yes, it is. But also more flexible. You are not committed to a time in advance to set it off.'

'So no one had to know what time we would be leaving Haydock. They would just have to see us go.'

'Yes . . . Or be told you had gone.'

I thought a bit. 'It does put a different slant, doesn't it?'

'I'd appreciate your thinking.'

'You must be thinking the same,' I protested. 'If the bomb could be set off at any hour, any day, any week even, it could have been put in the aircraft at any time after the last maintenance check.'

He smiled thinly. 'And that would let you halfway off the hook?'

'Half way,' I agreed.

'But only half.'

'Yes.'

He sighed. 'I've sprung this on you. I'd like you to think it over, from every angle. Seriously. Then tell me if anything occurs to you. If you care at all to find out what happened, that is, and maybe prevent it happening again.'

'You think I don't care?'

'I got the impression.'

'I would care now,' I said slowly, 'if Colin Ross were blown up.'

He smiled. 'You are less on your guard, today.'

'You aren't sniping at me from behind the bushes.'

'No . . .' He was surprised. 'You're very observant, aren't you?'

'More a matter of atmosphere.'

He hesitated. 'I have now read the whole of the transcript of your trial.'

'Oh.' I could feel my face go bleak. He watched me.

'Did you know,' he said, 'that someone has added to the bottom of it in pencil a highly libellous statement?'

'No,' I said. Waited for it.

'It says that the Chairman of Interport is of the undoubtedly correct opinion that the First Officer lied on oath throughout, and that it was because of the First Officer's own gross negligence, not that of Captain Shore, that the airliner strayed so dangerously off course.'

Surprised, shaken, I looked away from him, out of the window, feeling absurdly vindicated and released. If that postscript was there for anyone who read the transcript to see, then maybe my name hadn't quite so much mud on it as I'd thought. Not where it mattered anyway.

I said without heat, 'The Captain is always responsible. Whoever does what.'

'Yes.'

A silence lengthened. I brought my thoughts back from four years ago and my gaze from the empty airfield.

'Thank you,' I said.

He smiled very slightly. 'I wondered why you hadn't lost your licence . . . or your job. It didn't make sense to me that you hadn't. That's why I read the transcript, to see if there was any reason.'

'You're very thorough.'

'I like to be.'

'Interport knew one of us was lying . . . we both said the other had put the ship in danger . . . but I was the Captain. It inevitably came back to me. It was, in fact, my fault.'

'He wilfully disobeyed your instructions . . .'

'And I didn't find out until it was nearly too late.'

'Quite . . . but he need not have lied about it.'

'He was frightened,' I sighed. 'Of what would happen to his career.'

He let half a minute slip by without comment. Then he cleared his throat and said, 'I suppose you wouldn't like to tell me why you left the South American people?'

I admired his delicate approach. 'Gap in the dossier?' I suggested.

His mouth twitched. 'Well, yes.' A pause. 'You are of course not obliged . . .'

'No,' I said. 'Still . . .' Something for something. 'I refused to take off one day because I didn't think it was safe. They got another pilot who said it was. So he took off, and nothing happened. And they sacked me. That's all.'

'But,' he said blankly, 'it's a Captain's absolute right not to take off if he thinks it's unsafe.'

'There's no BALPA to uphold your rights there, you know. They said they couldn't afford to lose custom to other airlines because their Captains were cowards. Or words to that effect.'

'Good gracious.'

I smiled. 'Probably the Interport business accounted for my refusal to take risks.'

'But then you went to Africa and took them,' he protested.

'Well . . . I needed money badly, and the pay was fantastic. And you don't have the same moral obligation to food and medical supplies as to airline passengers.'

'But the refugees and wounded, coming out?'

'Always easier flying out than in. No difficulties finding the home base, not like groping for some jungle clearing on a black night.'

He shook his head wonderingly, giving me up as a bad job.

'What brought you back here to something as dull as crop spraying?'

I laughed. Never thought I could laugh in front of the Board of Trade. 'The particular war I was flying in ended. I was offered another one a bit further south, but I suppose I'd had enough of it. Also I was nearly solvent again. So I came back here, and crop spraying was the first thing handy.'

'What you might call a chequered career,' he commented.

'Mild compared with some.'

'Ah yes. That's true.' He stood up and threw his empty coffee beaker into the biscuit tin which served as a waste paper basket. 'Right then . . . You'll give a bit of thought to this bomb business?'

'Yes.'

'We'll be in touch with you again.' He fished in an inner pocket and produced a card. 'If you should want me, though, you can find me at this number.'

'OK.'

He made a wry face. 'I know how you must feel about us.'

'Never mind,' I said. 'Never mind.'

CHAPTER EIGHT

For most of that week I flew where I was told to, and thought about radio bombs, and sat on my own in the caravan in the evenings.

Honey didn't come back, but on the day after her visit I had returned from Rotterdam to find a large bag of groceries on the table: eggs, butter, bread, tomatoes, sugar, cheese, powdered milk, tins of soup. Also a pack of six half pints of beer. Also a note from Honey: 'Pay me next week.'

Not a bad guy, Honey Harley. I took up eating again. Old habits die hard.

Tuesday I took Colin and four assorted others to Wolverhampton races, Wednesday, after the Board of Trade departed, I took a politician to Cardiff to a Union strike meeting, and Thursday I took the racehorse trainer to various places in Yorkshire and Northumberland to look at some horses to see if he wanted to buy any.

Thursday evening I made myself a cheese and tomato sandwich and a cup of coffee, and ate them looking at the pin-ups, which were curling a bit round the edges. After I'd finished the sandwich I unstuck the Sellotape and took all the bosomy ladies down. The thrusting pairs of heavily ringed nipples regarded me sorrowfully, like spaniels' eyes. Smiling, I folded them decently over and dropped them in the rubbish bin. The caravan looked just as dingy, however, without them.

Friday morning, when I was in Harley's office filing flight records, Colin rang Harley and said he wanted me to stay overnight at Cambridge, ready again for Saturday.

Harley agreed. 'I'll charge Matt's hotel bill to your account.'

Colin said, 'Fine. But he can stay with me again if he likes.'

Harley relayed the message. Did I like? I liked.

Harley put down the receiver. 'Trying to save money,' he said disparagingly, 'having you to stay.' He brightened: 'I'll charge him the hangarage, though.'

I took the Cherokee over to Cambridge and fixed for them to give it shelter that night. When Colin came he was with four other jockeys: three I didn't know, and Kenny Bayst. Kenny said how was I. I was fine, how was he? Good as new, been riding since Newbury, he said.

Between them they had worked out the day's shuttle. All to Brighton, Colin to White Waltham for Windsor, aeroplane to return to Brighton, pick up the others, return to White Waltham, return to Cambridge.

'Is that all right?' Colin asked.

'Sure. Anything you say.'

He laughed. 'The fusses we used to have when we used to ask this sort of thing . . .'

'Don't see why,' I said.

'Larry was a lazy sod . . .'

They loaded themselves on board and we tracked down east of the London control zone and over the top of Gatwick to Shoreham airport for Brighton. When we landed Colin looked at his watch and Kenny nodded and said, 'Yeah, he's always faster than Larry. I've noticed it too.'

'Harley will give him the sack,' Colin said dryly, unfastening his seatbelt.

'He won't, will he?' Kenny sounded faintly anxious. Quicker journeys meant smaller bills.

'It depends on how many customers he pinches from Polyplanes through being fast.' Colin grinned at me. 'Am I right?'

'You could be,' I agreed.

They went off laughing about it to the waiting taxi. A couple of hours later Colin came back at a run in his breeches and colours and I whisked him over to White Waltham. He had won, it appeared, at Brighton. A close finish. He was still short of breath. A fast car drove right up to the aircraft as soon as I stopped and had him off down the road to Windsor in a cloud of dust. I went more leisurely back to Shoreham and collected the others at the end of their programme. It was a hot sunny day, blue and hazy. They came back sweating.

Kenny had ridden a winner and had brought me a

bottle of whisky as a present. I said he didn't need to give me a present.

'Look, sport, if it weren't for you, I wouldn't be riding any more bleeding winners. So take it.'

'All right,' I said. 'Thanks.'

'Thanks yourself.'

They were tired and expansive. I landed at White Waltham before Colin arrived back from Windsor, and the other four yawned and gossiped, opening all the doors and fanning themselves.

'. . . gave him a breather coming up the hill.'

'That was no breather. That was the soft bugger dropping his bit. Had to give him a sharp reminder to get him going again.'

'Can't stand that fellow Fossel . . .'

'Why do you ride for him then?'

'Got no choice, have I? Small matter of a retainer . . .'

'. . . What chance you got on Candlestick?'

'Wouldn't finish in the first three if it started now . . .'

'Hey,' said Kenny Bayst, leaning forward and tapping me on the shoulder. 'Got something that might interest you, sport.' He pulled a sheet of paper out of his trouser pocket. 'How about this, then?'

I took the paper and looked at it. It was a leaflet, high quality printing on good glossy paper. An invitation to all racegoers to join the Racegoers' Accident Fund.

'I'm not a racegoer,' I said.

'No, read it. Go on,' he urged. 'It came in the post this morning. I thought you'd be interested, so I brought it.'

I read down the page. 'Up to one thousand pounds for serious personal injury, five thousand pounds for accidental death. Premium five pounds. Double the premium double the insurance. The insurance everyone can afford. Stable lads, buy security for your missus. Jockeys: out of work but in the money. Race crowds, protect yourself against road accidents on the way home. Trainers who fly to meetings, protect yourself against bombs!'

'Damn it,' I said.

Kenny laughed. 'I thought you'd like it.'

I handed the leaflet back, smiling. 'Yeah. The so-and-sos.'

'Might not be a bad idea, at that.'

Colin's hired car drove up and decanted the usual spent force. He climbed wearily into his seat, clipped shut his belt, and said, 'Wake me at Cambridge.'

'How did it go?' Kenny asked.

'Got that sod Export home by a whisker . . . But as for Uptight,' he yawned, 'They might as well send him to the knackers. Got the slows right and proper, that one has.'

We woke him at Cambridge. It was a case of waking most of them, in point of fact. They stretched their way on to the tarmac, shirt necks open, ties hanging loose, jackets on their arms. Colin had no jacket, no tie: for him, the customary jeans, the rumpled sweat shirt, the air of being nobody, of being one in a crowd, instead of a crowd in one.

Nancy and Midge had come in the Aston Martin to pick us up.

'We brought a picnic,' Nancy said, 'as it's such a super evening. We're going to that place by the river.'

They had also brought swimming trunks for Colin and a pair of his for me. Nancy swam with us, but Midge said it was too cold. She sat on the bank wearing four watches on her left arm and stretching her long bare legs in the sun.

It was cool and quiet and peaceful in the river after the hot sticky day. The noise inside my head of engine throb calmed to silence. I watched a moorhen gliding along by the reeds, twisting her neck cautiously to fasten me with a shiny eye, peering suspiciously at Colin and Nancy floating away ahead. I pushed a ripple towards her with my arm. She rode on it like a cork. Simple being a moorhen, I thought. But it wasn't really. All of nature had its pecking order. Everywhere, someone was the pecked.

Nancy and Colin swam back. Friendly eyes, smiling faces. Don't get involved, I thought. Not with anyone. Not yet.

The girls had brought cold chicken and long crisp cos lettuce leaves with a tangy sauce to dip them in. We ate while the sun went down, and drank a cold bottle of Chablis, sitting on a large blue rug and throwing the chewed bones into the river for the fishes to nibble.

When she had finished Midge lay back on the rug and shielded her eyes from the last slanting rays.

'I wish this could go on for ever,' she said casually. 'The summer, I mean. Warm evenings. We get so few of them.'

'We could go and live in the south of France, if you like,' Nancy said.

'Don't be silly . . . Who would look after Colin?'

They smiled, all three of them. The unspoken things were all there. Tragic. Unimportant.

The slow dusk drained all colours into shades of grey. We lazed there, relaxing, chewing stalks of grass, watching the insects flick over the surface of the water, talking a little in soft summer evening murmuring voices.

'We both lost a stone in Japan, that year we went with Colin . . .'

'That was the food more than the heat.'

'I never did get to like the food . . .'

'Have you ever been to Japan, Matt?'

'Used to fly there for BOAC.'

'BOAC?' Colin was surprised. 'Why ever did you leave?'

'Left to please my wife. Long time ago, now, though.'

'Explains how you fly.'

'Oh sure . . .'

'I like America better,' Midge said. 'Do you remember Mr Kroop in Laurel, where you got those riding boots made in a day?'

'Mm . . .'

'And we kept driving round that shopping centre there and getting lost in the one way streets . . .'

'Super that week was . . .'

'Wish we could go again . . .'

There was a long regretful silence. Nancy sat up with a jerk and slapped her leg.

'Bloody mosquitoes.'

Colin scratched lazily and nodded. 'Time to go home.'

We wedged back into the Aston Martin. Colin drove. The twins sat on my legs, leaned on my chest and twined their arms behind my neck for balance. Not bad, not bad at all. They laughed at my expression.

'Too much of a good thing,' Nancy said.

When we went to bed they both kissed me goodnight, with identical soft lips, on the cheek.

Breakfast was brisk, businesslike, and accompanied throughout by telephone calls. Annie Villars rang to ask if there was still a spare seat on the Cherokee.

'Who for?' Colin asked cautiously. He made a face at us. 'Bloody Fenella,' he whispered over the mouthpiece. 'No, Annie, I'm terribly sorry, I've promised Nancy . . .'

'You have?' Nancy said. 'First I've heard of it.'

He put the receiver down. 'I rescue you from Chanter, now it's your turn.'

'Rescue my foot. You're in and out of the weighing room all day. Fat lot of good that is.'

'Do you want to come?'

'Take Midge,' she said. 'It's her turn.'

'No, you go,' Midge said. 'Honestly, I find it tiring. Especially as it's one of those rush from course to course days. I'll go along to the meeting here next week. That will do me fine.'

'Will you be all right?'

'Naturally I will. I'll lie in the sun in the garden and think of you all exhausting yourselves racing round in circles.'

When it turned out that there were two other empty seats as well, in spite of Nancy being there, Annie Villars gave Colin a reproachful look of carefully repressed annoyance and said it would have been useful to have had along Fenella to share the cost. Why else did Colin think she had suggested it?

'I must have miscounted,' said Colin happily. 'Too late to get her now.'

We flew to Bath without incident, Nancy sitting in the right-hand seat beside me and acting as co-pilot. It was clear that she intensely enjoyed it, and there was no pain in it for me either. I could see what Larry had meant about practising short landings, as the Bath runways were incredibly short, but we got down in fair order and parked alongside the opposition's Cessna.

Colin said, 'Lock the aeroplane and come into the races. You can't for ever stand on guard.'

The Polyplane pilot was nowhere to be seen. I hoped for the best, locked up, and walked with the others into the racecourse next door.

The first person we saw was Acey Jones, balancing on

his crutches with the sun making his pale head look fairer than ever.

'Oh yes. Colin,' Nancy said. 'Do you want me to send a fiver to the Accident Insurance people? You remember, the leaflet which came yesterday? That man reminded me . . . he got a thousand pounds from the fund for cracking his ankle. I heard him say so, at Haydock.'

'If you like,' he agreed. 'A fiver won't break the bank. May as well.'

'Bobbie Wessex is sponsoring it,' Annie commented.

'Yes,' Nancy added. 'It was on the leaflet.'

'Did you see the bit about the bombs?' I asked.

Annie and Nancy both laughed. 'Someone in insurance has got a sense of humour, after all.'

Annie hustled off to the weighing room to see her runner in the first race, and Colin followed her, to change.

'Lemonade?' I suggested to Nancy.

'Pints of it. Whew, it's hot.'

We drank it in a patch of shade, out on the grass. Ten yards away, loud and clear, Eric Goldenberg was conducting a row with Kenny Bayst.

'. . . And don't you think, sport, that you can set your guerrillas on me and expect me to do you favours afterwards, because if you think that you've got another think coming.'

'What guerrillas?' Goldenberg demanded, not very convincingly.

'Oh come off it. Set them to cripple me. At Redcar.'

'Must have been those bookmakers you swindled while you were busy double crossing us.'

'I never double crossed you.'

'Don't give me that crap,' Goldenberg said heavily. 'You know bloody well you did. You twisty little bastard.'

'If you think that, why the frigging hell are you asking me to set up another touch for you now?'

'Bygones are bygones.'

'Bygones bloody aren't.' Kenny spat on the ground at Goldenberg's feet and removed himself to the weighing room. Goldenberg watched him go with narrowed eyes and a venomous twist to his mouth. The next time I saw him he was holding a well-filled glass and adding substantially to his paunch, while muttering belligerently to a pasty slob who housed all his brains in his biceps. The slob wasn't one of the two who had lammed into Kenny at Redcar. I wondered if Goldenberg intended mustering reinforcements.

'What do you think of Kenny Bayst?' I asked Nancy.

'The big little Mister I-Am from Down Under,' she said. 'He's better than he used to be, though. He came over here thinking everyone owed him a living, as he'd had a great big successful apprenticeship back home.'

'Would he lose to order?'

'I expect so.'

'Would he agree to lose to order, take the money, back himself, and try to win?'

She grinned. 'You're learning fast.'

We watched Colin win the first race. Annie Villars' horse finished third from last. She stood glumly looking at its heaving sides while Kenny's successor made the best of explaining away his own poor showing.

'Annie should have kept Kenny Bayst,' Nancy said.

'He wanted out.'

'Like Colin doesn't want in,' she nodded. 'Annie's being a bit of a fool this season.'

Before the third race we went back to the aeroplane. The Polyplane pilot was standing beside it, peering in through the windows. He was not the stand off merchant from Redcar, but his colleague from Haydock.

'Good afternoon,' Nancy said.

'Good afternoon, Miss Ross.' He was polite in the way that is more insolent than rudeness. Not the best method, I would have thought, of seducing Colin's custom back from Derrydowns. He walked away, back to his Cessna, and I went over the Cherokee inch by inch looking for anything wrong. As far as I could see, there was nothing. Nancy and I climbed aboard and I started the engine to warm it up ready to take off.

Colin and Annie arrived in a hurry and loaded themselves in, and we whisked off across southern England to Shoreham. Colin and Annie again jumped into a waiting taxi and vanished. Nancy stayed with me and the Cherokee, and we sat on the warm grass and watched little aeroplanes landing and taking off, and talked now and then without pressure about flying, racing, life in general.

Towards the end of the afternoon she asked, 'Will you go on being a taxi pilot all your life?'

'I don't know. I don't look far ahead any more.'

'Nor do I,' she said.

'No.'

'We've been happy, these last few weeks, with Midge being so much better. I wish it would last.'

'You'll remember it.'

'That's not the same.'

'It's only special because of what's coming,' I said.

There was a long pause while she thought about it. At length she asked, disbelievingly, 'Do you mean that it is because Midge is dying that we are so happy now?'

'Something like that.'

She turned her head; considered me. 'Tell me something else. I need something else.'

'Comfort?'

'If you like.'

I said, 'You've all three been through the classic progression, these last two years. All together, not just Midge herself. Shock, disbelief, anger and in the end acceptance . . .' I paused. 'You've come through the dark tunnel. You're out in the sun the other end. You've done most of your grieving already. You are a most extraordinarily strong family. You'll remember this summer because it will be something worth remembering.'

'Matt . . .'

There were tears in her eyes. I watched the bright little dragonfly aeroplanes dart and go. They could heal me, the Ross family, I thought. Their strength could heal me. If it would take nothing away from them. If I could be sure.

'What was Colin's wife like?' I asked, after a while.

'Oh . . .' She gave a laugh which was half a sniff. 'A bit too much like Fenella. He was younger then. He didn't know how to duck. She was thirty-three and bossy and rich, and he was twenty and madly impressed by her. To be honest, Midge and I thought she was fabulous too. We were seventeen and still wet behind the ears. She thought it would be marvellous being married to a genius, all accolades and champagne and glamour. She didn't like it when it turned out to be mostly hard work and starvation and exhaustion . . . so she left him for a young actor who'd just had rave notices for his first film, and it took Colin months to get back to being himself from the wreck she'd made of him.'

'Poor Colin.' Or lucky Colin. Strong Colin. Months . . . it was taking me years.

'Yeah . . .' She grinned. 'He got over it. He's got some bird now in London. He slides down to see her every so often when he thinks Midge and I aren't noticing.'

'I must get me a bird,' I said idly. 'One of these days.'

'You haven't got one?'

I shook my head. I looked at her. Straight eyebrows,

straight eyes, sensible mouth. She looked back. I wanted to kiss her. I didn't think she would be angry.

'No,' I said absentmindedly. 'No bird.'

Take nothing away from them. Nothing from Midge.

'I'll wait a while longer,' I said.

Several days, several flights later I telephoned the Board of Trade. Diffidently. Sneering at myself for trying to do their job for them, for thinking I might have thought of something they hadn't worked out for themselves. But then, I'd been on the flight with the bomb, and they hadn't. I'd seen things, heard things, felt things that they hadn't.

Partly for my own sake, but mainly because of what Nancy had said about the bomb merchant still running around loose with his motives still rotting away inside him, I had finally found myself discarding the thought that it was none of my business, that someone else could sort it all out, and coming round to the view that if I could in fact come up with anything it might be a profitable idea.

To which end I wasted a lot of brain time chasing down labyrinths of speculation, and fetched up against a series of reasons why not.

There was Larry, for instance. Well, what about Larry? Larry had had every chance to put the bomb on board, right up to two hours before I set off to collect the passengers from White Waltham. But however strong a motive he had to kill Colin or ruin Derrydowns, and none had so far appeared bar a few trivial frauds, if it was true it was a radio and not a time bomb he couldn't have set it off because when it exploded he was in Turkey. If it had been Larry, a time bomb would have been the only simple and practical way.

Then Susan . . . Ridiculous as I thought it, I went over again what the Board of Trade man had said: she was going out occasionally with a demolitions expert. Well, good luck to her. The sooner she got married again the better off I'd be. Only trouble was, the aversion therapy of that last destructive six months seemed to have been just as successful with her as it had been with me.

I couldn't believe that any executive type in his right mind would bump off his occasional girlfriend's ex-husband for the sake of about six thousand pounds of insurance, especially as the longer I lived, the greater would be the sum she eventually collected. I had three years ago stopped paying any more premiums, but the value of the pay-off automatically went on increasing.

Apart from knowing her incapable of the cold-blooded murder of innocent people, I respected her mercenary instincts. The longer I lived the better off she would be on all counts. It was as simple as that.

Honey Harley . . . had said she would do 'anything' to keep Derrydowns in business, and the blowing up of the Cherokee had eased the financial situation. One couldn't sell things which were being bought on the hire purchase, and if one couldn't keep up the instalments the aircraft technically belonged to the HP company, who might sell it at a figure which did little more than cover themselves, leaving a molehill for Derrydowns to salvage. Insurance, on the other hand, had done them proud: paid off the HP and left them with capital in hand.

Yet killing Colin Ross would have ruined Derrydowns completely. Honey Harley would never have killed any of the customers, let alone Colin Ross. And the same applied to Harley himself, all along the line.

The Polyplane people, then? Always around, always belligerent, trying their damnedest to put Derrydowns out of business and win back Colin Ross. Well . . . the bomb would have achieved the first object but have put the absolute dampers on the second. I couldn't see even the craziest Polyplane pilot killing the golden goose.

Kenny Bayst . . . livid with Eric Goldenberg, Major Tyderman and Annie Villars. But as I'd said to Colin, where would he have got a bomb from in the time, and would he have killed Colin and me too? It didn't seem possible, any of it. No to Kenny Bayst.

Who, then?

Who?

Since I couldn't come up with anyone else, I went back over the possibilities all over again. Larry, Susan, the Harleys, Polyplanes, Kenny Bayst . . . Looked at them up, down, and sideways. Got nowhere. Made some coffee, went to bed, went to sleep.

Woke up at four in the morning with the moon

shining on my face. And one fact hitting me with a bang. Up, down and sideways. Look at things laterally. Start from the bottom.

I started from the bottom. When I did that, the answer rose up and stared me in the face. I couldn't believe it. It was too darned simple.

In the morning I made a lengthy telephone call to a long lost cousin, and two hours later got one back. And it was then, expecting a flat rebuff, that I rang up the Board of Trade.

The tall polite man wasn't in. He would, they said, call back later.

When he did, Harley was airborne with a pupil and Honey answered in the tower. She buzzed through to the crew room, where I was writing up records.

'The Board of Trade want you. What have you been up to?'

'It's only that old bomb,' I said soothingly.

'Huh.'

When the tall man came on the line, she was still listening on the tower extension.

'Honey,' I said. 'Quit.'

'I beg your pardon,' said the Board of Trade.

Honey giggled, but she put her receiver down. I heard the click.

'Captain Shore?' the voice said reprovingly.

'Er, yes.'

'You wanted me?'

'You said . . . if I thought of any angle on the bomb.'

'Indeed yes.' A shade of warmth.

'I've been thinking,' I said, 'about the transmitter which was needed to set it off.'

'Yes?'

'How big would the bomb have been?' I asked. 'All that plastic explosive and gunpowder and wires and solenoids?'

'I should think quite small . . . you would probably pack a bomb like that into a flat tin about seven inches by four by two inches deep. Possibly even smaller. The tighter they are packed the more fiercely they explode.'

'And how big would the transmitter have to be to send perhaps three different signals?'

'Nowadays, not very big. If size were important . . . a pack of cards, perhaps. But in this case I would have thought . . . larger. The transmissions must have had to carry a fairly long way . . . and to double the range of a signal you have to quadruple the power of the transmitter, as no doubt you know.'

'Yes . . . I apologize for going through all this the long way, but I wanted to be sure. Because although I don't know *why*, I've a good idea of *when* and *who*.'

'What did you say?' His voice sounded strangled.

'I said . . .'

'Yes, yes,' he interrupted. 'I heard. When . . . when, then?'

'It was put on board at White Waltham. Taken off again at Haydock. And put back on again at Haydock.'

'What do you mean?'

'It came with one of the passengers.'

'Which one?'

'By the way,' I said. 'How much would such a bomb cost?'

'Oh . . . about eighty pounds or so,' he said impatiently. 'Who? . . .'

'And would it take a considerable expert to make one?'

'Someone used to handling explosives and with a working knowledge of radio.'

'I thought so.'

'Look,' he said, 'look, will you please stop playing cat and mouse. I dare say it amuses you to tease the Board of Trade . . . I don't say I absolutely blame you, but will you please tell me which of the passengers had a bomb with him?'

'Major Tyderman,' I said.

'Major . . .' He took an audible breath. 'Are you meaning to say now that it wasn't the bomb rolling around on the elevator wires which caused the friction which persuaded you to land? . . . That Major Tyderman was carrying it around unknown to himself all the afternoon? Or what?'

'No,' I said, 'And no.'

'For God's sake . . .' He was exasperated. 'I suppose you couldn't simplify the whole thing by telling me exactly who planted the bomb on Major Tyderman? Who intended to blow him up?'

'If you like.'

He took a shaking grip. I smiled at the crew room wall.

'Well, who?'

'Major Tyderman,' I said. 'Himself.'

Silence. Then a protest.

'Do you mean suicide? It can't have been. The bomb went off when the aeroplane was on the ground . . .'

'Precisely,' I said.

'What?'

'If a bomb goes off in an aeroplane, everyone automatically thinks it was intended to blow up in the air and kill all the people on board.'

'Yes, of course.'

'Suppose the real intended victim was the aeroplane itself, not the people?'

'But why?'

'I told you, I don't know why.'

'All right,' he said. 'All right.' He took a deep breath. 'Let's start from the beginning. You are saying that Major Tyderman, intending to blow up the aeroplane for reasons unknown, took a bomb with him to the races.'

'Yes.'

'What makes you think so?'

'Looking back . . . He was rigidly tense all day, and he wouldn't be parted from his binocular case, which was large enough to contain a bomb of the size you described.'

'That's absurdly circumstantial,' he protested.

'Sure,' I agreed. 'Then it was the Major who borrowed the keys from me, to go over to the aircraft to fetch the *Sporting Life* which he had left there. He wouldn't let me go, though I offered. He came back saying he had locked up again, and gave me back the keys. Of course he hadn't locked up. He wanted to create a little confusion. While he was over there he unscrewed the back panel of the luggage bay and put the bomb behind it, against the fuselage. Limpet gadget, I expect, like I said before, which came unstuck on the bumpy flight.'

'He couldn't have foreseen you'd land at East Midlands . . .'

'It didn't matter where we landed. As soon as everyone was clear of the aircraft, he was ready to blow it up.'

'That's sheer guess work.'

'He did it in front of my eyes, at East Midlands. I saw him look round, to check there was no one near it. Then he was fiddling with his binocular case . . . sending the signals. They could have been either very low or superhigh frequencies. They didn't have very far to go. But more important, the transmitter would have been very low powered . . . and very small.'

'But . . . by all accounts . . . and yours too . . . he was severely shocked after the explosion.'

'Shocked by the sight of the disintegration he had been sitting on all day. And acting a bit, too.'

He thought it over at length. Then he said, 'Wouldn't someone have noticed that the Major wasn't using binoculars although he was carrying the case?'

'He could say he'd just dropped them and they were broken . . . and anyway, he carries a flask in that case normally as well as the race glasses . . . lots of people must have seen him taking a swig, as I have . . . they wouldn't think it odd . . . they might think he'd brought the flask but forgotten the glasses.'

I could imagine him shaking his head. 'It's a fantastic theory altogether. And not a shred of evidence. Just a guess.' He paused. 'I'm sorry, Mr Shore, I'm certain you've done your best, but . . .'

I noticed he'd demoted me from Captain. I smiled thinly.

'There's one other tiny thing,' I said gently.

'Yes?' He was slightly, very slightly apprehensive, as if expecting yet more fantasy.

'I got in touch with a cousin in the army, and he looked up some old records for me. In World War Two Major Tyderman was in the Royal Engineers, in charge of a unit which spent nearly all of its time in England.'

'I don't see . . .'

'They were dealing,' I said, 'with unexploded bombs.'

CHAPTER NINE

It was the next day that Nancy flew Colin to Haydock. They went in the four-seater 140 horse power small version Cherokee which she normally hired from her flying club for lessons and practice, and they set off from Cambridge shortly before I left there myself with a full load in the replacement Six. I had been through her flight plan with her and helped her all I could with the many technicalities and regulations she would meet in the complex Manchester control zone. The weather forecast was for clear skies until evening, there would be radar to help her if she got lost, and I would be listening to her nearly all the time on the radio as I followed her up.

Colin grinned at me. 'Harley would be horrified at the care you're taking to look after her. "Let them frighten themselves silly," he'd say, "then he'll fly with us all the time, with none of this do-it-yourself nonsense".'

'Yeah,' I agreed. 'And Harley wants you safe, too, don't forget.'

'Did he tell you to help us?'

'Not actually, no.'

'Thought not.'

Harley had said crossly, 'I don't want them making a habit of it. Persuade Colin Ross she isn't experienced enough.'

Colin didn't need persuading: he knew. He also wanted to please Nancy. She set off with shining eyes, like a child being given a treat.

The Derrydowns Six had been hired by an un-clued-up trainer who had separately agreed to share the trip with both Annie Villars and Kenny Bayst. Even diluted by the hiring trainer, the large loud-voiced owner of the horse he was running, and the jockey who was to ride it, the atmosphere at loading time was poisonous.

Jarvis Kitch, the hiring trainer, who could have helped, retreated into a huff.

'How was I to know,' he complained to me in aggrieved anger, 'that they loathe each other's guts?'

'You couldn't,' I said soothingly.

'They just rang up and asked if there was a spare seat. Annie yesterday, Bayst the day before. I said there was. How was I to know? . . .'

'You couldn't.'

The loud-voiced owner, who was evidently footing the bill, asked testily what the hell it mattered, they would be contributing their share of the cost. He had a north country accent and a bullying manner, and he was the sort of man who considered that when he bought a man's services he bought his soul. Kitch subsided hastily: the small attendant jockey remained cowed and silent throughout. The owner, whose name I later discovered from the racecard was Ambrose, then told me to get a move on as he hadn't hired me to stand around all day on the ground at Cambridge.

Annie Villars suggested in embarrassment that the captain of an aircraft was like the captain of a ship.

'Nonsense,' he said, 'In a two bit little outfit like this he's only a chauffeur. Taking me from place to place isn't he? For hire?' He nodded. 'Chauffeur.' His voice left no one in any doubt about his opinion on the proper place of chauffeurs.

I sighed, climbed aboard, strapped myself in. Easy to ignore him, as it was far from the first time in my life I'd met that attitude. All the same, hardly one of the jolliest of trips.

The Cherokee Six cruised at fifty miles an hour faster than the One Forty, so that I passed Nancy somewhere on the way up. I could hear her calling the various flight information regions on the radio, as she could hear me. It was companionable, in an odd sort of way. And she was doing all right.

I landed at Haydock a few minutes before her, and unloaded the passengers in time to watch her come in. She put on a show to impress the audience, touching down like a feather on the grass. I grinned to myself. Not bad for a ninety-hour amateur. It hadn't been the easiest of trips either. There would be no holding her, after this.

She rolled to a stop a little way along the rails from me and I finished locking the Six and walked over to tell her she would smash the undercarriage next time she thumped an aeroplane down like that.

She made a face at me, excited and pleased. 'It was super. Great. The Liverpool radar people were awfully kind. They told me exactly which headings to fly round the control zone and then told me they would put me smack overhead the racecourse, and they did.'

Colin was proud of her and teased her affectionately. 'Sure, we've got here, but we've got to go home yet.'

'Going home's always easier,' she said confidently. 'And there are none of those difficult control zone rules round Cambridge.'

We walked together across the track to the paddock, ducking under the rails. Nancy talked the whole way, as high as if she'd taken benzedrine. Colin grinned at me. I grinned back. Nothing as intoxicating as a considerable achievement.

We left him at the weighing room and went off to have some coffee.

'Do you know it's only four weeks since we were at Haydock before?' she said. 'Since the bomb. Only four weeks. I seem to have known you half my life.'

'I hope you'll know me for the other half,' I said.

'What did you say?'

'Nothing . . . Turkey sandwiches all right?'

'Mm, lovely.' She looked at me, unsure. 'What did you mean?'

'Just one of those pointless things people say.'

'Oh.'

She bit into the soft thick sandwich. She had good straight teeth. I was being a fool, I thought. A fool to get involved, a fool to grow fond of her. I had nothing but a lot of ruins to offer anyone, and she had the whole world to choose from, the sister of Colin Ross. If I was an iceberg, as Honey said, I'd better stay an iceberg. When ice melted, it made a mess.

'You've clammed up,' she said, observing me.

'I haven't.'

'Oh yes, you have. You do, sometimes. You look relaxed and peaceful, and then something inside goes snap shut and you retreat out into the stratosphere. Somewhere very cold.' She shivered. 'Freezing.'

I drank my coffee and let the stratosphere do its stuff. The melting edges safely refroze.

'Will Chanter be here today?' I asked.

'God knows.' She shrugged. 'Do you want him to be?'

'No.' It sounded more vehement than I meant.

'That's something, anyhow,' she said under her breath.

I let it go. She couldn't mean what it sounded like. We finished the sandwiches and went out to watch Colin ride, and after that while we were leaning against the parade ring rails Chanter appeared out of nowhere and smothered Nancy in hair and fringes and swirling fabric, as closely as if he were putting out a fire with a carpet.

She pushed him away. 'For God's sake . . .'

He was unabashed. 'Aw Nancy. C'mon now. You and me, we'd have everything going for us if you'd just loosen up.'

'You're a bad trip, Chanter, as far as I'm concerned.'

'You've never been on any real trip, chick, that's your problem.'

'And I'm not going,' she said firmly.

'A little acid lets you into the guts of things.'

'Components,' I agreed. 'Like you said before. You see things in fragments.'

'Huh?' Chanter focussed on me. 'Nancy, you still got this creep in tow? You must be joking.'

'He sees things whole,' she said. 'No props needed.'

'Acid isn't a prop, it's a doorway,' he declaimed.

'Shut the door,' she said. 'I'm not going through.'

Chanter scowled at me. The green chenille tablecloth had been exchanged for a weird shapeless tunic made of irregular shaped pieces of fabrics, fur, leather and metal all stapled together instead of sewn.

'This is your doing, man, you're bad news.'

'It's not his doing,' Nancy said. 'The drug scene is a drag. It always was. Maybe at art school I thought getting woozy on pot was a gas, but not any more. I've grown up, Chanter. I've told you before, I've grown up.'

'He's brainwashed you.'

She shook her head. I knew she was thinking of

Midge. Face something big enough, and you always grow up.

'Don't you have any classes today?' she asked.

He scowled more fiercely. 'The sods are out on strike.'

She laughed. 'Do you mean the students?'

'Yeah. Demanding the sack for the deputy Head for keeping a record of what demos they go to.'

I asked ironically, 'Which side are you on?'

He peered at me. 'You bug me, man, you do really.'

For all that, he stayed with us all afternoon, muttering, scowling, plonking his hands on Nancy whenever he got the chance. Nancy bore his company as if she didn't altogether dislike it. As for me, I could have done without it. Easily.

Colin won two races, including the day's biggest. Annie Villars' horse came second, Kenny Bayst won a race on an objection. The loud voiced Ambrose's horse finished fourth, which didn't bode well for sweetness and light on the way home.

The way home was beginning to give me faint twinges of speculation. The weak warm front which had been forecast for late evening looked as if it were arriving well before schedule. From the south-west the upper winds were drawing a strip of cloud over the sky like a sheet over a bed.

Nancy looked up when the sun went in.

'Golly, where did all that cloud come from?'

'It's the warm front.'

'Damn . . . do you think it will have got to Cambridge?'

'I'll find out for you, if you like.'

I telephoned to Cambridge and asked them for their actual and forecast weather. Nancy stood beside me inside the telephone box and Chanter fumed suspiciously outside. I had to ask Cambridge to repeat what they'd said. Nancy smelled faintly of a fresh flowering scent. 'Did you say two thousand feet?' Yes, said Cambridge with exaggerated patience, we've told you twice already.

I put down the receiver. 'The front isn't expected there for three or four hours, and the forecast cloud base even then is as high as two thousand feet, so you should be all right.'

'Anyway,' she said, 'I've done dozens of practice let-downs at Cambridge. Even if it should be cloudy by the time we get back, I'm sure I could do it in earnest.'

'Have you ever done it without an instructor?'

She nodded. 'Several times. On fine days, of course.'

I pondered. 'You aren't legally qualified yet to carry passengers in clouds.'

'Don't look so fraught. I won't have to. They said it was clear there now, didn't they? And if the base is two thousand feet when I get there, I can keep below that easily.'

'Yes, I suppose you can.'

'And I've got to get back, haven't I?' she said reasonably.

'Mm . . .'

Chanter pulled open the telephone box door. 'You taking a lease on that space, man?' he inquired. He put his arm forward over Nancy's chest a millimetre south of her breasts and scooped her out. She half disappeared into the enveloping fuzz and re-emerged blushing.

'Chanter, for God's sake, we're at the races!'

'Transfer to my pad, then.'

'No, thank you.'

'Women,' he said in disgust. 'Goddamn women. Don't know what's good for them.'

'How's that for a right-wing reactionary statement?' I inquired of the air in general.

'You cool it, man. Just cool it.'

Nancy smoothed herself down and said, 'Both of you cool it. I'm going back to the aeroplane now to get set for going home, and you're not coming with me, Chanter. I can't concentrate with you crawling all over me.'

He stayed behind with a bad grace, complaining bitterly when she took me with her.

'He's impossible,' she said as we walked across the track. But she was smiling.

Spreading the map out on the wing I went through the flight plan with her, step by step, as that was what she wanted. She was going back as we'd come, via the radio beacon at Lichfield: not a straight line but the easiest way to navigate. As she had said, it was a simpler business going home. I worked out the times between points for her and filled them in on her planning sheet.

'You are five times as quick at it as I am,' she sighed.

'I've had a spot more practice.'

I folded the map and clipped the completed plan on to it. 'See you at Cambridge,' I said. 'With a bit of luck.'

'Meany.'

'Nancy . . .'

'Yes?'

I didn't exactly know what I wanted to say. She waited.

After a while I said earnestly, 'Take care.'

She half smiled. 'I will, you know.'

Colin came across the track dragging his feet. 'God, I'm tired,' he said. 'How's my pilot?'

'Ready, willing, and if it's your lucky day, able.'

I did the external checks for her while they climbed aboard. No bombs to be seen. Didn't expect any. She started the engine after I'd given her the all clear, and they both waved as she taxied off. She turned into the wind at the far end of the field, accelerated quickly, and lifted off into the pale-grey sky. The clouds were a shade lower than they had been. Nothing to worry about. Not if it was clear at Cambridge. I strolled across to the Derrydowns Six. Annie Villars and Kenny Bayst were both there already, studiously looking in opposite directions. I unlocked the doors, and Annie embarked without a word. Kenny gave her a sour look and stayed outside on the ground. I congratulated him on his winner. It all helped, he said.

Ambrose's trainer and jockey trickled back looking pensive, and finally Ambrose came himself, reddish in the face and breathing out beer fumes in a sickly cloud. As soon as he reached the aircraft he leaned towards me and gave me the full benefit.

'I've left me hat in the cloakroom,' he said. 'Hop over and fetch it for me.'

Kenny and the other two were all of a sudden very busy piling themselves aboard and pretending they hadn't heard. Short of saying 'Fetch it yourself' and losing Harley a customer, I was stuck with it. I trudged back across the track, through the paddock, into the members' gents, and collected the hat off the peg it was hanging on. Its band was so greasy that I wondered how Ambrose had the nerve to let anyone see it.

Turned, made for the door. Felt my arm clutched in a fiercely urgent grip.

I swung round. The hands holding on to my arm like steel grabs belonged to Major Tyderman.

'Major,' I exclaimed in surprise. I hadn't seen him there all through the afternoon.

'Shore!' He was far more surprised to see me. And more than surprised. Horrified. The colour was draining out of his face while I watched.

'Shore . . . What are you doing here? Did you come back?'

Puzzled, I said, 'I came over for Mr Ambrose's hat.'

'But . . . you flew . . . you took off with Colin and Nancy Ross.'

I shook my head. 'No, I didn't. Nancy was flying.'

'But . . . you came with them.' He sounded agonized.

'I didn't. I flew the Six here with five passengers.' The extreme state of his shock got through to me like a tidal wave. He was clinging on to my arm now more for support than to attract my attention.

'Major,' I said, the terrible, terrifying suspicion shaking in my voice, 'you haven't put another bomb on that aircraft? Not . . . oh God . . . another bomb?'

'I . . . I . . .' His voice strangled in his throat.

'Major.' I disengaged my arm and seized both of his. Ambrose's hat fell and rolled unnoticed on the dirty floor. 'Major.' I squeezed him viciously. '*Not another bomb?*'

'No . . . but . . .'

'But *what*?'

'I thought . . . you were flying them . . . I thought you were with them . . . you would be able to cope . . .'

'Major.' I shook him, gripping as if I'd pull his arms in two. 'What have you done to that aeroplane?'

'I saw you . . . come with them, when they came. And go back . . . and look at the map . . . and do the checks . . . I was sure . . . it was you that was flying . . . and you . . . you . . . could deal with . . . but Nancy Ross . . . Oh my God . . .'

I let go one of his arms and slapped him hard in the face.

'*What have you done to that aeroplane?*'

'You can't . . . do anything . . .'

'I'll get her back. Get her down on the ground at once.'

He shook his head. 'You won't . . . be able to . . . She'll have no radio . . . I put . . .' He swallowed and put his hand to his face where I'd hit him. 'I put . . . a plaster . . . nitric acid . . . on the lead . . . to the master switch . . .'

I let go of his other arm and simply looked at him, feeling the coldness sink in. Then I blindly picked up Ambrose's hat and ran out of the door. Ran. Ran across the paddock, across the track, down to the aircraft. I didn't stop to slap it out of the Major what he'd done it for. Didn't think of it. Thought only of Nancy with her limited experience having to deal with a total electrical failure.

She could do it, of course. The engine wouldn't stop. Several of the instruments would go on working. The altimeter, the air-speed indicator, the compass, none of those essentials would be affected. They worked on magnetism, air pressure and engine driven gyroscopes, not electricity.

All the engine instruments would read zero, and the fuel gauge would register empty. She wouldn't know how much fuel she had left. But she did know, I thought, that she had enough for at least two hours' flying.

The worst thing was the radio. She would have no communication with the ground, nor could she receive any signals from the navigation beacons. Well . . . dozens of people flew without radio, without even having it installed at all. If she was worried about getting lost, she could land at the first suitable airfield.

It might not have happened yet, I thought. Her radio might still be working. The nitric acid might not yet have eaten through the main electrical cable.

While I was on the ground I was too low down for them to hear me, but if I got up in the air fast enough I could tell the Manchester control people the situation, get them to relay the facts to her, tell her to land at an airfield as soon as she could . . . A fairly simple matter to repair the cable, once she was safe on the ground.

I gave Ambrose his hat. He was still outside on the grass, waiting for me to climb through to the left hand seat. I shifted myself across on to it with no seconds wasted and he hauled himself up after me. By the time he'd strapped himself in I had the engine running, my head-set in place, and the radios warming up.

'What's the rush?' Ambrose inquired, as we taxied at just under take-off speed down to the far end.

'Have to send a radio message to Colin Ross, who's in the air ahead of us.'

'Oh . . .' He nodded heavily. He knew the Rosses had come up when we had, knew that Nancy was flying. 'All right then.'

I thought fleetingly that if he thought I couldn't even hurry without getting his permission first he was in for a moderate shock. I wasn't taking him back to Cambridge until I was certain Nancy and Colin were safe.

As there was only one head-set on board Ambrose couldn't hear any incoming transmissions, and with the microphone close against my lips I doubted if he could hear over the engine noise anything I sent outwards. I thought I would delay as long as possible inviting his objections.

Two hundred feet off the ground I raised the Air Traffic Controller at Liverpool. Explained that Nancy's radio might be faulty; asked if he had heard her.

Yes, he had. He'd given her radar clearance out of the control zone, and handed her on to Preston Information. Since I had to stay on his frequency until I was out of the zone myself, I asked him to find out from Preston if they still had contact with her.

'Stand by,' he said.

After a long two minutes he came back. 'They did have,' he said briefly. 'They lost her in the middle of one of her transmissions. They can't raise her now.'

Sod the Major, I thought violently. Stupid, dangerous little man.

I kept my voice casual. 'Did they have her position?'

'Stand by.' A pause. He came back. 'She was on track to Lichfield, ETA Lichfield five three, flying visual on top at flight level four five.'

'On top?' I repeated with apprehension.

'Affirmative.'

We had been climbing steadily ourselves. We went

into thin cloud at two thousand feet and came through it into the sunshine at four thousand. Everywhere below us in all directions spread the cottonwool blanket, hiding the earth beneath. She would have to climb to that height as well, because the Pennines to the east of Manchester rose to nearly three thousand feet and the high ridges would have been sticking up into the clouds. With no room for her between the clouds and the hills she would have had either to go back, or go up. She wouldn't see any harm in going up. With radio navigation and a good forecast for Cambridge it was merely the sensible thing to do.

'Her destination is Cambridge,' I said. 'Can you check the weather there?'

'Stand by.' A much longer pause. Then his voice, dead level, spelling it out. 'Cambridge actual weather, cloud has spread in fast from the south-west, now eight eighths cover, base twelve hundred feet, tops three thousand five hundred.'

I didn't acknowledge him at once: was digesting the appalling implications.

'Confirm weather copied,' he said baldly.

'Weather copied.'

'Latest meteorological reports indicate total cloud cover over the entire area south of the Tees.' He knew exactly what he was saying. The laconic non-panic voice was deliberately unexcited. Nancy was flying above the cloud layer with no means of telling where she was. She couldn't see the ground and couldn't ask anyone for directions. Eventually she would have to come down, because she would run out of fuel. With the gauge out of action, she couldn't tell exactly how long she could stay airborne, and it was essential for her to go down through the clouds while the engine was still running, so that she could find somewhere to land once she was underneath. But if she went down too soon, or in the wrong place, she could all too easily fly into a cloud-covered hill. Even for a highly experienced pilot it was a sticky situation.

I said, with the same studied artificial calm, 'Can the RAF radar stations find her and trace her where she goes? I know her flight plan . . . I made it out for her. She is likely to stick to it, as she thinks it is still clear at Cambridge. I could follow . . . and find her.'

'Stand by.' Again the pause for consultations. 'Change frequency to Birmingham radar on one one eight zero five.'

'Roger,' I said. 'And thanks very much.'

'Good luck,' he said. 'You'll need it.'

CHAPTER TEN

He had explained the situation to Birmingham. I gave the radar controller Nancy's planned track and air speed and estimated time for Lichfield, and after a few moments he came back and said there were at least ten aircraft on his screen which were possibles, but he had no way of telling who they were. 'I'll consult with the RAF Wymeswold . . . they may not be as busy as we are . . . they can concentrate on it more.'

'Tell them that at about five three she will change her heading to one two five.'

'Roger,' he said. 'Stand by.'

He came back. 'RAF Wymeswold say they will watch for her.'

'Great,' I said.

After a few moments he said in an incredulous voice, 'We have a report that Colin Ross is aboard the non-radio aircraft. Can you confirm?'

'Affirmative,' I said. 'The pilot is his sister.'

'Good God,' he said. 'Then we'd better find her.'

I had got them to route me straight through the

control zone instead of round it, and was making for Northwich, and then the Lichfield beacon. We had taken off, I calculated, a good thirty minutes behind her, and in spite of the short cut and the Six's superior speed it would be barely possible to overtake her before Cambridge. I looked at my watch for about the twentieth time. Five-fifty. At five fifty-three she would be turning over Lichfield . . . except that she wouldn't know she was at Lichfield. If she turned as scheduled, it would be on her part simply blind faith.

Birmingham radar called me up. 'Cambridge report a steady deterioration in the weather. The cloud base is now eight hundred feet.'

'Roger,' I said flatly.

After another five minutes, during which five fifty-three came and went in silence, he said, 'Wymeswold report that an aircraft on their screen has turned from one six zero on to one two five, but it is five miles north-east of Lichfield. The aircraft is unidentified. They will maintain surveillance.'

'Roger,' I said.

She could be drifting north-east, I thought, because the wind from the south-west was stronger than it had been on the northward journey, and I hadn't made enough allowance for it on the flight plan. I pressed the transmit button and informed the radar man.

'I'll tell them,' he said.

We flew on. I looked round at the passengers. They looked variously bored, thoughtful and tired. Probably none of them would notice when we left our direct course to go and look for Nancy: but they'd certainly notice if or when we found her.

'Wymeswold report the aircraft they were watching has turned north on to zero one zero.'

'Oh no,' I said.

'Stand by . . .'

Too easy, I thought despairingly. It had been too easy. The aircraft which had turned on to the right heading at the right time at roughly the right place hadn't been the right aircraft after all. I took three deep deliberate breaths. Concentrated on the fact that wherever she was she was in no immediate danger. She could stay up for more than another hour and a half.

I had over an hour in which to find her. In roughly three thousand square miles of sky as featureless as the desert. Piece of cake.

'Wymeswold report that the first aircraft has apparently landed at East Midlands, but that they have another possibility ten miles east of Lichfield, present heading one two zero. They have no height information.'

'Roger,' I said again. No height information meant that the blip on their screen could be flying at anything up to thirty thousand feet or more, not four thousand five hundred.

'Stand by.'

I stood by. Metaphorically bit my nails. Slid a sidelong glance at Ambrose and went unhurriedly about checking our own height, speed, direction. Lichfield dead ahead, eleven minutes away. Forty minutes to Cambridge. Too long. Have to go faster. Pushed the throttle open another notch and came up against the stops. Full power. Nothing more to be done.

'Possible aircraft now tracking steady one zero five. Present track if maintained will take it thirty miles north of Cambridge at estimated time two zero.'

'Roger.' I looked at my watch. Did a brief sum. Pressed the transmit button. 'That's the wrong aircraft. It's travelling too fast. At ninety knots she couldn't reach the Cambridge area before three five or four zero.'

'Understood.' A short silence. 'Retune now to RAF Cottesmore, Northern Radar, one two two decimal one. I'm handing you on to them.'

I thanked him. Retuned. Cottesmore said they were in the picture, and looking. They had seven unidentified aircraft travelling from west to east to the south of them, all at heights unknown.

Seven. She could be any one of them. She could have gone completely haywire and turned round and headed back to Manchester. I felt my skin prickle. Surely she would have enough sense not to fly straight into a control zone without radio. And anyway, she still believed it was clear at Cambridge . . .

I reached the Lichfield beacon. Turned on to course for Cambridge. Informed Cottesmore radar that I had done so. They didn't have me on their screen yet, they said: I was still too far away.

I tracked doggedly on towards Cambridge over the cottonwool wastes. The sun shone hotly into the cabin, and all the passengers except Ambrose went to sleep.

'One unidentified aircraft has landed at Leicester,' Cottesmore radar said. 'Another appears to be heading directly for Peterborough.'

'That leaves five?' I asked.

'Six . . . there's another now farther to the west.'

'It may be me.'

'Turn left thirty degrees for identification.'

I turned, flew on the new heading.

'Identified,' he said. 'Return to former heading.'

I turned back on track, stifling the raw anxiety which mounted with every minute. They must find her, I thought. They *must*.

Cottesmore said, 'One aircraft which passed close to the south of us five minutes ago has now turned north.'

Not her.

'The same aircraft has now flown in a complete circle and resumed a track of one one zero.'

It might be her. If she had spotted a thin patch. Had gone to see if she could see the ground and get down safely to below the cloud. Had found she couldn't: had gone on again in what she thought was the direction of Cambridge.

'That might be her,' I said. Or someone else in the

same difficulties. Or someone simply practising turns. Or anything.

'That particular aircraft has now turned due south . . . slightly west . . . now round again to south-east . . . back to one one zero.'

'Could be looking for thin patches in the cloud,' I said.

'Could be. Stand by.' A pause. Then his voice, remote and careful. 'Cloud base in this area is down to six hundred feet. Eight eighths cover. No clear patches.'

Oh Nancy . . .

'I'm going to look for that one,' I said. 'Can you give me a steer to close on its present track?'

'Will do,' he said. 'Turn left on to zero nine five. You are thirty miles to the west. I estimate your ground speed at one fifty knots. The aircraft in question is travelling at about ninety-five knots.'

In the twelve minutes it would take me to reach the other aircraft's present position, it would have shifted twenty miles farther on. Catching up would take twenty-five to thirty minutes.

'The aircraft in question is circling again . . . now tracking one one zero . . .'

The more it circled, the sooner I'd catch it. But if it wasn't Nancy at all . . . I thrust the thought violently out of my mind. If it wasn't we might never find her.

Ambrose touched my arm, and I had been concentrating so hard that I jumped.

'We're off course,' he said dogmatically. He tapped

the compass. 'We're going due east. We'd better not be lost.'

'We're under radar control,' I said matter-of-factly.

'Oh . . .' He was uncertain. 'I see.'

I would have to tell him, I thought. Couldn't put it off any longer. I explained the situation as briefly as I could, leaving out Major Tyderman's part in it and shouting to make myself heard over the noise of the engine.

He was incredulous. 'Do you mean we're chasing all over the sky looking for Colin Ross?'

'Directed by radar,' I said briefly.

'And who,' he asked belligerently, 'is going to pay for this? I am certainly not. In fact you have been totally irresponsible in changing course without asking my permission first.'

Cottesmore reported, 'The aircraft is now overhead Stamford, and circling again.'

'Roger,' I said. And for God's sake, Nancy, I thought, don't try going down through the cloud just there. There were some hills round about and a radio mast five hundred feet high.

'Steer one zero zero to close.'

'One zero zero.'

'Aircraft has resumed its former heading.'

I took a considerable breath of relief.

'Did you hear what I said?' Ambrose demanded angrily.

'We have a duty to go to the help of an aircraft in trouble,' I said.

'Not at my expense, we don't.'

'You will be charged,' I said patiently, 'only the normal amount for the trip.'

'That's not the point. You should have asked my permission. I am seriously displeased. I will complain to Harley. We should not have left our course. Someone else should have gone to help Colin Ross. Why should we be inconvenienced?'

'I am sure he will be pleased to hear your views,' I said politely. 'And no doubt he will pay any expenses incurred in his rescue.'

He glared at me speechlessly, swept by fury.

Annie Villars leaned forward and tapped me on the shoulder.

'Did I hear you say that Colin Ross is lost? Up here, do you mean? On top of the clouds?'

I glanced round. They were all awake, all looking concerned.

'Yes,' I said briefly. 'With no radio. The radar people think they may have found him. We're going over to see . . . and to help.'

'Anything we can do . . .' Annie said. 'Of course, call on us.'

I smiled at her over my shoulder. Ambrose turned round to her and started to complain. She shut him up smartly. 'Do you seriously propose we make no attempt to help? You must be out of your mind. It is our clear and absolute duty to do whatever we can. And a captain doesn't have to consult his passengers before he goes to help another ship in distress.'

He said something about expense. Annie said crisply, 'If you are too mean to pay a few extra pounds as your share of perhaps saving the life of Colin Ross, I shall be pleased to contribute the whole amount myself.'

'Atta girl,' Kenny Bayst said loudly. Annie Villars looked startled, but not displeased. Ambrose swivelled to face forwards. He had turned a dark purplish red. I hoped it was shame and embarrassment, not an incipient thrombosis.

'The aircraft is circling again,' Cottesmore reported. 'Its position now is just south of Peterborough . . . Remain on your present heading . . . I am handing you on now to Wytton . . . no need for you to explain to them . . . they know the situation.'

'Thank you very much,' I said.

'Good luck . . .'

Wytton, the next in the chain, the RAF master station north-east of Cambridge, was crisp, cool, efficient.

'Cloud base at Cambridge six hundred feet, no further deterioration in past half-hour. Visibility three kilometres in light rain. Surface wind two four zero, ten knots.'

'Weather copied,' I said automatically. I was looking at the map. Another radio mast, this one seven hundred feet high, south of Peterborough. Go on, Nancy, I thought, go on, further east. Don't try there. Not there . . .

Wytton said, 'Aircraft now back on one one zero.'

I rubbed a hand round the back of my neck. I could feel the sweat.

'Steer zero nine five. You are now ten miles west of the aircraft.'

'I'm climbing to flight level eight zero. To see better.'

'Cleared to eight zero.'

The altimeter hands crept round to eight thousand feet. The blanket of white fleece spread out unbroken in all directions to the horizon, soft and pretty in the sun. The passengers murmured, perhaps realizing for the first time the extent of Nancy's predicament. Mile after mile after mile of emptiness, and absolutely no way of telling where she was.

'Aircraft's circling again . . . Maintain zero nine five. You are now seven miles to the west.'

I said over my shoulder to Annie Villars, 'We'll see them soon . . . Would you take this notebook . . .' I handed her the spiral bound reporters' notebook I used for jotting during flight, 'and make some letters out of the pages? As big as you can. We will need, you see, to hold them up in the window, so that Nancy and Colin can read what we want them to do.'

And let it be them, I thought coldly. Just let it be them, and not some other poor lost souls. Because we'd have to stay to help. We couldn't leave them to struggle and look somewhere else for the ones we wanted . . .

Annie Villars fumbled in her handbag and produced a small pair of scissors.

'Which letters?' she said economically. 'You say, and I'll write them down, and then make them.'

'Right . . . FOLWBASE. That will do to start with.'

I twisted my head and saw her start snipping. She was making them full page size and as bold as possible. Satisfied, I looked forward again, scanning the sunny waste, searching for a small black cigarette shape moving ahead.

'Turn on to one zero five,' Wytton said. 'The aircraft is now in your one o'clock position five miles ahead.'

I looked down over to the right of the aircraft's nose. Ambrose reluctantly looked out of the window in sulky silence.

'*There*,' Kenny Bayst said. 'Over there, down there.' I looked where he was pointing . . . and there it was, slightly more over to our right, beginning another circling sweep over a darker patch of cloud which might have been a hole, but wasn't.

'Contact,' I said to Wytton. 'Closing in now.'

'Your intentions?' he asked unemotionally.

'Lead them up to the Wash, descend over the sea, follow the river and railway from King's Lynn to Cambridge.'

'Roger. We'll advise Marham. They'll give you radar coverage over the sea.'

I put the nose down, built up the speed, and overhauled the other aircraft like an E-type catching a bicycle. The nearer we got the more I hoped . . . it was a low-winged aeroplane . . . a Cherokee . . . white with red markings . . . and finally the registration number . . . and someone frantically waving a map at us from the window.

The relief was overpowering.

'It's them,' Annie said, and I could only nod and swallow.

I throttled back and slowed the Six until it was down to Nancy's cruising speed, then circled until I came up on her left side, and about fifty yards away. She had never done any formation flying. Fifty yards was the closest it was safe to go to her and even fifty yards was risking it a bit. I kept my hand on the throttle, my eyes on her, and an extra pair of eyes I didn't know I had, fixed on the heading.

To Annie Villars I said, 'Hold up the letters for "follow". Slowly. One by one.'

'Right.' She held them flat against the window beside her. We could see Colin's head leaning back behind Nancy's. When Annie finished the word we saw him wave his hand, and after that Nancy waved her map against her window, which showed up better.

'Wytton,' I reported. 'Is it the right aircraft. They are following us to the Wash. Can you give me a steer to King's Lynn?'

'Delighted,' he said. 'Steer zero four zero, and call Marham on frequency one one nine zero.'

'Thanks a lot,' I said with feeling.

'You're very welcome.'

Good guys, I thought. Very good guys, sitting in their darkened rooms wearing headsets and staring at their little dark circular screens, watching the multitude of yellow dots which were aircraft swimming slowly across like tadpoles. They'd done a terrific job, finding the Rosses. Terrific.

'Can you make a figure four?' I asked Annie Villars.

'Certainly.' The scissors began to snip.

'When you have, would you hold up the O, then the four, then the O again?'

'With pleasure.'

She held up the figures. Nancy waved the map. We set off north-eastwards to the sea, Nancy staying behind us to the right, with me flying looking over my shoulder to keep a steady distance between us. I judged it would take thirteen minutes at her speed to reach the sea, five to ten to let down, and twenty or so more to return underneath the cloud base to Cambridge. Her fuel by the time she got there would be low, but there was less risk of her running dry than of hitting a hill or trees or a building by going down over the land. Letting down over the sea was in these circumstances the best procedure whenever possible.

'We're going to need some more letters,' I told Annie.

'Which?'

'Um . . . R, I, V, and N, D, C, and a T, and a nine.'

'Right.'

Out of the corner of my eye I could see Annie Villars snipping and Kenny Bayst, sitting behind her, sorting out the letters she had already made so that she could easily pick them out when they were needed. There was, I thought to myself, with a small internal smile, a truce in operation in that area.

Marham radar reported, 'You have four miles to run to the coast.'

'Hope the tide's in,' I said facetiously.

'Affirmative,' he said with deadpan humour. 'High water eighteen forty hours BST.'

'And . . . er . . . the cloud base?'

'Stand by.' Down in his dark room he couldn't see the sky. He had to ask the tower dwellers above.

'Cloud base between six and seven hundred feet above sea level over the entire area from the Wash to Cambridge. Visibility two kilometres in drizzle.'

'Nice,' I said with irony.

'Very.'

'Could I have the regional pressure setting?'

'Nine nine eight millibars.'

'Nine nine eight,' I repeated, and took my hand off the throttle enough to set that figure on the altimeter subscale. To Annie Villars I said, 'Can you make an eight, as well?'

'I expect so.'

'Crossing the coast,' Marham said.

'Right . . . Miss Villars, will you hold up SEA?'

She nodded and did so. Nancy waved the map.

'Now hold up SET, then nine nine eight, then MBS.'

'S . . . E . . . T,' she repeated, holding them against the window. 'Nine, nine, eight.' She paused. 'There's no M cut out.'

'W upside down,' Kenny Bayst said, and gave it to her.

'Oh yes. M . . . B . . . S. What does MBS mean?'

'Millibars,' I said.

Nancy waved the map, but I said to Annie, 'Hold up the nine nine eight again, it's very important.'

She held them up. We could see Nancy's head nodding as she waved back vigorously.

'Why is it so important?' Annie said.

'Unless you set the altimeter to the right pressure on the subscale, it doesn't tell you how high you are above the sea.'

'Oh.'

'Now would you hold up BASE, then six zero zero, then FT.'

'Right . . . Base . . . six hundred . . . feet.'

There was a distinct pause before Nancy waved, and then it was a small, half-hearted one. She must have been horrified to find that the clouds were so low: she must have been thanking her stars that she hadn't tried to go down through them. Highly frightening piece of information, that six hundred feet.

'Now,' I said to Annie, 'hold up FOLLOW RIVER AND RAIL ONE NINE ZERO TO CAMBRIDGE.'

'Follow . . . river . . . and . . . rail . . . one . . . nine . . .

zero . . . to . . . Cambridge . . . no G . . . never mind, C will do, then E.' She spelt it out slowly. Nancy waved.

'And just one more . . . four zero, then N, then M.'

'Forty nautical miles,' she said triumphantly. She held them up and Nancy waved.

'Now hold up FOLLOW again.'

'Right.'

I consulted Marham, took Nancy out to sea a little further, and led her round in a circle until we were both heading just west of south on one nine zero, and in a straight line to the railway and river from King's Lynn to Cambridge.

'Hold up DOWN,' I said.

She did it without speaking. Nancy gave a little wave. I put the nose of the Six down towards the clouds and accelerated to a hundred and forty knots so that there would be no possibility of her crashing into the back of us. The white fleecy layer came up to meet us, embraced us in sunlit feathery wisps, closed lightly around us, became denser, darker, an anthracite fog pressing on the windows. The altimeter unwound, the clock needles going backwards through 3,000 feet, 2,000 feet, 1,000 feet, still no break at 800 feet, 700 . . . and there, there at last the mist receded a little and became drizzly haze, and underneath us, pretty close underneath, were the restless rainswept dark greeny grey waves.

The passengers were all silent. I glanced round at them. They were all looking down at the sea in varying states of awe. I wondered if any of them knew I had just broken two laws and would undoubtedly be prosecuted again by the Board of Trade. I wondered if I would ever, ever, learn to keep myself out of trouble.

We crossed the coast over King's Lynn and flew down the river to Ely and Cambridge, just brushing through the misty cloud base at seven hundred feet. The forward visibility was bad, and I judged it silly to go back and wait for Nancy, because we might collide before we saw each other. I completed the journey as briefly as possible and we landed on the wet tarmac and taxied round towards the airport buildings. When I stopped the engine, everyone as if moved by one mind climbed out and looked upwards; even Ambrose.

The drizzle was light now, like fine mist. We stood quietly in it, getting damp, listening for the sound of an engine, watching for the shadow against the sky. Minutes ticked past. Annie Villars looked at me anxiously. I shook my head, not knowing exactly what I meant.

She couldn't have gone down too far . . . hit the sea . . . got disorientated in the cloud . . . lost when she came out of it . . . still in danger.

The drizzle fell. My heart also.

But she hadn't made any mistakes.

The engine noise crept in as a hum, then a buzz, then a definite rhythm. The little red and white aeroplane appeared suddenly against the right-hand sky, and she was circling safely round the outskirts of the field and coming sedately down to land.

'Oh . . .' Annie Villars said, and wiped two surprising tears of relief out of her eyes.

Ambrose said sulkily, 'That's all right then. Now I hope we can get off home,' and stomped heavily away towards the buildings.

Nancy taxied round and stopped her Cherokee a short distance away. Colin climbed out on the wing, grinned hugely in our direction, and waved.

'He's got no bloody nerves,' Kenny said. 'Not a bleeding nerve in his whole body.'

Nancy came out after him, jumping down on to the tarmac and staggering a bit as she landed on wobbly knees. I began to walk towards them. She started slowly to meet me, and then faster, and then ran, with her hair swinging out and her arms stretched wide. I held her round the waist and swung her up and round in the air and when I put her down she wrapped her arms behind my neck and kissed me.

'Matt . . .' She was half laughing, half crying, her eyes shining, her cheeks a burning red, the sudden release of tension making her tremble down to her fingertips.

Colin reached us and gave me a buffet on the shoulder.

'Thanks, chum.'

'Thank the RAF. They found you on their radar.'

'But how did you know? . . .'

'Long story,' I said. Nancy was still holding on to me as if she would fall down if she let go. I made the most of it by kissing her again, on my own account.

She laughed shakily and untwined her arms. 'When you came . . . I can't tell you . . . it was such a relief . . .'

Annie Villars came up and touched her arm and she turned to her with the same hectic overexcitement.

'Oh . . . *Annie.*'

'Yes, dear,' she said calmly. 'What you need now is a strong brandy.'

'I ought to see to . . .' she looked vaguely in my direction, and back to the Cherokee.

'Colin and Matt will see to everything.'

'All right, then . . .' She let herself be taken off by Annie Villars, who had recovered her poise and assumed total command as a good general should. Kenny and the other jockey and trainer meekly followed.

'Now,' said Colin. 'How on earth did you know we needed you?'

'I'll show you,' I said abruptly. 'Come and look.' I walked him back to the little Cherokee, climbed up on to the wing and lay down on my back across the two front seats, looking up under the control panel.

'What on earth . . .?'

The device was there. I showed it to him. Very neat, very small. A little polythene-wrapped packet swinging free on a rubber band which was itself attached to the cable leading to the master switch. Nearer the switch one wire of the two wire cable had been bared: the two severed ends of copper showed redly against the black plastic casing.

I left everything where it was and eased myself out on to the wing.

'What is it? What does it mean?'

'Your electric system was sabotaged.'

'For God's sake . . . why?'

'I don't know,' I sighed. 'I only know who did it. The same person who planted the bomb a month ago. Major Rupert Tyderman.'

He stared at me blankly. 'It doesn't make sense.'

'Not much. No.'

I told him how the Major had set off the bomb while we were safely on the ground, and that today he had thought I was flying Nancy's Cherokee and could get myself out of trouble.

'But that's . . . that means . . .'

'Yes,' I said.

'He's trying to make it look as though someone's trying to kill me.'

I nodded. 'While making damn sure you survive.'

CHAPTER ELEVEN

The Board of Trade came down like the hounds of Hell and it wasn't the tall reasonable man I faced this time in the crew room but a short hard-packed individual with an obstinate jaw and unhumorous eyes. He refused to sit down: preferred to stand. He had brought no silent note-taker along. He was strictly a one man band. And hot on percussion.

'I must bring to your attention the Air Navigation Order Nineteen sixty-six.' His voice was staccato and uncompromising, the traditional politeness of his department reduced to the thinnest of veneers.

I indicated that I was reasonably familiar with the order in question. As it ruled every cranny of a professional pilot's life, this was hardly surprising.

'We have been informed that on Friday last you contravened Article 25, paragraph 4, subsection a, and Regulation 8, paragraph 2.'

I waited for him to finish. Then I said, 'Who informed you?'

He looked at me sharply. 'That is beside the point.'

'Could it have been Polyplanes?'

His eyelids flickered in spite of himself. 'If we receive a complaint which can be substantiated we are bound to investigate.'

The complaint could be substantiated, all right. Saturday's newspapers were still strewn around the crew room this Monday morning, all full of the latest attempt on Colin Ross' life. Front page stuff. Also minute details from all my passengers about how we had led him out to sea and brought him home under the 700 foot cloud base.

Only trouble was, it was illegal in a single-engine aeroplane like the Six to take paying customers out over the sea as low as I had, and to land them at an airport where the cloud base was lower than one thousand feet.

'You admit that you contravened Section . . .'

I interrupted him. 'Yes.'

He opened his mouth and shut it again. 'Er, I see.' He cleared his throat. 'You will receive a summons in due course.'

'Yes,' I said again.

'Not your first, I believe.' An observation, not a sneer.

'No,' I said unemotionally.

A short silence. Then I said, 'How did that gadget work? The nitric acid package on the rubber band.'

'That is not your concern.'

I shrugged. 'I can ask any schoolboy who does chemistry.'

He hesitated. He was not of the stuff to give anything

away. He would never, as the tall man had, say or imply that there could be any fault in his Government or the Board. But having searched his conscience and no doubt his standing orders, he felt able after all to come across.

'The package contained fluffy fibreglass soaked in a weak solution of nitric acid. A section of wire in the cable to the master switch had been bared, and the fibreglass wrapped around it. The nitric acid slowly dissolved the copper wire, taking, at that concentration, probably about an hour and a half to complete the process.' He stopped, considering.

'And the rubber band?' I prompted.

'Yes . . . well, nitric acid, like water, conducts electricity, so that while the fibreglass was still in position the electrical circuit would be maintained, even though the wire itself had been completely dissolved. To break the circuit the fibreglass package had to be removed. This was done by fastening it under tension via the rubber band to a point further up the cable. When the nitric acid dissolved right through the wire and the two ends parted, there was nothing to stop the rubber band contracting and pulling the fibreglass package away. Er . . . do I make myself clear?'

'Indeed,' I agreed, 'you do.'

He seemed to give himself a little mental and physical shake, and turned with sudden energy towards the door.

'Right,' he said briskly. 'Then I need a word with Mr Harley.'

'Did you get a word with Major Tyderman?' I asked.

After the merest hiatus he said again, 'That is not your concern.'

'Perhaps you have seen him already?'

Silence.

'Perhaps, though, he is away from home?'

More silence. Then he turned to me in stiff exasperation. 'It is not your business to question me like this. I cannot answer you any more. It is I who am here to inquire into you, not the other way round.' He shut his mouth with a snap and gave me a hard stare. 'And they even warned me,' he muttered.

'I hope you find the Major,' I said politely, 'before he plants any more little devices in inconvenient places.'

He snorted and strode before me out of the crew room and along to Harley's office. Harley knew what he was there for and had been predictably furious with me ever since Friday.

'Mr Shore admits the contraventions,' the Board of Trade said.

'He'd be hard pushed not to,' Harley said angrily, 'considering every RAF base across the country told him about the low cloud base at Cambridge.'

'In point of fact,' agreed the Board of Trade, 'he should then have returned immediately to Manchester which was then still within the legal limit, and waited there until conditions improved, instead of flying all the way to East Anglia and leaving himself with too small a fuel margin to go to any cloud-free airport. The proper course was certainly to turn back right at the beginning.'

'And to hell with Colin Ross,' I said conversationally.

Their mouths tightened in chorus. There was nothing more to be said. If you jumped red traffic lights and broke the speed limit rushing someone to hospital to save his life, you would still be prosecuted for the offences. Same thing exactly. Same impasse. Humanity versus law, an age-old quandary. Make your choice and lie on it.

'I'm not accepting any responsibility for what you did,' Harley said heavily. 'I will state categorically, and in court if I have to, that you were acting in direct opposition to Derrydowns' instructions, and that Derrydowns disassociates itself entirely from your actions.'

I thought of asking him if he'd like a basin for the ritual washing of hands. I also thought that on the whole I'd better not.

He went on, 'And of course if there is any fine involved you will pay it yourself.'

Always my bad luck, I reflected, to cop it when the firm was too nearly bankrupt to be generous. I said merely, 'Is that all, then? We have a charter, if you remember . . .'

They waved me away in disgust and I collected my gear and flew off in the Aztec to take a clutch of businessmen from Elstree to The Hague.

*

By the time, the previous Friday, that Colin and I had locked Nancy's Cherokee and ensured that no one would touch it, the first cohorts of the local press had come galloping up with ash on their shirt fronts, and the Board of Trade, who neither slumbered nor slept, were breathing heavily down the STD.

Aircraft radios are about as private as Times Square: it appeared that dozens of ground-based but air-minded Midlands enthusiasts had been listening in to my conversation with Birmingham radar and had jammed the switchboard at Cambridge ringing up to find out if Colin Ross was safe. Undaunted, they had conveyed to Fleet Street the possibility of his loss. His arrival in one piece was announced on a television news broadcast forty minutes after we landed. The great British media had pulled out every finger they possessed. Nancy and Annie Villars had answered questions until their throats were sore and had finally taken refuge in the Ladies Cloaks. Colin was used to dealing with the press, but by the time he extricated himself from their ever increasing news-hungry numbers he too was pale blue from tiredness.

'Come on,' he said to me. 'Let's get Nancy out and go home.'

'I'll have to ring Harley . . .'

Harley already knew and was exploding like a firecracker. Someone from Polyplanes, it appeared, had telephoned at once to inform him with acid sweetness that his so highly qualified chief pilot had broken every law in sight and put Derrydowns thoroughly in the cart. The fact that his best customer was still alive to pay another day didn't seem to have got through to Harley at all. Polyplanes had made him smart, and it was all my fault.

I stayed in Cambridge by promising to foot the bill for hangarage again, and went home with Nancy and Colin.

Home.

A dangerous, evocative word. And the trouble was, it *felt* like home. Only the third time I'd been there, and it was already familiar, cosy, undemanding, easy . . . It was no good feeling I belonged there, because I didn't.

Saturday morning I spent talking to the police face to face in Cambridge and the Board of Trade in London on the telephone. Both forces cautiously murmured that they might perhaps ask Major Rupert Tyderman to help them with their inquiries. Saturday afternoon I flew Colin back to Haydock without incident, Saturday night I again stayed contentedly at Newmarket, Sunday I took him to Buckingham, changed over to the Aztec, and flew him to Ostend. Managed to avoid Harley altogether until I got back Sunday evening, when he lay in wait for me as I taxied down to the hangar and bitched on for over half an hour about sticking to the letter of the law. The gist of his argument was that left to herself Nancy would have come down safely somewhere over the flat land of East Anglia. Bound to have done. She wouldn't have hit any of the radio masts or power station chimneys which scattered the area and which had stuck up into the clouds like needles. They were all marked there, disturbing her, on the map. She had known that if she had to go down at random she had an average chance of hitting one. The television mast at Mendlesham stretched upwards for more than a thousand feet . . . But, said Harley, she would have missed the lot. Certain to have done.

'What would you have felt like, in her position?' I asked.

He didn't answer. He knew well enough. As pilot, as businessman, he was a bloody fool.

On Tuesday morning he told me that Colin had telephoned to cancel his trip to Folkestone that day, but that I would still be going in the Six, taking an owner and his friends there from Nottingham.

I imagined that Colin had changed his intention to ride at Folkestone and gone to Pontefract instead, but it wasn't so. He had, I found, flown to Folkestone. And he had gone in a Polyplane.

I didn't know he was there until after the races when he came back to the airport in a taxi. He climbed out of it in his usual wilted state, surveyed the row of parked aircraft, and walked straight past me towards the Polyplane.

'Colin,' I said.

He stopped, turned his head, gave me a straight stare. Nothing friendly in it, nothing at all.

'What's the matter?' I said puzzled. 'What's happened?'

He looked away from me, along to the Polyplane. I followed his glance. The pilot was standing there smirking. He was the one who had refused to help Kenny Bayst, and he had been smirking vigorously all afternoon.

'Did you come with him?' I asked.

'Yes, I did.' His voice was cold. His eyes also.

I said in surprise, 'I don't get it . . .'

Colin's face turned from cold to scorching. 'You . . . you . . . I don't think I can bear to talk to you.'

A feeling of unreality clogged my tongue. I simply looked at him in bewilderment.

'You've properly bust us up . . . Oh, I dare say you didn't mean to . . . but Nancy has lit off out of the house and I left Midge at home crying . . .'

I was appalled. 'But why? On Sunday morning when we left, everything was fine . . .'

'Yesterday,' he said flatly. 'Nancy found out yesterday, when she went to the airfield for a practice session. It absolutely overthrew her. She came home in a dreadful mood and raged round the house practically throwing things and this morning she packed a suitcase and walked out . . . neither Midge nor I could stop her and Midge is frantically distressed . . .' He stopped, clenched his jaw, and said with shut teeth, 'Why the hell didn't you have the guts to tell her yourself?'

'Tell her what?'

'*What?*' He thrust his hand into the pocket of his faded jeans and brought out a folded wad of newspaper. 'This.'

I took it from him. Unfolded it. Felt the woodenness take over in my face; knew that it showed.

He had handed me the most biting, the most damaging, of the tabloid accounts of my trial and conviction for negligently putting the lives of eighty seven people in jeopardy. A one-day wonder to the general public; long forgotten. But always lying there in the files, if anyone wanted to dig it up.

'That wasn't all,' Colin said. 'He told her also that you'd been sacked from another airline for cowardice.'

'Who told her?' I said dully. I held out the cutting. He took it back.

'Does it matter?'

'Yes, it does.'

'He had no axe to grind. That's what convinced her.'

'No axe . . . did he say that?'

'I believe so. What does it matter?'

'Was it a Polyplane pilot who told her? The one, for instance, who is flying you today?' Getting his own back, I thought, for the way I'd threatened him at Redcar.

Colin's mouth opened.

'No axe to grind,' I said bitterly. 'That's a laugh.

They've been trying to prise you loose from Derrydowns all summer and now it looks as if they've done it.'

I turned away from him, my throat physically closing. I didn't think I could speak. I expected him to walk on, to walk away, to take himself to Polyplanes and my future to the trash can.

Instead of that he followed me and touched my arm. 'Matt . . .'

I shook him off. 'You tell your precious sister,' I said thickly, 'that because of the rules I broke leading her back to Cambridge last Friday I am going to find myself in court again, and convicted and fined and in debt again . . . and this time I did it with my eyes open . . . not like that . . .' I pointed to the newspaper clipping with a hand that trembled visibly, 'when I had to take the rap for something that was mostly not my fault.'

'Matt!' He was himself appalled.

'And as for the cowardice bit, she's got her facts wrong . . . Oh, I've no doubt it sounded convincing and dreadful . . . Polyplanes had a lot to gain by upsetting her to the utmost . . . but I don't see . . . I don't see why she was more upset than just to persuade you not to fly with me . . .'

'Why didn't you tell her yourself?'

I shook my head. 'I probably might have done, one day. I didn't think it was important.'

'Not important!' He was fierce with irritation. 'She seems to have been building up some sort of hero image of you, and then she discovered you had clay feet in all directions . . . Of course you should have told her, as you were going to marry her. That was obviously what upset her most . . .'

I was speechless. My jaw literally dropped. Finally I said foolishly, 'Did you say *marry* . . . ?'

'Well, yes, of course,' he said impatiently, and then seemed struck by my state of shock. 'You were going to marry her, weren't you?'

'We've never . . . even talked about it.'

'But you must have,' he insisted. 'I overheard her and Midge discussing it on Sunday evening, after I got back from Ostend. "When you are married to Matt," Midge said. I heard her distinctly. They were in the kitchen, washing up. They were deciding you would come and live with us in the bungalow . . . They were sharing out the bedrooms . . .' His voice tailed off weakly. 'It isn't . . . it isn't true?'

I silently shook my head.

He looked at me in bewilderment. 'Girls,' he said. 'Girls.'

'I can't marry her,' I said numbly. 'I've hardly enough for a licence . . .'

'That doesn't matter.'

'It does to me.'

'It wouldn't to Nancy,' he said. He did a sort of double take. 'Do you mean . . . she wasn't so far out . . . after all?'

'I suppose . . . not so far.'

He looked down at the cutting in his hand, and suddenly screwed it up. 'It looked so bad,' he said with a tinge of apology.

'It was bad,' I said.

He looked at my face. 'Yes. I see it was . . .'

A taxi drew up with a jerk and out piled my passengers, all gay and flushed with a winner and carrying a bottle of champagne.

'I'll explain to her,' Colin said. 'I'll get her back . . .' His expression was suddenly horrified. Shattered.

'Where has she gone?' I asked.

He screwed up his eyes as if in pain.

'She said . . .' He swallowed. 'She went . . . to Chanter.'

I sat all evening in the caravan wanting to smash something. Smash the galley. Smash the windows. Smash the walls.

Might have felt better if I had.

Chanter . . .

Couldn't eat, couldn't think, couldn't sleep.

Never had listened to my own advice: don't get involved. Should have stuck to it, stayed frozen. Icy. Safe.

Tried to get back to the Arctic and not feel anything, but it was too late. Feeling had come back with a vengeance and of an intensity I could have done without. I hadn't known I loved her. Knew I liked her, felt easy with her, wanted to be with her often and for a long time to come. I'd thought I could stop at friendship, and didn't realize how far, how deep I had already gone.

Oh Nancy . . .

I went to sleep in the end by drinking half of the bottle of whisky Kenny Bayst had given me, but it didn't do much good. I woke up at six in the morning to the same dreary torment and with a headache on top.

There were no flights that day to take my mind off it.

Nancy and Chanter . . .

At some point in the morning I telephoned from the coinbox in the customers' lounges to the art school in Liverpool, to ask for Chanter's home address. A crisp secretarial female voice answered: very sorry, absolutely not their policy to divulge the private addresses of their staff. If I could write, they would forward the letter.

'Could I speak to him, then, do you think?' I asked: though what good that would do, Heaven alone knew.

'I'm afraid not, because he isn't here. The school is temporarily closed, and we are not sure when it will reopen.'

'The students,' I remembered, 'are on strike?'

'That . . . er . . . is so,' she agreed.

'Can't you possibly tell me how I could get in touch with Chanter?'

'Oh dear . . . You are the second person pressing me to help . . . but honestly, to tell you the truth we don't know where he lives... he moves frequently and seldom bothers to keep us up to date.' Secretarial disapproval and despair in the tidy voice. 'As I told Mr Ross, with all the best will in the world, I simply have no idea where you could find him.'

I sat in the crew room while the afternoon dragged by. Finished writing up all records by two-thirty, read through some newly arrived information circulars, calculated I had only three weeks and four days to run before my next medical, worked out that if I bought four cups of coffee every day from Honey's machine, I was drinking away one fifteenth of my total week's spending money, decided to make it water more often, looked up when Harley came stalking in, received a lecture on loyalty (mine to him), heard that I was on the next day to take a Wiltshire trainer to Newmarket races, and that if I gave Polyplanes any more grounds for reporting me or the firm to the Board of Trade, I could collect my cards.

'Do my best not to,' I murmured. Didn't please him.

Looked at the door swinging shut behind his back.

Looked at the clock. Three twenty-two.

Chanter and Nancy.

Back in the caravan, the same as the evening before. Tried turning on the television. Some comedy about

American suburban life punctuated by canned laughter. Stood five minutes of it, and found the silence afterwards almost as bad.

Walked halfway round the airfield, cut down to the village, drank half a pint in the pub, walked back. Total, four miles. When I stepped into the caravan it was still only nine o'clock.

Honey Harley was waiting for me, draped over the sofa with maximum exposure of leg. Pink checked cotton sun-dress, very low cut.

'Hi,' she said with self possession. 'Where've you been?'

'For a walk.'

She looked at me quizzically. 'Got the Board of Trade on your mind?'

I nodded. That, and other things.

'I shouldn't worry too much. Whatever the law says or does, you couldn't have just left the Rosses to flounder.'

'Your uncle doesn't agree.'

'Uncle,' she said dispassionately, 'is a nit. And anyway, play your cards right, and even if you do get a fine, Colin Ross will pay it. All you'd have to do would be to ask.'

I shook my head.

'You're daft,' she said. 'Plain daft.'

'You may be right.'

She sighed, stirred, stood up. The curvy body rippled in all the right places. I thought of Nancy: much flatter, much thinner, less obviously sexed and infinitely more desirable. I turned abruptly away from Honey. Like hitting a raw nerve, the thought of Chanter, with his hair and his fringes . . . and his hands.

'OK, iceberg,' she said, mistakenly, 'relax. Your virtue is quite safe. I only came down, to start with, to tell you there was a phone call for you, and would you please ring back.'

'Who? . . .' I tried hard to keep it casual.

'Colin Ross,' Honey said matter-of-factly. 'He wants you to call some time this evening, if you can. I said if it was about a flight I could deal with it, but apparently it's something personal.' She finished the sentence halfway between an accusation and a question and left me ample time to explain.

I didn't. I said, 'I'll go up now, then, and use the telephone in the lounge.'

She shrugged. 'All right.'

She walked up with me, but didn't quite have the nerve to hover close enough to listen. I shut the lounge door in front of her resigned and humorously rueful face.

Got the number.

'Colin? Matt.'

'Oh good,' he said. 'Look. Nancy rang up today while Midge and I were at the races . . . I took Midge along on the Heath because she was so miserable at home, and now of course she's even more miserable that she missed Nancy . . . anyway, our cleaning woman answered the telephone, and Nancy left a message.'

'Is she . . . I mean, is she all right?'

'Do you mean, is she with Chanter?' His voice was strained. 'She told our cleaner she had met an old art school friend in Liverpool and was spending a few days camping with her near Warwick.'

'*Her?*' I exclaimed.

'Well, I don't know. I asked our Mrs Williams, and she then said she *thought* Nancy said "her", but of course she would think that, wouldn't she?'

'I'm afraid she would.'

'But anyway, Nancy had been much more insistent that Mrs Williams tell me something else . . . it seems she has seen Major Tyderman.'

'She didn't!'

'Yeah . . . She said she saw Major Tyderman in the passenger seat of a car on the Stratford road out of Warwick. Apparently there were some roadworks, and the car stopped for a moment just near her.'

'He could have been going anywhere . . . from anywhere . . .'

'Yes,' he agreed in depression. 'I rang the police in Cambridge to tell them, but Nancy had already been through to them, when she called home. All she could remember about the driver was that he wore glasses. She thought he might have had dark hair and perhaps a moustache. She only glanced at him for a second because she was concentrating on Tyderman. Also she hadn't taken the number, and she's hopeless on the make of cars, so altogether it wasn't a great deal of help.'

'No . . .'

'Anyway, she told Mrs Williams she would be coming home on Saturday. She said if I would drive to Warwick races instead of flying, she would come home with me in the car.'

'Well . . . thank God for that.'

'If for nothing else,' he said aridly.

CHAPTER TWELVE

I flew the customers from Wiltshire to Newmarket and parked the Six as far as possible from the Polyplane. When the passengers had departed standwards, I got out of the fuggy cabin and into the free air, lay propped on one elbow on the grass, loosened my tie, opened the neck of my shirt. Scorching hot day, a sigh of wind over the Heath, a couple of small cumulus clouds defying evaporation, blue sky over the blue planet.

A suitable day for camping.

Wrenched my thoughts away from the profitless grind: Nancy despised me, despised herself, had chosen Chanter as a refuge, as a steadfast known quantity, had run away from the near-stranger who had not seemed what he seemed, and gone to where she knew she was wanted. Blind, instinctive, impulsive flight. Reckless, understandable, forgivable flight . . .

I could take Chanter, I thought mordantly. I could probably take the thought and memory of Chanter, if only she would settle for me in the end.

It was odd that you had to lose something you didn't

even know you had, before you began to want it more than anything on earth.

Down at the other end of the row of aircraft the Polyplane pilot was strolling about, smoking again. One of these fine days he would blow himself up. There was no smile in place that afternoon: even from a hundred yards one could detect the gloom in the heavy frowns he occasionally got rid of in my direction.

Colin had booked with Harley for the week ahead. Polyplanes must have been wondering what else they would have to do to get him back.

They played rough, no doubt of that. Informing on Derrydowns to the Board of Trade, discrediting their pilot, spreading smears that they weren't safe. But would they blow up a Derrydowns aircraft? Would they go as far as that?

They would surely have had to be certain they would gain from it, before they risked it. But in fact they hadn't gained. No one had demonstrably been frightened away from using Derrydowns, particularly not Colin Ross. If the bomb had been meant to look like an attack on Colin's life, why should Colin think he would be any safer in a Polyplane?

If they had blown up the aircraft with passengers aboard, that would have ruined Derrydowns. But even if they had been prepared to go that far, they wouldn't have chosen a flight with Colin Ross on it.

And why Major Tyderman, when their own pilots could get near the Derrydowns aircraft without much comment? That was easier . . . they needed a bomb expert. Someone completely unsuspectable. Someone even their pilots didn't know. Because if the boss of Polyplanes had taken the dark step into crime, he wouldn't want chatty employees like pilots spilling it into every aviation bar from Prestwick to Lydd.

The second aeroplane, though, that Tyderman had sabotaged, hadn't been one of the Derrydowns at all. On the other hand, he had thought it was. I stood up, stretched, watched the straining horses scud through the first race, saw in the distance a girl with dark hair and a blue dress and thought for one surging moment it was Nancy. It wasn't Nancy. It wasn't even Midge. Nancy was in Warwickshire, living in a tent.

I thrust my balled fists into my pockets. Not the slightest use thinking about it. Concentrate on something else. Start from the bottom again, as before. Look at everything the wrong way up.

No easy revelation this time. Just the merest flicker of speculation.

Harley? . . .

He had recovered ill-invested capital on the first occasion. He had known Colin would not rely often on his sister's skill after the second. But would Harley go so far? . . . And Harley had known I wasn't flying Colin, though Tyderman had thought I was.

Rats on treadwheels, I thought, go round and round in small circles and get nowhere, just like me.

I sighed. It wasn't much use trying to work it all

out when I obviously lacked about fifty pieces of vital information. Decision: did I or did I not start actively looking for some of the pieces? If I didn't, a successor to Major Tyderman might soon be around playing another lot of chemical tricks on aeroplanes, and if I did, I could well be heading myself for yet more trouble.

I tossed a mental coin. Heads you do, tails you don't. In mid-toss I thought of Nancy. All roads led back to Nancy. If I just let everything slide and lay both physically and metaphorically on my back on the grass in the sun, I'd have nothing to think about except what I hated to think about. Very poor prospect. Almost anything else was better.

Took the plunge, and made a start with Annie Villars. She was standing in the paddock in a sleeveless dark-red dress, her greying short hair curling neatly under a black straw hat chosen more for generalship than femininity. From ten paces the authority was clearly uppermost: from three, one could hear the incongruously gentle voice, see the non-aggression in the consciously curved lips, realize that the velvet glove was being given a quilted lining.

She was talking to the Duke of Wessex. She was saying, 'Then if you agree, Bobbie, we'll ask Kenny Bayst to ride it. This new boy has no judgement of pace, and for all his faults, Kenny does know how to time a race.'

The Duke nodded his distinguished head and smiled at her benevolently. They caught sight of me hovering near them and both turned towards me with friendly expressions, one deceptively, and one authentically vacant.

'Matt,' smiled the Duke. 'My dear chap. Isn't it a splendid day?'

'Beautiful, sir,' I agreed. As long as one could obliterate Warwickshire.

'My nephew Matthew,' he said. 'Do you remember him?'

'Of course I do, sir.'

'Well . . . it's his birthday soon, and he wants . . . he was wondering if for a birthday present I would give him a flight in an aeroplane. With you, he said. Especially with you.'

I smiled. 'I'd like to do that very much.'

'Good, good. Then . . . er . . . how do you suggest we fix it?'

'I'll arrange it with Mr Harley.'

'Yes. Good. Soon then. He's coming down to stay with me tomorrow as it's the end of term and his mother is off somewhere in Greece. So next week, perhaps?'

'I'm sure that will be all right.'

He beamed happily. 'Perhaps I'll come along too.'

Annie Villars said patiently, 'Bobbie, we ought to go and see about saddling your horse.'

He looked at his watch. 'By jove, yes. Amazing where the afternoon goes to. Come along, then.' He gave me another large smile, transferred it intact to Annie, and obediently moved off after her as she started purposefully towards the saddling boxes.

I bought a racecard. The Duke's horse was a two-year-old maiden called Thundersticks. I watched the Duke and Annie watch Thundersticks walk round the parade ring, one with innocent beaming pride, the other with judicious non-commitment. The pace-lacking boy rode a bad race, even to my unpractised eye: too far out in front over the first furlong, too far out the back over the last. Just as well the Duke's colours were inconspicuous, I thought. He took his disappointment with charming grace, reassuring Annie that the colt would do better next time. Sure to. Early days yet. She smiled at him in soft agreement and bestowed on the jockey a look which would have bored a hole through steel plating.

After they had discussed the sweating colt's performance yard by yard, and patted him and packed him off with his lad towards the stables, the Duke took Annie away to the bar for a drink. After that she had another loser for another owner and another thoughtful detour for refreshment, so that I didn't manage to catch her on her own until between the last two races.

She listened without comment to me explaining that I thought it might be possible to do something positive about solving the Great Bomb Mystery, if she would help.

'I thought it was solved already.'

'Not really. No one knows why.'

'No. Well, I don't see how I can help.'

'Would you mind telling me how well Major

Tyderman and Mr Goldenberg know each other, and how they come to have any say in how Rudiments should run in its various races?'

She said mildly, 'It's none of your business.'

I knew what the mildness concealed. 'I know that.'

'And you are impertinent.'

'Yes.'

She regarded me straightly, and the softness gradually faded out of her features to leave taut skin over the cheekbones and a stern set to the mouth.

'I am fond of Midge and Nancy Ross,' she said. 'I don't see how anything I can tell you will help, but I certainly want no harm to come to those two girls. That last escapade was just a shade too dangerous, wasn't it? And if Rupert Tyderman could do that . . .' She paused, thinking deeply. 'I will be obliged if you will keep anything I may tell you to yourself.'

'I will.'

'Very well . . . I've known Rupert for a very long time. More or less from my childhood. He is about fifteen years older . . . When I was a young girl I thought he was a splendid person, and I didn't understand why people hesitated when they talked about him.' She sighed. 'I found out, of course, when I was older. He had been wild, as a youth. A vandal when vandalism wasn't as common as it is now. When he was in his twenties he borrowed money from all his relations and friends for various grand schemes, and never paid them back. His family bought him out of one mess where he had sold a picture entrusted to him for safe keeping and spent the proceeds . . . Oh, lots of things like that. Then the war came and he volunteered immediately, and I believe all during the war he did very well. He was in the Royal Engineers, I think . . . but afterwards, after the war ended, he was quietly allowed to resign his commission for cashing dud cheques with his fellow officers.'

She shook her head impatiently. 'He has always been a fool to himself . . . Since the war he has lived on some money his grandfather left in trust, and on what he could cadge from any friends he had left.'

'You included?' I suggested.

She nodded. 'Oh yes. He's always very persuasive. It's always for something extremely plausible, but all the deals fall through . . .' She looked away across the Heath, considering. 'And then this year, back in February or March, I think, he turned up one day and said he wouldn't need to borrow any more from me, he'd got a good thing going which would make him rich.'

'What was it?'

'He wouldn't say. Just told me not to worry, it was all legal. He had gone into partnership with someone with a cast iron idea for making a fortune. Well, I'd heard that sort of thing from him so often before. The only difference was that this time he didn't want money . . .'

'He wanted something else?'

'Yes.' She frowned. 'He wanted me to introduce him to Bobbie Wessex. He said . . . just casually . . . how much he'd like to meet him, and I suppose I was so relieved not to find him cadging five hundred or so that I instantly agreed. It was very silly of me, but it didn't seem important . . .'

'What happened then?'

She shrugged. 'They were both at the Doncaster meeting at the opening of the flat season, so I introduced them. Nothing to it. Just a casual racecourse introduction. And then,' she looked annoyed, 'the next time Rupert turned up with that man Goldenberg, saying Bobbie Wessex had given him permission to decide how Rudiments should be run in all his races. I said he certainly wasn't going to do that, and telephoned to Bobbie. But,' she sighed, 'Rupert had indeed talked him into giving him carte blanche with Rudiments. Rupert is an expert persuader, and Bobbie, well, poor Bobbie is easily open to suggestion. Anyone with half an eye could see that Goldenberg was as straight as a corkscrew but Rupert said he was essential as someone had got to put the bets on, and he, Rupert, couldn't, as no bookmaker would accept his credit and you had to have hard cash for the Tote.'

'And then the scheme went wrong,' I said.

'The first time Rudiments won, they'd both collected a lot of money. I had told them the horse would win. Must win. It started at a hundred to six, first time out, and they were both as high as kites afterwards.'

'And next time Kenny Bayst won again when he wasn't supposed to, when they had laid it?'

She looked startled. 'So you did understand what they were saying.'

'Eventually.'

'Just like Rupert to let it out. No sense of discretion.'

I sighed. 'Well, thank you very much for being so frank. Even if I still can't see what connection Rudiments has with Major Tyderman blowing up one aircraft and crippling another.'

She twisted her mouth. 'I told you,' she said, 'right at the beginning, that nothing I said would be of any help.'

Colin stopped beside me in pink and green silks on his way from the weighing room to the parade ring for the last race. He gave me a concentrated inquiring look which softened into something like compassion.

'The waiting's doing you no good,' he said.

'Has she telephoned again?'

He shook his head. 'Midge won't leave the house, in case she does.'

'I'll be at Warwick races on Saturday . . . flying some people up from Kent . . . Will you ask her . . . just to talk to me?'

'I'll wring her stupid little neck,' he said.

I flew the customers back to Wiltshire and the Six back to Buckingham. Harley, waiting around with bitter eyes, told me the Board of Trade had let him know they were definitely proceeding against me.

'I expected they would.'

'But that's not what I wanted to speak to you about. Come into the office.' He was unfriendly, as usual. Snappy. He picked up a sheet of paper from his desk and waved it at me.

'Look at these times. I've been going through the bills Honey has sent out since you've been here. All the times are shorter. We've had to charge less . . . we're not making enough profit. It's got to stop. D'you understand? Got to stop.'

'Very well.'

He looked nonplussed: hadn't expected such an easy victory.

'And I'm taking on another pilot.'

'Am I out, then?' I found I scarcely cared.

He was surprised. 'No. Of course not. We simply seem to be getting too much taxi work just lately for you to handle on your own, even with Don's help.'

'Maybe we're getting more work because we're doing the jobs faster and charging less,' I suggested.

He was affronted. 'Don't be ridiculous.'

Another long evening in the caravan, aching and empty.

Nowhere to go, no way of going, and nothing to spend when I got there. That didn't matter, because wherever I went, whatever I spent, the inescapable thoughts lay in wait. Might as well suffer them alone and cheaply as anywhere else.

For something to do, I cleaned the caravan from end to end. When it was finished, it looked better, but I, on the whole, felt worse. Scrambled myself two eggs, ate them unenthusiastically on toast. Drank a dingy cup of dried coffee, dried milk.

Switched on the television. Old movie, circa 1950, pirates, cutlasses, heaving bosoms. Switched off.

Sat and watched night arrive on the airfield. Tried to concentrate on what Annie Villars had told me, so as not to think of night arriving over the fields and tents of Warwickshire. For a long time, had no success at all.

Look at everything upside down. Take absolutely nothing for granted.

The middle of the night produced out of a shallow restless sleep a singularly wild idea. Most sleep-spawned revelations from the subconscious wither and die of ridicule in the dawn, but this time it was different. At five, six, seven o'clock, it still looked possible. I traipsed in my mind through everything I had seen and heard since the day of the bomb, and added a satisfactory answer to why to the answer to who.

That Friday I had to set off early in the Aztec to Germany with some television cameramen from Denham, wait while they took their shots, and bring them home again. In spite of breaking Harley's ruling about speed into pin-sized fragments it was seven-thirty before I climbed stiffly out of the cockpit and helped Joe push the sturdy twin into the hangar.

'Need it for Sunday, don't you?' he asked.

'That's right. Colin Ross to France.' I stretched and yawned, and picked up my heavy flight bag with all its charts and documents.

'We're working you hard.'

'What I'm here for.'

He put his hands in his overall pockets. 'You're light on those aeroplanes, I'll give you that. Larry, now, Larry was heavy-handed. Always needing things repaired, we were, before you came.'

I gave him a sketch of an appreciative smile and walked up to fill in the records in the office. Harley and Don were both still flying, Harley giving a lesson, and Don a sight-seeing trip in the Six, and Honey was still traffic-copping up in the tower. I climbed up there to see her and ask her a considerable favour.

'Borrow my Mini?' she repeated in surprise. 'Do you mean now, this minute?'

I nodded. 'For the evening.'

'I suppose I could get Uncle to take me home,' she reflected. 'If you'll fetch me in the morning?'

'Certainly.'

'Well . . . all right. I don't really need it this evening. Just fill it up with petrol before you hand it back.'

'OK. And thanks a lot.'

She gave me a frankly vulgar grin. 'Minis are too small for what you want.'

I managed to grin back. 'Yeah . . .'

Given the wheels, make the appointment. A pleasant male voice answered the telephone, polite and quiet.

'The Duke of Wessex? Yes, this is his house. Who is speaking please?'

'Matthew Shore.'

'One moment, sir.'

The one moment stretched to four minutes, and I fed a week's beer money into the greedy box. At last the receiver at the other end was picked up and with slightly heavy breathing the Duke's unmistakable voice said, 'Matt? My dear chap, what can I do for you?'

'If you are not busy this evening, sir, could I call in to see you for a few minutes?'

'This evening? Busy? Hm . . . Is it about young Matthew's flight?'

'No, sir, something different. I won't take up much of your time.'

'Come by all means, my dear chap, if you want to. After dinner, perhaps? Nine o'clock, say?'

'Nine o'clock,' I confirmed. 'I'll be there.'

The Duke lived near Royston, west of Cambridge. Honey's Mini ate up the miles like Billy Bunter so that it was nine o'clock exactly when I stopped at a local garage to ask for directions to the Duke's house. On Honey's radio, someone was reading the news. I listened idly at first while the attendant finished filling up the car in front, and then with sharp and sickened attention. 'Racehorse trainer Jarvis Kitch and owner Dobson Ambrose, whose filly Scotchbright won the Oaks last month, were killed today in a multiple traffic accident just outside Newmarket. The Australian jockey Kenny Bayst, who was in the car with them, was taken to hospital with multiple injuries. His condition tonight is said to be fair. Three stable lads, trapped when a lorry crushed their car, also died in the crash.'

Mechanically I asked for, got, and followed, the directions to the Duke's house. I was thinking about poor large aggressive Ambrose and his cowed trainer Kitch, hoping that Kenny wasn't too badly hurt to race again, and trying to foresee the ramifications.

There was nothing else on the news except the weather forecast: heatwave indefinitely continuing.

No mention of Rupert Tyderman. But Tyderman, that day, had been seen by the police.

CHAPTER THIRTEEN

The Duke's manservant was as pleasant as his voice: a short, assured, slightly pop-eyed man in his later forties with a good deal of the Duke's natural benevolence in his manner. The house he presided over opened to the public, a notice read, every day between March 1st and November 30th. The Duke, I discovered, lived privately in the upper third of the south-west wing.

'The Duke is expecting you, sir. Will you come this way?'

I followed. The distance I followed accounted for the length of time I had waited for the Duke to come to the telephone and also his breathlessness when he got there. We went up three floors, along a two-furlong straight, and up again, to the attics. The attics in eighteenth-century stately homes were a long way from the front hall.

The manservant opened a white-painted door and gravely showed me in.

'Mr Shore, your Grace.'

'Come in, come in, my dear chap,' said the Duke.

I went in, and smiled with instant, spontaneous delight. The square low-ceilinged room contained a vast toy electric train set laid out on an irregular ring of wide green-covered trestle tables. A terminus, sidings, two small towns, a branch line, tunnels, gradients, viaducts, the Duke had the lot. In the centre of the ring, he and his nephew Matthew stood behind a large control table pressing the switches which sent about six different trains clanking on different courses round the complex.

The Duke nudged his nephew. 'There you are, what did we say? He likes it.'

Young Matthew gave me a fleeting glance and went back to some complicated point changing. 'He was bound to. He's got the right sort of face.'

The Duke said, 'You can crawl in here best under that table with the signal box and level crossing.' He pointed, so I went down on hands and knees and made the indicated journey. Stood up in the centre. Looked around at the rows of lines and remembered the hopeless passion I'd felt in toy shops as a child: my father had been an underpaid schoolmaster who had spent his money on books.

The two enthusiasts showed me where the lines crossed and how the trains could be switched without crashing. Their voices were filled with contentment, their eyes shining, their faces intent.

'Built this lot up gradually, of course,' the Duke said. 'Started when I was a boy. Then for years I never came up here. Not until young Matthew got old enough. Now, as I expect you can see, we have great times.'

'We're thinking of running a branch line right through that wall over there into the next attic,' Matthew said. 'There isn't much room in here.'

The Duke nodded. 'Next week, perhaps. For your birthday.'

Young Matthew gave him a huge grin and deftly let a pullman cross three seconds in front of a chugging goods. 'It's getting dark,' he observed. 'Lighting up time.'

'So it is,' agreed the Duke.

Matthew with a flourish pressed a switch, and they both watched my face. All round the track, and on all the stations and signal boxes and in the signals themselves, tiny electric lights suddenly shone out. The effect, to my eyes, was enchanting.

'There you are,' said the Duke. 'He likes it.'

'Bound to,' young Matthew said.

They played with the trains for another whole hour, because they had worked out a timetable and they wanted to see if they could keep to it before they pinned it up on the notice board in the terminal. The Duke apologized, not very apologetically, for keeping me waiting, but it was, he explained, Matthew's first evening out of school, and they had been waiting all through the term for this occasion.

At twenty to eleven the last shuttle service stopped at the buffers in the terminal and Matthew yawned.

With the satisfaction of a job well done the two railwaymen unfolded several large dustsheets and laid them carefully over the silent tracks, and then we all three crawled back under the table which held the level crossing.

The Duke led the way down the first flight and along the two furlongs, and we were then, it appeared, in his living quarters.

'You'd better cut along to bed, now, Matthew,' he said to his nephew. 'See you in the morning. Eight o'clock sharp, out in the stables.'

'Sure thing,' Matthew said. 'And after that, the races.' He sighed with utter content. 'Better than school,' he said.

The Duke showed me into a smallish white-painted sitting-room furnished with Persian rugs, leather armchairs, and endless sporting prints.

'A drink?' he suggested, indicating a tray.

I looked at the bottles. 'Whisky, please.'

He nodded, poured two, added water, gave me the glass and waved me to an armchair.

'Now, my dear chap? . . .'

It suddenly seemed difficult, what I had come to ask him, and what to explain. He was so transparently honest, so incapable of double dealing: I wondered if he could comprehend villainy at all.

'I was talking to Annie Villars about your horse Rudiments,' I said.

A slight frown lowered his eyebrows. 'She was

annoyed with me for letting her friend Rupert Tyderman advise me . . . I do so dislike upsetting Annie, but I'd promised . . . Anyway, she has sorted it all out splendidly, I believe, and now that her friend has turned out to be so extraordinary, with that bomb, I mean, I don't expect he will want to advise me about Rudiments any more.'

'Did he, sir, introduce to you any friend of his?'

'Do you mean Eric Goldenberg? Yes, he did. Can't say I really liked the fellow, though. Didn't trust him, you know. Young Matthew didn't like him, either.'

'Did Goldenberg ever talk to you about insurance?'

'Insurance?' he repeated. 'No, I can't remember especially that he did.'

I frowned. It had to be insurance.

It had to be.

'It was his other friend,' said the Duke, 'who arranged the insurance.'

I stared at him. 'Which other friend?'

'Charles Carthy-Todd.'

I blinked. 'Who?'

'Charles Carthy-Todd,' he repeated patiently. 'He was an acquaintance of Rupert Tyderman. Tyderman introduced us one day. At Newmarket races, I think it was. Anyway, it was Charles who suggested the insurance. Very good scheme, I thought it was. Sound. Very much needed. An absolute boon to a great many people.'

'The Racegoers' Accident Fund,' I said. 'Of which you are Patron.'

'That's right.' He smiled contentedly. 'So many people have complimented me on giving it my name. A splendid undertaking altogether.'

'Could you tell me a little more about how it was set up?'

'Are you interested in insurance, my dear chap? I could get you an introduction at Lloyd's . . . but . . .'

I smiled. To become an underwriter at Lloyd's one had to think of a stake of a hundred thousand pounds as loose change. The Duke, in his quiet good natured way, was a very rich man indeed.

'No sir. It's just the Accident Fund I'm interested in. How it was set up, and how it is run.'

'Charles sees to it all, my dear chap. I can't seem to get the hang of these things at all, you know. Technicalities, and all that. Much prefer horses, don't you see?'

'Yes, sir, I do see. Could you perhaps, then, tell me about Mr Carthy-Todd? What he's like, and so on.'

'He's about your height but much heavier and he has dark hair and wears spectacles. I think he has a moustache . . . yes, that's right, a moustache.'

I was jolted. The Duke's description of Charles Carthy-Todd fitted almost exactly the impression Nancy had had of Tyderman's companion. Dozens of men around, though, with dark hair, moustache, glasses . . .

'I really meant, sir, his . . . er . . . character.'

'My dear chap. Sound. Very sound. A thoroughly

good fellow. An expert in insurance, spent years with a big firm in the city.'

'And . . . his background?' I suggested.

'Went to Rugby. Then straight into an office. Good family, of course.'

'You've met them?'

He looked surprised at the question. 'Not actually, no. Business connection, that's what I have with Charles. His family came from Herefordshire, I think. There are photographs in our office . . . land, horses, dogs, wife and children, that sort of thing. Why do you ask?'

I hesitated. 'Did he come to you with the Accident Scheme complete?'

He shook his fine head. 'No, no, my dear chap. It arose out of conversation. We were saying how sad it was for the family of that small steeplechase trainer who was drowned on holiday and what a pity it was that there wasn't some scheme which covered everyone engaged in racing, not just the jockeys. Then of course when we really went into it we broadened it to include the racing public as well. Charles explained that the more premiums we collected the more we could pay out in compensation.'

'I see.'

'We have done a great deal of good already.' He smiled happily. 'Charles was telling me the other day that we have settled three claims for injuries so far, and that those clients are so pleased that they are telling everyone else to join in.'

I nodded. 'I've met one of them. He'd broken his ankle and received a thousand pounds.'

He beamed. 'There you are, then.'

'When did the scheme actually start?'

'Let me see. In May, I should think. Towards the end of May. About two months ago. It took a little while to organize, of course, after we'd decided to go ahead.'

'Charles did the organizing?'

'My dear chap, of course.'

'Did you take advice from any of your friends at Lloyd's?'

'No need, you know. Charles is an expert himself. He drew up all the papers. I just signed them.'

'But you read them first?'

'Oh yes,' he said reassuringly, then smiled like a child. 'Didn't understand them much, of course.'

'And you yourself guaranteed the money?' Since the collapse of cut-price car insurance firms, I'd read somewhere, privately run insurance schemes had to show a minimum backing of fifty thousand pounds before the Board of Trade would give them permission to exist.

'That's right.'

'Fifty thousand pounds?'

'We thought a hundred thousand might be better. Gives the scheme better standing, more weight, don't you see?'

'Charles said so?'

'He knows about such things.'

'Yes.'

'But of course I'll never have to find that money. It's only a guarantee of good faith, and to comply with the law. The premiums will cover the compensation and Charles' salary and all the costs. Charles worked it all out. And I told him right at the beginning that I didn't want any profit out of it, just for lending it my name. I really don't need any profit. I told him just to add my share into the paying out fund, and he thought that was a most sensible suggestion. Our whole purpose, you see, is to do good.'

'You're a singularly kind, thoughtful and generous man,' I said.

It made him uncomfortable. 'My dear chap . . .'

'And after tonight's news, I think several widows in Newmarket will bless you.'

'What news?'

I told him about the accident in which Kitch and Ambrose and the three stable lads had died. He was horrified.

'Oh, the poor fellows. The poor fellows. One can only hope that you are right, and that they had joined our scheme.'

'Will the premiums you have already collected be enough to cover many large claims all at once?'

He wasn't troubled. 'I expect so. Charles will have seen to all that. But even if they don't, I will make up the difference. No one will suffer. That's what guaranteeing means, do you see?'

'Yes, sir.'

'Kitch and Ambrose,' he said. 'The poor fellows.'

'And Kenny Bayst is in hospital, badly hurt.'

'Oh dear.' His distress was genuine. He really cared.

'I know that Kenny Bayst was insured with you. At least, he told me he was going to be. And after this I should think you would be flooded with more applications.'

'I expect you're right. You seem to understand things, just like Charles does.'

'Did Charles have any plans for giving the scheme a quick boost to begin with?'

'I don't follow you, my dear chap.'

'What happened to the Accident Fund,' I asked casually, 'after that bomb exploded in the aeroplane which had been carrying Colin Ross?'

He looked enthusiastic. 'Do you know, a lot of people told me they would join. It made them think, they said. I asked Charles if they had really done anything about it, and he said yes, quite a few inquiries had come in. I said that as no one had been hurt, the bomb seemed to have done the Fund a lot of good, and Charles was surprised and said so it had.'

Charles had met the Duke through Rupert Tyderman. Rupert Tyderman had set off the bomb. If ever there was a stone cold certainty, it was that Charles Carthy-Todd was the least surprised on earth that cash had followed combustion. He had reckoned it would. He had reckoned right.

'Charles sent out a pamphlet urging everyone to insure against bombs on the way home,' I said.

The Duke smiled. 'Yes, that's right. I believe it was very effective. We thought, do you see, that as no one had been hurt, there would be no harm in it.'

'And as it was Colin Ross who was on board, the bomb incident was extensively covered on television and in the newspapers . . . and had a greater impact on your Fund than had it been anyone else.'

The Duke's forehead wrinkled. 'I'm not sure I understand.'

'Never mind, sir. I was just thinking aloud.'

'Very easy habit to fall into. Do it myself, you know, all the time.'

Carthy-Todd and Tyderman's second sabotage, I thought to myself, hadn't been as good. Certainly by attacking Colin they'd achieved the same impact and national coverage, but I would have thought it was too obviously slanted at one person to have had much universal effect. Could be wrong, though . . .

'This has been the most interesting chat,' said the Duke. 'But my dear fellow, the evening is passing. What was it that you wanted to see me about?'

'Er . . .' I cleared my throat. 'Do you know, sir, I'd very much like to meet Mr Carthy-Todd. He sounds a most go-ahead, enterprising man.'

The Duke nodded warmly.

'Do you know where I could find him?'

'Tonight, do you mean?' He was puzzled.

'No, sir. Tomorrow will do.'

'I suppose you might find him at our office. He's sure to be there, because he knows I will be calling in myself. Warwick races, do you see?'

'The Accident Fund office . . . is in Warwick?'

'Of course.'

'Silly of me,' I said. 'I didn't know.'

The Duke twinkled at me. 'I see you haven't joined the Fund.'

'I'll join tomorrow. I'll go to the office. I'll be at Warwick too, for the races.'

'Great,' he said. 'Great. The office is only a few hundred yards from the racecourse.' He put two fingers into an inside pocket and brought out a visiting card. 'There you are, my dear chap. The address. And if you're there about an hour before the first race, I'll be there too, and you can meet Charles. You'll like him, I'm sure of that.'

'I'll look forward to it,' I said. I finished my whisky and stood up. 'It was kind of you to let me come . . . and I think your trains are absolutely splendid . . .'

His face brightened. He escorted me all the way down to the front door, talking about young Matthew and the plans they had for the holidays. Would I fix Matthew's flight for Thursday, he asked. Thursday was Matthew's birthday. He would be eleven.

'Thursday it is,' I agreed. 'I'll do it in the evening, if there's a charter fixed for that day.'

'Most good of you, my dear chap.'

I looked at the kind, distinguished, uncomprehending face. I knew that if his partner Charles Carthy-Todd skipped with the accumulated premiums before paying out the Newmarket widows, as I was privately certain he would, the honourable Duke of Wessex would meet every penny out of his own coffers. In all probability he could afford it, but that wasn't the point. He would be hurt and bewildered and impossibly distressed at having been tangled up in a fraud, and it seemed to me especially vicious that anyone should take advantage of his vulnerable simplicity and goodness.

Charles Carthy-Todd was engaged in taking candy from a mentally retarded child and then making it look as though the child had stolen it in the first place. One couldn't help but feel protective. One couldn't help but want to stop it.

I said impulsively, 'Take care of yourself, sir.'

'My dear chap . . . I will.'

I walked down the steps from his front door towards Honey's Mini waiting in the drive, and looked back to where he stood in the yellow oblong of light. He waved a hand gently and slowly closed the door, and I saw from his benign slightly puzzled expression that he was still not quite sure why I had come.

*

It was after one o'clock when I got back to the caravan. Tired, hungry, miserable about Nancy, I still couldn't stay asleep. Three o'clock, I was awake again, tangling the sheets as if in fever. I got up and splashed my itching eyes with cold water: lay down, got up, went for a walk across the airfield. The cool starry night came through my shirt and quietened my skin but didn't do much for the hopeless ache between my ears.

At eight in the morning I went to fetch Honey, filling her tank with the promised petrol at the nearest garage. She had made a gallon or two on the deal, I calculated. Fair enough.

What was not fair enough, however, was the news with which she greeted me.

'Colin Ross wants you to ring him up. He rang yesterday evening about half an hour after you'd buzzed off.'

'Did he say . . . what about?'

'He did ask me to write you a message, but honestly, I forgot. I was up in the tower until nine, and then Uncle was impatient to get home, and I just went off with him and forgot all about coming down here with the message . . . and anyway, what difference would a few hours make?'

'What was the message?'

'He said to tell you his sister didn't meet anyone called Chanter at Liverpool. Something about a strike, and this Chanter not being there. I don't know . . . there were two aircraft in the circuit and I wasn't paying all that much attention. Come to think of it, he did seem pretty anxious I should give you the message last night, but like I said, I forgot. Sorry, and all that. Was it important?'

I took a deep breath. Thinking about the past night, I could cheerfully have strangled her. 'Thanks for telling me.'

She gave me a sharp glance. 'You looked bushed. Have you been making love all night? You don't look fit to fly.'

'Seldom felt better,' I said with truth. 'And no, I haven't.'

'Save yourself for me.'

'Don't bank on it.'

'Louse.'

When I rang Colin's number from the telephone in the lounge it was Midge who answered. The relief in her voice was as overwhelming as my own.

'Matt! . . .' I could hear her gulp, and knew she was fighting against tears. 'Oh, Matt . . . I'm so glad you've rung. She didn't go after Chanter. She didn't. It's all right. Oh dear . . . just a minute . . .' She sniffed and paused, and when she spoke again she had her voice under control. 'She rang yesterday evening and we talked to her for a long time. She said she was sorry if she had upset us, she had really left because she was so angry with herself, so humiliated at having made up such silly dreams about you . . . she said it was all her own fault, that you hadn't deceived her in any way, she had deceived herself . . . she wanted to tell us that it wasn't because she was angry with you that she ran out, but because she felt she had made such a fool of herself . . . Anyway, she said she had cooled off a good deal by the time her train got to Liverpool and she was simply miserable by then, and then when she found Chanter had gone away because of the strike she said she was relieved, really. Chanter's landlady told Nancy where he had gone . . . somewhere in Manchester, to do a painting of industrial chimneys, she thought . . . but Nancy decided it wasn't Chanter she wanted . . . and she didn't know what to do, she still felt muddled . . . and then outside the art school she met a girl who had been a student with us in London. She was setting off for a camping holiday near Stratford and . . . well . . . Nancy decided to go with her. She said a few days' peace and some landscape painting would put her right . . . so she rang up here and it was our cleaning woman who answered . . . Nancy swears she told her it was Jill she was with, and not Chanter, but of course we never got that part of the message . . .' She stopped, and when I didn't answer immediately she said anxiously, 'Matt, are you still there?'

'Yes.'

'You were so quiet.'

'I was thinking about the last four days.'

Four wretched, dragging days. Four endless grinding nights. All unnecessary. She hadn't been with Chanter at all. If she'd suffered about what she'd imagined about me, so had I from what I'd imagined about her. Which made us, I guessed, about quits.

'Colin told her she should have asked you about that court case instead of jumping to conclusions,' Midge said.

'She didn't jump, she was pushed.'

'Yes. She knows that now. She's pretty upset. She doesn't really want to face you at Warwick . . . after making such a mess of things . . .'

'I shan't actually slaughter her.'

She half laughed. 'I'll defend her. I'm driving over with Colin. I'll see you there too.'

'That's marvellous.'

'Colin's out on the gallops just now. We're setting off after he's come in and had something to eat.'

'Tell him to drive carefully. Tell him to think of Ambrose.'

'Yes . . . Isn't it awful about that crash?'

'Have you heard what happened, exactly?'

'Apparently Ambrose tried to pass a slow lorry on a bend and there was another one coming the other way . . . he ran into it head on and one of the lorries overturned and crushed another car with three stable lads in it. There's quite a lot about it in today's *Sporting Life*.'

'I expect I'll see it. And Midge . . . thank Colin for his message last night.'

'I will. He said he didn't want you to worry any longer. He seemed to think you were almost as worried about her as we were.'

'Almost,' I agreed wryly. 'See you at Warwick.'

CHAPTER FOURTEEN

Honey had arranged for me to fly a Mr and Mrs Whiteknight and their two young daughters down to Lydd, where the daughters were to meet friends and leave on the car air ferry to Le Touquet for a holiday in France. After waving the daughters off, the Whiteknights wanted to belt back to see their horse run in the first race at Warwick, which meant, since there was no racecourse strip, landing at Coventry and hailing a cab.

Accordingly I loaded them up at Buckingham and pointed the nose of the Six towards Kent. The two daughters, about fourteen and sixteen, were world-weary and disagreeable, looking down their noses at everything with ingrained hostility. Their mother behaved to me with the cool graciousness of condescension, and autocratically bossed the family. Mr Whiteknight, gruff, unconsulted, a downtrodden universal provider, out of habit brought up the rear.

At Lydd, after carrying the daughters' suitcases unthanked into the terminal, I went back to the Six to wait through the farewells. Mr Whiteknight had obligingly left his *Sporting Life* on his seat. I picked it up and read it. There was a photograph of the Ambrose crash. The usual mangled metal, pushed to the side of the road, pathetic result of impatience.

I turned to the middle page, to see how many races Colin was riding at Warwick. He was down for five, and in most of them was favourite.

Alongside the Warwick programme, there was an advertisement in bold black letters.

'Colin Ross has insured with us. Why don't you?' Underneath in smaller type it went on, '*You* may not be lucky enough to survive two narrow escapes. Don't chance it. Cut out the proposal form printed below and send it with five pounds to the Racegoers' Accident Fund, Avon Street, Warwick. Your insurance cover starts from the moment your letter is in the post.'

I put the paper down on my knee, looked into space, and sucked my teeth.

Major Tyderman had told Annie Villars that he and a partner of his had something going for them that would make them rich. She had thought he meant control of Rudiments, but of course it hadn't been that. The manoeuvring with Rudiments had come about simply because Tyderman couldn't resist a small swindle on the side, even when he was engaged in a bigger one.

Tyderman had got Annie to introduce him to the Duke so that he in his turn could produce Carthy-Todd. Goldenberg was incidental, needed only for placing bets. Carthy-Todd was central, the moving mind, the instigator. Everyone else, Tyderman, the Duke, Colin, Annie, myself, all of us were pieces on his chess-board, to be shoved around until the game was won.

Clean up and clear out, that was how he must have decided to play. He hadn't waited for the Fund to grow slowly and naturally, he'd blown up an aeroplane and used Colin Ross for publicity. He would only have stayed anyway until the claims began mounting, and if the crash victims at Newmarket were in fact insured he would be off within the week. He would stay just long enough to collect the crash-inspired rush of new premiums, and that would be that. A quick transfer to a Swiss bank. A one-way ticket to the next happy hunting ground.

I didn't know how to stop him. There would be no proof that he meant to defraud until after he'd done it. I could produce nothing to back up my belief. No one was going to lurch into drastic action on what was little more than a guess. I could perhaps telephone to the Board of Trade . . . but the Board of Trade and I were hardly on speaking terms. The tall man might listen. He had, after all, once asked for my thoughts. Maybe the aircraft section had a hotline to the insurance section. And maybe not.

With a sigh I folded up Mr Whiteknight's newspaper and glanced again at the crash on the front page. Down in one corner in the left-hand column, beside the account of the accident, a paragraph heading caught my eye.

Tyderman, it said. I read the dry meagre lines underneath with a vague and then mounting feeling of alarm.

'A man believed to be Major Rupert Tyderman was found dead early yesterday beside the main London to South Wales railway line, between Swindon and Bristol. His death, at first attributed to a fall from a train, was later established as having been the result of a stab wound. The police, who had wanted to interview Major Tyderman, are making inquiries.'

The Whiteknight parents were walking back across the apron by the time I'd decided what to do. They were displeased when I met them and said I was going to make a telephone call. There wasn't time, they said.

'Check on the weather,' I lied. They looked up at the hazy heatwave sky and gave me deservedly bitter looks. All the same, I went on my way.

The Duke's polite manservant answered.

'No, Mr Shore, I'm very sorry, His Grace left for Warwick half an hour ago.'

'Was young Matthew with him?'

'Yes, sir.'

'Do you know if he was planning to go to the Accident Fund office before he went to the racecourse?'

'I believe so, sir. Yes.'

I put the receiver down, feeling increasingly fearful. Rupert Tyderman's death put the game into a different league. Lives had been at risk before, in the aeroplanes; the basic callousness was there; but on those occasions the intention had been expressly not to kill. But now, if

Carthy-Todd had decided to clear up behind him . . . if Tyderman's blunder with Nancy's aeroplane, which had led to his uncovering, had also led directly to his death . . . if Carthy-Todd had stopped Tyderman giving evidence against him . . . then would he, could he possibly, also kill the simple, honest, truth-spilling Duke . . .?

He wouldn't, I thought coldly. He couldn't.

I didn't convince myself one little bit.

The Whiteknights had no cause for complaint about the speed at which I took them to Coventry, though they consented only with bad grace when I asked to share their taxi to the races. I parted from them at the main gate and walked back towards the town centre, looking for the office of the Accident Fund. As the Duke had said, it wasn't far: less than a quarter of a mile.

It was located on the first floor of a small moderately well kept town house which fronted straight on to the pavement. The ground floor seemed to be uninhabited, but the main door stood open and a placard on the wall just inside announced 'Racegoers' Accident Fund. Please walk up.'

I walked up. On the first landing there was a wash room, a secretary's office, and, at the front of the house, a door with a Yale lock and a knocker in the shape of a horse's head. I flipped the knocker a couple of times and the door came abruptly open.

'Hello,' said young Matthew, swinging it wide. 'Uncle was just saying you would miss us. We're just going along to the races.'

'Come along in, my dear chap,' said the Duke's voice from inside the room.

I stepped into the office. At first sight a plushy one: wall to wall plum coloured carpet, but of penny-pinching quality, two fat looking easy chairs with cheap foam seats, a pair of shoulder high metal filing cabinets and a modern afrormosia desk. The atmosphere of a solid, sober, long established business came exclusively from the good proportions of the bay windowed room, the mouldings round the nineteenth-century ceiling, the carved wood and marble slab of the handsome fireplace, and some dark old gilt framed oils on the walls. The office had been chosen with genius to convince, to reassure, to charm. And as clients of insurance companies seldom if ever visited its office, this one must have been designed to convince, to reassure, to charm only the Duke himself.

The Duke introduced me to the man who had been sitting and who now stood behind the desk.

'Charles Carthy-Todd . . . Matthew Shore.'

I shook his hand. He'd seen me before, as I'd seen him. Neither of us gave the slightest sign of it. I hoped he had not distinguished in me the minute subsidence of tension which I saw in him. The tension I felt hadn't subsided in the slightest.

He was all the Duke had said: a man with good

presence, good voice, a thorough-going public school gent. He would have had to have been, to net the Duke; and there were all those silver framed photographs, which the Duke had mentioned, standing around to prove it.

He had dark hair with the merest sprinkling of grey, a compact little moustache, pinkish tan, slightly oily-looking skin, and heavy black-framed glasses assisting his greyish-blue eyes.

The Duke was sitting comfortably in an armchair in the bay window, his splendid head haloed by the shining day behind. His knees were crossed, his hands relaxed, and he was smoking a cigar. From his general air of pleased well-being, it was easy to see the pride he held in his beautiful benevolent fund. I wished sincerely for his sake that he wasn't going to have to wake up.

Charles Carthy-Todd sat down and continued with what he had been going to do when I arrived, offering young Matthew a piece of chocolate-covered orange peel from a half-empty round red and gold tin. Matthew took it, thanked him, ate it, and watched him with anxious reserve. Like the Duke, I trusted young Matthew's instinct. All too clearly, it had switched to amber, if not to red. I hoped for all our sakes that he would have the good manners to keep quiet.

'Give Matthew a proposal form, Charles,' the Duke said contentedly. 'That's what he's come for, you know, to join the Fund.'

Carthy-Todd obediently rose, crossed to the filing

cabinet, pulled open the top drawer, and lifted out two separate sheets of paper. One, it appeared, was the proposal form: the other, a lavishly curlicued certificate of insurance. I filled in the spaces on the ultra-simple proposal while Carthy-Todd inscribed my name and number on the certificate; then I handed over a fiver, which left me with enough to live on cornflakes until pay day, and the transaction was complete.

'Take care of yourself now, Matt,' joked the Duke, and I smiled and said I would.

The Duke looked at his watch. 'Good gracious!' He stood up. 'Come along now, everybody. Time we went along to the racecourse. And no more excuses, Charles, I insist on you lunching with me.' To me he explained, 'Charles very rarely goes to the races. He doesn't much care for it, do you see? But as the course is so very close . . .'

Carthy-Todd's aversion to race meetings was to my mind completely understandable. He wished to remain unseen, anonymous, unrecognizable, just as he'd been all along. Charles would choose which meetings he went to very carefully indeed. He would never, I imagined, turn up without checking with the Duke whether he was going to be there too.

We walked back to the racecourse, the Duke and Carthy-Todd in front, young Matthew and me behind. Young Matthew slowed down a little and said to me in a quiet voice, 'I say, Matt, have you noticed something strange about Mr Carthy-Todd?'

I glanced at his face. He was half anxious, half puzzled, wanting reassurance.

'What do you think is strange?'

'I've never seen anyone before with eyes like that.'

Children were incredibly observant. Matthew had seen naturally what I had known to look for.

'I shouldn't mention it to him. He might not care for it.'

'I suppose not.' He paused. 'I don't frightfully like him.'

'I can see that.'

'Do you?'

'No,' I said.

He nodded in satisfaction. 'I didn't think you would. I don't know why Uncle's so keen on him. Uncle,' he added dispassionately, 'doesn't understand about people. He thinks everyone is as nice as he is. Which they're not.'

'How soon can you become his business manager?'

He laughed. 'I know all about trustees. I've got them. Can't have this and can't do that, that's all they ever say, Mother says.'

'Does your Uncle have trustees?'

'No, he hasn't. Mother's always beefing on about Uncle not being fit to control all that lucre and one day he'll invest the lot in a South Sea Bubble. I asked Uncle about it and he just laughed. He told me he has a stockbroker who sees to everything and Uncle just goes on getting richer and when he wants some money for something he just tells the stockbroker and he sells some shares and sends it along. Simple. Mother fusses over nothing. Uncle won't get into much trouble about money because he knows that he doesn't know about it, if you see what I mean?'

'I wouldn't like him to give too much to Mr Carthy-Todd,' I said.

He gave me a flashing look of understanding. 'So that's what I felt . . . Do you think it would do any good if I sort of tried to put Uncle off him a bit?'

'Couldn't do much harm.'

'I'll have a go,' he said. 'But he's fantastically keen on him.' He thought deeply and came up with a grin. 'I must say,' he said, 'that he has awfully good chocolate orange peel.'

Annie Villars was upset about Kenny Bayst. 'I went to see him for a few moments this morning. He's broken both legs and his face was cut by flying glass. He won't be riding again before next season, he says. Luckily he's insured with the Racegoers' Fund. Sent them a tenner, he told me, so he's hoping to collect two thousand pounds at least. Marvellous thing, that Fund.'

'Did you join?'

'I certainly did. After that bomb. Didn't know it was Rupert, then, of course. Still, better to do things at once rather than put them off, don't you agree?'

'Were Kitch and the stable lads insured too, do you know?'

She nodded. 'They were all Kitch's own lads. He'd advised them all to join. Even offered to deduct the premium from their wages bit by bit. Everyone in Newmarket is talking about it, saying how lucky it was. All the stable lads in the town who hadn't already joined are sending their fivers along in the next few days.'

I hesitated. 'Did you read about Rupert Tyderman in the *Sporting Life*?'

A twinge of regret twisted her face: her mouth for the first time since I had known her took on a soft curve that was not consciously constructed.

'Poor Rupert . . . What an end, to be murdered.'

'There isn't any doubt, then?'

She shook her head. 'When I saw the report, I rang the local newspaper down at Kemble . . . that's where they found him. He was lying, they said, at the bottom of an embankment near a road bridge over the railway. The local theory is that he could have been brought there by car during the night, and not fallen from a train at all . . .' She shook her head in bewilderment. 'He had one stab wound below his left shoulder-blade, and he had been dead for hours when he was found.'

It took a good deal of lying-in-wait to catch the Duke without Carthy-Todd at his elbow, but I got him in the end.

'I've left my wallet in the Accident Fund office,' I said. 'Must have left it on the desk when I paid my premium . . . Do you think, sir, that you could let me have a key, if you have one, so that I can slip along and fetch it?'

'My dear chap, of course.' He produced a small bunch from his pocket and sorted out a bright new yale. 'Here you are. That's the one.'

'Very kind, sir. I won't be long.' I took a step away and then turned back, grinning, making a joke.

'What happens, sir, if it's you who gets killed in a car crash? What happens to the Fund then?'

He smiled back reassuringly in a patting-on-the-shoulder avuncular manner. 'All taken care of, my dear chap. Some of the papers I signed, they dealt with it. The Fund money would be guaranteed from a special arrangement with my estate.'

'Did Charles see to it?'

'Naturally. Of course. He understands these things, you know.'

Between the Duke and the main gate a voice behind me crisply shouted.

'Matt.'

I stopped and turned. It was Colin, hurrying towards me, carrying the saddle from the loser he'd partnered in the first race.

'Can't stop more than a second,' he said. 'Got to

change for the next. You weren't leaving, were you? Have you seen Nancy?'

'No. I've been looking. I thought . . . perhaps . . .'

He shook his head. 'She's here. Up there, on the balcony, with Midge.'

I followed where he was looking, and there they were, distant, high up, talking with their heads together, two halves of one whole.

'Do you know which is Nancy?' Colin asked.

I said without hesitation, 'The one on the left.'

'Most people can't tell.'

He looked at my expression and said with exasperation, 'If you feel like that about her, why the bloody hell don't you let her know? She thinks she made it all up . . . she's trying to hide it but she's pretty unhappy.'

'She'd have to live on peanuts.'

'For crying out loud, what does that matter? You can move in with us. We all want you. Midge wants you . . . and now, not some distant time when you think you can afford it. Time for us is now, this summer. There may not be much after this.' He hitched the saddle up on his arm and looked back towards the weighing room. 'I'll have to go. We'll have to talk later. I came after you now, though, because you looked as though you were leaving.'

'I'm coming back soon.' I turned and walked along with him towards the weighing room. 'Colin . . . I ought to tell someone . . . you never know . . .' He gave me a puzzled glance and in three brief sentences I told him why the Accident Fund was a fraud, how he and the bomb had been used to drum up business, and in what way Carthy-Todd was a fake.

He stopped dead in his tracks. 'Good God,' he said. 'The Fund was such a great idea. What a bloody shame.'

Saturday afternoon. The Board of Trade had gone home to its lawn mowing and the wife and kids. I put down the telephone and considered the police.

The police were there, on the racecourse, all ready and able. But willing? Hardly. They were there to direct the traffic; a crime not yet committed would not shift them an inch.

Both lots, if they believed me, might eventually arrive on Carthy-Todd's doorstep. By appointment, probably; especially the Board of Trade.

There would be no Carthy-Todd to welcome them in. No records. No Fund. Possibly no Duke . . .

I always told myself to stay out of trouble.

Never listened.

No clocks ticked in Carthy-Todd's office. The silence was absolute. But it was only in my mind that it was ominous and oppressive. Carthy-Todd was safe at the races and I should have a clear hour at least: or so my brain told me. My nerves had other ideas.

I found myself tiptoeing across to the desk.

Ridiculous. I half laughed at myself and put my feet down flat on the soundless carpet.

Nothing on the desk top except a blotter without blots, a tray of pens and pencils, a green telephone, a photograph of a woman, three children and a dog in a silver frame, a desk diary, closed, and the red and gold tin of chocolate orange peel.

The drawers contained stationery, paper clips, stamps, and a small pile of the 'insure against bombs on the way home' brochures. Two of the four drawers were completely empty.

Two filing cabinets. One unlocked. One locked. The top of the three drawers of the unlocked cabinet contained the packets of proposal forms and insurance certificates, and a third packet containing claim forms; in the second, the completed and returned forms of those insured, filed in a rank of folders from A–Z; and the third, almost empty, contained three folders only, one marked 'Claims settled', one 'Claims pending', and the other 'Receipts'.

'Claims settled' embraced the records of two separate outgoing payments of one thousand pounds, one to Acey Jones and one to a trainer in Kent who had been kicked in the face at evening stables. Three hundred pounds had been paid to a stable girl in Newmarket in respect of fracturing her wrist in a fall from a two-year-old at morning exercise. The claim forms, duly filled in, and with doctor's certificates attached, were stamped 'paid' with a date.

'Claims pending' was fatter. There were five letters of application for claim forms, annotated 'forms sent', and two forms completed and returned, claiming variously for a finger bitten off by a hungry hurdler and a foot carelessly left in the path of a plough. From the dates, the claimants had only been waiting a month for their money, and few insurance companies paid out quicker than that.

The thin file 'Receipts' was in many ways the most interesting. The record took the form of a diary, with the number of new insurers entered against the day they paid their premiums. From sporadic twos and threes during the first week of operation the numbers had grown like a mushroom.

The first great spurt was labelled in the margin in small tidy handwriting 'A. C. Jones, etc.' The second, an astronomical burst, was noted 'Bomb!' The third, a lesser spurt, 'Pamphlet'. The fourth, a noticeable upthrust, 'Electric failure'. After that, the daily average had gone on climbing steadily. The word, by then, had reached pretty well every ear.

The running total in two months had reached five thousand, four hundred and seventy-two. The receipts, since some insurers had paid double premiums for double benefits, stood at £28,040.

With the next inrush of premiums after the Kitch-Ambrose accident (which Carthy-Todd certainly had not engineered, as only non-claiming accidents were any good to him) there would almost have been enough in the kitty to settle all the claims. I sighed, frowning. It was, as Colin had said, a bloody shame. The Duke's view of the Fund was perfectly valid. Run by an honest man, and with its ratio of premiums to pay-off slightly adjusted, it could have done good all round.

I slammed the bottom drawer shut with irritation and felt the adrenalin race through my veins as the noise reverberated round the empty room.

No one came. My nerves stopped registering tremble; went back to itch.

The locked second cabinet was proof only against casual eyes. I tipped it against the wall and felt underneath, and sure enough it was the type worked on one connecting rod up the back: pushed the rod up from the bottom and all the drawers became unlocked.

I looked through all of them quickly, the noise I had made seeming to act as an accelerator. Even if I had all the time in the world, I wanted to be out of there, to be gone.

The top drawer contained more folders of papers. The middle drawer contained a large grey metal box. The bottom drawer contained two cardboard boxes and two small square tins.

Taking a deep breath I started at the top. The folders contained the setting-up documents of the Fund and the papers which the Duke had so trustingly signed. The legal language made perfect camouflage for what Carthy-Todd had done. I had to read them twice, to take a strong grip and force myself to concentrate, before I understood the two covenants the Duke had given him.

The first, as the Duke had said, transferred one hundred thousand pounds from his estate into a guarantee trust for the Fund, in the event of his death. The second one at first sight looked identical, but it certainly wasn't. It said in essence that if the Duke died within the first year of the Fund, a further one hundred thousand pounds from his estate was to be paid into it.

In both cases, Carthy-Todd was to be sole Trustee.

In both cases, he was given absolute discretion to invest or use the money in any way he thought best.

Two hundred thousand pounds . . . I stared into space. Two hundred thousand pounds if the Duke died. A motive to make tongue-silencing look frivolous.

The twenty-eight thousand of the Fund money was only the beginning. The bait. The jackpot lay in the dead Duke.

His heirs would have to pay. Young Matthew, to be precise. The papers looked thoroughly legal, with signatures witnessed and stamped, and in fact it seemed one hundred per cent certain that Carthy-Todd wouldn't have bothered with them at all if they were not foolproof.

He wouldn't waste much more time, I thought. Not with the claims for the Ambrose accident coming in. With the Duke dead, the two hundred thousand would have to be paid almost at once, because the covenants would be a first charge on his estate, like debts. There would be no having to wait around for probate. If Carthy-Todd could stave off the claims for a while, he could skip with both the Duke's money and the whole Fund.

I put the papers back in their folder, back in the drawer. Closed it. Gently. My heart thumped.

Second drawer. Large metal box. One could open it without removing it from the cabinet. I opened it. Lots of space, but few contents. Some cottonwool, cold cream, glue, and a half used stick of greasepaint. I shut the lid, shut the drawer. Only to be expected.

Bottom drawer. Knelt on the floor. Two small square tins, one empty, one full and heavy and fastened all round with adhesive tape. Looked inside the two cardboard boxes first and felt the breath go out of my body as if I'd been kicked.

The cardboard boxes contained the makings of a radio bomb. Solenoids, transmitters, fuse wire, a battery and a small container of gunpowder in the first box. Plastic explosive wrapped in tin foil in the other.

I sat on my heels looking at the small square heavy tin. Heard in my mind the tall man from the Board of Trade: the tighter you pack a bomb the more fiercely it explodes.

Decided not to open the small square tin. Felt the sweat stand out in cold drops on my forehead.

I shut the bottom drawer with a caution which seemed silly when I remembered the casual way I'd tilted the whole cabinet over to open it. But then the bomb wouldn't get the signal where it was, not with those precious documents in the cabinet just above.

I wiped my hand over my face. Stood up. Swallowed.

I'd found everything I came to find, and more. All except for one thing. I glanced round the office, looking for somewhere else. Somewhere to hide something big . . .

There was a door in the corner behind Carthy-Todd's desk which I assumed connected with the secretary's office next door. I went over to it. Tried the handle. It was locked.

I let myself out of Carthy-Todd's office and went into the secretary's room, whose door was shut but had no keyhole. Stared, in there, at an L-shaped blank wall. No connecting door to Carthy-Todd. It was a cupboard, with the door on his side.

I went back to Carthy-Todd's office and stood contemplating the door. If I broke it open, he would know. If I didn't, I could only guess at what was inside. Evidence of a fraud committed, that would spur the Board of Trade to action. Evidence that would make the Duke rescind his covenants, or at least re-write them so that they were no longer death warrants . . .

Carthy-Todd hadn't been expecting trouble. He had left the key to the cupboard on his desk in the tray of pens and pencils. I picked up the single key which lay there, and it fitted.

Opened the cupboard door. It squeaked on its hinges, but I was too engrossed to notice.

There he was. Mr Acey Jones. The crutches, leaning against the wall. The white plaster cast lying on the floor.

I picked up the cast and looked at it. It had been slit neatly down the inside leg from the top to the ankle. One could put one's foot into it like a boot, with the bare toes sticking out of the end and the metal walking support under the arch. There were small grip-clips like those used on bandages sticking into the plaster all down the opening. Put your foot into the cast, fasten the clips, and bingo, you had a broken ankle.

Acey Jones, loudly drumming up business for the Fund.

Acey Jones, Carthy-Todd. Confidence tricksters were the best actors in the world.

I didn't hear him come.

I put the cast back on the floor just where it had been, and straightened up and started to shut the cupboard door, and saw him moving out of the corner of my eye as he came into the room. I hadn't shut the office door behind me, when I'd gone back. I hadn't given myself any time at all.

His face went rigid with fury when he saw what I'd seen.

'Meddling pilot,' he said. 'When the Duke told me he'd given you the key . . .' He stopped, unable to speak for rage. His voice was different, neither the Eton of

Carthy-Todd, nor the Australian of Acey Jones. Just ordinary uninflected English. I wondered fleetingly where he came from, who he really was . . . a thousand different people, one for every crime.

Unblinking behind the black-framed glasses the pale blue-grey eyes all but sizzled. The incongruous white eyelashes, which Matthew had noticed, gave him now a fierce fanatical ruthlessness. The decision he was coming to wasn't going to be for my good.

He put his hand into his trouser pocket and briefly pulled it out again. There was a sharp click. I found myself staring at the knife which had snapped out, and thought with a horrific shiver of Rupert Tyderman tumbling down dead beside the railway line . . .

He took a step sideways and kicked shut the office door. I twisted round towards the mantelshelf to pick up whatever I could find there . . . a photograph, a cigarette box . . . anything I could use as a weapon or a shield.

I didn't even get as far as taking anything into my hand, because he didn't try to stab me with the knife.

He threw it.

CHAPTER FIFTEEN

It hit me below the left shoulder and the jolt threw me forward on my twisting legs so that I hit my forehead solidly on the edge of the marble slab mantelshelf. Blacking out, falling, I put out a hand to stop myself, but there was nothing there, only the empty black hollow of the fireplace, and I went on, right down, smashing and crashing amongst the brass fire irons . . . but I heard them only dimly . . . and then not at all.

I woke up slowly, stiffly, painfully, after less than a quarter of an hour. Everything was silent. No sound. No people. Nothing.

I couldn't remember where I was or what had happened. Not until I tried to get up. Then the tearing soreness behind my shoulder stung me straight back into awareness.

Had a knife sticking in my back.

Lying face down among the fire irons I felt gingerly round with my right hand. My fingers brushed like feathers against the hilt. I cried out at my own touch. It was frightful.

Stupid the things you think of in moments of disaster. I thought: damn it, only three weeks and one day to my medical. I'll never pass it . . .

Never pull knives out of wounds, they say. It makes the bleeding worse. You can die from pulling knives out of wounds. Well . . . I forgot all that. I could see only that Acey-Carthy-Todd had left me for dead and if he found me alive when he came back he would almost certainly finish the job. Therefore I had to get out of his office before he came back. And it seemed incongruous, really, to walk round Warwick with a knife in one's back. So I pulled it out.

I pulled it out in two stages and more or less fainted after each. Kidded myself it was concussion from the mantelshelf, but I was crying as well. No stoic, Matt Shore.

When it was out I lay where I was for a while, looking at it, snivelling weakly and feeling the sticky warmth slowly spread, but being basically reassured because I was pretty sure by then that the knife had not gone through into my lung. It must have been deflected by hitting my shoulder blade: it had been embedded to three or four inches, but slanting, not straight in deep. I wasn't going to die. Or not yet.

After a while I got up on to my knees. I didn't have all the time in the world. I put my right hand on Carthy-Todd's desk: pulled myself to my feet.

Swayed. Thought it would be much much worse if I

fell down again. Leant my hip against the desk and looked vaguely round the office.

The bottom drawer of the second filing cabinet was open.

Shouldn't be. I'd shut it.

Open.

I shifted myself off the desk and tried a few steps. Tottered. Made it. Leant gingerly against the wall. Looked down into the drawer.

The cardboard boxes were still there. The empty tin was still there. The small heavy tin wasn't.

Realized coldly that the future no longer meant simply getting myself to safety out of that office, but getting to the Duke before the bomb did.

It was only four hundred yards . . . Only . . .

I'd have to do it, I thought, because if I hadn't searched the office Carthy-Todd wouldn't now be in a tearing hurry. When I didn't turn up to ferry home the Whiteknights, or turn up anywhere again for that matter, except with a stab wound in a ditch, the Duke would say where I had been last . . . and Carthy-Todd would want to avoid a police investigation like a slug shrinking away from salt. He wouldn't wait for that. He would obliterate my tracks.

There was something else missing from the office. I didn't know what it was, just knew it was something. It niggled for a moment, but was gone. Didn't think it could be important . . .

Walked with deliberation to the door. Opened it,

went outside. Stopped dead at the top of the stairs, feeling dizzy and weak.

Well. Had to get down them somehow. Had to.

The handrail was on the left-hand side. I couldn't bear to lift my left arm. Turned round, hung on tightly, and went down backwards.

'There you are,' I said aloud. 'You bloody can.' Didn't convince myself. It took Carthy-Todd to convince.

I laughed weakly. I was a fully paid up insurer with the Fund. Like to see Carthy-Todd pay my claim . . . a thousand smackers for a knife in the back. Lovely.

Rolled out into the hot sunlit street as light headed as a blond.

Blond Acey Jones . . .

Acey Jones was being pushed. Hurried. Knowing I'd found him out but still believing he could retrieve the situation. Still make his two hundred thousand. If he kept his nerve. If he killed the Duke immediately, this afternoon, and somehow made it look like an accident. If he dumped me somewhere later, as he had the Major . . .

He would think he could still do it. He didn't know I'd told Colin, didn't know that Colin knew he was Carthy-Todd . . .

The empty street had got much longer during the afternoon. Also it wouldn't stay absolutely still. It shimmered. It undulated. The pavement was uneven. Every time I put my foot down the paving stones reached up and stabbed me in the back.

I passed only an elderly woman on the way. She was muttering to herself. I realized that I was, too.

Half-way. I squinted along at the gate of the car park. Had to make it. Had to. And that wasn't all. Had to find someone to go and fetch the Duke, so that I could explain . . . explain . . .

Felt myself falling and put a hand out towards the wall. Mustn't shut my eyes . . . I'd be done for . . . spun heavily against the bricks and shuddered at the result. Rested my head against the wall, trying not to weep. Couldn't spare the time. Had to get on.

I pushed myself back into a moderately upright walking position. My feet couldn't tell properly how far it was down to the pavement: half the time I was climbing imaginary steps.

Weird.

Something warm on my left hand. I looked down. My head swam. Blood was running down my fingers, dripping on to the pavement. Looked up again, along to the course. Head swam again. Didn't know if it was concussion or heat or loss of blood. Only knew it reduced the time factor. Had to get there. Quickly.

One foot in front of the other, I told myself . . . just go on doing that: one foot in front of the other. And you'll get there.

Concentrate.

I got there. Gate to the car park. And no official guarding it. At that time in the afternoon, they'd given up expecting further customers.

I said 'Ohh . . .' in weak frustration. Have to go still further. Have to find someone . . . I turned in to the car park. Through the car park there was a gate into the paddock. Lots of people there. Lots . . .

I went between the cars, staggering, holding on to them, feeling my knees bending, knowing the dizzy weakness was winning and caring less and less about the jagged pain of every step. Had to find someone. Had to.

Someone suddenly called to me from quite close.

'Matt!'

I stopped. Looked slowly round. Midge was climbing out of Colin's parked Aston Martin down the row and running to catch me up.

'Matt,' she said, 'We've been looking for you. I came back to the car because I was tired. Where have you been?'

She put her hand with friendship on my left arm.

I said thickly, 'Don't . . . touch me.'

She took her hand away with a jerk. 'Matt!'

She looked at me more closely, at first in puzzlement and then in anxiety. Then she looked at her fingers, and where she'd grasped my coat there were bright red smears.

'It's blood,' she said blankly.

I nodded a fraction. My mouth was dry. I was getting very tired.

'Listen . . . Do you know the Duke of Wessex?'

'Yes. But . . .' she protested.

'Midge,' I interrupted. 'Go and find him. Bring him

here . . . I know it sounds stupid . . . but someone is trying to kill him . . . with a bomb.'

'Like Colin? But that wasn't . . .'

'Fetch him, Midge,' I said. 'Please.'

'I can't leave you. Not like this.'

'You must.'

She looked at me doubtfully.

'Hurry.'

'I'll get you some help, too,' she said. She turned lightly on her heel and half walked, half ran towards the paddock. I leant the bottom of my spine against a shiny grey Jaguar and wondered how difficult it would be to prevent Carthy-Todd from planting his bomb. That tin . . . it was small enough to fit into a binocular case . . . probably identical with the one which had destroyed the Cherokee. I would have sweated at the thought of so much confined explosive power if I hadn't been sweating clammily already.

Why didn't they come? My mouth was drier . . . The day was airless . . . I moved restlessly against the car. After I'd told the Duke, he'd have to go off somewhere and stay safely out of sight until the Board of Trade had dealt with Carthy-Todd . . .

I dispassionately watched the blood drip from my fingers on to the grass. I could feel that all the back of my coat was soaked. Couldn't afford a new one, either. Have to get it cleaned, and have the slit invisibly mended. Get myself mended, too, as best I could. Harley wouldn't keep the job for me. He'd have to get someone else in my place. The Board of Trade doctors wouldn't let me fly again for weeks and weeks. If you gave a pint of blood as a donor, they grounded you for over a month . . . I'd lost more than a pint involuntarily, by the looks of things . . . though a pint would make a pretty good mess, if you spilled it.

I lifted my lolling head up with a jerk. Got to stay awake until they came. Got to explain to the Duke . . .

Things were beginning to fuzz round the edges. I licked my dry lips. Didn't do much good. Didn't have any moisture in my tongue either.

I finally saw them, and it seemed a long way off, coming through the gate from the paddock. Not just Midge and the Duke, but two others as well. Young Matthew, jigging along in front.

And Nancy.

Chanter had receded into the unimportant past. I didn't give him a thought. Everything was as it had been before, the day she flew to Haydock. Familiar, friendly, trusting. The girl I hadn't wanted to get involved with, who had melted a load of ice like an acetylene torch.

Across the sea of cars Midge pointed in my direction and they began to come towards me, crossing through the rows. When they were only twenty or so yards away, on the far side of the row in front of me, they unaccountably stopped.

Come on, I thought. For God's sake come on.

They didn't move.

With an effort I pushed myself upright from the

Jaguar and took the few steps past its bonnet, going towards them. On my left, six cars along, was parked what was evidently the Duke's Rolls. On the bonnet stood a bright red and gold tin. Matthew was pointing, wanting to cross over and fetch it, and Midge was saying urgently, 'No, come on, Matt said to come quickly, and he's bleeding . . .'

Matthew gave her a concerned look and then nodded, but at the last second temptation was too much and he ran over and picked up the tin and started back to join them.

Bright red and gold tin. Containing sticks of orange peel dipped in chocolate. It had been on the desk. And afterwards . . . not on the desk. Something missing. Red and gold tin.

Missing from Carthy-Todd's desk.

My heart bumped. I shouted, and my voice came out hopelessly weak.

'Matthew, throw it to me.'

He looked up doubtfully. The others began to walk through the rows of cars towards him. They would reach him before I could. They would be standing all together, Nancy and Midge and the Duke and young Matthew, who knew too that I'd been in Carthy-Todd's office that day.

I scanned the car park desperately, but he was there. He'd put the tin on the car and simply waited for them to come out of the races. The last race was about to start . . . the horses had gone down to the post and at that moment the loudspeakers were announcing 'They're under starter's orders' . . . He knew it wouldn't be long before they came . . . He was standing over nearer the rails of the course with his black head showing and the sun glinting on his glasses. He had meant just to kill young Matthew and the Duke, but now there were Nancy and Midge as well . . . and he didn't know he couldn't get away with it . . . didn't know Colin knew . . . and he was too far away for me to tell him . . . I couldn't shout . . . could barely talk.

'Matthew, throw me the tin.' It was a whisper, nothing more.

I began to walk towards him, holding out my right arm. Stumbled. Swayed. Frightened him.

The others were closing on him.

No more time. I took a breath. Straightened up.

'Matthew,' I said loudly. 'To save your life, throw me that tin. Throw it now. At once.'

He was upset, uncertain, worried.

He threw the tin.

It was taking Carthy-Todd several seconds to press the transmission buttons. He wasn't as adept at it as Rupert Tyderman. He wouldn't be able to see that he had missed his opportunity with the Duke, and that now there was only me. But whatever he did, he'd lost the game.

The red-gold tin floated towards me like a blazing sun and seemed to take an eternity crossing the fifteen feet from Matthew. I stretched my right arm forward to meet it and when it landed on my hand I flung it with a bowling action high into the air behind where I was standing, back as far as I could over the parked rows, because behind them, at the rear, there was empty space.

The bomb went off in the air. Three seconds out of my hand, six seconds out of Matthew's. Six seconds. As long a time as I had ever lived.

The red and gold tin disintegrated into a cracking fireball like the sun, and the blast of it knocked both young Matthew and me with a screeching jolt flat to the ground. The windows in most of the cars in the car park crashed into splinters, and the two Fords just below the explosion were thrown about like toys. Nancy and Midge and the Duke, still sheltered between two cars, rocked on their feet and clung to each other for support.

Along in the stands, we heard later, no one took much notice. The race had started and the commentator's voice was booming out, filling everyone's ears with the news that Colin Ross was lying handy and going nicely on the favourite half a mile from home.

Young Matthew picked himself smartly up and said in amazement, 'What was that?'

Midge completed the four bare steps to his side and held his hand.

'It was a bomb,' she said in awe. 'Like Matt said, it was a bomb.'

I was trying to get myself up off the grass. Even though the Duke was for the present safe, the Fund money was not. Might as well try for set and match . . .

On my knees, I said to Matthew, 'Can you see Carthy-Todd anywhere? It was his tin . . . his bomb . . .'

'Carthy-Todd?' repeated the Duke vaguely. 'It can't be. Impossible. He wouldn't do a thing like that.'

'He just did,' I said. I was having no success in getting up any further. Had nothing much left. A strong arm slid under my right armpit, helping me. A soft calm voice said in my ear, 'You look as if you'd be better staying down.'

'Nancy . . .'

'How did you get into this state?'

'Carthy-Todd . . . had a knife . . .'

'There he is!' Matthew suddenly shouted. 'Over there.'

I wobbled to my feet. Looked where Matthew was pointing. Carthy-Todd, running between the rows. Nancy looked too.

'But that's,' she said incredulously, 'that's the man I saw in the car with Major Tyderman. I'd swear to it.'

'You may have to,' I said.

'He's running to get out,' Matthew shouted. 'Let's head him off.'

It was almost a game to him, but his enthusiasm infected several other racegoers who had come early out of the races and found their windows in splinters.

'Head him off,' I heard a man shout, and another, 'There, over there. Head him off.'

I leaned in hopeless weakness against a car, and

dimly watched. Carthy-Todd caught sight of the growing number converging on him. Hesitated. Changed course. Doubled back on his tracks. Made for the only free and open space he could see. The green grass behind him. The racecourse itself.

'Don't . . .' I said. It came out a whisper, and even if I'd had a microphone he wouldn't have heard.

'Oh God,' Nancy said beside me. 'Oh no.'

Carthy-Todd didn't see his danger until it was too late. He ran blindly out across the course looking over his shoulder at the bunch of men who had suddenly, aghast, stopped chasing him.

He ran straight in front of the thundering field of three-year-olds sweeping round the last bend to their final flying effort up the straight.

Close bunched, they had no chance of avoiding him. He went down under the pounding hooves like a rag into a threshing machine, and a second later the flowing line of horses broke up into tumbling chaos . . . crashing at thirty miles an hour . . . legs whirling . . . jockeys thudding to the ground like bright blobs of paint . . . a groaning shambles on the bright green turf . . . and side-stepping, swaying, looking over their shoulders, the rear ones in the field swerved past and went on to a finish that no one watched.

Nancy said in anguish, 'Colin!' and ran towards the rails. The pink and white silks lay still, a crumpled bundle curled in a protective ball. I followed her, plod by plod, feeling that I couldn't go any further, I simply couldn't. One car short of the rails, I stopped. I clung on to it, sagging. The tide was going out.

The pink and white ball stirred, unrolled itself, stood up. Relief made me even weaker. Crowds of people had appeared on the course, running, helping, gawping . . . closing in like a screen round the strewn bodies . . . I waited for what seemed an age, and then Colin and Nancy reappeared through a thronging wall of people and came back towards the car park.

'Only stunned for a second,' I heard him say to a passing inquirer. 'I shouldn't go over there . . .' But the inquirer went on, looking avid.

Nancy saw me and waved briefly, and ducked under the rails with Colin.

'He's dead,' she said abruptly. She looked sick. 'That man . . . he . . . he was Acey Jones . . . Colin said you knew . . . his hair was lying on the grass . . . but it was a wig . . . and there was this bald white head and that pale hair . . . and you could see the line of grease paint . . . and the black moustache . . .' Her eyes were wide. Full of horror.

'Don't think about it,' Colin said. He looked at me. 'She shouldn't have come over . . .'

'I had to . . . you were lying there,' she protested. He went on looking at me. His expression changed. He said, 'Nancy said you were hurt. She didn't say . . . how badly.' He turned abruptly to Nancy and said, 'Fetch the doctor.'

'I tried to before,' she said. 'But he said he was on

duty and couldn't see to Matt before the race in case he was needed . . .' She tailed off and looked over at the crowd on the course. 'He'll be over there . . . seeing to those two jockeys . . .' She looked back at Colin with sudden fright. 'Midge said Matt had cut his arm . . . Is it worse? . . .'

'I'll fetch him,' Colin said grimly, and ran back to the battlefield. Nancy looked at me with such flooding anxiety that I grinned.

'Not as bad as all that,' I said.

'But you were walking . . . you threw that bomb with such force . . . I didn't realize . . . You do look ill . . .'

The Duke and young Matthew and Midge reappeared from somewhere. I hadn't seen them come. Things were getting hazier.

The Duke was upset. 'My dear chap,' he said over and over again. 'My dear chap . . .'

'How did you know it was a bomb?' Matthew asked.

'Just knew.'

'That was a pretty good throw.'

'Saved our lives,' said the Duke. 'My dear chap . . .'

Colin was back.

'He's coming,' he said. 'Immediately.'

'Saved our lives . . .' said the Duke again. 'How can we repay . . .'

Colin looked at him straightly. 'I'll tell you how, sir. Set him up in business . . . or take over Derrydowns . . . give him an air taxi business, based near Newmarket. He'll make you a profit. He'll have me for a customer, and Annie, and Kenny . . . and in fact the whole town, because the Fund can go on now, can't it?' He looked at me inquiringly, and I fractionally nodded. 'It may cost a bit to put right,' Colin said, 'but your Fund can go on, sir, and do all the good it was meant to . . .'

'An air taxi business. Take over Derrydowns,' the Duke repeated. 'My dear Colin, what a splendid idea. Of course. Of course.'

I tried to say something . . . anything . . . to begin to thank him for so casually thrusting the world into my fingers . . . but I couldn't say anything . . . couldn't speak. I could feel my legs collapsing. Could do nothing any more to stop them. Found myself kneeling on the grass, keeping myself from falling entirely by hanging on to a door handle of the car. Didn't want to fall. Hurt too much.

'Matt!' Nancy said. She was down on her knees beside me. Midge too. And Colin.

'Don't bloody die,' Nancy said.

I grinned at her. Felt light-headed. Grinned at Colin. Grinned at Midge.

'Want a lodger?' I asked.

'Soon as you like,' Colin said.

'Nancy,' I said. 'Will you . . . will you . . .'

'You nit,' she said. 'You great nit.'

My hand slipped out of the door handle. Colin caught me as I fell. Everything drifted quietly away, and by the time I reached the ground I couldn't feel anything at all.

DEAD CERT

Dick Francis has written forty-one international best-sellers and is widely acclaimed as one of the world's finest thriller writers. His awards include the Crime Writers' Association's Cartier Diamond Dagger for his outstanding contribution to the crime genre, and an honorary Doctorate of Humane Letters from Tufts University of Boston. In 1996 Dick Francis was made a Mystery Writers of America Grand Master for a lifetime's achievement and in 2000 he received a CBE in the Queen's Birthday Honours list.

Also by Dick Francis in Pan Books

THE SPORT OF QUEENS
(autobiography)

LESTER: The Official
Biography

DICK FRANCIS
OMNIBUS ONE:
Long Shot, Straight, High
Stakes

DICK FRANCIS
OMNIBUS TWO:
Forfeit, Risk,
Reflex

DICK FRANCIS
OMNIBUS THREE:
Slay-Ride, Banker, Proof

DICK FRANCIS
OMNIBUS FOUR:
Enquiry, Rat Race,
Smokescreen

SID HALLEY
OMNIBUS:
Odds Against, Whip Hand,
Come to Grief

NERVE
FOR KICKS
ODDS AGAINST
FLYING FINISH
BLOOD SPORT
FORFEIT
ENQUIRY
RAT RACE
BONECRACK
SMOKESCREEN
SLAY-RIDE
KNOCK DOWN
HIGH STAKES
IN THE FRAME
RISK
TRIAL RUN
WHIP HAND
REFLEX
TWICE SHY
BANKER
THE DANGER
PROOF
BREAK IN
BOLT
HOT MONEY
THE EDGE
STRAIGHT
LONGSHOT
COMEBACK
DRIVING FORCE
DECIDER
WILD HORSES
COME TO GRIEF
TO THE HILT
10lb PENALTY
FIELD OF THIRTEEN
SECOND WIND
SHATTERED

Dick Francis

DEAD CERT

PAN BOOKS

First published 1962 by Michael Joseph Ltd

This edition published 1976 by Pan Books
an imprint of Pan Macmillan Ltd
Pan Macmillan, 20 New Wharf Road, London N1 9RR
Basingstoke and Oxford
Associated companies throughout the world
www.panmacmillan.com

ISBN 0 330 24621 6

49 48

A CIP catalogue record for this book is available from the British Library.

Photoset by Intype London Ltd
Printed and bound in Great Britain by
Mackays of Chatham plc, Chatham, Kent

CHAPTER ONE

The mingled smells of hot horse and cold river mist filled my nostrils. I could hear only the swish and thud of galloping hooves and the occasional sharp click of horseshoes striking against each other. Behind me, strung out, rode a group of men dressed like myself in white silk breeches and harlequin jerseys, and in front, his body vividly red and green against the pale curtain of fog, one solitary rider steadied his horse to jump the birch fence stretching blackly across his path.

All, in fact, was going as expected. Bill Davidson was about to win his ninety-seventh steeplechase. Admiral, his chestnut horse, was amply proving he was still the best hunter 'chaser in the kingdom, and I, as often before, had been admiring their combined back view for several minutes.

Ahead of me the powerful chestnut hindquarters bunched, tensed, sprang: Admiral cleared the fence with the effortlessness of the really good performer. And he'd gained another two lengths, I saw, as I followed him over. We were down at the far end of Maidenhead racecourse with more than half a mile to go to the winning post. I hadn't a hope of catching him.

The February fog was getting denser. It was now impossible to see much farther than from one fence to the next, and the silent surrounding whiteness seemed to shut us, an isolated string of riders, into a private lonely limbo. Speed was the only reality. Winning post, crowds, stands, and stewards, left behind in the mist, lay again invisibly ahead, but on the long deserted mile and a half circuit it was quite difficult to believe they were really there.

It was an eerie, severed world in which anything might happen. And something did.

We rounded the first part of the bend at the bottom of the racecourse and straightened to jump the next fence. Bill was a good ten lengths in front of me and the other horses, and hadn't exerted himself. He seldom needed to.

The attendant at the next fence strolled across the course from the outside to the inside, patting the top of the birch as he went, and ducked under the rails. Bill glanced back over his shoulder and I saw the flash of his teeth as he smiled with satisfaction to see me so far behind. Then he turned his head towards the fence and measured his distance.

Admiral met the fence perfectly. He rose to it as if flight were not only for the birds.

And he fell.

Aghast, I saw the flurry of chestnut legs threshing the air as the horse pitched over in a somersault. I had a glimpse of Bill's bright-clad figure hurtling head downwards from the highest point of his trajectory, and I heard the crash of Admiral landing upside down after him.

Automatically I swerved over to the right and kicked my horse into the fence. In mid-air, as I crossed it, I looked down at Bill. He lay loosely on the ground with one arm outstretched. His eyes were shut. Admiral had fallen solidly, back downwards, across Bill's unprotected abdomen, and he was rolling backwards and forwards in a frantic effort to stand up again.

I had a brief impression that something lay beneath them. Something incongruous, which ought not to be there. But I was going too fast to see properly.

As my horse pressed on away from the fence, I felt as sick as if I'd been kicked in the stomach myself. There had been a quality about that fall which put it straight into the killing class.

I looked over my shoulder. Admiral succeeded in getting to his feet and cantered off loose, and the attendants stepped forward and bent over Bill, who still lay motionless on the ground. I turned back to attend to the race. I had been left in front and I ought to stay there. At the side of the course a black-suited, white-sashed First-Aid man was running towards and past me.

He had been standing at the fence I was now approaching, and was on his way to help Bill.

I booted my horse into the next three fences, but my heart was no longer in it, and when I emerged as the winner into the full view of the crowded stands, the mixed gasp and groan which greeted me seemed an apt enough welcome. I passed the winning post, patted my mount's neck, and looked at the stands. Most heads were still turned towards the last fence, searching the impenetrable mist for Admiral, the odds-on certainty who had lost his first race for two years.

Even the pleasant middle-aged woman whose horse I was riding met me with the question 'What happened to Admiral?'

'He fell,' I said.

'How lucky,' said Mrs Mervyn, laughing happily.

She took hold of the bridle and led her horse into the winner's unsaddling enclosure. I slid off and undid the girth buckles with fingers clumsy from shock. She patted the horse and chattered on about how delighted she was to have won, and how unexpected it was, and how fortunate that Admiral had tripped up for a change, though a great pity in another way, of course.

I nodded and smiled at her and didn't answer, because what I would have said would have been savage and unkind. Let her enjoy her win, I thought. They come seldom enough. And Bill might, after all, be all right.

I tugged the saddle off the horse and, leaving a beaming Mrs Mervyn receiving congratulations from all around, pressed through the crowd into the weighing room. I sat on the scales, was passed as correct, walked into the changing room, and put my gear down on the bench.

Clem, the racecourse valet who looked after my stuff, came over. He was a small elderly man, very spry and tidy, with a weatherbeaten face and wrists whose tendons stood out like tight strung cords.

He picked up my saddle and ran his hand caressingly over the leather. It was a habit he had grown into, I imagined, from long years of caring for fine-grained skins. He stroked a saddle as another man would a pretty girl's cheek, savouring the suppleness, the bloom.

'Well done, sir,' he said; but he didn't look overjoyed.

I didn't want to be congratulated. I said abruptly, 'Admiral should have won.'

'Did he fall?' asked Clem anxiously.

'Yes,' I said. I couldn't understand it, thinking about it.

'Is Major Davidson all right, sir?' asked Clem. He valeted Bill too and, I knew, looked upon him as a sort of minor god.

'I don't know,' I said. But the hard saddle-tree had hit him plumb in the belly with the weight of a big horse falling at thirty miles an hour behind it. What chance has he got, poor beggar, I thought.

I shrugged my arms into my sheepskin coat and went

along to the First-Aid room. Bill's wife, Scilla, was standing outside the door there, pale and shaking and doing her best not to be frightened. Her small neat figure was dressed gaily in scarlet, and a mink hat sat provocatively on top of her cloudy dark curls. They were clothes for success, not sorrow.

'Alan,' she said, with relief, when she saw me. 'The doctor's looking at him and asked me to wait here. What do you think? Is he bad?' She was pleading, and I hadn't much comfort to give her. I put my arm round her shoulders.

She asked me if I had seen Bill fall, and I told her he had dived on to his head and might be slightly concussed.

The door opened, and a tall slim well-groomed man came out. The doctor.

'Are you Mrs Davidson?' he said to Scilla. She nodded.

'I'm afraid your husband will have to go along to the hospital,' he said. 'It wouldn't be sensible to send him home without an X-ray.' He smiled reassuringly, and I felt some of the tension go out of Scilla's body.

'Can I go in and see him?' she said.

The doctor hesitated. 'Yes,' he said finally, 'but he's almost unconscious. He had a bit of a bang on the head. Don't try to wake him.'

When I started to follow Scilla into the First-Aid room the doctor put his hand on my arm to stop me.

'You're Mr York, aren't you?' he asked. He had given me a regulation check after an easy fall I'd had the day before.

'Yes.'

'Do you know these people well?'

'Yes. I live with them most of the time.'

The doctor closed his lips, tight, thinking. Then he said, 'It's not good. The concussion's not much, but he's bleeding internally, possibly from a ruptured spleen. I've telephoned the hospital to take him in as an emergency case as soon as we can get him there.'

As he spoke, one of the racecourse ambulances backed up towards us. The men jumped out, opened the rear doors, took out a big stretcher and carried it into the First-Aid room. The doctor went in after them. Soon they all reappeared with Bill on the stretcher. Scilla followed, the anxiety plain on her face, deep and well-founded.

Bill's firm brown humorous face now lolled flaccid, bluish-white, and covered with fine beads of sweat. He was gasping slightly through his open mouth, and his hands were restlessly pulling at the blanket which covered him. He was still wearing his green and red checked racing colours, the most ominous sign of all.

Scilla said to me, 'I'm going with him in the ambulance. Can you come?'

'I've a ride in the last race,' I said. 'I'll come along to

the hospital straight after that. Don't worry, he'll be all right.' But I didn't believe it, and nor did she.

After they had gone I walked along beside the weighing room building and down through the car park until I came to the bank of the river. Swollen from the recently melted snow, the Thames was flowing fast, sandy brown and grey with froths of white. The water swirled out of a mist a hundred yards to my right, churned round the bend where I stood and disappeared again into the fog. Troubled, confused, not seeing a clear course ahead. Just like me.

For there was something wrong about Bill's accident.

Back in Bulawayo where I got my schooling, the mathematics master spent hours (too many, I thought in my youth) teaching us to draw correct inferences from a few known facts. But deduction was his hobby as well as his job, and occasionally we had been able to side-track him from problems of geometry or algebra to those of Sherlock Holmes. He produced class after class of boys keenly observant of well-worn toe-caps on charwomen and vicars and calluses on the finger tips of harpists; and the mathematics standard of the school was exceptionally high.

Now, thousands of miles and seven years away from the sunbaked schoolroom, standing in an English fog and growing very cold, I remembered my master and took out my facts, and had a look at them.

Known facts . . . Admiral, a superb jumper, had

fallen abruptly in full flight for no apparent reason. The racecourse attendant had walked across the course behind the fence as Bill and I rode towards it, but this was not at all unusual. And as I had cleared the fence, and while I was looking down at Bill, somewhere on the edge of my vision there had been a dull damp gleam from something grey and metallic. I thought about these things for a long time.

The inference was there all right, but unbelievable. I had to find out if it was the correct one.

I went back into the weighing room to collect my kit and weigh out for the last race, but as I packed the flat lead pieces into my weight cloth to bring my weight up to that set by the handicapper, the loudspeakers were turned on and it was announced that owing to the thickening fog the last race had been abandoned.

There was a rush then in the changing room and the tea and fruit-cake disappeared at a quickened tempo. It was a long time since breakfast, and I stuffed a couple of beef sandwiches into my mouth while I changed. I arranged with Clem for my kit to go to Plumpton, where I was due to ride four days later, and set off on an uninviting walk. I wanted to have a close look at the place where Bill had fallen.

It is a long way on foot from the stands to the far end of Maidenhead racecourse, and by the time I got there my shoes, socks, and trouser legs were wet through from the long sodden grass. It was very cold, very foggy. There was no one about.

I reached the fence, the harmless, softish, easy-to-jump fence, made of black birch twigs standing upright. Three feet thick at the bottom slanting to half that size at the top, four feet six inches tall, about ten yards wide. Ordinary, easy.

I looked carefully along the landing side of the fence. There was nothing unusual. Round I went to the take-off side. Nothing. I poked around the wing which guides the horses into the fence, the one on the inside of the course, the side Bill had been when he fell. Still nothing.

It was down underneath the wing on the outside of the course that I found what I was looking for. There it lay in the long grass, half hidden, beaded with drops of mist, coiled and deadly.

Wire.

There was a good deal of it, a pale silver grey, wound into a ring about a foot across, and weighted down with a piece of wood. One end of it led up the main side post of the wing and was fastened round it two feet above the level of the top of the birch. Fastened, I saw, very securely indeed. I could not untwist it with my fingers.

I went back to the inside wing and had a look at the post. Two feet above the fence there was a groove in the wood. This post had once been painted white, and the mark showed clearly.

It was clear to me that only one person could have

fixed the wire in place. The attendant. The man whom I myself had seen walk across from one side of the course to the other. The man, I thought bitterly, whom I had left to *help* Bill.

In a three mile 'chase at Maidenhead one rode twice round the course. On the first circuit there had been no trouble at this fence. Nine horses had jumped it safely, with Admiral lying third and biding his time, and me riding alongside telling Bill I didn't think much of the English climate.

Second time round, Admiral was lengths out in front. As soon as the attendant had seen him land over the fence before this one, he must have walked over holding the free end of the wire and wound it round the opposite post so that it stretched there taut in the air, almost invisible, two feet above the birch. At that height it would catch the high-leaping Admiral straight across the shoulders.

The callousness of it awoke a slow deep anger which, though I did not then know it, was to remain with me as a spur for many weeks to come.

Whether the horse had snapped the wire when he hit it, or pulled it off the post, I could not be sure. But as I could find no separate pieces, and the coil by the outer wing was all one length, I thought it likely that the falling horse had jerked the less secure end down with him. None of the seven horses following me had been brought down. Like me, they must have jumped clear over the remains of the trap.

Unless the attendant was a lunatic, which could by no means be ruled out, it was a deliberate attack on a particular horse and rider. Bill on Admiral had normally reached the front by this stage in a race, often having opened up a lead of twenty lengths, and his red and green colours, even on a misty day, were easy to see.

At this point, greatly disturbed, I began to walk back. It was already growing dark. I had been longer at the fence than I had realized, and when I at length reached the weighing room, intending to tell the Clerk of the Course about the wire, I found everyone except the caretaker had gone.

The caretaker, who was old and bad-tempered, and incessantly sucking his teeth, told me he did not know where the Clerk of the Course could be found. He said the racecourse manager had driven off towards the town five minutes earlier. He did not know where the manager had been going, nor when he would be back; and with a grumbling tale that he had five separate stoves besides the central boiler to see to, and that the fog was bad for his bronchitis, the caretaker shuffled purposefully off towards the dim murky bulk of the grandstand.

Undecided, I watched him go. I ought, I knew, to tell someone in authority about the wire. But who? The

Stewards who had been at the meeting were all on their way home, creeping wearily through the fog, unreachable. The manager was gone; the Clerk of the Course's office, I discovered, was locked. It would take me a long time to locate any of them, persuade them to return to the racecourse and get them to drive down the course over the rough ground in the dark; and after that there would be discussion, repetition, statements. It would be hours before I could get away.

Meanwhile Bill was fighting for his life in Maidenhead hospital, and I wanted profoundly to know if he were winning. Scilla faced racking hours of anxiety and I had promised to be with her as soon as I could. Already I had delayed too long. The wire, fogbound and firmly twisted round the post, would keep until tomorrow, I thought; but Bill might not.

Bill's Jaguar was alone in the car park. I climbed in, switched on the side lights and the fog lights and drove off. I turned left at the gates, went gingerly along the road for two miles, turned left again over the river, twisted through Maidenhead's one way streets, and finally arrived at the hospital.

There was no sign of Scilla in the brightly lit busy hall. I asked the porter.

'Mrs Davidson? Husband a jockey? That's right, she's down there in the waiting room. Fourth door on the left.'

I found her. Her dark eyes looked enormous,

shadowed with grey smudges beneath them. All other colour had gone from her sad strained face, and she had taken off her frivolous hat.

'How is he?' I asked.

'I don't know. They just tell me not to worry.' She was very close to tears.

I sat down beside her and held her hand.

'You're a comfort, Alan,' she said.

Presently the door opened and a fair young doctor came in, stethoscope dangling.

'Mrs Davidson, I think . . .' he paused, 'I think you should come and sit with your husband.'

'How is he?'

'Not . . . very well. We are doing all we can.' Turning to me he said, 'Are you a relative?'

'A friend. I am going to drive Mrs Davidson home.'

'I see,' he said. 'Will you wait, or come back for her? Later this evening.' There was meaning in his careful voice, his neutral words. I looked closely into his face, and I knew that Bill was dying.

'I'll wait.'

'Good.'

I waited for four hours, getting to know intimately the pattern of the curtains and the cracks in the brown linoleum. Mostly, I thought about wire.

At last a nurse came, serious, young, pretty.

'I am so sorry . . . Major Davidson is dead.'

Mrs Davidson would like me to go and see him, she

said, if I would follow her. She took me down the long corridors, and into a white room, not very big, where Scilla sat beside the single bed.

Scilla looked up at me. She couldn't speak.

Bill lay there, grey and quiet, finished. The best friend a man could wish for.

CHAPTER TWO

Early next morning I drove Scilla, worn out from the vigil she had insisted on keeping all night beside Bill's body, and heavily drugged now with sedatives, home to the Cotswolds. The children came out and met her on the doorstep, their three faces solemn and round-eyed. Behind them stood Joan, the briskly competent girl who looked after them, and to whom I had telephoned the news the evening before.

There on the step Scilla sat down and wept. The children knelt and sat down beside her, putting their arms round her, doing their best to comfort a grief they could only dimly understand.

Presently Scilla went upstairs to bed. I drew the curtains for her and tucked her in, and kissed her cheek. She was exhausted and very sleepy, and I hoped it would be many hours before she woke again.

I went along to my own room and changed my clothes. Downstairs I found Joan putting coffee, bacon and eggs, and hot rolls for me on the kitchen table. I gave the children the chocolate bars I had bought for them the previous morning (how very long ago it seemed) and they sat with me, munching, while I ate my breakfast. Joan poured herself some coffee.

'Alan?' said William. He was five, the youngest, and he would never go on speaking until you said 'Yes?' to show you were listening.

'Yes?' I said.

'What happened to Daddy?'

So I told them about it, all of it except the wire.

They were unusually silent for a while. Then Henry, just eight, asked calmly, 'Is he going to be buried or burnt?'

Before I could answer, he and his elder sister Polly launched into a heated and astonishingly well-informed discussion about the respective merits of burial or cremation. I was horrified, but relieved too, and Joan, catching my eye, was hard put to it not to laugh.

The innocent toughness of their conversation started me on my way back to Maidenhead in a more cheerful frame of mind. I put Bill's car in the garage and set off in my own little dark blue Lotus. The fog had completely gone, but I drove slowly (for me), working out what was best to do.

First I called at the hospital. I collected Bill's clothes, signed forms, made arrangements. There was to be a routine post mortem examination the next day.

It was Sunday. I drove to the racecourse, but the

gates were locked. Back in the town the Clerk of the Course's office was shut and empty. I telephoned his home, but there was no answer.

After some hesitation I rang up the Senior Steward of the National Hunt Committee, going straight to the top steeplechase authority. Sir Creswell Stampe's butler said he would see if Sir Creswell was available. I said it was very important that I should speak with him. Presently he came on the line.

'I certainly hope what you have to say *is* very important, Mr York. I am in the middle of luncheon with my guests.'

'Have you heard, sir, that Major Davidson died yesterday evening?'

'Yes, I'm very sorry about it, very sorry indeed.' He waited. I took a deep breath.

'His fall wasn't an accident,' I said.

'What do you mean?'

'Major Davidson's horse was brought down by wire,' I said.

I told him about my search at the fence, and what I had found there.

'You have let Mr Dace know about this?' he asked. Mr Dace was the Clerk of the Course.

I explained that I had been unable to find him.

'So you rang me. I see.' He paused. 'Well, Mr York, if you are right, this is too serious to be dealt with entirely by the National Hunt Committee. I think you should inform the police in Maidenhead without delay. Let me know this evening, without fail, what is happening. I will try to get in touch with Mr Dace.'

I put down the receiver. The buck had been passed, I thought. I could imagine the Stampe roast beef congealing on the plate while Sir Creswell set the wires humming.

The police station in the deserted Sunday street was dark, dusty-looking and uninviting. I went in. There were three desks behind the counter, and at one of them sat a young constable reading a newspaper of the juicier sort. Keeping up with his crime, I reflected.

'Can I help you, sir?' he said, getting up.

'Is there someone here?' I asked. 'I mean, someone senior? It's about a . . . a death.'

'Just a minute, sir.' He went out of a door at the back, and returned to say, 'Will you come in here, please?'

He stood aside to let me into a little inner office, and shut the door behind me.

The man who rose to his feet was small for a policeman, thick-set, dark, and in his late thirties. He looked more of a fighter than a thinker, but I found later that his brain matched his physique. His desk was littered with papers and heavy-looking law books. The gas fire had made a comfortable warm fug, and his ashtray was overflowing. He, too, was spending his Sunday afternoon reading up crime.

'Good afternoon. I am Inspector Lodge,' he said. He

gestured to a chair facing his desk, asking me to sit down. He sat down again himself, and began to shape his papers into neat piles.

'You have come about a death?' My own words, repeated, sounded foolish, but his tone was matter-of-fact.

'It's about a Major Davidson . . .' I began.

'Oh yes. We had a report. He died in the hospital last night after a fall at the races.' He waited politely for me to go on.

'That fall was engineered,' I said bluntly.

Inspector Lodge looked at me steadily, then drew a sheet of paper out of a drawer, unscrewed his fountain pen, and wrote, I could see, the date and the time. A methodical man.

'I think we had better start at the beginning,' he said. 'What is your name?'

'Alan York.'

'Age?'

'Twenty-four.'

'Address?'

I gave Davidson's address, explaining whose it was, and that I lived there a good deal.

'Where is your own home?'

'In Southern Rhodesia,' I said. 'On a cattle station near a village called Induna, about fifteen miles from Bulawayo.'

'Occupation?'

'I represent my father in his London office.'

'And your father's business?'

'The Bailey York Trading Company.'

'What do you trade in?' asked Lodge.

'Copper, lead, cattle. Anything and everything. We're transporters mainly,' I said.

He wrote it all down, in quick distinctive script.

'Now then,' he put down the pen, 'what is all this about?'

'I don't know what it's about,' I said, 'but this is what happened.' I told him the whole thing. He listened without interrupting, then he said, 'What made you even begin to suspect that this was not a normal fall?'

'Admiral is the safest jumper there is. He's sure-footed, like a cat. He doesn't make mistakes.'

But I could see from his politely surprised expression that he knew little, if anything, about steeplechasing, and thought that one horse was as likely to fall as another.

I tried again. 'Admiral is brilliant over fences. He would never fall like that, going into an easy fence in his own time, not being pressed. He took off perfectly. I saw him. That fall was unnatural. It looked to me as though something had been used to bring him down. I thought it might be wire, and I went back to look and it was. That's all.'

'Hm. Was the horse likely to win?' asked Lodge.

'Certain,' I said.

'And who did win?'

'I did,' I said.

Lodge paused, and bit the end of his pen.

'How do the racecourse attendants get their jobs?' he asked.

'I don't really know. They are casual staff, taken on for the meeting, I think,' I said.

'Why would a racecourse attendant wish to harm Major Davidson?' He said this naïvely, and I looked at him sharply.

'Do you think I have made it all up?' I asked.

'No.' He sighed. 'I suppose I don't. Perhaps I should have said, how difficult would it be for someone who wished to harm Major Davidson to get taken on as a racecourse attendant?'

'Easy,' I said.

'We'll have to find out.' He reflected. 'It's a very chancy way to murder a man.'

'Whoever planned it can't have meant to kill him,' I said flatly.

'Why not?'

'Because it was so unlikely that he would die. I should think it was simply meant to stop him winning.'

'Why was such a fall unlikely to result in death?' said Lodge. 'It sounds highly dangerous to me.'

I said: 'It could have been meant to injure him, I suppose. Usually when a horse is going fast and hits a fence hard when you're not expecting it, you get catapulted out of the saddle. You fly through the air and hit the ground way out in front of where your horse falls. That may do a lot of damage, but it doesn't often kill. But Bill Davidson wasn't flung off forwards. His toe may have stuck in his stirrup, though that's not very likely. Perhaps the wire caught round his leg and pulled him back. Anyway, he fell straight down and his horse crashed on top of him. Even then it was sheer bad luck that the saddle tree hit him in the stomach. You couldn't even hope to kill a man like that on purpose.'

'I see. You seem to have given it some thought.'

'Yes.' The pattern of the hospital waiting room curtains, the brown linoleum, came back into my mind in association.

'Can you think of anyone who might wish to hurt Major Davidson?' asked Lodge.

'No,' I said. 'He was very well liked.'

Lodge got up and stretched. 'We'll go and have a look at your wire,' he said. He put his head out into the big office. 'Wright, go and see if Hawkins is there, and tell him I want a car if there's one available.'

There was a car. Hawkins (I presumed) drove; I sat in the back with Lodge. The main gates of the racecourse were still locked, but there were ways and means, I found. A police key opened another, inconspicuous gate in the wooden fence.

'In case of fire,' said Lodge, seeing my sideways look.

There was no one about in the racecourse buildings:

the manager was out. Hawkins drove over the course into the centre and headed down towards the farthest fence. We bumped a good deal on the uneven ground. The car drew up just short of the inside wing, and Lodge and I climbed out.

I led the way past the fence to the outer wing.

'The wire is over here,' I said.

But I was wrong.

There was the post, the wing, the long grass, the birch fence. And no coil of wire.

'Are you sure this is the right fence?' said Lodge.

'Yes,' I said. We stood looking at the course set out in front of us. We were at the very far end, the stands a blurred massive block in the distance. The fence by which we stood was alone on a short straight between two curves, and the nearest fence to us was three hundred yards to the left, round a shallow bend.

'You jump that fence,' I said, pointing away to it. 'Then there's quite a long run, as you can see, to this one.' I patted the fence beside us. 'Then twenty yards after we land over this one there is that sharpish left turn into the straight. The next fence is some way up the straight, to allow the horses to balance themselves properly after coming round the bend, before they have to jump. It's a good course.'

'You couldn't have made a mistake in the mist?'

'No. This is the fence,' I said.

Lodge sighed. 'Well, we'll take a closer look.'

But all there was to be seen was a shallow groove on the once white inner post, and a deeper groove on the outer post, where the wire had bitten into the wood. Both grooves needed looking for and would ordinarily have been unnoticed. Both were at the same level, six feet six inches, from the ground.

'Very inconclusive indeed,' said Lodge.

We went back to Maidenhead in silence. Glum and feeling foolish, I knew now that even though I could reach no one in authority, I should have found someone, anyone, even the caretaker, the day before, to go back to the fence with me, after I had found the wire, to see it in its place. A witness who had seen wire fastened to a fence, even though it would have been dark and foggy, even though perhaps he could not swear at which fence he had seen it, would definitely have been better than no witness at all. I tried to console myself with the possibility that the attendant had been returning to the fence with his wire clippers at the same time that I was walking back to the stands, and that even if I had returned at once with a witness, if would already have been too late.

From Maidenhead police station I called Sir Creswell Stampe. I had parted him this time, he said, from his toasted muffins. The news that the wire had disappeared didn't please him either.

'You should have got someone else to see it at once. Photographed it. Removed it. We can't proceed without evidence. I can't think why you didn't have sense enough to act more quickly, either. You have been very irresponsible, Mr York.' And with these few kind words he put down the receiver.

Depressed, I drove home.

I put my head quietly round Scilla's door. Her room was dark, but I could hear her even breathing. She was still sound asleep.

Downstairs Joan and the children were sitting on the floor in front of the welcoming log fire playing poker. I had introduced them to the game one rainy day when the children were tired of snap and rummy and had been behaving very badly, quarrelling and shouting and raising tempers all round. Poker, the hitherto mysterious game of the cowboys in Westerns, had worked a miracle.

Henry developed in a few weeks into the sort of player you wouldn't sit down with twice without careful thought. His razor-sharp mathematical mind knew the odds to a fraction against any particular card turning up; his visual memory was formidable; and his air of slight bewilderment, calculated to be misleading, led many an unsuspecting adult straight into his traps. I admired Henry. He could out-bluff an angel.

Polly played well enough for me to be sure she would never lose continually in ordinary company, and even William knew a running flush from a full house.

They had been at it for some time. Henry's pile of poker chips was, as usual, three times as big as anyone else's.

Polly said, 'Henry won all the chips a little while ago, so we had to share them out and start all over again.'

Henry grinned. Cards were an open book to him and he couldn't help reading.

I took ten of Henry's chips and sat in with them. Joan dealt. She gave me a pair of fives and I drew another one. Henry discarded and drew two cards only, and looked satisfied.

The others threw in during the first two rounds. Then I boldly advanced two more chips to join the two on the table. 'Raise you two, Henry,' I said.

Henry glanced at me to make sure I was looking at him, then made a great show of indecision, drumming his fingers on the table and sighing. Knowing his habit of bluffing, I suspected he had a whipper of a hand and was scheming how to get me to disgorge the largest possible number of chips.

'Raise you one,' he said at last.

I was just about to put another two chips firmly out, but I stopped and said, 'Oh no you don't, Henry. Not this time,' and I threw in my hand. I pushed the four chips across to him. 'This time you get four and no more.'

'What did you have, Alan?' Polly turned my cards over, showing the three fives.

Henry grinned. He made no attempt to stop Polly looking at his cards too. He had a pair of Kings. Just one pair.

'Got you that time, Alan,' he said happily.

William and Polly groaned heavily.

We played until I had won back my reputation and a respectable number of Henry's chips. Then it was the children's bedtime, and I went up to see Scilla.

She was awake, lying in the dark.

'Come in, Alan.'

I went over and switched on the bedside light. The first shock was over. She looked calm, peaceful.

'Hungry?' I asked. She had not eaten since lunch the day before.

'Do you know, Alan, I am,' she said as if surprised.

I went downstairs and with Joan rustled up some supper. I carried the tray up and ate with Scilla. Sitting propped up with pillows, alone in the big bed, she began to tell me about how she had met Bill, the things they had done together, the fun they had had. Her eyes shone with remembered happiness. She talked for a long time, all about Bill, and I did not stop her until her lips began to tremble. Then I told her about Henry and his pair of Kings, and she smiled and grew calm again.

I wanted very much to ask her whether Bill had been in any trouble or had been threatened in any way during the last few weeks, but it wasn't the right time to do it. So I got her to take another of the sedatives the hospital had given me for her, turned off her light, and said good night.

As I undressed in my own room the tiredness hit me. I had been awake for over forty hours, few of which could be called restful. I flopped into bed. It was one of those times when the act of falling asleep is a conscious, delicious luxury.

Half an hour later Joan shook me awake again. She was in her dressing-gown.

'Alan, wake up for goodness' sake. I've been knocking on your door for ages.'

'What's the matter?'

'You're wanted on the telephone. Personal call,' she said.

'Oh no,' I groaned. It felt like the middle of the night. I looked at my watch. Eleven o'clock.

I staggered downstairs, eyes bleary with sleep.

'Hello?'

'Mr Alan York?'

'Yes.'

'Hold on, please.' Some clicks on the line. I yawned.

'Mr York? I have a message for you from Inspector Lodge, Maidenhead police. He would like you to come here to the police station tomorrow afternoon, at four o'clock.'

'I'll be there,' I said. I rang off, went back to bed, and slept and slept.

*

Lodge was waiting for me. He rose, shook hands, pointed to a chair. I sat down. The desk was clear now of everything except a neat, quarto-sized folder placed squarely in front of him. Slightly behind me, at a small table in the corner, sat a constable in uniform, pencil in hand, shorthand notebook at the ready.

'I have some statements here,' Lodge tapped the file, 'which I will tell you about. Then I have some questions to ask.' He opened the file and took out two sheets of paper clipped together.

'This is a statement from Mr J. L. Dace, Clerk of the Course of Maidenhead racecourse. In it he says nine of the attendants, the men who stand by to make temporary repairs to the fences during the races, are regularly employed in that capacity. Three of them were new this meeting.'

Lodge laid down this statement, and took out the next.

'This is a statement from George Watkins, one of the regular attendants. He says they draw lots among themselves to decide which fence each of them shall stand by. There are two at some fences. On Friday they drew lots as usual, but on Saturday one of the new men volunteered to go down to the farthest fence. None of them likes having to go right down there, Watkins says, because it is too far to walk back between races to "have a bit" on a horse. So they were glad enough to let the stranger take that fence, and they drew lots for the rest.'

'What did this attendant look like?' I said.

'You saw him yourself,' said Lodge.

'No, not really,' I said. 'All he was to me was a man. I didn't look at him. There's at least one attendant at every fence. I wouldn't know any of them again.'

'Watkins says he thinks he'd know the man again, but he can't describe him. Ordinary, he says. Not tall, not short. Middle-aged, he thinks. Wore a cap, old grey suit, loose mackintosh.'

'They all do,' I said gloomily.

Lodge said, 'He gave his name as Thomas Cook. Said he was out of work, had a job to go to next week and was filling in time. Very plausible, nothing odd about him at all, Watkins says. He spoke like a Londoner though, not with a Berkshire accent.'

Lodge laid the paper down, and took out another.

'This is a statement from John Russell of the St John Ambulance Brigade. He says he was standing beside the first fence in the straight watching the horses go round the bottom of the course. Because of the mist he says he could see only three fences: the one he was standing beside, the next fence up the straight, and the farthest fence, where Major Davidson fell. The fence before that, which was opposite him on the far side of the course, was an indistinct blur.

'He saw Major Davidson race out of the mist after

he had jumped that fence. Then he saw him fall at the next. Major Davidson did not reappear, though his horse got up and galloped off riderless. Russell began to walk towards the fence where he had seen Major Davidson fall; then when you, Mr York, passed him looking over your shoulder, he began to run. He found Major Davidson lying on the ground.'

'Did he see the wire?' I asked eagerly.

'No. I asked him if he had seen anything at all unusual. I didn't mention wire specifically. He said there was nothing.'

'Didn't he see the attendant roll up the wire while he was running towards him?'

'I asked him if he could see either Major Davidson or the attendant as he ran towards them. He says that owing to the sharp bend and the rails round it he could not see them until he was quite close. I gather he ran round the course instead of cutting across the corner through the long rough grass because it was too wet.'

'I see,' I said despondently. 'And what was the attendant doing when he got there?'

'Standing beside Major Davidson looking down at him. He says the attendant looked frightened. This surprised Russell, because although he was knocked out Major Davidson did not appear to him to be badly injured. He waved his white flag, the next First-Aid man saw it and waved his, and the message was thus relayed through the fog all the way up the course to the ambulance.'

'What did the attendant do then?'

'Nothing particular. He stayed beside the fence after the ambulance had taken Major Davidson away, and Russell says he was there until the abandonment of the last race was announced.'

Clutching at straws, I said, 'Did he go back with the other attendants and collect his pay?'

Lodge looked at me with interest. 'No,' he said, 'he didn't.'

He took out another paper.

'This statement is from Peter Smith, head travelling lad for the Gregory stables, where Admiral is trained. He says that after Admiral got loose at Maidenhead he tried to jump a blackthorn hedge. He stuck in it and was caught beside it, scared and bleeding. There are cuts and scratches all over the horse's shoulders, chest and forelegs.' He looked up. 'If the wire left any mark on him at all, it is impossible to distinguish it now.'

'You have been thorough,' I said, 'and quick.'

'Yes. We were lucky, for once, to find everyone we wanted without delay.'

There was only one paper left. Lodge picked it up, spoke slowly.

'This is the report of the post mortem on Major Davidson. Cause of death with multiple internal injuries. Liver and spleen were both ruptured.'

He sat back in his chair and looked at his hands.

'Now, Mr York, I have been directed to ask you some questions which . . .' his dark eyes came up to mine suddenly, '. . . which I do not think you will like. Just answer them.' His half smile was friendly.

'Fire away,' I said.

'Are you in love with Mrs Davidson?'

I sat up straight, surprised.

'No,' I said.

'But you live with her?'

'I live with the whole family,' I said.

'Why?'

'I have no home in England. When I first got to know Bill Davidson he asked me to his house for a week-end. I liked it there, and I suppose they liked me. Anyway, they asked me often. Gradually the week-ends got longer and longer, until Bill and Scilla suggested I should make their house my headquarters. I spend a night or two every week in London.'

'How long have you lived at the Davidsons?' asked Lodge.

'About seven months.'

'Were your relations with Major Davidson friendly?'

'Yes, very.'

'And with Mrs Davidson?'

'Yes.'

'But you do not love her?'

'I am extremely fond of her. As an elder sister,' I

said, sitting tight on my anger. 'She is ten years older than I am.'

Lodge's expression said quite plainly that age had nothing to do with it. I was aware, just then, that the constable in the corner was writing down my replies.

I relaxed. I said, tranquilly, 'She was very much in love with her husband, and he with her.'

Lodge's mouth twitched at the corners. He looked, of all things, amused. Then he began again.

'I understand,' he said, 'that Major Davidson was the leading amateur steeplechase jockey in this country?'

'Yes.'

'And you yourself finished second to him, a year ago, after your first season's racing in England?'

I stared at him. I said, 'For someone who hardly knew steeplechasing existed twenty-four hours ago, you've wasted no time.'

'Were you second to Major Davidson on the amateur riders' list last year? And were you not likely to be second to him again? Is it not also likely that now, in his absence, you will head the list?'

'Yes, yes, and I hope so,' I said. The accusation was as plain as could be, but I was not going to rush unasked into protestations of my innocence. I waited. If he wanted the suggestion made that I had sought to injure or kill Bill in order to acquire either his wife or his racing prestige, or both, Lodge would have to make it himself.

But he didn't. A full minute ticked by, during which I sat still. Finally Lodge grinned.

'Well, I think that's all, then, Mr York. The information you gave us yesterday and your answers today will be typed together as one statement, and I shall be glad if you will read and sign it.'

The policeman with the notebook stood up and walked into the outer office. Lodge said, 'The coroner's inquest on Major Davidson is to be held on Thursday. You will be needed as a witness; and Mrs Davidson, too, for evidence of identification. We'll be getting in touch with her.'

He asked me questions about steeplechasing, ordinary conversational questions, until the statement was ready. I read it carefully and signed it. It was accurate and perfectly fair. I could imagine these pages joining the others in Lodge's tidy file. How fat would it grow before he found the accidental murderer of Bill Davidson.

If he ever did.

He stood up and held out his hand, and I shook it. I liked him. I wondered who had 'directed' him to find out if I might have arranged the crime I had myself reported.

CHAPTER THREE

I rode at Plumpton two days later.

The police had been very discreet in their enquiries, and Sir Creswell also, for there was no speculation in the weighing room about Bill's death. The grapevine was silent.

I plunged into the bustle of a normal racing day, the minor frustration of a lot of jockeys changing in a smallish space, the unprintable jokes, the laughter, the cluster of cold half-undressed men round the red-hot coke stove.

Clem gave me my clean breeches, some pants, a thin fawn under-jersey, a fresh white stock for my neck, and a pair of nylon stockings. I stripped and put on the racing things. On top of the nylon stockings (laddered, as always) my soft, light, close-fitting racing boots slid on easily. Clem handed me my racing colours, the thick woollen sweater of coffee and cream checks, and the brown satin cap. He tied my stock for me. I pulled on the jersey, and slid the cap on to my crash helmet, ready to put on later.

Clem said, 'Only the one ride today, sir?' He pulled two thick rubber bands from his large apron pocket and slipped them over my wrists. They were to anchor the sleeves of my jersey and prevent the wind blowing them up my arms.

'Yes,' I said. 'So far, anyway.' I was always hopeful.

'Will you be wanting to borrow a light saddle? The weight's near your limit, I should think.'

'No,' I said, 'I'd rather use my own saddle if I can. I'll get on the trial scales with that first, and see how much overweight I am.'

'Right you are, sir.'

I went over with Clem, picked up my six pound racing saddle with its girth and stirrup leathers wound round it, and weighed myself with it, my crash helmet perched temporarily and insecurely on the back of my head. The total came to ten stone, nine pounds, which was four pounds more than the handicapper thought my horse deserved.

Clem took back the saddle, and I put my helmet on the bench again.

'I'll think I'll carry the overweight, Clem,' I said.

'Right.' He hurried off to attend to someone else.

I could have got down to the proper weight – just – by using a three pound 'postage stamp' saddle and changing into silk colours and 'paper' boots.

But as I was riding my own horse I could please myself, and he was an angular animal whose ribs would probably have been rubbed raw by too small a saddle.

He, Forlorn Hope, my newest acquisition, was a strongly built brown gelding only five years old. He looked as though he would develop into a 'chaser in a year or two, but meanwhile I was riding him in novice hurdle races to give him some sorely needed experience.

His unreliability as a jumper had made Scilla, the evening before, beg me not to ride him at Plumpton, a course full of snares for the unwary.

Unbearably strung up, and facing her loss for the first time without the help of drugs, she was angry and pleading by turns.

'Don't, Alan. Not a novice hurdle at Plumpton. You know your wretched Forlorn Hope isn't safe. You haven't got to do it, so why do you?'

'I like it.'

'There never was a horse more aptly named,' she said, miserably.

'He'll learn,' I said. 'But not if I don't give him the opportunity.'

'Put someone else up. Please.'

'There isn't any point in having a horse if I don't ride it myself. That's really why I came to England at all, to race. You know that.'

'You'll be killed, like Bill.' She began to cry, helplessly, worn out. I tried to reason with her.

'No, I won't. If Bill had been killed in a motor crash you wouldn't expect me to stop driving. Steeplechasing's just as safe and unsafe as motoring.' I paused, but she went on crying. 'There are thousands more people killed on the roads than on the race-track,' I said.

At this outrageous statement she recovered enough to point out acidly the difference in the number of people engaged in the two pursuits.

'Very few people are killed by steeplechasing,' I tried again.

'Bill was . . .'

'Only about one a year, out of hundreds,' I went on.

'Bill was the second since Christmas.'

'Yes.' I looked at her warily. There were still tears in her eyes.

'Scilla, was Bill in any sort of trouble recently?'

'Why ever do you ask?' She was astounded by my question.

'Was he?'

'Of course not.'

'Not worried about anything?' I persisted.

'No. Did he seem worried to you?'

'No,' I said. It was quite true. Until the moment of his fall Bill had been the same as I had always known him, cheerful, poised, reliable. He had had, and enjoyed, a pretty wife, three attractive children, a grey stone manor house, a considerable fortune and the best hunter 'chaser in England. A happy man. And rack my memory as I would, I could not recall the slightest ruffling of the pattern.

'Then why do you ask?' said Scilla, again.

I told her as gradually, as gently as I could, that Bill's fall had not been an ordinary accident. I told her about the wire and about Lodge's investigations.

She sat like stone, absolutely stunned.

'Oh no,' she said. 'Oh no. Oh no.'

As I stood now outside the weighing room at Plumpton I could still see her stricken face. She had raised no more objections to my racing. What I had told her had driven every other thought out of her head.

A firm hand came down on my shoulder. I knew it well. It belonged to Peter Gregory, racehorse trainer, a burly man nearly six feet tall, running to fat, growing bald, but in his day, I had been told, the toughest man ever to put his foot in a racing stirrup.

'Hello, Alan me lad. I'm glad to see you're here. I've already declared you for your horse in the second race.'

'How is he?' I asked.

'All right. A bit thin, still.' Forlorn Hope had only been in his stable for a month. 'I should give him an "easy", coming up the hill the first time, or he'll blow up before the finish. He needs more time before we can hope for much.'

'OK,' I said.

'Come out and see what the going is like,' said Pete. 'I want to talk to you.' He hitched the strap of his binoculars higher on his shoulder.

We walked down through the gate on to the course and dug our heels experimentally into the turf. They sank in an inch.

'Not bad, considering all the snow that melted into it a fortnight ago,' I said.

'Nice and soft for you to fall on,' said Pete with elementary humour.

We went up the rise to the nearest hurdle. The landing side had a little too much give in it, but we knew the ground at the other end of the course was better drained. It was all right.

Pete said abruptly, 'Did you see Admiral fall at Maidenhead?' He had been in Ireland buying a horse when it happened and had only just returned.

'Yes. I was about ten lengths behind him,' I said, looking down the course, concentrating on the hurdle track.

'Well?'

'Well, what?' I said.

'What happened? Why did he fall?' There was some sort of urgency in his voice, more than one would expect, even in the circumstances. I looked at him. His eyes were grey, unsmiling, intent. Moved by an instinct I didn't understand, I retreated into vagueness.

'He just fell,' I said. 'When I went over the fence he was on the ground with Bill underneath him.'

'Did Admiral meet the fence all wrong, then?' he probed.

'Not as far as I could see. He must have hit the top of it.' This was near enough to the truth.

'There wasn't . . . anything else?' Pete's eyes were fierce, as if they would look into my brain.

'What do you mean?' I avoided the direct answer.

'Nothing.' His anxious expression relaxed. 'If you didn't see anything . . .' We began to walk back. It troubled me that I hadn't told Pete the truth. He had been too searching, too aware. I was certain he was not the man to risk destroying a great horse like Admiral, let alone a friend, but why was he so relieved now he believed I had noticed nothing?

I had just decided to ask him to explain his attitude, and to tell him what had really happened, when he began to speak.

'Have you got a ride in the Amateur 'Chase, Alan?' He was back to normal, bluff and smiling.

'No, I haven't,' I said. 'Pete, look . . .'

But he interrupted. 'I had a horse arrive in my yard five or six days ago, with an engagement in today's Amateur 'Chase. A chestnut. Good sort of animal, I should say. He seems to be fit enough – he's come from a small stable in the West Country – and his new owner is very keen to run him. I tried to ring you this morning about it, but you'd already left.'

'What's his name?' I asked, for all this preamble of Pete's was, I knew, his way of cajoling me into something I might not be too delighted to do.

'Heavens Above.'

'Never heard of him. What's he done?' I asked.

'Well, not much. He's young, of course . . .'

I interrupted. 'What *exactly* has he done?'

Pete sighed and gave in. 'He's only had two runs, both down in Devon last autumn. He didn't fall, but – er – he got rid of his jockey both times. But he jumped well enough over my schooling fences this morning. I don't think you'd have any difficulty getting him round safely, and that's the main thing at this stage.'

'Pete, I don't like to say no, but . . .' I began.

'His owner is so hoping you'll ride him. It's her first horse, and it's running for the first time in her brand new colours. I brought her to the races with me. She's very excited. I said I'd ask you . . .'

'I don't think . . .' I tried again.

'Well, at least meet her,' said Pete.

'If I meet her, you know it'll be far more difficult for me to refuse to ride her horse.'

Pete didn't deny it.

I went on, 'I suppose she's another of your dear old ladies about to go into a nursing home from which she is unlikely to return, and wants a final thrill before she meets her fate?'

This was the sad tale which Peter had used not long before to inveigle me on to a bad horse against my better judgement. And I often saw the old lady at the races afterwards. The nursing home and her fate were still presumably awaiting her.

'This one is not,' said Pete, 'a dear old lady.'

We came to a stop in the paddock, and Pete looked around him and beckoned to someone. Out of the corner of my eye I saw a woman begin to walk towards us. It was already, without unforgivable rudeness, too late to escape. I had time for one heart-felt oath in Pete's ear before I turned to be introduced to the new owner of the jockey-depositing Heavens Above.

'Miss Ellery-Penn, Alan York,' said Pete.

I was lost before she spoke a word. The first thing I said was, 'I'll be glad to ride your horse.'

Pete was laughing openly at me.

She was beautiful. She had clear features, wonderful skin, smiling grey eyes, dark glossy hair falling almost to her shoulders. And she was used to the effect she had on men: but how could she help it?

Pete said, 'Right, then. I'll declare you for the amateurs' – it's the fourth race. I'll give your colours to Clem.' He went off towards the weighing room.

'I am so glad you agreed to ride my horse,' the girl said. Her voice was low-pitched and unhurried. 'He's a birthday present. Rather a problem one, don't you think? My Uncle George, who is a dear fellow but just the slightest bit off the beat, *advertised* in *The Times* for a racehorse. My aunt says he received fifty replies and bought this horse without seeing it because he liked the name. He said it would be more amusing for me to have a horse for my birthday than the conventional string of pearls.'

'Your Uncle George sounds fascinating,' I said.

'But just a little devastating to live with.' She had a trick of lifting the last two or three words in a sentence so that they sounded like a question. As if she had added, 'Don't you agree?' to her remark.

'Do you in fact live with him?' I asked.

'Oh, yes. Parents divorced in the murky past. Scattered to the four winds, and all that.'

'I'm sorry.'

'Waste no sympathy. I can't remember either of them. They abandoned me on Uncle George's doorstep, figuratively speaking, at the tender age of two.'

'Uncle George has done a good job,' I said, looking at her with the frankest admiration.

She accepted this without gaucherie, almost as a matter of course.

'Aunt Deb, actually. She is faintly more on the ball than Uncle George. Absolute pets, the pair of them.'

'Are they here today?' I asked.

'No, they aren't,' said Miss Ellery-Penn. 'Uncle

George remarked that having given me a passport into a new world peopled entirely by brave and charming young men, it would defeat the object if my path were cluttered up with elderly relatives.'

'I am getting fonder of Uncle George every minute,' I said.

Miss Ellery-Penn gave me a heavenly smile which held no promises of any sort.

'Have you seen my horse? Isn't he a duck?' she said.

'I haven't seen him. I'm afraid I didn't know he existed until five minutes ago. How did Uncle George happen to send him to Pete Gregory? Did he pick the stable with a pin?'

She laughed. 'No, I don't think so. He had the stable all planned. He said I could get a Major Davidson to ride for me if the horse went to Mr Gregory's.' She reflected, wrinkling her brow. 'He was quite upset on Monday when he read in the paper that Major Davidson had been killed.'

'Did he know him?' I asked idly, watching the delicious curves at the corners of her red mouth.

'No, I'm sure he didn't know him personally. Probably he knew his father. He seems to know most people's fathers. He just said "Good God, Davidson's dead" in a shocked sort of way and went on eating his toast. But he didn't hear me or Aunt Deb until we had asked him four times for the marmalade!'

'And that was all?'

'Yes. Why do you ask?' said Miss Ellery-Penn, curiously.

'Oh, nothing special,' I said. 'Bill Davidson and I were good friends.'

She nodded. 'I see.' She dismissed the subject. 'Now what do I have to do in my new role as racehorse owner? I don't particularly want to make a frightful boob on my first day. Any comments and instructions from you will be welcome, Mr York.'

'My name is Alan,' I said.

She gave me an appraising look. It told me plainer than words that although she was young she was already experienced at fending off unwelcome attentions and not being rushed into relationships she was not prepared for.

But she finally smiled, and said, 'Mine is Kate.' She bestowed her name like a gift; I was pleased to receive it.

'How much do you know about racing?' I asked.

'Not a thing. Never set foot on the Turf before today.' She gave the capital letter its full value, ironically.

'Do you ride, yourself?'

'Positively not.'

'Perhaps your Uncle George is fond of horses? Perhaps he hunts?' I suggested.

'Uncle George is the most un-addicted man to horses I have ever met. He says one end kicks and the other bites, and as for hunting, he says that he has cosier things to do than chase bushy tailed vermin in the gravest discomfort over waterlogged countryside in the depths of winter.'

I laughed. 'Perhaps he bets. Off the course?' I asked.

'Uncle George has been known to ask, on Cup Final day, what has won the Derby.'

'Then why Heavens Above?'

'Wider horizons for me, Uncle George says. My education has been along the well-tramped lines of boarding school, finishing school, and an over-chaperoned tour of Europe. I needed to get the smell of museums out of my nose, Uncle George said.'

'So he gave you a racehorse for your twenty-first birthday,' I stated matter-of-factly.

'Yes,' she said: then she looked at me sharply. I grinned. I had jumped her defences, that time.

'There's nothing special for you to do as an owner,' I said, 'except to go along to those stalls over there,' I pointed, 'before the fourth race, to see your horse being saddled up. Then you'll go into the parade ring with Pete, and stand around making intelligent remarks about the weather until I arrive and mount and go out for the race.'

'What do I do if he wins?'

'Do you expect him to win?' I asked. I was not sure how much she really knew about her horse.

'Mr Gregory says he won't.'

I was relieved. I did not want her to be disappointed.

'We'll all know much more about him after the race. But if he should come in the first three, he will be unsaddled down there opposite the weighing room. Otherwise, you'll find us up here on the grass.'

It was nearly time for the first race. I took the delectable Miss Ellery-Penn on to the stands and fulfilled Uncle George's design by introducing her to several brave and charming young men. I unfortunately realized that by the time I came back from riding in the novice hurdle, I should probably be an 'also ran' in the race for Miss Ellery-Penn's attentions.

I watched her captivating a group of my friends. She was a vivid, vital person. It seemed to me that she had an inexhaustible inner fire battened down tight under hatches, and only the warmth from it was allowed to escape into the amused, slow voice. Kate was going to be potently attractive even in middle age, I thought inconsequently, and it crossed my mind that had Scilla possessed this springing vitality instead of her retiring, serene passiveness, Inspector Lodge's implications might not have been very far off the mark.

After we had watched the first race I left Kate deciding which of her new acquaintances should have the honour of taking her to coffee, and went off to weigh out for the novice hurdle. Looking back, I saw her setting off to the refreshment room with a trail of admirers, rather like a comet with a tail. A flashing, bewitching comet.

For the first time in my life I regretted that I was going to ride in a race.

CHAPTER FOUR

In the changing room Sandy Mason stood with his hands on his hips and laid about him with his tongue. His red hair curled strongly, his legs, firmly planted with the feet apart, were as rigid as posts. From top to toe he vibrated life. He was a stocky man in his thirties, on the short side, very strong, with dark brown eyes fringed disconcertingly by pale, reddish lashes.

As a jockey, a professional, he was not among the top dozen, but he had had a good deal of success, mainly owing to his fighting spirit. Nothing ever frightened him. He would thrust his sometimes unwilling mounts into the smallest openings, even occasionally into openings which did not exist until he made them by sheer force. His aggressiveness in races had got him into hot water more than once with the Stewards, but he was not particularly unpopular with the other jockeys, owing to his irrepressible, infectious cheerfulness.

His sense of humour was as vigorous as the rest of

him, and if I thought privately that some of his jokes were too unkindly practical or too revoltingly obscene, I appeared to be in a minority.

'Which of you sods has half-inched my balancing pole?' he roared in a voice which carried splendidly above the busy chatter to every corner of the room. To this enquiry into the whereabouts of his whip, he received no reply.

'Why don't you lot get up off your fannies and see if you're hatching it,' he said to three or four jockeys who were sitting on a bench pulling on their boots. They looked up appreciatively and waited for the rest of the tirade. Sandy kept up a flow of invective without repeating himself until one of the valets produced the missing whip.

'Where did you find it?' demanded Sandy. 'Who had it? I'll twist his bloody arm.'

'It was on the floor under the bench, in your own place.'

Sandy was never embarrassed by his mistakes. He roared with laughter and took his whip. 'I'll forgive you all this time, then.' He went out into the weighing room carrying his saddle and whacking the air with his whip as if to make sure it was as pliable as usual. He always used it a good deal in the course of a race.

As he passed me where I stood just inside the changing room door, his eyes lifted to mine with one of the darting, laughing glances which made him likeable in spite of his faults. I turned and watched him go over and sit on the scales, parking the whip on the table beside him. He said something I couldn't hear, and both the Clerk of the Scales and the Judge, who was sitting there learning the colours so that he could distinguish them at the finish, laughed as they checked him against their lists and passed him for the race.

There had been rumours, a while back, that Sandy had 'stopped' a few horses and had been rewarded handsomely by bookmakers for the service. But nothing had been proved, and the official enquiry had lasted barely an hour. Those who had felt the rough edge of Sandy's practical jokes believed him capable of anything. Everyone else pointed out that stopping a horse was entirely out of character for one who had been in trouble for trying too ruthlessly to win.

Watching the free and easy way he handled the two racing officials, I could understand that in the face of that friendly, open manner, the Stewards at the enquiry must have found it impossible, in the absence of solidly convincing evidence, to believe him guilty. The general opinion among the jockeys was that Sandy had 'strangled' a couple at one stage, but not during the past few months.

'Stopping' a horse can be done by missing the start, setting off some lengths behind, and staying at the back. Then the crooked jockey can ride a fairly honest finish from the second last fence, when he is closely under the eyes of the crowd, secure in the knowledge that he had left the horse far too much to do and cannot possibly win. It is rare enough, because a jockey seen to do it regularly soon finds himself unemployed.

During my one and a half seasons' racing I had seen it happen only twice. It was the same man both times, a fair, round-faced youth called Joe Nantwich. On the second occasion, about two months ago, he had been lucky to escape with his licence, for he had been foolish enough to try it in a race where one of the jockeys was David Stampe, the tale-bearing younger son of the Senior Steward.

Joe, and, I was sure, Sandy too, had both gone to the lengths of deliberately holding back horses which, without their interference, would have been certain to win. They had, in fact, been guilty of criminal fraud. But was I so very much better, I wondered, as I tied on my helmet and took my saddle over to the scales. For I proposed to take Forlorn Hope sensibly over the hurdles, concentrating on getting round the course; and I had no intention of riding him all out in the faint possibility that he might finish in the first three. He was not properly fit, and too hard a race would do him great harm. Of course if by some unforeseen circumstances, such as a lot of falls among the other horses, I found myself placed with a winning chance, I intended to seize it. There is a world of difference between 'stopping' and 'not trying hard, but willing to win': but the result for disgruntled backers is the same. They lose their money.

I took my saddle out to the saddling boxes, where Pete was already waiting with Forlorn Hope. He saddled up, and Rupert, the tiny stable lad, led the horse out into the parade ring. Pete and I strolled in after him, discussing the other horses in the race. There was no sign of Kate.

When the time came I mounted and rode out on to the course. The familiar excitement was in my blood again. Not Bill's death, nor Scilla's mourning, nor the thought of Kate making progress with someone else, could affect the gripping happiness I always felt when cantering down to the starting gate. The speed of racing, the quick decisions, the risks, these were what I badly needed to counteract the safeties of civilization. One can be too secure. Adventure is good for the soul, especially for someone like me, whose father stopped counting after the fourth million.

And my father, with an understanding based on his own much wilder youth, had given me unconditionally a fast car and three good horses and turned me loose in a country five thousand miles from home. He said, however, as he dispatched me with his blessing, that he thought steeplechasing was rather mild for one who had been taken crocodile hunting on the Zambezi every year since he was ten. My father's annual month away from his trading empire usually meant for us a dash across the veldt and a plunge into the primeval forest, sometimes equipped with the absolute minimum of kit and no one but ourselves to carry it. And I, for whom the deep jungle was a familiar playground, found the challenge I needed in a tamed land, on friendly animals, in a sport hemmed all about with rules and regulations. It was very odd, when one came to consider it.

The starter called the roll to make sure everyone had arrived, while he circled round and checked the tightness of the girths. I found Joe Nantwich guiding his horse along beside me. He was wearing his usual unpleasant expression, half petulance, half swank.

'Are you going back to the Davidsons' after the races, Alan?' he asked. He always spoke to me with a familiarity I slightly resented, though I tried not to.

'Yes,' I said. Then I thought of Kate. 'I may not go at once, though.'

'Will you give me a lift as far as Epsom?'

'I don't go that way,' I said, very politely.

'But you go through Dorking. I could get a bus on from there if you don't want to go to Epsom. I came with someone who is going on to Kent, so I've got to find some transport home.' He was persistent, and although I thought he could find someone going directly to Epsom if he tried hard enough, I agreed in the end to take him.

We lined up for the start. Joe was on one side of me and Sandy on the other, and from the looks they gave each other across me, there was no love lost between them. Sandy's smile was a nasty one: Joe's round baby face puckered up like a child trying not to cry. I imagined that Sandy had been puncturing Joe's inflated ego with one of those famous practical jokes, such as filling the feet of his racing boots with jam.

Then we were off, and I gave all my attention to getting Forlorn Hope round as neatly, quickly, and safely as I could. He was still very green and inclined to waver as he met the clattering hurdles, but the basic spring was there. He was going so well that for over half of the race I lay in third place, staying slightly towards the outside, to give him a clear view of the obstacles. The last quarter mile coming up the hill was too much for him, though, and we finished sixth. I was satisfied; and Scilla would be reassured.

Sandy Mason finished ahead of me. Then Joe Nantwich's horse galloped past loose, reins dangling, and looking back to the far end of the course I saw the tiny figure of Joe himself trudging back to the stands. No doubt I would be hearing a stride by stride account of the calamity all the way to Dorking.

I unsaddled, went back to the weighing-room, changed into Kate's brand new colours, got Clem to pack me a weight cloth with ten pounds of flat lead pieces, the weight I needed for the Amateur 'Chase, and went out to see what had become of Miss Ellery-Penn.

She was leaning on the parade ring rails, looking alternately at the horses and (with too much approval,

I thought) at Dane Hillman, one of the brave and charming young men I had introduced to her.

'Mr Hillman has been telling me,' said Kate, 'that that poor-looking bag of bones over there – the one with his head down by his knees and those floppy ears – is the fastest horse in the race. Am I to believe it, or is the mickey being gently taken?'

'No mickey,' I said. 'That's the best horse. Not on looks, I grant you, but he's a certainty today, in this company.'

Dane said, 'Horses who go along with their heads down like that are nearly always good jumpers. They look where they're going.'

'But I like this gorgeous creature coming round now,' said Kate, looking at a bay with an arched back and high head carriage. Most of his body was covered by a rug to keep out the February cold, but at the back his glossy rump swelled roundly.

'He's much too fat,' said Dane. 'He probably ate his head off during the snow and hasn't had enough exercise since. He'll blow up when he's asked to do anything.'

Kate sighed. 'Horses appear to be as full of paradoxes as G. K. Chesterton. The duds look good, and good looks duds.'

'Not always,' said Dane and I together.

'I shall be glad,' said Dane, 'to give you a prolonged course in racehorse recognition, Miss Ellery-Penn.'

'I am a slow learner, Mr Hillman.'

'All the better,' said Dane, cheerfully.

'Aren't you riding today, Dane?' I asked hopefully.

'In the last two, my lad. Don't worry, I shall be able to look after Miss Ellery-Penn for you while you ride her horse.' He grinned.

'Are you a jockey too, Mr Hillman?' asked Kate in a surprised voice.

'Yes,' said Dane, and left it at that. He was the rising star of the profession, clearly heading straight to the top. Pete Gregory had first claim on him, which, apart from natural affinity, brought us together a good deal. Strangers often mistook us for each other. We were the same age, both dark, both of middle height and medium build. On horseback the difference was greater; he was a better jockey than I would ever be.

'I thought all jockeys were instantly recognizable as having come straight from Lilliput,' said Kate, 'but you two are quite a decent size.' She had to look up to both of us, although she was tall enough herself.

We laughed. I said, 'Steeplechasing jockeys are nearly all a decent size. It's easier to stick on over big fences if you have long legs to grip with.'

'Several of the Flat chaps are as tall as us, too,' said Dane. 'But they are very skinny, of course.'

'All my illusions are being shattered,' said Kate.

Dane said, 'I like your new horse, Alan. He'll make a good 'chaser next year.'

'Are you riding your own horses today, too?' Kate asked Dane.

'No, I'm not. I haven't any,' said Dane. 'I'm a professional, so I'm not allowed to own racehorses.'

'A professional?' Kate's eyebrows went up. She had clearly taken in the superlative tailoring of the suit under the short camel overcoat, the pleasant voice, the gentle manners. Another illusion was being shattered, I was amused to see.

'Yes. I ride for my life,' said Dane, smiling. 'Unlike Alan, I haven't a stinking rich father. But I get paid for doing what I like best in the world. It's a very satisfactory state of affairs.'

Kate looked carefully from one to the other of us. 'Perhaps in time I shall understand what makes you want to risk your elegant necks,' she said.

'When you find out, please tell us,' said Dane. 'It's still a mystery to me.'

We wandered back to the stands and watched the third race. The poor-looking horse won in a canter by twenty lengths. Kate's fancy was tailed-off after a mile and refused at the third last fence.

'Don't imagine that we always know what's going to win,' said Dane. 'Jockeys are bad tipsters. But that one was a cert, a dead cert.'

A dead cert. The casual, everyday racing expression

jabbed in my mind like a needle. Bill Davidson's attacker had relied on Admiral's being a certainty.

A dead cert. Dead . . .

Kate's horse, for a pig in a poke, was not as bad as I feared. At the second fence he put in a short one and screwed in mid-air. I came clear out of the saddle and landed back in it more by luck than judgement. This was obviously the trick which had rid Heaven's Above of his former jockey, who now had all my sympathy. He did it again at the third open ditch, but the rest of our journey was uneventful. The horse even found an unsuspected turn of foot up the hill and, passing several tired animals, ran on into fourth place.

Kate was delighted.

'Bless Uncle George for a brainwave,' she said. 'I've never had such a happy day in my life.'

'I thought you were coming off at the second, Alan,' said Pete Gregory, as I undid the girth buckles.

'So did I,' I said, feelingly. 'It was sheer luck I didn't.'

Pete watched the way Heavens Above was breathing: the ribs were moving in and out a good deal, but not labouring. He said, 'He's remarkably fit, considering everything. I think we'll win a race or two with him before the end of the season.'

'Can't we all go and celebrate with the odd

magnum?' asked Kate. Her eyes were shining with excitement.

Pete laughed. 'Wait till you have a winner, for the magnum,' he said. 'I'd like to have drunk a more modest toast to the future with you, though, but I've a runner in the next. Alan will take you, no doubt.' He looked at me sideways, very amused still at my complete surrender to the charm of Miss Ellery-Penn.

'Will you wait for me, Kate?' I asked. 'I have to go and weigh in now, because we were fourth. I'll change and be out as quickly as I can.'

'I'll come down outside the weighing room,' promised Kate, nodding.

I weighed in, gave my saddle to Clem, washed, and changed back into ordinary clothes. Kate was waiting outside the weighing-room, looking at a group of girls standing near her chatting.

'Who are they?' asked Kate. 'They have been here all the time I have, just doing nothing.'

'Jockeys' wives, mostly,' I said, grinning. 'Waiting outside the weighing room is their chief occupation.'

'And jockeys' girl friends too, I suppose,' said Kate, wryly.

'Yes,' I said. 'And I've just found out how nice it is to know there is someone waiting for you outside.'

We went round to the bar, and settled for two cups of coffee.

'Uncle George will be shattered to hear we drank to

Heavens Above so non-alcoholically,' said Kate. 'Don't grain and grapes figure in your life?'

'Oh, yes, of course. But I've never got used to them at three o'clock in the afternoon. How about you?'

'Champers for breakfast is my passion,' said Kate, with smiling eyes.

I asked her then if she would spend the evening with me, but she said she could not. Aunt Deb, it appeared, was having a dinner party, and Uncle George would be agog to hear how the birthday present had got on.

'Tomorrow, then?'

Kate hesitated and looked down at her glass. 'I'm . . . er . . . I'm going out with Dane, tomorrow.'

'Blast him,' I said, exploding.

Kate positively giggled.

'Friday?' I suggested.

'That will be lovely,' said Kate.

We went up to the stands and watched Dane win the fifth race by a short head. Kate cheered him home uninhibitedly.

CHAPTER FIVE

A battle was raging in the car park. I walked out to the gate to go home after the last race, and came to a dead stop. In the open space between the gate and the first rank of parked cars, at least twenty men were fighting, and fighting to hurt. Even at first glance there was a vicious quality about the strictly non-Queensberry type blows.

It was astounding. Scuffles between two or three men are common on racecourses, but a clash of this size and seriousness had to be caused by more than a disagreement over a bet.

I looked closer. There was no doubt about it. Some of the men were wearing brass knuckles. A length of bicycle chain swung briefly in the air. The two men nearest to me were lying on the ground, almost motionless, but rigid with exertion, as if locked in some strange native ritual. The fingers of one were clamped round the wrist of the other, whose hand held a knife with a sharp three-inch blade. Not long enough to be readily lethal, it was designed to rip and disfigure.

There seemed to be two fairly equally matched sides fighting each other, but one could not distinguish which was which. The man with the knife, who was slowly getting the worst of it, I saw to be little more than a boy; but most of the men were in their full strength. The only older-looking fighter was on his knees in the centre with his arms folded over his head, while the fight raged on around him.

They fought in uncanny silence. Only their heavy breathing and a few grunts were to be heard. The semicircle of open-mouthed homeward-bound racegoers watching them was growing larger, but no one felt inclined to walk into the mêlée and try to stop it.

I found one of the newspaper sellers at my elbow.

'What's it all about?' I asked. Nothing much to do with racing escapes the newsboys.

'It's the taxi-drivers,' he said. 'There's two rival gangs of 'em, one lot from London and one lot from Brighton. There's usually trouble when they meet.'

'Why?'

'Couldn't tell you, Mr York. But this isn't the first time they've been at it.'

I looked back at the struggling mob. One or two of them still had peaked caps on. Some pairs were rolling about on the ground, some were straining and heaving against the sides of the taxis. There were two rows of taxis parked there. All the drivers were fighting.

The fists and what they held in the way of iron-mongery were doing a lot of damage. Two of the men were bent over, clasping their bellies in agony. There was blood on nearly all their faces, and the clothes of some of them had been torn off to the skin.

They fought on with appalling fury, taking no notice at all of the swelling crowd around them.

'They'll kill each other,' said a girl standing next to me, watching the scene in a mixture of horror and fascination.

I glanced up over her head at the man standing on the other side of her, a big man well over six feet tall, with a deeply tanned skin. He was watching the fight with grim disapproval, his strong profile bleak, his eyes narrowed. I could not remember his name, though I had a feeling I ought to know it.

The crowd was growing uneasy, and began looking round for the police. The girl's remark was not idle. Any of the men might die, if they were unlucky, from the murderous chopping, gouging, and slogging, which showed no signs of abating.

The fight had caused a traffic jam in the car park. A policeman came, took a look, and disappeared fast for reinforcements. He returned with four constables on foot and one on horseback, all armed with truncheons. They plunged into the battle, but it took them several minutes to stop it.

More police arrived. The taxi-drivers were dragged

and herded into two groups. Both lots appeared to be equally battered, and neither side seemed to have won. The battlefield was strewn with caps and torn pieces of coats and shirts. Two shoes, one brown, one black, lay on their sides ten feet apart. Patches of blood stained the ground. The police began making a small pile of collected weapons.

The main excitement over, people began drifting away. The little knot of prospective customers for the taxis moved across to ask the policeman how long the drivers would be detained. The tall sunburned man who had been standing near me went over to join them.

One of the racing journalists paused beside me, scribbling busily in his notebook.

'Who is that very big man over there, John?' I asked him. He looked up and focused his eyes. 'His name's Tudor, I think. Owns a couple of horses. A newly arrived tycoon type. I don't know much about him. He doesn't look too pleased about the transport situation.'

Tudor, in fact, looked heavily angry, his lower jaw jutting forward obstinately. I was still sure there was something about this man which I ought to remember, but I did not know what. He was not having any success with the policeman, who was shaking his head. The taxis remained empty and driverless.

'What's it all about?' I asked the journalist.

'Gang warfare, my spies tell me,' he said cheerfully.

Five of the taxi-drivers were now lying flat out on

the cold damp ground. One of them groaned steadily.

The journalist said, 'Hospital and police station in about equal proportions, I should say. What a story!'

The man who was groaning rolled over and vomited.

'I'm going back to phone this lot through to the office,' said the journalist. 'Are you off home now?'

'I'm waiting for that wretched Joe Nantwich,' I said. 'I promised him a lift to Dorking, but I haven't seen a sign of him since the fourth race. It would be just like him to get a lift right home with someone else and forget to let me know.'

'The last I saw of him, he was having a few unfriendly words with Sandy in the gents, and getting the worst of it.'

'Those two really hate each other,' I said.

'Do you know why?'

'No idea. Have you?' I asked.

'No,' said the journalist. He smiled good-bye and went back into the racecourse towards the telephone.

Two ambulances drove up to collect the injured drivers. A policeman climbed into the back of each ambulance with them, and another sat in front beside the driver. With full loads the ambulances trundled slowly up the road to the main gates.

The remaining drivers began to shiver as the heat of the battle died out of them and the raw February afternoon took over. They were stiff and bruised, but unrepentant. A man in one group stepped forward, gave the other group a sneer, and spat, insultingly, on the ground in their direction. His shirt was in ribbons and his face was swelling in lumps. The muscles of his forearm would have done credit to a blacksmith, and silky dark hair grew low on his forehead in a widow's peak. A dangerous-looking man. A policeman touched his arm to bring him back into the group and he jumped round and snarled at him. Two more policemen began to close in, and the dark-haired man subsided angrily.

I was just giving Joe up when he came out of the gate and hailed me with no apology for his lateness. But I was not the only person to notice his arrival.

The tall dark Mr Tudor strode towards us.

'Nantwich, be so good as to give me a lift into Brighton, will you?' he said, authoritatively. 'As you can see, the taxis are out of action, and I have an important appointment in Brighton in twenty minutes.'

Joe looked at the taxi-drivers with vague eyes.

'What's happened?' he said.

'Never mind that now,' said Tudor impatiently. 'Where is your car?'

Joe looked at him blankly. His brain seemed to be working at half speed. He said, 'Oh – er – it isn't here, sir. I've got a lift.'

'With you?' said Tudor to me. I nodded. Joe, typically, had not introduced us.

'I'll be obliged if you will take me into Brighton,' said Tudor, briskly. 'I'll pay you the regular taxi fare.'

He was forceful and in a hurry. It would have been difficult to refuse to do him a favour so small to me, so clearly important to him.

'I'll take you for nothing,' I said, 'but you'll find it a bit of a squeeze. I have a two-seater sports car.'

'If it's too small for all of us, Nantwich can stay here and you can come back for him,' said Tudor in a firm voice. Joe showed no surprise, but I thought that the dark Mr Tudor was too practised at consulting no one's convenience but his own.

We skirted the groups of battered taxi-drivers, and threaded our way to my car. Tudor got in. He was so large that it was hopeless to try to wedge Joe in as well.

'I'll come back for you, Joe,' I said, stifling my irritation. 'Wait for me up on the main road.'

I climbed into the car, nosed slowly out of the car park, up the racecourse road, and turned out towards Brighton. There was too much traffic for the Lotus to show off the power of the purring Climax engine, and going along at a steady forty gave me time to concentrate on my puzzling passenger.

Glancing down as I changed gear, I saw his hand resting on his knees, the fingers spread and tense. And suddenly I knew where I had seen him before. It was his hand, darkly tanned, with the faint bluish tint under the finger-nails, that I knew.

He had been standing in the bar at Sandown with his back towards me and his hand resting flat on the counter beside him, next to his glass. He had been talking to Bill; and I had waited there, behind him, not wanting to interrupt their conversation. Then Tudor finished his drink and left, and I had talked with Bill.

Now I glanced at his face.

'It's a great shame about Bill Davidson,' I said.

The brown hand jumped slightly on his knee. He turned his head and looked at me while I drove.

'Yes, indeed it is.' He spoke slowly. 'I had been hoping he would ride a horse for me at Cheltenham.'

'A great horseman,' I said.

'Yes indeed.'

'I was just behind him when he fell,' I said, and on an impulse added, 'There are a great many questions to be asked about it.'

I felt Tudor's huge body shift beside me. I knew he was still looking at me, and I found his presence overpowering. 'I suppose so,' he said. He hesitated, but added nothing more. He looked at his watch.

'Take me to the Pavilion Plaza Hotel, if you please. I have to attend a business meeting there,' he said.

'Is it near the Pavilion?' I asked.

'Fairly. I will direct you when we get there.' His tone relegated me to the status of chauffeur.

We drove for some miles in silence. My passenger sat apparently in deep thought. When we reached Brighton he told me the way to the hotel.

'Thank you,' he said, without warmth, as he lifted his

bulk clumsily out of the low-slung car. He had an air of accepting considerable favours as merely his due, even when done him by complete strangers. He took two steps away from the car, then turned back and said, 'What is your name?'

'Alan York,' I said. 'Good afternoon.' I drove off without waiting for an answer. I could be brusque too. Glancing in the mirror I saw him standing on the pavement looking after me.

I went back to the racecourse.

Joe was waiting for me, sitting on the bank at the side of the road. He had some difficulty opening the car door, and he stumbled into his seat, muttering. He lurched over against me, and I discovered that Joe Nantwich was drunk.

The daylight was almost gone. I turned on the lights. I could think of pleasanter things to do than drive the twisty roads to Dorking with Joe breathing alcohol all over me. I sighed, and let in the clutch.

Joe was nursing a grievance. He would be. Everything which went wrong for Joe was someone else's fault, according to him. Barely twenty, he was a chronic grumbler. It was hard to know which was worse to put up with, his grousing or his bragging, and that he was treated with tolerance by the other jockeys said much for their good nature. Joe's saving grace was his undoubted ability as a jockey, but he had put that to bad use already by his 'stopping' activities, and now he was threatening it altogether by getting drunk in the middle of the afternoon.

'I would have won that race,' he whined.

'You're a fool, Joe,' I said.

'No, honestly, Alan, I would have won that race. I had him placed just right. I had the others beat, I had 'em stone cold. Just right.' He made sawing motions with his hands.

'You're a fool to drink so much at the races,' I said.

'Eh?' He couldn't focus.

'Drink,' I said. 'You've had too much to drink.'

'No, no, no, no . . .' The words came dribbling out, as if once he had started to speak it was too much effort to stop.

'Owners won't put you on their horses if they see you getting drunk,' I said, feeling it was no business of mine, after all.

'I can win any race, drunk or not,' said Joe.

'Not many owners would believe it.'

'They know I'm good.'

'So you are, but you won't be if you go on like this,' I said.

'I can drink and I can ride and I can ride and I can drink. If I want to.' He belched.

I let it pass. What Joe needed was a firm hand applied ten years ago. He looked all set now on the road to ruin and he wasn't going to thank anyone for directions off it.

He was whining again. 'That bloody Mason . . .'

I didn't say anything. He tried again.

'That bloody Sandy, he tipped me off. He bloody well tipped me off over the bloody rails. I'd have won that race as easy as kiss your hand and he knew it and tipped me off over the bloody rails.'

'Don't be silly, Joe.'

'You can't say I wouldn't have won the race,' said Joe argumentatively.

'And I can't say you would have won it,' I said. 'You fell at least a mile from home.'

'I didn't fall. I'm telling you, aren't I? Sandy bloody Mason tipped me off over the rails.'

'How?' I asked idly, concentrating on the road.

'He squeezed me against the rails. I shouted at him to give me more room. And do you know what he did? Do you know? He laughed. He bloody well laughed. Then he tipped me over. He stuck his knee into me and gave a heave and off I went over the bloody rails.' His whining voice finished on a definite sob.

I looked at him. Two tears were rolling down his round cheeks. They glistened in the light from the dashboard, and fell with a tiny flash on to the furry collar of his sheepskin coat.

'Sandy wouldn't do a thing like that,' I said mildly.

'Oh yes he would. He told me he'd get even with me. He said I'd be sorry. But I couldn't help it, Alan, I really couldn't.' Two more tears rolled down.

I was out of my depth. I had no idea what he was talking about; but it began to look as though Sandy, if he had unseated him, had had his reasons.

Joe went on talking. 'You're always decent to me, Alan, you're not like the others. You're my friend . . .' He put his hand heavily on my arm, pawing, leaning over towards me and giving me the benefit of the full force of his alcoholic breath. The delicate steering of the Lotus reacted to his sudden weight on my arm with a violent swerve towards the curb.

I shook him off. 'For God's sake sit up, Joe, or you'll have us in the ditch,' I said.

But he was too immersed in his own troubles to hear me. He pulled my arm again. There was a lay-by just ahead. I slowed, turned into it, and stopped the car.

'If you don't sit up and leave me alone you can get out and walk,' I said, trying to get through to him with a rough tone.

But he was still on his own track, and weeping noisily now.

'You don't know what it's like to be in trouble,' he sobbed. I resigned myself to listen. The quicker he got his resentments off his chest, I thought, the quicker he would relax and go to sleep.

'What trouble?' I said. I was not in the least interested.

'Alan, I'll tell you because you're a pal, a decent pal.' He put his hand on my knee. I pushed it off.

Amid a fresh burst of tears Joe blurted, 'I was supposed to stop a horse and I didn't, and Sandy lost a lot of money and said he'd get even with me and he's been following me around saying that for days and days and I knew he'd do something awful and he has.' He paused for breath. 'Lucky for me I hit a soft patch or I might have broken my neck. It wasn't funny. And that bloody Sandy,' he choked on the name, 'was laughing. I'll make him laugh on the other side of his bloody face.'

That last sentence made me smile. Joe with his baby face, strong of body perhaps, but weak of character, was no match for the tough, forceful Sandy, more than ten years older and incalculably more self-assured. Joe's bragging, like his whining, sprang from feelings of insecurity. But the beginning of his outburst was something different.

'What horse did you not stop?' I asked. 'And how did Sandy know you were supposed to be going to stop one?'

For a second I thought action would silence him, but after the smallest hesitation he babbled on. The drink was still at the flood. So were the tears.

From the self-pitying, hiccuping, half incoherent voice I learned a sorry enough story. Shorn of blasphemy and reduced to essentials, it was this. Joe had been paid well for stopping horses on several occasions, two of which I had seen myself. But when David Stampe had told his father the Senior Steward about the last one, and Joe had nearly lost his licence, it gave him a steadying shock. The next time he was asked to stop a horse he said he would, but in the event, from understandable nerves, he had not done it thoroughly enough early in the race, and at the finish was faced with the plain knowledge that if he lost the race he would lose his licence as well. He won. This had happened ten days ago.

I was puzzled. 'Is Sandy the only person who has harmed you?'

'He tipped me over the rails . . .' He was ready to start all over again.

I interrupted. 'It wasn't Sandy, surely, who was paying you not to win?'

'No, I don't think so. I don't know,' he snivelled.

'Do you mean you don't know who was paying you? Ever?'

'A man rang up and told me when he wanted me to stop one, and afterwards I got a packet full of money through the post.'

'How many times have you done it?' I asked.

'Ten,' said Joe, 'all in the last six months.' I stared at him.

'Often it was easy,' said Joe defensively. 'The —s wouldn't have won anyway, even if I'd helped them.'

'How much did you get for it?'

'A hundred. Twice it was two-fifty.' Joe's tongue was still running away with him, and I believed him. It was big money, and anyone prepared to pay on that scale would surely want considerable revenge when Joe won against orders. But Sandy? I couldn't believe it.

'What did Sandy say to you after you won?' I asked.

Joe was still crying. 'He said he'd backed the horse I beat and that he'd get even with me,' said Joe. And it seemed that Sandy had done that.

'You didn't get your parcel of money, I suppose?'

'No,' said Joe, sniffing.

'Haven't you any idea where they come from?' I asked.

'Some had London postmarks,' said Joe. 'I didn't take much notice.' Too eager to count the contents to look closely at the wrappings, no doubt.

'Well, I said, 'surely now that Sandy has had his little revenge, you are in the clear? Can't you possibly stop crying about it? It's all over. What are you in such a state about?'

For answer Joe took a paper from his jacket pocket and gave it to me.

'You might as well know it all. I don't know what to do. Help me, Alan. I'm frightened.'

In the light of the dashboard I could see that this was true. And Joe was beginning to sober up.

I unfolded the paper and switched on the lights inside the car. It was a single sheet of thin, ordinary typing paper. In simple capital letters, written with a ball-point pen, were five words: BOLINGBROKE, YOU WILL BE PUNISHED.

'Bolingbroke is the horse you were supposed to stop and didn't?'

'Yes.' The tears no longer welled in his eyes.

'When did you get this?' I asked.

'I found it in my pocket, today, when I put my jacket on after I'd changed. Just before the fifth race. It wasn't there when I took it off.'

'And you spent the rest of the afternoon in the bar, in a blue funk, I suppose,' I said.

'Yes . . . and I went back there while you took Mr Tudor to Brighton. I didn't think anything was going to happen to me because of Bolingbroke, and I've been frightened ever since he won. And just as I was thinking it was all right Sandy pushed me over the rails and then I found this letter in my pocket. It isn't fair.' The self-pity still whined in his voice.

I gave him back the paper.

'What am I to do?' said Joe.

I couldn't tell him, because I didn't know. He had got himself into a thorough mess, and he had good reason to be afraid. People who manipulated horses and jockeys to that extent were certain to play rough. The time lag of ten days between Bolingbroke's win and the arrival of the note could mean, I thought, that there was a cat-and-mouse, rather than a straightforward, mentality at work. Which was little comfort to offer Joe.

Apart from some convulsive hiccups and sniffs, Joe seemed to have recovered from his tears, and the worst of the drunkenness was over. I switched off the inside lights, started the car up, and pulled back on the road. As I had hoped, Joe soon went to sleep. He snored loudly.

Approaching Dorking, I woke him up. I had some questions to ask.

'Joe, who is that Mr Tudor I took to Brighton? He knows you.'

'He owns Bolingbroke,' said Joe. 'I often ride for him.'

I was surprised. 'Was he pleased when Bolingbroke won?' I asked.

'I suppose so. He wasn't there. He sent me ten per cent afterwards, though, and a letter thanking me. The usual thing.'

'He hasn't been in racing long, has he?' I asked.

'Popped up about the same time you did,' said Joe, with a distinct return to his old brash manner. 'Both of you arrived with dark sun-tans in the middle of winter.'

I had come by air from the burning African summer to the icy reception of October in England: but after eighteen months my skin was as pale as an Englishman's. Tudor's, on the other hand, remained dark.

Joe was sniggering. 'You know why Mr Clifford

bloody Tudor lives at Brighton? It gives him an excuse to be sunburnt all the year round. Touch of the old tar, really.'

After that I had no compunction in turning Joe out at the bus stop for Epsom. Unloading his troubles on me seemed, for the present at least, to have restored his ego.

I drove back to the Cotswolds. At first I thought about Sandy Mason and wondered how he had got wind of Joe's intention to stop Bolingbroke.

But for the last hour of the journey I thought about Kate.

CHAPTER SIX

Scilla was lying asleep on the sofa with a rug over her legs and a half-full glass on a low table beside her. I picked up the glass and sniffed. Brandy. She usually drank gin and Campari. Brandy was for bad days only.

She opened her eyes. 'Alan! I'm so glad you're back. What time is it?'

'Half past nine,' I said.

'You must be starving,' she said, pushing off the rug. 'Why ever didn't you wake me? Dinner was ready hours ago.'

'I've only just got here, and Joan is cooking now, so relax,' I said.

We went in to eat. I sat in my usual place. Bill's chair, opposite Scilla, was empty. I made a mental note to move it back against the wall.

Half way through the steaks, Scilla said, breaking a long silence, 'Two policemen came to see me today.'

'Did they? About the inquest tomorrow?'

'No, it was about Bill.' She pushed her plate away.

'They asked me if he was in any trouble, like you did. They asked me the same questions in different ways for over half an hour. One of them suggested that if I was as fond of my husband as I said I was and on excellent terms with him, I ought to know if something was wrong in his life. They were rather nasty, really.'

She was not looking at me. She kept her eyes down, regarding her half-eaten, congealing steak, and there was a slight embarrassment in her manner, which was unusual.

'I can imagine,' I said, realizing what was the matter. 'They asked you, I suppose, to explain your relationship with me, and why I was still living in your house?'

She glanced up in surprise and evident relief. 'Yes, they did. I didn't know how to tell you. It seems so ordinary to me that you should be here, yet I couldn't seem to make them understand that.'

'I'll go tomorrow, Scilla,' I said. 'I'm not letting you in for any more gossip. If the police can think that you were cheating Bill with me, so can the village and the county. I've been exceedingly thoughtless, and I'm very very sorry.' For I, too, had found it quite natural to stay on in Bill's house after his death.

'You will certainly not leave tomorrow on my account, Alan,' said Scilla with more resolution that I would have given her credit for. 'I need you here. I shall do nothing but cry all the time if I don't have you to talk to, especially in the evenings. I can get through the days, with the children and the house to think about. But the nights . . .' And in her suddenly ravaged face I could read all the tearing, savage pain of a loss four days old.

'I don't care what anyone says,' she said through starting tears, 'I need you here. Please, please, don't go away.'

'I'll stay,' I said. 'Don't worry. I'll stay as long as you want me to. But you must promise to tell me when you are ready for me to go.'

She dried her eyes and raised a smile. 'When I begin to worry about my reputation, you mean? I promise.'

I had driven the better part of three hundred miles besides riding in two races, and I was tired. We went to our beds early, Scilla promising to take her sleeping pills.

But at two o'clock in the morning she opened my bedroom door. I woke at once. She came over and switched on my bedside light, and sat down on my bed.

She looked ridiculously young and defenceless. She was wearing a pale blue knee-length chiffon nightdress which flowed transparently about her slender body and fell like mist over the small round breasts.

I propped myself up on my elbow and ran my fingers through my hair.

'I can't sleep,' she said.

'Did you take the pills?' I asked.

But I could answer my own question. Her eyes

looked drugged, and in her right mind she would not have come into my room so unrevealingly undressed.

'Yes, I took them. They've made me a bit groggy, but I'm still awake. I took an extra one.' Her voice was slurred and dopey. 'Will you talk for a bit?' she said. 'Then perhaps I'll feel more sleepy. When I'm on my own I just lie and think about Bill . . . Tell me more about Plumpton . . . You said you rode another horse . . . Tell me about it. Please. . . .'

So I sat up in bed and wrapped my eiderdown round her shoulders, and told her about Kate's birthday present and Uncle George, thinking how often I had told Polly and Henry and William bedside stories to send them to sleep. But after a while I saw she was not listening, and presently the slow heavy tears were falling from her bent head on to her hands.

'You must think me a terrible fool to cry so much,' she said, 'but I just can't help it.' She lay down weakly beside me, her head on my pillow. She took hold of my hand and closed her eyes. I looked down at her sweet, pretty face with the tears trickling past her ears into her cloudy dark hair, and gently kissed her forehead. Her body shook with two heavy sobs. I lay down and slid my arm under her neck. She turned towards me and clung to me, holding me fiercely, sobbing slowly with her deep terrible grief.

And at last, gradually, the sleeping pills did their job. She relaxed, breathing audibly, her hand twisted into the jacket of my pyjamas. She was lying half on top of the bedclothes, and the February night was cold. I tugged the sheet and blankets gently from underneath her with my free hand and spread them over her, and pulled the eiderdown up over our shoulders. I switched off the light and lay in the dark, gently cradling her until her breath grew soft and she was soundly asleep.

I smiled to think of Inspector Lodge's face if he could have seen us. And I reflected that I should not have been content to be so passive a bedfellow had I held Kate in my arms instead.

During the night Scilla twisted uneasily several times, murmuring jumbled words that made no sense, seeming to be calmed each time by my hand stroking her hair. Towards morning she was quiet. I got up, wrapped her in the eiderdown and carried her to her own bed. I knew that if she woke in my room, with the drugs worn off, she would be unnecessarily ashamed and upset.

She was still sleeping peacefully when I left her.

A few hours later, after a hurried breakfast, I drove her to Maidenhead to attend the inquest. She slept most of the way and did not refer to what had happened in the night. I was not sure she even remembered.

Lodge must have been waiting for us, for he met us as soon as we went in. He was carrying a sheaf of papers, and looked businesslike and solid. I introduced him to Scilla, and his eyes sharpened appreciatively at the sight of her pale prettiness. But what he said was a surprise.

'I'd like to apologize,' he began, 'for the rather unpleasant suggestions which have been put to you and Mr York about each other.' He turned to me. 'We are now satisfied that you were in no way responsible for Major Davidson's death.'

'That's big of you,' I said lightly, but I was glad to hear it.

Lodge went on, 'You can say what you like to the Coroner about the wire, of course, but I'd better warn you that he won't be too enthusiastic. He hates anything fancy, and you've no evidence. Don't worry if you don't agree with his verdict – I think it's sure to be accidental death – because inquests can always be reopened, if need be.'

In view of this I was not disturbed when the coroner, a heavily moustached man of fifty, listened keenly enough to my account of Bill's fall, but dealt a little brusquely with my wire theory. Lodge testified that he had accompanied me to the racecourse to look for the wire I had reported, but that there had been none there.

The man who had been riding directly behind me when Bill fell was also called. He was an amateur rider who lived in Yorkshire, and he'd had to come a long way. He said, with an apologetic glance for me, that he had seen nothing suspicious at the fence, and that in his opinion it was a normal fall. Unexpected maybe, but not mysterious. He radiated common sense.

Had Mr York, the Coroner enquired in a doubtful voice, mentioned the possible existence of wire to anyone at all on the day of the race? Mr York had not.

The Coroner, summing up medical, police, and all other evidence, found that Major Davidson had died of injuries resulting from his horse having fallen in a steeplechase. He was not convinced, he said, that the fall was anything but an accident.

Owing to a mistake about the time, the local paper had failed to send a representative to the inquest, and from lack of detailed reporting the proceedings rated only small paragraphs in the evening and morning papers. The word ‘wire’ was not mentioned. This omission did not worry me one way or the other, but Scilla was relieved. She said she could not yet stand questions from inquisitive friends, let alone reporters.

Bill’s funeral was held quietly in the village on Friday morning, attended only by his family and close friends. Bearing one corner of his coffin on my shoulder and bidding my private good-byes, I knew for sure that I would not be satisfied until his death was avenged. I didn’t know how it was to be done, and, strangely enough, I didn’t feel any urgency about it. But in time, I promised him, in time, I’ll do it.

Scilla’s sister had come to the funeral and was to stay

with her for two or three days, so, missing lunch out of deference to the light weight I was committed to ride at on the following day, I drove up to London to spend some long overdue hours in the office, arranging the details of insurance and customs duty on a series of shipments of copper.

The office staff were experts. My job was to discuss with Hughes, my second in command, the day-to-day affairs of the company, to make decisions and agree to plans made by Hughes, and to sign my name to endless documents and letters. It seldom took me more than three days a week. On Sunday it was my weekly task to write to my father. I had a feeling he skipped the filial introduction and the accounts of my racing, and fastened his sharp brain only on my report of the week's trade and my assessment of the future.

Those Sunday reports had been part of my life for ten years. School homework could wait, my father used to say. It was more important for me to know every detail about the kingdom I was to inherit; and to this end he made me study continually the papers he brought home from his office. By the time I left school I could appraise at a glance the significance of fluctuations in the world prices of raw materials, even if I had no idea when Charles I was beheaded.

On Friday evening I waited impatiently for Kate to join me for dinner. Unwrapped from the heavy overcoat and woolly boots she had worn at Plumpton, she was more ravishing than ever. She wore a glowing red dress, simple and devastating, and her dark hair fell smoothly to her shoulders. She seemed to be alight from within with her own brand of effervescence. The evening was fun and, to me at least, entirely satisfactory. We ate, we danced, we talked.

While we swayed lazily round the floor to some dreamy slow-tempo music Kate introduced the only solemn note of the evening.

'I saw a bit about your friend's inquest in this morning's paper,' she said.

I brushed my lips against her hair. It smelled sweet. 'Accidental death,' I murmured vaguely. 'I don't think.'

'Hm?' Kate looked up.

'I'll tell you about it one day, when I know the whole story,' I said, enjoying the taut line of her neck as she tilted her face up to mine. It was strange, I thought, that it was possible to feel two strong emotions at once. Pleasure in surrendering to the seduction of the music with a dancing Kate balanced in my arms, and a tugging sympathy for Scilla trying to come to terms with her loneliness eighty miles away in the windy Cotswold hills.

'Tell me now,' said Kate with interest. 'If it wasn't accidental death, what was it?'

I hesitated. I didn't want too much reality pushing the evening's magic sideways.

'Come on, come on,' she urged, smiling. 'You can't stop here. I'll die of suspense.'

So I told her about the wire. It shocked her enough to stop her dancing, and we stood flat-footed in the middle of the floor with the other couples flowing round and bumping into us.

'Dear heavens,' she said, 'how . . . how wicked.'

She wanted me to explain why the inquest verdict had been what it was, and after I had told her that with the wire gone there was no evidence of anything else, she said, 'I can't bear to think of anyone getting away with so disgusting a trick.'

'Nor can I,' I said, 'and they won't, I promise you, if I can help it.'

'That's good,' she said seriously. She began to sway again to the music, and I took her in my arms and we drifted back into the dance. We didn't mention Bill again.

It seemed to me for long periods that evening as if my feet were not in proper contact with the floor, and the most extraordinary tremors constantly shook my knees. Kate seemed to notice nothing: she was friendly, funny, brimming over with gaiety, and utterly unsentimental.

When at length I helped her into the chauffeur-driven car which Uncle George had sent up from Sussex to take her home, I had discovered how painful it is to love. I was excited, keyed up. And also anxious;

for I was sure that she did not feel as intensely about me as I about her.

I already knew I wanted to marry Kate. The thought that she might not have me was a bitter one.

The next day I went to Kempton Park races. Outside the weighing room I ran into Dane. We talked about the going, the weather, Pete's latest plans for us, and the horses. Usual jockey stuff. Then Dane said, 'You took Kate out last night?'

'Yes.'

'Where did you go?'

'The River Club,' I said. 'Where did you take her?'

'Didn't she tell you?' asked Dane.

'She said to ask you.'

'River Club,' said Dane.

'Damn it,' I said. But I had to laugh.

'Honours even,' said Dane.

'Did she ask you down to stay with Uncle George?' I asked suspiciously.

'I'm going today, after the races,' said Dane, smiling. 'And you?'

'Next Saturday,' I said gloomily. 'You know, Dane, she's teasing us abominably.'

'I can stand it,' said Dane. He tapped me on the shoulder. 'Don't look so miserable, it may never happen.'

'That's what I'm afraid of,' I sighed. He laughed and went into the weighing room.

It was an uneventful afternoon. I rode my big black mare in a novice 'chase and Dane beat me by two lengths. At the end of the day we walked out to the car park together.

'How is Mrs Davidson bearing up?' Dane asked.

'Fairly well, considering the bottom has dropped out of her world.'

'Jockeys' wives' nightmare come true.'

'Yes,' I said.

'It makes you pause a bit, before you ask a girl to put up with that sort of constant worry,' said Dane, thoughtfully.

'Kate?' I asked. He looked round sharply and grinned.

'I suppose so. Do you mind?'

'Yes,' I said, keeping my voice light. 'I mind very much.'

We came to his car first, and he put his race glasses and hat on the seat. His suitcase was in the back.

'So long, mate,' he said. 'I'll keep you posted.'

I watched him drive off, answered his wave. I seldom felt envious of anybody, but at that moment I envied Dane sorely.

I climbed into the Lotus and pointed its low blue nose towards home.

It was on the road through Maidenhead Thicket that I saw the horse-box. It was parked in a lay-by on the near side, with tools scattered on the ground round it and the bonnet up. It was facing me as I approached, as if it had broken down on its way into Maidenhead. A man was walking a horse up and down in front of it.

The driver, standing by the bonnet scratching his head, saw me coming and gestured me to stop. I pulled up beside him. He walked round to talk to me through the window, a middle-aged man, unremarkable, wearing a leather jacket.

'Do you know anything about engines, sir?' he asked.

'Not as much as you, I should think,' I said, smiling. He had grease on his hands. If a horse-box driver couldn't find the fault in his own motor, it would be a long job for whoever did. 'I'll take you back into Maidenhead, though, if you like. There's bound to be someone there who can help you.'

'That's extremely kind of you, sir,' he said, civilly. 'Thank you very much. But – er – I'm in a bit of a difficulty.' He looked into the car and saw my binoculars on the seat beside me. His face lightened up. 'You don't possibly know anything about horses, sir?'

'A bit, yes,' I said.

'Well, it's like this, sir. I've got these two horses going to the London docks. They're being exported. Well, that one's all right.' He pointed to the horse walking up and down. 'But the other one, he don't seem so good. Sweating hard, he's been, the last hour or so, and biting at his stomach. He keeps trying to lie down. Looks ill.

The lad's in there with him now, and he's proper worried, I can tell you.'

'It sounds as though it might be colic,' I said. 'If it is, he ought to be walking round, too. It's the only way to get him better. It's essential to keep them on the move when they've got colic.'

The driver looked troubled. 'It's a lot to ask, sir,' he said, tentatively, 'but would you have a look at him? Motors are my fancy, not horses, except to back 'em. And these lads are not too bright. I don't want a rocket from the boss for not looking after things properly.'

'All right,' I said, 'I'll have a look. But I'm not a vet, you know, by a long way.'

He smiled in a relieved fashion. 'Thank you, sir. Anyway, you'll know if I've got to get a vet at once or not, I should think.'

I parked the car in the lay-by behind the horse-box. The door at the back of the horse-box opened and a hand, the stable lad's, I supposed, reached out to help me up. He took me by the wrist.

He didn't leave go.

There were three men waiting for me inside the horse-box. And no horse, sick or otherwise. After a flurried ten seconds during which my eyes were still unused to the dim light, I ended up standing with my back to the end post of one of the partition walls.

The horse-box was divided into three stalls with two partition walls between them, and there was a space across the whole width of the box at the back, usually occupied by lads travelling with their horses.

Two of the men held my arms. They stood on each side of the partition and slightly behind me, and they had an uncomfortable leverage on my shoulders. The post of the partition was padded with matting, as it always is in racehorse boxes, to save the horses hurting themselves while they travel. The mattress tickled my neck.

The driver stepped up into the box and shut the door. His manner, still incredibly deferential, held a hint of triumph. It was entitled to. He had set a neat trap.

'Very sorry to have to do this, sir,' he said politely. It was macabre.

'If it's money you want,' I said, 'you're going to be unlucky. I don't bet much and I didn't have a good day at the races today. I'm afraid you've gone to a lot of trouble for a measly eight quid.'

'We don't want your money, sir,' he said. 'Though as you're offering it we might as well take it, at that.' And still smiling pleasantly he put his hand inside my jacket and took my wallet out of the inside pocket.

I kicked his shin as hard as I could, but was hampered because of my position against the post. As soon as they felt me move the two men behind me jerked my arms painfully backwards.

'I shouldn't do that, sir, if I was you,' said the friendly

driver, rubbing his leg. He opened my wallet and took out the money, which he folded carefully and stowed inside his leather coat. He peered at the other things in the wallet, then stepped towards me, and put it back in my pocket. He was smiling, faintly.

I stood still.

'That's better,' he said, approvingly.

'What's all this about?' I asked. I had some idea that they intended to ransom me to my distant millionaire parent. Along the lines of 'Cable us ten thousand pounds or we post your son back to you in small pieces.' That would mean that they knew all along who I was, and had not just stopped any random motorist in a likely-looking car to rob him.

'Surely you know, sir?' said the driver.

'I've no idea.'

'I was asked to give you a message, Mr York.'

So he did know who I was. And he had not this minute discovered it from my wallet, which contained only money, stamps, and a cheque book in plain view. One or two things with my name on were in a flapped pocket, but he had not looked there.

'What makes you think my name is York?' I asked, trying a shot at outraged surprise. It was no good.

'Mr Alan York, sir, was scheduled to drive along this road on his way from Kempton Park to the Cotswolds at approximately five fifteen p.m. on Saturday, February 27th, in a dark blue Lotus Elite, licence number KAB

890. I must thank you, sir, for making it easy for me to intercept you. You could go a month on the road without seeing another car like yours. I'd have had a job flagging you down if you'd been driving, say, a Ford or an Austin.' His tone was still conversational.

'Get on with your message. I'm listening,' I said.

'Deeds speak louder than words,' said the driver, mildly.

He came close and unbuttoned my jacket, looking at me steadily with wide eyes, daring me to kick him. I didn't move. He untied my tie, opened the neck of my shirt. We looked into each other's eyes. I hoped mine were as expressionless as his. I let my arms go slack in the grip of the two men behind me, and felt them relax their hold slightly.

The driver stepped back and looked towards the fourth man, who had been leaning against the horse-box wall, silently. 'He's all yours, Sonny. Deliver the message,' he said.

Sonny was young, with sideboards. But I didn't look at his face, particularly. I looked at his hands.

He had a knife. The hilt lay in his palms, and his fingers were lightly curled round it, not gripping. The way a professional holds a knife.

There was nothing of the driver's mock deference in Sonny's manner. He was enjoying his work. He stood squarely in front of me and put the point of his short blade on my breastbone. It scarcely pricked, so light was his touch.

Oh bloody hell, I thought. My father would not be at all pleased to receive ransom messages reinforced by pleas from me for my own safety. I would never be able to live it down. And I was sure that this little melodrama was intended to soften me up into a suitably frightened state of mind. I sagged against the post, as if to shrink away from the knife, Sonny's grim mouth smiled thinly in a sneer.

Using the post as a springboard I thrust forwards and sideways as strongly as I knew how, bringing my knee up hard into Sonny's groin and tearing my arms out of the slackened grasp of the men behind me.

I leaped for the door and got it open. In the small area of the horse-box I had no chance, but I thought that if only I could get out into the thicket I might be able to deal with them. I had learned a nasty trick or two about fighting from my cousin, who lived in Kenya and had taken lessons from the Mau Mau.

But I didn't make it.

I tried to swing out with the door, but it was stiff and slow. The driver grabbed my ankle. I shook his hand off, but the vital second had gone. The two men who had held me clutched at my clothes. Through the open door I glimpsed the man who had been leading the horse up and down. He was looking enquiringly at the horse-box. I had forgotten about him.

I lashed out furiously with feet, fists and elbows, but they were too much for me. I ended up where I began, against the matting-padded post with my arms pulled backwards. This time the two men were none too gentle. They slammed me back against the post hard and put their weight on my arms. I felt the wrench in my shoulders and down my chest to my stomach. I shut my teeth.

Sonny, clutching his abdomen, was half sitting, half kneeling in the corner. He watched with satisfaction.

'That hurt the bastard, Peaky,' he said. 'Do it again.'

Peaky and his mate did it again.

Sonny laughed. Not a nice laugh.

A little more pressure and I should have some torn ligaments and a dislocated shoulder. There didn't seem to be much I could do about it.

The driver shut the horse-box door and picked the knife up from the floor, where it had fallen. He was not looking quite so calm as before. My fist had connected with his nose and blood was trickling out of it. But his temper was intact.

'Stop it. Stop it, Peaky,' he said. 'The boss said we weren't to hurt him. He made quite a point of it. You wouldn't want the boss to know you disobeyed him, would you?' There was a threat in his voice.

The tension on my arms slowly relaxed. Sonny's smile turned to a sullen scowl. It appeared I had the boss to thank for something, even if not much.

'Now, Mr York,' said the driver reproachfully, wiping his nose on a blue handkerchief, 'all that was quite unnecessary. We only want to give you a message.'

'I don't like listening with knives sticking into me,' I said.

The driver sighed. 'Yes, sir, I can see that was a mistake. It was meant for you to understand that the warning is serious, see. Take no notice of it, and you'll find you're in real trouble. I'm telling you, real trouble.'

'What warning?' I said, mystified.

'You're to lay off asking questions about Major Davidson,' he said.

'*What?*' I goggled at him. It was so unexpected. 'I haven't been asking questions about Major Davidson,' I said weakly.

'I don't know about that, I'm sure,' said the driver, mopping away, 'but that's the message, and you'd do well to take heed of it, sir. I'm telling you for your own good. The boss don't like people poking into his affairs.'

'Who is the boss?' I asked.

'Now, sir, you know better than to ask questions like that. Sonny, go and tell Bert we've finished here. We'll load up the horse.'

Sonny stood up with a groan and went over to the door, his hand still pressed to his groin. He yelled something out of the window.

'Stand still, Mr York, and you'll come to no harm,' said the driver, his politeness unimpaired. He mopped, and looked at his handkerchief to see if his nose was still bleeding. It was. I took his advice, and stood still. He opened the door and climbed down out of the horse-box. A little time passed during which Sonny and I exchanged glares and nobody said anything.

Then there was the noise of bolts and clips being undone, and the side of the horse-box which formed the ramp was lowered to the ground. The fifth man, Bert, led the horse up the ramp and fastened him into the nearest stall. The driver raised the ramp again and fastened it.

I used the brief period while what was left of the daylight flooded into the box, to twist my head round as far as I could and take a clear look at Peaky. I saw what I expected, but it only increased my bewilderment.

The driver climbed into the cab, shut the door, and started the engine.

Bert said, 'Take him over to the door.' I needed no urging.

The horse-box began to move. Bert opened the door. Peaky and his pal let go of my arms and Bert gave me a push. I hit the ground just as the accelerating horse-box pulled out of the lay-by on to the deserted road. It was as well I had had a good deal of practice at falling off horses. Instinctively, I landed on my shoulder and rolled.

I sat on the ground and looked after the speeding

horse-box. The number plate was mostly obscured by thick dust, but I had time to see the registration letters. They were APX.

The Lotus still stood in the lay-by. I picked myself up, dusted the worst off my suit, and walked over to it. I intended to follow the horse-box and see where it went. But the thorough driver had seen to it that I should not. The car would not start. Opening the bonnet to see how much damage had been done, I found that three of the four sparking plugs had been taken out. They lay in a neat row on the battery. It took me ten minutes to replace them, because my hands were trembling.

By then I had no hope of catching the horse-box or of finding anyone who had noticed its direction. I got back into the car and fastened the neck of my shirt. My tie was missing altogether.

I took out the AA book and looked up the registration letters PX. For what it was worth, the horse-box was originally registered in West Sussex. If the number plate were genuine, it might be possible to discover the present owner. For a quarter of an hour I sat and thought. Then I started the car, turned it, and drove back into Maidenhead.

The town was bright with lights, though nearly all the shops were shut. The door of the police station was open wide. I went in and asked for Inspector Lodge.

'He isn't in yet,' said the policeman at the enquiry

desk, glancing up at the clock. It was ten past six. 'He'll be here any minute, if you care to wait, sir.'

'He isn't in yet? Do you mean he is just starting work for the day?'

'Yes, sir. He's on late turn. Busy evening here, Saturday,' he grinned. 'Dance halls, pubs, and car crashes.' I smiled back, sat down on the bench and waited. After five minutes Lodge came in quickly, peeling off his coat.

'Evening, Small, what's new?' he said to the policeman at the enquiry desk.

'Gentleman here to see you, sir,' said Small, gesturing to me. 'He's only been waiting a few minutes.'

Lodge turned round. I stood up. 'Good evening,' I said.

'Good evening, Mr York.' Lodge gave me a piercing look but showed no surprise at seeing me. His eyes fell to the neck of my shirt, and his eyebrows rose a fraction. But he said only, 'What can I do for you?'

'Are you very busy?' I asked. 'If you have time, I would like to tell you . . . how I lost my tie.' In mid-sentence I funked saying baldly that I had been manhandled. As it was, Small looked at me curiously, clearly thinking me mad to come into a police station to tell an inspector how I lost my tie.

But Lodge, whose perception was acute, said, 'Come into my office, Mr York.' He led the way. He hung up his hat and coat on pegs and lit the gas fire, but its glowing bars couldn't make a cosy place of the austere, square, filing-cabineted little room.

Lodge sat behind his tidy desk, and I, as before, faced him. He offered me a cigarette and gave me a light. As the smoke went comfortingly down into my lungs, I was wondering where to begin.

I said, 'Have you got any further with the Major Davidson business since the day before yesterday?'

'No, I'm afraid not. It no longer has any sort of priority with us. Yesterday we discussed it in conference and consulted your Senior Steward, Sir Creswell Stampe. In view of the verdict at the inquest, your story is considered, on the whole, to be the product of a youthful and overheated imagination. No one but you saw any wire. The grooves on the posts of the fence may or may not have been caused by wire, but there is no indication *when* they were made. I understand it is fairly common practice for groundsmen to raise a wire across a fence so that members of the riding public shall not try to jump it and make holes in the birch.' He paused, then went on, 'Sir Creswell says the view of the National Hunt Committee, several of whom he has talked to on the telephone, is that you made a mistake. If you saw any wire, they contend, it must have belonged to the groundsman.'

'Have they asked him?' I said.

Lodge sighed. 'The head groundsman says he didn't leave any wire on the course, but one of his staff is old and vague, and can't be sure that he didn't.'

We looked at each other in glum silence.

'And what do you think, yourself?' I asked finally.

Lodge said, 'I believe you saw the wire and that Major Davidson was brought down by it. There is one fact which I personally consider significant enough to justify this belief. It is that the attendant who gave his name as Thomas Cook did not collect the pay due to him for two days' work. In my experience there has to be a very good reason for a workman to ignore his pay packet.' He smiled sardonically.

'I could give you another fact to prove that Major Davidson's fall was no accident,' I said, 'but you'll have to take my word for it again. No evidence.'

'Go on.'

'Someone has been to great pains to tell me not to ask awkward questions about it.' I told him about the events in and around the horse-box, and added, 'And how's that for the product of a youthful and overheated imagination?'

'When did all this happen?' asked Lodge.

'About an hour ago.'

'And what were you doing between then and the time you arrived here?'

'Thinking,' I said, stubbing out my cigarette.

'Oh,' said Lodge. 'Well, have you given any thought to the improbabilities in your story? My chief isn't going to like them when I make my report.'

'Don't make it then,' I said, smiling. 'But I suppose

the most glaring improbability is that five men, a horse, and a horse-box should all be employed to give a warning which might much more easily have been sent by post.'

'That certainly indicates an organization of unusual size,' said Lodge, with a touch of irony.

'There are at least ten of them,' I said. 'One or two probably in hospital, though.'

Lodge sat up straighter.

'What do you mean? How do you know?'

'The five men who stopped me today are all taxi-drivers. Either from London or Brighton, but I don't know which. I saw them at Plumpton races three days ago, fighting a pitched battle against a rival gang.'

'What?' Lodge exclaimed. Then he said, 'Yes, I saw a paragraph about it in a newspaper. Do you recognize them positively?'

'Yes,' I said. 'Sonny had his knife out at Plumpton, too, but he was pinned down by a big heavy man, and didn't get much chance to use it. But I saw his face quite clearly. Peaky you couldn't mistake, with that dark widow's peak growing down his forehead. The other three were all rounded up into the same group at Plumpton. I was waiting to give someone a lift, and I had a long time to look at the taxi-drivers after the fight was over. Bert, the man with the horse, had a black eye today, and the man who held my right arm, whose name I don't know, he had some sticking plaster on his forehead. But why were they all free? The last I saw of them, they were bound for the cells, I thought, for disturbing the peace.'

'They may be out on bail, or else they were let off with a fine. I don't know, without seeing a report,' said Lodge. 'Now why, in your opinion, were so many sent to warn you?'

'Rather flattering, sending five, when you come to think of it,' I grinned. 'Perhaps the taxi business is in the doldrums and they hadn't anything else to do. Or else it was, like the driver said, to ram the point home.'

'Which brings me,' said Lodge, 'to another improbability. Why, if you were faced with a knife at your chest, did you throw yourself forward? Wasn't that asking for trouble?'

'I wouldn't have been so keen if he'd held the point a bit higher up; but it was against my breast bone. You'd need a hammer to get a knife through that. I reckoned that I'd knock it out of Sonny's hand rather than into me, and that's what happened.'

'Didn't it cut you at all?'

'Not much,' I said.

'Let's see,' said Lodge, getting up and coming round the desk.

I opened my shirt again. Between the second and third buttons there was a shallow cut an inch or so long in the skin over my breastbone. Some blood had clotted on the cut and there was a dried rusty trail down my chest where a few drops had run. My shirt was spotted here and there. Nothing. I hadn't felt it much.

Lodge sat down again. I buttoned my shirt.

'Now,' he said, picking up his pen and biting the end of it. 'What questions have you been asking about Major Davidson, and of whom have you asked them?'

'That is really what is most surprising about the whole affair,' I said. 'I've hardly asked anything of anybody. And I certainly haven't had any useful answers.'

'But you must have touched a nerve somewhere,' said Lodge. He took a sheet of paper out of the drawer. 'Tell me the names of everyone with whom you have discussed the wire.'

'With you,' I said promptly. 'And with Mrs Davidson. And everyone at the inquest heard me say I'd found it.'

'But I noticed that the inquest wasn't properly reported in the papers. There was no mention of wire in the press,' he said. 'And anyone seeing you at the inquest wouldn't have got the impression that you were hell-bent on unravelling the mystery. You took the verdict very calmly and not at all as if you disagreed with it.'

'Thanks to your warning me in advance what to expect,' I said.

Lodge's list looked short and unsatisfactory on the large sheet of paper.

'Anyone else?' he said.

'Oh . . . a friend . . . a Miss Ellery-Penn. I told her last night.'

'Girl friend?' he asked bluntly. He wrote her down.

'Yes,' I said.

'Anyone else?'

'No.'

'Why not?' he asked, pushing the paper away.

'I reckoned you and Sir Creswell needed a clear field. I thought I might mess things up for you if I asked too many questions. Put people on their guard, ready with their answers – that sort of thing. But it seems, from what you've said about dropping your enquiries, that I might as well have gone ahead.' I spoke a little bitterly.

Lodge looked at me carefully. 'You resent being considered youthful and hot-headed,' he said.

'Twenty-four isn't young,' I said. 'I seem to remember England once had a Prime Minister of that age. He didn't do so badly.'

'That's irrelevant, and you know it,' he said.

I grinned.

Lodge said, 'What do you propose to do now?'

'Go home,' I said, looking at my watch.

'No, I meant about Major Davidson.'

'Ask as many questions as I can think of,' I said promptly.

'In spite of the warning?'

'Because of it,' I said. 'The very fact that five men were sent to warn me off means that there is a good deal to find out. Bill Davidson was a good friend, you know. I can't tamely let whoever caused his death get away with it.' I thought a moment. 'First, I'll find out who owns the taxis which Peaky and Co. drive.'

'Well, unofficially, I wish you luck,' said Lodge. 'But be careful.'

'Sure,' I said standing up.

Lodge came to the street door of the police station and shook hands. 'Let me know how you get on,' he said.

'Yes, I will.'

He raised his hand in a friendly gesture, and went in. I resumed my interrupted journey to the Cotswolds. My wrenched shoulders were aching abominably, but as long as I concentrated on Bill's accident I could forget them.

It struck me that both the accident and the affair of the horse-box should give some clue to the mind which had hatched them. It was reasonable to assume it was the same mind. Both events were elaborate, where some simpler plan would have been effective, and the word 'devious' drifted into my thoughts and I dredged around in my memory chasing its echo. Finally I traced it to Joe Nantwich and the threatening letter which had reached him ten days late, but decided that Joe's troubles had nothing to do with Bill's.

Both the attack on Bill and the warning to me had been, I was certain, more violent in the event than in the plan. Bill had died partly by bad luck, and I would have been less roughly handled had I not tried to escape. I came to the conclusion that I was looking for someone with a fanciful imagination, someone prepared to be brutal up to a point, and whose little squibs, because of their complicated nature, were apt to go off with bigger bangs than were intended.

And it was comforting to realize that my adversary was not a man of superhuman intelligence. He could make mistakes. His biggest so far, I thought, was to go to great lengths to deliver an unnecessary warning whose sole effect was to stir me to greater action.

For two days I did nothing. There was no harm in giving the impression that the warning was being taken to heart.

I played poker with the children and lost to Henry because half my mind was occupied with his father's affairs.

Henry said, 'You aren't thinking what you're doing, Alan,' in a mock sorrowful tone as he rooked me of ten chips with two pairs.

'I expect he's in love,' said Polly, turning on me an assessing female eye. There was that, too.

'Pooh,' said Henry. He dealt the cards.

'What's in love?' said William, who was playing tiddly-winks with his chips, to Henry's annoyance.

'Soppy stuff,' said Henry. 'Kissing, and all that slush.'

'Mummy's in love with me,' said William, a cuddly child.

'Don't be silly,' said Polly loftily, from her eleven years. 'In love means weddings and brides and confetti and things.'

'Well, Alan,' said Henry, in a scornful voice, 'you'd better get out of love quick or you won't have any chips left.'

William picked up his hand. His eyes and mouth opened wide. This meant he had at least two aces. They were the only cards he ever raised on. I saw Henry give him a flick of a glance, then look back at his own hand. He discarded three and took three more, and at his turn, he pushed away his cards. I turned them over. Two queens and two tens. Henry was a realist. He knew when to give in. And William, bouncing up and down with excitement, won only four chips with three aces and a pair of fives.

Not for the first time I wondered at the quirks of heredity. Bill had been a friendly, genuine man of many solid virtues. Scilla, matching him, was compassionate and loving. Neither was at all intellectually gifted; yet they had endowed their elder son with a piercing, exceptional intelligence.

And how could I guess, as I cut the cards for Polly and helped William straighten up his leaning tower of chips, that Henry already held in his sharp eight-year-old brain the key to the puzzle of his father's death.

He didn't know it himself.

CHAPTER SEVEN

The Cheltenham National Hunt Festival meeting started on Tuesday, 2 March.

Three days of superlative racing lay ahead, and the finest 'chasers in the world crowded into the racecourse stables. Ferries from Ireland brought them across by boat and plane load; dark horses from the bogs whose supernatural turn of foot was foretold in thick mysterious brogue, and golden geldings who had already taken prizes and cups galore across the Irish Sea.

Horse-boxes from Scotland, from Kent, from Devon, from everywhere, converged on Gloucestershire. Inside, they carried Grand National winners, champion hurdlers, all-conquering handicappers, splendid hunters: the aristocrats among jumpers.

With four big races in the three days reserved for them alone, every amateur jockey in the country who could beg, borrow, or buy a mount hurried to the course. A ride at Cheltenham was an honour: a win at Cheltenham an experience never to be forgotten. The amateur jockeys embraced the Festival with passionate fervour.

But one amateur jockey, Alan York, felt none of this passionate fervour as he drove into the car park. I could not explain it to myself, but for once the hum of the gathering crowd, the expectant faces, the sunshine of the cold invigorating March morning, even the prospect of riding three good horses at the meeting, stirred me not at all.

Outside the main gate I sought out the newspaper seller I had spoken to at Plumpton. He was a short, tubby little Cockney with a large moustache and a cheerful temperament. He saw me coming, and held out a paper.

'Morning, Mr York,' he said. 'Do you fancy your horse today?'

'You might have a bit on,' I said, 'but not your shirt. There's the Irishman to be reckoned with.'

'You'll do him, all right.'

'Well, I hope so.' I waited while he sold a newspaper to an elderly man with enormous race glasses. Then I said, 'Do you remember the taxi-drivers fighting at Plumpton?'

'Couldn't hardly forget it, could I?' He beamed.

'You told me one lot came from London and one from Brighton.'

'Yes, that's right.'

'Which lot were which?' I said. He looked mystified.

I said, 'Which lot came from London and which came from Brighton?'

'Oh, I see.' He sold a paper to two middle-aged ladies wearing thick tweeds and ribbed woollen stockings, and gave them change. Then he turned back to me.

'Which lot was which, like? Hm . . . I see 'em often enough, you know, but they ain't a friendly lot. They don't talk to you. Not like the private chauffeurs, see? I'd know the Brighton lot if I could see 'em, though. Know 'em by sight, see?' He broke off to yell 'Midday Special' at the top of his lungs, and as a result sold three more papers. I waited patiently.

'How do you recognize them?' I asked.

'By their faces, o'course.' He thought it a foolish question.

'Yes, but which faces? Can you describe them?'

'Oh, I see. There's all sorts.'

'Can't you describe just one of them?' I asked.

He narrowed his eyes, thinking, and tugged his moustache. 'One of 'em. Well, there's one nasty-looking chap with sort of slitty eyes. I wouldn't like a ride in his taxi. You'd know him by his hair, I reckon. It grows nearly down to his eyebrows. Rum-looking cove. What do you want him for?'

'I don't want him,' I said. 'I just want to know where he comes from.'

'Brighton, that's it.' He beamed at me. 'There's

another one I see sometimes, too. A young ted with sideboards, always cleaning his nails with a knife.'

'Thanks a lot,' I said. I gave him a pound note and his beam grew wider. He tucked it into an inside pocket.

'Best of luck, sir,' he said. I left him, with 'Midday Special' ringing in my ears, and went in to the weighing room, pondering on the information that my captors with the horse-box came from Brighton. Whoever had sent them could not have imagined that I had seen them before, and could find them again.

Preoccupied, I suddenly realized that Pete Gregory was talking to me. '. . . Had a puncture on the way, but they've got here safely, that's the main thing. Are you listening, Alan?'

'Yes, Pete. Sorry. I was thinking.'

'Glad to hear you can,' said Pete with a fat laugh. Tough and shrewd though he was, his sense of humour had never grown up. Schoolboy insults passed as the highest form of wit for him; but one got used to it.

'How is Palindrome?' I asked. My best horse.

'He's fine. I was just telling you, they had a puncture . . .' He broke off, exasperated. He hated having to repeat things. 'Oh well . . . do you want to go over to the stables and have a look at him?'

'Yes, please,' I said.

We walked down to the stables. Pete had to come with me because of the tight security rules. Even owners could not visit their horses without the trainer to vouch for them, and stable boys had passes with their photographs on, to show at the stable gate. It was all designed to prevent the doping or 'nobbling' of horses.

In his box I patted my beautiful 'chaser, an eight-year-old bay with black points, and gave him a lump of sugar. Pete clicked his tongue disapprovingly and said, 'Not before the race,' like a nanny who had caught her charge being given sweets before lunch. I grinned. Pete had a phobia on the subject.

'Sugar will give him more energy,' I said, giving Palindrome another lump and making a fuss of him. 'He looks well.'

'He ought to win if you judge it right,' said Pete. 'Keep your eyes on that Irishman, Barney. He'll try to slip you all with a sudden burst as you go into the water so that he can start up the hill six lengths in front. I've seen him do it time and again. He gets everyone else chasing him like mad up the hill using up all the reserves they need for the finish. Now, either you burst with him, and go up the hill at his pace and no faster, or, if you lose him, take it easy up the hill and pile on the pressure when you're coming down again. Clear?'

'As glass,' I said. Whatever one might think of Pete's jokes, his advice on how to ride races was invaluable, and I owed a great deal to it.

I gave Palindrome a final pat, and we went out into the yard. Owing to the security system, it was the quietest place on the racecourse.

'Pete, was Bill in any trouble, do you know?' I said, plunging in abruptly.

He finished shutting the door of Palindrome's box, and turned round slowly, and stood looking at me vaguely for so long that I began to wonder if he had heard my question.

But at last he said, 'That's a big word, trouble. Something happened . . .'

'What?' I said, as he lapsed into silence again.

But instead of answering, he said, 'Why should you think there was any . . . trouble?'

I told him about the wire. He listened with a calm, unsurprised expression, but his grey eyes were bleak.

He said, 'Why haven't we all heard about it before?'

'I told Sir Creswell Stampe and the police a week ago,' I said, 'but with the wire gone they've nothing tangible to go on, and they're dropping it.'

'But you're not?' said Pete. 'Can't say I blame you. I can't help you much, though. There's only one thing . . . Bill told me he'd had a telephone call which made him laugh. But I didn't listen properly to what he said – I was thinking about my horses, you know how it is. It was something about Admiral falling. He thought it was a huge joke and I didn't go into it with him to find out what I'd missed. I didn't think it was important. When Bill was killed I did wonder if there could possibly be anything odd about it, but I asked you, and you said you hadn't noticed anything . . .' His voice trailed off.

'Yes, I'm sorry,' I said. Then I asked, 'How long before his accident did Bill tell you about the telephone call?'

'The last time I spoke to him,' Pete said. 'It was on the Friday morning just before I flew to Ireland. I rang him to say that all was ready for Admiral's race at Maidenhead the next day.'

We began to walk back to the weighing room. On an impulse I said, 'Pete, do you ever use the Brighton taxis?' He lived and trained on the Sussex Downs.

'Not often,' he said. 'Why?'

'There are one or two taxi-drivers there I'd like to have a few words with,' I said, not adding that I'd prefer to have the words with them one at a time in a deserted back alley.

'There are several taxi lines in Brighton, as far as I know,' he said. 'If you want to find one particular driver, why don't you try the railway station? That's where I've usually taken a taxi from. They line up there in droves for the London trains.' His attention drifted off as an Irish horse passed us on its way into the paddock for the first race.

'That's Connemara Pal or I'm a Dutchman,' said Pete enviously. 'I took one of my owners over and tried to buy him, last August, but they wanted eight thousand for him. He was tucked away in a broken-down hut behind some pigsties, so my owner wouldn't pay that price. And now look at him. He won the Leopardstown novice 'chase on Boxing Day by twenty lengths and would have blown a candle out afterwards. Best young horse we'll see this year.' Pete's mind was firmly back in its familiar groove, and we talked about the Irish raid until we were back in the weighing room.

I sought out Clem, who was very busy, and checked with him that my kit was all right, and that he knew the weight I was due to carry on Palindrome.

Kate had told me she was not coming to Cheltenham, so I went in search of the next best thing: news of her.

Dane's peg and section of bench were in the smaller of the two changing rooms, and he was sitting only one place away from the roaring stove, a sure sign of his rise in the jockeys' world. Champions get the warmest places by unwritten right. Beginners shiver beside the draughty doors.

He was clad in his shirt and pants, and was pulling on his nylon stockings. There was a hole in each foot and both his big toes were sticking comically out of them. He had long narrow feet, and long, narrow delicately strong hands to match.

'It's all very well for you to laugh,' said Dane, pulling the tops of the stockings over his knees. 'They don't seem to make nylons for size eleven shoes . . .'

'Get Walter to get you some stretching ones,' I suggested. 'Have you a busy day?'

'Three, including the Champion Hurdle,' said Dane.

'Pete has entered half the stable here.' He grinned at me. 'I might just find time to tell you about the Penn household, though, if that's what you're after. Shall I start with Uncle George, or Aunt Deb, or . . .' He broke off to pull on his silk breeches and his riding boots. His valet, Walter, gave him his under-jersey and some particularly vile pink and orange colours. Whoever had chosen them had paid no regard to their effect against a manly complexion. '. . . Or do you want to hear about Kate?' finished Dane, covering up the sickening jersey with a windproof jacket.

The changing room was filling up, packed with the extra Irish jockeys who had come over for the meeting and were in high spirits and robust voice. Dane and I went out into the crowded weighing room, where at least one could hear oneself speak.

'Uncle George,' he said, 'is a gem. And I'm not going to spoil him for you by telling you about him. Aunt Deb is the Honourable Mrs Penn to you and me, mate, and Aunt Deb to Kate alone. She has a chilly sort of charm that lets you know she would be downright rude if she were not so well bred. She disapproved of me, for a start. I think she disapproves on principle of everything to do with racing, including Heavens Above and Uncle George's idea of a birthday present.'

'Go on,' I urged, anxious for him to come to the most interesting part of the chronicle before someone else buttonholed him.

'Ah yes. Kate. Gorgeous, heavenly Kate. Strictly, you know, her name is Kate Ellery, not Penn at all. Uncle George added the hyphen and the Penn to her name when he took her in. He said it would be easier for her to have the same surname as him – save a lot of explanations. I suppose it does,' said Dane, musingly, knowing full well how he was tantalizing me. He relented, and grinned. 'She sent you her love.'

I felt a warm glow inside. The Cheltenham Festival meeting suddenly seemed not a bad place to be, after all.

'Thanks,' I said, trying not to smile fatuously and scarcely succeeding. Dane looked at me speculatively; but I changed the subject back to racing, and presently I asked him if he had ever heard Bill Davidson spoken of in connection with any sort of odd happenings.

'No, I never did,' he said positively. I told him about the wire. His reaction was typical.

'Poor Bill,' he said with anger. 'Poor old Bill. What a bloody shame.'

'So if you hear anything which might have even the faintest significance . . .'

'I'll pass it on to you,' he promised.

At that moment Joe Nantwich walked straight into Dane as if he hadn't seen him. He stopped without apology, took a step back, and then went on his way to the changing room. His eyes were wide, unfocused, staring.

'He's drunk,' said Dane, incredulously. 'His breath smells like a distillery.'

'He has his troubles,' I said.

'He'll have more still before the afternoon's much older. Just wait, till one of the Stewards catches that alcoholic blast.'

Joe reappeared at our side. It was true that one could smell his approach a good yard away. Without preamble he spoke directly to me.

'I've had another one.' He took a paper out of his pocket. It had been screwed up and straightened out again, so that it was wrinkled in a hundred fine lines, but its ball-pointed message was still abundantly clear.

BOLINGBROKE. THIS WEEK, it said.

'When did you get it?' I asked.

'It was here when I arrived, waiting for me in the letter rack.'

'You've tanked up pretty quickly, then,' I said.

'I'm not drunk,' said Joe indignantly. 'I only had a couple of quick ones in the bar opposite the weighing room.'

Dane and I raised our eyebrows in unison. The bar opposite the weighing room had no front wall, and anyone drinking there was in full view of every trainer, owner, and Steward who walked out of the weighing room. There might be a surer way for a jockey to commit professional suicide than to have 'a couple of quick ones' at that bar before the first race, but I couldn't think of it off-hand. Joe hiccuped.

'Double quick ones, I imagine,' said Dane with a smile, taking the paper out of my hand and reading it. 'What does it mean, Bolingbroke this week? Why are you so steamed up about it?'

Joe snatched the paper away and stuffed it back into his pocket. He seemed for the first time to be aware that Dane was listening.

'It's none of your business,' he said rudely.

I felt a great impulse to assure him it was none of mine either. But he turned back to me and said, 'What shall I do?' in a voice full of whining self-pity.

'Are you riding today?' I asked.

'I'm in the fourth and the last. Those bloody amateurs have got two races all to themselves today. A bit thick, isn't it, leaving us only four races to earn our living in? Why don't the fat-arsed gentlemen riders stick to the point-to-points where they belong? That's all they're – well, fit for,' he added, alliteratively.

There was a small silence. Dane laughed. Joe was after all not too drunk to realize he was riding his hobby horse in front of the wrong man. He said weakly, in his smarmiest voice, 'Well, Alan, of course I didn't mean you personally . . .'

'If you still want my advice, in view of your opinion of amateur jockeys,' I said, keeping a straight face, 'you should drink three cups of strong black coffee and stay out of sight as long as you can.'

'I mean, what shall I do about this note?' Joe had a thicker skin than a coach-hide cabin trunk.

'Pay it no attention at all,' I said. 'I should think that whoever wrote it is playing with you. Perhaps he knows you like to drown your sorrows in whisky and is relying on you to destroy yourself without his having to do anything but send you frightening letters. A neat, bloodless, and effective revenge.'

The sullen pout on Joe's babyish face slowly changed into a mulish determination which was only slightly less repellent.

'No one's going to do that to me,' he said, with an aggressiveness which I guessed would diminish with the alcohol level in his blood. He weaved off out of the weighing room door, presumably in search of black coffee. Before Dane could ask me what was going on, he received a hearty slap on the back from Sandy Mason, who was staring after Joe with dislike.

'What's up with that stupid little clot?' he asked, but he didn't wait for an answer. He said, 'Look, Dane, be a pal and gen me up on this horse of Gregory's I'm riding in the first. I've never seen it before, as far as I know. It seems the owner likes my red hair or something.' Sandy's infectious laugh made several people look round with answering smiles.

'Sure,' said Dane. They launched into a technical discussion and I turned away from them. But Dane touched my arm.

He said, 'Is it all right for me to tell people, say Sandy for instance, about the wire and Bill?'

'Yes, do. You might strike oil with someone I wouldn't have thought of asking about it. But be careful.' I thought of telling him about the warning in the horse-box, but it was a long story and it seemed enough to say, 'Remember that you're stirring up people who can kill, even if by mistake.'

He looked startled. 'Yes, you're right. I'll be careful.'

We turned back to Sandy together.

'What are you two so solemn about? Has someone swiped that luscious brunette you're both so keen on?' he said.

'It's about Bill Davidson,' said Dane, disregarding this.

'What about him?'

'The fall that killed him was caused by some wire being strung across the top of the fence, Alan saw it.'

Sandy looked aghast. 'Alan saw it,' he repeated, and then, as the full meaning of what Dane had said sank in, 'But that's murder.'

I pointed out the reasons for supposing that murder had not been intended. Sandy's brown eyes stared at me unwinkingly until I had finished.

'I guess you're right,' he said. 'What are you going to do about it?'

'He's trying to find out what is behind it all,' said Dane. 'We thought you might be able to help. Have you heard anything that might explain it? People tell you things, you know.'

Sandy ran his strong brown hands through his unruly red hair, and rubbed the nape of his neck. This brain massage produced no great thoughts, however. 'Yes, but mostly they tell me about their girl friends or their bets or such like. Not Major Davidson though. We weren't exactly on a bosom pals basis, because he thought I strangled a horse belonging to a friend of his. Well,' said Sandy with an engaging grin, 'maybe I did, at that. Anyway, we had words, as they say, a few months ago.'

'See if your bookmaker friends have heard any whispers, then,' said Dane. 'They usually have their ears usefully to the ground.'

'OK,' said Sandy. 'I'll pass the news along and see what happens. Now come on, we haven't much time before the first and I want to know what this sod of a horse is going to do.' And as Dane hesitated, he said, 'Come on, you don't have to wrap it up. Gregory only asks me to ride for him when it's such a stinker that he daren't ask any sensible man to get up on it.'

'It's a mare,' said Dane, 'with a beastly habit of galloping into the bottoms of fences as if they weren't there. She usually ends up in the open ditch.'

'Well, thanks,' said Sandy, apparently undaunted by this news. 'I'll tan her hide for her and she'll soon change her ways. See you later, then.' He went into the changing room.

Dane looked after him. 'The horse isn't foaled that could frighten that blighter Sandy,' he said with admiration.

'Nothing wrong with his nerve,' I agreed. 'But why ever is Pete running an animal like that here, of all places?'

'The owner fancies having a runner at Cheltenham. You know how it is. Snob value, and so on,' he said indulgently.

We were being jostled continually, as we talked, by the throng of trainers and owners. We went outside. Dane was immediately appropriated by a pair of racing journalists who wanted his views on his mount in the Gold Cup, two days distant.

The afternoon wore on. The racing began. With the fine sunny day and the holiday mood of the crowd, the excitement was almost crackling in the air.

Sandy got the mare over the first open ditch but disappeared into the next. He came back with a broad smile, cursing hard.

Joe reappeared after the second race, looking less drunk but more frightened. I avoided him shamelessly.

Dane, riding like a demon, won the Champion Hurdle by a head. Pete, patting his horse and sharing with the owner the congratulations of the great crowd round the unsaddling enclosure, was so delighted he could hardly speak. Large and red-faced, he stood there with his hat pushed back showing his baldness, trying to look as if this sort of thing happened every day, when it was in fact the most important winner he had trained.

He was so overcome that he forgot, as we stood some time later in the parade ring before the amateurs' race, to make his customary joke about Palindrome going backwards as well as forwards. And when I, following his advice to the letter, stuck like a shadow to the Irishman when he tried to slip the field, lay a scant length behind him all the way to the last fence, and passed him with a satisfying spurt fifty yards from the winning post, Pete said his day was complete.

I could have hugged him, I was so elated. Although I had won several races back in Rhodesia and about thirty since I had been in England, this was my first win at Cheltenham. I felt as high as if I had already drunk the champagne which waited unopened in the changing-room, the customary crateful of celebration for Champion Hurdle day. Palindrome was, in my eyes, the most beautiful, most intelligent, most perfect horse in the world. I walked on air to the scales to weigh in, and changed into my ordinary clothes, and had still not returned to earth when I went outside again. The gloom I had arrived in seemed a thousand years ago. I was so happy I could have turned cartwheels like a child. Such total, unqualified fulfilment comes rarely enough: and unexpectedly, I wished that my father were there to share it.

The problem of Bill had receded like a dot in the distance, and it was only because I had earlier planned to do it that I directed my airy steps down to the horse-box parking ground.

It was packed. About twenty horses ran in each race that day, and almost every horse-box available must have been pressed into service to bring them. I sauntered along the rows, humming light-heartedly, looking at the number plates with half an eye and less attention.

And there it was.

APX 708.

My happiness burst like a bubble.

There was no doubt it was the same horse-box. Regulation wooden Jennings design. Elderly, with dull and battered varnish. No name of owner or trainer painted anywhere on the doors or bodywork.

There was no one in the driver's cab. I walked round to the back, opened the door, and climbed in.

The horse-box was empty except for a bucket, a hay net, and a rug, the normal travelling kit for racehorses. The floor was strewn with straw, whereas three days earlier it had been swept clean.

The rug, I thought, might give me a clue as to where the box had come from. Most trainers and some owners have their initials embroidered or sewn in tape in large letters on the corners of their horse rugs. If there were initials on this one, it would be easy.

I picked it up. It was pale fawn with a dark brown binding. I found the initials. I stood there as if turned to stone. Plainly in view, embroidered in dark brown silk, were the letters A.Y.

It was my own rug.

Pete, when I ran him to earth, looked in no mood to answer any questions needing much thought. He leaned back against the weighing-room wall with a glass of champagne in one hand and a cigar in the other, surrounded by a pack of friends similarly equipped. From their rosy smiling faces I gathered the celebration had already been going on for some time.

Dane thrust a glass into my hand.

'Where have you been? Well done on Palindrome. Have some bubbly. The owner's paying, God bless him.' His eyes were alight with that fantastic, top-of-the-world elation that I had so lately felt myself. It began to creep back into me too. It was, after all, a great day. Mysteries could wait.

I drank a sip of champagne and said, 'Well done yourself, you old son-of-a-gun. And here's to the Gold Cup.'

'No such luck,' said Dane. 'I haven't much chance in that.' And from his laughing face I gathered he didn't care, either. We emptied our glasses. 'I'll get another bottle,' he said, diving into the noisy, crowded changing room.

Looking around I saw Joe Nantwich backed up into a nearby corner by the enormous Mr Tudor. The big man was doing the talking, forcefully, his dark face almost merging with the shadows. Joe, still dressed in racing colours, listened very unhappily.

Dane came back with the bubbles fizzing out of a newly opened bottle and filled our glasses. He followed my gaze.

'I don't know whether Joe was sober or not, but didn't he make a hash of the last race?' he said.

'I didn't see it.'

'Brother, you sure missed something. He didn't try a yard. His horse damned nearly stopped altogether at the hurdle over on the far side, and it was second favourite, too. What you see now,' he gestured with the bottle, 'is, I should think, our Joe getting the well-deserved sack.'

'That man owns Bolingbroke,' I said.

'Yes, that's right. Same colours. What a fool Joe is. Owners with five or six goodish horses don't grow on bushes any more.'

Clifford Tudor had nearly done. As he turned away from Joe in our direction we heard the tail end of his remarks.

'... think you can make a fool of me and get away

with it. The Stewards can warn you off altogether, as far as I'm concerned.'

He strode past us, giving me a nod of recognition, which surprised me, and went out.

Joe leaned against the wall for support. His face was pallid and sweating. He looked ill. He took a few unsteady steps towards us and spoke without caution, as if he had forgotten that Stewards and members of the National Hunt Committee might easily overhear.

'I had a phone call this morning. The same voice as always. He just said, "Don't win the sixth race" and rang off before I could say anything. And then that note saying "Bolingbroke, this week" . . . I don't understand it . . . and I didn't win the race and now that bloody wog says he'll get another jockey . . . and the Stewards have started an inquiry about my riding . . . and I feel sick.'

'Have some champagne,' said Dane, encouragingly.

'Don't be so bloody helpful,' said Joe, clutching his stomach and departing towards the changing-room.

'What the hell's going on?' said Dane.

'I don't know,' I said, perplexed and more interested in Joe's troubles than I had been before. The phone call was inconsistent, I thought, with the notes. One ordered business as usual, the other promised revenge. 'I wonder if Joe always tells the truth,' I said.

'Highly unlikely,' said Dane, dismissing it.

One of the Stewards came and reminded us that even after the Champion Hurdle, drinking in the weighing room itself was frowned on, and would we please drift along into the changing room. Dane did that, but I finished my drink and went outside.

Pete, still attended by a posse of friends, had decided that it was time to go home. The friends were unwilling. The racecourse bars, they were saying, were still open.

I walked purposefully up to Pete, and he made me his excuse for breaking away. We went towards the gates.

'Whew, what a day!' said Pete, mopping his brow with a white handkerchief and throwing away the stub of his cigar.

'A wonderful day,' I agreed, looking at him carefully.

'You can take that anxious look off your face, Alan, my lad. I'm as sober as a judge and I'm driving myself home.'

'Good. In that case you'll have no difficulty in answering one small question for me?'

'Shoot.'

'In what horse-box did Palindrome come to Cheltenham?' I said.

'Eh? I hired one. I had five runners here today. The hurdler, the mare, and the black gelding came in my own box. I had to hire one for Palindrome and the novice Dane rode in the first.'

'Where did you hire it from?'

'What's the matter?' asked Pete. 'I know it's a bit old, and it had a puncture on the way, as I told you, but it didn't do him any harm. Can't have done, or he wouldn't have won.'

'No, it's nothing like that,' I said. 'I just want to know where that horse-box comes from.'

'It's not worth buying, if that's what you're after. Too old by half.'

'Pete, I don't want to buy it. Just tell me where it comes from.'

'The firm I usually hire a box from, Littlepeths of Steyning.' He frowned. 'Wait a minute. At first they said all their boxes were booked up; then they said they could get me a box if I didn't mind an old one.'

'Who drove it here?' I asked.

'Oh, one of their usual drivers. He was swearing a bit at having to drive such an old hen coop. He said the firm had got two good horse-boxes out of action in Cheltenham week and he took a poor view of the administration.'

'Do you know him well?'

'Not exactly well. He often drives the hired boxes, that's all. He's always grousing about something. Now, what is all this in aid of?'

'It may have something to do with Bill's death,' I said, 'but I'm not sure what. Can you find out where the box really comes from? Ask the hire firm? And don't mention me, if you don't mind.'

'Is it important?' asked Pete.

'Yes, it is.'

'I'll ring 'em tomorrow morning, then,' he said.

As soon as he saw me the next day, Pete said, 'I asked about that horse-box. It belongs to a farm near Steyning. I've got his name and address here.' He tucked two fingers into his breast pocket, brought out a slip of paper, and gave it to me. 'The farmer uses the box to take his hunters around, and his children's show jumpers in the summer. He sometimes lets the hire firm use it, if he's not needing it. Is that what you wanted?'

'Yes, thank you very much,' I said. I put the paper in my wallet.

By the end of the Festival meeting I had repeated the story of the wire to at least ten more people, in the hope that someone might know why it had been put there. The tale spread fast round the racecourse.

I told fat Lew Panake, the well-dressed bookmaker who took my occasional bets. He promised to 'sound out the boys' and let me know.

I told Calvin Bone, a professional punter, whose nose for the smell of dirty work was as unerring as a bloodhound's.

I told a sly little tout who made his living passing on

stray pieces of information to anyone who would pay for them.

I told the newspaper seller, who tugged his moustache and ignored a customer.

I told a racing journalist who could scent a doping scandal five furlongs away.

I told an army friend of Bill's; I told Clem in the weighing-room; I told Pete Gregory's head travelling lad.

From all this busy sowing in the wind I learned absolutely nothing. And I would still, I supposed, have to reap the whirlwind.

CHAPTER EIGHT

On Saturday morning as I sat with Scilla and the children and Joan round the large kitchen table having a solidly domestic breakfast, the telephone rang.

Scilla went to answer it, but came back saying, 'It's for you, Alan. He wouldn't give his name.'

I went into the drawing-room and picked up the receiver. The March sun streamed through the windows on to a big bowl of red and yellow striped crocuses which stood on the telephone table. I said, 'Alan York speaking.'

'Mr York, I gave you a warning a week ago today. You have chosen to ignore it.'

I felt the hairs rising on my neck. My scalp itched. It was a soft voice with a husky, whispering note to it, not savage or forceful, but almost mildly conversational.

I didn't answer. The voice said, 'Mr York? Are you still there?'

'Yes.'

'Mr York, I am not a violent man. Indeed, I dislike

violence. I go out of my way to avoid it, Mr York. But sometimes it is thrust upon me, sometimes it is the only way to achieve results. Do you understand me, Mr York?'

'Yes,' I said.

'If I were a violent man, Mr York, I would have sent you a rougher warning last week. And I'm giving you another chance, to show you how reluctant I am to harm you. Just mind your own business and stop asking foolish questions. That's all. Just stop asking questions, and nothing will happen to you.' There was a pause, then the soft voice went on, with a shade, a first tinge, of menace, 'Of course, if I find that violence is absolutely necessary, I always get someone else to apply it. So that I don't have to watch. So that it is not too painful to me. You do understand me, I hope, Mr York?'

'Yes,' I said again. I thought of Sonny, his vicious grin, and his knife.

'Good, then that's all. I do so hope you will be sensible. Good morning, Mr York.' There was a click as he broke the connexion.

I jiggled the telephone rest to recall the operator. When she answered I asked if she could tell me where the call had come from.

'One moment, please,' she said. She suffered from enlarged adenoids. She came back. 'It was routed through London,' she said, 'but I can't trace it beyond there. So sorry.'

'Never mind. Thank you very much,' I said.

'Pleasure, I'm sure,' said the adenoids.

I put down the receiver and went back to my breakfast.

'Who was that?' asked Henry, spreading marmalade thickly on his toast.

'Man about a dog,' I said.

'Or in other words,' said Polly, 'ask no questions and you'll be told no thumping lies.'

Henry made a face at her and bit deeply into his toast. The marmalade oozed out of one corner of his mouth. He licked it.

'Henry always wants to know who's ringing up,' said William.

'Yes, darling,' said Scilla absently, rubbing some egg off his jersey. 'I wish you would lean over your plate when you eat, William.' She kissed the top of his blond head.

I passed my cup to Joan for more coffee.

Henry said, 'Will you take us out to tea in Cheltenham, Alan? Can we have some of those squelchy cream things like last time, and ice-cream sodas with straws, and some peanuts for coming home?'

'Oh, yes,' said William, blissfully.

'I'd love to,' I said, 'but I can't today. We'll do it next week, perhaps.' The day of my visit to Kate's house had come at last. I was to stay there for two nights, and I planned to put in a day at the office on Monday.

Seeing the children's disappointed faces I explained, 'Today I'm going to stay with a friend. I won't be back until Monday evening.'

'What a bore,' said Henry.

The Lotus ate up the miles between the Cotswolds and Sussex with the deep purr of a contented cat. I covered the fifty miles of good road from Cirencester to Newbury in fifty-three minutes, not because I was in a great hurry, but out of sheer pleasure in driving my car at the speed it was designed for. And I was going towards Kate. Eventually.

Newbury slowed me to a crawl, to a halt. Then I zipped briefly down the Basingstoke road, past the American air base at Greenham Common, and from the twisty village of Kingsclere onwards drove at a sedate pace which seldom rose above sixty.

Kate lived about four miles from Burgess Hill, in Sussex.

I arrived in Burgess Hill at twenty-past one, found my way to the railway station, and parked in a corner, tucked away behind a large shooting brake. I went into the station and bought a return ticket to Brighton. I didn't care to reconnoitre in Brighton by car: the Lotus had already identified me into one mess, and I hesitated to show my hand by taking it where it could be spotted by a cruising taxi driven by Peaky, Sonny, Bert, or the rest.

The journey took sixteen minutes. On the train I asked myself, for at least the hundredth time, what chance remark of mine had landed me in the horse-box hornet's nest. Whom had I alarmed by not only revealing that I knew about the wire, but more especially by saying that I intended to find out who had put it there? I could think of only two possible answers; and one of them I didn't like a bit.

I remembered saying to Clifford Tudor on the way from Plumpton to Brighton that a lot of questions would have to be answered about Bill's death; which was as good as telling him straight out that I knew the fall hadn't been an accident, and that I meant to do something about it.

And I had made the same thing quite clear to Kate. To Kate. To Kate. To Kate. The wheels of the train took up the refrain and mocked me.

Well, I hadn't sworn her to secrecy, and I hadn't seen any need to. She could have passed on what I had said to the whole of England, for all I knew. But she hadn't had much time. It had been after midnight when she left me in London, and the horse-box had been waiting for me seventeen hours later.

The train slowed into Brighton station. I walked up the platform and through the gate in a cluster of fellow passengers, but hung back as we came through the booking hall and out towards the forecourt. There were about twelve taxis parked there, their drivers standing outside them, surveying the out-pouring passengers for custom. I looked at all the drivers carefully, face by face.

They were all strangers. None of them had been at Plumpton.

Not unduly discouraged, I found a convenient corner with a clear view of arriving taxis and settled myself to wait, resolutely ignoring the cold draught blowing down my neck. Taxis came and went like busy bees, bringing passengers, taking them away. The trains from London attracted them like honey.

Gradually a pattern emerged. There were four distinct groups of them. One group had a broad green line painted down the wings, with the name Green Band on the doors. A second group had yellow shields on the doors, with small letters in black on the shields. A third group were bright cobalt blue all over. Into the fourth group I put the indeterminate taxis which did not belong to the other lines.

I waited for nearly two hours, growing stiffer and stiffer, and receiving more and more curious looks from the station staff. I looked at my watch. The last train I could catch and still arrive at Kate's at the right time was due to leave in six minutes. I had begun to straighten up and massage my cold neck, ready to go and board it, when at last my patience was rewarded.

Empty taxis began to arrive and form a waiting line, which I now knew meant that another London train was due. The drivers got out of their cars and clustered in little groups, talking. Three dusty black taxis arrived in minor convoy and pulled up at the end of the line. They had faded yellow shields painted on the doors. The drivers got out.

One of them was the polite driver of the horse-box. A sensible, solid citizen, he looked. Middle-aged, unremarkable, calm. I did not know the others.

I had three minutes left. The black letters were tantalizingly small on the yellow shields. I couldn't get close enough to read them without the polite driver seeing me, and I had not time to wait until he had gone. I went over to the ticket office, hovered impatiently while a woman argued about half fares for her teenage child, and asked a simple question.

'What is the name of the taxis with yellow shields on the doors?' The young man in the office gave me an uninterested glance.

'Marconicars, sir. Radio cabs, they are.'

'Thank you,' I said, and sprinted for the platform.

Kate lived in a superbly proportioned Queen Anne house which generations of Gothic-ruin-minded Victorians had left miraculously unspoilt. Its graceful symmetry, its creamy gravelled drive, its tidy lawns already mown in early spring, its air of solid serenity, all spoke of a social and financial security of such long standing that it was to be taken entirely for granted.

Inside, the house was charming, with just a saving touch of shabbiness about the furnishings, as if, though rich, the inhabitants saw no need to be either ostentatious or extravagant.

Kate met me at the door and took my arm, and walked me across the hall.

'Aunt Deb is waiting to give you tea,' she said. 'Tea is a bit of a ritual with Aunt Deb. You will be in her good graces for being punctual, thank goodness. She is very Edwardian, you'll find. The times have moved without her in many ways.' She sounded anxious and apologetic, which meant to me that she loved her aunt protectively, and wished me to make allowances. I squeezed her arm reassuringly, and said, 'Don't worry.'

Kate opened one of the white panelled doors and we went into the drawing-room. It was a pleasant room, wood panelled and painted white, with a dark plum-coloured carpet, good Persian rugs, and flower-patterned curtains. On a sofa at right angles to a glowing log fire sat a woman of about seventy. Beside her stood a low round table bearing a silver tray with Crown Derby cups and saucers and a Georgian silver teapot and cream jug. A dark brown dachshund lay asleep at her feet.

Kate walked across the room and said with some formality, 'Aunt Deb, may I introduce Alan York?'

Aunt Deb extended to me her hand, palm downwards. I shook it, feeling that in her younger days it would have been kissed.

'I am delighted to meet you, Mr York,' said Aunt Deb. And I saw exactly what Dane meant about her chilly, well-bred manner. She had no warmth, no genuine welcome in her voice. She was still, for all her years, or even perhaps because of them, exceedingly good-looking. Straight eyebrows, perfect nose, clearly outlined mouth. Grey hair cut and dressed by a first-class man. A slim, firm body, straight back, elegant legs crossed at the ankles. A fine shirt under a casual tweed suit, hand-made shoes of soft leather. She had everything. Everything except the inner fire which would make Kate at that age worth six of Aunt Deb.

She poured me some tea, and Kate handed it to me. There were pâté sandwiches and a home-made Madeira cake, and although tea was usually a meal I avoided if possible, I found my jinks in Brighton and no lunch had made me hungry. I ate and drank, and Aunt Deb talked.

'Kate tells me you are a jockey, Mr York.' She said it as if it were as dubious as a criminal record. 'Of course I am sure you must find it very amusing, but when I was a gel it was not considered an acceptable occupation in acquaintances. But this is Kate's home, and she may ask whoever she likes here, as she knows.'

I said mildly, 'Surely Aubrey Hastings and Geoffrey Bennett were both jockeys and acceptable when you were – er – younger?'

She raised her eyebrows, surprised. 'But they were gentlemen,' she said.

I looked at Kate. She had stuffed the back of her hand against her mouth, but her eyes were laughing.

'Yes,' I said to Aunt Deb, with a straight face. 'That makes a difference, of course.'

'You may realize then,' she said, looking at me a little less frigidly, 'that I do not altogether approve of my niece's new interest. It is one thing to own a race-horse, but quite another to make personal friends of the jockeys one employs to ride it. I am very fond of my niece. I do not wish her to make an undesirable . . . alliance. She is perhaps too young, and has led too sheltered a life, to understand what is acceptable and what is not. But I am sure you do, Mr York?'

Kate, blushing painfully, said, 'Aunt Deb!' This was apparently worse than she was prepared for.

'I understand you very well, Mrs Penn,' I said, politely.

'Good,' she said. 'In that case, I hope you will have an enjoyable stay with us. May I give you some more tea?'

Having firmly pointed out to me my place and having received what she took to be my acknowledgement of it, she was prepared to be a gracious hostess.

She had the calm authority of one whose wishes had been law from the nursery. She began to talk pleasantly enough about the weather and her garden, and how the sunshine was bringing on the daffodils.

Then the door opened and a man came in. I stood up.

Kate said, 'Uncle George, this is Alan York.'

He looked ten years younger than his wife. He had thick well-groomed grey hair and a scrubbed pink complexion with a fresh-from-the-bathroom moistness about it, and when he shook hands his palm was soft and moist also.

Aunt Deb said, without disapproval in her voice, 'George, Mr York is one of Kate's jockey friends.'

He nodded. 'Yes, Kate told me you were coming. Glad to have you here.'

He watched Aunt Deb pour him a cup of tea, and took it from her, giving her a smile of remarkable fondness.

He was too fat for his height, but it was not a bloated-belly fatness. It was spread all over him as though he were padded. The total effect was of a jolly rotundity. He had the vaguely good-natured expression so often found on fat people, a certain bland, almost foolish, looseness of the facial muscles. And yet his fat-lidded eyes, appraising me over the rim of the teacup as he drank, were shrewd and unsmiling. He reminded me of so many businessmen I had met in my work, the slap-you-on-the-back, come-and-play-golf men who would ladle out the Krug '49 and caviar with one hand while they tried to take over your contracts with the other.

He put down his cup and smiled, and the impression faded. 'I am very interested to meet you, Mr York,' he said, sitting down and gesturing to me to do the same. He looked me over carefully, inch by inch, while he asked me what I thought of Heavens Above. We discussed the horse's possibilities with Kate, which meant that I did most of the talking, as Kate knew little more than she had at Plumpton, and Uncle George's total information about racing seemed to be confined to Midday Sun's having won the Derby in 1937.

'He remembers it because of Mad Dogs and Englishmen,' said Kate. 'He hums it all the time. I don't think he knows the name of a single other horse.'

'Oh, yes I do,' protested Uncle George. 'Bucephalus, Pegasus, and Black Bess.'

I laughed. 'Then why did you give a racehorse to your niece?'

Uncle George opened his mouth and shut it again. He blinked. Then he said, 'I thought she should meet more people. She has no young company here with us, and I believe we may have given her too sheltered an upbringing.'

Aunt Deb, who had been bored into silence by the subject of horses, returned to the conversation at this point.

'Nonsense,' she said briskly. 'She has been brought up as I was, which is the right way. Gels are given too much freedom nowadays, with the result that they lose their heads and elope with fortune hunters or men-about-town of unsavoury background. Gels need strictness and guidance if they are to behave as ladies, and make suitable, well-connected marriages.'

She at least had the grace to avoid looking directly at me while she spoke. She leaned over and patted the sleeping dachshund instead.

Uncle George changed the subject with an almost audible jolt, and asked me where I lived.

'Southern Rhodesia,' I said.

'Indeed?' said Aunt Deb. 'How interesting. Do your parents plan to settle there permanently?' It was a delicate, practised, social probe.

'They were both born there,' I answered.

'And will they be coming to visit you in England?' asked Uncle George.

'My mother died when I was ten. My father might come some time if he is not too busy.'

'Too busy doing what?' asked Uncle George interestedly.

'He's a trader,' I said, giving my usual usefully non-committal answer to his question. 'Trader' could cover anything from a rag-and-bone man to what he actually was, the head of the biggest general trading concern in the Federation. Both Uncle George and Aunt Deb looked unsatisfied by this reply, but I did not add to it. It would have embarrassed and angered Aunt Deb to have had my pedigree and prospects laid out before her after her little lecture on jockeys, and in any case for Dane's sake I could not do it. He had faced Aunt Deb's social snobbery without any of the defences I could muster if I wanted to, and I certainly felt myself no better man than he.

I made instead a remark admiring an arrangement of rose prints on the white panelled walls, which pleased Aunt Deb but brought forth a sardonic glance from Uncle George.

'We keep our ancestors in the dining-room,' he said.

Kate stood up. 'I'll show Alan where he's sleeping, and so on,' she said.

'Did you come by car?' Uncle George asked. I nodded. He said to Kate, 'Then ask Culbertson to put Mr York's car in the garage, will you, my dear?'

'Yes, Uncle George,' said Kate, smiling at him.

As we crossed the hall again for me to fetch my suitcase from the car, Kate said, 'Uncle George's chauffeur's name is not really Culbertson. It's Higgins, or something like that. Uncle George began to call him Culbertson because he plays bridge, and soon we all did it. Culbertson seems quite resigned to it now. Trust Uncle George,' said Kate, laughing, 'to have a chauffeur who plays bridge.'

'Does Uncle George play bridge?'

'No, he doesn't like cards, or games of any sort. He says there are too many rules to them. He says he doesn't like learning rules and he can't be bothered to keep them. I should think bridge with all those conventions would drive him dotty. Aunt Deb can play quite respectably, but she doesn't make a thing of it.'

I lifted my suitcase out of the car, and we turned back.

Kate said, 'Why didn't you tell Aunt Deb you were an amateur rider and rich, and so on?'

'Why didn't you?' I asked. 'Before I came.'

She was taken aback. 'I . . . I . . . er . . . because . . .' She could not bring out the truthful answer, so I said it for her.

'Because of Dane?'

'Yes, because of Dane.' She looked uncomfortable.

'That's quite all right by me,' I said lightly. 'And I like you for it.' I kissed her cheek, and she laughed and turned away from me, and ran up the stairs in relief.

After luncheon – Aunt Deb gave the word three syllables – on Sunday I was given permission to take Kate out for a drive.

In the morning Aunt Deb had been to church with Kate and me in attendance. The church was a mile distant from the house, and Culbertson drove us there in a well-polished Daimler. I, by Aunt Deb's decree, sat beside him. She and Kate went in the back.

While we stood in the drive waiting for Aunt Deb to come out of the house, Kate explained that Uncle George never went to church.

'He spends most of his time in his study. That's the little room next to the breakfast room,' she said. 'He talks to all his friends on the telephone for hours, and he's writing a treatise or a monograph or something about Red Indians, I think, and he only comes out for meals and things like that.'

'Rather dull for your aunt,' I said, admiring the way the March sunlight lay along the perfect line of her jaw and lit red glints in her dark eyelashes.

'Oh, he takes her up to Town once a week. She has her hair done, and he looks things up in the library of the British Museum. Then they have a jolly lunch at the Ritz or somewhere stuffy like that, and go to a matinée or an exhibition in the afternoon. A thoroughly debauched programme,' said Kate, with a dazzling smile.

After lunch, Uncle George invited me into his study to see what he called his 'trophies'. These were a collection of objects belonging to various primitive or barbaric peoples, and, as far as I could judge, would have done credit to any small museum.

Ranks of weapons, together with some jewellery, pots, and ritual objects were labelled and mounted on shelves inside glass cases which lined three walls of the room. Among others, there were pieces from Central Africa and the Polynesian Islands, from the Viking age of Norway, and from the Maoris of New Zealand. Uncle George's interest covered the globe.

'I study one people at a time,' he explained. 'It gives me something to do since I retired, and I find it enthralling. Did you know that in the Fiji Islands the men used to fatten women like cattle and eat them.'

His eyes gleamed, and I had a suspicion that part of the pleasure he derived from primitive peoples lay in contemplation of their primitive violences. Perhaps he needed a mental antidote to those lunches at the Ritz, and the matinées.

I said, 'Which people are you studying now? Kate said something about Red Indians . . .?'

He seemed pleased that I was taking an interest in his hobby.

'Yes. I am doing a survey of all the ancient peoples of the Americas, and the North American Indians were my last subject. Their case is over here.'

He showed me over to one corner. The collection of feathers, beads, knives, and arrows looked almost ridiculously like those in Western films, but I had no doubt that these were genuine. And in the centre hung a hank of black hair with a withered lump of matter dangling from it, and underneath was gummed the laconic lable, 'Scalp'.

I turned round, and surprised Uncle George watching me with a look of secret enjoyment. He let his gaze slide past me to the case.

'Oh, yes,' he said. 'The scalp's a real one. It's only about a hundred years old.'

'Interesting,' I said non-committally.

'I spent a year on the North American Indians because there are so many different tribes,' he went on. 'But I've moved on to Central America now. Next I'll do the South Americans, the Incas and the Fuegians and so on. I'm not a scholar, of course, and I don't do any field work, but I do write articles sometimes for various publications. At the moment I am engaged on a series about Indians for the *Boys' Stupendous Weekly.*' His fat cheeks shook as he laughed silently at what appeared to be an immense private joke. Then he straightened his lips and the pink folds of flesh grew still, and he began to drift back towards the door.

I followed him, and paused by his big, carved, black oak desk which stood squarely in front of the window. On it, besides two telephones and a silver pen tray, lay several cardboard folders with pale blue stick-on labels marked Arapaho, Cherokee, Sioux, Navajo, and Mohawk.

Separated from these was another folder marked Mayas, and I idly stretched out my hand to open it, because I had never heard of such a tribe. Uncle George's plump fingers came down firmly on the folder, holding it shut.

'I have only just started on this nation,' he said

apologetically. 'And there's nothing worth looking at yet.'

'I've never heard of that tribe,' I said.

'They were Central American Indians, not North,' he said pleasantly. 'They were astronomers and mathematicians, you know. Very civilized. I am finding them fascinating. They discovered that rubber bounced, and they made balls of it long before it was known in Europe. At the moment I am looking into their wars. I am trying to find out what they did with their prisoners of war. Several of their frescos show prisoners begging for mercy.' He paused, his eyes fixed on me, assessing me. 'Would you like to help me correlate the references I have so far collected?' he said.

'Well . . . er . . . er . . .' I began.

Uncle George's jowls shook again. 'I didn't suppose you would,' he said. 'You'd rather take Kate for a drive, no doubt.'

As I had been wondering how Aunt Deb would react to a similar suggestion, this was a gift. So three o'clock found Kate and me walking round to the big garage behind the house, with Aunt Deb's grudging consent to our being absent at tea-time.

'You remember me telling you, a week ago, while we were dancing, about the way Bill Davidson died?' I said casually, while I helped Kate open the garage doors.

'How could I forget?'

'Did you by any chance mention it to anyone the

next morning? There wasn't any reason why you shouldn't . . . but I'd like very much to know if you did.'

She wrinkled her nose. 'I can't really remember, but I don't think so. Only Aunt Deb and Uncle George, of course, at breakfast. I can't think of anyone else. I didn't think there was any secret about it, though.' Her voice rose at the end into a question.

'There wasn't,' I said, reassuringly, fastening back the door. 'What did Uncle George do before he retired and took up anthropology?'

'Retired?' she said. 'Oh, that's only one of his jokes. He retired when he was about thirty, I think, as soon as he inherited a whacking great private income from his father. For decades he and Aunt Deb used to set off round the world every three years or so, collecting all those gruesome relics he was showing you in the study. What did you think of them?'

I couldn't help a look of distaste, and she laughed and said, 'That's what I think too, but I'd never let him suspect it. He's so devoted to them all.'

The garage was a converted barn. There was plenty of room for the four cars standing in it in a row. The Daimler, a new cream coloured convertible, my Lotus, and after a gap, the social outcast, an old black eight-horse-power saloon. All of them, including mine, were spotless. Culbertson was conscientious.

'We use that old car for shopping in the village and so on,' said Kate. 'This georgeous cream job is mine.

Uncle George gave it to me a year ago when I came home from Switzerland. Isn't it absolutely rapturous?' She stroked it with love.

'Can we go out in yours, instead of mine?' I asked. 'I would like that very much, if you wouldn't mind.'

She was pleased. She let down the roof and tied a blue silk scarf over her head, and drove us out of the garage into the sunlight, down the drive, and on to the road towards the village.

'Where shall we go?' she asked.

'I'd like to go to Steyning,' I said.

'That's an odd sort of place to choose,' she said. 'How about the sea?'

'I want to call on a farmer in Washington, near Steyning, to ask him about his horse-box,' I said. And I told her how some men in a horse-box had rather forcefully told me not to ask questions about Bill's death.

'It was a horse-box belonging to this farm at Washington,' I finished. 'I want to ask him who hired it from him last Saturday.'

'Good heavens,' said Kate. 'What a lark.' And she drove a little faster. I sat sideways and enjoyed the sight of her. The beautiful profile, the blue scarf whipped by the wind, with one escaping wisp of hair blowing on her forehead, the cherry-red curving mouth. She could twist your heart.

It was ten miles to Washington. We went into the village and stopped, and I asked some children on their way home from Sunday school where farmer Lawson lived.

'Up by there,' said the tallest girl, pointing.

'Up by there' turned out to be a prosperous workmanlike farm with a mellow old farmhouse and a large new Dutch barn rising behind it. Kate drove into the yard and stopped, and we walked round through a garden gate to the front of the house. Sunday afternoon was not a good time to call on a farmer, who was probably enjoying his one carefree nap of the week, but it couldn't be helped.

We rang the door bell, and after a long pause the door opened. A youngish good-looking man holding a newspaper looked at us enquiringly.

'Could I speak to Mr Lawson, please?' I said.

'I'm Lawson,' he said. He yawned again.

I said I understood he had a horse-box for hire. He rubbed his nose with his thumb while he looked us over. Then he said, 'It's very old, and it depends when you want it.'

'Could we see it, do you think?' I asked.

'Yes,' he said. 'Hang on a moment.' He went indoors and we heard his voice calling out and a girl's voice answering him. Then he came back without the newspaper.

'It's round here,' he said, leading the way. The horse-box stood out in the open, sheltered only by the hay piled in the Dutch barn. APX 708. My old friend.

I told Lawson then that I didn't really want to hire his box, but I wanted to know who had hired it eight days ago. And because he thought this question decidedly queer and was showing signs of hustling us off at once, I told him why I wanted to know.

'It can't have been my box,' he said at once.

'It was,' I said.

'I didn't hire it to anyone eight days ago. It was standing right here all day.'

'It was in Maidenhead,' I said, obstinately.

He looked at me for a full half a minute. Then he said, 'If you are right, it was taken without me knowing about it. I and my family were all away last week-end. We were in London.'

'How many people would know you were away?' I asked.

He laughed. 'About twelve million, I should think. We were on one of those family quiz shows on television on Friday night. My wife, my eldest son, my daughter, and I. The younger boy wasn't allowed on because he's only ten. He was furious about it. My wife said on the programme that we were all going to the Zoo on Saturday and to the Tower of London on Sunday, and we weren't going home until Monday.'

I sighed. 'And how soon before you went up to the quiz show did you know about it?'

'A couple of weeks. It was all in the local papers, that we were going. I was a bit annoyed about it, really. It doesn't do to let every tramp in the neighbourhood know you'll be away. Of course, there are my cowmen about, but it's not the same.'

'Could you ask them if they saw anyone borrow your box?'

'I suppose I could. It's almost milking time, they'll be in soon. But I can't help thinking you've mistaken the number plate.'

'Have you a middleweight thoroughbred bay hunter, then,' I said, 'with a white star on his forehead, one lop ear, and a straggly tail?'

His scepticism vanished abruptly. 'Yes, I have,' he said. 'He's in the stable over there.'

'Surely your men would have missed him when they went to give him his evening feed?' I said.

'My brother – he lives a mile away – borrows him whenever he wants. The men would just assume he'd got him. I'll ask the cowmen.'

'Will you ask them at the same time if they found a necktie in the box?' I said. 'I lost one there, and I'm rather attached to it. I'd give ten bob to have it back.'

'I'll ask them,' said Lawson. 'Come into the house while you wait.' He took us through the back door, along a stone-flagged hall into a comfortably battered sitting-room, and left us. The voices of his wife and children and the clatter of teacups could be heard in the distance. A half-finished jigsaw puzzle was scattered on a table; some toy railway lines snaked round the floor.

At length Lawson came back. 'I'm very sorry,' he said, 'the cowmen thought my brother had the horse and none of them noticed the box had gone. They said they didn't find your tie, either. They're as blind as bats unless it's something of theirs that's missing.'

I thanked him all the same for his trouble, and he asked me to let him know, if I found out, who had taken his box.

Kate and I drove off towards the sea.

She said, 'Not a very productive bit of sleuthing, do you think? Anyone in the world could have borrowed the horse-box.'

'It must have been someone who knew it was there,' I pointed out. 'I expect it was because it was so available that they got the idea of using it at all. If they hadn't known it would be easy to borrow, they'd have delivered their message some other way. I dare say one of those cowmen knows more than he's telling. Probably took a quiet tenner to turn a blind eye, and threw in the horse for local colour. Naturally he wouldn't confess it in a hurry to Lawson this afternoon.'

'Well, never mind,' said Kate lightheartedly. 'Perhaps it's just as well Farmer Lawson had nothing to do with it. It would have been rather shattering if he had turned out to be the head of the gang. You would probably have been bopped behind the ear with a gun butt and dumped in a bag of cement out at sea and I would have been tied up on the railway lines in the path of oncoming diesels.'

I laughed. 'If I'd thought he could have possibly been the leader of the gang I wouldn't have taken you there.'

She glanced at me. 'You be careful,' she said, 'or you'll grow into a cosseting old dear like Uncle George. He's never let Aunt Deb within arm's length of discomfort, let alone danger. I think that's why she's so out of touch with modern life.'

'You don't think danger should be avoided, then?' I asked.

'Of course not. I mean, if there's something you've got to do, then to hell with the danger.' She gave an airy wave with her right hand to illustrate this carefree point of view, and a car's horn sounded vigorously just behind us. A man swept past glaring at Kate for her unintentional signal. She laughed.

She swung the car down to the sea in Worthing, and drove eastwards along the coast road. The smell of salt and seaweed was strong and refreshing. We passed the acres of new bungalows outside Worthing, the docks and the power stations of Shoreham, Southwick, and Portslade, the sedate façades of Hove, and came at length to the long promenade at Brighton. Kate turned deftly into a square in the town, and stopped the car.

'Let's go down by the sea,' she said. 'I love it.'

We walked across the road, down some steps, and

staggered across the bank of shingle on to the sand. Kate took her shoes off and poured out a stream of little stones. The sun shone warmly and the tide was out. We walked slowly along the beach for about a mile, jumping over the breakwaters, and then turned and went back. It was a heavenly afternoon.

As we strolled hand in hand up the road towards Kate's car, I saw for the first time that she had parked it only a hundred yards from the Pavilion Plaza Hotel, where I had driven Clifford Tudor from Plumpton ten days earlier.

And talk of the devil, I thought. There he was. The big man was standing on the steps of the hotel, talking to the uniformed doorman. Even at a distance there was no mistaking that size, that dark skin, that important carriage of the head. I watched him idly.

Just before we arrived at Kate's car a taxi came up from behind us, passed us, and drew up outside the Pavilion Plaza. It was a black taxi with a yellow shield on the door, and this time it was close enough for me to read the name: Marconicars. I looked quickly at the driver and saw his profile as he went past. He had a large nose and a receding chin, and I had never seen him before.

Clifford Tudor said a few last words to the doorman, strode across the pavement, and got straight into the taxi without pausing to tell the driver where he wanted to go. The taxi drove off without delay.

'What are you staring at?' said Kate, as we stood beside her car.

'Nothing much,' I said. 'I'll tell you about it if you'd like some tea in the Pavilion Plaza Hotel.'

'That's a dull dump,' she said. 'Aunt Deb approves of it.'

'More sleuthing,' I said.

'All right, then. Got your magnifying glass and bloodhound handy?'

We went into the hotel. Kate said she would go and tidy her hair. While she was gone I asked the young girl in the reception desk if she knew where I could find Clifford Tudor. She fluttered her eyelashes at me and I grinned encouragingly back.

'You've just missed him, I'm afraid,' she said. 'He's gone back to his flat.'

'Does he come here often?' I asked.

She looked at me in surprise. 'I thought you knew. He's on the board of governors. One of the chief shareholders. In fact,' she added with remarkable frankness, 'he very nearly owns this place and has more say in running it than the manager.' It was clear from her voice and manner that she thoroughly approved of Mr Tudor.

'Has he got a car?' I asked.

This was a very odd question, but she prattled on without hesitation. 'Yes, he's got a lovely big car with a long bonnet and lots of chromium. Real classy. But he doesn't use it, of course. Mostly it's taxis for him. Why. just this minute I rang for one of those radio cabs for him. Real useful, they are. You just ring their office and they radio a message to the taxi that's nearest here and in no time at all it's pulling up outside. All the guests use them . . .'

'Mavis!'

The talkative girl stopped dead and looked round guiltily. A severe girl in her late twenties had come into the reception desk.

'Thank you for relieving me, Mavis. You may go now,' she said.

Mavis gave me a flirting smile and disappeared.

'Now, sir, can I help you?' She was polite enough, but not the type to gossip about her employers.

'Er – can we have afternoon tea here?' I asked.

She glanced at the clock. 'It's a little late for tea, but go along into the lounge and the waiter will attend to you.'

Kate eyed the resulting fishpaste sandwiches with disfavour. 'This is one of the hazards of detecting, I suppose,' she said, taking a tentative bite. 'What did you find out about what?'

I said I was not altogether sure, but that I was interested in anything that had even the remotest connexion with the yellow shield taxis or with Bill Davidson, and Clifford Tudor was connected in the most commonplace way with both.

'Nothing in it, I shouldn't think,' said Kate, finishing the sandwich but refusing another.

I sighed. 'I don't think so, either,' I said.

'What next, then?'

'If I could find out who owns the yellow shield taxis . . .'

'Let's ring them up and ask,' said Kate, standing up. She led the way to the telephone and looked up the number in the directory.

'I'll do it,' she said. 'I'll say I have a complaint to make and I want to write directly to the owners about it.'

She got through to the taxi office and gave a tremendous performance, demanding the names and addresses of the owners, managers and the company's solicitors. Finally, she put down the receiver and looked at me disgustedly.

'They wouldn't tell me a single thing,' she said. 'He was a really patient man, I must say. He didn't get ruffled when I was really quite rude to him. But all he would say was, "Please write to us with the details of your complaint and we will look into it fully." He said it was not the company's policy to disclose the names of its owners and he had no authority to do it. He wouldn't budge an inch.'

'Never mind. It was a darned good try. I didn't really think they would tell you. But it gives me an idea . . .'

I rang up the Maidenhead police station and asked

for Inspector Lodge. He was off duty, I was told. Would I care to leave a message? I would.

I said, 'This is Alan York speaking. Will you please ask Inspector Lodge if he can find out who owns or controls the Marconicar radio taxi cabs in Brighton? He will know what it is about.'

The voice in Maidenhead said he would give Inspector Lodge the message in the morning, but could not undertake to confirm that Inspector Lodge would institute the requested enquiries. Nice official jargon. I thanked him and rang off.

Kate was standing close to me in the telephone box. She was wearing a delicate flowery scent, so faint that it was little more than a quiver in the air. I kissed her, gently. Her lips were soft and dry and sweet. She put her hands on my shoulders, and looked into my eyes, and smiled. I kissed her again.

A man opened the door of the telephone box. He laughed when he saw us. 'I'm so sorry . . . I want to telephone . . .' We stepped out of the box in confusion.

I looked at my watch. It was nearly half-past six.

'What time does Aunt Deb expect us back?' I asked.

'Dinner is at eight. We've got until then,' said Kate. 'Let's walk through the Lanes and look at the antique shops.'

We went slowly down the back pathways of Brighton, pausing before each brightly lit window to admire the contents. And stopping, too, in one or two corners in the growing dusk, to continue where we had left off in the telephone box. Kate's kisses were sweet and virginal. She was unpractised in love, and though her body trembled once or twice in my arms, there was no passion, no hunger in her response.

At the end of one of the Lanes, while we were discussing whether to go any further, some lights were suddenly switched on behind us. We turned round. The licensee of The Blue Duck was opening his doors for the evening. It looked a cosy place.

'How about a snifter before we go back?' I suggested.

'Lovely,' said Kate. And in this casual inconsequential way we made the most decisive move in our afternoon's sleuthing.

We went into The Blue Duck.

CHAPTER NINE

The bar was covered with a big sheet of gleaming copper. The beer handles shone. The glasses sparkled. It was a clean, friendly little room with warm lighting and original oils of fishing villages round the walls.

Kate and I leaned on the bar and discussed sherries with the innkeeper. He was a military-looking man of about fifty with a bristly moustache waxed at the ends. I put him down as a retired sergeant-major. But he knew his stuff, and the sherry he recommended to us was excellent. We were his first customers, and we stood chatting to him. He had the friendly manner of all good innkeepers, but underlying this I saw a definite wariness. It was like the nostril cocked for danger in a springbok; uneasy, even when all appeared safe. But I didn't pay much attention, for his troubles, I thought erroneously, had nothing to do with me.

Another man and a girl came in, and Kate and I turned to take our drinks over to one of the small scattered tables. As we did so she stumbled, knocked her glass against the edge of the bar and broke it. A jagged edge cut her hand, and it began to bleed freely.

The innkeeper called his wife, a thin, small woman with bleached hair. She saw the blood welling out of Kate's hand, and exclaimed with concern, 'Come and put it under the cold tap. That'll stop the bleeding. Mind you don't get it on your nice coat.'

She opened a hatch in the bar to let us through, and led us into her kitchen, which was as spotless as the bar. On a table at one side were slices of bread, butter, cooked meats, and chopped salads. We had interrupted the innkeeper's wife in making sandwiches for the evening's customers. She went across to the sink, turned on the tap, and beckoned to Kate to put her hand in the running water. I stood just inside the kitchen door looking round me.

'I'm so sorry to be giving you all this trouble,' said Kate, as the blood dripped into the sink. 'It really isn't a very bad cut. There just seems to be an awful lot of gore coming out of it.'

'It's no trouble at all, dear,' said the innkeeper's wife. 'I'll find you a bandage.' She opened a dresser drawer to look for one, giving Kate a reassuring smile.

I started to walk over from the doorway to take a closer look at the damage. Instantly there was a deadly menacing snarl, and a black Alsatian dog emerged from a box beside the refrigerator. His yellow eyes were fixed on me, his mouth was slightly open with the top lip drawn back, and the razor-sharp teeth were parted. There was a collar round his neck, but he was not chained up. Another snarl rumbled deep in his throat.

I stood stock still in the centre of the kitchen.

The innkeeper's wife took a heavy stick from beside the dresser and went over to the dog. She seemed flustered.

'Lie down, Prince. Lie down.' She pointed with the stick to the box. The dog, after a second's hesitation, stepped back into it and sat erect, still looking at me with the utmost hostility. I didn't move.

'I'm very sorry, sir. He doesn't like strange men. He's a very good guard dog, you see. He won't hurt you now, not while I'm here.' And she laid the stick on the dresser, and went over to Kate with cotton wool, disinfectant, and a bandage.

I took a step towards Kate. Muscles rippled along the dog's back, but he stayed in his box. I finished the journey to the sink. The bleeding had almost stopped, and, as Kate said, it was not a bad cut. The innkeeper's wife dabbed it with cotton wool soaked in disinfectant, dried it, and wound on a length of white gauze bandage.

I leaned against the draining board, looking at the dog and the heavy stick, and remembering the underlying edginess of the innkeeper. They added up to just one thing.

Protection.

Protection against what? Protection against Protection, said my brain, dutifully, in a refrain. Someone had been trying the Protection racket on mine host. Pay up or we smash up your pub . . . or you . . . or your wife. But this particular innkeeper, whether or not I was right about his sergeant-major past, looked tough enough to defy that sort of bullying. The collectors of Protection had been met, or were to be met, by an authentically lethal Alsatian. They were likely to need protection themselves.

The innkeeper put his head round the door.

'All right?' he said.

'It's fine, thank you very much,' said Kate.

'I've been admiring your dog,' I said.

The innkeeper took a step into the room. Prince turned his head away from me for the first time and looked at his master.

'He's a fine fellow,' he agreed.

Suddenly out of nowhere there floated into my mind a peach of an idea. There could not, after all, be too many gangs in Brighton, and I had wondered several times why a taxi line should employ thugs and fight pitched battles. So I said, with a regrettable lack of caution, 'Marconicars.'

The innkeeper's professionally friendly smile vanished, and he suddenly looked at me with appalling, vivid hate. He picked the heavy stick off the dresser and raised it to hit me. The dog was out of his box in one fluid stride, crouching ready to spring, with his ears flat and his teeth bared. I had struck oil with a vengeance.

Kate came to the rescue. She stepped to my side and said, without the slightest trace of alarm, 'For heaven's sake don't hit him too hard because Aunt Deb is expecting us for roast lamb and the odd potato within half an hour or so and she is very strict about us being back on the dot.'

This surprising drivel made the innkeeper hesitate long enough for me to say 'I don't belong to Marconicars. I'm against them. Do be a good chap and put that stick down, and tell Prince his fangs are not required.'

The innkeeper lowered the stick, but he left Prince where he was, on guard four feet in front of me.

Kate said to me, 'Whatever have we walked into?' The bandage was trailing from her hand, and the blood was beginning to ooze through. She wound up the rest of the bandage unconcernedly and tucked in the end.

'Protection, I think?' I said to the innkeeper. 'It was just a wild guess, about the taxis. I'd worked out why you need such an effective guard dog, and I've been thinking about taxi-drivers for days. The two things just clicked, that's all.'

'Some of the Marconicar taxi-drivers beat him up a bit a week ago,' said Kate conversationally to the innkeeper's wife. 'So you can't expect him to be quite sane on the subject.'

The innkeeper gave us both a long look. Then he

went to his dog and put his hand round its neck and fondled it under its chin. The wicked yellow eyes closed, the lips relaxed over the sharp teeth, and the dog leaned against his master's leg in devotion. The innkeeper patted its rump, and sent it back to its box.

'A good dog, Prince,' he said, with a touch of irony. 'Well now, we can't leave the bar unattended. Sue, dear, will you look after the customers while I talk to these young people?'

'There's the sandwiches not made yet,' protested Sue.

'I'll do them,' said Kate, cheerfully. 'And let's hope I don't bleed into them too much.' She picked up a knife and began to butter the slices of bread. The innkeeper and his wife looked less able to deal with Kate than with the taxi-drivers: but after hesitating a moment, the wife went out to the bar.

'Now, sir,' said the innkeeper.

I outlined for him the story of Bill's death and my close contact with the taxi-drivers in the horse-box. I said, 'If I can find out who's at the back of Marconicars, I'll probably have the man who arranged Major Davidson's accident.'

'Yes, I see that,' he said. 'I hope you have more luck than I've had. Trying to find out who owns Marconicars is like running head on into a brick wall. Dead end. I'll tell you all I can, though. The more people sniping at them, the sooner they'll be liquidated.' He leaned over and picked up two sandwiches. He gave one to me, and bit into the other.

'Don't forget to leave room for the roast lamb,' said Kate, seeing me eating. She looked at her watch. 'Oh, dear, we'll be terribly late for dinner and I hate to make Aunt Deb cross.' But she went on placidly with her buttering.

'I bought The Blue Duck eighteen months ago,' said the innkeeper. 'When I got out into civvy street.'

'Sergeant-major?' I murmured.

'Regimental,' he said, with justifiable pride. 'Thomkins, my name is. Well, I bought The Blue Duck with my savings and my retirement pay, and dead cheap it was too. Too cheap. I should have known there'd be a catch. We hadn't been here more than three weeks, and taking good money too, when this chap comes in one night and says as bold as brass that if we didn't pay up like the last landlord it'd be just too bad for us. And he picked up six glasses off the bar and smashed them. He said he wanted fifty quid a week. Well, I ask you, fifty quid! No wonder the last landlord wanted to get out. I was told afterwards he'd been trying to sell the place for months, but all the locals found out they would be buying trouble and left it alone for some muggins like me straight out of the army and still wet behind the ears to come along and jump in with my big feet.'

Innkeeper Thomkins chewed on his sandwich while he thought.

'Well, then, I told him to eff off. And he came back the next night with about five others and smashed the place to bits. They knocked me out with one of my own bottles and locked my wife in the heads. Then they smashed all the bottles in the bar and all the glasses, and all the chairs. When I came round I was lying on the floor in the mess, and they were standing over me in a ring. They said that was just a taste. If I didn't cough up the fifty quid a week they'd be back to smash every bottle in the store-room and all the wine in the cellar. After that, they said, it would be my wife.'

His face was furious, as he relived it.

'What happened?' I asked.

'Well, my God, after the Germans and the Japs I wasn't giving in meekly to some little runts at the English seaside. I paid up for a couple of months to give myself a bit of breathing space, but fifty quid takes a bit of finding, on top of overheads and taxes. It's a good little business, see, but at that rate I wasn't going to be left with much more than my pension. It wasn't on.'

'Did you tell the police?' I asked.

A curious look of shame came into Thomkins' face. 'No,' he said hesitantly, 'not then I didn't. I didn't know then where the men had come from, see, and they'd threatened God knows what if I went to the police. Anyway, it's not good army tactics to re-engage an enemy who has defeated you once, unless you've got reinforcements. That's when I started to think about a dog. And I did go to the police later,' he finished, a little defensively.

'Surely the police can close the Marconicar taxi line if it's being used for systematic crime,' I said.

'Well, you'd think so,' he said, 'but it isn't like that. It's a real taxi service, you know. A big one. Most of the drivers are on the up and up and don't even know what's going on. I told a couple of them once that they were a front for the protection racket and they refused to believe me. The crooked ones look so plausible, see? Just like the others. They drive a taxi up to your door at closing time, say, all innocent like, and walk in and ask quietly for the money; and as like as not they'll pick up a customer in the pub and drive him home for the normal fare as respectable as you please.'

'Couldn't you have a policeman in plain clothes sitting at the bar ready to arrest the taxi driver when he came to collect the money?' suggested Kate.

The innkeeper said bitterly, 'It wouldn't do no good, miss. It isn't only that they come in on different days, at different times, so that a copper might have to wait a fortnight to catch one, but there aren't any grounds for arrest. They've got an IOU with my signature on it for fifty pounds, and if there was any trouble with the police, all they'd have to do would be show it, and they couldn't be touched. The police'll help all right if you can give them something they can use in court, but when it's just one man's word against another, they can't do much.'

'A pity you signed the IOU,' I sighed.

'I didn't,' he said, indignantly, 'but it looks like my signature, even to me. I tried to grab it once, but the chap who showed it to me said it wouldn't matter if I tore it up, they'd soon make out another one. They must have had my signature on a letter or something, and copied it. Easy enough to do.'

'You do pay them, then,' I said, rather disappointed.

'Not on your nellie, I don't,' said the innkeeper, his moustache bristling. 'I haven't paid them a sou for a year or more. Not since I got Prince. He chewed four of them up in a month, and that discouraged them, I can tell you. But they're still around all the time. Sue and I daren't go out much, and we always go together and take Prince with us. I've had burglar alarm bells put on all the doors and windows and they go off with an awful clatter if anyone tries to break in while we're out or asleep. It's no way to live, sir. It's getting on Sue's nerves.'

'What a dismal story,' said Kate, licking chutney off her fingers. 'Surely you can't go on like that for ever?'

'Oh, no, miss, we're beating them now. It isn't only us, see, that they got money from. They had a regular round. Ten or eleven pubs like ours – free houses. And a lot of little shops, tobacconists, souvenir shops, that sort of thing, and six or seven little cafés. None of the big places. They only pick on businesses run by people who own them, like us. When I cottoned on to that I went round to every place I thought they might be putting the screws on and asked the owners straight out if they were paying protection. It took me weeks, it's such a big area. The ones that were paying were all dead scared, of course, and wouldn't talk, but I knew who they were, just by the way they clammed up. I told them we ought to stop paying and fight. But a lot of them have kids and they wouldn't risk it, and you can't blame them.'

'What did you do?' asked Kate, enthralled.

'I got Prince. A year old, he was then. I'd done a bit of dog handling in the army, and I trained Prince to be a proper fighter.'

'You did, indeed,' I said, looking at the dog who now lay peacefully in his box with his chin on his paws.

'I took him round and showed him to some of the other victims of the protection racket,' Thomkins went on, 'and told them that if they'd get dogs too we'd chase off the taxi-drivers. Some of them didn't realize the taxis were mixed up in it. They were too scared to open their eyes. Anyway, in the end a lot of them did get dogs and I helped to train them, but it's difficult, the dog's only got to obey one master, see, and I had to get them to obey someone else, not me. Still, they weren't too bad. Not as good as Prince, of course.'

'Of course,' said Kate.

The innkeeper looked at her suspiciously, but she was demurely piling sandwiches on to a plate.

'Go on,' I said.

'In the end I got some of the people with children to join in too. They bought Alsatians or bull terriers, and we arranged a system for taking all the kiddies to school by car. Those regular walks to school laid them wide open to trouble, see? I hired a judo expert and his car to do nothing but ferry the children and their mothers about. We all club together to pay him. He's expensive, of course, but nothing approaching the protection money.'

'How splendid,' said Kate warmly.

'We're beating them all right, but it isn't all plain sailing yet. They smashed up the Cockleshell Café a fortnight ago, just round the corner from here. But we've got a system to deal with that, too, now. Several of us went round to help clear up the mess, and we all put something into the hat to pay for new tables and chairs. They've got an Alsatian bitch at that café, and she'd come into season and they'd locked her in a bedroom. I ask you! Dogs are best,' said the innkeeper, seriously.

Kate gave a snort of delight.

'Have the taxi-drivers attacked any of you personally, or has it always been your property?' I asked.

'Apart from being hit on the head with my own bottle, you mean?' The innkeeper pulled up his sleeve and showed us one end of a scar on his forearm. 'That's about seven inches long. Three of them jumped me one evening when I went out to post a letter. It was just after Prince had sent one of their fellows off, and silly like, I went out without him. It was only a step to the pillar box, see? A mistake though. They made a mess of me, but I got a good look at them. They told me I'd get the same again if I went to the police. But I rang the boys in blue right up, and told them the lot. It was a blond young brute who slashed my arm and my evidence got him six months,' he said with satisfaction. 'After that I was careful not to move a step without Prince, and they've never got near enough to have another go at me.'

'How about the other victims?' I asked.

'Same as me,' he said. 'Three or four of them were beaten up and slashed with knives. After I'd got them dogs I persuaded some of them to tell the police. They'd had the worst of it by then, I thought, but they were still scared of giving evidence in court. The gang have never actually killed anyone, as far as I know. It wouldn't be sense, anyhow, would it? A man can't pay up if he's dead.'

'No,' I said, thoughtfully. 'I suppose he can't. They might reckon that one death would bring everyone else to heel, though.'

'You needn't think I haven't that in my mind all the time,' he said sombrely, 'but there's a deal of difference between six months for assault and a life sentence or a hanging, and I expect that's what has stopped 'em. This isn't Chicago after all, though you'd wonder sometimes.'

I said, 'I suppose if they can't get money from their old victims, the gang try "protecting" people who don't know about your systems and your dogs . . .'

The innkeeper interrupted, 'We've got a system for that, too. We put an advertisement in the Brighton paper every week telling anyone who has been threatened with Protection to write to a Box number and they will get help. It works a treat, I can tell you.'

Kate and I looked at him with genuine admiration.

'They should have made you a general,' I said, 'not a sergeant-major.'

'I've planned a few incidents in my time,' he said modestly. 'Those young lieutenants in the war, straight out of civvy street and rushed through an officer course, they were glad enough now and then for a suggestion from a regular.' He stirred. 'Well, how about a drink now?'

But Kate and I thanked him and excused ourselves, as it was already eight o'clock. Thomkins and I promised to let each other know how we fared in battle, and we parted on the best of terms. But I didn't attempt to pat Prince.

Aunt Deb sat in the drawing-room tapping her foot. Kate apologized very prettily for our lateness, and Aunt

Deb thawed. She and Kate were clearly deeply attached to each other.

During dinner it was to Uncle George that Kate addressed most of the account of our afternoon's adventures. She told him amusingly and lightly about the wandering horse-box and made a rude joke about the Pavilion Plaza's paste sandwiches, which drew a mild reproof from Aunt Deb to the effect that the Pavilion Plaza was the most hospitable of the Brighton hotels. I gave a fleeting thought to the flighty Mavis, whom I had suspected, perhaps unjustly, of dispensing her own brand of hospitality on the upper floors.

'And then we had a drink in a darling little pub called The Blue Duck,' said Kate, leaving out the telephone box and our walk through the Lanes. 'I cut my hand there—' she held it out complete with bandage, '—but not very badly of course, and we went into the kitchen to wash the blood off, and that's what made us late. They had the most terrifying Alsatian there that I'd ever seen in my life. He snarled a couple of times at Alan and made him shiver in his shoes like a jelly . . .' She paused to eat a mouthful of roast lamb.

'Do you care for dogs, Mr York?' said Aunt Deb, with a touch of disdain. She was devoted to her dachshund.

'It depends,' I said.

Kate said, 'You don't exactly fall in love with Prince. I expect they call him Prince because he's black. The

Black Prince. Anyway, he's useful if any dog is. If I told you two dears what the man who keeps The Blue Duck told Alan and me about the skulduggery that goes on in respectable little old Brighton, you wouldn't sleep sound in your beds.'

'Then please don't tell us, Kate dear?' said Aunt Deb. 'I have enough trouble with insomnia as it is.'

I looked at Uncle George to see how he liked being deprived of the end of the story, and saw him push his half-filled plate away with a gesture of revulsion, as if he were suddenly about to vomit.

He noticed I was watching, and with a wry smile said, 'Indigestion, I'm afraid. Another of the boring nuisances of old age. We're a couple of old crocks now, you know.'

He tried to raise a chuckle, but it was a poor affair. There was a tinge of grey in the pink cheeks, and fine beads of sweat had appeared on the already moist-looking skin. Something was deeply wrong in Uncle George's world.

Aunt Deb looked very concerned about it, and as sheltering her from unpleasant realities was for him so old and ingrained a habit, he made a great effort to rally his resources. He took a sip of water and blotted his mouth on his napkin, and I saw the tremor in his chubby hands. But there was steel in the man under all that fat, and he cleared his throat and spoke normally enough.

He said, 'It quite slipped my mind, Kate my dear, but while you were out Gregory rang up to talk to you about Heavens Above. I asked him how the horse was doing and he said it had something wrong with its leg and won't be able to run on Thursday at Bristol as you planned.'

Kate looked disappointed. 'Is he lame?' she asked.

Uncle George said, 'I could swear Gregory said the horse had thrown out a splint. He hadn't broken any bones though, has he? Most peculiar.' He was mystified, and so, I saw, was Kate.

'Horses' leg-bones sometimes grow knobs all of a sudden, and that is what a splint is,' I said. 'The leg is hot and tender while the splint is forming, but it usually lasts only two or three weeks. Heavens Above will be sound again after that.'

'What a pest,' said Kate. 'I was so looking forward to Thursday. Will you be going to Bristol, Alan, now that my horse isn't running?'

'Yes,' I said. 'I'm riding Palindrome there. Do try and come Kate, it would be lovely to see you.' I spoke enthusiastically, which made Aunt Deb straighten her back and bend on me a look of renewed disapproval.

'It is not good for a young gel's reputation for her to be seen too often in the company of jockeys,' she said.

*

At eleven o'clock, when Uncle George had locked the study door on his collection of trophies, and when Aunt Deb had swallowed her nightly quota of sleeping pills, Kate and I went out of the house to put her car away in the garage. We had left it in the drive in our haste before dinner.

The lights of the house, muted by curtains, took the blackness out of the night, so that I could still see Kate's face as she walked beside me.

I opened the car door for her, but she paused before stepping in.

'They're getting old,' she said, in a sad voice, 'and I don't know what I'd do without them.'

'They'll live for years yet,' I said.

'I hope so . . . Aunt Deb looks very tired sometimes, and Uncle George used to have so much more bounce. I think he's worried about something now . . . and I'm afraid it's Aunt Deb's heart, though they haven't said . . . They'd never tell me if there was anything wrong with them.' She shivered.

I put my arms round her and kissed her. She smiled.

'You're a kind person, Alan.'

I didn't feel kind. I wanted to throw her in the car and drive off with her at once to some wild and lonely hollow on the Downs for a purpose of which the cave men would thoroughly have approved. It was an effort for me to hold her lightly, and yet essential.

'I love you, Kate,' I said, and I controlled even my breathing.

'No,' she said, 'Don't say it. Please don't say it.' She traced my eyebrows with her finger. The dim light was reflected in her eyes as she looked at me, her body leaning gently against mine, her head held back.

'Why not?'

'Because I don't know . . . I'm not sure . . . I've liked you kissing me and I like being with you. But love is so big a word. It's too important. I'm . . . I'm not . . . ready . . .'

And there it was. Kate the beautiful, the brave, the friendly, was also Kate the unawakened. She was not aware yet of the fire that I perceived in her at every turn. It had been battened down from childhood by her Edwardian aunt, and how to release it without shocking her was a puzzle.

'Love's easy to learn,' I said. 'It's like taking a risk. You set your mind on it and refuse to be afraid, and in no time you feel terrifically exhilarated and all your inhibitions fly out of the window.'

'And you're left holding the baby,' said Kate, keeping her feet on the ground.

'We could get married first,' I said, smiling at her.

'No. Dear Alan. No. Not yet.' Then she said, almost in a whisper, 'I'm so sorry.'

She got into the car and drove slowly round to the barn garage. I followed behind the car and helped her shut the big garage doors, and walked back with her to the house. On the doorstep she paused and squeezed my hand, and gave me a soft, brief, sisterly kiss.

I didn't want it.

I didn't feel at all like a brother.

CHAPTER TEN

On Tuesday it began to rain, cold slanting rain which lashed at the opening daffodils and covered the flowers with splashed-up mud. The children went to school in shining black capes with sou'-westers pulled down to their eyes and gum boots up to their knees. All that could be seen of William was his cherubic mouth with milk stains at the corners.

Scilla and I spent the day sorting out Bill's clothes and personal belongings. She was far more composed than I would have expected, and seemed to have won through to an acceptance that he was gone and that life must be lived without him. Neither of us had mentioned, since it happened, the night she had spent in my bed, and I had become convinced that when she woke the next morning she had had no memory of it. Grief and drugs had played tricks with her mind.

We sorted Bill's things into piles. The biggest section was to be saved for Henry and William, and into this pile Scilla put not only cuff links and studs and two gold watches, but dinner jackets and a morning suit and grey top hat. I teased her about it.

'It isn't silly,' she said. 'Henry will be needing them in ten years, if not before. He'll be very glad to have them.' And she added a hacking jacket and two new white silk shirts.

'We might just as well put everything back into the cupboards and wait for Henry and William to grow,' I said.

'That's not a bad idea,' said Scilla, bequeathing to the little boys their father's best riding breeches and his warmly lined white mackintosh.

We finished the clothes, went downstairs to the cosy study, and turned our attention to Bill's papers. His desk was full of them. He clearly hated to throw away old bills and letters, and in the bottom drawer we found a bundle of letters that Scilla had written to him before their marriage. She sat on the window seat reading them nostalgically while I sorted out the rest.

Bill had been methodical. The bills were clipped together in chronological order, and the letters were in boxes and files. There were some miscellaneous collections in the pigeon-holes, and a pile of old, empty, used envelopes with day-to-day notes on the backs. They were reminders to himself, mostly, with messages like 'Tell Simpson to mend fence in five-acre field,' and 'Polly's birthday Tuesday.' I looked through them quickly, hovering them over the heap bound for the wastepaper basket.

I stopped suddenly. On one of them, in Bill's loopy sprawling handwriting, was the name Clifford Tudor, and underneath, a telephone number and an address in Brighton.

'Do you know anyone called Clifford Tudor?' I asked Scilla.

'Never heard of him,' she said without looking up.

If Tudor had asked Bill to ride for him, as he had told me when I drove him from Plumpton to Brighton, it was perfectly natural for Bill to have his name and address. I turned the envelope over. It had come from a local tradesman, whose name was printed on the top left-hand corner, and the postmark was date-stamped January, which meant that Bill had only recently acquired Tudor's address.

I put the envelope in my pocket and went on sorting. After the old envelopes I started on the pigeon-holes. There were old photographs and some pages the children had drawn and written on with straggly letters in their babyhood, address books, luggage labels, a birthday card, school reports, and various notebooks of different shapes and sizes.

'You'd better look through these, Scilla,' I said.

'You look,' she said, glancing up from her letters with a smile. 'You can tell me what's what, and I'll look at them presently.'

Bill had had no secrets. The notebooks mainly contained his day-to-day expenses, jotted down to help his accountant at the annual reckoning. They went back some years. I found the latest, and leafed through it.

School fees, hay for the horses, a new garden hose, a repair to the Jaguar's head-lamp in Bristol, a present for Scilla, a bet on Admiral, a donation to charity. And that was the end. After that came the blank pages which were not going to be filled up.

I looked again at the last entries. A bet on Admiral. Ten pounds to win, Bill had written. And the date was the day of his death. Whatever had been said to Bill about Admiral's falling, he had taken it as a joke and had backed himself to win in spite of it. I would dearly have liked to know what the 'joke' had been. He had told Pete, whose mind was with the horses. He had not told Scilla, nor any of his friends as far as I could find out. Possibly he had thought it so unimportant that after he spoke to Pete it had wholly slipped his mind.

I stacked up the notebooks and began on that last pigeon-hole full of oddments. Among them were fifteen or twenty of the betting tickets issued by bookmakers at race meetings. As evidence of bets lost, they are usually torn up or thrown away by disappointed punters, not carefully preserved in a tidy desk.

'Why did Bill keep these betting tickets?' I asked Scilla.

'Henry had a craze for them not long ago, don't you

remember?' she said. 'And after it wore off Bill still brought some home for him. I think he kept them in case William wanted to play bookmakers in his turn.'

I did remember. I had backed a lot of horses for halfpennies with Henry the bookmaker, the little shark. They never won.

The extra tickets Bill had saved for him were from several different bookmakers. It was part of Bill's pleasure at the races to walk among the bookmakers' stands in Tattersall's and put his actual cash on the best odds, instead of betting on credit with a bookmaker on the rails.

'Do you want to keep them for William still?' I asked.

'May as well,' said Scilla.

I put them back in the desk, and finished the job. It was late in the afternoon. We went into the drawing-room, stoked up the fire, and settled into armchairs.

She said, 'Alan, I want to give you something which belonged to Bill. Now, don't say anything until I've finished. I've been wondering what you'd like best, and I'm sure I've chosen right.'

She looked from me to the fire and held her hands out to warm them.

She said, 'You are to have Admiral.'

'No.' I was definite.

'Why not?' She looked up, sounding disappointed.

'Dearest Scilla, it's far too much,' I said. 'I thought

you meant something like a cigarette case, a keepsake. You can't possibly give me Admiral. He's worth thousands. You must sell him, or run him in your name if you want to keep him, but you can't give him to me. It wouldn't be fair to you or the children for me to have him.'

'He might be worth thousands if I sold him – but I couldn't sell him, you know. I couldn't bear to do that. He meant so much to Bill. How could I sell him as soon as Bill's back was turned? And if I keep him and run him, I'll have to pay the bills, which might not be easy for a while with death duties hanging over me. If I give him to you, he's in hands Bill would approve of, and you can pay for his keep. I've thought it all out, so you're not to argue. Admiral is yours.'

She meant it.

'Then let me lease him from you,' I said.

'No, he's a gift. From Bill to you, if you like.'

And on those terms I gave in, and thanked her as best I could.

The following morning, early, I drove to Pete Gregory's stables in Sussex to jump my green young Forlorn Hope over the schooling hurdles. A drizzling rain was falling as I arrived, and only because I had come so far did we bother to take the horses out. It was not a very satisfactory session, with Forlorn Hope slipping on the wet grass as we approached the first hurdle and not taking on the others with any spirit after that.

We gave it up and went down to Pete's house. I told him Admiral was to be mine and that I would be riding him.

He said, 'He's in the Foxhunters' at Liverpool, did you know?'

'So he is!' I exclaimed delightedly. I had not yet ridden round the Grand National course, and the sudden prospect of doing it a fortnight later was exciting.

'You want to have a go?'

'Yes, indeed,' I said.

We talked over the plans for my other horses, Pete telling me Palindrome was in fine fettle after his Cheltenham race and a certainty for the following day at Bristol. We went out to look at him and the others, and I inspected the splint which Heavens Above was throwing out. His leg was tender, but it would right itself in time.

When I left Pete's I went back to Brighton, parking the Lotus and taking a train as before. I walked out of Brighton station with a brief glance at the three taxis standing there (no yellow shields) and walked briskly in the direction of the headquarters of the Marconicars as listed in the telephone directory.

I had no particular plan, but I was sure the core of the mystery was in Brighton, and if I wanted to discover it, I would have to dig around on the spot. My feelers on the racecourse had still brought me nothing but a husky warning on the telephone.

The Marconicars offices were on the ground floor of a converted Regency terrace house. I went straight into the narrow hall.

The stairs rose on the right, and on the left were two doors, with a third, marked Private, facing me at the far end of the passage. A neat board on the door nearest the entrance said 'Enquiries'. I went in.

It had once been an elegant room and even the office equipment could not entirely spoil its proportions. There were two girls sitting at desks with typewriters in front of them, and through the half-open folded dividing doors I could see into an inner office where a third sat in front of a switchboard. She was speaking into a microphone.

'Yes, madam, a taxi will call for you in three minutes,' she said. 'Thank you.' She had a pleasant high voice of excellent carrying quality.

The two girls in the outer office looked at me expectantly. They wore tight sweaters and large quantities of mascara. I spoke to the one nearest the door.

'Er . . . I'm enquiring about booking some taxis . . . for a wedding. My sister's,' I added, improvising and inventing the sister I never had. 'Is that possible?'

'Oh, yes, I think so,' she said. 'I'll ask the manager. He usually deals with big bookings.'

I said, 'I'm only asking for an estimate . . . on behalf of my sister. She has asked me to try all the firms, to find out which will be most – er – reasonable. I can't give you a definite booking until I've consulted her again.'

'I see,' she said. 'Well, I'll ask Mr Fielder to see you.' She went out, down the passage, and through the door marked Private.

While I waited I grinned at the other girl, who patted her hair, and I listened to the girl at the switchboard.

'Just a minute, sir. I'll see if there's a taxi in your area,' she was saying. She flipped a switch and said, 'Come in, any car in Hove two. Come in, any car in Hove two.'

There was a silence and then a man's voice said out of the radio receiving set, 'It looks as though there's no one in Hove two, Marigold. I could get there in five minutes. I've just dropped a fare in Langbury Place.'

'Right, Jim.' She gave him the address, flipped the switch again, and spoke into the telephone. 'A taxi will be with you in five minutes, sir. I am sorry for the delay, we have no cars available who can reach you faster than that. Thank you, sir.' As soon as she had finished speaking the telephone rang again. She said, 'Marconicars. Can I help you?'

Down the hall came the clip clop of high heels on linoleum, and the girl came back from Mr Fielder. She said, 'The manager can see you now, sir.'

'Thank you,' I said. I went down the hall and through the open door at the end.

The man who rose to greet me and shake hands was a heavy, well-tailored, urbane man in his middle forties. He wore spectacles with heavy black frames, had smooth black hair and hard blue eyes. He seemed a man of too strong a personality to be sitting in the back office of a taxi firm, too high-powered an executive for the range of his job.

I felt my heart jump absurdly, and I had a moment's panic in which I feared he knew who I was and what I was trying to do. But his gaze was calm and business-like, and he said only, 'I understand you wish to make a block booking for a wedding.'

'Yes,' I said, and launched into fictitious details. He made notes, added up some figures, wrote out an estimate, and held it out to me. I took it. His writing was strong and black. It fitted him.

'Thank you,' I said. 'I'll give this to my sister, and let you know.'

As I went out of his door and shut it behind me, I looked back at him. He was sitting behind his desk staring at me through his glasses with unwinking blue eyes. I could read nothing in his face.

I went back into the front office and said, 'I've got the estimate I wanted. Thank you for your help.' I turned to go, and had a second thought. 'By the way, do you know where I can find Mr Clifford Tudor?' I asked.

The girls, showing no surprise at my enquiry, said they did not know.

'Marigold might find out for you,' said one of them. 'I'll ask her.'

Marigold, finishing her call, agreed to help. She pressed the switch. 'All cars. Did anyone pick up Mr Tudor today? Come in please.'

A man's voice said, 'I took him to the station this morning, Marigold. He caught the London train.'

'Thanks, Mike,' said Marigold.

'She knows all their voices,' said one of the girls, admiringly. 'They never have to tell her the number of their car.'

'Do you all know Mr Tudor well?' I asked.

'Never seen him,' said one girl, and the others shook their heads in agreement.

'He's one of our regulars. He takes a car whenever he wants one, and we book it here. The driver tells Marigold where he's taking him. Mr Tudor has a monthly account, and we make it up and send it to him.'

'Suppose the driver takes Mr Tudor from place to place and fails to report it to Marigold?' I asked conversationally.

'He wouldn't be so silly. The drivers get commission on regulars. Instead of tips, do you see? We put ten per cent on the bills to save the regulars having to tip the drivers every five minutes.'

'A good idea,' I said. 'Do you have many regulars?'

'Dozens,' said one of the girls. 'But Mr Tudor is about our best client.'

'And how many taxis are there?' I asked.

'Thirty-one. Some of them will be in the garage for servicing, of course, and sometimes in the winter we only have half of them on the road. There's a lot of competition from the other firms.'

'Who actually owns the Marconicars?' I asked casually.

They said they didn't know and couldn't care less.

'Not Mr Fielder?' I asked.

'Oh, no,' said Marigold. 'I don't think so. There's a Chairman, I believe, but we've never seen him. Mr Fielder can't be all that high up, because he sometimes takes over from me in the evenings and at week-ends. Though another girl comes in to relieve me on my days off, of course.'

They suddenly all seemed to realize that this had nothing to do with my sister's wedding. It was time to go, and I went.

I stood outside on the pavement wondering what to do next. There was a café opposite, across the broad street, and it was nearly lunch-time. I went over and into the café, which smelled of cabbage, and because I had arrived before the rush there was a table free by the window. Through the chaste net curtains of the Olde Oake Café I had a clear view of the Marconicar office. For what it was worth.

A stout girl with wispy hair pushed a typed menu card in front of me. I looked at it, depressed. English home cooking at its very plainest. Tomato soup, choice of fried cod, sausages in batter, or steak and kidney pie, with suet pudding and custard to follow. It was all designed with no regard for an amateur rider's weight. I asked for coffee. The girl said firmly I couldn't have coffee by itself at lunch-time, they needed the tables. I offered to pay for the full lunch if I could just have the coffee, and to this she agreed, clearly thinking me highly eccentric.

The coffee, when it came, was surprisingly strong and good. I was getting the first of the brew, I reflected, idly watching the Marconicar front door. No one interesting went in or out.

On the storey above the Marconicars a big red neon sign flashed on and off, showing little more than a flicker in the daylight. I glanced up at it. Across the full width of the narrow building was the name L. C. PERTH. The taxi office had 'Marconicars' written in bright yellow on black along the top of its big window, and looking up I saw that the top storey was decorated with a large blue board bearing in white letters the information 'Jenkins, Wholesale Hats'.

The total effect was colourful indeed, but hardly what the Regency architect had had in mind. I had a mental picture of him turning in his grave so often that he made knots in his winding sheet, and I suppose I smiled, for a voice suddenly said, 'Vandalism, isn't it?'

A middle-aged woman had sat down at my table, unnoticed by me as I gazed out of the window. She had a mournful horsey face with no make-up, a hideous brown hat which added years to her age, and an earnest look in her eyes. The café was filling up, and I could no longer have a table to myself.

'It's startling, certainly,' I agreed.

'It ought not to be allowed. All these old houses in this district have been carved up and turned into offices, and it's really disgraceful how they look now. I belong to the Architectural Preservation Group,' she confided solemnly, 'and we're getting out a petition to stop people descrating beautiful buildings with horrible advertisements.'

'Are you having success?' I asked.

She looked depressed. 'Not very much, I'm afraid. People just don't seem to care as they should. Would you believe it, half the people in Brighton don't know what a Regency house looks like, when they're surrounded by them all the time? Look at that row over there, with all those boards and signs. And that neon,' her voice quivered with emotion, 'is the last straw. It's only been there a few months. We've petitioned to make them take it down, but they won't.'

'That's very discouraging,' I said, watching the Marconicar door. The two typists came out and went chattering up the road, followed by two more girls whom I supposed to have come down from the upper floors.

My table companion chatted on between spoonfuls of tomato soup. 'We can't get any satisfaction from Perth's at all because no one in authority there will meet us, and the men in the office say they can't take the sign down because it doesn't belong to them, but they won't tell us who it does belong to so that we can petition him in person.' I found I sympathized with Perth's invisible ruler in his disinclination to meet the Architectural Preservation Group on the warpath. 'It was bad enough before, when they had their name just painted on the windows, but neon . . .' Words failed her, at last.

Marigold left for lunch. Four men followed her. No one arrived.

I drank my coffee, parted from the middle-aged lady without regret, and gave it up for the day. I took the train back to my car and drove up to London. After a long afternoon in the office, I started for home at the tail end of the rush-hour traffic. In the hold-ups at crossings and roundabouts I began, as a change from Bill's mystery, to tackle Joe Nantwich's.

I pondered his 'stopping' activities, his feud with Sandy Mason, his disgrace with Tudor, his obscure threatening notes. I thought about the internal workings of the weighing-room, where only valets, jockeys, and officials are allowed in the changing rooms, and trainers and owners are confined to the weighing room itself: while the press and the public may not enter at all.

If the 'Bolingbroke, this week' note was to be believed, Joe would already have received his punishment, because 'this. week' was already last week. Yet I came to the conclusion that I would see him alive and well at Bristol on the following day, even if not in the best of spirits. For, by the time I reached home, I knew I could tell him who had written the notes, though I wasn't sure I was going to.

Sleep produces the answers to puzzles in the most amazing way. I went to bed on Wednesday night thinking I had spent a more or less fruitless morning in Brighton. But I woke on Thursday morning with a name in my mind and the knowledge that I had seen it before, and where. I went downstairs in my dressing-gown to Bill's desk, and took out the betting tickets he had saved for Henry. I shuffled through them, and found what I wanted. Three of them bore the name L. C. PERTH.

I turned them over. On their backs Bill had pencilled the name of a horse, the amount of his bet, and the date. He was always methodical. I took all the tickets up to my room, and looked up the races in the form book. I remembered many casual snatches of conversation. And a lot of things became clear to me.

But not enough, not enough.

CHAPTER ELEVEN

It poured with rain at Bristol, a cold, steady unrelenting wetness which took most of the pleasure out of racing.

Kate sent a message that she was not coming because of the weather, which sounded unlike her, and I wondered what sort of pressure Aunt Deb had used to keep her at home.

The main gossip in the weighing-room concerned Joe Nantwich. The Stewards had held an inquiry into his behaviour during the last race on Champion Hurdle day, and had, in the official phrase, 'severely cautioned him as to his future riding'. It was generally considered that he was very lucky indeed to have got off so lightly, in view of his past record.

Joe himself was almost as cocky as ever. From a distance his round pink face showed no traces of the fear or drunkenness which had made a sodden mess of him at Cheltenham. Yet I was told that he had spent the preceding Friday and Saturday and most of Sunday in the Turkish baths, scared out of his wits. He had drunk himself silly and sweated it off alternately during the whole of that time, confiding to the attendants in tears that he was safe with them, and refusing to get dressed and go home.

The authority for this story, and one who gave it its full flavour, was Sandy, who had happened, he said, to go into the Turkish baths on Sunday morning to lose a few pounds for Monday's racing.

I found Joe reading the notices. He was whistling through his teeth.

'Well, Joe,' I said, 'what makes you so cheerful?'

'Everything.' He smirked. At close quarters I could see the fine lines round his mouth and the slightly bloodshot eyes, but his experiences had left no other signs of strain. 'I didn't get suspended by the Stewards. And I got paid for losing that race.'

'You what?' I exclaimed.

'I got paid. You know, I told you. The packet of money. It came this morning. A hundred quid.' I stared at him. 'Well, I did what I was told, didn't I?' he said aggrievedly.

'I suppose you did,' I agreed, weakly.

'And another thing, those threatening notes. I fooled them you know. I stayed in the Turkish baths all over the week-end, and they couldn't harm me there. I got off scot free,' said Joe triumphantly, as if 'this week' could not be altered to 'next week'. He did not realize either that he had already taken his punishment, that there are other agonies than physical ones. He had suffered a week of acute anxiety, followed by three days of paralysing fear, and he thought he had got off scot free.

'I'm glad you think so,' I said, mildly. 'Joe, answer me a question. The man who rings you up to tell you what horse not to win on, what does his voice sound like?'

'You couldn't tell who it is, not by listening to him. It might be anybody. It's a soft voice, and sort of fuzzy. Almost a whisper, sometimes, as if he were afraid of being overheard. But what does it matter?' said Joe. 'As long as he delivers the lolly he can croak like a frog for all I care.'

'Do you mean you'll stop another horse, if he asks you to?' I said.

'I might do. Or I might not,' said Joe, belatedly deciding that he had been speaking much too freely. With a sly, sidelong look at me he edged away into the changing room. His resilience was fantastic.

Pete and Dane were discussing the day's plans not far away, and I went over to them. Pete was cursing the weather and saying it would play merry hell with the going, but that Palindrome, all the same, should be able to act on it.

'Go to the front at half way, and nothing else will be able to come to you. They're a poor lot. As far as I can see, you're a dead cert.'

'That's good,' I said, automatically, and then

remembered with a mental wince that Admiral had been a dead cert at Maidenhead.

Dane asked me if I had enjoyed my stay with Kate and did not look too overjoyed by my enthusiastic answer.

'Curses on your head, pal, if you have cut me out with Kate.' He said it in a mock ferocious voice, but I had an uncomfortable feeling that he meant it. Could a friendship survive between two men who were in love with the same girl? Suddenly at that moment, I didn't know; for I saw in Dane's familiar handsome face a passing flash of enmity. It was as disconcerting as a rock turning to quicksand. And I went rather thoughtfully into the changing-room to find Sandy.

He was standing by the window, gazing through the curtain of rain which streamed down the glass. He had changed into colours for the first race, and was looking out towards the parade ring, where two miserable-looking horses were being led round by dripping, mackintoshed stable lads.

'We'll need windscreen wipers on our goggles in this little lot,' he remarked, with unabashed good spirits. 'Anyone for a mud bath? Blimey, it's enough to discourage ducks.'

'How did you enjoy your Turkish bath on Sunday?' I asked, smiling.

'Oh, you heard about that, did you?'

'I think everyone has heard about it,' I said.

'Good. Serve the little bastard right,' said Sandy, grinning hugely.

'How did you know where to find him?' I asked.

'Asked his mother . . .' Sandy broke off in the middle of the word, and his eyes widened.

'Yes,' I said. 'You sent him those threatening Bolingbroke notes.'

'And what,' said Sandy, with good humour, 'makes you think so?'

'You like practical jokes, and you dislike Joe,' I said. 'The first note he received was put into his jacket while it hung in the changing-room at Plumpton, so it had to be a jockey or a valet or an official who did it. It couldn't have been a bookmaker or a trainer or an owner or any member of the public. So I began to think that perhaps the person who planted the note in Joe's pocket was not the person who was paying him to stop horses. That person has, strangely enough, exacted no revenge at all. But I asked myself who else would be interested in tormenting Joe, and I came to you. You knew before the race that Joe was not supposed to win on Bolingbroke. When he won you told him you'd lost a lot of money, and you'd get even with him. And I guess you have. You even tracked him down to enjoy seeing him suffer.'

'Revenge is sweet, and all that. Well, it's a fair cop,' said Sandy. 'Though how you know such a lot beats me.'

'Joe told me most of it,' I said.

'What a blabbermouth. That tongue of Joe's will get him into a right mess one of these days.'

'Yes, it will,' I said, thinking of the incautious way Joe had spoken of his 'stopping' and its rewards.

'Did you tell him I had sent him those notes?' asked Sandy, with his first show of anxiety.

'No, I didn't. It would only stir up more trouble,' I said.

'Thanks for that, anyway.'

'And in reward for that small service, Sandy,' I said, 'will you tell me how you knew in advance that Bolingbroke was not supposed to win?'

He grinned widely, rocking gently on his heels, but he didn't answer.

'Go on,' I said. 'It isn't much to ask, and it might even give me a lead to that other mystery, about Bill Davidson.'

Sandy shook his head. 'It won't help you any,' he said. 'Joe told me himself.'

'What?' I exclaimed.

'He told me himself. In the washroom when we were changing before the race. You know how he can't help swanking? He wanted to show off, and I was handy, and besides, he knew I'd stopped a horse or two in my time.'

'What did he say?' I asked.

'He said if I wanted a lesson in how to choke a horse I'd better watch him on Bolingbroke. Well, a nod's as good as a wink to Sandy Mason. I got a punter to put fifty quid on Leica, which I reckoned was bound to win with Bolingbroke not trying. And look what happened. The little sod lost his nerve and beat Leica by two lengths. I could have throttled him. Fifty quid's a ruddy fortune, mate, as far as I'm concerned.'

'Why did you wait as long as ten days before you gave him that first note?' I asked.

'I didn't think of it until then,' he said, frankly. 'But it was a damn good revenge, wasn't it? He nearly got his licence suspended at Cheltenham, and he sweated his guts out for three days at the week-end, all in the screaming heeby-jeebies worked up by yours truly.' Sandy beamed. 'You should have seen him in the Turkish baths. A sodden, whining, clutching wreck. In tears, and begging me to keep him safe. Me! What a laugh. I was nearly sick, trying not to laugh. A cracking good revenge, that was.'

'And you put him over the rails at Plumpton, too,' I said.

'I never did,' said Sandy, indignantly. 'Did he tell you that? He's a bloody liar. He fell off, I saw him. I've a good mind to frighten him again.' His red hair bristled and his brown eyes sparkled. Then he relaxed. 'Oh, well . . . I'll think of something, sometime. There's no rush. I'll make his life uncomfortable – ants in his pants, worms in his boots, that sort of thing. Harmless,' and Sandy began to laugh. Then he said, 'As you're such a roaring success as a private eye, how are you getting on with that other business?'

'Not fast enough,' I said. 'But I know a lot more than I did at this time last week, so I haven't lost hope. You haven't heard anything useful?' He shook his head.

'Not a squeak anywhere. You're not giving it up, then?'

'No,' I said.

'Well, the best of British luck,' said Sandy, grinning.

An official poked his head round the door. 'Jockeys out, please,' he said. It was nearly time for the first race.

Sandy put his helmet on and tied the strings. Then he took out his false teeth, the two centre incisors of the upper jaw, wrapped them in a handkerchief and tucked them into the pocket of the coat hanging on his peg. He, like most jockeys, never rode races wearing false teeth, for fear of losing them, or even swallowing them if he fell. He gave me a gap-toothed grin, sketched a farewell salute, and dived out into the rain.

It was still raining an hour later when I went out to ride Palindrome. Pete was waiting for me in the parade ring, the water dripping off the brim of his hat in a steady stream.

'Isn't this a God-awful day?' he said. 'I'm glad it's you that's got to strip off and get soaked, and not me. I had a bellyful when I was riding. I hope you're good at swimming.'

'Why?' I asked, mystified.

'If you are, you'll know how to keep your eyes open under water.' I suspected another of Pete's rather feeble jokes, but he was serious. He pointed to the goggles slung round my neck. 'You won't need those, for a start. With all the mud that's being kicked up today, they'd be covered before you'd gone a furlong.'

'I'll leave them down, then,' I said.

'Take them off. They'll only get in your way,' he said.

So I took them off, and as I turned my head to ease the elastic over the back of my helmet, I caught a glimpse of a man walking along outside the parade ring. There were few people standing about owing to the rain, and I had a clear view of him.

It was Bert, the man in charge of the horse in the lay-by on Maidenhead Thicket. One of the Marconicar drivers.

He was not looking at me, but the sight of him was as unpleasant as an electric shock. He was a long way from base. He might have travelled the hundred and forty miles solely to enjoy an afternoon's racing in the rain. Or he might not.

I looked at Palindrome, plodding slowly round the parade ring in his waterproof rug.

A dead cert.

I shivered.

I knew I had made some progress towards my quarry, the man who had caused Bill's death, even though he himself was as unknown to me as ever. I had disregarded his two emphatic warnings and I feared I had left a broad enough trail for him to be well aware of my pursuit. Bert would not be at Bristol alone, I thought, and I could guess that a third deterrent message was on its way.

There are times when one could do without an intuition, and this was one of them. Palindrome, the dead cert. What had been done once would be tried again, and somewhere out on the rain-swept racecourse another strand of wire could be waiting. For no logical reason, I was certain of it.

It was too late to withdraw from the race. Palindrome was an odds-on favourite, and clearly in the best of health; he showed no lameness, no broken blood-vessels, none of the permitted excuses for a last minute cancellation. And if I myself were suddenly taken ill and couldn't ride, another jockey would be quickly found to take my place. I couldn't send someone out in my colours to take a fall designed for me.

If I refused point-blank, without explanation, to let Palindrome run in the race, my permit to ride would be withdrawn, and that would be the end of my steeple-chasing.

If I said to the Stewards, 'Someone is going to bring Palindrome down with wire,' they might possibly send an official round the course to inspect the fences: but he wouldn't find anything. I was quite sure that if a wire were rigged, it would be, as in Bill's case, a last minute job.

If I rode in the race, but kept Palindrome reined in behind other horses the whole way, the wire might not be rigged at all. But my heart sank as I regarded the faces of the jockeys who had already ridden, and remembered in what state they had come back from their previous race. Mud was splashed on their faces like thick khaki chicken-pox, and their jerseys were soaked and muddied to such an extent that their colours were almost unrecognizable from a few steps away, let alone the distance from one fence to the next. My own coffee and cream colours would be particularly indistinct. A man waiting with wire would not be able to tell for certain which horse was in front, but he would expect me and act accordingly.

I looked at the other jockeys in the parade ring, now reluctantly taking off their raincoats and mounting their horses. There were about ten of them. They were men who had taught me a lot, and accepted me as one of themselves, and given me a companionship I enjoyed almost as much as the racing itself. If I let one of them crash in my place, I couldn't face them again.

It was no good. I'd have to ride Palindrome out in front and hope for the best. I remembered Kate saying, 'If there's something you've go to do, then to hell with the danger.'

To hell with the danger. After all, I could fall any

day, without the aid of wire. If I fell today, with it, that would be just too bad. But it couldn't be helped. And I might be wrong; there might be no wire at all.

Pete said, 'What's the matter? You look as if you'd seen a ghost.'

'I'm all right,' I said, taking off my coat. Palindrome was standing beside me, and I patted him, admiring his splendid intelligent head. My chief worry from then on was that he, at least, should come out of the next ten minutes unscathed.

I swung up on to his back and looked down at Pete, and said, 'If . . . if Palindrome falls in this race, please will you ring up Inspector Lodge at Maidenhead police station, and tell him about it?'

'What on earth . . .?'

'Promise,' I said.

'All right. But I don't understand. You could tell him yourself, if you want to, and anyway, you won't fall.'

'No, perhaps not,' I said.

'I'll meet you in the winner's enclosure,' he said, slapping Palindrome's rump as we moved off.

The rain was blowing into our faces as we lined up for the start in front of the stands, with two circuits of the course to complete. The tapes went up, and we were off.

Two or three horses jumped the first fence ahead of me, but after that I took Palindrome to the front, and stayed there. He was at his best, galloping and jumping with the smooth flow of a top class 'chaser. On any other day, the feel of this power beneath me would have pleased me beyond words. As it was, I scarcely noticed it.

Remembering Bill's fall, I was watching for an attendant to walk across behind a fence as the horses approached it. He would be uncoiling the wire, raising it, fixing it . . . I planned when I saw that to try to persuade Palindrome to take off too soon before the fence, so that he would hit the wire solidly with his chest when he was already past the height of his spread. That way, I hoped he might break or pull down the wire and still stay on his feet; and if we fell, it should not be in a shattering somersault like Admiral's. But it is easier to plan than to do, and I doubted whether a natural jumper like Palindrome *could* be persuaded to take off one short stride too soon.

We completed the first circuit without incident, squelching on the sodden turf. About a mile from home, on the far side of the course, I heard hoofbeats close behind, and looked over my shoulder. Most of the field were bunched up some way back, but two of them were chasing me with determination and they were almost up to Palindrome's quarters.

I shook him up and he responded immediately, and we widened the gap from our pursuers to about five lengths.

No attendant walked across the course.

I didn't see any wire.

But Palindrome hit it, just the same.

It wouldn't have been too bad a fall but for the horses behind me. I felt the heavy jerk on Palindrome's legs as we rose over the last fence on the far side of the course, and I shot off like a bullet, hitting the ground with my shoulder several yards ahead. Before I had stopped rolling the other horses were jumping the fence. They would have avoided a man on the ground if they possibly could, but in this case, I was told afterwards, they had to swerve round Palindrome, who was struggling to get up, and found me straight in their path.

The galloping hooves thudded into my body. One of the horses kicked my head and my helmet split so drastically that it fell off. There were six seconds of bludgeoning, battering chaos, in which I could neither think nor move, but only feel.

When it was all over I lay on the wet ground, limp and growing numb, unable to get up, unable even to stir. I was lying on my back with my feet towards the fence. The rain fell on my face and trickled through my hair, and the drops felt so heavy on my eyelids that opening them was like lifting a weight. Through a slit, from under my rain-beaded lashes, I could see a man at the fence.

He wasn't coming to help me. He was very quickly coiling up a length of wire, starting on the outside of the course and working inwards. When he reached the inner post he put his hand in his raincoat pocket, drew out a tool, and clipped the wire where it was fastened eighteen inches above the fence. This time, he had not forgotten his wire cutters. He finished his job, hooked the coil over his arm, and turned towards me.

I knew him.

He was the driver of the horse-box.

The colour was going out of everything. The world looked grey to me, like an under-exposed film. The green grass was grey, the box driver's face was grey . . .

Then I saw that there was another man at the fence, and he was walking towards me. I knew him, too, and he was not a taxi-driver. I was so glad to find I had some help against the box driver that I could have wept with relief. I tried to tell him to look at the wire, so that this time there should be a witness. But the words could get no farther than my brain. My throat and tongue refused to form them.

He came over and stood beside me, and stooped down. I tried to smile and say hello, but not a muscle twitched. He straightened up.

He said, over his shoulder, to the box driver, 'He's been knocked out.' He turned back to me.

He said, 'You nosey bastard,' and he kicked me. I heard the ribs crack, and I felt the hot stab in my side. 'Perhaps that'll teach you to mind your own business.' He kicked me again. My grey world grew darker. I was nearly unconscious, but even in that dire moment some part of my mind went on working, and I knew why the attendant had not walked across with the wire. He had not needed to. He and his accomplice had stood on opposite sides of the course and had raised it between them.

I saw the foot drawn back a third time. It seemed hours, in my disjointed brain, until it came towards my eyes, growing bigger and bigger until it was all that I could see.

He kicked my face, and I went out like a light.

CHAPTER TWELVE

Hearing came back first. It came back suddenly, as if someone had pressed a switch. At one moment no messages of any sort were getting through the swirling, distorted dreams which seemed to have been going on inside my head for a very long time, and in the next I was lying in still blackness, with every sound sharp and distinct in my ears.

A woman's voice said, 'He's still unconscious.'

I wanted to tell her it was not true, but could not.

The sounds went on; swishing, rustling, clattering, the murmur of distant voices, the thump and rattle of water in pipes of ancient plumbing. I listened, but without much interest.

After a while I knew I was lying on my back. My limbs, when I became aware of them, were as heavy as lead and ached persistently, and ton weights rested on my eyelids.

I wondered where I was. Then I wondered who I

was. I could remember nothing at all. This seemed too much to deal with, so I went to sleep.

The next time I woke up the weights were gone from my eyes. I opened them, and found I was lying in a dim light in a room whose fuzzy lines slowly grew clear. There was a wash-basin in one corner, a table with a white cloth on it, an easy chair with wooden arms, a window to my right, a door straight ahead. A bare, functional room.

The door opened and a nurse came in. She looked at me in pleased surprise and smiled. She had nice teeth.

'Hello there,' she said. 'So you've come back at last. How do you feel?'

'Fine,' I said, but it came out as a whisper, and in any case it wasn't strictly true.

'Are you comfortable?' she asked, holding my wrist for the pulse.

'No,' I said, giving up the pretence.

'I'll go and tell Dr Mitcham you've woken up, and I expect he will come and see you. Will you be all right for a few minutes?' She wrote something on a board which lay on the table, gave me another bright smile, and swished out of the door.

So I was in hospital. But I still had no idea what had happened. Had I, I wondered, been run over by a steam roller? Or a herd of elephants?

Dr Mitcham, when he came, would solve only half the mystery.

'Why am I here?' I asked, in a croaky whisper.

'You fell off a horse,' he said.

'Who am I?'

At this question he tapped his teeth with the end of his pencil and looked at me steadily for some seconds. He was a blunt-featured young man with fluffy, already receding, fair hair, and bright intelligent pale blue eyes.

'I'd rather you remember that for yourself. You will, soon, I'm sure. Don't worry about it. Don't worry about anything. Just relax, and your memory will come back. Not all at once, don't expect that, but little by little you'll remember everything, except perhaps the fall itself.'

'What is wrong with me, exactly?' I asked.

'Concussion is what has affected your memory. As to the rest of you,' he surveyed me from head to foot, 'you have a broken collar-bone, four cracked ribs and multiple contusions.'

'Nothing serious, thank goodness,' I croaked.

He opened his mouth and gasped, and then began to laugh. He said, 'No, nothing serious. You lot are all the same. Quite mad.'

'Which lot?' I said.

'Never mind, you'll remember soon,' he said. 'Just go to sleep for a while, if you can, and you'll probably understand a great deal more when you wake up.'

I took his advice, closed my eyes and drifted to sleep. I dreamed of a husky voice which came from the centre of a bowl of red and yellow crocuses, whispering menacing things until I wanted to scream and run away, and then I realized it was my own voice whispering, and the crocuses faded into a vision of deep green forests with scarlet birds darting in the shadows. Then I thought I was very high up, looking to the ground, and I was leaning farther and farther forward until I fell, and this time what I said made perfect sense.

'I fell out of the tree.' I knew it had happened in my boyhood.

There was an exclamation beside me. I opened my eyes. At the foot of the bed stood Dr Mitcham.

'What tree?' he said.

'In the forest,' I said. 'I hit my head, and when I woke my father was kneeling beside me.'

There was an exclamation again at my right hand. I rolled my head over to look.

He sat there, sunburnt, fit, distinguished, and at forty-six looking still a young man.

'Hi, there,' I said.

'Do you know who this is?' asked Dr Mitcham.

'My father.'

'And what is your name?'

'Alan York,' I said at once, and my memory bounded back. I could remember everything up to the morning I was going to Bristol races. I remembered setting off, but what happened after that was still a blank.

'How did you get here?' I asked my father.

'I flew over. Mrs Davidson rang me up to tell me you had had a fall and were in hospital. I thought I'd better take a look.'

'How long . . .' I began, slowly.

'How long were you unconscious?' said Dr Mitcham. 'This is Sunday morning. Two and a half days. Not too bad, considering the crack you had. I kept your crash-helmet for you to see.' He opened a locker and took out the shell which had undoubtedly saved my life. It was nearly in two pieces.

'I'll need a new one,' I said.

'Quite mad. You're all quite mad,' said Dr Mitcham.

This time I knew what he meant. I grinned, but it was a lopsided affair, because I discovered that half my face was swollen as well as stiff and sore. I began to put up my left hand to explore the damage, but I changed my mind before I had raised it six inches, owing to the sudden pain which the movement caused in my shoulder. In spite of the tight bandages which arched my shoulders backwards, I heard and felt the broken ends of collar-bone grate together.

As if they had been waiting for a signal, every dull separate ache in my battered body sprang to vicious, throbbing life. I drew in a deep breath, and the broken ribs sharply rebelled against it. It was a bad moment.

I shut my eyes. My father said anxiously, 'Is he all right?' and Dr Mitcham answered, 'Yes, don't worry. I rather think his breakages have caught up with him. I'll give him something to ease it, shortly.'

'I'll be out of bed tomorrow,' I said. 'I've been bruised before, and I've broken my collar-bone before. It doesn't last long.' But I added ruefully to myself that *while* it lasted it was highly unpleasant.

'You will certainly not get up tomorrow,' said Dr Mitcham's voice. 'You'll stay where you are for a week, to give that concussion a chance.'

'I can't stay in bed for a week,' I protested. 'I shouldn't have the strength of a flea when I got up, and I'm going to ride Admiral at Liverpool.'

'When is that?' asked Dr Mitcham suspiciously.

'March twenty-fourth,' I said.

There was a short silence while they worked it out.

'That's only a week on Thursday,' said my father.

'You can put it right out of your head,' said Dr Mitcham severely.

'Promise me,' said my father.

I opened my eyes and looked at him, and when I saw the anxiety in his face I understood for the first time in my life how much I meant to him. I was his only child, and for ten years, after my mother died, he had reared me himself, not delegating the job to a succession of housekeepers, boarding schools, and tutors as many a rich man would have done, but spending time playing with me and teaching me, and making sure I learned in my teens how to live happily and usefully under the burden of extreme wealth. He himself had taught me how to face all kinds of dangers, yet I realized that it must seem to him that if I insisted on taking my first tilt at Liverpool when I was precariously unfit, I was risking more than I had any right to do.

'I promise,' I said. 'I won't ride at Liverpool this month. But I'm going on racing afterwards.'

'All right. It's a deal.' He relaxed, smiling, and stood up. 'I'll come again this afternoon.'

'Where are you staying? Where are we now?' I asked.

'This is Bristol Hospital, and I'm staying with Mrs Davidson,' he said.

I said, 'Did I get this lot at Bristol races? With Palindrome?' My father nodded. 'How is he? Was he hurt? What sort of fall did he have?'

'No, he wasn't hurt,' he said. 'He's back in Gregory's stables. No one saw how or why he fell because it was raining so hard. Gregory said you had a premonition you were going to fall, and he asked me to tell you he had done what you wanted.'

'I don't remember anything about it, and I don't know what it was I wanted him to do.' I sighed. 'It's very irritating.'

Dr Mitcham and my father went away and left me puzzling over the gap in my memory. I had an elusive feeling that I had known for a few seconds a fact of paramount significance, but grope as I would, my conscious life ended on the road to Bristol races and began again in Bristol Hospital.

The rest of the day passed slowly and miserably, with each small movement I made setting up a chorus of protest in every crushed muscle and nerve. I had been kicked by horses before, but never in so many places all at once, and I knew, though I couldn't see it, that my skin must be covered with large angry crimson patches which had spread and were turning black and finally yellow as the blood underneath congealed and dispersed. My face, I knew, must be giving the same rainbow performance, and I undoubtedly had two lovely black eyes.

The pills Dr Mitcham had sent via the nurse with pretty teeth made less difference than I would have liked, so I lay with my eyes shut and pretended I was floating on the sea in the sunshine, with my grating bones and throbbing head cushioned by a gentle swell. I filled in the scene with sea-gulls and white clouds and children splashing in the shallows, and it worked well each time until I moved again.

Late in the evening my headache grew worse and I slid in and out of weird troubled dreams in which I imagined that my limbs had been torn off by heavy weights, and I woke soaked in sweat to wiggle my toes and fingers in an agony of fear that they were missing. But no sooner had the feel of them against the sheets sent relief flooding over me than I was drifting away into the same nightmare all over again. The cycle of short awakenings and long dreams went on and on, until I was no longer sure what was real and what was not.

So shattering was the night passed in this fashion that when Dr Mitcham came into my room in the morning I implored him to show me that my hands and feet were in fact still attached to me. Without a word he stripped back the bedclothes, grasped my feet firmly, and lifted them a few inches so that I could see them. I raised my hands and looked at them, and laced my fingertips together over my stomach: and felt a complete idiot to have been so terrified over nothing.

'There's no need to be embarrassed,' said Mitcham. 'You can't expect your brain to be in perfect working order when you've been unconscious for so long. I promise you that you have no injuries you don't know about. No internal damage, no bits missing. You'll be as good as new in three weeks.' His steady pale blue eyes were reliable. 'Only,' he added, 'you'll have a scar on your face. We stitched up a cut over your left cheekbone.'

As I had not been exactly handsome before, this news did not disturb me. I thanked him for his forbearance, and he pulled the sheet and blankets over me again. His blunt face suddenly lit up with a mischievous smile, and he said, 'Yesterday *you* told *me* there was nothing seriously wrong with you and you'd be out of bed today, if I remember correctly.'

'Blast you,' I said weakly. 'I'll be out of bed tomorrow.'

In the end it was Thursday before I made it on my feet, and I went home to Scilla's on Saturday morning feeling more tottery than I cared to admit, but in good spirits nevertheless. My father, who was still there but planning to leave early the next week, came to fetch me.

Scilla and Polly clicked their tongues and made sympathetic remarks as I levered myself out of the Jaguar at one quarter my usual speed and walked carefully up the front steps. But young Henry, giving me a sweeping, comprehensive glance which took in my black and yellow face and the long newly healed cut across one cheek, greeted me with, 'And how's the horrible monster from outer space?'

'Go and boil your head,' I said, and Henry grinned delightedly.

At seven o'clock in the evening, just after the children had gone upstairs to bed, Kate rang up. Scilla and my father decided to bring some wine up from the cellar, and left me alone in the drawing-room to talk to her.

'How are the cracks?' she asked.

'Knitting nicely,' I said. 'Thank you for your letter, and for the flowers.'

'The flowers were Uncle George's idea,' she said. 'I said it was too much like a funeral, sending you flowers, and he thought that was so funny that he nearly choked. It didn't seem all that funny to me, actually, when I knew from Mrs Davidson that it very nearly was your funeral.'

'It was nowhere near that,' I said. 'Scilla was exaggerating. And whether it was your idea or Uncle George's, thank you anyway for the flowers.'

'Lilies, I expect I should have sent, not tulips,' Kate teased.

'You can send lilies next time,' I said, taking pleasure in hearing her slow attractive voice.

'Good heavens, is there going to be a next time?'

'Bound to be,' I said cheerfully.

'Well all right,' said Kate, 'I'll place a standing order with Interflora, for lilies.'

'I love you, Kate,' I said.

'I must say,' she said happily, 'it's nice hearing people say that.'

'People? Who else has said it? And when?' I asked, fearing the worst.

'Well,' she said, after a tiny pause. 'Dane, as a matter of fact.'

'Oh.'

'Don't be jealous,' she said. 'And Dane's just as bad

as you. He glowers like a thunderstorm if he hears your name. You're both being childish.'

'Yes, ma'am,' I said. 'When will I see you again?'

We fixed a luncheon date in London, and before she rang off I told her again that I loved her. I was about to put down my own receiver, when I heard the most unexpected sound on the telephone.

A giggle. A quickly suppressed, but definite giggle.

I knew she had disconnected; but I said into the dead mouthpiece in front of me, 'Hang on a minute, Kate, I – er – want to read you something . . . in the paper. Just a minute while I get it.' I put my receiver down on the table, went carefully out of the drawing-room, up the stairs, and into Scilla's bedroom.

There stood the culprits, grouped in a guilty huddle round the extension telephone. Henry, with the receiver pressed to his ear; Polly, her head close against his; and William, looking earnestly up at them with his mouth open. They were all in pyjamas and dressing-gowns.

'And just what do you think you're doing?' I asked, with a severe expression.

'Oh golly,' said Henry, dropping the receiver on to the bed as if it were suddenly too hot to hold.

'Alan!' said Polly, blushing deeply.

'How long have you been listening?' I demanded.

'Actually, right from the beginning,' said Polly shamefacedly.

'Henry always listens,' said William, proud of his brother.

'Shut up,' said Henry.

'You little beasts,' I said.

William looked hurt. He said again. 'But Henry always listens. He listens to everyone. He's checking up, and that's good, isn't it? Henry checks up all the time, don't you Henry?'

'Shut up William,' said Henry, getting red and furious.

'So Henry checks up, does he?' I said, frowning crossly at him. Henry stared back, caught out, but apparently unrepentant.

I advanced towards them, but the homily on the sacredness of privacy that I was about to deliver suddenly flew out of my mind. I stopped and thought.

'Henry, how long have you been listening to people on the telephone?' I asked mildly.

He looked at me warily. Finally he said, 'Quite some time.'

'Days? Weeks? Months?'

'Ages,' said Polly, taking heart again as I no longer seemed angry with them.

'Did you ever listen to your father?' I asked.

'Yes, often,' said Henry.

I paused, studying this tough, intelligent little boy. He was only eight, but if he knew the answers to what I was going to ask him, he would understand their significance and be appalled by his knowledge all his life. But I pressed on.

'Did you by any chance ever hear him talking to a man with a voice like this?' I asked. Then I made my voice husky and whispering, and said, 'Am I speaking to Major Davidson?'

'Yes,' said Henry without hesitation.

'When was that?' I asked, trying to show nothing of the excitement I felt. I was sure now that he had listened in to the telephone call which Bill had mentioned as a joke to Pete, who had not taken in what he said.

'It was that voice the last time I listened to Daddy,' said Henry, matter-of-factly.

'Do you remember what the voice said?' I forced myself to speak slowly, gently.

'Oh yes, it was a joke. It was two days before he was killed,' said Henry, without distress. 'Just when we were going to bed, like now. The phone rang and I scooted in here and listened as usual. That man with the funny voice was saying, "Are you going to ride Admiral on Saturday, Major Davidson?" and Daddy said he was.' Henry paused. I waited, willing him to remember.

He screwed up his eyes in concentration and went on. 'Then the man with the funny voice said, "You are not to win on Admiral, Major Davidson." Daddy just laughed, and the man said, "I'll pay you five hundred pounds if you promise not to win." And Daddy said, "Go to hell" and I nearly snorted because he was always telling me not to say that. Then the whispery man said he didn't want Daddy to win, and that Admiral would fall if Daddy didn't agree not to win, and Daddy said "You must be mad." And then he put down the telephone, and I ran back to my room in case he should come up and find me listening.'

'Did you say anything to your father about it?' I asked.

'No,' said Henry frankly, 'That's the big snag about listening. You have to be awfully careful not to know too much.'

'Yes, I can see that,' I said, trying not to smile.

Then I saw the flicker in Henry's eyes as the meaning of what he had heard grew clearer to him. He said jerkily, 'It wasn't a joke after all, was it?'

'No, it wasn't,' I said.

'But that man didn't make Admiral fall, did he? He couldn't . . . could he? Could he?' said Henry desperately, wanting me to reassure him. His eyes were stretched wide open and he was beginning to realize that he had listened to the man who had caused his father's death. Although he would have to know one day about the strand of wire, I didn't think I ought to tell him at that moment.

'I don't really know. I don't expect so,' I lied calmly. But Henry's wide eyes stared blindly at me as if he were looking at some inward horror.

'What's the matter?' said Polly. 'I don't understand

why Henry is so upset. Just because someone told Daddy they didn't want him to win is no reason for Henry to go off in a fit.'

'Does he always remember so clearly what people say?' I asked Polly. 'It's a month ago, now, since your father died.'

'I expect Daddy and that man said a lot of things that Henry has forgotten,' said Polly judiciously, 'but he doesn't make things up.' And I knew this was true. He was a truthful child.

He said stonily, 'I don't see how he could have done it.'

I was glad at least that Henry was dealing with his revelation practically and not emotionally. Perhaps I had not done him too much harm, after all, in making him understand what he had heard and disregarded.

'Come along to bed and don't worry about it, Henry,' I said, holding out my hand to him. He took it, and uncharacteristically held on to it all the way along the landing and into his bedroom.

CHAPTER THIRTEEN

While I was dressing myself at tortoise pace the following morning the front door bell rang downstairs, and presently Joan came up to say that an Inspector Lodge would like to see me, please.

'Tell him I'll be down as soon as possible,' I said, struggling to get my shirt on over the thick bracing bandage round my shoulders. I did up most of the buttons, but decided I didn't need a tie.

The strapping round my ribs felt tight and itched horribly, my head ached, large areas of flesh were black still and tender, I had slept badly, and I was altogether in a foul mood. The three aspirins I had swallowed in place of breakfast had not come up to scratch.

I picked up my socks, tried to bend to put them on with my one useful arm, found how far away my feet had become, and flung them across the room in a temper. The day before, in the hospital, the nurse with nice teeth had helped me to dress. Today perverseness stopped me asking my father to come and do it for me.

The sight of my smudgy, yellow, unshaven face in the looking-glass made matters no better. Henry's 'horrible monster from outer space' was not so far off the mark. I longed to scratch the livid scar on my cheek, to relieve its irritation.

I plugged in my electric razor and took off the worst, brushed my hair sketchily, thrust my bare feet into slippers, put one arm into my hacking jacket and swung it over the other shoulder, and shuffled gingerly downstairs.

Lodge's face when he saw me was a picture.

'If you laugh at me I'll knock your block off. Next week,' I said.

'I'm not laughing,' said Lodge, his nostrils twitching madly as he tried to keep a straight face.

'It's not funny,' I said emphatically.

'No.'

I scowled at him.

My father said, glancing at me from behind his Sunday newspaper in the depths of an armchair by the fire, 'You sound to me as if you need a stiff brandy.'

'It's only half-past ten,' I said crossly.

'Emergencies can happen at any time of the day,' said my father, standing up, 'and this would appear to be a grave one.' He opened the corner cupboard where Scilla kept a few bottles and glasses, poured out a third of a tumbler full of brandy, and splashed some soda into it. I complained that it was too strong, too early, and unnecessary.

My father handed me the glass. 'Drink it and shut up,' he said.

Furious, I took a large mouthful. It was strong and fiery, and bit into my throat. I rolled the second mouthful round my teeth so that the scarcely diluted spirit tingled on my gums, and when I swallowed I could feel it slide warmly down to my empty stomach.

'Did you have any breakfast?' asked my father.

'No,' I said.

I took another, smaller gulp. The brandy worked fast. My bad temper began draining away, and in a minute or two I felt reasonably sane. Lodge and my father were looking at me intently as though I were a laboratory animal responding to an experiment.

'Oh very well then,' I admitted grudgingly, 'I feel better.' I took a cigarette from the silver box on the table and lit it, and noticed the sun was shining.

'Good.' My father sat down again.

It appeared that he and Lodge had introduced themselves while they waited for me, and Lodge had told him, among other things, about my adventures in the horse-box outside Maidenhead, a detail I had omitted from my letters. This I considered to be treachery of the basest sort, and said so; and I told them how Kate and I had tracked down the horse-box, and that that particular line of enquiry was a dead end.

I took my cigarette and glass across the room and sat on the window seat in the sun. Scilla was in the garden, cutting flowers. I waved to her.

Lodge, dressed today not in uniform but in grey flannels, fine wool shirt, and sports jacket, opened his briefcase, which lay on the table, and pulled out some papers. He sat down beside the table and spread them out.

He said, 'Mr Gregory rang me up at the station on the morning after your fall at Bristol to tell me about it.'

'Why on earth did he do that?' I asked.

'You asked him to,' said Lodge. He hesitated, and went on, 'I understand from your father that your memory is affected.'

'Yes. Most bits of that day at Bristol have come back now, but I still can't remember going out of the weighing room to ride Palindrome, or the race or the fall, or anything.' My last mental picture was of Sandy walking out into the rain. 'Why did I ask Pete to tell you I fell?'

'You asked him before the race. You apparently thought you were likely to fall. So, unofficially, I checked up on that crash of yours.' He smiled suddenly. 'You've accounted for all my free time lately, and today is really my day off. Why I bother with you I really don't know!' But I guessed that he was as addicted to detecting as an alcoholic to drink. He couldn't help doing it.

He went on, 'I went down to Gregory's stables and

took a look at Palindrome. He had a distinct narrow wound across his front on those two pads of flesh . . .'

'Chest,' I murmured.

'. . . Chest, then; and I'll give you one guess at what cut him.'

'Oh, no,' I said, guessing, but not believing it.

'I checked up on the attendants at the fences,' he said. 'One of them was new and unknown to the others. He gave his name as Thomas Butler and an address which doesn't exist, and he volunteered to stand at the farthest fence from the stands, where you fell. His offer was readily accepted because of the rain and the distance of the fence from the bookmakers. The same story as at Maidenhead. Except that this time Butler collected his earnings in the normal way. Then I got the clerk of the course to let me inspect the fence, and I found a groove on each post, six feet six inches from the ground.'

There was a short silence.

'Well, well, well,' I said blankly. 'It looks as though I was luckier than Bill.'

'I wish you could remember something about it . . . anything. What made you suspect you would fall?' asked Lodge.

'I don't know.'

'It was something that happened while you were in the parade ring waiting to mount.' He leaned forward, his dark eyes fixed intently on my face, willing my sluggish memory to come to life. But I remembered nothing, and I still felt weary from head to foot. Concentration was altogether too much of an effort.

I looked out into the peaceful spring garden. Scilla held an armful of forsythia, golden yellow against her blue dress.

'I can't remember,' I said flatly. 'Perhaps it'll come back when my head stops aching.'

Lodge sighed and sat back in his hard chair.

'I suppose,' he said, a little bitterly, 'that you do at least remember sending me a message from Brighton, asking me to do your investigating for you?'

'Yes, I do,' I said. 'How did you get on?'

'Not very well. No one seems to know who actually owns the Marconicar taxi line. It was taken over just after the war by a business man named Clifford Tudor . . .'

'What?' I said in astonishment.

'Clifford Tudor, respectable Brighton resident, British subject. Do you know him?'

'Yes,' I said. 'He owns several racehorses.'

Lodge sorted out a paper from his briefcase. 'Clifford Tudor, born Khroupista Thasos, in Trikkala, Greece. Naturalized nineteen thirty-nine, when he was twenty-five. He started life as a cook, but owing to natural business ability he acquired his own restaurant that same year. He sold it for a large profit after the war, went to Brighton, and bought for next to nothing an old taxi business that had wilted from wartime restrictions and lack of petrol. Four years ago he sold the taxis, again at a profit, and put his money into the Pavilion Plaza Hotel. He is unmarried.'

I leaned my head back against the window and waited for these details to mean something significant, but all that happened was that my inability to think increased.

Lodge went on. 'The taxi line was bought from Tudor by nominees, and that's where the fog begins. There have been so many transfers of ownership from company to company, mostly through nominees who can't be traced, that no one can discover who is the actual present owner. All business matters are settled by a Mr Fielder, the manager. He says he consults with a person he calls "the Chairman" by telephone, but that "the Chairman" rings him up every morning, and never the other way round. He says the Chairman's name is Claud Thiveridge, but he doesn't know his address or telephone number.'

'It sounds very fishy to me,' said my father.

'It is,' said Lodge. 'There is no Claud Thiveridge on the electoral register, or in any other official list, including the telephone accounts department, in the whole of Kent, Surrey, or Sussex. The operators in the telephone exchange are sure the office doesn't receive a long distance call regularly every morning, yet the morning call has been standard office routine for the last four years.

As this means that the call must be a local one, it seems fairly certain that Claud Thiveridge is not the gentleman's real name.'

He rubbed the palm of his hand round the back of his neck and looked at me steadily. 'You know a lot more than you've told me, amnesia or not,' he said. 'Spill the beans, there's a good chap.'

'You haven't told me what the Brighton police think of the Marconicars,' I said.

Lodge hesitated. 'Well, they were a little touchy on the subject, I would say. It seems they have had several complaints, but not much evidence that will stand up in court. What I have just told you is the result of their inquiries over the last few years.'

'They would not seem,' said my father dryly, 'to have made spectacular progress. Come on, Alan, tell us what's going on.'

Lodge turned his head towards him in surprise. My father smiled.

'My son is Sherlock Holmes reincarnated, didn't you know?' he said. 'After he went to England I had to employ a detective to do the work he used to do in connexion with frauds and swindles. As one of my head clerks put it, Mr Alan has an unerring instinct for smelling out crooks.'

'Mr Alan's unerring instinct is no longer functioning,' I said gloomily. Clouds were building up near the sun, and Scilla's back disappeared through the macrocarpa hedge by the kitchen door.

'Don't be infuriating, Alan,' said my father. 'Elucidate.'

'Oh, all right.' I stubbed out my cigarette, began to scratch my cheek, and dragged my fingers away from the scar with a strong effort of will. It went on itching.

'There's a lot I don't know,' I said, 'but the general gist appears to be this. The Marconicars have been in the protection racket for the last four years, intimidating small concerns like cafés and free house pubs. About a year ago, owing to the strongmindedness of one particular publican, mine host of The Blue Duck, business in the protection line began to get unexpectedly rough for the protectors. He set Alsatians on them, in fact.' I told my fascinated father and an aghast Lodge what Kate and I had learned in The Blue Duck's kitchen, carefully watched by the yellow-eyed Prince.

'Ex-Regimental Sergeant-Major Thomkins made such serious inroads into the illicit profits of Marconicars,' I continued, 'that as a racket it was more or less defunct. The legitimate side hasn't been doing too well during the winter either, according to the typists who work in the office. There are too many taxis in Brighton for the number of fares at this time of year, I should think. Anyway, it seems to me that the Marconicar boss – the Chairman, your mysterious Claud Thiveridge – set about mending his fortunes by branching out into another form of crime. He bought, I think, the shaky bookmaking business on the floor above the Marconi-cars, in the same building.'

I could almost smell the cabbage in the Olde Oake Café as I remembered it. 'An earnest lady told me the bookmakers had been taken over by a new firm about six months ago, but that its name was still the same. L. C. Perth, written in neon. She was very wrought up about them sticking such a garish sign on an architectural gem, and she and her old buildings society, whose name I forget, had tried to reason with the new owners to take down what they had just put up. Only they couldn't find out who the new owner was. It's too much of a coincidence to have two businesses, both shady, one above the other, both with invisible and untraceable owners. They must be owned by the same person.'

'It doesn't follow, and I don't see the point,' said my father.

'You will in a minute,' I said. 'Bill died because he wouldn't stop his horse winning a race. I know his death wasn't necessarily intended, but force was used against him. He was told not to win by a husky-voiced man on the telephone. Henry, Bill's elder son, he's eight—' I explained to Lodge, 'has a habit of listening on the extension upstairs, and he heard every word. Two days before Bill died, Henry says, the voice offered him five hundred pounds to stop his horse winning, and when

Bill laughed at this, the voice told him he wouldn't win because his horse would fall.'

I paused, but neither Lodge nor my father said anything. Swallowing the last of the brandy, I went on. 'There is a jockey called Joe Nantwich who during the last six months, ever since L. C. Perth changed hands, has regularly accepted a hundred pounds, sometimes more, to stop a horse winning. Joe gets his instructions by telephone from a husky-voiced man he has never met.'

Lodge stirred on his hard, self-chosen chair.

I went on. 'I, as you know, was set upon by the Marconicar drivers, and a few days later the man with the husky voice rang me up and told me to take heed of the warning I had been given in the horse-box. One doesn't have to be Sherlock Holmes to see that the crooked racing and the Marconicar protection racket were being run by the same man.' I stopped.

'Finish it off, then,' said my father impatiently.

'The only person who would offer a jockey a large sum to lose a race is a crooked bookmaker. If he *knows* a well-fancied horse is not going to win, he can accept any amount of money on that horse without risk.'

'Enlarge,' said Lodge.

'Normally bookmakers try to balance their books so that whichever horse wins they come out on the winning side,' I said. 'If too many people want to back one horse, they accept the bets, but they back the horse themselves with another bookmaker; then if that horse wins, they collect their winnings from the second bookmaker, and pay it out to their customers. It's a universal system known as "laying off". Now suppose you were a crooked bookmaker and Joe Nantwich is to ride a fancied horse. You tip Joe the wink to lose. Then however much is betted with you on that horse, you do no laying off, because you know you won't have to pay out.'

'I would have thought that a hundred pounds would have been more than it was worth,' said Lodge, 'since bookmakers normally make a profit anyway.'

'Your friend wasn't satisfied with the legitimate gains from the taxis,' my father pointed out.

I sighed, and shifted my stiff shoulders against the frame of the window.

'There's a bit more to it, of course,' I said. 'If a bookmaker knows he hasn't got to pay out on a certain horse, he can offer better odds on it. Not enough to be suspicious, but just enough to attract a lot of extra custom. A point better than anyone else would go to – say eleven to four, when the next best offer was five to two. The money would roll in, don't you think?'

I stood up and went towards the door, saying, 'I'll show you something.'

The stairs seemed steeper than usual. I went up to my room and fetched the racing form book and the little bunch of bookmakers' tickets, and shuffled back to the drawing-room. I laid the tickets out on the table in front of Lodge, and my father came over to have a look.

'These,' I explained, 'are some tickets Bill kept for his children to play with. Three of them, as you see, were issued by L. C. Perth, and all the others are from different firms, no two alike. Bill was a methodical man. On the backs of all the tickets he wrote the date, the details of his bet, and the name of the horse he'd put his money on. He used to search around in Tattersall's for the best odds and bet in cash, instead of betting on credit with Tote Investors or one of the bookmakers on the rails – those,' I added for Lodge's benefit, as I could see the question forming on his lips, 'are bookmakers who stand along the railing between Tattersall's and the Club enclosures, writing down bets made by Club members and other people known to them. They send out weekly accounts, win or lose. Bill didn't bet in large amounts, and he thought credit betting wasn't exciting enough.'

Lodge turned over the three Perth tickets.

Bill's loopy writing was clear and unmistakable. I picked up the first ticket, and read aloud, ' "Peripatetic. 7 November. Ten pounds staked at eleven to ten." So he stood to win eleven pounds for his money.' I opened the detailed form book and turned to 7 November.

'Peripatetic,' I said, 'lost the two mile hurdle at Sandown that day by four lengths. He was ridden by

Joe Nantwich. The starting price was eleven to ten on – that is, you have to stake eleven pounds to win ten – and had earlier been as low as eleven to eight on. L. C. Perth must have done a roaring trade at eleven to ten against.'

I picked up the second card and read, 'Sackbut. 10 October. Five pounds staked at six to one.' I opened the form book for that day. 'Sackbut was unplaced at Newbury and Joe Nantwich rode it. The best price generally offered was five to one, and the starting price was seven to two.'

I put the Sackbut ticket back on the table, and read the third card where it lay. 'Malabar. 2 December. Eight pounds staked at fifteen to eight.' I laid the form book beside it, opened at 2 December. 'Malabar finished fourth at Birmingham. Joe Nantwich rode him. The starting price was six to four.'

Lodge and my father silently checked the book with the ticket.

'I looked up all the other cards as well,' I said. 'Of course, as Bill still had the tickets, all the horses lost; but on only one of them did he get better odds than you'd expect. Joe didn't ride it, and I don't think it's significant, because it was an outsider at a hundred to six.'

'I wish the racing fraternity would use only whole numbers and halves,' said Lodge plaintively.

'Haven't you heard,' I asked, 'about the keen gambler who taught his baby son to count? One, six-to-four, two . . .'

Lodge laughed, his dark eyes crinkling at the corners. 'I'll have to write down these figures on the Perth tickets alongside the form book information, and get it straightened out in my mind,' he said, unscrewing his pen and settling to the task.

My father sat down beside him and watched the tell-tale list grow. I went back to the window seat and waited.

Presently Lodge said, 'I can see why your father misses you as a fraud spotter.' He put his pen back in his pocket.

I smiled and said, 'If you want to read a really blatant fraud, you should look up the Irish racing in that form book. It's fantastic.'

'Not today. This is quite enough to be going on with,' said Lodge, rubbing his hand over his face and pinching his nose between thumb and forefinger.

'All that remains, as far as I'm concerned, is for you to tell us who is organizing the whole thing,' said my father with a touch of mockery, which from long understanding I interpreted as approval.

'That, dear Pa, I fear I cannot do,' I said.

But Lodge said seriously, 'Could it be anyone you know on the racecourse? It must be someone connected with racing. How about Perth, the bookmaker?'

'It could be. I don't know him. His name won't

actually be Perth of course. That name was sold with the business. I'll have a bet on with him next time I go racing and see what happens,' I said.

'You will do no such thing,' said my father emphatically, and I felt too listless to argue.

'How about a jockey, or a trainer, or an owner?' asked Lodge.

'You'd better include the Stewards and the National Hunt Committee,' I said, ironically. 'They were almost the first to know I had discovered the wire and was looking into it. The man we are after knew very early on that I was inquisitive. I didn't tell many people I suspected more than an accident, or ask many pointed questions, before that affair in the horse-box.'

'People you know . . .' said Lodge, musingly. 'How about Gregory?'

'No,' I said.

'Why not? He lives near Brighton, near enough for the Marconicar morning telephone call.'

'He wouldn't risk hurting Bill or Admiral,' I said.

'How can you be sure?' asked Lodge. 'People aren't always what they seem, and murderers are often fond of animals, until they get in the way. One chap I saw at the assizes lately killed a nightwatchman and showed no remorse at all. But when evidence was given that the nightwatchman's dog had had his head bashed in too, the accused burst into tears and said he was sorry.'

'Pathetic,' I said. 'But no dice. It isn't Pete.'

'Faith or evidence?' persisted Lodge.

'Faith,' I said grudgingly, because I was quite sure.

'Jockeys?' suggested Lodge, leaving it.

'None of them strikes me as being the type we're looking for,' I said, 'and I think you're overlooking the fact that racing came second on the programme and may even have been adopted solely because a shaky bookmaking business existed on the floor above the Marconicars. I mean, that in itself may have turned the boss of Marconicars towards racing.'

'You may be right,' admitted Lodge.

My father said, 'It's just possible that the man who originally owned Marconicars decided to launch out into crime, and faked a sale to cover his tracks.'

'Clifford Tudor, née Thasos, do you mean?' asked Lodge with interest. My father nodded, and Lodge said to me, 'How about it?'

'Tudor pops up all over the place,' I said. 'He knew Bill, and Bill had his address noted down on a scrap of paper.' I put my hand into my jacket pocket. The old envelope was still there. I drew it out and looked at it again. 'Tudor told me he had asked Bill to ride a horse for him.'

'When did he tell you that?' asked Lodge.

'I gave him a lift from Plumpton races into Brighton, four days after Bill died. We talked about him on the way.'

'Anything else?' asked Lodge.

'Well . . . Tudor's horses have been ridden – up until lately – by our corrupted friend Joe Nantwich. It was on Tudor's horse Bolingbroke that Joe won once when he had been instructed to lose . . . but at Cheltenham he threw away a race on a horse of Tudor's, and Tudor was very angry about it.'

'Camouflage,' suggested my father.

But I rested my aching head against the window, and said, 'I don't think Tudor can possibly be the crook we're looking for.'

'Why not?' asked Lodge. 'He has the organizing ability, he lives in Brighton, he owned the taxis, he employs Joe Nantwich, and he knew Major Davidson. He seems the best proposition so far.'

'No,' I said tiredly. 'The best lead we've had is the taxis. If I hadn't recognized that the men who stopped me in the horse-box were also taxi-drivers, I'd never have found out anything at all. Whoever put them on to me can't possibly have imagined I would know them, or he wouldn't have done it. But if there's one person who knew I would recognize them, it's Clifford Tudor. He was standing near me while the taxi-drivers fought, and he knew I'd had time to look at them after the police had herded them into two groups.'

'I don't rule him out altogether, even so,' said Lodge, gathering his papers together, and putting them back into his briefcase. 'Criminals often make the stupidest mistakes.'

I said, 'If we ever do find your Claud Thiveridge, I think he will turn out to be someone I've never met and never heard of. A complete stranger. It's far more likely.'

I wanted to believe it.

I did not want to have to face another possibility, one that I shied away from so uncomfortably that I could not bring myself even to lay it open for Lodge's inspection.

Who, besides Tudor, knew before the horse-box incident that I wanted Bill's death avenged? Kate. And to whom had she passed this on? To Uncle George. Uncle George, who, I suspected, housed a lean and hungry soul in his fat body, behind his fatuous expression.

Uncle George, out of the blue, had bought a horse for his niece. Why? To widen her interests, he had said. But through her, I thought, he would learn much of what went on at the races.

And Uncle George had sent Heavens Above to be trained in the stable which housed Bill's horse. Was it a coincidence . . . or the beginning of a scheme which Bill's unexpected death had cut short?

It was nebulous, unconvincing. It was based only on supposition, not on facts, and bolstered only by memory of the shock on Uncle George's face when Kate told him we had been to The Blue Duck – shock which he had called indigestion. And perhaps it had been indigestion, after all.

And all those primitive weapons in his study, the ritual objects and the scalp . . . were they the playthings of a man who relished violence? Or who loathed it? Or did both at the same time?

Scilla came into the drawing-room, carrying a copper bowl filled with forsythia and daffodils. She put it on the low table near me, and the spring sun suddenly shone on the golden flowers, so that they seemed like a burst of light, reflecting their colour upwards on to her face as she bent over them, tweaking them into order.

She gave me a sharp glance, and turned round to the others.

'Alan looks very tired,' she said. 'What have you been doing?'

'Talking,' I said, smiling at her.

'You'll find yourself back in hospital if you're not careful,' she scolded mildly, and without pausing offered mid-morning coffee to Lodge and my father.

I was glad of the interruption, because I had not wished to discuss with them what was to be done next in pursuit of Mr Claud Thiveridge. Every small advance I had made in his direction had brought its retribution, it was true; yet in each of his parries I had found a clue. My faulty memory was still cheating me of the information I had paid for with the drubbing at Bristol, but it did not deter me from wanting to see the business through.

I would get closer to Thiveridge. He would hit out again, and in doing it show me the next step towards him, like the flash of a gunshot in the dark revealing the hiding-place of a sniper.

CHAPTER FOURTEEN

Joe Nantwich found the sniper first.

Eight days after Lodge's visit I drove down to West Sussex races, having put in a short morning at the office. My bruises had faded and gone; the ribs and collar-bone were mended and in perfect working order, and even my stubborn headache was losing its grip. I whistled my way into the changing-room and presented to Clem my brand new crash-helmet, bought that morning from Bates of Jermyn Street for three guineas.

The weighing room was empty, and distant oohs and ahs proclaimed that the first race was in progress. Clem, who was tidying up the changing-room after the tornado of getting a large number of jockeys out of their ordinary clothes, into racing colours, past the scales, and out to the parade ring, greeted me warmly and shook hands.

'Glad to see you back, sir,' he said, taking the helmet. With a ball-point pen he wrote my name on a piece of adhesive tape and stuck it on to the shiny shell. 'Let's hope you won't be needing another new one of these in a hurry.' He pressed his thumb firmly on to the adhesive tape.

'I'm starting again tomorrow, Clem,' I said. 'Can you bring my gear? Big saddle. There's no weight problem, I'm riding Admiral.'

'Top flipping weight,' said Clem, resignedly. 'And a lot of lead, which Admiral isn't used to. Major Davidson hardly ever needed any.' Clem gave me an assessing sideways look and added, 'You've lost three or four pounds, I shouldn't wonder.'

'All the better,' I said cheerfully, turning to the door.

'Oh, just a minute, sir,' said Clem. 'Joe Nantwich asked me to let you know, if you came, that he has something to tell you.'

'Oh, yes?' I said.

'He was asking for you on Saturday at Liverpool, but I told him you'd probably be coming here, as Mr Gregory mentioned last week that you'd be riding Admiral tomorrow,' said Clem, absent-mindedly picking up a saddle and smoothing his hand over the leather.

'Did Joe say what it was he wanted to tell me?' I asked.

'Yes, he wants to show you a bit of brown wrapping paper with something written on it. He said you'd be interested to see it, though I can't think why – the word I saw looked like something to do with chickens. He had the paper out in the changing-room at Liverpool, and folded it up flat on the bench into a neat shape, and tucked it into the inside pocket of his jacket. Giggling over it, he was. He'd had a drink or two I reckon, but then most people had, it was after the National. He said what was written on the paper was double Dutch to him, but it might be a clue, you never knew. I asked him a clue to what? But he wouldn't say, and anyway, I was too busy to bother with him much.'

'I'll see him, and find out what it's all about,' I said. 'Has he still got the paper with him, do you know?'

'Yes, he has. He patted his pocket just now when he asked me if you were here, and I heard the paper crackle.'

'Thanks, Clem,' I said.

I went outside. The race was over, the winner was being led towards the unsaddling enclosure in front of the weighing-room, and down from the stands streamed the hundreds of chattering racegoers. I stood near the weighing-room door, waiting for Joe and catching up with the latest gossip. Liverpool, I learned, had been disappointing, fabulous, bloody, a dead loss, and the tops, according to who told it. I had not been there. I had been too busy getting intensive treatment on my shoulder muscles to help my strength back.

Sandy clapped me soundly on the back as he passed, remarking that it was 'Bloody good to see your old physog on the horizon again, even if you do look like an understudy for Scarface.' He went on, 'Have you seen Joe? The little drip's been squealing for you.'

'So I hear,' I said. 'I'm waiting for him now.'

A couple of press men asked me my riding plans, and made notes about Admiral for their morning edition. Sir Creswell Stampe noticed my existence with a nod of his distinguished head and the characteristic puffing up of his top lip which passed with him for a smile.

My content at being back in my favourite environment was somewhat marred by the sight of Dane strolling across the grass, talking intently to a slender, heart-catchingly beautiful girl at his side. Her face was turned intimately towards his, and she was laughing. It was Kate.

When they saw me they quickened their steps and approached me smiling, a striking pair evenly matched in grace and dark good looks.

Kate, who had got used to my battered face over lunch some days earlier, greeted me with a brisk 'Hi, there,' from which all undertones of love and longing were regrettably absent. She put her hand on my arm and asked me to walk down the course with her and Dane to watch the next race from beside the water jump.

I glanced at Dane. His smile was faint, and his dark eyes looked at me inscrutably, without welcome. My own muscles had tensed uncontrollably when I saw him and Kate together; so now I knew exactly how he felt about me.

It was as much unease over the low ebb of our friendship as desire to chase Claud Thiveridge which made me say, 'I can't come at this instant. I must find Joe Nantwich first. How about later on . . . if you'd like to walk down again?'

'All right, Alan,' she said. 'Or maybe we could have tea together?' She turned away with Dane and said, 'See you later,' over her shoulder with a mischievous grin, in which I read her mockery of the jealousy she could arouse in me.

Watching them go, I forgot to look out for Joe, and went in to search for him through the weighing- and changing-rooms again. He wasn't there.

Pete towered over me as I returned to my post outside the door and greeted me like a long-lost friend. His hat tipped back on his big head, his broad shoulders spreading apart the lapels of his coat, he gazed with good humour at my face, and said, 'They've made a good job of sewing you up, you know. You were a very gory sight indeed last time I saw you. I suppose you still can't remember what happened?'

'No,' I said, regretfully. 'Sometimes I think . . . but I can't get hold of it . . .'

'Perhaps it's just as well,' he said comfortingly, hitching the strap of his race glasses higher on to his shoulder and preparing to go into the weighing-room.

'Pete,' I said, 'have you seen Joe anywhere? I think he's been asking for me.'

'Yes, he said. 'He was looking for you at Liverpool, too. He was very keen to show you something, an address I think, written on some brown paper.'

'Did you see it?' I asked.

'Yes, as a matter of fact I did, but he annoys me and I didn't pay much attention. Chichester, I think the place was.'

'Do you know where Joe is now?' I asked. 'I've been waiting for him for some time, but there isn't a sign of him.'

Pete's thin lips showed contempt. 'Yes, I saw the little brute going into the bar, about ten minutes ago.'

'Already!' I exclaimed.

'Drunken little sod,' he said dispassionately. 'I wouldn't put him up on one of my horses if he was the last jockey on earth.'

'Which bar?' I pressed.

'Eh? Oh, the one at the back of Tattersall's, next to the Tote. He and another man went in with that dark fellow he rides for . . . Tudor, isn't that his name?'

I gaped at him. 'But Tudor finished with Joe at Cheltenham . . . and very emphatically, too.'

Pete shrugged. 'Tudor went into the bar with Joe and the other chap a few steps behind him. Maybe it was only coincidence.'

'Thanks, anyway,' I said.

It was only a hundred yards round one corner to the bar where Joe had gone. It was a long wooden hut backing on to the high fence which divided the racecourse from the road. I wasted no time, but nonetheless when I stepped into the building and threaded my way through the overcoated, beer-drinking customers, I found that Joe was no longer there. Nor was Clifford Tudor.

I went outside again. The time for the second race was drawing near, and long impatient queues waited at the Tote next door to the bar, eyes flickering between racecards and wrist watches, money clutched ready in hopeful hands. The customers from the bar poured out, hurrying past me. Men were running across the grass towards the stands, coat-tails flapping. Bells rang loudly in the Tote building, and the queues squirmed with the compulsion to push their money through the little windows before the shutters came down.

I hovered indecisively. There was no sign of Joe in all this activity, and I decided to go up to the jockeys' box in the stands and look for him there. I put my head into the bar for a final check, but it was now empty except for three ageing young ladies mopping up the beer-slopped counter.

It was only because I was moving so slowly that I found Joe at all.

Owing to the curve of the road behind them, the Tote and bar buildings did not stand in a perfectly straight line. The gap between the two was narrow at the front, barely eighteen inches across; but it widened farther back until, by the high fence itself, the Tote and bar walls were four or five feet apart.

I glanced into this narrow area as I passed. And there was Joe. Only I did not know it was Joe until I got close to him.

At first I saw only a man lying on the ground in the corner made by the boundary fence and the end wall of the Tote, and thinking he might be ill, or faint, or even plain drunk, went in to see if he needed help.

He lay in shadow, but something about his shape and rag-doll relaxedness struck me with shocking recognition as I took the five or six strides across to him.

He was alive, but only just. Bright red frothy blood trickled from his nose and the corner of his mouth, and a pool of it lay under his cheek on the weedy gravel. His round young face still wore, incredibly, a look of sulky petulance, as if he did not realize that what had happened to him was more than a temporary inconvenience.

Joe had a knife in his body. Its thick black handle protruded incongruously from his yellow and white checked shirt, slanting downwards from underneath his breastbone. A small patch of blood stained the cloth round it, a mild enough indication of the damage the blade was doing inside.

His eyes were open, but vague and already glazing.

I said, urgently, 'Joe!'

His eyes came round to mine and I saw them sharpen into focus and recognize me. A muscle moved in his cheek and his lips opened. He made a great effort to speak.

The scarlet blood suddenly spilled in a gush from his nostrils and welled up in a sticky, bottomless pool in his open mouth. He gave a single choking sound that was almost indecently faint, and over his immature face spread a look of profound astonishment. Then his flesh blanched and his eyes rolled up, and Joe was gone. For several seconds after he died his expression said clearly, 'It's not fair.' The skin settled in this crisis into the lines most accustomed to it in life.

Fighting nausea at the sweet smell of his blood, I shut the eyes with my fingers, and sat back on my heels, looking at him helplessly.

I knew it was useless, but after a moment or two I opened his coat and felt in his pockets for the brown paper he had wanted to show me. It was not there, and his death would not have made sense if it had been. The brown paper was, I thought, the wrapping from Joe's last payment for stopping a horse. It had to be. With something about it which he thought would disclose who had sent it. A postmark? An address? Something to do with chickens, Clem had said; and Pete said it was Chichester. Neither of these held any significance at all for me. According to Clem it meant nothing to Joe either, and he was simply going to show it to me because he had said he would.

He had always been too talkative for his own good. Not quick or quiet. Prudently and privately he could have telephoned to tell me his discovery as soon as he made it. But instead he had flourished the paper at Liverpool. Someone had taken drastic steps to make sure he did not show it to me.

'Poor, silly blabbermouth,' I said softly, to his still body.

I got to my feet, and went back to the narrow entrance of the little area. There was no one about. The voice of the commentator boomed over the loud-speakers that the horses were approaching the second open ditch, which meant that the race was already half over and that I would have to hurry.

I ran the last fifty yards to the Clerk of the Course's office and thrust open the door. A nondescript, grey-haired man in glasses, sitting at a desk, looked up, startled, his pen in mid-air and the paper he was writing on pressed under the palm of his hand. He was the Clerk of the Course's secretary.

'Mr Rollo isn't here?' I asked unnecessarily, glancing round the otherwise empty office.

'He's watching the race. Can I help you?' A dry voice, a dry manner. Not the sort of man one would choose to announce a murder to. But it had to be done. Suppressing all urgency from my voice I told him plainly and quietly that Joe Nantwich was lying dead between the Tote and the bar with a knife through his lungs. I suggested that he send for a canvas screen to put across the gap between the two buildings, as when the crowds began to stream towards the bar and the paying-out Tote windows after the race, someone would be certain to see him. The ground round his body would be well trodden over. Clues, if there were any, would be lost.

The eyes behind the spectacles grew round and disbelieving.

'It's not a joke,' I said desperately. 'The race is nearly over. Tell the police then. I'll find a screen.' He still did not move. I could have shaken him, but I could not spare the time. 'Hurry,' I urged. But his hand had still not gone out to his telephone when I shut the door.

The ambulance room was attached to the end of the weighing-room building. I went in in a hurry, to find two motherly St John's nurses drinking tea. I spoke to the younger one, a middle-aged soul of ample proportions.

'Put that down and come with me quickly,' I said, hoping she would not argue. I picked up a stretcher which was standing against the wall, and as she put her cup down slowly, I added, 'Bring a blanket. There's a man hurt. Please hurry.'

The call to duty got my nurse moving without demur,

and picking up a blanket she followed me across the paddock, though at under half speed.

The commentator's voice rose slightly as he described the race from the last fence, and crisply into the silence when the cheers died away came another voice announcing the winner. I reached the gap by the Tote building as he spoke the names of the second and third horses.

The first stalwart punters began to drift back towards the bar. I looked in at Joe. He had not been disturbed.

I set the stretcher up on end on its handles, to make a sort of screen across the gap. The nurse came up to me, breathing audibly. I took the blanket from her and hung it over the stretcher so that no one could see into the area at all.

'Listen,' I said, trying to speak slowly. 'There is a man between these two buildings. He is dead, not hurt. He has been killed with a knife. I am going to make sure that the police are coming, and I want you to stand here holding the stretcher up like this. Don't let anyone past you until I come back with a policeman. Do you understand?'

She did not answer. She twisted the stretcher a little so that she could peer through the gap. She took a long look. Then, drawing up her considerable bosom and with the light of battle in her eyes, she said firmly, 'No one shall go in, I'll see to that.'

I hurried back to the Clerk of the Course's office. Mr

Rollo was there himself this time, and after I had told him what had happened things at last began to move.

It is always difficult to find a place to be alone at the races. After I had taken a policeman along to where Joe lay, and seen the routine bustle begin, I needed a pause to think. I had had an idea while I crouched beside Joe's body, but it was not one to be acted upon headlong.

People thronged everywhere in the paddock and the racecourse buildings, and to get away from them I walked out on to the course and over the rough grass in the centre until the stands were some way behind. Distance, I hoped, would give me a sense of proportion as well as solitude.

I thought about Bill and Scilla, and also about what I owed to my father, now back in Rhodesia. I thought about the terrorized pub-keepers in Brighton and the bloody face of Joe Nantwich.

It was no use pretending that Joe's murder had not made a great deal of difference to the situation, for until now I had blithely pursued Mr Claud Thiveridge in the belief that though he might arrange for people to be beaten up, he did not purposely kill. Now the boundary was crossed. The next killing would come easier, and the next easier still. The plucky, dog-owning rebels against protection were in greater danger than before, and I was probably responsible.

Joe had shown his brown paper to several people, and no one, including apparently himself, had immediately seen the meaning of what was written on it. Yet he had been killed before he could show it to me. To me, then, the words would have told their tale. Perhaps to me alone.

I watched the rising wind blowing the grass in flattening ripples across the course, and heard the distant voices of the bookmakers as they shouted the odds for the next race.

The question to be answered was simple. Was I, or was I not, going on with the chase? I'm no hero. I did not want to end up dead. And there was no doubt that the idea I had had beside Joe's body was as safe as a stick of dynamite in a bonfire.

The horses for the third race came out and cantered down to the start. Idly I watched them. The race was run: the horses returned to the paddock: and still I stood in the centre of the course, dithering on top of my mental fence.

At last I walked back to the paddock. The jockeys were already out in the parade ring for the fourth race, and as I reached the weighing-room one of the racecourse officials grabbed my arm, saying the police had been looking everywhere for me. They wanted me to make a statement, he said, and I would find them in the Clerk of the Course's office.

I went along there, and opened the door.

Mr Rollo, spare and short, leaned against the window wearing a worried frown. His grey-haired bespectacled secretary still sat at his desk, his mouth slightly open as if even yet he had not grasped the reality of what had happened.

The police inspector, who introduced himself as Wakefield, had established himself at Mr Rollo's table, and was attended by three constables, one of them armed with shorthand notebook and pencil. The racecourse doctor was sitting on a chair by the wall, and a man I did not know stood near him.

Wakefield was displeased with me for what he called my irresponsibility in disappearing for over half an hour at such a time. Big and thick, he dominated the room. Authority exuded from his short upspringing grey hair, his narrow eyes, his strong stubby fingers. A policeman to put the fear of God into evildoers. His baleful glare suggested that at the moment I should be included in this category.

'If you're quite ready, Mr York,' he began sarcastically, 'we'll take your statement.'

I looked round the crowded little office, and said, 'I prefer to make my statement to you alone.'

The inspector growled and erupted and argued; but finally everyone left except Wakefield, myself, and the notebook constable, to whom I agreed as a compromise. I told Wakefield exactly what had happened. The whole truth, and nothing but the truth.

Then I went back to the weighing-room, and to every one of the dozens who clustered round asking for an eye-witness account, I said I had found Joe alive. Yes, I agreed steadily, he had spoken to me before he died. What did he say? Well, it was only two or three words, and I preferred not to discuss it at present, if they did not mind. I added that I had not actually mentioned it to the police yet, but of course I would if I thought it would be important. And I put on a puzzled, thoughtful expression, hoping I looked as if I had a key in my hand and was on the point of finding the right lock to put it in.

I took Kate to tea, and Pete, catching sight of us, came over to join us. To them, too, I told the same story, feeling ashamed, but not caring to risk their broadcasting the truth, that Joe had died without uttering a syllable.

Shortly before the sixth race I left the meeting. The last thing I saw, as I glanced back from the gate, was Wakefield and Clifford Tudor standing outside the door of the Clerk of the Course's office, shaking hands. Tudor, who had been with Joe so soon before his death, had apparently been 'assisting the police with their investigations'. Satisfactorily, it seemed.

I went through the car park to the Lotus, started up, and drove out towards the west, and along the straight secondary roads of the South Downs I opened up the engine and sent the little car along at over a hundred. No Marconicars, I thought with satisfaction, could compete with that. But to make quite certain I was not being followed I stopped once at a vantage point on top of a rise, and studied the road behind me with raceglasses. It was deserted. There was nothing on my tail.

About thirty miles from the racecourse I stopped at an undistinguished roadhouse and booked a room for the night. I insisted also on a lock-up garage for the car. It was too far from Brighton to be within the normal reach of the Marconicars, but I was taking no chances. I wanted to be invisible. It is one thing to stick your neck out; but quite another to go to sleep in full view of the axe.

After a dull dinner I went to my room and wrote a letter to my father. A difficult one. I told him about Joe's death, and that I was trying to use it to entice Mr Thiveridge out of his lair. I asked him, as lightly as I could, to forgive me. I am, I wrote, only hunting another crocodile.

I finished the letter, sealed it, went early to bed, and lay awake for a long time before I slept.

On the way back to the racecourse in the morning I stopped at a post office and air-mailed my letter. I also acquired four shillings' worth of pennies, which I stacked into a paper-wrapped roll. I took the spare pair of socks out of my overnight case and slid the roll of pennies down into the foot of one of them, knotting them there securely. I swung my little cosh experimentally on to the palm of my hand. It was heavy enough, I thought, to knock a man out. I put it in my trouser pocket and finished the journey to the course.

I asked a constable on duty in the paddock where I could find Inspector Wakefield if I wanted him. The constable said that Wakefield was at the station, he thought, and was not coming to the course that afternoon, although he had been there in the morning. I thanked him, and went into the weighing-room, and asked several people in a loud voice to tell me if they saw Inspector Wakefield about, as I wanted to have a word with him about what Joe had said to me before he died.

The awareness of danger, though I had brought it on myself, had a noticeable effect on my nerves. The wrought-up, quickened pulse I always felt to some extent when cantering down to the start of a race was unduly magnified, so that I could hear my own heart beating. Every noise seemed louder, every chance remark more significant, every light brighter. But I was not so much afraid as excited.

I was careful only about what I turned my back to, having no intention of being attacked from behind. It was more likely, I thought, that someone would try to cajole me into an out-of-the-way place as they must have done with Joe, because most of the racecourse was too public for murder.

A knife in the ribs seemed what I should be most wary of. Effective in Joe's case, it had the advantages – to its wielder – of being silent and accurate. Moreover the weapon was left with the body, so that there was no subsequent difficulty in getting rid of it. The black handle protruding from Joe had had the familiar knobbed shape of the sort of French steel cooking knife on sale in any hardware shop. Too common to be a clue of any kind, I suspected, and easy to replace with another to stick into the guts of a second victim. If anyone tried that I intended to be ready. My fingers closed comfortably on the pennies in my pocket.

I hoped to be able to deliver an attacker (unconscious from a four-shilling bump behind the ear) to Inspector Wakefield, to be charged with attempted murder. I had great faith that Wakefield's bulldog personality would shake information out of the toughest criminal in those circumstances, and that with reasonable luck a firm clue to Thiveridge's identity might disclose itself. It was too much to hope that Thiveridge would appear himself. I believed his husky avowal to me on the telephone that he hated personal violence and ordered others to do his dirty work for him, out of his squeamish sight.

I changed, and weighed on the trial scales, and chatted, and went about my ordinary business, and waited.

Nothing happened.

No one asked me to step into dim corners to discuss private business. No one showed any particular interest in what Joe was supposed to have told me before he died. Naturally his murder was still the chief topic of conversation, but it lost ground as the day wore on, and the living horses became more interesting to the inmates of the weighing-room than the dead jockey.

Admiral was to run in the fifth race. By the time the fourth was over my nerves had calmed down and my tense readiness had evaporated. I had expected action before this. I had been at the meeting for nearly three hours, a man with essential information inviting to have his mouth permanently shut, and no move had been made against me.

It crossed my mind, not for the first time, that cause and effect in the Thiveridge organization never followed closely on each other. Joe's death happened two whole days after he showed his brown paper at Liverpool. The warning to me on the telephone was delivered two days after I had spread at Cheltenham the news of the wire which had killed Bill. The horse-box affair had taken at least a day to arrange. The Bristol wire was rigged to bring me down two days after my excursion into the Marconicar office.

I had begun to suspect that the whole organization was still geared to the telephone call Thiveridge made every morning to Fielder, and that Fielder had no other way of getting urgent messages to his 'Chairman', or of receiving instructions from him. Presumably Thiveridge still felt the delay in his news service was a lesser evil than providing an address or telephone number at which he could be reached and perhaps discovered.

Depressed, I was coming to believe that my carefully acted lies had not at all reached the ears for which they were meant, and felt that offering myself as bait to a predator who did not know he should be hunting me was a bit idiotic.

Trying to shake off this deflation, I went out to the parade ring to join Pete and mount Admiral. Bill's horse, now mine, looked as splendid as ever. With his intelligent head, deep chest, straight hocks, and good bone below the knee, he was a perfect example of what a top class steeplechaser should be.

'Even though he hasn't been on a racecourse since that ghastly day at Maidenhead, he's at the top of his form,' said Pete, admiring him beside me. 'You can't lose the race, so go along quietly for a while, getting used to him. You'll find he has plenty in reserve. You'll never get to the bottom of him. Bill used to take him to the front early on, as you know, but you don't need to. He's got a terrific turn of foot from the last.'

'I'll do as you say,' I said.

Pete gave me a leg-up. 'Admiral's odds-on, again,' he said. 'If you make a mess of this race the crowd'll murder you. So will I.' He grinned.

'I'll try to stay alive,' I said, grinning back cheerfully.

Admiral was as superb to ride as he looked. He put himself right before every fence, making his spring at exactly the right moment and needing no help from the saddle. He had the low, flowing galloping stride of the really fast mover, and from the first fence onward I found racing on his back an almost ecstatic pleasure. Following Pete's advice I went round the whole course without forcing the pace, but riding into the last fence alongside two others, I gave Admiral a kick in the ribs and shook up the reins. He took off from just inside the wings and landed as far out on the other side, gaining two lengths in the air and shedding the other two horses like dead leaves. We came home alone, easy winners, to warm cheers from the stands.

In the winner's unsaddling enclosure, where I dismounted and undid the girths, Admiral behaved as if he had only been out for an exercise gallop, his belly hardly moving as he breathed. I patted his glossy chestnut neck, noticed that he was hardly sweating at all, and asked Pete, 'What on earth can he do if he really tries?'

'The National, no less,' said Pete, rocking back on his heels, and tipping his hat off his face, as he collected his due congratulations from all around.

I grinned, pulled the saddle off over my arm, and went into the weighing-room to weigh-in and change. The familiar joy of winning flushed through my limbs, as warming as a hot bath, and I could have done handsprings down the changing-room if I hadn't known it was the horse to whom all credit was due, not the jockey.

Pete called to me to hurry up and we'd have a celebration drink together, so I changed quickly and went outside to join him. He steered me towards the bar next to the Tote building, and we stopped at the gap, looking in to where Joe had died. There was a shoulder-high wooden fence across the entrance now, to keep sensation seekers out. A rusty brown stain on the gravel was all that was left of Joe.

'A terrible thing, that,' Pete said, as we stepped into the bar. 'What did he say to you before he died?'

'I'll tell you sometime,' I said idly. 'But just now I'm more interested in where Admiral runs next.' And over our drinks we talked solely about horses.

Returning to the weighing-room we found two men in belted raincoats waiting for us near the door. They wore trilby hats and large shoes, and gave off that indefinable aura of solid menace which characterizes many plain-clothes policemen.

One of them put his hand inside his coat, drew out a folded warrant and flipped it in my direction.

'Mr York?'

'Yes.'

'Inspector Wakefield's compliments, and will you come down to the police station to help his inquiries, please.' The 'please' he tacked on as an afterthought.

'Very well,' I said, and asked Pete to see Clem about my kit.

'Sure,' he said.

I walked with the two men across to the gate and through the car park.

'I'll get my car and follow you to the station,' I said.

'There's a police car waiting for us in the road, sir,' said the larger of the two. 'Inspector Wakefield did say to bring you in it, and if you don't mind, sir, I'd rather do as the Inspector says.'

I grinned. If Inspector Wakefield were my boss I'd do as he said, too. 'All right,' I agreed.

Ahead of us the sleek black Wolseley was parked outside the gate, with a uniformed driver standing beside it and another man in a peaked cap in the front passenger's seat.

Away towards my right, in front of the ranks of parked horse-boxes, several of the runners from Admiral's race were being led up and down to get the stiffness out of their limbs before they were loaded up for the journey home. Admiral was among them, with Victor, his lad, walking proudly at his head.

I was telling the man on my right, the smaller of the two, that there was my horse and wasn't he a beauty, when I got a shock which knocked the breath out of me as thoroughly as a kick in the stomach.

To cover myself I dropped my race glasses on to the turf and bent slowly to pick them up, my escort stopping a pace ahead of me to wait. I grasped the strap and slung it over my shoulder, straightening and looking back at the same time to where we had come from. Forty yards of grass separated us from the last row of cars. There was no one about except some distant people going home. I looked at my watch. The last race was just about to begin.

I turned round unhurriedly, letting my eyes travel blankly past the man on my right and on towards Admiral, now going away from me. As usual after a race, he was belted into a rug to avoid cooling down too quickly, and he still wore his bridle. Victor would change that for a head collar when he put him in the horse-box.

Victor's great drawback was his slow wits. Endowed with an instinctive feeling for horses and an inborn skill in looking after them, he had never risen above 'doing his two' in forty years of stable life, and never would. I would have to do without much help from him.

'Victor,' I shouted, and when he turned round I signalled to him to bring Admiral over.

'I just want to make sure the horse's legs are all right,' I explained to the two men. They nodded and waited beside me, the larger one shifting from foot to foot.

I did not dare to take a third look, and in any case I knew I was not mistaken.

The man on my right was wearing the tie I had lost in the horse-box on Maidenhead Thicket.

It was made from a piece of silk which had been specially woven and given to me on my twenty-first birthday by a textile manufacturer who wanted to do business with my father. I had two other ties like it, and a scarf, and the pattern of small red and gold steamships interlaced with the letter Y on a dark green background was unique.

How likely was it that a junior CID officer should have come honestly by my tie, I asked myself urgently. Farmer Lawson had not found it, and none of his men admitted to having seen it. It was too much of a coincidence to be innocent that it should reappear round the throat of a man who was asking me to step into a car and go for a ride with him.

Here was the attack I had been waiting for, and I had damn nearly walked meekly into the trap. Getting out of it, when it was so nearly sprung, was not going to be easy. The 'police' car was parked across the gateway barely twenty paces ahead, with the driver standing by the bonnet and looking in our direction. The menacing aura of my two tough escorts now revealed itself to be something a great deal more sinister than a manner assumed to deal with crooks. One of them, perhaps, had killed Joe.

If I gave the slightest sign of doubting them, I was sure the three of them would hustle me into the car and drive off in a cloud of dust, leaving only Victor to report doubtfully what he had seen. And that, as far as I was concerned, would be that. It was to be one of those rides from which the passenger did not return.

My plan to present Wakefield with an attempted

murderer was no good. One, I could have managed. But not three, and another sitting in the car.

When Victor was within fifteen paces of me I let the strap of my race-glasses slip from my shoulder, down my arm and into my hand. Abruptly, with all my strength, I swung the glasses like a scythe round the legs of the larger man and overbalanced him, tripped the smaller man with the one elementary judo throw I knew, and sprinted for Admiral.

The five seconds it took them to recover from the unexpected assault were enough. As they started after me with set faces I leaped on to Admiral's back, picked up the reins which lay loosely on his neck, and turned him round sharply out of Victor's grasp.

The third man was running towards me from the car. I kicked Admiral into a canter in two strides, swerving round the advancing chauffeur, and set him towards the hedge which formed the boundary of the car park. He cleared it powerfully, landing on the grass verge of the road a few yards in front of the black car. The fourth man had the door open and was scrambling out. I looked back quickly.

Victor was standing stock-still with his mouth open. The three men were all running towards the gate with purposeful strides. They had nearly reached it. I had barely time to hope they were not carrying guns, since I presented a large and close target, when I saw the sun glint on something bright in the hand of the man who was wearing my tie. It hardly seemed the moment to stop and discover whether the glint came from a black-handled chef's knife: but I nearly found out the hard way, because he drew back his arm and threw it at me. I flung myself flat on the horse's neck and it missed, and I heard it clatter on to the road beyond.

I urged Admiral straight across the road, ignoring the squeal of brakes from a speeding lorry, and jumped him into the field opposite. The land sloped upwards, so that when I reined-in about halfway up it and turned round to see what was happening, the road and the car park were spread out below like a map.

The men were making no attempt to follow. They had moved the Wolseley away from the gate and were now drawing to a halt some yards further along the verge. It looked as if all four were inside the car.

Victor still stood in the car park, scratching his head as he looked up towards me. I could imagine his bewilderment. I wondered how long it would be before he went to tell Pete what had happened.

Once the last race was over the car park would be buzzing with people, and the cars would pour out of the now unobstructed gateway. I thought that then I would be able to return safely to the racecourse without being abducted.

At this point another black car drew up behind the Wolseley, and then another, and several others, until a line of eight or more stretched along the side of the road. There was something rather horribly familiar about the newcomers.

They were Marconicars.

CHAPTER FIFTEEN

All the drivers climbed out of the taxis and walked along towards the Wolseley. With its low expensive lines and its efficient-looking aerial on top, it sill looked every inch a police car; but the reinforcements it had called up dispelled any last doubts it was possible to have about the nature of the 'CID officers'.

The men stood in a dark group on the road, and I sat on Admiral half-way up the field watching them. They seemed to be in no hurry, but having seen their armoury of bicycle chains, knives, and assorted knuckledusters when they fought the London gang at Plumpton, and with Joe's fate constantly in mind, I had no doubt what would happen if I let them catch me.

I was in a good position. They could not drive the taxis up the field because there was no gate into it from the road, nor could they hope to reach me on foot, and I was still confident that when the race crowd flocked out I could evade the enemy and return to the course.

Two things quickly happened to change the picture.

First, the men began looking and pointing towards the side of the field I was in. Turning my head to the right I saw a car driving downhill on the farther side of the hedge, and realized that there was a road there. Twisting round, I now took note for the first time that a large house with out-buildings and gardens spread extensively across the skyline.

Three of the taxis detached themselves from the line and drove round into the road on my right, stopping at intervals along it. I now had taxi drivers to the right and ahead, and the big house at my back, but I was still not unduly dismayed.

Then yet another Marconicar came dashing up and stopped with a jerk in front of the Wolseley. A stocky man swung open the door and raised himself out of the driver's seat. He strode across the road to the hedge, and stood there pointing up at me with his arm extended. I was still wondering why when I heard the low whine of a bullet passing at the level of my feet. There was no sound of a shot.

As I turned Admiral to gallop off across the field, a bullet hit the ground with a phut in front of me. Either the range was too far for accurate shooting with a gun fitted with a silencer, or . . . I began to sweat . . . the marksman was aiming deliberately low, not at me but at Admiral.

It was only an eight or ten acre field, nothing like big enough for safety. I used precious moments to pull the horse up and take a look at the ragged sprawling hedge on the far side of the field. It was threaded half-way up with barbed wire. Over my shoulder I could see the man with the gun running along the road parallel to the course I had just taken. He would soon be within range again.

I took Admiral back a little way, faced him towards the hedge and urged him to jump. He cleared the whole thing, wire and all, without bending so much as a twig. We landed in another field, this time occupied by a herd of cows but again small and much too open to the road. Also, I discovered, trotting along the top boundary, that barbed wire had been laid lavishly in three strong strands all round it. All pastures have a gate, however, and I came to it in the farthest corner. I opened it, guided Admiral through into the next field, and shut it behind me.

This field was fenced with posts and wire only, and it was the extent of the barbed wire which decided me then to put as much space as I could between me and my pursuers in the shortest possible time. If I let the taxi-drivers follow me slowly from field to field I might find myself in a corner that even Admiral could not jump out of.

I was glad the sun was shining, for at least I could tell in which direction I was going. Since I was already headed towards the east, and because it seemed sensible to have a definite destination to aim for, I decided to take Admiral back to his own stable in Pete's yard.

I reckoned I had about twelve miles to cover, and I racked my brains to remember what the country was like in between. I knew the patchwork farmland which I was then grappling with gave way at some point ahead to Forestry Commission plantations. Then there would be a short distance of bare downland before I reached the hollow and the small village where Pete trained. Of the roads which crossed this area I had but the vaguest idea, and on any of them I could be spotted by a cruising Marconicar.

With this thought uncomfortably in mind, I found another by-road ahead. I let myself out on to it through a gate, and was trotting down it, looking for an opening in the neglected growth on the other side, when a squat black car swept round a distant bend and sped uphill towards me. Without giving Admiral a good chance to sight himself I turned him sharply towards the overgrown hedge and kicked his ribs.

It was too high for him, and too unexpected, but he did his best. He leaped straight into the tangle of sagging wire and beech saplings, crashed his way heavily through, and scrambled up almost from his knees on to the higher ground of the next field. It had been ploughed and planted with mangolds and made heavy going, but I urged him into a canter, hearing behind me the screech of brakes forcefully applied. A glance showed me the driver thrusting through the hole Admiral had made, but he did not try to chase me and I realized thankfully that he was not the man with the gun.

All the same, he had his radio. My whereabouts would be known to all the Marconicars within a minute.

I put another field between us and the taxi before pulling up and dismounting to see what damage Admiral had done himself. To my relief there were only a few scratches and one jagged cut on his stifle from which a thread of blood was trickling. I left it to congeal.

Patting his neck and marvelling at how he retained his calm sensible nature in very upsetting circumstances, I grasped the leather roller he wore round his middle, and sprang up again on to his back. The rug he was wearing now gaped in a right-angled tear on one side, but I decided not to take it off as it gave more purchase for my legs than riding him completely bareback.

Three or four fields farther on the arable land began to give way to bracken, and ahead lay the large enclosures of the Forestry Commission.

The trees, mostly conifers, were being grown in large orderly expanses with rough tracks between each section. These acted both as convenient roadways for the foresters and as breaks in case of fire. They occurred about one in each half-mile, and were crossed at intervals by tracks leading in the opposite direction.

I wanted to set a course towards the south-east, but by consulting my watch and the sun in conjunction, found that the tracks ran from almost due north to south, and from east to west. Fretting at the extra mileage this was going to cost me, I steered Admiral into an eastbound track, took the next turning right to the south, then the next left to the east, and so on, crabwise across the forest.

The sections of trees were of varying ages and stages of growth, and turning again to the south, I found the area on my left was planted with trees only two feet high. This did not specially alarm me until I saw, a hundred yards to my left, a red and white motor coach speeding along apparently through the middle of the plantation.

I pulled Admiral up. Looking carefully I could see the posts and the high wire fence which formed the boundary between the little trees and the road beyond. If I turned east at the next track according to schedule, I would be facing straight down to the road.

The far side of the road looked similar to the section I was in: regular rows of conifers, put there by careful design.

At some point, I knew, I would have to cross a road of some sort. If I retreated back into the part of the forest I had crossed and took no risks, I would have to stay there all night. All the same, I thought, as I cantered Admiral along the southbound track and turned into the east one, I could have wished for more cover just at that moment.

Ahead of me the wire gates to the road were open, but before going through them I stopped and took a look at the other side of the road. Not all the plantations were surrounded by high mesh wire like the one I was in, and opposite only three strands of plain wire threaded through concrete posts barred the way.

The road had to be crossed quickly because where I was I felt as sheltered as a cock pheasant on a snow field. The heads in all the passing cars turned curiously towards me. But I saw nothing which looked like a Marconicar, and waiting only for a gap in the traffic, I clicked my tongue and set Admiral towards the wire fence opposite. His hooves clattered loudly on the tarmac, drummed on the firm verge, and he lifted into the air like a bird. There was no track straight ahead, only some fairly sparsely growing tall pines, and as Admiral landed I reined him in to a gentle trot before beginning to thread a way through them.

Coming eventually to another track I checked again with my watch and the sun to make sure it was still running from east to west, which it was, and set off along it at a good pace. The going underfoot was perfect, dry and springy with loam and pine needles, and Admiral, though he had completed a three mile race and covered several miles of an unorthodox cross-country course, showed no signs of flagging.

We made two more turns and the sky began to cloud over, dulling the brilliant spring afternoon; but it was not the fading of beauty which bothered me so much as the fact that you cannot use a wrist watch as a compass unless the sun is shining. I would have to be careful not to get lost.

Just ahead, to my right, a small grass-grown hill rose sharply to its little rounded summit, the conifer forest flowing round its edges like sea round a rock. I had now left the bigger trees and was cantering through sections of young feathery pines only slightly taller than the top of my head, and I could see the hill quite clearly. A man, a black distant silhouetted man, was standing on the top, waving his arms.

I did not connect him with myself at all because I thought I had slipped my pursuers, so that what happened next had the full shock of a totally unexpected disaster.

From a track to the right, which I had not yet reached and could not see, a sleek black shape rolled out across my path and stopped, blocking the whole width of the track. It was the Wolseley.

The young pines on each side of me were too thick and low-growing to be penetrated. I flung a look over my shoulder. A squat black Marconicar was bumping up the track behind me.

I was so close to the Wolseley that I could see one of the men looking out of the rear window with a gloating grin on his face, and I decided then that even if I broke Admiral's neck and my own in trying to escape, it would be a great deal better than tamely giving in.

There was scarcely a pause between the arrival of the Wolseley and my legs squeezing tight into Admiral's sides.

I had no reason to suppose he would do it. A horse can dare just so much and no more. He had had a hard day already. He might be the best hunter-'chaser in England, but . . . The thoughts flickered through my brain in a second and were gone. I concentrated wholly, desperately, on getting Admiral to jump.

He scarcely faltered. He put in a short stride and a long one, gathered the immense power of his hind-quarters beneath him, and thrust himself into the air. Undeterred even by the opening doors and the threatening shouts of the men scrambling out of the Wolseley, he jumped clear over its gleaming black bonnet. He did not even scratch the paint.

I nearly came off when we landed. Admiral stumbled, and I slipped off the rug round on to his shoulder, clinging literally for dear life to the leather roller with one hand and Admiral's plaited mane with the other. The reins hung down, swaying perilously near his galloping feet, and I was afraid he would put his foot through them and trip. I still had one leg half across his rump, and, bumping heavily against his side, I hauled myself inch by inch on to his back. A warning twinge in my shoulder told me my newly mended collar-bone could not be relied upon for too much of this, but leaning along his neck and holding on with all my strength, I reached the reins, gathered them up, and finally succeeded in reducing Admiral to a less headlong pace.

When I got my breath back I looked to see if the Wolseley was following, but it was so far behind that I was not sure whether it was moving or not. I could not spare time to stop and find out.

I realized that I had underestimated the Marconi-cars, and that it was only thanks to Admiral's splendid courage that I was still free. They had had an advantage in knowing the lie of the land, and had used the little hill as a spotting point. I suspected that its summit commanded quite a large area, and that as soon as I had entered the young pines I had been seen.

I was forced to admit that they had guessed which direction I would take and had circled round in front of me. And that being so, they probably knew I had been making for Pete's stable. If I went on I should find them in my way again, with perhaps as little warning and less chance of escape.

I had left the hill behind me, and turned right again on the next track, seeing in the distance a section of taller trees. The horse cantered along tirelessly, but he could not keep it up for ever. I had to reach shelter as quickly as I could, out of sight of the man still standing on the hill-top, and out of the danger of being ambushed on another of the straight and suddenly uninviting tracks. Once we were hidden in the big trees, I promised Admiral, he should have a rest.

The light was dim under the tall pines. They had been allowed to grow close together to encourage their bare trunks to height, and the crowns of foliage far above were matted together like a roof, shutting out most of the daylight. I was glad for the obscurity. I slowed Admiral to a walk and dismounted as we entered the trees, and we went quietly and deeply into them. It was like walking through a forest of telegraph poles. Which of course, I thought fleetingly, perhaps they were destined to be.

The forest felt like home, even though it was different from those I was schooled in. It was very quiet, very dark. No birds at all. No animals. The horse and I went steadily on, silent on the thick pine needles, relying on instinct to keep us on a straight course.

I did not find our situation particularly encouraging. Whichever way I went in this extensive plantation I would have to come to a road in the end, and within three or four square miles the Marconicars knew exactly where I was. They had only to stand round the forest like hounds waiting for the fox to break cover, then it would be view tally-ho over the radio intercoms and the hunt would be on again.

There was a track ahead. A narrow one. I tied the reins round a tree and went forward alone. Standing still on the edge of the track and giving, I hoped, a good imitation of a tree trunk in my tweed suit, I slowly turned my head both ways. The daylight was much stronger on the track owing to the gap in the trees overhead, and I could see quite clearly for several hundred yards. There was no one in sight.

I went back for Admiral, made a final check, and led him across the track. There was no alarm. We walked steadily on. Admiral had begun to sweat long ago and had worked up a lather after our dash away from the Wolseley, damping large patches of the rug. Now that he was cooling down it was not good for him to keep it on, but I hadn't a dry one to give him. I decided that a damp rug was better than no rug, and trudged on.

Eventually I began to hear the hum of traffic and the occasional toot of a horn, and as soon as I could see the road in the distance I tied Admiral to a tree and went on alone again.

The end of the plantation was marked by a fence made of only two strands of stout wire, looking as if it were designed mainly to prevent picnickers driving their cars farther in than the verge. I chose a tree as near to the fence as I could get, dropped down on to my belly behind it, and wriggled forward until I could look along the road. There was only sporadic traffic on it.

On the far side of the road there were no plantations, and no fence either. It was unorganized woodland, a mixture of trees, rhododendrons, and briars. Perfect cover, if I could reach it.

A heavy lorry ground past five feet from my nose, emitting a choking cloud of diesel fumes. I put my face down into the pine needles and coughed. Two saloon cars sped by in the other direction, one trying to pass the other, followed by a single-decker country bus full of carefree people taking home their Tuesday afternoon's shopping. A pair of schoolgirls in green uniform cycled past without noticing me, and when their high twittering voices had faded into the distance and the road was empty, I put my hands under my chest to heave myself up and go back for Admiral.

At that moment two Marconicars came into sight round a bend. I dropped my face down again and lay absolutely still. They drove past my head slowly, and though I did not look at them, I guessed they must be staring keenly into the forest. I hoped wholeheartedly that I had left Admiral far enough back to be invisible, and that he would not make a noise.

The Marconicars swerved across the road and pulled up on the opposite verge barely twenty-five yards away. The drivers got out of the taxis and slammed the doors. I risked a glance at them. They were lighting cigarettes, leaning casually against the taxis, and chatting. I could hear the mumble of their voices, but not what they were saying.

They had not seen me, or Admiral. Yet. But they

seemed to be in no hurry to move on. I glanced at my watch. It was six o'clock. An hour and a half since I had jumped off the racecourse. More important, there was only one hour of full daylight left. When it grew dark my mobility on Admiral would end and we should have to spend the night in the forest, as I could not get him to jump a fence if he could not see it.

There was a sudden clattering noise from one of the taxis. A driver put his hand through the window and brought out a hand microphone attached to a cord. He spoke into it distinctly, and this time I could make out what he said.

'Yeah, we got the road covered. No, he ain't crossed it yet.' There was some more clattering on the taxi radio, and the driver answered, 'Yeah, I'm sure. I'll let you know the second we see him.' He put the microphone back in the taxi.

I began to get the glimmerings of an idea of how to use the manhunt I had caused.

But first things first, I thought; and slowly I started to slither backwards through the trees, pressing close to the ground and keeping my face down. I had left Admiral a good way inside the forest, and I was now certain that the taxi-drivers could not see him. It was uncomfortable travelling on my stomach, but I knew if I stood up the drivers would see me moving among the bare tree trunks. When finally I got to my feet my suit was filthy peat brown, clogged with prickling pine needles. I brushed off the dirt as best I could, went over to Admiral and untied his reins.

Out in the daylight on the road I could still catch glimpses, between the tree trunks, of the two taxis and their drivers, but knowing that they could not see me, I set off towards the west, keeping parallel with the road and at some distance from it. It was, I judged, a little more than a quarter of a mile before I saw another Marconicar parked at the side of the road. I turned back and, as I went along, began to collect an armful of small dead branches. About half way between the parked taxis, where they were all out of my sight, I took Admiral right up to the wire fence to give him a look at it. Although extremely simple in construction, it was difficult to see in the shade of the trees. I set the dead branches up on end in a row to make it appear more solid; then jumped on to Admiral's back, and taking him back a few paces, faced him towards the fence and waited for a heavy vehicle to come along. In still air the sound of hooves on tarmacadam would carry clearly, and I did not want the taxi-drivers round the nearby bends to hear me crossing the road. The longer they believed I was still in the pine forest, the better. But how long the taxis would *remain* parked I did not know, and the palms of my hands grew damp with tension.

A motor bike sped past, and I stayed still with an effort; but then, obligingly, a big van loaded with empty milk bottles came rattling round the bend on my right.

It could not have been better. As it went past me I trotted Admiral forward. He made nothing of the dead-wood patch of fence, popped over on to the grass verge, took three loping strides over the tarmac, and in an instant was safely in the scrub on the far side. The milk lorry rattled out of sight.

I pulled up behind the first big rhododendron, dismounted, and peered round it.

I had not been a second too soon. One of the Marconicars was rolling slowly along in the wake of the milk lorry, and the driver's head was turned towards the forest I had left.

If one driver believed me still there, they all did. I walked Admiral away from the road until it was safe to mount, then jumped on to his back and broke him into a slow trot. The ground now was unevenly moulded into little hillocks and hollows and overgrown with brambles, small conifers, and the brown remains of last year's bracken, so I let the horse pick his own footing to a great extent while I worked out what I was going to do. After a little way he slowed to a walk and I left him to it, because if his limbs felt as heavy and tired as mine he was entitled to crawl.

As nearly as I could judge I travelled west, back the way I had come. If there is one thing you can be sure of in England, it is that a straight line in any direction will bring you to a road without much delay, and I had covered perhaps a mile when I came to the next one. Without going too close I followed it to the north.

I was hunting a prey myself, now. A taxi, detached from the herd.

Admiral was picking his way silently across a bare patch of leaf-moulded earth when I suddenly heard the now familiar clatter of a Marconicar radio, and the answering voice of its driver. I pulled up in two strides, dismounted, and tied Admiral to a nearby young tree. Then I climbed up into the branches.

Some way ahead I saw a white four-fingered signpost, and beside it stood a Marconicar, of which only the roof and the top half of the windows were visible. The rest was hidden from me by the rhododendrons, trees, and undergrowth which crowded the ground ahead. My old friend the pine forest rose in a dark green blur away to the right.

I climbed down from the tree and felt in my pocket for the roll of pennies. I also found two lumps of sugar, which I fed to Admiral. He blew down his nostrils and nuzzled my hand, and I patted his neck gently and blessed Scilla for giving him to me.

With so much good cover it was easy enough to approach the cross-roads without being seen, but when, from the inside of an old rhododendron, I at length had a clear view of the taxi, the driver was not in it. He was a youngish sallow-faced man in a bright blue suit, and he was standing bareheaded in the middle of the crossroads with his feet well apart, jingling some coins in his pocket. He inspected all four directions, saw nothing, and yawned.

The radio clattered again, but the driver took no notice. I had intended to creep up to his taxi and knock him out before he could broadcast that I was there; but now I waited, and cursed him, and he stood still and blew his nose.

Suddenly he began to walk purposefully in my direction.

For an instant I thought he had seen me, but he had not. He wheeled round a large patch of brambles close in front of me, turned his back towards my hiding place, and began to relieve himself. It seemed hardly fair to attack a man at such a moment, and I know I was smiling as I stepped out of the rhododendron, but it was an opportunity not to be missed. I took three quick steps and swung, and the sock-wrapped roll of pennies connected solidly with the back of his head. He collapsed without a sound.

I put my wrists under his shoulders and dragged him back to where I had left Admiral. Working as quickly as I could I ripped all the brown binding off the edge of the horse rug and tested it for strength. It seemed strong enough. Fishing my penknife out of my trouser pocket I cut the binding into four pieces and tied together the driver's ankles and knees with two of them. Then I dragged him closer to the tree and tied his wrists behind him. The fourth piece of binding knotted him securely to the trunk.

I patted his pockets. His only weapon was a spiked metal knuckleduster, which I transferred to my own jacket. He began to wake up. His gaze wandered fuzzily from me to Admiral and back again, and then his mouth opened with a gasp as he realized who I was.

He was not a big man in stature, nor, I now discovered, in courage. The sight of the horse looming so close above him seemed to worry him more than his trussed condition or the bump on the head.

'He'll tread on me,' he yelled, fright drawing back his lips to show a nicotine-stained set of cheap artificial teeth.

'He's very particular what he walks on,' I said.

'Take him away. Take him away,' he shouted. Admiral began to move restlessly at the noise.

'Be quiet and he won't harm you,' I said sharply to the driver, but he took no notice and shouted again. I stuffed my handkerchief unceremoniously into his mouth until his eyes bulged.

'Now shut up,' I said. 'If you keep quiet he won't harm you. If you screech you'll frighten him and he might lash out at you. Do you understand?'

He nodded. I took out the handkerchief, and he began to swear vindictively, but fairly quietly.

I soothed Admiral and lengthened his tether so that

he could get his head down to a patch of grass. He began munching peacefully.

'What is your name?' I asked the taxi driver.

He spat and said nothing.

I asked him again, and he said, 'What the ruddy hell has it got to do with you?'

I needed particularly to know his name and I was in a hurry.

With no feelings of compunction I took hold of Admiral's reins and turned him round so that the driver had a good close view of a massive pair of hindquarters. My captive's newfound truculence vanished in a flash. He opened his mouth to yell.

'Don't,' I said. 'Remember he'll kick you if you make a noise. Now, what is your name?'

'John Smith.'

'Try again,' I said, backing Admiral a pace nearer.

The taxi-driver gave in completely, his mouth trembling and sweat breaking out on his forehead.

'Blake.' He stumbled on the word.

'First name?'

'Corny. It's a nickname, sort of.' His eyes flickered fearfully between me and Admiral's hind legs.

I asked him several questions about the working of the radio, keeping the horse handy. When I had learned all I wanted I untied the reins from the tree and fastened them to a sapling a few feet away, so that when it grew dark the horse would not accidentally tread on the taxi-driver.

Before leaving them I gave Blake a final warning. 'Don't start yelling for help. For one thing there's no one to hear you, and for another, you'll upset the horse. He's a thoroughbred, which means nervous, from your point of view. If you frighten him by yelling he's strong enough to break his reins and lash out at you. Shut up and he'll stay tied up. Get it?' I knew if Admiral broke his reins he would not stop to attack the man, but luckily, Blake did not. He nodded, his body sagging with fear and frustration.

'I won't forget you're here,' I said. 'You won't have to stay here all night. Not that I care about you, but the horse needs to be in a stable.'

Admiral had his head down to the grass. I gave his rump a pat, made sure the knots were still tight on the demoralized driver, and picked my way quickly through the bushes to the taxi.

The signpost was important, for I would have to come back and find it in the dark in miles of haphazard woodland. I wrote down all the names and mileages on all of its four arms, just to make sure. Then I got into the taxi and sat in the driver's seat.

Inside the taxi one could hear the radio as a voice and not as a clatter. The receiver was permanently tuned in so that each driver could hear all messages and replies going from taxis to base and base to taxis.

A man was saying, 'Sid, here. No sign of him. I've got a good mile and a half of the road in view from up here, nearly the whole side of that wood he's in. I'll swear he hasn't got across here. The traffic's too thick for him to do it quickly. I'm sure to see him if he tries it.' Sid's voice came out of the radio small and tinny, like a voice on the telephone, and he spoke casually, as if he were looking for a lost dog.

While he spoke I started the engine, sorted out the gears, and drove off along the road going south. The daylight was just beginning to fade. Half an hour of twilight, I calculated, and perhaps another ten minutes of dusk. I put my foot down on the accelerator.

There was a short silence on the radio. Then someone said, 'He has got to be found before dark.'

Even though I had been half-hoping, half-expecting it, the husky timbre-less whisper made me jerk in my seat. I gripped the steering wheel tightly and the muscles round my eyes contracted. The voice was so close it seemed suddenly as if the danger it spelled for me were close as well, and I had to reassure myself by looking out sideways at the deserted heathland, and backwards in the driving mirror at the empty road astern.

'We're doing our best, sir,' said a quiet voice, respectfully. 'I've been driving up and down this ruddy road for nearly an hour. Two miles up and two miles back. All the parked cars in my section are still in position.'

'How many of you have guns?' said the whisper.

'Four altogether, sir. We could do with more, to be sure of him.'

There was a pause. Then the husky voice said, 'I have one here, but you haven't time to come in for it. You'll have to manage with what you've got.'

'Yes, sir.'

'Pay attention, all drivers. Aim for the horse. Shoot the horse. The man is not to be found with bullets in him. Do you understand?'

There was a chorus of assent.

'Fletcher, repeat your orders.'

The polite taxi-driver said, 'As soon as we spot him either in the trees or breaking cover, we shoot, aiming for the horse. Call up all drivers, chase and catch the man. We are to – er – restrain him as necessary, place him in one of the taxis, and wait for your instructions.'

Half-way through this recital of plans for my disposal, I recognized his voice. The polite tone, in the first instance, gave him away. I had heard it on the Maidenhead road, luring me with its false respectability into a waiting trap: he was the driver of the horse-box. Fletcher. I made a note of it.

Suddenly, as if someone had pressed a switch, a light flooded into my brain and I remembered the fence at Bristol. I remembered the pouring rain on my face and the greyness of everything, and now clearly I remembered the horse-box driver cutting the wire down from the fence, rolling it up, and hanging it over his arm.

There was something else, too . . . but before I could pin it down I came to a halt sign at a main road. I turned left from my empty by-road into a stream of traffic, and began to look for a signpost which would tell my how far away I was from Brighton. After half a mile I found one. Eleven miles. Say, twenty minutes to my destination.

I thought back to the Bristol fence, but the shade had come down again in my memory, and now I was not even sure that any gaps in it remained. My fingers wandered of their own accord to the scar on my cheek and traced along it gently, but it was a gesture I had caught myself in once or twice before, and I attached no importance to it. Besides, the immediate future needed all my thought.

All the way to Brighton I listened to the husky voice. Its tone grew both more urgent and more violent. I found it weird at first to eavesdrop on a man-hunt of which I was myself the quarry, but after a few minutes I got used to it and paid it less and less attention, and this could have been a catastrophic mistake.

'Have you anything to report, twenty-three?' said the husky whisper. There was no reply on the radio. I was only half aware of it. More sharply the voice said, 'Twenty-three, Blake, have you anything to report?'

I came back to the present with a jerk. I picked up the microphone, clicked over the switch, and said 'No' in as bored and nasal a tone as I could muster.

'Answer more quickly next time,' said the husky voice severely. He was apparently checking that all the outlying taxis were still in position, for he went on to ask three more drivers whether they had anything to report. I thanked heaven, as I switched off the microphone, that I had not had to impersonate Blake's voice for more than one second, for any attempt at conversation would have found me out. As it was, I listened more intently than before to the exchanges on the radio.

The whispering voice began to acquire tone and characteristics as I became more familiar with it, until it formed a pattern of phrasing and emphasis which tantalized me at first because I could not remember its origin.

Then I knew. I knew for sure, at last.

You can start on a plan that you think touches the limit of what you can do; and then you have to do much, much more. Once more into the breach . . . only the breach had got bigger. Stiffen the sinews, summon up the blood . . . and bend up every spirit to his full height. There was no one like Bill Shakespeare for bounding things in a nutshell.

I drove into the outskirts of Brighton very thoughtfully indeed.

CHAPTER SIXTEEN

A taxi-driver asking the way to the main police station would be enough to arouse suspicion in a moron. I parked the taxi in a side street and hurried round the corner to ask directions in the nearest shop.

It was a tobacconist's, and busy, so I buttonholed one of the customers, an elderly man with watery eyes and a cloth cap. He told me the way quite clearly, though with frequent sniffs.

'You in trouble, mate?' he enquired inquisitively, eyeing my dirty, dishevelled appearance as I thanked him.

'Lost my dog,' I said, smiling, pulling out the most unexciting reason I could think of for wanting the police.

The watery-eyed man lost interest. I walked quickly back to the taxi and found two small boys listening open-mouthed to the radio. I got into the taxi, winked at them, and said, 'It's a thrilling story on children's hour, isn't it?' Their little faces cleared and they grinned.

I drove off. The husky voice was saying, '. . . at all costs. I don't care how you do it. He must not get away. If you can't catch him alive you must kill him. No bullets, though.'

'It would be more certain if you would let us shoot him sir,' said the polite voice of Fletcher.

Following the watery-eyed man's instructions I found the police station without trouble. Lights shone inside it as I drove past. The daylight was going quickly.

I circled the police station until I found a quiet side turning a hundred yards away. There I stopped, close to the kerb. I turned on the side-lights and shut the windows. The radio was still chattering, and the man with the husky voice could no longer keep his fury in control. For a last moment I listened to him conceding, now that time was running out, to Fletcher's plea that they should be allowed to shoot on sight. Then with a grimace I got out of the taxi, shut the door, and walked away from it.

The Marconicars office, I reckoned, was not more than half a mile off. I half-walked, half-ran towards it, looking, as I went, for a telephone. The street lamps were suddenly turned on, the bulbs glowing palely in the fading light.

The red telephone box outside a sub-post-office was lit up inside, too, and although my reason told me I was in no danger, instinct would have made me stay in darkness. The whispering voice had done my nerves no good.

Though I knew I was still out of sight of the Marconicar office, I went into the telephone box with a conscious effort. I asked Enquiries for the number of the Maidenhead police station, and without delay was put through to the desk sergeant. Inspector Lodge, he told me, had left an hour earlier, but after some urging he parted with Lodge's home number. I thanked him and rang off.

Fumbling with haste, I fed more coins into the machine, and gave the operator the new number. It rang and rang. My heart sank, for if I couldn't get hold of Lodge quickly I did not stand nearly so good a chance of cleaning up the Marconicars the way I wanted. But at last a voice answered. A woman's.

'Inspector Lodge? Just a minute, I'll see if I can find him.'

A pause. And, finally, Lodge's voice.

'Mr York?'

I explained briefly what had happened. I said, 'I've left the taxi in Melton Close, a hundred yards back from the main police station here. I want you to ring the Brighton police and get them to send someone responsible to fetch it in. Tell them to listen carefully to the radio in the taxi. Our friend with the husky voice is speaking on it, inciting all the drivers to kill me. That should settle the Marconicars once and for all, I should think. One of the drivers out looking for me is called Fletcher. He's the one who drove the horse-box at Maidenhead, and he also rigged that wire for me at Bristol. I've remembered about it. It's likely he did the same for Bill Davidson, don't you think?'

'Yes, I do. Where are you now?' asked Lodge.

'In a 'phone box,' I said.

'Well, go back to the taxi and wait there while I telephone the Brighton police. I don't really understand why you didn't go straight to them and explain it at first hand yourself.'

'I thought it would have more weight, coming from you. And anyway . . .' I broke off, realizing just in time that I could not tell Lodge what I was going to do next. I said instead, 'Don't tell the Brighton police to expect me back at the taxi. I've a few phone calls to make . . . er . . . I must tell Scilla I'll be late, and things like that. But you won't waste any time, will you? Mr Claud Thiveridge won't go on talking for ever, especially after it gets dark.'

'I'll ring at once,' promised Lodge, disconnecting. I put down the receiver and pushed out into the street.

I went on my way, totting up the time I could count on before Lodge sent the Brighton police to the Marconicar office. He had to ring them up and give them a fairly lengthy account of what was going on. Then they had to find the taxi, listen to the radio, and make a shorthand record of what they heard, to be used as proof a court would accept that the whole organization was illegal. Very shortly after that they would come chasing round to apprehend the owner of the voice. Ten minutes altogether perhaps, if they hustled; perhaps a quarter of an hour.

When the Marconicar office was in sight I stayed close to the buildings so that I should not be seen from the Marconicar window. The street was nearly empty, and across the road the Olde Oake Café had closed its doors for the night. Through the glass I could see the plump waitress tiredly piling the old oak chairs on to the old oak tables.

A small black car was parked by the kerb ahead. I glanced at it cursorily, and then with sudden recognition, I stopped. I purposely had not told Lodge whose face I had attached to the husky voice, though I knew I ought to have done. The sight of his car, parked flagrantly barely twenty yards from the Marconicar door, gave me a chance to square things with my conscience. I lifted the bonnet, unclipped the distributor lid, and took off the rocker arm, which I put in my pocket. Whatever happened now, there would be no quick getaway for Mr Thiveridge.

There were no lights on in the Marconicar office, nor in any of the floors above. The neon sign, L. C. Perth, was flashing steadily on and off at two-second intervals, wasting its message on the empty road. The only gambler in sight, I reflected, was myself.

Reaching the Marconicar window I bent double below the sill and edged past as close to the wall as I could press. The street door was closed, but opened readily at a touch. I stepped very quietly into the hall, leaving the door open behind me. The silence in the house was tensely oppressive, and for a cowardly instant I was tempted to go out into the street again and wait like a sensible citizen for the police.

Stepping cautiously I went down the hall and pressed my ear to the door of Fielder's room. I could hear nothing. I opened the door gently and looked in. The room was tidy and empty. Next I tried the door on my left, which led into the back office where Marigold by day presided over her radio switchboard.

Through the thick door I could hear nothing, but when I opened it an inch a faint hum reached my ears. There was no one in the office. I went quietly in.

The hum was coming from the radio equipment. A small red brightly glowing circle in the control panel indicated that it was switched on, and through a crack in the casing the tiny light of a valve shone blue-white. The microphone lay casually on its side on its ledge.

For a sickening moment I thought that my bird had flown during the time it had taken me to ring Lodge and travel the half mile from the taxi; then I remembered the car outside, and at the same time, looking for wires leading out of the radio, saw a narrow plastic-covered cable running up the far wall and into the ceiling.

Praying that the stairs in the old house would not creak, I went up them lightly and quickly, and pressed my ear to the panels of the door of the main office of L. C. Perth. There were some large painted capital letters beside my nose. I squinted across at them while I listened. They said PLEASE ENTER.

Owing to the solidity of the Regency door I could hear only a fierce hissing sound, but by this time the whisper was so familiar to me that an inch of mahogany could not disguise it.

He was there.

The hair on the back of my neck began to itch.

I judged it must have been seven or eight minutes since I spoke to Lodge. As I had to give the Brighton police time to find the taxi and record something of what they would hear on its radio, I could not risk interrupting the husky voice too soon. But neither did I intend to hover where I was until the police arrived. I made myself count one hundred slowly, and it seemed the longest three minutes of my life. Then I rubbed the palm of my hand on my trousers, and gingerly took hold of the ornate glass doorknob.

It turned silently and I eased the door open a few inches. It made no noise at all. I could see straight into that unlit room.

He was sitting at a desk with his back turned squarely towards me, and he seemed to be looking out into the street. The neon sign flashed off and on outside the window, illuminating the whole of the room and lighting up his dusky outline with a red glow. Red reflections winked on chromium ashtrays and slid along the metal edges of filing cabinets. A row of black telephones, ranked like an army on a long desk, threw curious angular shadows on the wall.

At close quarters the husky whisper lost some of its disembodied menace, even though what it was saying was now almost hysterically violent.

The open door can have stirred no current of air, for the man at the desk went on talking into his microphone, completely unaware that I was standing behind him.

'Kill him,' he said. 'Kill him. He's in that wood somewhere. He's an animal. Hunt him. Turn your cars towards the wood and put the headlights on. You'd better start beating through the trees. Fletcher, organize it. I want York dead, and quickly. Shoot him down. Smash him.'

The man paused and drew in so sharp a breath that it gagged in his throat. His hand stretched out for a glass of water, and he drank.

Fletcher's voice came tinnily into the room through an extension loud-speaker on the desk. 'We haven't seen a sign of him since he went into the wood. I think he might have got past us.'

The man at the desk shook with fury. He began to whisper again with a rough burring rasp.

'If he escapes, you'll pay for it. You'll pay, I tell you. I want him dead. I want him smashed. You can do what you like with him. Use those chains to good purpose, and the spiked knuckles. Tear him to pieces. If he lives it will be the end for all of us, remember that.' The whisper rose in tone to a thin sound like a strangled shriek. 'Rip his guts out . . . smash . . . destroy . . .'

He went on for some time elaborating on the way I should be killed, until it was clear that his mind was very nearly unhinged.

Abruptly I had heard enough. I opened the door wide, and put my hand on the light switch, and pressed it down. The room was suddenly brilliantly flooded with light.

The man at the desk whirled round and gaped at me.

'Good evening, Uncle George,' I said softly.

CHAPTER SEVENTEEN

His eyes scorched with hate. The vacuous expression was torn away, the hidden personality now out in the open and as mean and savage as any crocodile. He was still Kate's amusing Uncle George in corpulent outline and country-gentleman tweeds, the Uncle George who had written for boys' magazines and taken his wife to matinées, but the face was the one which had had a knife stuck into Joe Nantwich and had urged a blood-thirsty mob to tear me to bits.

His hand snaked out across the desk and came up with a gun. It was a heavy, old-fashioned pistol, cumbersome, but deadly enough, and it was pointing straight at my chest. I resolutely looked at Uncle George's eyes, and not at the black hole in the barrel. I took a step towards him.

Then it came, the instant on which I had gambled my safety.

Uncle George hesitated.

I saw the flicker, the drawing back. For all his sin, for

all the horror he had spread into the lives of others, he had never himself committed an act of violence. When he had delivered his threatening warning to me on the telephone on the very morning that I went to stay in his house, he had told me that he hated even to watch violence; and in spite of, or perhaps because of, his vicarious pleasure in the brutalities of primitive nations, I believed him. He was the sort of man, I thought, who liked to contemplate atrocities he could never inflict himself. And now, in spite of the fury he felt against me, he couldn't immediately, face to face, shoot me down.

I gave him no time to screw himself up. One fast stride and I had my hand on his wrist. He was trying to stand up. Too late he found the power to kill and squeezed the trigger; but the bullet smashed harmlessly into the wall. I bent his arm outwards with force, and twisted the gun out of his grasp. His muscles were soft and without strength, and he didn't know how to fight.

I flung him back hard into his chair, knocking the wind out of him, and then I reached over and switched off his microphone. I wasn't anxious that either the police or the taxi-drivers should overhear what I was going to say.

There was a crackle as I brushed against his coat. I pulled it open. A folded piece of brown paper protruded from an inner pocket, and I tugged it out and spread it open on the desk. He was gasping for breath and didn't try to stop me. I read what was on it.

Joe's address.

I turned it over. In one corner on the other side, scribbled carelessly as if someone were not sure of the spelling and had used the nearest piece of paper to try them out on, were the words:

Chichen Itza;
Chitchen Itsa
Chitsen

Not chickens, not Chichester. Chichen Itza. I had the vaguest memory of having heard it before. It was the name of an emperor I thought; and it meant nothing to me, nothing. Yet Joe had died for it.

I left the paper on the desk, and hoped that the police would find it useful.

The hysteria had drained out of Uncle George. He looked suddenly ill and old, now that his day was done. I could summon no compassion for him, all the same: but then it was not regard for Kate's uncle that had brought me into the Marconicar office, but love for Kate herself.

'The police will be here in less than a minute,' I said, speaking slowly and distinctly. He shifted in his seat and made a sharp helpless gesture with his pudgy hands. I went on, 'They have been listening in to what you have been saying on the radio.'

Uncle George's eyes widened. 'Twenty-three,' he

said, with a remnant of anger. 'Twenty-three hasn't answered my last few calls.'

I nodded. I said, 'You will be charged with incitement to murder. Gaol for life, at least.' I paused. 'Think,' I said with emphasis. 'Think of your wife. You did it all for her, didn't you, so that she could go on living in the luxury she was used to?' I was guessing, but I felt sure it was true, and he didn't deny it.

'You have shielded her from reality too long,' I said. 'What will it do to her, if you are arrested and tried, and maybe hanged?'

Or to Kate either, I added hopelessly to myself.

Uncle George listened and stared at me, and slowly his gaze fell to the pistol I still held in my hand.

'It's quicker,' I said.

There was a short silence.

Very faintly in the distance I heard an alarm bell. Uncle George heard it too. He looked up. He hated me still, but he had come to the end of the line, and he knew it.

'The police,' I said. The bell grew perceptibly louder.

I took the three steps across to the door, turned, and tossed the gun back into Uncle George's lap. As his stubby fingers fumbled and clutched it I went through the door, closed it, and ran down the stairs. The front door was still open. I hurried through that and pulled it shut behind me. The police alarm bells were no longer ringing.

In the shadow of the building I slipped along into the dark porch of the next-door house; and I was only just in time. Two police cars slowed, crawled, and halted in front of the Marconicar building.

Over in the Olde Oake Café the lights were out. The plump waitress had gone home.

There had been no sound from upstairs. I shivered, struck by the horrifying thought that Uncle George, having already screwed himself once to pull the trigger, might just possibly shoot a policeman instead of himself. With the gun I had so thoughtfully given back to him.

As the doors of the police cars slammed open and the black figures poured out I took the first step towards them to warn them that their quarry was armed. But Uncle George's devotion to Aunt Deb's interests remained steadfast after all. I thought that the single crashing shot in the room behind the neon sign was the best thing he had ever done for her sake.

I waited for a few minutes in my dark doorway, and while I stood there a small crowd began to collect on the pavement, drawn by the noise of the shots and the presence of the police cars. I slipped unhurriedly among them, and after a little while walked quietly away.

Round two or three turnings I found a telephone box and stepped inside, feeling in my pocket for coins. The calls to Lodge had taken all my small change, and for a moment I looked blankly at the threepenny piece and two halfpennies which were all I could dredge from my trouser pocket. Then I remembered my cosh. I untied the sock, tipped some of the pennies out on to my hand, pushed four of them into the slot, and asked the operator for Pete's number.

He answered at the second ring.

He said, 'Thank God you've rung. Where the hell have you been?'

'Touring Sussex.'

'And where's Admiral?'

'Well . . . I left him tied to a tree somewhere in the heathland,' I said.

Pete began to splutter, but I interrupted him.

'Can you send the horse-box to collect him? Get the driver to come down to Brighton and pick me up on the sea-front, near the main pier. And Pete . . . have you got a decent map of Sussex?'

'A map? Are you mad? Don't you know where you left him? Have you really just tied the best hunter-'chaser in the country to a tree and forgotten where?' He sounded exasperated.

'I'll find him easily if you send a map. Don't be too long, will you? I'll tell you all about it later. It's a bit complicated.'

I put down the receiver, and after some thought, rang up The Blue Duck. Ex-Regimental Sergeant-Major Thomkins answered the phone himself.

'The enemy is routed, Sergeant-Major,' I said. 'The Marconicars are out of business.'

'A lot of people will be thankful to hear it,' said the strong deep voice, with a good deal of warmth.

I went on, 'However, the mopping up operations are still in progress. Would you be interested in taking charge of a prisoner and delivering him to the police?'

'I would indeed,' he said.

'Meet me down at the main pier, then, at the double, and I'll gen you up.'

'I'm on my way,' said the sergeant-major.

He joined me by the sea wall soon after I got there myself. It was quite dark by then, and the lights along the front barely lit the ghostly grey lines of the breaking waves.

We had not long to wait for the horse-box, and when it came, Pete himself poked his big bald head out of the passenger seat and called to me. He, I and the sergeant-major got into the back and sat on a couple of straw bales, and as we swayed to the movement of the box on its way west I told them all that had happened since the day Bill died at Maidenhead. All, that is, up to my last conversation with Lodge. Of my visit to the Marconicar office and the true identity of Claud Thiveridge, I said nothing. I didn't know how English law viewed the crime of inciting to suicide, and for various reasons had decided to tell no one about it.

Parts of the story Pete already knew, and part Thomkins knew, but I had to go over the whole thing for them both to get it clear from first to last.

The horse-box driver had been given my note of the all-important signpost, and by comparing it with the map Pete had brought, he drove us back to it in remarkably short time.

Both Admiral and Corny Blake were still attached to their various trees, and we led one and frog-marched the other into the horse-box. Admiral was overjoyed to see us, but Blake's emotions seemed slightly mixed, especially when he recognized Thomkins. It appeared that it was Blake who had bashed the sergeant-major on the head with one of his own bottles.

With a grin I fished Blake's brass knuckleduster out of my pocket and handed it to Thomkins. 'The prisoner's armoury,' I said.

Thomkins tossed the wicked-looking weapon in his hand and tried it on for size, and Blake gave one agonized look at it and rolled off his bale of straw in a dead faint.

'We had better go round by West Sussex racecourse, if you don't mind,' I said. 'My car is still in the car park there; I hope.'

It was there, all alone in the big field, the rising moon glinting on its low dark shape. I stepped down into the road, shook hands with Thomkins and Pete, wished them luck, and watched the red tail-lights of the horsebox until they disappeared into the darkness.

Then I went over and started my car, turned my back firmly on what was doubtless my duty – the answering of interminable questions in Brighton police station – and with a purring roar set off for the Cotswolds.

Driven by an irresistible curiosity, I made a detour along the coast to Portsmouth, taking a chance that the public library would still be open there; and it was. In the reference department I hefted out a volume of an encyclopedia and looked up Chichen Itza. The first spelling on the paper was the right one.

Chichen Itza, I found, was not an emperor; it was a capital city. It was the ancient Yucatán capital of the Mayas, an Indian nation who had flourished in Central America fifteen hundred years ago.

I stared at the page until the words faded into a blur.

What happened next was partly, I supposed, delayed reaction from the abysmal fear I felt when I looked into the barrel of Uncle George's gun; and partly it was hunger and a wave of deathly tiredness, and the sudden letting up of the stresses of the past weeks. My hands, my whole body, began to shake. I braced my foot against the leg of the table I was sitting at and gripped the big book hard to stop it. It went on for minutes, until I could have cried with weakness, but gradually the spasm lessened, and the tension went out of my muscles, and I was just plain cold.

Chichen Itza. I stood up stiffly and closed the book

and put it back on the shelf, and went soberly out to the car. I had set a better trap than I knew, pretending to be on the point of understanding what Joe might have said before he died.

I remembered clearly the study lined with glass cases. I could see the heavy carved oak desk, the folders devoted to Indian tribes, and the one separate folder clearly marked 'Mayas'. Uncle George had told me too much about the Mayas: and he'd known that Chichen Itza would lead me conclusively to him.

CHAPTER EIGHTEEN

What I had not managed to do for Kate by loving her, I had done by tearing her world apart.

She stood in front of me, rigidly controlling herself, with a look of such acrid unrelenting hatred that I tasted my misery literally as a bitterness in the mouth. The banked fires were burning fiercely at last. There was a new depth and maturity in her face, as if in two weeks she had become wholly a woman. It made her more desirable than ever.

The inquest and inquiry into the life and death of George Penn had been adjourned twice, and had just ended; and police, witnesses, and Kate and I were standing in the hall of the Brighton court buildings, preparing to leave.

The verdict of temporary insanity was merciful, but there had been no hiding from news-scenting journalists the extent of Uncle George's criminal activities, and L. C. Perth and Marconicars had been front page news, on and off, for a fortnight.

My getting Uncle George to kill himself had been no help after all to Aunt Deb. It had been impossible to keep the truth from her, and shock and distress had brought on a series of heart attacks, of which the fourth was fatal. But for Kate, though she knew nothing about it, it was still the best thing. She had had to face the knowledge of his guilt, but not his trial and punishment.

But my letters of condolence had been unanswered. My telephone calls had regularly found her 'out'. And now I saw why. She blamed me alone for the sorrows which had come to her.

'I loathe you,' she said implacably. 'You nauseate me. You wormed your way into our house and accepted everything we gave you . . .' I thought of those gentle kisses, and so, from the extra flash in her eyes, did Kate . . . 'and all you have done in return is to hound a poor old man to his death, and kill a defenceless old woman as a result. I have no uncle and no aunt. I have no one anywhere at all. I have no one.' She spoke in anguish. 'Why did you do it? Why couldn't you leave them alone? Why did you have to destroy my home? You knew how much I loved them. I can't bear to look at you, I loathe you so much . . .'

I swallowed, and tried to work some saliva into my dry mouth. I said, 'Do you remember the children who had to be driven to school by a judo expert to keep them safe?'

But Kate stared blackly back as if she hadn't heard.

'You are the most beastly person I have ever known, and although you have made it impossible for me to forget you, I shall never think of you without . . . without . . .' Her throat moved convulsively as if she were going to be sick. She turned away abruptly and walked unsteadily out through the big main door into the street.

The flash of camera bulbs met her and caught her unawares, and I saw her throw up her arm in a forlorn attempt to hide her face. The vulnerability and the loneliness in the droop of her shoulders cried out for comfort, and I, who most wanted to give it, was the only person she wouldn't accept it from. I watched her walk quickly through the questioning newspapermen and get into the hired car which was waiting for her.

It drove off. I stared after it, numbly.

Presently I became aware that Lodge was standing at my elbow and had been talking for some seconds. I hadn't heard a word he said, and he appeared to be waiting for a reply.

'I beg your pardon,' I said. 'What did you say?'

Lodge glanced out through the door where Kate had gone and sighed. 'It wasn't very important . . . Look, she'll see things more reasonably in a little while, when she begins to think straight again. I heard a good deal of what she said . . . but you aren't to blame because her uncle took to crime.'

'If I had known . . .' I stopped, on the verge of adding

the give-away words 'for sure': 'If I had known that George Penn was Claud Thiveridge, I would have done things differently.'

'Things worked out well for the Penns, I think,' said Lodge. 'A quick end has its merits.'

His tone was loaded with meaning, and I knew that he half guessed what part I had played in Uncle George's death. He had several times earlier remarked that my disappearance from Brighton at the moment of success was out of character, and had shown polite scepticism over my excuse that I was growing anxious about my horse. He had mentioned pointedly that the Brighton police, listening in the Marconicar taxi to Uncle George's ravings, had heard a faint murmur (indistinguishable) in the background, a single shot, and nothing more. They had not been able to account for this, apart from later finding the microphone switched off and a bullet in the wall, and had come to the conclusion that Uncle George had been testing the old pistol to see if it were in working order. The shot had, however, brought them in haste to the Marconicar buildings.

'You may be right,' I said non-committally to Lodge. His eyelids flickered, and he smiled and changed the subject.

'The Marconicar drivers come up in court again this week. You'll be there to give evidence, I suppose,' he said.

'Yes,' I agreed, not liking the prospect.

All the drivers who had been looking for me had been alarmed by the shot and the silence on their radios. Some had begun to drive back to Brighton, some had made for London, and one or two had left their taxis and started out on foot. But all had quickly been rounded up, as following the rather vague directions I had phoned to Lodge, the police had begun making road blocks round them while they were still listening to Uncle George. Now the drivers faced charges ranging from intimidation and grievous bodily harm to murder itself.

Records discovered in Uncle George's study, inside a folder marked with gory humour 'Notes on Human Sacrifices', made it clear that Joe Nantwich had indeed been knifed by the man who had been wearing my tie.

And Uncle George's motives were now clear too. Keeping up old standards of luxury had been too much for his income after the war, and instead of making Aunt Deb face reality, or facing it himself, he had gradually spent most of his capital. With almost the last of it he had bought Marconicars and launched into crime. He had directed everything through Fielder and had apparently never seen with his own eyes the brutal results of his orders. I doubted whether his misdeeds had seemed either more or less real to him than the primitive barbarities he spent his time studying.

The police had found neat lists, in files going back

four years, of the money he had collected from the little terrorized businesses; and occasionally against the name of a café or a shop or a pub, Lodge told me, was written the single word, 'Persuaded'.

The racing record was shorter and contained lists of sums of money which the police did not know the purpose of; but one sheet headed 'Joe Nantwich' was clear enough. It was a list of dates and amounts, of which the smallest was one hundred pounds. And underneath was drawn a thick line, with the words: 'Account closed' printed in Uncle George's neat handwriting.

With Kate gone, the press men had drifted away. Their fun was over.

'Are you ready to go?' I asked Lodge. I had picked him up in Maidenhead on my way down. He nodded, and we went out to my car.

I drive faster when I'm happy. That day I had no trouble at all in keeping within the speed limit through all the twisty Sussex villages; and Lodge endured my gloomy silence without comment half the way back to Maidenhead.

Finally he said, 'Miss Ellery-Penn was very useful to her uncle. Everything you did in pursuing him went straight back to him through her. No wonder he was so well informed about your movements.'

I had lived with this thought for a long time now; but hearing someone else speak it aloud had a most extraordinary effect. A tingle ran up my spine and set my brain suddenly alive, as if an alarm bell were ringing in my subconscious.

We were running through shrub and heathland. I slowed, swung the car off the road on to the peaty verge, and stopped. Lodge looked at me questioningly.

'What you said . . . I want to think,' I said.

He waited a while in silence, and then said, 'What's worrying you? The case is over. There are no more mysteries.'

I shook my head. 'There's someone else,' I said.

'What do you mean?'

'There's someone else we don't know about. Someone in Uncle George's confidence.' In spite of everything, I still thought of him as Uncle George.

Lodge said, 'Fielder, the manager, was rounded up. So were all the L. C. Perth operators, though they have been freed again. Only two of the clerks had any idea of what was going on, one who went to the race tracks and one in the office. They received their instructions through Fielder about which horses to accept unlimited money on. There are no niggers left in the woodpile.'

'Joe was stopping horses for months before Uncle George gave Heavens Above to Kate, and she had never been racing before that. Someone else who goes racing must have been working for Uncle George,' I said with conviction.

'Penn would need only the morning paper and a form book for choosing a horse to stop. He wouldn't need to go to the races himself. He didn't need an accomplice at the races apart from his bookmaker – Perth. You're imagining things.'

'Uncle George didn't know enough about horses,' I said.

'So he made out,' said Lodge sceptically.

'Kate told me that for as long as she remembers he was a dead loss on the subject. He started the Marconicar Protection racket only four years ago, and the racing racket less than a year ago. Before that he had no reason to pretend. Therefore his ignorance of horses was genuine.'

'I'll give you that,' he said, 'But I don't see that it proves anything.'

'He *must* have had a contact on the racecourse. How else did he manage to pick on the one jockey who could most easily be corrupted?' I said.

'Perhaps he tried several, until he found a taker,' suggested Lodge.

'No. Everyone would have talked about it, if he had.'

'He tried Major Davidson,' said Lodge. 'That looks like a very bad mistake from your mythical adviser.'

'Yes,' I conceded. I changed to another tack. 'There have been one or two things which have been relayed recently to Uncle George which Kate herself didn't know. How do you explain that?'

'What things?'

'Joe's bit of brown wrapping paper, for instance. He

told everyone in the weighing-room at Liverpool about it. Kate wasn't at the meeting. But two days later, on Uncle George's instructions, Joe was killed and the paper taken away from him.'

Lodge pondered. 'Someone might have rung her up on the Sunday and mentioned it in passing.'

I thought fleetingly of Dane. I said, 'Even then, it was surely not interesting enough for her to have told Uncle George.'

'You never know,' he said.

I started up and drove on in silence for some miles. I was loath to produce for his scepticism the most deep-rooted of my reasons for believing an enemy still existed: the near-certainty that in the concussed gap in my memory I already knew who it was.

When at last I tentatively told him this, he treated it more seriously than I expected. And after some minutes of thought he pierced and appalled me by saying, 'Perhaps your subconscious won't let you remember who this enemy of yours is *because you like him*.'

I dropped Lodge at Maidenhead and went on to the Cotswolds.

Entering the old stone house with the children noisily tumbling through the hall on their way to tea was like stepping into a sane world again. Scilla was coming down the stairs with her arms full of Polly's summer dresses: I went over and met her on the bottom step and kissed her cheek.

'Joan and I will have to lengthen all these,' she said, nodding at the dresses. 'Polly's growing at a rate of knots.'

I followed her into the drawing-room and we sat down on the hearthrug in front of a newly lit fire.

'Is it all over?' asked Scilla, pushing the dresses off her lap on to the floor.

'Yes, I think so.' Too much was all over.

I told her about the inquest and the verdict. I said, 'It was only because of Bill that George Penn was ever found out. Bill didn't die for nothing.'

She didn't answer for a long time, and I saw the yellow flames glinting on the unshed tears in her eyes. Then she sniffed and shook her head as if to free herself from the past, and said, 'Let's go and have tea with the children.'

Polly wanted me to mend a puncture on her bicycle. Henry said he'd worked out some gambits in chess and would I play against him after tea. William gave me a sticky kiss and pressed an aged fruit drop into my palm as a present. I was home again.

CHAPTER NINETEEN

The almost unbearable belief that I had lost Kate grew very little easier as the days passed. I couldn't get her out of my mind. When I woke in the morning the ache rushed in to spoil the day: when I slept I dreamed continually that she was running away down a long dark tunnel. I thought it unlikely I would ever see her again, and tried to make myself be sensible about it.

Then, a week after the inquest on Uncle George, I went to ride at Banbury races, and Kate was there. She was dressed in dark navy blue and there were big grey hollows round her eyes. Her face was pale and calm, and her expression didn't change when she saw me. She was waiting outside the weighing-room, and spoke to me as soon as I drew near.

'Alan, I think I should apologize for what I said to you the other day.' The words were clearly an effort.

'It's all right,' I said.

'No . . . it's not. I thought about what you said . . . about those children going to school with the judo expert . . . and I realize Uncle George had got to be stopped.' She paused. 'It was not your fault Aunt Deb died. I'm sorry I said it was.' She let out a breath as if she had performed an intolerable duty.

'Did you come all the way here especially to say that?' I asked.

'Yes. It has been worrying me that I was so unjust.'

'My dear precious Kate,' I said, the gloom of the past week beginning to vanish like morning mist, 'I would have given anything for it not to have been Uncle George, believe me.' I looked at her closely. 'You look very hungry. Have you had anything to eat today?'

'No,' she said, in a small voice.

'You must have some lunch,' I said, and giving her no chance to refuse, took her arm and walked her briskly to the luncheon-room. There I watched her eat, pecking at first but soon with ravenous appetite, until some colour came back into her cheeks and a faint echo of her old gaiety to her manner.

She was well into her second helping of hot game pie when she said in a friendly tone, 'I wish you'd eat something too.'

I said, 'I'm riding.'

'Yes, I know, I saw in the paper. Forlorn Hope, isn't it?' she asked between forkfuls.

'Yes,' I said.

'You will be careful, won't you? He's not a very good jumper, Pete says.'

I looked at her with delighted astonishment, and she blushed deeply.

'Kate!' I said.

'Well . . . I thought you'd never forgive me for being so abysmally beastly. I've spent the most vile week of my life regretting every word I said. But at least it brought me to my senses about you. I tried to tell myself I'd be delighted never to see you again and instead I got more and more miserable. I . . . I didn't think you'd come back for a second dose, after the way you looked at Brighton. So I thought if I wanted you to know I was sorry I'd have to come and tell you, and then I could see how . . . how you reacted.'

'How did you expect me to react?'

'I thought you'd be rather toffee-nosed and cool, and I wouldn't have blamed you.' She stuffed an inelegant amount of pie-crust into her mouth.

'Will you marry me, then, Kate?' I asked.

She said, 'Yes' indistinctly with her mouth full and went on uninterruptedly cutting up her food. I waited patiently while she finished the pie and made good time with a stack of cheese and biscuits.

'When did you eat last?' I asked, as she eventually put down her napkin.

'Can't remember.' She looked across at me with a new joy in her face and the old sadness beneath it, and I knew from that and from her remark about Forlorn

Hope – the first concern she had ever shown for my safety – that she had indeed grown up.

I said, 'I want to kiss you.'

'Racecourses were not designed for the convenience of newly affianced lovers,' she said. 'How about a horse-box?'

'We've only got ten minutes,' I said. 'I'm riding in the second race.'

We borrowed Pete's horse-box without more ado. I took her in my arms, and found this time on Kate's lips a satisfactorily unsisterly response.

The ten minutes fled in a second, and the races wouldn't wait. We walked back, and I went into the weighing room and changed into colours, leaving Kate, who looked a bit dazed and said she felt it, sitting on a bench in the sun.

It was the first time I had been racing since Uncle George's inquest. I glanced uneasily round the changing room at the well-known faces, refusing to believe that any was the go-between who had brought death to Joe. Perhaps Lodge was right, and I didn't want to find out. I had liked Uncle George himself, once. Did I shrink from seeing the façade stripped from another friend to reveal the crocodile underneath?

Clem handed me my lead-packed weight cloth. I looked at his patient wrinkled face, and thought, 'Not you, not you.'

It was a sort of treachery to reflect that Clem heard

all that went on and that no event of any significance ever escaped his ears. 'The oracle,' some of the lads called him . . .

A hearty thump on the back cut off my speculations.

'Wotcher, me old cock sparrow, how's the sleuthing business?' bellowed Sandy, pausing and balancing his saddle on one knee while he looped up the girths. 'How's Sherlock these days?'

'Retired,' I said, grinning.

'No, really? After such grade A results?'

'I'll stick to steeplechasing, I think. It's less risky.'

Sandy's friendly gaze strayed to the scar on my cheek.

'You're welcome to your little illusions, chum,' he said. 'You'll change your mind when you've broken as many bones as I have.' He wound the girths round the saddle, tucked in the buckles, and with his helmet pushed far back on his head and his cheerful voice drawing heads round like a magnet, made his way out to the scales.

From across the changing room I had a good view of Dane's back solidly and deliberately turned towards me. Talking to someone by the gate, he had unfortunately seen Kate and me returning from the horse-box parking ground. He had had a good look at our radiant faces before we knew he was there, and he didn't need to have things spelled out for him. He had congratulated Kate in two clipped sentences, but to me he had still spoken not a word.

I went past his unyielding back and out to the paddock. He followed. Pete trained both the horses we were riding, and we both had to join him.

Pete jumped in with both feet.

'Alan, Kate's told me your news. Well done.'

He received a fierce glower from Dane, and hastily began to assess the race. He was talking about Dane's mount, and my attention wandered.

There, ten yards away, stood the craggy Clifford Tudor, opulently rolling a cigar round his mouth and laying down the law to his trainer and jockey. Odd, I thought, how often I had come across that man. I watched him make heavy chopping motions with his dark hands to emphasize his points, and caught the young jockey, Joe's substitute, wrinkling his forehead in acute anxiety.

My gaze slid beyond him to where Sir Creswell Stampe was superintending the raising of his unamiable son David into the saddle, before going to take his judicial position in the Stewards' box. Beyond him again were other groups of owners and trainers planning their plans, hoping their hopes, giving their jockeys instructions (and counter-instructions) and calculating their last-minute bets.

So many people I knew. So many people I liked.

Which of them . . . which of them was not what he seemed?

Pete gave me a leg up on to Forlorn Hope's narrow back, and I waved to Kate, who was standing by the parade ring rails, and cantered down towards the start.

On the way Dane came past briskly, turning his head in my direction as he drew level. With cold eyes he said, 'Blast you,' giving both words equal punch, and shook up his horse to get away from me and give me no chance to reply. I let him go. Either he would get over it or he wouldn't; and in either case there wasn't much I could do about it.

There were eleven runners in the race. We circled round while the starter's assistant tightened girths and the starter himself called the roll. Sandy asked his permission to dismount in order to straighten his saddle, which had slipped forwards on the way down to the gate. The starter nodded, looking at his wristwatch and telling Sandy not to be too long. This particular starter hated to start his races late and grew fidgety over every minor delay.

Sandy unbuckled the girths, pulling his saddle straight, and tightened it up again. I was watching him instead of concentrating wholly on Forlorn Hope, so that what happened was entirely my own fault.

An attendant flapped open under my horse's nose the white flag which it was his job to wave aloft, to signal to the stands that the horses were about to start.

My green young hurdler took fright, reared up like a circus horse, twisted sideways, and threw me off. I hit the ground almost flat on my back, winding myself, and I saw Forlorn Hope kick up his heels and depart at a smart pace up the course.

For a few seconds I lay there trying to get my breath back, and Sandy walked over with his hand outstretched to help me up, laughing and making some rude remarks about my sudden descent.

The most extraordinary dizziness suddenly swept over me, and my senses began to play fantastic tricks. Lying in the spring sun, I felt rain on my face. Winded but unhurt, my body was momentarily invaded by shocking pain. In my whirling brain it seemed as if past and present had become confused, and that two completely different events were somehow happening at the same time.

I stared up into Sandy's face. There was the familiar wide gap-toothed grin, the false incisors removed for safety; there were the devil-may-care expression. The sunshine bathed his face in light. And what I saw as well was the same face looming towards me in pouring rain, with cruel eyes and a grim mouth. I heard a voice say, 'You nosey bastard, perhaps that'll teach you to mind your own business;' and I threw up my hand to shield my cheek against the kick which was coming . . .

My sight cleared and steadied, and Sandy and I were

looking straight into each other's eyes as if a battle were being fought there. He dropped the hand outstretched to help me, and the friendliness went out of his face with the completeness of an actor shedding a role when the play is over.

I found my palm was still pressed against my cheek. I let it drop away, but the gesture had told its tale. I had remembered what had happened by the fence at Bristol, and Sandy knew it.

Strength returned to my limbs, and I stood up. The starter, consulting his watch in barely concealed annoyance, asked if I was all right. I replied that I was, and apologized for holding up the race. Some way down the course someone had caught Forlorn Hope, and as I watched he was turned round to be led back to the starting gate.

Sandy, showing no haste to remount, stood his ground in front of me.

'You can't prove a thing,' he said, characteristically taking the bull by the horns. 'No one can connect me with Penn.'

'Fletcher,' I said at once.

'He'll keep his mouth shut,' said Sandy, with conviction. 'He is my cousin.'

Uncle George's racing venture, I now saw, had not been inspired solely by the availability of a shaky bookmaking business. The existence of an easily recruited ally on the racecourse might have been the very factor which decided him, in the first place, to buy L. C. Perth.

I mentally reviewed the rest of the gang.

'How abut Fielder?' I suggested after a short pause.

'I'm a voice on the phone to him. A voice called Smith. He doesn't know me from Adam,' said Sandy.

Temporarily, I gave up. I said, 'What did you do it for?'

'Money. What else?' he said scornfully, clearly thinking the question foolish.

'Why didn't you stop the horses yourself? Why let Joe collect the big fat fees for losing?'

Sandy seemed perfectly willing to explain. 'I did stop a couple myself. The Stewards had me in over the second one, and I got off by the skin of my bloody teeth. I saw the red light, mate. I tipped the boss to try that little bastard Joe instead. Let him lose his licence, not me, I told him. But mind you, I was on to a bloody good percentage every time he strangled one.'

'Which made you all the more angry when he won against orders on Bolingbroke,' I said.

'That's right.'

'Then Joe didn't tell you in the washroom he was going to pull Bolingbroke. You knew already.'

'Proper little Sherlock,' mocked Sandy.

'And you put him over the rails at Plumpton, I suppose?'

'He bloody well deserved it. He lost me fifty quid on Leica as well as my bonus from the boss.'

'Did he deserve to die, as well?' I asked bitterly.

The man leading Forlorn Hope back was now only a hundred yards away.

'The stupid little sod couldn't keep his mouth shut,' said Sandy violently. 'Waving that brown paper at Liverpool and yelling for you. I saw what was written on it, and told Fielder, that's all. I didn't know what it meant, but it was a ton to a tanner the boss wouldn't like it. Joe was asking for it.'

'And after he'd got it, you rang Fielder and told him the job had been bungled, and Joe had lived long enough to talk to me?'

'Yes,' said Sandy morosely. 'I heard you telling every bloody body in the weighing-room.'

I couldn't resist it. I said, 'I was lying. Joe died without saying a word.'

As the full significance of this slowly dawned on him, his jaw dropped, and I saw him waver in some secret inner place as if an axe had hacked into the roots of his colossal self-confidence. He turned on his heel, strode across to where the starter's assistant held his horse, and swung abruptly into the saddle.

I went to meet Forlorn Hope, thanked the man who had brought him back, and remounted. The starter's patience had run out.

'Get into line, please,' he said, and the circling horses began to straighten out across the course. I came up from behind and took a place alongside Sandy. I had one more question to ask.

'Tell me,' I said, 'why on earth did you get Penn to try to bribe Major Davidson? You must have known he wouldn't have stopped Admiral winning for all the money in the world.'

'It was the boss's idea, not mine,' said Sandy roughly. 'I warned Fielder to tell him it wouldn't work, but the boss knew bee-all about horses and was pig-headed besides. Fielder said he wouldn't listen, because he thought if he fixed a cert it would be worth a fortune. He made a packet out of it, all right. He thought up the wire himself. And I'd be a ruddy sight better off if the wire had killed you too,' he added, with a sudden spurt of venom.

The starter's hand swept down on the lever. The tape flew up, and, five minutes late, the horses bounded forwards towards the first hurdle.

I don't know exactly when Sandy decided to put me over the rails. Perhaps the thought of all the money he would not be getting overwhelmed him, and perhaps I had brought it on myself by recalling that he had done it to Joe when Joe, as he saw it, had cheated him.

In any case, as we approached the second hurdle, he swerved his horse towards me. We were both in the group just behind the leaders, and I was on the inside, with the rails on my left.

I glanced at Sandy's face. His slitted eyes were concentrated on the jump ahead, but with every stride his horse drew nearer to mine. He wasn't leaving me much room, I thought.

Only just in time did I realize that he intended to leave me no room at all. He was aiming to crowd my horse so closely that I would be thrust into the six foot high wing leading up to the hurdles. A crash through the wings, I had been told, was one of the most dangerous of all falls. The time had clearly come for rapid evasive action if I were not to find this out for myself.

I literally hauled on the reins. Forlorn Hope lost impetus dramatically, and as soon as the quarters of Sandy's horse were past his shoulder I pulled his head unceremoniously to the right. It was only just in time. The hurdles were beneath his feet before he had time to see them, and he knocked one flat with his forelegs. The horse following us, going faster, bumped hard into the back of him, and the jockey yelled at me to mind what I was doing.

Forlorn Hope was too much of a novice to stand this sort of thing, and I decided that if I were not to ruin his nerve for good, I would have to keep him out of Sandy's way for the rest of the race.

But Sandy was not content with that. Along the straight in front of the stands he gradually worked himself back to my side. He was a better jockey than I and his horse was more experienced. When I tried to go faster, he kept pace, and when I slowed down, he slowed too. I could not shake him off. In front of the crowds, apart from keeping pace with me, he rode fairly enough; but round the next bend lay the long curved leg out into the comparatively deserted country, and what he might do there I hated to think.

I did consider pulling up and dropping out of the race altogether, but that seemed an even more ignominious defeat than being put over the rails.

As the field swept round the bend in a bunch, Sandy tried again. He closed his horse tight up against mine and very slightly behind. On my left I was jammed against Dane. He glanced across and shouted, 'Get over, Sandy. Give us some room.'

Sandy did not answer. Instead I felt his knee slide along under my thigh until he was pressing fiercely on my hamstrings. Then he gave a sudden violent jerk forwards and upwards with his whole leg.

My foot flew out of the stirrup and I lost my balance completely. I swayed wildly over to the left, my head tipping down beside my horse's neck, my fingers clutching frantically at his mane. I looked down and saw the blur of hooves pounding tight-packed round the bend, and I struggled to prevent myself slipping off among them. But all my weight was too far forward, and the jolt of the horse's galloping stride tended to tip me farther forward still. I knew that in a few seconds I would be off.

It was Dane who saved me. He put his hand on my side and literally pushed me back into my saddle.

'Thanks,' I gasped, feeling with my right foot for the dangling stirrup.

Not far round the bend lay the next flight of hurdles, and I fought to get myself and the horse properly balanced before we met it. As we came round the bend the sun had shone straight into our faces, but swinging out towards the country it lay on our right. Glancing to see if Sandy was still beside me I caught the sunshine full in the eyes and was for a second dazzled. He was there. He appeared to me as a black silhouette against the sun.

I remembered then that on such bright days on this course the sun shone straight into the eyes of the crowds on the stands also, and that it was difficult for them to distinguish what was happening on the far side of the course. Whatever Sandy did, he could be fairly sure the Stewards would not be able to see.

I gained a yard or two on Sandy and Dane at the next hurdle, but over my shoulder I could hear Sandy clicking with his tongue to hurry his horse, and in a few more strides he was beside me again. His shadow lay across my horse's withers.

Suddenly he swung his arm; and had I not been so acutely ready he would have had me. He swung his right arm round his body in a chop at my face, slashing with his riding whip. I ducked in a reflex, without actually seeing the whip at all. The heavy blow landed across my helmet just above the peak, and knocked it clean off my head. It bounced away on the turf.

I felt, rather than saw, Sandy draw back his arm for another try. I slipped my own whip and the reins into my left hand, and when he struck, threw up my right. More by luck than design my fingers fastened on the stick and I gripped and twisted and pulled with the strength of desperation.

I had him half out of his saddle and I almost exulted; but at the vital moment he let go of his stick and regained his balance. Rebounding, his horse swerved away from me, leaving a gap, and I looked hopefully over my shoulder for one of the other runners to come up between us. But most of them had gone on in front, and there was no one close. I threw Sandy's stick away.

The next hurdle lay ahead. I kept well away from the rails and tried to steady Forlorn Hope so that he should have a fair chance at it, but I was all too aware that Sandy was beginning to close on me again with a burst of extra speed.

My horse jumped the hurdle in reasonable style. Sandy kicked his horse into a tremendous leap, and as he landed he pulled straight across in front of me.

Forlorn Hope crashed into the rails.

By some miracle he did not fall. He bounced off, staggered, faltered, and galloped on. My leg, which had been crushed just below the knee between his body and the rails, was completely numb. I looked down at it: it appeared to be doing its job all right, even though I no longer seemed to be connected to it. My silk breeches were ripped open across the knee, and in my new extremely expensive made-to-measure racing boots flapped a large triangular tear.

Illogically, this made me very angry.

Sandy was some lengths ahead and had not so far managed to pull back again. Dane came up on my right, and I was glad to see him there.

He yelled, 'What the hell's going on? What the blazes does Sandy think he's playing at?'

'He's not playing,' I shouted. 'He wants to get me off.'

'Why?' yelled Dane.

'He was working for George Penn. He was making a lot of money. Now he isn't. He blames me,' I shouted in snatches, the wind picking the words out of my mouth and blowing them back over my shoulder.

'With reason,' shouted Dane.

'Yes,' I agreed. I glanced at him, but now it was he who was outlined against the sun, and I could not see his expression clearly. If he felt badly enough about Kate to carry on where Sandy had for the moment left off, I should have no chance at all. He could ride rings round me, and Sandy, too.

We raced in silence towards the next hurdle, the last on the far side. Sandy was gradually slowing to wait for me.

Then Dane said, 'Alan?'

'Yes?' I shouted back.

'Do you want to give Sandy some of his own medicine?'

'Yes.' I suddenly had no reservations. It was a terrible thing to do, and if the Stewards saw me I'd lose my permit; but I had taken just about enough from Uncle George's assorted strong-arm boys.

Dane shouted, 'I'll go up on his outside. You come outside me. Then I'll get away and leave him between you and the rails. OK?'

I nodded. I tried to foresee the future. If I unseated Sandy he would not dare to complain to the Stewards; and I, as he said, could give no tangible evidence against him to the police. There could be an uneasy truce between us. And fall for fall, the score would be equal.

'Come on, then,' Dane shouted.

He kicked his horse and began to take his place on Sandy's right. I pulled away from the rails and urged Forlorn Hope to the outside. There was nearly a mile to go to the finish, and as no one had yet begun to put on the pressure the field was still fairly closely bunched just ahead of us. There was no one behind. After the hurdle lay the long oval bend leading round into the straight. If either Sandy or I were to get the other off, it would have to be done on the bend, once we were round into the straight the Stewards would have too clear a view of our behaviour.

Dane jumped the hurdle alongside Sandy with me not far behind. As soon as I was level with them both, Dane shook up his horse and sped clear away from us, leaving me, as he had promised, with Sandy between me and the rails.

I swung Forlorn Hope over roughly on to Sandy's horse, bumping him against the rails. Sandy yelled and lashed out with his fist. I hit his arm sharply with my stick.

I had got to unseat him without hurting his horse. I was being unfair enough already to the owner in trying to lose him the race by dislodging his jockey: if I could not do it without damaging the horse, I must not do it at all.

Shifting the reins into my right hand, I planted my left abruptly on Sandy's boot just behind his armpit, and shoved. But I was too far away to get enough force behind it. He swayed in his saddle, but kept his balance. He began to swear at me.

We were on the crown of the bend. It had to be now or never. I pushed Sandy's horse harder against the rails. He yelled again. His leg, I knew, must be being crushed, pounded, even torn by the white-painted wood. With my own leg numb from the same treatment, I had no sympathy for him. Then his foot crashed into one of the uprights with an audible snap.

He screamed.

I gritted my teeth, shot out my arm, and pushed him with all my might. I knew if he had not gone then I would not have had the resolution to try again. But he began to topple, slowly, it seemed, at first, and then with an accelerating rush, as if he had been sucked away by a slipstream.

I caught a final glimpse of his face, eyes staring widely, mouth twisted with agony, as he fell into the long grass on the other side of the rails. Then I was round the bend into the straight, bruised, breathless, tattered, and helmetless, but still on board.

Sandy's loose horse, relieved of his weight, spurted forward through the other runners.

Dane saw him, and turned round in his saddle and grinned at me, and jerked up his thumb.

Hot Money

Dick Francis has written thirty-nine international bestsellers and is widely acclaimed as one of the world's finest thriller writers. His awards include the Crime Writers' Association's Cartier Diamond Dagger for his outstanding contribution to the crime genre, and an honorary Doctorate of Humane Letters from Tufts University of Boston. In 1996 Dick Francis was made a Mystery Writers of America Grand Master for a lifetime's achievement and in 2000 he received a CBE in the Queen's Birthday Honours list.

Also by Dick Francis in Pan Books

THE SPORT OF QUEENS
(autobiography)

LESTER:The Official
Biography

DEAD CERT
NERVE
FOR KICKS
ODDS AGAINST
FLYING FINISH
BLOOD SPORT
FORFEIT
ENQUIRY
RAT RACE
BONECRACK
SMOKESCREEN
SLAY-RIDE
KNOCK DOWN
HIGH STAKES
LONGSHOT
DECIDER

IN THE FRAME
RISK
TRIAL RUN
WHIP HAND
REFLEX
TWICE SHY
BANKER
THE DANGER
PROOF
BREAK IN
BOLT
THE EDGE
STRAIGHT
COMEBACK
DRIVING FORCE
WILD HORSES
COME TO GRIEF
TO THE HILT
10lb PENALTY
FIELD OF THIRTEEN
SECOND WIND
SHATTERED

DICK FRANCIS OMNIBUS ONE:
Long Shot, Straight, High Stakes

DICK FRANCIS OMNIBUS TWO: Forfeit, Risk, Reflex

DICK FRANCIS OMNIBUS THREE:
Slay-Ride, Banker, Proof

DICK FRANCIS OMNIBUS FOUR:
Enquiry, Rat Race, Smokescreen

SID HALLEY OMNIBUS:
Odds Against, Whip Hand, Come to Grief

Dick Francis

HOT MONEY

PAN BOOKS

First published 1987 by Michael Joseph Ltd

This edition first published 1988 by Pan Books
an imprint of Pan Macmillan Ltd
Pan Macmillan, 20 New Wharf Road, London N1 9RR
Basingstoke and Oxford
Associated companies throughout the world
www.panmacmillan.com

ISBN 0 330 30505 0

39

A CIP catalogue record for this book is available from the British Library.

Printed and bound in Great Britain by
Mackays of Chatham plc, Chatham, Kent

With love and thanks as usual

to

MERRICK and FELIX

THE PEMBROKES

MALCOLM PEMBROKE

HIS WIVES	1	**Vivien**
	2	**Joyce**
	3	**Alicia**
	4	**Coochie**
	5	**Moira**
VIVIEN'S CHILDREN	1	**Donald**, married to Helen
	2	**Lucy**, married to Edwin
	3	**Thomas**, married to Berenice
JOYCE'S CHILD	1	**Ian**, unmarried
ALICIA'S CHILDREN	1	**Gervase**, married to Ursula
	2	**Ferdinand**, married to Debs
	3	**Serena**, unmarried
COOCHIE'S CHLDREN	1	**Robin**
	2	**Peter**, dead

CHAPTER ONE

I intensely disliked my father's fifth wife, but not to the point of murder.

I, the fruit of his second ill-considered gallop up the aisle, had gone dutifully to the next two of his subsequent nuptials, the changes of 'mother' punctuating my life at six and fourteen.

At thirty however I'd revolted: wild horses couldn't have dragged me to witness his wedding to the sharp-eyed honey-tongued Moira, his fifth choice. Moira had been the subject of the bitterest quarrel my father and I ever had and the direct cause of a non-speaking wilderness which had lasted three years.

After Moira was murdered, the police came bristling with suspicion to my door, and it was by the merest fluke that I could prove I'd been geographically elsewhere when her grasping little soul had left her carefully tended body. I didn't go to her funeral, but I wasn't alone in that. My father didn't go either.

A month after her death he telephoned me, and it

was so long since I'd heard his voice that it seemed that of a stranger.

'Ian?'

'Yes,' I said.

'Malcolm.'

'Hello,' I said.

'Are you doing anything?'

'Reading the price of gold.'

'No, dammit,' he said testily. 'In general, are you busy?'

'In general,' I said, 'fairly.'

The newspaper lay on my lap, an empty wine glass at my elbow. It was late evening, after eleven, growing cold. I had that day quit my job and put on idleness like a comfortable coat.

He sighed down the line. 'I suppose you know about Moira?'

'Front page news,' I agreed. 'The price of gold is on . . . er . . . page thirty-two.'

'If you want me to apologize,' he said, 'I'm not going to.'

His image stood sharp and clear in my mind: a stocky, grey-haired man with bright blue eyes and a fizzing vitality that flowed from him in sparks of static electricity in cold weather. He was to my mind stubborn, opinionated, rash and often stupid. He was also financially canny, intuitive, quick-brained and courageous, and hadn't been nicknamed Midas for nothing.

'Are you still there?' he demanded.

'Yes.'

'Well . . . I need your help.'

He said it as if it were an everyday requirement, but I couldn't remember his asking anyone for help ever before, certainly not me.

'Er . . .' I said uncertainly. 'What sort of help?'

'I'll tell you when you get here.'

'Where is "here"?'

'Newmarket,' he said. 'Come to the sales tomorrow afternoon.'

There was a note in his voice which couldn't be called entreaty but was far from a direct order, and I was accustomed only to orders.

'All right,' I said slowly.

'Good.'

He disconnected immediately, letting me ask no questions: and I thought of the last time I'd seen him, when I'd tried to dissuade him from marrying Moira, describing her progressively, in the face of his implacable purpose, as a bad misjudgement on his part and as a skilful, untruthful manipulator and, finally, as a rapacious blood-sucking tramp. He'd knocked me down to the floor with one fast, dreadful blow, which he'd been quite capable of at sixty-five, three years ago. Striding furiously away, he'd left me lying dazed on my carpet and had afterwards behaved as if I no longer existed, packing into boxes everything I'd left in my old room in his house and sending them by public carrier to my flat.

Time had proved me right about Moira, but the unforgivable words had remained unforgiven to her death and, it had seemed, beyond. On this October evening, though, perhaps they were provisionally on ice.

I, Ian Pembroke, the fourth of my father's nine children, had from the mists of infancy loved him blindly through thunderous years of domestic infighting which had left me permanently impervious to fortissimo voices and slammed doors. In a totally confused chaotic upbringing, I'd spent scattered unhappy periods with my bitter mother but had mostly been passed from wife to wife in my father's house as part of the furniture and fittings, treated by him throughout with the same random but genuine affection he gave to his dogs.

Only with the advent of Coochie, his fourth wife, had there been peace, but by the time she took over I was fourteen and world-weary, cynically expecting a resumption of hostilities within a year of the honeymoon.

Coochie, however, had been different. Coochie of all of them had been my only real mother, the only one who'd given me a sense of worth and identity, who'd listened and encouraged and offered good advice. Coochie produced twin boys, my half-brothers Robin and Peter, and it had seemed that at last Malcolm Pembroke had achieved a friendly family unit, albeit a sort of sunny clearing surrounded by jungle thickets of ex-wives and discontented siblings.

I grew up and left home but went back often, never feeling excluded. Coochie would have seen Malcolm into a happy old age but, when she was forty and the twins eleven, a hit-and-run driver swerved her car off the road and downhill onto rocks. Coochie and Peter had been killed outright. Robin, the elder twin, suffered brain damage. I had been away. Malcolm was in his office: a policeman went to him to tell him, and he let me know soon after. I'd learned the meaning of grief on that drizzly afternoon, and still mourned them all, their loss irreparable.

On the October evening of Malcolm's telephone call, I glanced at them as usual as I went to bed, their three bright faces grinning out from a silver frame on my chest of drawers. Robin lived – just – in serene twilight in a nursing home. I went to see him now and again. He no longer looked like the boy in the photograph, but was five years older, growing tall, empty-eyed.

I wondered what Malcolm could possibly want. He was rich enough to buy anything he needed, maybe – only maybe – excluding the whole of Fort Knox. I couldn't think of anything I could do for him that he couldn't get from anyone else.

Newmarket, I thought. The sales.

Newmarket was all very well for me because I'd been working as an assistant to a racehorse trainer. But Newmarket for Malcolm? Malcolm never gambled on horses, only on gold. Malcolm had made several immense consecutive fortunes from buying and selling the hard yellow stuff, and had years ago reacted to my stated choice of occupation by saying merely, 'Horses? Racing? Good Lord! Well, if that's what you want, my boy, off you go. But don't expect me to know the first thing about anything.' And, as far as I knew, he was still as ignorant of the subject as he'd been all along.

Malcolm and Newmarket bloodstock sales simply didn't mix. Not the Malcolm I'd known, anyway.

I drove the next day to the isolated Suffolk town whose major industry was the sport of kings, and among the scattered purposeful crowd found my father standing bareheaded in the area outside the sale-ring building, eyes intently focused on a catalogue.

He looked just the same. Brushed grey hair, smooth brown vicuna knee-length overcoat, charcoal business suit, silk tie, polished black shoes; confidently bringing his City presence into the casual sophistication of the country.

It was a golden day, crisp and clear, the sky a cold cloudless blue. I walked across to him in my own brand of working clothes: cavalry twill trousers, checked wool shirt, padded olive-green jacket, tweed cap. A surface contrast that went personality deep.

'Good afternoon,' I said neutrally.

He raised his eyes and gave me a stare as blue as the sky.

'So you came.'

'Well . . . yes.'

He nodded vaguely, looking me over. 'You look older,' he said.

'Three years.'

'Three years and a crooked nose.' He observed it dispassionately. 'I suppose you broke that falling off a horse?'

'No . . . You broke it.'

'Did I?' He seemed only mildly surprised. 'You deserved it.'

I didn't answer. He shrugged. 'Do you want some coffee?'

'OK.'

We hadn't touched each other, I thought. Not a hug, not a handshake, not a passing pat on the arm. Three years' silence couldn't easily be bridged.

He set off not in the direction of the regular refreshment room, but towards one of the private rooms set aside for the privileged. I followed in his footsteps, remembering wryly that it took him roughly two minutes any time to talk himself into the plushest recesses, wherever.

The Newmarket sales building was in the form of an amphitheatre, sloping banks of seats rising all round from the ground-level ring where each horse was led round while being auctioned. Underneath the seating and in a large adjacent building were rooms used as offices by auctioneers and bloodstock agents, and as entertainment rooms by commercial firms, such as Ebury Jewellers, Malcolm's present willing hosts.

I was used only to the basic concrete boxes of the bloodstock agents' offices. Ebury's space was decorated in contrast as an expensive showroom, with well-lit glass display cases round three walls shining with silver and sparkling with baubles, everything locked away safely but temptingly visible. Down the centre of the room, on brown wall-to-wall carpeting, stood a long polished table surrounded with armed, leather-covered dining chairs. Before each chair was neatly laid a leather-edged blotter alongside a gold-tooled tub containing pens, suggesting that all any client needed to provide here was his cheque book.

A smooth young gentleman welcomed Malcolm with enthusiastic tact and offered drinks and goodies from the well-stocked buffet table which filled most of the fourth wall. Lunch, it seemed, was an all-day affair. Malcolm and I took cups of coffee and sat at the table, I, at any rate, feeling awkward. Malcolm fiddled with his spoon. A large loud lady came in and began talking to the smooth young man about having one of her dogs modelled in silver. Malcolm raised his eyes to them briefly and then looked down again at his cup.

'What sort of help?' I said.

I suppose I expected him to say he wanted help in

some way with horses, in view of the venue he'd chosen, but it seemed to be nothing as straightforward.

'I want you beside me,' he said.

I frowned, puzzled. 'How do you mean?'

'Beside me,' he said. 'All the time.'

'I don't understand.'

'I don't suppose you do,' he said. He looked up at my face. 'I'm going to travel a bit. I want you with me.'

I made no fast reply and he said abruptly, explosively, 'Dammit, Ian, I'm not asking the world. A bit of your time, a bit of your attention, that's all.'

'Why now, and why me?'

'You're my son.' He stopped fiddling with the spoon and dropped it onto the blotter where it left a round stain. He leaned back in his chair. 'I trust you.' He paused. 'I need someone I can trust.'

'Why?'

He didn't tell me why. He said, 'Can't you get some time off from work? Have a holiday?'

I thought of the trainer I'd just left, whose daughter had made my job untenable because she wanted it for her fiancé. There was no immediate need for me to find another place, save for paying the rent. At thirty-three, I'd worked for three different trainers, and had lately come to feel I was growing too old to carry on as anyone's assistant. The natural progression was towards becoming a trainer myself, a dicey course without money.

'What are you thinking?' Malcolm asked.

'Roughly whether you would lend me half a million quid.'

'No,' he said.

I smiled. 'That's what I thought.'

'I'll pay your fares and your hotel bills.'

Across the room the loud lady was giving the smooth young man her address. A waitress had arrived and was busy unpacking fresh sandwiches and more alcohol onto the white-clothed table. I watched her idly for a few seconds, then looked back to Malcolm's face, and surprised there an expression that could only be interpreted as anxiety.

I was unexpectedly moved. I'd never wanted to quarrel with him: I'd wanted him to see Moira as I did, as a calculating, sweet-talking honeypot who was after his money, and who had used the devastation of Coochie's death to insinuate herself with him, turning up constantly with sympathy and offers to cook. Malcolm, deep in grief, had been helpless and grateful and seemed hardly to notice when she began threading her arm through his in company, and saying 'we'. I had for the whole three silent years wanted peace with my father, but I couldn't bear to go to his house and see Moira smirking in Coochie's place, even if he would have let me in through the door.

Now that Moira was dead, peace was maybe possible, and it seemed now as though he really wanted it also. I thought fleetingly that peace wasn't his prime object, that peace was only a preliminary necessary for some other purpose, but all the same it was enough.

'Yes,' I said, 'all right. I can take time off.'

His relief was visible. 'Good! Good! Come along then, I may as well buy a horse.' He stood up, full of sudden energy, waving his catalogue. 'Which do you suggest?'

'Why on earth do you want a horse?'

'To race, of course.'

'But you've never been interested . . .'

'Everyone should have a hobby,' he said briskly, though he'd never had one in his life. 'Mine is racing.' And, as an afterthought, he added, 'Henceforth,' and began to walk to the door.

The smooth young man detached himself from the dog lady and begged Malcolm to come back any time. Malcolm assured him he would, then wheeled round away from him again and marched across to one of the display cabinets.

'While I was waiting for you, I bought a cup,' he said to me over his shoulder. 'Want to see? One rather like that.' He pointed. 'It's being engraved.'

The cup in question was a highly-decorated and graceful elongated jug, eighteen inches tall and made undoubtedly of sterling silver.

'What's it for?' I asked.

'I don't know yet. Haven't made up my mind.'

'But . . . the engraving?'

'Mm. The Coochie Pembroke Memorial Challenge Trophy. Rather good, don't you think?'

'Yes,' I said.

He gave me a sidelong glance. 'I thought you'd think so.' He retraced his steps to the door. 'Right, then, a horse.'

Just like old times, I thought with half-forgotten pleasure. The sudden impulses which might or might not turn out to be thoroughly sensible, the intemperate enthusiasms needing instant gratification . . . and sometimes, afterwards, the abandoning of a débâcle as if it didn't exist. The Coochie Pembroke Memorial Challenge Trophy might achieve worldwide stature in competition or tarnish unpresented in an attic: with Malcolm it was always a toss-up.

I called him Malcolm, as all his children did, on his own instructions, and had grown up thinking it natural. Other boys might have Dad: I had my father, Malcolm.

Outside Ebury's room, he said, 'What's the procedure, then? How do we set about it?'

'Er . . .' I said. 'This is the first day of the Highflyer Sales.'

'Well?' he demanded as I paused. 'Go on.'

'I just thought you ought to know . . . the minimum opening bid today is twenty thousand guineas.'

It rocked him only slightly. 'Opening bid? What do they sell them for?'

'Anything from a hundred thousand up. You'll be lucky today to get a top-class yearling for under a quarter of a million. This is generally the most expensive day of the year.'

He wasn't noticeably deterred. He smiled. 'Come on, then,' he said. 'Let's go and start bidding.'

'You need to look up the breeding first,' I said. 'And then look at the animals, to see if you like them, and then get the help and advice of an agent . . .'

'Ian,' he said with mock sorrow, 'I don't know anything about the breeding, I can just about tell if a thing's got four legs, and I don't trust agents. So let's get on and bid.'

It sounded crazy to me, but it was his money. We went into the sale-ring itself where the auction was already in progress, and Malcolm asked me where the richest bidders could be found, the ones that really meant business.

'In those banks of seats on the left of the auctioneers, or here, in the entrance, or just round there to the left . . .'

He looked and listened and then led the way up to a section of seats from where we could watch the places I'd pointed out. The amphitheatre was already more than three-quarters full, and would later at times be crammed, especially whenever a tip-top lot came next.

'The very highest prices will probably be bid this evening,' I said, half teasing him, but all he said was, 'Perhaps we should wait, then.'

'If you buy ten yearlings,' I said, 'six might get to a

racecourse, three might win a race and one might be pretty good. If you're lucky.'

'Cautious Ian.'

'You,' I said, 'are cautious with gold.'

He looked at me with half-shut eyes. 'Not many people say that.'

'You're fast and flamboyant,' I said, 'but you sit and wait for the moment.'

He merely grunted and began paying attention to the matter in hand, intently focusing not on the merchandise but on the bidders on the far side of the ring. The auctioneers in the box to our left were relaxed and polished, the one currently at the microphone elaborately unimpressed by the fortunes passing. 'Fifty thousand, thank you, sir; sixty thousand, seventy... eighty? Shall I say eighty? Eighty, thank you, sir. Against you, sir. Ninety? Ninety. One hundred thousand. Selling now. I'm selling now. Against you, sir? No? All done? All done?' A pause for a sweep round to make sure no new bidder was frantically waving. 'Done, then. Sold to Mr Siddons. One hundred thousand guineas. The next lot...'

'Selling now,' Malcolm said. 'I suppose that means there was a reserve on it?'

I nodded.

'So until the fellow says "selling now", it's safe to bid, knowing you won't have to buy?'

'Yours might be the bid that reaches the reserve.'

He nodded. 'Russian roulette.'

We watched the sales for the rest of the afternoon, but he aimed no bullets at his own head. He asked who people were. 'Who is that Mr Siddons? That's the fourth horse he's bought.'

'He works for a bloodstock agency. He's buying for other people.'

'And that man in navy, scowling. Who's he?'

'Max Jones. He owns a lot of horses.'

'Every time that old woman bids, he bids against her.'

'It's a well-known feud.'

He sniffed. 'It must cost them fortunes.' He looked around the amphitheatre at the constantly changing audience of breeders, trainers, owners and the simply interested. 'Whose judgement would you trust most?'

I mentioned several trainers and the agents who might be acting on their behalf, and he told me to tell him when someone with good judgement was bidding, and to point them out. I did so many times, and he listened and passed no comment.

After a while, we went out for a break, an Ebury scotch, a sandwich and fresh air.

'I suppose you know,' Malcolm said casually, watching yearlings skittering past in the grasp of their handlers, 'that Moira and I were divorcing?'

'Yes, I heard.'

'And that she was demanding the house and half my possessions?'

'Mm.'

'And half my future earnings?'

'Could she?'

'She was going to fight for it.'

I refrained from saying that whoever had murdered Moira had done Malcolm a big favour, but I'd thought it several times.

I said instead, 'Still no clues?'

'No, nothing new.'

He spoke without regret. His disenchantment with Moira, according to his acid second wife, my own mother Joyce, had begun as soon as he'd stopped missing Coochie; and as Joyce was as percipient as she was catty, I believed it.

'The police tried damned hard to prove I did it,' Malcolm said.

'Yes, so I heard.'

'Who from? Who's your grapevine?'

'All of them,' I said.

'The three witches?'

I couldn't help smiling. He meant his three living ex-wives, Vivien, Joyce and Alicia.

'Yes, them. And all of the family.'

He shrugged.

'They were all worried that you might have,' I said.

'And were you worried?' he asked.

'I was glad you weren't arrested.'

He grunted noncommittally. 'I suppose you do know that most of your brothers and sisters, not to mention the witches, told the police you hated Moira?'

'They told me they'd told,' I agreed. 'But then, I did.'

'Lot of stinkers I've fathered,' he said gloomily.

Malcolm's personal alibi for Moira's death had been as unassailable as my own, as he'd been in Paris for the day when someone had pushed Moira's retroussé little nose into a bag of potting compost and held it there until it was certain she would take no more geranium cuttings. I could have wished her a better death, but it had been quick, everyone said. The police still clung to the belief that Malcolm had arranged for an assassin, but even Joyce knew that that was nonsense. Malcolm was a creature of tempest and volatility, but he'd never been calculatingly cruel.

His lack of interest in the horses themselves didn't extend to anything else at the sales: inside the salering he had been particularly attentive to the flickering electronic board which lit up with the amount as each bid was made, and lit up not only in English currency but in dollars, yen, francs, lire and Irish punts at the current exchange rates. He'd always been fascinated by the workings of money, and had once far more than doubled a million pounds simply by banking it in the United States at two dollars forty cents to the pound, waiting five years, and bringing it back when the rate stood at one dollar twenty cents, which neatly gave him twice the capital he'd started with and the interest besides. He thought of the money market, after gold, as a sort of help-yourself cornucopia.

None of his children had inherited his instinct for timing and trends, a lack he couldn't understand. He'd told me directly once or twice to buy this or sell that, and he'd been right, but I couldn't make money the way he did without his guidance.

He considered that the best years of his talent had been wasted: all the years when, for political reasons, the free movement of capital had been restricted and when gold bullion couldn't be bought by private Britons. Always large, Malcolm's income, once the controls were lifted, went up like a hot air balloon, and it was at the beginning of that period, when he'd woken to the possibilities and bought his first crock of gold for sixty pounds an ounce to sell it presently for over a hundred, that he'd first been called Midas.

Since then, he'd ridden the yellow roller-coaster several times, unerringly buying when the price sank ever lower, selling as it soared, but before the bubble burst, always seeming to spot the wobbling moment when the market approached trough or peak.

Coochie had appeared wearing ever larger diamonds. The three witches, Vivien, Joyce and Alicia, each with a nice divorce settlement agreed in less sparkling days, unavailingly consulted their lawyers.

There was a second electronic board outside the sale-ring showing the state of the sale inside. Malcolm concentrated on the flickering figures until they began to shine more brightly in the fading daylight, but he still paid no close attention to the merchandise itself.

'They all look very small,' he said reprovingly, watching a narrow colt pass on its way from stable to sale-ring.

'Well, they're yearlings.'

'One year old, literally?'

'Eighteen months, twenty months: about that. They race next year, when they're two.'

He nodded and decided to return to the scene of the action, and again found us seats opposite the big-money crowd. The amphitheatre had filled almost to capacity while we'd been outside, and soon, with every seat taken, people shoved close-packed into the entrance and the standing-room sections: the blood of Northern Dancer and Nijinsky and of Secretariat and Lyphard was on its regal way to the ring.

A hush fell in the building at the entrance of the first of the legend-bred youngsters, the breath-held expectant hush of the knowledgeable awaiting a battle among financial giants. A fat cheque on this sales evening could secure a Derby winner and found a dynasty, and it happened often enough to tempt belief each time that this . . . *this* . . . was the one.

The auctioneer cleared his throat and managed the introduction without a quiver. 'Ladies and gentlemen, we now have Lot No 76, a bay colt by Nijinsky . . .' He recited the magical breeding as if bored, and asked for an opening bid.

Malcolm sat quiet and watched while the numbers flew high on the scoreboard, the price rising in jumps of fifty thousand; watched while the auctioneer scanned the bidding faces for the drop of an eyelid, the twitch of a head, the tiny acknowledgements of intent.

' . . . against you, sir. No more, then? All done?' The auctioneer's eyebrows rose with his gavel, remained poised in elevation, came smoothly, conclusively down. 'Sold for one million seven hundred thousand guineas to Mr Siddons . . .'

The crowd sighed, expelling collective breath like a single organism. Then came rustling of catalogues, movement, murmuring and rewound expectation.

Malcolm said, 'It's a spectator sport.'

'Addictive,' I agreed.

He glanced at me sideways. 'For one million . . . five million . . . there's no guarantee the colt will ever race, isn't that what you said? One could be throwing one's cash down the drain?'

'That's right.'

'It's a perfectly blameless way of getting rid of a lot of money very fast, wouldn't you say?'

'Well . . .' I said slowly, 'is that what you're at?'

'Do you disapprove?'

'It's your money. You made it. You spend it.'

He smiled almost secretively at his catalogue and said, 'I can hear the "but" in your voice.'

'Mm. If you want to enjoy yourself, buy ten next-best horses instead of one super-colt, and get interested in them.'

'And pay ten training fees instead of one?'

I nodded. 'Ten would drain the exchequer nicely.'

He laughed in his throat and watched the next half-grown blue-blood reach three million guineas before Mr Siddons shook his head. ' . . . sold for three million and fifty thousand guineas to Mrs Terazzini . . .'

'Who's she?' Malcolm asked.

'She owns a worldwide bloodstock empire.'

He reflected. 'Like Robert Sangster?'

'Yep. Like him.'

He made a noise of understanding. 'An industry.'

'Yes.'

The following lot, a filly, fetched a more moderate sum, but the hush of expectancy returned for the next offering. Malcolm, keenly tuned by now to the atmosphere, watched the bidders as usual, not the nervous chestnut colt.

The upward impetus stopped at a fraction over two million and the auctioneer's eyebrows and gavel rose. 'All done?'

Malcolm raised his catalogue.

The movement caught the eye of the auctioneer, who paused with the gavel raised, using his eyebrows as a question, looking at Malcolm with surprise. Malcolm sat in what could be called the audience, not with the usual actors.

'You want to bid, sir?' asked the auctioneer.

'And fifty,' Malcolm said clearly, nodding.

There was a fluttering in the dovecot of auctioneers as head bent to head among themselves, consulting. All round the ring, necks stretched to see who had spoken, and down in the entrance-way the man who'd bid last before Malcolm shrugged, shook his head and turned his back to the auctioneer. His last increase had been for twenty thousand only: a last small raise over two million, which appeared to have been his intended limit.

The auctioneer himself seemed less than happy. 'All done, then?' he asked again, and with no further replies, said, 'Done then. Sold for two million and seventy thousand guineas to . . . er . . . the bidder opposite.'

The auctioneer consulted with his colleagues again and one of them left the box, carrying a clipboard. He hurried down and round the ring to join a minion on our side, both of them with their gaze fastened on Malcolm.

'Those two auctioneers won't let you out of their sight,' I observed. 'They suffered badly from a vanishing bidder not so long ago.'

'They look as if they're coming to arrest me,' Malcolm said cheerfully; and both of the auctioneers indeed made their way right to his side, handing him the clipboard and politely requiring him to sign their bill of sale, in triplicate and without delay. They retired to ground level but were still waiting for us with steely intent when, after three further sales had gone through as expected, we made our way down.

They invited Malcolm civilly to the quieter end of their large office, and we went. They computed what he owed and deferentially presented the total. Malcolm wrote them a cheque.

They politely suggested proof of identity and a reference. Malcolm gave them an American Express card and the telephone number of his bank manager. They took the cheque gingerly and said that although Mr . . . er . . . Pembroke should if he wished arrange insurance on his purchase at once, the colt would not be available for removal until . . . er . . . tomorrow.

Malcolm took no offence. He wouldn't have let anyone he didn't know drive off with a horsebox full of gold. He said tomorrow would be fine, and in high good spirits told me I could ferry him back to his Cambridge hotel, from where he'd come that morning in a taxi, and we would have dinner together.

After we'd called in at an insurance agent's office and he'd signed some more papers and another cheque, we accordingly walked together to the car park from where people were beginning to drift home. Night had fallen, but there were lights enough to see which car was which, and as we went I pointed out the row ahead where my wheels stood.

'Where are you going to send your colt?' I asked, walking.

'Where would you say?'

'I should think,' I said . . . but I never finished the answer, or not at that actual moment.

A car coming towards us between two rows of parked cars suddenly emitted two headlight beams, blinding us; and at the same moment it seemed to accelerate fiercely, swerving straight towards Malcolm.

I leaped . . . flung myself . . . at my father, my flying weight spinning him off balance, carrying him off his feet, knocking him down. I fell on top of him, knowing that the pale speeding bulk of the car had caught me, but not sure to what extent. There was just a bang and a lot of lights curving like arcs, and a whirling view of gleams on metal, and a fast crunch into darkness.

We were on the ground then between two silent parked cars, our bodies heavy with shock and disorientation, in a sort of inertia.

After a moment, Malcolm began struggling to free himself from under my weight, and I rolled awkwardly onto my knees and thankfully thought of little but bruises. Malcolm pushed himself up until he was sitting with his back against a car's wheel, collecting his wits but looking as shaken as I felt.

'That car,' he said eventually, between deep breaths, 'was aiming . . . to kill me.'

I nodded speechlessly. My trousers were torn, thigh grazed and bleeding.

'You always had . . . quick reactions,' he said. 'So now . . . now you know . . . why I want you beside me . . . all the time.'

CHAPTER TWO

It was the second time someone had tried to kill him, he said.

I was driving towards Cambridge a shade more slowly than usual, searching anxiously in the rear-view mirror for satanically-minded followers but so far thankfully without success. My right leg was stiffening depressingly from the impact of twenty minutes ago, but I was in truth fairly used to that level of buffet through having ridden over the years in three or four hundred jump races, incurring consequent collisions with the ground.

Malcolm didn't like driving for reasons Coochie had deftly diagnosed as impatience. Coochie hadn't liked his driving either, for reasons (she said) of plain fear, and had taken over as family chauffeur. I too had been used to driving Malcolm from the day I gained my licence: I would need to have been delirious to ask him to take the wheel just because of some grazed skin.

The second time someone had tried to kill him . . .

'When was the first time?' I asked.

'Last Friday.'

It was currently Tuesday evening. 'What happened?' I said.

He took a while over answering. When he did there was more sadness in his voice than anger, and I listened to his tone behind the words and slowly understood his deepest fears.

'One moment I was walking the dogs . . . well, I think I was, but that's it, I don't really remember.' He paused. 'I think I had a bang on the head . . . Anyway, the last thing I remember is calling the dogs and opening the kitchen door. I meant to take them through the garden to that field with the stream and the willows. I don't know how far I went. I shouldn't think far. Anyway, I woke up in Moira's car in the garage . . . it's still there . . . and it's damn lucky I woke up at all . . . the engine was running . . .' He stopped for a few moments. 'It's funny how the mind works. I knew absolutely at once that I had to switch off the engine. Extraordinary. Like a flash. I was in the back seat, sort of tumbled . . . toppled over . . . half lying. I got up and practically fell through between the front seats to reach the key in the ignition, and when the engine stopped I just lay there, you know, thinking that I was bloody uncomfortable but not having any more energy to move.'

'Did anyone come?' I said, when he paused.

'No . . . I felt better after a while. I stumbled out of the car and was sick.'

'Did you tell the police?'

'Sure, I told them.' His voice sounded weary at the recollection. 'It must have been about five when I set off with the dogs. Maybe seven by the time I called the police. I'd had a couple of stiff drinks by then and stopped shaking. They asked me why I hadn't called them sooner. Bloody silly. And it was the same lot who came after Moira. They think I did it, you know. Had her killed.'

'I know.'

'Did the witches tell you that too?'

'Joyce did. She said you couldn't have. She said you might have . . . er . . .' I baulked from repeating my mother's actual words, which were 'throttled the little bitch in a rage', and substituted more moderately, ' . . . been capable of killing her yourself, but not of paying someone else to do it.'

He made a satisfied noise but no comment, and I added, 'That seems to be the family concensus.'

He sighed. 'It's not the police concensus. Far from it. I don't think they believed anyone had tried to kill me. They made a lot of notes and took samples . . . I ask you . . . of my vomit, and dusted over Moira's car for fingerprints, but it was obvious they were choked with doubts. I think they thought I'd been going to commit suicide and thought better of it . . . or else that I'd staged it in the hope people would believe I couldn't have killed Moira if someone was trying to kill *me* . . .'

He shook his head. 'I'm sorry I told them at all, and that's why we're not reporting tonight's attempt either.'

He had been adamant, in the sales car park, that we shouldn't.

'What about the bump on your head?' I asked.

'I had a swelling above my ear. Very tender, but not very big. The word I heard the police use about that was "inconclusive".'

'And if you'd died . . .' I said thoughtfully.

He nodded. 'If I'd died, it would have wrapped things up nicely for them. Suicide. Remorse. Implicit admission of guilt.'

I drove carefully towards Cambridge, appalled and also angry. Moira's death hadn't touched me in the slightest, but the attacks on my father showed me I'd been wrong. Moira had had a right to live. There should have been rage, too, on her behalf.

'What happened to the dogs?' I said.

'What? Oh, the dogs. They came back . . . they were whining at the kitchen door. I let them in while I was waiting for the police. They were muddy . . . heaven knows where they'd been. They were tired anyway. I fed them and they went straight to their baskets and went to sleep.'

'Pity they couldn't talk.'

'What? Yes, I suppose so. Yes.' He fell into silence, sighing occasionally as I thought over what he'd told me.

'Who,' I said eventually, 'knew you were going to Newmarket Sales?'

'Who?' He sounded surprised at the question, and then understood it. 'I don't know.' He was puzzled. 'I've no idea. I didn't know myself until yesterday.'

'Well, what have you been doing since the police left you last Friday night?'

'Thinking.' And the thoughts, it was clear, had been melancholic: the thoughts now saddening his voice.

'Mm,' I said, 'along the lines of why was Moira killed?'

'Along those lines.'

I said it plainly. 'To stop her taking half your possessions?'

He said unwillingly, 'Yes.'

'And the people who had a chief interest in stopping her were your likely heirs. Your children.'

He was silent.

I said, 'Also perhaps their husbands and wives, also perhaps even the witches.'

'I don't want to believe it,' he said. 'How could I have put a murderer into the world.'

'People do,' I said.

'*Ian*!'

The truth was that, apart from poor Robin, I didn't know my half-brothers and half-sisters well enough to have any certainty about any of them. I was usually on speaking terms with them all, but didn't seek them out. There had been too much fighting, too many rows:

Vivien's children disliked Alicia's, Alicia's disliked them and me, Vivien hated Joyce and Joyce hated Alicia very bitterly indeed. Under Coochie's reign, the whole lot had been banned from sleeping in the house, if not from single-day visits, with the result that a storm of collective resentment had been directed at me whom she had kept and treated as her own.

'Apart from thinking,' I said, 'what have you been doing since Friday night?'

'When the police had gone, I . . . I . . .' he stopped.

'The shakes came back?' I suggested.

'Yes. Do you understand that?'

'I'd have been scared silly,' I said. 'Stupid not to be. I'd have felt that whoever had tried to kill me was prowling about in the dark waiting for me to be alone so he could have another go.'

Malcolm audibly swallowed. 'I telephoned to the hire firm I use now and told them to send a car to fetch me. Do you know what panic feels like?'

'Not that sort, I guess.'

'I was sweating, and it was cold. I could feel my heart thumping . . . banging away at a terrible rate. It was awful. I packed some things . . . I couldn't concentrate.'

He shifted in his seat as the outskirts of Cambridge came up in the headlights and began to give me directions to the hotel where he said he'd spent the previous four nights.

'Does anyone know where you're staying?' I asked,

turning corners. 'Have you seen any of your old chums?'

Malcolm knew Cambridge well, had been at university there and still had friends at high tables. It must have seemed to him a safe city to bolt to, but it was where I would have gone looking for him, if not much else failed.

'Of course I have,' he said in answer to my question. 'I spent Sunday with the Rackersons, dined with old Digger in Trinity last night . . . it's nonsense to think they could be involved.'

'Yes,' I agreed, pulling up outside his hotel. 'All the same, go and pack and check out of here, and we'll go somewhere else.'

'It's not necessary,' he protested.

'You appointed me as minder, so I'm minding,' I said.

He gave me a long look in the dim light inside the car. The doorman of the hotel stepped forward and opened the door beside me, an invitation to step out.

'Come with me,' my father said.

I was both astounded by his fear and thought it warranted. I asked the doorman where I should park, and turned at his suggestion through an arch into the hotel's inner courtway. From there, through a back door and comfortable old-fashioned hallways, Malcolm and I went up one flight of red-carpeted stairs to a lengthy winding corridor. Several people we passed glanced down at my torn trouser-leg with the dried-blood scenery inside, but no one said anything: was it still British politeness, I wondered, or the new creed of not getting involved? Malcolm, it seemed, had forgotten the problem existed.

He brought his room key out of his pocket and, with it raised, said abruptly, 'I suppose *you* didn't tell anyone I would be at the sales.'

'No, I didn't.'

'But you knew.' He paused. 'Only you knew.'

He was staring at me with the blue eyes and I saw all the sudden fear-driven question marks rioting through his mind.

'Go inside,' I said. 'The corridor isn't the place for this.'

He looked at the key, he looked wildly up and down the now empty corridor, poised, almost, to run.

I turned my back on him and walked purposefully away in the direction of the stairs.

'*Ian*,' he shouted.

I stopped and turned round.

'Come back,' he said.

I went back slowly. 'You said you trusted me,' I said.

'I haven't seen you for three years . . . and I broke your nose . . .'

I took the key out of his hand and unlocked the door. I supposed I might have been suspicious of me if I'd been attacked twice in five days, considering I came into the high-probability category of son. I switched on the light and went forward into the room which was free from lurking murderers that time at least.

Malcolm followed, only tentatively reassured, closing the door slowly behind him. I drew the heavy striped curtains across the two windows and briefly surveyed the spacious but old-fashioned accommodation: reproduction antique furniture, twin beds, pair of armchairs, door to bathroom.

No murderer in the bathroom.

'Ian . . .' Malcolm said.

'Did you bring any scotch?' I asked. In the old days, he'd never travelled without it.

He waved a hand towards a chest of drawers where I found a half-full bottle nestling among a large number of socks. I fetched a glass from the bathroom and poured him enough to tranquillize an elephant.

'For God's sake . . .' he said.

'Sit down and drink it.'

'You're bloody arrogant.'

He did sit down, though, and tried not to let the glass clatter against his teeth from the shaking of his hand.

With much less force, I said, 'If I'd wanted you dead, I'd have let that car hit you tonight. I'd have jumped the other way . . . out of trouble.'

He seemed to notice clearly for the first time that there had been any physical consequences to our escape.

'Your leg,' he said, 'must be all right?'

'Leg is. Trousers . . . can I borrow a pair of yours?'

He pointed to a cupboard where I found a second suit almost identical to the one he was wearing. I was three inches taller than he and a good deal thinner but, belted and slung round the hips, whole cloth was better than holey.

He silently watched me change and made no objection when I telephoned down to the reception desk and asked them to get his bill ready for his departure. He drank more of the scotch, but nowhere was he relaxed.

'Shall I pack for you?' I asked.

He nodded, and watched some more while I fetched his suitcase, opened it on one of the beds and began collecting his belongings. The things he'd brought spoke eloquently of his state of mind when he'd packed them: about ten pairs of socks but no other underwear, a dozen shirts, no pyjamas, two towelling bath-robes, no extra shoes. The clearly new electric razor in the bathroom still bore a stick-on price tag, but he had brought his antique gold-and-silver-backed brushes, all eight of them, including two clothes brushes. I put everything into the case, and closed it.

'Ian,' he said.

'Mm?'

'People can pay assassins . . . You could have decided not to go through with it tonight . . . at the last moment . . .'

'It wasn't like that,' I protested. Saving him had been utterly instinctive, without calculation or counting of risks: I'd been lucky to get off with a graze.

He said almost beseechingly, with difficulty, 'It wasn't you, was it, who had Moira . . . Or me, in the garage . . .? Say it wasn't you.'

I didn't know really how to convince him. He'd known me better, lived with me longer than with any of his other children, and if his trust was this fragile then there wasn't much future between us.

'I didn't have Moira killed,' I said. 'If you believe it of me, you could believe it of yourself.' I paused. 'I don't want you dead, I want you alive. I could never do you harm.'

It struck me that he really needed to hear me say I loved him, so although he might scoff at the actual words, and despite the conditioned inhibitions of my upbringing, I said, feeling that desperate situations needed desperate remedies, 'You're a great father . . . and . . . er . . . I love you.'

He blinked. Such a declaration pierced him, one could see. I'd probably overdone it, I thought, but his distrust had been a wound for me too.

I said much more lightly, 'I swear on the Coochie Pembroke Memorial Challenge Trophy that I would never touch a hair on your head . . . nor Moira's either, though I did indeed loathe her.'

I lifted the suitcase off the bed.

'Do I go on with you or not?' I said. 'If you don't trust me, I'm going home.'

He was looking at me searchingly, as if I were a stranger, which I suppose in some ways I was. He had never before, I guessed, had to think of me not as a son but as a man, as a person who had led a life separate from his, with a different outlook, different desires, different values. Sons grew from little boys into their own adult selves: fathers tended not to see the change clearly. Malcolm, I was certain, thought of me basically as still having the half-formed personality I'd had at fifteen.

'You're different,' he said.

'I am the same. Trust your instinct.'

Some of the tension at last slackened in his muscles. His instinct had been trust, an instinct strong enough to carry him to the telephone after three silent years. He finished the scotch and stood up, filling his lungs with a deep breath as if making resolves.

'Come with me, then,' he said.

I nodded.

He went over to the chest of drawers and from the bottom drawer, which I hadn't checked, produced a briefcase. I might have guessed it would be there somewhere: even in the direst panic, he wouldn't have left behind the lists of his gold shares or his currency exchange calculator. He started with the briefcase to the door, leaving me to bring the suitcase, but on impulse I went over again to the telephone and asked for a taxi to be ready for us.

'But your car's here,' Malcolm said.

'Mm. I think I'll leave it here, for now.'

'But why?'

'Because if I didn't tell anyone you were going to Newmarket Sales, and nor did you, then it's probable you were followed there, from . . . er . . . here. If you think about it . . . the car that tried to kill you was waiting in the sales car park, but you didn't have a car. You went there by taxi. Whoever drove at you must have seen you and me together, and known who I was, and guessed you might leave with me, so although I didn't see anyone following us tonight from Newmarket, whoever-it-was probably knew we would come here, to this hotel, so . . . well . . . so they might be hanging about in the courtyard where we parked, where it's nice and dark outside the back door, waiting to see if we come out again.'

'My God!'

'It's possible,' I said. 'So we'll leave through the front with the doorman in attendance, don't you think?'

'If you say so,' he said weakly.

'From now on,' I said, 'we take every exaggerated precaution we can think of.'

'Well, where are we going in this taxi?'

'How about somewhere where we can rent a car?'

The taxi-driver, however, once we'd set off without incident from the hotel, bill paid, luggage loaded, doorman tipped, informed us doubtfully that nine o'clock on a Tuesday night wasn't going to be easy. All the car-hire firms' offices would be closed.

'Chauffeur-driven car, then,' Malcolm said. 'Fellows who do weddings, that sort of thing. Twenty quid in it for you if you fix it.'

Galvanized by this offer, the taxi-driver drove us down some back streets, stopped outside an unpromising little terraced house and banged on the door. It opened, shining out a melon-slice of light, and gathered the taxi-driver inside.

'We're going to be mugged,' Malcolm said.

The taxi-driver returned harmlessly, however, accompanied by a larger man buttoning the jacket of a chauffeur's uniform and carrying a reassuring peaked cap.

'The firm my brother-in-law works for does mostly weddings and funerals,' the taxi-driver said. 'He wants to know where you want to go.'

'London,' I said.

London appeared to be no problem at all. The driver and his brother-in-law climbed into the front of the taxi which started off, went round a corner or two, and pulled up again outside a lock-up garage. We sat in the taxi as asked while the two drivers opened the garage, disclosing its contents. Which was how Malcolm and I proceeded to London in a very large, highly-polished black Rolls-Royce, the moonlighting chauffeur separated from us discreetly by a glass partition.

'Why did you go to the sales at all?' I asked Malcolm. 'I mean, why Newmarket? Why the sales?'

Malcolm frowned. 'Because of Ebury's, I suppose.'

'The jewellers?'

'Yes... well... I knew they were going to have a showroom there. They told me so last week when I went to see them about Coochie's jewellery. I mean, I know them pretty well, I bought most of her things from there. I was admiring a silver horse they had, and they said they were exhibiting this week at Newmarket Sales. So then yesterday when I was wondering what would fetch you... where you would meet me... I remembered the sales were so close to Cambridge, and I decided on it not long before I rang you.'

I pondered a bit. 'How would you set about finding where someone was, if you wanted to, so to speak?'

To my surprise he had a ready answer. 'Get the fellow I had for tailing Moira.'

'Tailing...'

'My lawyer said to do it. It might save me something, he said, if Moira was having a bit on the side, see what I mean?'

'I do indeed,' I agreed dryly. 'But I suppose she wasn't?'

'No such luck.' He glanced at me. 'What do you have in mind?'

'Well... I just wondered if he could check where everyone in the family was last Friday and tonight.'

'Everyone!' Malcolm exclaimed. 'It would take weeks.'

'It would put your mind at rest.'

He shook his head gloomily. 'You forget about assassins.'

'Assassins aren't so frightfully easy to find, not for ordinary people. How would you set about it, for instance, if you wanted someone killed? Put an ad in *The Times*?'

He didn't seem to see such a problem as I did, but he agreed that 'the fellow who tailed Moira' should be offered the job of checking the family.

We discussed where we should stay that night: in which hotel, in fact, as neither of us felt like returning home. Home, currently, to me, was a rather dull suburban flat in Epsom, not far from the stable I'd been working for. Home for Malcolm was still the house where I'd been raised, from which Moira had apparently driven him, but to which he had returned immediately after her death. 'Home' for all the family was that big house in Berkshire which had seen all five wives come and go: Malcolm himself had been brought up there, and I could scarcely imagine what he must have felt at the prospect of losing it.

'What happened between you and Moira?' I said.

'None of your goddam business.'

We travelled ten miles in silence. Then he shifted, sighed, and said, 'She wanted Coochie's jewellery and I wouldn't give it to her. She kept on and on about it, rabbit, rabbit. Annoyed me, do you see? And then . . . well . . .' he shrugged, 'she caught me out.'

'With another woman?' I said without surprise.

He nodded, unashamed. He'd never been monogamous and couldn't understand why it should be expected. The terrible rows in my childhood had all been centred on his affairs: while he'd been married to Vivien and then to Joyce, he had maintained Alicia all the time as his mistress. Alicia bore him two children while he was married to Vivien and Joyce, and also one subsequently, when he'd made a fairly honest woman of her, at her insistence.

I liked to think he had been faithful finally to Coochie, but on the whole it was improbable, and I was never going to ask.

Malcolm favoured our staying at the Dorchester, but I persuaded him he was too well known there, and we settled finally on the Savoy.

'A suite,' Malcolm said at the reception desk. 'Two bedrooms, two bathrooms and a sitting room, and send up some Bollinger right away.'

I didn't feel like drinking champagne, but Malcolm did. He also ordered scrambled eggs and smoked salmon for us both from room service, with a bottle of Hine Antique brandy and a box of Havana cigars for comforts.

Idly I totted up the expenses of his day: one solid silver trophy, one two-million-guinea thoroughbred, insurance for same, Cambridge hotel bill, tip for the taxi-driver, chauffeured Rolls-Royce, jumbo suite at the Savoy with trimmings. I wondered how much he was really worth, and whether he intended to spend the lot.

We ate the food and drank the brandy still not totally in accord with each other. The three years' division had been, it seemed, a chasm not as easy to cross as I'd thought. I felt that although I'd meant it when I said I loved him, it was probably the long memories of him that I really loved, not his physical presence here and now, and I could see that if I was going to stay close to him, as I'd promised, I would be learning him again and from a different viewpoint; that each of us, in fact, would newly get to know the other.

'Any day now,' Malcolm said, carefully dislodging ash from his cigar, 'we're going to Australia.'

I absorbed the news and said, 'Are we?'

He nodded. 'We'll need visas. Where's your passport?'

'In my flat. Where's yours?'

'In the house.'

'Then I'll get them both tomorrow,' I said, 'and you stay here.' I paused. 'Are we going to Australia for any special reason?'

'To look at gold mines,' he said. 'And kangaroos.'

After a short silence, I said, 'We don't just have to escape. We do have to find out who's trying to kill you, in order to stop them succeeding.'

'Escape is more attractive,' he said. 'How about a week in Singapore on the way?'

'Anything you say. Only . . . I'm supposed to ride in a race at Sandown on Friday.'

'I've never understood why you like it. All those cold wet days. All those falls.'

'You get your rush from gold,' I said.

'Danger?' His eyebrows rose. 'Quiet, well-behaved, cautious Ian? Life is a bore without risk, is that it?'

'It's not so extraordinary,' I said.

I'd ridden always as an amateur, unpaid, because something finally held me back from the total dedication needed for turning professional. Race riding was my deepest pleasure, but not my entire life, and in consequence I'd never developed the competitive drive necessary for climbing the pro ladder. I was happy with the rides I got, with the camaraderie of the changing room, with the wide skies and the horses themselves, and yes, one had to admit it, with the risk.

'Staying near me,' Malcolm said, 'as you've already found out, isn't enormously safe.'

'That's why I'm staying,' I said.

He stared. He said, 'My God,' and he laughed. 'I thought I knew you. Seems I don't.'

He finished his brandy, stubbed out his cigar and decided on bed; and in the morning he was up before me, sitting on a sofa in one of the bathrobes and reading the *Sporting Life* when I ambled out in the underpants and shirt I'd slept in.

'I've ordered breakfast,' he said. 'And I'm in the paper – how about that?'

I looked where he pointed. His name was certainly there, somewhere near the end of the detailed lists of yesterday's sales. 'Lot 79, ch. colt, 2,070,000 gns. Malcolm Pembroke'.

He put down the paper, well pleased. 'Now, what do we do today?'

'We summon your private eye, we fix a trainer for the colt, I fetch our passports and some clothes, and you stay here.'

Slightly to my surprise, he raised no arguments except to tell me not to be away too long. He was looking rather thoughtfully at the healing graze down my right thigh and the red beginnings of bruising around it.

'The trouble is,' he said, 'I don't have the private eye's phone number. Not with me.'

'We'll get another agency, then, from the yellow pages.'

'Your mother knows it, of course. Joyce knows it.'

'How does she know it?'

'She used him,' he said airily, 'to follow me and Alicia.'

There was nothing, I supposed, which should ever surprise me about my parents.

'When the lawyer fellow said to have Moira tailed, I got the private eye's name from Joyce. After all, he'd done a good job on me and Alicia all those years ago. Too bloody good, when you think of it. So get through to Joyce, Ian, and ask her for the number.'

Bemused, I did as he said.

'Darling,' my mother shrieked down the line. 'Where's your father?'

'I don't know,' I said.

'Darling, do you know what he's bloody *done*?'

'No . . . what?'

'He's given a *fortune*, darling, I mean literally *hundreds* of *thousands*, to some wretched little film company to make some absolutely *ghastly* film about tadpoles or something. Some bloody fool of a man telephoned to find out where your father was, because it seems he promised them even *more* money which they'd like to have . . . I ask you! I know you and Malcolm aren't talking, but you've got to do something to stop him.'

'Well,' I said, 'it's his money.'

'Darling, don't be so *naive*. Someone's going to inherit it, and if only you'd swallow all that bloody pride, as I've told you over and over, it would be *yours*. If you go on and on with this bloody quarrel, he'll leave it all to Alicia's beastly brood, and I cannot *bear* the prospect of her gloating for ever more. So make it up with Malcolm *at once*, darling, and get him to see sense.'

'Calm down,' I said. 'I have.'

'*What?*'

'Made it up with him.'

'Thank God, at *last*!' my mother shrieked. 'Then, darling, what are you waiting for? Get onto him *straight* away and stop him spending your inheritance.'

CHAPTER THREE

Malcolm's house, after three years of Moira's occupancy, had greatly changed.

Malcolm's Victorian house was known as 'Quantum' because of the Latin inscription carved into the lintel over the front door. QUANTUM IN ME FUIT – roughly, 'I did the best I could.'

I went there remembering the comfortable casualness that Coochie had left and not actually expecting that things would be different: and I should have known better, as each wife in turn, Coochie included, had done her best to eradicate all signs of her predecessor. Marrying Malcolm had, for each wife, involved moving into his house, but he had indulged them all, I now understood, in the matter of ambience.

I let myself in through the kitchen door with Malcolm's keys and thought wildly for a moment that I'd come to the wrong place. Coochie's pinewood and red-tiled homeliness had been swept away in favour of glossy yellow walls, glittering white appliances and shelves crowded with scarlet and deep pink geraniums cascading from white pots.

Faintly stunned, I looked back through time to the era before Coochie, to Alicia's fluffy occupancy of broderie anglaise frills on shimmering white curtains with pale blue work-tops and white floor tiles; and back further still to the starker olive and milk-coffee angularities chosen by Joyce. I remembered the day the workmen had torn out my mother's kitchen, and how I'd gone howling to Malcolm: he'd packed me off to Joyce immediately for a month, which I didn't like either, and when I returned I'd found the white frills installed, and the pale blue cupboards, and I thought them all sissy, but I'd learned not to say so.

For the first time ever, I wondered what the kitchen had looked like in Vivien's time, when forty-five or so years ago young Malcolm had brought her there as his first bride. Vivien had been dispossessed and resentful by the time I was born, and I'd seldom seen her smiling. She seemed to me the least positive of the five wives and the least intelligent but, according to her photographs, she had been in her youth by streets the most beautiful. The dark sweep of her eyebrows and the high cheekbones remained, but the thick black hair had thinned now in greying, and entrenched bitterness had soured the once sweet mouth. Vivien's marriage, I'd guessed, had died through Malcolm's boredom with her, and although they now still met occasionally at events to do with their mutual children and grandchildren, they were more apt to turn their backs than to kiss.

Vivien disliked and was plaintively critical of almost everybody while at the same time unerringly interpreting the most innocent general remarks of others as being criticism of herself. It was impossible to please her often or for long, and I, like almost all the extended family, had long ago stopped trying. She had indoctrinated her three offspring with her own dissatisfactions to the point where they were nastily disparaging of Malcolm behind his back, though not to his face, hypocrites that they were.

Malcolm had steadfastly maintained them through young adulthood and then cast them loose, each with a trust fund that would prevent them from actually starving. He had treated all seven of his normally surviving children in the same way; his eighth child, Robin, would be looked after for ever. None of us seven could have any complaints: he had given us all whatever vocational training we'd chosen and afterwards the cushion against penury, and at that point in each of our lives had considered his work done. Whatever became of us in the future, he said, had to be in our own hands.

With the family powerfully in mind, I went from the kitchen into the hall where I found that Moira had had the oak panelling painted white. Increasingly amused, I thought of the distant days when Alicia had painstakingly bleached all the old wood, only to have Coochie stain it dark again: and I supposed that perhaps Malcolm enjoyed change around him in many ways, not just in women.

His own private room, always called the office although more like a comfortable cluttered sitting room, seemed to have escaped the latest refit except in the matter of gold velvet curtains replacing the old green. Otherwise, the room as always seemed filled with his strong personality, the walls covered with dozens of framed photographs, the deep cupboards bulging with files, the bookshelves crammed, every surface bearing mementoes of his journeyings and achievements, nothing very tidy.

I went over to the desk to find his passport and half-expected to hear his voice at any minute even though I'd left him forty miles away persuasively telephoning to 'the fellow who tailed Moira'.

His passport, he'd said, was in the second drawer down on the right-hand side, and so it was, among a large clutter of bygone travel arrangements and expired medical insurances. Malcolm seldom threw much away, merely building another cupboard for files. His filing system was such that no one but he had the slightest idea where any paper or information could be found, but he himself could put his finger on things unerringly. His method, he'd told me once long ago, was always to put everything where he would first think of looking for it; and as a child, I'd seen such sense in that that I had copied him ever since.

Looking around again, it struck me that although

the room was crammed with objects, several familiar ones were missing. The gold dolphin, for instance, and the gold tree bearing amethysts, and the Georgian silver candelabras. Perhaps at last, I thought, he had stored them prudently in the bank.

Carrying the passport, I went upstairs to fetch clothes to add to his sketchy packing and out of irresistible curiosity detoured into the room which had been mine. I expected a bright Moira-style transformation, but in fact nothing at all had been changed, except that nothing of me remained.

The room was without soul; barren. The single bed, stripped, showed a bare mattress. There were no cobwebs, no dust, no smell of neglect, but the message was clear: the son who had slept there no longer existed.

Shivering slightly, I closed the door and wondered whether the absolute rejection had been Malcolm's or Moira's and, shrugging, decided I didn't now mind which.

Moira's idea of the perfect bedroom turned out to be plum and pink with louvred doors everywhere possible. Malcolm's dressing room next door had received the same treatment, as had their joint bathroom, and I set about collecting his belongings with a strong feeling of intruding upon strangers.

I found Moira's portrait only because I kicked it while searching for pyjamas: it was underneath Malcolm's chest of drawers in the dressing room. Looking to see what I'd damaged, I pulled out a square gold frame which fitted a discoloured patch on the wall and, turning it over, found the horrible Moira smiling at me with all her insufferable complacency.

I had forgotten how young she had been, and how pretty. Thirty years younger than Malcolm; thirty-five when she'd married him and, in the painting anyway, unlined. Reddish-gold hair, pale unfreckled skin, pointed chin, delicate neck. The artist seemed to me to have caught the calculation in her eyes with disconcerting clarity, and when I glanced at the name scrawled at the bottom I understood why. Malcolm might not have given her diamonds, but her portrait had been painted by the best.

I put her back face down under the chest of drawers as I'd found her, where Malcolm, I was sure, had consigned her.

Fetching a suitcase from the boxroom (no decor changes there), I packed Malcolm's things and went downstairs, and in the hall came face to face with a smallish man carrying a large shotgun, the business end pointing my way.

I stopped abruptly, as one would.

'Put your hands up,' he said hoarsely.

I set the suitcase on the floor and did as he bid. He wore earth-stained dark trousers and had mud on his hands, and I asked him immediately, 'Are you the gardener?'

'What if I am? What are you doing here?'

'Collecting clothes for my father . . . er . . . Mr Pembroke. I'm his son.'

'I don't know you. I'm getting the police.' His voice was belligerent but quavery, the shotgun none too steady in his hands.

'All right,' I said.

He was faced then with the problem of how to telephone while aiming my way.

I said, seeing his hesitation, 'I can prove I'm Mr Pembroke's son, and I'll open the suitcase to show you I'm not stealing anything. Would that help?'

After a pause, he nodded. 'You stay over there, though,' he said.

I judged that if I alarmed him there would be a further death in my father's house, so I very slowly and carefully opened the suitcase, removed the underpants and the rest, and laid them out on the hall floor. After that, I equally slowly took my own wallet out of my pocket, opened it, removed a credit card and laid it on the floor face upwards. Then I retreated backwards from the exhibits, ending with my back against the closed and locked front door.

The elderly gardener came suspiciously forward and inspected the show, dropping his eyes only in split seconds, raising them quickly, giving me no chance to jump him.

'That's his passport,' he said accusingly.

'He asked me to fetch it.'

'Where is he?' he said. 'Where's he gone?'

'I have to meet him with his passport. I don't know where he's going.' I paused. 'I really am his son. You must be new here. I haven't seen you before.'

'Two years,' he said defensively. 'I've worked here two years.' He seemed to come quite suddenly to a decision to believe me, and almost apologetically lowered the gun. 'This house is supposed to be locked up,' he said. 'Then I see you moving about upstairs.'

'Upsetting,' I agreed.

He gestured to Malcolm's things. 'You'd better pack them again.'

I began to do so under his still watchful eye.

'It was brave of you to come in here,' I said, 'if you thought I was a burglar.'

He braced his shoulders in an old automatic movement. 'I was in the army once.' He relaxed and shrugged. 'Tell you the truth, I was coming in quietly-like to phone the police, then you started down the stairs.'

'And . . . the gun?'

'Brought it with me just in case. I go after rabbits . . . I keep the gun handy.'

I nodded. It was the gardener's own gun, I thought. Malcolm had never owned one, as far as I knew.

'Has my father paid you for the week?' I said.

His eyes at once brightened hopefully. 'He paid me last Friday, same as usual. Then Saturday morning he phoned my house to tell me to come round here to see to the dogs. Take them home with me, same as I always do when he's away. So I did. But he was gone off the line before I could ask him how long he'd be wanting me to have them.'

I pulled out my cheque-book and wrote him a cheque for the amount he specified. Arthur Bellbrook, he said his name was. I tore out the cheque and gave it to him and asked him if there was anyone else who needed wages.

He shook his head. 'The cleaner left when Mrs Pembroke was done in . . . er . . . murdered. Said she didn't fancy the place any more.'

'Where exactly was Mrs Pembroke . . . er . . . murdered?'

'I'll show you if you like.' He stored the cheque away in a pocket. 'Outside in the greenhouse.'

He took me, however, not as I'd imagined to the rickety old familiar greenhouse sagging against a mellowed wall in the kitchen garden, but to a bright white octagonal wrought-iron construction like a fancy birdcage set as a summer-house on a secluded patch of lawn. From far outside, one could clearly see the flourishing geraniums within.

'Well, well,' I said.

Arthur Bellbrook uttered 'Huh' as expressing his disapproval and opened the metal-and-glass door.

'Cost a fortune to heat, will this place,' he observed. 'And it got too hot in the summer. The only thing as will survive in it is geraniums. Mrs Pembroke's passion, geraniums.'

An almost full sack of potting compost lay along one of the work surfaces, the top side of it slit from end to end to make the soil mixture easy to reach. A box of small pots stood nearby, some of them occupied by cuttings.

I looked at the compost with revulsion. 'Is that where . . .?' I began.

'Yes,' he said. 'Poor lady. There's no one ought to die like that, however difficult they could be.'

'No,' I agreed. A thought struck me. 'It was you who found her, wasn't it?'

'I went home like always at four o'clock, but I was out for a stroll about seven, and I thought I would just come in to see what state she'd left the place in. See, she played at gardening. Never cleaned the tools, things like that.' He looked at the boarded floor as if still seeing her there. 'She was lying face down, and I turned her over. She was dead all right. She was white like always but she had these little pink dots in her skin. They say you get those dots from asphyxiation. They found potting compost in her lungs, poor lady.' He had undoubtedly been shocked and moved at the time, but there was an echo of countless repetitions in his voice now and precious little feeling.

'Thank you for showing me,' I said.

He nodded and we both went out, shutting the door behind us.

'I don't think Mr Pembroke liked this place much,' he said unexpectedly. 'Last spring, when she chose it, he said she could have it only if he couldn't see it from the house. Otherwise he wouldn't pay the bill. I wasn't supposed to hear, of course, but there you are, I did. They'd got to shouting, you see.'

'Yes,' I said, 'I do see.' Shouting, slammed doors, the lot.

'They were all lovey-dovey when I first came here,' he said, 'but then I reckon her little ways got to him, like, and you could see it all going downhill like a runaway train. I'm here all day long, see, and in and out of the house, and you couldn't miss it.'

'What little ways?' I asked casually.

He glanced at me sideways with reawakening suspicions. 'I thought you were his son. You must have known her.'

'I didn't come here. I didn't like her.'

He seemed to find that easily believable.

'She could be as sweet as sugar . . .' He paused, remembering. 'I don't know what you'd call it, really, what she was. But for instance last year, as well as the ordinary vegetables for the house, I grew a special little patch separately . . . fed them, and so on . . . to enter in the local show. Just runner beans, carrots and onions, for one of the produce classes. I'm good at that, see? Well, Mrs Pembroke happened to spot them a day or two before I was ready to harvest. On the Thursday, with the show on the Saturday. "What huge vegetables," she says, and I tell her I'm going to exhibit them on Saturday. And she looks at me sweet as syrup and says, "Oh no, Arthur. Mr Pembroke and I both like vegetables, as you know. We'll have some of these for dinner tomorrow and I'll freeze the rest. They are *our* vegetables, aren't they, Arthur? If you want to grow vegetables to show, you must do it in your own garden in your own time." And blow me, when I came to work the next morning, the whole little patch had been picked over, beans, carrots, onions, the lot. She'd taken them, right enough. Pounds and pounds of them, all the best ones. Maybe they ate some, but she never did bother with the freezing. On the Monday, I found a load of the beans in the dustbin.'

'Charming,' I said.

He shrugged. 'That was her sort of way. Mean, but within her rights.'

'I wonder you stayed,' I said.

'It's a nice garden, and I get on all right with Mr Pembroke.'

'But after he left?'

'He asked me to stay on to keep the place decent. He paid me extra, so I did.'

Walking slowly, we arrived back at the kitchen door. He smelled faintly of compost and old leaves and the warm fertility of loam, like the gardener who'd reigned in this place in my childhood.

'I grew up here,' I said, feeling nostalgia.

He gave me a considering stare. 'Are you the one who built the secret room?'

Startled, I said, 'It's not really a room. Just a sort of triangular-shaped space.'

'How do you open it?'

'You don't.'

'I could use it,' he said obstinately, 'for an apple store.'

I shook my head. 'It's too small. It's not ventilated. It's useless, really. How do you know of it?'

He pursed his lips and looked knowing. 'I could see the kitchen garden wall looked far too thick from the back down at the bottom corner and I asked old Fred about it, who used to be gardener here before he retired. He said Mr Pembroke's son once built a sort of shed there. But there's no door, I told him. He said it was the son's business, he didn't know anything about it himself, except that he thought it had been bricked up years ago. So if it was you who built it, how do you get in?'

'You can't now,' I said. 'I did brick it up soon after I built it to stop one of my half-brothers going in there and leaving dead rats for me to find.'

'Oh.' He looked disappointed. 'I've often wondered what was in there.'

'Dead rats, dead spiders, a lot of muck.'

He shrugged. 'Oh well, then.'

'You've been very helpful,' I said. 'I'll tell my father.'

His lined face showed satisfaction. 'You tell him I'll keep the dogs and everything in good nick until he comes back.'

'He'll be grateful.'

I picked up the suitcase from inside the kitchen door, gave a last look at Moira's brilliant geraniums, vibrantly alive, shook the grubby hand of Arthur Bellbrook, and (in the car hired that morning in London) drove away towards Epsom.

Collecting my own things from my impersonal suburban flat took half the time. Unlike Malcolm, I liked things bare and orderly and, meaning always to move to somewhere better but somehow never going out to search, I hadn't decked the sitting room or the two small bedrooms with anything brighter than new patterned curtains and a Snaffles print of Sergeant Murphy winning the 1923 Grand National.

I changed from Malcolm's trousers into some of my own, packed a suitcase and picked up my passport. I had no animals to arrange for, nor any bills pressing. Nothing anywhere to detain me.

The telephone answering machine's button glowed red, announcing messages taken. I rewound the tape and listened to the disembodied voices while I picked out of the fridge anything that would go furry and disgusting before my return.

Something, since I'd left the day before, had galvanized the family into feverish activity, like stirring an anthill with a stick.

A girlish voice came first, breathless, a shade anxious. 'Ian, this is Serena. Why are you always out? Don't you sleep at home? Mummy wants to know where Daddy is. She knows you and he aren't speaking, she's utterly thick to expect you to know, but anyway she insisted I ask you. So if you know, give me a ring back, OK?'

Serena, my half-sister, daughter of Alicia, the one child born to Alicia in wedlock. Serena, seven years my junior, lay in my distant memory chiefly as a small fair-haired charmer who'd followed me about like a shadow, which had flattered my twelve-year-old ego disgracefully. She liked best to sit on Malcolm's lap, his arms protectively around her, and from him, it had seemed to me, she could conjure a smile when he was angry and pretty dresses when she had a cupboardful.

Alicia, in sweeping out of the house when Serena was six, taking with her not only Serena but her two older boys, had left me alone in the suddenly quiet house, alone in the frilly kitchen, alone and untormented in the garden. There had been a time then when I would positively have welcomed back Gervase, the older boy, despite his dead rats and other rotten tricks; and it had actually been in the vacuum after his departure that I contrived the bricking up of my kitchen-wall room, not while he was there to jeer at it.

Grown up, Gervase still displayed the insignia of a natural bully: mean tightening of the mouth, jabbing forefinger, cold patronizing stare down the nose, visible enjoyment of others' discomfiture. Serena, now tall and slim, taught aerobic dancing for a living, bought clothes still by the cartload and spoke to me only when she wanted something done.

'Mummy wants to know where Daddy is . . .' The childish terms sat oddly in the ear, somehow, coming from someone now twenty-six; and she alone of all his children had resisted calling Malcolm, Malcolm.

The next caller was Gervase himself. He started crossly, 'I don't like these message contraptions. I tried to get you all evening yesterday and I hear nothing but your priggish voice telling me to leave my name and telephone number, so this time I'm doing it, but under protest. This is your brother Gervase, as no doubt you realize, and it is imperative we find Malcolm at once. He has gone completely off his rocker. It's in your own interest to find him, Ian. We must all bury our differences and stop him spending the family money in this reckless way.' He paused briefly. 'I suppose you do know he has given half a million . . . *half a million* . . . to a busload of retarded children? I got a phone call from some stupid gushing female who said, "Oh Mr Pembroke, however can we thank you?" and when I asked her what for, she said wasn't I *the* Mr Pembroke who had solved all their problems, Mr Malcolm Pembroke? Madam, I said, what are you talking about? So she told me. *Half a million pounds.* Are you listening, Ian? He's irresponsible. It's out of proportion. He's got to be prevented from giving way to such ridiculous impulses. If you ask me, it's the beginning of senility. You must find him and tell us where he's got to, because so far as I can discover he hasn't answered his telephone since last Friday morning when I rang him to say Alicia's alimony had not been increased by the rate of inflation in this last quarter. I expect to hear from you without delay.'

His voice stopped abruptly on the peremptory order and I pictured him as he was now, not the muscular thick-set black-haired boy but the flabbier, overweight thirty-five-year-old stockbroker, over-bearingly pompous beyond his years. In a world increasingly awash with illegitimate children, he increasingly resented his own illegitimacy, referring to it ill-temperedly on inappropriate occasions and denigrating the father who, for all his haste into bed with Alicia, had accepted Gervase publicly always as his son, and given him his surname with legal adoption.

Gervase had nonetheless been taunted early on by cruel schoolmates, developing an amorphous hatred then which later focused itself on me, Ian, the half-brother who scarcely valued or understood the distinction between his birth and mine. One could understand why he'd lashed out in those raw adolescent days, but it was a matter of regret, I thought, that he'd never outgrown his bitterness. It remained with him, festering, colouring his whole personality, causing people often to wriggle away from his company, erupting in didactic outbursts and wretched unjustified jealousies.

Yet his wife appeared to love him forgivingly, and had produced two children, both girls, the first of them appearing a good three years after the well-attended marriage. Gervase had said a little too often that he himself would never in any circumstances have burdened a child with what he had suffered. Gervase, to my mind, would spend his last-ever moments worrying that the word 'illegitimate' would appear on his death certificate.

Ferdinand, his brother, was quite different, taking illegitimacy as of little importance, a matter of paperwork, no more.

Three years younger than Gervase, a year younger than myself, Ferdinand looked more like Malcolm than any of us, a living testimony to his parentage. Along with the features, he'd inherited the financial agility but lacking Malcolm's essential panache had carved himself a niche in an insurance company, not a multi-million fortune.

Ferdinand and I had been friends while we both lived in the house as children, but Alicia had thoroughly soured all that when she'd taken him away, dripping into all her children's ears the relentless spite of her dispossession. Ferdinand now looked at me with puzzlement as if he couldn't quite remember why he disliked me, and then Alicia would remind him sharply that if he wasn't careful I would get my clutches on his, Gervase's and Serena's rightful shares of Malcolm's money, and his face would darken again into unfriendliness.

It was a real pity about Ferdinand, I thought, but I never did much about it.

After Gervase on my answering machine came my mother, Joyce, very nearly incoherent with rage. Someone, it appeared, had already brought the *Sporting Life* to her notice. She couldn't *believe* it, she said. Words failed her. (They obviously didn't.) How *could* I have done anything as stupid as taking Malcolm to Newmarket Sales, because obviously I would have been there with him, it wasn't his scene otherwise, and why had I been so *deceitful* that morning when I'd talked to her, and would I without fail ring her *immediately*, this was a *crisis*, Malcolm had got to be stopped.

The fourth and last message, calmer after Joyce's hysteria, was from my half-brother Thomas, the third of Malcolm's children, born to his first wife, Vivien.

Thomas, rising forty, prematurely bald, pale skinned, sporting a gingerish moustache, had married a woman who acidly belittled him every time she opened her mouth. ('Of course, Thomas is absolutely useless when it comes to . . .' [practically anything] and 'if only poor Thomas was capable of commanding a suitable salary' and 'Dear Thomas is one of life's failures, aren't you, darling?') Thomas bore it all with hardly a wince, though after years of it I observed him grow less effective and less decisive, not more, almost as if he had come to believe in and to act out his Berenice's opinion of him.

'Ian,' Thomas said in a depressed voice, 'this is

Thomas. I've been trying to reach you since yesterday lunchtime but you seem to be away. When you've read my letter, please will you ring me up.'

I'd picked up his letter from my front doormat but hadn't yet opened it. I slit the envelope then and found that he too had a problem. I read:

Dear Ian,

Berenice is seriously concerned about Malcolm's wicked selfishness. She, well, to be honest, she keeps on and on about the amounts he's throwing away these days, and to be honest the only thing which has pacified her for a long time now is the thought of my eventual share of Malcolm's money, and if he goes on spending at this rate, well my life is going to be pretty *intolerable*, and I wouldn't be telling you this if you weren't my brother and the best of the bunch, which I suppose I've never said until now, but sometimes I think you're the only sane one in the family even if you do ride in those dangerous races, and, well, can you do anything to reason with Malcolm, as you're the only one he's likely to listen to, even though you haven't been talking for ages, which is unbelievable considering how you used to be with each other, and I blame that money-grubbing Moira, I really do, though Berenice used to think that anything or anyone who came between you and Malcolm could only be to my benefit, because Malcolm might with luck cut you out of his will.

Well, I didn't mean to say that, old chap, but it's what Berenice thought, to be honest, until Moira was going to take half of everything in the divorce settlement, and I really thought Berenice would have a seizure when she heard that, she was so furious. It really would save my sanity, Ian, if you could make Malcolm see that we all *NEED* that money. I don't know what will happen if he goes on spending it at this rate. I do *BEG* you, old chap, to stop him.

Your brother Thomas.

I looked at the letter's general incoherence and at the depth of the plea in the last few sentences with their heavily underlined words and thought of the non-stop barrage of Berenice's disgruntlement, and felt more brotherly towards Thomas than ever before. True, I still thought he should tell his wife to swallow her bile, not spill it all out on him, corroding his self-confidence and undermining his prestige with everyone within earshot; but I did at least and perhaps at last see how he could put up with it, by soothing her with the syrup of prosperity ahead.

I understood vaguely why he didn't simply ditch her and decamp: he couldn't face doing what Malcolm had done, forsaking wife and children when the going got rough. He had been taught from a very young age to despise Malcolm's inconstancy. He stayed grimly glued to Berenice and their two cheeky offspring and suffered for his virtue; and it was from fear of making the same calamitous mistake, I acknowledged, that I had married no one at all.

Thomas's was the last message on the tape. I took it out of the machine and put it in my pocket, inserting a fresh tape for future messages. I also, after a bit of thought, sorted through a boxful of family photographs, picking out groups and single pictures until I had a pretty comprehensive gallery of Pembrokes. These went into my suitcase along with a small cassette player and my best camera.

I did think of answering some of the messages, but decided against it. The arguments would all have been futile. I did truly believe in Malcolm's absolute right to do what he liked with the money he had made by his own skill and diligence. If he chose to give it in the end to his children, that was our good luck. We had no rights to it; none at all. I would have had difficulty in explaining that concept to Thomas or Joyce or Gervase or Serena, and apart from not wanting to, I hadn't the time.

I put my suitcase in the car, along with my racing saddle, helmet, whip and boots and drove back to the Savoy, being relieved to find Malcolm still there, unattacked and unharmed.

He was sitting deep in an armchair, dressed again as for the City, drinking champagne and smoking an oversize cigar. Opposite him, perched on the front edge of an identical armchair, sat a thin man of much Malcolm's age but with none of his presence.

'Norman West,' Malcolm said to me, waving the cigar vaguely at his visitor; and to the visitor he said, 'My son, Ian.'

Norman West rose to his feet and shook my hand briefly. I had never so far as I knew met a private detective before, and it wouldn't have been the occupation I would have fitted to this damp-handed nervous threadbare individual. Of medium height, he had streaky grey hair overdue for a wash, dark-circled brown eyes, greyish unhealthy skin and a day's growth of greying beard. His grey suit looked old and uncared for and his shoes had forgotten about polish. He looked as much at home in a suite in the Savoy as a punk rocker in the Vatican.

As if unerringly reading my mind he said, 'As I was just explaining to Mr Pembroke, I came straight here from an all-night observation job, as he was most insistent that it was urgent. This rig fitted my observation point. It isn't my normal gear.'

'Clothes for all seasons?' I suggested.

'Yes, that's right.'

His accent was the standard English of bygone radio announcers, slightly plummy and too good to be true. I gestured to him to sit down again, which he did as before, leaning forward from the front edge of the seat cushion and looking enquiringly at Malcolm.

'Mr West had just arrived when you came,'

Malcolm said. 'Perhaps you'd better explain to him what we want.'

I sat on the spindly little sofa and said to Norman West that we wanted him to find out where every single member of our extended family had been on the previous Friday from, say, four o'clock in the afternoon onwards, and also on Tuesday, yesterday, all day.

Norman West looked from one to the other of us in obvious dismay.

'If it's too big a job,' Malcolm said, 'bring in some help.'

'It's not really *that*,' Norman West said unhappily. 'But I'm afraid there may be a conflict of interest.'

'What conflict of interest?' Malcolm demanded.

Norman West hesitated, cleared his throat and hummed a little. Then he said, 'Last Saturday morning I was hired by one of your family to find *you*, Mr Pembroke. I've already been working, you see, for one of your family. Now you want me to check up on *them*. I don't think I should, in all conscience, accept your proposition.'

'*Which* member of my family?' Malcolm demanded.

Norman West drummed his fingers on his knee, but decided after inner debate to answer.

'Mrs Pembroke,' he said.

CHAPTER FOUR

Malcolm blinked. 'Which one?' he asked.

'Mrs Pembroke,' Norman West repeated, puzzled.

'There are nine of them,' I said. 'So which one?'

The detective looked uncomfortable. 'I spoke to her only on the telephone. I thought . . . I assumed . . . it was the Mrs Malcolm Pembroke for whom I worked once before, long ago. She referred me to that case, and asked for present help. I looked up my records . . .' He shrugged helplessly. 'I imagined it was the same lady.'

'Did you find Mr Pembroke,' I asked, 'when you were looking for him?'

Almost unwillingly, West nodded. 'In Cambridge. Not too difficult.'

'And you reported back to Mrs Pembroke?'

'I really don't think I should be discussing this any further.'

'At least, tell us how you got back in touch with Mrs Pembroke to tell her of your success.'

'I didn't,' he said. 'She rang me two or three times

a day, asking for progress reports. Finally on Monday evening, I had news for her. After that, I proceeded with my next investigation, which I have now concluded. This left me free for anything Mr Pembroke might want.'

'I want you to find out which Mrs Pembroke wanted to know where I was.'

Norman West regretfully shook his unkempt head. 'A client's trust . . .' he murmured.

'A client's trust, poppycock!' Malcolm exploded. 'Someone who knew where to find me damn near killed me.'

Our detective looked shocked but rallied quickly. 'I found you, sir, by asking Mrs Pembroke for a list of places you felt at home in, as in my experience missing people often go to those places, and she gave me a list of five such possibilities, of which Cambridge was number three. I didn't even go to that city looking for you. As a preliminary, I was prepared to telephone to all the hotels in Cambridge asking for you, but I tried the larger hotels first, as being more likely to appeal to you, sir, and from only the third I got a positive response. If it was as easy as that for me to find you, it was equally easy for anyone else. And, sir, if I may say so, you made things easy by registering under your own name. People who want to stay lost shouldn't do that.'

He spoke with a touching air of dignity ill-matched to his seedy appearance and for the first time I thought he might be better at his job than he looked. He must have been pretty efficient, I supposed, to have stayed in the business so long, even if catching Malcolm with his trousers off couldn't have taxed him sorely years ago.

He finished off the glass of champagne that Malcolm had given him before my arrival, and refused a refill.

'How is Mrs Pembroke paying you?' I asked.

'She said she would send a cheque.'

'When it comes,' I said, 'you'll know which Mrs Pembroke.'

'So I will.'

'I don't see why you should worry about a conflict of interests,' I said. 'After all, you've worked pretty comprehensively for various Pembrokes. You worked for my mother, Joyce Pembroke, to catch my father with the lady who gave her grounds for divorce. You worked for my father, to try to catch his fifth wife having a similar fling. You worked for the unspecified Mrs Pembroke to trace my father's whereabouts. So now he wants you to find out where all his family were last Friday and yesterday so as to be sure it was none of his close relatives who tried to kill him, as it would make him very unhappy if it were. If you can't square that with your conscience, of course with great regret he'll have to retain the services of someone else.'

Norman West eyed me with a disillusionment which again encouraged me to think him not as dim as he looked. Malcolm was glimmer-eyed with amusement.

'Pay you well, of course,' he said.

'Danger money,' I said, nodding.

Malcolm said, 'What?'

'We don't want him to step on a rattlesnake, but in fairness he has to know he might.'

Norman West looked at his short and grimy nails. He didn't seem unduly put out, nor on the other hand eager.

'Isn't this a police job?' he asked.

'Certainly,' I said. 'My father called them in when someone tried to kill him last Friday, and he'll tell you all about it. And you have to bear in mind that they're also enquiring into the murder of Moira Pembroke, whom you followed through blameless days. But you would be working for my father, not for the police, if you take his cash.'

'Pretty decisive, aren't you, sir?' he said uneasily.

'Bossy,' Malcolm agreed, 'in his quiet way.'

All those years, I thought, of getting things done in a racing stable, walking a tightrope between usurping the power of the head lad on one hand and the trainer himself on the other, like a lieutenant between a sergeant-major and a colonel. I'd had a lot of practice, one way and another, at being quietly bossy.

Malcolm unemotionally told West about his abortive walk with the dogs and the brush with carbon monoxide, and after that described also the near-miss at Newmarket.

Norman West listened attentively with slowly

blinking eyes and at the end said, 'The car at Newmarket could have been accidental. Driver looking about for cigarettes, say. Not paying enough attention. Seeing you both at the last minute . . . swerving desperately.'

Malcolm looked at me. 'Did it seem like that to you?'

'No.'

'Why not?' West asked.

'The rate of acceleration, I suppose.'

'Foot on accelerator going down absent-mindedly during search for cigarettes?'

'Headlights, full beam,' I said.

'A sloppy driver? Had a few drinks?'

'Maybe.' I shook my head. 'The real problem is that if the car *had* hit us – or Malcolm – there might have been witnesses. The driver might have been stopped before he could leave the sales area. The car number might have been taken.'

West smiled sorrowfully. 'It's been done successfully before now, in broad daylight in a crowded street.'

'Are you saying,' Malcolm demanded of me, 'that the car *wasn't* trying to kill me?'

'No, only that the driver took a frightful risk.'

'Did any witnesses rush to pick us up?' Malcolm asked forcefully. 'Did anyone so much as pass a sympathetic remark? No, they damned well didn't. Did anyone try to stop the driver or take his number? The hell they did.'

'All the same,' West said, 'your son is right. Hit-and-run in a public place has its risks. If it was tried here, and, sirs, I'm not saying it wasn't, the putative gain must have outweighed the risk, or, er, in other words – '

'In other words,' Malcolm interrupted with gloom, 'Ian is right to think they'll try again.'

Norman West momentarily looked infinitely weary, as if the sins of the world were simply too much to contemplate. He had seen, I supposed, as all investigators must, a lifetime's procession of sinners and victims; and, moreover, he looked roughly seventy and hadn't slept all night.

'I'll take your job,' he said without enthusiasm, radiating minimum confidence, and I glanced at Malcolm to see if he really thought this was the best we could do in detectives, signs of intelligence or not. Malcolm appeared to have no doubts, however, and spent the next five minutes discussing fees which seemed ominously moderate to me.

'And I'll need a list,' West said finally, 'of the people you want checked. Names and addresses and normal habits.'

Malcolm showed unexpected discomfort, as if checking that amorphous entity 'the family' was different from checking each individual separately, and it was I who found a piece of Savoy writing paper to draw up the list.

'OK,' I said, 'first of all there's Vivien, my father's first wife. Mrs Vivien Pembroke.'

'Not her,' Malcolm objected. 'It's ridiculous.'

'Everyone,' I said firmly. 'No exceptions. That makes it fair on everyone . . . because there are going to be some extremely angry relations when they all realize what's happening.'

'They won't find out,' Malcolm said.

Fat chance, I thought.

To West, I said, 'They all telephone each other all the time, not by any means always out of friendship but quite often out of spite. They won't gang up against you because they seldom form alliances among themselves. Some of them are pretty good liars. Don't believe everything they say about each other.'

'*Ian!*' Malcolm said protestingly.

'I'm one of them, and I know,' I said.

After Vivien's name on the list I wrote the names of her children:

Donald

Lucy

Thomas

'Thomas,' I said, 'is married to Berenice.' I added her name beside his. 'He is easy to deal with, she is not.'

'She's a five-star cow,' Malcolm said.

West merely nodded.

'Lucy,' I said, 'married a man called Edwin Bugg. She didn't like that surname, and persuaded him to change it to hers, and she is consequently herself a Mrs Pembroke.'

West nodded.

'Lucy is a poet,' I said. 'People who know about poetry say her stuff is the real thing. She makes a big production of unworldliness which Edwin, I think, has grown to find tiresome.'

'Huh,' Malcolm said. 'Edwin's an out-and-out materialist, always tapping me for a loan.'

'Do you give them to him?' I said interestedly.

'Not often. He never pays me back.'

'Short of money, are they?' West asked.

'Edwin Bugg,' Malcolm said, 'married Lucy years ago because he thought she was an heiress, and they've scraped along ever since on the small income she gets from a trust fund I set up for her. Edwin's never done a stroke of work in his parasitic life and I can't stand the fellow.'

'They have one teenage schoolboy son,' I said, smiling, 'who asked me the last time I saw him how to set about emigrating to Australia.'

West looked at the list and said to Malcolm, 'What about Donald, your eldest?'

'Donald,' said his father, 'married a replica of his mother, beautiful and brainless. A girl called Helen. They live an utterly boring virtuous life in Henley-on-Thames and are still billing and cooing like newlyweds although Donald must be nearly forty-five, I suppose.'

No one commented. Malcolm himself, rising sixty-nine, could bill and coo with the best, and with a suppressed shiver I found myself thinking for the first time about the *sixth* marriage, because certainly, in the future, if Malcolm survived, there would be one. He had never in the past lived long alone. He liked rows better than solitude.

'Children?' Norman West asked into the pause.

'Three,' Malcolm said. 'Pompous little asses.'

West glanced at me questioningly, and yawned.

'Are you too tired to take all this in?' I asked.

'No, go ahead.'

'Two of Donald's children are too young to drive a car. The eldest, a girl at art school, is five foot two and fragile, and I cannot imagine her being physically capable of knocking Malcolm out and carrying his body from garden to garage and inserting him into Moira's car.'

'She hasn't the courage either,' Malcolm said.

'You can't say that,' I disagreed. 'Courage can pop up anywhere and surprise you.'

West gave me a noncommittal look. 'Well,' he said, taking the list himself and adding to it, 'this is what we have so far. Wife number one: Vivien Pembroke. Her children: Donald (44), wife Helen, three offspring. Lucy, husband Edwin (née Bugg), school-age son. Thomas, wife Berenice . . .?'

'Two young daughters.'

'Two young daughters,' he repeated, writing.

'My grandchildren,' Malcolm protested, 'are all too young to have murdered anybody.'

'Psychopaths start in the nursery,' West said laconically. 'Any sign in any of them of abnormal violent behaviour? Excessive cruelty, that sort of thing? Obsessive hatreds?'

Malcolm and I both shook our heads but with a touch of uncertainty; his maybe because of something he did know, mine because of all I didn't know, because of all the things that could be hidden.

'Does greed, too, begin in the nursery?' I said.

'I wouldn't say so, would you?' West answered.

I shook my head again. 'I'd say it was nastily adult and grows with opportunity. The more there is to grab, the greedier people get.'

Malcolm said, only half as a question, 'My fortune corrupts . . . geometrically?'

'You're not alone,' I said dryly. 'Just think of all those multi-billionaire families where the children have already had millions settled on them and still fight like cats over the pickings when their father dies.'

'Bring it down to thousands,' West said unexpectedly. 'Or to hundreds. I've seen shocking spite over hundreds. And the lawyers rub their hands and syphon off the cream.' He sighed, half disillusionment, half weariness. 'Wife number two?' he asked, and answered his own question, 'Mrs Joyce Pembroke.'

'Right,' I said. 'I'm her son. She had no other children. And I'm not married.'

West methodically wrote me down.

'Last Friday evening,' I said, 'I was at work in a racing stable at five o'clock with about thirty people as witnesses, and last night I was certainly not driving the car that nearly ran us over.'

West said stolidly, 'I'll write you down as being cleared of primary involvement. That's all I can do with any of your family, Mr Pembroke.' He finished the sentence looking at Malcolm who said, 'Hired assassin' between his teeth, and West nodded. 'If any of them hired a good professional, I doubt if I'll discover it.'

'I thought good assassins used rifles,' I said.

'Some do. Most don't. They pick their own way. Some use knives. Some garotte. I knew of one who used to wait at traffic lights along his victim's usual route to work. One day, the lights would be red, the victim would stop. The assassin tapped on the window, asking a question . . . or so it's supposed. The victim wound down the window and the assassin shot him point blank in the head. By the time the lights turned green and the cars behind started tooting their horns, the assassin had long gone.'

'Did they ever catch him?' I asked.

West shook his head. 'Eight prominent businessmen were killed that way within two years. Then it stopped. No one knows why. My guess is the assassin lost his nerve. It happens in every profession.'

I thought of jump jockeys to whom it had happened

almost overnight, and I supposed it occurred in stockbrokers also. Any profession, as he said.

'Or someone bumped him off because he knew too much,' Malcolm said.

'That too is possible.' West looked at the list. 'After Mrs Joyce?'

Malcolm said sourly, 'The lady you so artfully photographed me with at the instigation of, as you call her, Mrs Joyce.'

The West eyebrows slowly rose. 'Miss Alicia Sandways? With, if I remember, two little boys?'

'The little boys are now thirty-five and thirty-two,' I said.

'Yes.' He sighed. 'As I said, I recently dug out that file. I didn't realize that . . . er . . . Well, so we have wife number three, Mrs Alicia Pembroke. And her children?'

Malcolm said, 'The two boys, Gervase and Ferdinand. I formally adopted them when I married their mother, and changed their surname to Pembroke. Then we had little Serena,' his face softened, 'and it was for her I put up with Alicia's tantrums the last few years we were together. Alicia was a great mistress but a rotten wife. Don't ask me why. I indulged her all the time, let her do what she liked with my house, and in the end nothing would please her.' He shrugged. 'I gave her a generous divorce settlement, but she was very bitter. I wanted to keep little Serena . . . and Alicia screamed that she supposed I didn't want the boys because they were illegitimate. She fought in the courts for Serena, and she won . . . She filled all her children's heads with bad feelings for me.' The old hurt plainly showed. 'Serena did suggest coming back to look after me when Coochie was killed, but it wasn't necessary because Moira was there. When Moira was killed, she offered again. It was kind of Serena. She's a nice girl, really, but Alicia tries to set her against me.'

West, in a pause that might or might not have been sympathetic, wrote after Alicia's name:

Gervase. Illegitimate at birth, subsequently adopted

Ferdinand. The same

Serena. Legitimate

'Are they married?' he asked.

'Gervase has a wife called Ursula,' I said. 'I don't know her well, because when I see them they're usually together and it's always Gervase who does the talking. They too, like Thomas, have two little girls.'

West wrote it down.

'Ferdinand,' I said, 'has married two raving beauties in rapid succession. The first, American, has gone back to the States. The second one, Deborah, known as Debs, is still in residence. So far, no children.'

West wrote.

'Serena,' I said, 'is unmarried.'

West completed that section of the list. 'So we have wife number three, Mrs Alicia Pembroke. Her children are Gervase, wife Ursula, two small daughters.

Ferdinand, current wife Debs, no children. Serena, unmarried . . . er . . . a fiancé, perhaps? Live-in-lover?'

'I don't know of one,' I said, and Malcolm said he didn't know either.

'Right,' West said. 'Wife number four?'

There was a small silence. Then I said, 'Coochie. She's dead. She had twin sons. One was killed with her in a car crash, the other is brain-damaged and lives in a nursing home.'

'Oh.' The sound carried definite sympathy this time. 'And wife number five, Mrs Moira Pembroke, did she perhaps have any children from a previous marriage?'

'No,' Malcolm said. 'No previous marriage, no children.'

'Right.' West counted up his list. 'That's three ex-wives . . . er, by the way, did any of them remarry?'

I answered with a faint smile, 'They would lose their alimony if they did. Malcolm was pretty generous in their settlements. None of them has seen any financial sense in remarrying.'

'They all should have done,' Malcolm grumbled. 'They wouldn't be so warped.'

West said merely, 'Right. Then, er, six sons, two daughters. Four current daughters-in-law, one son-in-law. Grandchildren . . . too young. So, er, discounting the invalid son and Mr Ian here, there are fourteen adults to be checked. That will take me a week at least. Probably more.'

'As fast as you can,' I said.

He looked actually as if he had barely enough strength or confidence to get himself out of the door let alone embark on what was clearly an arduous task.

'Can I tell them all why I'm making these enquiries?' he asked.

'Yes, you damned well can,' Malcolm said positively. 'If it's one of them, and I hope to God it isn't, it might put the wind up them and frighten them off. Just don't tell them where to find me.'

I looked down at the list. I couldn't visualize any of them as being criminally lethal, but then greed affected otherwise rational people in irrational ways. All sorts of people . . . I knew of a case when two male relatives had gone into a house where an old woman had been reported newly dead, and taken the bedroom carpet off the floor, rolling it up and making off with it and leaving her lying alone in her bed above bare boards, all to seize her prize possession before the rest of the family could get there. Unbelievable, I'd thought it. The old woman's niece, who cleaned my flat every week, had been most indignant, but not on her aunt's account. 'It was the only good carpet in the house,' she vigorously complained. 'Nearly new. The only thing worth having. It should have come to me, by rights. Now I'll never get it.'

'I'll need all their addresses,' West said.

Malcolm waved a hand. 'Ian can tell you. Get him to write them down.'

Obediently I opened my suitcase, took out my

address book and wrote the whole list, with telephone numbers. Then I got out the pack of photographs and showed them to West.

'Would they help you?' I asked. 'If they would, I'll lend them to you, but I want them back.'

West looked through them one by one, and I knew that he could see, if he were any detective at all, all the basic characters of the subjects. I liked taking photographs and preferred portraits, and somehow taking a camera along gave me something positive to do whenever the family met. I didn't like talking to some of them; photography gave me a convincing reason for disengagements and drifting around.

If there was one common factor in many of the faces it was discontent, which I thought was sad. Only in Ferdinand could one see real lightheartedness, and even in him, as I knew, it could come and go; and Debs, his second wife, was a stunning blonde, taller than her husband, looking out at the world quizzically as if she couldn't quite believe her eyes, not yet soured by disappointment.

I'd caught Gervase giving his best grade-one bullying down-the-nose stare, and saw no good purpose in ever showing him the reflection of his soul. Ursula merely looked indeterminate and droopy and somehow guilty, as if she thought she shouldn't even have her photo taken without Gervase's permission.

Berenice, Thomas's wife, was the exact opposite, staring disapprovingly straight into the lens, bold and sarcastic, unerringly destructive every time she uttered. And Thomas, a step behind her, looking harried and anxious. Another of Thomas alone, smiling uneasily, defeat in the sag of his shoulders, desperation in his eyes.

Vivien, Joyce and Alicia, the three witches, dissimilar in features but alike in expression, had been caught when they weren't aware of the camera, each of them watching someone else with disfavour.

Alicia, fluffy and frilly, still wore her hair brought youthfully high to a ribbon bow on the crown, from where rich brown curls tumbled in a cascade to her shoulders. Nearly sixty, she looked in essence younger than her son Gervase, and she would still have been pretty but for the pinched hardness of her mouth.

She had been a fair sort of mother to me for the seven years of her reign, seeing to my ordinary needs like food and new clothes and treating me no different from Gervase and Ferdinand, but I'd never felt like going to her for advice or comfort. She hadn't loved me, nor I her, and after the divorce we had neither felt any grief in separation. I'd detested what she'd done afterwards to Gervase, Ferdinand and Serena, twisting their minds with her own spite. I would positively have liked to have had friendly brothers and sisters as much as Malcolm would have valued friendly children. After nearly twenty years, Alicia's intense hurt still spread suffering outward in ripples.

Serena's picture showed her as she had been a year

earlier, before aerobic dancing had slimmed her further to a sexless-looking leanness. The fair hair of childhood had slightly darkened, and was stylishly cut in a short becoming cap-shape which made her look young for her twenty-six years. A leggy Peter Pan, I thought, not wanting to grow up: a girl-woman with a girlish voice saying 'Mummy and Daddy', and an insatiable appetite for clothes. I wondered briefly whether she were still a virgin and felt faintly surprised to find that I simply didn't know and, moreover, couldn't tell.

'These are very interesting,' West said, glancing at me. 'I should certainly like to borrow them.' He shuffled them around and sorted them out. 'Who are these? You haven't put their names on the back, like the others.'

'That's Lucy and Edwin, and that's Donald and Helen.'

'Thanks.' He wrote the identification carefully in small neat letters.

Malcolm stretched out a hand for the photographs which West gave him. Malcolm looked through them attentively and finally gave them back.

'I don't remember seeing any of these before,' he said.

'They're all less than three years old.'

His mouth opened and shut again. He gave me a brooding look, as if I'd just stabbed him unfairly in the ribs.

'What do you think of them?' I asked.

'A pity children grow up.'

West smiled tiredly and collected the lists and photographs together.

'Right, Mr Pembroke. I'll get started.' He stood up and swayed slightly, but when I took a step forward to steady him he waved me away. 'Just lack of sleep.' On his feet, he looked even nearer to exhaustion, as if the outer greyness had penetrated inwards to the core. 'First thing in the morning, I'll be checking the Pembrokes.'

It would have been churlish to expect him to start that afternoon, but I can't say I liked the delay. I offered him another drink and a reviving lunch, which he declined, so I took him to the hotel's front door and saw him safely into a taxi, watching him sink like a collapsing scarecrow into the seat cushions.

Returning to the suite, I found Malcolm ordering vodka and Beluga caviar from room service with the abandon to which I was becoming accustomed. That done, he smoothed out the *Sporting Life* and pointed to one section of it.

'It says the Arc de Triomphe race is due to be run this Sunday in Paris.'

'Yes, that's right.'

'Then let's go.'

'All right,' I said.

Malcolm laughed. 'We may as well have some fun. There's a list here of the runners.'

I looked where he pointed. It was a bookmaker's advertisement showing the ante-post prices on offer.

'What are the chances,' Malcolm said, 'of my buying one of these horses?'

'Er,' I said. 'Today, do you mean?'

'Of course. No good buying one *after* the race, is there?'

'Well . . .'

'No, of course not. The winner will be worth millions and the others peanuts. *Before* the race, that's the thing.'

'I don't suppose anyone will sell,' I said, 'but we can try. How high do you want to go? The favourite won the Epsom Derby and is reported to be going to be syndicated for ten million pounds. You'd have to offer a good deal more than that before they'd consider selling him now.'

'Hm,' Malcolm said. 'What do you think of him as a horse?'

I smothered a gasp or two and said with a deadpan face, 'He's a very good horse but he had an exceptionally exhausting race last time out. I don't think he's had enough time to recover, and I wouldn't back him this time.'

'Have you backed him before?' Malcolm asked curiously.

'Yes, when he won the Derby, but he was favourite for that, too.'

'What do you think will win the Arc de Triomphe, then?'

'Seriously?' I said.

'Of course seriously.'

'One of the French horses, Meilleurs Voeux.'

'Can we buy him?'

'Not a hope. His owner loves his horses, loves winning more than profit and is immensely rich.'

'So am I,' Malcolm said simply. 'I can't help making money. It used to be a passion, now it's a habit. But this business about Moira jolted me, you know. It struck me that I may not have a hell of a lot of time left, not with enough health and strength to enjoy life. I've spent all these years amassing the stuff, and for what? For my goddam children to murder me for it? Sod that for a sad story. You buy me a good horse in this race on Sunday and we'll go and yell it home, boy, at the top of our lungs.'

It took all afternoon and early evening to get even a tinge of interest from anyone. I telephoned to the trainers of the English – or Irish – runners, asking if they thought their owners might sell. I promised each trainer that he would go on training the horse, and that my father would send him also the two-million-guinea colt he'd bought yesterday. Some of the trainers were at the Newmarket Sales and had to be tracked down to hotels, and once tracked, had to track and consult with their owners. Some simply said no, forget it.

Finally, at seven forty-five, a trainer from Newmarket rang back to say his owner would sell a half-share if his price was met. I relayed the news and the price to Malcolm.

'What do you think?' he said.

'Um . . . the horse is quite good, the price is on the high side, the trainer's in the top league.'

'OK.' Malcolm said. 'Deal.'

'My father accepts,' I said. 'And, er, the colt is still in the sales stables. Can you fetch it tomorrow, if we clear it with the auctioneers?'

Indeed he could. He sounded quite cheerful altogether. He would complete his paperwork immediately if Malcolm could transfer the money directly to his bloodstock account, bank and account number supplied. I wrote the numbers to his dictation. Malcolm waved a hand and said, 'No problem. First thing in the morning. He'll have it by afternoon.'

'Well,' I said, breathing out as I put the receiver down, 'you now own half of Blue Clancy.'

'Let's drink to it,' Malcolm said. 'Order some Bollinger.'

I ordered it from room service, and while we waited for it to arrive I told him about my encounter with his gardener, Arthur Bellbrook.

'Decent chap,' Malcolm said, nodding. 'Damned good gardener.'

I told him wryly about Moira and the prize vegetables, which he knew nothing about.

'Silly bitch,' he said. 'Arthur lives in a terrace house

with a pocket handkerchief garden facing north. You couldn't grow prize stuff there. If she'd asked me I'd have told her that, and told her to leave him alone. Good gardeners are worth every perk they get.'

'He seemed pretty philosophical,' I said, 'and, incidentally, pretty bright. He'd spotted that the kitchen garden wall is thicker than it should be at the corner. He'd asked old Fred, and heard about the room I built there. He wanted to know how to get in, so he could use it as an apple store.'

Malcolm practically ejected from his armchair, alarm widening his eyes, his voice coming out strangled and hoarse. 'My God, you didn't tell him, did you?'

'No, I didn't,' I said slowly. 'I told him it was empty and was bricked up twenty years ago.' I paused. 'What have you put in there?'

Malcolm subsided into his chair, not altogether relieved of anxiety.

'Never you mind,' he said.

'You forget that I could go and look.'

'I don't forget it.'

He stared at me. He'd been interested, all those summers ago, when I'd designed and built the pivoting brick door. He'd come down the garden day after day to watch, and had patted me often on the shoulder, and smiled at the secret. The resulting wall looked solid, felt solid, *was* solid. But at one point there was a thick vertical steel rod within it, stretching from a concrete underground foundation up into the beam supporting the roof. Before I'd put the new roof on, I'd patiently drilled round holes in bricks (breaking many) and slid them into the rod, and arranged and mortared the door in neat courses, so that the edges of it dovetailed into the fixed sections next to it.

To open the room, when I'd finished everything, one had first to remove the wedge-like wooden sill which gave extra support to the bottom course of the door when it was closed, and then to activate the spring latch on the inner side by poking a thin wire through a tiny hole in the mortar at what had been my thirteen-year-old waist height. The design of the latch hadn't been my own, but something I'd read in a book: at any rate, when I'd installed it, it worked obligingly at once.

It had pleased me intensely to build a door that Gervase would never find. No more dead rats. No more live birds, shut in and fluttering with fright. No more invasions of my own private place.

Gervase had never found the door and nor had anyone else and, as the years passed, grass grew long in front of the wall, and nettles, and although I'd meant to give the secret to Robin and Peter some day, I hadn't done so by the time of the crash. Only Malcolm knew how to get in – and Malcolm had used the knowledge.

'What's in there?' I repeated.

He put on his airiest expression. 'Just some things I didn't want Moira to get her hands on.'

I remembered sharply the objects missing from his study.

'The gold dolphin, the amethyst tree, the silver candelabra . . . those?'

'You've been looking,' he accused.

I shook my head. 'I noticed they were gone.'

The few precious objects, all the same, hardly accounted for the severity of his first alarm.

'What else is in there?' I said.

'Actually,' he said, calmly now, 'quite a lot of gold.'

CHAPTER FIVE

'Some people buy and sell gold without ever seeing it,' he said. 'But I like possessing the actual stuff. There's no fun in paper transactions. Gold is beautiful on its own account, and I like to see it and feel it. But it's not all that easy to store it in banks or safety deposits. Too heavy and bulky. And insurance is astronomical. Takes too much of the profit. I never insure it.'

'You're storing it there in the wall . . . waiting for the price to rise?'

'You know me, don't you?' He smiled. 'Buy low, bide your time, sell high. Wait a couple of years, not often more. The price of gold itself swings like a pendulum, but there's nothing, really, like gold shares. When gold prices rise, gold shares often rise by two or three times as much. I sell the gold first and the shares a couple of months later. Psychological phenomenon, you know, that people go on investing in gold mines, pushing the price up, when the price of gold itself is static or beginning to drop. Illogical, but invaluable to people like me.'

He sat looking at me with the vivid blue eyes, teaching his child.

'Strategic Minerals, now. There never was anything like the Strategic Minerals Corporation of Australia. This year, the price of gold itself rose twenty-five per cent, but Strats – shares in Strategic Minerals – rose nearly a thousand per cent before they dropped off the top. Incredible, I got in near the beginning of those and sold at nine hundred and fifty per cent profit. But don't be fooled, Strats happen only once or twice in a lifetime.'

'How much,' I said, fascinated, 'did you invest in Strats?'

After a brief pause he said, 'Five million. I had a feeling about them . . . they just smelled right. I don't often go in so deep, and I didn't expect them to fly so high, no one could, but there you are, all gold shares rose this year, and Strats rose like a skylark.'

'How are they doing now?' I asked.

'Don't know. I'm concerned with the present. Gold mines, you see, don't go on for ever. They have a life: exploration, development, production, exhaustion. I get in, wait a while, take a profit, forget them. Never stay too long with a rising gold share. Fortunes are lost by selling too late.'

He did truly trust me, I thought. If he'd doubted me still, he wouldn't have told me there was gold behind the brick door, nor that even after tax he had made approximately thirty million pounds on one deal. I stopped worrying that he was overstretching himself in buying the colt and a half-share in Blue Clancy. I stopped worrying about practically everything except how to keep him alive and spending.

I'd talked to someone once whose father had died when she was barely twenty. She regretted that she hadn't ever known him adult to adult, and wished she could meet him again, just to talk. Watching Malcolm, it struck me that in a way I'd been given her wish: that the three years' silence had been a sort of death, and that I could talk to him now adult to adult, and know him as a man, not as a father.

We spent a peaceful evening together in the suite, talking about what we'd each done during the hiatus, and it was difficult to imagine that outside, somewhere, a predator might be searching for the prey.

At one point I said, 'You gave Joyce's telephone number on purpose to the film man, didn't you? And Gervase's number to the retarded-children lady? You wanted me with you to see you buy the colt . . . You made sure that the family knew all about your monster outlays as soon as possible, didn't you?'

'Huh,' he said briefly, which after a moment I took as admission. One misdirected telephone call had been fairly possible: two stretched credibility too far.

'Thomas and Berenice,' I said, 'were pretty frantic over some little adventure of yours. What did you do to stir *them* up?'

'How the hell do you know all this?'

I smiled and fetched the cassette player, and re-ran for him the message tape from my telephone. He listened grimly but with an undercurrent of amusement to Serena, Gervase and Joyce and then read Thomas's letter, and when he reached Thomas's intense closing appeal I waited for explosions.

They didn't come. He said wryly, 'I suppose they're what I made them.'

'No,' I said.

'Why not?'

'Personality is mysterious, but it's born in you, not made.'

'But it can be brainwashed.'

'Yes, OK,' I said. 'But you didn't do it.'

'Vivien and Alicia did . . . because of me.'

'Don't wallow in guilt so much. It isn't like you.'

He grinned. 'I don't feel guilty, actually.'

Joyce, I thought, had at least played fair. A screaming fury she might have been on the subject of Alicia, but she'd never tried to set me against Malcolm. She had agreed in the divorce settlement when I was six that he should have custody of me: she wasn't basically maternal, and infrequent visits from her growing son were all she required. She'd never made great efforts to bind me to her, and it had always been clear to me that she was relieved every time at my departure. Her life consisted of playing, teaching, and writing about bridge, a game she played to international tournament standard, and she was often abroad. My visits had always disrupted the acute concentration she needed for winning, and as winning gave her the prestige essential for lecture tours and magazine articles, I had more often raised impatience in her than comradeship, a feeling she had dutifully tried to stifle.

She had given me unending packs of cards to play with and had taught me a dozen card games, but I'd never had her razor memory of any and every card played in any and every game, a perpetual disappointment to her and a matter for impatience in itself. When I veered off to make my life in a totally different branch of the entertainment industry, she had been astonished at my choice and at first scornful, but had soon come round to checking the racing pages during the steeplechase season to see if I was listed as riding.

'What did you tell Thomas and Berenice?' I asked Malcolm again, after a pause.

With satisfaction he said, 'I absentmindedly gave their telephone number to a wine merchant who was to let me know the total I owed him for the fifty or so cases of 1979 Pol Roger he was collecting for me to drink.'

'And, er, roughly how much would that cost?'

'The 1979, the Winston Churchill vintage, is quite exceptional, you know.'

'Of course it would be,' I said.

'Roughly twenty-five thousand pounds, then, for fifty cases.'

Poor Thomas, I thought.

'I also made sure that Alicia knew I'd given about a quarter of a million pounds to fund scholarships for bright girls at the school Serena went to. Alicia and I haven't been talking recently. I suppose she's furious I gave it to the school and not to Serena herself.'

'Well, why did you?'

He looked surprised. 'You know my views. You must all carve your own way. To make you all rich too young would rob you of incentive.'

I certainly did know his views, but I wasn't sure I always agreed with them. I would have had bags of incentive to make a success of being a racehorse trainer if he'd lent, advanced or given me enough to start, but I also knew that if he did, he'd have to do as much for the others (being ordinarily a fair man), and he didn't believe in it, as he said.

'Why did you want them all to know how much you've been spending?' I asked. 'Because of course they all will know by now. The telephone wires will have been red hot.'

'I suppose I thought . . . um . . . if they believed I was getting rid of most of it there would be less point in killing me . . . do you see?'

I stared at him. 'You must be crazy,' I said. 'It sounds to me like an invitation to be murdered without delay.'

'Ah well, that too has occurred to me of late.' He smiled vividly. 'But I have you with me now to prevent that.'

After a speechless moment I said, 'I may not always be able to see the speeding car.'

'I'll trust your eyesight.'

I pondered. 'What else have you spent a bundle on, that I haven't heard about?'

He drank some champagne and frowned, and I guessed that he was trying to decide whether or not to tell me. Finally he sighed and said, 'This is for your ears only. I didn't do it for the same reason, and I did it earlier . . . several weeks ago, in fact, before Moira was murdered.' He paused. 'She was angry about it, though she'd no right to be. It wasn't her money. She hated me to give anything to anyone else. She wanted everything for herself.' He sighed. 'I don't know how you knew right from the beginning what she was like.'

'Her calculator eyes,' I said.

He smiled ruefully. He must have seen that look perpetually, by the end.

'The nursing home where Robin is,' he said unexpectedly, 'needed repairs. So I paid for them.'

He wasn't talking, I gathered, in terms of a couple of replaced window-frames.

'Of course, you know it's a private nursing home?' he said. 'A family business, basically.'

'Yes.'

'They needed a new roof. New wiring. A dozen urgent upgradings. They tried raising the residential fees too high and lost patients, familiar story. They asked my advice about fund-raising. I told them not to bother. I'd get estimates, and all I'd want in return was that they'd listen to a good business consultant who I'd send them.' He shifted comfortably in his armchair. 'Robin's settled there. Calm. Any change upsets him, as you know. If the whole place closed and went out of business, which was all too likely, I'd have to find somewhere else for him, and he's lost enough . . .'

His voice tapered off. He had delighted in Robin and Peter when they'd been small, playing with them on the carpet like a young father, proud of them as if they were his first children, not his eighth and ninth. Good memories: worth a new roof.

'I know you still go to visit him,' he said. 'The nurses tell me. So you must have seen the place growing threadbare.'

I nodded, thinking about it. 'They used to have huge vases of fresh flowers everywhere.'

'They used to have top quality everything, but they've had to compromise to patch up the building. Country houses are open money drains when they age. I can't see the place outliving Robin, really. You will look after him, when I've gone?'

'Yes,' I said.

He nodded, taking it for granted. 'I appointed you his trustee when I set up the fund for him, do you remember? I've not altered it.'

I was glad that he hadn't. At least, somewhere, obscurely, things had remained the same between us.

'Why don't we go and see him tomorrow?' he said. 'No one will kill me there.'

'All right,' I agreed: so we went in the hired car in the morning, stopping in the local town to buy presents of chocolate and simple toys designed for three-year-olds, and I added a packet of balloons to the pile while Malcolm paid.

'Does he like balloons?' he asked, his eyebrows rising.

'He gets frustrated sometimes. I blow the balloons up, and he bursts them.'

Malcolm looked surprised and in some ways disturbed. 'I didn't know he could feel frustration.'

'It seems like that. As if sometimes he half remembers us . . . but can't quite.'

'Poor boy.'

We drove soberly onwards and up the drive of the still splendid-looking Georgian house which lay mellow and symmetrical in the autumn sunshine. Inside, its near fifty rooms had been adapted and transformed in the heyday of private medicine into a highly comfortable hospital for mostly chronic, mostly old, mostly rich patients. Short-stay patients came and went, usually convalescing after major operations performed elsewhere, but in general one saw the same faces month after month: the same faces ageing, suffering, waiting for release. Dreadfully depressing, I found it, but for Robin, it was true, it seemed the perfect haven, arrived at after two unsuccessful stays in more apparently suitable homes involving other children, bright colours, breezy nurses and jollying atmospheres. Robin seemed better with peace, quiet and no demands, and Malcolm had finally acted against professional advice to give them to him.

Robin had a large room on the ground floor with French doors opening on to a walled garden. He seldom went out into the garden, but he preferred the doors open in all weathers, including snow-storms. Apart from that, he was docile and easy to deal with, and if anyone had speculated on the upheavals that might happen soon if puberty took its natural course, they hadn't mentioned it in my hearing.

He looked at us blankly, as usual. He seldom spoke, though he did retain the ability to make words: it was just that he seemed to have few thoughts to utter. Brain damage of that magnitude was idiosyncratic, we'd been told, resulting in behaviour individual to each victim. Robin spoke rarely and then only to himself, in private, when he didn't expect to be overheard: the nurses sometimes heard him, and had told us, but said he stopped as soon as he saw them.

I'd asked them what he said, but they didn't know, except for words like 'shoes' and 'bread' and 'floor': ordinary words. They didn't know why he wouldn't speak at other times. They were sure, though, that he understood a fair amount of what others said, even if in a haze.

We gave him some pieces of chocolate which he ate,

and unwrapped the toys for him which he fingered but didn't play with. He looked at the balloon packet without emotion. It wasn't a frustration day: on those, he looked at the packet and made blowing noises with his mouth.

We sat with him for quite a while, talking, telling him who we were while he wandered around the room. He looked at our faces from time to time, and touched my nose once with his finger as if exploring that I was really there, but there was no connection with our minds. He looked healthy, good looking, a fine boy: heart-breaking, as always.

A nurse came in the end, middle-aged, kind-faced, to take him to a dining room for lunch, and Malcolm and I transferred to the office where my father was given a saviour's welcome and offered a reviving scotch.

'Your son, slow progress, I'm afraid.' Earnest, dedicated people.

Malcolm nodded. No progress would have been more accurate.

'We do our best for him always.'

'Yes, I know.' Malcolm drank the scotch, shook their hands, made our farewells. We left, as I always left, in sadness, silence and regret.

'So bloody unfair,' Malcolm said halfway back to London. 'He ought to be laughing, talking, roaring through life.'

'Yes.'

'I can't bear to see him, and I can't bear not to. I'd give all my money to have him well again.'

'And make a new fortune afterwards,' I said.

'Well, yeah, why not?' He laughed, but still with gloom. 'It would have been better if he'd died with the others. Life's a bugger, sometimes, isn't it?'

The gloom lasted back to the Savoy and through the next bottle of Bollinger, but by afternoon Malcolm was complaining of the inactivity I'd thrust upon him and wanting to visit cronies in the City. Unpredictability be our shield, I prayed, and kept my eyes open for speeding cars; but we saw the day out safely in offices, bars, clubs and a restaurant, during which time Malcolm increased his wealth by gambling a tenner at evens on the day's closing price of gold which fell by two pounds when the trend was upwards. 'It'll shoot right up next year, you watch.'

On Friday, despite my pleas for sanity, he insisted on accompanying me to Sandown Park races.

'You'll be safer here,' I protested, 'in the suite.'

'I shan't *feel* safer.'

'At the races, I can't stay beside you.'

'Who's to know I'll be there?'

I gazed at him. 'Anyone who guesses we are now together could know. They'll know how to find *me*, if they look in the papers.'

'Then don't go.'

'I'm going. You stay here.'

I saw, however, that the deep underlying apprehension which he tried to suppress most of the time would erupt into acute nervous anxiety if I left him alone in the suite for several hours, and that he might, out of boredom, do something much sillier than going to the races, like convincing himself that anyone in his family would keep a secret if he asked it.

Accordingly I drove him south of London and took him through the jockeys' entrance gate to the weighing room area where he made his afternoon a lot safer by meeting yet another crony and being instantly invited to lunch in the holy of holies.

'Do you have cronies all over the world?' I asked.

'Certainly,' he said, smiling broadly. 'Anyone I've known for five minutes is a crony, if I get on with them.'

I believed him. Malcolm wasn't easy to forget, nor was he hard to like. I saw the genuine pleasure in his immediate host's face as they walked away together, talking, and reflected that Malcolm would have been a success in whatever career he had chosen, that success was part of his character, like generosity, like headlong rashness.

I was due to ride in the second race, a steeplechase for amateurs, and as usual had arrived two prudent hours in advance. I turned away from watching Malcolm and looked around for the owner of the horse I was about to partner, and found my path blocked by a substantial lady in a wide brown cape. Of all the members of the family, she was the last I would have expected to see on a racecourse.

'Ian,' she said accusingly, almost as if I'd been pretending to be someone else.

'Hello.'

'Where have you been? Why don't you answer your telephone?'

Lucy, my elder half-sister. Lucy, the poet.

Lucy's husband Edwin was, as always, to be found at her side, rather as if he had no separate life. The leech, Malcolm had called him unkindly in the past. From a Bugg to a leech.

Lucy was blessed with an unselfconsciousness about her weight which stemmed both from unworldliness and an overbelief in health foods. 'But nuts and raisins are *good* for you,' she would say, eating them by the kilo. 'Bodily vanity, like intellectual arrogance, is a sickness of the soul.'

She was forty-two, my sister, with thick straight brown hair uncompromisingly cut, large brown eyes, her mother's high cheek-bones and her father's strong nose. She was as noticeable in her own way as Malcolm was himself, and not only because of her shapeless clothes and dedicated absence of cosmetics. Malcolm's vitality ran in her too, though in different directions, expressing itself in vigour of thought and language.

I had often, in the past, wondered why someone as talented and strongminded as she shouldn't have made a marriage of equal minds, but in recent years had come to think she had settled for a nonentity like Edwin because the very absence of competition freed her to be wholly herself.

'Edwin is concerned,' she said, 'that Malcolm is leaving his senses.'

For Edwin, read Lucy, I thought. She had a trick of ascribing her own thoughts to her husband if she thought they would be unwelcome to her audience.

Edwin stared at me uneasily. He was a good-looking man in many ways, but mean spirited, which if one were tolerant one would excuse because of the perpetual knife-edge state of his and Lucy's finances. I wasn't certain any more whether it was he who had actually failed to achieve employment, or whether Lucy had in some way stopped him from trying. In any event, she earned more prestige than lucre for her writing, and Edwin had grown tired of camouflaging the frayed elbows of his jackets with oval patches of thin leather badly sewn on.

Edwin's concern, it seemed, was real enough although if it had been his alone they wouldn't have come.

'It isn't fair of him,' he said, meaning Malcolm. 'Lucy's trust fund was set up years ago before inflation and doesn't stretch as far as it used to. He really ought to put that right. I've told him so several times, and he simply ignores me. And now he's throwing his money away in this profligate way as if his heirs had no rights at all.' Indignation shook in his voice, along with, I could see, a very definite fear of a rocky future if the fortune he'd counted on for so long should be snatched away in the last furlong, so to speak.

I sighed and refrained from saying that I thought that Malcolm's heirs had no rights while he was alive. I said merely, soothingly, 'I'm sure he won't let you starve.'

'That's not the point,' Edwin said with thin fury. 'The point is that he's given an *immense* amount of money to Lucy's old college to establish post-graduate scholarships for poets.'

I looked from his pinch-lipped agitated mouth to Lucy's face and saw shame where there should perhaps have been pride. Shame, I thought, because she found herself sharing Edwin's views when they ran so contrary to her normal disdain for materialism. Perhaps even Lucy, I thought, had been looking forward to a comfortably off old age.

'You should be honoured,' I said.

She nodded unhappily. 'I am.'

'No,' Edwin said. 'It's disgraceful.'

'The Lucy Pembroke Scholarships,' I said slowly.

'Yes. How did you know?' Lucy asked.

And there would be the Serena Pembroke Scholarships, of course. And the Coochie Pembroke Memorial Challenge Trophy . . .

'What are you smiling at?' Lucy demanded. 'You can't say you've made much of a success of your life so far, can you? If Malcolm leaves us all nothing, you'll end up carting horse-muck until you drop from senility.'

'There are worse jobs,' I said mildly.

There were horses around us, and racecourse noises, and a skyful of gusty fresh air. I could happily spend my life, I knew, in almost any capacity that took me to places like Sandown Park.

'You've wasted every talent you have,' Lucy said.

'My only talent is riding horses.'

'You're blind and stupid. You're the only male Pembroke with decent brains and you're too lazy to use them.'

'Well, thanks,' I said.

'It's not a compliment.'

'No, so I gathered.'

'Joyce says you're sure to know where Malcolm is as you've finally made up your quarrel, though you'll lie about it as a matter of course,' Lucy said. 'Joyce said you would be here today on this spot at this time, if I wanted to reach you.'

'Which you did, rather badly.'

'Don't be so obtuse. You've got to stop him. You're the only one who can, and Joyce says you're probably the only one who won't try . . . and you *must* try, Ian, and succeed, if not for yourself, then for the rest of the family.'

'For you?' I asked.

'Well . . .' She couldn't openly abandon her principles, but they were bending, it seemed. 'For the others,' she said stalwartly.

I looked at her with new affection. 'You're a hypocrite, my dear sister,' I said.

In smarting retaliation, she said sharply, 'Vivien thinks you're trying to cut the rest of us out and ingratiate yourself again with Malcolm.'

'I expect she would,' I said. 'I expect Alicia will think it also, when Vivien has fed it to her.'

'You really are a bastard.'

'No,' I said, my lips twitching, 'that's Gervase.'

'*Ian!*'

I laughed. 'I'll tell Malcolm you're concerned. I promise I will, somehow. And now I've got to change my clothes and ride in a race. Are you staying?'

Lucy hesitated but Edwin said, 'Will you win?'

'I don't think so. Save your money.'

'You're not taking it seriously,' Lucy said.

I looked straight at her eyes. 'Believe me,' I said, 'I take it very seriously indeed. No one had a right to murder Moira to stop her taking half Malcolm's money. No one has a right to murder Malcolm to stop him spending it. He is fair. He will leave us all provided for, when the time comes, which I hope may be twenty years from now. You tell them all to stop fretting, to ease off, to have faith. Malcolm is teasing you all and I think it's dangerous, but he is dismayed by everyone's greed, and is determined to teach us a lesson. So you tell them, Lucy, tell Joyce and Vivien and everyone, that the more we try to grab, the less we will get. The more we protest, the more he will spend.'

She looked back silently. Eventually she said, 'I am ashamed of myself.'

'Rubbish,' Edwin said to me vehemently. 'You must stop Malcolm. You must.'

Lucy shook her head. 'Ian's right.'

'Do you mean Ian won't even try?' Edwin demanded incredulously.

'I'm positive he won't,' Lucy said. 'Didn't you hear what he said? Weren't you listening?'

'It was all rubbish.'

Lucy patted my arm. 'We may as well see you race, while we're here. Go and get changed.'

It was a more sisterly gesture and tone than I was used to, and I reflected with a shade of guilt that I'd paid scant attention to her own career for a couple of years.

'How is the poetry going?' I asked. 'What are you working on?'

The question caught her unprepared. Her face went momentarily blank and then filled with what seemed to be an odd mixture of sadness and panic.

'Nothing just now,' she said. 'Nothing for quite a while,' and I nodded almost apologetically as if I had intruded, and went into the weighing room and through to the changing room reflecting that poets, like mathematicians, mostly did their best work when young. Lucy wasn't writing; had maybe stopped altogether.

And perhaps, I thought, the frugality she had for so long embraced had begun to seem less worthy and less worth it, if she were losing the inner sustaining comfort of creative inspiration.

Poor Lucy, I thought. Life could be a bugger, as Malcolm said. She had already begun to value the affluence she had long despised or she wouldn't have come on her mission to Sandown Park, and I could only guess at the turmoil in her spiritual life. Like a nun losing her faith, I thought. But no, not a nun. Lucy, who had written explicitly of sex in a way I could never believe had anything to do with Edwin (though one could be wrong), wouldn't ever have been a nun.

With such random thoughts, I took off my ordinary clothes and put on white breeches and a scarlet jersey with blue stripes on the sleeves, and felt the usual battened-down excitement which made me breathe deeply and feel intensely happy. I rode in about fifty races a year, if I was lucky . . . and I would have to get another job fairly soon, I reflected, if I were to ride exercise regularly and stay fit enough to do any good.

Going outside, I talked for a while to the trainer and owner of the horse I was to ride, a husband and wife who had themselves ridden until twenty years earlier in point-to-point races and who liked to re-live it all vicariously through me. The husband, George, was now a public trainer on a fairly grand scale, but the wife, Jo, still preferred to run her own horses in amateur races. She currently owned three steeplechasers, all pretty good. It did me no harm at all to be seen on them and to be associated in racing minds with that stable.

'Young Higgins is jumping out of his skin,' Jo said.

Young Higgins was the name of that day's horse. Young Higgins was thirteen, a venerable gentleman out to disprove rumours of retirement. We all interpreted 'jumping out of his skin' as meaning fit, sound and pricking his ears with enthusiasm, and at his age one couldn't ask for much more. Older horses than he had won the Grand National, but Young Higgins and I had fallen in the great race the only time we'd tried it, and to my regret Jo had decided on no more attempts.

'We'll see you in the parade ring, then, Ian, before the race,' George said, and Jo added, 'And give the old boy a good time.'

I nodded, smiling. Giving all of us a good time was the point of the proceedings. Young Higgins was definitely included.

The minute George and Jo turned away to go off towards the grandstands, someone tapped me on the back of the shoulder. I turned round to see who it was and to my total astonishment found myself face to face with Lucy's older brother, Malcolm's first child, my half-brother Donald.

'Good heavens,' I said. 'You've never been to the races in your life.'

He often told me he hadn't, saying rather superciliously that he didn't approve of the sordid gambling.

'I haven't come for the races,' he said crossly. 'I've come to see you about Malcolm's taking leave of his senses.'

'How . . . er . . .?' I stopped. 'Did Joyce send you?' I said.

'What if she did? We are all concerned. She told us where to find you, certainly.'

'Did she tell the whole family?' I asked blankly.

'How do I know? She telephoned us. I daresay she telephoned everyone she could get hold of. You know what she's like. She's your mother, after all.'

Even so late in his life, he couldn't keep out of his voice the old resentments, and perhaps also, I reflected, they were intensifying with age. My mother had supplanted his, he was saying, and any indiscretion my mother ever committed was in some way my fault. He had thought in that illogical way for as long as I'd been aware of him, and nothing had changed.

Donald was, in the family's opinion, the brother nearest in looks to myself, and I wasn't sure I liked it. Irrefutably, he was the same height and had blue eyes less intense in colour than Malcolm's. Agreed, Donald had middling brown curly hair and shoulders wider than his hips. I didn't wear a bushy moustache though, and I just hoped I didn't walk with what I thought of as a self-important strut; and I sometimes tried to make sure, after I'd been in Donald's company, that I absolutely didn't.

Donald's life had been so disrupted when Malcolm

had ousted Vivien, Donald always told us, that he had never been able to decide properly on a career. It couldn't have been easy, I knew, to survive such an upheaval, but Donald had only been nine at the time, a bit early for life decisions. In any event, as an adult he had drifted from job to job in hotels, coming to harbour at length as secretary of a prestigious golf club near Henley-on-Thames, a post which I gathered had proved ultimately satisfactory in social standing, which was very important to his self-esteem.

I didn't either like or dislike Donald particularly. He was eleven years older than I was. He was *there.*

'Everyone insists you stop Malcolm squandering the family money,' he said, predictably.

'It's *his* money, not the family's,' I said.

'What?' Donald found the idea ridiculous. 'What you've got to do is explain that he owes it to us to keep the family fortune intact until we inherit it. Unfortunately we know he won't listen to any of us except you, and now that you appear to have made up your quarrel with him, you are elected to be our spokesman. Joyce thinks we have to convince you first of the need to stop Malcolm, but I told her it was ridiculous. You don't need convincing, you want to be well off one day just the same as the rest of us, of course you do, it's only natural.'

I was saved from both soul-searching and untrue disclaimers by the arrival of Helen, Donald's wife, who had apparently been buying a racecard.

'We're not staying,' Donald said disapprovingly, eyeing it.

She gave him a vague smile. 'You never know,' she said.

Beautiful and brainless, Malcolm had said of her, and perhaps he was right. Tall and thin, she moved with natural style and made cheap clothes look expensive: I knew they were cheap because she had a habit of saying where they'd come from and how much she'd paid for them, inviting admiration of her thriftiness. Donald always tried to shut her up.

'Do tell us where to watch the races from,' she said.

'We're not here for that,' Donald said.

'No, dear, we're here because we need money now that the boys have started at Eton.'

'No, dear,' Donald said sharply.

'But you know we can't afford . . .'

'Do be quiet, dear,' Donald said.

'Eton costs a bomb,' I said mildly, knowing that Donald's income would hardly stretch to one son there, let alone two. Donald had twin boys, which seemed to run in the family.

'Of course it does,' Helen said, 'but Donald puts such store by it. "My sons are at Eton," that sort of thing. Gives him *standing* with the people he deals with in the golf club.'

'Helen, dear, do be quiet.' Donald's embarrassment showed, but she was undoubtedly right.

'We thought Donald might have inherited before the

boys reached thirteen,' she said intensely. 'As he hasn't, we're borrowing every penny we can to pay the fees, the same as we borrowed for the prep school and a lot of other things. But we've borrowed against Donald's expectations . . . so you see it's essential for us that there really is plenty to inherit, as there are so many people to share it with. We'll be literally bankrupt if Malcolm throws too much away . . . and I don't think Donald could face it.'

I opened my mouth to answer her but no sound came out. I felt as if I'd been thrust into a farce over which I had no control.

Walking purposefully to join us came Serena, Ferdinand and Debs.

CHAPTER SIX

'Stay right here,' I said to all of them. 'I have to go into the weighing room to deal with a technicality. Stay right here until I come out.'

They nodded with various frowns, and I dived into privacy in a desperate search for a sheet of paper and an envelope.

I wrote to Malcolm:

> Half the family have turned up here, sent by Joyce. For God's sake stay where you are, keep out of sight and wait until I come to fetch you.

I stuck the note into the envelope, wrote Malcolm's name on the outside, and sought out an official who had enough rank to send someone to deliver it.

'My father is lunching in the Directors' dining room,' I said. 'And it's essential that he gets this note immediately.'

The official was obliging. He was going up to the Stewards' room anyway, he said, and he would take it himself. With gratitude and only a minor lessening of despair – because it would be just like Malcolm to come down contrarily to confront the whole bunch – I went out again into the sunlight and found the five of them still faithfully waiting exactly where I'd left them.

'I say,' Debs said, half mocking, 'you do look dashing in all that kit.'

Donald looked at her in surprise, and I had a vivid impression of his saying soon in his golf club, 'My brother, the amateur jockey . . .' knowing that if I'd been a professional he would have hushed it up if he could. A real snob, Donald: but there were worse sins.

Debs, Ferdinand's second wife, had come to the races in a black leather coat belted at the waist, with shoulder-length blonde hair above and long black boots below. Her eyelids were purple, like her fingernails. The innocence I'd photographed in her a year ago was in danger of disappearing.

Ferdinand, shorter than Debs and more like Malcolm than ever, appeared to be in his usual indecision over whether I was to be loved or hated. I smiled at him cheerfully and asked what sort of a journey he'd had.

'A lot of traffic,' he said lamely.

'We didn't come here to talk about traffic,' Serena said forbiddingly. 'We want to know where Daddy is.'

Malcolm's little Serena, now taller than he, was dressed that day in royal blue with white frills at neck and wrists, a white woollen hat with a pompom on top covering her cap of fair hair. She looked a leggy sixteen, not ten years older. Her age showed only in the coldness of her manner towards me, which gave no sign of thawing.

In her high-pitched, girlish voice she said, 'We want him to settle very substantial sums on us all right now. Then he can go to blazes with the rest.'

I blinked. 'Who are you quoting?' I asked.

'Myself,' she said loftily, and then more probably added, 'Mummy too. And Gervase.'

It had Gervase's thuggish style stamped all over it.

Donald and Helen looked distinctly interested in the proposal. Ferdinand and Debs had of course heard it before.

'Gervase thinks it's the best solution,' Ferdinand said, nodding.

I doubted very much that Malcolm would agree, but said only, 'I'll pass on your message next time he gets in touch with me.'

'But Joyce is sure you know where he is,' Donald objected.

'Not exactly,' I said. 'Do you know that Lucy and Edwin are here too?'

They were satisfactorily diverted, looking over their shoulders to see if they could spot them in the growing crowds.

'Didn't Joyce tell you she was sending so many of you here?' I asked generally, and it was Ferdinand, sideways, his face turned away, who answered.

'She told Serena to come here. She told Serena to tell me, which she did, so we came together. I didn't know about Donald and Helen or Lucy and Edwin. I expect she wanted to embarrass you.'

His eyes swivelled momentarily to my face, wanting to see my reaction. I don't suppose my face showed any. Joyce might call me 'darling' with regularity but could be woundingly unkind at the same time, and I'd had a lifetime to grow armour.

Ferdinand happened to be standing next to me. I said on impulse into his ear, 'Ferdinand, who killed Moira?'

He stopped looking for Lucy and Edwin and transferred his attention abruptly and wholly to me. I could see calculations going on in the pause before he answered, but I had no decoder for his thoughts. He was the most naturally congenial to me of all my brothers, yet the others were open books compared with him. He was secretive, as perhaps I was myself. He had wanted to build his own kitchen-wall hidey-hole when I'd built mine, only Malcolm had said we must share, that one was enough. Ferdinand had sulked and shunned me for a while, and smirked at Gervase's dead rats. I wondered to what extent people remained the same as they'd been when very young: whether it was safe to assume they hadn't basically changed, to believe that if one could peel back the layers of living one would come to the known child. I wanted Ferdinand to be as I had known him at ten, eleven, twelve

– a boy dedicated to riding a bicycle while standing on his head on the saddle – and not in a million years a murderer.

'I don't know who killed Moira,' he said finally. 'Alicia says you did. She told the police it *had* to be you.'

'I couldn't have.'

'She says the police could break your alibi if they really tried.'

I knew that they had really tried: they'd checked every separate five minutes of my day, and their manner and their suspicions had been disturbing.

'And what do *you* think?' I asked curiously.

His eyelids flickered. 'Alicia says . . .'

I said abruptly, 'Your mother says too damned much. Can't you think for yourself?'

He was offended, as he would be. He hooked his arms through those of Debs and Serena and made an announcement. 'We three are going to have a drink and a sandwich. If you fall off and kill yourself, no one will miss you.'

I smiled at him, though his tone had held no joke.

'And don't be so bloody forgiving,' he said.

He whirled the girls away from me and marched them off. I wondered how he'd got the day off from work, though I supposed most people could if they tried. He was a statistician, studying to be an actuary in his insurance company. What were the probabilities, I wondered, of a thirty-two-year-old statistician whose wife had purple fingernails being present when his brother broke his neck at Sandown Park?

Donald and Helen said that they too would run a sandwich to earth (Donald's words) and Helen added earnestly that *she* would care that I finished the race safely, whatever Ferdinand said.

'Thanks,' I said, hoping I could believe her, and went back into the changing room for an interval of thought.

Lucy and Edwin might leave before the end of the afternoon, and so might Donald and Helen, but Ferdinand wouldn't. He liked going racing. He'd said on one mellow occasion that he'd have been quite happy being a bookmaker; he was lightning fast at working out relative odds.

The problem of how to extract Malcolm unseen from the racecourse didn't end, either, with those members of the family I'd talked to. If they were all so certain I knew where Malcolm was, one of the others, more cunning, could be hiding behind trees, waiting to follow me when I left.

There were hundreds of trees in Sandown Park.

The first race came and went, and in due course I went out to partner Young Higgins in the second.

Jo as usual had red cheeks from pleasure and hope. George was being gruffly businesslike, also as usual, telling me to be especially careful at the difficult first fence and to go easy up the hill past the stands the first time.

I put Malcolm out of my mind, and also murder,

and it wasn't difficult. The sky was a clear distant blue, the air crisp with the coming of autumn. The leaves on all those trees were yellowing, and the track lay waiting, green and springy, with the wide fences beckoning to be flown. Simple things; and out there one came starkly face to face with oneself, which I mostly found more exhilarating than frightening. So far, anyway.

Jo said, 'Only eight runners, just a perfect number,' and George said, as he always did, 'Don't lie too far back coming round the last long bend.'

I said I would try not to.

Jo's eyes were sparkling like a child's in her sixty-year-old face, and I marvelled that she had never in all that time lost the thrill of expectation in moments like these. There might be villains at every level in horse racing, but there were also people like Jo and George whose goodness and goodwill shone out like search-lights, who made the sport overall good fun and wholesome.

Life and death might be serious in the real world, but life and death on a fast steeplechaser on a Friday afternoon in the autumn sunshine was a lighthearted toss-up, an act of health on a sick planet.

I fastened the strap of my helmet, was thrown up on Young Higgins and rode him out onto the track. Perhaps if I'd been a professional and ridden up to ten times as often I would have lost the swelling joy that that moment always gave me: one couldn't grin like a maniac, even to oneself, at a procession of bread-and-butter rides on cold days, sharp tracks, bad horses.

Young Higgins was living up to his name, bouncing on his toes and tossing his head in high spirits. We lined up with the seven others, all of whose riders I happened to know from many past similar occasions. Amateurs came in all guises: there was a mother, an aunt and a grandfather riding that afternoon, besides a journalist, an earl's son, a lieutenant colonel, a showjumper and myself. From the stands, only a keen eye could have told one from the other without the guidance of our colours, and that was what amateur racing was all about: the equality, the levelling anonymity of the starting gate.

The tapes went up and we set off with three miles to go, almost two whole circuits, twenty-two jumps and an uphill run to the winning post.

The aunt's horse, too strong for her, took hold of the proceedings and opened up an emphatic lead, which no one else bothered to cut down. The aunt's horse rushed into the difficult downhill first fence and blundered over it, which taught him a lesson and let his rider recover control, and for about a mile after that there were no dramatic excitements. The first race I'd ever ridden in had seemed to pass in a whirling heaving flurry leaving me breathless and exhausted, but time had stretched out with experience until one could watch and think and even talk.

'Give me room, blast you,' shouted the lieutenant colonel on one side of me.

'Nice day,' said the earl's son chattily on the other, always a clown who enlivened his surroundings.

'Shift your *arse*!' yelled the mother to her horse, giving him a crack round that part of his anatomy. She was a good rider, hated slow horses, hated not to win, weighed a muscular ten stone and was scornful of the showjumper, whom she had accused often of incompetence.

The showjumper, it was true, liked to set his horse right carefully before jumps, as in the show ring, and hadn't managed to speed up in the several steeplechase races he'd ridden so far. He wasn't in consequence someone to follow into a fence and I avoided him whenever possible.

The journalist was the best jockey in the race, a professional in all but status, and the grandfather was the worst but full of splendid reckless courage. More or less in a bunch, the whole lot of us came round the bottom bend and tackled the last three jumps of the first circuit. The aunt was still in front, then came the lieutenant colonel, myself and the earl's son in a row, then the mother just behind, with the showjumper and the grandfather beside her. I couldn't see the journalist: somewhere in the rear, no doubt, biding his wily time.

The lieutenant colonel's mount made a proper hash of the last of the three fences, jogging both of his rider's feet out of the irons and tipping the military backside into the air somewhere in the region of the horse's mane. Landing alongside and gathering my reins, I saw that the lieutenant colonel's balance was hopelessly progressing down the horse's galloping shoulder as he fought without success to pull himself back into the saddle.

I put out an arm, grasped his jersey and yanked him upwards and backwards, shifting his disastrous centre of gravity into a more manageable place and leaving him slowing and bumping in my wake as he sat down solidly in the saddle, trying to put his feet back into his flying stirrups, which was never very easy at thirty miles an hour.

He had breathing space to collect things going up the hill, though, as we all did, and we swept round the top bend and down to the difficult fence again with not much change in order from the first time.

Someone had once long ago pulled me back into the saddle in that same way: it was fairly common in jump racing. Someone had also once tipped me straight into the air with an upward wrench of my heel, but that was another story. The lieutenant colonel was saying 'Thanks' and also 'Move over, you're crowding me,' more or less in the same breath.

After crossing the water jump for the second time over on the far side of the track, the showjumper made a spurt to the front and then slowed almost to a standstill on landing over the next fence, having jumped especially pedantically, and the aunt crashed into the back of him with some singularly un-aunt-like language.

'Lovely lady,' said the earl's son, appreciatively, as we passed the débâcle. 'How are you going yourself?'

'Not bad,' I said. 'How are you?'

We jumped the last of the seven far-side fences together and in front, and put all our energies into staying there round the long last bend and over the three last fences. I could hear horses thudding behind me and the mother's voice exhorting her slowcoach. Approaching the Pond fence, I could sense the earl's son's horse beginning to tire, I could see that precious winning post far ahead and the way to it clear, and for at least a few moments I thought I might win. But then the lieutenant colonel reappeared fast at my elbow, still shouting for room, and between the last two fences, as I'd feared he would, the journalist materialized from the outback and made it look easy, and Young Higgins tired into Middle-Aged Higgins on the hill.

He and I finished third, which wasn't too bad, with the earl's son, persevering, not far away fourth.

'A nice afternoon out,' he said happily as we trotted back together, and I looked at the lights in his eyes and saw it was the same for him as for me, a high that one couldn't put into words, an adventure of body and spirit that made of dismounting and walking on the ground a literal coming down to earth.

Jo was pleased enough, patting Young Higgins hard.

'Ran a great race, didn't you, old boy? Jumped like a stag.'

'You'd have been second,' said George, who had good binoculars, 'if you'd let the lieutenant colonel fall off.'

'Yeah, well,' I said, unbuckling the girths, 'there were a lot of hooves down there.'

George smiled. 'Don't forget to weigh in.' (He said it every time.) 'Come for a drink in the Owners' bar when you've changed.'

I accepted. It was part of the ritual, part of the bargain. They liked to re-live Young Higgins' outing fence for fence in return for having given me the ride. They were still standing in the unsaddling enclosure talking to friends when I went out again in street clothes, and with welcoming smiles waved me into their group. None of my own family being in sight, I went with them without problems and, over glasses of Jo's favourite brandy and ginger ale, earned my afternoon's fun by describing it.

I returned to the weighing room area afterwards and found that not only were all the same family members still on the racecourse, but that they had coalesced into an angry swarm and had been joined by one of the queen bees herself, my mother Joyce.

Joyce, in fur and a green hat, was a rinsed blonde with greenish eyes behind contact lenses which seldom missed a trick in life as in cards. Dismayed but blank-faced, I gave her a dutiful peck on her smooth cheek which, it seemed, she was in no mood to receive.

'Darling,' she said, the syllables sizzling with displeasure, 'did you or did you not send that weasel Norman West to check up on my whereabouts last Friday?'

'Er,' I said.

'Did you or did you not send him sniffing round Vivien on the same errand?'

'Well,' I said, half smiling, 'I wouldn't have put it as crudely, but I suppose so, yes.'

The battery of eyes from the others was as friendly as napalm.

'Why?' Joyce snapped.

'Didn't Norman West tell you?'

She said impatiently, 'He said something nonsensical about Malcolm being attacked. I told him if Malcolm had been attacked, I would have heard of it.'

'Malcolm was very nearly killed,' I said flatly. 'He and I asked Norman West to make sure that none of you could have done it.'

Joyce demanded to be told what had happened to Malcolm, and I told her. She and all the others listened with open mouths and every evidence of shock, and if there was knowledge, not ignorance, behind any of the horrified eyes, I couldn't discern it.

'Poor Daddy!' Serena exclaimed. 'How *beastly*.'

'A matter for the police,' Donald said forcefully.

'I agree,' I said. 'I'm surprised they haven't been to see all of you already, as they did when Moira died.'

Edwin said, with a shake of the head, 'How near, how near,' and then, hearing the regret in his voice as clearly as I did, added hurriedly, 'What a blessing he woke up.'

'When the police make their enquiries,' I said, 'they don't exactly report the results to Malcolm. He wants to make sure for himself that none of the family was at Quantum last Friday afternoon. If you cooperate with Norman West when he gets to you, you'll set Malcolm's mind at rest.'

'And what if we can't prove where we were?' Debs asked.

'Or even remember?' Lucy said.

'Malcolm will have to live with it,' Joyce said crisply.

'Living with it would present him less problem,' I said dryly. 'It's dying he wants to avoid.'

They stared at me in silence. The reality of Moira's murder had been to them, I guessed, as to me, a slow-burning fuse, with seemingly no bad consequences at first, but with accelerating worries as time passed. Perhaps they, as I had done, had clung to the motive-less-intruder-from-outside theory at first because the alternative was surely unthinkable, but in the weeks since then, they must at least have begun to wonder. The fuse would heat soon into active suspicions, I saw, which might tear apart and finally scatter for ever the fragile family fabric.

Would I mind, I thought? Not if I still had Malcolm . . . and perhaps Ferdinand . . . and Joyce . . . and maybe Lucy, or Thomas . . . Serena . . . would I care if I never again laid eyes on Gervase?

The answer, surprisingly enough, was yes, I would mind. Imperfect, quarrelsome, ramshackle as it was, the family were origins and framework, the geography of living. Moira, ungrieved, was already rewriting that map, and if her murderer remained for ever undiscovered, if Malcolm himself – I couldn't think of it – were killed, there would be no healing, no reforming, no telephone network for information, no contact, just a lot of severed galaxies moving inexorably apart.

The big bang, I thought, still lay ahead. The trick was to smother the fuse before the explosion, and that was all very well, but where was the burning point, and how long had we got?

'Buy me a drink, darling,' Joyce commanded. 'We're in deep trouble.'

She began to move off, but the others showed no signs of following. I looked at the seven faces all expressing varying degrees of anxiety and saw them already begin to move slightly away from each other, not one cohesive group, but Donald and Helen as a couple, Lucy and Edwin, a pair, and Ferdinand, Debs and Serena, the youngest trio.

'I'll tell Malcolm your fears,' I said. 'And your needs.'

'Oh yes, please do,' Helen said intensely.

'And Gervase's plan,' Ferdinand added.

'Do come on, darling,' Joyce said peremptorily over her shoulder. 'Which way is the bar?'

'Run along, little brother,' Lucy said with irony. Serena said, 'Mumsie's waiting,' and Debs fairly tittered. I thought of sticking my toes in and making Joyce come back, but what did it matter? I could put up with the jibes, I'd survived them for years, and I understood what prompted them. I shrugged ruefully and went after Joyce, and could feel the pitying smiles on the back of my neck.

I steered Joyce into the busy Members' bar which had a buffet table along one side with salads and breads and a large man in chef's clothes carving from turkeys, haunches of beef and hams on the bone. I was hungry after riding and offered Joyce food, but she waved away the suggestion as frivolity. I bought her instead a large vodka and tonic with a plain ginger ale for myself, and we found spare seats at a table in a far corner where, after the merest glance around to make sure she wouldn't be overheard among the general hubbub, she leaned forward until the brim of the green hat was practically touching my forehead and launched into her inquisition.

'Where is your father?' she said.

'When did you last see your father?' I amended.

'What on earth are you talking about?'

'That picture by Orchardson.'

'Stop playing games. Where is Malcolm?'

'I don't know,' I said.

'You're lying.'

'Why do you want to find him?'

'*Why?*' She was astonished. 'Because he's out of his mind.' She dug into her capacious handbag and brought out an envelope, which she thrust towards me. 'Read that.'

I opened the envelope and found a small piece of newspaper inside, a snipped paragraph without headline or provenance.

It said:

> Second-string British contender is Blue Clancy, second in last year's Derby and winner this year of Royal Ascot's King Edward VII Stakes. Owner Ramsey Osborn yesterday hedged his Arc bets by selling a half-share in his four-year-old colt to arbitrageur Malcolm Pembroke, who launched into bloodstock only this week with a two million guineas yearling at the Premium Sales.

Ouch, I thought.

'Where did it come from?' I asked.

'What does it matter where it came from? That new "Racing Patter" column in the *Daily Towncrier*, as a matter of fact. I was drinking coffee this morning when I read it and nearly choked. The point is, is it true?'

'Yes,' I said.

'*What*?'

'Yes,' I said again. 'Malcolm bought half of Blue Clancy. Why shouldn't he?'

'Sometimes,' my mother said forcefully, 'you are so stupid I could hit you.' She paused for breath. 'And what exactly is an arbitrageur?'

'A guy who makes money by buying low and selling high.'

'Oh. Gold.'

'And foreign currencies. And shares. And maybe racehorses.'

She was unmollified. 'You know perfectly well he's just throwing his money away to spite everybody.'

'He didn't like Moira being killed. He didn't like being attacked himself. I shouldn't think he'll stop spending until he knows whether we have or haven't a murderer in the family, and even then . . .' I smiled, 'he's getting a taste for it.'

Joyce stared. 'Moira was murdered by an intruder,' she said.

I didn't answer.

She took a large swallow of her vodka and tonic and looked at me bleakly. She had been barely twenty when I was born, barely nineteen when Malcolm had whisked her headlong from an antique shop in Kensington and within a month installed her in his house with a new wedding ring and too little to do.

Malcolm, telling me now and again about those days, had said, 'She understood figures, you see. And she could beat me at cards. And she looked so damned demure. So young. Not bossy at all, like she was later. Her people thought me an upstart, did you know? Their ancestors traced back to Charles II, mine traced back to a Victorian knife-grinder. But her people weren't rich, you know. More breeding than boodle. It was an impulse, marrying Joyce. There you are, I admit it. Turned out she didn't like sex much, more's the pity. Some women are like that. No hormones. So I went on seeing Alicia. Well, I would, wouldn't I? Joyce and I got on all right, pretty polite to each other and so on, until she found out about Alicia. Then we had fireworks, all hell let loose for months on end, do you remember? Don't suppose you remember, you were only four or five.'

'Five and six, actually.'

'Really? Joyce liked being mistress of the house, you know. She learned about power. Grew up, I suppose. She took up bridge seriously, and started voluntary work. She hated leaving all that, didn't much mind leaving me. She said Alicia had robbed her of her self-esteem and ruined her position in the local community. She's never forgiven her, has she?'

Joyce had returned to the small Surrey town where her parents had lived and later died, their social mantle falling neatly onto her able shoulders. She bullied the local people into good works, made continual bridge-tournament forays, earned herself a measure of celebrity, and no, had never forgiven Alicia.

In the bar at Sandown she was dressed, as always,

with a type of businesslike luxury: mink jacket over grey tailored suit, neat white silk shirt, long strings of pearls, high-heeled shoes, green felt hat, polished calf handbag. 'A well-dressed, well-bred, brassy blonde' Alicia had once called her, which was both accurate and unfair, as was Joyce's tart tit-for-tat opinion of Alicia as 'White meat of chicken aboard the gravy train'.

Joyce drank most of the rest of her vodka and said, 'Do you really think one of the family is capable of murder?'

'I don't know.'

'But *who*?'

'That's the question.'

'It isn't possible,' she insisted.

'Well,' I said. 'Take them one by one. Tell me why it's impossible in each individual case, according to each person's character. Start at the beginning, with Vivien.'

'No, Ian,' she protested.

'Yes,' I said. 'Help me. Help Malcolm. Help us all.'

She gave me a long worried look, oblivious to the movement and noise going on all around us. The next race was already in progress but without noticeable thinning of the crowd who were watching it on closed circuit television above our heads.

'Vivien,' I prompted.

'Impossible, just impossible. She's practically dim-witted. If she was ever going to murder anybody, it would have been long ago and it would have been Alicia. Alicia ruined Vivien's marriage, just like mine. Vivien's a sniffler, full of self-pity. And why would she do it? For those three wimpish offspring?'

'Perhaps,' I said. 'They all need money. She hasn't enough herself to bail them out of their holes.'

'It's still impossible.'

'All right,' I said. 'How about Donald? And Helen?'

Donald had been ten, more than half Joyce's age, when she had married Malcolm, and he had been in and out of Quantum, as had Lucy and Thomas, whenever Malcolm had exercised his joint-custody rights and had them to stay. Joyce's lack of interest in children had definitely extended to her step-children, whom she'd found noisy, bad tempered and foul mannered, though Malcolm disagreed.

'Donald's a pompous, snobbish ass,' she said now, 'and as insecure as hell under the bluster. Malcolm thinks Helen's as brainless as she's pretty, but I'd say you don't need brains to murder, rather the opposite. I'd think Helen would fight like a fury to save her cubs from physical harm. But Moira wasn't threatening her cubs, not directly. I'd think Helen could be only a hot-blood killer, but so could most people, driven hard enough to defend themselves or their young.'

I wondered if she knew about the school-fees crisis: if they hadn't directly told her, she had got them remarkably right.

'Lucy?' I said.

'Lucy thinks everyone is inferior to herself, especially if they have more money.'

Poor Lucy, I thought. 'And Edwin?' I said.

Joyce frowned. 'Edwin . . .'

'Edwin isn't impossible?' I asked.

'He never gets time off from running errands. Not enough time anyway for waiting around to catch Moira alone in her glass house.'

'But in character?'

'I don't know enough about him,' Joyce confessed. 'He yearns for money, that's for sure, and he's earned it, picking up after Lucy all these years. I don't know his impatience level.'

'All right then,' I said, 'what about Thomas?'

'Thomas!' Joyce's face looked almost sad. 'He wasn't as insufferable as Donald and Lucy when he was little. I liked him best of the three. But that damned Vivien screwed him up properly, didn't she? God knows why he married Berenice. She'll badger him into the grave before he inherits, and then where will she be?'

Joyce finished the vodka and said, 'I don't like doing this, Ian, and I'm stopping right here.'

Thomas, I thought. She wasn't sure about Thomas, and she doesn't want to say so. The analysis had all of a sudden come to an unwelcome, perhaps unexpected, abyss.

'Another drink?' I suggested.

'Yes. Gervase is drinking, did you know?'

'He always drinks.'

'Ursula telephoned me to ask for advice.'

'Did she really?' I was surprised. 'Why didn't she ask Alicia?'

'Ursula detests her mother-in-law,' Joyce said. 'We have that in common. Ursula and I have become quite good friends.'

Amazing, I thought, and stood up to fetch the refills.

Joyce's eyes suddenly widened in disbelief, looking beyond me.

'I knew you were lying,' she said bitterly. 'There's Malcolm.'

CHAPTER SEVEN

I turned, not knowing whether to be frightened or merely irritated.

Malcolm hadn't seen Joyce, and he wasn't looking for her or for me but solely for a drink. I made my way to the bar to meet him there and took him by the arm.

'Why aren't you bloody upstairs?' I said.

'I was outstaying my welcome, old chap. It was getting very awkward. They had an ambassador to entertain. I've been up there three bloody hours. Why didn't you come and fetch me?'

'Joyce,' I said grimly, 'is sitting over there in the corner. I am buying her a drink, and she saw you come in.'

'Joyce!' He turned round and spotted her as she looked balefully in our direction. 'Damn it.'

'Prowling around outside we also have Donald and Helen, Lucy and Edwin, Ferdinand and Debs, and Serena.'

'Christ,' he said. 'Hunting in pairs.'

'You may joke,' I said, 'and you may be right.'

'I couldn't stay up there. They were waiting for me to leave, too polite to tell me to go.'

He looked apprehensive, as well he might.

'Will Joyce tell them all that I'm here?'

'We'll see if we can stop it,' I said. 'What do you want to drink? Scotch?'

He nodded and I squeezed through the throng by the bar and eventually got served. He helped me carry the glasses and bottles back to the table, and sat where I'd been sitting, facing Joyce. I fetched another chair from nearby and joined my ever non-loving parents.

'Before you start shouting at each other,' I said, 'can we just take two things for granted? Joyce wants Malcolm to stop scattering largesse, Malcolm wants to go on living. Both ends are more likely to be achieved if we discover who murdered Moira, in case it is Moira's murderer who wishes also to kill Malcolm.' I paused. 'OK for logic?'

They both looked at me with the sort of surprise parents reserve for unexpected utterances from their young.

Malcolm said, 'Surely it's axiomatic that it's Moira's murderer who's trying to kill me?'

I shook my head. 'Ever heard of copycat crime?'

'My God,' he said blankly. 'One possible murderer in the family is tragedy. Two would be . . .'

'Statistically improbable,' Joyce said.

Malcolm and I looked at her with respect.

'She's right,' Malcolm said, sounding relieved, as if one killer were somehow more manageable than two.

'OK,' I agreed, wondering what the statistical probabilities really were, wondering whether Ferdinand could work them out, 'OK, the police failed to find Moira's murderer although they tried very hard and are presumably still trying . . .'

'Trying to link me with an assassin,' muttered Malcolm darkly.

'We might, as a family,' I said, 'have been able to overcome Moira's murder by making ourselves believe in the motiveless unknown outside-intruder theory . . .'

'Of course we believe it,' Joyce said faintly.

'Not now, we can't. Two unknown outside-intruder motiveless murders – because Malcolm was meant to die – are so statistically improbable as to be out of sight. The police haven't found Moira's murderer, but we have now got to try to do it ourselves. It's no longer safe not to, which is why we engaged Norman West.' I looked directly at Joyce. 'Stop fussing over what Malcolm is spending and start thinking of ways to save his life, if only so that he can make more money, which he can do, but only if he's alive.'

'Ian . . .' She was shocked.

'You roused the whole family this morning on the telephone, telling them where to find me, and now seven of them that we know of are here, and others may be who've kept out of sight. Much though we hate the idea, Moira's murderer may be here.'

'No, no,' Joyce exclaimed.

'Yes,' I said. 'Malcolm's primary defence against being murdered is staying out of reach of lethal instruments, which means people not knowing where to find him. Well, you, my darling mother, brought the whole pack here to the races, so now you'd better help Malcolm to leave before they catch him.'

'I didn't know he'd be here,' she protested.

'No, but he is. It's time to be practical.'

No one pointed out that if she *had* known he'd be there, she would have sent everyone with even more zeal.

'Do you have any ideas?' Malcolm asked me hopefully.

'Yes, I do. But we have to have Joyce's help, plus her promise of silence.'

My mother was looking less than her normal commanding self and gave assurances almost meekly.

'This is not a private bar,' I said, 'and if any of the family have bought Club passes, they may turn up in here at any moment, so we'd best lose no time. I'm going to leave you both here for a few minutes, but I'll be back. Stay in this corner. Whatever happens, stay right here. If the family find you, still stay here. OK?'

They both nodded, and I left them sitting and looking warily at each other in the first tête-à-tête they'd shared for many a long year.

I went in search of the overall catering director whom I knew quite well because one of his daughters rode against me regularly in amateur races, and found him by sending urgent messages via the manager of the Members' bar.

'Ian,' he said ten slow minutes later, coming to the bar from the back, where the bottles were, 'what's the trouble?'

He was a company director, head of a catering division, a capable man in his fifties, sprung from suburbia, upwardly mobile from merit, grown worldly wise.

I said the trouble was private, and he led me away from the crowds, through the back of the bar and into a small area of comparative quiet, out of sight of the customers.

My father, I told him, badly needed an immediate inconspicuous exit from the racecourse and wanted to know if a case of vintage Bollinger would ease his passage.

'Not skipping his bookie, I hope?' the caterer said laconically.

'No, he wants to elope with my mother, his ex-wife, from under the eyes of his family.'

The caterer, amused, agreed that Bollinger might be nice. He also laughed at my plan, told me to put it into operation, he would see it went well, and to look after his Rosemary whenever she raced.

I went back through the bar to collect Malcolm and to ask Joyce to fetch her car and to drive it to where the caterers parked their vans, giving her directions. The two of them were still sitting alone at the table, not exactly gazing into each other's eyes with rapture but at least not drawn apart in frost. They both seemed relieved at my reappearance, though, and Joyce picked up her handbag with alacrity to go to fetch her car.

'If you see any of the others,' I said, 'just say you're going home.'

'I wasn't born yesterday, darling,' she replied with reviving sarcasm. 'Run along and play games, and let me do my part.'

The game was the same one I'd thought of earlier in the changing-room, modified only by starting from a different point. It was just possible that the wrong eyes had spotted Malcolm in his brief passage outside from the exit door of the Directors' rooms to the entrance door of the bar, but even if so, I thought we could fool them.

In the quiet private space at the rear of the bar, the catering director was watching the large chef remove his white coat and tall hat.

'A case of vintage Bollinger for the caterer, a handout for the chef,' I murmured in Malcolm's ear. 'Get Joyce to drop you at a railway station, and I'll see you in the Savoy. Don't move until I get there.'

Malcolm, looking slightly dazed, put on the chef's coat and hat and pulled out his wallet. The chef looked delighted with the result and went back to slicing his turkeys in temporary shirtsleeves. Malcolm and the catering director left through the bar's rear door and set off together through the racecourse buildings to go outside to the area where the caterers' vans were parked. I waited quite a long anxious time in the bar, but eventually the catering director returned, carrying the white disguise, which he restored to its owner.

'Your father got off safely,' he assured me. 'He didn't see anyone he knew. What was it all about? Not really an elopement, was it?'

'He wanted to avoid being assassinated by his disapproving children.'

The caterer smiled, of course not believing it. I asked where he would like the fizz sent and he took out a business card, writing his private address on the back.

'Your father lunched with the Directors, didn't he?' he said. 'I thought I saw him up there.' His voice implied that doing favours for people who lunched with the Directors was doubly vouched for, like backing up a cheque with a credit card, and I did my best to reinforce further his perception of virtue.

'He's just bought a half share in an Arc de Triomphe runner,' I said. 'We're going over for the race.'

'Lucky you,' he said, giving me his card. He frowned suddenly, trying to remember. 'Didn't Rosemary tell me something about your father's present wife being pointlessly murdered some weeks ago? His late wife, I suppose I should say. Dreadful for him, dreadful.'

'Yes,' I said. 'Well . . . some people connected with

her turned up here today unexpectedly, and he wanted to escape meeting them.'

'Ah,' he said with satisfied understanding. 'In that case, I'm glad to have been of help.' He chuckled. 'They didn't really look like elopers.'

He shook my hand and went away, and with a couple of deep breaths I left the Members' bar and walked back to the weighing room to pick up my gear. There was still one more race to be run but it already felt like a long afternoon.

George and Jo were there when I came out carrying saddle, helmet, whip and holdall, saying they'd thought they'd catch me before I left.

'We've decided to run Young Higgins again two weeks tomorrow at Kempton,' Jo said. 'You'll be free for that, won't you?'

'Yes, indeed.'

'And Park Railings, don't forget, at Cheltenham next Thursday.'

'Any time, any place,' I said, and they laughed, conspirators in addiction.

It occurred to me as they walked away, looking back and waving, that perhaps I'd be in Singapore, Australia or Timbuktu next week or the week after; life was uncertain, and that was its seduction.

I saw none of the family on my way to the exit gate, and none between there and my car. With a frank sigh of relief, I stowed my gear in the boot and without much hurry set off towards Epsom, a detour of barely ten miles, thinking I might as well pick up my mail and listen to messages.

The telephone answering machine did have a faculty for listening to messages from afar, but it had never worked well, and I'd been too lazy to replace the remote controller which, no doubt, needed new batteries anyway.

With equally random thoughts I drove inattentively onwards, and it wasn't until I'd gone a fair distance that I realized that every time I glanced in the rear-view mirror I could see the same car two or three cars back. Some cars passed me: it never did, nor closed a gap to catch up.

I sat up, figuratively and literally, and thought, 'What do you know?' and felt my heart beat as at the starting gate.

What I didn't know was whose car it was. It looked much like the hired one I was driving, a middle-rank four-door in underwashed cream; ordinary, inconspicuous, no threat to Formula One.

Perhaps, I thought sensibly, the driver was merely going to Epsom, at my own pace, so at the next traffic lights I turned left into unknown residential territory, and kept on turning left at each crossroads thereafter, reasoning that in the end I would complete the circle and end up facing where I wanted to go. I didn't hurry nor continually look in the rear-view mirror, but when I was back again on a road – a different one – with signposts to Epsom, the similar car was still somewhere on my tail, glimpsed tucked in behind a van.

If he had only a minimal sense of direction, I thought, he would realize what I had done and guess I now knew he was following. On the other hand, the back roads between Sandown Park and Epsom were a maze, like most Surrey roads, and he might possibly not have noticed, or thought I was lost, or . . .

Catching at straws, I thought. Face facts. I knew he was there and he knew I knew and what should I do next?

We were already on the outskirts of Epsom and almost automatically I threaded my way round corners, going towards my flat. I had no reason not to, I thought. I wasn't leading my follower to Malcolm, if that was what he had in mind. I also wanted to find out who he was, and thought I might outsmart him through knowing some ingenious short cuts round about where I lived.

Many of the houses in that area, having been built in the thirties without garages, had cars parked permanently on both sides of the streets. Only purpose-built places, like my block of flats, had adequate parking, except for two or three larger houses converted to flats which had cars where once there had been lawns.

I drove on past my home down the narrow roadway and twirled fast into the driveway of one of the large houses opposite. That particular house had a narrow exit drive also into the next tree-lined avenue: I drove straight through fast, turned quickly, raced round two more corners and returned to my own road to come up behind the car which had been following me.

He was there, stopped, awkwardly half-parked in too small a space with his nose to the kerb, rear sticking out, brake lights still shining: indecision showing all over the place. I drew to a halt right behind him, blocking his retreat, put on my brakes, climbed out, took three or four swift strides and opened the door on the driver's side.

There was a stark moment of silence.

Then I said, 'Well, well, well,' and after that I nodded up towards my flat and said, 'Come on in,' and after that I said, 'If I'd known you were coming, I'd have baked a cake.'

Debs giggled. Ferdinand, who had been driving, looked sheepish. Serena, unrepentant, said, 'Is Daddy here?'

They came up to my flat where they could see pretty clearly that no, Daddy wasn't. Ferdinand looked down from the sitting room window to where his car was now parked beside mine in neat privacy, and then up at the backs of houses opposite over a nearby fence.

'Not much of a view,' he said disparagingly.

'I'm not here much.'

'You knew I was following you, didn't you?'

'Yes,' I said. 'Like a drink?'

'Well . . . scotch?'

I nodded and poured him some from a bottle in the cupboard.

'No ice,' he said, taking the glass. 'After that drive, I'll take it neat.'

'I didn't go fast,' I said, surprised.

'Your idea of fast and mine round those goddam twisty roads are about ten miles an hour different.'

The two girls were poking about in the kitchen and bedrooms and I could hear someone, Serena no doubt, opening doors and drawers in a search for residues of Malcolm.

Ferdinand shrugged, seeing my unconcern. 'He hasn't been here at all, has he?' he said.

'Not for three years.'

'Where is he?'

I didn't answer.

'We'll have to torture you into telling,' said Ferdinand. It was a frivolous threat we'd used often in our childhood for anything from 'Where are the cornflakes?' to 'What is the time?' and Ferdinand himself looked surprised that it had surfaced.

'Mm,' I said. 'As in the tool shed?'

'Shit,' Ferdinand said. 'I didn't mean . . .'

'I should absolutely hope not.'

We both remembered, though, the rainy afternoon when Gervase had put the threat into operation, trying to make me tell him where I'd hidden my new cricket bat which he coveted. I hadn't told him, out of cussedness. Ferdinand had been there, too frightened of

Gervase to protest, and also Serena, barely four, wide-eyed and uncomprehending.

'I thought you'd forgotten,' Ferdinand said. 'You've never mentioned it.'

'Boys will be bullies.'

'Gervase still is.'

Which of us, I thought, was not as we had been in the green garden? Donald, Lucy, Thomas, Gervase, Ferdinand, Serena – all playing there long ago, children's voices calling through the bushes, the adults we would become already forming in the gangling limbs, smooth faces, groping minds. None of those children . . . *none of us* . . . I thought protestingly, could have killed.

Serena came into the sitting room carrying a white lace negligée and looking oddly shocked.

'You've had a woman here!' she said.

'There's no law against it.'

Debs, following her, showed a more normal reaction. 'Size ten, good perfume, expensive tastes, classy lady,' she said. 'How am I doing?'

'Not bad.'

'Her face cream's in the bathroom,' Serena said. 'You didn't tell us you had a . . . a . . .'

'Girlfriend,' I said. 'And do you have . . . a boy-friend?'

She made an involuntary face of distaste and shook her head. Debs put a sisterly arm round Serena's shoulders and said, 'I keep telling her to go to a sex therapist or she'll end up a dry old stick, but she won't listen, will you love?'

Serena wriggled free of Debs' arm and strode off with the negligée towards the bedrooms.

'Has anyone ever assaulted her?' I asked Ferdinand. 'She has that look.'

'Not that I know of.' He raised his eyebrows. 'She's never said so.'

'She's just scared of sex,' Debs said blithely. 'You wouldn't think anyone would be, these days. Ferdinand's not, are you, bunny?'

Ferdinand didn't react, but said, 'We've finished here, I think.' He drained his scotch, put down his glass and gave me a cold stare as if to announce that any semi-thaw I might have perceived during the afternoon's exchanges was now at an end. The ice-curtain had come down again with a clang.

'If you cut us out with Malcolm,' he said, 'you'll live to regret it.'

Hurt, despite myself, and with a touch of acid, I asked, 'Is that again what Alicia says?'

'Damn you, Ian,' he said angrily, and made for the door, calling, 'Serena, we're going,' giving her no choice but to follow.

Debs gave me a mock gruesome look as she went in their wake. 'You're Alicia's number one villain, too bad, lovey. You keep your hooks off Malcolm's money or you won't know what hit you.'

There was a fierce last-minute threat in her final

words, and I saw, as the jokey manner slipped, that it was merely a façade which hid the same fears and furies of all the others, and her eyes, as she went, were just as unfriendly.

With regret, I watched from the window as the three of them climbed into Ferdinand's car and drove away. It was an illusion to think one could go back to the uncorrupted emotions of childhood, and I would have to stop wishing for it. I turned away, rinsed out Ferdinand's glass, and went into my bedroom to see how Serena had left it.

The white negligée was lying on my bed. I picked it up and hung it in its cupboard, rubbing my cheek in the fabric and smelling the faint sweet scent of the lady who came occasionally for lighthearted interludes away from a husband who was all but impotent but nevertheless loved. We suited each other well: perfectly happy in ephemeral passion, with no intention of commitment.

I checked round the flat, opened a few letters and listened to the answering machine: there was nothing of note. I spent a while thinking about cars. I had arranged on the telephone two days earlier that the hotel in Cambridge would allow my own car to remain in their park for a daily fee until I collected it, but I couldn't leave it there for ever. If I took a taxi to Epsom station, I thought, I could go up to London by train. In the morning, I would go by train to Cambridge, fetch my car, drive back to the flat, change to the hired car and drive that back to London. It might even be a shade safer, I thought, considering that Ferdinand, and through him the others, would know its colour, make and number, to turn that car in and hire a different one.

The telephone rang. I picked up the receiver and heard a familiar voice, warm and husky, coming to the point without delay.

'How about now?' she said. 'We could have an hour.'

I could seldom resist her. Seldom tried.

'An hour would be great. I was just thinking of you.'

'Good,' she said. 'See you.'

I stopped worrying about cars and thought of the white lace negligée instead; more enticing altogether. I put two wine glasses on the table by the sofa and looked at my watch. Malcolm would scarcely have reached the Savoy, I thought, but it was worth a try; and in fact he picked up the telephone saying he had that minute walked into the suite.

'I'm glad you're safely back,' I said. 'I've been a bit detained. I'll be two or three hours yet. Don't get lost.'

'Your mother is a cat,' he said.

'She saved your skin.'

'She called me a raddled old roué done up like a fifth-rate pastrycook.'

I laughed and could hear his scowl down the line.

'What do you want after caviar,' he said, 'if I order dinner?'

'Chef's special.'

'God rot you, you're as bad as your mother.'

I put the receiver down with amusement and waited through the twenty minutes it would take until the doorbell rang.

'Hello,' she said, as I let her in. 'How did the races go?'

I kissed her. 'Finished third.'

'Well done.'

She was older than I by ten or twelve years, also slender, auburn-haired and unselfconscious. I fetched the always-waiting champagne from the refrigerator, popped off the cork and poured our drinks. They were a ritual preliminary, really, as we'd never yet finished the bottle and, as usual, after half a glass, there was no point in sitting around on the sofa making small talk.

She exclaimed over the long black bruise down my thigh. 'Did you fall off a horse?'

'No, hit a car.'

'How careless.'

I drew the bedroom curtains to dim the setting western sun and lay with her naked between the sheets. We were practised lovers and comfortable with each other, philosophical over the fact that the coupling was usually better for one than the other, rarely earth-moving for both simultaneously. That day, like the time before, it turned out ecstatic for her, less so for me, and I thought the pleasure of giving such pleasure enough in itself.

'Was it all right for you?' she said finally.

'Yes, of course.'

'Not one of your great times.'

'They don't come to order. Not your turn, my turn. It's luck.'

'A matter of friction and angles,' she teased me, repeating what I'd once said. 'Who's showering first?'

She liked to return clean to her husband, acknowledging the washing to be symbolic. I showered and dressed, and waited for her in the sitting room. She was an essential part of my life, a comfort to the body, a contentment in the mind, a bulwark against loneliness. I usually said goodbye with regret, knowing she would return, but on that particular afternoon I said, 'Stay,' knowing all the same that she couldn't.

'What's the matter?' she said.

'Nothing.'

'You shivered.'

'Premonition.'

'What of?' She was preparing to go, standing by the door.

'That this will be the last time.'

'Don't be silly,' she said. 'I'll be back.'

She kissed me with what I knew was gratitude, the way I too kissed her. She smiled into my eyes. 'I'll be back.'

I opened the door for her and she went away light-heartedly, and I knew that the premonition had been not for her, but for myself.

*

I ferried the cars in the morning, going from London to Cambridge and Epsom and back to the hire firm, and no one followed me anywhere, as far as I could see.

When I'd departed, Malcolm had been full of rampaging indignation over the non-availability of first-class seats on any flight going to Paris the following day for the Arc de Triomphe.

'Go economy,' I said, 'it's only half an hour.'

It appeared that there were no economy seats either. I left him frowning but returned to find peace. He had chartered a private jet.

He told me that snippet later, because he was currently engaged with Norman West who had called to give a progress report. The detective still seemed alarmingly frail but the grey on-the-point-of-death look had abated to fawn. The dustbin clothes had been replaced by an ordinary dark suit, and the greasy hair, washed, was revealed as almost white and neatly brushed.

I shook his hand: damp, as before.

'Feeling better, Mr West?' I asked.

'Thank you, yes.'

'Tell my son what you've just said,' Malcolm commanded. 'Give him the bad news.'

West gave me a small apologetic smile and then looked down at the notepad on his knee.

'Mrs Vivien Pembroke can't remember what she did on the Friday,' he said. 'And she spent Tuesday alone at home sorting through piles of old magazines.'

'What's bad news about that?' I asked.

'Don't be obtuse,' Malcolm said impatiently. 'She hasn't an alibi. None of the whole damn bunch has an alibi.'

'Have you checked them all?' I said, surprised. 'You surely haven't had time.'

'I haven't,' he agreed.

'Figure of speech.' Malcolm waved a hand. 'Go on telling him, Mr West.'

'I called on Mrs Berenice Pembroke.' West sighed expressively. 'She found me unwelcome.'

Malcolm chuckled sourly. 'Tongue like a rhinoceros-hide whip.'

West made a small squirming movement as if still feeling the lash, but said merely, with restraint, 'She was completely uncooperative.'

'Was Thomas there, when you called?' I asked.

'No, sir, he wasn't. Mrs Pembroke said he was at work. I later telephoned his office, to the number you gave me, hoping he could tell me where both his wife and himself had been at the relevant times, and a young lady there said that Mr Pembroke left the firm several weeks ago, and she knew nothing of his present whereabouts.'

'Well,' I said, stumped. 'I didn't know.'

'I telephoned Mrs Pembroke again to ask where her husband worked now, and she told me to . . . er . . . drop dead.'

Thomas, I thought, had worked for the same firm of

biscuit makers from the day he'd finished a course in bookkeeping and accountancy. Berenice referred disparagingly to his occupation as 'storekeeping' but Thomas said he was a quantity surveyor whose job it was to estimate the raw materials needed for each large contract, and cost them, and pass the information to the management. Thomas's promotions within the firm had been minor, such as from second assistant to first assistant, and at forty he could see, I supposed, that he would never be boardroom material. How bleak, I thought, to have to face his mid-life limitations with Berenice cramming them down his throat at every turn. Poor old Thomas . . .

'Mrs Joyce Pembroke,' West said, 'is the only one who is definite about her movements. On each relevant day, she was playing bridge. She didn't like me snooping, as she called it, and she wouldn't say who she was playing bridge with as she didn't want those people bothered.'

'You can leave Mrs Joyce Pembroke out,' I said.

'Huh?' Malcolm said.

'You know perfectly well,' I told him, 'that Joyce wouldn't kill you. If you'd had any doubts, you wouldn't have gone off in a car with her yesterday.'

'All right, all right,' he said, grumbling. 'Cross Joyce off.'

I nodded to West, and he put a line through Joyce.

'Yesterday I called on Mrs Alicia Pembroke and then later on Mrs Ursula Pembroke.' West's face showed no joy over the encounters. 'Mrs Alicia Pembroke told me to mind my own business, and Mrs Ursula Pembroke had been crying and wouldn't speak to me.' He lifted his hands out in a gesture of helplessness. 'I couldn't persuade either of them of the advantage of establishing alibis.'

'Did you get any impression,' I asked, 'that the police had been there before you, asking the same questions?'

'None at all.'

'I told you,' Malcolm said. 'They didn't believe I was attacked. They thought I'd just staged the whole thing.'

'Even so . . .'

'They checked everyone out over Moira, as you no doubt remember, and came up with a load of clean slates. They're just not bothering to do it again.'

'Do you happen to have their telephone number with you?'

'Yes I do,' he said, bringing a diary out of an inner pocket and flicking over the pages. 'But they won't tell you anything. It's like talking to a steel door.'

I dialled the number all the same and asked for the superintendent.

'In what connection, sir?'

'About the attempted murder of Mr Malcolm Pembroke a week ago yesterday.'

'One moment, sir.'

Time passed, and a different voice came on the line, plain and impersonal.

'Can I help you, sir?'

'About the attempted murder of Mr Malcolm Pembroke . . .'

'Who are you, sir?'

'His son.'

'Er . . . which one?'

'Ian.'

There was a brief rustling of paper.

'Could you tell me your birth date, as proof of identity?' Surprised, I gave it.

Then the voice said, 'Do you wish to give information, sir?'

'I wanted to find out how the investigation was going.'

'It isn't our custom to discuss that.'

'But . . .'

'But I can tell you, sir, that investigations into the alleged attack are being conducted with thoroughness.'

'*Alleged!*' I said.

'That's right, sir. We can find no evidence at all that there was another party involved.'

'I don't believe it.'

With slightly exaggerated patience but also a first flicker of sympathy, he said, 'I can tell you, sir, that there was no evidence of Mr Pembroke being dragged from the garden to the garage, which he alleged must have happened. No marks on the path. No scrapes on the heels of Mr Pembroke's shoes, which we examined at the time. There were no fingerprints except his own on the door handles of the car, no fingerprints except his anywhere. He showed no signs of carbon monoxide poisoning, which he explained was because he had delayed calling us. We examined the scene thoroughly the following morning, after Mr Pembroke had left home, and we found nothing at all to indicate the presence of an assailant. You can be sure we are not closing the case, but we are not at this time able to find grounds for suspicion of any other person.'

'He was nearly killed,' I said blankly.

'Yes, sir, well I'm sorry, sir, but that's how things stand.' He paused briefly. 'I can understand your disbelief, sir. It can't be easy for you.' He sounded quite human, offering comfort.

'Thank you at least for talking to me,' I said.

'Right, sir. Goodbye.'

'Goodbye,' I said slowly, but he had already gone.

'*Now* what's the matter?' Malcolm asked, watching my face.

I repeated what I'd just heard.

'Impossible!' Malcolm said explosively.

'No.'

'What then?'

'Clever.'

CHAPTER EIGHT

'Which door did you go out of, with the dogs?' I asked.

'The kitchen door, like I always do.'

'The kitchen door is about five steps along that covered way from the rear door into the garage.'

'Yes, of course it is,' Malcolm said testily.

'You told me that you set off down the garden with the dogs, and I suppose you told the police the same thing?'

'Yes, of course I did.'

'But you can't really remember actually going. You remember that you meant to, isn't that what you told me?'

He frowned. 'I suppose it is.'

'So what if you never made it to the garden, but were knocked out right there by the kitchen door? And what if you weren't dragged from there into the garage, but *carried*?'

His mouth opened. 'But I'm . . .'

'You're not too heavy,' I said. 'I could carry you easily in a fireman's lift.'

He was five foot seven, stocky but not fat. He weighed ten stone something, I would have guessed.

'And the fingerprints?' Norman West asked.

'In a fireman's lift,' I said, 'you sling the person you want to carry over your left shoulder, don't you, with his head hanging down your back. Then you grasp his knees with your left arm, and hold his right wrist in your own right hand, to stop him slipping off?'

They both nodded.

'So if you're holding someone's wrist, you can put his hand easily onto any surface you like, including car door handles . . . particularly,' I said, thinking, 'if you've opened the doors yourself first with gloves on, so that your victim's prints will be on top of any smudges you have made.'

'You should have been an assassin,' Malcolm said. 'You'd have been good at it.'

'So now we have Malcolm slumped in the back seat, half lying, like you said. So next you switch on the engine and leave the doors open so that all the nice fumes pour into the car quickly.'

'Doors?' Malcolm interrupted.

'The driver's door and one of the rear doors, at the least.'

'Oh, yes.'

'And then you have,' I said, 'a suicide.'

'And when I woke up,' Malcolm said gloomily, 'I put my prints all over the place. On the ignition key . . . everywhere.'

'No one could have counted on that.'

'It just looked bad to the police.'

We contemplated the scenario.

'If it happened like that,' West said, 'as indeed it could have done, whoever attacked you had to know that you would go out of the kitchen door at around that time.'

Malcolm said bleakly, 'If I'm at home, I always go for a walk with the dogs about then. Take them out, bring them back, give them their dinners, pour myself a drink. Routine.'

'And . . . er . . . is there anyone in your family who doesn't know when you walk the dogs?'

'Done it all my life, at that time,' Malcolm said.

There was a short silence, then I said, 'I wish I'd known all this when that car nearly killed us at Newmarket. We really ought to have told the police.'

'I was fed up with them,' Malcolm said. 'I've spent hours and hours with the suspicious buggers since Moira's death. I'm allergic to them. They bring me out in a rash.'

'You can't blame them, sir. Most murdered wives are killed by their husbands,' West said. 'And frankly, you appeared to have an extremely strong motive.'

'Rubbish,' Malcolm said. 'I don't see how people can kill people they've loved.'

'Unfortunately it's common.' West paused. 'Do you want me to continue with your family, sir, considering how little progress I've been able to make with them?'

'Yes,' Malcolm said heavily. 'Carry on. I'll get Joyce to tell them all to answer your questions. She seems to be able to get them to do what she wants.'

To get them to do what *they* want, I thought. She couldn't stir them into courses they didn't like.

Norman West put his notebook into his jacket pocket and shifted his weight forward on his chair.

'Before you go,' I said, 'I thought you might like to know that I asked the telephonist of the Cambridge hotel if anyone besides yourself had asked if a Mr Pembroke was staying there last weekend. She said they'd definitely had at least three calls asking for Mr Pembroke, two men and a woman, and she remembered because she thought it odd that no one wanted to talk to him, or would leave a message; they only wanted to know if he was there.'

'*Three!*' Malcolm exclaimed.

'One would be Mr West,' I pointed out. To West, I said, 'In view of that, could you tell us who asked you to find my father?'

West hesitated. 'I don't positively know which Mrs Pembroke it was. And . . . er . . . even if I became sure during these investigations, well, no sir, I don't think I could.'

'Professional ethics,' Malcolm said, nodding.

'I did warn you, sir,' West said to me, 'about a conflict of interests.'

'So you did. Hasn't she paid you yet, then? No name on any cheque?'

'No, sir, not yet.'

He rose to his feet, no one's idea of Atlas, though world-weary all the same. He shook my hand damply, and Malcolm's, and said he would be in touch. When he'd gone, Malcolm sighed heavily and told me to pour him some scotch.

'Don't you want some?' he said, when I gave him the glass.

'Not right now.'

'What did you think of Mr West?'

'He's past it.'

'You're too young. He's experienced.'

'And no match for the female Pembrokes.'

Malcolm smiled with irony. 'Few are,' he said.

We flew to Paris in the morning in the utmost luxury and were met by a chauffeured limousine which took its place with regal slowness in the solid traffic jam moving as one entity towards Longchamp.

The French racecourse, aflutter with flags, seemed to be swallowing *tout le monde* with insatiable appetite, until no one could walk in a straight line through the public areas where the crowds were heavy with guttural vowels and garlic.

Malcolm's jet/limousine package also included, I found, an invitation from the French Jockey Club, passes to everywhere and a Lucullan lunch appointment with the co-owner of Blue Clancy, Mr Ramsey Osborn.

Ramsey Osborn, alight with the *joie de vivre* gripping the whole place, turned out to be a very large sixtyish American who towered over Malcolm and took to him at once. Malcolm seemed to see the same immediate signals. They were cronies within two minutes.

'My son, Ian,' Malcolm said eventually, introducing me.

'Glad to know you.' He shook my hand vigorously. 'The one who fixed the sale, right?' His eyes were light grey and direct. 'Tell you the truth, there's a colt and a filly I want to buy for next year's Classics, and this way Blue Clancy will finance them very nicely.'

'But if Blue Clancy wins the Arc?' I said.

'No regrets, son.' He turned to Malcolm. 'You've a cautious boy, here.'

'Yeah,' Malcolm said. 'Cautious like an astronaut.'

The Osborn grey eyes swivelled back my way. 'Is that so? Do you bet?'

'Cautiously, sir.'

He laughed, but it wasn't unalloyed good humour. Malcolm, I thought, was much more to his liking. I left them sitting down at table together and, confident enough that no assassin would penetrate past the eagle-eyed doorkeepers of the upper citadel of the French Jockey Club, went down myself to ground level, happier to be with the action.

I had been racing in France a good deal, having for

some years been assistant to a trainer who sent horses across the Channel as insouciantly as to York. Paris and Deauville were nearer anyway, he used to say, despatching me from Epsom via nearby Gatwick airport whenever he felt disinclined to go himself. I knew in consequence a smattering of racecourse French and where to find what I wanted, essential assets in the vast stands bulging with hurrying, vociferous, uninhibited French racegoers.

I loved the noise, the smell, the movement, the quick angers, the gesticulations, the extravagance of ground-level French racing. British jockeys tended to think French racegoers madly aggressive, and certainly once I'd actually had to defend with my fists a jockey who'd lost on a favourite I'd brought over. Jockeys in general had been insulted and battered to the extent that they no longer had to walk through crowds when going out or back from races at many tracks, and at Longchamp made the journey from weighing room to horse by going up an escalator enclosed with plastic walls like a tunnel, across a bridge, and down a similar plastic-tunnel escalator on the other side.

I wandered around, greeting a few people, watching the first race from the trainers' stand, tearing up my losing pari-mutuel ticket, wandering some more, and feeling finally, without any work to do, without any horse to saddle, purposeless. It was an odd feeling. I couldn't remember when I'd last gone racing without being actively involved. Racing wasn't my playground, it was my work; without work it felt hollow.

Vaguely depressed, I returned to Malcolm's eyrie and found him blossoming in his new role as racehorse owner. He was referring to Le Prix de l'Arc de Triomphe familiarly as 'the Arc' as if it hadn't swum into his consciousness a bare half-week earlier, and discussing Blue Clancy's future with Ramsey Osborn as if he knew what he was talking about.

'We're thinking of the Breeders' Cup,' he said to me, and I interpreted the glint in his eyes as a frantic question as well as an instant decision.

'If he runs well today,' Osborn put in, qualifying it.

'It's a long way to California,' I said, agreeing with him. 'To the world championships, one might say.'

Malcolm was grateful for the information and far from dismayed by it. Pretty well the opposite, I saw. It would be to California we would go on the way to Australia, I guessed, rather than Singapore.

Lunch seemed to be continuing all afternoon, in the way French lunches do, with tidy circles of chateaubriand appearing, the empty plates to be cleared before small bundles of beans and carrots were served, followed by fresh little cheeses rolled in chopped nuts, and tiny strawberry tartlets with vanilla coulis. According to the menu, I had through my absence missed the *écrevisses*, the consommé, the *crêpes de volaille*, the *salade verte* and the sorbet. Just as well, I thought, eyeing the *friandises* which arrived with the coffee. Even amateur jockeys had to live by the scales.

Malcolm and Ramsey Osborn passed mellowly to cognac and cigars and watched the races on television. No one was in a hurry: the Arc was scheduled for five o'clock and digestion could proceed until four-thirty.

Ramsey Osborn told us he came from Stamford, Connecticut, and had made his money by selling sports clothes. 'Baseball caps by the million,' he said expansively. 'I get them made, I sell them to retail outlets. And shoes, shirts, jogging suits, whatever goes. Health is big business, we'd be nowhere without exercise.'

Ramsey looked as if he didn't exercise too much himself, having pads of fat round his eyes, a heavy double chin and a swelling stomach. He radiated goodwill, however, and listened with kind condescension as Malcolm said reciprocally that he himself dealt modestly in currency and metal.

Ramsey wasn't grasping Malcolm's meaning, I thought, but then for all his occasional flamboyance Malcolm never drew general attention to his wealth. Quantum was a large comfortable Victorian family house, but it wasn't a mansion: when Malcolm had reached mansion financial status, he'd shown no signs of wanting to move. I wondered briefly whether that would change in future, now that he'd tasted prodigality.

In due course, the three of us went down to the saddling boxes and met both Blue Clancy and his trainer. Blue Clancy looked aristocratic, his trainer more so. Malcolm was visibly impressed with the trainer, as indeed was reasonable, as he was a bright young star, now rising forty, who had already trained six Classic winners and made it look easy.

Blue Clancy was restless, his nostrils quivering. We watched the saddling ritual and the final touches; flick of oil to shine the hooves, sponging of nose and mouth to clean and gloss, tweaking of forelock and tack to achieve perfection. We followed him into the parade ring and were joined by his English jockey who was wearing Ramsey's white, green and crimson colours and looking unexcited.

Malcolm was taking with alacrity to his first taste of big-time ownership. The electricity was fairly sparking. He caught my eye, saw what I was thinking, and laughed.

'I used to think you a fool to choose racing,' he said. 'Couldn't understand what you saw in it.'

'It's better still when you ride.'

'Yes . . . I saw that at Sandown. And about time, I suppose.'

Ramsey and the trainer claimed his attention to discuss tactics with the jockey, and I thought of the summer holidays when we were children, when Gervase, Ferdinand and I had all learned to ride. We'd learned on riding-school ponies, cycling to the nearby stables and spending time there grooming, feeding and mucking out. We'd entered local gymkhanas, and booted the poor animals in pop-the-balloon races. We'd ridden them backwards, bareback and with our knees on the saddle, and Ferdinand, the specialist, standing briefly on his head. The ponies had been docile and no doubt tired to death, but for two or three years we had been circus virtuosi: and Malcolm had paid the bills uncomplainingly, but had never come to watch us. Then Gervase and Ferdinand had been whisked away by Alicia, and in the lonely vacuum afterwards I'd ridden almost every possible morning, laying down a skill without meaning it seriously, not realizing, in the flurry of academic school examinations, that it was the holiday pastime that would beckon me for life.

Blue Clancy looked as well as any of the others, I thought, watching the runners walk round, and the trainer was displaying more confidence than uncertainty. He thanked me for fixing the sale (from which he'd made a commission) and assured me that the two-million-guinea yearling was now settled snugly in a prime box in his yard. He'd known me vaguely until then as another trainer's assistant, a dogsbody, but as son and go-between of a new owner showing all signs of being severely hooked by the sport, I was now worth cultivation.

I was amused and far from minding. Life was like that. I might as well make the most of Malcolm's coat-tails while I was on them, I thought. I asked if I could see round the trainer's yard next time I was in Newmarket, and he said sure, he'd like it, and almost seemed to mean it.

'I'm sometimes there with George and Jo,' I said. 'Schooling their few jumpers. I ride them in amateur 'chases.' Everyone in Newmarket knew who George and Jo were: they were the equivalent of minor royalty.

'Oh, that's you, is it?' He put a few things together. 'Didn't realize that was you.'

'Mm.'

'Then come any time.' He sounded warmer, more positive. 'I mean it,' he said.

The way upwards in racing, I thought, ironic at myself, could lead along devious paths. I thanked him without effusiveness, and said 'Soon.'

Blue Clancy went out to the parade and the rest of us moved to the owners' and trainers' stand, which was near the core of things and buzzing with other similar groups locked in identical tensions.

'What chance has he got?' Malcolm demanded of me. 'Seriously.' His eyes searched my face as if for truth, which wasn't what I thought he wanted to hear.

'A bit better than he had on Thursday, since the second favourite has been scratched.' He wanted me to tell him more, however unrealistic, so I said, 'He's got a good chance of being placed. Anything can happen. He could win.'

Malcolm nodded, not knowing whether or not to believe me, but wanting to. Well and truly hooked, I thought, and felt fond of him.

I thought in my heart of hearts that the horse would finish sixth or seventh, not disgraced but not in the money. I'd backed him on the pari-mutuel but only out of loyalty: I'd backed the French horse Meilleurs Voeux out of conviction.

Blue Clancy moved well going down to the start. This was always the best time for owners, I thought, while the heart beat with expectation and while the excuses, explanations, disappointments were still ten minutes away. Malcolm lifted my binoculars to his eyes with hands that were actually trembling.

The trainer himself was strung up, I saw, however he might try to disguise it. There was only one 'Arc' in a year, of course, and too few years in a lifetime.

The horses seemed to circle for an interminable time at the gate but were finally fed into the slots to everyone's satisfaction. The gates crashed open, the thundering rainbow poured out, and twenty-six of Europe's best thoroughbreds were out on the right-hand circuit straining to be the fastest, strongest, bravest over one and a half miles of grass.

'Do you want your binoculars?' Malcolm said, hoping not.

'No. Keep them, I can see.'

I could see Ramsey Osborn's colours on the rails halfway back in the field, the horse moving easily, as were all the others at that point of the race. In the 'Arc', the essentials were simple: to be in the first ten coming round the last long right-hand bend, not to swing too wide into the straight and, according to the horse's stamina, pile on the pressure and head for home. Sometimes in a slow-starting 'Arc', one jockey would slip the field on the bend and hang on to his lead; in others, there would be war throughout to a whisker verdict. Blue Clancy's 'Arc' seemed to be run at give-no-quarter speed, and he came into the finishing straight in a bunch of flying horses, lying sixth or eighth, as far as I could see.

Malcolm shouted 'Come on,' explosively as if air had backed up in his lungs from not breathing, and the ladies around us in silk dresses and hats, and the men in grey morning suits, infected by the same urgency, yelled and urged and cursed in polyglot babel. Malcolm put down the raceglasses and yelled louder, totally involved, rapt, living through his eyes.

Blue Clancy was doing his bit, I thought. He hadn't blown up. In fact, he was hanging on to fifth place. Going faster. Fourth . . .

The trainer, more restrained than owners, was now saying, 'Come on, come *on*' compulsively under his breath, but two of the horses already in front suddenly came on faster than Blue Clancy and drew away from the field, and the real hope died in the trainer with a sigh and a sag to the shoulders.

The finish the crowd watched was a humdinger which only a photograph could decide. The finish Malcolm, Ramsey, the trainer and I watched was two lengths further back, where Blue Clancy and his jockey, never giving up, were fighting all out to the very end, flashing across the line absolutely level with their nearest rival, only the horse's nose in front taking his place on the nod.

'On the nod,' the trainer said, echoing my thought.

'What does that mean?' Malcolm demanded. He was high with excitement, flushed, his eyes blazing. 'Were we third? Say we were third.'

'I think so,' the trainer said. 'There'll be a photograph.'

We hurried down from the stand to get to the unsaddling enclosure, Malcolm still short of breath and slightly dazed. 'What does on the nod mean?' he asked me.

'A galloping horse pokes his head out forward with each stride in a sort of rhythm, forward, back, forward, back. If two horses are as close as they were, and one horse's nose is forward when it passes the finishing line, and the other horse's happens to be back . . . well, that's on the nod.'

'Just luck, you mean?'

'Luck.'

'My God,' he said, 'I never thought I'd feel like that. I never thought I'd *care.* I only did it for a jaunt.'

He looked almost with wonderment at my face, as if I'd been before him into a far country and he'd now discovered the mystery for himself.

Ramsey Osborn, who had roared with the best, beamed with pleasure when an announcement confirmed Blue Clancy's third place, saying he was sure glad the half-share sale had turned out fine. There were congratulations all round, with Malcolm and Ramsey being introduced to the owners of the winner, who were Italian and didn't understand Ramsey's drawl. Press photographers flashed like popping suns. There were television cameras, enquiring journalists, speeches, presentations. Malcolm looked envious of the Italian owners: third was fine but winning was better.

The four of us went for a celebratory drink; champagne, of course.

'Let's go for it,' Ramsey said. 'The Breeders' Cup. All the way.'

'We'll have to see how he is after today,' the trainer said warningly. 'He had a hard race.'

'He'll be all right,' Ramsey said with hearty confidence. 'Did you see the distance? Two lengths behind the winner. That's world class and no kidding.'

The trainer looked thoughtful but didn't argue. The favourite, undeniably world class, had finished second, victory snatched away no doubt by his earlier exhausting outing. He might not come back at all after his gruelling 'Arc'. The French favourite (and mine), Meilleurs Voeux, had finished fifth which made Blue Clancy better than I'd thought. Maybe he wouldn't be disgraced in the Breeders' Cup, if we went. I hoped we would go, but I was wary of hope.

The afternoon trickled away with the champagne, and Malcolm, almost as tired as his horse, sank euphorically into the limousine going back to the airport and closed his eyes in the jet.

'My first ever runner,' he said sleepily. 'Third in the "Arc". Not bad, eh?'

'Not bad.'

'I'm going to call the yearling Chrysos.'

'Why Chrysos?' I said.

He smiled without opening his eyes. 'It's Greek for gold.'

Malcolm was feeling caged in the Savoy.

On Sunday night, when we returned from Paris, he'd hardly had the energy to undress. By Monday morning, he was pacing the carpet with revitalized energy and complaining that another week in the suite would drive him bonkers.

'I'm going back to Quantum,' he said. 'I miss the dogs.'

I said with foreboding, 'It would take the family half a day at most to find out you were there.'

'I can't help it. I can't hide for ever. You can come and stay close to me there.'

'Don't go,' I said. 'You're safe here.'

'Keep me safe at Quantum.'

He was adamant and began packing, and short of roping him to the bedstead, I couldn't stop him.

Just before we left, I telephoned Norman West and found him at home – which didn't bode well for the investigations. He was happy to tell me, he said, that it was now certain Mrs Deborah Pembroke, Ferdinand's wife, couldn't have been at Newmarket Bloodstock Sales, as on that day she had done a photo-modelling session. He had checked up with the magazine that morning, as Mrs Deborah had told him he could, and they had provided proof.

'Right,' I said. 'What about Ferdinand himself?'

'Mr Ferdinand was away from his office on both those days. Working at home on the Friday. The next week, he attended a course on the statistical possibilities of insurance fraud. He says that after registration on the Monday, they kept no record of attendance. I checked there too, and no one clearly remembers, they're all half strangers to each other.'

I sighed. 'Well . . . my father and I are going back to Quantum.'

'That's not wise, surely.'

'He's tired of imprisonment. Report to us there, will you?'

He said he would, when he had more news.

Cross off Debs, I thought. Bully for Debs.

I drove us down to Berkshire, stopping at Arthur Bellbrook's house in the village to collect the dogs. The two full-grown Dobermanns greeted Malcolm like puppies, prancing around him and rubbing against his legs as he slapped and fondled them. Real love on both sides, I saw. Uncomplicated by greed, envy or rejection.

Malcolm looked up and saw me watching him.

'You should get a dog,' he said. 'You need something to love.'

He could really hit home, I thought.

He bent back to his friends, playing with their muzzles, letting them try to snap at his fingers, knowing they wouldn't bite. They weren't guard dogs as such: he liked Dobermanns for their muscular agility, for their exuberance. I'd been brought up with relays of them around me, but it wasn't the affection of dogs I wanted, and I'd never asked for one of my own.

I thought of the afternoon he'd let them out of the kitchen and then been hit on the head. The dogs must have seen or sensed someone there. Though not guard dogs, they should still have warned Malcolm.

'Do those two dogs bark when strangers call?' I asked.

'Yes, of course.' Malcolm straightened, still smiling, letting the lithe bodies press against his knees. 'Why?'

'Did they bark a week last Friday, when you set out to walk them?'

The smile died out of his face. With almost despair he said, 'No. I don't think so. I don't remember. No . . . not especially. They were pleased to be going out.'

'How many of the family do they know well?' I said.

'Everyone's been to the house several times since Moira died. All except you. I thought at first it was to support me, but . . .' he shrugged with disillusion, 'they were all busy making sure none of the others ingratiated themselves with me and cut them out.'

Every possibility led back to the certainty we couldn't accept.

Malcolm shuddered and said he would walk through the village with the dogs. He would meet people he knew on the way, and there were people in that village who'd been close friends with Vivien, Alicia and Joyce and had sided with them, and had since fed them inflammatory half-lies about Malcolm's doings.

'You know the village grapevine is faster than telex,' I said. 'Put the dogs in the car.'

He wouldn't listen. It was only six days since the second time someone had tried to kill him, but he was already beginning to believe there would be no more attempts. Well, no more that morning, I supposed. He walked a mile and a half with the dogs, and I drove slowly ahead, looking back, making sure at each turn that he was coming into sight. When he reached the house safely, he said I was being over-protective.

'I thought that was what you wanted,' I said.

'It is and it isn't.'

Surprisingly, I understood him. He was afraid and ashamed of it, and in consequence felt urged to bravado. Plain straightforward fear, I thought, would have been easier to deal with. At least I got him to wait outside with the dogs for company while I went into the house to reconnoitre, but no one had been there laying booby traps, no one was hiding behind doors with raised blunt instruments, no one had sent parcel bombs in the post.

I fetched him, and we unpacked. We both took it for granted I would sleep in my old room, and I made up the bed there. I had bought provisions in London to the extent of bread, milk, lemons, smoked salmon and caviar, a diet both of us now considered normal. There was champagne in the cellar and a freezer full of post-Moira TV dinners in cardboard boxes. We weren't going to starve, I thought, inspecting them, though we might get indigestion.

Malcolm spent the afternoon in his office opening letters and talking to his stockbroker on the telephone, and at the routine time proposed to give the dogs their pre-dinner walk.

'I'll come with you,' I said.

He nodded without comment, and in the crisp early October air we set off down the garden, through the gate into the field, and across to the willow-lined stream he had been aiming for ten days earlier.

We had all sailed toy boats down that stream when we'd been children, and picked watercress there, and got thoroughly wet and muddy as a matter of course. Alicia had made us strip, more than once, before she would let us into her bridal-white kitchen.

'Last Monday,' Malcolm said casually, watching the dogs sniff for water rats round the tree roots, 'I made a new will.'

'Did you?'

'I did. In Cambridge. I thought I might as well. The old one left a lot to Moira. And then, after that

Friday . . . well, I wanted to put things in order, in case . . . just in case.'

'What did you do with it?' I asked.

He seemed amused. 'The natural question is surely, "What's in it? What have you left to *me*?" '

'Mm,' I said dryly. 'I'm not asking that, ever. What I'm asking is more practical.'

'I left it with the solicitor in Cambridge.'

We were wandering slowly along towards the stream, the dogs quartering busily. The willow leaves, yellowing, would fall in droves in the next gale, and there was bonfire smoke drifting somewhere in the still air.

'Who knows where your will is?' I asked.

'I do. And the solicitor.'

'Who's the solicitor?'

'I saw his name on a brass plate outside his office and went in on impulse. I've got his card somewhere. We discussed what I wanted, he had it typed up, and I signed it with witnesses in his office and left it there for safekeeping.'

'For a brilliant man,' I said peaceably, 'you're as thick as two planks.'

CHAPTER NINE

Malcolm said explosively, 'You're bloody rude,' and, after a pause, 'In what way am I thick? A new will was essential.'

'Suppose you died without telling me or anybody else you'd made it, or where it could be found?'

'Oh.' He was dismayed, then brightened. 'The solicitor would have produced it.'

'If he knew you by reputation, if he had any idea of the sums involved, if he heard you were dead, if he were conscientious, and if he knew who to get in touch with. If he were lazy, he might not bother, he's under no obligation. Within a month, unless you boasted a bit about your wealth, he'll have forgotten your will's in his files.'

'You seem to know an awful lot about it.'

'Joyce worked for years for the Citizens Advice Bureau, do you remember? I used to hear lurid tales of family squabbles because no one knew where to find a will they were sure had been made. And equally lurid tales of family members knowing where the will was and burning it before anyone else could find it, if they didn't like what was in it.'

'That's why I left it in safekeeping,' Malcolm said. 'Precisely because of that.'

We reached the far boundary of the field. The stream ran on through the neighbour's land, but at that point we turned back.

'What should I do then?' he asked. 'Any ideas?'

'Send it to the probate office at Somerset House.'

'How do you mean?'

'Joyce told me about it, one time. You put your will in a special envelope they'll send you if you apply for it, then you take it or send it to the central probate office. They register your will there and keep it safe. When anyone dies and any solicitor anywhere applies for probate, the central probate office routinely checks its files. If it has ever registered a will for that person, that's the envelope that will be opened, and that's the will that will be proved.'

He thought it over. 'Do you mean, if I registered a will with the probate office, and then changed my mind and wrote a new one, it wouldn't be any good?'

'You'd have to retrieve the old will and re-register the new one. Otherwise the old will would be the one adhered to.'

'Good God. I didn't know any of this.'

'Joyce says not enough people know. She says if people would only register their wills, they couldn't be pressured into changing them when they're gaga or frightened or on their deathbeds. Or at least, wills made like that would be useless.'

'I used to laugh, rather, at Joyce's voluntary work. Felt indulgent.' He sighed. 'Seems it had its uses.'

The Citizens Advice Bureau, staffed by knowledgeable armies of Joyces, could steer one from the cradle to the grave, from marriage to divorce to probate, from child allowance to old age supplements. I'd not always listened attentively to Joyce's tales, but I'd been taken several times to the Bureau, and I seemed to have absorbed more than I'd realized.

'I kept a copy of my new will,' Malcolm said. 'I'll show it to you when we go in.'

'You don't need to.'

'You'd better see it,' he said.

I didn't argue. He whistled to the dogs who left the stream reluctantly, and we made our way back to the gate into the garden.

'Just wait out here while I check the house,' I said.

He was astonished. 'We've only been out for half an hour. And we locked the doors.'

'You regularly go out for half an hour at this time. And how many of the family still have keys to the house?'

He was silent. All of the people who had ever lived there could have kept their keys to the house, and there had never been any need, before now, to change the locks.

'Stay here, then?' I asked, and he nodded sadly.

The kitchen door was still locked. I let myself in and went all through the house again, but it was quiet and undisturbed, and doors that I'd set open at certain angles were still as I'd left them.

I called Malcolm and he came into the kitchen and began getting the food for the dogs.

'Are you going through this checking rigmarole every single time we leave the house?' he said, sounding as if he didn't like it.

'Yes, until we get the locks changed.'

He didn't like that either, but expressed his disapproval only in a frown and a rather too vigorous scraping of dog food out of a tin.

'Fill the water bowls,' he said rather crossly, and I did that and set them down again on the floor.

'It isn't so easy to change the locks,' he said. 'They're all mortice locks, as you know, set into the doors. The one on the front door is antique.'

The front door keys were six inches long and ornate, and there had never been more than three of them, as far as I knew.

'All right,' I said. 'If we keep the front door bolted and the keys in your safe, we won't change that one.'

A little pacified, he put the filled dinner bowls on the floor, wiped his fingers and said it was time for a noggin. I bolted the kitchen door on the inside and then followed him through the hall to the office, where he poured scotch into two glasses and asked if I wanted to desecrate mine with ice. I said yes and went back to the kitchen to fetch some. When I returned, he had taken some sheets of paper from his open briefcase and was reading them.

'Here you are. Here's my will,' he said, and passed the papers over.

He had made the will, I reflected, before he had telephoned me to put an end to our quarrel, and I expected not to figure in it in consequence, but I'd done him an injustice. Sitting in an armchair and sipping the whisky, I read through all the minor bequests to people like Arthur Bellbrook, and all the lawyerly gobbledegook 'upon trust' and without commas, and came finally to the plain language.

'To each of my three divorced wives Vivien Joyce and Alicia I bequeath the sum of five hundred thousand pounds.

'My son Robin being provided for I direct that the residue of my estate shall be divided equally among my children Donald Lucy Thomas Gervase Ian Ferdinand and Serena.'

A long clause followed with provisions for 'if any of my children shall pre-decease me', leaving 'his or her share' to the grandchildren.

Finally came two short sentences:

'I bequeath to my son Ian the piece of thin wire to be found on my desk. He knows what he can do with it.'

Surprised and more moved than I could say, I looked up from the last page and saw the smile in Malcolm's eyes deepen to a throaty chuckle.

'The lawyer chap thought the last sentence quite obscene. He said I shouldn't put that sort of thing in a will.'

I laughed. 'I didn't expect to be in your will at all.'

'Well . . .' He shrugged. 'I'd never have left you out. I've regretted for a long while . . . hitting you . . . everything.'

'Guess I deserved it.'

'Yes, at the time.'

I turned back to the beginning of the document and re-read one of the preliminary paragraphs. In it, he had named me as his sole executor, when I was only his fifth child. 'Why me?' I said.

'Don't you want to?'

'Yes. I'm honoured.'

'The lawyer said to name someone I trusted.' He smiled lopsidedly. 'You got elected.'

He stretched out an arm and picked up from his desk a leather pot holding pens and pencils. From it, he pulled a wire about ten inches long and about double the thickness of the sort used by florists for stiffening flower stalks.

'If this one should get lost,' he said, 'just find another.'

'Yes. All right.'

'Good.' He put the wire back in the pot and the pot back on the desk.

'By the time you pop off,' I said, 'the price of gold

might have risen out of sight and all I'd find in the wall would be spiders.'

'Yeah, too bad.'

I felt more at one with him than at any time since he'd telephoned, and perhaps he with me. I hoped it would be a very long time before I would have to execute his will.

'Gervase,' I said, 'suggests that you should distribute some of your money now, to . . . er . . . reduce the estate tax.'

'Does he? And what do you think?'

'I think,' I said, 'that giving it to the family instead of to scholarships and film companies and so on might save your life.'

The blue eyes opened wide. 'That's immoral.'

'Pragmatic.'

'I'll think about it.'

We dined on the caviar, but the fun seemed to have gone out of it.

'Let's have shepherd's pie tomorrow,' Malcolm said. 'There's plenty in the freezer.'

We spent the next two days uneventfully at Quantum being careful, but with no proof that care was needed.

Late on Tuesday afternoon, out with the dogs and having made certain that Arthur Bellbrook had gone home, we walked round behind the kitchen wall and came to the treasure house.

A veritable sea of nettles guarded the door. Malcolm looked at them blankly. 'The damn things grow overnight.'

I pulled my socks over the bottoms of my trousers and assayed the traverse; stamped down an area by the bottom of the door and with fingers all the same stinging felt along to one end of the wooden sill and with some effort tugged it out. Malcolm leaned forward and gave me the piece of wire, and watched while I stood up and located the almost invisible hole. The wire slid through the tiny tube built into the mortar and, under pressure, the latch inside operated as smoothly as it had when I'd installed it. The wire dislodged a metal rod out of a slot, allowing the latch to spring open.

'I oiled it,' Malcolm said. 'The first time I tried, it was as rusty as hell.'

I pushed the edge of the heavy narrow door and it opened inwards, its crenellated edges disengaging from the brick courses on each side with faint grating noises but with no pieces breaking off.

'You built it well,' Malcolm said. 'Good mortar.'

'You told me how to mix the mortar, if you remember.'

I stepped into the small brick room which was barely four feet across at the far end and about eight feet long, narrowing in a wedge-shape towards the door which was set into one of the long walls. The wider end wall was stacked to waist height with flat wooden boxes like those used for château-bottled wines. In front, there were two large cardboard boxes with heavily taped-down tops. I stepped further in and tried to open one of the wine-type boxes, but those were nailed shut. I turned round and took a couple of steps back and stood in the doorway, looking out.

'Gold at the back, treasures in front,' Malcolm said, watching me with interest.

'I'll take your word for it.'

The air in the triangular room smelled faintly musty. There was no ventilation, as I'd told Arthur Bellbrook, and no damp course, either. I reset the rod into the latch on the inside, as it wouldn't shut unless one did, and stepped outside. My teenage design limitations meant that one had to go down on one's knees to close the door the last few inches, hooking one's fingers into a hollow under the bottom row of bricks and pulling hard. The door and walls fitted together again like pieces of jigsaw, and the latch inside clicked into place. I replaced the sill under the door, kicking it home, and tried to encourage the crushed nettles to stand up again.

'They'll be flourishing again by morning,' Malcolm said. 'Rotten things.'

'Those cardboard boxes are too big to come out through the door,' I observed, rubbing stings on my hands and wrists.

'Oh, sure. I took them in empty and flat, then set them up, and filled them bit by bit.'

'You could take those things out again now.'

There was a pause, then he said, 'I'll wait. As things are at present, they might as well stay there.'

I nodded. He whistled to the dogs and we went on with the walk. We had given up referring explicitly to fear of the family, but it still hung around us like grief. On our return from the field, Malcolm waited outside without comment until I checked through the house, and prosaically began feeding the dogs on my report of all clear.

Neither of us discussed how long all the precautions were going to have to go on. Norman West's latest report had been as inconclusive as his first, and by Wednesday evening the pitiful summary I'd been making of his results read as follows:

DONALD:	busy about the golf club. Cannot pinpoint any times.
HELEN:	working at home making Henley souvenirs.
LUCY:	reading, walking, writing, meditating.
EDWIN:	housework, shopping for groceries, going to public library.
THOMAS:	looking for new job, suffering headaches.
BERENICE:	housekeeping, looking after children, uncooperative.
GERVASE:	commuting to London, in and out of his office, home late.

URSULA:	looking after daughters, unhappy.
FERDINAND:	on statistics course, no attendance records.
DEBS:	photo-session vouched for on Newmarket Sales day.
SERENA:	teaching aerobics mornings and most evenings, shopping for clothes afternoons.
VIVIEN:	pottering about, can't remember.
ALICIA:	probably the same, unhelpful.
JOYCE:	playing bridge.

All one could say, I thought, was that no one had made any effort to produce alibis for either relevant time. Only Debs had a firm one, which had been arranged and vouched for by others. All the rest of the family had been moving about without timing their exits and entrances: normal behaviour for innocent people.

Only Joyce and I lived beyond half an hour's drive from Quantum. All of the others, from Donald at Henley to Gervase at Maidenhead, from Thomas near Reading to Lucy near Marlow, from Ferdinand in Wokingham to Serena in Bracknell, and even Vivien in Twyford and Alicia near Windsor, all of them seemed to have put down roots in a ring round the parent house like thistledown blown on the wind and reseeding.

The police had remarked on it when investigating

Moira's murder, and had checked school runs and train timetables until they'd been giddy. They had apparently caught no one lying, but that seemed to me inconclusive in a family which had had a lot of practice in misrepresentation. The fact had been, and still was, that anybody could have got to Quantum and home again without being missed.

I spent a short part of that Wednesday wandering around Moira's greenhouse, thinking about her death.

The greenhouse was invisible from the house, as Arthur Bellbrook had said, set on a side lawn which was bordered with shrubs. I wondered whether Moira had been alarmed to see her killer approach. Probably not. Quite likely, she had herself arranged the meeting, stating time and place. Malcolm had once mentioned that she didn't like casual callers, preferring them to telephone first. Perhaps it had been an unforeseen killing, an opportunity seized. Perhaps there had been a quarrel. Perhaps a request denied. Perhaps one of Moira's specials in acid-sweet triumphs, like picking Arthur Bellbrook's vegetables.

Moira in possession of Quantum, about to take half of everything Malcolm owned. Moira smugly satisfied, oblivious to her danger. I doubted if she had believed in her nightmare death even while it was happening.

Malcolm spent the day reading the *Financial Times* and making phone calls: yen, it appeared from snatches I overheard, were behaving gruesomely from Malcolm's point of view.

Although making calls outward, neither of us was keen to answer inward calls since that morning, when Malcolm had been drenched by a shower of recriminations from Vivien, all on the subject of meanness. He had listened with wry pain and given me a resumé once Vivien had run out of steam.

'One of the cats in the village told her we were here, so now the whole family will know,' he said gloomily. 'She says Donald is bankrupt, Lucy is starving and Thomas got the sack and can't deal with unemployment. Is it all true? It can't be. She says I should give them twenty thousand pounds each immediately.'

'It wouldn't hurt,' I said. 'It's Gervase's idea watered down.'

'But I don't believe in it.'

I explained about Donald's school fees crisis, Lucy's crumbling certainties, Thomas with Berenice chipping away at his foundations. He said their troubles lay in their own characters, which was true enough. He said if he gave those three a hand-out, he would have to do it for us all, or there would be a shooting civil war among Vivien, Joyce and Alicia. He made a joke of it, but he was stubborn. He had provided for us through our trust funds. The rest was up to us. He hadn't changed his mind. He'd thought over Vivien's suggestion, and the answer was no.

He telephoned back to Vivien and to her fury told her so. I could hear her voice calling him wicked, mean, cruel, vindictive, petty, sadistic, tyrannical and evil. He took offence, shouted at her to shut up, shut up, and finally slammed down the receiver while she was still in full flood.

All Vivien had achieved, I thought, was to make him dig his toes in further.

I thought him pig-headed, I thought him asking to be murdered. I looked at the unrelenting blue eyes daring me to argue, and wondered if he thought giving in would be weakness, if he thought baling out his children would diminish his own self-respect.

I said nothing at all. I was in a bad position to plead for the others, as I stood to gain myself. I hoped for many reasons that he would be able to change his mind, but it had to come from inside. I went out to Moira's greenhouse to give him time to calm down, and when I returned neither of us mentioned what had passed.

On the dogs' walk that afternoon, I reminded him that I was due to ride at Cheltenham the following day, and asked if he had any cronies in that direction with whom he could spend the time.

'I'd like to see you ride again,' he said.

He constantly surprised me.

'What if the family come too?'

'I'll dress up as another chef.'

I didn't know that it was wise, but again he had his own way, and I persuaded myself he would come to no harm on a racecourse. When we got there, I introduced him to George and Jo who congratulated him on Blue Clancy and took him off to lunch.

I looked around apprehensively all afternoon for brothers, sisters, mother and step-mothers, but saw none. The day was cold and windy with everyone turning up collars and hunching shoulders to keep warm, with hats on every head, felt, tweed, wool and fur. If anyone had wanted to hide inside their clothes, the weather was great for it.

Park Railings gave me a splendid ride and finished fourth, less tired than his jockey, who hadn't sat on a horse for six days. George and Jo were pleased enough, and Malcolm, who had been down the track with them to watch one of the other steeplechases from beside one of the jumps, was thoughtful.

'I didn't realize you went so fast,' he said, going home. 'Such speed over those jumps.'

'About thirty miles an hour.'

'I suppose I could buy a steeplechaser,' he said, 'if you'd ride it.'

'You'd better not. It would be favouritism.'

'Huh.'

We went thirty miles towards Berkshire and came to a hostelry he liked where we stopped for the late afternoon noggins (Arthur Bellbrook was taking the dogs home with him for the night) and waited lazily until dinner.

We talked about racing, or rather Malcolm asked questions and I answered them. His interest seemed inexhaustible, and I wondered if it would die as fast as it had sprung up. He couldn't wait to find out what Chrysos might do next year.

We ate without hurrying, lingering over coffee, and went on home, pulling up yawning outside the garage, sleepy from fresh air and French wine.

'I'll check the house,' I said without enthusiasm.

'Oh, don't bother, it's late.'

'I'd better check it. Honk the horn if you see something you don't like.'

I left him in the car, let myself into the kitchen and switched on the lights. The door to the hall was closed as usual, to keep the dogs, when they were there, from roaming through the house. I opened the door to the hall and switched on the hall lights.

I stopped there briefly, looking round.

Everything looked quiet and peaceful, but my skin began to crawl just the same, and my chest felt tight from suddenly suspended breath.

The door to the office and the door to the sitting room were not as I had left them. The door to the office was more than half open, the door to the sitting room all but closed; neither standing at the precise narrow angle at which I'd set them every time we'd been out.

I tried to remember whether I'd actually set the doors before leaving that morning, or whether I'd forgotten. But I *had* set them. I knew I had. I'd picked up my saddle and other gear in the hall after doing it, and shut the hall-to-kitchen door, and locked the outside door, leaving the dogs with Arthur Bellbrook in the garden.

I hadn't until then thought of myself as a coward, but I felt dead afraid of going further into the house. It was so large, so full of dark corners. There were two cellars, and the several unlit attic bedrooms of long-gone domestic servants, and the boxroom deep with shadows. There were copious cupboards everywhere and big empty wardrobes. I'd been round them all three or four times during the past few days, but not at night, and not with the signals standing at danger.

With an effort, I took a few steps into the hall, listening. I had no weapon. I felt nakedly vulnerable. My heart thumped uncomfortably. The house was silent.

The heavy front door, locked and bolted like a fortress, had not been touched. I went over to the office, reached in with an arm, switched on the light and pushed the half-open door wider.

There was no one in there. Everything was as Malcolm had left it in the morning. The windows shone blackly, like threats. Taking a deep breath, I repeated the procedure with the sitting room, but also checking the bolts on the French windows, and after that with the dining room, and the downstairs cloakroom, and then with worse trepidation went down the passage beside the stairs to the big room that had been our playroom when we were children and a billiard room in times long past.

The door was shut. Telling myself to go on with it, I opened the door, switched on the light, pushed the door open.

There was no one there. It wasn't really a relief, because I would have to go on looking. I checked the storeroom opposite, where there were stacks of garden furniture, and also the door at the end of the passage, which led out into the garden: securely bolted on the inside. I went back to the hall and stood at the bottom of the stairs, looking upward.

It was stupid to be so afraid, I thought. It was home, the house I'd been brought up in. One couldn't be frightened by home.

One was.

I swallowed. I went up the stairs. There was no one in my bedroom. No one in five other bedrooms, nor in the boxroom, no one in the bathrooms, no one in the plum and pink lushness of Malcolm's own suite. By the end, I was still as scared as I'd been at the beginning, and I hadn't started on cellars or attics or small hiding places.

I hadn't looked under the beds. Demons could be waiting anywhere to jump out on me, yelling. Giving in, I switched off all the upstairs lights and went cravenly back to the hall.

Everything was still quiet, mocking me.

I was a fool, I thought.

Leaving the hall and kitchen lights on, I went back to Malcolm who started to get out of the car when he saw me coming. I waved him back and slid in beside him, behind the driving wheel.

'What's the matter?' he said.

'Someone may be here.'

'What do you mean?'

I explained about the doors.

'You're imagining things.'

'No. Someone has used their key.'

We hadn't yet been able to have the locks changed, although the carpenter was due to be bringing replacements the following morning. He'd had difficulty finding good new locks to fit into such old doors, he'd said, and had promised them for Thursday, but I'd put him off until Friday because of Cheltenham.

'We can't stay out here all night,' Malcolm protested. 'It's bound to be the wind or something that moved the doors. Let's go to bed, I'm whacked.'

I looked at my hands. They weren't actually shaking. I thought for a while until Malcolm grew restless.

'I'm getting cold,' he said. 'Let's go in, for God's sake.'

'No . . . we're not sleeping here.'

'What? You can't mean it.'

'I'll lock the house, and we'll go and get a room somewhere else.'

'At this time of night?'

'Yes.' I made to get out of the car and he put a hand on my arm to catch my attention.

'Fetch some pyjamas, then, and washing things.'

I hesitated. 'No, I don't think it's safe.' I didn't say I couldn't face it, but I couldn't.

'Ian, all this is crazy.'

'It would be crazier still to be murdered in our beds.'

'But just because two doors . . .'

'Yes. Because.'

He seemed to catch some of my own uneasiness because he made no more demur, but when I was headed again for the kitchen he called after me, 'At least bring my briefcase from the office, will you?'

I made it through the hall again with only a minor tremble in the gut; switched on the office light, fetched his briefcase without incident and set the office door again at its usual precise angle. I did the same to the sitting room door. Perhaps they would tell us in the morning, I thought, whether or not we had had a visitor who had hidden from my approach.

I went back through the hall, switched the lights off, shut the hall-to-kitchen door, let myself out, left the house dark and locked and put the briefcase on the car's back seat.

On the basis that it would be easiest to find a room in London, particularly at midnight, for people without luggage, I drove up the M4 and on Malcolm's instructions pulled up at the Ritz. We might be refugees, he said, but we would be staying in no camp, and he explained to the Ritz that he'd decided to stay overnight in London as he'd been delayed late on business.

'Our name is Watson,' I said impulsively, thinking suddenly of Norman West's advice and picking out of the air the first name I could think of. 'We will pay with travellers' cheques.'

Malcolm opened his mouth, closed it again, and kept blessedly quiet. One could write whatever name one wanted onto travellers' cheques.

The Ritz batted no eyelids, offered us connecting rooms (no double suites available) and promised razors, toothbrushes and a bottle of scotch.

Malcolm had been silent for most of the journey, and so had I, feeling with every heart-calming mile that I had probably over-reacted, that maybe I hadn't set the doors, that if any of the family had let themselves into the house while we were out, they'd been gone long before we returned. We had come back hours later than anyone could have expected, if they were judging the time it would take us to drive from Cheltenham.

I could have sat at the telephone in the house and methodically checked with all the family to make sure they were in their own homes. I hadn't thought of it, and I doubted if I could have done it, feeling as I had.

Malcolm, who held that sleeping pills came a poor second to scotch, put his nightcap theory to the test and was soon softly snoring. I quietly closed the door between our two rooms and climbed between my own sheets, but for a long time lay awake. I was ashamed of my fear in the house which I now thought must have been empty. I had risked my neck without a qualm over big fences that afternoon: I'd been petrified in the house that someone would jump out on me from the dark. The two faces of courage, I thought mordantly: turn one face to the wall.

We went back to Berkshire in the morning and couldn't reach Quantum by car because the whole village, it seemed, was out and blocking the road. Cars and people everywhere: cars parked along the roadsides, people walking in droves towards the house.

'What on earth's going on?' Malcolm said.

'Heaven knows.'

In the end I had to stop the car, and we finished the last bit of the journey on foot.

We had to push through crowds and were unpopular until people recognized Malcolm, and made way for him, and finally we reached the entrance to the drive . . . and there literally rocked to a stop.

To start with there was a rope stretched across it, barring our way, with a policeman guarding it. In front of the house, there were ambulances, police cars, fire engines . . . swarms of people in uniform moving purposefully about.

Malcolm swayed with shock, and I felt unreal,

disconnected from my feet. Our eyes told us: our brains couldn't believe.

There was an immense jagged gaping hole in the centre of Quantum.

People standing near us in the gateway, round-eyed, said, 'They say it was the gas.'

CHAPTER TEN

We were in front of the house, talking to policemen. I couldn't remember walking up the drive.

Our appearance on the scene had been a shock to the assembled forces, but a welcome one. They had been searching for our remains in the rubble.

They told us that the explosion had happened at four-thirty in the morning, the *wumph* and reverberation of it waking half the village, the shockwaves breaking windows and setting dogs howling. Several people had called the police, but when the force had reached the village, everything had seemed quiet. No one knew where the explosion had occurred. The police drove round the extended neighbourhood until daylight, and it was only then that anyone saw what had happened to Quantum.

The front wall of the hall, the antique front door with it, had been blown out flat onto the drive, and the centre part of the upper storey had collapsed into the hall. The glass in all the windows had disappeared.

'I'm afraid it's worse at the back,' a policeman said

phlegmatically. 'Perhaps you'd come round there, sir. We can at least tell everyone there are no bodies.'

Malcolm nodded mechanically and we followed the policeman round to the left, between the kitchen and garage, through to the garden and along past the dining-room wall. The shock when we rounded onto the terrace was, for all the warning, horrific and sickening.

Where the sitting room had been, there was a mountain of jumbled dusty bricks, plaster, beams and smashed furniture spilling outwards onto the grass. Malcolm's suite, which had been above the sitting room, had vanished, had become part of the chaos. Those of the attic rooms that had been above his head had come down too. The roof, which had looked almost intact from the front, had at the rear been stripped of tiles, the old sturdy rafters standing out against the sky like picked ribs.

My own bedroom had been on one side of Malcolm's bedroom: all that remained of it were some shattered spikes of floorboards, a strip of plaster cornice and a drunken mantle clinging to a cracked wall overlooking a void.

Malcolm began to shake. I took off my jacket and put it round his shoulders.

'We don't have gas,' he said to the policeman. 'My mother had it disconnected sixty years ago because she was afraid of it.'

There was a slight spasmodic wind blowing, enough

to lift Malcolm's hair and leave it awry. He looked suddenly frail, as if the swirling air would knock him over.

'He needs a chair,' I said.

The policeman gestured helplessly to the mess. No chairs left.

'I'll get one from the kitchen. You look after him.'

'I'm quite all right,' Malcolm said faintly.

'The outside kitchen door is locked, sir, and we can't allow you to go in through the hall.'

I produced the key, showed it to him, and went along and in through the door before he could stop me. In the kitchen, the shiny yellow walls themselves were still standing, but the door from the hall had blown open, letting in a glacier tongue of bricks and dust. Dust everywhere, like a veil. Lumps of plaster had fallen from the ceiling. Everything glass, everything china in the room had cracked apart. Moira's geraniums, fallen from their shelves, lay in red farewell profusion over her all-electric domain.

I picked up Malcolm's pine armchair, the one thing he had insisted on keeping through all the changes, and carried it out to where I'd left him. He sank into it without seeming to notice it and put his hand over his mouth.

There were firemen and other people tugging at movable parts of the ruins, but the tempo of their work had slowed since they'd seen we were alive. Several of them came over to Malcolm, offering sympathy, but mostly wanting information, such as were we certain there had been no one else in the house?

As certain as we could be.

Had we been storing any gas in the house? Bottled gas? Butane? Propane? Ether?

No.

Why ether?

It could be used for making cocaine.

We looked at them blankly.

They had already discovered, it seemed, that there had been no mains gas connected. They were asking about other possibilities because it nevertheless looked like a gas explosion.

We'd had no gas of any sort.

Had we been storing any explosive substances whatsoever?

No.

Time seemed disjointed.

Women from the village, as in all disasters, had brought hot tea in thermos flasks for the men working. They gave some to Malcolm and me, and found a red blanket for Malcolm so that I could have my jacket back in the chill gusty air. There was grey sheet cloud overhead: the light was grey, like the dust.

A thick ring of people from the village stood in the garden round the edges of the lawn, with more arriving every minute across the fields and through the garden gate. No one chased them away. Many were taking photographs. Two of the photographers looked like Press.

A police car approached, its siren wailing ever louder as it made slow progress along the crowded road. It wailed right up the drive, and fell silent, and presently a senior-looking man not in uniform came round to the back of the house and took charge.

First, he stopped all work on the rubble. Then he made observations and wrote in a notebook. Then he talked to the chief of the firemen. Finally he came over to Malcolm and me.

Burly and black moustached, he said, as to an old acquaintance, 'Mr Pembroke.'

Malcolm similarly said, 'Superintendent,' and everyone could hear the shake he couldn't keep out of his voice. The wind died away for a while, though Malcolm's shakes continued within the blanket.

'And you, sir?' the superintendent asked me.

'Ian Pembroke.'

He pursed his mouth below the moustache, considering me. He was the man I'd spoken to on the telephone, I thought.

'Where were you last night, sir?'

'With my father in London,' I said. 'We've just . . . returned.'

I looked at him steadily. There were a great many things to be said, but I wasn't going to rush into them.

He said noncommittally, 'We will have to call in explosive experts as the damage here on preliminary inspection, and in the absence of any gas, seems to have been caused by an explosive device.'

Why didn't he say bomb, I thought irritably. Why shy away from the word? If he'd expected any reaction from Malcolm or me, he probably got none as both of us had come to the same conclusion from the moment we'd walked up the drive.

If the house had merely been burning, Malcolm would have been dashing about, giving instructions, saving what he could, dismayed but full of vigour. It was the implications behind a bomb which had knocked him into shivering lassitude: the implications and the reality that if he'd slept in his own bed, he wouldn't have risen to bath, read the *Sporting Life*, go to his bank for travellers' cheques and eat breakfast at the Ritz.

And nor, for that matter, would I.

'I can see you're both shocked,' the superintendent said unemotionally. 'It's clearly impossible to talk here, so I suggest you might come to the police station.' He spoke carefully, giving us at least theoretically the freedom of refusing.

'What about the house?' I said. 'It's open to the four winds. Apart from this great hole, all the windows are broken everywhere else. There's a lot of stuff still inside . . . silver . . . my father's papers in his office . . . some of the furniture.'

'We will keep a patrol here,' he said. 'If you'll give the instructions, we'll suggest someone to board up the windows, and we'll contact a construction firm with a tarpaulin large enough for the roof.'

'Send me the bill,' Malcolm said limply.

'The firms concerned will no doubt present their accounts.'

'Thanks anyway,' I said.

The superintendent nodded.

A funeral for Quantum, I thought. Coffin windows, pall roof. Lowering the remains into the ground would probably follow. Even if any of the fabric of the house should prove sound enough, would Malcolm have the stamina to rebuild, and live there, and remember?

He stood up, the blanket clutched around him, looking infinitely older than his years, a sag of defeat in the cheeks. Slowly, in deference to the shaky state of his legs, Malcolm, the superintendent and I made our way along past the kitchen and out into the front drive.

The ambulances had departed, also one of the fire engines, but the rope across the gateway had been overwhelmed, and the front garden was full of people, one young constable still trying vainly to hold them back.

A bunch in front of the rest started running in our direction as soon as we appeared, and with a feeling of unreality I saw they were Ferdinand, Gervase, Alicia, Berenice, Vivien, Donald, Helen . . . I lost count.

'Malcolm,' Gervase said loudly, coming to a halt in front of us, so that we too had to stop. 'You're alive!'

A tiny flicker of humour appeared in Malcolm's eyes at this most obvious of statements, but he had no chance of answering as the others set up a clamour of questions.

Vivien said, 'I heard from the village that Quantum had blown up and you were both dead.' Her strained voice held a complaint about having been given erroneous news.

'So did I,' Alicia said. 'Three people telephoned . . . so I came at once, after I'd told Gervase and the others, of course.' She looked deeply shocked, but then they all did, mirroring no doubt what they could see on my own face but also suffering from the double upset of misinformation.

'Then when we all get here,' Vivien said, 'we find you *aren't* dead.' She sounded as if that too were wrong.

'What did happen?' Ferdinand asked. 'Just look at Quantum.'

Berenice said, 'Where were you both, then, when it exploded?'

'We thought you were dead,' Donald said, looking bewildered.

More figures pushed through the crowd, horror opening their mouths. Lucy, Edwin and Serena, running, stumbling, looking alternately from the wounded house to me and Malcolm.

Lucy was crying, 'You're alive, you're alive!' Tears ran down her cheeks. 'Vivien said you were dead.'

'I was told they were dead,' Vivien said defensively. Dim-witted . . . Joyce's judgement came back.

Serena was swaying, pale as pale. Ferdinand put an arm round her and hugged her. 'It's all right, girl, they're not dead after all. The old house's a bit knocked about, eh?' He squeezed her affectionately.

'I don't feel well,' she said faintly. 'What happened?'

'Too soon to say for certain,' Gervase said assertively. 'But I'd say one can't rule out a bomb.'

They repudiated the word, shaking their heads, covering their ears. Bombs were for wars, for wicked schemes in aeroplanes, for bus stations in far places, for cold-hearted terrorists . . . for other people. Bombs weren't for a family house outside a Berkshire village, a house surrounded by quiet green fields, lived in by an ordinary family.

Except that we weren't an ordinary family. Ordinary families didn't have fifth wives murdered while planting geraniums. I looked around at the familiar faces and couldn't see on any of them either malice or dismay that Malcolm had escaped. They were all beginning to recover from the shock of the wrongly reported death and also beginning to realize how much damage had been done to the house.

Gervase grew angry. 'Whoever did this shall pay for it!' He sounded pompous more than effective.

'Where's Thomas?' I asked.

Berenice shrugged waspishly. 'Dear Thomas went out early on one of his useless job-hunting missions.

I've no idea where he was going. Vivien telephoned after he'd left.'

Edwin said, 'Is the house insured against bombs, Malcolm?'

Malcolm looked at him with dislike and didn't answer.

Gervase said masterfully, 'You'd better come home with me, Malcolm. Ursula will look after you.'

None of the others liked that. They all instantly made counter-proposals. The superintendent, who had been listening with attentive eyes, said at this point that plans to take Malcolm home would have to be shelved for a few hours.

'Oh, really?' Gervase stared down his nose. 'And who are you?'

'Detective Superintendent Yale, sir.'

Gervase raised his eyebrows but didn't back down. 'Malcolm's done nothing wrong.'

'I want to talk to the superintendent myself,' Malcolm said. 'I want him to find out who tried to destroy my house.'

'Surely it was an accident,' Serena said, very upset.

Ferdinand still had his arm round her. 'Face facts, girl.' He hesitated, looking at me. 'Vivien and Alicia told everyone you were both living here again . . . so how come you escaped being hurt?'

'Yes,' Berenice said. 'That's what I asked.'

'We went to London for a night out and stayed there,' I said.

'Very lucky,' Donald said heartily, and Helen, who stood at his elbow and hadn't spoken so far at all, nodded a shade too enthusiastically and said, 'Yes, yes.'

'But if we'd been in the office,' I said, 'we would have been all right.'

They looked along the front of the house to the far corner where the office windows were broken but the walls still stood.

'You wouldn't be in the office at four-thirty in the morning,' Alicia said crossly. 'Why should you be?'

Malcolm was growing tired of them. Not one had hugged him, kissed him, or made warm gestures over his survival. Lucy's tears, if they were genuine, had come nearest. The family obviously could have accommodated his death easily, murmuring regrets at his graveside, maybe even meaning them, but looking forward also with well-hidden pleasure to a safely affluent future. Malcolm dead could spend no more. Malcolm dead would free them to spend instead.

'Let's go,' he said to the superintendent, 'I'm cold.'

An unwelcome thought struck me. 'Did any of you,' I asked the family, 'tell Joyce . . . about the house?'

Donald cleared his throat. 'Yes, I . . . er . . . broke it to her.'

His meaning was clear. 'You told her we were dead?'

'Vivien said you were dead,' he said, sounding as defensive as she had. 'She said I should tell Joyce, so I did.'

'My God,' I said to the superintendent, 'Joyce is my mother. I'll have to phone her at once.'

I turned instinctively back to the house, but the superintendent stopped me, saying the telephones weren't working.

He, I and Malcolm began to move towards the gate, but we had gone only halfway when Joyce herself pushed through the crowd and ran forward, frantically, fearfully distraught.

She stopped when she saw us. Her face went white and she swayed as Serena had done, and I sprinted three or four long strides and caught her upright before she fell.

'It's all right,' I said, holding her. 'It's all right. We're alive.'

'Malcolm . . .'

'Yes, we're both fine.'

'Oh, I thought . . . Donald said . . . I've been crying all the way here, I couldn't see the road . . .' She put her face against my jacket and cried again with a few deep gulps, then pushed herself off determinedly and began searching her tailored pockets for a handkerchief. She found a tissue and blew her nose. 'Well, darling,' she said, 'as you're alive, what the hell's been going on?'

She looked behind Malcolm and me and her eyes widened.

'The whole bloody tribe come to the wake?' To

Malcolm she said, 'You've the luck of the devil, you old bugger.'

Malcolm grinned at her, a distinct sign of revival.

The three ex-wives eyed each other warily. Any mushy idea that the near-death of the man they'd all married and the near-destruction of the house they'd all managed might have brought them to sisterly sympathy was a total non-starter.

'Malcolm can come and stay with me,' Joyce said.

'Certainly not,' Alicia said instantly, clearly alarmed. 'You can take your precious Ian. Malcolm can go with Gervase.'

'I won't have it,' Vivien said sharply. 'If Malcolm's going anywhere, it's fitting he should stay with Donald, his eldest son.'

Malcolm looked as if he didn't know whether to laugh or scream.

'He's staying with me,' I said. 'If he wants to.'

'In your flat?' Ferdinand asked.

I had an appalling vision of my flat disintegrating like Quantum but, unlike Quantum, killing people above and below.

'No, not there,' I said.

'Then where, darling?' Joyce asked.

'Wherever we happen to be.'

Lucy smiled. It was the sort of thing she was happy with. She pulled her big brown cloak closer round her large form and said that it sounded a thoroughly sensible proposal. The others looked at her as if she were retarded instead of the brains of the tribe.

'I'll go wherever I want to,' Malcolm said flatly, 'and with Ian.'

I collected a battery of baleful glares, all of them as ever afraid I would scoop their shares of the pool: all except Joyce, who wanted me to.

'As that's settled,' she said with a hint of maternal smugness which infuriated all the others, 'I want to see just how bad the damage is to the house.' She looked at me briefly. 'Come along, darling, you can show me.'

'Run along, mummy's boy,' Gervase said spitefully, smarting from having been spurned by Malcolm.

'Poor dear Ian, tied to mummy's apron strings.' Berenice's effort came out thick with detestation. 'Greedy little Ian.'

'It isn't fair,' Serena said plaintively. 'Ian gets everything, always. I think it's beastly.'

'Come on, darling,' Joyce said. 'I'm waiting.'

I felt rebellious, tried to smother it, and sought for a different solution.

'You can all come,' I said to them. 'Come and see what really happened here.'

The superintendent had in no way tried to break up the family party but had listened quietly throughout. I happened to catch his eye at that point, and he nodded briefly and walked back beside Malcolm as everyone slowly moved round to the rear of the house.

The extent and violence of the damage there

silenced even Gervase. All of the mouths gaped: in all eyes, horrified awe.

The chief fireman came over and with a certain professional relish began in a strong Berkshire accent to point out the facts.

'Blast travels along the lines of least resistance,' he said. 'This is a good strong old house, which I reckon is why so much of it is still standing. The blast, see, travelled outwards, front and back from a point somewhere near the centre of the main upper storey. Some of the blast went upwards into the roof, bringing down some of those little attic bedrooms, and a good bit of blast, I'd reckon, blew downwards, making a hole that the upper storey and part of the attic just collapsed into, see what I mean?'

Everyone saw.

'There's this wall here,' he pointed to the one between what had been the sitting room and what was still the dining room, 'this wall here, with the chimney built into it, this is one of the main load-bearing walls. It goes right up to the roof. Same the other side, more or less. Those two thick walls stopped the blast travelling sideways, except a bit through the doorways.' He turned directly to Malcolm. 'I've seen a lot of wrecked buildings, sir, mostly burned, it's true, but some gas explosions, and I'd say, and mind you, you'd have to get a proper survey done, but I'd say, on looking at this house, that although it got a good shaking you could think of rebuilding it. Good solid Victorian house, otherwise it would have folded up like a pack of cards.'

'Thank you,' Malcolm said faintly.

The fireman nodded. 'Don't you let any fancy demolition man tell you different, sir. I don't like people being taken advantage of when they're overcome by disasters. I've seen too much of that, and it riles me. What I'm telling you is a straight opinion. I've nothing to gain one way or the other.'

'We're all grateful,' I said.

He nodded, satisfied, and Gervase finally found his voice.

'What sort of bomb was it?' he asked.

'As to that, sir, I wouldn't know. You'd have to wait for the experts.' The fireman turned to the superintendent. 'We shut off the electricity at the meter switch in the garage when we got here, and likewise turned off the mains water under a man-hole cover out by the gate. The storage tank in the roof had emptied through the broken pipes upstairs and water was still running when we got here, and all that water's now underneath the rubble. There's nothing I can see can start a fire. If you want to go into the upper storey at the sides, you'll need ladders, the staircase is blocked. I can't vouch for the dividing walls up there, we looked through the windows but we haven't been inside, you'd have to go carefully. We didn't go up to the attic much, bar a quick look from up the ladder. But down here, you should be all right in the dining room and in that big room the other side of this mess, and also in the kitchen and the front room on the far side.'

'My office,' Malcolm said.

The superintendent nodded, and I reflected that he already knew the layout of the house well from earlier repeated visits.

'We've done as much as we can here,' the fireman said. 'All right if we shove off now?'

The superintendent, agreeing, went a few steps aside with him in private consultation and the family began to come back from suspended animation.

The Press photographers moved in closer, and took haphazard pictures of us, and a man and a woman from different papers approached with insistent questions. Only Gervase seemed to find those tolerable and did all the answering. Malcolm sat down again on the pine chair, which was still there, and gathered his blanket around him, retreating into it up to his eyes like a Red Indian.

Vivien, spotting him, went over and told him she was tired of standing and needed to sit down and it was typically selfish of him to take the only seat, and an insult to her, as she was the senior woman present. Glancing at her with distaste, Malcolm got to his feet and moved a good distance away, allowing her to take his place with a self-satisfied smirk. My dislike of Vivien rose as high as her cheekbones and felt as shrewish as her mouth.

Alicia, recovered, was doing her fluttery feminine act

for the reporters, laying out charm thickly and eclipsing Serena's little-girl ploy. Seeing them together, I thought that it must be hard for Serena to have a mother who refused to mature, who in her late fifties still dressed and behaved like an eighteen-year-old, who for years had blocked her daughter's natural road to adulthood. Girls needed a motherly mother, I'd been told, and Serena didn't have one. Boys needed one too, and Joyce wasn't one, but I'd had a father all the time and in the end I'd also had Coochie, and Serena hadn't had either, and there lay all the difference in the world.

Edwin was having as hard a time as Donald in putting on a show of rejoicing over Malcolm's deliverance.

'It's all very well for you,' he said to me bitterly, catching my ironic look in his direction. 'Malcolm despises me – and don't bother to deny it, he makes it plain enough – and I don't see why I should care much for him. Of course, I wouldn't wish him dead . . .'

'Of course not,' I murmured.

' . . . but, well, if it had happened . . .' he stopped, not actually having the guts to say it straight out.

'You'd have been glad?' I said.

'No.' He cleared his throat. 'I could have faced it,' he said.

I almost laughed. 'Bully for you, Edwin,' I said. 'Hang in there, fellow.'

'I could have faced your death, too,' he said stuffily.

Oh well, I thought. I asked for that.

'How much do you know about bombs?' I asked.

'That's a ridiculous question,' he said, and walked off, and I reflected that Norman West had reported Edwin as spending an hour most days in the public library, and I betted one could find out how to make bombs there, if one persevered.

Berenice said to me angrily, 'It's all your fault Thomas is out of work.'

I blinked. 'How do you make that out?'

'He's been so worried about Malcolm's behaviour that he couldn't concentrate and he made mistakes. He says you could get Malcolm to help us, but of course I tell him you won't, why should you, you're Malcolm's pet.' She fairly spat the last word, the rage seething also in her eyes and tightening all the cords in her neck.

'You told Thomas that?' I said.

'It's true,' she said furiously. 'Vivien says you've always been Malcolm's favourite and he's never been fair to Thomas.'

'He's always been fair to all of us,' I said positively, but of course she didn't believe it.

She was older than Thomas by four or five years and had married him when she was well over thirty and (Joyce had said cattily) desperate for any husband that offered. Ten years ago, when I'd been to their wedding, she had been a thin, moderately attractive woman lit up by happiness. Thomas had been proud of himself and proprietary. They had looked, if not an exciting couple, stable and full of promise, embarking on a good adventure.

Ten years and two daughters later, Berenice had put on weight and outward sophistication and lost whatever illusions she'd had about marriage. I'd long supposed it was basic disappointment which had made her so destructive of Thomas, but hadn't bothered to wonder about the cause of it. Time I did, I thought. Time I understood the whole lot of them, because perhaps in that way we might come to know who could and who couldn't murder.

To search through character and history, not through alibis. To listen to what they said and didn't say, to learn what they could control, and what they couldn't.

I knew, as I stood there looking at the bunch of them, that only someone in the family itself could go that route, and that if I didn't do it, no one else would.

Norman West and Superintendent Yale could dig into facts. I would dig into the people. And the problem with that, I thought, mocking my own pretension, was that the people would do anything to keep me out.

I had to recognize that what I was going to do could produce more trouble than results. Spotting the capability of murder could elude highly-trained psychiatrists, who had been known to advise freedom for reformed characters only to have them go straight out and kill. A highly-trained psychiatrist I was not. Just someone who could remember how we *had* been, and could learn how we were now.

I looked at the monstrously gutted house and shivered. We had returned unexpectedly on Monday; today was Friday. The speed of planning and execution was itself alarming. Never again were we likely to be lucky. Malcolm had survived three attacks by sheer good fortune, but Ferdinand wouldn't have produced healthy statistics about a fourth. The family looked peacefully normal talking to the reporters, and I was filled with a sense of urgency and foreboding.

CHAPTER ELEVEN

One of Malcolm's dogs came bounding across the grass towards him, followed a few seconds later by the other. Malcolm put a hand out of his blanket and patted them, but with more absentmindedness than welcome. After them came Arthur Bellbrook with a face of consternation and concern which lightened considerably when he set eyes on Malcolm. In his grubby trousers and ancient tweed jacket, he came at a hobbling run in old army boots and fetched up very out of breath at Malcolm's side.

'Sir! You're alive! I went to Twyford to fetch some weedkiller. When I got back, they told me in the village . . .'

'Gross exaggeration,' Malcolm said, nodding.

Arthur Bellbrook turned to me, panting. 'They said you were both dead. I couldn't get down the road . . . had to come across the fields. Look at the house!'

I explained about our going to London, and asked him what time he'd gone home the previous day.

'Four o'clock, same as always. Say three-forty, then.

About then.' He was beginning to get his breath back, his eyes round with disbelief as he stared at the damage.

Nearer to three-thirty, I privately reckoned, if he was admitting to going home early at all.

'Did you go in the house at any time during the day?' I asked.

He switched his gaze from the ruins to me and sounded aggrieved. 'No, I didn't. You know I couldn't have. You've been locking the place like it's a fortress since you came back, and I didn't have a key. Where could I have got a key from?'

I said placatingly, 'It's just that we're anxious . . . someone got in, they must have.'

'Not me.' He was slightly mollified. 'I was working in the kitchen garden all day, digging potatoes and such like. I had the two dogs with me, tied up on their leads. If anyone had tried to get in the house, they'd have barked for sure, but they didn't.'

Malcolm said, 'Arthur, could you keep the dogs with you for another day or two?'

'Yes, I . . .' He looked helplessly at the heap of rubble spilling out across the terrace and onto the lawn. 'What do you want me to do about the garden?'

'Just . . . carry on,' Malcolm said. 'Keep it tidy.' It didn't seem incongruous to him to polish the setting, though I thought that perhaps, left to its own, nature would scatter leaves and grow longer grass and soften the raw brutality of the jagged edges.

The superintendent, seeing Arthur Bellbrook, came

across to him and asked the same questions that I had. Again, they seemed to know each other well, undoubtedly from Moira's investigations, and if there didn't seem to be friendship, there was clearly a mutual respect.

The reporters, having sucked the nectar from Gervase, advanced on Malcolm and on the gardener and the superintendent. I moved away, leaving them to it, and tried to talk to Ferdinand.

He was unfriendly and answered with shrugs and monosyllables.

'I suppose,' I said bitterly, 'you would rather I was lying in shreds and bloody tatters under all that lot.'

He looked at the tons of fallen masonry. 'Not really,' he said coolly.

'That's something.'

'You can't expect us to like it that you've an inside edge with Malcolm.'

'You had three years,' I pointed out, 'during which he wouldn't speak to me. Why did you waste them? Why didn't you get an inside edge yourself?'

'We couldn't get past Moira.'

I half smiled. 'Nor could I.'

'It's now we're talking about,' he said. He looked greatly like Malcolm, right down to the stubbornness in the eyes.

'What do you want me to do, walk away and let him be murdered?' I said.

'Walk away . . .?'

'That's why he wants me with him, to try to keep him safe. He asked me to be his bodyguard, and I accepted.'

Ferdinand stared. 'Alicia said . . .'

'Alicia is crazy,' I interrupted fiercely. 'So are you. Take a look at yourself. Greed, jealousy and spite, you've let them all in. I won't cut you out with Malcolm, I'd never attempt it. Try believing that instead, brother, and save yourself a lot of anxiety.'

I turned away from him in frustration. They were all illogical, I thought. They had almost begged me to use any influence I had with Malcolm to stop him spending and bale them out, and at the same time they believed I would ditch them to my own advantage. But then people had always been able to hold firmly to two contradictory ideas at the same time, as when once, in racing's past, Stewards, Press and public alike had vilified one brilliant trainer as 'most crooked', and elected one great jockey as 'most honest', blindly and incredibly ignoring that it was the self-same trusted jockey who for almost all of his career rode the brilliant trainer's horses. I'd seen a cartoon once that summed it up neatly: 'Entrenched belief is never altered by the facts.'

I wished I hadn't lashed out at Ferdinand. My idea of detection from the inside wasn't going to be a riotous success if I let my own feelings get in the way so easily. I might think the family unjust, they might think me conniving: OK, I told myself, accept all that and forget it. I'd had to put up with their various resentments for much of my life and it was high time I developed immunity.

Easier said than done, of course.

Superintendent Yale had had enough of the reporters. The family had by this time divided into two larger clumps, Vivien's and Alicia's, with Joyce and I hovering between them, belonging to neither. The superintendent went from group to group asking that everyone should adjourn to the police station. 'As you are all here,' he was saying, 'we may as well take your statements straight away, to save you being bothered later.'

'Statements?' Gervase said, eyebrows rising.

'Your movements yesterday and last night, sir.'

'Good God,' Gervase said. 'You don't think any of us would have done this, do you?'

'That's what we have to find out.'

'It's preposterous.'

None of the others said anything, not even Joyce.

The superintendent conferred with a uniformed colleague who was busy stationing his men round the house so that the ever-increasing spectators shouldn't get too close. The word must have spread, I thought. The free peepshow was attracting the next villages, if not Twyford itself.

Much of the family, including Malcolm, Joyce and myself, packed into the three police cars standing in the front drive, and Gervase, Ferdinand and Serena set off on foot to go back to the transport they had come in.

'I wouldn't put it past Alicia,' Joyce said darkly to the superintendent as we drove past them towards the gate, 'to have incited that brood of hers to blow up Quantum.'

'Do you have any grounds for that statement, Mrs Pembroke?'

'Statement? It's an opinion. She's a bitch.'

In the front passenger seat, Yale's shoulders rose and fell in a sigh.

The road outside was still congested with cars, with still more people coming on foot. Yale's driver stopped beside Joyce's car, which she'd left in the centre of the road in her haste, and helped to clear room for her to turn in. With her following, we came next to the hired car Malcolm and I had arrived in, but as it was hopelessly shut in on three sides by other locked vehicles, we left it there and went on in the police car.

In his large modern police station with its bullet-proofed glass enquiry desk, the superintendent ushered us through riot-proofed doors to his office and detailed a policewoman to take Joyce off for some tea. Joyce went protestingly, and Yale with another sigh sat us down in his bare-looking Scandinavian-type place of business.

He looked at us broodingly from behind a large desk. He looked at his nails. He cleared his throat. Finally he said to Malcolm, 'All right. You don't have to say it. I do not believe you would blow up your house just to make me believe that someone is trying to kill you.'

There was a long pause.

'That being so,' he said, as we both sat without speaking, 'we must take the attack in the garage more seriously.'

He was having a hard time, I thought. He ran a finger and thumb down his large black moustache and waited for comments from us that still didn't come.

He cleared his throat again. 'We will redouble our efforts to find Mrs Moira Pembroke's killer.'

Malcolm finally stirred, brought out his cigar case, put a cigar in his mouth and patted his pockets to find matches. There was a plastic notice on Yale's desk saying NO SMOKING. Malcolm, his glance resting on it momentarily, lit the match and sucked the flame into the tobacco.

Yale decided on no protest and produced a glass ashtray from a lower drawer in his desk.

'I would be dead twice over,' Malcolm said, 'if it weren't for Ian.'

He told Yale about the car roaring straight at us at Newmarket.

'Why didn't you report this, sir?' Yale said, frowning.

'Why do you think?'

Yale groomed his moustache and didn't answer.

Malcolm nodded. 'I was tired of being disbelieved.'

'And . . . er . . . last night?' Yale asked.

Malcolm told him about our day at Cheltenham, and

about Quantum's inner doors. 'I wanted to sleep in my own bed. I was tired. Ian absolutely wouldn't have it, and drove us to London.'

Yale looked at me steadily. 'Did you have a premonition?'

'No, I don't think so.' I hadn't felt a shiver, as I had in my flat. Perhaps the premonition in the flat had been for the house. 'I was just . . . frightened,' I said.

Malcolm glanced at me with interest.

Yale said, 'What of?'

'Not of bombs,' I said. 'I never considered that. Frightened there was someone in the house. I couldn't have slept there, that's all.' I paused. 'I saw the way the car drove at my father at Newmarket – it hit my leg, after all – and I believed him, of course, about being attacked and gassed in the garage. I knew he wouldn't have murdered Moira, or have had her murdered by anyone else. I believe absolutely in his extreme danger. We've been moving around, letting no one know where to find us, until this week.'

'My fault,' Malcolm said gloomily. 'I insisted on coming back here. Ian didn't want to.'

'When the doors were moved,' I said, 'it was time to go.'

Yale thought it over without comment for a while and then said, 'When you were in the house looking round, did you see anything unusual except for the doors?'

'No, nothing.'

'Nothing where it shouldn't be? Or absent from where it should have been?'

I thought back to that breathless heart-thumping search. Whoever had moved the doors must at least have looked into the office and the sitting room. I hadn't bothered with the position of any of the other doors except closing the one from the kitchen to the hall. Someone could have looked into all the rooms in the house, for all I knew.

'No,' I said in the end. 'Nothing else seemed out of place.'

Yale sighed again. He sighed a lot, it seemed to me. 'If you think of anything later, let me know.'

'Yes, all right.'

'The time-frame we're looking at,' he said, 'is between about three-forty p.m., when the gardener went home taking the dogs, and ten-thirty p.m., when you returned from Cheltenham.' He pursed his lips. 'If you hadn't stayed out to dinner, what time would you have been home?'

'We meant to stay out to dinner,' Malcolm said. 'That's why Arthur had the dogs.'

'Yes, but if . . .'

'About six-thirty,' I said. 'If we'd gone straight home after the last race.'

'We had a drink at the racecourse after the last race,' Malcolm said. 'I had scotch, Ian had some sort of fizzy gut-rot.' He tapped ash into the ashtray. He was enjoying having Yale believe him at last, and seemed to be feeling expansive.

'Ian thinks,' he said, 'that I was probably knocked out just outside the kitchen door that day, and that I was carried from there straight into the garage, not dragged, and that it was someone the dogs knew, as they didn't bark. They were jumping up and down by the kitchen door, I can remember that, as they do if someone they know has come. But they do that anyway when it's time for their walk, and I didn't give it a thought.' He inhaled a lot of smoke and let it out into the superintendent's erstwhile clean air. 'Oh yes, and about the fingerprints . . .' He repeated what I'd said about firemen's lifts.

Yale looked at me neutrally and polished his moustache. He was difficult to read, I thought, chiefly because he didn't want to be read. All policemen, I supposed, raised barriers and, like doctors and lawyers, tended not to trust what they were told, which could be bitterly infuriating to the truthful.

He must have been forty or forty-five, I supposed, and had to be competent to have reached that rank. He looked as if he habitually had too little exercise and too many sandwiches, and gave no impression of wallowing in his own power. Perhaps now he'd dropped his over-smart suspicions of Malcolm, he could actually solve his case, though I'd heard the vast majority of criminals were in jail because of having been informed on, not detected. I did very much want him to succeed.

I wished he could spontaneously bring himself to share what he was thinking, but I supposed he'd been trained not to. He kept his counsel anyway on that occasion, and I kept mine, and perhaps it was a pity.

A policewoman came in and said, looking harassed, that she didn't know where to put the Pembroke family.

Yale thought briefly and told her to show them all to his office. Malcolm said, 'Oh God,' and dragged on his cigar, and presently the whole troop arrived.

I got to my feet and Alicia immediately sat on my chair. Vivien and Joyce both glared at Malcolm, still seated, willing him to rise, which he didn't. Which of them could he possibly give his chair to, I thought, stifling laughter, without causing exmarital bloodshed?

With a straight face, Yale asked the policewoman to fetch two more chairs, and I couldn't even tell if he were amused or simply practical. When Vivien and Joyce were suitably enthroned, he looked around and counted us all: thirteen.

'Who's missing?' he asked.

He got various answers: 'My wife, Debs', 'Thomas, my husband', 'Ursula, of course.'

'Very well. Now, if any of you know anything or guess anything about the explosion at Quantum House, I want to hear about it.'

'Terrorists,' Vivien said vaguely.

Everyone ignored her and no one else made any suggestion.

'While you are here,' Yale said, 'I'll ask you all to

answer certain questions. I'll have my personnel write down your answers, and of course after that you can leave. The questions are, what were you doing yesterday between three in the afternoon and midnight, what were you doing a week last Tuesday between the same hours, and what were you doing two weeks ago today, Friday, also between three p.m. and midnight?'

Edwin said crossly, 'We've already answered most of those questions for that wretched man, West. It's too much to go over it all again.'

Several of the others nodded.

Yale looked blank. 'Who is West?'

'A detective,' Berenice said. 'I sent him away with a flea in his ear, I can tell you.'

'He was awfully persistent,' Helen said, not liking the memory. 'I told him I couldn't possibly remember exactly, but he went on prying.'

'Dreadful little man,' Serena said.

'He said I was illegitimate,' Gervase complained sourly. 'It's thanks to Joyce that he knew.'

Yale's mouth opened and closed again and he took a deep breath. 'Who is West?' he asked intensely.

'Fellow I hired,' Malcolm said. 'Private detective. Hired him to find out who was trying to kill me, as I reckoned the police weren't getting anywhere.'

Yale's composure remained more or less intact. 'All the same,' he said, 'please answer the questions again. And those of you without husband and wife here, please answer for them as best you can.' He looked around at all the faces, and I would have sworn he was puzzled. I looked to see what he had seen, and I saw the faces of ordinary people, not murderers. Ordinary people with problems and hang-ups, with quirks and grievances. People anxious and disturbed by the blasting of the house that most had lived in and all had visited. Not one of them could possibly be a murderer, I thought. It had after all to be someone from outside.

I felt a lot of relief at this conclusion until I realized I was raising any excuse not to have to find a murderer among ourselves; yet we did have to find one, if Malcolm were to live. The dilemma was permanent.

'That's all for now,' Yale said, rising to his feet. 'My staff will take your statements in the interview rooms. And Mr Pembroke senior, will you stay here a moment? And Mr Ian Pembroke also? There are the arrangements to be made about the house.'

The family left me behind with bad grace. 'It's my job, not Ian's, to see to things. I am the eldest.' That was Donald. 'You need someone with know-how.' That was Gervase, heavily. 'It's not Ian's house.' Petulance from Edwin.

Yale managed however to shovel them all out, and immediately the door had closed, I said, 'While they're all in the interview rooms, I'm taking my father out of here.'

'The house . . .' Malcolm began.

'I'll see to the house later. We're leaving here now,

this minute. If Superintendent Yale will lend us a police car, fine; otherwise we'll catch buses or taxis.'

'You can have a police car within reason,' Yale said.

'Great. Then . . . um . . . just take my father to the railway station. I'll stay here.'

'All right.'

To Malcolm, I said, 'Go to London. Go to where we were last night. Use the same name. Don't telephone anyone. Don't for God's sake let anyone know where you are.'

'You're bloody arrogant.'

'Yes. This time, listen to me.'

Malcolm gave me a blue glare, stubbed out his cigar, stood up and let the red blanket drop from his shoulders to the floor.

'Where will you be?' Yale asked him.

'Don't answer,' I said brusquely.

Malcolm looked at me, then at the superintendent. 'Ian will know where I am. If he doesn't want to tell you, he won't. Gervase tried to burn some information out of him once, and didn't succeed. He still has the scars . . .' he turned to me ' . . . don't you?'

'Malcolm!' I protested.

Malcolm said to Yale, 'I gave Gervase a beating he'll never forget.'

'And he's never forgiven me,' I said.

'Forgiven you? For what? You didn't snitch to me. Serena did. She was so young she didn't really understand what she'd been seeing. Gervase could be a proper bully.'

'Come on,' I said, 'we're wasting time.'

Superintendent Yale followed us out of his office and detailed a driver to take Malcolm.

'I'll come in the car, once I can move it,' I said to him. 'Don't go shopping, I'll buy us some things later. Do be sensible, I beg you.'

'I promise,' he said; but promises with Malcolm weren't necessarily binding. He went out with the driver and I stood on the police station steps watching his departure and making sure none of the family had seen him or could follow.

Yale made no comment but waved me back to his office. Here he gave me a short list of reputable building contractors and the use of his telephone. I chose one of the firms at random and explained what was needed, and Yale took the receiver himself and insisted that they were to do minimum weather-proofing only, and were to move none of the rubble until the police gave clearance.

'When the driver returns from taking your father,' he said to me, disconnecting, 'we can spare him to ferry you back to your car.'

'Thank you.'

'I'm trusting you, you know, to maintain communications between me and your father.'

'I'll telephone here every morning, if you like.'

'I'd much rather know where he is.'

I shook my head. 'The fewer people know, the safer.'

He couldn't exactly accuse me of taking unreasonable precautions, so he left it, and asked instead, 'What did your half-brother burn you with?'

'A cigarette. Nothing fancy.'

'And what information did he want?'

'Where I'd hidden my new cricket bat,' I answered: but it hadn't been about cricket bats, it had been about illegitimacy, which I hadn't known at the time but had come to understand since.

'How old were you both?'

'I was eleven. Gervase must have been thirteen.'

'Why didn't you give him the bat?' Yale asked.

'It wasn't the bat I wouldn't give him. It was the satisfaction. Is this part of your enquiries?'

'Everything is,' he said laconically.

The hired car was movable when I got back to it and as it was pointing in that direction I drove it along to Quantum. There were still amazing numbers of people there, and I couldn't get past the now more substantial barrier across the drive until the policeman guarding it had checked with Superintendent Yale by radio.

'Sorry, sir,' one of them said, finally letting me in. 'The superintendent's orders.'

I nodded and drove on, parking in front of the house beside two police cars which had presumably returned from taking the many family members to their various cars.

I had already grown accustomed to the sight of the house; it still looked as horrific but held no more shocks. Another policeman walked purposefully towards me as I got out of the car and asked what I wanted. To look through the downstairs windows, I said.

He checked by radio. The superintendent replied that I could look through the windows as long as the constable remained at my side, and as long as I would point out to him anything I thought looked wrong. I readily agreed to that. With the constable beside me, I walked towards the place where the hall could still be discerned, skirting the heavy front door, which had been blown outwards, frame and all, when the brick-work on either side of it had given way.

QUANTUM IN ME FUIT lay face downwards on the gravel. I did the best I could. Someone's best, I thought, grateful to be alive, hadn't quite been good enough.

'Don't go in, sir,' the young constable said warningly. 'There's more could come down.'

I didn't try to go in. The hall was full of ceilings and floors and walls from upstairs, though one could see daylight over the top of the heap, the daylight from the back garden. Somewhere in the heap were all of Malcolm's clothes except the ones he'd worn to Chel-tenham, all his vicuna coats and handmade shoes, all of the gold-and-silver brushes he'd packed on his flight to Cambridge, and somewhere, too, the portrait of Moira.

Jagged arrows of furniture stuck up from the devastation like the arms of the drowning, and pieces of dusty unrecognizable fabric flapped forlornly when a gust of wind took them. Tangled there, too, was everything I'd brought with me from my flat, save only my racing kit – saddle, helmet and holdall – which was still in the boot of the car along with Malcolm's briefcase. Everything was replaceable, I supposed; and I felt incredibly glad I hadn't thought of bringing the silver-framed picture of Coochie and the boys.

There was glass everywhere along the front of the house, fallen from the shattered windows. With the constable in tow, I crunched along towards the office, passing the ruins of the downstairs cloakroom on the way, where a half-demolished wall had put paid to the plumbing.

The office walls themselves, like those of the kitchen, were intact, but the office door that I'd set at such a careful angle was wide open with another brick and plaster glacier spilling through it. The shockwave that must have passed through the room to smash its way out through the windows had lifted every unweighted sheet of paper and redistributed it on the floor. Most of the pictures and countless small objects were down there also, including, I noticed, the pen pot holding the piece of wire. Apart from the ancient bevelled glass of a splendid breakfront bookcase which stood along one wall, everything major looked restorable, though getting rid of the dust would be a problem in itself.

I spent a good deal of time gazing through the open spaces of the office windows, but in the end had to admit defeat. The positions of too much had been altered for me to see anything inexplicably wrong. I'd seen nothing significant in there the previous evening when I'd fetched Malcolm's briefcase, when I'd been wide awake with alarm to such things.

Shaking my head I moved on round the house, passing the still shut and solidly bolted garden door which marked the end of the indoor passage. The blast hadn't shifted it, had dissipated on nearer targets. Past it lay the long creeper-covered north wall of the old playroom, and I walked along there and round into the rear garden.

The police had driven stakes into the lawn and tied ropes to them, making a line for no one to cross. Behind the rope the crowd persisted, open-eyed, chattering, pointing, coming to look and moving away to trail back over the fields. Among them Arthur Bellbrook, the dogs at his side, was holding a mini-court in a semi-circle of respectful listeners. The reporters and Press photographers seemed to have vanished but other cameras still clicked in a barrage. There was a certain restrained orderliness about everything which struck me hard as incongruous.

Turning my back to the gawpers, I looked through

the playroom window, seeing it, like the office, from the opposite angle to the previous night. Apart from the boxroom and my bedroom, it was the only room unmetamorphosed by Moira, and it still looked what it had been for forty years, the private domain of children.

The old battered armchairs were still there, and the big table that with a little imagination had been fort, boat, spaceship and dungeon in its time. The long shelves down the north wall still bore generations of train sets, building sets, board games and stuffed toys. Robin and Peter's shiny new bicycles were still propped there, that had been the joy of their lives in the week before the crash. There were posters of pop groups pinned to the walls and a bookcase bulging with reprehensible tastes.

The explosion on the other side of the thick load-bearing wall had done less damage to the playroom than to anywhere else I'd seen; only the broken windows and the ubiquitous dust, which had flooded in from the passage, showed that anything had happened. A couple of teddy bears had tumbled off the shelves, but the bicycles were still standing.

Anything there that shouldn't be there, anything not there that should be, Yale had said. I hadn't seen anything the night before in those categories, and I still couldn't.

With a frustrated shrug, I skirted the poured-out guts of the house and on the far side looked through the dining-room windows. Like the playroom, the dining room was relatively undamaged, though here the blast had blown in directly from the hall, leaving the now familiar tongue of rubble and covering everything with a thick grey film. For ever after, I would equate explosions with dust.

The long table, primly surrounded by high-backed chairs, stood unmoved. Some display plates held in wires on the wall had broken and fallen off. The sideboard was bare, but then it had been before. Malcolm had said the room had hardly been used since he and Moira had taken to shouting.

I continued round to the kitchen and went in through the door, to the agitation of the constable. I told him I'd been in there earlier to fetch the pine chair, which someone had since brought back, and he relaxed a very little.

'That door,' I said, pointing to one in a corner, 'leads to the cellars. Do you know if anyone's been down there?'

He didn't think so. He was pretty sure not. He hadn't heard anyone mention cellars.

The two underground rooms lay below the kitchen and dining room, and without electric lights I wasn't keen to go down there. Still . . . what excuse did I have not to?

Malcolm kept some claret in racks there, enough to grieve him if the bottles were broken. Coochie had used the cellars romantically for candlelit parties with red-checked tablecloths and gypsy music, and the folding tables and chairs were still stacked there, along with the motley junk of ages that was no longer used but too valuable to throw away.

'Do you have a torch, constable?' I asked.

No, he hadn't. I went to fetch the one I'd installed by habit in the hired car and, in spite of his disapproval, investigated downstairs. He followed me, to do him justice.

To start with, the cellars were dry, which was a relief as I'd been afraid the water from the storage tank and the broken pipes would have drained down and flooded them.

None of Malcolm's bottles was broken. The chimney wall, continuing downwards as sturdy foundations, had sheltered everything on its outer side as stalwartly below as it had above.

The dire old clutter of pensioned-off standard lamps, rocking chair, pictures, tin trunk, tiger skin, bed head-board, tea trolley, all took brief life in the torchlight and faded back to shadow. Same old junk, undisturbed.

All that one could say again was that nothing seemed to be there in the cellar that shouldn't be, and nothing not there that should. Shrugging resignedly, I led the way upstairs and closed the door.

Outside again, I looked into the garage, which seemed completely untouched, and walked round behind it to the kitchen garden. The glass in the old greenhouse was broken, and I supposed Moira's little folly, away on the far side of the garden, would have suffered the same fate.

I dearly wanted to go down to the far end of the kitchen garden to make sure the gold store was safe, but was deterred by the number of interested eyes already swivelled my way, and particularly by Arthur Bellbrook's.

The wall itself looked solid enough. The crowds were nowhere near it, as it was away to the left, while they were coming in from the fields on the right.

The constable stood by my side, ready to accompany me everywhere.

Shrugging, I retreated. Have faith, I thought, and drove away to London.

CHAPTER TWELVE

Malcolm had achieved a double suite at the Ritz with views of Green Park. He had lunched on Strasbourg pâté and Dover sole, according to the remains on the white-clothed room-service table, and had reached the lower half of a bottle of Krug.

'How are the shakes?' I said, putting his briefcase down beside him.

'Were you followed here?' he asked.

'I was not.'

He was doing his best to pretend he had regained total command of himself, yet I guessed the train journey had been an anxious and lonely ordeal. It was difficult for me to imagine the escalating trauma within him. How could anyone be the target of deadly unrelenting virulence and not in the end break down? I'd got to invent something better for him, I thought, than cooping him up in millionaire cells. Make him safe, give him back his lightheartedness, set him free.

'Um,' I said. 'I hope your passport's still in your briefcase.'

'Yes, it is.' He had taken it in his briefcase to Paris.

'Good.'

An unfortunate thought struck him. 'Where's yours?' Malcolm asked.

'In the rubble. Don't worry, I'll get a replacement. Do you have a visa for America?'

'Yes. I also had one for Australia once, but they only last a year. If we go, we'll have to get new visas from Australia House.'

'How about if you go to America tomorrow?' I said.

'*Tomorrow*? How can I?'

'I'll take you safely to Heathrow and see you off.'

'Dammit, that's not what I meant.'

'No,' I said. 'Well . . . the Breeders' Cup races are three weeks tomorrow at Santa Anita. Why don't we phone Ramsey Osborn? Why don't we phone Blue Clancy's trainer? Why don't you fly to Los Angeles tomorrow and have a fine old time at the races for three weeks? They have racing every day on the same track. If I know you, you'll be cronies with the racetrack committee immediately. Ramsey Osborn will send introductions. You can stay where the Breeders' Cup organizers do, at the Beverly Wilshire hotel which I've heard is right at the end of Rodeo Drive where there's a man's shop so expensive you have to make an appointment to be let in. Buy a few shirts there, it'll make a nice dent in your bankroll. Forget Quantum. Forget the bloody family. They won't know where you are and they'll never find you.'

I stopped only a fraction for breath, not long enough for him to raise objections. 'On the Tuesday after the Breeders' Cup, they're running the Melbourne Cup in Melbourne, Australia. That's their biggest race. The whole country stops for it. A lot of the people from the Breeders' Cup will go on to Australia. You'll have made cronies among them by the dozen. I've heard it's all marvellous. I've never been, and I'd love to. I'll join you as soon as my passport's renewed and I'll go on minding your back – if you still want me to.'

He had listened at first with apathy, but by the end he was smiling. I'd proposed the sort of impulsive behaviour that had greatly appealed to him in the past, and it still did, I was grateful to see.

'A damn sight better than rotting at the Ritz,' he announced.

'Great,' I said. 'Get out your diary for the numbers.'

It was soon settled. Blue Clancy would go over for the Breeders' Cup as long as he was fit. Ramsey Osborn, booming away in Stamford, Connecticut, promised introductions galore to a score of very dear friends he'd met a couple of times out West. Why didn't Malcolm stop off at Lexington on the way and feast his eyes on some real bloodstock? Ramsey had some very good friends in Lexington who would be delighted to have Malcolm stay with them. Ramsey would call them and fix it. Stay by the phone, you guys, he said. He would fix it and call back. It was breakfast time in Connecticut, he said. It would be an hour earlier in Lexington. He would see if the lazy so and so's were out of bed.

Whether they were or they weren't, Ramsey phoned back within twenty minutes. As before, Malcolm talked on the sitting-room telephone, I on the extension in my bedroom.

'All set,' Ramsey said. 'They're expecting you, Malcolm, tomorrow, and I'm flying down Sunday. They're real sweet guys, you'll love them. Dave and Sally Cander. Dogwood Drift Farm, outside of Lexington.' He read out the telephone number. 'You got that?'

Malcolm had got it.

Ramsey asked where Malcolm was planning to stay for the Breeders' Cup. 'Beverly Wilshire? Couldn't be better. Centre of the universe. I'll make reservations right away.'

Malcolm explained he needed a two-bedroom suite for himself and me. Sure thing, Ramsey agreed. No problem. See you, he said. We had made his day, he said, and to have a good one.

The sitting room seemed smaller and quieter when he'd gone off the line, but Malcolm had revitalized remarkably. We went at once by taxi to Australia House where Malcolm got his visa without delay, and on the way back stopped first at his bank for more travellers' cheques and then in Piccadilly a little short of the Ritz to shop in Simpson's for replacement clothes from the skin up, not forgetting suitcases to pack them in.

Malcolm paid for all of mine with his credit card, which was a relief. I hardly liked to ask him outright for my fare to California, but he'd thought of my other finances himself already and that evening gave me a bumper cheque to cover several additional destinations.

'Your fare and so on. Pay Arthur Bellbrook. Pay Norman West. Pay the contractors for weatherproofing Quantum. Pay for the hired car. Pay your own expenses. Anything else?'

'Tickets to Australia?'

'We'll get those in the morning. I'll pay for them here, with mine to Lexington. If we can get you a Los Angeles ticket without a date on, I can pay for that too.'

We made plans about telephone calls. He was not to phone me, I would phone him.

We dined in good spirits, the dreadful morning at least overlaid. He raised his glass: 'To Blue Clancy' and 'To racing' and 'To life.'

'To life,' I said.

I drove him to Heathrow in the morning safely as promised, and saw him on his way to Lexington via New York and Cincinnati. He was fizzing at least at half strength and gave me a long blue look before he departed.

'Don't think I don't know what I owe you,' he said.

'You owe me nothing.'

'Bloody Moira,' he said unexpectedly, and looked back and waved as he went.

Feeling good about him, I telephoned from the airport to Superintendent Yale but got one of his assistants: his chief was out at Quantum and had left a message that if I phoned I was to be asked if I could join him. Yes, I could, I agreed, and arrived in the village about forty minutes later.

The road to the house wasn't as congested as the day before, but fresh waves of sightseers still came and went continuously. I drove up to the gate and after radio consultation the constable there let me pass. Another policeman was at my side the moment I stopped in front of the house. Different men, both of them, from the day before.

Superintendent Yale appeared from the direction of the kitchen, having been alerted by the gateman, I surmised.

'How is Mr Pembroke?' he asked, shaking hands with every sign of having adopted humanity as a policy.

'Shaken,' I said.

He nodded understandingly. He was wearing an overcoat and looked cold in the face, as if he'd been out of doors for some time. The mild wind of yesterday had intensified rawly and the clouds looked more threatening, as if it would rain. Yale glanced with anxiety at the heavens and asked me to go round with him to the back garden.

The front of the house looked sad and blind, with

light brown plywood hammered over all the windows and a heavy black tarpaulin hanging from under the roof to hide the hole in the centre. At the rear, the windows were shuttered and the bare roof rafters were covered but the devastated centre was still open to the elements. Several men in hard hats and overalls were working there, slowly picking up pieces from the huge jumble and carrying them to throw them into a rubbish skip which stood a short distance away across the lawn.

'Do they propose to move all that by hand?' I asked.

'As much as is necessary,' Yale said. 'We've got a surprise for you.' He waved to a man in beige overalls with a blue hard hat who came over to us and asked me my name.

'Ian Pembroke,' I said obligingly.

He unzipped the front of his overalls, put a hand inside and drew out a battered navy-blue object which he held out to me with a small satisfied smile. 'You may need this,' he said.

Never a truer word. It was my passport.

'Where on earth did you find it?' I said, delighted.

He shrugged and pointed to the mess. 'We always come across a few things unharmed. We're making a pile of them for you, but don't get your hopes up.'

I zipped the passport into my new Simpson's Barbour and thought gratefully that I wouldn't have to trail around getting a new one.

'Have you found any gold-and-silver-backed brushes?' I asked.

'Not so far.'

'They're my father's favourite things.'

'We'll look out for them,' he said. 'Now, we'd like you to help us in return.'

'Anything I can.'

He was a lean, highly professional sort of man, late forties I guessed, giving an impression of army. He said his name was Smith. He was an explosives expert.

'When you first came here yesterday morning,' he said, 'did you smell anything?'

I was surprised. I thought back.

'Brick dust,' I said. 'The wind was stirring it up. It was in my throat.'

He grunted. 'This looks like a gas explosion, but you're quite certain, aren't you, that there was no gas in the house?'

'Absolutely certain.'

'Do you know what cordite smells like?' he asked.

'Cordite? Like after a gun's been fired, do you mean?'

'That's right.'

'Well, yes, I know what it smells like.'

'And you didn't smell that here yesterday morning?'

I looked at him, puzzled. 'No one was shot,' I said.

He smiled briefly. 'Do you know what cordite is?' he asked.

'Not really.'

'It was used very commonly as a general explosive,' he said, 'before Nobel invented dynamite in 1867. It's less fierce than dynamite. It's sort of high-grade gun-powder, and it's still used in some types of quarries. It explodes comparatively slowly, at about two thousand five hundred metres per second, or a little over. It explodes like a gas. It doesn't punch small holes through walls like a battering ram. It's rather like an expanding balloon that knocks them flat.'

I looked at the house.

'Yes, like that,' Smith said.

'Cordite . . .' I frowned. 'It means nothing.'

'Its strong smell lingers,' he said.

'Well . . . we didn't get here until ten, and the explosion was at four-thirty in the morning, and it was fairly windy, though not as rough as today. I should think any smell had blown away.' I paused. 'What about all the people who were here before us? What do they say?'

'They're not here today,' Smith said succinctly. 'I haven't asked them.'

'No one said anything to me about a smell,' I said.

Smith shrugged. 'We'll do microscopic tests. We would do, anyway. But it looks to me as if cordite is a strong possibility.'

'Can you buy cordite?' I asked vaguely. 'Can anyone?'

'No, they definitely can't,' Smith said with decision. 'Twenty years or so ago, maybe, but not now. Since terrorism became a part of life, most sorts of explosives are highly regulated. It's extremely difficult for the general public to get hold of them. There are a few explosive substances on the open market, but detonators to set them off are not.'

I found I was thinking of cordite in terms of the small quantities used in firearms, whereas to knock down half a house . . .

'How much cordite would that have taken?' I asked, gesturing to the results.

'I haven't yet worked it out. A good deal.'

'What would it have been in?'

'Anything.'

'What does it look like? Is it like jelly?'

'No, you're thinking of high-explosive TNT. That's liquid when it's fed into bomb cases, then it gels inside. Bombs dropped from aircraft are that sort. Cordite is loose grains, like gunpowder. To get a useful result, you have to compress it. Confine it. Then you need heat to start off the chemical reaction, which proceeds at such a rate that the ingredients appear to explode.'

'Appear!' I said, and added hastily, 'OK, I take your word for it, don't explain.'

He gave me a slightly pitying look but let up on the lecture and went back to searching in the ruins. Superintendent Yale asked if any of the Pembrokes had ever had any connection whatever with quarries. None that I knew of, I said. It was most improbable.

'Or had friends who had quarries, or who worked in quarries?'

I didn't know. I'd never heard of any.

My gaze wandered away from Smith and his fellow diggers after truth, and I became more aware of the audience beyond the rope in the garden. There weren't anything like as many as the day before, but clearly the work in progress was a draw in itself.

Arthur Bellbrook was there again, talking away. He must enjoy the celebrity, I thought. He'd been the one who'd found Moira, and now there was the house . . . Arthur was talking as if he owned the news, rocking back on his heels and sticking his stomach out. The dogs on their leads patiently waited. It didn't matter to them, I supposed, that Arthur was into maybe the twentieth account of life and death with the Pembrokes.

A stray piece of memory connected Arthur to the smell of cordite, and I couldn't think why that should be until I remembered him carrying his shotgun into the house on the day he'd thought I was a burglar.

I cast the stray thought out but it sauntered back, telling me it was nothing to do with Arthur and shotguns.

What then?

I frowned, trying to remember.

'What's the matter?' Yale said, watching me.

'Nothing, really.'

'You've thought of something. One of your family does have a quarry connection, is that it?'

'Oh no,' I half laughed. 'Not that. The smell of cordite . . .'

The smell of cordite on a misty morning, and the gardener . . . not Arthur, but old Fred before him . . . telling us children to keep out of the way, to go right back out of the field, he didn't want our heads blown off . . .

I remembered abruptly, like a whole scene springing to life on a film screen. I walked across to where Smith in his hard blue hat bent to his task and said, without preamble, 'Does cordite have another name?'

He straightened, with a piece of brick and plaster in his hand.

'I suppose so,' he said. 'It's commonly called "black powder".'

Black powder.

'Why?' he said.

'Well, we had some here once. But long ago, when we were children. Twenty years ago at least, probably more. But I suppose . . . some of the family could have remembered . . . as I just have.'

Yale, who had followed me to listen, said, 'Remember what?'

'There used to be four or five great old willow trees down by the stream, across the field.' I pointed. 'Those you can see now are only twenty years old or so. They grow very fast . . . they were planted after they took the old trees down. They were splendid old trees, huge, magnificent.'

Yale made hurrying-up motions with his hands, as if to say the state of long-gone willows, however patrician, was immaterial.

'They were at the end of their lives,' I said. 'If there was a gale, huge branches would crack off. Old Fred, who was the gardener for years here before Arthur, told my father they weren't safe and they'd have to come down, so he got some foresters to come and fell them. It was dreadful seeing them come down . . .' I didn't think I'd tell Yale that half the family had been in tears. The trees had been friends, playground, climbing frames, deepest purple imaginary rain forests: and, afterwards, there was too much daylight and the dead bodies being sawn up for firewood and burned on bonfires. The stream hadn't looked the same when open to bright sunshine; rather ordinary, not running through dappled mysterious shade.

'Go on,' Yale said with half-stifled impatience. 'What's all this about trees?'

'The stumps,' I said. 'The tree men sawed the trees off close to the ground but left the stumps, and no one could get them out. A tractor came from a nearby farm and tried . . .' We'd had a great time then, having rides all day. 'Anyway, it failed. Nothing else would move the stumps, and Fred didn't want to leave them there to rot, so he decided to blow them up . . . with black powder.'

'Ah,' Yale said.

Black powder had sounded, somehow, as if it ought

to belong to pirates. We'd been most impressed. Fred had got his powder and he'd dug a hole down below the stubborn roots of the first stump, and filled it and set off one enormous explosion. It was just as well he'd cleared us out of the field first because the blast had knocked Fred himself flat although he'd been about a hundred feet away. The first tree stump had come popping out of the ground looking like a cross between an elephant and an octopus, but Malcolm, who came running in great alarm to see what had happened, forbade Fred to blow up the others.

As I told the gist of this to Yale and Smith, the second reel of the film was already unrolling in my mind, and I stopped fairly abruptly when I realized what I was remembering.

'Fred,' I said, 'carried the box of black powder back to the tool shed and told us never to touch it. We were pretty foolish but not that crazy. We left it strictly alone. And there the box stayed until it got covered over with other junk and we didn't notice it or think of it any more . . .' I paused, then said, 'Wouldn't any explosive be useless after all this time?'

'Dynamite wouldn't last much more than a year in a tool shed,' Smith said. 'One hot summer would ruin it. But black powder – cordite – is very stable, and twenty years is immaterial.'

'What are we waiting for?' Yale said, and walked towards the tool shed which lay behind the garage on the near side of the kitchen garden.

The tool shed was a place I hadn't thought of looking into the day before: but even if I had, I doubted if I would have remembered the black powder. Its memory had been too deep.

'Where is this box?' Yale asked.

I looked at the contents of the tool shed in perplexity. I hadn't been in there for years, and in that time it had passed from Fred to Arthur. Fred had had an upturned orange box to sit on while he waited through heavy showers: Arthur had an old fireside chair. Fred had had a tray with a cracked mug and a box of sugar cubes and had come indoors to fetch his tea: Arthur had an electric kettle. Fred had tended old tools lovingly: Arthur had shiny new ones with paint still on the handles.

Beyond the tools and the chair, in the centre section of the spacious shed, were things like mowers, chainsaws and hedgeclippers and, at the furthest shadowy end, the flotsam by-passed by time, like the stuff in the cellar, stood in forgotten untidy heaps.

It all looked unpromisingly undisturbed, but Yale called up a pair of young policemen and told them to take everything out of the tool shed and lay each object separately on the ground. Smith went back to the rubble, but Yale and I watched the policemen and so did Arthur Bellbrook, who came hurrying across the moment he saw what was happening.

'What's going on?' he said suspiciously.

'When did you last clean out the tool shed?' Yale asked.

Arthur was put out and beginning to bridle.

'Just say,' I said to him. 'We just want to know.'

'I've been meaning to,' he said defensively. 'That's Fred's old rubbish, all that at the back.'

The superintendent nodded, and we all watched the outgoing procession of ancient, rusting, broken and neglected tat. Eventually one of the men came out with a dirty wooden box which I didn't recognize at first because it was smaller than I'd seen in my memory. He put it on the ground beside other things, and I said doubtfully, 'I think that's it.'

'Mr Smith,' Yale called.

Mr Smith came. Yale pointed at the box, which was about the size of crates used for soft drink bottles, and Smith squatted beside it.

The lid was nailed shut. With an old chisel, Smith prised it open and peeled back the yellowish paper which was revealed. Inside the paper, half-filling the box, there was indeed black powder.

Smith smelled it and poked it around. 'It's cordite, all right, and in good condition. But as it's here, it obviously hasn't been used. And anyway, there wouldn't have been anything like enough in this box to have caused that much damage to the house.'

'Well,' I said weakly, 'it was only an idea.'

'Nothing wrong with the idea,' Smith said. He looked

around at the growing collection of discards. 'Did you find any detonators?'

He had everyone open every single packet and tin: a lot of rusty staples and nails saw daylight, and old padlocks without keys and rotting batteries, but nothing he could identify as a substance likely to set off an explosion.

'Inconclusive,' he said, shrugging, and returned to his rubble.

Yale told Arthur to leave the cordite where it was and do what he liked with the rest, and Arthur began throwing the decaying rubbish into the skip.

I tried to apologize for all the waste of time, but the superintendent stopped me.

'When you saw the tree stump blown up, which of your brothers and sisters were there?'

I sighed, but it had to be faced. 'Gervase, Ferdinand and I were always together at that time, but some of the older ones were there too. They used to come for weekends still after they were grown up. Vivien used to make them, so that Malcolm wouldn't cut them out. Alicia hated it. Anyway, I know Lucy was there, because she wrote a poem about roots shrieking blindly to the sky.'

Yale looked sceptical.

'She's a poet.' I said lamely. 'Published.'

'The roots poem was published?'

'Yes.'

'All right, then. She was there. Who else?'

'Someone was carrying Serena on his shoulders when we had to leave the field for the explosion. I think it must have been Thomas. He used to make her laugh.'

'How old were you all at that time?' Yale asked.

'I don't know exactly.' I thought back. Alicia had swept out not very long after. 'Perhaps I was thirteen. Gervase is two years older, Ferdinand one year younger. Lucy would have been . . . um . . . twenty-two, about, and Thomas nineteen. Serena must have been six, at that rate, and Donald . . . I don't know if he was there or not . . . he would have been twenty-four.'

Yale thoughtfully pulled out his notebook and asked me to repeat the ages, starting with Donald.

'Donald twenty-four, Lucy twenty-two, Thomas nineteen, Gervase fifteen, myself thirteen, Ferdinand twelve, Serena six.'

'Right,' he said, putting a full-stop.

'But what does it matter, if the cordite is still here?' I said.

'They all saw the force of the explosion,' he said. 'They all saw it knock the gardener over from a hundred feet away, isn't that what you said?'

I looked at the shattered house and said forlornly, 'None of them could have done it.'

Yale put his notebook away. 'You might be right,' he said.

Smith again came over to join us. 'You've given me an idea,' he said to me. 'You and your tree roots. Can you draw me a plan of where the rooms were, exactly, especially those upstairs?'

I said I thought so, and the three of us went into the garage out of the wind, where I laid a piece of paper on the bonnet of Moira's car and did my best.

'The sitting room stretched all the way between the two thick walls, as you know,' I said. 'About thirty feet. Above that . . .' I sketched, 'there was my room, about eight feet wide, twelve deep, with a window on the short side looking out to the garden. Malcolm's bedroom came next, I suppose about fifteen feet wide and much deeper than mine. The passage outside bent round it . . . and then his bathroom, also looking out to the garden, with a sort of dressing room at the back of it which also led out of the bedroom . . .' I drew it. 'Malcolm's whole suite would have been about twenty-two feet wide facing the garden, by about seventeen or eighteen feet deep.'

Yale studied the drawing. 'Your room and the suite together were more or less identical with the sitting room, then?'

'Yes, I should think so.'

'A big house,' he commented.

'It used to be bigger. The kitchen was once a morning room, and where the garage is now there were kitchens and servants' halls. And on the other side, where the passage now goes out into the garden, there were gun rooms and flower rooms and music rooms, a bit of a rabbit warren. I never actually saw the wings, only photographs of them. Malcolm had them pulled down when he inherited the house, to make it easier to deal with without the droves of servants his mother had.'

'Hm,' he said. 'That explains why there are no sideways-facing windows on the ground floor.'

'Yes,' I agreed.

He borrowed my pen and did some calculations and frowned.

'Where exactly was your father's bed?'

I drew it in. 'The bed was against the wall between his room and the large landing, which was a sort of upstairs place to sit in, over the hall.'

'And your bed?'

'Against the wall between my room and Malcolm's.'

Smith considered the plan for some time and then said, 'I think the charge here was placed centrally. Did your father by any chance have a chest, or anything, at the foot of his bed?'

'Yes, he did,' I said, surprised. 'A long box with a padded top for a seat. He kept his tennis things in it, when he used to play.'

'Then I'd think that would be where the explosion occurred. Or under your father's bed. But if there was a box at the foot, I'd bet on that.' Smith borrowed the pen again for some further calculations and looked finally undecided.

'What's the matter?' I asked.

'Mm . . . well, because of your tree roots, I was

thinking of an explosive that farmers and landowners use sometimes which is safer than cordite. They blow up tree trunks, clear blocked ditches, that sort of thing. You can buy the ingredients anywhere without restrictions and mix it yourself.'

'That sounds extraordinary,' I said.

He smiled slightly. 'It's not so easy to get the detonators to set it off.'

'What is it, then?' I asked.

Yale, too, was listening with great interest.

'Fertilizer and diesel oil,' Smith said.

'What?' I sounded disappointed and Smith's smile expanded.

'Ammonium nitrate,' he said. 'You can buy it in fine granules from seed merchants and garden centres, places like that. Mix it with fuel oil. Dead simple. As far as I remember, but I'd have to look it up to be sure, it would be sixteen parts fertilizer to one part oil. The only problem is,' he scratched his nose, 'I think you'd need a good deal of it to do the sort of damage we have here. I mean, again I'd have to look it up, but I seem to remember it'll be volume in cubic metres over three, answer in kilos.'

'What volume?' I asked.

'The volume of the space you want cleared by the explosion.'

He looked at the mixed emotions I could feel on my face and dealt at least with the ignorance.

'Say you want effective destruction of everything

within a space three metres by three metres by three metres. Twenty-seven cubic metres, OK? Volume of your bedroom, near enough. Divide by three, equals nine. Nine kilos of explosive needed.'

'Is that,' I said slowly, 'why reports of terrorist attacks are often so definite about the weight of the bomb used?'

'Absolutely. The area cleared directly relates to the size of the . . . er . . . bomb. If you can analyse the type of explosive and measure the area affected, you can tell how much explosive was needed.'

Superintendent Yale was nodding as if he knew all that.

'But you don't think this bomb went off in my bedroom,' I said.

'No, I don't. Nine kilos of ammonium nitrate in your bedroom would have annihilated it and made a nasty hole all round, but I wouldn't have thought it would bring half a house down. So if we locate the device in that foot-of-the-bed box, we are looking at something in the region of . . .' he did some more calculations '. . . say at least seventy-five cubic metres for your father's bedroom . . . that's twenty-five kilos of explosive.'

'That's heavy,' I said blankly.

'Yes. A large suitcaseful. But then you'd need a suitcaseful also if you were using cordite. For demolishing this whole house, you'd have needed four times that amount, placed in about four places on the ground floor right against the thickest walls. People often think a small amount of explosive will do a tremendous lot of damage, but it doesn't.'

'What sets it off, then?' I asked.

'Ah.' He smiled the professional smile that wasn't about to give away its secrets. 'Let's just say fulminate of mercury, plus, I should say, an electrical circuit.'

'Please do explain,' I said.

He hesitated, then shrugged. 'ANFO won't explode on its own, it's very stable.'

'What's ANFO?' I interrupted.

'Ammonium nitrate fuel oil. The first letters. ANFO for short.'

'Oh yes. Sorry.'

'So you stick into it a package of something that explodes fast: the detonator, in fact. Then you arrange to heat the detonating substance, either with a burning fuse, or by an electrical circuit which can be achieved by ordinary batteries. The heat sets off the detonator, the detonator detonates the ANFO. And bingo . . .'

'Bang, you're dead.'

'Quite right.'

'At four-thirty in the morning,' I said, 'it would probably be a time-bomb, wouldn't it?'

Mr Smith nodded happily. 'That's what we're looking for. If it was an alarm clock, for instance, we'll probably find the pieces. We usually do if we look hard enough. They don't vaporize in the explosion, they scatter.'

CHAPTER THIRTEEN

I drove unhurriedly to Epsom but as soon as I let myself into my flat, I knew I wouldn't stay there. It was too negative, too empty, too boring. I wouldn't live there much longer, I thought.

There were a few letters, a few bills, a few messages on the answering machine, but nothing of great interest. If I'd been blown up at Quantum along with Malcolm, it wouldn't have made any vital difference to anybody, and I didn't like that thought very much.

I went into the bedroom to see what I'd got left in the way of clothes and came to the white lace negligée. Well, maybe *she* would have been sorry for a while. I wished I could phone her, but it was forbidden: her husband would answer as he had once before when I'd tried, and too many 'sorry, I've got the wrong number' messages would raise the suspicions of the dimmest of men, which he reputedly wasn't.

Apart from her, I thought, making a mental inventory, I mostly knew a lot of racing people on the borderline between acquaintance and friend. Enough to be asked to parties, enough for contentment at work. I knew I wasn't in general unpopular. It was enough, I guessed. Or it had seemed enough, up to now.

I had enjoyed being with Malcolm more than I'd realized. I missed him already, and in the twelve days I'd spent with him, I'd developed a taste for spontaneity which made sitting around in my flat impossible. I packed a pair of breeches and a sweater, added some limp old shirts to the new ones in the Simpson's suitcase, closed up the flat and went down to the car park.

My own car stood there, but I took the hired one again, meaning to turn it in some time and return for my own by train. First stop was at the bank to drop through the letter box an envelope containing Malcolm's cheque, with a paying-in slip to lodge it in my account. After that, I set off again in the overall direction of Quantum, but without really knowing where I was going.

I felt an awful aversion to the task of searching the psyches of the family, but I ended up in a place from where visiting them all would be easy, taking by impulse a turn onto the road to the village of Cookham and booking a room there in an old inn friendly with dark oak beams and log fires.

Norman West was out. I phoned him on the hour at four and five and reached him at six. He said apologetically that he had stopped working on the Pembroke case, there was nothing else he could do. He was sorry he hadn't been able to solve the . . . er . . . problem, and should he send his account to Mr Pembroke at the Savoy, or at Quantum House?

'Neither,' I said. 'We'd like you to carry on working.' And I told him what had happened to Quantum and very nearly to ourselves.

'Dear me,' he said.

I laughed internally, but I supposed 'dear me' was as apt a comment as any.

'So would you mind traipsing all the way round again to ask what everyone was doing the day before yesterday between three p.m. and midnight?'

He was silent for an appreciable interval. Then, he said, 'I don't know that it would be useful, you know. Your family were unhelpful before. They would be doubly unhelpful again. Surely this time the police will make exhaustive enquiries? I think I must leave it to them.'

I was more dismayed than I expected. 'Please do reconsider,' I said. 'If the police go asking the family their movements, and then you do also, I agree they won't like it. But if after that I too go and ask, they may be upset enough or angry enough to let out things that could tell us . . . one way or another.' I paused. 'I suppose I'm not making much sense.'

'Do you remember what you said to me about stepping on a rattlesnake?' he said.

'Well, yes.'

'You're proposing to stir up one with a stick.'

'We absolutely have to know who the rattlesnake is.'

I heard him sigh and could feel his disinclination.

'Look,' I said, 'could you just meet me somewhere? You gave my father and me summaries of what all the family were doing on those two days we asked about, but there must be much more you could tell me. If you don't want to visit them again, could you just . . . help me?'

'I don't mind doing that,' he said. 'When?'

'Tonight? Tomorrow?'

Tonight he was already working. Tomorrow he was taking his wife to visit their grandchildren all day as it was Sunday, but his evening would be free. He knew the pub I was staying in, he would come there, he said; he would meet me in the bar at seven.

I thanked him for that anyway, and next telephoned two stables along on the Downs to ask the trainers if I could ride exercise on their horses for several mornings, if it would be useful to them. The first said no, the second said yes, he was a couple of lads short and he'd be glad of the free help. Start Monday, first lot, pull out at seven-thirty, could I be there by seven-fifteen?

'Yes,' I said appreciatively.

'Stay to breakfast.'

Sanity lay in racing stables, I thought, thanking him. Their brand of insanity was my sort of health. I couldn't stay away for long. I felt unfit, not riding.

I spent the evening in the bar in the pub, mostly listening to a lonely man who felt guilty because his wife was in hospital having her guts rearranged. I never did discover the reason for the guilt but while he grew slowly drunk, I learned a lot about their financial troubles and about his anxieties over her illness. Not a riotously amusing evening for me, though he said he felt better himself from being able to tell a perfect stranger all the things he'd been bottling up. Was there anyone at all, I wondered, going to bed, who went through life feeling happy?

I dawdled Sunday away pleasurably enough, and Norman West, true to his word, appeared at seven.

His age was again very apparent from the grey-white hair downwards, and when I remarked that he looked tired, he said he'd been up most of the previous night but not to worry, he was used to it. Had he been to see his grandchildren? Yes, he had: lively bunch. He accepted a double scotch with water and, under its reviving influence, opened the large envelope he was carrying and pulled out some papers.

'Your photographs of the family are in here,' he said, patting the envelope, 'and I've also brought these copies of all my notes.' He laid the notes on the small table between us. 'You can have them to keep. The originals are in my files. Funny thing,' he smiled fleetingly, 'I used to think that one day I'd write a book about all my cases, but there they are, all those years of work, sitting in their files, and there they'll stay.'

'Why don't you write it?' I asked.

'I'm better at following people.'

I reflected that following people was what he'd been

good at when Joyce had first employed him, and that probably we'd expected too much of him, setting him to unravel attempted murders.

He said, 'You'll find there's a definite pattern about the movements of your family, and at the same time an absence of pattern. The murder of Mrs Moira and the gassing of Mr Pembroke both took place at about five in the evening, and at five almost all your family are habitually on the move. Mind you, so is most of the working population. It's a time of day when it's easy to lose an hour or so without anyone noticing. Traffic jams, left work late, stopped for a drink, watched television in shop windows . . . I've heard all those from erring husbands. The list is limitless of things people think up as excuses for getting home late. With a family like yours, where practically no one has a set time for leaving a place of work, it's even easier. That's why it's been almost hopeless establishing alibis, and I'm pretty sure the police found the same thing over Mrs Moira. When there's no expectation of anyone arriving at a regular time, no one looks at the clock.'

'I do understand,' I said thoughtfully.

'Newmarket was a bit different,' he said, 'because it meant someone being away from their normal environment for a whole day, assuming that Mr Pembroke was followed from his hotel when he left at lunchtime for Newmarket. And one has to assume that a follower would be in position much earlier than that, because he wouldn't know when Mr Pembroke would leave, or where he would go.' He cleared his throat and sipped his whisky. 'I thought it would be simple in those circumstances to discover which family member had been away all of that Tuesday, but in fact it wasn't, as you'll read. Now, if the explosive device was planted in Quantum House between four when the gardener usually left and six, when you might have returned from the races, we're back to the . . . er . . .'

'Five o'clock shadow,' I said.

He looked mildly shocked. It wasn't a laughing matter. 'I've no doubt the same pattern will be found,' he said. 'No one will be able, or willing, to say exactly where they were or where anyone else was during that period.'

'We may be lucky,' I said.

He said maybe, and looked unconvinced.

'Couldn't you please tell me,' I said, 'which Mrs Pembroke got you to find Malcolm? I know all about your ethics, but after this bomb . . . can't you? Whose name was on the cheque?'

He considered, staring at his drink as if to find wisdom in the depths. He sighed heavily, and shrugged.

'I didn't get paid,' he said. 'The cheque never came. I'm not sure, but I think . . . I think it was the voice of Mrs Alicia Pembroke.' He shook his head. 'I asked her if it was her, when I interviewed her. She said it wasn't but I think she was lying. But two other people found out on their own account, don't forget, by doing exactly as I did, telephoning around.'

'I won't forget.'

He looked at me sombrely. 'I hope Mr Pembroke can't be found as easily at this moment.'

'I don't think so,' I said.

'Can I give you some advice?'

'Please do.'

'Carry a weapon with you.'

'Mr West!'

'Even if it's only a pot of pepper,' he said, 'or a can of spray paint. There's a good deal of enmity towards you in your family because of your favoured status with Mr Pembroke. You were supposed to die with him in the house, I should imagine. So don't go unprepared.'

I swallowed and thanked him. He nodded and prosaically produced a smaller envelope from an inner pocket, which contained his account. I wrote him his cheque. He took it, inspected it, and put it away.

He rose wearily to his feet and shook my hand. 'Any time you want to,' he said, 'phone me. I don't mind talking, if it will help.'

I thanked him again and he went greyly away, leaving me on my own with his notes and a feeling of nakedness.

I began reading the notes. It so happened that he had reversed his original working order, or perhaps the order had become reversed during the copying: in any event, the eldest-to-youngest progression had been transposed, and it was Serena's notes which came first.

Norman West had written all his notes in longhand

with aides-mémoire to himself, and I could almost hear his radio-announcer voice in my head as I read.

Miss Serena Pembroke (26) unmarried, lives at 14 Mossborough Court, Bracknell, a block of flats just off the Easthampstead Road, turn left by the pub. Flats built during Bracknell's new-town expansion, middle-income, business people tenants, keep themselves to themselves. Pretty girl, one of the neighbours said (No. 12) but don't know her name. Miss S. has lived there three months. One bedroom, one sitting room, kit, bath, all small.

Miss S. works at Deanna's Dance and Aerobics Studio, High Street, Bracknell, teaching aerobics. Private business, sloppily run (my opinion), owned by Mrs Deanna Richmond (45?) whose mind is on a younger gent with a hairy chest, gold chain showing, rubbish.

Miss S. works mornings Monday to Friday 8.00 to 1.30 pm, taking classes, first office workers, then housewives. Miss S. and another girl (Sammy Higgs) work in rotation, half hour on, half off. Miss S.'s times are 8–8.30, 9–9.30, 10–10.30, 11–11.30, 12–12.30, 1–1.30 most days.

Miss S. and Sammy H. are both good workers. The clients I spoke to said classes v. good. Continuous, therefore popular. A girl can drop in on way to office, on way home after taking children to school, etc. Sign in, pay on way out. Clients come from all over – large clientele.

Evening classes, Monday to Friday, 7 pm–8.30 only. Miss S. does these alone. (S. Higgs does afternoons 1.30–4 pm.) Evenings quite social – rests for clients' drinks etc. Well attended.

Miss S. has bad menstrual cramps every month. Can't dance or exercise. Always two days off. The Tuesday of Newmarket Sales was one of these days – the second. Miss S. called in Monday morning in pain, didn't work, no one expected her Tuesday, she returned Wednesday. Mrs Deanna Richmond's daughter stands in on these occasions and also if either girl especially asks for time off otherwise. No records kept of these times.

Miss S. leads sober, hard-working, regulated life.

Likes pretty clothes, a bit immature (my opinion), has few friends. Goes to her brother's house (Mr Ferdinand) a good deal at weekends, or to her mother's (Mrs Alicia).

No ascertainable love life.

Miss S. likes shopping and window-shopping. On the Friday of attack on Mr Pembroke she says she bought food and frilly white blouse at Marks and Spencers, she thinks. (Not sure of the day.) She buys something to wear about four times a week probably – tights, leotards, sweaters, etc. 'Has to look nice for her clients.'

Miss S. owns two-year-old grey/silver Ford Escort,

but usually jogs one mile to work to warm up. Drives only if cold or wet. Car clean from automatic car wash: Miss S. goes through same car wash approx every two weeks. Car wash people corroborate, but can't remember exact dates.

Miss S. says Mr Ian must have killed Mrs Moira because she (Mrs Moira) took away both Mr Pembroke and his (Mr Ian's) inheritance, and he hated her. She says Mr Ian must have tried to kill Mr Pembroke for the money. The police are fools not to arrest him, she says. I told her Mr Ian couldn't have killed Moira or attacked his father as he was seeing round a racehorse training stable forty miles away at both times, with thirty or more witnesses. I said he obviously hadn't been driving the car which nearly ran him down. She says he could have arranged it. In my opinion, Miss S. doesn't want to be convinced of Mr Ian's innocence. She wants the killer to be Mr Ian because she doesn't want to find any others in her family guilty. If it is Mr Ian, she can bear it, she says, because it would serve him right for being Daddy's pet. (Muddled thinking!)

End of enquiry.

The three pages of notes on Serena were held together with a paperclip. I shuffled Serena to the bottom of the pack and came to the next paperclip, holding notes on Debs and Ferdinand.

Norman West used grey paperclips, not silver. Most appropriate, I thought.

The first page read:

Mrs Deborah Pembroke (27) second wife of Mr Ferdinand, lives with him at Gables Cottage, Reading Road, Wokingham, Berkshire.

Mrs Deborah works as a photographic model chiefly for mail-order catalogues, and was engaged in London on the Tuesday of Newmarket Sales modelling a succession of swimsuits. There were two other models there, also a photographer and two assistants, also a dresser, a representative of the mail-order firm and a notetaker. The swimsuit session went on until 6 pm. Mrs D. was there until the end. Vouched for without possibility of doubt. Mrs Debs has no firm alibi for the previous Friday evening. She finished work early in London at 3.30 (corroborated by mail-order people) and drove home. No witness to arrival (Mr Ferdinand was out).

Owing to her Tuesday engagement Mrs Debs could not have been at Newmarket. Friday, inconclusive.

Mrs Debs drives her own car, a scarlet Lancia. When I inspected it, it was dusty overall, with no sign of contact with Mr Ian.

Mrs Debs appeared undisturbed in the main by my questions and gave the following answers. She says her husband is the only good one in the

Pembroke family, the only one with any sense of humour. She says he listens to his mother too much, but she'll change that in time. She says they'll be well off one day as long as Mr Ian doesn't queer their pitch. She said that she was happy enough and is in no hurry to have children. She objected to my asking about such a personal matter.

End of enquiry.

I turned over the page and on the next one found:

Mr Ferdinand Pembroke (32) married to Deborah (2nd wife), lives at Gables Cottage, Reading Road, Wokingham, Berks.

Mr Ferdinand is a statistician/actuary for the Merchant General Insurance Company, head office in Reading, Berks. He works about a third of the time at home, where he has a computer with a link to the one in the insurance company offices. Both he and his company like the arrangement which means he can do exacting work without constant interruption. In addition, his company arranged for him to go on an anti-fraud course, as they are pleased with his ability.

I visited his office and explained to his boss that Mr Pembroke senior wanted to prove his children couldn't have been implicated in attacking him. Mr Ferdinand's boss wanted to be helpful, but in the end couldn't satisfy me.

Mr F. was not in the office on Friday afternoon, nor on the following Tuesday. On the Friday he'd worked at home, on Tuesday he was on the course.

I checked with the course at the Bingham Business Institute, City of London. Mr F. signed in on the first day, Monday, but after that no stringent attendance records were kept. Mr F. couldn't suggest anyone on the course who knew him well enough to swear he was there on Tuesday. I asked if he had made notes on the lectures. He said he didn't take any: the Tuesday lectures were about statistical probabilities and how to calculate them; basic stuff which he knew about. I checked this on the course schedule. The Tuesday lectures were as he said.

Mr Ferdinand drives a cream/grey Audi. It was clean when I saw it. Mr F. says he washes it himself with a brush on a hose (he showed it to me) and he does it frequently. He says he likes things to be clean.

Although he was working at home on the Friday afternoon, he was not in when Mrs Debs arrived from London. He says he had finished the job he'd been working on and decided to drive over to Henley and feed the ducks on the Thames. He found it peaceful. He liked the fresh air. He often did it, had done all his life, he said. He didn't know Mrs Debs was finishing work as early as 3.30 that day, but he said that wouldn't have stopped him going out. They were independent people and not accountable to each other for every minute.

I stopped reading and lifted my head. It was true that Ferdinand had always been attracted to the ducks. I couldn't count the number of times we'd walked along the Henley towpath, scattering bread and listening to the rude laughter of the mallards. Malcolm was the one who took us, whenever Alicia started throwing plates. She squawked rather like the ducks, I'd thought, and had had enough sense not to say so.

I went on reading:

Mr Ferdinand is hard working and successful, going to be more so. (My opinion and his boss's.) He has planning ability and energy. He is physically like his father, stocky and strong. (I remember Mr Pembroke 28 years ago. He threatened to throw me over his car when he found out I'd been following him, and I believed he could do it. Mr Ferdinand is the same.)

Mr F. can be very funny and good company, but his moods change to black disconcertingly fast. He is casual with his wife, not possessive. He is protective of his sister Serena. He is attentive to his mother, Mrs Alicia. He seems to have ambivalent feelings about Mr Pembroke and Mr Ian; I gathered from his inconsistent attitude that he liked them both in the past but no longer trusts them. Mr F. is capable of hate, I think.

End of enquiry.

I put Debs and Ferdinand to the back of the pile but had no mental stamina left for the next section on Ursula and Gervase. I put all the notes into the envelope and ate some pub steak instead and decided I would see the family in the age-reversed order Norman West had handed me, taking the easy ones first. Where was the bravado that had led me to tell Malcolm at Cambridge that I would stay with him just because it was dangerous?

Where indeed.

Somewhere under the rubble of Quantum.

In the morning, I rode out on the windy Downs, grateful for the simplicity of horses and for the physical pleasure of using one's muscles in the way they were trained for. Vigour seemed to flow of its own accord in my arms and legs, and I thought that maybe it was the same for a pianist sitting down after a few days to play; there was no need to work out what to do with one's fingers, it was easy, it was embedded in one's brain, the music came without thought.

I thanked my host sincerely after breakfast and drove towards Quantum thinking of the telephone call I'd made to Malcolm the evening before. It had been nearly midnight for me: nearly six, early evening, for him.

He had arrived safely, he said, and Dave and Sally Cander were true blue cronies. Ramsey Osborn had flown down. The Canders were giving a party, starting in five minutes. He'd seen some good horses. He'd had some great new ideas for spending money (wicked chuckle). How were things in England?

He sounded satisfactorily carefree, having shed depression with the miles, and I said things were the same as when he left except that the house was wrapped up in tarpaulins. The state of the house troubled him for roughly ten seconds, and after that he said he and Ramsey might be leaving Lexington on Tuesday or Wednesday; he wasn't sure.

'Wherever you go,' I said, 'will you please give the Canders a telephone number where I can reach you?'

'I promise,' he said blithely. 'Hurry up with your passport, and come over.'

'Soon.'

'I've got used to you being with me. Keep looking round for you. Odd. Must be senile.'

'Yes, you sound it.'

He laughed. 'It's a different world here, and I like it.'

He said goodbye and disconnected, and I wondered how many horses he would have bought by the time I reached him.

Back at the pub in Cookham, I changed out of riding clothes and dutifully telephoned Superintendent Yale.

He had nothing to tell me, nor I to tell him: the call was short.

'Where is your father?' he asked conversationally.

'Safe.'

He grunted. 'Phone me,' he said, and I said, 'Yes.'

With a heavy lack of enthusiasm I returned to the car and pointed its nose towards Bracknell, parking in one of the large featureless car parks and walking through to the High Street.

The High Street, long before, had been the main road through a minor country town; now it was a pedestrian backwater surrounded by the factories, offices and convoluted ring roads of mushroom progress. 'Deanna's Dance and Aerobics Studio' looked like a wide shop front flanked by a bright new shiny newsagent on one side and on the other a photographic shop whose window display seemed to consist chiefly of postcard-sized yellow fluorescent labels with prices on, mostly announcing '20% OFF'.

Deanna's studio consisted firstly of a reception area with a staircase on one side leading upwards. A young girl sitting behind the reception desk looked up and brightened when I pushed open the glass entrance door and stepped onto some thick grey carpet, but lost interest when I asked for Serena, explaining I was her brother.

'Back there,' she said. 'She's taking class at the moment.'

Back there was through white-painted double doors.

I went through and found myself in a windowless but brightly lit and attractive area of small tables and chairs, where several women sat drinking from polystyrene cups. The air vibrated with the pulse of music being played somewhere else, and when I again asked for Serena and was directed onwards, I came to its source.

The studio itself ran deeply back to end in a wall of windows overlooking a small strip of garden. The floor was of polished wood, sprung somehow so that it almost bounced underfoot. The walls were white except for the long left-hand one, which was entirely of looking-glass. The music, warm and insistent, invited rhythmic response.

Serena herself danced with her back to the mirror. Facing her, in three spread-out rows, was a collection of clients, all female, bouncing in unison on springy ankles, arms and legs swinging in circles and kicks. On every face, concentration and sweat. 'Go for the burn,' Serena commanded, looking happy, and her class with an increase of already frenetic energy, presumably went.

'Great, ladies, that's great,' Serena said eventually, stopping jumping and switching off the music machine which stood in a corner near where I'd come in. She gave me an unfriendly glance but turned with radiance back to the customers. 'If any of you want to continue, Sammy will be here within a minute. Take a rest, ladies.'

A few of the bodies stayed. Most looked at the

clock on the wall and filed panting into a door marked 'changing rooms'.

Serena said, 'What do you want?'

'Talk.'

She looked colourful but discouraging. She wore a bright pink long-sleeved body stocking with white bouncing shoes, pink and white leg-warmers and a scarlet garment like a chopped off vest. 'I'll give you five minutes,' she said.

She was hardly out of breath. A girl who was apparently Sammy Higgs came in in electric blue and started taking charge, and Serena with bad grace led me back through the refreshment area and the entrance hall and up the stairs.

'There are no classes up here just now. Say what you've come for and then go.'

Upstairs, according to a notice on the wall, Deanna offered ballroom dancing tuition, also 'ballet and posture'. Serena stood with her hands on her skinny pink hips and waited.

'Malcolm wants me to find out who bombed Quantum,' I said.

She glowered at me. 'Well, I didn't.'

'Do you remember the day old Fred blew up the tree stump?'

'No,' she said. She didn't bother to think, hadn't tried to remember.

'Thomas gave you a ride on his shoulders out of the

field, and the blast of the explosion knocked old Fred over.'

'I don't know what you're talking about.'

'Why are you so hostile?'

'I'm not. Where's Daddy?'

'With friends,' I said. 'It saddens him that you're hostile.'

She said bitterly, 'That's a laugh. He's rejected all of us except you. And I'll bet you killed Moira.'

'He hasn't rejected you,' I said. 'And I didn't.'

'He kicked us all out. I loved him when I was little.' Tears appeared suddenly in her eyes and she shook them angrily away. 'He couldn't wait to get rid of me.'

'He tried to keep you, but Alicia wouldn't have it. She fought him in the courts for custody, and won.'

'He didn't want me,' she said fiercely. 'He only said so to spite Mummy, to make her suffer. I know all about it.'

'Alicia told you?'

'Of course she did. Daddy couldn't wait to get rid of us, to get rid of Mummy, to get married again, to . . . to . . . throw everything about us out of the house, to tear out all the pretty rooms . . . blot us out.'

She was deeply passionate with the old feelings, still smouldering after twenty years. I remembered how upset I'd been when Alicia tore out my own mother's kitchen, how I'd felt betrayed and dispossessed. I had been six, as Serena had been, and I still remembered it clearly.

'Give him a chance,' I suggested.

'I did give him a chance. I offered to help him after Moira died and he still didn't want me. And look at the way he's behaving,' she said. 'Throwing money away. If he thinks I care a tuppenny damn about his stupid scholarships, he's a fool. You can toady up to him all you like, but I'm not going to. He can keep his damned money. I can manage without it.'

She looked hard-eyed and determinedly stubborn. The old man in all of us, I thought.

'You've had your five minutes,' she said. She side-stepped me in swift movements and made for the stairs. 'See you at the funeral.'

'Whose funeral?' I asked, following her.

'Anyone's,' she said darkly, and ran weightlessly down the stairs as if skimming were more normal than walking.

When I reached the entrance hall, she was vanishing through the white double doors. It was pointless to pursue her. I left Deanna's studio feeling I had achieved nothing, and with leaden spirits went back to the car and drove to Wokingham to call on Ferdinand.

I half-hoped he wouldn't be in, but he was. He came to the door frowning because I had interrupted him at his computer, and grudgingly let me in.

'We've nothing to say,' he said, but he sounded more resigned than forbidding; half-relaxed, as he'd been in my flat.

He led the way into the front room of the bungalow

he and Debs had bought on the road to Reading. The front room was his office, a perfectly natural arrangement to Ferdinand, since Malcolm's office had always been at home.

The rest of the bungalow, which I'd visited two or three times before, was furnished sparsely in accordance with Debs' and Ferdinand's joint dislike of dirt and clutter. One of the three bedrooms was completely empty, one held a single bed and a chest of drawers (for Serena's visits), and in the third, the couple's own, there was a mattress on a platform and a wall of cupboards and enclosed shelves that Ferdinand had put together himself. The sitting room held two chairs, a standard lamp, a lot of floor cushions and a television set. In the tidy kitchen, there was a table with four stools. All visible life was in the office, though even there, in direct contrast to Malcolm's comfortable shambles, a spartan order of neatness ruled.

Ferdinand's computer bore a screenful of graphics. He glanced at it and then looked with some impatience back to me.

'What do you want?' he asked. 'I've a lot to do after being away on a course.'

'Can't you save all that,' I gestured to the screen, 'or whatever it is you do? Record it, and come out to a pub for lunch.'

He shook his head and looked at his watch. Then, in indecision, said, 'I suppose I have to eat,' and fiddled about with the computer. 'All right. Half an hour, max.'

I drove us to the town centre and he pointed out a pub with a car park. The bar was full of business people similarly out for lunch breaks, and I bought scotch and sandwiches after a good deal of polite elbowing. Ferdinand had secured a table from which he was clearing the past customer's detritus with a finicky expression.

'Look,' I said, handing him his drink as we sat down, 'Malcolm wants me to find out who's trying to kill him.'

'It isn't me,' he said. He took a swallow, unconcerned.

'Do you remember old Fred blowing up the tree roots, that time? When we were about twelve or thirteen? When the blast blew old Fred flat?'

He stared. 'Yes, I do,' he said slowly, 'but that's years ago. It can't have anything to do with the house.'

'Why not?' I asked. 'That bang made a big impression on us. Memories last more or less for ever, they just need digging up. The explosives expert working at Quantum asked if I knew what cordite was, and I remembered old Fred.'

Ferdinand did his own digging. 'Black powder . . . in a box.'

'Yes, it's still there in the tool shed. Still viable, but not used on the house. They're working now on its being a homemade explosive called ANFO.'

Ferdinand was visibly shaken and after a minute said, 'I suppose I hadn't considered . . . what it was.'

'Do you know what ANFO is?' I asked.

He said no uncertainly, and I thought he wasn't being truthful. Perhaps he felt that knowing could be considered guilt. I needed to jolt him into being more positive. Into being an ally, if I could.

'Malcolm's made a new will,' I said.

'And left you the lot, I suppose,' he sneered bitterly.

'No,' I said. 'If he dies from normal causes, we all inherit equally.' I paused, and added an invention. 'If someone murders him, it all goes to charities. So how about you getting on the telephone and telling the whole tribe to help me find out who's trying to do them out of their future?'

CHAPTER FOURTEEN

In my room at Cookham in the evening, I read Norman West's notes on Gervase and Ursula.

Gervase first:

Mr Gervase Pembroke (35) lives with Mrs Ursula at 14 Grant St, Maidenhead, a detached house with a quarter-acre garden in good residential neighbourhood. They have been married for 11 years and have 2 daughters (8 and 6) both attending a private school.

Mr G. is a stockbroker who commutes to the City firm of Wells, Gibson & Cathcart. (Wells, Gibson and Cathcart have all died or retired long ago, but the respected name is kept.) Mr Gervase works for his own commission within the firm: each partner does. He has flexible working hours; he's his own boss to a great extent. He used to work harder than he does now but has become erratic of late, according to the firm's lady receptionist. She didn't like to say outright, but I gathered Mr G. sometimes returns from lunch the worse for drink, and sometimes doesn't return at all.

She didn't of course note down such times. She said she'd heard two of the other partners discussing Mr G., saying he'd lost his nerve and was selling his clients only gilts. They thought that too much playing safe was bad stockbroking. She had no qualms in denigrating Mr G., who she said has a filthy temper when things don't go his way, and never appreciates how hard she works (!)

I requested to interview Mr G. at his place of work. I was shown into his office and explained who I was. He said he knew. I said as a preliminary that I understood he was the illegitimate son of Mrs Alicia Pembroke, and the interview ended immediately. He physically hustled me out (bruise on left arm). He said I'd insulted him. Perhaps I did! I managed to say that if he could produce office records – letters written, brokerage transactions – for the Tuesday in question, he would be in the clear. He said to consult his secretary, which I did. Mr G. went into the office that morning, she confirmed, and dictated two letters. Mr G. told her he was going to see a new client, and left at 10.30 am. She didn't know who the client was, he was not listed on Mr G.'s office diary. It was more usual for new clients to come to the office, but not invariable. Mr G. didn't return to the office that day, but returned Wednesday in bad mood (with a hangover?).

Mr G. left the office the previous Friday (secretary's notes) at midday, didn't return. (Mr G. worked normally all day Monday.)

Mr G. commutes by train, leaves off-white Rover in station car park. His car clean and unmarked when I saw it.

Visited Mr G. at his home to ask about the client on Tuesday re solid alibi. Mr G. said none of my business. Guess: client was either a mistress or a bottle, or else Mr G. wants me to believe that.

Mr G.'s alcohol problem is serious (my opinion) but not incapacitating. He has strong masterful manner, but must have insecurities (illegitimacy??) to make him drink and treat people badly. (His secretary does not love him.) Mr G. appears to make good income, no sign of financial straits.

Attentive to Mrs Alicia. Bossy and possessive with his wife and children. Jealous of Mr Ian and (my judgement) fears him. (I don't know why this is. Something in the past? Mr Pembroke's preference?) Despises but also fears Mr Pembroke. (A lot of bluster when he talked of him.)

Mr G. is physically strong but getting less so, I'd think. Takes little exercise, somewhat overweight. Difficult personality. A bully.

End of enquiry.

I paperclipped Gervase together with a sigh. Norman West, for all his ineffective appearance, had a way of getting to the heart of things pretty smartly.

What had he made of Ursula, I wondered. Ursula, the quiet wife, who had talked in tears to Joyce. Pretty enough in an insipid way, she was like an unfinished painting, without highlights. Pleasant enough to me whenever Gervase allowed, she had never told me her thoughts. I turned with unexpected interest to the West view of Gervase's wife.

Mrs Ursula Pembroke (35) wife of Mr Gervase, lives with him at 14 Grant St, Maidenhead. She has no employment beyond looking after children and household. A cleaner comes in Monday to Friday mornings, 9 am to 1 pm, stays Tuesdays and Thursdays until 4 pm, also babysits whenever asked. (I had to make two visits to Mrs U. On the first occasion she had been crying and wouldn't talk. On the second she was cooperative.)

The daughters' school is at the other end of Maidenhead. Mrs U. shares the school run with a family nearby; Mrs U.'s mornings are Tuesday and Thursday; afternoons Mon., Wed. and Fri. Mrs U.'s car is a cream Austin. Clean.

On the Friday of the attack on Mr Pembroke, the daughters were invited to tea by the other school run family (the mother corroborates). Mrs U. left the daughters there after school (4 pm). Picked them up about 6.30.

On the following Tuesday, Mrs U. arranged for the cleaner to stay and give the daughters their tea as she wanted a day out in London. The cleaner told me Mrs U. did the school run, came back and changed, and drove away to the station to catch the train. She (Mrs U.) said she would be back late as she would go to the cinema after she'd done her shopping. Mrs U. has done this several times lately. She returned at 10 pm. Cleaner went home. (Mrs U. gave me permission to consult the cleaner.) Mrs U. says she didn't go to the cinema, she didn't like the look of the films, she just had dinner in a steak house. She also said she had been into a church to pray. She hadn't bought anything (nothing fitted).

Mrs U. nervous and evasive about trip to London. Did she go to Newmarket? Possible (my opinion) that she goes to London to meet someone, doesn't want cleaner or husband to know. Who? Lover? Not possible, she hasn't the air, they can't hide that inner excitement. Priest? Friend unacceptable to Mr G.? Doctor? Some sort of solace, I would say.

Mrs U. unhappy woman but wouldn't unbutton. Loyal. Any wife of Mr G. liable to be unhappy (my opinion). Mrs U. doesn't like having the cleaner around for so long. Mr G. insists on cleanliness. Mrs U. gets tired of the cleaner's incessant chatter. All adds to Mrs U.'s stress. Mrs U. would like a job or to do voluntary work. Mr G. won't have it. 'The children come first.' (Mrs U. obviously very fond of the children.)

Mrs U. wishes Mr Pembroke would give all the family a lot of money now so that they would stop griping about it. She sees nothing wrong in Mr Ian, but her husband won't let her talk to him. She could like Mr Pembroke, she thinks he's funny and generous, but her husband ditto. She can't go against her husband. She has no money of her own, I'd say. She's in a trap. (Can't support children herself, couldn't leave without them.)

Does she believe killing Mr Pembroke could solve her problems? Does she believe if Mr G. becomes richer it will make things right? I could tell her it won't.

End of enquiry.

Poor Mrs U. Poor Ursula. Could she have blown up Quantum? Perhaps, if she'd wanted to. She sounded desperate enough for anything, but if she had any sense, her desperation should drive her to beg from Malcolm, not to kill him.

I clipped Ursula behind Gervase: forever in his shadow.

I wondered why she'd married him, but then I'd attended their wedding also, and if one hadn't in the past been on the wrong end of his glowing cigarette, one could have taken him as he seemed on the surface, confident, good looking, positive and strong. A rising young stockbroker. A catch.

I put Gervase and Ursula back in the envelope but they wouldn't stay there, they stuck like burrs in my mind.

There must be thousands, hundreds of thousands of sad marriages like that, I thought, where the unhappiness came from inside. Probably one could more easily withstand disasters that came from without, survive wars, poverty, illness, grief. Much harder to find any good way forward when personality disintegrated. Each of them was disintegrating, Ursula because of Gervase, Gervase because of . . .

Because of Malcolm? Because of Malcolm's boredom with Vivien, his affair with Alicia, his quick marriage to Joyce? Because of illegitimacy? But Ferdinand had been a product of the same process, and Ferdinand was whole.

There were questions without answers. The most likely answers were often wrong. I didn't know why Gervase was disintegrating: I thought only that the process had already begun when we both lived at Quantum; had maybe begun in the womb.

I slept with troubled dreams and went to ride the next morning as if for therapy and release. Solace, Norman West's word, met the case. The raw morning, the moving horses, the filthy language and the crude jokes, a daily fix of the sort of reality I'd chosen at eighteen. I didn't know why I'd liked horses so much.

Choice sprang from deep needs, but where did the needs come from?

I wasn't accustomed to thinking in that way. I usually coasted along, not worrying much, doing my job, enjoying riding in races, making love without strings. Lazy in many respects, I dared say, but uncomplicated. An opt-out that had come to an abrupt end with meeting Malcolm at Newmarket.

It was Tuesday.

Ursula's cleaner, I thought, driving back to Cookham, would currently be chatting away with no respite for Ursula until the girls got back from school. I wondered if Ursula was quietly going bananas at 14 Grant St, Maidenhead. I changed into ordinary clothes and went along there to find out.

The cleaner came to the door; middle-aged, in a flowered overall, with an inquisitive face. Mrs Pembroke was lying down with a headache, she said, and yes, perhaps she could go upstairs and ask her if her brother-in-law might take her out to lunch. Perhaps I would like to wait in the hall.

I waited, and presently Ursula came downstairs looking wan and wearing a coat and gloves.

'Oh!' she said faintly when she saw me. 'I thought it was Ferdinand.'

I'd hoped she would. I said, 'Where would you best like to go?'

'Oh.' She was irresolute. She looked back up the stairs and saw the cleaner watching interestedly from the landing. If she didn't come out with me, she'd be stuck with explaining.

'Come on,' I said persuasively. 'The car's warm.'

It sounded a silly thing to say, but I suppose she listened to the intention, not the words. She continued across the hall and came with me out of the front door, closing it behind us.

'Gervase won't like this,' she said.

'Why should he know?'

'She'll find a way of telling him.' She gestured back to the house, to the cleaner. 'She likes to make trouble. It brightens up her life.'

'Why do you keep her?'

She shrugged. 'I hate housework. If I sack her, I'd have to do it. Gervase thinks she's thorough, and he pays her. He said he wouldn't pay anyone else.'

She spoke matter-of-factly, but I was startled by the picture of domestic tyranny. We got into the car and I drove out of the town and towards the village of Bray, and twice more on the way she said, 'Gervase won't like this.' We stopped at a small roadside restaurant and she chose homemade soup and moussaka, several times looking over her shoulder as if her husband would materialize and pounce.

I ordered a carafe of red wine. Not for her, she protested, but when it came she drank it almost absent-mindedly. She had removed the coat and gloves to reveal a well-worn grey skirt topped by a blue sweater with a cream shirt underneath. She wore a string of pearls. Her dark hair was held back at one side by a tortoiseshell slide, and there was no lipstick on her pale mouth. The sort of appearance, I supposed, that Gervase demanded.

When the soup came, she said, 'Ferdinand phoned last night and told Gervase that Malcolm had made a new will, according to you.'

'Yes, he made one,' I agreed. 'He showed it to me.'

'Gervase didn't tell me,' she said. 'He phoned Alicia and told her, and I listened. That's what usually happens. He doesn't tell me things, he tells his mother.'

'How do you get on with Alicia?' I asked.

She very carefully drank the soup already in her spoon. She spoke as if picking her way through a minefield.

'My mother-in-law,' she said intensely, 'has caused more trouble than anyone since Eve. I can't talk about her. Drink your soup.'

I had the impression that if she once started talking about Alicia, she would never stop. I wondered how to start her, but when I tentatively asked what she meant about trouble, she shook her head vehemently.

'Not here,' she said.

I left it. She talked about her children, which she could do without strain, looking almost animated, which saw us through to the moussaka.

'What do you do on your trips to London?' I asked casually.

She looked amazed, then said, 'Oh yes, that

wretched Mr West. Gervase was furious with him. Then Gervase was annoyed with me also, and wanted to know where I'd been. I'd been wandering around, that's all.' She ate her moussaka methodically. 'Ferdinand told Gervase and Gervase told Alicia something about a tree stump. What was that all about?'

I explained about the cordite.

She nodded. 'Gervase told Alicia he'd had a good laugh when old Fred was knocked flat.'

She seemed undisturbed by the thought of explosives. We finished the lunch, I paid the bill, and we set off on the short road back to Maidenhead. A little way along there, I stopped the car in a lay-by and switched off the engine.

She didn't ask why we'd stopped. After a pause she said, 'Alicia is ruining our marriage, I suppose you know that?'

I murmured an assent.

'I'd known Gervase for only four months when we got married. I didn't realize . . . She's twisted him from birth, hasn't she? With her awful lies and spite. She sets him against you all the time. Gervase says terrible things about you sometimes . . . I mean, violent . . . I hate it. I try to tell him not to, but he doesn't listen to me, he listens to her. She says you sneer at him, you think you're much superior, because you're legitimate. I know you don't. Gervase believes her though. She tells him over and over that Malcolm threw them out and never loved them. She's wicked. And look what she's done to Serena. Gervase says she was a bright girl, but Alicia wouldn't let her stay on at school, Alicia wanted her to be a little girl, not to grow up. And Serena hates all men, and it's Alicia's fault. The only men Serena will let touch her are Ferdinand and Gervase. It's such a waste. Alicia got rid of Ferdinand's first wife, did you know? Went on and on at her until she couldn't stand it and left. I don't know how Debs puts up with her. It's driving me insane, you know, her drip, drip, drip. She's the worst enemy you'll ever have. If it was you that had been murdered, she would have done it.'

'She wasn't always like that,' I said, as she paused. 'When she lived at Quantum, she treated me the same as Ferdinand and Gervase.'

'Then it must have started when Malcolm kept you there on your own, and as she's got older it's got worse. She's much worse now than she was when we got married, and she was bad enough then. She hated Coochie, you know, and Coochie was nice, wasn't she? I was sorry when Coochie died. But Coochie banned all the family from staying in the house except you, and I should think that's when Alicia turned against you. Or let it all out. I bet it was there inside all the time. Like Gervase keeps things in and lets them out violently . . . so does Serena, and Ferdinand too . . . they're all like that. I wish Alicia would die. I can understand people wanting to kill. I would like to kill Alicia.'

She stopped abruptly, the raw truth quivering in her voice.

'Drive me home,' she said. 'I shouldn't have said that.'

I didn't immediately restart the engine. I said, 'Is it Alicia that's causing Gervase to drink?'

'Oh!' Ursula gulped, the flow of anger ending, the misery flooding back. 'It's just . . . everything. I can see he's unhappy, but he won't let me help him, he won't talk to me, he just talks to *her*, and she makes it worse.'

I sighed and set off towards Grant Street. Alicia hadn't quite reached sixty: the worst of the witches could outlive them all.

'I shouldn't have told you all this,' Ursula said, when I stopped at the door. 'Gervase won't like it.'

'Gervase won't know what you've said.'

She fished a handkerchief out of her handbag and blew her nose.

'Thank you for the lunch. Did your mother tell you we've had lunch a few times in London, she and I? She gives me good advice. I can't tell Gervase, he'd be furious.'

I nodded. 'Joyce told me you were friends.'

'She's awfully catty about Alicia. It cheers me up no end.' She gave me a wan smile and got out of the car. She waved as she opened her front door: I waved back and drove away, and covered the few miles to Cookham.

I thought it might be interesting to see what Norman West had made of Alicia, and I searched through the notes until I came to her.

West had written:

Mrs Alicia Pembroke (59) refused to speak to me at all on my first visit and was ungracious and edgy on my second.

Mrs Alicia lives at 25 Lions Court, London Road, Windsor, a block of flats. She still maintains she can't remember what she was doing on the Friday or the Tuesday: she was pottering about, she says. 'One day is much like another.' I think she's being obstructive for the sake of it.

Mrs A. drives a big silver/grey Fiat. Clean, no damage.

Mrs A. antagonistic to me personally because of my following her in Mrs Joyce's divorce case, although in the end she benefited.

Twenty-eight years ago! She remembers every detail of that time. Can't remember last Tuesday . . .

I asked her if she had ever engaged me to work for her. She said no. (?)

Mrs A. has changed from the Miss A. I followed. Miss A. was full of giggles, very little-girl. Mrs A. still dresses very young, acts young, but is embittered. Odd how some women flower in love affairs and wither in marriage. Seen it often. Seems as if the spice of secrecy and naughtiness is what they love, not the man himself.

Mrs A. very bitter on subject of Mr Pembroke spending money. Mr Ian's name brought angry looks. Mrs A. turned me out.

End of enquiry.

Short and unsweet, I thought.

I couldn't face going to see Alicia at that moment. I didn't think her physically capable of carrying Malcolm while he was unconscious, and I didn't think her efficient enough to construct a bomb: good enough reasons for avoiding something I wanted to do as much as jump into a crocodile-infested swamp.

I didn't want to talk to Gervase either, but that couldn't be as easily avoided.

I drove back to Grant Street in the early evening and parked along the road from No 14 waiting for the master to return. It wasn't until I was sitting there that I remembered Norman West's advice about defence. Pepper... paint... I couldn't see myself throwing either in Gervase's eyes, or anyone else's for that matter. Gervase was, goddammit, my brother. Half-brother. Cain killed Abel. Abel hadn't had his pepper ready, or his paint.

Upon that sober reflection, Gervase came home.

His Rover turned into his house's short driveway and pulled up outside the garage. Gervase, carrying a briefcase, let himself in through the front door. Five minutes later, I walked along the road and rang the bell.

The door was opened by one of the children, who called over her shoulder, 'It's Ian.'

Gervase, still in his City suit, came immediately into the hall from his sitting room, looking inhospitable and carrying a cut-glass tumbler half filled with what I expected was scotch.

'Ferdinand phoned me,' he said authoritatively. 'It's the police's business to look into the bombing of Quantum, not yours.'

'Malcolm asked me to,' I said.

'You'd better come in, I suppose.' He was grudging, but pointed me to the room he'd left. 'Do you want a drink?'

'Yes, please.'

He poured from the scotch bottle into a duplicate tumbler, and handed me the glass, gesturing to the matching jug of water which stood on a silver tray. I diluted my drink and sipped it, and said, 'Thanks.'

He nodded, busy with his own.

There was no sign of Ursula, but I could hear the two girls' high voices in the kitchen and supposed she was with them. They would tell her I had come, and she would be worrying about her lunch.

'Ferdinand told me about Malcolm's new will,' Gervase said with annoyance. 'It's ridiculous putting in that clause about being murdered. What if some random mugger bumps him off? Do we all lose our inheritance?'

'Some random mugger is unlikely. A paid assassin might not be.'

Gervase stared. 'That's rubbish.'

'Who killed Moira?' I said. 'Who's tried three times to kill Malcolm?'

'How should I know?'

'I think you should put your mind to it.'

'No. It's for the police to do that.' He drank. 'Where is he now?'

'Staying with friends.'

'I offered him a bed here,' he said angrily, 'but I'm not good enough, I suppose.'

'He wanted to be away from the family,' I said neutrally.

'But he's with you.'

'No, not any more.'

He seemed to relax a little at the news. 'Did you quarrel again?' he said hopefully.

We were still standing in the centre of the room, as the offer of a drink hadn't extended to a chair also. There were fat chintz-covered armchairs in a stylized flower pattern on a mottled grey carpet, heavy red curtains and a brick fireplace with a newly-lit fire burning. I'd been in his house about as seldom as in Ferdinand's, and I'd never been upstairs.

'We haven't quarrelled,' I said. 'Do you remember when old Fred blew up the tree stump?'

He found no difficulty in the change of subject.

'Ferdinand said you'd asked that,' he said. 'Yes, of course I remember.'

'Did Fred show you how he set off the explosive?'

'No, he damn well didn't. You're not trying to make out that I blew up the house, are you?' His anger, always near the surface, stoked up a couple of notches.

'No,' I said calmly. 'I should have said, did Fred show you or anyone else how he set off the explosive.'

'I can only speak for myself,' he said distinctly, 'and the answer is no.'

Gervase was heavy and, I thought, getting heavier. His suit looked filled. I had never quite grown to his height. He was the tallest and biggest of all Malcolm's children and easily the most forceful. He looked a strong successful man, and he was cracking up for lack of a piece of paper that no one gave a damn about except himself.

Perhaps, I thought, there was something of that obsessiveness in us all. In some it was healthy, in others destructive, but the gene that had given Malcolm his Midas obsession with gold had been a dominant strain.

Gervase said, 'Will Malcolm ante up anything before he dies?'

His voice was as usual loud and domineering, but I looked at him speculatively over my glass. There had been an odd sub-note of desperation, as if it weren't just of academic interest to him, but essential. Norman West's notes recycled themselves: ' . . . lost his nerve and was selling only gilts. Too much playing safe was bad stockbroking . . .' Gervase, who had seemed comfortably fixed, might all of a sudden not be.

I answered the words of the question, not the implications. 'I did ask him to. He said he would think about it.'

'Bloody old fool,' Gervase said violently. 'He's playing bloody games with us. Chucking the stuff away just to spite us. Buying bloody *horses.* I could strangle him.' He stopped as if shocked at what he'd more or less shouted with conviction. 'Figure of speech,' he said, hard-eyed.

'I'll try again,' I said, ignoring it, 'but Vivien tried, and rubbed him up the wrong way so that he stuck his toes in. Malcolm's obstinate, the way we all are, and the more anyone tries to push him, the harder he'll resist.'

'It's you that got him to buy horses. He wouldn't have thought of it on his own.' He was glaring at me. 'Two million pounds for a bloody *colt.* Do you realize what two million pounds means? Have you any idea? *Two million pounds* for a four-legged nothing? He's raving mad. Two million pounds invested in any one of us would give us freedom from worry for the rest of our lives, and he goes and spends it on a *horse.* Retarded children are bad enough, half a million for retarded children . . . but that's not enough for him, is it? Oh no. He buys that bloody horse Blue Clancy, and how many more millions did that cost him? How many?' He was insistent, belligerent, demanding, his chin thrust aggressively forward.

'He can afford it,' I said. 'I think he's very rich.'

'Think!' Gervase grew even angrier. 'How do you know he isn't flinging away every penny? I'll find a way of stopping him. He's *got* to be stopped.'

He suddenly stretched out his free hand and plucked my half-full glass from my grasp.

'Go on, get out of here,' he said. 'I've had enough.'

I didn't move. I said, 'Throwing me out won't solve any problems.'

'It'll make a bloody good start.' He put both glasses on the table and looked ready to put thought into action.

'When Malcolm fled to Cambridge,' I said, 'did Alicia tell you where he was?'

'What?' It stopped him momentarily. 'I don't know what you're talking about. Go on, get out.'

'Did you telephone to Malcolm's hotel in Cambridge?'

He hardly listened. He embarked on a heartfelt tirade. 'I'm fed up with your sneers and your airs and graces. You think you're better than me, you always have, and you're *not*. You've always weaselled into Malcolm's good books and set him against us and he's blind and stupid about you . . . and get out.' He stepped forward threateningly, one hand in a fist.

'But you still want me to plead your case,' I said, standing still.

His mouth opened but no words came out.

'Alicia tells you I sneer at you,' I said, 'but I don't. She tells you lies, you believe them. I've never set Malcolm against you. You hit me now, and I might think of it. If you want me to try to get him to cough up, you'll put that fist down and give me my scotch back, and I'll drink it and go.'

After a long staring pause, he turned his back on me. I took it as agreement to the terms and picked up one of the glasses, not sure whether it was mine or his.

It was his. The drink was much stronger, hardly any water in it at all. I put it down and picked up the other. He didn't turn round, didn't notice.

'Gervase,' I said dispassionately, 'try a psychiatrist.'

'Mind your own bloody business.'

I drank a mouthful of scotch but as a token only, and put the glass down again.

'Goodbye,' I said.

He still showed me his back, and was silent. I shrugged wryly and went out into the hall. Ursula and the two girls stood in the kitchen doorway looking anxious. I smiled at them lopsidedly and said to Ursula, 'We'll get through it somehow.'

'I hope so.' Forlorn hope, she was saying.

'I'll be back,' I said, not knowing if I meant it, but meaning anyway that anything I could do to help her or Gervase, I would do.

I let myself out of the front door quietly, and back

at Cookham telephoned to the Canders in Lexington. I talked to Mrs Cander; Sally.

Malcolm had gone to Stamford, Connecticut with Ramsey, she said. She thought they were fixing some kind of deal. She and Dave had really enjoyed Malcolm's visit and Malcolm had just loved the horse farms. Yes, of course she had Ramsey's phone number, he was an old friend. She read it out to me. I thanked her and she said sure thing and to have a nice day.

Ramsey and Malcolm were out. A woman who answered said to try at five-thirty. I tried at five-thirty Connecticut time and they were still out. The woman said Mr Osborn was a busy man and would I like to leave a message. I asked her to tell Mr Pembroke that his son Ian had phoned, but that there was no special news. She would do that, she said.

I went to bed and in the morning rode out on the Downs, and afterwards, from the house of the trainer whose horses I was riding, got through to Superintendent Yale's police station. He was there and came on the line.

'Where are you?'

'At the moment in a racing stable near Lambourn.'

'And your father?'

'I don't know.'

He made a disbelieving grunt. 'What time could you meet me at Quantum House?'

I looked at my watch. 'In riding clothes,' I said, 'in

forty-five minutes. If you want me to change, add on an hour.'

'Come as you are,' he said. 'Mr Smith says there's something to see.'

CHAPTER FIFTEEN

At Quantum, the heap of rubble had reduced to merely a mess.

I walked round to the back of the house and found two men in hard hats barely ankle deep as they methodically removed debris brick by brick from house to rubbish skip. The wind had abated and the clouds had relented to the extent that a pale sunshine washed the scene, making it to my eyes more of a wasteland than ever.

Superintendent Yale stood beside a trestle table that had been erected on the lawn, with the explosives expert Smith in his beige overalls and blue hat standing close beside him, heads bent in conference. There were no spectators any more on the far side of the rope across the lawn, not even Arthur Bellbrook. I walked over to the experts and said good morning.

'Good morning,' they said, looking up. 'Glad you came,' Smith said.

He stretched out a casual hand and picked up an object from the table, holding it out to me.

'We've found this,' he said. 'What do you think?'

I took the thing from him. It had been a coil of thin plastic-coated wire, but the coils had been stretched so that the wire was straighter, but still curled. It was about eighteen inches long. The plastic coating had been white, I thought. About an inch of bare wire stuck out of the plastic at each end. Onto the plastic, near one end, someone had bonded a hand from a clock. The hand pointed to the bare wire, so that the wire was an extension of the hand.

I looked at it with despair, though not with shock. I'd been fearing and hoping . . . trying not to believe it possible.

When I didn't ask what it was, Yale said with awakening suspicion, 'Does your silence mean that you know what it is?'

I looked up at the two men. They hadn't expected me to know, were surprised by my reaction, even astonished.

'Yes,' I said drearily. 'I do know. Did you find any other bits?'

Smith pointed to a spot on the table. I took a step sideways and stared down. There were some pieces of metal and plastic, but not those I'd expected. No cogwheels or springs. A grey plastic disc with a small hole in the centre.

'Was this a clock?' I said dubiously.

'A battery-driven clock,' Smith said. 'There's the coil from the electric motor.'

The coil was tiny, about a centimetre in diameter.

'How did you find it in all this rubbish?' I asked.

'We found various remains of the padded box which used to stand at the foot of Mr Pembroke's bed. These small pieces became embedded in the lid when the box blew apart. The wire with the clock's hand on it, and this . . .' he picked up the flat plastic disc ' . . . were in the same area.' He turned the plastic disc over to reveal a clock face on the other side. 'There should also be at least one other piece of wire somewhere, and some of the clock case and a battery or two, but we haven't found those yet. This was not actually an alarm clock, I don't think. We've found no sign of an alarm mechanism.'

'No, it won't have been an alarm clock,' I said.

The superintendent had been growing restive during Smith's account and could contain himself no longer.

'Will you please explain your familiarity with this device,' he said formidably. 'Did the gardener use this sort of thing for blowing up the tree trunk?'

'No, I don't think so. This device wasn't meant for setting off bombs. It was a toy.'

'What sort of toy?'

'Well . . . it was for switching things on. Torch bulbs, mostly. Like the lights we had on a station in a train set. A buzzer, sometimes. It was incredibly simple.'

'Explain,' Yale commanded.

I glanced at Smith. He was nodding resignedly.

'You get an old or cheap clock,' I said. 'We had

wind-up clocks, not a battery clock. You fix a length of wire to one of the hands, like this, so that a bare bit of wire sticks out and makes the hand much longer.'

'The hands are still on the clock, I take it?'

'Oh yes. Though sometimes we'd pull the minute hand off and just use the hour hand, because it's stronger, even though it's shorter. All you need is for the bare wire to reach out beyond the edge of the clock face. We used glue to stick the wire to the hand. Then you have a long bit of wire coming out from the centre of the front of the clock, and you fasten the free end of that to a battery. One of those nine-volt batteries with things like press-studs at the end.'

Smith was still nodding. Yale looked very much as if I shouldn't know such things.

'We made quite a lot of other gadgets,' I said, hearing the defensiveness in my voice. 'Buzzers for morse codes. Rudimentary telephones. Not just time switches. I made a lock once which could only be operated with a straight piece of wire.' And it still worked fine, although I wasn't going to show him.

Yale sighed. 'So in this case, we've got the wire fixed to the clock's hand at one end and to a battery at the other, right? Go on from there.'

'You need two more lengths of wire. One goes from the battery to whatever you want to activate. In our case, it was usually a torch bulb screwed into a metal holder. We fastened a bare end of wire to the metal holder. Then the third wire went back from the metal holder to the clock. We fixed this wire with glue to the clock case itself, not to the hands, in such a way that the bare end of wire was pointing out forwards, towards you if you were facing the clock like this.' I demonstrated with the clock face. 'We usually stuck it on over the number twelve, at the top, but you could fix it anywhere you liked. Then you wind up the clock and set the hand with the wire where you want it, and just wait. The wired hand travels round towards the jutting out wire and eventually hits against it at right angles. The circuit is thus complete from the clock wires to the battery to the light and back to the clock, so the light goes on. The clock hand keeps on trying to go round and the jutting wire keeps stopping it, so the light stays on. Well . . .' I finished lamely, 'that's what happened when we made them.'

'Them?' Yale said with apprehension.

'They were easy to make. They were interesting. I don't know how many we had, but quite a few.'

'My God.'

'There might be one still in the playroom,' I said. 'The old train sets are there.'

Yale looked at me balefully. 'How many of your family saw these devices?' he asked.

'Everyone.'

'Who made them?'

'I did, Gervase did, and Ferdinand. Thomas did. I don't remember who else.'

'But your whole family knows how to make a simple time switch?'

'Yes, I should think so.'

'And why,' he said, 'haven't you mentioned this before?'

I sighed and twisted the wired clock hand round in my fingers. 'Because,' I said, 'for starters I didn't think of it until after I'd left here the other day. After we'd been digging out the black powder and so on, and I'd been looking back to the past. I didn't want you to find this. I wanted you to find something sophisticated, that no one in the family could have thought up.'

'Hm,' he said, seeming to accept it. 'How many people outside your family knew about these clocks?'

'Several did, I suppose, but it was such a long time ago. No one would remember, would they?'

'They might.' Yale turned to Smith. 'This toy, is this really what set off the bomb?'

Smith nodded. 'It sounds just right. Wire in a detonator where the Pembroke children had a torch bulb . . .' He spread his hands. 'It wouldn't need more current than that.'

Not surprisingly, they decided to take a look in the playroom. They picked their way cautiously across the ankle-twisting rubble and headed for the passage which was comparatively clear by this time. The playroom, when we reached it, was shadowy inside, with the windows boarded up. Light of sorts seeped in through the door, but it took a few minutes for eyes to acclimatize, during which Yale bumped into the bicycles, knocking them over. I helped him pick them up. He wanted to know whose they were, and I told him about Peter and Robin.

He made no especial comment but watched while I went over to the shelves and began peering into boxes. I hadn't been in the room at all since the twins had gone, and their own playthings had overlaid those outgrown and abandoned by their elder brothers and sisters so that most of what I was looking at was unfamiliar and seemed to belong to strangers. It took several minutes to locate the box I thought I wanted, and to pick it off the shelves and put it on the table.

Someone, Coochie I dared say, had packed the trains away for good after Gervase and Ferdinand had left and I'd been busy with school and horses. At one time, the tracks had run permanently round half the room, but Peter and Robin had been television-watchers more than the rest of us, and hadn't dragged them out again. I opened the box and found the old treasures undisturbed, looking more battered than I'd thought, with rust on the much-used wheels.

I lifted out a couple of engines and some coaches, then followed them with a tunnel, a signal box with green and red bulbs and a brown plastic railway station adorned with empty bulb-holders among the advertisement stickers. I suppose to any adult, his childhood's rediscovered toys look smaller, deader, less appealing than he remembers. The trains were dusty and sad, relics ready for the skip outside, melancholic. The little lights had long gone out.

I took everything out of the box, but there were no clocks.

'Sorry,' I said. 'They could be in anything, really. If they're here.'

Smith began looking into any box whose contents weren't easily identifiable by the picture on top. Yale, with a no-hope expression, followed suit. I packed the trains back into oblivion with regret.

'Well, just look here,' Smith said suddenly. 'Gold mine.'

He had produced from a jumble of Lego constructions a bright new-looking clock with a Mickey Mouse face in unfaded technicolour. Mickey's hands in fat white gloves were the hands of the clock. To the minute hand was fixed a coil of white plastic-covered wire. A second white coil was stuck to the scarlet clock casing, its bared end jutting out over noon. When Smith held it all up, the white coils stretched out and down like curling streamers.

I looked at it blankly.

'I've never seen that one before,' I said. 'We didn't make them decorative. Ours were . . .' I sought for the word ' . . . utilitarian.'

Smith picked away among the Lego. 'Can't find a battery,' he reported. 'Nor a torch bulb, for that matter.' A pause. 'Wait a minute . . .' He rattled around and, finally, triumphantly produced a red and white Lego tower with a bulb-holder lodged inside near the top.

'A lighthouse, wouldn't you say?' he asked, standing it upright. 'Neat.'

'Someone made this for your twin brothers,' Yale said. 'Are you sure you never saw it?'

I shook my head. 'I didn't live here then, only visited. The twins had a short attention span, anyway. They tired of new toys pretty quickly. Always wanted to get on with the next thing.'

'I'll find out who made it,' Yale said. 'Can you sort out a box to put it in? I'll give you a receipt, of course.'

Smith found him an empty Lego box and into it they packed the bright co-star of an act that had brought half the house down. There was room in the box for the lighthouse, so they took that, too. Yale solemnly wrote a receipt on a page of his notebook and gave it to me, and with him carrying the box we went out into the daylight, blinking as our eyes adjusted after the gloom.

As we walked back in the general direction of the trestle table, Smith said, 'We've put all the clothes we've found on a table in the garage. I'm afraid they're mostly torn and unwearable, but you might want to see. All the personal things we've salvaged are in a cardboard carton. Do you want to take those today, or wait until we're finished?'

'Look now, take later,' I said.

Smith half smiled. 'They're in that box under the table.'

I squatted down beside the brown cardboard carton and opened the top flaps. Inside there was quite a good collection of dusty bits and pieces, more than I would have imagined. I picked out one of Malcolm's precious brushes and ran my finger over the gold and silver chased backing. The dust came off and the metal shone in the sunlight. He would be pleased, I thought.

'We've found five of those,' Smith observed. 'Two are badly dented, the others look all right.'

'There were eight,' I said. 'In his dressing room.'

He shrugged. 'We might find more.'

I turned over a few things in the box. Mostly they were uninteresting, like a bottle of aspirins from the bathroom. At the bottom, I came across one or two things of my own – an empty spongebag and the tape recorder.

I lifted the recorder out, straightened up and put it on the table. Pressed the start button. Absence of results.

'It was just a chance you might want it,' Smith said philosophically. 'It doesn't work as it is, but you might want to get it mended.'

'Probably cheaper to buy a new one,' I said. I pressed the rewind and fast-forward buttons pointlessly, and then the eject button, which worked. The plastic lid staggered open, revealing a tape within. I had to think for a minute which tape it was and then remembered it was only the one from my answering machine; nothing interesting. I shut the lid and put the recorder back in the box under the table.

'If you find my camera, now that would be good news,' I said, straightening again.

Yale had lost interest and was preparing to leave.

'Was it yours?' said Mr Smith. 'It's in the skip, I'm afraid. Badly smashed.'

'Oh well . . .'

'Were you insured?'

I shook my head. 'Never thought of it.'

Smith made sympathetic gestures and went back to the rubble. The superintendent said I should telephone him the following morning without fail. He ran his thumb and finger down his moustache and asked me if I now knew who had bombed the house.

'No,' I said. 'I don't. Do you?'

He wouldn't say he didn't, but he didn't. He picked up the Lego box and marched off with it, and I went to look at the clothes in the garage.

Nothing was worth saving, I thought. All highly depressing. My jodhpur boots with the toes flattened, Malcolm's vicuna coats with triangular tears. I left it all as it lay and started out on a quick hike round the garden to make sure all was well with the gold, and came upon Arthur Bellbrook digging potatoes within six feet of it. My heart jumped a bit. His was undisturbed.

We exchanged good mornings and remarks about

the weather. He asked what he should do with the potatoes and I told him to take them home. He nodded his thanks. He complained that the pick-up trucks for the rubbish skips were ruining the lawn. He said souvenir hunters had stripped Mrs Pembroke's fancy greenhouse of every single geranium, including the cuttings, but not to worry, without glass in the windows they would have died in the first frost. It had been a mild autumn, but frost would come soon.

He looked along the length of the kitchen garden, his back towards the end wall. He would dig everything over, he said, ready for winter.

I left him bending again to his task, not sure whether he was a guardian of the gold or a threat to it. Malcolm had a nerve, I thought, hiding his stockpile in that place and seeing Arthur work close to it day after day. Malcolm had more nerve than was good for him.

I drove to the pub in Cookham, where they were getting used to my hours, took a bath, put on trousers, shirt and jersey and, accompanied by Norman West's notes, went down to the bar for a drink before lunch. I read:

> Mr Thomas Pembroke (39) lives with his wife Berenice at 6 Arden Haciendas, Sonning, Nr. Reading, in the strip of new townhouses where old Arden House used to be. Two daughters (9 and 7) go to comprehensive school.
>
> Mr T. used to work as quantity surveyor for

Reading firm of biscuit makers, Shutleworth Digby Ltd. He got sacked for wrong estimates several weeks ago. I was told unofficially at the firm that he'd cost them thousands by ordering six times the glacé cherries needed for a run of 'dotted pinks'. (Had to laugh!) No laughing matter when tons of sliced almonds turned up after 'nut fluffs' had been discontinued. Mr T. didn't contest sacking, just left. Firm very relieved. Mr T. had been getting more and more useless, but had long service.

Mr T. didn't tell his wife he'd lost his job, but went off as if to work every day. (Common reaction.) On Newmarket Sales Tuesday he was 'walking about', same as the previous Friday. Pressed, he says he probably went to the public library in Reading, he did that most days; also sat around wherever there were seats, doing nothing. He read the job-offer pages in newspapers, but apparently did little to find work. No heart. (My opinion.)

Mr T. on brink of nervous breakdown (my opinion). I interviewed him in coffee shop. His hands trembled half the time, rattling cup against teeth, and he's not yet forty. Alcohol? Don't think so. Nerves shot to hell.

Mr T. drives old grey Austin 1100. Has slight dent in front wing. Mr T. says it's been there weeks. Car dirty, could do with wash, Mr T. says he has no energy for things like that.

Mr T.'s opinion of Mr Ian is very muddled (like

the rest of him). Mr Ian is 'best of bunch, really', but also Mr T. says Mr Ian is Mr Pembroke's favourite and it isn't fair. (!)

End of enquiry.

With a sigh, I put Thomas to the back and read about Berenice; no happy tale.

Mrs Berenice Pembroke (44 according to Mrs Joyce), wife of Mr Thomas, lives at 6 Arden Haciendas. No job. Looks after daughters, spends her days doing housework and reading trashy romances (according to Mrs Joyce again!).

Mrs B. very hard to interview. First visit, nothing. Second visit, a little, not much. She couldn't produce alibi for either day.

I asked about children and school journeys. Mrs B. doesn't drive them, they go by bus. They walk alone along pavement in residential side road to and from bus stop, which is about one-third of mile away, on the main thoroughfare. Mrs B.'s mother lives actually on the bus route. The girls get off the bus there most afternoons and go to their grandmother's for tea.

Interviewed Mrs B.'s mother. Not helpful. Agreed girls go there most days. Sometimes (if cold, wet or dark) she drives them home at about 7 pm. Other days, they finish journey by bus. I asked why they go there for tea so often and stay so late. Told to mind my own business. Younger girl said Granny makes better teas, Mummy gets cross. Told to shut up by older girl. Mrs B.'s mother showed me out.

Mrs B. drives old white Morris Maxi, clean, no marks on it.

Mrs B. gave no opinion of Mr Ian when asked, but looked as if she could spit. Says Mr Pembroke is wicked. Mrs B. slammed her front door (she hadn't asked me in!).

End of enquiry.

I put Berenice, too, back in the packet, and cheered myself up just a fraction with a slice of pork pie and a game of darts.

From the outside, Arden Haciendas were dreadful: tiny houses of dark brown-red brick set at odd angles to each other, with dark-framed windows at odd heights and dark front doors leading from walled front gardens one could cross in one stride. Nevertheless, Arden Haciendas, as Joyce had informed me a year earlier when Thomas had moved there, were socially the in thing, as they had won a prize for the architect.

God help architecture, I thought, ringing the bell of No 6. I hadn't been to this house before: had associated Thomas and Berenice always with the rather ordinary bungalow they'd bought at the time of their wedding.

Berenice opened the door and tried to close it again

when she saw me, but I pushed from my side and put my shoe over the threshold, and finally, with ill grace, she stepped back.

'We don't want to see you,' she said. 'Dear Thomas isn't well. You've no right to shove your way in here. I hate you.'

'Well, hate or not, I want to talk to Thomas.'

She couldn't say he wasn't there, because I could see him. Inside, the Haciendas were open plan with rooms at odd angles to each other, which explained the odd-angled exteriors. The front door led into an angled off-shoot of the main room, which had no ceiling where one would expect it, but soared to the rafters. Windows one couldn't see out of let daylight in at random points in the walls. Horrible, I thought, but that was only, as Mr West would say, my opinion.

Thomas rose to his feet from one of the heavily-stuffed armchairs brought from the bungalow, old comfortable chairs looking incongruous in all the aggressive modernity. There was no carpet on the woodblock floor; Thomas's shoes squeaked on it when he moved.

'Come in, old chap,' he said.

'We don't want him,' Berenice objected.

Thomas was looking haggard and I was shocked. I hadn't seen him, I realized, for quite a long time. All youth had left him, and I thought of him as he had been at eighteen or nineteen, laughing and good-humoured, coming for weekends and making Serena giggle.

Twenty years on, he looked middle-aged, the head balder than when I'd last taken his photograph, the ginger moustache less well tended, the desperation all-pervading. Norman West's assessment of early breakdown seemed conservative. It looked to me as if it had already happened. Thomas was a lot further down the line to disintegration than Gervase.

Ferdinand, he confirmed in answer to my question, had told him about Malcolm's will and about Malcolm's wish that I should try to find out who wanted to kill him. Thomas couldn't help, he said.

I reminded him of the day old Fred blew up the tree stump. Ferdinand had mentioned that too, he said. Thomas had been there. He remembered it clearly. He had carried Serena on his shoulders, and Fred had been blown flat.

'And do you remember the time switches we used to make, with wire on the clocks' hands?'

He stared, his eyes gaunt. After a long pause, he said, 'Yes.'

'Thomas, after Gervase and Ferdinand left Quantum, did you or they make any more of them?'

Berenice interrupted, 'Dear Thomas couldn't make a time switch to save his life, could you, darling?' Her voice was pitying, sneering, unkind. Thomas sent her a haunted look but no protest.

'Someone gave Robin and Peter a Mickey Mouse clock with white plastic-covered wires stuck on it,' I said. 'Very bright and attractive.'

Thomas shook his head helplessly.

'In the rubble at Quantum, they've found a clock hand stuck onto some white plastic-covered wire.'

'Oh, my God,' Thomas said miserably.

'So what?' Berenice demanded. 'Dear Thomas does overact so.'

'So,' I said, 'someone who knew how to make these time switches blew up Quantum.'

'What of it?' she said. 'I can't see Thomas doing it. Not enough nerve, have you, darling?'

Thomas said to me, 'Have a drink?'

Berenice looked disconcerted. Asking me to have a drink had been for Thomas an act of rebellion against her wishes. There hadn't been many of them, I guessed. I accepted with thanks, although it was barely five-thirty and to my mind too early. I'd chosen the hour on purpose, hoping both that Thomas would have returned from his day's wanderings and that the daughters would stop at their grandmother's house on their way home from school.

Thomas squeaked across the floor to the kitchen, which was divided from the main room only by a waist-high counter, and began opening cupboards. He produced three tumblers which he put clumsily on the counter, and then sought in the fridge interminably for mixers. Berenice watched him with her face screwed into an expression of long-suffering impatience and made no move to help.

'We have some gin somewhere,' he said vaguely,

having at last found the tonic. 'I don't know where Berenice puts things. She moves them about.'

'Dear Thomas couldn't find a book in a library.'

Thomas gave her a look of black enmity which she either didn't see or chose to ignore. He opened another cupboard, and another, and in his wife's continued unhelpful silence finally found a nearly full bottle of Gordon's gin. He came round into the main room and poured from the bottle into three glasses, topping up inadequately from a single bottle of tonic.

He handed me a glass. I didn't much care for gin, but it was no time to say so.

He held out the second glass to Berenice.

'I don't want any,' she said.

Thomas's hand was trembling. He made an awkward motion as if to raise the glass to his own lips, then put it down with a bang on the counter, and in an uncoordinated movement accidentally knocked the gin bottle over so that it fell to the floor, smashing into green shiny pieces, the liquid spreading in a pool.

Thomas bent down to pick up the bits. Berenice didn't help.

She said, 'Thomas can't get anything right, can you, darling?' The words were no worse than others, but the acid sarcasm in her voice had gone beyond scathing to unbearable.

Thomas straightened with a face filled with passionate hatred, the worm turning at last, and by the neck he held the top part of the green bottle, the broken edges jagged as teeth.

He came up fast with his hand rising. Berenice, cushioned in complacency, wasn't even looking at him and seemed not to begin to understand her danger.

Malcolm said I had fast reactions . . . I dropped my own drink, grasped Berenice by both arms and swung her violently round and out of the slicing track of the razor-sharp weapon. She was furiously indignant, protesting incredulously, sprawling across the floor where I'd almost thrown her, still unaware of what had been happening.

Thomas looked at the damage he'd done to me for a long blank second, then he dropped the fearsome bottle and turned to stumble off blindly towards his front door. I took two strides and caught him by the arm.

'Let me go . . .' He struggled, and I held on. 'Let me go . . . I can't do anything right . . . she's right.'

'She's bloody wrong.'

I was stronger than he. I practically dragged him across the room and flung him into one of the armchairs.

'I've cut you,' he said.

'Yes, well, never mind. You listen to me. You both listen to me. You're over the edge. You're going to have to face some straight facts.'

Berenice had finally realized how close she'd come to needing stitches. She looked with anger at the point of my left shoulder where jersey and shirt had been ripped away, where a couple of cuts were bleeding. She turned to Thomas with a bitterly accusing face and opened her mouth.

'Shut up,' I said roughly. 'If you're going to tell him he's incompetent, don't do it. If you're going to complain that he could have cut you instead, yes he could, he was trying to. Sit down and *shut up*.'

'Trying to?' She couldn't believe it. She sat down weakly, her hair awry, her body slack, eyes shocked.

'You goaded him too far. Don't you understand what you've been doing to him? Putting him down, picking him to pieces every time you open your mouth? You have now completely succeeded. He can't function any more.'

'Dear Thomas – ' she began.

'Don't say that. You don't mean it.'

She stared.

'If he were your dear Thomas,' I said, 'you would help him and encourage him, not sneer.'

'I'm not listening to this.'

'You just think what you stirred up in Thomas today, and if I were you, I'd be careful.' I turned to Thomas, 'And it's not all her fault. You've let her do it, let her carp all this time. You should have stopped her years ago. You should have walked out. You've been loyal to her beyond reason and she's driven you to want to kill her, because that's what I saw in your face.'

Thomas put a hand over his eyes.

'You were dead lucky you didn't connect with her mouth or her throat or whatever you were going for. There would have been no going back. You just think what would have happened, both of you. The consequences to yourselves, and to your girls. *Think!*' I paused. 'Well, it's beyond facing.'

'I didn't mean it,' Thomas mumbled.

'I'm afraid you did,' I said.

'He couldn't have done,' Berenice said.

'He did mean it,' I said to her. 'It takes quite a force to tear away so much woollen jersey. Your only hope is to believe to the depths of your soul that he put all his goaded infuriated strength behind that blow. I'll tell you, I was lucky too. I was moving away fast trying to avoid being cut, and it can have been only the points of the glass that reached my skin, but I'll remember the speed of them . . .' I broke off, not knowing how else to convince her. I didn't want to say, 'It bloody hurts,' but it did.

Thomas put his head in his hands.

'Come on,' I said to him, 'I'm taking you out of here. On your feet, brother.'

'Don't be ridiculous,' Berenice said.

'If I leave him here, will you cuddle him?'

The negative answer filled her whole face. She wouldn't have thought of it. She was aggrieved. It would have taken little time for her to stoke up the recriminations.

'When the firemen have gone,' I said, 'fires often start again from the heat in the embers.'

I went over to Thomas. 'Come on. There's still life ahead.'

Without looking up, he said in a dull sort of agony, 'You don't know . . . It's too late.'

I said 'No' without great conviction, and then the front door opened with a bang to let in the two girls.

'Hello,' they said noisily, bringing in swirls of outside air. 'Granny turned us out early. What's going on? What's all this glass on the floor? What's all the blood on your arm?'

'A bottle got broken,' I said, 'and I fell on it.'

The young one looked at the bowed head of her father, and in a voice that was a devastating mimic of her mother's, vibrating with venom and contempt, she said, 'I'll bet it was Dear Thomas who broke it.'

Berenice heard for herself what she'd been doing to her husband. Heard what she was implanting in her own children. The revelation seemed to overwhelm her, and she sought for excuses.

'If we had more money . . . If only Malcolm . . . It's not fair . . .'

But they had two cars, thanks to their trust fund, and a newly-built townhouse, and Thomas's unemployment had brought no immediate financial disaster: money wasn't their trouble, nor would it cure it.

'Why didn't you get a job?' I said. 'What did you

ever expect of Thomas? That he'd set the world alight? He did the best he could.'

Quantum in me fuit . . .

'I wanted a son,' she said flatly. 'Thomas got a vasectomy. He said two children were enough, we couldn't afford any more. It wasn't fair. Malcolm should have given us more money. *I always wanted a son.*'

Dear God, I thought: flat simple words at the absolute heart of things, the suppurating disappointment that she had allowed to poison their lives. Just like Gervase, I thought. So much unhappiness from wanting the unobtainable, so much self-damage.

I could think of nothing to say. Nothing of help. It was too late.

I went across to Thomas and touched him on the shoulder. He stood up. He didn't look at his family, or at me. I put my hand lightly under his elbow and steered him to the front door, and in unbroken silence we left the wasteland of his marriage.

CHAPTER SIXTEEN

I took Thomas to Lucy's house.

It seemed to me, as I drove away from the pretentious Haciendas, that Lucy's particular brand of peace might be just what Thomas needed. I couldn't take him to Vivien, who would demolish him further, and Joyce, who was fond of him, would be insufferably bracing. I frankly didn't want him with me in Cookham; and Donald, influenced by Berenice, tended to despise him.

Lucy was in, to my relief, and opened the front door of the farm cottage where she and Edwin led the simple life near Marlow.

She stared at us. At my red arm. At Thomas's hanging head.

'Sister, dear,' I said cheerfully. 'Two brothers needing succour come knocking at thy gate. Any chance of hot sweet tea? Loving looks? A sticking plaster?'

Edwin appeared behind her, looking peevish. 'What's going on?'

To Lucy, I said, 'We cracked a bottle of gin, and I fell on it.'

'Are you drunk?' she said.

'Not really.'

'You'd better come in.'

'Ferdinand has been on the telephone,' Edwin said without welcome, staring with distaste at my blood as we stepped over his threshold. 'He warned us you'd be turning up some time. You might have had the courtesy to let us know in advance.'

'Sorry,' I said dryly.

Lucy glanced swiftly at my face. 'This is trouble?'

'Just a spot.'

She took Thomas by the arm and led him out of the tiny entrance hall into her book-filled sitting room. Edwin's and Lucy's cottage consisted of two rooms downstairs, which had been partly knocked into one, with a modern bathroom tacked on at the back. The stairs, which were hidden behind a latched door, led up to three rooms where one had to inch round the beds, bending one's head so as not to knock it on the eaves. Laura Ashley wallpaper everywhere covered uneven old plaster, and rag rugs provided warmth underfoot. Lucy's books were stacked in columns on the floor along one wall in the sitting room, having overflowed the bookcases, and in the kitchen there were wooden bowls, pestles and mortar, dried herbs hanging.

Lucy's home was unselfconscious, not folksy. Lucy herself, large in dark trousers and thick handknitted sweater, sat Thomas in an armchair and in a very short time thrust a mug of hot liquid into his unwilling hand.

'Drink it, Thomas,' I said. 'How about some gin in it?' I asked Lucy.

'It's in.'

I smiled at her.

'Do you want some yourself?' she said.

'Just with milk.' I followed her into the kitchen. 'Have you got any tissues I could put over this mess?'

She looked at my shoulder. 'Are tissues enough?'

'Aspirins?'

'I don't believe in them.'

'Ah.'

I drank the hot tea. Better than nothing. She had precious few tissues, when it came to the point, and far too small for the job. I said I would leave it and go along to the hospital later to get it cleaned up. She didn't argue.

She said, 'What's all this about?' and dipped into a half-empty packet of raisins and then offered me some, which I ate.

'Thomas has left Berenice. He's in need of a bed.'

'Not here,' she protested. 'Take him with you.'

'I will if you won't keep him, but he'd be better off here.'

She said her son, my nephew, was up in his bedroom doing his homework.

'Thomas won't disturb him,' I said.

She looked at me doubtfully. 'There's something you're not telling me.'

'The last straw,' I said, 'has just broken Thomas. If someone doesn't treat him kindly, he'll end up in the nut house or the suicide statistics and I am not, repeat not, joking.'

'Well . . .'

'That's my girl.'

'I'm not your girl,' she said tartly. 'Perhaps I'm Thomas's.' Her face softened slightly. 'All right, he can stay.'

She ate another handful of raisins and went back to the sitting room, and I again followed. Edwin had taken the second armchair. Lucy lowered her bulk onto a leather stool beside Thomas, which left me on my feet looking around. There were no other seats. Resignedly I sat on the floor and rested my back against a wall. Neither Lucy nor Edwin commented. Neither had invited me to sit.

'As I'm here,' I said, 'I may as well ask the questions I was going to come and ask tomorrow.'

'We don't want to answer,' Edwin said. 'And if you get blood on the wallpaper you can pay for redecorating.'

'The police will come,' I said, twisting slightly out of harm's way. 'Why not practise on me? They'll ask about the timing device that set off the bomb at Quantum.'

Thomas stirred. 'I made it, you know. The Mickey Mouse clock.'

It was the first time he'd spoken since we'd left his house. Lucy looked as if she thought him delirious, then raised her eyebrows and started to concentrate.

'Not that,' she said, troubled.

'Do you remember those clocks?' I asked.

'Of course I do. We've got one upstairs, that Thomas made for our son.'

'What sort of face has it got?'

'A sailing ship. Did the Mickey Mouse clock explode . . .?'

'No,' I said. 'The one actually used had a grey plastic dial with white numbers. The Mickey Mouse clock was intact, in the playroom.'

Thomas said dully, 'I haven't made one for years.'

'When did you make the Mickey Mouse for Robin and Peter?' I asked.

'I didn't make it for them. I made it a long time ago for Serena. She must have given it to them. It made her laugh, when I made it.'

'You were a nice boy, Thomas,' Lucy said. 'Funny and kind.'

Edwin said restlessly, 'I would have thought any timing device would have been blown to unrecognizable fragments by such a big bomb.'

'It seems they often find pieces,' I said.

'Do you mean,' he demanded, 'that they've actually sifted through all those tons of rubbish?'

'More or less. They know it was a battery clock. They found part of the motor.'

'It serves Malcolm right the house was blown up,' Edwin said with barely suppressed violence. 'Flinging money about on ridiculous scholarships. Keeping us poor. I suppose *you're* all right, aren't you?' There was a sneer there for me, openly. 'He's never been fair to Lucy. You've always been in the way, smarming him up, taking the lion's share. He gives you whatever you ask for while we have to struggle along on a pittance.'

'Is that the authentic voice of Vivien?' I asked.

'It's the truth!'

'No,' I said. 'It's what you have been told over and over again, but it's not the truth. Most people believe a lie if they're told it often enough. It's easy enough after all to believe a lie if you've heard it only once. Especially if you want to believe it.'

Lucy looked at me intently. 'You care about this, don't you?'

'About being cast perpetually as the family villain? Yes, I dare say I do. But I was thinking also of Thomas. He's been told ad infinitum that he's useless, and now he believes it. I'm going now, Lucy.' I stood up without haste. 'You tell Thomas over and over that he's a worthwhile person, and maybe he'll begin to believe that instead. You have to believe in yourself to get anywhere.'

'Oh yes,' she said quietly. 'You do.'

'What you've written,' I said, 'is for ever.'

Her eyes widened. 'How do you know . . . that I've lost . . .'

'I guessed.' I bent and kissed her cheek, to her surprise. 'Are you seriously in need?'

'Financially?' She was startled. 'No worse than usual.'

'Of course we are,' Edwin said to her waspishly. 'You're earning almost nothing now and you still spend a fortune on books.'

Lucy looked only mildly embarrassed, as if she'd heard that often before.

'If I held the purse-strings,' Edwin complained, 'you'd use the public library, as I do.'

'Why don't you work, Edwin?' I asked.

'Lucy doesn't like bustle.' He seemed to think it explanation enough. 'We'd be perfectly happy if Malcolm trebled Lucy's trust fund, as he ought to. He has millions, we live in a hovel. It's not fair.'

'Doesn't Lucy despise money?' I asked. 'And people who have it? Do you want her to become what she despises?'

Edwin glared.

Lucy looked at me blandly. 'There's no such state as perfection,' she said.

I drove back to Reading, to the hospital that had an emergency room open all evening, and there got my shoulder and upper arm cleaned and stitched. There were three cuts, it seemed, variously deep but nothing frightful, and they had long stopped bleeding: with the stitches, they would heal almost instantly. The staff advised pain-killers pro tem. I thanked them and eventually drove to Cookham feeling more than slightly tired but chiefly hungry, and having remedied both conditions satisfactorily, set off again next morning to ride. There was no problem there with the stitches: they were tender to the touch and stiff when I lifted my arm, but that was all.

Restored yet again in spirit by the dose of fresh air, I took a lazy day off from the emotional battering of the family and went to London to get my American and Australian visas. It was only a week since I'd ridden Park Railings at Cheltenham and it felt like eternity. I bought a new sweater and had my hair cut and thought about Ursula 'wandering about' through days of escape. One could wander for hours in London, thinking one's thoughts.

On an impulse, I telephoned Joyce, not expecting her to be in.

'Darling,' she yelled. 'I'm going out. Bridge. Where are you?'

'In a phone box.'

'Where's your father?'

'I don't know.'

'Darling, you're *infuriating*. What did you ring for?'

'I suppose . . . just to hear your voice.'

It seemed to stump her entirely. 'Are you out of your head? You tell that old bugger . . . tell him . . .' She choked on it.

'That you're glad he's alive?' I suggested.

'Don't let the old sod get blown up.'

'No,' I said.

'Must rush, darling. Don't break your neck. 'Bye . . .'

''Bye now,' I said.

I wondered if she ever talked on the telephone except at the top of her voice. The decibels were comforting, somehow. At least she never sounded bored. I would rather infuriate her than bore her, I thought.

I went unhurriedly back to Cookham and in the evening bent again to Norman West's notes.

Of Edwin, he had said:

Mr Edwin Pembroke (53) née Bugg, lives with his wife Lucy in No 3 Wrothsay Farm Cottages, near Marlow. One son (15), attends state school, bicycles to school, has latchkey, gets his own tea, goes upstairs, does homework, working for exams, conscientious, doesn't know if his parents were around on the Friday or Tuesday at specified hours, doesn't expect so. He comes downstairs about 8 or 9 pm, they all eat vegetarian meal then. (No TV!) Mrs L. cooks in a wok. Mr E. washes up.

Mr E. does the housework (not much) and shopping, mostly vegetables. He spends hours reading in public library (librarians agree). Goes to pub, spends more hours over one beer (barman indignant). Takes laundry to laundromat. Listens to radio.

Spends hours doing crossword puzzles. (The garden's untidy. Mr E. doesn't like gardening. They grow only runner beans, they're easy.)

Mr E. and Mrs L. share an old Hillman, which Mr E. mostly drives. (Mrs L. has licence.) Car dusty and rusty, no dents.

Mr E. good-looking man, complete drone (my opinion). Idle life suits him. Mr E.'s idle life seems to suit Mrs L. also – no accounting for people. She does less than he does, come to think. Mr E. has sharp sarcastic manner on occasions. Detests Mr Ian, curses Mr Pembroke but at same time wants money from him (!). Definitely thinks of Mr Pembroke's money too much, broods on it, talked about it all the time.

End of enquiry.

Of Lucy, among other things, he had written:

Mrs L. spends large parts of the day unaware of what's going on around her (my opinion). I had to repeat several questions. It seemed she didn't hear me, but nothing wrong with her ears. She listens to things going on in her own head (can't put it very well). Has no alibis for Friday or Tuesday. Can't remember where she was. (I believe it.) Goes for rambling walks. Mrs L. very troubled over something, but wouldn't say what. She ate a tinful of peanuts while I was there, looked surprised when they'd gone.

So much for Lucy and Edwin, I thought. What about Donald and Helen?

Donald Pembroke (44) eldest of Mr Pembroke's offspring, lives at Marblehill House, detached chalet-style house which goes with his job, Secretary, Marblehill Golf Club (rich club, high fees) near Henley-on-Thames. Long waiting list for membership, rich members.

Mr D. has staff (green keeper, club steward, etc). He himself oversees and runs the whole place, is said to be good at it, members like him, say he gets things done, runs tight ship, decent bar, club rooms, tournaments etc, always listens to and deals with complaints, seen as friend, authority figure, social equal. Mr D. likes his work. His social standing extremely important to him (my opinion). Keeps up high appearances.

As to alibis for the Friday and Tuesday in question: no alibis ascertainable. Is always 'round the place', never at any place at set hours except first thing in the mornings (9 am) to see to post with office staff. Has Mondays off, works Saturdays and Sundays.

Walks to work (barely 100 yds). Usually returns home at 7 pm (much earlier in winter), sometimes stays until bar closes. Often walks round later to see all is well everywhere. Dedicated.

Mr D. has daughter in art school, high fees. Also twin sons who have started this term at Eton, previously at good prep. school. (How does he afford it?)

Mr D. drives silver Mercedes, 2 years old. Clean. No marks of collision with Mr Ian.

Mr D. thinks it's very bad news Mr Ian is back in Mr Pembroke's favour. Certain to mean less inheritance for him (Mr D.). He's angry about that. But he also thinks Mr Ian the only one who can persuade Mr Pembroke to distribute some wealth now. Sees no inconsistency in these beliefs. (He'll use Mr Ian, doesn't have to trust him, he said.) Thinks Mr Pembroke's recent expenditure unreasonable, 'insane' (!). Says he's senile.

Mr D. gave me rapid answers; busy. Says his financial affairs were none of my business, edgy on subject. Is he in debt? (My opinion, considering his expenses, probably.) Champagne lifestyle.

End of enquiry.

And Helen?

Mrs Helen Pembroke (43) wife of Mr D. Very good-looking lady. Very worried, wouldn't say what about.

I interviewed her in Marblehill House – big name

for fairly ordinary-sized three-bedroom, nice sitting room, though, over-looking golf course. Good furniture, appearance of wealth.

Mrs H. works at home (on dustsheet in dining room) painting views of Henley by hand onto plates, jugs, boxes; all china. Very quick, very good (to my eyes), nice pictures. They go off to be glazed, she said, then sell in local shops. Reasonably paid, she says. (What's reasonable? She says her work was to be seen as a hobby. Mr D. refers to it in that way.)

Mrs H. works alone nearly every day, no alibis for Friday or Tuesday. Sometimes drives into Henley to shop, no regular pattern. Mrs H. has white Cavalier, clean, no dents.

No children at home. Daughter shares flat with friends near art school (more expense).

Mrs H. ultra-loyal to Mr D. Says my enquiries unnecessary. Says it's ridiculous to suppose Mr D. would attack his father. Out of the question. (My opinion, she wasn't too sure.) They need more cash badly (my opinion).

Mrs H. mostly shares Mr D.'s opinion of Mr Ian, but doesn't seem to dislike him personally.

End of enquiry.

On Friday morning, I called in on a public library and looked up 'explosives' in encyclopaedias. Ammonium nitrate was there, also the proportion of fertilizer to diesel oil needed, also the formula for relating volume to kilos. The knowledge was available to anyone who sought it.

On Friday after lunch I went to the Marblehill Golf Club and found Donald in the clubroom placating a foursome who had arrived late and missed their game.

'Go over to the house,' he said when he saw me. 'I can't talk here.' He turned decisively back to the problem in hand and I did what I was told, like a good little brother.

Helen was resigned more than annoyed to see me. 'Ferdinand said you would come, and we had the police here yesterday. Not that we could tell them anything, or you either.'

She was wearing a painter's smock over jeans and looked dressed by Dior. She took me into the sitting room and pointed to a chair, and with unconscious grace sat herself half-on, half-off a polished table, raising her wrists to keep her paint-smudged hands away from the furniture.

Donald came bustling in, telling me he could give me ten minutes. 'Don't see what you can do,' he said. 'Leave it to the police.'

'What did they ask you?'

'About Fred blowing up the tree stump. I said yes, of course we'd been there. Helen and I weren't then married. It was the first time she'd met Malcolm, she was staying the weekend.'

'Saturday morning,' she said, nodding. 'The gardener came in specially to blow up the tree trunks. Not something one would forget, seeing him knocked flat. I took a photograph of the tree roots afterwards. It's still in one of our albums.'

'And the time switch clocks, do you remember those?' I asked.

'Naturally,' Donald said.

Helen added, 'Dear Thomas made two for our boys for their birthday once, when they could just tell the time.' She had said Dear Thomas, I noticed, as if she had meant it, not as Berenice said it. 'They got lost in one of our moves.'

'Where's Malcolm?' Donald asked brusquely.

'I don't know.'

'You're lying,' he said, but for once I wasn't. Malcolm and Ramsey Osborn had left the Osborn residence, according to the female voice on the line the evening before, and had given her no number at which they could be reached. I could try again tomorrow, she said. Mr Osborn should have let her know by then; he usually did.

'Did either of you,' I asked, 'trace Malcolm to Cambridge the weekend he was put in the car?'

I hadn't expected any answer but negative, but the question came at them unexpectedly and Helen practically jumped.

'Did you?' I said to her.

'No, of course not,' Donald said quickly. 'We had no

way of knowing he would go to Newmarket Sales, if that's what you're inferring.'

'The hotel at Cambridge said three people – two men and a woman – had asked if Malcolm was staying there,' I said. 'One was Norman West, who were the others? I'm not saying you went to Newmarket Sales, just did one of you trace Malcolm?'

They looked at me glumly. Then Helen said, 'I suppose so.'

'Why?' I asked.

Donald cleared his throat. 'I needed his signature on a guarantee.'

'Go on, what guarantee?'

'For a temporary bank loan.' He swallowed. 'I thought he might . . .'

'We had to have the money in a hurry,' Helen said. 'The bank manager told Donald we could borrow it if Malcolm would guarantee it. Then we couldn't get hold of Malcolm. We had to think where he might be, and he's always going to Cambridge. Donald and I just talked about it, guessing, wondering . . . And then, well, Donald went over to the club house and I just picked up the AA book and found those hotels in Cambridge, and without really believing in it I tried two . . . only two . . . and he was there, at the second. When Donald came home I told him and the extraordinary thing was, he'd had the same idea and got the same result.' She paused. 'We were pretty desperate, you see.'

'Don't say that,' Donald said. ' "Desperate" gives the wrong picture.'

'What did you need the money for?' I asked.

They looked at each other, foreheads wrinkled in worry. Finally, reluctantly, but as if coming to a decision, Donald said, 'We had some interest to pay unexpectedly. I had negotiated three months' deferment of interest on a loan, or at least I thought I had, and then I got a threatening demand. I had to pay at once or they'd start proceedings.' The desperation he said wasn't there, definitely had been; it still echoed in his voice. 'I couldn't have it getting around the golf club, could I?' he demanded. 'No one in the family could lend me a large sum in a hurry. Our ordinary bank overdraft is always at maximum. The finance company was inflexible. I knew Malcolm wouldn't *give* me the money, he has those stupid warped views, but I did think he might guarantee . . . just for a short while . . .'

To save the whole pack of cards collapsing, perhaps he might. Malcolm wasn't cruel. He'd lent Edwin money sometimes in the past. Donald, I thought, had stood a good chance.

'But when you'd found where he was, you didn't get in touch with him, did you?'

'No,' Donald said. 'I didn't relish telling Malcolm our troubles. I didn't want to look a fool, and Helen thought of a different way out.'

I looked at her enquiringly.

'Popped my baubles,' she said with a brave attempt

at lightness. 'Took them to London. All my lovely rocks.' She held her head high, refusing to cry.

'Pawned them?' I said.

'We'll get them back,' she said valiantly, trying to believe it.

'What day did you pop them?'

'Wednesday. Donald took the money in cash to the finance company, and that gives us a three-months' breather.'

Wednesday, I thought. The day after someone had failed to kill Malcolm at Newmarket.

'When did the finance company start threatening you?'

'The Thursday before,' Helen said. 'They gave us a week. They were utterly beastly, Donald said.'

'Vivien tried to get Malcolm to give us some money,' Donald said with resentment, 'and he flatly refused.'

'Well,' I said, half-smiling, 'she called him an evil, wicked, vindictive tyrant, and that's not the best way in the world to persuade Malcolm to be generous. If she'd used honey, she might have succeeded.'

Helen said, 'You're the only one he'll listen to. I don't care if you get millions more than us. All the others are furious about it, they don't believe it about equal shares in his will, but I don't care. If you could just . . . I mean . . .'

'I'll try,' I promised, 'but the equal shares are true.'

It fell on deaf ears. They believed what they believed, the whole lot of them, feeding and reinforcing their fears every time they consulted.

I left Donald and Helen among their antique furniture and behind their shaky façade and trundled along to Quantum to see how things were developing.

Not fast, was the answer. The place was abandoned except for a solitary uniformed policeman sitting in a police car outside what had been the front door. One could see right through the house now. The tarpaulin that had hung from the roof had come down. The policeman was the one who had accompanied me on my tour of peering in through the windows, and I gathered he was pleased to have a visitor to enliven a monotonous stint.

He picked up his car radio and spoke into it to the effect that Mr Ian Pembroke had come by. A request came back, which he relayed to me: would Mr Pembroke please drop in at the police station when he left? Mr Pembroke would.

The policeman and I walked round to the back of the house. Mr Smith had gone, also his helpers. The last of the rubble was away from the house and overflowing a skip. A flat black plastic sheet, the sort used for roofing hayricks, lay where a week ago the walls of my bedroom had come tumbling down. The interior doors had been sealed with plywood, like the windows, to deter looters, and the broken end of the staircase had been barred off. A house with its centre torn out; a thirty-foot yawn between surviving flanks.

'It looks terrible,' I said, and the policeman agreed.

Arthur Bellbrook was cleaning his spades, getting

ready to leave. I gave him a cheque for his wages for that week and the next, and added a chunk for the care of the dogs. He gave me dignified thanks. He hoped Mr Pembroke was all right, poor man, and I said I thought so.

'I had my picture in the paper,' he said. 'Did you see it?'

I said I was sorry I hadn't.

'Oh, well. I did.' He shrugged disappointedly and set off homewards, and I walked down to where he'd earlier been digging potatoes, and then further, to check that the nettles were still untrampled on the far side of the wall.

The green sea looked dusty and ageing but upright. They too, I supposed, would die with the frost.

The policeman was watching me incuriously. I stopped and stared at the house from a distance, giving the impression that that's why I had gone as far as I had, and then walked back and took my leave. The house from a distance looked just as bad, if not worse.

Superintendent Yale shook my hand. Things were almost friendly at the police station but they were no nearer discovering who had planted the bomb. Enquiries were proceeding, the superintendent said and perhaps I could help.

'Fire away,' I said.

'We interviewed the former gardener, Fred Perkins,' Yale said. 'We asked him about the tree stump and what he used to blow it up. Besides cordite, that is. What sort of a fuse.'

I was interested. 'What did he say? Does he remember?'

'He said he'd got the black powder and some detonators and some fuse cord from a quarryman friend of his. The black powder was in the box which we saw, the detonators were in a separate tin with the cord and the instructions.'

'The instructions!' I repeated incredulously.

'Yes.' He sighed. 'Fred Perkins says he followed the instructions because he'd never blown anything up before. He said he used a bit of extra black powder just to make sure.'

'It was quite an explosion.'

'Yes. We asked him what he'd done with the other detonators. He says Mr Pembroke took them away from him that morning, when he came running out of the house. We need to ask Mr Pembroke what he did with them, so . . . er . . . where is he?'

'I really don't know,' I said slowly, 'and that's the truth. I can probably find him, but it'll take a day or two.' I thought for a moment, then said, 'Surely he would have thrown away those detonators years ago.'

'If he had any sense he wouldn't have thrown them anywhere,' Yale said. 'Mr Smith says you handle detonators with extreme caution if you don't want to lose a finger or an eye. They can explode if you knock or drop them or make them too warm. Mr Pembroke's correct course would have been to turn them over to the police.'

'Maybe he did,' I said.

'We'd like to find out.'

'But would detonators still detonate after twenty years?' I asked.

'Mr Smith thinks it possible, perhaps likely. He wouldn't take any liberties, he said.'

'What does a detonator look like?' I asked.

He hesitated, but said, 'Mr Smith said we might be looking for a small aluminium tube about the thickness of a pencil or slightly less, about six centimetres long. He says that's what the army used. He used to be in the Royal Engineers. He says the tube contains fulminate of mercury, and the word "fulminate" means to flash like lightning.'

'He should know.'

'Fred Perkins can't clearly remember what his detonators looked like. He remembers he had to fasten the cord into the end of the tube with pliers. Crimp it in. Mr Smith says civilians who touch explosives should be certified.'

I reflected. 'Did Mr Smith find out exactly what the Quantum bomb was made of?'

'Yes. ANFO, as he thought. He said the whole thing was amateur in the extreme.'

'Amateurs,' I said dryly, 'run faster than anyone else.'

As an amateur, I went to Kempton Park the next day and on Young Higgins beat the hell out of a lot of professionals.

I didn't know what possessed me. It seemed that I rode on a different plane. I knew it was the horse who had to be fast enough; the jockey, however determined, couldn't do it on his own. Young Higgins seemed inspired and against more formidable opponents than at Sandown produced a totally different race.

There were no aunts riding this time, no lieutenant colonels falling off. No earl's son to chat to. No journalist to make it look easy. For some reason, George and Jo had entered Young Higgins in a high-class open three-mile steeplechase, and I was the only amateur in sight.

I'd ridden against an all-professional field of top jockeys a few times before, and it was usually a humbling experience. I had the basic skills and a good deal of touch. I could get horses settled and balanced. I liked speed, I liked the stretch of one's spirit: but there was always a point against top professionals at which that wasn't enough.

George and Jo were unfussed. Young Higgins was fitter than at Sandown, they thought, and at Kempton there was no hill to tire him. They were bright-eyed and enthusiastic, but not especially hopeful. 'We didn't want to change you for a professional,' they said in explanation. 'It wouldn't have been fair.'

Maybe not fair, but prudent, I thought. The top pros raced with sharper eyes, better tactics, more strength, quicker reactions. Theirs was an intenser determination, a fiercer concentration. Humour was for before and after, not during. Race-riding was their business, besides their pleasure, and some of them thought of amateur opponents as frivolous unfit nuisances who caused accidents and endangered lives.

Perhaps because of an arrogant desire to prove them wrong, perhaps because of the insights and realities I'd faced in a traumatic week, perhaps because of Young Higgins himself: I rode anyway with a new sharp revelationary perception of what was needed for winning, and the horse and I came home in front by four lengths to a fairly stunned silence from the people on the stands who'd backed everything else on the card but us.

George and Jo were vindicated and ecstatic. Young Higgins tossed his head at the modest plaudits. A newspaperman labelled the result as a fluke.

I'd cracked it, I thought. I'd graduated. That had been real professional riding. Satisfactory. But I was already thirty-three. I'd discovered far too late the difference between enjoyment and fire. I'd needed to know it at nineteen or twenty. I'd idled it away.

'This is no time,' Jo said laughing, 'to look sad.'

CHAPTER SEVENTEEN

I flew to New York two days later, still not knowing where to find Malcolm.

The voice at Stamford, Connecticut, always helpful but uninformed, had thought, the previous evening, that the gentlemen might have gone back to Kentucky: they'd been talking of buying a horse that they'd seen there a week earlier. Another horse, not the one they'd bought yesterday.

It was just as well, I thought, that Donald and Helen and Thomas and Berenice and Edwin and Lucy and Vivien and Joyce didn't know. That Gervase, Ursula, Alicia, Ferdinand, Debs and Serena hadn't heard. All fourteen of them would have fallen upon Malcolm and torn him apart.

I chose New York for the twin reasons that Stamford, Connecticut, was barely an hour and a half's drive away (information from the voice) and that everyone should see New York some time. My journeys before that had been only in Europe, to places like Paris,

Rome, Athens and Oslo. Beaches and race-meetings and temples. Horses and gods.

I was heading for a hotel on 54th Street, Manhattan, that the voice had recommended: she would tell Mr Pembroke I would be there, as soon as she knew where Mr Pembroke was. It seemed as good an arrangement as any.

Superintendent Yale didn't know I'd left England, nor did any of the family. I sighed with deep relief on the aeroplane and thought about the visits I'd made the day before to Alicia and Vivien. Neither had wanted to see me and both had been abrasive, Alicia in the morning, Vivien in the afternoon.

Alicia's flat outside Windsor was spacious and overlooked the Thames, neither of which pleasures seemed to please her. She did reluctantly let me in, but was unplacated by my admiration of her view.

She was, in fact, looking youthfully pretty in a white wool dress and silver beads. Her hair was pulled high in a velvet bow on the crown, and her neat figure spoke of luck or dieting. She had a visitor with her already when I called, a fortyish substantial-looking man introduced coquettishly as Paul, who behaved with unmistakable lordliness, the master in his domain. How long, I wondered, had this been going on?

'You might have said you were coming,' Alicia complained. 'Ferdinand said you would, some time. I told him to tell you not to.'

'It seemed best to see everyone,' I said neutrally.

'Then hurry up,' she said. 'We're going out to lunch.'

'Did Ferdinand tell you about Malcolm's new will?'

'He did, and I don't believe a word of it. You've always been Malcolm's wretched little pet. He should have sent you back to Joyce when I left. I told him to. But would he listen? No, he wouldn't.'

'That was twenty years ago,' I protested.

'And nothing's changed. He does what he likes. He's utterly selfish.'

Paul listened to the conversation without stirring and with scant apparent interest but he did, it seemed, have his influence. With an arch look at him, Alicia said, 'Paul says Gervase should force Malcolm to give him power of attorney.'

I couldn't offhand think of anything less likely to happen.

'Have you two known each other long?' I asked.

'No,' Alicia said, and the look she gave Paul was that of a flirt of sixteen.

I asked her if she remembered the tree stump. 'Of course. I was furious with Malcolm for letting Fred do anything so ridiculous. The boys might have been hurt.'

And did she remember the switches? How could she forget them, she said, they'd been all over the house. Not only that, Thomas had made another one for Serena some time later. It had sat in her room gathering dust. Those clocks had all been a pest.

'You were good to me in those old days,' I said.

She stared. There was almost a softening round her

eyes, but it was transitory. 'I had to be,' she said acidly. 'Malcolm insisted.'

'Weren't you ever happy?' I asked.

'Oh, yes.' Her mouth curled in a malicious smile. 'When Malcolm came to see me, when he was married to Joyce. Before that weaselly detective spoiled it.'

I asked her if she had engaged Norman West to find Malcolm in Cambridge.

She looked at me with wide empty eyes and said blandly, 'No, I didn't. Why would I want to? I didn't care where he was.'

'Almost everyone wanted to find him to stop him spending his money.'

'He's insane,' she said. 'Paranoid. He should hand control over to Gervase, and make sure that frightful Ursula isn't included. She's the wrong wife for Gervase, as I've frequently told him.'

'But you didn't ask Norman West to find Malcolm?'

'No, I didn't,' she said very sharply. 'Stop asking that stupid question.' She turned away from me restlessly. 'It's high time you went.'

I thought so too, on the whole. I speculated that perhaps the presence of Paul had inhibited her from saying directly to my face the poison she'd been spreading behind my back. They would dissect me when I'd gone. He nodded coolly to me as I left. No friend of mine, I thought.

If my visit to Alicia had been unfruitful, my call on Vivien was less so. Norman West's notes had been minimal: name, address, sorting magazines, no alibis. She wouldn't answer any of my questions either, or discuss any possibilities. She said several times that Malcolm was a fiend who was determined to destroy his children, and that I was the devil incarnate helping him. She hoped we would both rot in hell. (I thought devils and fiends might flourish there, actually.)

Meanwhile, I said, had she employed Norman West to find Malcolm in Cambridge? Certainly not. She wanted nothing to do with that terrible little man. If I didn't remove myself from her doorstep she would call in the police.

'It can't be much fun,' I said, 'living with so much hatred in your head.'

She was affronted. 'What do you mean?'

'No peace. All anger. Very exhausting. Bad for your health.'

'Go away,' she said, and I obliged her.

I drove back to Cookham and spent a good deal of the evening on the telephone, talking to Lucy about Thomas and to Ferdinand about Gervase. 'We are all our brothers' keepers,' Lucy said, and reported that Thomas was spending most of the time asleep. 'Retreating,' Lucy said.

Lucy had spoken to Berenice. 'Whatever did you say to her, Ian? She sounds quite different. Subdued.

Can't see it lasting long, can you? I told her Thomas was all right and she started blubbing.'

Lucy said she would keep Thomas for a while, but not for his natural span.

Ferdinand, when he heard my voice, said, 'Where the hell have you been? All I get is your answering machine. Did you find out who killed Moira?' There was anxiety, possibly, in his voice.

'I found out a few who didn't,' I said.

'That's not what I asked.'

'Well,' I said, 'like you with your computer, I've fed in a lot of data.'

'And the result?'

'The wheels are turning.'

'Computers don't have wheels. Come to think of it, though, I suppose they do. Anyway, you've left a whole trail of disasters behind you, haven't you? I hear Thomas has left Berenice, and as for Gervase, he wants your guts for taking Ursula out to lunch. Did you do that? Whatever for? You know how possessive he is. There's a hell of a row going on.'

'If you want to hang on to Debs,' I said, 'don't listen to Alicia.'

'What the hell's that got to do with Gervase and Ursula having a row?' he demanded.

'Everything.'

He was furious. 'You've always got it in for Alicia.'

'The other way round. She's a dedicated trouble-maker who's cost you one wife already.' He didn't immediately answer. I said, 'Gervase is knocking back a fortune in scotch.'

'What's that got to do with anything?'

'How do you cope so well with illegitimacy?'

'*What?*'

'Everything's linked. So long, pal. See you.' I put the receiver down with a sigh, and ate dinner, and packed.

In the morning, having paid a few bills, I took the hired car to Heathrow and turned it in there and, with a feeling of shackles dropping off, hopped into the air.

I spent four nights in New York before I found Malcolm; or before he found me, to be more precise.

In daily consultations, the Stamford voice assured me that I wasn't forgotten, that the message would one day get through. I had a vision of native bearers beating through jungles, but it wasn't like that, it transpired. Malcolm and Ramsey had simply been moving from horse farm to horse farm through deepest Kentucky, and it was from there he finally phoned at eight-ten in the morning.

'What are you doing in New York?' he demanded.

'Looking at skyscrapers,' I said.

'I thought we were meeting in California.'

'Well, we are,' I said. 'When?'

'What's today?'

'Friday.'

'Hang on.'

I heard him talking in the background, then he returned. 'We're just going out to see some horses breeze. Ramsey reserved the rooms from tomorrow through Saturday at the Beverly Wilshire, he says, but he and I are going to spend a few more days here now. You go to California tomorrow and I'll join you, say, on Wednesday.'

'Couldn't you please make it sooner? I do need to talk to you.'

'Did you find something out?' His voice suddenly changed gear, as if he'd remembered almost with shock the world of terrors he'd left behind.

'A few things.'

'Tell me.'

'Not on the telephone. Not in a hurry. Go and see the horses breeze and meet me tomorrow.' I paused. 'There are horses in California. Thousands of them.'

He was quiet for a few moments, then he said, 'I owe it to you. I'll be there,' and disconnected.

I arranged my air ticket and spent the rest of the day as I'd spent all the others in New York, wandering around, filling eyes and ears with the city . . . thinking painful private thoughts and coming to dreadful conclusions.

Malcolm kept his word and, to my relief, came without Ramsey who had decided Stamford needed him if Connecticut were to survive. Ramsey, Malcolm said, would be over on Wednesday, we would all have three days at the races and go to Australia on Saturday night.

He was crackling with energy, the eyes intensely blue. He and Ramsey had bought four more horses in partnership, he said in the first three minutes, and were joining a syndicate to own some others down under.

A forest fire out of control, I thought, and had sympathy for my poor brothers.

The Beverly Wilshire gave us a suite with brilliant red flocked wallpaper in the sitting room and vivid pink and orange flowers on a turquoise background in the bedrooms. There were ornate crimson curtains, filmy cream inner curtains, a suspicion of lace, an air of Edwardian roguishness brought up to date. Rooms to laugh in, I thought. And with little wrought-iron balconies outside the bowed windows looking down on a pool with a fountain and gardens and orange trees, not much to complain of.

We dined downstairs in a bar that had tables at one end and music, and Malcolm said I looked thinner.

'Tell me about the horses,' I said; and heard about them through the smoked salmon, the salad, the veal and the coffee.

'Don't worry,' he said, near the beginning. 'They're not all as expensive as Blue Clancy and Chrysos. We got all four for under a million dollars, total, and they're two-year-olds ready to run. Good breeding; the best. One's by Alydar, even.'

I listened, amused and impressed. He knew the

breeding of all his purchases back three generations, and phrases like 'won a stakes race' and 'his dam's already produced Group I winners' came off his tongue as if he'd been saying them all his life.

'Do you mind if I ask you something?' I said eventually.

'I won't know until you ask.'

'No . . . um . . . just how rich *are* you?'

He laughed. 'Did Joyce put you up to that question?'

'No. I wanted to know for myself.'

'Hm.' He thought. 'I can't tell you to the nearest million. It changes every day. At a rough estimate, about a hundred million pounds. It would grow now of its own accord at the rate of five million a year if I never lifted a finger again, but you know me, that would be boring, I'd be dead in a month.'

'After tax?' I said.

'Sure.' He smiled. 'Capital gains tax usually. I've spent a year's investment income after tax on the horses, that's all. Not as much as that on all those other projects that the family were going bananas about. I'm not raving mad. There'll be plenty for everyone when I pop off. More than there is now. I just have to live longer. You tell them that.'

'I told them you'd said in your will that if you were murdered, it would all go to charity.'

'Why didn't I think of that?'

'Did you think any more of letting the family have some of the lucre before you . . . er . . . pop off?'

'You know my views on that.'

'Yes, I do.'

'And you don't approve.'

'I don't disapprove in theory. The trust funds were generous when they were set up. Many fathers don't do as much. But your children aren't perfect and some of them have got into messes. If someone were bleeding, would you buy them a bandage?'

He sat back in his chair and stared moodily at his coffee.

'Have they sent you here to plead for them?' he asked.

'No. I'll tell you what's been happening, then you can do what you like.'

'Fair enough,' he said, 'but not tonight.'

'All right.' I paused. 'I won a race at Kempton, did you know?'

'Did you really?' He was instantly alive with interest, asking for every detail. He didn't want to hear about his squabbling family with its latent murderer. He was tired of being vilified while at the same time badgered to be bountiful. He felt safe in California although he had, I'd been interested to discover, signed us into the hotel as Watson and Watson.

'Well, you never know, do you?' he'd said. 'It may say in the British papers that Blue Clancy's coming over, and Ramsey says this hotel is the centre for the Breeders' Cup organizers. They're having reception rooms here, and buffets. By Wednesday, he says, this place will be teeming with the international racing crowd. So where, if someone wanted to find me, do you think they'd look first?'

'I think Norman West gave us good advice.'

'So do I.'

The Watsons, father and son, breakfasted the following morning out in the warm air by the pool, sitting in white chairs beside a white table under a yellow sun umbrella, watching the oranges ripen amid dark green leaves, talking of horrors.

I asked him casually enough if he remembered Fred and the tree roots.

'Of course I do,' he said at once. 'Bloody fool could have killed himself.' He frowned. 'What's that got to do with the bomb at Quantum?'

'Superintendent Yale thinks it may have given someone the idea.'

He considered it. 'I suppose it might.'

'The superintendent, or some of his men, asked old Fred what he'd used to set off the cordite . . .' I told Malcolm about the cordite still lying around in the tool shed ' . . . and Fred said he had some detonators, but after that first bang, you came out and took them away.'

'Good Lord, I'd forgotten that. Yes, so I did. You were all there, weren't you? Pretty well the whole family?'

'Yes, it was one of those weekends. Helen says it

was the first time she met you, she was there too, before she was married to Donald.'

He thought back. 'I don't remember that. I just remember there being a lot of you.'

'The superintendent wonders if you remember what happened to the detonators after you'd taken them away.'

He stared. 'It's twenty years ago, must be,' he protested.

'It might be the sort of thing you wouldn't forget.'

He shook his head doubtfully.

'Did you turn them over to the police?'

'No.' He was definite about that, anyway. 'Old Fred had no business to have them, but I wouldn't have got him into trouble, or the friend he got them from, either. I'll bet they were nicked.'

'Do you remember what they looked like?' I asked.

'Well, yes, I suppose so.' He frowned, thinking, pouring out more coffee. 'There was a row of them in a tin, laid out carefully in cotton wool so that they shouldn't roll about. Small silverish tubes, about two and a half inches long.'

'Fred says they had instructions with them.'

He laughed. 'Did he? A do-it-yourself bomb kit?' He sobered suddenly. 'I suppose it was just that. I don't remember the instructions, but I dare say they were there.'

'You did realize they were dangerous, didn't you?'

'I probably did, but all those years ago ordinary

people didn't know so much about bombs. I mean, not terrorist bombs. We'd been bombed from the air, but that was different. I should think I took the detonators away from Fred so he shouldn't set off any more explosions, not because they were dangerous in themselves, if you see what I mean?'

'Mm. But you did know you shouldn't drop them?'

'You mean if I'd dropped them, I wouldn't be here talking about it?'

'According to the explosives expert working at Quantum, quite likely not.'

'I never worked with explosives, being an adjutant.' He buttered a piece of croissant, added marmalade and ate it. His service as a young officer in his war had been spent in arranging details of troop movements and as assistant to camp commanders, often near enough to the enemy but not seeing the whites of their eyes. He never spoke of it much: it had been history before I was born.

'I remembered where the cordite was, even after all this time,' I said. 'If you imagine yourself going into the house with this tin of detonators, where would you be likely to put it? You'd put it where you would think of looking for it first, wouldn't you?'

'Yes,' he nodded, 'always my system.' A faraway unfocused look appeared in his eyes, then he suddenly sat bolt upright.

'I know where they are! I saw the tin not so very long ago, when I was looking for something else. I didn't pay much attention. It didn't even register what was in it, but I'm pretty sure now that that's what it was. It's a sort of sweet tin, not very big, with a picture on top.'

'Where was it, and how long ago?'

'Surely,' he said, troubled, 'they'd be duds by this time?'

'Quite likely not.'

'They're in the office.' He shrugged self-excusingly. 'You know I never tidy that place up. I'd never find anything ever again. I'm always having to stop people tidying it.'

'Like Moira?'

'She could hardly bear to keep her hands off.'

'Where in the office?' I remembered the jumble in his desk drawer when I'd fetched his passport. The whole place was similar.

'On top of some of the books in the breakfront bookcase. Bottom row, right over on the right-hand side, more or less out of sight when the door's closed. On top of the Dickens.' His face suddenly split into a huge grin. 'I remember now, by God. I put it there because the picture on the tin's lid was The Old Curiosity Shop.'

I rubbed my hand over my face, trying not to laugh. Superintendent Yale was going to love it.

'They're safe enough there,' Malcolm said reasonably, 'behind glass. I mean, no one can pick them up accidentally, can they? That's where they are.'

I thought it highly likely that that's where they weren't, but I didn't bother to say so. 'The glass in the breakfront is broken,' I said.

He was sorry about that. It had been his mother's, he said, like all the books.

'When did you see the tin there?' I asked.

'Haven't a clue. Not all that long ago, I wouldn't have thought, but time goes so quickly.'

'Since Moira died?'

He wrinkled his forehead. 'No, probably not. Then, before that, I was away from the house for a week or ten days when I couldn't stand being in the same place with her and she obdurately wouldn't budge. Before that, I was looking for something in a book. Not in Dickens, a shelf or two higher. Can't remember what book, though I suppose I might if I went back and stood in front of them and looked at the titles. Altogether, over three months ago, I should say.'

I reflected a bit and drank my coffee. 'I suppose the bookcase must have been moved now and then for redecorating. The books taken out . . .'

'Don't be ridiculous,' Malcolm interrupted with amusement. 'It weighs more than a ton. The books stay inside it. Redecorating goes on around it, and not at all if I can help it. Moira tried to make me take everything out so she could paint the whole office dark green. I stuck my toes in. She had the rest of the house. That room is mine.'

I nodded lazily. It was pleasant in the sunshine. A

few people were sunbathing, a child was swimming, a waiter in a white jacket came along with someone else's breakfast. All a long way away from the ruins of Quantum.

From that quiet Sunday morning and on until Wednesday, Malcolm and I led the same remote existence, being driven round Los Angeles and Hollywood and Beverly Hills in a stretch-limousine Malcolm seemed to have hired by the yard, neck-twisting like tourists, going out to Santa Anita racetrack in the afternoons, dining in restaurants like Le Chardonnay.

I gradually told him what was happening in the family, never pressing, never heated, never too much at one time, stopping at once if he started showing impatience.

'Donald and Helen should send their children to state schools,' he said moderately.

'Maybe they should. But you sent Donald to Marlborough, and you went there yourself. Donald wants the best for his boys. He's suffering to give them what you gave him effortlessly.'

'He's a snob to choose Eton.'

'Maybe, but the Marlborough fees aren't much less.'

'What if it was Donald and Helen who've been trying to kill me?'

'If they had plenty of money they wouldn't be tempted.'

'You've said that before, or something like it.'

'Nothing has changed.'

Malcolm looked out of the long car's window as we were driven up through the hills of Bel Air on the way to the racetrack.

'Do you see those houses perched on the cliffs, hanging out over space? People must be mad to live like that, on the edge.'

I smiled. 'You do,' I said.

He liked Santa Anita racetrack immediately and so did I; it would have been difficult not to. Royal palms near the entrances stretched a hundred feet upward, all bare trunks except for the crowning tufts, green fronds against the blue sky. The buildings were towered and turreted, sea-green in colour, with metal tracery of stylized palm leaves along the balconies and golden shutters over rear-facing windows. It looked more like a château than a racecourse, at first sight.

Ramsey Osborn had given Malcolm fistfuls of instructions and introductions and, as always, Malcolm was welcomed as a kindred spirit upstairs in the Club. He was at home from the first minute, belonging to the scene as if he'd been born there. I envied him his ease and didn't know how to acquire it. Maybe time would do it. Maybe millions. Maybe a sense of achievement.

While he talked easily to almost strangers (soon to be cronies) about the mixing of European and American bloodlines in thoroughbreds, I thought of the phone call I'd made at dawn on Monday morning to Superintendent Yale. Because of the eight-hour time difference, it was already afternoon with him, and I thought it unlikely I would reach him at first try. He was there, however, and came on the line with unstifled annoyance.

'It's a week since you telephoned.'

'Yes, sorry.'

'Where are you?'

'Around,' I said. His voice sounded as clear to me as if he were in the next room, and presumably mine to him, as he didn't at all guess I wasn't in England. 'I found my father,' I said.

'Oh. Good.'

I told him where Malcolm had stored the detonators. 'On top of *The Old Curiosity Shop*, as appropriate.'

There was a shattered silence. 'I don't believe it,' he said.

'The books are all old and leatherbound classics standing in full editions. Poets, philosophers, novelists, all bought years ago by my grandmother. We were all allowed to borrow a book occasionally to read, but we had to put it back. My father had us well trained.'

'Are you saying that anyone who borrowed a book from that bookcase could have seen the detonators?'

'Yes, I suppose so, if they've been there for twenty years.'

'Did you know they were there?'

'No. I didn't read those sort of books much. Spent my time riding.'

Lucy, I thought, had in her teens plunged into poets as a fish into its native sea, but twenty years ago she had been twenty-two and writing her own immortality. None of the rest of us had been scholars. Some of grandmother's books had never been opened.

'It is incredible that when someone thought of making a bomb, the detonators were to hand,' Yale complained.

'Other way round, wouldn't you think?' I said. 'The availability of the detonators suggested the bomb.'

'The pool of common knowledge in your family is infuriating,' he said. 'No one can be proved to have special access to explosives. No one has a reliable alibi . . . except Mrs Ferdinand . . . Everyone can make a timing device and nearly all of you have a motive.'

'Irritating,' I agreed.

'That's the wrong word,' he said sourly. 'Where's your father?'

'Safe.'

'You can't stay in hiding for ever.'

'Don't expect to see us for a week or two. What chance is there of your solving the case?'

Enquiries were proceeding, he said with starch. If I came across any further information, I would please give it to him.

Indeed, I said, I would.

'When I was younger,' he said to my surprise, 'I used to think I had a nose for a villain, that I could always tell. But since then, I've met embezzlers I would have trusted my savings to, and murderers I'd have let marry my daughter. Murderers can look like harmless ordinary people.' He paused. 'Does your family know who killed Moira Pembroke?'

'I don't think so.'

'Please enlarge,' he said.

'One or two may suspect they know, but they're not telling. I went to see everyone. No one was even guessing. No one accusing. They don't want to know, don't want to face it, don't want the misery.'

'And you?'

'I don't want the misery either, but I also don't want my father killed, or myself.'

'Do you think you're in danger?'

'Oh, yes,' I said. '*In loco* Moira.'

'As chief beneficiary?'

'Something like that. Only I'm not chief, I'm equal. My father made a new will saying so. I've told the family but they don't believe it.'

'Produce the will. Show it to them.'

'Good idea,' I said. 'Thank you.'

'And you,' he paused, 'do you know, yourself?'

'I don't know.'

'Guess, then.'

'Guessing is one thing, proof is another.'

'I might remind you it's your duty . . .'

'It's not my duty,' I interrupted without heat, 'to go off half-cocked. My duty to my family is to get it right or do nothing.'

I said goodbye to him rather firmly and concluded, from his tone as much as his words, that the police had no more information than I had, and perhaps less: that they hadn't managed (if they'd tried) to find out where the grey plastic clock had come from or who had bought it, which was their only lead as far as I could see and a pretty hopeless proposition. It had been a cheap mass-production clock, probably on sale in droves.

Malcolm said on one of our car journeys, after I'd been telling him about Berenice, 'Vivien, you know, had this thing about sons.'

'But she had a boy first. She had two.'

'Yes, but before Donald was born, she said she wouldn't look at the baby if it was a girl. I couldn't understand it. I'd have liked a girl. Vivien's self-esteem utterly depended on having a boy. She was obsessed with it. You'd have thought she'd come from some dreadful tribe where it really mattered.'

'It did matter,' I said. 'And it matters to Berenice. All obsessions matter because of their results.'

'Vivien never loved Lucy, you know,' he said thoughtfully. 'She shoved her away from her. I always thought that was why Lucy got fat and retreated into poetic fantasies.'

'Berenice shoves off her daughters onto her mother as much as she can.'

'Do you think Berenice murdered Moira?' he said doubtfully.

'I think she thinks that having more money would make her happier, which it probably would. If you were going to think of any . . . er . . . distribution, I'd give it to the wives as well as the husbands. Separately, I mean. So they had independence.'

'Why?' he said.

'Gervase might value Ursula more if she didn't need him financially.'

'Ursula's a mouse.'

'She's desperate.'

'They're all desperate,' he said with irritation. 'It's all their own faults. The fault, dear Brutus, is not in our stars but in ourselves, that we are underlings.'

'I dare say,' I said.

'The bell captain at the hotel gave me a tip for the fourth race.'

Back to horses.

Another day, another journey.

Malcolm said, 'What did Serena say, when you saw her?'

'She said you could stuff your money, or words to that effect.'

Malcolm laughed.

'She also said,' I went on, 'that Alicia told her you'd only tried to get custody of her that time so as to be cruel to Alicia.'

'Alicia's a real bitch.'

'She's got a lover, did you know?' I said.

He was thunderstruck. 'Who is he?'

'Someone else's husband, I should think. That's what she likes, isn't it?'

'Don't be so bloody accurate.'

Further down the road we were talking about the time switch clocks, which had been an unwelcome piece of news to him also.

'Thomas was best at making them, wasn't he?' Malcolm said. 'He could do them in a jiffy. They were his idea originally, I think. Serena brought one over for Robin and Peter which Thomas had made for her years ago.'

I nodded. 'A Mickey Mouse clock. It's still there in the playroom.'

'Serena made them a lighthouse of Lego to go with it, I remember.' He sighed deeply. 'I miss Coochie still, you know. The crash happened not long after that.' He shook his head to rid it of sadness. 'What race shall we choose for the Coochie Memorial Trophy? What do you think?'

On another day, I asked why Ferdinand didn't mind being illegitimate when Gervase did, to the brink of breakdown.

'I don't know,' Malcolm said. 'Gervase always thinks people are sneering and laughing, even now. Someone rubbed his nose in it when he was young, you know. Told him he was rubbish, a mistake, should have been aborted. Boys can be bloody cruel. Gervase got aggressive to compensate, I suppose. Nothing ever worried Ferdinand very much. He's like me in more than looks.'

'Only two wives so far,' I said incautiously.

'Why don't you get married?' he asked.

I was flippant. 'Haven't met the one and only. Don't want five.'

'Don't you trust yourself?' he said.

Christ, I thought, that was sharp, that was penetrating. That was unfair. It was because of him that I didn't trust myself: because in inconstancy, I felt I was very much his son.

His imprint, for better or worse, was on us all.

CHAPTER EIGHTEEN

On Wednesday, the Beverly Wilshire came alive as Ramsey had prophesied and Ramsey himself blew in with gusto and plans. We would go to parties. We would go round the horse barns. We would go to a Hollywood Gala Ball.

The Breeders' Cup organizers opened their reception room where everyone concerned with the races could have breakfast and cocktails (together if they liked) and talk about horses, could arrange cars and tickets and talk about horses, could meet the people they'd met at Epsom and Longchamp and talk about horses. Well-mannered people in good suits and silk dresses, owners whose enthusiasm prompted and funded the sport. Big bucks, big business, big fun.

Malcolm adored it. So did I. Life in high gear. Early on Friday, we went out to the racecourse to see Blue Clancy in his barn and watch him breeze round the track in his last warm-up before the big one. His English trainer was with him, and his English lad. There was heady excitement, a lot of anxiety. The orderly bustle of stable life, the smells, the swear words, the earthy humour, the pride, the affection, the jealousies, the injustices, the dead disappointments, all the same the world over.

Blue Clancy looked fine, worked well, threw Malcolm and Ramsey into back-slapping ecstasies. 'Wait until tomorrow,' the trainer said cautiously, watching them. 'We're taking on the best in the world, don't forget. The hot money is for a California-bred horse.'

'What's hot money?' Malcolm demanded.

'The bets made by people in the know. People with inside information.'

Who cared, Malcolm said. He couldn't remember ever having more fun in his life: and I thought his euphoria was at least partly due to his three close approaches to losing it.

Along with a thousand others, we went to the ball, though in the stretch-limo, not a converted pumpkin, and in the vast sound stage which had lately held a split-open aeroplane for filming cabin dramas, Malcolm danced with several ladies he'd known well for two days. He spent his time laughing. He was infectious. Everyone around him lit up like nightlights, banishing gloom.

We slept, we ate breakfast, we went to the races. The smog that all week had covered the mountains everyone swore were there on the far side of the track, relented and evaporated and disclosed a sunlit rocky backdrop worthy of the occasion. Tables with tablecloths had appeared overnight throughout the Club stands, and overworked black-coated waiters sweated under huge trays of food, threading through ever-moving racegoers, never dropping the lot.

There were seven Breeders' Cup races; various distances, variously aged horses. The first five each offered a total purse (for first, second, third and so on) of one million dollars. Blue Clancy's race, the one-and-a-half-mile Turf, had a purse of two million, and the climactic event, the Breeders' Cup Classic, promised three. They weren't racing for peanuts. The owner of the winner of Blue Clancy's race would be personally richer by six hundred and twenty-nine thousand dollars, enough to keep him in Bollinger for weeks.

We cheered home the first five winners. We went down to the saddling stalls and saw Blue Clancy prepared. We went up to the stands and bit our nails.

Five of the seven races were run on the dirt track, two on grass, of which this was the second; and most of the European horses were running on grass, the green stuff of home. Blue Clancy was taking on the Epsom Derby winner, the Arc de Triomphe winner and the winner of the Italian Derby. On paper, he looked to have an outside chance of coming fourth. In Malcolm's and Ramsey's eyes, he was a shoo-in. (Malcolm had learned the local jargon.)

Blue Clancy broke cleanly from the gate away on the far side of the course and his English jockey held him handily in sixth place all down the far side. Ramsey and Malcolm were looking through binoculars and muttering encouragements. Blue Clancy, not hearing them, swung into the long left-hand bottom bend in no better position and was still lying sixth when the field crossed the dirt track as they turned for home. Malcolm's muttering grew louder. 'Come on, you bugger. Come on.'

There was no clear leader. Three horses raced together in front, followed by a pair together, then Blue Clancy alone. Too much to do, I thought: and the agile colt immediately proved me wrong. His jockey swung him wide of the others to allow him a clear run and gave him unmistakable signals that now was the time that mattered, now, this half-minute, if never again.

Blue Clancy accelerated. Malcolm was shouting, Ramsey was speechless. Blue Clancy in third place, all the crowds roaring. Blue Clancy still faster, second now. Malcolm silent, mouth open, eyes staring. The incredible was happening, awesome, breathtaking . . . and Blue Clancy had definitely, indubitably won.

Malcolm's eyes were like sapphires lit from inside. He still couldn't speak. Ramsey grabbed him by the arm and pulled him, and the two of them ran, almost dancing, weaving through slowcoaches, making their way down to greet their champion's return. I followed close on their heels, marvelling. Some owners were always lucky, some owners always weren't; it was an inexplicable fact of racing life. Malcolm's luck was stupendous. It always had been, in everything except wives. I should have known, I supposed, that it would come with him onto the track. King Midas had touched him, and Blue Clancy was his latest gold.

I wondered ironically what the family would say. The fortune he'd flung away on horses had already come back: Blue Clancy was worth at least double what he'd been before the Arc.

Chrysos, I daydreamed, would win the Derby. The tadpole film (about sharks actually, Malcolm had told me) would win at Cannes. The Pol Roger would appreciate. Everyone would see the point of not murdering the golden goose (Wrong sex, never mind. It was a lightheaded day.) We could return home to welcomes and safety.

Only it wasn't like that. We would return home to an unassessable danger, and it was essential to be aware of it, and to plan.

Sobered as always by what lay ahead, I nevertheless went to a post-race party in fine spirits, and after that to Los Angeles airport to fly through the night to Australia. The party, the people came with us. Melbourne took up the impetus, pressing forward to its own Cup, always held on the first Tuesday in November. Everything, they told us there, stopped for the race. Schoolchildren had a holiday and the Melbourne shops closed. The Hyatt Hotel, where we stayed (Watson and Watson), had a lobby criss-crossed by people known better in Newmarket, all with the ready grins of kids out of school.

Ramsey had surpassed himself in the matter of reservations. Even to reach our floor, we had to use a special key in the elevator, and there was a private lounge up there for cocktails and breakfast (but separately). Malcolm appreciated it, took it all in his stride, ordered champagne, breathed Melbourne air and became an instant Australian.

Out at Flemington racecourse (no château), there was less sophistication than at Santa Anita, just as much enthusiasm, very good food, a much better parade ring. Malcolm found the day's racing less compulsive than Paris or California through not owning a runner. He'd tried to remedy this on arrival, but no one would sell one of the top bunch, and he wanted nothing less. Instead, he set about gambling with method but only in tens and soon tired of it, win or lose. I left him and Ramsey in the Committee rooms and wandered down to the crowd as in Paris, and wondered how many in the throng struggled with intractable problems in their shirtsleeves, no shirts, carnival hats. When the party was over, Malcolm would grow restless and want to move on, and I wasn't ready. Under the shade of trees, surrounded by beer cans, listening to the vigorous down-under language, I searched for the solution that would cause us least grief.

There was no truly easy way out. No overlooking or dodging what had been done to Moira. But if someone could plead guilty and plead diminished responsibility owing to stress, there might be a quiet trial and a lifetime for us of visiting a sort of hospital instead of a rigorous prison. Either way, any way, there were tears in our future.

On top of that I had to be right, and I had to convince Malcolm beyond any doubt that I was. Had to convince all the family, and the police, without any mistake. Had to find a way of doing it that was peaceful and simple, for all our sakes.

I watched the Melbourne Cup from ground level, which meant in effect that I didn't see much of it because of the other thousands doing the same. On the other hand, I was closer to the horses before and after, watching them walk, listening to comments, mostly unflattering, from knowledgeable elbowers striving for a view.

The Melbourne Cup runners were older and more rugged than stars back home. Some were eight or nine. All raced far more often, once a week not being unusual. The favourite for that day's race had won on the course three days earlier.

They were racing for a purse of a million Australian dollars, of which sixty-five per cent went to the winner, besides a handsome gold cup. Thwarted this year, Malcolm, I imagined, would be back next year. He'd met in Paris and California several of the owners now standing in the parade ring and I could guess the envy he was feeling. No one was as passionate as a new convert.

When the race was finally off, I couldn't hear the commentary for the exhortations around me, but it didn't much matter: the winner was owned by one of the international owners and afterwards I found Malcolm beside the winner's enclosure looking broody and thinking expensive thoughts.

'Next year,' he said.

'You're addicted.'

He didn't deny it. He and Ramsey slapped each other on the back, shook hands and promised like blood brothers to meet regularly on every major race-course in the world. Ramsey, the bulky manufacturer of millions of baseball caps, had somewhere along the line realized what 'metal' really meant in Malcolm's vocabulary and from cronies they had become comfortable friends, neither feeling at an advantage over the other.

They discussed staying on in Australia but Ramsey said the baseball caps needed guidance. Malcolm wavered about going to see some gold mines in Kalgoorlie but decided on a gold share broker in Melbourne instead. We spent Melbourne Cup night in a farewell dinner, and when Ramsey had departed in the morning and left us alone in the quiet breakfast room upstairs, Malcolm looked at me as if coming down to earth for the first time since we'd left England. With a touch of despondency, he asked for how long he was to be exiled for safety's sake.

'But you've enjoyed it,' I said.

'God, yes.' The remembrance flashed in his eyes. 'But it's not real life. We have to go back. I know I've avoided talking about it, it's all dreadful. I know you've been thinking about it all this time. I could see it in your face.'

'I've come to know them all so much better,' I said, 'my brothers and my sisters. I didn't care for them all that much, you know, before Moira died. We've always met of course from time to time, but I'd forgotten to a great extent what we had been like as children.' I paused for a bit, but he didn't comment. 'Since the bomb went off at Quantum,' I said, 'a great deal of the past has come back. And I've seen, you know, how the present has grown out of that past. How my sisters-in-law and my brother-in-law have been affected by it. How people easily believe lies, old and new. How destructive it is to yearn for the unobtainable, to be unsatisfied by anything else. How obsessions don't go away, they get worse.'

He was silent for a while, then said, 'Bleak.' Then he sighed and said, 'How much do they need, then? How much should I give them? I don't believe in it, but I see it's necessary. Their obsessions have got worse as I've grown richer. If the money wasn't there, they'd have sorted themselves out better. Is that what you're saying?'

'Yes, partly.' It hadn't been, entirely, but as it had

produced a reaction I'd wanted but hadn't expected, I kept quiet.

'All right, then,' he said. 'I've had a bloody good holiday and I'm feeling generous, so draw up a list of who's to get what.'

'All equal,' I said.

He began to protest, but sighed instead. 'What about you, then?'

'I don't know. We'll decide about that later.'

'I thought you wanted half a million to set up as a trainer.'

'I've changed my mind. For now, anyway. There's something else I want to do first.'

'What's that?'

I hesitated. I'd barely admitted it to myself, had certainly told no one else.

'Go on,' he urged.

'Be a jockey. Turn professional.'

'Good Lord,' he said, astonished, 'haven't you left it too late?'

'Maybe. We'll see. I'll have three or four years, perhaps. Better than not trying.'

'You amaze me.' He reflected. 'Come to think of it, you've constantly amazed me since you came to Newmarket Sales. It seems I hardly knew you before.'

'That's how I feel about you,' I said, 'and about all of the family.'

*

We set off homewards later the same day, travelling west via Singapore. Malcolm's gold share broker happened to be going there at the same time, so I changed places with him on the aeroplane and let the two of them say things like 'percussion and rotary air blast drilling to get a first idea' and 'diamond core drilling is necessary for estimating reserves accurately', which seemed to entertain them for hours.

I thought meantime about invitations. About invitations like meat over bear pits. The right invitation would bring the right visitor. The problem was how to make the invitation believable.

Part of the trouble was time. When we reached England, Malcolm would have been out of harm's way for four weeks, and I for almost three. We'd been safe, and I'd had time to reflect: those on the plus side. On the minus, as far as the invitation was concerned, was the fact that it would be six weeks since Malcolm had survived in the garage, and ten since Moira had died. Would a classic trap invitation work after so long an interval? Only one thing to do: try it and see.

Malcolm's voice was saying, ' . . . a section assaying five point eight grams per tonne' and a bit later, ' . . . Big Bell's plant milling oxide and soft rock', and ' . . . the future is good in Queensland, with those epithermal gold zones at Woolgar'. The broker listened and nodded and looked impressed. My old man, I thought, really knows his stuff. He'd told me at one point on our journeyings that there were roughly twenty-five hundred active gold mines in Australia and that it would soon rival or even surpass Canada as a producer. I hadn't known gold was big in Canada. I was ignorant, he said. Canada had so far come regularly second to South Africa in the non-communist world.

We'd taught each other quite a lot, I thought, in one way and another.

I would need someone to deliver the invitation. Couldn't do it myself.

'Market capitalization per ounce . . .' I heard the broker saying in snatches, and ' . . . in situ reserves based on geological interpretation . . .'

I knew who could deliver the invitation. The perfect person.

'As open-cut mining cost as little as two hundred Australian dollars an ounce . . .'

Bully for open-cut mining, I thought, and drifted to sleep.

We left spring behind in Australia on Wednesday and came home to winter on Friday in England. Malcolm and I went back to the Ritz as Mr and Mr Watson and he promised with utmost sincerity that he wouldn't telephone anyone, not even his London broker. I went shopping in the afternoon and then confounded him at the brandy and cigar stage late that evening by getting through to Joyce.

'But you said . . .' he hissed as he heard her voice jump as usual out of the receiver.

'Listen,' I hissed back. 'Hello, Joyce.'

'Darling! Where are you? What are you doing? Where's your father?'

'In Australia,' I said.

'*What?*' she yelled.

'Looking at gold mines,' I said.

It made sense to her, as it would make sense to them all.

'He went to California, I saw it in the paper,' she said. 'Blue Clancy won a race.'

'We went to Australia afterwards.'

'*We?* Darling, where are you now?'

'It doesn't matter where I am,' I said. 'To make it safe for us to come home, will you help to find out who killed Moira?'

'But darling, the police have been trying for weeks . . . and anyway, Ferdinand says it has to be Arthur Bellbrook.'

'It's not Arthur Bellbrook,' I said.

'Why not?' She sounded argumentative, still wanting it to be Arthur, wanting it to be the intruder from outside. 'He could have done it easily. Ferdinand says he could have done everything. It has to be him. He had a shotgun, Ferdinand says.'

I said, 'Arthur didn't use his shotgun. More importantly, he wouldn't have made a timing device exactly like we'd made as children, and he hadn't a motive.'

'He could have detested Moira.'

'Absolutely,' I said, 'but why should he want to kil Malcolm, whom he liked? I saw his face when he found Malcolm was alive that morning after the bomb and he was genuinely glad.'

'Everyone wants it to be Arthur Bellbrook,' she saic obstinately. 'He found her body.'

'If the police thought he'd done it, they wouldn' have been so suspicious of Malcolm.'

'You've got an answer for everything,' she com plained.

I had myself for a while wished it to be Arthur After all, there had been the affair of the prize vege tables (but he'd sounded philosophical about them, anc would anyone kill for so little?) and he'd been in the army and might know about explosives. But he stooc to lose rather than gain from Malcolm's death, and i was beyond believing that he would trace Malcolm tc Cambridge, follow him to Newmarket Sales and try to run him down. That was the work of obsession Arthur placidly digging potatoes; Arthur enjoying the temporary fame; Arthur looking after the dogs. Arthur had been the personification of stolid, sensible balance

Besides, whoever had tried to run Malcolm down a Newmarket had guessed Malcolm would leave the sale with me and would come to the car park, and at tha point Arthur would have had no reason to think sc He didn't know me. Hadn't met me until he came intc the house with his shotgun, thinking I was a burglar. I'd had to exclude Arthur, although with regret.

Joyce said, 'Darling, how do you expect to succeed where the police have failed?'

'The police can't do what we can do.'

'What do you mean? What can we do?'

I told her. Malcolm's mouth opened and there was a long silence from Joyce.

'Let me get this straight,' she said eventually. 'You want me to telephone to everyone in the family . . .'

'*Everyone*,' I said emphatically. 'If a husband answers, tell him, then ask to speak to the wife, and tell her too. And vice versa.'

'Yes,' she said. 'I'm to say you're in Australia, both of you. Right?'

'Yes.'

'I'm to gush. Dreadful word, where *did* you learn it? I'm to let all this drip out as if it were of absolutely no importance but something I've just thought of? Darling, you can't mean I have to ring up *Alicia*?'

'Especially Alicia. Tell her I told you she has a boy-friend. That should stir her up nicely.'

'Darling, you don't mean it!'

'Ask her. And . . . er . . . do you know if the police are still guarding Quantum?'

'They told Donald that if he wanted constant guards, he'd have to get his own now. No one in the family wants to spend the money, so the police just have it on their occasional surveillance list, apparently.'

'And has anything else much happened in the family since we've been away?'

'No, nothing new. Thomas left Berenice, did you know that?'

'Yes . . . Is he still with Lucy?'

'Yes, darling, I think so. Do you want me to tell him too?'

'You might as well.'

'I'm to think of something to phone them about and gossip a bit, and then I'm to say that I don't really care who killed Moira, but I don't think the police were thorough. Is that right? They never thought of looking for her notepad, the one she used to keep in the kitchen, in one of the drawers of those dazzling white cabinets. When anyone telephoned when she was in the kitchen, which was a lot of the time, she doodled their names with stars and things round it and wrote notes like "Donald, Sunday, noon" when people were coming to visit. I'm to say the police could never have found it but I've just remembered it, and I wonder if it's still there. I'm thinking of telling the police about it after the weekend. Is that right?'

'That's right,' I said.

'And I'm to say, what if she wrote down the name of her murderer?'

'Yes,' I said.

'Darling, why do you think her murderer telephoned? To make an appointment to kill her? You don't mean that, do you?'

'To make an appointment to see her, yes. To kill her, I don't know.'

'But why, darling? Why do you think the killer telephoned?'

'Because Malcolm told me she didn't like people just dropping in,' I said. 'She preferred people to telephone first. And because Moira's greenhouse can't be seen from the road, the drive, or from any windows of Quantum. Malcolm made her put it where it was well out of sight on that patch of lawn surrounded by shrubs, because he didn't like it. If anyone had come to see Moira unannounced that evening, they'd have found the house empty. If they'd telephoned first, she'd have said to come round to the greenhouse, that's where she'd be.'

'I suppose that's logical, darling. The police always did say she knew her killer, but I didn't want to believe it unless it was Arthur Bellbrook. He knew her. He fits all round, darling.'

'If Arthur had killed her, why would he go back later and find her body?'

'Darling, are you *sure* it wasn't Arthur Bellbrook?'

'Positive.'

'Oh dear. All right then, darling. You want me to start those phone calls tomorrow but definitely not before ten o'clock, and to go on all day until I've reached everyone? You do realize, I hope, that I'm playing in a sort of exhibition bridge game tomorrow evening?'

'Just keep plugging along.'

'What if they're out, or away?'

'Same thing. If nothing happens and we get no results, I'll phone you on Monday evening.'

'Darling, let me go to Quantum with you.'

'No, definitely not.' I was alarmed. 'Joyce, promise me you'll stay in Surrey. Promise!'

'Darling, don't be so vehement. All right, I promise,' She paused. 'Was that old bugger in good nick when you last saw him?'

'In excellent nick,' I said.

'Can't help being fond of him, darling, but don't bloody tell him I said so. Can't go back, of course. But well, darling, if there's one thing I regret in my life it's getting that frightful man West to catch him with Alicia. If I'd had any bloody *sense*, darling, I'd have turned a blind eye and let him have his bit on the side. But there it is, I was too young to know any better.'

She said goodbye cheerfully, however, promising to do all the phone calls in the morning, and I put the receiver down slowly.

'Did you hear any of that last bit?' I asked Malcolm.

'Not a lot. Something about if she'd had any sense, she wouldn't have done something or other.'

'Wouldn't have divorced you,' I said.

He stared incredulously. 'She insisted on it.'

'Twenty-seven years later, she's changed her mind.'

He laughed. 'Poor old Joyce.' He spent no more

thought on it. 'Moira didn't doodle on notepads that I know of.'

'I dare say she didn't. But if you were a murderer, would you bet on it?'

He imagined it briefly. 'I'd be very worried to hear from Joyce. I would think long and hard about going to Quantum to search for the notepad before she told the police.'

'And would you go? Or would you think, if the police didn't find it when Moira was first murdered, then it isn't there? Or if it is there, there's nothing incriminating on it?'

'I don't know if I would risk it. I think I would go. If it turned out to be a silly trap of Joyce's, I could say I'd just come to see how the house was doing.' He looked at me questioningly. 'Are we both going down there?'

'Yes, but not until morning. I'm jet-lagged. Don't know about you. I need a good sleep.'

He nodded. 'Same for me.'

'And that shopping you were doing?' he eyed the several Fortnum & Mason carrier bags with tall parcels inside. 'Essential supplies?'

'Everything I could think of. We'll go down by train and . . .'

He waved his cigar in a negative gesture. 'Car and chauffeur.' He fished out his diary with the phone numbers. 'What time here?'

Accordingly, we went in the morning in great comfort and approached Quantum circumspectly from the far side, not past the eyes of the village.

The chauffeur goggled a bit at the sight of the house, with its missing centre section and boarded-up windows and large new sign saying: 'Keep out. Building unsafe.'

'Reconstructions,' Malcolm said.

The chauffeur nodded and left, and we carried the Fortnum & Mason bags across the windy central expanse and down the passage on the far side of the staircase, going towards the playroom.

Black plastic sheeting still covered all the exposed floor space, not taut and pegged down, but wrinkled and slack. Our feet made soft crunching noises on the grit under the plastic and there were small puddles here and there as if rain had blown in. The boarded-up doors and the barred stairs looked desolate, and far above, over the roof, the second black plastic sheet flapped like sails between the rafters.

Sad, sad house. Malcolm hadn't seen it like that, and was deeply depressed. He looked at the very solid job the police had made of hammering the plywood to the door frame of the playroom and asked me politely how I proposed to get in.

'With your fingernails?' he suggested.

I produced a few tools from one of the bags. 'There are other shops in Piccadilly,' I said. 'Boy scouts come prepared.'

I'd thought it likely that I wouldn't be able to get

the plywood off easily as I understood they'd used four-inch nails, so I'd brought a hammer and chisel and a saw, and before Malcolm's astonished gaze proceeded to dig a hole through the plywood and cut out a head-high, body-wide section instead. Much quicker, less sweat.

'You didn't think of all this since yesterday, did you?' he asked.

'No. On the plane. There were a lot of hours then.'

I freed the cut-out section and put it to one side, and we went into the playroom. Nothing had changed in there. Malcolm fingered the bicycles when his eyes had adjusted to the partial light, and I could see the sorrow in his body.

It was by that time nine-thirty. If Joyce by any chance phoned the right person first, the earliest we could have a visitor was about half past ten. After that, anything was possible. Or nothing.

Malcolm had wanted to know what we would do if someone came.

'All the family have keys to the outside kitchen door,' I said. 'We never had the locks changed, remember? Our visitor will go into the kitchen that way and we will go round and . . . er . . .'

'Lock him in,' Malcolm said.

'Roughly, yes. And then talk about confessing. Talk about what to do with the future.'

I went round myself to the kitchen door and made sure it did still unlock normally, which it did. I locked it again after a brief look inside. Still a mess in there, unswept.

I returned to the playroom and from the bags produced two stick-on mirrors, each about eight inches by ten.

'I thought you'd brought champagne,' Malcolm grumbled. 'Not saws and bloody looking-glasses.'

'The champagne's there. No ice.'

'It's cold enough without any bloody ice.' He wandered aimlessly round the playroom, finally slumping into one of the armchairs. We had both worn layers of the warmest clothes we had, leaving the suitcases in the Ritz, but the raw November air looked as if it would be a match for the Simpson's vicuna overcoat and my new Barbour, and the gloves I had bought for us in the same shop the day before. We were at least out of the wind which swirled round and through the house, but there was no heat but our own.

I stuck one of the mirrors onto the cut-out piece of plywood, and the other at the same height onto the wall which faced the playroom door, the side wall of the staircase: stuck it not exactly opposite the door but a little further along towards the hall.

'What are you doing?' Malcolm asked.

'Just making it possible for us to see anyone come up the drive without showing ourselves. Would you mind sitting in the other chair, and telling me when the mirrors are at the right angle? Look into the one on the stair wall. I'll move the other. OK?'

He rose and sat in the other chair as I'd asked, and I moved the plywood along and angled it slightly until he said, 'Stop. That's it. I can see a good patch of drive.'

I went and took his place and had a look for myself. It would have been better if the mirrors had been bigger, but they served the purpose. Anyone who came to the house that way would be visible.

If they came across the fields we'd have to rely on our ears.

By eleven, Malcolm was bored. By eleven-thirty, we'd temporarily unbolted and unlocked the door at the end of the passage and been out into the bushes to solve the problem posed by no plumbing. By twelve, we were into Bollinger in disposable glasses (disgusting, Malcolm said) and at twelve-thirty ate biscuits and pâté.

No one came. It seemed to get colder. Malcolm huddled inside his overcoat in the armchair and said it had been a rotten idea in the first place.

I had had to promise him that we wouldn't stay overnight. I thought it unlikely anyway that someone would choose darkness rather than daylight for searching for a small piece of paper that could be anywhere in a fairly large room, and I'd agreed to the chauffeur returning to pick us up at about six. Left to myself, I might have waited all night, but the whole point of the exercise was that Malcolm himself should be there. We would return in the morning by daybreak.

He said, 'This person we're waiting for . . . you know who it is, don't you?'

'Well . . . I think so.'

'How sure are you, expressed as a percentage?'

'Um . . . ninety-five.'

'That's not enough.'

'No, that's why we're here.'

'Edwin,' he said. 'It's Edwin, isn't it?'

I glanced across at him, taking my gaze momentarily off the mirrors. He wanted it to be Edwin. He could bear it to be Edwin. In Edwin's own words, he could have faced it. Edwin might possibly have been capable of killing Moira, I thought: an unplanned killing, shoving her head into the potting compost because the open bag of it gave him the idea. I didn't think he had the driving force, the imagination or the guts to have attempted the rest.

When I didn't contradict him, Malcolm began saying, 'If Edwin comes . . .' and it was easier to leave it that way.

Time crept on. It was cold. By two-thirty, to stoke our internal fires, we were eating rich dark fruit cake and drinking claret. (Heresy, Malcolm said. We should have had the claret with the pâté and the champagne with the cake. As at weddings? I asked. God damn you, he said.)

I didn't feel much like laughing. It was a vigil to which there could be no good end. Malcolm knew as well as I did that he might be going to learn something he fervently didn't want to know. He didn't deep down want anyone to come. And I wanted it profoundly.

By three-thirty, he was restless. 'You don't really mean to go through all this again tomorrow, do you?'

I watched the drive. No change, as before. 'The Ritz might give us a packed lunch.'

'And Monday? Not Monday as well.' He'd agreed on three days before we'd started. The actuality was proving too much.

'We'll give up on Monday when it gets dark,' I said.

'You're so bloody persistent.'

I watched the mirrors. Come, I thought. *Come.*

'Joyce might have forgotten the phone calls,' Malcolm said.

'She wouldn't forget.'

'Edwin might have been out.'

'That's more likely.'

A light-coloured car rolled up the drive, suddenly there.

No attempt at concealment. No creeping about, looking suspicious. All confidence. Not a thought given to entrapment.

I sat still, breathing deeply.

She stood up out of the car, tall and strong. She went round to the passenger side, opened the door, and lifted out a brown cardboard box which she held in front of her, with both arms round it, as one holds groceries. I'd expected her to go straight round to the kitchen door, but she didn't do that, she walked a few steps into the central chasm, looking up and around her as if with awe.

Malcolm noticed my extreme concentration, rose to his feet and put himself between me and the mirrors so that he could see what I was looking at. I thought he would be stunned and miserably silent, but he was not in the least.

'Oh, no,' he said with annoyance. 'What's *she* doing here?'

Before I could stop him, he shot straight out of the playroom and said, 'Serena, do go away, you're spoiling the whole thing.'

I was on his heels, furious with him. Serena whirled round when she heard his voice. She saw him appear in the passage. I glimpsed her face, wide-eyed and scared. She took a step backwards, and tripped on a fold of the black plastic floor covering, and let go of the box. She tried to catch it . . . touched it . . . knocked it forward.

I saw the panic on her face. I had an instantaneous understanding of what she'd brought.

I yanked Malcolm back with an arm round his neck, twisting and flinging us both to find shelter behind the wall of the staircase.

We were both still falling when the world blew apart.

CHAPTER NINETEEN

I lay short of the playroom door trying to breathe. My lungs felt collapsed. My head rang from the appalling noise, and the smell of the explosive remained as a taste as if my mouth were full of it.

Malcolm, on his stomach a few feet away, was unconscious.

The air was thick with dust and seemed to be still reverberating, though it was probably my concussion. I felt pulped. I felt utterly without strength. I felt very lucky indeed.

The house around us was still standing. We weren't under tons of new rubble. The tough old load-bearing walls that had survived the first bomb had survived the second – which hadn't anyway been the size of a suitcase.

My chest gave a heave, and breath came back. I moved, struggled to get up, tried things out. I felt bruised and unwell, but there were no broken bones; no blood. I rolled to my knees and went on them to Malcolm. He was alive, he was breathing, he was not bleeding from ears or nose: at that moment, it was enough.

I got slowly, weakly, to my feet, and walked shakily into the wide centre space. I could wish to shut my eyes, but one couldn't blot it out. One had to live through terrible things if they came one's way.

At the point where the bomb had exploded, the black floor covering had been ripped right away, and the rest was doubled over and convoluted in large torn pieces. Serena – the things that had been Serena – lay among and half under the black folds of plastic: things in emerald and frilly white clothes, pale blue leg-warmers, dark blue tights; torn edges of flesh, scarlet splashes . . . a scarlet pool.

I went round covering the parts of her completely with the black folds, hiding the harrowing truth from anyone coming there unprepared. I felt ill. I felt as if my head were full of air. I was trembling uncontrollably. I thought of people who dealt often with such horrors and wondered if they ever got hardened.

Malcolm groaned in the passage. I went back to him fast. He was trying to sit up, to push himself off the floor. There was a large area already beginning to swell on his forehead, and I wondered if he'd simply been knocked out through hitting the wood floor at high speed.

'God,' he said in anguish. 'Serena . . . oh dear God.'

I helped him to his groggy feet and took him out into the garden through the side door, and round past the office to the front of the house. I eased him into the passenger seat of Serena's car.

Malcolm put his head in his hands and wept for his daughter. I stood with my arms on top of the car and my head on those, and felt wretched and sick and unutterably old.

I'd hardly begun to wonder what to do next when a police car came into the drive and rolled slowly, as if tentatively, towards us.

The policeman I'd looked through the windows with stopped the car and stepped out. He looked young, years younger than I was.

'Someone in the village reported another explosion . . .' He looked from us to the house questioningly.

'Don't go in there,' I said. 'Get word to the superintendent. Another bomb has gone off here, and this time someone's been killed.'

Dreadful days followed, full of questions, formalities, explanations, regrets. Malcolm and I went back to the Ritz where he grieved for the lost child who had tried hard to kill him.

'But you said . . . she didn't care about my money. *Why* . . . why did she do it all?'

'She wanted . . .' I said. 'To put it at its simplest, I think she wanted to live at Quantum with you. That's what she's longed for since she was six, when Alicia took her away. She might perhaps have grown up sweet and normal if the courts had given you custody, but courts favour mothers, of course. She wanted to have back what had been wrenched away from her. I saw her cry about it, not long ago. It was still sharp and real to her. She wanted to be your little girl again. She refused to grow up. She dressed very often like a child.'

He was listening with stretched eyes, as if seeing familiar country haunted by devils.

'Alicia was no help to her,' I said. 'She filled her with stories of how you'd rejected her, and she actively discouraged her from maturing, because of her own little-girl act.'

'Poor Serena.' He looked tormented. 'She didn't have much luck.'

'No, she didn't.'

'But Moira . . .?' he said.

'I think Serena made herself believe that if she got rid of Moira, you would go back to Quantum and she would live there with you and look after you, and her dream would come true.'

'It doesn't make sense . . .'

'Murder has nothing to do with sense. It has to do with obsession. With compulsion, irresistible impulse, morbid drive. An act beyond reason.'

He shook his head helplessly.

'It's impossible to know,' I said, 'whether she intended to kill Moira on that day. I wish we could know, but we can't . . . she can't have meant to kill her the way she did, because no one could know there'd be a slit-open nearly full sack of potting compost waiting there, handy. If she meant to kill Moira that day, she'd have taken some sort of weapon. I've been wondering, you know, if she meant to hit her over the head and put her in the car, the way she did you.'

'God . . .'

'Anyway, after Moira was out of the way, Serena offered to live with you at Quantum and look after you, but you wouldn't have it.'

'But it wouldn't have worked, you know. I didn't even consider it seriously. It was nice of her, I thought, but I didn't want her, it's true.'

'And I expect you made it clear in a fairly testy way?'

He thought about it. 'I suppose in the end I did. She kept on about it, you see. Asked me several times. Came to Quantum to beg me. I got tired of it and said no pretty definitely. I told her not to keep bothering me . . .' He looked shattered. 'She began to hate me then, do you think?'

I nodded unhappily. 'I'd think so. I think she finally believed she would never have what she craved for. You could have given it to her, and you wouldn't. The rejection was ultimate. Absolute. Extreme. She believed it, as she'd never really believed it before. She told me she'd given you a chance, but you'd turned her down.'

He put a hand over his eyes.

'So she set out to kill you, and finally to kill the house as well . . . to destroy what she couldn't have.'

I still wondered, as I'd wondered in New York, whether it was because I, Ian, had gone back to live at Quantum with Malcolm that she'd come to that great violent protest. I had too often had what she'd yearned for. The bomb had been meant as much for me as for Malcolm, I thought.

'Do you remember that morning when she found we weren't dead?' I asked. 'She practically fainted. Everyone supposed it was from relief, but I'll bet it wasn't. She'd tried three times to kill you and it must have seemed intolerable to her that you were still alive.'

'She must have been . . . well . . . insane.'

Obsessed . . . insane. Sometimes there wasn't much difference.

Malcolm had given up champagne and gone back to scotch. The constant bubbles, I saw, had been a sort of gesture, two fingers held up defiantly in the face of danger, a gallant crutch against fear. He poured a new drink of the old stuff and stood by the window looking over Green Park.

'You knew it was Serena . . . who would come.'

'If anyone did.'

'How did you know?'

'I saw everyone, as you know. I saw what's wrong with their lives. Saw their desperations. Donald and Helen are desperate for money, but they were coping the best way they could. Bravely, really, pawning her jewellery. They thought you might help them with guaranteeing a loan, if they could find you. That's a long way from wanting to kill you.'

Malcolm nodded and drank, and watched life proceeding outside.

'Lucy,' I said, 'may have lost her inspiration but not her marbles. Edwin is petulant but not a planner, not dynamic. Thomas . . .' I paused. 'Thomas was absolutely desperate, but for peace in his house, not for the money itself. Berenice has made him deeply ineffective. He's got a long way to go, to climb back. He seemed to me incapable almost of tying his shoelaces, let alone making a time bomb, even if he did invent the wired-up clocks.'

'Go on,' Malcolm said.

'Berenice is obsessed with herself and her desires, but her grudge is against Thomas. Money would make her quieter, but it's not money she really wants, it's a son. Killing Moira and you wouldn't achieve that.'

'And Gervase?'

'He's destroying himself. It takes all his energies. He hasn't enough left to go around killing people for money. He's lost his nerve. He drinks. You have to be courageous and sober to mess with explosives. Ursula's desperation takes her to churches and to lunches with Joyce.'

He grunted in his throat, not quite a chuckle.

Joyce had been thanked by us on the telephone on the Saturday night when we'd come back exhausted.

She'd been devastated to the point of silence about what had happened and had put the phone down in tears. We phoned her again in the morning. 'I got Serena first,' she said sorrowfully. 'She must have gone out and bought all the stuff . . . I can't bear it. That dear little girl, so sweet when she was little, even though I hated her mother. So *awful.*'

'Go on, then,' Malcolm said. 'You keep stopping.'

'It couldn't have been Alicia or Vivien, they're not strong enough to carry you. Alicia's new boyfriend would be, but why should he think Alicia would be better off with you dead? And I couldn't imagine any of them constructing a bomb.'

'And Ferdinand?'

'I really couldn't see it, could you? He has no particular worries. He's good at his job. He's easy-going most of the time. Not him. Not Debs. That's the lot.'

'So did you come to Serena just by elimination?' He turned from the window, searching my face.

'No,' I said slowly. 'I thought of them all together, all their troubles and heart-aches. To begin with, when Moira died, I thought, like everyone else did, that she was killed to stop her taking half your money. I thought the attacks on you were for money, too. It was the obvious thing. And then, when I'd seen them all, when I understood all the turmoils going on under apparently normal exteriors, I began to wonder whether the money really mattered at all . . . And when I was in New York,

I was thinking of them all again but taking the money out . . . and with Serena . . . everything fitted.'

He stirred restlessly and went to sit down.

'It wouldn't have convinced the police,' he said.

'Nor you either,' I agreed. 'You had to see for yourself.' We fell silent, thinking what in fact he had seen, his daughter come to blast out the kitchen rather than search it for a notepad.

'But didn't you have any proof?' he said eventually. 'I mean, any real reason to think it was her? Something you could put your finger on.'

'Not really. Nothing that would stand up in court. Except that I think it was Serena who got Norman West to find you in Cambridge, not Alicia, as West himself thought.'

He stared. 'Why do you think that?'

'Alicia said she hadn't done it. Both West and I thought she was lying, but I think now she was telling the truth. Do you remember the tape from my telephone answering machine? Do you remember Serena's voice? "Mummy wants to know where Daddy is. I told her you wouldn't know, but she insisted I ask." That's what she said. Alicia told me positively that she herself hadn't wanted to know where you were. If Alicia's telling the truth, it was *Serena* who wanted to know, and she wanted to know because she'd lost us after failing to run you over. Lost us because of us scooting up to London in the Rolls.'

'My God,' he said. 'What happened to the tape? I suppose it got lost in the rubble.'

'No, it's in a box in the garage at Quantum. A few things were saved. Several of your gold-and-silver brushes are there too.'

He waved the thought away, although he was pleased enough. 'I suppose Serena did sound like Alicia on the telephone. I sometimes thought it was Alicia when she phoned. Breathless and girlish. You know Norman West just got it wrong.'

'She did call herself Mrs Pembroke,' I pointed out. 'Just to confuse matters. Or maybe she said Ms and he didn't hear clearly.'

'It doesn't much matter.' He was quiet for a while. 'Although it was terrible yesterday, it was the best thing really. We'll grieve and get over this. She couldn't have borne to be locked up, could she, not with all that energy . . . not in drab clothes.'

On that Sunday morning also, we began telephoning to the family to tell them what had happened. I expected to find that Joyce had already told them, but she hadn't. She'd talked to them all the day before, they said, but that was all.

We left a lot of stunned silences behind us. A lot of unstoppable tears.

Malcolm told Alicia first, and asked if she'd like him to come to see her, to comfort her. When she could speak, she said no. She said Serena didn't kill Moira, Ian did. Everything was Ian's fault. Malcolm put the receiver down slowly, rubbed his hand over his face, and told me what she'd said.

'It's very hard,' he said, excusing her, 'to face that you've given birth to a murderer.'

'She helped to make her a murderer,' I said.

I spoke to my four brothers and to Lucy. Malcolm told Vivien last.

They all asked where we were: Joyce had told them we were in Australia. In London, we said, but didn't add where. Malcolm said he couldn't face having them all descend on him before he was ready. By the end, I was dropping with fatigue and Malcolm had finished off half a bottle. Long before bedtime, we were asleep.

We went back to Quantum on Monday, as we'd promised the police, and found Mr Smith poking around like old times.

All physical signs of Serena had mercifully been taken away, and all that remained were the torn flaps of black plastic that hadn't been near her.

Mr Smith shook hands with us dustily and after a few commiserating platitudes came out with his true opinions.

'Anyone who carries a fully-wired explosive device from place to place is raving mad. You don't connect the battery until the device is where you want it to go off. If you're me, you don't insert the detonator, either. You keep them separate.'

'I don't suppose she meant to drop it,' I said.

'Mind you, she was also unlucky,' Mr Smith said judiciously. 'It is possible, but I myself wouldn't risk it, to drop ANFO with a detonator in it and have it not explode. But maybe dropping it caused the clock wires to touch.'

'Have you found the clock?' I asked.

'Patience,' he said, and went back to looking.

A policeman fending away a few sensation seekers told us that Superintendent Yale had been detained, and couldn't meet us there: please would we go to the police station. We went, and found him in his office.

He shook hands. He offered sympathy.

He asked if we knew why Serena had gone to Quantum with a second bomb, and we told him. Asked if we knew why she should have killed Moira and tried to kill Malcolm. We told him my theories. He listened broodingly.

'There will be an inquest,' he said. 'Mr Ian can formally identify the remains. You won't need to see them . . . her . . . again, though. The coroner's verdict will be death by misadventure, I've no doubt. You may be needed to give an account of what happened. You'll be informed of all that in due course.' He paused. 'Yesterday, we went to Miss Pembroke's flat and conducted a search. We found a few items of interest. I am going to show you some objects and I'd be glad if you'd say whether you can identify them or not.'

He reached into a carton very like the one Serena had been carrying, which stood on his desk. He brought out a pile of twenty or thirty exercise books with spiral bindings and blue covers and after that a tin large enough to contain a pound of sweets, with a picture on top.

'*The Old Curiosity Shop*,' Malcolm said sadly.

'No possibility of doubt,' Yale nodded. 'The title's printed across the bottom of the picture.'

'Are there any detonators in it?' I asked.

'No, just cotton wool. Mr Smith wonders if she used more than one detonator for each bomb, just to make sure. He says amateurs are mad enough to try anything.'

I picked up one of the notebooks and opened it.

'Have you seen those before, sirs?' Yale asked.

'No,' I said, and Malcolm shook his head.

In Serena's looping handwriting, I read:

'Daddy and I had such fun in the garden this morning. He was teaching the dogs to fetch sticks and I was throwing the sticks. We picked a lot of beautiful daffodils and when we went indoors I put them all in vases in all the rooms. I cooked some lamb chops for lunch and made mint sauce and peas and roast potatoes and gravy and for pudding we had ice cream and peaches. Daddy is going to buy me some white boots with zips and silver tassels.

He calls me his princess, isn't that lovely? In the afternoon, we went down to the stream and picked some watercress for tea. Daddy took his socks off and rolled up his trousers and the boys *no* the boys weren't there I won't have them in my stories it was Daddy who picked the watercress and we washed it and ate it with brown bread. This evening I will sit on his lap and he will stroke my hair and call me his little princess, his little darling, and it will be lovely.'

I flicked through the pages. The whole book was full. Speechlessly I handed it to Malcolm, open where I'd read.

'All the notebooks are like that,' Yale said. 'We've had them all read right through. She's been writing them for years, I would say.'

'But you don't mean . . . they're recent?' I said.

'Some of them are, certainly. I've seen several sets of books like these in my career. Compulsive writing, I believe it's called. These of your sister's are wholesome and innocent by comparison. You can't imagine the pornography and brutality I've read. They make you despair.'

Malcolm, plainly moved, flicking over pages, said, 'She says I bought her a pretty red dress . . . a white sweater with blue flowers on it . . . a bright yellow leotard – I hardly know what a leotard is. Poor girl. Poor girl.'

'She bought them herself,' I said. 'Three or four times a week.'

Yale tilted the stack of notebooks up, brought out the bottom one and handed it to me. 'This is the latest. It changes at the end. You may find it interesting.'

I turned to the last entries in the book and with sorrow read:

'Daddy is going away from me and I don't want him any more. I think perhaps I will kill him. It isn't so difficult. I've done it before.'

There was a space on the page after that, and then, lower down: 'Ian is back with Daddy.'

Another space, and then,

'IAN IS AT QUANTUM WITH DADDY. I CAN'T BEAR IT.'

After yet another space, she had written my name again in larger-still capitals 'IAN' and surrounded it with a circle of little lines radiating outwards: an explosion with my name in the centre.

That was the end. The rest of the notebook was empty.

Malcolm read the page over my arm and sighed deeply. 'Can I have them?' he said to Yale. 'You don't need them, do you? There won't be a trial.'

Yale hesitated but said he saw no reason to retain them. He pushed the pile of books towards Malcolm and put the sweet tin on top.

'And the lighthouse and clock,' I said. 'Could we have those?'

He produced the Lego box from a cupboard, wrote

a list of what we were taking on an official-looking receipt and got Malcolm to sign it.

'All very upsetting, Mr Pembroke,' he said, again shaking hands, 'but we can mark our case closed.'

We took the sad trophies back to the Ritz, and that afternoon Malcolm wrote and posted cheques that would solve every financial problem in the Pembrokes' repertoire.

'What about the witches?' he said. 'If Helen and that dreadful Edwin and Berenice and Ursula and Debs are all having their own share, what about those other three?'

'Up to you,' I said. 'They're your wives.'

'*Ex*-wives.' He shrugged and wrote cheques for them also. 'Easy come, easy go,' he said. 'Bloody Alicia doesn't deserve it.'

'Engines work better with a little oil,' I said.

'Greasing their palms, you mean.' He still didn't believe in it. Still felt he was corrupting them by giving them wealth. Still thinking that *he* could stay sane and reasonably sensible when he had millions, but nobody else could.

He wrote a final cheque and gave it to me. I felt awkward taking it, which he found interesting.

'You should have had double,' he said.

I shook my head, reeling at noughts. 'You've post-dated it,' I said.

'Of course I have. I've post-dated all of them. I don't have that much in readies lying around in the bank.

Have to sell a few shares. The family can have the promise now and the cash in a month.'

He licked the envelopes. Not a cruel man, I thought.

On Tuesday, because I wished it, we went to see Robin.

'He won't remember Serena,' Malcolm said.

'No, I don't expect so.'

We went in the car I'd hired the day before for going to Quantum, and on the way stopped again to buy toys and chocolate and a packet of balloons.

I had taken with us the Lego lighthouse and the Mickey Mouse clock, thinking they might interest Robin, over which Malcolm shook his head.

'He won't be able to make them work, you know.'

'He might remember them. You never know. They used to be his and Peter's, after all. Serena gave them the clock and made them the lighthouse.'

Robin's room was very cold because of the open French windows. Malcolm tentatively went across and closed them, and Robin at once flung them open. Malcolm patted Robin's shoulder and moved away from the area, and Robin looked at him searchingly, in puzzlement, and at me the same way, as he sometimes did: trying, it seemed, to remember, and never quite getting there.

We gave him the new toys which he looked at and put down again, and after a while I opened the Lego box and brought out the old ones.

He looked at them for only a moment and then went on a long wander round and round the room, several times. Then he came to me, pointed at the packet of balloons and made a puffing noise.

'Good Lord,' Malcolm said.

I opened the packet and blew up several balloons, tying knots in the necks, as I always did. Robin went on making puffing noises until I'd blown up every balloon in the packet. His face looked agitated. He puffed harder to make me go faster.

When they were all scattered round the room, red, yellow, blue, green and white, bobbing about in stray air currents, shiny and festive, he went round bursting them with furious vigour, sticking his forefinger straight into some, pinching others, squashing the last one against the wall with the palm of his hand, letting out the anger he couldn't express.

Most times, after this ritual, he was released and at peace, and would retreat into a corner and sit staring into space or huddled up, rocking.

This time, however, he went over to the table, picked up the lighthouse, pulled it roughly apart into four or five pieces and threw them forcefully out of the wide-open window. Then he picked up the clock and with violence yanked the wires off, including the Mickey Mouse hands.

Malcolm was aghast. Docile Robin's rage shouted out of his mute body. His strength was a revelation.

He took the clock in his hand and walked round the

room smashing it against the wall at each step. Step, *smash*, step, *smash*, step, *smash*.

'Stop him,' Malcolm said in distress.

'No . . . he's talking,' I said.

'He's not talking.'

'He's telling us . . .'

Robin reached the window and threw the mangled clock far and high into the garden. Then he started shouting, roaring without words, his voice rough from disuse and hoarse with the change taking place from boy into man. The sound seemed to excite him until his body was reverberating, pouring out sound, the dam of silence swept away. 'Aaah . . . aaah . . . aaah . . .' and then real words, 'No . . . No . . . No . . . Serena . . . No . . . Serena . . . No . . . Serena . . . No . . .' He shouted to the skies, to the fates, to the wicked unfairness of the fog in his brain. Shouted in fury and frenzy. 'Serena . . . No . . . Serena . . . No . . .' and on and on until it became mindless, without meaning, just words.

I stepped close beside him in the end and yelled in his ear, 'Serena's dead.'

He stopped shouting immediately. 'Serena's dead,' I repeated. 'Like the clock. Smashed. Finished. Dead.'

He turned and looked at me vaguely, his mouth open, no sound coming out, the sudden silence as unnerving as the shouting had been.

'Serena-is-dead,' I said, making each word separate, giving it weight.

'He doesn't understand,' Malcolm said: and Robin went away and sat in a corner with his arms round his knees and his head down, and began rocking.

'The nurses think he understands quite a lot,' I said. 'Whether he understands that Serena is dead, I don't know. But at least we've tried to tell him.' Robin went on rocking as if we weren't there.

'What does it matter?' Malcolm said helplessly.

'It matters because if he does understand, it may give him rest. I brought the lighthouse and the clock because I wondered if Robin remembered anything at all. I thought it worth trying . . . didn't expect quite these results . . . but I think he smashed the clock Serena gave him because it reminded him of her, because she gave it to him and Peter shortly before the car crash. Somewhere in that woolly head, things sometimes connect.'

Malcolm nodded, puzzled and instinctively alarmed.

'One could almost think it was that afternoon,' I said, 'seeing the twins happy at Quantum where she hungered to be, seeing you there with them, loving them; perhaps it was that afternoon which finally tipped her over into the insanity of trying to make her fantasy come true. It didn't come true . . . you met Moira . . . but I'm certain she tried.'

Malcolm was staring saying 'No! Don't say it! *Don't!*'

I said it anyway. 'I think Robin saw the hit-and-run driver who forced their car off the road. In whatever mangled dreamlike way, he knows who it was. No

Serena, no Serena, no . . . You heard him. I've thought ever since New York that it could possibly have happened that way. Serena's obsession was full-blown a long time ago, long before she got rid of Moira. I think she killed Peter . . . and Coochie.'

EPILOGUE

We all went back to Quantum a year later for the Grand Reopening Ceremony, the house bedecked with garlands and champagne corks popping.

After much soul-searching, Malcolm had decided to rebuild. Without Quantum as its centre, the family would have fallen apart, and he didn't want that to happen. When he told everyone of his intention, there was great communal relief, and he saw without question that it was the right thing to do.

The rancour level lessened dramatically after the arrival of the cheques and the production of his will for inspection, and I was suddenly not everyone's villain, though still and forever Alicia's. Malcolm, having deleted Serena by codicil, sent his will to the Central Probate Office for registration and let everyone know it.

Malcolm still felt that he had pampered and corrupted his children, but he had to admit they were happier because of it. Dramatically happier in some cases, like Donald and Helen whose problems had all been financial. Helen redeemed her baubles and stopped painting china, and Donald paid off the finance company and the bank and ran the golf club with a light heart.

A few weeks after Serena's death, Helen asked me over to Marblehill House. 'A drink before dinner,' she said. I went on a freezing evening in December and she surprised me by kissing me in greeting. Donald was standing with his back to a roaring fire, looking contentedly pompous.

'We wanted to thank you,' Helen said. 'And I suppose . . . to apologize.'

'There's no need.'

'Oh, yes. We all know there is. Not everyone will say so, but they know.'

'How's Malcolm?' Donald asked.

'He's fine.'

Donald nodded. Even the fact that Malcolm and I were still together seemed no longer to worry him, and later, when we'd sat round the fire drinking for a while, he asked me to stay on for dinner. I stayed, and although we were never going to be in and out of each other's houses every five minutes, at least on that evening we reached a peaceful plateau as brothers.

Some time later, I went to see Lucy. She and Edwin had made no changes to their cottage and had no plans to move, much to Edwin's disgust.

'We should live somewhere more *suitable*,' he said

to her crossly. 'I never thought we would stay here when you inherited.'

Lucy looked at him with affection. 'If you want to leave, Edwin, you can, now that you have money of your own.'

He was disconcerted; open mouthed. 'I don't want to leave,' he said, and it was clearly the truth.

Lucy said to me, 'I'll find a good use for my money: keep the capital, give away most of the income. We have no anxieties now, and that's a relief, I agree, but I haven't changed altogether. I don't believe in luxurious living. It's bad for the soul. I'm staying here.' She ate a handful of raisins determinedly, the old man looking out of her eyes.

Thomas was no longer her guest. Thomas, against all advice, had gone back to Berenice.

I called at Arden Haciendas one dark cold afternoon and Thomas opened the front door himself, looking blank when he saw me.

'Berenice is out,' he said, letting me in.

'I came to see you. How are you doing?'

'Not so bad,' he said, but he still looked defeated.

He gave me a drink. He knew where the gin was, and the tonic. He said Berenice and he had been going to marriage guidance sessions, but he didn't know that they were doing much good.

'You can get vasectomies reversed sometimes,' I said.

'Yes, but I don't really want to. Suppose I did, and

we had another girl? Unless Berenice can get over not having sons, I'm going to leave her again. I told her.'

I gazed at him, awestruck. 'What did she say?'

'Nothing much. I think she's afraid of me, really.'

As long as it didn't go to his head, I thought that might not be at all a bad thing.

I went to see Gervase and Ursula soon after. The change in Ursula, who let me in, was like unwrapping a brown paper parcel and finding Christmas inside. The old skirt, shirt, pullover and pearls had vanished. She wore narrow scarlet trousers, a huge white sweater and a baroque gold chain. She smiled at me like a shy conspirator and came with me into the sitting room. Gervase, if not overpoweringly friendly, seemed ready for neutrality and a truce.

'I told Gervase,' Ursula said sweetly, 'that now that I can afford to leave him and take the girls with me, I'm staying because I want to, not because I have to. I'm staying as long as he gets help with this ridiculous fixation about his birth. Who *cares* that Malcolm wasn't married to Alicia at the time? I certainly don't. No one does. Ferdinand doesn't. Ferdinand's been very good, he's been over here several times giving Gervase advice.'

Gervase, who in the past would have shouted her down, listened almost with gratitude. The bear that had run himself into a thicket was being led out by compassionate hands.

Ferdinand, when I called, was in rocketing good

spirits. He and Debs had moved immediately from their small bare bungalow into a large bare bungalow with a tennis court, a swimming pool and a three-car garage. Affluence was fun, he said; but one of the new house's rooms was also his office. He was going on with his job.

'I took your remarks to heart, you know,' he said. 'Took a look at what Alicia had done to us. I don't listen to her any more. She won't get rid of Debs and she won't get rid of Ursula. Have you seen Ursula? Transformation! I've told Gervase he has a wife in a million and a mother who's nothing but trouble. I've been talking to him about illegitimacy . . . isn't that what you wanted?' He punched my arm lightly. 'Stay to dinner?' he said.

I didn't go to see either Alicia or Vivien. I stayed a few nights with Joyce.

'Darling, how's that old fool getting along?'

'He spends a lot of time at Quantum with the builders.'

'Don't let him catch pneumonia. It's bitter outside.'

'He does what he likes,' I said.

'Darling, when did he not?'

Joyce rushed busily away to a bridge tournament in Paris, kissing my cheek, patting me with approval, telling me to be careful not to break my neck in those frightful races I insisted on riding.

I gave her the assurances and went back to Lambourn, now my home instead of Epsom. I'd asked the trainer I'd been riding exercise for if he knew of anyone needing a second-string stable jockey, if I should take the giant step of turning professional.

He stared. 'I heard you don't need to. Didn't you come into money?'

'Forget the money. What chance would I have?'

'I saw you win that race at Kempton,' he said. 'If you turn pro, if you come to Lambourn, I'll give you plenty of rides.'

He was as good as his word, and George and Jo, astonished but happy, entered their few horses to fit in.

I bought a house in Lambourn and Malcolm came to live in it while Quantum was rebuilt. Malcolm loved Lambourn. He went often up to the Downs with the trainer I was riding for to watch the horses work, and far from losing interest in racing, grew more and more involved. When I won my first professional race, the Bollinger ran through Lambourn like a river.

By the day the following November that we all went to the house for the Grand Reopening (with embossed invitation cards and an army of caterers), everyone's lives had settled into the new patterns.

Malcolm had been to the 'Arc' again, and round the world with Ramsey Osborn. Chrysos had won the Futurity at Doncaster and was tipped for the next year's Derby. Blue Clancy had gone to stud, syndicated for millions.

I had ended my first professional season with a respectable score and at the start of my second had become the chief retained jockey for the stable. I would be a trainer in the end, I supposed. Meantime, I felt alive and fulfilled as never before.

Lucy and Edwin were still eating healthily in the cottage. Lucy, coming to terms with not writing more poetry herself, had started on a scholarly biography and commentary on the Life and Work of Thomas Stearns Eliot. Edwin was still doing the shopping.

Donald and Helen, arm in arm, wandered round the garden like lovers.

Ferdinand fussed over Debs, who was pregnant.

Gervase had recovered most of his bullishness, which seemed to reassure Ursula rather than cow her. She came in a mink coat, laughing with pleasure.

In Berenice, the fire had gone out: in Thomas, it had been faintly rekindled. No longer needing a job, he was learning to play golf. Berenice was house-hunting, with Thomas's approval.

Alicia came looking girlish, trilling away in a voice like an echo of Serena's, and everyone made polite remarks to her with closed teeth.

Vivien complained that Malcolm had re-done the house too much in Coochie's taste. Joyce made diplomatic friends with the married couple he had engaged to look after him. He – and they – had been living in the house for a week.

All of the grandchildren were there, re-exploring the place: children's voices again in the garden. Robin, far away, had fallen silent once more and had never since that violent day wanted me to blow up balloons.

Malcolm and I walked out through the new sitting-room windows and from the lawn looked up at the house. It felt whole again, not just physically, but at peace.

'I don't feel Serena's here, do you?' Malcolm said.

'No, she isn't.'

'I was afraid she might be. I'm glad she's not.'

We went further down the lawn.

'Did you notice I'd taken the golden dolphin and the amethyst tree and so on out of the wall and put them in the sitting room?' he asked casually.

'Yes, I did.'

'I sold the gold too.'

I glanced at him. He looked quizzically back.

'The price rose sharply this year, as I thought it would. I took the profit. There's nothing in the wall now except spiders and dust.'

'Never mind.'

'I'm leaving the clause in the will though.' The family had been curious about his leaving me the piece of wire, and he'd refused to explain. 'I'll buy more gold, and sell it. Buy and sell. Forward and backward. One of these days . . .' his blue eyes gleamed ' . . . you may win on the nod.'

COME TO GRIEF

Dick Francis has written forty-one international bestsellers and is widely acclaimed as one of the world's finest thriller writers. His awards include the Crime Writers' Association's Cartier Diamond Dagger for his outstanding contribution to the crime genre, and an honorary Doctorate of Humane Letters from Tufts University of Boston. In 1996 Dick Francis was made a Mystery Writers of America Grand Master for a lifetime's achievement and in 2000 he received a CBE in the Queen's Birthday Honours list.

Also by Dick Francis in Pan Books

DEAD CERT
NERVE
FOR KICKS
ODDS AGAINST
FLYING FINISH
BLOOD SPORT
FORFEIT
ENQUIRY
RAT RACE
BONECRACK
SMOKESCREEN
SLAY-RIDE
KNOCK DOWN
HIGH STAKES
IN THE FRAME
RISK
TRIAL RUN
WHIP HAND
REFLEX
TWICE SHY
BANKER
THE DANGER
PROOF
BREAK IN
BOLT
HOT MONEY
THE EDGE
STRAIGHT
LONGSHOT
COMEBACK
DRIVING FORCE
DECIDER
WILD HORSES
TO THE HILT
10lb PENALTY
FIELD OF THIRTEEN
SECOND WIND
SHATTERED

THE SPORT OF QUEENS
(autobiography)

LESTER: The Official
Biography

DICK FRANCIS
OMNIBUS ONE:
Long Shot, Straight,
High Stakes

DICK FRANCIS
OMNIBUS TWO:
Forfeit, Risk, Reflex

DICK FRANCIS
OMNIBUS THREE:
Slay-Ride, Banker, Proof

DICK FRANCIS
OMNIBUS FOUR:
Enquiry, Rat Race,
Smokescreen

SID HALLEY OMNIBUS:
Odds Against, Whip Hand,
Come to Grief

Dick Francis

COME TO GRIEF

PAN BOOKS
In association with Michael Joseph Ltd

First published 1995 by Michael Joseph Ltd

This edition published 1996 by Pan Books
an imprint of Pan Macmillan Ltd
Pan Macmillan, 20 New Wharf Road, London N1 9RR
Basingstoke and Oxford
Associated companies throughout the world
www.panmacmillan.com

In association with Michael Joseph Ltd

ISBN 0 330 34777 2

21 23 25 27 29 28 26 24 22

A CIP catalogue record for this book is available from
the British Library.

Phototypeset by Intype London Ltd
Printed and bound in Great Britain by
Mackays of Chatham plc, Chatham, Kent

In November 1994, as part of the BBC's Children in Need Appeal, Radio 2 gave an auction of opportunities 'that money can't buy'. One of the lots was 'To have one's name used as a character in Dick Francis's next book'.

The lot was secured by Mrs Patricia Huxford. It has given Dick Francis great pleasure to include her in *Come to Grief.*

CHAPTER ONE

I had this friend, you see, that everyone loved.

(My name is Sid Halley.)

I had this friend that everyone loved, and I put him in the dock.

The trouble with working as an investigator, as I had been doing for approaching five years, was that occasionally one turned up facts that surprised and appalled and smashed peaceful lives for ever.

It had taken days of inner distress for me to decide to act on what I'd learned. Miserably, by then, I'd suffered through disbelief, through denial, through anger and at length through acceptance; all the stages of grief. I grieved for the man I'd known. For the man I *thought* I'd known, who had all along been a façade. I grieved for the loss of a friendship, for a man who still looked the same but was different, alien . . . despicable. I could much more easily have grieved for him dead.

The turmoil I'd felt in private had on public disclosure become universal. The press, jumping instinctively and strongly to his defence, had given me, as his accuser, a severely rough time. On racecourses, where I chiefly worked, long-time acquaintances had turned their backs. Love, support and comfort poured out towards my friend. Disbelief and denial and anger prevailed: acceptance lay a long way ahead. Meanwhile I, not he, was seen as the target for hatred. It would pass, I knew. One had simply to endure it, and wait.

On the morning set for the opening of his trial, my friend's mother killed herself.

The news was brought to the law courts in Reading, in Berkshire, where the presiding judge, gowned, had already heard the opening statements and where I, a witness for the prosecution, waited alone in a soulless side-room to be called. One of the court officials came to give me the suicide information and to say that the judge had adjourned the proceedings for the day, and I could go home.

'Poor woman,' I exclaimed, truly horrified.

Even though he was supposed to be impartial, the official's own sympathies were still with the accused. He eyed me without favour and said I should return the following morning, ten o'clock sharp.

I left the room and walked slowly along the corridor towards the exit, fielded on the way by a senior lawyer who took me by the elbow and drew me aside.

'His mother took a room in a hotel and jumped from the sixteenth floor,' he said without preamble. 'She left a note saying she couldn't bear the future. What are your thoughts?'

I looked at the dark, intelligent, eyes of Davis Tatum, a clumsy fat man with a lean agile brain.

'You know better than I do,' I said.

'*Sid!*' A touch of exasperation. 'Tell me your thoughts.'

'Perhaps he'll change his plea.'

He relaxed and half smiled. 'You're in the wrong job.'

I wryly shook my head. 'I catch the fish. You guys gut them.'

He amiably let go of my arm and I continued to the outside world to catch a train for the thirty-minute ride to the terminus in London, flagging down a taxi for the last mile or so home.

Ginnie Quint, I thought, travelling through London. Poor, poor Ginnie Quint, choosing death in preference to the everlasting agony of her son's disgrace. A lonely slamming exit. An end to tears. An end to grief.

The taxi stopped outside the house in Pont Square (off Cadogan Square), where I currently lived on the first floor, with a balcony overlooking the central leafy railed garden. As usual, the small secluded square was quiet, with little passing traffic and only a few people on foot. A thin early October wind shook the dying leaves on the lime trees, floating a few of them sporadically to the ground like soft yellow snowflakes.

I climbed out of the cab and paid the driver through his open window, and, as I turned to cross the pavement and go up the few steps to the front door, a man who was apparently quietly walking past suddenly sprang at me in fury, raising a long black metal rod with which he tried to brain me.

I sensed rather than saw the first wicked slash and moved enough to catch the weight of it on my shoulder, not my head. He was screaming at me, half demented, and I fielded a second brutal blow on a raised defensive forearm. After that I seized his wrist in a pincer grip and rolled the bulk of his body backward over the leg I pushed out rigidly behind his knees, and felled him, sprawling, iron bar and all, onto the hard ground. He yelled bitter words; cursing, half incoherent, threatening to kill.

The taxi still stood there, diesel engine running, the driver staring wide-mouthed and speechless, a state of affairs that continued while I yanked open the black rear door and stumbled in again onto the seat. My heart thudded. Well, it would.

'*Drive*,' I said urgently. 'Drive on.'

'But . . .'

'Just drive. Go *on*. Before he finds his feet and breaks your windows.'

The driver closed his mouth fast and meshed his gears, and wavered at something above running pace along the road.

'Look,' he said, protesting, half turning his head back to me, 'I didn't see nothing. You're my last fare today, I've been on the go eight hours and I'm on my way home.'

'Just drive,' I said. Too little breath. Too many jumbled feelings.

'Well . . . but, drive where *to*?'

Good question. Think.

'He didn't look like no mugger,' the taxi driver observed aggrievedly. 'But you never can tell these days. D'you want me to drop you off at the police? He hit you something shocking. You could *hear* it. Like he broke your arm.'

'Just drive, would you?'

The driver was large, fiftyish and a Londoner, but no John Bull, and I could see from his head movements and his repeated spiky glances at me in his rear-view mirror that he didn't want to get involved in my problems and couldn't wait for me to leave his cab.

Pulse eventually steadying, I could think of only one place to go. My only haven, in many past troubles.

'Paddington,' I said. 'Please.'

'St Mary's, d'you mean? The hospital?'

'No. The trains.'

'But you've just come from there!' he protested.

'Yes, but please go back.'

Cheering a little he rocked round in a U-turn and set off for the return to Paddington Station where he assured me again that he hadn't seen nothing, nor heard nothing neither, and he wasn't going to get involved, did I see?

I simply paid him and let him go, and if I memorised

his cab-licensing number it was out of habit, not expectation.

As part of normal equipment I wore a mobile phone on my belt and, walking slowly into the high airy terminus, I pressed the buttons to reach the man I trusted most in the world, my ex-wife's father, Rear Admiral Charles Roland, Royal Navy, retired, and to my distinct relief he answered at the second ring.

'Charles,' I said. My voice cracked a bit, which I hadn't meant.

A pause, then, 'Is that you, Sid?'

'May I . . . visit?'

'Of course. Where are you?'

'Paddington. I'll come by train and taxi.'

He said calmly, 'Use the side-door. It's not locked,' and put down his receiver.

I smiled, reassured as ever by his steadiness and his brevity with words. An unemotional, undemonstrative man, not paternal towards me and very far from indulgent, he gave me nevertheless a consciousness that he cared considerably about what happened to me and would proffer rocklike support if I needed it. Like I needed it at that moment, for several variously dire reasons.

Trains to Oxford being less frequent in the middle of the day, it was four in the afternoon by the time the country taxi, leaving Oxford well behind, arrived at Charles's vast old house at Aynsford and decanted me at the side-door. I paid the driver clumsily owing to stiffening bruises, and walked with relief into the pile I really thought of as home, the one unchanging constant in a life that had tossed me about, rather, now and then.

Charles sat, as often, in the large leather armchair that I found too hard for comfort but that he, in his uncompromising way, felt appropriate to accommodate his narrow rump. I had sometime in the past moved one of the softer but still fairly formal old gold brocade armchairs from the drawing-room into the smaller room, his 'wardroom', as it was there we always sat when the two of us were alone. It was there that he kept his desk, his collection of flies for fishing, his nautical books, his racks of priceless old orchestral recordings and the gleaming marble and steel wonder of a custom-built, frictionless turntable on which he played them. It was there on the dark green walls that he'd hung large photographs of the ships he'd commanded, and smaller photos of shipmates, and there, also, that he'd lately positioned a painting of me as a jockey riding over a fence at Cheltenham racecourse, a picture that summed up every ounce of vigour needed for race-riding, and which had hung for years less conspicuously in the dining-room.

He had had a strip of lighting positioned along the top of the heavy gold frame, and when I got there that evening, it was lit.

He was reading. He put his book face down on his lap when I walked in, and gave me a bland noncommittal inspection. There was nothing, as usual, to be read in his eyes: I could often see quite clearly into other people's minds, but seldom his.

'Hullo,' I said.

I could hear him take a breath and trickle it out through his nose. He spent all of five seconds looking me over, then pointed to the tray of bottles and glasses which stood on the table below my picture.

'Drink,' he said briefly. An order, not invitation.

'It's only four o'clock.'

'Immaterial. What have you eaten today?'

I didn't say anything, which he took to be answer enough.

'Nothing,' he said, nodding. 'I thought so. You look thin. It's this *bloody* case. I thought you were supposed to be in court today.'

'It was adjourned until tomorrow.'

'Get a drink.'

I walked obediently over to the table and looked assessingly at the bottles. In his old-fashioned way he kept brandy and sherry in decanters. Scotch – Famous Grouse, his favourite – remained in the screw-topped bottle. I would have to have Scotch, I thought, and doubted if I could pour even that.

I glanced upwards at my picture. In those days, six years ago, I'd had two hands. In those days I'd been British steeplechasing's champion jockey: whole, healthy and, I dared say, fanatical. A nightmare fall had resulted in a horse's sharp hoof half ripping off my left hand: the end of one career and the birth, if you could call it that, of another. Slow lingering birth of a detective, while I spent two years pining for what I'd lost and drifted rudderless like a wreck that didn't quite sink but was unseaworthy, all the same. I was ashamed of those two years. At the end of them a ruthless villain had smashed beyond mending the remains of the useless hand and had galvanised me into a resurrection of the spirit and the impetus to seek what I'd had since, a myoelectric false hand that worked on nerve impulses from my truncated forearm and looked and behaved so realistically that people often didn't notice its existence.

My present problem was that I couldn't move its thumb far enough from its fingers to grasp the large heavy cut-glass brandy decanter, and my right hand wasn't working too well either. Rather than drop alcohol all over Charles's Persian rug, I gave up and sat in the gold armchair.

'What's the matter?' Charles asked abruptly. 'Why did you come? Why don't you pour a drink?'

After a moment I said dully, knowing it would hurt him, 'Ginnie Quint killed herself.'

'*What?*'

'This morning,' I said. 'She jumped from sixteen floors up.'

His fine-boned face went stiff and immediately looked much older. The bland eyes darkened, as if retreating into their sockets. Charles had known Ginnie

Quint for thirty or more years, and had been fond of her and had been a guest in her house often.

Powerful memories lived in my mind also. Memories of a friendly, rounded, motherly woman happy in her role as a big-house wife, inoffensively rich, working genuinely and generously for several charities and laughingly glowing in reflected glory from her famous, good-looking successful only child, the one that everyone loved.

Her son, Ellis, that I had put in the dock.

The last time I'd seen Ginnie she'd glared at me with incredulous contempt, demanding to know how I could *possibly* seek to destroy the golden Ellis, who counted me his friend, who liked me, who'd done me favours, who would have trusted me with his life.

I'd let her molten rage pour over me, offering no defence. I knew exactly how she felt. Disbelief and denial and anger . . . The idea of what he'd done was so sickening to her that she rejected the guilt possibility absolutely, as almost everyone else had done, though in her case with anguish.

Most people believed I had got it all wrong, and had ruined *myself*, not Ellis. Even Charles, at first, had said doubtfully, 'Sid, are you *sure*?'

I'd said I was certain. I'd hoped desperately for a way out . . . for *any* way out . . . as I knew what I'd be pulling down on myself if I went ahead. And it had been at least as bad as I'd feared, and in many ways worse. After the first bombshell solution – a proposed solution – to a crime that had had half the country baying for blood (but not *Ellis*'s blood, no *no*, it was *unthinkable*), there had been the first court appearance, the remand into custody (a *scandal*, he should of *course* be let out immediately on bail), and after that there had fallen a sudden press silence, while the *sub judice* law came into effect.

Under British *sub judice* law, no evidence might be publicly discussed between the remand and the trial. Much investigation and strategic trial planning could go on behind the scenes, but neither potential jurors nor John Smith in the street was allowed to know details. Uninformed, public opinion had consequently stuck at the 'Ellis is innocent' stage, and I'd had nearly three months, now, of obloquy.

Ellis, you see, was a Young Lochinvar, in spades. Ellis Quint, once champion amateur jump jockey, had flashed onto television screens like a comet, a brilliant, laughing, able, funny performer, the draw for millions on sports quiz programmes, the ultimate chat-show host, the model held up to children, the glittering star that regularly raised the nation's happiness level, to whom everyone, from tiara to baseball cap worn backwards, responded.

Manufacturers fell over themselves to tempt him to endorse their products, and half the kids in England strode about with machismo in glamorised jockey-type riding boots over their jeans. And it was this man, this *paragon* that I sought to eradicate.

No one seemed to blame the tabloid columnist who'd written, 'The once-revered Sid Halley, green with envy, tries to tear down a talent he hasn't a prayer of matching . . .' There had been inches about 'A spiteful little man trying to compensate for his own inadequacies.' I hadn't shown any of it to Charles, but others had.

The telephone at my waist buzzed suddenly, and I answered its summons.

'Sid . . . Sid . . .'

The woman on the other end was crying. I'd heard her crying often.

'Are you at home?' I asked.

'No . . . In the hospital.'

'Tell me the number and I'll phone straight back.'

I heard murmuring in the background; then another voice came on, efficient, controlled, reading out a number, repeating it slowly. I tapped the digits onto my mobile so that they appeared on the small display screen.

'Right,' I said, reading the number back. 'Put down your receiver.' To Charles I said, 'May I use your phone?'

He waved a hand permissively towards his desk, and I pressed the buttons on his phone to get back to where I'd been.

The efficient voice answered immediately.

'Is Mrs Ferns still there?' I said. 'It's Sid Halley.'

'Hang on.'

Linda Ferns was trying not to cry. 'Sid . . . Rachel's worse. She's asking for you. Can you come? Please.'

'How bad is she?'

'Her temperature keeps going up.' A sob stopped her. 'Talk to Sister Grant.'

I talked to the efficient voice, Sister Grant. 'How bad is Rachel?'

'She's asking for you all the time,' she said. 'How soon can you come?'

'Tomorrow.'

'Can you come this evening?'

I said, 'Is it that bad?'

I listened to a moment of silence, in which she couldn't say what she meant because Linda was beside her.

'Come this evening,' she repeated.

This evening. Dear God. Nine-year-old Rachel Ferns lay in a hospital in Kent a hundred and fifty miles away. Ill to death, this time, it sounded like.

'Promise her,' I said, 'that I'll come tomorrow.' I explained where I was. 'I have to be in court tomorrow morning, in Reading, but I'll come to see Rachel as soon as I get out. Promise her. Tell her I'm going to be there. Tell her I'll bring six wigs and an angel fish.'

The efficient voice said, 'I'll tell her,' and then added, 'Is it true that Ellis Quint's mother has killed herself? Mrs Ferns says someone heard it on the radio news and repeated it to her. She wants to know if it's true.'

'It's true.'

'Come as soon as you can,' the nurse said, and disconnected.

I put down the receiver. Charles said, 'The child?'

'It sounds as if she's dying.'

'You knew it was inevitable.'

'It doesn't make it any easier for the parents.' I sat down again slowly in the gold armchair. 'I would go tonight if it would save her life, but I . . .' I stopped, not knowing what to say, how to explain that I wouldn't go. Couldn't go. Not except to save her life, which no one could do however much they ached to.

Charles said briefly, 'You've only just got here.'

'Yeah.'

'And what else is there, that you haven't told me?'

I looked at him.

'I know you too well, Sid,' he said. 'You didn't come all this way just because of Ginnie. You could have told me about her on the telephone.' He paused. 'From the look of you, you came for the oldest of reasons.' He paused again, but I didn't say anything. 'For sanctuary,' he said.

I shifted in the chair. 'Am I so transparent?'

'Sanctuary from what?' he asked. 'What is so sudden . . . and urgent?'

I sighed. I said with as little heat as possible, 'Gordon Quint tried to kill me.'

Gordon Quint was Ginnie's husband. Ellis was their son.

It struck Charles silent, open mouthed: and it took a great deal to do that.

After a while I said, 'When they adjourned the trial I went home by train and taxi. Gordon Quint was waiting there in Pont Square for me. God knows how long he'd been there, how long he would have waited, but anyway, he was there, with an iron bar.' I swallowed. 'He aimed it at my head, but I sort of ducked, and it hit my shoulder. He tried again . . . Well, this mechanical hand has its uses. I closed it on his wrist and put into practice some of the judo I've spent so many hours learning, and I tumbled him onto his back . . . and he was screaming at me all the time that I'd killed Ginnie . . . I'd killed her.'

'*Sid.*'

'He was half mad . . . raving, really . . . He said I'd destroyed his whole family. I'd destroyed all their lives . . . he swore I would die for it . . . that he would get me . . . get me . . . I don't think he knew what he was saying, it just poured out of him.'

Charles said dazedly, 'So what did you do?'

'The taxi driver was still there, looking stunned, so . . . er . . . I got back into the taxi.'

'You got back . . .? But . . . what about Gordon?'

'I left him there. Lying on the pavement. Screaming revenge . . . starting to stand up . . . waving the iron bar. I . . . er . . . I don't think I'll go home tonight, if I can stay here.'

Charles said faintly, 'Of course you can stay. It's

taken for granted. You told me once that this was your home.'

'Yeah.'

'Then believe it.'

I did believe it, or I wouldn't have gone there. Charles and his certainties had in the past saved me from inner disintegration, and my reliance on him had oddly been strengthened, not evaporated, by the collapse of my marriage to his daughter Jenny, and our divorce.

Aynsford offered respite. I would go back soon enough to defuse Gordon Quint; I would swear an oath in court and tear a man to shreds; I would hug Linda Ferns and, if I were in time, make Rachel laugh; but for this one night I would sleep soundly in Charles's house in my own accustomed room – and let the dry well of mental stamina refill.

Charles said, 'Did Gordon . . . er . . . hurt you, with his bar?'

'A bruise or two.'

'I know your sort of bruises.'

I sighed again. 'I think . . . um . . . he's cracked a bone. In my arm.'

His gaze flew instantly to the left arm, the plastic job.

'No,' I said, 'the other one.'

Aghast, he said, 'Your *right* arm?'

'Well, yeah. But only the ulna, which goes from the little finger side of the wrist up to the elbow. Not the radius as well, luckily. The radius will act as a natural splint.'

'But *Sid* . . .'

'Better than my skull. I had the choice.'

'How can you *laugh* about it?'

'A bloody bore, isn't it?' I smiled without stress. 'Don't *worry* so, Charles. It'll heal. I broke the same bone worse once before, when I was racing.'

'But you had two hands then.'

'Yes, so I did. So would you mind picking up that damned heavy brandy decanter and sloshing half a pint of anaesthetic into a glass?'

Wordlessly he got to his feet and complied. I thanked him. He nodded. End of transaction.

When he was again sitting down, he said, 'So the taxi driver was a witness.'

'The taxi driver is a "don't-get-involved" man.'

'But if he *saw* . . . He must have heard . . .'

'Blind and deaf, he insisted he was.' I drank fiery neat liquid gratefully. 'Anyway, that suits me fine.'

'But, Sid . . .'

'Look,' I said reasonably, 'what would you have me do? Complain? Prosecute? Gordon Quint is normally a level-headed worthy sixty-ish citizen. He's not your average murderer, Besides, he's your own personal long-time friend, and I, too, have eaten in his house. But he already hates me for attacking Ellis, the light of his life, and he'd not long learned that Ginnie, his adored wife, had killed herself because she couldn't bear what lies ahead. So how do you think Gordon feels?' I paused. 'I'm just glad he didn't succeed in smashing my brains in. And, if you can believe it, I'm almost as glad for *his* sake that he didn't, as for my own.'

Charles shook his head resignedly.

'Grief can be dangerous,' I said.

He couldn't dispute it. Deadly revenge was as old as time.

We sat companionably in silence. I drank brandy and felt marginally saner. Knots of tension relaxed in my stomach. I made various resolutions to give up chasing the deadlier crooks – but I'd made resolutions like that before, and hadn't kept them.

I'd stopped asking myself why I did it. There were hundreds of other ways of passing the time and earning one's keep. Other ex-jockeys became trainers or commentators or worked in racing in official capacities and only I, it seemed, felt impelled to swim round the hidden fringes, attempting to sort out doubts and worries for people who for any reason didn't want to bother the police or the racing authorities.

There was a need for me and what I could do, or I would have sat around idle, twiddling my thumbs. Instead, even in the present general climate of ostracism, I had more offers of work than I could accept.

Most jobs took me less than a week, particularly those that involved looking into someone's credit and credibility rating: bookmakers asked me to do that frequently, before taking on new account customers, and trainers paid me fees to assure them that if they bought expensive two-year-olds for new owners at the Sales, they wouldn't be left with broken promises and a mountain of debt. I'd checked on all sorts of proposed business plans and saved a lot of people from confidence tricksters, and I'd uncovered absconding debtors, and thieves of all sorts, and had proved a confounded nuisance to imaginative felons.

People had sobbed on my shoulders from joy and deliverance: others had threatened and battered to make me quit: Linda Ferns would hug me and Gordon Quint hate me; and I also had two more investigations in hand that I'd spent too little time on. So why didn't I give it up and change to a life of quiet safe financial management, which I wasn't bad at either? I felt the effects of the iron bar from neck to fingers . . . and didn't know the answer.

The mobile phone on my belt buzzed and I answered it as before, finding on the line the senior lawyer I'd talked to in the corridor in the law courts.

'Sid, this is Davis Tatum. I've news for you,' he said.

'Give me your number and I'll call you back.'

'Oh? Oh, OK.' He read off his number, which I copied as before, and also as before I borrowed Charles's phone on the desk to get back to square one.

'Sid,' said Tatum, coming as usual straight to the point, 'Ellis Quint is changing his plea from not guilty to guilty by reason of diminished responsibility. It seems his mother's powerful statement of no confidence in his innocence has had a laxative effect on the bowels of the counsel for the defence.'

'Jeez,' I said.

Tatum chuckled. I imagined his double chin wobbling. He said, 'The trial will now be adjourned for a week to allow expert psychiatric witnesses to be briefed. In other words, you don't have to turn up tomorrow.'

'Good.'

'But I hope you will.'

'How do you mean?'

'There's a job for you.'

'What sort of job?'

'Investigating, of course. What else? I'd like to meet you somewhere privately.'

'All right,' I said, 'but sometime tomorrow I have to go to Kent to see the child, Rachel Ferns. She's back in hospital and it doesn't sound good.'

'Hell.'

'Yeah.'

'Where are you?' he asked. 'The Press are looking for you.'

'They can wait a day.'

'I told the people from *The Pump* that after the mauling they've given you they haven't a prayer of you talking to them.'

'I appreciate that,' I said, smiling.

He chuckled. 'About tomorrow . . .'

'I'll go to Kent in the morning,' I said. 'I don't know how long I'll stay, it depends on Rachel. How about five o'clock in London? Would that do you? The end of your business day.'

'Right. Where? Not in my office. How about your place? No, perhaps not, if *The Pump*'s after you.'

'How about, say, the bar leading to the second-floor restaurant of the Le Meridien Hotel in Piccadilly?'

'I don't know it.'

'All the better.'

'If I need to change it,' he said, 'can I still get you on your mobile phone?'

'Always.'

'Good. See you tomorrow.'

I replaced Charles's receiver and sat on the gold armchair as before. Charles looked at the mobile instrument I'd lain this time on the table beside my glass and asked the obvious question.

'Why do you ring them back? Why don't you just talk?'

'Well,' I said, 'someone is listening to this gadget.'

'*Listening?*'

I explained about the insecurity of open radio transmission, that allowed anyone clever and expert to hear what they shouldn't.

Charles said, 'How do you know someone's listening to you?'

'A lot of small things people have recently learned that I haven't told them.'

'Who is it?'

'I don't actually know. Someone has also accessed my computer over the phone lines. I don't know who did that, either. It's disgustingly easy nowadays – but again, only if you're expert – to suss out people's private passwords and read their secret files.'

He said with slight impatience, 'Computers are beyond me.'

'I've had to learn,' I said, grinning briefly. 'A bit different from scudding over hurdles at Plumpton on a wet day.'

'Everything you do astounds me.'

'I wish I was still racing.'

'Yes, I know. But if you were, you'd anyway be coming to the end of it soon, wouldn't you? How old are you now? Thirty-four?'

I nodded. Thirty-five loomed.

'Not many top jump jockeys go on much after that.'

'You put things so delightfully bluntly, Charles.'

'You're of more use to more people the way you are.'

Charles tended to give me pep talks when he thought I needed them. I could never work out how he knew. He'd said something once about my looking like a brick wall: that when I shut out the world and retreated into myself, things were bad. Maybe he was right. Retreat inwards meant for me not retreating outwardly, and I supposed I'd learned the technique almost from birth.

Jenny, my loved and lost wife, had said she couldn't

live with it. She'd wanted me to give up race-riding and become a softer shelled person, and when I wouldn't – or couldn't – we had shaken acridly apart. She had recently remarried, and this time she'd tied herself not to a thin dark-haired risk-taking bundle of complexes, but to a man to fit her needs, a safe, greying, sweet-natured uncomplicated fellow with a knighthood. Jenny, the warring unhappy Mrs Halley, was now serenely Lady Wingham. A photograph of her with her handsome beaming Sir Anthony stood in a silver frame next to the telephone on Charles's desk.

'How's Jenny?' I asked politely.

'Fine,' Charles answered without expression.

'Good.'

'He's a bore, after you,' Charles observed.

'You can't say such things.'

'I can say what I bloody well like in my own house.'

In harmony and mutual regard we passed a peaceful evening, disturbed only by five more calls on my mobile phone, all demanding to know, with varying degrees of peremptoriness, where they could find Sid Halley.

I said each time, 'This is an answering service. Leave your number and we'll pass on your message.'

All of the callers, it seemed, worked for newspapers, a fact that particularly left me frowning.

'I don't know where they all got this number from,' I told Charles. 'It's not in any directory. I give it only to people I'm working for, so they can reach me day or night, and only to others whose calls I wouldn't want to miss. I tell them it's a private line for their use only. I don't hand this number out on printed cards, and I don't have it on my writing paper. Quite often I re-route calls to this phone from my phone in the flat, but I didn't today because of Gordon Quint bashing away outside and preventing me from going in. So how do half the newspapers in London know it?'

'How will you find out?' Charles asked.

'Um . . . engage Sid Halley to look into it, I dare say'.

Charles laughed. I felt uneasy, all the same. Someone had been listening on that number, and now someone had broadcast it. It wasn't that my phone conversations were excessively secret – and I'd started the semi-exclusive number anyway solely so that the machine didn't buzz unnecessarily at awkward moments – but now I had a sense that someone was deliberately crowding me. Tapping into my computer – which wouldn't get anyone far, as I knew a lot of defences. Assaulting me electronically. *Stalking.*

Enough was enough. Five newspapers were too much. Sid Halley, as I'd said, would have to investigate his own case.

Charles's long-time live-in housekeeper, Mrs Cross, all dimples and delight, cooked us a simple supper and fussed over me comfortably like a hen. I guiltily found her a bit smothering sometimes, but always sent her a card for her birthday.

I went to bed early and found that, as usual, Mrs

Cross had left warm welcoming lights on in my room and had put out fresh pyjamas and fluffy towels.

A pity the day's troubles couldn't be as easily cosseted into oblivion.

I undressed and brushed my teeth and eased off the artificial hand. My left arm ended uselessly four inches below the elbow; a familiar punctuation, but still a sort of bereavement.

My right arm now twinged violently at every use.

Damn the lot, I thought.

CHAPTER TWO

The morning brought little improvement.

I sometimes used a private chauffeur-driven car hire firm based in London to ferry around people and things I wanted to keep away from prying eyes and, consequently, waking to a couple of faulty arms, I telephoned from Charles's secure number and talked to my friends at TeleDrive.

'Bob?' I said. 'I need to get from north-west of Oxford to Kent, Canterbury. There'll be a couple of short stops on the journey. And, sometime this afternoon, a return to London. Can anyone do it at such short notice?'

'Give me the address,' he said briefly. 'We're on our way.'

I breakfasted with Charles. That is to say, we sat in the dining-room where Mrs Cross, in her old-fashioned way, had set out toast, coffee and cereals and a warming dish of scrambled eggs.

Charles thought mornings hadn't begun without scrambled eggs. He ate his on toast and eyed me drinking coffee left-handedly. From long acquaintance with my preference for no fuss, he made no comment on the consequences of iron bars.

He was reading a broad-sheet newspaper which, as he showed me, was making a good-taste meal of Ginnie Quint's death. Her pleasant, smiling face inappropriately spread across two columns. I shut out of my mind any image of what she might look like sixteen floors down.

Charles said, reading aloud, ' "Friends say she appeared depressed about her son's forthcoming trial. Her husband, Gordon, was unavailable for comment." In other words, the Press couldn't find him.'

Ordeal by newsprint, I thought; the latter-day torture.

'Seriously, Sid,' Charles said in his most calm civilised voice, 'was Gordon's rage at you transient or . . . er . . . obsessive?'

'Seriously,' I echoed him, 'I don't know.' I sighed. 'I should think it's too soon to tell. Gordon himself probably doesn't know.'

'Do take care, Sid.'

'Sure.' I sorted through the flurry of impressions I'd gathered in the brief seconds of violence in Pont Square. 'I don't know where Ginnie was when she jumped,' I said, 'but I don't think Gordon was with her. I mean, when he leaped at me he was wearing country clothes. Work-day clothes: mud on his boots, corduroy trousers, old tweed jacket, open-necked blue shirt. He hadn't been staying in any sixteen-storey hotel. And the metal bar he hit me with . . . it wasn't a smooth rod, it was a five-foot piece of angle iron, the sort you thread wire through or fencing. I saw the holes in it.'

Charles stared.

I said, 'I'd say he was at home in Berkshire when he was told about Ginnie. I think if I'd loitered around to search, I would have found Gordon's Land-Rover parked near Pont Square.'

Gordon Quint, though a landowner, was a hands-on custodian of his multiple acres. He drove tractors, scythed weeds to clear streams, worked alongside his men to repair his boundaries, re-fence his sheep fields and thin out his woodlands, enjoying both the physical labour and the satisfaction of a job most competently done.

I knew him also as self-admiring and as expecting – and receiving – deference from everyone, including Ginnie. It pleased him to be a generous host while leaving his guests in no doubt of his superior worth.

The man I'd seen in Pont Square, all 'squire' manner stripped away, had been a raw, hurt, *outraged* and oddly more genuine person than the Gordon I'd known before: but until I learned for sure which way the explosively tossed-up bricks of his nature would come down, I would keep away from fencing posts and any other agricultural hardware he might be travelling with.

I told Charles I'd engaged TeleDrive to come and pick me up. To his raised eyebrows I explained I would put the cost against expenses. Whose expenses? General running expenses, I said.

'Is Mrs Ferns paying you?' Charles neutrally asked.

'Not any more.'

'Who is, exactly?' He liked me to make a profit. I did, but he seldom believed it.

'I don't starve,' I said, drinking my coffee. 'Have you ever tried three or four eggs whipped up in mushroom soup? Instant mushroom omelette, not at all bad.'

'Disgusting,' Charles said.

'You get a different perspective, living alone.'

'You need a new wife,' Charles said. 'What about that girl who used to share a flat with Jenny in Oxford?'

'Louise McInnes?'

'Yes. I thought you and she were having an affair.'

No one had affairs any more. Charles's words were half a century out of date. But though the terms might now be different, the meaning was eternal.

'A summer picnic,' I said. 'The frosts of winter killed it off.'

'Why?'

'What she felt for me was more curiosity than love.'

He understood that completely. Jenny had talked about me so long and intimately to her friend Louise, mostly to my detriment, that I recognised – in retrospect – that the friend had chiefly been fascinated in checking out the information personally. It had been a lighthearted passage from mating to parting. Nice while it lasted, but no roots.

When the car came for me I thanked Charles for his sanctuary.

'Any time,' he said, nodding.

We parted as usual without physically touching. Eye contact said it all.

Getting the driver to thread his way back and forth through the maze of shopping dead-ends in the town of Kingston in Surrey, I acquired six dressing-up party wigs from a carnival store and an angel fish in a plastic tub from a pet shop; and, thus armed, arrived eventually at the children's cancer ward that held Rachel Ferns.

Linda greeted my arrival with glittering tears, but her daughter still lived. Indeed, in one of those unpredictable quirks that made leukaemia such a roller-coaster of hope and despair, Rachel was marginally better. She was awake, semi-sitting up in bed and pleased at my arrival.

'Did you bring the angel fish?' she demanded by way of greeting.

I held up the plastic bucket, which swung from my plastic wrist. Linda took it and removed the watertight lid, showing her daughter the shining black-and-silver fish that swam vigorously inside.

Rachel relaxed. 'I'm going to call him Sid,' she said.

She'd been a lively, blonde, pretty child once, according to her photographs: now she seemed all huge eyes in a bald head. Lassitude and anaemia had made her frighteningly frail.

When her mother had first called me in to investigate an attack on Rachel's pony, the illness had been in remission, the dragon temporarily sleeping. Rachel had become someone special to me and I'd given her a fish tank complete with lights, aeration, water plants, Gothic castle arches, sand and brilliant tropical swimming inhabitants. Linda had wept. Rachel had spent hours getting to know her new friends' habits; the ones that skulked in corners, the one who bossed all the rest. Half of the fish were called Sid.

The fish tank stood in the Ferns' sitting-room at home and it seemed uncertain now whether Rachel would see the new Sid among his mates.

It was there, in the comfortable middle-sized room furnished with unaggressively expensive modern sofas, with glass-topped end tables and stained-glass Tiffany lamps, that I had first met my clients, Linda and Rachel Ferns.

There were no books in the room, only a few magazines; dress fashions and horses. Shiny striped curtains in crimson and cream; geometrically patterned carpet in merging fawn and grey; flower prints on pale pink walls. Overall the impression was a degree of lack of coordination which probably indicated impulsive inhabitants without strongly formed characters. The Ferns weren't 'old' money, I concluded, but there appeared to be plenty of it.

Linda Ferns, on the telephone, had begged me to come. Five or six ponies in the district had been attacked by vandals, and one of the ponies belonged to her daughter, Rachel. The police hadn't found out who the vandals were and now months had gone by, and her daughter was still very distressed and would I *please*, *please*, come and see if I could help.

'I've heard you're my only hope. I'll pay you, of course. I'll pay you *anything* if you help Rachel. She has these terrible nightmares. *Please*.'

I mentioned my fee.

'Anything,' she said.

She hadn't told me, before I arrived in the far-flung village beyond Canterbury, that Rachel was ill unto death.

When I met the huge-eyed bald-headed slender child she shook hands with me gravely.

'Are you really Sid Halley?' she asked.

I nodded.

'Mum said you would come. Daddy said you didn't work for kids.'

'I do sometimes.'

'My hair is growing,' she said; and I could see the thin fine blonde fuzz just showing over the pale scalp.

'I'm glad.'

She nodded. 'Quite often I wear a wig, but they itch. Do you mind if I don't?'

'Not in the least.'

'I have leukaemia,' she said calmly.

'I see.'

She studied my face, a child old beyond her age, as I'd found all sick young people to be.

'You will find out who killed Silverboy, won't you?'

'I'll try,' I said. 'How did he die?'

'No, no,' Linda interrupted. 'Don't ask her. I'll tell you. It upsets her. Just say you'll sort them out, those *pigs*. And Rachel, you take Pegotty out into the garden and push him round so that he can see the flowers.'

Pegotty, it transpired, was a contented-looking baby strapped into a buggy. Rachel without demur pushed him out into the garden and could presently be seen through the window giving him a close-up acquaintance with an azalea.

Linda Ferns watched and wept the first of many tears.

'She needs a bone marrow transplant,' she said, trying to suppress sobs. 'You'd think it would be simple, but no one so far can find a match to her, not even in the international register set up by the Anthony Nolan Trust.'

I said inadequately, 'I'm sorry.'

'Her father and I are divorced,' Linda said. 'We divorced five years ago, and he's married again.' She spoke without bitterness. 'These things happen.'

'Yes,' I said.

I was at the Ferns' house early in a June of languorous days and sweet-smelling roses, a time for the lotus, not horrors.

'A bunch of vandals,' Linda said with a fury that set her whole body trembling, 'they maimed a lot of ponies in Kent . . . in this area particularly . . . so that poor loving kids went out into their paddocks and found their much loved ponies *mutilated*. What sick, sick mind would *blind* a poor inoffensive pony that had never done anyone any harm? Three ponies round here were blinded and others had had knives stuck up their back passages.' She blinked on her tears. 'Rachel was terribly upset. All the children for miles were crying inconsolably. And the police couldn't find who'd done any of it.'

'Was Silverboy blinded?' I asked.

'No . . . no . . . It was worse . . . For Rachel, it was worse. She found him, you see . . . out in the paddock . . .' Linda openly sobbed. 'Rachel wanted to sleep in a makeshift stable . . . a lean-to shed, really. She wanted to sleep there at nights with Silverboy tied up there beside her, and I wouldn't let her. She's been ill for nearly three years. It's such a *dreadful* disease, and I feel so helpless . . .' She wiped her eyes, plucking a tissue from a half-empty box. 'She keeps saying it wasn't my fault, but I know she thinks Silverboy would be alive if I'd let her sleep out there.'

'What happened to him?' I asked neutrally.

Linda shook her head miserably, unable still to tell me. She was a pretty woman in a conventional thirty-something way: trim figure, well-washed short fair hair, all the health and beauty magazine tips come to admirable life. Only the dullness in the eyes and the intermittent vibrations in many of her muscles spoke plainly of the long strain of emotional buffeting still assailing her.

'She went out,' she said eventually, 'even though it was bitter cold, and beginning to rain . . . February . . . she always went to see that his water trough was filled and clean and not frozen over . . . and I'd made her put on warm clothes and gloves and a scarf and a real thick woolly hat . . . and she came back running, and screaming . . . *screaming* . . .'

I waited through Linda's unbearable memories.

She said starkly, 'Rachel found his *foot*.'

There was a moment of utter stillness, an echo of the stunned disbelief of that dreadful morning.

'It was in all the papers,' Linda said,

I moved and nodded. I'd read – months ago – about the blinded Kent ponies. I'd been busy, inattentive: hadn't absorbed names or details, hadn't realised that one of the ponies had lost a foot.

'I've found out since you telephoned,' I said, 'that round the country, not just here in Kent, there have been another half a dozen or so scattered vandalising attacks on ponies and horses in fields.'

She said unhappily, 'I did see a paragraph about a horse in Lancashire, but I threw the paper away so that Rachel wouldn't read it. Every time anything reminds her of Silverboy, she has a whole week of nightmares. She wakes up sobbing. She comes into my bed, shivering, crying. Please, please find out why . . . find out *who* . . . She's so ill . . . and although she's in remission just now and able to live fairly normally, it almost certainly won't last. The doctors say she needs the transplant.'

I said, 'Does Rachel know any of the other children whose ponies were attacked?'

Linda shook her head. 'Most of them belonged to the Pony Club, I think, but Rachel didn't feel well enough to join the Club. She loved Silverboy – her father gave him to her – but all she could do was sit in the saddle while we led her round. He was a nice quiet pony, a very nice-looking grey with a darker smoky-coloured mane. Rachel called him Silverboy, but he had a long pedigree name really. She needed something to *love*, you see, and she wanted a pony so *much*.'

I asked, 'Did you keep any of the newspaper accounts of Silverboy and the other local ponies being attacked? If you did, can I see them?'

'Yes,' she answered doubtfully, 'but I don't see how they could help. They didn't help the police.'

'They'd be a start,' I said.

'All right, then.' She left the room and after a while returned with a small blue suitcase, the size for stowing under the seats of aircraft. 'Everything's in here,' she said, passing me the case, 'including a tape of a programme a television company made. Rachel and I are in it. You won't lose it, will you? We never show it, but I wouldn't want to lose it.' She blinked against tears. 'It was actually the only good thing that happened.

Ellis Quint came to see the children and he was utterly sweet with them. Rachel loved him. He was so *kind.*'

'I know him quite well,' I said. 'If anyone could comfort the children, he could.'

'A really *nice* man,' Linda said.

I took the blue suitcase with its burden of many small tragedies back with me to London and spent indignant hours reading muted accounts of a degree of vandalism that must have been mind-destroying when fresh and bloody and discovered by loving children.

The twenty-minute video tape showed Ellis Quint at his best: the gentle sympathetic healer of unbearable sorrows; the sensible, caring commentator urging the police to treat these crimes with the seriousness given to murders. How good he was, I thought, at pitching his responses exactly right. He put his arms round Rachel and talked to her without sentimentality, not mentioning, until right at the end of the programme when the children were off the screen, that for Rachel Ferns the loss of her pony was just one more intolerable blow in a life already full of burdens.

For that programme, Rachel had chosen to wear the pretty blonde wig that gave her back her pre-chemotherapy looks. Ellis, as a final dramatic impact, had shown for a few seconds a photo of Rachel bald and vulnerable: an ending poignant to devastation.

I hadn't seen the programme when it had been broadcast: from the March date on the tape, I'd been away in America trying to find an absconding owner who'd left a monstrous training account unpaid. There were, anyway, many of Ellis's programmes I hadn't seen: he presented his twenty-minute twice-weekly journalistic segments as part of an hour-long sports news medley, and was too often on the screen for any one appearance to be especially fanfared.

Meeting Ellis, as I often did at the races, I told him about Linda Ferns calling me in, and asked him if he'd learned any more on the subject of who had mutilated the Kent ponies.

'My dear old Sid,' he said, smiling, 'all of that was months ago, wasn't it?'

'The ponies were vandalised in January and February and your programme was aired in March.'

'And it's now June, right?' He shook his head, neither distressed nor surprised. 'You know what my life's like, I have *researchers* digging out stories for me. Television is insatiably hungry. Of course, if there were any more discoveries about these ponies, I would have been told, and I would have done a follow-up, but I've heard nothing.'

I said, 'Rachel Ferns, who has leukaemia, still has nightmares.'

'Poor little kid.'

'She said you were very kind.'

'Well . . .' He made a ducking, self-deprecating movement of his head, 'It isn't so very difficult. Actually that programme did marvels for my ratings.' He paused. 'Sid, do you know anything about this bookmaker kickback scandal I'm supposed to be doing an exposé on next week?'

'Nothing at all,' I regretted. 'But Ellis, going back to the mutilations, did you chase up those other scattered cases of foals and two-year-old thoroughbreds that suffered from vandalism?'

He frowned lightly, shaking his head. 'The researchers didn't think them worth more than a mention or two. It was copycat stuff. I mean, there wasn't anything as strong as that story about the children.' He grinned. 'There were no heartstrings attached to the others.'

'You're a cynic,' I said.

'Aren't we all?'

We had been close friends for years, Ellis and I. We had ridden against each other in races, he as a charismatic amateur, I as a dedicated pro, but both with the inner fire that made hurtling over large jumps on semi-wild half-ton horses at thirty miles an hour seem a wholly reasonable way of passing as many afternoons as possible.

Thinking, after three or four months of no results from the police or the Ellis Quint programme, that I would probably fail also in the search for vandals, I nevertheless did my best to earn my fee by approaching the problem crabwise, from the side, not by asking questions of the owners of the ponies, but of the newspapermen who had written the columns in the papers.

I did it methodically on the telephone, starting with

the local Kent papers, then chasing up the by-line reporters in the London dailies. Most of the replies were the same: the story had originated from a news agency that supplied all papers with condensed factual information. Follow-ups and interpretation were the business of the papers themselves.

Among the newspapers Linda Fern had given me, *The Pump* had stirred up most disgust, and after about six phone calls I ran to earth the man who'd practically burned holes in the page with the heat of his prose; Kevin Mills, *The Pump*'s chief bleeding hearts reporter.

'A jar?' he said, to my invitation. 'Don't see why not.'

He met me in a pub (nice anonymous surroundings) and he told me he'd personally been down to Kent on that story. He'd interviewed all the children and their parents and also a fierce lady who ran one of the branches of the Pony Club, and he'd pestered the police until they'd thrown him out.

'Zilch,' he said, downing a double gin and tonic. 'No one saw a thing. All those ponies were out in fields and all of them were attacked some time between sunset and dawn, which in January and February gave the vandals hours and hours to do the job and vamoose.'

'All dark, though,' I said.

He shook his head. 'They were all done over on fine nights, near the full moon in each month.'

'How many, do you remember?'

'Four altogether in January. Two of them were

blinded. Two were mares with torn knife wounds up their . . . well, *birth passages*, as our squeamish editor had me put it.'

'And February?'

'One blinded, two more chopped up mares, one cut-off foot. A poor little girl found the foot near the water trough where her pony used to drink. Ellis Quint did a brilliant TV programme about it. Didn't you see it?'

'I was in America, but I've heard about it since.'

'There were trailers of that programme all week. Almost the whole nation watched it. It made a hell of an impact. That pony was the last one in Kent, as far as I know. The police think it was a bunch of local thugs who got the wind up when there was so much fuss. And people stopped turning ponies out into unguarded fields, see?'

I ordered him another double. He was middle-aged, half bald, doing nicely as to paunch. He wiped an untidy moustache on the back of his hand and said that in his career he'd interviewed so many parents of raped and murdered girls that the ponies had been almost a relief.

I asked him about the later copycat attacks on thoroughbreds in other places, not Kent.

'Copycat?' he repeated. 'So they say.'

'But?' I prompted.

He drank, thought it over, confided.

'All the others,' he said, 'are not in bunches, like Kent. As far as I know – and there may be still others – there were about five very young horses, foals and yearlings, that had things done to them, bad enough mostly for them to have to be put down, but none of them was blinded. One had his muzzle hacked off. None of them were mares. But . . .' He hesitated, sure of his facts, I thought, but not of how I would react to them.

'Go on.'

'See, three others were two-year-olds, and all of those had a foot off.'

I felt the same revulsion that I saw in his face.

'One in March,' he said. 'One in April. One last month.'

'Not,' I said slowly, 'at the full moon?'

'Not precisely. Just on moonlit nights.'

'But why haven't you written about it?'

'I get sent to major disasters,' he said patiently. 'Air crashes, multiple deaths, dozens of accidents and murders. Some nutter driving around chopping off a horse's foot now and again – it's not my absolute priority, but maybe I'll get round to it. The news agency hasn't picked up on it, but I tend to read provincial papers. Old habit. There has been just a par or two here and there about animal vandals. It's always happening. Horses, sheep, dogs – weirdos get their mucky hands on them. Come to think of it, though, if there's another one this month I'll insist on giving it the both-barrel treatment. And now don't you go feeding this to other papers. I want my scoop.'

'Silence,' I promised, 'if . . .'

He asked suspiciously 'If what?'

'If you could give me a list of the people whose thoroughbreds have been damaged.'

He said cautiously, 'It'll cost you.'

'Done,' I said, and we agreed both on a fee and on my giving him first chance at any story I might come up with.

He fulfilled his commitment that same afternoon by sending a motorbike courier bearing a sealed brown envelope containing photocopies of several inconspicuous small paragraphs culled from provincial papers in Liverpool, Reading, Shrewsbury, Manchester, Birmingham and York. All the papers gave the names and vague addresses of the owners of vandalised thoroughbreds, so I set off by car and visited them.

Four days later, when I returned to Linda Ferns' house in Kent, I had heard enough about man's inhumanity to horses to last me for life. The injuries inflicted, from the hacked-off muzzle onwards, were truly beyond comprehension but, compared with the three two-year-olds, were all random and without pattern. It was the severed feet that were connected.

'I came across his foot by the water trough in the field,' one woman said, her eyes screwing up at the memory. 'I couldn't *believe* it. Just a *foot.* Tell you the truth, I brought up my breakfast. He was a really nice two-year-old colt.' She swallowed. 'He wasn't standing anywhere near his foot. The off-fore, it was. He'd wandered away on three legs and he was eating grass. Just *eating*, as if nothing had happened. He didn't seem to feel any pain.'

'What did you do?' I asked.

'I called the vet. He came . . . He gave *me* a tranquilliser. He said I needed it more than the colt did. He looked after everything for me.'

'Was the colt insured?' I asked.

She took no offence at the question. I guessed it had been asked a dozen times already. She said there had been no insurance. They had bred the two-year-old themselves. They had been going to race him later in the year. They had been to Cheltenham races and had backed the winner of the Gold Cup, a great day, and the very next morning . . .

I asked her for the vet's name and address, and I went to see him at his home.

'How was the foot taken off?' I asked.

He wrinkled his forehead. 'I don't rightly know. It was neat. The colt had bled very little. There was a small pool of blood on the grass about a yard away from the foot, and that was all. The colt himself let me walk right up to him. He looked calm and normal, except that his off-fore ended at the fetlock.'

'Was it done with an axe?'

He hesitated. 'I'd say more like a machete. Just the one cut, fast and clean. Whoever did it knew just where to aim for, unless he was simply lucky.'

'Did you tell the police?'

'Sure. A detective sergeant came out. He vomited

too. Then I called the knackers and put the colt down. Bloody vandals! I'd like to cut off *their* foot, see if they liked life with a stump.' He remembered suddenly about my own sliced off hand, and reddened, looking confused and embarrassed. There had been a much publicised court case about my hand. Everyone knew what had happened. I had finally stopped wincing visibly when people referred to it.

'It's all right,' I said mildly.

'I'm sorry. My big mouth . . .'

'Do you think the colt's amputation was done by a vet? By any sort of surgical expert? Was it done with a scalpel? Was the colt given a local anaesthetic?'

He said, disturbed, 'I don't know the answers. I'd just say that whoever did it was used to handling horses. That colt was loose in the field, though wearing a head-collar.'

I went to see the detective sergeant, who looked as if he might throw up again at the memory.

'I see a lot of injured people. Dead bodies, too,' he said, 'but that was different. Mindless. Fair turned my stomach.'

The police had found no culprit. It had been an isolated event, not part of a pattern. The only report they'd had was of the presence of a blue Land-Rover driving away along the lane from the colt's field; and Land-Rovers were two a penny in the countryside. Case not closed, but also not being actively investigated. The colt and his hoof had long gone to the glue factory.

'Are there any photographs?' I asked.

The sergeant said that the photographs were a police matter, not open to the general public.

'I do know who you are,' he said, not abrasively, 'but to us you're the general public. Sorry.'

The colt's owner, consulted, said she had been too upset to want photographs.

I drove onwards, northwards to Lancashire, into a gale of anger. Big, blustery and impressively furious, a hard competent large-scale farmer let loose his roaring sense of injustice, yelling in my face, spraying me with spittle, jabbing the air with a rigid forefinger, pushing his chin forward in a classic animal gesture of aggression.

'Best colt I ever owned,' he bellowed. 'He cost me a packet, but he was a good 'un. Breeding, conformation, the lot. And he was *fast*, I'll tell you. He was going to Newmarket the next week.' He mentioned a prestigious trainer who I knew wouldn't have accepted rubbish. 'A good 'un,' the farmer repeated. 'And then the sodding police asked if I'd killed him for the insurance. I ask you! He wasn't insured, I told them. They said I couldn't *prove* he wasn't insured. Did you know that? Did you know you can prove something *is* insured, but you can't prove it *isn't*? Did you know that?'

I said I'd heard it was so.

'I told them to bugger off. They weren't interested in finding who took my colt's foot off, only in proving

I did it myself. They made me that *angry* . . .' His words failed him. I'd met many people unjustly accused of setting fires, battering children, stealing, and taking bribes, and by then I knew the vocal vibrations of truly outraged innocence. The angry farmer, I would have staked all on it, had not taken the foot off his own colt, and I told him so. Some of his anger abated into surprise. 'So you *believe* me?'

'I sure do,' I nodded. 'The point is, who knew you'd bought a fine fast colt that you had at your farm in a field?'

'Who knew?' He suddenly looked guilty, as if he'd already had to face an unpalatable fact. 'I'd blown my mouth off a bit. Half the country knew. And I'd been boasting about him at Aintree, the day before the Grand National. I was at one of those sponsors' lunch things – Topline Foods, it was – and the colt was fine that night. I saw him in the morning. And it was the next night, after the National, that he was got at.'

He had taken his own colour photographs (out of distrust of the police) and he showed them to me readily.

'The off-fore,' he said, pointing to a close-up of the severed foot. 'He was cut just below the fetlock. Almost through the joint. You can see the white ends of the bones.'

The photographs jolted. It didn't help that I'd seen my own left wrist in much the same condition. I said, 'What was your vet's opinion?'

'Same as mine.'

I went to see the vet. One chop, he said. Only one. No missed shots. Straight through at the leg's most vulnerable point.

'What weapon?'

He didn't know.

I pressed onwards to Yorkshire where, barely a month earlier, at the time of the York Spring Meeting, a dark brown two-year-old colt had been deprived of his off-fore foot on a moonlit night. One chop. No insurance. Sick and angry owners. No clues.

These owners were a stiff-upper-lip couple with elderly manners and ancient immutable values who were as deeply bewildered as repelled by the level of evil that would for no clear reason destroy a thing of beauty; in this case, the fluid excellence of a fleet glossy equine princeling.

'*Why?*' they asked me insistently. '*Why* would anyone do such a pointlessly wicked thing?'

I had no answer. I prompted them only to talk, to let out their pain and deprivation. I got them to talk, and I listened.

The wife said, 'We had such a lovely week. Every year we have people to stay for the York Spring Meeting . . . because, as you can see, this is quite a large house . . . so we have six or eight friends staying, and we get in extra staff and have a party – such fun, you see – and this year the weather was perfect and we all had a great time.'

'Successful, don't you know,' said her husband, nodding.

'Dear Ellis Quint was one of our guests,' smiled the hostess, 'and he lifted everyone's spirits in that easy way of his so that it seemed we spent the whole week laughing. He was filming for one of his television programmes at York races, so we were all invited behind the scenes and enjoyed it all so much. And then . . . then . . . the very night after all our guests had left . . . well . . .'

'Jenkins came and told us – Jenkins is our groom – he told us while we were sitting at breakfast, that our colt . . . our colt . . .'

'We have three brood-mares,' his wife said. 'We love to see the foals and yearlings out in the fields, running free, you know . . . and usually we sell the yearlings, but that colt was so beautiful that we kept him, and he was going into training soon . . . All our guests had admired him.'

'Jenkins had made a splendid job of breaking him in.'

'Jenkins was in *tears*,' the wife said. 'Jenkins! A tough leathery old man. In *tears*.'

The husband said with difficulty, 'Jenkins found the foot by the gate, beside the water trough.'

His wife went on. 'Jenkins told us that Ellis had done a programme a few months ago about a pony's foot being cut off and the children being so devastated. So we wrote to Ellis about our colt and Ellis telephoned at once to say how *awful* for us. He couldn't have been nicer. Dear Ellis. But there wasn't anything he could do, of course, except sympathise.'

'No,' I agreed, and I felt only the faintest twitch of surprise that Ellis hadn't mentioned the York colt when I'd been talking to him less than a week earlier about Rachel Ferns.

CHAPTER THREE

Back in London I met Kevin Mills, the journalist from *The Pump*, at lunchtime in the same pub as before.

'It's time for both barrels,' I said.

He swigged his double gin. 'What have you discovered?'

I outlined the rest of the pattern, beyond what he'd told me about two-year-old colts on moonlit nights. One chop from something like a machete. Always the off-fore foot. Always near a water trough. No insurance. And always just after a major local race meeting: Cheltenham, the Gold Cup Festival; the Grand National at Liverpool; the Spring Meeting at York.

'And this Saturday, two days from now,' I said levelly, 'we have the Derby.'

He put his glass down slowly, and after a full silent minute said, 'What about the kid's pony?'

I shrugged resignedly. 'It was the first that we know of.'

'And it doesn't fit the pattern. Not a two-year-old colt, was he? And no major race meeting, was there?'

'The severed foot was by the water trough. The off-fore foot. Moon in the right quarter. One chop. No insurance.'

He frowned, thinking. 'Tell you what,' he said eventually, 'it's worth a *warning*. I'm not a sports writer, as you know, but I'll get the message into the paper somewhere. "Don't leave your two-year-old colts unguarded in open fields during and after the Epsom meeting." I don't think I can do more than that.'

'It might be enough.'

'Yeah. *If* all the owners of colts read *The Pump*.'

'It will be the talk of the racecourse. I'll arrange that.'

'On Derby Day?' he looked sceptical. 'Still, it will be better than nothing.' He drank again. 'What we really need to do is catch the bugger red-handed.'

We gloomily contemplated that impossibility. Roughly fifteen thousand thoroughbred foals were born each year in the British Isles. Half would be colts. Many of those at two would already be in training for Flat racing, tucked away safely in stables; but that still left a host unattended out of doors. By June, also, yearling colts, growing fast, could be mistaken at night for two-year-olds.

Nothing was safe from a determined vandal.

Kevin Mills went away to write his column and I travelled on to Kent to report to my clients.

'Have you found out *who*?' Linda demanded.

'Not yet.'

We sat by the sitting-room window again, watching Rachel push Pegotty in his buggy round the lawn, and I told her about the three colts and their shattered owners.

'Three more,' Linda repeated numbly. 'In March, April and May? And Silverboy in February?'

'That's right.'

'And what about *now*? This month . . . *June*?'

I explained about the warning to be printed in *The Pump*.

'I'm not going to tell Rachel about the other three,' Linda said. 'She wakes up screaming as it is.'

'I enquired into other injured horses all over England,' I said, 'but they were all hurt differently from each other. I think . . . well . . . that there are several different people involved. And, I don't think the thugs that blinded and cut the ponies round here had anything to do with Silverboy.'

Linda protested. 'But they must have done! There couldn't be *two* lots of vandals.'

'I think there were.'

She watched Rachel and Pegotty, the habitual tears not far away. Rachel was tickling the baby to make him laugh.

'I'd do anything to save my daughter,' Linda said. 'The doctor said that if only she'd had several sisters, one of them might have had the right tissue type. Joe

– Rachel's father – is half Asian. It seems harder to find a match. So I had the baby. I had Pegotty five months ago.' She wiped her eyes. 'Joe has his new wife and he wouldn't sleep with me again, not even for Rachel. So he donated sperm and I had artificial insemination, and it worked at once. It seemed an omen . . . and I had the baby . . . but he doesn't match Rachel. There was only ever one chance in four that he would have the same tissue type and antigens . . . I hoped and prayed . . . but he *doesn't*.' She gulped, her throat closing. 'So I have Pegotty . . . he's Peter, really, but we call him Pegotty . . . but Joe won't bond with him . . . and we still can't find a match anywhere for Rachel and there isn't much time for me to try with another baby . . . and Joe *won't* anyway. His wife objects . . . and he didn't want to do it the first time.'

'I'm so sorry,' I said.

'Joe's wife goes on and on about Joe having to pay child support for Pegotty . . . and now she's pregnant herself.'

Life, I thought, brought unlimited and complicated cruelties.

'Joe isn't mean,' Linda said. 'He loves Rachel and he bought her the pony and he keeps us comfortable, but his wife says I could have *six* children without getting a match . . .' Her voice wavered and stopped, and after a while she said, 'I don't know why I burdened you with all that. You're so easy to talk to.'

'And interested.'

She nodded, sniffing and blowing her nose. 'Go out and talk to Rachel. I told her you were coming back today. She liked you.'

Obediently I went out into the garden and gravely shook hands with Rachel, and we sat side by side on a garden bench like two old buddies.

Though still warm, the golden days of early June were greying and growing damp: good for roses perhaps, but not for the Derby.

I apologised that I hadn't yet found out who had attacked Silverboy.

'But you will in the end, won't you?'

'I hope so,' I said.

She nodded. 'I told Daddy yesterday that I was sure you would.'

'Did you?'

'Yes. He took me out in his car. He does that sometimes, when Didi goes to London to do shopping.'

'Is Didi his wife?'

Rachel's nose wrinkled in a grimace, but she made no audible judgement. She said, 'Daddy says someone chopped your hand off, just like Silverboy.'

She regarded me gravely, awaiting confirmation.

'Er,' I said, unnerved, 'not exactly like Silverboy.'

'Daddy says the man who did it was sent to prison, but he's out again now on parole.'

'Do you know what "on parole" means?' I asked curiously

'Yes. Daddy told me.'

'Your daddy knows a lot.'

'Yes, but it is *true* that someone chopped your hand off?'

'Does it matter to you?'

'Yes, it does,' she said. 'I was thinking about it in bed last night. I have awful dreams. I tried to stay awake because I didn't want to go to sleep and dream about you having your hand chopped off.'

She was trying to be grown up and calm, but I could feel screaming hysteria too near the surface; so, stifling my own permanent reluctance to talk about it, I gave her an abbreviated account of what had happened.

'I was a jockey,' I began.

'Yes, I know. Daddy said you were the champion for years.'

'Well, one day my horse fell in a race, and while I was on the ground another horse landed over a jump straight onto my wrist and . . . um . . . tore it apart. It got stitched up, but I couldn't use my hand much. I had to stop being a jockey, and I started doing what I do now, which is finding out things, like who hurt Silverboy.'

She nodded.

'Well, I found out something that an extremely nasty man didn't want me to know, and he . . . er . . . he hit my bad wrist and broke it again, and that time the doctors couldn't stitch it up, so they decided that I'd be better off with a useful plastic hand instead of the useless old one.'

'So he didn't really . . . not *really* chop it off. Not like with an axe or anything?'

'No. So don't waste dreams on it.'

She smiled with quiet relief and, as she was sitting on my left, put her right hand down delicately but without hesitation on the replacement parts. She stroked the tough plastic unfeeling skin and looked up with surprise at my eyes.

'It isn't *warm*,' she said.

'Well, it isn't cold, either.'

She laughed with uncomplicated fun. 'How does it work?'

'I tell it what to do,' I said simply. 'I send a message from my brain down my arm saying open thumb from fingers, or close thumb to fingers, to grip things, and the messages reach very sensitive terminals called electrodes, which are inside the plastic and against my skin.' I paused, but she didn't say she didn't understand. I said, 'My real arm ends about there' – I pointed – 'and the plastic arm goes up round my elbow. The electrodes are up in my forearm, there, against my skin. They feel my muscles trying to move. That's how they work.'

'Is the plastic arm tied on, or anything?'

'No. It just fits tightly and stays on by itself. It was specially made to fit me.'

Like all children she took marvels for granted, although to me, even though by then I'd had the false arm for nearly three years, the concept of nerve messages moving machinery was still extraordinary.

'There are three electrodes,' I said. 'One for opening the hand, one for closing, and one for turning the wrist.'

'Do electrodes work on electricity?' It puzzled her. 'I mean, you're not plugged into the wall, or anything?'

'You're a clever girl,' I told her. 'It works on a special sort of battery which slots into the outside above where I wear my watch. I charge up the batteries on a charger which *is* plugged into the wall.'

She looked at me assessingly. 'It must be pretty useful to have that hand.'

'It's brilliant,' I agreed.

'Daddy says Ellis Quint told him that you can't tell you have a plastic hand unless you touch it.'

I asked, surprised, 'Does your daddy know Ellis Quint?'

She nodded composedly. 'They go to the same place to play squash. He helped Daddy buy Silverboy. He was really really sorry when he found out it was Silverboy himself that he was making his programme about.'

'Yes, he would be.'

'I wish . . .' she began, looking down at my hand, 'I do wish Silverboy could have had a new foot . . . with electrodes and a battery.'

I said prosaically, 'He might have been able to have a false foot fitted, but he wouldn't have been able to trot or canter, or jump. He wouldn't have been happy just limping around.'

She rubbed her own fingers over the plastic ones, not convinced.

I said, 'Where did you keep Silverboy?'

'The other side of that fence at the end of the garden.' She pointed. 'You can't see it from here because of those trees. We have to go through the house and out and down the lane.'

'Will you show me?'

There was a moment of drawing back, then she said, 'I'll take you if I can hold your hand on the way.'

'Of course.' I stood up and held out my real, warm, normal arm.

'No . . .' She shook her head, standing up also. 'I mean, can I hold this hand that you can't feel?'

It seemed to matter to her that I wasn't whole; that I would understand someone ill, without hair.

I said lightly, 'You can hold which hand you like.'

She nodded, then pushed Pegotty into the house, and matter of factly told Linda she was taking me down to the field to show me where Silverboy had lived. Linda gave me a wild look but let us go, so the bald-headed child and the one-handed man walked in odd companionship down a short lane and leaned against a five-barred gate across the end.

The field was a lush paddock of little more than an acre, the grass growing strongly, uneaten. A nearby standing pipe with an ordinary tap on it stood ready to fill an ordinary galvanised water trough. The ground round the trough was churned up, the grass growing more sparsely, as always happened round troughs in fields.

'I don't want to go in,' Rachel said, turning her head away.

'We don't need to.'

'His foot was by the trough,' she said jerkily, 'I mean . . . you could see *blood* . . . and white bones.'

'Don't talk about it.' I pulled her with me and walked back along the lane, afraid I should never have asked her to show me.

She gripped my unfeeling hand in both of hers, slowing me down.

'It's all right,' she said. 'It was a long time ago. It's all right now when I'm awake.'

'Good.'

'I don't like going to sleep.'

The desperation of that statement was an open appeal, and had to be addressed.

I stopped walking before we reached the door of the house. I said, 'I don't usually tell anyone this, but I'll tell you. I still sometimes have bad dreams about my hand. I dream I can clap with two hands. I dream I'm still a jockey. I dream about my smashed wrist. Rotten dreams can't be helped. They're awful when they happen. I don't know how to stop them. But one does wake up.'

'And then you have leukaemia . . . or a plastic arm.'

'Life's a bugger,' I said.

She put her hand over her mouth and, in a fast release of tension, she giggled. 'Mum won't let me say that.'

'Say it into your pillow.'

'Do you?'

'Pretty often.'

We went on into the house and Rachel again pushed Pegotty into the garden. I stayed in the sitting-room with Linda and watched through the window.

'Was she all right?' Linda asked anxiously.

'She's a very brave child.'

Linda wept.

I said, 'Did you hear anything at all the night Silverboy was attacked?'

'Everyone asks that. I'd have said if I had.'

'No car engines?'

'The police said they must have stopped the car in the road and walked down the lane. My bedroom window doesn't face the lane, nor does Rachel's. But that lane doesn't go anywhere except to the field. As you saw, it's only a track really, it ends at the gate.'

'Could anyone see Silverboy from the road?'

'Yes, the police asked that. You could see him come to drink. You can see the water trough from the road, if you know where to look. The police say the thugs must have been out all over this part of Kent looking for unguarded ponies like Silverboy. Whatever you say about two-year-olds, Silverboy *must* have been done by thugs. Why don't you ask the police?'

'If you wholeheartedly believed the police, you wouldn't have asked me for help.'

'Joe just telephoned,' she confessed, wailing, 'and he says that calling you in to help is a waste of money.'

'Ah.'

'I don't know what to think.'

I said, 'You're paying me by the day, plus expenses. I can stop right now, if you like.'

'No. Yes. I don't *know*.' She wiped her eyes, undecided, and said, 'Rachel dreams that Silverboy is standing in the field and he's glowing bright and beautiful in the moonlight. He's *shining*, she says. And there's a dark mass of monsters oozing down the lane . . . oozing is what she says . . . and they are shapeless and devils and they're going to kill Silverboy. She says she is trying to run fast to warn him, and she can't get through the monsters, they clutch at her like cobwebs. She can't get through them and they reach Silverboy and smother his light, and all his hair falls out, and she wakes up and screams. It's always the same nightmare. I thought if you could find out who cut the poor thing's foot off, the monsters would have names and faces and would be in the papers, and Rachel would know who they were and stop thinking they're lumps that ooze without eyes and won't let her through.'

After a pause, I said, 'Give me another week.'

She turned away from me sharply and, crossing to a desk, wrote me a cheque. 'For two weeks, one gone, one ahead.'

I looked at the amount. 'That's more than we agreed on.'

'Whatever Joe says, I want you to go on trying.'

I gave her tentatively a small kiss on the cheek. She smiled, her eyes still dark and wet. 'I'll pay anything for Rachel,' she said.

I drove slowly back to London thinking of the cynical old ex-policemen who had taught me the basics of investigation. 'There are two cardinal rules in this trade,' he said. 'One. Never believe everything a client tells you, and always believe they could have told you more if you'd asked the right questions. And two. Never, never get emotionally involved with your client.'

Which was all very well, except when your client was a bright truthful nine-year-old fighting a losing battle against a rising tide of lymphoblasts.

I bought a take-out curry on the way home and ate it before spending the evening on overdue paperwork.

I much preferred the active side of the job, but clients wanted, and deserved, and paid for, detailed accounts of what I'd done on their behalf, preferably with results they liked. With the typed recital of work done, I sent also my final bill, adding a list of itemised expenses supported by receipts. I almost always played fair, even with clients I didn't like: investigators had been known to charge for seven days' work when, with a little application, they could have finished the job in three. I didn't want that sort of reputation. Speed succeeded in my new occupation as essentially as in my old.

Besides bathroom and kitchen, my pleasant (and frankly, expensive) flat consisted of three rooms; bedroom, big sunny sitting-room and a third, smaller, room that I used as an office. I had no secretary or helper; no one read the secrets I uncovered except the client and myself, and whatever the client did with the information he'd paid for was normally his or her own business. Privacy was what drove many people to consult me, and privacy was what they got.

I listened to some unexciting messages on my answering machine, typed a report on my secure word-processor, printed it and put it ready for posting. For reports and anything personal I used a computer system that wasn't connected to any phone line. No one could in consequence tap into it and, as a precaution against thieves, I used also unbreakable passwords. It was my second system that could theoretically be accessed; the one connected by modem to the big wide world of universal information. Any snooper was welcome to anything found there.

On the subject of the management of secrecy, my cynical mentor had said, 'Never ever tell your right hand what your left hand is doing. Er . . .' he added, 'whoops. Sorry, Sid.'

'It'll cost you a pint.'

'And,' he went on later, drinking, 'keep back-up copies of completed sensitive enquiries in a bank vault, and wipe the information from any computer systems in your office. If you use random passwords, and change them weekly, you should be safe enough while you're actually working on something, but once you've finished, get the back-up to the bank and wipe the office computer, like I said.'

'All right.'

'Never forget,' he told me, 'that the people you are investigating may go to violent lengths to stop you.'

He had been right about that.

'Never forget that you don't have the same protection as the police do. You have to make your own protection. You have to be careful.'

'Maybe I should look for another job.'

'No, Sid,' he said earnestly, 'you have a gift for this. You listen to what I tell you and you'll do fine.'

He had taught me for the two years I'd spent doing little but drift in the old Radnor detection agency after the end of my racing life and, for nearly three years since, I'd lived mostly by his precepts. But he was dead now, and Radnor himself also, and I had to look inwards for wisdom, which could be a variable process, not always ultra-productive.

I could try to comfort Rachel by telling her I had bad dreams also, but I could never have told her how vivid and liquefying they could be. That night, after I'd eased off the arm and showered and gone peacefully to bed, I fell asleep thinking of her, and descended after midnight into a familiar dungeon.

It was always the same.

I dreamed I was in a big dark space, and some people were coming to cut off both my hands.

Both.

They were making me wait, but they would come. There would be agony and humiliation and helplessness . . . and no way out.

I semi-awoke in shaking, sweating heart-thudding terror and then realised with flooding relief that it wasn't true, I was safe in my own bed: and then remembered that it had already half happened in fact, and also that I'd come within a fraction once of a villain's shooting the remaining hand off. As soon as I was awake enough to be clear about the present actual not-too-bad state of affairs I slid back reassured into sleep, and that night the whole appalling nightmare cycled again . . . and again.

I forced myself to wake up properly, to sit up and get out of bed and make full consciousness take over. I stood under the shower again and let cool water run through my hair and down my body. I put on a towelling bathrobe and poured a glass of milk, and sat in an armchair in the sitting-room with all the lights on.

I looked at the space where a left hand had once been, and I looked at the strong whole right hand that held a glass, and I acknowledged that often, both waking as well as sleeping, I felt, and could not repress, stabs of savage petrifying fear that one day it would indeed be both. The trick was not to let the fear show, nor to let it conquer, nor rule my life.

It was pointless to reflect that I'd brought the terrors on myself. I had chosen to be a jockey. I had chosen to go after violent crooks. I was at that moment actively seeking out someone who knew how to cut off a horse's foot with one chop.

My own equivalent of the off-fore held a glass of milk.

I had to be mentally deranged.

But then there were people like Rachel Ferns.

In one way or another I had survived many torments, and much could have been avoided but for my own obstinate nature. I knew by then that whatever came along, I would deal with it. But that child had had her hair fall out and had found her beloved pony's foot, and none of that was her fault. No nine-year-old mind could sleep sweetly under such assaults.

Oh God, Rachel, I thought, I would dream your nightmares for you, if I could.

In the morning I made a working analysis in five columns of the Ferns pony and the three two-year-olds. The analysis took the form of a simple graph, ruled in boxes. Across the top of the page I wrote: Factors, Ferns, Cheltenham, Aintree, York, and down the left-hand column, Factors, I entered 'date', 'name of owner', 'racing programme', 'motive', and finally, 'who knew of victim's availability?' I found that although I could *think* of answers to that last question, I hadn't the wish to write them in, and after a bit of indecision I phoned Kevin Mills at *The Pump* and, by persistence, reached him.

'Sid,' he said heartily, 'the warning will be in the paper tomorrow. You've done your best. Stop agitating.'

'Great,' I said, 'but could you do something else? Something that could come innocently from *The Pump*, but would raise all sorts of reverberations if I asked directly myself.'

'Such as what?'

'Such as ask Topline Foods for a list of the guests they entertained at a sponsors' lunch at Aintree the day before the National.'

'What the *hell* for?'

'Will you do it?'

He said, 'What are you up to?'

'The scoop is still yours. Exclusive.'

'I don't know why I trust you.'

'It pays off,' I said, smiling.

'It had better.' He put down his receiver with a crash, but I knew he would do what I asked.

It was Friday morning. At Epsom that day they would be running the Coronation Cup and also the Oaks, the fillies' equivalent of the Derby. It was also lightly raining: a weak warm front, it seemed, was slowly blighting southern England.

Racecourses still drew me as if I were tethered to them with bungy elastic, but before setting out I telephoned the woman whose colt's foot had been amputated during the night after the Cheltenham Gold Cup.

'I'm sorry to bother you again, but would you mind a few more questions?'

'Not if you can catch the bastards.'

'Well, was the two-year-old alone in his field?'

'Yes, he was. It was only a paddock. Railed, of course. We kept him in the paddock nearest to the house, that's what is so infuriating. We had two old hacks turned out in the field beyond him, but the vandals left them untouched.'

'And,' I said neutrally, 'how many people knew the colt was accessible? And how accessible was he?'

'Sid,' she exclaimed, 'don't think we haven't racked our brains. The trouble is, all our friends knew about him. We were excited about his prospects. And then, at the Cheltenham meeting, we had been talking to people about *trainers.* Old Gunners, who used to train for us in the past, has died, of course, and we don't like that uppity assistant of his that's taken over the stable, so we were asking around, you see.'

'Yeah. And did you decide on a trainer?'

'We did, but, of course . . .'

'Such a bloody shame,' I sympathised. 'Who did you decide on?'

She mentioned a first-class man. 'Several people said that with him we couldn't go wrong.'

'No.' I mentally sighed, and asked obliquely, 'What did you especially enjoy about the Festival meeting?'

'The Queen came,' she said promptly. 'I had thick warm boots on, and I nearly fell over them, curtseying.' She laughed. 'And oh, also, I suppose you do know you're in the Hall of Fame there?'

'It's an honour,' I said. 'They gave me an engraved glass goblet that I can see across the room right now from where I'm sitting.'

'Well, we were standing in front of that big exhibit they've put together of your life, and we were reading the captions, and dear Ellis Quint stopped beside us and put his arm round my shoulders and said that our Sid was a pretty great guy, all in all.'

Oh *shit*, I thought.

Her warm smile was audible down the line. 'We've known Ellis for years, of course. He used to ride our horses in amateur races. So he called in at our house for a drink on his way home after the Gold Cup. Such a *lovely* day.' She sighed. 'And then those *bastards* . . . You will catch them, won't you, Sid?'

'If I can,' I said.

I left a whole lot of the boxes empty on my chart, and drove to Epsom Downs, spirits as grey as the skies. The bars were crowded. Umbrellas dripped. The brave colours of June dresses hid under drabber raincoats, and only the geraniums looked happy.

I walked damply to the parade ring before the two-year-old colts' six-furlong race and thoughtfully watched all the off-fore feet plink down lightheartedly. The young spindly bones of those forelegs thrust 450-kilo bodies forward at sprinting speeds near forty miles an hour. I had mostly raced on the older mature horses of steeplechasing, half a ton in weight, slightly slower, capable of four miles and thirty jumps from start to finish, but still on legs scarcely thicker than a big man's wrist.

The anatomy of a horse's foreleg consisted, from the shoulder down, of forearm, knee, cannon bone, fetlock joint (also known as the ankle), pastern bone, and hoof. The angry Lancashire farmer's coloured photograph had shown the amputation to have been effected straight through the narrowest part of the whole leg, just at the base of the fetlock joint, where the pastern emerged from it. In effect, the whole pastern and the hoof had been cut off.

Horses had very fast instincts for danger and were easily scared. Young horses seldom stood still. Yet one single chop had done the job each time. *Why* had all those poor animals stood quietly while the deed was done? None of them had squealed loud enough to alert his owner.

I went up on the stands and watched the two-year-olds set off from the spur away to the left at the top of the hill; watched them swoop down like a flock of starlings round Tattenham Corner, and sort themselves out into winner and losers along the straight with its deceptively difficult camber that could tilt a horse towards the rails if his jockey were inexperienced.

I watched, and I sighed. Five long years had passed since I'd ridden my last race. Would regret, I wondered, ever fade?

'Why so pensive, Sid, lad?' asked an elderly trainer, grasping my elbow. 'A Scotch and water for your thoughts!' He steered me round towards the nearest bar and I went with him unprotestingly, as custom came my way quite often in that casual manner. He was great with horses and famously mean with his money.

'I hear you're damned expensive,' he began inoffensively, handing me a glass. 'What will you charge me for a day's work?'

I told him.

'Too damned much. Do it for nothing, for old times' sake.'

I added, smiling, 'How many horses do you train for nothing?'

'That's different.'

'How many races would you have asked me to ride for nothing?'

'Oh, all *right* then. I'll pay your damned fee. The fact is, I think I'm being *had*, and I want you to find out.'

It seemed he had received a glowing testimonial from the present employer of a chauffeur/houseman/handyman who'd applied for a job he'd advertised. He wanted to know if it was worth bringing the man up for an interview.

'She–' he said, 'his employer is a woman – I phoned her when I got the letter, to check the reference, you see. She couldn't have been more complimentary about the man if she'd tried, but . . . I don't know . . . She was *too* complimentary, if you see what I mean.'

'You mean you think she might be glad to see the back of him?'

'You don't hang about, Sid. That's exactly what I mean.'

He gave me the testimonial letter of fluorescent praise.

'No problem,' I said, reading it. 'One day's fee, plus travel expenses. I'll phone you, then send you a written report.'

'You still *look* like a jockey,' he complained. 'You're a damned sight more expensive on your feet.'

I smiled, put the letter away in a pocket, drank his Scotch and applauded the string of winners he'd had recently, cheering him up before separating him from his cash.

I drifted around pleasurably but unprofitably for the rest of the day, slept thankfully without nightmares and found on a dry and sunny Derby Day morning that my friendly *Pump* reporter had really done his stuff.

'Lock up your colts,' he directed in the paper. 'You've heard of foot-fetishists? This is one beyond belief.'

He outlined in succinct paragraphs the similarities in 'the affair of the four severed fetlocks' and pointed out that on that very night after the Derby – the biggest race of all – there would be moonlight enough at 3.00 a.m. for torches to be unnecessary. All two-year-old colts should, like Cinderella, be safe indoors by mid-night. 'And if . . .' he finished with a flourish, '. . . you should spy anyone creeping through the fields armed with a machete, phone ex-jockey turned gumshoe Sid Halley, who provided the information gathered here and can be reached via *The Pump*'s special Hotline. Phone *The Pump*! Save the colts! Halley to the rescue!'

I couldn't imagine how he had got that last bit – including a telephone number – past any editor, but I needn't have worried about spreading the message on the racecourse. No one spoke to me about anything else all afternoon.

I phoned *The Pump* myself and reached someone eventually who told me that Kevin Mills had gone to a train crash; sorry.

'Damn,' I said. 'So how are you re-routing calls about colts to me? I didn't arrange this. How will it work?'

'Hold on.'

I held on. A different voice came back.

'As Kevin isn't available, we're re-routing all Halley Hotline calls to this number,' he said, and he read out my own Pont Square number.

'Where's your bloody Mills? I'll wring his neck.'

'Gone to the train crash. Before he left he gave us this number for reaching you. He said you would want to know at once about any colts.'

That was true enough – but hell's bloody bells, I thought, I could have set it up better if he'd warned me.

I watched the Derby with inattention. An outsider won.

Ellis teased me about the piece in *The Pump*.

'Hotline Halley,' he said, laughing and clapping me on the shoulder, tall and deeply friendly and wiping out in a flash the incredulous doubts I'd been having about him. 'It's an extraordinary coincidence, Sid, but I actually *saw* one of those colts. Alive, of course. I was staying with some chums for York, and after we'd gone home someone vandalised their colt. Such fun people. They didn't deserve anything like that.'

'No one does.'

'True.'

'The really puzzling thing is motive,' I said. 'I went to see all the owners. None of the colts was insured. Nor was Rachel Ferns' pony, of course.'

He said interestedly, 'Did you think it was an insurance scam?'

'It jumps to mind, doesn't it? Theoretically it's possible to insure a horse and collect the lucre without the owner knowing anything about it. It's been done. But if that's what this is all about, perhaps someone in an insurance company somewhere will see the piece in

The Pump and connect a couple of things. Come to think of it,' I finished slowly, 'I might send a copy to every likely insurance company's board of directors, asking, and warning them.'

'Good idea,' he said. 'Does insurance and so on really take the place of racing? It sounds a pretty dull life for you, after what we used to do.'

'Does television replace it for you?'

'Not a hope.' He laughed. 'Danger is addictive, wouldn't you say? The only dangerous job in television is reporting wars and – have you noticed – the same few war reporters get out there all the time, talking with their earnest committed faces about this or that month's little dust-up, while bullets fly and chip off bits of stone in the background to prove how brave they are.'

'You're jealous,' I smiled.

'I get sodding bored sometimes with being a chat-show celebrity, even if it's nice being liked. Don't you ache for speed?'

'Every day,' I said.

'You're about the only person who understands me. No one else can see that fame's no substitute for danger.'

'It depends what you risk.'

Hands, I thought. One could risk hands.

'Good luck, Hotline,' Ellis said.

It was the owners of two-year-old colts that had the good luck. My telephone jammed and rang non-stop all evening and all night when I got home after the Derby, but the calls were all from people enjoying their shivers and jumping at shadows. The moonlight shone on quiet fields, and no animal, whether colt or two-year-old thoroughbred or children's pony, lost a foot.

In the days that followed, interest and expectation dimmed and died. It was twelve days after the Derby, on the last night of the Royal Ascot meeting, that the screaming heeby-jeebies reawoke.

CHAPTER FOUR

On the Monday after the Derby I trailed off on the one-day dig into the overblown reference and, without talking to the lady-employer herself (which would clearly have been counter-productive) I uncovered enough to phone the tight-fisted trainer with sound advice.

'She wants to get rid of him without the risk of being accused of unfair dismissal,' I said. 'He steals small things from her house which pass through a couple of hands and turn up in the local antique shop. She can't prove they were hers. The antique shop owner is whining about his innocence. The lady has apparently said she won't try to prosecute her houseman if he gets the heck out. Her testimonial is part of the bargain. The houseman is a regular in the local betting shop, and gambles heavily on horses. Do you want to employ him?'

'Like hell.'

'The report I'll write and send to you,' I told him, 'will say only, "Work done on recruitment of staff." You can claim tax relief on it.'

He laughed dryly. 'Any time you want a reference,' he said, pleased, 'I'll write you an affidavit.'

'You never know,' I said, 'and thanks.'

I had phoned the report from the car park of a motorway service station on my way home late in the dusky evening, but it was when I reached Pont Square that the day grew doubly dark. There was a two-page fax waiting on my machine and I read it standing in the sitting-room with all thoughts of a friendly glass of Scotch evaporating into disbelief and the onset of misery.

The pages were from Kevin Mills. 'I don't know why you want this list of the great and good,' he wrote, 'but for what it's worth and because I promised, here is a list of the guests entertained by Topline Foods at lunch at Aintree on the day before the Grand National.'

The list contained the name of the angry Lancashire farmer, as was expected, but it was the top of the list that did the psychological damage.

'Guest of Honour,' it announced, 'Ellis Quint.'

All the doubts I'd banished came roaring back with double vigour. Back too came self-ridicule and every defence mechanism under the sun.

I couldn't, didn't, *couldn't* believe that Ellis could maim – and effectively kill – a child's pony and three young racehorses. Not Ellis! It was *impossible.*

There had to be *dozens* of other people who could have learned where to find all four of those vulnerable unguarded animals. It was *stupid* to give any weight to an unreliable coincidence. All the same, I pulled my box chart out of a drawer, and in very small letters, as if in that way I could physically diminish the implication, I wrote in each 'who knew of victim's availability?' space the unthinkable words, Ellis Quint.

The 'motive' boxes had also remained empty. There was no apparent rational motive. Why did people poke out the eyes of ponies? Why did they stalk strangers and write poison pen letters? Why did they torture and kill children and tape-record their screams?

I wrote 'self gratification', but it seemed too weak. Insanity? Psychosis? The irresistible primordial upsurge of a hunger for pointless, violent destruction?

It didn't fit the Ellis I knew. Not the man I'd raced against and laughed with, and had deemed a close friend for years. One couldn't know someone that well, and yet not know them at all.

Could one?

No.

Relentless thoughts kept me awake all night and in the morning I sent Linda Ferns' cheque back to her, uncashed.

'I've got no further,' I wrote. 'I'm exceedingly sorry.'

Two days later the same cheque returned.

'Dear Sid,' Linda replied, 'Keep the money. I know you'll find the thugs one day. I don't know what you said to Rachel but she's much happier and she hasn't had any bad dreams since you came last week. For that alone I would pay you double. Affectionately, Linda Ferns.'

I put the cheque in a pending file, caught up with paperwork and attended my usual judo training session.

The judo I practised was the subtle art of self-defence, the shifting of balance that used an attacker's own momentum to overcome him. Judo was rhythm, leverage and speed; a matter sometimes of applying pressure to nerves and always, in the way I learned, a quiet discipline. The yells and the kicks of karate, the arms slapped down on the padded mat to emphasise aggression, they were neither in my nature nor what I needed. I didn't seek physical domination. I didn't by choice start fights. With the built-in drawbacks of half an arm, a light frame and a height of about five feet seven, my overall requirement was survival.

I went through the routines absentmindedly. They were at best a mental crutch. A great many dangers couldn't be wiped out by an ability to throw an assailant over one's shoulder.

Ellis wouldn't leave my thoughts.

I was wrong. Of *course* I was wrong.

His face was universally known. He wouldn't risk being seen sneaking around fields at night armed with anything like a machete.

But he was bored with celebrity. Fame was no substitute for danger, he'd said. Everything he had was not enough.

All the same . . . *he couldn't.*

*

In the second week after the Derby I went to the four days of the Royal Ascot meeting, drifting around in a morning suit, admiring the gleaming coats of the horses and the women's extravagant hats. I should have enjoyed it, as I usually did. Instead, I felt as if the whole thing were a charade taking illusory place over an abyss.

Ellis, of course, was there every day: and, of course, he sought me out.

'How's it going, Hotline?'

'The Hotline is silent.'

'There you are, then,' Ellis said with friendly irony, 'you've frightened your foot merchant off.'

'For ever, I hope.'

'What if he can't help it?' Ellis said.

I turned my head: looked at his eyes. 'I'll catch him,' I said.

He smiled and looked away. 'Everyone knows you're a whiz at that sort of thing, but I'll bet you—'

'Don't,' I interrupted. 'Don't bet on it. It's bad luck.'

Someone came up to his other elbow, claiming his attention. He patted my shoulder, said with the usual affection, 'See you, Sid,' and was drawn away; and I couldn't believe, I *couldn't*, that he had told me *why*, even if not how.

'What if he can't help it?'

Could compulsion lead to cruel senseless acts?

No . . .

Yes, it could, and yes, it often did.

But not in Ellis. Not, *not* in Ellis.

Alibis, I thought, seeking for a rational way out. I would find out – somehow – exactly where Ellis had been on the nights the horses had been attacked. I would prove to my own satisfaction that it couldn't have been Ellis, and I would return with relief to the beginning, and admit I had no pointers at all, and would never find the thugs for Linda, and would quite happily chalk up a failure.

At five-thirty in the morning on the day after the Ascot Gold Cup, I sleepily awoke and answered my ringing telephone to hear a high agitated female voice saying, 'I want to reach Sid Halley.'

'You have,' I said, pushing myself up to sitting and squinting at the clock.

'What?'

'You are talking to Sid Halley.' I stifled a yawn. Five-bloody-thirty.

'But I phoned *The Pump* and asked for the Hotline!'

I said patiently, 'They re-route the Hotline calls direct to me. This is Sid Halley you're talking to. How can I help you?'

'Christ,' she said, sounding totally disorganised. 'We have a colt with a foot off.'

After a breath-catching second I said, 'Where are you?'

'At home. Oh, I see, Berkshire.'

'Where, exactly?'

'Combe Bassett, south of Hungerford.'

'And . . . um . . .' I thought of asking, 'What's the state of play?' and discarded it as less than tactful. 'What is . . . happening?'

'We're all up. Everyone's yelling and crying.'

'And the vet?'

'I just phoned him. He's coming.'

'And the police?'

'They're sending someone. Then we decided we'd better call you.'

'Yes,' I replied. 'I'll come now, if you like.'

'That's why I phoned you.'

'What's your name then? Address?'

She gave them. 'Betty Bracken, Manor House, Combe Bassett' – stumbling on the words as if she couldn't remember.

'Please,' I said, 'ask the vet not to send the colt or his foot off to the knackers until I get there.'

'I'll try,' she said jerkily. 'For God's sakes, *why*? Why our colt?'

'I'll be there in an hour,' I said.

What if he can't help it . . .

But it took such planning. Such stealth. So many crazy risks. Someone, sometime, would see him.

Let it not be Ellis, I thought. Let the compulsion be some other poor bastard's ravening subconscious. Ellis would be able to control such a vicious appetite, even if he felt it.

Let it not be Ellis.

Whoever it was, he had to be stopped: and I would stop him, if I could.

I shaved in the car (a Mercedes), clasping the battery-driven razor in the battery-driven hand, and I covered the eighty miles to south-west Berkshire in a time down the comparatively empty M4 that had the speedometer needle quivering where it had seldom been before. The radar speed traps slept. Just as well.

It was a lovely high June morning, fine and fresh. I curled through the gates of Combe Bassett Manor, cruised to a stop in the drive and at six-thirty walked into a house where open doors led to movement, loud voices and a general gnashing of teeth.

The woman who'd phoned rushed over when she saw me, her hands flapping in the air, her whole demeanour in an out-of-control state of fluster.

'Sid Halley? Thank God. Punch some sense into this lot.'

This lot consisted of two uniformed policemen and a crowd of what later proved to be family members, neighbours, ramblers and half a dozen dogs.

'Where's the colt?' I asked. 'And where's his foot?'

'Out in the field. The vet's there. I told him what you wanted but he's an opinionated Scot. God knows if he'll wait, he's a cantankerous old devil. He—'

'Show me where,' I said abruptly, cutting into the flow.

She blinked. 'What? Oh, yes. This way.'

She set off fast, leading me through big-house, unevenly painted hinterland passages reminiscent of those of Aynsford, of those of any house built with servants in mind. We passed a gun-room, flower-room, and mud-room (ranks of green wellies) and emerged at last through a rear door into a yard inhabited by dustbins. From there, through a green wooden garden door, she led the way fast down a hedge-bordered grass path and through a metal-railing gate at the far end of it. I'd begun to think we were off to limbo when suddenly, there before us, was a lane full of vehicles and about ten people leaning on paddock fencing.

My guide was tall, thin, fluttery, at a guess about fifty, dressed in old cord trousers and a drab olive sweater. Her greying hair flopped, unbrushed, over a high forehead. She had been, and still was, beyond caring how she looked, but I had a powerful impression that she was a woman to whom looks mattered little anyway.

She was deferred to. The men leaning on the paddock rails straightened and all but touched their forelocks, 'Morning, Mrs Bracken.'

She nodded automatically and ushered me through the wide metal gate that one of the men swung open for her.

Inside the field, at a distance of perhaps thirty paces,

stood two more men, also a masculine-looking woman and a passive colt with three feet. All, except the colt, showed the facial and body language of impatience.

One of the men, tall, white-haired, wearing black-rimmed glasses, took two steps forward to meet us.

'Now, Mrs Bracken, I've done what you asked, but it's past time to put your poor boy out of his misery. And you'll be Sid Halley, I suppose,' he said, peering down as from a mountain top. 'There's little you can do.' He shook hands briefly as if it were a custom he disapproved of.

He had a strong Scottish accent and the manner of one accustomed to command. The man behind him, unremarkably built, self-effacing in manner, remained throughout a silent watcher on the fringe.

I walked over to the colt and found him wearing a head-collar, with a rope halter held familiarly by the woman. The young horse watched me with calm bright eyes, unafraid. I stroked my hand down his nose, talking to him quietly. He moved his head upwards against the pressure and down again as if nodding, saying hello. I let him whiffle his black lips across my knuckles. I stroked his neck and patted him. His skin was dry: no pain, no fear, no distress.

'Is he drugged?' I asked.

'I'd have to run a blood test,' the Scotsman said.

'Which you are doing, of course?'

'Of course.'

One could tell from the faces of the other man

and the woman that no blood test had so far been considered.

I moved round the colt's head and squatted down for a close look at his off-fore, running my hand down the back of his leg, feeling only a soft area of no resistance where normally there would be the tough bowstring tautness of the leg's main tendon. Pathetically, the fetlock was tidy, not bleeding. I bent up the colt's knee and looked at the severed end. It had been done neatly, sliced through, unsplintered ends of bone showing white, the skin cleanly cut as if a practised chef had used a disjointing knife.

The colt jerked his knee, freeing himself from my grasp.

I stood up.

'Well?' the Scotsman challenged.

'Where's his foot?'

'Over yon, out of sight behind the water trough.' He paused, then as I turned away from him, suddenly added, 'It wasn't found there. I put it there, out of sight. It was they ramblers that came to it first.'

'Ramblers?'

'Aye.'

Mrs Bracken, who had joined us, explained. 'One Saturday every year in June, all the local rambling clubs turn out in force to walk the footpaths in this part of the country, to keep them legally open for the public.'

'If they'd stay on the footpaths,' the Scot said forbiddingly, 'they be within their rights.'

Mrs Bracken agreed. 'They bring their children and their dogs and their picnics, and act as if they own the place.'

'But . . . what on earth time did they find your colt's foot?'

'They set off soon after dawn,' Mrs Bracken observed morosely. 'In the middle of June, that's four-thirty in the morning, more or less. They gather before five o'clock while it is still cool, and set off across my land first, and they were hammering on my door by five-fifteen. Three of the children were in full-blown hysteria, and a man with a beard and a pony-tail was screaming that he blamed the élite. What élite? One of the ramblers phoned the Press and then someone fanatical in animal rights, and a carload of activists arrived with "ban horse racing" banners.' She rolled her eyes. 'I *despair*,' she said. 'It's bad enough losing my glorious colt. These people are turning it into a *circus*.'

Hold on to the real tragedy at the heart of the farce, I thought briefly, and walked over to the water trough to look at the foot that lay behind it. There were horse-feed nuts scattered everywhere around. Without expecting much emotion, I bent and picked the foot up.

I hadn't seen the other severed feet. I'd actually thought some of the reported reactions excessive. But the reality of that poor, unexpected, curiously lonely lump of bone, gristle and torn ends of blood vessels, that wasted miracle of anatomical elegance, moved me close to the fury and grief of all the owners.

There was a shoe on the hoof; the sort of small light shoe fitted to youngsters to protect their fore feet out in the field. There were ten small nails tacking the shoe to the hoof. The presence of the shoe brought its own powerful message: civilisation had offered care to the colt's foot, barbarity had hacked it off.

I'd loved horses always: it was hard to explain the intimacy that grew between horses and those who tended or rode them. Horses lived in a parallel world, spoke a parallel language, were a mass of instincts, lacked human perceptions of kindness or guilt, and allowed a merging on an untamed, untamable mysterious level of spirit. The Great God Pan lived in racehorses. One cut off his foot at one's peril.

On a more prosaic level I put the hoof back on the ground, unclipped the mobile phone I wore on my belt and, consulting a small diary/notebook for the number, connected myself to a veterinary friend who worked as a surgeon in an equine hospital in Lambourn.

'Bill?' I said. 'This is Sid Halley.'

'Go to sleep,' he said.

'Wake up. It's six-fifty and I'm in Berkshire with the severed off-fore hoof of a two-year-old colt.'

'Jesus.' He woke up fast.

'I want you to look at it. What do you advise?'

'How long has it been off? Any chance of sewing it back on?'

'It's been off at least three hours, I'd say. Probably more. There's no sign of the achilles tendon. It's contracted up inside the leg. The amputation is through the fetlock joint itself.'

'One blow, like the others?'

I hesitated. 'I didn't see the others.'

'But something's worrying you?'

'I want you to look at it,' I said.

Bill Ruskin and I had worked on other, earlier puzzles, and got along together in a trusting undemanding friendship that remained unaltered by periods of non-contact.

'What shape is the colt in generally?' he asked.

'Quiet. No visible pain.'

'Is the owner rich?'

'It looks like it.'

'See if he'll have the colt – and his foot, of course – shipped over here.'

'She,' I said. 'I'll ask her.'

Mrs Bracken gaped at me mesmerised when I relayed the suggestion, and said 'Yes' faintly.

Bill said, 'Find a sterile surgical dressing for the leg. Wrap the foot in another dressing and a polythene bag and pack it in a bucket of ice cubes. Is it clean?'

'Some early morning ramblers found it.'

He groaned. 'I'll send a horse ambulance,' he said. 'Where to?'

I explained where I was, and added, 'There's a Scots

vet here that's urging to put the colt down at once. Use honey-tongued diplomacy.'

'Put him on.'

I returned to where the colt still stood and, explaining who he would be talking to, handed my phone to the vet. The Scot scowled. Mrs Bracken said 'Anything, anything,' over and over again. Bill talked.

'Very well,' the Scot said frostily, finally, 'but you do understand, don't you, Mrs Bracken, that the colt won't be able to race, even if they do succeed in reattaching his foot, which is very, very doubtful.'

She said simply, 'I don't want to lose him. It's worth a try.'

The Scot, to give him his due, set about enclosing the raw leg efficiently in a dressing from his surgical bag and in wrapping the foot in a businesslike bundle. The row of men leaning on the fence watched with interest. The masculine-looking woman holding the head-collar wiped a few tears from her weatherbeaten cheeks while crooning to her charge, and eventually Mrs Bracken and I returned to the house, which still rang with noise. The ramblers, making the most of the drama, seemed to be rambling all over the ground floor and were to be seen assessing their chances of penetrating upstairs. Mrs Bracken clutched her head in distraction and said, 'Please will everyone leave,' but without enough volume to be heard.

I begged one of the policemen, 'Shoo the lot out, can't you?' and finally most of the crowd left, the ebb revealing a large basically formal pale green and gold drawing-room inhabited by five or six humans, three dogs and a clutter of plastic cups engraving wet rings on ancient polished surfaces. Mrs Bracken, like a somnambulist, drifted around picking up cups from one place only to put them down in another. Ever tidy-minded, I couldn't stop myself twitching up a waste-paper basket and following her, taking the cups from her fingers and collecting them all together.

She looked at me vaguely. She said, 'I paid a quarter of a million for that colt.'

'Is he insured?'

'No. I don't insure my jewellery either.'

'Or your health?'

'No, of course not.'

She looked unseeingly round the room. Five people now sat on easy chairs, offering no help or succour.

'Would someone make a cup of tea?' she asked.

No one moved.

She said to me, as if it explained everything, 'Esther doesn't start work until eight.'

'Mm,' I said. 'Well . . . er . . . who is everybody?'

'Goodness, yes. Rude of me. That's my husband.' Her gaze fell affectionately on an old bald man who looked as if he had no comprehension of anything. 'He's deaf, the dear man.'

'I see.'

'And that's my aunt, who mostly lives here.'

The aunt was also old and proved unhelpful and selfish.

'Our tenants.' Mrs Bracken indicated a stolid couple. 'They live in part of the house. And my nephew.'

Even her normal good manners couldn't keep the irritation from either her voice or her face at this last identification. The nephew was a teenager with a loose mouth and an attitude problem.

None of this hopeless bunch looked like an accomplice in a spite attack on a harmless animal, not even the unsatisfactory boy, who was staring at me intensely as if demanding to be noticed: almost, I thought fleetingly, as if he wanted to tell me something by telepathy. It was more than an interested inspection, but also held neither disapproval nor fear, as far as I could see.

I said to Mrs Bracken, 'If you tell me where the kitchen is, I'll make you some tea.'

'But you've only one hand.'

I reassured her, 'I can't climb Everest but I can sure make tea.'

A streak of humour began to banish the morning's shocks from her eyes. 'I'll come with you,' she said.

The kitchen, like the whole house, had been built on a grand scale for a cast of dozens. Without difficulties we made tea in a pot and sat at the well-scrubbed old wooden central table to drink it from mugs.

'You're not what I expected,' she said. 'You're *cosy*.'

I liked her: couldn't help it.

She went on, 'You're not like my brother said. I'm afraid I didn't explain that it is my brother who is out in the field with the vet. It was he who said I should phone you. He didn't say you were cosy, he said you were flint. I should have introduced you to him, but you can see how things are . . . Anyway, I rely on him dreadfully. He lives in the next village. He came at once when I woke him.'

'Is he,' I asked neutrally, 'your nephew's father?'

'Goodness, no. My nephew . . . Jonathan . . .' She stopped, shaking her head. 'You don't want to hear about Jonathan.'

'Try me.'

'He's our sister's son. Fifteen. He got into trouble, expelled from school . . . on probation . . . his step-father can't stand him. My sister was at her wits' end so I said he could come here for a bit. It's not working out, though. I can't get through to him.' She looked suddenly aghast. 'You don't think he had anything to do with the colt?'

'No, no. What trouble did he get into? Drugs?'

She sighed, shaking her head. 'He was with two other boys. They stole a car and crashed it. Jonathan was in the back seat. The boy driving was also fifteen and broke his neck. Paralysed. Joy-riding, they called it. Some joy! Stealing, that's what it was. And Jonathan isn't repentant. Really, he can be a *pig*. But not the colt . . . not that?'

'No,' I assured her, 'positively not.' I drank hot tea

and asked, 'Is it well known hereabouts that you have this great colt in that field?'

She nodded. 'Eva, who looks after him, she talks of nothing else. All the village knows. That's why there are so many people here. Half the men from the village, as well as the ramblers. Even so early in the morning.'

'And your friends?' I prompted.

She nodded gloomily. 'Everyone. I bought him at the Premium Yearling Sales last October. His breeding is a dream. He was a late foal – end of April – he's . . . he *was* going into training next week. Oh *dear*.'

'I'm so sorry,' I said. I screwed myself unhappily to ask the unavoidable question, 'Who, among your friends, came here in person to admire the colt?'

She was far from stupid, and also vehement. 'No one who came here could *possibly* have done this! People like Lord and Lady Dexter? Of course not! Gordon and Ginnie Quint, and darling Ellis? Don't be silly. Though I suppose,' she went on doubtfully, 'they could have mentioned him to other people. He wasn't a *secret*. Anyone since the Sales would know he was here, like I told you.'

'Of course,' I said.

Ellis.

We finished the tea and went back to the drawing-room. Jonathan, the nephew, stared at me again unwaveringly, and after a moment, to test my own impression, I jerked my head in the direction of the door, walking that way; and, with hardly a hesitation, he stood up and followed.

I went out of the drawing-room, across the hall and through the still wide-open front door onto the drive.

'Sid Halley,' he said behind me.

I turned. He stopped four paces away, still not wholly committed. His accent and general appearance spoke of expensive schools, money and privilege. His mouth and his manner said slob.

'What is it that you know?' I asked.

'Hey! Look here! What do you mean?'

I said without pressure, 'You want to tell me something, don't you?'

'I don't know. Why do you think so?'

I'd seen that intense bursting-at-the-seams expression too often by then to mistake it. He knew something that he ought to tell: it was only his own contrary rebelliousness that had kept him silent so far.

I made no appeal to a better nature that I wasn't sure he had.

I said, guessing, 'Were you awake before four o'clock?'

He glared, but didn't answer.

I tried again. 'You hate to be helpful, is that it? No one is going to catch you behaving well – that sort of thing? Tell me what you know. I'll give you as bad a press as you want. Your obstructive reputation will remain intact.'

'Sod you,' he said.

I waited.

'She'd kill me,' he said. 'Worse, she'd pack me off home.'

'Mrs Bracken?'

He nodded. 'My Aunt Betty.'

'What have you done?'

He used a few old Anglo-Saxon words: bluster to impress me with his virility, I supposed. Pathetic, really. Sad.

'She has these effing stupid rules,' he said. 'Be back in the house at night by eleven-thirty.'

'And last night,' I suggested, 'you weren't?'

'I got probation,' he said. 'Did she tell you?'

'Yeah.'

He took two more steps towards me, into normal talking distance.

'If she knew I went out again,' he said, 'I could get youth custody.'

'If she shopped you, you mean?'

He nodded. 'But . . . sod it . . . to cut a foot off a horse . . .'

Perhaps the better nature was somewhere there after all. Stealing cars was OK, maiming racehorses wasn't. He wouldn't have blinded those ponies: he wasn't that sort of lout.

'If I fix it with your aunt, will you tell me?' I asked.

'Make her promise not to tell Archie. He's worse.'

'Er,' I said, 'who is Archie?'

'My uncle. Aunt Betty's brother. He's Establishment, man. He's the flogging classes.'

I made no promises. I said, 'Just spill the beans.'

'In three weeks I'll be sixteen.' He looked at me intently for reaction, but all he'd caused in me was puzzlement. I thought the cut-off age for crime to be considered 'juvenile' was two years older. He wouldn't be sent to an adult jail.

Jonathan saw my lack of understanding. He said impatiently, 'You can't be under age for sex if you're a man, only if you're a girl.'

'Are you sure?'

'*She* says so.'

'Your Aunt Betty?' I felt lost.

'No, stupid. The woman in the village.'

'Oh . . . ah.'

'Her old man's a long-distance lorry driver. He's away for nights on end. He'd kill me. Youth custody would be apple-pie.'

'Difficult,' I said.

'She *wants* it, see? I'd never done it before. I bought her a gin in the pub.' Which, at fifteen, was definitely illegal to start with.

'So . . . um . . .' I said, 'last night you were coming back from the village . . . When, exactly?'

'It was dark. Just before dawn. There had been more moonlight earlier, but I'd left it late. I was *running*. She – Aunt Betty – she wakes with the cocks. She lets the dogs out before six.' His agitation, I thought, was producing what sounded like truth.

I thought, and asked, 'Did you see any ramblers?'

'No. I was earlier than them.'

I held my breath. I had to ask the next question, and dreaded the answer.

'So, who was it that you saw?'

'It wasn't a "who", it was a "what".' He paused and reassessed his position. 'I didn't go to the village.' He said, 'I'll deny it.'

I nodded. 'You were restless. Unable to sleep. You went for a walk.'

He said, 'Yeah, that's it,' with relief.

'And you saw?'

'A Land-Rover.'

Not a who. A what. I said, partly relieved, partly disappointed, 'That's not so extraordinary, in the country.'

'No, but it wasn't Aunt Betty's Land-Rover. It was much newer, and blue, not green. It was standing in the lane not far from the gate into the field. There was no one in it. I didn't think much of it. There's a path up to the house from the lane. I always go out and in that way. It's miles from Aunt Betty's bedroom.'

'Through the yard with all the dustbins?' I asked.

He was comically astounded. I didn't explain that his aunt had taken me out that way. I said, 'Couldn't it have been a rambler's Land-Rover?'

He said sullenly, 'I don't know why I bothered to tell you.'

I asked, 'What else did you notice about the Land-Rover, except for its colour?'

'Nothing. I told you, I was more interested in getting back into the house without anyone spotting me.'

I thought a bit and said, 'How close did you get to it?'

'I touched it. I didn't see it until I was almost on top of it. Like I told you, I was running along the lane. I was mostly looking at the ground, and it was still almost dark.'

'Was it facing you, or did you run into the back of it?'

'Facing. There was still enough moonlight to reflect off the windscreen. That's what I saw first, the reflection.'

'What part of it did you touch?'

'The bonnet.' Then he added as if surprised by the extent of his memory, 'It was quite hot.'

'Did you see a number plate?'

'Not a chance. I wasn't hanging about for things like that.'

'What else did you see?'

'Nothing.'

'How did you know there was no one in the cab? There might have been a couple lying in there snogging.'

'Well, there wasn't. I looked through the window.'

'Open or shut windows?'

'Open.' He surprised himself again. 'I looked in fast, on the way past. No people, just a load of machinery behind the front seats.'

'What sort of machinery?'

'How the eff do I know? It had handles sticking up. Like a lawn mower. I didn't look. I was in a hurry. I didn't want to be seen.'

'No,' I agreed. 'How about an ignition key?'

'Hey?' It was a protest of hurt feelings. 'I didn't drive it away.'

'Why not?'

'I don't take every car I see. Not alone, ever.'

'There's no fun in it if you're alone?'

'Not so much.'

'So there *was* a key in the ignition?'

'I suppose so. Yah.'

'Was there one key, or a bunch?'

'Don't know.'

'Was there a key-ring?'

'You don't ask much!'

'Think, then.'

He said unwillingly, 'See, I *notice* ignition keys.'

'Yes.'

'It was a bunch of keys, then. They had a silver horseshoe dangling from them on a little chain. A little horseshoe. Just an ordinary key-ring.'

We stared at each other briefly.

He said, 'I didn't think anything of it.'

'No,' I agreed. 'You wouldn't. Well, go back a bit. When you put your hand on the bonnet, were you looking at the windscreen?'

'I must have been.'

'What was on it?'

'Nothing. What do you mean?'

'Did it have a tax disc?'

'It must have done, mustn't it?' he said.

'Well, did it have anything else? Like, say, a sticker saying "Save the Tigers"?'

'No, it didn't.'

'Shut your eyes and think,' I urged him. 'You're running. You don't want to be seen. You nearly collide with a Land-Rover. Your face is quite near the windscreen—'

'There was a red dragon,' he interrupted. 'A red circle with a dragon thing in it. Not very big. One of those sort of transparent transfers that stick to glass.'

'Great,' I said. 'Anything else?'

For the first time he gave it concentrated thought, but came up with nothing more.

'I'm nothing to do with the police,' I said, 'and I won't spoil your probation and I won't give you away to your aunt, but I'd like to write down what you've told me, and if you agree that I've got it right, will you sign it?'

'Hey. I don't know. I don't know why I told you.'

'It might matter a lot. It might not matter at all. But

I'd like to find this bugger . . .' God help me, I thought. I have to.

'So would I.' He meant it. Perhaps there was hope for him yet.

He turned on his heel and went rapidly alone into the house, not wanting to be seen in even semi-reputable company, I assumed. I followed more slowly. Jonathan had not returned to the drawing-room, where the tenants still sat stolidly, the difficult old aunt complained about being woken early, the deaf husband said, 'Eh?' mechanically at frequent intervals and Betty Bracken sat looking into space. Only the three dogs, now lying down and testing their heads on their front paws, seemed fully sane.

I said to Mrs Bracken, 'Do you by any chance have a typewriter?'

She said incuriously, 'There's one in the office.'

'Er . . .'

'I'll show you.' She rose and led me to a small, tidy back room containing the bones of communication but an impression of under-use.

'I don't know how anything works,' Betty Bracken said frankly. 'We have a part-time secretary, once a week. Help yourself.'

She left, nodding, and I thanked her, and I found an electric typewriter under a fitted dust-cover, plugged ready into the current.

I wrote:

> Finding it difficult to sleep I went for a short walk in the grounds of Combe Bassett Manor at about three-thirty in the morning. [I inserted the date.] In the lane near to the gate of the home paddock I passed a Land-Rover that was parked there. The vehicle was blue. I did not look at the number plate. The engine was still hot when I touched the bonnet in passing. There was a key in the ignition. It was one of a bunch of keys on a key-ring which had a silver horseshoe on a chain. There was no one in the vehicle. There was some sort of equipment behind the front seat, but I did not take a close look. On the inside of the windscreen I observed a small transfer of a red dragon in a red circle. I went past the vehicle and returned to the house.

Under another fitted cover I located a copier, so I left the little office with three sheets of paper and went in search of Jonathan, running him to earth eating a haphazard breakfast in the kitchen. He paused over his cereal, spoon in air, while he read what I'd written. Wordlessly, I produced a ballpoint pen and held it out to him.

He hesitated, shrugged and signed the first of the papers with loops and a flourish.

'Why *three*?' he asked suspiciously, pushing the copies away.

'One for you,' I said calmly. 'One for my records.

One for the on-going file of bits and pieces which may eventually catch our villain.'

'Oh.' He considered. 'All right then.' He signed the other two sheets and I gave him one to keep. He seemed quite pleased with his civic-mindedness. He was re-reading his edited deposition over his flakes as I left.

Back in the drawing-room, looking for her, I asked where Mrs Bracken had gone. The aunt, the tenants and the deaf husband made no reply.

Negotiating the hinterland passage and the dustbin yard again, I arrived back at the field, to see Mrs Bracken herself, the fence-leaners, the Scots vet and her brother watching the horse ambulance drive into the field and draw up conveniently close to the colt.

The horse ambulance consisted of a narrow low-slung trailer pulled by a Range Rover. There was a driver and a groom used to handling sick and injured horses and, with crooning noises from the solicitous Eva, the poor young colt made a painful-looking, head-bobbing stagger up a gentle ramp into the waiting stall.

'Oh *dear*, oh *dear*,' Mrs Bracken whispered beside me. 'My dear, dear, young fellow . . . how *could* they?'

I shook my head. Rachel Ferns' pony and four prized colts . . . How could *anyone*.

The colt was shut into the trailer, the bucket containing the foot was loaded, and the pathetic twelve-mile journey to Lambourn began.

The Scots vet patted Betty Bracken sympathetically on the arm, gave her his best wishes for the colt, claimed his car from the line of vehicles in the lane and drove away.

I unclipped my mobile phone and got through to *The Pump*, who forwarded my call to an irate newspaperman at his home in Surrey.

Kevin Mills yelled, 'Where the hell are you? They say all anyone gets on the Hotline now is your answering machine, saying you'll call back. About fifty people have phoned. They're all rambling.'

'Ramblers,' I said.

'What?'

I explained.

'It's supposed to be my day off,' he grumbled. 'Can you meet me in the pub? What time? Five o'clock?'

'Make it seven,' I suggested.

'It's no longer a *Pump* exclusive, I suppose you realise?' he demanded. 'But save yourself for me alone, will you, buddy? Give me the inside edge?'

'It's yours.'

I closed my phone and warned Betty Bracken to expect the media on her doorstep.

'Oh no!'

'Your colt is one too many.'

'Archie!' She turned to her brother for help with a beseeching gesture of the hand and, as if for the thousandth time in their lives, he responded with comfort and competent solutions.

'My dear Betty,' he said, 'if you can't bear to face the Press, simply don't be here.'

'But . . .' she wavered.

'I shouldn't waste time,' I said.

The brother gave me an appraising glance. He himself was of medium height, lean of body, grey in colour, a man to get lost in a crowd. His eyes alone were notable: brown, bright and *aware.* I had an uncomfortable feeling that, far beyond having his sister phone me, he knew a good deal about me.

'We haven't actually met,' he said to me civilly. 'I'm Betty's brother. I'm Archie Kirk.'

I said, 'How do you do,' and I shook his hand.

CHAPTER FIVE

Betty Bracken, Archie Kirk and I returned to the house, again circumnavigating the dustbins. Archie Kirk's car was parked outside the Manor's front door, not far from my own.

The lady of the Manor refusing to leave without her husband, the uncomprehending old man, still saying 'Eh?', was helped with great solicitude across the hall, through the front door and into an ancient Daimler, an Establishment-type conservative-minded political statement if ever I saw one.

My own Mercedes, milk-coffee-coloured, stood beyond: and what, I thought astringently, was it saying about *me*? Rich enough, sober enough, preferring reliability to flash? All spot on, particularly the last. And speed, of course.

Betty spooned her beloved into the back seat of the Daimler and folded herself in beside him, patting him gently. Touch, I supposed, had replaced speech as their means of communication. Archie Kirk took his place behind the wheel as natural commander-in-chief, and drove away, leaving for me the single short parting remark, 'Let me know.'

I nodded automatically. Let him know *what*? Whatever I learned, I presumed.

I returned to the drawing-room. The stolid tenants, on their feet, were deciding to return to their own wing of the house. The dogs snoozed. The cross aunt crossly demanded Esther's presence. Esther, on duty at eight and not a moment before, come ramblers, police or whatever, appeared forbiddingly in the doorway, a small, frizzy-haired worker, clear about her 'rights'.

I left the two quarrelsome women pitching into each other and went in search of Jonathan. What a household! The media were welcome to it. I looked but couldn't find Jonathan, so I just had to trust that his boorishness would keep him well away from inquisitive reporters with microphones. The Land-Rover he'd seen might have brought the machete to the colt, and I wanted, if I could, to find it before its driver learned there was a need for rapid concealment.

The first thing in my mind was the colt himself. I started the car and set off north to Lambourn, driving thoughtfully, wondering what was best to do concerning the police. I had had varying experiences with the Force, some good, some rotten. They did not, in general, approve of freelance investigators like myself, and could be downright obstructive if I appeared to be working on something they felt belonged to them alone. Sometimes, though, I'd found them willing to take over if I'd come across criminal activity that couldn't go unprosecuted. I stepped gingerly round their sensitive areas, and also those of racing's own security services run by the Jockey Club and the British Horse-racing Board. I was careful always not to claim credit for clearing up three-pipe problems. Not even one-pipe problems, hardly worthy of Sherlock Holmes.

Where the Jockey Club itself was concerned, I fluctuated in their view between flavour of the month and anathema, according as to who currently reigned as Senior Steward. With the police, collaboration depended very much on which individual policeman I reached and his private-life stress level at the moment of contact.

The rules governing evidence, moreover, were growing ever stickier. Juries no longer without question believed the police. For an object to be admitted for consideration in a trial it had to be ticketed, docketed and continuously accounted for. One couldn't, for instance, flourish a machete and say, 'I found it in X's Land-Rover, therefore it was X who cut off a colt's foot.' To get even within miles of conviction one needed a specific search warrant before one could even *look* in the Land-Rover for a machete, and search warrants weren't granted to Sid Halleys, and sometimes not to the police.

The police force as a whole was divided into autonomous districts, like the Thames Valley Police, who solved crimes in their own area but might not take much notice outside. A maimed colt in Lancashire might not have been heard of in Yorkshire. Serial rapists had gone for years uncaught because of the slow flow of information. A serial horse maimer might have no central file.

Dawdling along up the last hill before Lambourn I became aware of a knocking in the car and pulled over to the side with gloomy thoughts of broken shock absorbers and misplaced trust in reliability, but after the car stopped the knocking continued. With awakening awareness, I climbed out, went round to the back and with difficulty opened the boot. There was something wrong with the lock.

Jonathan lay curled in the space for luggage. He had one shoe off, with which he was assaulting my milk-coffee bodywork. When I lifted the lid he stopped banging and looked at me challengingly.

'What the hell are you doing there?' I demanded.

Silly question. He looked at his shoe. I rephrased it. 'Get out.'

He manoeuvred himself out onto the road and calmly replaced his shoe with no attempt at apology. I slammed the boot lid shut at the second try and returned to the driver's seat. He walked to the passenger side, found the door there locked and tapped on the window to draw my attention to it. I started the engine, lowered the electrically controlled window a little, and shouted to him, 'It's only three miles to Lambourn.'

'No. Hey! You can't leave me here!'

Want to bet, I thought, and set off along the deserted downland road. I saw him, in the rear-view mirror, running after me determinedly. I drove slowly, but faster than he could run. He went on running, nevertheless.

After nearly a mile a curve in the road took me out of his sight. I braked and stopped. He came round the bend, saw my car and put on a spurt, racing this time up to the driver's side. I'd locked the door but lowered the window three or four inches.

'What's all that for?' he demanded.

'What's all what for?'

'Making me run.'

'You've broken the lock on my boot.'

'What?' He looked baffled. 'I only gave it a clout. I didn't have a key.' No key; a clout. Obvious, his manner said.

'Who's going to pay to get it mended?' I asked.

He said impatiently, as if he couldn't understand such small-mindedness, 'What's that got to do with it?'

'With what?'

'With the colt.'

Resignedly I leaned across and pulled up the locking knob on the front passenger door. He went round there and climbed in beside me. I noted with interest that he was hardly out of breath.

Jonathan's haircut, I thought as he settled into his seat and neglected to buckle the seat-belt, shouted an indication of his adolescent insecurity, of his desire to shock or at least to be *noticed.* He had, I thought, bleached inexpert haphazard streaks into his hair with a comb dipped in something like hydrogen peroxide. Straight and thick, the mop was parted in the centre with a wing each side curving down to his cheek, making a curtain beside his eye. From one ear backwards, and round to the other ear, the hair had been sliced off in a straight line. Below the line, his scalp was shaven. To my eyes it looked ugly, but then I wasn't fifteen.

Making a statement through hairstyle was universal, after all. Men with bald crowns above pigtails, men with plaited beards, women with severely scraped back pinnings, all were saying 'This is *me*, and I'm *different*.' In the days of Charles I, when long male hair was normal, rebellious sons had cut off their curls to have roundheads. Archie Kirk's grey hair had been short, neat and controlled. My own dark hair would have curled girlishly if allowed to grow. A haircut was still the most unmistakable give-away of the person inside.

Conversely, a wig could change all that.

I asked Jonathan, 'Have you remembered something else?'

'No, not really.'

'Then why did you stow away?'

'Come on, man, give me a break. What am I supposed to do all day in that graveyard of a house? The aunt's whinging drives me insane and even Karl Marx would have throttled Esther.'

He did, I suppose, have a point.

I thoughtfully coasted down the last hill towards Lambourn.

'Tell me about your uncle, Archie Kirk,' I said.

'What about him?'

'You tell me. For starters, what does he do?'

'He works for the government.'

'What as?'

'Some sort of civil servant. Dead boring.'

Boring, I reflected, was the last adjective I would have applied to what I'd seen in Archie Kirk's eyes.

'Where does he live?' I asked.

'Back in Shelley Green, a couple of miles from Aunt Betty. She can't climb a ladder unless he's holding it.'

Reaching Lambourn itself I took the turn that led to the equine hospital. Slowly though I had made the journey, the horse-ambulance had been slower. They were still unloading the colt.

From Jonathan's agog expression, I guessed it was in fact the first view he'd had of a shorn-off leg, even if all he could now see was a surgical dressing.

I said to him, 'If you want to wait half an hour for me, fine. Otherwise, you're on your own. But if you try stealing a car, I'll personally see you lose your probation.'

'Hey. Give us a break.'

'You've had your share of good breaks. Half an hour. OK?'

He glowered at me without words. I went across to where Bill Ruskin, in a white coat, was watching his patient's arrival. He said, 'Hello, Sid,' absentmindedly, then collected the bucket containing the foot and, with me following, led the way into a small laboratory full of weighing and measuring equipment and microscopes.

Unwrapping the foot, he stood it on the bench and looked at it assessingly.

'A good clean job,' he said.

'There's nothing good about it.'

'Probably the colt hardly felt it.'

'How was it done?' I asked.

'Hm.' He considered. 'There's no other point on the leg that you could amputate a foot without using a saw to cut through the bone. I doubt if a single swipe with a heavy knife would achieve this precision. And achieve it several times, on different animals, right?'

I nodded.

'Yes, well, I think we might be looking at game shears.'

'*Game shears?*' I exclaimed. 'Do you mean those sort of heavy scissors that will cut up duck and pheasant?'

'Something along those lines, yes.'

'But those shears aren't anywhere near big enough for this.'

He pursed his mouth. 'How about a gralloching

knife, then? The sort used for disembowelling deer out on the mountains?'

'Jeez.'

'There are signs of *compression*, though. On balance, I'd hazard heavy game shears. How did he get the colt to stand still?'

'There were horse-nuts on the ground.'

He nodded morosely. 'Slime ball.'

'There aren't any words for it.'

He peered closely at the raw red and white end of the pastern. 'Even if I can reattach the foot, the colt will never race.'

'His owner knows that. She wants to save his life.'

'Better to collect the insurance.'

'No insurance. A quarter of a million down the drain. But it's not the money she's grieving over. What she's feeling is guilt.'

He understood. He saw it often.

Eventually he said, 'I'll give it a try. I don't hold out much hope.'

'You'll photograph this as it is?'

He looked at the foot. 'Oh, sure. Photos, X-rays, blood tests on the colt, micro-stitching, every luxury. I'll get on with anaesthetising the colt as soon as possible. The foot's been off too long . . .' He shook his head. 'I'll try.'

'Phone my mobile.' I gave him the number. 'Any time.'

'See you, Sid. And catch the bugger.'

He bustled away, taking the foot with him, and I returned to my car to find Jonathan not only still there but jogging around with excitement.

'What's up?' I asked.

'That Range Rover that pulled the trailer that brought the colt . . .'

'What about it?'

'It's got a red dragon on the windscreen!'

'What? But you said a *blue*—'

'Yeah, yeah, it wasn't the vet's Range Rover I saw in the lane, but it's got a red dragon transfer on it. Not exactly the same, I don't think, but definitely a red dragon.'

I looked round, but the horse-ambulance was no longer in sight.

'They drove it off,' Jonathan said, 'but I saw the transfer close to, and it has *letters* in it.' His voice held triumph, which I allowed was justified.

'Go on, then,' I said. 'What letters?'

'Aren't you going to say "well done"?'

'Well done. What letters?'

'E.S.M. They were cut out of the red circle. Gaps, not printed letters.' He wasn't sure I understood.

'I do see,' I assured him.

I returned to the hospital to find Bill and asked him when he'd bought his Range Rover.

'Our local garage got it for us from a firm in Oxford.'

'What does E.S.M. stand for?'

'God knows.'

'I can't ask God. What's the name of the Range-Rover firm in Oxford?'

He laughed and thought briefly. 'English Sporting Motors. E.S.M. Good Lord.'

'Can you give me the name of someone there? Who did you actually deal with?'

With impatience he said, 'Look, Sid, I'm trying to scrub up to see what I can do about sticking the colt's foot back on.'

'And I'm trying to catch the bugger that took it off. And it's possible he travelled in a Land-Rover sold by English Sporting Motors.'

He said 'Christ' wide-eyed and headed for what proved to be the hospital's record office, populated by filing cabinets. Without much waste of time he flourished a copy of a receipted account, but shook his head.

'Ted James in the village might help you. I paid *him.* He dealt direct with Oxford. You'd have to ask Ted James.'

I thanked him, collected Jonathan, drove into the small town of Lambourn and located Ted James, who would do a lot for a good customer like Bill Ruskin, it seemed.

'No problem,' he assured me. 'Ask for Roger Brook in Oxford. Do you want me to phone him?'

'Yes, please.'

'Right-oh.' He spoke briefly on the phone and reported back. 'He's busy. Saturday's always a busy sales day. He'll help you if it doesn't take long.'

The morning seemed to have been going on for ever, but it was still before eleven o'clock when I talked to Roger Brook, tubby, smooth and self-important in the carpeted sales office of English Sporting Motors.

Roger Brook pursed his lips and shook his head; not the firm's policy to give out information about its customers.

I said ruefully, 'I don't want to bother the police . . .'

'Well . . .'

'And, of course, there would be a fee for your trouble.'

A fee was respectable where a bribe wasn't. In the course of life I disbursed a lot of fees.

It helpfully appeared that the red-dragon transparent transfers were slightly differently designed each year: *improved* as time went on, did I see?

I fetched Jonathan in from outside for Roger Brook to show him the past and present dragon logos, and Jonathan with certainty picked the one that had been, Brook said, that of the year before last.

'Great,' I said with satisfaction. 'How many blue Land-Rovers did you sell in that year? I mean, what are the names of the actual buyers, not the middlemen like Ted James?'

An open-mouthed silence proved amenable to a larger fee. 'Our Miss Denver' helped with a computer print-out. Our Miss Denver got a kiss from me. Roger Brook with dignity took his reward in readies, and Jonathan and I returned to the Mercedes with the names and addresses of two hundred and eleven purchasers of blue Land-Rovers a little back in time.

Jonathan wanted to read the list when I'd finished. I handed it over, reckoning he'd deserved it. He looked disappointed when he reached the end, and I didn't point out to him the name that had made my gut contract.

One of the Land-Rovers had been delivered to Twyford Lower Farms Ltd.

I had been to Twyford Lower Farms to lunch. It was owned by Gordon Quint.

Noon, Saturday. I sat in my parked car outside English Sporting Motors, while Jonathan fidgeted beside me, demanding 'What next?'

I said, 'Go and eat a hamburger for your lunch and be back here in twenty minutes.'

He had no money. I gave him some. 'Twenty minutes.'

He promised nothing, but returned with three minutes to spare. I spent his absence thinking highly unwelcome thoughts and deciding what to do, and when he slid in beside me smelling of raw onions and chips I set off southwards again, on the roads back to Combe Bassett.

'Where are we going?'

'To see your Aunt Betty.'

'But hey! She's not at home. She's at Archie's.'

'Then we'll go to Archie's. You can show me the way.'

He didn't like it, but he made no attempt to jump ship when we were stopped by traffic lights three times on the way out of Oxford. We arrived together in due course outside a house an eighth the size of Combe Bassett Manor; a house, moreover, that was frankly modern and not at all what I'd expected.

I said doubtfully, 'Are you sure this is the place?'

'The lair of the wolf. No mistake. He won't want to see me.'

I got out of the car and pressed the thoroughly modern doorbell beside a glassed-in front porch. The woman who came to answer the summons was small and wrinkled like a drying apple, and wore a sleeveless sundress in blue and mauve.

'Er . . .' I said to her enquiring face, 'Archie Kirk?'

Her gaze lengthened beyond me to include Jonathan in my car, a sight that pinched her mouth and jumped her to an instant wrong conclusion. She whirled away and returned with Archie, who said repressively, 'What is *he* doing here?'

'Can you spare me half an hour?' I asked.

'What's Jonathan done?'

'He's been extraordinarily helpful. I'd like to ask your advice.'

'*Helpful!*'

'Yes. Could you hold your disapproval in abeyance for half an hour while I explain?'

He gave me an intense inspection, the brown eyes

sharp and knowing, as before. Decision arrived there plainly.

'Come in,' he said, holding his front door wide.

'Jonathan's afraid of you,' I told him. 'He wouldn't admit it but he is. Could I ask you not to give him the normal tongue-lashing? Will you invite him in and leave him alone?'

'You don't know what you're asking.'

'I do,' I said.

'No one speaks to me like this.' He was, however, only mildly affronted.

I smiled at his eyes. 'That's because they know you. But I met you only this morning.'

'And,' he said, 'I've heard about your lightning judgements.'

I felt, as on other occasions with people of his sort, a deep thrust of mental satisfaction. Also, more immediately, I knew I had come to the right place.

Archie Kirk stepped out from his door, took the three paces to my car, and said through the window, 'Jonathan, please come into the house.'

Jonathan looked past him to me. I jerked my head, as before, to suggest that he complied, and he left the safe shelter and walked to the house, even if reluctantly and frozen-faced.

Archie Kirk led the way across a modest hallway into a middle-sized sitting-room where Betty Bracken, her husband, and the small woman who'd answered my ring were sitting in armchairs drinking cups of coffee.

The room's overall impression was of old oak and books, a room for dark winter evenings and lamps and log fires, not fitted to the dazzle of June. None of the three faces turned towards us could have looked welcoming to the difficult boy.

The small woman, introducing herself as Archie's wife, stood up slowly and offered me coffee, 'And . . . er . . . Jonathan . . . Coca-Cola?'

Jonathan, as if reprieved, followed her out to the next door kitchen, and I told Betty Bracken that her colt was at that moment being operated on, and that there should be news of him soon. She was pathetically pleased: too pleased, I was afraid.

I said casually to Archie, 'Can I talk to you in private?' and without question he said, 'This way,' and transferred us to a small adjacent room, again all dark oak and books, that he called his study.

'What is it?' he asked.

'I need a policeman,' I said.

He gave me a long level glance and waved me to one of the two hard oak chairs, himself sitting in the other, beside a paper-strewn desk.

I told him about Jonathan's night walk (harmless version) and about our tracing the Land-Rover to the suppliers at Oxford. I said that I knew where the Land-Rover might now be, but that I couldn't get a search warrant to examine it. For a successful prosecution, I mentioned, there had to be integrity of evidence; no chance of tampering or substitution. So I needed a policeman, but one that would listen and cooperate, not one that would either brush me off altogether or one that would do the police work sloppily.

'I thought you might know someone,' I finished. 'I don't know who else to ask, as at the moment this whole thing depends on crawling up to the machine-gun nest on one's belly, so to speak.'

He sat back in his chair staring at me vacantly while the data got processed.

At length he said, 'Betty called in the local police this morning early, but . . . ' he hesitated, 'they hadn't the clout you need.' He thought some more, then picked up an address book. He leafed through it for a number and made a phone call.

'Norman, this is Archie Kirk.'

Whoever Norman was, it seemed he was unwilling.

'It's extremely important,' Archie said.

Norman apparently capitulated, but with protest, giving directions.

'You had better be right,' Archie said to me, disconnecting. 'I've just called in about a dozen favours he owed me.'

'Who is he?'

'Detective Inspector Norman Picton, Thames Valley Police.'

'Brilliant,' I said.

'He's off duty. He's on the gravel pit lake. He's a clever and ambitious young man. And I,' he added with a glimmer, 'am a magistrate, and I may sign a search warrant myself, if he can clear it with his superintendent.'

He rendered me speechless, which quietly amused him.

'You didn't know?' he asked.

I shook my head and found my voice, 'Jonathan said you were a civil servant.'

'That too,' he agreed. 'How did you get that boorish young man to talk?'

'Er . . .' I said. 'What is Inspector Picton doing on the gravel pit lake?'

'Water ski-ing,' Archie said.

There were speedboats, children, wet-suits, picnics. There was a club house in a sea of scrubby grass and people sliding over the shining water pulled by strings.

Archie parked his Daimler at the end of a row of cars, and I, with Jonathan beside me, parked my Mercedes alongside. We had agreed to bring both cars so that I could go on eventually to London, with Archie ferrying Jonathan back to pick up the Brackens and take them all home to Combe Bassett. Jonathan hadn't warmed to the plan, but had ungraciously accompanied me as being a lesser horror than spending the afternoon mooching aimlessly round Archie's aunt-infested house.

Having got as far as the lake, he began looking at the harmless physical activity all around him, not with a sneer but with something approaching interest. On the shortish journey from Archie's house he had asked three moody questions, two of which I answered.

First: 'This is the best day for a long time. How come you get so much done so quickly?'

No answer possible.

And second: 'Did you ever steal anything?'

'Chocolate bars,' I said.

And third: 'Do you mind having only one hand?'

I said coldly, 'Yes.'

He glanced with surprise at my face and I saw that he'd expected me to say no. I supposed he wasn't old enough to know it was a question one shouldn't ask; but then, perhaps he would have asked it anyway.

When we climbed out of the car at the water-ski club I said, 'Can you swim?'

'Do me a favour.'

'Then go jump in the lake.'

'Sod you,' he said, and actually laughed.

Archie had meanwhile discovered that one of the scudding figures on the water was the man we'd come to see. We waited a fair while until a large presence in a blue wet-suit with scarlet stripes down arms and legs let go of the rope pulling him and skied free and gracefully to a sloping landing place on the edge of the water. He stepped off his skis grinning, knowing he'd shown off his considerable skill, and wetly shook Archie's hand.

'Sorry to keep you waiting,' he said, 'but I reckoned once you got here I'd have had it for the day.'

His voice, with its touch of Berkshire accent, held self-confidence and easy authority.

Archie said formally, 'Norman, this is Sid Halley.'

I shook the offered hand, which was cold besides wet. I received the sort of slow searching inspection I'd had from Archie himself: and I had no idea what the policeman thought.

'Well,' he said finally, stirring, 'I'll get dressed.'

We watched him walk away, squelching, gingerly barefooted, carrying his skis. He was back within five minutes, clad now in jeans, sneakers, open-necked shirt and sweater, his dark hair still wet and spiky, uncombed.

'Right,' he said to me. 'Give.'

'Er . . .' I hesitated. 'Would it be possible for Mr Kirk's nephew, Jonathan, to go for a ride in a speedboat?'

Both he and Archie looked over to where Jonathan, not far away, lolled unprepossessingly against my car. Jonathan did himself no favours, I thought; self-destruction rampant in every bolshie tilt of the anti-authority haircut.

'He doesn't deserve any ride in a speedboat,' Archie objected.

'I don't want him to overhear what I'm saying.'

'That's different,' Norman Picton decided. 'I'll fix it.'

Jonathan ungraciously allowed himself to be driven

round the lake by Norman Picton's wife in Norman Picton's boat, accompanied by Norman Picton's son. We watched the boat race past with a roar, Jonathan's streaky mop blown back in the wind.

'He's on the fence,' I said mildly to Archie. 'There's a lot of good in him.'

'You're the only one who thinks so.'

'He's looking for a way back without losing face.'

Both men gave me the slow assessment and shook their heads.

I said, bringing Jonathan's signed statement from my pocket, 'Try this on for size.'

They both read it, Picton first, Archie after.

Archie said in disbelief, 'He never talks. He wouldn't have said all this.'

'I asked him questions,' I explained. 'Those are his answers. He came with me to the Land-Rover central dealers in Oxford who put that red dragon transfer on the windscreen of every vehicle they sell. And we wouldn't know of the Land-Rover's presence in the lane, or its probable owner and whereabouts now, except for Jonathan. So I really do think he's earned his ride on the lake.'

'What exactly do you want the search warrant *for*?' Picton asked. 'One can't get search warrants unless one can come up with a good reason – or at least a convincing possibility or probability of finding something material to a case.'

'Well,' I said, 'Jonathan put his hand on the bonnet

of the vehicle standing right beside the gate to the field where Betty Bracken's colt lost his foot. If you search a certain Land-Rover and find Jonathan's hand-print on the bonnet, would that be proof enough that you'd found the right wheels?'

Picton said, 'Yes.'

'So,' I went on without emphasis, 'if we leave Jonathan here by the lake while your people fingerprint the Land-Rover, there could be no question of his having touched it this afternoon, and not last night.'

'I've heard about you,' Picton said.

'I think,' I said, 'that it would be a good idea to fingerprint that bonnet before it rains, don't you? Or before anyone puts it through a car-wash?'

'Where is it?' Picton asked tersely.

I produced the English Sporting Motors' print-out, and pointed. 'There,' I said. 'That one.'

Picton read it silently, Archie aloud.

'But I know the place. You're quite *wrong*. I've been a guest there. They're friends of Betty's.'

'And of mine,' I said.

He listened to the bleakness I could hear in my own voice.

'Who are we talking about?' Picton asked.

'Gordon Quint,' Archie said. 'It's rubbish.'

'Who is Gordon Quint?' Picton asked again.

'The father of Ellis Quint,' Archie said. 'And you must have heard of *him*.'

Picton nodded. He had indeed.

'I suppose it's possible,' I suggested tentatively, 'that someone *borrowed* the Land-Rover for the night.'

'But you don't believe it,' Picton remarked.

'I wish I did.'

'But where's the connection?' Picton asked. 'There has to be *more.* The fact that Twyford Lower Farms Ltd owned a blue Land-Rover of the relevant year isn't enough on its own. We cannot search that vehicle for hand-prints unless we have good reason to believe that it was that one and no other that we are looking for.'

Archie said thoughtfully, 'Search warrants have been issued on flimsier grounds before now.'

He and Picton walked away from me, the professionals putting their distance between themselves and Sid Public. I thought that if they refused to follow the trail it would be a relief, on the whole. It would let me off the squirming hook. But there could be another month and another colt . . . and an obsession feeding and fattening on success.

They came back, asking why I should link the Quint name to the deed. I described my box chart. Not conclusive, Archie said judiciously, and I agreed, no.

Picton repeated what I'd just said, 'Rachel's pony was bought by her father, Joe, on the advice of Ellis Quint?'

I said, 'Ellis did a broadcast about Rachel's pony losing his foot.'

'I saw it,' Picton said.

They didn't want to believe it any more than I did. There was a fairly long indeterminate silence.

Jonathan came back looking uncomplicatedly happy from his fast laps round the lake, and Norman Picton abruptly went into the club house, returning with a can of Coke which he put into Jonathan's hands. Jonathan held it in his left hand to open it and his right hand to drink. Norman took the empty can from him casually but carefully by the rim, and asked if he would like to try the skiing itself, not just a ride in the boat.

Jonathan, on the point of enthusiastically saying, '*Yes*,' remembered his cultivated disagreeableness and said, 'I don't mind. If you insist, I suppose I'll have to.'

'That's right,' Picton said cheerfully. 'My wife will drive. My son will watch the rope. We'll find you some swimming trunks and a wet-suit.'

He led Jonathan away. Archie watched inscrutably.

'Give him a chance,' I murmured. 'Give him a challenge.'

'Pack him off to the colonies to make a man of him?'

'Scoff,' I smiled. 'But long ago it often worked. He's bright and he's bored and he's not yet a totally confirmed delinquent.'

'You'd make a soft and rotten magistrate.'

'I expect you're right.'

Picton returned, saying, 'The boy will stay here until I get back, so we'd better get started. We'll take two cars, mine and Mr Halley's. In that way he can go on to London when he wants. We'll leave your car here, Archie. Is that all right?'

Archie said he didn't trust Jonathan not to steal it.

'He doesn't think stealing's much fun without his pals,' I said.

Archie stared. 'That boy never says *anything*.'

'Find him a dangerous job.'

Picton, listening, said, 'Like what?'

'Like,' I said, unprepared, 'like . . . well . . . on an oil rig. Two years of that. Tell him to keep a diary. Tell him to write.'

'Good God,' Archie said, shaking his head, 'he'd have the place in flames.'

He locked his car and put the keys in his pocket, climbing into the front passenger seat beside me as we followed Norman Picton into Newbury, to his official place of work.

I sat in my car outside the police station while Archie and Picton, inside, arranged the back-ups: the photographer, the fingerprinter, the detective constable to be Inspector Picton's note-taking assistant.

I sat with the afternoon sun falling through the windscreen and wished I were anywhere else, engaged on any other mission.

All the villains I'd caught before hadn't been people I knew. Or people – one had to face it – people I'd thought I'd known. I'd felt mostly satisfaction, sometimes relief, occasionally even regret, but never anything approaching this intensity of entrapped despair.

Ellis was loved. I was going to be hated.

Hatred was inevitable.

Could I bear it?

There was no choice, really.

Archie and Picton came out of the police station followed by their purposeful troop.

Archie, sliding in beside me, said the search warrant was signed, the Superintendent had given the expedition his blessing, and off we could go to the Twyford Lower Farms.

I sat without moving, without starting the car.

'What's the matter?' Archie demanded, looking at my face.

I said with pain, 'Ellis is my friend.'

CHAPTER SIX

Ginnie Quint was gardening in a large straw hat, businesslike gloves and grey overall dungarees, waging a losing war on weeds in flower beds in front of the comfortable main house of Twyford Lower Farms.

'Hello, dear Sid!' She greeted me warmly, standing up, holding the dirty gloves wide and putting her soft cheek forward for a kiss of greeting. 'What a nice surprise. But Ellis isn't here, you know. He went to the races, then he was going up to the Regent's Park flat. That's where you'll find him, dear.'

She looked in perplexity over my shoulder to where the Norman Picton contingent were erupting from their transport.

Ginnie said uncertainly, 'Who are your friends, dear?' Her face cleared momentarily in relief, and she exclaimed, 'Why, it's Archie Kirk! My dear man. How nice to see you.'

Norman Picton, carrying none of Archie's or my social-history baggage, came rather brutally to the point.

'I'm Detective Inspector Picton, madam, of the Thames Valley Police. I've reason to believe you own a blue Land-Rover, and I have a warrant to inspect it.'

Ginnie said in bewilderment, 'It's no secret we have a Land-Rover. Of course we have. You'd better talk to my husband. Sid . . . Archie . . . what's all this about?'

'It's possible,' I said unhappily, 'that someone borrowed your Land-Rover last night and . . . er . . . committed a crime.'

'Could I see the Land-Rover, please, madam?' Picton insisted.

'It will be in the farmyard,' Ginnie said. 'I'll get my husband to show you.'

The scene inexorably unwound. Gordon, steaming out of the house to take charge, could do nothing but protest in the fact of a properly executed search warrant. The various policemen went about their business, photographing, fingerprinting and collecting specimens of dusty earth from the tyre treads. Every stage was carefully documented by the assisting constable.

The warrant apparently covered the machinery and anything else behind the front seat. The two sticking up handles that had looked to Jonathan like those of a lawn mower were, in fact, the handles of a lawn mower – a light electric model. There were also a dozen or so angled iron posts for fencing, also a coil of fencing wire and the tools needed for fastening the wire through the posts. There was an opened bag of horse-feed nuts. There was a rolled leather apron, like those used by farriers. There were two spades, a heavy four-pronged fork and a large knife like a machete wrapped in sacking.

The knife was clean, sharp and oiled.

Gordon, questioned, growled impatiently that a good workman looked after his tools. He picked up a rag and a can of oil, to prove his point. What was the knife for? Clearing ditches, thinning woodland, a hundred small jobs around the fields.

There was a second, longer bundle of sacking lying beneath the fencing posts. I pointed to it non-committally, and Norman Picton drew it out and unwrapped it.

Inside there were two once-varnished wooden handles a good metre in length, with, at the business end, a heavy arrangement of metal.

'Lopping shears,' Gordon pronounced. 'For lopping off small branches of trees in the woods. Have to keep young trees pruned, you know, or you get a useless tangle where nothing will grow.'

He took the shears from Picton's hands to show him how they worked. The act of parting the handles widely away from each other opened heavy metal jaws at the far end; sharp, clean and oiled jaws with an opening wide enough to grip a branch three inches thick. Gordon, with a strong quick motion, pulled the handles towards each other, and the metal jaws closed with a snap.

'Very useful,' Gordon nodded, and rewrapped the shears in their sacking.

Archie, Picton and I said nothing.

I felt faintly sick.

Archie walked away speechless and Gordon, not understanding, laid the sacking parcel back in the Land-Rover and walked after him, saying, puzzled, 'Archie! What is it?'

Picton said to me, 'Well?'

'Well,' I said, swallowing, 'what if you took those shears apart? They look clean, but in the jaws . . . in that hinge . . . just one drop of blood . . . or one hair . . . that would do, wouldn't it?'

'So these shears fit the bill?'

I nodded faintly. 'Mr Kirk saw the colt's leg, like I did. And he saw the foot.' I swallowed again. '*Lopping* shears. Oh Christ.'

'It was only a *horse*,' he protested.

'Some people love their horses like they do their children,' I said. 'Suppose someone lopped off your son's foot?'

He stared. I said wryly, 'Betty Bracken is the fifth bereaved owner I've met in the last three weeks. Their grief gets to you.'

'My son,' he said slowly, 'had a dog that got run over. He worried us sick . . . wouldn't eat properly . . .' He stopped, then said, 'You and Archie Kirk are too close to this.'

'And the Great British public,' I reminded him, 'poured their hearts out to those cavalry horses maimed by terrorists in Hyde Park.'

He was old enough to remember the carnage that had given rise to the daily bulletins and to medals and hero-status bestowed on Sefton, the wonderful survivor of heartless bombs set off specifically to kill harmless horses used by the army solely as a spectacle in plumed parades.

This time the Great British public would vilify the deed, but wouldn't, and couldn't, believe a national idol guilty. Terrorists, yes. Vandals, yes. Idol . . . *no.*

Picton and I walked in the wake of Archie and Gordon, returning to Ginnie in front of the house.

'I don't understand,' Ginnie was saying plaintively. 'When you say the Land-Rover may have been taken and used in a crime . . . what crime do you mean?'

Gordon jumped in without waiting for Picton to explain.

'It's always for robbery,' he said confidently. 'Where did the thieves take it?'

Instead of answering, Norman Picton asked if it was Gordon Quint's habit to leave the ignition key in the Land-Rover.

'Of course not,' Gordon said, affronted. 'Though a little thing like no ignition key never stops a practised thief.'

'If you did by any chance leave the key available – which I'm sure you didn't, sir, please don't get angry – but if anyone could have found and used your key, would it have been on a key-ring with a silver chain and a silver horseshoe?'

'Oh no,' Ginnie interrupted utterly guilelessly. 'That's Ellis's key-ring. And it's not a silver horseshoe, it's white gold. I had it made especially for him last Christmas.'

I drove Archie Kirk back to Newbury. The unmarked car ahead of us carried the four policemen and a variety of bagged, docketed, documented objects for which receipts had been given to Gordon Quint.

Lopping shears in sacking. Machete, the same. Oil rag and oil-can. Sample of horse-feed nuts. Instant photos of red-dragon logo. Careful containers of many lifted fingerprints, including one sharply defined right full hand-print from the Land-Rover's bonnet that, on first inspection, matched exactly the right hand-print from the Coke can held by Jonathan at the lake.

'There's no doubt that it was the Quint Land-Rover in my sister's lane,' Archie said. 'There's no doubt Ellis's keys were in the ignition. But there's no proof that Ellis himself was anywhere near.'

'No,' I agreed. 'No one saw him.'

'Did Norman ask you to write a report?'

'Yes.'

'He'll give your report and Jonathan's statement to the Crown Prosecution Service, along with his own findings. After that, it's up to them.'

'Mm.'

After a silence, as if searching for words of comfort, Archie said, 'You've done wonders.'

'I hate it.'

'But it doesn't stop you.'

What if he can't help it . . .? What if I couldn't help it, either?

At the police station, saying goodbye, Archie said, 'Sid . . . you don't mind if I call you Sid? And I'm Archie, of course, as you know . . . I do have some idea of what you're facing. I just wanted you to know.'

'I . . . er . . . thanks,' I said. 'If you wait a minute, I'll phone the equine hospital and find out how the colt is doing.'

His face lightened but the news was moderate.

'I've re-attached the tendon,' Bill reported. 'I grafted a couple of blood vessels so there's now an adequate blood supply to the foot. Nerves are always difficult. I've done my absolute best and, bar infection, the foot could technically stay in place. The whole leg is now in a cast. The colt is semi-conscious. We have him in slings. But you know how unpredictable this all is. Horses don't recover as easily as humans. There'll be no question of racing, of course, but breeding . . . I understand he's got the bloodlines of champions. Absolutely no promises, mind.'

'You're brilliant,' I said.

'It's nice,' he chuckled, 'to be appreciated.'

I said, 'A policeman will come and collect some of the colt's hair and blood.'

'Good. Catch the bugger,' he said.

I drove willy nilly without haste in heavy traffic to London. By the time I reached the pub I was half an hour late for my appointment with Kevin Mills of *The Pump*, and he wasn't there. No balding head, no paunch, no drooping beer-frothed moustache, no cynical world-weariness.

Without regret I mooched tiredly to the bar, bought some whisky and poured into it enough London tap water to give the distiller fits.

All I wanted was to finish my mild tranquilliser, go home, find something to eat, and sleep. Sleep, I thought, yawning, had overall priority.

A woman's voice at my side upset those plans.

'Are you Sid Halley?' it said.

I turned reluctantly. She had shining black shoulder-length hair, bright light-blue eyes and dark red lipstick, sharply edged. Naturally unblemished skin had been given a matt porcelain powdering. Black eyebrows and eyelashes gave her face strong definition, an impression her manner reinforced. She wore black clothes in June. I found it impossible to guess her age, within ten years, from her face, but her manicured red-nailed hands said no more than thirty.

'I'm from *The Pump*,' she said. 'My colleague, Kevin Mills, has been called away to a rape.'

I said, 'Oh,' vaguely.

'I'm India Cathcart,' she said.

I said 'Oh' again, just as vaguely, but I knew her by her name, by her reputation and by her writing. She was a major columnist, a ruthless interviewer, a deconstructing nemesis, a pitiless exposer of pathetic human secrets. They said she kept a penknife handy for sharpening her ballpoints. She was also funny, and I, like every *Pump* addict, avidly read her stuff and laughed even as I winced.

I did not, however, aim to be either her current or future quarry.

'I came to pick up our exclusive,' she said.

'Ah. 'Fraid there isn't one.'

'But you *said*.'

'I hoped,' I agreed.

'And you haven't answered your phone all day.'

I unclipped my mobile phone and looked at it as if puzzled, which I wasn't. I said, making a discovery, 'It's switched off.'

She said, disillusioned, 'I was warned you weren't dumb.'

There seemed to be no answer to that, so I didn't attempt one.

'We tried to reach you. Where have you been?'

'Just with friends,' I said.

'I went to Combe Bassett. What did I find? No colt,

with or without feet. No Sid Halley. No sobbing colt-owner. I find some batty old fusspot who says everyone went to Archie's house.'

I gazed at her with a benign expression. I could do a benign expression rather well.

'So,' continued India Cathcart with visible disgust, 'I go to the house of a Mr Archibald Kirk in the village of Shelley Green, and what do I find *there*?'

'What?'

'I find about five other newspapermen, sundry photographers, a Mrs Archibald Kirk and a deaf old gent saying "Eh?" '

'So then what?'

'Mrs Kirk is lying, all wide-eyed and helpful. She's saying she doesn't know where anyone is. After three hours of that, I went back to Combe Bassett to look for ramblers.'

'Did you find any?'

'They had rambled twenty miles and had climbed a stile into a field with a resident bull. A bunch of ramblers crashed out in panic through a hedge backwards and the rest are discussing suing the farmer for letting a dangerous animal loose near a public footpath. A man with a pony-tail says he's also suing Mrs Bracken for not keeping her colt in a stable, thus preventing an amputation that gave his daughter hysterics.'

'Life's one long farce,' I said.

A mistake. She pounced on it. 'Is that your comment on the maltreatment of animals?'

'No.'

'Your opinion of ramblers?'

'Footpaths are important,' I said.

She looked past me to the bartender. 'Sparkling mineral water, ice and lemon, please.'

She paid for her own drink as a matter of course. I wondered how much of her challenging air was unconscious and habitual, or whether she volume-adjusted it according to who she was talking to. I often learned useful things about people's characters by watching them talk to others than myself, and comparing the response.

'You're not playing fair,' she said, judging me over the wedge of lemon bestriding the rim of her glass. 'It was *The Pump*'s Hotline that sent you to Combe Bassett. Kevin says you pay your debts. So pay.'

'The Hotline was his own idea. Not a bad one, except for about a hundred false alarms. But there's nothing I can tell you this evening.'

'Not can't. Won't.'

'It's often the same thing.'

'Spare me the philosophy!'

'I enjoy reading your page every week,' I said.

'But you don't want to figure in it?'

'That's up to you.'

She raised her chin. 'Strong men *beg* me not to print what I know.'

I didn't want to antagonise her completely and I could forgo the passing pleasure of banter, so I gave her the benign expression and made no comment.

She said abruptly, 'Are you married?'

'Divorced.'

'Children?'

I shook my head. 'How about you?'

She was more used to asking questions than answering. There was perceptible hesitation before she said, 'The same.'

I drank my Scotch. I said, 'Tell Kevin I'm very sorry I can't give him his inside edge. Tell him I'll talk to him on Monday.'

'Not good enough.'

'No, well . . . I can't do more.'

'Is someone *paying* you?' she demanded. 'Another paper?'

I shook my head. 'Maybe Monday,' I said. I put my empty glass on the bar. 'Goodbye.'

'Wait!' She gave me a straight stare, not overtly or aggressively feminist, but one that saw no need to make points in a battle that had been won by the generation before her. I thought that perhaps India Cathcart wouldn't have made it a condition of continued marriage that I should give up the best skill I possessed. I'd married a loving and gentle girl and turned her bitter: the worst, the most miserable failure of my life.

India Cathcart said, 'Are you hungry? I've had nothing to eat all day. My expense account would run to two dinners.'

There were many worse fates. I did a quick survey of the possibility of being deconstructed all over page fifteen, and decided as usual that playing safe had its limits. Take risks with caution: a great motto.

'Your restaurant or mine?' I said, smiling, and was warned by the merest flash of triumph in her eyes that she thought the tarpon hooked and as good as landed.

We ate in a noisy brightly lit large and crowded black-mirrored restaurant that was clearly the in-place for the in-crowd. India's choice. India's habitat. A few sycophantic hands shot out to make contact with her as we followed a lisping young greeter to a central, noteworthy table. India Cathcart acknowledged the plaudits and trailed me behind her like a comet's tail (Halley's?) while introducing me to no one.

The menu set out to amaze, but from long habit I ordered fairly simple things that could reasonably be dealt with one-handed: watercress mousse, then duck curry with sliced baked plantains. India chose baby aubergines with oil and pesto, followed by a large mound of crisped frogs' legs that she ate uninhibitedly with her fingers.

The best thing about the restaurant was that the decibel level made private conversation impossible: everything anyone said could be overheard by those at the next table.

'So,' India raised her voice, teeth gleaming over a herb-dusted *cuisse*, 'was Betty Bracken in tears?'

'I didn't see any tears.'

'How much was the colt worth?'

I ate some plantain and decided they'd overdone the caramel. 'No one knows,' I said.

'Kevin told me it cost a quarter of a million. You're simply being evasive.'

'What it cost and what it was worth are different. It might have won the Derby. It might have been worth millions. No one knows.'

'Do you always play word games?'

'Quite often,' I nodded. 'Like you do.'

'Where did you go to school?'

'Ask Kevin,' I said, smiling.

'Kevin's told me things about you that you wouldn't want me to know.'

'Like what?'

'Like it's easy to be taken in by your peaceful front. Like you having tungsten where other people have nerves. Like you being touchy about losing a hand. That's for starters.'

I would throttle Kevin, I thought. I said, 'How are the frogs' legs?'

'Muscular.'

'Never mind,' I said. 'You have sharp teeth.'

Her mind quite visibly changed gears from patronising to uncertain, and I began to like her.

Risky to like her, of course.

After the curry and the frogs we drank plain black coffee and spent a pause or two in eye-contact appraisal. I expected she saw me in terms of adjectives and paragraphs. I saw her with appeased curiosity. I now knew what the serial reputation-slasher looked like at dinner.

In the way one does, I wondered what she looked like in bed; and in the way that one doesn't cuddle up to a potential cobra, I made no flicker of an attempt to find out.

She seemed to take this passivity for granted. She paid for our meal with a *Pump* business credit card, as promised, and crisply expected I would kick in my share on Monday as an exclusive for Kevin.

I promised what I knew I wouldn't be able to deliver, and offered her a lift home.

'But you don't know where I live!'

'Wherever,' I said.

'Thanks. But there's a bus.'

I didn't press it. We parted on the pavement outside the restaurant. No kiss. No handshake. A nod from her. Then she turned and walked away, not looking back: and I had no faith at all in her mercy.

On Sunday morning I reopened the small blue suitcase Linda had lent me, and read again through all the clippings that had to do with the maimed Kent ponies.

I played again the video tape of the twenty-minute programme Ellis had made of the child owners, and watched it from a different, and sickened, perspective.

There on the screen he looked just as friendly, just as charismatic, just as expert. His arms went round

Rachel in sympathy. His good-looking face filled with compassion and outrage. Blinding ponies, cutting off a pony's foot, he said, those were crimes akin to murder.

Ellis, I thought in wretchedness, how *could* you?

What if he can't help it?

I played the tape a second time, taking in more details and attentively listening to what he had actually said.

His instinct for staging was infallible. In the shot where he'd commiserated with the children all together, he had had them sitting around on hay bales in a tack room, the children dressed in riding breeches, two or three wearing black velvet riding hats. He himself had sat on the floor among them, casual in a dark open-necked jogging suit, a peaked cap pushed back on his head, sunglasses in pocket. Several of the children had been in tears. He'd given them his handkerchief and helped them cope with grief.

There were phrases he had used when talking straight to camera that had brought the children's horrors sharply to disturbingly visual life: 'pierced empty sockets, their eyesight running down their cheeks', and 'a pure-bred silver pony proud and shining in the moonlight'.

His caring tone of voice alone had made the word-pictures bearable.

'A silver pony shining in the moonlight.' The basis of Rachel's nightmare.

'In the moonlight.' He had *seen* the pony in the moonlight.

I played the tape a third time, listening with my eyes shut, undistracted by the familiar face, or by Rachel in his comforting hug.

He said, 'A silver pony trotting trustfully across the field lured by a handful of horse-nuts.'

He shouldn't have known that.

He could have known it if any of the Ferns had suggested it.

But the Ferns themselves wouldn't have said it. They hadn't fed Silverboy on nuts. The agent of destruction that had come by night had brought the nuts.

Ellis would say, of course, that he had made it up, and the fact that it might be true was simply a coincidence. I rewound the tape and stared for a while into space. Ellis would have an answer to everything. Ellis would be believed.

In the afternoon I wrote a long, detailed report for Norman Picton: not a joyous occupation.

Early Monday morning, as he had particularly requested it, I drove to the police station in Newbury and personally delivered the package into the Detective Inspector's own hands.

'Did you talk about this to anybody?' he asked.

'No.'

'Especially not to Quint?'

'Especially not. But . . .' I hesitated, 'they're a close family. It's more than likely that on Saturday evening or yesterday, Ginnie and Gordon told Ellis that you and I and Archie were sniffing round the Land-Rover and that you took away the shears. I think you must consider that Ellis knows the hunt is on.'

He nodded disgustedly. 'And as Ellis Quint officially lives in the Metropolitan area, we in the Thames Valley district cannot pursue our enquiries . . .'

'You mean, you can't haul him down to the local Regent's Park nick and ask him awkward questions, like what was he doing at 3.00 a.m. on Saturday?'

'That's right. We can't ask him ourselves.'

'I thought these divisions were being done away with.'

'Everything takes time.'

I left him to sort out his problems and set off to drive to Kent. On the way, wanting to give Rachel Ferns a cheering-up present, I detoured into the maze of Kingston and, having parked, walked around the precincts looking for inspiration in the shops.

A windowful of tumbling puppies made me pause; perhaps Rachel needed an animal to love, to replace the pony. And perhaps Linda would *not* be pleased at having to house-train a growing nuisance that moulted and chewed the furniture. I went into the pet shop, however, and that's how I came to arrive at Linda Fern's house with my car full of fish tank, water weeds, miniature ruined castle walls, electric pump, lights, fish food, instructions, and three large lidded buckets of tropical fish.

Rachel was waiting by the gate for my arrival.

'You're half an hour late,' she accused. 'You said you'd be here by twelve.'

'Have you heard of the M25?'

'*Everyone* makes that motorway an excuse.'

'Well, sorry.'

Her bald head was still a shock. Apart from that she looked well, her cheeks full and rounded by steroids. She wore a loose sundress and clumpy trainers on stick-like legs. It was crazy to love someone else's child so comprehensively, yet for the first time ever, I felt the idea of fatherhood take a grip.

Jenny had refused to have children on the grounds that any racing day could leave her a widow, and at the time I hadn't cared one way or another. If ever I married again, I thought, following Rachel into the house, I would long for a daughter.

Linda gave me a bright bright smile, a pecking kiss and the offer of a gin and tonic while she threw together some pasta for our lunch. The table was laid. She set out steaming dishes.

'Rachel was out waiting for you two hours ago!' she said. 'I don't know what you've done to the child.'

'How are things?'

'Happy.' She turned away abruptly, tears as ever near the surface. 'Have some more gin. You said you'd got news for me.'

'Later. After lunch. And I've brought Rachel a present.'

The fish tank after lunch was the ultimate success. Rachel was enthralled, Linda interested and helpful. 'Thank goodness you didn't give her a dog,' she said. 'I can't stand animals under my feet. I wouldn't let Joe give her a dog. That's why she wanted a pony.'

The vivid fish swam healthily through the Gothic ruins, the water weeds rose and swelled, the lights and bubbles did their stuff. Rachel sprinkled fish food and watched her new friends eat. The pet shop owner had persuaded me to take a bigger tank than I'd thought best, and he had undoubtedly been right. Rachel's pale face glowed. Pegotty, in a baby-bouncer, sat wide eyed and open mouthed beside the glass. Linda came with me into the garden.

'Any news about a transplant?' I asked.

'It would have been the first thing I'd told you.'

We sat on the bench. The roses bloomed. It was a beautiful day, heartbreaking.

Linda said wretchedly, 'In acute lymphoblastic leukaemia, which is what Rachel's got, chemotherapy causes remission almost always. More than ninety per cent of the time. In seven out of ten children, the remission lasts for ever, and after five years they can be thought of as cured for life. And girls have a better chance than boys, isn't that odd? But in thirty per cent of children, the disease comes back.'

She stopped.

'And it has come back in Rachel?'

'Oh, *Sid*!'

'Tell me.'

She tried, the tears trickling while she spoke. 'The disease came back in Rachel after less than two years, and that's not good. Her hair was beginning to grow, but it came out again with the drugs. They re-established her again in remission, and they're so good, it isn't so easy the second time. But I know from their faces – and they don't suggest transplants unless they have to, because only about half of bone marrow transplants are successful. I always talk as if a transplant will definitely save her, but it only *might.* If they found a tissue match they'd kill all her own bone marrow with radiation, which makes the children terribly nauseous and wretched, and then when the marrow's all dead they transfuse new liquid marrow into the veins and hope it will migrate into the bones and start making leukaemia-free blood there, and quite often it *works* . . . and sometimes a child can be born with one blood group and be transfused with another. It's extraordinary. Rachel now has type A blood, but she might end up with type O, or something else. They can do so *much* nowadays. One day they may cure *everybody.* But oh . . . oh . . .'

I put my arm round her shoulders while she sobbed. So many disasters were for ever. So many Edens lost.

I waited until the weeping fit had passed, and then I told her I'd discovered who had maimed and destroyed Silverboy.

'You're not going to like it,' I said, 'and it might be

best if you can prevent Rachel from finding out. Does she ever read the newspapers?'

'Only Peanuts.'

'And the television news?'

'She doesn't like news of starving children.' Linda looked at me fearfully. 'I've *wanted* her to know who killed Silverboy. That's what I'm paying you for.'

I took out of my pocket and put into her hands an envelope containing her much-travelled cheque torn now into four pieces.

'I don't like what I found, and I don't want your money. Linda . . . I'm so very sorry . . . but it was Ellis Quint himself who cut off Silverboy's foot.'

She sprang in revulsion to her feet, her immediate anger filling her, the shock hard and physical, the enormity of what I'd said making her literally shake.

I should have broken it more slowly, I thought, but the words had had to be said.

'How can you say such a thing?' she demanded. 'How *can* you? You've got it all wrong. He couldn't possibly! You're *crazy* to say such a thing.'

I stood up also. 'Linda . . .'

'Don't say anything. I won't listen. I *won't*. He is so *nice*. You're *truly* crazy. And of course I'm not going to tell Rachel what you've accused him of, because it would upset her, and you're *wrong*. And I know you've been kind to her . . . and to me . . . but I wouldn't have asked you here if I'd thought you could do so much awful harm. So please . . . *go*. Go, just *go*.'

I shrugged a fraction. Her reaction was extreme, but her emotions were always at full stretch. I understood her, but that didn't much help.

I said persuasively, 'Linda, *listen*.'

'No!'

I said, 'Ellis has been my own friend for years. This is terrible for me, too.'

She put her hands over her ears and turned her back, screaming, 'Go away. Go away.'

I said uncomfortably, 'Phone me, then,' and got no reply.

I touched her shoulder. She jerked away from me and ran a good way down the lawn, and after a minute I turned and went back into the house.

'Is Mummy crying?' Rachel asked, looking out of the window. 'I heard her shout.'

'She's upset.' I smiled, though not feeling happy. 'She'll be all right. How are the fish?'

'Cool.' She went down on her knees, peering into the wet little world.

'I have to go now,' I said.

'Goodbye.' She seemed sure I would come back. It was a temporary farewell, between friends. She looked at the fishes, not turning her head.

'Bye,' I said, and drove ruefully to London knowing that Linda's rejection was only the first: the beginning of the disbelief.

In Pont Square the telephone was ringing when I opened my front door, and continued to ring while

I poured water and ice from a jug in the refrigerator, and continued to ring while I drank thirstily after the hot afternoon, and continued to ring while I changed the battery in my left arm.

In the end, I picked up the receiver.

'Where the bloody hell have you *been*?'

The Berkshire voice filled my ear, delivering not contumely, but information. Norman Picton, Detective Inspector, Thames Valley Police.

'You've heard the news, of course.'

'What news?' I asked.

'Do you live with your head in the sand? Don't you own a radio?'

'What's happened?'

'Ellis Quint is in custody,' he said.

'He's *what*?'

'Yes, well, hold on, he's sort of in custody. He's in hospital, under guard.'

'Norman,' I said, disoriented. 'Start at the beginning.'

'Right.' He sounded over-patient, as if talking to a child. 'This morning two plain clothes officers of the Metropolitan Police went to Ellis Quint's flat overlooking Regent's Park intending to interview him harmlessly about his whereabouts early Saturday morning. He came out of the building before they reached the main entrance, so, knowing him by sight, they approached him, identifying themselves and showing him their badges. At which point,' Picton cleared his throat but didn't seem able to clear his account of pedestrian police phraseology, '. . . at which point Mr Ellis Quint pushed one of the officers away so forcefully that the officer overbalanced into the roadway and was struck by a passing car. Mr Quint himself then ran into the path of traffic as he attempted to cross the road to put distance between himself and the police officers. Mr Quint caused a bus to swerve. The bus struck Mr Quint a glancing blow, throwing him to the ground. Mr Quint was dazed and bruised. He was taken to hospital where he is now in a secure room while investigations proceed.'

I said, 'Are you reading that from a written account?'

'That's so.'

'How about an interpretation in your own earthy words?'

'I'm at work. I'm not alone.'

'OK,' I said. 'Did Ellis panic or did he think he was being mugged?'

Picton half laughed. 'I'd say the first. His lawyers will say the second. But, d'you know what? When they emptied his pockets at the hospital, they found a thick packet of cash – and his passport.'

'No!'

'It isn't illegal.'

'What does he say?'

'He hasn't said anything yet.'

'How's the officer he pushed?'

'Broken leg. He was lucky.'

'And . . . when Ellis's daze wears off?'

'It'll be up to the Met. They can routinely hold him for seventy-two hours while they frame a charge. I'd say that's a toss-up. With the clout he can muster, he'll be out in hours.'

'What did you do with my report?'

'It went to the proper authorities.'

Authorities was such a vague word. Whoever described their occupation as 'an authority'?

'Thanks for phoning,' I said.

'Keep in touch.' An order, it sounded like.

I put down the receiver and found a handwritten scrawl from Kevin Mills on *Pump* note-headed paper in my fax.

He'd come straight to the point.

Sid, you're a shit.

CHAPTER SEVEN

The week got worse, slightly alleviated only by a letter from Linda on Thursday morning. Variably slanting handwriting. Jerky. A personality torn this way and that.

Dear Sid,

I'm sorry I talked to you the way I did. I still cannot believe that Ellis Quint would cut off Silverboy's foot, but I remember thinking when he came here to do the TV programme that he already knew a lot about what had happened. I mean things that hadn't been in the papers, like Silverboy liking horse-nuts, which we never gave him, so how did he know, we didn't know ourselves, and I did wonder who had told him, but of course Joe asked Ellis who to buy a pony from, so of course I thought Ellis knew things about him from way back, like Silverboy being fed on horse-nuts before he came to us.

Anyway, I can see how you got it wrong about

Ellis, and it was very nice of you to bring the fish tank for Rachel, I can't tear her away from it. She keeps asking when you will come back and I don't like to tell her you won't, not as things are, so if you'll visit us again I will not say any more about you being wrong about Ellis. I ask you for Rachel.

We are glad Ellis wasn't hurt today by that horrid bus.

Yours sincerely,

Linda Ferns.

I wrote back thanking her for her letter, accepting her invitation and saying I would phone her soon.

On Tuesday Ellis was charged with 'actual bodily harm' for having inadvertently and without intention pushed 'an assailant' into the path of potential danger (under the wheels of a speeding motor) and was set free 'pending enquiries'.

Norman Picton disillusionedly reported, 'The only approximately good thing is that they confiscated his passport. His lawyers are pointing their fingers up any police nose they can confront, screeching that it's a scandal.'

'Where's Ellis now?'

'Look to your back. Your report is with the Crown Prosecution Service, along with mine.'

'Do you mean you don't know where he is?'

'He's probably in Britain or anywhere he can get to where he doesn't need a passport. He told the magistrates in court that he'd decided to do a sports programme in Australia, and he had to have his passport with him because he needed it to get a visa for Australia.'

'Never underestimate his wits,' I said.

'And he'd better look out for yours.'

'He and I know each other too well.'

On Wednesday afternoon Ellis turned up at his regular television studio as if life were entirely normal and, on completion of an audience-attended recording of a sports quiz, was quietly arrested by three uniformed police officers. Ellis spent the night in custody, and on Thursday morning was charged with severing the foot of a colt: to be exact, the off-fore foot of an expensive two-year-old thoroughbred owned by Mrs Elizabeth Bracken of Combe Bassett Manor, Berkshire. To the vociferous fury of most of the nation, the magistrates remanded him in custody for another seven days, a preliminary precaution usually applied to those accused of murder.

Norman Picton phoned me privately on my home number.

'I'm not telling you this,' he said. 'Understand?'

'I've got cloth ears.'

'It would mean my job.'

'I hear you,' I said. 'I won't talk.'

'No,' he said, 'that, I believe.'

'Norman?'

'Word gets around. I looked up the transcript of the trial of that man that smashed off your hand. You didn't tell *him* what he wanted to know, did you?'

'No . . . well . . . everyone's a fool sometimes.'

'Some fool. Anyway, pin back the cloth ears. The reason why Ellis Quint is remanded for seven days is because after his arrest he tried to hang himself in his cell with his tie.'

'He *didn't!*'

'No one took his belt or tie away, because of who he was. No one in the station *believed* in the charge. There's all hell going on now. The top brass are passing the parcel like a children's party. No one's telling anyone outside anything on pain of death, so Sid . . .'

'I promise,' I said.

'They'll remand him next week for another seven days, partly to stop him committing suicide and partly because . . .' He faltered on the brink of utter trust, his whole career at risk.

'I *promise*,' I said again quickly. 'And if I know what it is you want to keep quiet, then I'll know what not to guess at publicly, won't I?'

'God,' he said, half the anxiety evaporating, 'then . . . there's horse blood in the hinges of the shears, and horse blood and hairs on the oily rag, and horse blood and hairs in the sacking. They've taken samples from the colt in the hospital at Lambourn, and everything's gone away for DNA testing. The results will be back next week.'

'Does Ellis know?'

'I imagine that's why he tried the quick way out. It was an Hermès tie, incidentally, with a design of horseshoes. The simple knot he tied slid undone because the tie was pure smooth silk.'

'For God's sake . . .'

'I keep forgetting he's your friend. Anyway, his lawyers have got to him. They're six deep. He's now playing the lighthearted celebrity, and he's sorrowful about *you*, Sid, for having got him all wrong. His lawyers are demanding proof that Ellis himself was ever at Combe Bassett by night, and we are asking for proof that he wasn't. His lawyers know we would have to drop the case if they can come up with a trustable alibi for any of the other amputations, but so far they haven't managed it. It's early days, though. They'll dig and dig, you can bet on it.'

'Yeah.'

'None of the Land-Rover evidence will get into the papers because the *sub judice* rule kicked in the minute they remanded him. Mostly, that helps us but you, as Sid Halley, won't be able to justify yourself in print until after the trial.'

'Even if I can then.'

'Juries are unpredictable.'

'And the law is, frequently, an ass.'

'People in the Force are already saying you're off your rocker. They say Ellis is too well known. They say that wherever he went he would be recognised, therefore if no one recognised him, that in itself is proof he wasn't there.'

'Mm,' I said. 'I've been thinking about that. Do you have time off at the weekend?'

'Not this weekend, no. Monday do you?'

'I'll see if I can fix something up with Archie . . . and Jonathan.'

'And there's another thing,' Norman said, 'the Land-Rover's presence at Combe Bassett is solid in itself, but Jonathan, if he gets as far as the witness box, will be a *meal* for Ellis's lawyers. On probation for stealing cars! What sort of witness is that?'

'I understood the jury isn't allowed to know anything about a witness. I was at a trial once in the Central Law Courts – the Old Bailey – when a beautifully dressed and blow-dried twenty-six-year-old glamour boy gave evidence – all lies – and the jury weren't allowed to know that he was already serving a sentence for confidence tricks and had come to court straight from jail, via the barber and the wardrobe room. The jury thought him a *lovely* young man. So much for juries.'

'Don't you believe in the jury system?'

'I would believe in it if they were told more. How can a jury come to a prison-or-freedom decision if half the facts are withheld? There should be *no* inadmissable evidence.'

'You're naive.'

'I'm Sid Public, remember? The law bends over backwards to give the accused the benefit of the slightest doubt. The *victim* of murder is never there to give evidence. The colt in Lambourn can't talk. It's safer to kill animals. I'm sorry, but I can't stand what Ellis has become.'

He said flatly, 'Emotion works against you in the witness box.'

'Don't worry. In court, I'm a block of ice.'

'So I've heard.'

'You've heard too damned much.'

He laughed. 'There's an old-boy internet,' he said. 'All you need is the password and a whole new world opens up.'

'What's the password?'

'I can't tell you.'

'Don't bugger me about. What's the password?'

'Archie,' he said.

I was silent for all of ten seconds, remembering Archie's eyes the first time I met him, remembering the *awareness*, the message of knowledge. Archie knew more about me than I knew about him.

I asked, 'What exactly does Archie do in the Civil Service?'

'I reckon,' Norman said, amused, 'that he's very like

you, Sid. What he don't want you to know, he don't tell you.'

'Where can I reach you on Monday?'

'Police station. Say you're John Paul Jones.'

Kevin Mills dominated the front page of *The Pump* on Friday – a respite from the sexual indiscretions of cabinet ministers but a demolition job on myself. '*The Pump*', he reminded readers, 'had set up a Hotline to Sid Halley to report attacks on colts. Owners had been advised to lock their stable doors, and to great effect had done so after the Derby. *The Pump* disclaims all responsibility for Sid Halley now ludicrously fingering Ellis Quint as the demon responsible for torturing defenceless horses. Ellis Quint, whose devotion to thoroughbreds stretches back to his own starry career as the country's top amateur race-rider, the popular hero who braved all perils in the ancient tradition of gentlemen sportsmen . . .'

More of the same.

'See also "Analysis" on page 10, and India Cathcart, page 15.'

I supposed one had to know the worst. I read the leader column – 'Should an ex-jockey be allowed free rein as pseudo sleuth? (Answer: no, of course not.)' – and then, dredging deep for steel, I finally turned to India Cathcart's piece.

> Sid Halley, smugly accustomed to acclaim as a champion, in short time lost his career, his wife and his left hand, and then weakly watched his friend soar to super-celebrity and national star status, all the things that he considered should be his. Who does this pathetic little man think he's kidding? He's no Ellis Quint. He's a has-been with an ego problem, out to ruin what he envies.

That was for starters. The next section pitilessly but not accurately dissected the impulse that led one to compete at speed (ignoring the fact that presumably Ellis himself had felt the same power-hungry inferiority complex).

My ruthless will to win, India Cathcart had written, had destroyed everything good in my own life. The same will to win now aimed to destroy my friend Ellis Quint. This was ambition gone mad.

The Pump would not let it happen. Sid Halley was a beetle ripe for squashing. *The Pump* would exterminate. The Halley myth was curtains.

Damn and blast her, I thought and, for the first time in eighteen years, got drunk.

On Saturday morning, groaning around the flat with a headache, I found a message in my fax machine.

Handwritten scrawl, *Pump*-headed paper same as before . . . Kevin Mills.

Sid, sorry, but you asked for it.

You're still a shit.

Most of Sunday I listened to voices on my answering machine delivering the same opinion.

Two calls relieved the gloom.

One from Charles Roland, my ex-father-in-law. 'Sid, if you're in trouble, there's always Aynsford,' and a second from Archie Kirk, 'I'm at home. Norman Picton says you want me.'

Two similar men, I thought gratefully. Two men with cool dispassionate minds who would listen before condemning.

I phoned back to Charles, who seemed relieved I sounded sane.

'I'm all right,' I said.

'Ellis is a knight in shining armour, though.'

'Yeah.'

'Are you *sure*, Sid?'

'Positive.'

'But Ginnie . . . and Gordon . . . they're *friends*.'

'Well,' I said, 'if *I* cut the foot off a horse, what would you do?'

'But you *wouldn't*.'

'No.'

I sighed. That was the trouble. No one could believe it of Ellis.

'Sid, come, any time,' Charles said.

'You're my rock,' I said, trying to make it sound light. 'I'll come if I need to.'

'Good.'

I phoned Archie and asked if Jonathan were still staying with Betty Bracken.

Archie said, 'I've been talking to Norman. Jonathan is now addicted to water ski-ing and spends every day at the lake. Betty is paying hundreds and says it's worth it to get him out of the house. He'll be at the lake tomorrow. Shall we all meet there?'

We agreed on a time, and met.

When we arrived, Jonathan was out on the water.

'That's him,' Norman said, pointing.

The flying figure in a scarlet wet-suit went up a ramp, flew, turned a somersault in the air and landed smoothly in the water on two skis.

'*That*,' Archie said in disbelief, 'is *Jonathan*?'

'He's a natural,' Norman said. 'I've been out here for a bit most days. Not only does he know his spatial balance and attitude by instinct, but he's fearless.'

Archie and I silently watched Jonathan approach the shore, drop the rope and ski confidently up the sloping landing place with almost as much panache as Norman himself.

Jonathan grinned. Jonathan's streaky hair blew wetly back from his forehead. Jonathan, changed, looked blazingly *happy*.

A good deal of the joy dimmed with apprehension as he looked at Archie's stunned and expressionless face. I took a soft sports bag out of my car and held it out to him, asking him to take it with him to the dressing-rooms.

'Hi,' he said. 'OK.' He took the grip and walked off barefooted, carrying his skis.

'Incredible,' Archie said, 'but he can't ski through life.'

'It's a start,' Norman said.

After we'd stood around for a few minutes discussing Ellis we were approached by a figure in a dark blue tracksuit, wearing also black running shoes, a navy baseball cap and sunglasses and carrying a sheet of paper. He came to within fifteen feet of us and stopped.

'Yes?' Norman asked, puzzled, as to a stranger. 'Do you want something?'

I said, 'Take off the cap and the glasses.'

He took them off. Jonathan's streaky hair shook forward into its normal startling shape and his eyes stared at my face. I gave him a slight jerk of the head, and he came the last few paces and handed the paper to Norman.

Archie for once looked wholly disconcerted. Norman read aloud what I'd written on the paper.

' "Jonathan, this is an experiment. Please put on the clothes you'll find in this bag. Put on the baseball cap, peak forward, hiding your face. Wear the sunglasses. Bring this paper. Walk towards me, stop a few feet away, and don't speak. OK. Thanks, Sid." '

Norman lowered the paper, looked at Jonathan and said blankly, 'Bloody hell.'

'Is that the lot?' Jonathan asked me.

'Brilliant,' I said.

'Shall I get dressed now?'

I nodded, and he walked nonchalantly away.

'He looked totally different,' Archie commented, still amazed. 'I didn't know him at all.'

I said to Norman, 'Did you look at the tape of Ellis's programme, that one I put in with my report?'

'The tape covered with stickers saying it was the property of Mrs Linda Ferns? Yes, I did.'

'When Ellis was sitting on the floor with those children,' I said, 'he was wearing a dark tracksuit, open at the neck. He had a peaked cap pushed back on his head. He looked young. Boyish. The children responded to him . . . touched him . . . *loved* him. He had a pair of sunglasses tucked into a breast pocket.'

After a silence Norman said, 'But he *wouldn't*. He wouldn't wear those clothes on television if he'd worn them to mutilate the Ferns pony.'

'Oh yes he would. It would deeply amuse him. There's nothing gives him more buzz than taking risks.'

'A baseball cap,' Archie said thoughtfully, 'entirely changes the shape of someone's head.'

I nodded. 'A baseball cap and sports clothes can reduce any man of status to anonymity.'

'We'll never prove it,' Norman said.

Jonathan slouched back in his own clothes and with

his habitual half-sneering expression firmly in place. Archie's exasperation with him sharply returned.

'This is not the road to Damascus,' I murmured.

'Damn you, Sid.' Archie glared, and then laughed.

'What are you talking about?' Norman asked.

'St Paul's conversion on the road to Damascus happened like a thunderclap,' Archie explained. 'Sid's telling me not to look for instant miracles by the gravel pit lake.'

Jonathan, now listening, handed me the grip. 'Cool idea,' he said. 'No one knew me.'

'They would, close to.'

'It was still a risk,' Norman objected.

'I told you,' I said, 'the risk is the point.'

'It doesn't make sense.'

'Cutting off a horse's foot doesn't make sense. Half of human actions don't make sense. Sense is in the eye of the beholder.'

I drove back to London.

My answer-phone had answered so many calls that it had run out of recording tape.

Among the general abuse, three separate calls were eloquent about the trouble I'd stirred up. All three of the owners of the other colt victims echoed Linda Ferns' immovable conviction.

The lady from Cheltenham: 'I can't believe you can be so misguided. Ellis is absolutely innocent. I wouldn't have thought of you as being jealous of him, but all the papers say so. I'm sorry, Sid, but you're not welcome here any more.'

The angry Lancashire farmer: 'You're a moron, do you know that? Ellis Quint! You're stupid. You were all right as a jockey. You should give up this pretence of being Sherlock Holmes. You're pitiful, lad.'

The lady from York. 'How *can* you? Dear Ellis! He's worth ten of you, I have to say.'

I switched off the critical voices, but they went on reverberating in my brain.

The Press had more or less uniformly followed *The Pump*'s lead. Pictures of Ellis at his most handsome smiled confidently from news stands everywhere. Trial by media found Ellis Quint the wronged and innocent hero, Sid Halley the twisted jealous cur snapping at his heels.

I'd known it would be bad: so why the urge to bang my head against the wall? Because I was human, and didn't have tungsten nerves, whatever anyone thought. I sat with my eyes shut, ostrich fashion.

Tuesday was much the same. I still didn't bang my head. Close run thing.

On the Wednesday Ellis appeared again before magistrates, who that time set him free on bail.

Norman phoned.

'Cloth ears?' he said. 'Same as before?'

'Deaf,' I assured him.

'It was fixed beforehand. Two minutes in court. Different time than posted. The Press arrived just after it was over. Ellis greeted them, free, smiling broadly.'

'Shit.'

Norman said, 'His lawyers have done their stuff. It's rubbish to think that the well-balanced personality intended to kill himself – his tie got caught somehow but he managed to free it. The policeman he pushed failed to identify himself adequately and is now walking about comfortably in a cast. The colt Ellis is accused of attacking is alive and recovering well. As bail is granted in cases of manslaughter, it is unnecessary to detain Ellis Quint any longer on far lesser charges. So . . . he's walked.'

'Is he still to be tried?'

'So far. His lawyers have asked for an early trial date so that he can put this unpleasantness behind him. He will plead not guilty, of course. His lawyers are already patting each other on the back. And . . . I think there's a heavyweight manoeuvring someone in this case.'

'A heavyweight? Who?'

'Don't know. It's just a feeling.'

'Could it be Ellis's father?'

'No, no. Quite different. It's just . . . since our reports, yours and mine, reached the Crown Prosecution Service, there's been a new factor. Political, perhaps. It's difficult to describe. It's not exactly a cover-up. There's already been too much publicity, it's more a sort of re-direction. Even officially, and not just to the Press, someone with muscles is trying to get you thoroughly, and I'm afraid I must say, *malignantly* discredited.'

'Thanks a bunch.'

'Sid, seriously, look out for yourself.'

I felt as prepared as one could be for some sort of catastrophic pulverisation to come my way, but in the event the process was subtler and long drawn out.

As if nothing had happened, Ellis resumed his television programme and began making jokes about Sid Halley – 'Sid Halley? That friend of mine! Have you heard that he comes from Halifax? Halley facts – he makes them up.'

And 'I like halibut – I eat it.' And the old ones that I was used to, 'Halitosis' and 'Hallelujah'.

Hilarious.

When I went to the races, which I didn't do as often as earlier, people either turned their backs or *laughed*, and I wasn't sure which I disliked more.

I took to going only to jumping meetings, knowing Ellis's style took him to the most fashionable meetings on the Flat. I acknowledged unhappily to myself that in my avoidance of him there was an element of cringe. I despised myself for it. All the same, I shrank from a confrontation with him and truly didn't know whether it was because of an ever-deepening aversion to what he had done, or because of the fear – the certainty – that he would publicly mock me.

He behaved as if there were never going to be a trial; as if awkward details like Land-Rovers, lopping shears, and confirmed matching DNA tests tying the shears to the Bracken colt were never going to surface, once the *sub judice* silence ended.

Norman, Archie and also Charles Roland worried that, for all the procedural care we had taken, Ellis's lawyers would somehow get the Land-Rover disallowed. Ellis's lawyers, Norman said, backed by the heavy unseen presence that was motivating them and possibly even paying the mounting fees, now included a defence counsel whose loss rate for the previous seven years was nil.

Surprisingly, despite the continuing barrage of ignominy, I went on being offered work. True, the approach was often tentative and apologetic – 'Whether you're right or pigheaded about Ellis Quint . . .' and 'Even if you've got Ellis Quint all wrong . . .' The nitty-gritty seemed to be that they needed me and there was no one else.

Well, hooray for that. I cleaned up minor mysteries, checked credit ratings, ditto characters, found stolen horses, caught sundry thieves, all the usual stuff.

July came in with a deluge that flooded rivers and ruined the shoes of racegoers, and no colt was attacked at the time of the full moon, perhaps because the nights were wet and windy and black dark with clouds.

The Press finally lost interest in the daily trashing of Sid Halley and Ellis Quint's show wrapped up for the summer break. I went down to Kent a couple of times, taking new fish for Rachel, sitting on the floor with her, playing draughts. Neither Linda nor I mentioned Ellis. She hugged me goodbye each time and asked when I would be coming back. Rachel, she said, had had no more nightmares. They were a thing of the past.

August came quietly and left in the same manner. No colts were attacked. The Hotline went cold. India Cathcart busied herself with a cabinet member's mistress but still had a routinely vindictive jab at me each Friday. I went to America for two short weeks and rode horses up the Teton mountains in Wyoming, letting the wide skies and the forests work their peace.

In September, one dew-laden early autumn English Saturday morning after a calm moonlit night, a colt was discovered with a foot off.

Nauseated, I heard the announcement on the radio in the kitchen while I made coffee.

Listeners would remember, the cool newsreader said, that in June Ellis Quint had been notoriously accused by ex-jockey Sid Halley of a similar attack. Quint was laughing off this latest incident, affirming his total ignorance on the matter.

There were no Hotline calls from *The Pump*, but Norman Picton scorched the wires.

'Have you heard?' he demanded.

'Yes. But no details.'

'It was a yearling colt this time. Apparently, there aren't many two-year-olds in the fields just now, but there are hundreds of yearlings.'

'Yes,' I agreed. 'The yearling sales are starting.'

'The yearling in question belonged to some people near Northampton. They're frantic. Their vet put the colt out of his misery. But get this. Ellis Quint's lawyers have already claimed he has an alibi.'

I stood in silence in my sitting-room, looking out to the unthreatening garden.

'Sid?'

'Mm.'

'You'll have to break that alibi. Otherwise, it will break *you*.'

'Mm.'

'Say something else, dammit.'

'The police can do it. Your lot.'

'Face it. They're not going to try very hard. They're going to believe in his alibi, if it's anything like solid.'

'Do you think, do you *really* think,' I asked numbly, 'that an ultra-respected barrister would connive with his client to mutilate . . . to kill . . . a colt – or pay someone else to do it – to cast doubt on the prosecution's case in the matter of a *different* colt?'

'Put like that, no.'

'Nor do I.'

'So Ellis Quint has set it up himself, and what he has set up, you can knock down.'

'He's had weeks – more than two months – to plan it.'

'Sid,' he said, 'it's not like you to sound defeated.'

If he, I thought, had been on the receiving end of a long pitiless barrage of systematic denigration, he might feel as I did, which, if not comprehensively defeated, was at least battle weary before I began.

'The police at Northampton,' I said, 'are not going to welcome me with open arms.'

'That's never stopped you before.'

I sighed. 'Can you find out from the Northampton police what his alibi actually is?'

'Piece of cake. I'll phone you back.'

I put down the receiver and went over to the window. The little square looked peaceful and safe, the railed garden green and grassy, a tree-dappled haven where generations of privileged children had run and played while their nursemaids gossiped. I'd spent my own childhood in Liverpool's back streets, my father dead and my mother fighting cancer. I in no way regretted the contrast in origins. I had learned self-sufficiency and survival there. Perhaps because of the back streets I now valued the little garden more. I wondered how the children who'd grown up in that garden would deal with Ellis Quint. Perhaps I could learn from them. Ellis had been that sort of child.

Norman phoned back later in the morning.

'Your friend,' he said, 'reportedly spent the night at a private dance in Shropshire, roughly a hundred miles to the north-west of the colt. Endless friends will testify to his presence, including his hostess, a duchess. It was a dance given to celebrate the twenty-first birthday of the heir.'

'Damn.'

'He could hardly have chosen a more conspicuous or more watertight alibi.'

'And some poor bitch will swear she lay down for him at dawn.'

'Why dawn?'

'It's when it happens.'

'How do you know?'

'Never you mind,' I said.

'You're a bad boy, Sid.'

Long ago, I thought. Before Jenny. Summer dances, dew, wet grass, giggles and passion. Long ago and innocent.

Life's a bugger, I thought.

'Sid,' Norman's voice said, 'do you realise the trial is due to start two weeks on Monday?'

'I do realise.'

'Then get a move on, with this alibi.'

'Yes, sir, Detective Inspector.'

He laughed. 'Put the bugger back behind bars.'

On the Tuesday I went to see the Shropshire duchess, for whom I had ridden winners in that former life. She even had a painting of me on her favourite horse, but I was no longer her favourite jockey.

'Yes, of *course* Ellis was here all night,' she confirmed. Short, thin, and at first unwelcoming, she led me through the armour-dotted entrance hall of her draughty old house to the sitting-room where she had been watching the jump racing on television when I arrived.

Her front door had been opened to me by an arthritic old manservant who had hobbled away to see if Her Grace was in. Her Grace had come into the hall clearly anxious to get rid of me as soon as possible, and had then relented, her old kindness towards me resurfacing like a lost but familiar habit.

A three-mile steeplechase was just finishing, the jockeys kicking side by side to the finish line, the horses tired and straining, the race going in the end to the one carrying less weight.

The duchess turned down the volume, the better to talk.

'I cannot *believe*, Sid,' she said, 'that you've accused dear Ellis of something so *disgusting*. I know you and Ellis have been friends for years. Everyone knows that. I do think he's been a bit unkind about you on television, but you did *ask* for it, you know.'

'But he *was* here . . .?' I asked.

'Of course. All night. It was five or later when everyone started to leave. The band was playing still . . . we'd all had breakfast . . .'

'When did the dance start?' I asked.

'*Start?* The invitations were for ten. But you know how people are. It was eleven or midnight before most people came. We had the fireworks at three-thirty because rain was forecast for later, but it was fine all night, thank goodness.'

'Did Ellis say goodnight when he left?'

'My dear Sid, there were over three hundred people here last Friday night. A *succès fou*, if I say it myself.'

'So you don't actually remember when Ellis left?'

'The last I saw of him he was dancing an eightsome with that gawky Raven girl. Do drop it, Sid. I'm seeing you now for old times' sake, but you're not doing yourself any good, are you?'

'Probably not.'

She patted my hand. 'I'll always *know* you, at the races and so on.'

'Thank you,' I said.

'Yes. Be a dear and find your own way out. Poor old Stone has such bad arthritis these days.'

She turned up the volume in preparation for the next race, and I left.

The gawky Raven girl who had danced an eightsome reel with Ellis turned out to be the third daughter of an earl. She herself had gone off to Greece to join someone's yacht, but her sister (the second daughter) insisted that Ellis had danced with dozens of people after that, and wasn't I, Sid Halley, being a teeny weeny *twit*?

I went to see Miss Richardson and Mrs Bethany, joint owners of the Windward Stud Farm, home of the latest colt victim: and to my dismay found Ginnie Quint there as well.

All three women were in the stud farm's office, a building separate from the rambling one-storey dwelling house. A groom long-reining a yearling had directed me incuriously and I drew up outside the pinkish brick new-looking structure without relish for my mission, but not expecting a tornado.

I knocked and entered, as one does with such offices, and found myself in the normal clutter of desks, computers, copiers, wall charts and endless piles of paper.

I'd done a certain amount of homework before I went there, so it was easy to identify Miss Richardson as the tall bulky dominant figure in tweed jacket, worn cord trousers and wiry grey short cropped curls. Fifty, I thought; despises men. Mrs Bethany, a smaller, less powerful version of Miss Richardson, was reputedly the one who stayed up at night when the mares were foaling, the one on whose empathy with horses the whole enterprise floated.

The women didn't own the farm's two stallions (they belonged to syndicates) nor any of the mares: Windward Stud was a cross between a livery stable and a maternity ward. They couldn't afford the bad publicity of the victimised yearling.

Ginnie Quint, sitting behind one of the desks, leapt furiously to her feet the instant I appeared in the doorway and poured over me an accumulated concentration of verbal volcanic lava, scalding, shrivelling, sticking my feet to the ground and my tongue in dryness to the roof of my mouth.

'He *trusted* you. He would have *died* for you.'

I sensed Miss Richardson and Mrs Bethany listening in astonishment, not knowing who I was nor what I'd done to deserve such an onslaught; but I had eyes only for Ginnie, whose long fondness for me had fermented to hate.

'You're going to go into court and try to send your best friend to prison . . . to destroy him . . . pull him down . . . ruin him. You're going to *betray* him. You're not fit to live.'

Emotion twisted her gentle features into ugliness. Her words came out spitting.

It was her own son who had done this. Her golden idolised son. He had made of me finally the traitor that would deliver the kiss.

I said absolutely nothing.

I felt, more intensely than ever, the by now accustomed and bitter awareness of the futility of rebellion. Gagged by *sub judice*, I'd been unable all along to put up any defence, especially because the Press had tended to pounce on my indignant protests and label them as 'whining' and 'diddums', and 'please teacher, he hit me . . .' and 'it's not fair, I hit him first'.

A quick check with a lawyer had confirmed that though trying to sue one paper for libel might have been possible, suing the whole lot was not practical. Ellis's jokes were not actionable and, unfortunately, the fact that I was still profitably employed in my chosen occupation meant that I couldn't prove the criticism had damaged me financially.

'Grit your teeth and take it,' he'd advised cheerfully, and I'd paid him for an opinion I gave myself free every day.

As there was no hope of Ginnie's listening to anything I might say, I unhappily but pragmatically turned to retreat, intending to return another day to talk to Miss Richardson and Mrs Bethany, and found my way barred by two new burly arrivals, known already to the stud owners as policemen.

'Sergeant Smith reporting, madam,' one said to Miss Richardson.

She nodded. 'Yes, sergeant?'

'We've found an object hidden in one of the hedges round the field where your horse was done in.'

No one objected to my presence, so I remained in the office, quiet and riveted.

Sergeant Smith carried a long narrow bundle which

he laid on one of the desks. 'Could you tell us, madam, if this belongs to *you*?'

His manner was almost hostile: accusatory. He seemed to expect the answer to be yes.

'What is it?' Miss Richardson asked, very far from guilty perturbation.

'This, madam,' the sergeant said with a note of triumph, and lifted back folds of filthy cloth to reveal their contents, which were two long wooden handles topped by heavy metal clippers.

A pair of lopping shears.

Miss Richardson and Mrs Bethany stared at them unmoved. It was Ginnie Quint who turned slowly white and fainted.

CHAPTER EIGHT

So here we were in October, with the leaves weeping yellowly from the trees.

Here I was, perched on the end of Rachel Ferns' bed, wearing a huge fluffy orange clown wig and a red bulbous nose, making sick children laugh while feeling far from merry inside.

'Have you hurt your arm?' Rachel asked conversationally.

'Banged it,' I said.

She nodded. Linda looked surprised. Rachel said, 'When things hurt it shows in people's eyes.'

She knew too much about pain for a nine-year-old. I said, 'I'd better go before I tire you.'

She smiled, not demurring. She, like the children wearing the other wigs I'd brought, all had very short bursts of stamina. Visiting was down to ten minutes maximum.

I took off the clown wig and kissed Rachel's forehead. 'Bye,' I said.

'You'll come back?'

'Of course.'

She sighed contentedly, knowing I would. Linda walked with me from the ward to the hospital door.

'It's . . . *awful*,' she said, forlorn, on the exit steps. Cold air. The chill to come.

I put my arms round her. Both arms. Hugged her.

'Rachel asks for you all the time,' she said. 'Joe cuddles her, and cries. She cuddles *him*, trying to comfort him. She's her daddy's little girl. She loves him. But you . . . you're her *friend*. You make her laugh, not cry. It's you she asks for all the time – not Joe.'

'I'll always come if I can.'

She sobbed quietly on my shoulder and gulped, 'Poor Mrs Quint.'

'Mm,' I said.

'I haven't told Rachel about Ellis . . .'

'No. Don't,' I said.

'I've been beastly to you.'

'No, far from it.'

'The papers have said such *dreadful* things about you.' Linda shook in my arms. 'I knew you weren't like that . . . I told Joe I have to believe you about Ellis Quint and he thinks I'm stupid.'

'Look after Rachel, nothing else matters.'

She went back into the hospital and I rode dispiritedly back to London in the TeleDrive car.

Even though I'd returned with more than an hour to spare I decided against Pont Square and took the sharp memory of Gordon Quint's attack straight to the bar in the Piccadilly hotel where I'd agreed to meet the lawyer Davis Tatum.

With a smile worth millions, the French lady in charge of the restaurant arranged for me to have coffee and a sandwich in the tiny bar while I waited for my friend. The bar, in fact, looked as if it had been wholly designed as a meeting place for those about to lunch. There were no more than six tables, a bartender who brought drinks to one's elbow, and a calm atmosphere. The restaurant itself was full of daylight, with huge windows and green plants, and was sufficiently hidden from the busy artery of Mayfair downstairs as to give peace and privacy and no noisy passing trade.

I sat at a bar table in the corner with my back to the entrance, though in fact few were arriving: more were leaving after long hours of talk and lunch. I took some ibuprofen, and waited without impatience. I spent hours in my job, sometimes, waiting for predators to pop out of their holes.

Davis Tatum arrived late and out of breath from having apparently walked up the stairs instead of waiting for the lift. He wheezed briefly behind my back, then came round into view and lowered his six foot three inch bulk into the chair opposite.

He leaned forward and held out his hand for a shake. I gave him a limp approximation, which raised his eyebrows but no comment.

He was a case of an extremely agile mind in a totally unsuitable body. There were large cheeks, double chins, fat-lidded eyes and a small mouth. Dark smooth hair had neither receded nor greyed. He had flat ears, a neck like a weight-lifter and a charcoal pin-striped suit straining over a copious belly. He might have difficulty, I thought, in catching sight of certain parts of his own body. Except in the brain-box, nature had dealt him a sad hand.

'First of all,' he said, 'I have some bad news, and I possibly shouldn't be here talking to you at all, according to how you read *Archbold*.'

'*Archbold* being the dos and don'ts manual for trial lawyers?'

'More or less.'

'What's the bad news, then?' I asked. There hadn't been much that was good.

'Ellis Quint has retracted his "guilty" plea, and has gone back to "not guilty".'

'*Retracted?*' I exclaimed. 'How can one retract a confession?'

'Very easily.' He sighed. 'Quint says he was upset yesterday about his mother's death, and what he said about feeling guilty was misinterpreted. In other words, his lawyers have got over the shock and have had a re-think. They apparently know you have so far not been able to break Ellis Quint's alibi for the night that last colt was attacked in Northamptonshire, and they think they can therefore get the Bracken colt charge dismissed, despite the Land-Rover and circumstantial evidence, so they are aiming for a complete acquittal, not psychiatric treatment, and, I regret to tell you, they are likely to succeed.'

He didn't have to tell me that my own reputation would never recover if Ellis emerged with his intact.

'And *Archbold*?'

'If I were the crown prosecuting counsel in this case I could be struck off for talking to you, a witness. As you know, I am the senior barrister in the chambers where a colleague prosecuting Ellis Quint works. I have seen his brief and discussed the case with him. I can absolutely properly talk to you, though perhaps some people might not think it prudent.'

I smiled. 'Bye bye, then.'

'I may not discuss with you a case in which I may be examining you as a witness. But of course I will not be examining you. Also, we can talk about anything else. Like, for instance, a recent game of golf.'

'I don't play golf.'

'Don't be obtuse, my dear fellow. Your perceptions are acute.'

'Are we talking about angles?'

His eyes glimmered behind the folds of fat. 'I saw the report package that you sent to the CPS.'

'The Crown Prosecution Service?'

'The same. I happened to be talking to a friend. I said your report had surprised me, both by its thoroughness and by your deductions and conclusions. He said I shouldn't be surprised. He said you'd had the whole top echelon of the Jockey Club hanging on your every word. He said that, about a year ago, you'd cleared up two major racing messes at the same time. They've never forgotten it.'

'A year last May,' I said. 'Is that what he meant?'

'I expect so. He said you had an assistant then that isn't seen around any more. The job I'd like you to do might need an assistant for the leg-work. Don't you have your assistant nowadays?'

'Chico Barnes?'

He nodded. 'A name like that.'

'He got married,' I said briefly. 'His wife doesn't like what I do, so he's given it up. He teaches judo. I still see him – he gives me a judo lesson most weeks, but I can't ask him for any other sort of help.'

'Pity.'

'Yes. He was good. Great company and bright.'

'And he got *deterred*. That's why he gave it up.'

I went, internally, very still. I said, 'What do you mean?'

'I heard,' he said, his gaze steady on my face, 'that he got beaten with some sort of thin chain to deter him from helping you. To deter him from all detection. And it worked.'

'He got married,' I said.

David Tatum leaned back in his chair, which creaked under his weight.

'I heard,' he said, 'that the same treatment was doled out to you, and in the course of things the Jockey Club mandarins made you take your shirt off. They said they had never seen anything like it. The whole of your upper body, arms included, was black with bruising, and there were vicious red weals all over you. And with your shirt hiding all that you'd calmly explained to them how and why you'd been attacked and how one of their number, who had arranged it, was a villain. You got one of the big shots chucked out.'

'Who told you all that?'

'One hears things.'

I thought in unprintable curses. The six men who'd seen me that day with my shirt off had stated their intention of never talking about it. They'd wanted to keep to themselves the villainy I'd found within their own walls; and nothing had been more welcome to me than that silence. It had been bad enough at the time. I didn't want continually to be reminded.

'Where does one hear such things?' I asked.

'Be your age, Sid. In the clubs . . . Buck's, the Turf, the RAC, the Garrick . . . these things get mentioned.'

'How often . . . do they get mentioned? How often have you heard that story?'

He paused as if checking with an inner authority, and then said, 'Once.'

'Who told you?'

'I gave my word.'

'One of the Jockey Club?'

'I gave my word. If you'd given your word, would *you* tell *me*?'

'No.'

He nodded. 'I asked around, about you. And that's what I was told. Told in confidence. If it matters to you, I've heard it from no one else.'

'It matters.'

'It reflects to your credit,' he protested. 'It obviously didn't stop you.'

'It could give other villains ideas.'

'And do villains regularly attack you?'

'Well, no,' I said. 'Physically no one's laid a finger on me since that time.' Not until yesterday, I thought. 'If you're talking about non-physical assaults . . . Have you read the papers?'

'Scurrilous.' Davis Tatum twisted in his seat until he could call the barman. 'Tanqueray and tonic, please – and for you, Sid?'

'Scotch. A lot of water.'

The barman brought the glasses, setting them out on little round white mats.

'Health,' Davis Tatum toasted, raising his gin.

'Survival,' I responded, and drank to both.

He put down his glass and came finally to the point.

'I need someone,' he said, 'who is clever, unafraid and able to think fast in a crisis.'

'No one's like that.'

'What about you?'

I smiled. 'I'm stupid, scared silly a good deal of the time, and I have nightmares. What you think you see, is not what you get.'

'I get the man who wrote the Quint report.'

I looked benignly at my glass and not at his civilised face.

'If you're going to do something to a small child that you know he won't like,' I said, 'such as sticking a needle into him, you *first* tell him what a brave little boy he is – in the hope that he'll then let you make a pincushion of him without complaint.'

There was a palpable silence, then he chuckled, the low rich timbre filling the air. There was embarrassment in there somewhere; a ploy exposed.

I said prosaically, 'What's the job?'

He waited while four businessmen arrived, arranged their drinks and sank into monetary conversation at the table furthest from where we sat.

'Do you know who I mean by Owen Yorkshire?' Tatum asked, looking idly at the newcomers, not at me.

'Owen Yorkshire,' I rolled the name around in memory and came up with only doubts. 'Does he own a horse or two?'

'He does. He also owns Topline Foods.'

'Topline . . . as in sponsored race at Aintree? As in Ellis Quint, guest of honour at the Topline Foods lunch the day before the Grand National?'

'That's the fellow.'

'And the enquiry?'

'Find out if he's manipulating the Quint case to his own private advantage.'

I said thoughtfully, 'I did hear that there's a heavy-weight abroad.'

'Find out who it is, and why.'

'What about poor old Archbold? He'd turn in his grave.'

'So you'll do it!'

'I'll try. But why me? Why not the police? Why not the old boy internet?'

He looked at me straightly. 'Because you include silence in what you sell.'

'And I'm expensive,' I said.

'Retainer and refreshers,' he promised.

'Who's paying?'

'The fees will come through me.'

'And it's agreed,' I said, 'that the results, if any, are yours. Prosecution or otherwise will normally be your choice.'

He nodded.

'In case you're wondering,' I said, 'when it comes to Ellis Quint, I gave the client's money back, in order to be able to stop him myself. The client didn't at first believe in what he'd done. I made my own choice. I have to tell you that you'd run that risk.'

He leaned forward and extended his pudgy hand.

'We'll shake on it,' he said, and grasped my palm with a firmness that sent a shockwave fizzing clear up to my jaw.

'What's the matter?' he said, sensing it.

'Nothing.'

He wasn't getting much of a deal, I thought. I had a reputation already in tatters, a crackled ulna playing up, and the prospect of being chewed to further shreds by Ellis's defence counsel. He'd have done as well to engage my pal Jonathan of the streaky hair.

'Mr Tatum,' I began.

'Davis. My name's Davis.'

'Will you give me your *assurance* that you won't speak of that Jockey Club business around the clubs?'

'Assurance?'

'Yes.'

'But I told you . . . it's to your credit.'

'It's a private thing. I don't like *fuss*.'

He looked at me thoughtfully. He said, 'You have my assurance.' And I wanted to believe in it, but I wasn't sure that I did. He was too intensely a club man, a filler of large armchairs in dark panelled rooms full of old exploded reputations and fruitily repeated secrets. 'Won't say a word, old boy.'

'Sid.'

'Mm?'

'Whatever the papers say, where it really counts, you are respected.'

'Where's that?'

'The clubs are good for gossip, but these days that's not where the power lies.'

'Power wanders round like the magnetic North Pole.'

'Who said that?'

'I just did,' I said.

'No, I mean, did you make it up?'

'I've no idea.'

'Power, these days, is fragmented,' he said.

I added, 'And where the power is at any one time is not necessarily where one would want to be.'

He beamed proprietorially as if he'd invented me himself.

There was a quick rustle of clothes beside my ear and a drift of flowery scent, and a young woman tweaked a chair round to join our table and sat in it, looking triumphant.

'Well, well, well,' she said. 'Mr Davis Tatum and Sid Halley! What a surprise!'

I said, to Davis Tatum's mystified face, 'This is Miss India Cathcart, who writes for *The Pump*. If you say nothing you'll find yourself quoted repeating things you never thought, and if you say anything at all, you'll wish you hadn't.'

'Sid,' she said mock-sorrowfully, 'can't you take a bit of kicking around?'

Tatum opened his mouth indignantly and, as I was afraid he might try to defend me, I shook my head. He stared at me, then with a complete change of manner said in smooth lawyerly detachment, 'Miss Cathcart, why are you here?'

'Why? To see you, of course.'

'But why?'

She looked from him to me and back again, her appearance just as I remembered it: flawless porcelain skin, light-blue eyes, cleanly outlined mouth, black shining hair. She wore brown and red, with amber beads.

She said, 'Isn't it improper for a colleague of the Crown Prosecutor to be seen talking to one of the witnesses?'

'No, it isn't,' Tatum said, and asked me, 'Did you tell her we were meeting here?'

'Of course not.'

'Then how . . . why, Miss Cathcart, are you here?'

'I told you. It's a story.'

'Does *The Pump* know you're here?' I asked.

A shade crossly she said, 'I'm not a child. I'm allowed out on my own, you know. And anyway, the paper sent me.'

'*The Pump* told you we'd be here?' Tatum asked.

'My editor said to come and see you. And he was right!'

Tatum said, 'Sid?'

'Mm,' I said. 'Interesting.'

India said to me, 'Kevin says you went to school in Liverpool.'

Tatum, puzzled, asked, 'What did you say?'

She explained, 'Sid wouldn't tell me where he went to school, so I found out.' She looked at me accusingly. 'You don't sound like Liverpool.'

'Don't I?'

'You sound more like Eton. How come?'

'I'm a mimic,' I said.

If she really wanted to, she could find out also that

between the ages of sixteen and twenty-one I'd been more or less adopted by a Newmarket trainer (who *had* been to Eton) who made me into a good jockey and by his example changed my speech and taught me how to live and how to behave and how to manage the money I earned. He'd been already old then, and he died. I often thought of him. He opened doors for me still.

'Kevin told me you were a slum child,' India said.

'Slum is an attitude, not a place.'

'Prickly, are we?'

Damn, I thought. I will *not* let her goad me. I smiled, which she didn't like.

Tatum, listening with disapproval, said, 'Who is Kevin?'

'He works for *The Pump*,' I told him.

India said, 'Kevin Mills is *The Pump*'s chief reporter. He did favours for Halley and got kicked in the teeth.'

'Painful,' Tatum commented dryly.

'This conversation's getting nowhere,' I said. 'India, Mr Tatum is not the prosecutor in any case where I am a witness, and we may talk about anything we care to, including, as just now before you came, golf.'

'You can't play golf with one hand.'

It was Tatum who winced, not I. I said, 'You can watch golf on television without arms, legs or ears. Where did your editor get the idea that you might find us here?'

'He didn't say. It doesn't matter.'

'It is of the essence,' Tatum said.

'It's interesting,' I said, 'because to begin with it was *The Pump* that worked up the greatest head of steam about the ponies mutilated in Kent. That was why I got in touch with Kevin Mills. Between us we set up a Hotline, as a "Save the *Tussilago farfara*" sort of thing.'

India demanded, 'What did you say?'

'*Tussilago farfara*,' Tatum repeated, amused. 'It's the botanical name of the wildflower, coltsfoot.'

'How did you know that?' she asked me fiercely.

'I looked it up.'

'Oh.'

'Anyway, the minute I linked Ellis Quint, even tentatively, to the colts, and to Rachel Ferns' pony, *The Pump* abruptly changed direction and started tearing me apart with crusading claws. I can surely ask, India, why do you write about me so ferociously? Is it just your way? Is it that you do so many hatchet jobs that you can't do anything else? I didn't expect kindness, but you are . . . every week . . . extreme.'

She looked uncomfortable. She did what she had one week called me 'diddums' for doing: she defended herself.

'My editor gives me guidelines.' She almost tossed her head.

'You mean he tells you what to write?'

'Yes. No.'

'Which?'

She looked from me to Tatum and back.

She said, 'He subs my piece to align it with overall policy.'

I said nothing. Tatum said nothing. India, a shade desperately, said, 'Only saints get themselves burned at the stake.'

Tatum said with gravitas, 'If I read any lies or innuendoes about my having improperly talked to Sid Halley about the forthcoming Quint trial, I will sue you personally for defamation, Miss Cathcart, and I will ask for punitive damages. So choose your stake. Flames seem inevitable.'

I felt almost sorry for her. She stood up blankly, her eyes wide.

'Say we weren't here,' I said.

I couldn't read her frozen expression. She walked away from us and headed for the stairs.

'A confused young woman,' Tatum said. 'But how did she – or her paper – know we would be here?'

I asked, 'Do you feed your appointments into a computer?'

He frowned. 'I don't do it personally. My secretary does it. We have a system which can tell where all the partners are, if there's a crisis. It tells where each of us can be found. I did tell my secretary I was coming here, but not who I was going to meet. That still doesn't explain . . .'

I sighed. 'Yesterday evening you phoned my mobile number.'

'Yes, and you phoned me back.'

'Someone's been listening on my mobile phone's frequency. Someone heard you call me.'

'Hell! But you called me back. They heard almost nothing.'

'You gave your name . . . How secure is your office computer?'

'We change passwords every three months.'

'And you use passwords that everyone can remember easily?'

'Well . . .'

'There are people who crack passwords just for the fun of it. And others hack into secrets. You wouldn't believe how *careless* some firms are with their most private information. Someone has recently accessed my own on-line computer – during the past month. I have a detector program that tells me. Much good it will do any hacker as I never keep anything personal there. But a combination of my mobile phone and your office computer must have come up with the *possibility* that your appointment was with me. Someone in *The Pump* did it. So they sent India along to find out . . . and here we are. And because they succeeded, we now know they tried.'

'It's incredible.'

'Who runs *The Pump*? Who sets the policy?'

Tatum said thoughtfully, 'The editor is George Godbar. The proprietor's Lord Tilepit.'

'Any connection with Ellis Quint?'

He considered the question and shook his head. 'Not that I know of.'

'Does Lord Tilepit have an interest in the television company that puts on Ellis Quint's programme? I think I'd better find out.'

Davis Tatum smiled.

Reflecting that, as about thirty hours had passed since Gordon Quint had jumped me in Pont Square, he was unlikely still to be hanging about there with murderous feelings and his fencing post (not least because with Ginnie dead he would have her inquest to distract him) and also feeling that one could take self-preservation to shaming lengths, I left the Piccadilly restaurant in a taxi and got the driver to make two reconnoitring passes round the railed central garden.

All seemed quiet. I paid the driver, walked without incident up the steps to the front door, used my key, went up to the next floor and let myself into the haven of home.

No ambush. No creaks. Silence.

I retrieved a few envelopes from the wire basket clipped inside the letter box and found a page in my fax. It seemed a long time since I'd left, but it had been only the previous morning.

My cracked arm hurt. Well, it would. I'd ridden races – and winners – now and then with cracks: disguising them, of course, because the betting public deserved healthy riders to carry their money. The odd thing was that in the heat of a race one didn't feel an injury. It was in the cooler ebbing of excitement that the discomfort returned.

The best way, always, to minimise woes was to concentrate on something else. I looked up a number and phoned the handy acquaintance who had set up my computers for me.

'Doug,' I said, when his wife had fetched him in from an oil change, 'tell me about listening in to mobile phones.'

'I'm covered in grease,' he complained. 'Won't this do another time?'

'Someone is listening to my mobile.'

'Oh.' He sniffed. 'So you want to know how to stop it?'

'You're dead right.'

He sniffed again. 'I've got a cold,' he said, 'my wife's mother is coming to dinner and my sump is filthy.'

I laughed: couldn't help it. 'Please, Doug.'

He relented. 'I suppose you've got an analog mobile. They have radio signals that can be listened to. It's difficult, though. Your average bloke in the pub couldn't do it.'

'Could you?'

'I'm not your average bloke in the pub. I'm a walking mid-life crisis halfway through an oil change. I could do it if I had the right gear.'

'How do I deal with it?'

'Blindingly simple.' He sneezed and sniffed heavily. 'I need a tissue.' There was a sudden silence on the line, then the distant sound of a nose being vigorously blown, then the hoarse voice of wisdom in my ear.

'OK,' he said. 'You ditch the analog, and get a digital.'

'I do?'

'Sid, being a jockey does not equip the modern man to live in tomorrow's world.'

'I do see that.'

'Everyone,' he sniffed, 'if they had any sense, would go digital.'

'Teach me.'

'The digital system,' he said, 'is based on two numbers, nought and one. Nought and one have been with us from the dawn of computers, and no one has ever invented anything better.'

'They haven't?'

He detected my mild note of irony. 'Has anyone,' he asked, 're-invented the wheel?'

'Er, no.'

'Quite. One cannot improve on an immaculate conception.'

'That's blasphemous.' I enjoyed him always.

'Certainly not,' he said, 'Some things are perfect to begin with. $E = mc^2$, and all that.'

'I grant that. How about my mobile?'

'The signal sent to a digital telephone,' he said, 'is

not one signal, as in analog, but is eight simultaneous signals, each transmitting one eighth of what you hear.'

'Is that so?' I asked dryly.

'You may bloody snigger,' he said, 'but I'm giving you the goods. A digital phone receives eight simultaneous signals, and it is *impossible* for anyone to decode them, except the receiving mobile. Now, because the signal arrives in eight pieces, the reception isn't always perfect. You don't get the crackle or the fading in and out that you get on analog phones, but you do sometimes get bits of words missing. Still, *no one* can listen in. Even the police can never tap a digital mobile number.'

'So,' I said, fascinated, 'where do I get one?'

'Try Harrods,' he said.

'*Harrods?*'

'Harrods is just round the corner from where you live, isn't it?'

'More or less.'

'Try there, then. Or anywhere else that sells phones. You can use the same number that you have now. You just need to tell your service provider. And, of course, you'll need an SIM card. You have one, of course?'

I said meekly, 'No.'

'Sid!' he protested. He sneezed again. 'Sorry. An SIM card is a Subscribers Identity Module. You can't live without one.'

'I can't?'

'Sid, I despair of you. Wake up to technology.'

'I'm better at knowing what a horse thinks.'

Patiently he enlightened me, 'An SIM card is like a credit card. It actually *is* a credit card. Included on it are your name and mobile phone number and other details, and you can slot it into any mobile that will take it. For instance, if you are someone's guest in Athens and he has a mobile that accepts an SIM card, you can slot *your* card into *his* phone and the charge will appear on your account, not his.'

'Are you serious?' I asked.

'With my problems, would I joke?'

'Where do I get an SIM card?'

'Ask Harrods.' He sneezed. 'Ask anyone who travels for a living. Your service provider will provide.' He sniffed. 'So long, Sid.'

Amused and grateful, I opened my post and read the fax. The fax being most accessible got looked at first.

Handwritten, it scrawled simply, 'Phone me,' and gave a long number.

The writing was Kevin Mills', but the fax machine he'd sent it from was anonymously not *The Pump*'s.

I phoned the number given, which would have connected me to a mobile, and got only the infuriating instruction, 'Please try later.'

There were a dozen messages I didn't much want on my answering machine and a piece of information I *definitely* didn't want in a large brown envelope from Shropshire.

The envelope contained a copy of a glossy county magazine, one I'd sent for as I'd been told it included lengthy coverage of the heir-to-the-dukedom's coming-of-age dance. There were, indeed, four pages of pictures, mostly in colour, accompanied by prose gush about the proceedings and a complete guest list.

A spectacular burst of fireworks filled half a page, and there in a group of heaven-gazing spectators, there in white dinner jacket and all his photogenic glory, there unmistakably stood Ellis Quint.

My heart sank. The fireworks had started at three-thirty. At three-thirty, when the moon was high, Ellis had been a hundred miles north-west of the Windward Stud's yearling.

There were many pictures of the dancing, and a page of black and white shots of the guests, names attached. Ellis had been dancing. Ellis smiled twice from the guests' page, carefree, having a good time.

Damn it to hell, I thought. He had to have taken the colt's foot off early. Say by one o'clock. He could then have arrived for the fireworks by three-thirty. I'd found no one who'd seen him *arrive*, but several who swore to his presence after five-fifteen. At five-fifteen he had helped the heir to climb onto a table to make a drunken speech. The heir had poured a bottle of champagne over Ellis's head. Everyone remembered *that*. Ellis could not have driven back to Northampton before dawn.

For two whole days the previous week I'd traipsed

round Shropshire, and next door Cheshire, handed on from grand house to grander, asking much the same questions (according to sex) – did you dance with Ellis Quint or did you drink/eat with him. The answers at first had been freely given, but, as time went on, news of my mission spread before me until I was progressively met by hostile faces and frankly closed doors. Shropshire was solid Ellis country. They'd have stood on their heads to prove him unjustly accused. They were not going to say that they didn't know when he'd arrived.

In the end I returned to the duchess's front gates, and from there drove as fast as prudence allowed, to the Windward Stud Farm, timing the journey at two hours and five minutes. On empty roads at night, Northampton to the duchess might have taken ten minutes less. I'd proved nothing except that Ellis had had time.

Enough time was not enough.

As always before gathering at such dances, the guests had given and attended dinner parties both locally and further away. No one that I'd asked had entertained Ellis to dinner.

No dinner was not enough.

I went through the guest list crossing off the people I'd seen. There were still far more than half unconsulted, most of whom I'd never heard of.

Where was Chico? I needed him often. I hadn't the time, or to be frank, the appetite to locate and question all the guests, even if they would answer. There must have been people – local people – helping with the parking of cars that night. Chico would have chatted people up in the local pubs and found out if any of the car-parkers remembered Ellis's arrival. Chico was good at pubs, and I wasn't in his class.

The police might have done it, but they wouldn't. The death of a colt still didn't count like murder.

The police.

I phoned Norman Picton's police station number and gave my name as John Paul Jones.

He came on the line in a good humour and listened to me without protest.

'Let me get this straight,' he said. 'You want me to ask favours of the Northamptonshire police? What do I offer in return?'

'Blood in the hinges of lopping shears.'

'They'll have made their own tests.'

'Yes, and that Northamptonshire colt is dead and gone to the glue factory. An error, wouldn't you say? Might they not do you a favour in exchange for commiseration?'

'You'll have my head off. What is it you actually *want*?'

'Er . . .' I began, 'I was there when the police found the lopping shears in the hedge.'

'Yes, you told me.'

'Well, I've been thinking. Those shears weren't wrapped in sacking, like the ones we took from the Quints.'

'No, and the shears weren't the same, either. The

ones at Northampton are a slightly newer model. They're on sale everywhere in garden centres. The problem is that Ellis Quint hasn't been reported as buying any, not in the Northamptonshire police district, nor ours.'

'Is there any chance,' I asked, 'of my looking again at the material used for wrapping the shears?'

'If there are horse hairs in it, there's nothing left to match them to, same as the blood.'

'All the same, the cloth might tell us where the shears came from. *Which* garden centre, do you see?'

'I'll see if they've done that already.'

'Thanks, Norman.'

'Thank Archie. He drives me to help you.'

'Does he?'

He heard my surprise. 'Archie has *influence*,' he said, 'and I do what the magistrate tells me.'

When he'd gone off the line I tried Kevin Mills again and reached the same electronic voice: 'Please try later.'

After that I sat in an armchair while the daylight faded and the lights came on in the peaceful square. We were past the equinox, back in winter thoughts, the year dying ahead. Autumn for me had for almost half my life meant the longed-for resurgence of major jump racing, the time of big winners and speed and urgency in the blood. Winter now brought only nostalgia and heating bills. At thirty-four I was growing old.

I sat thinking of Ellis and the wasteland he had made of my year. I thought of Rachel Ferns and Silverboy, and lymphoblasts. I thought of the Press, and especially *The Pump* and India Cathcart and the orchestrated months of vilification. I thought of Ellis's relentless jokes.

I thought for a long time about Archie Kirk, who had drawn me to Combe Bassett and given me Norman Picton. I wondered if it had been from Archie that Norman had developed a belief in a heavy presence behind the scenes. I wondered if it could possibly be Archie who had prompted Davis Tatum to engage me to find that heavyweight. I wondered if it could possibly have been Archie who told Davis Tatum about my run-in with the bad hat at the Jockey Club, and if so, how did *he* know?

I trusted Archie. He could pull my strings, I thought, as long as I was willing to go where he pointed, and as long as I was sure no one was pulling *his*.

I thought about Gordon Quint's uncontrollable rage, and the practical difficulties his fencing post had inflicted. I thought of Ginnie Quint and despair and sixteen floors down.

I thought of the colts and their chopped-off feet.

When I went to bed I dreamed the same old nightmare.

Agony. Humiliation. Both hands.

I awoke sweating.

Damn it all to hell.

CHAPTER NINE

In the morning, when I'd failed yet again to get an answer from Kevin Mills, I shunted by tube across central London and emerged not far from Companies House at 55 City Road, E.C.

Companies House, often my friend, contained the records of all public and private limited companies active in the United Kingdom, including the audited annual balance sheets, investment capital, fixed assets and the names of major shareholders and the directors of the boards.

Topline Foods, I soon learned, was an old company recently taken over by a few new big investors and a bustling new management. The chief shareholder and managing director was listed as Owen Cliff Yorkshire. There were fifteen non-executive directors, of whom one was Lord Tilepit.

The premises at which business was carried out were located at Frodsham in Cheshire. The registered office was at the same address.

The product of the company was foodstuffs for animals.

After Topline, I looked up Village Pump Newspapers (they'd dropped the 'Village' in about 1900, but retained the idea of a central meeting place for gossip) and found interesting items, and after Village Pump Newspapers I looked up the TV company that aired Ellis's sports programme, but found no sign of Tilepit or Owen Yorkshire in its operations.

I travelled home (safely) and phoned Archie, who was, his wife reported, at work.

'Can I reach him at work?' I asked.

'Oh no, Sid. He wouldn't like it. I'll give him a message when he gets back.'

Please try later.

I tried Kevin Mills later and this time nearly got my eardrums perforated. 'At last!'

'I've tried you a dozen times,' I said.

'I've been in an old people's home.'

'Well, bully for you.'

'A nurse hastened three harpies into the hereafter.'

'Poor old sods.'

'If you're in Pont Square,' he said, 'can I call round and see you? I'm in my car not far away.'

'I thought I was *The Pump*'s number one all-time shit.'

'Yeah. Can I come?'

'I suppose so.'

'Great.' He clicked off before I could change my mind and he was at my door in less than ten minutes.

'This is *nice*,' he said appreciatively, looking round my sitting-room. 'Not what I expected.'

There was a Sheraton writing-desk and buttoned brocade chairs and a couple of modern exotic wood inlaid tables by Mark Boddington. The overall colours were greyish blue, soft and restful. The only brash intruder was an ancient fruit machine that worked on tokens.

Kevin Mills made straight towards it, as most visitors did. I always left a few tokens haphazardly on the floor, with a bowl of them nearby on a table. Kevin picked a token from the carpet, fed it into the slot, and pulled the handle. The wheels clattered and clunked. He got two cherries and a lemon. He picked up another token and tried again.

'What wins the jackpot?' he asked, achieving an orange, a lemon and a banana.

'Three horses with jockeys jumping fences.'

He looked at me sharply.

'It used to be the bells,' I said. 'That was boring, so I changed it.'

'And do the three horses ever come up?'

I nodded. 'You get a fountain of tokens all over the floor.'

The machine was addictive. It was my equivalent of the psychiatrist's couch. Kevin played throughout our conversation but the nearest he came was two horses and a pear.

'The trial has started, Sid,' he said, 'so give us the scoop.'

'The trial's only technically started. I can't tell you a thing. When the adjournment's over, you can go to court and listen.'

'That's not exclusive,' he complained.

'You know damned well I can't tell you.'

'I gave you the story to begin with.'

'I sought you out,' I said. 'Why did *The Pump* stop helping the colt owners and shaft me instead?'

He concentrated hard on the machine. Two bananas and a blackberry.

'Why?' I asked.

'Policy.'

'Whose policy?'

'The public wants demolition, they gobble up spite.'

'Yes, but—'

'Look, Sid, we get the word from on high. And don't ask *who* on high. I don't know. I don't like it. None of us likes it. But we have the choice, go along with overall policy or go somewhere else where we feel more in tune. And do you know where that gets you? I work for *The Pump* because it's a good paper with, on the whole, fair comment. OK, so reputations topple. Like I said, that's what Mrs Public wants. Now and then we get a *request*, such as "lean hard on Sid Halley". I did it without qualms, as you'd clammed up on me.'

He looked all the time at the machine, playing fast.

'And India Cathcart?' I asked.

He pulled the lever and waited until two lemons and a jumping horse came to rest in a row.

'India . . .' he said slowly. 'For some reason she didn't want to trash you. She said she'd enjoyed her dinner with you and you were quiet and kind. Kind! I ask you! Her editor had to squeeze the poison out of her drop by drop for that first long piece. In the end he wrote most of her page himself. She was furious the next day when she read it, but it was out on the streets by then and she couldn't do anything about it.'

I was more pleased than I would have expected, but I wasn't going to let Kevin see it. I said, 'What about the continued stab wounds almost every week?'

'I guess she goes along with the policy. Like I said, she has to eat.'

'Is it George Godbar's policy?'

'The big white chief himself? Yes, you could say the editor of the paper has the final say.'

'And Lord Tilepit?'

He gave me an amused glance. Two pears and a lemon. 'He's not a hands-on proprietor of the old school. Not a Beaverbrook or a Harmsworth. We hardly know he's alive.'

'Does he give the overall policy to George Godbar?'

'Probably.' A horse, a lemon and some cherries. 'Why do I get the idea that *you* are interviewing *me*, instead of the other way round?'

'I cannot imagine. What do you know about Owen Cliff Yorkshire?'

'Bugger all. Who is he?'

'Quite likely a friend of Lord Tilepit.'

'Sid,' he protested. 'I do my job. Rapes, murders, little old ladies smothered in their sleep. I do *not* chew off the fingernails of my pay cheque.'

He banged the fruit machine frustratedly. 'The bloody thing hates me.'

'It has no soul,' I said. I fed in a stray token myself with my plastic fingers and pulled the handle. Three horses. Fountains of love. Life's little irony.

Kevin Mills took his paunch, his moustache and his disgusted disgruntlement off to his word-processor, and I again phoned Norman as John Paul Jones.

'My colleagues now think John Paul Jones is a snitch,' he said.

'Fine.'

'What is it this time?'

'Do you still have any of those horse-nuts I collected from Betty Bracken's field, and those others we took from the Land-Rover?'

'Yes, we do. And as you know, they're identical in composition.'

'Then could you find out if they were manufactured by Topline Foods Ltd, of Frodsham in Cheshire?'

After a short silence he said cautiously, 'It could be done, but is it necessary?'

'If you could let me have some of the nuts I could do it myself.'

'I can't let you have any. They are bagged and counted.'

'Shit.' And I could so easily have kept some in my own pocket. Careless. Couldn't be helped.

'Why does it matter where they came from?' Norman asked.

'Um . . . You know you told me you thought there might be a heavyweight somewhere behind the scenes? Well, I've been asked to find out.'

'Jeez,' he said. 'Who asked you?'

'Can't tell you. Client confidentiality and all that.'

'Is it Archie Kirk?'

'Not so far as I know.'

'Huh!' He sounded unconvinced. 'I'll go this far. If you get me some authenticated Topline nuts I'll see if I can run a check on them to find out if they match the ones we have. That's the best I can do, and that's stretching it, and you wouldn't have a prayer if you hadn't been the designer of our whole prosecution – and you can *not* quote me on that.'

'I'm truly grateful. I'll get some Topline nuts, but they probably won't match the ones you have.'

'Why not?'

'The grains – the balance of ingredients – will have changed since those were manufactured. Every batch must have its own profile, so to speak.'

He well knew what I meant, as an analysis of ingredients could reveal their origins as reliably as grooves on a bullet.

'What interests you in Topline Foods?' Norman asked.

'My client.'

'Bugger your client. Tell me.' I didn't answer and he sighed heavily. 'All right. You can't tell me now. I hate amateur detectives. I've got you a strip off that dirty Northampton material. At least, it's promised for later today. What are you going to do about it, and have you cracked Ellis Quint's alibi yet?'

'You're *brilliant*,' I said. 'Where can I meet you? And no, I haven't cracked the alibi.'

'Try harder.'

'I'm only an amateur.'

'Yeah, yeah. Come to the lake at five o'clock. I'm picking up the boat to take it home for winter storage. OK?'

'I'll be there.'

'See you.'

I phoned the hospital in Canterbury. Rachel, the ward sister told me, was 'resting comfortably'.

'What does that mean?'

'She's no worse than yesterday, Mr Halley. When can you return?'

'Sometime soon.'

'Good.'

I spent the afternoon exchanging my old vulnerable analog mobile cellular telephone for a digital receiving eight splintered transmissions that would baffle even the Thames Valley stalwarts, let alone *The Pump.*

From my flat I then phoned Miss Richardson of Northamptonshire, who said vehemently that *no*, I certainly might *not* call on her again. Ginnie and Gordon Quint were her dear friends and it was *unthinkable* that Ellis could harm horses, and I was foul and *wicked* even to think it. Ginnie had told her about it. Ginnie had been very distressed. It was all my fault that she had killed herself.

I persevered with two questions, however, and did get answers of sorts.

'Did your vet say how long he thought the foot had been off when the colt was found at seven o'clock?'

'No, he didn't.'

'Could you give me his name and phone number?'

'No.'

As I had over the years accumulated a whole shelfful of area telephone directories, it was not so difficult, via the Northamptonshire Yellow Pages, to find and talk to Miss Richardson's vet. He would, he said, have been helpful if he could. All he could with confidence say was that neither the colt's leg nor the severed foot had shown signs of recent bleeding. Miss Richardson herself had insisted he put the colt out of his misery immediately, and, as it was also his own judgement, he had done so.

He had been unable to suggest to the police any particular time for the attack; earlier rather than later was as far as he could go. The wound had been clean: one chop. The vet said he was surprised a yearling would have stood still long enough for shears to be applied. Yes, he confirmed, the colt had been lightly shod, and yes, there had been horse-nuts scattered around, but Miss Richardson often gave her horses nuts as a supplement to grass.

He'd been helpful, but no help.

After that I had to decide how to get to the lake, as the normal taken-for-granted act of driving now had complications. I had a knob fixed on the steering wheel of my Mercedes which gave me a good grip for one-(right)handed operation. With my left unfeeling hand I shifted the automatic gear lever.

I experimentally flexed and clenched my right hand. Sharp protests. Boring. With irritation I resorted to ibuprofen and drove to the lake wishing Chico were around to do it.

Norman had winched his boat onto its trailer by the edge of the water. Big, competent and observant, he watched my slow emergence to upright and frowned.

'What hurts?' he asked.

'Self-esteem.'

He laughed. 'Give me a hand with the boat, will you? Pull when I lift.'

I looked at the job and said briefly that I couldn't.

'You only need one hand for pulling.'

I told him unemotionally that Gordon Quint had aimed for my head and done lesser but inconvenient damage. 'I'm telling you in case he tries again and succeeds. He was slightly out of his mind over Ginnie.'

Norman predictably said I should make an official complaint.

'No,' I said. 'This is unofficial, and ends right here.'

He went off to fetch a friend to help him with the boat, and then busied himself with enclosing his powerful outboard engine into a fitted zipped cover.

I said, 'What first gave you the feeling that there was some heavyweight meandering behind the scenes?'

'First?' He went on working while he thought. 'It's months ago. I talked it over with Archie. I expect it was because one minute I was putting together an ordinary case – even if Ellis Quint's fame made it newsworthy – and the next I was being leaned on by the Superintendent to find some reason to drop it, and when I showed him the strength of the evidence, he said the Chief Constable was unhappy, and the reason for the Chief Constable's unhappiness was always the same, which was political pressure from outside.'

'What sort of political?'

Norman shrugged. 'Not party politics especially. A pressure group. Lobbying. A bargain struck somewhere, along the lines of "Get the Quint prosecution aborted and such-and-such a good thing will come your way!" '

'But not a direct cash advantage?'

'Sid!'

'Well, sorry.'

'I should frigging well hope so.' He wrapped thick twine round the shrouded engine. 'I'm not asking cash for a strip of rag from Northamptonshire.'

'I grovel,' I said.

He grinned. 'That'll be the day.' He climbed into his boat and secured various bits of equipment against movement en route.

'No one has entirely given in to the pressure,' he pointed out. 'The case against Ellis Quint has not been dropped. True, it's now in a ropey state. You yourself have been relentlessly discredited to the point where you're almost a liability to the prosecution, and even though that's brutally unfair, it's a fact.'

'Mm.'

In effect, I thought, I'd been commissioned by Davis Tatum to find out who had campaigned to defeat me. It wasn't the first time I'd faced campaigns to enforce my inactivity, but it was the first time I'd been offered a fee to save myself. To save myself, in this instance, meant to defeat Ellis Quint: so I was being paid for *that*, in the first place. And for what *else*?

Norman backed his car up to the boat trailer and hitched them together. Then he leaned through the open front passenger window of the car, unlocked the glove compartment there, and drew out and handed me a plastic bag.

'One strip of dirty rag,' he said cheerfully. 'Cost to you, six grovels before breakfast for a week.'

I took the bag gratefully. Inside, the filthy strip, about

three inches wide, had been loosely folded until it was several layers thick.

'It's about a metre long,' Norman said. 'It was all they would let me have. I had to sign for it.'

'Good.'

'What are you going to do with it?'

'Clean it, for a start.'

Norman said doubtfully, 'It's got some sort of pattern in it but there wasn't any printing on the whole wrapping. Nothing to say where it came from. No garden centre name, or anything.'

'I don't have high hopes,' I said, 'but, frankly, just now every straw's worth clutching.'

Norman stood with his legs apart and his hands on his hips. He looked like a pillar of every possible police strength but what he was actually feeling turned out to be indecision.

'How far can I trust you?' he asked.

'For silence?'

He nodded.

'I thought we'd discussed this already.'

'Yes, but that was months ago.'

'Nothing's changed,' I said.

He made a decision, stuck his head into his car again and this time brought out a business-sized brown envelope which he held out to me.

'It's a copy of the analysis done on the horse-nuts,' he said. 'So read it and shred it.'

'OK. And thanks.'

I held the envelope and plastic bag together and knew I couldn't take such trust lightly. He must be very sure of me, I thought; and felt not complimented but apprehensive.

'I've been thinking,' I said, 'do you remember, way back in June, when we took those things out of Gordon Quint's Land-Rover?'

'Of course I remember.'

'There was a farrier's apron in the Land-Rover. Rolled up. We didn't take that, did we?'

He frowned. 'I don't remember it, but no, it's not among the things we took. What's significant about it?'

I said, 'I've always thought it odd that the colts should stand still long enough for the shears to close round the ankle, even with head-collars and those nuts. But horses have an acute sense of smell . . . and all those colts had shoes on – I checked with their vets – and they would have known the smell of a blacksmith's apron. I think Ellis might have worn that apron to reassure the colts. They may have thought he was the man who shod them. They would have *trusted* him. He could have lifted a fetlock and gripped it with the shears.'

He stared.

'What do you think?' I asked.

'It's you who knows horses.'

'It's how I might get a two-year-old to let me near his legs.'

'As far as I'm concerned,' he said, 'that's how it was done.'

He held out his hand automatically to say goodbye, then remembered Gordon Quint's handiwork, shrugged, grinned, and said instead, 'If there's anything interesting about that strip of rag, you'll let me know?'

'Of course.'

'See you.'

He drove off with a wave, trailing his boat, and I returned to my car, stowed away the bag and the envelope and made a short journey to Shelley Green, the home of Archie Kirk.

He had returned from work. He took me into his sitting-room while his smiling wife cooked in the kitchen.

'How's things?' Archie asked. 'Whisky?'

I nodded. 'A lot of water . . .'

He indicated chairs, and we sat. The dark room looked right in October: imitation flames burnt imitation coals in the fireplace, giving the room a life that the sun of June hadn't achieved.

I hadn't seen Archie since then. I absorbed again the probably deliberate greyness of his general appearance, and I saw again the whole internet in the dark eyes.

He said casually, 'You've been having a bit of a rough time.'

'Does it show?'

'Yes.'

'Never mind,' I said. 'Will you answer some questions?'

'It depends what they are.'

I drank some of his undistinguished whisky and let my muscles relax into the ultimate of non-aggressive, non-combative postures.

'For a start, what do you do?' I said.

'I'm a civil servant.'

'That's not . . . well . . . specific.'

'Start at the other end,' he said.

I smiled. I said, 'It's a wise man who knows who's paying him.'

He paused with his own glass halfway to his lips.

'Go on,' he said.

'Then . . . do you know Davis Tatum?'

After a pause he answered, 'Yes.'

It seemed to me he was growing wary; that he, as I did, had to sort through a minefield of facts one could not or should not reveal that one knew. The old dilemma – does he know I know he knows – sometimes seemed like child's play.

I said, 'How's Jonathan?'

He laughed. 'I hear you play chess,' he said. 'I hear you're a whiz at misdirection. Your opponents think they're winning, and then . . . wham.'

I played chess only with Charles at Aynsford, and not very often.

'Do you know my father-in-law?' I asked. 'Ex-father-in-law, Charles Roland?'

With a glimmer he said, 'I've talked to him on the telephone.'

At least he hadn't lied to me, I thought; and, if he hadn't lied he'd given me a fairly firm path to follow. I asked about Jonathan, and about his sister, Betty Bracken.

'That wretched boy is still at Combe Bassett and now that the water ski-ing season is over he is driving everyone *mad*. You are the only person who sees any good in him.'

'Norman does.'

'Norman sees a talented water-skier with criminal tendencies.'

'Has Jonathan any money?'

Archie shook his head. 'Only the very little we gave him for toothpaste and so on. He's still on probation. He's a mess.' He paused. 'Betty has been paying for the water ski-ing. She's the only one in our family with real money. She married straight out of school. Bobby's thirty years older – he was rich when they married and he's richer than ever now. As you saw, she's still devoted to him. Always has been. They had no children; she couldn't. Very sad. If Jonathan had any sense he would be *nice* to Betty.'

'I don't think he's that devious. Or not yet, anyway.'

'Do you like him?' Archie asked curiously.

'Not much, but I hate to see people go to waste.'

'Stupid boy.'

'I checked on the colt,' I said. 'The foot stayed on.'

Archie nodded. 'Betty's delighted. The colt is permanently lame, but they're going to see if, with his breeding, he's any good for stud. Betty's offering him free next year to good mares.'

Archie's sweet wife came in and asked if I would stay to dinner; she could easily cook extra. I thanked her but stood up to go. Archie shook my hand. I winced through not concentrating, but he made no comment. He came out to my car with me as the last shreds of daylight waned to dark.

He said, 'In the Civil Service, I work in a small unacknowledged off-shoot department which was set up sometime ago to foretell the probable outcome of any high political appointment. We also predict the future inevitable consequences of pieces of proposed legislation.' He paused and went on wryly, 'We call ourselves the Cassandra outfit. We see what will happen and no one believes us. We are always on the look out for exceptional independent investigators with no allegiances. They're hard to find. We think you are one.'

I stood beside my car in the dying light looking into the extraordinary eyes. An extraordinary man of unimaginable insights. I said, 'Archie, I'll work for you to the limit as long as I'm sure you're not sending me into a danger that you know exists but are not telling me about.'

He took a deep breath but gave no undertaking.

'Goodnight,' I said mildly.

'Sid.'

'I'll phone you.' It was as firm a promise, I thought, as 'let's do lunch'.

He was still standing on his gravel as I drove out through his gates. A true civil servant, I thought ruefully. No positive assurances could ever be given because the rules could at any time be changed under one's feet.

I drove north across Oxfordshire to Aynsford and rang the bell of the side entrance of Charles's house. Mrs Cross came in answer to the summons, her enquiring expression melting to welcome as she saw who had arrived.

'The Admiral's in the wardroom,' she assured me, when I asked if he were at home, and she bustled along before me to give Charles the news.

He made no reference to the fact that it was the second time in three days that I had sought his sanctuary. He merely pointed to the gold brocade chair and poured brandy into a tumbler without asking.

I sat and drank and looked gratefully at the austerity and restraint of this thin man who'd commanded ships and was now my only anchor.

'How's the arm?' he asked briefly, and I said lightly, 'Sore.'

He nodded and waited.

'Can I stay?' I said.

'Of course.'

After a longish pause, I said, 'Do you know a man called Archibald Kirk?'

'No, I don't think so.'

'He says he talked to you on the telephone. It was months ago, I think. He's a civil servant and a magistrate. He lives near Hungerford, and I've come here from his house. Can you remember? Way back. I think he may have been asking you about *me.* Like sort of checking up, like a reference. You probably told him that I play chess.'

He thought about it, searching for the memory.

'I would always give you a good reference,' he said. 'Is there any reason why you'd prefer I didn't?'

'No, definitely not.'

'I've been asked several times about your character and ability. I always say if they're looking for an investigator they couldn't do better.'

'You're . . . very kind.'

'Kind, my foot. Why do you ask about this Archibald Church?'

'Kirk.'

'Kirk, then.'

I drank some brandy and said, 'Do you remember that day you came with me to the Jockey Club? The day we got the head of the Security section sacked?'

'I could hardly forget it, could I?'

'You didn't tell Archie Kirk about it, did you?'

'Of course not. I *never* talk about it. I gave you my word I wouldn't.'

'Someone has,' I said morosely.

'The Jockey Club didn't actually swear an oath of silence.'

'I know.' I thought a bit and asked, 'Do you know a barrister called Davis Tatum? He's the head of chambers of the prosecution counsel at Ellis's trial.'

'I know *of* him. Never met him.'

'You'd like him. You'd like Archie, too.' I paused, and went on, 'They both know about that day at the Jockey Club.'

'But Sid . . . does it really matter? I mean, you did the Jockey Club a tremendous favour, getting rid of their villain.'

'Davis Tatum and, I'm sure, Archie, have engaged me to find out who is moving behind the scenes to get the Quint trial quashed. And I'm not telling you that.'

He smiled. 'Client confidentiality?'

'Right. Well, Davis Tatum made a point of telling me that he knew all about the mandarins insisting I took off my shirt, and why. I think he and Archie are trying to reassure themselves that if they ask me to do something dangerous, I'll do it.'

He gave me a long slow look, his features still and expressionless.

Finally he said, 'And will you?'

I sighed, 'Probably.'

'What sort of danger?'

'I don't think they know. But realistically, if someone has an overwhelming reason for preventing Ellis's trial from ever starting, who is the person standing chiefly in the way?'

'*Sid!*'

'Yes. So they're asking me to find out if anyone might be motivated enough to ensure my permanent removal from the scene. They want me to find out *if* and *who* and *why*.'

'God, Sid.'

From a man who never blasphemed, those were strong words.

'So . . .' I sighed. 'Davis Tatum gave me a name, Owen Yorkshire, and told me he owned a firm called Topline Foods. Now Topline Foods gave a sponsored lunch at Aintree on the day before the Grand National. Ellis Quint was guest of honour. Also among the guests was a man called Lord Tilepit, who is both on the Board of Topline Foods and the proprietor of *The Pump*, which has been busy mocking me for months.'

He sat as if frozen.

'So,' I said, 'I'll go and see what Owen Yorkshire and Lord Tilepit are up to, and if I don't come back you can kick up a stink.'

When he'd organised his breath, he said, 'Don't do it, Sid.'

'No . . . but if I don't, Ellis will walk out laughing, and my standing in the world will be down the tubes for ever, if you see what I mean.'

He saw.

After a while he said, 'I do vaguely remember talking to this Archie fellow. He asked about your *brains.* He said he knew about your physical resilience. Odd choice of words – I remember them. I told him you played a wily game of chess. And it's true, you do. But it was a long time ago. Before all this happened.'

I nodded. 'He already knew a lot about me when he got his sister to phone at five-thirty in the morning to tell me she had a colt with his foot off.'

'So that's who he is? Mrs Bracken's brother?'

'Yeah.' I drank brandy and said, 'If you're ever talking to Sir Thomas Ullaston, would you mind asking him – and don't make a drama of it – if he told Archie Kirk or Davis Tatum about that morning in the Jockey Club?'

Sir Thomas Ullaston had been Senior Steward at the time, and had conducted the proceedings which led to the removal of the head of the Security section who had arranged for Chico and me to be thoroughly deterred from investigating anything ever again. As far as I was concerned it was all past history, and I most emphatically wanted it to remain so.

Charles said he would ask Sir Thomas.

'Ask him not to let *The Pump* get hold of it.'

Charles contemplated that possibility with about as much horror as I did myself.

The bell of the side-door rang distantly, and Charles frowned at his watch.

'Who can that be? It's almost eight o'clock.'

We soon found out. An ultra-familiar voice called

'Daddy?' across the hall outside, and an ultra-familiar figure appeared in the doorway. Jenny . . . Charles's younger daughter . . . my sometime wife. My still-embittered wife, whose tongue had barbs.

Smothering piercing dismay I stood up, and Charles also.

'Jenny,' Charles said, advancing to greet her. 'What a lovely surprise.'

She turned her cheek coolly, as always, and said, 'We were passing. It seemed impossible not to call in.' She looked at me without much emotion and said, 'We didn't know *you* were here until I saw your car outside.'

I took the few steps between us and gave her the sort of cheek to cheek salutation she'd bestowed on Charles. She accepted the politeness, as always, as the civilised acknowledgement of adversaries after battle.

'You look thin,' she observed, not with concern but with criticism, from habit.

She, I thought, looked as beautiful as always, but there was nothing to be gained by saying so. I didn't want her to sneer at me. To begin with, it ruined the sweet curve of her mouth. She could hurt me with words whenever she tried, and she'd tried often. My only defence had been – and still was – silence.

Her handsome new husband had followed her into the room, shaking hands with Charles and apologising for having appeared without warning.

'My dear fellow, any time,' Charles assured him.

Anthony Wingham turned my way and with self-conscious affability said, 'Sid . . .' and held out his hand.

It was extraordinary, I thought, enduring his hearty embarrassed grasp, how often one regularly shook hands in the course of a day. I'd never really noticed it before.

Charles poured drinks and suggested dinner. Anthony Wingham waffled a grateful refusal. Jenny gave me a cool look and sat in the gold brocade chair.

Charles made small talk with Anthony until they'd exhausted the weather. I stood with them but looked at Jenny, and she at me. Into a sudden silence, she said, 'Well, Sid, I don't suppose you want me to say it, but you've got yourself into a proper mess this time.'

'No.'

'No what?'

'No, I don't want you to say it.'

'Ellis Quint! Biting off more than you can chew. And back in the summer the papers pestered me too. I suppose you know?'

I unwillingly nodded.

'That reporter from *The Pump*,' Jenny complained. 'India Cathcart, I couldn't get rid of her. She wanted to know all about you and about our divorce. Do you know what she wrote? She wrote that I'd told her that quite apart from being crippled, you weren't man enough for me.'

'I read it,' I said briefly.

'Did you? And did you like it? Did you like that, Sid?'

I didn't reply. It was Charles who fiercely protested. '*Jenny!* Don't.'

Her face suddenly softened, all the spite dissolving and revealing the gentle girl I'd married. The transformation happened in a flash, like prison bars falling away. Her liberation, I thought, had dramatically come at last.

'I didn't say that,' she told me, as if bewildered. 'I really didn't. She made it up.'

I swallowed. I found the re-emergence of the old Jenny harder to handle than her scorn.

'What *did* you say?' I said.

'Well . . . I . . . I . . .'

'*Jenny*,' Charles said again.

'I told her,' Jenny said to him, 'that I couldn't live in Sid's hard world. I told her that whatever she wrote she wouldn't smash him or disintegrate him because no one had ever managed it. I told her that he never showed his feelings and that steel was putty compared to him, and that I couldn't live with it.'

Charles and I had heard her say much the same thing before. It was Anthony who looked surprised. He inspected my harmless-looking self from his superior height and obviously thought she had got me wrong.

'India Cathcart didn't believe Jenny either,' I told him soothingly.

'*What?*'

'He reads minds, too,' Jenny said, putting down her glass and rising to her feet. 'Anthony, darling, we'll go now. OK?' To her father she said, 'Sorry it's such a short visit,' and to me, 'India Cathcart is a bitch.'

I kissed Jenny's cheek.

'I still love you,' I said.

She looked briefly into my eyes. 'I couldn't live with it. I told her the truth.'

'I know.'

'Don't let her break you.'

'No.'

'Well,' she said brightly, loudly, smiling. 'When birds fly out of cages they sing and rejoice. So . . . goodbye, Sid.'

She looked happy. She laughed. I ached for the days when we'd met, when she looked like that always; but one could never go back.

'Goodbye, Jenny,' I said.

Charles, uncomprehending, went with them to see them off and came back frowning.

'I simply don't understand my daughter,' he said. 'Do you?'

'Oh, yes.'

'She tears you to pieces. *I* can't stand it, even if you can. Why don't you ever fight back?'

'Look what I did to her.'

'She knew what she was marrying.'

'I don't think she did. It isn't always easy, being married to a jockey.'

'You forgive her too much! And then, do you know what she said just now, when she was leaving? I don't understand her. She gave me a hug – a hug – not a dutiful peck on the cheek, and she said, "Take care of Sid." '

I felt instantly liquefied inside: too close to tears.

'Sid . . .'

I shook my head, as much to retain composure as anything else.

'We've made our peace,' I said.

'When?'

'Just now. The old Jenny came back. She's free of me. She felt free quite suddenly . . . so she'll have no more need to . . . to tear me to pieces, as you put it. I think that all that destructive anger has finally gone. Like she said, she's flown out of the cage.'

He said, 'I hope so,' but looked unconvinced. 'I need a drink.'

I smiled and joined him, but I discovered, as we later ate companionably together, that even though his daughter might no longer despite or torment me, what I perversely felt wasn't relief, but loss.

CHAPTER TEN

Leaving Aynsford early I drove back to London on Thursday morning and left the car, as I normally did, in a large public underground car park near Pont Square. From there I walked to the laundry where I usually took my shirts and waited while they fed my strip of rag from Northampton twice through the dry-cleaning cycle.

What emerged was a stringy looking object, basically light turquoise in colour, with a non-geometric pattern on it of green, brown and salmon pink. There were also black irregular stains that had stayed obstinately in place.

I persuaded the cleaners to iron it, with the only result that I had a flat strip instead of a wrinkled one.

'What if I wash it with detergent and water?' I asked the burly half-interested dry cleaner.

'You couldn't exactly *harm* it,' he said sarcastically.

So I washed it and ironed it and ended as before: turquoise strip, wandering indeterminate pattern, stubborn black stain.

With the help of Yellow Pages I visited the wholesale showrooms of a well-known fabric designer. An infinitely polite old man there explained that my fabric pattern was *woven*, while theirs – the wholesaler's – was *printed*. Different market, he said. The wholesaler aimed at the upper end of the middle-class market. I, he said, needed to consult an interior decorator, and with kindness he wrote for me a short list of firms.

The first two saw no profit in answering questions. At the third address I happened on an underworked twenty-year-old who ran pale long fingers through clean shoulder-length curls while he looked with interest at my offering. He pulled out a turquoise thread and held it up to the light.

'This is silk,' he said.

'Real silk?'

'No possible doubt. This was expensive fabric. The pattern is woven in. See.' He turned the piece over to show me the back. 'This is remarkable. Where did you get it? It looks like a very old lampas. Beautiful. The colours are organic, not mineral.'

I looked at his obvious youth and asked if he could perhaps seek a second opinion.

'Because I'm straight out of design school?' he guessed without umbrage. 'But I studied *fabrics*. That's why they took me on here. I *know* them. The designers don't weave them, they use them.'

'Then tell me what I've got.'

He fingered the turquoise strip and held it to his lips

and his cheek and seemed to commune with it as if it were a crystal ball.

'It's a modern copy,' he said. 'It's very skilfully done. It is lampas, woven on a Jacquard loom. There isn't enough of it to be sure, but I think it's a copy of a silk hanging made by Philippe de Lasalle in about 1760. But the original hadn't a blue-green background, it was cream with this design of ropes and leaves in greens and red and gold.'

I was impressed. 'Are you sure?'

'I've just spent three years learning this sort of thing.'

'Well, who makes it now? Do I have to go to France?'

'You could try one or two English firms but, you know what—'

He was brusquely interrupted by a severe-looking woman in a black dress and huge Aztec-type necklace who swept in and came to rest by the counter on which lay the unprepossessing rag.

'What are you doing?' she asked. 'I asked you to catalogue the new shipment of *passementerie*.'

'Yes, Mrs Lane.'

'Then please get on with it. Run along now.'

'Yes, Mrs Lane.'

'Do you want help?' she asked me briskly.

'Only the names of some weavers.'

On his way to the *passementerie*, my source of knowledge spoke briefly over his shoulder. 'It looks like a solitary weaver, not a firm. Try Saul Marcus.'

'Where?' I called.

'London.'

'Thanks.'

He went out of sight. Under Mrs Lane's inhospitable gaze I picked up my rag, smiled placatingly and departed.

I found Saul Marcus first in the telephone directory and then in white-bearded person in an airy artist's studio near Chiswick in west London where he created fabric patterns.

He looked with interest at my rag but shook his head.

I urged him to search the far universe.

'It might be Patricia Huxford's work,' he said at length, dubiously. 'You could try her. She does – or did – work like this sometimes. I don't know of anyone else.'

'Where would I find her?'

'Surrey. Sussex. Somewhere like that.'

'Thank you very much.'

Returning to Pont Square I looked for Patricia Huxford in every phone book I possessed for Surrey and Sussex and, for good measure, the bordering southern counties of Hampshire and Kent. Of the few Huxfords listed, none turned out to be Patricia, a weaver.

I really *needed* an assistant, I thought, saying goodbye to Mrs Paul Huxford, wife of a double-glazing salesman. This sort of search could take hours. Damn Chico, and his dolly-bird protective missus.

With no easy success from the directories I started on directory enquiries, the central computerised number-finder. As always, to get a number one had to give an address, but the computer system contemptuously spat out Patricia Huxford, Surrey, as being altogether too vague.

I tried Patricia Huxford, Guildford (Guildford being Surrey's county town) but learned only of the two listed P. Huxfords that I'd already tried. Kingston, Surrey: same lack of results. I systematically tried all the other main areas: Sutton, Epsom, Leatherhead, Dorking . . . Surrey might be a small county in square-mile size, but large in population. I drew a uniform blank.

Huxfords were fortunately rare. A good job she wasn't called Smith.

Sussex, then. There was East Sussex (county town Lewes) and West Sussex (Chichester). I flipped a mental coin and chose Chichester, and could hardly believe my lucky ears.

An impersonal voice told me that the number of Patricia Huxford was ex-directory and could only be accessed by the police, in an emergency. It was not even in the C.O. grade one class of ex-directory, where one could sweet-talk the operator into phoning the number on one's behalf (C.O. stood for Calls Offered). Patricia Huxford valued absolute grade two privacy and couldn't be reached that way.

In the highest, third grade, category, there were the numbers that weren't on any list at all, that the exchanges and operators might not know even existed; numbers for government affairs, the Royal Family and spies.

I yawned, stretched and ate cornflakes for lunch.

While I was still unenthusiastically thinking of driving to Chichester, roughly seventy more miles of arm-ache, Charles phoned from Aynsford.

'So glad to catch you in,' he said. 'I've been talking to Thomas Ullaston, I thought you'd like to know.'

'Yes,' I agreed with interest. 'What did he say?'

'You know, of course, that he's no longer Senior Steward of the Jockey Club? His term of office ended.'

'Yes, I know.'

I also regretted it. The new Senior Steward was apt to think me a light-weight nuisance. I supposed he had a point, but it never helped to be discounted by the top man if I asked for anything at all from the department heads in current power. No one was any longer thanking me for ridding them of their villain: according to them, the whole embarrassing incident was best forgotten, and with that I agreed, but I wouldn't have minded residual warmth.

'Thomas was dumbfounded by your question,' Charles said. 'He protested that he'd meant you no harm.'

'Ah!' I said.

'Yes. He didn't deny that he'd told someone about that morning, but he assured me that it had been only *one* person, that that person was someone of utterly good standing, a man of the utmost probity. I asked if it was Archibald Kirk, and he *gasped*, Sid. He said it was early in the summer when Archie Kirk sought him out to ask about you. Archie Kirk told him he'd heard you were a good investigator and he wanted to know *how* good. It seems Archie Kirk's branch of the Civil Service occasionally likes to employ independent investigators quietly, but that it's hard to find good ones they can trust. Thomas Ullaston told him to trust *you*. Archie Kirk apparently asked more and more questions, until Thomas found himself telling about that chain and those awful marks . . . I mean, sorry, Sid.'

'Yeah,' I said, 'go on.'

'Thomas told Archie Kirk that with your jockey constitution and physical resilience – he said physical resilience, Thomas did, so that's exactly where Kirk got that phrase from – with your natural inborn physical resilience you'd shaken off the whole thing as if it had never happened.'

'Yes,' I said, which wasn't entirely true. One couldn't ever forget. One could, however, ignore. And it was odd, I thought, that I never had nightmares about whippy chains.

Charles chuckled. 'Thomas said he wouldn't want young master Halley on his tail if he'd been a crook.'

Young master Halley found himself pleased.

Charles asked, 'Is there anything else I can do for you, Sid?'

'You've been great.'

'Be careful.'

I smiled as I assured him I would. Be careful was hopeless advice to a jockey, and at heart I was as much out to win as ever.

On my way to the car I bought some robust adhesive bandage and, with my right forearm firmly strapped and a sufficient application of ibuprofen, drove to Chichester in West Sussex, about seven miles inland from the coast.

It was a fine spirits-lifting afternoon. My milk-coffee Mercedes swooped over the rolling South Downs and sped the last flat mile to the cathedral city of Chichester, wheels satisfyingly fast but still not as fulfilling as a horse.

I sought out the public library and asked to see the electoral roll.

There was masses of it: all the names and addresses of registered voters in the county, divided into electoral districts.

Where was Chico, blast him?

Resigned to a long search that could take two or three hours, I found Patricia Huxford within a short fifteen minutes. A record. I hated electoral rolls: the small print made me squint.

Huxford, Patricia Helen, Bravo House, Lowell.

Hallelujah.

I followed my road map, and asked for directions in the village of Lowell, and found Bravo House, a small converted church with a herd of cars and vans outside.

It didn't look like the reclusive lair of an ex-directory hermit.

As people seemed to be walking in and out of the high heavy open west door, I walked in too. I had arrived, it was soon clear, towards the end of a photographic session for a glossy magazine.

I said to a young woman hugging a clipboard, 'Patricia Huxford?'

The young woman gave me a radiant smile. 'Isn't she *wonderful*?' she said.

I followed the direction of her gaze. A small woman in an astonishing dress was descending from a sort of throne that had been built on a platform situated where the old transepts crossed the nave. There were bright theatrical spotlights that began to be switched off, and there were photographers unscrewing and dismantling and wrapping cables into hanks. There were effusive thanks in the air and satisfied excitement and the overall glow of a job done well.

I waited, looking about me, discovering the changes from church to modern house. The window glass, high up, was clear, not coloured. The stone-flagged nave had rugs, no pews, comfortable modern sofas pushed back against the wall to accommodate the crowd, and a large-screen television set.

A white-painted partition behind the throne platform cut off the view of what had been the altar area, but nothing had been done to spoil the sweep of the vaulted ceiling, built with soaring stone arches to the glory of God.

One would have to have a very secure personality, I thought, to choose to live in that place.

The media flock drifted down the nave and left with undiminished goodwill. Patricia Huxford waved to them and closed her heavy door and, turning, was surprised to find me still inside.

'So sorry,' she said, and began to open the door again.

'I'm not with the photographers,' I said. 'I came to ask you about something else.'

'I'm tired,' she said. 'I must ask you to go.'

'You look beautiful,' I told her, 'and it will only take a minute.' I brought my scrap of rag out and showed it to her. 'If you are Patricia Huxford, did you weave this?'

'Trish,' she said absently. 'I'm called Trish.'

She looked at the strip of silk and then at my face.

'What's your name?' she asked.

'John.'

'John what?'

'John Sidney.'

John Sidney were my real two first names, the ones my young mother had habitually used. 'John Sidney, give us a kiss.' 'John Sidney, wash your face.' 'John Sidney, have you been fighting again?'

I often used John Sidney in my job: whenever, in fact, I didn't want to be known to be Sid Halley. After the past months of all-too-public drubbing I wasn't sure that Sid Halley would get me anything anywhere but a swift heave-ho.

Trish Huxford, somewhere, I would have guessed, in the middle to late forties, was pretty, blonde (natural?), small-framed and cheerful. Bright observant eyes looked over my grey business suit, white shirt, unobtrusive tie, brown shoes, dark hair, dark eyes, unthreatening manner; my usual working confidence-inspiring exterior.

She was still on a high from the photo session. She needed someone to help her unwind, and I looked – and was – safe. Thankfully I saw her relax.

The amazing dress she had worn for the photographs was utterly simple in cut, hanging heavy and straight from her shoulders, floor length and sleeveless with a soft ruffled frill round her neck. It was the cloth of the dress that staggered: it was blue and red and silver and gold, and it *shimmered.*

'Did you weave your dress?' I asked.

'Of course.'

'I've never seen anything like it.'

'No, you wouldn't, not nowadays. Can I do anything for you? Where did you come from?'

'London. Saul Marcus suggested you might know who wove my strip of silk.'

'Saul! How is he?'

'He has a white beard,' I said. 'He seemed fine.'

'I haven't seen him for years. Will you make me some tea? I don't want marks on this dress.'

I smiled. 'I'm quite good at tea.'

She led the way past the throne and round the white-painted screen. There were choir stalls beyond, old and untouched, and an altar table covered by a cloth that brought me to a halt. It was of a brilliant royal blue with shining gold Greek motifs woven into its deep hem. On the table, in the place of religious altar furniture, stood an antique spinning wheel, good enough for Sleeping Beauty. Above the table, arched clear glass windows rose to the roof.

'This way,' Patricia Huxford commanded, and, leading me past the choir stalls, turned abruptly through a narrow doorway which opened onto what could only probably have been a vestry and was now a small modern kitchen with a bathroom beside it.

'My bed is in the south transept,' she told me, 'and my looms are in the north. You might expect us to be going to drink China tea with lemon out of a silver teapot, but in fact I don't have enough time for that sort of thing, so the tea bags and mugs are on that shelf.'

I half filled her electric kettle and plugged it in, and she spent the time walking around watching the miraculous colours move and mingle in her dress.

Intrigued, waiting for the water to boil, I asked, 'What is it made of?'

'What do you think?'

'Er, it looks like . . . well . . . gold.'

She laughed. 'Quite right. Gold, silver thread, and silk.'

I rather clumsily filled the mugs.

'Milk?' she suggested.

'No, thank you.'

'That's lucky. The crowd that's just left finished it off.' She gave me a brilliant smile, picked up a mug by its handle and returned to the throne, where she sat neatly on the vast red velvet chair and rested a thin arm delicately along gilt carving. The dress fell into sculptured folds over her slender thighs.

'The photographs,' she said, 'are for a magazine about a festival of the arts that Chichester is staging all next summer.'

I stood before her like some mediaeval page: stood chiefly because there was no chair nearby to sit on.

'I suppose,' she said, 'that you think me madly eccentric?'

'Not madly.'

She grinned happily. 'Normally I wear jeans and an old smock.' She drank some tea. 'Usually I work. Today is play-acting.'

'And magnificent.'

She nodded. 'No one, these days, makes cloth of gold.'

'The Field of the Cloth of Gold,' I exclaimed.

'That's right. What do you know of it?'

'Only that phrase.'

'The field was the meeting place at Guines, France,

in June 1520, of Henry VIII of England and Francis I of France. They were supposed to be making peace between England and France but they hated each other and tried to outdo each other in splendour. So all their courtiers wore cloth woven out of gold and they gave each other gifts you'd never see today. And I thought it would be historic to weave some cloth of gold for the festival . . . so I did. And this dress weighs a ton, I may tell you. Today is the only time I've worn it and I can't bear to take it off.'

'It's breathtaking,' I said.

She poured out her knowledge. 'In 1476 the Duke of Burgundy left behind a hundred and sixty gold cloths when he fled from battle against the Swiss. You make gold cloth – like I made this – by supporting the soft gold on threads of silk, and you can recover the gold by burning the cloth. So when I was making this dress, that's what I did with the pieces I cut out to make the neck and armholes. I burnt them and collected the melted gold.'

'Beautiful.'

'You know something?' she said. 'You're the only person who's seen this dress who hasn't asked how much it cost.'

'I did wonder.'

'And I'm not telling. Give me your strip of silk.'

I took her empty mug and tucked it under my left arm, and in my right hand held out the rag, which she took; and I found her looking with concentration at my left hand. She raised her eyes to meet my gaze.

'Is it . . .?' she said.

'Worth its weight in gold,' I said flippantly. 'Yes.'

I carried the mugs back to the kitchen and returned to find her standing and smoothing her fingers over the piece of rag.

'An interior decorator,' I said, 'told me it was probably a modern copy of a hanging made in 1760 by . . . um . . . I think Philippe de Lasalle.'

'How clever. Yes, it is. I made quite a lot of it at one time.' She paused, then said abruptly, 'Come along,' and dived off again, leaving me to follow.

We went this time through a door in another white-painted partition and found ourselves in the north transept, her workroom.

There were three looms of varying construction, all bearing work in progress. There was also a business section with filing cabinets and a good deal of office paraphernalia, and another area devoted to measuring, cutting and packing.

'I make fabrics you can't buy anywhere else,' she said. 'Most of it goes to the Middle East.' She walked towards the largest of the three looms, a monster that rose in steps to double our height.

'This is a Jacquard loom,' she said. 'I made your sample on this.'

'I was told this piece was . . . a lampas? What's a lampas?'

She nodded. 'A lampas is a compound weave with extra warps and wefts which put patterns and colours on the face of the fabric only, and are tucked into the back.' She showed me how the design of ropes and branches of leaves gleamed on one side of the turquoise silk but hardly showed on the reverse. 'It takes ages to set up,' she said. 'Nowadays almost no one outside the Middle East thinks the beauty is worth the expense, but once I used to sell quite a lot of it to castles and great houses in England, and all sorts of private people. I only make it to order.'

I said neutrally, 'Would you know who you made this piece for?'

'My dear man. No, I can't remember. But I probably still have the records. Why do you want to know? Is it important?'

'I don't know if it is important. I was given the strip and asked to find its origin.'

She shrugged. 'Let's find it then. You never know, I might get an order for some more.'

She opened cupboard doors to reveal many ranks of box files, and ran her fingers along the labels on the spines until she came to one that her expression announced as possible. She lifted the box file from the shelf and opened it on a table.

Inside were stiff pages with samples of fabric stapled to them, with full details of fibres, dates, amount made, names of purchasers and receipts.

She turned the stiff pages slowly, holding my strip

in one hand for comparison. She came to several versions of the same design, but all in the wrong colour.

'That's it!' she exclaimed suddenly. 'That's the one. I see I wove it almost thirty years ago. How time flies. I was so young then. It was a hanging for a four-poster bed. I see I supplied it with gold tassels made of gimp.'

I asked without much expectation, 'Who to?'

'It says here a Mrs Gordon Quint.'

I said, '. . . Er . . .' meaninglessly, my breath literally taken away.

Ginnie? *Ginnie* had owned the material.

'I don't remember her or anything about it,' Trish Huxford said. 'But all the colours match. It must have been this one commission. I don't think I made these colours for anyone else.' She looked at the black stains disfiguring the strip I'd brought. 'What a pity! I think of my fabrics as going on for ever. They could easily last two hundred years. I love the idea of leaving something beautiful in the world. I expect you think I'm a sentimental old bag.'

'I think you're splendid,' I said truthfully, and asked, 'Why are you ex-directory, with a business to run?'

She laughed. 'I hate being interrupted when I'm setting up a design. It takes vast concentration. I have a mobile phone for friends – I can switch it off – and I have an agent in the Middle East who gets orders for me. Why am I telling you all this?'

'I'm interested.'

She closed the file and put it back on the shelf, asking, 'Does Mrs Quint want some more fabric to replace this damaged bit, do you think?'

Mrs Quint was sixteen floors dead.

'I don't know,' I said.

On the drive back to London I pulled off the road to phone Davis Tatum at the number he'd given me, his home.

He was in and, it seemed, glad to hear from me, wanting to know what I'd done for him so far.

'Tomorrow,' I said, 'I'll give Topline Foods a visit. Who did you get Owen Yorkshire's name from?'

He said, stalling, 'I beg your pardon?'

'Davis,' I said mildly, 'you want me to take a look at Owen Yorkshire and his company, so why? Why *him*?'

'I can't tell you.'

'Do you mean you promised not to, or you don't know?'

'I mean . . . just go and take a look.'

I said, 'Sir Thomas Ullaston, Senior Steward last year of the Jockey Club, told Archie Kirk about that little matter of the chains, and Archie Kirk told *you*. So did the name Owen Yorkshire come to you from Archie Kirk?'

'Hell,' he said.

'I like to know what I'm getting into.'

After a pause he said, 'Owen Yorkshire has been seen twice in the boardroom of *The Pump*. We don't know why.'

'Thank you,' I said.

'Is that enough?'

'To be going on with. Oh, and my mobile phone is now safe. No more leaks. See you later.'

I drove on to London, parked in the underground garage and walked along the alleyway between tall houses that led into the opposite side of the square from my flat.

I was going quietly and cautiously in any case, and came to a dead stop when I saw that the street light almost directly outside my window was not lit.

Boys sometimes threw stones at it to break the glass. Normally its darkness wouldn't have sent shudders up my spine and made my right arm remember Gordon Quint from fingers to neck. Normally I might have crossed the square figuratively whistling while intending to phone in the morning to get the light fixed.

Things were not normal.

There were two locked gates into the central garden, one opposite the path I was on, and one on the far side, opposite my house. Standing in shadow I sorted out the resident-allocated garden key, went quietly across the circling roadway and unlocked the near gate.

Nothing moved. I eased the gate open, slid through, and closed it behind me. No squeaks. I moved slowly from patch to patch of shaded cover, the half-lit tree branches moving in a light breeze, yellow leaves drifting down like ghosts.

Near the far side I stopped and waited.

There could be no one there. I was foolishly afraid over nothing.

The street light was out.

It had been out at other times . . .

I stood with my back to a tree, waiting for alarm to subside to the point where I would unlock the second gate and cross the road to my front steps. The sounds of the city were distant. No cars drove into the cul-de-sac square.

I couldn't stand there all night, I thought . . . *and then I saw him.*

He was in a car parked by one of the few meters. His head – unmistakably Gordon Quint's head – moved behind the window. He was looking straight ahead, waiting for me to arrive by road or pavement.

I stood immobile as if stuck to the tree. It had to be obsession with him, I thought. The burning fury of Monday had settled down not into grief but revenge. I hadn't been in my flat for about thirty hours. How long had he been sitting there waiting? I'd had a villain wait almost a week for me once, before I'd walked unsuspectingly into his trap.

Obsession – fixation – was the most frightening of enemies and the hardest to escape.

I retreated, frankly scared, expecting him to see my movement, but he hadn't thought of an approach by garden. From tree to tree, round the patches of open grass, I regained the far gate, eased through it, crossed the road and drifted up the alleyway, cravenly expecting a bellow and a chase and, as he was a farmer, perhaps a shotgun.

Nothing happened. My shoes, soled and heeled for silence, made no sound. I walked back to my underground car and sat in it, not exactly trembling but nonetheless stirred up. So much, I thought, for Tatum's myth of a clever, unafraid investigator.

I kept always in the car an overnight bag containing the personality-change clothes I'd got Jonathan to wear; dark two-piece tracksuit (trousers and zip-up jacket) navy blue trainers, and a baseball cap. The bag also contained a long-sleeved open-necked shirt, two or three charged-up batteries for my arm, and a battery charger, to make sure. Habitually round my waist I wore a belt with a zipped pocket big enough for a credit card and money.

I had no weapons nor defences like mace. In America I might have carried both.

I sat in the car considering the matter of distance and ulnas. It was well over two hundred miles from my London home to Liverpool, city of my birth. Frodsham, the base of Topline Foods, wasn't quite as far as Liverpool, but still over two hundred miles. I had already, that day, steered a hundred and fifty – Chichester and back. I'd never missed Chico so much.

I considered trains. Too inflexible. Airline? Ditto.

TeleDrive? I lingered over the comfort of TeleDrive but decided against, and resignedly set off northwards.

It was an easy drive normally; a journey on wide fast motorways taking at most three hours. I drove for only one hour, then stopped at a motel to eat and sleep, and at seven o'clock in the morning wheeled on again, trying to ignore both the obstinately slow-mending fracture and India Cathcart's column that I'd bought from the motel's news stand.

Friday mornings had been a trial since June. Page fifteen in *The Pump* – trial by the long knives of journalism, the blades that ripped the gut.

She hadn't mentioned at all seeing Tatum and me in the Le Meridien bar. Perhaps she'd taken my advice and pretended we hadn't been there. What her column said about me was mostly factually true but spitefully wrong. I wondered how she could do it? Had she no sense of humanity?

Most of her page concerned yet another politician caught with his trousers at half-mast, but the far-right column said:

> Sid Halley, illegitimate by-blow of a nineteen-year-old window cleaner and a packer in a biscuit factory, ran amok as a brat in the slums of Liverpool. Home was a roach-infested council flat. Nothing wrong with that! But this same Sid Halley now puts on airs of middle-class gentility. A flat in Chelsea? Sheraton furniture? Posh accent? Go back to your roots, lad.

No wonder Ellis Quint thinks you funny. Funny pathetic!

The slum background clearly explains the Halley envy. Halley's chip on the shoulder grows more obvious every day. Now we know why!

The Halley polish is all a sham, just like his pathetic left hand.

Christ, I thought, how much more? Why did it so bloody *hurt*?

My father had been killed in a fall eight months before my birth and a few days before he was due to marry my eighteen-year-old mother. She'd done her best as a single parent in hopeless surroundings. 'Give us a kiss, John Sidney . . .'

I hadn't ever run amok. I'd been a quiet child, mostly. 'Have you been fighting again, John Sidney . . .?' She hadn't liked me fighting, though one had to sometimes, or be bullied.

And when she knew she was dying she'd taken me to Newmarket, because I'd been short for my age, and had left me with the king of trainers to be made into a jockey, as I'd always wanted.

I couldn't possibly go back to Liverpool 'roots'. I had no sense of ever having grown any there.

I had never envied Ellis Quint. I'd always liked him. I'd been a better jockey than he, and we'd both known it. If anything, the envy had been the other way round. But it was useless to protest, as it had been all along.

Protests were used regularly to prove *The Pump*'s theories of my pitiable inadequacy.

My mobile phone buzzed. I answered it.

'Kevin Mills,' a familiar voice said. 'Where are you? I tried your flat. Have you seen today's *Pump* yet?'

'Yes.'

'India didn't write it,' he said. 'I gave her the info, but she wouldn't use it. She filled that space with some parts on sexual stress and her editor rubbed them out.'

Half of my muscles unknotted, and I hadn't realised they'd been tense. I forced unconcern into my voice even as I thought of hundreds of thousands of readers sniggering about me over their breakfast toast.

'Then you wrote it yourself,' I said. 'So who's a shit now? You're the only person on *The Pump* who's seen my Sheraton desk.'

'Blast you. Where are you?'

'Going back to Liverpool. Where else?'

'Sid, look, I'm sorry.'

'Policy?'

He didn't answer.

I asked, 'Why did you phone to tell me India didn't write today's bit of demolition?'

'I'm getting soft.'

'No one's listening to this phone any more. You can say what you like.'

'Jeez.' He laughed. 'That didn't take you long.' He paused. 'You might not believe it, but most of us on

The Pump don't any more like what we've been doing to you.'

'Rise up and rebel,' I suggested dryly.

'We have to eat. And you're a tough bugger. You can take it.'

You just try it, I thought.

'Listen,' he said, 'the paper's received a lot of letters from readers complaining that we're not giving you a fair deal.'

'How many is a lot?'

'Two hundred or so. Believe me, that's a *lot*. But we're not allowed to print any.'

I said with interest, 'Who says so?'

'That's just it. The Ed, Godbar himself, says so, and he doesn't like it either, but the policy is coming from the very top.'

'Tilepit?'

'Are you *sure* this phone's not bugged?'

'You're safe.'

'You've had a bloody raw mauling, and you don't deserve it. I know that. We all know it. I'm sorry for my part in it. I'm sorry I wrote today's venom, especially that bit about your hand. Yes, it's Tilepit. The proprietor himself.'

'Well . . . thanks.'

He said, 'Did Ellis Quint *really* cut off those feet?'

I smiled ruefully. 'The jury will decide.'

'Sid, look here,' he protested, 'you *owe* me!'

'Life's a bugger,' I said.

CHAPTER ELEVEN

Nine o'clock Friday morning I drove into the town of Frodsham and asked for Topline Foods.

Not far from the river, I was told. Near the river; the Mersey.

The historic docks of Liverpool's Mersey waterfront had long been silent, the armies of tall cranes dismantled, the warehouses converted or pulled down. Part of the city's heart has stopped beating. There had been by-pass surgery of sorts, but past muscle would never return. The city had a vast red-brick cathedral, but faith, as in much of Britain, had dimmed.

For years I'd been to Liverpool only to ride there on Aintree racecourse. The road I'd once lived in lay somewhere under a hyper-market. Liverpool was a place, but not home.

At Frodsham there was a 'Mersey View' vantage point with, away to the distant north, some still-working docks at Runcorn on the Manchester Ship Canal. One of those docks (I'd been told earlier by telephone from the dockmaster's office) was occupied by Topline

Foods. A ship lying alongside bearing the flag and insignia of Canada had been unloading Topline grain.

I'd stopped the car from where I could see the sweep of river with the seagulls swooping and the stiff breeze tautening flags at the horizontal. I stood in the cold open air, leaning on the car, smelling the salt and the mud, and hearing the drone of traffic on the road below.

Were these roots? I'd always loved wide skies, but it was the wide sky of Newmarket Heath that I thought of as home. When I'd been a boy there'd been no wide skies, only narrow streets, the walk to school, and rain. 'John Sidney, wash your face. Give us a kiss.'

The day after my mother died I'd ridden my first winner, and that evening I'd got drunk for the first and only time until the arrest of Ellis Quint.

Soberly, realistically, in the Mersey wind I looked at the man I had become: a jumble of self-doubt, ability, fear and difficult pride. I had grown as I was from the inside out. Liverpool and Newmarket weren't to blame.

Stirring and getting back into the car I wondered where to find all those tungsten nerves I was supposed to have.

I didn't know what I was getting into. I could still at that point retreat and leave the field to Ellis. I could – and I couldn't. I would have myself to live with, if I did.

I'd better simply get on with it, I thought.

I drove down from the vantage point, located the Topline Foods factory, and passed through its twelve foot high but hospitably open wire-mesh gates. There was a guard in a gatehouse who paid me no attention.

Inside there were many cars tidily parked in ranks. I added myself to the end of one row and decided on a clothing compromise of suit trousers, zipped up tracksuit top, white shirt, no tie, ordinary shoes. I neatly combed my hair forward into a young-looking style and looked no threat to anybody.

The factory, built round three sides of a big central area, consisted of loading bays, a vast main building and a new-looking office block. Loading and unloading took place under cover, with articulated lorries backing into the bays. In the one bay I could see into clearly, the cab section had been disconnected and removed; heavy sacks that looked as if they might contain grain were being unloaded from a long container by two large men who slung the sacks onto a moving conveyor belt of rollers.

The big building had a row of windows high up: there was no chance of looking in from outside.

I ambled across to the office building and shouldered open a heavy glass door that led into a large but mostly bare entrance hall, and found there the reason for the unguarded front gates. The security arrangements were all inside.

Behind a desk sat a purposeful-looking middle-aged woman in a green jumper. Flanking her were two men in navy blue security-guard suits with Topline Foods insignia on their breast pockets.

'Name, please,' said the green jumper. 'State your business. All parcels, carriers and handbags must be left here at the desk.'

She had a distinct Liverpool accent. With the same inflection in my own voice, I told her that, as she could see, I had no bag, carrier or handbag with me.

She took the accent for granted and unsmilingly asked again for my name.

'John Sidney.'

'Business?'

'Well,' I said as if perplexed by the reception I was getting. 'I was asked to come here to see if you made some horse-nuts.' I paused. 'Like,' I lamely finished, dredging up the idiom.

'Of course we make horse-nuts. It's our business.'

'Yes,' I told her earnestly, 'but this farmer, like, he asked me to come in, as I was passing this way, to see if it was you that made some horse-nuts that someone had given him, that were very good for his young horse, like, but he was given them loose and not in a bag and all he has is a list of what's in the nuts and he wanted to know if you made them, see?' I half pulled a sheet of paper from an inside pocket and pushed it back.

She was bored by the rigmarole.

'If I could just *talk* to someone,' I pleaded. 'See, I owe this farmer a favour and it wouldn't take no more than a minute, if I could talk to someone. Because this farmer, he'll be a big customer if these are the nuts he's looking for.'

She gave in, lifted a telephone, and repeated a shortened version of my improbable tale.

She inspected me from head to foot. 'Couldn't hurt a fly,' she reported.

I kept the suitably feeble half-anxious smile in place.

She put down the receiver. 'Miss Rowse will be down to help you. Raise your hands.'

'Eh?'

'Raise your hands . . . please.'

Surprised, I did as I was told. One of the security guards patted me all over in the classic way of their job, body and legs. He missed the false hand and the cracked bone. 'Keys and mobile phone,' he reported. 'Clean.'

Green jumper wrote 'John Sidney' onto a clip-on identity card and I clipped it dutifully on.

'Wait by the lift,' she said.

I waited.

The doors finally parted to reveal a teenage girl with wispy fair hair who said she was Miss Rowse. 'Mr Sidney? This way, please.'

I stepped into the lift with her, and rode to the third floor.

She smiled with bright inexperienced encouragement and led me down a newly carpeted passage to an office conspicuously labelled 'Customer Relations' on its open door.

'Come in,' Miss Rowse said proudly. 'Please sit down.'

I sat in a Scandinavian-inspired chair of blond wood with arms, simple lines, blue cushioning and considerable comfort.

'I'm afraid I didn't really understand your problem,' Miss Rowse said trustingly. 'If you'll explain again, I can get the right person to talk to you.'

I looked round her pleasant office, which showed almost no sign of work in progress.

'Have you been here long?' I asked. (Guileless Liverpool accent, just like hers.) 'Nice office. They must think a lot of you here.'

She was pleased, but still honest. 'I'm new this week. I started on Monday – and you're my second enquiry.'

No wonder, I thought, that she'd let me in.

I said, 'Are all the offices as plush as this?'

'Yes,' she said enthusiastically. 'Mr Yorkshire, he likes things nice.'

'Is he the boss?'

'The managing director,' she nodded. The words sounded stiff and unfamiliar, as if she'd only newly learned them.

'Nice to work for, is he?' I suggested.

She confessed, 'I haven't met him yet. I know what he looks like, of course, but . . . I'm new here, like I said.'

I smiled sympathetically and asked what Owen Yorkshire looked like.

She was happy to tell me. 'He's ever so *big*. He's got a big head and a lovely lot of hair, wavy like.'

'Moustache?' I suggested. 'Beard?'

'No,' she giggled. 'And he's not *old*. Not a grandad. Everyone gets out of his way.'

Do they indeed, I thought.

She went on, 'I mean, Mrs Dove, she's my boss really, she's the office manager, she says not to make him angry, whatever I do. She says just to do my job. She has a lovely office. It used to be Mr Yorkshire's own, she says.'

Miss Rowse, shaped like a woman, chattered like a child.

'Topline Foods must be doing all right to have rich new offices like these,' I said admiringly.

'They've got the TV cameras coming tomorrow to set up for Monday. They brought dozens of potted plants round this morning. Ever so keen on publicity, Mrs Dove says, Mr Yorkshire is.'

'The plants do make it nice and homey,' I said. 'Which TV company, do you know?'

She shook her head. 'All the Liverpool big noises are coming to a huge reception on Monday. The TV cameras are going all over the factory. Of course, although they're going to have all the machines running, they won't really make any nuts on Monday. It will all be pretend.'

'Why's that?'

'Security. They have to be security mad, Mrs Dove says. Mr Yorkshire worries about people putting things in the feed, she says.'

'What things?'

'I don't know. Nails and safety-pins and such. Mrs Dove says all the searching at the entrance is Mr Yorkshire's idea.'

'Very sensible,' I said.

An older and more cautious woman came into the office, revealing herself to be the fount of wisdom, Mrs Dove. Middle-aged and personally secure, I thought. Status, ability and experience all combining in priceless efficiency.

'Can I help you?' she said to me civilly, and to the girl, 'Marsha dear, I thought we'd agreed you would always come to me for advice.'

'Miss Rowse has been really helpful,' I said. 'She's going to find someone to answer my question. Perhaps you could, yourself?'

Mrs Dove (grey hair pinned high under a flat black bow, high heels, customer-relations neat satin shirt, cinched waist and black tights) listened with slowly glazing eyes to my expanding tale of the nutty farmer.

'You need our Willy Parrot,' she said when she could insert a comment. 'Come with me.'

I waggled conspiratorial fingers at Marsha Rowse and followed Mrs Dove's busy backview along the expensive passage with little partitioned but mostly empty offices on each side. She continued through a thick fire-door at the end, to emerge on a gallery round an atrium in the main factory building, where the nuts came from.

Rising from the ground, level almost to the gallery, were huge mixing vats, all with paddles circulating, activated from machinery stretching down from above. The sounds were an amalgam of whirr, rattle and slurp: the air bore fine particles of cereal dust and it looked like a brewery, I thought. It smelled rather the same also, but without the fermentation.

Mrs Dove passed me thankfully on to a man in brown overalls who inspected my dark clothes and asked if I wanted to be covered in fall-out.

'Not particularly.'

He raised patient eyebrows and gestured to me to follow him, which I did, to find myself on an iron staircase descending one floor, along another gallery and ending in a much-used battered little cubby-hole of an office, with a sliding glass door that he closed behind us.

I commented on the contrast from the office building.

'Fancy fiddle-faddle,' he said. 'That's for the cameras. This is where the work is done.'

'I can see that,' I told him admiringly.

'Now, lad,' he said, looking me up and down, unimpressed, 'what is it you want?'

He wasn't going to be taken in very far by the farmer twaddle. I explained in a shorter version and produced the folded paper bearing the analysis of the nuts from the Combe Bassett and the Land-Rover, and asked if it was a Topline formula.

He read the list that by then I knew by heart.

Wheat, oatfeed, ryegrass, straw, barley, maize, molasses, salt, linseed.

Vitamins, selenium, copper, other substances and probably the antioxidant Ethoxyquin.

'Where did you get this?' he asked.

'From a farmer, like I told you.'

'This list isn't complete,' he said.

'No . . . but is it enough?'

'It doesn't give percentages. I can't possibly match it to any of our products.' He folded the paper and gave it back. 'Your cubes might be our supplement feed for horses out at grass. Do you know anything about horses?'

'A little.'

'Then the more oats you give them, the more energy they expend. Racehorses need more oats. I can't tell you for sure if these cubes were for racehorses in training unless I know the proportion of oats.'

'They weren't racehorses in training.'

'Then your farmer friend couldn't do better than our Sweetfield mix. They do contain everything on your list.'

'Are other people's cubes much different?'

'There aren't very many manufacturers. We're perhaps fourth on the league table but after this advertisement campaign we expect that to zoom up. The new management aims for the top.'

'But . . . um . . . do you have enough space?'

'Capacity?'

I nodded.

He smiled. 'Owen Yorkshire has plans. He talks to us man to man.' His face and voice were full of approval. 'He's brought the old place back to life.'

I said inoffensively, 'Mrs Dove seems in awe of his anger.'

Willy Parrott laughed and gave me a male chauvinist-type wink. 'He has a flaming temper, has our Owen Yorkshire. And the more a man for that.'

I looked vaguely at some charts taped to a wall. 'Where does he come from?' I asked.

'Haven't a clue,' Willy told me cheerfully. 'He knows bugger all about nutrition. He's a salesman, and *that's* what we needed. We have a couple of nerds in white coats working on what we put in all the vats.'

He was scornful of scientists as well as women. I turned back from the wall charts and thanked him for his time. Very interesting job, I told him. Obviously he ran the department that mattered most.

He took the compliment as his due and saved me the trouble of asking by offering to let me tag along with him while he went to his next task, which was to check a new shipment of wheat. I accepted with an enthusiasm that pleased him. A man good at his job often enjoyed an audience, and so did Willy Parrott.

He gave me a set of over-large brown overalls and told me to clip the identity card on the outside, like his own.

'Security is vital,' he said to me. 'Owen's stepped it all up. He lectures us on not letting strangers near the mixing vats. I can't let you any nearer than this. Our competitors wouldn't be above adding foreign substances that would put us out of business.'

'D'you mean it?' I said, looking avid.

'You have to be specially careful with horse feed,' he assured me, sliding open his door when I was ready. 'You can't mix cattle food in the same vats, for instance. You can put things in cattle feed that are prohibited for racehorses. You can get traces of prohibited substances in the horse-cubes just by using the same equipment, even if you think you've cleaned everything thoroughly.'

There had been a famous example in racing of a trainer getting into trouble by unknowingly giving his runners contaminated nuts.

'Fancy,' I said.

I thought I might have overdone the impressed look I gave him, but he accepted it easily.

'We do nothing else except horse-cubes here,' Willy said. 'Owen says when we expand we'll do cattle feed and chicken pellets, and all sorts of other muck, but I'll be staying here, Owen says, in charge of the equine branch.'

'A top job,' I said with admiration.

He nodded. 'The best.'

We walked along the gallery and came to another fire-door, which he lugged open.

'All these internal doors are locked at night now, and there's a watchman with a dog. Very thorough, is Owen.' He looked back to make sure I was following, then stopped at a place from which we could see bags marked with red maple leaves travelling upwards on an endless belt of bag-sized ledges, only to be tumbled off the top and be manhandled by two smoothly swinging muscular workers.

'I expect you saw those two security men in the entrance hall?' Willy Parrott said, the question of security not yet exhausted.

'They frisked me,' I grinned. 'Going a bit far, I thought.'

'They're Owen's private bodyguards,' Willy Parrott said with a mixture of awe and approval. 'They're real hard men from Liverpool. Owen says he needs them in case the competitors try to get rid of him the old-fashioned way.'

I frowned disbelievingly. 'Competitors don't kill people.'

'Owen says he's taking no risks because he definitely is trying to put other firms out of business, if you look at it that way.'

'So you think he's right to need bodyguards?'

Willy Parrott turned to me and said, 'It's not the

world I was brought up in, lad. But we have to live in this new one, Owen says.'

'I suppose so.'

'You won't get far with that attitude, lad.' He pointed to the rising bags. 'That's this year's wheat straight from the prairie. Only the best is good enough, Owen says, in trade wars.'

He led the way down some nearby concrete stairs and through another heavy door, and I realised we were on ground level just off the central atrium. With a smile of satisfaction he pushed through one more door and we found ourselves amid the vast mixing vats, pygmies surrounded by giants.

He enjoyed my expression.

'Awesome,' I said.

'You don't need to go back upstairs to get out,' he said. 'There's a door out to the yard just down here.'

I thanked him for his advice about the nuts for the farmer, and for showing me round. I'd been with him for half an hour and couldn't reasonably stretch it further, but while I was in mid-sentence he looked over my shoulder and his face changed completely from man-in-charge to subservient subject.

I turned to see what had caused this transformation and found it not to be a Royal Person but a large man in white overalls accompanied by several anxious blue-clad attendants who were practically walking back-wards.

'Morning, Willy,' said the man in white. 'Everything going well?'

'Yes, Owen. Fine.'

'Good. Has the Canadian wheat come up from the docks?'

'They're unloading it now, Owen.'

'Good. We should have a talk about future plans. Come up to my new office at four this afternoon. You know where it is? Top floor, turn right from the lift, like my old office.'

'Yes, Owen.'

'Good.'

The eyes of the businessman glanced my way briefly and incuriously, and passed on. I was wearing brown overalls and an identity card, after all, and looked an employee. Not an employee of much worth, either, with my over-big overalls wrinkling around my ankles and drooping down my arms to the fingers. Willy didn't attempt to explain my presence, for which I was grateful. Willy was almost on his knees in reverence.

Owen Yorkshire was, without doubt, impressive. Easily over six foot tall, he was simply large, but not fat. There was a lot of heavy muscle in the shoulders, and a trim, sturdy belly. Luxuriant closely-waving hair spilled over the collar, with the beginnings of grey in the lacquered wings sweeping back from above his ears. It was a hairstyle that in its way made as emphatic a statement as Jonathan's. Owen Yorkshire intended not only to rule but to be remembered.

His accent was not quite Liverpool and not at all London, but powerful and positive. His voice was unmistakably an instrument of dominance. One could imagine that his rages might in fact shake the building. One could have sympathy with his yes-men.

Willy said, 'Yes, Owen,' several more times.

The man-to-man relationship that Willy Parrott prized so much extended, I thought, not much farther than the use of first names. True, Owen Yorkshire's manner to Willy was of the 'we're all in this together' type of management technique, and seemed to be drawing the best out of a good man; but I could imagine the boss also finding ways of getting rid of his Willy Parrott, if it pleased him, with sad shrugs and 'You know how it is these days, we no longer *need* a production manager just for horse-cubes; your job is computerised and phased out. Redundancy money? Of course. See my secretary. No hard feelings.'

I hoped it wouldn't happen to Willy.

Owen Yorkshire and his satellites swept onwards. Willy Parrott looked after him with pride tinged very faintly with anxiety.

'Do you work tomorrow?' I asked. 'Is the factory open on Saturdays?'

He reluctantly removed his gaze from the Yorkshire backview and began to think I'd been there too long.

'We're opening on Saturdays from next week,' he said. 'Tomorrow they're making more advertising films. There will be cameras all over the place, and on

Monday too. We won't get anything useful done until Tuesday.' He was full of disapproval, but he would repress all that, it was clear, for man-to-man Owen. 'Off you go then, lad. Go back to the entrance and leave the overalls and identity tag there.'

I thanked him again and this time went out into the central yard which, since my own arrival, had become clogged with vans and truckloads of television and advertising people. The television contingent were from Liverpool. The advertisement makers, according to the identification on their vans, were from Intramind Imaging (Manchester) Ltd.

One of the Intramind drivers, in the unthinking way of his kind, had braked and parked at an angle to all the other vehicles. I walked across to where he still sat in his cab and asked him to straighten up his van.

'Who says so?' he demanded belligerently.

'I just work here,' I said, still in the brown overalls that, in spite of Willy Parrott's instructions, I was not going to return. 'I was sent out to ask you. Big artics have to get in here.' I pointed to the unloading bays.

The driver grunted, started his engine, straightened his vehicle, switched off and jumped down to the ground beside me.

'Will that do?' he asked sarcastically.

'You must have an exciting job,' I said enviously. 'Do you see all those film stars?'

He sneered. 'We make *advertising* films, mate. Sure,

sometimes we get big names, but mostly they're endorsing things.'

'What sort of things?'

'Sports gear, often. Shoes, golf clubs.'

'And horse-cubes?'

He had time to waste while others unloaded equipment. He didn't mind a bit of showing off.

He said, 'They've got a lot of top jockeys lined up to endorse the horse-nuts.'

'Have they?' I asked interestedly. 'Why not trainers?'

'It's the jockeys the public know by their faces. That's what I'm told. I'm a football man myself.'

He didn't, I was grateful to observe, even begin to recognise my own face, that in years gone by had fairly taken up space on the nation's sports pages.

Someone in the team called him away and I walked off, sliding into my own car and making an uneventful exit through the tall unchecked outward gates. Odd, I thought, that the security-paranoid Owen Yorkshire didn't have a gate bristling with electronic barriers and ominous name-gatherers; and the only reason I could think of for such laxity was that he didn't always *want* name-takers to record everyone's visits.

Blind-eye country, I thought, like the private backstairs of the great before the India Cathcarts of the world floodlit the secretive comings and goings, and rewarded promiscuity with taint.

Perhaps Owen Yorkshire's backstairs was the lift to

the fifth floor. Perhaps Mrs Green Jumper and the bouncers in blue knew who to admit without searching.

Perhaps this, perhaps that. I'd seen the general layout and been near the power running the business, but basically I'd done little there but reconnoitre.

I stopped in a public car park, took off the brown overalls and decided to go to Manchester.

The journey was quite short, but it took me almost as long again to find Intramind Imaging (Manchester) Ltd which, although in a back street, proved to be a much bigger outfit than I'd pictured; I shed the tracksuit top and the Liverpool accent and approached the reception desk in suit, tie and business aura.

'I've come from Topline Foods,' I said. 'I'd like to talk to whoever is in charge of their account.'

Did I have an appointment?

No, it was a private matter.

If one pretended sufficient authority, I'd found doors got opened, and so it was at Intramind Imaging. A Mr Gross would see me. An electric door-latch buzzed and I walked from the entrance lobby into an inner hallway, where cream paint had been used sparingly and there was no carpet underfoot. Ostentation was out.

Mr Gross was 'third door on the left'. Mr Gross's door had his name and a message on it, 'Nick Gross. What the F do you want?'

Nick Gross looked me up and down. 'Who the hell

are *you*? You're not Topline Foods top brass, and you're over-dressed.'

He himself wore a black satin shirt, long hair and a gold earring. Forty-five disintegrating to fifty, I thought, and stuck in a time warp of departing youth. Forceful, though. Strong lines in his old-young face. Authority.

'You're making advertising films for Topline,' I said.

'So what? And if you're another of their whinging accountants sent to beg for better terms, the answer is up yours, mate. It isn't our fault you haven't been able to use those films you spent millions on. They're all brilliant stuff, the best. So you creep back to your Mr Owen effing Yorkshire and tell him there's no deal. Off you trot, then. If he wants his jockey series at the same price as before he has to send us a cheque every week. *Every week* or we yank the series, got it?'

I nodded.

Nick Gross said, 'And tell him not to forget that in ads the magic is the *cutting*, and the cutting comes *last*. No cheque, no cutting. No cutting, no magic. No magic, no message. No message, we might as well stop right now. Have you got it?'

I nodded again.

'Then you scurry right back to Topline and tell them no cheque, no cutting. And that means no campaign. Got it?'

'Yes.'

'Right. Bugger off.'

I meekly removed myself but, seeing no urgent

reason to leave altogether, I turned the wrong way out of his office and walked as if I belonged there down a passage between increasingly technical departments.

I came to an open door through which one could see a screen showing startlingly familiar pieces of an ad campaign currently collecting critical acclaim as well as phenomenally boosting sales. There were burst of pictures as short as three seconds followed by longer intervals of black. Three seconds of fast action. Ten of black.

I stopped, watching, and a man walked into my sight and saw me standing there.

'Yes?' he said. 'Do you want something?'

'Is that,' I said, nodding towards the screen, 'one of the mountain bike ads?'

'It will be when I cut it together.'

'Marvellous,' I said. I took half a step unthreateningly over his threshold. 'Can I watch you for a bit?'

'Who are you exactly?'

'From Topline Foods. I came to see Nick Gross.'

'Ah.' There was a world of comprehension in the monosyllable: comprehension that I immediately aimed to transfer from his brain to mine.

He was younger than Nick Gross and not so mock-rock-star in dress. His certainty shouted from the zany speed of his three-second flashes and the wit crackling in their juxtaposition: he had no need for earrings.

I said, quoting the bike campaign's slogan, 'Every kid under fifty wants a mountain bike for Christmas.'

He fiddled with reels of film and said cheerfully, 'There'll be hell to pay if they don't.'

'Did you work on the Topline ads?' I asked neutrally.

'No, thank Christ. A colleague did. Eight months of award-worthy brilliant work sitting idle in cans on the shelves. No prizes for us, and your top man's shitting himself, isn't he? All that cabbage spent and bugger all back. And all because some twisted little pipsqueak gets the star attraction arrested for something he didn't do.'

I held my breath, but he had no flicker of an idea what the pipsqueak looked like. I said I'd better be going and he nodded vaguely without looking up from his problems.

I persevered past his domain until I came to two big doors, one saying 'Sound Stage. Keep Out' and one, opening outwards with a push-bar, marked 'Backlot'. I pushed that door half open and saw outside in the open air a huge yellow crane dangling a red sports car by a rear axle. Film cameras and crews were busy round it. Work in progress.

I retreated. No one paid me any attention on the way out. This was not, after all, a bank vault, but a dream factory. No one could steal dreams.

The reception lobby, as I hadn't noticed on my way in, bore posters round the walls of past and current purse-openers, all prestigious prize-winning campaigns. Ad campaigns, I'd heard, were now considered an OK step on the career ladder for both directors and actors.

Sell cornflakes one day, play Hamlet the next. Intramind Imagining could speed you on your way.

I drove into the centre of Manchester and anonymously booked into a spacious restful room in the Crown Plaza Hotel. Davis Tatum might have a fit over the expense but if necessary I would pay for it myself. I wanted a shower, room-service and cosseting, and hang the price.

I phoned Tatum's home number and got an answering machine. I asked him to call back to my mobile number and repeated it, and then sat in an armchair watching racing on television – Flat racing at Ascot.

There was no sight of Ellis on the course. The commentator mentioned that his 'ludicrous' trial was due to resume in three days' time, on Monday. Sid Halley, he said, was sensibly keeping his head down as half Ellis's fan club was baying for his blood.

This little tit-bit came from a commentator who'd called me a wizard and a force for good not long ago. Times changed: did they ever. There were smiling close-ups of Ellis's face, and of mine, both helmetless but in racing colours, side by side. 'They used to be the closest of friends,' said the commentator sadly. 'Now they slash and gore each other like bulls.'

Sod him, I thought.

I also hoped that none of Mrs Green Jumper, Marsha Rowse, Mrs Dove, Willy Parrott, the Intramind van driver, Nick Gross and the film cutter had switched on to watch racing at Ascot. I didn't think Owen Yorkshire's sliding glance across my overalls would have left an imprint, but the others would remember me for a day or two. It was a familiar risk, sometimes lucky, sometimes not.

When the racing ended I phoned Intramind Imaging and asked a few general questions that I hadn't thought of in my brief career on the spot as a Topline Foods employee.

Were advertising campaigns originally recorded on film or on disks or on tape, I wanted to know, and could the public buy copies. I was answered helpfully: Intramind usually used film, especially for high-budget location-based ads and no, the public could *not* buy copies. The finished film would eventually be transferred onto Broadcast Quality video tape, known as BETACAM. These tapes then belonged to the clients, who paid television companies for air time. Intramind did not act as an agent.

'Thanks very much,' I said politely, grateful always for knowledge.

Davis Tatum phoned soon after.

'Sid,' he said, 'where are you?'

'Manchester, city of rain.'

It was sunny that day.

'Er . . .' Davis said. 'Any progress?'

'Some,' I said.

'And, er . . .' he hesitated again. 'Did you read India Cathcart this morning?'

'She didn't write that she'd seen us at Le Meridien,' I said.

'No. She took your excellent advice. But as to the rest . . .!'

I said, 'Kevin Mills phoned especially to tell me that she didn't write the rest. He did it himself. Policy. Pressure from above. Same old thing.'

'But wicked.'

'He apologised. Big advance.'

'You take it so lightly,' Davis said.

I didn't disillusion him. I said, 'Tomorrow evening – would you be able to go to Archie Kirk's house?'

'I should think so, if it's important. What time?'

'Could you arrange that with him? About six o'clock, I should think. I'll arrive there sometime myself. Don't know when.'

With a touch of complaint he said, 'It sounds a bit vague.'

I thought I'd better not tell him that with burglary, times tended to be approximate.

CHAPTER TWELVE

I phoned *The Pump*, asking for India Cathcart. Silly me.

Number one, she was never in the office on Fridays.

Number two, *The Pump* never gave private numbers to unknown callers.

'Tell her Sid Halley would like to talk to her,' I said, and gave the switchboard operator my mobile number, asking him to repeat it so I could make sure he had written it down right.

No promises, he said.

I sat for a good while thinking about what I'd seen and learned, and planning what I would do the next day. Such plans got altered by events as often as not, but I'd found that no plan at all invited nil results. If all else failed try Plan B. Plan B, in my battle strategy, was to escape with skin intact. Plan B had let me down a couple of times but disasters were like falls in racing; you never thought they'd happen until you were nose down to the turf.

I had some food sent up and thought some more, and at ten-fifteen my mobile buzzed.

'Sid?' India said nervously.

'Hello.'

'Don't say anything! I'll cry if you say anything.' After a pause she said, 'Sid! Are you there?'

'Yes. But I don't want you to cry so I'm not saying anything.'

'Oh, God.' It was half a choke, half a laugh. 'How can you be so . . . so *civilised*?'

'With enormous difficulty,' I said. 'Are you busy on Sunday evening? Your restaurant or mine?'

She said disbelievingly, 'Are you asking me out to dinner?'

'Well,' I said, 'it's not a proposal of marriage. And no knife through the ribs. Just food.'

'How can you *laugh*?'

'Why are you called India?' I asked.

'I was conceived there. What has that got to do with anything?'

'I just wondered,' I said.

'Are you *drunk*?'

'Unfortunately not. I'm sitting soberly in an armchair contemplating the state of the universe, which is C minus, or thereabouts.'

'Where? I mean, where is the armchair?'

'On the floor,' I said.

'You don't trust me!'

'No,' I sighed, 'I don't. But I do want to have dinner with you.'

'Sid,' she was almost pleading, 'be sensible.'

Rotten advice, I'd always thought. But then if I'd been sensible I would have two hands and fewer scars, and I reckoned one had to be *born* sensible, which didn't seem to have happened in my case.

I said, 'Your proprietor – Lord Tilepit – have you met him?'

'Yes.' She sounded a bit bewildered. 'He comes to the office party at Christmas. He shakes everyone's hand.'

'What's he like?'

'Do you mean to look at?'

'For a start.'

'He's fairly tall. Light-brown hair.'

'That's not much,' I said, when she stopped.

'He's not part of my day-to-day life.'

'Except that he burns saints,' I said.

A brief silence, then, 'Your restaurant, this time.'

I smiled. Her quick mind could reel in a tarpon where her red mouth couldn't. 'Does Lord Tilepit,' I asked, 'wear an obvious cloak of power? Are you aware of his power when you're in a room with him?'

'Actually . . . no.'

'Is anyone . . . *could* anyone be physically in awe of him?'

'No.' It was clear from her voice that she thought the idea laughable.

'So his leverage,' I said, 'is all economic?'

'I suppose so.'

'Is there anyone that *he* is in awe of?'

'I don't know. Why do you ask?'

'That man,' I said, 'has spent four months directing his newspaper to . . . well . . . ruin me. You must allow, I have an interest.'

'But you aren't ruined. You don't sound in the least ruined. And anyway, your ex-wife said it was impossible.'

'She said *what* was impossible?'

'To . . . to . . .'

'Say it.'

'To reduce you to rubble. To make you beg.'

She silenced me.

She said, 'Your ex-wife's still in love with you.'

'No, not any more.'

'I'm an expert on ex-wives,' India said. 'Wronged wives, dumped mistresses, women curdled with spite, women angling for money. Women wanting revenge, women breaking their hearts. I know the scenery. Your Jenny said she couldn't live in your purgatory, but when I suggested you were a selfish brute she defended you like a tigress.'

Oh *God*, I thought. After nearly six years apart the same old dagger could pierce us both.

'Sid?'

'Mm.'

'Do you still love *her*?'

I found a calm voice. 'We can't go back, and we don't want to,' I said. 'I regret a lot, but it's now finally over. She has a better husband, and she's happy.'

'I met her new man,' India said. 'He's sweet.'

'Yes.' I paused. 'What about your own ex?'

'I fell for his looks. It turned out he wanted an admiration machine in an apron. End of story.'

'Is his name Cathcart?'

'No,' she said. 'Patterson.'

Smiling to myself I said, 'Will you give me your phone number?'

She said, 'Yes,' and did so.

'Kensington Place restaurant. Eight o'clock.'

'I'll be there.'

When I was alone, which was usual nowadays, since Louise McInnes and I had parted, I took off my false arm at bedtime and replaced it after a shower in the morning. I couldn't wear it in showers, as water wrecked the works. Taking it off after a long day was often a pest, as it fitted tightly and tended to cling to my skin. Putting it on was a matter of talcum powder, getting the angle right and pushing hard.

The arm might be worth its weight in gold, as I'd told Trish Huxford, but even after three years, whatever lighthearted front I might now achieve in public, in private the management of amputation still took me a positive effort of the 'get on with it' ethos. I didn't know why I continued to feel vulnerable and sensitive. Too much pride, no doubt.

I'd charged up the two batteries in the charger overnight, so I started the new day, Saturday, with a fresh battery in the arm and a spare in my pocket.

It was by then five days since Gordon Quint had cracked my ulna, and the twinges had become less acute and less frequent. Partly it was because one naturally found the least painful way of performing any action, and partly because the ends of bone were beginning to knit. Soft tissue grew on the site of the break and on the eighth day it would normally begin hardening, the whole healing process being complete within the next week. Only splintered displaced ends caused serious trouble, which hadn't occurred in this case.

When I'd been a jockey the feel of a simple fracture had been an almost twice-yearly familiarity. One tended in jump racing to fall on one's shoulder, quite often at thirty miles an hour, and in my time I'd cracked my collar bones six times each side: only once had it been distinctly bad.

Some jockeys had stronger bones than others, but I didn't know anyone who'd completed a top career unscathed. Anyway, by Saturday morning, Monday's crack was no real problem.

Into my overnight bag I packed the battery charger, washing things, pyjamas, spare shirt, business suit and shoes. I wore both pieces of the tracksuit, white shirt, no tie and the dark trainers. In my belt I carried money and a credit card, and in my pocket a bunch of six keys on a single ring, which bore also a miniature torch. Three of the keys were variously for my car and the entry doors of my flat. The other three, looking misleadingly simple, would between them open any ordinary lock, regardless of the wishes of the owners.

My old teacher had had me practise until I was quick at it. He'd shown me also how to open the simple combination locks on suitcases; the method used by airport thieves.

I checked out of the hotel and found the way back to Frodsham, parking by the kerb within sight of the Topline Foods' wire-mesh gates.

As before, the gates were wide open and, as before, no one going in and out was challenged by the gatekeeper. No one, in fact, seemed to have urgent business in either direction and there were far fewer cars in the central area than on the day before. It wasn't until nearly eleven o'clock that the promised film crews arrived in force.

When getting on for twenty assorted vans and private cars had come to a ragged halt all over the place, disgorging film cameras (Intramind Imaging), a television camera (local station) and dozens of people looking purposeful with heavy equipment and chest-hugged clipboards, I got out of my car and put on the ill-fitting brown overalls, complete with identity badge. Into the boot I locked my bag and also the mobile phone, first taking the SIM card out of it and stowing it in my belt.

'Get into the habit of removing the SIM card,' my supplier had advised. 'Then if someone steals your phone, too bad, they won't be able to use it.'

'Great,' I'd said.

I started the car, drove unhesitatingly through the gates, steered a course round the assorted vans and stopped just beyond them, nearest to the unloading bays. Saturday or not, a few other brown-overall hands were busy on the rollers and the shelf escalator, and I simply walked straight in past them, saying 'Morning' as if I belonged.

They didn't answer, didn't look up, took me for granted.

Inside, I walked up the stairs I'd come down with Willy Parrott and, when I reached the right level, ambled along the gallery until I came to his office.

The sliding glass door was closed and locked and there was no one inside.

The paddles were silent in the vats. None of the day before's hum and activity remained, and almost none of the smells. Instead, there were cameras being positioned below, with Owen Yorkshire himself directing the director, his authoritative voice telling the experts their job.

He was too busy to look up. I went on along the gallery, coming to the fire-door up the flight of metal stairs. The fire-doors were locked at night. Willy had said. By day, they were open. Thankful, I reached in the end the plush carpet of the offices.

There was a bunch of three media people in there, measuring angles and moving potted plants. Office work, I gathered, was due for immortality on Monday. Cursing internally at their presence, I walked on towards the lift, passing the open door of 'Customer Relations'. No Marsha Rowse.

To the right of the lift there was a door announcing 'Office Manager, A. Dove', fastened with businesslike locks.

Looking back, I saw the measuring group taking their damned time. I needed them out of there and they infuriatingly dawdled.

I didn't like to hover. I returned to the lift and, to fill in time, opened a nearby door which proved to enclose fire-stairs, as I'd hoped.

Down a floor, and through the fire-door there, I found an expanse of open space, unfurnished and undecorated, the same in area as the office suite above. Up two storeys, above the offices, there was similar quiet, undivided, clean-swept space. Owen Yorkshire had already built for expansion, I gathered.

Cautiously, I went on upwards to the fifth floor, lair of the boss.

Trusting that he was still down among the vats, I opened the fire-door enough to put my head through.

More camera people moved around. Veritable banks of potted plants blazed red and gold. To the left, open opulently-gleaming double doors led into an entertaining and boardroom area impressive enough for a major industry of self-importance. On the right, more double doors led to Yorkshire's own new office; not, from what I could see, a place of paperwork. Polished wood gleamed. Plants galore. A tray of bottles and glasses.

I retreated down the unvarnished nitty-gritty fire-stairs until I was back on the working-office floor, standing there indecisively, wondering if the measurers still barred my purpose.

I heard voices, growing louder and stopping on the other side of the door. I was prepared to go into a busy-employee routine, but it appeared they preferred the lift to the stairs. The lifting machinery whirred on the other side of the stairwell, the voices moved into the lift and diminished to zero. I couldn't tell whether they'd gone up or down, and I was concerned only that they'd *all* gone up and not left one behind.

There was no point in waiting. I opened the fire-door, stepped onto the carpet and looked left and right towards Mrs Dove's domain.

I had the whole office floor to myself.

Great.

Mrs Dove's door was locked twice: an old-looking mortise and a new knob with a keyhole in the centre. These were locks I liked. There could be no nasty surprises like bolts or chains or wedges on the inside: also the emphatic statement of *two* locks probably meant that there were things of worth to guard.

The mortise lock took a whole minute, with the ghost of my old master breathing disapprovingly down my neck. The modern lock took twenty seconds of delicate probing. One had to 'feel' one's way through. False fingers for that, as for much else, were useless.

Once inside Mrs Dove's office I spent time relocking the door so that anyone outside trying it for security would find it as it should be. If anyone came in with keys, I would have warning enough to hide.

Mrs Dove's cote was large and comfortable with a wide desk, several of the Scandinavian-design armchairs and grainy blow-up black and white photographs of racing horses round the walls. Along one side there were the routine office machines – fax, copier and large print-out calculator, and, on the desk, a computer, shrouded for the weekend in a fitted cover. There were multiple filing cabinets and a tall white-painted and – as I discovered – locked cupboard.

Mrs Dove had a window with louvred blinds and a distant view of the Mersey. Mrs Dove's office was managing director stuff.

I had only a vague idea of what I was looking for. The audited accounts I'd seen in Companies House seemed not to match the actual state of affairs at Frodsham. The audit did, of course, refer to a year gone by, to the first with Owen Yorkshire in charge, but the fragile bottom-line profit, as shown, would not suggest or justify expensive publicity campaigns or televised receptions for the notables of Liverpool.

The old French adage 'look for the lady' was a century out of date, my old teacher had said. In modern times it should be 'look for the money'; and, shortly before he died, he had amended that to 'follow the paper'. Shady or doubtful transactions, he said, always left a paper trail. Even in the age of computers, he'd insisted that paper showed the way; and over and over again I'd proved him right.

The paper in Mrs Dove's office was all tidied away in the many filing cabinets, which were locked.

Most filing cabinets, like these, locked all drawers simultaneously with a notched vertical rod out of sight within the right-hand front corner, operated by a single key at the top. Turning the key raised the rod, allowing all the drawers to open. I wasn't bad at opening filing cabinets.

The trouble was that Topline Foods had little to hide, or at least not at first sight. Pounds of paper referred to orders and invoices for incoming supplies; pounds more to sales, pounds more to the expenses of running an industry, from insurance to wages, to electricity to general maintenance.

The filing cabinets took too long and were a waste of time. What they offered was the entirely respectable basis of next year's audit.

I locked them all again and, after investigating the desk drawers themselves, which held only stationery, took the cover off the computer and switched it on, pressing the buttons for 'List Files', and 'Enter'. Scrolls of file names appeared and I tried one at random: 'Aintree'.

Onto the screen came details of the lunch given the day before the Grand National, the guest list, the menu, a summary of the speeches and a list of the coverage given to the occasion in the press.

Nothing I could find seemed any more secret. I switched off, replaced the cover and turned my lock-pickers to the tall white cupboard.

The feeling of time running out, however irrational, shortened my breath and made me hurry. I always envied the supersleuths in films who put their hands on the right papers in the first ten seconds and, this time, I didn't know if the right paper even existed.

It turned out to be primarily not a paper but a second computer.

Inside the white cupboard, inside a drop-down desk arrangement in there, I came across a second keyboard and a second screen. I switched the computer on and nothing happened, which wasn't astounding as I found an electric lead lying alongside, disconnected. I plugged it into the computer and tried again, and with a grumble or two the machine became ready for business.

I pressed 'List Files' again, and this time found myself looking not at individual subjects, but at 'Directories', each of which contained file names such as 'Formula A'.

What I had come across were the more private records, the electronic files, some very secret, some not.

In quick succession I highlighted the 'Directories' and brought them to the screen until one baldly listed

'Quint': but no amount of button-pressing got me any further.

Think.

The reason I couldn't get the Quint information onto the screen must be because it wasn't in the computer.

OK? OK. So where was it?

On the shelf above the computer stood a row of box-files, numbers 1 to 9, but not one labelled Quint.

I lifted down Number 1 and looked inside. There were several letters filed in there, also a blue computer floppy disk in a clear cover. According to the letters, box-file No. 1 referred to loans made to Topline Foods, loans not repaid on the due date. There was also a mention of 'sweeteners' and 'quid pro quos'. I fed the floppy disk into the drive slot in the computer body and got no further than a single unhelpful word on the screen: PASSWORD?

Password? Heaven knew. I looked into the box-files one by one and came to 'Quint' in No. 6. There were three floppies in there, not one.

I fed in the first.

PASSWORD?

Second and third disks – PASSWORD?

Bugger, I thought.

Searching for anything helpful I lifted down a heavy white cardboard box, like a double-height shoebox, that filled the rest of the box-file shelf. In there was a row of big black high-impact plastic protective coverings. I picked out one and unlatched its fastening, and found inside it a video tape, but a tape of double the ordinary width. A label on the tape said 'Broadcast Quality Videotape'. Underneath that was the single word BETACAM. Under that was the legend 'Quint series. 15 × 30 secs.'

I closed the thick black case and tried another one. Same thing. Quint series. 15 × 30 secs. All of the cases held the same.

These double-size tapes needed a special tape player not available in Mrs Dove's office. To see what was on these expensive tapes meant taking one with me.

I could, of course, simply put one of them inside my tracksuit jacket and walk out with it. I could take all the 'PASSWORD' disks. If I did I was a) stealing, b) in danger of being found carrying the goods, and c) making it impossible for any information they held to be used in any later legal enquiry. I would steal the information itself, if I could, but not the hardware.

Think.

As I'd told Charles at Aynsford, I'd had to learn a good deal about computers just to keep a grip on the accelerating world, but the future became the present so fast that I could never get ahead.

Someone tried to open the door.

There was no time to restore the room to normal. I could only speed across the carpet and stand where I would be hidden by the door when it swung inwards. Plan B meant simply running – and I was wearing running shoes.

The knob turned again and rattled, but nothing else happened. Whoever was outside had presumably been either keyless or reassured: in either case it played havoc with my breathing.

Oddly, the pumping adrenalin brought me my computer answer which was, if I couldn't bring the contents of a floppy disk to the screen, I could transfer it whole to *another* computer, one that would give me all the time I needed to crack the password, or to get help from people who could.

Alongside the unconnected electric cable there had been a telephone cable, also unattached. I snapped it into the telephone socket on the computer, thereby connecting Mrs Dove's modem to the world-wide Internet.

It needed a false start or two while I desperately tried to remember half-learned techniques, but finally I was rewarded by the screen prompting: 'Enter telephone number.'

I tapped in my own home number in the flat in Pont Square, and pressed 'Enter', and the screen announced nonchalantly 'dialling in progress', then 'call accepted', then 'transfer', and finally 'transfer complete'.

Whatever was on the first guarded 'Quint' disk was now in my own computer in London. I transferred the other two 'Quint' floppies in the same way, and then the disk from box-file No. 1, and for good measure another from Box 3, identified as 'Tilepit'.

There was no way that I knew of transferring the

BETACAM tapes. Regretfully I left them alone. I looked through the paper pages in the 'Quint' box and make a photocopy of one page – a list of unusual racecourses – folding it and hiding it within the zipped pocket of my belt.

Finally I disconnected the electric and telephone cables again, closed the computer compartment, checked that the box-files and BETACAM tapes were as they should be, relocked the white cupboard, then unlocked and gently opened the door to the passage.

Silence.

Breathing out with relief I relocked Mrs Dove's door and walked along through the row of cubby-hole offices and came to the first setback: the fire-door leading to brown-overalls territory was not merely locked but had a red light shining above it.

Shining red lights often meant alarm systems switched on with depressingly loud sirens ready to screech.

I'd been too long in Mrs Dove's office. I retreated towards her door again and went down the fire-stairs beside the lift, emerging into the ground-floor entrance hall with its glass doors to the parking area beyond.

One step into the lobby proved to be one step too far. Something hit my head rather hard and one of the beefy body-guards in blue flung a sort of strap round my body and effectively pinned my upper arms to my sides.

I plunged about a bit and got another crack on the

head which left me unable to help myself and barely able to think. I was aware of being in the lift, but wasn't quite sure how I'd got there. I was aware of having my ankles strapped together and of being dragged ignominiously over some carpet and dropped in a chair.

Regulation Scandinavian chair with wooden arms, like all the others.

'Tie him up,' a voice said, and a third strap tightened across my chest, so that when the temporary mist cleared I woke to a state of near physical immobility and a mind full of curses.

The voice belonged to Owen Yorkshire. He said, 'Right. Good. Well done. Leave the wrench on the desk. Go back downstairs and don't let anyone up here.'

'Yes, sir.'

'Wait,' Yorkshire commanded, sounding uncertain. 'Are you sure you've got the right man?'

'Yes, sir. He's wearing the identity badge we issued to him yesterday. He was supposed to return it when he left, but he didn't.'

'All right. Thanks. Off you go.'

The door closed behind the bodyguards and Owen Yorkshire plucked the identity badge from my overalls, read the name and flung it down on his desk.

We were in his fifth-floor office. The chair I sat in was surrounded by carpet. Marooned on a desert island, feeling dim and stupid.

The man-to-man all-pals-together act was in abeyance. The Owen Yorkshire confronting me was very angry, disbelieving and, I would have said, *frightened.*

'What are you doing here?' he demanded, bellowing.

His voice echoed and reverberated in the quiet room. His big body loomed over me, his big head close to mine. All his features, I thought, were slightly oversized: big nose, big eyes, wide forehead, large flat cheeks, square jaw, big mouth. The collar-length black waving hair with its grey-touched wings seemed to vibrate with vigour. I would have put his age at forty; maybe a year or two younger.

'Answer,' he yelled. 'What are you doing here?'

I didn't reply. He snatched up from his desk a heavy fifteen-inch-long silvery wrench and made as if to hit my head with it. If that was what his boys-in-blue had used on me, and I gathered it was, then connecting it again with my skull was unlikely to produce any answer at all. The same thought seemed to occur to him, because he threw the wrench down disgustedly onto the desk again, where it bounced slightly under its own weight.

The straps round my chest and ankles were the sort of fawn close-woven webbing often used round suitcases to prevent them from bursting open. There was no elasticity in them, no stretch. Several more lay on the desk.

I felt a ridiculous desire to chatter, a tendency I'd noticed in the past in mild concussion after racing falls, and sometimes on waking up from anaesthetics. I'd learned how to suppress the garrulous impulse, but it was still an effort, and in this case, essential.

Owen Yorkshire was wearing man-to-man togs; that is to say, no jacket, a man-made-fibre shirt (almost white with vertical stripes made of interlocking beige-coloured horseshoes), no tie, several buttons undone, unmissable view of manly hairy chest, gold chain and medallion.

I concentrated on the horseshoe stripes. If I could count the number of horseshoes from shoulder to waist I would not have any thoughts that might dribble out incautiously. The boss was talking. I blanked him out and counted horseshoes and managed to say nothing.

He went abruptly out of the room, leaving me sitting there looking foolish. When he returned he brought two people with him: they had been along in the reception area, it seemed, working out table placements for Monday's lunch.

They were a woman and a man; Mrs Dove and a stranger. Both exclaimed in surprise at the sight of my trussed self. I shrank into the chair and looked mostly at their waists.

'Do you know who this is?' Yorkshire demanded of them furiously.

The man shook his head, mystified. Mrs Dove, frowning, said to me, 'Weren't you here yesterday? Something about a farmer?'

'This,' Yorkshire said with scorn, 'is Sid Halley.'

The man's face stiffened, his mouth forming an O.

'*This*, Verney,' Yorkshire went on with biting sarcasm, 'is the feeble creature you've spent months thundering on about. *This!* And Ellis said he was dangerous! Just look at him! All those big guns to frighten a mouse.'

Verney *Tilepit*. I'd looked him up in *Burke's Peerage*. Verney Tilepit, 3rd Baron, aged forty-two, a director of Topline Foods, proprietor – by inheritance – of *The Pump*.

Verney Tilepit's grandfather, created a baron for devoted allegiance to the then prime minister, had been one of the old roistering, powerful opinion-makers who'd had governments dancing to their tune. The first Verney Tilepit had put his shoulder to history and given it a shove. The third had surfaced after years of quiescence, primarily, it seemed, to discredit a minor investigator. Policy! His bewildered grandfather would have been speechless.

He was fairly tall, as India had said, and he had brown hair. The flicking glance I gave him took in also a large expanse of face with small features bunched in the middle: small nose, small mouth, small sandy moustache, small eyes behind large, light-framed glasses. Nothing about him seemed physically threatening. Perhaps I felt the same disappointment in my adversary as he plainly did about me.

'How do you know he's Sid Halley?' Mrs Dove asked.

Owen Yorkshire said disgustedly, 'One of the TV crew knew him. He swore there was no mistake. He'd filmed him often. He *knows* him.'

Bugger, I thought.

Mrs Dove pulled up the long left sleeve of my brown overalls, and looked at my left hand. 'Yes. It must be Sid Halley. Not much of a champion now, is he?'

Owen Yorkshire picked up the telephone, pressed numbers, waited and forcefully spoke.

'Get over here quickly,' he said. 'We have a crisis. Come to my new office.' He listened briefly. 'No,' he said, 'just get over here.' He slammed down the receiver and stared at me balefully. 'What the sod are you doing here?'

The almost overwhelming urge to tell him got as far as my tongue and was only over-ridden by clamped-shut teeth. One could understand why people confessed. The itch to unburden outweighed the certainty of retribution.

'Answer,' yelled Yorkshire. He picked up the wrench again. 'Answer, you little cuss.'

I did manage an answer of sorts.

I spoke to Verney Tilepit directly in a weak, mock-respectful tone, 'I came to see you . . . sir.'

'My lord,' Yorkshire told me. 'Call him my lord.'

'My lord,' I said.

Tilepit said, 'What for?' and 'What made you think I would be here?'

'Someone told me you were a director of Topline

Foods, my lord, so I came here to ask you to stop and I don't know why I've been dragged up here and tied up like this.' The last twenty words just dribbled out. Be *careful*, I thought. *Shut up*.

'To stop *what*?' Tilepit demanded.

'To stop your paper telling lies about me.' Better.

Tilepit didn't know how to answer such naivety. Yorkshire properly considered it barely credible. He spoke to Mrs Dove, who was dressed for Saturday morning, not in office black and white, but in bright red with gold buttons.

'Go down and make sure he hasn't been in your office.'

'I locked it when I left last night, Owen.'

Mrs Dove's manner towards her boss was interestingly like Will Parrott's. All-equals-together; up to a point.

'Go and look,' he said. 'And check that cupboard.'

'No one's opened that cupboard since you moved offices up here this week. And you have the only key.'

'Go and check anyway,' he said.

She had no difficulty with obeying him. I remembered Marsha Rowse's ingenuous statement – 'Mrs Dove says never to make Mr Yorkshire angry.'

Mrs Dove, self-contained, confident, was taking her own advice. She was not, I saw, in love with the man, nor was she truly afraid of him. His temper, I would have thought, was to her more of a nuisance than life – or even job – threatening.

As things stood, or rather as I sat, I saw the wisdom of following Mrs Dove's example for as long as I could.

She was gone a fair time, during which I worried more and more anxiously that I'd left something slightly out of place in that office, that she would know by some sixth sense that someone had been in there, that I'd left some odour in the air despite never using after-shave, that I'd closed the filing cabinets incorrectly, that I'd left visible fingerprints on a shiny surface, that I'd done *anything* that she knew she hadn't.

I breathed slowly, trying not to sweat.

When she finally came back she said, 'The TV crews are leaving. Everything's ready for Monday. The florists are bringing the Lady Mayoress's bouquet at ten o'clock. The red-carpet people are downstairs now measuring the lobby. And, oh, the man from Intramind Imaging says they want a cheque.'

'What about the office?'

'The office? Oh, the office is all right.' She was unconcerned. 'It was all locked. Just as I left it.'

'And the cupboard?' Yorkshire insisted.

'Locked.' She thought he was over-reacting. I was concerned only to show no relief.

'What are you going to do with *him*?' she asked, indicating me. 'You can't keep him here, can you? The TV crew downstairs were talking about him being here. They want to interview him. What shall I say?'

Yorkshire with black humour said, 'Tell them he's all tied up.'

She wasn't amused. She said, 'I'll say he went out the back way. And I'll be off, too. I'll be here by eight, Monday morning.' She looked at me calmly and spoke to Yorkshire, 'Let him go,' she said unemotionally. 'What harm can he do? He's pathetic.'

Yorkshire, undecided, said, 'Pathetic? Why pathetic?'

She paused composedly halfway through the door, and dropped a pearl beyond price.

'It says so in *The Pump*.'

Neither of these two men, I thought, listening to them, was a full-blown criminal. Not yet. Yorkshire was too near the brink.

He still held the heavy adjustable wrench, slapping its head occasionally against his palm, as if it helped his thoughts.

'Please untie me,' I said. At last I found the fatal loquaciousness had abated. I no longer wanted to gabble, but just to talk my way out.

Tilepit himself might have done it. He clearly was unused to – and disturbed by – even this level of violence. His power base was his grandfather's name. His muscle was his hire-and-fire clout. There were only so many top editorships in the British Press and George Godbar, editor of *The Pump*, wasn't going to lose his hide to save mine. Matters of principle were all too often an unaffordable luxury, and I didn't believe that in George Godbar's place, or even in Kevin Mills' or India's, I would have done differently.

Yorkshire said, 'We wait.'

He opened a drawer in his desk and drew out what looked bizarrely like a jar of gherkins. Dumping the wrench temporarily, he unscrewed the lid, put the jar on the desk, pulled out a green finger and bit it, crunching it with large white teeth.

'Gherkin?' he offered Tilepit.

The third baron averted his nose.

Yorkshire, shrugging, chewed uninhibitedly and went back to slapping his palm with the wrench.

'I'll be missed,' I said mildly, 'if you keep me much longer.'

'Let him go,' Tilepit said with a touch of impatience. 'He's right, we can't keep him here indefinitely.'

'We wait,' Yorkshire said heavily, fishing out another gherkin and, to the accompaniment of noisy munching, we waited.

I could smell the vinegar.

The door opened finally behind me and both Yorkshire and Tilepit looked welcoming and relieved.

I didn't. The newcomer, who came round in front of me blankly, was Ellis Quint.

Ellis, in open-necked white shirt; Ellis, handsome, macho, vibrating with showmanship; Ellis, the nation's darling, farcically accused. I hadn't seen him since Ascot races, and none of his radiance had waned.

'What's *Halley* doing here?' he demanded, sounding alarmed. 'What has he learned?'

'He was wandering about,' Yorkshire said, pointing a gherkin at me. 'I had him brought up here. He can't have learned a thing.'

Tilepit announced, 'Halley says he came to ask me to stop *The Pump*'s campaign against him.'

Ellis said positively, 'He wouldn't have done that.'

'Why not?' Yorkshire asked. 'Look at him. He's a wimp.'

'A *wimp*!'

Despite my precarious position I smiled involuntarily at the depth of incredulity in his voice. I even grinned at him sideways from below half-lowered eyelids, and saw the same private smile on his face: the acknowledgment of brotherhood, of secrecy, of shared esoteric experience, of cold winter afternoons, perils embraced, disappointments and injuries taken lightly, of indescribable triumphs. We had hugged each other standing in our stirrups, ecstatic after winning posts. We had trusted, bonded, and twinned.

Whatever we were now, we had once been more than brothers. The past – our past – remained. The intense and mutual memories could not be erased.

The smiles died. Ellis said, 'This *wimp* comes up on your inside and beats you in the last stride. This wimp could ruin us all if we neglect our inside rail. This wimp was champion jockey for five or six years and might have been still, and we'd be fools to forget it.'

He put his face close to mine. 'Still the same old Sid, aren't you? Cunning. Nerveless. Win at all costs.'

There was nothing to say.

Yorkshire bit into a gherkin. 'What do we do with him, then?'

'First we find out why he's here.'

Tilepit said, 'He came to get *The Pump* to stop—'

'Balls,' Ellis interrupted. 'He's lying.'

'How can you tell?' Tilepit protested.

'I know him.' He said it with authority, and it was true.

'What, then?' Yorkshire asked.

Ellis said to me, 'You'll not get me into court, Sid. Not Monday. Not ever. You haven't been able to break my Shropshire alibi, and my lawyers say that without that the prosecution won't have a chance. They'll withdraw the charge. Understand? I know you *do* understand. You'll have destroyed your own reputation, not mine. What's more, my father's going to kill you.'

Yorkshire and Tilepit showed, respectively, pleasure and shock.

'Before Monday?' I asked.

The flippancy fell like lead. Ellis strode round behind me and yanked back the right front of my brown overalls, and the tracksuit beneath. He tore a couple of buttons off my shirt, pulling that back after, then he pressed down strongly with his fingers.

'Gordon says he broke your collar-bone,' he said.

'Well, he didn't.'

Ellis would see the remains of bruising and he could feel the bumps of callus formed by earlier breaks, but it was obvious to him that his father had been wrong.

'My father will kill you,' he repeated. 'Don't you care?'

Another unanswerable question.

It seemed to me as if the cruel hidden side of Ellis suddenly took over, banishing the friend and becoming the threatened star who had everything to lose. He roughly threw my clothes together and continued round behind me until he stood on my left side.

'You won't defeat me,' he said. 'You've cost me half a million. You've cost me lawyers. You've cost me *sleep*.'

He might insist that I couldn't defeat him, but we both knew I would in the end, if I tried, because he was guilty.

'You'll pay for it,' he said.

He put his hands on the hard shell of my left forearm and raised it until my elbow formed a right angle. The tight strap round my upper arms and chest prevented me from doing anything to stop him. Whatever strength that remained in my upper left arm (and it was, in fact, quite a lot) was held in uselessness by that strap.

Ellis peeled back the brown sleeve, and the blue one underneath. He tore open my shirt cuff and pulled that sleeve back also. He looked at the plastic skin underneath.

'I know something about that arm,' he said. 'I got a

brochure on purpose. That skin is a sort of glove, and it comes off.'

He felt up my arm until, by the elbow, he came to the top of the glove. He rolled it down as far as the wrist and then, with concentration, pulled it off finger by finger, exposing the mechanics in all their detail.

The close-fitting textured glove gave the hand an appearance of life, with knuckles, veins and shapes like finger nails. The works inside were gears, springs and wiring. The bared forearm was bright pink, hard and shiny.

Ellis smiled.

He put his own strong right hand on my electrical left and pressed and twisted with knowledge and then, when the works clicked free, unscrewed the hand round several turns until it came right off.

Ellis looked into my eyes as at a feast. 'Well?' he said.

'You *shit*.'

He smiled. He opened his fingers and let the unscrewed hand fall onto the carpet.

CHAPTER THIRTEEN

Tilepit looked shocked enough to vomit, but not Yorkshire: in fact, he laughed.

Ellis said to him sharply, 'This man is not funny. Everything that has gone wrong is because of *him*, and don't you forget it. It's this Sid Halley that's going to ruin you, and if you think he doesn't care about what I've just done' – he put his toe against the fallen hand and moved it a few inches – 'if you think it's something to laugh at, I'll tell you that for *him* it's almost unbearable . . . but *not* unbearable, is it, Sid?' He turned to ask me, and told Yorkshire at the same time. 'No one yet has invented anything you've found actually unbearable, have they, Sid?'

I didn't answer.

Yorkshire protested, 'But he's only—'

'Don't say *only*,' Ellis interrupted, his voice hard and loud. 'Don't you understand it yet? What do you think he's doing here? How did he get here? What does he know? He's not going to tell you. His nickname's tungsten carbide – that's the hardest of all metals and it saws through steel. I *know* him. I've almost loved him. You have no idea what you're dealing with, and we've got to decide what to do with him. How many people know he's here?'

'My bodyguards,' Yorkshire said. 'They brought him up.'

It was Lord Tilepit who gave him the real bad news. 'It was a TV crew who told Owen that Sid Halley was in the building.'

'A TV crew!'

'They wanted to interview him. Mrs Dove said she would tell them he'd gone.'

'*Mrs Dove!*'

If Ellis had met Mrs Dove he would know, as I did, that she wouldn't lie for Yorkshire. Mrs Dove had seen me, and she would say so.

Ellis asked furiously, 'Did Mrs Dove see him tied in that chair?'

'Yes,' Tilepit said faintly.

'You *stupid* . . .' Words failed Ellis, but for only a few short seconds. 'Then,' he said flatly, 'you can't kill him here.'

'*Kill* him?' Tilepit couldn't believe what he'd heard. His whole large face blushed pink. 'I'm not . . . are you talking about *murder*?'

'Oh yes, my lord,' I said dryly, 'they are. They're thinking of putting your lordship behind bars as an accessory. You'll love it in the slammer.'

I'd meant only to get Tilepit to see the enormity of

what Ellis was proposing. but in doing so I'd made the mistake of unleashing Yorkshire's rage.

He took two paces and kicked my unscrewed hand with such force that it flew across the room and crashed against the wall. Then he realised the wrench was still in his hand and swung it at my head.

I saw the blow coming but couldn't get my head back far enough to avoid it altogether. The wrench's heavy screw connected with my moving cheekbone and tore the skin, but didn't this time knock me silly.

In Owen Yorkshire, the half-slipping brakes came wholly off. Perhaps the very sight of me, left-handless and bleeding and unable to retaliate, was all it took. He raised his arm and the wrench again, and I saw the spite in his face and the implacably murderous intention and I thought of nothing much at all, which afterwards seemed odd.

It was Ellis who stopped him. Ellis caught the descending arm and yanked Owen Yorkshire round sideways, so that although the heavy weapon swept on downwards, it missed me altogether.

'You're *brainless*,' Ellis shouted. 'I said *not in here*. You're a raving lunatic. Too many people know he came here. Do you want to splatter his blood and brains all over your new carpet? You might as well go and shout from the rooftops. Get a grip on that frigging temper and find a tissue.'

'A what?'

'Something to stop him bleeding. Are you terminally

insane? When he doesn't turn up wherever he's expected, you're going to get the police in here looking for him. TV crew! Mrs Dove! The whole frigging country! You get one drop of his blood on anything in here, you're looking at twenty-five years.'

Yorkshire, bewildered by Ellis's attack and turning sullen, said there weren't any tissues. Verney Tilepit tentatively produced a handkerchief; white, clean and embroidered with a coronet. Ellis snatched it from him and slapped it on my cheek, and I wondered if ever, in any circumstances, I could, to save myself, deliberately kill *him*, and didn't think so.

Ellis took the handkerchief away briefly, looked at the scarlet staining the white, and put it back, pressing.

Yorkshire strode about, waving the wrench as if jerked by strings. Tilepit looked extremely unhappy. I considered my probable future with gloom and Ellis, taking the handkerchief away again and watching my cheek critically, declared that the worst of the bleeding had stopped.

He gave the handkerchief back to Tilepit, who put it squeamishly in his pocket, and he snatched the wrench away from Yorkshire and told him to cool down and *plan*.

Planning took them both out of the office, the door closing behind them. Verney Tilepit didn't in the least appreciate being left alone with me and went to look out of the window, to look anywhere except at me.

'Untie me,' I said with force.

No chance. He didn't even show he'd heard.

I asked, 'How did you get yourself into this mess?'

No answer.

I tried again. I said, 'If I walk out of here free, I'll forget I ever saw you.'

He turned round, but he had his back to the light and I couldn't see his eyes clearly behind the spectacles.

'You really are in deep trouble,' I said.

'Nothing will happen.'

I wished I believed him. I said, 'It must have seemed pretty harmless to you, just to use your paper to ridicule someone week after week. What did Yorkshire tell you? To save Ellis at all costs. Well, it *is* going to cost you.'

'You don't understand. Ellis is blameless.'

'I understand that you're up to your noble neck in shit.'

'I can't do anything.' He was worried, unhappy and congenitally helpless.

'Untie me,' I said again, with urgency.

'It wouldn't help. I couldn't get you out.'

'Untie me,' I said. 'I'll do the rest.'

He dithered. If he had been capable of reasoned decisions he wouldn't have let himself be used by Yorkshire, but he wasn't the first or last rich man to stumble blindly into a quagmire. He couldn't make up his mind to attempt saving himself by letting me free and, inevitably, the opportunity passed.

Ellis and Yorkshire came back, and neither of them would meet my eyes.

Bad sign.

Ellis, looking at his watch, said, 'We wait.'

'What for?' Tilepit asked uncertainly.

Yorkshire answered, to Ellis's irritation, 'The TV people are on the point of leaving. Everyone will be gone in fifteen minutes.'

Tilepit looked at me, his anxieties showing plainly. 'Let Halley go,' he begged.

Ellis said comfortingly, 'Sure, in a while.'

Yorkshire smiled. His anger was preferable, on the whole.

Verney Tilepit wanted desperately to be reassured, but even he could see that if freeing me was the intention, why did we have to wait.

Ellis still held the wrench. He wouldn't get it wrong, I thought. He wouldn't spill my blood. I would probably not know much about it. I might not consciously learn the reciprocal answer to my self-searching question: could *he* personally kill *me*, to save himself? How deep did friendship go? Did it ever have absolute taboos? Had I already, by accusing him of evil, melted his innermost restraints? He wanted to get even. He would wound me any way he could. But *kill* . . . I didn't know.

He walked round behind me.

Time, in a way, stood still. It was a moment in which to plead, but I couldn't. The decision, whatever I said, would be *his*.

He came eventually round to my right-hand side and murmured, 'Tungsten,' under his breath.

Water, I thought, I had water in my veins.

He reached down suddenly and clamped his hand round my right wrist, pulling fiercely upwards.

I jerked my wrist out of his grasp and without warning he bashed the wrench across my knuckles. In the moment of utter numbness that resulted he slid the open jaws of the wrench onto my wrist and tightened the screw. Tightened it further, until the jaws grasped immovably, until they squeezed the upper and lower sides of my wrist together, compressing blood vessels, nerves and ligaments, bearing down on the bones inside.

The wrench was heavy. He balanced its handle on the arm of the chair I was sitting in and held it steady so that my wrist was up at the same level. He had two strong hands. He persevered with the screw.

I said, 'Ellis,' in protest, not from anger or even fear, but in disbelief that he could do what he was doing: in a lament for the old Ellis, in a sort of passionate sorrow.

For the few seconds that he looked into my face, his expression was flooded with awareness . . . and shame. Then the feelings passed, and he returned in deep concentration to an atrocious pleasure.

It was extraordinary. He seemed to go into a kind of trance, as if the office and Yorkshire and Tilepit didn't exist, as if there were only one reality, which was the clench of forged steel jaws on a wrist and the extent to which he could intensify it.

I thought: if the wrench had been lopping shears, if its jaws had been knives instead of flat steel, the whole devastating nightmare would have come true. I shut my mind to it: made it cold. Sweated, all the same.

I thought: what I see in his face is the full-blown addiction; not the cruel satisfaction he could get from unscrewing a false hand, but the sinful fulfilment of cutting off a live hoof.

I glanced very briefly at Yorkshire and Tilepit and saw their frozen bottomless astonishment, and I realised that until that moment of revelation they hadn't wholly believed in Ellis's guilt.

My wrist hurt. Somewhere up my arm the ulna grumbled.

I said, '*Ellis*,' sharply, to wake him up.

He got the screw to tighten another notch.

I yelled at him, '*Ellis*,' and again, '*Ellis*.'

He straightened, looking vaguely down at fifteen inches of heavy stainless steel wrench incongruously sticking out sideways from its task. He tied it to the arm of the chair with another strap from the desk and went over to the window, not speaking, but not rational either.

I tried to dislodge myself from the wrench but my hand was too numb and the grip too tight. I found it difficult to think. My hand was pale blue and grey. Thought was a crushed wrist and an abysmal shattering fear that if the damage went on too long, it would be permanent. Hands could be lost.

Both hands . . . Oh God. Oh *God.*

'Ellis,' I said yet again, but in a lower voice this time: a plea for him to return to the old self, that was there all the time, somewhere.

I waited. Acute discomfort and the terrible anxiety continued. Ellis's thoughts seemed far out in space. Tilepit cleared his throat in embarrassment and Yorkshire, as if in unconscious humour, crunched a gherkin.

Minutes passed.

I said, 'Ellis . . .'

I closed my eyes. Opened them again. More or less prayed.

Time and nightmare fused. One became the other. The future was a void.

Ellis left the window and crossed with bouncing steps to the chair where I sat. He looked into my face and enjoyed what he could undoubtedly see there. Then he unscrewed and untied the wrench with violent jerks and dropped the abominable ratchet from a height onto the desk.

No one said anything. Ellis seemed euphoric, high, full of good spirits, striding round the room as if unable to contain his exhilaration.

I got stabbing pins and needles in my fingers, and thanked the fates for it. My hand felt dreadful but turned slowly yellowish pink.

Thought came back from outer space and lodged again earthily in my brain.

Ellis, coming down very slightly, looked at his watch. He plucked from the desk the cosmetic glove from my false arm, came to my right side, shoved the glove inside my shirt against my chest and, with a theatrical flourish, zipped up the front of my blue tracksuit to keep his gift from falling out.

He looked at his watch again. Then he went across the room, picked up the unscrewed hand, returned to my side, and slapped the dead mechanism into my living palm. There was a powerful impression all round that he was busy making sure no trace of Sid Halley remained in the room.

He went round behind me and undid the strap fastening me into the chair. Then he undid the second strap that held my upper arms against my body.

'Screw the hand back on,' he instructed.

Perhaps because they had bent from being kicked around, or perhaps because my real hand was eighty per cent useless, the screw threads wouldn't mesh smoothly, and after three half turns they stuck. The hand looked re-attached, but wouldn't work.

'Stand up,' Ellis said.

I stood, swaying, my ankles still tied together.

'You're letting him go,' Tilepit exclaimed, with grateful relief.

'Of course,' Ellis said.

Yorkshire was smiling.

'Put your hands behind your back,' Ellis told me.

I did so, and he strapped my wrists tight together.

Last, he undid my ankles.

'This way.' He pulled me by the arm over to the door and through into the passage. My feet walked like automatons.

Looking back, I saw Yorkshire put his hand on the telephone. Beyond him, Tilepit was happy with foolish faith.

Ellis pressed the call button for the lift, and the door opened immediately.

'Get in,' he said.

I looked briefly at his now unsmiling face. Expressionless. That made two of us, I thought, two of us thinking the same thing and not saying it.

I stepped into the lift and he leaned in quickly and pressed the button for the ground floor, then jumped back. The door closed between us. The lift began its short journey down.

To tie together the wrists of a man who could unscrew one of them was an exercise in futility. All the same, the crossed threads and my fumbling fingers gave me trouble and some severe moments of panic before the hand slipped free. The lift had already reached its destination by the time I'd shed the tying strap, leaving no chance to emerge from the opening door with everything anywhere near normal.

I put the mechanical hand deep into my right-hand tracksuit trousers pocket. Surreal, I grimly thought. The long sleeve of brown overall covered the void where it belonged.

Ellis had given me a chance. Not much of one, probably, but at least I did have the answer to my question, which was no, he wouldn't personally kill me. Yorkshire definitely would.

The two blue-clad bodyguards were missing from the lobby.

The telephone on the desk was ringing, but the bodyguards were outside, busily positioning a Topline Foods van. One guard was descending from the driver's seat. The other was opening the rear doors.

A van, I understood, for abduction. For a journey to an unmarked grave. A bog job, the Irish called it. How much, I wondered, were they being paid.

Ellis's timing had given me thirty seconds. He'd sent me down too soon. In the lobby I had no future. Out in the open air . . . some.

Taking a couple of deep breaths, I shot out through the doors as fast as I could, and sprinted: and I ran out to the right towards my own car, but veered left round the van toward the open gates.

There was a shout from one of the blue figures, a yell from the second and I thought for a moment that I could avoid them, but to my dismay the gatekeeper himself came to unwelcome life, emerging from his kiosk and barring my exit. Big man in another blue uniform, over-confident.

I ran straight at him. He stood solidly, legs apart, his

weight evenly balanced. He wasn't prepared for or expecting my left foot to knock aside the inside of his knee or for my back to bend and curl like a cannon ball into his stomach: he fell over backwards and I was on my way before he struggled to his knees. The other two, though, had gained ground.

The sort of judo Chico had taught me was in part the stylised advances and throws of a regulated sport and in part an individual style for a one-handed victim. For a start, I never wore, in my private sessions with him, the loose white judogi uniform. I never fought in bare feet but always in ordinary shoes or trainers. The judo I'd learned was how to save my life, not how to earn a black belt.

Ordinary judo needed two hands. Myoelectric hands had a slow response time, a measurable pause between instruction and action. Chico and I had scrapped all grappling techniques for that hand and substituted clubbing; and I used all his lessons at Frodsham as if they were as familiar as walking.

We hadn't exactly envisaged no useful hands at all, but it was amazing what one could do if one wanted to live. It was the same as it had been in races: win now, pay later.

My opponents were straight muscle men with none of the subtlety of the Japanese understanding of lift and leverage and speed. Chico could throw me every time, but Yorkshire's watch-dogs couldn't.

The names of the movements clicked like a litany in

my brain – shintai, randori, tai-sabaki. Fighting literally to live, I stretched every technique I knew and adapted others, using falling feints that involved my twice lying on the ground and sticking a foot into a belly to fly its owner over my head. It ended with one blue uniform lying dazed on its back, one complaining I'd broken his nose, and one haring off to the office building with the bad news.

I stumbled out onto the road, feeling that if I went back for my car the two men I'd left on the ground would think of getting up again and closing the gates.

In one direction lay houses, so I staggered that way. Better cover. I needed cover before anyone chased me in the Topline Foods van.

The houses, when I reached them, were too regular, the gardens too tidy and small. I chose one house with no life showing, walked unsteadily up the garden path, kept on going, found myself in the back garden with another row of houses over the back fence.

The fence was too high to jump or vault, but there was an empty crate lying there, a gift from the gods.

No one came out of any of the houses to ask me what I thought I was doing. I emerged into the next street and began to think about where I was going and what I looked like.

Brown overalls. Yorkshire would be looking for brown overalls.

I took them off and dumped them in one of the houses' brown-looking beech hedges.

Taking off the overalls revealed the non-existence of a left hand.

Damn it, I thought astringently. Things are never easy, so *cope.*

I put the pink exposed end of arm, with its bare electrical contacts, into my left-hand jacket pocket, and walked, not ran, up the street. I wanted to run, but hadn't the strength. Weak . . . Stamina, a memory: a laugh.

There was a boy in the distance roller-blading, coming towards me and wearing not the ubiquitous baseball cap but a striped woollen hat. That would do, I thought. I fumbled some money out of the zip pocket in my belt and stood in his way.

He tried to avoid me, swerved, overbalanced and called me filthy names until his gaze fell on the money in my hand.

'Sell me your hat,' I suggested.

'Yer wha?'

'Your hat,' I said, 'for the money.'

'You've got blood on your face,' he said.

He snatched the money and aimed to roller-blade away. I stuck out a foot and knocked him off his skates. He gave me a bitter look, and a choice of swear words, but also the hat, sweeping it off and throwing it at me.

It was warm from his head and I put it on hoping he didn't have lice. I wiped my face gingerly on my sleeve and slouched along towards the road with traffic that crossed the end of the residential street . . . and saw the Topline Foods van roll past.

Whatever they were looking for, it didn't seem to be a navy tracksuit with a striped woollen hat.

Plan B – run away. OK.

Plan C – where to?

I reached the end of the houses and turned left into what might once have been a shopping street, but which now seemed to offer only estate agents, building societies and banks. Marooned in this unhelpful landscape were only two possible refuges – a betting shop and a place selling ice-cream.

I chose the ice-cream. I was barely through the door when outside the window my own Mercedes went past.

Ellis was driving.

I still had its keys in my pocket. Jonathan, it seemed, wasn't alone in his car-stealing skill.

'What do you want?' a female voice said behind me.

She was asking about ice-cream: a thin young woman, bored.

'Er . . . that one,' I said, pointing at random.

'Tub or cone? Large or small?'

'Cone. Small.' I felt disoriented, far from reality. I paid for the ice-cream and licked it, and it tasted of almonds.

'You've cut your face,' she said.

'I ran into a tree.'

There were four or five tables with people sitting at them, mostly adolescent groups. I sat at a table away from the window and within ten minutes saw the Topline van pass twice more and my own car, once.

Tremors ran in my muscles. Fear, or over-exertion, or both.

There was a door marked Gents at the back of the shop. I went in there when I'd finished the ice-cream and looked at my reflection in the small mirror over the wash basin.

The cut along my left cheekbone had congealed into a blackening line, thick and all too visible. Dampening a paper towel I dabbed gently at the mess, trying to remove the clotted blood without starting new bleeding, but making only a partial improvement.

Locked in a cubicle I had another try at screwing my wandering hand into place, and this time at length got it properly aligned and fastened, but it still wouldn't work. Wretchedly depressed, I fished out the long covering glove and with difficulty, because of no talcum powder and an enfeebled right hand, pulled that too into the semblance of reality.

Damn Ellis, I thought mordantly. He'd been right about some things being near to unbearable.

Never mind. Get on with it.

I emerged from the cubicle and tried my cheek again with another paper towel, making the cut paler, fading it into skin colour.

Not too bad.

The face below the unfamiliar woollen hat looked strained. Hardly a surprise.

I went out through the ice-cream shop and walked along the street. The Topline Foods van rolled past quite slowly, driven by one of the blue guards, who was intently scanning the other side of the road. That bodyguard meant, I thought, that Yorkshire himself might be out looking for me in a car I couldn't recognise.

Perhaps all I had to do was go up to some sensible-looking motorist and say, 'Excuse me, some people are trying to kill me. Please will you drive me to the police station?' And then, 'Who are these people?' 'The managing director of Topline Foods, and Ellis Quint.' 'Oh *yes*?? And *you* are . . .??'

I did go as far as asking someone the way to the police station – 'Round there, straight on, turn left – about a mile' – and for want of anything better I started walking that way; but what I came to first was a bus shelter with several people standing in a queue, waiting. I added myself to the patient half dozen and stood with my back to the road, and a woman with two children soon came up behind me, hiding me well.

Five long minutes later my Mercedes pulled up on the far side of the road with a white Rolls Royce behind it. Ellis stepped out of my car and Yorkshire out of the Rolls. They conferred together, furiously stabbing the air, pointing up and down the street while I bent my head down to the children and prayed to remain unspotted.

The bus came while the cars were still there.

Four people got off. The waiting queue, me included, surged on. I resisted the temptation to look out of the window until the bus was travelling again, and then saw with relief that the two men were still talking.

I had no idea where the bus was going.

Who cared? Distance was all I needed. I'd paid to go to the end of the line, wherever that was.

Peaceful Frodsham in Cheshire, sometime Saturday, people going shopping in the afternoon. I felt disconnected from that sort of life; and I didn't know what the time was, as the elastic metal bracelet watch I normally wore on my left wrist had come off in Yorkshire's office and was still there, I supposed.

The bus slowly filled at subsequent stops. Shopping baskets. Chatter. Where was I going?

The end of the line proved to be the railway station in Runcorn, halfway to Liverpool, going north when I needed to go south.

I got off the bus and went to the station. There was no Mercedes, no Rolls Royce, no Topline Foods van in sight, which didn't mean they wouldn't think of buses and trains eventually. Runcorn railway station didn't feel safe. There was a train to Liverpool due in four minutes, I learned, so I bought a ticket and caught it.

The feeling of unreality continued, also the familiar aversion to asking for help from the local police. They didn't approve of outside investigators. If I ever got into messes, besides, I considered it my own responsibility to get myself out. Norman Pictons were rare. In Liverpool, moreover, I was probably counted a local boy who'd been disloyal to his 'roots'.

At Liverpool station I read the well-displayed timetable for trains going south.

An express to London, I thought; then backtrack to Reading and get a taxi to Shelley Green, Archie Kirk's house.

No express for hours. What else, then?

The incredible words took a time to penetrate: Liverpool to Bournemouth, departing at 3.10 pm. A slow train, meandering southwards across England, right down to the Channel, with many stops on the way . . . and one of the stops was *Reading*.

I sprinted, using the last shreds of strength. It was already, according to the big station clock, ticking away at 3.07. Whistles were blowing when I stumbled into the last carriage in the long train. A guard helped thrust me in and close the door. The wheels rolled. I had no ticket and little breath, but a marvellous feeling of escape. That feeling lasted only until the first of the many stops, which I discovered with horror to be Runcorn.

Square one: where I'd started. All fear came flooding back. I sat stiff and immobile, as if movement itself would give me away.

Nothing happened. The train quietly rolled onwards. Out on the platform a blue-clad Topline Foods security guard was speaking into a hand-held telephone and shaking his head.

*

Crewe, Stafford, Wolverhampton, Birmingham, Coventry, Leamington Spa, Banbury, Oxford, Didcot, Reading.

It took four hours. Slowly, in that time, the screwed-tight wires of tension slackened to manageable if not to ease. At every stop, however illogical I might tell myself it was, dread resurfaced. Oversize wrenches could kill when one wasn't looking . . . Don't be a fool, I thought. I'd bought a ticket from the train conductor between Runcorn and Crewe, but every subsequent appearance of his dark uniform as he checked his customers bumped my heart muscles.

It grew dark. The train clanked and swayed into realms of night. Life felt suspended.

There were prosaically plenty of taxis at Reading. I travelled safely to Shelley Green and rang Archie Kirk's bell.

He came himself to open the door.

'Hello,' I said.

He stood there staring, then said awkwardly, 'We'd almost given you up.' He led the way into his sitting-room. 'He's here,' he said.

There were four of them. Davis Tatum, Norman Picton, Archie himself, and Charles.

I paused inside the doorway. I had no idea what I looked like, but what I saw on their faces was shock.

'Sid,' Charles said, recovering first and standing up. 'Good. Great. Come and sit down.'

The extent of his solicitude always measured the

depth of his alarm. He insisted I take his place in a comfortable chair and himself perched on a hard one. He asked Archie if he had any brandy and secured for me a half-tumblerful of a raw-tasting own-brand from a supermarket.

'Drink it,' he commanded, holding out the glass.

'Charles . . .'

'Drink it. Talk after.'

I gave in, drank a couple of mouthfuls and put the glass on a table beside me. He was a firm believer in the life-restoring properties of distilled wine and I'd proved him right oftener than enough.

I remembered that I still wore the soft stripey hat, and took it off; and its removal seemed to make my appearance more normal to them, and less disturbing.

'I went to Topline Foods,' I said.

I thought: I don't feel well; what's wrong with me?

'You've cut your face,' Norman Picton said.

I also ached more or less all over from the desperate exertions of the judo. My head felt heavy and my hand was swollen and sore from Ellis's idea of entertainment. On the bright side, I was alive and home, safe . . . and reaction was all very well but I was *not* at this point going to faint.

'Sid!' Charles said sharply, putting out a hand.

'Oh . . . yes. Well, I went to Topline Foods.'

I drank some brandy. The weak feeling of sickness abated a bit. I shifted in my chair and took a grip on things.

Archie said, 'Take your time,' but sounded as if he didn't mean it.

I smiled. I said, 'Owen Yorkshire was there. So was Lord Tilepit. So was Ellis Quint.'

'Quint!' Davis Tatum exclaimed.

'Mm. Well . . . you asked me to find out if there was a heavyweight lumbering about behind the Quint business, and the answer is yes, but it is Ellis Quint himself.'

'But he's a playboy,' Davis Tatum protested. 'What about the big man, Yorkshire?' Tatum's own bulk quivered. 'He's getting known. One hears his name.'

I nodded. 'Owen Cliff Yorkshire is a heavyweight in the making.'

'What do you mean?'

I ached. I hadn't really noticed the wear and tear until then. Win now, pay later.

'Megalomania,' I said. 'Yorkshire's on the edge. He has a violent unpredictable temper and an uncontrolled desire to be a tycoon. I'd call it incipient megalomania because he's spending far beyond sanity on self-aggrandisement. He's built an office block fit for a major industry – and it's mostly empty – before building the industry first. He's publicity mad – he's holding a reception for half of Liverpool on Monday. He has plans – a *desire* – to take over the whole horse-feed nuts industry. He employs at least two bodyguards who will murder to order because he fears his competitors will assassinate him . . . which is paranoia.'

I paused, then said, 'It's difficult to describe the impression he gives. Half the time he sounds reasonable, and half the time you can see that he will simply get rid of anyone who stands in his way. And he is desperate . . . *desperate* . . . to save Ellis Quint's reputation.'

Archie asked 'Why?' slowly.

'Because,' I said, 'he has spent a colossal amount of money on an advertising campaign featuring Ellis, and if Ellis is found guilty of cutting off a horse's foot, that campaign can't be shown.'

'But a few advertisements can't have cost that much,' Archie objected.

'With megalomania,' I said, 'you don't just make a few economically priced advertisements. You really go to town. You engage an expensive highly prestigious firm – in this case, Intramind Imaging of Manchester – and you travel the world.'

With clumsy fingers I took from my belt the folded copy of the paper in the Quint box-file in Mrs Dove's office.

'This is a list of racecourses,' I said. 'These racecourses are where they filmed the commercials. A thirty-second commercial gleaned from each place. The expense is phenomenal.'

Archie scanned the list uncomprehendingly and passed it to Charles, who read it aloud.

'Flemington, Germiston, Sha Tin, Churchill Downs, Woodbine, Longchamps, K.L., Fuchu . . .'

There were fifteen altogether. Archie looked lost.

'Flemington,' I said, 'is where they run the Melbourne Cup in Australia. Germiston is outside Johannesburg. Sha Tin is in Hong Kong. Churchill Downs is where they hold the Kentucky Derby. K.L. is Kuala Lumpur in Malaysia, Woodbine is in Canada, Longchamps is in Paris, Fuchu is where the Japan Cup is run in Tokyo.'

They all understood.

'Those commercials are reported to be brilliant,' I said, 'and Ellis himself wants them shown as much as Yorkshire does.'

'Have you seen them?' Davis asked.

I explained about the box of BETACAM tapes. 'Making those special Broadcasting Quality tapes themselves must have been fearfully expensive – and they need special playing equipment which I didn't find at Topline Foods, so no, I haven't seen them.'

Norman Picton, with his policeman's mind, asked, 'Where did you see the tapes? Where did you get that list of racecourses?'

I said without emotion, 'In an office at Topline Foods.'

He gave me a narrow inspection.

'My car,' I told him, 'is still somewhere in Frodsham. Could you get your pals up there to look out for it?' I gave him its registration number, which he wrote down.

'Why did you leave it?' he asked.

'Er . . . I was running away at the time.' For all that I tried to say it lightly, the grim reality reached them.

'Well,' I sighed, 'I'd invaded Yorkshire's territory. He found me there. It gave him the opportunity to get rid of the person most likely to send Ellis to jail. I accepted that possibility when I went there but, like you, I wanted to know what was causing terrible trouble behind the scenes. And it is the millions spent on those ads.' I paused, and went on, 'Yorkshire and Ellis set out originally, months ago, not to kill me but to discredit me so that nothing I said would get Ellis convicted. They used a figurehead, Topline Foods director Lord Tilepit, because he owned *The Pump*. They persuaded Tilepit that Ellis was innocent and that I was all that *The Pump* has maintained. I don't think Tilepit believed Ellis guilty until today. I don't think *The Pump* will say a word against me from now on.' I smiled briefly. 'Lord Tilepit was duped by Ellis, and so, also, to some extent, was Owen Yorkshire himself.'

'How, Sid?' Davis asked.

'I think Yorkshire too believed in Ellis. Ellis dazzles people. Knowing Ellis, to Yorkshire, was a step up the ladder. Today they planned together to . . . er . . . wipe me out of the way. Yorkshire would have done it himself in reckless anger. Ellis stopped him, but left it to chance that the bodyguards might do it . . . but I escaped them. Yorkshire now knows Ellis is guilty, but he doesn't care. He cares only to be able to show that brilliant ad campaign, and make himself king of the horse-nuts. And, of course, it's not just horse-nuts that it's all about. They're a stepping stone. It's about being the Big Man with the power to bring mayors to his doorstep. If Yorkshire isn't stopped you'll find him manipulating more than *The Pump*. He's the sort of man you get in the kitchens of political clout.'

After a moment, Archie asked, 'So how do we stop him?'

I shifted wearily in the chair and drank some brandy, and said, 'I can, possibly, give you the tools.'

'What tools?'

'His secret files. His financial manoeuvrings. His debts. Details of bribes, I'd guess. Bargains struck. You scratch my back, I'll scratch yours. Evidence of leverage. Details of all his dealings with Ellis, and all his dealings with Tilepit. I'll give you the files. You can take it from there.'

'But,' Archie said blankly, 'where are these files?'

'In my computer in London.'

I explained the Internet transfer and the need for password cracking. I couldn't decide whether they were gladdened or horrified by what I'd done. A bit of both, I thought.

Charles looked the most shocked, Archie the least.

Archie said, 'If I ask you, will you work for me another time?'

I looked into the knowing eyes, and smiled, and nodded.

'Good,' he said.

CHAPTER FOURTEEN

I went home to Aynsford with Charles.

It had been a long evening in Archie's house. Archie, Davis, Norman and Charles had all wanted details, which I found as intolerable to describe as to live through. I skipped a lot.

I didn't tell them about Ellis's games with my hands. I didn't know how to explain to them that, for a jockey, his hands were at the heart of his existence . . . of his skill. One knew a horse by the feel of the bit on the reins, one listened to the messages, one interpreted the vibrations, one *talked* to a horse through one's hands. Ellis understood more than most people what the loss of a hand had meant to me, and that day he'd been busy punishing me in the severest way he could think of for trying to strip him of what he himself now valued most, his universal acclaim.

I didn't know how to make them understand that to Ellis the severing of a horse's foot had become a drug more addictive than any substance invented, that the risk and the power were intoxicating; that I'd been lucky he'd had only a wrench to use on me.

I didn't know how near he had come in his own mind to irrevocably destroying the right hand. I only knew that to me it had seemed possible that he would. I couldn't tell them that I'd intensely lived my own nightmare and still shook from fear inside.

I told them only that an adjustable wrench in Yorkshire's hands had cut my face.

I told them a little about the escape by judo, and all about the boy on roller-blades and the ice-cream cone and catching the bus within sight of Yorkshire and Ellis. I made it sound almost funny.

Archie understood that there was a lot I hadn't said, but he didn't press it. Charles, puzzled, asked, 'But did they *hurt* you, Sid?' and I half laughed and told him part of the truth. 'They scared me witless.'

Davis asked about Ellis's Shropshire alibi. His colleague, the Crown Prosecutor, was increasingly concerned, he said, that Ellis's powerful lawyers would prevent the trial from resuming.

I explained that I hadn't had time to find out at what hour Ellis had arrived at the dance.

'Someone must know,' I said. 'It's a matter of asking the local people, the people who helped to park the cars.' I looked at Norman. 'Any chance of the police doing it?'

'Not much,' he said.

'Round the pubs,' I suggested.

Norman shook his head.

'There isn't much time,' Davis pointed out. 'Sid, couldn't you do it tomorrow?'

Tomorrow, Sunday. On Monday, the trial.

Archie said firmly, 'No, Sid can't. There's a limit . . . I'll try and find someone else.'

'Chico would have done it,' Charles said.

Chico had undisputedly saved my pathetic skin that day. One could hardly ask more.

Archie's wife, before she'd driven over to spend the evening with her sister-in-law Betty Bracken, had, it appeared, made a mound of sandwiches. Archie offered them diffidently. I found the tastes of cheese and of chicken strange, as if I'd come upon them new from another world. It was weird the difference that danger and the perception of mortality made to familiar things. Unreality persisted even as I accepted a paper napkin to wipe my fingers.

Archie's doorbell rang. Archie went again to the summons and came back with a pinched displeased expression, and he was followed by a boy that I saw with surprise to be Jonathan.

The rebel wings of hair were much shorter. The yellow streaks had all but grown out. There were no shaven areas of scalp.

'Hi,' he said, looking round the room and fastening his attention on my face. 'I came over to see you. The aunts said you were here. Hey, man, you look different.'

'Three months older,' I nodded, 'so do you.'

Jonathan helped himself to a sandwich, disregarding Archie's disapproval.

'Hi,' he said nonchalantly to Norman. 'How's the boat?'

'Laid up for winter storage.'

Jonathan chewed and told me, 'They won't take me on an oil-rig until I'm eighteen. They won't take me in the navy. I've got good pecs. What do I do with them?'

'Pecs?' Charles asked, mystified.

'Pectoral muscles,' Norman explained. 'He's strong from weeks of water ski-ing.'

'Oh.'

I said to Jonathan, 'How did you get here from Combe Bassett?'

'Ran.'

He'd walked into Archie's house not in the least out of breath.

'Can you ride a motor-bike,' I asked, 'now that you're sixteen?'

'Do me a favour!'

'He hasn't got one,' Archie said.

'He can hire one.'

'But . . . what for?'

'To go to Shropshire,' I said.

I was predictably drowned by protests. I explained to Jonathan what was needed. 'Find someone – anyone – who saw Ellis Quint arrive at the dance. Find the people who parked the cars.'

'He can't go round the pubs,' Norman insisted. 'He's under age.'

Jonathan gave me a dark look which I steadfastly returned. At fifteen he'd bought gin for a truck-driver's wife.

'Hey,' he said. 'Where do I go?'

I told him in detail. His uncle and everyone else disapproved. I took all the money I had left out of my belt and gave it to him. 'I want receipts,' I said. 'Bring me paper. A signed statement from a witness. It's all got to be solid.'

'Is this,' he asked slowly, 'some sort of test?'

'Yes.'

'OK.'

'Don't stay longer than a day,' I said. 'Don't forget, you may be asked to give evidence this week at the trial.'

'As if I could forget.'

He took a bunch of sandwiches, gave me a wide smile, and without more words departed.

'You *can't*,' Archie said to me emphatically.

'What do *you* propose to do with him?'

'But . . . he's . . .'

'He's bright,' I said. 'He's observant. He's athletic. Let's see how he does in Shropshire.'

'He's only *sixteen*.'

'I need a new Chico.'

'But Jonathan steals cars.'

'He hasn't stolen one all summer, has he?'

'That doesn't mean . . .'

'An ability to steal cars,' I said with humour, 'is in my eyes an asset. Let's see how he does tomorrow, with this alibi.'

Archie, still looking affronted, gave in.

'Too much depends on it,' Davis said heavily, shaking his head.

I said, 'If Jonathan learns nothing, I'll go myself on Monday.'

'That will be too late,' Davis said.

'Not if you get your colleague to ask for one more day's adjournment. Invent flu or something.'

David said doubtfully, 'Are you totally committed to this trial? *The Pump* – or Ellis Quint – they haven't got to you in any way, have they? I mean . . . the hate campaign . . . do you want to back out?'

Charles was offended on my behalf. 'Of course he doesn't,' he said.

Such faith! I said plainly to Davis, 'Don't let your colleague back down. That's the real danger. Tell him to insist on prosecuting, alibi or no alibi. Tell the prosecution service to dredge up some guts.'

'Sid!' He was taken aback. 'They're realists.'

'They're shit-scared of Ellis's lawyers. Well, I'm not. Ellis took the foot off Betty Bracken's colt. I wish like hell that he hadn't, but he did. He has no alibi for that night. You get your colleague to tell Ellis's lawyers that the Northampton colt was a copycat crime. If we can't break Ellis's alibi, copycat is our story and we're sticking to it, and if you have any influence over your colleague the prosecutor, you make sure he gives me a chance in court to say so.'

Davis said faintly, 'I must not instruct him to do anything like that.'

'Just manage to get it dripped into his mind.'

'So there you are, Davis,' Archie said dryly, 'our boy shows no sign of the hate campaign having been successful. Rather the opposite, wouldn't you say?'

'Our boy' stood up, feeling a shade fragile. It seemed to have been a long day. Archie came out into the hall with Charles and me and offered his hand in farewell. Charles shook it warmly. Archie lifted my wrist and looked at the swelling and the deep bruising that was already crimson and black.

He said, 'You've had difficulty holding your glass all evening.'

I shrugged a fraction, long resigned to occupational damage. My hand was still a hand, and that was all that mattered.

'No explanation?' Archie asked.

I shook my head.

'Stone walls tell more,' Charles informed him calmly.

Archie, releasing my wrist, said to me, 'The British Horseracing Board wants you to double-check some of their own members for loyalty. Ultra-secret digging.'

'They wouldn't ask *me*.' I shook my head. 'I'm not the new people's idea of reliable.'

'They asked *me*,' he said, the eyes blazing with amusement. 'I said it would be you or nobody.'

'Nobody,' I said.

He laughed. 'You start as soon as the Quint thing is over.'

The trouble, I thought, as I sat quietly beside Charles as he drove to Aynsford, was that for me the Quint thing would never be over. Ellis might or might not go to jail . . . but that wouldn't be the end for either of us. Gordon's obsession might deepen. Ellis might maim more than horses. In both of them lay a compulsive disregard of natural law.

No one could ever be comprehensively protected from obsession. One simply had to live as best one could and disregard the feral threat lying in wait: and I would somehow have to shake Gordon loose from staking out my Pont Square door.

Charles said, 'Do you consider that transferring Yorkshire's secret files to your own computer was at all immoral? Was it . . . theft?'

He spoke without censure, but censure was implied. I remembered a discussion we'd had once along the lines of what was honourable and what was not. He'd said I had a vision of honour that made my life a purgatory and I'd said he was wrong, and that purgatory was abandoning your vision of honour and knowing you'd done it. 'Only for you, Sid,' he'd said. 'The rest of the world has no difficulty at all.'

It seemed he was applying to me my own rash judgement. Was stealing knowledge ever justified, or was it not?

I said without self-excuse, 'It was theft, and dishonourable, and I would do it again.'

'And purgatory can wait?'

I said with amusement, 'Have you read *The Pump*?'

After about five miles he said, 'That's specious.'

'Mm.'

'*The Pump*'s a different story of purgatory.'

I nodded and said idly, 'The anteroom to hell.'

He frowned, glancing across in distaste. 'Has hell arrived, then?' He hated excess emotion. I cooled it.

I said, 'No. Sorry. It's been a long day.'

He drove another mile, then asked, 'How *did* you hurt your hand?'

I sighed. 'I don't want a fuss. Don't *fuss*, Charles, if I tell you.'

'No. All right. No fuss.'

'Then . . . Ellis had a go at it.'

'*Ellis?*'

'Mm. Lord Tilepit and Owen Yorkshire watched Ellis enjoy it. That's how they now know he's guilty as charged with the colts. If Ellis had had shears instead of a wrench to use on my wrist, I would now have no hands – and for God's sake, Charles, keep your eyes on the road.'

'But *Sid* . . .'

'No fuss. You promised. There'll be no lasting harm.' I paused. 'If he'd wanted to kill me today, he could have done it, but instead he gave me a chance to escape. He wanted . . .' I swallowed, 'he wanted to make me pay for defeating him . . . and he did make me pay . . . and on Monday in court I'll try to disgrace him for ever . . . and I *loathe* it.'

He drove to Aynsford in a silence I understood to be at least empty of condemnation. Braking outside the door he said regretfully, 'If you and Ellis hadn't been such good friends . . . no wonder poor Ginnie couldn't stand it.'

Charles saw the muscles stiffen in my face.

'What is it, Sid?' he asked.

'I . . . I may have made a wrong assumption.'

'What assumption?'

'Mm?' I said vaguely. 'Have to think.'

'Then think in bed,' he said lightly. 'It's late.'

I thought for half the night. Ellis's revenge brutally throbbed in my fingers. Ellis had tied my wrists and given me thirty seconds . . . I would be dead, I thought, if we hadn't been friends.

At Aynsford I kept duplicates of all the things I'd lost in my car – battery charger, razor, clothes and so on – all except the mobile phone. I did have the SIM card, but nothing to use it in.

The no-car situation was solved again by TeleDrive who came to pick me up on Sunday morning.

To Charles's restrained suggestion that I pass the

day resting with him – 'A game of chess, perhaps?' – I replied that I was going to see Rachel Ferns. Charles nodded.

'Come back,' he said, 'if you need to.'

'Always.'

'Take care of yourself, Sid.'

Rachel, Linda told me on the telephone, was home from the hospital for the day.

'Oh, do come,' she begged. 'Rachel *needs* you.'

I went empty-handed with no fish or wigs, but it didn't seem to matter.

Rachel herself looked bloodless, a white wisp of a child in the foothills of a far country. In the five days since I'd seen her, the bluish shadows under her eyes had deepened, and she had lost weight so that the round cheeks of the steroids under the bald head and the big shadowed eyes gave her the look of an exotic little bird, unlike life.

Linda hugged me and cried on my shoulder in the kitchen.

'It's good news, really,' she said, sobbing. 'They've found a donor.'

'But that's *marvellous*.' Like a sunburst of hope, I thought, but Linda still wept.

'He's a Swiss,' she said. 'He's coming from Switzerland. He's coming on Wednesday. Joe is paying his air fare and the hotel bills. Joe says money's no object for his little girl.'

'Then stop crying.'

'Yes . . . but it may not work.'

'And it *may*,' I said positively. 'Where's the gin?'

She laughed shakily. She poured two glasses. I still didn't much care for gin but it was all she liked. We clinked to the future and she began talking about paella for lunch.

Rachel was half sitting, half lying, on a small sofa that had been repositioned in the sitting-room so that she could look straight and closely into the fish tank. I sat beside her and asked how she felt.

'Did my mum tell you about the transplant?' she said.

'Terrific news.'

'I might be able to run again.'

Running, it was clear from her pervading lassitude, must have seemed at that point as distant as the moon.

Rachel said, 'I begged to come home to see the fishes. I have to go back tonight, though. I hoped you would come. I begged God.'

'You knew I would come.'

'I meant *today*, while I'm home.'

'I've been busy since I saw you on Tuesday.'

'I know, Mummy said so. The nurses tell me when you phone every day.'

Pegotty was crawling all round the floor, growing in

size and agility and putting everything unsuitable in his mouth; making his sister laugh.

'He's so *funny*,' she said. 'They won't let him come to the hospital. I begged to see him and the fishes. They told me the transplant is going to make me feel sick, so I wanted to come home first.'

'Yes,' I said.

Linda produced steamy rice with bits of chicken and shrimps in, which we all ate with spoons.

'What's wrong with your hand?' Linda asked. 'In places it's almost black.'

'It's only a bruise. It got a bit squashed.'

'You've got sausage fingers,' Rachel said.

'They'll be all right tomorrow.'

Linda returned to the only important subject. 'The Swiss donor,' she said, 'is older than I am! He has three children of his own. He's a school teacher . . . he sounds a nice man, and they say he's so pleased to be going to give Rachel some of his bone marrow.'

Rachel said, 'I wish it had been Sid's bone marrow.'

I'd had myself tested, right at the beginning, but I'd been about as far from a match as one could get. Neither Linda nor Joe had been more than fifty per cent compatible.

'They say he's a ninety per cent match,' Linda said. 'You never get a hundred per cent, even from siblings. Ninety per cent is great.'

She was trying hard to be positive. I didn't know

enough to put a bet on ninety per cent. It sounded fine to me; and no one was going to kill Rachel's own defective bone marrow if they didn't believe they could replace it.

'They're going to put me into a bubble,' Rachel said. 'It's a sort of plastic tent over my bed. I won't be able to touch the Swiss man, except through the plastic. And he doesn't speak English, even. He speaks German. *Danke schön.* I've learned that, to say to him. Thank you very much.'

'He's a lucky man,' I said.

Linda, clearing the plates and offering ice-cream for pudding, asked if I would stay with Rachel while she took Pegotty out for a short walk in fresh air.

'Of course.'

'I won't be long.'

When she'd gone, Rachel and I sat on the sofa and watched the fish.

'You see that one?' Rachel pointed. 'That's the one you brought on Tuesday. Look how fast he swims! He's faster than all the others.'

The black and silver angel fish flashed through the tank, fins waving with vigour.

'He's you,' Rachel said. 'He's Sid.'

I teased her, 'I thought half of them were Sid.'

'Sid is always the fastest one. That's Sid,' she pointed. 'The others aren't Sid any more.'

'Poor fellows.'

She giggled. 'I wish I could have the fishes in the hospital. Mummy asked, but they said no.'

'Pity.'

She sat loosely cuddled by my right arm but held my other hand, the plastic one, pulling it across towards her. That hand still wasn't working properly, though a fresh battery and a bit of tinkering had restored it to half-life.

After a long silent pause, she said, 'Are you afraid of dying?'

Another pause. 'Sometimes,' I said.

Her voice was quiet, almost murmuring. It was a conversation all in a low key, without haste.

She said, 'Daddy says when you were a jockey you were never afraid of anything.'

'Are you afraid?' I asked.

'Yes, but I can't tell Mummy. I don't like her crying.'

'Are you afraid of the transplant?'

Rachel nodded.

'You will die without it,' I said matter-of-factly. 'I know you know that.'

'What's dying like?'

'I don't know. No one knows. Like going to sleep, I should think.' If you were lucky, of course.

'It's funny to think of not being here,' Rachel said. 'I mean, to think of being a *space*.'

'The transplant will work.'

'Everyone says so.'

'Then believe it. You'll be running by Christmas.'

She smoothed her fingers over my hand. I could feel the faint vibrations distantly in my forearm. Nothing, I thought, was ever entirely lost.

She said, 'Do you know what I'll be thinking, lying there in the bubble feeling awfully sick?'

'What?'

'Life's a bugger.'

I hugged her, but gently. 'You'll do fine.'

'Yes, but tell me.'

'Tell you what?'

'How to be brave.'

What a question, I thought. I said, 'When you're feeling awfully sick, think about something you like doing. You won't feel as bad if you don't think about how bad you feel.'

She thought it over. 'Is that all?'

'It's quite a lot. Think about fishes. Think about Pegotty pulling off his socks and putting them in his mouth. Think about things you've enjoyed.'

'Is that what *you* do?'

'It's what I do if something hurts, yes. It does work.'

'What if nothing hurts yet, but you're going into something scary!'

'Well . . . it's all right to be frightened. No one can help it. You just don't have to let being frightened stop you.'

'Are you ever frightened?' she asked.

'Yes.' Too often, I thought.

She said lazily, but with certainty, 'I bet you've never

been so frightened you didn't do something. I bet you're always brave.'

I was startled. 'No . . . I'm not.'

'But Daddy said . . .'

'I wasn't afraid of riding in races,' I agreed. 'Try me in a pit full of snakes, though, and I wouldn't be so sure.'

'What about a bubble?'

'I'd go in there promising myself I'd come out running.'

She smoothed my hand. 'Will you come and see me?'

'In the bubble?' I asked. 'Yes, if you like.'

'You'll make me brave.'

I shook my head. 'It will come from inside you. You'll see.'

We went on watching the fish. My namesake flashed his fins and seemed to have endless stamina.

'I'm going into the bubble tomorrow,' Rachel murmured. 'I don't want to cry when they put me in there.'

'Courage is lonely,' I said.

She looked up into my face. 'What does that mean?'

It was too strong a concept, I saw, for someone of nine. I tried to make things simpler.

'You'll be alone in the bubble,' I said. 'So make it your own palace. The bubble is to keep you safe from infection – safe from dragons. You won't cry.'

She snuggled against me; happier, I hoped. I loved

her incredibly. The transplant had a fifty-fifty chance of success. Rachel would run again. She *had* to.

Linda and Pegotty came back laughing from their walk and Linda built towers of bright plastic building blocks for Pegotty to knock down, a game of endless enjoyment for the baby. Rachel and I sat on the floor, playing draughts.

'You always let me be white,' Rachel complained, 'and then you sneak up with the black counters when I'm not looking.'

'You can play black, then.'

'It's disgusting,' she said, five minutes later. 'You're cheating.'

Linda looked up and said, astounded, 'Are you two *quarrelling*?'

'He always wins,' Rachel objected.

'Then don't play with him,' Linda said reasonably.

Rachel set up the white pieces as her own. I neglected to take one of them halfway through the game and with glee she huffed me, and won.

'Did you *let* me win?' she demanded.

'Winning's more fun.'

'I hate you.' She swept all the pieces petulantly from the board and Pegotty put two of them in his mouth.

Rachel, laughing, picked them out again and dried them and set up the board again, with herself again as white, and peacefully we achieved a couple of close finishes until, suddenly as usual, she tired.

Linda produced tiny chocolate cakes for tea and

talked happily of the Swiss donor and how everything was going to be *all right.* Rachel was convinced, I was convinced, Pegotty smeared chocolate all over his face. Whatever the next week might bring to all of us, I thought, that afternoon of hope and ordinariness was an anchor in reality, an affirmation that small lives mattered.

It wasn't until after she'd fastened both children into the back of her car to drive to the hospital that Linda mentioned Ellis Quint.

'That trial is on again tomorrow, isn't it?' she asked.

We stood in the chilly air a few paces from her car. I nodded. 'Don't let Rachel know.'

'She doesn't. It hasn't been hard to keep it all away from her. She never talks about Silverboy any more. Being so ill . .. she hasn't much interest in anything else.'

'She's terrific.'

'Will Ellis Quint go to prison?'

How could I say 'I hope so'? And *did* I hope so? Yet I had to stop him, to goad him, to make him fundamentally wake up.

I said, dodging it, 'It will be for the judge to decide.'

Linda hugged me. No tears. 'Come and see Rachel in her bubble?'

'You couldn't keep me away.'

'God . . . I hope . . .'

'She'll be all right,' I said. 'So will you.'

*

Patient TeleDrive took me back to London and, because of the fixed hour of Linda's departure to the hospital, I again had time to spare before meeting India for dinner.

I again ducked being dropped in Pont Square in the dark evening, and damned Gordon for his vigilance. He had to sleep *sometime* . . . but when?

The restaurant called Kensington Place was near the northern end of Church Street, the famous road of endless antique shops, stretching from Kensington High Street in the south, up to Notting Hill Gate, north. Teledrive left me and my overnight bag on the north-west corner of Church Street where I dawdled a while looking in the brightly lit windows of Waterstone's bookshop, wondering if Rachel would be able to hear the store's advertised children's audio tapes in her bubble. She enjoyed the subversive *Just William* stories. Pegotty, she thought, would grow up to be like him.

A large number of young Japanese people were milling around on the corner, all armed with cameras, taking flash pictures of each other. I paid not much attention beyond noticing that they all had straight black hair, short padded jackets, and jeans. As far as one could tell, they were happy. They also surged between me and Waterstone's windows.

They bowed to me politely, I bowed unenthusiastically in return.

They seemed to be waiting, as I was, for some pre-arranged event to occur. I gradually realised from their quiet chatter, of which I understood not a word, that half of them were men, and half young women.

We all waited. They bowed some more. At length, one of the young women shyly produced a photograph that she held out to me. I took it politely and found I was looking at a wedding. At a mass wedding of about ten happy couples wearing formal suits and western wedding dresses. Raising my head from the photo I was met by twenty smiles.

I smiled back. The shy young woman retrieved her photo, nodded her head towards her companions and clearly told me that they were all on their honeymoon. More smiles all round. More bows. One of the men held out his camera to me and asked – I gathered – if I would photograph them all as a group.

I took the camera and put my bag at my feet, and they arranged themselves in pairs neatly, as if they were used to it.

Click. Flash. The film wound on, quietly whirring.

All the newly-weds beamed.

I was presented, one by one, with nine more cameras. Nine more bows. I took nine more photos. Flash. Flash. Group euphoria.

What was it about me, I wondered, that encouraged such trust? Even without language there seemed to be no doubt on their part of my willingness to give pleasure. I mentally shrugged. I had the time, so what the hell. I took their pictures and bowed, and waited for eight o'clock.

I left the happy couples on Waterstone's corner and, carrying my bag, walked fifty yards down Church Street towards the restaurant. There was a narrow side street beside it, and opposite, on the other side of Church Street, one of those quirks of London life, a small recessed area of pavement with a patch of scrubby grass and a park bench, installed by philanthropists for the comfort of footsore shoppers and other vagrants. I would sit there, I decided, and watch for India. The restaurant doors were straight opposite the bench. A green-painted bench made of horizontal slats.

I crossed Church Street to reach it. The traffic on Sunday evening was sporadic to non-existent. I could see a brass plate on the back of the bench: the name of the benefactor who'd paid for it.

I was turning to sit when at the same time I heard a bang and felt a searing flash of pain across my back and into my right upper arm. The impact knocked me over and round so that I ended sprawling on the bench, half lying, half sitting, facing the road.

I thought incredulously, I've been *shot.*

I'd been shot once before. I couldn't mistake the *thud.* Also I couldn't mistake the shudder of outrage that my invaded body produced. Also . . . there was a great deal of blood.

I'd been shot by Gordon Quint.

He walked out of the shadows of the side street opposite and came towards me across Church Street. He carried a hand-gun with its black round mouth pointing my way. He was coming inexorably to finish what he'd started, and he appeared not to care if anyone saw him.

I didn't seem to have the strength to get up and run away.

There was nowhere to run to.

Gordon looked like a farmer from Berkshire, not an obsessed murderer. He wore a checked shirt and a tie and a tweed jacket. He was a middle-aged pillar of the community, a judge and jury and a hangman . . . a raw, primitive walking act of revenge.

There was none of the screaming out-of-control obscenity with which he'd attacked me the previous Monday. This killer was cold and determined and *reckless.*

He stopped in front of me and aimed at my chest.

'This is for Ginnie,' he said.

I don't know what he expected. He seemed to be waiting for something. For me to protest, perhaps. To plead.

His voice was hoarse.

'For Ginnie,' he repeated.

I was silent. I wanted to stand. Couldn't manage it.

'Say something!' He shouted in sudden fury. The gun wavered in his hand, but he was too close to miss. 'Don't you *understand*?'

I looked not at his gun but at his eyes. Not the best view, I thought inconsequentially, for my last on earth.

Gordon's purpose didn't waver. I might deny him

any enjoyment of my fear, but that wasn't going to stop him. He stared at my face. He didn't blink. No hesitancy there. No withdrawal or doubt. None.

Now, I thought frozenly. It's going to be *now.*

A voice was shouting in the road, urgent, frantic, coming nearer, far too late.

The voice shouted one despairing word.

'*Dad.*'

Ellis . . . *Ellis* . . . Running across the road waving a five-foot piece of black angled iron fencing and shouting in frenzy at his father, '*Dad* . . . Dad . . . Don't . . . Don't do it.'

I could see him running. Nothing seemed very clear. Gordon could hear Ellis shouting but it wasn't going to stop him. The demented hatred simply hardened in his face. His arm straightened until his gun was a bare yard from my chest.

Perhaps I won't feel it, I thought.

Ellis swung the iron fencing post with two hands and all his strength and *hit his father on the side of the head.*

The gun went off. The bullet hissed past my ear and slammed into a shop window behind me. There were razor splinters of glass and flashes of light and shouting and confusion everywhere.

Gordon fell silently unconscious face down on the scrubby patch of grass, his right hand with the gun underneath him. My blood ran into a scarlet and widening pool below the slats of the bench. Ellis stood for an eternity of seconds holding the fencing post and staring at my eyes as if he could see into my soul, as if he would show me his.

For an unmeasurable hiatus blink of time it seemed there was between us a fusing of psyche, an insight of total understanding. It could have been a hallucination, a result of too much stress, but it was unmistakably the same for him.

Then he dropped the fencing post beside his father, and turned, and went away at a slow run, across Church Street and down the side road, loping, not sprinting, until he was swallowed by shadow.

I was suddenly surrounded by Japanese faces all asking unintelligible questions. They had worried eyes. They watched me bleed.

The gunshots brought more people, but cautiously. Gordon's attack, that to me had seemed to happen in slow motion, had in reality passed to others with bewildering speed. No one had tried to stop Ellis. People thought he was going to bring help.

I lost further account of time. A police car arrived busily, lights flashing, the first manifestation of all that I most detested – questions, hospitals, forms, noise, bright lights in my eyes, clanging and banging and being shoved around. There wasn't a hope of being quietly stitched up and left alone.

I told a policeman that Gordon, though unconscious at present, was lying over a loaded gun.

He wanted to know if Gordon had fired the shots in self-defence.

I couldn't be bothered to answer.

The crowd grew bigger and an ambulance made an entrance.

A young woman pushed the uniforms aside, yelling that she was from the Press. India . . . India . . . come to dinner.

'Sorry,' I said.

'*Sid* . . .' Horror in her voice and a sort of despair.

'Tell Kevin Mills . . .' I said. My mouth was dry from loss of blood. I tried again. She bent her head down to mine to hear above the hubbub.

With humour I said, 'Those Japanese people took a load of photos . . . I saw the flashes . . . so tell Kevin to get moving. Get those photos . . . and he can have . . . his exclusive.'

CHAPTER FIFTEEN

India wasn't a newspaperwoman for nothing. The front page of Monday's *Pump* bore the moderately accurate headline '*Shot in the Back*', with, underneath, a picture taken of Gordon Quint aiming his gun unequivocally at my heart.

Gordon's half-backview was slightly out of focus. My own face was sharp and clear with an expression that looked rather like polite interest, not the fatalistic terror I'd actually felt.

Kevin and *The Pump* had gone to town. *The Pump* acknowledged that its long campaign of denigration of Sid Halley had been a mistake.

Policy, I saw cynically, had done a one-eighty U-turn. Lord Tilepit had come to such senses as he possessed and was putting what distance he could between himself and Ellis Quint.

There had been twenty eyewitnesses to the shooting of J. S. Halley. Kevin, arming himself with a Japanese interpreter, had listened intently, sorted out what he'd been told, and got it right. Throughout his piece there was an undercurrent of awe that no one was going to be able to dispute the facts. He hadn't once said 'It is *alleged*.'

Gordon Quint, though still unconscious, would in due course be 'helping the police with their enquiries'. Kevin observed that Ellis Quint's whereabouts were unknown.

Inside the paper there were more pictures. One showed Ellis Quint, arms and fence post raised, on the point of striking his father. The Japanese collectively, and that one photographer in particular, had not known who Ellis Quint was. Ellis didn't appear on the TV screens in Japan.

Why had there been so much photo coverage? Because Mr Halley, Kevin said, had been kind to the honeymooners, and many of them had been watching him as he walked away down Church Street.

I read *The Pump* while sitting upright in a high bed in a small white side-room in Hammersmith Hospital, thankfully alone except for a constant stream of doctors, nurses, policemen and people with clipboards.

The surgeon who'd dealt with my punctures came to see me at nine in the morning, before he went off duty for the day. He looked a lot worse for wear by then than I did, I thought.

'How are you doing?' he asked, coming in wearily in a sweat-stained green gown.

'As you see . . . fine, thanks to you.'

He looked at the newspaper lying on the bed. 'Your

bullet,' he said, 'ploughed along a rib and in and out of your arm. It tore a hole in the brachial artery, which is why you bled so much. We repaired that and transfused you with three units of blood and saline, though you may need more later. We'll see how you go. There's some muscle damage but with physiotherapy you should be almost as good as new. You seem to have been sideways on, when he shot you.'

'I was turning. I was lucky.'

'You could put it like that,' he said dryly. 'I suppose you do know you've also got a half-mended fracture of the forearm? And some fairly deep trauma to the wrist?'

I nodded.

'And we've put a few stitches in your face.'

'Great.'

'I watched you race,' he said. 'I know how fast jockeys heal. Ex-jockeys too, no doubt. You can leave here when you feel ready.'

I said, 'Thanks,' sincerely, and he smiled exhaustedly and went away.

I could definitely move the fingers of my right hand, even though only marginally at present. There had been a private moment of sheer cowardice in the night when I'd woken gradually from anaesthesia and been unable to feel anything in my arm from the shoulder down. I didn't care to confess or remember the abject dread in which I'd forced myself to *look*. I'd awoken once before to a stump. This time the recurrent nightmare of helplessness and humiliation and no hands had drifted horrifyingly in and out, but when I did finally look, there was no spirit-pulverising void but a long white-wrapped bundle that discernibly ended in fingernails. Even so, they didn't seem to be connected to me. I had lain for a grim while trying to consider paralysis, and when at length pain had roared back it had been an enormous relief: only whole healthy nerves felt that like. I had an arm . . . and a hand . . . and a life.

Given those, nothing else mattered.

In the afternoon Archie Kirk and Norman Picton argued themselves past the NO VISITORS sign on the door and sat in a couple of chairs bringing good news and bad.

'The Frodsham police found your car,' Norman said, 'but I'm afraid it's been stripped. It's up on bricks – no wheels.'

'Contents?' I asked resignedly.

'No. Nothing.'

'Engine?'

'Most of it's there. No battery, of course. Everything movable's missing.'

Poor old car. It had been insured though, for a fortune.

Archie said, 'Charles sends his regards.'

'Tell him thanks.'

'He said you would be looking as though nothing much had happened. I didn't believe him. Why aren't you lying down?'

'It's more comfortable sitting up.'

Archie frowned.

I amplified mildly. 'There's a bullet burn across somewhere below my shoulder blade.'

Archie said, 'Oh.'

They both looked at the tall contraption standing beside the bed with a tube leading from a high bag to my elbow. I explained that too.

'It's one of those "painkiller on demand" things,' I said. 'If I get a twinge I press a button, and bingo, it goes away.'

Archie picked up the copy of *The Pump*. 'All of a sudden,' he commented, 'you're Saint Sid who can do no wrong.'

I said, 'It's enough to make Ellis's lawyers weep.'

'But you don't think, do you,' Archie said doubtfully, 'that Ellis's lawyers *connived* at the hate-Halley campaign?'

'Because they are ethical people?' I asked.

'Yes.'

I shrugged and left it.

'Is there any news of Ellis?' I asked. 'Or of Gordon?'

'Gordon Quint,' Norman said in a policeman's voice, 'was, as of an hour ago, still unconscious in a secure police facility and suffering from a depressed skull fracture. He is to have an operation to relieve the pressure on his brain. No one is predicting when he'll wake up or what mental state he'll be in, but as soon as he can understand, he'll be formally charged with attempted murder. As you know, there's a whole flock of eye-witnesses.'

'And Ellis?' I asked.

Archie said, 'No one knows where he is.'

'It's very difficult,' I said, 'for him to go anywhere without being recognised.'

Norman nodded. 'Someone may be sheltering him. But we'll find him, don't worry.'

'What happened this morning,' I asked, 'about the trial?'

'Adjourned. Ellis Quint's bail is rescinded as he didn't turn up, and also he'll be charged with grievous bodily harm to his father. A warrant for his arrest has been issued.'

'He wanted to prevent his father from murdering,' I said. 'He can't have meant to hurt him seriously.'

Archie nodded. 'It's a tangle.'

'And Jonathan,' I asked, 'did he go to Shropshire?'

Both of them looked depressed.

'Well,' I said, 'didn't he go?'

'Oh yes, he went,' Norman said heavily. 'And he found the car-parkers.'

'Good boy,' I said.

'It's *not* so good.' Archie, like a proper civil servant, had brought with him a briefcase, from which he now produced a paper that he brought over to the bed. I pinned it down with the weight of my still-sluggish left hand and took in its general meaning.

The car-parkers had signed a statement saying that

Ellis Quint had dined with media colleagues and had brought several of them with him to the dance at about eleven-thirty. The parkers remembered him – of course – not only because of who he was (there had been plenty of other well-known people at the party, starting with members of the Royal Family) but chiefly because he had given them a tip and offered them his autograph. They knew it was before midnight, because their employment as car-parkers had ended then. People who arrived later had found only one car-parker – a friend of those who'd gone off duty.

Media colleagues! Damn it, I thought. I hadn't checked those with the duchess.

'It's an unbreakably solid alibi,' Norman observed gloomily. 'He was in Shropshire when the yearling was attacked.'

'Mm.'

'You don't seem disappointed, Sid,' Archie said, puzzled.

'No.'

'But why not?'

'I think,' I said, 'that you should phone Davis Tatum. Will he be in his office right now?'

'He might be. What do you want him for?'

'I want him to make sure the prosecutors don't give up on the trial.'

'You told him that on Saturday.' He was humouring me, I thought.

'I'm not light-headed from bullets, Archie, if that's

what you think. Since Saturday I've worked a few things out, and they are not as they may seem.'

'What things?'

'Ellis's alibi, for one.'

'But Sid—'

'Listen,' I said. 'This isn't all that easy to say, so don't look at me, look at your hands or something.' They showed no sign of doing so, so I looked at my own instead. I said, 'I have to explain that *I* am not as I seem. When people in general look at me they see a harmless person, youngish, not big, not tall, no threat to anyone. Self-effacing. I'm not complaining about that. In fact, I choose to be like that because people then *talk* to me, which is necessary in my job. They tend to think I'm cosy, as your sister Betty told me, Archie. Owen Yorkshire considers me a wimp. He said so. Only . . . I'm not really like that.'

'A *wimp*!' Archie exclaimed.

'I can look it, that's the point. But Ellis knows me better. Ellis calls me cunning and ruthless, and I probably am. It was he who years ago gave me the nickname of tungsten carbide because I wasn't easy to . . . er . . . intimidate. He thinks I can't be terrified, either, though he's wrong about that. But I don't mind him thinking it. Anyway, unlikely though it may seem, all this past summer, Ellis has been afraid of me. That's why he made jokes about me on television and got Tilepit to set his paper onto me. He wanted to defeat me by ridicule.'

I paused. Neither of them said a word.

I went on. 'Ellis is not what he seems, either. Davis Tatum thinks him a playboy. Ellis is tall, good-looking, outgoing, charming and *loved*. Everyone thinks him a delightful entertainer with a knack for television. But he's not only that. He's a strong, purposeful and powerful man with enormous skills of manipulation. People underestimate both of us for various and different reasons – I look weak and he looks frivolous – but we don't underestimate each other. On the surface, the easy surface, we've been friends for years. But in our time we rode dozens of races against each other, and racing, believe me, strips your soul bare. Ellis and I know each other's minds on a deep level that has nothing to do with afternoon banter or chit-chat. We've been friends on that level too. You and Davis can't believe that it is Ellis himself who is the heavyweight, not Yorkshire, but Ellis and I both know it. Ellis has manipulated everyone – Yorkshire, Tilepit, *The Pump*, public opinion, and also those so-smart lawyers of his who think they're dictating the pace.'

'And you, Sid?' Norman asked. 'Has he pulled your strings too?'

I smiled ruefully, not looking at him. 'He's had a go.'

'I'd think it was impossible,' Archie said. 'He would have to put you underground to stop you.'

'You've learned a lot more about me, Archie,' I said lazily. 'I do like to win.'

He said, 'So why aren't you disappointed that Ellis's Shropshire alibi can't be broken?'

'Because Ellis set it up that way.'

'How do you mean?'

'Ever since the Northampton yearling was attacked, Ellis's lawyers have been putting it about that if Ellis had an unbreakable alibi for that night, which I bet he assured them he had, it would invalidate the whole Combe Bassett case. They put pressure on the Crown Prosecution Service to withdraw, which they've been tottering on the brink of doing. Never mind that the two attacks were separate, the strong supposition arose that if Ellis couldn't have done one, then he hadn't done the other.'

'Of course,' Norman said.

'No,' I contradicted. 'He made for himself a positively unbreakable alibi in Shropshire, and he got someone else to go to Northampton.'

'But no one *would*.'

'One person would. And did.'

'But *who*, Sid?' Archie asked.

'Gordon. His father.'

Archie and Norman both stiffened as if turned to pillars of salt.

The nerves in my right arm woke up. I pressed the magic button and they went slowly back to sleep. Brilliant. A lot better than in days gone by.

'He *couldn't* have done,' Archie said in revulsion.

'He did.'

'You're just *guessing*. And you're *wrong*.'

'No.'

'But *Sid* . . .'

'I know,' I sighed. 'You, Charles and I have all been guests in his house. But he shot me last night. See it in *The Pump*.'

Archie said weakly, 'But that doesn't mean . . .'

'I'll explain,' I said. 'Give me a moment.'

My skin was sweating. It came and went a bit, now and then. An affronted body, letting me know.

'A moment?'

'I'm not made of iron.'

Archie breathed on a smile. 'I thought it was tungsten?'

'Mm.'

They waited. I said, 'Gordon and Ginnie Quint gloried in their wonderful son, their only child. I accused him of a crime that revolted them. Ginnie steadfastly believed in his innocence; an act of faith. Gordon, however reluctantly, faced with all the evidence we gathered from his Land-Rover, must have come to acknowledge to himself that the unthinkable was true.'

Archie nodded.

I went on, 'Ellis's wretched persecution of me didn't really work. Sure, I hated it, but I was still *there*, and meanwhile the time of the trial was drawing nearer and nearer. Whatever odium I drew onto myself by doing it, I was going to describe in court, with all the Press and public listening, just how Ellis could have cut off the foot of Betty's colt. The outcome of the trial – whether or not the jury found Ellis guilty, and whether or not the judge sent him to jail – that wasn't the prime point. The trial itself, and all that evidence, would have convinced enough of the population of his guilt to destroy for ever the shining-knight persona. Topline Foods couldn't have – and, in fact, won't be able to – use those diamond-plated round-the-world ads.'

I took a deep couple of lungfuls of air. I was talking too much. Not enough oxygen, not enough blood.

I said, 'The idea of the Shropshire alibi probably came about gradually, and heaven knows to which of them first. Ellis received an invitation to the dance. The plan must have started from that. They saw it as the one effective way to stop the trial from taking place.'

Hell, I thought, I don't feel well. I'm getting old.

I said, 'You have to remember that Gordon is a farmer. He's used to the idea of the death of animals being profitable. I dare say that the death of one insignificant yearling was as nothing to him when set beside the saving of his son. And he knew where to find such a victim. He would have to have long replaced the shears taken by the police. It must have seemed quite easy, and in fact he carried out the plan without difficulty.'

Archie and Norman listened as if not breathing.

I started again. 'Ellis is many things, but he's not a murderer. If he had been, perhaps he would have been a serial killer of humans, not horses. That urge to do evil – I don't understand it, but it *happens*. Wings off butterflies and so on.' I swallowed. 'Ellis has given me a hard time, but in spite of several opportunities he hasn't let me be killed. He stopped Yorkshire doing it. He stopped his father last night.'

'People can hate until they make themselves ill,' Archie nodded. 'Very few actually murder.'

'Gordon Quint tried it,' Norman pointed out, 'and all but succeeded.'

'Yes,' I agreed, 'but that wasn't to help Ellis.'

'What was it, then?'

'Have to go back a bit.'

I'm too tired, I thought, but I'd better finish it.

I said to Norman, 'You remember that piece of rag you gave me?'

'Yes. Did you do anything with it?'

I nodded.

'What rag?' Archie asked.

Norman outlined for him the discovery at Northampton of the lopping shears wrapped in dirty material.

'The local police found the shears hidden in a hedge,' I said, 'and they brought them into the stud farm's office while I was there. The stud farm's owners, Miss Richardson and Mrs Bethany, were there, and so was Ginnie Quint, who was a friend of theirs and who had gone there to comfort them and sympathise. Ginnie forcibly said how much she despised me for falsely accusing her paragon of a son. For accusing my *friend*. She more or less called me Judas.'

'Sid!'

'Well, that's how it seemed. Then she watched the policeman unwrap the shears that had cut off the yearling's foot and, quite slowly, she went white . . . and fainted.'

'The sight of the shears,' Norman said, nodding.

'It was much more than that. It was the sight of the *material.*'

'How do you mean?'

'I spent a whole day . . . last Thursday, it seems a lifetime away . . . I chased all over London with that little piece of cloth, and I finished up in a village near Chichester.'

'Why Chichester?' Archie asked.

'Because that filthy old cloth had once been part of some bed hangings. They were woven as a special order by a Mrs Patricia Huxford, who's a doll of the first rank. She has looms in Lowell, near Chichester. She looked up her records and found that that fabric had been made nearly thirty years ago especially – and exclusively – for a Mrs Gordon Quint.'

Archie and Norman both stared.

'Ginnie recognised the material,' I said. 'She'd just been giving me the most frightful tongue-lashing for believing Ellis capable of maiming horses, and she suddenly saw, because that material was wrapped round shears, that I'd been right. Not only that, she knew that Ellis had been in Shropshire the night Miss Richardson's colt was done. She knew the importance of his alibi . . . and she saw – she understood – that the only other person who could or would have wrapped lopping shears in that unique fabric was Gordon. Gordon wouldn't have thought twice about snatching up any old rag to wrap his shears in – and I'd guess he decided to dump them because we might have checked Quint shears again for horse DNA if he'd taken them home. Ginnie saw that *Gordon* had maimed the yearling. It was too big a shock . . . and she fainted.'

Archie and Norman, too, looked shocked.

I sighed. 'I didn't understand that then, of course. I didn't understand it until the night before last, when everything sort of *clicked*. But now . . . I think it wasn't just because of Ellis's terrible guilt that Ginnie killed herself last Monday, but because it was Gordon's guilt and reputation as well . . . and then the trial was starting in spite of everything . . . and it was all too much . . . too much to bear.'

I paused briefly and went on, 'Ginnie's suicide sent Gordon berserk. He'd set out to help his son. He'd caused his wife's death. He blamed me for it, for having destroyed his family. He tried to smash my brains in, the morning she'd died. He lay in wait for me outside my flat . . . he was screaming that I'd killed her. Then, last night, in the actual moment that the picture in *The Pump* was taken, he was telling me the bullets were for Ginnie . . . it was my life for hers. He meant . . . he meant to do it.'

I stopped talking.

The white room was silent.

Later in the day I phoned the hospital in Canterbury and spoke to the ward sister.

'How is Rachel?' I asked.

'Mr Halley! But I thought . . . I mean, we've all read *The Pump*.'

'But you didn't tell Rachel, did you?' I asked anxiously.

'No . . . Linda – Mrs Ferns – said not to.'

'Good.'

'But are you—'

'I'm absolutely OK,' I assured her. 'I'm in Hammersmith Hospital. Du Cane Road.'

'The best!' she exclaimed.

'I won't argue. How's Rachel?'

'You know that she's a very sick little girl, but we're all hopeful of the transplant.'

'Did she go into the bubble?'

'Yes, very bravely. She says it's her palace and she's its queen.'

'Give her my love.'

'How soon . . . oh dear, I shouldn't ask.'

'I'll make it by Thursday.'

'I'll tell her.'

*

Kevin Mills and India came to visit before ten o'clock the following morning, on their way to work.

I was again sitting up in the high bed but by then felt much healthier. In spite of my protests my shot and mending arm was still held immobile in a swaddle of splint and bandages. Give it another day's rest, I'd been told, and just practise wiggling your fingers: which was all very well, except that the nurses had been too busy with an emergency that morning to reunite me with my left hand, which lay on the locker beside me. For all that it didn't work properly, I felt naked without it, and could do nothing for myself, not even scratch my nose.

Kevin and India both came in looking embarrassed by life in general and said far too brightly how glad they were to see me awake and recovering.

I smiled at their feelings. 'My dear children,' I said, 'I'm not a complete fool.'

'Look, mate . . .' Kevin's voice faded. He wouldn't meet my eyes.

I said, 'Who told Gordon Quint where to find me?'

Neither of them answered.

'India,' I pointed out, 'you were the only person who knew I would turn up at Kensington Place at eight o'clock on Sunday evening.'

'Sid!' She was anguished, as she had been in Church Street when she'd found me shot; and she wouldn't look at my face, either.

Kevin smoothed his moustache. 'It wasn't her fault.'

'Yours, then?'

'You're right about your not being a fool,' Kevin said. 'You've guessed what happened, otherwise you'd be flinging us out of here right now.'

'Correct.'

'The turmoil started Saturday evening,' Kevin said, feeling secure enough to sit down. 'Of course, as there's no daily *Pump* on Sundays there was hardly anyone in the office. George Godbar wasn't. No one was. Saturday is our night off. The shit really hit the fan on Sunday morning at the editorial meeting. You know editorial meetings . . . well, perhaps you don't. All the department editors – news, sport, gossip, features, whatever, and the senior reporters – meet to decide what stories will be run in the next day's paper, and there was George Godbar in a positive *lather* about reversing policy on S. Halley. I mean, Sid mate, you should've heard him swear. I never knew so many orifices and sphincters existed.'

'The boss had leaned on him?'

'*Leaned!* There was a panic. Our lord the proprietor wanted you *bought off.*'

'How nice,' I said.

'He'd suggested ten thousand smackers, George said. Try ten million, I said. George called for copies for everyone of the complete file of everything *The Pump* has published about you since June, nearly all of it in India's column on Fridays. I suppose you've kept all those pieces?'

I hadn't. I didn't say so.

'Such *poison*,' Kevin said. 'Seeing it all together like that. I mean, it silenced the whole meeting, and it takes a lot to do that.'

'I wasn't there,' India said. 'I don't go to those meetings.'

'Be fair to India,' Kevin told me, 'she didn't write most of it. I wrote some. You know I did. Six different people wrote it.'

India still wouldn't meet my eyes and still wouldn't sit in the one empty chair. I knew about 'policy' and being burned at the stake and all that, yet week after week I'd dreaded her by-line. Try as I would, I still felt sore from that savaging.

'Sit down,' I said mildly.

She perched uneasily.

'If we make another dinner date,' I said, 'don't tell anyone.'

'Oh, Sid.'

'She didn't mean to get you *shot*, for Chrissakes,' Kevin protested. 'The Tilepit wanted you found. Wanted! He was shitting himself, George said. *The Pump*'s lawyer had passed each piece week by week as being just on the safe side of actionable, but at the meeting, when he read the whole file at once, he was *sweating*, Sid. He says *The Pump* should settle out of court for whatever you ask.'

'And I suppose you're not supposed to be telling me that?'

'No,' Kevin confessed, 'but you did give me the exclusive of the decade.'

'How did Gordon Quint find me?' I asked again.

'George said our noble lord was babbling on about you promising not to send him to jail if you walked out free from somewhere or other, and you *had* walked out free, and he wanted to keep you to your promise. George didn't know what he was talking about, but Tilepit made it crystal that George's job depended on finding you within the next five minutes, if not sooner. So George begged us all to find you, to say *The Pump* would confer sainthood immediately and fatten your bank balance, and I phoned India on the off-chance, and she said not to worry, she would tell you herself . . . and I asked her how . . . and where. There didn't seem to be any harm in it.'

'And you told George Godbar?' I said.

Kevin nodded.

'And he,' I said, 'told Lord Tilepit? And *he* told Ellis, I suppose . . . because Ellis turned up too.'

'George Godbar phoned Ellis's father's house, looking for Ellis. He got an answering machine telling him to try a mobile number, and he reached Gordon Quint in a car somewhere . . . and he told Gordon where you would be, if Ellis wanted to find you.'

Round and round in circles, and the bullets come out *here*.

I sighed again. I was lucky to be alive. I would settle for that. I also wondered how much I would screw out of *The Pump*. Only enough, I decided, to keep his lordship grateful.

Kevin, the confession over, got restlessly to his feet and walked round the room, stopping when he reached the locker on my left side.

He looked a little blankly at the prosthesis lying there and, after a moment, picked it up. I wished he wouldn't.

He said, surprised, 'It's bigger than I pictured. And heavier. And *hard*.'

'All the better to club you with,' I said.

'Really?' he asked interestedly. 'Straight up?'

'It's been known,' I said, and after a moment he put the arm down.

'It's true what they say of you, isn't it? You may not look it, but you're one tough bugger, Sid, mate, like I told you before.'

I said, 'Not many people look the way they are inside.'

India said, 'I'll write a piece about that.'

'There you are then, Sid.' Kevin was ready to go. 'I've got a rape waiting. Thanks for those Japs. Makes us even, right?'

'Even,' I nodded.

India stood up as if to follow him. 'Stay a bit,' I suggested.

She hesitated. Kevin said, 'Stay and hold his bloody hand. Oh shit. Well . . . sorry, mate. *Sorry*.'

'Get out of here,' I said.

India watched him go.

'I'm really sorry,' she said helplessly, 'about getting you shot.'

'I'm alive,' I pointed out, 'so forget it.'

Her face looked softer. At that hour in the morning she hadn't yet put on the sharply outlined lipstick nor the matt porcelain make-up. Her eyebrows were as dark and positive, and her eyes as light blue and clear, but this was the essential India I was seeing, not the worldly package. How different, I wondered, was the inner spirit from the cutting brain of her column.

She too, as if compelled, came over to my left side and looked at the plastic arm.

'How does it work?' she asked.

I explained about the electrodes, as I had for Rachel.

She picked up the arm and put her fingers inside, touching the electrodes. Nothing happened. No movement in the thumb.

I swallowed. I said, 'It probably needs a fresh battery.'

'Battery?'

'It clips into the side. That box-like thing . . .' I nodded towards the locker. '. . . that's a battery charger. There's a recharged battery in there. Change them over.'

She did so, but slowly, because of the unfamiliarity. When she touched the electrodes again, the hand obeyed the signals.

'Oh,' she said.

She put the hand down and looked at me.

'Do you,' she said, 'have a steel rod up your backbone? I've never seen anyone more tense. And your forehead's sweating.'

She picked up the box of tissues lying beside the battery charger and offered it to me.

I shook my head. She looked at the immobilised right arm and at the left one on the locker, and a wave of understanding seemed to leave her without breath.

I said nothing. She pulled a tissue out of the box and jerkily dabbed at a dribble of sweat that ran down my temple.

'Why don't you put this arm on?' she demanded. 'You'd be better with it on, obviously.'

'A nurse will do it.' I explained about the emergency. 'She'll come when she can.'

'Let *me* do it,' India said.

'No.'

'Why not?'

'Because.'

'Because you're too bloody *proud*.'

Because it's too private, I thought.

I was wearing one of those dreadful hospital gowns like a barber's smock that fastened at the back of the neck and shapelessly covered the body. A white flap covered my left shoulder, upper arm, elbow, and what remained below. Tentatively India lifted and turned back the flap so that we both could see my elbow and the short piece of forearm.

'You hate it, don't you?' India said.

'Yes.'

'I would hate it, too.'

I can't bear this, I thought. I can bear Ellis unscrewing my hand and mocking me. I can't bear love.

India picked up the electric arm.

'What do I do?' she asked.

I said with difficulty, nodding again at the locker, 'Talcum powder.'

'Oh.' She picked up the prosaic white tinful of comfort for babies. 'In the arm, or on you?'

'On me.'

She sprinkled powder on my forearm. 'Is this right? More?'

'Mm.'

She smoothed the powder all over my skin. Her touch sent a shiver right down to my toes.

'And now?'

'Now hold it so that I can put my arm into it.'

She concentrated. I put my forearm into the socket, but the angle was wrong.

'What do I do?' she asked anxiously.

'Turn the thumb towards you a bit. Not too far. That's right. Now push up while I push down. That top bit will slide over my elbow and grip – and keep the hand on.'

'Like that?' She was trembling.

'Like that,' I said. The arm gripped where it was designed to.

I sent the messages. We both watched the hand open and close.

India abruptly left my side and walked over to where she'd left her handbag, picking it up and crossing to the door.

'Don't go,' I said.

'If I don't go, I'll cry.'

I thought that might make two of us. The touch of her fingers on the skin of my forearm had been a caress more intimate than any act of sex. I felt shaky. I felt more moved than ever in my life.

'Come back,' I said.

'I'm supposed to be in the office.'

'India,' I said, 'please . . .' Why was it always so impossible to plead? 'Please . . .' I looked down at my left hand. 'Please don't *write* about this.'

'Don't *write* about it?'

'No.'

'Well, I won't, but why not?'

'Because I don't like pity.'

She came halfway back to my side with tears in her eyes.

'Your Jenny,' she said, 'told me that you were so afraid of being pitied that you would never ask for help.'

'She told you too much.'

'Pity,' India said, coming a step nearer, 'is actually about as far from what I feel for you as it's possible to get.'

I stretched out my left arm and fastened the hand on her wrist.

She looked at it. I tugged, and she took the last step to my side.

'You're strong,' she said, surprised.

'Usually.'

I pulled her nearer. She saw quite clearly what I intended, and bent her head and put her mouth on mine as if it were not the first time, as if it were natural.

A pact, I thought.

A beginning.

Time drifted when she'd gone.

Time drifted to the midday news.

A nurse burst into my quiet room. 'Don't you have your television on? You're on it.'

She switched on knobs, and there was my face on the screen, with a newsreader's unemotional voice saying, 'Sid Halley is recovering in hospital.' There was a widening picture of me looking young and in racing colours: a piece of old film taken years ago of me weighing-in after winning the Grand National. I was holding my saddle in two hands and my eyes were full of the mystical wonder of having been presented with the equivalent of the Holy Grail.

The news slid to drought and intractable famine.

The nurse said 'Wait,' and twiddled more knobs,

and another channel opened with the news item and covered the story in its entirety.

A woman announcer whose lugubrious voice I had long disliked put on her portentous-solemn face and intoned:

'Police today found the body of Ellis Quint in his car deep in the New Forest in Hampshire . . .'

Frozen, I heard her saying, as if from a distance, 'Foul play is not suspected. It is understood that the popular broadcaster left a note for his father, still unconscious after an accidental blow to the head on Sunday night. Now over to our reporter in Hampshire, Buddy Bowes.'

Buddy Bowes, microphone in hand, filled the foreground of the screen with, slightly out of focus in the distance behind him, woodland and activity and a rear view of a white car.

'This is a sad ending,' Buddy Bowes said, appearing at least to show genuine regret, 'to a fairytale life. Ellis Quint, thirty-eight, who gave pleasure to millions with his appearances on television, will also be remembered as the dashing champion amateur steeplechase jockey whose courage and gallantry inspired a whole generation to get out there and *achieve.* In recent months he has been troubled by accusations of cruelty to animals from his longtime colleague and supposed friend, Sid Halley, ex-professional top jockey. Quint was due to appear in court yesterday to refute those charges . . .'

There was a montage of Ellis winning races, striding

about in macho riding boots, wowing a chat-show audience, looking glowingly alive and handsome.

'Ellis will be mourned by millions,' Buddy Bowes finished. 'And now back to the studio . . .'

The nurse indignantly switched off the set. 'They didn't say anything about you being shot.'

'Never mind.'

She went away crossly. The reputation Ellis had manufactured for me couldn't be reversed in a night, whatever *The Pump* might now say. Slowly perhaps. Perhaps never.

Ellis was dead.

I sat in the quiet white room.

Ellis was *dead.*

An hour later a hospital porter brought me a letter that he said had been left by hand on the counter of the hospital's main reception desk and overlooked until now.

'Overlooked since when?'

Since yesterday, he thought.

When he'd gone I held the envelope in the pincer fingers and tore it open with my teeth.

The two-page letter was from Ellis, his handwriting strong with life.

It said:

Sid, I know where you are. I followed the ambulance. If you are reading this, you are alive and I am dead. I didn't think you would catch me. I should have known you would.

If you're wondering why I cut off those feet, don't *you* ever want to break out? I was tired of goody goody. I wanted the dark side. I wanted to smash. To explode. To mutilate. I wanted to laugh at the fools who fawned on me. I hugged myself. I mocked the proles.

And that *scrunch*.

I did that old pony to make a good programme. The kid had leukaemia. Sob-stuff story, terrific. I needed a good one. My ratings were slipping.

Then I lusted to do it again. The danger. The risk, the difficulty. And that *scrunch*. I can't describe it. It gives me an ecstasy like nothing else. Cocaine is for kids. Sex is nothing. I've had every woman I ever wanted. The scrunch of bones is a million-volt orgasm.

And then there's you. The only one I've ever envied. I wanted to corrupt you too. No one should be unbendable.

I know all you fear is helplessness. I know you. I wanted to make you helpless in Owen Yorkshire's office but all you did was sit there watching your hand turn blue. I could feel you willing me to be my real self but my real self wanted to hear your wrist bones *crunch* to dust. I wanted to prove that no one was good. I wanted you to crumble. To be like me.

And then, you'll think I'm crazy, I was suddenly glad you weren't sobbing and whining and I was proud of you that you really were how you are, and I felt happy and higher than a kite. And I didn't want you to die, not like that, not for anything. Not because of me.

I see now what I've done. What infinite damage.

My father did that last colt. I talked him into it.

It's cost my mother's life. If my father lives they'll lock him up for trying to kill you. They should have let me hang, back in June, when I tried with my tie.

They say people want to be caught. They go on and on sinning until someone stops them.

The letter ended there except for three words much lower down the page:

You win, Sid.

The two sheets of paper lay on the white bedclothes. No one else would see them, I thought.

I remembered Rachel saying how odd it would be to be dead. To be a *space*.

The whole white room was space.

Good and evil, he had been my friend. An enemy: but finally a friend.

The sour, cruel, underside of him receded.

I had the win, but there was no one standing in the stirrups to share it with.

Regret, loss, acceptance and relief; I felt them all.

I grieved for Ellis Quint.

TO THE HILT

Dick Francis has written thirty-nine international bestsellers and is widely acclaimed as one of the world's finest thriller writers. His awards include the Crime Writers' Association's Cartier Diamond Dagger for his outstanding contribution to the crime genre, and an honorary Doctorate of Humane Letters from Tufts University of Boston. In 1996 Dick Francis was made a Mystery Writers of America Grand Master for a lifetime's achievement.

Also by Dick Francis in Pan Books

DEAD CERT
NERVE
FOR KICKS
ODDS AGAINST
FLYING FINISH
BLOOD SPORT
FORFEIT
ENQUIRY
RAT RACE
BONECRACK
SMOKESCREEN
SLAY-RIDE
KNOCK DOWN
HIGH STAKES
IN THE FRAME
RISK
TRIAL RUN
WHIP HAND
REFLEX
TWICE SHY
BANKER
THE DANGER
PROOF
BREAK IN
BOLT
HOT MONEY
THE EDGE
STRAIGHT
LONGSHOT
COMEBACK
DRIVING FORCE
DECIDER
WILD HORSES
COME TO GRIEF
10lb PENALTY
FIELD OF THIRTEEN
SECOND WIND
SHATTERED

THE SPORT OF QUEENS
(autobiography)

LESTER: The Official
Biography

DICK FRANCIS
OMNIBUS ONE:
Long Shot, Straight, High
Stakes

DICK FRANCIS
OMNIBUS TWO:
Forfeit, Risk,
Reflex

Dick Francis

TO THE HILT

PAN BOOKS

First published 1996 by Michael Joseph Ltd

This edition published 1997 by Pan Books
an imprint of Pan Macmillan Ltd
Pan Macmillan, 20 New Wharf Road, London N19RR
Basingstoke and Oxford
Associated companies throughout the world
www.panmacmillan.com

ISBN 0 330 35225 3

'Disobedience' from *When We Were Very Young* by A. A. Milne, first published by
Methuen Children's Books (1924), by permission of Reed Consumer Books

21 23 25 27 29 28 26 24 22 20

A CIP catalogue record for this book is available from
the British Library.

Typeset by CentraCet Limited, Cambridge
Printed by Mackays of Chatham plc, Chatham, Kent

BEDE'S DEATH SONG

Fore thaem neidfaerae   naenig uuirthit
thoncsnotturra,   than him tharf sie
to ymbhycggannae aer   his hiniongae
hwaet his gastae   godaes aeththae yflaes
aefter deothdaege   doemid uueorthae.

Before that sudden journey no one is wiser in thought than he needs to be, in considering, before his departure, what will be adjudged to his soul, of good or evil, after his death-day.

From *The Earliest English Poems*,
translated by Michael Alexander
(Penguin Books, Third Edition 1991)

CHAPTER ONE

I don't think my stepfather much minded dying. That he almost took me with him wasn't really his fault.

My mother sent me a postcard – 'Perhaps I'd better tell you your stepfather has had a heart attack' – which I read in disbelief outside the remote Scottish post office where I went every two weeks to collect my letters. The postcard had lain there unread for approximately ten days.

Somewhat distractedly, though my stepfather and I were hardly intimate, I went back into the cluttered little shop and begged use of the telephone.

'You'll be reimbursing us as usual, Mr Kinloch?'

'Of course.'

Dour old Donald Cameron, nodding, lifted a flap of counter and allowed me through to his own jealously protected and wall-mounted instrument. As the official public telephone, thoughtfully provided outside for the few surrounding inhabitants, survived vandalism for roughly thirty minutes each time it was mended, old Donald was accustomed to extending to customers the courtesy of his own phone. Since he charged an extra fee for its use, I privately reckoned it was Donald himself who regularly disabled the less profitable technology on his doorstep.

'Mother?' I said, eventually connected to her in London. 'This is Al.'

'Alexander,' she corrected automatically, not liking my abbreviation, 'are you in Scotland?'

'I am, yes. What about the old man?'

'Your stepfather,' she said reprovingly, 'is resting.'

'Er . . . *where* is he resting?' In hospital? In *peace*?

'In bed,' she said.

'So he is alive?'

'Of course he's alive.'

'But your postcard . . .'

'There's nothing to panic about,' she said calmly. 'He had some chest pains and spent a week in the Clinic for stabilisation and tests, and now he is home with me, resting.'

'Do you want me to come?' I asked blankly. 'Do you need any help?'

'He has a nurse,' she said.

My mother's unvarying composure, I sometimes thought, stemmed from a genuine deficiency of emotion. I had never seen her cry, had never heard tears in her voice, not even after her first husband, my father, had been killed in a shooting accident out on the moors. To me, at seventeen, his sudden loss had been devastating. My mother, dry-eyed, had told me to pull myself together.

A year later, still cool at the ceremony, she had married Ivan George Westering, baronet, brewer, pillar of the British Jockey Club, my stepfather. He was not domineering; had been generous, even; but he disapproved of the way I lived. We were polite to each other.

'How ill is he?' I asked.

'You can come if you like,' my mother said. 'It's entirely up to you.'

Despite the casual voice, the carefully maintained distance, it sounded closer to a plea than I was used to.

'I'll arrive tomorrow,' I said, making up my mind.

'If you're sure?' She betrayed no relief, however; no welcome.

'I'm sure.'

'Very well.'

I paid the phone call's ransom into Donald's stringy outstretched palm and returned to my laden, ancient and battered four-wheel drive outside. It had good gears, good brakes, good tyres and little remaining colour on its thin metal flanks. It contained, at that moment, food for two weeks, a big cylinder of butane gas, supplies of batteries, bottled water and insect killer and three brown cardboard boxes, parcel delivery, replenishing the tools of my trade.

I painted pictures. I lived in a broken down long-deserted shepherd's hut, known as a bothy, out on a windy Scottish mountainside, without electricity. My hair grew to my shoulders. I played the bagpipes. My many and fairly noble relations thought me weird.

Some are born weird, some achieve it, others have weirdness thrust upon them. I preferred solitude and paint to out-thinking salmon and shooting for food; I had only half inherited the country skills and courtesies of my ancestors. I was the twenty-nine-year-old son of the (dead) fourth son of an earl and I had no unearned wealth. I had three uncles, four aunts and twenty-one cousins. Someone in such a large (and conventional) family had to be weird, and it seemed I'd been elected.

I didn't mind. Mad Alexander. Messes about with paints. And not even *oils*, my dear, but those frightfully common *acrylics*.

If Michelangelo could have laid his hands on acrylics, I said, he would have joyfully used them. Acrylics were endlessly versatile and never faded. They out-virtued oils by furlongs.

Don't be *ridiculous*, Alexander.

I paid my uncle (the present earl, known as 'Himself') a painting a year as rent for the ruin I inhabited on his estate. The painting was done to his choice. He mostly asked for portraits of his horses and dogs. I quite liked to please him.

Outside the post office, on that dry cloudy cold morning in September, I sat in my old jeep-type jalopy and did my paperwork, opening my letters, answering them and sending off the replies. There were two cheques that day for work delivered, which I despatched to the bank, and an order from America for six more paintings to be done at once – like yesterday. Ridiculous, mad Alexander, in his weird way, actually, quietly prospered; and I kept that fact to myself.

The paperwork done, I drove my wheels northwards, at first along a recognisable road, then a roughly gravelled stretch, then up a long, rutted and indistinct track which led nowhere but to my unnamed home in the Monadhliath Mountains. 'Between Loch Ness and Aviemore,' I usually explained, and no, I hadn't seen the monster.

Whoever in the mists of time had first built my bothy had chosen its position well: it backed straight into an elbowed granite outcrop that sheltered it from the north and east, so that winter blizzards mostly leapfrogged over the top. In front lay a sort of small stony plateau that on the far side dropped away steeply, giving me long views of valleys and rocky hills and of a main road far below.

The only problem with the road, that served to remind me that an outside world existed, was that my dwelling was visible *from* it, so that far too often I found strangers on my doorstep, hikers equipped with shorts, maps, half-ton walking boots and endless energy. There was nowhere left in the world unpenetrated by inquisitive legs.

On the day of my mother's postcard I returned to

find four of the nosy species poking around without inhibitions. Male. Blue, scarlet, orange backpacks. Glasses. English regional voices.

The days when I'd offered tea, comforts and conversation were long gone. Irritated by the invasion I drove onto the plateau, stopped the engine, removed my keys from the ignition and walked towards my front (and only) door.

The four men stopped peering into things and ranged themselves into a ragged line ahead of me, across my path.

'There's no one in,' one of them called. 'It's all locked up.'

I replied without heat, 'What do you want?'

'Him as lives here,' one said loudly.

'Maybe that's you,' said another.

I felt the first tremble of something wrong. Their manner wasn't the awkwardness of trespassers caught in the act. There was no shuffling from foot to foot. They met my eyes not with placating apology, but with fierce concentration.

I stopped walking and said again, 'What do you want?'

The first speaker said, 'Where is it?'

I felt a strong primitive impulse to turn tail and run, and wished afterwards that I'd listened to the wisdom of prehistory, but somehow one doesn't easily equate knobbly-kneed hikers with positive danger.

I said, 'I don't know what you mean,' and I made

the mistake of turning my back on them and retracing my steps towards the jeep.

I heard their heavy feet scrunching on the stony ground behind me but still didn't truly believe in disaster until they clutched and spun me round and purposefully and knowledgeably punched. I had a sort of splintered composite view of intent malevolent faces, of grey daylight reflecting on their incongruous glasses, of their hard bombarding fists and of a wildly slanting horizon of unhelpful mountains as I doubled forward over a debilitating pain in the abdomen. Neck chop. Jabs to the ribs. Classic pattern. Over and over. Thud, merciless thud.

I was wearing jeans, shirt and sweater: they might as well have been gossamer for all the protection they offered. As for meaningful retaliation, read non-existent. I couldn't find breath. I swung at them in anger but fought an octopus. Bad news.

One of the men kept saying insistently, 'Where is it? Where is it?' but his colleagues made it impossible for me to answer.

I wondered vaguely if by 'it' they meant money, of which I carried little. They were welcome to it, I thought groggily, if they would stop their attentions. I unintentionally dropped my small bunch of keys and lost it to a hand that grabbed it up with triumph.

Somehow or other I ended with my back against the jeep: no further retreat. One of them snatched handfuls of my hair and banged my head against metal. I clawed blood down his cheek and got a head-butt in return that went straight from my skull to my knees, buckling them like butter.

Events became unclear. I slid to the ground, face down. I had a close view of grey granite stones and short dry struggling blades of grass, more brown than green.

'Where is it?'

I didn't answer. Didn't move. Shut my eyes. Drifted.

'He's out,' a voice said. 'Fat lot of help you are.'

I felt hands roughly searching my pockets. Resistance, as an option, promised only more bruises. I lay still, not wholly conscious, inertia pervading, angry but helplessly passive, nothing coordinating, no strength, no will.

After a time of floating I felt their hands on me again.

'Is he alive?'

'No thanks to you, but yes, he is. He's breathing.'

'Just leave him.'

'Chuck him over there.'

'Over there' turned out to be the edge of the plateau, but I didn't realise it until I'd been dragged across the stones and lifted and flung over. I went rolling fast and inexorably down the steep mountain slope, almost bouncing from rock to rock, still incapable of helping myself, unable to stop, dimly aware of flooding with whirling comprehensive pain.

I slammed down onto a larger rock and did stop

there, half on my side, half on my stomach. I felt no gratitude. I felt pulverised. Winded. Dazed. Thought vanished.

Some sort of consciousness soon came crazily back, but orderly memory took much longer.

Those bastard hikers, I thought eventually. I remembered their faces. I could draw them. They were demons in a dream.

The accurate knowledge of who I was and where I was arrived quietly.

I tried to move. A mistake.

Time would take care of it, perhaps. Give it time.

Those bastards had been *real*, I realised, demons or not. Their fists had been real. 'Where is it?' had been real. In spite of everything, I ruefully smiled. I thought it possible that they hadn't known what they were actually looking for. 'It' could have been whatever their victim valued most. There was no guarantee in any case that delivering up 'it' would save one from being thrown down a mountain.

It occurred to me to wonder what time it was. I looked at my left wrist, but my watch had gone.

It had been about eleven o'clock when I'd got back from the post office . . .

Hell's teeth, I thought abruptly. *Mother. Ivan. Heart attack.* I was supposed to be going to London. Or the moon.

The worst thing I might feel, I considered, was nothing.

Not the case.

With fierce concentration, I could move all my fingers and all my toes. Anything more hurt too much for enthusiasm. Outraged muscles went into breath-stopping spasms to protect themselves.

Wait. Lie still. I felt cold.

Bloody stupid, being mugged on one's own doorstep. Embarrassing. A helpless little old lady I was not, but a pushover – literally – just the same.

I found the casual callousness of the walkers extraordinary. They had appeared not to care whether I lived or died, and had in fact left it to chance. I supposed they could truthfully say, 'He was alive when we saw him last.' They could dodge the word murder.

The ebb tide in my body finally turned. Movement could at last be achieved without spasm. All I had to do from then on was scrape myself off the mountain and go and catch a train. Even the thought was exhausting.

I was sure, after a while, that by immense good fortune I had broken no bones in my helter-skeltering fall. I'd been a rag doll. Babies got lucky through not trying to help themselves. Same principle, I supposed.

With an unstoical groan, I raised from prone to kneeling on my rock and took a look up at where I'd come down. The edge of the plateau was hidden behind outcrops but was alarmingly far above. Looking down was almost worse, though from five or more years of living there, I understood at once where I was in relation to the bothy above. If I could traverse to the right without losing my footing and plunging down another slope, I would come eventually to the uneven but definable path that meandered from the road below up to my home: the challenging half-hidden ascent that brought walkers to my door.

The four hiker-demons had probably come up that way. I certainly didn't want to meet them if they were on their way down. Hours had probably passed, though. I knew I had lain helpless for a long time. They must surely by then have left.

Realistically, I was going nowhere except uncontrollably downwards again unless I could reach that path. Hikers or not, it was the only possible route. Trying to go in the opposite direction, to reach the track up from the post office, was pointless, as it involved an overhang and a perpendicular rock climb, neither of which could be managed without gear.

I was well used to moving alone in the mountains, and I was always careful. I would never normally have attempted what now confronted me without an axe and crampons, let alone with every move a wince, but fear of a less lucky fall, of a broken leg or worse, kept me stuck like glue, with fingernails and tiny cautious shifts of weight, to every protruding scrap of solid rock. Loose stones rattled and bounced away. Scrubby earth gave too little purchase. Rock was all.

I made the journey sitting down, looking out over the perilous drops to the valley, digging in with my heels; careful, careful . . . *careful*.

The path, when at last I reached it, was by comparison a broad highway. I sat on one of its rocky steps and felt as weak as thankful: sat with my forearms on my knees, head hanging, trying to be cool about a degree of strain and discomfort far beyond the easily bearable.

Those *bastards*, I thought. The helpless rage of all victims shook in my gut. My physical state was shaming and infuriating. Somehow or other I should surely have put up a better fight.

From where I sat I could see most of the long path down to the road. No scarlet, orange or blue backpacks moved on it anywhere. Curse them, I thought; and damn them; and *shit*.

There was silence behind and above me and I had no sense of anyone being there. The inescapability of having to go up for a look was only a shade worse than actually making the effort; but I couldn't stay where I was for ever.

With reluctant muscles and a fearful mind I got laboriously to my feet and began the climb.

No evil faces grinned over the plateau above. My instinct that I was alone proved a true one, and I crawled the last bit on hands and knees and raised my head for a cautious look without anyone pouncing on me with a yell and kicking me back into space.

The reason for the silence and the absence of attackers was immediately obvious: my jeep had gone.

I stood erect on the plateau, figuratively groaning. Not only had I lost my transport, but the door of my home stood wide open with heaps of my belongings spilling out of it – a chair, clothes, books, bedclothes. I walked wearily across the plateau and looked in at a sickening mess.

Like all who live purposefully alone without provision for guests, my actual household goods were few. I tended to eat straight out of the frying pan, and to drink all liquids from a mug. Living without electricity, I owned none of the routinely stolen things like television, stereo or computer, nor did I have a mobile phone because of not being able to recharge the batteries. I did own a portable radio cassette for checking that interstellar war hadn't broken out, and for playing taped music if I felt like it, but it was no grand affair with resale value. I had no antique silver. No Chippendale chairs.

What I did have was paint.

When I'd moved into the tumbledown building five and a half years earlier I'd made only the centre and largest of its three divisions habitable. About fifteen feet by nine, my room had been given a businesslike new roof, a large double-glazed window, and a host of anti-damp preservation measures in its rebuilt walls and flooring. Light, heat and cooking were achieved with gas. Running water came from a small clear burn trickling through nearby rocks, and for a bathroom I had a weathered privy a short walk away. I'd meant at first to stay on the mountain only during the long northern summer days, but in the end had left my departure later and later that first year until suddenly the everlasting December nights were shortening again, and I'd stayed snug through a freezing January and February and had never since considered leaving.

Apart from a bed, a small table, a chest of drawers and one comfortable chair, the whole room was taken up by three easels, stacked canvases, a work stool, a wall of shelves and the equivalent of a kitchen table covered with pots and tubes of paints, and other essentials of my work like jugs of brushes and painting knives and jamjars full of clear or dirty water.

Lack of space and my own instincts dictated order and overall tidiness, but chiefly the disciplined organisation was the result of the very nature of the acrylics themselves: they dried so fast when exposed to air that lids *had* to be replaced, tubes had to be capped, only small quantities could be squeezed onto a palette at a time, brushes had to be constantly rinsed clean, knives wiped, hands washed. I kept large amounts of clean and dirty water in separate buckets under the table and used tissues by the jeep-load for keeping mess at bay.

Despite all care, I had few clothes free of paint stains and had to sand down the woodblock floor now and then to get rid of multicoloured sludge.

The mess the four demons had made of all this was spectacularly awful.

I had left work in progress on all three easels as I often painted three pictures simultaneously. All three were now face down on the floor, thoroughly saturated by the kicked-over buckets. My work table lay on its side, pots, brushes and paints spilling wide. Burst paint tubes had been squashed underfoot. My bed had been tipped over, chest of drawers ransacked, box files pulled down from the shelves, ditto books, every container emptied, sugar and coffee granules scattered in a filthy jumbled chaos.

Bastards.

I stood without energy in the doorway looking at the depressing damage and working out what to do. The clothes I was wearing were torn and dirty and I'd been bleeding from many small scrapes and scratches. The bothy had been robbed, as far as I could see, of everything I could have raised money on. Also my wallet had gone and my watch had gone. My chequebook had been in the jeep.

I had said I would go to London.

Well . . . so I bloody well *would.*

Mad Alexander. Might as well live up to the name.

Apart from moving back into the room the chair and other things that were half out of the doorway, I left the scene mostly as it was. I sorted out only the cleanest jeans, jersey and shirt from the things emptied out of the chest of drawers, and I changed into them out by the burn, rinsing off the dried trickles of blood in the cold clean water.

I ached deeply all over.

Bloody bastards.

I walked along to the privy, but there had been nothing to steal there, and they had left it alone. Of the two original but ruined flanks to my habitable room, one was now a carport with a grey camouflage-painted roof of corrugated iron, the other, still open to the skies, was where I kept the gas cylinders (in a sort of bunker) and also rubbish bins, now empty, as I had taken the filled black bags down to the post office for disposal that morning. Let into one tumbledown wall there were the remains of what might have been a fireplace with a small oven above. Perhaps the place had once been a kitchen or bakehouse, but I'd been happier with gas.

Nothing in these two side sections had been vandalised. Lucky, I suppose.

From the jumble on the main bothy floor I harvested a broken stick of charcoal and slid pieces of it into my shirt pocket, and I found a sketch-pad with some clean pages; and armed with such few essentials I left home and set off down the wandering path to the road.

The Monadhliath Mountains, rising sharply to between 2500 and 3000 feet, were rounded rather than acutely jagged, but were bare of trees and starkly, unforgivingly grey. The steep path led down to heather-clad valley slopes and finally to a few pine trees and patches of grass. The transition from my home to the road was always more than a matter of height above sea level: up in the wild taxing granite wilderness, life – to me at any rate – felt simple, complete and austere. I could work there with concentration. The clutching 'normal' life of the valley diminished my awareness of something elemental that I took from the palaeolithic silence and converted into paint: yet the canvases I sold for my bread and butter were usually full of colour and light-heartedness and were, in fact, mostly pictures of golf.

By the time I reached the road there was a hint in the quality of light of dusk hovering in the wings getting ready to draw together the skirts of evening. It was the time of day when I stopped painting. As it was then September, watch or no watch, I could pretty accurately guess at six thirty.

Even though it had been by-passed by the busy A9 artery from Inverness to Perth, there was enough traffic on the road for me to hitch a ride without much difficulty, but it was a shade disconcerting to find that the driver who stopped to pick up a long-haired jeans-clad young male stranger was an expectant-eyed forty-ish woman who put her hand caressingly on my knee half a mile into the ride.

Lamely I said, 'I only want to go to Dalwhinnie railway station.'

'Boring, aren't you, dear.'

'Ungrateful,' I agreed. And bruised, tired and laughing inside.

She took the hand away with a shrug. 'Where do you want to go?' she asked. 'I could take you to Perth.'

'Just Dalwhinnie.'

'Are you gay, dear?'

'Er,' I said. 'No.'

She gave me a sideways glance. 'Have you banged your face?'

'Mm,' I said.

She gave me up as a prospect and dumped me half a mile from the trains. I walked, ruefully thinking of the offer I'd declined. I'd been celibate too long. It had become a habit. Bloody feeble, all the same, to pass up a free lunch. My ribs hurt.

Lights were going on everywhere when I reached the station and I was glad of the minimum shelter of its bare ticket office, as the air temperature was dropping alarmingly towards night. Shivering and blowing on my fingers I made a telephone call, endlessly grateful that this instrument at least was in fine working order and not suffering from a clone of Donald Cameron.

A reverse charge call via the operator.

A familiar Scots voice spluttered at the far end, talking first to the operator, then to me. 'Yes, of course I'll pay for the call . . . Is that really you, Al? What the heck are you doing at Dalwhinnie?'

'Catching the night train to London. The Royal Highlander.'

'It doesn't go for hours.'

'No . . . What are you doing at this moment?'

'Getting ready to leave the office and drive home to Flora and a good dinner.'

'Jed . . .'

He heard more in my voice than just his name. He said sharply, 'Al? What's the matter?'

'I . . . um . . . I've been burgled,' I said. 'I'd . . . um . . . I'd be very glad of your help.'

After a short silence he said briefly, 'I'm on my way,' and the line went quiet.

Jed Parlane was my uncle's factor, the man who managed the Kinloch Scottish estates. Though he'd been in the job less than four years we had become the sort of friends that took goodwill from each other for granted. He would come. He was the only one I would have asked.

He was forty-six, a short stocky Lowland Scot from Jedburgh (hence his name), whose plain common sense had appealed to my uncle after the turmoil stirred up by an arrogant predecessor. Jed had calmed the resentful tenants and spent maintenance money oiling many metaphorical gates, so that the huge enterprise now ran at a peaceful profit. Jed, the wily Lowlander, understood and used the Highlander's stubborn pride; and I'd learned more from him about getting my own way than perhaps he realised.

He came striding into Dalwhinnie station after his twelve or more mile drive to reach me, and stood four-square in front of where I sat on a brown-painted bench against a margarine wall.

'You've hurt your face,' he announced. 'And you're cold.'

I stood up stiffly, the overall pain no doubt showing. I said, 'Does the heater work in your car?'

He nodded without speaking and I followed him outside to where he'd parked. I sat in his front passenger seat while he re-started the engine and twiddled knobs to bring out hot air, and I found myself unexpectedly shuddering from the physical relief.

'OK,' he said, switching on the car's internal light, 'so what's happened to your face? You're going to have a hell of a black eye. That left-hand side of your forehead and temple is all swollen . . .' He stopped, sounding uncertain. I was not, I guessed, my usual picture of glowing good health.

'I got head-butted,' I said. 'I got jumped on and bashed about and robbed, and don't laugh.'

'I'm not laughing.'

I told him about the four pseudo hill-walkers and the devastation in the bothy.

'The door isn't locked,' I said. 'They took my keys. So tomorrow maybe you'll take your own key along there – though there's nothing left worth stealing . . .'

'I'll take the police,' he said firmly, aghast.

I nodded vaguely.

Jed pulled a notebook and pen from inside his jacket and asked for a list of things missing.

'My jeep,' I said gloomily, and told him its number. 'Everything in it . . . food and stores, and so on. From the bothy they took my binoculars and camera and all my winter padded clothes and four finished paintings and climbing gear and some Glenlivet . . . and my golf clubs.'

'*Al!*'

'Well, look on the bright side. My bagpipes are in Inverness having new bits fitted, and I've sent my passport away for renewal.' I paused. 'They took all my cash and my credit card . . . I don't know its number, though it's somewhere on file in your office – will you alert them? – and they took my father's old gold watch. Anyway,' I finished, 'if you have a credit card with you, will you lend me a ticket to London?'

'I'll take you to a hospital.'

'No.'

'Then come home to Flora and me. We'll give you a bed.'

'No . . . but thanks.'

'Why *London*?'

'Ivan Westering had a heart attack.' I paused briefly, watching him assimilate the consequences. 'You know my mother . . . though I suppose you don't actually know her all that well . . . she would never ask me to help her but she didn't say *not* come, which was as good as an SOS . . . so I'm going.'

'The police will want you to give a statement.'

'The bothy is a statement.'

'Al, don't go.'

'Will you lend me the fare?'

He said, 'Yes, but—'

'Thanks, Jed.' I fished a piece of charcoal stick out of my shirt pocket and opened the sketch-pad I still carried. 'I'll draw them. It'll be better than just describing them.'

He watched me start and with a touch of awkwardness said, 'Were they looking for anything special?'

I glanced across at him with half a smile. 'One of them kept saying "Where is it?"'

Anxiously he said, 'Did you tell them?'

'Of course not.'

'If you'd told them, they might have stopped hitting you.'

'And they might have made sure I was dead, before they left.'

I drew the four men in a row, face on: knees, boots, glasses, air of threat.

'Anyway,' I said, 'they didn't *say* what they were looking for. They just said "Where is *it*?" so *it* might have been *anything*. They might have been fishing for anything I valued. For what I valued most, if you see what I mean?'

He nodded.

I went on, 'They didn't call me by name. They'll know it now, because it was all over things in the jeep.' I finished the composite sketch and turned to a clean page. 'Do you remember those hikers who preyed on holidaymakers last year in the Lake District? They robbed trailers, mobile homes.'

'The police caught them,' Jed agreed, nodding. 'But those hikers didn't *beat* people and throw them down mountains.'

'Might be the same sort of thing, though. I mean, just opportunist theft.'

I drew the head of the 'Where is it?' man, as I remembered him the most clearly. I drew him without glasses.

'This is their leader,' I explained, shading planes into the bony face. 'I'm not good at voices and accents, but I'd say his was sloppy south-east England. Same with them all.'

'Hard men?'

'They'd all done time in a boxing gym, I'd say. Short-arm jabs, like at a punch-bag.' I swallowed. 'Out of my league.'

'Al . . .'

'I felt an utter fool.'

'That's illogical. No one could fight four at once.'

'Fight? I couldn't even *connect.*' I broke off, remembering. 'I scratched one of their faces . . . He was the one who crashed his head against mine.' I turned to a fresh page in the sketch-pad and drew again, and his face came out with a clawed cheek, eyes glaring through round glasses and a viciousness that leaped off the paper.

'You'd know him again,' Jed said with awe.

'I'd know them all.'

I gave him the sketch-pad. He looked from drawing to drawing, troubled and kind.

'Come home with Flora and me,' he repeated. 'You look bad.'

I shook my head. 'I'll be all right by tomorrow.'

'The next day is always the worst.'

'You're a laugh a minute.'

After a while he sighed heavily, went into the station and returned with tickets.

'I got you a sleeper for tonight, and an open return for whenever you come back. Ten oh one from here, arrives at Euston at seven forty-three in the morning.'

'Thanks, Jed.'

He gave me cash from his pockets. 'Phone me tomorrow evening.'

I nodded.

He said, 'They've put the heater on in the waiting-room here.'

I shook his hand gratefully and waved him away home to his comfortable Flora.

CHAPTER TWO

Best to forget that night.

The face that looked back from an oblong of mirror as the train clattered over the points on the approach to Euston was, I realised, going to appeal to my mother's fastidious standards even less than usual. The black eye was developing inexorably, my chin bristled, and even I could see that a comb would be a good idea.

I righted what I could with the help of Jed's cash and a chemist's shop in the station but my Mama predictably eyed me up and down with a pursed mouth before dispensing a minimum hug on her doorstep.

'Really, Alexander,' she said. 'Haven't you *any* clothes free of paint?'

'Few.'

'You look thin. You look . . . well, you'd better come in.'

I followed her into the prim polished hallway of the architectural gem she and Ivan inhabited in the semicircle of Park Crescent, by Regent's Park.

As usual, she herself looked neat, pretty, feminine and disciplined, with short shining dark hair, and a hand-span waist, and as usual I wanted to tell her how much I loved her, but didn't, because she found such emotion excessive.

I'd grown tall, like my father, and had been taught by him from birth to look after the delicately boned sweet-natured centre of his devotion, to care for her and serve her and to consider it not a duty but a delight. I remembered a childhood of gusty laughter from him and small pleased smiles from her, and he'd lived long enough for me to sense their joint bewilderment that the boy they'd carefully furnished with a good education and Highland skills like shooting, fishing and stalking was showing alarming signs of non-conformity.

At sixteen, I'd said one day, 'Dad . . . I don't want to go to university.' (*Heresy*.) 'I want to paint.'

'A good hobby, Al,' he'd said, frowning. He'd praised for years the ease with which I could draw, but never taken it seriously. He never did, to the day he died.

'I'm just telling you, Dad.'

'Yes, Al.'

He hadn't minded my liking for being alone. In Britain the word 'loner' flew none of the danger signals it did over in the United States, where the desirability of being 'one of a team' was indoctrinated from pre-school. 'Loners' there, I'd discovered, were people who went off their heads. So maybe I was off mine, but anything else felt wrong.

'How's Ivan?' I asked my mother.

'Would you like coffee?' she said.

'Coffee, eggs, toast . . . anything.'

I followed her down to the basement-kitchen where I cooked and ate a breakfast that worked a change for the better.

'Ivan?' I said.

She looked away as if refusing to hear the question and asked instead, 'What's the matter with your eye?'

'I walked into . . . well, it doesn't matter. Tell me about Ivan.'

'I er . . .' She looked uncharacteristically uncertain. 'His doctors say he should slowly be resuming his normal activities . . .'

'But?' I said, as she stopped.

'But he won't.'

After a pause I said, 'Well, tell me.'

There was then this subtle thing between us: that shadowy moment when the generations shift and the child becomes the parent. And perhaps it was happening to us at an earlier age than in most families because of my long training in care of her, a training that had been in abeyance since she'd married Ivan, but which now resurfaced naturally and with redoubled force across her kitchen table.

I said, 'James James Morrison Morrison Weatherby George Dupree . . .'

She laughed, and went on, 'Took great care of his Mother, though he was only three.'

I nodded. 'James James said to his Mother, "Mother," he said, said he, "You must never go down to the end of the town if you don't go down with me."'

'Oh, *Alexander.*' A whole lifetime of restraint quivered in her voice, but the dammed up feelings didn't break.

'Just tell me,' I said.

A pause. Then she said, 'He's so *depressed.*'

'Er . . . *clinically* depressed?'

'I don't know what that means. But I don't know how to deal with it. He lies in bed most of the time. He won't get dressed. He hardly eats. I want him to go back into the Clinic but he won't do that either, he says he doesn't like it there, and Dr Robbiston doesn't seem to be able to prescribe anything that will pull him out of it.'

'Well . . . has he a good reason for being depressed? Is his heart in a bad state?'

'They said there wasn't any need for by-passes or a pacemaker. They used one of those balloon things on one of his arteries, that's all. And he has to take pills, of course.'

'Is he afraid he's going to die?'

My mother wrinkled her smooth forehead. 'He just tells me not to worry.'

'Shall I . . . um . . . go up and say hello?'

She glanced at the big kitchen clock, high on the wall above an enormous cooker. Five to nine.

'His nurse is with him now,' she said. 'A male nurse. He doesn't really *need* a nurse, but he won't let him go. Wilfred, the nurse – and I don't like him, he's too obsequious – he sleeps on our top floor here in those old attics, and Ivan has had an intercom installed so that he can call him if he has chest pains in the night.'

'And does he have chest pains in the night?'

My mother said with perplexity, 'I don't know. I don't think so. But he did, of course, when he had the attack. He woke up with it at four in the morning, but at the time he thought it was only bad indigestion.'

'Did he wake you?'

She shook her head. She and Ivan had always slept in adjoining but separate bedrooms. Not from absence of love; they simply preferred it.

She said, 'I went in to say good morning to him and give him the papers, as I always do, and he was sweating and pressing his chest with his fist.'

'You should have got a message to me at once,' I said. 'Jed would have driven over with it. You shouldn't have had to deal with all this by yourself.'

'Patsy came . . .'

Patsy was Ivan's daughter. Sly eyes. Her chief and obsessive concern was to prevent Ivan leaving his fortune and his brewery to my mother and not to herself. Ivan's assurances got nowhere: and Patsy's feelings for me, as my mother's potential heir, would have curdled sulphuric acid. I always smiled at her sweetly.

'What did Patsy do?' I asked.

'Ivan was in the Clinic when she came here. She used the telephone.' My mother stopped for effect.

'Who did she want?' I prompted helpfully.

Amusement glimmered in my mother's dark eyes. 'She telephoned Oliver Grantchester.'

Oliver Grantchester was Ivan's lawyer.

'How blatant was she?' I asked.

'Oh, straight to the jugular, darling.' Patsy called everyone darling. She would murder, I surmised, with a 'Sorry, darling' while she slid the stiletto into the heart. 'She told Oliver,' smiled my mother, 'that if Ivan tried to change his Will, she would contest it.'

'And she meant you to hear.'

'If she hadn't wanted me to, she could have called him from anywhere else. And naturally she was sugar-candy all over the Clinic. The loving daughter. She's good at it.'

'And she said there was no need for you to bring me all the way from Scotland while she was there to look after things.'

'Oh dear, you know how *positive* she is . . .'

'A tidal wave.'

Civility was a curse, I often thought. Patsy needed someone to be brusquely rude about the way she bullied everyone with saccharine; but if ever openly crossed she could produce so intense an expression of 'poor little me-dom' that potential critics found themselves comforting her instead. Patsy at thirty-four had a husband, three children, two dogs and a nanny all anxiously twitching to please her.

'And,' my mother said, 'there's some sort of serious trouble at the brewery, and also I think he's worried about the Cup.'

'What cup?'

'The King Alfred Cup, what else?'

I frowned. 'Do you mean the race?' The King Alfred Gold Cup, sponsored by Ivan's brewery as a great advertisement for King Alfred Gold beer, was a splendid two-mile steeplechase run every October, a regular part now of the racing year.

'The race, or the Cup itself,' my mother said. 'I'm not sure.'

At that inconclusive point the kitchen was abruptly invaded by two large middle-aged ladies who heavily plodded down the outside iron steps from road level to basement and let themselves in with familiarity.

'Morning, Lady Westering,' they said. A double act. Sisters, perhaps. They looked from my mother to me expectantly, awaiting an explanation, I thought, as much as an introduction. My gentle mother could be far too easily intimidated.

I stood and said mildly, 'I am Lady Westering's son. And you are?'

My mother told me, 'Edna and Lois. Edna cooks for us. Lois cleans.'

Edna and Lois gave me stares in which disapproval sheltered sketchily behind a need to keep their jobs. Disapproval? I wondered if Patsy had been at work.

Edna looked with a critical eye at the evidence of my cooking, an infringement of her domain. Too bad. She would have to get used to it. My father and I had historically always done the family meals because we'd liked it that way. It had started with my mother breaking a wrist: by the time it was mended, feeding the three of us had forever changed hands; and as I'd understood very early the chemistry of cooking, good food had always seemed easy.

My mother and Ivan had from the beginning employed a cook, though Edna – and also Lois – was new since my last visit.

I said to my mother, 'Wilfred notwithstanding, I'll go up now and see Ivan. I expect I'll find you upstairs in your sitting-room.'

Edna and Lois hovered visibly between allegiances. I gave them my most cheerful non-combative smile, and found my mother following me gratefully up the stairs to the main floor, quiet now but grandly formal with dining-room and drawing-room for entertaining.

'Don't tell me,' I teased her, once we were out of the kitchen's earshot, 'Patsy employed them.'

She didn't deny it. 'They're very efficient.'

'How long have they worked here?'

'A week.'

She came with me up to the next floor, where she and Ivan each had a bedroom, bathroom and personal day-room, in his case a study-cum-office, in hers the refuge they used most, a comfortable pink and green matter of fat armchairs and television.

'Lois cleans very well,' my mother sighed as we went in there, 'but she will *move* things. It's almost as if she moves them deliberately, just to prove to me that she's dusted.'

She shifted two vases back to their old familiar position of one at each end of the mantelshelf. Silver candlesticks were returned to flank the clock.

'Just tell her not to,' I said, but I knew she wouldn't. She didn't like to upset people: the opposite of Patsy.

I went along to see Ivan, who was sitting palely in his study while noises from his bedroom next door suggested bed-making and the tidying of bottles.

He wore a crimson woollen dressing-gown and brown leather slippers and showed no surprise at my presence.

'Vivienne said you were coming,' he said neutrally. Vivienne was Mother.

'How are you feeling?' I asked, sitting in a chair opposite him and realising with misgiving that he looked older, greyer and a good deal thinner than he had been on my last visit in the spring. Then, I'd been on my way to America with my mind full of the commercial part of my life. He had made, I now remembered, an unexpected invitation for my advice, and I had been too preoccupied, too impatient and too full of doubt of his sincerity to listen properly to what he'd wanted. It had been something to do with his horses, his steeplechasers in training at Lambourn, and I'd had other reasons than press of business to avoid going there.

I repeated my question, 'How are you feeling?'

He asked merely, 'Why don't you cut your hair?'

'I don't know.'

'Curls are girlish.'

He himself had the short-cut shape that went with the businessman personality: with the baronetcy and membership of the Jockey Club. I knew him to be fair-minded and well respected, a middling man who had inherited a modest title from a cousin and a large brewery from his father and had done his best by both.

It was a sadness with him that he had neither son nor any male relative: he was resigned to the baronetcy dying with him.

I'd often flippantly asked him, 'How's the beer, then?', but on that morning it seemed inappropriate. I said instead, 'Is there anything I can do for you?' and regretted it before the last words were out of my mouth. Not Lambourn, I thought. Anything else.

But 'Look after your mother,' was what he said first.

'Yes, of course.'

'I mean . . . after I've gone.' His voice was quiet and accepting.

'You're going to live.'

He surveyed me with the usual lack of enthusiasm and said dryly, 'You've had a word with God, have you?'

'Not yet.'

'You wouldn't be so bad, Alexander, if you would come down off your mountain and rejoin the human race.'

He had offered, when he'd married my mother, to take me into the brewery and teach me the business, and at eighteen, with chaotic visions of riotous colours intoxicating my inner eye, I'd learned the first great lesson of harmonious stepsonship, how to say no without giving offence.

I wasn't ungrateful and I didn't dislike him: we were just entirely different. As far as one could see, he and my mother were quietly happy together and there was nothing wrong with his care of her.

He said, 'Have you seen your uncle Robert during the last few days?'

'No.'

My uncle Robert was the earl – 'Himself'. He came to Scotland every year in late August and stayed north for the shooting and fishing and the Highland Games. He sent for me every year to visit him, but although I knew from Jed that he was now in residence, I hadn't so far been summoned.

Ivan pursed his lips. 'I thought he might have wanted to see you.'

'Any time soon, I expect.'

'I've asked him—' He broke off, then continued, 'he'll tell you himself.'

I felt no curiosity. Himself and Ivan had known each other for upwards of twenty years, drawn together by a fondness for owning racehorses. They still had their steeplechasers trained in the same yard in Lambourn.

Himself had approved of the match between Ivan and the widow of his much-loved youngest brother. He'd stood beside me at the wedding ceremony and told me to go to him if I ever needed help; and considering that he had five children of his own and half a clan of other nephews and nieces, I'd felt comforted in the loss of my father and in a deep way secure.

I had managed on my own, but I'd known that he was *there*.

I said to Ivan, 'Mother thinks you may be worried about the Cup.'

He hesitated over an answer, then asked, 'What about it?'

'She doesn't know if it's troubling you and making you feel worse.'

'Your dear mother!' he deeply sighed.

I said, 'Is there something wrong with this year's race? Not enough entries, or something?'

'Look after her.'

She'd been right, I thought, about his depression. A

malaise of the soul, outwardly discernible in weak movements of his hands and the lack of vigour in his voice. I didn't think there was much I could do to improve things, if his own doctor couldn't.

As if on cue a fifty-to-sixty, thin, moustached, busy-busy person hurried into the room in a dark flapping suit announcing that as he was passing on his way to the Clinic he had called in for five minutes to check on his patient. 'Morning, Ivan. How's things?'

'Good of you to come, Keith.'

Ivan drifting a limp hand in my direction, I stood up with parent-inculcated politeness and was identified as 'My stepson'.

Dr Keith Robbiston rose in my regard by giving me a sharp glance and a sharper question, 'What analgesic have you been taking for that eye?'

'Aspirin.' Euston station aspirin, actually.

'Huh.' Scorn. 'Are you allergic to any drugs?'

'I don't think so.'

'Are you taking any other drugs?'

'No.'

'Then try these.' He produced a small packet from an inner suit pocket and held it out to me. I accepted it with gratitude.

Ivan, mystified, asked what was going on.

His doctor briskly answered while at the same time producing from other pockets a stethoscope and blood-pressure monitor. 'Your stepson . . . name?'

'Alexander Kinloch,' I said.

'. . . Alexander, your stepson, can't move without pain.'

'What?'

'You haven't noticed? No, I suppose not.' To me he said, 'The reduction and management of pain is my speciality. It can't be disguised. How did you get like this? It can't be organic if you're not taking medicine. Car crash?'

I said with a flicker of amusement, 'Four thugs.'

'Really?' He had bright eyes, very alert. 'Bad luck.'

'What are you talking about?' Ivan said.

I shook my head at Dr Robbiston and he checked around his heart-threatened patient with effective economy of movement but no comment on my own state.

'Well done, Ivan,' he said cheerfully, whisking his aids out of sight. 'The ticker's banging away like a baby's. Don't strain yourself, though. But walk around the house a bit. Use this strong stepson as a crutch. How's your dear wife?'

'In her sitting-room,' I said.

'Great.' He departed as abruptly as he'd arrived. 'Hang in there, Ivan.'

He gave me a brief smile on his quick way out. I sat down again opposite Ivan and swallowed one of the tablets the doctor had given me. His assessment had been piercingly on target. Punch-bags led a rotten life.

'He's a good doctor, really,' Ivan told me defensively.

'The best,' I agreed. 'Why do you doubt him?'

'He's always in a hurry. Patsy wants me to change . . .' He tapered off indecisively; only a shadow seemed left of his former chief-executive decisiveness.

'Why change?' I asked. 'He wants you to be well, and he makes house calls, a miracle these days.'

Ivan frowned. 'Patsy says he's hasty.'

I said mildly, 'Not everyone thinks or moves at the same speed.'

Ivan took a tissue out of a flat box on the table beside him and blew his nose, then dropped the used tissue carefully into a handy waste-paper basket. Always neat, always precise.

He said, 'Where would you hide something?'

I blinked.

'Well?' Ivan prompted.

'Er . . . it would depend what it was.'

'Something of value.'

'How big?'

He didn't directly answer, but I found what he said next more unusual than anything he'd said to me since I'd known him.

'You have a quirky mind, Alexander. Tell me a safe hiding place.'

Safe.

'Um,' I said, 'who would be looking?'

'Everyone. After my death.'

'You're not dying.'

'Everyone dies.'

'It's essential to tell *someone* where you've hidden something, otherwise it may be lost for ever.'

Ivan smiled.

I said, 'Are we talking about your Will?'

'I'm not telling you what we are talking about. Not yet. Your uncle Robert says you know how to hide things.'

That put me into a state of breathlessness. How *could* they? Those two well-intentioned men must have said something to someone somewhere that had got me beaten to buggery and thrown over the next best thing to a cliff. Nephew of one, stepson of the other . . . I shifted in undeniable pain in that civilised room and acknowledged that for all their worldliness they had no true conception of the real voracious jungle of greed and cruelty roughly known as mankind.

'Ivan,' I said, 'put whatever it is in a bank vault and send a letter of instruction to your lawyers.'

He shook his head.

Don't give anything to me to hide, I thought. Please don't. Let me off. I'm not hiding anything else. Every battered muscle protested.

'Suppose it's a horse,' he said.

I stared.

He said, 'You can't put a horse in a bank vault.'

'What horse?'

He didn't say. He asked, 'How would you hide a horse?'

'A racehorse?' I asked.

'Certainly.'

'Then . . .' I paused a moment, 'in a racing stable.'

'Not in an obscure barn miles away from anywhere?'

'Definitely not. Horses have to be fed. Regular visits to an obscure barn would be as good as a sign saying "treasure here".'

'Do you believe in hiding things where everyone can see them but they don't realise what they're looking at?'

I said, 'The snag with that is that in the end someone *does* understand what they're looking at. *Someone* spots the rare stamp on the envelope. Someone spots the real pearls when the mistletoe berries wither.'

'But you would still put a racehorse among others?'

'And move it often,' I said.

'And the snag to that?'

'The snag,' I said obligingly, 'is that the horse can't be raced without disclosing its whereabouts. Unless, of course, you're a crook with a ringer, which would be unlike you, Ivan.'

'Thank you for that, Alexander.' His voice was dryly amused.

'And if you didn't race the horse,' I went on, 'you would waste its life and its value, until in the end it wouldn't be worth hiding.'

Ivan sighed. 'Any more snags?'

'Horses are as recognisable as people. They have faces.'

'And legs . . .'

After a pause I said, 'Do you want me to hide a horse?' and I thought, What the *hell* am I saying?

'Would you?'

'If you had a good reason.'

'For money?'

'Expenses.'

'Why?'

'Do you mean, why would I do it?' I asked.

He nodded.

I said feebly, 'For the interest,' but in fact it would be because it might lighten his depression to have something other than his illness to think about. I would do it because of my mother's anxiety.

He said, 'What if I asked you to *find* a horse?'

He was playing games, I thought.

'I suppose I would look for it,' I said.

The telephone on the table by his elbow rang but he merely stared at it apathetically and made no attempt to pick up the receiver. He simply waited until it stopped ringing and then showed exasperated fatigue when my mother appeared in the doorway to tell him that someone to do with the brewery wanted him.

'I'm ill. I've told them not to bother me.'

'It's Tobias Tollright, dear. He says it's essential he talks to you.'

'No, no.'

'Please, Ivan. He sounds so worried.'

'I don't want to talk to him,' Ivan said tiredly. 'Let Alexander talk to him.'

Both my mother and I thought the suggestion pointless, but once he got the idea in his head Ivan wouldn't be budged. In the end I walked over and picked up the phone and explained who I was.

'But I *must* speak to Sir Ivan himself,' said an agitated voice. 'You simply don't understand.'

'No,' I agreed, 'but if you'll tell me what's the matter, I'll relay it to him for an answer.'

'It's ridiculous.'

'Yes, but um . . . fire away.'

'Do you know who I am?' the voice demanded.

'No, I'm afraid not.'

'I am Tobias Tollright, a partner in a firm of chartered accountants. We audit the King Alfred Brewery accounts.'

'Right,' I said.

'There are discrepancies . . . Really, Sir Ivan is Chairman and managing director and majority shareholder . . . it is *unethical* for me to speak to you instead of him.'

'Mm,' I said, 'I do see that. Perhaps you'd better write to him.'

'The matter is too urgent. Remind him it is illegal for a limited company to go on trading when it is insolvent, and I fear . . . I really fear that measures must be taken at once, and only he can authorise them.'

'Well, Mr Tollright, er . . . hold on, while I explain.'

'What is it?' my mother asked anxiously. Ivan didn't ask but looked deeply exhausted.

He knew.

I said to him, 'There are things that only you can sign.'

Ivan shook his head.

I went back to Tollright, 'Can any of your urgent measures save the day?'

'I have to discuss it with Sir Ivan. But perhaps, yes.'

'What if he gives me power of attorney to act for him in this matter? Would that do the trick?'

He hesitated. It might be a legal move, but he didn't like it.

I said, 'Sir Ivan is still at an early stage of convalescence.'

I couldn't say in front of Ivan that too much worry might kill him, but it seemed as if Tobias's mental cogs abruptly engaged in a higher gear. How soon, he wanted to know without any more protest, could he expect to see me.

'Tomorrow?' I suggested.

'This afternoon,' he contradicted positively. 'Come to our main offices in Reading.' He told me the address. 'This matter is very urgent.'

'Ultra?'

He cleared his throat and repeated the word as if he'd never used it before. 'Well . . . yes . . . ultra.'

'Just hold on, would you?' I lowered the receiver

and spoke to my unwilling stepfather. 'I can sign things if you give me the authority. Is that what you really want? I mean, you'll have to trust me a lot.'

He said wearily, 'I do trust you.'

'But this is . . . well, *extreme* trust.'

He simply flapped his hand.

I said into the phone, 'Mr Tollright, I'll see you as soon as I can.'

'Good.'

I put down the receiver and told Ivan that such trust was unwise.

He smiled faintly. 'Your uncle Robert said I could trust you with my life.'

'You just more or less did.' I did a double-take. '*When* did he say that?'

'A few days ago. He'll tell you about it.'

And *who else* had they told? Alexander can hide things . . . *Shit.*

'Ivan,' I said, 'It's more solid if a power of attorney is signed and witnessed in front of a lawyer.'

'Phone Oliver Grantchester. I'll talk to him.'

He was vague, however, with his lawyer, telling him only that he wanted to draw up a power of attorney, but not saying what for. Extremely urgent, though, he emphasised; and, as he still felt wretchedly ill, would Oliver please come to his house so that everything could be completed at once.

Oliver Grantchester, it seemed, easily agreed to instant action, but Ivan's gloom nevertheless intensified. How on earth, I wondered, but didn't ask, had a brewery as well known as King Alfred's tied itself in financial knots?

Standing close outside Wantage, the ancient town of the great king's birth, King Alfred's Brewery supplied most of southern England and half of the Midlands with King Alfred's Gold (a fine light brew) and King Alfred's Bronze (a brew more bitter) which flowed by the frothy lakeful down grateful throats.

Ivan had shown me round his brewery. I'd seen the Kingdom and the Crown that I'd declined. He had offered them again and yet again, and he couldn't understand why I went back to the mountains every time.

The phone call done, Ivan seemed grateful when a thin man in a short white cotton jacket came in from the next-door bedroom and told him respectfully that everything was clean and tidy for the day. The obsequious Wilfred, I presumed.

Out in the hallway a vacuum cleaner began whining. At the noise Ivan's fragile tolerance looked on the absolute brink of disintegration. Wilfred went out into the hallway. The vacuuming stopped but an aggrieved female voice could be heard saying, 'It's all very well, but I've got my job to do, you know.'

'Oh dear,' my mother said, and went to pour oil.

'I can't stand it all,' Ivan said.

He stood up, swaying unsteadily and knocking the box of tissues from the table to the floor. I picked up the box, noticing it had numbers written on its underside, one a series that I recognised as Himself's phone number in Scotland.

Seeing me looking at it, Ivan said, 'There's a pencil by the phone but that new cleaner keeps moving my notepad over onto the desk. It drives me mad. So I use the tissue-box instead.'

'Why don't you tell her?'

'Yes, I suppose I should.'

I offered him my arm for balance, which he accepted.

'Think I'll just rest until Oliver comes,' he said, and I went with him through to his wide bed, where he lay down on the covers in his dressing-gown and slippers and closed his eyes.

I went back into his study and eased down into the chair I'd occupied before. Dr Robbiston's tablet had at least diminished the persistently acute stabs of muscular pain to an overall ache. I could no longer feel anything but a general soreness round my left eye. Think of something else, I told myself. Think of how to hide a bankruptcy . . .

I was a *painter*, dammit. Not a fixer. Not a universal rock. I should cultivate an ability to say no.

My mother came back. The vacuum remained silent. She perched in Ivan's chair and said, 'You see? You see?'

I nodded. 'I see a man who loves you.'

'That's not . . .'

'That's what's the matter. He knows his brewery is in trouble, is maybe on the edge. The brewery is the base of his life. It may be that the brewery's troubles brought on his heart attack in the first place. He may feel a loss of prestige. He may think he's failed you. He can't bear that.' I paused. 'He told me to look after you.'

She stared at me. 'But,' she said, 'I would live with him in poverty, and comfort him.'

'I think you need to tell him.'

'But—'

'I know you find it hard to put feelings into words, but I think you should do it now.'

'Perhaps . . .'

'No,' I said, 'I mean *now*. This minute. He talks about dying as if it would be a haven. He's told me twice to look after you. I will, but if that's not what you want, go and put your arms round him. I think he's ashamed because of the brewery. He's a good man – he needs saving.'

'I don't . . .'

'Go and love him,' I said.

She gave me a wild look and walked into Ivan's bedroom as if not sure of her footing.

I sat in a sort of hiatus, waiting for the next buffet of fate and wishing that all I had to decide that day was whether to pick Hooker's green or emerald for the colour of the grass of the eighteenth hole at Pebble Beach. Golf was peaceful and well mannered and tested one's honesty to disintegration. I painted the passions of golf as much as its physical scenery, and I'd learned it was the raw emotion, the conflict within the self, that sold the pictures. If I painted pretty scenery without feeling moral tension in my own mind, it quite likely wouldn't sell. It was golfers who bought my work, and they bought it for its core of struggle.

The four completed paintings stolen from the bothy had all been views of play on the great courses at Pebble Beach, California, and represented not only time spent and future income, but also an ingredient of anguish that I couldn't quantify or explain. Along with the canvas and the paint, the demon hikers had taken psychic energy, and although I could produce other and similar work again and again, never exactly *those* brushstrokes, *those* slanting shadows, *those* understandings of the flow of determination in the seconds before the striking of the ball.

The comparative peace of half an hour came to an end with the arrival of Oliver Grantchester who brought with him a frail-looking young woman hung around with computer, printer and bag of office necessities.

Oliver Grantchester and I had met about twice over the years, neither of us showing regret that it hadn't been oftener. My presence in Ivan's study was stiffeningly unwelcome to him, raising not a smile but a scowl.

He said not 'Good morning' but, 'I thought you were in Scotland.'

Ivan and my mother, hearing his voice, came through from the bedroom and gave him the friendly welcome he hadn't got from me.

'Oliver!' my mother exclaimed, offering her cheek for a routine kiss. 'So good of you to come.'

'Yes, good of you,' Ivan echoed pianissimo, taking his customary chair.

'Any time, Ivan,' Oliver Grantchester said heavily. 'You know that.'

The lawyer's large grey-suited body and authoritative voice somehow took up a lot of room and made the study seem smaller. Perhaps fifty, he had a bald crown surrounded by greying dark hair and a large fleshy mouth with chins to match. I wouldn't have been able to make him look out of a portrait as a friendly, warm-eyed philanthropist, but that could have been because I, Alexander, prompted no smile in *him*.

He introduced his assistant dismissively as 'Miranda', and it was my mother who settled her helpfully at Ivan's desk against one wall, and made space for her to set out her portable machines.

Grantchester said to Ivan, 'You want to draw up a power of attorney? Very wise of you, if I may say so, in view of your health. I brought with me a basic document. You have that ready, Miranda?' Miranda meekly nodded. Grantchester went on, 'It's a pity more people aren't as thoughtful as you, my old friend. Life must go on. A temporary power of attorney will smooth things over nicely until you're back to your old self again.'

Ivan meekly agreed.

'So who is to act for you?' Grantchester asked. 'You know I would be honoured to help you in any way I can. However, you might prefer to have Patsy. Yes, your daughter will be eminently suitable. I expect you've already discussed it with her.' He looked round the room as if expecting her to materialise. 'Patsy it is, then.' To Miranda he said in explanation, 'Draw up the document, naming Mrs Patsy Benchmark, Sir Ivan's daughter.'

Ivan cleared his throat and said to her, 'No. Not Mrs Benchmark. I'm giving the power of attorney to my stepson, here. Write Alexander Kinloch.'

Oliver Grantchester's mouth opened wide, but no sound came out. He looked utterly astounded and also angry.

'Alexander Robert Kinloch,' Ivan repeated to Miranda, and spelled out my last name letter by letter so that there should be no mistake.

The lawyer, finally finding his voice, said, 'You *can't*.'

'Why not?' Ivan asked.

'But he's . . . he's . . . *look* at him.'

'He has long hair,' Ivan agreed. 'I wish he would cut it. All the same—'

'But your *daughter*,' Grantchester protested, 'what will she say?'

What Patsy would say raised anxious lines on Ivan's forehead. He gave me a long look of doubt, and I looked back with calm, allowing the decision to be his alone. If Patsy got her busy fingers on his affairs, I thought, he would never get them back.

Ivan looked at my mother. 'Vivienne, what do you think?'

She clearly felt, as I did, that he would have to make up his own mind. She said, 'The choice is yours, my dear. Your judgment is best.'

Ivan said to me, 'Alexander?'

'Whatever you want.'

'I advise Mrs Benchmark,' Oliver Grantchester said firmly. 'She's the natural person. She's your heir.'

Ivan dithered. The post-heart-attack Ivan dithered where once he would have dominated. The brewery's predicament had knocked his certainties to pulp.

'Alexander,' he said finally, 'I want *you*.'

I nodded, giving him a tacit promise.

'Alexander,' he said to Grantchester. 'I'll give the power of attorney to *him*.'

'You could have both of them,' his lawyer said, desperately. 'You could have both of them, acting jointly.'

Even he could see, though, that such a path would lead to chaos.

'Only Alexander,' Ivan said.

His lawyer wouldn't accept it without a struggle. I listened to him trying to persuade Ivan with heavy legal arguments to change his decision, and I thought frivolously that, never mind my stepfather, it was Oliver himself who didn't want to have to deal with Patsy raging.

Ivan, true at least to part of his nature, wouldn't be budged. Miranda typed my name on the document and Grantchester told me crossly to sign it, which I did. Ivan, of course, signed it also.

'Make certified copies,' Ivan said. 'Make ten.'

With irritation, the lawyer waved at Miranda who made ten copies on a portable fax machine. Grantchester himself signed them all, thereby, I gathered, certifying that the power of attorney had been properly drawn.

'Also,' Ivan said tiredly, 'I will write a letter to the brewery's Company Secretary making Alexander my Alternate Director, which will give him authority to act on my behalf in all business decisions at the brewery, not just my personal affairs, that are covered by the power of attorney.'

'You can't!' Grantchester said explosively. 'He knows nothing at all about business.'

Ivan looked at me calmly. 'I think he does,' he said.

'But he's . . . he's an *artist*.' Grantchester filled the word with an opinion near contempt.

Ivan said obstinately, 'Alexander will be my Alternate Director. I'll write the letter at once.'

The lawyer scowled. 'No good will come of it,' he said.

CHAPTER THREE

My mother gave me her National Westminster Bank card for getting cash from machines and told me her secret number: a very extreme manifestation of trust.

I used the card and then bought a train ticket to Reading although I didn't, as she'd begged, acquire some 'decent' clothes before arriving at the offices of Pierce, Tollright and Simmonds.

I took with me from Ivan's study a folder containing the power of attorney, the certified copies, and a copy of Ivan's handwritten letter appointing me his Alternate Director.

Tobias Tollright looked me up and down, inspected the power of attorney and Ivan's letter and telephoned my mother.

'This person who says he's your son,' he asked her, 'would you please describe him.'

He had his office phone switched to conference, so I could hear her resigned reply.

'He's about six feet tall. Thin. He has chestnut hair,

wavy, curling onto his shoulders. And, oh yes, he has a black eye.'

Tobias thanked her and disconnected, his enthusiasm for my appearance still bumping along at zero in a way that I was used to from men in suits.

'What is wrong,' I asked, plunging in, 'at the brewery?'

Once he'd come to terms with the way I looked, he proved both astute and helpful. In my turn I ignored his fussy little mannerism of digging round his teeth with a succession of wooden picks and making sucking noises, and concentrated on understanding the mumbled nasal voice that by-passed the cleaning. He was barely ten years older than myself, I reckoned. Not enough age gap, anyway for him to pull much advantage of seniority. After the first ten minutes we got on fine.

His office was a boring functional box with a view of railway lines from a stark window, and strip lighting overhead that developed bags under the youngest eyes. Interesting to paint (a thin glaze of ultramarine perhaps, over yellow ochre) but terrible to live with.

'Basically,' he said, 'the man in charge of the brewery's finances has milked the cow and done a bunk to Brazil or some such haven with no extradition treaties. The brewery cannot in consequence meet its obligations. The creditors are restive, to put it mildly, and as auditor I cannot at the moment give King Alfred an OK to continue trading.'

More than enough, I thought, to give Ivan a heart attack.

I asked, 'How much is missing?'

He smiled. 'How big is a fog?'

'You mean, you don't know?'

'Our embezzler was the *Finance Director*. He worked the three-card trick. Find the queen . . . but she's gone to a nice anonymous bank account for ever and all you have left is debts.'

I frowned. 'You're not being awfully precise.'

'I warned Sir Ivan last year that I thought he had an open drain somewhere, but he didn't want to believe it. Now he's so ill, he still won't face it. I'm sorry to say it, but there it is. And he would rather cover up the theft, if he can, than admit to the world that he – and his whole board of directors – has been careless and even stupid.'

'And he's not the first down that road.'

'Far, far from it.'

'So, what are your life-belt measures?'

He hesitated, picking away at the teeth. 'I can *advise* you,' he said, 'but I cannot act for you. As an auditor I must keep a certain distance from my clients' affairs. In effect, I can only point out a course of action you might wish to take.'

'Then please point.'

He fiddled some more with his mouth and I felt sore and in need of sleep and not scintillatingly bright.

'I would suggest,' he said carefully, 'that you might call in an insolvency practitioner.'

'A who?'

'Insolvency practitioner. Someone to negotiate for you.'

'I didn't know such people existed.'

'Lucky you.'

'Where do I find one?' I asked blankly.

'I'll give you a name. I can do that at least.'

'And,' I asked gratefully, 'what will he do?'

'She.'

'Oh, well, what will she do?'

'If she thinks the brewery can be saved – and to do that she will have to make her own independent assessment of the position – if she thinks there's still life in the corpse she'll set up a CVA.'

He looked at my face. 'A CVA,' he explained patiently, 'is a company voluntary arrangement. In other words, she will try to call together a meeting of creditors. She'll explain to them the scope of the losses, and if she can persuade them that the brewery can go back to trading at a profit, they will together work out a rate at which the debts can be paid off bit by bit. Creditors will always do that if possible, because if they force a firm into total liquidation, they don't get paid much at all.'

'That,' I said, 'I understand.'

'Then,' Tobias went on, 'if the committee, acting

with the brewery, can produce to me a budget and a forecast that will satisfy me as auditor that the brewery has a viable future, then I can sign the audited accounts, and it can continue to trade.'

'Well . . .' I thought for a bit, then said, 'What are the chances?'

'Fairly reasonable.'

'No higher?'

'It depends on the creditors.'

'And . . . er . . . who are they?'

'The usual. The bank. The Inland Revenue. The pension fund. The suppliers.'

'The bank?'

'The Finance Director organised a line of credit for expansion. The money's gone. There's no expansion and nothing in the bank to service the loan. To pay the interest, that is to say. The bank has given notice that they will not honour any more cheques.'

'And the tax people?'

'The brewery hasn't paid its employees' national insurance contributions for six months. The money's vanished. As for the pension fund, it's evaporated. The suppliers, in comparison, are small beer – if you'll excuse the dreadful pun – but the can suppliers are berserk.'

'What a mess,' I said. 'Aren't there any . . . er . . . *assets*?'

'Sure. The brewery itself. But there's an outstanding

loan on that too, and nothing left to service it with. The bank would foreclose at a loss.'

'What about the pubs the brewery owns?' I asked.

'The tied houses? The Finance Director mortgaged the lot. To put it briefly, that money's gone too.'

'It sounds *hopeless*.'

'I've known worse.'

'And what about the King Alfred Cup?'

'Ah.' He concentrated on his teeth. 'You might ask Sir Ivan where it is.'

'At Cheltenham,' I said, puzzled. 'They run it at Cheltenham a month on Saturday.'

'Ah,' he said again, 'you're talking about the *race*.'

'Yes. What else?'

'The Cup itself,' he said earnestly. 'The King Alfred Gold Cup. The chalice. Medieval, I believe.'

I rubbed a hand over my face. Bruises were catching up.

'It's extremely valuable,' Tobias said. 'Sir Ivan should really consider selling it to offset some of the debt. But there is some doubt as to whether it belongs to the brewery or to Sir Ivan personally and . . . I say,' he broke off, 'are you feeling all right?'

'Yes.'

'You don't look it. Would you like some coffee?'

'Very much.'

He bustled about, organising what turned out to be tea.

I took another of Keith Robbiston's pills and slowly stopped sweating. The tea was fine. I smiled feebly to allay Tobias's kind concern and explained I'd travelled all night on the train, which seemed to him reason enough for faintness in the afternoon, even without the rainbowed eye.

'Actually,' I said, getting a better grip on things, 'I was wondering about the race itself, not the trophy. The race is part of the brewery's prestige. A sign of its success. Would . . . er . . . would the creditors agree to go ahead on the basis of keeping up public confidence in the brewery, even though the prize money will have to be found, and also the money for an entertaining tent and lunch and drinks for maybe a hundred guests? It's the brewery's best advertisement, that race. Cancelling it now, at this late stage, when the entries are already in, would send a massive message to all and sundry that the company's in a shaky state . . . and there's nothing like an ill wind for blowing a dicky house to rubble.'

He gazed at me. 'You'll need to say all that to the committee.'

'She . . . your insolvency angel, couldn't she say it?'

His gaze wandered over my hair and down to my paint-marked jeans, and I could see him thinking that the race had a better chance of survival with a more conventional advocate.

'You'll need to convince her.' He smiled briefly. 'You've convinced *me*.' He paused. 'Incidentally, among the brewery's possible assets there is a *race-horse*. That's to say, it's unclear again whether it belongs to the brewery or to Sir Ivan himself. I'd be glad if you could clarify it.'

'I?'

'You are in total charge. Your comprehensive powers of attorney make that unquestionably clear.'

'Oh.'

'Sir Ivan must have absolute faith in you.'

'In spite of how I look?'

'Well . . .' He gave me suddenly a broad grin. 'Since you mention it, yes.'

'I'm a painter,' I explained, 'and I look like one. You don't find droves of painters in pinstripes.'

'I suppose not.'

I drank a second cup of tea and asked idly, 'What is the name of the horse?'

'How do you hide a horse, Alexander . . .?'

Hide a horse. Ye gods.

'It's called Golden Malt,' Tobias said.

Yesterday morning, I thought morosely, I was leading the peaceful if eccentric life of a chronicler of the equally eccentric compulsion to hit a small white ball a furlong or two and tap it over lovingly landscaped grass until it dropped into a small round hole. Yesterday morning's sensible madness now lay the other side of a violent robbery, an aching body, an edge-of-the-grave stepfather, his ordeal by domesticity and his shift onto my shoulders of ever-expanding troubles.

Ivan, I saw, wanted me to keep his horse hidden away from the clutches of bankruptcy. Ivan had given me the legal right to commit an illegal act.

'What are you thinking?' Tobias asked.

'Um ... um ... How is the brewery going to pay its workers this week?'

He sighed. 'You do have a way of cutting down to the essentials.'

'Will the bank cough up?'

'They say not. Not a penny more.'

'Do I have to go to them on my knees?'

He said with compassion, 'Yes.'

It was by then Wednesday afternoon. Payroll day at the brewery, as in most business enterprises, was Friday. On the Tollright telephone I engaged the professional services of the lady negotiator and also made an appointment with the bank for the following morning.

I asked Tobias how much was needed to keep the ship afloat until the creditors could set up the rescue operation – if they would – and he obligingly referred to King Alfred's ledgers and told me a sum that made Ivan's heart attack seem a reasonable response to the information.

'You can only do your best,' Tobias observed, busy with a toothpick. 'None of this is your fault. It appears you've just been dumped into it up to the hilt.'

I didn't know whether to wince or smile at the familiar phrase. Up to the hilt – in one particular way

I'd been in jeopardy up to the hilt for the last five years. It had taken five years for the demons to arrive at my door.

I said, 'About that horse – Golden Malt, did you say? – why is there a doubt about who owns it?'

Tobias frowned. 'You'll have to ask Sir Ivan. The horse isn't listed as an actual asset of the brewery. There's been no annual claim for depreciation, as if it were office equipment, but the brewery has paid the training fees and claimed them against tax as an advertising expense. As I said, you'll need to sort it out.'

For the next hour he tracked with me through the past year's accounts, item by item. I could see, as he demonstrated, that but for the perfidy of the man in charge of the cash flow, the beer business would have fermented its yeast to its usual profitable heights.

'The head brewer's the best asset,' Tobias said. 'Don't lose him.'

I said helplessly, 'I know nothing about brewing beer.'

'You don't have to. You are the overall strategist. I'm simply advising you as an outsider, and I can tell you the brewery's share of the market has risen perceptibly since they appointed this particular brewmaster.'

'Thank you.'

'You do look exhausted,' he said.

'I was never that good at maths.'

'You're doing all right.'

He produced papers for me to sign. I read them and did my best to understand, but trusted a lot to his good faith. As Ivan had trusted his Finance Director, no doubt.

'Good luck with the bank tomorrow,' Tobias said, shuffling the papers together and sucking his toothpick. 'Don't let them mug you.'

They wouldn't be the first, I thought. 'Will you come with me?'

He shook his head. 'It's your job, not mine. I wish you good luck.'

I said, 'There's one other thing . . .'

'Yes?'

'How do I get from here to Lambourn nowadays, without a car?'

'Taxi.'

'And without much money.'

'Ah,' he said. 'Same as ever. Bus to Newbury. Bus from there to Lambourn.' He summoned a timetable from reception. 'Bus from Newbury to Lambourn leaves at five forty-five.'

'Thanks.'

'What you need,' he said, 'is the out-patients department of the Royal Berkshire Hospital.'

I caught the bus instead. I even had time at Newbury to spend some of my mother's cash on a new pair of jeans and to discard the old paint-stained denims in the bus station's gents. In fractionally more respectable mode, therefore, I arrived on a Lambourn doorstep that I would have been happier to avoid.

My stepfather's horses – and that included Golden Malt – and also my uncle Robert 'Himself's' horses, were trained at the racing town of Lambourn by a young woman, Emily Jane Cox.

She said at the sight of me, 'What the hell are you doing here?'

'Slumming.'

'I hate you, Alexander.'

The problem was that she didn't, any more than what I felt for her could at worst be described as lust, and at best as unrealistic Round Table chivalry. Worse than hate or love, we had come near to apathy.

I had walked, feet metaphorically dragging, from the bus stop to the stable on Upper Lambourn Road. I had arrived as she was completing her evening rounds of the stable, checking on the welfare of each of the fifty or so horses entrusted to her care.

It was true, as jealous detractors pointed out, that she had inherited the yard as a going concern from a famous father, but it was her own skill that continued to turn out winners trained by Cox.

She loved the life. She loved the horses. She was respected and successful. She might once also have loved Alexander Kinloch, but she was not going to dump a busy and fulfilled career for solitude on a bare cold mountain.

'If you love me,' she'd said, 'live in Lambourn.'

I'd lived with her in Lambourn for nearly six months, once, and I'd painted nothing worth looking at.

'It doesn't matter,' she'd consoled me early on. 'Marry me and be content.'

I had married her and after a while left her. She'd never used my name, but had become simply Mrs Cox.

'What are you doing here?' she repeated.

'Er . . . Ivan has had a heart attack.'

She frowned. 'Yes, I read about it in the papers. But he's all right, isn't he? I telephoned. Your mother said not to worry.'

'He's not well. He asked me to look after his horses.'

'You? Look after them? You don't know all that much about horses.'

'He just said . . .'

She shrugged. 'Oh, all right then. You may as well set his mind at rest.'

She turned away from me and walked back across her stable yard to an open door where a lad was positioning a bucket of water.

She had dark hair cut like a cap and the sort of figure that looked good in trousers. We were the same age almost to the day, and at twenty-three had married without doubts.

She'd always had a brisk authoritative way of talking that now had intensified with the years of responsibility and success. I had admired – loved – her positive energy, but it had drained my own. Even if I'd still loved her physically, I couldn't have forever bowed to her natural habit of command. We would have quarrelled if I'd stayed. We would have fought if I'd ever tried to return. We existed in a perpetual uncontested truce. We had met four times since I'd left, but never alone and never in Lambourn.

Ivan had three horses in training in Emily's yard. She showed me two unremarkable bays and one bright chestnut, Golden Malt. Somewhat to my dismay he had noticeably good looks, two white socks and a bright white blaze down his nose: great presence as an advertisement for a brewery, not such a good idea for disappearing without trace.

'He's entered for the King Alfred Gold Cup,' Emily said with pride, patting the horse's glossy neck. 'Ivan wants to win his own race.'

'And will he?'

'Win?' She pursed her lips. 'Let's say Golden Malt's running for the news value. He won't disgrace himself, can't put it higher than that.'

I said absently, 'I'm sure he'll do fine.'

'What's the matter with your eye?'

'I got mugged.'

She nearly laughed, but not quite. 'Do you want a drink?'

'Good idea.'

I followed her into her house, where she led the way through the much lived-in kitchen, past her efficient office and into the larger sitting-room where she entertained visiting owners and, it seemed, revenant husbands.

'Still Campari?' she enquired, hands hovering over a tray of bottles and glasses.

'Anything.'

'I'll get some ice.'

'Don't bother,' I said, but she went all the same to the kitchen.

I walked across the unchanged room with its checked wool sofas and dark oak side tables and stood before a painting she'd hung on the wall. It showed a view of windswept links with a silver slit of sea in the background; with grey scudding clouds and two golfers doggedly leaning face-against the gale, trudging and pulling their golf clubs behind them on trolleys. In the foreground, where long dry grass bent away from the wind, there lay a small white ball, invisible still to the players.

I'd sent the painting as a sort of peace offering: it was one of the first I'd painted in the bothy after I'd left, and seeing it again brought sharply back not just the feel of the paint going onto the canvas but also all the guilt and joyous sense of freedom of that time.

Emily said behind me, 'One of my owners brought a friend with him a few weeks ago who spotted that painting from across the room and said, "I say, is that an Alexander?"'

I turned. She was carrying two tumblers with ice in

and looking at the picture. 'You'd signed it just Alexander,' she said.

I nodded. 'I always do, as you know.'

'Nothing else?'

'Alexander's long enough.'

'Anyway, he recognised it. I was very surprised, but he turned out to be some sort of art critic. He'd seen quite a lot of your work.'

'What was his name?'

She shrugged. 'Can't remember. I said you always painted golf, and he said no you didn't, you painted the perseverance of the human spirit.'

God, I thought, and I asked again, 'What was his name?'

'I told you, I can't remember. I didn't know I was going to see you so soon, did I?' She walked over to the bottles and poured Campari and soda onto ice. 'He also said you might be going to be a great painter one day. He said you had both the technique and the courage. The courage, I ask you! I said what courage did it take to paint golf and he said it took courage to succeed at *anything*. Like training horses, he said.'

'I wish you could remember his name.'

'Well, I can't. He was a round little man. I told him I knew you and he went on a bit about how you'd got those tiny red flecks into the stems of the dry grass in the foreground.'

'Did he tell you how?'

'No.' She wrinkled her forehead. 'I think the owner asked me about his horse.'

She poured gin and tonic for herself, sat down and waved me to a sofa. It felt extraordinarily odd to be a guest where once I'd been host. The house had always been hers, as it had been her father's, but it had felt like my home when I'd lived there.

'That art man,' Emily said after a large swallow of gin, 'also said that your paintings were too attractive at present to be taken seriously.'

I smiled.

'Don't you mind?' she asked.

'No. Ugly is *in*. Ugly is considered *real*.'

'But I don't want ugly paintings on my walls.'

'Well . . . in the art world I'm sneered at because my paintings sell. I can do portraits, I accept commissions, I can draw – all unforgivable.'

'You don't seem bothered.'

'I paint what I like. I earn my bread. I'll never be Rembrandt. I settle for what I can do, and if that is to give pleasure, well, it's better than nothing.'

'You never said anything like that when you were here.'

'Too much emotion got in the way.'

'Actually,' she rose to her feet and crossed back to the picture, 'since that Sunday morning I've been looking at the grass. So how did you get those tiny red flecks on the stalks? And the brown flecks and the yellow flecks, come to that.'

'You'd be bored.'

'No, actually, I wouldn't.'

Campari tasted sweet and bitter, a lot like life. I said, 'Well, first I painted the whole canvas bright red.'

'Don't be silly.'

'I did,' I assured her. 'Bright solid cadmium red, all over.' I rose and walked over to join her. 'You can still see horizontal faint streaks of red in the silver of the sea. There's even some red in the grey of the clouds. Red in those two figures. All the rest is overpainted with the colours you can see now. That's the chief beauty of acrylic paint. It dries so fast you can paint layer on layer without having to wait days, like with oils. If you try to overpaint oils too soon the layers can mix and go muddy. Anyway, that grass . . . I overpainted that once with raw umber, which is a dark yellowish brown, and on top of that I put mixtures of yellow ochre, and then I scratched through all the layers with a piece of metal comb.'

'With *what*?'

'A comb. I scratched the metal teeth through the layers right down to the red. The scratches lean as if with the wind . . . they are the stalks. The scratches show red flecks and brown flecks from the layers. And then I laid a very thin transparent glaze of purple over parts of the yellow, which is what gives it all that ripple effect that you get in long grass in a strong wind.'

She stared silently at the canvas that had hung on

her wall for more than five years, and she said eventually, 'I didn't know.'

'What didn't you know?'

'Why you left. Why you couldn't paint here.'

'Em . . .' The old fond abbreviation arose naturally.

'You did try to tell me. I was too hurt to understand. And too young.' She sighed. 'And nothing's changed, has it?'

'Not really.'

She smiled vividly, without pain. 'For a marriage that lasted barely four months, ours wasn't so bad.'

I felt a great and undeserved sense of release. I hadn't wanted to come to Lambourn again: I'd avoided it from guilt and unwillingness to risk stirring Emily to an ill will she had in fact never shown. I had shied away habitually from the memory of her baffled eyes.

Her actual words to me had been tough. 'All right then, if you want to live on a mountain, bugger off.' It had been her eyes that had begged me to stay.

She'd said, 'If you care more for bloody paint than you do for me, bugger off.'

Now, more than five tranquillising years later, she said, 'I wouldn't have given up training racehorses, not for anything.'

'I know.'

'And you couldn't give up painting.'

'No.'

'So there we are. It's OK now between us, isn't it?'

'You're generous, Em.'

She grinned. 'I quite enjoy saintly forbearance. Do you want something to eat?'

It was she who made mushroom omelettes in the kitchen, though when I'd lived there I'd done most of the cooking. We ate at the kitchen table. She still had a passion for ice cream: strawberry, that evening.

She said, 'Do you want a divorce? Is that why you came here?'

Startled, I said, 'No. Hadn't thought of it! Do you?'

'You can have one any time.'

'Do you want one?'

'Actually,' she said calmly, 'I find it quite useful sometimes to be able to mention a husband, even if he's never around.' She sucked her ice-cream spoon. 'I'm used to being in charge. I no longer want a live-in husband, to be frank.'

She stacked our plates in the dishwasher, and said, 'If you don't want a divorce, why did you come?'

'Ivan's horses.'

'That's crap. You could have asked on the phone.'

The Emily I'd known had been forthrightly honest. She had rid herself of some of the owners she'd inherited from her father because they'd sometimes wanted her to instruct her jockeys not to win. There was a world of difference, she'd said, between giving a young horse an easy race to get him to like the game, and trying to cheat the racing public by stopping a horse from winning in order to come home next time out at better odds. 'My horses run to win,' she said robustly, and the racing world, with clear-eyed judgment, gave her its trust.

It was tentatively, therefore, that I said, 'Ivan wants me to make Golden Malt disappear.'

'What on earth are you talking about? Do you want some coffee?'

She made the coffee in a drip-feed pot, a new one since my days.

I explained about the brewery's financial predicament.

'The brewery,' Emily said tartly, 'owes me four months' training fees for Golden Malt. I wrote to Ivan personally about it not long before his heart attack. I don't like to bitch, but I want my money.'

'You'll get it,' I promised. 'But he wants me to take the horse away from here, so that it doesn't get sucked in and sold prematurely.'

She frowned, 'I can't let you take it.'

'Well . . . yes you can.'

I stretched down the table to reach the folder I'd brought with me and handed her one of the certified copies of the power of attorney, explaining that it gave me authority to do as I thought best regarding Ivan's property, which one way or another definitely included Golden Malt.

She read the whole thing solemnly and at the end said merely, 'All right. What do you want to do?'

'To ride the horse away from here tomorrow morning, when the town and the Downs are alive with horses going in all directions.'

She stared. 'Firstly,' she said, 'he's not an easy ride.'

'And I'd fall off?'

'You might. And secondly, where would you go?'

'If I tell you where, you'll be involved more than maybe you'd want to be.'

She thought it over. She said, 'I don't see how you can do it without my help. At the very least you need me to tell the lads not to worry when one of the horses goes missing.'

'Much easier with your help,' I agreed.

We drank the coffee, not talking.

'I like Ivan,' she said finally. 'Technically he's still my stepfather-in-law, same as Vivienne is still my mother-in-law. I see them at the races. We're on good terms, though she's never effusive. We send each other Christmas cards.'

I nodded. I knew.

'If Ivan wants the horse hidden,' Emily said, 'I'll help you. So where do you plan to go?'

'I bought a copy of *Horse and Hound* in Newbury,' I said, taking the magazine out of the folder and opening at the pages of classified advertisements. 'There's a man here, over the Downs from here, saying he looks after hunters at livery and prepares horses for hunter 'chases and point-to-points. I thought about phoning him and asking him to take my hack for a few weeks. For four weeks, in fact, until a day or two before the King Alfred Gold Cup. The horse would have to come back here, wouldn't he, so he could run with you as trainer?'

She nodded absently, looking where my finger pointed.

'I'm not sending Golden Malt to *him*,' she announced. 'That man's a bully, horses go sour on him, and he thinks he's God's gift to women.'

'Oh.'

She thought briefly. 'I have a friend, a woman, who offers the same service and is a damn sight better.'

'Is she within riding distance?'

'About eight miles across the Downs. You'd get lost on the Downs, though.'

'Er . . . you used to have a map of the tracks and gallops.'

'Yes, the Ordnance Survey map. But my map must be seven years old. There are a lot of new roads.'

'Roads may change, but the tracks are seven *thousand* years old. They'll still be there.'

She laughed and fetched the map from the office, spreading it out on the kitchen table. 'Her yard is west of here,' Emily said, pointing. 'She's quite a good way away from Mandown, where most people exercise the Lambourn strings. She's *there*, see, outside the village of Foxhill.'

'I could find that,' I said.

Emily looked doubtful, but phoned her friend.

'My yard's so full,' she said, 'could you take an overflow for me for a week or two? Keep him fit. He'll be racing later on . . . You can? Good . . . I'll send one of my lads over with him in the morning. The horse's name? Oh, just call him Bobby. Send me the bills. How are your kids?'

After the chit-chat she put down the receiver.

'There you are,' she said. 'One conjuring trick done to order.'

'You're brilliant.'

'Absolutely right. Where are you sleeping?'

'I'll find a room in Lambourn.'

'Not unless you want to advertise your presence. Don't forget you lived here for six months. People know you. We got married in Lambourn church. I don't want tongues wagging that you've come back to me. You can sleep here, on a sofa, out of sight.'

'How about,' I said impulsively, 'in your bed?'

'No.'

I didn't try to persuade her. Instead, I borrowed her telephone for two calls, one to my mother to tell her I would be away for the night but hoped to have good news for Ivan the next day, and one to Jed Parlane in Scotland.

'How are you?' he said anxiously.

'Living at a flat-out gallop.'

'I meant . . . anyway, I took the police to the bothy. What a *mess*.'

'Mm.'

'I gave them your drawings. The police haven't had any other complaints about hikers robbing people around here.'

'Not surprising.'

'Himself wants to see you as soon as you return. He says I'm to meet you off the train and take you straight to the castle. When are you coming back?'

'With luck, on tomorrow night's Highlander. I'll let you know.'

'How is Sir Ivan?'

'Not good.'

'Take care, then,' he said. 'So long.'

Emily, deep in thought, said, as I put down the receiver, 'I'll send my head lad out with the first lot, as usual, but I'll tell him not to take Golden Malt. I'll tell him that the horse is going away for a bit of remedial treatment to his legs. There's nothing wrong with his legs, actually, but my lads know better than to argue.'

They always had, I reflected. Also, they faithfully stayed. She trained winners; the lads prospered, and did as she said.

She wrote, as she always did, a list of which lad would ride which horse when the first lot of about twenty horses pulled out for exercise at seven o'clock the next morning, and which lad would ride which horse in the second lot, after breakfast, and which lad would go out again later in the morning with every horse not yet exercised. She employed about twenty lads – men and women – for the horses, besides two secretaries, a housekeeper and a yard man. Jockeys came for breakfast and to school the horses over jumps. Vets called. People delivered hay and feed and removed manure. Owners visited. I'd learned to ride, but not well. The telephone trilled incessantly. Messages whizzed in and out by computer. No one ever for long sat still.

I had been absorbed into the busy scenery as general cook/dogsbody, and runner of errands, and although I'd fitted in as best I could, and for a while happily, my own internal life had shrivelled to zero. There had been weeks of self-doubt, of wondering if my compulsion to paint was mere selfishness, if the belief in my talent was a delusion, if I should deny the promptings of my nature and be forever the lieutenant that Emily wanted.

Now, more than five years later, she put her newly written list for the head lad in the message box outside the back door. She let out her two Labradors for a last run and walked round the stable yard to make sure that all was well. Then she came in, whistled for the dogs to return to their baskets in the kitchen, and locked her doors against the night.

All so familiar. All so long ago.

She gave me two travelling rugs to keep warm on the sofa and said calmly, 'Goodnight.'

I put my arms round her tentatively. 'Em?'

'No,' she said.

I kissed her forehead, holding her close. 'Em?'

'Oh,' she said in exasperation. 'All *right.*'

CHAPTER FOUR

She no longer slept in the big bedroom we'd shared, but in the old guest room, in a new queen-sized romping ground suitable for passing fancies.

She had slotted a new luxurious bathroom into what had once been her father's dressing-room. Downstairs the house might be as I remembered it, but upstairs it was not.

'This is not a precedent,' Emily said, taking off layers down to a white lace bra. 'And I don't think it's wise.'

'Bugger wise.'

'You obviously haven't been getting enough.'

'No, I haven't.' I switched off the lights and drew back the curtains, as I'd always done. 'How about you?'

'I'm known as a dragon. There aren't many with the guts of St George.'

'Do you regret it?'

She rustled out of the rest of her clothes and slid naked between the sheets, her curved shape momentarily silhouetted against a window oblong of stars. I took off my clothes and felt ageless.

'Rumours run round Lambourn like the pox,' she said. 'I'm bloody careful who I let into this room.'

We stopped talking. We had never, I supposed, been inventive or innovative lovers. There had been no need. Front to front with hands and lips and tongues we had shivered with sensual intense arousal, and that at least hadn't changed. Her body to my touch was long known and long forgotten, like going back to an abandoned building: a newly explored breast, familiar concave abdomen, hard mound of pelvis, soft dark warm mystery below and beyond, known secretly but never explored by spotlight since, in spite of her forthright public face, she was privately shy.

I did what I knew she liked, and as ever my own intensest pleasure came in pleasing her. Entry was easy, her readiness receptive. Movement strong and rhythmic, an instinct shared. When I felt her deep pulse beating, then too I took my own long moment; sometimes in the past it had been as good as that, but not always. It seemed that in that way also we had grown up.

'I've missed you,' she said.

'I, too.'

We slept peacefully side by side, and it was in the morning in the shower that she looked at my collection of bruises with disbelief.

'I told you,' I said mildly. 'I got mugged.'

'Trampled by a stampede of cows, more like.'

'Bulls.'

'OK, then. Bulls. Don't come downstairs until the first lot has gone out.'

I'd almost forgotten I was there to steal a horse. I waited until the scrunching hooves outside had diminuendoed into the distance and went down for coffee and toast.

Emily came in from the yard, saying, 'I've saddled and bridled Golden Malt. He's all ready for you, but he's pretty fresh. For God's sake, don't let him whip round and buck you off. The last thing I want is to have him loose on the Downs.'

'I've been thinking about anonymity,' I said, spreading honey on toast. 'Have you still got any of those nightcaps you put over their heads in very cold weather? A nightcap would hide that very white blaze down his nose. And perhaps boots for his white socks . . .'

She nodded, amused. 'And you'd better borrow a helmet from the cloakroom, and anything else you need.'

I thanked her and went into the large downstairs cloakroom where there was always a haphazard collection of jackets, boots, gloves and helmets for kitting out visitors. I found some jodhpur boots to fit me (better than trainers for the job) and tied my hair up on the top of my head with a shoelace before hiding the lot under a shiny blue helmet. I slung round my neck a pair of jockeys' goggles, the big mica jobs they used against rain and mud . . . fine disguise for a black eye.

Emily, still amused, said no one would recognise the result. 'And do borrow one of those padded jackets. It's cold on the Downs these mornings.'

I fetched a dark-coloured jacket and said, 'If anyone comes looking for the horse, say I had authority to take him, and I took him, and you don't know where he is.'

'Do you think anyone will come?' She was curious more than worried, it seemed.

'Hope not.'

Golden Malt eyed me with disillusion from inside his nightcap. Emily gave me a leg-up onto his back and at this point looked filled with misgiving.

'When the hell did you last sit on a horse?' she asked, frowning.

'Er . . . some time ago.' But I got my feet into the stirrups and collected the reins into a reasonable bunch.

'How often have you actually ridden since you left here?' Emily demanded.

'It's all in the mind,' I said. Golden Malt skittered around unhelpfully. It looked a long way down to the ground.

'You're a bloody fool,' she said.

'I'll phone you if anything goes wrong . . . and thanks, Em.'

'Yes. Go on, then. Bugger off.' She was smiling. 'I'll kill you if you let him get loose.'

I'd reckoned that the first three hundred yards might be the most difficult from the point of view of my deficient riding ability as I had to go that distance along a public road to reach the track that led up to the Downs; but I was lucky, there were few cars on the road and those that were had drivers who slowed down for racehorses. I touched my helmet repeatedly in thanks and managed to steer a not-too-disgraceful course.

No one wound down a window and called to me by name or linked the camouflaged horse to Emily. I was just on one of hundreds of Lambourn equine residents, large as life but also invisible.

Golden Malt thought he knew where he was going, which helped at first but not later. He tossed his head with pleasure and trotted jauntily up the rutted access to the downlands which spread for fifty miles east to west across central southern England – from the Chilterns to Salisbury Plain. I felt more at home on the Downs than in Lambourn itself, but even there solitude was rare: strings of horses cluttered every skyline and trainers' Land Rovers bumped busily in their wake. Lambourn's industry lay out there on the sweeping green uplands in the wind and the prehistoric mornings. I had thought that they would be world enough: that I could live and work there . . . and I'd been wrong.

Golden Malt began to fight when I turned him to the west at the top of the hill, instead of continuing to the east. He ran backwards, he turned in small circles, he obstinately refused to go where I tried to point his head. I didn't know whether expert horsemen with legs of iron would have forced him to obey in a long battle of wills: I only knew that I was losing.

I remembered suddenly that one day I'd stood beside Emily on the trainers' stand at a race meeting watching one of her horses refuse to go down to the start. The horse had run backwards, cantered crabwise, turned in circles, ignored every instruction and used his vast muscle power to make a fool of the slight man on his back. And that man had been a tough experienced jockey.

Across the years I heard Emily's furious comment, 'Why doesn't the bloody fool get off and *lead* him?'

Oh *Em*, I thought. My dear wife. Thank you.

I slid off the stubborn brute's back and pulled the reins over his head, and *walked* towards the west, and as if his entire nature had done an abracadabra, Golden Malt ambled along peacefully beside me so that all I had to worry about was not letting him step on my heels.

Emily's anxiety that I would get lost on the bare rolling grassland didn't take into consideration the boyhood training I'd had in following deer across unmapped Scottish moorlands. The first great rule was to determine the direction of the wind, and to steer by its angle on one's face. Stalking a deer was only possible if one were down wind of him, so that he couldn't smell one's presence.

The wind on that particular September day was blowing steadily from the north. I headed at first straight into it and then, when Golden Malt was used to its feel, veered slightly to the left, plodding purposefully across the green featureless sea as if I knew my bearings exactly.

I could see glimpses of villages in the lower distances, but no horses. When I'd walked about a mile I tried riding again, scrambling clumsily back into the saddle and gathering the reins; and this time, as if unsure in his isolation from sight and sound of his own kind, Golden Malt walked docilely where I asked.

I risked another trot.

No problem.

I crossed a footpath or two and skirted a few farms, setting dogs barking. There was no great need for pinpoint accuracy at that stage of the journey because somewhere ahead lay the oldest path in Britain, the Ridgeway, that still ran east–west between the Thames at Goring Gap to West Kennet, a village south-west of Swindon. Although from there on it had disappeared, it was likely the Druids had walked it to reach Stonehenge. True to its name, it ran along the highest ground of the hills because once, long before the Romans came with Julius Caesar, the valleys had been wooded and prowled by bears.

In the age of cars, the Ridgeway path beckoned walkers, and to lone horse-thieves it was a broad highway.

When I reached it I almost missed it: trotted straight across and only belatedly realised that I'd been expecting more of a production than a simple rutted track. Indeed, I retraced my steps and stopped Golden Malt for a rest while I looked around for helpful signposts, and found none. I was on high ground. The track ran from east to west, according to the wind. It was definitely a *path*. It had to be the right one.

Shrugging, I committed the enterprise and turned left, to the west, and trotted hopefully on. All paths, after all, led *somewhere*, even if not to Stonehenge.

I had chosen a longer route than essential in order to avoid roads, and it was true that the Ridgeway didn't represent the straightest line from A to B, but as I didn't want to get lost and have to ask the way and draw attention to myself, I considered the extra time and miles well spent.

The path turned south-west at roughly where I expected and led across a minor road or two and, to my relief, proving to be the real thing, delivered me to Foxhill.

Emily's friend took my quiet arrival for granted.

'Mrs Cox,' I said, 'says she will call by in a day or two to pick up the saddle and bridle.'

'Fine.'

'I'll be off, then.'

'Right. Thanks. We'll look after the old boy.' She patted the chestnut neck with maternal and expert fondness, and nodded to me cheerfully as I left, not querying my assertion of thumbing a lift back to Lambourn.

I thumbed a lift to Swindon instead, however, and caught a train to Reading, and called on a powerful area bank manager who wasn't expecting a padded jacket, jodhpur boots and a shiny blue riding helmet with jockeys' goggles.

'Er . . .' he said.

'Yes. Well, I'm sorry about the presentation but I'm acting for my stepfather, Sir Ivan Westering, and this is not my normal world.'

'I know Sir Ivan well,' he said. 'I'm sorry he's ill.'

I handed him a certified copy of the power of attorney and Ivan's Alternate Director letter which, although much creased by now through having been folded into my shirt pocket for the cross-country expedition, worked its customary suspension of prompt ejection, and, smooth man that he was, he listened courteously to my plea for the workers at the brewery to receive their wages as usual for this present week, and for the pensioners to be paid also, while the insolvency practitioner, Mrs Morden, tried to put together a committee of creditors for a voluntary arrangement.

He nodded. 'I've already been approached by Mrs Morden.' He paused thoughtfully, then said, 'I've also talked to Tobias Tollright. He told me you would come here on your knees.'

'I'll kneel if you like.'

The faintest of smiles twitched in his eye muscles, and vanished. He said, 'What do you get out of this personally?'

Surprised, I didn't know what to say, so I didn't say

anything, a feeble absence of answer that seemed not to bother him.

'Hmph.' He sniffed. He looked at his fingers. He said, 'All right. The wages cheques will be honoured for this week. We'll allow the pensioners seventy-five per cent. Then we'll see.' He stood up, holding out a smooth white hand. 'A revelation doing business with you, Mr Kinloch.'

I shook his hand and breathed deeply with relief on the way out.

With an hour and a half to spare before the intimidating prospect of my appointment with Mrs Margaret Morden, fairy godmother to near-bankrupt Cinderellas, I bought more throwaway razors, a small tube of shaving cream and another comb – the Euston collection being still in London – and in a pub tried to put a tidier face on things. Nothing but time, though, would unblack the eye. I drank half a pint of King Alfred Gold to get reacquainted with what I was trying to save and turned up promptly on the lady's threshold.

A word or two had gone ahead of me, I gathered, as she knew at once who I was and welcomed me without blinking. The power of attorney was yet again carefully inspected, a certified copy accepted and ready to be filed away, and a copy of Ivan's letter taken, as had been done also at Tollright's firm, and the bank. Mrs Morden gave me back Ivan's open-sesames and requested me, in my turn, to sign an authorisation for her to act for the brewery. This was not handshake-gentleman's-agreement-land, this was paper-trail responsibility.

Mrs Margaret Morden looked somewhere in the ageless forties, and was not the severe businesswoman I'd expected. True, her manner was based on self-confidence, and formidable intelligence shone in steady grey eyes, but she was dressed not in a suit but in a soft calf-length dress of pink and violet printed silk, with a ruffle round the neck.

Involuntarily I smiled, and from her satisfied change of expression realised that that was exactly the aim of her clothes; to encourage, to soften prejudice, to mediate, to persuade.

Her office was spacious, a cross between functional grey and leather-bound law books, with a desk-like shelf the whole length of one wall, bearing six or seven computer monitors, all showing different information. A chair on castors stood ready before them waiting, it seemed, to roll her from screen to screen.

She sat down in a large black chair behind a separate executive-sized desk and waved me to the clients' (slightly smaller) chair facing. There were brewery papers already spread out on the desk: she and Tobias between them had obviously wasted no time.

She said, 'We have here a serious situation . . .'

The serious situation was abruptly made worse by the door crashing open to admit a purposeful missile of a man, with a flustered secretary behind him bleating (as in a thousand film scripts), 'I'm very sorry, Mrs Morden, I couldn't stop him.'

The intruder, striding into centre-stage, pointed a sharp finger at my face and said, 'You've no right to be here. *Out.*' He jerked the finger towards the door. 'Any negotiations needed by the King Alfred Brewery will be performed by *me.*'

He was quivering with rage, a thin fiftyish man going extensively bald and staring fiercely through large glasses with silvery metal rims. He had a scrawny neck, a sharp Adam's apple and megawatt mental energy. He told me again to leave.

Mrs Morden asked calmly, 'And you are . . .?'

'Madam,' he said furiously, 'in the absence of Sir Ivan Westering I am in charge of the brewery. I am the acting managing director. This wretched young man hasn't the slightest authority to go round interviewing our auditor and our bank manager, as I hear he's been doing. You will disregard him and get rid of him, and *I* will decide whether or not we need your services at all, which I doubt.'

Mrs Morden asked non-committally, 'Your name?'

He gasped as if amazed that she shouldn't know it. 'Finch,' he said sharply, 'Desmond Finch.'

'Ah, yes.' Mrs Morden looked down at the papers. 'It mentions you here. But I'm sorry, Mr Finch, Mr Kinloch has an undoubted right to act in Sir Ivan's stead.'

She waved a hand towards the certified copy of the power of attorney, which lay on her desk. Finch snatched it up, glanced at it, and tore the page across. 'Sir Ivan's too ill to know what he's doing,' he pronounced. 'This farce has got to stop. *I* am in charge of the brewery's affairs and I alone.'

Mrs Morden put her head on one side and invited my comment. 'Mr Kinloch?'

Ivan, I reflected, had deliberately by-passed Desmond Finch in giving me his trust, and I wondered why. It would have been normal for him to have passed his power to his second-in-command. If he hadn't done so – if he had very pointedly not done so – then my obligation to my stepfather was absolute.

'Please continue with your work, Mrs Morden,' I said without heat. 'I will check again with Sir Ivan, and if he wants me to withdraw from his affairs, then of course I will.'

She smiled gently at Finch.

'It's not good enough,' he said furiously. 'I want this . . . this usurper out *now*. This minute. At *once*. Mrs Benchmark is adamant.'

Mrs Morden lifted her eyebrows in my direction, no doubt seeing the arrival of total comprehension in my face.

'Mrs Benchmark,' I explained, 'is Patsy Benchmark, Sir Ivan's daughter. She would prefer me out of her father's life. She would prefer me . . . er . . . to evaporate.'

'Let me get this right,' Margaret Morden said patiently, 'Sir Ivan is Mrs Benchmark's actual father, and you are his stepson?'

I nodded. 'Sir Ivan had a daughter, Patsy, with his first wife, who died. He then married my widowed mother when I was eighteen, so I am his stepson.'

Finch, loudly and waspishly, added, 'And he is trying to worm his way into Sir Ivan's fortune and cut out Mrs Benchmark.'

'No,' I said.

I couldn't blame Margaret Morden for looking doubtful. Patsy's fear was obsessive but real.

'Please try to save the brewery,' I said to Mrs Morden. 'Sir Ivan's health may depend on it. Also, the brewery will be Patsy's one day. Save it for her, not for me. And she won't thank *you*, Mr Finch, if it goes down the tubes.'

It silenced them both.

Finch gaped and made for the door, and then stopped dead and came back to accuse with venom: 'Mrs Benchmark says you have stolen the King Alfred Gold Cup. You've stolen the golden chalice and you're hiding it, and if necessary she will take it back by force.'

Hell's teeth. '*Where is it?*'

My ribs ached.

The King Alfred Gold Cup. *It*. The *it* that the demons had been looking for. The *it* that I didn't have, not the *it* that I did have.

'You look tired, Mr Kinloch,' Mrs Morden said.

'*Tired!*' Finch was deeply sarcastic. 'If he's tired he can go back to Scotland and sleep for a week. Better, a month.'

Good suggestion, I thought. I said, 'Was the Cup kept at the brewery?'

Desmond Finch opened and closed his mouth without answering.

'Don't you know?' I asked with interest. 'Has there been a rumpus, with policemen flourishing handcuffs? Or did Patsy just *tell* you I'd taken it? She does have a galvanic way of neutralising people's common sense.'

The second-in-command of the brewery made an exit as unheralded as his entry. When the air had settled after his departure, Mrs Morden asked if by any chance I had a replacement certified copy of the power of attorney which, owing to Ivan's foresight in giving me ten, I had. I gave her one: five left.

'I need further instructions,' she said.

'Such as, carry on?'

'I am willing to, if you will give me a handwritten assurance releasing me from any proceedings arising from work done on your say-so. This is by no means a normal request, but little about this particular insolvency now seems normal.'

I wrote the release to her dictation, and signed it, and she had it witnessed by her secretary as being supplemental to the authorities to act that I'd already given her.

'I hope to bring together the brewery's main creditors on Monday,' she said. 'Telephone me tomorrow for a progress report.'

'Thank you, Mrs Morden.'

'Margaret,' she said. 'Now, these depressing numbers . . .'

I walked back to Pierce, Tollright and Simmonds, where the auditor and I became Tobe and Al and went out for an early beer.

I told Tobias of Desmond Finch's visit to Margaret Morden, a tale that resulted in much vicious chewing of an innocent toothpick but an otherwise diplomatic silence.

'Have you met him?' I asked, prompting.

'Oh yes. Quite often.'

'What do you think of him?'

'Off the record?'

'This whole pub,' I said, 'is off the record.'

Even so, his caution took its time. Then he said, 'Desmond Finch gets things done. He's a very effective lieutenant. Give him a programme he understands, and he will unswervingly carry it out. His energy pumps the blood round the brewery, and it is his persistence that makes sure that everything that ought to be done, is done.'

'You approve of him, then?'

He grinned. 'I applaud his work. I can't stand the man.'

I laughed. 'Thank God for that.'

We drank in harmony. I said, 'What was Norman Quorn like?' Norman Quorn was the Finance Director that had vanished with the cash. 'You must have known him well.'

'I thought I did. I'd worked with him for years.' Tobias took out a toothpick and swallowed beer. 'The last person, I would have thought, to do what he did. But then, that's what they always say.'

'Why was he the last person?'

'Oh. He was coming up to retirement. Sixty-five. A grey, meticulous accountant. No fun in him. Dry. We went through the firm's books together every year. Never a decimal out of place. It's my job of course to pull out invoices at random and make sure that the transactions referred to did in fact take place, and in Quorn's work there was never the slightest discrepancy. I'd have bet my reputation on his honesty.'

'He was saving everything up for the big one.'

Tobias sighed. Another toothpick took a mauling. 'He was clever, I'll give him that.'

'How did he actually steal so much? I've been reeling at the figures with Margaret Morden.'

'He didn't go round to the bank with a sack, if that's what you mean. He didn't shovel the readies into a suitcase and disappear through the Channel Tunnel. He did it the new-fashioned way, by wire.' He sucked noisily. 'He did it by electronic transfer, by routing money all over the place via ABA numbers – those are international bank identification numbers – and by backing up the transactions with faxed authorisations, all bearing the right identifying codes. He was too damned clever. I may have believed I could follow any tracks, but I've lost him somewhere in Panama. It's a job for the serious fraud people, though Sir Ivan wants to hush up the whole thing and won't call them in, and of course it wouldn't save the brewery if he did. Margaret Morden is the best hope for that. The only hope, I'd say.'

We refilled the half-pints in suitable gloom.

I said tentatively, 'Do you think Quorn could have stolen the King Alfred Cup? The actual gold chalice?'

'*What?*' He was astonished. 'No. Not his style.'

'But electronic transfers *were* his style?'

'I see what you mean.' He sighed deeply. 'All the same . . .'

'Desmond Finch says that Patsy Benchmark – have you met Ivan's daughter? – is accusing *me* of having stolen the Cup. She's persuasive. I may yet find myself in Reading Gaol.'

'Writing ballads à la Oscar Wilde?'

'You may jest.'

'I've met her,' Tobias said. He thought through another toothpick. 'The fact that no one seems to know where this priceless gold medieval goblet actually *is*, does not mean that it's been stolen.'

'I drink to clarity of mind.'

He laughed. 'You'd make a good auditor.'

'A better slosher-on of paint.'

I considered his friendly harmless-looking face and imagined the analytical wheels whirring round as fast in him as they were in me. Benevolent versions of Uncle Joe Stalin's vulpine smirk hid unsmiling intents from presidents to peasants and all points in between. Yet trust had to begin somewhere, or at least a belief in it.

I asked, 'What happened first? The disappearance of Norman Quorn, or your realisation that the books were cooked, or my stepfather's heart attack? And when was the Cup first said to be missing?'

He frowned, trying to remember. 'They were all more or less at the same time.'

'They can't have been simultaneous.'

'Well, no.' He paused. 'No one seems to have seen the Cup for ages. Of the other three . . . I told Sir Ivan one morning about two weeks ago . . . he was in his London house . . . that the brewery was insolvent, and why. He told me to cover it up and keep quiet. Quorn had already gone away for a few days' leave, or so the brewery secretaries said. Sir Ivan collapsed in the afternoon. I could get no instructions after that from anyone until you came along. The whole financial mess simply got worse while Sir Ivan was in hospital because no one except him could make decisions and he wouldn't talk to me. But the bank wouldn't wait any longer.'

'What about Desmond Finch?'

'What about him?' Tobias asked. 'Like I told you, he's a great lieutenant but he needs a general to tell him what to do. He may say now he's in charge, but without Mrs Benchmark prodding him from behind he'd be doing the same as he's been doing for the past two weeks, which is telling me he can't act without Sir Ivan's orders.'

It all, in a way, made sense.

I said, 'Margaret Morden says I don't have to go to the creditors' meeting on Monday.'

'No, better not. She'll persuade them if anyone can.'

'I asked her to root for the race.'

'Race? Oh yes. King Alfred Gold Cup. But no trophy.'

'The winner only ever gets a gold-plated replica. Never the real thing.'

'Life,' he said, 'is full of disillusion.'

When I reached the house in Park Crescent, Dr Keith Robbiston was just leaving, and we spoke on the steps outside with my mother holding the door open, smiling while she waited for me to go in.

'Hello,' Robbiston greeted me fast and cheerfully. 'How's things?'

'I finished the pills you gave me.'

'Did you? Do you want some more?'

'Yes, please.'

He instantly produced another small packet: it

seemed he carried an endless supply. 'When was it,' he asked, 'that you fell among thieves?'

'The day before yesterday.' It felt more like a decade. 'How is Ivan?'

The doctor glanced at my mother and, clearly because she could hear, said briefly, 'He needs rest.' His gaze switched intensely back to me. 'Perhaps you, you strong young man, can see he gets it. I have given him a powerful sedative. He needs to sleep. Good day to you now.' He flapped a hand in farewell and hurried off in a life taken always at a run.

'What did he mean about rest?' I asked my mother, giving her a token hug and following her indoors.

She sighed. 'Patsy is here. So is Surtees.'

Surtees was not the great nineteenth-century story-teller of that name, but Patsy's husband, whose parents had been bookworms. Surtees Benchmark, tall, lean and of the silly-ass school of mannerism, could waffle apologetically while he did you a bad turn, rather like his wife. He saw me through her eyes. His own never twinkled when he smiled.

My mother and I went upstairs. I could hear Patsy's voice from the floor above.

'I *insist*, Father. He's got to go.'

An indistinct rumble in return.

As her voice was coming from Ivan's study I went up and along there with my neat mother following.

Patsy saw my arrival with predictable rage. She too

was tall and lean, and stunningly beautiful when she wanted to charm. The recipients of her 'Darling!' greetings opened to her like sunflowers: only those who knew her well looked wary, with Surtees no exception.

'I have been telling Father,' she said forcefully, 'that he must revoke that stupid power of attorney he made out in your name and give it to *me*.'

I put up no opposition but said mildly, 'He can of course do what he likes.'

Ivan looked alarmingly pale and weak, sitting as ever in his dark red dressing-gown in his imposing chair. The heavy sedative drooped already in his eyelids, and I went across to him, offering my arm and suggesting he should lie down on his bed.

'Leave him alone,' Patsy said sharply. 'He has a nurse for that.'

Ivan however put both hands on my offered forearm and pulled himself to his feet. His frailty had worsened, I thought, since the day before.

'Lie down,' he said vaguely. 'Good idea.'

He let me help him towards his bedroom and, short of physically attacking me, Patsy and Surtees couldn't stop me. Four practised thugs had been beyond my fighting capabilities, but Patsy and her husband weren't, and they had sense enough to know it.

As I went past him, Surtees said spitefully, 'Next time you'll *scream*.'

My mother's eyes widened in surprise. Patsy's head

snapped round towards her husband and with scorn she shrivelled him verbally, 'Will you keep your silly mouth *shut*.'

I went on walking with Ivan into his bedroom, where my mother and I helped him out of his dressing-gown and into the wide bed where he relaxed gratefully, closing his eyes and murmuring, 'Vivienne ... Vivienne.'

'I'm here.' She stroked his hand. 'Go to sleep, my dear.'

He couldn't with so powerful a drug have stayed awake. When he was breathing evenly my mother and I went out into the study and found that Patsy and Surtees had gone.

'What did he mean?' she asked perplexed. 'Why did Surtees say, "Next time you'll scream"?'

'I dread to think.'

'It didn't sound like a joke.' She looked doubtful and worried. 'There's something about Surtees that isn't . . . oh dear . . . that isn't *normal*.'

'Dearest Ma,' I said, teasing her, 'almost no one is normal. Look at your son, for a start.'

Her worry dissolved into a laugh and from there to visible happiness when from the study phone I told Jed Parlane that I would be staying down south for another twenty-four hours.

'I'll catch tomorrow night's train,' I said. 'I'm afraid it gets to Dalwhinnie at a quarter past seven in the morning. Saturday morning.'

Jed faintly protested. 'Himself wants you back here as soon as possible.'

'Tell him my mother needs me.'

'So do the police.'

'Too bad. See you, Jed.'

My mother and I ate the good meal Edna had cooked and left ready, and spent a peaceful, rare and therapeutic evening alone together in her sitting-room, not talking much, but companionable.

'I saw Emily,' I said casually, at one point.

'Did you?' She was unexcited. 'How is she?'

'Well. Busy. She asked after Ivan.'

'Yes, she telephoned. Nice of her.'

I smiled. My mother's reaction to my leaving my wife had been as always calm, unjudgmental and accepting. It was our own business, she had implied. She had also, I thought, understood. Her sole comment to me had been, 'Solitary people are never alone,' an unexpected insight that she wouldn't enlarge or explain, but she had long been accustomed to the solitary nature of her son's instincts, that I had tried – and failed – to stifle.

In the morning, when everyone had slept well, I talked for much longer than previously with Ivan.

He looked better. He still wore pyjamas, dressing-gown and slippers, but there was muscle tone and colour in his face, and clarity in his mind.

I told him in detail what I'd learned and done over the two days I'd spent in Reading. He faced unwillingly the whole frightening extent of the plundering of the brewery and approved of the appointment of Margaret Morden as captain of the lifeboat to save the wreck.

'It's my own fault things got so bad,' Ivan sighed. 'But, you know, I couldn't believe that Norman Quorn would rob the firm. I've known him for years, moved him up from the accounts department, made him Finance Director, gave him a seat on the Board . . . I *trusted* him. I wouldn't listen to or believe Tobias Tollright. I'll never be able to trust my own judgment again.'

I said, intending to console, 'The same thing happens to firms every year.'

He nodded heavily. 'They say the greater the trust the safer the opportunity. But *Norman* . . . how *could* he . . .?'

His pain was more personal than financial, the treachery and rejection harder to bear than the actual loss, and it was the heartlessness of that personal treachery that he couldn't endure.

'I wish,' he said with feeling, 'that you would take over and run the brewery. I've always known you could do it. I hoped when you married that efficient and attractive young woman that you would change your mind and come in with me. So *suitable*. You could live in Lambourn in her training stables and manage the brewery in Wantage, only seven miles away. *Perfect*. A life most young men would jump at. But no, you have to be different. You have to go off and live on your own, and *paint*.' His voice wasn't exactly contemptuous, but he found my compulsion wholly incomprehensible. 'Your dear mother seems to understand you. She says you can't keep mountain mist in a cage.'

'I'm sorry,' I said inadequately. I could see the sense of the life path he'd offered. I didn't know why I couldn't take it. I did know it would result in meltdown.

I changed the subject and said I'd asked Margaret Morden to get the creditors if possible to keep the Cheltenham race alive; to get them to realise that the seventeenth running of the King Alfred Gold Cup would underpin public faith in the brewery and boost the sales that would generate the income that alone would save the day.

Ivan smiled. 'The Devil would like you on his side.'

'But it's true.'

'Truth can subvert,' he said. 'I wish you were my son.'

That silenced me completely. He looked as though he were surprised he had said it, but he let it stand. A silence grew.

In the end I said tentatively, 'Golden Malt . . .?'

'My horse.' His gaze sharpened on my face. 'Did you hide it?'

'Did you mean me to?'

'Of course I did. I hoped you would, but . . .'

'But,' I finished when he stopped, '*you* are a member of the Jockey Club and can't afford to be in the wrong, and the creditors may want to count Golden Malt an asset and sell him. And yes, I did steal him out of Emily's yard but any sleuth worth his salt could find him, and if he has to vanish for more than a week I'll have to move him.'

'Where is he?'

'If you don't know, you can't tell.'

'Who does know, besides you?'

'At present, Emily. If I move him, it will be to shield her.' I paused. 'Do you have any proof that you personally own him? Bill of sale?'

'No. I bought him as a foal for cash to help out a needy friend. He paid no tax on the gain.'

'Tut.'

'You can't see that six years down the road your good turn will bite you.'

The telephone buzzed at his elbow, and he made a gesture asking me to answer it for him. I said 'Hello?' and found Tobias Tollright at the other end.

'Is that you, Al?' he asked. 'This is Tobe.' Fluster and insecurity in his voice.

'Hi, Tobe. What's up?'

'I've had this man on the phone who says Sir Ivan has revoked your powers of attorney.'

'What man?'

'Someone called Oliver Grantchester. A solicitor. He says he's in charge of Sir Ivan's affairs.'

'He certified all the copies of the power of attorney,' I said. 'What's wrong with them?'

'He says they were a mistake. Apparently Patsy Benchmark got Sir Ivan to say so.'

'Hold on,' I said, 'while I talk to my stepfather.'

I rested the receiver on the table and explained the situation to Ivan. He picked up the receiver and said, 'Mr Tollright, what is your opinion of my stepson's business sense?'

He smiled through the reply, then said, 'I stand by every word I signed.' He listened, then went on, 'My daughter misinformed Mr Grantchester. Alexander acts for me in everything, and I give my trust to no one else. Clear?' He gave me back the telephone and I said to Tobias, 'OK?'

'My God. That woman. She's dangerous, Al.'

'Mm . . . Tobe, do you know any good, honest, discreet private investigators?'

He chuckled. 'Good, honest and discreet. Hang on . . .' There was a rustle of pages. 'Got a pencil?'

There was a pencil on the table but no notepad. I turned over the box of tissues, in Ivan's fashion, and wrote on the bottom of it the name and phone number of a firm in Reading. 'Thanks, Tobe.'

'Any time, Al.'

I disconnected and said to Ivan, 'Patsy is also going around telling people I've stolen the chalice, the King Alfred Cup.'

'But,' he said, undisturbed, 'you do have it, don't you?'

CHAPTER FIVE

After a moment of internal chill I said carefully, 'Why do you think I have the Cup?'

He looked astonished but not yet alarmed. 'Because I sent it to you, of course. You are good at hiding things, Robert said. I sent it to you, to keep it safe.'

Hell's teeth, I thought. Oh God. Oh *no*.

I said 'How? How did you send it to me?'

For the first time he seemed to realise that however good his plans had been, somewhere along the line the points had got switched. He frowned, but still not with anxiety.

'I gave it to Robert to give to you. That's to say, I told him where to find it. Are you listening? Stop looking so blank. I asked your uncle Robert to take the damned Cup to Scotland for you to take care of. So don't tell me you don't have it.'

'Er . . .' I said, clearing my throat, 'when did you send it to Scotland?'

'I don't know.' He waved a hand as if the detail were

unimportant. 'Ask Robert. If you haven't got the Cup, then he has.'

I breathed slowly and deeply, and said, 'Who else knew you were sending the Cup to me?'

'Who? No one else. What does it matter? Robert will pass the Cup to you when you go back to Scotland, and you can keep it safe for me until the brewery's affairs are settled because, like the horse, the Cup belongs to *me*, and I don't want to see it counted as a brewery asset and sold for a drop in the ocean.'

'Bill of sale?' I suggested hopelessly.

'Don't be ridiculous.'

'No.'

I asked with artificial absence of urgency, 'When did all this happen? When did you ask Himself to take the Cup to Scotland?'

'When? Oh, sometime last week.'

'Last week . . . while you were still in the Clinic?'

'Of course while I was in the Clinic. You're being very dense, Alexander. I was feeling very ill and I'd had so many drugs and injections, I was *thinking* double, let alone seeing, and Robert came to visit me while I was worried sick by Tobias Tollright, and he, Robert, of course, not Tollright, said he was leaving the next day for Scotland for his annual shooting and fishing, and for the Games, and it made sense to ask him to look after the Cup, and he said he would, but better still he would entrust it to *you*. I asked if he trusted you enough . . . and he said he would trust you with his life.'

Hell, I thought, and asked, 'Which day was that?'

'I can't possibly remember. Why do you think it matters?'

His own illness had been painful and traumatic but he hadn't, I thought, had a lot of fists thudding like ramrods into his ribs and abdomen until he could hardly breathe, he hadn't been head-butted and bounced half unconscious down a mountain and he hadn't spent three days bruised, aching and sorry for himself, swallowing Keith Robbiston's pills to make life tolerable.

By that Friday morning, as it happened, the waves of overall malaise had receded; only individual spots were at that point sore to the touch. I felt more or less normal.

Next time you'll scream.

I relaxed into my chair and asked conversationally, 'Did you tell Patsy that I was looking after the Cup?'

Ivan said, 'I do wish you and Patsy could like each other. Your dear mother and I are so fond of each other, but with our children we are not a successful family. You and Patsy both have such strong characters, it's such a shame you can't be friends.'

'Yes, I'm sorry,' I said, and it was true that I was. I would actually have liked to have a sister. I went on, 'She did, though, tell Desmond Finch that I'd stolen the Cup, and he believes it and is spreading it about, which is unfortunate.'

'Oh, Desmond,' Ivan said indulgently. 'Such a good

man in so many ways. I rely on him, you know, to get things done. He's thorough, which so many people are not these days. At least through all this troubling time I can be sure that the brewing and sales are running as they should.'

'Yes,' I said.

The spurt of returning health that had carried Ivan through the morning began to fade, and we sat quietly together, taking life at his pace, which was slow to negligible. I asked him if I could bring him anything, like coffee, but he said not.

After a while, in which he briefly dozed, he said with weakness, 'Patsy couldn't have been sweeter when I was in the Clinic. She came every day, you know. She looked after my flowers . . . I had so many plants, people were so kind. Everyone in the Clinic said how lucky I was to have such a loving, thoughtful and beautiful daughter . . . and perhaps she was in and out when Robert came, but I can't think how she thought you had *stolen* the Cup. You must be mistaken about that, you know.'

'Don't worry about it,' I said.

Armed with generous cash from my mother I trekked back by rail to Reading and went to see the firm of Young and Uttley, the investigators recommended by Tobias. An unprepossessing male voice on the telephone having given me a time and a place, I found a soulless box of an office – outer room, inner room, desks, filing cabinets, computers and coat stand – with an inhabitant, a man of about my own age dressed in jeans, black hard boots, a grubby singlet with cut-out armholes and a heavy black hip-slung belt shining with aggressive studs. He had an unshaven chin, close-cropped dark hair, one earring dangling – right ear – and the word HATE in black letters across the backs of the fingers of both hands.

'Yeah?' he said, when I went in. 'Want something?'

'I'm looking for Young and Uttley. I telephoned—'

'Yeah,' said the voice I'd heard on the phone. 'See. Young and Uttley are *partners*. That's their pictures on the wall, there. Which one do you want?'

He pointed to two glossy eight-by-ten-inch black-and-white photographs drawing-pinned to a framed cork board hanging on a dingy wall. Alongside hung a framed certificate giving Young and Uttley licence to operate as private investigators, though to my understanding no such licence was necessary in Britain, nor existed. A ploy to impress ignorant clients, I supposed.

Mr Young and Mr Uttley were, first, a sober dark-suited man with a heavy moustache, a striped tie and a hat, and secondly, a wholesome fellow in a pale blue jogging suit, carrying a football and a whistle and looking like a dedicated schoolteacher going out to coach children.

I turned away, smiling, and said to the skinhead watching me, 'I'll take you as you are.'

'What do you mean?'

'Those pictures are both you.'

'Quick, aren't you?' he said tartly. 'And Tobe warned me, and all.'

'I asked him for someone good, honest and discreet.'

'You got him. What do you want done?'

I said, 'Where did you learn your trade?'

'Reform school. Various nicks. Do you want me or not?'

'I want the discreet bit most of all.'

'Priority.'

'Then I want you to follow someone and find out if he meets, or knows where to find, four other people.'

'Done,' he said easily. 'Who are they?'

I drew them for him in a mixture of pencil and ball-point, having somewhere lost my charcoal. He looked at the drawings, one of Surtees Benchmark, and one of each of my four attackers.

I told him Surtees's name and address. I said I knew nothing about the others except their ability to punch.

'Are those four how you got that eye?'

'Yes. They robbed my house in Scotland, but they have south-east England voices.'

He nodded. 'When did they hit you?'

'Tuesday morning.'

He mentioned his fee and I paid him a retainer for a week. I gave him Jed's phone number and asked him to report.

'What do I call you?' I asked.

'Young or Uttley, take your pick.'

'Young and Utterly Outrageous, more like.'

'You're so sharp, you'll cut yourself.'

I went grinning to the train.

I spent the later part of the afternoon shopping, accompanied by my long-suffering mother, who paid for everything with her credit cards.

'I suppose,' she said at one point, 'you weren't *insured* against the loss of your winter clothes and your climbing gear and your paints?'

I looked at her sideways, amused.

She sighed.

'I did insure the jeep,' I said.

'That's something, at least.'

Back at Park Crescent I changed into some of the new things and left the jodhpur boots, padded jacket, crash helmet and goggles for return to Emily sometime, and I told Ivan (having checked with Margaret Morden) that so far the brewery's creditors were earning haloes and had agreed to meet on Monday.

'Why don't you stay here?' he said, a shade petulantly. 'Your mother would like it.'

I hadn't told him about the attack on the bothy so as not to trouble him and he hadn't persisted in asking how I'd hurt my eye. I explained my departure in the one way that would satisfy him.

'Himself wants me up there . . . and I'd better do something about the Cup.'

Relaxing, he nodded. 'Keep it safe.'

The three of us tranquilly ate an Edna-cooked dinner, then I shook Ivan's hand, hugged my mother warmly, humped my bags and boxes along to Euston, boarded the Royal Highlander and slept my way to Scotland.

Even the air at Dalwhinnie smelled different. Smelled like home. Cold. Fresh. A promise of mountains.

Jed Parlane was striding up and down to keep warm and blowing on his fingers. He helped carry my clutter out to his car and said he was relieved to see me and how was I feeling

'Good as new.'

'That's more than can be said for the bothy.'

'Did you lock it?' I asked, trying not to sound anxious.

'Relax. Yes, I did. In fact I got a new lock for it. Whatever was there when you left is still there. Himself asks me to drive over and check every day. No one is sniffing around, that I can see. The police want to interview you, of course.'

'Sometime.'

Jed drove me not to the bothy but, as arranged, straight to Kinloch Castle to talk to Himself.

The castle was no fairy-tale confection of Disney spires and white-sugar icing, but like all ancient Scottish castles had been heavily constructed to keep out both enemies and weather. It was of thick and plain perpendicular grey stone with a minimum of narrow windows that had once been arrow slots for archers. Built on a rise to command views of the valley at its foot, it looked dour and inhospitable and threatening even on sunny days, and could chill the soul under nimbostratus.

My father had grown up there, and as a grandson of the old earl I'd played there as a child until it held no terrors: but times had changed and the castle itself no longer belonged to the Kinloch family but was the property of Scotland, administered and run as a tourist attraction by one of the conservation organisations. Himself, who had effected the transfer, had pronounced the roof upkeep and the heating bills too much for even the Kinloch coffers, and had negotiated a retreat to a smaller snugger home in what had once been the kitchen wing with living quarters for a retinue of dozens.

Himself would on occasion dress in historic Highland finery and act as host to visiting monarchs in the castle's vast main dining-hall, and it had been after one such grand evening, about six years earlier, that an enterprising band of burglars in the livery of footmen had lifted and borne away an irreplaceable gold-leafed eighteenth-century dinner service for fifty. Not a side plate, not a charger, had surfaced since.

It had been less than a year later, when a second theft had deprived the castle of several tapestry wall-hangings, that Himself had thought of a way of keeping safe the best known and most priceless of the many Kinloch treasures, the jewel-encrusted solid gold hilt of the ceremonial sword of Prince Charles Edward Stuart, Bonnie Prince Charlie.

It had, of course, meant taking the hilt out of its supposedly thief-proof display case and replacing the real thing with a replica. Ever since he had whisked the genuine article to safety, Himself had politely refused to tell the castle's administrators where to find it. It belonged to *him*, he maintained, as it had been given personally by Prince Charles Edward to his ancestor, the Earl of Kinloch at the time, and had been handed down to him, the present earl, in the direct male line.

So had the castle, the administrators said. The hilt belonged to the nation.

Not so, Himself argued. The castle transfer documents had not included personal property and had in fact specifically excluded the hilt.

There had been hot debates in newspapers and on television as to when, if ever, a gift to one man became the property of all.

Moreover, as Himself pointed out, the hilt had been given as thanks and appreciation for hospitality, horses and provisions. The facts were well attested. Prince Charles Edward, on his long retreat northwards (after his nearly successful campaign to win the English crown) had stayed for two nights at Kinloch Castle, had been comforted and revictualled, his retinue rested and re-horsed, for which services he had passed on to the then earl the hilt of his ceremonial sword, the blade having been earlier snapped off short in an accident.

The sword had never been used in nor intended for battle: it was too heavy and too ornate, a symbol of power and pomp only. The Prince, his dreams shattered like the blade, had left it behind and ridden on towards Inverness, to what proved to be his army's last decisive defeat at Culloden.

The Prince, tougher in flight, had famously escaped across Scotland to the Western Isles, making it safely back to France. The Earl of Kinloch, not so lucky, had been beheaded by the English for his allegiance (like poor fat old Lord Lovat) but had by then passed the splendid hilt to his son, who passed it to *his* son, and so on down the generations. It had become known as the 'Honour of the Kinlochs', and Himself, the present earl, though he had had to cede his castle, had finally won a declaration in the courts (still disputed) that the hilt, for his lifetime at least, belonged to *him*.

Since he had 'disappeared' the hilt, the castle had been further robbed of a display of Highland artifacts: shields, claymores and brooches. Himself, in residence in London at the time of that break-in, had made sarcastic remarks about bureaucrats being hopeless custodians of treasures. Ill-feeling flew like barbs in the air. The castle's bruised administrators were now hell-bent on finding the hilt, to prove that Himself was no better at guarding things than they were.

Under guise of rewiring and refurbishing the castle, including Himself's wing, they were inching with probes everywhere, determined on uncovering the cache. All they had wrung out of Himself was a promise that the Honour of the Kinlochs had not left his property. The ill-feeling and the search went on.

Jed having decanted me at the private wing's seldom-locked door I went inside and found my uncle in his dining-room, dressed in tweeds despite the early hour and pouring coffee from a pot on the sideboard.

He gave me, as always when we met after an interval, the salutation of my whole name, to which I replied with old and easy formality.

'Alexander.'

'My lord.'

He nodded, smiled faintly, and gestured to the coffee.

'Breakfast?'

'Thank you.'

He took his cup over to the table and began eating toast. Two places had been laid at the table, and he waved me to the free one.

'That's laid for you,' he said. 'Your aunt stayed in London.' I sat and ate toast and he asked me if I'd had a good journey.

'I slept all the way.'

'Good.'

He was a tall man, topping me by at least four

inches, and broad and large without looking fat. At sixty-five he had grey hair showing a white future, a strong nose, heavy chin and guarded eyes. His physical movements tended to be uncoordinated and clumsy; his mind was as tough and solid as an oak. If it were true that he'd told Ivan he would trust me with his life, then the reverse in general was also true, but like many good men he tended to trust too many people, and I wouldn't have staked my life on his absolute silence, even though any indiscretion would have been unintentional.

He said, spreading marmalade, 'Jed told me what happened at the bothy.'

'Boring.'

He wanted me to tell him in detail what had happened, so I did, though with distaste. I told him also about Ivan giving me the power of attorney, and my experiences in Reading.

He drank three cups of coffee, stretching as if absently for slice after slice of toast.

Eventually I asked him calmly, 'So do you have the King Alfred Gold Cup? Is it here?'

He answered broodingly, 'I did tell Ivan you were good at hiding things.'

'Mm.' I paused. 'Probably someone heard you.'

'God, Al.'

I said, 'I think it was the chalice, not the hilt, that those men were trying to find at the bothy. I also think they hadn't been told precisely what they were looking for. They kept saying "Where is it?" but they didn't say what they meant by *it*. I thought at the time they meant the hilt, because I didn't know Ivan had given you the Cup, but also it seemed possible they were simply fishing for anything I valued.' I sighed. 'Anyway, I'd say now the *it* was definitely the Cup.'

He said heavily, 'Jed said they'd hurt you badly.'

'That was Tuesday. Today's Saturday, and I'm fine. Don't worry about it.'

'Was it my fault?'

'It was the Finance Director's fault for running off with the brewery's cash.'

'But mine for suggesting you to Ivan.'

'It's history.'

He hesitated. 'I still have to decide what to do with that damned lump of gold.'

I did not make instant glad-eyed offers to keep it safe.

He listened to my silence and gave me a rueful shake of the head.

'I can't ask it of you, I suppose,' he said.

Next time you'll scream . . . There would be no next time.

I said, 'Patsy has told a few people that I already have the Cup. She's saying I stole it from the brewery.'

'But that's nonsense!'

'People believe her.'

'But you've never been to the brewery. Not for years, anyway.'

I agreed. 'Not for years.'

'Anyway,' said my uncle, 'it was Ivan himself who took the Cup out of the brewery, on the day before his heart attack. He told me he was feeling deeply upset and depressed. His firm of auditors – what's that chap's name . . . Tollright? – were warning him he was on the point of losing everything. And you know Ivan . . . he was worried both about his workpeople losing their jobs and about himself losing face and credibility. He takes his baronetcy and his membership of the Jockey Club very seriously . . . he could not bear having his whole life collapse in failure.'

'But it wasn't his fault.'

'He appointed Norman Quorn to be Finance Director. He says he no longer trusts his own judgment. He's taking too much guilt onto his own shoulders.'

'Yes.'

'So when he could see bankruptcy and disgrace ahead, he simply walked out with the Cup. Sick at heart was the phrase he used. Sick at heart.'

Poor Ivan. Poor sick heart.

I asked, 'Did he take the Cup to Park Crescent? Is that where you collected it from?'

My uncle half laughed. 'Ivan said he was afraid it would be as accessible in Park Crescent as in the brewery. He wanted to keep it out of any asset-pool and he didn't want to leave a paper-trail, like renting a bank vault, so he left it . . . you'll laugh . . . he left the treasure in a cardboard box in the cloakroom of his club. Left it in the care of the door-keeper.'

'Hell's teeth.'

'I fetched it from his club. Gave the doorman a thank you. Brought the Cup up here, in my car. James and I drove up here together as usual, you see. The family flew up, of course.'

James was his eldest son, his heir.

'I didn't tell James what I'd got,' Himself observed thoughtfully. 'James doesn't understand the word secret.'

James, a friendly fellow, liked to talk. Life, to my cousin James, was mostly a lark. He had a pretty wife and three wild children, 'all away sailing this week,' explained Himself, 'when they should be back at school.'

My uncle and I left the dining-room and walked outside round the whole ancient complex, as he liked to do, our feet quiet on the sheep-cropped grass.

'I asked Ivan how much the King Alfred Cup was actually worth,' he said. 'Everyone tends to refer to it as priceless, but it isn't, of course. Not like the hilt.'

'How much did Ivan say?'

'He said it was a symbol. He says you can't put a price on a symbol.'

'I suppose he's right.'

We walked a way in silence, then he said, 'I told Ivan I wanted to get the Cup valued. If he wanted me to get you to look after it, I had to know its worth.'

'What did he say?'

'He got very agitated. He said if I took it to a reputable valuer he would end up losing it. He said it was too well known. He began panting with distress. I had to assure him I wouldn't take it to anyone that would recognise it.'

'But,' I said, 'no one else could give you a reliable estimate.'

He smiled. We rounded the southernmost corner and turned our faces into the endless wind.

'This afternoon,' he said, raising his voice, 'we'll find out.'

The valuer summoned to the castle was neither an auctioneer nor a jeweller, but a thin eighty-year-old woman, a retired lecturer in English from St Andrew's University, Dr Zoë Lang, with a comet tail of distinguished qualifications after her name.

My uncle explained he had met her 'at some function or other', and when she arrived, gushing but overwhelmingly intellectual, he waved a vague hand in my direction and introduced me as 'Al, one of my many nephews'.

'How do you do?' Dr Lang asked politely, giving me a strong bony handshake with her gaze elsewhere. 'Cold day, isn't it?'

Himself made practised small-talk and led the way

into the dining-room, where with gentle ceremony he sat his guest at the table.

'Al,' he said to me, 'there's a box in the sideboard, right-hand cupboard. Put it on the table, would you?'

I found and carried across a large brown cardboard box stuck all over with sticky tape and conspicuously marked in big black handwritten capitals, 'Books. Property of Sir I. Westering'.

'Open it, Al,' Himself instructed without excitement. 'Let's see what we've got.'

Dr Lang looked politely interested, but no more.

'I have to warn you again, Lord Kinloch,' she said in her pure Scots voice, 'that almost no significant works of goldsmiths' art survive from the ninth century in England. I have done as you asked and kept your request private, which has been no hardship as the last thing you want, I'm sure, is ridicule.'

'The last,' Himself agreed gravely.

Dr Zoë Lang had straight grey hair looped back into a loose bun on her neck. She wore glasses and lipstick, and clothes too large for her thin frame. There was a small gold brooch but no rings. Something about her, all the same, warned one not to think in terms of dry old virginal spinster.

I ripped off the sticky tape and opened the box, and found inside, as promised, books: old editions of Dickens, to be precise.

'Keep going, Al,' my uncle said.

I lifted out the books and underneath came to a grey duster-cloth draw-string bag enclosing another box. I lifted that out also.

The inner box, in size a twelve-inch cube, was of black leather with gold clasps. Between the clasps, stamped in small gold letters, were the words MAXIM, London. I freed the box from its protecting bag and pushed it across the table to Himself.

'Dr Lang,' he said courteously, pushing the box on further into her reach, 'do us the honour.'

Without flourish she undid the clasps and opened the box, and then sat as still as marble while I felt her surprise in mental gusts across the table.

'Well,' she said finally, and again, '*Well . . .*'

Inside the box, supported by white satin-covered cushioning, the King Alfred Gold Cup lay on its side. I had never actually seen it before and nor, from his expression, had my uncle Robert.

No wonder, I thought, that Ivan had wanted to keep that Cup for his own. No wonder he wanted it hidden and kept safe. That Cup must have come to mean as much to him as Prince Charles Edward's sword hilt had come to mean to the earls of Kinloch, the affirmation that the personal stewardship of symbolic treasures should not be whisked away by ephemeral grey-faces, who wouldn't, down the decades, care a jot.

King Alfred's Cup, bigger than I'd imagined, was in shape a wide round bowl on a sturdy neck with a spreading foot. The rim of the bowl was crenellated like many castles (Windsor, but not the Kinlochs'): its sides glittered with red, blue and green inlaid stones and overall it shone with the warm unmistakable golden glow of twenty-two carats at least.

With almost reverence Dr Lang lifted out the astonishing object and stood it on the polished wood of the table, where it gleamed as if with inner light.

Dr Lang cleared her throat and said as if pulling herself down to earth, 'King Alfred never saw this, of course. It's shaped like a chalice, but if King Alfred ever used anything like this to take communion, it would have been much smaller and, of course, very much lighter. This cup must weigh five or more pounds. No . . . sad as I am to say it, this cup is modern.'

'*Modern?*' Himself echoed, surprised.

'Certainly not medieval,' regretted the expert. 'Almost certainly Victorian. Eighteen-sixty, or thereabouts. Very handsome. Beautiful, even. But not old.'

The cup had what looked like a pattern engraved right round the top below the crenellations and again round the lower third of the bowl. Dr Lang looked attentively at the patterns and smiled with obvious enjoyment.

'The cup is engraved with a poem in Anglo-Saxon,' she said. 'No trouble spared. But it's still Victorian. And I doubt if those coloured stones are rubies and emeralds, though you'd need to get an informed opinion for that.'

'Can you read the poem?' I asked.

She glanced at me briefly. 'Of course. I taught Anglo-Saxon for years. Wonderful vigorous poetry, what little's left of it. No printing presses or copying machines then, of course.' She fingered the bands of engraving. 'This is Bede's Death Song. Very famous. Bede died in 735, long before Alfred was born.' She turned the cup round, searching with her fingers for the beginning of the verse. 'In literal translation it says, "Before that sudden journey no one is wiser in thought than he needs to be, in considering, before his departure, what will be adjudged to his soul, of good or evil, after his death-day."'

Her old voice held the echo of years of lecturing to students; the authority of confident scholarship. At seventeen I had run away from that sort of slightly didactic tone and deprived myself of much enlightenment in consequence, and all these years later I found I still irrationally resented her perfectly justifiable consciousness of the high ground of superior knowledge.

Be ashamed of yourself, Al, I thought. Be humble. Bede's Death Song's message was of taking stock of the good and evil one did on earth because hell after death was a certainty. Unimaginable centuries later I believed that the only real hell was on earth and usually undeserved: and I was not going to discuss it with Zoë Lang.

I took it for a certainty that Ivan knew what teaching was engraved on his Cup. He had judged and found himself culpable and was harder on himself precisely because his standard for his own probity had been set so high. I wondered if he valued the Cup more for what was inscribed on it than for its intrinsic worth.

'So how much,' Himself was asking his expert, 'should one insure this Cup for?'

'Insure?' She pursed her lips. 'You could weigh it and multiply by the current price of gold, or you could maintain it is a valuable and interesting example of Victorian romanticism, or you could say it's worth dying for.'

'Not that.'

'People die in defence of their property all the time. It's a powerful instinct.' She nodded as if to emphasise the point. 'I don't think you could insure this Cup for any more than its worth in gold.'

Its weight in gold wouldn't save the brewery or go anywhere near subtracting even a significant nought.

My uncle thoughtfully restored the Cup to its box and closed the lid. The whole room looked a little darker at its eclipse.

'The accounts of King Alfred burning the cakes and suffering from haemorrhoids were all tosh,' Dr Lang said in her lecturing voice. 'King Alfred suffered from spin-doctors. But the fact remains, he is the only king in Britain ever to be called great. Alfred the Great. Born in Wantage, Berkshire. He was the fifth son, you know. Primogeniture wasn't supreme. They chose the fittest. Alfred was a scholar. He could read and write, both in Latin and his native tongue, Anglo-Saxon. He freed southern England – Wessex – from the rule of the invading Danes, first by appeasement and sly negotiation, then by battle. He was *clever.*' Her old face shone. 'People now try to make him a twentieth-century thinking social worker who founded schools and wrote new good laws, and the probabilities are that he did both, but only in the context of his own times. He died in 899, and no other well-authenticated king of that whole first millennium is so revered or honoured, or even remembered. It's a great pity this remarkable gold chalice here isn't a genuine ninth-century treasure, but of course it would have been either stolen or lost when Henry VIII devastated the churches. So many old treasures were buried in the fifteen-thirties to keep them safe, and the buriers died or were killed without telling where the treasures were hidden, and all over England farmers still to this day find gold deep in their fields, but not this Cup. Alas, it wasn't around in the days of Henry VIII. I think, actually, that the proper place for it now is in a museum. All such treasures should be cared for and displayed in museums.'

She stopped. Himself, who disagreed with her, thanked her warmly for her trouble and offered her wine or tea.

'What I would like,' she said, 'is to see the Kinloch hilt.'

Himself blinked. 'We have only the replica on show.'

'The real one,' she said. 'Show me the real one.'

After less than three seconds he said, smiling, 'We have to keep it safe from Henry VIII.'

'What do you mean?'

'I mean we have had to bury it to keep it.' He was making a joke of it and, unwillingly, she smiled tightly and settled for a sight of the copy.

We walked down the long passage where once relays of footmen had hurried with steaming dishes from kitchen to Great Hall, and Himself unlocked the weighty door that let us into the castle proper.

The Great Hall's walls, thanks to the theft of all the tapestries, were now for the most part grimly bare. The display cases, since the disappearance of the priceless dinner service, were unlit and empty. The long centre table, where once fifty guests had dined in splendour, bore a thin film of dust. Without comment my uncle walked down the long room under its high vaulted ceiling until he came to the imposing grilled glass display unit at the far end that had once held the true Honour of the Kinlochs.

Himself flicked a switch. Lights inside the glass case came to brilliant life and beamed onto the gold-looking object inside.

The replica hilt lay on black velvet and, even though one knew it was not the real thing, it looked impressive.

'It is gold plated,' its owner said. 'The red stones are

spinel, not ruby. The blue stones are lapis lazuli, the green ones are peridots. I commissioned it and paid for it, and no one disputes that this is mine.'

Dr Zoë Lang studied it carefully and in silence.

The hilt itself, though larger than a large man's fist, looked remarkably like the King Alfred Gold Cup, except that there were no crenellations and no engraving. There was instead the pommel, the grip that fitted into the palm of the hand: and instead of the circular foot, only the neck into which the snapped-off blade had been fastened.

The ceremonial sword that Prince Charles Edward had hoped to use at his coronation as rightful King of England and Scotland had been made for him in France (and, amazingly, paid for by him personally) in 1740. It had been his own to give, and on impulse, in gratitude and despair, he had given it.

Dr Lang, with fervour and unexpected fanaticism, said intensely, 'This imitation may be your own, but I agree with the castle's custodians that the real Honour of the Kinlochs belongs to Scotland.'

'Do you think so?' Himself asked politely, good manners and jocularity in his voice. 'I would argue with you, of course, and I would defend my right of ownership . . .' He paused provocatively.

'Yes?' she prompted.

He smiled sweetly. 'To the hilt.'

CHAPTER SIX

'Al,' Himself asked thoughtfully, as we walked back from seeing Zoë Lang out to her taxi, 'how far would you actually go in defending the Honour of the Kinlochs?'

'Up to and including the hilt?'

'I'm not joking, Al.'

I glanced at his heavy troubled face.

'The answer,' I said, 'is that I don't know.'

After a pause he asked, 'Would you have given up the hilt to the four men who attacked you if they'd told you what they wanted and had used more than their fists?'

'I don't know.'

'But how much urge did you have anyway to tell them where to look?'

'None,' I said. 'I didn't like them.'

'Al, be serious.'

'They made me angry. They made me feel futile. I would have denied them anything I could.'

'I don't ask for you to suffer to keep that thing safe.

If they attack you again, don't let them hurt you. Tell them what they want to know.'

I said with humour, 'You wouldn't have said that two hundred years ago.'

'Times change.'

We went peacefully into his house and into his dining-room, where the black cube containing the King Alfred Gold Cup still lay on the table. We checked briefly to make sure that the gold prize was still inside, and I ran a finger over the faint indentations of Bede's Death Song: consider the evil one does on earth, because a reckoning awaits.

Was it good or evil, in changing times, to pay for physical relief on earth with one's eternal honour?

Where did common sense begin?

At what point did one duck the scream?

I had no need to ask such questions aloud. Himself – my august uncle, my hereditary clan chief – was the product of the same ancient ethos and conditioning that I had received from his brother, and I had willy nilly inherited the mainstream Kinloch mind, stubbornness and all.

Himself and I re-enclosed the black cube in its drawstring bag and replaced it in the cardboard box with the copies of Dickens on top. I restuck it all as best I could with the wide brown fastening tape, though the result couldn't be called secure, and we put the box back in the sideboard for the want of anywhere better.

'We can't leave it there for ever,' my uncle said.

'No.'

'Do you trust Dr Lang?'

I was surprised by the question, but said, 'I would trust her to be true to her beliefs.'

'Think of somewhere better for the Cup, Al.'

'I'll try.'

At his own request I hadn't told him to the inch where to find the hilt, though he knew it was somewhere at the bothy. After much consideration we had, as a precaution against us both inconveniently dying with our secret untold, like Henry VIII's evaders, entrusted Jed with the basic information.

'If you have to,' Himself had said to him, 'dig around and pull the bothy apart stone by stone. Otherwise, forget what we've told you.'

Jed couldn't, of course, forget it although he had never alluded to it since except to say once that he felt overwhelmed by our faith in his loyalty. If Jed had been going to betray us to the castle's administrators he could have done it at any time in the past few years, but instead had taken the game of hide and seek into his own private world in enjoyment, and it was certainly the basis of the solid friendship between the two of us.

Jed came back to the castle late in the afternoon, still with my gear in the boot of his car, wanting to know if he could drive me home to the bothy.

'No,' Himself said decisively. 'Al will stay here tonight. Sit down, Jed. Get yourself a drink.'

We were by then in the room my uncle considered

his own private domain, a severe predominantly brown room with walls bearing stuffed fish in glass cases and deers' antlers from long-past battles on the hills. There were also three of my paintings of his racehorses and one painting of his favourite gun-dog, much loved but now dead.

Jed fixed a glass of whisky and water and sat down on one of the elderly hard-stuffed chairs.

Himself as usual made the decisions. 'I see Al seldom enough. He will stay here tonight and tomorrow night to please me, and on Monday morning you can take him to the bothy and the police station, and anywhere else you care to. I'll be fishing the Spey next week. I have guests Monday, Tuesday and Wednesday. Thursday and Friday I'll be out on the moor with the guns . . .' He outlined his plans. 'James returns from sailing tomorrow. He'll be staying on here. His wife will take the children back to school. All clear, Jed?'

'Yes, sir.'

Jed and he discussed estate affairs for a while and I listened with half an ear and tried to imagine a good temporary home for Bede's Death Song engraved in gold.

I had asked Zoë Lang to read the poem aloud in Anglo-Saxon, and with enjoyment she had done so, her love of the old language giving the words shape and meaning and new life. I couldn't understand a syllable, but I could hear the throb and the pulse and the strong alliteration, and when I commented on it she'd told me a shade patronisingly that all Anglo-Saxon poetry had been written to be spoken, not read. The excitement, even the *intoxication*, she said, was engendered by the rhythmic beat as much as by the vivid imagery of the words. The poems describing battle could set sword-arms twitching. 'The Dream of the Rood' would make a Christian of an atheist.

Himself and I had listened respectfully, and I thought how much the outward appearance of age could colour one's expectation of a person's character. I wanted to paint her as young, vibrant, fanatical, with the ghost of the way she looked now superimposed in thin light grey lines, like age's cobwebs.

I strongly sensed a singular individual powerful entity that might have intensified with time, not faded. We were dealing with that inner woman, and should not forget it.

If I underpainted thickly in Payne's grey mixed with titanium white, I thought, and then brought the essential person to glowing life with strong bone structure in a faithful portrait, no colour tricks or linear gimmicks, and then scratched down into the grey for the unthinkable future ... then with a steady hand and a strong vision I might produce a statement of terrible truth – or I might finish with a disaster fit only for the bin. To have the technique and the courage weren't always enough. Apart from vision as well, one needed luck.

Hide King Alfred's Gold Cup . . . my mind wandered back to the task in hand.

Hiding the Cup, for all its worth in gold, wasn't in the same sphere as hiding the hilt. Ivan might prize the Cup for reasons of his own, but as a symbol it wasn't entangled with history and an earl's beheading and generations of clan honour. The King Alfred Gold Cup had been fashioned a thousand years after the great king's days of glory: a tribute to him, undoubtedly, but never his own property.

The King Alfred Cup might be worth killing for . . . but not suffering for, or dying.

And yet . . . I asked myself again if I would have given the demon walkers that Cup if I'd known what they were looking for, if I'd had it to give, and I thought quite likely not. Anger . . . pride . . . *cussedness.*

Mad, weird, ridiculous Alexander.

The problem with hiding anything in the castle was that Himself was rarely in residence, while the administrators were not only in and out all the time but were also actively hunting treasure. In the family's private wing lived a full-time overall caretaker with his housekeeper wife, a conscientious worker who eviscerated private cupboards in the name of spring cleaning. The sideboard in the dining-room wouldn't shelter even a peanut for long. The discovery on the premises of a golden wonder, even if not the hilt, would have leaked into informed circles like burst pipes. If hiding the Cup involved hiding also any awareness of its existence, as I supposed it did, then the castle was out.

The castle grounds were out also, thanks to an efficient gardener.

So where?

Any thoughts anyone might have had about a peaceful evening were at that point blasted apart by the earthquake arrival of my friendly cousin James, who had listened to a gale-and-rain weather forecast and decided to run for port a day early, along with his boisterous family, who habitually lived fortissimo at Indy-car speed.

When the invasion stampeded upstairs to arrange bedrooms, I telephoned my mother and asked after Ivan. Things were no worse. There had been no further agitated crisis in the brewery's affairs: insolvency had gone into hiatus for the weekend.

'And Patsy?' I asked.

'Not a sound from her since yesterday morning.'

'My uncle Robert sends his regards.'

'And ours to him,' my mother said.

James, red haired and freckled, wandering by with gin and tonic in fist, asked amiably how the 'old boy' was doing.

'Depressed,' I said.

'Father says someone decamped with the brewery's nest egg.'

'Nest egg, chickens, battery hens, the lot.'

'What a lark, eh? How long are you staying?'

'Till Monday.'

'Great. Father's always saying we don't see enough of you. How are the daubs?'

'In abeyance,' I said, and gave him a lightweight account of the trouble at the bothy.

'Good Lord!' He stared. 'I didn't think you had much there worth stealing.'

'Jeep and golf clubs, and bits and pieces.'

'What rotten luck.'

His sympathy was genuine enough. James would always summon nurses to patch up one's wounds.

'Did they take your pipes?' he asked, concerned.

'Luckily they're in Inverness. The bag had sprung a leak.'

'Are you entering the contests this year?'

'I'm not good enough.'

'You don't practise enough, that's all.'

'The winners are nearly always army pipe majors. You know that. Why do I bother to say it?'

'I just like to encourage people,' he said, beaming; and I thought that that in truth was his great gift, to make people feel better about their lives.

The piping contests, held every autumn, took place from the far north all the way south to London. I had once or twice tried my hand in a piobaireachd competition, but it had been like a novice downhill skier taking on Klammer or Killy, an interesting experience memorable only for not having made an absolute fool of oneself.

Besides, I had political problems with some of the

pibrochs, the ancient laments for the deaths and defeats of history. I couldn't – wouldn't – play 'My King has landed at Moidart', because the King that had landed was Prince Charles Edward, rightful King of England by descent, but disqualified (since Henry VIII's quarrel with the Pope) because of being Roman Catholic. Prince Charles Edward landed at Moidart in the Western Isles to begin his fateful march towards London, a thrust for the Crown, however understandable, that had led to the ruination of Scotland. In the wake of Prince Charles Edward's defeat at Culloden, the English, to remove the threat of a third upheaval (the 1715 and 1745 rebellions having been barely unsuccessful), had notoriously chased the Scots from their lands and had tried to wipe out nationhood by outlawing the speaking of Gaelic, the wearing of the tartan and the playing of the pipes. Scotland had never recovered. Sure, the tartan, the pipes and the slightly sentimental allegiances had crept back, but they were tourist attractions contrasting affectedly with the drab slab functional housing round the commercially regenerated modern city of Glasgow.

The direct descendant of Mary, Queen of Scots, had brought ruin, still unresolved, to most of Scotland – though even at Culloden, sixty per cent of those fighting *against* the Bonny Prince had been Scots themselves, not English – and although to please my uncle I guarded the lethal gift to my ancestor, I couldn't feel anything but fury for the inept, selfish, vain and ultimately faint-hearted Prince. I played laments for those he'd damaged. I played laments for the damage he'd done. I never felt love for the man.

Saturday evening passed in the chaos indigenous to James's family, and in the morning when I went downstairs in search of coffee I found Himself in the dining-room looking around him as if in bewilderment at an empty cardboard box, old faded leather-bound copies of Dickens, an empty black cube with white satin lining and a grey draw-string duster bag all lying about haphazardly on the floor.

The sideboard door stood open. The King Alfred Gold Cup had gone.

There were squeals from the kitchen next door. Children's voices. High.

Dazedly my uncle opened the connecting door and I followed him into the large unmodernised kitchen, an expanse of black and white tiling still called on old castle plans 'the cold preparation room'. Shades of old vegetables, I thought. Food nowadays mostly arrived at the castle in caterers' vans, wrapped in film and ready to heat and eat.

James was leaning against the sink, coffee mug in hand, indulgent smile in place.

His three unruly children – two boys and a girl – scrambled around on the floor, all of them wearing large saucepans on their heads with the handles pointing backwards. Spacewatch good guys, we were told.

The King Alfred Cup also stood on the floor, upside

down. Himself bent from the waist and picked it up, finding it heavier than he expected.

'Hey,' objected his elder grandson, standing up to face him, 'that's the galactic core of M.100 with all its Cepheid variables in those red stones. We have to keep it safe from the black-hole suction mob.'

'I'm glad to hear it,' his grandfather said dryly.

The boy – Andrew – was eleven years old and already rebellious, hard-eyed and tough. If time took its normal course he would one day succeed James as earl. James might be open to soft persuasion but I wanted to know for sure about his son.

I said, 'Andrew, if you had a favourite toy, something you really valued, and someone tried very hard to take it away from you . . . suppose he even threatened to hurt you if you didn't give it to him, what would you do?'

He said promptly, as if he thought the question feeble, 'Bash his face in.'

My uncle smiled. James said with mild protest, 'Andy, you would talk it over and make a deal.'

His son repeated stalwartly, 'I'd bash his face in. Can we have the Cepheid monitor back?'

'No,' his grandfather said. 'You shouldn't have taken it out of its box.'

'We were looking for something worth fighting for,' Andrew said.

James defended them. 'They haven't done it any harm. What is it, anyway? It can't be real gold.'

Himself thrust the Cup into my arms, where its weight again surprised. 'Put it away safely,' he said.

'OK.'

'It's a racing challenge trophy,' my uncle explained unexcitedly to his son. 'I can't keep it for more than a year and I need to give it back without dents in.'

The explanation satisfied James entirely and he told his children to look for a substitute galactic goody.

On an impulse I asked him if he would like to spend some of the day playing golf. We both belonged to the local club where, with varying success, I quite often walked after the elusive white ball, but there were seldom days when we could go out together.

He looked pleased, but said, 'I thought you said your clubs were stolen.'

'I might buy some new ones.'

'Great, then.'

He phoned the club, who found a slot for us in the afternoon, and we drove over in good time for the pro shop to kit me out with better clubs than the ones I'd lost: and, for good measure, I acquired snazzy black-and-white shoes with spikes on, and gloves and balls and umbrellas: also a lightweight blue waterproof bag to carry things in and a trolley like James's to pull everything along on wheels. Thus re-equipped I went out with my cousin into the wind and rain, which had arrived as forecast, and got happily soaked to the skin despite the umbrellas.

'Will you paint this?' James asked, squelching on wet grass.

'Yes, of course.'

'You're not really as weird as we all think, are you?'

I putted a ball to the rim of a hole, where it obstinately stopped.

'I paint frustration,' I said, and gave the ball a kick.

James laughed, and in good spirits we finished the eighteen holes and went back to the castle for the nineteenth.

My hands-on relationship with golf was essential to my work, I'd found. It wasn't that I had much skill, but in a way the failures were more revelatory than success: and I particularly liked to play with James who laughed and lost or won with equal lack of seriousness.

The only really warm room in the whole castle complex (apart from the caretaker's quarters) was the home of the vast hot water tank, where ranks of airers dried out the persistent Scottish rains. James and I accordingly showered, changed, and left all our wet things steaming, including my sopping new shoes and golf bag, and then ambled back to the dining-room for tinctures.

James's children were in there. The King Alfred Cup, though still in its white satin nest, lay in full glorious view on the polished table under a chandelier's light.

'You didn't say we couldn't *look* at it,' Andy

objected to his father's mild rebuke. 'We couldn't find *anything* else worth fighting a space war for.'

I said to James, 'What about the hilt?'

'Oh yes.' He thought it over. 'But we'd only see the replica, and anyway, I can't let the children through into the castle proper. I promised Himself I wouldn't.'

'Let's ask him,' I said. So we found him in his own room and asked, with the result that all of us, Himself, James, James's wife and children and I, walked the length of the Great Hall and stood round the grilled glass cage, staring down at its floodlit treasure.

'*That*,' Andrew decided, 'would be worth fighting a galactic space war for. If it was real, of course.'

'And you, James,' Himself asked, 'would you too fight for it?'

James, no fool, answered soberly, making what must have been to him an unwelcome commitment, 'If I had to, I suppose so, yes.'

'Good. Let's hope it's never necessary.'

'Where is the real one?' Andrew asked.

His grandfather said, 'We have to keep it safe from the black-hole suction mob.'

Andy's face was an almost unpaintable mixture of glee and understanding. A boy worth fighting for, I thought.

Himself carefully didn't look at me once.

*

It was still raining on Monday morning. James took his family to set off south, Himself left to meet his guests and ghillies at Crathie to bother the silver swimmers in the Spey, and Jed arrived to pick me up and set my normal life back on course.

He brought with him a replacement credit card and cheque-book which he had had sent to his house for me, and he'd heard from Inverness that my bagpipes were ready for collection. He had freed one of the estate's Land Rovers for my temporary use, and he lent me a fully charged portable phone to put me in touch with events in London and Reading. Reception was poor in the mountains, but better than nothing, he said.

I said inadequately, 'Thanks, Jed,' and he shook his head and grinned, shrugging it off.

'There's a new lock on the bothy, like I told you, and here are two keys,' he said, handing them over. 'I have a third. There aren't any others.'

I nodded and went out of doors with him, and found the boxes from London that I'd left in his car on Saturday evening already piled into the Land Rover. I'd taken into Himself's house only clothes in a paper carrier and I left with them (dry) in an all-purpose heavy duty duffle bag from the gun-room. The bag smelled of cartridges, moors and old tweed: very Edwardian, very lost world.

Jed commented on my new clubs.

'Yes,' I said, 'but this time I'm storing my kit in the

club house. Where do you propose I should keep my pipes?'

Jed said awkwardly, 'Are you afraid the robbers will come back?'

'Would you be?'

'You can always stay with Flora and me.'

'Have you noticed,' I asked, 'how people tend to rebuild their earthquaked houses in the same place on the San Andreas fault? Or in the path of hurricanes?'

'You don't have to.'

'Call it blind faith,' I said.

'Call it obstinacy.'

I grinned. 'Definitely. But don't worry. This time I'll install a few burglar alarms.'

'There isn't any electricity.'

'Tins on strings with stones in.'

Jed shook his head. 'You're mad.'

'So they say.'

He gave up. 'The police are expecting you. Ask for Detective Sergeant Berrick. He came out with me to the bothy. He knows what the vandalism looks like.'

'OK.'

'Take care, Al. I mean it. Take care.'

'I will,' I said.

We drove off together but parted at the estate gates, from where I headed towards the bothy, stopping only once, briefly, to pay with a replacement cheque for the new golf gear, and unload it into a locker, which I would have done better to have done oftener in the past.

The new keys to the bothy door opened my way into the same old devastation that I'd left there six days earlier.

Nothing looked better. The only overall improvement was that it no longer hurt to move, a plus, I had to concede, of significant worth. With a sigh I dug out of the mess an unused plastic rubbish bag and, instead of its normal light load of paint-cleaning tissues, filled it with the debris of ruined acrylics and everything small but broken.

It was still raining out of doors. Indoors my mattress and bedding were soaked and smelling from a bucketful of dirty paint water. I wasn't sure what they'd done to my armchair, but it, too, smelled revolting.

Bastards.

Out of rainy-day habit I'd run the Land Rover into the shelter of the carport when I'd arrived, but at that point I backed it out again, and bit by bit stacked my ruined possessions in the dry space, painstakingly looking for anything *not* mine that might have been left behind by my attackers. When I'd finished, all that was left in the room was the bare metal and coiled wire bedstead, the chest of drawers (empty), one shelf of salvaged books, a frying pan with cooking tools and one easel (two broken). I swept the floor and collected coffee, sugar and sundry debris into a dustpan and gloomily looked at the dozens of superimposed paint-laden footprints on my wood-blocks, all left by the types of trainers sold by the million throughout Britain and useless for identifying the wearers.

In spite of the thoroughness of my search, the only thing I found that I hadn't had before was not a helpful half-used matchbook printed with the address and phone number of a boxing gym, but a pair of plastic-framed glasses.

I put them on and everything close went blurry. For long distances, they were sharp.

The prescription was stamped into one of the ear-pieces: −2.

They were, I thought, the sort of aid one could buy off revolving-stand displays all over the world. They were the sort of glasses worn by my attackers. A disguise. A theatrical prop. I wrapped them in a piece of tinfoil from a roll I sometimes used for instant makeshift palettes: one didn't have to scrape off old dry paint but could simply scrunch the whole thing up and throw it away. Some poverty-afflicted painters used old phone books that way all the time.

I carted the bags and boxes of new gear into the bothy from the Land Rover and stacked everything unopened on the bare springs of the bed. Then I locked the door, sat for a while in the Land Rover, thinking, and finally drove off in search of Detective Sergeant Berrick.

Within five minutes of my arrival, the Detective

Sergeant had told me he implacably disliked drug dealers, prostitutes, Englishmen, the Celtic football team, the Conservative party, anyone educated beyond sixteen, all superior officers, paperwork, rules forbidding him to beat up suspects, long-haired gits – and in particular long-haired gits who lived on mountains and got themselves cuffed up while eating handouts from people with titles who ought to be abolished. Detective Sergeant Berrick, in fact, revealed himself as a typical good-hearted aggressive Scot with a strong sense of justice.

He was thin, somewhere in the tail-end thirties, and would probably soon be promoted to become one of the superiors he despised. His manner to me was artificially correct and a touch self-righteous, a long way from the paternal instincts of his friendly old neighbourhood predecessor who had turned bad boys into good citizens for years but was now flying a desk in far off Perth, made useless by age regulations and the reclassification of paternalism as a dirty word.

Sergeant Berrick told me not to expect to get my goods back.

I said, 'I was wondering if you might have some luck with the paintings.'

'What paintings?' He peered at a list. 'Oh yes, here we are. Four paintings of scenes of golf courses.' He looked up. 'There was paint all over your place.'

'Yes.'

'And you painted those pictures yourself?'

'Yes.'

'Is there any way we could recognise them?'

'They had stickers on the back, in the top left-hand corner,' I said. 'Copyright stickers giving my name, Alexander, and this year's date.'

'Stickers can be pulled off,' he said.

'These stickers can't. The glue bonds with the canvas.'

He gave me a don't-bother-me stare but punched up my file on a computer.

'Copyright stickers on backs,' he said aloud, typing in the words. He shrugged. 'You never know.'

'Thanks,' I said.

'You could put another sticker over the top,' he said.

'Yes, you could,' I agreed, 'but you might not know my name is printed in an ink that shows up in X-rays.'

He stared. 'Tricky, aren't you?'

'It's a wicked world,' I said, and got an unpremeditated smile in return.

'We'll see what we can do,' he promised. 'How's that?'

'I'll paint your portrait if you find my pictures.'

He spread out on his desk the drawings I'd done at Dalwhinnie station of my assailants, and changed his challenging attitude to one of convinced interest.

'Paint my wife,' he said.

'Done.'

*

A few doors along from the police station I visited a shop that was a campers' heaven aimed at tourists, and there acquired a sleeping bag and enough essentials to make living in the stripped bothy possible, and then drove a long detour to Donald Cameron's far-flung post office to see if any letters had arrived for me in the past week, and to stock up, as I usually did, with food and a full gas cylinder.

'Will you be wanting to use my telephone, Mr Kinloch?' old Donald asked hopefully. 'There's something amiss with the one outside.'

I bet there is, I thought; but to please the old beggar I made one call on his instrument, asking the bagpipe restorers if there was any chance of their delivering my pipes either to Jed Parlane's house or to Donald Cameron's shop.

Old Donald practically snatched the receiver out of my hand and told the pipe people he would be going to Inverness on Wednesday and would collect my pipes for me personally: and so it was arranged. Donald, restoring the phone to its cradle, beamed at me with expectation.

'How much?' I asked, resigned, and negotiated a minor king's ransom.

'Always at your service, Mr Kinloch.'

It rained all the way up the muddy track to the bothy. Once there I sat in the comparative comfort of the Land Rover outside my locked front door and made inroads into the battery power of Jed's portable phone. Poor reception, but possible.

It was still office hours in Reading. I tried Tobias Tollright first with trepidation, but he was reasonably reassuring.

'Mrs Morden wants to talk to you. She held the meeting of creditors. They did at least attend.'

'And that's good?'

'Encouraging.'

I said, 'Tobe . . .'

'What is it?'

'Young and Uttley.'

Tobias laughed. 'He's a genius. Wait and see. I wouldn't recommend him to everyone, or everyone to him, but you're two of a kind. You both think sideways. You'll get on well together. Give him a chance.'

'Did he tell you that I engaged him?'

'Er . . .' The guilt of his voice raised horrible doubts in my mind.

'He surely didn't tell you what I asked him to do?' I said.

'Er . . .'

'So much for discretion.'

Tobias said again, lightheartedly, 'Give him a chance, Al.'

It was too late by then, I thought ruefully, to do anything else.

I phoned Margaret Morden and listened to her crisp voice.

'I laid out all the figures. The creditors all needed smelling salts. Norman Quorn took off with every last available cent, a really remarkable job. But I've persuaded the bank and the Inland Revenue to try to come up with solutions, and we are meeting again on Wednesday, when they've had a chance to consult their head offices. The best that one can say is that the brewery is basically still trading at a profit, and while it still has the services of Desmond Finch and the present brewmaster, it should go on doing so.'

'Did you . . . did you ask the creditors about the race?'

'They see your point. They'll discuss it on Wednesday.'

'There's hope, then?'

'But they want Sir Ivan back in charge.'

I said fervently, 'So do I.'

'Meanwhile you may still sign for him. He is adamant it should be you and no one else.'

'Not his daughter?'

'I asked him myself. He agreed to speak to me. Alexander, he said. No one else.'

'Then I'll do anything you need, and . . . Margaret . . .'

'Yes?'

'What are you wearing today?'

She gasped, and then laughed. 'Coffee and cream.'

'Soft and pretty?'

'It gets subliminal results. Wednesday – a gentle practical dark blue, touches of white. Businesslike but not threatening.'

'Appearances help.'

'Indeed they do . . .' her voice tailed off hesitantly. 'There's something odd, though.'

'Odd about what?'

'About the appearance of the brewery's accounts.'

Alarmed, I said, 'What exactly is odd?'

'I don't know. I can't identify it. You know when you can smell something but you don't know what it is? It's like that.'

'You worry me,' I said.

'It's probably nothing.'

'I trust your instincts.'

She sighed. 'Tobias Tollright drew up the audit. He's very reliable. If there were anything incongruous, he would have noticed.'

'Don't alarm the creditors,' I pleaded.

'They are interested only in the future. In getting their money. What I feel – a whisper of disquiet – is in the past. I'll sleep on it. Solutions often come in the night.'

I wished her useful dreams, and sat on my Scottish mountainside in the rain-spattered Land Rover realising how little I knew, and how much I relied on Tobe and Margaret and Young (or Uttley) for answers to questions I hadn't the knowledge to ask.

I wanted to paint.

I could feel the compulsion, the fusing of mental vision with the physical longing to feel the paint in my hands that came always before I did any picture worth looking at: the mysterious impetus that one had to call creation, whether the results were worth the process or not.

Inside the bothy there was an old familiar easel and the new painting supplies from London, and I had to instruct myself severely that two more phone calls had to be made before I could light a lamp (new from the camping shop) and prepare a canvas ready for morning.

Tack cotton duck onto a stretched frame. Prime three times with gesso to produce a good surface, let it dry. Lay on the Payne's grey mixed with titanium white. Make working drawings. Plan. Sleep. Dream.

I phoned my mother.

Ivan was no worse, no better. He had agreed to talk to some woman or other about saving the brewery, but he still wanted me to act for him, as he couldn't yet summon the strength.

'OK,' I said.

'The real trouble at present,' my mother said, 'is Surtees.'

'What about him?'

'He is *paranoid*. Patsy is furious with him. Patsy is furious about *everything*. I do wish you would come back. Alexander, you're the only person she can't bully.'

'Is she bullying Ivan?'

'She bullies him terribly, but he can't see it. He told Oliver Grantchester he wants to write a codicil to his Will, and it seems Oliver mentioned it to Patsy, and now Patsy is demanding to know what Ivan wants a codicil for, and for once Ivan won't tell me, and oh *dear*, it's so bad for Ivan. And she's practically *living* here, she's at his elbow every minute.'

'And Surtees? Why is he paranoid?'

'He says he's being followed everywhere by a skinhead.'

I said weakly, '*What?*'

'I know. It's stupid. No one else has seen this skinhead. Surtees says the skinhead disappears whenever he, Surtees, is with other people. Patsy's livid with him. I do wish they wouldn't crowd in here all the time. Ivan needs rest and quiet. Come back, Alexander ... please.'

The overt uncharacteristic plea was almost too much. Too many people wanted too much. I could see that they needed someone to decide things – Ivan, my mother, Tobias, Margaret, even my uncle Robert – but I didn't feel strong enough myself to give them all strength.

I wanted to *paint*.

To my mother I said, 'I'll come back soon.'

'When?'

Dear heaven, I thought, and said helplessly, 'Wednesday night.'

We said goodbye and, finally, I phoned Jed.

He said, 'All hell has broken loose at the castle.'

'What sort of hell?'

'Andy – Himself's young grandson – has run off with the King Alfred Gold Cup.'

CHAPTER SEVEN

I laughed.

'Well,' Jed said, 'I suppose it's quite funny.'

'What exactly happened?'

It seemed that soon after Himself and his guests returned to the castle for a good Scots afternoon tea of hot scones and fortified cups, Dr Zoë Lang had made an unheralded return visit, bringing with her an expert in precious and semi-precious stones. She couldn't rest, she said, while her evaluation of the King Alfred Cup had been incomplete.

Himself, Dr Lang, the jeweller and the fishing guests had all accordingly gone into the dining-room in the quest for truth.

The cardboard box had been retrieved from the sideboard and the copies of Dickens removed. The black leather cube had been lifted out and the gold clasp undone, and in the white satin nest . . . nothing.

My cousin James, who had returned from seeing his family onto the air shuttle from Glasgow to London, had instantly said he would tan the hide off his elder son, who had been fascinated by the Cup, but the Spacewatch good guy could not at that moment be reached for questioning, as he was by then somewhere on the road back to boarding school with his mother, who had no phone in her car.

Jed said, 'I called in to see Himself about estate business, and I found this old lady rather rudely telling him he shouldn't be trusted to keep the Kinloch hilt safe from robbers if he couldn't guard things from his own grandson, and Himself just stood there benevolently agreeing with her, which seemed to make her even crosser. Anyway, after she'd gone, he asked me to ask you if you thought he ought to worry about Andrew, so do you?'

'No.'

Jed's sigh was half a chuckle.

'I told Himself you had carried out of the castle one of those big old game-bags from the gun-room, and he beamed. But what's it all about? They were saying that that Cup is a racing challenge trophy, that's all. Is it really worth a lot?'

'It depends where you stand,' I said. 'It's gold. If you're rich, it's just an expensive bauble. If you're a thief, it's worth murder. In between – you balance the greed against the risks.'

'And to you? To Himself? To Sir Ivan?'

When I didn't reply at once, he said, 'Al, are you still there?'

'Yes . . . I don't know the answer, and I don't want to find out.'

On Tuesday morning a cold front swept the sky dramatically, clearing away the grey rain and leaving a high washed pale blue cosmos with a northern yellowish tint of sunlight. The bothy faced west, which often gave me long mornings of near-perfect painting light, followed by warm afternoon glows that I'd at first subconsciously translated into mellowing glazes and then, when I found out those pictures sold most quickly, into commercial technique. I did paint for a living: I also earned money so that I could paint to please only myself, when I wanted to.

On that Tuesday, on the grey-white underpainting, I lightly drew in pencil the head of a still-young woman, with a face already strongly defined by character, a face of good bone structure, of intelligence, of purpose. I drew her not looking straight ahead but as though she saw something to her right, and I drew her not smiling, not disapproving, not arrogant, not self-conscious, but simply *being*.

When the proportions and the expression were near to what I intended, I painted the whole head in light and dark intensities of ultramarine blue, mostly transparent, mixed with water. I painted dark blue shadows round the edges of the canvas, leaving light areas round the head itself, and worked dark shadows round the eyes and under the chin until I had a fairly complete monochrome portrait in blue on light grey.

She looked as I thought Dr Lang might have looked forty years earlier.

I had learned my trade from four different painters, one in Scotland, one in England, one in Rome and one in California, and had watched and assimilated and practised until I knew what paint would do, and what it wouldn't. Unable to afford art school, with a father dead and a mother newly married and rebuilding her own life, I had offered my services as cook, cleaner, gofer and dogsbody to the four accomplished painters in turn, asking only for payment in food, a patch of floor to sleep on, and scraps of paper and paint.

After three years of such profitable drudgery I'd received a surprise enquiry from my uncle: what, he wanted to know, would I like for a twenty-first coming-of-age birthday present? I'd asked for the use of a tumbledown shed on the mountainous part of his estate and a pass to give me an occasional game on the local golf course (which he owned).

He'd given me the use of the hut (once an overnight shelter for shepherds at lambing time), full membership of the golf club and some money for paints. Two years later he'd sent me to Lambourn to make portraits of the horses he had in training with Emily Jane Cox.

After I'd run from Lambourn he'd moved me from

the hut to the sturdier but ruined bothy and had paid for it to be made habitable; and a year after that he'd asked me to take care of the Honour of the Kinlochs.

I couldn't have refused him, even if I'd wanted to, which I hadn't.

I had all my younger life been in awe of him. It was only during the last five years that I'd grown old enough for a more adult understanding. He had of course taken the place of the father I'd lost, but much more than that he had become friend, partner and ally: and never would I trade on that privilege, either with him or within the family.

Brooding over my blue woman, I ate a cheese and chutney sandwich and in the afternoon overpainted the background with browns and crimsons, glazing and rubbing together the colours in the method called scumbling until I had a deep rich background that wasn't identifiably blue or brown or red but which receded from the eye, leaving the face itself startlingly near and clear.

Tuesday night I slept again on the floor in the sleeping bag and dreamed of colours, and early on Wednesday, as soon as it was light, began overpainting flesh onto the blue bones, working from light areas to dark, giving her strength and brain but not a peach-skin luminous beauty. By afternoon she was a woman who would both excel in an academic world and comfort a strong man in bed . . . or so, in my mind, I saw her.

At about the time when every day Jed could be found in the estate office writing notes on current affairs, I phoned him.

'Are you OK?' he asked.

'Any news of Andrew and the Cup?'

'The poor little bugger swore he didn't take it. Himself says he believes him. Anyway, the damned thing seems to have vanished.'

'Are you alone in the office?' I asked.

'You guessed right. I'm not.'

'Well, listen. I'm going back to London tonight from Dalwhinnie. Can you meet me there, and if so, when? And could you bring with you an old bedsheet?'

'Er . . .'

'A bedsheet,' I repeated. 'People I see in London will know I am not in the bothy. While I'm in London, the bothy is as secure as one blow from a sledgehammer on that nice new lock.'

'*Al.*'

'I've been painting a picture that I really do *not* want stolen or ruined. Please could you bring a sheet to wrap it in? Please will you keep it safe for me?'

'Yes, of course,' he said hesitantly, 'but what about . . . anything else?'

'No one will find anything else. I just don't want to lose the picture.'

After barely a pause he said, 'How about nine thirty?'

'Perfect. Could you bring Flora, to drive your own car home? You can have the estate's Land Rover back.'

'How long will you be gone?'

'How long is a piece of string . . .?'

Reliable as always, he brought Flora and a bedsheet to the station, and drove away in the Land Rover with the well-wrapped picture and all my new climbing gear and paints and winter clothes (in duffle bag) and also my bagpipes, newly ransomed from the old fleecer, Donald Cameron, on his return from Inverness.

Jed swore on his mother's grave to keep my belongings safe (she was still alive) and Flora laughed and kissed me, and with minimum luggage I yet again rocked down the rails and hugged my mother before breakfast.

The Park Crescent house felt as claustrophobic as it had the previous week. The cleaner, Lois, relentlessly vacuumed, her expression mulish. She and Ivan's male nurse, Wilfred, had reached head-tossing terms. Edna the cook tut-tutted over the evidence of my hot fried breakfast. My mother put up with it all instead of chucking the whole lot out.

Although it was by then more than three weeks since Ivan's heart attack, he had still not summoned will or strength enough to dress in day clothes. As if time had been suspended since I'd left, I found him, in gown and slippers, looking equally exhausted in his armchair. He greeted me with a weak smile and an instant and relieved transference to me of all decision-making.

'That woman wants you to phone her,' he said, pointing at the tissue-box, so I turned it over and found Margaret Morden's number written beside the one-word message – NOW.

I phoned her 'now'.

'Sir Ivan said you'd be coming to London.'

'I'm here.'

'Oh, good.' She sounded relieved. 'Can you hop down to my office?'

'How did it go yesterday?'

'Quite well. I need Sir Ivan's agreement. If he can't come here, perhaps you could carry papers to London for his signature.'

'Great idea,' I said with enthusiasm, but Ivan flapped a no-no hand and said into the receiver when I held it out for him, 'Alexander will sign things. Advise him as you would advise me. He's fairly bright . . .' He waved the telephone away and Margaret Morden said in my ear, 'But your daughter . . .'

'You're talking to Al,' I said. 'What about Patsy?'

'She and that brewery manager, Desmond Finch, very nearly wrecked the negotiations yesterday by crashing the creditors' meeting. And she had her husband with her . . . he's a menace. I shouldn't say it, but if the brewery survives it will be in spite of Mrs Benchmark. I don't understand her. The brewery will be hers, you'd think she would be the first to want the rescue operation to succeed.'

'She wants me, personally, dead.'

'You don't mean that!' she protested.

'Well, she doesn't want me to be instrumental in saving the day.'

'I can agree with *that.* How soon can you get here?'

'An hour and a half.'

'Right,' she said. 'I'll clear the decks.'

I spent over half an hour with Ivan, during which he told me several times not to bother him with details (such as, would his brewery survive), but to stick to *essentials* (namely, the safe-keeping of his best horse and his Gold Cup).

'Bede's Death Song,' I said casually, and watched astounded as my stepfather's eyes filled with tears.

'Look after your mother,' he said.

'You are *not* going to die.'

'I think so.' He wiped the tears away with his finger. 'Probably.'

'No. She needs you.'

'I am adding a codicil to my Will,' he said. 'Don't let anyone stop me.'

'By "anyone", do you mean Patsy?'

'Patsy,' he nodded. 'And Surtees, and Oliver.'

'Oliver Grantchester?' I asked. 'Your lawyer?'

'Patsy gets him to tell her things.'

I said with dismay, 'Did you tell Oliver Grantchester you wanted to add a codicil, and *he* told Patsy?'

'Yes.' His voice held defeated acceptance. 'Oliver says she's family.'

'He should be struck off.'

'He won't be, though, will he? I asked him to come tomorrow morning, so please, Alexander . . .'

'I'll be here,' I promised, frowning, 'but—'

'She's so *strong*, you see,' he interrupted. 'So sweet and kind. But she gets her own way.'

'If I were you,' I said, 'I would take a piece of paper here and now and simply write down in your own handwriting what you want, and then get Wilfred and Lois in here to witness you signing – unless of course they are recipients—' he shook his head '—and then the codicil would be done and legal and you wouldn't have to endure any arguments tomorrow.'

He wasn't a man to whom simple solutions came naturally. He relied on accountants and lawyers and formality. His first strong instinct was to disregard my suggestion as frivolous, and it was only after about five quiet minutes, during which I did nothing to persuade him, that he saw the attraction of the peaceful path.

'The only thing is,' I said, 'don't leave *me* anything. If you do the codicil will be declared void, as Patsy will say I influenced you.'

'But . . .'

'Don't,' I said.

He shook his head.

'I don't want you dead,' I said. 'Live and leave me nothing. Give me your word.'

He smiled weakly. 'You're as bossy as Patsy.'

I fetched paper and a pen from his desk and from across the room watched him write a scant half-page.

Then I sought out Wilfred and Lois, and Ivan himself lightly asked them to witness him signing and dating a simple legal document.

Ivan signed his paper and held his arm across the wording itself so that his witnesses couldn't read the details while they themselves signed: and, at his request, they added their home addresses.

Ivan thanked them courteously, giving their service little weight. With luck, I thought, Lois wouldn't report within five minutes to Patsy.

When Wilfred and Lois had gone (heads tossing at each other) I gave Ivan an envelope for his codicil; from cautious habit, when he'd stuck down its flap, he signed his name and the date twice across the join.

He held out the sealed envelope for me to take.

'Look after it,' he said.

'Ivan . . .'

'Who else?'

'If you promise I'm not in it.'

'You're not.'

'OK then.' I took the envelope. Horse, Cup, codicil, what else?

I was fifteen minutes later than I'd said for Margaret Morden but she made no comment. She wore a widely belted soft printed wool dress of dark reds and blues, accentuating the fairness of her fine and flyaway hair, and making sure one noticed the slenderness of her waist.

The creditors, she reported, had worked out a rate of payment that they would accept. Their terms were stringent, which I should expect, but just about possible, if sales held up. The creditors conceded that good sales depended on the brewery's solid reputation, and they had included the King Alfred Gold Cup race's expenses in their calculations.

'*Great*,' I said. 'You're *brilliant*.'

'Yes, but they want a guarantee that if there is any shortfall in the expected receipts for the next six months, Sir Ivan will forfeit the Cup itself. The gold chalice is to be considered as an asset of the brewery, and may be sold.'

'Is that a fair arrangement?'

'I'd say so. I agreed subject to your approval. The same applies to the horse, Golden Malt.' She paused. 'Some of the creditors insisted the Cup and the horse be sold at once, but the certainty of negative publicity persuaded them to wait. Also no one at the brewery seems to know exactly where either the horse or Cup have got to.'

'Who's looking?'

'Desmond Finch. He is complaining bitterly about the creditors' terms. I told you he crashed the meeting. It is he who will have to implement the stringent measures. The creditors want the workforce reduced. Downsized – that's the fashionable term for sacked. Desmond Finch says he can't run the brewery with fewer people. He wants to sell the Cup.'

'Um.'

'You don't look convinced.'

'Well, when Ivan took the Cup out of the brewery he made it into the equivalent of a freely bouncing ball. I mean ... anyone who caught it might throw it on safely into trustworthy hands, who might bounce it some more ... but in its free state it could be caught by someone who would keep it for its value in gold. That Cup isn't worth enough to pay the brewery's debts but it is definitely worth stealing.'

Margaret listened without moving.

I went on, 'Ivan took his Cup and had a heart attack, so he gave his treasure into the keeping of his long-time friend, my uncle, Robert Kinloch. The two men decided to give the Cup to me to look after, but in their trusting way they spoke of that plan in front of listening ears, with the result that four robbers came to my door to find and steal the Cup.'

'So it's gone?'

'No. It wasn't there. It hadn't reached me. The four robbers ... er ... damaged me a bit.'

'That black eye last week? And all those winces?'

'Mm ... Well, the Cup's still bouncing, so to speak, and I wouldn't stake my life on Desmond Finch returning it to the brewery if he got his hands on it.'

'That's probably slanderous – what would he do with it?'

'I'd say he would think it reasonable, if not proper, to give it to Patsy Benchmark.'

Margaret Morden's mouth opened.

I sighed. 'Patsy heard her father and my uncle plan to give the Cup to me.'

'My God. But ... surely ... she wouldn't send people to *harm* you.'

'She might. She might not. But how about Surtees, her husband?'

Margaret said, looking horrified, 'He was violent enough at that meeting yesterday for anything. But funnily enough, his violent way of speaking, and Mrs Benchmark's furious denunciation of you personally as a ruthless adventurer out for whatever you could get, well, they worked *against* them, and *for* you. When they'd gone the very senior bank manager put all his weight behind your trustworthiness, and it was he, too, who pushed for the race to be run. He said the bank would make the funds available.'

I could think of nothing to say.

'Fortunately the receivables are enough to more than cover the running costs this week. The pay cheques will be issued and honoured. You have to sign the agreements drawn up yesterday, but, if you do, Tobias Tollright will OK the audit, and King Alfred's Brewery will stay in business.'

I stood up blindly and walked to her window, and heard her voice behind me, 'Al?'

'Mm?'

'I thought you would be pleased.'

I didn't answer her, and she came questioningly to stand beside me. I put my arms round her silently and hugged her, and finally found voice enough to thank her in a more businesslike fashion.

She said, 'The bank manager said that nothing you have done is for your own benefit.'

'He's wrong. What benefits the brewery benefits Ivan, and what benefits Ivan benefits my mother, which benefits me.'

'Yes,' she said gravely, mocking me, 'I do see.'

She spread out the agreement papers on her desk and showed me where to put my name, bringing in her secretary to witness every signature. She then said she would have copies run off for all the creditors, which I would initial, and for Ivan and for Tobias, and for the brewery in the shape of Desmond Finch.

While all the copying was in hand she asked me why Ivan and my uncle had planned to send the King Alfred Gold Cup to *me*. Why to Alexander on his mountain?

I said I supposed it was because of Prince Charles Edward's sword hilt, and I told her of the ancient Honour of the Kinlochs, and about my uncle's ongoing disagreement with the castle's administrators.

'I'm afraid,' I said lightly, 'that now, owing to the incautious tongues of two men who would never knowingly harm me, any number of people may learn that whether or not I may know where to find the King Alfred chalice, I do have in my care the Kinloch golden hilt, which is infinitely more valuable, as apart from its historical uniqueness, it is oozing with emeralds and rubies.'

'Al!'

'So it looks as if it is time to bounce that on to someone else.'

'Immediately!'

Immediately. But to whom?

Not to James: and Andrew was too young.

Himself would have to decide.

Margaret's secretary returned with the copy agreements for copious initialling, and I asked if protocol would stretch to a pub lunch for three, Margaret, Tobias and me.

Margaret thought it might. Tobe, when telephoned, agreed. Accordingly we sat round a small table in a dark discreet corner and toasted the brewery's survival in a bottle of good Bordeaux.

I said to Margaret, 'You mentioned something to me about a twitch of unease. Is it for our auditor's ears?'

Margaret considered Tobias and slowly nodded. 'He might help.'

'What twitch of unease?' he asked, searching his

pockets for toothpicks. 'To do with the brewery's prospects?'

'No, with its past.'

His search drew a blank. He walked over to the bar and returned with a whole small pot of picks. 'Go on, then,' he said. 'What twitch?'

'I think,' Margaret said tentatively, 'that Norman Quorn may have done a trial run.'

Tobias blinked. 'A what?'

'You remember I asked you for the accounts for the past five years?'

'Yes, you had them.'

Margaret nodded. 'Immaculate work. But I just got a teeniest whiff of what I call a "beach towel and hotel" job, only *that* one seems to have gone full circle, which of course doesn't usually happen, and didn't happen this time.'

'You've lost me,' I said. 'What's a "beach towel and hotel" job?'

I looked enquiringly at Tobias, but he shook his head. 'Never heard of it.'

Margaret, smiling, explained. 'I got the idea one day on holiday, while I was lying sunbathing on a beach chair round a hotel pool, watching people come and go. They would put a towel on a chair and go off and leave it, maybe for hours, and then come back and pick it up and wander off . . . and no one working for the hotel would think of asking who the towel belonged to. Do you see?'

'No,' I said, but Tobias thoughtfully nodded.

'Suppose,' Margaret said, 'that you were Norman Quorn, and you wanted to retire with a pension big enough to give you all the luxuries you'd never had – not just a bungalow on the south coast, counting the cost of things like postage stamps – but round-the-world cruises and a big new car and a bejewelled companion and caviare and playing the tables in a casino or whatever excites his dry conventional old bachelor mind. Suppose you got the sparkling explosive idea of taking enough for a glorious sunset, and you know how easy and fast it is now to send money whizzing round the world impersonally by wire . . . then you open small banking accounts here and there . . . you sort of book into hotels . . . and every so often you leave a beach towel on a sunbed for a while . . . and then move it onward to another hotel . . . and no one pays much notice, because the beach towel never goes missing, and comes safely home.'

'Only one day it doesn't,' Tobias said. 'I lost him in Panama.'

We drank the substantial red wine and ordered fried brie and cranberries with another half-bottle.

Margaret's job fascinated her. 'Almost everyone sees when their bankruptcy's looming,' she said, 'and nearly everyone makes the giveaway mistake of removing their most valuable possessions before torching the premises. Insurance fraud is the worst way out of bankruptcy. It never works. I won't take those cases. I tell them to go to jail and get it over with. Most insolvencies are caused by bad luck, bad management and changing times. Last year's rage is this year's ruin. And then sometimes you get a Norman Quorn. Ingenious, careful. A small trial run, to get the hotels used to the arrival of his beach towel . . . and they give the towel a sunbed to lie on for a day or so, and send it on unsuspectingly when the right instruction arrives – right codes, right signatures . . . lovely job.'

'And no one asks questions?' I said.

'Of course not. Millions of transactions take place round the world every day. Hotel guests arrive and leave by the hundred thousand.'

'And beach towels,' Tobias grinned, 'get sent to the laundry.'

I went to see Young and Uttley.

Neither Mr Young (moustache, suit and hat) nor Mr Uttley (football coach, ball and whistle) was in the office, and nor was the skinhead. Alone in occupation I found a secretary at work at a computer, a young woman with dark curly hair, black tights, short black skirt, loose bright blue sweater, scarlet lips and fingernails.

Giving me a flick of a glance, she said, 'Can I help you?' and went on working.

'Well . . .' I looked at her carefully, 'you can tell me why the hell you made sure Surtees Benchmark saw you following him.'

The busy fingers stilled. The bright eyes looked at my face. The familiar voice deepened and said in exasperation, 'How the shit do you *know*?'

'Eye sockets.'

'What?'

'I draw people. I look at their bones. Your eye sockets slant down in a particular way at the outer corners. Also your wrists are male. You should wear frilled cuffs.'

'Bugger you.'

I laughed. 'So why did you let Surtees see you?'

'Let him? I made sure he did, like you said, I got him real worried. See, if someone knows they're being followed, they're dead careful, but when they *don't* see their shadow they think they're safe, so they go at once and do what you could wait weeks for them to do otherwise, and you'd never know, either, what things he didn't care about anyone watching, and what he really wanted to keep hidden. See?'

'I guess I do.'

'So I got him busy looking out for a skinhead.'

'And,' I suggested, 'he then doesn't notice a secretary in a dark brown wig?'

'You got it.'

'What did the secretary see?'

'Ah.' Young, Uttley (and associates) enjoyed himself. 'Yon bonnie Surtees has a lady wife who keeps him on a throttling leash. Some men enjoy subjugation, I'm not saying they don't, but Wednesday afternoons it seems Mrs Surtees chairs some sort of local women's action committee and her Mister bolts into Guildford to consult his business colleague. Seems Surtees runs a stud farm that's half owned by his wife and half by someone else, the business colleague. Anyway, Wednesday afternoon – yesterday – Surtees drives round in a circle or two looking out for the skinhead, and when he thinks it's safe he steers not to any business office but to a terrace house on the outskirts of Guildford. That's to say, he parks in the next street and looks all around carefully – a dead giveaway, he's stupid – and then he walks to the little house and opens the front door with a key.'

I sighed.

'Don't you want to hear about it?'

'Yes, but I'd rather he'd visited four thugs in a gym.'

'Sorry about that. Anyway, yesterday Mr Young paid a visit to the house at Guildford, as soon as Surtees had left.'

'Mr Young in suit, hat, moustache?'

He nodded. 'The lot.'

'And?'

'And there's a poor little cow lives there that lets inadequates like Surtees pay to spank her before sex.'

'Damn.'

'Not what you hoped?'

'Too simple.'

'Do you want me to carry on?'

'Yes.' I brought a foil-wrapped packet out of a pocket and gave it to him. 'This is a pair of glasses left behind by one of the four robbers. They're the strength people take off when they want to read. I don't suppose they'll be much use, but it's all they left.'

He/she unwrapped the glasses without excitement.

'Also,' I said, 'see what you can find out about a goldsmith working in London in around 1850 or 60, called Maxim.'

After a short stare, he said, 'Anything else?'

'How do you rate as a bodyguard?'

'That's extra.'

I paid him another week's retainer. Expenses and extras, he said, would fall due at the end.

CHAPTER EIGHT

When Ivan spread out the creditors' agreements on his table and slowly took each of them onto his lap to read them carefully one by one, his overall reaction was one of relieved gloom.

When my mother came into his room, though, he lifted his head to her and smiled, and for the first time since his illness the worry dissolved from the lines on her forehead. She smiled back with the deep understanding friendship of a strong marriage, and I thought inconsequentially that if the area bank bighead had seen that exchange he would have counted it benefit enough for anything I had done.

'Our boy,' Ivan said (and I was usually '*your*' boy), 'has signed the brewery into chains and penury.'

'But . . .' my mother asked, 'why are you pleased?'

He picked up a thick batch of paper in a blue cover and waved it at her.

'This,' he said, 'is our annual audit. Tobias Tollright has signed it. It is our passport to continue trading. The creditors' terms for payment are tough, very tough, but they've been fair. We ought to be able to win our way back. And they've factored in the Cheltenham race! I was sure we'd have to cancel it. But the chalice and Golden Malt are still at risk ... I'll not give them up. We *must* meet the payments. Increase sales ... I'll call a board meeting.'

One could actually see his resolution trickling back.

'Well done, Alexander,' he said.

I shook my head. 'Thank Mrs Morden. It was all her work.'

We spent an easy, companionable evening, the three of us, but by morning Ivan's euphoria had mostly vanished and he was complaining that the brewery's shareholders would be receiving only tiny token dividends for the next three years. To do him justice he wasn't thinking of himself, although he was by far the major shareholder, but of various widows and relations left behind by time and mergers from the days before he'd inherited. Several widows relied on their dividends for existence, he said.

'If you'd have gone bankrupt,' I pointed out, 'they'd be lucky to get anything at all. A tiny lump sum and no dividends for ever.'

'But still ...'

I'd hoped he would have had energy enough to dress, but he fretted instead about the widows. 'Perhaps I can afford ... out of my own funds ... heating bills this winter ...'

My mother stroked his hand fondly.

I had expected, since he had written his codicil the day before, that he would have told his lawyer not to bother to come, but it seemed he had forgotten to cancel the meeting, and Oliver Grantchester, with his loud voice, bulky frame and room-filling presence arrived punctually at ten o'clock, the meek Miranda in tow.

Ivan began stuttering an embarrassed apology, to which Grantchester didn't listen.

The lawyer looked me up and down without favour and told Ivan that they didn't need my presence. He pointed to me and then to the door, giving me an unmistakable order. I might in fact have gone, but at that moment Patsy arrived like a ship in full sail, Surtees floundering foolishly in her wake.

Surtees the spanker: weak, pathetic and vicious.

'You are not making any codicil, Father, unless I'm sure Alexander' – Patsy spat the word – 'doesn't in any way benefit.'

'My dear,' Ivan told her pleasantly, 'I'm not writing any codicil this morning. None at all.'

'But you said ... You arranged for Oliver to come ...'

'Yes, I know, I'm sorry I forgot to tell him, but I wrote my codicil yesterday. It's all done. We can just have some coffee now.'

Ivan was naive if he thought coffee would quell a

tempest. Patsy and Oliver both berated him. My mother stood like a shield beside him. Surtees glared at me as if his brains had seized up.

'It's perfectly simple,' Grantchester boomed. 'You can tear up yesterday's codicil and write another one.'

Ivan looked at me as if for help. 'But I don't need to write another one,' he said, 'do I?'

I shook my head.

The bombardment of voices went on. Ivan, upset, nevertheless held to his position: he had written his codicil, it expressed what he wanted, and there was no need to write it again.

'At least let me check it from the legal point of view,' Grantchester said.

Ivan with a touch of starch told him that he, Ivan, knew when a document had been correctly executed, and his codicil had.

'But perhaps I can see it . . .?'

'No,' Ivan said, regretfully polite.

'I don't understand you.'

'I *do*,' Patsy said forcefully. 'It's quite clear that Alexander is manipulating you, Father, and you're so blind you can't see that everything he does is aimed at taking my place as your heir.'

Ivan looked at me with such troubled indecision that I quietly went out of his study and climbed the stairs to the room I'd slept in, to put together the few things I'd brought with me, ready for leaving. I'd done my best for the brewery – for Ivan, for my mother – but the biggest difference between my stepfather and me was the ease and extent of his mood swings and changes of opinions, and, good and honourable man though he might be, I never quite knew what he believed of me from one hour to the next.

It had seemed, since his illness, that he had relied on and believed in and made use of my good faith, but it had been a frail belief after all.

I could hear shouting going on downstairs, though I'd thought my departure would at least have stopped Patsy haranguing her father.

I stood at the window looking out towards Regent's Park and didn't hear my mother come upstairs until she spoke behind me.

'Alexander, Ivan needs you.'

I turned. 'I can't. I'm not fighting Patsy.'

'It's not just Patsy. That man who runs the brewery is here now too. Desmond Finch. Ivan thinks the world of him but he's a terrific fusspot, and he trots to Patsy with every complaint. They're all telling Ivan . . . yelling at him . . . that the terms you signed with the creditors are disgraceful and they could all have done better, and they want him to cancel your power of attorney retrospectively so that your signature on everything is void.'

I asked, 'Did Ivan send you to fetch me?'

'Well, no. But last night he was so *pleased* . . .'

I sighed and put my arm round her slender waist. 'And,' I said, 'he can't legally make my signature void.'

We went down. Ivan looked hunted, harried by the

pack. They all resented my reappearance, and I looked at them one by one, trying to put reasons to their antagonism.

Patsy, tall, good-looking, fierce and obsessed, had been an unappeasable foe since the day her father had fallen in love with my mother. Young women who felt possessive of their widowed fathers usually hated the usurper who displaced them, but Patsy's rage had skipped over her sweet-natured unthreatening step-mother and fastened inexorably on me. If she had ever stopped to make a sensible reckoning she would know that she had never lost anything at all because of me, let alone her father's love, but emotion ruled her entirely, and, after twelve years of her steadfast detestation, I didn't expect her to change.

She'd married Surtees two years after her father had married my mother, and in the weak, good-looking Hooray-Henry had chosen a mate she could indoctrinate.

I looked at Surtees as he stood behind Ivan's chair; he was a person, I thought, who would always seek such a shield, who would never have the steel to stand out in the open and say; 'Here I am. Judge me as I am.' Patsy had married a man she could bully and it had been very bad for both of them.

I found it less easy to understand Desmond Finch. He stood there glaring at me, thin, aggressive, flashing his large silver-rimmed glasses in sharp little head movements, his Adam's apple actively jumping in his neck. I had no reason to doubt the general assessment I'd been given that he was efficient and energetic in his job, but I believed also in the evaluation that he would act only if given directions. It seemed plain that he danced to Patsy's instructions: plain also that he'd made no objective overview on the brewery's troubles, in spite of his own whole career being bound up in its financial health.

A limited man, I thought. Short-sighted mentally as well as optically. A voice baying in the pack. Not one to sink the teeth in first.

And Oliver Grantchester? He'd never liked me; I'd never liked him.

There he balefully stood, bulky, going bald, Ivan's legal adviser from way-back, consulted, wise – and enchanted by Patsy to the extent that his manner to me was always of suspicion, distrust and obstruction.

Ivan said weakly, 'Couldn't you have got a better deal for the brewery, Alexander?'

I smiled grimly. 'I'm sick of the brewery,' I said. 'Ivan, let Patsy loose on the creditors. I don't give a damn about the fact that she'll ruin her inheritance. Why should I care? The brewery is yours. It's rescued; it has problems that are basically solved, but which you can muck up in a moment. I'm a painter and I'm going back to my own work, and goodbye . . . a heartfelt goodbye to you all.'

Ivan said miserably, 'Alexander . . .'

'For you,' I said to him plainly, 'I've taken risks that

I'll take again, and I've begged and persuaded and bargained to save your good name. Because you sent me the chalice' – and I glanced at Patsy and Surtees, who stared as if transfixed – 'I got beaten beyond a joke. And I've had enough. I'll do anything on earth for my mother, but that's where it now ends. Do what you like, Ivan. Just count me out.'

My mother said, barely audibly, 'Oh no . . . *please*, Alexander,' and Ivan looked exhaustedly strained.

Grantchester said heavily, 'Ivan tells us he gave you his codicil for safe-keeping. He now sees that this was a mistake. So hand it over.'

Into the silence that followed I said, 'Ivan?'

His eyes looked deep in their sockets. I understood the impossibility he faced. His faith in me was a disloyalty to his daughter; a disloyalty I had no right to coerce, even if I could.

'I'll get it,' I said, letting him off. 'It's upstairs.'

I went up and fetched the sealed envelope, and returning, put it into his hands.

'I'll take it,' Grantchester said authoritatively, but Ivan put the envelope on his knees and folded his hands on it, and shook his head.

'I'll keep it here, Oliver,' he said.

'But—'

'Then I can tear it up if I change my mind.'

I smiled into Ivan's troubled eyes and without weight said I would be upstairs for an hour or two more if he wanted me.

'He doesn't want you,' Surtees said spitefully. 'None of us do.'

I shrugged and left them and, shaking my head to my mother's pleading eyes, went back upstairs, looking out of the window and waiting.

They went on shouting, downstairs, but finally the angry voices came out of Ivan's study and descended to street level and left by the front door. When all was quiet I went out of my room and onto the stairs, and found Ivan on the landing below me, looking up. He made a gesture towards his study, a flip of the hand that was unmistakably an invitation, so I went down and followed him into his room, and sat opposite him in my usual chair.

My mother, looking as frail as her husband, stood beside Ivan, touching him as if to give him strength.

He said to me, 'Did you mean it, that you've had enough?'

For answer I asked, 'Did you cancel the power of attorney?'

'I . . . I don't know what to do.'

'No, he didn't,' my mother said. 'Ivan, tell Alexander . . . *Beg* Alexander to go on acting for you.' To me she said, 'Don't leave us.'

I had so recently vowed I would do anything on earth for my mother. So small a thing, to stay and field a few insults. I wilted inside from disinclination.

'What did you mean about being beaten?' Ivan said.

'That black eye I had last week . . .'

He frowned. 'Keith Robbiston said you were hurt.'

I told them about the robbers. 'I didn't want to worry you when you were so ill . . . so I didn't tell you.'

'Oh my God,' he said, 'I've done so much harm.'

'Nothing that isn't being put right.'

I poured brandy into two glasses standing ready on a nearby silver tray and handed one to Ivan, one to my mother. They both drank without protest, as if I'd given them medicine.

I said to Ivan, 'If you just leave things as they are, the brewery should be out of debt in three years. I know some of the terms are hard. They have to be. The debts are truly enormous. Mrs Morden has done a marvellous job, but she says the future depends greatly on keeping the services of your present brewmaster and on the managing energies of Desmond Finch. Desmond Finch wouldn't take a diamond-studded suggestion from me, but he's used to following your instructions, so that's what you have to do, Ivan. Go back to the brewery and instruct him.'

My stepfather nodded with resolution. And how long, I morosely considered, would that resolution last?

The telephone rang. Ivan's hand asked me to answer it, so I did.

A confident voice said, 'This is Detective Constable Thompson of the Leicestershire police. I want to speak to Sir Ivan Westering.'

Ivan, of course, wanted me to deal with whatever it

was. I explained that Sir Ivan was recovering from a heart attack, and offered my services.

'And you are, sir?'

'His son.' Well, near enough.

After a pause a different voice, just as confident, identified himself as Detective Chief Inspector Reynolds.

'What is this about?' I asked.

The voice enquired whether Sir Ivan knew anyone named Norman Quorn.

'Yes, he does.'

The voice impersonally explained. I listened blankly. The Leicestershire police had for two weeks been trying to identify a body that they now had reason to believe was that of a Mr Norman Quorn. The Chief Inspector wanted Sir Ivan Westering, as Mr Quorn's long-term employer, to assist in making a positive identification, yes or no.

With shortened breath, I said, 'Doesn't he have any relations?'

'Only his sister, sir, and she is . . . *distressed.* The body is partly decomposed. The sister gave us Sir Ivan's name. So we would be grateful, sir . . .'

'He isn't well,' I said.

'Perhaps you, then?'

'I didn't know him.' I thought briefly. 'I'll tell my father. Give me a number to phone you back.' He told me a number, which I wrote out of habit on the bottom of the box of tissues. 'Right,' I said, 'five minutes.'

As emotionlessly as possible I gave Ivan the news.

'Norman!' he said disbelievingly. '*Dead?*'

'They want to know for sure. They ask you to go.'

'I'll go with you,' my mother said.

I phoned the Chief Inspector, told him I would be driving, and wrote his directions on the bottom of the tissue-box.

In the end four of us went to Leicestershire in Ivan's Rover (retrieved from an underground garage), Ivan and my mother in the back with Wilfred sitting in the front beside me, a box of heart-attack remedies on his lap. Wilfred read out the directions on the tissue-box so that fairly early in the afternoon we arrived at a featureless building in Leicester that housed a mortuary and investigating laboratories.

The Detective Chief Inspector met us, shook hands with Ivan and my mother and me and was impressed into solicitude by Wilfred's presence and medical precautions. Ivan, though in suit and tie, looked almost greyer than in his dressing-gown.

Inside the building, in a small reception area that doubled as waiting-room, a large weeping woman was being comforted in the arms of an equally large uniformed policewoman. The Chief Inspector indicated that we should wait there while he took Ivan to see the body, but Ivan clutched my arm and wouldn't go without me, so, shrugging, the senior policeman settled for taking me too.

We were all then issued with disposable gowns, with

gloves, overshoes and masks for our noses and mouths. Dead bodies, it seemed, could infect the living.

I hadn't been in such a place before, but it was curiously familiar from pictures. We went down a passage into a white painted room that was clean, brightly lit, not very large and smelled not unpleasantly of disinfectant. On a high centre table, under a white cover, lay a long quiet shape.

Ivan's hand shook on my arm but civic duty won the day. He looked steadily at the white face revealed when a gowned and masked mortuary attendant pulled back one end of the covering sheet, and he said without wavering, 'Yes, that's Norman.'

'Norman Quorn?'

'Yes, Chief Inspector. Norman Quorn.'

'Thank you, sir.'

I said, 'What did he die of?'

There was a pause. The policeman and the mortuary attendant exchanged eyebrow signals that I hadn't the code to read, and the policeman also looked assessingly at Ivan's physical state, and at mine, and came to a decision.

'I'll take you back to your wife, sir,' he said to Ivan, and offered his arm instead of mine, neatly leaving me behind alone to hear the answer to my question.

The mortuary attendant first of all identified himself as the pathologist who had carried out the original post mortem.

'Sorry,' I said.

'Don't be.' He casually pulled down his mask, revealing a young face, competent.

'So . . . what did he die of?' I asked.

'We're not sure.' He shrugged. 'There are no obvious causes of death. No gunshots, no stab wounds, no fractures of the skull, no signs of strangulation, no household poisons. No evidence of murder. He had been dead about two weeks when he was discovered. He didn't die where he was found, which was in a rubbish dump. I saw him *in situ*. He had been placed there after death.'

'Well . . .' I frowned, 'was he simply ill? Heart attack? Stroke? Pneumonia?'

'More likely one of the first two, though we can't know for sure. But there is an abnormality . . .' He hesitated. 'We showed it to his sister, and she fainted.'

'I'm not his sister.'

'No.'

He stripped back the sheet as far as the body's waist, showing the dark discolorations of decomposition and the efforts made to tidy up the radical post mortem incisions. I thought it no wonder the sister had fainted and hoped I wouldn't copy her.

'Look at his back,' the pathologist instructed, and with his gloved hands gripped the shoulders and half rolled the body towards him.

There were about a dozen or more rows of darker marks in the darkened flesh, and flecks of white.

The pathologist eased the body flat again.

'Those white bits – did you see them? – are his ribs.'

I felt nauseous, and swallowed.

The pathologist said, 'Those darker marks are burns.'

'*Burns?*'

'Yes. The skin and flesh have been burned away in a few places down to the ribs. He must have fallen into something very hot when he died. Something like a grating. People fall on electric fires in that way. Terrible burns, sometimes. This is like that. Any thoughts?'

My chief thought was how soon I could leave the mortuary.

'He was wearing a nylon shirt,' the pathologist said chattily, 'and there were man-made fibres in the lining and cloth of his suit jacket. They melted to some extent into his skin.'

In another minute, I thought, I would vomit.

I said, 'Could he have died from the burns?'

'I don't think so. As you saw, the burns extended only from below his shoulder blades to his waist. Several local burns, but not lethal, I don't think. It's most likely they occurred just after death, or anyway at about the same time. I would guess he had a stroke, fell unconscious on the fire, and died.'

'Oh.'

'Anyway,' the pathologist said with satisfaction, 'now that we have a positive identification we can have an inquest. The coroner's verdict will be "cause of death unknown" and the poor man can have a decent burial. I'll be glad to get him out of here, to be honest.'

I left him with relief and, stripping off the protective clothing, rejoined the group in the entrance area.

'Please tell us,' I said to the Chief Inspector, 'where exactly you found Mr Quorn.'

Instead of directly answering he explained that the still quietly weeping woman was Norman Quorn's sister. My mother had taken over from the policewoman the role of comforter although, true to form, she looked as if she would prefer saying 'Pull yourself together' to 'There, there.'

'Mr Quorn,' the Chief Inspector told us conversationally, 'was found by council workers who went to clear away a decaying rubbish dump left behind on a farmer's land when a band of travellers moved on. We made lengthy enquiries among the travellers at their next place, but drew a total blank. We spent a great deal of time on it. The travellers pointed out that they were all much younger – we had told them the unknown body was elderly—'

'Sixty-five,' the sister sobbed.

'On the other hand, these travellers were accustomed to cook on home-made barbecues of brick supports with metal rods across, and there were signs that perhaps Mr Quorn had overbalanced backwards onto something like that. None of their current barbecues matched Mr Quorn's burns, but it was all inconclusive.

There are absolutely no indications at all of foul play. So now we have your identifications, we can close the case. I'm sorry, but it isn't always possible to determine how things happened, and unless any other facts turn up . . .'

He left the sentence unfinished. Neither Ivan nor my mother told him that the brewery's funds had vanished with the Finance Director, and nor did I. Ivan would have to think it through, and decide.

Because of Wilfred's presence we were silent on the way back to London but spent the evening discussing nothing else.

Ivan was inclined to be glad that Norman Quorn hadn't after all run off with the money.

'We misjudged him,' he said sorrowfully. 'My dear old friend . . .'

'Your dear old friend,' I corrected regretfully, 'certainly did transfer the money out of the brewery. I've seen copies of about six huge withdrawals that he made just before he left. He did indeed, I'm afraid, send all the funds on their way to destinations still unknown.'

'But he didn't *go*!'

'No. He died. He didn't die on the rubbish tip. Someone put him there. Wherever he died, someone didn't report it to anyone, but just dumped him.'

Ivan's beliefs and intentions swung widely to and fro, but his chief instinct, as before, was not to make public the brewery's loss. Norman Quorn dead, Norman Quorn living under palm trees . . . it made no difference. The theft existed and either way would be covered up.

I said, 'But don't you care who dumped him? Don't you want to know where he died?'

'What does it really matter? And as Norman was homosexual—' Ivan saw my surprise. 'Didn't you know? No, I suppose you didn't, he was always discreet . . . but, you see, suppose he died where it was *awkward* for someone . . . do you see what I mean?'

I saw.

'And it wouldn't do Norman or the brewery any good to disclose his sexual preference or, oh dear, his theft.'

It was astounding, I thought, to find my starchy stepfather so tolerant of homosexuality, but my mother, who after all knew him better, took it for granted. 'Quite a lot of Ivan's friends,' she told me later, 'were "that way". Delightful friends,' she added. 'Good company always.'

Ivan asked me, 'If we tell the police that Norman stole the funds and was homosexual, would it affect the creditors' arrangements?'

'Well, I don't know. The creditors do know he stole the funds. They signed the agreements knowing that.'

'Well, then?'

'But they believe he skipped the country. They believe he's alive. They believe the money is with him . . . and it isn't.'

'So?'

'So where is it?'

A long silence.

By ten in the evening Ivan was saying we needed someone else's advice.

'OK,' I agreed, 'whose?'

'Perhaps . . . Oliver's?'

I said mildly, 'Oliver would ask you what I, Alexander, suggested, and then give you an opposite opinion.'

'But he knows the law!'

I had been careful always not to belittle Patsy to her father. Oliver was Patsy's man. So was Desmond Finch.

I asked, 'What did Patsy think of Norman Quorn?'

'She didn't like him. Always a sadness. Why do you want to know?'

'What would she expect you to do?'

Ivan dithered.

By midnight he had decided, in his law-abiding Jockey Club persona, that I should ask Margaret Morden whether Norman Quorn's death made any difference to the creditors, and that I, not Ivan, should tell Detective Chief Inspector Reynolds that the now-identified corpse had been probably an embezzler about to leave the country.

'Probably?' I echoed with scepticism.

'We don't know for sure.'

I thought he would have changed his mind again by morning, but it seemed my sensible mother had fortified his decision, as she agreed with it; so at nine o'clock Ivan, again in dressing-gown and slippers, instructed me to phone Leicestershire.

Slight snag. The policeman's phone number was written on the tissue-box. The tissue-box was still in the car. I trailed off to retrieve it and finally reached the necessary ear.

'Tell me on the phone,' he commanded when I suggested meeting.

'Better face to face.'

'I'm off duty at noon.'

'I'll get there. Where?'

'Do you remember the way to the mortuary? There then. It's on my way home.'

I refrained – just – from observing that the mortuary was on everyone's way home, and managed to trace Margaret Morden to hers.

'It's Saturday,' she said tartly.

'I do know.'

'Then it had better be important.'

'The King Alfred Brewery's Finance Director has turned up, still in England – but dead.'

'I agree,' she said slowly, 'that that is Saturday news. How did he die?'

'Stroke or heart attack, the pathologist thinks.'

'When?'

'About the time he disappeared.'

She thought briefly and said, 'Phone me in the office on Monday. And tell Tobias. But if what's bothering you most is the status of the creditors' agreements, my first impression is that they will stand.'

'You're a doll.'

'No, I'm definitely *not*.'

I put down the receiver with a smile and drove to Leicester.

The chief inspector's reaction was as expected. 'Why didn't you tell me this yesterday?'

'The brewery has hushed up the theft.'

'The body,' he said reflectively, 'was dressed in suit, shirt, tie, underpants, socks and shoes, all unremarkable. There was nothing in his pockets.'

'How did you identify him in the end?'

'One of our clever young constables took another look at the clothes. The shoes were new – on the sole of one was the name of a shop and the price. The shop was in Wantage, and they remembered the sale . . . Mr Quorn was a regular customer. He was away from home, but a neighbour had the sister's address.'

'Neat.'

'But what he was doing in Leicestershire . . .?' He shrugged. 'It's possible he died out of doors, in a garden. There were a few blades of mown grass in his clothes. That would gel with him falling back onto a barbecue of some sort.'

'Hardly the right clothes for a barbecue.'

He looked me up and down in amusement. 'While you, sir, if I may say so, look more like a traveller.'

I acknowledged it in good humour.

'I'll complete my case notes with what you've told me,' the policeman said. 'It isn't by any means unknown for people to get rid of bodies when they've died inconveniently. I appreciate your help. Give my regards to Sir Ivan. He looks so ill himself.'

It was by then three and a half weeks since Ivan's heart attack (and four weeks and a day since Quorn had skipped with the cash) and what Ivan badly still needed and wasn't getting was complete untroubled rest. I drove back to London and for the remainder of that day and all of the next kept the house tranquil with the telephone switched into an answering machine and with simple meals, cooked by me, that needed no decisions. I gave Wilfred the rest of the weekend off and did his jobs: it was all peaceful and curative and its own reward.

On Monday I went by train again to Reading and did the rounds of the offices.

Life had moved on for Tobias and Margaret, who were already dealing with the next unfortunates down the line, but they each gave me half an hour and information.

'Old Quorn's dead!' Tobias exclaimed. 'Then where's the money?'

I said, 'I thought you might be able to work it out.'

He gave me his best blank outer stare concealing furious activity within.

'I followed him to Panama . . .' he said thoughtfully.

'How many stops to Panama?' I asked.

'Wait.' He turned to one of his three computer monitors, sorted out a disc from an indexed box, and fed it into a slot, pressing keys. 'Here we are. Wire transfer from the brewery to a bank in Guernsey . . . six transfers in one day, each from a different brewery account – it was as if he'd collected everything available into those six accounts, then he sent all six separately into the same account in Guernsey, and the bank there already had instructions to transfer the whole amount – multiple millions – to a bank in New York, which already held instructions to wire the money onward to a bank in Panama, and that bank cannot say where the money went from there.'

'Can't or won't?' I asked.

'Quite likely both. All these banks have unbreakable privacy laws. We only know the path to Panama because Norman Quorn had scribbled the ABA numbers on some rough paper and neglected to shred it.'

'Remind me about ABA numbers.'

Tobias chewed a toothpick. 'They identify all banks in the United States and roundabout areas like the Caribbean. They're part of the Fedwire system.'

'Tobe – what's Fedwire?'

'There are three huge worldwide organisations

dealing with the international transfer of funds and information,' he said. 'Fedwire – ABA included – is the Federal Reserve Bank's institution. They have nine-digit routing numbers, so any transfer with a nine-digit code is likely to have been seen to by Fedwire.'

I sighed.

'Then,' Tobe said, 'there's SWIFT – the Society for Worldwide Interbank Financial Telecommunication. And third, there's CHIPS, Clearing House Interbank Payments System, which is operated also through New York and has special identifier codes unique to their customers, ultra secret.'

'God.'

'Take your pick,' Tobias said. 'All the systems have identifying codes. The codes will tell you the bank, but not the account number. We know the brewery money went to a branch of Global Credit in Panama, but not into which account there.'

'But they must know,' I said. 'I mean, they can't have millions sent to them every day from New York. The amount, the dispatcher, the date . . . they could surely work it out.'

'Perhaps, but it's against their law to pass the information on.'

'Not to the police? Or the tax people?'

'Especially not to the police or the tax people. A lot of banks would be out of business at once if they did that.' Tobe smiled. 'You're an infant, Al.'

I acknowledged it. 'But,' I said, 'what if the money

just sits in Panama for ever, now Norman Quorn is dead?'

'It may do,' Tobias nodded. 'There are billions and trillions of loot in unclaimed accounts sitting in banks all over the world, and you can bet your soul the banks profit from them and are in no hurry to look for heirs.'

'Henry VIII syndrome,' I said.

'What?'

I explained about gold church treasures hidden in fields.

'Just like that,' he said.

I left him pulverising a toothpick over someone else's problems and presented myself on Margaret Morden's doorstep.

I told her what few details I knew of Norman Quorn's exit. 'Poor man,' she said.

'So you don't think,' I asked, 'that the wages of sin is death?'

'*Are* death, surely? And where have you been for the last fifty years? The wages of sin nowadays are a few years of full board and lodging at the country's expense with a chance to study for a degree, followed by tender loving care from ex-prisoners' aid societies.'

'Cynical.'

'Realistic.'

'What about the victims?'

'The wages of a victim is to be blamed if at all possible for a crime committed against her – I regret it's often a her – and seldom to be offered compensation, let alone free board and lodging and a university education. The wages of a victim are poverty, oblivion and a lonely grave. It's the sinners the tabloids pursue with their cheque-books.'

'Margaret!'

'So now you know me better,' she said. 'Norman Quorn robbed little old widows of their pathetic dividends and I don't give a shit if he died of a guilty conscience.'

'Little old widows are a bit mawkish . . .'

'Not if you happen to be one.'

'Well . . . if the little old widows' dividends are languishing in a foreign bank somewhere, how do we find them?'

She said, 'What's in it for you?'

I looked at my hands. What could I say? She would consider it mawkish in the extreme whatever I said.

'I don't mean that, Al. I'm in a bad mood today. I'm dealing with yet another deliberate bankruptcy whose sole aim is to dodge paying small-scale creditors, who may themselves go out of business through the loss. The people I'm dealing with will dump the suppliers in the shit, declare the business bankrupt and closed, and go off and start all over again under another name.'

'But,' I said, 'is that legal?'

'Legal, yes. Moral, you must be kidding. I'm not used to people like you. Go away and leave me to my disillusions.'

'I wanted to ask you,' I said, 'about that possible

trial run. Do you remember any of the trial's destinations?'

She frowned, then, as Tobias had done, consulted one of her row of computer faces and tapped instructions into the keys.

'It's possible,' she said finally, but with doubts, 'that Quorn sent a fairly small sum to a bank on an island in the Bahamas, who forwarded it to a bank in Bermuda, who sent it back to Wantage. The transactions weren't backed up by signed documentation, and half the information – like the actual account numbers – is missing. If the brewery's money is in either of those banks, which is doubtful, you're not going to find it.'

'Thanks a bunch.'

'Cheer up. First thing this morning I consulted your committee of creditors. The agreements they signed with you will remain unaltered by Norman Quorn's death.'

CHAPTER NINE

I walked to the office of Young and Uttley, half expecting to find it locked, but when I knocked and turned the handle, the door opened.

I walked in. The occupant that day wasn't a skinhead or a secretary or Mr Young with moustache or even the football coach Uttley, but a straightforward-looking man of about my own age dressed much as I was myself in jeans, shirt and sweater: no tie, unaggressive trainers and clean hands. The chief difference between us was that he had very short light brown hair, while mine still curled on my shoulders.

I smiled at him slowly, and I said, 'Hello.'

'Hello.'

'What's your name?' I asked.

'Chris.'

'Chris Young?'

He nodded. 'I've done a bit of let-your-fingers-do-the-walking for you,' he said.

His accent was unchanged. The skinhead, the secretary and Chris Young all spoke with the same voice.

'And?' I asked.

'There was a goldsmith name of Maxim working in London in the eighteen hundreds. Like Garrard's or Asprey's today. Good name. Ritzy. Made fancy things like peacocks for table ornaments, gold filigree feathers with real jewels in.'

'Tobe promised me you were good,' I said.

'Just good?'

'Brilliant. A genius, actually.'

He grinned immodestly. 'Tobe told me you were a walking brain and not to be put off by your good manners.'

'I'll kill him.'

'Tobe told me you were raised in a castle.'

'It was cold.'

'Yeah. I drew an orphanage. Warm.'

We got on fine. I made a drawing of King Alfred's golden chalice, and he phoned back to his goldsmith informant with a detailed description. 'And it has engraved lines round it that look just like random patterns but are some sort of verse in Anglo-Saxon. Yeah, yeah, that's what I said, Anglo-bloody-Saxon. See what you can do.'

He put down the receiver. 'Those specs you gave me,' he said, 'you can buy them anywhere.'

I nodded.

'I'd use them myself for disguises, if I could see through them.'

'I reckon that's why the robber took them off.'

'That's another thing,' Chris Young said. 'Boxing gyms. Your spanking pal Surtees never goes near a gym. He's as unfit as a leaking balloon. I've tailed him until I've had it up to here with him, and besides, none of the gyms in his area have ever heard of him.'

'Fingers doing the walking?'

'Sure.'

'Suppose he uses a different name?'

Chris Young sighed. 'He's not the gym type, I'm telling you. Which leaves me – and don't point it out – with no option but to flash your drawings of your robbers all over the place hoping for a fist in the guts.'

I stared.

'An adverse reaction,' he said carefully, in his incongruous voice, 'is a positive indication of a nerve touched.'

'You've been reading books!'

'I've been bashed a few times. It always tells me something. Like being bashed told you quite a lot, didn't it?'

'I suppose it did.'

'See? If anyone bashes you again, learn from it.'

'I don't intend to be bashed again.'

'No? That's why you asked about bodyguards?'

'Exactly why.'

He grinned. 'I've a friend who's a jockey over the jumps. He's broken his bones about twenty times. It'll never happen again, he says. He says it every time.'

'Mad,' I agreed.

'Have you ever met a jump jockey?'

'I was married once to a trainer in Lambourn.'

'Emily Cox,' he said.

I was still.

'I like to know who I'm working for,' he said.

'And to check up on whether I would lie to you?'

'Most of my clients do.'

I would, I acknowledged to myself, have lied to him if I'd wanted to.

His telephone rang and he answered it formally, 'Young and Uttley, can I help you?'

He listened and said, 'Thank you' half a dozen times, and wrote a few words onto a notepad, and disconnected.

'Your chalice,' he said, 'was inscribed with something called Bede's Death Song. It sounds a right laugh. It was made in 1867 to the order of a Mr Hanworth Hill of Wantage, Berkshire, probably to impress the neighbours. It cost an arm and a leg because it was solid gold inlaid with emeralds, sapphires and rubies.'

'Real ones?' I exclaimed, surprised.

Chris consulted his notes. 'Cabochon gems, imperfect.' He looked up. 'What does cabochon mean?'

'It means polished but uncut. No facets. Rounded, like pebbles. Not made to sparkle.' I paused. 'They don't look real. They're big.'

'You mean, you've actually seen this thing?'

'I think it's what I got bashed for.'

'So where is it now?'

'You,' I said smiling, 'are – I hope – going to prevent anyone else from trying to bash that information out of me.'

'Oh.' He blinked. 'How difficult would it be to make you tell?'

'Fairly easy.' But, I thought, it might depend on who was asking.

'You'd fold? You surprise me.'

'The chalice isn't mine.'

'Reasonable. OK. I'll start on the gyms.'

'Be careful,' I said.

'Sure.' He sounded lighthearted. 'Black eyes will cost you extra.'

He wanted to know if I were serious about a bodyguard, and we agreed that identifying my robbers took priority.

Ah well.

Returning by train, tube and legs to Park Crescent I was met by my mother in a state of agitation: that is to say, she was looking out for me and told me calmly but at once that I should telephone Emily immediately.

'What about?'

'Golden Malt got loose.'

Damnation, I thought; *fuck it.*

'How's Ivan?' I asked.

'Not bad. Phone Emily, won't you?'

I phoned her.

'Golden Malt got loose on the Downs at Foxhill,' she said. 'He's not an easy ride, as you know. He bucked off the exercise lad and got loose and they couldn't catch him.'

'But racehorses often go home by themselves, don't they? Surely he'll turn up—'

'He *has* turned up,' she interrupted. 'He's found his way back *here*. Don't ask me how. He's been in this yard for five years, ever since Ivan bought him as a foal, and, first chance he got, he came home.'

'Bugger.'

'The thing is, what do you want me to do?'

'Keep him. I'll think.'

'I've had a phone call from Surtees. He says he's coming to collect him.'

'He said *what*?'

'He says the horse is Patsy's.'

I took a steadying breath. 'The horse is Ivan's.'

'Surtees says Patsy's going to sell the horse to prevent you getting your hands on it. He says you've stolen the King Alfred Cup and you'll steal Golden Malt and rob Patsy and the brewery. I said you wouldn't do that, but he's bringing a trailer to collect Golden Malt and take him to his stud farm for safe keeping.'

I tried to organise scattered thoughts.

'When do you expect him?' I asked.

'He'll be on his way already.'

I groaned. I'd just come from Reading, about thirty

miles from Lambourn, and now, in London, it was nearer eighty.

'How did Surtees know you have the horse back?' I asked.

'I don't know. But he also knows he was in Foxhill. All my lads know, too. I can't send the horse back there.'

'Well, I'll come as soon as I can. Don't let Surtees take Golden Malt.'

She said despairingly, 'But how do I stop him?'

'Let down the tyres of the trailer. Build a Great Wall. Anything.'

I explained the problem briefly to my mother, who said at once that I could borrow Ivan's car.

Two hours at least by car. Roadworks and hold-ups in tortoise-slow traffic. Also, remembering the gauge from Saturday, I would have to stop for petrol.

I chose a train. I wasn't bad at trains. I ran and was lucky, catching an underground without waiting and a non-stop express from Paddington to Didcot junction and a taxi driver who hurried his wheels to Lambourn for a bonus. I took with me my mother's cash card and her phone card and all her available money, and my own new credit card and cheques, and also a zipped bag containing the things I'd borrowed ten days earlier from Emily – helmet, padded jacket, jodhpur boots – that my mother hadn't yet returned to her.

Helter-skelter though I went, Surtees had arrived

first. He had brought with him not only a trailer for the horse but an assistant horse-handler in the shape of his nine-year-old daughter, Xenia.

Surtees, Emily, Xenia and Golden Malt were all out in the stable yard, Emily holding the horse by his bridle and arguing angrily with the others.

Emily's Land Rover stood in the driveway behind Surtees's trailer, effectively blocking his way out. The exit on the far side of the yard, the wide earth track used by the horses on their way out to exercise, was at present impassable as it seemed a lorry delivering hay had carelessly shed its load of bales there.

I paid the taxi driver his bonus and with reluctance walked into the angry scene. Emily looked relieved to see me, Surtees furious. Xenia gave me a head-to-toe sneer and in a voice just like her mother's said, 'What *do* you think you look like?'

'Good afternoon, Surtees,' I said. 'Having trouble?'

Surtees said with unthrottled rage, 'Tell your wife to get out of my way. That horse is Patsy's, and I'm taking it.'

I said, 'It's Ivan's, and I'm looking after Ivan's things, as you know.'

'Get out of my way!'

'The horse is officially in training here with Emily. It can't race from your stud farm. You surely know the rules.'

'Bugger the rules!'

Xenia, giving me the insolent stare she'd learned from her parents, said, 'You're a thief. Mummy says so.'

She was dressed in riding breeches, navy hacking jacket, polished boots and black velvet helmet, as if for a showground. Not a bad kid. Fair haired, blue eyed, hopelessly spoiled.

'Why aren't you in school?' I asked.

'I have riding lessons on Monday afternoons,' she answered automatically, and then added, 'and it's none of your business.'

Surtees, presumably deciding that argument would get him nowhere, made a sudden rugger charge at me while my head and attention were turned towards Xenia, and with his shoulder cannon-balling into my stomach, knocked me over.

He fell on top of me, seeking to damage. Neither rugger nor any form of contact sport had ever been my choice or capability. I rolled over and over in the gravelly dirt with Surtees, scrambling for a weight advantage, trying to disconnect myself and stand up.

I could sense Xenia jumping up and down and screaming, 'Kill him, Daddy. Kill him.'

The whole situation was idiotic. Farcical. Killing me was definitely outside Surtees's imagination, but the prospect of offering Golden Malt to Patsy as a symbol of his virility and superiority over the hated step-brother lent him a strength and viciousness hard to deal with.

Neither of us landed a decisive punch. Surtees, as Chris Young had sworn, wasn't the boxing-gym type.

Add in Xenia who, as befitted her clothes, carried a riding crop, and we arrived at a childish form of warfare in which a bodyguard would have lightened the load.

Surtees clutched my hair and tried to bang my head on the ground, which gave me the idea of doing it to him, with equal lack of effectiveness, while Xenia danced around us lashing out with the riding crop which usually landed on me though occasionally on her father, to his bellowing disgust.

I scrambled finally to my feet, but dragged Surtees up with me as he wouldn't leave go. Xenia hit my legs. Surtees tried a sweeping too-slow wide-armed clout to my head that gave me a chance to both duck the blow and get hold of his clothes and fling him with all my strength away from me so that he overbalanced and staggered backwards and, falling, cracked his head against a brick stable wall.

It stunned him. He slid to his knees. Xenia screamed, 'You've killed my Daddy,' though I clearly hadn't, and I wrapped my arms round her writhing little body, lifting her off her feet, and yelled to Emily, 'Are any of these boxes empty?'

'The end two,' she shouted, and struggled to hold Golden Malt in control, the horse stamping around, upset by the noise.

The top half door of the end box stood open, the bottom half closed and bolted. I carried the frantically struggling child over there and dropped her over the lower half of the door, closing the top half and sliding home a bolt before she could climb out.

I unbolted and opened both halves of the vacant box next door and, grabbing the groggy Surtees by the back of his collar and by his belt, half ran him, half flung him into the space, closing both halves of the door and slapping home the bolts.

Xenia screeched and kicked her door. Surtees had yet to find his voice. Out of breath, I went over to Emily, whose expression was a mixture of outrage and laugh.

'Now what?' she said.

'Now I bolt you into Golden Malt's box so that none of this is your fault, and decamp with the horse.'

She stared. 'Are you serious?'

'None of this is serious, but it's not very funny, either.'

We could both hear Xenia's muffled shrieks.

'She'll upset all the horses,' Emily said, calming Golden Malt with small pats. 'I did think you might ride this fellow away again,' she said. 'I was just saddling him when Surtees came. The saddle is over there, in his box.'

I walked across the yard and found the saddle, which I carried back and fixed in place. There was a full net of hay in the box also, and a head collar for tying up a horse more comfortably than with a bridle. I carried them out and threaded them together with the zipped bag I'd brought, taking out the helmet but slinging the rest over the withers of the horse, in front of the saddle; like saddle bags of yore.

Then I took the reins from Emily and walked with her to the empty box. She went inside and I bolted the bottom half of the door.

'You'd better hurry,' she said calmly. 'The lads will arrive in less than half an hour for evening stables, and Surtees will have the police looking for you five minutes after that.'

I kissed her over the stable door.

'It will be dark in the next hour,' she said. 'Where will you go?'

'God knows.'

I kissed her again and bolted her into her temporary prison, and hauled myself into Golden Malt's saddle and, buckling on the helmet, set off again onto the Downs.

I needed the helmet for anonymity more than safety. So universal was the wearing of helmets that a head without one would have been remembered, even in a part of the country where horses were commoner than cows.

Golden Malt, to my relief, showed no reluctance to go along the stretch of road leading to the familiar track up to the training grounds, and seemed, if I understood him at all, to be reassured by being ridden and directed, not running loose and having to find his own way home.

Even at four in the afternoon there were other horses around in the distance. Golden Malt whinnied loudly and received an echoing response from afar, which caused him to nod his head as if in satisfaction: he went along sweetly, not trying to buck me off.

The problem was that I didn't know where to go. Surtees might indeed send the police after me, and although they wouldn't try to catch me on horseback like a Wild West posse, at some point or other I would very likely find myself vulnerably back on a road. Out of sight – that was the thing.

I tried to remember the map Emily and I had spread out in the kitchen, but I'd been concentrating on the way to Foxhill then, and I certainly couldn't go back there. Emily had a Patsy-informant in her yard – one of her lads making a little extra money from Surtees – and so, now, maybe, had her Foxhill friend. No good risking it.

The rolling sea of grass on Lambourn Downs was to my eyes featureless. I'd been up there fairly often with Emily in her Land Rover, but it had been five or six years ago. I looked back and could no longer distinguish the track home.

Think.

Monday, late afternoon. Time for all horses to go to their stables for food, for night.

I decided to be ordinary; to conform. It would be the abnormal, like an unhelmeted head, that would draw comment and attention and questions.

I thought again of the Ridgeway. I wouldn't get lost on it.

I might get *found* on it.

Golden Malt trotted happily the length of Mandown, his regular exercise ground. It was when I stopped at the far end and didn't turn his head back towards home that he grew restive.

I patted his neck and talked to him, as Emily would have done.

'Never mind, old fellow, we're safe out here,' I murmured over and over, and it was the lack of panic in the voice of confidence, that I think calmed him. I was afraid he would by-pass the false front and go instinctively for the underlying doubt, but he slowly relaxed and waited patiently, twitching his ears forward and back as untroubled horses do, leaving his future in my hands.

Unwelcome though the thought had been, I'd accepted that we might have to stay out on the Downs all night. I could otherwise amble into someone's stable yard or farm and ask for stabling until morning, but this wasn't normal any longer in the age of cars. There were motels but no horsetels; not anyway for unannounced strangers on thoroughbreds.

Shelter.

The weather was fine, though chilly. It wasn't too cold for Golden Malt's survival, but he was used to a snug box with food and drink provided, and perhaps a rug. An animal of racehorse calibre wouldn't stand quiet for even an hour if one simply tied his reins to a railing. He would break free and kick up his heels in a V sign as he galloped to the horizon. While red carpets might be out, four walls and water were essential.

There were two hours left until darkness. It took me nearly all of that time to find a place that Golden Malt would enter.

There were various huts on the Downs where the groundsmen kept equipment, but none of those would be big enough or empty enough, or would have running water. What I needed was the sort of shelter farmers built at a distance from their home yards, providing walls and roofs against hail and gales, and troughs for their stock to drink from.

The first two such shelters I came to were both filthy inside, thick with droppings. More importantly, Golden Malt wouldn't drink the water. He whiffled his nose and lips over the surface and turned his fastidious head away: and it was no good getting angry, I had to trust to his equine sense.

The third shelter I came to looked just as unappetising, but Golden Malt walked into it amiably and then came out and drank from the trough even before I'd removed bits and pieces from the water's surface.

Much relieved, I waited until he'd drunk his fill and then walked back in with him, and found a comfort in the shape of an iron ring let into the wall. Exchanging the head collar for the bridle I fastened the horse into his new quarters and positioned the hay net where he could eat when he wanted. I unsaddled him and took the saddle outside where he couldn't step on it, and finally – and resignedly – took stock of my own situation.

Like almost all such shelters, its windowless walls faced chiefly north and west and south against the prevailing winds. The east wall was pierced by the entry, which of course had no door. By good luck, although the air was always on the move on the uplands, there was no strong wind that evening, and although the temperature dropped with darkness, I felt more at home in the open than inside with the horse.

I unzipped the holdall and thankfully put on the padded jacket, which alone made the night enterprise feasible. Then I folded the holdall thickly to make a cushion and propped the saddle against the wall for a chair back, and reckoned I'd spent far worse hours on Scottish mountains.

After dark, the clear sky blazed with depths of stars, and in the folds of the Downs below me, little clumps of distant lights assured me that this solitude was relative: and solitude, to me, anyway, was natural.

Inside the shelter, Golden Malt steadily chomped on his hay and made me feel hungry. I'd eaten breakfast in London and a chocolate bar on the train to Didcot, but I hadn't had the foresight to fill the holdall with enough for dinner.

It couldn't be helped. I scooped a handful of water out of the trough and smelled it, and although it wasn't the cleanest ever, judged that if the horse had passed it fit, it wouldn't kill me. Cold water was never bad at anaesthetising hunger: and hunger was an odd sort of thing, not so much a grind in the stomach as an overall feeling of lassitude, and a headache.

I put my hands into the jacket pockets for warmth and slept sitting up, and soon after two o'clock (according to the luminous hands on the cheap watch I'd bought to replace my father's stolen gold one) awoke from cold. Everything was so quiet inside the shelter that I went in in some alarm, but Golden Malt was still there, safely tied up, asleep, resting a hock in mental twilight, his eyes open but no thoughts showing.

I walked around quietly outside to unstiffen and warm myself and after a while drank more water and sat down again to wait for dawn.

None of my thoughts was hilariously funny.

Surtees's second-hand dislike and spite towards me would now certainly have intensified into personal hatred, because he would think I had made a fool of him in front of his daughter. No matter that he had belligerently chosen to come to remove Ivan's horse, no matter that it was he who had rushed me first to knock me down, he would care only that Xenia had seen him fail on both fronts: the obnoxious Alexander had made off with the goods and left her father imprisoned in a box for horses, looking stupid.

Xenia, with whom I had no quarrel, could now be counted a foe for life. Her mother's consequently increased antagonism might really give a bodyguard work. *Someone* had sent the robbers to my bothy.

Next time you'll scream . . .

Bugger it, I thought. Even if I should dump Ivan and all his concerns (and with him, my mother) I wouldn't necessarily free myself from Patsy's obsession or revenge.

Surtees was Ivan's son-in-law. I was Ivan's stepson. Which of us, I wondered vaguely, took legal priority? Did priority exist?

I itched to paint, I longed to go back to my easel, to my silent room. Zoë Lang filled crevices in my mind to such an extent that in the middle of wondering if water were drinkable I would see the hollow under her cheekbone and think 'purple glaze on turquoise thinned with medium'. The face of the inner woman had to be built of glazes, of colour not as opaque as outer living skin might be, but still to be unmistakably the person who lived in that flesh, who thought and believed and confronted doubt.

I had set myself an unattainable ideal. Such human skill as I could summon wasn't enough for the job. I felt the suicidal despair of all who longed to do what they couldn't, what only a few in each century could – whether blessed or cursed in spirit. No achievement was ever finite. There was no absolute summit. No peak of Everest to plant a flag on. Success was someone else's opinion.

I drifted and dozed and woke again shivering in the

first grey promise of light. Golden Malt was pawing the ground, his hooves thudding heavily on dirt, giving me the prosaic news that he had finished his hay. I undid his head collar and took him outside for a drink, and felt, if not exactly a communion with him, at least an awareness of being a fellow creature on a lonely planet.

Deciding that grass would do for breakfast he walked around a bit, head down, munching, while I held his rope and thought of coffee and toast. Then, as daylight more positively arrived, I saddled and bridled him in the shelter, and changed my trainers for jodhpur boots, to look and ride better, and finally, when the morning's first exercise strings would be peopling the landscape, heaved myself and gear onto his back and set about completing the disappearing trick.

I rode to the east, towards the strengthening light. I knew that the Ridgeway path lay to the north of me, also running west to east. Not far ahead I would come to the road from Wantage going south to Hungerford, and I wanted to cross that to reach the next wide expanse of open downland on the far side, where many trainers had their yards but wouldn't know by sight a conspicuous horse from Lambourn. Neither Emily nor I, in my rush to be gone before the lads arrived for evening stables, had given a thought this time to a hood and boots for hiding Golden Malt's white features.

I came to the main road and dismounted to walk the horse across, needing to open and shut gates on either side but, that done, I was free on the wide lands south of Wantage, with five or six miles available in most directions to find a suitable string of horses to attach myself to and follow.

I was looking for a small string of no more than four or five, as I reckoned I would get a more hospitable reception from a small-scale trainer: and so it proved. Just when I thought I'd drawn a blank and was in trouble I came across four horses plodding homeward, one of them being led by a lad on foot.

I followed at a distance and tried not to feel disconcerted when my leaders headed towards the heart of a village from where I could see ahead the huge swathe of the main north–south arterial road, the A34: impassable, if not impossible, for horses to walk across.

The road into the village led downhill. The string of four marched on, undaunted, and I found we were crossing the road *beneath* it, to a second half of the village on the far side. On through the village, the horses turned in between the peeling gates of a small stable yard.

A motor horsebox stood in the yard with a trainer's name and phone number painted on it. I retraced Golden Malt's steps to a phone box we had passed in the village and, juggling reins and coins, took the trainer away from his breakfast.

I was, I explained, an owner who was also an amateur jockey. I had just had a blazing row on the Downs with my trainer and had ridden off in a fury, and I was looking for somewhere to park my horse while I sorted things out. Could he help?

'Glad to,' he said heartily, and showed no less enthusiasm when I shortly arrived on a good-looking thoroughbred, offering generous cash for its board and lodging.

When I asked the trainer ('Call me Phil') the quickest way to London he said, 'By taxi to Didcot,' and I thought it ironic that I'd travelled three parts of an oval on Golden Malt and ended in the underpass village of East Ilsley which was actually nearer to Surtees's stud farm than to Emily's yard.

I would come to fetch my horse later that day, I told Phil, and he said not to hurry. He phoned for a taxi for me. We shook hands, in tune.

Back in London I met Ivan's and my mother's anxiety with perhaps more reassurance than I truly felt. Golden Malt, I assured them, was secure and well looked after, but it might be better to move him right away from the Berkshire Downs area where, to horse-educated eyes, he was as recognisable as a film star.

I asked Ivan to lend me his copy of *Horses in Training*, which gave the location amongst other details of every licensed trainer and permit holder in Britain, and I asked my mother to phone Emily and get her to go out shopping in Swindon or Newbury, as she often did, and to phone back to Park Crescent from a public phone there.

'But why?' my mother asked, puzzled.

'Emily's walls have ears, and Surtees is listening.' My mother looked disbelieving. 'And,' I added, 'please don't tell Emily I'm here.'

My obliging parent talked to Emily, who cheerfully said she would be going shopping soon, and forty-five minutes later she was telling my mother the number she was calling from in Swindon. I took the number and my mother's phone card and jogged to the nearest outside line; and Emily wanted to know if all this cloak and dagger stuff were necessary.

'Probably not,' I said, 'but just in case.' I paused. 'What happened when I left?'

Emily almost laughed. 'The lads came for evening stables and let us all out. Xenia's tantrums turned to tears. Surtees was purple with fury and phoned the police, who arrived with a siren wailing that upset all the horses. Surtees told them that you'd stolen Golden Malt but fortunately the police had been to my yard before when we had a lot of saddles and bridles stolen, and they believed me when I said the horse was Ivan's and you had absolute authority to look after it in any way you thought best. I showed them the copy you gave me of the power of attorney and they told Surtees they wouldn't start a police hunt for you, which sent him practically berserk. He was yelling at the police, which did him no good at all with them, but I begged them to stay until he had gone because he was so violent I was afraid he would attack me or some of the horses. So they tried to quieten him and finally got him to drive his trailer away, but Xenia was crying out of control, and if Surtees reached home without causing an accident it will have been a miracle.'

'He's a fool.'

'He's a dangerous fool,' Emily said. 'All that silly-ass front of his has changed to pure poison. So take care, Al. I'm serious. You made him look stupid and he'll never forgive you.'

I said lightly, 'I'm engaging a bodyguard.'

'Al!' She sounded exasperated. 'Look out for Surtees. I mean it.'

'Yes,' I said. 'I want to talk to you, though, about Golden Malt.'

'Where is he?'

'Safe enough, but it will be better if I move him again, and I need your knowledge and advice. I've borrowed Ivan's copy of *Horses in Training* and sorted out four trainers who look possible, so if I tell you who they are, will you give me your opinion?'

'Fire away.'

I named the four trainers and again asked what she thought.

'Two of them would be OK,' she said slowly, 'but look up Jimmy Jennings.'

I looked him up and objected, 'He has too many horses.' I counted. 'Thirty-six.'

'Not any more. He's been ill. He's halved his yard . . . told some of the owners to take their horses away temporarily, but it looks as if it might be for ever. He and I are good friends. The real advantage of going to him is that he has two yards, and one of them is now standing empty. Tell me his phone number and I'll see what he says.'

I read out the phone number and asked, 'Would the horse be able to race from there in your own name as its trainer?'

'Well, Jimmy's a licensed trainer himself; no problem there. The horse could detour to my yard in Lambourn on the day of the race to pick up the colours and tack and his usual lad. I could inform the Jockey Club in advance, and as the owner, Ivan, is a member, I can't see there being any difficulty.' She thought briefly. 'From the secrecy point of view it's always the lads that are the leaky sieves. It's not deliberate disloyalty, they just talk in the pubs.'

'And one of your lads talks to Surtees.'

She sighed. 'If I knew which one, I would give him disinformation.'

'That's a thought.'

'Give me ten minutes and I'll phone you back.'

I waited quite a while by the phone, loitering and repelling a resentful woman who wanted to use the *end* instrument of the row, not one of the vacant others. She had fierce words to say. When Emily at last rang, the resentful woman still hovered, black beady eyes full of ill will.

'It's all fixed,' Emily said. 'Sorry I was so long. I told Jimmy the whole situation. He's a hundred per cent trustable if you trust him first. He says he'll put Golden Malt in his empty yard, and to avoid the chatty lad business, the horse will be cared for and exercised by Jimmy's sixteen-year-old daughter, who's already an amateur jockey and knows when to keep quiet. There's no need for his regular lads even to know Golden Malt is there. The yards are at opposite ends of the village. What's more, it's not a busy training area. Jimmy's gallops aren't the best, though it hasn't stopped him training a lot of winners in his time. I said you'd get there sometime this afternoon, and ... er ... I promised the training fee would be inflated. Jimmy didn't want to hear of it, but I insisted. He could do with a bit extra, though he's too proud to ask.'

'He'll get it,' I said.

'Yes. I knew you would agree.'

She gave me directions to the Hampshire village and said Jimmy had said I should look for a square white house with bronze flaming-torch gateposts, and I should ring the front door bell, not go round to the back.

'OK.'

'I'll phone Jimmy later for news. Don't worry, I won't do it from home. And I told him *not* to phone me.'

'Brilliant.'

'Do you *really* think my phone is bugged?'

'Don't take the risk.'

We said goodbye and the baleful old witch shouldered me out of the way to reach her preferred public phone. Everyone to their own obsession, I supposed. Impossible to dislodge fixed ideas. There were six unoccupied instruments she could have used.

I returned to Ivan's house, detouring to a newsagent for a copy of *Horse and Hound* and an up-to-date road map, and to my mother's and stepfather's bemusement I told them in detail about the shenanigans in Emily's yard and my travels with Golden Malt.

I said, 'Emily has arranged for a trainer friend of hers to look after your horse and keep him fit so he can run in the King Alfred Gold Cup. If you agree with what we've planned, I'll transfer Golden Malt to the trainer this afternoon. The horse will be in very good hands and it would be only by exceptionally bad luck that Surtees would discover where he is.'

Ivan said slowly, 'You've gone to a lot of trouble.'

'Well, the horse is yours. You asked me to look after your affairs, so . . . er . . . I try.'

'For your mother's sake.' A statement, not a question.

'Yes, but for yours, also. You don't approve of the way I live, but you have never been ungenerous to me, and you would have taken me into the brewery, and I don't forget that.'

He looked at his hands and I couldn't read his thoughts, but when I asked if I could borrow his car for the afternoon, he agreed without conditions.

Via the classified advertisements in *Horse and Hound* and the road map and the telephone, I arranged to meet a four-horse travelling horsebox (the smallest of a prestigious firm) in Phil's yard in East Ilsley, and there loaded Golden Malt for the last leg of his journey.

Phil and I shook hands again, mutually pleased and, asking the box driver of the top-class transport firm to follow Ivan's car as arranged, I led him southwards and eastwards along secondary roads until we arrived somewhere near Basingstoke in a village that looked as if it had never seen a racehorse. But there, in the village's main street, stood a square white house with bronze flaming torches on the gateposts.

I stopped the car, the horsebox braking to a halt behind me, and went to ring the front door bell, as instructed.

A thin, smiling middle-aged man opened the door in welcome. His skin had the grey tautness of terminal illness but his handshake was strong. A pace or two behind him stood a short fine-boned girl whom he introduced as his daughter, saying she would drive through the village in the horsebox and settle Golden Malt into his new home. He watched approvingly as she climbed into the high cab beside the driver for the journey, and he invited me into his house, eyeing Ivan's expensive car with reassurance and telling me that

Emily had said she was sending her 'special lad' to ensure the safe transit of a special horse.

Jimmy Jennings asked why I was smiling. Was I not Emily's 'special lad'?

'I'm married to her,' I said.

'*Really?*' He looked me up and down. 'Are you that painter feller who ran off and left her?'

'I'm afraid so.'

'Good Lord! Come this way. Come this way.'

He hurried down a hallway, beckoning me to follow, and led me into his office, furnished, like most trainers' such rooms, with ranks of framed photographs on the walls. He stood and pointed in silence, but I didn't need his directing finger: among the clutter hung a painting I'd done and sold four or more years earlier.

As always when I saw my own work freshly after an interval, I felt a mixture of excitement and shock. The picture was of a jockey plodding back to the stands after a fall, disappointment in his shoulders, a tear in his grass-stained breeches. I remembered the intensity of feeling in the brushstrokes, the stoicism and the loneliness of that man's defeat.

'Feller I trained for couldn't pay his bill,' Jimmy Jennings explained. 'He offered me that picture instead. He swore it would be worth a fortune one day, but I took it because I liked it. Whether you realise it or not, that picture just about sums up a jump jockey's life. Endurance. Courage. Persistence. All those things. Do you see?'

I said lamely, 'I'm glad you like it.'

He thrust out his chin, a defiant gesture against an imminent and inevitable fate.

'That picture keeps me going,' he said.

I drove back to London, having briefly checked on Golden Malt in his isolated splendour, Jimmy Jennings's daughter tending him with years of experience showing.

The horsebox driver had already unloaded and gone, as agreed with his firm. The hiding of Ivan's horse should, barring accidents, be complete.

I left Ivan's car in its underground lair and returned to his house to learn that Patsy had spent the afternoon with him, complaining that I had attacked Surtees so murderously as to leave him concussed, that I had committed child abuse against Xenia, and had brazenly stolen Golden Malt for my own illegal ends, such as holding him for ransom.

'I listened to her,' Ivan said judiciously. 'Is my horse safe?'

'Yes.'

'And a ransom?'

I said tiredly, 'Don't be silly.'

He actually laughed. 'I listened to her, and she's my daughter, but when she went on and on about how devious and dishonest you are, I slowly realised that I've truly been trusting you all along, that my inner instinct has held firm, even though to you I may sometimes have shown indecision. I love my daughter, but I think she's wrong. I said once impulsively that I wished you were my son. I didn't think I meant it when I said it. I do mean it now.'

My mother embraced him with uncharacteristic delight and he stroked her arm happily, content to have pleased her. I saw in them both the youthful faces they had left behind, and thought I might paint that perception, one day soon.

There was time after that for the three of us to eat dinner calmly before I left for the night train. We drank wine in friendship, Ivan and I, and had come nearer than ever before to an appreciative and lasting understanding. I did believe, against all previous experience, that Patsy could not henceforth sow overthrowing doubts of me in his decent mind.

He insisted on returning to my care the unopened envelope containing the codicil to his Will.

'Don't argue, Alexander,' he said. 'It will be safest with you.'

'We won't need it for years. By then it will be out of date.'

'Yes. Perhaps. Anyway, I've decided to tell you what's in it.'

'You don't have to.'

'I need to,' he said, and told me.

I smiled and hugged him for the first time ever.

I hugged my mother, and went to Scotland.

CHAPTER TEN

To my surprise Jed was waiting at Dalwhinnie in the dawn. Himself had telephoned my mother late the previous evening, he said, and she'd told him I was on the train. Himself wanted me to go directly from train to castle, a command automatically to be obeyed.

On the way Jed told me that I now had a new bed and a new armchair in the bothy (chosen by Jed, paid for by Himself) and I was to write a list of other things I would need. My uncle would foot the bill unconditionally.

'But he doesn't have to,' I protested.

'If you ask me, he feels guilty. Let him atone.'

I glanced at Jed sideways. 'A shrink, are you?' I asked.

'He told me you wouldn't think, let alone suggest, that he ought to make good your losses. I explained that you'd cleared out the bothy and he had me get that pile of muck removed. I hope to God the hilt wasn't hidden in it.'

'Your prayers are answered. Where's the painting, the one in the sheet?'

'In my house, with all the other things you gave me.'

I sighed with relief.

'Flora looked at it,' he said. 'She says it's the portrait of a ghost.'

Flora, his wife, had 'the sight', the ability deep in the Scottish gene-pool of being able sometimes to see the future.

'The word ghost means spirit,' I said. 'If Flora sees a spirit, that's what I painted.'

'You make it sound so prosaic.'

'It isn't finished,' I said.

'No. Flora said not.' He paused. 'She said she saw that ghost weeping.'

'*Weeping?*'

'She said so.' He sounded apologetic. 'You know how she gets, sometimes.'

I nodded.

Weeping and Dr Zoë Lang weren't concepts that sat easily together, and I had no intention of trying to paint regret, but only a statement that while the outer shell aged, the inner spirit might not. The task was hard enough already. Weeping for lost youth would have to be a sequel.

As before I found Himself in his dining-room eating toast. He raised his big head at my entrance and gave me his formal greeting.

'Alexander.'

'My lord.'

'Breakfast?' He waved a hand.

'Thank you.'

There were three places laid that morning, one used. James, I learned, had already gone out on the moors.

'He wants a round of golf,' Himself said. 'How about this afternoon? He's leaving tomorrow. I've asked Jed to fix you up with wheels, and also with a portable telephone of your own, and don't object that you can't recharge the batteries, Jed is getting you extra ones and he'll call on you every day with replacements. It may not be to your liking for solitude, but please humour me in this.'

He looked at my silent face and smiled. 'You would no doubt die for me as your clan chief. You can suffer a portable telephone.'

'Put like that . . .'

'You can go back to your damned paints tomorrow.'

Resignedly, I ate toast. The old feudal obligations might be thought to be extinct, but in fact were not. The freedom of the wild mountains that I so prized was my uncle's gift. I owed him an allegiance both decreed by my ancestry and reinforced by present favours and, besides, I liked him very much.

He wanted to know what I'd been doing in the south, and he kept prodding me for details. I told him fairly fully about the codicil, about Patsy's chatty involvement with Oliver Grantchester, about the discovery of Norman Quorn's body, and about my fracas with Surtees in Emily's yard.

'Two things emerge from all that,' he said eventually. 'Surtees is a dangerous fool, and where is the brewery's money?'

'The brewery's auditor can't find it.'

'No,' he said thoughtfully, 'but can *you*?'

'I?' I no doubt sounded as surprised as I felt. 'If the accountant and the insolvency lady say finding it is impossible, how can I, who know next to nothing about international transfers, how can I even know where to begin?'

'It will come to you,' he said.

'But I don't have access . . .'

'What to?' he said, when I stopped.

'Well . . . to whatever is left of Norman Quorn's office in the brewery.'

He wrinkled his forehead. 'Would there be anything still there?'

'If the dragons didn't guard the gates, I'd take a look.'

'Dragons?'

'Patsy, and the brewery's manager, Desmond Finch.'

'You would think they would *want* the money found.'

'But not by me.'

'That woman,' he said, meaning Patsy, 'is a menace.'

I told him of the friendly evening I'd spent with

Ivan, and he said that my stepfather seemed to have come to his silly senses at last.

'He's a good man,' I observed mildly. 'If your son James told you over and over again for years and years that I was trying to worm my way into your regard and your Will, would you believe him?'

Himself thought long and intensely. 'I might,' he at last acknowledged.

'Patsy is afraid of losing her father's love,' I said. 'Not just her inheritance.'

'She's in danger of bringing about what she fears.'

'People do,' I agreed.

The two of us made a complete circuit outside of the whole castle and its wings, as he liked to do, only to find on our return, outside the entrance door the family now used, a small white car that drew from him frowns and disgust.

'That bloody woman.'

'Who?'

'That Lang woman. She lives on my doorstep! Why did I ever ask her here?'

Himself might rue the day, but I was fascinated to see her again. She and her eighty-year-old wrinkles climbed out of the car and stood stalwartly in our path.

'She has joined the conservationists who look after the castle,' Himself said. 'Joined them? She *rules* them. This past week she's somehow got herself appointed chief custodian of the castle's historic contents . . . and you can guess what she's chiefly after.'

'The hilt,' I said.

'The hilt.' He raised his voice as we approached the white car. 'Good morning, Dr Lang.'

'Lord Kinloch.' She shook his hand, then looked me briefly up and down, unsure of my name.

'My nephew,' Himself said.

'Oh, yes.' She extended her hand again and shook mine perfunctorily. 'Lord Kinloch, I've come to discuss the Treasures of Scotland exhibition being planned for the Edinburgh Festival next year . . .'

Himself with faultless courtesy showed her not into the dining-room this time, nor into his private room, but into the fairly grand drawing-room into which his best pieces of furniture had been moved at the time of the handover. Dr Lang eyed two French commodes with a mixture of admiration for their beauty and workmanship and disapproval of their private ownership. She believed, as she said later, that they should have been included in the transfer, despite their having been personally bought and imported by a nineteenth-century Kinloch earl with cultured taste.

My uncle offered sherry. Dr Lang accepted.

'Al?' he enquired.

'Not right now.'

Himself took a polite tokenful. 'The flying eagle,' he said cheerfully, 'will look magnificent in the Treasures of Scotland.'

The flying eagle stood in the castle's main entrance hall, a splendid treble-life-sized marble sculpture with wing feathers shining with gold leaf, the wings high and wide as if the fabulous bird were about to alight on the onyx ball at its feet. Transporting the flying eagle to the Edinburgh exhibition would mean cranes and crates and a slow low-loader. Himself had been heard to remark (tactlessly) that the castle's conservationists still had charge of the eagle only because its weight made stealing it difficult.

'We must insist,' Dr Lang said crisply, 'on taking charge of the Kinloch hilt.'

'Mm,' my uncle made a non-committal humming noise and offered nothing more.

'You can't hide it away for ever.'

Himself said with regret, 'Thieves grow more ingenious every year.'

'You know my views,' she told him crossly. 'The hilt belongs to Scotland.'

Zoë Lang looked half the size of her adversary, and was neat and precise where he moved clumsily. Belief in their cause stiffened them both. While he controlled the whereabouts of his treasure, she couldn't claim it: if once she'd found it, she would never relinquish it. I could see that for each of them it was all hardening into a relentless battle of wills, a mortal duel fought over dry La Ina sherry in cut lead crystal.

I said to Zoë Lang, 'Do you mind if I draw you?'

'*Draw* me?'

'Just a pencil sketch.'

She looked astonished. 'Whatever for?'

'He's an artist,' Himself explained casually. 'He painted that large picture over there.' He pointed briefly. 'Al, if you want any paper, there's some in my room, in the desk drawers.'

Gratefully I went to fetch some: high grade typing paper, but anything would do. I sorted out a reasonable pencil and returned to the drawing-room to find my uncle and his enemy standing side by side in front of the gloomiest painting I'd ever attempted.

'Glen Coe,' Dr Lang said with certainty. 'The sun never shines.'

It was true that the shape of the terrain caused orographic cloud formation more days than not over the unhappy valley, but the dark grey morning when the perfidious Campbells murdered their hosts the Macdonalds – thirty-seven of them, including women and children – seemed to brood forever over the heather-clad hills. A place of shivers, of horror, of betrayal.

Zoë Lang stepped closer to the picture for a long inspection, then turned my way.

'The shadows,' she told me, 'the dark places round the roots of the heather, they're all painted like tiny patches of *tartan*, the red of the Macdonalds and the yellow of the Campbells, little ragged lines of shading. You can only see them when you're up close . . .'

'He knows,' my uncle said calmly.

'Oh.' She looked from me to the picture and back again. There were glazes of shadow over the hillsides and atmospheric double shadows over many of the tartan pools round the heather roots. I'd felt ill all the time, painting it. The massacre of Glen Coe could still churn in the gut of a world that had seen much worse genocide in plenty since.

She said, 'Where do you want me to sit?'

'Oh.' I was grateful. 'By the window, if you would.'

I got her to sit where the light fell on her face at the same angle as I'd painted her, and I drew the face in pencil as it appeared now to my eyes, an old face with folds and lines in the skin and taut sinews in the neck. It was clear and accurate, and predictably she didn't like it.

'You're cruel,' she said.

I shook my head. 'It's time that's cruel.'

'Tear it up.'

Himself peered at the drawing and shrugged, and said in my defence, 'He usually paints nice-looking golf scenes, all sunshine with people enjoying themselves. Sells them to America faster than he can paint them, don't you, Al?'

'Why *golf*?' Zoë Lang demanded. 'Why America?'

I answered easily, 'Golf courses in America are built to look good, with lots of water hazards. Water looks great in paintings.' I painted water-washed pebbles in metal paints, gold, silver and copper, and they always sold instantly. 'American golfers buy more golf pictures than British golfers do. So I paint what sells. I paint to live.'

She looked as if she thought the commercial attitude all wrong, as if any painter not starving in a garret were somehow reprehensible. I wondered what she would think if I told her I amplified my income nicely via royalties from postcards, thousands of copies of my paintings for golfers to send to each other from places like Augusta (the Masters) and from Pebble Beach and Oakland Hills (the Open) and even, in Britain, from Muirfield, St Andrews and The Belfry.

She sparred a little more with my uncle. He offered unstinting help with the eagle and smiled blandly to all else. She asked if King Alfred's chalice had turned up, as her friend was still waiting to put a value on the 'glass ornaments' (her words) embedded in the gold.

'Not yet,' Himself said unworriedly. 'One of my family will no doubt have it safe.'

She couldn't understand his carefree attitude, and it wasn't until after she had left that I told him the glass ornaments, if they were the original gems, were in fact genuine sapphires, emeralds and rubies.

'The King Alfred Gold Cup,' I said, 'is almost certainly worth far more intrinsically than the hilt. There's far more gold by weight, and the gems are nearly double the carats.'

'You don't mean it! How do you know?'

'I had it traced to the firm that made it. It cost an absolute fortune.'

'My God. My God. And young Andrew was playing with it on the kitchen floor!'

'Upside down,' I agreed, smiling.

'Does Ivan know where it is?'

'Not exactly,' I said, and told him where to look.

'You're a rogue, Alexander.'

I had put him in great good humour. He marched us into his own room for a 'decent drink' – Scotch whisky – and I stunned him speechless by suggesting that next time Zoë Lang vowed the hilt belonged to the nation he tell her then OK, the nation would lose on the deal.

'How do you mean?'

'Generation by generation – ever since the invention of inheritance taxes – the Kinlochs have paid for that hilt. The same object, but taxed after a death and retaxed and taxed again. It never ends. If you give it into public ownership, the country forfeits the tax. It's a case of kill the goose . . . Dr Lang never thinks of the golden tax eggs.'

He said thoughtfully, 'James will not have to pay crippling death duties on the castle, as I did. It was my greatest reason for handing it over.'

'One is taxed for giving a big present to one's son,' I smiled, 'but not for losing the same amount at the casino. Nor for winning. Screwy. But that's spite and envy for you. All feeling and no addition.'

'What brought all this on?'

'Thinking about the hilt.'

'Do you seriously think we should surrender it?'

'No,' I said, 'but arithmetic might cool Dr Lang's ardour.'

'I'll try it.' He lavishly poured more gold into my glass. 'By God, Al.'

'If you get me drunk,' I said, 'James will beat me at golf.'

James beat me at golf.

'Whatever did you say to Himself?' he asked. 'Nothing but catching a twenty-pound salmon puts him into such a high mood.'

'He's good to me.'

'The sun shines out of your arse.'

The difference between James and Patsy was that my cousin felt secure enough to make a joke of his father's occasional glance in my direction. James would inherit his title and an entailed estate. He had none of Patsy's devilish doubts sitting bleakly on his sunny shoulders.

As always we went amicably round eighteen holes, laughing, cursing, helplessly incompetent, racking up scores we would never confess to, happy in each other's undemanding company, cousins in the simplest sense, family attitudes and loyalties taken for granted.

We pulled our golf bags along behind us on their little trolleys, and if I were careful replacing my clubs each time, sliding them gently into the bag instead of ramming them home, it was because the handles rested not on the firm base of the bag but in the wide bowl of the grey cloth-wrapped shape within it, the jewelled gold treasure fashioned by Maxim in 1867.

We finished our round lightheartedly, and in the club house I wiped clean my woods and irons and stowed them upright in the bag in the locker, sentinels guarding King Alfred's Gold Cup.

Owing to the rigid divisions at the top of the golf bags, which held the clubs apart to prevent their damaging each other, I had had to buy a bag that could be taken apart at the bottom – for cleaning – and in the castle's drying-room I had undone the necessary screws to take the bag apart, and had lodged the Cup inside. It fitted there snugly: and as a bonus for having to undo the bag to get it out again, it could never be tipped out by accident.

The locker's flat grey doors were uniform and anonymous. Changing my shoes, I put the black-and-white studs on the shelf and closed everything unremarkably away, and with amusement returned with James to the castle.

By mid-morning the next day my life in the bothy had taken shape again, and in greater comfort than before when it came to mattress and armchair. A hired jeep stood outside my front door, the portable phone (with spare batteries) was working, and Zoë Lang's portrait stood unwrapped on the easel.

With a thankful feeling of coming home I set out the paints I needed, feeling their texture on knife and brush, darkening the background again, adding the shadows that had flashed into imagination in my travels, putting a glow on the skin and life-lights in the water-like surfaces of the eyes.

The woman lived on the canvas, as vital as I knew how to make her.

At five o'clock, when the quality of the light subtly changed, I put down the brushes, washed them for the last time that day and made sure that all the brilliant colours were airtight in their pots and tubes, a routine as natural as breathing. Then I lit my lamp and put it by the window, and took my bagpipes out of their case, and walked with them up the rocky hillside until the bothy lay far below.

It was weeks since I'd played the pipes. My fingers were rusty on the chanter. I filled the bag with air and tuned the drones, swinging them along my shoulder and waiting for such skill as I had to reawaken in my ear; and at length began to feel and to remember the fingering of one of the long ancient laments of a time earlier than Prince Charles Edward. The sadness that had enveloped Scotland for centuries before him, the untamable independence that no Act of Union could undo, all the dark Celtic mysteries pulsed in the old elemental endlessly recurring tunes that slowly wove a mood more of endurance than hope.

I had learned to play laments – the pibrochs – as a boy, chiefly for the unromantic reason that their slowness meant I had more time to get the notes right. I'd progressed to marches later, but a lament suited my painting of Zoë Lang better, and I stood on the Monadhliath Mountains while the moon rose, and played for her a mixture of an old tune called 'The King's Taxes' and a new one that I made up as I went along. And it was just as well, I thought, as stray squeaks and wrong notes made me wince, that my old army teacher wasn't there to hear.

Scottish piping laments could go on for hours, but earthly hunger put a stop to them usually in my case, and I returned in the dark to the bothy, filled with a pleasant melancholy but with no feeling of despair, and cooked paella in contentment.

I always woke early in the mountains, even in the dark winters, and the next day I sat in front of the easel watching the slow change of light on that face; the growth, as it almost seemed, of the emerging personality taking place before me; and I wondered if anyone would ever again see that gradual birth. If the picture were successful, if it ever hung in a gallery, passing visitors might give it a glance under a bright light and view it as a conjuring trick: now you see youth, now you don't.

When daylight was fully established I still sat comfortably in my new armchair, trying to tap into that courage I was supposed to have. It was one thing to imagine, another to *do*. And if I didn't do, I would know for ever that I'd failed in courage, even though, as it now stood, the portrait of an unknown woman was complete and workmanlike.

I had ransacked my mother's kitchen for a sharp-pointed knife, and in the end I'd borrowed from her not a knife but a meat thermometer. This unlikely tool had proved to have a spike whose tip was both sharp and abrasive. The spike was for sticking into joints of meat: the round dial from which it protruded measured the inner heat and the state of cooking – rare, medium, well done.

'Of course you can borrow it,' my mother said, puzzled, 'but whatever for?'

'It's scratchy. It's rigid. The dial gives it good grip. It's pretty well perfect.'

She sweetly humoured her unfathomable son.

So I had the perfect tool. I had the light. I had the vision.

I sat and quaked.

I had the pencil drawing of the real Zoë Lang. I'd drawn her at the same angle. It should have been easy.

I had to see the old face over the young.

I had to see it clearly, unmistakably, down to the soul.

I had to play the lament for time past. I had to play the lament as a fact but not necessarily as a tragedy. I had to depict the persistence of the spirit inside the transient flesh.

I couldn't.

Time passed.

When I finally picked up the meat thermometer and stood in front of Zoë Lang and made the first scratch down to the Payne's grey, it was as if I had surrendered to an inner force.

I started with the neck, conscious that if the whole concept were in fact beyond my ability, I could overpaint a fluffy scarf or jewel decoration to conceal the failure.

I saw the outer shell of age as larger than the face within, as if the external presentation were the cage, the prison, of the spirit. I held the pencil drawing beside the painting and put dots of reference at pivotal points: at the outer lines of the eye sockets, at the upper edges of the jaw bones, at the rear extension of the skull.

With almost an abandonment of rational thought I swept the sharp scratching point across my careful painting. I let go with instinct. I drew the old Zoë in grey scratches, as if the flesh colours weren't anything but background; I scratched the prison bars with the cruelty she'd sensed in me, with the inability to soften or compromise the brutal conception.

I left as little to chance as I could. I traced the direction of each line in my mind until I could see the effect, and that could take ten minutes or half an hour. The result might be a sweeping stroke that looked spontaneous and inevitable, but in nerving myself each time to scrape down to the grey I was cravenly aware that a mistake couldn't be put right.

It was a cold day, and I sweated.

By five o'clock the shape of Zoë Lang's old face was clearly established over the inner spirit. I put down the meat thermometer, stretched and flexed my cramped fingers, took the portable phone with me and went for a walk outside.

Sitting on a granite boulder, looking down on the bothy, looking away down the valley to the tiny cars crawling along the distant road, I phoned my mother. Bad reception: crackle and static.

Ivan, she assured me, was at last and slowly shedding his depression. He had dressed. He was talking of not needing Wilfred any longer. Keith Robbiston had paid one of his flying visits and had been pleased with the patient's progress. She herself felt more settled and less anxious.

'Great,' I said.

She wanted to know how the meat-thermometer picture was coming along.

'Medium rare,' I said.

She laughed and said she was pleased Himself had insisted on a phone.

I told her the number.

She was calm, cool and collected, her normal serene self.

I said I would call her again on Sunday, the day after tomorrow, when I had finished the picture.

'Take care of yourself, Alexander.'

'You too,' I said.

I went down again to the bothy and ate the remaining half of the paella, and sat outside in the dark thinking of what needed to be done to the picture to complete its meaning; and chiefly I thought of not muddling the outlines by too many more strong grey scratches but of not going down so deep, not nearly down to the canvas, but only as far as the ultramarine blue layer, so that the wrinkles and sagging areas of old skin would be gentler, though still unmistakable, and I would end, if I could manage it, with a blue-grey mist-like top portrait, so that the eye could see both portraits separately, the outer or the inner, according to the chosen focus, or could see both together as an interpretation of what all life was like, the outward relentless change of cell-structure decreed by the passing of time.

I slept only in snatches that night and dreamed a lot and in the morning again watched the light grow on Zoë Lang, and spent the day with rigidly governed finger muscles until my arms and neck ached with tension, but by late afternoon I had gone to the limit of what I could understand and show, and whatever the picture might be judged to lack, it was because the lack was in *me*.

Only the eyes of the finished portrait looked blazingly young, whichever other aspect one chose to see. I put suggestions of bags under the lower lids with a few blue lines, and drooped upper lids in faintly, but that unchanging spirit of Zoë Lang looked out, present and past identical.

I couldn't sleep. I lay for a while in the dark wondering what I could have done better, and coming to a realisation that I would probably go on wondering that for weeks and months, if not for my whole life.

I would wrap the picture in its sheet and put its face to the wall, and when I looked at it again, when I'd forgotten the strength and direction and feeling of each individual brushstroke or scratch, when I could see the whole with time's perspective, then I would know if I'd done something worth keeping, or whether the whole idea had been a mistake and beyond me.

Restlessly I got up at about four in the morning and, locking my door behind me, took my bagpipes up into the mountains, seeing my way by starlight, humbled by the distance of those flaming unvisited worlds, melancholy with the insignificance of one self in the cosmos and thinking such unoriginal thoughts as that it was much easier to do harm than good, even unintentionally.

As always the melancholy drifted away into space and left acceptance. Some people clung to angst as if it were a virtue. I let it go with relief. Optimism was a gift at birth. Bottles were half full, not half empty. When I took up the pipes in the dawn and blew the bag full of air, it was marches and strathspeys I played into the brightening silence, no longer the sad regrets of the piobaireachd.

Zoë Lang, the real Zoë Lang, now lived in an old body. Through all her ages, persisting into her fanaticism, the essence of Zoë Lang had triumphed. The shell was but a crab's carapace, grown, hardened, shed and grown again. I played marches for her this time as a salutation.

She would never find the Kinloch hilt if I could prevent it, but I would pay my foe the most intense respect (short of capitulation) that I could.

I never counted time up there on the granite heights. The grey dawn turned to a brilliant blue sparkling day and I reckoned I would go down to the bothy only when the lack of breakfast gave me a shove. Meanwhile I played the pipes and marched to the beat and filled the whole optimism bottle slowly with uncomplicated joy at being there in that wilderness, alive.

Too good to last, I supposed.

I was aware first of a buzzing noise that increasingly interfered with the drone of the pipes, and then a helicopter rose fast over the ridge of the mountain at my back and flew overhead, drowning out all sound but the deafening roar of its rotor.

I stopped playing. The helicopter swooped and wheeled and clattered and circled, and while I still half-cursed its insistent penetrating din and half wondered what on earth anyone would be looking for in that deserted area at that early time on a Sunday, the helicopter seemed like a falcon spotting a kill, and dropped purposefully towards its prey.

The prey, I realised in dismay, was the bothy. I sat down and folded the pipes across my knees, and watched.

The helicopter made a sort of circuit and approached the bothy from in front, hovering unsteadily over the small plateau there, sliding through the air to one side of my parked replacement jeep and finally settling onto the ground the longitudinal bars of the landing support.

The noise of the engine faded, and the speed of the rotor fell away.

I watched in extreme apprehension. I sat as motionless as the mountain itself, aware that unless I moved or put my head above the skyline I was invisible from below against the jumble of rocks.

If the four robbers had come . . .

If the four robbers had come they wouldn't catch me up in the mountains, but they could again break into my house.

They could destroy my painting.

I felt as if it were a child I'd left there. A sleeping child. Irreplaceable. I wondered how I could bear it, if they destroyed it.

After what seemed time for several deaths the rotor blades came to rest. The side door of the helicopter opened and one man jumped out. A small figure, far below.

One.

Not four.

He looked around him then walked forward out of my sight, and I knew he must be trying the front door of the bothy. He reappeared, looked into the truck, stuck his head into the helicopter door as if talking to someone there, and then in obvious frustration walked to the edge of the plateau and stood looking down the valley towards the road.

Something about the set of his shoulders as he turned back towards the helicopter brought me recognition and floods of relief.

Jed, I thought. It's Jed.

Blowing a scant lungful of air into the bag on my knees I squeezed it and played four or five random notes on the chanter.

In the clear silent air Jed heard them immediately. He whirled and looked up towards the mountains, shading his eyes against the eastern sun. I stood up and waved, and after a few moments he spotted me, and made huge circular movements with an arm, beckoning, beseeching me to come down.

Not good news, I thought. Helicopters were extreme.

I went down to join him, though not with happy haste.

'Where the hell have you been?' he demanded, as soon as I was within earshot. 'We've been trying to phone you for hours.'

'Good morning,' I said.

'Oh, shut up. Why do you think you've got that portable phone?'

'Not for lugging around on the mountains. What's happened?'

'Well . . .' he hesitated.

'You'd better tell me.'

'It's Sir Ivan. He's had another heart attack.'

'No! How bad?'

'He's dead.'

I stood motionless, just staring at him.

I said stupidly, 'He can't be dead. He was better.'

'I'm sorry.'

I hadn't thought I would care so much but I found I cared very much indeed. I'd grown fond of the old guy in the past three weeks without realising the depth of my feeling.

'When?' I said. As if it mattered.

'Some time late yesterday. I don't know exactly. Your mother phoned Himself before six this morning. She said you'd given her your number but she'd phoned you from five onwards and you didn't answer.'

I said blankly, 'I'd better phone her at once.'

'Himself said to tell you that Sir Ivan's daughter is now re-routing all calls, and she wouldn't let him get back to your mother. He says she has taken complete charge and is being unreasonable. So he told me to find you by helicopter and fly you direct to Edinburgh to catch the first flight south. He said you could do without arguing with Patsy Benchmark.'

He was right.

We went into the bothy. Jed seemed struck dumb by the painting but agreed to take care of it again, wrapped in its sheet. We loaded it into the jeep; also my pipes and other belongings. I collected a few travelling things into the duffle bag. We locked the bothy door.

'Jed,' I said awkwardly, aware of how much I owed him.

'Get going.'

We didn't need, I supposed, to say more. He waved me away into the helicopter and watched until it was circling in the air before setting off homewards in the jeep.

CHAPTER ELEVEN

My mother wept.

I held her tight while she shook with near-silent sobs, the grief deep and terrible.

I wondered if she had ever cried in the dark for my father, privately broken up under the public composure. I'd been too young then to be of understanding comfort to her, and also I'd been too immersed in my own feelings.

This time, when I arrived at Park Crescent, she turned to me on every level, and there was no doubt at all that her emotions were intense and overwhelming.

From life-long habit, though, after the first revealing half-hour, she stiffened her whole body, damped all movements, powdered her face and presented, at least to the world if no longer to me, the outward semblance of serenity.

Ivan was not in the house.

When she could talk, she told me that at bedtime the previous evening she'd heard Ivan cry out, and she'd found him lying on the stairs.

'Such pain . . .'

'Don't talk,' I said.

She told me at intervals.

She had been in her nightclothes, and he in his. She didn't know why he had been downstairs. There was no need for him to go down to the kitchen for anything. He had water and a glass beside his bed, and there was the tray of other drinks in his study. He hadn't told her why he was coming upstairs. He seemed to be out of breath, as if he'd been *hurrying*, but why should he have been hurrying, it was after ten o'clock?

He had said her name, 'Viv . . . Vivienne . . .'

I squeezed my mother's hand.

She said, 'I loved him.'

'I know.'

A long pause. She had been very frightened. They had given Wilfred the night off because Ivan had been so much better. They had said they wouldn't need him much longer. He had left the box of heart-attack remedies at hand on Ivan's bedside table and my mother had run to fetch them. She had put one of the tiny nitroglycerine tablets under Ivan's tongue, and although he had tried to cling to her she had run to the telephone and had miraculously reached Keith Robbiston at his home, and he had said he would send an ambulance immediately.

She had put a second pill under Ivan's tongue, and then a third.

They hadn't stopped the pain.

She had sat on the stairs, holding him.

When the front door bell had rung she had had to go down to answer it as there was no one else in the house. The ambulancemen had been very quick. They had carried a stretcher upstairs and had given him an injection and oxygen, and had put him on the stretcher and had fastened straps round him and carried him down.

She was wearing only her nightdress.

The men were kind to her. They said that they were taking him just along the road to the London Clinic, as he had been a patient there and Dr Robbiston had arranged it. They were a private firm. They gave my mother a card.

'A *card*,' she said blankly.

She had gone down the stairs with Ivan, holding his hand.

Keith Robbiston had arrived.

He had waited while she put some clothes on, and he had driven her to the Clinic.

A long, long pause.

'I wasn't with him when he died,' she said.

I squeezed her hand.

'Keith said they did everything possible.'

'I'm sure they did.'

'He died before they could get him to the operating theatre.'

I simply held her.

'*What am I going to do?*'

It was the unanswerable cry, I guessed, of all the bereaved. It wasn't until the next day, Monday, that Patsy swept in. She wasn't pleased to see me but seemed to realise my presence was inevitable.

She was brisk, decisive, the manager. Her grief for her father, and to be charitable one had to believe her own description of her feelings as 'distraught' (that excellent but over-used word) were chiefly expressed by a white tissue clutched valiantly ready for stemming tears.

'Darling Father,' she announced, 'will be cremated . . .' she applied the tissue gently to her nose, '. . . on Thursday at Cockfosters crematorium, where they have a slot at ten o'clock owing to someone else's postponement. It's so difficult to arrange this sort of thing, you would be appalled . . . but I agreed to that, so I hope, Vivienne, that you don't mind the early hour? And of course I've asked everyone to come here afterwards, and I've booked a caterer for drinks and a buffet lunch . . .'

She went on talking about the arrangements and the announcements in the papers and the seating in the chapel, and she'd notified the Jockey Club and invited Ivan's colleagues to the wake; and it seemed she had done most of all this that morning, while I had been seeing to breakfast. I had to admit to relief not to be doing it all myself, and my mother, who seemed mesmerised, simply said, 'Thank you, Patsy,' over and over.

'Do you want flowers?' Patsy demanded of her. 'I've put "no flowers" in the announcement to the papers. Just a wreath from you on the coffin, don't you think? And one from me, of course. Do you want me to arrange it? I've asked the caterers to bring flowers here for the buffet table, of course . . . And I'll just go down now and talk to Lois about cleaning the silver . . .'

My mother looked exhausted when Patsy left.

'She loved him,' she said weakly, as if defending her.

I nodded. 'All the activity is her way of showing it.'

'I don't know how you understand her, when she's always so beastly to you.'

I shrugged. No amount of understanding would make her a friend.

We struggled through the next few days somehow. I cooked for my mother; Edna tossed her head. When my mother asked forlornly if I thought she should wear a black hat to the funeral, because she couldn't face shopping, I went out and bought her one, and pinned a big white silk rose to its sweeping brim so that she looked good enough to paint, though I just refrained from saying so.

We went one afternoon to see Ivan in his coffin at the undertaker. He looked pale and peaceful; my mother kissed his forehead and said on the way home how icy cold he was; nothing like life; and I didn't tell her that it wasn't the chill of death but of efficient refrigeration.

For Thursday morning I engaged a car with a

chauffeur to take the two of us to the crematorium and back again. I had personally asked a fair number of Ivan's friends and business people to turn up at Park Crescent even if they couldn't face the crematorium but, in the event, the old boy drew a full house at Cockfosters, an eloquent and moving tribute to a good man.

'All the brewery people are here,' my mother murmured. 'All the workpeople!'

They had come in a chartered bus, we found, and were working extra hours to make up.

The racing people had come. Many bigwigs and owners. Several lads from her yard accompanied Emily.

Himself came, with his countess. Jamie came, ever cheerful, with his pretty wife.

Patsy, with husband and daughter, received everyone graciously.

My mother looked ethereal and shed no tears.

Chris Young showed up at my shoulder, dressed as the secretary, lighthearted about his task of guarding my back against Surtees.

Patsy, at her administrative best, had briefed the presiding cleric thoroughly, so that he spoke knowledgeably and well about Ivan's life; and Himself, delivering a eulogy, quoted, to my surprise, from the translation of Bede's Death Song: 'No one is wiser in thought than he needs to be, in considering, before his departure, what will be adjudged to his soul, of good or evil, after his death-day,' he said, and declared that

Ivan Westering had behaved on earth with such uprightness that only good would be adjudged to him now, after his death-day.

All in all, impressive.

The grand drawing-room at Park Crescent was packed afterwards with mourners, and I had to acknowledge that Patsy had been far more accurate in her estimation than I would have been. The caterers nevertheless sent their van away early for re-inforcements.

Tobias Tollright came, and also Margaret Morden. I asked them both to linger for a while after the crush had cleared to discuss a brewery plan of action, and I was reminded triumphantly by Desmond Finch that all my powers of attorney had been cancelled by Ivan's death, and nothing I might say or do mattered any more in Ivan's or the brewery's affairs.

Oliver Grantchester made his large presence benevolently felt both at the crematorium and Park Crescent, behaving rather as if Ivan had been his own personal achievement; as if he, Oliver, had been responsible for all Ivan's good decisions and successes. 'Of course Ivan regularly took my advice,' I heard him saying, and he saw me listening and gave me a sideways Patsy-inspired glare of disapproval. I had no need to ask him to stay on for a conference; he showed every sign of wanting to conduct one.

I had invited Lois and Edna to join the gathering, but they stayed obstinately below stairs. Wilfred took a brief glass of farewell champagne, spoke a few words to Patsy and descended to join them. Wilfred thought I hadn't appreciated his services sufficiently: Edna had told me Wilfred thought it was my fault he hadn't been there when Ivan had needed him. The fact that I'd been in Scotland didn't excuse me.

Emily's lads ate and drank with an eye on the scales, made awkward but genuine little speeches to my mother, and left Emily behind when they departed.

Emily eyed Chris with obvious speculation, not doubting his/her gender but wondering if the tall leggy dark-haired presence in black tights, short inappropriate skirt and baggy black sweater, were a serious girlfriend, in view of the glue that kept her ever and only a short pace away from my side.

Chris wore white frilled shirt-cuffs over the thick wrists, and a small discreet white frill round his neck. He carried a small black handbag. Tobias attempted to chat him up. They could both hardly speak for laughing. 'This is a *funeral*, for God's sake,' I told them.

Keith Robbiston dashed in, glancing at his watch. He kissed my mother's cheek and murmured comfort quietly into her ear, so that she smiled at him gratefully. He shook my hand, nodding, and made a sort of sketchy bow to Patsy, who looked forbidding, as if Ivan's death were the doctor's fault. She had said, in fact, during the past few days, that clearly Ivan should have stayed in the Clinic and been shielded from stress, though she hadn't said it when he was alive, and had herself generated a good deal of the stress.

Keith Robbiston shook hands with Oliver Grantchester, their mutual disregard stiff in their spines, then, duty done, the doctor gave my mother another cheek-to-cheek fondness and hurried away.

I wandered round the room, thanking people for coming, carrying a glass of champagne that I didn't feel like drinking.

The champagne was good. So were the canapé snacks. Patsy had ordered the best.

There was a woman standing apart in a far corner of the room, talking to no one and looking a little lost, so I drifted that way to draw her in.

'You have no champagne,' I said.

'It's all right.'

She was undemanding and not at home among Ivan's friends. She wore a tweed skirt, a shiny pale blue blouse, a brown cardigan, flat shoes and pearls. Sixty, or thereabouts.

'Take my champagne,' I said, holding it out to her. 'I haven't drunk any. I'll get some more.'

'Oh no, I couldn't.' She took the glass, though, and sipped, eyeing me over the rim.

'I'm Lady Westering's son,' I said.

'Yes, I know. I've seen you coming and going.' Then, seeing my surprise, added, 'I live next door. I'm the caretaker there, you see. I've just popped in to pay my respects to Sir Ivan. Lady Westering invited me. Always so kind to me, both of them. Really nice people.'

'Yes.'

'I'm ever so sorry Sir Ivan died. Did he find what he was looking for?'

'Er . . .' I said. 'What was he looking for?'

'Ever so distressed he was, poor man.'

'Was he?' I asked, only half interested. 'When was that?'

'Why, the night he died, of course.'

She sensed in me the sudden acute sharpening of attention and began to look nervous.

'It's all right, Mrs . . . er . . .' I assured her, calming us both. 'I'm sorry, I'm afraid I don't know your name.'

'Hall. Connie Hall.'

'Mrs Hall. Please do tell me about the night Sir Ivan died.'

'I was walking my little dog, you see, same as I always do before going to bed.'

'Yes, of course,' I said, nodding.

Reassured, she went on, 'When I got back to the house – next door, that is, of course – there was Sir Ivan down in the road, and in his pyjamas and dressing-gown poor man, and *frantic*, there's no other word for it. *Frantic*.'

'Mrs Hall,' I said intensely, 'what was he frantic *about*?'

She began to lose her nervousness and to enjoy telling me her tale.

'It was ever so unlike him, you see. I mean, I never thought of him in *pyjamas* like everyone else, and I didn't recognise him at first and told him pretty sharply to take himself off and leave the black plastic rubbish bags alone, because he was scrabbling about in them, and it wasn't until he turned and spoke to me that I realised who he was, and he said, "Oh, Mrs Hall, when do they collect the rubbish?" I mean, it was after ten o'clock at night! So I told him they collected the bags every Monday, Wednesday and Friday morning – we have a good service round here, this being a wealthy sort of place and not a once-a-week-if-you're-lucky back street – and he was tearing open some of the bags with his *fingernails* . . . and looking inside them . . . he was ever so . . . *upset* . . . and I asked him if I could help him, and . . . and . . .'

Connie Hall stopped, herself distressed at the memory, and emptied her glass.

I pivoted one-eighty degrees, aware of Chris close behind me, and fielded his full glass of bubbles.

'Hey!' he objected.

'Get some more.'

I turned back to Connie Hall and exchanged Chris's glass for the empty one she held.

'You'll get me tiddly,' she said.

'What was Sir Ivan looking for in the black bags?' I asked. 'Did he tell you?'

'I mean,' she said, 'it didn't make sense, him emptying some of the bags like that.'

I waited, smiling vaguely, while she sipped.

'He said he was looking for an empty box,' she frowned. 'I asked him what empty box and he said Lois must have thrown it away. He was so fearfully upset . . .'

'What sort of box?'

'I think he said a tissue-box. I *think* that's what he said. But why should anyone worry so much about an empty tissue-box?'

Dear God, I thought: *what had been written on it*?

I said, 'Have you told my mother about this?'

'No.' She shook her grey-haired head. 'I didn't want to upset her. Sir Ivan left all the rubbish just lying there and went in through his front door, which was open, of course, and said he would look in the kitchen, and I said goodnight to him and went in myself with my little dog, and it was a terrible shock the next day when I heard Sir Ivan had died.'

'It must have been . . . I suppose Sir Ivan didn't tell you why he was looking for the box?'

'No, but he was sort of talking to himself. I think it was something about Lois always moving things.'

'Nothing else?'

'No, poor man. He can't have been himself, can he, poor Sir Ivan, to be scrabbling about in a rubbish bag in his nightclothes?'

'Well . . . Thank you for telling me, Mrs Hall. Would you like some smoked salmon?'

I collected a plate of goodies for her and found her another Park Crescent neighbour to talk to, but later on I saw her talking to Patsy, and from her gestures and her pleasure in the drama I suspected she was telling her the same story, and felt a deep thrust of unease, but wasn't quite sure why.

Surtees stood beside Patsy, listening, and when he saw me looking at him he gave me a stare of such high-voltage malevolence that Chris said '*Jeeze*' into my ear.

Maddened and murderous, I thought. It wasn't the restrained and sensible who sought to kill. Surtees might, to my mind, be a fool, but I felt him also to be as unstable and volatile as hydrogen.

Himself also fielded Surtees's raw exhibition of an obsessional hatred fast ballooning past Patsy's enduring antagonism and, startled, asked, 'Whatever did you do to deserve that?'

'Probably didn't care being shut in the box in Emily's yard.'

'In retrospect, a bad move.'

'Mm.' I shrugged. 'It can't be helped.'

'Introduce me to your friend,' my uncle said, looking at Chris.

'Oh . . . er . . . Lord Kinloch,' I said to Chris, and to my uncle, 'Christina.'

Himself said, 'How do you do?'

Chris shook his head, silently, though shooting a frilled cuff with panache. My uncle looked at me quizzically. I smiled back without explanation. Chris stuck to my back.

The room gradually cleared until only those close to Ivan and his affairs were left. There was to be no formal reading of his Will as its general provisions had been much discussed and were well-known – the brewery to Patsy, everything else to my mother for her lifetime, reverting to Patsy on her death. For all her fears, Ivan had never swerved from his promises to his daughter, though all she displayed to me was triumph, not apology.

Oliver Grantchester who, true to his loud-voiced authoritative manner, had taken it as his natural province to orchestrate the semi-business meeting, cleared his throat noisily and said, 'I say, I say' a few times until everyone was listening. 'I suggest we all sit down,' he said, 'and discuss the immediate future.'

Everyone acted on his suggestion, and I looked round at the haphazard circle of sofas, chairs and footstools, and at my mother, with me on one side of her and Emily on the other, then at Patsy and at Surtees (scowling) and Xenia (fidgeting), and at Margaret Morden and at Tobe, at Himself (alone, having sent his countess off with James and his wife), at Oliver (in charge), at Desmond Finch (smirking) and finally at Chris, beside me.

Chris crossed his long legs in their black tights,

showing a stretch of thigh. The legs ended below the ankles in black patent medium-heeled court shoes. ('Don't worry, I can run in them,' he'd said.)

Oliver stared at him with displeasure. 'You may leave now,' he said.

I started to say, 'I want him to stay . . .' and almost choked on the 'him', turning it to 'her' at the last fraction of credibility. 'I asked Christina to stay,' I repeated. 'She is my guest in my mother's house.'

No one protested further. Tobe put his face in his hands. His body shook.

Oliver said with satisfaction, 'We all know that the power of attorney that Ivan gave to Alexander expired with his death. Alexander has no authority from now on to conduct any business for Ivan's estate. Patsy, indeed, forbids it.'

Patsy nodded vigorously. Surtees sneered. Xenia, not old enough to understand the words, simply transmitted secondhand hate.

I said mildly, 'There's the codicil . . .'

Oliver interrupted, 'Ivan may have written a codicil, but it can't be found. We can assume he tore it up, as he suggested he would.'

'He didn't tear it up. He gave it to me for safekeeping.'

'Yes, we know that,' Oliver said impatiently, 'and he made you give it back again. We were all there. He made you give it back.'

'It isn't in this house,' Patsy said.

'Have you searched?' I asked with interest.

She glared.

'It isn't in my office,' Grantchester said smoothly. 'We can safely assume it no longer exists.'

'No, we can't,' I said. 'Ivan gave it back to me again later, and I have got it here today.'

Both Patsy and Grantchester looked furiously disconcerted. My mother was nodding, 'Ivan gave it back to Alexander,' and no one else seemed to mind one way or another.

'Give it to me, then, and I'll read it out,' Grantchester said.

I hesitated. 'I think,' I said politely, 'that I'll give it to Tobias to read out. If you don't mind, Tobe?'

He had with difficulty stopped laughing. He said he would be of any service he could.

I put a hand out towards Chris, who opened his black leather handbag and took out the codicil in its envelope. Also in the handbag, I knew, were a scent-laden lace handkerchief, a lipstick and a thoroughly illegal set of brass knuckles. It wasn't only Tobe who had trouble with giggles.

I took the envelope and crossed to Tobias, saying, 'Ivan signed and dated this twice across the stick-down flap. You can verify that I haven't tampered with it.'

Soberly Tobias examined the envelope, reported on its secure state, and ripped it open, pulling out the single sheet of paper inside.

He read the introduction, then:

'I bequeath my racehorses to Emily Jane Kinloch, known as Emily Jane Cox.'

Emily gasped, wide-eyed, moved beyond tears.

Tobias continued, 'I bequeath the chalice known as King Alfred's Gold Cup to my friend Robert, Earl of Kinloch.'

Himself looked stricken dumb.

Tobias read, 'I appoint Alexander Kinloch, my step-son, to be my executor, in conjunction with my two executors already appointed in my Will, namely Oliver Grantchester and Robert, Earl of Kinloch.'

Patsy stood up, stiffly angry, and demanded, 'What does that mean, appointing Alexander as executor?'

'It means,' Himself told her neutrally, 'that Alexander has a duty to help bring your father's estate to probate.'

'Are you telling me he still has any say in the brewery's affairs?'

'Yes. Until your father's estate is wound up, he does.'

'It's impossible.' She turned to the lawyer. 'Oliver! Say he's wrong.'

Grantchester said regretfully, 'If the codicil was properly drawn and witnessed, then Lord Kinloch is correct.'

Tobias stood and walked round the room, showing the paper to everyone in turn. 'It is written in Sir Ivan's own handwriting,' he said.

'But the witnesses?' Patsy demanded, before he reached her. 'Who were *they*?'

'The witnesses,' my mother said, 'were Wilfred, his nurse, and Lois, our cleaner. I watched them witness Ivan's signature. It was all done properly. Ivan was very careful.'

Patsy stared long at the paper. 'He had no *right* . . .'

'He had every right,' Himself said. 'Alexander will work with Mr Grantchester and me to do the best we can for a good resolution to your father's affairs. Why do you not acknowledge that the continued existence of the brewery today is altogether thanks to Alexander's efforts, in conjunction with Mr Tollright and Mrs Morden . . .' he gave them one of his little bows, '. . . and why do you not realise that your father knew what he was doing when he put his trust in Alexander's integrity . . .?'

'Don't,' I said, trying to stop him.

'You never stand up for yourself, Al.'

'Let it be.'

He shook his head at me.

I reflected that Ivan's trust had wandered in and out a bit, and also that he'd trusted Norman Quorn, but anything that might dampen Patsy's animosity, I supposed, couldn't be bad.

Oliver Grantchester moved smoothly back to his intended overview, this time accepting the codicil's provisions as fact, whatever he privately thought of them.

'The horse Golden Malt—' he began.

'Will run in the King Alfred Gold Cup a week on Saturday,' Emily said firmly.

Grantchester raised his eyebrows and said, 'No one seems to know where the horse is.'

Surtees stood up convulsively and pointed at me in accusation. 'He knows where it is.' He was unnecessarily shouting. 'Make him tell you.'

Himself said, 'After probate the horse will belong to Emily. Until then it can run in races by order of the executors.'

Surtees obstinately shouted, 'It belongs to the brewery. Alexander stole it. I'll see he goes to jail.'

Even the lawyer began to lose patience with him. He said, 'Whether Mrs Cox or the brewery is ultimately judged to be the owner, the executors can still authorise the horse to race, as it may lose value as an asset if it doesn't, for which the executors might be held accountable. If Mrs Cox can assure us that she can produce the horse at Cheltenham while complying with all racing regulations, then as executors, Lord Kinloch, Alexander and I will, at the appropriate time, declare him a runner.'

Well, bravo, I thought.

Surtees seethed.

Emily said sweetly that she was sure she could abide by all the regulations.

Surtees sat down like a cocked volcano, steaming, ever ready to erupt.

'Now,' Oliver Grantchester said, moving along the agenda majestically, 'The prize, the King Alfred chalice. Where is it?'

No one answered.

My mother said eventually, almost weakly, 'Ivan never sends . . . oh dear, *sent* . . . the real chalice to the races. It's far too valuable to risk. But he had several smaller replicas made only a few years ago. There must be one or two left. A replica is given to the winning owner each year.'

Desmond Finch made throat-clearing noises and flashed the silver frames of his glasses as he reported that two replicas remained in the locked glass-fronted cabinet in Sir Ivan's office.

'That's the trophy settled, then,' Himself said cheerfully, but Patsy told him with spite, 'Your precious Alexander stole the real one. Make him give it back. And whatever my father said, the chalice belongs to the brewery. It belongs to *me*.'

'I'm sure,' Himself said with courteous worldliness, 'that we can come to a civilised solution to our differences out of court. It would be so unwise, don't you agree, to hang out the brewery's private troubles on the public washing line? That's why your father thought it best to swallow in silence the frightful financial losses. He wouldn't, I feel sure, want you to discard out of pique the fortune he worked so hard to give you.'

I didn't look at Patsy. Her hatred of me always drastically interfered with her common sense. I'd taken so many insults from her over the years that it was only for Ivan's memory that I now cared what happened to the brewery. I wanted to go back to the mountains. It was like a physical ache.

Oliver Grantchester droned on, a committee man to his fingertips. The executors would be doing this and the executors would be doing that, and as my uncle made no protest or suggestion, nor did I.

Tobias finally broke up the session by parking a chewed toothpick and apologising to my mother that he had a plane to catch: he was off to Paris for the weekend.

'I'll be back on Monday,' he said to me. 'In the office on Tuesday, if you have any brilliant ideas.'

Patsy, overhearing, demanded to know what I could possibly have brilliant ideas about.

'Finding the brewery's lost millions,' he said and, correctly interpreting and anticipating her automatic denigration, added, 'and you should pray, Mrs Benchmark, that he does have a brilliant idea, because those lost millions are yours now, don't you understand? See you,' he finished, lightly punching my arm. 'Don't play on the railway lines.'

When Tobias had gone, Chris asked me what I wanted him to do.

'Follow Surtees,' I said promptly. 'I want to know where he is.'

Chris looked down at his clothes. 'He knows what I look like.'

'Go up two floors,' I said. 'Turn right up there. You'll find my room. Take what you need. There's money on the chest of drawers. Take it.'

He nodded and quietly left the room, and only Emily, appearing at my elbow, seemed to notice.

'Are you bedding Christina?' she asked blandly. 'She knows you well.'

I nearly laughed but made it a smile. 'She's not my bed mate and never will be.'

'She never takes her eyes off you.'

'How's Golden Malt?'

'Fine. You're exasperating.'

'Has Surtees bothered you?'

Emily glanced at him where he stood across the room talking to Grantchester and stabbing the air with a vigorous forefinger. 'He hasn't found the horse. He won't, either. I've driven over to Jimmy Jennings's place twice. It's all quiet there. And actually I think the change of scene is doing the horse good. He was really on his toes two days ago.'

'He's yours now.'

She blinked hard. 'Did you know Ivan was going to do that?'

I nodded. 'He told me.'

'I liked him.'

It seemed natural to me to put my arms round her. She hugged me back.

'Jimmy showed me your painting of the jockey,' she said. 'He told me you gave him courage.'

I silently kissed her hair. We had said everything we needed to. She stepped back, composed, and went to comfort my mother.

People gradually left. Himself (positively grinning) patted me on the shoulder, told me he would be in residence in his London home for the following ten days, asserted his intention of going to Cheltenham races and kissed my mother's cheek affectionately, calling her 'my dear, dear Vivienne'.

Emily waved goodbye. Fussy Desmond Finch twittered away. Margaret Morden paid her respects. Oliver Grantchester ponderously closed his briefcase.

Chris Young ran lightly down the stairs, crossed past the open door of the drawing-room and left quickly by the front door.

'Who was that?' asked my mother unsuspiciously, watching through the window as the fleeting backview of cropped light brown hair, loose jacket, rolled up jeans and too-big trainers made a fast sloppy shuffle out of sight.

'One of the caterers?' I casually guessed.

She lost interest. 'Did you talk to Connie Hall from next door?'

'Yes, I did.'

She looked distressed. 'Patsy told me what Connie Hall said about Ivan searching the rubbish bags.'

Patsy *would*. I said, 'Mrs Hall didn't want to upset you.'

My mother said unhappily, 'I think Patsy has gone down to the kitchen to talk to Lois about it.'

I glanced round the room. Surtees, Xenia, Grantchester still, but no Patsy.

'Let's go down, then,' I suggested, and moved her with me below stairs, where Lois was tossing her head and bridling with umbrage at any insinuation that her work wasn't perfect. Edna stood beside her, nodding rhythmically in support.

The caterers, spread all around the extensive room, were packing away their equipment. I threaded a path through them, my mother following, and fetched up by Patsy's side in time to hear Lois saying indignantly, '. . . of course I threw the box away. There were only a couple of tissues left in it, which I used. I gave Sir Ivan a fresh box, what's wrong with *that*?'

'Didn't you check whether anything was written on the bottom of the box you threw away?'

'Of course not,' Lois said scornfully. 'Whoever looks on the bottom of empty tissue-boxes?'

'But you must have known my father wrote on the bottom of a tissue-box all the time.'

'Why should I know that?'

'You kept moving his notepad onto the desk, out of his reach.'

Patsy was right, of course, but predictably (like most legislation) she achieved the opposite result to that intended.

Lois inflated her lungs and stuck out her considerable frontage, her hoity-toity level at boiling-over point. 'Sir Ivan never complained,' she announced with self-righteousness, 'and if you're implying some stupid tissue-box gave him a heart attack and that it's my fault I'll . . . I'll . . . I'll consult my lawyer!'

She tossed her head grandly. Everyone knew she didn't *have* a lawyer. Even Patsy wasn't fool enough to point it out.

My mother, looking exhausted, said soothingly, 'Of course it wasn't your fault, Lois.' Turning to go, she stopped and said to me, 'I think I'll go up to my sitting-room. Alexander, would you bring me some tea?'

'Of course.'

'Patsy . . .' My mother hesitated, '. . . thank you, dear, for arranging everything so well. I couldn't have done it. Ivan would have been so pleased.'

She went slowly and desolately out of the kitchen and Patsy spoiled the moment by giving me the grim glare of habit.

'Go on, say it,' she said. 'You could have done it better.'

'No, I couldn't. It was a brilliantly managed funeral, and she's right, Ivan would have been proud.' I meant it sincerely, which she didn't believe.

She said bitterly over her shoulder, stalking away, 'I can do without your sarcasm,' and Edna, touching my arm, said kindly, 'You go on up, I'll make Lady Westering's tea.'

Lois, in unspent pique, slammed a few pots together to make a noise. She had been Patsy's appointee and, I guessed, Patsy's informant as to my comings and goings in that house, but she was discovering, as everyone did in the end, that Patsy's beauty and charm were questionable pointers to her core nature.

I followed her up the stairs to where my mother was bidding goodbye on the doorstep to Oliver Grantchester and, after him, to Patsy, Surtees and Xenia.

A taxi cruised past slowly on the road outside. Chris Young didn't look our way out of the window, but I saw his profile clearly. I wouldn't have known how to begin to follow Surtees, but when Chris was trying he seldom lost him. Since the dust-up in Emily's yard, Surtees hadn't often left home without a tail.

I went up to my mother's sitting-room where she soon joined me, followed by Edna with the tea. When Edna had gone I poured the hot liquid and squeezed lemon slices and handed the tea as she liked it to a woman who looked frail and spent and unable to answer questions.

She told me what I wanted to know, however, without my asking.

'You're bursting to know if I saw what Ivan wrote on that terrible box of tissues. Do you really think he was frantic to find it? I can't bear it, Alexander. *I* would have looked for the box, if he'd told me. But we'd kissed goodnight . . . he didn't say anything then about the box. I'm certain it wasn't in his mind. He'd been so much better . . . calmer . . . saying he relied on your strength . . . we were truly *happy* that evening . . .'

'Yes.'

'Connie Hall didn't say anything about Ivan being in the street, not until today.'

'She would have caused you pain if she had.'

She drank the tea and said slowly, reluctantly, 'Whatever was written on the box of tissues . . . I wrote it.'

'My dearest Ma . . .'

'But I don't remember what it was. I haven't given it a thought. I wish I'd known . . .'

The cup rattled in its saucer. I took them from her and kneeled beside her.

'I wish he was *here*,' she said.

I waited through the inconsolable bout of grief. I knew, after four days, that it would sweep through her like a physical disturbance, making her tremble, and then would subside back into a general state of misery.

'Someone telephoned – it was a woman,' she said, 'and she wanted to speak to Ivan, and he was in the bathroom or something, and I said he would phone her back, and you know how there was never a notepad beside the phone, so I wrote what she said on the back of the box, like Ivan does, and I told him . . . but . . .' She stopped, trying to remember, and shook her head. 'I didn't think it was important.'

'It probably wasn't,' I said.

'But if he went down to the street to find it . . .'

'Well . . . when did the woman phone? What time of day?'

She thought. 'She phoned in the morning, when Ivan was dressing. He did phone her back, but she was out, I think. There was no reply.'

'And Lois was cleaning?'

'Yes. She always comes on Saturday mornings, just to tidy up.' She drank her tea, thinking. 'All I wrote on the box was the woman's phone number.'

'And you don't know who she was?'

She frowned. 'I remember that she wouldn't say.' A few moments passed, then she exclaimed, 'She said it was something to do with Leicestershire.'

'Leicestershire?'

'I think so.'

Leicestershire to me at that time meant Norman Quorn, and anything to do with Norman Quorn would have caught Ivan's attention.

I said slowly, 'Do you think it could possibly have been Norman Quorn's sister, that we met in Leicestershire, at that mortuary?'

'That poor woman! She wouldn't stop crying.'

She had just seen something pretty frightful, I thought. Enough to make me feel sick. 'Could it have been her?'

'I don't know.'

'Do you by any chance remember her name?'

My mother looked blank. 'No, I don't.'

I couldn't remember having heard it at all, though I suppose I must have been told. Perhaps, I speculated, it had been only when he was going to bed that Ivan remembered that he hadn't phoned back again to Norman Quorn's sister, and had then discovered that he had lost her phone number, and had gone to look for the box . . . and had thought of something to upset him badly.

How could I find Norman Quorn's sister if I didn't know her name . . .?

I phoned the brewery.

Total blank. No one even seemed to know he had had a sister at all.

Who else?

Via directory enquiries (because yet another tissue-box was long gone) I asked for Detective Chief Inspector Reynolds. Off duty. Impossible to be given his home number. Try in the morning.

I sought out and telephoned the mortuary. All they could or would tell me was the name of the undertaker to whom they had released the body of Norman Quorn. I phoned the undertaker, asking who had arranged cremation and paid the bills. Sir Ivan Westering, I was told, had written them a single cheque to cover all expenses.

How like him, I thought.

CHAPTER TWELVE

I reached Chief Inspector Reynolds in the morning. He hummed and hahhed and told me to phone him back in ten minutes, and when I did he told me the answers.

Norman Quorn's sister was a Mrs Audrey Newton, widow, living at 4, Minton Terrace, in the village of Bloxham, Oxfordshire. Telephone number supplied.

I thanked him wholeheartedly. Let him know, he said, if I found anything he should add to his files.

'Like, where did Norman Quorn die?' I asked.

'Exactly like that.'

I promised.

Using the portable phone, as I had for all the calls I'd made from the Park Crescent house, I tried Mrs Audrey Newton's number and found her at home. She agreed that yes, nearly a week ago she had tried to talk to Sir Ivan Westering, but he hadn't called back, and she would have quite understood if he didn't want to talk to her, but he'd been ever so kind in paying for the cremation, and she'd thought things over, and since her brother couldn't get into any more trouble, poor man, she had decided to give Sir Ivan something Norman had left with her.

'What thing?' I asked.

'A paper. A list really. Very short. But Norman thought it important.'

I cleared my throat, trying to disregard sudden breathlessness, and asked if she would give the list to me instead. After a pause she said, 'I'll give it to Lady Westering. Ever so kind, she was, that day I had to identify Norman.'

Her voice shook at the memory.

I said I would bring Lady Westering to her house, and please could she tell me how to find it.

My mother disliked the project.

'*Please,*' I said. 'And the drive will do you good.'

I drove her north-west out of London in Ivan's car and came to a large village, almost a small town, not far from the big bustling spread of modern Banbury, where no fair lady would be allowed anywhere near the Cross on a white horse, bells on her toes notwithstanding.

Minton Terrace proved to be a row of very small cottages with thatched roofs, and at No. 4 the front door was opened by the rounded woman we'd met at the mortuary.

She invited us in. She was nervous. She had set out sherry glasses and a plate of small cakes on round white crocheted mats which smelled of cedar, for deterring moths.

Audrey Newton, plain and honest, was ashamed of the brother she had spent years admiring. It took a great deal of sherry-drinking and cake-eating to bring her, not just to give the list to my mother, but to explain how and why Norman had given it to *her*.

'I was over in Wantage, staying with him for a few days. I did that sometimes, there was only the two of us, you see. He never married, of course. Anyway, he was going away on holiday, he always liked to go alone, and he was going that day, and I was going to catch a bus to start on my way home.'

She paused to see if we understood. We nodded.

'He was going to go in a taxi to Didcot railway station, but someone, I think from the brewery, came to collect him first. We happened to be both standing by the window on the upstairs landing when the car drew up at the gate.' She frowned. 'Norman wasn't pleased. It's extraordinary, but looking back I might almost say he was *frightened*, though at the time it didn't occur to me. I mean, the brewery was his *life*.'

And his death, I thought.

'Norman said he'd better go,' she went on, 'but all of a sudden he took an envelope out of the inner pocket of his jacket – and I saw his passport there because he was going to Spain for his holiday, as he usually did – and he pushed the envelope into my hands and told me to keep it for him until he sent for it . . . and of course he never sent for it. And it wasn't until I was clearing out his house after the cremation that I remembered the envelope and wondered what was in it, so I opened it when I got home here and found this little list, and I wondered if it had anything to do with the brewery . . . if I should give it to Sir Ivan, as he had been so good to me, paying for everything he didn't need to, considering Norman stole all that money, which I can hardly believe, even now.'

I sorted my way through the flood of words.

I said, 'You brought the envelope home with you—'

'That's right,' she interrupted. 'Norman told me to take his taxi, which he'd ordered, when it came, and he gave me the money for it to take me all the way home – such a *treat*, he was so generous – and I would never get him into trouble if he was alive.'

'We do know that, Mrs Newton,' I said. 'So you only opened the envelope one day last week . . .?'

'Yes, that's right.'

'And you phoned Sir Ivan . . .'

'But I didn't get him.'

'And you still have the list.'

'Yes.' She crossed to a sideboard and took an envelope out of a drawer. 'I do hope I'm doing right,' she said, handing the envelope to my mother. 'The brewery man telephoned only about an hour ago asking if Norman had left anything with me, and I said only a small list, nothing important, but he said he would send someone over for it early this afternoon.'

I looked at my watch. It was then twelve o'clock, noon.

I asked my mother, 'Did you tell anyone we were coming here?'

'Only Lois.' She was puzzled by the question. 'I said we were going to see a lady in Bloxham and wouldn't be needing lunch.'

I looked at her and at Audrey Newton. Neither woman had the slightest understanding of the possible consequences of what they had just said.

I turned to Mrs Newton. 'The brewery told me they didn't know your name. They said they didn't know Norman Quorn *had* a sister.'

She said, surprised, 'But of course I'm known there. Norman sometimes used to take me to the Directors' parties. Ever so proud, he was, of being made Director of Finance.'

'Who was it at the brewery who phoned you today?'

'Desmond Finch.' She made a face. 'I've never liked him much. But he definitely knows me, even if no one else does.'

I took the envelope from my mother and removed the paper from inside which was, as Audrey Newton had said, a short list. There were two sections, one of six lines, each line a series of numbers, and another section, also of six lines, each line either a personal or corporate name. I put the list back into the envelope and held it loosely.

A silence passed, which seemed long to me, in which I did some very rapid thinking.

I said to Audrey Newton, 'I think it would be a

marvellous idea if you would go away for a lovely long weekend at the seaside.' And I said to my mother, 'And it would be a marvellous idea if you would go with Mrs Newton, and get away just for a few days from the sadness of Park Crescent.'

My mother looked astonished. 'I don't want to go,' she said.

'I so seldom ask anything,' I said. 'I wouldn't ask this if it were not important.' To Audrey Newton I said, 'I'll pay for you to go to a super hotel if you would go upstairs now and pack what you would need for a few days.'

'But it's so sudden,' she objected.

'Yes, but spur-of-the-moment treats are often the best, don't you think?'

She responded almost girlishly and, with an air of growing excitement, went upstairs out of earshot.

My mother said, 'What on earth is all this about?'

'Keeping you safe,' I said flatly. 'Just do it, Ma.'

'I haven't any clothes!'

'Buy some.'

'You're truly eccentric, Alexander.'

'Just as well,' I said.

I picked up my mobile phone and pressed the numbers of the pager Chris carried always and spoke the message, 'This is Al, phone me at once.'

We waited barely thirty seconds before my mobile buzzed, 'It's Chris.'

'Where are you?'

'Outside Surtees's house.'

'Is he home?'

'I saw him five minutes ago, wandering around, looking at his horses.'

'Good. Can Young and Uttley do a chauffeur-and-nice-car job?'

'No problem.'

'Chauffeur's hat. Comfortable car for three ladies.'

'When and where?'

'Like five minutes ago. Leave Surtees's, get the chauffeur to Emily Cox's yard in Lambourn. I'll meet you there.'

'Urgent?'

'Ultra urgent.'

'I'm on my way.'

My mother fluttered her hands. 'What is ultra urgent?'

'Have you by any chance got a safety pin?'

She looked at me wildly.

'Have you? You always used to have, in a baby sewing kit.' She dug into her handbag and produced the credit-card-sized travelling sewing kit that she carried for emergencies from life-long habit, and speechlessly she opened it and gave me the small safety pin it contained.

I was as usual wearing a shirt under a sweater. I put the Quorn envelope in my shirt pocket, pinned it to the shirt to prevent its falling out, and pulled my sweater down over it.

'And paper,' I said. 'Have you anything I could draw on?'

She had a letter from a friend in her handbag. I took the envelope, opened it out flat, and on its clean inside, with my mother's ball point pen, had time to make nine small outline drawings of familiar people – Desmond Finch, Patsy, Surtees, Tobias included – before Audrey Newton came happily downstairs in holiday mood carrying a suitcase.

I showed her the page of small heads. 'The person who came to pick up your brother on the first day of his holiday . . . was it one of these?'

She looked carefully and, as if the request were nothing out of the ordinary, pointed firmly. 'That one,' she said.

'You're sure?'

'Positive.'

'Let's get going,' I said.

Audrey Newton having locked her house, we drove away and headed for Lambourn.

'Why Lambourn?' my mother asked.

'I want to talk to Emily.'

'What's wrong with a telephone?'

'Insects,' I said. 'Bugs.'

Friday lunchtime. If Emily had gone to the races it would have complicated things a little, but she was at home, in her office, busy at paperwork with her secretary.

Nothing I did surprised her any more, she said. She

agreed easily to my making lunch and pouring wine for her unexpected guests but adamantly refused to join them in any flight from Egypt. She was not, she pointed out, Moses.

I persuaded her to go as far as her drawing-room and there explained the explosive dangers of the present situation.

'You're exaggerating,' she objected.

'Well, I hope so.'

'And anyway, I'm not afraid.'

'But I am,' I said.

She stared.

'Em,' I said, 'if someone were standing behind you now with a knife, threatening to cut your throat if I didn't shoot myself, and I believed it, then . . .' I hesitated.

'Then what?'

'Then,' I said matter-of-factly, 'I would shoot myself.'

After a long pause, she said, 'It won't come to that.'

'Please, Em.'

'What about my horses?'

'Your head lad must have a home number. You can phone him.'

'Where from?'

'I don't know yet,' I said. 'But wherever you are, use your portable phone.'

'It's all mad.'

'I wish I were in Scotland,' I said. 'I wish I were

painting. But I'm here. I'm walking over an abyss that no one else seems to see. I want you safe.'

'Al . . .' She breathed out on a long, capitulating sigh. 'Why you?'

Why me?

The cry of ages.

Unanswerable.

Why did I care about right and wrong?

What made a policeman a policeman?

Emily went quickly out of the room and left me looking at the painting I had given her, that was not about an amateur game of golf in bad weather, but about the persistence of the human spirit.

After a while I unpinned the Quorn envelope from my shirt pocket. I lifted the golf picture off its hook and turned it over, and I slotted the envelope between the canvas and the frame, in the lower left-hand corner, so that it was held there securely, out of sight.

I hung the picture back on its hook and went out to see how lunch and life was passing in the kitchen.

Although not natural friends my mother and Audrey were being punctiliously civil to each other and were talking about how to pot cuttings from geraniums. I listened with the disjointed unreality-perception of an alien. At any minute the brewery might be breaking into the house in Bloxham. One should dip the slant-cut stem into fertiliser, Audrey said, and stick it into a peat container full of potting compost.

A large car rolled up the drive and stopped outside the kitchen window. The driver, a chauffeur in a dark navy blue suit, flat cap with shiny peak, and black leather gloves, climbed out and looked enquiringly at the building, and I went out to talk to him.

'Where am I going?' he said.

'Somewhere like Tor Bay. Find a good hotel with a sea view. Make them happy.'

'They?'

'My mother, my wife and the sister of the man who stole the brewery's money. Hide them.'

'Safe from Surtees?'

'And other thugs.'

'Your mother and your wife might recognise me.'

'Not without the wig, the rouge, the mascara, the high heels and the white frills.'

Chris Young grinned. 'I'll phone you when I've parked them,' he said.

'What's your name today?'

'Uttley.'

When I went back into the kitchen Emily, having made herself a sandwich, was talking to the head lad on the telephone.

'I'll be away this weekend . . . no, I'll phone you . . .' She gave her instructions about the horses. 'Severance runs at Fontwell tomorrow. I'll talk to the owners, don't forget to send the colours . . .'

She finished the details and hung up; not happy, not reassured.

'My dears,' I said lightly, looking at all three women, 'just have a good time.'

My mother asked, 'But why are we going? I don't really understand.'

'Um ... Emily knows. It's to do with hostages. A hostage is a lever. If you hold a hostage you hold a lever. I'm afraid, if any of you were taken hostage, that I might have to do what I don't want to do, so I want you safely out of sight, and if that sounds a bit improbable and melodramatic, then it's better than being sorry. So go and enjoy yourselves ... and please don't tell *anyone* where you are, and only use Emily's mobile phone if you *have* to phone someone, like Emily to her head lad, because it wouldn't be much fun to be taken hostage.'

'You might get your throat cut,' Emily said nonchalantly, munching her sandwich, and although my mother and Audrey Newton looked suitably horrified, it seemed Emily's words did the trick.

'How long are we going for?' my mother asked.

'Monday or Tuesday,' I said. Or Wednesday or Thursday. I had no idea.

I hugged my mother goodbye and kissed Emily and warmly clasped Audrey Newton's soft hand.

'The chauffeur's name is Mr Uttley,' I told them.

'Call me C.Y.,' he said, and winked at me, and drove them cheerfully away.

*

I sat in Ivan's car in a shopping centre's car park and tried to reach Margaret Morden by phone.

She was at a meeting, her office reported, and no, they couldn't break in with an urgent message, the meeting was out of town, and she would not be available until Monday, and even then she had meetings all day.

So kind.

Tobias had said he was going to Paris: back in the office on Tuesday.

I hated weekends. Other people's weekends. In my usual life, weekends flowed indistinguishably, work continuing regardless of the day. I sat indecisively, working out what to do next, and jumped when the mobile phone rang in my hand.

It was, surprisingly, Himself.

'Where are you?' he said.

'In the car somewhere. God knows where.'

'And your mother?'

'Gone away for a long weekend with friends.'

'So, if you're alone, come for a drink.'

'Do you mean in London?'

'Of course in London.'

'I'll be an hour or so.'

I drove to Chesham Place, home of the Earl in the capital, and parked on a meter.

Himself had a single malt ready, a sign of good humour.

'A good send-off, yesterday,' he observed, pouring generously. 'Ivan would have approved.'

'Yes.'

After a long silence he said, 'What's on your mind, Al?' I didn't answer at once and he said, 'I know your silences, so what gives?'

'Well . . .' I said, searching for an image, something pictorial, 'it's as if there's a high wall with a path along each side of it, stretching into the distance,' I said, 'and I am on one side of the wall and Patsy and some other people are on the other side, and we are all trying to go in the same direction to find the same pot of gold at the end, and I can't see what they are doing and they can't see what I am doing. The way forward on both sides of the wall is difficult and full of pot-holes and one keeps making mistakes.'

He listened, frowning.

I went on, 'Yesterday at the wake, Mrs Connie Hall, who lives next door to Ivan, told me that, on the night he died, Ivan was very upset because he couldn't find a tissue-box that had a phone number written on the bottom of it. He couldn't find it because it had been thrown away. Mrs Hall, the neighbour, told Patsy the same thing, so there we are, Patsy and I, one on each side of the wall, starting off together.' I paused. 'My mother told me that it was she who had written the telephone number on the bottom of the box, and it was something to do with someone we met in Leicestershire. She had forgotten all about it until yesterday, because of Ivan dying. The woman we had met in Leicestershire was Norman Quorn's sister, but I didn't know her name, so I phoned the brewery and asked them for it, which was a very stupid mistake.'

'But, Al,' Himself said, 'how could it have been a mistake?'

'Because,' I said, 'it set an alarm bell somewhere jangling.'

'What alarm bell?'

'It gave rise to the question – *Why* did I suddenly want to know Norman Quorn's sister's name and phone number? And I think that, on Patsy's side of the wall, messages and speculations began fizzing about.'

Himself sat still, listening.

I said, 'This morning I found out Norman Quorn's sister's name and address from the police in Leicestershire, where Norman Quorn's body was found, and I took my mother to see her, because she said she had a list that her brother had given her, that she had been going to give to Ivan. She said she would give it to my mother, and she did.' I drank some whisky. 'On the other side of the wall, which I can only guess at, someone decided to ask Norman Quorn's sister if her brother had given her anything to look after before he went on his holidays, and she told them that yes he had, but it was nothing very important, only some little list.' I stopped.

Himself said, 'What little list?'

'I think it is the signpost to the pot of gold. In fact, I don't think the gold can be found without it.'

Himself stared.

'So here I am on one side of the wall and, on the other side of the wall, they will know by now I have the list. So if you want to know what's troubling me, it is how to find the treasure safely.'

'But Al . . .'

'They know I've had a lot of practice in hiding things, starting with the Kinloch hilt.'

'I'm sorry about that. Sorry, I mean, that I talked to Ivan about it when Patsy could hear.'

'It can't be helped.'

'And you've hidden the list?'

'Sort of.'

'And – am I understanding you right – you think that list alone will lead to the brewery's lost money?'

'It's possible.'

'But surely . . . Patsy will want that money, won't she, to put the brewery back on its feet?'

'The problem is,' I sighed, 'that the brewery will survive *without* that money, partly as a result of my own efforts. The coffers will slowly fill up again, the pensioners will eventually get back to their old levels, the poor little widows will be able to stop recycling their teabags, the brewery may re-employ the workers they are having to sack and the firm will be as prosperous as it was before. There's no guarantee, really, that Patsy, or anyone else who finds the money, will use it to pay off the brewery's debts.'

Himself looked horrified.

'Theoretically,' I said, 'after a year or two of prosperity, the brewery could be plundered again.'

'Al . . .!'

'That would be the end of the brewery, because the creditors would not stand for it twice.'

'But you surely don't think Patsy is as dishonest as that?'

'Perhaps not Patsy, but Surtees . . .? People do often kill the golden goose.'

'Is Surtees bright enough?'

'He's dumb enough to think a double whammy a good idea.'

'But *Patsy*. I simply can't believe it.'

My uncle's goodness interfered with his perception of sin.

I said, 'Patsy has henchmen. She has people she talks to, who are entranced by her and lead her on. There are people like Desmond Finch and Oliver Grantchester and others, who scramble to please her. There's Lois who cleans at Park Crescent. Patsy gave her that job, and Lois has been faithful to her, even though yesterday I think Lois began to see the stiletto behind the smile. But she has the *habit* of reporting to Patsy, and I would expect that to go on, at least for a while, so I don't think I'll go back to Ivan's house just now.'

Himself said, as if baffled, 'But Patsy must know you have the good of the brewery at heart!'

I shook my head. 'She's resented me for twelve years and feared I would cut her out with Ivan, and although she now knows I didn't, I'm sure she's wide open to the suggestion that I'm trying to find the brewery's millions in order to hide them away for myself.'

'Oh no, Al.'

'Why not? She tells everyone I stole the King Alfred Gold Cup. I don't know if she really believes that. But I'm certain she can be persuaded I'm after the money.'

'But who would persuade her?'

'Anyone who's looking for it, who wants her attention and ill will fixed on *me.* A bit of distraction, as in conjuring tricks – watch my right hand while I vanish your wallet with my left.'

Himself said, frowning, 'Why don't you try telling her all that?'

I smiled. 'I paid her a compliment yesterday on how well she'd organised the funeral. She automatically thought I was being sarcastic. In her eyes, I'm a villain, so anything I do is suspect.' I shrugged. 'Don't worry, I'm used to it. But just now it's one big complication.'

'She's an idiot.'

'Not in her own estimation.'

He poured more whisky.

'You'll get me drunk,' I said.

'James says it's the only way he can beat you at golf.'

It wasn't golf that I was presently engaged in. I had better stay sober, I thought.

I declined my uncle's offer of a bed for the night and stayed instead in one of the hundreds of small hotels catering for London tourists. I ate a hamburger for dinner and wandered around under the bright lights among the back-packing youth of Europe. No demons. I felt old.

I took with me the portable phone and spoke to Chris while I sat beside the fountains and bronze lions in Trafalgar Square.

'I'm back home,' he said. 'My passengers have nice sea-view rooms in a hotel in Paignton, in Devon.'

'Which hotel?'

'The Redcliffe. Your mother wouldn't stay at the Imperial in Torquay because she'd been there with Sir Ivan. The Redcliffe is about three miles from there, round Tor Bay. They all seemed quite happy. They talked about *shopping*.'

'My mother had no suitcase.'

'So I gathered. So, anyway, what do you want done next? More Surtees-watching? That's the most unproductive job on earth, bar looking for your four thugs.'

He had had no luck with the boxing gyms. Had I

any idea how many of them there were in south-east England? Sorry, I'd said.

'You can charge me double-time,' I promised, 'if you watch Surtees all weekend.'

'Right,' he said, 'you're on.'

He had assured me, laughing, that if Surtees spent all his time looking out of his front gate, which he didn't, he would seldom see the same person there. There were cyclists with baseball caps on backwards, there were council employees measuring the road, there were housewives waiting for a bus, there were aged gentlemen walking dogs; there were beer drinkers sitting on the wall outside the pub up the road, and there were people tinkering with the innards of a variety of rented cars. Surtees never saw the skinhead or the secretary-bird.

Patsy and Surtees's stud farm lay on the outskirts of a village south of Hungerford. I had never been there myself, but I felt I knew it well from Chris's reports.

I tried to phone Margaret Morden at her home, but there was no reply. I tried again in the morning, and reached her.

'It's Saturday,' she objected.

'It's always Saturday.'

'It had better be worth it.'

'How about some numbers and names that Norman Quorn gave to his sister?'

After a silent moment she said, 'Are you talking about routes and destinations?'

'I think so.'

'We can't do anything until Monday.'

Bugger weekends, I thought.

'I can't change my Monday meetings. It'll have to be Tuesday.'

'Tobias said he was going to Paris and wouldn't be back in his office until Tuesday.'

'On Monday morning,' Margaret said, 'I will liaise with Tobias's office for an appointment and I will rope in the big bank cheese. Say ten o'clock, Tuesday, at the bank? Will you bring the numbers?'

I agreed resignedly to what seemed to me an endless and endlessly dangerous delay. The weekend stretched ahead like a boring monochrome desert, so it was quite a relief when, early in the afternoon, Himself decided to give me a buzz.

'Where are you?' he said.

'Little Venice, looking at the narrow boats, and thinking about paddling.' Thinking about the mountains, thinking about paint. Ah well.

'I have been talking to Patsy,' my uncle said.

'Who phoned who?' I asked.

'She phoned me. What does it matter? She wanted to know if I knew where you were.'

'What did you say?'

'I said you could be anywhere. She sounded quite different, Al. She sounded as if she had suddenly woken up. I told her that you had been working for her all along, at the brewery, and that she had misjudged you, and you had never tried to cause trouble between her and her father, very much the opposite, and that she had been grossly unfair to you all these years.'

'What did she say?'

'She said she wanted to talk to you. Al, do talk to her, at least it's a beginning.'

'Do you mean,' I said, 'talk to her on the phone?'

'It would be a start. She said she would be at home all afternoon. Do you have her number?' He read it out to me.

'I can't believe this,' I said.

'Give her a chance,' my uncle pleaded. 'It can't do any harm just to talk to her.'

I said, 'Any olive branch is worth the grasping.' And, ten minutes later, I was talking to her.

She sounded, as Himself had said, quite different. She *apologised*. She said that my uncle had given her a proper ticking-off for never seeing that I was no threat to her, and she was willing, if I were, to try and sort things out between us. She asked if I would let bygones be bygones, and perhaps we could come to an understanding for the future.

'What sort of understanding?' I asked.

'Well,' she said, 'just that we don't fight all the time.'

I agreed to a truce.

Would I, she suggested diffidently, would I come for a drink?

'Where?' I asked.

'Well . . . here?'

'Where is here?'

'At home,' she said. She mentioned the name of the village.

'Do you really mean it?' I asked.

'Oh, Alexander, your uncle has made me see how prejudiced I have been about you. I just want to start to put things right.'

I told her I would turn up for a drink at about six thirty and then, disconnecting, I phoned Chris's pager. He called back.

I said, 'Are you outside Surtees's house?'

'You betya.'

'Is anything happening?'

'Bugger all.'

'I have been invited for a drink.'

'Belladonna? Aconite? Gin and toadstools?'

I sighed. 'But if she is genuine . . .'

'She is never genuine, you said.'

I was truly undecided. 'I think I'll go for the drink,' I said.

'Bad choice.'

'I'll take you with me. Have you got the "secretary" handy?'

'In the car, zipped bag number five.'

I laughed. 'What are in numbers one, two, three and four?'

'The skinhead. Various Mr Youngs, various Mr Uttleys.'

'And at present?'

'I'm in a jogging suit, in a rented car, reading a map.'

'I'll pick up the "secretary" in the road at half past six.'

'Fair enough.'

I spent a couple of hours wondering if it were possible that Patsy had undergone a sea-change. I had either to believe it or not believe it. I had either to try for peace or fear a trap.

I would go, I thought, and take Chris with me. Peace treaties had to start somewhere, after all. So, in the late afternoon, I followed the map and arrived in Patsy's village at dusk and came across a long black-legged figure thumbing a lift.

I stopped beside him and he oozed into the car, wafting billows of expensive scent and doubling up with chuckles.

'Is anything happening?' I asked.

'Half an hour ago Surtees and his missus came out of the house, got into the car, and drove down the road, and I followed them in my car and I was just about to phone you when they turned into the gates of a house about half a mile away from here. They have got fairy lights all around the garden in the trees there, and several cars outside, and it looks as if it's some sort of party. So what do you want to do, try the house where Surtees lives, or join the party?'

'The house,' I said.

I walked from the road to the front door with Chris a step behind me and rang the bell. A young woman opened it. Beside her stood Xenia, unforgiving as always, with, behind, two younger children.

'Mrs Benchmark is expecting you,' the young woman said when I introduced myself. 'She says that she is very sorry but, when she was talking to you earlier, she forgot that she and Mr Benchmark were going to a drinks party. It's through the village, past the pub, along on the right-hand side, and you can't miss it. It is all decorated with lights. Mrs Benchmark asked me just to phone when you got here, so that she can meet you when you arrive at the party.'

I thanked her, and Chris and I walked back to the car.

'What do you think?' I asked.

'A toss-up.'

I tossed up mentally, heads you win, tails you lose, and lost.

CHAPTER THIRTEEN

Chris and I drove along past the pub and came to the house with the lights. When we reached the driveway, which was full of cars, we parked in the roadway. As we climbed out, Chris stumbled and broke the heel off one of his high-heeled patents. He swore, stopped, and said he would break off the other one to level himself up. I laughed, and set off towards the house a few steps ahead of him.

It was as if the bushes themselves erupted.

One moment I was walking unsuspectingly along, and the next I was being enmeshed in nets and ropes and being overwhelmed and pushed and dragged, not into the looming shadowy house but through some sort of rustic gate from the drive into a garden.

The garden, I was hazily aware, was lit by more festoons of fairy lights and by big multicoloured bulbs installed against many trees which, shining upwards, made canopies of illuminated branches and leaves; it was all strikingly theatrical, dramatically magnificent, a brilliant setting for a party.

No party that I'd been to before had started with one of the guests being tied to the trunk of a maple tree next to a bunch of red light bulbs that shone upwards into autumn-red leaves, creating a scarlet canopy above his head. My back was against the tree. There was rope round my ankles, and round my wrists, drawing them backwards, and – worst – round my neck.

At no party that I'd attended before had there been four familiar thugs as guests, one of them busy putting on boxing gloves.

Red leather boxing gloves.

The only other guests were Patsy and Surtees and Oliver Grantchester.

Surtees looked triumphant, Grantchester serious and Patsy astounded.

I looked round the garden for possible exits and could see precious few. There was a lawn ringed with bushes, lit on the garden side, shadowy beyond. There was a flower bed with straggling chrysanthemums. There was an ornamental goldfish pond with an artificial stream running down into it over a pile of rocks.

There was a big house to the left, mostly dark, but with a brightly lit conservatory facing the garden.

There was Oliver Grantchester.

Oliver Grantchester.

The one crucial piece of information I hadn't learned was that he had a place in the country half a mile along the road from Patsy's house. The only address and telephone number for Oliver Grantchester in Ivan's address book had been in London.

Audrey Newton had firmly pointed to Oliver Grantchester's sketched head as the person who had collected her brother on the day he left Wantage to go on holiday.

I'd known *who* would be looking for me, but not *where*.

There weren't swear words bad enough to describe my stupidity.

Patsy would never change. Why had I ever thought that she would?

I'd *wanted* to believe that she had. I'd wanted an end to the long pointless feud.

Serve me right.

Grantchester stood six feet away from me and said, 'Where is the Kinloch hilt?'

I looked at him in bewilderment. I could think of no reason why he would want to know. He made some sort of signal to the wearer of the boxing gloves, who hit me low down, in the abdomen, which hurt.

My neck jerked forwards against the rope. Dire.

Grantchester said, 'Where is the King Alfred Gold Cup?'

Golf bag. Locker. Club house. Scotland. Out of his grasp.

A bash in the ribs. Reverberations. Altogether too much, and quite likely only the beginning. *Shit.*

'Ivan sent you the Cup. Where is it?'

Ask Himself.

Another fast, hard, pin-pointed bash. Shudder country.

Where the hell, I wondered, was my bodyguard?

Surtees strode to Grantchester's side.

'Where's the horse?' he yelled. 'Make him tell you where he's put the horse.'

The thug with the gloves was the one who had been demanding 'Where is it?' at the bothy.

'Where's the horse?' Grantchester said.

I didn't tell him. Painful decision.

Surtees positively jumped up and down.

'Make him tell you. Hit him harder.'

I thought detachedly that I would quite likely prefer to die than give in to Surtees.

Oliver Grantchester hadn't the same priorities as Patsy's husband.

He said to me, 'Where's your mother?'

In Devon, I thought: thank God.

Bash.

He had to be mad, if he thought I would tell him.

'Where's Emily Cox?'

Safe. Same thing.

Bash.

'Where is Norman Quorn's sister?'

I was by then fairly breathless. It would have been difficult to tell him even if I'd wanted to.

He stepped forward to within three feet of me, and with quiet intensity said, 'Where's the list?'

The list.

The point of all the battering, I supposed, was to make it more likely that I would answer the one question that really mattered.

'Where's the list?'

He had never liked me, he had seen me always as a threat to his domination of Ivan. He had encouraged Patsy's obsessive suspicions of me. I remembered his dismay and fury when Ivan had given his powers of attorney to me, not to Patsy or himself. He hadn't wanted me looking into the brewery's affairs. He had been right to fear it.

His big body, his heavy personality faced me now with thunderous malevolence. He didn't care how much he hurt me. He was enjoying it. He might not be hitting me himself, but he was swaying in a sort of ecstasy as each blow landed. He wanted my surrender, but wanted it difficult; intended that I should crumble, but not too soon.

I saw the pleasure in his eyes. The full lips smiled. I hated him. Shook with hate.

'Tell me,' he said.

I saw it was my defeat he wanted almost as much as the list itself: and I saw also that he was wholly confident of achieving both. If I could deny him . . . then I would.

'Where's the list?'

The boxing gloves thudded here and there. Face, ribs, belly. Head. I lost count.

'Where's the list?'

Such a pretty garden, I groggily thought.

The punch-bag practice stopped. Grantchester went away. The four thugs stood around me watchfully, as if I could slide out of their ropes and knots, which I couldn't, but not for lack of trying.

Patsy's face swam into my close vision.

'What list?' she said.

It made no sense. Surely she knew what list.

I would have said she looked worried. Horrified even. But she'd lured me there. My own fault.

'Why,' she said, 'why did Oliver ask where your mother and Emily are?'

I dredged up an answer, 'How does he know they are not at home?' My face felt stiff. The rest just felt.

'Alexander,' Patsy said in distress, not working it out, 'whatever Oliver wants, for God's sake give it to him. This . . . this . . .' she gestured to my trussed state, and to the thugs, '. . . this is *awful.*'

I agreed with her. I also couldn't believe she didn't know what her friendly neighbourhood lawyer wanted. I'd done believing Patsy. Finished for life. Finished for what was left of life.

Oliver Grantchester was playing for millions, and boxing gloves were getting him nowhere. He returned from the direction of his house, pulling behind him a barbecue cooker on wheels.

Oh God, I thought. Oh no.

I can't do this. I'll tell him. I know I will. They're not my millions.

Grantchester took the grill grid off the barbecue and propped it against one of the wheeled legs. Then he went back into his bright conservatory and returned carrying a bag of charcoal briquettes and a bottle of lighter fuel. He poured briquettes from the bag into the fire-box of the barbecue and then poured the whole bottleful of lighter fuel over the briquettes.

He struck a match and tossed it onto the fuel.

Flame rushed upward in a roaring plume, scarlet and gold and eternally untamed. The flame was reflected in Grantchester's eyes, so that for a moment it looked as if the fire were inside his head, looking out.

Then, satisfied, he picked up the grill with a pair of long tongs and settled it in place, to get hot.

I could see the thugs' faces. They showed no surprise. One showed sickened revulsion, but still no surprise.

I thought: *they've seen this before.*

They'd seen Norman Quorn.

Norman Quorn . . . burned in a garden, with grass cuttings in his clothes . . .

Patsy looked merely puzzled. So did Surtees.

The briquettes flamed, heating up quickly.

I would tell him, I thought. Enough was enough. My entire body already hurt abominably. There was a point beyond which it wasn't sensible to go. There were out-of-date abstractions like the persistence of the human spirit, and they might be all right for paintings but didn't apply in pretty country gardens in the evening of the second Saturday in October.

Norman Quorn had burned down to his ribs, and died, and he hadn't told.

I wasn't Norman Quorn. I hadn't millions to lose. They were Patsy's millions. God damn her soul.

Grantchester waited with lip-licking anticipation for frightful ages while the heat built up, and when the briquettes glowed a bright searing red, he lifted the barred grill off the fire with his pair of long tongs and dropped it flat on the lawn, where it sizzled and singed the grass.

'You'll lie on that if you don't tell me,' he said. He was enjoying himself. 'Where's the list?'

Cussed, rebellious, stubborn . . . I might be all those by nature: but I knew I would tell him.

Defeat lay there at my feet, blackening the grass. Money was of no importance. The decision was a matter of will. Of pride, even. And such pride came too expensive.

Tell him . . . you have to.

'Where is it?' he said.

I meant to tell him. I tried to tell him. But when it came to the point, I couldn't.

So I burned.

*

Some of the marks will be there always, but I can't see them unless I look in a mirror.

I could hear someone screaming and I remembered Surtees promising 'next time you'll scream', but it wasn't I, after all, who was screaming; it was Patsy.

Her high urgent voice, screaming.

'No. No. You can't. For God's sake, stop it. Oliver. Surtees. You can't do this. Stop it. For God's sake. Stop it . . .'

The noise I made wasn't a scream. From deep inside, like an age-old recognition of a primeval torment, starting low in my gut and ending like a growl in the throat, the sound I heard in myself, that was at one with myself, that was all there was of existence, that unified every feeling, every nerve's message into one consuming elemental protest, that noise was a deep sort of groan.

I could hear him repeating, 'Where is it? Where is it?'

Irrelevant.

It all lasted, I dare say, not much more than a minute. Two minutes, perhaps.

Half a lifetime, condensed.

I'd gone beyond speech when the scene blew apart.

With crashes and bangs and shrieking metal the driving cab and entire front half of a large travelling coach smashed down the fence and gate between the drive and the garden. Out of the bus and onto the lawn poured a half-drunk mob of football supporters, all dressed in orange (it seemed) with orange scarves and heavy boots and raucous shouting voices.

'Where's the beer, then? Where's the beer?'

Scrambling through the demolished fence came more and more orange scarves. Hooligan faces. 'Where's the beer?'

The four thugs who'd been pinning down my arms and legs decided to quit and took their weight off me so that I was blessedly able to roll off the grill and lie face down on the cool grass: and a pair of long legs in black tights appeared in my limited field of vision, with a familiar voice above me saying, 'Jesus Christ, Al,' and I tried to say, 'What took you so long?' but it didn't come out.

The brightly lit garden went on filling with noise and orange scarves and demands for beer. Surrealism, I thought.

Chris went away and came back and poured a container of cold water over me, and squatted down beside me and said, 'Your sweater was *smouldering*, for God's sake,' and I agreed with him silently that water was better than fire any day.

'Al,' he said worriedly, 'are you OK?'

'Yuh.'

A goldfish flapped on the grass. Poor little bugger. A goldfish out of the pond. Pond water, that Chris had used.

Goldfish pond. Cold water.

Great idea.

I made an attempt to crawl and stagger there, and Chris, seeing the point, unwound the ropes from my arms and legs and neck and hooked an arm under my armpit and gave me a haul, so that somehow or other I crossed the short distance of grass and lay down full-length in the cold pond, my head using the surrounding stones like a pillow, leaves of waterlilies on my chest, the overall relief enormous.

'Did bloody Surtees do this?' Chris demanded with fury.

'Bloody Grantchester.'

He went away.

There were more people in the garden. Policemen. Uniforms. The monstrous front half of the coach rose over the scene like a giant incarnation of Chaos, yellow, white and silver with windows like eyes. I lay in the pond and watched the football fans scurry about looking for free beer and turning violent when they couldn't find any, and I watched the police slapping handcuffs on everyone moving, including the four thugs, who had over-estimated the window of escape, and I watched Patsy's bewilderment and Surtees's swings from glee to noncomprehension and back.

I heard one of the football crowd telling policemen that it was a *girl* who had stolen the coach from outside the pub where they had pulled up for some refreshment; a girl who had yelled that there was free beer at the party along the road, a girl – 'a bit of all right', 'a knock-out' – who'd said she was up for grabs for the quickest pair of boots after her into the garden.

When they'd drifted away, Chris came back.

'I caught bloody Grantchester trying to sneak out through the garage,' he said with satisfaction. 'He'll be going nowhere for a while.'

'Chris,' I said. 'Get lost.'

'Do you mean it?'

'The police are looking for the young woman who drove the bus.'

A shiny object splashed down onto my chest.

A set of brass knuckles, gleaming wetly. I swept them off my chest into deeper, concealing water.

Chris's hand briefly squeezed my shoulder and I had only one more glimpse of his dark shape as he passed from the lit side of the bushes into the shadows.

The farce continued. A large uniformed policeman told me to get out of the pond, and when I failed to obey he clicked a pair of handcuffs on my wrists and walked off, deaf to protests.

It gradually appeared that a couple of people in the garden were neither uniformed police nor uniformed fanatics but the law in plain clothes or, in other words, tweed jackets with leather patches on the elbows.

The artificial waterfall splashed cold water over my throbbing head. I lifted my handcuffed hands and steered the water delicately over my face.

A new voice said, 'Get out of the pond.'

I opened my closed eyes. The voice held police authority. Just behind him stood Patsy.

He was a middle-aged man, not unkind, but my occupancy of the pond, the length of my wet hair and the presence of the handcuffs could hardly have been encouraging.

'Get out,' he said. 'Stand up.'

'I don't know if he can,' Patsy said worriedly. 'They were hitting him . . .'

'Who were?'

She looked over to where bunches of handcuffed figures sat gloomily on the grass. No beer. No fun at all.

'And they burnt him,' Patsy said. 'I couldn't stop them.'

The policeman looked at the barbecue with its glowing coals.

'No,' Patsy said, pointing, 'on that grill thing, over there.'

One of the uniformed policemen bent down to pick the grill up and snatched his hand away, cursing and sucking his fingers.

I laughed.

Patsy said as if shattered, 'Alexander, it's not *funny*.'

The policeman said, 'Mrs Benchmark, do you know this man?'

'Of course I know him.' She stared down at me. I looked expressionlessly back, resigned to the usual abuse. 'He's . . . *he's my brother*,' she said.

It came nearer to breaking me up than all Grantchester's attentions.

She saw that it did, and it made her cry.

Patsy, my implacable enemy, wept.

She brushed the tears away brusquely and told the policeman she would point out my attackers among the football crowd, and when they moved off their place was taken by Surtees, who was very far from a change of heart and had clearly enjoyed the earlier entertainment.

'Where's the horse?' he said. He sneered. His feet quivered, I thought he might kick my head.

I said with threat, 'Surtees, any more shit from you and I'll tell Patsy where you go on Wednesday afternoons. I'll tell her the address of the little house on the outskirts of Guildford and I'll tell her the name of the prostitute who lives there, and I'll tell her what sort of sex you go there for.'

Surtees's mouth opened in absolute horror. When he could control his throat, he stuttered.

'How . . . how . . . how . . .? I'll deny it.'

I said, smiling, 'I paid a skinhead to follow you.'

His eyes seemed to bulge.

'So you keep your hands to yourself as far as I'm concerned, and your mouth *shut*, Surtees,' I said, 'and if you're still what Patsy wants, I won't disillusion her.'

He looked sick. He physically backed away from me, as if I'd touched him with the plague. I gazed up peacefully at the bright coloured lights in the trees. Life had its sweet moments, after all.

No one had actually seen Oliver Grantchester being attacked and tied up securely in his own garage. He had been swiftly knocked out and had seen no one. He was found, when he recovered consciousness, to be suffering not only from a blow to the back of the skull but also from a broken nose, a broken jaw, and extensive damage to his lower abdomen and genitals, as if he'd been well kicked while knowing nothing about it.

Whoever would do such a thing! Tut tut.

The police put him in a prison hospital and provided him with a doctor.

Patsy organised things, which she was good at.

Patsy organised me into a private hospital that specialised in burns with an elderly woman doctor able to deal with anything on a Saturday evening.

'Dear me,' she said. 'Nasty. Very painful. But you're a healthy young man. You'll heal.'

She wrapped me in bio-synthetic burn-healing artificial skin and large bandages and in her grandmotherly way enquired, 'And a couple of cracked ribs, too, wouldn't you say?'

'I would.'

She smiled. 'I'll see that you sleep.'

She efficiently drugged me out until six in the morning, when I phoned Chris's bleeper and got his return call five minutes later.

'Where the hell are you?' he demanded aggrievedly.

I told him.

'That hospital's strictly for millionaires,' he objected.

'Then get me out. Bring some clothes.'

He brought my own clothes, the ones he'd borrowed for his departure from the wake at Park Crescent three days earlier, and he arrived to find me standing by the window watching the grey dawn return to the perilous earth.

'Hospital gowns,' he said, as I turned to greet him, 'shouldn't be visited even on the damned.'

'They cut my clothes off last night.'

'Sue them.'

'Mm.'

'To be frank,' he said, almost awkwardly, 'I didn't expect you to be on your feet.'

'More comfortable,' I said succinctly. 'That bus, if I may say so, was brilliant.'

He grinned. 'Yes, it was, wasn't it?'

'Go on then, tell me all.'

He dumped the carrier bag with the clothes in and came over to join me by the window, the familiar face alight with enjoyment. High cheekbones, light brown hair, bright brown eyes, natural air of impishness. Solemnity sat unnaturally upon him, and he couldn't tell me what had happened without making light-hearted jokes about it.

'Those thugs that jumped out of the bushes at you, they were the real McCoy. Brutal bastards. There was no mistaking they were the ones I'd been looking for. And to be honest, Al, I couldn't handle four of them at once on my own, any more than you could.'

I nodded, understanding.

'So,' Chris said, 'I thought the best thing to do would be to find out how big a posse would be needed to round up the outlaws, so to speak, so I shunted round in the shelter of a sort of high wooden fence that's all round that garden, until I could see through the bushes. All those lights . . . and there they were, your four thugs, tying you up to that tree and bashing you about, and there were three other people there too, which made seven, and I couldn't manage seven . . .'

'No,' I said.

'There was that big fat slob, the lawyer from your stepfather's funeral.'

'Yes,' I said.

'And bloody Surtees . . .'

'Yes,' I said again.

'And his wife.'

I nodded.

'So,' Chris said again, 'I had to go for reinforcements,

and I ran down the road to the pub and used their telephone and told the police there was a riot going on, and those bastards told me there were a dozen riots going on every Saturday evening, and they wanted to know *where* exactly, so I asked the barman in the pub if he knew whose house it was with all those lights in the garden, and he said it belongs to Mr Oliver Grantchester, a very well-known lawyer, so I told the police, but they didn't show up, or anything, and to tell you the truth, mate, I was jumping up and down a bit by that time.'

So would I have been, I thought.

'So then,' Chris said, 'this bloody big coachload of fervent psychos in orange scarves invaded the bar, and I thought then, "manna dropped from heaven", so I went outside where half of them were still in the bus, and I yelled at them that there was free beer down the road at a party, and I just got into the driver's seat and drove that damned jumbo straight through Grantchester's fence into the garden.'

'It did the trick,' I said, smiling.

'Yes, but . . . my God . . .!'

'Best forgotten,' I said.

'I'll never forget it,' he said, 'and nor will you.'

'You came, though.'

'So did the bloody police, in the end. Too many of them.'

'What exactly,' I asked him contentedly, 'did you do to Oliver Grantchester?'

'Kicked him a good many times in the goolies.' Chris had been wearing, I remembered, pointed black patent shoes, sharp enough even without heels. 'And I smashed him round the face a bit with the hard knuckles. I mean, there's villains, and there's villains. Boxing gloves is one thing, but burning people . . . that's diabolical. I could have killed him. Lucky I didn't.'

'The police asked me,' I said, 'if I knew who had tied him up. I said how could I possibly know anything. I was lying in the pond.'

Chris laughed. 'I'll work for you any time,' he said. 'Attending to Grantchester will be extra.'

Patsy arrived silently while I was sitting on the edge of the bed, dressed in trousers and shirt, head hanging, feeling rotten. Of all the people I would have preferred not to see me like that, she would have been tops.

'Go away,' I said, and she went, and the next person through the door was a nurse with a syringeful of relief.

Around mid-morning I had a visit from a Detective Inspector Vernon, whom I'd met, it transpired, in the garden.

'Mrs Benchmark said you were dressed,' he remarked, not shaking hands.

'Do you know her well?'

'She's a patron of local police charities.'

'Oh.'

He joined me by the window. There were scudding clouds in the sky. A good day for mountains.

'Mrs Benchmark says that Mr Grantchester, who is another of our patrons, was instructing four other men to ill-treat you.'

'You could put it like that,' I agreed.

He was a bulky short man, going grey: never, at that rank, at that age, going to climb high in police hierarchy, but maybe a more down-to-earth and dogged investigator because of it.

'Can you tell me why?' he said.

'You'll have to ask Mr Grantchester.'

'His lower jaw's badly broken. This morning he can't speak. He's badly bruised in the abdomen, too. Doubled over. Black and blue.'

Vernon asked me again if I knew who had attacked him. I'd been in the pond, I repeated. As he knew.

I said helpfully, however, that the same four thugs had battered me earlier in Scotland, and told him where I'd given a statement to the police there. I suggested that he might also talk to Chief Inspector Reynolds of the Leicestershire police about people being burned on barbecue grills on mown grass. Vernon wrote everything down methodically. If I had recovered enough, he said, he would appreciate it if I would attend his police station the following morning. They could send an unmarked car for me, he offered.

'See you down the nick,' Chris would have said, but all I raised was 'OK'.

The day passed somehow, and the night.

Bruises blackened. The cracked ribs were all on my right side: a south-paw puncher's doing.

The burns got inspected again. No sign of infection. Very lucky, I was told, considering the unsterile nature of goldfish ponds.

On Monday morning I discharged myself from the hospital against their advice. I had too much to do, I said.

A plain-clothes police car came to transport me to Vernon's official stamping ground, where I was instantly invited to look through a window into a brightly lit room, and to say if I'd seen any of eight men at any earlier time in my life.

'No problem. Numbers one, three, seven and eight.'

'They deny they touched you.'

I gave Vernon a glowering come-off-it glare. 'You saw them yourself in that garden. You arrested them there.'

'I didn't see them in the act of committing grievous bodily harm.'

I closed my eyes briefly, took a grip on my pain-driven temper, and said, on a deep breath, 'Number three wore boxing gloves and caused the damage you can see in my face. He is left-handed. The others watched. All four assisted in compelling me to lie on that hot grill. All four also attacked me outside my home in Scotland. I don't know their names, but I do know their faces.'

It had seemed to me on other occasions that the great British police force not only never apologised, but also never saw the need for it: however, Inspector Vernon ushered me politely into a bare interview room and offered me coffee, which in his terms came into the category of tender loving care.

'Mrs Benchmark couldn't identify them for certain,' he observed.

I asked if he had talked to Sergeant Berrick in Scotland, and to Chief Inspector Reynolds in Leicestershire. They had been off duty, he said.

Bugger weekends.

Could I use a telephone, I asked.

Who did I want to talk to? Long-distance calls were not free.

'A doctor in London,' I said.

I reached, miraculously, Keith Robbiston; alert, in a hurry.

'Could I have a handful of your wipe-out pills?' I asked.

'What's happened?' he said.

'I got bashed again.'

'More thugs?'

'The same ones.'

'Oh . . . as bad as before?'

'Well, actually . . . worse.'

'How much worse?'

'Cracked ribs and some burns.'

'*Burns?*'

'Nothing to do with "Auld Lang Syne".'

He laughed, and talked to Inspector Vernon, and said my mother would kill him if he failed me, and pills would be motor-biked door to door within two hours.

If nothing else, Keith Robbiston's speed impressed the Inspector. He went off to telephone outside. When the coffee came, it was in a pot, on a tray.

I sat and waited for unmeasurable time, thinking. When Vernon returned I told him that number seven in the line-up had been wearing what looked like my father's gold watch, stolen from me in Scotland.

'Also,' I said, 'number seven didn't relish the burning.'

'That won't excuse him.'

'No . . . but if you could make it worth his while, he might tell you what happened to a Norman Quorn.'

The Inspector didn't say, 'Who?' He went quietly away. A uniformed constable brought me a sandwich lunch.

My pills arrived. Things got better.

After another couple of hours Inspector Vernon came into the room, sat down opposite me across the table and told me that the following conversation was not taking place. Positively *not.* It was his private thanks. Understood?

'OK,' I said.

'First of all, can you identify your father's gold watch?'

'It has an engraving on the back, "Alistair from Vivienne".'

Vernon faintly smiled. In all the time I spent with him it was the nearest he came to showing pleasure.

'Number seven in the line-up may be known as Bernie,' he said. 'Bernie, as you saw, is a worried man.' He paused. 'Can I totally trust you not to repeat this? Can I rely on you?'

I said dryly, 'To the hilt,' which he didn't understand beyond the simple words, but he took them as I meant them: utterly. 'But,' I added, 'why all this cloak-and-dagger stuff?'

He spent a moment thinking, then said, 'In Britain one isn't, as you may or may not know, allowed to make bargains with people accused of crimes. One can't *promise* a light sentence in return for information. That's a myth. You can persuade someone unofficially to plead guilty to a lesser charge, like in this case, *actual* bodily harm, rather than *grievous* bodily harm, GBH, which is a far more serious crime, and can carry a long jail sentence. But some authorities can be perverse, and if they suspect a deal has been struck, they're perfectly capable of upsetting it. Follow?'

'I follow.'

'Also the business of what is and what isn't admissible evidence is a minefield.'

'So I've heard.'

'If you hadn't told me to ask Bernie questions about Norman Quorn I wouldn't have thought of doing it. But Bernie split wide open, and now my superiors here are patting me on the back and thinking of going to the Crown Prosecution Service – who, of course, decide whether or not a trial should take place – not with a GBH involving *you*, but with a charge against Oliver Grantchester for manslaughter. The manslaughter of Norman Quorn.'

'Hell's teeth.'

'At this point in such proceedings everyone gets very touchy indeed about who knows what, in order not to jeopardise any useful testimony. It wouldn't do for you to have heard Bernie's confession. It could have compromised the case. So I'll tell you what he said . . . but I shouldn't.'

'You're safe.'

He nevertheless looked around cautiously, as if listeners had entered unseen.

'Bernie said,' he finally managed, 'that they – the four you call the thugs – all go to a gym in London, east of the City, which Oliver Grantchester has been visiting for fitness sessions for the past few years. Grantchester goes on the treadmill, lifts a few weights and so on, but isn't a boxer.'

'No.'

'So when he wanted a rough job done, he recruited your four thugs. Bernie was willing. The up-front money was good. So was the pay-off afterwards, though the job went wrong.'

'Quorn died.'

Vernon nodded.

'Grantchester,' he said, 'told them to turn up at his house in the country. He told them the name of the village and said they would know his house because it had Christmas lights all over the driveway, and he would turn them on, even though it would be daylight and not Christmas. Grantchester arrived at his house with an older man, who was Norman Quorn, and he took him through the gate in the fence into the garden. The four thugs tied the man – whose name they didn't yet know – to the same tree as they tied you, but they didn't belt him, like you. Grantchester lit the barbecue and told Quorn he would burn him if he didn't come across with some information.'

Vernon paused, then went on. 'Bernie didn't know what the information was, and still doesn't. Quorn was shitting himself, Bernie says, and Grantchester waited until the fire was very hot, and then he threw the grill onto the grass, and told Quorn he would lie on it until he told him – Grantchester – what he wanted to know. Quorn told him he would tell him at once, but Grantchester got the four thugs to throw Quorn onto the grill anyway, and hold him there, and although he was screaming and hollering that he would tell, Grantchester wouldn't let him up, and seemed to be enjoying it, and when he did let him up, Quorn dropped down dead.'

Vernon stopped. I listened in fascinated horror.

'Bernie,' Vernon said, 'was near to puking, describing it.'

'I'm not surprised.'

'Grantchester was furious. There was this dead body on the ground and he hadn't found out what he wanted to know. He got Bernie and the others to put Quorn into the boot of his car in the garage, and in the house he made them put their hands round empty glasses, so that he had all their fingerprints, and he threatened that if they ever spoke of what they'd seen they would be in mortal trouble. Then he paid them and told them to go away, which they did. Bernie doesn't know what Grantchester did with Quorn's body.'

After a while I said, 'Did you ask Bernie about Scotland?'

Vernon nodded. 'Grantchester paid them again to go to your house and beat you up a bit until you gave them something to give to him. He didn't tell them what it was. He just told them to say, "Where is it?" to you, and you would know what it was. Bernie said you didn't give them anything, and Grantchester was furious, and told them they should have made sure you were dead before they threw you down the mountain.'

'Well, well,' I said.

'Bernie says he complained that beating up people

was one thing, but murder was another, and Grantchester threatened that Bernie would do as he was told, because of his fingerprints.'

'Bernie is simple,' I said.

Vernon nodded. 'Just as well, from our point of view. Anyway, the pay was good, so when Grantchester told them to turn up again at his house the day before yesterday, they did.'

'Yes.'

'Grantchester told them that you would be coming, and that they were to tie you to the same tree, like Quorn before, only this time there was no talk of burning.' He paused. 'The one with the boxing gloves is known as Jazzo. He thought you got knocked out too soon in Scotland. He told Grantchester you wouldn't like another dose. He said he wouldn't knock you out and he would guarantee you would answer any question you were asked.'

I listened without comment.

'Of course, it didn't turn out that way,' Vernon said. 'So Grantchester brought out his barbecue again, because it had worked the first time, and that's when Bernie's bottle deserted him, he says.'

'It didn't stop him sitting on my legs,' I remarked with satire.

'He didn't mention sitting on your legs.'

'You don't say.'

'He said Mrs Benchmark was there, and she was

screaming and screaming to Grantchester to stop, and he wouldn't. I asked Bernie if you were screaming too.'

'That's an unfair bloody question.'

Vernon gave me a sideways glance. 'He said the only noise you made was a sort of moan.'

Charming, I thought.

'And that's when the bus crashed into the garden.' Vernon paused and looked at me straight. 'Is Bernie's account of things accurate?'

'As far as I'm concerned, yes.'

Vernon stood up and walked around the room twice, as if disturbed.

'Mrs Benchmark,' he said, 'called you her brother, but you're not, are you?'

'Her father was married to my mother. He died a week ago.'

Vernon nodded. 'Mrs Benchmark is devastated by what happened in the garden. She doesn't understand it. The poor lady is very upset.'

I again made no comment.

'She said your girlfriend was there. We released all the football supporters yesterday, but half of them agreed that the bus was driven from the pub to the garden by a young woman. Was she your girlfriend?'

I said, 'She is a friend. She was walking a few steps behind me when the thugs hustled me into the garden. They didn't notice her. She told me yesterday that when she saw what was happening she ran down to the pub and called the police. Then, it seems, the busload of happy revellers arrived, so she drove the bus to the rescue, for which I'll always be grateful.'

'In other words,' Vernon said, 'you are not going to get her into trouble.'

'Quite right.'

He gave me a long slow look. 'And you're not going to give us her name and address.'

'She lives with a man,' I said, 'who wouldn't like to see her in court. You don't really need her, do you?'

'Probably not.'

'If there was any damage to the bus,' I said, 'I'll pay for it.'

Vernon went over to the door, opened it, and shouted to someone outside to bring tea. When he came back he said, 'We obtained a warrant yesterday to search Grantchester's house.'

He waited for me to ask if he'd found anything useful, so I did.

He didn't answer straightforwardly. He said, 'The policeman in Scotland sent us faxes today of the drawings you did of the thugs the day they attacked you at your home. Bernie almost collapsed when we showed them to him. Your policeman also sent the list of things that were stolen from you. In Grantchester's house we found four paintings of golf courses.'

'You didn't!'

Vernon nodded. 'Your policeman, Sergeant Berrick, said that the pictures had stickers on the backs, and if other stickers had been stuck over them, your name would still be visible under X-ray. So this afternoon we X-rayed the stickers.' He almost smiled. 'Your Scottish policeman said that you promised to paint a portrait of his wife if he helped to find your pictures.'

'I did,' I said. 'And I will.'

Vernon suggested, 'Mine, too?'

'A pleasure,' I said.

CHAPTER FOURTEEN

On Tuesday morning I went to the bank meeting in Reading and was shown into a small private conference room where the area bank manager, Margaret Morden and Tobias were already sitting round a table with coffee cups in front of them.

When I went in, they stood up.

'Don't,' I said awkwardly. 'Am I late?'

'No,' Tobe said.

They all sat. I took the one empty chair.

'Did you bring the list?' the bank man said.

I was wearing an open-necked white shirt with no tie, and carrying a jacket. I dug into a jacket pocket and handed Norman Quorn's envelope to Tobias.

They were staring at me, rather.

'Sorry about the bruises,' I said, making a gesture towards my face. 'I got a bit clobbered again. Very careless.'

Tobias said, 'I've talked to Chris. He told me about . . . Grantchester's barbecue.'

'Oh.'

Tobias had also, clearly, relayed to the bank man and to Margaret what Chris had said. All of them were embarrassed. I too. Very British.

'Well,' I said, 'can we find the money?'

They had no doubt of it. With a relieved air of eagerness and satisfaction they passed to each other the piece of paper, the riddle that Quorn had left; it soon became apparent that, although the numbers and names belonged to bank accounts, the brewery's Finance Director had been coy about setting down on paper which account referred to which bank. The list had been an aide memoire to himself. He had never meant anyone else to have to decipher it.

Thoughtfully they each copied out for themselves the whole list, numbers and names. (He wouldn't trust it to the office copier, the bank man said; the information was so hot it would not be allowed to leave that room.)

Each of them had brought a personal computer that was not connected to anything else and could not be hacked into from outside. Each of them fed into their separate computer a disc recording what each of them, separately, knew. The bank had supplied a fax machine dedicated to this one job.

The room grew silent except for the tapping of keys and the drumming of thoughtful fingers when the solutions didn't quickly appear.

I waited without fret. They knew their business, and I didn't.

Tobias and the bank man wore the suits of their trade, dark confidence-builders with gravitas. Margaret had come in flowery printed wool, soft and rose-red and disarming, hiding the steel-hard brain. How ridiculous, I thought, that the male mind could often accept a female as equal only if she pretended to be in need of help. Margaret amused me. She caught me looking at her, read my thought, and winked. Men were right to be afraid of women, I concluded: the witch lived near the surface in all of them.

They burned witches . . . God help them.

I moved stiffly on my chair, leaning forward, resting my elbows on the table, taking shallow breaths. Body management, learned fast.

At the police station the previous afternoon Inspector Vernon had told me that Ivan's car (the wheels I'd driven to the party) had been identified by Mrs Benchmark and towed by the police and was, in fact, at that moment right outside in the station's car park.

'Can I take it?' I asked, surprised.

'If you think you're fit to drive.'

I had the car keys, among other things, in my restored trousers pocket.

Fit or not, I drove the car to Lambourn, found Emily's spare house key on its old familiar nail in the tack room, made inroads into her whisky and spent a disturbed night lying on my side in my clothes on the sofa in her drawing-room, lacking energy for anything else, feeling shivery and sick.

In the morning I'd made it upstairs to the bathroom, found a throw-away razor, combed my hair and rinsed my mouth. Well, I told myself, my physical state was my own stubborn fault: just put up with it. Swallow the tablets and be grateful for mercies.

I phoned Chris who said he'd been trying without success to reach my mobile number.

'The phone's in the car,' I said. 'I expect the battery's flat.'

'For hell's sake, charge it.'

'Yes.'

'Are you all right, Al? And where are you?'

'Lambourn. Could you drive to Paignton and then come here?'

'Today? Bring all three ladies?'

'If you can. I'll phone the hotel.'

'Chauffeur's togs coming up. Zipped bag nine.'

We disconnected on a smile. I phoned the Redcliffe and left messages for Emily and my mother. Then I retrieved the Quorn list from the back of the golf picture and drove to Reading.

By lunchtime the experts had got nowhere nearer the end of the rainbow.

They sent out for sandwiches, and we drank more coffee.

'The trouble is,' the bank man explained to me, 'that we have here three lots of variables. We have to match the account numbers on the list with a name on the list and with a bank identification number that we already have, and then we have to send that combination to the bank in question and hope to get a response from them to acknowledge that that account exists. We haven't so far been able to do that. The nearest we have come is matching one of the account numbers to one of the banks, but we supplied the wrong name for the account, and the bank told us by return fax, just now, that as our enquiry is incomplete, they cannot answer it. No one is being helpful. On top of that, the account numbers are the wrong way round.'

I said, 'How do you mean, the wrong way round?'

'All the numbers on the list end with two zeros. As a rule account numbers *begin* with two zeros. We have tried reversing the numbers, so far without success. I am still sure that all of the numbers have been reversed, but if Quorn jumbled them up further, or multiplied by two, for instance, we are in real trouble.'

Tobias and Margaret nodded in depression.

Tobias said, 'Quorn may have sent the money on a circular route involving all of these numbers – like the beach towels on the poolside chairs – or he may have sent it direct from Panama to any one place, but so far we haven't found a single trace of it. I have been working on the belief that one of these numbers or names must mean something to the Global Bank in Panama, but they will not admit it.'

'All banks are secretive,' the big bank man said. 'And so are we.'

'Don't despair,' Margaret said, 'we'll find the money. It's just taking longer than we hoped.'

By the end of the afternoon, however, they themselves were looking cast down; they said they would think of a new strategy for the next day. The time change alone was making things difficult. It was already mid-afternoon in Reading when the bank in Panama opened for business.

They carefully shredded every scrap of used fax and working paper and locked Norman Quorn's list into the manager's private safe. I drove a shade dispiritedly back to Lambourn and found that Emily, my mother and Audrey Newton had arrived a bare five minutes before me.

C. Y. Uttley was busy unloading suitcases from the boot.

I gave my mother a minimum hug, kissed Emily and planted an air kiss beside Audrey Newton's buxom cheek.

'We've had a lovely weekend,' she said, beaming. 'Thank you ever so much. You've bruised your face, dear, did you know?'

'Walked into a door.'

Emily took Audrey and my mother into the house and Chris gave me an assessing inspection.

'You look lousy,' he said. 'Worse than Sunday.'

'Thanks.'

'Your bus-stealing Grantchester-immobilising friend

no longer exists,' he assured me. 'I dumped her today, bit by bit, in a succession of wheelybins on my way to Devon.'

'So wise.'

'How do blonde bubble curls and D-cup knockers grab you?'

'I wouldn't be seen dead with her.'

'At least the lawyer didn't cauterise your sense of humour.'

'A close-run thing.'

'Do you want anything else done?'

'Just take Audrey Newton home to Bloxham.'

'After that?'

We stared at each other.

'A friend for life,' I suggested.

'I'll send my bill.'

Emily proposed that my mother and I stay the night in Lambourn and met with little resistance.

The telephone rang in the kitchen while we were sitting round the big table watching Emily search for supper in the freezer. Emily picked up the receiver and in a moment said with surprise, 'Yes, he's here. So is Vivienne.' She held out the receiver in my direction. 'It's Himself. He's been looking for you.'

I took the instrument and said, 'My lord.'

'Al, where have you been? I've had Patsy on the line all day. She sounds practically hysterical. She wants to talk to you. She says you signed yourself out of some hospital she put you in. She won't tell me why she put you in hospital. What the hell's happened?'

'Er . . . I ran out of wall.'

'Al, talk sense.'

My mother and Emily could both hear what I said. I thought through five seconds of silence and said, 'Can I come for a drink with you at about six tomorrow evening?'

'Of course.'

'Well . . . please don't tell Patsy where I am. Ask her if she'll meet me at two o'clock tomorrow afternoon in the car park of the brewery's bank's head office in Reading. And tell her . . .' I paused. 'Tell her thanks for the help.'

Emily said, astounded, as I put the phone down, 'Patsy *helped* you?'

'Mm.'

They would have to know, so I told them as unemotionally as possible that Oliver Grantchester had been trying to lay his hands on the brewery's missing millions. 'He had either conspired with Norman Quorn to steal the money in the first place, or tried to wrest it from him afterwards,' I said. 'I'm not yet sure which.'

'Not *Oliver*!' my mother protested in total disbelief. 'We've known him for years. He's always been Ivan's solicitor, and the brewery's too . . .' her voice faded. 'Ivan trusted him.'

I said, 'Ivan trusted Norman Quorn. Quorn and

Grantchester . . . they were two normal men, good at their jobs, but fatally attracted by what looked like an easy path to a bucket of gold – and I'm not talking about the literal bucket of gold, the King Alfred Gold Cup, which Grantchester thought he could lay his hands on as a consolation when the serious prize slipped through his fingers. Grantchester may have been a good lawyer but he's an inefficient crook. He hasn't got the Gold Cup and he hasn't got the brewery's money, and Patsy has woken up to the fact that her dear darling avuncular Oliver had been trying his damnedest to rob *her*, as she now owns the brewery complete with its losses.'

My mother had her own concern, 'You didn't really walk into a door, did you, Alexander?'

I smiled. 'I walked into Grantchester's fist man. You'd think I'd know better.'

'And no one took hostages,' Emily said thoughtfully, with much understanding.

We went to bed. Emily expected and invited me between her sheets, but I simply had no stamina left for the oldest of games.

She asked what was under the bandages that was making me sweat.

'The wages of pride,' I said. 'Go to sleep.'

I drove my mother to Reading in the morning and saw her onto the London train, promising to spend the evening and night in Park Crescent after my six o'clock date with Himself.

Frail from grief, my calm and exquisite parent showed me in a single trembling hug on the railway platform how close we both were to being stretched too far. I understood suddenly that it was from her I had learned the way to hide fear and pain and humiliation, and that if I'd extended that ability into material things like hilts and chalices and dynamite lists, it had been because of her ultra-controlled outer face that I had all my life taken to be an absence – or at least a deficiency – of emotion.

'Ma,' I said on Reading station, 'I adore you.'

The train came, quiet and rapid, slowing to whisk her away.

'Alexander,' she said, 'don't be ridiculous.'

In the bank Tobias, Margaret and the big financial cheese were gloomily studying the electronic messages on the one machine they had left alive to receive them overnight.

Useful information from around the globe: zero.

The experts had drawn up ways of approaching the problem from so far untried angles, but nothing worked. By lunchtime they were saying they couldn't dedicate more than that afternoon to the search, as they had other unbreakable commitments ahead.

When I asked if I could bring Patsy to the afternoon

session they said I could do anything I liked but Tobias, chewing hard on a toothpick, asked if I remembered what had happened to me four days ago, on the one time I'd believed in her good faith.

I was leaning forward, elbows on table, the morning's pills wearing off. I remembered, I said, and I would rely on Tobe to defend me from the maiden.

I could joke, he said, but I should also remember the sirens whose seductive songs lured foolish sailors to shipwreck and death.

Not in this bank, I said.

I met her in the car park, as arranged.

'Hello,' I said.

'Alexander . . .'

She was unsure of herself. Awkward. I'd never seen her like that.

She wore a shirt, a cardigan, long skirt, flat shoes: wholesome, well-groomed.

I explained that she should come into the bank with me and listen to the difficulties that had arisen in finding the brewery's millions.

For someone whose main fears for twelve years or so had been that I would somehow manage to rob her, she seemed less than anxious about the success of the search.

'I promise you,' I said, 'they are trying everything they know to find your money.'

'My father's money,' she said. 'Everything you have done was for him, wasn't it?'

'I suppose so.'

'You would never have done it for *me*.'

I said, 'His whole life was the brewery. He built it up. It was his pride. The heartless betrayal of Norman Quorn devastated him, and yes, I believe it killed him. And for his sake, and for my mother's sake I would have done anything to put things right. I've tried. I haven't managed it. I want the bank people to tell you that I am not trying to steal from you. I am trying to restore what Ivan built.'

'Alexander . . .'

'I did believe on Saturday,' I said, 'that you were sincerely offering a truce. I hope you didn't know exactly what you were beckoning me into. I know you tried to stop that little lark with the barbecue . . . I could hear you. I know you got me help. Anyway,' I finished, running out of impetus, 'will you come into the bank?'

She nodded speechlessly and went with me into the conference room, where of course her looks and natural charm immediately enslaved the bank man who hadn't encountered her before. He fussed over a chair for her and offered her coffee, and she smiled at him sweetly, as she could.

We all sat down round the table. The bank man obligingly outlined all the measures so far taken to keep the brewery alive, and he explained that they were trying to find the missing millions by using the list.

'That list!' she murmured. 'What's on that list?'

'Don't let her see it,' Tobe said abruptly.

The bank man asked, 'Why ever not?'

'Because of what it cost to bring it here. Al may sit at this table with us hour after hour pretending there's nothing the matter, but he's halfway to fainting most of the time . . .'

'No,' I objected.

'Yeah, yeah.' He waved his toothpick in my direction. 'It was Oliver Grantchester, I'll bet you, who got Patsy to offer you a truce and to inveigle you into that garden. He may be in the lock-up at this moment, but he'll get out sometime, and he may know a way of using this list that we haven't fathomed, and he may have told her what to look for, so don't let her see it.'

There was an intense silence.

Patsy slowly stood up.

'Oliver used me,' she said. 'You are right. It's not easy to admit it.' She swallowed. 'I didn't know anything about any list before Oliver tried to make Alexander give it to him. Don't show it to me. I don't want to see it.' She looked directly at me, and said, 'I'm sorry.'

I stood up also. She gave me a long look, and a nod, and went away.

At the end of the afternoon that produced nothing but baffling frustration I drove back to London and Chesham Place and told my uncle, over a tumblerful of single malt, that three clever financial brains had spent two whole working days trying to make sense of Norman Quorn's list of bank accounts, and failing.

'They'll succeed tomorrow,' he said encouragingly.

I shook my head. 'They've given up. They've got other things they have to do.'

'You've done your best, Al.'

I was sitting forward, forearms on knees, holding my glass with both hands, trying not to sound as spent as I felt. I told him about Patsy's visit to the bank and about her understanding of Oliver Grantchester's intention of robbing the brewery. 'But between them,' I said, 'he and Norman Quorn have fumbled the ball. The millions are lost. I'm glad Ivan didn't know.'

After a while Himself asked, 'What were you doing in hospital? Patsy wouldn't tell me.'

'Sleeping, mostly.'

'Al!'

'Well . . . it was Grantchester who sent the thugs to the bothy, thinking you'd given me the King Alfred Gold Cup to look after. He didn't tell them exactly what they were looking for, I suppose because he was afraid they would steal it for themselves if they knew how valuable it was. Anyway, when he found out I had that damned list, that has proved useless, he got the same thugs to persuade me to hand it over, but I still didn't like them – or him – so I didn't.'

He looked aghast.

'Some of my ribs are cracked. Grantchester's in a police hospital ward. Patsy and I may come to that truce in the end. You're making me drunk.'

My mother and I ate an Edna-cooked dinner and afterwards played Scrabble.

My mother won.

I took a pill at bedtime and stayed asleep for hours, and was astounded to meet Keith Robbiston on the stairs when I dawdled on my way down to breakfast.

'Come in here,' he said, pointing me into Ivan's lifeless study. 'Your uncle and your mother are both worried about you.'

I said, 'Why?'

'Your mother said she beat you at Scrabble and your uncle says you're not telling him the whole truth.' He studied my face, from which the swelling and bruises had largely faded, but which did, as I had to acknowledge, show grey fatigue and strain. 'You didn't tell either of them about any burns.'

'They worry too much.'

'So where are these burns?'

I took off my shirt, and he unwound the bandages. His silence, I thought, was ominous.

'They told me,' I said, 'that there wasn't any sign of infection, and that I would heal OK.'

'Well, yes.'

He got from me the name of the hospital and on

Ivan's phone traced the grandmotherly doctor. He listened to her for quite a long time, staring at me throughout, his gaze slowly intensifying and darkening. 'Thank you,' he said eventually. 'Thank you very much.'

'Don't tell my mother,' I begged him. 'It's too soon after Ivan.'

'All right.'

He said he would not disturb the synthetic skin dressings, and re-wrapped the damage from armpits to waist.

'They gave you several injections of morphine in the hosptal,' he said. 'And those pills I've given you, they too contain morphine.'

'I thought they were pretty strong.'

'You'll get addicted, Al. And I'm not being funny.'

'I'll deal with that later.'

He gave me enough pills for another four days. I thanked him, and meant it.

'Don't take more than you can help. And driving a car,' he observed, 'is only making things worse.'

I phoned Tobe's office and didn't get him. He had gone away for the weekend.

'But it's only Thursday,' I protested.

He would probably be back on Monday.

God damn him, I thought.

Margaret was 'unavailable'.

The big bank cheese had left me a message. 'All the King Alfred Gold Cup race expenses will be honoured by the bank, working closely with Mrs Benchmark who is now organising everything for the day at Cheltenham.'

Bully for Patsy. Big cheeses were putty in her hands.

I drifted through a quiet morning and companionable lunch with my mother and in the afternoon drove to Lambourn, arriving in the hour of maximum bustle; evening stables.

Emily, in her natural element, walked confidently around her yard in her usual fawn cavalry twill trousers, neat and businesslike, instructing the lads, feeling horses' legs, patting necks and rumps, offering treats of carrots, delivering messages of positive love to the powerful shining creatures that rubbed their noses against her in response.

I watched her for some time before she realised I was there, and I vividly understood again how comprehensively she belonged in that life, and how essential it was to her mind's well-being.

While I was still sitting in Ivan's car, a horsebox drove into the yard and unloaded Golden Malt.

He came out forwards, muscles quivering, hooves placed delicately on the ramp as he sought for secure footing, the whole process jerky and precarious: once out, he moved with liquid perfection, his feet on springs, his chestnut coat like fire in the evening sun, the arrogance of great thoroughbreds in every toss of his head.

Impossible not to be moved. He had twice let me lead him into misty unknown distances, taking me on faith. Looking at his splendid homecoming, I didn't know how I'd dared.

I stood up out of the car. Emily, seeing me, came to stand beside me, and together we watched the horse being led a few times round the yard to loosen his leg muscles after the confines of his journey.

'He looks great,' I said.

Emily nodded. 'The short change of scene suited him.'

'And Saturday?'

'He won't disgrace himself.' Her words were judicious, but trembled with the hard-to-control excitement of any trainer who felt there was a chance of winning a big race.

We went into the house where it proved impossible for her to do anything as ordinary as cooking dinner. I hadn't the energy, either.

We ate bread and cheese.

At ten o'clock she went out into her stable yard, as she was accustomed, to check that all her charges were happily settled for the night. I followed her and stood irresolutely in the yard looking up at the stars and the rising moon.

'Em,' I said, as she came towards me, 'will you lend me a horse?'

'What horse?' she asked, puzzled.

'Any.'

'But . . . what for?'

'I want . . .' How could I explain it? 'I want to go up onto the Downs . . . to be alone.'

'*Now?*'

I nodded.

'Even for you,' she said, 'you've been very silent this evening.'

'Things need thinking out,' I said.

'And it's a matter of the hundred and twenty-first psalm?'

'What?'

'I will lift up mine eyes unto the hills,' she said, 'from whence cometh my help.'

'*Em.*'

'And the Downs will have to do, instead of your mountains.'

Her understanding took my voice away entirely.

Without questions, without arguing, she went across to the tack room and reappeared with a saddle and a bridle. Then she crossed to one of the boxes in the yard and switched on its internal light.

I joined her there.

'This is one of Ivan's other horses. He's not much good, but he's a friendly old fellow. I suppose he's mine now . . . and as you're Ivan's executor, you've every right to ride him . . . but don't let him get loose if you can help it.'

'No.'

She saddled the horse expertly, pulling the girth tight.

'Wait,' she said, and made a fast detour back to the house, returning with the blue crash helmet and a padded jacket. Looking at my cotton shirt, she said, 'It'll be cold up there.'

She held the jacket for me to put on. Even though she was careful, it hurt.

'Oliver Grantchester can burn in hell,' she said.

'Em . . . how do you know?'

'Margaret Morden phoned me today to ask how you were feeling. She told me. She thought I knew.'

She bridled up the horse and unemotionally gave me a leg-up onto his back. She offered me the helmet, but made no fuss when I shook my head. She knew I preferred free air, and I was not going out to gallop.

'Thanks, Em,' I said.

She understood that it was a comprehensive sort of gratitude.

'Get going,' she said.

King Alfred, I thought, had perhaps sat on a horse on the exact place where I'd reined to a halt after a slow walk uphill from Lambourn.

I was on one of the highest points of the Downs, looking east to the valleys where the uplands slid away towards the Thames, that hadn't been a grand waterway in Alfred's lifetime, more a long winding drainage system from the Cotswolds to the North Sea.

King Alfred had been a scholar, a negotiator, a poet, a warrior, a strategist, a historian, an educator, a law-giver. I wished a fraction of him could be inhaled to give me wisdom, but he had ridden this land eleven hundred and more years ago, when villainy wore its selfsame face but nothing much else was familiar.

It was odd to reflect that it was, of all things, *ale* that was least changed. The brewery named for the king still flowed with the drink that had sustained and comforted his people.

Ivan's horse walked onwards, plodding slowly, going nowhere under my aimless direction.

The clear sky and weak moonlight were millions of years old. Chill threads of the earth's wind moved in my hair. The perspective of time could cool any fever if one gave it a chance.

One could learn, perhaps, that failure was bearable: make peace with the certainty that all wasn't enough.

I came to the long fallen tree trunk that many trainers on the Downs made use of to give young horses an introduction to jumping. I slid off Ivan's horse to let him rest and sat on the log, holding the reins loosely while the horse bent his head unexcitedly to graze. His presence was in its own way a balm, an undemanding kinship with the natural ancient world.

I had caused in myself more pain than I really knew

how to deal with, and the fact that it had been for nothing had to be faced.

It was five days now since I'd been dragged into Grantchester's garden. Five days since the thug called Jazzo, with his boxing gloves and his well-trained technique, had cracked my ribs and hit me with such force that I flinched from the memory as sorely as I still ached in places. I hadn't been able to dodge or in any way defend myself, and the helplessness had only added to the burden.

I could call him a bastard.

Bastard.

It didn't make anything better. Cracked ribs were like daggers stabbing at every movement. Much better not to cough.

As for the grill . . .

I looked out over the quiet age of the Downs.

Even with the pills, I was spending too long on the absolute edge of normal behaviour. I didn't want to retreat to a drugged inertia while my skin grew back, but it was an option with terrible temptations. I wanted not oblivion but fortitude. More fortitude than I found easy.

The horse scrunched and munched, the bit clinking.

What I had done had been irrational.

I should have told Grantchester where to find the list.

There was no saying, of course, that even if I'd told

him the minute I'd set foot in his garden, he would have let me walk out of there untouched. I had seen the sickening enjoyment in his face ... I'd heard from Bernie's confession to the police that Grantchester had burned Norman Quorn even though the frantic Finance Director would have told him anything to escape the fire. Grantchester's pleasure in prolonging Quorn's agony had directly led to Quorn's sudden death ... from heart failure, from stroke or from shock; one or another. Grantchester's pleasure had in itself denied him the knowledge he sought. The only bright outcome of the whole mess.

Poor Norman Quorn, non-violent embezzler, had been sixty-five and frightened.

I'd been twenty-nine ... and frightened ... and irrational ... and I'd been let off in time not to die.

I'd been let off with multiple bars of first, second and third degree burns, that would heal.

I'd been let off in time to know that burning had been a gesture for nothing, because whatever information Norman Quorn had entrusted to his sister in that benighted envelope, it hadn't turned out to be an indication of what he'd done with the brewery's money.

I could admit to myself that I'd burned from pride.

Harder to accept that it had been pointless.

Essential to accept that it had been pointless, and to go on from there.

I stood up stiffly and walked for a while, leading the horse.

If I'd been in Scotland I would have gone up into the mountains and let the wild pipes skirl out the raw sorrow, as they always had in turbulent history. Yet . . . would a lament be enough? A pibroch would cry for the wounded man but I needed more – I needed something tougher. Something to tell me, well OK, too bad, don't whine, you did it to yourself. Get out the paints.

When I went back to the mountains, I would play a march.

I rode for a while and walked by turns through the consoling night, and when the first grey seeped into the dark sky I turned the horse westwards and let him amble that way until we came to landmarks we both recognised as the right way home.

CHAPTER FIFTEEN

Friday morning, Lambourn, Emily's house.

I telephoned Margaret Morden.

No, she said, no one had thought of any new way of finding the money. The list, if it held the secret, had humbled them so far, but . . .

'It was a false hope,' I said. 'Useless. Forget it. Give it up.'

'Don't talk like that!'

'It's all right. Truly. Will you come to the races?'

'If you want me . . .'

'Of course we want you. Without you, there would be no race.'

'Without *you.*'

'We're brilliant,' I said, laughing, 'but no one will give us our due.'

'You do sound better.'

'I promise you, I'm fine.'

I was floating on a recent pill. Well, one had to, sometimes.

Inspector Vernon telephoned. 'Oliver Grantchester,' he said.

'What about him?'

'Someone viciously assaulted him last Saturday, in his garage . . . as you know.'

'The poor fellow.'

'Was it your girlfriend who kicked hell out of him?'

'Inspector,' I said reasonably, 'I was lying in that pond. How could I know?'

'She might have told you who did it.'

'No, she didn't – and, anyway, I don't repeat what I'm told.'

After a moment he said, 'Fair enough.'

I smiled. He could hear it in my voice. 'I do hope,' I said, 'that poor Mr Grantchester is still in a bad way.'

'I can tell you, off the record,' he said austerely, 'that the testicular damage inflicted on Mr Grantchester was of a severity that involved irreparable rupture and . . . er . . . surgical removal.'

'What a shame,' I said happily.

'Mr Kinloch!'

'My friend has gone abroad, and she won't be back,' I said. 'Don't bother looking. She wouldn't have attacked anyone, I'm sure.'

Vernon didn't sound convinced, but apart from no witnesses, it seemed he had no factual clues. The unknown assailant seemed to be getting away with it.

'How awful,' I said.

I supposed that, when Chris found out, the gelding

of Oliver Grantchester would cost me extra. Money well spent.

I said to Vernon, 'Give Grantchester my best regards for a falsetto future.'

'That's heartless.'

'You don't say.'

I slept on the pill for three or four hours. Out in the yard life bustled along in the same old way, and by lunchtime I found myself falling into the same old role of general dogsbody, 'popping' down to the village for such-and-such, ferrying blood samples to the vet's office, collecting tack from repair.

Emily and I ate dinner together and went to bed together, and even though this time I easily raised the necessary enthusiasm, she lay in my arms afterwards and told me it broke her heart.

'What does?' I asked.

'Seeing you try to be a husband.'

'But I am . . .'

'No.' She kissed my shoulder above the bandages. 'You know you don't belong here. Just come back sometimes. That'll do.'

Patsy had organised the race day. Patsy had consulted with the tent-erectors and caterers who were out to please. At Patsy's command, the hundred or so commercial guests – creditors, suppliers, landlords of tied houses – were given a big welcome, unlimited drinks, free racecards, tickets to every enclosure, press-release photographs, lunch, tea.

Cheltenham's racecourse, always forward-looking, had extended to King Alfred's brewery, in Ivan's memory, every red-carpet courtesy they could give to the chief sponsor of one of their top crowd-pulling early-season afternoons. Patsy had the whole race-course executive committee tumbling over themselves to please her. Patsy's social gifts were priceless.

To Patsy had been allocated the Sponsors' Box in the grandstand, next best thing to the plushed-up suite designed for crowned heads and other princes.

Patsy had organised, in the Sponsors' Box, a private family lunch for my mother, her stepmother, so that Ivan's widow could be both present and apart.

Having met my mother at the Club entrance, I walked with her to the Sponsors' Box. Patsy faultlessly welcomed her with kisses. Patsy was dressed in dark grey, in mourning for her father but with a bright Hermès silk scarf round her neck. She looked grave, businesslike, and in full control of the day.

Behind her stood Surtees, who would not meet my eyes. Surtees shifted from foot to foot, gave my mother a desultory peck on the cheek, and altogether behaved as if he wished he weren't there.

'Hello, Surtees,' I said, to be annoying.

He gave me a silent, frustrated look, and took two paces backwards. What a grand change, I thought, from days gone by.

Patsy gave us both a puzzled look, and at one point later in the afternoon said, 'What have you said to Surtees? He won't talk about you at all. If I mention you he finds some reason for leaving the room, I don't understand it.'

'Surtees and I,' I said, 'have come to an understanding. He keeps his mouth shut, and so do I.'

'What about?'

'On my side about his behaviour in Oliver Grantchester's garden.'

'He didn't really mean what he said.'

I clearly remembered Surtees urging Jazzo to hit me harder, when Jazzo was already hitting me as hard as he could. Surtees had meant it, all right: his revenge for my making him look foolish in Emily's yard.

I said, 'For quite a while I believed it was Surtees who sent those thugs to my house in Scotland, to find the King Alfred Gold Cup.'

It shook her. 'But why?'

'Because he said, "Next time you'll scream".'

Her eyes darkened. She said slowly, 'He was wrong about that.'

I shrugged. 'You were telling everyone that I'd stolen the Cup. Surtees, of course, believed it.'

'You wouldn't steal.'

I listened to the certainty in her voice, and asked, trying to suppress bitterness, 'How long have you known that?'

Obliquely she told me the truth, opening to my

understanding her own long years of unhappy fear. She said, 'He would have given you anything you asked for.'

'Ivan?'

She nodded.

I said, 'I would never have taken anything that was yours.'

'I thought you would.' She paused. 'I did hate you.'

She made no more admissions, nor any excuses, but in the garden she had called me her brother, and in the bank she had said, 'I'm sorry.' Perhaps, just perhaps, things had really changed.

'I suppose,' she began, 'that it's too late . . .' She left the sentence unfinished, but it was a statement of acceptance, not a plea.

'Call it quits,' I said, 'if you like.'

When Himself and his countess arrived to keep my mother company, I went down to find out how things were going in the hospitality tent, and found that the mood, in spite of the brewery's troubles, was up-beat, alcoholic and forgiving.

Margaret Morden greeted me with the sort of embrace that would have been over the top in any office but seemed appropriate to the abandon of a race day. Dressed in soft blue, with a reliable-looking husband by her side, she said she knew nothing about horses but would back Golden Malt.

She followed my gaze across the tent to where Patsy,

flanked not by Surtees but by the perfect lieutenant, Desmond Finch, was encouraging everyone's future.

'You know,' I said to Margaret, 'Patsy will make a great success of running the brewery. She's a born manager. Better than her father. He was conscientious and a good man. She can bend and manipulate people to achieve her own ends . . . and I'd guess she'll lug the brewery out of the threat of bankruptcy faster than you can imagine.'

'How can you *possibly* forgive her?'

'I didn't say I forgave her. I said she would be a good manager.'

'It was in your voice.'

I smiled into the clever eyes. 'Find out for me,' I said, 'whether Oliver Grantchester suggested the embezzlement, or just stumbled across it and muscled in. Not that it really matters, I just wonder, that's all.'

'I can tell you now. It was Grantchester's idea all along. Then Norman Quorn did some fancy footwork to keep the loot himself, and misjudged the strength and cruelty of his partner.'

'How do you know?' I asked entranced.

'That weasel Desmond Finch told me. I leaned on him the tiniest bit. I said that as deputy managing director he should have spotted irregularities in the finance department, and he fell over himself to tell me that Norman Quorn had practically cried on his shoulder. I think – and to be honest I don't see how we can prove it unless Grantchester confesses, which I can't see him doing . . .'

'He's not the man he used to be,' I murmured.

'I think,' Margaret said, not hearing, or at least not understanding, 'that Norman Quorn must have said in all good faith to Ivan's trusted friend and lawyer Oliver, how easy it would be in these days of electronic transfers to make oneself seriously rich. I think they worked it out together, maybe even as an academic exercise to begin with, and then, when the trial run succeeded, they did it in earnest, and then Quorn tried at the last minute to back out.'

'He did steal the money,' I said flatly. 'He tried to cut his partner out.'

She agreed bleakly. 'They both did.'

We drank champagne. Sweetish. Patsy was no spendthrift fool.

I sighed. 'I wish Tobe could have been here today,' I said.

Margaret hesitated. 'He couldn't bear that we hadn't been able to find the money with that list, when you suffered so much to bring it to us.'

'Tell him not to be so soft.'

She bent forward and unexpectedly kissed my cheek. 'Soft,' she said, 'is the last word I would apply to Alexander Kinloch.'

*

Himself and I, as two of the executors in whose name the horse was running, stood by the saddling boxes and watched Emily fasten the racing-size saddle onto Golden Malt.

Himself said to me conversationally, 'Word gets around, you know.'

'What word?'

'What Oliver Grantchester put you through in his garden.'

'Forget it.'

'If you say so. But it is rippling outward, and you can't stop it.'

(He was right to the extent that a short while later I got a postcard from young Andrew at his prep school. 'Is it true you were lying fully clothed in a goldfish pond one cold night in October?' – and I sent him back a single-word answer, 'Yes.')

Mad, weird Alexander. Who cared? Some have weirdness thrust upon them.

'Al,' Himself said, 'would you have burned for the Kinloch hilt?'

'It wasn't for the list,' I said.

He smiled. He knew. He was the one person who wholly understood.

We stood in the parade ring with Emily, watching Golden Malt stride round, led by his lad.

Emily's jockey joined us, dressed in Ivan's racing colours of gold, green checks, gold cap.

Emily was all business, no excitement obvious, a shortness of breath the only sign. She told the jockey to be handy in fourth place all the way, if he could, and make his move only after he'd rounded the last bend and straightened up for the uphill run to the winning post.

'Don't forget,' she said, 'that he won't accelerate on a curve. Wait, even though it hurts. He'll deliver if you do. He's a great fighter uphill.'

When the horses had gone out onto the track, Himself, Emily and I joined my mother up in the Sponsors' Box.

My mother, in the black clothes she had worn to Ivan's funeral, and the black sweeping hat with the white rose, gazed out over the autumnal racecourse and yearned for her lost consort, for the steadfast man of no great fire who had been all she needed as a companion.

It was Ivan's race. Ivan's day. Nothing would comfort her.

Patsy arrived, with Surtees. Patsy's manner to her husband was impatient: she was looking at him with the fresh cold eyes of disillusion. I would give that marriage another year at most, I thought. The Surtees looks wouldn't for ever make up for the void inside.

Golden Malt looked splendid on the turf, but he

faced no easy task: the generous money prize alongside the prestige of taking home the King Alfred Gold Cup, even in replica, had drawn out the best. Of the nine provenly fast steeplechasers lining up, Golden Malt was generally counted only fourth or fifth in the hierarchy.

White knuckle time. Emily watched the start through race-glasses without trembling. Probably no one else in the box could have managed it. Emily stood rock still for nearly all of the two miles.

It was one of those races at Cheltenham when neither the fences nor the undulating curves sorted the runners out into a straggling line: all nine runners went round in a bunch, no one fell, the crowd on the grandstands yelled and drowned out the commentator, and Golden Malt came round the last bend in close fourth place and headed for glory up the hill.

Emily put down her race-glasses and breathlessly watched.

Himself was shouting with powerful lungs. My mother clasped her hands over her heart.

Patsy murmured, 'Oh, come *on* . . .'

Three horses crossed the line together.

One couldn't tell by eye which head had nodded forward. We all went down to the unsaddling area for first, second and third, and none of the little group could disguise the agony of the wait for the photograph.

When the result came it was in the impersonal voice of the course announcer.

'First, number five.'

Number five: Golden Malt.

There was a lot of kissing. Patsy gave me an uncomplicated smile, with no acid. Emily's eyes outshone the stars.

Patsy had ordained that the trophy should be presented to the winning owner by my mother, as Ivan's wife; so it happened that at the ceremony my mother presented the replica of the King Alfred Gold Cup to Emily, to universal cheers and a blaze of flashing cameras.

Ivan would have loved it.

When my mother and I were placidly breakfasting and reading congratulatory newspapers, my uncle Robert telephoned with a full-head of steam.

'Whatever you're doing, stop doing it. I've had Jed on the line. He is more or less foaming at the mouth. The conservationists have invaded the bothy with spades and pickaxes and metal detectors, and are tearing everything apart. He has told them they are trespassing, but it makes no difference, they won't go away, and Zoë Lang is there, with the light of battle in her eyes as if she were on a crusade.'

'Does Jed mean they are there now?'

'Indeed he does,' he said. 'They intend to stay all day and they are digging up all the ground round the bothy. He begs me to fly up there at once.'

'Do you want me to come with you?'

'Of course I do,' he bellowed. 'Meet me at Heathrow, terminal one, as soon as you can.'

I explained to my mother that I would have to go. Resignedly, she told me to finish my toast.

I laughed and hugged her, and found a taxi which would go to Heathrow on a Sunday morning.

Himself was striding up and down, an awesome sight. We caught a flight to Edinburgh where we were met by the helicopter pilot who had risked the bothy's plateau once before.

Our arrival alarmed the crowd at the bothy who scattered outwards like ants under an insect-killing spray. When the rotor stopped, the ants came back, led by Jed but with Zoë Lang close on his heels.

'How dare you?' Himself thundered to the fanatical lady.

She straightened, as if she would add inches to her stature. 'This bothy,' she insisted, 'was given to the nation with the castle.'

'It certainly was not,' my uncle said furiously. 'It comes under the heading of my private apartment.'

Behind both of their backs, Jed raised his eyebrows to heaven.

No doubt the courts would decide, I thought, but meanwhile the conservationists were making almost as much mess of my home as the four thugs had done in the first place. There were holes in the ground everywhere. Beside each hole lay a little heap of empty Coke cans and other metal debris.

In the ruined section of bothy that housed the rubbish bins, the corner that held the old bread oven had been excavated to a depth of three feet and the oven left belly up. At the carport end, the earth had more or less been ploughed, revealing old spanners and ancient pieces of iron machinery.

Staggered by the extent of the ruthless search, I left Himself arguing with Zoë Lang and went into my home to see what damage had been done inside.

To my surprise and relief, very little. Jed had brought back my pipes. The place looked tidy. The picture, wrapped in its sheet, stood on the easel. It seemed the searchers had left the core of the search until last.

I went out to protest to Zoë Lang about the work of her fanatical friends, about ten of whom were still digging holes in every direction, but as I approached her my mobile phone, which I by now carried around out of habit, buzzed weakly in my hand, demanding attention.

Because of the bad reception in the mountains, and the whining noise of the metal detectors and yelling all around of the conservationists, I could hear nothing in the receiver but a crackle, with the faintest of voices in the background.

To obliterate at least some of the noise, I carried the mobile phone into the bothy and closed the door.

I said loudly into the receiver, 'Whoever you are, shout.'

I heard an earful of crackle, and one word, 'Tobias.'

I shouted, unbelieving, 'Tobias?'

Crackle.

His faint voice said, 'I've found it.'

Another load of static.

His voice said again, 'Al, I've found the money.'

I couldn't believe it. His voice said, 'Are you there?'

I bellowed, 'Yes. Where are you?'

Crackle. Crackle. 'In Bogota. In Columbia.'

I still couldn't believe it. There was a sudden clearing of the static and I could hear his voice plainly. 'The money is all here. I found it by accident. The account here had three names on it, not just one or two. A person's name and two corporate names. I put them all on an application form by mistake, and it was like pressing a button, a door opened, and they are asking for my onward directions. The money will be back in Reading next week.'

'I can't believe it. I thought you went away for the weekend.'

He laughed. 'I went to Panama. We were getting nowhere electronically. I went to bang a fist . . . and the trail led to Bogota.'

'Tobe . . .'

'See you soon,' he said.

The crackle came back. I switched off the telephone

and felt my knees weakening as in the phrase 'weak at the knees' which I had never believed in before.

After a while I took the wrapping sheet off the picture, and even to me the force of it filled the small room.

I had thought I would need time's perspective to know what I'd done, but the power of the concept seemed to have taken over and made me its instrument. The picture might not comfort, but one wouldn't forget it.

During the past few weeks I had painted that picture, the brewery's money had been found, and I'd discovered how far – how deep – I could go into myself.

I had met Tobe and Margaret and Chris.

I'd slept again with Emily and would stay married for as long as she wanted.

I had come to a compact with Patsy.

There wasn't a great deal I would undo.

Shakily, I went out of the bothy and walked on the weak knees to where Himself and Zoë Lang were gesticulating in each other's air-space with none too gentlemanly fury.

Himself stopped abruptly, alerted by whatever he saw in my face.

'What is it?' he said.

'The money is found.'

'What money?' Zoë Lang demanded.

Himself didn't answer her. He stared at me alone

with the realisation that what had been paid for had been miraculously delivered.

Zoë Lang, thinking that I had found some treasure or other within the bothy, strode off in that direction and disappeared inside.

'Tobias found the money in Bogota,' I said.

'Using the list?'

'Yes.'

Himself's rejoicing was like my own; unexpressed except in the eyes, a matter of central warmth rather than triumphal whoops.

'Prince Charles Edward's hilt,' he said, 'is irrelevant.'

We looked around at the determined searchers. None of them was now metal-detecting in the right place, but they might succeed if they went on long enough. The prize had been within their reach: they had dug quite near it.

I thought ruefully that this lot wouldn't burn me to make me tell them where to look. Zoë Lang wouldn't strike a match. I wouldn't have wanted her to be Grantchester.

'Will they find it, Al?' my uncle asked.

'Would you mind it very much?'

'Of course I would. That woman would crow.'

I said, 'If she perseveres long enough . . . she will.'

'No, Al,' he protested.

'When I hid it,' I said, 'it was from burglars, not from a zealot with a mission. When her cohorts give up, that's when she'll start thinking. Up until now, I'd guess she believes she's dealing with simple minds, yours and mine. She suffers from the arrogance of the very brainy. She doesn't expect anyone to keep up with her on level terms.'

'Your mind is far from simple.'

'She doesn't know that. And my mind is simpler than hers. She will find the hilt. We could go away and not watch her gloat.'

'Leave the battlefield?' He was outraged. 'Defeat may be unavoidable, but we will meet it with pride.'

Spoken like a true Kinloch, I thought, and remembered briquettes flaming.

Zoë Lang came out of the bothy and walked towards us still carrying a metal detector, basically a long black stick with a white control box near the top and a flat white plate at the bottom.

When she reached us she ignored Himself and spoke directly and with penetration to me alone. 'You will tell me the truth,' she said in her old voice. 'I am sure you are a very good liar, but this time you will tell me the truth.'

I made no reply. She took it as assent, which it was.

She said, 'I saw that picture. Did you paint it?'

'Yes.'

'Is it you who has hidden the Kinloch hilt?'

'Yes.'

'Is it here . . . in your bothy? And would I find it?'

I said, after a pause, 'Yes . . . and yes.'

My uncle's mouth opened in protest. Zoë Lang

flicked him a glance and thrust the metal detector into his arms.

'You can keep the hilt,' she said. 'I'll look for it no longer.'

Himself watched in bewilderment while she told one of her helpers to round up the searchers, that they were leaving.

'But, Dr Lang . . .' her helper objected.

'The hilt isn't here,' she said. 'We are going home.'

We watched while they picked up their spades and pickaxes and metal detectors and drifted across to their mini-van transport, and when they'd gone Zoë Lang said to Himself, 'Don't you understand?'

'No, I frankly don't.'

'He hasn't seen the picture,' I said.

'Oh.' She blinked. 'What is it called? Does it have a name?'

'Portrait of Zoë Lang.'

A tear appeared in each of her eyes and ran down her wrinkled old cheeks, as Jed's wife Flora had foreseen.

'I will not fight you,' she said to me. 'You have made me immortal.'

Himself looked long at the picture when Zoë Lang had driven away in her small white car.

'Immortal,' he said thoughtfully. 'Is it?'

'Time will tell.'

'Mad Alexander, who messes about with paints . . .'

I smiled. 'One has to be slightly mad to do almost anything such as hiding a treasure.'

'Yes,' he said. 'Where is it?'

'Well,' I said, 'when you gave me the hilt to hide all those years ago, the first thing I thought about was metal detectors because those things find gold almost more easily than any other metal. So I had to think of a hiding place safe from metal detectors, which is actually almost impossible unless you dig down six feet or more . . . and under water is no good because water is no barrier.'

He interrupted. 'How does a metal detector *work*?'

'Well,' I said, 'inside that flat white plate thing there is a coil of very thin wire. The batteries in that white box, when you switch them on, produce a high-frequency alternating current in the coil, which in turn produces an oscillating magnetic field which will induce a responding current in any metal near it, which will, in turn, excite the coil even more, whose increased activity can be interpreted as a whine – and that's putting it simply.'

'You've lost me,' Himself said.

'I had to look it up,' I agreed. 'It's a bit hard to understand.'

He looked around at all the little dug up heaps of unprecious metal.

'Well, yes,' I grinned. 'I buried a lot of things to keep searchers busy.'

'Really, Al.'

'The childish mind,' I said. 'I couldn't help it. I did it five years ago. I might not do it now.'

'So where is the hilt?'

'It's where I hid it when you gave it to me.'

'But *where*?'

'Everyone talks about buried treasure . . .' I said, 'so I didn't bury it.'

He stared.

I said, 'The metal that most confuses a detector is a sheet of aluminium foil. So to start with I wrapped the hilt in several loose layers of foil, until it was a shapeless bundle about the size of a pillow. Then I took a length of cotton duck – that's the stuff I paint the pictures on – and I primed it with several coats of gesso to stiffen it and make it waterproof, and then I painted it all over with burnt-umber acrylic paint, which is a dark brown colour and also waterproof.'

'Go *on*,' he said when I paused. 'What then?'

'Then I wrapped the foil bundle in the cotton duck, and super-glued it so that it wouldn't fall undone. Then all over the surface I super-glued pieces of granite.' I waved a hand at the grey stony ground of the plateau. 'And then . . . well, the more metal you offer to a detector the more it gets confused, so I put the hilt bundle where it was more or less surrounded by metal . . .'

'But,' he objected, 'they dug up that whole old oven and the hilt wasn't in it . . .'

'I told you,' I said, 'I didn't bury it. I glued it onto the mountain.'

'You did . . . *what*?'

'I glued it granite to granite, and covered it with more granite pieces until you can't distinguish it by eye from the rock around it. I check it fairly often. It never moves.'

He looked at the metal detector in his hands.

'Turn it upside down,' I said.

He did as I said, waving the flat round plate in the air.

'Now I'll switch it on,' I said, and did so. 'And,' I said formally, laughing, 'my lord, follow me.'

I walked not up onto the hill, as he obviously expected, but into my corrugated iron-topped carport.

The waving upside-down metal detector whined non-stop.

'If you go to the rear wall,' I said, 'and stand just there,' I pointed, 'you will hear the indistinguishable noise of the Honour of the Kinlochs, which is up on the carport roof where it joins the mountain. If you stand just there, the hilt of Prince Charles Edward Stuart's ceremonial sword will be straight above your head.'

All Pan Books are available at your local bookshop or newsagent, or can be ordered direct from the publisher. Indicate the number of copies required and fill in the form below.

Send to: Macmillan General Books C.S.
Book Service By Post
PO Box 29, Douglas I-O-M
IM99 1BQ

or phone: 01624 675137, quoting title, author and credit card number.

or fax: 01624 670923, quoting title, author, and credit card number.

or Internet: http://www.bookpost.co.uk

Please enclose a remittance* to the value of the cover price plus 75 pence per book for post and packing. Overseas customers please allow £1.00 per copy for post and packing.

*Payment may be made in sterling by UK personal cheque, Eurocheque, postal order, sterling draft or international money order, made payable to Book Service By Post.

Alternatively by Access/Visa/MasterCard

Card No. | | | | | | | | | | | | | | | | |

Expiry Date | | | | | | | | | | | | | | | | |

Signature ______________________

Applicable only in the UK and BFPO addresses.

While every effort is made to keep prices low, it is sometimes necessary to increase prices at short notice. Pan Books reserve the right to show on covers and charge new retail prices which may differ from those advertised in the text or elsewhere.

NAME AND ADDRESS IN BLOCK CAPITAL LETTERS PLEASE

Name ______________________

Address ______________________

____

____

____

8/95

Please allow 28 days for delivery.
Please tick box if you do not wish to receive any additional information. ☐

BREAK IN

Dick Francis has written thirty-nine international best-sellers and is widely acclaimed as one of the world's finest thriller writers. His awards include the Crime Writers' Association's Cartier Diamond Dagger for his outstanding contribution to the crime genre, and an honourary Doctorate of Humane Letters from Tufts University of Boston. In 1996 Dick Francis was made a Mystery Writers of America Grand Master for a lifetime's achievement and in 2000 he received a CBE in the Queen's Birthday Honours List.

Also by Dick Francis in Pan Books

DICK FRANCIS
OMNIBUS ONE:
Long Shot, Straight,
High Stakes

DICK FRANCIS
OMNIBUS TWO:
Forfeit, Risk, Reflex

DICK FRANCIS
OMNIBUS THREE:
Slay-Ride, Banker, Proof

THE SID HALLEY
OMNIBUS:
Odds Against, Whip Hand,
Come to Grief

THE SPORT OF
QUEENS (autobiography)

LESTER: The Official Biography

DEAD CERT
NERVE
FOR KICKS
ODDS AGAINST
FLYING FINISH
BLOOD SPORT
FORFEIT
ENQUIRY
RAT RACE
BONECRACK
SMOKESCREEN
SLAY-RIDE
KNOCK DOWN
HIGH STAKES
IN THE FRAME
RISK
TRIAL RUN
WHIP HAND
REFLEX
TWICE SHY
BANKER
THE DANGER
PROOF
BOLT
HOT MONEY
STRAIGHT
LONGSHOT
COMEBACK
DRIVING FORCE
DECIDER
WILD HORSES
COME TO GRIEF
TO THE HILT
10lb PENALTY
FIELD OF THIRTEEN
SECOND WIND
SHATTERED

Dick Francis

BREAK IN

PAN BOOKS

First published 1985 by Michael Joseph Ltd

This edition published 1987 by Pan Books
an imprint of Pan Macmillan Ltd
Pan Macmillan, 20 New Wharf Road, London N1 9RR
Basingstoke and Oxford
Associated companies throughout the world
www.panmacmillan.com

In association with Michael Joseph Ltd

ISBN 0 330 29380 X

34 36 38 39 37 35 33

A CIP catalogue record for this book is available from the British Library.

Printed and bound in Great Britain by
Mackays of Chatham plc, Chatham, Kent

With love and thanks
to my son
MERRICK
racehorse trainer

and to

NANCY BROOKS GILBERT
bureau coordinator
for WSVN

CHAPTER ONE

Blood ties can mean trouble, chains and fatal obligation. The tie of twins, inescapably strongest. My twin, my bond.

My sister Holly, sprung into the world ten minutes after myself on Christmas morning with bells ringing over frosty fields and hope still wrapped in beckoning parcels, my sister Holly had through thirty years been cot-mate, puppy-companion, boxing target and best friend. Consecutively, on the whole.

My sister Holly came to Cheltenham races and intercepted me between weighing room and parade ring when I went out to ride in a three-mile steeplechase.

'Kit!' she said intensely, singling me out from among the group of other jockeys with whom I walked, and standing four-square and portentously in my way.

I stopped. The other jockeys walked on, parting like water round a rock. I looked at the lines of severe strain in her normally serene face and jumped in before she could say why she'd come.

'Have you any money with you?' I said.

'What? What for?' She wasn't concentrating on my question but on some inner scenario of obvious doom.

'Have you?' I insisted.

'Well . . . but that's not . . .'

'Go to the Tote,' I said. 'Put all you've got on my horse to win. Number eight. Go and do it.'

'But I don't . . .'

'Go and do it,' I interrupted. 'Then go to the bar and with what's left buy yourself a triple gin. Then come and meet me in the winners' enclosure.'

'No, that's not . . .'

I said emphatically, 'Don't put your disaster between me and that winning post.'

She blinked as if awakening, taking in my helmet and the colours I wore beneath my husky, looking towards the departing backs of the other jockeys and understanding what I meant.

'Right?' I said.

'Right.' She swallowed. 'All right.'

'Afterwards,' I said.

She nodded. The doom, the disaster, dragged at her eyes.

'I'll sort it out,' I promised. 'After.'

She nodded dumbly and turned away, beginning almost automatically to open her shoulder bag to look for money. Doing what her brother told her, even after all these years. Coming to her brother, still, for her worst troubles to be fixed. Even though she was four years married, those patterns of behaviour, established in a parentless childhood, still seemed normal to us both.

I'd sometimes wondered what difference it would have made to her if she had been the elder by that crucial ten minutes. Would she have been motherly? Bossy, perhaps. She felt safer, she'd said, being the younger.

I walked on towards the parade ring, putting consciously out of my mind the realization that whatever the trouble this time, it was bad. She had come, for a start, one hundred and fifty miles from Newmarket to see me, and she disliked driving.

I shook my head physically throwing her out. The horse ahead, the taxing job in hand, had absolute and necessary priority. I was primarily no one's brother. I was primarily Kit Fielding, steeplechase jockey, some years champion, some years not, sharing the annual honour with another much like myself, coming out top when my bones didn't break, bowing to fate when they did.

I wore the colours of a middle-aged princess of a dispossessed European monarchy, a woman of powerful femininity whose skin was weathering towards sunset like cracked glaze on porcelain. Sable coat, as usual, swinging from narrow shoulders. Glossy dark hair piled high. Plain gold earrings. I walked towards her across the parade-ring grass; smiled, bowed, and briefly shook the offered glove.

'Cold day,' she said; her consonants faintly thick,

vowel sounds pure English, intonation as always pleasant.

I agreed.

'And will you win?' she asked.

'With luck.'

Her smile was mostly in the eyes. 'I will expect it.'

We watched her horse stalk round the ring, its liver chestnut head held low, the navy rug with gold embroidered crest covering all else from withers to tail. North Face, she'd named it, from her liking for mountains, and a suitably bleak, hard and difficult customer he'd turned out to be. Herring-gutted, ugly, bad-tempered, moody. I'd ridden him in his three-year-old hurdles, his first races, and on over hurdles at four, five and six. I'd ridden him in his novice steeplechases at seven and through his prime at eight and nine. He tolerated me when he felt like it and I knew his every mean move. At ten he was still an unpredictable rogue, and as clever a jumper as a cat. He had won thirty-eight races over the years and I'd ridden him in all but one. Twice to my fury he had purposefully dropped his shoulder and dislodged me in the parade ring. Three times we had fallen together on landing, he each time getting unhurt to his feet and departing at speed with indestructible legs, indestructible courage, indestructible will to win. I loved him and hated him and he was as usual starting favourite.

The princess and I had stood together in such a way in parade rings more often than one could count, as she rarely kept fewer than twenty horses in training and I'd ridden them constantly for ten years. She and I had come to the point of almost monosyllabic but perfectly understood conversation and, as far as I could tell, mutual trust and regard. She called me 'Kit', and I called her 'Princess' (at her request) and we shared a positive and quite close friendship which nevertheless began and ended at the racecourse gates. If we met outside, as occasionally happened, she was considerably more formal.

We stood alone together in the parade ring, as so often, because Wykeham Harlow, who trained North Face, suffered from migraine. The headaches, I'd noticed, occurred most regularly on the coldest days, which might have been a truly physical phenomenon, but also they seemed to develop in severity in direct ratio to the distance between his armchair and the day's racing. Wykeham Harlow trained south of London and very seldom now made the north-westerly traverse to Cheltenham: he was growing old and wouldn't confess he was nervous about driving home in the winter dark.

The signal was given for jockeys to mount, and Dusty, the travelling head lad who nowadays deputized for Wykeham more often than not, removed North Face's rug with a flick and gave me a deft leg-up into the saddle.

The princess said, 'Good luck,' and I said cheerfully, 'Thank you.'

No one in jump racing said 'Break a leg' instead of

'Good luck', as they did in the theatre. Break a leg was all too depressingly possible.

North Face was feeling murderous: I sensed it the moment I sat on his back and put my feet in the irons. The telepathy between that horse and myself was particularly strong always, and I simply cursed him in my mind and silently told him to shut up and concentrate on winning, and we went out on to the windy track with the mental dialogue continuing unabated.

One had to trust that the urge to race would overcome his grouchiness once the actual contest started. It almost always did, but there had been days in the past when he'd refused to turn on the enthusiasm until too late. Days, like this one, when his unfocused hatred flowed most strongly.

There was no way of cajoling him with sweet words, encouraging pats, pulling his ears. None of that pleased him. A battle of wills was what he sought, and that, from me, was what he habitually got.

We circled at the starting point, seven runners in all, while the roll was called and girths were tightened. Waited, with jockeys' faces turning pale blue in the chilly November wind, for the seconds to tick away to start time, lining up in no particular order as there were no draws or stalls in jump races, watching for the starter to raise the tapes and let us go.

North Face's comment on the proceedings took the form of a lowered head and arched back, and a kick like a bronco. The other riders cursed and kept out of his way, and the starter told me to stay well to the rear.

It was the big race of the day, though heavier in prestige than prize money, an event in which the sponsors, a newspaper, were getting maximum television coverage for minimum outlay. The Sunday Towncrier Trophy occurred annually on a Saturday afternoon (naturally) for full coverage in the *Sunday Towncrier* itself the next morning, with self-congratulatory prose and dramatic pictures jostling scandals on the front page. Dramatic pictures of Fielding being bucked off before the start were definitely not going to be taken. I called the horse a bastard, a sod and a bloody pig, and in that gentlemanly fashion the race began.

He was mulish and reluctant and we got away slowly, trailing by ten lengths after the first few strides. It didn't help that the start was in plain view of the stands instead of decently hidden in some far corner. He gave another two bronco kicks to entertain the multitude, and there weren't actually many horses who could manage that while approaching the first fence at Cheltenham.

He scrambled over that fence, came almost to a halt on landing and bucked again before setting off, shying against coercion from the saddle both bodily and clearly in mind.

Two full circuits ahead. Nineteen more jumps. A gap between me and the other runners of embarrassing and lengthening proportions. I sent him furious messages:

Race, you bastard, race, or you'll end up as dogmeat, I'll personally kill you, you bastard, and if you think you'll get me off, think again, you're taking me all the way, you sod, so get on with it, start racing, you sod, you bastard, you know you like it, so get going . . .

We'd been through it before, over and over, but he'd never been worse. He ignored all take-off signals at the second fence and made a mess of it and absolutely refused to gallop properly round the next bend.

Once in the past when he'd been in this mood I'd tried simply not fighting him but letting him sort out his own feelings, and he'd brought himself to a total halt within a few strides. Persevering was the only way: waiting until the demonic fit burned itself out.

He stuck his toes in as we approached the next fence as if the downhill slope there alarmed him, which I knew it didn't; and over the next, the water jump, he landed with his head down by his feet and his back arched, a configuration almost guaranteed to send a jockey flying. I knew his tricks so well that I was ready for him and stayed in the saddle, and after that jolly little manoeuvre we were more than three hundred yards behind the other horses and seriously running out of time.

My feelings about him rose to somewhere near absolute fury. His sheer pigheadedness was again going to lose us a race we could easily have won, and as on other similar occasions I swore to myself that I'd never ride the brute again, never. Not ever. Never. I almost believed I meant it.

As if he'd been a naughty child who knew its tantrums had gone too far, he suddenly began to race. The bumpy uneven stride went smooth, the rage faded away, the marvellous surge of fighting spirit returned, as it always did in the end. But we were a furlong and a half to the rear, and to come from more than three hundred yards behind and still win meant theoretically that one could have won by the same margin if one had tried from the start. A whole mile had been wasted; two left for retrieval. Hopeless.

Never give up, they say.

Yard by flying yard over the second circuit we clawed back the gap, but we were still ten lengths behind the last tired and trailing horse in front as we turned towards the final two fences. Passed him over the first of them. No longer last, but that was hardly what mattered. Five horses in front, all still on their feet after the long contest, all intent on the final uphill battle.

All five went over the last fence in front of North Face. He must have gained twenty feet in the air. He landed and strode away with smooth athletic power as if sticky bronco jumps were the peccadillo of another horse altogether.

I could dimly hear the crowd roaring, which one usually couldn't. North Face put his ears back and galloped with a flat, intense, bloody-minded stride, accelerating towards the place he knew was his, that he'd so wilfully rejected, that he wanted in his heart.

I flattened myself forward to the line of his neck to cut the wind resistance; kept the reins tight, my body still, my weight steady over his shoulders, all the urging a matter of mind and hands, a matter of giving that fantastic racing creature his maximum chance.

The others were tiring, the incline slowing them drastically, as it did always to so many. North Face swept past a bunch of them as they wavered and there was suddenly only one in front, one whose jockey thought he was surely winning and had half dropped his hands.

One could feel sorry for him, but he was a gift from heaven. North Face caught him at a rush a bare few strides from the winning post, and I heard his agonized cry as I passed.

Too close for comfort, I thought, pulling up. Reprieved on the scaffold.

There was nothing coming from the horse's mind: just a general sort of haze that in a human one would have interpreted as smugness. Most good horses knew when they'd won: filled their lungs and raised their heads with pride. Some were definitely depressed when they lost. Guilt they never felt, nor shame nor regret nor compassion: North Face would dump me next time if he could.

The princess greeted us in the unsaddling enclosure with starry eyes and a flush on her cheeks. Stars for success, I diagnosed, and the flush from earlier embarrassment. I unbuckled the girths, slid the saddle over my arm and paused briefly before going to weigh in, my head near to hers.

'Well done,' she said.

I smiled slightly. 'I expected curses.'

'He was especially difficult.'

'And brilliant.'

'There's a trophy.'

'I'll come right out,' I said, and left her to the flocking newsmen, who liked her and treated her reverently, on the whole.

I passed the scales. The jockey I'd beaten at the last second was looking ashamed, but it was his own fault, as well he knew. The Stewards might fine him. His owners might sack him. No one else paid much attention either to his loss or to my win. The past was the past: the next race was what mattered.

I gave my helmet and saddle to the valet, changed into different colours, weighed out, put the princess's colours back on, on top of those I would carry in the next race, combed my hair and went out dutifully for the speeches. It always seemed a shame to me when the presentation photographs were taken with the jockey not wearing the winner's colours, and for owners I cared for I did whenever possible appear with the right set on top. It cost me nothing but a couple of minutes, and it was more satisfactory, I thought.

The racecourse (in the shape of the chairman of directors) thanked the *Sunday Towncrier* for its generosity and the *Sunday Towncrier* (in the shape of its proprietor, Lord Vaughnley) said it was a pleasure to support National Hunt racing and all who sailed in her.

Cameras clicked.

There was no sign anywhere of Holly.

The proprietor's lady, thin, painted and good-natured, stepped forward in smooth couturier clothes to give a foot-high gilded statue of a towncrier (medieval version) to the princess, amid congratulation and hand shaking. The princess accepted also a smaller gilt version on behalf of Wykeham Harlow, and in my turn I received the smile, the handshake, the congratulations and the attentions of the cameras, but not, to my surprise, my third set of golden towncrier cufflinks.

'We were afraid you might win them again,' Lady Vaughnley explained sweetly, 'so this year it's a figure like the others,' and she pressed warmly into my hands a little golden man calling out the news to the days before printing.

I genuinely thanked her. I had more cufflinks already than shirts with cuffs to take them.

'What a finish you gave us,' she said, smiling. 'My husband is thrilled. Like an arrow from nowhere, he said.'

'We were lucky.'

I looked automatically to her shoulder, expecting to greet also her son, who at all other Towncriers had accompanied his parents, hovering around and running errands, willing, nice-natured, on the low side of average for brains.

'Your son isn't with you?' I asked.

Most of Lady Vaughnley's animation went into eclipse. She glanced swiftly and uncomfortably across to her husband, who hadn't heard my remark, and said unhappily, 'No, not today.'

'I'm sorry,' I said; not for Hugh Vaughnley's absence, but for the obvious row in the family. She nodded and turned away, blinking, and I thought fleetingly that the trouble must be new and bad, near the surface of tears.

The princess invited Lord and Lady Vaughnley to her box and they happily accepted.

'You as well, Kit,' she said.

'I'm riding in the next race.'

'Come after.'

'Yes. Thank you.'

Everyone left their trophies on the presentation table to be taken away for engraving and I returned to the changing room as the princess moved away with the Vaughnleys.

She always asked me to her box because she liked to discuss her horses and what they'd done, and she had a loving and knowledgeable interest in all of them. She liked most to race where she rented a private box, namely at Cheltenham, Ascot, Sandown and Lingfield, and she went only to other courses where she had standing invitations from box-endowed friends. She was not democratic to the point of standing on the open stands and yelling.

I came out in the right colours for the next race and found Holly fiercely at my elbow immediately.

'Have you collected your winnings?' I asked.

'I couldn't reach you,' she said disgustedly. 'All those officials, keeping everyone back, and the crowds . . .'

'Look, I'm sorry. I've got to ride again now.'

'Straight after, then.'

'Straight after.'

My mount in that race, in contrast to North Face, was unexciting, unintelligent and of only run-of-the-mill ability. Still, we tried hard, finished third, and seemed to give moderate pleasure to owners and trainer. Bread and butter for me: expenses covered for them. The basic fabric of jump racing.

I weighed in and changed rapidly into street clothes, and Holly was waiting when I came out.

'Now, Kit . . .'

'Um,' I said. 'The princess is expecting me.'

'No! Kit!' She was exasperated.

'Well . . . it's my job.'

'Don't come to the office, you mean?'

I relented. 'OK. What's the matter?'

'Have you seen this?' She pulled a page torn from a newspaper called the *Daily Flag* out of her shoulder bag. 'Has anyone said anything in the weighing room?'

'No and no,' I said, taking the paper and looking

where she was pointing with an agitated stabbing finger. 'I don't read that rag.'

'Nor do we, for God's sake. Just look at it.'

I glanced at the paragraph which was boxed by heavy red lines on a page entitled 'Intimate Details', a page well known to contain information varying from stale to scurrilous and to be intentionally geared to stirring up trouble.

'It's yesterday's,' I said, looking at the date.

'Yes, yes. Read it.'

I read the piece. It said:

Folk say the skids are under Robertson (Bobby) Allardeck (32), racehorse-trainer son of tycoon Maynard Allardeck (50). Never Daddy's favourite (they're not talking), Bobby's bought more than he can pay for, naughty boy, and guess who won't be coming to the rescue. Watch this space for more.

Robertson (Bobby) Allardeck (32) was my sister Holly's husband.

'It's libellous,' I said. 'Bobby can sue.'

'What with?' Holly demanded. 'We can't afford it. And we might not win.'

I looked at the worry in her normally unlined face.

'Is it true, then?' I said.

'No. Yes. In a way. Of course he's bought things he can't pay for. Everyone does. He's bought horses. It's yearling sale time, dammit. Every trainer buys yearlings he can't pay for. It's natural, you know that.'

I nodded. Trainers bought yearlings at auction for their owners, paying compulsorily for them on the spot and relying on the owners to reimburse them fairly soon. Sometimes the owners backed out after a yearling had been bought; sometimes trainers bought an extra animal or two to bring on themselves and have ready for a later sale at a profit. Either way, at sale time, it was more common than not to borrow thousands short-term from the bank.

'How many has Bobby bought that he can't sell?' I asked.

'He'll sell them in the end, of course,' she said, staunchly.

Of course. Probably. Perhaps.

'But now?'

'Three. We've got three.'

'Total damage?'

'More than a hundred thousand.'

'The bank paid for them?'

She nodded. 'It's not that it won't be all right in the end, but where did that disgusting rag get the information from? And why put it in the paper at all? I mean, it's pointless.'

'And what's happened?' I asked.

'What's happened is that everyone we owe money to has telephoned demanding to be paid. I mean, horrible threats, really, about taking us to court. All day yesterday . . . and this morning the feed-merchant rang and said he wouldn't deliver any more feed unless we paid our bill and we've got thirty horses munching their heads off, and the owners are on the line non-stop asking if Bobby's going to go on training or not and making veiled hints about taking their horses away.'

I was sceptical. 'All this reaction from that one little paragraph?'

'Yes.' She was suddenly close to tears. 'Someone pushed the paper through the letter box of half the tradesmen in Newmarket, open at that page with that paragraph outlined in red, just like this. The blacksmith showed me. It's his paper. He came to shoe some of the horses and made us pay him first. Made a joke of it. But all the same, he meant it. Not everyone's been so nice.'

'And I suppose you can't simply just pay everyone off and confound them?'

'You know we can't. The bank manager would bounce the cheques. We have to do it gradually, like we always do. Everyone will get paid, if they wait.'

Bobby and Holly lived in fairly usual fashion at permanent full stretch of their permitted overdraft, juggling the incoming cheques from the owners with the outgoing expenses of fodder, wages, overheads and taxes. Owners sometimes paid months late, but the horses had to be fed and the lads' wages found to the minute. The cash flow tended to suffer from air locks.

'Well,' I said, 'go for another triple gin while I talk to the princess.'

CHAPTER TWO

The Princess Casilia, Mme de Brescou (to give her her full style), had as usual asked a few friends to lunch with her to watch the races, and her box contained, besides herself and the Vaughnleys, a small assortment of furs and tweeds, all with inhabitants I'd formerly met on similar occasions.

'You know everyone, don't you?' the princess said, and I nodded 'Yes', although I couldn't remember half their names.

'Tea?' she asked.

'Yes, thank you.'

The same waitress as usual smoothly gave me a full cup, smiling. No milk, no sugar, slice of lemon, as always.

The princess had had a designer decorate her boxes at the racecourses and they were all the same: pale peach hessian on the walls, coffee-coloured carpet and a glass-topped dining table surrounded by comfortable chairs. By late afternoon, my habitual visiting time, the table had been pushed to one side and bore not lunch but plates of sandwiches, creamy pastries, assorted alcohol, a box of cigars. The princess's friends tended to linger long after the last races had been run.

One of the women guests picked up a plate of small delicious-looking cakes and offered it to me.

'No, thank you,' I said mildly. 'Not this minute.'

'Not ever,' the princess told her friend. 'He can't eat those. And don't tempt him. He's hungry.'

The friend looked startled and confused. 'My dear, I never thought. And he's so tall.'

'I eat a lot,' I said. 'But just not those.'

The princess, who had some idea at least of the constant struggle I had to stay down at a body weight of ten stone, gave me a glimmering look through her eyelashes, expressing disbelief.

The friend was straightforwardly curious. 'What do you eat most of,' she asked, 'if not cake?'

'Lobster, probably,' I said.

'Good heavens.'

Her male companion gave me a critical glance from above a large moustache and long front teeth.

'Left it a bit late in the big race, didn't you, what?' he said.

'I'm afraid so, yes.'

'Couldn't think what you were doing out there, fiddling about at the back. You nearly bungled it entirely, what? The princess was most uncomfortable, I can tell you, as we all had our money on you, of course.'

The princess said, 'North Face can behave very

badly, Jack. I told you. He has such a mind of his own. Sometimes it's hard to get him to race.'

'It's the jockey's job to get him to race,' Jack said to me with a touch of belligerence. 'Don't you agree, what?'

'Yes,' I said. 'I do agree.'

Jack looked fractionally disconcerted and the princess's lips twitched.

'And then you set him alight,' said Lord Vaughnley, overhearing. 'Gave us a rousing finish. The sort of thing a sponsor prays for, my dear fellow. Memorable. Something to talk about, to refer to. North Face's finish in the Towncrier Trophy. Splendid, do you see?'

Jack saw, chose not to like it, drifted away. Lord Vaughnley's grey eyes looked with bonhomie from his large bland face and he patted me with kindly meant approval on the shoulder.

'Third time in a row,' he said. 'You've done us proud. Would you care, one Saturday night, to see the paper put to bed?'

'Yes,' I said, surprised. 'Very much.'

'We might print a picture of you watching a picture of yourself go through the presses.'

More than bonhomie, I thought, behind the grey eyes: a total newspaperman's mentality.

He was the proprietor of the *Towncrier* by inheritance, the fiftyish son of one of the old-style newspaper barons who had muscled on to the scene in the nineteen thirties and brought new screaming life to millions of breakfasts. Vaughnley Senior had bought a dying provincial weekly and turned it into a lusty voice read nationwide. He'd taken it to Fleet Street, seen the circulation explode, and in due course had launched a daily version which still prospered despite sarcastic onslaughts from newer rivals.

The old man had been a colourful buccaneering entrepreneur. The son was quieter, a manager, an advertising man at heart. The *Towncrier*, once a raucous newsheet, had over the last ten years developed Establishment leanings, a remarkable testimony of the hand-over from the elder personality to the younger.

I thought of Hugh Vaughnley, the son, next in the line: the sweet-tempered young man without strength, at present at odds, it appeared, with his parents. In his hands, if it survived at all, the *Towncrier* would soften to platitude, waffle and syrup.

The *Daily Flag*, still at the brassiest stage, and among the *Towncrier*'s most strident opposition, had been recently bought, after bitter financial intrigues, by a thrusting financier in the ascendant, a man hungry, it was said, for power and a peerage, and taking a well-tried path towards both. The *Flag* was bustling, go-getting, stamping on sacrosanct toes and boasting of new readers daily.

Since I'd met Lord Vaughnley several times at various racing presentation dinners where annual honours were dished out to the fortunate (like champion jockeys, leading trainers, owners-of-the-year, and so on) and with Holly's distress sharp in my mind, I asked him if he knew who was responsible for 'Intimate Details' in the *Flag*.

'Responsible?' he repeated with a hint of holier-than-thou distaste. 'Irresponsible, more like.'

'Irresponsible, then.'

'Why, precisely?' he asked.

'They've made an unprovoked and apparently pointless attack on my brother-in-law.'

'Hm,' Lord Vaughnley said. 'Too bad. But, my dear fellow, pointless attacks are what the public likes to read. Destructive criticism sells papers, back-patting doesn't. My father used to say that, and he was seldom wrong.'

'And to hell with justice,' I said.

'We live in an unkind world. Always have, always will. Christians to the lions, roll up, buy the best seats in the shade, gory spectacle guaranteed. People buy newspapers, my dear fellow, to see victims torn limb from limb. Be thankful it's physically bloodless, we've advanced at least that far.' He smiled as if talking to a child. 'Intimate Details, as you must know, is a composite affair, with a whole bunch of journalists digging out nuggets and also a network of informants in hospitals, mortuaries, night clubs, police stations and all sorts of less savoury places, telephoning in with the dirt and collecting their dues. We at the *Towncrier* do the same sort of thing. Every paper does. Gossip columns would be non-starters, my dear fellow, if one didn't.'

'I'd like to know where the piece about my brother-in-law came from. Who told who, if you see what I mean. And why.'

'Hm.' The grey eyes considered. 'The editor of the *Flag* is Sam Leggatt. You could ask him of course, but even if he finds out from his staff, he won't tell you. Head against brick wall, I'm afraid, my dear fellow.'

'And you approve,' I said, reading his tone. 'Closing ranks, never revealing sources, and all that.'

'If your brother-in-law has suffered real positive harm,' he nodded blandly, 'he should get his solicitor to send Sam Leggatt a letter announcing imminent prosecution for libel unless a retraction and an apology are published immediately. It sometimes works. Failing that, your brother-in-law might get a small cash settlement out of court. But do advise him, my dear fellow, against pressing for a fully fledged libel action with a jury. The *Flag* retains heavyweight lawyers and they play very rough. They would turn your brother-in-law's most innocent secrets inside out and paint them dirty. He'd wish he'd never started. Friendly advice, my dear fellow, I do assure you.'

I told him about the paragraph being outlined in red and delivered by hand to the houses of tradespeople.

Lord Vaughnley frowned. 'Tell him to look for the informant on his own doorstep,' he said. 'Gossip column items often spring from local spite. So do stories about vicars and their mistresses.' He smiled briefly.

'Good old spite. Whatever would the newspaper industry do without it!'

'Such a confession!' I said with mockery.

'We clamour for peace, honesty, harmony, common sense and equal justice for all,' he said. 'I assure you we do, my dear fellow.'

'Yes,' I said. 'I know.'

The princess touched Lord Vaughnley's arm and invited him to go out on to the balcony to see the last race. He said, however, that he should return to the *Towncrier*'s guests whom he had temporarily abandoned in a sponsors' hospitality room, and, collecting his wife, he departed.

'Now, Kit,' said the princess, 'while everyone is outside watching the race, tell me about North Face.'

We sat, as so often, in two of the chairs, and I told her without reservation what had happened between her horse and myself.

'I do wish,' she said thoughtfully, at the end, 'that I had your sense of what horses are thinking. I've tried putting my head against their heads,' she smiled almost self-consciously, 'but nothing happens. I get nothing at all. So how do you do it?'

'I don't know,' I said. 'I don't think head to head would work, anyway. It's just when I'm riding them, I seem to know. It's not in words, not at all. It's just there. It just seems to come. It happens to very many riders. Horses are telepathic creatures.'

She looked at me with her head on one side. 'But

you, Kit, you're telepathic with people as well as horses. Quite often you've answered a question I was just going to ask. Quite disconcerting. How do you do it?'

I was startled. 'I don't know how.'

'But you know you do?'

'Well . . . I used to. My twin sister Holly and I were telepathic between ourselves at one time. Almost like an extra way of talking. But we've grown out of it, these last few years.'

'Pity,' she said. 'Such an interesting gift.'

'It can't logically exist.'

'But it does.' She patted my hand. 'Thank you for today, although you and North Face between you almost stopped my heart.'

She stood up without haste, adept from some distant training at ending a conversation gracefully when she wished, and I stood also and thanked her formally for her tea. She smiled through the eyelashes, as she often did with everybody: not out of coquetry but in order, it seemed to me, to hide her private feelings.

She had a husband to whom she went home daily; Monsieur Roland de Brescou, a Frenchman of aristocratic lineage, immense wealth and advanced age. I had met him twice, a frail white-haired figure in a wheelchair with an autocratic nose and little to say. I asked after his health occasionally: the princess replied always that he was well. Impossible ever to tell from her voice or demeanour what she felt about him: love, anxiety, frustration, impatience, joy . . . nothing showed.

'We run at Devon and Exeter, don't we?' she said.

'Yes, Princess. Bernina and Icicle.'

'Good. I'll see you there on Tuesday.'

I shook her hand. I'd sometimes thought, after a win such as that day's, of planting a farewell kiss on her porcelain cheek. I liked her very much. She might consider it the most appalling liberty, though, and give me the sack, so in her own disciplined fashion I made her merely a sketch of a bow, and went away.

'You've been a hell of a long time,' Holly complained. 'That woman treats you like a lap dog. It's sickening.'

'Yeah . . . well . . . here I am.'

She had been waiting for me on her feet outside the weighing room in the cold wind, not snugly in a chair in the bar. The triple gin anyway had been a joke because she seldom drank alcohol, but that she couldn't even sit down revealed the intensity of her worry.

The last race was over, the crowds streaming towards the car parks. Jockeys and trainers, officials and valets and pressmen bade each other goodnight all around us although it was barely three-forty in the afternoon and not yet dusk. Time to go home from the office. Work was work, even if the end product was entertainment. Leisure was a growth industry, so they said.

'Will you come home with me?' Holly asked.

I had known for an hour that that was what she would want.

'Yes,' I said.

Her relief was enormous but she tried to hide it with a cough, a joke and a jerky laugh. 'Your car or mine?'

I'd thought it over. 'We'll both go to the cottage. I'll drive us in your car from there.'

'OK.' She swallowed. 'And Kit . . .'

'Save it,' I said.

She nodded. We'd had an ancient pact: never say thank you out loud. Thanks came in help returned, unstintingly and at once, when one needed it. The pact had faded into abeyance with her marriage but still, I felt, existed: and so did she, or she wouldn't have come.

Holly and I were more alike in looks than many fraternal twins, but nowhere near the identical Viola and Sebastian: Shakespeare, most rarely, got it wrong. We each had dark hair, curly. Each, lightish brown eyes. Each, flat ears, high foreheads, long necks, easily tanned skin. We had different noses and different mouths, though the same slant to the bone above the eye socket. We had never had an impression of looking into a mirror at the sight of the other, although the other's face was more familiar to us than our own.

When we were two years old our young and effervescent parents left us with our grandparents, went for a winter holiday in the Alps, and skied into an avalanche. Our father's parents, devastated, had kept us and brought us up and couldn't in many ways have been better, but Holly and I had turned inward to each other more than might have happened in a normal family. We had invented and spoken our own private language, as many such children do, and from there had progressed to a speechless communication of minds. Our telepathy had been more a matter of knowing what the other was thinking rather than of deliberately planting thoughts in the other's head. More reception than transmission, one might say: and it happened also without us realizing it, as over and over again when we'd been briefly apart we had done things like writing in the same hour to our Australian aunt, getting the same book out of the library, and buying identical objects on impulse. We had both, for instance, one day gone separately home with roller skates as a surprise birthday present for the other and hidden them in our grandmother's wardrobe. Grandmother herself by that time hadn't found it strange as we'd done similar things too often, and she'd said that right from when we could talk if she asked, 'Kit, where's Holly?' or, 'Holly, where's Kit?' we would always know, even if logically we couldn't.

The telepathy between us had not only survived the stresses and upheavals of puberty and adolescence but had actually become stronger: also we were more conscious of it, and used it purposely when we wanted, and grew in young adulthood into a new dimension of friendship. Naturally we put up a front to the world of banter, sarcasm and sibling rivalry, but underneath we were solid, never doubting our private certainty.

When I'd left our grandparents' house to buy a place

of my own with my earnings, Holly had from time to time lived there with me, working away in London most of the time but returning as of right whenever she wished, both of us taking it for granted that my cottage was now her home also.

That state of affairs had continued until she fell in love with Bobby Allardeck and married him.

Even before the wedding the telepathy had begun to fade and fairly soon afterwards it had more or less stopped. I wondered for a while if she had shut down deliberately, and then realized it had been also my own decision: she was off on a new life and it wouldn't have been a good idea to try to cling to her, or to intrude.

Four years on, the old habit had vanished to such an extent that I hadn't felt a flicker of her present distress, where once I would somehow have had it in my mind and would have telephoned to find out if she was all right.

On our way out to the car park I asked her how much she'd won on North Face.

'My God,' she said, 'you left that a bit late, didn't you?'

'Mm.'

'Anyway, I went to put my money on the Tote but the queues were so long I didn't bother and I went down on to the lawn to watch the race. Then when you were left so far behind I was glad I hadn't backed you. Then those bookies on the rails began shouting five to one North Face. Five to one! I mean, you'd started at odds-on. There was a bit of booing when you came past the stands and it made me cross. You always do your best, they didn't have to boo. So I walked over and got one of the bookies to take all my money at fives. It was a sort of gesture, I suppose. I won a hundred and twenty-five, which will pay the plumber, so thanks.'

'Did the plumber get Intimate Details?'

'Yes, he did.'

'Someone knows your life pretty thoroughly,' I said.

'Yes. But who? We were awake half the night wondering.' Her voice was miserable. 'Who could hate us that much?'

'You haven't just kicked out any grievance-laden employees?'

'No. We've a good lot of lads this year. Better than most.'

We arrived at her car and she drove me to where mine was parked.

'Is that house of yours finished yet?' she asked.

'Getting on.'

'You're bizarre.'

I smiled. Holly liked things secure, settled and planned in advance. She thought it crazy that I'd bought on impulse the roofless shell of a one-storey house from a builder who was going broke. He'd been in the local pub one night when I'd gone in for a steak: leaning on the bar and morosely drowning his sorrows in beer.

He'd been building the house for himself, he said, but he'd no money left. All work on it had stopped.

I'd ridden horses for him in his better-off days and had known him for several years, so the next morning I'd gone with him to see the house; and I'd liked its possibilities and bought it on the spot, and engaged him to finish it for me, paying him week by week for work done. It was going to be a great place to live and I was going to move into it, finished or not, well before Christmas, as I'd already exchanged contracts on my old cottage and would have to leave there willy nilly.

'I'll follow you to the cottage,' Holly said. 'And don't drive like you won the Towncrier.'

We proceeded in sedate convoy to the racehorse-training village of Lambourn on the Berkshire Downs, leaving my car in its own garage there and setting off together on the hundred miles plus to the Suffolk town of Newmarket, headquarters of the racing industry.

I liked the informality of little Lambourn. Holly and Bobby swam easily in the grander pond. Or had done, until a pike came along to snap them up.

I told her what Lord Vaughnley had said about demanding a retraction from the *Flag*'s editor but not suing, and she said I'd better tell Bobby. She seemed a great deal more peaceful now that I was actually on the road with her, and I thought she had more faith in my ability to fix things than I had myself. This was a lot different from beating up a boy who pinched her bottom twice at school. A little more shadowy than making a salesman take back the rotten car he'd conned her into buying.

She slept most of the way to Newmarket and I had no idea at all what I was letting myself in for.

We drove into the Allardeck stableyard at about eight o'clock and found it ablaze with lights and movement when it should have been quiet and dark. A large horsebox was parked in the centre, all doors open, loading ramp down. Beside it stood an elderly man watching a stable-lad lead a horse towards the ramp. The door of the place where the horse had been dozing the night away shone as a wide open oblong of yellow behind him.

A few steps away from the horsebox, lit as on a stage, were two men arguing with fists raised, arms gesticulating, voices clearly shouting.

One of them was my brother-in-law, Bobby. The other . . .?

'Oh my God,' Holly said. 'That's one of our owners. Taking his horses. And he owes us a fortune.'

She scrambled out of the car almost before I'd braked to a halt, and ran towards the two men. Her arrival did nothing, as far as I could see, to cool the flourishing row, and to all intents they simply ignored her.

My calm-natured sister was absolutely no good at stalking into any situation and throwing her weight about. She thought privately that it was rather pleasant to cook and keep house and be a gentle old-fashioned woman: but then she was of a generation for whom that way was a choice, not a drudgery oppressively imposed.

I got out of the car and walked across to see what could be done. Holly ran back to meet me.

'Can you stop him?' she said urgently. 'If he takes the horses, we'll never get his money.'

I nodded.

The lad leading the horse had reached the ramp but the horse was reluctant to board. I walked over to the lad without delay, stood in his way, on the bottom of the ramp, and told him to put the horse back where he'd brought it from.

'What?' he said. He was young, small, and apparently astonished to see anyone materialize from the dark.

'Put it back in the box, switch off the light, close the door. Do it now.'

'But Mr Graves told me . . .'

'Just do it,' I said.

He looked doubtfully across to the two shouting men.

'Do you work here?' I said. 'Or did you come with the horsebox?'

'I came with the horsebox.' He looked at the elderly man standing there who had so far said and done nothing. 'What should I do, Jim?'

'Who are you?' I asked him.

'The driver,' he said flatly. 'Keep me out of it.'

'Right,' I said to the lad. 'The horse isn't leaving. Take it back.'

'Are you Kit Fielding?' he said doubtfully.

'That's right. Mrs Allardeck's brother. Get going.'

'But Mr Graves . . .'

'I'll deal with Mr Graves,' I said. 'His horse isn't leaving tonight.'

'Horses,' the boy said, correcting me. 'I loaded the other one already.'

'OK,' I said. 'They're both staying here. When you've put back the one you're loading, unload the first one again.'

The boy gave me a wavering look, then turned the horse round and began to plod it back towards its rightful quarters.

The change of direction broke up the slanging match at once. The man who wasn't Bobby broke away and shouted to the lad across the yard, 'Hey, you, what the shit do you think you're doing? Load the horse this minute.'

The lad stopped. I walked fast over to him, took hold of the horse's head-collar and led the bemused animal back into its own home. The lad made no move at all to stop me. I came out. Switched off the light. Shut and bolted the door.

Mr Graves (presumably) was advancing fast with flailing arms and an extremely belligerent expression.

'Who the shit do you think you are?' he shouted. 'That's my horse. Get it out here at once!'

I stood, however, in front of the bolted door, leaning my shoulders on it, crossing one ankle over the other, folding my arms. Mr Graves came to a screeching and disbelieving halt.

'Get away from there,' he said thunderously, stabbing the night air with a forefinger. 'That's my horse. I'm taking it, and you can't stop me.'

His pudgy face rigid with obstinacy, he stood about five feet five from balding crown to polished toecaps. He was perhaps fifty, plump, already out of breath. There was no way whatever that he was going to shift my five feet ten by force.

'Mr Graves,' I said calmly, 'you can take your horses away when you've paid your bill.'

His mouth opened speechlessly. He took a step forward and peered at my face, which I dare say was in shadow.

'That's right,' I said. 'Kit Fielding. Holly's brother.'

The open mouth snapped shut. 'And what the shit has all this to do with you? Get out of my way.'

'A cheque,' I said. 'You do have your chequebook with you?'

His gaze grew calculating. I gave him little time to slide out.

I said, 'The *Daily Flag* is always hungry for tit-bits for its Intimate Details. Owners trying to sneak their horses away at dead of night without paying their bills would be worth a splash, don't you think?'

'That's a threat!' he said furiously.

'Quite right.'

'You wouldn't do that.'

'Oh yes, I certainly would. I might even suggest that if you can't pay this one bill, maybe you can't pay others. Then all your creditors would be down like vultures in a flash.'

'But that's . . . that's . . .'

'That's what's happening to Bobby, yes. And if Bobby has a cash-flow problem, and I'm only saying if, then it's partly due to you yourself and others like you who don't pay when you should.'

'You can't talk to me like that,' he said furiously.

'I don't see why not.'

'I'll report you to the Jockey Club.'

'Yes, you do that.'

He was blustering, his threat a sham. I looked over his shoulder towards Bobby and Holly, who had been near enough to hear the whole exchange.

'Bobby,' I said, 'go and fetch Mr Graves's account. Make sure every single item he owes is on it, as you may not have a second chance.'

Bobby went at a half-run, followed more tentatively by Holly. The lad who had come with the horsebox retreated with the driver into the shadows. Mr Graves and I stood as if in a private tableau, waiting.

While a horse remained in a trainer's yard the trainer had a good chance of collecting his due, because the law firmly allowed him to sell the horse and deduct from the proceeds what he was owed. With the horse whisked away his prospects were a court action and a lengthy wait, and if the owner went bankrupt, nothing at all.

Graves's horses were Bobby's security, plain and simple.

Bobby eventually returned alone bringing a lengthy bill which ran to three sheets.

'Check it,' I said to Graves, as he snatched the pages from Bobby's hand.

Angrily he read the bill through from start to finish and found nothing to annoy him further until he came to the last item. He jabbed at the paper and again raised his voice.

'Interest? What the shit do you mean, interest?'

'Um,' Bobby said, 'on what I've had to borrow because you hadn't paid me.'

There was a sudden silence. Respectful, on my part. I wouldn't have thought my brother-in-law had it in him.

Graves suddenly controlled his anger, pursed his lips, narrowed his eyes, and delved into an inner pocket for his chequebook. Without any sign of fury or haste he carefully wrote a cheque, tore it out, and handed it to Bobby.

'Now,' he said to me. 'Move.'

'Is it all right?' I asked Bobby.

'Yes,' he said as if surprised. 'All of it.'

'Good,' I said, 'then go and unload Mr Graves's other horse from the horsebox.'

CHAPTER THREE

'Do what?' Bobby said, astonished.

I remarked mildly, 'A cheque is only a piece of paper until it's been through the bank.'

'That's slander!' Graves said furiously, all his earlier truculence reappearing.

'It's an observation,' I said.

Bobby shoved the cheque quickly into his trouser pocket as if fearing that Graves would try to snatch it back, not an unreasonable suspicion in view of the malevolence facing him.

'Once the cheque's been cleared,' I said to Graves, 'you can come and pick up the horses. Thursday or Friday should do. Bobby will keep them for nothing until then, but if you haven't removed them by Saturday he will begin charging training fees again.'

Bobby's mouth opened slightly and shut purposefully, and he walked without more ado towards the horsebox. Graves scuttled a few steps after him, protesting loudly, and then reversed and returned to me, shouting and practically dancing up and down.

'I'll see the Stewards hear about this!'

'Most unwise,' I said.

'I'll stop that cheque.'

'If you do,' I said calmly, 'Bobby will have you put on the forfeit list.'

This most dire of threats cut off Graves's ranting miraculously. A person placed on the Jockey Club's forfeit list for non-payment of training fees was barred in disgrace from all racecourses, along with his horses. Mr Graves, it seemed, was not quite ready for such a social blight.

'I won't forget this,' he assured me viciously. 'You'll regret you meddled with me, I'll see to that.'

Bobby had succeeded in unloading Graves's first horse and was leading it across to its stable, while the lad and the driver closed the ramp and bolted it shut.

'Off you go, then, Mr Graves,' I said. 'Come back in the daytime and telephone first.'

He gave me a bullish stare and then suddenly went into the same routine as earlier: pursed his mouth, narrowed his eyes and abruptly quietened his rage. I had guessed, the first time, watching him write his cheque without further histrionics, that he had decided he might as well write it because he would tell his bank not to cash it.

It looked very much now as if he were planning something else. The question was, what?

I watched him walk calmly over to the horsebox and wave an impatient hand at the lad and the driver, telling them to get on board. Then he himself climbed clumsily up into the cab after them and slammed the door.

The engine started. The heavy vehicle throbbed, shuddered, and rolled away slowly out of the yard, Graves looking steadfastly ahead as if blinkered.

I detached myself from the stable door and walked across towards Bobby.

'Thanks,' he said.

'Be my guest.'

He looked round. 'All quiet. Let's go in. It's cold.'

'Mm.'

We walked two steps and I stopped.

'What is it?' Bobby asked, turning.

'Graves,' I said. 'He went too meekly.'

'He couldn't have done much else.'

'He could have gone shouting and kicking and uttering last-minute threats.'

'I don't know what you're worrying about. We've got his cheque and we've got his horses . . . er, thanks to you.'

His horses.

The breath in my lungs went out in a whoosh, steaming in a vanishing plume against the night sky.

'Bobby,' I said, 'have you any empty boxes?'

'Yes, there are some in the fillies' yard.' He was puzzled. 'Why?'

'We might just put Graves's horses in them, don't you think?'

'You mean . . . he might come back?' Bobby shook

his head. 'I'd hear him. I heard him before, though I admit that was lucky because we should have been out at a party, but we were too worried about things to go.'

'Could Graves have known you would be out?' I asked.

He looked startled. 'Yes, I suppose he could. The invitation is on the mantelpiece in the sitting room. He came in there last Sunday for a drink. Anyway, I'd hear a horsebox coming back. Couldn't miss it.'

'And if it parked at three in the morning on that strip of grass along from your gate, and the horses were led out in rubber boots to deaden the noise of their hooves?'

Bobby looked nonplussed. 'But he wouldn't. Not all that. Would he?'

'He was planning something. It showed.'

'All right,' Bobby said. 'We'll move them.'

On my way back to fetch the horse I'd been guarding I reflected that Bobby was uncommonly amenable to advice. He usually considered any suggestion from me to be criticism of himself and defensively found sixteen reasons for not doing what I'd mentioned: or at least not until I was well out of sight and wouldn't know. This evening things were different. Bobby had to be very worried indeed.

We walked Graves's horses round to Bobby's second yard behind the main quadrangle and installed them there in two empty boxes, which happened (all to the good, I thought) not to be side by side.

'Does Graves know his horses by sight?' I asked Bobby; which was not by any means a stupid question, as many owners didn't.

'I don't know,' he said dubiously. 'It's never come up.'

'In other words,' I said, 'he always knows them because they're where he expects to see them?'

'Yes. I should think so. But it's not certain. He might know them better than I think.'

'Well . . . in that case, how about rigging some sort of alarm?'

Bobby didn't say certainly not, it wasn't necessary, he said, 'Where?'

Incredible.

'On one of the boxes they are normally in,' I said.

'Yes. I see. Yes.' He paused. 'What sort of alarm? I haven't any electric gadgets here. If I need any special tight security before a big race I hire a man with a dog.'

I did a quick mental review of his house and its contents. Saucepan lids? Metal trays? Something to make a noise.

'The bell,' I said. 'Your old school bell.'

'In the study.' He nodded. 'I'll fetch it.'

Bobby's study contained shelves of tidily arranged mementoes of his blameless early life: cricket caps, silver cups won at school sports, team photographs, a rugger ball . . . and the hand bell which as a prefect he had rung noisily through his House to send the younger boys to bed. Bobby had been the sort of steadfast team-spirited boy that made the British public school system work: that he had emerged complacent and slightly pompous was probably owing to his many good qualities being manifest to all, including himself.

'Bring a hammer,' I said. 'And some staples if you have any. Nails, if not. And some heavy-duty string.'

'Right.'

He went away and in due course returned carrying the bell quietly by its clapper in one hand and a toolbox in the other. Between us we installed the bell as near to Bobby's house as possible and rigged it in such a way that a good tug to the string tied to its handle would send it toppling and jangling. Then we led the string through a long line of staples to the usual home of one of Graves's horses, and fastened the end of it out of sight to the top of the closed door.

'OK,' I said. 'Go into the house. I'll open this door and you see if you can hear the bell.'

He nodded and went away, and after a fair interval I opened the stable door. The bell fell with a satisfying clamour and Bobby came back saying it would wake the dead. We returned it to its precarious pre-toppling position and with rare accord walked together into the house.

There had been Fieldings and there had been Allardecks in racing further back than anyone could remember: two families with some land and some money and a bitter mutual persisting hatred.

There had been a Fielding and an Allardeck knifing each other for favour with King Charles II when he held court not in London but in Newmarket, thereby making foreign ambassadors travel wearily north-east by coach to present their credentials.

There had been an Allardeck who had wagered three hundred sovereigns on a two-horse race on Queen Anne's own racecourse on Ascot Heath and lost his money to a Fielding, who had been killed and robbed before he reached home.

There had been a Mr Allardeck in the Regency years who had challenged a Mr Fielding to a cross-country contest over fearsome jumps, the winner to take the other's horse. Mr Allardeck (who lost) accused Mr Fielding (an easy victor) of taking a cheating short cut, and the dispute went to pistols at dawn, when they each shot carefully at the other and died of their wounds.

There had been a Victorian gentleman rider named Fielding with a wild moustache and a wilder reputation, and an Allardeck who had fallen off, drunk, at the start of the Grand National. Fielding accused Allardeck of being a coward, Allardeck accused Fielding of seducing his (Allardeck's) sister. Both charges were true: and those two settled their differences by fisticuffs on Newmarket Heath, Fielding half killing the (again) drunk and frightened Allardeck.

By Edwardian times the two families were inextricably locked into inherited hostility and would accuse each other of anything handy. A particularly aggressive Fielding had bought an estate next door to the Allardecks on purpose to irritate, and bitter boundary disputes led to confrontations with shotguns and (more tamely) writs.

Bobby's great-grandfather burned down Great-grandfather Fielding's hay-barn (Great-grandfather Fielding having built it where it most spoiled the Allardeck's view) only to find his favourite hunter shot dead in its field a week later.

Bobby's grandfather and Grandfather Fielding had naturally been brought up to hate each other, the feud in their case extending later to bitter professional rivalry, as each (being a second son and not likely to inherit the family estate) had decided to set up as a licensed racehorse trainer. They each bought training stables in Newmarket and paid their lads to spy and report on the other. They cockily crowed when their horses won and seethed when the other's did, and, if coming first and second in the same race, lodged objections against each other almost as a matter of course.

Holly and I, being brought up in Grandfather Fielding's tempestuous household, were duly indoctrinated with the premise that all Allardecks were villainous madmen (or worse) who were to be cut dead at all times in Newmarket High Street.

Bobby and I, I dare say, each having been taught from birth to detest the other, might in our turn have come to fists or fire, were it not for my father dying, and Bobby's father leaving Newmarket with his family and going off into property and commodities. Not that Bobby's father, Maynard, could bear even the mention of the word Fielding: and the reason he was not speaking to Bobby (as truthfully noted in Intimate Details) was because Bobby Allardeck had dared, despite a promise of disinheritance, to defy his father's fury and walk up the aisle with Holly Fielding.

When Holly was thirteen her one absolute heroine had been Juliet in *Romeo and Juliet*. She learned almost the whole play by heart, but Juliet's part particularly, and became hopelessly romantic about the dead young lovers uniting the warring families of Montague and Capulet. Bobby Allardeck, I reckoned, was her Romeo, and she had been powerfully predisposed to fall in love with him, even if he hadn't been, as he was, tall, fair-haired and good-looking.

They had met by chance (or did she seek him out?) in London after several years of not seeing each other, and within a month were inseparable. The marriage had succeeded in its secret purpose to the extent that Bobby and I were now almost always polite to each other and that our children, if we had any, could, if they would, be friends.

Bobby and Holly had returned to Newmarket, Bobby hoping to take over as trainer in his by then ailing grandfather's yard, but the quarrelsome old man, calling his grandson a traitor to the family, had made him pay full market price for the property, and had then died, not leaving him a penny.

Bobby's current financial troubles were not simple. His house and yard (such small part of it as was free from mortgage) would as a matter of course be held by the bank as security for the extra loans they'd made him for the buying of yearlings. If the bank called in the loans, he and Holly would be left with no home, no livelihood, and an extremely bleak future.

As in many racing houses, a great deal of life went on in the kitchen, which in Holly and Bobby's case was typically furnished with a long dining table and a good number of comfortable chairs. A friendly room, with a lot of light pine, warmly lit and welcoming. When Bobby and I went in from the yard Holly was whisking eggs in a bowl and frying chopped onions and green peppers in a large pan.

'Smells good,' I said.

'I was starving.' She poured the eggs over the onions and peppers. 'We must all be.'

We ate the omelette with hot French bread and wine and talked of nothing much until we had finished.

Then Holly, making coffee, said, 'How did you get Jermyn Graves to go?'

'Jermyn? Is that his name? I told him if he stopped the cheque Bobby would put him on the forfeit list.'

'And don't think I haven't thought of it,' Bobby said.

'But of course it's a dead loss from our point of view really.'

I nodded. The Jockey Club would refrain from putting an owner on the forfeit list if he (or she) paid all training fees which had been owing for three months or more. Unfortunately, though, the forfeit list leverage applied to basic training fees only, and not to vets' or blacksmiths' fees or to the cost of transporting horses to race meetings. Bobby had had to pay out for all those things already for Graves's horses, and putting the owner on the forfeit list wouldn't get them reimbursed.

'Why is he in such a hurry to take his horses away?' I asked.

'He's just using our troubles as an excuse,' Holly said.

Bobby nodded. 'He's done something like this to at least two other trainers. All young and trying to get going, like us. He runs up big bills and then one day the trainer comes home and finds the horses gone. Then Graves pays the bare training fees to avoid the forfeit list, and the trainer's left with no horses as security and all the difficulties and expense of going to court to try to get what he's owed, and of course it's seldom worth it, and Graves gets away with it.'

'Why did you accept his horses in the first place?' I said.

'We didn't know about him, then,' Holly said gloomily. 'And we're not exactly going to turn away people who ask us to take two horses, are we?'

'No,' I said.

'Anyway,' Holly said, 'Jermyn's just another blow. The worst crisis is the feed-merchant.'

'Give him Graves's cheque,' I said.

Holly looked pleased but Bobby said dubiously, 'Our accountant doesn't like us doing that sort of thing.'

'Yeah, but your accountant hasn't got thirty hungry horses on his doorstep staring at him reproachfully.'

'Twenty-nine, really,' Holly said.

'Twenty-seven,' Bobby sighed, 'when Graves's have gone.'

'Does that include the three unsold yearlings?' I asked.

'Yes.'

I rubbed my nose. Twenty-four paying inmates were basically a perfectly viable proposition, even if in his grandfather's day there had been nearer forty. They were, moreover, just about to enter their annual rest period (as Bobby trained only on the Flat) and would no longer be incurring the higher expenses of the season.

Conversely they could not until the following March win any prize money, but then nor would they be losing any bets.

Winter, in flat-racing stables, was time for equilibrium, for holidays, for repainting, and for breaking in the yearlings, sold or not.

'Apart from the unsold yearlings, how much do you owe?' I asked.

I didn't think Bobby would tell me, but after a pause, reluctantly, he did.

I winced.

'But we can pay everything,' Holly said. 'At our own pace. We always do.'

Bobby nodded.

'And it's so unfair about the yearlings,' my sister said passionately. 'One of our owners told Bobby to go up to fifty thousand to get one particular yearling, and Bobby did, and now the owner's telephoned to say he's very sorry he can't afford it after all; he just hasn't got the money. And if we send it back to the next sale, we'll make a loss. It's always that way. People will think there's something wrong with it.'

'I'll probably be able to syndicate it,' Bobby said. 'Sell twelve equal shares. But it takes time to do that.'

'Well,' I said, 'surely the bank will give you time.'

'The bank manager's panic-stricken by that damned newspaper.'

'Did someone deliver it to him too?' I asked.

Holly said gloomily, 'Someone did.'

I told Bobby what Lord Vaughnley had said about the *Flag*'s informant being someone local with a grudge.

'Yes, but who?' Bobby said. 'We really haven't any enemies.' He gave me a sidelong look in which humour was definitely surfacing. 'Once upon a time it would have been a Fielding.'

'Too true.'

'Grandfather!' Holly said. 'It couldn't be him, could it? He's never forgiven me, but surely . . . he wouldn't?'

We thought of the obstinate old curmudgeon who still trained a yardful of horses half a mile away and bellowed at his luckless lads on the Heath every morning. He was still, at eighty-two, a wiry, vigorous, cunningly intelligent plotter whose chief regret these days was that Bobby's grandfather was no longer alive to be outsmarted.

It was true that Grandfather Fielding had been as outraged as Grandfather Allardeck by the unthinkable nuptials, but the man who brought us up had loved us in his own testy way, and I couldn't believe he would actively try to destroy his granddaughter's future. Not unless old age was warping him into malice, as it sadly could sometimes.

'I'll go and ask him,' I said.

'Tonight?' Holly looked at the clock. 'He'll be in bed. He goes so early.'

'In the morning.'

'I don't want it to be him,' Holly said.

'Nor do I.'

We sat over the coffee for a while, and at length I said, 'Make a list of all the people who you know had the *Flag* delivered to them with that paragraph marked, and I'll go and call on some of them tomorrow. All I can get to on a Sunday.'

'What for?' Bobby said. 'They won't change their

minds. I've tried. They just say they want their money at once. People believe what they read in newspapers. Even when it's all lies, they believe it.'

'Mm,' I said. 'But apart from telling them again that they'll be paid OK I'll ask them if any of them saw the paper being delivered. Ask them what time it came. Get a picture of what actually went on.'

'All right,' Holly said. 'We'll make the list.'

'And after that,' I said, 'work out who could possibly know who you deal with. Who could have written the same list. Unless, of course,' I reflected, 'dozens of other people who you don't owe money to got the paper delivered to them as well.'

'I've no idea,' Holly said. 'We never thought of that.'

'We'll find out tomorrow.'

Bobby yawned. 'Scarcely slept last night,' he said.

'Yes. Holly told me.'

There was suddenly a loud clanging from outside, a fierce and urgent alarm, enough to reawaken all the houses, if not the dead.

'God!' Bobby leapt to his feet, crashing his chair over backwards. 'He came back!'

We pelted out into the yard, all three of us, intent on catching Jermyn Graves in the act of trying to steal away his own property; and we did indeed find an extremely bewildered man holding open a stable door.

It was not, however, Jermyn Graves, but Nigel,

Bobby's ancient head lad. He had switched on the light inside the empty box and turned his weatherbeaten face to us as he heard us approach, the light carving deep canyons in his heavy vertical wrinkles.

'Sooty's gone,' he said anxiously. 'Sooty's gone, guv'nor. I fed him myself at half-six, and all the doors were shut and bolted when I went home.' There was a detectable tinge of defensiveness in his voice which Bobby also heard and laid to rest.

'I moved him,' he said easily. 'Sooty's fine.'

Sooty was not the real name of Graves's horse, but the real names of some horses tended to be hopeless mouthfuls for their attendant lads. It was hard to sound affectionate when saying (for instance) Nettleton Manor. Move over Nettleton Manor. Nettleton Manor, you old rogue, have a carrot.

'I was just taking a last look round,' Nigel said. 'Going home from the pub, like.'

Bobby nodded. Nigel, like most head lads, took the welfare of the horses as a personal pride. Beyond duty, their horses could be as dear to head lads as their own children, and seeing they were safely tucked up last thing at night was a parental urge that applied to both species.

'Did you hear a bell ring?' Holly said.

'Yes.' He wrinkled his forehead. 'Near the house.' He paused. 'What was it?'

'A new security system we're trying out,' Bobby said.

'The bell rings to tell us someone's moving about the yard.'

'Oh?' Nigel looked interested. 'Works a treat then, doesn't it?'

CHAPTER FOUR

Work a treat the bell might, but no one came in the small hours to tug it again to its sentinel duty. I slept undisturbed in jeans and sweater, ready for battle but not called, and Bobby went out and disconnected the string before the lads arrived for work in the morning.

He and Holly had written out the list of *Flag* recipients, and after coffee, when it was light, I set off in Holly's car to seek them out.

I went first, though, as it was Sunday and early, to every newsagent, both in the town and within a fair radius of the outskirts, asking if they had sold a lot of copies of the *Flag* to any one person two days ago, on Friday, or if anyone had arranged for many extra copies to be delivered on that morning.

The answer was a uniform negative. Sales of the *Flag* on Friday had been the same as Thursday, give or take. None of the shops, big or small, had ordered more copies than usual, they said, and no one had sold right out of the *Flag*. The boys had done their regular delivery rounds, nothing more.

Dead end to the first and easiest trail.

I went next to seek out the feed-merchant, who was not the one who supplied my grandfather. I had been struck at once, in fact, by the unfamiliarity of all the names of Bobby's suppliers, though when one thought about it, it was probably only to be expected. Bobby, taking over from his grandfather, would continue to use his grandfather's suppliers: and never, it seemed, had the lifelong antagonists used the same blacksmith, the same vet, the same anything. Each had always believed the other would spy on him, given the slightest opportunity. Each had been right.

No feed-merchant in Newmarket, with several thousand horses round about, would find it strange to have his doorbell rung on his theoretical day of rest. The feed-merchant who waved me into the brick office annexe to his house was young and polished; and in an expensive accent and with crispness he told me it was not good business to allow accounts to run on overdue, he had his own cash-flow to consider, and Allardeck's credit had run out.

I handed him Jermyn Graves's cheque, duly endorsed by Bobby on the back.

'Ah,' said the feed-merchant, brightening. 'Why ever didn't you say so?'

'Bobby hoped you might wait, as usual.'

'Sorry. No can do. Cash on delivery from now on.'

'That cheque is for more than your account,' I pointed out.

'So it is. Right then. Bobby shall be supplied until this runs out.'

'Thank you,' I said, and asked him if he had seen his copy of the *Flag* delivered.

'No. Why?'

I explained why. 'This was a large scale and deliberate act of spite. One tends to want to know who.'

'Ah.'

I waited. He considered.

'It must have been here fairly early Friday morning,' he said finally. 'And it was delivered here to the office, not to the house, as the papers usually are. I picked it up with the letters when I came in. Say about eight-thirty.'

'And it was open at the gossip page with the paragraph outlined in red?'

'That's right.'

'Didn't you wonder who'd sent it?'

'Not really . . .' He frowned. 'I thought someone was doing me a good turn.'

'Mm,' I said. 'Do you take the *Flag* usually?'

'No, I don't. *The Times* and the *Sporting Life*.'

I thanked him and left, and took Holly's winnings to the plumber, who greeted me with satisfaction and gave me some of the same answers as the feed-merchant. The *Flag* had been inside his house on the front door mat by seven o'clock, and he hadn't seen who brought it. Mr Allardeck owed him for some pipe-work done way back in the summer, and he would admit, he said, that he had telephoned and threatened him pretty strongly with a county court action if he didn't pay up at once.

Did the plumber take the *Flag* usually?

Yes, he did. On Friday, he got two.

'Together?' I asked. 'I mean, were they both there on the mat at seven?'

'Yes. They were.'

'Which was on top of the other?'

He shrugged, thought, and said, 'As far as I remember, the one marked in red was underneath. Funny, I thought it was, that the boy had delivered two. Then I saw the paragraph, and I reckoned one of my neighbours was tipping me off.'

I said it was all very hard on Bobby.

'Yes, well, I suppose so.' He sniffed. 'He's not the only bad payer, by a long shot.' He gave me the beginnings of a sardonic smile. 'They pay up pretty quick when their pipes burst. Come a nice heavy freeze.'

I tried three more creditors on the list. Still unpaid, they were more brusque and less helpful, but an overall pattern held good. The marked papers had been delivered before the newsboys did their rounds and no one had seen who delivered them.

I went back to the largest of the newsagents and asked the earliest time their boys set out.

'The papers reach us here by van at six. We sort them into the rounds, and the boys set off on their bicycles before six-thirty.'

'Thanks,' I said.

They nodded. 'Any time.'

Disturbed by the stealth and thoroughness of the operation I drove finally to see my grandfather in the house where I'd been brought up: a large brick-built place with gables like comic eyebrows peering down at a barbed-wire-topped boundary fence.

The yard was deserted when I drove in, all the horses in their boxes with the top doors closed against the cold. On the day after the last day of the Flat season, no one went out to gallop on the Heath. Hibernation, which my grandfather hated, was already setting in.

I found him in his stable office, typing letters with concentration, the result, I surmised, of the departure of yet another beleaguered secretary.

'Kit!' he said, glancing up momentarily. 'I didn't know you were coming. Sit down. Get a drink.' He waved a thin hand. 'I won't be long. Damned secretary walked out. No consideration, none at all.'

I sat and watched while he hammered the keys with twice the force necessary, and felt the usual slightly exasperated affection for him, and the same admiration.

He loved horses beyond all else. He loved Grandmother next best and had gone very silent for a while the winter she'd died, the house eerily quiet after the years they'd spent shouting at each other. Within a few months he had begun shouting at Holly and me instead, and later, after we'd left, at the secretaries. He didn't intend to be unkind. In an imperfect world he was a perfectionist irritated by minor incompetencies, which meant most of the time.

The typing stopped. He stood up, the same height as myself, white-haired, straight and trim in shirt, tie and excellently cut tweed jacket. Casual my grandfather was not, not in habits or manners or dress, and if he was obsessive by nature it was probably just that factor which had brought him notable success over almost sixty years.

'There's some cheese,' he said, 'for lunch. Are you staying tonight?'

'I'm, er, staying with Holly.'

His mouth compressed sharply. 'Your place is here.'

'I wish you'd make it up with her.'

'I talk to her now,' he said, 'which is more than can be said for that arrogant Maynard with his rat of a son. She comes up here some afternoons. Brings me stews and things sometimes. But I won't have him here and I won't go there, so don't ask.' He patted my arm, the ultimate indication of approval. 'You and I, we get along all right, eh? That's enough.'

He led the way to the dining room where two trays lay on the table, each covered with a cloth. He removed one cloth to reveal a carefully laid single lunch: cheeses, biscuits under clingfilm, pats of butter, dish of chutney, a banana and an apple with a silver fruit knife. The other tray was for dinner.

'New housekeeper,' he said succinctly. 'Very good.'

Long may she last, I thought. I removed the clingfilm and brought another knife and plate, and the two of us sat there politely eating very little, he from age, I from necessity.

I told him about the paragraph in the *Flag* and knew at once with relief that he'd had no hand in it.

'Nasty,' he said. 'Mind you, my old father could have done something like that, if he'd thought of it. Might have done it myself,' he chuckled, 'long ago. To Allardeck.' Allardeck, to Grandfather, was Bobby's grandfather, Maynard's father, the undear departed. Grandfather had never in my hearing called him anything but plain Allardeck.

'Not to Holly,' my grandfather said. 'Couldn't do it to Holly. Wouldn't be fair.'

'No.'

He looked at me searchingly. 'Did she think it might be me?'

'She said it couldn't be, and also that she very much didn't want it to be you.'

He nodded, satisfied and unhurt. 'Quite right. Little Holly. Can't think what possessed her, marrying that little rat.'

'He's not so bad,' I said.

'He's like Allardeck. Just the same. Smirking all over his face when his horse beat mine at Kempton two weeks ago.'

'But you didn't lodge an objection, I noticed.'

'Couldn't. No grounds. No bumping, boring or

crossing. His horse won by three lengths.' He was disgusted. 'Were you there? I didn't see you.'

'Read it in the paper.'

'Huh.' He chose the banana. I ate the apple. 'I saw you win the Towncrier yesterday on television. Rotten horse, full of hate. You could see it.'

'Mm.'

'You get people like that, too,' he observed. 'Chockful of ability and too twisted up to do anything worthwhile.'

'He did win,' I pointed out.

'Just. Thanks to you. And don't argue about that, it's something I enjoy, watching you ride. There never was an Allardeck anywhere near your class.'

'And I suppose that's what you said to Allardeck himself?'

'Yes, of course. He hated it.' Grandfather sighed. 'It's not the same since he's gone. I thought I'd be glad, but it's taken some of the point out of life. I used to enjoy his sour looks when I got the better of him. I got him barred from running his horse in the St Leger once, because my spies told me it had ringworm. Did I tell you that? He would have killed me that day if he could. But he'd stolen one of my gullible lady owners with a load of lies about me never entering her horses where they could win. They didn't win for him either, as I never let him forget.' He cut the peeled banana into neat pieces and sat looking at them. 'Maynard, now,' he said, 'Maynard hates my guts too, but he's not worth the ground Allardeck stood on. Maynard is a power-hungry egomaniac, just the same, but he's also a creeper, which his father never was, for all his faults.'

'How do you mean, a creeper?'

'A bully to the weak but a boot-licker to the strong. Maynard boot-licked his way up every ladder, stamping down on all the people he passed. He was a hateful child. Smarmy. He had the cheek to come up to me once on the Heath and tell me that when he grew up he was going to be a lord, because then I would have to bow to him, and so would everyone else.'

'Did he really?'

'He was quite small. Eight or nine. I told him he was repulsive and clipped his ear. He snitched to his father, of course, and Allardeck sent me a stiff letter of complaint. Long ago, long ago.' He ate a slice of banana without enthusiasm. 'But that longing for people to bow to him, he's still got it, I should think. Why else does he take over all those businesses?'

'To win,' I said. 'Like we win, you and I, if we can.'

'We don't trample on people doing it. We don't want to be bowed to.' He grinned. 'Except by Allardecks, of course.'

We made some coffee and while we drank I telephoned some of Grandfather's traditional suppliers, and his vet and blacksmith and plumber. All were surprised at my question, and no, none of them had received a marked copy of the *Flag*.

'The little rat's got a traitor right inside his camp,'

Grandfather said without noticeable regret. 'Who's his secretary?'

'No one. He does everything himself.'

'Huh. Allardeck had a secretary.'

'You told me about fifty times Allardeck had a secretary only because you did. You boasted in his hearing that you needed a secretary as you had so many horses to train, so he got one too.'

'He never could bear me having more than he did.'

'And if I remember right,' I said, 'you were hopping up and down when he got some practice starting stalls, until you got some too.'

'No one's perfect.' He shrugged dismissively. 'If the little rat hasn't got a secretary, who else knows his life inside out?'

'That,' I said, 'is indeed the question.'

'Maynard,' Grandfather said positively. 'That's who. Maynard lived in that house, remember, until long after he was married. He married at eighteen . . . stupid, I thought it, but Bobby was on the way. And then he was in and out for at least another fifteen years, when he was supposed to be Allardeck's assistant, but was always creeping off to London to do all those deals. Cocoa! Did you ever hear of anyone making a fortune out of cocoa? That was Maynard. Allardeck smirked about it for weeks, going on and on about how smart his son was. Well, my son was dead, as I reminded him pretty sharply one day, and he shut up after that.'

'Maynard wouldn't destroy Bobby's career,' I said.

'Why not? He hasn't spoken to him since he took up with Holly. Holly told me if Maynard wants to say anything to Bobby he gets his tame lawyer to write, and all the letters so far have been about Bobby repaying some money Maynard lent him to buy a car when he left school. Holly says Bobby was so grateful he wrote his father a letter thanking him and promising to repay him one day, and now Maynard's holding him to it.'

'I can't believe it.'

'Absolutely true.'

'What a bastard.'

'The one thing Maynard is actually not,' Grandfather said dryly, 'is a bastard. He's got Allardeck's looks stamped all over him. The same sneer. The same supercilious smirk. Lanky hair. No chin. The little rat's just like them, too.'

Bobby, the little rat, was to any but a Fielding eye a man with a perfectly normal chin and a rather pleasant smile, but I let it pass. The sins and shortcomings of the Allardecks, past and present, could never be assessed impartially in a Fielding house.

I stayed with Grandfather all afternoon and walked round the yard with him at evening stables at four-thirty, the short winter day already darkening and the lights in the boxes shining yellow.

The lads were busy, as always, removing droppings, carrying hay and water, setting the boxes straight. The long-time head lad (at whom Grandfather never shouted) walked round with us, both of them briefly discussing details of each of the fifty or so horses. Their voices were quiet, absorbed and serious, and also in a way regretful, as the year's expectations and triumphs were all over, excitement put away.

I dreaded the prospect of those excitements being put away for ever: of Grandfather ill or dying. He wouldn't retire before he had to, because his job was totally his life, but it was expected that at some point not too very far ahead I would return to live in that house and take over the licence. Grandfather expected it, the owners were prepared for it, the racing world in general thought it a foregone conclusion; and I knew that I was far from ready. I wanted four more years, or five, at the game I had a passion for. I wanted to race for as long as my body was fit and uninjured and anyone would pay me. Jump jockeys never went on riding as long as flat jockeys because crunching to the ground at thirty miles an hour upwards of thirty times a year is a young man's sport, but I'd always thought of thirty-five as approximately hanging-up-the-boots time.

By the time I was thirty-five, Grandfather would be eighty-seven, and even for him . . . I shivered in the cold air and thrust the thought away. The future would have to be faced, but it wasn't upon me yet.

To Grandfather's great disgust I left him after stables and went back to the enemy house, to find the tail end of the same evening ritual still in progress. Graves's horses were still in the fillies' yard, and Bobby was feeling safer because Nigel had told him that Graves had at least twice mistaken other horses for his own when he'd called to see them on Sunday mornings.

I watched Bobby with his horses as he ran his hand down their legs to feel for heat in strained tendons, and peered at the progress of minor skin eruptions, and slapped their rumps as a friendly gesture. He was a natural-born horseman, there was no doubt, and the animals responded to him in the indefinable way that they do to someone they feel comfortable with.

I might find him a bit indecisive sometimes, and not a razor-brain, but he was in truth a good enough fellow, and I could see how Holly could love him. He had, moreover, loved her enough himself to turn his back on his ancestors and estrange himself from his powerful father, and it had taken strength, I reckoned, to do that.

He stood up from feeling a leg and saw me watching him, and with an instinct straight from the subconscious stretched to his full height and gave me a hawk-like look of vivid antagonism.

'Fielding,' he said flatly, as if the word itself was an accusation and a curse: a declaration of continuing war.

'Allardeck,' I replied, in the same way. I grinned slightly. 'I was thinking, as a matter of fact, that I liked you.'

'Oh!' He relaxed as fast as he'd tensed, and looked confused. 'I don't know . . . for a moment . . . I felt . . .'

'I know,' I said, nodding. 'Hatred.'

'Your eyes were in shadow. You looked . . . hooded.'

It was an acceptable explanation and a sort of apology; and I thought how irrational it was that the deep conditioning raised itself so quickly to the surface, and in myself on occasions just the same, however I might try to stop it.

He finished the horses without comment and we walked back towards the house.

'I'm sorry,' he said then, with a touch of awkwardness. 'Back there . . .' He waved a hand. 'I didn't mean it.'

I asked curiously, 'Do you ever think of Holly in that way? As a Fielding? If her eyes are in shadow, does she seem a menace?'

'No, of course not. She's different.'

'How is she different?'

He glanced at my face and seemed to find it all right to explain. 'You,' he said, 'are strong. I mean, in your mind, not just muscles. No one who's talked to you much could miss it. It makes you . . . I don't know . . . somehow people notice when you're there, like in the weighing room, or somewhere. People would be able to say if you'd been at a particular race meeting or not, or at a party, even though you don't try. I suppose I'm not making sense. It's what's made you a champion jockey, I should think, and it's totally *Fielding*. Well, Holly's not like that. She's gentle and calm and she hasn't an ounce of aggressiveness or ambition, and she doesn't want to go out and beat the world on horses, so she isn't really a Fielding at heart.'

'Mm.' It was a dry noise from the throat more than a word. Bobby gave me another quick glance. 'It's all right,' I said. 'I'll plead guilty to my inheritance, and also exonerate her from it. But she does have ambition.'

'No.' He shook his head positively.

'For you,' I said. 'For you to be a lasting success. For you both to be. To prove you were right to get married.'

He paused with his hand on the knob of the door which led from the yard to the kitchen. 'You were against it, like all the others.'

'Yes, for various reasons. But not now.'

'Not on the actual day,' he said with fairness. 'You were the only one that turned up.'

'She couldn't walk up that aisle by herself, could she?' I said. 'Someone had to go with her.'

He smiled as instinctively as before he'd hated.

'A Fielding giving a Fielding to an Allardeck,' he said. 'I wondered at the time if there would be an earthquake.'

He opened the door and we went in. Holly, who bound us together, had lit the log fire in the sitting room and was trying determinedly to be cheerful.

We sat in armchairs and I told them about my morning travels, and also assured them of Grandfather's non-involvement.

'The marked copies of the *Flag* were on people's mats at least by six,' I said, 'and they came from outside, not from Newmarket. I don't know what time the papers get to the shops in Cambridge, but not a great deal before five, I shouldn't think, and there couldn't have been much time for anyone to buy twenty or so papers in Cambridge and deliver them, folded and marked, to addresses all over Newmarket, twenty miles away, before the newsboys here started on their rounds.'

'London?' Holly said. 'Do you think someone brought them up direct?'

'I should think so,' I nodded. 'Of course that doesn't necessarily mean that it wasn't someone from here who arranged it, or even did it personally, so we're not much further ahead.'

'It's all so pointless,' Holly said.

'No one seems to have been looking out of their windows by six,' I went on. 'You'd think someone would be, in this town. But no one that I asked had seen anyone walking up to anyone's door with a newspaper at that time. It was black dark, of course. They said they hardly ever see the newsboys themselves, in winter.'

The telephone on the desk beside Bobby's chair rang, and Bobby stretched out a hand to pick up the receiver with a look of apprehension.

'Oh . . . hello, Seb,' he said. There was some relief in his voice, but not much.

'Friend,' Holly said to me. 'Has a horse with us.'

'You saw it, did you?' Bobby made a face. 'Someone

sent you a copy . . .' He listened, then said, 'No, of course I don't know who. It's sheer malice. No, of course it's not true. I'm here in business to stay, and don't worry, your mare is very well and I was just now feeling her tendon. It's cool and firm and doing fine. What? Father? He won't guarantee a penny, he said so. Yes, you may well say he's a ruthless swine . . . No, there's no hope of it. In fact on the contrary he's trying to squeeze out of me some money he lent me to buy a car about fourteen years ago. Yes, well . . . I suppose it's that sort of flint that's made him rich. What? No, not a fortune, it was a second-hand old banger, but my first. I suppose I'll have to pay him in the end just to get his lawyers off my back. Yes, I told you, everything's fine. Pay no attention to the *Flag*. Sure, Seb, any time. Bye.'

He put down the receiver, his air nowhere near as confident as his telephone voice.

'Another owner full of doubt. Load of rats. Half of them are thinking of leaving without waiting to see if the ship will sink. Half of them, as well, haven't paid their last month's bills.'

'Has Seb?' asked Holly.

Bobby shook his head.

'He's got a cheek, then.'

'That wretched paragraph reached him by post yesterday: just the Intimate Details column. A clipping, he said, not the whole paper. In an ordinary brown envelope, typed. From London, like the others.'

'Did all the owners get a clipping?' I asked.

'It looks like it. Most of them have been on the phone. I haven't exactly rung the rest to ask.'

We sat around for a while, and I borrowed the telephone to pick up my messages from the answering machine in the cottage, and to call in return a couple of trainers who'd offered rides during the week, and to talk to a couple of jockeys who lived in Newmarket, asking for a lift down to Plumpton in Sussex for racing the next day. Two of them were already going together, they said, and would take me.

'Will you come back here?' Holly said, when all was fixed.

I looked at the anxiety in her face and the lack of opposition in Bobby's. I wouldn't have expected him to want me even in the first place, but it seemed I was wrong.

'Stay,' he said briefly, but with invitation, not grudge.

'I haven't been much help.'

'We feel better,' Holly said, 'with you here.'

I didn't much want to stay because of practical considerations. I was due to ride in Devon on the Tuesday, and one reason I preferred to live in Lambourn, not Newmarket, was that from Lambourn one could drive to every racecourse in England and return home on the same day. Lambourn was central.

I said apologetically, 'I'll have to get a lift back to Lambourn from Plumpton, because I need my car to go to Devon on Tuesday. When I get back to Lambourn on Tuesday evening, we'll see how things are here.'

Holly said, 'All right,' dispiritedly, not attempting to persuade.

I looked at her downcast face, more beautiful, as often, in sorrow than in joy. A thought came unexpectedly into my head and I said without reflection, 'Holly, are you pregnant?'

CHAPTER FIVE

Bobby was dumbstruck.

Holly gave me a piercing look from the light brown eyes in which I read both alarm and stimulation.

'Why did you say that?' Bobby demanded.

'She's only a short while overdue. We haven't had any tests done yet,' Bobby said; and to Holly, 'You must have told him.'

'No, I haven't.' She shook her head. 'But I was thinking just then how happy I was first thing on Friday, when I woke up feeling sick. I was thinking how ironic it would be. All those months of trying, and the first time it may really have happened, we are in such trouble that the very last thing we need is a baby.'

Bobby frowned. 'You must have told him,' he repeated, and he sounded definitely upset, almost as if he were jealous.

'Well, no, I didn't,' Holly said uncertainly.

'On the way back here yesterday,' he insisted.

'Look,' I said. 'Forget I said it. What does it matter?'

Bobby looked at me with resentment and then more

forgivingly at Holly, as if some thought had struck him. 'Is this the sort of thing you meant,' he said doubtfully, 'when you told me once about you and Kit reading each other's minds when you were kids?'

She reluctantly nodded. 'We haven't done it for years, though.'

'It doesn't happen nowadays,' I agreed. 'I mean, this was just a one-off. A throw-back. I don't suppose it will happen again.'

And if it did happen again, I thought, I would be more careful what I said. Stray thoughts would be sieved.

I understood Bobby's jealousy perfectly well because I had felt it myself, extraordinarily strongly, when Holly first told me she had fallen in love. The jealousy had been quickly overlaid by a more normal dismay when she'd confessed just who it was she'd set her heart on, but I still remembered the sharpness of not wanting to share her, not wanting my status as her closest friend to be usurped by a stranger.

I'd been slightly shocked at my jealousy and done a fair amount of soul-searching, never before having questioned my feelings for my sister: and I'd made the reassuring but also rueful discovery that she could sleep with Bobby all she liked and leave me undisturbed: it was the mental intimacy I minded losing.

There had been sexual adventures of my own, of course, both before and after her marriage, but they had been short-lived affairs with no deep involvement, nothing anywhere approaching Holly's commitment to Bobby. Plenty of time, I thought, and maybe, one of these days; and platitudes like that.

Bobby made at least a show of believing that telepathy between me and Holly wouldn't happen again, although both she and I, giving each other the merest flick of a glance, guessed differently. If we chose to tune in, so to speak, the old habit would come back.

The three of us spent the evening trying not to return over and over to the central questions of who and why, and in the end went wearily to bed without any possible answers. I lay down again in jeans, jersey and socks in case Graves should return, but I reckoned that if he'd ever planned it, he had had second thoughts.

I was wrong.

The bell woke me with a clatter at three-thirty-five in the morning, and I was into my shoes, out of the house and running down the drive, in the strategy that Bobby and I had discussed the night before, almost before it stopped ringing.

Out of the open gateway, turn left; and sure enough, on a stretch of roadside grass that sometimes accommodated gypsies, stood the wherewithal for shifting horses. A car, this time, towing a two-horse trailer. A trailer with its rear ramp lowered; ready, but not yet loaded.

I ran straight up to the car and yanked open the driver's door, but there was no one inside to be taken by surprise. Just keys in the ignition; unbelievable.

I lifted up the trailer's ramp and bolted it shut, then

climbed into the car, started up, and drove a couple of hundred yards to a side road. I turned into there, parked a short way along, left the keys in the ignition as before, and sprinted back to Bobby's yard.

The scene was almost a repeat of the time before, at least as far as the lights, the shouting and obscenity went. Bobby and Jermyn Graves were standing outside the empty box where the alarm had been rigged and had all but come to blows. A thin boy of perhaps sixteen stood a short distance away, holding a large carrier bag, shifting from foot to foot and looking unhappy.

'Give me my property,' Graves yelled. 'This is stealing.'

'No, it's not,' I said in his ear. 'Stealing is an intention permanently to deprive.'

'What?' He swung round to glare at me. 'You again!'

'If you're talking law,' I said, 'it is within the law to withhold property upon which money is owed, until the debt is discharged.'

'I'll ruin you,' he said vindictively. 'I'll ruin you both.'

'Be sensible, Mr Graves,' I said. 'You're in the wrong.'

'Who the shit cares. I won't have some pipsqueak jockey and some bankrupt little trainer get the better of me, I'll tell you that.'

The attendant boy said nervously, 'Uncle . . .'

'You shut up,' Graves snapped.

The boy dropped the carrier and and fell over his feet picking it up.

'Go away, Mr Graves,' I said. 'Calm down. Think it over. Come and fetch your horses when your cheque's been cleared, and that'll be the end of it.'

'No, it won't.'

'Up to you,' I said, shrugging.

Bobby and I watched him try to extricate himself without severe loss of face, which could hardly be done. He delivered a few more threats with a good deal of bluster, and then finally, saying 'Come on, come on' irritably to his nephew, he stalked away down the drive.

'Did you immobilize his horsebox?' Bobby asked.

'It was a car and a trailer, and the key was in it. I just drove it out of sight round the nearest corner. Wonder if they'll find it.'

'I suppose we needn't have bothered,' Bobby said. 'As Graves went to the alarm box first.'

We had thought he might go to his other horse's box first, find it empty, think he had the wrong place, and perhaps remove one of the horses from either side. We thought he might have brought more men. In the event, he hadn't done either. But the precaution, all the same, might have been worth it.

We closed the empty stable and Bobby kicked against something on the ground. He bent to pick it up, and held it out for me to see: a large piece of thick felt with pieces of velcro attached. A silencer for a hoof. Fallen out of the carrier, no doubt.

'Not leather boots,' Bobby said, grimly. 'Home-made.'

He switched off the yard lights and we stood for a while near the kitchen door, waiting. We would hear the car and trailer drive off, we thought, in the quiet night. What we heard instead, however, were hesitant footsteps coming back into the yard.

Bobby turned the lights on again, and the boy stood there, blinking and highly embarrassed.

'Someone's stolen Uncle's car,' he said.

'What's your name?' I asked.

'Jasper.'

'Graves?'

He nodded and swallowed. 'Uncle wants me to ring the police and get a taxi.'

'If I were you,' I said, 'I'd go out of the gate here, turn left, take the first turn to the left along the road a bit, and use the public telephone box you'll find down there.'

'Oh,' he said. 'All right.' He looked at us almost beseechingly. 'It was only supposed to be a lark,' he said. 'It's all gone wrong.'

We gave him no particular comfort, and after a moment he turned and went away again down the drive, his footsteps slowly receding.

'What do you think?' Bobby said.

'I think we should rig the bell so that anyone coming up the drive sets it off.'

'So do I. And I'll disconnect it first thing when I get up.'

We began to run a blackened string tightly across the drive at knee level, and heard Graves's car start up in the distance.

'He's found it,' Bobby said. He smiled. 'There's no telephone box down that road, did you know?'

We finished the elementary alarm system and went yawning indoors to sleep for another couple of hours, and I reflected, as I lay down, about the way a feud could start, as with Graves, and continue through centuries, as with Allardecks and Fieldings, and could expand into political and religious persecutions on a national scale, permanently persisting as a habit of mind, a destructive hatred stuck in one groove. I would make a start in my own small corner, I thought sardonically, drifting off, and force my subconscious to love the Allardecks, of which my own sister, God help her, was one.

Persistence raised its ugliest head first thing in the morning.

I answered the telephone when it rang at eight-thirty because Bobby was out exercising his horses and Holly was again feeling sick: and it was the feed-merchant calling in his Etonian accent to say that he had received a further copy of the *Daily Flag*.

'I've just picked it up,' he said. 'It's today's paper. Monday. There's another piece outlined in red.'

'What does it say?' I asked, my heart sinking.

'I think . . . well . . . you can come and fetch it, if you like. It's longer, this time. And there's a picture of Bobby.'

'I'll be there.'

I drove straight round in Holly's car and found the feed-merchant in his office as before. Silently he handed me the paper, and with growing dismay I looked at the picture which made Bobby seem a grinning fool, and read the damage in Intimate Details.

Money troubles abound for Robertson (Bobby) Allardeck (32), still training a few racehorses in his grandfather's once-bustling stables in Newmarket. Local traders threaten court action over unpaid bills. Bobby weakly denies the owners of the remaining horses should be worried, although the feed-merchant has stopped deliveries. Where will it end?

Not with manna from heaven from Daddy.

Maynard 'Moneybags' Allardeck (50), cross with Bobby for marrying badly, won't come to the rescue.

Maynard, known to be fishing for a knighthood, gives all his spare cash to charity.

Needy Bobby's opinion? Unprintable.

Watch this space for more.

'If Bobby doesn't sue for libel,' I said, 'his father surely will.'

'Greater the truth, greater the libel,' the feed-merchant said dryly, and added, 'Tell Bobby his credit's good with me again. I've been thinking it over. He's always paid me regularly, even if always late. And I don't like being manipulated by muck like that.' He pointed to the paper. 'So tell Bobby I'll supply him as before. Tell him to tell his owners.'

I thanked him and went back to Bobby's house, and read Intimate Details again over a cup of coffee in the kitchen. Then I pensively telephoned the feed-merchant.

'Did you,' I said, 'actually tell anyone that you intended to stop making deliveries to Bobby?'

'I told Bobby.' He sounded equally thoughtful. 'No one else.'

'Positive.'

'Not even your secretary? Or your family?'

'I admit that on Friday I was very annoyed and wanted my money immediately, but no one overheard my giving Bobby a talking to about it, I'm quite certain. My secretary doesn't come in until eleven on Fridays, and as you know, my office is an annexe. I was alone when I telephoned him, I assure you.'

'Well, thanks,' I said.

'The informant must be at Bobby's end,' he insisted.

'Yes. I think you're right.'

We disconnected and I began to read the *Daily Flag*

from start to finish, which I'd never done before, seeking enlightenment perhaps on what made a newspaper suddenly attack an inoffensive man and aim to destroy him.

The *Flag*'s overall and constant tone, I found, was of self-righteous spite, its message a sneer, its aftertaste guaranteed to send a reader belligerently out looking for an excuse to take umbrage or to spread ill will.

Any story that would show someone in a poor light was in. Praise was out. The put-down had been developed to a minor art, so that a woman, however prominent or successful, did not 'say'; instead she 'trilled', or she 'shrilled', or she 'wailed'. A man 'chortled', or he 'fumed', or he 'squeaked'.

The word 'anger' appeared on every single page. All sorts of things were 'slammed', but not doors. People were reported as denying things in a way that interpreted 'deny' as 'guilty but won't own up'; and the word 'claims', in the *Flag*'s view, as, for instance, in 'He claims he saw . . .' was synonymous with 'He is lying when he says he saw . . .'

The *Flag* thought that respect was unnecessary, envy was normal, all motives were loved; and presumably it was what people wanted to read, as the circulation (said the *Flag*) was increasing daily.

On the premise that a newspaper ultimately reflected the personality of its owner, as the *Towncrier* did Lord Vaughnley's, I thought the proprietor of the *Daily Flag* to be destructive, calculating, mean-spirited and dangerous. Not a good prospect. It meant one couldn't with any hope of success appeal to the *Flag*'s better nature to let up on Bobby, because a better nature it didn't have.

Holly came downstairs looking wan but more cheerful, Bobby returned from the Heath with reviving optimism, and I found the necessity of demolishing their fragile recovery just one more reason to detest the *Flag*.

Holly began to cry quietly and Bobby strode about the kitchen wanting to smash things, and still there was the unanswerable question: Why?

'This time,' I said, 'you consult your lawyer, and to hell with the cost. Also this time we are going to pay all your worst bills at once, and we are going to get letters from all your creditors saying they have been paid, and we'll get those letters photocopied by the dozen, and we'll send a set of them out to everyone who got a copy of the *Flag*, and to the *Flag* itself, to Sam Leggatt, the editor, special delivery, and to all the owners, and to anyone else we can think of, and we'll accompany these with a letter of your own saying you don't understand why the *Flag* is attacking you but the attacks have no foundation, the stable is in good shape and you are certainly not going out of business.'

'But,' Holly said, gulping, 'the bank manager won't honour our cheques.'

'Get the worst bills,' I said to Bobby, 'and let's have a look at them. 'Specially the blacksmith, the vets and the transport people. We'll pay those and any others that are vital.'

'What with?' he said irritably.

'With my money.'

They were both suddenly still, as if shocked, and I realized with a thrust of pleasure that that plain solution simply hadn't occurred to them. They were not askers, those two.

Holly couldn't disguise her upsurge of hope, but she said doubtfully, 'Your new house, though. It must be taking you all you've saved. You haven't been paid for the cottage yet.'

'There's enough,' I assured her. 'And let's get started because I'll have to be off to Plumpton pretty soon.'

'But we can't . . .' Bobby said.

'Yes, you must. Don't argue.'

Bobby looked pole-axed but he fetched the bunch of accounts and I made out several cheques.

'Take these round yourself this morning and get watertight receipts, and in a minute we'll write the letter to go with them,' I said. 'And see if you can get them all photocopied and clipped into sets in time to catch this afternoon's post. I know it's a bit of a job, but the sooner very much the better, don't you think?'

'And one set to Graves?' Bobby asked.

'Certainly to Graves.'

'We'll start immediately,' Holly said.

'Don't forget the feed-merchant,' I said. 'He'll write

you something good. He didn't like being made use of by the *Flag*.'

'I don't like to mention it . . .' Holly began slowly.

'The bank?' I asked.

She nodded.

'Leave the bank for now. Tomorrow maybe you can go to the manager with a set of letters and see if he will reinstate you. He darned well ought to. His bank's making enough out of you in interest, especially on the yearling loans. And you do still have the yearlings as security.'

'Unfortunately,' Bobby said.

'One step at a time,' I said.

'I'll telephone my solicitor straight away,' he said, picking up the receiver and looking at his watch. 'He'll be in by now.'

'No, I shouldn't,' I said.

'But you said . . .'

'You've got an informant right inside this house.'

'What do you mean?'

'Your telephone,' I said, 'I should think.'

He looked at it with disgusted understanding and in a half-groan said, 'Oh, God.'

'It's been done before,' I said: and there had in fact been a time in Lambourn when everyone had been paranoid about being overheard and had gone to elaborate lengths to avoid talking on their home telephones. Illegal it might well be to listen uninvited, but it was carried on nevertheless, as everyone knew.

Without more ado we unscrewed all the telephones in the house, but found no limpet-like bugs inside. Horses, however, not electronics, were our speciality, and Bobby said he would go out to a public box and ring up the telephone company and ask them to come themselves to see what they could find.

It happened at one point that Bobby was on his knees by the kitchen wall screwing together the telephone junction there and Holly and I were standing side by side in the centre of the room, watching him, so that when the newcomer suddenly arrived among us unannounced it was my sister and I that he saw first.

A tall man with fair hair fading to grey, immensely well brushed. Neat, good-looking features, smoothly shaven rounded chin; trim figure inside a grey City suit of the most impeccable breeding. A man of fifty, a man of power whose very presence filled the kitchen, a man holding a folded copy of the *Daily Flag* and looking at Holly and me with open loathing.

Maynard Allardeck; Bobby's father.

Known to me, as I to him, as the enemy. Known to each other by frequent sight, by indoctrination, by professional repute. Ever known, never willingly meeting.

'Fieldings,' he said with battering hate; and to me directly, 'What do you think you're doing in this house?'

'I asked him,' Bobby said, straightening up.

His father turned abruptly in his direction, seeing

his son for the first time closely face to face for more than four years.

They stared at each other for a long moment as if frozen, as if relearning familiar features, taking physical stock. Seeing each other perhaps as partial strangers, freshly. Whatever any of us might have expected or wished for in the way of reconciliation, it turned out to be the opposite of what Maynard had in mind. He had come neither to help nor even to commiserate, but to complain.

Without any form of greeting he said, 'How dare you drag me into your sordid little troubles.' He waved his copy of the *Flag*. 'I won't have you whining to the Press about something that's entirely your own fault. If you want to marry into a bunch of crooks, take your consequences and keep me out of it.'

I imagine we all blinked, as Bobby was doing. Maynard's voice was thick with anger and his sudden onslaught out of all proportion, but it was his reasoning above all which had us stunned.

'I didn't,' Bobby said, almost rocking on his feet. 'I mean, I haven't talked to the Press. I wouldn't. They just wrote it.'

'And this part about me refusing you money? How else would they know, if you hadn't told them? Answer me that.'

Bobby swallowed. 'You've always said . . . I mean, I thought you meant it, that you wouldn't.'

'Of course I mean it.' His father glared at him. 'I

won't. That's not the point. You've no business snivelling about it in public and I won't have it. Do you hear?'

'I haven't,' Bobby protested, but without conviction.

I thought how much father and son resembled each other in looks, and how little in character. Maynard had six times the force of Bobby but none of his sense of fair play. Maynard could make money work for him, Bobby worked to be paid. Maynard could hold a grudge implacably for ever, Bobby could waver and crumble and rethink. The comparative weaknesses in Bobby, I thought, were also his strength.

'You must have been blabbing.' Maynard was uncompromisingly offensive in his tone, and I thought that if Bobby ever wanted to announce to the whole world that his father would let him sink, he would have every provocation and every right.

Bobby said with a rush, 'We think someone may have been tapping our telephone.'

'Oh, you do, do you?' Maynard said ominously, casting an angry look at the silent instrument. 'So it's on the telephone you've been bleating about me, is it?'

'No,' Bobby said, half stuttering. 'I mean, no I haven't. But one or two people said ask your father for money, and I told them I couldn't.'

'And this bit,' Maynard belted the air furiously with the newspaper, 'about me fishing for a knighthood. I won't have it. It's a damned lie.'

It struck me forcibly at that point, perhaps because

of an undisguisable edge of fear in his voice, that it was the bit about the knighthood which lay at the real heart of Maynard's rage.

It was no lie, I thought conclusively. It was true. He must indeed be trying actively to get himself a title. Grandfather had said that Maynard at nine had wanted to be a lord. Maynard at fifty was still the same person, but now with money, with influence, with no doubt a line to the right ears. Maynard might be even then in the middle of delicate but entirely unlawful negotiations.

Sir Maynard Allardeck. It certainly rolled well off the tongue. Sir Maynard. Bow down to me, you Fieldings. I am your superior, bow low.

'I didn't say anything about a knighthood,' Bobby protested with more force. 'I mean, I didn't know you wanted one. I never said anything about it. I never thought of it.'

'Why don't you sue the newspaper?' I said.

'You keep quiet,' he said to me vehemently. 'Keep your nose out.' He readdressed himself to Bobby. 'If you didn't mention a knighthood on the telephone, how did they get hold of it? Why did they write that . . . that damned lie? Answer me that.'

'I don't know,' Bobby said, sounding bewildered. 'I don't know why they wrote any of it.'

'Someone has put you up to stirring up trouble against me,' Maynard said, looking hard and mean and deadly in earnest.

We all three stared at him in amazement. How anyone could think that was beyond me.

Bobby said with more stuttering, ‘Of course not. I mean, that’s stupid. It’s not you that’s in trouble because of what they wrote, it’s me. I wouldn’t stir up trouble against myself. It doesn’t make sense.’

‘Three people telephoned me before seven this morning to tell me there was another paragraph in today’s *Flag*,’ Maynard said angrily. ‘I bought a copy on my way here. I was instantly certain it was your poisonous brother-in-law or his pig of a grandfather who was at the back of it, it’s just their filthy sort of thing.’

‘No,’ Holly said.

Maynard ignored her as if she hadn’t spoken.

‘I came in here to tell you it served you right,’ he said to Bobby, ‘and to insist on your forcing the Fieldings to get a full retraction printed in the paper.’

‘But,’ Bobby said, shaking his head as if concussed, ‘it wasn’t Kit. He wouldn’t do that. Nor his grandfather.’

‘You’re soft,’ Maynard said contemptuously. ‘You’ve never understood that someone can smile into your face while they shove a knife through your ribs.’

‘Because of Holly,’ Bobby insisted, ‘they wouldn’t.’

‘You’re a naive fool,’ his father said. ‘Why shouldn’t they try to break up your marriage? They never wanted it, any more than I did. They’re a wily, shifty, vengeful family, the whole lot of them, and if you trust any one of them, you deserve what you get.'

Bobby gave me a quick glance in which I read only discomfort, not doubt. Neither Holly nor I offered any sort of defence because mere words wouldn't dent the opinions that Maynard had held all his life, and nor would hitting him. Moreover we had heard the same sort of invective too often from Grandfather on the subject of the Allardecks. We were more or less immune, by then, to violent reaction. It was Bobby, interestingly, who protested.

'Kit and Holly care what becomes of me,' he said. 'You don't. Kit came to help, and you didn't. So I'll judge as I find, and I don't agree with what you say.'

Maynard looked as if he could hardly believe his ears, and nor, to be honest, could I. It wasn't just that what Bobby was expressing was a heretical defection from his upbringing, but that he also had the courage to stand up to his father and say it to his face.

He looked, as a matter of fact, slightly nervous. Maynard, it was said, inspired wholesale nervousness in the boardroom of any business his eye fell on, and as of that morning I understood why. The unyielding ruthlessness in him, clearly perceptible to all three of us, was central to his success, and for us at least he made no attempt to disguise it or dress it with a façade of charm.

Bobby made a frustrated gesture with both hands, walked over to the sink and began to fill the kettle.

'Do you want any coffee?' he said to his father.

'Of course not.' He spoke as if he'd been insulted. 'I've a committee meeting at the Jockey Club.' He looked at his watch, and then at me. 'You,' he said, 'have attacked me. And you'll suffer for it.'

I said calmly but distinctly, 'If I hear you have said in the Jockey Club that a Fielding is responsible for what has appeared in the *Flag*, I will personally sue you for slander.'

Maynard glared. He said, 'You're filth by birth, you're not worth the fuss that's made of you, and I'd be glad to see you dead.'

I felt Holly beside me begin to spring forward in some passionate explosion of feeling and gripped her wrist tight to stop her. I was actually well satisfied. I had read in Maynard's eyes that he was inclined to take me seriously, but he didn't want me to know it, and I understood also, for the first time, and with unease, that the very fact of my being successful, of being champion, was to him, in his obsession, intolerable.

Along at the Jockey Club, which had its ancient headquarters in Newmarket's main street, and where he had been one of its members for four or five years, Maynard would with luck now pass off the whole *Flag* thing with a grouchy joke. There, in the organization which ruled the racing industry, he would show all courtesy and hide the snarl. There, where he served on dogsbody committees while he made his determined way up that particular ladder, aiming perhaps to be a Steward, one of the top triumvirate, before long, he would now perhaps be careful to say nothing that could get back to my ears.

There were no active professional jockeys in the Jockey Club, nor any licensed trainers, though a few retired practitioners of both sorts sprinkled the ranks. There were many racehorse owners, among whom I had real friends. The approximately 140 members, devoted to the welfare of racing, were self-perpetuating, self-elected. If Maynard had ever campaigned quietly to be chosen for membership it might have helped him to be a member of an old-established racing family, and it might have helped him to be rich, but one thing was certain: he would never have unsheathed for the civilized inspection of his peers the raw, brutal anti-Fielding prejudice he had given spleen to in the kitchen. Nothing alienated the courteous members more than ill-mannered excess.

The preserving of Maynard's public good manners was very much my concern.

He went as he'd come, private manners non-existent, walking out of the kitchen without a farewell. We listened to the firm footsteps recede and to the distant slam of a car door, and his engine starting.

'Do you realize,' Bobby said to me slowly, 'that if he's made a Steward and you're still a jockey . . . you'd be horribly vulnerable . . .?'

'Mm,' I said dryly. 'Very nasty indeed.'

CHAPTER SIX

I rode at Plumpton. A typical day of four rides; one win, one third, one nowhere, one very nearly last, with owner reactions to match.

Far more people than in the previous week seemed to have seen the pieces in Intimate Details, and I spent a good deal of the day assuring all who asked that, no, Bobby wasn't bankrupt, and yes, I was certain, and no, I couldn't say for sure what Bobby's father's intentions were in any respect.

There was the usual small scattering of racing journalists at the meeting, but no one from the *Flag*. The racing column in the *Flag* was most often the work of a sharp young man who wrote disparagingly about what was to come and critically of what was past, and who was avoided whenever possible by all jockeys. On that day, however, I would have been satisfied enough to see him, but had to make do with his equivalent on the *Towncrier*.

'You want to know about the *Flag*? Whatever for? Disgusting rag.' Large and benevolent, Bunty Ireland, the *Towncrier*'s man, spoke with the complacency of a more respectful rag behind him. 'But if you want to know if the parts about your brother-in-law are the work of our sharp-nosed colleague, then no, I'm pretty sure they're not. He was at Doncaster on Friday and he didn't know at first what was in the gossip column. Slightly put out, he was, when he found out. He said the gossip people hadn't consulted him and they should have done. He was his usual endearing sunny self.' Bunty Ireland beamed. 'Anything else?'

'Yes,' I said. 'Who runs Intimate Details?'

'Can't help you there, old son. I'll ask around, if you like. But it won't do Bobby much good, you can't just go and bop us fellows on the nose, however great the provocation.'

Never be too sure, I thought.

I cadged a lift home to Lambourn, ate some lobster and an orange, and thought about telephoning Holly.

Someone, it was certain, would be listening in on the line. Someone had probably been listening in on that line for quite a long period. Long enough to make a list of people Bobby dealt with in Newmarket, long enough to know where he banked, long enough to know how things stood between him and his father. The owner who had telephoned to say he couldn't afford to pay fifty thousand for his yearling must have been listened to, and so must Bobby's unsuccessful attempts to sell it to anyone else.

Someone must indeed have listened also to Bobby's

racing plans and to his many conversations with owners and jockeys. There was no trainer alive who wouldn't in the fullness of time have passed unflattering or downright slanderous opinions about jockeys to owners and vice versa, but nothing of that nature had been used in the paper. No 'inside' revelations of betting coups. No innuendoes about regulations broken or crimes committed, such as giving a horse an easy race, a common practice for which one could be fined or even have one's licence suspended if found out. The target hadn't in fact been Bobby's training secrets, but his financial status alone.

Why?

Too many whys.

I pressed the necessary buttons and the bell rang only once at the other end.

'Kit?' Holly said immediately.

'Yes.'

'Did you try earlier?'

'No,' I said.

'That's all right, then. We've left the receiver off for most of the day, the calls were so awful. But it just occurred to me that you might be trying to ring, so I put it back less than a minute ago . . .' Her voice faded away as she realized what she was saying. 'We've done it again,' she said.

'Yes.'

She must have heard the smile in my voice, because it was in hers also when she replied.

'Look,' she said. 'I've been thinking . . . I've got to go out, now. I'll ring you later, OK?'

'Sure,' I said.

'Bye.'

'Bye,' I said, and disconnected. I also waited, wondering where she would go. Where she'd planned. She called back within fifteen minutes and it was unexpectedly from the feed-merchant's office. The feed-merchant, it appeared, had let her in, switched on the heater, and left her in private.

'He's been terribly good,' Holly explained. 'I think he'd been feeling a bit guilty, though he's no need to really. Anyway I told him we thought our telephone might be bugged and he said he thought it highly possible, and I could come in here and use the phone whenever I liked. I said I'd like to ring you this evening . . . and anyway, here I am.'

'Great,' I said. 'How are things going?'

'We spent the whole day doing those letters and we're frankly bushed. Bobby's asleep on his feet. Everyone took your cheque without question and gave us paid-in-full letters, and we photocopied those and also the rebuttal letter we all wrote before you went to Plumpton, and by the time we'd finished putting everything in the envelopes the last post was just going, and in fact the postman actually waited at the post office while I stuck on the last ten stamps, and I saw him take the special delivery one to the editor of the *Flag*, so with luck, with luck, it will be all over.'

'Mm,' I said. 'Let's hope so.'

'Oh, and Bobby went to see the solicitor, who said he would write a strong letter of protest to the editor and demand a retraction in the paper, like Lord Vaughnley told you, but Bobby says he isn't sure that that letter will have gone today, he says the solicitor didn't seem to think it was frantically urgent.'

'Tell Bobby to get a different solicitor.'

Holly almost laughed. 'Yes. OK.'

We made plans and times for me to talk to her again the next evening after I got home from Devon, but it was at eight in the morning when my telephone rang and her voice came sharp and distressed into my ear.

'It's Holly,' she said. 'Get a copy of the *Flag*. I'll be along where I was last night. OK?'

'Yes,' I said.

She disconnected without another word, and I drove to the village for the paper.

The column would have been printed during the past night. The special delivery envelope wouldn't reach the editor until later in the present morning. I thought in hindsight it would have been better for Bobby to have driven the letter to London and specially delivered it himself, which might just possibly have halted the campaign.

The third broadside read:

Don't pity Robertson (Bobby) Allardeck (32), strapped for cash but still trying to train racehorses in Newmarket. It's the small trader who suffers when fat cats run up unpaid bills.

In his luxury home yesterday Bobby refused to comment on reports he came to blows with the owner of one of the horses in the stable, preventing the owner taking his horse away by force. 'I deny everything,' Bobby fumed.

Meanwhile Daddy Maynard ('Moneybags') Allardeck (50) goes on record as prize skinflint of the month. 'My son won't get a penny in aid from me,' he intoned piously. 'He doesn't deserve it.'

Instead Moneybags lavishes ostentatious handouts on good deserving charities dear to the Government's heart. Can knighthoods be bought nowadays? Of course not!

Bobby wails that while Daddy lashes out the loot on the main chance, he (Bobby) gets threatening letters from Daddy's lawyers demanding repayment of a fourteen-year-old loan. Seems Moneybags advanced a small sum for 18-year-old Bobby to buy a banger on leaving school. With the wheels a long-ago memory on the scrapheap, Daddy wants his money back. Bobby's opinion of Daddy? 'Ruthless swine.'

Can stingy Maynard be extorting interest on top? Watch this space.

Thoughtfully I got the feed-merchant's number from directory enquiries and pressed the buttons: Holly was waiting at the other end.

'What are we going to do?' she said miserably. 'They're such pigs. All those quotes . . . they just made them up.'

'Yes,' I said. 'If you could bear to put together another batch of those letters you sent yesterday, it might do some good to send them to the editors of the other national newspapers, and to the *Sporting Life*. None of them likes the *Flag*. A spot of ridicule from its rivals might make the *Flag* shut up.'

'Might,' Holly said, unconvinced.

'Doing everything one can think of is better than doing nothing,' I said. 'You never know which pellet might kill the bird when you loose off the shot.'

'Poetic,' Holly said sardonically. 'All right. We'll try.'

'And what about the solicitor?' I asked.

'Bobby says he'll find a better one today. Not local. In a London firm. High powered.'

'Some of his owners may know who's best,' I said. 'If not, I could get him a name from one of the people I ride for.'

'Great.'

'But do you know something?' I said.

'What?'

'I'm not so sure that Maynard was very far wrong. All this aggro is aimed as much at him as at Bobby.'

'Yes,' Holly said slowly. 'When we read today's bit of dirt, that's what Bobby thought too.'

'I wouldn't mind betting,' I said, 'that a fair few copies of Intimate Details, episodes one, two and three, will find their way to the attention of the Honours' Secretary in Downing Street. And that this was chiefly what was at the bottom of Maynard's anger yesterday. If Maynard is really being considered for a knighthood, Intimate Details could have put the lid on his chances, at least for just now.'

'Do you think it would? Just a few words in a paper?'

'You never know. The whole Honours thing is so sensitive. Anyway it's about now that they send out those ultra-secret letters asking Mr Bloggs if he would accept a medal if invited. They'll be drawing up the New Year's Honours' List at this moment. And the sixty-four dollar question is, if you were the Honours' Secretary drawing up a list for the Prime Minister's approval, would you put Maynard on it?'

'But we don't know that anything like that is happening.'

'No, we sure don't.'

'It's probably just the *Flag* being its typically vicious, mean, destructive self.'

'Perhaps,' I said.

'You know how nasty the Press can be, if they want to. And the *Flag* seems to want to, all the time, as a matter of policy.'

'Mm,' I said. 'Maybe you're right.'

'But you don't think so?'

'Well . . . It would make more sense if we could see a purpose behind these attacks, and stopping Maynard getting a knighthood would be a purpose. But why they'd want to stop it, and how they got to hear of it . . . hell alone knows.'

'They didn't hear about any knighthood from our telephone,' Holly said positively. 'So perhaps they're just making it up.'

'Everything else in those stories is founded on things that have happened or been said,' I pointed out. 'They've taken the truth and distorted it. Shall I write to the Honours' Secretary and ask if Maynard's on his provisional list?'

'Yes, yes, funny joke.'

'Anyway,' I said. 'How did Bobby get on with the telephone people?'

'They said they would look into it. They said telephone tapping is illegal as of 1985. They didn't send anyone here yesterday looking for bugs. They said something about checking our exchange.'

'The exchange? I didn't know people could tap into an exchange.'

'Well, apparently they can.'

'So no actual bugs?'

'We told them we couldn't find any and they said we probably didn't know where to look.'

'Well, at least they're paying attention.'

'They said a lot of people think they're being bugged when they aren't,' Holly said. 'All the same, they did say they would look.'

'Keep them up to it.'

'I'll ring you this evening when I get back from

Devon,' I said. 'If I don't get back... I'll ring sometime.'

'Yes,' she said. 'Take care of yourself.'

'Always do,' I said automatically; and both she and I knew it was impossible. If a steeplechase jockey took too much care of himself, he didn't win races, and there were days occasionally when one couldn't drive oneself home. I was superstitious to the extent of not making binding commitments for the evenings of race days, and like most other jump jockeys accepted invitations with words like 'If I can' and 'With luck'.

I drove the two hours to the Devon and Exeter meeting with my mind more on Holly and Bobby and Maynard than on the work ahead. None of the five horses I was due to ride posed the problems of North Face, and I'd ridden all of them often enough to know their little quirks and their capabilities. All I had to do was help them turn in the best they could do on the day.

The Devon and Exeter racecourse lay on the top of Halden Moor, a majestic sweep of bare countryside with the winds blowing vigorously from the Channel to the Atlantic. The track itself, with its long circuit of almost two miles, stretched away as a green undulating ribbon between oceans of scrub and heather, its far deserted curves as private a place as one could imagine for contest of horse and man.

Unfashionable in Ascot terms, distant geographically, drawing comparatively small crowds, it was still one of my favourite courses; well run, well kept, with welcoming locals, nice people.

The princess liked to go there because friends of hers maintained one of the few private boxes, friends who had a house down by a Devon beach and who invited her to stay regularly for the meetings.

She was there, lunched, fur-coated and discreetly excited, in good time for the first race, accompanied in the parade ring by a small bunch of the friends. Three friends, to be exact. The couple she stayed with, and a young woman.

The princess made introductions. 'Kit . . . you know Mr and Mrs Inscombe . . .' We shook hands. ' . . . And my niece. Have you met my niece, Danielle?'

No, I hadn't. I shook the niece's hand.

'Danielle de Brescou,' the niece said. 'Hi. How're you doing?' And in spite of her name she was not French but audibly American.

I took in briefly the white wool short coat, the black trousers, the wide band of what looked like flowered chintz holding back a lot of dark hair. I got in return a cool look of assessment; half interest, half judgement deferred, topped by a bright smile of no depth.

'What shall we expect?' the princess asked. 'Will Bernina win?'

Wykeham, naturally, had not made the journey to Devon. Moreover he had been vague when I'd talked to him on the telephone, seeming almost unclear as to Bernina's identity, let alone her state of readiness, and it had been Dusty, when I'd handed him my saddle to put on to the mare before the race, who had told me she was 'jumping out of her skin and acting up something chronic'.

'She's fit and ready,' I said to the princess.

'And Wykeham's riding instructions?' Mr Inscombe enquired genially. 'What are those?'

Wykeham's instructions to me were zero, as they had been for several years. I said diplomatically, 'Stay handy in fourth place or thereabouts and kick for home at the second last hurdle.'

Inscombe nodded benevolent approval and I caught the ghost of a grin from the princess, who knew quite well that Wykeham's instructions, if any, would have taken the form of 'Win if you can', an uncomplicated declaration of honesty by no means universal among trainers.

Wykeham produced his horses fighting fit from a mixture of instinct, inherited wisdom, and loving them individually as athletes and children. He knew how to bring them to a peak and understood their moods and preferences, and if nowadays he found the actual races less interesting than the preparation, he was still, just, one of the greats.

I had been his retained jockey for the whole of the main part of my career and he frequently called me by the name of my predecessor. He quite often told me I would be riding horses long dead. 'Polonium in the big race at Sandown,' he would say, and, mystified, I would ask who owned the horse as I'd never heard of it. 'Polonium? Don't be stupid. Big chestnut. Likes mints. You won on him last week.' 'Oh . . . Pepperoni?' 'What? Yes, Pepperoni, of course, that's what I said. Big race at Sandown.'

He was almost as old as my grandfather, and gradually, through their eyes, I was coming to see the whole of racing as a sort of stream that rolled onwards through time, the new generations rising and the old floating slowly away. Racing had a longer history than almost any other sport and changed less, and sometimes I had a powerful feeling of repeating in my own person the experience of generations of jockeys before me and of being a transient speck in a passing pageant; vivid today, talked about, fêted, but gone tomorrow, a memory fading into a footnote, until no one alive had seen me race or cared a damn whether I'd won or lost.

Dead humbling, the whole thing.

Bernina, named after the mountain to the south of St Moritz, had by four years old produced none of the grandeur of the Alps, and to my mind was never going to. She could, however, turn in a respectable performance in moderate company, which was all she was faced with on this occasion, and I hoped very much to win on her, as much for the princess's sake as my own. I understood very well that she liked to be able to please the various hosts around the country who offered her multiple invitations, and was always slightly anxious for her horses to do well where she felt they might contribute to her overnight bread and butter. I thought that if people like the Inscombes didn't enjoy her company for its own sake they wouldn't keep on asking her to stay. The princess's inner insecurities were sometimes astonishing.

Bernina, without any of the foregoing complications of intent, took me out of the parade ring and down to the start in her best immoderate fashion which included a display of extravagant head-shaking and some sideways dancing on her toes. These preliminaries were a good sign: on her off days she went docilely to the starting gate, left it without enthusiasm and took her time about finishing. Last time out she'd had me hauled in front of the Stewards and fined for not trying hard enough to win, and I'd said they should have understood that a horse that doesn't want to race won't race; and that mares have dull days like anyone else. They listened, unimpressed. Pay the fine, they said.

The princess had insisted on reimbursing me for that little lot, where other owners might have raged. 'If she wouldn't go, she wouldn't go,' she'd said with finality. 'And she's my horse, so I'm responsible for her debts.' Owners didn't come more illogical or more generous than the princess.

I'd told her never to let her friends back Bernina on the days she went flat-footed to the start, and she'd acknowledged the advice gravely. I hoped, sitting on top of the bravura performance going on in Devon, that she, the Inscombes and the niece would all be at that moment trekking to the bookmakers or the Tote. The mare was feeling good, and, beyond that, competitive.

The event was a two-mile hurdle race, which meant eight jumps over the sort of fencing used for penning sheep: hurdles made of wood and threaded with gorse or brushwood, each section unattached to the hurdle on either side, so that if a horse hit one, it could be knocked over separately. Good jumpers flowed over hurdles easily, rising little in the air but bending up their forelegs sharply; the trick was to get them to take off from where the hurdle could be crossed in mid-stride.

Bernina, graciously accepting my guidance in that matter, went round the whole course without touching a twig. She also attacked the job of beating her opponents with such gusto that one mightn't have blamed the Stewards this time for testing her for dope, such was the contrast.

She would, if she'd had serious talent, have won by twenty lengths, especially as the chief danger had fallen in a flurry of legs about halfway round. As it was, she made enough progress, when I gave her an encouraging kick between the last two hurdles, to reach the last jump upsides of the only horse still in front, and on the run-in she produced a weak burst of speed for just long enough to pass and demoralize her tiring opponent.

Accepting my congratulatory pats on her victorious neck as totally her due, she pulled up and pranced back to the winners' enclosure, and skittered about there restlessly, sweating copiously and rolling her eyes, up on a high like any other triumphant performer.

The princess, relieved and contented, kept out of the way of the powerful body as I unbuckled the girths and slid my saddle off on to my arm. She didn't say much herself as the Inscombes were doing a good deal of talking, but in any case she didn't have to. I knew what she thought and she knew I knew: we'd been through it all a couple of hundred times before.

The niece said, 'Wow,' a little thoughtfully.

I glanced briefly at her face and saw that she was surprised: I didn't know what she was surprised at, and didn't have time to find out as there was the matter of weighing in, changing, and weighing out for the next race. Icicle, the princess's other runner, didn't go until the fourth race, but I had two other horses to ride before that.

Those two, undisgraced, finished fifth and second, and were both for a local trainer who I rode for when I could: besides Wykeham I also often rode for a stable in Lambourn, and when neither of them had a runner, for anyone else who asked. After, that is, having looked up the offered horse in the form book. Constant fallers I refused, saying Wykeham wouldn't give his approval. Wykeham was a handy excuse.

Icicle, like his name, was the palest of greys; also long-backed, angular and sweet-natured. He had been fast and clever over hurdles, the younger horses' sport, but at a mature eight years and running over bigger fences, was proving more cautious than carefree, more dependable than dazzling, willing but no whirlwind.

I went out to the parade ring again in the princess's colours and found her and the friends deep in a discussion that had nothing to do with horses but which involved a good deal of looking at watches.

'The train from Exeter is very fast,' Mrs Inscombe was saying comfortingly; and the niece was giving her a bright look of stifled impatience.

'Most unfortunate,' Mr Inscombe said in a bluff voice. 'But the train, that's the thing.'

The princess said carefully as if for the tenth time, 'But my dears, the train goes too late . . .' She broke off to give me an absent-minded smile and a brief explanation.

'My niece Danielle was going to London by car with friends but the arrangement has fallen through.' She paused. 'I suppose you don't know anyone who is driving straight from here to London after this race?'

'Sorry, I don't,' I said regretfully.

I looked at the niece: at Danielle. She looked worriedly back. 'I have to be in London by six-thirty,' she said. 'In Chiswick. I expect you know where that is? Just as you reach London from the west?'

I nodded.

'Could you possibly ask,' she waved a hand towards the busy door of the weighing room, 'in there?'

'Yes, I'll ask.'

'I have to be at work.'

I must have showed surprise, because she added, 'I work for a news bureau. This week I'm on duty in the evenings.'

Icicle stalked methodically round the parade ring with two and a half miles of strenuous jumping ahead of him. After that, in the fifth race, I would be riding another two miles over hurdles.

After that . . .

I glanced briefly at the princess, checking her expression, which was benign, and I thought of the fine she'd paid for me when she didn't have to.

I said to Danielle, 'I'll take you myself straight after the fifth race . . . if, er, that would be of any use to you.'

Her gaze intensified fast on my face and the anxiety cleared like sunrise.

'Yes,' she said decisively. 'It sure would.'

Never make positive commitments on race days . . .

'I'll meet you outside the weighing room, after the fifth, then,' I said. 'It's a good road. We should get to Chiswick in time.'

'Great,' she said, and the princess seemed relieved that we could now concentrate on her horse and the immediate future.

'Kind of you, Kit,' she said, nodding.

'Any time.'

'How do you think my old boy will do today?'

'He's got bags of stamina,' I said. 'He should run well.'

She smiled. She knew 'bags of stamina' was a euphemism for 'not much finishing speed'. She knew Icicle's ability as well as I did, but like all owners, she wanted good news from her jockey.

'Do your best.'

'Yes,' I said.

I mounted and took Icicle out on to the track.

To hell with superstition, I thought.

CHAPTER SEVEN

It wasn't Icicle I had trouble with.

Icicle jumped adequately but without inspiration and ran on doggedly at one pace up the straight, more by good luck than anything else hanging on to finish second.

'Dear old slowcoach,' the princess said to him proudly in the unsaddling enclosure, rubbing his nose. 'What a gentleman you are.'

It was the hurdler afterwards that came to grief: an experienced racer but unintelligent. The one horse slightly ahead and to the right of us hit the top of the second hurdle as he rose to the jump and stumbled on to his nose on landing, and my horse, as if copying, promptly did exactly the same.

As falls went, it wasn't bad. I rolled like a tumbler on touching the ground, a circus skill learned by every jump jockey, and stayed curled, waiting for all the other runners to pass. As standing up in the middle of a thundering herd was the surest way to get badly injured, staying on the ground, where horses could more easily avoid one, was almost the first lesson in survival. The bad thing about falls near the start of hurdle races, however, was that the horses were going faster than in steeplechases, and were often bunched up together, with the result that they tended not to see a fallen rider until they were on top of him, by which time there was nowhere else to put their feet.

I was fairly used to hoof-shaped bruises. In the quiet that came after the buffeting I stood slowly and stiffly up with the makings of a new collection, and found the other fallen jockey doing the same.

'You all right?' I said.

'Yeah. You?'

I nodded. My colleague expressed a few obscene opinions of his former mount and a car came along to pick us up and deliver us to the ambulance room to be checked by the doctor on duty. In the old days jockeys had got away easily with riding with broken bones, but nowadays the medical inspections had intensified to safeguard the interests not altogether of the men injured but of the people who bet on them. Appeasing the punter was priority stuff.

Bruises didn't count. Doctors never stopped one from riding for those, and in any case bruises weren't visible when very new. I proved to the local man that all the bits of me that should bend, did, and all the bits that shouldn't bend, didn't, and got passed fit to ride again from then on.

One of the two volunteer nurses went to answer a

knock on the door and came back slightly bemused to say I was wanted outside by a woman who said she was a princess.

'Right,' I said, thanking the doctor and turning to go.

'Is she?' the nurse asked dubiously.

'A princess? Yes. How often do you come to race meetings?'

'Today's my first.'

'She's been leading owner three times in the past six jumping seasons, and she's a right darling.'

The young nurse grinned. 'Makes you sick.'

I went outside to find the right darling looking first worried and then relieved at my reappearance. She was certainly not in the habit of enquiring after my health by waiting around outside ambulance room doors, and of course it wasn't my actual well-being which mattered at that point, but my being well enough to drive the niece to work.

The niece was also there and also relieved and also looking at her watch. I said I would change into street clothes and be ready shortly, and the princess kissed the niece and patted my arm, and went away saying she would see me at Newbury on the morrow.

I changed, found the niece waiting outside the weighing room, and took her to my car. She was fairly fidgeting with an impatience which slightly abated when she found the car was a Mercedes, but changed to straight anxiety when she saw me wince as I edged into the driving seat.

'Are you OK? You're not going to pass out, or anything, are you?' she said.

'I shouldn't think so.'

I started the car and extricated ourselves from the close-packed rows. A few other cars were leaving, but not enough to clog the entrance or the road outside. We would have a clear run, barring accidents.

'I guess I thought you'd be dead,' the niece said without emotion. 'How does anyone survive being trampled that way by a stampede?'

'Luck,' I said succinctly.

'My aunt was sure relieved when you stood up.'

I made an assenting noise in my throat. 'So was I.'

'Why do you do it?' she said.

'Race?'

'Uh-huh.'

'I like it.'

'Like getting trampled?'

'No,' I said. 'That doesn't happen all that often.'

We swooped down the hill from the moor and sped unhindered along roads that in the summer were busy with holiday crises. No swaying overloaded caravans being towed that day, no children being sick at the roadside, no radiators boiling and burst, with glum groups on the verges waiting for help. Devon roads in November were bare and fast and led straight to the motorways which should take us to Chiswick with no problems.

'Tell me truthfully,' she said, 'why do you do it?'

I glanced at her face, seeing there a quality of interest suitable for a newsgatherer. She had also large grey eyes, a narrow nose, and a determined mouth. Good-looking in a well-groomed way, I thought.

I had been asked the same question many times by other newsgatherers, and I gave the standard answer.

'I do it because I was born to it. I was brought up in a racing stable and I can't remember not being able to ride. I can't remember not wanting to ride in races.'

She listened with her head on one side and her gaze on my face.

'I guess I never met a jockey until now,' she said reflectively. 'And we don't have much jump racing in America.'

'No,' I agreed. 'In England there are probably more jump races than Flat. Just as many, anyway.'

'So why do you do it?'

'I told you,' I said.

'Yeah.'

She turned her head away to look out at the passing fields.

I raced, I thought fancifully, as one might play a violin, making one's own sort of music from coordinated muscles and intuitive spirit. I raced because the partnership with horses filled my mind with perfections of cadence and rhythmic excitement and intensities of communion: and I couldn't exactly say aloud such pretentious rubbish.

'I feel alive,' I said, 'on a horse.'

She looked back, faintly smiling. 'My aunt says you read their thoughts.'

'Everyone close to horses does that.'

'But some more than others?'

'I don't really know.'

She nodded. 'That makes sense. My aunt says you read the thoughts of people also.'

I glanced at her briefly. 'Your aunt seems to have said a lot.'

'My aunt,' she said neutrally, 'wanted me to understand, I think, that if I went in your car I should arrive unmolested.'

'Good God.'

'She was right, I see.'

'Mm.'

Molesting Danielle de Brescou, I thought, would be my quickest route to unemployment. Not that in other circumstances and with her willing cooperation I would have found it unthinkable. Danielle de Brescou moved with understated long-legged grace and watched the world from clear eyes, and if I found the sheen and scent of her hair and skin fresh and pleasing, it did no more than change the journey from a chore to a pleasure.

Between Exeter and Bristol, while dusk dimmed the day, she told me that she had been in England for three weeks and was staying with her uncle and aunt while she found herself an apartment. She had come because she'd been posted to London by the national broadcasting company she worked for: she was the bureau coordinator, and as it was only her second week there it was essential not to be late.

'You won't be late,' I assured her.

'No . . . Do you always drive at eighty miles an hour?'

'Not if I'm in a real hurry.'

'Very funny.'

She told me Roland de Brescou, the princess's husband, was her father's eldest brother. Her father had emigrated to California from France as a young man and had married an American girl, Danielle being their only child.

'I guess there was a family ruckus when Dad left home, but he never told me the details. He's been sending greetings cards lately though, nostalgic for his roots, I guess. Anyway, he told Uncle Roland I was coming to London and the princess wrote me to say come visit. I hadn't met either of them before. It's my first trip to Europe.'

'How do you like it?'

She smiled. 'How would you like being cosseted in a sort of mansion in Eaton Square with a cook and maids and a butler? And a chauffeur. All last week the chauffeur drove me to work and picked me up after. Same thing yesterday. Aunt Casilia says it's not safe here after midnight on the subway, the same as it isn't in New York. She fusses worse than my own mother. But I can't live with them for too long. They're both sweet to me. I like her a lot and we get along fine. But I need a place of my own, near the office. And I'll get a car. I guess I'll have to.'

'How long will you be in England?' I asked.

'Don't know. Three years, maybe. Maybe less. The company can shift you around.'

She said I didn't need to tell her much about myself on account of information from her aunt.

She said she knew I lived in Lambourn and came from an old racing family and had a twin sister married to a racehorse trainer in Newmarket. She said she knew I wasn't married. She left the last observation dangling like a question mark, so I answered the unasked query.

'Not married. No present girlfriend. A couple in the past.'

I could feel her smile.

'And you?' I asked.

'Same thing.'

We drove for a good while in silence on that thought, and I rather pensively wondered what the princess would say or think if I asked her niece out to dinner. The close but arms-length relationship I'd had with her for so many years would change subtly if I did, and perhaps not for the better.

Between Bristol and Chiswick, while we sped with headlights on up the M4 motorway, Danielle told me about her job, which was, she said, pretty much a matter of logistics: she sent the camera crews and interviewers to wherever the news was.

'Half the time I'm looking at train schedules and road maps to find the fastest route, and starting from when we did, and taking the road we're on right now, I expected to be late.' She glanced at the speedometer. 'I didn't dream of ninety.'

I eased the car back to eighty-eight. A car passed us effortlessly. Danielle shook her head. 'I guess it'll take a while,' she said. 'How often do you get speeding tickets?'

'I've had three in ten years.'

'Driving like this every day?'

'Pretty much.'

She sighed. 'In dear old US of A we think seventy is sinful. Have you ever been there?'

'America?' I nodded. 'Twice. I rode there once in the Maryland Hunt Cup.'

'That's an amateurs' race,' she said without emphasis, careful, it seemed, not to appear to doubt my word.

'Yes. I started as an amateur. It seemed best to find out if I was any good before I committed my future to what I do.'

'And if it hadn't worked out?'

'I had a place at college.'

'And you didn't take it?' she said incredulously.

'No. I started winning, and that was what I wanted

most. I tried for the place at college only in case I couldn't make it as a jockey. Sort of insurance.'

'What subject?'

'Veterinary science.'

It shocked her. 'You mean you passed up being a veterinarian to be a jockey?'

'That's right,' I said. 'Why not?'

'But . . . but . . .'

'Yeah,' I said. 'All athletes . . . sportsmen . . . whatever . . . find themselves on the wrong side of thirty-five with old age staring them point-blank in the face. I might have another five years yet.'

'And then?'

'Train them, I suppose. Train horses for others to ride.' I shrugged. 'It's a long way off.'

'It came pretty close this afternoon,' Danielle said.

'Not really.'

'Aunt Casilia says the Cresta Run is possibly more dangerous than the life of a jump jockey. Possibly. She wasn't sure.'

'The Cresta Run is a gold medal or the fright of a lifetime, not a career.'

'Have you been down it?'

'Of course not. It's dangerous.'

She laughed. 'Are all jockeys like you?'

'No. All different. Like princesses.'

She took a deep breath, as if of sea air. I removed my attention from the motorway for a second's inspection of her face, for whatever her aunt might think of my ability to read minds I never seemed to be able to do it with any young woman except Holly . . . I was aware also that I wanted to, that without it, any loving was incomplete. I thought that if I hadn't had Holly I might have married one of the two girls I'd most liked: as it was, I hadn't reached the living-in stage with either of them.

I hadn't wanted to marry Holly, nor to sleep with her, but I'd loved her more deeply. It seemed that sex and telepathy couldn't co-exist in me, and until or unless they did, I probably would stay single.

'What are you thinking?' Danielle asked.

I smiled wryly. 'About not knowing what you were thinking.'

After a pause she said, 'I was thinking that when Aunt Casilia said you were exceptional, I can see what she meant.'

'She said what?'

'Exceptional. I asked her in what way, but she just smiled sweetly and changed the subject.'

'Er . . . when was that?'

'On our way down to Devon this morning. She's been wanting me to go racing with her ever since I came over, so today I did, because she'd arranged that ride back for me, although she herself was staying with the Inscombes tonight for some frantically grand party. She hoped I would love racing like she does, I think. Do you think sometimes she's lonesome, travelling all those miles to racemeets with just her chauffeur?'

'I don't think she felt lonesome until you came.'

'Oh!'

She fell silent for a while, and eventually I said prosaically, 'We'll be in Chiswick in three minutes.'

'Will we?' She sounded almost disappointed. 'I mean, good. But I've enjoyed the journey.'

'So have I.'

My inner vision was suddenly filled very powerfully with the presence of Holly, and I had a vivid impression of her face, screwed up in deep distress.

I said abruptly to Danielle, 'Is there a public telephone anywhere near your office?'

'Yeah, I guess so.' She seemed slightly puzzled by the urgency I could hear in my voice. 'Sure . . . use the one on my desk. Did you remember something important?'

'No . . . er, I . . .' I drew back from the impossibility of rational explanation. 'I have a feeling,' I said lamely, 'that I should telephone my sister.'

'A feeling?' she asked curiously. 'You looked as if you'd forgotten a date with the President, at least.'

I shook my head. 'This is Chiswick. Where do we go from here?'

She gave me directions and we stopped in a parking space labelled 'Staff Only' outside a warehouse-like building in a side street. Six-twenty on the clock; ten minutes to spare.

'Come on in,' Danielle said. 'The least I can do is lend you a phone.'

I stood up stiffly out of the car, and she said with contrition, 'I guess I shouldn't have let you drive all this way.'

'It's not much further than going home.'

'You lie in your teeth. We passed the exit to Lambourn fifty miles back.'

'A bagatelle.'

She watched me lock the car door. 'Seriously, are you OK?'

'It's nothing that a hot bath won't put right.'

She nodded and turned to lead the way into the building, which proved to have glass entrance doors into a hallway furnished with armchairs, potted plants and a uniformed guard behind a reception desk. She and he signed me into a book, gave me a pass to clip to my clothes, and ushered me through a heavy door that opened to an electronic buzz.

'Sorry about the fortress syndrome,' Danielle said. 'The company is currently paranoid about bombs.'

We went down a short corridor into a wide open office inhabited by six or seven desks, mostly with people behind them showing signs of packing up to go home. There was also a sea of green carpet, a dozen or so computers, and on one long wall a row of television screens above head height, all showing different programmes and none of them emitting a sound.

Danielle and the other inhabitants exchanged a few 'Hi's, and 'How're you doing's, and no one questioned my presence. She took me across the room to her own domain, an area of two large desks set at right angles with a comfortable-looking swivelling chair serving both. The desk tops bore several box files, a computer, a typewriter, a stack of newspapers and a telephone. On the wall behind the chair there was a large chart on which things could be written in chinagraph and rubbed off: a chart with columns labelled along the top as SLUG, TEAM, LOCATION, TIME, FORMAT.

'Sit down,' Danielle said, pointing to the chair. She picked up the receiver and pressed a lighted button on the telephone. 'OK. Make your call.' She turned to look at the chart. 'Let's see what's been happening in the world since I left it.' She scanned the segments. Under SLUG someone had written 'Embassy' in large black letters. Danielle called across the room, 'Hank, what's this embassy story?' and a voice answered, 'Someone painted "Yanks Go Home" in red on the US embassy steps and there's a stink about security.'

'Good grief.'

'You'll need to do a follow-up for *Nightline*.'

'Right . . . has anyone interviewed the Ambassador?'

'We couldn't reach him earlier.'

'Guess I'll try again.'

'Sure. It's your baby, baby. All yours.'

Danielle smiled vividly down at me, and I recognized with some surprise that her job was of far higher status than I'd guessed, and that she herself came alive also when she was working.

'Make your call,' she said again.

'Yes.'

I pressed the buttons and at the first ring Holly picked up the receiver.

'Kit,' she said immediately, full of stress.

'Yes,' I said.

Holly's voice had come explosively out of the telephone, loudly enough to reach Danielle's ears.

'How did she know?' she asked. Then her eyes widened. 'She was waiting . . . you knew.'

I half nodded. 'Kit,' Holly was saying. 'Where are you? Are you all right? Your horse fell . . .'

'I'm fine. I'm in London. What's the matter?'

'Everything's worse. Everything's terrible. We're going to lose . . . lose the yard . . . everything . . . Bobby's out walking somewhere . . .'

'Holly, remember the telephone,' I said.

'What? Oh, the bugs? I simply don't care any more. The telephone people are coming to look for bugs in the morning, they've promised. But what does it matter? We're finished . . . It's over.' She sounded exhausted. 'Can you come? Bobby wants you. We need you. You hold us together.'

'What's happened?' I asked.

'It's the bank. The new manager. We went to see him today and he says we can't even have the money for the wages on Friday and they're going to make us sell up . . . he says we haven't enough security to cover all we owe them . . . and we're just slipping further into debt because we aren't making enough profit to pay the interest on the loan for those yearlings, and do you know how much he's charging us for that now? Seven per cent over base rate. Seven. That's about seventeen per cent right now. And he's adding the interest on, so now we're paying interest on the interest . . . it's like a snowball . . . it's monstrous . . . it's bloody unfair.'

A shambles, I thought. Banks were never in the benefaction business.

'He admitted it was because of the newspaper articles,' Holly said wretchedly. 'He said it was unfortunate . . . unfortunate! . . . that Bobby's father wouldn't help us, not even a penny . . . I've caused Bobby all this trouble . . . it's because of me . . .'

'Holly, stop it,' I said. 'That's nonsense. Sit tight and I'll come. I'm at Chiswick. It will take me an hour and a half.'

'The bank manager says we will have to tell the owners to take their horses away. He says we're not the only trainers who've ever had to sell up . . . he says it happens, it's quite common . . . he's so hard-hearted I could kill him.'

'Mm,' I said. 'Well, don't do anything yet. Have a drink. Cook me some spinach or something, I'm starving. I'll be on my way . . . See you soon.'

I put down the receiver with a sigh. I didn't really want to drive on to Newmarket with stiffening bruises and an echoingly empty stomach, and I didn't really want to shoulder all the Allardeck troubles again, but a pact was a pact and that was the end of it. My twin, my bond, and all that.

'Trouble?' Danielle said, watching.

I nodded. I told her briefly about the attacks in the *Flag* and their dire financial consequences and she came swiftly to the same conclusion as myself.

'Bobby's father is crass.'

'Crass,' I said appreciatively, 'puts it in a nutshell.'

I stood up slowly from her chair and thanked her for the telephone.

'You're in no shape for all this,' she said objectively.

'Never believe it.' I leaned forward and kissed her fragrant cheek. 'Will you come racing again, with your aunt?'

She looked at me straightly. 'Probably,' she said.

'Good.'

Bobby and Holly were sitting in silence in the kitchen, staring into space, and turned their heads towards me apathetically when I went in.

I touched Bobby on the shoulder and kissed Holly and said, 'Come on, now, where's the wine? I'm dying of various ills and the first thing I need is a drink.'

My voice sounded loud in their gloom. Holly got heavily to her feet and went over to the cupboard where they kept glasses. She put her hand out towards it and then let it fall again. She turned towards me.

'I had my test results since you phoned,' she said

blankly. 'I definitely am pregnant. This should have been the happiest night of our lives.' She put her arms around my neck and began quietly to cry. I wrapped my arms round her and held her, and Bobby stayed sitting down, too defeated, it seemed, to be jealous.

'All right,' I said. 'We'll drink to the baby. Come on, loves, businesses come and go, and this one hasn't gone yet, but babies are for ever, God rot their dear little souls.'

I disentangled her arms and picked out the glasses while she silently wiped her eyes on the sleeve of her jersey.

Bobby said dully, 'You don't understand,' but I did, very well. There was no fight in him, the deflation was too great; and I'd had my own agonizing disappointments now and then. It could take a great effort of will not to sit around and mope.

I said to Holly, 'Put on some music, very loud.'

'No,' Bobby said.

'Yes, Bobby. Yes,' I said. 'Stand up and yell. Stick two fingers up at fate. Break something. Swear your guts out.'

'I'll break your neck,' he said with a flicker of savagery.

'All right, then, do it.'

He raised his head and stared at me and then rose abruptly to his feet, power crowding back into his muscles and vigour and exasperation into his face.

'All right then,' he shouted, 'I'll break your fucking Fielding neck.'

'That's better,' I said. 'And give me something to eat.'

Instead he went over to Holly and enfolded her and the two of them stood there half weeping, half laughing, entwined in privacy and back with the living. I resignedly dug in the freezer for something fast and unfattening and transferred it to the microwave oven, and I poured some red wine and drank it at a gulp.

Over the food Bobby admitted that he'd been too depressed to walk round at evening stables, so after coffee he and I both went out into the yard for a last inspection. The night was windy and cold and moonlit behind scurrying clouds. Everything looked normal and quiet, all the horses dozing behind closed doors, scarcely moving when we looked in on them, checking.

The boxes that had contained Jermyn Graves's horses were still empty, and the string which led to the bell had been detached from the door and hung limply from its last guiding staple. Bobby watched while I attached it to the door again.

'Do you think it's still necessary?' he asked dubiously.

'Yes, I do,' I said positively. 'The feed-merchant will have paid in Graves's cheque yesterday, but it won't have been cleared yet. I wouldn't trust Graves out of sight and I'd rig as many strings to the bell as we can manage.'

'He won't come back again,' Bobby said, shaking his head.

'Do you want to risk it?'

He stared at me for a while and then said, 'No.'

We ran three more strings, all as tripwires across pathways, and made sure the bell would fall if any one of them was tugged. It was perhaps not the most sophisticated of systems, but it had twice proved that it worked.

It worked for the third time at one in the morning.

CHAPTER EIGHT

My first feeling, despite what I'd said to Bobby, was of incredulity. My second, that springing out of bed was a bad idea, despite the long hot soaking I'd loosened up with earlier; and I creaked and groaned and felt sore.

As I took basic overnight things with me permanently in a bag in the car – razor, clean shirt, toothbrush – I was sleeping (as usual in other people's houses) in bright blue running shorts. I would have dressed, I think, if I'd felt more supple. Instead I simply thrust my feet into shoes and went out on to the landing, and found Bobby there, bleary-eyed, indecisive, wearing the top half of his pyjamas.

'Was that the bell?' he said.

'Yes. I'll take the drive again. You take the yard.'

He looked down at his half-nakedness and then at mine.

'Wait.' He dived back into his and Holly's bedroom and reappeared with a sweater for me and trousers for himself, and, struggling into these garments en route, we careered down the stairs and went out into the windy night. There was enough moonlight to see by, which was as well, as we hadn't brought torches.

At a shuffle more than a run I hurried down the drive, but the string across that route was still stretched tight. If Graves had come, he hadn't come that way.

I turned back and went to help Bobby in the yard, but he was standing there indecisively in the semi-darkness, looking around him, puzzled. 'I can't find Graves,' he said. 'Do you think the bell just blew off in the wind?'

'It's too heavy. Have you checked all the strings?'

'All except the one across the gate from the garden. But there's no one here. No one's come that way.'

'All the same . . .' I set off down the path to the gate to the garden, Bobby following: and we found the rustic wooden barrier wide open. We both knew it couldn't have blown open. It was held shut normally with a loop of chain, and the chain hung there on the gatepost, lifted off the gate by human hands.

We couldn't hear much for the wind. Bobby looked doubtfully back the way we had come and made as if to return to the yard.

I said, 'Suppose he's in the garden.'

'But what for? And how?'

'He could have come through the hedge from the road into the paddock, and over the paddock fence, and then down this path, and he'd have missed all the strings except this one.'

'But it's pointless. He can't get horses out through the garden. There are walls all round it. He wouldn't try.'

I was inclined to agree, but all the same, someone had opened the gate.

The walled garden of Bobby's house was all and only on one side, with the drive, stable yard and outhouses wrapping round the other three; and apart from the gate where we now stood, the only way into the garden was through French windows from the drawing room of the house.

Maybe Bobby was struck by the same unwelcome thought as myself. In any case he followed me instantly through the gate and off the paving-stone path inside on to the grass which would be quieter underfoot.

We went silently, fast, the short distance towards the French windows, but they appeared shut, the many square glass frames reflecting the pale light from the sky.

We were about to go over to try them to make sure they were still locked when a faint click and a rattle reached my ears above the breeze, followed by a sharp and definite 'Bugger'.

Bobby and I stood stock still. We could see no one, even with eyes fast approaching maximum night vision.

'Get down,' a voice said. 'I don't like it.'

'Shut up.'

Feeling highly visible in my long bare legs and electric blue shorts I moved across the grass in the direction of the shadows which held the voices, and as policemen will tell you, you should not do that; one should go indoors and telephone the force.

We found, Bobby and I, a man standing at the bottom of a ladder, looking upwards. He wore no mask, no hood, simply an ordinary suit – incongruous as a burglar kit.

He was not Jermyn Graves, and he was not the nephew, Jasper.

He was under forty, dark haired, and a stranger.

He didn't see us at all until we were near him, so firmly fixed upwards was his attention, and when I said loudly, 'What the hell do you think you're doing?' he jumped a foot.

Bobby made a flying rugby tackle at his knees and I took hold of the ladder and pushed it sideways. There was a yell from above and a good deal of clattering, and a second stranger tumbled down from the eaves and fell with a thud on to an uninhabited flower bed.

I pounced on that one and pushed his face down into the November mud and with one hand tried to search his pockets for a weapon, with him heaving and threshing about beneath me, and then when I found no weapon, for some sort of identification, for a diary or a letter, for anything. People who came to burgle dressed as for going to the office might not have taken all suitable precautions.

I couldn't get into his pockets – it was too dark and there was too much movement – but somehow I found myself grasping the collar of his jacket, and I pulled it backwards and downwards with both hands, temporarily fastening his arms to his sides. He plunged and kicked and managed to throw my weight off his back, but I held fiercely on to the jacket, which was entangling his arms and driving him frantic.

To get loose he slid right out of the jacket, leaving it in my hands, and before I could do anything he was up from his knees to his feet, and running.

Instead of chasing him I turned towards Bobby, who was rolling on the ground exchanging short jabbing blows and breathless grunts with the man who'd been holding the ladder. Throwing the jacket into the deep shadow against the house wall I went to Bobby's help, and between the two of us we managed to pin the intruder face down on to the grass, Bobby astride his legs and I with a foot on his neck. Bobby delivered several meaningful blows to the kidneys, designed to hurt.

'Something to tie him with,' he said.

I bent down, gripped the collar of that jacket also, and pulled it as before backwards over the burglar's shoulders, pinning his arms, and then yanking it right off, I took my foot off the neck and said to Bobby, 'That's enough.'

'What? Don't be stupid.'

The intruder rolled under him still full of fight. Bobby punched him wickedly on the ear and again in the small of his back.

I shoved a hand into an inside pocket of the jacket and drew out a wallet.

'See,' I said to Bobby, pushing it under his nose. He shook his head, ignoring it, not wanting to be deterred.

I put the wallet back into the jacket and threw that jacket too into the shadows, and for a second watched Bobby and the now shirt-sleeved intruder tearing at each other and punching again, half standing, half falling, the one trying to cling on and hit, the other to escape.

Bobby was tall and strong and angry at having his house attacked, and no doubt erupting also with the suppressed and helpless fury of the past traumatic days: in any case he was hitting his adversary with tangible hatred and very hard, and I thought with spurting sudden alarm that it was too much, he was beating the man viciously and murderously and not merely capturing a burglar.

I caught Bobby's raised wrist and pulled his bunched fist backwards, upsetting his balance, and his victim twisted out of his grasp and half fell on his knees, coughing, retching, clutching his stomach.

Bobby shouted 'You bugger' bitterly and hit me instead, and the intruder got unsteadily to his feet and staggered towards the gate.

Bobby tried to follow and when I grasped at him to stop him he jabbed his fist solidly into my ribs, calling me a bloody Fielding, a bloody sod, a fucking bastard.

'Bobby . . . Let him go.'

I got a frightful cuff on the head and another clout in the ribs along with some more obscene opinions of my character and ancestors, and he didn't calm down, he kicked my shin and shoved me off him, tearing himself away with another direct hit to my head which rattled my teeth.

I caught him again in a couple of strides and he swung at me, swearing and increasingly violent, and I said to him, 'For God's sake, Bobby . . .' and just tried to hang on to his lethal fists and parry them and survive until the fireball had spent itself.

The generations were all there in his intent face: Allardecks and Fieldings fighting with guns and swords and bare knuckles in malice and perpetuity. He had transferred the intruder-born fury on to the older enemy and all rational restraints had vanished. It was me, his blood's foe, that he was at that point trying to smash, I the focus of his anger and fear and despair.

Locked in this futile archaic struggle we traversed the lawn all the way to the gate; and it was there, when I was wedged against the heavy post and finally in serious trouble, that the killing rage went out of his hands from one second to the next, and he let them fall, the passion dying, the manic strength draining away.

He gave me a blank look, his eyes like glass reflecting the moonlight, and he said 'Bastard', but without much force, and he turned and walked away along the path to the yard.

I said 'God Almighty' aloud, and took a few deep

breaths of rueful and shaky relief, standing for a while to let my hammering heart settle before shoving off the gatepost to go and fetch the burglars' coats. Bobby's fists hadn't had the same weight as the hurdlers' hooves, but I could well have done without them. Heigh ho, I thought, in about twelve hours I would ride three tricky jumpers at Newbury.

The coats lay where I had thrown them, in the angle of the empty flower bed and the brick wall of the house. I picked them up and stood there looking at the silvery ladder which had reached high up the wall, and then at the wall itself, which stretched in that section right to the roof, smooth and unbroken.

No windows.

Why would burglars try to break into a house at a point where there were no windows?

I frowned, tipping my head back, looking upwards. Beyond the line of the roof, above it, rising like a silhouette against the night sky, there was a sturdy brick chimney, surmounted by a pair of antique pots. It was, I worked out, the chimney from the fireplace in the drawing room. The fireplace was right through the wall from where I stood.

Irresolutely I looked from the ladder to the chimney pots and shivered in the wind. Then, shrugging, I put the jackets back into the shadow, propped the ladder up against the eaves, rooted its feet firmly in the flower bed, and climbed.

The ladder was aluminium, made in telescopic sections. I hoped none of them would collapse.

I didn't much like heights. Halfway up I regretted the whole enterprise. What on earth was I doing climbing an unsteady ladder in the dark? I could fall and hurt myself and not be able to race. It was madness, the whole thing. Crazy.

I reached the roof. The top of the ladder extended beyond that, four or five more rungs going right up to the chimney. On the tiles of the roof lay an opened tool kit, a sort of cloth roll with spanners, screwdrivers, pliers and so on, all held in stitched pockets. Beside it lay a coil of what looked like dark cord, with one end leading upwards to a bracket on the chimney.

I looked more closely at the chimney and almost laughed. One takes so many things for granted, sees certain objects day by day and never consciously sees them at all. Fixed to the chimney was the bracket and mounted on the bracket were the two terminals of the telephone wires leading to Bobby's house. I had seen them a hundred times and never noticed they were fixed to the chimney.

The wire itself stretched away into darkness, going across the telephone pole out on the road; the old above-ground wiring system of all but modern housing.

Attached to the telephone bracket, at the end of the dark cord leading from the coil, there appeared to be a small square object about the size of a sugar cube, with a thin rod about the length of a finger extending downwards. I stretched out a hand precariously to touch it and found it wobbled as if only half attached.

The moon seemed to be going down just when I needed it most. I fumbled around the small cube and came to what felt like a half-undone screw. I couldn't see it, but it turned easily anti-clockwise and in a few moments slipped out into my hand.

The cube and the rod fell straight off the bracket, and I would have lost them in the night if it hadn't been for the coil of stiff cord attached to them. Some of the cord unwound before I caught it, but not a great deal, and I put the coil, the cube and the rod on to the row of tools and rolled up the canvas kit and fastened it with its buckle.

The flower bed, I thought, wouldn't hurt the tool kit, so I dropped the rolled bundle straight below, and went down the ladder as slowly as I'd gone up, careful to balance and not to fall. There was no doubt I felt more at home on horses.

Retrieving the jackets and the tool kit but leaving the ladder, I went out of the garden and walked along the path and round to the kitchen door. Holly in a dressing gown and with wide frightened eyes was standing there, shivering with cold and anxiety.

'Thank goodness,' she said when I appeared. 'Where's Bobby?'

'I don't know. Come on in. Let's make a hot drink.'

We went into the kitchen where it was always

warmest and I put the kettle on while Holly looked out of the window for her missing husband.

'He'll come soon,' I said. 'He's all right.'

'I saw two men running . . .'

'Where did they go?'

'Over the fence into the paddock. One first, then the other a bit later. The second one was . . . well . . . groaning.'

'Mm,' I said. 'Bobby hit him.'

'Did he?' She sounded proud. 'Who were they? They weren't Jermyn. Did they come for his horses?'

'Which do you want,' I asked, 'coffee, tea or chocolate?'

'Chocolate.'

I made chocolate for her and tea for myself and brought the steaming cups to the table.

'Come and sit down,' I said. 'He'll be back.'

She came reluctantly and then watched with awakening curiosity while I unbuckled and unrolled the tool kit.

'See that?' I said. 'That tiny little box with its rod and its coil of cord? I'll bet anything that that's what's been listening to your telephone.'

'But it's minute.'

'Yes. I wish I knew more. Tomorrow we'll find out just how it works.' I looked at my watch. 'Today, I suppose one should say.' I told her where I'd found the bug, and about Bobby and me disturbing the intruders.

She frowned. 'These two men . . . Were they fixing this to our telephone?'

'Taking it away, perhaps. Or changing its battery.'

She reflected. 'I did say to you this evening on the telephone that the telephone people were coming tomorrow to look for bugs.'

'So you did.'

'So perhaps if they heard that, they thought . . . those two men . . . that if they took their bug away first, there wouldn't be anything to find, and we'd never know for sure.'

'Yes,' I said. 'I think you're right.' I picked up the first of the jackets and went through the pockets methodically, laying the contents on the table.

Holly, watching in amazement, said, 'They surely didn't leave their coats?'

'They didn't have much choice.'

'But all those things . . .'

'Dead careless,' I said. 'Amateurs.'

The first jacket produced a notepad, three pens, a diary, a handkerchief, two toothpicks and the wallet I had shown to Bobby in the garden. The wallet contained a moderate amount of money, five credit cards, a photograph of a young woman, and a reminder to go to the dentist. The name on the credit cards was Owen Watts. The diary not only gave the same name but also an address (home) and telephone number (office). The pages were filled with appointments and memos, and spoke of a busy and orderly life.

'Why are you purring like a cat with cream?' Holly said.

'Take a look.'

I pushed Owen Watts's belongings over to her and emptied the pockets of the second jacket. These revealed another notepad, more pens, a comb, cigarettes, throwaway lighter, two letters and a chequebook. There was also, tucked into the outside breast pocket, a small plastic folder containing a gold-coloured card announcing that Mr Jay Erskine was member number 609 of The Press Club, London EC4A 3JB; and Mr Jay Erskine's signature and address were on the back.

Just as well to make absolutely certain, I thought.

I telephoned to Owen Watts's office number, and a man's voice answered immediately.

'*Daily Flag*,' he said.

Satisfied, I put the receiver down without speaking.

'No answer?' Holly said. 'Not surprising, at this hour.'

'The *Daily Flag* neither slumbers nor sleeps. The switchboard, anyway, was awake.'

'So those two really are . . . those pigs.'

'Well,' I said. 'They work for the *Flag*. One can't say if they actually wrote those pieces. Not tonight. We'll find out in the morning.'

'I'd like to smash their faces.'

I shook my head. 'You want to smash the face of whoever sent them.'

'Him too.' She stood up restlessly. 'Where is Bobby? What's he doing?'

'Probably making sure that everything's secure.'

'You don't think those men came back?' she said, alarmed.

'No, I don't. Bobby will come in when he's ready.'

She was worried, however, and went to the outside door and called him, but the wind snatched her voice away so that one could scarcely have heard her from across the yard.

'Go and look for him, will you?' she said anxiously. 'He's been out there so long.'

'All right.' I collected the bugging device, the tools and the pressmen's things together on the table. 'Could you find a box for these, and put them somewhere safe.'

She nodded and began to look vaguely about, and I went out into the yard on the unwelcome errand. Wherever Bobby was, I was probably the last person he wanted to have come after him. I thought that I would simply set about rigging the alarm bell again, and if he wanted to be found, he would appear.

I rigged the bell and got back some night vision, and came across him down by the gate into the garden. He had brought the ladder out so that it lay along the path, and he was simply standing by the gatepost, doing nothing.

'Holly's wondering where you've got to,' I said easily.

He didn't answer.

'Do you think you can hear the bell from here?' I

said. 'Would you climb up someone's house if you'd heard an alarm bell?'

Bobby said nothing. He watched in flat calm while I found the string and shut the gate, fastening everything as before so that the bell would fall on the far side of the house if the gate was opened.

Bobby watched but did nothing. Shrugging, I opened the gate.

One could hear the bell if one was listening for it. On a still night it would have been alarming, but in the breeze the intruders had ignored it.

'Let's go in,' I said. 'Holly's anxious.'

I turned away to walk up the path.

'Kit,' he said stiffly.

I turned back.

'Did you tell her?' he asked.

'No.'

'I'm sorry,' he said.

'Come on in. It doesn't matter.'

'Yes, it does matter.' He paused. 'I couldn't help it. That makes it worse.'

'Tell you what,' I said, 'let's go in out of this bloody cold wind. My legs are freezing. If you want to talk, we'll talk tomorrow. But it's OK. Come on in, you old bugger, it's OK.'

I put the journalists' belongings under my bed for safety before I went achingly back to sleep, but their owners seemed to make no attempt to break in to get them back. I derived a great deal of yawning pleasure from picturing their joint states of mind and body, and thought that anything that had happened to them served them very well right.

Owen Watts and Jay Erskine. Jay Erskine, Owen Watts.

They were going to be, I decided hazily, trying to find an unbruised area to lie on, the lever with which to shift the world. Careless, sneaky, callous Owen Watts, battered half unconscious by Bobby, and stupid, snooping, flint-hearted Jay Erskine, fallen off his ladder with his face pressed into the mud. Served them bloody well right.

I dreamed of being run over by a tractor and felt like it a bit when I woke up. The morning after falls like the day before's were always a bore.

It was nearly nine when I made it to the kitchen, but although the lights were on against the grey morning, there was no one else there. I heated myself some coffee and began to read Bobby's daily paper, which was the *Towncrier*, not the *Flag*.

On page seven, which was wholly devoted to the Wednesday comments and opinions of a leading and immensely influential lady columnist, the central headline read:

WHAT PRICE FATHERLY LOVE?

And underneath, in a long spread unmissable by any *Towncrier* reader, came an outline of Maynard Allardeck's upwardly thrusting career.

He had journeyed from commodity broker, she said, to multi-storey magnate, sucking in other people's enterprises and spitting out the husks.

His *modus operandi*, she explained, was to advance smilingly towards an over-extended business with offers of loans of life-saving cash. Easy terms, pay when you can, glad to help. His new partners, the journalist said, welcomed him with open arms and spoke enthusiastically of their benefactor. But oh, the disillusionment! Once the business was running smoothly, Maynard would very pleasantly ask for his money back. Consternation! Disaster! Impossible to pay him without selling up and closing. The workforce redundant. Personal tragedies abounding. Can't have that, Maynard agreed genially. He would take the business instead of the money, how was that? Everyone still had their job. Except, hard luck, the proprietor and the managing director. Maynard presently would sell his now financially stable newly acquired business at a comfortable profit to any big fish looking out for manageable minnows: and so back, one might say, to the start, with Maynard appreciably richer.

How do I know all this? the lady journalist asked; and answered herself; less than three weeks ago on the TV programme *How's Trade*, Maynard himself told us. Classic takeover procedure, he smugly called it.

Anyone could do the same. Anyone could make a fortune the same way that he had.

It now seemed, she wrote, that one particular over-extended business in dire need of easy-terms cash was the racehorse training enterprise of Maynard's own and only son, Robertson (32).

Maynard was on record in this one instance as obstinately refusing to offer help.

My advice to someone in Robertson's (known as Bobby) position, said the lady firmly, would be to not touch Daddy's money with a bargepole. To count his rocky blessings. Daddy's fond embrace could find him presently sweeping the streets. Don't forget, she said, this parent is still grasping for car money he lent his son as a kid.

Is Maynard, she asked finally, worth a knighthood for services to industry? And she answered herself again: in her own opinion, definitely not.

There was a photograph of Maynard, polished and handsome, showing a lot of teeth. The word 'shark' sprang to mind. Maynard, I thought, would be apoplectic.

Bobby's first lot of horses clattered back into the yard from their morning exercise on the Heath, and Bobby himself came into the kitchen looking intensely depressed. He fixed himself a cup of coffee and wouldn't look at me, and drank standing by the window, staring out.

'How's Holly?' I asked.

'Sick.'

'Your father's in the paper,' I said.

'I don't want to read it.' He put down his cup. 'I expect you'll be going.'

'Yes. I'm riding at Newbury.'

'I meant . . . because of last night.'

'No, not because of that.'

He came over to the table and sat down, looking not at me but at his hands. There were grazes on the knuckles of both fists, red-raw patches where he'd smashed off his own skin.

'Why didn't you fight?' he said.

'I didn't want to.'

'You could have hurt me to hell and gone. I know that now. Why didn't you? I could have killed you.'

'Over my dead body,' I said dryly.

He shook his head. I looked at his face, at the downcast blue eyes, seeing the trouble, the self-doubt, the confusion.

'What I fight,' I said, 'is being brainwashed. Why should we still jump to that old hate? It was a Fielding you were trying to kill. Any Fielding. Not me, Kit, your brother-in-law who actually likes you, though I can't quite see why after last night. I'll fight my indoctrination, I'll fight my bloody ancestors, but I won't fight you, my sister's husband, with whom I have no quarrel.'

He sat for a while without speaking, still looking at his hands, then in a low voice he said, 'You're stronger than me.'

'No. If it makes you feel better, I don't know what I'd have done if I'd been through all you have in the past week and there had been an Allardeck handy to let it all out on.'

He raised his head, the very faintest of glimmers reappearing. 'Truce, then?' he said.

'Yeah,' I agreed; and wondered if our subconscious minds would observe it.

CHAPTER NINE

The vans swept into the yard as if conducting a race; one red, one yellow. Out of each emerged more slowly a man in dark clothes carrying, from the red van, the day's letters, and from the yellow, a clipboard. The Royal Mail and British Telecom side by side.

Bobby went to the door, accepted the letters, and brought the phone company man back with him into the kitchen.

'Bug-hunting,' the latter said heartily, as the red van roared away again outside. 'Got termites in the telephone, have you? Been hearing clicking noises on the line? No end of people hear them. False alarms, you know.'

He was large, moustached, and too full of unnecessary bonhomie. Bobby, making a great effort, offered tea or coffee, and I went upstairs to fetch the non-imaginary equipment from the chimney.

I could hear the phone man's voice long before I could see him on my way back.

'You get your M15, of course, but your average left-wing militant, they call us in regular. In Cambridge, now, false alarms all the time.'

'This is not,' Bobby said through gritted teeth, 'a false alarm.'

'We found this,' I said calmingly, putting the tool kit on the table, unrolling it, and producing for inspection the small metal cube with its rod and its coil of attached stiff cord.

'Ah now,' the telephone man's interest came to life, 'now you know what this is, don't you?'

'A bug,' I said.

'Now that,' he said, 'is your transformer stroke transmitter and your earth. Where's the rest?'

'What rest?'

He looked at us with pity. 'You got to have the tap itself. Where did you get this little lot?'

'From the chimney stack, where the phone wires reach the house.'

'Did you now.' He blew down his nose. 'Then that's where we'd better look.'

We took him outside the house rather than through the drawing room, walking down the path from the yard and through the gate. The telescopic aluminium ladder still lay on the path, but the phone man, eyeing the height of the chimney, decided against its fragile support and went back to his van for much sturdier rungs. He returned also with a busy tool-belt buckled round his rotund middle.

Planting and extending his workmanlike ladder he

lumbered up it as casually as walking. To each his own expertise.

At the top, with his stomach supported, he reached out to where the telephone wire divided to the two terminals, and with tools from his belt spent some time clamping, clipping and refastening before returning unruffled to earth.

'A neat little job,' he said appreciatively. 'Superior bit of wire-tapping. Looks like it's been in place for a couple of weeks. Grimy, but not too bad, see? Been up there just a while in the soot and rain.'

He held out a large palm on which rested a small cylinder with two short wires leading from it.

'See, this picks up the currents from your phone wire and leads them into that transformer you took down last night. See, voice frequencies run at anywhere between fifty Hertz and three kiloHertz, but you can't transmit that by radio, you have to transform it up to about three thousand megaHertz. You need an amplifier which modulates the frequency to something a microwave transmitter can transmit.' He looked at our faces. 'Not exactly electronics experts, are you?'

'No,' we said.

With complacent superiority he led the way back to the yard, carrying his heavy ladder with ease. In the kitchen he put the newly gathered cylinder alongside the previous night's spoils and continued with the lecture.

'These two wires from the cylinder plug into the transformer and this short little rod is the aerial.'

'What's all that cord?' I asked.

'Cord?' He smiled largely. 'That's not cord, it's wire. See? Fine wire inside insulation. That's an earth wire, to complete the circuit.'

We looked no doubt blank.

'If you'd have closely inspected your brickwork below your chimney these last weeks you'd have seen this so-called cord lying against it. Running through clips, even. Going down from the transmitter into the earth.'

'Yes,' Bobby said. 'We're never out there much this time of the year.'

'Neat little job,' the telephone man said again.

'Is it difficult to get?' I asked. 'This sort of equipment.'

'Dead easy,' he said pityingly. 'You can send for it from your electronic mail order catalogue any day.'

'And what then?' I asked. 'We've got the tap and the transmitter. Where would we find the receiver?'

The phone man said judiciously, 'This is a low-powered transmitter. Has to be, see, being so small. Runs on a battery, see? So you'd need a big dish-receiver to pick up the signals. Line of sight. Say a quarter-mile away? And no buildings to distort things. Then I'd reckon you'd get good results.'

'A big dish-receiver a quarter of a mile away?' I repeated. 'Everyone would see it.'

'Not inside a van, they wouldn't.' He touched the cube transmitter reflectively. 'Nice high chimney you've got there. Most often we find these babies on the poles out on the road. But the higher you put the transmitter, of course, the further you get good reception.'

'Yes,' I said, understanding that at least.

'This is an unofficial bit of snooping,' he said, happy to instruct. 'Private. You won't get no clicks from this, neither. You'd never know it was there.' He hitched up his tool-belt. 'Right then, you just sign my sheet and I'll be off. And you want to take your binoculars out there now and then and keep a watch on your chimney and your pole in the road, and if you see any more little strangers growing on your wires, you give me a ring and I'll be right back.'

Bobby signed his sheet and thanked him and saw him out to his van; and I looked at the silent bug and wondered vaguely whose telephone I could tap with it, if I learned how.

Holly came in as the yellow van departed, Holly looking pale in jeans and sloppy sweater, with hair still damp from the shower.

'Morning sickness is the pits,' she said. 'Did you make any tea?'

'Coffee in the pot.'

'Couldn't face it.' She put the kettle on. 'What happened out there last night between you and Bobby? He said you would never forgive him, but he wouldn't say what for. I don't think he slept at all. He was up walking round the house at five. So what happened?'

'There's no trouble between us,' I said. 'I promise you.'

She swallowed. 'It would just be the end if you and Bobby quarrelled.'

'We didn't.'

She was still doubtful but said no more. She put some bread in the toaster as Bobby came back, and the three of us sat round the table passing the marmalade and thinking our own thoughts, which in my case was a jumble of journalists, Bobby's bank manager, and how was I going to warm and loosen my muscles before the first race.

Bobby with apprehension began opening the day's letters, but his fears were unfounded. There was no blast from the bank and no demands for payment with menaces. Three of the envelopes contained cheques.

'I don't believe it,' he said, sounding stunned. 'The owners are paying.'

'That's fast,' I said. 'They can only have got those letters yesterday. Their consciences must be pricking overtime.'

'Seb's paid,' Bobby said. He mentally added the three totals and then pushed the cheques across to me. 'They're yours.'

I hesitated.

'Go on,' he said. 'You paid our bills on Monday. If

those cheques had come on Monday you wouldn't have had to.'

Holly nodded.

'What about the lads' wages this Friday?' I asked.

Bobby shrugged frustratedly. 'God knows.'

'What did your bank manager actually say?' I said.

'Sadistic bully,' Bobby said. 'He sat there with a smirk on his prim little face telling me I should go into voluntary liquidation immediately. Voluntary! He said if I didn't, the bank would have no choice but to start bankruptcy proceedings. No choice! Of course they have a choice. Why did they ever lend the money for the yearlings if they were going to behave like this five minutes later?'

The probable answer to that was because Bobby was Maynard's son. Maynard's millions might have seemed security enough, before the *Flag* fired its broadside.

'Isn't there any trainer in Newmarket who would buy the yearlings from you?' I said.

'Not a chance. Most of them are in the same boat. They can't sell their own.'

I pondered. 'Did the bank manager say anything about bailiffs?'

'No,' Bobby said, and Holly, if possible, went paler.

We might have a week, I thought. I didn't know much about liquidation or bankruptcy: I didn't know the speed of events. Perhaps we had no time at all. No one, however, could expect Bobby to be able to sell all his property overnight.

'I'll take the cheques,' I said, 'and I'll get them cashed. We'll pay your lads this week out of the proceeds and keep the rest for contingencies. And don't tell the bank manager, because he no doubt thinks this money belongs to the bank.'

'They lent it to us quick enough,' Holly said bitterly. 'No one twisted their arm.'

It wasn't only Maynard, I thought, who could lend with a smile and foreclose with a vengeance.

'It's hopeless,' Bobby said. 'I'll have to tell the owners to take their horses. Sack the lads.' He stopped abruptly. Holly, too, had tears in her eyes. 'It's such a mess,' Bobby said.

'Yeah . . . well . . . hold tight for a day or two,' I said.

'What's the point?'

'We might try a little fund-raising.'

'What do you mean?'

I knew only vaguely what I meant and I didn't think I would discuss it with Bobby. I said instead, 'Don't break up the stable before the dragon's breathing fire right in the yard.'

'St George might come along,' Holly said.

'What?' Bobby looked uncomprehending.

'In the story,' Holly said. 'You know. Kit and I had a pop-up book where St George came along and slew the dragon. We used to read it with a torch under the bedclothes and scare ourselves with shadows.'

'Oh.' He looked from one of us to the other, seeing

dark-haired twins with a shared and private history. He may have felt another twinge of exclusion because he smothered some reaction with a firming of the mouth, but after a while, with only a hint of sarcasm and as if stifling any hope I might have raised, he came up with an adequate reply. 'OK, St George. Get on your horse.'

I drove to Newbury and solved the stiff muscle problem by borrowing the sauna of a local flat race jockey who spent every summer sweating away his body in there and had thankfully come out for the winter. I didn't like water-shedding in saunas as a daily form of weight-control (still less diuretics), but after twenty minutes of its hot embrace on that cold morning I did feel a good deal fitter.

My first two mounts were for the Lambourn stable I normally rode for, and, given a jockey with smoothly working limbs, they both cleared the obstacles efficiently without covering themselves with either mud or glory. One could say to the hopeful owners afterwards that yes, their horses would win one day; and so they might, when the weights were favourable and the ground was right and a few of the better opponents fell. I'd ridden duds I wouldn't have taken out of the stable and had them come in first.

My final mount of the day belonged to the princess, who was waiting, alone as usual, for me to join her in the parade ring. I was aware of being faintly disappointed that Danielle wasn't with her, even though I hadn't expected it: most illogical. The princess, sable coat swinging, wore a pale yellow silk scarf at her neck with gold and citrine earrings, and although I'd seen her in them often before I thought she was looking exceptionally well and glowing. I made the small bow; shook her hand. She smiled.

'How do you think we'll do today?' she said.

'I think we'll win.'

Her eyes widened. 'You're not usually so positive.'

'Your horses are all in form. And . . .' I stopped.

'And what?'

'And . . . er . . . you were thinking, yourself, that we would win.'

She said without surprise, 'Yes, I was.' She turned to watch her horse walk by. 'What else was I thinking?'

'That . . . well . . . that you were happy.'

'Yes.' She paused. 'Do you think the Irish mare will beat us? Several people have tipped it.'

'She's got a lot of weight.'

'Lord Vaughnley thinks she'll win.'

'Lord Vaughnley?' I repeated, my interest quickening. 'Is he here?'

'Yes,' she said. 'He was lunching in a box near mine. I came down the stairs with him just now.'

I asked her if she remembered which box, but she didn't. I said I would like to talk to him, if I could find him.

'He'll be glad to,' she said, nodding. 'He's still

delighted about the Towncrier Trophy. He says literally hundreds of people have congratulated him on this year's race.'

'Good,' I said. 'If I ask him a favour, I might get it.'

'You could ask the world.'

'Not that much.'

The signal came for jockeys to mount, and I got up on her horse to see what we could do about the Irish mare: and what we did was to start out at a fast pace and maintain it steadily throughout, making the mare feel every extra pound she was carrying every stride of the way, and finally to beat off her determined challenge most satisfactorily by a length and a half.

'Splendid,' the princess exclaimed in the winners' enclosure, sparkling. 'Beautiful.' She patted her excited 'chaser. 'Come up to the box, Kit, when you've changed.' She saw my very faint and stifled hesitation and interpreted it. 'I saw Lord Vaughnley up there again. I asked him to my box also.'

'You're amazingly kind.'

'I'm amazingly pleased with winning races like this.'

I changed into street clothes and went up to her familiar box high above the winning post. For once she was there alone, not surrounded by guests, and she mentioned that she was on her way back from Devon, her chauffeur having driven her up that morning.

'My niece telephoned yesterday evening from her bureau to say she had arrived promptly,' the princess said. 'She was most grateful.'

I said I'd been very pleased to help. The princess offered tea, pouring it herself, and we sat on adjacent chairs, as so often, as I described the past race to her almost fence by fence.

'I could see,' she said contentedly. 'You were pushing along just ahead of the mare all the way. When she quickened, you quickened, when she took a breather down the bottom end, so did you. And then I could see you just shake up my horse when her jockey took up his whip . . . I knew we'd win. I was sure of it all the way round. It was lovely.'

Such sublime confidence could come crashing down on its nose at the last fence, but she knew that as well as I did. There had been times when it had. It made the good times better.

She said, 'Wykeham says we're giving Kinley his first try over hurdles at Towcester tomorrow. His first ever race.'

'Yes,' I nodded. 'And Dhaulagiri's taking his first start at a novice 'chase. I rode both of them schooling at Wykeham's last week, did he tell you? They both jumped super. Er . . . will you be there?'

'I wouldn't miss it.' She paused. 'My niece says she will come with me.'

I lifted my head. 'Will she?'

'She said so.'

The princess regarded me calmly and I looked straight back, but although it would have been useful I couldn't read what she was thinking.

'I enjoyed driving her,' I said.

'She said the journey went quickly.'

'Yes.'

The princess patted my arm non-committally, and Lord and Lady Vaughnley appeared in the doorway, looking in with enquiring faces and coming forward with greetings. The princess welcomed them, gave them glasses of port, which it seemed they liked particularly on cold days, and drew Lady Vaughnley away with her to admire something out on the viewing balcony, leaving Lord Vaughnley alone inside with me.

He said how truly delighted he'd been with everyone's response to last Saturday's race, and I asked if he could possibly do me a favour.

'My dear man. Fire away. Anything I can.'

I explained again about Bobby and the attacks in the *Flag*, which by now he himself knew all about.

'Good Lord, yes. Did you see the comment page in our own paper this morning? That woman of ours, Rose Quince, she has a tongue like a rattlesnake, but when she writes, she makes sense. What's the favour?'

'I wondered,' I said, 'if the *Towncrier* would have a file of clippings about Maynard Allardeck. And if you have one, would you let me see it.'

'Good Lord,' he said. 'You'll have a reason, no doubt?'

I said we had concluded that Bobby had been a casualty in a campaign mainly aimed at his father. 'And it would be handy to know who might have enough of a grudge against Maynard to kill off his chance of a knighthood.'

Lord Vaughnley smiled benignly. 'Such as anyone whose business was pulled from beneath them?'

'Such as,' I agreed. 'Yes.'

'You're suggesting that the *Flag* could be pressured into mounting a hate campaign?' He pursed his mouth, considering.

'I wouldn't have thought it would take much pressure,' I said. 'The whole paper's a hate campaign.'

'Dear, dear,' he said with mock reproof. 'Very well. I can't see how it will directly help your brother-in-law, but yes, I'll see you get access to our files.'

'That's great,' I said fervently. 'Thank you very much.'

'When would suit you?'

'As soon as possible.'

He looked at his watch. 'Six o'clock?'

I shut my mouth on a gasp. He said, 'I have to be at a dinner in the City this evening. I'll be dropping into the *Towncrier* first. Ask for me at the front desk.'

I duly asked at his front desk in Fleet Street and was directed upwards to the editorial section on the third floor, arriving, it seemed, at a point of maximum bustle as the earliest editions of the following day's papers were about to go to press.

Lord Vaughnley, incongruous in tweed jacket, dress

trousers, stiff shirt and white tie, stood at the shoulder of a coatless man seated at a central table, both of them intent on the newspaper before them. Around them, in many bays half separated from each other by shoulder-high partitions, were clumps of three or four desks, each bay inhabited by telephones, typewriters, potted plants and people in a faint but continuous state of agitation.

'What do you want?' someone said to me brusquely as I hovered, and when I said Lord Vaughnley, he merely pointed. Accordingly I walked over to the centre of the activity and said neutrally to Lord Vaughnley, 'Excuse me . . .'

He raised his eyes but not his head. 'Ah yes, my dear chap, be with you directly,' he said, and lowered the eyes again, intently scanning what I saw to be tomorrow's front page, freshly printed.

I waited with interest while he finished, looking around at a functional scene which I guessed hadn't changed much since the days of that rumbustious giant, the first Lord Vaughnley. Desks and equipment had no doubt come and gone, but from the brown floor to the yellowing cream walls the overall impression was of a working permanence, slightly old-fashioned.

The present Lord Vaughnley finished reading, stretched himself upwards and patted the shirt-sleeved shoulder of the seated man, who was, I discovered later, that big white chief, the editor.

'Strong stuff, Marty. Well done.'

The seated man nodded and went on reading. Lord Vaughnley said to me, 'Rose Quince is here. You might like to meet her.'

'Yes,' I said, 'I would.'

'Over here.' He set off towards one of the bays, the lair, it proved, of the lady of the rattlesnake tongue who could nevertheless write sense, and who had written that day's judgement on Maynard.

'Rose,' said the paper's proprietor, 'take care of Kit Fielding, won't you?' and the redoubtable Rose Quince assured him that yes, she would.

'Files,' Lord Vaughnley said. 'Whatever he wants to see, show him.'

'Right.'

To me he said, 'We have a box at Ascot. The *Towncrier* has, I mean. I understand from the princess that you'll be riding there this Friday and Saturday. No point, I suppose, my dear chap, in asking you to lunch with me on Saturday, which is the day I'll be there, but do come up for a drink when you've finished. You'll always be welcome.'

I said I'd be glad to.

'Good. Good. My wife will be delighted. You'll be in good hands with Rose, now. She was born in Fleet Street the same as I was, her father was Conn Quince who edited the old *Chronicle*; she knows more of what goes on than the Street itself. She'll give you the gen, won't you, Rose?'

Rose, who looked to me to be bristling with

reservations, agreed again that yes, she would; and Lord Vaughnley, with the nod of a man who knows he's done well, went away and left me to her serpent mercies.

She did not, it is true, have Medusa snakes growing out of her head, but whoever had named her Rose couldn't have foreseen its incongruity.

A rose she was not. A tiger-lily, more like. She was tall and very thin and fifteen to twenty years older than myself. Her artfully tousled and abundant hair was dark but streaked throughout with blonde, the aim having clearly been two contrasting colours, not overall tortoiseshell. The expertly painted sallow face could never have been pretty but was strongly good-looking, the nose masculine, the eyes noticeably pale blue; and from several feet away one could smell her sweet and heavy scent.

A quantity of bracelets, rings and necklaces decorated the ultimate in fashionable outlines, complemented by a heavy bossed and buckled belt round the hips, and I wondered if the general overstatement was a sort of stockade to frighten off the encroachment of the next generation of writers, a battlement against time.

If it was, I knew how she felt. Every jump jockey over thirty felt threatened by the rising nineteen-year-olds who would supplant them sooner or later. Every jockey, every champion had to prove race by race that he was as good as he'd ever been, and it was tough at the top only because of those hungry to take over one's saddle. I didn't need bangles, but I pulled out grey hairs when they appeared.

Rose Quince looked me up and down critically and said, 'Big for a jockey, aren't you?' which was hardly original, as most people I met said the same.

'Big enough.'

Her voice had an edge to it more than an accent, and was as positive as her appearance.

'And your sister is married to Maynard Allardeck's son.'

'Yes, that's right.'

'The source of Daddy's disapproval.'

'Yes.'

'What's wrong with her? Was she a whore?'

'No, a Capulet.'

Rose took barely three seconds to comprehend, then she shook her head in self-disgust.

'I missed an angle,' she said.

'Just as well.'

She narrowed her eyes and looked at me with her head tilted.

'I watched the Towncrier Trophy on television last Saturday,' she said. 'It would more or less have been treason not to.' She let her gaze wander around my shoulders. 'Left it a bit late, didn't you?'

'Probably.'

She looked back to my face. 'No excuses?'

'We won.'

'Yes, dammit, after you'd given everyone cardiac

arrest. Did you realize that half the people in this building had their pay packets on you?'

'No, I didn't.'

'The Sports Desk told us you couldn't lose.'

'Bunty Ireland?'

'Precisely, Bunty Ireland. He thinks the sun shines out of your arse.' She shook an armful of baubles to express dismissal of Bunty's opinions. 'No jockey is that smart.'

'Mm,' I said. 'Could we talk about Maynard?'

Her dark eyebrows rose. 'On first name terms, are you?'

'Maynard Allardeck.'

'A prize shit.'

'Olympic gold.'

She smiled, showing well-disciplined teeth. 'You read nothing in the paper, buddy boy. Do you want to see the tape?'

'What tape?'

'The tape of *How's Trade*. It's still here, downstairs. If you want to see it, now's the time.'

'Yes,' I said.

'Right. Come along. I've got the unexpurgated version, the one they cut from to make the programme. Ready for the rough stuff? It's dynamite.'

CHAPTER TEN

She had acquired, it appeared, both the ten-minute edition which had been broadcast as well as the half-hour original.

'Did you see the programme on the box?' Rose said.

I shook my head.

'You'd better see that first, then.'

She had taken me to a small room which contained a semi-circle of comfortable chairs grouped in front of a television set. To each side of the set various makes of video machine sat on tables, with connecting cables snaking about in apparent disorder.

'We get brought or sent unsolicited tapes of things that have happened,' Rose explained casually. 'All sorts of tapes. Loch Ness monsters by the pailful. Mostly rubbish, but you never know. We've had a scoop or sixteen this way. The big white chief swears by it. Then we record things ourselves. Some of our reporters like to interview with video cameras, as I do sometimes. You get the flavour back fresh if you don't write the piece for a week or so.'

While she talked she connected a couple of wandering cable ends to the back of the television set and switched everything on. Her every movement was accompanied by metallic clinks and jingles, and her lily scent filled the room. She picked up a tape cassette which had been lying on the table behind one of the video machines and fed it into the slot.

'Right. Here we go.'

We sat in two of the chairs, she sprawling sideways so she could see my face, and the screen sprang immediately to life with an interesting arrangement of snow. Total silence ensued for ten seconds before the Maynard segment of *How's Trade* arrived in full sharp colour with sound attached. Then we had the benefit of Maynard looking bland and polished through a voice-over introduction, with time to admire the hand-sewn lapels and silk tie.

The interviewer asked several harmless questions, Maynard's slightly condescending answers being lavishly interrupted by views of the interviewer nodding and smiling. The interviewer himself, unknown as far as I was concerned, was perhaps in his mid-thirties, with forgettable features except for calculating eyes of a chilling detachment. A prosecutor, I thought; and disliked him.

In reply to a question about how he got rich Maynard said that 'once or twice' he had come to the rescue of an ailing but basically sound business, had set it back on its feet with injections of liquidity and had subsequently acquired it to save it from closure when it had been unable to repay him. To the benefit, he suavely insisted, of all concerned.

'Except the former owners?' the interviewer asked; but the question was put as merely fact-finding, without bite.

Maynard's voice said that generous compensation was of course paid to the owners.

'And then what?' asked the interviewer, in the same way.

Naturally, Maynard said, if a good offer came along, he would in his turn sell: he could then lend the money to rescue another needy firm. The buying, selling and merging of businesses was advisable when jobs could be saved and a sensible profit made. He had done his modest best for industry and had ensured employment for many. It had been most rewarding in human terms.

Neither Maynard nor the interviewer raised his voice above a civilized monotone, and as an entertainment it was a drag. The segment ended with the interviewer thanking Maynard for a most interesting discussion, and there was a final shot of Maynard looking noble.

The screen, as if bored silly, reverted to black and white snow.

'Allardeck the philanthropist,' Rose said, jangling the bracelets and recrossing her long legs. 'Have you met him?'

'Yes.'

'Well, now for Allardeck the rapacious bully.'

'I've met him too,' I said.

She gave me a quizzical look and watched me watch the snowstorm until we were suddenly alive again with Maynard's charm and with the introduction and the first few harmless questions. It wasn't until the interviewer started asking about takeovers that things warmed up; and in this version the interviewer's voice was sharp and critical, designed to raise a prickly defensive response.

Maynard had kept his temper for a while, reacting self-righteously rather than with irritation, and these answers had been broadcast. In the end however his courtesy disintegrated, his voice rose and a forefinger began to wag.

'I act within the law,' he told the interviewer heavily. 'Your insinuations are disgraceful. When a debtor can't pay, one is entitled to take his property. The state does it. The courts enforce it. It's the law. Let me tell you that in the horse racing business, if a man can't pay his training fees, the trainer is entitled to sell the horse to recover his money. It's the law, and what's more, it's natural justice.'

The interviewer mentioned villainous mortgage holders who foreclosed and evicted their tenants. Hadn't Maynard, he asked, lent money to a hard-pressed family business that owned a block of flats which was costing more to maintain than the rental income, and couldn't afford the repairs required by the authorities? And after the repairs were done, hadn't

Maynard demanded his money back? And when the family couldn't pay, hadn't he said he would take the flats instead, which were a loss to the family anyway? And after that, hadn't mysterious cracks developed in the fabric, so that the building was condemned and all the poor tenants had to leave? And after that, hadn't he demolished the flats and sold the freehold land to a development company for ten times his original loan for repairs?

The inquisitional nature of the interviewer was by now totally laid bare, and the questions came spitting out as accusations, to which Maynard answered variously with growing fury:

'It's none of your business.'

'It was a long time ago.'

'The building subsided because of underground trains.'

'The family was glad to be rid of a millstone liability.'

'I will not answer these questions.'

The last statement was practically a shout. The interviewer made calming motions with his hand, leaning back in his chair, appearing to relax, all of which cooling behaviour caused Maynard to simmer rather than seethe. A mean-looking scowl, however, remained in place. Nobility was nowhere to be seen.

The interviewer with subterranean cunning said pleasantly, 'You mentioned racehorses. Am I right in thinking your own father was a racehorse trainer and that you at one time were his assistant?'

Maynard said ungraciously, 'Yes.'

'Give us your opinion of investing in bloodstock.'

Maynard said profits could be made if one took expert advice.

'But in your case,' the interviewer said, 'you must be your own expert.'

Maynard shrugged. 'Perhaps.'

The interviewer said very smoothly, 'Will you tell us how you acquired your racehorse Metavane?'

Maynard said tightly, 'I took him in settlement of a bad debt.'

'In the same way as your other businesses?'

Maynard didn't answer.

'Metavane proved to be a great horse, didn't he? And you syndicated him for at least four million pounds . . . which must be your biggest coup ever – bigger than the Bourne Brothers' patents. Shall we talk about those two enterprises? First, tell me how much you allow either Metavane's former owners or the Bourne Brothers out of the continuing fruits of your machinations.'

'Look here,' Maynard said furiously, 'if you had a fraction of my business sense you'd be out doing something useful instead of sitting here green with envy picking holes.'

He stood up fiercely and abruptly and walked decisively off the set, tearing off the microphone he had been wearing on his tie and flinging it on the ground. The interviewer made no attempt to stop him. Instead he faced the camera and with carefully presented distaste said that some of the other businesses, big and small, known to have benefited from Mr Allardeck's rescue missions were Downs and Co. (a printing works), Benjy's Fast Food Takeout, Healthy Life (sports goods manufacturers), Applewood Garden Centre, Purfleet Electronics and Bourne Brothers (light engineers).

The Bourne Brothers' assets, he said, had proved to include some long overlooked patents for a special valve which had turned out to be just what industry was beginning to need. As soon as it was his, Maynard Allardeck had offered the valve on a royalty basis to the highest bidder, and had been collecting handsomely ever since. The Bourne Brothers? The interviewer shook his head. The Bourne Brothers hadn't realized what they'd owned until they'd irrevocably parted with it. But did Maynard Allardeck know what he was getting? Almost certainly yes. The interviewer smiled maliciously and pushed the knife right in. If Allardeck had told the Bourne Brothers what they owned, collecting dust in a file, they could have saved themselves several times over.

The interviewer's smugly sarcastic face vanished into another section of blizzard, and Rose Quince rose languidly to switch everything off.

'Well?' she said.

'Nasty.'

'Is that all?'

'Why didn't they show the whole tape on *How's Trade*? They obviously meant to needle Maynard. Why did they smother the results?'

'I thought you'd never ask.' Rose hitched a hip on to one of the tables and regarded me with acid amusement. 'I should think Allardeck paid them not to show it.'

'What?'

'Pure as a spring lamb, aren't you? That interviewer and his producer have before this set up a pigeon and then thoroughly shot him down, but without the brawl ever reaching the screen. One politician, I know for certain, was invited by the producer to see his hopelessly damaging tape before it was broadcast. He was totally appalled and asked if there was any way he could persuade the producer to edit it. Sure, the producer said, the oldest way in the world, through your wallet.'

'How do you know?'

'The politician told me himself. He wanted me to write about it, he was so furious, but I couldn't. He wouldn't let me use his name.'

'Maynard,' I said slowly, 'has a real genius for acquiring assets.'

'Oh, sure. And nothing illegal. Not unless he helped the trains to shake the block of flats' foundations.'

'One could never find out.'

'Not a chance.'

'How did the interviewer rake all that up?'

Rose shrugged. 'Out of files. Out of archives. Same as we all do when we're on a story.'

'He'd done a great deal of work.'

'Expecting a great deal of pay-off.'

'Mm,' I said, 'if Maynard was already angling for a knighthood, he'd have paid the earth. They could probably have got more from him than they did.'

'They'll curl up like lemon rind now that they know.' The idea pleased Rose greatly.

'How did you get this tape?' I asked curiously.

'From the producer himself, sort of. He owed me a big favour. I told him I wanted to do a shredding job on Allardeck, and asked to see the interview again, uncut if possible, and he was as nice as pie. I wouldn't tell him I knew about his own little scam, now would I?'

'I suppose,' I said slowly, 'that I couldn't have a copy?'

Rose gave me a long cool look while she considered it. Her eyelids, I noticed, were coloured purple, dark contrast to the pale blue eyes.

'What would you do with it?' she said.

'I don't know yet.'

'It's under copyright,' she said.

'Mm.'

'You shouldn't have it.'

'No.'

She bent over the video machine and pressed the eject button. The large black cassette slid quietly and smoothly into her hand. She slotted it into its case and held it out to me, gold chains tinkling.

'Take this one. This is a copy. I made it myself. The originals never left the building, they're hot as hell about that in that television company, but I'm fairly quick with these things. They left me alone in an editing room to view, with some spare tapes stacked in a corner, which was their big mistake.'

I took the box, which bore a large white label saying 'Do not touch'.

'Now listen to me, buddy boy, if you're found with this, you don't get me into trouble, right?'

'Right,' I said. 'Do you want it back?'

'I don't know why I trust you,' she said plaintively. 'A goddamn jockey. If I want it back I'll ask. You keep it somewhere safe. Don't leave it lying about, for God's sake. Though I suppose I should tell you it won't play on an ordinary video. The tape is professional tape three-quarters of an inch wide, it gives better definition. You'll need a machine that takes that size.'

'What were you going to do with it yourself?' I asked.

'Wipe it off,' she said decisively. 'I got it yesterday morning and played it several times here to make sure I didn't put the uncut version's words into Allardeck's mouth in the paper. I don't need suing. Then I wrote my piece, and I've been busy today . . . but if you'd come one day later, it would all have been wiped.'

'Lucky,' I said.

'Yes. What else? Files? There's more on the tape, but Bill said files, so files you can have.'

'Bill?'

'Bill Vaughnley. We worked together when we were young. Bill started at the bottom, the old Lord made him. So did I. You don't call someone sir when you've shared cigarette butts on a night stint.'

They had been lovers, I thought. It was in her voice.

'He says I have a tongue like a viper,' she said without offence. 'I dare say he told you?'

I nodded. 'Rattlesnake.'

She smiled. 'When he's a pompous fool, I let him know it.'

She stood up, tawny and tinkling like a mobile in a breeze, and we went out of the television room, down a corridor, round a few corners, and found ourselves in an expanse like a library with shelves to the ceiling bearing not books but folders of all sorts, the whole presided over by a severe looking youth in spectacles who signed us in, looked up the indexing and directed us to the section we needed.

The file on Maynard Allardeck was, as Rose had said, less informative than the tape. There were sundry photographs of him, black and white glossy prints, chiefly taken at race meetings, where I supposed he was more accessible. There were three, several years old now, of him leading in his great horse Metavane after its win in the 2000 Guineas, the Goodwood Mile and the Champion Stakes. Details and dates were on flimsy paper strips stuck to the back of the prints.

There were two bunches of newspaper clippings, one from the *Towncrier*, one from other sources such as the *Financial Times* and the *Sporting Life*. Nothing critical had been written, it seemed, before the onslaught in the *Flag*. The paragraphs were mainly dull: Maynard, from one of the oldest racing families . . . Maynard, proud owner . . . Maynard, member of the Jockey Club . . . Maynard, astute businessman . . . Maynard, supporter of charity . . . Maynard the great and good. Approving adjectives like bold, compassionate, far-sighted and responsible occurred. The public persona at its prettiest.

'Enough to make you puke,' Rose said.

'Mm,' I said. 'Do you think you could ask your producer friend why he hit on Maynard as a target?'

'Maybe. Why?'

'Someone's got it in for Maynard. That TV interview might be an attack that didn't work, God bless bribery and corruption. The attack in the *Flag* has worked well. You've helped it along handsomely yourself. So who got to the *Flag*, and did they also get to the producer?'

'I take it back,' she said. 'Some jockeys are smarter than others.'

'Very few are dumb.'

'They just talk a different language?'

'Dead right.'

She returned the file to its place. 'Anything else? Any dinky little thing?'

'Yes,' I said. 'How would I get to talk to Sam Leggatt, who edits the *Flag*?'

She let out a breath, a cross between a cough and a laugh. 'Sam Leggatt? You don't.'

'Why not?'

'He walks around in a bullet-proof vest.'

'Seriously?'

'Metaphorically.'

'Do you know him?'

'Sure, I know him. Can't say I like him. He was political correspondent on the *Record* before he went to the *Flag*, and he's always thought he was God's gift to Fleet Street. He's a mocker by nature. He and the *Flag* are soulmates.'

'Could you reach him on the telephone?' I asked.

She shook her head over my naivety. 'They'll be printing the first edition by now, but he'll be checking everything again for the second. Adding stuff. Changing it round. There's no way he'd talk to Moses let alone a . . . a jumping bean.'

'You could say,' I suggested, 'that you were your editor's secretary, and it was urgent.'

She looked at me in disbelief. 'And why the hell should I?'

'Because you trade in favours.'

'Jee-sus.' She blinked the pale blue eyes.

'Any time,' I said. 'I'll pay. I took it for granted that this . . .' I held up the tape, 'was on account.'

'The telephone,' she said, 'makes it two favours.'

'All right.'

She said with amusement, 'Is this how you win your races?' She turned without waiting for an answer and led the way back roughly to where we had started from but ending in a small, bare little room furnished only with three or four chairs, a table and a telephone.

'Interview room,' Rose said. 'General purposes. Not used much. I'm not having anyone hear me make this call.'

She sat on one of the chairs looking exotically sensuous and behaving with middle-class propriety, the baroque façade for frighteners, the sensible woman beneath.

'You'll have about ten seconds, if that,' she said, stretching out the bracelets for the telephone. 'Leggatt will know straight away you're not our editor. Our editor comes from Yorkshire and still sounds like it.'

I nodded.

She got an outside line and with long red nails tapped in the *Flag*'s number, which she knew by heart; and within a minute, after out-blarneying the Irish, she handed me the receiver silently.

'Hello, Martin, what goes?' an unenthusiastic voice said.

I said slowly and clearly, 'Owen Watts left his credit cards in Bobby Allardeck's garden.'

'What? I don't see . . .' There was a sudden silence. 'Who is this?'

'Jay Erskine,' I said, 'left his Press Club card in the same place. To whom should I report these losses? To the Press Council, the police or my member of parliament?'

'Who is that?' he asked flatly.

'I'm speaking from a telephone in the *Towncrier*. Will you talk to me in your office, or shall I give the *Towncrier* a scoop?'

There was a long pause. I waited. His voice then said, 'I'll ring you back. Give me your extension.'

'No,' I said. 'Now or never.'

A much shorter pause. 'Very well. Come to the front desk. Say you're from the *Towncrier*.'

'I'll be there.'

He crashed the telephone down as soon as I'd finished speaking, and Rose was staring at me as if alarmed for my wholeness of mind.

'No one speaks to editors like that,' she said.

'Yeah . . . well, I don't work for him. And somewhere along the way I've learned not to be afraid of people. I was never afraid of horses. People were more difficult.'

She said with a touch of seriousness, 'People can harm you.'

'They sure can. But I'd get nowhere with Leggatt by being soft.'

'Where do you want to be?' she asked. 'What's this scoop you're not giving the *Towncrier*?'

'Nothing much. Just some dirty tricks the *Flag* indulged in to get their Allardeck story for Intimate Details.'

She shrugged. 'I doubt if we'd print that.'

'Maybe not. What's the limit journalists will go to to get a story?'

'No limit. Up Everest, into battlefields, along the gutters, anywhere a scandal leads. I've done my crusading time in rotten health farms, corrupt local governments, nutty religions. I've seen more dirt, more famine, more poverty, more tragedy than I need. I've sat through nights with parents of murdered children and I've been in a village of lifeboatmen's widows weeping for their dead. And then some damn fool man expects me to go sit on a prissy gilt chair and swoon over skirt lengths in some goddam Paris salon. I've never been a women's writer and I'm bloody well not starting now.'

She stopped, smiled twistedly, 'My feminism's showing.'

'Say you won't go,' I said. 'If it's a demotion, refuse it. You've got the clout. No one expects you to write about fashion, and I agree with you, you shouldn't.'

She gave me a long look. 'I wouldn't be fired, but he's new, he's a chauvinist, he could certainly make life difficult.'

'You,' I said, 'are one very marketable lady. Get out the famous poison fangs. A little venom might work wonders.'

She stood up, stretching tall, putting her hands on her heavily belted hips. She looked like an Amazon equipped for battle but I could still sense the indecision inside. I stood also, to the same height, and kissed her cheek.

'Very brotherly,' she said dryly. 'Is that all?'

'That's all you want, isn't it?'

'Yes,' she said, mildly surprised. 'You're goddam right.'

The *Daily Flag*, along Fleet Street from the *Towncrier*, had either been built much later or had been done over in Modern Flashy.

There was a fountain throwing out negative ions in the foyer and ceiling-wide chandeliers of thin vertical shimmering glass rods, each emitting light at its downward tip. Also a marble floor, futuristic seating and a security desk populated by four large men in intimidating uniforms.

I told one of them I'd come from the *Towncrier* to see Mr Leggatt and half expected to be thrown out bodily into the street. All that happened, however, was that after a check against a list on the desk I was directed upwards with the same lack of interest as I'd met with on friendlier territory.

Upstairs the decorative contrast continued. Walls in the *Flag* were pale orange with red flecks, the desks shining green plastic, the floor carpeted with busy orange and red zigzags, the whole a study in unrestfulness. Anger on every page, I thought, and no wonder.

Sam Leggatt's office had an opaque glass door marked 'editor' in large lower-case white letters, followed some way below by smaller but similar letters telling callers to ring bell and wait.

I rang the bell and waited, and presently with a buzz the door swung inwards a few inches. Sam Leggatt might not actually wear a bullet-proof vest but his defences against people with grievances were impressive.

I pushed the door open further and went in to another brash display of rotten taste: black plastic desk, red wallpaper flecked in a geometric pattern, and a mottled green carpet, which as a working environment would have sent me screaming to the bottle.

There were two shirt-sleeved men in there, both standing, both apparently impervious to their surroundings. One was short, stubby and sandy-haired, the other taller, stooped, bespectacled and going bald. Both about fifty, I thought. A third man, younger, sat in a corner, in a suit, watchful and quiet.

'Mr Leggatt?' I said.

The short sandy-haired one said, 'I'm Leggatt. I'll give you five minutes.' He inclined his head towards the taller man beside him. 'This is Tug Tunny, who edits Intimate Details. That is Mr Evans from our legal department. So who are you, and what do you want?'

Tug Tunny snapped his fingers. 'I know who he is,'

he said. 'Jockey. That jockey.' He searched for the name in his memory and found it. 'Fielding. Champion jockey.'

I nodded, and it seemed to me that they all relaxed. There was a trace of arrogance all the same in the way Leggatt stood, and a suggestion of pugnaciousness, but not more, I supposed, than his eminence and the circumstances warranted, and he spoke and behaved without bluster throughout.

'What do you want?' Leggatt repeated, but lacking quite the same tension as when I'd entered; and it crossed my mind as he spoke that with his passion for security they would be recording the conversation, and that I was speaking into an open microphone somewhere out of sight.

I said carefully, 'I came to make arrangements for returning the property of two of your journalists, Owen Watts and Jay Erskine.'

'Return it then,' Leggatt said brusquely.

'I would be so glad,' I said, 'if you would tell me why they needed to climb a ladder set against Bobby Allardeck's house at one in the morning.'

'What's it to you?'

'We found them, you understand, with telephone tapping equipment. Up a ladder, with tools, at the point where the telephone wires enter the Allardecks' house. What were they doing there?'

There was a pause, then Tunny flicked his fingers again.

'He's Allardeck's brother-in-law. Mrs Allardeck's brother.'

'Quite right,' I said. 'I was staying with them last night when your men came to break in.'

'They didn't break in,' Leggatt said. 'On the contrary, they were, I understand, quite savagely attacked. Allardeck should be arrested for assault.'

'We thought they were burglars. What would you think if you found people climbing a ladder set against your house at dead of night? It was only after we'd chased them off that we found they weren't after the silver.'

'Found? How found?'

'They left their jackets behind, full of credit cards and other things with their names on.'

'Which you propose to return.'

'Naturally. But I'd like a proper explanation of why they were there at all. Wire-tapping is illegal, and we disturbed them in the act of removing a tap which had been in place for at least two weeks, according to the telephone engineer who came this morning to complete the dismantling.'

They said nothing, just waited with calculating eyes.

I went on. 'Your paper mounted an unprovoked and damaging attack on Bobby Allardeck, using information gleaned by illegal means. Tell me why.'

They said nothing.

I said, 'You were sent, Mr Leggatt, a special delivery letter containing proof that all of Bobby Allardeck's creditors had been paid and he was not going bankrupt. Why don't you now try to undo a fraction of the misery you've caused him and my sister? Why don't you print conspicuously in Intimate Details an apology for misrepresenting Bobby's position? Why don't you outline the paragraph in red and get your two busy nocturnal journalists to scoot up to Newmarket with the edition hot off the presses like before, and while the town is asleep deliver a copy personally to every recipient who was on their earlier round? And why don't you send a red-inked copy to each of Bobby's owners, as before? That would be most pleasing, don't you think?'

They didn't looked pleased in the slightest.

'It's unfortunate,' I said mildly, 'that it's one's duty as a citizen to report illegal acts to the relevant authorities.'

Without any show of emotion Sam Leggatt turned his head towards the silent Mr Evans. After a pause Mr Evans briefly nodded.

'Do it,' Sam Leggatt said to Tunny.

Tunny was thunderstruck. 'No.'

'Print the apology and get the papers delivered.'

'But . . .'

'Don't you know a barrel when you see one?' He looked back at me. 'And in return?'

'Watts's credit cards and Erskine's Press Club pass.'

'And you'll still have . . .?'

'Their jackets, a chequebook, photos, letters, notebooks, a diary and a neat little bugging system.'

He nodded. 'And for those?'

'Well,' I said slowly, 'how about if you asked your lawyers what you would be forced to pay to Bobby if the wire-tapping came to court? If you cared to compensate him at that level now we would press no charges and save you the bad publicity and the costs and the penalties of a trial.'

'I have no authority for that.'

'But you could get it.'

He merely stared, without assent or denial.

'Also,' I said, 'the answer to why the attack was made. Who suggested it? Did you direct your journalists to break the law? Did they do it at their own instigation? Were they paid to do it, and if so by whom?'

'Those questions can't be answered.'

'Do you yourself know the answers?'

He said flatly, 'Your bargaining position is strong enough only for the apology and the delivery of the apology, and you shall have those, and I will consult on the question of compensation. Beyond that, nothing.'

I knew a stone wall when I saw one. The never-reveal-your-sources syndrome at its most flexible. Leggatt was telling me directly that answering my questions would cause the *Flag* more trouble than my reporting them for wire-tapping, which being so I would indeed get nothing else.

'We'll settle for the compensation,' I said. 'We would have to report the wire-tapping quite soon. Within a few days.' I paused. 'When a sufficient apology appears in the paper on Friday morning, and I've checked on the Newmarket deliveries, I'll see that the credit cards and the Press Club pass reach you here at your front desk.'

'Acceptable,' Leggatt said, smothering a protest from Tunny. 'I agree to that.'

I nodded to them and turned and went out through the door, and when I'd gone three steps felt a hand on my arm and found Leggatt had followed me.

'Off the record,' he said, 'what would you do if you discovered who had suggested the Allardeck attacks?'

I looked into sandy brown eyes, at one with the hair. At the businesslike outward presentation of the man who daily printed sneers, innuendo, distrust and spite, and spoke without showing a trace of them.

'Off the record,' I said, 'bash his face in.'

CHAPTER ELEVEN

I didn't suppose an apology printed in the *Flag* would melt Bobby's bank manager's cash register heart, and I was afraid that the *Flag*'s compensation, if they paid it, wouldn't be enough, or soon enough, to make much difference.

I thought with a sigh of the manager in my own bank, who had seen me uncomplainingly through bad patches in the past and had stuck out his neck later to lend me capital for one or two business excursions, never pressing prematurely for repayment. Now that I looked like being solvent for the foreseeable future he behaved the same as ever, friendly, helpful, a generous source of advice.

Getting the apology printed was more a gesture than an end to Bobby's troubles, but at least it should reassure the owners and put rock back under the quick-sands for the tradespeople in Newmarket. If the stable could be saved, it would be saved alive, not comatose.

I'd got from Sam Leggatt a tacit admission that the *Flag* had been at fault, and the certainty that he knew the answers to my questions. I needed those answers immediately and had no hope of unlocking his tongue.

With a sense of failure and frustration I booked into a nearby hotel for the night, feeling more tired than I liked to admit and afraid of falling asleep on the seventy dark miles home. I ordered something to eat from room service and made a great many telephone calls between yawns.

First, to Holly.

'Well done, today,' she said.

'What?'

'Your win, of course.'

'Oh, yes.' It seemed a lifetime ago. 'Thanks.'

'Where are you?' she said. 'I tried the cottage.'

'In London.' I told her the hotel and my room number. 'How are things?'

'Awful.'

I told her about the *Flag* promising to print the apology, which cheered her a little but not much.

'Bobby's out. He's gone walking on the Heath. It's all dreadful. I wish he'd come back.'

The anxiety was raw in her voice and I spent some time trying to reassure her, saying Bobby would certainly return soon, he would know how she worried; and privately wondering if he wasn't sunk so deep in his own despair that he'd have no room for imagining Holly's.

'Listen,' I said after a while. 'Do something for me, will you?'

'Yes. What?'

'Look up in the form books for Maynard's horse Metavane. Do you remember, it won the 2000 Guineas about eight years ago?'

'Vaguely.'

'I want to know who owned it before Maynard.'

'Is it important?' She sounded uninterested and dispirited.

'Yes. See if you can find out, and ring me back.'

'All right.'

'And don't worry.'

'I can't help it.'

No one could help it, I thought, disconnecting. Her unhappiness settled heavily on me as if generated in my own mind.

I telephoned Rose Quince at the home number she had given me on my way out, and she answered breathlessly at the eighth ring saying she had just that minute come through the door.

'So they didn't throw you to the presses?' she said.

'No. But I fear I got bounced off the flak jacket.'

'Not surprising.'

'All the same, read Intimate Details on Friday. And by the way, do you know a man called Tunny? He edits Intimate Details.'

'Tunny,' she said. 'Tug Tunny. A memory like a floppy disc, instant recall at the flick of a switch. He's been in the gossip business all his life. He probably pulled the wings off butterflies as a child and he's fulfilled if he can goad any poor slob to a messy divorce.'

'He didn't look like that,' I said dubiously.

'Don't be put off by the parsonage exterior. Read his column. That's *him*.'

'Yes. Thanks. And what about Owen Watts and Jay Erskine?'

'The people who left their belongings in your sister's garden?'

'That's right.'

'Owen Watts I've never heard of before today,' Rose said. 'Jay Erskine . . . if it's the same Jay Erskine, he used to work on the *Towncrier* as a crime reporter.'

There were reservations in her voice, and I said persuasively, 'Tell me about him.'

'Hm.' She paused, then seemed to make up her mind. 'He went to jail some time ago,' she said. 'He was among criminals so much because of his job, he grew to like them, like policemen sometimes do. He got tried for conspiracy to obstruct the course of justice. Anyway, if it's the same Jay Erskine, he was as hard as nails but a terrific writer. If he wrote those pieces about your brother-in-law, he's sold out for the money.'

'To eat,' I said.

'Don't get compassionate,' Rose said critically. 'Jay Erskine wouldn't.'

'No,' I said. 'Thanks. Have you been inside the *Flag* building?'

'Not since they did it up. I hear it's gruesome. When

Pollgate took over he let loose some decorator who'd been weaned on orange kitchen plastic. What's it like?'

'Gruesome,' I said, 'is an understatement. What's Pollgate like himself?'

'Nestor Pollgate, owner of the *Flag* as of a year ago,' she said, 'is reported to be a fairly young upwardly mobile shit of the first water. I've never met him myself. They say a charging rhinoceros is safer.'

'Does he have editorial control?' I asked. 'Does Sam Leggatt print to Pollgate's orders?'

'In the good old days proprietors never interfered,' she said nostalgically. 'Now, some do, some still don't. Bill Vaughnley gives general advice. The old Lord edited the *Towncrier* himself in the early years, which was different. Pollgate bought the *Flag* over several smarting dead bodies and you'll see old-guard *Flag* journalists weeping into their beer in Fleet Street bars over the whipped-up rancour they have to dip their pens in. The editor before Sam Leggatt threw in the sponge and retired. Pollgate has certainly dragged the *Flag* to new heights of depravity, but whether he stands over Leggatt with a whip, I don't know.'

'He wasn't around tonight, I don't think,' I said.

'He spends his time putting his weight about in the City, so I'm told. Incidentally, compared with Pollgate, your man Maynard is a babe in arms with his small takeovers and his saintly front. They say Pollgate doesn't give a damn what people think of him, and his financial bullying starts where Maynard's leaves off.'

'A right darling.'

'Sam Leggatt I understand,' she said. 'Pollgate I don't. If I were you I wouldn't twist the *Flag*'s tail any further.'

'Perhaps not.'

'Look what they did to your brother-in-law,' she said, 'and be warned.'

'Yes,' I said soberly. 'Thank you.'

'Any time.'

She said goodbye cheerfully and I sat drinking a glass of wine and thinking of Sam Leggatt and the fearsome manipulator behind him: wondering if the campaign against Maynard had originated from the very top, or from Leggatt or from Tunny, or from Watts and Erskine, or from outside the *Flag* altogether, or from one of Maynard's comet-trail of victims.

The telephone rang and I picked up the receiver, hearing Holly's voice saying without preamble, 'Maynard got Metavane when he was an unraced two-year-old, and I couldn't find the former owners in the form book. But Bobby has come back now, and he says he thinks they were called Perryside. He's sure his grandfather used to train for them, but they seem to have dropped right out of racing.'

'Um,' I said. 'Have you got any of those old *Racing Who's Who*s? They had pages of owners in them, with addresses. I've got them, but they're in the cottage, which isn't much good tonight.'

'I don't think we've got any from ten years ago,' she

said doubtfully, and I heard her asking Bobby. 'No, he says not.'

'Then I'll ring up Grandfather and ask him. I know he's kept them all, back to the beginning.'

'Bobby wants to know what's so important about Metavane after all these years.'

'Ask him if Maynard still owns any part of Metavane.'

The murmuring went on and the answer came back. 'He thinks Maynard still owns one share. He syndicated the rest for millions.'

I said, 'I don't know if Metavane's important. I'll know tomorrow. Keep the chin up, won't you?'

'Bobby says to tell you the dragon has started up the drive.'

I put the receiver down smiling. If Bobby could make jokes he had come back whole from the Heath.

Grandfather grumbled that he was ready for bed but consented to go downstairs in his pyjamas. 'Perryside,' he said, reading, 'Major Clement Perryside, The Firs, St Albans, Hertfordshire, telephone number attached.' Disgust filled the old voice. 'Did you know the fella had his horses with Allardeck?'

'Sorry, yes.'

'To hell with him, then. Anything else? No? Then goodnight.'

I telephoned to the Perryside number he'd given me and a voice at the other end said, Yes, it was The Firs, but the Perrysides hadn't lived there for about seven years. The voice had bought the house from Major and Mrs Perryside, and if I would wait they might find their new address and telephone number.

I waited. They found them. I thanked them; said goodnight.

At the new number another voice said, No, Major and Mrs Perryside don't live here any more. The voice had bought the bungalow from them several months back. They thought the Perrysides had gone into sheltered housing in Hitchin. Which sheltered housing? They couldn't say, but it was definitely in Hitchin. Or just outside. They thought.

Thank you, I said, sighing, and disconnected.

Major and Mrs Perryside, growing older and perhaps poorer, knowing Maynard had made millions from their horse: could they still hold a grievance obsessional enough to set them tilting at him at this late stage? But even if they hadn't, I thought it would be profitable to talk to them.

If I could find them; in Hitchin, or outside.

I telephoned to my answering machine in the cottage and collected my messages: four from various trainers, the one from Holly, and a final unidentified man asking me to ring him back, number supplied.

I got through to Wykeham Harlowe first because he, like my grandfather, went early to bed, and he, too, said he was in his pyjamas.

We talked for a while about that day's runners and those for the next day and the rest of the week, normal more or less nightly discussions. And as usual nowadays he said he wouldn't be coming to Towcester tomorrow, it was too far. Ascot, he said, on Friday and Saturday. He would go to Ascot, perhaps only on one day, but he'd be there.

'Great,' I said.

'You know how it is, Paul,' he said. 'Old bones, old bones.'

'Yes,' I said. 'I know. This is Kit.'

'Kit? Of course you're Kit. Who else would you be?'

'No one,' I said. 'I'll ring you tomorrow night.'

'Good, good. Take care of those novices. Goodnight, then, Paul.'

'Goodnight,' I said.

I talked after that with the three other trainers, all on the subject of the horses I'd be riding for them that week and next, and finally, after ten o'clock and yawning convulsively, I got through to the last, unidentified, number.

'This is Kit Fielding,' I said.

'Ah.' There was a pause, then a faint but discernible click. 'I'm offering you,' said a civilized voice, 'a golden opportunity.'

He paused. I said nothing. He went on, very smoothly, 'Three thousand before, ten thousand after.'

'No,' I said.

'You haven't heard the details.'

I'd heard quite enough. I disconnected without

saying another word and sat for a while staring at walls I didn't see.

I'd been propositioned before, but not quite like that. Never for such a large sum. The before-and-after merchants were always wanting jockeys to lose races to order, but I hadn't been approached by any of them seriously for years. Not since they'd tired of being told no.

Tonight's was an unknown voice, or one I hadn't heard often enough to recognize. High in register. Education to match. Prickles wriggled up my spine. The voice, the approach, the amount, the timing, all of them raised horrid little suggestions of entrapment.

I sat looking at the telephone number I'd been given.

A London number. The exchange 722. I got through to the operator and asked whereabouts in London one would find exchange 722, general information printed in London telephone directories. Hold on, she said, and told me almost immediately; 722 was Chalk Farm stroke Hampstead.

I thanked her. Chalk Farm stroke Hampstead meant absolutely nothing, except that it was not an area known for devotion to horse racing. Very much the reverse, I would have thought. Life in Hampstead tended to be intellectually inward-looking, not raucously open-air.

Why Hampstead . . .

I fell asleep in the chair.

*

After a night spent at least half in bed I drank some coffee in the morning and went out shopping, standing in draughty doorways in Tottenham Court Road, waiting for the electronic wizards to unbolt their steel-mesh shutters.

I found a place that would re-record Rose's professional three-quarter-inch tape of Maynard on to a domestic size to fit my own player, no copyright questions asked. The knowingly obliging youth who performed the service seemed disgusted and astounded that the contents weren't pornographic, but I cheered him up a little by buying a lightweight video-recording camera, a battery pack to run it off and a number of new tapes. He showed me in detail how to work everything and encouraged me to practise in the shop. He could point me to a helpful little bachelor club, he said, if I needed therapy.

I declined the offer, piled everything in the car, and set off north to Hitchin, which was not exactly on the direct route to Towcester but at least not in a diametrically opposite direction.

Finding the Perrysides when I got there was easy: they were in the telephone book. Major C. Perryside, 14 Conway Retreat, Ingle Barton. Helpful locals pointed me to the village of Ingle Barton, three miles outside the town, and others there explained how to find number 14 in the retirement homes.

The houses themselves were several long terraces of small one-storey units, each with its own brightly painted front door and strip of minute flower bed. Paths alone led to the houses: one had to park one's car on a tarmac area and walk along neatly paved ways between tiny segments of grass. Furniture removal men, I thought, would curse the lay-out roundly, but it certainly led to an air of unusual peace, even on a cold damp morning in November.

I walked along to number 14, carrying the video camera in its bag. Pressed the bell push. Waited.

Everywhere was quiet, and no one answered the door. After two or three more unsuccessful attempts at knocking and ringing I went to the door of the right-hand neighbour and tried there.

An old lady answered, round, bright-eyed, interested.

'They walked round to the shop,' she said.

'Do you know how long they'll be?'

'They take their time.'

'How would I know them?' I asked.

'The Major has white hair and walks with a stick. Lucy will be wearing a fishing hat, I should think. And if you're thinking of carrying their groceries home for them, young man, you'll be welcomed. But don't try to sell them encyclopaedias or life insurance. You'll be wasting your time.'

'I'm not selling,' I assured her.

'Then the shop is past the car park and down the lane to the left.' She gave me a sharp little nod and retreated behind her lavender door, and I went where she'd directed.

I found the easily recognizable Perrysides on the point of emerging from the tiny village stores, each of them carrying a basket and moving extremely slowly. I walked up to them without haste and asked if I could perhaps help.

'Decent of you,' said the Major gruffly, holding out his basket.

'What are you selling?' Lucy Perryside said suspiciously, relinquishing hers. 'Whatever it is, we're not buying.'

The baskets weren't heavy: the contents looked meagre.

'I'm not selling,' I said, turning to walk with them at the snail's pace apparently dictated by the Major's shaky legs. 'Would the name Fielding mean anything to you?'

They shook their heads.

Lucy under the battered tweed fishing hat had a thin imperious-looking face, heavily wrinkled with age but firm as to mouth. She spoke with clear upper-class diction and held her back ramrod straight as if in defiance of the onslaughts of time. Lucy Perryside, in various guises and various centuries, had pitched pride against bloody adversity and come through unbent.

'My name is Kit Fielding,' I said. 'My grandfather trains horses in Newmarket.'

The Major stopped altogether. 'Fielding. Yes. I remember. We don't like to talk about racing. Better keep off the subject, there's a good chap.'

I nodded slightly and we moved on as before, along the cold little lane with the bare trees fuzzy with the foreboding of drizzle; after a while Lucy said, 'That's why he came, Clement, to talk about racing.'

'Did you?' asked the Major apprehensively.

'I'm afraid so, yes.'

This time, however, he went on walking, with, it seemed to me, resignation; and I had an intense sense of the disappointments and downward adjustments he had made, swallowing his pain and behaving with dignity, civil in the face of disasters.

'Are you a journalist?' Lucy asked.

'No . . . a jockey.'

She gave me a sweeping glance from head to foot. 'You're too big for a jockey.'

'Steeplechasing,' I said.

'Oh.' She nodded. 'We didn't have jumpers.'

'I'm making a film,' I said. 'It's about hard luck stories in racing. And I wondered if you would help with one segment. For a fee, of course.'

They glanced at each other, searching each other's reactions, and in their private language apparently decided not to turn down the offer without listening.

'What would we have to do?' Lucy asked prosaically.

'Just talk. Talk to my camera.' I indicated the bag I

was carrying along with the baskets. 'It wouldn't be difficult.'

'Subject?' the Major asked, and before I could tell him he sighed and said, 'Metavane?'

'Yes,' I said.

They faced up to it as to a firing squad, and Lucy said eventually, 'For a fee. Very well.'

I mentioned an amount. They made no audible comment, but it was clear from their nods of acceptance that it was enough, that it was a relief, that they badly needed the money.

We made our slow progress across the car park and down the path and through their bright blue front door, and at their gestured invitation I brought out the camera and fed in a tape.

They grouped themselves naturally side by side on the sofa whose chintz cover had been patched here and there with different fabrics. They sat in a room unexpectedly spacious, facing large sliding windows which let out on to a tiny secluded paved area where in summer they could sit in the sun. There was a bedroom, Lucy said, and a kitchen and a bathroom, and they were comfortable, as I could see.

I could see that their furniture, although sparse, was antique, and that apart from that it looked as if everything saleable had been sold.

I adjusted the camera in the way I'd been taught and balanced it on a pile of books on a table, kneeling behind it to see through the viewfinder.

'OK,' I said, 'I'll ask you questions. Would you just look into the camera lens while you talk?'

They nodded. She took his hand: to give courage, I thought, rather than to receive.

I started the camera silently recording and said, 'Major, would you tell me how you came to buy Metavane?'

The Major swallowed and blinked, looking distinguished but unhappy.

'Major,' I repeated persuasively, 'please do tell me how you bought Metavane.'

He cleared his throat. 'I er . . . we . . . always had a horse, now and then. One at a time. Couldn't afford more, do you see? But loved them.' He paused. 'We asked our trainer . . . he was called Allardeck . . . to buy us a yearling at the sales. Not too expensive, don't you know. Not more than ten thousand. That was always the limit. But at that price we'd had a lot of fun, a lot of good times. A few thousand for a horse every four or five years, and the training fees. Comfortably off, do you see.'

'Go on, Major,' I said warmly as he stopped. 'You're doing absolutely fine.'

He swallowed. 'Allardeck bought us a colt that we liked very much. Not brilliant to look at, rather small, but good blood lines. Our sort of horse. We were delighted. He was broken in during the winter and during the spring he began to grow fast. Allardeck said we shouldn't race him then until the autumn, and of course we took his advice.' He paused. 'During the summer he developed splendidly and Allardeck told us he was very speedy and that we might have a really good one on our hands if all went well.'

The ancient memory of those heady days lit a faint glow in the eyes, and I saw the Major as he must have been then, full of boyish enthusiasm, inoffensively proud.

'And then, Major, what happened next?'

The light faded and disappeared. He shrugged. He said, 'Had a bit of bad luck, don't you know.'

He seemed at a loss to know how much to say, but Lucy, having contracted for gain, proved to have fewer inhibitions.

'Clement was a member of Lloyd's,' she said. 'He was in one of those syndicates which crashed . . . many racing people were, do you remember? He was called upon, of course, to make good his share of the losses.'

'I see,' I said, and indeed I did. Underwriting insurance was fine as long as one never actually had to pay out.

'A hundred and ninety-three thousand pounds,' the Major said heavily, as if the shock was still starkly fresh, 'over and above my Lloyd's deposit, which was another twenty-five. Lloyd's took that, of course, straight away. And it was a bad time to sell shares. The market was down. We cast about, do you see, to know what to do.' He paused gloomily, then went on, 'Our house was already mortgaged. Financial advisers, you understand, had always told us it was best to mortgage one's house and use the money for investments. But the investments had gone badly down . . . some of them never recovered.'

The flesh on his old face drooped at the memory of failure. Lucy looked at him anxiously, protectively stroking his hand with one finger.

'It does no good to dwell on it,' she said uneasily. 'I'll tell you what happened. Allardeck got to hear of our problems and said his son Maynard could help us, he understood finance. We'd met Maynard once or twice and he'd been charming. So he came to our house and said if we liked, as we were such old owners of his father, he would lend us whatever we needed. The bank had agreed to advance us fifty thousand on the security of our shares, but that still left a hundred and forty. Am I boring you?'

'No, you are not,' I said with emphasis. 'Please go on.'

She sighed. 'Metavane was going to run in about six weeks and I suppose we were clutching at straws, we hoped he would win. We needed it so badly. We didn't want to have to sell him unraced for whatever we could get. If he won he would be worth very much more. So we were overwhelmed by Maynard's offer. It solved all our problems. We accepted. We were overjoyed. We banked his cheque and Clement paid off his losses at Lloyd's.'

Sardonic bitterness tugged at the corners of her mouth, but her neck was still stretched high.

'Was Maynard charging you interest?' I asked.

'Very low,' the Major said. 'Five per cent. Damned good of him, we thought.' The downward curve of his mouth matched his wife's. 'We knew it would be a struggle, but we were sure we would get back on our feet somehow. Economize, do you see. Sell things. Pay him back gradually. Sell Metavane, when he'd won.'

'Yes,' I said. 'What happened next?'

'Nothing much for about five weeks,' Lucy said. 'Then Maynard came to our house again in a terrible state and told us he had two very bad pieces of news for us. He said he would have to call in some of the money he had just lent us as he was in difficulties himself, and almost worse, his father had asked him to tell us that Metavane had lamed himself out at exercise so badly that the vet said he wouldn't be fit to run before the end of the season. It was late September by then. We'd counted on him running in October. We were absolutely, completely shattered, because of course we couldn't afford any longer to pay training fees for six months until racing started again in March, and worse than that, a lame unraced two-year-old at the end of the season isn't worth much. We wouldn't be able to sell him for even what we'd paid for him.'

She paused, staring wretchedly back to the heartbreak.

'Go on,' I said.

She sighed. 'Maynard offered to take Metavane off our hands.'

'Is that how he put it?'

'Yes. Exactly. Take him off our hands is what he said. He said moreover he would knock ten thousand off our debt, just as if the colt was still worth that much. But, he said, he desperately needed some cash, and couldn't we possibly raise a hundred thousand for him at once.' She looked at me bleakly. 'We simply couldn't. We went through it all with him, explaining. He could see that we couldn't pay him without borrowing from a moneylender at a huge interest and he said in no way would he let us do that. He was understanding and charming and looked so worried that in the end we found ourselves comforting him in his troubles, and assuring him we'd do everything humanly possible to repay him as soon as we could.'

'And then?'

'Then he said we'd better make it all legal, so we signed papers transferring ownership of Metavane to him. He changed the amount we owed him from a hundred and forty to a hundred and thirty thousand, and we signed a banker's order to pay him regularly month by month. We were all unhappy, but it seemed the best that could be done.'

'You let him have Metavane without contingencies?' I asked. 'You didn't ask for extra relief on your debt if the horse turned out well?'

Lucy shook her head wearily. 'We didn't think about

contingencies. Who thinks about contingencies for a lame horse?'

'Maynard said he would have to put our interest payments up to ten per cent,' the Major said. 'He kept apologizing, said he felt embarrassed.'

'Perhaps he was,' I said.

Lucy nodded. 'Embarrassed at his own wickedness. He went away leaving us utterly miserable, but it was nothing to what we felt two weeks later. Metavane ran in a two-year-old race at Newmarket and won by three lengths. We couldn't believe it. We saw the result in the paper. We telephoned Allardeck at once. And I suppose you'll have guessed what he said?'

I half nodded.

'He said he couldn't think why we thought Metavane was lame. He wasn't. He never had been. He had been working brilliantly of late on the Heath.'

CHAPTER TWELVE

'You hadn't thought, I suppose,' I said gently, 'to ask to see the vet's report? Or even to check with Allardeck?'

Lucy shook her head. 'We took Maynard's word.'

The Major nodded heavily. 'Trusted him. Allardeck's son, do you see.'

Lucy said, 'We protested vigorously, of course, that Maynard had told us a deliberate lie, and Maynard said he hadn't. He just denied he'd ever told us Metavane wouldn't run before spring. Took our breath away. Clement complained to the Jockey Club, and got nowhere. Maynard charmed them too. Told them we had misunderstood. The Stewards were very cool to Clement. And do you know what I think? I think Maynard told them we were trying to screw yet more money out of him, when he'd been so generous as to help us out of a dreadful hole.'

They were both beginning to look distressed and I had a few twinges of conscience of my own. But I said, 'Please tell me the state of your debt now, and how much Maynard shared with you out of his winnings and the syndication of Metavane as a stallion.'

They both stared.

The Major said as if surprised, 'Nothing.'

'How do you mean, nothing?'

'He didn't give us a farthing.'

'He syndicated the horse for several millions,' I said.

The Major nodded. 'We read about it.'

'I wrote to him,' Lucy said, her cheeks slightly pink. 'I asked him to at least release us from what we owed him.'

'And?'

'He didn't answer.'

'Lucy wrote twice,' the Major said uncomfortably. 'The second time, she sent it special delivery, to be handed to him personally, so we know he must have received it.'

'He didn't reply,' Lucy said.

'We borrowed the money and that's that,' the Major said with resignation. 'Repayments and interest take most of our income, and I don't think we will ever finish.'

Lucy stroked his hand openly. 'We are both eighty-two, you see,' she said.

'And no children?' I asked.

'No children,' Lucy said regretfully. 'It wasn't to be.'

I packed away the camera, thanking them and giving them the cash I'd collected for paying Bobby's lads, proceeds of cashing one of Bobby's cheques with my valet at Newbury. My valet, a walking bank, had found the service routine and had agreed to bring cash for the other cheques to Towcester.

The Major and Lucy accepted the money with some embarrassment but more relief, and I wondered if they had feared I might not actually pay them once I'd got what I wanted. They'd learned in a hard school.

I looked at my watch and asked if I could make a quick credit card call on their telephone. They nodded in unison, and I got through to the manager where I banked.

'John,' I said.

'Kit.'

'Look, I'm in a hurry, on my way to ride at Towcester, but I've been thinking . . . It's true, isn't it, that money can be paid into my account without my knowing?'

'Yes, by direct transfer from another bank, like your riding fees. But you'd see it on your next statement.'

'Well,' I said, 'except for my riding fees, could you see to it that nothing gets paid in? If anything else arrives, can you refuse to put it into my account?'

'Yes, I can,' he said doubtfully, 'but why?'

'Someone offered me a bribe last night,' I said. 'It felt too much like a set-up. I don't want to find I've been sneakily paid by a back door for something I don't intend to do. I don't want to find myself trying to tell the Stewards I didn't take the money.'

He said after a short pause, 'Is this one of your intuitions?'

'I just thought I'd take precautions.'

'Yes,' he said. 'All right. If anything comes, I'll check with you before crediting your account.'

'Thanks,' I said. 'Until further notice.'

'And perhaps you would drop me a line putting your instructions in writing? Then you would be wholly safe, if it came to the Stewards.'

'I do not know,' I said, 'what I would do without you.'

I said goodbye to the Perrysides and drove away, reflecting that it was their own total lack of sensible precautions which had crystallized in me the thought that I should prudently take my own.

They should have insured in the first place against a catastrophic loss at Lloyd's and they should have brought in an independent vet to examine Metavane. It was easy to see these things after the event. The trick for survival was to imagine them before.

Towcester was a deep-country course, all rolling green hills sixty miles to the north-west of London. I drove there with my mind on anything except the horses ahead.

Mostly I thought about precautions.

With me in the car, besides my overnight bag, I had the tapes of Maynard, the tape of the Perrysides, the video camera and a small hold-all of Holly's containing the jackets and other belongings of Jay Erskine and Owen Watts. Without all those things I would not be able to get any sort of compensation or future for Bobby and Holly, and it occurred to me that I should make sure that no one stole them.

Sam Leggatt or anyone else at the *Flag* would see that repossessing the journalists' belongings would be a lot cheaper and less painful than coughing up cash and printing and distributing humble apologies.

Owen Watts and Jay Erskine were bound to be revengeful after the damage they had suffered, and they could be literally anywhere, plotting heaven knew what.

I was driving to a time and place printed in more than half the daily newspapers: my name plain to see on the racing pages, declared overnight for the one-thirty, two o'clock, three o'clock and three-thirty races.

If I were Jay Erskine, I thought, I would be jemmying open Kit Fielding's Mercedes at one-thirty, two o'clock, three o'clock or three-thirty.

If I were Owen Watts, perhaps at those times, I would be breaking into Kit Fielding's cottage in Lambourn.

They might.

They might not.

I didn't think a little active breaking and entering would disturb their consciences in the least, especially as the current penalties for a conviction for wire-tapping ran to a two thousand pound fine or up to two years in prison, or both.

I didn't know that I would recognize them from the mêlée in the dark. They could however make it their business to know me. To watch for my arrival in the jockeys' car park. To note my car.

It took forty-five minutes to drive from the Perry-sides' village to Towcester racecourse and for half the journey I thought I was being unnecessarily fanciful.

Then abruptly I drove into the centre of the town of Bletchley and booked myself into an old and prosperous looking hotel, the Golden Lion. They took an impression of my credit card and I was shown to a pleasant room, where I hung Watt's and Erskine's jackets in the closet, draped my night things around the bathroom and stowed everything else in a drawer. The receptionist nodded pleasantly and impersonally when I left the key at the desk on my way out, and no one else took any notice; and with a wince at my watch but feeling decidedly safer I broke the speed limit to Towcester.

The princess's novices were the first and last of my booked rides, with another for Wykeham and one for the Lambourn trainer in between.

The princess was waiting with her usual lambent patina in the parade ring when I went out there, and so was Danielle, dressed on that damp day in a blazing red shiny coat over the black trousers. I suppose my pleasure showed. Certainly both of them smiled down their noses in the way women do when they know they're admired, and Danielle, instead of shaking my hand, gave me a brief peck of a kiss on the cheek, a half touch of skin to skin, unpremeditated, the sensation lingering surprisingly in my nerve endings.

She laughed. 'How're you doing?' she said.

'Fine. And you?'

'Great.'

The princess said mildly, 'What do we expect from Kinley, Kit?'

I had a blank second of non-comprehension before remembering that Kinley was her horse. The one I was about to ride: three years old, still entire, a dappled grey going to the starting gate as second favourite for the first race of his life. High time, I thought, that I concentrated on my job.

'Dusty says he's travelled well; he's excited but not sweating,' I said.

'And that's good?' Danielle asked.

'That's good,' said the princess, nodding.

'He's mature for three, he jumps super at home and I think he's fast,' I said.

'And it all depends, I suppose, on whether he enjoys it today.'

'Yes,' I said. 'I'll do my best.'

'Enjoys it?' Danielle asked, surprised.

'Most horses enjoy it,' I said. 'If they don't, they won't race.'

'Do you remember Snowline?' the princess said. I

nodded, and she said to Danielle, 'Snowline was a mare I had a long time ago. She was beautiful to look at and had won two or three times on the Flat, and I bought her to be a hurdler, partly, I must confess, because of her name, but she didn't like jumping. I kept her in training for two years because I had a soft spot for her, but it was a waste of money and hope.' She smiled. 'Wykeham tried other jockeys, do you remember, Kit? For the second of those she wouldn't even start. I learned a great lesson. If a horse doesn't like racing, cut your losses.'

'What became of Snowline?' Danielle said.

'I sold her as a brood mare. Two of her foals have been winners on the Flat.'

Danielle looked from her aunt to me and back again. 'You both totally love it, don't you?'

'Totally,' said the princess.

'Totally,' I agreed.

I got up on Kinley and walked him slowly up past the stands to let him take in the sounds and smells, and then down towards the start, giving him a long close look at a flight of hurdles, letting him stand chest-high, almost touching, looking out over the top. He pricked his ears and extended his nostrils, and I felt the instinct stir in him most satisfactorily, the in-bred compulsion that ran in the blood like a song, the surging will to race and win.

You, Kinley, I thought, know all I've been able to teach you about jumping, and if you mess it up today you'll be wasting all those mornings I've spent with you on the schooling grounds this autumn.

Kinley tossed his head. I smoothed a hand down his neck and took him on to the start, mingling there with two or three other complete novices and about ten who had run at least once before but never won. The youngest a horse was allowed to go jump racing in Britain was in the August of its three-year-old year, and Kinley's was a two-mile event for three-year-olds who hadn't yet won.

Some jockeys avoided doing schooling sessions, but I'd never minded, on the basis that if I'd taught the horse myself I'd know what it could and wouldn't do. Some trainers sent green horses to crash around racecourses with only the haziest idea of how to meet a jump right, but Wykeham and I were in accord: it was no good expecting virtuoso jumping in public without arpeggios at home.

Wykeham was in the habit of referring to Kinley as Kettering, a horse he'd trained in the distant past. It was amazing, I sometimes thought, that the right horses turned up at the meetings: Dusty's doing, no doubt.

Kinley circled and lined up with only an appropriate amount of nervousness and when the tapes went up, set off with a fierce plunge of speed. Everything was new to him, everything unknown; nothing on the home gallops ever prepared a horse for the first rocketing reality. I settled him gradually with hands and mind, careful not to do it too much, not to teach him that what he was really feeling was wrong but just to control it, to keep it simmering, to wait.

He met the first hurdle perfectly and jumped it cleanly and I clearly felt his reaction of recognition, his increase in confidence. He let me shorten his stride a little approaching the second hurdle so as to meet it right and avoid slowing to jump, and at the third flight he landed so far out on the other side that my spirits rose like a bird. Kinley was going to be good. One could tell sometimes right from the beginning, like watching a great actor in his first decent role.

I let him see every obstacle clearly, mostly by keeping him to the outside. Technically the inside was the shortest way, but also the more difficult. Time for squeezing through openings when he could reliably run straight.

Just keep it going, Kinley old son, I told him; you're doing all right. Just take a pull here, that's right, to get set for the next jump, and now go for it, go for it . . . dear bloody hell, Kinley, you'll leave me behind, jumping like that, just wait while I get up here over your shoulders, I don't see why we can't kick for home, first time out, why not, it's been done, get on there, Kinley, you keep jumping like that and we'll damned near win.

I gave him a breather on the last uphill section and he was most aggrieved at my lack of urging, but once round the last bend, with one jump left before the run-in, I shook him up and told him aloud to get on with it, squeezing him with the calves of my legs, sending him rhythmic messages through my hands, telling him OK, my son, now fly, now run, now stretch out your bloody neck, this is what it's all about, this is your future, take it, embrace it, it's all yours.

He was bursting with pride when I pulled him up, learning at once that he'd done right, that the many pats I gave him were approval, that the applause greeting his arrival in the winners' enclosure was the curtain call for a smash hit. Heady stuff for a novice; and I reckoned that because of that day he would run his guts out to win all his life.

'He enjoyed it,' the princess said, glowing with pleasure.

'He sure did.'

'Those jumps . . .'

I unbuckled my saddle and drew it off on to my arm.

'He's very good,' I said. 'You have seriously got a good horse.'

She looked at me with speculation, and I nodded. 'You never know. Too soon to be sure.'

'What on earth are you talking about?' Danielle demanded.

'The Triumph Hurdle,' said her aunt.

I went to weigh in, change and weigh out and go through the whole rigmarole again with Wykeham's second runner, which didn't belong to the princess but to a couple in their seventies who cared just as much.

They owned only the one horse, an ageing 'chaser who'd been retired once and had pined until he'd been sent back into training, and I was truly pleased for them when, because of his experience, he stood up throughout the three miles as others fell, and against all the odds thundered along insouciantly into first place.

Wykeham might not go to the meetings, I thought, gratefully pulling up, he might have his mental grooves stuck in the past, but he sure as hell could still train winners.

I watched the next race after that from the jockeys' stand, and won the one after for the Lambourn trainer. One of those days, I thought contentedly. A treble. It happened once or twice a season, not much more.

It occurred to me as I was unbuckling my saddle in the winners' enclosure that Eric Olderjohn, the owner of the horse, who was present and quietly incandescent with delight, was something to do with the Civil Service on a high level, a fact I knew only because he occasionally lamented that government business would keep him away from seeing his pride and joy run.

I asked him on an impulse if I could talk to him for a few minutes after I'd weighed in and changed for the next race, and rather in the Vaughnley mould he said 'Anything' expansively, and was waiting there as promised when I went out.

We talked for a bit about his win, which was uppermost in his mind, and then he asked what I wanted. I wanted, I said, the answers to a couple of questions, and I wondered if he could – or would – get them for me.

'Fire away,' he said. 'I'm listening.'

I explained about the newspaper attacks on Bobby and Maynard, and to my surprise he nodded.

'I've heard about this, yes. What are your questions?'

'Well, first, whether Maynard was in fact being considered for a knighthood, and second, if he was, who would have known?'

He half laughed. 'You don't want much, do you?' He shook his head. 'Patronage is not my department.' He looked up at the sky and down at the colours I wore, which were by then the princess's. 'What good would it do you to find out?'

'I don't know,' I said frankly. 'But someone ought to make reparation to Bobby and my sister.'

'Hm. Why don't they ask these questions themselves?'

I said blankly, 'But they wouldn't.'

'They wouldn't, but you would.' His eyes were half assessing, half amused.

'Those newspaper articles were maliciously unfair,' I said positively. 'Bobby and my sister Holly are gentle well-intentioned people trying to make a success of training and doing no harm to anyone.'

'And the newspaper attack on them makes you angry?'

'Yes, it does. Wouldn't it you?'

He considered it. 'An attack on my daughter would, yes.' He nodded briefly. 'I don't promise, but I'll ask.'

'Thank you very much,' I said.

He smiled, turned to go and said, 'Win for me again next time out.'

I said I hoped to, and wondered why I'd described Bobby as gentle when the marks of his fists lay scattered on my body among the dark red attentions of the hurdlers. Bobby was brother to the wind, the seed of the tornado dormant in the calm.

I went back into the changing room for my helmet and stick and then out to the parade ring again for the sixth and last race of the day, the two-mile novice 'chase.

'Totally awesome,' Danielle said, standing there.

'What is?' I asked.

'We went down in the medic's car to one of the fences. We stood right by there watching you jump. That speed . . . so fast . . . you don't realize, from the stands.'

'In the three-mile 'chase,' the princess said, nodding.

'The medic said you were all going over there at better than thirty miles an hour. He says you're all crazy. He's right.'

The princess asked me if I thought I'd be making it four for the day, but I thought it unlikely: this one, Dhaulagiri, hadn't as much talent as Kinley.

'There's a woman riding in this race,' Danielle observed, watching the other jockeys standing in groups with the owners. She looked at me without archness. 'What do you think if you're beaten in a race by a woman?'

'That she had a faster horse,' I said.

'Ouch.'

The princess smiled but made no comment. She knew I didn't like racing against the very few women who rode professionally over jumps, not for fear of a male ego-battering, but because I couldn't rid myself of protectiveness. A male opponent could take his bumps, but I'd never learned to ride ruthlessly against a female; and moreover I didn't like the idea of what falls and horses' hooves could do to their faces and bodies. The women jockeys despised my concern for them, and took advantage of it if they could.

Dhaulagiri was looking well, I thought, watching him walk round. Better than when I'd schooled him the previous week. Tauter. A new lean line of muscle on the haunch. Something in the carriage of the head.

'What is it, Kit?' the princess asked.

I looked from the horse to her enquiring face. 'He's improved since last week,' I said.

'Wykeham said he seemed to like jumping fences better than hurdles.'

'Yes, he did.'

Her eyes smiled. 'Do you think, then . . .?'

'It would be nice, wouldn't it?'

'Exquisite,' she said.

I nodded and went away on Dhaulagiri to the start,

and in some odd way it seemed a jaunt to the horse as much as to me. Three winners raised my spirits euphorically. Dhaulagiri could jump. So why not, why bloody not make it four. Dhaulagiri took the mood from his jockey, as all horses do. I reckon Dhaulagiri on that afternoon would have light-heartedly jumped off a cliff if I'd asked him.

It wasn't the most advisable tactic for a horse running for the first time over the bigger fences and I dared say Wykeham would have deplored it, but Dhaulagiri and I went round the whole two miles in friendly, fully stretched recklessness, and at the winning post I thought for nearly the thousandth time in my life that there was nothing in existence comparable to the shared intense joy of victory. Better perhaps, but comparable, no. I was laughing aloud when we pulled up.

The exhilaration lasted all the way back to the changing room and in and out of the shower, and only marginally began to abate when my valet handed me a zipped webbing belt stuffed full of Bobby's money. Jockeys' valets washed one's breeches and took one's saddles and other belongings from racecourse to racecourse, turning up with everything clean every day. Besides that they were the grapevine, the machine oil, the comforters and the bank. My valet said he was lending me the money-belt he used himself on holidays, as he didn't like the idea of me walking around with all those thousands in my pockets.

Bobby, I thought, sighing. I would drive to Bletchley and collect my stuff from the Golden Lion, and then go on to Newmarket to give the money to Bobby so he could pay his lads at the normal time the next day and stack the rest away in his safe. I would sleep there and go direct to Ascot in the morning.

I strapped the belt against my skin and buttoned my shirt over it, the valet nodding approval. It didn't show, he said.

I thanked him for his thoughtfulness, finished dressing, and went out for a briefer than usual talk with the princess, whose eyes were still sparkling behind the sheltering lashes.

Vague thoughts I'd had of asking Danielle to help celebrate my four winners over dinner disintegrated when she said she was again due at her bureau at six-thirty, and they would be leaving for London at any moment.

'Do you work at weekends?' I asked.

'No.'

'Could . . . er, could I ask you out on Saturday evening?'

She glanced at her aunt, and so did I, but as usual one could tell nothing from the princess's face that she didn't want one to see. I felt no withdrawal, though, coming from her mind, and nor, it seemed, did her niece.

'Yes,' Danielle said, 'you could. I'll be coming to Ascot. After the races, we might make plans.'

Extraordinary, I thought. She understood. She had of course come close to seeing her ride from Devon to London evaporate at the third hurdle two days ago. Two days. That too was extraordinary. I seemed to have known her for longer.

'Tomorrow at Ascot,' the princess said to me, shaking my hand in goodbye. 'How long can we go on winning?'

'Until Christmas.'

She smiled. 'Christmas Fielding.'

'Yes.'

Danielle said, 'What do you mean, Christmas Fielding?'

'It's my name,' I said.

'What? I mean, I know it says C. Fielding on the number boards, but I took it for granted that Kit was for Christopher.'

I shook my head. 'We were born on Christmas morning. Christmas and Holly. No accounting for parents.'

There was warmth in her eyes as well as in the princess's. I left them saying their thanks to their hosts for the day before starting home, and with swelling contentment walked out to my own car.

At the sight of it most of the contentment vanished into anger. All four tyres were flat, the window on the driver's side was broken, and the lid of the boot hovered halfway open.

I said aloud and precisely about four obscene words

and then shrugged and turned to go back into the racecourse to telephone. The AA could deal with it. I could hire another car. The things I'd feared losing were safe in the Golden Lion and if that was what the vandals had been looking for, they were out of luck.

Most people had already left, but there were still a few cars in the park, still a person or two moving about. I was thinking chiefly of inconvenience and paying little attention to anything else, and very suddenly there was a voice at my left ear saying, 'Stand still, Fielding', and another man crowding against my right elbow with the same message.

I did stand still, too taken by surprise to think of doing anything else.

From each side the message reached me clearly.

Reached through my jacket, through my shirt and into my skin, somewhere above the money-belt.

'That's right,' said the one who'd spoken before. 'We've come to repossess some property. You don't want to get cut, do you?'

CHAPTER THIRTEEN

I certainly didn't.

'See that grey Ford over there right by the road,' said the man on my left. 'We're going to get into it, nice and easy. Then you'll tell us where to go for some jackets and the things in the pockets. We'll be sitting one each side of you on the back seat, and we're going to tie your hands, and if you make any sudden moves we'll slice your tendons so you won't stand again, never mind ride horses. You got that?'

Dry mouthed, I nodded.

'You've got to learn there's people you can't push around. We're here to teach you. So now walk.'

They were not Owen Watts and Jay Erskine. Different build, different voices, older and much heavier. They underlined their intentions with jabs against my lower ribs, and I did walk. Walked stiff-legged towards the grey Ford.

I would give them what they wanted: that was simple. Owen Watts's credit cards and Jay Erskine's Press Club pass weren't worth being crippled for. It was what would happen after the Golden Lion that seized up the imagination and quivered in the gut. They weren't going to release me with a handshake and a smile. They had as good as said so.

There was a third man, a driver, sitting in the Ford. At our approach he got out of the car and opened both rear doors. The car itself was pointing in the direction of the way out to the main road.

There seemed to be no one within shouting distance. No one near enough to help. I decided sharply and suddenly that all the same I wouldn't get into the car. I would run. Take my chances in the open air. Better under the sky than in some little dark corner; than on the back seat of a car with my hands tied. I would have given them the jackets but their priority was damage, and their intention of it was reaching me like shock waves.

It came to the point of now or never, and I was already tensing my muscles for it to be now, when a large quiet black car rolled along the road towards the racecourse exit and stopped barely six feet away from where I stood closely flanked. The nearside rear window slid down and a familiar voice said, 'Are you in trouble, Kit?'

I never was more pleased to see the princess in all my life.

'Say no,' the man on the left directed into my ear, screwing his knife round a notch. 'Get rid of them.'

'Kit?'

'Yes,' I said.

The princess's face didn't change. The rear door of her Rolls swung widely open and she said economically, 'Get in.'

I leapt. I jumped. I dived into her car head first, landing on my hands as lightly as possible across her ankles and Danielle's, flicking from there to the floor.

The car was moving forward quite fast even before the princess said, 'Drive on, Thomas' to her chauffeur, and I saw the angry faces of my three would-be captors staring in through the windows, heard their fists beating on the glossy bodywork, their hands trying to open the already centrally locked doors.

'They've got knives,' Danielle said in horror. 'I mean . . . *knives*.'

Thomas accelerated further, setting the heavy men running alongside and then leaving them behind, and I fumbled my way up on to one of the rear-facing folding seats and said I was sorry.

'Sorry!' Danielle exclaimed.

'For involving you in such a mess,' I said to the princess. I rubbed my hand across my face. 'I'm very sorry.'

Thomas said without noticeable alarm, 'Madam, those three men are intending to follow us in a grey Ford car.'

I looked out through the tinted rear window and saw that he was right. The last of them was scrambling in, fingers urgently pointing.

'Then we'd better find a policeman,' the princess said calmly; but as on every other racing day the police had left the racecourse as soon as the crowds had gone. There was no one at the racecourse gate directing traffic, since there was no longer any need. Thomas slowed and turned in the direction of London and put his foot smoothly on the accelerator.

'If I might suggest, madam?' he said.

'Yes. Go on.'

'You would all be safer if we kept going. I don't know where the police station is in Stony Stratford, which is the first town we come to. I would have to stop to ask directions.'

'If we go to a police station,' Danielle said anxiously, 'they'll keep us there for ages, taking statements, and I'll be terribly late.'

'Kit?' the princess asked.

'Keep going,' I said. 'If that's all right.'

'Keep going then, Thomas,' said the princess, and Thomas, nodding, complied. 'And now, Kit,' she said, 'tell us why you needed to be rescued in such a melodramatic fashion.'

'They had knives on him,' Danielle said.

'So I observed. But why?'

'They wanted something I've got.' I took a deep breath, trying to damp down the incredible relief of not being a prisoner in the car behind, trying to stop myself trembling. 'It started with some newspaper articles about my brother-in-law, Bobby Allardeck.'

She nodded. 'I heard about those from Lord Vaughnley yesterday, after you'd gone.'

'I've got blood on my leg,' Danielle said abruptly. 'How did I get . . .' She was looking down at her ankles, and then lifted her head suddenly and said to me, 'When you flew in like an acrobat, were you bleeding? Are you still bleeding?'

'I suppose so.'

'What do you mean, you suppose so? Can't you feel it?'

'No.' I looked inside my jacket, right and left.

'Well?' Danielle demanded.

'A bit,' I said.

Maybe the heavies hadn't expected me to jump with their knives already in. Certainly they'd reacted too slowly to stop me, ripping purposefully, but too late. The sting had been momentary, the aftermath ignorable. A little blood, however, went a long way.

The princess said resignedly, 'Don't we carry a first-aid box, Thomas?'

Thomas said 'Yes, madam' and produced a black box from a built-in compartment. He held it over his shoulder, and I took it, opened it, and found it contained useful-sized padded absorbent sterile dressings and all manner of ointments and sticky tapes. I took out one of the thick dressings and found two pairs of eyes watching.

'Excuse me,' I said awkwardly.

'You're embarrassed!' Danielle said.

'Mm.'

I was embarrassed by the whole situation. The princess turned her head away and studied the passing fields while I groped around under my shirt for somewhere to stick the dressing. The cuts, wherever they were, proved to be too far round for me to see them.

'For heaven's sake,' Danielle said, still watching, 'let me do it.'

She removed herself from the rear seat facing me to the folding seat by my side, took the dressing out of my hand and told me to hold my shirt and jacket up so that she could see the action. When I did she lifted her head slowly and looked at me directly.

'I simply don't believe you can't feel that.'

I smiled into her eyes. Whatever I felt was a pinprick to what I'd been facing. 'Stick the dressing on,' I said.

'All right.'

She stuck it on, and we changed places so she could do the other one, on my left. 'What a mess,' she said, wiping her hands and returning to the rear seat while I tucked my shirt untidily into my trousers. 'That first cut is long and horribly deep and needs stitches.'

The princess stopped staring out of the window and looked at me assessingly.

'I'll be all right for racing tomorrow,' I said.

Her mouth twitched. 'I would expect you to say that, if you had two broken legs.'

'I probably would.'

'Madam,' Thomas said, 'we're approaching the motorway and the grey Ford is still on our tail.'

The princess made an indecisive gesture with her hands. 'I suppose we'd better go on,' she said. 'What do you think?'

'On,' Danielle said positively, and Thomas and I nodded.

'Very well. On to London. And now, Kit, tell us what was happening.'

I told them about Bobby and me finding the journalists dismantling their wire-tap, and about removing their jackets before letting them go.

The princess blinked.

I said I had offered to return the jackets if the *Flag* would print an apology to Bobby and also pay some compensation. I explained about finding my car broken into, and about the suddenness with which my assailants had appeared.

'They wanted those jackets,' I said. 'And although I'd thought about robbery, I hadn't expected violence.' I couldn't think why not, after the violence of Bobby's assault on Owen Watts. I paused. 'I can't thank you enough.'

'Thank Thomas,' the princess said. 'Thomas said you were in trouble. I wouldn't have known.'

'Thank you, Thomas.'

'You could see it a mile off,' he said.

'You were pretty quick getting away.'

'I went to a lecture once about how not to get your employer kidnapped.'

'Thomas!' said the princess. 'Did you really?'

He said seriously, 'I wouldn't want to lose you, madam.'

The princess was moved and for once without an easy surface answer. Thomas, who had driven her devotedly for years, was a large quiet middle-aged Londoner with whom I talked briefly most days in racecourse car parks, where he sat and read books in the Rolls. I'd asked him once long ago if he didn't get bored going to the races every day when he wasn't much interested in horses and didn't gamble, and he'd said no, he liked the long journeys, he liked his solitude and most of all he liked the princess. He and I both, in many ways opposites, would I dare say have died for the lady.

I thought, all the same, that she wouldn't much care for the alarms of the continuing present. I looked back to the grey car still steadfastly following and began to consider what to do to vanish. I was thinking about perhaps diving down into thick undergrowth once we'd left the motorway, when the car behind suddenly swerved dangerously from the centre lane, cut across the slow lane to a wild blowing of horns and disappeared down a side road.

Thomas made a sort of growl in his throat and said with relief, 'They've gone into the service station.'

'You mean we've lost them?' Danielle said, twisting to look back.

'They peeled off.' To telephone, I supposed, a no-success story.

The princess said 'Good' as if that ended the matter entirely, and, greatly released, began to talk of her horses, of the day's triumphs, of more pleasing excitements, tracking with intent and expertise away from the alien violent terror of maiming steel back to the safe familiar danger of breaking one's neck.

By the time we reached central London she had returned the atmosphere to a semblance of full normality, behaving as if my presence in her car were commonplace, the tempestuous entrance overlooked. She would have gone with good manners to the scaffold, I thought, and was grateful for the calm she had laid upon us.

Within the last mile home, with dusk turning to full night, the princess asked Thomas if he would drive her niece to Chiswick as usual and return for her when she'd finished work.

'Certainly, madam.'

'Perhaps,' I said, 'I could fetch Danielle instead? Save Thomas the trip.'

'At two in the morning?' Danielle said.

'Why not?'

'OK.'

The princess made no comment, showed no feeling. 'It seems you have the night off, Thomas' was all she said; and to me, 'If you are wanting to go to the police, Thomas will drive you.'

I shook my head. 'I'm not going to the police.'

'But,' she said doubtfully, 'those horrid men . . .'

'If I go to the police, you will be in the newspapers.'

She said 'Oh' blankly. Cavorting about saving her jockey from a bunch of knife-wielding heavies was not the sort of publicity she yearned for. 'Do what you think best,' she said faintly.

'Yes.'

Thomas braked to a halt outside her house in Eaton Square and opened the car door for us to disembark. On the pavement I thanked the princess for the journey. Politeness conquered all. With the faintest gleam of amusement she said she would no doubt see me at Ascot, and as on ordinary days held out her hand for a formal shake, accepting the sketch of a bow.

'I don't believe it,' Danielle said.

'If you get the form of things right,' the princess said to her sweetly, 'every peril can be tamed.'

I bought a shirt and an anorak and booked into a hotel for the night, stopping in the lobby to rent a car from an agency booth there.

'I want a good one,' I said. 'A Mercedes, if you have one.'

They would try, they assured me.

Upstairs I changed from the slashed bloodstained

shirt and jacket into the new clothes, and began another orgy of telephoning.

The Golden Lion via directory enquiries said there was no problem, they would hold my room for another day, they had my credit card number, too bad I'd been unexpectedly detained, my belongings would be perfectly safe.

The AA said not to worry, they would rescue my car from Towcester racecourse within the hour. If I phoned in the morning, they would tell me where they'd taken it for repairs.

My answering system in the cottage had been hard-worked with please-ring-back messages from the police, my neighbour, my bank manager, Rose Quince, three trainers and Sam Leggatt.

My neighbour, an elderly widow, sounded uncommonly agitated, so I called her back first.

'Kit, dear, I hope I did right,' she said. 'I saw a strange man moving about in your cottage and I told the police.'

'You did right,' I agreed.

'It was lunchtime and I knew you'd be at Towcester, I always follow your doings. Four winners! It was on the radio just now. Well done.'

'Thanks . . . What happened at the cottage?'

'Nothing, really. I went over when the police came to let them in with my key. They couldn't have been more than five minutes getting there, but there wasn't anyone in the cottage. I felt so foolish, but then one of the policemen said a window was broken, and when they looked around a bit more they said someone had been in there searching. I couldn't see anything missing. Your racing trophies weren't touched. Just the window broken in the cloakroom.'

I sighed. 'Thank you,' I said. 'You are a dear.'

'I got Pedro from down the road to mend the window. I didn't like to leave it. I mean, anyone could get in.'

'I'll take you for a drink in the pub when I get back.'

She chuckled. 'Thank you, dear. That'll be nice.'

The police themselves had nothing to add. I should return, they said, to check my losses.

I got through to my bank manager at his home and listened to him chewing while he spoke. 'Sorry. Piece of toast,' he said. 'A man came into the bank at lunch-time to pay three thousand pounds into your account.'

'What man?'

'I didn't see him, unfortunately. I was out. It was a banker's draft, not a personal cheque.'

'Damn,' I said feelingly.

'Don't worry, it won't appear on your account. I've put a stop on anything being paid into it, as we agreed. The banker's draft is locked in the safe in my office. What do you want me to do with it?'

'Tear it up in front of witnesses,' I said.

'I can't do that,' he protested. 'Someone paid three thousand pounds for it.'

'Where was it issued?'

'At a bank in the City.'

'Can you ask them if they remember who bought it?'

'Yes, I'll try tomorrow. And be a good chap, let me have the no-paying-in instruction in writing pronto.'

'Yes,' I said.

'And well done with the winners. It was on the radio.'

I thanked him and disconnected, and after some thought left the hotel, walked down the street to an Underground station and from a public phone rang Sam Leggatt at the *Flag*.

There was no delay this time. His voice came immediately on the line, brisk and uncompromising.

'Our lawyers say that what you said here yesterday was tantamount to blackmail.'

'What your reporters did at my brother-in-law's house was tantamount to a jail sentence.'

'Our lawyers say if your brother-in-law thinks he has a case for settlement out of court, his lawyers should contact our lawyers.'

'Yeah,' I said. 'And how long would that take?'

'Our lawyers are of the opinion that no compensation should be paid. The information used in the column was essentially true.'

'Are you printing the apology?'

'Not yet. We haven't gone to press yet.'

'Will you print it?'

He paused too long.

'Did you know,' I said, 'that today someone searched

my cottage, someone smashed their way into my car, two men attacked me with knives, and someone tried to bribe me with three thousand pounds, paid directly into my bank account?'

More silence.

'I'll be telling everyone I can think of about the wire-tapping,' I said. 'Starting now.'

'Where are you?' he said.

'At the other end of the telephone line.'

'Wait,' he said. 'Ring me back, will you?'

'How long?'

'Fifteen minutes.'

'All right.'

I put the receiver down and stood looking at it, drumming my fingers and wondering if the *Flag* really did have equipment which could trace where I'd called from, or whether I was being fanciful.

I couldn't afford, I thought, any more punch-ups. I left the Underground station, walked along the street for ten minutes, went into a pub, rang the *Flag*. My call was again expected: the switchboard put me straight through.

When Sam Leggatt said 'Yes' there were voices raised loudly in the backgound.

'Fielding,' I said.

'You're early.' The backgound voices abruptly stopped.

'Your decision,' I said.

'We want to talk to you.'

'You're talking.'

'No. Here, in my office.'

I didn't answer immediately, and he said sharply, 'Are you still there?'

'Yes,' I said. 'What time do you go to press?'

'First edition, six-thirty, to catch the West Country trains. We can hold until seven. That's the limit.'

I looked at my watch. Fourteen minutes after six. Too late, to my mind, for talking.

'Look,' I said. 'Why don't you just print and distribute the apology? It's surely no big deal. It'll cost you nothing but the petrol to Newmarket. I'll come to your office when you assure me that you're doing that.'

'You'd trust my word?'

'Do you trust mine?'

He said grudgingly, 'Yes, I suppose I do expect you to return what you said.'

'I'll do it. I'll act in good faith. But so must you. You seriously did damage Bobby Allardeck, and you must at least try to put it right.'

'Our lawyers say an apology would be an acknowledgment of liability. They say we can't do it.'

'That's it, then,' I said. 'Goodbye.'

'No, Fielding, wait.'

'Your lawyers are fools,' I said, and put down the receiver.

I went out into the street and rubbed a hand over my head, over my hair, feeling depressed and a loser.

Four winners, I thought. It happened so seldom. I

should be knee-deep in champagne, not banging myself against a brick wall that kicked back so viciously.

The cuts on my ribs hurt. I could no longer ignore them.

I walked dispiritedly along to yet another telephone and rang up a long-time surgical ally.

'Oh, hello,' he said cheerfully. 'What is it this time? A little clandestine bone-setting?'

'Sewing,' I said.

'Ah. And when are you racing?'

'Tomorrow.'

'Toddle round, then.'

'Thanks.'

I went in a taxi and got stitched.

'That's not a horseshoe slash,' he observed, dabbing anaesthetic into my right side. 'That's a knife.'

'Yeah.'

'Did you know the bone is showing?'

'I can't see it.'

'Don't tear it open again tomorrow.'

'Then fix it up tight.'

He worked for a while before patting my shoulder. 'It's got absorbable stitches, also clips and gripping tape, but whether it would stand another four winners is anyone's guess.'

I turned my head. I'd said nothing about the winners.

'I heard it on the news,' he said.

He worked less lengthily on the other cut and

said lightly, 'I didn't think getting knifed was your sort of thing.'

'Nor did I.'

'Want to tell me why it happened?'

He was asking, I saw, for reassurance. He would come to my aid on the quiet, but it was important to him that I should be honest.

'Do you mean,' I said, 'have I got myself into trouble with gamblers and race-fixers and such?'

'I suppose so.'

'Then no, I promise you.' I told him briefly of Bobby's problems and felt his reservations fade.

'And the bruises?' he said.

'I fell under some hurdlers the day before yesterday.'

He nodded prosaically. I paid his fee in cash and he showed me to his door.

'Good luck,' he said. 'Come back when you need.'

I thanked him, caught a taxi and rode back to the hotel thinking of the *Flag* thundering off the presses at that moment without carrying the apology. Thinking of Leggatt and the people behind him; lawyers, Nestor Pollgate, Tug Tunny, Owen Watts and Jay Erskine. Thinking of the forces and the furies I had somehow unleashed. You've got to learn there's people you can't push around, one of the knifemen had said.

Well, I was learning.

The rented car booth in the lobby told me I was in luck, they'd got me a Mercedes; here were the keys, it was in the underground car park; the porter would show me when I wanted to go out. I thanked them. We try harder, they said.

Up in my room I ordered some food from room service and telephoned Wykeham to tell him how his winners had won, catching at least an echo of the elation of the afternoon.

'Did they get home all right?' I asked.

'Yes, they all ate up. Dhaulagiri looks as if he had a hard race but Dusty said he won easy.'

'Dhaulagiri ran great,' I said. 'They all did. Kinley's as good as any you've got.'

We talked of Kinley's future and of the runners at Ascot the next day and Saturday. For Wykeham the months of October, November and December were the peak: his horses came annually into their best form then, the present flourish of successes expected and planned for.

Between 30 September and New Year's Day he ran every horse in his charge as often as he could. 'Seize the moment,' he would say. After Christmas, with meetings disrupted by frost and snow, he let his stable more or less hibernate, resting, regrouping, aiming for a second intense flowering in March. My life followed his rhythms to a great extent, as natural to me as to his horses.

'Get some rest, now,' he said jovially. 'You've got six rides tomorrow, another five on Saturday. Get some good sleep.'

'Yes,' I said. 'Goodnight, Wykeham.'

'Goodnight, Paul.'

My food came and I ate bits of it and drank some wine while I got through to the other trainers who'd left messages, and after that I rang Rose Quince.

'Four winners,' she said. 'Laying it on a bit thick, aren't you?'

'These things happen.'

'Oh, sure. Just hold on to your moment of glory, buddy boy, because I've some negative news for you.'

'How negative?'

'A firm and positive thumbs down from the producer of *How's Trade*. There's no way on earth he's going to say who sicked him on to Maynard Allardeck.'

'But someone did?'

'Oh, sure. He just won't say who. I'd guess he got paid to do it as well as paid not to, if you see what I mean.'

'Whoever paid him to do it must be feeling betrayed.'

'Too bad,' she said. 'See you.'

'Listen,' I said hastily, 'what did Jay Erskine go to jail for?'

'I told you. Conspiracy to obstruct the course of justice.'

'But what did he actually do?'

'As far as I remember, he put some frighteners on to a chief prosecution witness who then skipped the country and never gave evidence, so the villain got off. Why?'

'I just wondered. How long did he get?'

'Five years, but he was out in a lot less.'

'Thanks.'

'You're welcome. And by the way, one of the favours you owed me is cancelled. I took your advice. The venom worked a treat and I'm freed, I'm no longer under the jurisdiction of the chauvinist. So thanks, and goodnight.'

'Goodnight.'

If the *Flag* wanted frighteners, Jay Erskine could get them.

I sighed and rubbed my eyes and thought about Holly, who had been hovering in my mind for ages, telling me to ring her up. She would want the money I still wore round my waist and I was going to have to persuade her and Bobby to come to London or Ascot in the morning to fetch it.

I was going to have to tell her that I hadn't after all managed to get the apology printed. That hers and Bobby's lawyers could grind on for ever and get nothing. That reporting the wire-tapping to all and sundry might inconvenience the *Flag*, but would do nothing to change their bank manager's mind. I put the call through to Holly reluctantly.

'Of course we'll come to fetch the money,' she said. 'Will you please stop talking about it and listen.'

'OK.'

'Sam Leggatt telephoned. The editor of the *Flag*.'

'Did he? When?'

'About an hour ago. An hour and a half. About seven o'clock. He said you were in London, somewhere in the Knightsbridge area, and did I know where you would be staying?'

'What did you say?' I asked, alarmed.

'I told him where you stayed last night. I told him to try there. He said that wasn't in Knightsbridge and I said of course not, but hadn't he heard of taxis. Anyway he wanted to get a message to you urgently, he said. He wanted me to write it down. He said to tell you the apology was being printed at that moment and will be delivered.'

'What! Why on earth didn't you say so?'

'But you told me last night it was going to happen. I mean, I thought you knew.'

'Christ Almighty,' I said.

'Also,' Holly said, 'he wants you to go to the *Flag* tonight. He said if you could get there before ten there would be someone there you wanted to meet.'

CHAPTER FOURTEEN

When I pressed the buzzer and walked unannounced through his unlatching door he was sitting alone in his office, shirt-sleeved behind his shiny black desk, reading the *Flag*.

He stood up slowly, his fingers spread on the paper as if to give himself leverage, a short solid man with authority carried easily, as of right.

I was not who he'd expected. A voice behind me was saying, 'Here it is, Sam', and a man came walking close, waving a folder.

'Yes, Dan, just leave it with me, will you?' Leggatt said, stretching out a hand and taking it. 'I'll get back to you.'

'Oh? OK.' The man Dan went away, looking at me curiously, closing the door with a click.

'I got your message,' I said.

He looked down at his copy of the *Flag*, turned a page, reversed the paper and pushed it towards me across the desk.

I read the Intimate Details that would be titillating

a few million Friday breakfasts and saw that at least he'd played fair. The paragraph was in bold black type in a black-outlined box.

It said:

The Daily Flag *acknowledges that the Newmarket racing stable of Robertson (Bobby) Allardeck (32) is a sound business and is not in debt to local traders. The* Daily Flag *apologizes to Mr Allardeck for any inconvenience he may have suffered in consequence of reports to the contrary printed in this column earlier.*

'Well,' he said, when I'd read.

'Thank you.'

'Bobby Allardeck should thank God for his brother-in-law.'

I looked at him in surprise, and I thought of Bobby's schizophrenic untrustable regard for me, and of my sister, for whom I truly acted. That paragraph should at least settle the nerves of the town and the owners and put the stable back into functionable order: given, of course, that its uneasy underlying finances could be equally sorted out.

'What changed your mind?' I asked.

He shrugged. 'You did. The lawyers said you would back down. I said you wouldn't. They think they can intimidate anybody with their threats of long expensive lawsuits.' He smiled twistedly. 'I said you'd be real poisonous trouble if we didn't print, and you would have been, wouldn't you?'

'Yes.'

He nodded. 'I persuaded them we didn't want Jay Erskine and Owen Watts in court, where you would put them.'

'Particularly as Jay Erskine has a criminal record already.'

He was momentarily still. 'Yes,' he said.

It had been that one fact, I thought, that had swayed them.

'Did Jay Erskine write the attacks on Bobby?' I asked.

After a slight hesitation he nodded. 'He wrote everything except the apology. I wrote that myself.'

He pressed a button on an intercom on his desk and said, 'Fielding's here' neutrally to the general air.

'Where are the credit cards, now we've printed?' he asked.

'You'll get them tomorrow, after the newspapers have been delivered, like I said.'

'You never let up, do you? Owen Watts has set off to Newmarket already and the others are in the post.' He looked at me broodingly. 'How did you find out about the bank?'

'I thought you might try to discredit me. I put a stop on all ingoing payments.'

He compressed his mouth. 'They can't see what they're dealing with,' he said.

The buzzer on his door sounded and he pushed the release instantly. I turned and saw a man I didn't know walking in with interest and no caution. Fairly tall, with a receding hairline over a pale forehead, he wore an ordinary dark suit with a brightly striped tie and had a habit of rubbing his fingers together, like a schoolmaster brushing off chalk.

'David Morse, head of our legal department,' said Sam Leggatt briefly.

No one offered to shake hands. David Morse looked me over as an exhibit, up and down, gaze wandering over the unzipped anorak and the blue shirt and tie beneath.

'The jockey,' he said coolly. 'The one making the fuss.'

I gave no reply, as none seemed useful, and through the open door behind him came another man who brought power with him like an aura and walked softly on the outsides of his feet. This one, as tall as the lawyer, had oiled dark hair, olive skin, a rounded chin, a small mouth and eyes like bright dark beads: also heavy shoulders and a flat stomach in smooth navy suiting. He was younger than either Sam Leggatt or Morse and was indefinably their boss.

'I'm Nestor Pollgate,' he announced, giving me a repeat of the Morse inspection and the same absence of greeting. 'I am tired of your antics. You will return my journalists' possessions immediately.'

His voice, like his body, was virile, reverberatingly bass in unaccented basic English.

'Did you ask me here just for that?' I said.

Don't twist their tail, Rose Quince had said. Ah well.

Pollgate's mouth contracted and he moved round to Leggatt's side of the desk, and the lawyer also, so that they were ranged there in a row like a triumvirate of judges with myself before them, as it were, on the carpet.

I had stood before the racing Disciplinary Stewards once or twice in that configuration, and I'd learned to let neither fright nor defiance show. Every bad experience, it seemed, could bring unexpected dividends. I stood without fidgeting and waited.

'Your contention that we mounted a deliberate campaign to ruin your brother-in-law is rubbish,' Pollgate said flatly. 'If you utter that opinion in public we will sue you.'

'You mounted a campaign to ruin Maynard Allardeck's chance of a knighthood,' I said. 'You aimed to destroy his credibility and you didn't give a damn who else you hurt in the process. Your paper was ruthlessly callous. It often is. I will utter that opinion as often as I care to.'

Pollgate perceptibly stiffened. The lawyer's mouth opened a little and Leggatt looked on the verge of inner amusement.

'Tell me why you wanted to wreck Maynard Allardeck,' I said.

'None of your business.' Pollgate answered with the finality of a bank-vault door, and I acknowledged that if I ever found out it wouldn't be by straightforward questions put to anyone in that room.

'You judged,' I said instead, 'that a sideways swipe at Maynard would be most effective, and you decided to get at him through his son. You gave not a thought to the ruin you were bringing on the son. You used him. You should compensate him for that use.'

'No,' Pollgate said.

'We admit nothing,' the lawyer said. A classically lawyer-like phrase. We may be guilty but we'll never say so. He went on, 'If you persist in trying to extort money by menaces, the *Daily Flag* will have you arrested and charged.'

I listened not so much to the words as to the voice, knowing I'd heard it somewhere recently, sorting out the distinctive high pitch and the precision of consonants and the lack of belief in any intelligence I might have.

'Do you live in Hampstead?' I said thoughtfully.

'What's that got to do with anything?' Pollgate said, coldly impatient.

'Three thousand before, ten after.'

'You're talking gibberish,' Pollgate said.

I shook my head. David Morse was looking as if he'd bitten a wasp.

'You were clumsy,' I said to him. 'You don't know the first thing about bribing a jockey.'

'What is the first thing?' Sam Leggatt asked.

I almost smiled. 'The name of the horse.'

'You admit you take bribes, then,' Morse said defensively.

'No I don't, but I've been propositioned now and then, and you didn't sound right. Also you were recording your offer on tape. I heard you start the machine. True would-be corrupters wouldn't do that.'

'I did advise caution,' Sam Leggatt said mildly.

'You've no proof of any of this,' Pollgate said with finality.

'My bank manager's holding a three thousand pound draft issued in the City. He intends on my behalf to ask questions about its origins.'

'He'll get nowhere,' Pollgate said positively.

'Then perhaps he'll do what I asked him first, which is to tear it up.'

There was a short stark silence. If they asked for the draft back they would admit they'd delivered it, and if they didn't, their failed ploy would have cost them the money.

'Or it could be transferred to Bobby Allardeck, as a first small instalment of compensation.'

'I've heard enough,' Pollgate said brusquely. 'Return the property of our journalists immediately. There will be no compensation, do you understand? None. You will come to wish, I promise you, that you had never tried to extort it.'

Under the civilized suiting he hunched his shoulders like a boxer, rotating them as a physical warning of an imminent onslaught, a flexing of literal muscles before an explosion of mental aggression. I saw in his face all the brutality of his newspaper and also the arrogance of absolute power. No one, I thought, could have defied him for too long, and he didn't intend that I should be an exception.

'If you make trouble for us in the courts,' he said grittily, 'I'll smash you. I mean it. I'll see to it that you yourself are accused of some crime that you'll hate, and I'll get you convicted and sent to prison, and you'll go down, I promise you, dishonoured and reviled, with maximum publicity and disgrace.'

The final words were savagely biting, the intention vibratingly real.

Both Leggatt and Morse looked impassive and I wondered what any of them could read on my own face. Show no fright . . . ye gods.

He surely wouldn't do it, I thought wildly. The threat must be only to deter. Surely a man in his position wouldn't risk his own status to frame and jail an adversary who wanted so little, who represented no life-or-death danger to his paper or to himself, who wielded no corporate power.

All the same, it looked horrible. Jockeys were eternally vulnerable to accusations of dishonesty and it took little to disillusion a cynical public. The assumption of guilt would be strong. He could try harder and more subtly to frame me for taking bribes, and certainly for things worse. What his paper had already set their hand to, they could do again and more thoroughly. A crime I would hate.

I could find no immediate words to reply to him, and while I stood there in the lengthening silence the door alarm buzzed fiercely, making Morse jump.

Sam Leggatt flicked a switch. 'Who is it?' he said.

'Erskine.'

Leggatt looked at Pollgate, who nodded. Leggatt pressed the button that unlatched the door, and the man I'd shaken off the ladder came quietly in.

He was of about my height, reddish haired going bald, with a drooping moustache and chillingly unsmiling eyes. He nodded to the triumvirate as if he'd been talking to them earlier and turned to face me directly, chin tucked in, stomach thrust out, a man with a ruined life behind him and a present mind full of malice.

'You'll give me my stuff,' he said. Not a question, not a statement: more a threat.

'Eventually,' I said.

There was a certain quality of stillness, of stiffening, on the far side of Leggatt's desk. I looked at Pollgate's thunderous expression and realized that I had almost without intending it told him with that one word that his threat, his promise, hadn't immediately worked.

'He's yours, Jay,' he said thickly.

I didn't have time to wonder what he meant. Jay Erskine caught hold of my right wrist and twisted my arm behind my back with a strength and speed that spoke of practice. I had done much the same to him in Bobby's garden, pressing his face into the mud, and into my ear with the satisfaction of an account paid he said, 'You tell me where my gear is or I'll break your shoulder so bad you'll ride no more races this side of Doomsday.'

His vigour hurt. I checked the three watching faces. No surprise, not even from the lawyer. Was this, I wondered fleetingly, a normal course of events in the editor's office of the *Daily Flag*?

'Tell me,' Erskine said, shoving.

I took a sharp half-pace backwards, cannoning into him. I went down in a crouch, head nearly to the floor, then straightened my legs with the fiercest possible jerk, pitching Jay Erskine bodily forwards over my shoulders, where he let go of my wrist and sailed sprawlingly into the air. He landed with a crash on a potted palm against the far wall while I completed the rolling somersault and ended upright on my feet. The manoeuvre took a scant second in the execution: the stunned silence afterwards lasted at least twice as long.

Jay Erskine furiously tore a leaf from his mouth and struggled pugnaciously to right himself, almost pawing the carpet like a bull for a second charge.

'That's enough,' I said. 'That's bloody enough.'

I looked directly at Nestor Pollgate. 'Compensation,' I said. 'Another of your banker's drafts. One hundred thousand pounds. Tomorrow. Bobby Allardeck will be coming to Ascot races. You can give it to him there. It could cost you about that much to manufacture a crime I didn't commit and have me convicted. Why not save yourself the trouble.'

Jay Erskine was upright and looking utterly malignant.

I said to him, 'Pray the compensation's paid . . . Do you want another dose of the slammer?'

I walked to the door and looked briefly back. Pollgate, Leggatt and Morse had wiped-slate faces: Jay Erskine's was glitteringly cold.

I wondered fearfully for a second if the door's unlatching mechanism also locked and would keep me in; but it seemed not. The handle turned easily, came smoothly towards me, opening the path of escape.

Out of the office, along the passage to the lifts my feet felt alarmingly detached from my legs. If I believed Pollgate's threats I was walking into the bleakest of futures: if I believed Erskine's malevolence it would be violent and soon. Why in God's name, I thought despairingly, hadn't I given in, given them the jackets, let Bobby go bust.

There were running footsteps behind me across the mock-marble hallway outside the lifts, and I turned fast, expecting Erskine and danger, but finding, as once before, Sam Leggatt.

His eyes widened at the speed with which I'd faced him.

'You expected another attack,' he said.

'Mm.'

'I'll come down with you.' He pressed the button for descent and stared at me for a while without speaking while we waited.

'One hundred thousand,' he said finally, 'is too much. I thought you meant less.'

'Yesterday, I did.'

'And today?'

'Today I met Pollgate. He would sneer at a small demand. He doesn't think in peanuts.'

Sam Leggatt went back to staring, blinking his sandy lashes, not showing his unspoken thoughts.

'That threat,' I said slowly, 'about sending me to prison. Has he used that before?'

'What do you mean?'

'On someone else.'

'What makes you think so?'

'You and your lawyer,' I said, 'showed no surprise.'

The lift purred to a halt inside the shaft and the doors opened. Leggatt and I stepped inside.

'Also,' I said, as the doors closed, 'the words he used sounded almost rehearsed. "You'll go down, I promise you, dishonoured and reviled, with maximum publicity and disgrace." Like a play, don't you think?'

He said curiously, 'You remember the exact words?'

'One wouldn't easily forget them.' I paused. 'Did he mean it?'

'Probably.'

'What happened before?'

'He wasn't put to the test.'

'Do you mean, the threat worked?' I asked.

'Twice.'

'Jesus,' I said.

I absent-mindedly rubbed my right shoulder, digging in under the anorak with the left thumb and fingers to massage. 'Does he always get his way by threats?'

Leggatt said evenly, 'The threats vary to suit the circumstances. Does that hurt?'

'What?'

'Your shoulder.'

'Oh. Yes, I suppose so. Not much. No worse than a fall.'

'How did you do that? Fling him off you, like that?'

I half grinned. 'I haven't done it since I was about fifteen, same as the other guy. I wasn't sure it would work with a grown man, but it did, a treat.'

We reached the ground floor and stepped out of the lift.

'Where are you staying?' he asked casually.

'With a friend,' I said.

He came with me halfway across the ornate entrance hall, stopping beside the small fountain.

'Why did Nestor Pollgate want to crunch Maynard Allardeck?' I said.

'I don't know.'

'Then it wasn't your idea or Erskine's? It came from the top?'

'From the top.'

'And beyond,' I said.

'What do you mean?'

I frowned. 'I don't know. Do you?'

'As far as I know, Nestor Pollgate started it.'

I said ruefully, 'Then I didn't exactly smash his face in.'

'Not far off.'

There was no shade of disloyalty in his voice, but I had the impression that he was in some way apologizing: the chief's sworn lieutenant offering comfort to the outcast. The chief's man, I thought. Remember it.

'What do you plan to do next?' he said.

'Ride at Ascot.'

He looked steadily into my eyes and I looked right back. I might have liked him, I thought, if he'd steered any other ship.

'Goodbye,' I said.

He seemed to hesitate a fraction but in the end said merely, 'Goodbye' and turned back to the lifts: and I went out into Fleet Street and breathed great gulps of free air under the stars.

I walked the two miles back to the hotel and sat in my room for a while there contemplating the walls, and then I went down to find the rented Mercedes in the underground park and drove it out to Chiswick.

'You're incredibly early,' Danielle said, faintly alarmed at my arrival. 'I did say two a.m., not half after eleven.'

'I thought I might just sit here and watch you, as no one seemed to mind me being here last time.'

'You'll be bored crazy.'

'No.'

'OK.'

She pointed to a desk and chair close to hers. 'No one's using that tonight. You'll be all right there. Did you get that cut fixed?'

'Yes, it's fine.'

I sat in the chair and listened to the mysteries of newsgathering, American style, for the folks back home. The big six-thirty evening slot, eastern US time, was being aired at that moment, it appeared. The day's major hassle had just ended. From now until two, Danielle said, she would be working on anything new and urgent which might make the eleven o'clock news back home, but would otherwise be on the screens at breakfast.

'Does much news happen here at this time of night?' I asked.

'Right now we've got an out-of-control fire in an oil terminal in Scotland and at midnight Devil-Boy goes on stage at a royal charity gala to unveil a new smash.'

'Who?' I said.

'Never mind. A billion teenagers can't be wrong.'

'And then what?' I said.

'After we get the pictures? Transmit them back here from a mobile van, edit them, and transmit the finished article to the studios in New York. Sometimes at midday here we do live interviews, mostly for the seven-to-nine morning show back home, but nothing live at nights.'

'You do edit the tapes here?'

'Sure. Usually. Want to see?'

'Yes, very much.'

'After I've made these calls.' She gestured to the telephone and I nodded, and subsequently listened to her talking to someone at the fire.

'The talent is on his way back by helicopter from the race riot and should be with you in ten minutes. Get him to call me when he can. How close to the blaze are you? OK, when Cervano gets to you try to go closer, from that distance a volcano would look like a sparkler. OK, tell him to call me when he's reached you. Yeah, OK, get him to call me.'

She put down the receiver, grimacing. 'They're a good mile off. They might as well be in Brooklyn.'

'Who's the talent?' I said.

'Ed Cervano. Oh . . . the talent is any person behind a microphone talking to the camera. News reporter, anchor, anyone.'

She looked along the headings on the board on the

wall behind her chair. 'Slug. That's the story we're working on. Oil fire. Devil-Boy. Embassy. So on.'

'Yes,' I said.

'Locations, obvious. Time, obvious. Crew. That's the camera crew which is allocated to that story, and also the talent. Format, that's how fully we're covering a story. Package means the works, camera crew, talent, interviews, the lot. Voice-over is just a cameraman, with the commentary tagged on later. So on.'

'And it's you who decides who goes where for what?'

She half nodded. 'The bureau chief, and the other coordinators, who work in the daytime, and me, yes.'

'Some job,' I said.

She smiled with her eyes. 'If we do well, the company's ratings go up. If we do badly, we get fired.'

'The news is the news, surely,' I said.

'Oh yes? Which would you prefer, an oil fire from a mile off or to think you feel the flames?'

'Mm.'

Her telephone rang. 'News,' she said, and listened. 'Look,' she said, sounding exasperated, 'if he's late, it's news. If he's sick, it's news. If he doesn't make it on to the stage at a royal gala, it's news. You just stay there, whatever happens is news, OK? Get some shots of royalty leaving, if all else fails.' She put down the receiver. 'Devil-Boy hasn't arrived at the theatre and it takes him a good hour to dress.'

'The joys of the non-event.'

'I don't want to be scooped by one of the other broadcasting companies, now do I?'

'Where do you get the news from in the first place?'

'Oh . . . the press agencies, newspapers, police broadcasts, publicity releases, things like that.'

'I guess I never wondered before how the news arrived on the box.'

'Ten seconds' worth can take all day to gather.'

Her telephone rang again, with the helicoptering Ed Cervano now down to earth at the other end. Danielle asked him in gentle tones to go get himself a first degree burn, and from her smile it seemed he was willing to go up in flames entirely for her sake.

'A sweet-talking guy,' she said, putting down the receiver. 'And he writes like a poet.' Her eyes were shining over the talent's talents, her mouth curving from his honey.

'Writes?' I said.

'Writes what he says on the news. All our news reporters write their own stuff.'

Another message came through from the royal gala: Devil-Boy, horns and all, was reported on his way to the theatre in a bell-ringing ambulance.

'Is he sick?' Danielle asked. 'If it's a stunt, make sure you catch it.' She disconnected, shrugging resignedly. 'The hip-wriggling imp of Satan will get double the oil fire exposure. Real hell stands no chance against the fake. Do you want to see the editing rooms?'

'Yes,' I said, and followed her across the large office and down a passage, admiring the neatness of her walk and wanting to put my hands deep into her cloud of dark hair, wanting to kiss her, wanting quite fiercely to take her to bed.

She said, 'I'll show you the studio first, it's more interesting,' and veered down a secondary passage towards a door warningly marked 'If red light shows, do not enter'. No red light shone. We went in. The room was moderate in size, furnished barely with a couple of armchairs, a coffee table, a television camera, a television set, a teleprompter and a silent coffee machine with paper cups. The only surprise was the window, through which one could see a stretch of the Thames and Hammersmith Bridge, all decked with lights and busily living.

'We do live interviews in here in front of the window,' Danielle said. 'Mostly politicians but also actors, authors, sportsmen, anyone in the news. Red buses go across the bridge in the background. It's impressive.'

'I'm sure,' I said.

She gave me a swift look. 'Am I boring you?'

'Absolutely not.'

She wore pink lipstick and had eyebrows like wings. Dark smiling eyes, creamy skin, long neck to hidden breasts like apples on a slender stem . . . For Christ's sake, Kit, I thought, drag your mind off it and ask some sensible questions.

'How does your stuff get from here to America?' I said.

'From in here.' She walked over to a closed door in one of the walls, and opened it. Beyond it was another room, much smaller, dimly lit, which was warm and hummed faintly with walls of machines.

'This is the transmitter room,' she said. 'Everything goes from in here by satellite, but don't ask me how, we have a man with a haunted expression twiddling the knobs and we leave it to him.'

She closed the transmitter room door and we went through the studio, into the passage and back to the editing rooms, of which there were three.

'OK,' she said, switching a light on and revealing a small area walled on one side by three television screens, several video recorders and racks of tape cassettes, 'this is what we still use, though I'm told there's a load of new technology round the corner. Our guys here like these machines, so I guess we'll have them around for a while yet.'

'How do they work?' I asked.

'You run the unedited tape through on the left-hand screen and pick out the best bits, then you record just those on to the second tape, showing on the second screen. You can switch it all around until it looks good and you get a good feeling. We transmit it like that, but New York often cuts it shorter. Depends how much else they've got to fit in.'

'Can you work these machines yourself?' I asked.

'I'm slow. If you really want to know now, you can watch Joe later when we get the oil fire and Devil-Boy tapes – he's one of the best.'

'Great,' I said.

'I'm surprised you're so interested.'

'Well, I've some tapes I want to edit myself. It would be nice to learn how.'

'Is that why you came here so early?' She sounded as if I might say yes without at all offending her.

I said, 'Partly. Mostly to see you . . . and what you do.'

She was close enough to hug and I had no insight at all into what she was thinking. A brick wall between minds. Disconcerting.

She looked with friendliness but nothing else into my face, and the only thing I was sure of was that she didn't feel as I did about a little uninhibited love-making on the spot.

She asked if I would like to see the library and I said yes please: and the library turned out to be not books but rows and rows of recorded tapes, past years of news stories forgotten but waiting like bombs in the dark, records of things said, undeniable.

'Mostly used for obituaries,' Danielle said. 'Reactivated scandals. Things like that.'

We returned to her news desk, where over the next hour I sat and listened to the progress of events (Devil-Boy had arrived at the stage door, fit, well and fully made-up in a blaze of technicolor lights to the gratified hysterics of a streetful of fans) and met Danielle's working companions, the bureau chief, Joe the editor, the gaunt transmitter expert, two spare cameramen and a bored and unallocated female talent. About sixty people altogether worked for the bureau, Danielle said, but of course never all at one time. The day shift, from ten to six-thirty, was much bigger: in the daytime there were two to do her job.

At one o'clock Ed Cervano telephoned to say they'd gotten a whole load of spectacular shots of the oil fire but the blaze was now under control and the story was as dead as tomorrow's ashes.

'Bring back the tapes anyway,' Danielle said. 'We don't have any oil fire stock shots in the library.'

She put down the receiver resignedly. 'So it goes.'

The crew from the royal gala returned noisily bearing Devil-Boy's capers themselves, and at the same time a delivery man brought a stock of morning newspapers to put on Danielle's desk for her to look through for possible stories. The *Daily Flag*, as it happened, lay on top, and I opened it at Intimate Details to re-read Leggatt's words.

'What are you looking at?' Danielle asked.

I pointed. She read the apology and blinked.

'I didn't think you stood a chance,' she said frankly. 'Did they agree to the compensation also?'

'Not so far.'

'They'll have to,' she said. 'They've practically admitted liability.'

I shook my head. 'British courts don't award huge damages for libel. It's doubtful whether Bobby would actually win if he sued, and even if he won, unless the *Flag* was ordered to pay his costs, which also isn't certain, he simply couldn't afford the lawyers' fees.'

She gazed at me. 'Back home you don't pay the lawyers unless you win. Then the lawyers take their slice of the damages. Forty per cent, sometimes.'

'It's not like that here.'

Here, I thought numbly, one bargained with threats. On the one side: I'll get your wrist slapped by the Press Council, I'll get questions asked in Parliament, I'll see your ex-convict journalist back in the dock. And on the other, I'll slice your tendons, I'll lose you your jockey's licence for taking bribes, I'll put you in prison. Reviled, dishonoured, and with publicity, disgraced.

Catch me first, I thought.

CHAPTER FIFTEEN

I watched Joe the editor, dark-skinned and with rapid fingers, sort his way through a mass of noisy peacock footage, clicking his tongue as a sort of commentary to himself, punctuating the lifted sections he was stringing together to make the most flamboyant impact. Kaleidoscope arrival of Devil-Boy, earlier entrance of royals, wriggling release of new incomprehensible song.

'Thirty seconds,' he said, running through the finished sequence. 'Maybe they'll use it all, maybe they won't.'

'It looks good to me.'

'Thirty seconds is a long news item.' He took the spooled tape from the machine, put it into an already labelled box and handed it to the gaunt transmitter man, who was waiting to take it away. 'Danielle says you want to learn to edit, so what do you want to know?'

'Er . . . what these machines will do, for a start.'

'Quite a lot.' He fluttered his dark fingers over the banks of controls, barely touching them. 'They'll take any size tape, any make, and record on any other. You can bring the sound up, cut it out, transpose it, superimpose any sounds you like. You can put the sound from one tape on to the pictures of another, you can cut two tapes together so that it looks as if the people are talking to each other when they were recorded hours and miles apart, you can tell lies and goddam lies and put a false face on truth.'

'Anything else?'

'That about covers it.'

He showed me how to achieve some of his effects, but his speed confounded me.

'Have you got an actual tape you want to edit?' he asked finally.

'Yes, but I want to add to it first, if I can.'

He looked at me assessingly, a poised black man of perhaps my own age with a touch of humour in the eyes but a rarely smiling mouth. I felt untidy in my anorak beside his neat suit and cream shirt; also battered and sweaty and dim. It had been, I thought ruefully, too long a day.

'Danielle says you're OK,' he said surprisingly. 'I don't see why you can't ask the chief to rent you the use of this room some night we're not busy. You tell me what you want, and I'll edit your tapes for you, if you like.'

*

'Joe's a nice guy,' Danielle said, stretching lazily beside me in the rented Mercedes on her way home. 'Sure, if he said he'd edit your tape, he means it. He gets bored. He waited three hours tonight for the Devil-Boy slot. He loves editing. Has a passion for it. He wants to work in movies. He'll enjoy doing your tape.'

The bureau chief, solicited, had proved equally generous. 'If Joe's using the machines, go ahead.' He'd looked over to where Danielle was eyes down marking paragraphs in the morning papers. 'I had New York on the line this evening congratulating me on the upswing of our output recently. That's her doing. She says you're OK, you're OK.'

For her too it had been a long day.

'Towcester,' she said, yawning, 'seems light years back.'

'Mm,' I said. 'What did Princess Casilia say after you went in, when you got back to Eaton Square?'

Danielle looked at me with amusement. 'In the hall she told me that good manners were a sign of strength, and in the drawing room she asked if I thought you would really be fit for Ascot.'

'What did you say?' I asked, faintly alarmed.

'I said yes, you would.'

I relaxed. 'That's all right, then.'

'I did not say,' Danielle said mildly, 'that you were insane, but only that you didn't appear to notice when you'd been injured. Aunt Casilia said she thought this to be fairly typical of steeplechase jockeys.'

'I do notice,' I said.

'But?'

'Well . . . if I don't race, I don't earn. Almost worse, if I miss a race on a horse and it wins, the happy owner may put up that winning jockey the next time, so I can lose not just the one fee but maybe the rides on that horse for ever.'

She looked almost disappointed. 'So it's purely economic, this refusal to look filleted ribs in the face?'

'At least half.'

'And the rest?'

'What you feel for your job. What Joe feels for his. Much the same.'

She nodded, and after a pause said, 'Aunt Casilia wouldn't do that, though. Keep another jockey on, after you were fit again.'

'No, she never has. But your aunt is special.'

'She said,' Danielle said reflectively, 'that I wasn't to think of you as a jockey.'

'But I am.'

'That's what she said this morning on the way to Towcester.'

'Did she explain what she meant?'

'No. I asked her. She said something vague about essences.' She yawned. 'Anyway, this evening she told Uncle Roland all about those horrid men with knives, as she put it, and although he was scandalized and said she shouldn't get involved in such sordid brawls, she seemed quite serene and unaffected. She may look like porcelain, but she's quite tough. The more I get to know her, the more, to be honest, I adore her.'

The road from Chiswick to Eaton Square, clogged by day with stop-go traffic, was at two-fifteen in the morning regrettably empty. Red lights turned green at our approach and even sticking rigidly to the speed limit didn't much seem to lengthen the journey. We slid to a halt outside the princess's house far too soon.

Neither of us made a move to spring at once out of the car: we sat rather for a moment letting the day die in peace.

I said, 'I'll see you then, on Saturday.'

'Yes,' she sighed for no clear reason. 'I guess so.'

'You don't have to,' I said.

'Oh no,' she half laughed. 'I suppose I meant... Saturday's some way off.'

I took her hand. She let it lie in mine, passive, waiting.

'We might have,' I said, 'a lot of Saturdays.'

'Yes, we might.'

I leaned over and kissed her mouth, tasting her pink lipstick, feeling her breath on my cheek, sensing the tremble somewhere in her body. She neither drew back nor clutched forward, but kissed as I'd kissed, as an announcement, as a promise perhaps; as an invitation.

I sat away from her and smiled into her eyes, and then got out of the car and went round to open her door.

We stood briefly together on the pavement.

'Where are you sleeping?' she said. 'It's so late.'

'In a hotel.'

'Near here?'

'Less than a mile.'

'Good . . . you won't have far to drive.'

'No distance.'

'Goodnight, then,' she said.

'Goodnight.'

We kissed again, as before. Then, laughing, she turned away, walked across the pavement and let herself through the princess's porticoed front door with a latchkey: and I drove away thinking that if the princess had disapproved of her jockey making approaches to her niece, she would by now have let both of us know.

I slept like the dead for five hours, then rolled stiffly out of bed, blinked blearily at the heavy cold rain making a mess of the day, and pointed the Mercedes towards Bletchley.

The Golden Lion was warm and alive with the smells of breakfast, and I ate there while the desk processed my bill. Then I telephoned the AA for news of my car (ready Monday) and to Holly to check that the marked *Flag* copies had been delivered as promised (which they had: the feed-merchant had telephoned) and after that I packed all my gear into the car and headed straight back towards the hotel I'd slept in.

No problem, they said helpfully at reception, I could retain my present room for as long as I wanted, and yes, certainly, I could leave items in the strongroom for safe-keeping.

Upstairs I put Jay Erskine's Press Club pass and Owen Watts's credit cards into an envelope and wrote 'URGENT DELIVER TO MR LEGGATT IMMEDIATELY' in large letters on the outside. Then I put the video recordings and all of the journalists' other possessions, except their jackets, into one of the hotel's laundry bags, rolling it into a neat bundle which downstairs was fastened with sticky-tape and labelled before vanishing into the vault.

After that I drove to Fleet Street, parked where I shouldn't, ran through the rain to leave the envelope for Sam Leggatt at the *Flag* front desk, fielded the car from under the nose of a traffic warden, and went lightheartedly to Ascot.

It was a rotten afternoon there in many ways. Sleet fell almost ceaselessly, needle-sharp, ice-cold and slanting, soaking every jockey to the skin before the start and proving a blinding hazard thereafter. Goggles were useless, caked with flying mud; gloves slipped wetly on the reins; racing boots clung clammily to waterlogged feet. A day for gritting one's teeth and getting round safely, for meeting fences exactly right and not slithering along on one's nose on landing. Raw November at its worst.

The crowd was sparse, deterred before it started out by the visible downpour and the drenching forecast, and the few people standing in the open were huddled inside dripping coats looking like mushrooms with their umbrellas.

Holly and Bobby both came but wouldn't stay, arriving after I'd won the first race more by luck than inspiration, and leaving before the second. They took the money out of the money-belt, which I returned to the valet with thanks.

Holly hugged me. 'Three people telephoned, after I'd talked to you, to say they were pleased about the apology,' she said. 'They're offering credit again. It's made all the difference.'

'Take care how you go with running up bills,' I said.

'Of course we will. The bank manager haunts us.'

I said to Bobby, 'I borrowed some of that money. I'll repay it next week.'

'It's all yours, really.' He spoke calmly in friendship, but the life-force was again at a low ebb. No vigour. Too much apathy. Not what was needed.

Holly looked frozen and was shivering. 'Keep the baby warm,' I said. 'Go into the trainers' bar.'

'We're going home.' She kissed me with cold lips. 'We would stay to watch you, but I feel sick. I feel sick most of the time. It's the pits.'

Bobby put his arm round her protectively and took her away under a large umbrella, both of them leaning head down against the icy wind, and I felt depressed for them, and thought also of the risks that lay ahead, before they could be safe.

The princess had invited to her box the friends of hers that I cared for least, a quartet of aristocrats from her old country, and as always when they were there I saw little of her. With two of them she came in red oilskins down to the parade ring before the first of her two runners, smiling cheerfully through the freezing rain and asking what I thought of her chances, and with the other two she repeated the enquiry an hour and a half later.

In each case I said, 'Reasonable.' The first runner finished reasonably fourth, the second runner, second. Neither time did she come down to the unsaddling enclosure, for which one couldn't blame her, and nor did I go up to her box, partly because it was a perfunctory routine when those friends were there, but mostly on account of crashing to the ground on the far side of the course in the last race. By the time I got in and changed, she would be gone.

Oh well, I thought dimly, scraping myself up; six rides, one winner, one second, one fourth, two also-rans, one fall. You can't win four every day, old son. And nothing broken. Even the stitches had survived without leaking. I waited in the blowing sleet for the car to pick me up, and took off my helmet to let the water run through my hair, embracing in a way the wild day, feeling at home. Winter and horses, the old song in the blood.

There was no fruit cake left in the changing room.

'Rotten buggers,' I said.

'But you never eat cake,' my valet said, heaving off my sodden boots.

'Every so often,' I said, 'like on freezing wet Fridays after a fall in the last race.'

'There's some tea still. It's hot.'

I drank the tea, feeling the warmth slide down, heating from inside. There was always tea and fruit cake in the changing rooms; instant energy, instant comfort. Everyone ate cake now and then.

An official put his head through the door: someone to see you, he said.

I pulled on a shirt and shoes and went out to the door from the weighing room to the outside world. No one all day had appeared with a banker's draft from Pollgate, and I suppose I went out with an incredulous flicker of hope. Hope soon extinguished. It was only Dusty, huddled in the weighing room doorway, blue of face, eyes watering with cold.

'Is the horse all right?' I asked. 'I heard you caught him.'

'Yes. Useless bugger. What about you?'

'No damage. I got passed by the doctor. I'll be riding tomorrow.'

'Right, I'll tell the guv'nor. We'll be off, then. So long.'

'So long.'

He scurried away into the leaden early dusk, a small dedicated man who liked to check for himself after I'd fallen that I was in good enough shape to do his charges justice next time out. He had been known to advise Wykeham to stand me down. Wykeham had been known to take the advice. Passing Dusty was sometimes harder than passing the medics.

I showered and dressed and left the racecourse via the cheaper enclosures, walking from there into the darkening town, where I'd left the rented Mercedes in a public parking place in the morning. Maybe it was unlikely that a repeat ambush would be set in the nearly deserted jockeys' car park long after the last race, but I was taking no chances. I climbed unmolested into the Mercedes and drove in safety to London.

There in my comfortable bolthole I again made additions to my astronomical phone bill, arranging first for my obliging neighbour to go into my cottage in the morning and pack one of my suits and some shirts and other things into a suitcase.

'Of course I will, Kit dear, but I thought you'd be back here for sure tonight, after riding at Ascot.'

'Staying with friends,' I said. 'I'll get someone to pick up the suitcase from your place tomorrow morning to take it to Ascot. Would that be all right?'

'Of course, dear.'

I persuaded another jockey who lived in Lambourn to collect the case and bring it with him, and he said sure he would, if he remembered.

I telephoned Wykeham when I judged he'd be indoors after his evening tour of the horses and told him his winner had been steadfast, the princess's two as good as could be hoped for, and one of the also-rans disappointing.

'And Dusty says you made a clear balls-up of the hurdle down by Swinley Bottom in the last.'

'Yeah,' I said. 'If Dusty can see clearly half a mile through driving sleet in poor light he's got better eyesight than I thought.'

'Er . . .' Wykeham said. 'What happened?'

'The one in front fell. Mine went down over him. He wouldn't have won, if that's any consolation. He was beginning to tire already, and he was hating the weather.'

Wykeham grunted assent. 'He's a sun-lover, true-bred. Kit, tomorrow there's Inchcape for the princess in the big race and he's in grand form, jumping out of his skin, improved a mile since you saw him last week.'

'Inchcape,' I said resignedly, 'is dead.'

'What? Did I say Inchcape? No, not Inchcape. What's the princess's horse?'

'Icefall.'

'Icicle's full brother,' he said, not quite making it a question.

'Yes.'

'Of course.' He cleared his throat. 'Icefall. Naturally. He should win, Kit, seriously.'

'Will you be there?' I asked. 'I half expected you today.'

'In that weather?' He sounded surprised. 'No, no, Dusty and you and the princess, you'll do fine.'

'But you've had a whole bunch of winners this week and you haven't seen one of them.'

'I see them here in the yard. I see them on video tapes. You tell Inchcape he's the greatest, and he'll jump Ben Nevis.'

'All right,' I said. Icefall, Inchcape, what did it matter?

'Good. Great. Goodnight, Kit.'

'Goodnight, Wykeham,' I said.

I got through to my answering machine and collected the messages, one of which was from Eric Olderjohn, the civil servant owner of the horse I'd won on for the Lambourn trainer at Towcester.

I called him back without delay at the London number he'd given, and caught him, it seemed, on the point of going out.

'Oh, Kit, yes. Look, I suppose you're in Lambourn?'

'No, actually. In London.'

'Really? That's fine. I've something you might be interested to see, but I can't let it out of my hands.' He paused for thought. 'Would you be free this evening after nine?'

'Yes,' I said.

'Right. Come round to my house, I'll be back by then.' He gave me directions to a street south of Sloane Square, not more than a mile from where I was staying. 'Coffee and brandy, right? Got to run. Bye.'

He disconnected abruptly and I put down my own receiver more slowly saying 'Wow' to myself silently. I hadn't expected much action from Eric Olderjohn, civil servant, and certainly none with such speed.

I sat for a while thinking of the tape of Maynard, and of the list of companies at the end, of those who had suffered from Maynard's philanthropy. Short of finding somewhere to replay the tape, I would have to rely on memory, and the only name I could remember for certain was Purfleet Electronics; chiefly because I'd spent a summer sailing holiday with a schoolfriend there long ago.

Purfleet Electronics, directory enquiries told me, was not listed.

I sucked my teeth a bit and reflected that the only way to find things was to look in the right place. I would go to Purfleet, as to Hitchin, in the morning.

I filled in the evening with eating and more phone calls, and by nine had walked down Sloane Street and found Eric Olderjohn's house. It was narrow, two storeys, one of a long terrace built for low-income early Victorians, now inhabited by the affluent as pieds-à-terre: or so Eric Olderjohn affably told me, opening his dark green front door and waving me in.

From the street one stepped straight into the sitting room, which stretched from side to side of the house; all of four metres. The remarkably small space glowed with pinks and light greens, textured trellised wall-paper, swagged satin curtains, round tables with skirts, china birds, silver photograph frames, fat buttoned arm-chairs, Chinese creamy rugs on the floor. There were softly glowing lamps, and the trellised wallpaper covered the ceiling also, enclosing the crowded contents in an impression of a summer grotto.

My host watched my smile of appreciation as if the reaction were only what he would have expected.

'It's great,' I said.

'My daughter did it.'

'The one you would defend from the *Flag*?'

'My only daughter. Yes. Sit down. Has it stopped raining? You'd like a brandy, I dare say?' He moved the one necessary step to a silver tray of bottles on one of the round tables and poured cognac into two modest balloon glasses. 'I've set some coffee ready. I'll just fetch it. Sit down, do.' He vanished through a rear door camouflaged by trellis and I looked at the photographs in the frames, seeing a well-groomed young woman who might be his daughter, seeing the horse that he owned, with myself on its back.

He returned with another small tray, setting it alongside the first.

'My daughter,' he said, nodding, as he saw I'd been looking. 'She lives here part of the time, part with her mother.' He shrugged. 'One of those things.'

'I'm sorry.'

'Yes. Well, it happens. Coffee?' He poured into two small cups and handed me one. 'Sugar? No, I suppose not. Sit down. Here's the brandy.'

He was neat in movement as in dress, and I found myself thinking 'dapper'; but there was purposefulness there under the surface, the developed faculty of getting things done. I sat in one of the armchairs with coffee and brandy beside me, and he sat also, and sipped, and looked at me over his cup.

'You were in luck,' he said finally. 'I put out a few feelers this morning and was told a certain person might be lunching at his club.' He paused. 'I was sufficiently interested in your problem to arrange for a friend of mine to meet and sound out that person, whom he knows well, and their conversation was, one might say, fruitful. As a result I myself went to a certain person's office this afternoon, and the upshot of that meeting was some information which I'll presently show you.'

His care over the choice of words was typical, I supposed, of the stratosphere of the civil service: the wheeler-dealers in subtlety, obliqueness and not saying quite what one meant. I never discovered the exact identity of the certain person, on the basis no doubt that it wasn't something I needed to know, and in view of what he'd allowed me a sight of, I could scarcely complain.

'I have some letters,' Eric Olderjohn said. 'More precisely, photocopies of letters. You can read them, but I am directly commanded not to let you take them away. I have to return them on Monday. Is all that . . . er . . . quite clear?'

'Yes,' I said.

'Good.'

Without haste he finished his coffee and put down

the cup. Then, raising the skirt of the table which bore the trays, he bent and brought out a brown leather attaché case, which he rested on his knees. He snapped open the locks, raised the lid and paused again.

'They're interesting,' he said, frowning.

I waited.

As if coming to a decision which until that moment he had left open, he drew a single sheet of paper out of the case and passed it across.

The letter had been addressed to the Prime Minister and had been sent in September from a company which made fine china for export. The chairman, who had written the letter, explained that he and the other directors were unanimous in suggesting some signal honour for Mr Maynard Allardeck, in recognition of his great and patriotic services to industry.

Mr Allardeck had come generously to the aid of the historic company, and thanks entirely to his efforts the jobs of two hundred and fifty people had been saved. The skills of many of these people were priceless and included the ability to paint and gild porcelain to the world's highest standards. The company was now exporting more than before and was looking forward to the brightest of futures.

The board would like to propose a knighthood for Mr Allardeck.

I finished reading and looked over at Eric Olderjohn.

'Is this sort of letter normal?' I asked.

'Entirely.' He nodded. 'Most awards are the result

of recommendations to the Prime Minister's office. Anyone can suggest anyone for anything. If the cause seems just, an award is given. The patronage people draw up a list of awards they deem suitable, and the list is passed to the Prime Minister for approval.'

I said, 'So all these people in the honours lists who get medals . . . firefighters, music teachers, postmen, people like that, it's because their mates have written in to suggest it?'

'Er, yes. More often their employers, but sometimes their mates.'

He produced a second letter from his briefcase and handed it over. This one also was from an exporting company and stressed Maynard's invaluable contributions to worthwhile industry, chief among them the saving of very many jobs in an area of great local unemployment.

It was impossible to overestimate Mr Allardeck's services to his country in industry, and the firm unreservedly recommended that he should be offered a knighthood.

'Naturally,' I said, 'the patronage people checked that all this was true?'

'Naturally,' Eric Olderjohn said.

'And of course it was?'

'I am assured so. The certain person with whom I talked this afternoon told me that occasionally, if they receive six or seven similar letters all proposing someone unknown to the general public, they may begin to suspect that the person is busily proposing himself by persuading his friends to write in. The writers of the two letters I've shown you were specifically asked, as their recommendations were so similar, if Maynard himself had suggested they write. Each of them emphatically denied any such thing.'

'Mm,' I said. 'Well they would, wouldn't they, if they stood to gain from Maynard for his knighthood.'

'That's a thoroughly scurrilous remark.'

'So it is,' I said cheerfully. 'And your certain person, did he put Maynard down for his Sir?'

He nodded. 'Provisionally. To be considered. Then they received a third letter, emphasizing substantial philanthropy that they already knew about, and the question mark was erased. Maynard Allardeck was definitely in line for his K. The letter inviting him to accept the honour was drafted, and would have been sent out in about ten days from now, at the normal time for the New Year's list.'

'Would have been?' I said.

'Would have been.' He smiled twistedly. 'It is not now considered appropriate, as a result of the stories in the *Daily Flag* and the opinion page in the *Towncrier*.'

'Rose Quince,' I said.

He looked uncomprehending.

'She wrote the piece in the *Towncrier*,' I said.

'Oh . . . yes.'

'Would your, er, certain person,' I asked, 'really take notice of those bits in the newspapers?'

'Oh, definitely. Particularly as in each case the paragraphs were delivered by hand to his office, outlined in red.'

'They weren't!'

Eric Olderjohn raised an eyebrow. 'That means something to you?' he asked.

I explained about the tradespeople and the owners all receiving similarly marked copies.

'There you are, then. A thorough job of demolition. Nothing left to chance.'

'You mentioned a third letter,' I said. 'The clincher.'

He peered carefully into his case and produced it. 'This one may surprise you,' he said.

The third letter was not from a commercial firm but from a charitable organization with a list of patrons that stretched half the way down the left side of the page. The recipients of the charity appeared to be the needy dependants of dead or disabled public servants. Widows, children, the old and the sick.

'How do you define a public servant?' I asked.

'The Civil Service, from the top down.'

Maynard Allardeck, the letter reported, had worked tirelessly over several years to improve the individual lives of those left in dire straits through no fault of their own. He unstintingly poured out his own fortune in aid, besides giving his time and extending a high level of compassionate ongoing care to families in need. The charitable organization said it would itself feel honoured if the reward of a knighthood should be given to one of its most stalwart pillars: to the man they had unanimously chosen to be their next chairman, the appointment to be effective from 1 December of that year.

The letter had been signed by no fewer than four of the charity's officers: the retiring chairman, the head of the board of management, and two of the senior patrons. It was the fourth of these signatures which had me lifting my head in astonishment.

'Well?' Eric Olderjohn asked, watching.

'That's odd,' I said blankly.

'Yes, curious, I agree.'

He held out his hand for the letters, took them from me, snapped them safely back into his case. I sat with thoughts tumbling over themselves and unquestioned assumptions melting like wax.

Was it true, I had wanted to know, if Maynard Allardeck was being considered for a knighthood, and if so, who knew?

The people who had proposed him; they knew.

The letter from the charity, dated 1 October, had been signed by Lord Vaughnley.

CHAPTER SIXTEEN

'Why,' I said, 'did your certain person allow you to show these letters to me?'

'Ah.' Eric Olderjohn joined his fingers together in a steeple and studied them for a while. 'Why do you think?'

'I would suppose,' I said, 'he might think it possible I would stir up a few ponds, get a few muddy answers, without him having to do it himself.'

Eric Olderjohn switched his attention from his hands to my face. 'Something like that,' he said. 'He would like to know for sure Maynard Allardeck isn't just the victim of a hate campaign, for instance. He wants to do him justice. To put him back on the list, perhaps, for a knighthood next time around, in the summer.'

'He wants proof?' I asked.

'Can you supply it?'

'Yes, I think so.'

'What are you planning to do,' he asked with dry humour, 'when you have to give up race-riding?'

'Jump off a cliff, I dare say.'

I stood up, and he also. I thanked him sincerely for the trouble he'd taken. He said he would expect me to win again on his horse next time out. Do my best, I said, and took a last appreciative glance round his bower of a sitting room before making my way back to the hotel.

Lord Vaughnley, I thought.

On 1 October he had recommended Maynard for a knighthood. By the end of that month or the beginning of November there had been a tap on Bobby's telephone.

The tap had been installed by Jay Erskine, who had listened for two weeks and then written the articles in the *Flag*.

Jay Erskine had once worked for Lord Vaughnley, as crime reporter on the *Towncrier*.

But if Lord Vaughnley had got Jay Erskine to attack Maynard Allardeck, why was Nestor Pollgate so aggressive?

Because he didn't want to have to pay compensation, or to admit his paper had done wrong.

Well . . . perhaps.

I went round in circles and came back always to the central and unexpected question: Was it really Lord Vaughnley who had prompted the attacks, and if so, why?

From my hotel room I telephoned Rose Quince's home, catching her again soon after she had come in.

'Bill?' she said. 'Civil Service charity? Oh, sure, he's

a patron of dozens of things. All sorts. Keeps him in touch, he says.'

'Mm,' I said. 'When you wrote that piece about Maynard Allardeck, did he suggest it?'

'Who? Bill? Yes, sure he did. He put the clippings from the *Flag* on my desk and said it looked my sort of thing. I may know him from way back, but he's still the ultimate boss. When he wants something written, it gets written. Martin, our big white chief, always agrees to that.'

'And, er, how did you get on to the *How's Trade* interview? I mean, did you see the programme when it was broadcast?'

'Do me a favour. Of course not.' She paused. 'Bill suggested I try the television company, to ask for a private re-run.'

'Which you did.'

'Yes, of course. Look,' she demanded, 'what's all this about? Bill often suggests subjects to me. There's nothing strange in it.'

'No,' I said. 'Sleep well, Rose.'

'And goodnight to you, too.'

I slept soundly and long, and early in the morning took the video camera and drove to Purfleet along the flat lands just north of the Thames estuary. The rains of the day before had drawn away, leaving the sky washed and pale, and there were seagulls wheeling high over the low-tide mud.

I asked in about twenty places, post office and shops,

before I found anyone who had heard of Purfleet Electronics, but was finally pointed towards someone who had worked there. 'You want George Tarker . . . he owned it,' he said.

Following a few further instructions from helpful locals, I eventually pulled up beside a shabby old wooden boatshed optimistically emblazoned with a signboard saying 'George Tarker Repairs All'.

Out of the car and walking across the pot-holed entrance yard to the door one could see that the sign had once had a bottom half, which had split off and was lying propped against the wall, and which read 'Boats and Marine Equipment'.

With a sinking feeling of having come entirely to the wrong place I pushed open the rickety door and stepped straight into the untidiest office in the world, a place where every surface and every shelf was covered with unidentifiable lumps of ships' hardware in advanced age, and where every patch of wall was occupied by ancient calendars, posters, bills and instructions, all attached not by drawing pins but by nails.

In a sagging old chair, oblivious to the mess, sat an elderly grey-bearded man with his feet up on a desk, reading a newspaper and drinking from a cup.

'Mr Tarker?' I said.

'That's me.' He lowered the paper, looking at me critically from over the soles of his shoes. 'What do you want repaired?' He looked towards the bag I was carrying which contained the camera. 'A bit off a boat?'

'I'm afraid I've come to the wrong place,' I said. 'I was looking for Mr George Tarker who used to own Purfleet Electronics.'

He put his cup down carefully on the desk, and his feet on the floor. He was old, I saw, from an inner weariness as much as from age: it lay in the sag of his shoulders and the droop of his eyes and shouted from the disarray of everything around him.

'That George Tarker was my son,' he said.

Was.

'I'm sorry,' I said.

'Do you want anything repaired, or don't you?'

'No,' I said. 'I want to talk about Maynard Allardeck.'

The cheeks fell inwards into shadowed hollows and the eyes seemed to recede darkly into the sockets. He had scattered grey hair, uncombed, and below the short beard, in the thin neck inside the unbuttoned and tieless shirt, the tendons tightened and began to quiver.

'I don't want to distress you,' I said: but I had. 'I'm making a film about the damage Maynard Allardeck has done to many people's lives. I hoped you . . . I hoped your son . . . might help me.' I gestured vaguely with one hand. 'I know it wouldn't sway you one way or another, but I'm offering a fee.'

He was silent, staring at my face but seeing, I thought, another scene altogether, looking back into memory and finding it almost past bearing. The strain in his face deepened to the point when I did actively regret having come.

'Will it destroy him, your film?' he said huskily.

'In some ways, yes.'

'He deserves hellfire and damnation.'

I took the video camera out of its bag and showed it to him, explaining about talking straight at the lens.

'Will you tell me what happened to your son?' I asked.

'Yes, I will.'

I balanced the camera on a heap of junk and started it running; and with few direct questions from me he repeated in essence the familiar story. Maynard had come smiling to the rescue in a temporary cash crisis caused by a rapid expansion of the business. He had lent at low rates, but at the last and worst moment demanded to be repaid; had taken over the firm and ousted George Tarker, and after a while had stripped the assets, sold the freehold and put the workforce on the dole.

'Charming,' George Tarker said. 'That's what he was. Like a con man, right to the end. Reasonable. Friendly. Then he was gone, and everything with him. My son's business, gone. He started it when he was only eighteen and worked and worked . . . and after twenty-three years it was growing too fast.'

The gaunt face stared starkly into the lens, and water stood in the corner of each eye.

'My son George . . . my only child . . . he blamed himself for everything . . . for all his workers losing their jobs. He began to drink. He knew such a lot about electricity.' The tears spilled over the lower eyelids and rolled down the lined cheeks to be lost in the beard. 'My son wired himself up . . . and hit the switch . . .'

The voice stopped as if with the jolt that had stopped his son's heart. I found it unbearable. I wished with an intensity of pity that I hadn't come. I turned off the camera and stood there in silence, not knowing how to apologize for such an intrusion.

He brushed the tears away with the back of his hand. 'Two years ago, just over,' he said. 'He was a good man, you know, my son George. That Allardeck . . . just destroyed him.'

I offered him the same amount that I'd given the Perrysides, setting it down in front of him on the desk. He stared at the flat bunch of banknotes for a while, and then pushed it towards me.

'I didn't tell you for money,' he said. 'You take it back. I told you for George.'

I hesitated.

'Go on,' he said. 'I don't want it. Doesn't feel right. Any time you have a boat, you pay me then for repairs.'

'All right,' I said.

He nodded and watched while I picked up the notes.

'You make your film good,' he said. 'Make it for George.'

'Yes,' I said; and he was still sitting there, staring with pain into the past, when I left.

I went to Ascot with the same precautions as before, leaving the Mercedes down in the town and walking into the racecourse from the opposite direction to the jockeys' official car park. No one that I could see took any notice of my arrival, beyond the gatemen with their usual good mornings.

I had rides in the first five of the six races; two for the princess, two others for Wykeham, one for the Lambourn trainer. Dusty reported Wykeham to have a crippling migraine headache which would keep him at home watching on television. Icefall, Dusty said, should zoom in, and all the lads had staked their wages. Dusty's manner to me was as usual a mixture of deference and truculence, a double attitude I had long ago sorted into components: I might do the actual winning for the stable, but the fitness of the horses was the gift of the lads in the yard, and I wasn't to forget it. Dusty and I had worked together for ten years in a truce founded on mutual need, active friendship being neither sought nor necessary. He said the guv'nor wanted me to give the princess and the other owners his regrets about his headache. I'd tell them, I said.

I rode one of Wykeham's horses in the first race with negligible results, and came third in the second race, for the Lambourn trainer. The third race was

Icefall for the princess, and she and Danielle were both waiting in the parade ring, rosily lunched and sparkling-eyed, when I went out there to greet them.

'Wykeham sends his regrets,' I said.

'The poor man.' The princess believed in the migraines as little as I did, but was willing to pretend. 'Will we give him a win to console him?'

'I'm afraid he expects it.'

We watched Icefall walk round, grey and well muscled under his coroneted rug, more compact than his full brother Icicle.

'I schooled him last week,' I said. 'Wykeham says he's come on a ton since then. So there's hope.'

'Hope!' Danielle said. 'He's hot favourite.'

'Odds on,' nodded the princess. 'It never makes one feel better.'

She and I exchanged glances of acknowledgement of the extra pressure that came with too much expectation, and when I went off to mount she said only, 'Get round safely, that's all.'

Icefall at six was at the top of his hurdling form with a string of successes behind him, and his race on that day was a much publicized, much sponsored two-mile event which had cut up, as big-prize races tended occasionally to do, into no more than six runners: Icefall at the top of the handicap, the other five at the bottom, the centre block having decided to duck out for less taxing contests.

Icefall was an easy horse to ride, as willing as his

brother and naturally courageous, and the only foreseeable problem was the amount of weight he carried in relation to the others: twenty pounds and more. Wykeham never liked his horses to be front runners and had tried to dissuade me sometimes from running Icefall in that way; but the horse positively preferred it and let me know it at every start, and even with the weights so much against us, when the tapes went up we were there where he wanted to be, setting the pace.

I'd learned in my teens from an American flat-race jockey how to start a clock in my head, to judge the speed of each section of the race against the clock, and to judge how fast I could go in each section in order to finish at or near the horse's own best time for the distance.

Icefall's best time for two miles at Ascot at almost the same weights on the same sort of wet ground was three minutes forty-eight seconds, and I set out to take him to the finish line in precisely that period, and at a more or less even speed the whole way.

It seemed to the crowd on the stands, I was told afterwards, that I'd set off too fast, that some of the lightweights would definitely catch me; but I'd looked up their times also in the form book, and none of them had ever completed two miles as fast as I aimed to.

All Icefall had to do was jump with perfection, and that he did, informing me of his joy in mid-air at every hurdle. The lightweights never came near us, and we finished ahead, without slackening, by eight lengths, a margin that would do Icefall's handicap no good at all next time out.

Maybe, I thought, pulling up and patting the grey neck hugely, it would have been better for the future not to have won by so far, but the present was what mattered, and with those weights one couldn't take risks.

The princess was flushed and laughing and delighted, and as usual intensified my own pleasure in winning. Victories for glum and grumbling owners were never so sweet.

'My friends say it's sacrilege,' she said, 'for a top-weight to set off so fast and try to make all the running after rain like yesterday's. They were pitying me up in the box, telling me you were mad.'

I smiled at her, unbuckling my saddle. 'When he jumps like today, he can run this course even on wet gound in three minutes forty-eight seconds. That's what we did, more or less.'

Her eyes widened. 'You planned it! You didn't tell me. I didn't expect you to go off so fast, even though he likes it in front.'

'If he'd made a hash of any of the hurdles, I'd have looked a right idiot.' I patted the grey neck over and over. 'He understands racing,' I said. 'He's a great horse to ride. Very generous. He enjoys it.'

'You talk as if horses were people,' Danielle said, standing behind her aunt, listening.

'Yes, they are,' I said. 'Not human, but individuals, all different.'

I took the saddle in and sat on the scales, and changed into other colours and weighed out again for the next race. Then put the princess's colours back on, on top of the others, and went out bareheaded for the sponsors' presentations.

Lord Vaughnley was among the crowd round the sponsors' table of prizes, and he came straight over to me when I went out.

'My dear chap, what a race! I thought you'd gone off your rocker, I'm sorry to say. Now, you are coming to our box, aren't you? Like we agreed?'

He was a puzzle. His grey eyes smiled blandly in the big face, full of friendliness, empty of guile.

'Yes,' I said. 'Thank you. After the fifth race, when I'll have finished for the day, if that's all right?'

Lady Vaughnley appeared at his elbow, reinforcing the invitation. 'Delighted to have you. Do come.'

The princess, overhearing, said, 'Come along to me after,' taking my compliance for granted, not expecting an answer. 'Did you know,' she said with humour, 'the time Icefall took?'

'No, not yet.'

'Three minutes forty-nine seconds.'

'We were one second late.'

'Yes, indeed. Next time, go faster.'

Lady Vaughnley looked at her in astonishment.

'How can you say that?' she protested, and then understood it was merely a joke. 'Oh. For a moment . . .'

The princess patted her arm consolingly, and I watched Danielle, on the far side of the green-baized pot-laden table, talking to the sponsors as to the winning habit born. She turned her head and looked straight at me, and I felt the tingle of that visual connection run right down my spine. She's beautiful, I thought. I want her in bed.

It seemed that she had broken off in the middle of whatever she was saying. The sponsor spoke to her enquiringly. She looked at him blankly, and then with another glance at me seemed to sort out her thoughts and answer whatever he'd asked.

I looked down at the trophies, afraid that my feelings were naked. I had two races and a lot of box-talk to get through before we could be in any real way together, and the memory of her kisses was no help.

The presentations were made, the princess and the others melted away, and I peeled off the princess's colours and went out and rode another winner for Wykeham, scrambling home that time by a neck, all elbows, no elegance, practically throwing the horse ahead of himself, hard on him, squeezing him, making him stretch beyond where he thought he could go.

'Bloody hell,' said his owner, in the winners' unsaddling area. 'Bloody hell, I'd not like you on my back.' He seemed pleased enough all the same, a Sussex farmer, big and forthright, surrounded by chattering friends. 'You're a bloody demon, lad, that's what you are. Hard as bloody nails. He'll know he's had a race, I'll tell you.'

'Yes, well, Mr Davis, he can take it, he's tough, he'd not thank you to be soft. Like his owner, wouldn't you say, Mr Davis?'

He gave a great guffaw and clapped me largely on the shoulder, and I went and weighed in, and changed into the princess's colours again for the fifth race.

The princess's runner, Allegheny, was the second of her only two mares (Bernina being the other), as the princess, perhaps because of her own femininity, had a definite preference for male horses. Not as temperamental as Bernina, Allegheny was a friendly old pudding, running moderately well always but without fire. I'd tried to get Wykeham to persuade the princess to sell her but he wouldn't: Princess Casilia, he said, knew her own mind.

Allegheny's seconds, thirds, fourths, fifths, sixths, also-rans never seemed to disappoint her. It wasn't essential to her, he said, for all her children to be stars.

Allegheny and I set off amicably but as usual my attempts to jolly her into *joie de vivre* got little response. We turned into the straight for the first time lying fourth, going easily, approaching a plain fence, meeting it right, launching into the air, landing, accelerating away . . .

In one of her hind legs a suspensory ligament tore apart at the fetlock, and Allegheny went lame in three strides, all rhythm gone; like driving a car on a suddenly flat tyre. I pulled her up and jumped off her back, and walked her a few paces to make sure she hadn't broken a bone.

Just the tendon, I thought in relief. Bad enough, but not a death sentence. Losing a horse to the bolt of a humane killer upset everyone for days. Wykeham had wept sometimes for dead horses, and I also, and the princess. One couldn't help it, sometimes.

The vet sped round in his car, looked her over and pronounced her fit to walk, so I led her back up the course, her head nodding every time she put the injured foot to the ground. The princess and Danielle came down anxiously to the unsaddling area and Dusty assured them the guv'nor would get a vet to Allegheny as soon as possible.

'What do you think?' the princess asked me in depression, as Dusty and the mare's lad led her, nodding, away.

'I don't know.'

'Yes, you do. Tell me.'

The princess's eyes were deep blue. I said, 'She'll be a year off the racecourse, at least.'

She sighed. 'Yes, I suppose so.'

'You could patch her up,' I said, 'and sell her as a brood mare. She's got good blood lines. She could breed in the spring.'

'Oh!' She seemed pleased. 'I'm fond of her, you know.'

'Yes, I know.'

'I do begin to see,' Danielle said, 'what racing is all about.'

My neighbour and the Lambourn fellow jockey having come up trumps in the matter of a suitcase of clothes, I went up to Lord Vaughnley's box in a change for the better. I appeared to have chosen, though, the doldrums of time between events when everyone had gone down to look at the horses or to bet, and not yet returned to watch the race.

There was only one person in there, standing nervously beside the table now laid for tea, shifting from foot to foot: and I was surprised to see it was Hugh Vaughnley, Lord Vaughnley's son.

'Hello,' I said. 'No one's here . . . I'll come back.'

'Don't go.'

His voice was urgent. I looked at him curiously, thinking of the family row which had so clearly been in operation on the previous Saturday, seeing only trouble still in the usually cheerful face. Much thinner than his father, more like his mother in build, he had neat features well placed, two disarming dimples, and youth still in the indecision of his mouth. Around nineteen, I thought. Maybe twenty. Not more.

'I . . . er . . .' he said. 'Do stay. I want someone here, to be honest, when they come back.'

'Do you?'

'Er . . .' he said. 'They don't know I'm here. I mean . . . Dad might be furious, and he can't be, can he, in front of strangers? That's why I came here, to the races. I mean, I know you're not a stranger, but you know what I mean.'

'Your mother will surely be glad to see you.'

He swallowed. 'I hate quarrelling with them. I can't bear it. To be honest, Dad threw me out almost a month ago. He's making me live with Saul Bradley, and I can't bear it much longer, I want to go home.'

'He threw you out?' I must have sounded as surprised as I felt. 'You always seemed such a solid family. Does he think you should stand on your own two feet? Something like that?'

'Nothing like that. I just wish it was. I did something . . . I didn't know he'd be so desperately angry . . . not really . . .'

I didn't want to hear what it was, with so much else on my mind.

'Drugs?' I said, without sympathy.

'What?'

'Did you take drugs?'

I saw from his face that it hadn't been that. He was simply bewildered by the suggestion.

'I mean,' he said plaintively, 'he thought so much of him. He said so. I mean, I thought he approved of him.'

'Who?' I said.

He looked over my shoulder however and didn't answer, a fresh wave of anxiety blotting out all else.

I turned. Lord and Lady Vaughnley had come through the door from the passage and were advancing towards us. I saw their expressions with clarity when they caught sight of their son. Lady Vaughnley's face lifted into a spontaneous uncomplicated smile.

Lord Vaughnley looked from his son to myself, and his reaction wasn't forgiveness, apathy, irritation or even anger.

It was alarm. It was horror.

CHAPTER SEVENTEEN

He recovered fast to some extent. Lady Vaughnley put her arms around Hugh and hugged him, and her husband looked on, stony-faced and displeased. Others of their guests came in good spirits back to the box, and Hugh was proved right to the extent that his father was not ready to fight with him in public.

Lord Vaughnley, in fact, addressed himself solely to me, fussing about cups of tea and making sure I talked no more to his son, seemingly unaware that his instant reaction and his current manner were telling me a good deal more than he probably meant.

'There we are,' he said heartily, getting a waitress to pass me a cup. 'Milk? Sugar? No? Princess Casilia's mare is all right, isn't she? So sad when a horse breaks down in a race. Sandwich?'

I said the mare wouldn't race again, and no thanks to the sandwich.

'Hugh been bothering you with his troubles, has he?' he said.

'Not really.'

'What did he say?'

I glanced at the grey eyes from where the blandness had flown and watchfulness taken over.

'He said he had quarrelled with you and wanted to make it up.'

'Hmph.' An unforgiving noise from a compressed mouth. 'As long as he didn't bother you?'

'No.'

'Good. Good. Then you'll be wanting to talk to Princess Casilia, eh? Let me take your cup. Good of you to come up. Yes. Off you go, then. Can't keep her waiting.'

Short of rudeness I couldn't have stayed, and rudeness at that point, I thought, would accomplish no good that I could think of. I went obediently along to the princess's well-populated box and drank more tea and averted my stomach from another sandwich, and tried not to look too much at Danielle.

'You're abstracted,' the princess said. 'You are not here.'

'I was thinking of Lord Vaughnley . . . I just came from his box.'

'Such a nice man.'

'Mm.'

'And for Danielle, this evening, what are your plans?'

I shut out the thoughts of what I would like. If I could read the princess's mind, she could also on occasion read mine.

'I expect we'll talk, and eat, and I'll bring her home.'

She patted my arm. She set me to talk to her guests, most of whom I knew, and I worked my way round to Danielle scattering politeness like confetti.

'Hi,' she said. 'Am I going back with Aunt Casilia, or what?'

'Coming with me from here, if you will.'

'OK.'

We went out on to the balcony with everyone else to watch the sixth race, and afterwards said goodbye correctly to the princess and left.

'Where are we going?' Danielle asked.

'For a walk, for a drink, for dinner. First of all we're walking to Ascot town, where I left the car, so as not to be carved up again in the car park.'

'You're too much,' she said.

I collected my suitcase from the changing room and we walked down through the cheaper enclosures to the furthest gate, and from there again safely to the rented Mercedes.

'I guess I never gave a thought to it happening again,' she said.

'And next time there would be no princess to the rescue.'

'Do you seriously think they'd be lying in wait?'

'I still have what they wanted.' And I'd twisted their tail fiercely, besides. 'I just go where they don't know I'm going, and hope.'

'Yes, but,' she said faintly, 'for how long?'

'Um,' I said, 'I suppose Joe doesn't work on Sundays?'

'No. Not till Monday night, like me. Not weekends. What's that got to do with how long?'

'Tuesday or Wednesday,' I said.

'You're not making much sense.'

'It's because I don't know for sure.' We got into the car and I started the engine. 'I feel like a juggler. Half a dozen clubs in the air and all likely to fall in a heap.'

'With you underneath?'

'Not,' I said, 'if I can help it.'

I drove not very fast to Henley, and stopped near a telephone box to try to reach Rose Quince, who was out. She had an answering machine which invited me to give a number for her to call back. I would try later, I said.

Henley-on-Thames was bright with lights and late Saturday afternoon shopping. Danielle and I left the car in a parking place and walked slowly along in the bustle.

'Where are we going?' she asked.

'To buy you a present.'

'What present?'

'Anything you'd like.'

She stopped walking. 'Are you crazy?'

'No.' We were outside a shop selling sport goods. 'Tennis racket?'

'I don't play tennis.'

I waved at the next shop along. 'Piano?'

'I can't play a piano.'

'Over there,' I pointed at a flower shop. 'Orchids?'

'In their place, but not to pin on me.'

'And over there, an antique chair?'

She laughed, her eyes crinkling. 'Tell me, too, what you like, and what you don't.'

'All right.'

We walked along the shopfronts, looking and telling. She liked blues and pinks but not yellow, she liked things with flowers and birds on, not geometric patterns, she liked baskets and nylon-tipped pens and aquamarines and seedless grapes and books about Leonardo da Vinci. She would choose for me, she said, something simple. If I were giving her a present, I would have to have one as well.

'OK,' I said. 'Twenty minutes. Meet me back at the car. Here's the key, in case you get there first.'

'And not expensive,' she said, 'or I'm not playing.'

'All right.'

When I returned with my parcel she was sitting in the car already, and smiling.

'You've been half an hour,' she said. 'You're disqualified.'

'Too bad.'

I climbed into the car beside her and we sat looking at each other's packages, mine to her in brown paper, hers to me flatter, in a carrier bag.

'Guess,' she said.

I tried to, and nothing came. I said with regret, 'I don't know.'

She eyed the brown-wrapped parcel in my hands. 'Three books? Three pounds of chocolates? A jack-in-a-box?'

'All wrong.'

We exchanged the presents and began to unwrap them. 'More fun than Christmas,' she said. 'Oh. How odd. I'd forgotten it was your name.' She paused very briefly for thought and said it the other way round. 'Christmas is more fun.'

It sounded all right in American. I opened the paper carrier she'd given me and found that our walk along the street had taught her a good deal about me, too. I drew out a soft brown leather zipped-around case which looked as if it would hold a pad of writing paper and a few envelopes: and it had KIT stamped in gold on the top.

'Go on, open it,' she said. 'I couldn't resist it. And you like neat small things, the way I do.'

I unzipped the case, opened it flat, and smiled with pure pleasure. It contained on one side a tool kit and on the other pens, a pocket calculator and a notepad; all in slots, all of top quality, solidly made.

'You do like it,' she said with satisfaction. 'I thought you would. It had your name on it, literally.'

She finished taking off the brown paper and showed me that I had pleased her also, and as much. I'd given her a baby antique chest of drawers which smelled faintly of polish, had little brass handles, and ran smoothly as silk. Neat, small, well-crafted, useful, good-looking, efficient: like the kit.

She looked long at the implications of the presents, and then at my face.

'That,' she said slowly, 'really is amazing, that we should both get it right.'

'Yes, it is.'

'And you broke the rules. That chest's not cheap.'

'So did you. Nor's the kit.'

'God bless credit cards.'

I kissed her, the same way as before, the gifts still on our laps. 'Thank you for mine.'

'Thank you for mine.'

'Well,' I said, reaching over to put my tool kit on the back seat. 'By the time we get there, the pub might be open.'

'What pub?'

'Where we're going.'

'Anyone who wants to know what you're not about to tell them,' she said, 'has a darned sticky time.'

I drove in contentment to the French Horn at Sonning, where the food was legendary and floodlights shone on willow trees drooping over the Thames. We went inside and sat on a sofa, and watched ducks roast on a spit over an open fire, and drank champagne. I stretched and breathed deeply, and felt the tensions of the long week relax: and I'd got to phone Rose Quince.

I went and phoned her. Answering machine again. I

said, 'Rose, Rose, I love you. Rose, I need you. If you come home before eleven, please, I beg you, ring me at the French Horn Hotel, the number is 0734 692204, tell them I'm in the restaurant having dinner.'

I telephoned Wykeham. 'Is the headache better?' I said.

'What?'

'Never mind. How's the mare?'

The mare was sore but eating, Mr Davis's horse was exhausted, Inchcape hardly looked as if he'd had a race.

'Icefall,' I said.

'What? I wish you wouldn't ride him from so far in front.'

'He liked it. And it worked.'

'I was watching on TV. Can you come and school on Tuesday? We have no runners that day, I'm not sending any to Southwell.'

'Yes, all right.'

'Well done, today,' he said with sincerity. 'Very well done.'

'Thanks.'

'Yes. Er. Goodnight then, Paul.'

'Goodnight, Wykeham,' I said.

I went back to Danielle and we spent the whole evening talking and later eating in the restaurant with silver and candlelight gleaming on the tables and a living vine growing over the ceiling; and at the last minute Rose Quince called me back.

'It's after eleven,' she said, 'but I just took a chance.'

'You're a dear.'

'I sure am. So what is so urgent, buddy boy?'

'Um,' I said. 'Does the name Saul Bradfield or Saul Bradley . . . something like that . . . mean anything to you?'

'Saul Bradley? Of course it does. What's so urgent about him?'

'Who is he?'

'He used to be the sports editor of the *Towncrier*. He retired last year . . . everyone's universal father-figure, an old friend of Bill's.'

'Do you know where he lives?'

'Good heavens. Wait while I think. Why do you want him?'

'In the general area of demolishing our business friend of the tapes.'

'Oh. Well, let's see. He moved. He said he was taking his wife to live by the sea. I'd've thought it would drive him mad but no accounting for taste. Worthing, or somewhere. No. Selsey.' Her voice strengthened. 'I remember, Selsey, in Sussex.'

'Terrific,' I said. 'And Lord Vaughnley. Where does he live?'

'Mostly in Regent's Park, in one of the Nash terraces. They've a place in Kent too, near Sevenoaks.'

'Could you tell me exactly?' I said. 'I mean . . . I'd like to write to thank him for my Towncrier trophy, and for all his other help.'

'Sure,' she said easily, and told me both his addresses

right down to the postal codes, tacking on the telephone numbers for good measure. 'You might need those. They're not in the directory.'

'I'm back in your debt,' I said, writing it all down.

'Deep, deep, buddy boy.'

I replaced the receiver feeling perfidious but unrepentant, and went to fetch Danielle to drive her home. It was midnight, more or less, when I pulled up in Eaton Square: and it wasn't where I would have preferred to have taken her, but where it was best.

'Thank you,' she said, 'for a great day.'

'What about tomorrow?'

'OK.'

'I don't know what time,' I said. 'I've something to do first.'

'Call me.'

'Yes.'

We sat in the car looking at each other, as if we hadn't been doing that already for hours. I've known her since Tuesday, I thought. In five days she'd grown roots in my life. I kissed her with much more hunger than before, which didn't seem to worry her, and I thought not long, not long . . . but not yet. When it was right, not before.

We said goodnight again on the pavement, and I watched her go into the house, carrying her present and waving as she closed the door. Princess Casilia, I thought, you are severely inhibiting, but I said I'd bring your niece home, and I have; and I don't even know what Danielle wanted, I can't read her mind and she didn't tell me in words, and tomorrow . . . tomorrow maybe I'd ask.

Early in the morning I drove to Selsey on the South Coast and looked up Saul Bradley in the local telephone book, and there he was, address and all, 15 Sea View Lane.

His house was on two floors and looked more suburban than seaside with mock-Tudor beams in its cream plastered gables. The mock-Tudor door, when I rang the bell, was opened by a grey-haired bespectacled motherly looking person in a flowered overall, and I could smell bacon frying.

'Hugh?' she said in reply to my question. 'Yes, he's still here, but he's still in bed. You know what boys are.'

'I'll wait,' I said.

She looked doubtful.

'I do very much want to see him,' I said.

'You'd better come in,' she said. 'I'll ask my husband. I think he's shaving, but he'll be down soon.'

She led me across the entrance hall into a smallish kitchen, all yellow and white tiles, with sunlight flooding in.

'A friend of Hugh's?' she said.

'Yes . . . I was talking to him yesterday.'

She shook her head worriedly. 'It's all most upsetting.

He shouldn't have gone to the races. He was more miserable than ever when he came back.'

'I'll do my best,' I said, 'to make things better.'

She attended to the breakfast she was frying, pushing the bacon round with a spatula. 'Did you say Fielding, your name was?' She turned from the cooker, the spatula in the air, motion arrested. 'Kit Fielding? The jockey?'

'Yes.'

She didn't know what to make of it, which wasn't surprising. She said uncertainly, 'I'm brewing some tea,' and I said I'd wait until after I'd seen her husband and Hugh.

Her husband came enquiringly into the kitchen, hearing my voice, and he knew me immediately by sight. A sports editor would, I supposed. Bunty Ireland's ex-boss was comfortably large with a bald head and shrewd eyes and a voice grown fruity, as from beer.

My presence nonplussed him, as it had his wife.

'You want to help Hugh? I suppose it's all right. Bill Vaughnley was speaking highly of you a few days ago. I'll go and get Hugh up. He's not good in the mornings. Want some breakfast?'

I hesitated.

'Like that, is it?' He chuckled. 'Starving and daren't put on an ounce.'

He went away into the house and presently returned,

followed shortly by Hugh, tousle-haired, in jeans and a T-shirt, his eyes puffed from sleep.

'Hello,' he said, bewildered. 'How did you find me?'

'You told me where you were staying.'

'Did I? I suppose I did. Er . . . sorry and all that, but what do you want?'

I wanted, I said, to take him out for a drive, to talk things over and see what could be done to help him: and with no more persuasion, he came.

He didn't seem to realize that his father had made sure he didn't speak to me further on the previous day. It had been done too skilfully for him to notice, especially in the anxiety he'd been suffering.

'Your father made you come back here,' I said, as we drove along Sea View Lane. 'Wouldn't let you go home?'

'It's so unfair.' There was self-pity in his voice, and also acceptance. The exile had been earned, I thought, and Hugh knew it.

'Tell me, then,' I said.

'Well, you know him. He's your father-in-law. I mean, no, he's your sister's father-in-law.'

I breathed deeply. 'Maynard Allardeck.'

'Yes. He caused it all. I'd kill him, if I could.'

I glanced at the good-looking immature face, at the dimples. Even the word kill came oddly from that mouth.

'I mean,' he said in an aggrieved voice, 'he's a member of the Jockey Club. Respected. I thought it was all right. I mean, he and Dad are patrons of the same charity. How was I to know? How was I?'

'You weren't,' I said. 'What happened?'

'He introduced me to his bookmaker.'

Whatever I'd imagined he might say, it wasn't that. I rolled the car to a halt in a parking place which at that time on a Sunday November morning was deserted. There was a distant glimpse of shingle banks and scrubby grass and sea glittering in the early sun, and nearby there was little but an acre of tarmac edged by a low brick wall, and a summer ice cream stall firmly shut.

'I've got a video camera,' I said. 'If you'd care to speak into that, I'll show the tape to your father, get him to hear your side of things, see if I can persuade him to let you go home.'

'Would you?' he said, hopefully.

'Yes, I would.'

I stretched behind my seat for the bag with the camera. 'Let's sit on the wall,' I said. 'It might be a bit chilly, but we'd get a better picture than inside the car.'

He made no objection, but came and sat on the wall, where I steadied the camera on one knee bent up, framed his face in the viewfinder and asked him to speak straight at the lens.

'Say that again,' I prompted, 'about the bookmaker.'

'I was at the races with my parents one day and having a bet, and a bookmaker was saying I wasn't old enough and making a fuss, and Maynard Allardeck was there and he said not to worry, he would introduce me to his own bookmaker instead.'

'How do you mean, he was there?'

Hugh's brow furrowed. 'He was just standing there. I mean, I didn't know who he was, but he explained he was a friend of my father.'

'And how old were you, and when did this happen?'

'That's what's so silly. I was twenty. I mean, you can bet on your eighteenth birthday. Do I look seventeen?'

'No,' I said truthfully. 'You look twenty.'

'I was twenty-one, actually, in August. It was right back in April when I met Maynard Allardeck.'

'So you started betting with Maynard Allardeck's bookmaker . . . regularly?'

'Well, yes,' Hugh said unhappily. 'He made it so easy, always so friendly, and he never seemed to worry when I didn't pay his accounts.'

'There isn't a bookmaker born who doesn't insist on his money.'

'This one didn't,' Hugh said defensively. 'I used to apologize. He'd say never mind, one day, I know you'll pay when you can, and he used to joke . . . and let me bet again . . .'

'He let you bet until you were very deeply in debt?'

'Yes. Encouraged me. I mean, I suppose I should have known . . . but he was so friendly, you see. All the summer . . . Flat racing, every day . . . on the telephone.'

'Until all this happened,' I said, 'did you bet much?'

'I've always liked betting. Studying the form. Picking

the good things, following hunches. Never any good, I suppose, but probably any money I ever had went on horses. I'd get someone to put it on for me, on the Tote, when I was ten, and so on. Always. I mean, I won often too, of course. Terrific wins, quite often.'

'Mm.'

'Everyone who goes racing bets,' he said. 'What else do they go for? I mean, there's nothing wrong with a gamble, everyone does it. It's fun.'

'Mm,' I said again. 'But you were betting every day, several bets a day, even though you didn't go.'

'I suppose so, yes.'

'And then one day,' I said, 'it stopped being fun?'

'The Hove Stakes at Brighton,' he said. 'In September.'

'What about it?'

'Three runners. Slateroof couldn't be beaten. Maynard Allardeck told me. Help yourself, he said. Recoup your losses.'

'When did he tell you?'

'Few days before. At the races. Ascot. I went with my parents, and he happened to be there too.'

'And did you go to Brighton?'

'No.' He shook his head. 'Rang up the bookmaker. He said he couldn't give me a good price, Slateroof was a certainty, everyone knew it. Five to one on, he said. If I bet twenty, I could win four.'

'So you bet twenty pounds?'

'No.' Hugh looked surprised. 'Twenty thousand.'

'Twenty . . . thousand.' I kept my voice steady, unemotional. 'Was that, er, a big bet, for you, by that time?'

'Biggish. I mean, you can't win much in fivers, can you?'

You couldn't lose much either, I thought. I said, 'What was normal?'

'Anything between one thousand and twenty. I mean, I got there gradually, I suppose. I got used to it. Maynard Allardeck said one had to think big. I never thought of how much they really were. They were just numbers.' He paused, looking unhappy. 'I know it sounds stupid to say it now, but none of it seemed real. I mean, I never had to pay anything out. It was all done on paper. When I won, I felt great. When I lost I didn't really worry. I don't suppose you'll understand. Dad didn't. He couldn't understand how I could have been so stupid. But it just seemed like a game . . . and everyone smiled . . .'

'So Slateroof got beaten?'

'He didn't even start. He got left flat-footed in the stalls.'

'Oh yes,' I said. 'I remember reading about it. There was an enquiry and the jockey got fined.'

'Yes, but the bets stood, of course.'

'So what happened next?' I said.

'I got this frightful account from the bookmaker. He'd totted up everything, he said, and it seemed to be getting out of hand, and he'd like to be paid. I mean, there were pages of it.'

'Records of all the bets you'd made with him?'

'Yes, that's right. Winners and losers. Many more losers. I mean, there were some losers I couldn't remember backing; though he swore I had, he said he would produce his office records to prove it, if I liked, but he said I was ungenerous to make such a suggestion when he'd been so accommodating and patient.' Hugh swallowed. 'I don't know if he cheated me, I just don't. I mean, I did bet on two horses in the same race quite often, I know that, but I didn't realize I'd done it so much.'

'And you'd kept no record, yourself, of how much you'd bet, and what on?'

'I didn't think of it. I mean, I could remember. I mean, I thought I could.'

'Mm. Well, what next?'

'Maynard Allardeck telephoned me at home and said he'd heard from our mutual bookmaker that I was in difficulties, and could he help, as he felt sort of responsible, having introduced me, so to speak. He said we could meet somewhere and perhaps he could suggest some solutions. So I met him for lunch in a restaurant in London, and talked it all over. He said I should confess to my father and get him to pay my debts but I said I couldn't, he would be so angry, he'd no idea I'd gambled so much, he was always lecturing me about taking care of money. And I didn't want to disappoint him, if you can understand that? I didn't want him to be upset. I mean, I expect it sounds silly, but it wasn't really out of fear, it was, well, sort of love, really, only it's difficult to explain.'

'Yes,' I said, 'go on.'

'Maynard Allardeck said not to worry, he could see why I couldn't tell my father, it reflected well on me, he said, and he would lend me the money himself, and I could pay him back slowly, and he would just charge me a little over, if I thought that was fair. And I did think it was fair, of course. I was so extremely relieved. I thanked him a lot, over and over.'

'So Maynard Allardeck paid your bookmaker?'

'Yes.' Hugh nodded. 'I got a final account from him marked "Paid with thanks", and a note saying it would be best if I laid off betting for a while, but if I needed him in the future, he would accommodate me again. I mean, I thought it very fair and kind, wouldn't you?'

'Mm,' I said dryly. 'And then after a while Maynard Allardeck told you he was short of money himself and would have to call in the debt?'

'Yes,' Hugh said in surprise. 'How did you know? He was so apologetic and embarrassed I almost felt sorry for him, though he was putting me in a terrible hole. Terrible. And then he suggested a way round it, which was so easy . . . so simple . . . like the sun coming out. I couldn't think why I hadn't thought of it myself.'

'Hugh,' I asked slowly, 'what did you have, that he wanted?'

'My shares in the *Towncrier*,' he said.

CHAPTER EIGHTEEN

He took my breath away. Oh my Christ, I thought. Bloody bingo.

Talk about the sun coming out. So simple, so easy. Why hadn't I thought of it myself.

'Your shares in the *Towncrier* . . .'

'Yes,' Hugh said. 'They were left to me by my grandfather. I mean, I didn't know I had them, until I was twenty-one.'

'In August.'

'Yes. That's right. Anyway, it seemed to solve everything. I mean it did solve everything, didn't it? Maynard Allardeck looked up the proper market value and everything, and gave me two or three forms to sign, which I did, and then he said that was fine, we were all square, I had no more debts. I mean, it was so easy. And it wasn't all of my shares. Not even half.'

'How much were the shares worth, that you gave Allardeck?'

He said as if such figures were commonplace, 'Two hundred and fifty-four thousand pounds.'

After a pause I said, 'Didn't it upset you . . . so much money?'

'Of course not. It was only on paper. And Maynard Allardeck laughed and said if I ever felt like gambling again, well, I had the collateral, and we could always come to the same arrangement again, if it was necessary. I begged him not to tell my father, and he said no, he wouldn't.'

'But your father found out?'

'Yes, it was something to do with voting shares, or preference shares or debentures. I'm really not sure, I didn't know what they were talking about, but they were busy fending off a takeover. They're always fending off takeovers, but this one had them all dead worried, and somewhere in the *Towncrier* they discovered that half of my shares had gone, and Dad made me tell him what I'd done . . . and he was so angry . . . I'd never seen him angry . . . never like that . . .'

His voice faded away, his eyes stark with remembrance.

'He sent me here to Saul Bradley and he said if I ever bet on anything ever again I could never go home . . . I want him . . . I do . . . to forgive me. I want to go home.'

He stopped. The intensity of his feelings stared into the lens. I let the camera run for a few silent seconds, and then turned it off.

'I'll show him the film,' I said.

'Do you think . . .?'

'In time he'll forgive you? Yes, I'd say so.'

'I could go back to just the odd bet in cash on the Tote.' His eyes were speculative, his air much too hopeful. The infection too deep in his system.

'Hugh,' I said, 'would you mind if I gave you some advice?'

'No. Fire away.'

'Take some practical lessons about money. Go away without any, find out it's not just numbers on a page, learn it's the difference between eating and hunger. Bet your dinner, and if you lose, see if it's worth it.'

He said earnestly, 'Yes, I do see what you mean. But I might win.' And I wondered doubtfully whether one could ever reform an irresponsible gambler, be he rich, poor, or the heir to the *Towncrier.*

I drove back to London, added the Hugh Vaughnley tape to the others in the hotel's care, and went upstairs for another session of staring blindly at the walls. Then I telephoned Holly, and got Bobby instead.

'How's things?' I said.

'Not much different. Holly's lying down, do you want to talk to her?'

'You'll do fine.'

'I've had some more cheques from the owners. Almost everyone's paid.'

'That's great.'

'They're a drop in the ocean.' His voice sounded tired. 'Will your valet cash them again?'

'Sure to.'

'Even then,' he said, 'we're right at the end.'

'I suppose,' I said, 'you haven't heard any more from the *Flag*? No letter? No money?'

'Not a thing.'

I sighed internally and said, 'Bobby, I want to talk to your father.'

'It won't do any good. You know what he was like the other day. He's stubborn and mean, and he hates us.'

'He hates me,' I said, 'and Holly. Not you.'

'One wouldn't guess it,' he said bitterly.

'I've no rides on Tuesday,' I said. 'Persuade him to come to your house on Tuesday afternoon. I'm schooling at Wykeham's place in the morning.'

'It's impossible. He wouldn't come here.'

'He might,' I said, 'if you tell him he was right all along, every Fielding is your enemy, and you want his help in getting rid of me, out of your life.'

'Kit!' He was outraged. 'I can't do that. It's the last thing I want.'

'And if you can bring yourself to it, tell him you're getting tired of Holly, as well.'

'No. How can I? I love her so much . . . I couldn't make it sound true.'

'Bobby, nothing less will bring him. Can you think

of anything else? I've been thinking for hours. If you can get him there some other way, we'll do it your way.'

After a pause he said, 'He would come out of hate. Isn't that awful? He's my father . . .'

'Yes. I'm sorry.'

'What do you want to talk to him about?'

'A proposition. Help for you in return for something he'd want. But don't tell him that. Don't tell him I'm coming. Just get him there, if you can.'

He said doubtfully, 'He'll never help us. Never.'

'Well, we'll see. At least give it a try.'

'Yes, all right, but for heaven's sake, Kit . . .'

'What?'

'It's dreadful to say it, but where you're concerned . . . I think he's dangerous.'

'I'll be careful.'

'It goes back so far . . . When I was little he taught me to hit things . . . with my fists, with a stick, anything, and he told me to think I was hitting Kit Fielding.'

I took a breath. 'Like in the garden?'

'God, Kit . . . I've been so sorry.'

'I told you. I mean it. It's all right.'

'I've been thinking about you, and remembering so much. Things I'd forgotten, like him telling me the Fieldings would eat me if I was naughty . . . I must have been three or four. I was scared stiff.'

'When you were four, I was two.'

'It was your father and your grandfather who would eat me. Then when you were growing up he told me to hit Kit Fielding, he taught me how, he said one day it would be you and I, we would have to fight. I'd forgotten all that . . . but I remember it now.'

'My grandfather,' I sighed, 'gave me a punchbag and taught me how to hit it. That's Bobby Allardeck, he said. Bash him.'

'Do you mean it?'

'Ask Holly. She knows.'

'Bloody, weren't they.'

'It's finished now,' I said.

We disconnected and I got through to Danielle and said how about lunch and tea and dinner.

'Are you planning to eat all those?' she said.

'All or any.'

'All, then.'

'I'll come straight round.'

She opened the Eaton Square front door as I braked to a halt and came across the pavement with a spring in her step, an evocation of summer in a flower-patterned jacket over cream trousers, the chintz band holding back the fluffy hair.

She climbed into the car beside me and kissed me as if from old habit.

'Aunt Casilia sends her regards and hopes we'll have a nice day.'

'And back by midnight?'

'I would think so, wouldn't you?'

'Does she notice?'

'She sure does. I go past their rooms to get to mine

– she and Uncle Roland sleep separately – and the floors creak. She called me in last night to ask if I'd enjoyed myself. She was sitting in bed, reading, looking a knock-out as usual. I told her what we'd done and showed her the chest of drawers . . . we had quite a long talk.'

I studied her face. She looked seriously back.

'What did she say?' I asked.

'It matters to you, doesn't it, what she thinks?'

'Yes.'

'I guess she'd be glad.'

'Tell me, then.'

'Not yet.' She smiled swiftly, almost secretly. 'What about this lunch?'

We went to a restaurant up a tower and ate looking out over half of London. 'Consommé and strawberries . . . you'll be good for my figure,' she said.

'Have some sugar and cream.'

'Not if you don't.'

'You're thin enough,' I said.

'Don't you get tired of it?'

'Of not eating much? I sure do.'

'But you never let up?'

'A pound overweight in the saddle,' I said wryly, 'can mean a length's difference at the winning post.'

'End of discussion.'

Over coffee I asked if there was anywhere she'd like to go, though I apologized that most of London seemed to shut on Sundays, especially in November.

'I'd like to see where you live,' she said. 'I'd like to see Lambourn.'

'Right,' I said, and drove her there, seventy miles westwards down the M4 motorway, heading back towards Devon, keeping this time law-abidingly within the speed limit, curling off into the large village, small town, where the church stood at the main crossroads and a thousand thoroughbreds lived in boxes.

'It's quiet,' she said.

'It's Sunday.'

'Where's your cottage?'

'We'll drive past there,' I said. 'But we're not going in.'

She was puzzled, and, it seemed, disappointed, looking across at me lengthily. 'Why not?'

I explained about the break in, and the police saying the place had been searched. 'The intruders found nothing they wanted, and they stole nothing. But I'd bet they left something behind.'

'What do you mean?'

'Creepy-crawlies.'

'Bugs?'

'Mm,' I said. 'That's it over there.'

We went past slowly. There was no sign of life. No sign of heavy men lying in the bushes with sharp knives, which they wouldn't be by then, not after three days. Too boring, too cold. Listening somewhere, though, those two, or others.

The cottage was brick-built, rather plain, and would perhaps have looked better in June, with the roses.

'It's all right inside,' I said.

'Yuh.' She sounded downcast. 'OK. That's that.'

I drove around and up a hill and took her to the new house instead.

'Whose is this?' she said. 'This is great.'

'This is mine.' I got out of the car, fishing for keys. 'It's empty. Come and look.'

The bright day was fading but there was enough direct sunlight to shine horizontally through the windows and light the big empty rooms, and although the air inside was cold, the central heating, when I switched it on, went into smooth operation with barely a hiccup. There were a few light sockets with bulbs in, but no shades. No curtains. No carpets. Wood-block floor everywhere, swept but not polished. Signs of builders all over the place.

'They're just starting to paint,' I said, opening the double doors from the hall to the sitting room. 'I'll move in alongside, if they don't hurry up.'

There were trestles in the sitting room set up for reaching the ceiling, and an army of tubs of paint, and dustsheets all over the flooring to avoid spatters.

'It's huge,' she said. 'Incredible.'

'It's got a great kitchen. An office. Lots of things.' I explained about the bankrupt builder. 'He designed it for himself.'

We went around and through everywhere and ended

in the big room which led directly off the sitting room, the room where I would sleep. It seemed that the decorators had started with that: it was clean, bare and finished, the bathroom painted and tiled, the woodblocks faintly gleaming with the first layer of polish, the western sun splashing in patches on the white walls.

Danielle stood by the window looking out at the muddy expanse which by summer would be a terrace, with geraniums in pots. The right person . . . in the right place . . . at the right time.

'Will you lie in my bedroom?' I said.

She turned, silhouetted against the sun, her hair like a halo, her face in shadow, hard to read. It seemed that she was listening still to what I'd said, as if to be sure that she had heard right and not misunderstood.

'On the bare floor?' Her voice was steady, uncommitted, friendly and light.

'We could, er, fetch some dustsheets, perhaps.'

She considered it.

'OK,' she said.

We brought a few dustsheets from the sitting room and arranged them in a rough rectangle, with pillows.

'I've seen better marriage beds,' she said.

We took all our clothes off, not hurrying, dropping them in heaps. No real surprises. She was as I had thought, flat and rounded, her skin glowing now in the sun. She stretched out her fingers, touching lightly the stitches, the fading bruises, the known places.

She said, 'When you looked at me at the races yesterday, over those cups, were you thinking of this?'

'Something like this. Was it so obvious?'

'Blinding.'

'I was afraid so.'

We didn't talk a great deal after that. We stood together for a while, and lay down, and on the hard cotton surface learned the ultimate things about each other, pleasing and pleased, with advances and retreats, with murmurs and intensities and breathless primeval energy.

The sunlight faded slowly, the sky lit still with afterglow, gleams reflecting in her eyes and on her teeth, darknesses deepening in hollows and in her hair.

At the end of a long calm afterwards she said prosaically, 'I suppose the water's not hot?'

'Bound to be,' I said lazily. 'It's combined with the heating. Everything's working, lights, plumbing, the lot.'

We got up and went into the bathroom, switching on taps but not lights. It was darker in there and we moved like shadows, more substance than shape.

I turned on the shower, running it warm. Danielle stepped into it with me, and we made love again there in the spray, with tenderness, with passion and in friendship, her arms round my neck, her stomach flat on mine, united as I'd never been before in my life.

I turned off the tap, in the end.

'There aren't any towels,' I said.

'Always the dustsheets.'

We took our bed apart and dried ourselves, and got dressed, and kissed again with temperance, feeling clean. In almost full darkness we dumped the dust sheets in the sitting room, switched off the heating, and went out of the house, locking it behind us.

Danielle looked back before getting into the car. 'I wonder what the house thinks,' she said.

'It thinks holy wow.'

'As a matter of fact, so do I.'

We drove back to London along the old roads, not the motorway, winding through the empty Sunday evening streets of a string of towns, stopping at traffic lights, stretching the journey. I parked the car in central London and we walked for a while, stopping to read menus, and eating eventually in a busy French bistro with red checked tablecloths and an androgynous guitarist; sitting in a corner, holding hands, reading the bill of fare chalked on a blackboard.

'Aunt Casilia,' Danielle said, sometime later over coffee, her eyes shining with amusement, 'said last night, among other things, that while decorum was essential, abstinence was not.'

I laughed in surprise, and kissed her, and in a while and in decorum drove her back to Eaton Square.

I raced at Windsor the next day, parking the car at the railway station and taking a taxi from there right to the jockeys' entrance gate near the weighing room on the racecourse.

The princess had no runners and wasn't expected; I rode two horses each for Wykeham and the Lambourn trainer and got all of them round into the first or second place, which pleased the owners and put grins on the stable lads. Bunty Ireland, beaming, told me I was on the winning streak of all time, and I calculated the odds that I'd come crashing down again by Thursday, and hoped that I wouldn't, and that he was right.

My valet said, sure, he would return me to the station in his van – a not too abnormal service. He was reading aloud from the *Flag* with disfavour. 'Reality is sweaty armpits, sordid sex, junkies dead in public lavatories, it says here.' He threw the paper on to the bench. 'Reality is the gas bill, remembering the wife's birthday, a beer with your mates, that's more like it. Get in the van, Kit, it's right outside the weighing room. I've just about finished here.'

Reality, I thought, going out, was speed over fences, a game of manners, love in a shower: to each his own.

I travelled without incident back to the hotel and telephoned on time to Wykeham.

'Where are you?' he said. 'People keep asking for you.'

'Who?' I said.

'They don't say. Four fellows, at least. All day. Where are you?'

'Staying with friends.'

'Oh.' He didn't ask further. He himself didn't care. We talked about his winner and his second, and discussed the horses I would be schooling in the morning.

'One of those fellows who rang wanted you for some lunch party or other in London,' he said, as if suddenly remembering. 'They invited me, too. The sponsors of Inchcape's race, last Saturday. The princess is going, and they wanted us as well. They said it was a great opportunity as they could see from tomorrow's race programmes that we hadn't any runners.'

'Are you going?'

'No, no. I said I couldn't. But it might be better if you came here early, and do the schooling in good time.'

I agreed, and said goodnight.

'Goodnight, Kit,' he said.

I got through to my answering machine, and there among the messages were the sponsors of Icefall's race, inviting me to lunch the next day. They would be delighted if I could join them and the princess in celebrating our victory in their race, please could I ring back at the given number.

I rang the number and got an answering machine referring me on, reaching finally the head of the sponsors himself.

'Great, great, you can come?' he said. 'Twelve-thirty at the Guineas restaurant in Curzon Street. See you there. That's splendid.'

Sponsors got advertising from racing and in return

pumped in generous cash. There was an unspoken understanding among racing people that sponsors were to be appreciated, and that jockeys should turn up if possible where invited. Part of the job. And I wanted to go, besides, to talk to the princess.

I answered my other messages, none of which were important, and then got through to Holly.

'Bobby spoke to his father,' she said. 'The beast said he would come only if you were there. Bobby didn't like it.'

'Did Bobby say I would be there anyway?'

'No, he waited to know what you wanted him to say. He has to ring back to his father.'

I didn't like it any more than Bobby. 'Why does Maynard want me?' I said. 'I didn't think he would come at all if he knew I'd be there.'

'He said he would help Bobby get rid of you once and for all, but that you had to be there.'

Bang, I thought, goes any advantage of surprise. 'All right,' I said. 'Tell Bobby to tell him I'll be coming. At about four o'clock, I should think. I'm going to a sponsors' lunch in London.'

'Kit . . . whatever you're planning, don't do it.'

'Must.'

'I've a feeling . . .'

'Stifle it. How's the baby?'

'Never have one,' she said. 'It's the pits.'

*

I collected all four recorded video tapes from the hotel's vaults and took them with six others, unused, to Chiswick: and kissed Danielle with circumspection at her desk.

'Hi,' she said, smiling deeply in her eyes.

'Hi, yourself.'

'How did it go, today?'

'Two wins, two seconds.'

'And no crunches.'

'No crunches.'

She seemed to relax. 'I'm glad you're OK.'

Joe appeared from the passage to the editing rooms saying he was biting his fingernails with inactivity and had I by any chance brought my tapes. I picked the four recorded tapes off Danielle's desk and he pounced on them, bearing them away.

I followed him with the spare tapes into an editing room and sat beside him while he played the interviews through, one by one, his dark face showing shock.

'Can you stick them together?' I asked, when he'd finished.

'I sure can,' he said sombrely. 'What you need is some voice-over linkage. You got anything else? Shots of scenery, anything like that?'

I shook my head. 'I didn't think of it.'

'It's no good putting a voice-over on a black screen,' he explained. 'You've got to have pictures, to hold interest. We're bound to have something here in the library that we can use.'

Danielle appeared at the doorway, looking enquiring.

'How's it going?' she said.

'I guess you know what's on these tapes,' Joe said.

'No. Kit hasn't told me.'

'Good,' Joe said. 'When I've finished, we'll try it out on you. Get a reaction.'

'OK,' she said. 'It's a quiet night for news, thank goodness.'

She went away and Joe got me to speak into a microphone, explaining who the Perrysides were, giving George Tarker a location, introducing Hugh Vaughnley. I wanted them in that order, I said.

'Right,' he said. 'Now you go away and talk to Danielle and leave it to me, and if you don't like the result, no problem, we can always change it.'

'I brought these unused tapes,' I said, giving them to him. 'Once we've settled on the final version, could we make copies?'

He took one of the new tapes, peeled off the cellophane wrapping and put it into a machine. 'A breeze,' he said.

He spent two or three hours on it, coming out whistling a couple of times to see if the station chief was still happy (which he appeared to be), telling me Spielberg couldn't do better, drinking coffee from a machine, going cheerfully back.

Danielle worked sporadically on a story about a police hunt for a rapist who lurked in bus shelters and had just been arrested, which she said would probably not make it on to network news back home, but kept everyone working, at least. No Devil-Boys, no oil fires that night.

Aunt Casilia, Danielle said, was looking forward to tomorrow's lunch party and hoped I would be there.

'Will you be going?' I asked.

'Nope. Aunt Casilia would have gotten me invited, but I've a college friend passing through London. We're having lunch. Long time date, I can't break it.'

'Pity.'

'You're going? Shall I tell her?'

I nodded. 'I'm schooling some of her horses in the morning, and I'll be coming along after.'

Joe came out finally, stretching his backbone and flexing his fingers.

'Come on, then,' he said. 'Come and see.'

We all went, the station chief as well, sitting in chairs collected from adjoining rooms. Joe started his machine, and there, immediately, was the uncut version of the television interview of Maynard and his tormentor, followed by the list of firms Maynard had acquired. At the end of that the tape returned to repeat the interviewer's outline of Metavane's story, and then came my voice, superimposed on views of horses exercising on Newmarket Health, explaining who Major and Mrs Perryside were, and where they now lived.

The Perrysides appeared in entirety, poignant and

brave; and at the end the tape returned to the television interviewer again repeating the takeover list. This time it stopped after the mention of Purfleet Electronics, and then, over a view of mudflats in the Thames estuary, my voice introduced George Tarker. The whole of that interview was there also, and when he said in tears about his son wiring himself up, Danielle's own eyes filled . . .

Joe left the shot of George Tarker's ravaged face running as long as I'd taped it, and then there was my voice again, this time over a printing press in full production, explaining that the next person to appear would be the son of Lord Vaughnley, who owned the *Daily* and *Sunday Towncrier* newspapers.

All of Hugh's tape was there, ending with his impassioned plea to come home. On the screen after that came a long shot taken from the cut televised version of *How's Trade*, of Maynard smiling and looking noble. The soundtrack of that had been erased, so that one saw him in silence. Then the screen went silently into solid black for about ten seconds before reverting to snow and background crackle.

Even though I'd recorded three of the main segments myself, the total effect was overpowering. Run together they were a punch to the brain, emotional, damning the wicked.

The station chief said, 'Christ', and Danielle blew her nose.

'It runs for one hour, thirteen minutes,' Joe said to me, 'if you're interested.'

'I can't thank you enough.'

'I hope the bastard burns,' he said.

In the morning I went to Wykeham's place south of London and on the Downs there spent two profitable hours teaching his absolute novices how to jump and refreshing the memories of others. We gave the one who had fallen at Ascot a pop to help him get his confidence back after being brought down, and talked about the runners for the rest of that week.

'Thank you for coming,' he said. 'Good of you.'

'A pleasure.'

'Goodbye, P . . . er . . . Kit.'

'Goodbye, Wykeham,' I said.

I went back to London, showered, dressed in grey suit, white shirt, quiet tie, presenting a civilized face to the sponsors.

I put one of the six copies Joe had made of the Allardeck production into a large envelope, sticking it shut, and then zipped a second of them into the big inside pocket of my blue anorak. The other four I took downstairs and lodged in the hotel vault, and carrying both the envelope and the anorak went by taxi to Eric Olderjohn's terrace house behind Sloane Square.

The taxi waited while I rang the bell beside the green door, and not much to my surprise there was no one at home. I wrote on the envelope: 'Mr Olderjohn, Please give this to a Certain Person, for his eyes only. Regards, Kit Fielding' and pushed it through the letter box.

'Right,' I said to the taxi driver. 'The Guineas restaurant, Curzon Street.'

The Guineas, where I'd been several times before, was principally a collection of private dining rooms of various sizes, chiefly used for private parties such as the one I was bound for. Opulent and discreet, it went in for dark green flocked wallpaper, gilded cherubs and waiters in gloves. Every time I had been there, there had been noisettes of lamb.

I left my anorak in the cloakroom downstairs and put the ticket in my pocket, walked up the broad stairs to the next floor, turned right, went down a passage and ended, as directed, at the sponsors' party in the One Thousand Room.

The sponsors greeted me effusively. 'Come in, come in. Have some champagne.' They gave me a glass.

The princess was there, dressed in a cream silk suit with gold and citrines, dark hair piled high, smiling.

'I'm so pleased you've come,' she said, shaking my hand.

'I wouldn't have missed it.'

'How are my horses? How is Icefall? How is my

poor Allegheny? Did you know that Lord Vaughnley is here?'

'Is he?'

I looked around. There were about thirty people present, more perhaps than I'd expected. From across the room Lady Vaughnley saw me, and waved.

'The *Towncrier* joined forces with the Icefall people,' the princess said. 'It's a double party, now.'

The Icefall sponsors came to bear her away. 'Do come . . . may I present . . .'

Lord Vaughnley approached, looking blander than bland.

'Now, everybody,' said one of the sponsors loudly, 'we're all going into another room to see films of our two races, both won by our most honoured guest, Princess Casilia.'

There was a little light applause, and everyone began to move to the door. Lord Vaughnley stood at my elbow. The princess looked back. 'You're coming, Kit?'

'In a minute,' Lord Vaughnley said. 'Just want to ask him something.'

The princess smiled and nodded and went on. Lord Vaughnley shepherded everyone out, and when the room was empty, closed the door and stood with his back to it.

'I wanted to reach you,' I said; but I don't think he heard. He was looking towards a second door, set in a side wall.

The door opened, and two people came through it.

Nestor Pollgate.

Jay Erskine.

Pollgate looked satisfied and Jay Erskine was smirking.

CHAPTER NINETEEN

'Neatly done,' Pollgate said to Lord Vaughnley.

'It worked out well,' he replied, his big head nodding.

He still stood four-square in front of the door. Erskine stood similarly, with folded arms, in front of the other.

There were chairs and tables round the green walls, tables with white cloths bearing bowls of nuts and cigarette-filled ashtrays. Champagne goblets all over the place, some still with bubble contents. There would be waiters, I thought, coming to clear the rubble.

'We won't be disturbed,' Pollgate told Lord Vaughnley. 'The "do not enter" signs are on both doors, and Mario says we have the room for an hour.'

'The lunch will be before that,' Lord Vaughnley said. 'The films take half an hour, no more.'

'He's not going to the lunch,' Pollgate said, meaning me.

'Er, no, perhaps not. But I should be there.'

I thought numbly: catch me first.

It had taken five days . . . and the princess.

'You are going to give us,' Pollgate said to me directly, 'the wire-tap and my journalists' belongings. And that will be the end of it.'

The power of the man was such that the words themselves were a threat. What would happen if I didn't comply wasn't mentioned. My compliance was assumed; no discussion.

He walked over to Jay Erskine, producing a flat box from a pocket and taking Jay Erskine's place guarding the door.

Jay Erskine's smirk grew to a twisted smile of anticipation. I disliked intensely the cold eyes, the drooping moustache, his callous pen and his violent nature; and most of all I disliked the message in his sneer.

Pollgate opened the box and held it out to Jay Erskine, who took from it something that looked like the hand-held remote control of a television set. He settled it into his hand and walked in my direction. He came without the wariness one might have expected after I'd thrown him across a room, and he put the remote control thing smoothly between the open fronts of my jacket, on to my shirt.

I felt something like a thud, and the next thing I knew I was lying flat on my back on the floor, wholly disorientated, not sure where I was or what had happened.

Jay Erskine and Lord Vaughnley bent down, took my arms, helped me up, and dropped me on to a chair.

The chair had arms. I held on to them. I felt dazed, and couldn't work out why.

Jay Erskine smiled nastily and put the black object again against my shirt.

The thud had a burn to it that time. And so fast. No time to draw breath.

I would have shot out of the chair if they hadn't held me in it. My wits scattered instantly to the four winds. My muscles didn't work. I wasn't sure who I was or where I was, and nor did I care. Time passed. Time was relative. It was minutes, anyway. Not very quick.

The haze in my brain slowly resolved itself to the point where I knew I was sitting in a chair, and knew the people round me were Nestor Pollgate, Lord Vaughnley and Jay Erskine.

'Right,' Pollgate said. 'Can you hear me?'

I said, after a pause, 'Yes.' It didn't sound like my voice. More a croak.

'You're going to give us the wire-tap,' he said. 'And the other things.'

Some sort of electricity, I thought dimly. Those thuds were electric shocks. Like touching a cold metal door-knob after walking on nylon carpet, but magnified monstrously.

'You understand?' he said.

I didn't answer. I understood, but I didn't know whether I was going to give him the things or not.

'Where are they?' he said.

To hell with it, I thought.

'Where are they?'

Silence.

I didn't even see Jay Erskine put his hand against me the third time. I felt a great burning jolt and went shooting into space, floating for several millennia in a disorientated limbo, ordinary consciousness suspended, living as in dream-state, docile and drifting. I could see them in a way, but I didn't know who they were. I didn't know anything. I existed. I had no form.

Whatever would be done, wherever they might take me, whatever God-awful crime they might plant me in, I couldn't resist.

Thought came back again slowly. There were burns somewhere, stinging. I heard Lord Vaughnley's voice saying something, and Pollgate answering, 'Five thousand volts.'

'He's awake,' Erskine said.

Lord Vaughnley leaned over me, his face close and worried. 'Are you sure he's all right?'

'Yes,' Pollgate said. 'There'll be no permanent harm.'

Thank you, I thought wryly, for that. I felt dizzy and sick. Just as well that with lunch in view I had missed breakfast.

Pollgate was looking at his watch and shaking his head. 'He was dazed for twelve minutes that time. A three-second shock is too much. The two-second is better, but it's taking too long. Twenty minutes already.' He glared down at me. 'I can't waste any more time. You'll give me those things, now, at once.'

It was he who held the electric device now, not Erskine.

I thought I could speak. Tried it. Something came out: the same sort of croak. I said 'It will take . . . days.'

It wasn't heroics. I thought vaguely that if they believed it would take days they would give up trying, right there and then. Logic, at that point, was at a low ebb.

Pollgate stepped within touching distance of me and showed me five thousand volts at close range.

'Stun gun,' he said.

It had two short flat metal prongs protruding five centimetres apart from one end of a flat plastic case. He squeezed some switch or other, and between the prongs leapt an electric spark the length of a thumb, bright blue, thick and crackling.

The spark fizzed for a long three seconds of painful promise and disappeared as fast as it had come.

I looked from the stun gun up to Pollgate's face, staring straight at the shiny-bead eyes.

'Weeks,' I said.

It certainly nonplussed him. 'Give us the wire-tap,' he said; and he seemed to be looking, as I was, at a long, tiring battle of wills, much of which I would half sleep through, I supposed.

Lord Vaughnley said to Pollgate uncomfortably, 'You can't go on with this.'

A certain amount of coherence returned to my brain.

The battle of wills, I thought gratefully, shouldn't be necessary.

'He's going to give us those things,' Pollgate said obstinately. 'I'm not letting some clod like this get the better of me.' Pride, loss of face, all the deadly intangibles.

Lord Vaughnley looked down at me anxiously.

'I'll give you,' I said to him, 'something better.'

'What?'

My voice was steadier. Less hoarse, less slow. I moved in the chair, arms and legs coming back into coordination. It seemed to alarm Jay Erskine but I was still a long way from playing judo.

'What will you give us?' Lord Vaughnley said.

I concentrated on making my throat and tongue work properly. 'It's in Newmarket,' I said. 'We'll have to go there for it. Now, this afternoon.'

Pollgate said with impatience. 'That's ridiculous.'

'I'll give you,' I said to Lord Vaughnley, 'Maynard Allardeck.'

A short burst of stun couldn't have had more effect.

'How do you mean?' he said; not with puzzlement, but with hope.

'On a plate,' I said. 'In your power. Where you want him, don't you?'

They both wanted him. I could see it in Pollgate's face just as clearly as in Lord Vaughnley's. I suppose that I had guessed in a way that it would be both.

Jay Erskine said aggressively, 'Are our things in Newmarket, then?'

I said with an effort, 'That's where you left them.'

'All right, then.'

He seemed to think that the purpose of their expedition had been achieved, and I didn't tell him differently.

Nestor Pollgate said, 'Jay, fetch the car to the side entrance, will you?' and the obnoxious Erskine went away.

Pollgate and Lord Vaughnley agreed that Mario, whoever he was, should tell Icefall's sponsors not to expect their guests back for lunch, saying I'd had a bilious attack and Lord Vaughnley was helping me. 'But Mario can't tell them until after we've gone,' Lord Vaughnley said, 'or you'll have my wife and I daresay the princess out here in a flash to mother him.'

I sat and listened lethargically, capable of movement but not wanting to move, no longer sick, all right in my head, peaceful, extraordinarily, and totally without energy.

After a while Jay Erskine came back, the exasperating smirk still in place.

'Can you walk?' Pollgate asked me.

I said, 'Yes' and stood up, and we went out of the side door, along a short passage and down some gilded deeply carpeted backstairs, where no doubt many a Guineas visitor made a discreet entrance and exit, avoiding public eyes in the front hall.

I went down the stairs shakily, holding on to the rail.

'Are you all right?' Lord Vaughnley said solicitously, putting his hand supportively under my elbow.

I glanced at him. How he could think I would be all right was beyond me. Perhaps he was remembering that I was used to damage, to falls, to concussion: but bruises and fractures were different from that day's little junket.

'I'm all right,' I said though, because it was true where it counted, and we went safely down to the bottom.

I stopped there. The exit door stood open ahead, a passage stretching away indoors to the right.

'Come along,' Pollgate said, gesturing to the door. 'If we're going, let's go.'

'My anorak,' I said, 'is in the cloakroom.' I produced the ticket from my pocket. 'Anorak,' I said.

'I'll get it,' Lord Vaughnley said, taking the ticket. 'And I'll see Mario. Wait for me in the car.'

It was a large car. Jay Erskine was driving. Nestor Pollgate sat watchfully beside me on the back seat, and Lord Vaughnley, when he returned, sat in the front.

'Your anorak,' he said, holding it out, and I thanked him and put it by my feet, on the floor.

'The films of the races have just ended, Mario says,' he reported to Pollgate. 'He's going straight in to make our apologies. It's all settled. Off we go.'

It took ages to get out of London, partly because of thick traffic, mostly because Jay Erskine was a rotten driver, all impatience and heavy on the brakes. An hour and a half to Newmarket, at that rate: and I would have to be better by then.

No one spoke much. Jay Erskine locked all the doors centrally and Nestor Pollgate put the stun gun in its case in his right-hand jacket pocket, hidden but available; and I sat beside him in ambiguity, half prisoner, half ringmaster, going willingly but under threat, waiting for energy to return, physical, mental and psychic.

Stun guns, I thought. I'd heard of them, never seen one before. Used originally by American police to subdue dangerous violent criminals without shooting them. Instantaneous. Effective. You don't say.

I remembered from long-ago physics lessons that if you squeezed piezoelectric crystals you got sparks, as in the flickering lighters used for gas cookers. Maybe stun guns were like that, multiplied. Maybe not. Maybe I would ask someone. Maybe not. Five thousand volts . . .

I looked with speculation at the back of Lord Vaughnley's head, wondering what he was thinking. He was eager, that was for sure. They had agreed to the journey like thirsty men in a drought. They were going without knowing for sure why, without demanding to be told. Anything that could do Maynard Allardeck harm must be worth doing, in their eyes: that had to be why, at the beginning, Lord Vaughnley had been happy enough to introduce me to Rose Quince, to let me loose on the files. The destruction of Maynard's credibility could only be helped along, he might have thought, by pin pricks from myself.

I dozed, woke with a start, found Pollgate's face turned my way, his eyes watching. He was looking, if anything, puzzled.

In my rag-doll state I could think of nothing useful to say, so I didn't, and presently he turned his head away and looked out of the window, and I still felt very conscious of his force, his ruthlessness, and of the ruin he could make of my life if I got the next few hours wrong.

I thought of how they had set their trap in the Guineas.

Icefall's sponsors, on my answering machine, inviting me to lunch. The sponsors hadn't said where, but they'd said tomorrow, Tuesday: today. The message would have been overheard and despatched to Pollgate, and sent from him to Lord Vaughnley, who would have said, Nothing simpler, my dear fellow, I'll join forces with those sponsors, which they can hardly refuse, and Kit Fielding will definitely come, he'd do anything to please the princess . . .

Pollgate had known the Guineas. Known Mario. Known he could get an isolated room for an hour. The sort of place he would know, for sure.

Maybe Lord Vaughnley had suggested the Guineas to Icefall's sponsors. Maybe he hadn't had to. There were often racing celebration parties at the Guineas.

The sponsors would very likely have chosen it themselves, knowing they could show the films there.

Unprofitable thoughts. However it had been planned, it had worked.

I thought also about the alliance between Lord Vaughnley and Nestor Pollgate, owners of snapping rival newspapers, always at each other's throats in print, and acting in private accord.

Allies, not friends. They didn't move comfortably around each other, as friends did.

On 1 October Lord Vaughnley had signed the charity letter recommending Maynard for a knighthood: signed it casually perhaps, not knowing him well.

Then later in October his son Hugh had confessed to his dealings with Maynard, and Lord Vaughnley, outraged, had sought to unzip Maynard's accolade by getting Pollgate and his *Flag* to do the demolition; because it was the *Flag*'s sort of thing . . . and Jay Erskine, who had worked for Lord Vaughnley once, was in place there in the *Flag*, and was known not to be averse to an illegal sortie, now and then.

I didn't know why Lord Vaughnley should have gone to Pollgate, should have expected him to help. Somewhere between them there was a reason. I didn't suppose I would get an answer, if I asked.

Lord Vaughnley, I thought, could have been expected to tell the charity he wanted to recant his approval of Maynard Allardeck's knighthood: but they might have said too bad, your son was a fool, but

Allardeck definitely helped him. Lord Vaughnley might as a newspaperman have seen a few destructive paragraphs as more certain, and more revengefully satisfying, besides.

Before that, though, I guessed it had been he who had gone to the producers of *How's Trade*, who said dig up what you can about Allardeck, discredit him, I'll pay you: and had been defeated by the producer himself, who according to Rose Quince was known for taking more money in return for helping his victims off the hook.

The *How's Trade* programme on Maynard had gone out loaded in Maynard's favour, which hadn't been the plan at all. And it was after that, I thought, that Lord Vaughnley had gone to Pollgate.

I shut my eyes and drifted. The car hummed. They had the heater on. I thought about horses; more honest than men. Tomorrow I was due to ride at Haydock. Thank God the racecourse doctor hadn't been at the Guineas.

Takeovers, I thought inconsequentially. Always fending off takeovers.

Pollgate would bury me if I didn't get it right.

Towards the end of the journey both mental and physical power came seeping slowly back, like a tide rising, and it was an extraordinary feeling: I hadn't known how much power I did have until I'd both lost it and felt its return. Like not realizing how ill one had been, until one was well.

I stretched thankfully with the renewed strength in my muscles and breathed deeply from the surge in my mind, and Pollgate, for whom the consciousness of power must have been normal, sensed in some way the vital recharging in me and sat up more tensely himself.

Erskine drove into Bobby's stableyard at five minutes past three, and in the middle of what should have been a quiet snooze in the life of the horses, it seemed that there were people and movement all over the place. Erskine stopped the car with his accustomed jerk, and, Pollgate having told him to unlock the doors, we climbed out.

Holly was looking distractedly in our direction, and there were besides three or four cars, a horse trailer with the ramp down and grooms wandering about with head-collars.

There was also, to my disbelief, Jermyn Graves.

Holly came running across to me and said, 'Do something, he's a madman, and Bobby's indoors with Maynard, he came early and they've been shouting at each other and I don't want to go in, and thank God you're here, it's a farce.'

Jermyn Graves, seeing me, followed Holly. His gaze swept over Pollgate, Jay Erskine and Lord Vaughnley and he said belligerently, 'Who the hell are these people? Now see here, Fielding, I've had enough of your smart-arse behaviour, I've come for my horses.'

I put my arm around Holly. 'Did his cheque go through?' I asked her.

'Yes, it bloody well did,' Graves said furiously.

Holly nodded. 'The feed-merchant told us. The cheque was cleared yesterday. He has his money.'

'Just what is all this?' Pollgate said heavily.

'You keep out of it,' Graves said rudely. 'It's you, Fielding, I want. You give me my bloody horses or I'll fetch the police to you.'

'Calm down, Mr Graves,' I said. 'You shall have your horses.'

'They're not in their boxes.' He glared with all his old fury; and it occurred to me that his total disregard of Pollgate was sublime. Perhaps one had to know one should be afraid of someone before one was.

'Mr Graves,' I said conversationally to the two proprietors and one journalist, 'is removing his horses because of what he read in Intimate Details. You see here in action the power of the Press.'

'Shut your trap and give me my horses,' Graves said.

'Yes, all right. Your grooms are going in the wrong direction.'

'Jasper,' Graves yelled. 'Come here.'

The luckless nephew approached, eyeing me warily.

'Come on,' I jerked my head. 'Round the back.'

Jay Erskine would have prevented my going, but Pollgate intervened. I took Jasper round to the other yard and pointed out the boxes that contained Graves's horses. 'Awfully sorry,' Jasper said.

'You're welcome,' I said, and I thought that but for him and his uncle we wouldn't have rigged the bell, and but for the bell we wouldn't have caught Jay Erskine up the ladder, and I felt quite grateful to the Graveses, on the whole.

I went back with Jasper walking behind me leading the first of the horses, and found them all standing there in much the same places, Jermyn Graves blustering on about not having faith when the trainer couldn't meet his bills.

'Bobby's better off without you, Mr Graves,' I said. 'Load your horses up and hop it.'

Apoplexy hovered. He opened and shut his mouth a couple of times and finally walked over to his trailer to let out his spleen on the luckless Jasper.

'Thank God for that,' Holly said. 'I can't stand him. I'm so glad you're here. Did you have a good time at your lunch?'

'Stunning,' I said.

They all heard and looked at me sharply.

Lord Vaughnley said, mystified, 'How can you laugh . . .?'

'What the hell,' I said. 'I'm here. I'm alive.'

Holly looked from one to the other of us, sensing something strongly, not knowing what. 'Something happened?' she said, searching my face.

I nodded a fraction. 'I'm OK.'

She said to Lord Vaughnley, 'He risks his life most days of the week. You can't frighten him much.'

They looked at her speechlessly, to my amusement.

I said to her, 'Do you know who you're talking to?'

and she shook her head slightly, half remembering but not sure.

'This is Lord Vaughnley who owns the *Towncrier*. This is Nestor Pollgate who owns the *Flag*. This is Jay Erskine who wrote the paragraphs in Intimate Details and put the tap on your telephone.' I paused, and to them I said, 'My sister, Bobby's wife.'

She moved closer beside me, her eyes shocked.

'Why are they here? Did you bring them?'

'We sort of brought each other,' I said. 'Where are Maynard and Bobby?'

'In the drawing room, I think.'

Jasper was crunching across the yard with the second horse, Jermyn shouting at him unabated. The other groom who had come with them was scurrying in and out of the trailer, attempting invisibility.

Nestor Pollgate said brusquely, 'We're not standing here watching all this.'

'I'm not leaving Holly alone to put up with that man,' I said. 'He's a menace. It's because of you that he's here, so we'll wait.'

Pollgate stirred restlessly, but there was nowhere particular for him to go. We waited in varying intensities of impatience while Jasper and the groom raised the ramp and clipped it shut, and while Jermyn Graves walked back several steps in our direction and shook his fist at me with the index finger sticking out, jabbing, and said no one messed with him and got away with it, and he'd see I'd be sorry. I'd pay for what I'd done.

'Kit,' Holly said, distressed.

I put my arm round her shoulders and didn't answer Graves, and after a while he turned abruptly on his heel, went over to his car, climbed in, slammed the door, and overburdened his engine, starting with a jerk that must have rocked his horses off their feet in the trailer.

'He's a pig,' Holly said. 'What will he do?'

'He's more threat than action.'

'I,' Pollgate said, 'am not.'

I looked at him, meeting his eyes.

'I do know that,' I said.

The time, I thought, had inescapably come.

Power when I needed it. Give me power, I thought.

I let go of Holly and leaned into the car we had come in, picking up my anorak off the floor.

I said to Holly, 'Will you take these three visitors into the sitting room? I'll get Bobby . . . and his father.'

She said with wide apprehensive eyes, 'Kit, do be careful.'

'I promise.'

She gave me a look of lingering doubt, but set off with me towards the house. We went in by long habit through the kitchen: I don't think it occurred to either of us to use the formal front door.

Pollgate, Lord Vaughnley and Jay Erskine followed, and in the hall Holly peeled them off into the sitting room, where in the evenings she and Bobby watched television sometimes. The larger drawing room lay ahead, and there were voices in there, or one voice, Maynard's, continuously talking.

I screwed up every inner resource to walk through that door, and it was a great and appalling mistake. Bobby told me afterwards that he saw me in the same way as in the stable and in the garden, the hooded, the enemy, the old foe of antiquity, of immense and dark threat.

Maynard was saying monotonously as if he had already said it over and over, '. . . And if you want to get rid of him you'll do it, and you'll do it today . . .'

Maynard was holding a gun, a hand gun, small and black.

He stopped talking the moment I went in there. His eyes widened. He saw, I supposed, what Bobby saw: Fielding, satanic.

He gave Bobby the pistol, pressing it into his hand.

'Do it,' he said fiercely. 'Do it now.'

His son's eyes were glazed, as in the garden.

He wouldn't do it. He couldn't . . .

'Bobby,' I said explosively, beseechingly: and he raised the gun and pointed it straight at my chest.

CHAPTER TWENTY

I turned my back on him.

I didn't want to see him do it; tear our lives apart, mine and his, and Holly's and the baby's. If he was going to do it, I wasn't going to watch.

Time passed, stretched out, uncountable. Danielle, I thought.

I heard his voice, close behind my shoulder.

'Kit . . .'

I stood rigidly still. You can't frighten him much, Holly had said. Bobby with a gun frightened me into immobility and despair.

He came round in front of me, as white as I felt. He looked into my face. He was holding the gun flat, not aiming, and put it into my hand.

'Forgive me,' he said.

I couldn't speak. He turned away blindly and made for the door. Holly appeared there, questioning, and he enfolded her and hugged her as if he had survived an earthquake, which he had.

I heard a faint noise behind me and turned, and

found Maynard advancing, his face sweating, his teeth showing, the charming image long gone. I turned holding the gun, and he saw it in my hand and went back a pace, and then another and another, looking fearful, looking sick.

'You incited,' I said bitterly, 'your own son to murder. Brainwashed him.'

'It would have been an accident,' he said.

'An Allardeck killing a Fielding would not have been believed as an accident.'

'I would have sworn it,' he said.

I loathed him. I said, 'Go into the sitting room,' and I stood back to let him pass, keeping the gun pointing his way all the while.

He hadn't had the courage to shoot me himself. Making Bobby do it . . . that crime was worse.

It hadn't been a good idea to draw him there with the express purpose of getting rid of me once and for all. He'd too nearly succeeded. My own stupid fault.

We went down the hall and into the sitting room. Pollgate and Erskine and Lord Vaughnley were all there, standing in the centre, with Bobby and Holly, still entwined, to one side. I went in there feeling I was walking into a cageful of tigers, and Holly said later that with the gun in my hand I looked so dangerous she hardly recognized me as her brother.

'Sit down,' I said. 'You,' I pointed to Maynard, 'over there in that chair at the end.' It was a deep chair, enveloping, no good for springing out of suddenly. 'You next, beside him,' I said to Erskine. 'Then Lord Vaughnley, on the sofa.'

Pollgate looked at the spare place beside Lord Vaughnley and took it in silence.

'Take out the stunner,' I said to him. 'Put it on the floor. Kick it this way.'

I could feel the refusal in him, see it in his eyes. Then he shrugged, and took out the flat black box, and did as I'd said.

'Right,' I said, 'you're all going to watch a video.' I glanced down at the pistol. 'I'm not a good shot. I don't know what I'd hit. So stay sitting down.' I held out the anorak in Bobby's direction. 'The tape's zipped into one of the pockets.'

'Put it on now?' he said, finding it and bringing it out. His hands were shaking, his voice unsteady. Damn Maynard, I thought.

'Yes, now,' I said. 'Holly, close the curtains and put on a lamp, it'll be dark before we're finished.'

No one spoke while she shut out the chilly day, while Bobby switched on the video machine and the television, and fed the tape into the slot. Pollgate looked moodily at the anorak which Bobby had laid on a chair and Lord Vaughnley glanced at the gun, and at my face, and away again.

'Ready,' Bobby said.

'Start it off,' I said, 'and you and Holly sit down and watch.'

I shut the door and leaned against it as Lord

Vaughnley had done in the Guineas, and Maynard's face came up bright and clear and smiling on the television screen.

He started to struggle up from his deep chair.

'Sit down,' I said flatly.

He must have guessed that what was coming was the tape he thought he'd suppressed. He looked at the gun in my hand and judged the distance he would have to cover to reach me, and he subsided into the cushions as if suddenly weak.

The interview progressed and went from smooth politeness into direct attack, and Lord Vaughnley's mouth slowly opened.

'You've not seen this before?' I said to him.

He said, 'No, no' with his gaze uninterruptedly on the screen, and I supposed that Rose wouldn't have seen any need to go running to the proprietor with her purloined tape, the two days she had had it in the *Towncrier* building.

I looked at all their faces as they watched. Maynard sick, Erskine blank, Lord Vaughnley riveted, Pollgate awakening to acute interest, Bobby and Holly horrified. Bobby, I thought ruefully, was in for some frightful shocks: it couldn't be much fun to find one's father had done so much cruel damage.

The interview finished, to be replaced by the Perrysides telling how they'd lost Metavane, with George Tarker and his son's suicide after, and Hugh Vaughnley, begging to go home; and finally Maynard again, smugly smiling.

The impact of it all on me was still great, and in the others produced something like suspended animation. Their expressions at the end of the hour and thirteen minutes were identical, of total absorption and stretched eyes, and I thought Joe would have been satisfied with the effect of his cutting, and of his hammer blow of final silence.

The trial was over: the accused, condemned. The sentence alone remained to be delivered.

The screen ran from black into snow, and no one moved.

I peeled myself off the door and walked across and switched off the set.

'Right,' I said, 'now listen.'

The eyes of all of them were looking my way with unadulterated concentration, Maynard's dark with humiliation, his body slack and deep in the chair.

'You,' I said to Lord Vaughnley, 'and you,' I said to Nestor Pollgate. 'You or your newspapers will each pay to Bobby the sum of fifty thousand pounds in compensation. You'll write promissory notes, here and now, in this room, in front of witnesses, to pay the money within three days, and those notes will be legal and binding.'

Lord Vaughnley and Nestor Pollgate simply stared.

'And in return,' I said, 'you shall have the wire-tap and the other evidence of Jay Erskine's criminal activity. You shall have complete silence from me about your various assaults on me and my property. You shall have back the draft for three thousand pounds now lodged in my bank manager's safe. And you shall have the tape you've just watched.'

Maynard said, 'No' in anguished protest, and no one took any notice.

'You,' I said to Maynard, 'will write a promissory note promising to pay to Bobby within three days the sum of two hundred and fifty thousand pounds, which will wipe out the overdrafts and the loans and mortgages on this house and stables, which you and your father made Bobby pay for, and which should rightfully be his by inheritance.'

Maynard's mouth opened, but no sound came out.

'You will also,' I said, 'give to Major and Mrs Perryside the one share you still own in Metavane.'

He began to shake his head weakly.

'And in return,' I said, 'you will have my assurance that many copies of this tape will not turn up simultaneously in droves of sensitive places, such as with the Senior Steward of the Jockey Club, or among the patrons of the civil service charity of which you are the new chairman, or in a dozen places in the City.' I paused. 'When Bobby has the money safe in the bank, you will be safe from me also. But that safety will always be conditional on your doing no harm either to Bobby and Holly or to me in future. The tapes will always exist.'

Maynard found his voice, hoarse and shaken.

'That's extortion,' he said aridly. 'It's blackmail.'

'It's justice,' I said.

There was silence. Maynard shrank as if deflated into the chair, and neither Pollgate nor Lord Vaughnley said anything at all.

'Bobby,' I said, 'take the tape out of the machine and out of this room and put it somewhere safe, and bring back some writing paper for the notes.'

Bobby stood up slowly, looking numb.

'You said we could have the tape,' Pollgate said, demurring.

'So you can, when Bobby's been paid. If the money's all safely in the bank by Friday, you shall have it then, along with Erskine's escape from going to jail.'

Bobby took the tape away, and I contemplated Pollgate's and Lord Vaughnley's expressionless faces and thought they were being a good deal too quiet. Maynard, staring at me blackly from his chair, was simple by comparison, his reactions expected. Erskine looked his usual chilling self, but without the smirk, which was an improvement.

Bobby came back with some large sheets of the headed writing paper he used for the bills for the owners, and gave a sheet each to Nestor Pollgate and Lord Vaughnley, and with stiff legs and an arm outstretched as far as it would go, gave the third to his father with his head turned away, not wanting to look at his face.

I surveyed the three of them sitting there stonily holding the blank sheets, and into my head floated various disjointed words and phrases.

'Wait,' I said. 'Don't write yet.'

The words were 'invalid', and 'obtained by menaces', and 'invalid by reason of having been extorted at gun-point'.

I wondered if the thought had come on its own or been generated somewhere else in that room, and I looked at their faces carefully, one by one, searching their eyes.

Not Maynard. Not Erskine. Not Lord Vaughnley.

Nestor Pollgate's eyelids flickered.

'Bobby,' I said, 'pick that black box up off the floor and drop it out of the window, into the garden.'

He looked bewildered, but did as I asked, the November air blowing in a great gust through the curtains into the room.

'Now the gun,' I said, and gave it to him.

He took it gingerly and threw it out, and shut the window again.

'Right,' I said, putting my hands with deliberation into my pockets, 'you've all heard the propositions. If you accept them, please write the notes.'

For a long moment no one moved. Then Lord Vaughnley stretched out an arm to the coffee table in front of him and picked up a magazine. He put the sheet of writing paper on the magazine for support. With a slightly pursed mouth but in continued quiet he lifted a pen from a pocket inside his jacket, pressed the top of it with a click, and wrote a short sentence, signing his name and adding the date.

He held it out towards Bobby, who stepped forward hesitantly and took it.

'Read it aloud,' I said.

Bobby's voice said shakily, 'I promise to pay Robertson Allardeck fifty thousand pounds within three days of this date.' He looked up at me. 'It is signed William Vaughnley, and the date is today's.'

I looked at Lord Vaughnley.

'Thank you,' I said neutrally.

He gave the supporting magazine to Nestor Pollgate, and offered his own pen. Nestor Pollgate took both with a completely unmoved face and wrote in his turn.

Bobby took the paper from him, glanced at me, and read aloud, 'I promise to pay Robertson Allardeck fifty thousand pounds within three days of this date. It's signed Nestor Pollgate. It's dated today.'

'Thank you,' I said to Pollgate.

Bobby looked slightly dazedly at the two documents he held. They would clear the debt for the unsold yearlings, I thought. When he sold them, anything he got would be profit.

Lord Vaughnley and Jay Erskine, as if in some ritual, passed the magazine and the pen along to Maynard.

With fury he wrote, the pen jabbing hard on the paper. I took the completed page from him myself and read it aloud, 'I promise to pay my son Robertson two hundred and fifty thousand pounds within three days. Maynard Allardeck. Today's date.'

I looked up at him. 'Thank you,' I said.

'Don't thank me. Your thanks are an insult.'

I was careful, in fact, to show no triumph, though in his case I did feel it: and I had to admit to myself ruefully that in that triumph there was a definite element of the old feud. A Fielding had got the better of an Allardeck, and I dared say my ancestors were gloating.

I gave Maynard's note to Bobby. It would clear all his debts and put him on a sure footing to earn a fair living as a trainer, and he held the paper unbelievingly, as if it would evaporate before his eyes.

'Well, gentlemen,' I said cheerfully, 'bankers' drafts by Friday, and you shall have the notes back, properly receipted.'

Maynard stood up, his greying fair hair still smooth, his face grimly composed, his expensive suit falling into uncreased shape; the outer shell intact, the man inside in shreds.

He looked at nobody, avoiding eyes. He walked to the door, opened it, went out, didn't look back. A silence lengthened behind his exit like the silence at the end of the tape; the enormity of Maynard struck one dumb.

Nestor Pollgate rose to his feet, tall, frowning, still with his power intact. He looked at me judiciously, gave me a brief single nod of the head, and said to Holly, 'Which way do I go out?'

'I'll show you,' she said, sounding subdued, and led the way into the hall.

Erskine followed, his face pinched, the drooping reddish moustache in some way announcing his continuing inflexible hatred of those he had damaged.

Bobby went after him, carrying his three notes carefully as if they were brittle, and Lord Vaughnley, last of all, stood up to go. He shook his head, shrugged his shoulders, spread his hands in a sort of embarrassment.

'What can I say?' he said. 'What am I to say when I see you on racecourses?'

'Good morning, Kit,' I said.

The grey eyes almost smiled before awkwardness returned. 'Yes, but,' he said, 'after what we did to you in the Guineas . . .'

I shrugged. 'Fortunes of war,' I said. 'I don't resent it, if that's what you mean. I took the war to the *Flag*. Seek the battle, don't complain of the wounds.'

He said curiously, 'Is that how you view race-riding? How you view life?'

'I hadn't thought of it, but yes, perhaps.'

'I'm sorry all the same,' he said. 'I had no idea what it would be like. Jay Erskine got the stun gun . . . he said two short shocks and you'd be putty. I don't think Nestor realized himself how bad it would be . . .'

'Yeah,' I said dryly, 'but he agreed to it.'

'That was because,' Lord Vaughnley explained with

a touch of earnestness, wanting me to understand, perhaps to absolve, 'because you ignored all his threats.'

'About prison?' I said.

He nodded. 'Sam Leggatt warned him you were intelligent . . . he said an attempt to frame you could blow up in their faces, that you would get the *Flag* and Nestor himself into deep serious gritty trouble . . . David Morse, their lawyer, was of the same opinion, so he agreed not to try. Sam Leggatt told me. But you have to understand Nestor. He doesn't like to be crossed. He said he wasn't going to be beaten by some . . . er . . . jockey.'

Expletives deleted, I thought, amused.

'You were elusive,' he said. 'Nestor was getting impatient . . .'

'And he had a tap on my telephone?'

'Er, yes.'

'Mm,' I said. 'Is it Maynard Allardeck who is trying to take over the *Towncrier*?'

He blinked, and said 'Er – ' and recovered. 'You guessed?'

'It seemed likely, Maynard got half of Hugh's shares by a trick. I thought it just might be him who was after the whole thing.'

Lord Vaughnley nodded. 'A company . . . Allardeck is behind it. When Hugh confessed, I got people digging up Allardeck's contacts. Just digging for dirt. I'd no idea until then that he owned the company . . . his name hadn't surfaced. All I knew was that it was the same company that nearly acquired the *Flag* a year ago. Very aggressive. It cost Nestor a fortune to cap their bid, far more than he would have had to pay otherwise.'

Holy wow, I thought.

'So when you found out that Maynard was the ultimate enemy,' I said, 'and knew also that he'd recently been proposed for a knighthood, you thought at least you could put paid to that, and casually asked Pollgate to do it in the *Flag*?'

'Not all that casually. Nestor said he'd be pleased to, if it was Allardeck who had cost him so much.'

'Didn't you even consider what hell you were manufacturing for Bobby?'

'Erskine found he couldn't get at Allardeck's phone system . . . they decided on his son.'

'Callous,' I said.

'Er . . . yes.'

'And appallingly spiteful to deliver all those copies to Bobby's suppliers.'

He said without much apology, 'Nestor thought the story would make more of a splash that way. Which it did.'

We began to walk from the sitting room into the hall. He'd told me what I hadn't asked: where the alliance began. In common enmity to Maynard, who had cost them both dear.

'Will you use the tape,' I asked, 'to stop Maynard now in his tracks?'

He glanced at me. 'That would be blackmail,' he said mildly.

'Absolutely.'

'Fifty thousand pounds,' he said. 'That tape's cheap at the price.'

We went into the kitchen and paused again.

'The *Towncrier* is the third newspaper,' he said, 'that has had trouble with Allardeck's company. One paper after another . . . he won't give up till he's got one.'

'He's obsessive,' I said. 'And besides, he's wanted all his life to have power over others . . . to be kowtowed to. To be a lord.'

Lord Vaughnley's mouth opened. I told him about my grandfather, and Maynard at nine. 'He hasn't changed,' I said. 'He still wants those things. Sir first, Lord after. And don't worry, he won't get them. I sent a copy of the tape to where you sent your charity letter.'

He was dumbstruck. He said weakly, 'How did you know about that letter?'

'I saw it,' I said. 'I was shown it. I wanted to know who knew Maynard might be up for a knighthood, and there it was, with your name.'

He shook his head: at life in general, it seemed.

We went on through the kitchen and out into the cold air. All the lights were on round the yard and some of the box doors were open, the lads working there in the routine of evening stables.

'Why did you try to stop me talking to Hugh?' I asked.

'I was wrong, I see that now. But at the time . . . by then you were pressing Nestor for large compensation. He wanted us simply to get back the wire-tap and shut you up.' He spread his hands. 'No one imagined, you see, that you would do all that you've done. I mean, when it was just a matter of disgracing Allardeck in the public eye, no one could have foreseen . . . no one even thought of your existence, let alone considered you a factor. No one knew you would defend your brother-in-law, or be . . . as you are.'

We walked across the yard to the car where Pollgate and Erskine were waiting, shadowy figures behind glass.

'If I were you,' I said, 'I'd find out if Maynard owns the bookmakers that Hugh bet with. If he does, you can threaten him with fraud, and get Hugh's shares back, I should think.'

We stopped a few feet from the car.

'You're generous,' he said.

We stood there, face to face, not knowing whether or not to shake hands.

'Hugh had no chance against Maynard,' I said.

'No.' He paused. 'I'll let him come home.'

He looked at me lengthily, the mind behind the grey eyes perhaps totting up, as I was, where we stood.

Even if he hadn't intended it, he had set in motion the attacks on Bobby; yet because of them Bobby would be much better off. From the dirt, gold.

If he offered his hand, I thought, I would take it.

Tentatively, unsure, that's what he did. I shook it briefly; an acknowledgement, a truce.

'See you at the races,' I said.

When they had gone I went and found the pistol and the stun gun outside the sitting-room window, and with them in my pockets returned to the kitchen, where Holly and Bobby were looking more dazed than happy.

'Tea?' I said hopefully.

They didn't seem to hear. I put the kettle on and got out some cups.

'Kit . . .' Holly said. 'Bobby told me . . .'

'Yeah . . . well . . . have you a lemon?' I said.

She dumbly fetched me one from the refrigerator, and sliced it.

Bobby said, 'I nearly killed you.'

His distress, I saw, was still blotting out any full realization – or celebration – of the change in his fortunes. He still looked pale, still gaunt round the eyes.

'But you didn't,' I said.

'No . . . when you turned your back on me, I thought, I can't shoot him in the back . . . not in the back . . . and I woke up. Like waking from a nightmare. I couldn't . . . how could I . . . I stood there with that gun, sweating at how near I'd come . . .'

'You frightened me silly,' I said. 'Let's forget it.'

'How can we?'

'Easily.' I punched his arm lightly. 'Concentrate, my old chum, on being a daddy.'

The kettle boiled and Holly made the tea; and we heard a car driving into the yard.

'They've come back,' Holly said in dismay.

We went out to see, all of us fearful.

The car was large and bewilderingly familiar. Two of its doors opened and from one came Thomas, the princess's chauffeur, in his best uniform, and from the other, scrambling and running, Danielle.

'Kit . . .' She ran headlong into my arms, her face screwed up with worry. 'Are you . . . are you really OK?'

'Yes, I am. You can see.'

She put her head on my shoulder and I held her close, and felt her trembling, and kissed her hair.

Thomas opened a third door of the car and helped out the princess, holding the sable coat for her to put on over the silk suit against the cold.

'I am glad, Kit,' she said calmly, snuggling into the fur, 'to see you are alive and well.' She looked from me to Bobby and Holly. 'You are Bobby, you are Holly, is that right?' She held out her hand to them, which they blankly shook.

'We are here,' she said, 'because my niece Danielle insisted that we come.' She was explaining, half apologizing for her presence. 'When I went home after the Icefall luncheon,' she said to me, 'Danielle was waiting on the pavement. She said you were in very great danger, and that you were at your sister's house in Newmarket. She didn't know how she knew, but she was certain. She said that we must come at once.'

Bobby and Holly looked astounded.

'As I know that with you, Kit, telepathy definitely exists,' the princess said, 'and as you had disappeared from the lunch and were reported to be ill, and as Danielle was distraught . . . we came. And I see she was right in part at least. You are here, at your sister's house.'

'She was right about the rest,' Holly said soberly. 'He was in that danger . . . a split second from dying.' She looked at my face. 'Did you think of her then?'

I swallowed. 'Yes, I did.'

'Holy wow,' Holly said.

'Kit says that too,' Danielle said, lifting her head from my neck and beginning to recover. 'It's awesome.'

'We always did,' Holly said. She looked at Danielle with growing interest and understanding, and slowly smiled with pleasure.

'She's like us, isn't she?' she said.

'I don't know,' I said. 'I've never known what she was thinking.'

'You might, after this'; and to Danielle, with friendship, she said, 'Think of something. See if he can tell what it is.'

'OK.'

There was a silence. The only thought in my head

was that telepathy was unpredictable and only sometimes worked to order.

I looked at the princess, and at Bobby and Holly, and saw in their faces the same hope, the same expectation, the same realization that this moment might matter in all our futures.

I smiled into Danielle's eyes. I knew, for a certainty.

'Dustsheets,' I said.

DICK FRANCIS

To the Hilt

£6.99

'Another one for the winner's enclosure'
Daily Telegraph

Alexander Kinloch found solitude and a steady income painting in a bothy on a remote Scottish mountain. Until the morning the strangers arrived to rough him up, and Alexander was dragged reluctantly back into the real and violent world he thought he had left behind.

Millions of pounds are missing from his stepfather's business. A valuable racehorse is under threat. Then comes the first ugly death and the end of all Alexander's doubts. For the honour of the Kinlochs he will face the strangers . . . committed up to the hilt . . .

'The book is a cracker . . . the former champion jockey is still taking jumps with consummate grace'
Sunday Telegraph

'Fast-moving, readable and beautifully constructed . . . a cracking yarn'
Country Life

DICK FRANCIS

Wild Horses

£6.99

'A marvellous storyteller and an immaculate craftsman'
Daily Mail

Movie director Thomas Lyon came to Newmarket to rake the ashes of an old Jockey Club scandal for a new Hollywood film. Too late, he found himself listening to a blacksmith's dying confession. Found himself watching as the past came violently back to life.

Capturing the shockwaves over one woman's macabre death nearly thirty years before is drama. But a frenzied knife attack on the set of *Unstable Times* is definitely attempted murder. Who stood to gain from the threats? Between truth and shadowy fiction, Thomas Lyon already knew too much.

Following the real story could mean the difference between life and death. His own . . .

'Still the best bet for a winning read'
Mail on Sunday

DICK FRANCIS

For Kicks

£5.99

'Absolutely first class . . . warmly recommended'
Sunday Times

Proprietor of a stud farm in the breathtaking region of Australia's Snowy Mountains? Or muck-raking stable boy in Yorkshire?

The Earl of October persuades young Australian Danny Roke to accept the English alternative. It's the change of scene and the challenge that pushes Danny undercover, on the scent of a suspected racehorse dope scandal.

But the pain involved, dealing with vicious swindlers and the Earl's two attractive daughters, could overturn all his pleasure in the chase . . .

'Very lively, hard-bitten account . . . some jolting action scenes'
Financial Times

DICK FRANCIS

In the Frame

£5.99

'A writer of champion class'
The Times

Charles Todd makes a living as a painter of horses. Someone else is making a lot more, forging paintings by masters such as Stubbs and Munnings. And selling them to people like Charles' cousin and his wife. People who usually end up dead.

When Charles arrives in Australia, he's not there for the surf at Bondi beach. He's right on the trail of the ruthless fraudsters, to whom violence and corruption are part of normal business practice. And he's right in the frame for murder . . .

'When the gloves are off it's very gritty indeed'
Daily Telegraph

Dick Francis

STRAIGHT

PAN BOOKS

First published in Great Britain 1989 by Michael Joseph Ltd

This edition published 1990 by Pan Books
an imprint of Pan Macmillan Ltd
Pan Macmillan, 20 New Wharf Road, London N1 9RR
Basingstoke and Oxford
www.panmacmillan.com

Associated companies throughout the world

In association with Michael Joseph

ISBN 0 330 31442 4

24 26 28 29 27 25

A CIP catalogue record for this book is available from
the British Library.

Phototypeset by Intype London Ltd
Printed and bound in Great Britain by
Mackays of Chatham PLC, Chatham, Kent

STRAIGHT

Dick Francis has written forty-one international bestsellers and is widely acclaimed as one of the world's finest thriller writers. His awards include the Crime Writers' Association's Cartier Diamond Dagger for his outstanding contribution to the crime genre, and an honorary Doctorate of Humane Letters from Tufts University of Boston. In 1996 Dick Francis was made a Mystery Writers of America Grand Master for a lifetime's achievement and in 2000 he received a CBE in the Queen's Birthday Honours list.

Also by Dick Francis in Pan Books

THE SPORT OF QUEENS
(autobiography)

LESTER: The Official
Biography

DEAD CERT
NERVE
FOR KICKS
ODDS AGAINST
FLYING FINISH
BLOOD SPORT
FORFEIT
ENQUIRY
RAT RACE
BONECRACK
SMOKESCREEN
SLAY-RIDE
KNOCK DOWN
HIGH STAKES
LONGSHOT
IN THE FRAME
RISK
TRIAL RUN
WHIP HAND
REFLEX
TWICE SHY
BANKER
THE DANGER
PROOF
BREAK IN
BOLT
HOT MONEY
THE EDGE
DRIVING FORCE
DECIDER
WILD HORSES
COME TO GRIEF
TO THE HILT
COMEBACK
10lb PENALTY
FIELD OF THIRTEEN
SECOND WIND
SHATTERED

My thanks especially to

JOSEPH and DANIELLE ZERGER
of ZARLENE IMPORTS
dealers in semi-precious stones

and also to

MARY BROMILEY – ankle specialist

BARRY PARK – veterinary surgeon

JEREMY THOMPSON – doctor, pharmacologist

ANDREW HEWSON – literary agent

and as always to

MERRICK and FELIX, our sons.

All the people in this story are imaginary.
All the gadgets exist.

CHAPTER ONE

I inherited my brother's life. Inherited his desk, his business, his gadgets, his enemies, his horses and his mistress. I inherited my brother's life, and it nearly killed me.

I was thirty-four at the time and walking about on elbow crutches owing to a serious disagreement with the last fence in a steeplechase at Cheltenham. If you've never felt your ankle explode, don't try it. As usual it hadn't been the high-speed tumble that had done the damage but the half-ton of one of the other runners coming over the fence after me, his forefoot landing squarely on my boot on the baked earth of an Indian summer. The hoof mark was imprinted on the leather. The doctor who cut the boot off handed it to me as a souvenir. Medical minds have a macabre sense of humour.

Two days after this occurrence, while I was reluctantly coming to terms with the fact that I was going to miss at least six weeks of the steeplechasing season and with them possibly my last chance of making it to champion again (the middle thirties being the beginning of the end for jump jockeys), I answered the telephone for about the tenth time that morning and found it was not another friend ringing to commiserate.

'Could I speak,' a female voice asked, 'to Derek Franklin?'

'I'm Derek Franklin,' I said.

'Right.' She was both brisk and hesitant, and one could understand why. 'We have you listed,' she said, 'as your brother Greville's next of kin.'

Those three words, I thought with an accelerating heart, must be among the most ominous in the language.

I said slowly, not wanting to know, 'What's happened?'

'I'm speaking from St Catherine's Hospital, Ipswich. Your brother is here, in the intensive care unit . . .'

At least he was alive, I thought numbly.

'. . . and the doctors think you should be told.'

'How is he?'

'I'm sorry I haven't seen him. This is the almoner's office. But I understand that his condition is very serious.'

'What's the matter with him?'

'He was involved in an accident,' she said. 'He has multiple injuries and is on life support.'

'I'll come,' I said.

'Yes. It might be best.'

I thanked her, not knowing exactly what for, and put

down the receiver, taking the shock physically in light-headedness and a constricted throat.

He would be all right, I told myself. Intensive care meant simply that he was being carefully looked after. He would recover, of course.

I shut out the anxiety to work prosaically instead on the practicalities of getting from Hungerford in Berkshire, where I lived, to Ipswich in Suffolk, about a hundred and fifty miles across country, with a crunched ankle. It was fortunately the left ankle, which meant I would soon be able to drive my automatic gears without trouble, but it was on that particular day at peak discomfort and even with painkillers and icepacks was hot, swollen and throbbing. I couldn't move it without holding my breath, and that was partly my own fault.

Owing to my hatred – not to say phobia – about the damaging immobility of plaster of Paris I had spent a good deal of the previous day persuading a long-suffering orthopaedic surgeon to give me the support of a plain crêpe bandage instead of imprisonment in a cast. He was himself a plate-and-screw man by preference and had grumbled as usual at my request. Such a bandage as I was demanding might be better in the end for one's muscles, but it gave no protection against knocks, as he had reminded me on other occasions, and it would be more painful, he said.

'I'll be racing much quicker with a bandage.'

'It's time you stopped breaking your bones,' he said, giving in with a shrug and a sigh and obligingly winding the crêpe on tightly. 'One of these days you'll crack something serious.'

'I don't actually like breaking them.'

'At least I haven't had to pin anything this time,' he said. 'And you're mad.'

'Yes. Thanks very much.'

'Go home and rest it. Give those ligaments a chance.'

The ligaments took their chance along the back seat of my car while Brad, an unemployed welder, drove it to Ipswich. Brad, taciturn and obstinate, was unemployed by habit and choice but made a scratchy living doing odd jobs in the neighbourhood for anyone willing to endure his moods. As I much preferred his long silences to his infrequent conversation, we got along fine. He looked forty, hadn't reached thirty, and lived with his mother.

He found St Catherine's Hospital without much trouble and at the door helped me out and handed me the crutches, saying he would park and sit inside the reception area and I could take my time. He had waited for me similarly for hours the day before, expressing neither impatience nor sympathy but simply being restfully and neutrally morose.

The intensive care unit proved to be guarded by brisk nurses who looked at the crutches and said I'd come to the wrong department, but once I'd persuaded them of my identity they kitted me sympathetically with a mask and gown and let me in to see Greville.

I had vaguely expected Intensive Care to involve a

lot of bright lights and clanging bustle, but I found that it didn't, or at least not in that room in that hospital. The light was dim, the atmosphere peaceful, the noise level, once my ears adjusted to it, just above silence but lower than identification.

Greville lay alone in the room on a high bed with wires and tubes all over the place. He was naked except for a strip of sheeting lying loosely across his loins and they had shaved half the hair off his head. Other evidences of surgery marched like centipede tracks across his abdomen and down one thigh, and there were darkening bruises everywhere.

Behind his bed a bank of screens showed blank rectangular faces, as the information from the electrodes fed into other screens in a room directly outside. He didn't need, they said, an attendant constantly beside him, but they kept an eye on his reactions all the time.

He was unconscious, his face pale and calm, his head turned slightly towards the door as if expecting visitors. Decompression procedures had been performed on his skull, and that wound was covered by a large padded dressing which seemed more like a pillow to support him.

Greville Saxony Franklin, my brother. Nineteen years my senior: not expected to live. It had to be faced. To be accepted.

'Hi, guy,' I said.

It was an Americanism he himself used often, but it produced no response. I touched his hand, which was warm and relaxed, the nails, as always, clean and cared for. He had a pulse, he had circulation: his heart beat by electrical stimulus. Air went in and out of his lungs mechanically through a tube in his throat. Inside his head the synapses were shutting down. Where was his soul, I wondered: where was the intelligent, persistent, energetic spirit? Did he know that he was dying?

I didn't want just to leave him. No one should die alone. I went outside and said so.

A doctor in a green overall replied that when all the remaining brain activity had ceased, they would ask my consent before switching off the machines. I was welcome to be with my brother at this crisis point as well as before. 'But death,' he said austerely, 'will be for him an infinitesimal process, not a definitive moment.' He paused. 'There is a waiting room along the hall, with coffee and things.'

Bathos and drama, I thought: his everyday life. I crutched all the way down to the general reception area, found Brad, gave him an update and told him I might be a long time. All night, perhaps.

He waved a permissive hand. He would be around, he said, or he would leave a message at the desk. Either way, I could reach him. I nodded and went back upstairs, and found the waiting room already occupied by a very young couple engulfed in grief, whose baby was hanging on to life by threads not much stronger than Greville's.

The room itself was bright, comfortable and impersonal, and I listened to the mother's slow sobs and thought of the misery that soaked daily into those walls. Life has a way of kicking one along like a football, or so I've found. Fate had never dealt me personally a particularly easy time, but that was OK, that was normal. Most people, it seemed to me, took their turn to be football. Most survived. Some didn't.

Greville had simply been in the wrong place at the wrong time. From the scrappy information known to the hospital, I gleaned that he had been walking down Ipswich High Street when some scaffolding that was being dismantled had fallen on him from a considerable height. One of the construction workers had been killed, and a second had been taken to hospital with a broken hip.

I had been given my brother's clinical details. One metal bar had pierced his stomach, another had torn into his leg, something heavy had fallen on his head and caused brain damage with massive cerebral bleeding. It had happened late the previous afternoon, he had been deeply unconscious from the moment of the impact and he hadn't been identified until workmen dealing with the rubble in the morning had found his diary and given it to the police.

'Wallet?' I asked.

No, no wallet. Just the diary with, neatly filled in on the first page, next of kin, Derek Franklin, brother; telephone number supplied. Before that, they had no clue except the initials G.S.F. embroidered above the pocket of his torn and blood-stained shirt.

'A *silk* shirt,' a nurse added disapprovingly, as if monogrammed silk shirts were somehow immoral.

'Nothing else in his pockets?' I asked.

'A bunch of keys and a handkerchief. That was all. You'll be given them, of course, along with the diary and his watch and signet ring.'

I nodded. No need to ask when.

The afternoon stretched out, strange and unreal, a time-warped limbo. I went again to spend some time with Greville, but he lay unmoving, oblivious in his dwindling twilight, already subtly not himself. If Wordsworth were right about immortality, it was the sleep and the forgetting that were slipping away and reawakening that lay ahead, and maybe I should be glad for him, not grieve.

I thought of him as he had been, and of our lives as brothers. We had never lived together in a family unit because, by the time I was born, he was away at university, building a life of his own. By the time I was six, he had married, by the time I was ten, he'd divorced. For years he was a semi-stranger whom I met briefly at family gatherings, celebrations which grew less and less frequent as our parents aged and died, and which stopped altogether when the two sisters who bridged the gap between Greville and me both emigrated, one to Australia and one to Japan.

It wasn't until I'd reached twenty-eight myself that

after a long Christmas-and-birthday-card politeness we'd met unexpectedly on a railway platform and during the journey ahead had become friends. Not close time-sharing friends even then, but positive enough for telephoning each other sporadically and exchanging restaurant dinners and feeling good about it.

We had been brought up in different environments, Greville in the Regency London house which went with our father's job as manager of one of the great landowning estates, I in the comfortable country cottage of his retirement. Greville had been taken by our mother to museums, art galleries and the theatre: I had been given ponies.

We didn't even look much alike. Greville, like our father, was six feet tall, I three inches shorter. Greville's hair, now greying, had been light brown and straight, mine darker brown and curly. We had both inherited amber eyes and good teeth from our mother and a tendency to leanness from our father, but our faces, though both tidy enough, were quite different.

Greville best remembered our parents' vigorous years; I'd been with them through their illnesses and deaths. Our father had himself been twenty years older than our mother, and she had died first, which had seemed monstrously unfair. The old man and I had lived briefly together after that in tolerant mutual non-comprehension, though I had no doubt that he'd loved me, in his way. He had been sixty-two when I was born and he died on my eighteenth birthday, leaving me a fund for my continued education and a letter of admonitions and instructions, some of which I'd carried out.

Greville's stillness was absolute. I shifted uncomfortably on the crutches and thought of asking for a chair. I wouldn't see him smile again, I thought: not the lightening of the eyes and the gleam of teeth, the quick appreciation of the black humour of life, the awareness of his own power.

He was a magistrate, a justice of the peace, and he imported and sold semi-precious stones. Beyond these bare facts I knew few details of his day-to-day existence, as whenever we met it seemed that he was always more interested in my doings than his own. He had himself owned horses from the day he telephoned to ask my opinion: someone who owed him money had offered his racehorse to settle the debt. What did I think? I told him I'd phone back, looked up the horse, thought it was a bargain and told Greville to go right ahead if he felt like it.

'Don't see why not,' he'd said. 'Will you fix the paperwork?'

I'd said yes, of course. It wasn't hard for anyone to say yes to my brother Greville: much harder to say no.

The horse had won handsomely and given him a taste for future ownership, though he seldom went to see his horses run, which wasn't particularly unusual in an owner but always to me mystifying. He refused absolutely to own jumpers on the grounds that he might buy something that would kill me. I was too big for Flat races; he'd felt safe with those. I couldn't persuade him that I would like to ride for him and in the end I stopped trying. When Greville made up his mind he was unshakable.

Every ten minutes or so a nurse would come quietly into the room to stand for a short while beside the bed, checking that all the electrodes and tubes were still in order. She gave me brief smiles and commented once that my brother was unaware of my presence and could not be comforted by my being there.

'It's as much for me as for him,' I said.

She nodded and went away, and I stayed for a couple more hours, leaning against a wall and reflecting that it was ironic that it was he who should meet death by chance when it was I who actively risked it half the days of the year.

Strange to reflect also, looking back now to that lengthening evening, that I gave no thought to the consequences of his death. The present was vividly alive still in the silent diminishing hours, and all I saw in the future was a pretty dreary programme of form-filling and funeral arrangements, which I didn't bother to think about in any detail. I would have to telephone the sisters, I vaguely supposed, and there might be a little long-distance grief, but I knew they would say, 'You can see to it, can't you? Whatever you decide will be all right with us,' and they wouldn't come back halfway round the world to stand in mournful drizzle at the graveside of a brother they'd seen perhaps twice in ten years.

Beyond that, I considered nothing. The tie of common blood was all that truly linked Greville and me, and once it was undone there would be nothing left of him but memory. With regret I watched the pulse that flickered in his throat. When it was gone I would go back to my own life and think of him warmly sometimes, and remember this night with overall sorrow, but no more.

I went along to the waiting room for a while to rest my legs. The desperate young parents were still there, hollow-eyed and entwined, but presently a sombre nurse came to fetch them, and in the distance, shortly after, I heard the rising wail of the mother's agonized loss. I felt my own tears prickle for her, a stranger. A dead baby, a dying brother, a universal uniting misery. I grieved for Greville most intensely then because of the death of the child, and realized I had been wrong about the sorrow level. I would miss him very much.

I put my ankle up on a chair and fitfully dozed, and sometime before daybreak the same nurse with the same expression came to fetch me in my turn.

I followed her along the passage and into Greville's room. There was much more light in there this time, and more people, and the bank of monitoring screens behind the bed had been switched on. Pale greenish lines moved across them, some in regular spasms, some uncompromisingly straight.

I didn't need to be told, but they explained all the same. The straight lines were the sum of the activity in Greville's brain. None at all.

There was no private goodbye. There was no point. I was there, and that was enough. They asked for, and received, my agreement to the disconnection of the machines, and presently the pulsing lines straightened out also, and whatever had been in the quiet body was there no longer.

It took a long time to get anything done in the morning because it turned out to be Sunday.

I thought back, having lost count of time. Thursday when I broke my ankle, Friday when the scaffolding fell on Greville, Saturday when Brad drove me to Ipswich. It all seemed a cosmos away: relativity in action.

There was the possibility, it seemed, of the scaffolding constructors being liable for damages. It was suggested that I should consult a solicitor.

Plodding through the paperwork, trying to make decisions, I realized that I didn't know what Greville would want. If he'd left a will somewhere, maybe he had given instructions that I ought to carry out. Maybe no one but I, I thought with a jolt, actually knew he was dead. There had to be people I should notify, and I didn't know who.

I asked if I could have the diary the police had found in the rubble, and presently I was given not only the diary but everything else my brother had had with him: keys, watch, handkerchief, signet ring, a small amount of change, shoes, socks, jacket. The rest of his clothes, torn and drenched with blood, had been incinerated, it appeared. I was required to sign for what I was taking, putting a tick against each item.

Everything had been tipped out of the large brown plastic bag in which they had been stored. The bag said 'St Catherine's Hospital' in white on the sides. I put the shoes, socks, handkerchief and jacket back into the bag and pulled the strings tight again, then I shovelled the large bunch of keys into my own trouser pocket, along with the watch, the ring and the money, and finally consulted the diary.

On the front page he had entered his name, his London home telephone number and his office number, but no addresses. It was near the bottom, where there was a space headed 'In case of accident please notify', that he had written 'Derek Franklin, brother, next of kin.'

The diary itself was one I had sent him at Christmas: the racing diary put out by the Jockeys' Association and the Injured Jockeys' Fund. That he should have chosen to use that particular diary when he must have been given several others I found unexpectedly moving. That he had put my name in it made me wonder what he had really thought of me; whether there was much we might have been to each other, and had missed.

With regret I put the diary into my other trouser pocket. The next morning, I supposed, I would have to telephone his office with the dire news. I couldn't forewarn anyone as I didn't know the names, let alone the phone numbers, of the people who worked for him. I knew only that he had no partners, as he had said several times that the only way he could run his business was by himself. Partners too often came to blows, he said, and he would have none of it.

When all the signing was completed, I looped the strings of the plastic bag a couple of times round my wrist and took it and myself on the crutches down to the reception area, which was more or less deserted on that early Sunday morning. Brad wasn't there, nor was there any message from him at the desk, so I simply sat down and waited. I had no doubt he would come back in his own good time, glowering as usual, and eventually he did, slouching in through the door with no sign of haste.

He saw me across the acreage, came to within ten feet, and said, 'Shall I fetch the car, then?' and when I nodded, wheeled away and departed. A man of very few words, Brad. I followed slowly in his wake, the plastic bag bumping against the crutch. If I'd thought faster I would have given it to Brad to carry, but I didn't seem to be thinking fast in any way.

Outside, the October sun was bright and warm. I breathed the sweet air, took a few steps away from the door and patiently waited some more, and was totally unprepared to be savagely mugged.

I scarcely saw who did it. One moment I was upright, leaning without concentration on the crutches, the next I'd received a battering-ram shove in the back and was sprawling face forward onto the hard black surface of the entrance drive. To try to save myself, I put my left foot down instinctively and it twisted beneath me, which was excruciating and useless. I fell flat down on my stomach in a haze and I hardly cared when someone kicked one of the fallen crutches away along the ground and tugged at the bag around my wrist.

He . . . it had to be a he, I thought, from the speed and strength . . . thumped a foot down on my back and put his weight on it. He yanked my arm up and back roughly, and cut through the plastic with a slash that took some of my skin with it. I scarcely felt it. The messages from my ankle obliterated all else.

A voice approached saying, 'Hey! Hey!' urgently, and my attacker lifted himself off me as fast as he'd arrived and sped away.

It was Brad who had come to my rescue. On any other day there might have been people constantly coming and going, but not on Sunday morning. No one else seemed to be around to notice a thing. No one but Brad had come running.

'Friggin' hell,' Brad said from above me. 'Are you all right?'

Far from it, I thought.

He went to fetch the scattered crutch and brought it

back. 'Your hand's bleeding,' he said with disbelief. 'Don't you want to stand up?'

I wasn't too sure that I did, but it seemed the only thing to do. When I'd made it to a moderately vertical position he looked impassively at my face and gave it as his opinion that we ought to go back into the hospital. As I didn't feel like arguing, that's what we did.

I sat on the end of one of the empty rows of seats and waited for the tide of woe to recede, and when I had more command of things I went across to the desk and explained what had happened.

The woman behind the reception window was horrified.

'Someone stole your plastic bag!' she said, round-eyed. 'I mean, everyone around here knows what those bags signify, they're always used for the belongings of people who've died or come here after accidents. I mean, everyone knows they can contain wallets and jewellery and so on, but I've never heard of one being snatched. How awful! How much did you lose? You'd better report it to the police.'

The futility of it shook me with weariness. Some punk had taken a chance that the dead man's effects would be worth the risk, and the police would take notes and chalk it up among the majority of unsolved muggings. I reckoned I'd fallen into the ultra-vulnerable bracket which included little old ladies, and however much I might wince at the thought, I on my crutches had looked and been a pushover, literally.

I shuffled painfully into the washroom and ran cold water over my slowly bleeding hand, and found that the cut was more extensive than deep and could sensibly be classified as a scratch. With a sigh, I dabbed a paper towel on the scarlety oozing spots and unwound the cut-off pieces of white and brown plastic which were still wrapped tightly round my wrist, throwing them in the bin. What a bloody stupid anti-climactic postscript, I thought tiredly, to the accident that had taken my brother.

When I went outside Brad said with a certain amount of anxiety, 'You going to the police, then?' and he relaxed visibly when I shook my head and said, 'Not unless you can give them a detailed description of who-ever attacked me.'

I couldn't tell from his expression whether he could or not. I thought I might ask him later, on the way home, but when I did, all that he said was, 'He had jeans on, and one of them woolly hats. And he had a knife. I didn't see his face, he sort of had his back turned my way, but the sun flashed on the knife, see? It all went down so fast. I did think you were a goner. Then he ran off with the bag. You were dead lucky, I'd say.'

I didn't feel lucky, but all things were relative.

Brad, having contributed what was for him a long speech, relapsed into his more normal silence, and I wondered what the mugger would think of the worth-less haul of shoes, socks, handkerchief and jacket whose loss hadn't been realistically worth reporting. Whatever of value Greville had set out with would have been in his wallet, which had fallen to an earlier predator.

I had been wearing, was still wearing, a shirt, tie and sweater, but no jacket. A sweater was better with the crutches than a jacket. It was pointless to wonder whether the thief would have dipped into my trouser pockets if Brad hadn't shouted. Pointless to wonder if he would have put his blade through my ribs. There was no way of knowing. I did know I couldn't have stopped him, but his prize in any case would have been meagre. Apart from Greville's things I was carrying only a credit card and a few notes in a small folder, from a habit of travelling light.

I stopped thinking about it and instead, to take my mind off the ankle, wondered what Greville had been doing in Ipswich.

Wondered if, ever since Friday, anyone had been waiting for him to arrive. Wondered how he had got there. Wondered if he had parked his car somewhere there and, if so, how I would find it, considering I didn't know its number and wasn't even sure if he still had a Porsche. Someone else would know, I thought easily. His office, his local garage, a friend. It wasn't really my worry.

By the time we reached Hungerford three hours later, Brad had said, in addition, only that the car was running out of juice (which we remedied) and, half an hour from home, that if I wanted him to go on driving me during the following week, he would be willing.

'Seven-thirty tomorrow morning?' I suggested, reflecting, and he said 'Yerss' on a growl which I took to mean assent.

He drove me to my door, helped me out as before, handed me the crutches, locked the car and put the keys into my hand all without speaking.

'Thanks,' I said.

He ducked his head, not meeting my eyes, and turned and shambled off on foot towards his mother's house. I watched him go; a shy difficult man with no social skills who had possibly that morning saved my life.

CHAPTER TWO

I had for three years rented the ground floor of an old house in a turning off the main road through the ancient country town. There was a bedroom and bathroom facing the street and the sunrise, and a large all-purpose room to the rear into which the sunset flooded. Beyond that, a small stream-bordered garden which I shared with the owners of the house, an elderly couple upstairs.

Brad's mother had cooked and cleaned for them for years; Brad mended, painted and chopped when he felt like it. Soon after I'd moved in, mother and son had casually extended their services to me, which suited me well. It was all in all an easy uncluttered existence, but if home was where the heart was, I really lived out on the windy Downs and in stable yards and on the raucous racetracks where I worked.

I let myself into the quiet rooms and sat with ice-packs along a sofa, watching the sun go down on the far side of the stream and thinking I might have done better to stay in the Ipswich hospital. From the knee down my left leg was hurting abominably, and it was still getting clearer by the minute that falling had intensified Thursday's damage disastrously. My own surgeon had been going off to Wales for the weekend, but I doubted that he would have done very much except say 'I told you so', so in the end I simply took another Distalgesic and changed the icepacks and worked out the time zones in Tokyo and Sydney.

At midnight I telephoned to those cities where it was already morning and by good luck reached both of the sisters. 'Poor Greville,' they said sadly, and, 'Do whatever you think best.' 'Send some flowers for us.' 'Let us know how it goes.'

I would, I said. Poor Greville, they repeated, meaning it, and said they would love to see me in Tokyo, in Sydney, whenever. Their children, they said, were all fine. Their husbands were fine. Was I fine? Poor, poor Greville.

I put the receiver down ruefully. Families did scatter, and some scattered more than most. I knew the sisters by that time only through the photographs they sometimes sent at Christmas. They hadn't recognized my voice.

Taking things slowly in the morning, as nothing was much better, I dressed for the day in shirt, tie and sweater as before, with a shoe on the right foot, sock alone on the left, and was ready when Brad arrived five minutes early.

'We're going to London,' I said. 'Here's a map with the place marked. Do you think you can find it?'

'Got a tongue in my head,' he said, peering at the maze of roads. 'Reckon so.'

'Give it a go, then.'

He nodded, helped me inch onto the back seat, and drove seventy miles through the heavy morning traffic in silence. Then, by dint of shouting at street vendors via the driver's window, he zig-zagged across Holborn, took a couple of wrong turns, righted himself, and drew up with a jerk in a busy street round the corner from Hatton Garden.

'That's it,' he said, pointing. 'Number fifty-six. That office block.'

'Brilliant.'

He helped me out, gave me the crutches, and came with me to hold open the heavy glass entrance door. Inside, behind a desk, was a man in a peaked cap personifying security who asked me forbiddingly what floor I wanted.

'Saxony Franklin,' I said.

'Name?' he asked, consulting a list.

'Franklin.'

'Your name, I mean.'

I explained who I was. He raised his eyebrows, picked up a telephone, pressed a button and said, 'A Mr Franklin is on his way up.'

Brad asked where he could park the car and was told

there was a yard round the back. He would wait for me, he said. No hurry. No problem.

The office building, which was modern, had been built rubbing shoulders to the sixth floor with Victorian curlicued neighbours, soaring free to the tenth with a severe lot of glass.

Saxony Franklin was on the eighth floor, it appeared. I went up in a smooth lift and elbowed my way through some heavy double doors into a lobby furnished with a reception desk, several armchairs for waiting in and two policemen.

Behind the policemen was a middle-aged woman who looked definitely flustered.

I thought immediately that news of Greville's death had already arrived and that I probably hadn't needed to come, but it seemed the Force was there for a different reason entirely.

The flustered lady gave me a blank stare and said, 'That's not Mr Franklin. The guard said Mr Franklin was on his way up.'

I allayed the police suspicions a little by saying again that I was Greville Franklin's brother.

'Oh,' said the woman. 'Yes, he does have a brother.'

They all swept their gaze over my comparative immobility.

'Mr Franklin isn't here yet,' the woman told me.

'Er . . .' I said, 'what's going on?'

They all looked disinclined to explain. I said to her, 'I'm afraid I don't know your name.'

'Adams,' she said distractedly. 'Annette Adams. I'm your brother's personal assistant.'

'I'm sorry,' I said slowly, 'but my brother won't be coming at all today. He was involved in an accident.'

Annette Adams heard the bad news in my voice. She put a hand over her heart in the classic gesture as if to hold it still in her chest and with anxiety said, 'What sort of accident? A car crash? Is he hurt?'

She saw the answer clearly in my expression and with her free hand felt for one of the armchairs, buckling into it with shock.

'He died in hospital yesterday morning,' I said to her and to the policemen, 'after some scaffolding fell on him last Friday. I was with him in the hospital.'

One of the policemen pointed at my dangling foot. 'You were injured at the same time, sir?'

'No. This was different. I didn't see his accident. I meant, I was there when he died. The hospital sent for me.'

The two policemen consulted each other's eyes and decided after all to say why they were there.

'These offices were broken into during the weekend, sir. Mrs Adams here discovered it when she arrived early for work, and she called us in.'

'What does it matter? It doesn't matter now,' the lady said, growing paler.

'There's a good deal of mess,' the policeman went on, 'and Mrs Adams doesn't know what's been stolen. We were waiting for your brother to tell us.'

'Oh dear, oh dear,' said Annette, gulping.

'Is there anyone else here?' I asked her. 'Someone who could get you a cup of tea?' Before you faint, I thought, but didn't say it.

She nodded a fraction, glancing at a door behind the desk, and I swung over there and tried to open it. It wouldn't open: the knob wouldn't turn.

'It's electronic,' Annette said weakly. 'You have to put in the right numbers . . .' She flopped her head back against the chair and said she couldn't remember what today's number was; it was changed often. She and the policemen had come through it, it seemed, and let it swing shut behind them.

One of the policemen came over and pounded on the door with his fist, shouting 'Police' very positively which had the desired effect like a reflex. Without finesse he told the much younger woman who stood there framed in the doorway that her boss was dead and that Mrs Adams was about to pass out and was needing some strong hot sweet tea, love, like five minutes ago.

Wild-eyed, the young woman retreated to spread more consternation behind the scenes and the policeman nullified the firm's defences by wedging the electronic door open, using the chair from behind the reception desk.

I took in a few more details of the surroundings, beyond my first impression of grey. On the light greenish-grey of the carpet stood the armchairs in charcoal and the desk in matt black unpainted and unpolished wood. The walls, palest grey, were hung with a series of framed geological maps, the frames black and narrow and uniform in size. The propped-open door, and another similar door to one side, still closed, were painted the same colour as the walls. The total effect, lit by recessed spotlights in the ceiling, looked both straightforward and immensely sophisticated, a true representation of my brother.

Mrs Annette Adams, still flaccid from too many unpleasant surprises on a Monday morning, wore a cream shirt, a charcoal grey skirt and a string of knobbly pearls. She was dark haired, in her late forties, perhaps, and from the starkness in her eyes, just beginning to realize, I guessed, that the upheaval of the present would be permanent.

The younger woman returned effectively with a scarlet steaming mug and Annette Adams sipped from it obediently for a while, listening to the policemen telling me that the intruder had not come in this way up the front lift, which was for visitors, but up another lift at the rear of the building which was used by the staff of all floors of offices, and for freight. That lift went down into a rear lobby which, in its turn, led out to the yard where cars and vans were parked: where Brad was presumably waiting at that moment.

The intruder had apparently ridden to the tenth floor, climbed some service stairs to the roof, and by some means had come down outside the building to the eighth floor, where he had smashed a window to let himself in.

'What sort of means?' I asked.

'We don't know, sir. Whatever it was, he took it with him. Maybe a rope.' He shrugged. 'We've had only a quick preliminary look around up there. We wanted to know what's been stolen before we . . . er . . . See, we don't want to waste our time for nothing.'

I nodded. Like Greville's stolen shoes, I thought.

'This whole area round Hatton Garden is packed with the jewel trade. We get break-ins, or attempted break-ins, all the time.'

The other policeman said, 'This place here is loaded with stones, of course, but the vault's still shut and Mrs Adams says nothing seems to be missing from the other stock-rooms. Only Mr Franklin has a key to the vault which is where their more valuable faceted stones are kept.'

Mr Franklin had no keys at all. Mr Franklin's keys were in my own pocket. There was no harm, I supposed, in producing them.

The sight of what must have been a familiar bunch brought tears to Annette Adams's eyes. She put down the mug, searched around for a tissue and cried, 'He really is dead, then,' as if she hadn't thoroughly believed it before.

When she'd recovered a little I asked her to point out the vault key, which proved to be the longest and slenderest of the lot, and shortly afterwards we were all walking through the propped-open door and down a central corridor with spacious offices opening to either side. Faces showing shock looked out at our passing. We stopped at an ordinary-looking door which might have been mistaken for a cupboard and certainly looked nothing like a vault.

'That's it,' Annette Adams insisted, nodding; so I slid the narrow key into the small ordinary keyhole, and found that it turned unexpectedly anti-clockwise. The thick and heavy door swung inwards to the right under pressure and a light came on automatically, shining in what did indeed seem exactly like a large walk-in cupboard, with rows of white cardboard boxes on several plain white-painted shelves stretching away along the left-hand wall.

Everyone looked in silence. Nothing seemed to have been disturbed.

'Who knows what should be in the boxes?' I asked, and got the expected answer: my brother.

I took a step into the vault and took the lid off one of the nearest boxes which bore a sticky label saying $MgA1_20_4$, Burma. Inside the box there were about a dozen glossy white envelopes, each taking up the whole width. I lifted one out to open it.

'Be careful!' Annette Adams exclaimed, fearful of my clumsiness as I balanced on the crutches. 'The packets unfold.'

I handed to her the one I held, and she unfolded it carefully on the palm of her hand. Inside, cushioned by white tissue, lay two large red translucent stones, cut and polished, oblong in shape, almost pulsing with intense colour under the lights.

'Are they rubies?' I asked, impressed.

Annette Adams smiled indulgently. 'No, they're spinel. Very fine specimens. We rarely deal in rubies.'

'Are there any diamonds in here?' one of the policemen asked.

'No, we don't deal in diamonds. Almost never.'

I asked her to look into some of the other boxes, which she did, first carefully folding the two red stones into their packet and restoring them to their right place. We watched her stretch and bend, tipping up random lids on several shelves to take out a white packet here and there for inspection, but there were clearly no dismaying surprises, and at the end she shook her head and said that nothing at all was missing, as far as she could see.

'The real value of these stones is in quantity,' she said. 'Each individual stone isn't worth a fortune. We sell stones in tens and hundreds . . .' Her voice trailed off into a sort of forlornness. 'I don't know what to do,' she said, 'about the orders.'

The policemen weren't affected by the problem. If nothing was missing, they had other burglaries to look into, and they would put in a report, but goodbye for now, or words to that effect.

When they'd gone, Annette Adams and I stood in the passage and looked at each other.

'What do I do?' she said. 'Are we still in business?'

I didn't like to tell her that I hadn't the foggiest notion. I said, 'Did Greville have an office?'

'That's where most of the mess is,' she said, turning away and retracing her steps to a large corner room near the entrance lobby. 'In here.'

I followed her and saw what she meant about mess. The contents of every wide-open drawer seemed to be out on the floor, most of it paper. Pictures had been removed from the walls and dropped. One filing cabinet lay on its side like a fallen soldier. The desk top was a shambles.

'The police said the burglar was looking behind the pictures for a safe. But there isn't one . . . just the vault.' She sighed unhappily. 'It's all so pointless.'

I looked around. 'How many people work here altogether?' I said.

'Six of us. And Mr Franklin, of course.' She swallowed. 'Oh dear.'

'Mm,' I agreed. 'Is there anywhere I can meet everyone?'

She nodded mutely and led the way into another large office where three of the others were already gathered, wide-eyed and rudderless. Another two came when called; four women and two men, all worried and uncertain and looking to me for decisions.

Greville, I perceived, hadn't chosen potential leaders to work around him. Annette Adams herself was no aggressive waiting-in-the-wings manager but a true second-in-command, skilled at carrying out orders, incapable of initiating them. Not so good, all things considered.

I introduced myself and described what had happened to Greville.

They had liked him, I was glad to see. There were tears on his behalf. I said that I needed their help because there were people I ought to notify about his death, like his solicitor and his accountant, for instance, and his closest friends, and I didn't know who they were. I would like, I said, to make a list, and sat beside one of the desks, arming myself with paper and pen.

Annette said she would fetch Greville's address book from his office but after a while returned in frustration: in all the mess she couldn't find it.

'There must be other records,' I said. 'What about that computer?' I pointed across the room. 'Do you have addresses on that?'

The girl who had brought the tea brightened a good deal and informed me that this was the stock control room, and the computer in question was programmed to record 'stock in, stock out', statements, invoices and accounts. But, she said encouragingly, in her other domain across the corridor there was another computer which she used for letters. She was out of the door by the end of the sentence and Annette remarked that June was a whirlwind always.

June, blonde, long-legged, flat-chested, came back with a fast print-out of Greville's ten most frequent correspondents (ignoring customers) which included not only the lawyers and the accountants but also the bank, a stockbroker and an insurance company.

'Terrific,' I said. 'And could one of you get through to the big credit card companies, and see if Greville was a customer of theirs and say his cards have been stolen, and he's dead.' Annette agreed mournfully that she would do it at once.

I then asked if any of them knew the make and number of Greville's car. They all did. It seemed they saw it every day in the yard. He came to work in a ten-year-old Rover 3500 without radio or cassette player because the Porsche he'd owned before had been broken into twice and finally stolen altogether.

'The old car's still bursting with gadgets, though,' the younger of the two men said, 'but he keeps them all locked in the boot.'

Greville had always been a sucker for gadgets, full of enthusiasm for the latest fidgety way of performing an ordinary task. He'd told me more about those toys of his, when we'd met, than ever about his own human relationships.

'Why did you ask about his car?' the young man said. He had rows of badges attached to a black leather jacket and orange spiky hair set with gel. A need to prove he existed, I supposed.

'It may be outside his front door,' I said. 'Or it may be parked somewhere in Ipswich.'

'Yeah,' he said thoughtfully. 'See what you mean.'

The telephone rang on the desk beside me, and Annette after a moment's hesitation came and picked up the receiver. She listened with a worried expression and then, covering the mouthpiece, asked me, 'What shall I do? It's a customer who wants to give an order.'

'Have you got what he wants?' I asked.

'Yes, we're sure to have.'

'Then say it's OK.'

'But do I tell him about Mr Franklin?'

'No,' I said instinctively, 'just take the order.'

She seemed glad of the direction and wrote down the list, and when she'd disconnected I suggested to them all that for that day at least they should take and send out orders in the normal way, and just say if asked that Mr Franklin was out of the office and couldn't be reached. We wouldn't start telling people he was dead until after I'd talked to his lawyers, accountants, bank and the rest, and found out our legal position. They were relieved and agreed without demur, and the older man asked if I would soon get the broken window fixed, as it was in the packing and despatch room, where he worked.

With a feeling of being sucked feet first into quicksand I said I would try. I felt I didn't belong in that place or in those people's lives, and all I knew about the jewellery business was where to find two red stones in a box marked $MgA1_20_4$, Burma.

At the fourth try among the Yellow Pages I got a promise of instant action on the window and after that, with office procedure beginning to tick over again all around me, I put a call through to the lawyers.

They were grave, they were sympathetic, they were at my service. I asked if by any chance Greville had made a will, as specifically I wanted to know if he had left any instructions about cremation or burial, and if he hadn't, did they know of anyone I should consult, or should I make whatever arrangements I thought best.

There was a certain amount of clearing of throats and a promise to look up files and call back, and they kept their word almost immediately, to my surprise.

My brother had indeed left a will: they had drawn it up for him themselves three years earlier. They couldn't swear it was his *last* will, but it was the only one they had. They had consulted it. Greville, they said, pedantically, had expressed no preference as to the disposal of his remains.

'Shall I just . . . go ahead, then?'

'Certainly,' they said. 'You are in fact named as your brother's sole executor. It is your duty to make the decisions.'

Hell, I thought, and I asked for a list of the beneficiaries so that I could notify them of the death and invite them to the funeral.

After a pause they said they didn't normally give out that information on the telephone. Could I not come to their office? It was just across the City, at Temple.

'I've broken an ankle,' I said, apologetically. 'It takes me all my time to cross the room.'

Dear, dear, they said. They consulted among themselves in guarded whispers and finally said they supposed there was no harm in my knowing. Greville's will was extremely simple; he had left everything he possessed to Derek Saxony Franklin, his brother. To my good self, in fact.

'What?' I said stupidly. 'He can't have.'

He had written his will in a hurry, they said, because he had been flying off to a dangerous country to buy stones. He had been persuaded by the lawyers not to go intestate, and he had given in to them, and as far as they knew, that was the only will he had ever made.

'He can't have meant it to be his last,' I said blankly.

Perhaps not, they agreed: few men in good health expected to die at fifty-three. They then discussed probate procedures discreetly and asked for my instructions, and I felt the quicksands rising above my knees.

'Is it legal,' I asked, 'for this business to go on running, for the time being?'

They saw no impediment in law. Subject to probate, and in the absence of any later will, the business would be mine. If I wanted to sell it in due course, it would be in my own interest to keep it running. As my brother's executor it would also be my duty to do my best for the estate. An interesting situation, they said with humour.

Not wholeheartedly appreciating the subtlety, I asked how long probate would take.

Always difficult to forecast, was the answer. Anything between six months or two years, depending on the complexity of Greville's affairs.

'Two years!'

More probably six months, they murmured soothingly. The speed would depend on the accountants and the Inland Revenue, who could seldom be hurried. It was in the lap of the gods.

I mentioned that there might be work to do over claiming damages for the accident. Happy to see to it, they said, and promised to contact the Ipswich police. Meanwhile, good luck.

I put the receiver down in sinking dismay. This business, like any other, might run on its own impetus for two weeks, maybe even for four, but after that . . . After that I would be back on horses, trying to get fit again to race.

I would have to get a manager, I thought vaguely, and had no idea where to start looking. Annette Adams with furrows of anxiety across her forehead asked if it would be all right to begin clearing up Mr Franklin's office, and I said yes, and thought that her lack of drive could sink the ship.

Please would someone, I asked the world in general, mind going down to the yard and telling the man in my car that I wouldn't be leaving for two or three hours; and June with her bright face whisked out of the door again and soon returned to relate that my man would lock the car, go on foot for lunch, and be back in good time to wait for me.

'Did he say all that?' I asked curiously.

June laughed. 'Actually he said, "Right. Bite to eat," and off he stomped.'

She asked if I would like her to bring me a sandwich when she went out for her own lunch and, surprised and grateful, I accepted.

'Your foot hurts, doesn't it?' she said judiciously.

'Mm.'

'You should put it up on a chair.'

She fetched one without ado and placed it in front of me, watching with a motherly air of approval as I lifted my leg into place. She must have been all of twenty, I thought.

A telephone rang beside the computer on the far side of the room and she went to answer it.

'Yes, sir, we have everything in stock. Yes, sir, what size and how many? A hundred twelve-by-ten millimetre ovals . . . yes . . . yes . . . yes.'

She tapped the lengthy order rapidly straight on to the computer, not writing in longhand as Annette had done.

'Yes, sir, they will go off today. Usual terms, sir, of course.' She put the phone down, printed a copy of the order and laid it in a shallow wire tray. A fax machine simultaneously clicked on and whined away and switched off with little shrieks, and she tore off the emergent sheet and tapped its information also into the computer, making a print-out and putting it into the tray.

'Do you fill all the orders the day they come in?' I asked.

'Oh, sure, if we can. Within twenty-four hours without fail. Mr Franklin says speed is the essence of good business. I've known him stay here all evening by himself packing parcels when we're swamped.'

She remembered with a rush that he would never come back. It did take a bit of getting used to. Tears welled in her uncontrollably as they had earlier, and she stared at me through them, which made her blue eyes look huge.

'You couldn't help liking him,' she said. 'Working with him, I mean.'

I felt almost jealous that she'd known Greville better than I had; yet I could have known him better if I'd tried. Regret stabbed in again, a needle of grief.

Annette came to announce that Mr Franklin's room was at least partially clear so I transferred myself into there to make more phone calls in comparative privacy. I sat in Greville's black leather swivelling chunk of luxury and put my foot on the typist's chair June carried in after me, and I surveyed the opulent carpet, deep armchairs and framed maps as in the lobby, and smoothed a hand over the grainy black expanse of the oversized desk, and felt like a jockey, not a tycoon.

Annette had picked up from the floor and assembled at one end of the desk some of the army of gadgets, most of them matt black and small, as if miniaturization were part of the attraction. Easily identifiable at a glance were battery-operated things like pencil sharpener, hand-held copier, printing calculator, dictionary-thesaurus, but most needed investigation. I stretched out a hand to the nearest and found that it was a casing with a dial face, plus a head like a microphone on a lead.

'What's this?' I asked Annette who was picking up a stack of paper from the far reaches of the floor. 'Some sort of meter?'

She flashed a look at it. 'A Geiger counter,' she said matter-of-factly, as if everyone kept a Geiger counter routinely among their pens and pencils.

I flipped the switch from off to on, but apart from a couple of ticks, nothing happened.

Annette paused, sitting back on her heels as she knelt among the remaining clutter.

'A lot of stones change colour for the better under gamma radiation,' she said. 'They're not radioactive afterwards, but Mr Franklin was once accidentally sent a batch of topaz from Brazil that had been irradiated in a nuclear reactor and the stones were bordering on dangerous. A hundred of them. There was a terrible lot of trouble because, apart from being unsaleable, they had come in without a radioactivity import licence, or something like that, but it wasn't Mr Franklin's fault, of course. But he got the Geiger counter then.' She paused. 'He had an amazing flair for stones, you know. He just felt there was something wrong with that topaz.

Such a beautiful deep blue they'd made it, when it must have been almost colourless to begin with. So he sent a few of them to a lab for testing.' She paused again. 'He'd just been reading about some old diamonds that had been exposed to radium and turned green, and were as radioactive as anything . . .'

Her face crumpled and she blinked her eyes rapidly, turning away from me and looking down to the floor so that I shouldn't see her distress. She made a great fuss among the papers and finally, with a sniff or two, said indistinctly, 'Here's his desk diary,' and then, more slowly, 'That's odd.'

'What's odd?'

'October's missing.'

She stood up and brought me the desk diary, which proved to be a largish appointments calendar showing a week at a glance. The month on current display was November, with a few of the daily spaces filled in but most of them empty. I flipped back the page and came next to September.

'I expect October's still on the floor, torn off,' I said.

She shook her head doubtfully, and in fact couldn't find it.

'Has the address book turned up?' I asked.

'No.' She was puzzled. 'It hasn't.'

'Is anything else missing?'

'I'm not really sure.'

It seemed bizarre that anyone should risk breaking in via the roof simply to steal an address book and some pages from a desk diary. Something else had to be missing.

The Yellow-Pages glaziers arrived at that point, putting a stop to my speculation. I went along with them to the packing room and saw the efficient hole that had been smashed in the six-by-four-foot window. All the glass that must have been scattered over every surface had been collected and swept into a pile of dagger-sharp glittering triangles, and a chill breeze ruffled papers in clipboards.

'You don't break glass this quality by tapping it with a fingernail,' one of the workmen said knowledgeably, picking up a piece. 'They must have swung a weight against it, like a wrecking ball.'

CHAPTER THREE

While the workmen measured the window frame, I watched the oldest of Greville's employees take transparent bags of beads from one cardboard box, insert them into bubble-plastic sleeves and stack them in another brown cardboard box. When all was transferred he put a list of contents on top, crossed the flaps and stuck the whole box around with wide reinforced tape.

'Where do the beads come from?' I asked.

'Taiwan, I dare say,' he said briefly, fixing a large address label on the top.

'No . . . I meant, where do you keep them here?'

He looked at me in pitying astonishment, a white-haired grandfatherly figure in storemen's brown overalls. 'In the stock-rooms, of course.'

'Of course.'

'Down the hall,' he said.

I went back to Greville's office and in the interests of good public relations asked Annette if she would show me the stock-rooms. Her heavyish face lightened with pleasure and she led the way to the far end of the corridor.

'In here,' she said with obvious pride, passing through a central doorway into a small inner lobby, 'there are four rooms.' She pointed through open doorways. 'In there, mineral cabochons, oval and round; in there, beads; in there, oddities, and in there, organics.'

'What are organics?' I asked.

She beckoned me forward into the room in question, and I walked into a windowless space lined from floor to shoulder height with column after column of narrow grey metal drawers, each presenting a face to the world of about the size of a side of a shoebox. Each drawer, above a handle, bore a label identifying what it contained.

'Organics are things that grow,' Annette said patiently, and I reflected I should have worked that out for myself. 'Coral, for instance.' She pulled open a nearby drawer which proved to extend lengthily backwards, and showed me the contents: clear plastic bags, each packed with many strings of bright red twiglets. 'Italian,' she said. 'The best coral comes from the Mediterranean.' She closed that drawer, walked a few paces, pulled open another. 'Abalone, from abalone shells.' Another: 'Ivory. We still have a little, but we can't sell it now.' Another: 'Mother of pearl. We sell tons of it.' 'Pink mussel.' 'Freshwater pearls.' Finally, 'Imitation pearls. Cultured pearls are in the vault.'

Everything, it seemed, came in dozens of shapes and

sizes. Annette smiled at my bemused expression and invited me into the room next door.

Floor to shoulder height metal drawers, as before, not only lining the walls this time but filling the centre space with aisles, as in a supermarket.

'Cabochons, for setting into rings, and so on,' Annette said. 'They're in alphabetical order.'

Amethyst to turquoise via garnet, jade, lapis lazuli and onyx, with dozens of others I'd only half heard of. 'Semi-precious,' Annette said briefly. 'All genuine stones. Mr Franklin doesn't touch glass or plastic.' She stopped abruptly. Let five seconds lengthen. 'He didn't touch them,' she said lamely.

His presence was there strongly, I felt. It was almost as if he would walk through the door, all energy, saying 'Hello, Derek, what brings you here?' and if he seemed alive to me, who had seen him dead, how much more physical he must still be to Annette and June.

And to Lily too, I supposed. Lily was in the third stock-room pushing a brown cardboard box around on a thing like a tea-trolley, collecting bags of strings of beads and checking them against a list. With her centre-parted hair drawn back into a slide at her neck, with her small pale mouth and rounded cheeks, Lily looked like a Charlotte Brontë governess and dressed as if immolation were her personal choice. The sort to love the master in painful silence, I thought, and wondered what she'd felt for Greville.

Whatever it was, she wasn't letting it show. She raised

downcast eyes briefly to my face and at Annette's prompting told me she was putting together a consignment of rhodonite, jasper, aventurine and tiger eye, for one of the largest firms of jewellery manufacturers.

'We import the stones,' Annette said. 'We're wholesalers. We sell to about three thousand jewellers, maybe more. Some are big businesses. Many are small ones. We're at the top of the semi-precious trade. Highly regarded.' She swallowed. 'People trust us.'

Greville, I knew, had travelled the world to buy the stones. When we'd met he'd often been on the point of departing for Arizona or Hong Kong or had just returned from Israel, but he'd never told me more than the destinations. I at last understood what he'd been doing, and realized he couldn't easily be replaced.

Depressed, I went back to his office and telephoned to his accountant and his bank.

They were shocked and they were helpful, impressively so. The bank manager said I would need to call on him in the morning, but Saxony Franklin, as a limited company, could go straight on functioning. I could take over without trouble. All he would want was confirmation from my brother's lawyers that his will was as I said.

'Thank you very much,' I said, slightly surprised, and he told me warmly he was glad to be of service. Greville's affairs, I thought with a smile, must be amazingly healthy.

To the insurance company, also, my brother's death

seemed scarcely a hiccup. A limited company's insurance went marching steadily on, it seemed: it was the company that was insured, not my brother. I said I would like to claim for a smashed window. No problem. They would send a form.

After that I telephoned to the Ipswich undertakers who had been engaged to remove Greville's body from the hospital, and arranged that he should be cremated. They said they had 'a slot' at two o'clock on Friday: would that do? 'Yes,' I said, sighing. 'I'll be there.' They gave me the address of the crematorium in a hushed obsequious voice, and I wondered what it must be like to do business always with the bereaved. Happier by far to sell glittering baubles to the living or to ride jump-racing horses at thirty miles an hour, win, lose or break your bones.

I made yet another phone call, this time to the orthopaedic surgeon, and as usual came up against the barrier of his receptionist. He wasn't in his own private consulting rooms, she announced, but at the hospital.

I said, 'Could you ask him to leave me a prescription somewhere, because I've fallen on my ankle and twisted it, and I'm running out of Distalgesic.'

'Hold on,' she said, and I held until she returned. 'I've spoken to him,' she said. 'He'll be back here later. He says can you be here at five?'

I said gratefully that I could, and reckoned that I'd have to leave soon after two-thirty to be sure of making it. I told Annette, and asked what they did about locking up.

'Mr Franklin usually gets here first and leaves last.' She stopped, confused. 'I mean . . .'

'I know,' I said. 'It's all right. I think of him in the present tense too. So go on.'

'Well, the double front doors bolt on the inside. Then the door from the lobby to the offices has an electronic bolt, as you know. So does the door from the corridor to the stock-rooms. So does the rear door, where we all come in and out. Mr Franklin changes . . . changed . . . the numbers at least every week. And there's another electronic lock, of course, on the door from the lobby to the showroom, and from the corridor into the showroom . . .' She paused. 'It does seem a lot, I know, but the electronic locks are very simple, really. You only have to remember three digits. Last Friday they were five, three, two. They're easy to work. Mr Franklin installed them so that we shouldn't have too many keys lying around. He and I both have a key, though, that will unlock all the electronic locks manually, if we need to.'

'So you've remembered the numbers?' I asked.

'Oh, yes. It was just, this morning, with everything . . . they went out of my head.'

'And the vault,' I said. 'Does that have any electronics?'

'No, but it has an intricate locking system in that heavy door, though it looks so simple from the outside. Mr Franklin always locks . . . locked . . . the vault before he left. When he went away on long trips, he made the key available to me.'

I wondered fleetingly about the awkward phrase, but didn't pursue it. I asked her instead about the showroom, which I hadn't seen and, again with pride, she went into the corridor, programmed a shining brass doorknob with the open sesame numbers, and ushered me into a windowed room that looked much like a shop, with glass-topped display counters and the firm's overall ambience of wealth.

Annette switched on powerful lights and the place came to life. She moved contentedly behind the counters, pointing out to me the contents now bright with illumination.

'In here are examples of everything we stock, except not all the sizes, of course, and not the faceted stones in the vault. We don't really use the showroom a great deal, only for new customers mostly, but I like being in here. I love the stones. They're fascinating. Mr Franklin says stones are the only things the human race takes from the earth and makes more beautiful.' She lifted a face heavy with loss. 'What will happen without him?'

'I don't know yet,' I said, 'but in the short term we fill the orders and despatch them, and order more stock from where you usually get it. We keep to all the old routines and practices. OK?'

She nodded, relieved at least for the present.

'Except,' I added, 'that it will be you who arrives first and leaves last, if you don't mind.'

'That's all right. I always do when Mr Franklin's away.'

We stared briefly at each other, not putting words to the obvious, then she switched off the showroom lights almost as if it were a symbolic act, and as we left pulled the self-locking door shut behind us.

Back in Greville's office I wrote down for her my own address and telephone number and said that if she felt insecure, or wanted to talk, I would be at home all evening.

'I'll come back here tomorrow morning, after I've seen the bank manager,' I said. 'Will you be all right until then?'

She nodded shakily. 'What do we call you? We can't call you Mr Franklin, it wouldn't seem right.'

'How about Derek?'

'Oh no.' She was instinctively against it. 'Would you mind, say . . . Mr Derek?'

'If you prefer it.' It sounded quaintly old-fashioned to me, but she was happy with it and said she would tell the others.

'About the others,' I said, 'sort everyone out for me, with their jobs. There's you, June, Lily . . .'

'June works the computers and the stock control,' she said. 'Lily fills the orders. Tina, she's a general assistant, she helps Lily and does some of the secretarial work. So does June. So do I, actually. We all do what's needed, really. There are few hard and fast divisions.

Except that Alfie doesn't do much except pack up the orders. It takes him all his time.'

'And that younger guy with the spiky orange halo?'

'Jason? Don't worry about the hair, he's harmless. He's our muscles. The stones are very heavy in bulk, you know. Jason shifts boxes, fills the stock-rooms, does odd jobs and hoovers the carpets. He helps Alfie sometimes, or Lily, if we're busy. Like I said, we all do anything, whatever's needed. Mr Franklin has never let anyone mark out a territory.'

'His words?'

'Yes, of course.'

Collective responsibility, I thought. I bowed to my brother's wisdom. If it worked, it worked. And from the look of everything in the place, it did indeed work, and I wouldn't disturb it.

I closed and locked the vault door with Greville's key and asked Annette which of his large bunch overrode the electronic locks. That one, she said, pointing, separating it.

'What are all the others, do you know?'

She looked blank. 'I've no idea.'

Car, house, whatever. I supposed I might eventually sort them out. I gave her what I hoped was a reassuring smile, sketched a goodbye to some of the others and rode down in the service lift to find Brad out in the yard.

'Swindon,' I said. 'The medical centre where we were on Friday. Would you mind?'

'Course not.' Positively radiant, I thought.

It was an eighty-mile journey, ten miles beyond home. Brad managed it without further communication and I spent the time thinking of all the things I hadn't yet done, like seeing to Greville's house and stopping delivery of his daily paper, wherever it might come from, and telling the post office to divert his letters . . . To hell with it, I thought wearily, why did the damned man have to die?

The orthopod X-rayed and unwrapped my ankle and tut-tutted. From toes to shin it looked hard, black and swollen, the skin almost shiny from the stretching.

'I advised you to rest it,' he said, a touch crossly.

'My brother died . . .' and I explained about the mugging, and also about having to see to Greville's affairs.

He listened carefully, a strong sensible man with prematurely white hair. I didn't know a jockey who didn't trust him. He understood our needs and our imperatives, because he treated a good many of us who lived in or near the training centre of Lambourn.

'As I told you the other day,' he said when I'd finished, 'you've fractured the lower end of the fibula, and where the tibia and fibula should be joined, they've sprung apart. Today, they are further apart. They're now providing no support at all for the talus, the heel bone. You've now completely ripped the lateral ligament which normally binds the ankle together. The whole joint is insecure and coming apart inside, like a mortise joint in a piece of furniture when the glue's given way.'

'So how long will it take?' I asked.

He smiled briefly. 'In a crêpe bandage it will hurt for about another ten days, and after that you can walk on it. You could be back on a horse in three weeks from now, if you don't mind the stirrup hurting you, which it will. About another three weeks after that, the ankle might be strong enough for racing.'

'Good,' I said, relieved. 'Not much worse than before, then.'

'It's worse, but it won't take much longer to mend.'

'Fine.'

He looked down at the depressing sight. 'If you're going to be doing all this travelling about, you'd be much more comfortable in a rigid cast. You could put your weight on it in a couple of days. You'd have almost no pain.'

'And wear it for six weeks? And get atrophied muscles?'

'Atrophy is a strong word.' He knew all the same that jump jockeys needed strong leg muscles above all else, and the way to keep them strong was to keep them moving. Inside plaster they couldn't move at all and weakened rapidly. If movement cost a few twinges, it was worth it.

'Delta-cast is lightweight,' he said persuasively. 'It's a polymer, not like the old plaster of Paris. It's porous, so air circulates, and you don't get skin problems. It's good.

And I could make you a cast with a zip in it so you could take it off for physiotherapy.'

'How long before I was racing?'

'Nine or ten weeks.'

I didn't say anything for a moment or two and he looked up fast, his eyes bright and quizzical.

'A cast, then?' he said.

'No.'

He smiled and picked up a roll of crêpe bandage. 'Don't fall on it again in the next month, or you'll be back to square one.'

'I'll try not to.'

He bandaged it all tight again from just below the knee down to my toes and back, and gave me another prescription for Distalgesic. 'No more than eight tablets in twenty-four hours and not with alcohol.' He said it every time.

'Right.'

He considered me thoughtfully for a moment and then rose and went over to a cabinet where he kept packets and bottles of drugs. He came back tucking a small plastic bag into an envelope which he held out to me.

'I'm giving you something known as DF 1–1–8s. Rather appropriate, as they're your own initials! I've given you three of them. They are serious painkillers, and I don't want you to use them unless something like yesterday happens again.'

'OK,' I said, putting the envelope in my pocket. 'Thanks.'

'If you take one, you won't feel a thing.' He smiled. 'If you take two at once, you'll be spaced out, high as a kite. If you take all three at once, you'll be unconscious. So be warned.' He paused. 'They are a last resort.'

'I won't forget,' I said, 'and I truly am grateful.'

Brad drove to a chemist's, took my prescription in, waited for it to be dispensed, and finished the ten miles home, parking outside my door.

'Same time tomorrow morning?' I asked. 'Back to London.'

'Yerss.'

'I'd be in trouble without you,' I said, climbing out with his help. He gave me a brief haunted glance and handed me the crutches. 'You drive great,' I said.

He was embarrassed, but also pleased. Nowhere near a smile, of course, but a definite twitch in the cheeks. He turned away, ducking my gaze, and set off doggedly towards his mother.

I let myself into the house and regretted the embargo on a large scotch. Instead, with June's lunchtime sandwich a distant memory, I refuelled with sardines on toast and ice-cream after, which more or less reflected my habitual laziness about cooking.

Then, aligned with icepacks along the sofa, I

telephoned the man in Newmarket who trained Greville's two racehorses.

He picked up the receiver as if he'd been waiting for it to ring.

'Yes?' he said. 'What are they offering?'

'I've no idea,' I said. 'Is that Nicholas Loder?'

'What? Who are you?' He was brusque and impatient, then took a second look at things and with more honey said, 'I beg your pardon, I was expecting someone else. I'm Loder, yes, who am I talking to?'

'Greville Franklin's brother.'

'Oh yes?'

It meant nothing to him immediately. I pictured him as I knew him, more by sight than face to face, a big light-haired man in his forties with enormous presence and self-esteem to match. Undoubtedly a good-to-great trainer, but in television interviews occasionally overbearing and condescending to the interviewer, as I'd heard he could be also to his owners. Greville kept his horses with him because the original horse he'd taken as a bad debt had been in that stable. Nicholas Loder had bought Greville all his subsequent horses and done notably well with them, and Greville had assured me that he got on well with the man by telephone, and that he was perfectly friendly.

The last time I'd spoken to Greville myself on the telephone he'd been talking of buying another two-year-old, saying that Loder would get him one at the October sales, perhaps.

I explained to Loder that Greville had died and after the first sympathetic exclamations of dismay he reacted as I would have expected, not as if missing a close friend but on a practical business level.

'It won't affect the running of his horses,' he said. 'They're owned in any case by the Saxony Franklin company, not by Greville himself. I can run the horses still in the company name. I have the company's Authority to Act. There should be no problem.'

'I'm afraid there may be,' I began.

'No, no. Dozen Roses runs on Saturday at York. In with a great chance. I informed Greville of it only a few days ago. He always wanted to know when they were running, though he never went to see them.'

'The problem is,' I said, 'about my being his brother. He has left the Saxony Franklin company to me.'

The size of the problem suddenly revealed itself to him forcibly. 'You're not his brother *Derek* Franklin? That brother? The jockey?'

'Yes. So . . . could you find out from Weatherby's whether the horses can still run while the estate is subject to probate?'

'My God,' he said weakly.

Professional jockeys, as we both knew well, were not allowed to own runners in races. They could own other horses such as brood mares, foals, stallions, hacks, hunters, show-jumpers, anything in horseshoes; they could even own racehorses, but they couldn't run them.'

'Can you find out?' I asked again.

'I will.' He sounded exasperated. 'Dozen Roses should trot up on Saturday.'

Dozen Roses was currently the better of Greville's two horses whose fortunes I followed regularly in the newspapers and on television. A triple winner as a three-year-old, he had been disappointing at four, but in the current year, as a five-year-old, he had regained all his old form and had scored three times in the past few weeks. A 'trot-up' on Saturday was a reasonable expectation.

Loder said, 'If Weatherby's give the thumbs down to the horse running, will you sell it? I'll find a buyer by Saturday, among my owners.'

I listened to the urgency in his voice and wondered whether Dozen Roses was more than just another trot-up, of which season by season he had many. He sounded a lot more fussed than seemed normal.

'I don't know whether I can sell before probate,' I said. 'You'd better find that out, too.'

'But if you can, will you?'

'I don't know,' I said, puzzled. 'Let's wait and see, first.'

'You won't be able to hang on to him, you know,' he said, forcefully. 'He's got another season in him. He's still worth a good bit. But unless you do something like turn in your licence, you won't be able to run him, and he's not worth turning in your licence for. It's not as if he were favourite for the Derby.'

'I'll decide during the week.'

'But you're not thinking of turning in your licence, are you?' He sounded almost alarmed. 'Didn't I read in the paper that you're on the injured list but hope to be back racing well before Christmas?'

'You did read that, yes.'

'Well, then.' The relief was as indefinable as the alarm, but came clear down the wires. I didn't understand any of it. He shouldn't have been so worried.

'Perhaps Saxony Franklin could lease the horse to someone,' I said.

'Oh. Ah. To me?' He sounded as if it were the perfect solution.

'I don't know,' I said cautiously. 'We'll have to find out.'

I realized that I didn't totally trust him, and it wasn't a doubt I'd have felt before the phone call. He was one of the top five Flat race trainers in the country, automatically held to be reliable because of his rock-solid success.

'When Greville came to see his horses,' I asked, 'did he ever bring anyone with him? I'm trying to reach people he knew, to tell them of his death.'

'He never came here to see his horses. I hardly knew him personally myself, except on the telephone.'

'Well, his funeral is on Friday at Ipswich,' I said. 'What if I called in at Newmarket that day, as I'll be over your way, to see you and the horses and complete any paperwork that's necessary?'

'No,' he said instantly. Then, softening it, 'I always

discourage owners from visiting. They disrupt the stable routine. I can't make any exceptions. If I need you to sign anything I'll arrange it another way.'

'All right,' I agreed mildly, not crowding him into corners. 'I'll wait to hear from you about what Weatherby's decide.'

He said he would get in touch and abruptly disconnected, leaving me thinking that on the subject of his behaviour I didn't know the questions let alone the answers.

Perhaps I had been imagining things: but I knew I hadn't. One could often hear more nuances in someone's voice on the telephone than one could face to face. When people were relaxed, the lower vibrations of their voices came over the wires undisturbed; under stress, the lower vibrations disappeared because the vocal cords involuntarily tightened. After Loder had discovered I would be inheriting Dozen Roses, there had been no lower vibrations at all.

Shelving the enigma I pondered the persisting difficulty of informing Greville's friends. They had to exist, no one lived in a vacuum; but if it had been the other way round, I supposed that Greville would have had the same trouble. He hadn't known my friends either. Our worlds had scarcely touched except briefly when we met, and then we had talked a bit about horses, a bit about gadgets, a bit about the world in general and any interesting current events.

He'd lived alone, as I did. He'd told me nothing about any love life. He'd said merely, 'Bad luck' when three years earlier I'd remarked that my live-in girlfriend had gone to live-in somewhere else. It didn't matter, I said. It had been a mutual agreement, a natural ending. I'd asked him once about his long-ago divorced wife. 'She remarried. Haven't seen her since,' was all he'd said.

If it had been I that had died, I thought, he would have told the world I worked in: he'd have told, perhaps, the trainer I mostly rode for and maybe the racing papers. So I should tell his world: tell the semi-precious stone fraternity. Annette could do it, regardless of the absence of Greville's address book, because of June's computer. The computer made more and more nonsense of the break-in. I came back to the same conviction: something else had been stolen, and I didn't know what.

I remembered at about that point that I did have Greville's pocket diary, even if his desk diary had lost October, so I went and fetched it from the bedroom where I'd left it the night before. I thought I might find friends' names and phone numbers in the addresses section at the back, but he had been frugal in that department as everywhere in the slim brown book. I turned the pages, which were mostly unused, seeing only short entries like 'R arrives from Brazil' and 'B in Paris' and 'Buy citrine for P'.

In March I was brought up short. Because it was a racing diary, the race-meetings to be held on each day of the year were listed under the day's date. I came to Thursday 16 March which listed 'Cheltenham'. The word Cheltenham had been ringed with a ball-point pen, and Greville had written 'Gold Cup' in the day's space; and then, with a different pen, he had added the words 'Derek won it!!'

It brought me to sudden tears. I couldn't help it.

I longed for him to be alive so I could get to know him better. I wept for the lost opportunities, the time wasted. I longed to know the brother who had cared what I did, who had noted in his almost empty diary that I'd won one of the top races of the year.

CHAPTER FOUR

There were only three telephone numbers in the addresses section at the back, all identified merely by initials. One, NL, was Nicholas Loder's. I tried the other two, which were London numbers, and got no reply.

Scattered through the rest of the diary were three more numbers. Two of them proved to be restaurants in full evening flood, and I wrote down their names, recognizing one of them as the place I'd last dined with Greville, two or three months back. On 25 July, presumably, as that was the date on which he'd written the number. It had been an Indian restaurant, I remembered, and we had eaten ultra-hot curry.

Sighing, I turned the pages and tried a number occurring on 2 September, about five weeks earlier. It wasn't a London number, but I didn't recognize the code. I listened to the bell ringing continuously at the other end and had resigned myself to another blank when someone lifted the distant receiver and in a low breathy voice said, 'Hello?'

'Hello,' I replied. 'I'm ringing on behalf of Greville Franklin.'

'Who?'

'Greville Franklin.' I spoke the words slowly and clearly.

'Just a moment.'

There was a long uninformative silence and then someone else clattered on sharp heels up to the receiver and decisively spoke, her voice high and angry.

'How dare you!' she said. 'Don't ever do this again. I will not have your name spoken in this house.'

She put the receiver down with a crash before I could utter a word, and I sat bemusedly looking at my own telephone and feeling as if I'd swallowed a wasp.

Whoever she was, I thought wryly, she wouldn't want to send flowers to the funeral, though she might have been gladdened by the death. I wondered what on earth Greville could have done to raise such a storm, but that was the trouble, I didn't know him well enough to make a good guess.

Thankful on the whole that there weren't any more numbers to be tried I looked again at what few entries he had made, more out of curiosity than looking for helpful facts.

He had noted the days on which his horses had run, again only with initials. DR, Dozen Roses, appeared most, each time with a number following, like 300 at 8s, which I took to mean the amounts he'd wagered at what odds. Below the numbers he had put each time another number inside a circle which, when I compared them with the form book, were revealed as the placings of the horse at the finish. Its last three appearances, all with 5 in the circle, seemed to have netted Greville respectively 500 at 14s, 500 at 5s, 1000 at 6/4. The trot-up scheduled for Saturday, I thought, would be likely to be at odds-on.

Greville's second horse, Gemstones appearing simply as G, had run six times, winning only once but profitably: 500 at 100/6.

All in all, I thought, a moderate betting pattern for an owner. He had made, I calculated, a useful profit overall, more than most owners achieved. With his prize money in addition to offset both the training fees and the capital cost of buying the horses in the first place, I guessed that he had come out comfortably ahead, and it was in the business sense, I supposed, that owning horses had chiefly pleased him.

I flicked casually forward to the end of the book and in the last few pages headed 'NOTES' came across a lot of doodling and then a list of numbers.

The doodling was the sort one does while listening on the telephone, a lot of boxes and zig-zags, haphazard and criss-crossed with lines of shading. On the page facing, there was an equation: CZ=C × 1.7. I supposed it had been of sparkling clarity to Greville, but of no use to me.

Overleaf I found the sort of numbers list I kept in my own diary: passport, bank account, national insurance.

After those, in small capital letters further down the page, was the single word DEREK. Another jolt, seeing it again in his writing.

I wondered briefly whether, from its placing, Greville had used my name as some sort of mnemonic, or whether it was just another doodle: there was no way of telling. With a sigh I riffled back through the pages and came to something I'd looked at before, a lightly-pencilled entry for the day before his death.. Second time around, it meant just as little.

Koningin Beatrix? he had written. Just the two words and the question mark. I wondered idly if it were the name of a horse, if he'd been considering buying it; my mind tended to work that way. Then I thought that perhaps he'd written the last name first, such as Smith, Jane, and that maybe he'd been going to Ipswich to meet a Beatrix Koningin.

I returned to the horse theory and got through to the trainer I rode for, Milo Shandy, who enquired breezily about the ankle and said would I please waste no time in coming back.

'I could ride out in a couple of weeks,' I said.

'At least that's something, I suppose. Get some massage.'

The mere thought of it was painful. I said I would, not meaning it, and asked about Koningin Beatrix, spelling it out.

'Don't know of any horse called that, but I can find out for you in the morning. I'll ask Weatherby's if the name's available, and if they say yes, it means there isn't a horse called that registered for racing.'

'Thanks a lot.'

'Think nothing of it. I heard your brother died. Bad luck.'

'Yes . . . How did you know?'

'Nicholas Loder rang me just now, explaining your dilemma and wanting me to persuade you to lease him Dozen Roses.'

'But that's crazy. His ringing you, I mean.'

He chuckled. 'I told him so. I told him I could bend you like a block of teak. He didn't seem to take it in. Anyway, I don't think leasing would solve anything. Jockeys aren't allowed to own racing horses, period. If you lease a horse, you still own it.'

'I'm sure you're right.'

'Put your shirt on it.'

'Loder bets, doesn't he?' I asked. 'In large amounts?'

'So I've heard.'

'He said Dozen Roses would trot up at York on Saturday.'

'In that case, do you want me to put a bit on for you?'

Besides not being allowed to run horses in races, jockeys also were banned from betting, but there were always ways round that, like helpful friends.

'I don't think so, not this time,' I said, 'but thanks anyway.'

'You won't mind if I do?'

'Be my guest. If Weatherby's let it run, that is.'

'A nice little puzzle,' he said appreciatively. 'Come over soon for a drink. Come for evening stables.'

I would, I said.

'Take care.'

I put down the phone, smiling at his easy farewell colloquialism. Jump jockeys were paid not to take care, on the whole. Not too much care.

Milo would be horrified if I obeyed him.

In the morning, Brad drove me to Saxony Franklin's bank to see the manager who was young and bright and spoke with deliberate slowness, as if waiting for his clients' intelligence to catch up. Was there something about crutches, I wondered, that intensified the habit? It took him five minutes to suspect that I wasn't a moron. After that he told me Greville had borrowed a sizeable chunk of the bank's money, and he would be looking to me to repay it. 'One point five million United States dollars in cash, as a matter of fact.'

'One point five million dollars,' I repeated, trying not to show that he had punched most of the breath out of me. '*What for?*'

'For buying diamonds. Diamonds from the DTC of the CSO are, of course, normally paid for in cash, in dollars.'

Bank managers around Hatton Garden, it seemed, saw nothing extraordinary in such an exercise.

'He doesn't . . . didn't deal in diamonds,' I protested.

'He had decided to expand and, of course, we made the funds available. Your brother dealt with us for many years and as you'll know was a careful and conscientious businessman. A valued client. We have several times advanced him money for expansion and each time we have been repaid without difficulty. Punctiliously, in fact.' He cleared his throat. 'The present loan, taken out three months ago, is due for repayment progressively over a period of five years, and of course as the loan was made to the company, not to your brother personally, the terms of the loan will be unchanged by his death.'

'Yes,' I said.

'I understood from what you said yesterday that you propose to run the business yourself?' He seemed happy enough where I might have expected a shade of anxiety. So why no anxiety? What wasn't I grasping?

'Do you hold security for the loan?' I asked.

'An agreement. We lent the money against the stock of Saxony Franklin.'

'All the stones?'

'As many as would satisfy the debt. But our best security has always been your brother's integrity and his business ability.'

I said, 'I'm not a gemmologist. I'll probably sell the business after probate.'

He nodded comfortably. 'That might be the best course. We would cxpect the Saxony Franklin loan to be repaid on schedule, but we would welcome a dialogue with the purchasers.'

He produced papers for me to sign and asked for extra specimen signatures so that I could put my name to Saxony Franklin cheques. He didn't ask what experience I'd had in running a business. Instead, he wished me luck.

I rose to my crutches and shook his hand, thinking of the things I hadn't said.

I hadn't told him I was a jockey, which might have caused a panic in Hatton Garden. And I hadn't told him that, if Greville had bought one and a half million dollars' worth of diamonds, I didn't know where they were.

'Diamonds?' Annette said. 'No. I told you. We never deal in diamonds.'

'The bank manager believes that Greville bought some recently. From something called the DTC of the CSO.'

'The Central Selling Organization? That's De Beers. The DTC is their diamond trading company. No, no.' She looked anxiously at my face. 'He can't have done. He never said anything about it.'

'Well, has the stock-buying here increased over the past three months?'

'It usually does,' she said, nodding. 'The business always grows. Mr Franklin comes back from world trips with new stones all the time. Beautiful stones. He can't resist them. He sells most of the special ones to a jewellery designer who has several boutiques in places like Knightsbridge and Bond Street. Gorgeous costume jewellery, but with real stones. Many of his pieces are one-offs, designed for a single stone. He has a great name. People prize some of his pieces like Fabergé's.'

'Who is he?'

'Prospero Jenks,' she said, expecting my awe at least.

I hadn't heard of him, but I nodded all the same.

'Does he set the stones with diamonds?' I asked.

'Yes, sometimes. But he doesn't buy those from Saxony Franklin.'

We were in Greville's office, I sitting in his swivel chair behind the vast expanse of desk, Annette sorting yesterday's roughly heaped higgledy-piggledy papers back into the drawers and files that had earlier contained them.

'You don't think Greville would ever have kept diamonds in this actual office, do you?' I asked.

'Certainly not.' The idea shocked her. 'He was always very careful about security.'

'So no one who broke in here would expect to find anything valuable lying about?'

She paused with a sheaf of papers in one hand, her brow wrinkling.

'It's odd, isn't it? They wouldn't expect to find anything valuable lying about in an office if they knew anything about the jewellery trade. And if they didn't know anything about the jewellery trade, why pick this office?'

The same old unanswerable question.

June with her incongruous motherliness brought in the typist's chair again for me to put my foot on. I thanked her and asked if her stock control computer kept day-to-day tabs on the number and value of all the polished pebbles in the place.

'Goodness, yes,' she said with amusement. 'Dates and amounts in, dates and amounts out. Prices in, prices out, profit margin, VAT, tax, you name it, the computer will tell you what we've got, what it's worth, what sells slowly, what sells fast, what's been hanging around here wasting space for two years or more, which isn't much.'

'The stones in the vault as well?'

'Sure.'

'But no diamonds?'

'No, we don't deal in them.' She gave me a bright incurious smile and swiftly departed, saying over her shoulder that the Christmas rush was still going strong and they'd been bombarded by fax orders overnight.

'Who reorders what you sell?' I asked Annette.

'I do for ordinary stock. June tells me what we need. Mr Franklin himself ordered the faceted stones and anything unusual.'

She went on sorting the papers, basically unconcerned because her responsibility ended on her way home. She was wearing that day the charcoal skirt of the day before but topped with a black sweater, perhaps out of respect for Greville. Solid in body, but not large, she had good legs in black tights and a settled, well-groomed, middle-aged air. I couldn't imagine her being as buoyant as June even in her youth.

I asked her if she could lay her hands on the company's insurance policy and she said as it happened she had just refiled it. I read its terms with misgivings and then telephoned the insurance company. Had my brother, I asked, recently increased the insurance? Had he increased it to cover diamonds to the value of one point five million dollars? He had not. It had been discussed only. My brother had said the premium asked was too high, and he had decided against it. The voice explained that the premium had been high because the stones would be often in transit, which made them vulnerable. He didn't know if Mr Franklin had gone ahead with buying the diamonds. It had been an enquiry only, he thought, three or four months ago. I thanked him numbly and put down the receiver.

The telephone rang again immediately and as Annette seemed to be waiting for me to do so, I answered it.

'Hello?' I said.

A male voice said, 'Is that Mr Franklin? I want to speak to Mr Franklin, please.'

'Er . . . could I help? I'm his brother.'

'Perhaps you can,' he said. 'This is the clerk of the West London Magistrates Court. Your brother was due here twenty minutes ago and it is unlike him to be late. Could you tell me when to expect him?'

'Just a minute.' I put my hand over the mouthpiece

and told Annette what I'd just heard. Her eyes widened and she showed signs of horrified memory.

'It's his day for the Bench! Alternate Tuesdays. I'd clean forgotten.'

I returned to the phone and explained the situation.

'Oh. Oh. How dreadfully upsetting.' He did indeed sound upset, but also a shade impatient. 'It really would have been more helpful if you could have alerted me in advance. It's very short notice to have to find a replacement.'

'Yes,' I agreed, 'but this office was broken into during the weekend. My brother's appointments diary was stolen, and in fact we cannot alert anybody not to expect him.'

'How extremely inconvenient.' It didn't seem an inappropriate statement to him. I thought Greville might find it inconvenient to be dead. Maybe it wasn't the best time for black humour.

'If my brother had personal friends among the magistrates,' I said, 'I would be happy for them to get in touch with me here. If you wouldn't mind telling them.'

'I'll do that, certainly.' He hesitated. 'Mr Franklin sits on the licensing committee. Do you want me to inform the chairman?'

'Yes, please. Tell anyone you can.'

He said goodbye with all the cares of the world on his shoulders and I sighed to Annette that we had better begin telling everyone else as soon as possible, but the trade was to expect business as usual.

'What about the papers?' she asked. 'Shall we put it in *The Times* and so on?'

'Good idea. Can you do it?'

She said she could, but in fact showed me the paragraph she'd written before phoning the papers. 'Suddenly, as the result of an accident, Greville Saxony Franklin JP, son of . . .' She'd left a space after 'son of' which I filled in for her: 'the late Lt. Col. and Mrs Miles Franklin'. I changed 'brother of Derek' to 'brother of Susan, Miranda and Derek', and I added a few final words, 'Cremation, Ipswich, Friday'.

'Have you any idea,' I asked Annette, 'what he could have been doing in Ipswich?'

She shook her head. 'I've never heard him mention the place. But then he didn't ever tell me very much that wasn't business.' She paused. 'He wasn't exactly secretive, but he never chatted about his private life.' She hesitated. 'He never talked about you.'

I thought of all the times he'd been good company and told me virtually nothing, and I understood very well what she meant.

'He used to say that the best security was a still tongue,' she said. 'He asked us not to talk too much about our jobs to total strangers, and we all know it's safer not to, even though we don't have precious stones here. All the people in the trade are security mad and the diamantaires can be paranoid.'

'What,' I said, 'are diamantaires?'

'Not what, who,' she said. 'They're dealers in rough

diamonds. They get the stones cut and polished and sell them to manufacturing jewellers. Mr Franklin always said diamonds were a world of their own, quite separate from other gemstones. There was a ridiculous boom and a terrible crash in world diamond prices during the eighties and a lot of the diamantaires lost fortunes and went bankrupt and Mr Franklin was often saying that they must have been mad to over-extend the way they had.' She paused. 'You couldn't help but know what was happening all round us in this area, where every second business is in gemstones. No one in the pubs and restaurants talked of much else. So you see, I'm sure the bank manager must be wrong. Mr Franklin would never buy diamonds.'

If he hadn't bought diamonds, I thought, what the hell had he done with one point five million dollars in cash?

Bought diamonds. He had to have done. Either that or the money was still lying around somewhere, undoubtedly carefully hidden. Either the money or diamonds to the value were lying around uninsured, and if my semi-secretive ultra-security-conscious brother had left a treasure-island map with X marking the precious spot, I hadn't yet found it. Much more likely, I feared, that the knowledge had died under the scaffolding. If it had, the firm would be forfeited to the bank, the last thing Greville would have wanted.

If it had, a major part of the inheritance he'd left me had vanished like morning mist.

He should have stuck to his old beliefs, I thought gloomily, and let diamonds strictly alone.

The telephone on the desk rang again and this time Annette answered it, as she was beside it.

'Saxony Franklin, can I help you?' she said, and listened. 'No, I'm very sorry, you won't be able to talk to Mr Franklin personally . . . Could I have your name, please?' She listened. 'Well, Mrs Williams, we must most unhappily inform you that Mr Franklin died as a result of an accident over the weekend. We are however continuing in business. Can I help you at all?'

She listened for a moment or two in increasing puzzlement, then said, 'Are you there? Mrs Williams, can you hear me?' But it seemed as though there was no reply, and in a while she put the receiver down, frowning. 'Whoever it was hung up.'

'Do I gather you don't know Mrs Williams?'

'No, I don't.' She hesitated. 'But I think she rang yesterday, too. I think I told her yesterday that Mr Franklin wasn't expected in the office all day, like I told everyone. I didn't ask for her name yesterday. But she has a voice you don't forget.'

'Why not?'

'Cut glass,' she said succinctly. 'Like Mr Franklin, but more so. Like you too, a bit.'

I was amused. She herself spoke what I thought of as unaccented English, though I supposed any way of speaking sounded like an accent to someone else. I wondered briefly about the cut-glass Mrs Williams who had received the news of the accident in silence and hadn't asked where, or how, or when.

Annette went off to her own office to get through to the newspapers and I picked Greville's diary out of my trouser pocket and tried the numbers that had been unreachable the night before. The two at the back of the book turned out to be first his bookmaker and second his barber, both of whom sounded sorry to be losing his custom, though the bookmaker less so because of Greville's habit of winning.

My ankle heavily ached; the result, I dared say, of general depression as much as aggrieved bones and muscle. Depression because whatever decisions I'd made to that point had been merely common sense, but there would come a stage ahead when I could make awful mistakes through ignorance. I'd never before handled finances bigger than my own bank balance and the only business I knew anything about was the training of racehorses, and that only from observation, not from hands-on experience. I knew what I was doing around horses: I could tell the spinel from the ruby. In Greville's world, I could be taken for a ride and never know it. I could lose badly before I'd learned even the elementary rules of the game.

Greville's great black desk stretched away to each side of me, the wide knee-hole flanked to right and left by twin stacks of drawers, four stacks in all. Most of them now contained what they had before the break-in, and I began desultorily to investigate the nearest on the left, looking vaguely for anything that would prompt me as to what I'd overlooked or hadn't known was necessary to be done.

I first found not tasks but the toys: the small black gadgets now tidied away into serried ranks. The Geiger counter was there, also the hand-held copier and a variety of calculators, and I picked out a small black contraption about the size of a paperback book and, turning it over curiously, couldn't think what it could be used for.

'That's an electric measurer,' June said, coming breezily into the office with her hands full of paper. 'Want to see how it works?'

I nodded and she put it flat on its back on the desk. 'It'll tell you how far it is from the desk to the ceiling,' she said, pressing knobs. 'There you are, seven feet five and a half inches. In metres,' she pressed another knob, 'two metres twenty-six centimetres.'

'I don't really need to know how far it is to the ceiling,' I said.

She laughed. 'If you hold it flat against a wall, it measures how far it is to the opposite wall. Does it in a flash, as you saw. You don't need to mess around with tape measures. Mr Franklin got it when he was redesigning the stock-rooms. And he worked out how much carpet we'd need, and how much paint for the walls. This gadget tells you all that.'

'You like computers, don't you?' I said.

'Love them. All shapes, all sizes.' She peered into the

open drawer. 'Mr Franklin was always buying the tiny ones.' She picked out a small grey leather slip-cover the size of a pack of cards and slid the contents onto her palm. 'This little dilly is a travel guide. It tells you things like phone numbers for taxis, airlines, tourist information, the weather, embassies, American Express.' She demonstrated, pushing buttons happily. 'It's an American gadget, it even tells you the TV channels and radio frequencies for about a hundred cities in the US, including Tucson, Arizona, where they hold the biggest gem fair every February. It helps you with fifty other cities round the world, places like Tel Aviv and Hong Kong and Taipei where Mr Greville was always going.'

She put the travel guide down and picked up something else. 'This little round number is a sort of telescope, but it also tells you how far you are away from things. It's for golfers. It tells you how far you are away from the flag on the green, Mr Franklin said, so that you know which club to use.'

'How often did he play golf?' I said, looking through the less than four-inch-long telescope and seeing inside a scale marked GREEN on the lowest line with diminishing numbers above, from 200 yards at the bottom to 40 yards at the top. 'He never talked about it much.'

'He sometimes played at weekends, I think,' June said doubtfully. 'You line up the word GREEN with the actual green, and then the flag stick is always eight feet high, I think, so wherever the top of the stick is on the scale, that's how far away you are. He said it was a good gadget for amateurs like him. He said never to be ashamed of landing in life's bunkers if you'd tried your best shot.' She blinked a bit. 'He always used to show these things to me when he bought them. He knew I liked them too.' She fished for a tissue and without apology wiped her eyes.

'Where did he get them all from?' I asked.

'Mail order catalogues, mostly.'

I was faintly surprised. Mail order and Greville didn't seem to go together, somehow, but I was wrong about that, as I promptly found out.

'Would you like to see our own new catalogue?' June asked, and was out of the door and back again before I could remember if I'd ever seen an old one and decide I hadn't. 'Fresh from the printers,' she said. 'I was just unpacking them.'

I turned the glossy pages of the 50-page booklet, seeing in faithful colours all the polished goodies I'd met in the stock-rooms and also a great many of lesser breeding. Amulets, heart shapes, hoops and butterflies: there seemed to be no end to the possibilities of adornment. When I murmured derogatorily that they were a load of junk, June came fast and strongly to their defence, a mother-hen whose chickens had been snubbed.

'Not everyone can afford diamonds,' she said sharply, 'and, anyway, these things are pretty and we sell them in thousands, and they wind up in hundreds of High Street shops and department stores and I often see people buying the odd shapes we've had through here. People do like them, even if they're not your taste.'

'Sorry,' I said.

Some of her fire subsided. 'I suppose I shouldn't speak to you like that,' she said uncertainly, 'but you're not Mr Franklin . . .' She stopped with a frown.

'It's OK,' I said. 'I am, but I'm not. I know what you mean.'

'Alfie says,' she said slowly, 'that there's a steeple-chase jockey called Derek Franklin.' She looked at my foot as if with new understanding. 'Champion jockey one year, he said. Always in the top ten. Is that . . . you?'

I said neutrally, 'Yes.'

'I *had* to ask you,' she said. 'The others didn't want to.'

'Why not?'

'Annette didn't think you could be a jockey. You're too tall. She said Mr Franklin never said anything about you being one. All she knew was that he had a brother he saw a few times a year. She said she was going to ignore what Alfie thought, because it was most unlikely.' She paused. 'Alfie mentioned it yesterday, after you'd gone. Then he said . . . they all said . . . they didn't see how a jockey could run a business of this sort. If you were one, that is. They didn't want it to be true, so they didn't want to ask.'

'You tell Alfie and the others that if the jockey doesn't run the business their jobs will be down the tubes and they'll be out in the cold before the week's over.'

Her blue eyes widened. 'You sound just like Mr Franklin!'

'And you don't need to mention my profession to the customers, in case I get the same vote of no confidence I've got from the staff.'

Her lips shaped the word 'Wow' but she didn't quite say it. She disappeared fast from the room and presently returned, followed by all the others who were only too clearly in a renewed state of anxiety.

Not one of them a leader. What a pity.

I said, 'You all look as if the ship's been wrecked and the lifeboat's leaking. Well, we've lost the captain, and I agree we're in trouble. My job is with horses and not in an office. But, like I said yesterday, this business is going to stay open and thrive. One way or another, I'll see that it does. So if you'll all go on working normally and keep the customers happy, you'll be doing yourselves a favour because if we get through safely you'll all be due for a bonus. I'm not my brother, but I'm not a fool either, and I'm a pretty fast learner. So just let's get on with the orders, and, er, cheer up.'

Lily, the Charlotte Brontë lookalike, said meekly, 'We don't really doubt your ability . . .'

'Of course we do,' interrupted Jason. He stared at me with half a snigger, with a suggestion of curling lip. 'Give us a tip for the three-thirty, then.'

I listened to the street-smart bravado which went with the spiky orange hair. He thought me easy game.

I said, 'When you are personally able to ride the winner of any three-thirty, you'll be entitled to your jeer. Until then, work or leave, it's up to you.'

There was a resounding silence. Alfie almost smiled. Jason looked merely sullen. Annette took a deep breath, and June's eyes were shining with laughter.

They all drifted away still wordless and I couldn't tell to what extent they'd been reassured, if at all. I listened to the echo of my own voice saying I wasn't a fool, and wondering ruefully if it were true: but until the diamonds were found or I'd lost all hope of finding them, I thought it more essential than ever that Saxony Franklin Ltd should stay shakily afloat. All hands, I thought, to the pumps.

June came back and said tentatively, 'The pep talk seems to be working.'

'Good.'

'Alfie gave Jason a proper ticking off, and Jason's staying.'

'Right.'

'What can I do to help?'

I looked at her thin alert face with its fair eyelashes and blonde-to-invisible eyebrows and realized that without her the save-the-firm enterprise would be a non-starter. She, more than her computer, was at the heart of things. She more than Annette, I thought.

'How long have you worked here?' I asked.

'Three years. Since I left school. Don't ask if I like the job, I love it. What can I do?'

'Look up in your computer's memory any reference to diamonds,' I said.

She was briefly impatient. 'I told you, we don't deal in diamonds.'

'All the same, would you?'

She shrugged and was gone. I got to my feet – foot – and followed her, and watched while she expertly tapped her keys.

'Nothing at all under diamonds,' she said finally. 'Nothing. I told you.'

'Yes.' I thought about the boxes in the vault with the mineral information on the labels. 'Do you happen to know the chemical formula for diamonds?'

'Yes, I do,' she said instantly. 'It's C. Diamonds are pure carbon.'

'Could you try again, then, under C?'

She tried. There was no file for C.

'Did my brother know how to use this computer?' I asked.

'He knew how to work all computers. Given five minutes or so to read the instructions.'

I pondered, staring at the blank unhelpful screen.

'Are there,' I asked eventually, 'any secret files in this?'

She stared. 'We never use secret files.'

'But you could do?'

'Of course. Yes. But we don't need to.'

'If,' I said, 'there were any secret files, would you know that they were there?'

She nodded briefly. 'I wouldn't know, but I could find out.'

'How?' I asked. 'I mean, please would you?'

'What am I looking for? I don't understand.'

'Diamonds.'

'But I told you, we don't . . .'

'I know,' I said, 'but my brother said he was going to buy diamonds and I need to know if he did. If there's any chance he made a private entry on this computer some day when he was first or last in this office, I need to find it.'

She shook her head but tapped away obligingly, bringing what she called menus to the screen. It seemed a fairly lengthy business but finally, frowning, she found something that gave her pause. Then her concentration increased abruptly until the screen was showing the word 'Password?' as before.

'I don't understand,' she said. 'We gave this computer a general password which is Saxony, though we almost never use it. But you can put in any password you like on any particular document to supersede Saxony. This entry was made only a month ago. The date is on the menu. But whoever made it didn't use Saxony as the password. So the password could be anything, literally any word in the world.'

I said, 'By document you mean file?'

'Yes, file. Every entry has a document name, like, say,

"oriental cultured pearls". If I load "oriental cultured pearls" onto the screen I can review our whole stock. I do it all the time. But this document with an unknown password is listed under pearl in the singular, not pearls in the plural, and I don't understand it. I didn't put it there.' She glanced at me. 'At any rate, it doesn't say diamonds.'

'Have another try to guess the password.'

She tried Franklin and Greville without result. 'It could be *anything*,' she said helplessly.

'Try Dozen Roses.'

'Why Dozen Roses?' She thought it extraordinary.

'Greville owned a horse – a racehorse – with that name.'

'Really? He never said. He was so nice, and awfully private.'

'He owned another horse called Gemstones.'

With visible doubt she tried 'Dozen Roses' and then 'Gemstones'. Nothing happened except another insistent demand for the password.

'Try "diamonds", then,' I said.

She tried 'diamonds'. Nothing changed.

'You knew him,' I said. 'Why would he enter something under "pearl"?'

'No idea.' She sat hunched over the keys, drumming her fingers on her mouth. 'Pearl. Pearl. Why pearl?'

'What is a pearl?' I said. 'Does it have a formula?'

'Oh.' She suddenly sat up straight. 'It's a birthstone.'

She typed in 'birthstone', and nothing happened.

Then she blushed slightly.

'It's one of the birthstones for the month of June,' she said. 'I could try it, anyway.'

She typed 'June', and the screen flashed and gave up its secrets.

CHAPTER FIVE

We hadn't found the diamonds.

The screen said:

> June, if you are reading this, come straight into my office for a rise. You are worth your weight in your birthstone, but I'm only offering to increase your salary by twenty per cent. Regards, Greville Franklin.

'Oh!' She sat transfixed. 'So that's what he meant.'

'Explain,' I said.

'One morning . . .' She stopped, her mouth screwing up in an effort not to cry. It took her a while to be able to continue, then she said, 'One morning he told me he'd invented a little puzzle for me and he would give me six months to solve it. After six months it would self-destruct. He was smiling so much.' She swallowed. 'I asked him what sort of puzzle and he wouldn't tell me. He just said he hoped I would find it.'

'Did you look?' I asked.

'Of course I did. I looked everywhere in the office, though I didn't know what I was looking for. I even looked for a new document in the computer, but I just never gave a thought to its being filed as a secret, and my eyes just slid over the word "pearl", as I see it so often. Silly of me. Stupid.'

I said, 'I don't think you're stupid, and I'll honour my brother's promise.'

She gave me a swift look of pleasure but shook her head a little and said, 'I didn't find it. I'd never have solved it except for you.' She hesitated. 'How about ten per cent?'

'Twenty,' I said firmly. 'I'm going to need your help and your knowledge, and if Annette is Personal Assistant, as it says on the door of her office, you can be Deputy Personal Assistant, with the new salary to go with the job.'

She turned a deeper shade of rose and busied herself with making a print-out of Greville's instruction, which she folded and put in her handbag.

'I'll leave the secret in the computer,' she said with misty fondness. 'No one else will ever find it.' She pressed a few buttons and the screen went blank, and I wondered how many times in private she would call up the magic words that Greville had left her.

I wondered if they would really self-destruct: if one could programme something on a computer to erase itself on a given date. I didn't see why not, but I thought

Greville might have given her strong clues before the six months were out.

I asked her if she would print out first a list of everything currently in the vault and then as many things as she thought would help me understand the business better, like the volume and value of a day's, a week's, a month's sales; like which items were most popular, and which least.

'I can tell you that what's very popular just now is black onyx. Fifty years ago they say it was all amber, now no one buys it. Jewellery goes in and out of fashion like everything else.' She began tapping keys. 'Give me a little while and I'll print you a crash course.'

'Thanks.' I smiled, and waited while the printer spat out a gargantuan mouthful of glittering facets. Then I took the list in search of Annette, who was alone in the stock-rooms, and asked her to give me a quick canter round the vault.

'There aren't any diamonds there,' she said positively.

'I'd better learn what is.'

'You don't seem like a jockey,' she said.

'How many do you know?'

She stared. 'None, except you.'

'On the whole,' I said mildly, 'jockeys are like anyone else. Would you feel I was better able to manage here if I were, say, a piano tuner? Or an actor? Or a clergyman?'

She said faintly, 'No.'

'OK, then. We're stuck with a jockey. Twist of fate. Do your best for the poor fellow.'

She involuntarily smiled a genuine smile which lightened her heavy face miraculously. 'All right.' She paused. 'You're really like Mr Franklin in some ways. The way you say things. Deal with honour, he said, and sleep at night.'

'You all remember what he said, don't you?'

'Of course.'

He would have been glad, I supposed, to have left so positive a legacy. So many precepts. So much wisdom. But so few signposts to his personal life. No visible signpost to the diamonds.

In the vault Annette showed me that, besides its chemical formula, each label bore a number: if I looked at that number on the list June had printed, I would see the formula again, but also the normal names of the stones, with colours, shapes and sizes and country of origin.

'Why did he label them like this?' I asked. 'It just makes it difficult to find things.'

'I believe that was his purpose,' she answered. 'I told you, he was very security conscious. We had a secretary working here once who managed to steal a lot of our most valuable turquoise out of the vault. The labels read "turquoise" then, which made it easy, but now they don't.'

'What do they say?'

She smiled and pointed to a row of boxes. I looked

at the labels and read $CuAl_6(PO_4)_4(OH)_8{\cdot}4\text{–}5(H_2O)$ on each of them.

'Enough to put anyone off for life,' I said.

'Exactly. That's the point. Mr Franklin could read formulas as easily as words, and I've got used to them myself now. No one but he and I handle these stones in here. We pack them into boxes ourselves and seal them before they go to Alfie for despatch.' She looked along the rows of labels and did her best to educate me. 'We sell these stones at so much per carat. A carat weighs two hundred milligrams, which means five carats to a gram, a hundred and forty-two carats to an ounce and five thousand carats to the kilo.'

'Stop right there,' I begged.

'You said you learned fast.'

'Give me a day or two.'

She nodded and said if I didn't need her any more she had better get on with the ledgers.

Ledgers, I thought, wilting internally. I hadn't even started on those. I thought of the joy with which I'd left Lancaster University with a degree in Independent Studies, swearing never again to pore dutifully over books and heading straight (against my father's written wishes) to the steeplechase stable where I'd been spending truant days as an amateur. It was true that at college I'd learned fast, because I'd had to, and learned all night often enough, keeping faith with at least the first half of my father's letter. He'd hoped I would grow out of the lure he knew I felt for race-riding, but it was all I'd ever wanted and I couldn't have settled to anything else. There was no long-term future in it, he'd written, besides a complete lack of financial security along with a constant risk of disablement. I ask you to be sensible, he'd said, to think it through and decide against.

Fat chance.

I sighed for the simplicity of the certainty I'd felt in those days, yet, given a second beginning, I wouldn't have lived any differently. I had been deeply fulfilled in racing and grown old in spirit only because of the way life worked in general. Disappointments, injustices, small betrayals, they were everyone's lot. I no longer expected everything to go right, but enough had gone right to leave me at least in a balance of content.

With no feeling that the world owed me anything, I applied myself to the present boring task of opening every packet in every box in the quest for little bits of pure carbon. It wasn't that I expected to find the diamonds there: it was just that it would be so stupid not to look, in case they were.

I worked methodically, putting the boxes one at a time on the wide shelf which ran along the right-hand wall, unfolding the stiff white papers with the soft inner linings and looking at hundreds of thousands of peridots, chrysoberyls, garnets and aquamarines until my head spun. I stopped in fact when I'd done only a third of the stock because apart from the airlessness of the vault it was physically tiring standing on one leg all the time, and the crutches got in the way as much as they helped. I refolded the last of the $XY_3Z_6[(O,OH,F)_4(BO_3)_3Si_6O_{18}]$ (tourmaline) and gave it best.

'What did you learn?' Annette asked when I reappeared in Greville's office. She was in there, replacing yet more papers in their proper files, a task apparently nearing completion.

'Enough to look at jewellery differently,' I said.

She smiled. 'When I read magazines I don't look at the clothes, I look at the jewellery.'

I could see that she would. I thought that I might also, despite myself, from then on. I might even develop an affinity with black onyx cufflinks.

It was by that time four o'clock in the afternoon of what seemed a very long day. I looked up the racing programme in Greville's diary, decided that Nicholas Loder might well have passed over going to Redcar, Warwick and Folkestone, and dialled his number. His secretary answered, and yes, Mr Loder was at home, and yes, he would speak to me.

He came on the line with almost none of the previous evening's agitation, bass resonances positively throbbing down the wire.

'I've been talking to Weatherby's and the Jockey Club,' he said easily, 'and there's fortunately no problem. They agree that before probate the horses belong to Saxony Franklin Limited and not to you, and they will not bar them from racing in that name.'

'Good,' I said, and was faintly surprised.

'They say of course that there has to be at least one registered agent appointed by the company to be responsible for the horses, such appointment to be sealed with the company's seal and registered at Weatherby's. Your brother appointed both himself and myself as registered agents, and although he has died I remain a registered agent as before and can act for the company on my own.'

'Ah,' I said.

'Which being so,' Loder said happily, 'Dozen Roses runs at York as planned.'

'And trots up?'

He chuckled. 'Let's hope so.'

That chuckle, I thought, was the ultimate in confidence.

'I'd be grateful if you could let Saxony Franklin know whenever the horses are due to run in the future,' I said.

'I used to speak to your brother personally at his home number. I can hardly do that with you, as you don't own the horses.'

'No,' I agreed. 'I meant, please will you tell the company? I'll give you the number. And would you ask for Mrs Annette Adams? She was Greville's second-in-command.'

He could hardly say he wouldn't, so I read out the number and he repeated it as he wrote it down.

'Don't forget though that there's only a month left of the Flat season,' he said. 'They'll probably run only once more each. Two at the very most. Then I'll sell them for you, that would be best. No problem. Leave it to me.'

He was right, logically, but I still illogically disliked his haste.

'As executor, I'd have to approve any sale,' I said, hoping I was right. 'In advance.'

'Yes, yes, of course.' Reassuring heartiness. 'Your injury,' he said, 'what exactly is it?'

'Busted ankle.'

'Ah. Bad luck. Getting on well, I hope?' The sympathy sounded more like relief to me than anything else, and again I couldn't think why.

'Getting on,' I said.

'Good, good. Goodbye then. The York race should be on the television on Saturday. I expect you'll watch it?'

'I expect so.'

'Fine.' He put down the receiver in great good humour and left me wondering what I'd missed.

Greville's telephone rang again immediately, and it was Brad to tell me that he had returned from his day's visit to an obscure aunt in Walthamstow and was downstairs in the front hall: all he actually said was, 'I'm back.'

'Great. I won't be long.'

I got a click in reply. End of conversation.

I did mean to leave almost at once but there were two more phone calls in fairly quick succession. The first was from a man introducing himself as Elliot Trelawney, a colleague of Greville's from the West London Magistrates Court. He was extremely sorry, he said, to hear about his death, and he truly sounded it. A positive voice, used to attention: a touch of plummy accent.

'Also,' he said, 'I'd like to talk to you about some projects Greville and I were working on. I'd like to have his notes.'

I said rather blankly, 'What projects? What notes?'

'I could explain better face to face,' he said. 'Could I ask you to meet me? Say tomorrow, early evening, over a drink? You know that pub just round the corner from Greville's house? The Rook and Castle? There. He and I often met there. Five-thirty, six, either of those suit you?'

'Five-thirty,' I said obligingly.

'How shall I know you?'

'By my crutches.'

It silenced him momentarily. I let him off embarrassment.

'They're temporary,' I said.

'Er, fine, then. Until tomorrow.'

He cut himself off, and I asked Annette if she knew him, Elliot Trelawney? She shook her head. She couldn't honestly say she knew anyone outside the office who was known to Greville personally. Unless you counted Prospero Jenks, she said doubtfully. And even then, she herself had never really met him, only talked to him frequently on the telephone.

'Prospero Jenks . . . alias Fabergé?'

'That's the one.'

I thought a bit. 'Would you mind phoning him now?' I said. 'Tell him about Greville and ask if I can go to see him to discuss the future. Just say I'm Greville's brother, nothing else.'

She grinned. 'No horses? Pas de gee-gees?'

Annette, I thought in amusement, was definitely loosening up.

'No horses,' I agreed.

She made the call but without results. Prospero Jenks wouldn't be reachable until morning. She would try then, she said.

I levered myself upright and said I'd see her tomorrow. She nodded, taking it for granted that I would be there. The quicksands were winning, I thought. I was less and less able to get out.

Going down the passage I stopped to look in on Alfie whose day's work stood in columns of loaded cardboard boxes waiting to be entrusted to the post.

'How many do you send out every day?' I asked, gesturing to them.

He looked up briefly from stretching sticky tape round yet another parcel. 'About twenty, twenty-five regular, but more from August to Christmas.' He cut off the tape expertly and stuck an address label deftly on the box top. 'Twenty-eight so far today.'

'Do you bet, Alfie?' I asked. 'Read the racing papers?'

He glanced at me with a mixture of defensiveness

and defiance, neither of which feeling was necessary. 'I *knew* you was him,' he said. 'The others said you couldn't be.'

'You know Dozen Roses too?'

A tinge of craftiness took over in his expression. 'Started winning again, didn't he? I missed him the first time, but yes, I've had a little tickle since.'

'He runs on Saturday at York, but he'll be odds-on,' I said.

'Will he win, though? Will they be trying with him? I wouldn't put my shirt on that.'

'Nicholas Loder says he'll trot up.'

He knew who Nicholas Loder was: didn't need to ask. With cynicism, he put his just-finished box on some sturdy scales and wrote the result on the cardboard with a thick black pen. He must have been well into his sixties, I thought, with deep lines from his nose to the corners of his mouth and pale sagging skin everywhere from which most of the elasticity had vanished. His hands, with the veins of age beginning to show dark blue, were nimble and strong however, and he bent to pick up another heavy box with a supple back. A tough old customer, I thought, and essentially more in touch with street awareness than the exaggerated Jason.

'Mr Franklin's horses run in and out,' he said pointedly. 'And as a jock you'd know about that.'

Before I could decide whether or not he was intentionally insulting me, Annette came hurrying down the passage calling my name.

'Derek . . . Oh there you are. Still here, good. There's another phone call for you.' She about-turned and went back towards Greville's office, and I followed her, noticing with interest that she'd dropped the Mister from my name. Yesterday's unthinkable was today's natural, now that I was established as a jockey, which was OK as far as it went, as long as it didn't go too far.

I picked up the receiver which was lying on the black desk and said, 'Hello? Derek Franklin speaking.'

A familiar voice said, 'Thank God for that. I've been trying your Hungerford number all day. Then I remembered about your brother . . .' He spoke loudly, driven by urgency.

Milo Shandy, the trainer I'd ridden most for during the past three seasons: a perpetual optimist in the face of world evidence of corruption, greed and lies.

'I've a crisis on my hands,' he bellowed, 'and can you come over? Will you pull out all stops to come over first thing in the morning?'

'Er, what for?'

'You know the Ostermeyers? They've flown over from Pittsburgh for some affair in London and they phoned me and I told them Datepalm is for sale. And you know that if they buy him I can keep him here, otherwise I'll lose him because he'll have to go to auction. And they want you here when they see him work on the Downs and they can only manage first lot tomorrow, and they think the sun twinkles out of your backside, so for God's sake *come.*'

Interpreting the agitation was easy. Datepalm was the horse on which I'd won the Gold Cup: a seven-year-old gelding still near the beginning of what with luck would be a notable jumping career. Its owner had recently dropped the bombshell of telling Milo she was leaving England to marry an Australian, and if he could sell Datepalm to one of his other owners for the astronomical figure she named, she wouldn't send it to public auction and out of his yard.

Milo had been in a panic most of the time since then because none of his other owners had so far thought the horse worth the price, his Gold Cup success having been judged lucky in the absence through coughing of a couple of more established stars. Both Milo and I thought Datepalm better than his press, and I had as strong a motive as Milo for wanting him to stay in the stable.

'Calm down,' I assured him. 'I'll be there.'

He let out a lot of breath in a rush. 'Tell the Ostermeyers he's a really good horse.'

'He is,' I said, 'and I will.'

'Thanks, Derek.' His voice dropped to normal decibels. 'Oh, and by the way, there's no horse called Koningin Beatrix, and not likely to be. Weatherby's say Koningin Beatrix means Queen Beatrix, as in Queen Beatrix of the Netherlands, and they frown on people naming racehorses after royal persons.'

'Oh,' I said. 'Well, thanks for finding out.'

'Any time. See you in the morning. For God's sake

don't be late. You know the Ostermeyers get up before larks.'

'What I need,' I said to Annette, putting down the receiver, 'is an appointments book, so as not to forget where I've said I'll be.'

She began looking in the drawerful of gadgets.

'Mr Franklin had an electric memory thing he used to put appointments in. You could use that for now.' She sorted through the black collection, but without result. 'Stay here a minute,' she said, closing the drawer, 'while I ask June if she knows where it is.'

She went away busily and I thought about how to convince the Ostermeyers, who could afford anything they set their hearts on, that Datepalm would bring them glory if not necessarily repay their bucks. They had had steeplechasers with Milo from time to time, but not for almost a year at the moment. I'd do a great deal, I thought, to persuade them it was time to come back.

An alarm like a digital watch alarm sounded faintly, muffled, and to begin with I paid it no attention, but as it persisted I opened the gadget drawer to investigate and, of course, as I did so it immediately stopped. Shrugging, I closed the drawer again, and Annette came back bearing a sheet of paper but no gadget.

'June doesn't know where the Wizard is, so I'll make out a rough calendar on plain paper.'

'What's the Wizard?' I asked.

'The calculator. Baby computer. June says it does everything but boil eggs.'

'Why do you call it the Wizard?' I asked.

'It has that name on it. It's about the size of a paper-back book and it was Mr Franklin's favourite object. He took it everywhere.' She frowned. 'Maybe it's in his car, wherever that is.'

The car. Another problem. 'I'll find the car,' I said, with more confidence than I felt. Somehow or other I would have to find the car. 'Maybe the Wizard was stolen out of this office in the break-in,' I said.

She stared at me with widely opening eyes. 'The thief would have to have known what it was. It folds up flat. You can't see any buttons.'

'All the gadgets were out on the floor, weren't they?'

'Yes.' It troubled her. 'Why the address book? Why the engagements for October? Why the Wizard?'

Because of diamonds, I thought instinctively, but couldn't rationalize it. Someone had perhaps been looking, as I was, for the treasure map marked X. Perhaps they'd known it existed. Perhaps they'd found it.

'I'll get here a couple of hours later tomorrow,' I said to Annette. 'And I must leave by five to meet Elliot Trelawney at five-thirty. So if you reach Prospero Jenks, ask him if I could go to see him in between. Or failing that, any time Thursday. Write off Friday because of the funeral.'

Greville died only the day before yesterday, I thought. It already seemed half a lifetime.

Annette said, 'Yes, Mr Franklin,' and bit her lip in dismay.

I half smiled at her. 'Call me Derek. Just plain Derek. And invest it with whatever you feel.'

'It's confusing,' she said weakly, 'from minute to minute.'

'Yes, I know.'

With a certain relief I rode down in the service lift and swung across to Brad in the car. He hopped out of the front seat and shovelled me into the back, tucking the crutches in beside me and waiting while I lifted my leg along the padded leather and wedged myself into the corner for the most comfortable angle of ride.

'Home?' he said.

'No. Like I told you on the way up, we'll stop in Kensington for a while, if you don't mind.'

He gave the tiniest of nods. I'd provided him in the morning with a detailed large-scale map of West London, asking him to work out how to get to the road where Greville had lived, and I hoped to hell he had done it, because I was feeling more drained than I cared to admit and not ready to ride in irritating traffic-clogged circles.

'Look out for a pub called The Rook and Castle, would you?' I asked, as we neared the area. 'Tomorrow at five-thirty I have to meet someone there.'

Brad nodded and with the unerring instinct of the beer drinker quickly found it, merely pointing vigorously to tell me.

'Great,' I said, and he acknowledged that with a wiggle of the shoulders.

He drew up so confidently outside Greville's address that I wondered if he had reconnoitred earlier in the day, except that his aunt lived theoretically in the opposite direction. In any case, he handed me the crutches, opened the gate of the small front garden and said loquaciously, 'I'll wait in the car.'

'I might be an hour or more. Would you mind having a quick recce up and down this street and those nearby to see if you can find an old Rover with this number?' I gave him a card with it on. 'My brother's car,' I said.

He gave me a brief nod and turned away, and I looked up at the tall townhouse that Greville had moved into about three months previously, and which I'd never visited. It was creamy-grey, gracefully proportioned, with balustraded steps leading up to the black front door, and businesslike but decorative metal grilles showing behind the glass in every window from semi-basement to roof.

I crossed the grassy front garden and went up the steps, and found there were three locks on the front door. Cursing slightly I yanked out Greville's half-ton of keys and by trial and error found the way into his fortress.

Late afternoon sun slanted yellowly into a long main drawing room which was on the left of the entrance hall, throwing the pattern of the grilles in shadows on the greyish-brown carpet. The walls, pale salmon, were adorned with vivid paintings of stained-glass cathedral windows, and the fabric covering sofa and armchairs was of a large broken herringbone pattern in dark brown and white, confusing to the eye. I reflected ruefully that I didn't know whether it all represented Greville's own taste or whether he'd taken it over from the past owner. I knew only his taste in clothes, food, gadgets and horses. Not very much. Not enough.

The drawing room was dustless and tidy; unlived in. I returned to the front hall from where stairs led up and down, but before tackling those I went through a door at the rear which opened into a much smaller room filled with a homely clutter of books, newspapers, magazines, black leather chairs, clocks, chrysanthemums in pots, a tray of booze and framed medieval brass rubbings on deep green walls. This was all Greville, I thought. This was home.

I left it for the moment and hopped down the stairs to the semi-basement, where there was a bedroom, unused, a small bathroom and decorator-style dining room looking out through grilles to a rear garden, with a narrow spotless kitchen alongside.

Fixed to the fridge by a magnetic strawberry was a note.

Dear Mr Franklin,

I didn't know you'd be away this weekend. I brought in the papers, they're in the back room. You didn't leave your laundry out, so I haven't taken it. Thanks for the money. I'll be back next Tuesday as usual.

Mrs P

I looked around for a pencil, found a ball-point, pulled the note from its clip and wrote on the back, asking Mrs P to call the following number (Saxony Franklin's) and speak to Derek or Annette. I didn't sign it, but put it back under the strawberry where I supposed it would stay for another week, a sorry message in waiting.

I looked in the fridge which contained little but milk, butter, grapes, a pork pie and two bottles of champagne.

Diamonds in the ice cubes? I didn't think he would have put them anywhere so chancy: besides, he was security conscious, not paranoid.

I hauled myself upstairs to the hall again and then went on up to the next floor where there was a bedroom and bathroom suite in self-conscious black and white. Greville had slept there: the built-in cupboards and drawers held his clothes, the bathroom closet his privacy. He had been sparing in his possessions, leaving a single row of shoes, several white shirts on hangers, six assorted suits and a rack of silk ties. The drawers were tidy with sweaters, sports shirts, underclothes, socks. Our mother, I thought with a smile, would have been proud of him. She'd tried hard and unsuccessfully to instil tidiness into both of us as children, and it looked as if we'd both got better with age.

There was little else to see. The drawer in the bedside table revealed indigestion tablets, a torch and a paperback, John D. MacDonald. No gadgets and no treasure maps.

With a sigh I went into the only other room on that floor and found it unfurnished and papered with garish metallic silvery roses which had been half ripped off at one point. So much for the decorator.

There was another flight of stairs going upwards, but I didn't climb them. There would only be, by the looks of things, unused rooms to find there, and I thought I would go and look later when stairs weren't such a sweat. Anything deeply interesting in that house seemed likely to be found in the small back sitting room, so it was to there that I returned.

I sat for a while in the chair that was clearly Greville's favourite, from where he could see the television and the view over the garden. Places that people had left for ever should be seen through their eyes, I thought. His presence was strong in that room, and in me.

Beside his chair there was a small antique table with, on its polished top, a telephone and an answering machine. A red light for messages received was shining on the machine, so after a while I pressed a button marked 'rewind', followed by another marked 'play'.

A woman's voice spoke without preamble.

'Darling, where are you? Do ring me.'

There was a series of between-message clicks, then the same voice again, this time packed with anxiety.

'Darling, please please ring. I'm very worried. Where are you, darling? *Please* ring. I love you.'

Again the clicks, but no more messages.

Poor lady, I thought. Grief and tears waiting in the wings.

I got up and explored the room more fully, pausing by two drawers in a table beside the window. They contained two small black unidentified gadgets which baffled me and which I stowed in my pockets, and also a slotted tray containing a rather nice collection of small bears, polished and carved from shaded pink, brown and charcoal stone. I laid the tray on top of the table beside some chrysanthemums and came next to a box made of greenish stone, also polished and which, true to Greville's habit, was firmly locked. Thinking perhaps that one of the keys fitted it I brought out the bunch again and began to try the smallest.

I was facing the window with my back to the room, balancing on one foot and leaning a thigh against the table, my arms out of the crutches, intent on what I was doing and disastrously unheeding. The first I knew of anyone else in the house was a muffled exclamation behind me, and I turned to see a dark-haired woman coming through the doorway, her wild glance rigidly fixed on the green stone box. Without pause she came fast towards me, pulling out of a pocket a black object like a long fat cigar.

I opened my mouth to speak but she brought her hand round in a strong swinging arc, and in that travel the short black cylinder more than doubled its length into a thick silvery flexible stick which crashed with shattering force against my left upper arm, enough to stop a heavyweight in round one.

CHAPTER SIX

My fingers went numb and dropped the box. I swayed and spun on the force of the impact and overbalanced, toppling, thinking sharply that I mustn't this time put my foot on the ground. I dropped the bunch of keys and grabbed at the back of an upright black leather chair with my right hand to save myself, but it turned over under my weight and came down on top of me onto the carpet in a tangle of chair legs, table legs and crutches, the green box underneath and digging into my back.

In a spitting fury I tried to orientate myself and finally got enough breath for one single choice, charming and heartfelt word.

'*Bitch.*'

She gave me a baleful glare and picked up the telephone, pressing three fast buttons.

'Police,' she said, and in as short a time as it took the emergency service to connect her, 'Police, I want to report a burglary. I've caught a burglar.'

'I'm Greville's brother,' I said thickly, from the floor.

For a moment it didn't seem to reach her. I said again, more loudly, 'I'm Greville's brother.'

'What?' she said vaguely.

'For Christ's sake, are you deaf? I'm not a burglar, I'm Greville Franklin's brother.' I gingerly sat up into an L-shape and found no strength anywhere.

She put the phone down. 'Why didn't you say so?' she demanded.

'What chance did you give me? And who the hell are you, walking into my brother's house and belting people?'

She held at the ready the fearsome thing she'd hit me with, looking as if she thought I'd attack her in my turn, which I certainly felt like. In the last six days I'd been crunched by a horse, a mugger and a woman. All I needed was a toddler to amble up with a coup de grâce. I pressed the fingers of my right hand on my forehead and the palm against my mouth and considered the blackness of life in general.

'What's the matter with you?' she said after a pause.

I slid the hand away and drawled, 'Absolutely bloody nothing.'

'I only tapped you,' she said with criticism.

'Shall I give you a hefty clip with that thing so you can feel what it's like?'

'You're angry.' She sounded surprised.

'Dead right.'

I struggled up off the floor, straightened the fallen chair and sat on it. 'Who are you?' I repeated. But I knew who she was: the woman on the answering machine. The same voice. The cut-crystal accent. Darling, where are you? I love you.

'Did you ring his office?' I said. 'Are you Mrs Williams?'

She seemed to tremble and crumple inwardly and she walked past me to the window to stare out into the garden.

'Is he really dead?' she said.

'Yes.'

She was forty, I thought. Perhaps more. Nearly my height. In no way tiny or delicate. A woman of decision and power, sorely troubled.

She wore a leather-belted raincoat, though it hadn't rained for weeks, and plain black businesslike court shoes. Her hair, thick and dark, was combed smoothly back from her forehead to curl under on her collar, a cool groomed look achieved only by expert cutting. There was no visible jewellery, little remaining lipstick, no trace of scent.

'How?' she said eventually.

I had a strong impulse to deny her the information, to punish her for her precipitous attack, to hurt her and get even. But there was no point in it, and I knew I would end up with more shame than satisfaction, so after a struggle I explained briefly about the scaffolding.

'Friday afternoon,' I said. 'He was unconscious at once. He died early on Sunday.'

She turned her head slowly to look at me directly. 'Are you Derek?' she said.

'Yes.'

'I'm Clarissa Williams.'

Neither of us made any attempt to shake hands. It would have been incongruous, I thought.

'I came to fetch some things of mine,' she said. 'I didn't expect anyone to be here.'

It was an apology of sorts, I supposed: and if I had indeed been a burglar she would have saved the bric-à-brac.

'What things?' I asked.

She hesitated, but in the end said, 'A few letters, that's all.' Her gaze strayed to the answering machine and there was a definite tightening of muscles round her eyes.

'I played the messages,' I said.

'Oh God.'

'Why should it worry you?'

She had her reasons, it seemed, but she wasn't going to tell me what they were: or not then, at any rate.

'I want to wipe them off,' she said. 'It was one of the purposes of coming.'

She glanced at me, but I couldn't think of any urgent reason why she shouldn't, so I didn't say anything. Tentatively, as if asking my forbearance every step of the way, she walked jerkily to the machine, rewound the tape and pressed the record button, recording silence over what had gone before. After a while she rewound the tape again and played it, and there were no desperate appeals any more.

'Did anyone else hear . . .?'

'I don't think so. Not unless the cleaner was in the habit of listening. She came today, I think.'

'Oh God.'

'You left no name.' Why the hell was I reassuring her, I wondered. I still had no strength in my fingers. I could still feel that awful blow like a shudder.

'Do you want a drink?' she said abruptly. 'I've had a dreadful day.' She went over to the tray of bottles and poured vodka into a heavy tumbler. 'What do you want?'

'Water,' I said. 'Make it a double.'

She tightened her mouth and put down the vodka bottle with a clink. 'Soda or tonic?' she asked starchily.

'Soda.'

She poured soda into a glass for me and tonic into her own, diluting the spirit by not very much. Ice was downstairs in the kitchen. No one mentioned it.

I noticed she'd left her lethal weapon lying harmlessly beside the answering machine. Presumably I no longer represented any threat. As if avoiding personal contact, she set my soda water formally on the table beside me between the little stone bears and the chrysanthemums and drank deeply from her own glass. Better than tranquillizers, I thought. Alcohol loosened the stress, calmed the mental pain. The world's first anaesthetic. I could have done with some myself.

'Where are your letters?' I asked.

She switched on a table light. The on-creeping dusk in the garden deepened abruptly towards night and I wished she would hurry up because I wanted to go home.

She looked at a bookcase which covered a good deal of one wall.

'In there, I think. In a book.'

'Do start looking, then. It could take all night.'

'You don't need to wait.'

'I think I will,' I said.

'Don't you trust me?' she demanded.

'No.'

She stared at me hard. 'Why not?'

I didn't say that because of the diamonds I didn't trust anyone. I didn't know who I could safely ask to look out for them, or who would search to steal them, if they knew they might be found.

'I don't know you,' I said neutrally.

'But I . . .' She stopped and shrugged. 'I suppose I don't know you either.' She went over to the bookshelves. 'Some of these books are hollow,' she said.

Oh Greville, I thought. How would I ever find anything he had hidden? I liked straight paths. He'd had a mind like a labyrinth.

She began pulling out books from the lower shelves and opening the front covers. Not methodically book by book along any row but always, it seemed to me, those with predominantly blue spines. After a while, on her knees, she found a hollow one which she laid open on the floor with careful sarcasm, so that I could see she wasn't concealing anything.

The interior of the book was in effect a blue velvet box with a close-fitting lid that could be pulled out by a tab. When she pulled the lid out, the shallow blue velvet-lined space beneath was revealed as being entirely empty.

Shrugging, she replaced the lid and closed the book, which immediately looked like any other book, and returned it to the shelves: and a few seconds later found another hollow one, this time with red velvet interiors. Inside this one lay an envelope.

She looked at it without touching it, and then at me. 'It's not my letters,' she said. 'Not my writing paper.'

I said, 'Greville made a will leaving everything he possessed to me.'

She didn't seem to find it extraordinary, although I did: he had done it that way for simplicity when he was in a hurry, and he would certainly have changed it, given time.

'You'd better see what's in here, then,' she said calmly, and she picked the envelope out and stretched across to hand it to me.

The envelope, which hadn't been stuck down, contained a single ornate key, about four inches long, the top flattened and pierced like metal lace, the business end narrow with small but intricate teeth. I laid it on my palm and showed it to her, asking her if she knew what it unlocked.

She shook her head. 'I haven't seen it before.' She paused. 'He was a man of secrets,' she said.

I listened to the wistfulness in her voice. She might be strongly controlled at that moment, but she hadn't been before Annette told her Greville was dead. There had been raw panicky emotion on the tape. Annette had simply confirmed her frightful fears and put what I imagined was a false calmness in place of escalating despair. A man of secrets . . . Greville had apparently not opened his mind to her much more than he had to me.

I put the key back in its envelope and handed it across.

'It had better stay in the book for now,' I said, 'until I find a keyhole it fits.'

She put the key in the book and returned it to the shelves, and shortly afterwards found her letters. They were fastened not with romantic ribbons but held together by a prosaic rubber band; not a great many of them by the look of things but carefully kept.

She stared at me from her knees. 'I don't want you to read them,' she said. 'Whatever Greville left you, they're mine, not yours.'

I wondered why she needed so urgently to remove all traces of herself from the house. Out of curiosity I'd have read the letters with interest if I'd found them myself, but I could hardly demand now to see her love letters . . . if they were love letters.

'Show me just a short page,' I said.

She looked bitter. 'You really don't trust me, do you? I'd like to know why.'

'Someone broke into Greville's office over the weekend,' I said, 'and I'm not quite sure what they were looking for.'

'Not my letters,' she said positively.

'Show me just a page,' I said, 'so I know they're what you say.'

I thought she would refuse altogether, but after a moment's thought she slid the rubber band off the letters and fingered through them, finally, with all expression repressed, handing me one small sheet.

It said:

> . . . and until next Monday my life will be a desert. What am I to do? After your touch I shrink from him. It's dreadful. I am running out of headaches. I adore you.
>
> C.

I handed the page back in silence, embarrassed at having intruded.

'Take them,' I said.

She blinked a few times, snapped the rubber band back round the small collection, and put them into a plain black leather handbag which lay beside her on the carpet.

I felt down onto the floor, collected the crutches and stood up, concentrating on at least holding the hand support of the left one, even if not putting much weight on it. Clarissa Williams watched me go over towards Greville's chair with a touch of awkwardness.

'Look,' she said, 'I didn't realize . . . I mean, when I came in here and saw you stealing things I thought you were stealing things . . . I didn't notice the crutches.'

I supposed that was the truth. Bona fide burglars didn't go around peg-legged, and I'd laid the supports aside at the time she'd come storming in. She'd been too fired up to ask questions: propelled no doubt by grief, anxiety and fear of the intruder. None of which lessened my contrary feeling that she damned well *ought* to have asked questions before waging war.

I wondered how she would have explained her presence to the police, if they had arrived, when she was urgent to remove all traces of herself from the house. Perhaps she would have realized her mistake and simply departed, leaving the incapacitated burglar on the floor.

I went over to the telephone table and picked up the brutal little man-tamer. The heavy handle, a black cigar-shaped cylinder, knurled for a good grip, was under an inch in diameter and about seven inches long. Protruding beyond that was a short length of solidly thick chromium-plated closely-coiled spring, with a similar but narrower spring extending beyond that, the whole tipped with a black metal knob, fifteen or sixteen inches overall. A kick as hard as a horse.

'What is this?' I said, holding it, feeling its weight.

'Greville gave it to me. He said the streets aren't safe. He wanted me to carry it always ready. He said all women should carry them because of muggers and rapists ... as a magistrate he heard so much about women being attacked ... he said one blow would render the toughest man helpless and give me time to escape.'

I hadn't much difficulty in believing it. I bent the black knob to one side and watched the close heavy spring flex and straighten fast when I let it go. She got to her feet and said, 'I'm sorry. I've never used it before, not in anger. Greville showed me how ... he just said to swing as hard as I could so that the springs would shoot out and do the maximum damage.'

My dear brother, I thought. Thank you very much.

'Does it go back into its shell?' I asked.

She nodded. 'Twist the bigger spring clockwise ... it'll come loose and slide into the casing.' I did that, but the smaller spring with the black knob still stuck out. 'You have to give the knob a bang against something, then it will slide in.'

I banged the knob against the wall, and like a meek lamb the narrower spring slid smoothly into the wider, and the end of the knob became the harmless-looking end of yet another gadget.

'What makes it work?' I asked, but she didn't know.

I found that the end opposite the knob unscrewed if one tried, so I unscrewed it about twenty turns until the inch-long piece came off, and I discovered that the whole end section was a very strong magnet.

Simple, I thought. Ordinarily the magnet held the heavy springs inside the cylinder. Make a strong flicking arc, in effect throw the springs out, and the magnet couldn't hold them, but let them go, letting loose the full whipping strength of the thing.

I screwed back the cap, held the cylinder, swung it hard. The springs shot out, flexible, shining, horrific.

Wordlessly, I closed the thing up again and offered it to her.

'It's called a kiyoga,' she said.

I didn't care what it was called. I didn't care if I never saw it again. She put it familiarly into her raincoat pocket, every woman's ultimate reply to footpads, maniacs and assorted misogynists.

She looked unhappily and uncertainly at my face. 'I suppose I can't ask you to forget I came here?' she said.

'It would be impossible.'

'Could you just . . . not speak of it?'

If I'd met her in another way I suppose I might have liked her. She had generous eyes that would have looked better smiling, and an air of basic good humour which persisted despite her jumbling emotions.

With an effort she said, 'Please.'

'Don't beg,' I said sharply. It made me uncomfortable and it didn't suit her.

She swallowed. 'Greville told me about you. I guess . . . I'll have to trust to his judgement.'

She felt in the opposite pocket to the one with the kiyoga and brought out a plain keyring with three keys on it.

'You'd better have these,' she said. 'I won't be using them any more.' She put them down by the answering machine and in her eyes I saw the shininess of sudden tears.

'He died in Ipswich,' I said. 'He'll be cremated there on Friday afternoon. Two o'clock.'

She nodded speechlessly in acknowledgement, not looking at me, and went past me, through the doorway and down the hall and out of the front door, closing it with a quiet finality behind her.

With a sigh, I looked round the room. The book-box that had contained her letters still lay open on the floor and I bent down, picked it up, and restored it to the shelves. I wondered just how many books were hollow. Tomorrow evening, I thought, after Elliot Trelawney, I would come and look.

Meanwhile I picked up the fallen green stone box and put it on the table by the chrysanthemums, reflecting that the ornate key in the red-lined book-box was far too large to fit its tiny lock. Greville's bunch of keys was down on the carpet also. I returned to what I'd been doing before being so violently interrupted, but found that the smallest of the bunch was still too big for the green stone.

A whole load of no progress, I thought moodily.

I drank the soda water, which had lost its fizz.

I rubbed my arm, which didn't make it much better.

I wondered what judgement Greville had passed on me, that could be trusted.

There was a polished cupboard that I hadn't investigated underneath the television set and, not expecting much, I bent down and pulled one of the doors open by its brass ring handle. The other door opened of its own accord and the contents of the cupboard slid outwards as a unit; a video machine on top with, on two shelves below, rows of black boxes holding recording tapes. There were small uniform labels on the boxes bearing, not formulas this time, but dates.

I pulled one of the boxes out at random and was stunned to see the larger label stuck to its front: 'Race Video Club', it said in heavy print, and underneath, in typing, 'July 7th, Sandown Park, Dozen Roses.'

The Race Video Club, as I knew well, sold tapes of races to owners, trainers and anyone else interested. Greville, I thought in growing amazement as I looked further, must have given them a standing order: every race his horses had run in for the past two years, I judged, was there on his shelves to be watched.

He'd told me once, when I asked why he didn't go to see his runners, that he saw them enough on television;

and I'd thought he meant on the ordinary scheduled programmes, live from the racetracks in the afternoons.

The front doorbell rang, jarring and unexpected. I went along and looked through a small peephole and found Brad standing on the doorstep, blinking and blinded by two spotlights shining on his face. The lights came from above the door and lit up the whole path and the gate. I opened the door as he shielded his eyes with his arm.

'Hello,' I said. 'Are you all right?'

'Turn the lights off. Can't see.'

I looked for a switch beside the front door, found several, and by pressing them all upwards indiscriminately, put out the blaze.

'Came to see you were OK,' Brad explained. 'Those lights just went on.'

Of their own accord, I realized. Another manifestation of Greville's security, no doubt. Anyone who came up the path after dark would get illuminated for his pains.

'Sorry I've been so long,' I said. 'Now you're here, would you carry a few things?'

He nodded as if he'd let out enough words already to last the evening, and followed me silently, when I beckoned him, towards the small sitting room.

'I'm taking that green stone box and as many of those video tapes as you can carry, starting from that end,' I said, and he obligingly picked up about ten recent tapes, balancing the box on top.

I found a hall light, switched that on, and turned off the lamp in the sitting room. It promptly turned itself on again, unasked.

'Cor,' Brad said.

I thought that maybe it was time to leave before I tripped any other alarms wired direct after dark to the local constabulary. I closed the sitting-room door and we went along the hall to the outer world. Before leaving I pressed all the switches beside the front door downwards, and maybe I turned more on than I'd turned off: the spotlights didn't go on, but a dog started barking noisily behind us.

'Strewth,' Brad said, whirling round and clutching the video tapes to his chest as if they would defend him.

There was no dog. There was a loudspeaker like a bull horn on a low hall table emitting the deep-throated growls and barks of a determined Alsatian.

'Bleeding hell,' Brad said.

'Let's go,' I said in amusement, and he could hardly wait.

The barking stopped of its own accord as we stepped out into the air. I pulled the door shut, and we set off to go down the steps and along the path, and we'd gone barely three paces when the spotlights blazed on again.

'Keep going,' I said to Brad. 'I daresay they'll turn themselves off in time.'

It was fine by him. He'd parked the car round the corner, and I spent the swift journey to Hungerford wondering about Clarissa Williams; her life, love and adultery.

During the evening I failed both to open the green stone box and to understand the gadgets.

Shaking the box gave me no impression of contents and I supposed it could well be empty. A cigarette box, I thought, though I couldn't remember ever seeing Greville smoking. Perhaps a box to hold twin packs of cards. Perhaps a box for jewellery. Its tiny keyhole remained impervious to probes from nail scissors, suitcase keys and a piece of wire, and in the end I surrendered and laid it aside.

Neither of the gadgets opened or shut. One was a small black cylindrical object about the size of a thumb with one end narrowly ridged, like a coin. Turning the ridged end a quarter-turn clockwise, its full extent of travel, produced a thin faint high-pitched whine which proved to be the unexciting sum of the thing's activity. Shrugging, I switched the whine off again and stood the small tube upright on the green box.

The second gadget didn't even produce a whine. It was a flat black plastic container about the size of a pack of cards with a single square red button placed centrally on the front. I pressed the button: no results. A round chromiumed knob set into one of the sides of the cover revealed itself on further inspection as the end of a telescopic aerial. I pulled it out as far as it would go, about ten inches, and was rewarded with what I presumed was a small transmitter which transmitted I didn't know what to I didn't know where.

Sighing, I pushed the aerial back into its socket and added the transmitter to the top of the green box, and after that I fed Greville's tapes one by one into my video machine and watched the races.

Alfie's comment about in-and-out running had interested me more than I would have wanted him to know. Dozen Roses, from my own reading of the results, had had a long doldrum period followed by a burst of success, suggestive of the classic 'cheating' pattern of running a horse to lose and go on losing until he was low in the handicap and unbacked, then setting him off to win at long odds in a race below his latent abilities and wheeling away the winnings in a barrow.

All trainers did that in a mild way sometimes, whatever the rules might say about always running flat out. Young and inexperienced horses could be ruined by being pressed too hard too soon: one had to give them a chance to enjoy themselves, to let their racing instinct develop fully.

That said, there was a point beyond which no modern trainer dared go. In the bad old days before universal camera coverage, it had been harder to prove a horse hadn't been trying: many jockeys had been artists at waving their whips while hauling on the reins. Under the eagle lenses and fierce discipline of the current scene, even natural and unforeseen fluctuations in a horse's form could find the trainer yanked in before the Stewards for an explanation, and if the trainer couldn't explain why his short-priced favourite had turned leaden footed it could cost him a depressing fine.

No trainer, however industrious, was safe from suspicion, yet I'd never read or heard of Nicholas Loder getting himself into that sort of trouble. Maybe Alfie, I thought dryly, knew something the Stewards didn't. Maybe Alfie could tell me why Loder had all but panicked when he'd feared Dozen Roses might not run on Saturday next.

Brad had picked up the six most recent outings of Dozen Roses, interspersed by four of Gemstones's. I played all six of Dozen Roses's first, starting with the earliest, back in May, checking the details with what Greville had written in his diary.

On the screen there were shots of the runners walking round the parade ring and going down to the start, with Greville's pink and orange colours bright and easy to see. The May race was a ten-furlong handicap for three-year-olds and upwards, run at Newmarket on a Friday. Eighteen runners. Dozen Roses ridden by a second-string jockey because Loder's chief retained jockey was riding the stable's other runner which started favourite.

Down at the start there was some sort of fracas involving Dozen Roses. I rewound the tape and played it through in slow motion and couldn't help laughing.

Dozen Roses, his mind far from racing, had been showing unseemly interest in a mare.

I remembered Greville saying once that he thought it a shame and unfair to curb a colt's enthusiasm: no horse of his would ever be gelded. I remembered him vividly, leaning across a small table and saying it over a glass of brandy with a gleam in which I'd seen his own enjoyment of sex. So many glimpses of him in my mind, I thought. Too few, also. I couldn't really believe I would never eat with him again, whatever my senses said.

Trainers didn't normally run mares that had come into season, but sometimes one couldn't tell early on. Horses knew, though. Dozen Roses had been aroused. The mare was loaded into the stalls in a hurry and Dozen Roses had been walked around until the last minute to cool his ardour. After that, he had run without sparkle and finished mid-field, the mare to the rear of him trailing in last. Loder's other runner, the favourite, had won by a length.

Too bad, I thought, smiling, and watched Dozen Roses's next attempt three weeks later.

No distracting attractions this time. The horse had behaved quietly, sleepily almost, and had turned in the sort of moderate performance which set owners wondering if the game was worth it. The next race was much the same, and if I'd been Greville I would have decided it was time to sell.

Greville, it seemed, had had more faith. After seven weeks' rest Dozen Roses had gone bouncing down to the start, raced full of zest and zoomed over the finishing line in front, netting 14/1 for anyone ignorant enough to have backed him. Like Greville, of course.

Watching the sequence of tapes I did indeed wonder why the Stewards hadn't made a fuss, but Greville hadn't mentioned anything except his pleasure in the horse's return to his three-year-old form.

Dozen Roses had next produced two further copybook performances of stamina and determination, which brought us up to date. I rewound and removed the last tape and could see why Loder thought it would be another trot-up on Saturday.

Gemstones's tapes weren't as interesting. Despite his name he wasn't of much value, and the one race he'd won looked more like a fluke than constructive engineering. I would sell them both, I decided, as Loder wanted.

CHAPTER SEVEN

Brad came early on Wednesday and drove me to Lambourn. The ankle was sore in spite of Distalgesics but less of a constant drag that morning and I could have driven the car myself if I'd put my mind to it. Having Brad around, I reflected on the way, was a luxury I was all too easily getting used to.

Clarissa Williams's attentions had worn off completely except for a little stiffness and a blackening bruise like a bar midway between shoulder and elbow. That didn't matter. For much of the year I had bruises somewhere or other, result of the law of averages operating in steeplechasing. Falls occurred about once every fourteen races, sometimes oftener, and while a few of the jockeys had bodies that hardly seemed to bruise at all, mine always did. On the other hand I healed everywhere fast, bones, skin and optimism.

Milo Shandy, striding about in his stable yard as if incapable of standing still, came over to my car as it rolled to a stop and yanked open the driver's door. The words he was about to say didn't come out as he stared first at Brad, then at me on the back seat, and what he eventually said was, 'A chauffeur, by God. Coddling yourself, aren't you?'

Brad got out of the car, gave Milo a neanderthal look and handed me the crutches as usual.

Milo, dark, short and squarely built, watched the proceedings with disgust.

'I want you to ride Datepalm,' he said.

'Well, I can't.'

'The Ostermeyers will want it. I told them you'd be here.'

'Gerry rides Datepalm perfectly well,' I said, Gerry being the lad who rode the horse at exercise as a matter of course most days of the week.

'Gerry isn't you.'

'He's better than me with a groggy ankle.'

Milo glared. 'Do you want to keep the horse here or don't you?'

I did.

Milo and I spent a fair amount of time arguing at the best of times. He was pugnacious by nature, mercurial by temperament, full of instant opinions that could be reversed the next day, didactic, dynamic and outspoken. He believed absolutely in his own judgement and was sure that everything would turn out all right in the end. He was moderately tactful to the owners, hard on his work-force and full of swearwords for his horses, which he produced as winners by the dozen.

I'd been outraged by the way he'd often spoken to

me when I first started to ride for him three years earlier, but one day I lost my temper and yelled back at him, and he burst out laughing and told me we would get along just fine, which in fact we did, though seldom on the surface.

I knew people thought ours an unlikely alliance, I neat and quiet, he restless and flamboyant, but in fact I liked the way he trained horses and they seemed to run well for him, and we had both prospered.

The Ostermeyers arrived at that point and they too had a chauffeur, which Milo took for granted. The bullishness at once disappeared from his manner to be replaced by the jocular charm that had owners regularly mesmerized, that morning being no exception. The Ostermeyers responded immediately, she with a roguish wiggle of the hips, he with a big handshake and a wide smile.

They were not so delighted about my crutches.

'Oh dear,' Martha Ostermeyer exclaimed in dismay. 'What have you done? Don't say you can't ride Datepalm. We only came, you know, because dear Milo said you'd be here to ride it.'

'He'll ride it,' Milo said before I had a chance of answering, and Martha Ostermeyer clapped her small gloved hands with relief.

'If we're going to buy him,' she said, smiling, 'we want to see him with his real jockey up, not some exercise rider.'

Harley Ostermeyer nodded in agreement, benignly.

Not really my week, I thought.

The Ostermeyers were all sweetness and light while people were pleasing them, and I'd never had any trouble liking them, but I'd also seen Harley Ostermeyer's underlying streak of ruthless viciousness once in a racecourse car-park where he'd verbally reduced to rubble an attendant who had allowed someone to park behind him, closing him in. He had had to wait half an hour. The attendant had looked genuinely scared. 'Goodnight, Derek,' he'd croaked as I went past, and Ostermeyer had whirled round and cooled his temper fifty per cent, inviting my sympathy in his trouble. Harley Ostermeyer liked to be thought a good guy, most of the time. He was the boss, as I understood it, of a giant supermarket chain. Martha Ostermeyer was also rich, a fourth-generation multi-millionaire in banking. I'd ridden for them often in the past years and been well rewarded, because generosity was one of their pleasures.

Milo drove them and me up to the Downs where Datepalm and the other horses were already circling, having walked up earlier. The day was bright and chilly, the Downs rolling away to the horizon, the sky clear, the horses' coats glossy in the sun. A perfect day for buying a champion chaser.

Milo sent three other horses down to the bottom of the gallop to work fast so that the Ostermeyers would know where to look and what to expect when Datepalm came up and passed them. They stood out on the grass, looking where Milo pointed, intent and happy.

Milo had brought a spare helmet with us in the big-wheeled vehicle that rolled over the mud and ruts on the Downs, and with an inward sigh I put it on. The enterprise was stupid really, as my leg wasn't strong enough and if anything wild happened to upset Datepalm, he might get loose and injure himself and we'd lose him surely one way or another.

On the other hand, I'd ridden races now and then with cracked bones, not just exercise gallops, and I knew one jockey who in the past had broken three bones in his foot and won races with it, sitting with it in an ice bucket in the changing room betweentimes and literally hopping out to the parade ring, supported by friends. The authorities had later brought in strict medical rules to stop that sort of thing as being unfair to the betting public, but one could still get away with it sometimes.

Milo saw me slide out of the vehicle with the helmet on and came over happily and said, 'I knew you would.'

'Mm,' I said. 'When you give me a leg up, put both hands round my knee and be careful, because if you twist my foot there'll be no sale.'

'You're such a wimp,' he said.

Nevertheless, he was circumspect and I landed in the saddle with little trouble. I was wearing jeans, and that morning for the first time I'd managed to get a shoe on, or rather one of the wide soft black leather moccasins I used as bedroom slippers. Milo threaded the stirrup over the moccasin with unexpected gentleness and I wondered if he were having last-minute doubts about the wisdom of all this.

One look at the Ostermeyers' faces dispelled both his doubts and mine. They were beaming at Datepalm already with proprietary pride.

Certainly he looked good. He filled the eye, as they say. A bay with black points, excellent head, short sturdy legs with plenty of bone. The Ostermeyers always preferred handsome animals, perhaps because they were handsome themselves, and Datepalm was well-mannered besides, which made him a peach of a ride.

He and I and two others from the rest of the string set off at a walk towards the far end of the gallop but were presently trotting, which I achieved by standing in the stirrups with all my weight on my right foot while cursing Milo imaginatively for the sensations in my left. Datepalm, who knew how horses should be ridden, which was not lopsided like this, did a good deal of head and tail shaking but otherwise seemed willing to trust me. He and I knew each other well as I'd ridden him in all his races for the past three years. Horses had no direct way of expressing recognition, but occasionally he would turn his head to look at me when he heard my voice, and I also thought he might know me by scent as he would put his muzzle against my neck sometimes and make small whiffling movements of his nostrils. In any case we did have a definite rapport and that morning it stood us in good stead.

At the far end the two lads and I sorted out our three horses ready to set off at a working gallop back towards Milo and the Ostermeyers, a pace fast enough to be interesting but not flat out like racing.

There wasn't much finesse in riding a gallop to please customers, one simply saw to it that one was on their side of the accompanying horses, to give them a clear view of the merchandise, and that one finished in front to persuade them that that's what would happen in future.

Walking him around to get in position I chatted quietly as I often did to Datepalm, because in common with many racehorses he was always reassured by a calm human voice, sensing from one's tone that all was well. Maybe horses heard the lower resonances: one never knew.

'Just go up there like a pro,' I told him, 'because I don't want to lose you, you old bugger. I want us to win the National one day, so shine, boy. Dazzle. Do your bloody best.'

I shook up the reins as we got the horses going, and in fact Datepalm put up one of his smoothest performances, staying with his companions for most of the journey, lengthening his stride when I gave him the signal, coming away alone and then sweeping collectedly past the Ostermeyers with fluid power; and if the jockey found it an acutely stabbing discomfort all the way, it was a fair price for the result. Even before I'd pulled up, the Ostermeyers had bought the horse and shaken hands on the deal.

'Subject to a veterinarian's report, of course,' Harley was saying as I walked Datepalm back to join them. 'Otherwise, he's superb.'

Milo's smile looked as if it would split his face. He held the reins while Martha excitedly patted the new acquisition, and went on holding them while I took my feet out of the stirrups and lowered myself very carefully to the ground, hopping a couple of steps to where the crutches lay on the grass.

'What did you do to your foot?' Martha asked unworriedly.

'Wrenched it,' I said, slipping the arm cuffs on with relief. 'Very boring.'

She smiled, nodded and patted my arm. 'Milo said it was nothing much.'

Milo gave me a gruesome look, handed Datepalm back to his lad, Gerry, and helped the Ostermeyers into the big-wheeled vehicle for the drive home. We bumped down the tracks and I took off the helmet and ran my fingers through my hair, reflecting that although I wouldn't care to ride gallops like that every day of the week, I would do it again for as good an outcome.

We all went into Milo's house for breakfast, a ritual there as in many other racing stables, and over coffee, toast and scrambled eggs Milo and the Ostermeyers planned Datepalm's future programme, including all the top races with of course another crack at the Gold Cup.

'What about the Grand National?' Martha said, her eyes like stars.

'Well, now, we'll have to see,' Milo said, but his dreams too were as visible as searchlights. First thing on our return, he'd telephoned to Datepalm's former owner and got confirmation that she agreed to the sale and was pleased by it, and since then one had almost needed to pull him down from the ceiling with a string like a helium-filled balloon. My own feelings weren't actually much lower. Datepalm really was a horse to build dreams on.

After the food and a dozen repetitions of the horse's virtues, Milo told the Ostermeyers about my inheriting Dozen Roses and about the probate saga, which seemed to fascinate them. Martha sat up straighter and exclaimed, 'Did you say York?'

Milo nodded.

'Do you mean this Saturday? Why, Harley and I are going to York races on Saturday, aren't we, Harley?'

Harley agreed that they were. 'Our dear friends Lord and Lady Knightwood have asked us to lunch.'

Martha said, 'Why don't we give Derek a ride up there to see his horse run? What do you say, Harley?'

'Be glad to have you along,' Harley said to me genuinely. 'Don't give us no for an answer.'

I looked at their kind insistent faces and said lamely, 'I thought of going by train, if I went at all.'

'No, no,' Martha said. 'Come to London by train and we'll go up together. Do say you will.'

Milo was looking at me anxiously: pleasing the Ostermeyers was still an absolute priority. I said I'd be glad to accept their kindness and Martha, mixing gratification with sudden alarm, said she hoped the inheritance wouldn't persuade me to stop riding races.

'No,' I said.

'That's positive enough.' Harley was pleased. 'You're part of the package, fella. You and Datepalm together.'

Brad and I went on to London, and I was very glad to have him drive.

'Office?' he asked, and I said, 'Yes,' and we travelled there in silent harmony.

He'd told me the evening before that Greville's car wasn't parked anywhere near Greville's house: or rather he'd handed me back the piece of paper with the car's number on it and said, 'Couldn't find it.' I thought I'd better get on to the police and other towers-away in Ipswich, and I'd better start learning the company's finances and Greville's as well, and I had two-thirds of the vault still to check and I could feel the suction of the quicksands inexorably.

I took the two baffling little gadgets from Greville's sitting room upstairs to Greville's office and showed them to June.

'That one,' she said immediately, pointing to the

thumb-sized tube with the whine, 'is a device to discourage mosquitoes. Mr Franklin said it's the noise of a male mosquito, and it frightens the blood-sucking females away.' She laughed. 'He said every man should have one.'

She picked up the other gadget and frowned at it, pressing the red button with no results.

'It has an aerial,' I said.

'Oh yes.' She pulled it out to its full extent. 'I think . . .' She paused. 'He used to have a transmitter which started his car from a distance, so he could warm the engine up in cold weather before he left his house, but the receiver bit got stolen with his Porsche. Then he bought the old Rover, and he said a car-starter wouldn't work on it because it only worked with direct transmission or fuel injection, or something, which the Rover doesn't have.'

'So this is the car-starter?'

'Well . . . no. This one doesn't do so much. The car-starter had buttons that would also switch on the headlights so that you could see where your car was, if you'd left it in a dark car-park.' She pushed the aerial down again. 'I think this one only switches the lights on, or makes the car whistle, if I remember right. He was awfully pleased with it when he got it, but I haven't seen it for ages. He had so many gadgets, he couldn't take them all in his pockets and I think he'd got a bit tired of carrying them about. He used to leave them in his desk, mostly.'

'You just earned your twenty per cent all over again,' I said.

'What?'

'Let's just check that the batteries work,' I said.

She opened the battery compartment and discovered it was empty. As if it were routine, she then pulled open a drawer in one of the other tiers of the desk and revealed a large open box containing packet after packet of new batteries in every possible size. She pulled out a packet, opened it and fed the necessary power packs into the slots, and although pressing the red button still provided no visible results, I was pretty confident we were in business.

June said suddenly, 'You're going to take this to Ipswich, aren't you? To find his car? Isn't that what you mean?'

I nodded. 'Let's hope it works.'

'Oh, it must.'

'It's quite a big town, and the car could be anywhere.'

'Yes,' she said, 'but it must be *somewhere*. I'm sure you'll find it.'

'Mm.' I looked at her bright, intelligent face. 'June,' I said slowly, 'don't tell anyone else about this gadget.'

'Why ever not?'

'Because,' I said, 'someone broke into this office looking for something and we don't know if they found it. If they didn't, and it is by any chance in the car, I don't want anyone to realize that the car is still lost.' I paused. 'I'd much rather you said nothing.'

'Not even to Annette?'

'Not to anyone.'

'But that means you think . . . you think . . .'

'I don't really think anything. It's just for security.'

Security was all right with her. She looked less troubled and agreed to keep quiet about the car-finder; and I hadn't needed to tell her about the mugger who had knocked me down to steal Greville's bag of clothes, which to me, in hindsight, was looking less and less a random hit and more and more a shot at a target.

Someone must have known Greville was dying, I thought. Someone who had organized or executed a mugging. I hadn't the faintest idea who could have done either, but it did seem to me possible that one of Greville's staff might have unwittingly chattered within ear-shot of receptive ears. Yet what could they have said? Greville hadn't told any of them he was buying diamonds. And why hadn't he? Secretive as he was, gems were his business.

The useless thoughts squirrelled around and got me nowhere. The gloomiest of them was that someone could have gone looking for Greville's car at any time since the scaffolding fell, and although I might find the engine and the wheels, the essential cupboard would be bare.

Annette came into the office carrying a fistful of papers which she said had come in the morning post and needed to be dealt with – by me, her manner inferred.

'Sit down, then,' I said, 'and tell me what they all mean.'

There were letters from insurance people, fund raisers, dissatisfied customers, gemmology forecasters, and a cable from a supplier in Hong Kong saying he didn't have enough African 12 mm amethyst AA quality round beads to fill our order and would we take Brazilian amethyst to make it up.

'What's the difference?' I asked. 'Does it matter?'

Annette developed worry lines over my ignorance. 'The best amethyst is found in Africa,' she said. 'Then it goes to Hong Kong or Taiwan for cutting and polishing into beads, then comes here. The amethyst from Brazil isn't such a good deep colour. Do you want me to order the Brazilian amethyst or wait until he has more of the African?'

'What do you think?' I said.

'Mr Franklin always decided.'

She looked at me anxiously. It's hopeless, I thought. The simplest decision was impossible without knowledge.

'Would the customers take the Brazilian instead?' I asked.

'Some would, some wouldn't. It's much cheaper. We sell a lot of the Brazilian anyway, in all sizes.'

'Well,' I said, 'if we run out of the African beads, offer the customers Brazilian. Or offer a different size of African. Cable the Chinese supplier to send just the

African AA 12 mm he's got now and the rest as soon as he can.'

She looked relieved. 'That's what I'd have said.'

Then why didn't you, I thought, but it was no use being angry. If she gave me bad advice I'd probably blame her for it: it was safer from her viewpoint, I supposed, not to stick her neck out.

'Incidentally,' she said, 'I did reach Prospero Jenks. He said he'd be in his Knightsbridge shop at two-thirty today, if you wanted to see him.'

'Great.'

She smiled. 'I didn't mention horses.'

I smiled back. 'Fine.'

She took the letters off to her own office to answer them, and I went from department to department on a round trip to the vault, watching everyone at work, all of them capable, willing and beginning to settle obligingly into the change of regime, keeping their inner reservations to themselves. I asked if one of them would go down and tell Brad I'd need him at two, not before: June went and returned like a boomerang.

I unlocked the vault and started on topaz: thousands of brilliant translucent slippery stones in a rainbow of colours, some bigger than acorns, some like peas.

No diamonds.

After that, every imaginable shape and size of garnet which could be yellow and green, I found, as well as red, and boxes of citrine.

Two and a half hours of unfolding and folding glossy white packets, and no diamonds.

June swirled in and out at one point with a long order for faceted stones which she handed to me without comment, and I remembered that only Greville and Annette packed orders from the vault. I went in search of Annette and asked if I might watch while she worked down the list, found what was needed from twenty or more boxes and assembled the total on the shelf. She was quick and sure, knowing exactly where to find everything. It was quite easy, she said, reassuring me. I would soon get the hang of it. God help me, I thought.

At two, after another of June's sandwich lunches, I went down to the car and gave Prospero Jenks's address to Brad. 'It's a shop somewhere near Harrods,' I said, climbing in.

He nodded, drove through the traffic, found the shop.

'Great,' I said. 'Now this time you'll have to answer the car phone whether you like it or not, because there's nowhere here to park.'

He shook his head. He'd resisted the suggestion several times before.

'Yes,' I said. 'It's very easy. I'll switch it on for you now. When it rings pick it up and press this button, SND, and you'll be able to hear me. OK? I'll ring when I'm ready to leave, then you just come back here and pick me up.'

He looked at the telephone as if it were contaminated.

It was a totally portable phone, not a fixture in the car, and it didn't receive calls unless one switched it on, which I quite often forgot to do and sometimes didn't do on purpose. I put the phone ready on the passenger seat beside him, to make it easy, and hoped for the best.

Prospero Jenks's shop window glittered with the sort of intense lighting that makes jewellery sparkle, but the lettering of his name over the window was neat and plain, as if ostentation there would have been superfluous.

I looked at the window with a curiosity I would never have felt a week earlier and found it filled not with conventional displays of rings and wristwatches but with joyous toys: model cars, aeroplanes, skiing figures, racing yachts, pheasants and horses, all gold and enamel and shining with gems. Almost every passer-by, I noticed, paused to look.

Pushing awkwardly through the heavy glass front door I stepped into a deep-carpeted area with chairs at the ready before every counter. Apart from the plushness, it was basically an ordinary shop, not very big, quiet in decor, all the excitement in the baubles.

There was no one but me in there and I swung over to one of the counters to see what was on display. Rings, I found, but not simple little circles. These were huge, often asymmetric, all colourful eyecatchers supreme.

'Can I help you?' a voice said.

A neutral man, middle-aged, in a black suit, coming from a doorway at the rear.

'My name's Franklin,' I said. 'Came to see Prospero Jenks.'

'A minute.'

He retreated, returned with a half-smile and invited me through the doorway to the privacies beyond. Shielded from customers' view by a screening partition lay a much longer space which doubled as office and workroom and contained a fearsome-looking safe and several tiers of little drawers like the ones in Saxony Franklin. On one wall a large framed sign read: 'NEVER TURN YOUR BACK TO CUSTOMERS. ALWAYS WATCH THEIR HANDS.' A fine statement of no trust, I thought in amusement.

Sitting on a stool by a workbench, a jeweller's lens screwed into one eye, was a hunched man in pale pink and white striped shirtsleeves, fiddling intently with a small gold object fixed into a vice. Patience and expert workmanship were much on view, all of it calm and painstaking.

He removed the lens with a sigh and rose to his feet, turning to inspect me from crown to crutches to toecaps with growing surprise. Whatever he'd been expecting, I was not it.

The feeling, I supposed, was mutual. He was maybe fifty but looked younger in a Peter Pan sort of way; a boyish face with intense bright blue eyes and a lot of lines developing across the forehead. Fairish hair, no beard, no moustache, no personal display. I had expected someone fancier, more extravagant, temperamental.

'Grev's brother?' he said. 'What a turn-up. There I was, thinking you'd be his age, his height.' He narrowed his eyes. 'He never said he had a brother. How do I know you're legit?'

'His assistant, Annette Adams, made the appointment.'

'Yes, so she did. Fair enough. Told me Grev was dead, long live the King. Said his brother was running the shop, life would go on. But I'll tell you, unless you know as much as Grev, I'm in trouble.'

'I came to talk to you about that.'

'It don't look like tidings of great joy,' he said, watching me judiciously. 'Want a seat?' He pointed at an office chair for me and took his place on the stool. His voice was a long way from cut-glass. More like East End London tidied up for West; the sort that came from nowhere with no privileges and made it to the top from sheer undeniable talent. He had the confident manner of long success, a creative spirit who was also a tradesman, an original artist without airs.

'I'm just learning the business,' I said cautiously. 'I'll do what I can.'

'Grev was a genius,' he said explosively. 'No one like him with stones. He'd bring me oddities, one-offs from all over the world, and I've made pieces . . .' He stopped and spread his arms out. 'They're in palaces,' he said, 'and museums and mansions in Palm Beach. Well, I'm in business. I sell them to wherever the money's coming from. I've got my pride, but it's in the pieces. They're good, I'm expensive, it works a treat.'

'Do you make everything you sell?' I asked.

He laughed. 'No, not myself personally, I couldn't. I design everything, don't get me wrong, but I have a workshop making them. I just make the special pieces myself, the unique ones. In between, I invent for the general market. Grev said he had some decent spinel, have you still got it?'

'Er,' I said, 'red?'

'Red,' he affirmed. 'Three, four or five carats. I'll take all you've got.'

'We'll send it tomorrow.'

'By messenger,' he said. 'Not post.'

'All right.'

'And a slab of rock crystal like the Eiger. Grev showed me a photo. I've got a commission for a fantasy . . . Send the crystal too.'

'All right,' I said again, and hid my doubts. I hadn't seen any slab of rock crystal. Annette would know, I thought.

He said casually, 'What about the diamonds?'

I let the breath out and into my lungs with conscious control.

'What about them?' I said.

'Grev was getting me some. He'd got them, in fact.

He told me. He'd sent a batch off to be cut. Are they back yet?'

'Not yet,' I said, hoping I wasn't croaking. 'Are those the diamonds he bought a couple of months ago from the Central Selling Organization that you're talking about?'

'Sure. He bought a share in a sight from a sight-holder. I asked him to. I'm still running the big chunky rings and necklaces I made my name in, but I'm setting some of them now with bigger diamonds, making more profit per item since the market will stand it, and I wanted Grev to get them because I trust him. Trust is like gold dust in this business, even though diamonds weren't his thing really. You wouldn't want to buy two- to three-carat stones from just anyone, even if they're not D or E flawless, right?'

'Er, right.'

'So he bought the share of the sight and he's having them cut in Antwerp as I require them, as I expect you know.'

I nodded. I did know, but only since he'd just told me.

'I'm going to make stars of some of them to shine from the rock crystal . . .' He broke off, gave a self-deprecating shrug of the shoulders, and said, 'And I'm making a mobile, with diamonds on gold trembler wires that move in the lightest air. It's to hang by a window and flash fire in the sunlight.' Again the self-deprecation, this time in a smile. 'Diamonds are ravishing in sunlight, they're at their best in it, and all the social snobs in this city scream that it's so frightfully vulgar, darling, to wear diamond earrings or bracelets in the daytime. It makes me sick, to be honest. Such a waste.'

I had never thought about diamonds in sunlight before, though I suppose I would in future. Vistas opened could never be closed, as maybe Greville would have said.

'I haven't caught up with everything yet,' I said, which was the understatement of the century. 'Have any of the diamonds been delivered to you so far?'

He shook his head. 'I haven't been in a hurry for them before.'

'And . . . er . . . how many are involved?'

'About a hundred. Like I said, not the very best colour in the accepted way of things but they can look warmer with gold sometimes if they're not ultra blue-white. I work with gold mostly. I like the feel.'

'How much,' I said slowly, doing sums, 'will your rock crystal fantasy sell for?'

'Trade secret. But then, I guess you're trade. It's commissioned, I've got a contract for a quarter of a million if they like it. If they don't like it, I get it back, sell it somewhere else, dismantle it, whatever. In the worst event I'd lose nothing but my time in making it, but don't you worry, they'll like it.'

His certainty was absolute, built on experience.

I said, 'Do you happen to know the name of the Antwerp cutter Greville sent the diamonds to? I mean, it's bound to be on file in the office, but if I know who to look for . . .' I paused. 'I could try to hurry him up for you, if you like.'

'I'd like you to, but I don't know who Grev knew there, exactly.'

I shrugged. 'I'll look it up, then.'

Exactly where was I going to look it up, I wondered? Not in the missing address book, for sure.

'Do you know the name of the sightholder?' I asked.

'Nope.'

'There's a ton of paper in the office,' I said in explanation. 'I'm going through it as fast as I can.'

'Grev never said a word he didn't have to,' Jenks said unexpectedly. 'I'd talk, he listened. We got on fine. He understood what I do better than anybody.'

The sadness of his voice was my brother's universal accolade, I thought. He'd been liked. He'd been trusted. He would be missed.

I stood up and said, 'Thank you, Mr Jenks.'

'Call me Pross,' he said easily. 'Everyone does.'

'My name's Derek.'

'Right,' he said, smiling. 'Now I'll keep on dealing with you, I won't say I won't, but I'm going to have to find me another traveller like Grev, with an eye like his . . . He's been supplying me ever since I started on my own, he gave me credit when the banks wouldn't, he had faith in what I could do . . . Near the beginning he brought me two rare sticks of watermelon tourmaline that were each over two inches long and were half pink, half green mixed all the way up and transparent with the light shining through them and changing while you watched. It would have been a sin to cut them for jewellery. I mounted them in gold and platinum to hang and twist in sunlight.' He smiled his deprecating smile. 'I like gemstones to have life. I didn't have to pay Grev for that tourmaline ever. It made my name for me, the piece was reviewed in the papers and won prizes, and he said the trade we'd do together would be his reward.' He clicked his mouth. 'I do go on a bit.'

'I like to hear it,' I said. I looked down the room to his workbench and said, 'Where did you learn all this? How does one start?'

'I started in metalwork classes at the local comprehensive,' he said frankly. 'Then I stuck bits of glass in gold-plated wire to give to my mum. Then her friends wanted some. So when I left school I took some of those things to show to a jewellery manufacturer and asked for a job. Costume jewellery, they made. I was soon designing for them, and I never looked back.'

CHAPTER EIGHT

I borrowed Prospero's telephone to get Brad, but although I could hear the ringing tone in the car, he didn't answer. Cursing slightly, I asked Pross for a second call and got through to Annette.

'Please keep on trying this number,' I said, giving it to her. 'When Brad answers, tell him I'm ready to go.'

'Are you coming back here?' she asked.

I looked at my watch. It wasn't worth going back as I had to return to Kensington by five-thirty. I said no, I wasn't.

'Well, there are one or two things . . .'

'I can't really tie this phone up,' I said. 'I'll go to my brother's house and ring you from there. Just keep trying Brad.'

I thanked Pross again for the calls. Any time, he said vaguely. He was sitting again in front of his vice, thinking and tinkering, producing his marvels.

There were customers in the shop being attended to by the black-suited salesman. He glanced up very briefly in acknowledgement as I went through and immediately returned to watching the customers' hands. A business without trust; much worse than racing. But then, it was probably impossible to slip a racehorse into a pocket when the trainer wasn't looking.

I stood on the pavement and wondered pessimistically how long it would take Brad to answer the telephone but in the event he surprised me by arriving within a very few minutes. When I opened the car door, the phone was ringing.

'Why don't you answer it?' I asked, wriggling my way into the seat.

'Forgot which button.'

'But you came,' I said.

'Yerss.'

I picked up the phone myself and talked to Annette. 'Brad apparently reckoned that if the phone rang it meant I was ready, so he saw no need to answer it.'

Brad gave a silent nod.

'So now we're setting off to Kensington.' I paused. 'Annette, what's a sightholder, and what's a sight?'

'You're back to diamonds again!'

'Yes. Do you know?'

'Of course I do. A sightholder is someone who is permitted to buy rough diamonds from the CSO. There aren't so many sightholders, only about a hundred and fifty world-wide, I think. They sell the diamonds then to other people. A sight is what they call the sales CSO hold every five weeks, and a sight-box is a packet of stones they sell, though that's often called a sight too.'

'Is a sightholder the same as a diamantaire?' I asked.

'All sightholders are diamantaires, but all diamantaires are not sightholders. Diamantaires buy from the sightholders, or share in a sight, or buy somewhere else, not from De Beers.'

Ask a simple question, I thought.

Annette said, 'A consignment of cultured pearls has come from Japan. Where shall I put them?'

'Um . . . Do you mean where because the vault is locked?'

'Yes.'

'Where did you put things when my brother was travelling?'

She said doubtfully, 'He always said to put them in the stock-room under "miscellaneous beads".'

'Put them in there, then.'

'But the drawer is full with some things that came last week. I wouldn't want the responsibility of putting the pearls anywhere Mr Franklin hadn't approved.' I couldn't believe she needed direction over the simplest thing, but apparently she did. 'The pearls are valuable,' she said. 'Mr Franklin would never leave them out in plain view.'

'Aren't there any empty drawers?'

'Well, I . . .'

'Find an empty drawer or a nearby empty drawer and put them there. We'll see to them properly in the morning.'

'Yes, all right.'

She seemed happy with it and said everything else could wait until I came back. I switched off the telephone feeling absolutely swamped by the prospect she'd opened up: if Greville hid precious things under 'miscellaneous beads', where else might he not have hidden them? Would I find a hundred diamonds stuffed in at the back of rhodocrosite or jasper, if I looked?

The vault alone was taking too long. The four big stock-rooms promised a nightmare.

Brad miraculously found a parking space right outside Greville's house, which seemed obscurely to disappoint him.

'Twenty past five,' he said, 'for the pub?'

'If you wouldn't mind. And . . . er . . . would you just stand there now while I take a look-see?' I had grown cautious, I found.

He ducked his head in assent and watched me manoeuvre the few steps up to the front door. No floodlights came on and no dog barked, presumably because it was daylight. I opened the three locks and pushed the door.

The house was still. No movements of air. I propped the door open with a bronze horse clearly lying around for the purpose and went down the passage to the small sitting room.

No intruders. No mess. No amazons waving riot sticks, no wrecking balls trying to get past the grilles on the windows. If anyone had attempted to penetrate Greville's fortress, they hadn't succeeded.

I returned to the front door. Brad was still standing beside the car, looking towards the house. I gave him a thumbs-up sign, and he climbed into the driver's seat while I closed the heavy door, and in the little sitting room, started taking all of the books off the shelves methodically, riffling the pages and putting each back where I found it.

There were ten hollow books altogether, mostly with titles like *Tales of the Outback* and *With a Mule in Patagonia.* Four were empty, including the one which had held Clarissa Williams's letters. One held the big ornate key. One held an expensive-looking gold watch, the hands pointing to the correct time.

The watch Greville had been wearing in Ipswich was one of those affairs with more knobs than instructions. It lay now beside my bed in Hungerford emitting bleeps at odd intervals and telling me which way was north. The slim gold elegance in the hollow box was for a different mood, a different man, and when I turned it over on my palm I found the inscription on the back: G my love C.

She couldn't have known it was there, I thought. She hadn't looked for it. She'd looked only for the letters, and by chance had come to them first. I put the watch back into the box and back on the shelf. There was no way I could return it to her, and perhaps she wouldn't want it, not with that inscription.

Two of the remaining boxes contained large keys, again unspecified, and one contained a folded instruction leaflet detailing how to set a safe in a concrete nest. The last revealed two very small plastic cases containing baby recording tapes, each adorned with the printed legend 'microcassette'. The cassette cases were all of two inches long by one and a half wide, the featherweight tapes inside a fraction smaller.

I tossed one in my hand indecisively. Nowhere among Greville's tidy belongings had I so far found a microcassette player, which didn't mean I wouldn't in time. Sufficient to the day, I thought in the end, and left the tiny tapes in the book.

With the scintillating titles and their secrets all back on the shelves I stared at them gloomily. Not a diamond in the lot.

Instructions for concrete nests were all very well, but where was the safe? Tapes were OK, but where was the player? Keys were fine, but where were the keyholes? The most frustrating thing about it was that Greville hadn't meant to leave such puzzles. For him, the answers were part of his fabric.

I'd noticed on my way in and out of the house that mail was accumulating in the wire container fixed inside the letter-box on the front door, so to fill in the time before I was due at the pub I took the letters along to the sitting room and began opening the envelopes.

It seemed all wrong. I kept telling myself it was necessary but I still felt as if I were trespassing on ground Greville had surrounded with keep-out fences. There were bills, requests from charities, a bank statement for his private account, a gemmology magazine and two invitations. No letters from sightholders, diamantaires or cutters in Antwerp. I put the letters into the gemmology magazine's large envelope and added to them some similar unfinished business that I'd found in the drawer under the telephone, and reflected ruefully, putting it all ready to take to Hungerford, that I loathed paperwork at the best of times. My own had a habit of mounting up into increasingly urgent heaps. Perhaps having to do Greville's would teach me some sense.

Brad whisked us round to The Rook and Castle at five-thirty and pointed to the phone to let me know how I could call him when I'd finished, and I saw from his twitch of a smile that he found it a satisfactory amusement.

The Rook and Castle was old fashioned inside as well as out, an oasis of drinking peace without a juke-box. There was a lot of dark wood and tiffany lampshades and small tables with beer mats. A clientele of mostly business-suited men was beginning to trickle in and I paused inside the door both to get accustomed to the comparative darkness and to give anyone who was interested a plain view of the crutches.

The interest level being nil, I judged Elliot Trelawney to be absent. I went over to the bar, ordered some Perrier and swallowed a Distalgesic, as it was time. The morning's gallop had done no good to the ankle department but it wasn't to be regretted.

A bulky man of about fifty came into the place as if

familiar with his surroundings and looked purposefully around, sharpening his gaze on the crutches and coming without hesitation to the bar.

'Mr Franklin?'

I shook his offered hand.

'What are you drinking?' he said briskly, eyeing my glass.

'Perrier. That's temporary also.'

He smiled swiftly, showing white teeth. 'You won't mind if I have a double Glenlivet? Greville and I drank many of them together here. I'm going to miss him abominably. Tell me what happened.'

I told him. He listened intently, but at the end he said merely, 'You look very uncomfortable propped against that stool. Why don't we move to a table?' And without more ado he picked up my glass along with the one the bartender had fixed for him, and carried them over to two wooden armchairs under a multicoloured lampshade by the wall.

'That's better,' he said, taking a sip and eyeing me over the glass. 'So you're the brother he talked about. You're Derek.'

'I'm Derek. His only brother, actually. I didn't know he talked about me.'

'Oh, yes. Now and then.'

Elliot Trelawney was big, almost bald, with half-moon glasses and a face that was fleshy but healthy looking. He had thin lips but laugh lines around his eyes, and I'd have said on a snap judgement that he was a realist with a sense of humour.

'He was proud of you,' he said.

'Proud?' I was surprised.

He glimmered. 'We often played golf together on Saturday mornings and sometimes he would be wanting to finish before the two o'clock race at Sandown or somewhere, and it would be because you were riding and it was on the box. He liked to watch you. He liked you to win.'

'He never told me,' I said regretfully.

'He wouldn't, would he? I watched with him a couple of times and all he said after you'd won was, "That's all right then." '

'And when I lost?'

'When you lost?' He smiled. 'Nothing at all. Once you had a crashing fall and he said he'd be glad on the whole when you retired, as race-riding was so dangerous. Ironic, isn't it?'

'Yes.'

'By God, I'll miss him.' His voice was deep. 'We were friends for twenty years.'

I envied him. I wanted intolerably what it was too late to have, and the more I listened to people remembering Greville the worse it got.

'Are you a magistrate?' I asked.

He nodded. 'We often sat together. Greville introduced me to it, but I've never had quite his gift. He seemed to know the truth of things by instinct. He said goodness was visible, therefore in its absence one sought for answers.'

'What sort of cases did . . . do you try?'

'All sorts.' He smiled again briefly. 'Shoplifters. Vagrants. Possession of drugs. TV licence fee evaders. Sex offenders . . . that's prostitution, rape, sex with minors, kerb crawlers. Greville always seemed to know infallibly when those were lying.'

'Go on,' I said, when he stopped. 'Anything else?'

'Well, there are a lot of diplomats in West London, in all the embassies. You'd be astonished what they get away with by claiming diplomatic immunity. Greville hated diplomatic immunity, but we have to grant it. Then we have a lot of small businessmen who "forget" to pay the road tax on the company vehicles, and there are TDAs by the hundred – that's Taking and Driving Away cars. Other motoring offences, speeding and so on, are dealt with separately, like domestic offences and juveniles. And then occasionally we get the preliminary hearings in a murder case, but of course we have to refer those to the Crown Court.'

'Does it all ever depress you?' I said.

He took a sip and considered me. 'It makes you sad,' he said eventually. 'We see as much inadequacy and stupidity as downright villainy. Some of it makes you laugh. I wouldn't say it's depressing, but one learns to see the world from underneath, so to speak. To see the dirt and the delusions, to see through the offenders' eyes and understand their weird logic. But one's disillusion is sporadic because we don't have a bench every day. Twice a month, in Greville's and my cases, plus a little committee work. And that's what I really want from you: the notes Greville was making on the licensing of a new-style gambling club. He said he'd learned disturbing allegations against one of the organizers and he was going to advise turning down the application at the next committee meeting even though it was a project we'd formerly looked on favourably.'

'I'm afraid,' I said, 'that I haven't so far found any notes like that.'

'Damn . . . Where would he have put them?'

'I don't know. I'll look for them, though.' No harm in keeping an eye open for notes while I searched for C.

Elliot Trelawney reached into an inner jacket pocket and brought out two flat black objects, one a notebook, the other a folded black case a bit like a cigarette case.

'These were Greville's,' he said. 'I brought them for you.' He put them on the small table and moved them towards me with plump and deliberate fingers. 'He lent me that one,' he pointed, 'and the notebook he left on the table after a committee meeting last week.'

'Thank you,' I said. I picked up the folded case and opened it and found inside a miniature electronic chess set, the sort that challenged a player to beat it. I looked up. Trelawney's expression, unguarded, was intensely sorrowful. 'Would you like it?' I said. 'I know it's not much, but would you like to keep it?'

'If you mean it.'

I nodded and he put the chess set back in his pocket. 'Greville and I used to play . . . *dammit* . . .' he finished explosively. 'Why should such a futile thing happen?'

No answer was possible. I regretfully picked up the black notebook and opened it at random.

'The bad scorn the good,' I read aloud, 'and the crooked despise the straight.'

'The thoughts of Chairman Mao,' Trelawney said dryly, recovering himself. 'I used to tease him . . . he said it was a habit he'd had from university when he'd learned to clarify his thoughts by writing them down. When I knew he was dead I read that notebook from cover to cover. I've copied down some of the things in it, I hope you won't mind.' He smiled. 'You'll find parts of it especially interesting.'

'About his horses?'

'Those too.'

I stowed the notebook in a trouser pocket which was already pretty full and brought out from there the racing diary, struck by a thought. I explained what the diary was, showing it to Trelawney.

'I phoned that number,' I said, turning pages and pointing, 'and mentioned Greville's name, and a woman told me in no uncertain terms never to telephone again as she wouldn't have the name Greville Franklin spoken in her house.'

Elliot Trelawney blinked. 'Greville? Doesn't sound like Greville.'

'I didn't think so, either. So would it have had something to do with one of your cases? Someone he found guilty of something?'

'Hah. Perhaps.' He considered. 'I could probably find out whose number it is, if you like. Strange he would have had it in his diary, though. Do you want to follow it up?'

'It just seemed so odd,' I said.

'Quite right.' He unclipped a gold pencil from another inner pocket and in a slim notebook of black leather with gold corners wrote down the number.

'Do you make enemies much, because of the court?' I asked.

He looked up and shrugged. 'We get cursed now and then. Screamed at, one might say. But usually not. Mostly they plead guilty because it's so obvious they are. The only real enemy Greville might have had is the gambling club organizer who's not going to get his licence. A drugs baron is what Greville called him. A man suspected of murder but not tried through lack of evidence. He might have had very hard feelings.' He hesitated. 'When I heard Greville was dead, I even wondered about Vaccaro. But it seems clear the scaffolding was a sheer accident . . . wasn't it?'

'Yes, it was. The scaffolding broke high up. One man working on it fell three storeys to his death. Pieces just rained down on Greville. A minute earlier, a minute later . . .' I sighed. 'Is Vaccaro the gambling-licence man?'

'He is. He appeared before the committee and

seemed perfectly straightforward. Subject to screening, we said. And then someone contacted Greville and uncovered the muck. But we don't ourselves have any details, so we need his notes.'

'I'll look for them,' I promised again. I turned more pages in the diary. 'Does Koningin Beatrix mean anything to you?' I showed him the entry. 'Or CZ = C × 1.7?'

C, I thought, looking at it again, stood for diamond.

'Nothing,' Elliot Trelawney said. 'But as you know, Greville could be as obscure as he was clear-headed. And these were private notes to himself, after all. Same as his notebook. It was never for public consumption.'

I nodded and put away the diary and paid for Elliot Trelawney's repeat Glenlivet but felt waterlogged myself. He stayed for a while, seeming to be glad to talk about Greville, as I was content to listen. We parted eventually on friendly terms, he giving me his card with his phone number for when I found Greville's notes.

If, I silently thought. If I find them.

When he'd gone I used the pub's telephone to ring the car, and after five unanswered brr-brrs disconnected and went outside, and Brad with almost a grin reappeared to pick me up.

'Home,' I said, and he said, 'Yerss,' and that was that.

On the way I read bits of Greville's notebook, pausing often to digest the passing thoughts which had clearly been chiefly prompted by the flotsam drifting through the West London Magistrates Court.

'Goodness is sickening to the evil,' he wrote, 'as evil is sickening to the good. Both the evil and the good may be complacent.'

'In all income groups you find your average regulation slob who sniggers at anarchy but calls the police indignantly to his burglarized home, who is actively anti-authority until he needs to be saved from someone with a gun.'

'The palm outstretched for a hand-out can turn in a flash into a cursing fist. A nation's palm, a nation's fist.'

'Crime to many is not crime but simply a way of life. If laws are inconvenient, ignore them, they don't apply to you.'

'Infinite sadness is not to trust an old friend.'

'Historically, more people have died of religion than cancer.'

'I hate rapists. I imagine being anally assaulted myself, and the anger overwhelms me. It's essential to make my judgement cold.'

Further on I came unexpectedly to what Elliot Trelawney must have meant.

Greville had written, 'Derek came to dinner very stiff with broken ribs. I asked him how he managed to live with all those injuries. "Forget the pain and get on with the party," he said. So we drank fizz.'

I stopped reading and stared out at the autumn countryside which was darkening now, lights going on. I remembered that evening very well, up to a point. Greville had been good fun. I'd got pretty high on the cocktail of champagne and painkillers and I hadn't felt a thing until I'd woken in the morning. I'd driven myself seventy miles home and forgotten it, which frightening fact was roughly why I was currently and obediently sticking to water.

It was almost too dark to read more, but I flicked over one more page and came to what amounted to a prayer, so private and impassioned that I felt my mouth go dry. Alone on the page were three brief lines:

May I deal with honour.
May I act with courage.
May I achieve humility.

I felt as if I shouldn't have read it; knew he hadn't meant it to be read. May I achieve humility . . . that prayer was for saints.

When we reached my house I told Brad I would go to London the next day by train, and he looked devastated.

'I'll drive you for nowt,' he said, hoarsely.

'It isn't the money.' I was surprised by the strength of his feelings. 'I just thought you'd be tired of all the waiting about.'

He shook his head vigorously, his eyes positively pleading.

'All right, then,' I said. 'London tomorrow, Ipswich on Friday. OK?'

'Yerss,' he said with obvious relief.

'And I'll pay you, of course.'

He looked at me dumbly for a moment, then ducked his head into the car to fetch the big brown envelope from Greville's house, and he waited while I unlocked my door and made sure that there were no unwelcome visitors lurking.

Everything was quiet, everything orderly. Brad nodded at my all-clear, gave me the envelope and loped off into the night more tongue-tied than ever. I'd never wondered very much about his thoughts during all the silent hours; had never tried, I supposed, to understand him. I wasn't sure that I wanted to. It was restful the way things were.

I ate a microwaved chicken pie from the freezer and made an unenthusiastic start on Greville's letters, paying his bills for him, closing his accounts, declining his invitations, saying sorry, sorry, very sorry.

After that, in spite of good resolutions, I did not attack my own backlog but read right through Greville's notebook looking for diamonds. Maybe there were some solid gold nuggets, maybe some pearls of wisdom, but no helpful instructions like turn right at the fourth apple tree, walk five paces and dig.

I did however find the answer to one small mystery, which I read with wry amusement.

> The green soapstone box pleases me as an exercise in misdirection and deviousness. The keyhole has no key because it has no lock. It's impossible to unlock men's minds with keys, but guile and pressure will do it, as with the box.

Even with the plain instruction to be guileful and devious it took me ages to find the secret. I tried pressing each of the two hinges, pressing the lock, twisting, pressing everything again with the box upside down. The green stone stayed stubbornly shut.

Misdirection, I thought. If the keyhole wasn't a lock, maybe the hinges weren't hinges. Maybe the lid wasn't a lid. Maybe the whole thing was solid.

I tried the box upside down again, put my thumbs on its bottom surface with firm pressure and tried to push it out endways, like a slide. Nothing happened. I reversed it and pushed the other way and as if with a sigh for the length of my stupidity the bottom of the box slid out reluctantly to halfway, and stopped.

It was beautifully made, I thought. When it was shut one couldn't see the bottom edges weren't solid stone, so closely did they fit. I looked with great curiosity to see what Greville had hidden in his ingenious hiding place, not really expecting diamonds, and brought out two well-worn chamois leather pouches with drawstrings, the sort jewellers use, with the name of the jeweller indistinctly stamped on the front.

Both of the pouches were empty, to my great disappointment. I stuffed them back into the hole and shut the box, and it sat on the table beside the telephone all evening, an enigma solved but useless.

It wasn't until I'd decided to go to bed that some switch or other clicked in my brain and a word half-seen became suddenly a conscious thought. Van Ekeren, stamped in gold. Perhaps the jeweller's name stamped on the chamois pouches was worth another look.

I opened the box and pulled the pouches out again and in the rubbed and faded lettering read the full name and address.

Jacob van Ekeren
Pelikanstraat 70
Antwerp

There had to be, I thought, about ten thousand jewellers in Antwerp. The pouches were far from new, certainly not only a few weeks old. All the same . . . better find out.

I took one and left one, closing the box again, and in the morning bore the crumpled trophy to London and through international telephone enquiries found Jacob van Ekeren's number.

The voice that answered from Antwerp spoke either Dutch or Flemish, so I tried in French, '*Je veux parler avec Monsieur Jacob van Ekeren, s'il vous plaît.*'

'*Ne quittez pas.*'

I held on as instructed until another voice spoke, this time in French, of which I knew far too little.

'*Monsieur van Ekeren n'est pas ici maintenant, monsieur.*'

'*Parlez vous anglais*?' I asked. 'I'm speaking from England.'

'*Attendez.*'

I waited again and was rewarded with an extremely English voice asking if he could help.

I explained that I was speaking from Saxony Franklin Ltd, gemstone importers in London.

'How can I help you?' He was courteous and non-committal.

'Do you,' I said baldly, 'cut and polish rough diamonds?'

'Yes, of course,' he answered. 'But before we do business with any new client we need introductions and references.'

'Um,' I said. 'Wouldn't Saxony Franklin Ltd be a client of yours already? Or Greville Saxony Franklin, maybe? Or just Greville Franklin? It's really important.'

'May I have your name?'

'Derek Franklin. Greville's brother.'

'One moment.' He returned after a while and said he would call me back shortly with an answer.

'Thank you very much,' I said.

'*Pas du tout.*' Bilingual besides.

I put down the phone and asked both Annette and June, who were busily moving around, if they could find

Jacob van Ekeren anywhere in Greville's files. 'See if you can find any mention of Antwerp in the computer,' I added to June.

'Diamonds again!'

'Yup. The van Ekeren address is 70 Pelikanstraat.'

Annette wrinkled her brow. 'That's the Belgian equivalent of Hatton Garden,' she said.

It disrupted their normal work and they weren't keen, but Annette was very soon able to say she had no record of any Jacob van Ekeren, but the files were kept in the office for only six years, and any contact before that would be in storage in the basement. June whisked in to confirm that she couldn't find van Ekeren or Pelikanstraat or Antwerp in the computer.

It wasn't exactly surprising. If Greville had wanted his diamond transaction to be common knowledge in the office he would have conducted it out in the open. Very odd, I thought, that he hadn't. If it had been anyone but Greville one would have suspected him of something underhand, but as far as I knew he always had dealt with honour, as he'd prayed.

The telephone rang and Annette answered it. 'Saxony Franklin, can I help you?' She listened. 'Derek Franklin? Yes, just a moment.' She handed me the receiver and I found it was the return of the smooth French–English voice from Belgium. I knew as well as he did that he had spent the time between the two calls getting our number from international enquiries so that he could check back and be sure I was who I'd said. Merely prudent. I'd have done the same.

'Mr Jacob van Ekeren has retired,' he said. 'I am his nephew Hans. I can tell you now after our researches that we have done no business with your firm within the past six or seven years, but I can't speak for the time before that, when my uncle was in charge.'

'I see,' I said. 'Could you, er, ask your uncle?'

'I will if you like,' he said civilly. 'I did telephone his house, but I understand that he and my aunt will be away from home until Monday, and their maid doesn't seem to know where they went.' He paused. 'Could I ask what all this is about?'

I explained that my brother had died suddenly, leaving a good deal of unfinished business which I was trying to sort out. 'I came across the name and address of your firm. I'm following up everything I can.'

'Ah,' he said sympathetically. 'I will certainly ask my uncle on Monday, and let you know.'

'I'm most grateful.'

'Not at all.'

The uncle, I thought morosely, was a dead-end.

I went along and opened the vault, telling Annette that Prospero Jenks wanted all the spinel. 'And he says we have a piece of rock crystal like the Eiger.'

'The what?'

'Sharp mountain. Like Mont Blanc.'

'Oh.' She moved down the rows of boxes and chose a heavy one from near the bottom at the far end. 'This is it,' she said, humping it on to the shelf and opening the lid. 'Beautiful.'

The Eiger, filling the box, was lying on its side and had a knobbly base so that it wouldn't stand up, but I supposed one could see in the lucent faces and angled planes that, studded with diamond stars and given the Jenks's sunlight treatment, it could make the basis of a fantasy worthy of the name.

'Do we have a price for it?' I asked.

'Double what it cost,' she said cheerfully. 'Plus VAT, plus packing and transport.'

'He wants everything sent by messenger.'

She nodded. 'He always does. Jason takes them in a taxi. Leave it to me, I'll see to it.'

'And we'd better put the pearls away that came yesterday.'

'Oh, yes.'

She went off to fetch them and I moved down to where I'd given up the day before, feeling certain that the search was futile but committed to it all the same. Annette returned with the pearls, which were at least in plastic bags on strings, not in the awkward open envelopes, so while she counted and stored the new intake, I checked my way through the old.

Boxes of pearls, all sizes. No diamonds.

'Does CZ mean anything to you?' I asked Annette idly.

'CZ is cubic zirconia,' she said promptly. 'We sell a fair amount of it.'

'Isn't that, um, imitation diamond?'

'It's a manufactured crystal very like diamond,' she said, 'but about ten thousand times cheaper. If it's in a ring, you can't tell the difference.'

'Can't anyone?' I asked. 'They must do.'

'Mr Franklin said that most high-street jewellers can't at a glance. The best way to tell the difference, he said, is to take the stones out of their setting and weigh them.'

'*Weigh* them?'

'Yes. Cubic zirconia's much heavier than diamond, so one carat of cubic zirconia is smaller than a one-carat diamond.'

'CZ equals C times one point seven,' I said slowly.

'That's right,' she said, surprised. 'How did you know?'

CHAPTER NINE

From noon on, when I closed the last box-lid unproductively on the softly changing colours of rainbow opal from Oregon, I sat in Greville's office reading June's print-out of a crash course in business studies, beginning to see the pattern of a cash flow that ended on the side of the angels. Annette, who as a matter of routine had been banking the receipts daily, produced a sheaf of cheques for me to sign, which I did, feeling that it was the wrong name on the line, and she brought the day's post for decisions, which I strugglingly made.

Several people in the jewellery business telephoned in response to the notices of Greville's death which had appeared in the papers that morning. Annette, reassuring them that the show would go on, sounded more confident than she looked. 'They all say Ipswich is too far, but they'll be there in spirit,' she reported.

At four there was a phone call from Elliot Trelawney, who said he'd cracked the number of the lady who didn't want Greville's name spoken in her house.

'It's sad, really,' he said with a chuckle. 'I suppose I

shouldn't laugh. That lady can't and won't forgive Greville because he sent her upper-crust daughter to jail for three months for selling cocaine to a friend. The mother was in court, I remember her, and she talked to the press afterwards. She couldn't believe that selling cocaine to a friend was an offence. Drug peddlers were despicable, of course, but that wasn't the same as selling to a friend.'

'If a law is inconvenient, ignore it, it doesn't apply to you.'

'What?'

'Something Greville wrote in his notebook.'

'Oh yes. It seems Greville got the mother's phone number to suggest ways of rehabilitation for the daughter, but mother wouldn't listen. Look,' he hesitated. 'Keep in touch now and then, would you? Have a drink in The Rook and Castle occasionally?'

'All right.'

'And let me know as soon as you find those notes.'

'Sure,' I said.

'We want to stop Vaccaro, you know.'

'I'll look everywhere,' I promised.

When I put the phone down I asked Annette.

'Notes about his cases?' she said. 'Oh no, he never brought those to the office.'

Like he never bought diamonds, I thought dryly. And there wasn't a trace of them in the spreadsheets or the ledgers.

The small insistent alarm went off again, muffled

inside the desk. Twenty past four, my watch said. I reached over and pulled open the drawer and the alarm stopped, as it had before.

'Looking for something?' June said, breezing in.

'Something with an alarm like a digital watch.'

'It's bound to be the world clock,' she said. 'Mr Franklin used to set it to remind himself to phone suppliers in Tokyo, and so on.'

I reflected that as I wouldn't know what to say to suppliers in Tokyo I hardly needed the alarm.

'Do you want me to send a fax to Tokyo to say the pearls arrived OK?' she said.

'Do you usually?'

She nodded. 'They worry.'

'Then please do.'

When she'd gone Jason with his orange hair appeared through the doorway and without any trace of insolence told me he'd taken the stuff to Prospero Jenks and brought back a cheque, which he'd given to Annette.

'Thank you,' I said neutrally.

He gave me an unreadable glance, said, 'Annette said to tell you,' and took himself off. An amazing improvement, I thought.

I stayed behind that evening after they'd all left and went slowly round Greville's domain looking for hiding places that were guileful and devious and full of misdirection.

It was impossible to search the hundreds of shallow

drawers in the stock-rooms and I concluded he wouldn't have used them because Lily or any of the others might easily have found what they weren't meant to. That was the trouble with the whole place, I decided in the end. Greville's own policy of not encouraging private territories had extended also to himself, as all of his staff seemed to pop in and out of his office familiarly whenever the need arose.

Hovering always was the uncomfortable thought that if any pointer to the diamonds' whereabouts had been left by Greville in his office, it could have vanished with the break-in artist, leaving nothing for me to find; and indeed I found nothing of any use. After a fruitless hour I locked everything that locked and went down to the yard to find Brad and go home.

The day of Greville's funeral dawned cold and clear and we were heading east when the sun came up. The run to Ipswich taking three hours altogether, we came into the town with generous time to search for Greville's car.

Enquiries from the police had been negative. They hadn't towed, clamped or ticketed any ancient Rover. They hadn't spotted its number in any public road or car-park, but that wasn't conclusive, they'd assured me. Finding the car had no priority with them as it hadn't been stolen but they would let me know if, if.

I explained the car-finder to Brad en route, producing a street map to go with it.

'Apparently when you press this red button the car's lights switch on and a whistle blows,' I said. 'So you drive and I'll press, OK?'

He nodded, seeming amused, and we began to search in this slightly bizarre fashion, starting in the town centre near to where Greville had died and very slowly rolling up and down the streets, first to the north, then to the south, checking them off on the map. In many of the residential streets there were cars parked nose to tail outside houses, but nowhere did we get a whistle. There were public car-parks and shop car-parks and the station car-park, but nowhere did we turn lights on. Rover 3500s in any case were sparse: when we saw one we stopped to look at the plates, even if the paint wasn't grey, but none of them was Greville's.

Disappointment settled heavily. I'd seriously intended to find that car. As lunchtime dragged towards two o'clock I began to believe that I shouldn't have left it so long, that I should have started looking as soon as Greville died. But last Sunday, I thought, I hadn't been in any shape to, and anyway it wasn't until Tuesday that I knew there was anything valuable to look for. Even now I was sure that he wouldn't have left the diamonds themselves vulnerable, but some reason for being in Ipswich at all . . . given luck, why not?

The crematorium was set in a garden with neatly planted rose trees: Brad dropped me at the door and drove away to find some food. I was met by two blacksuited men, both with suitable expressions, who introduced themselves as the undertaker I'd engaged and one of the crematorium's officials. A lot of flowers had arrived, they said, and which did I want on the coffin.

In some bemusement I let them show me where the flowers were, which was in a long covered cloister beside the building, where one or two weeping groups were looking at wreaths of their own.

'These are Mr Franklin's,' the official said, indicating two long rows of bright bouquets blazing with colourful life in that place of death.

'All of these?' I said, astonished.

'They've been arriving all morning. Which do you want inside, on the coffin?'

There were cards on the bunches, I saw.

'I sent some from myself and our sisters,' I said doubtfully. 'The card has Susan, Miranda and Derek on it. I'll have that.'

The official and the undertaker took pity on the crutches and helped me find the right flowers; and I came first not to the card I was looking for but to another that shortened my breath.

'I will think of you every day at four-twenty. Love, C.'

The flowers that went with it were velvety red roses arranged with ferns in a dark green bowl. Twelve sweet-smelling blooms. Dozen Roses, I thought. Heavens above.

'I've found them,' the undertaker called, picking up a large display of pink and bronze chrysanthemums. 'Here you are.'

'Great. Well, we'll have these roses as well, and this wreath next to them, which is from the staff in his office. Is that all right?'

It appeared to be. Annette and June had decided on all-white flowers after agonizing and phoning from the office, and they'd made me promise to notice and tell them that they were pretty. We had decided that all the staff should stay behind and keep the office open as trade was so heavy, though I'd thought from her down-cast expression that June would have liked to have made the journey.

I asked the official where all the other flowers had come from: from businesses, he said, and he would collect all the cards afterwards and give them to me.

I supposed for the first time that perhaps I should have taken Greville back to London to be seen off by colleagues and friends, but during the very quiet half-hour that followed had no single regret. The clergyman engaged by the undertakers asked if I wanted the whole service read as I appeared to be the only mourner, and I said yes, go ahead, it was fitting.

His voice droned a bit. I half listened and half watched the way the sunshine fell onto the flowers on the coffin from the high windows along one wall and thought mostly not of Greville as he'd been alive but what he had become to me during the past week.

His life had settled on my shoulders like a mantle. Through Monday, Tuesday, Wednesday and Thursday I'd learned enough of his business never to forget it.

People who'd relied on him had transferred their reliance onto me, including in a way his friend Elliot Trelawney who wanted me as a Greville substitute to drink with. Clarissa Williams had sent her flowers knowing I would see them, wanting me to be aware of her, as if I weren't already. Nicholas Loder aimed to manipulate me for his own stable's ends. Prospero Jenks would soon be pressing hard for the diamonds for his fantasy, and the bank loan hung like a thundercloud in my mind.

Greville, lying cold in the coffin, hadn't meant any of it to happen.

A man of honour, I thought. I mentally repeated his own prayer for him, as it seemed a good time for it. May I deal with honour. May I act with courage. May I achieve humility. I didn't know if he'd managed that last one; I knew that I couldn't.

The clergyman droned to a halt. The official removed the three lots of flowers from the coffin to put them on the floor and, with a whirring and creaking of machinery that sounded loud in the silence, the coffin slid away forward, out of sight, heading for fire.

Goodbye, pal, I said silently. Goodbye, except that you are with me now more than ever before.

I went outside into the cold fresh air and thanked everyone and paid them and arranged for all of the flowers to go to St Catherine's Hospital, which seemed to be no problem. The official gave me the severed cards and asked what I wanted to do with my brother's ashes, and I had a ridiculous urge to laugh, which I saw from his hushed face would be wildly inappropriate. The business of ashes had always seemed to me an embarrassment.

He waited patiently for a decision. 'If you have any tall red rose trees,' I said finally, 'I daresay that would do, if you plant one along there with the others. Put the ashes there.'

I paid for the rose tree and thanked him again, and waited for a while for Brad to return, which he did looking smug and sporting a definite grin.

'I found it,' he said.

'What?' I was still thinking of Greville.

'Your brother's wheels.'

'You didn't!'

He nodded, highly pleased with himself.

'Where?'

He wouldn't say. He waited for me to sit and drove off in triumph into the centre of town, drawing up barely three hundred yards from where the scaffolding had fallen. Then, with his normal economy, he pointed to the forecourt of a used car sales business where under strips of fluttering pennants rows of offerings stood with large white prices painted on their windscreens.

'One of those?' I asked in disbelief.

Brad gurgled; no other word for the delight in his throat. 'Round the back,' he said.

He drove into the forecourt, then along behind the cars, and turned a corner, and we found ourselves outside the wide-open doors of a garage advertising repairs, oil changes, MOT tests and Ladies and Gents. Brad held the car-finder out of his open window and pressed the red button, and somewhere in the shadowy depths of the garage a pair of headlights began flashing on and off and a piercing whistle shrieked.

A cross-looking mechanic in oily overalls came hurrying out. He told me he was the foreman in charge and he'd be glad to see the back of the Rover 3500, and I owed him a week's parking besides the cleaning of the sparking plugs of the V.8 engine, plus a surcharge for inconvenience.

'What inconvenience?'

'Taking up space for a week when it was meant to be for an hour, and having that whistle blast my eardrums three times today.'

'Three times?' I said, surprised.

'Once this morning, twice this afternoon. This man came here earlier, you know. He said he'd bring the Rover's new owner.'

Brad gave me a bright glance. The car-finder had done its best for us early on in the morning, it seemed: it was our own eyes and ears that had missed it, out of sight as the car had been.

I asked the foreman to make out a bill and, getting out of my own car, swung over to Greville's. The Rover's doors would open, I found, but the boot was locked.

'Here,' said the foreman, coming over with the

account and the ignition keys. 'The boot won't open. Some sort of fancy lock. Custom made. It's been a bloody nuisance.'

I mollifyingly gave him a credit card in settlement and he took it off to his cubby-hole of an office.

I looked at the Rover. 'Can you drive that?' I asked Brad.

'Yerss,' he said gloomily.

I smiled and pulled Greville's keys out of my pocket to see if any of them would unlock the boot; and one did, to my relief, though not a key one would normally have associated with cars. More like the keys to a safe, I thought; and the lock revealed was intricate and steel. Its installation was typically Greville, ultra security-conscious after his experiences with the Porsche.

The treasure so well guarded included an expensive-looking set of golf clubs, with a trolley and a new box of golf balls, a large brown envelope, an overnight bag with pyjamas, clean shirt, toothbrush and a scarlet can of shaving cream, a portable telephone like my own, a personal computer, a portable fax machine, an opened carton of spare fax paper, a polished wooden box containing a beautiful set of brass scales with featherlight weights, an anti-thief device for locking onto the steering wheel, a huge torch, and a heavy complicated-looking orange metal contraption that I recognized from Greville's enthusiastic description as a device for sliding under flat tyres so that one could drive to a garage on it instead of changing a wheel by the roadside.

'Cor,' Brad said, looking at the haul, and the foreman too, returning with the paperwork, was brought to an understanding of the need for the defences.

I shut the boot and locked it again, which seemed a very Greville-like thing to do, and took a quick look round inside the body of the car, seeing the sort of minor clutter which defies the tidiest habit: matchbooks, time-clock parking slips, blue sunglasses, and a cellophane packet of tissues. In the door pocket on the driver's side, jammed in untidily, a map.

I picked it out. It was a road map of East Anglia, the route from London to Ipswich drawn heavily in black with, written down one side, the numbers of the roads to be followed. The marked route, I saw with interest, didn't stop at Ipswich but went on beyond, to Harwich.

Harwich, on the North Sea, was a ferry port. Harwich to the Hook of Holland; the route of one of the historic crossings, like Dover to Calais, Folkestone to Ostend. I didn't know if the Harwich ferries still ran, and I thought that if Greville had been going to Holland he would certainly have gone by air. All the same he had, presumably, been going to Harwich.

I said abruptly to the foreman, who was showing impatience for our departure, 'Is there a travel agent near here?'

'Three doors along,' he said, pointing, 'and you can't park here while you go there.'

I gave him a tip big enough to change his mind, and left Brad keeping watch over the cars while I peg-legged along the street. Right on schedule the travel agents came up, and I went in to enquire about ferries for the Hook of Holland.

'Sure,' said an obliging girl. 'They run every day and every night. Sealink operate them. When do you want to go?'

'I don't know, exactly.'

She thought me feeble. 'Well, the *St Nicholas* goes over to Holland every morning, and the *Koningin Beatrix* every night.'

I must have looked as stunned as I felt. I closed my open mouth.

'What's the matter?' she said.

'Nothing at all. Thank you very much.'

She shrugged as if the lunacies of the travelling public were past comprehension, and I shunted back to the garage with my chunk of new knowledge which had solved one little conundrum but posed another, such as what was Greville doing with Queen Beatrix, not a horse but a boat.

Brad drove the Rover to London and I drove my own car, the pace throughout enough to make a snail weep. Whatever the Ipswich garage had done to Greville's plugs hadn't cured any trouble, the V.8 running more like a V.4 or even a V.1½ as far as I could see. Brad stopped fairly soon after we'd left the town and, cursing, cleaned the plugs again himself, but to no avail.

'Needs new ones,' he said.

I used the time to search thoroughly through the golf bag, the box of golf balls, the overnight bag and all the gadgets.

No diamonds.

We set off again, the Rover going precariously slowly in very low gear up hills, with me staying on its tail in case it petered out altogether. I didn't much mind the slow progress except that resting my left foot on the floor sent frequent jabs up my leg and eventually reawoke the overall ache in the ankle, but in comparison with the ride home from Ipswich five days earlier it was chickenfeed. I still mended fast, I thought gratefully. By Tuesday at the latest I'd be walking. Well, limping, maybe, like Greville's car.

There was no joy in reflecting, as I did, that if the sparking plugs had been efficient he wouldn't have stopped to have them fixed and he wouldn't have been walking along a street in Ipswich at the wrong moment. If one could foresee the future, accidents wouldn't happen. 'If only' were wretched words.

We reached Greville's road eventually and found two spaces to park, though not outside the house. I'd told Brad in the morning that I would sleep in London that night to be handy for going to York with the Ostermeyers the next day. I'd planned originally that if we found the Rover he would take it on the orbital route direct to Hungerford and I would drive into London and go on home from there after I got back from York. The plugs having changed that plan near Ipswich, it was now Brad who would go to Hungerford in my car, and I would finish the journey by train. Greville's car, ruin that it was, could decorate the street.

We transferred all the gear from Greville's boot into the back of my car, or rather Brad did the transferring while I mostly watched. Then, Brad carrying the big brown envelope from the Rover and my own overnight grip, we went up the path to the house in the dark and set off the lights and the barking. No one in the houses around paid any attention. I undid the three locks and went in cautiously but, as before, once I'd switched the dog off the house was quiet and deserted. Brad, declining food and drink, went home to his mum, and I, sitting in Greville's chair, opened the big brown envelope and read all about Vaccaro who had been a very bad boy indeed.

Most of the envelope's contents were a copy of Vaccaro's detailed application, but on an attached sheet in abbreviated prose Greville had hand-written:

> Ramón Vaccaro, wanted for drug-running, Florida, USA.
>
> Suspected of several murders, victims mostly pilots, wanting out from flying drug crates. Vaccaro leaves no mouths alive to chatter. My info from scared-to-death pilot's widow. She won't come to the committee meeting but gave enough insider details for me to believe her.

Vaccaro seduced private pilots with a big pay-off, then when they'd done one run to Colombia and got away with it, they'd be hooked and do it again and again until they finally got rich enough to have cold feet. Then the poor sods would die from being shot on their own doorsteps from passing cars, no sounds because of silencers, no witnesses and no clues. But all were pilots owning their own small planes, too many for coincidence. Widow says her husband scared stiff but left it too late. She's remarried, lives in London, always wanted revenge, couldn't believe it was the same man when she saw local newspaper snippet, Vaccaro's Family Gaming, with his photo. Family! She went to Town Hall anonymously, they put her on to me.

We don't have to find Vaccaro guilty. We just don't give him a gaming licence. Widow says not to let him know who turned his application down, he's dangerous and vengeful, but how can he silence a whole committee? The Florida police might like to know his whereabouts. Extradition?

I telephoned Elliot Trelawney at his weekend home, told him I'd found the red-hot notes and read them to him, which brought forth a whistle and a groan.

'But Vaccaro didn't kill Greville,' I said.

'No.' He sighed. 'How did the funeral go?'

'Fine. Thank you for your flowers.'

'Just sorry I couldn't get there – but on a working day, and so far . . .'

'It was fine,' I said again, and it had been. I'd been relieved, on the whole, to be alone.

'Would you mind,' he said, diffidently, 'if I arranged a memorial service for him? Sometime soon. Within a month?'

'Go right ahead,' I said warmly. 'A great idea.'

He hoped I would send the Vaccaro notes by messenger on Monday to the Magistrates Court, and he asked if I played golf.

In the morning, after a dream-filled night in Greville's black and white bed, I took a taxi to the Ostermeyers' hotel, meeting them in the foyer as arranged on the telephone the evening before.

They were in very good form, Martha resplendent in a red wool tailored dress with a mink jacket, Harley with a new English-looking hat over his easy grin, binoculars and racing paper ready. Both of them seemed determined to enjoy whatever the day brought forth and Harley's occasional ill-humour was far out of sight.

The driver, a different one from Wednesday, brought a huge super-comfortable Daimler to the front door exactly on time, and with all auspices pointing to felicity, the Ostermeyers arranged themselves on the rear seat, I sitting in front of them beside the chauffeur.

The chauffeur, who announced his name as Simms,

kindly stowed my crutches in the boot and said it was no trouble at all, sir, when I thanked him. The crutches themselves seemed to be the only tiny cloud on Martha's horizon, bringing a brief frown to the proceedings.

'Is that foot still bothering you? Milo said it was nothing to worry about.'

'No, it isn't, and it's much better,' I said truthfully.

'Oh, good. Just as long as it doesn't stop you riding Datepalm.'

'Of course not,' I assured her.

'We're so pleased to have him. He's just darling.'

I made some nice noises about Datepalm, which wasn't very difficult, as we nosed through the traffic to go north on the M1.

Harley said, 'Milo says Datepalm might go for the Charisma 'Chase at Kempton next Saturday. What do you think?'

'A good race for him,' I said calmly. I would kill Milo, I thought. A dicey gallop was one thing, but no medic on earth was going to sign my card in one week to say I was fit; and I wouldn't be, because half a ton of horse over jumps at thirty-plus miles an hour was no puffball matter.

'Milo might prefer to save him for the Mackeson at Cheltenham next month,' I said judiciously, sowing the idea. 'Or of course for the Hennessy Cognac Gold Cup two weeks later.' I'd definitely be fit for the Hennessy, six weeks ahead. The Mackeson, at four weeks, was a toss-up.

'Then there's that big race the day after Christmas,' Martha sighed happily. 'It's all so exciting. Harley promises we can come back to see him run.'

They talked about horses for another half hour and then asked if I knew anything about a Dick Turpin.

'Oh, sure.'

'Some guy said he was riding to York. I didn't understand any part of it.'

I laughed. 'It happened a couple of centuries ago. Dick Turpin was a highwayman, a real villain, who rode his mare Black Bess north to escape the law. They caught him in York and flung him in gaol and for a fortnight he held a sort of riotous court in his cell, making jokes and drinking with all the notables of the city who came to see the famous thief in his chains. Then they took him out and hanged him on a piece of land called the Knavesmire, which is now the racecourse.'

'Oh, my,' Martha said, ghoulishly diverted. 'How perfectly grisly.'

In time we left the M1 and travelled north-east to the difficult old A1, and I thought that no one in their senses would drive from London to York when they could go by train. The Ostermeyers, of course, weren't doing the driving.

Harley said as we neared the city, 'You're expected at lunch with us, Derek.'

Expected, in Ostermeyer speech, meant invited. I protested mildly that it wasn't so.

'It sure is. I talked with Lord Knightwood yesterday

evening, told him we'd have you with us. He said right away to have you join us for lunch. They're giving their name to one of the races, it'll be a big party.'

'Which race?' I asked with curiosity. Knightwood wasn't a name I knew.

'Here it is.' Harley rustled the racing newspaper. 'The University of York Trophy. Lord Knightwood is the University's top man, president or governor, some kind of figurehead. A Yorkshire VIP. Anyway, you're expected.'

I thanked him. There wasn't much else to do, though a sponsor's lunch on top of no exercise could give me weight problems if I wasn't careful. However, I could almost hear Milo's agitated voice in my ear: 'Whatever the Ostermeyers want, for Christ's sake give it to them.'

'There's also the York Minster Cup,' Harley said, reading his paper, 'and the Civic Pride Challenge. Your horse Dozen Roses is in the York Castle Champions.'

'My brother's horse,' I said.

Harley chuckled. 'We won't forget.'

Simms dropped us neatly at the Club entrance. One could get addicted to chauffeurs, I thought, accepting the crutches gravely offered. No parking problems. Someone to drive one home on crunch days. But no spontaneity, no real privacy . . . No thanks, not even long-term Brad.

Back the first horse you see, they say. Or the first jockey. Or the first trainer.

The first trainer we saw was Nicholas Loder. He

looked truly furious and, I thought in surprise, alarmed when I came face to face with him after he'd watched our emergence from the Daimler.

'What are you doing here?' he demanded brusquely. 'You've no business here.'

'Do you know Mr and Mrs Ostermeyer?' I asked politely, introducing them. 'They've just bought Datepalm. I'm their guest today.'

He glared; there wasn't any other word for it. He had been waiting for a man, perhaps one of his owners, to collect a Club badge from the allotted window and, the transaction achieved, the two of them marched off into the racecourse without another word.

'Well!' Martha said, outraged. 'If Milo ever behaved like that we'd whisk our horses out of his yard before he could say goodbye.'

'It isn't my horse,' I pointed out. 'Not yet.'

'When it is, what will you do?'

'The same as you, I think, though I didn't mean to.'

'Good,' Martha said emphatically.

I didn't really understand Loder's attitude or reaction. If he wanted a favour from me, which was that I'd let him sell Dozen Roses and Gemstones to others of his owners either for the commission or to keep them in his yard, he should at least have shown an echo of Milo's feelings for the Ostermeyers.

If Dozen Roses had been cleared by the authorities to run, why was Loder scared that I was there to watch it?

Crazy, I thought. The only thing I'd wholly learned was that Loder's ability to dissimulate was underdeveloped for a leading trainer.

Harley Ostermeyer said the York University's lunch was to be held at one end of the Club members' dining room in the grandstand, so I showed the way there, reflecting that it was lucky I'd decided on a decent suit for that day, not just a sweater. I might have been a last-minute addition to the party but I was happy not to look it.

There was already a small crowd of people, glasses in hand, chatting away inside a temporary white-lattice-fenced area, a long buffet set out behind them with tables and chairs to sit at for eating.

'There are the Knightwoods,' said the Ostermeyers, clucking contentedly, and I found myself being introduced presently to a tall white-haired kindly-looking man who had benevolence shining from every perhaps seventy-year-old wrinkle. He shook my hand amicably as a friend of the Ostermeyers with whom, it seemed, he had dined on a reciprocal visit to Harley's alma mater, the University of Pennsylvania. Harley was endowing a Chair there. Harley was a VIP in Pittsburgh, Pennsylvania.

I made the right faces and listened to the way the world went round, and said I thought it was great of the city of York to support its industry on the turf.

'Have you met my wife?' Lord Knightwood said vaguely. 'My dear,' he touched the arm of a woman with her back to us, 'you remember Harley and Martha Ostermeyer? And this is their friend Derek Franklin that I told you about.'

She turned to the Ostermeyers smiling and greeting them readily, and she held out a hand for me to shake, saying, 'How do you do. So glad you could come.'

'How do you do, Lady Knightwood,' I said politely. She gave me a very small smile, in command of herself.

Clarissa Williams was Lord Knightwood's wife.

CHAPTER TEN

She had known I would be there, it was clear, and if she hadn't wanted me to find out who she was she could have developed a strategic illness in plenty of time.

She was saying graciously, 'Didn't I see you on television winning the Gold Cup?' and I thought of her speed with that frightful kiyoga and the tumult of her feelings on Tuesday, four days ago. She seemed to have no fear that I would give her away, and indeed, what could I say? Lord Knightwood, my brother was your wife's lover? Just the right sort of thing to get the happy party off to a good start.

The said Lord was introducing the Ostermeyers to a professor of physics who with twinkles said that as he was the only true aficionado of horse-racing among the teaching academics he had been pressed into service to carry the flag, although there were about fifty undergraduates out on the course ready to bet their socks off in the cause.

'Derek has a degree,' Martha said brightly, making conversation.

The professorial eyeballs swivelled my way speculatively. 'What university?'

'Lancaster,' I said dryly, which raised a laugh. Lancaster and York had fought battles of the red and white roses for many a long year.

'And subject?'

'Independent Studies.'

His desultory attention sharpened abruptly.

'What are Independent Studies?' Harley asked, seeing his interest.

'The student designs his own course and invents his own final subject,' the professor said. 'Lancaster is the only university offering such a course and they let only about eight students a year do it. It's not for the weak-willed or the feeble-minded.'

The Knightwoods and the Ostermeyers listened in silence and I felt embarrassed. I had been young then, I thought.

'What did you choose as your subject?' asked the professor, intent now on an answer. 'Horses, in some way?'

I shook my head. 'No. . . er. . . "Roots and Results of War".'

'My dear chap,' Lord Knightwood said heartily, 'sit next to the professor at lunch.' He moved away benignly, taking his wife and the Ostermeyers with him, and the professor, left behind, asked what I fancied for the races.

Clarissa, by accident or design, remained out of

talking distance throughout the meal and I didn't try to approach her. The party broke up during and after the first race, although everyone was invited to return for tea, and I spent most of the afternoon, as I'd spent so many others, watching horses stretch and surge and run as their individual natures dictated. The will to win was born and bred in them all, but some cared more than others: it was those with the implacable impulse to lead a wild herd who fought hardest and oftenest won. Sports writers tended to call it courage but it went deeper than that, right down into the gene pool, into instinct, into the primordial soup on the same evolutionary level as the belligerence so easily aroused in Homo sapiens, that was the taproot of water.

I was no stranger to the thought that I sought battle on the turf because, though the instinct to fight and conquer ran strong, I was averse to guns. Sublimation, the pundits would no doubt call it. Datepalm and I both, on the same primitive plane, wanted to win.

'What are you thinking?' someone asked at my shoulder.

I would have known her voice anywhere, I thought. I turned to see her half-calm half-anxious expression, the Lady Knightwood social poise explicit in the smooth hair, the patrician bones and the tailoring of her clothes, the passionate woman merely a hint in the eyes.

'Thinking about horses,' I said.

'I suppose you're wondering why I came today, after I learned last night that you'd not only be at the races, which I expected you might be anyway because of Dozen Roses, but actually be coming to our lunch . . .' She stopped, sounding uncertain.

'I'm not Greville,' I said. 'Don't think of me as Greville.'

Her eyelids flickered. 'You're too damned perceptive.' She did a bit of introspection. 'Yes, all right, I wanted to be near you. It's a sort of comfort.'

We were standing by the rails of the parade ring watching the runners for the next race walk round, led by their lads. It was the race before the University Trophy, two races before that of Dozen Roses, a period without urgency for either of us. There were crowd noises all around and the clip-clop of horses walking by, and we could speak quietly as in an oasis of private space without being overheard.

'Are you still angry with me for hitting you?' she said a shade bitterly, as I'd made no comment after her last remark.

I half smiled. 'No.'

'I did think you were a burglar.'

'And what would you have explained to the police, if they'd come?'

She said ruefully, 'I hope I would have come to my senses and done a bunk before they got there.' She sighed. 'Greville said if I ever had to use the kiyoga in earnest to escape at once and not worry what I'd done to my attacker, but he never thought of a burglar in his own house.'

'I'm surprised he gave you a weapon like that,' I said mildly. 'Aren't they illegal? And him a magistrate.'

'I'm a magistrate too,' she said unexpectedly. 'That's how we originally met, at a magistrates' conference. I've not enquired into the legality of kiyogas. If I were prosecuted for carrying and using an offensive weapon, well, that would be much preferable to being a victim of the appalling assaults that come before us every week.'

'Where did he get it?' I asked curiously.

'America.'

'Do you have it with you here?'

She nodded and touched her handbag. 'It's second nature, now.'

She must have been thirty years younger than her husband, I thought inconsequentially, and I knew what she felt about him. I didn't know whether or not I liked her, but I did recognize there was a weird sort of intimacy between us and that I didn't resent it.

The jockeys came out and stood around the owners in little groups. Nicholas Loder was there with the man he'd come in with, a thickset powerful-looking man in a dark suit, the pink cardboard Club badge fluttering from his lapel.

'Dozen Roses,' I said, watching Loder talking to the owner and his jockey, 'was he named for you?'

'Oh, God,' she said, disconcerted. 'How ever . . .?'

I said, 'I put your roses on the coffin for the service.'

'Oh . . .' she murmured with difficulty, her throat closing, her mouth twisting, 'I . . . can't . . .'

'Tell me how York University came to be putting its name to a race.' I made it sound conversational, to give her composure time.

She swallowed, fighting for control, steadying her breathing. 'I'm sorry. It's just that I can't even mourn for him except inside; can't let it show to anyone except you, and it sweeps over me, I can't help it.' She paused and answered my unimportant question. 'The Clerk of the Course wanted to involve the city. Some of the bigwigs of the University were against joining in, but Henry persuaded them. He and I have always come here to meetings now and then. We both like it, for a day out with friends.'

'Your husband doesn't actually lecture at the University, does he?'

'Oh, no, he's just a figurehead. He's chairman of a fair number of things in York. A public figure here.'

Vulnerable to scandal, I thought: as she was herself, and Greville also. She and he must have been unwaveringly discreet.

'How long since you first met Greville?' I asked noncommittally.

'Four years.' She paused. 'Four marvellous years. Not enough.'

The jockeys swung up onto the horses and moved away to go out onto the course. Nicholas Loder and his owner, busily talking, went off to the stands.

'May I watch the race with you?' Clarissa said. 'Do you mind?'

'I was going to watch from the grass.' I glanced down apologetically at the crutches. 'It's easier.'

'I don't mind the grass.'

So we stood side by side on the grass in front of the grandstand and she said, 'Whenever we could be together, he bought twelve red roses. It just . . . well . . .' She stopped, swallowing again hard.

'Mm,' I said. I thought of the ashes and the red rose tree and decided to tell her about that another time. It had been for him, anyway, not for her.

Nicholas Loder's two-year-old won the sprint at a convincing clip and I caught a glimpse of the owner afterwards looking heavily satisfied but unsmiling. Hardly a jolly character, I thought.

Clarissa went off to join her husband for the University race and after that, during their speeches and presentations, I went in search of Dozen Roses who was being led round in the pre-parade ring before being taken into a box or a stall to have his saddle put on.

Dozen Roses looked docile to dozy, I thought. An unremarkable bay, he had none of the looks or presence of Datepalm, nor the chaser's alert interest in his surroundings. He was a good performer, of that there was no question, but he didn't at that moment give an impression of going to be a 'trot-up' within half an hour, and he was vaguely not what I'd expected. Was this the colt that on the video tapes had won his last three races full of verve? Was this the young buck who had tried to mount a filly at the starting gate at Newmarket?

No, I saw with a sense of shock, he was not. I peered under his belly more closely, as it was sometimes difficult to tell, but there seemed to be no doubt that he had lost the essential tackle; that he had in fact been gelded.

I was stunned, and I didn't know whether to laugh or be furious. It explained so much: the loss of form when he had his mind on procreation rather than racing, and the return to speed once the temptation was removed. It explained why the Stewards hadn't called Loder in to justify the difference in running: horses very often did better after the operation.

I unfolded my racecard at Dozen Roses's race, and there, sure enough, against his name stood not c for colt or h for horse, but g for gelding.

Nicholas Loder's voice, vibrating with fury, spoke from not far behind me, 'That horse is not your horse. Keep away from him.'

I turned. Loder was advancing fast with Dozen Roses's saddle over his arm and full-blown rage in his face. The heavily unjoyful owner, still for some reason in tow, was watching the proceedings with puzzlement.

'Mine or not, I'm entitled to look at him,' I said. 'And look at him I darned well have, and either he is not Dozen Roses or you have gelded him against my brother's express wishes.'

His mouth opened and snapped shut.

'What's the matter, Nick?' the owner said. 'Who is this?'

Loder failed to introduce us. Instead he said to me

vehemently, 'You can't do anything about it. I have an Authority to Act. I am the registered agent for this horse and what I decide is none of your business.'

'My brother refused to have any of his horses gelded. You knew it well. You disobeyed him because you were sure he wouldn't find out, as he never went to the races.'

He glared at me. He was aware that if I lodged a formal complaint he would be in a good deal of trouble, and I thought he was certainly afraid that as my brother's executor I could and quite likely would do just that. Even if I only talked about it to others, it could do him damage: it was the sort of titbit the hungry racing press would pounce on for a giggle, and the owners of all the princely colts in his prestigious stable would get cold feet that the same might happen to their own property without their knowledge or consent.

He had understood all that, I thought, in the moment I'd told him on the telephone that it was I who would be inheriting Dozen Roses. He'd known that if I ever saw the horse I would realize at once what had been done. No wonder he'd lost his lower resonances.

'Greville was a fool,' he said angrily. 'The horse has done much better since he was cut.'

'That's true,' I agreed, 'but it's not the point.'

'How much do you want, then?' he demanded roughly.

My own turn, I thought, to gape like a fish. I said feebly, 'It's not a matter of money.'

'Everything is,' he declared. 'Name your price and get out of my way.'

I glanced at the attendant owner who looked more phlegmatic than riveted, but might remember and repeat this conversation, and I said merely, 'We'll discuss it later, OK?' and hitched myself away from them without aggression.

Behind me the owner was saying, 'What was that all about, Nick?' and I heard Loder reply, 'Nothing, Rollo. Don't worry about it,' and when I looked back a few seconds later I saw both of them stalking off towards the saddling boxes followed by Dozen Roses in the grasp of his lad.

Despite Nicholas Loder's anxious rage, or maybe because of it, I came down on the side of amusement. I would myself have had the horse gelded several months before the trainer had done it out of no doubt unbearable frustration: Greville had been pigheaded on the subject from both misplaced sympathy and not knowing enough about horses. I thought I would make peace with Loder that evening on the telephone, whatever the outcome of the race, as I certainly didn't want a fight on my hands for so rocky a cause. Talk about the roots of war, I thought wryly: there had been sillier reasons for bloody strife in history than the castration of a thoroughbred.

At York some of the saddling boxes were open to public view, some were furnished with doors. Nicholas

Loder seemed to favour the privacy and took Dozen Roses inside away from my eyes.

Harley and Martha Ostermeyer, coming to see the horses saddle, were full of beaming anticipation. They had backed the winner of the University Trophy and had wagered all the proceeds on my, that was to say, my *brother*'s horse.

'You won't get much return,' I warned them. 'It's favourite.'

'We know that, dear,' Martha said happily, looking around. 'Where is he? Which one?'

'He's inside that box,' I pointed, 'being saddled.'

'Harley and I have had a marvellous idea,' she said sweetly, her eyes sparkling.

'Now, Martha,' Harley said. He sounded faintly alarmed as if Martha's marvellous ideas weren't always the best possible news.

'We went you to dine with us when we get back to London,' she finished.

Harley relaxed, relieved. 'Yes. Hope you can.' He clearly meant that this particular marvellous idea was passable, even welcome. 'London at weekends is a graveyard.'

With a twitching of an inward grin I accepted my role as graveyard alleviator and, in the general good cause of cementing Ostermeyer–Shandy–Franklin relations, said I would be very pleased to stay to dinner. Martha and Harley expressed such gratification as to make me wonder whether when they were alone they bored each other to silence.

Dozen Roses emerged from his box with his saddle on and was led along towards the parade ring. He walked well, I thought, his good straight hocks encouraging lengthy strides, and he also seemed to have woken up a good deal, now that the excitement was at hand.

In the horse's wake hurried Nicholas Loder and his friend Rollo, and it was because they were crowding him, I thought, that Dozen Roses swung round on his leading rein and pulled backwards from his lad, and in straightening up again hit the Rollo man a hefty buffet with his rump and knocked him to his knees.

Martha with instinctive kindness rushed forward to help him, but he floundered to his feet with a curse that made her blink. All the same she bent and picked up a thing like a blue rubber ball which had fallen out of his jacket and held it towards him, saying, 'You dropped this, I think.'

He ungraciously snatched it from her, gave her an unnecessarily fierce stare as if she'd frightened the horse into knocking him over, which she certainly hadn't, and hurried into the parade ring after Nicholas Loder. He, looking back and seeing me still there, reacted with another show of fury.

'What perfectly horrid people,' Martha said, making a face. 'Did you hear what that man said? Disgusting! Fancy saying it aloud!'

Dear Martha, I thought, that word was everyday

coinage on racecourses. The nicest people used it: it made no one a villain. She was brushing dust off her gloves fastidiously as if getting rid of contamination and I half expected her to go up to Rollo and in the tradition of the indomitable American female to tell him to wash his mouth out with soap.

Harley had meanwhile picked something else up off the grass and was looking at it helplessly. 'He dropped this too,' he said. 'I think.'

Martha peered at his hands and took the object out of them.

'Oh, yes,' she said with recognition, 'that's the other half of the baster. You'd better have it, Derek, then you can give it back to that obnoxious friend of your trainer, if you want to.'

I frowned at what she'd given me, which was a rigid plastic tube, semi-transparent, about an inch in diameter, nine inches long, open at one end and narrowing to half the width at the other.

'A baster,' Martha said again. 'For basting meat when it's roasting. You know them, don't you? You press the bulb thing and release it to suck up the juices which you then squirt over the meat.'

I nodded. I knew what a baster was.

'What an extraordinary thing to take to the races,' Martha said wonderingly.

'Mm,' I agreed. 'He seems an odd sort of man altogether.' I tucked the plastic tube into an inside jacket pocket, from which its nozzle end protruded a couple of inches, and we went first to see Dozen Roses joined with his jockey in the parade ring and then up onto the stands to watch him race.

The jockey was Loder's chief stable jockey, as able as any, as honest as most. The stable money was definitely on the horse, I thought, watching the forecast odds on the information board change from 2/1 on to 5/2 on. When a gambling stable didn't put its money up front, the whisper went round and the price eased dramatically. The whisper where it mattered that day had to be saying that Loder was in earnest about the 'trot-up', and Alfie's base imputation would have to wait for another occasion.

Perhaps as a result of his year-by-year successes, Loder's stable always, it was well-known in the racing world, attracted as owners serious gamblers whose satisfaction was more in winning money than in winning races: and that wasn't the truism it seemed, because in steeplechasing the owners tended to want to win the races more than the money. Steeplechasing owners only occasionally made a profit overall and realistically expected to have to pay for their pleasure.

Wondering if the Rollo man was one of the big Loder gamblers, I flicked back the pages of the racecard and looked up his name beside the horse of his that had won the sprint. Owner, Mr T. Rollway, the card read. Rollo for short to his friends. Never heard of him, I thought, and wondered if Greville had.

Dozen Roses cantered down to the start with at least

as much energy and enthusiasm as any of the seven other runners and was fed into the stalls without fuss. He'd been striding out well, I thought, and taking a good hold of the bit. An old hand at the game by now, of course, as I was also, I thought dryly.

I'd ridden in several Flat races in my teens as an amateur, learning that the hardest and most surprising thing about the unrelenting Flat race crouch over the withers was the way it cramped one's lungs and affected one's breathing. The first few times I'd almost fallen off at the finish from lack of oxygen. A long time ago, I thought, watching the gates fly open in the distance and the colours spill out, long ago when I was young and it all lay ahead.

If I could find Greville's diamonds, I thought, I would in due course be able to buy a good big yard in Lambourn and start training free of a mortgage and on a decent scale, providing of course I could get owners to send me horses, and I had no longer any doubt that one of these years, when my body packed up mending fast, as everyone's did in the end, I would be content with the new life, even though the consuming passion I still felt for race-riding couldn't be replaced by anything tamer.

Dozen Roses was running with the pack, all seven bunched after the first three furlongs, flying along the far side of the track at more than cruising speed but with acceleration still in reserve.

If I didn't find Greville's diamonds, I thought, I

would just scrape together whatever I could and borrow the rest, and still buy a place and set my hand to the future. But not yet, not yet.

Dozen Roses and the others swung left-handed into the long bend round the far end of the track, the bunch coming apart as the curve element hit them. Turning into the straight five furlongs from the winning post Dozen Roses was in fourth place and making not much progress. I wanted him quite suddenly to win and was surprised by the strength of the feeling; I wanted him to win for Greville, who wouldn't care anyway, and perhaps also for Clarissa, who would. Sentimental fool, I told myself. Anyway, when the crowd started yelling home their fancy I yelled for mine also, and I'd never done that before as far as I could remember.

There was not going to be a trot-up, whatever Nicholas Loder might have thought. Dozen Roses was visibly struggling as he took second place at a searing speed a furlong from home and he wouldn't have got the race at all if the horse half a length in front, equally extended and equally exhausted, hadn't veered from a straight line at the last moment and bumped into him.

'Oh dear,' Martha exclaimed sadly, as the two horses passed the winning post. 'Second. Oh well, never mind.'

'He'll get the race on an objection,' I said. 'Which I suppose is better than nothing. Your winnings are safe.'

'Are you sure?'

'Certain,' I said, and almost immediately the loudspeakers were announcing 'Stewards' enquiry'.

More slowly than I would have liked to be able to manage, the three of us descended to the area outside the weighing room where the horse that was not my horse stood in the place for the unsaddling of the second, a net rug over his back and steam flowing from his sweating skin. He was moving about restlessly, as horses often do after an all-out effort, and his lad was holding tight to the reins, trying to calm him.

'He ran a great race,' I said to Martha, and she said, 'Did he, dear?'

'He didn't give up. That's really what matters.'

Of Nicholas Loder there was no sign: probably inside the Stewards' room putting forward his complaint. The Stewards would show themselves the views from the side camera and the head-on camera, and at any moment now . . .

'Result of Stewards' enquiry,' said the loudspeakers. 'Placing of first and second reversed.' Hardly justice, but inevitable: the faster horse had lost. Nicholas Loder came out of the weighing room and saw me standing with the Ostermeyers, but before I could utter even the first conciliatory words like, 'Well done,' he'd given me a sick look and hurried off in the opposite direction. No Rollo in his shadow, I noticed.

Martha, Harley and I returned to the luncheon room for the University's tea where the Knightwoods were being gracious hosts and Clarissa, at the sight of me, developed renewed trouble with the tear glands. I left the Ostermeyers taking cups and saucers from a waitress and drifted across to her side.

'So silly,' she said crossly, blinking hard as she offered me a sandwich. 'But wasn't he great?'

'He was.'

'I wish . . .' She stopped. I wished it too. No need at all to put it into words. But Greville never went to the races.

'I go to London fairly often,' she said. 'May I phone you when I'm there?'

'Yes, if you like.' I wrote my home number on my racecard and handed it to her. 'I live in Berkshire,' I said, 'not in Greville's house.'

She met my eyes, hers full of confusion.

'I'm not Greville,' I said.

'My dear chap,' said her husband boomingly, coming to a halt beside us, 'delighted your horse finally won. Though, of course, not technically your horse, what?'

'No, sir.'

He was shrewd enough, I thought, looking at the intelligent eyes amid the bonhomie. Not easy to fool. I wondered fleetingly if he'd ever suspected his wife had a lover, even if he hadn't known who. I thought that if he had known who, he wouldn't have asked me to lunch.

He chuckled. 'The professor says you tipped him three winners.'

'A miracle.'

'He's very impressed.' He looked at me benignly. 'Join us at any time, my dear chap.' It was the sort of vague invitation, not meant to be accepted, that was a mild seal of approval, in its way.

'Thank you,' I said, and he nodded, knowing he'd been understood.

Martha Ostermeyer gushed up to say how marvellous the whole day had been, and gradually from then on, as such things always do, the University party evaporated.

I shook Clarissa's outstretched hand in farewell, and also her husband's who stood beside her. They looked good together, and settled, a fine couple on the surface.

'We'll see you again,' she said to me, and I wondered if it were only I who could hear her smothered desperation.

'Yes,' I said positively. 'Of course.'

'My dear chap,' her husband said. 'Any time.'

Harley, Martha and I left the racecourse and climbed into the Daimler, Simms following Brad's routine of stowing the crutches.

Martha said reproachfully, 'Your ankle's broken, not twisted. One of the guests told us. I said you'd ridden a gallop for us on Wednesday and they couldn't believe it.'

'It's practically mended,' I said weakly.

'But you won't be able to ride Datepalm in that race next Saturday, will you?'

'Not really. No.'

She sighed. 'You're very naughty. We'll simply have to wait until you're ready.'

I gave her a fast smile of intense gratitude. There weren't many owners who would have dreamed of waiting. No trainer would; they couldn't afford to. Milo was currently putting up one of my arch-rivals on the horses I usually rode, and I just hoped I would get all of them back once I was fit. That was the main trouble with injuries, not the injury itself but losing one's mounts to other jockeys. Permanently, sometimes, if they won.

'And now,' Martha said as we set off south towards London, 'I have had another simply marvellous idea, and Harley agrees with me.'

I glanced back to Harley who was sitting behind Simms. He was nodding indulgently. No anxiety this time.

'We think,' she said happily, 'that we'll buy Dozen Roses and send him to Milo to train for jumping. That is,' she laughed, 'if your brother's executor will sell him to us.'

'Martha!' I was dumbstruck and used her first name without thinking, though I'd called her Mrs Ostermeyer before, when I'd called her anything.

'There,' she said, gratified at my reaction, 'I told you it was a marvellous idea. What do you say?'

'My brother's executor is speechless.'

'But you will sell him?'

'I certainly will.'

'Then let's use the car phone to call Milo and tell him.' She was full of high good spirits and in no mood for waiting, but when she reached Milo he apparently didn't immediately catch fire. She handed the phone to me with a frown, saying, 'He wants to talk to you.'

'Milo,' I said, 'what's the trouble?'

'That horse is an entire. They don't jump well.'

'He's a gelding,' I assured him.

'You told me your brother wouldn't ever have it done.'

'Nicholas Loder did it without permission.'

'You're kidding!'

'No,' I said. 'Anyway the horse got the race today on a Stewards' enquiry but he ran gamely, and he's fit.'

'Has he ever jumped?'

'I shouldn't think so. But I'll teach him.'

'All right then. Put me back to Martha.'

'Don't go away when she's finished. I want another word.'

I handed the phone to Martha who listened and spoke with a return to enthusiasm, and eventually I talked to Milo again.

'Why,' I asked, 'would one of Nicholas Loder's owners carry a baster about at the races?'

'A what?'

'Baster. Thing that's really for cooking. You've got one. You use it as a nebuliser.'

'Simple and effective.'

He used it, I reflected, on the rare occasions when it was the best way to give some sort of medication to a horse. One dissolved or diluted the medicine in water and filled the rubber bulb of the baster with it. Then one fitted the tube onto that, slid the tube up the horse's nostril, and squeezed the bulb sharply. The liquid came out in a vigorous spray straight onto the mucous membranes and from there passed immediately into the bloodstream. One could puff out dry powder with the same result. It was the fastest way of getting some drugs to act.

'At the races?' Milo was saying. 'An owner?'

'That's right. His horse won the five-furlong sprint.'

'He'd have to be mad. They dope-test two horses in every race, as you know. Nearly always the winner, and another at random. No owner is going to pump drugs into his horse at the races.'

'I don't know that he did. He had a baster with him, that's all.'

'Did you tell the Stewards?'

'No, I didn't. Nicholas Loder was with his owner and he would have exploded as he was angry with me already for spotting Dozen Roses's alteration.'

Milo laughed. 'So that was what all the heat was about this past week?'

'You've got it.'

'Will you kick up a storm?'

'Probably not.'

'You're too soft,' he said, 'and oh yes, I almost forgot. There was a phone message for you. Wait a tick. I wrote it down.' He went away for a bit and returned. 'Here you are. Something about your brother's diamonds.' He sounded doubtful. 'Is that right?'

'Yes. What about them?'

He must have heard the urgency in my voice because he said, 'It's nothing much. Just that someone had been trying to ring you last night and all day today, but I said you'd slept in London and gone to York.'

'Who was it?'

'He didn't say. Just said that he had some info for you. Then he hummed and hahed and said if I talked to you would I tell you he would telephone your brother's house, in case you went there, at about ten tonight, or later. Or it might have been a she. Difficult to tell. One of those middle-range voices. I said I didn't know if you would be speaking to me, but I'd tell you if I could.'

'Well, thanks.'

'I'm not a message service,' he said testily. 'Why don't you switch on your answer phone like everyone else?'

'I do sometimes.'

'Not enough.'

I switched off the phone with a smile and wondered who'd been trying to reach me. It had to be someone who knew Greville had bought diamonds. It might even be Annette, I thought: her voice had a mid-range quality.

I would have liked to have gone to Greville's house as soon as we got back to London, but I couldn't exactly renege on the dinner after Martha's truly marvellous idea, so the three of us ate together as planned and I tried to please them as much as they'd pleased me.

Martha announced yet another marvellous idea during dinner. She and Harley would get Simms or another of the car firm's chauffeurs to drive us all down to Lambourn the next day to take Milo out to lunch, so that they could see Datepalm again before they went back to the States on Tuesday. They could drop me at my house afterwards, and then go on to visit a castle in Dorset they'd missed last time around. Harley looked resigned. It was Martha, I saw, who always made the decisions, which was maybe why the repressed side of him needed to lash out sometimes at car-park attendants who boxed him in.

Milo, again on the telephone, told me he'd do practically anything to please the Ostermeyers, definitely including Sunday lunch. He also said that my informant had rung again and he had told him/her that I'd got the message.

'Thanks,' I said.

'See you tomorrow.'

I thanked the Ostermeyers inadequately for everything and went to Greville's house by taxi. I did think of asking the taxi driver to stay, like Brad, until I'd reconnoitred, but the house was quiet and dark behind the impregnable grilles, and I thought the taxi driver would think me a fool or a coward or both, so I paid him off and, fishing out the keys, opened the gate in the hedge and went up the path until the lights blazed on and the dog started barking.

Everyone can make mistakes.

CHAPTER ELEVEN

I didn't get as far as the steps up to the front door. A dark figure, dimly glimpsed in the floodlight's glare, came launching itself at me from behind in a cannonball rugger tackle and when I reached the ground something very hard hit my head.

I had no sensation of blacking out or of time passing. One moment I was awake, and the next moment I was awake also, or so it seemed, but I knew in a dim way that there had been an interval.

I didn't know where I was except that I was lying face down on grass. I'd woken up concussed on grass several times in my life, but never before in the dark. They couldn't have all gone home from the races, I thought, and left me alone out on the course all night.

The memory of where I was drifted back quietly. In Greville's front garden. Alive. Hooray for small mercies.

I knew from experience that the best way to deal with being knocked out was not to hurry. On the other hand, this time I hadn't come off a horse, not on

Greville's pocket handkerchief turf. There might be urgent reasons for getting up quickly, if I could think of them.

I remembered a lot of things in a rush and groaned slightly, rolling up onto my knees, wincing and groping about for the crutches. I felt stupid and went on behaving stupidly, acting on fifty per cent brainpower. Looking back afterwards, I thought that what I ought to have done was slither silently away through the gate to go to any neighbouring house and call the police. What I actually did was to start towards Greville's front door, and of course the lights flashed on again and the dog started barking and I stood rooted to the spot expecting another attack, swaying unsteadily on the crutches, absolutely dim and pathetic.

The door was ajar, I saw, with lights on in the hall, and while I stood dithering it was pulled wide open from inside and the cannonball figure shot out.

The cannonball was a motor-cycle helmet, shiny and black, its transparent visor pulled down over the face. Behind the visor the face also seemed to be black, but a black balaclava, I thought, not black skin. There was an impression of jeans, denim jacket, gloves, black running shoes, all moving fast. He turned his head a fraction and must have seen me standing there insecurely, but he didn't stop to give me another unbalancing shove. He vaulted the gate and set off at a run down the street and I simply stood where I was in the garden waiting for my head to clear a bit more and start working.

When that happened to some extent, I went up the short flight of steps and in through the front door. The keys, I found, were still in the lowest of the locks; the small bunch of three keys that Clarissa had had, which I'd been using instead of Greville's larger bunch as they were easier. I'd made things simple for the intruder, I thought, by having them ready in my hand.

With a spurt of alarm I felt my trouser pocket to find if Greville's main bunch had been stolen, but to my relief they were still there, clinking.

I switched off the floodlights and the dog and in the sudden silence closed the front door. Greville's small sitting room, when I reached it, looked like the path of a hurricane. I surveyed the mess in fury rather than horror and picked the tumbled phone off the floor to call the police. A burglary, I said. The burglar had gone.

Then I sat in Greville's chair with my head in my hands and said '*Shit*' aloud with heartfelt rage and gingerly felt the sore bump swelling on my scalp. A bloody pushover, I thought. Like last Sunday. Too like last Sunday to be a coincidence. The cannonball had known both times that I wouldn't be able to stand upright against a sudden unexpected rush. I supposed I should be grateful he hadn't smashed my head in altogether this time while he had the chance. No knife, this time, either.

After a bit I looked wearily round the room. The pictures were off the walls, most of the glass smashed. The drawers had been yanked out of the tables and the tables themselves overturned. The little pink and brown stone bears lay scattered on the floor, the chrysanthemum plant and its dirt were trampled into the carpet, the chrysanthemum pot itself was embedded in the smashed screen of the television, the video recorder had been torn from from its unit and dropped, the video cassettes of the races lay pulled out in yards of ruined tape. The violence of it all angered me as much as my own sense of failure in letting it happen.

Many of the books were out of the bookshelves, but I saw with grim satisfaction that none of them lay open. Even if none of the hollow books had contained diamonds, at least the burglar hadn't known the books were hollow. A poor consolation, I thought.

The police arrived eventually, one in uniform, one not. I went along the hall when they rang the doorbell, checked through the peep-hole and let them in, explaining who I was and why I was there. They were both of about my own age and they'd seen a great many break-ins.

Looking without emotion at Greville's wrecked room, they produced notebooks and took down an account of the assault in the garden. (Did I want a doctor for the bump? No, I didn't.) They knew of this house, they said. The new owner, my brother, had installed all the window grilles and had them wired on a direct alarm to the police station so that if anyone tried to enter that way they would be nicked. Police specialists had given their advice over the defences and had considered the house as secure as was possible, up to now: but shouldn't there have been active floodlights and a dog alarm? They'd worked well, I said, but before they came I'd turned them off.

'Well, sir,' they said, not caring much, 'what's been stolen?'

I didn't know. Nothing large, I said, because the burglar had had both hands free, when he vaulted the gate.

Small enough to go in a pocket, they wrote.

What about the rest of the house? Was it in the same state?

I said I hadn't looked yet. Crutches. Bang on head. That sort of thing. They asked about the crutches. Broken ankle, I said. Paining me, perhaps? Just a bit.

I went with them on a tour of the house and found the tornado had blown through all of it. The long drawing room on the ground floor was missing all the pictures from the walls and all the drawers from chests and tables.

'Looking for a safe,' one of the policemen said, turning over a ruined picture. 'Did your brother have one here, do you know?'

'I haven't seen one,' I said.

They nodded and we went upstairs. The black and white bedroom had been ransacked in the same fashion and the bathroom also. Clothes were scattered everywhere. In the bathroom, aspirins and other pills were scattered on the floor. A toothpaste tube had been squeezed flat by a shoe. A can of shaving cream lay in the wash basin, with some of the contents squirted out in loops on the mirror. They commented that as there was no graffiti and no excrement smeared over everything, I had got off lightly.

'Looking for something small,' the non-uniformed man said. 'Your brother was a gem merchant, wasn't he?'

'Yes.'

'Have you found any jewels here yourself?'

'No, I haven't.'

They looked into the empty bedroom on that floor, still empty, and went up the stairs to look round above, but coming down reported nothing to see but space. It's one big attic room, they explained, when I said I hadn't been up there. Might have been a studio once, perhaps.

We all descended to the semi-basement where the mess in the kitchen was indescribable. Every packet of cereal had been poured out, sugar and flour had been emptied and apparently sieved in a strainer. The fridge's door hung open with the contents gutted. All liquids had been poured down the sinks, the cartons and bottles either standing empty or smashed by the draining boards. The ice cubes I'd wondered about were missing, presumably melted. Half of the floor of carpet tiles had been pulled up from the concrete beneath.

The policemen went phlegmatically round looking at things but touching little, leaving a few footprints in the floury dust.

I said uncertainly, 'How long was I unconscious? If he did all this . . .'

'Twenty minutes, I'd say,' one said, and the other nodded. 'He was working fast, you can see. He was probably longest down here. I'd say he was pulling up these tiles looking for a floor safe when you set the alarms off again. I'd reckon he panicked then, he'd been here long enough. And also, if it's any use to you, I'd guess that if he was looking for anything particular, he didn't find it.'

'Good news, is that?' asked the other, shrewdly, watching me.

'Yes, of course.' I explained about the Saxony Franklin office being broken into the previous weekend. 'We weren't sure what had been stolen, apart from an address book. In view of this,' I gestured to the shambles, 'probably nothing was.'

'Reasonable assumption,' one said.

'When you come back here another time in the dark,' the other advised, 'shine a good big torch all around the garden before you come through the gate. Sounds as if he was waiting there for you, hiding in the shadow of the hedge, out of range of the body-heat detecting mechanism of the lights.'

'Thank you,' I said.

'And switch all the alarms on again, when we leave.'

'Yes.'

'And draw all the curtains. Burglars sometimes wait about outside, if they haven't found what they're after, hoping that the householders, when they come home, will go straight to the valuables to check if they're there. Then they come rampaging back to steal them.'

'I'll draw the curtains,' I said.

They looked around in the garden on the way out and found half a brick lying on the grass near where I'd woken up. They showed it to me. Robbery with violence, that made it.

'If you catch the robber,' I said.

They shrugged. They were unlikely to, as things stood. I thanked them for coming and they said they'd be putting in a report, which I could refer to for insurance purposes when I made a claim. Then they retreated to the police car doubled-parked outside the gate and presently drove away, and I shut the front door, switched on the alarms, and felt depressed and stupid and without energy, none of which states was normal.

The policemen had left lights on behind them everywhere. I went slowly down the stairs to the kitchen meaning merely to turn them off, but when I got there I stood for a while contemplating the mess and the reason for it.

Whoever had come had come because the diamonds were still somewhere to be found. I supposed I should be grateful at least for that information; and I was also inclined to believe the policeman who said the burglar hadn't found what he was looking for. But could I find it, if I looked harder?

I hadn't particularly noticed on my first trip downstairs that the kitchen's red carpet was in fact carpet tiles, washable squares that were silent and warmer underfoot than conventional tiles. I'd been brought up on such flooring in our parents' house.

The big tiles, lying flat and fitting snugly, weren't stuck to the hard surface beneath, and the intruder had had no trouble in pulling them up. The intruder hadn't been certain there was a safe, I thought, or he wouldn't have sieved the sugar. And if he'd been successful and found a safe, what then? He hadn't given himself time to do anything about it. He hadn't killed me. Hadn't tied me. Must have known I would wake up.

All it added up to, I thought, was a frantic and rather unintelligent search, which didn't make the bump on my head or my again knocked-about ankle any less sore. Mincing machines had no brains either. Nor, I thought dispiritedly, had the mince.

I drew the curtains as advised and bent down and pulled up another of the red tiles, thinking about Greville's security complex. It would be just like him to build a safe into the solid base of the house and cover it with something deceptive. Setting a safe in concrete, as the pamphlet had said. People tended to think of safes as being built into walls: floors were less obvious and more secure, but far less convenient. I pulled up a few more tiles, doubting my conclusions, doubting my sanity.

The same sort of feeling as in the vaults kept me

going. I didn't expect to find anything but it would be stupid not to make sure, just in case. This time it took half an hour, not three days, and in the end the whole area was up except for a piece under a serving table on wheels. Under that carpet square, when I'd moved the table, I found a flat circular piece of silvery metal flush with the hard base floor, with a recessed ring in it for lifting.

Amazed and suddenly unbearably hopeful I knelt and pulled the ring up and tugged, and the flat piece of metal came away and off like the lid of a biscuit-tin, revealing another layer of metal beneath: an extremely solid-looking circular metal plate the size of a dinner plate in which there was a single keyhole and another handle for lifting.

I pulled the second handle. As well try to pull up the house by its roots. I tried all of Greville's bunch of keys in the keyhole but none of them came near to fitting.

Even Greville, I thought, must have kept the key reasonably handy, but the prospect of searching anew for anything at all filled me with weariness. Greville's affairs were a maze with more blind alleys than Hampton Court.

There were keys in the hollow books, I remembered. Might as well start with those. I shifted upstairs and dug out *With a Mule in Patagonia* and the others, rediscovering the two businesslike keys and also the decorative one which looked too flamboyant for sensible use. True to Greville's mind, however, it was that one whose wards slid easily into the keyhole of the safe and under pressure turned the mechanism inside.

Even then the circular lid wouldn't pull out. Seesawing between hope and frustration I found that, if one turned instead of pulling, the whole top of the safe went round like a wheel until it came against stops; and at that point it finally gave up the struggle and came up loose in my grasp.

The space below was big enough to hold a case of champagne but to my acute disappointment it contained no nest-egg, only a clutch of business-like brown envelopes. Sighing deeply I took out the top two and found the first contained the freehold deeds of the house and the second the paperwork involved in raising a mortgage to buy it. I read the latter with resignation. Greville's house belonged in essence to a finance company, not to me.

Another of the envelopes contained a copy of his will, which was as simple as the lawyers had said, and in another there was his birth certificate and our parents' birth and marriage certificates. Another yielded an endowment insurance policy taken out long ago to provide him with an income at sixty-five: but inflation had eaten away its worth and he had apparently not bothered to increase it. Instead, I realized, remembering what I'd learned of his company's finances, he had ploughed back his profits into expanding his business which would itself ride on the tide of inflation and provide him with a munificent income when he retired and sold.

A good plan, I thought, until he'd knocked the props out by throwing one point five million dollars to the winds. Only he hadn't, of course. He'd had a sensible plan for a sober profit. Deal with honour . . . He'd made a good income, lived a comfortable life and run his racehorses, but he had stacked away no great personal fortune. His wealth, whichever way one looked at it, was in the stones.

Hell and damnation, I thought. If I couldn't find the damned diamonds I'd be failing him as much as myself. He would long for me to find them, but where the bloody *hell* had he put them?

I stuffed most of the envelopes back into their private basement, keeping out only the insurance policy, and replaced the heavy circular lid. Turned it, turned the key, replaced the upper piece of metal and laid a carpet tile on top. Fireproof the hiding place undoubtedly was, and thiefproof it had proved, and I couldn't imagine why Greville hadn't used it for jewels.

Feeling defeated, I climbed at length to the bedroom where I found my own overnight bag had, along with everything else, been tipped up and emptied. It hardly seemed to matter. I picked up my sleeping shorts and changed into them and went into the bathroom. The mirror was still half covered with shaving cream and by the time I'd wiped that off with a face cloth and swallowed a Distalgesic and brushed my teeth and swept a lot of the crunching underfoot junk to one side with a towel, I had used up that day's ration of stamina pretty thoroughly.

Even then, though it was long past midnight. I couldn't sleep. Bangs on the head were odd, I thought. There had been one time when I'd dozed for a week afterwards, going to sleep in mid-sentence as often as not. Another time I'd apparently walked and talked rationally to a doctor but hadn't any recollection of it half an hour later. This time, in Greville's bed, I felt shivery and unsettled, and thought that that had probably as much to do with being attacked as concussed.

I lay still and let the hours pass, thinking of bad and good and of why things happened, and by morning felt calm and much better. Sitting on the lid of the loo in the bathroom I unwrapped the crêpe bandage and by hopping and holding on to things took a long, luxurious and much needed shower, washing my hair, letting the dust and debris and the mental tensions of the week run away in the soft bombardment of water. After that, loin-clothed in a bath towel, I sat on the black and white bed and more closely surveyed the ankle scenery.

It was better than six days earlier, one could confidently say that. On the other hand, it was still black, still fairly swollen and still sore to the touch. Still vulnerable to knocks. I flexed my calf and foot muscles several times: the bones and ligaments still violently protested, but none of it could be helped. To stay strong, the muscles had to move, and that was that. I kneaded the calf muscle a bit to give it some encouragement and thought about borrowing an apparatus called Electrovet which Milo had tucked away somewhere, which he used on his horses' legs to give their muscles electrical stimuli to bring down swelling and get them fit again. What worked on horses should work on me, I reckoned.

Eventually I wound the bandage on again, not as neatly as the surgeon, but I hoped as effectively. Then I dressed, borrowing one of Greville's clean white shirts and, down in the forlorn little sitting room, telephoned to Nicholas Loder.

He didn't sound pleased to hear my voice.

'Well done with Dozen Roses,' I said.

He grunted.

'To solve the question of who owns him,' I continued, 'I've found a buyer for him.'

'Now look here!' he began angrily. 'I—'

'Yes, I know,' I interrupted, 'you'd ideally like to sell him to one of your own owners and keep him in your yard, and I do sympathize with that, but Mr and Mrs Ostermeyer, the people I was with yesterday at York, they've told me they would like the horse themselves.'

'I strongly protest,' he said.

'They want to send him to Milo Shandy to be trained for jumping.'

'You owe it to me to leave him here,' he said obstinately. 'Four wins in a row . . . it's downright dishonourable to take him away.'

'He's suitable for jumping, now that he's been

gelded.' I said it without threat, but he knew he was in an awkward position. He'd had no right to geld the horse. In addition, there was in fact nothing to stop Greville's executor selling the horse to whomever he pleased, as Milo had discovered for me, and which Nicholas Loder had no doubt discovered for himself, and in the racing world in general the sale to the Ostermeyers would make exquisite sense as I would get to ride the horse even if I couldn't own him.

Into Loder's continued silence I said, 'If you find a buyer for Gemstones, though, I'll give my approval.'

'He's not as good.'

'No, but not useless. No doubt you'd take a commission, I wouldn't object to that.'

He grunted again, which I took to mean assent, but he also said grittily, 'Don't expect any favours from me, ever.'

'I've done one for you,' I pointed out, 'in not lodging a complaint. Anyway, I'm lunching with the Ostermeyers at Milo's today and we'll do the paperwork of the sale. So Milo should be sending a box to collect Dozen Roses sometime this week. No doubt he'll fix a day with you.'

'Rot you,' he said.

'I don't want to quarrel.'

'You're having a damn good try.' He slammed down his receiver and left me feeling perplexed as much as anything else by his constant rudeness. All trainers lost horses regularly when owners sold them and, as he'd said himself, it wasn't as if Dozen Roses were a Derby hope. Nicholas Loder's stable held far better prospects than a five-year-old gelding, prolific winner though he might be.

Shrugging, I picked up my overnight bag and felt vaguely guilty at turning my back on so much chaos in the house. I'd done minimum tidying upstairs, hanging up Greville's suits and shirts and so on, and I'd left my own suit and some other things with them because it seemed I might spend more nights there, but the rest was physically difficult and would have to wait for the anonymous Mrs P, poor woman, who was going to get an atrocious shock.

I went by taxi to the Ostermeyers' hotel and again found them in champagne spirits, and it was again Simms, fortyish, with a moustache, who turned up as chauffeur. When I commented on his working Sunday as well as Saturday he smiled faintly and said he was glad of the opportunity to earn extra; Monday to Friday he developed films in the dark.

'Films?' Martha asked. 'Do you mean movies?'

'Family snapshots, madam, in a one-hour photo shop.'

'Oh.' Martha sounded as if she couldn't envisage such a life. 'How interesting.'

'Not very, madam,' Simms said resignedly, and set off smoothly into the sparse Sunday traffic. He asked me for directions as we neared Lambourn and we arrived without delay at Milo's door, where Milo himself greeted me with the news that Nicholas Loder wanted me to phone him at once.

'It sounded to me,' Milo said, 'like a great deal of agitation pretending to be casual.'

'I don't understand him.'

'He doesn't want me to have Dozen Roses, for some reason.'

'Oh, but,' Martha said to him anxiously, overhearing, 'you are going to, aren't you?'

'Of course, yes, don't worry. Derek, get it over with while we go and look at Datepalm.' He bore the Ostermeyers away, dazzling them with twinkling charm, and I went into his kitchen and phoned Nicholas Loder, wondering why I was bothering.

'Look,' he said, sounding persuasive. 'I've an owner who's very interested in Dozen Roses. He says he'll top whatever your Ostermeyers are offering. What do you say?'

I didn't answer immediately, and he said forcefully, 'You'll make a good clear profit that way. There's no guarantee the horse will be able to jump. You can't ask a high price for him, because of that. My owner will top their offer and add a cash bonus for you personally. Name your figure.'

'Um,' I said slowly, 'this owner wouldn't be yourself, would it?'

He said sharply, 'No, certainly not.'

'The horse that ran at York yesterday,' I said even more slowly, 'does he fit Dozen Roses's passport?'

'That's slanderous!'

'It's a question.'

'The answer is yes. The horse is Dozen Roses. Is that od enough for you?'

'Yes.'

'Well, then,' he sounded relieved, 'name your figure.'

I hadn't yet discussed any figure at all with Martha d Harley and I'd been going to ask a bloodstock agent end for a snap valuation. I said as much to Nicholas der who, sounding exasperated, repeated that his ner would offer more, plus a tax-free sweetener for self.

I had every firm intention of selling Dozen Roses to Ostermeyers and no so-called sweetener that I uld think of would have persuaded me otherwise.

'Please tell your owner I'm sorry,' I said, 'but the termeyers have bought Datepalm, as I told you, and m obligated to them, and loyalty to them comes first. n sure you'll find your owner another horse as good Dozen Roses.'

'What if he offered double what you'd take from the termeyers?'

'It's not a matter of money.'

'Everyone can be bought,' he said.

'Well, no. I'm sorry, but no.'

'Think it over,' he said, and slammed the receiver wn again. I wondered in amusement how often he oke them. But he hadn't in fact been amusing, and the uation as a whole held no joy. I was going to have to

meet him on racecourses for ever once I was a train
myself, and I had no appetite for chronic feuds.

I went out into the yard where, seeing me, Mi
broke away from the Ostermeyers who were feastin
their eyes as Datepalm was being led round on th
gravel to delight them.

'What did Loder want?' Milo demanded, comin
towards me.

'He offered double whatever I was asking the Oste
meyers to pay for Dozen Roses.'

Milo stared. 'Double! Without knowing what
was?'

'That's right.'

'What are you going to do?'

'What do you think?' I asked.

'If you've accepted, I'll flatten you.'

I laughed. Too many people that past week ha
flattened me and no doubt Milo could do it with th
best.

'Well?' he said belligerently.

'I told him to stuff it.'

'Good.'

'Mm, perhaps. But you'd better arrange to fetch th
horse here at once. Like tomorrow morning, as we don
want him having a nasty accident and ending up at th
knackers, do you think?'

'Christ!' He was appalled. 'He wouldn't! Not Nich
las Loder.'

'One wouldn't think so. But no harm in removing the temptation.'

'No.' He looked at me attentively. 'Are you all right?' he asked suddenly. 'You don't look too well.'

I told him briefly about being knocked out in Greville's garden. 'Those phone calls you took,' I said, 'were designed to make sure I turned up in the right place at the right time. So I walked straight into an ambush and, if you want to know, I feel a fool.'

'Derek!' He was dumbfounded, but also of course practical. 'It's not going to delay your getting back on a horse?'

'No, don't worry.'

'Did you tell the Ostermeyers?'

'No, don't bother them. They don't like me being unfit.'

He nodded in complete understanding. To Martha, and to Harley to a lesser but still considerable extent, it seemed that proprietorship in the jockey was as important as in the horse. I'd met that feeling a few times before and never undervalued it: they were the best owners to ride for, even if often the most demanding. The quasi-love relationship could however turn to dust and damaging rejection if one ever put them second, which was why I would never jeopardize my place on Datepalm for a profit on Dozen Roses. It was hard to explain to more rational people, but I rode races, as every jump jockey did, from a different impetus than making money, though the money was nice enough and thoroughly earned besides.

When Martha and Harley at length ran out of questions and admiration of Datepalm we all returned to the house, where over drinks in Milo's comfortable sitting room we telephoned to the bloodstock agent for an opinion and then agreed on a price which was less than he'd suggested. Milo beamed. Martha clapped her hands together with pleasure. Harley drew out his chequebook and wrote in it carefully, 'Saxony Franklin Ltd.'

'Subject to a vet's certificate,' I said.

'Oh yes, dear,' Martha agreed, smiling. 'As if you would ever sell us a lemon.'

Milo produced the 'Change of Ownership' forms which Martha and Harley and I all signed, and Milo said he would register the new arrangements with Weatherby's in the morning.

'Is Dozen Roses ours, now?' Martha asked, shiny-eyed.

'Indeed he is,' Milo said, 'subject to his being alive and in good condition when he arrives here. If he isn't the sale is void and he still belongs to Saxony Franklin.'

I wondered briefly if he were insured. Didn't want to find out the hard way.

With business concluded, Milo drove us all out to lunch at a nearby restaurant which as usual was crammed with Lambourn people: Martha and Harley held splendid court as the new owners of Gold Cup winner Datepalm and were pink with gratification over the compliments to their purchase. I watched their stimulated faces, hers rounded and still pretty under the blonde-rinsed grey hair, his heavily handsome, the square jaw showing the beginning of jowls. Both now looking sixty, they still displayed enthusiasms and enjoyments that were almost childlike in their simplicity, which did no harm in the weary old world.

Milo drove us back to rejoin the Daimler and Simms, who'd eaten his lunch in a village pub, and Martha in farewell gave Milo a kiss with flirtation but also real affection. Milo had bound the Ostermeyers to his stable with hoops of charm and all we needed now was for the two horses to carry on winning.

Milo said 'Thanks' to me briefly as we got into the car, but in truth I wanted what he wanted, and securing the Ostermeyers had been a joint venture. We drove out of the yard with Martha waving and then settling back into her seat with murmurs and soft remarks of pleasure.

I told Simms the way to Hungerford so that he could drop me off there, and the big car purred along with Sunday afternoon somnolence.

Martha said something I didn't quite catch and I turned my face back between the headrests, looking towards her and asking her to say it again. I saw a flash of raw horror begin on Harley's face, and then with a crash and a bang the car rocketed out of control across the road towards a wall and there was blood and shredded glass everywhere and we careered off the wall back onto the road and into the path of a fifty-seater touring coach which had been behind us and was now bearing down on us like a runaway cliff.

CHAPTER TWELVE

In a split second before the front of the bus hit the side of the car where I was sitting, in the freeze-frame awareness of the tons of bright metal thundering inexorably towards us, I totally believed I would be mangled to pulp within a breath.

There was no time for regrets or anger or any other emotion. The bus plunged into the Daimler and turned it again forwards and both vehicles screeched along the road together, monstrously joined wheel to wheel, the white front wing of the coach buried deep in the black Daimler's engine, the noise and buffeting too much for thinking, the speed of everything truly terrifying and the nearness of death an inevitability merely postponed.

Inertia dragged the two vehicles towards a halt, but they were blocking the whole width of the road. Towards us, round the bend, came a family car travelling too fast to stop in the space available. The driver in a frenzy braked so hard that his rear end swung round and hit the front of the Daimler broadside with a sickening jolt and a crunching bang and behind us, somewhere, another car ran into the back of the bus.

About that time I stopped being clear about the sequence of events. Against all catastrophe probability, I was still alive and that seemed enough. After the first stunned moments of silence when the tearing of metal had stopped, there were voices shouting everywhere, and people screaming and a sharp petrifying smell of raw petrol.

The whole thing was going to burn, I thought. Explode. Fireballs coming. Greville had burned two days ago. Greville had at least been dead at the time. Talk about delirious. I had half a car in my lap and in my head the warmed-up leftovers of yesterday's concussion.

The heat of the dead engine filled the cracked-open body of the car, forewarning of worse. There would be oil dripping out of it. There were electrical circuits . . . sparks . . . there was dread and despair and a vision of hell.

I couldn't escape. The glass had gone from the window beside me and from the windscreen, and what might have been part of the frame of the door had bent somehow across my chest, pinning me deep against the seat. What had been the fascia and the glove compartment seemed to be digging into my waist. What had been ample room for a dicky ankle was now as constricting as any cast. The car seemed to have wrapped itself around me in an iron-maiden embrace and the only parts free to move at all were my head and the arm nearest Simms. There was intense pressure rather than active agony, but what I felt most was fear.

Almost automatically, as if logic had gone on working on its own, I stretched as far as I could, got my fingers on the keys, twisted and pulled them out of the ignition. At least, no more sparks. At most, I was breathing.

Martha, too, was alive, her thoughts probably as abysmal as my own. I could hear her whimpering behind me, a small moaning without words. Simms and Harley were silent; and it was Simms's blood that had spurted over everything, scarlet and sticky. I could smell it under the smell of petrol; it was on my arm and face and clothes and in my hair.

The side of the car where I sat was jammed tight against the bus. People came in time to the opposite side and tried to open the doors, but they were immovably buckled. Dazed people emerged from the family car in front, the children weeping. People from the coach spread along the roadside, all of them elderly, most of them, it seemed to me, with their mouths open. I wanted to tell them all to keep away, to go further to safety, far from what was going to be a conflagration at any second, but I didn't seem to be able to shout, and the croak I achieved got no further than six inches.

Behind me Martha stopped moaning. I thought wretchedly that she was dying, but it seemed to be the opposite. In a quavery small voice she said, 'Derek?'

'Yes.' Another croak.

'I'm frightened.'

So was I, by God. I said futilely, hoarsely, 'Don't worry.'

She scarcely listened. She was saying 'Harley? Harley, honey?' in alarm and awakening anguish. 'Oh, get us out, please, someone get us out.'

I turned my head as far as I could and looked back sideways at Harley. He was cold to the world but his eyes were closed, which was a hopeful sign on the whole.

Simms's eyes were half open and would never blink again. Simms, poor man, had developed his last one-hour photo. Simms wouldn't feel any flames.

'Oh God, honey. Honey, wake up.' Her voice cracked, high with rising panic. 'Derek, get us out of here, can't you smell the gas?'

'People will come,' I said, knowing it was of little comfort. Comfort seemed impossible, out of reach.

People and comfort came, however, in the shape of a works foreman-type of man, used to getting things done. He peered through the window beside Harley and was presently yelling to Martha that he was going to break the rear window to get her out and she should cover her face in case of flying glass.

Martha hid her face against Harley's chest, calling to him and weeping, and the rear window gave way to determination and a metal bar.

'Come on, Missis,' encouraged the best of British

workmen. 'Climb up on the seat, we'll have you out of there in no time.'

'My husband . . .' she wailed.

'Him too. No trouble. Come on, now.'

It appeared that strong arms hauled Martha out bodily. Almost at once her rescuer was himself inside the car, lifting the still unconscious Harley far enough to be raised by other hands outside. Then he put his head forward near to mine, and took a look at me and Simms.

'Christ,' he said.

He was smallish, with a moustache and bright brown eyes.

'Can you slide out of there?' he asked.

'No.'

He tried to pull me, but we could both see it was hopeless.

'They'll have to cut you out,' he said, and I nodded. He wrinkled his nose. 'The smell of petrol's very strong in here. Much worse than outside.'

'It's vapour,' I said. 'It ignites.'

He knew that, but it hadn't seemed to worry him until then.

'Clear all those people further away,' I said. I raised perhaps a twitch of a smile. 'Ask them not to smoke.'

He gave me a sick look and retreated through the rear window, and soon I saw him outside delivering a warning which must have been the quickest crowd control measure on record.

Perhaps because with more of the glass missing there

was a through current of air, the smell of petrol did begin to abate, but there was still, I imagined, a severed fuel line somewhere beneath me, with freshly-released vapour continually seeping through the cracks. How much liquid bonfire, I wondered numbly, did a Daimler's tank hold?

There were a great many more cars now ahead in the road, all stopped, their occupants out and crash-gazing. No doubt to the rear it would be the same thing. Sunday afternoon entertainment at its worst.

Simms and I sat on in our silent immobility and I thought of the old joke about worrying, that there was no point in it. If one worried that things would get bad and they didn't, there was no point in worrying. If they got bad and one worried they would get worse, and they didn't, there was no point in worrying. If they got worse and one worried that one might die, and one didn't, there was no point in worrying, and if one died one could no longer worry, so why worry?

For worry read fear, I thought; but the theory didn't work. I went straight on being scared silly.

It was odd, I thought, that for all the risks I took, I very seldom felt any fear of death. I thought about physical pain, as indeed one often had to in a trade like mine, and remembered things I'd endured, and I didn't know why the imagined pain of burning should fill me with a terror hard to control. I swallowed and felt lonely, and hoped that if it came it would be over quickly.

There were sirens at length in the distance and the best sight in the world, as far as I was concerned, was the red fire-engine which slowly forced its way forward, scattering spectator cars to either side of the road. There was room, just, for three cars abreast; a wall on one side of the road, a row of trees on the other. Behind the fire-engine I could see the flashing blue light of a police car and beyond that another flashing light which might betoken an ambulance.

Figures in authority uniforms appeared from the vehicles, the best being in flameproof suits lugging a hose. They stopped in front of the Daimler, seeing the bus wedged into one side of it and the family car on the other and one of them shouted to me through the space where the windscreen should have been.

'There's petrol running from these vehicles,' he said. 'Can't you get out?'

What a damn silly question, I thought. I said, 'No.'

'We're going to spray the road underneath you. Shut your eyes and hold something over your mouth and nose.'

I nodded and did as I was bid, managing to shield my face inside the neck of my jersey. I listened to the long whooshing of the spray and thought no sound could be sweeter. Incineration faded progressively from near certainty to diminishing probability to unlikely outcome, and the release from fear was almost as hard to manage as the fear itself. I wiped blood and sweat off my face and felt shaky.

After a while some of the firemen brought up metal-cutting gear and more or less tore out of its frame the buckled door next to where Harley had been sitting. Into this new entrance edged a policeman who took a preliminary look at Simms and me and then perched on the rear seat where he could see my head. I turned it as far as I could towards him, seeing a serious face under the peaked cap: about my own age, I judged, and full of strain.

'A doctor's coming,' he said, offering crumbs. 'He'll deal with your wounds.'

'I don't think I'm bleeding,' I said. 'It's Simms's blood that's on me.'

'Ah.' He drew out a notebook and consulted it. 'Did you see what caused this . . . all this?'

'No,' I said, thinking it faintly surprising that he should be asking at this point. 'I was looking back at Mr and Mrs Ostermeyer, who were sitting where you are now. The car just seemed to go out of control.' I thought back, remembering. 'I think Harley . . . Mr Ostermeyer . . . may have seen something. For a second he looked horrified . . . then we hit the wall and rebounded into the path of the bus.'

He nodded, making a note.

'Mr Ostermeyer is now conscious,' he said, sounding carefully noncommittal. 'He says you were shot.'

'We were *what*?'

'Shot. Not all of you. You, personally.'

'No.' I must have sounded as bewildered as I felt. 'Of course not.'

'Mr and Mrs Ostermeyer are very distressed but he is quite clear he saw a gun. He says the chauffeur had just pulled out to pass a car that had been in front of you for some way, and the driver of that car had the window down and was pointing a gun out of it. He says the gun was pointing at you, and you were shot. Twice at least, he says. He saw the spurts of flame.'

I looked from the policeman to Simms, and at the chauffeur's blood over everything and at the solidly scarlet congealed mess below his jaw.

'No,' I protested, not wanting to believe it. 'It can't be right.'

'Mrs Ostermeyer is intensely worried that you are sitting here bleeding to death.'

'I feel squeezed, not punctured.'

'Can you feel your feet?'

I moved my toes, one foot after another. There wasn't the slightest doubt, particularly about the left.

'Good,' he said. 'Well, sir, we are treating this from now on as a possible murder enquiry, and apart from that I'm afraid the firemen say it may be some time before they can get you loose. They need more gear. Can you be patient?' He didn't wait for a reply, and went on, 'As I said, a doctor is here and will come to you, but if you aren't in urgent need of him there are two other people back there in a very bad way, and I hope you can be patient about that also.'

I nodded slightly. I could be patient for hours if I wasn't going to burn.

'Why,' I asked, 'would anyone shoot at us?'

'Have you no idea?'

'None at all.'

'Unfortunately,' he said, 'there isn't always an understandable reason.'

I met his eyes. 'I live in Hungerford,' I said.

'Yes, sir, so I've been told.' He nodded and slithered out of the car, and left me thinking about the time in Hungerford when a berserk man had gunned down many innocent people, including some in cars, and turned the quiet country town into a place of horror. No one who lived in Hungerford would ever discount the possibility of being randomly slaughtered.

The bullet that had torn into Simms would have gone through my own neck or head, I thought, if I hadn't turned round to talk to Martha. I'd put my head between the headrests, the better to see her. I tried to sort out what had happened next, but I hadn't seen Simms hit. I'd heard only the bang and crash of the window breaking and felt the hot spray of the blood that had fountained out of his smashed main artery in the time it had taken him to die. He had been dead, I thought, before anyone had started screaming: the jet of blood had stopped by then.

The steering wheel was now rammed hard against his chest with the instrument panel slanting down across his knees, higher my end than his. The edge of it pressed comfortably into my stomach, and I could see that if had travelled back another six inches, it would have t me in half.

A good many people arrived looking official with easuring tapes and cameras, taking photographs of nms particularly and consulting in low tones. A police rgeon solemnly put a stethoscope to Simms's chest d declared him dead, and without bothering with the thoscope declared me alive.

How bad was the compression, he wanted to know. ncomfortable, I said.

'I know you, don't I?' he said, considering me. ren't you one of the local jockeys? The jumping ys?'

'Mm.'

'Then you know enough about being injured to give an assessment of your state.'

I said that my toes, fingers and lungs were OK and at I had cramp in my legs, the trapped arm was aching d the instrument panel was inhibiting the digestion of good Sunday lunch.

'Do you want an injection?' he asked, listening.

'Not unless it gets worse.'

He nodded, allowed himself a small smile and wrig-ed his way out onto the road. It struck me that there s much less leg-room for the back seat than there had en when we set out. A miracle Martha's and Harley's s hadn't been broken. Three of us, I thought, had en incredibly lucky.

Simms and I went on sitting quietly side by side fo what seemed several more ages but finally the extr gear to free us appeared in the form of winches, cran and an acetylene torch, which I hoped they would us around me with discretion.

Large mechanics scratched their heads over th problems. They couldn't get to me from my side the car because it was tight against the bus. The decided that if they tried to cut through the suppo under the front seats and pull them backwards the might upset the tricky equilibrium of the engine an instead of freeing my trapped legs bring the whol weight of the front of the car down to crush them. I wa against the idea, and said so.

In the end, working from inside the car in fireproo suits and with thick foam pumped all around, using well-sheltered but still scorching hot acetylene flam which roared and threw terrifying sparks around lik matches, they cut away most of the driver's side, an after that, because he couldn't feel or protest, the forcefully pulled Simms's stiffening body out and laid on a stretcher. I wondered greyly if he had a wife, wh wouldn't know yet.

With Simms gone, the mechanics began fixing chai and operating jacks and I sat and waited without both ering them with questions. From time to time they sai 'You all right, mate?' and I answered 'Yes,' and wa grateful to them.

After a while they fastened chains and a winch to th

family car still impacted broadside on the Daimler's wing and with inching care began to pull it away. There was almost instantly a fearful shudder through the Daimler's crushed body and also through mine, and the pulling stopped immediately. A little more head-scratching went on, and one of them explained to me that their crane couldn't get a good enough stabilizing purchase on the Daimler because the family car was in the way, and they would have to try something else. Was I all right? Yes, I said.

One of them began calling me Derek. 'Seen you in Hungerford, haven't I,' he said, 'and on the telly?' He told the others, who made jolly remarks like, 'Don't worry, we'll have you out in time for the three-thirty tomorrow. Sure to.' One of them seriously told me that it sometimes did take hours to free people because of the dangers of getting it wrong. Lucky, he said, that it was a Daimler I was in, with its tank-like strength. In anything less I would have been history.

They decided to rethink the rear approach. They wouldn't disturb the seat anchorages from their pushed-back position: the seats were off their runners, they said, and had dug into the floor. Also the recliner-mechanism had jammed and broken. However they were going to cut off the back of Simms's seat to give themselves more room to work. They were then going to extract the padding and springs from under my bottom and see if they could get rid of the back of my seat also, and draw me out backwards so that they wouldn't have to manoeuvre me out sideways past the steering column, which they didn't want to remove as it was the anchor for one of the chief stabilizing chains. Did I understand? Yes, I did.

They more or less followed this plan, although they had to dismantle the back of my seat before the cushion, the lowering effect of having the first spring removed from under me having jammed me even tighter against the fascia and made breathing difficult. They yanked padding out from behind me to relieve that, and then with a hacksaw took the back of the seat off near the roots; and, finally, with one of them supporting my shoulders, another pulled out handfuls of springs and other seat innards, the bear-hug pressure on my abdomen and arm and legs lessened and went away, and I had only blessed pins and needles instead.

Even then the big car was loath to let me go. With my top half free the two men began to pull me backwards, and I grunted and stiffened, and they stopped at once.

'What's the matter?' one asked anxiously.

'Well, nothing. Pull again.'

In truth, the pulling hurt the left ankle but I'd sat there long enough. It was at least an old, recognizable pain, nothing threateningly new. Reassured, my rescuers hooked their arms under my armpits and used a bit of strength, and at last extracted me from the car's crushing embrace like a breeched calf from a cow.

Relief was an inadequate word. They gave me a minute's rest on the back seat, and sat each side of me, all three of us breathing deeply.

'Thanks,' I said briefly.

'Think nothing of it.'

I guessed they knew the depths of my gratitude, as I knew the thought and care they'd expended. Thanks, think nothing of it: it was enough.

One by one we edged out onto the road, and I was astonished to find that after all that time there was still a small crowd standing around waiting: policemen, firemen, mechanics, ambulance men and assorted civilians, many with cameras. There was a small cheer and applause as I stood up free, and I smiled and moved my head in a gesture of both embarrassment and thanksgiving.

I was offered a stretcher but said I'd much rather have the crutches that might still be in the boot, and that caused a bit of general consternation, but someone brought them out unharmed, about the only thing still unbent in the whole mess. I stood for a bit with their support simply looking at all the intertwined wreckage; at the bus and the family car and above all at the Daimler's buckled-up roof, at its sheared-off bonnet, its dislodged engine awry at a tilted angle, its gleaming black paintwork now unrecognizable scrap, its former shape mangled and compressed like a stamped-on toy. I thought it incredible that I'd sat where I'd sat and lived. I reckoned that I'd used up a lifetime's luck.

The Ostermeyers had been taken to Swindon Hospital and treated for shock, bruises and concussion. From there, recovering a little, they had telephoned Milo and told him what had happened and he, reacting I guessed with spontaneous generosity but also with strong business sense, had told them they must stay with him for the night and he would collect them. All three were on the point of leaving when I in my turn arrived.

There was a predictable amount of fussing from Martha over my rescue, but she herself looked as exhausted as I felt and she was pliably content to be supported on Harley's arm on their way to the door.

Milo, coming back a step, said, 'Come as well, if you like. There's always a bed.'

'Thanks, I'll let you know.'

He stared at me. 'Is it true Simms was shot?'

'Mm.'

'It could have been you.'

'Nearly was.'

'The police took statements here from Martha and Harley, it seems.' He paused, looking towards them as they reached the door. 'I'll have to go. How's the ankle?'

'Be back racing as scheduled.'

'Good.'

He bustled off and I went through the paperwork

routines, but there was nothing wrong with me that a small application of time wouldn't fix and I got myself discharged pretty fast as a patient and was invited instead to give a more detailed statement to the police. I couldn't add much more than I'd told them in the first place, but some of their questions were in the end disturbing.

Could we have been shot at for any purpose?

I knew of no purpose.

How long had the car driven by the man with the gun been in front of us?

I couldn't remember: hadn't noticed.

Could anyone have known we would be on that road at that time? I stared at the policeman. Anyone, perhaps, who had been in the restaurant for lunch. Anyone there could have followed us from there to Milo's house, perhaps, and waited for us to leave, and passed us, allowing us then to pass again. But why ever should they?

Who else might know?

Perhaps the car company who employed Simms.

Who else?

Milo Shandy, and he'd have been as likely to shoot himself as the Ostermeyers.

Mr Ostermeyer said the gun was pointing at you, sir.

With all due respect to Mr Ostermeyer, he was looking through the car and both cars were moving, and at different speeds presumably, and I didn't think one could be certain.

Could I think of any reason why anyone should want to kill me?

Me, personally? No . . . I couldn't.

They pounced on the hesitation I could hear in my own voice, and I told them I'd been attacked and knocked out the previous evening. I explained about Greville's death. I told them he had been dealing in precious stones as he was a gem merchant and I thought my attacker had been trying to find and steal part of the stock. But I had no idea why the would-be thief should want to shoot me today when he could easily have bashed my head in yesterday.

They wrote it down without comment. Had I any idea who had attacked me the previous evening?

No, I hadn't.

They didn't say they didn't believe me, but something in their manner gave me the impression they thought anyone attacked twice in two days had to know who was after him.

I would have liked very much to be able to tell them. It had just occurred to me, if not to them, that there might be more to come.

I'd better find out soon, I thought.

I'd better not find out too late.

CHAPTER THIRTEEN

I didn't go to Milo's house nor to my own bed, but stayed in an anonymous hotel in Swindon where unknown enemies wouldn't find me.

The urge simply to go home was strong, as if one could retreat to safety into one's den, but I thought I would probably be alarmed and wakeful all night there, when what I most wanted was sleep. All in all it had been a rough ten days, and however easily my body usually shook off bumps and bangs, the accumulation was making an insistent demand for rest.

RICE, I thought wryly, RICE being the acronym of the best way to treat sports injuries: rest, ice, compression, elevation. I rarely seemed to be managing all of them at the same time, though all, in one way or another, separately. With elevation in place, I phoned Milo from the hotel to say I wouldn't be coming and asked how Martha and Harley were doing.

'They're quavery. It must have been some crash. Martha keeps crying. It seems a car ran into the back of the bus and two people in the car were terribly injured.

She saw them, and it's upsetting her almost as much as knowing Simms was shot. Can't you come and comfort her?'

'You and Harley can do it better.'

'She thought you were dying too. She's badly shocked. You'd better come.'

'They gave her a sedative at the hospital, didn't they?'

'Yes,' he agreed grudgingly. 'Harley too.'

'Look . . . persuade them to sleep. I'll come in the morning and pick them up and take them back to their hotel in London. Will that do?'

He said unwillingly that he supposed so.

'Say goodnight to them from me,' I said. 'Tell them I think they're terrific.'

'Do you?' He sounded surprised.

'It does no harm to say it.'

'Cynic.'

'Seriously,' I said, 'they'll feel better if you tell them.'

'All right then. See you at breakfast.'

I put down the receiver and on reflection a few minutes later got through to Brad.

'Cor,' he said, 'you were in that crash.'

'How did you hear about it?' I asked, surprised.

'Down the pub. Talk of Hungerford. Another madman. It's shook everyone up. My mum won't go out.'

It had shaken his tongue loose, I thought in amusement. 'Have you still got my car?' I said.

'Yerss.' He sounded anxious. 'You said keep it here.'

'Yes. I meant keep it there.'

'I walked down your house earlier. There weren't no one there then.'

'I'm not there now,' I said. 'Do you still want to go on driving?'

'Yerss.' Very positive. 'Now?'

'In the morning.' I said I would meet him at eight outside the hotel near the railway station at Swindon, and we would be going to London. 'OK?'

'Yerss,' he said, signing off, and it sounded like a cat purring over the resumption of milk.

Smiling and yawning, a jaw-cracking combination, I ran a bath, took off my clothes and the bandage and lay gratefully in hot water, letting it soak away the fatigue along with Simms's blood. Then, my overnight bag having survived unharmed along with the crutches, I scrubbed my teeth, put on sleeping shorts, rewrapped the ankle, hung a 'Do not disturb' card outside my door and was in bed by nine and slept and dreamed of crashes and fire and hovering unidentified threats.

Brad came on the dot in the morning and we went first to my place in a necessary quest for clean clothes. His mum, Brad agreed, would wash the things I'd worn in the crash.

My rooms were still quiet and unransacked and no

dangers lurked outside in daylight. I changed uneventfully and repacked the travelling bag and we drove in good order to Lambourn, I sitting beside Brad and thinking I could have done the driving myself, except that I found his presence reassuring and I'd come to grief on both of the days he hadn't been with me.

'If a car passes us and sits in front of us,' I said, 'don't pass it. Fall right back and turn up a side road.'

'Why?'

I told him that the police thought we'd been caught in a deliberate moving ambush. Neither the Ostermeyers nor I, I pointed out, would be happy to repeat the experience, and Brad wouldn't be wanting to double for Simms. He grinned, an unnerving sight, and gave me to understand with a nod that he would follow the instruction.

The usual road to Lambourn turned out to be still blocked off, and I wondered briefly, as we detoured, whether it was because of the murder enquiry or simply technical difficulties in disentangling the omelette.

Martha and Harley were still shaking over breakfast, the coffee cups trembling against their lips. Milo with relief shifted the burden of their reliance smartly from himself to me, telling them that now Derek was here, they'd be safe. I wasn't so sure about that, particularly if both Harley and the police were right about me personally being yesterday's target. Neither Martha nor Harley seemed to suffer such qualms and gave me the instant status of surrogate son/nephew, the one to be naturally leaned on, psychologically if not physically, for succour and support.

I looked at them with affection. Martha had retained enough spirit to put on lipstick. Harley was making light of a sticking plaster on his temple. They couldn't help their nervous systems' reaction to mental trauma, and I hoped it wouldn't be long before their habitual preference for enjoyment resurfaced.

'The only good thing about yesterday,' Martha said with a sigh, 'was buying Dozen Roses. Milo says he's already sent a van for him.'

I'd forgotten about Dozen Roses. Nicholas Loder and his tizzies seemed a long way off and unimportant. I said I was glad they were glad, and that in about a week or so, when he'd settled down in his new quarters, I would start teaching him to jump.

'I'm sure he'll be brilliant,' Martha said bravely, trying hard to make normal conversation. 'Won't he?'

'Some horses take to it better than others,' I said neutrally. 'Like humans.'

'I'll believe he'll be brilliant.'

Averagely good, I thought, would be good enough for me: but most racehorses could jump if started patiently over low obstacles like logs.

Milo offered fresh coffee and more toast, but they were ready to leave and in a short while we were on the road to London. No one passed us and slowed, no one ambushed or shot us, and Brad drew up with a flourish outside their hotel, at least the equal of Simms.

Martha with a shine of tears kissed my cheek in goodbye, and I hers: Harley gruffly shook my hand. They would come back soon, they said, but they were sure glad to be going home tomorrow. I watched them go shakily into the hotel and thought uncomplicated thoughts, like hoping Datepalm would cover himself with glory for them, and Dozen Roses also, once he could jump.

'Office?' I suggested to Brad, and he nodded, and made the now familiar turns towards the environs of Hatton Garden.

Little in Saxony Franklin appeared to have changed. It seemed extraordinary that it was only a week since I'd walked in there for the first time, so familiar did it feel on going back. The staff said, 'Good morning, Derek,' as if they'd been used to me for years, and Annette said there were letters left over from Friday which needed decisions.

'How was the funeral?' she asked sadly, laying out papers on the desk.

A thousand light years ago, I thought. 'Quiet,' I said. 'Good. Your flowers were good. They were on top of his coffin.'

She looked pleased and said she would tell the others, and received the news that there would be a memorial service with obvious satisfaction. 'It didn't seem right, not being at his funeral, not on Friday. We had a minute's silence here at two o'clock. I suppose you'll think us silly.'

'Far from it.' I was moved and let her see it. She smiled sweetly in her heavy way and went off to relay to the others and leave me floundering in the old treacle of deciding things on a basis of no knowledge.

June whisked in looking happy with a pink glow on both cheeks and told me we were low in blue lace agate chips and snowflake obsidian and amazonite beads.

'Order some more, same as before.'

'Yes, right.'

She turned and was on her way out again when I called her back and asked her if there was an alarm clock among all the gadgets. I pulled open the deep drawer and pointed downwards.

'An alarm clock?' She was doubtful and peered at the assorted black objects. 'Telescopes, dictionaries, Geiger counter, calculators, spy juice . . .'

'What's spy juice?' I asked, intrigued.

'Oh, this.' She reached in and extracted an aerosol can. 'That's just my name for it. You squirt this stuff on anyone's envelopes and it makes the paper transparent so you can read the private letters inside.' She looked at my face and laughed. 'Banks have got round it by printing patterns all over the insides of their envelopes. If you spray their envelopes, all you see is the pattern.'

'Whatever did Greville use it for?'

'Someone gave it to him, I think. He didn't use it much, just to check if it was worth opening things that looked like advertisements.'

She put a plain sheet of paper over one of the letters

lying on the desk and squirted a little liquid over it. The plain paper immediately became transparent so that one could read the letter through it, and then slowly went opaque again as it dried.

'Sneaky,' she said, 'isn't it?'

'Very.'

She was about to replace the can in the drawer but I said to put it on top of the desk, and I brought out all the other gadgets and stood them around in plain sight. None of them, as far as I could see, had an alarm function.

'You mentioned something about a world clock,' I said, 'but there isn't one here.'

'I've a clock with an alarm in my room,' she said helpfully. 'Would you like me to bring that?'

'Um, yes, perhaps. Could you set it to four-fifteen?'

'Sure, anything you like.'

She vanished and returned fiddling with a tiny thing like a black credit card which turned out to be a highly versatile timepiece.

'There you are,' she said. 'Four-fifteen – pm, I suppose you mean.' She put the clock on the desk.

'This afternoon, yes. There's an alarm somewhere here that goes off every day at four-twenty. I thought I might find it.'

Her eyes widened. 'Oh, but that's Mr Franklin's watch.'

'Which one?' I asked.

'He only ever wore one. It's a computer itself, a calendar and a compass.'

That watch, I reflected, was beside my bed in Hungerford.

'I think,' I said, 'that he may have had more than one alarm set to four-twenty.'

The fair eyebrows lifted. 'I did sometimes wonder why,' she said. 'I mean, why four-twenty? If he was in the stock-room and his watch alarm went off he would stop doing whatever it was for a few moments. I sort of asked him once, but he didn't really answer, he said it was a convenient time for communication, or something like that. I didn't understand what he meant, but that was all right, he didn't mean me to.'

She spoke without resentment and with regret. I thought that Greville must have enjoyed having June around him as much as I did. All that bright intelligence and unspoiled good humour and common sense. He'd liked her enough to make puzzles for her and let her share his toys.

'What's this one?' I asked, picking up a small grey contraption with black ear sponges on a headband with a cord like a walkabout cassette player, but with no provision for cassettes in what might have been a holder.

'That's a sound-enhancer. It's for deaf people, really, but Mr Franklin took it away from someone who was using it to listen to a private conversation he was having with another gem merchant. In Tucson, it was. He said he was so furious at the time that he just snatched the amplifier and headphones off the man who was listening and walked away with them uttering threats about commercial espionage, and he said the man hadn't even tried to get them back.' She paused. 'Put the earphones on. You can hear everything everyone's saying anywhere in the office. It's pretty powerful. Uncanny, really.'

I put on the ultra-light earphones and pressed the ON switch on the cigarette-packet-sized amplifier and sure enough I could straightaway hear Annette across the hallway talking to Lily about remembering to ask Derek for time off for the dentist.

I removed the earphones and looked at June.

'What did you hear?' she asked. 'Secrets?'

'Not that time, no.'

'Scary, though?'

'As you say.'

The sound quality was in fact excellent, astonishingly sensitive for so small a microphone and amplifier. Some of Greville's toys, I thought, were decidedly unfriendly.

'Mr Franklin was telling me that there's a voice transformer that you can fix on the telephone that can change the pitch of your voice and make a woman sound like a man. He said he thought it was excellent for women living alone so that they wouldn't be bothered by obscene phone calls and no one would think they were alone and vulnerable.'

I smiled. 'It might disconcert a bona fide boyfriend innocently ringing up.'

'Well, you'd have to warn them,' she agreed. 'Mr Franklin was very keen on women taking precautions.'

'Mm,' I said wryly.

'He said the jungle came into his court.'

'Did you get a voice changer?' I asked.

'No. We were only talking about it just before . . .' She stopped. 'Well . . . anyway, do you want a sandwich for lunch?'

'Yes, please.'

She nodded and was gone. I sighed and tried to apply myself to the tricky letters and was relieved at the interruption when the telephone rang.

It was Elliot Trelawney on the line, asking if I would messenger round the Vaccaro notes at once if I wouldn't mind as they had a committee meeting that afternoon.

'Vaccaro notes,' I repeated. I'd clean forgotten about them. I couldn't remember, for a moment, where they were.

'You said you would send them this morning,' Trelawney said with a tinge of civilized reproach. 'Do you remember?'

'Yes.' I did, vaguely.

Where the hell were they? Oh yes, in Greville's sitting room. Somewhere in all that mess. Somewhere there, unless the thief had taken them.

I apologized. I didn't actually say I'd come near to being killed twice since I'd last spoken to him and it was playing tricks with my concentration. I said things had cropped up. I was truly sorry. I would try to get them to the court by . . . when?

'The committee meets at two and Vaccaro is first on the agenda,' he said.

'The notes are still in Greville's house,' I replied, 'but I'll get them to you.'

'Awfully good of you.' He was affable again. 'It's frightfully important we turn this application down.'

'Yes, I know.'

Vaccaro, I thought uncomfortably, replacing the receiver, was alleged to have had his wanting-out cocaine-smuggling pilots murdered by shots from moving cars.

I stared into space. There was no reason on earth for Vaccaro to shoot me, even supposing he knew I existed. I wasn't Greville, and I had no power to stand in the way of his plans. All I had, or probably had, were the notes on his transgressions, and how could he know that? And how could he know I would be in a car between Lambourn and Hungerford on Sunday afternoon? And couldn't the notes be gathered again by someone else besides Greville, even if they were now lost?

I shook myself out of the horrors and went down to the yard to see if Brad was sitting in the car, which he was, reading a magazine about fishing.

Fishing? 'I didn't know you fished,' I said.

'I don't.'

End of conversation.

Laughing inwardly I invited him to go on the journey. I gave him the simple keyring of three keys and explained about the upheaval he would find. I described the Vaccaro notes in and out of their envelope and wrote down Elliot Trelawney's name and the address of the court.

'Can you do it?' I asked, a shade doubtfully.

'Yerss.' He seemed to be slighted by my tone and took the paper with the address with brusqueness.

'Sorry,' I said.

He nodded without looking at me and started the car, and by the time I'd reached the rear entrance to the offices he was driving out of the yard.

Upstairs, Annette said there had just been a phone call from Antwerp and she had written down the number for me to ring back.

Antwerp.

With an effort I thought back to Thursday's distant conversations. What was it I should remember about Antwerp?

Van Ekeren. Jacob. His nephew, Hans.

I got through to the Belgian town and was rewarded with the smooth bilingual voice telling me that he had been able now to speak to his uncle on my behalf.

'You're very kind,' I said.

'I'm not sure that we will be of much help. My uncle says he knew your brother for a long time, but not very well. However, about six months ago your brother telephoned my uncle for advice about a sightholder.' He paused. 'It seems your brother was considering buying diamonds and trusted my uncle's judgement.'

'Ah,' I said hopefully. 'Did your uncle recommend anyone?'

'Your brother suggested three or four possible names. My uncle said they were all trustworthy. He told your brother to go ahead with any of them.'

I sighed. 'Does he possibly remember who they were?'

Hans said, 'He knows one of them was Guy Servi here in Antwerp, because we ourselves do business with him often. He can't remember the others. He doesn't know which one your brother decided on, or if he did business at all.'

'Well, thank you, anyway.'

'My uncle wishes to express his condolences.'

'Very kind.'

He disconnected with politeness, having dictated to me carefully the name, address and telephone number of Guy Servi, the one sightholder Greville had asked about that his uncle remembered.

I dialled the number immediately and again went through the rigmarole of being handed from voice to voice until I reached someone who had both the language and the information.

Mr Greville Saxony Franklin, now deceased, had been my brother? They would consult their files and call me back.

I waited without much patience while they went through whatever security checks they considered necessary but finally, after a long hour, they came back on the line.

What was my problem, they wanted to know.

'My problem is that our offices were ransacked and a lot of paperwork is missing. I've taken over since Greville's death, and I'm trying to sort out his affairs. Could you please tell me if it was your firm who bought diamonds for him?'

'Yes,' the voice said matter-of-factly. 'We did.'

Wow, I thought. I quietened my breath and I tried not to sound eager.

'Could you, er, give me the details?' I asked.

'Certainly. Your brother wanted colour H diamonds of approximately three carats each. We bought a normal sight-box of mixed diamonds at the July sight at the CSO in London and from it and from our stocks chose one hundred colour H stones, total weight three hundred and twenty carats, which we delivered to your brother.'

'He . . . er . . . paid for them in advance didn't he?'

'Certainly. One point five million United States dollars in cash. You don't need to worry about that.'

'Thank you,' I said, suppressing irony. 'Um, when you delivered them, did you send any sort of, er, packing note?'

It seemed he found the plebeian words 'packing note' faintly shocking.

'We sent the diamonds by personal messenger,' he said austerely. 'Our man took them to your brother at his private residence in London. As is our custom, your brother inspected the merchandise in our messenger's presence and weighed it, and when he was satisfied he signed a release certificate. He would have the carbon copy of that release. There was no other – uh – packing note.'

'Unfortunately I can't find the carbon copy.'

'I assure you, sir . . .'

'I don't doubt it,' I said hastily. 'It's just that the tax people have a habit of wanting documentation.'

'Ah.' His hurt feelings subsided. 'Yes, of course.'

I thought a bit and asked, 'When you delivered the stones to him, were they rough or faceted?'

'Rough, of course. He was going to get them cut and polished over a few months, as he needed them, I believe, but it was more convenient for us and for him to buy them all at once.'

'You don't happen to know who he was getting to polish them?'

'I understood they were to be cut for one special client who had his own requirements, but no, he didn't say who would be cutting them.'

I sighed. 'Well, thank you anyway.'

'We'll be happy to send you copies of the paperwork of the transaction, if it would be of any use?'

'Yes, please,' I said. 'It would be most helpful.'

'We'll put them in the post this afternoon.'

I put the receiver down slowly. I might now know where the diamonds had come *from* but was no nearer knowing where they'd gone *to*. I began to hope that they were safely sitting somewhere with a cutter who would kindly write to tell me they were ready for delivery. Not an impossible dream, really. But if Greville had sent them to a cutter, why was there no record?

Perhaps there had been a record, now stolen. But if the record had been stolen the thief would know the diamonds were with a cutter, and there would be no point in searching Greville's house. Unprofitable thoughts, chasing their own tails.

I straightened my neck and back and eased a few of the muscles which had developed small aches since the crash.

June came in and said, 'You look fair knackered,' and then put her hand to her mouth in horror and said, 'I'd never have said that to Mr Franklin.'

'I'm not him.'

'No, but . . . you're the boss.'

'Then think of someone who could supply a list of cutters and polishers of diamonds, particularly those specializing in unusual requirements, starting with Antwerp. What we want is a sort of Yellow Pages directory. After Antwerp, New York, Tel Aviv and Bombay, isn't that right? Aren't those the four main centres?' I'd been reading his books.

'But we don't deal—'

'Don't say it,' I said. 'We do. Greville bought some

for Prospero Jenks who wants them cut to suit his sculptures or fantasy pieces, or whatever one calls them.'

'Oh.' She looked first blank and then interested. 'Yes, all right, I'm sure I can do that. Do you want me to do it now?'

'Yes, please.'

She went as far as the door and looked back with a smile. 'You still look fair . . .'

'Mm. Go and get on with it.'

I watched her back view disappear. Grey skirt, white shirt. Blonde hair held back with combs behind the ears. Long legs. Flat shoes. Exit June.

The day wore on. I assembled three orders in the vault by myself and got Annette to check they were all right, which it seemed they were. I made a slow tour of the whole place, calling in to see Alfie pack his parcels, watching Lily with her squashed governess air move endlessly from drawer to little drawer collecting orders, seeing Jason manhandle heavy boxes of newly arrived stock, stopping for a moment beside strong-looking Tina, whom I knew least, as she checked the new intake against the packing list and sorted it into trays.

None of them paid me great attention. I was already wallpaper. Alfie made no more innuendoes about Dozen Roses and Jason, though giving me a dark sideways look, again kept his cracks to himself. Lily said, 'Yes, Derek,' meekly, Annette looked anxious, June was busy. I returned to Greville's office and made another effort with the letters.

By four o'clock, in between her normal work with the stock movements on the computer, June had received answers to her 'feelers', as she described them, in the shape of a long list of Antwerp cutters and a shorter one so far for New York. Tel Aviv was 'coming' but had language difficulties and she had nothing for Bombay, though she didn't think Mr Franklin would have sent anything to Bombay because with Antwerp so close there was no point. She put the lists down and departed.

At the rate all the cautious diamond-dealers worked, I thought, picking up the roll call, it would take a week just to get yes or no answers from the Antwerp list. Maybe it would be worth trying. I was down to straws. One of the letters was from the bank, reminding me that interest on the loan was now due.

June's tiny alarm clock suddenly began bleeping. All the other mute gadgets on top of the desk remained unmoved. June returned through my doorway at high speed and paid them vivid attention.

'Five minutes to go,' I said calmingly. 'Is every single gadget in sight?'

She checked all the drawers swiftly and peered into filing cabinets, leaving everything wide open, as I asked.

'Can't find any more,' she said. 'Why does it matter?'

'I don't know,' I said. 'I try everything.'

She stared. I smiled lopsidedly.

'Greville left me a puzzle too,' I said. 'I try to solve it, though I don't know where to look.'

'Oh.' It made a sort of sense to her, even without more explanation. 'Like my rise?'

I nodded. 'Something like that.' But not so positive, I thought. Not so certain. He had at least assured her that the solution was there to find.

The minutes ticked away and at four-twenty by June's clock the little alarm duly sounded. Very distant, not at all loud. Insistent. June looked rather wildly at the assembled gadgets and put her ear down to them.

'I will think of you every day at four-twenty.'

Clarissa had written it on her card at the funeral. Greville had apparently done it every day in the office. It had been their own private language, a long way from diamonds. I acknowledged with regret that I would learn nothing from whatever he'd used to jog his awareness of loving and being loved.

The muffled alarm stopped. June raised her head, frowning.

'It wasn't any of these,' she said.

'No. It was still inside the desk.'

'But it can't have been.' She was mystified. 'I've taken everything out.'

'There must be another drawer.'

She shook her head, but it was the only reasonable explanation.

'Ask Annette,' I suggested.

Annette, consulted, said with a worried frown that she knew nothing at all about another drawer. The three of us looked at the uninformative three-inch-deep slab of black grainy wood that formed the enormous top surface. There was no way it could be a drawer, but there wasn't any other possibility.

I thought back to the green stone box. To the keyhole that wasn't a keyhole, to the sliding base.

To the astonishment of Annette and June I lowered myself to the floor and looked upwards at the desk from under the knee-hole part. The wood from there looked just as solid, but in the centre, three inches in from the front, there was what looked like a sliding switch. With satisfaction I regained the black leather chair and felt under the desk top for the switch. It moved away from one under pressure, I found. I pressed it, and absolutely nothing happened.

Something had to have happened, I reasoned. The switch wasn't there for nothing. Nothing about Greville was for nothing. I pressed it back hard again and tried to raise, slide or otherwise move anything else I could reach. Nothing happened. I banged my fist with frustration down on the desk top, and a section of the front edge of the solid-looking slab fell off in my lap.

Annette and June gasped. The piece that had come off was like a strip of veneer furnished with metal clips for fastening it in place. Behind it was more wood, but this time with a keyhole in it. Watched breathlessly by Annette and June, I brought out Greville's bunch of keys and tried those that looked the right size: and one of them turned obligingly with hardly a click. I pulled the key, still in the hole, towards me, and like silk a wide shallow drawer slid out.

We all looked at the contents. Passport. Little flat black gadgets, four or five of them.

No diamonds.

June was delighted. 'That's the Wizard,' she said.

CHAPTER FOURTEEN

'Which is the Wizard?' I asked.

'That one.'

She pointed at a black rectangle a good deal smaller than a paperback, and when I picked it up and turned it over, sure enough, it had WIZARD written on it in gold. I handed it to June who opened it like a book, laying it flat on the desk. The right-hand panel was covered with buttons and looked like an ultra-versatile calculator. The left-hand side had a small screen at the top and a touch panel at the bottom with headings like 'expense record', 'time accounting', 'reports' and 'reference'.

'It does everything,' June said. 'It's a diary, a phone directory, a memo pad, an appointments calendar, an accounts keeper . . . a world clock.'

'And does it have an alarm system set to four-twenty?'

She switched the thing on, pressed three keys and showed me the screen. Daily alarm, it announced. 4.20 pm, set.

'Fair enough.'

For Annette the excitement seemed to be over. There were things she needed to see to, she said, and went away. June suggested she should tidy away all the gadgets and close all the doors, and while she did that I investigated further the contents of the one drawer we left open.

I frowned a bit over the passport. I'd assumed that in going to Harwich, Greville had meant to catch the ferry. The *Koningin Beatrix* sailed every night . . .

If one looked at it the other way round, the *Koningin Beatrix* must sail from Holland to Harwich every day. If he hadn't taken the passport with him, perhaps he'd been going to *meet* the *Koningin Beatrix*, not leave on her.

Meet *who*?

I looked at his photograph which, like all passport photographs, wasn't very good but good enough to bring him vividly into the office; his office, where I sat in his chair.

June looked over my shoulder and said, 'Oh,' in a small voice. 'I do miss him, you know.'

'Yes.'

I put the passport with regret back into the drawer and took out a flat square object hardly larger than the Wizard, that had a narrow curl of paper coming out of it.

'That's the printer,' June said.

'A printer? So small?'

'It'll print everything stored in the Wizard.'

She plugged the printer's short cord into a slot in the side of the Wizard and dexterously pressed a few keys. With a whirr the tiny machine went into action and began printing out a strip of half the telephone directory, or so it seemed.

'Lovely, isn't it?' June said, pressing another button to stop it. 'When he was away on trips, Mr Franklin would enter all his expenses on here and we would print them out when he got home, or sometimes transfer them from the Wizard to our main computer through an interface . . . oh, dear.' She smothered the uprush of emotion and with an attempt at controlling her voice said, 'He would note down in there a lot of things he wanted to remember when he got home. Things like who had offered him unusual stones. Then he'd tell Prospero Jenks, and quite often I'd be writing to the addresses to have the stones sent.'

I looked at the small black electronic marvel. So much information quiescent in its circuits.

'Is there an instruction manual?' I asked.

'Of course. All the instruction manuals for everything are in this drawer.' She opened one on the outer right-hand stack. 'So are the warranty cards, and everything.' She sorted through a rank of booklets. 'Here you are. One for the Wizard, one for the printer, one for the expenses organizer.'

'I'll borrow them,' I said.

'They're yours now,' she replied blankly. 'Aren't they?'

'I can't get used to it any more than you can.'

I laid the manuals on top of the desk next to the Wizard and the printer and took a third black object out of the secret drawer.

This one needed no explanation. This was the microcassette recorder that went with the tiny tapes I'd found in the hollowed-out books.

'That's voice activated,' June said, looking at it. 'It will sit quietly around doing nothing for hours, then when anyone speaks it will record what's said. Mr Franklin used it sometimes for dictating letters or notes because it let him say a bit, think a bit, and say a bit more, without using up masses of tape. I used to listen to the tapes and type straight onto the word processor.'

Worth her weight in pearls, Greville had judged. I wouldn't quarrel with that.

I put the microcassette player beside the other things and brought out the last two gadgets. One was a tiny Minolta camera which June said Greville used quite often for pictures of unusual stones for Prospero Jenks, and the last was a grey thing one could hold in one's hand that had an on/off switch but no obvious purpose.

'That's to frighten dogs away,' June said with a smile. 'Mr Franklin didn't like dogs, but I think he was ashamed of not liking them, because at first he didn't want to tell me what that was, when I asked him.'

I hadn't known Greville didn't like dogs. I fiercely wanted him back, if only to tease him about it. The real trouble with death was what it left unsaid: and knowing that that thought was a more or less universal regret made it no less sharp.

I put the dog frightener back beside the passport and also the baby camera, which had no film in it. Then I closed and locked the shallow drawer and fitted the piece of veneer back in place, pushing it home with a click. The vast top again looked wholly solid, and I wondered if Greville had bought that desk simply because of the drawer's existence, or whether he'd had the whole piece especially made.

'You'd never know that drawer was there,' June said. 'I wonder how many fortunes have been lost by people getting rid of hiding places they didn't suspect?'

'I read a story about that once. Something about money stuffed in an old armchair that was left to someone.' I couldn't remember the details: but Greville had left me more than an old armchair, and more than one place to look, and I too could get rid of the treasure from not suspecting the right hiding place, if there were one at all to find.

Meanwhile there was the problem of staying healthy while I searched. There was the worse problem of sorting out ways of taking the war to the enemy, if I could identify the enemy in the first place.

I asked June if she could find something I could carry the Wizard and the other things in and she was back in a flash with a soft plastic bag with handles. It reminded me fleetingly of the bag I'd had snatched at Ipswich but this time, I thought, when I carried the booty to the car,

I would take with me an invincible bodyguard, a long-legged flat-chested twenty-one-year-old blonde half in love with my brother.

The telephone rang. I picked up the receiver and said, 'Saxony Franklin' out of newly acquired habit.

'Derek? Is that you?'

'Yes, Milo, it is.'

'I'm not satisfied with this horse.' He sounded aggressive, which wasn't unusual, and also apologetic, which was.

'Which horse?' I asked.

'Dozen Roses, of course. What else?'

'Oh.'

'What do you mean, oh? You knew damn well I was fetching it today. The damn thing's half asleep. I'm getting the vet round at once and I'll want urine and blood tests. The damn thing looks doped.'

'Maybe they gave him a tranquillizer for the journey.'

'They've no right to, you know that. If they have, I'll have Nicholas Loder's head on a platter, like you should, if you had any sense. The man does what he damn well likes. Anyway, if the horse doesn't pass my vet he's going straight back, Ostermeyers or no Ostermeyers. It's not fair on them if I accept shoddy goods.'

'Um,' I said calmingly, 'perhaps Nicholas Loder wants you to do just that.'

'What? What do you mean?'

'Wants you to send him straight back.'

'Oh.'

'And,' I said, 'Dozen Roses was the property of Saxony Franklin Ltd, not Nicholas Loder, and if you think it's fair to the Ostermeyers to void the sale, so be it, but my brother's executor will direct you to send the horse anywhere else but back to Loder.'

There was a silence. Then he said with a smothered laugh, 'You always were a bright tricky bastard.'

'Thanks.'

'But get down here, will you? Take a look at him. Talk to the vet. How soon can you get here?'

'Couple of hours. Maybe more.'

'No, come on, Derek.'

'It's a long way to Tipperary,' I said. 'It never gets any nearer.'

'You're delirious.'

'I shouldn't wonder.'

'Soon as you can, then,' he said. 'See you.'

I put down the receiver with an inward groan. I did not want to go belting down to Lambourn to a crisis, however easily resolved. I wanted to let my aches unwind.

I telephoned the car and heard the ringing tone, but Brad, wherever he was, didn't answer. Then, as the first step towards leaving, I went along and locked the vault. Alfie in the packing room was stretching his back, his day's load finished. Lily, standing idle, gave me a repressed look from under her lashes. Jason goosed Tina in the doorway to the stock-rooms, which she didn't seem to mind. There was a feeling of afternoon ending, of abeyance in the offing, of corporate activity drifting to suspense. Like the last race on an October card.

Saying goodnights and collecting the plastic bag I went down to the yard and found Brad there waiting.

'Did you find those papers OK?' I asked him, climbing in beside him after storing the crutches on the back seat.

'Yerss,' he said.

'And delivered them?'

'Yerss.'

'Thanks. Great. How long have you been back?'

He shrugged. I left it. It wasn't important.

'Lambourn,' I said, as we turned out of the yard. 'But on the way, back to my brother's house to collect something else. OK?'

He nodded and drove to Greville's house skilfully, but slowed just before we reached it and pointed to Greville's car, still standing by the kerb.

'See?' he said. 'It's been broken into.'

He found a parking place and we went back to look. The heavily locked boot had been jemmied open and now wouldn't close again.

'Good job we took the things out,' I said. 'I suppose they are still in my car.'

He shook his head. 'In our house, under the stairs. Our Mum said to do it, with your car outside our door all night. Dodgy neighbourhood, round our part.'

'Very thoughtful,' I said.

He nodded. 'Smart, our Mum.'

He came with me into Greville's garden, holding the gate open.

'They done this place over proper,' he said, producing the three keys from his pocket. 'Want me to?'

He didn't wait for particular assent but went up the steps and undid the locks. Daylight: no floods, no dog.

He waited in the hall while I went along to the little sitting room to collect the tapes. It all looked forlorn in there, a terrible mess made no better by time. I put the featherweight cassettes in my pocket and left again, thinking that tidying up was a long way down my urgency list. When the ankle had altogether stopped hurting; maybe then. When the insurance people had seen it, if they wanted to.

I had brought with me a note which I left prominently on the lowest step of the staircase, where anyone coming into the house would see it.

'Dear Mrs P. I'm afraid there is bad news for you. Don't clean the house. Telephone Saxony Franklin Ltd instead.'

I'd added the number in case she didn't know it by heart, and I'd warned Annette to go gently with anyone ringing. Nothing else I could do to cushion the shock.

Brad locked the front door and we set off again to Lambourn. He had done enough talking for the whole journey and we travelled in customary silence, easy if not comrades.

Milo was striding about in the yard, expending

energy to no purpose. He yanked the passenger side door of my car open and scowled in at Brad, more as a reflection of his general state of mind, I gathered, than from any particular animosity.

I retrieved the crutches and stood up, and he told me it was high time I threw them away.

'Calm down,' I said.

'Don't patronize me.'

'Is Phil here?'

Phil was Phil Urquhart, veterinary surgeon, pill pusher to the stable.

'No, he isn't,' Milo said crossly, 'but he's coming back. The damned horse won't give a sample. And for a start, you can tell me whether it is or isn't Dozen Roses. His passport matches, but I'd like to be sure.'

He strode away towards a box in one corner of the yard and I followed and looked where he looked, over the bottom half of the door.

Inside the box were an obstinate-looking horse and a furious red-faced lad. The lad held a pole which had on one end of it an open plastic bag on a ring, like a shrimping net. The plastic bag was clean and empty.

I chuckled.

'It's all right for you,' Milo said sharply. 'You haven't been waiting for more than two hours for the damned animal to stale.'

'On Singapore racecourse, one time,' I said, 'they got a sample with nicotine in it. The horse didn't smoke, but the lad did. He got tired of waiting for the horse and just supplied the sample himself.'

'Very funny,' Milo said repressively.

'This often takes hours, though, so why the rage?'

It sounded always so simple, of course, to take a regulation urine sample from two horses after every race, one nearly always from the winner. In practice, it meant waiting around for the horses to oblige. After two hours of non-performance, blood samples were taken instead, but blood wasn't as easy to come by. Many tempers were regularly lost while the horses made up their minds.

'Come away,' I said, 'he'll do it in the end. And he's definitely the horse that ran at York. Dozen Roses without doubt.'

He followed me away reluctantly and we went into the kitchen where Milo switched lights on and asked me if I'd like a drink.

'Wouldn't mind some tea,' I said.

'Tea? At this hour? Well, help yourself.' He watched me fill the kettle and set it to boil. 'Are you off booze for ever?'

'No.'

'Thank God.'

Phil Urquhart's car scrunched into the yard and pulled up outside the window, and he came breezing into the kitchen asking if there were any results. He read Milo's scowl aright and laughed.

'Do you think the horse is doped?' I asked him.

'Me? No, not really. Hard to tell. Milo thinks so.'

He was small and sandy-haired, and about thirty, the grandson of a three-generation family practice, and to my mind the best of them. I caught myself thinking that when I in the future trained here in Lambourn, I would want him for my horses. An odd thought. The future planning itself behind my back.

'I hear we're lucky you're still with us,' he said. 'An impressive crunch, so they say.' He looked at me assessingly with friendly professional eyes. 'You've a few rough edges, one can see.'

'Nothing that will stop him racing,' Milo said crisply.

Phil smiled. 'I detect more alarm than sympathy.'

'Alarm?'

'You've trained more winners since he came here.'

'Rubbish,' Milo said.

He poured drinks for himself and Phil, and I made my tea; and Phil assured me that if the urine passed all tests he would give the thumbs up to Dozen Roses.

'He may just be showing the effects of the hard race he had at York,' he said. 'It might be that he's always like this. Some horses are, and we don't know how much weight he lost.'

'What will you get the urine tested for?' I asked.

He raised his eyebrows. 'Barbiturates, in this case.'

'At York,' I said thoughtfully, 'one of Nicholas Loder's owners was walking around with a nebulizer in his pocket. A kitchen baster, to be precise.'

'An owner?' Phil asked, surprised.

'Yes. He owned the winner of the five-furlong sprint. He was also in the saddling box with Dozen Roses.'

Phil frowned. 'What are you implying?'

'Nothing. Merely observing. I can't believe he interfered with the horse. Nicholas Loder wouldn't have let him. The stable money was definitely on. They wanted to win, and they knew if it won it would be tested. So the only question is, what could you give a horse that wouldn't disqualify it? Give it via a nebulizer just before a race?'

'Nothing that would make it go faster. They test for all stimulants.'

'What if you gave it, say, sugar? Glucose? Or adrenalin?'

'You've a criminal mind!'

'I just wondered.'

'Glucose would give energy, as to human athletes. It wouldn't increase speed, though. Adrenalin is more tricky. If it's given by injection you can see it, because the hairs stand up all round the puncture. But straight into the mucous membranes . . . well, I suppose it's possible.'

'And no trace.'

He agreed. 'Adrenalin pours into a horse's bloodstream naturally anyway, if he's excited. If he wants to win. If he feels the whip. Who's to say how much? If you suspected a booster, you'd have to take a blood sample in the winner's enclosure, practically, and even then you'd have a hard job proving any reading was excessive.

Adrenalin levels vary too much. You'd even have a hard job proving extra adrenalin made any difference at all.' He paused and considered me soberly. 'You do realize that you're saying that if anything was done, Nicholas Loder condoned it?'

'Doesn't seem likely, does it?'

'No, it doesn't,' he said. 'If he were some tin-pot little crook, well then, maybe, but not Nicholas Loder with his Classic winners and everything to lose.'

'Mm.' I thought a bit. 'If I asked, I could get some of the urine sample that was taken from Dozen Roses at York. They always make it available to owners for private checks. To my brother's company, that is to say, in this instance.' I thought a bit more. 'When Nicholas Loder's friend dropped his baster, Martha Ostermeyer handed the bulb part back to him, but then Harley Ostermeyer picked up the tube part and gave it to me. But it was clean. No trace of liquid. No adrenalin. So I suppose it's possible he might have used it on his own horse and still had it in his pocket, but did nothing to Dozen Roses.'

They considered it.

'You could get into a lot of trouble making unfounded accusations,' Phil said.

'So Nicholas Loder told me.'

'Did he? I'd think twice, then, before I did. It wouldn't do you much good generally in the racing world, I shouldn't think.'

'Wisdom from babes,' I said, but he echoed my thoughts.

'Yes, old man.'

'I kept the baster tube,' I said, shrugging, 'but I guess I'll do just what I did at the races, which was nothing.'

'As long as Dozen Roses tests clean both at York and here, that's likely best,' Phil said, and Milo, for all his earlier pugnaciousness, agreed.

A commotion in the darkening yard heralded the success of the urine mission and Phil went outside to unclip the special bag and close its patented seal. He wrote and attached the label giving the horse's name, the location, date and time and signed his name.

'Right,' he said, 'I'll be off. Take care.' He loaded himself, the sample and his gear into his car and with economy of movement scrunched away. I followed soon after with Brad still driving, but decided again not to go home.

'You saw the mess in London,' I said. 'I got knocked out by whoever did that. I don't want to be in if they come to Hungerford. So let's go to Newbury instead, and try The Chequers.'

Brad slowed, his mouth open.

'A week ago yesterday,' I said, 'you saved me from a man with a knife. Yesterday someone shot at the car I was in and killed the chauffeur. It may not have been your regulation madman. So last night I slept in Swindon, tonight in Newbury.'

'Yerss,' he said, understanding.

'If you'd rather not drive me any more, I wouldn't blame you.'

After a pause, with a good deal of stalwart resolution, he made a statement. 'You need me.'

'Yes,' I said. 'Until I can walk properly, I do.'

'I'll drive you, then.'

'Thanks,' I said, and meant it wholeheartedly, and he could hear that, because he nodded twice to himself emphatically and seemed even pleased.

The Chequers Hotel having a room free, I booked in for the night. Brad took himself home in my car, and I spent most of the evening sitting in an armchair upstairs learning my way round the Wizard.

Computers weren't my natural habitat like they were Greville's and I hadn't the same appetite for them. The Wizard's instructions seemed to take it for granted that everyone reading them would be computer-literate, so it probably took me longer than it might have done to get results.

What was quite clear was that Greville had used the gadget extensively. There were three separate telephone and address lists, the world-time clock, a system for entering daily appointments, a prompt for anniversaries, a calendar flashing with the day's date, and provision for storing oddments of information. By plugging in the printer, and after a few false starts, I ended with long printed lists of everything held listed under all the headings, and read them with growing frustration.

None of the addresses or telephone numbers seemed to have anything to do with Antwerp or with diamonds, though the 'Business Overseas' list contained many gem merchants' names from all round the world. None of the appointments scheduled, which stretched back six weeks or more, seemed to be relevant, and there were no entries at all for the Friday he'd gone to Ipswich. There was no reference to *Koningin Beatrix*.

I thought of my question to June the day she'd found her way to 'pearl': what if it were all in there, but stored in secret?

The Wizard's instruction manual, two hundred pages long, certainly did give lessons in how to lock things away. Entries marked 'secret' could only be retrieved by knowing the password which could be any combination of numbers and letters up to seven in all. Forgetting the password meant bidding farewell to the entries: they could never be seen again. They could be deleted unseen, but not printed or brought to the screen.

One could tell if secret files were present, the book said, by the small symbol s, which could be found on the lower right-hand side of the screen. I consulted Greville's screen and found the s there, sure enough.

It would be, I thought. It would have been totally unlike him to have had the wherewithal for secrecy and not used it.

Any combination of numbers or letters up to seven . . .

The book suggested 1234, but once I'd sorted out the

opening moves for unlocking and entered 1234 in the space headed 'Secret Off', all I got was a quick dusty answer, 'Incorrect Password'.

Damn him, I thought, wearily defeated. Why couldn't he make any of it easy?

I tried every combination of letters and numbers I thought he might have used but got absolutely nowhere. Clarissa was too long, 12Roses should have been right but wasn't. To be right, the password had to be entered exactly as it had been set, whether in capital letters or lower case. It all took time. In the end I was ready to throw the confounded Wizard across the room, and stared at its perpetual 'Incorrect Password' with hatred.

I finally laid it aside and played the tiny tape recorder instead. There was a lot of office chat on the tapes and I couldn't think why Greville should have bothered to take them home and hide them. Long before I reached the end of the fourth side, I was asleep.

I woke stiffly after a while, unsure for a second where I was. I rubbed my face, looked at my watch, thought about all the constructive thinking I was supposed to be doing and wasn't, and rewound the second of the baby tapes to listen to what I'd missed. Greville's voice, talking business to Annette.

The most interesting thing, the only interesting thing about those tapes, I thought, was Greville's voice. The only way I would ever hear him again.

'. . . going out to lunch,' he was saying. 'I'll be back by two-thirty.'

Annette's voice said, 'Yes, Mr Franklin.'

A click sounded on the tape.

Almost immediately, because of the concertina-ing of time by the voice-activated mechanism, a different voice said, 'I'm in his office now and I can't find them. He hides everything, he's security mad, you know that.' Click. 'I can't ask. He'd never tell me, and I don't think he trusts me.' Click. 'Po-faced Annette doesn't sneeze unless he tells her to. She'd never tell me anything.' Click. 'I'll try. I'll have to go, he doesn't like me using this phone, he'll be back from lunch any second.' Click.

End of tape.

Bloody hell, I thought. I rewound the end of the tape and listened to it again. I knew the voice, as Greville must have done. He'd left the recorder on, I guessed by mistake, and he'd come back and listened, with I supposed sadness, to treachery. It opened up a whole new world of questions and I went slowly to bed groping towards answers.

I lay a long time awake. When I slept, I dreamed the usual surrealist muddle and found it no help, but around dawn, awake again and thinking of Greville, it occurred to me that there was one password I hadn't tried because I hadn't thought of his using it.

The Wizard was across the room by the armchair. Impelled by curiosity I turned on the light, rolled out of bed and hopped over to fetch it. Taking it back with me, I switched it on, pressed the buttons, found 'Secret Off' and into the offered space typed the word Greville had written on the last page of his racing diary, below the numbers of his passport and national insurance.

DEREK, all in capital letters.

I typed DEREK and pressed Enter, and the Wizard with resignation let me into its data.

CHAPTER FIFTEEN

I began printing out everything in the secret files as it seemed from the manual that, particularly as regarded the expense organizer, it was the best way to get at the full information stored there.

Each category had to be printed separately, the baby printer clicking away line by line and not very fast. I watched its steady output with fascination, hoping the small roll of paper would last to the end, as I hadn't any more.

From the Memo section, which I printed first, came a terse note, 'Check, don't trust.'

Next came a long list of days and dates which seemed to bear no relation to anything. Monday, 30 January, Wednesday, 8 March ... Mystified I watched the sequence lengthen, noticing only that most of them were Mondays, Tuesdays or Wednesdays, five or six weeks apart, sometimes less, sometimes longer. The list ended five weeks before his death, and it began ... It began, I thought blankly, four years earlier. Four years ago; when he first met Clarissa.

I felt unbearable sadness for him. He'd fallen in love with a woman who wouldn't leave home for him, whom he hadn't wanted to compromise: he'd kept a record, I was certain, of every snatched day they'd spent together, and hidden it away as he had hidden so much else. A whole lot of roses, I thought.

The Schedule section, consulted next, contained appointments not hinted at earlier, including the delivery of the diamonds to his London house. For the day of his death there were two entries: the first, 'Ipswich. Orwell Hotel, P. 3.30 pm', and the second, 'Meet *Koningin Beatrix* 6.30 pm, Harwich.' For the following Monday he had noted, 'Meet C King's Cross 12.10 Lunch Luigi's.'

Meet C at King's Cross . . . He hadn't turned up, and she'd telephoned his house, and left a message on his answering machine, and sometime in the afternoon she'd telephoned his office to ask for him. Poor Clarissa. By Monday night she'd left the ultra-anxious second message, and on Tuesday she had learned he was dead.

The printer whirred and produced another entry, for the Saturday after. 'C and Dozen Roses both at York! Could I go? Not wise. Check TV.'

The printer stopped, as Greville's life had done. No more appointments on record.

Next I printed the Telephone sections, Private, Business and Business Overseas. Private contained only Knightwood. Business was altogether empty, but from Business Overseas I watched with widening eyes the emergence of five numbers and addresses in Antwerp. One was van Ekeren, one was Guy Servi: three were so far unknown to me. I breathed almost painfully with exultation, unable to believe Greville had entered them there for no purpose.

I printed the Expense Manager's secret section last as it was the most complicated and looked the least promising, but the first item that emerged was galvanic.

Antwerp say 5 of the first
batch of rough are CZ.
Don't want to believe it.
Infinite sadness.
Priority 1.
Arrange meetings. Ipswich?
Undecided. Damnation!

I wished he had been more explicit, more specific, but he'd seen no need to be. It was surprising he'd written so much. His feelings must have been strong to have been entered at all. No other entries afterwards held any comment but were short records of money spent on courier services with a firm called Euro-Securo, telephone number supplied. In the middle of those the paper ran out. I brought the rest of the stored information up on to the screen and scrolled through it, but there was nothing else disturbing.

I switched off both baby machines and reread the long curling strip of printing from the beginning, afterwards flattening it out and folding it to fit a shirt pocket. Then I dressed, packed, breakfasted, waited for Brad and travelled to London hopefully.

The telephone calls to Antwerp had to be done from the Saxony Franklin premises because of the precautionary checking back. I would have preferred more privacy than Greville's office but couldn't achieve it, and one of the first things I asked Annette that morning was whether my brother had had one of those gadgets that warned you if someone was listening to your conversation on an extension. The office phones were all interlinked.

'No, he didn't,' she said, troubled.

'He could have done with one,' I said.

'Are you implying that we listened when he didn't mean us to?'

'Not you,' I assured her, seeing her resentment of the suggestion. 'But yes, I'd think it happened. Anyway, at some point this morning, I want to make sure of not being overheard, so when that call comes through perhaps you'll all go into the stock-room and sing Rule Britannia.'

Annette never made jokes. I had to explain I didn't mean sing literally. She rather huffily agreed that when I wanted it, she would go round the extensions checking against eavesdroppers.

I asked her why Greville hadn't had a private line in any case, and she said he had had one earlier but they now used that for the fax machine.

'If he wanted to be private,' she said, 'he went down to the yard and telephoned from his car.'

There, I supposed, he would have been safe also from people with sensitive listening devices, if he'd suspected their use. He had been conscious of betrayal, that was for sure.

I sat at Greville's desk with the door closed and matched the three unknown Antwerp names from the Wizard with the full list June had provided, and found that all three were there.

The first and second produced no results, but from the third, once I explained who I was, I got the customary response about checking the files and calling back. They did call back, but the amorphous voice on the far end was cautious to the point of repression.

'We at Maarten-Pagnier cannot discuss anything at all with you, monsieur,' he said. 'Monsieur Franklin gave express orders that we were not to communicate with anyone in his office except himself.'

'My brother is dead,' I said.

'So you say, monsieur. But he warned us to beware of any attempt to gain information about his affairs and we cannot discuss them.'

'Then please will you telephone to his lawyers and get their assurance that he's dead and that I am now managing his business?'

After a pause the voice said austerely, 'Very well, monsieur. Give us the name of his lawyers.'

I did that and waited for ages during which time

three customers telephoned with long orders which I wrote down, trying not to get them wrong from lack of concentration.

Then there was a frantic call from a nearly incoherent woman who wanted to speak to Mr Franklin urgently.

'Mrs P?' I asked tentatively.

Mrs P it was. Mrs Patterson, she said. I gave her the abysmal news and listened to her telling me what a fine nice gentleman my brother had been, and oh dear, she felt faint, had I seen the mess in the sitting room?

I warned her that the whole house was the same. 'Just leave it,' I said. 'I'll clean it up later. Then if you could come after that to hoover and dust, I'd be very grateful.'

Calming a little, she gave me her phone number. 'Let me know, then,' she said. 'Oh dear, oh dear.'

Finally the Antwerp voice returned and, begging him to hold on, I hopped over to the door, called Annette, handed her the customers' orders and said this was the moment for securing the defences. She gave me a disapproving look as I again closed the door.

Back in Greville's chair I said to the voice, 'Please, monsieur, tell me if my brother had any dealings with you. I am trying to sort out his office but he has left too few records.'

'He asked us particularly not to send any records of the work we were doing for him to his office.'

'He, er, what?' I said.

'He said he could not trust everyone in his office as he would like. Instead, he wished us to send anything necessary to the fax machine in his car, but only when he telephoned from there to arrange it.'

'Um,' I said, blinking, 'I found the fax machine in his car but there were no statements or invoices or anything from you.'

'I believe if you ask his accountants, you may find them there.'

'Good grief.'

'I beg your pardon, monsieur?'

'I didn't think of asking his accountants,' I said blankly.

'He said for tax purposes . . .'

'Yes, I see.' I hesitated. 'What exactly were you doing for him?'

'Monsieur?'

'Did he,' I asked a shade breathlessly, 'send you a hundred diamonds, colour H, average uncut weight three point two carats, to be cut and polished?'

'No, monsieur.'

'Oh.' My disappointment must have been audible.

'He sent twenty-five stones, monsieur, but five of them were not diamonds.'

'Cubic zirconia,' I said, enlightened.

'Yes, monsieur. We told Monsieur Franklin as soon as we discovered it. He said we were wrong, but we were not, monsieur.'

'No,' I agreed. 'He did leave a note saying five of the first batch were CZ.'

'Yes, monsieur. He was extremely upset. We made several enquiries for him, but he had bought the stones from a sightholder of impeccable honour and he had himself measured and weighed the stones when they were delivered to his London house. He sent them to us in a sealed Euro-Securo courier package. We assured him that the mistake could not have been made here by us, and it was then, soon after that, that he asked us not to send or give any information to anyone in his . . . your . . . office.' He paused. 'He made arrangements to receive the finished stones from us, but he didn't meet our messenger.'

'Your messenger?'

'One of our partners, to be accurate. We wished to deliver the stones to him ourselves because of the five disputed items, and Monsieur Franklin thought it an excellent idea. Our partner dislikes flying, so it was agreed he should cross by boat and return the same way. When Monsieur Franklin failed to meet him he came back here. He is elderly and had made no provision to stay away. He was . . . displeased . . . at having made a tiring journey for nothing. He said we should wait to hear from Monsieur Franklin. Wait for fresh instructions. We have been waiting, but we've been puzzled. We didn't try to reach Monsieur Franklin at his office as he had forbidden us to do that, but we were considering asking someone else to try on our behalf. We are very sorry to hear of his death. It explains everything, of course.'

I said, 'Did your partner travel to Harwich on the *Koningin Beatrix*?'

'That's right, monsieur.'

'He brought the diamonds with him?'

'That's right, monsieur. And he brought them back. We will now wait your instructions instead.'

I took a deep breath. Twenty of the diamonds at least were safe. Five were missing. Seventy-five were . . . *where*?

The Antwerp voice said, 'It's to be regretted that Monsieur Franklin didn't see the polished stones. They cut very well. Twelve tear drops of great brilliance, remarkable for that colour. Eight were not suitable for tear drops, as we told Monsieur Franklin, but they look handsome as stars. What shall we do with them, monsieur?'

'When I've talked to the jeweller they were cut for, I'll let you know.'

'Very good, monsieur. And our account? Where shall we send that?' He mentioned considerately how much it would be.

'To this office,' I said, sighing at the prospect. 'Send it to me marked "Personal".'

'Very good, monsieur.'

'And thank you,' I said. 'You've been very helpful.'

'At your service, monsieur.'

I put the receiver down slowly, richer by twelve

glittering tear drops destined to hang and flash in sunlight, and by eight handsome stars that might twinkle in a fantasy of rock crystal. Better than nothing, but not enough to save the firm.

Using the crutches, I went in search of Annette and asked her if she would please find Prospero Jenks, wherever he was, and make another appointment for me, that afternoon if possible. Then I went down to the yard, taking a tip from Greville, and on the telephone in my car put a call through to his accountants.

Brad, reading a golfing magazine, paid no attention.

Did he play golf, I asked?

No, he didn't.

The accountants helpfully confirmed that they had received envelopes both from my brother and from Antwerp, and were holding them unopened, as requested, pending further instructions.

'You'll need them for the general accounts,' I said. 'So would you please just keep them?'

Absolutely no problem.

'On second thoughts,' I said, 'please open all the envelopes and tell me who all the letters from Antwerp have come from.'

Again no problem: but the letters were all either from Guy Servi, the sightholder, or from Maarten-Pagnier, the cutters. No other firms. No other safe havens for seventy-five rocks.

I thanked them, watched Brad embark on a learned

comparison of Ballesteros and Faldo, and thought about disloyalty and the decay of friendship.

It was restful in the car, I decided. Brad went on reading. I thought of robbery with violence and violence without robbery, of being laid out with a brick and watching Simms die of a bullet meant for me, and I wondered whether, if I were dead, anyone could find what I was looking for, or whether they reckoned they now couldn't find it if I were alive.

I stirred and fished in a pocket and gave Brad a cheque I'd written out for him upstairs.

'What's this?' he said, peering at it.

I usually paid him in cash, but I explained I hadn't enough for what I owed him, and cash dispensers wouldn't disgorge enough all at once and we hadn't recently been in Hungerford when the banks were open, as he might have noticed.

'Give me cash later,' he said, holding the cheque out to me. 'And you paid me double.'

'For last week and this week,' I nodded. 'When we get to the bank I'll swap it for cash. Otherwise, you could bring it back here. It's a company cheque. They'd see you got cash for it.'

He gave me a long look.

'Is this because of guns and such? In case you never get to the bank?'

I shrugged. 'You might say so.'

He looked at the cheque, folded it deliberately and stowed it away. Then he picked up the magazine and stared blindly at a page he'd just read. I was grateful for the absence of comment or protest, and in a while said matter-of-factly that I was going upstairs for a bit, and why didn't he get some lunch.

He nodded.

'Have you got enough money for lunch?'

'Yerss.'

'You might make a list of what you've spent. I've enough cash for that.'

He nodded again.

'OK, then,' I said. 'See you.'

Upstairs, Annette said she had opened the day's post and put it ready for my attention, and she'd found Prospero Jenks and he would be expecting me in the Knightsbridge shop any time between three and six.

'Great.'

She frowned. 'Mr Jenks wanted to know if you were taking him the goods Mr Franklin bought for him. Grev – he always calls Mr Franklin, Grev. I do wish he wouldn't – I asked what he meant about goods and he said you would know.'

'He's talking about diamonds,' I said.

'But we haven't . . .' She stopped and then went on with a sort of desperate vehemence. 'I *wish* Mr Franklin was here. Nothing's the same without him.'

She gave me a look full of her insecurity and doubt of my ability and plodded off into her own domain and I thought that with what lay ahead I'd have preferred a vote of confidence: and I too, with all my heart, wished Greville back.

The police from Hungerford telephoned, given my number by Milo's secretary. They wanted to know if I had remembered anything more about the car driven by the gunman. They had asked the family in the family car if they had noticed the make and colour of the last car they'd seen coming towards them before they rounded the bend and crashed into the Daimler, and one of the children, a boy, had given them a description. They had also, while the firemen and others were trying to free me, walked down the row of spectator cars asking them about the last car they'd seen coming towards them. Only the first two drivers had seen a car at all, that they could remember, and they had no helpful information. Had I any recollection, however vague, as they were trying to piece together all the impressions they'd been given?

'I wish I could help,' I said, 'but I was talking to Mr and Mrs Ostermeyer, not concentrating on the road. It winds a bit, as you know, and I think Simms had been waiting for a place where he could pass the car in front, but all I can tell you, as on Sunday, is that it was a greyish colour and fairly large. Maybe a Mercedes. It's only an impression.'

'The child in the family car says it was a grey Volvo travelling fast. The bus driver says the car in question was travelling slowly before the Daimler tried to pass it, and he was aiming to pass also at that point, and was accelerating to do so, which was why he rammed the Daimler so hard. He says the car was silver grey and accelerated away at high speed, which matched what the child says.'

'Did the bus driver,' I asked, 'see the gun or the shots?'

'No, sir. He was looking at the road ahead and at the Daimler, not at the car he intended to pass. Then the Daimler veered sharply, and bounded off the wall straight into his path. He couldn't avoid hitting it, he said. Do you confirm that, sir?'

'Yes. It happened so fast. He hadn't a chance.'

'We are asking in the neighbourhood for anyone to come forward who saw a grey four-door saloon, possibly a Volvo, on that road on Sunday afternoon, but so far we have heard nothing new. If you remember anything else, however minor, let us know.'

I would, I said.

I put the phone down wondering if Vaccaro's shot-down pilots had seen the make of car from which their deaths had come spitting. Anyone seeing those murders would, I supposed, have been gazing with uncomprehending horror at the falling victims, not dashing into the road to peer at a fast disappearing number plate.

No one had heard any shots on Sunday. No one had heard the shots, the widow had told Greville, when her husband was killed. A silencer on a gun in a moving car . . . a swift pfftt . . . curtains.

It couldn't have been Vaccaro who shot Simms. Vaccaro didn't make sense. Someone with the same anti-social habits, as in Northern Ireland and elsewhere. A copycat. Plenty of precedent.

Milo's secretary had been busy and given my London number also to Phil Urquhart who came on the line to tell me that Dozen Roses had tested clean for barbiturates and he would give a certificate of soundness for the sale.

'Fine,' I said.

'I've been to examine the horse again this morning. He's still very docile. It seems to be his natural state.'

'Mm.'

'Do I hear doubt?'

'He's excited enough every time cantering down to the start.'

'Natural adrenalin,' Phil said.

'If it was anyone but Nicholas Loder . . .'

'He would never risk it,' Phil said, agreeing with me. 'But look . . . there are things that potentiate adrenalin, like caffeine. Some of them are never tested for in racing, as they are not judged to be stimulants. It's your money that's being spent on the tests I've done for you. We have some more of that sample of urine. Do you want me to get different tests done, for things not usually looked for? I mean, do you really think Nicholas Loder gave the horse something, and if you do, do you want to know about it?'

'It was his owner, a man called Rollway, who had the baster, not Loder himself.'

'Same decision. Do you want to spend more, or not bother? It may be money down the drain, anyway. And if you get any results, what then? You don't want to get the horse disqualified, that wouldn't make sense.'

'No . . . it wouldn't.'

'What's your problem?' he asked. 'I can hear it in your voice.'

'Fear,' I said. 'Nicholas Loder was afraid.'

'Oh.' He was briefly silent. 'I could get the tests done anonymously, of course.'

'Yes. Get them done, then. I particularly don't want to sell the Ostermeyers a lemon, as she would say. If Dozen Roses can't win on his own merits, I'll talk them out of the idea of owning him.'

'So you'll pay for negative results?'

'I will indeed.'

'While I was at Milo's this morning,' he said, 'he was talking to the Ostermeyers in London, asking how they were and wishing them a good journey. They were still a bit wobbly from the crash, it seems.'

'Surprising if they weren't.'

'They're coming back to England though to see Datepalm run in the Hennessy. How's your ankle?'

'Good as new by then.'

'Bye then.' I could hear his smile. 'Take care.'

He disconnected and left me thinking that there still were good things in the world, like the Ostermeyers' faith and riding Datepalm in the Hennessy, and I stood up and put my left foot flat on the floor for a progress report.

It wasn't so bad if I didn't lean any weight on it, but there were still jabbingly painful protests against attempts to walk. Oh well, I thought, sitting down again, give it another day or two. It hadn't exactly had a therapeutic week and was no doubt doing its best against odds. On Thursday, I thought, I would get rid of the crutches. By Friday, definitely. Any day after that I'd be running. Ever optimistic. It was the belief that cured.

The ever-busy telephone rang again, and I answered it with 'Saxony Franklin?' as routine.

'Derek?'

'Yes,' I said.

Clarissa's unmistakable voice said, 'I'm in London. Could we meet?'

I hadn't expected her so soon, I thought. I said, 'Yes, of course. Where?'

'I thought . . . perhaps . . . Luigi's. Do you know Luigi's bar and restaurant?'

'I don't,' I said slowly, 'but I can find it.'

'It's in Swallow Street near Piccadilly Circus. Would you mind coming at seven, for a drink?'

'And dinner?'

'Well . . .'

'And dinner,' I said.

I heard her sigh, 'Yes. All right,' as she disconnected, and I was left with a vivid understanding both of her compulsion to put me where she had been going to meet Greville and of her awareness that perhaps she ought not to.

I could have said no, I thought. I could have, but hadn't. A little introspection revealed ambiguities in my response to her also, like did I want to give comfort, or to take it.

By three-thirty I'd finished the paperwork and filled an order for pearls and another for turquoise and relocked the vault and got Annette to smile again, even if faintly. At four, Brad pulled up outside Prospero Jenks's shop in Knightsbridge and I put the telephone ready to let him know when to collect me.

Prospero Jenks was where I'd found him before, sitting in shirtsleeves at his workbench. The discreet dark-suited man, serving customers in the shop, nodded me through.

'He's expecting you, Mr Franklin.'

Pross stood up with a smile on his young-old Peter Pan face and held out his hand, but let it fall again as I waggled a crutch handle at him instead.

'Glad to see you,' he said, offering a chair, waiting while I sat. 'Have you brought my diamonds?' He sat down again on his own stool.

'No. Afraid not.'

He was disappointed. 'I thought that was what you were coming for.'

'No, not really.'

I looked at his long efficient workroom with its little drawers full of unset stones and thought of the marvels he produced. The big notice on the wall still read 'NEVER TURN YOUR BACK TO CUSTOMERS. ALWAYS WATCH THEIR HANDS.'

I said, 'Greville sent twenty-five rough stones to Antwerp to be cut for you.'

'That's right.'

'Five of them were cubic zirconia.'

'No, no.'

'Did you,' I asked neutrally, 'swap them over?'

The half-smile died out of his face, which grew stiff and expressionless. The bright blue eyes stared at me and the lines deepened across his forehead.

'That's rubbish,' he said. 'I'd never do anything stupid like that.'

I didn't say anything immediately and it seemed to give him force.

'You can't come in here making wild accusations. Go on, get out, you'd better leave.' He half-rose to his feet.

I said, not moving, 'When the cutters told Greville five of the stones were cubic zirconia, he was devastated. Very upset.'

I reached into my shirt pocket and drew out the print-out from the Wizard.

'Do you want to see?' I asked. 'Read there.'

After a hesitation he took the paper, sat back on the stool and read the entry:

> Antwerp say 5 of the first
> batch of rough are CZ.

Don't want to believe it.
Infinite sadness.
Priority 1.
Arrange meetings. Ipswich?
Undecided. Damnation!

'Greville used to write his thoughts in a notebook,' I said. 'In there it says, "Infinite sadness is not to trust an old friend." '

'So what?'

'Since Greville died,' I said, 'someone has been trying to find his diamonds, to steal them from me. That someone had to be someone who knew they were there to be found. Greville kept the fact that he'd bought them very quiet for security reasons. He didn't tell even his staff. But of course you yourself knew, as it was for you he bought them.'

He said again, 'So what?'

'If you remember,' I said, still conversationally, 'someone broke into Greville's office after he died and stole things like an address book and an appointments diary. I began to think the thief had also stolen any other papers which might point to where the diamonds were, like letters or invoices. But I know now there weren't any such papers to be found there, because Greville was full of distrust. His distrust dated from the day the Antwerp cutters told him five of his stones were cubic zirconia, which was about three weeks before he died.'

Pross, Greville's friend, said nothing.

'Greville bought the diamonds,' I went on, 'from a sightholder based in Antwerp who sent them by messenger to his London house. There he measured them and weighed them and signed for them. Then it would be reasonable to suppose that he showed them to you, his customer. Or showed you twenty-five of them, perhaps. Then he sent that twenty-five back to Antwerp by the Euro-Securo couriers. Five diamonds had mysteriously become cubic zirconia, and yes, it was an entirely stupid thing to do, because the substitution was bound to be discovered almost at once, and you knew it would be. Had to be. I'd think you reckoned Greville would never believe it of you, but would swear the five stones had to have been swapped by someone in the couriers or the cutters in Antwerp, and he would collect the insurance in due course, and that would be that. You would be five diamonds to the good, and he would have lost nothing.'

'You can't prove it,' he said flatly.

'No, I can't prove it. But Greville was full of sorrow and distrust, and why should he be if he thought his stones had been taken by strangers?'

I looked with some of Greville's own sadness at Prospero Jenks. A likeable, entertaining genius whose feelings for my brother had been strong and long-lasting, whose regret at his death had been real.

'I'd think,' I said, 'that after your long friendship, after all the treasures he'd brought you, after the pink and green tourmaline, after your tremendous success, that he could hardly bear your treachery.'

'Stop it,' he said sharply. 'It's bad enough . . .'

He shut his mouth tight and shook his head, and seemed to sag internally.

'He forgave me,' he said.

He must have thought I didn't believe him.

He said wretchedly, 'I wished I hadn't done it almost from the beginning, if you want to know. It was just an impulse. He left the diamonds here while he went off to do a bit of shopping, and I happened to have some rough CZ the right size in those drawers, as I often do, waiting for when I want special cutting, and I just . . . exchanged them. Like you said. I didn't think he'd lose by it.'

'He knew, though,' I said. 'He knew you, and he knew a lot about thieves, being a magistrate. Another of the things he wrote was, "If laws are inconvenient, ignore them, they don't apply to you." '

'Stop it. Stop it. He forgave me.'

'When?'

'In Ipswich. I went to meet him there.'

I lifted my head. 'Ipswich. Orwell Hotel, P. 3.30 pm,' I said.

'What? Yes.' He seemed unsurprised that I should know. He seemed to be looking inwards to an unendurable landscape.

'I saw him die,' he said.

CHAPTER SIXTEEN

'I saw the scaffolding fall on him,' he said.

He'd stunned me to silence.

'We talked in the hotel. In the lounge there. It was almost empty . . . then we walked down the street to where I'd left my car. We said goodbye. He crossed the road and walked on, and I watched him. I wanted him to look back and wave . . . but he didn't.'

Forgiveness was one thing, I thought, but friendship had gone. What did he expect? Absolution and comfort? Perhaps Greville in time would have given those too, but I couldn't.

Prospero Jenks with painful memory said, 'Grev never knew what happened . . . There wasn't any warning. Just a clanging noise and metal falling and men with it. Crashing down fast. It buried him. I couldn't see him . . . I ran across the road to pull him and there were bodies . . . and he . . . he . . . I thought he was dead already. His head was bleeding . . . there was a metal bar in his stomach and another had ripped into his leg . . . it was . . . I can't . . . I try to forget but I see it all the time.'

I waited and in a while he went on.

'I didn't move him. Couldn't. There was so much blood . . . and a man lying over his legs . . . and another man groaning. People came running . . . then the police . . . it was just chaos . . .'

He stopped again, and I said, 'When the police came, why didn't you stay with Greville and help him? Why didn't you identify him to them, even?'

His genuine sorrow was flooded with a shaft of alarm. The dismay was momentary, and he shrugged it off.

'You know how it is.' He gave me a little-boy shame-faced look, much the same as when he'd admitted to changing the stones. 'Don't get involved. I didn't want to be dragged in . . . I thought he was dead.'

Somewhere along the line, I thought, he was lying to me. Not about seeing the accident: his description of Greville's injuries had been piercingly accurate.

'Did you simply . . . drive off?' I asked bleakly.

'No, I couldn't. Not for ages. The police cordoned off the street and took endless statements. Something about criminal responsibility and insurance claims. But I couldn't help them. I didn't see why the scaffolding fell. I felt sick because of the blood . . . I sat in my car till they let us drive out. They'd taken Grev off in an ambulance before that . . . and the bar was still sticking out of his stomach . . .'

The memory was powerfully reviving his nausea.

'You knew by then that he was still alive,' I said.

He was shocked. 'How? How could I have known?'

'They hadn't covered his face.'

'He was dying. Anyone could see. His head was dented . . . and bleeding . . .'

Dead men don't bleed, I thought, but didn't say it. Prospero Jenks already looked about to throw up, and I wondered how many times he actually had, in the past eleven days.

Instead, I said, 'What did you talk about in the Orwell Hotel?'

He blinked. 'You know what.'

'He accused you of changing the stones.'

'Yes.' He swallowed. 'Well, I apologized. Said I was sorry. Which I was. He could see that. He said why did I do it when I was bound to be found out, but when I did it, it was an impulse, and I didn't think I'd be found out, like I told you.'

'What did he say?'

'He shook his head as if I were a baby. He was sad more than angry. I said I would give the diamonds back, of course, and I begged him to forgive me.'

'Which he did?'

'Yes, I told you. I asked if we could go on trading together. I mean, no one was as good as Grev at finding marvellous stones, and he always loved the things I made. It was good for both of us. I wanted to go back to that.'

Going back was one of life's impossibilities, I thought. Nothing was ever the same.

'Did Greville agree?' I asked.

'Yes. He said he had the diamonds with him but he had arrangements to make. He didn't say what. He said he would come here to the shop at the beginning of the week and I would give him his five stones and pay for the tear drops and stars. He wanted cash for them, and he was giving me a day or two to find the money.'

'He didn't usually want cash for things, did he? You sent a cheque for the spinel and rock crystal.'

'Yes, well . . .' Again the quick look of shame, 'He said cash in future, as he couldn't trust me. But you didn't know that.'

Greville certainly hadn't trusted him, and it sounded as if he'd said he had the diamonds with him when he knew they were at that moment on a boat crossing the North Sea. Had he said that, I wondered? Perhaps Prospero Jenks had misheard or misunderstood, but he'd definitely believed Greville had had the diamonds with him.

'If I give you those diamonds now, then that will be the end of it?' he said. 'I mean, as Grev had forgiven me, you won't go back on that and make a fuss, will you? Not the police . . . Grev wouldn't have wanted that, you know he wouldn't.'

I didn't answer. Greville would have to have balanced his betrayed old friendship against his respect for the law, and I supposed he wouldn't have had Prospero prosecuted, not for a first offence, admitted and regretted.

Prospero Jenks gave my silence a hopeful look, rose from his stool and crossed to the ranks of little drawers. He pulled one open, took out several apparently unimportant packets and felt deep inside with a searching hand. He brought out a twist of white gauze fastened with a band of sticky tape and held it out for me.

'Five diamonds,' he said. 'Yours.'

I took the unimpressive little parcel which most resembled the muslin bag of herbs cooks put in stews, and weighed it in my hand. I certainly couldn't myself tell CZ from C and he could see the doubt in my face.

'Have them appraised,' he said with unjustified bitterness, and I said we would weigh them right there and then and he would write out the weight and sign it.

'Grev didn't . . .'

'More fool he. He should have done. But he trusted you. I don't.'

'Come on, Derek.' He was cajoling; but I was not Greville.

'No. Weigh them,' I said.

With a sigh and an exaggerated shrug he cut open the little bag when I handed it back to him, and on small fine scales weighed the contents.

It was the first time I'd actually seen what I'd been searching for, and they were unimposing, to say the least. Five dull-looking greyish pieces of crystal the size of large misshapen peas without a hint of the fire waiting within. I watched the weighing carefully and took them myself off the scales, wrapping them in a fresh square of gauze which Prospero handed me and fastening them safely with sticky tape.

'Satisfied?' he said with a touch of sarcasm, watching me stow the bouquet garni in my trouser pocket.

'No. Not really.'

'They're the genuine article,' he protested. He signed the paper on which he'd written their combined weight, and gave it to me. 'I wouldn't make that mistake again.' He studied me. 'You're much harder than Grev.'

'I've reason to be.'

'What reason?'

'Several attempts at theft. Sundry assaults.'

His mouth opened.

'Who else?' I said.

'But I've never . . . I didn't . . .' He wanted me to believe him. He leaned forward with earnestness. 'I don't know what you're talking about.'

I sighed slightly. 'Greville hid the letters and invoices dealing with the diamonds because he distrusted someone in his office. Someone that he guessed was running to you with little snippets of information. Someone who would spy for you.'

'Nonsense.' His mouth seemed dry, however.

I pulled out of a pocket the microcassette recorder and laid it on his workbench.

'This is voice activated,' I said. 'Greville left it switched on one day when he went to lunch, and this is what he found on the tape when he returned.' I pressed the switch and the voice that was familiar to both of us spoke revealing forth:

'I'm in his office now and I can't find them. He hides everything, he's security mad, you know that. I can't ask. He'd never tell me, and I don't think he trusts me. Po-faced Annette doesn't sneeze unless he tells her to . . .'

Jason's voice, full of the cocky street-smart aggression that went with the orange spiky hair, clicked off eventually into silence. Prospero Jenks worked some saliva into his mouth and carefully made sure the recorder was not still alive and listening.

'Jason wasn't talking to me,' he said unconvincingly. 'He was talking to someone else.'

'Jason was the regular messenger between you and Greville,' I said. 'I sent him round here myself last week. Jason wouldn't take much seducing to bring you information along with the merchandise. But Greville found out. It compounded his sense of betrayal. So when you and he were talking in the Orwell at Ipswich, what was his opinion of Jason?'

He made a gesture of half-suppressed fury.

'I don't know how you know all this,' he said.

It had taken nine days and a lot of searching and a good deal of guessing at possibilities and probabilities, but the pattern was now a reliable path through at least part of the maze, and no other interpretation that I could think of explained the facts.

I said again, 'What did he say about Jason?'

Prospero Jenks capitulated. 'He said he'd have to leave Saxony Franklin. He said it was a condition of us ever doing business again. He said I was to tell Jason not to turn up for work on the Monday.'

'But you didn't do that,' I said.

'Well, no.'

'Because when Greville died, you decided to try to steal not only five stones but the lot.'

The blue eyes almost smiled. 'Seemed logical, didn't it?' he said. 'Grev wouldn't know. The insurance would pay. No one would lose.'

Except the underwriters, I thought. But I said, 'The diamonds weren't insured. Are not now insured. You were stealing them directly from Greville.'

He was almost astounded, but not quite.

'Greville told you that, didn't he?' I guessed.

Again the little-boy shame. 'Well, yes, he did.'

'In the Orwell?'

'Yes.'

'Pross,' I said, 'did you ever grow up?'

'You don't know what growing up is. Growing up is being ahead of the game.'

'Stealing without being found out?'

'Of course. Everyone does it. You have to make what you can.'

'But you have this marvellous talent,' I said.

'Sure. But I make things for money. I make what people like. I take their bread, whatever they'll pay. Sure, I get a buzz when what I've made is brilliant, but I wouldn't starve in a garret for art's sake. Stones sing to me. I give them life. Gold is my paintbrush. All that, sure. But I'll laugh behind people's backs. They're gullible. The day I understood all customers are suckers is the day I grew up.'

I said, 'I'll bet you never said all that to Greville.'

'Do me a favour. Grev was a saint, near enough. The only truly good person through and through I've ever known. I wish I hadn't cheated him. I regret it something rotten.'

I listened to the sincerity in his voice and believed him, but his remorse had been barely skin deep, and nowhere had it altered his soul.

'Jason,' I said, 'knocked me down outside St Catherine's Hospital and stole the bag containing Greville's clothes.'

'No.' The Jenks' denial was automatic, but his eyes were full of shock.

I said, 'I thought at the time it was an ordinary mugging. The attacker was quick and strong. A friend who was with me said the mugger wore jeans and a woolly hat, but neither of us saw his face. I didn't bother to report it to the police because there was nothing of value in the bag.'

'So how can you say it was Jason?'

I answered his question obliquely.

'When I went to Greville's firm to tell them he was dead,' I said, 'I found his office had been ransacked. As you know. The next day I discovered that Greville had bought diamonds. I began looking for them, but there was no paperwork, no address book, no desk diary, no reference to or appointments with diamond dealers. I couldn't physically find the diamonds either. I spent three days searching in the vault, with Annette and June, her assistant, telling me that there never were any diamonds in the office, Greville was far too security-conscious. You yourself told me the diamonds were intended for you, which I didn't know until I came here. Everyone in the office knew I was looking for diamonds, and at that point Jason must have told you I was looking for them, which informed you that I didn't know where they were.'

He watched my face with his mouth slightly open, no longer denying, showing only the stunned disbelief of the profoundly found out.

'The office staff grew to know I was a jockey,' I said, 'and Jason behaved to me with an insolence I thought inappropriate, but I now think his arrogance was the result of his having had me face down on the ground under his foot. He couldn't crow about that, but his belief in his superiority was stamped all over him. I asked the office staff not to unsettle the customers by telling them that they were now trading with a jockey not a gemmologist, but I think it's certain that Jason told *you*.'

'What makes you think that?' He didn't say it hadn't happened.

'You couldn't get into Greville's house to search it,' I

said, 'because it's a fortress. You couldn't swing any sort of wrecking ball against the windows because the grilles inside made it pointless, and anyway they're wired on a direct alarm to the police station. The only way to get into that house is by key, and I had the keys. So you worked out how to get me there, and you set it up through the trainer I ride for, which is how I know you were aware I was a jockey. Apart from the staff, no one else who knew I was a jockey knew I was looking for diamonds, because I carefully didn't tell them. Come to the telephone in Greville's house for information about the diamonds, you said, and I obediently turned up, which was foolish.'

'But I never went to Greville's house . . .' he said.

'No, not you, Jason. Strong and fast in the motorcycle helmet which covered his orange hair, butting me over again just like old times. I saw him vault the gate on the way out. That couldn't have been you. He turned the house upside down but the police didn't think he'd found what he was looking for, and I'm sure he didn't.'

'Why not?' he asked, and then said, 'That's to say . . .'

'Did you mean Jason to kill me?' I asked flatly.

'No! Of course not!' The idea seemed genuinely to shock him.

'He could have done,' I said.

'I'm not a murderer!' His indignation, as far as I could tell, was true and without reservation, quite different from his reaction to my calling him a thief.

'What were you doing two days ago, on Sunday afternoon?' I said.

'What?' He was bewildered by the question but not alarmed.

'Sunday afternoon,' I said.

'What about Sunday afternoon? What are you talking about?'

I frowned. 'Never mind. Go back to Saturday night. To Jason giving me concussion with half a brick.'

The knowledge of that was plain to read. We were again on familiar territory.

'You can kill people,' I said, 'hitting them with bricks.'

'But he said . . .' He stopped dead.

'You might as well go on,' I said reasonably, 'we both know that what I've said is what happened.'

'Yes, but . . . what are you going to do about it?'

'I don't know yet.'

'I'll deny everything.'

'What did Jason say about the brick?'

He gave a hopeless little sigh. 'He said he knew how to knock people out for half an hour. He'd seen it done in street riots, he said, and he'd done it himself. He said it depended on where you hit.'

'You can't time it,' I objected.

'Well, that's what he said.'

He hadn't been so wrong, I supposed. I'd beaten his estimate by maybe ten minutes, not more.

'He said you'd be all right afterwards,' Pross said.

'He couldn't be sure of that.'

'But you are, aren't you?' There seemed to be a tinge of regret that I hadn't emerged punch drunk and unable to hold the present conversation. Callous and irresponsible, I thought, and unforgivable, really. Greville had forgiven treachery; and which was worse?

'Jason knew which office window to break,' I said, 'and he came down from the roof. The police found marks up there.' I paused. 'Did he do that alone, or were you with him?'

'Do you expect me to tell you?' he said incredulously.

'Yes, I do. Why not? You know what plea bargaining is, you just tried it with five diamonds.'

He gave me a shattered look and searched his common sense; not that he had much of it, when one considered.

Eventually, without shame, he said, 'We both went.'

'When?'

'That Sunday. Late afternoon. After he brought Grev's things back from Ipswich and they were a waste of time.'

'You found out which hospital Greville was in,' I said, 'and you sent Jason to steal his things because you believed they would include the diamonds which Greville had told you he had with him, is that right?'

He rather miserably nodded. 'Jason phoned me from the hospital on the Saturday and said Grev wasn't dead yet but that this brother had turned up, some frail old creature on crutches, and it was good because he'd be an easy mark . . . which you were.'

'Yes.'

He looked at me and repeated, 'Frail old creature,' and faintly smiled, and I remembered his surprise at my physical appearance when I'd first come into this room. Jason, I supposed, had seen only my back view and mostly at a distance. I certainly hadn't noticed anyone lurking, but I probably wouldn't at the time have noticed half a ship's company standing at attention. Being with the dying, seeing the death, had made ordinary life seem unreal and unimportant, and it had taken me until hours after Jason's attack to lose that feeling altogether.

'All right,' I said, 'so Jason came back empty-handed. What then?'

He shrugged. 'I thought I'd probably got it wrong. Grev couldn't have meant that he had the diamonds with him.' He frowned. 'I thought that was what he said, though.'

I enlightened him. 'Greville was on his way to Harwich to meet a diamond cutter coming from Antwerp by ferry, who was bringing your diamonds with him. Twelve tear drops and eight stars.'

'Oh.' His face cleared momentarily with pleasure but gloom soon returned. 'Well, I thought it was worth looking in his office, though Jason said he never kept anything valuable there. But for diamonds . . . so many diamonds . . . it was worth a chance. Jason didn't take much persuading. He's a violent young bugger . . .'

I wondered fleetingly if that description mightn't be positively and scatologically accurate.

'So you went up to the roof in the service lift,' I said, 'and swung some sort of pendulum at the packing room window.'

He shook his head. 'Jason brought grappling irons and a rope ladder and climbed down that to the window, and broke the glass with a baseball bat. Then when he was inside I threw the hooks and the ladder down into the yard, and went down in the lift to the eighth floor, and Jason let me in through the staff door. But we couldn't get into the stock-rooms because of Grev's infernal electronic locks or into the showroom, same reason. And that vault . . . I wanted to try to beat it open with the bat but Jason said the door is six inches thick.' He shrugged. 'So we had to make do with papers . . . and we couldn't find anything about diamonds. Jason got angry . . . we made quite a mess.'

'Mm.'

'And it was all a waste of time. Jason said what we really needed was something called a Wizard, but we couldn't find that either. In the end, we simply left. I gave up. Grev had been too careful. I got resigned to not having the diamonds unless I paid for them. Then Jason said you were hunting high and low for them, and I got interested again. Very. You can't blame me.'

I could and did, but I didn't want to switch off the fountain.

'And then,' he said, 'like you guessed, I inveigled you into Grev's garden, and Jason had been waiting ages there getting furious you took so long. He let his anger out on the house, he said.'

'He made a mess there too, yes.'

'Then you woke up and set the alarms off and Jason said he was getting right nervous by then and he wasn't going to wait around for the handcuffs. So Grev had beaten us again . . . and he's beaten you too, hasn't he?' He looked at me shrewdly. 'You haven't found the diamonds either.'

I didn't answer him. I said, 'When did Jason break into Greville's car?'

'Well . . . when he finally found it in Greville's road. I'd looked for it at the hotel and round about in Ipswich, but Grev must have hired a car to drive there because his own car won't start.'

'When did you discover that?'

'Saturday. If the diamonds had been in it, we wouldn't have needed to search the house.'

'He wouldn't have left a fortune in the street,' I said.

Pross shook his head resignedly. 'You'd already looked there, I suppose.'

'I had.' I considered him. 'Why Ipswich?' I said.

'What?'

'Why the Orwell Hotel at Ipswich, particularly? Why did he want you to go there?'

'No idea,' he said blankly. 'He didn't say. He'd often ask me to meet him in odd places. It was usually because he'd found some heirloom or other and wanted to know if the stones would be of use to me. An ugly old tiara once, with a boring yellow diamond centrepiece filthy from neglect. I had the stone recut and set it as the crest of a rock crystal bird and hung it in a golden cage . . . it's in Florida, in the sun.'

I was shaken with the pity of it. So much soaring priceless imagination and such grubby, perfidious greed.

I said, 'Had he found you a stone in Ipswich?'

'No. He told me he'd asked me to come there because he didn't want us to be interrupted. Somewhere quiet, he said. I suppose it was because he was going to Harwich.'

I nodded. I supposed so also, though it wasn't on the most direct route which was further south, through Colchester. But Ipswich was where Greville had chosen, by freak mischance.

I thought of all Pross had told me, and was struck by one unexplored and dreadful possibility.

'When the scaffolding fell,' I said slowly, 'when you ran across the road and found Greville lethally injured . . . when he was lying there bleeding with the metal bar in him . . . did you steal his wallet?'

Pross's little-boy face crumpled and he put up his hands to cover it as if he would weep. I didn't believe in the tears and the remorse. I couldn't bear him any longer. I stood up to go.

'You thought he might have diamonds in his wallet,' I said bitterly. 'And then, even then, when he was dying, you were ready to rob him.'

He said nothing. He in no way denied it.

I felt such anger on Greville's behalf that I wanted suddenly to hurt and punish the man before me with a ferocity I wouldn't have expected in myself, and I stood there trembling with the self-knowledge and the essential restraint, and felt my throat close over any more words.

Without thinking, I put my left foot down to walk out and felt the pain as an irrelevance, but then after three steps used the crutches to make my way to his doorway and round the screen into the shop and through there out onto the pavement, and I wanted to yell and scream at the bloody injustice of Greville's death and the wickedness of the world and call down the rage of angels.

CHAPTER SEVENTEEN

I stood blindly on the pavement oblivious to the passers-by finding me an obstacle in their way. The swamping tidal wave of fury and desolation swelled and broke and gradually ebbed, leaving me still shaking from its force, a tornado in the spirit.

I loosened a jaw I hadn't realized was clamped tight shut and went on feeling wretched.

A grandmotherly woman touched my arm and said, 'Do you need help?' and I shook my head at her kindness because the help I needed wasn't anyone's to give. One had to heal from the inside: to knit like bones.

'Are you all right?' she asked again, her eyes concerned.

'Yes.' I made an effort. 'Thank you.'

She looked at me uncertainly, but finally moved on, and I took a few sketchy breaths and remembered with bathos that I needed a telephone if I were ever to move from that spot.

A hairdressing salon having (for a consideration) let me use their instrument, Brad came within five minutes to pick me up. I shoved the crutches into the back and climbed wearily in beside him, and he said, 'Where to?' giving me a repeat of the grandmotherly solicitude in his face if not his words.

'Uh,' I said. 'I don't know.'

'Home?'

'No . . .' I gave it a bit of thought. I had intended to go to Greville's house to change into my suit that was hanging in his wardrobe before meeting Clarissa at seven, and it still seemed perhaps the best thing to do, even if my energy for the project had evaporated.

Accordingly we made our way there, which wasn't far, and when Brad stopped outside the door, I said, 'I think I'll sleep here tonight. This house is as safe as anywhere. So you can go on to Hungerford now, if you like.'

He didn't look as if he liked, but all he said was, 'I come back tomorrow?'

'Yes, please,' I agreed.

'Pick you up. Take you to the office?'

'Yes, please.'

He nodded, seemingly reassured that I still needed him. He got out of the car with me and opened the gate, brought my overnight bag and came in with me to see, upstairs and down, that the house was safely empty of murderers and thieves. When he'd departed I checked that all the alarms were switched on and went up to Greville's room to change.

I borrowed another of his shirts and a navy silk tie,

and shaved with his electric razor which was among the things I'd picked up from the floor and had put on his white chest of drawers, and brushed my hair with his brushes for the same reason, and thought with an odd frisson that all of these things were mine now, that I was in his house, in his room, in his clothes . . . in his life.

I put on my own suit, because his anyway were too long, and came across the tube of the baster, still there in an inner breast pocket. Removing it, I left it among the jumble on the dressing chest and checked in the looking glass on the wall that Franklin, Mark II, wouldn't entirely disgrace Franklin, Mark I. He had looked in that mirror every day for three months, I supposed. Now his reflection was my reflection and the man that was both of us had dark marks of tiredness under the eyes and a taut thinness in the cheeks, and looked as if he could do with a week's lying in the sun. I gave him a rueful smile and phoned for a taxi, which took me to Luigi's with ten minutes to spare.

She was there before me all the same, sitting at a small table in the bar area to one side of the restaurant, with an emptyish glass looking like vodka on a prim mat in front of her. She stood up when I went in and offered me a cool cheek for a polite social greeting, inviting me with a gesture to sit down.

'What will you drink?' she asked formally, but battling, I thought, with an undercurrent of diffidence.

I said I would pay for our drinks and she said no, no, this was her suggestion. She called the waiter and said,

'Double water?' to me with a small smile and when I nodded ordered Perrier with ice and fresh lime-juice for both of us.

I was down by then to only two or three Distalgesics a day and would soon have stopped taking them, though the one I'd just swallowed in Greville's house was still an inhibitor for the evening. I wondered too late which would have made me feel better, a damper for the ankle or a large scotch everywhere else.

Clarissa was wearing a blue silk dress with a double-strand pearl necklace, pearl, sapphire and diamond ear-rings and a sapphire and diamond ring. I doubted if I would have noticed those, in the simple old jockey days. Her hair, smooth as always, curved in the expensive cut and her shoes and handbag were quiet black calf. She looked as she was, a polished, well-bred woman of forty or so, nearly beautiful, slender, with generous eyes.

'What have you been doing since Saturday?' she asked, making conversation.

'Peering into the jaws of death. What have you?'

'We went to . . .' She broke off. '*What* did you say?'

'Martha and Harley Ostermeyer and I were in a car crash on Sunday. They're OK, they went back to America today, I believe. And I, as you see, am here in one piece. Well . . . almost one piece.'

She was predictably horrified and wanted to hear all the details, and the telling at least helped to evaporate any awkwardness either of us had been feeling at the meeting.

'Simms was *shot*?'

'Yes.'

'But . . . do the police know who did it?'

I shook my head. 'Someone in a large grey Volvo, they think, and there are thousands of those.'

'Good heavens.' She paused. 'I didn't like to comment, but you look . . .' She hesitated, searching for the word.

'Frazzled?' I suggested.

'Smooth.' She smiled. 'Frazzled underneath.'

'It'll pass.'

The waiter came to ask if we would be having dinner and I said yes, and no argument, the dinner was mine. She accepted without fuss, and we read the menus.

The fare was chiefly Italian, the decor cosmopolitan, the ambience faintly European tamed by London. A lot of dark red, lamps with glass shades, no wallpaper music. A comfortable place, nothing dynamic. Few diners yet, as the hour was early.

It was not, I was interested to note, a habitual rendezvous place for Clarissa and Greville: none of the waiters treated her as a regular. I asked her about it and, startled, she said they had been there only two or three times, always for lunch.

'We never went to the same place often,' she said. 'It wouldn't have been wise.'

'No.'

She gave me a slightly embarrassed look. 'Do you disapprove of me and Greville?'

'No,' I said again. 'You gave him joy.'

'Oh.' She was comforted and pleased. She said with a certain shyness, 'It was the first time I'd fallen in love. I suppose you'll think that silly. But it was the first time for him, too, he said. It was . . . truly *wonderful.* We were like . . . as if twenty years younger . . . I don't know if I can explain. Laughing. Lit up.'

'As far as I can see,' I said, 'the thunderbolt strikes at any age. You don't have to be teenagers.'

'Has it . . . struck you?'

'Not since I was seventeen and fell like a ton of bricks for a trainer's daughter.'

'What happened?'

'Nothing much. We laughed a lot. Slept together, a bit clumsily at first. She married an old man of twenty-eight. I went to college.'

'I met Henry when I was eighteen. He fell in love with me . . . pursued me . . . I was flattered . . . and he was so very good looking . . . and kind.'

'He still is,' I said.

'He'd already inherited his title. My mother was ecstatic . . . she said the age difference didn't matter . . . so I married him.' She paused. 'We had a son and a daughter, both grown up now. It hasn't been a bad life, but before Greville, incomplete.'

'A better life than most,' I said, aiming to comfort.

'You're very like Greville,' she said unexpectedly. 'You look at things straight, in the same way. You've his sense of proportion.'

'We had realistic parents.'

'He didn't speak about them much, only that he became interested in gemstones because of the museums his mother took him to. But he lived in the present and he looked outward, not inward, and I loved him to distraction and in a way I didn't know him . . .' She stopped and swallowed and seemed determined not to let emotion intrude further.

'He was like that with me too,' I said. 'With everyone, I think. It didn't occur to him to give running commentaries on his actions and feelings. He found everything else more interesting.'

'I do miss him,' she said.

'What will you eat?' I asked.

She gave me a flick of a look and read the menu without seeing it for quite a long time. In the end she said with a sigh, 'You decide.'

'Did Greville?'

'Yes.'

'If I order fried zucchini as a starter, then fillet steak in pepper sauce with linguine tossed in olive oil with garlic, will that do?'

'I don't like garlic. I like everything else. Unusual. Nice.'

'OK. No garlic.'

We transferred to the dining room before seven-thirty and ate the proposed programme, and I asked if she were returning to York that night: if she had a train to catch, if that was why we were eating early.

'No, I'm down here for two nights. Tomorrow I'm going to an old friend's wedding, then back to York on Thursday morning.' She concentrated on twirling linguine onto her fork. 'When Henry and I come to London together we always stay at the Selfridge Hotel, and when I come alone I stay there also. They know us well there. When I'm there alone they don't present me with an account, they send it to Henry.' She ate the forkful of linguine. 'I tell him I go to the cinema and eat in snack bars . . . and he knows I'm always back in the hotel before midnight.'

There was a good long stretch of time between this dinner and midnight.

I said, 'Every five weeks or so, when you came down to London alone, Greville met you at King's Cross, isn't that right, and took you to lunch?'

She said in surprise, 'Did he tell you?'

'Not face to face. Did you ever see that gadget of his, the Wizard?'

'Yes, but . . .' She was horrified. 'He surely didn't put me in it?'

'Not by name, and only under a secret password. You're quite safe.'

She twiddled some more with the pasta, her eyes down, her thoughts somewhere else.

'After lunch,' she said, with pauses, 'if I had appointments, I'd keep them, or do some shopping . . . something to take home. I'd register at the hotel and change, and go to Greville's house. He used to have the flat, of course, but the house was much better. When he came, we'd have drinks . . . talk . . . maybe make love. We'd go to dinner early, then back to his house.' Her voice stopped. She still didn't look up.

I said, 'Do you want to go to his house now, before midnight?'

After a while, she said, 'I don't know.'

'Well . . . would you like coffee?'

She nodded, still not meeting my eyes, and pushed the linguine away. We sat in silence while waiters took away the plates and poured into cups, and if she couldn't make up her mind, nor could I.

In the end I said, 'If you like, come to Greville's house now. I'm sleeping there tonight, but that's not a factor. Come if you like, just to be near him, to be with him as much as you can for maybe the last time. Lie on his bed. Weep for him. I'll wait for you downstairs . . . and take you safely to your hotel before the fairy coach changes back to a pumpkin.'

'Oh!' She turned what had been going to be a sob into almost a laugh. 'Can I really?'

'Whenever you like.'

'Thank you, then. Yes.'

'I'd better warn you,' I said, 'it's not exactly tidy.' I told her what she would find, but she was inconsolable at the sight of the reality.

'He would have hated this,' she said. 'I'm so glad he didn't see it.'

We were in the small sitting room, and she went

round picking up the pink and brown stone bears, restoring them to their tray.

'I gave him these,' she said. 'He loved them. They're rhodonite, he said.'

'Take them to remember him by. And there's a gold watch you gave him, if you'd like that too.'

She paused with the last bear in her hand and said, 'You're very kind to me.'

'It's not difficult. And he'd have been furious with me if I weren't.'

'I'd love the bears. You'd better keep the watch, because of the engraving.'

'OK,' I said.

'I think,' she said with diffidence, 'I'll go upstairs now.'

I nodded.

'Come with me,' she said.

I looked at her. Her eyes were wide and troubled, but not committed, not hungry. Undecided. Like myself.

'All right,' I said.

'Is there chaos up there too?'

'I picked some of it up.'

She went up the stairs ahead of me at about four times my speed, and I heard her small moan of distress at the desecration of the bedroom. When I joined her, she was standing forlornly looking around, and with naturalness she turned to me and put her arms loosely round my waist, laying her head on my shoulder. I shed the confounded crutches and hugged her tight in grief for her and for Greville and we stood there for a long minute in mutual and much needed comfort.

She let her arms fall away and went over to sit on the bed, smoothing a hand over the black and white chequer-board counterpane.

'He was going to change this room,' she said. 'All this drama . . .' She waved a hand at the white furniture, the black carpet, one black wall . . . 'It came with the house. He wanted me to choose something softer, that I would like. But this is how I'll always remember it.'

She lay down flat, her head on the pillows, her legs toward the foot of the bed, ankles crossed. I half-hopped, half-limped across the room and sat on the edge beside her.

She watched me with big eyes. I put my hand flat on her stomach and felt the sharp internal contraction of muscles.

'Should we do this?' she said.

'I'm not Greville.'

'No . . . Would he mind?'

'I shouldn't think so.' I moved my hand, rubbing a little. 'Do you want to go on?'

'Do you?'

'Yes,' I said.

She sat up fast and put her arms round my neck in a sort of released compulsion.

'I do want this,' she said. 'I've wanted it all day. I've been pretending to myself, telling myself I shouldn't, but yes, I do want this passionately, and I know you're not Greville, I know it will be different, but this is the only way I can love him . . . and can you bear it, can you understand it, if it's him I love?'

I understood it well, and I minded not at all.

I said, smiling, 'Just don't *call* me Greville. It would be the turn-off of the century.'

She took her face away from the proximity of my ear and looked me in the eyes, and her lips too, after a moment, were smiling.

'Derek,' she said deliberately, 'make love to me. Please.'

'Don't beg,' I said.

I put my mouth on hers and took my brother's place.

As a memorial service it was quite a success. I lay in the dark laughing in my mind at that disgraceful pun, wondering whether or not to share it with Clarissa.

The catharsis was over, and her tears. She lay with her head on my chest, lightly asleep, contented, as far as I could tell, with the substitute loving. Women said men were not all the same in the dark, and I knew both where I'd surprised her and failed her, known what I'd done like Greville and not done like Greville from the instinctive releases and tensions of her reactions.

Greville, I now knew, had been a lucky man, though whether he had himself taught her how to give exquisite pleasure was something I couldn't quite ask. She knew, though, and she'd done it, and the feeling of her featherlight tattooing fingers on the base of my spine at the moment of climax had been a revelation. Knowledge marched on, I thought. Next time, with anyone else, I'd know what to suggest.

Clarissa stirred and I turned my wrist over, seeing the fluorescent hands of my watch.

'Wake up,' I said affectionately. 'It's Cinderella time.'

'Ohh . . .'

I stretched out a hand and turned on a bedside light. She smiled at me sleepily, no doubts remaining.

'That was all right,' she said.

'Mm. Very.'

'How's the ankle?'

'What ankle?'

She propped herself on one elbow, unashamed of nakedness, and laughed at me. She looked younger and sweeter, and I was seeing, I knew, what Greville had seen, what Greville had loved.

'Tomorrow,' she said, 'my friend's wedding will be over by six or so. Can I come here again?' She put her fingers lightly on my mouth to stop me answering at once. 'This time was for him,' she said. 'Tomorrow for us. Then I'll go home.'

'For ever?'

'Yes, I think so. What I had with Greville was unforgettable and unrepeatable. I decided on the train coming down here that whatever happened with you, or didn't happen, I would live with Henry, and do my best there.'

'I could easily love you,' I said.

'Yes, but don't.'

I knew she was right. I kissed her lightly.

'Tomorrow for us,' I agreed. 'Then goodbye.'

When I went into the office in the morning, Annette told me crossly that Jason hadn't turned up for work, nor had he telephoned to say he was ill.

Jason had been prudent, I thought. I'd have tossed him down the lift shaft, insolence, orange hair and all, given half an ounce of provocation.

'He won't be coming back,' I said, 'so we'll need a replacement.'

She was astonished. 'You can't sack him for not turning up. You can't sack him for anything without paying compensation.'

'Stop worrying,' I said, but she couldn't take that advice.

June came zooming into Greville's office waving a tabloid newspaper and looking at me with wide incredulous eyes.

'Did you know you're in the paper? Lucky to be alive, it says here. You didn't say anything about it!'

'Let's see,' I said, and she laid the *Daily Sensation* open on the black desk.

There was a picture of the smash in which one could more or less see my head inside the Daimler, but not recognizably. The headline read: 'Driver shot, jockey lives', and the piece underneath listed the lucky-to-be-alive passengers as Mr and Mrs Ostermeyer of Pittsburgh, America, and ex-champion steeplechase jockey Derek Franklin. The police were reported to be interested in a grey Volvo seen accelerating from the scene, and also to have recovered two bullets from the bodywork of the Daimler. After that titbit came a rehash of the Hungerford massacre and a query, 'Is this a copycat killing?' and finally a picture of Simms looking happy: 'Survived by wife and two daughters who were last night being comforted by relatives'.

Poor Simms. Poor family. Poor every shot victim in Hungerford.

'It happened on Sunday,' June exclaimed, 'and you came here on Monday and yesterday as if nothing was wrong. No wonder you looked knackered.'

'June!' Annette disapproved of the word.

'Well, he did. Still does.' She gave me a critical, kindly, motherly-sister inspection. 'He could have been killed, and then what would we all have done here?'

The dismay in Annette's face was a measure, I supposed, of the degree to which I had taken over. The place no longer felt like a quicksand to me either and I was beginning by necessity to get a feel of its pulse.

But there was racing at Cheltenham that day. I turned the pages of the newspaper and came to the runners and riders. That was where my name belonged, not on Saxony Franklin cheques. June looked over my shoulder and understood at least something of my sense of exile.

'When you go back to your own world,' she said, rephrasing her thought and asking it seriously, 'what will we do here?'

'We have a month,' I said. 'It'll take me that time to get fit.' I paused. 'I've been thinking about that problem, and, er, you might as well know, both of you, what I've decided.'

They both looked apprehensive, but I smiled to reassure them.

'What we'll do,' I said, 'is this. Annette will have a new title, which will be Office Manager. She'll run things generally and keep the keys.'

She didn't look displeased. She repeated 'Office Manager' as if trying it on for size.

I nodded. 'Then I'll start looking from now on for a business expert, someone to oversee the cash flow and do the accounts and try to keep us afloat. Because it's going to be a struggle, we can't avoid that.'

They both looked shocked and disbelieving. Cash flow seemed never to have been a problem before.

'Greville did buy diamonds,' I said regretfully, 'and so far we are only in possession of a quarter of them. I can't find out what happened to the rest. They cost the firm altogether one and a half million dollars, and we'll still owe the bank getting on for three-quarters of that sum when we've sold the quarter we have.'

Their mouths opened in unhappy unison.

'Unless and until the other diamonds turn up,' I said, 'we have to pay interest on the loan and persuade the bank that somehow or other we'll climb out of the hole. So we'll want someone we'll call the Finance Manager, and we'll pay him out of part of what used to be Greville's own salary.'

They began to understand the mechanics, and nodded.

'Then,' I said, 'we need a gemmologist who has a feeling for stones and understands what the customers like and need. There's no good hoping for another Greville, but we will create the post of Merchandise Manager, and that,' I looked at her, 'will be June.'

She blushed a fiery red. 'But I can't . . . I don't know enough.'

'You'll go on courses,' I said. 'You'll go to trade fairs. You'll travel. You'll do the buying.'

I watched her expand her horizons abruptly and saw the sparkle appear in her eyes.

'She's too young,' Annette objected.

'We'll see,' I said, and to June I added, 'You know what sells. You and the Finance Manager will work together to make us the best possible profit. You'll still work the computer, and teach Lily or Tina how to use it for when you're away.'

'Tina,' she said, 'she's quicker.'

'Tina, then.'

'What about you?' she asked.

'I'll be General Manager. I'll come when I can, at

least twice a week for a couple of hours. Everyone will tell me what's going on and we will all decide what is best to be done, though if there's a disagreement I'll have the casting vote. Right or wrong will be my responsibility, not yours.'

Annette, nevertheless troubled, said, 'Surely you yourself will need Mr Franklin's salary.'

I shook my head. 'I earn enough riding horses. Until we're solvent here, we need to save every penny.'

'It's an adventure!' June said, enraptured.

I thought it might be a very long haul and even in the end impossible, but I couldn't square it with the consciousness of Greville all around me not to try.

'Well,' I said, putting a hand in a pocket and bringing out a twist of gauze, 'we have here five uncut diamonds which cost about seventy-five thousand dollars altogether.'

They more or less gasped.

'How do we sell them?' I said.

After a pause, Annette said, 'Interest a diamantaire.'

'Do you know how to do that?'

After another moment's hesitation, she nodded.

'We can give provenance,' I said. 'Copies of the records of the original sale are on their way here from Guy Servi in Antwerp. They might be here tomorrow. Sight-box number and so on. We'll put these stones in the vault until the papers arrive, then you can get cracking.'

She nodded, but fearfully.

'Cheer up,' I said. 'It's clear from the ledgers that Saxony Franklin is normally a highly successful and profitable business. We'll have to cut costs where we can, that's all.'

'We could cut out Jason's salary,' Annette said unexpectedly. 'Half the time Tina's been carrying the heavy boxes, anyway, and I can do the hoovering myself.'

'Great,' I said with gratitude. 'If you feel like that, we'll succeed.'

The telephone rang and Annette answered it briefly.

'A messenger has left a packet for you down at the front desk,' she said.

'I'll go for it,' June said, and was out of the door on the words, returning in her usual short time with a brown padded jiffy bag, not very large, addressed simply to Derek Franklin in neat handwriting, which she laid before me with a flourish.

'Mind it's not a bomb,' she said facetiously as I picked it up, and I thought with an amount of horror that it was a possibility I hadn't thought of.

'I didn't mean it,' she said teasingly, seeing me hesitate. 'Do you want me to open it?'

'And get your hands blown off instead?'

'Of course it's not a bomb,' Annette said uneasily.

'Tell you what,' June said, 'I'll fetch the shears from the packing room.' She was gone for a few seconds. 'Alfie says,' she remarked, returning, 'we ought to put it in a bucket of water.'

She gave me the shears, which were oversized scissors that Alfie used for cutting cardboard, and for all her disbelief she and Annette backed away across the room while I sliced the end off the bag.

There was no explosion. Complete anti-climax. I shook out the contents which proved to be two objects and one envelope.

One of the objects was the microcassette recorder that I'd left on Prospero Jenks's workbench in my haste to be gone.

The other was a long black leather wallet almost the size of the Wizard, with gold initials G.S.F. in one corner and an ordinary brown rubber band holding it shut.

'That's Mr Franklin's,' Annette said blankly, and June, coming to inspect it, nodded.

I peeled off the rubber band and laid the wallet open on the desk. There was a business card lying loose inside it with Prospero Jenks's name and shops on the front, and on the reverse the single word, 'Sorry.'

'Where did he get Mr Franklin's wallet from?' Annette asked, puzzled, looking at the card.

'He found it,' I said.

'He took his time sending it back,' June said tartly.

'Mm.'

The wallet contained a Saxony Franklin chequebook, four credit cards, several business cards and a small pack of banknotes, which I guessed were fewer in number than when Greville set out.

The small excitement over, Annette and June went off to tell the others the present and future state of the nation, and I was alone when I opened the envelope.

CHAPTER EIGHTEEN

Pross had sent me a letter and a certified bank draft: instantly cashable money.

I blinked at the numbers on the cheque and reread them very carefully. Then I read the letter.

It said:

Derek,

This is a plea for a bargain, as you more or less said. The cheque is for the sum I agreed with Grev for the twelve tear drops and eight stars. I know you need the money, and I need those stones.

Jason won't be troubling you again. I'm giving him a job in one of my workrooms.

Grev wouldn't have forgiven the brick, though he might the wallet. For you it's the other way round. You're very like him. I wish he hadn't died.

Pross.

What a mess, I thought. I did need the money, yet if I accepted it I was implicitly agreeing not to take any action against him. The trouble about taking action against him was that however much I might want to I didn't know that I could. Apart from difficulties of evidence, I had more or less made a bargain that for information he would get inaction, but that had been before the wallet. It was perceptive of him, I thought, to see that it was betrayal and attacks on our *brother* that would anger both Greville and me most.

Would Greville want me to extend, if not forgiveness, then at least suspended revenge? Would Greville want me to confirm his forgiveness or to rise up in wrath and tear up the cheque . . .

In the midst of these sombre squirrelling thoughts the telephone rang and I answered it.

'Elliot Trelawney here,' the voice said.

'Oh, hello.'

He asked me how things were going and I said life was full of dilemmas. Ever so, he said with a chuckle.

'Give me some advice,' I said on impulse, 'as a magistrate.'

'If I can, certainly.'

'Well. Listen to a story, then say what you think.'

'Fire away.'

'Someone knocked me out with a brick . . .' Elliot made protesting noises on my behalf, but I went on, 'I know now who it was, but I didn't then, and I didn't see his face because he was masked. He wanted to steal a particular thing from me, but although he made a mess in the house searching, he didn't find it, and so didn't rob me of anything except consciousness. I guessed later who it was, and I challenged another man with having sent him to attack me. That man didn't deny it to me, but he said he would deny it to anyone else. So . . . what do I do?'

'Whew.' He pondered. 'What do you want to do?'

'I don't know. That's why I need the advice.'

'Did you report the attack to the police at the time?'

'Yes.'

'Have you suffered serious after-effects?'

'No.'

'Did you see a doctor?'

'No.'

He pondered some more. 'On a practical level you'd find it difficult to get a conviction, even if the prosecution service would bring charges of actual bodily harm. You couldn't swear to the identity of your assailant if you didn't see him at the time, and as for the other man, conspiracy to commit a crime is one of the most difficult charges to make stick. As you didn't consult a doctor, you're on tricky ground. So, hard as it may seem, my advice would be that the case wouldn't get to court.'

I sighed. 'Thank you,' I said.

'Sorry not to have been more positive.'

'It's all right. You confirmed what I rather feared.'

'Fine then,' he said. 'I rang to thank you for sending the Vaccaro notes. We held the committee meeting and turned down Vaccaro's application, and now we find we needn't have bothered because on Saturday night he was arrested and charged with attempting to import illegal substances. He's still in custody, and America is asking for him to be extradited to Florida where he faces murder charges and perhaps execution. And we nearly gave him a gambling licence! Funny old world.'

'Hilarious.'

'How about our drink in The Rook and Castle?' he suggested. 'Perhaps one evening next week?'

'OK.'

'Fine,' he said. 'I'll ring you.'

I put the phone down thinking that if Vaccaro had been arrested on Saturday evening and held in custody, it was unlikely he'd shot Simms from a moving car in Berkshire on Sunday afternoon. But then, I'd never really thought he had.

Copycat. Copycat, that's what it had been.

Pross hadn't shot Simms either. Had never tried to kill me. The Peter-Pan face upon which so many emotions could be read had shown a total blank when I'd asked him what he was doing on Sunday afternoon.

The shooting of Simms, I concluded, had been random violence like the other murders in Hungerford. Pointless and vicious; malignant, lunatic and impossible to explain.

I picked up the huge cheque and looked at it. It would solve all immediate problems: pay the interest already due, the cost of cutting the diamonds and more than a fifth of the capital debt. If I didn't take it, we would no doubt sell the diamonds later to someone else, but they had been cut especially for Prospero Jenks's fantasies and might not easily fit necklaces and rings.

A plea. A bargain. A chance that the remorse was at least half real. Or was he taking me again for a sucker?

I did some sums with a calculator and when Annette came in with the day's letters I showed her my figures and the cheque and asked her what she thought.

'That's the cost price,' I pointed. 'That's the cost of cutting and polishing. That's for delivery charges. That's for loan interest and VAT. If you add those together and subtract them from the figure on this cheque, is that the sort of profit margin Greville would have asked?'

Setting prices was something she well understood, and she repeated my steps on the calculator.

'Yes,' she said finally; 'it looks about right. Not over-generous, but Mr Franklin would have seen this as a service for commission, I think. Not like the rock crystal, which he bought on spec, which had to help pay for his journeys.' She looked at me anxiously. 'You understand the difference?'

'Yes,' I said. 'Prospero Jenks says this is what he and Greville agreed on.'

'Well then,' she said, relieved, 'he wouldn't cheat you.'

I smiled with irony at her faith. 'We'd better bank this cheque, I suppose,' I said, 'before it evaporates.'

'I'll do it at once,' she declared. 'With a loan as big as you said, every minute costs us money.'

She put on her coat and took an umbrella to go out

with, as the day had started off raining and showed no signs of relenting.

It had been raining the previous night when Clarissa had been ready to leave, and I'd had to ring three times for a taxi, a problem Cinderella didn't seem to have encountered. Midnight had come and gone when the wheels had finally arrived, and I'd suggested meanwhile that I lend her Brad and my car for going to her wedding.

I didn't need to, she said. When she and Henry were in London, they were driven about by a hired car firm. The car was already ordered to take her to the wedding which was in Surrey. The driver would wait for her and return her to the hotel, and she'd better stick to the plan, she said, because the bill for it would be sent to her husband.

'I always do what Henry expects,' she said, 'then there are no questions.'

'Suppose Brad picks you up from the Selfridge after you get back?' I said, packing the little stone bears and giving them to her in a carrier. 'The forecast is lousy and if it's raining you'll have a terrible job getting a taxi at that time of day.'

She liked the idea except for Brad's knowing her name. I assured her he never spoke unless he couldn't avoid it, but I told her I would ask Brad to park somewhere near the hotel. Then she could call the car phone's number when she was ready to leave, and Brad would beetle up at the right moment and not need to know her name or ask for her at the desk.

As that pleased her, I wrote down the phone number and the car's number plate so that she would recognize the right pumpkin, and described Brad to her; going bald, a bit morose, an open-necked shirt, a very good driver.

I couldn't tell Brad's own opinion of the arrangement. When I'd suggested it in the morning on the rainy way to the office, he had merely grunted which I'd taken as preliminary assent.

When he'd brought Clarissa, I thought as I looked through the letters Annette had given me, he could go on home, to Hungerford, and Clarissa and I might walk along to the restaurant at the end of Greville's street where he could have been known but I was not, and after an early dinner we would return to Greville's bed, this time for us, and we'd order the taxi in better time . . . perhaps.

I was awoken from this pleasant daydream by the ever-demanding telephone, this time with Nicholas Loder on the other end spluttering with rage.

'Milo says you had the confounded cheek,' he said, 'to have Dozen Roses dope-tested.'

'For barbiturates, yes. He seemed very sleepy. Our vet said he'd be happier to know the horse hadn't been tranquillized for the journey before he gave him an all-clear certificate.'

'I'd never give a horse tranquillizers,' he declared.

'No, none of us really thought so,' I said pacifyingly, 'but we decided to make sure.'

'It's shabby of you. Offensive. I expect an apology.'

'I apologize,' I said sincerely enough, and thought guiltily of the further checks going on at that moment.

'That's not good enough,' Nicholas Loder said huffily.

'I was selling the horse to good owners of Milo, people I ride for,' I said reasonably. 'We all know you disapproved. In the same circumstances, confronted by a sleepy horse, you'd have done the same, wouldn't you? You'd want to be sure what you were selling.'

Weigh the merchandise, I thought. Cubic zirconia, size for size, was one point seven times heavier than diamond. Greville had carried jewellers' scales in his car on his way to Harwich, presumably to check what the *Koningin Beatrix* was bringing.

'You've behaved disgustingly,' Nicholas Loder said. 'When did you see the horse last? And when next?'

'Monday evening, last. Don't know when next. As I told you, I'm tied up a bit with Greville's affairs.'

'Milo's secretary said I'd find you in Greville's office,' he grumbled. 'You're never at home. I've got a buyer for Gemstones, I think, though you don't deserve it. Where will you be this evening, if he makes a definite offer?'

'In Greville's house, perhaps.'

'Right, I have the number. And I want a written apology from you about those dope tests. I'm so angry I can hardly be civil to you.'

He hardly was, I thought, but I was pleased enough about Gemstones. The money would go into the firm's coffers and hold off bankruptcy a little while longer. I still held the Ostermeyers' cheque for Dozen Roses, waiting for Phil Urquhart's final clearance before cashing it. The horses would make up for a few of the missing diamonds. Looking at it optimistically, saying it quickly, the millstone had been reduced to near one million dollars.

June out of habit brought me a sandwich for lunch. She was walking with an extra bounce, with unashamed excitement. Way down the line, I thought, if we made it through the crisis, what then? Would I simply sell the whole of Saxony Franklin as I'd meant or keep it and borrow against it to finance a stable, as Greville had financed the diamonds? I wouldn't hide the stable! Perhaps I would know enough by then to manage both businesses on a sound basis: I'd learned a good deal in ten days. I had also, though I found it surprising, grown fond of Greville's firm. If we saved it, I wouldn't want to let it go.

If I went on riding until solvency dawned I might be the oldest jump jockey in history . . .

Again the telephone interrupted the daydreams, and I'd barely made a start on the letters.

It was a man with a long order for cabochons and beads. I hopped to the door and yelled for June to pick up the phone and to put the order on the computer, and Alfie came along to complain we were running out of heavy duty binding tape and to ask why we'd ever needed Jason. Tina did his work in half the time without the swear words.

Annette almost with gaiety hoovered everywhere, though I thought I would soon ask Tina to do it instead. Lily came with downcast eyes to ask meekly if she could have a title also. Stock-room Manager? she suggested.

'Done!' I said with sincere pleasure; and before the day was out we had a Shipment Manager (Alfie) and an Enabling Manager (Tina), and it seemed to me that such a spirit had been released there that the enterprise was now flying. Whether the euphoria would last or not was next week's problem.

I telephoned Maarten-Pagnier in Antwerp and discussed the transit of twelve tear drops, eight stars and five fakes.

'Our customer has paid us for the diamonds,' I said. 'I'd like to be able to tell him when we could get them to him.'

'Do you want them sent direct to him, monsieur?'

'No. Here to us. We'll pass them on.' I asked if he would insure them for the journey and send them by Euro-Securo; no need to trouble his partner again personally as we did not dispute that five of the stones sent to him had been cubic zirconia. The real stones had been returned to us, I said.

'I rejoice for you, monsieur. And shall we expect a further consignment for cutting? Monsieur Franklin intended it.'

'Not at the moment, I regret.'

'Very well, monsieur. At any time, we are at your service.'

After that I asked Annette if she could find Prospero Jenks to tell him his diamonds would be coming. She ran him to earth in one of his workrooms and appeared in my doorway saying he wanted to speak to me personally.

With inner reluctance I picked up the receiver. 'Hello, Pross,' I said.

'Truce, then?' he asked.

'We've banked the cheque. You'll get the diamonds.'

'When?'

'When they get here from Antwerp. Friday, maybe.'

'Thanks.' He sounded fervently pleased. Then he said with hesitation, 'You've got some light blue topaz, each fifteen carats or more, emerald cut, glittering like water . . . can I have it? Five or six big stones, Grev said. I'll take them all.'

'Give it time,' I said, and God, I thought, what unholy nerve.

'Yes, well, but you and I need each other,' he protested.

'Symbiosis?' I said.

'What? Yes.'

It had done Greville no harm in the trade, I'd gathered, to be known as the chief supplier of Prospero Jenks. His firm still needed the cachet as much as the cash. I'd taken the money once. Could I afford pride?

'If you try to steal from me one more time,' I said, 'I not only stop trading with you, I make sure everyone knows why. Everyone from Hatton Garden to Pelikanstraat.'

'Derek!' He sounded hurt, but the threat was a dire one.

'You can have the topaz,' I said. 'We have a new gemmologist who's not Greville, I grant you, but who knows what you buy. We'll still tell you what special stones we've imported. You can tell us what you need. We'll take it step by step.'

'I thought you wouldn't!' He sounded extremely relieved. 'I thought you'd never forgive me the wallet. Your face . . .'

'I don't forgive it. Or forget. But after wars, enemies trade.'

It always happened, I thought, though cynics might mock. Mutual benefit was the most powerful of bridge-builders, even if the heart remained bitter. 'We'll see how we go,' I said again.

'If you find the other diamonds,' he said hopefully, 'I still want them.' Like a little boy in trouble, I thought, trying to charm his way out.

Disconnecting, I ruefully smiled. I'd made the same inner compromise that Greville had, to do business with the treacherous child, but not to trust him. To supply the genius in him, and look to my back.

June came winging in and I asked her to go along to the vault to look at the light blue large-stone topaz which I well remembered. 'Get to know it while it's still here. I've sold it to Prospero Jenks.'

'But I don't go into the vault,' she said.

'You do now. You'll go in there every day from now on at spare moments to learn the look and feel of the faceted stones, like I have. Topaz is slippery, for instance. Learn the chemical formulas, learn the cuts and the weights, get to know them so that if you're offered unusual faceted stones anywhere in the world, you can check them against your knowledge for probability.'

Her mouth opened.

'You're going to buy the raw materials for Prospero Jenks's museum pieces,' I said. 'You've got to learn fast.'

Her eyes stretched wide as well, and she vanished.

With Annette I finished the letters.

At four o'clock I answered the telephone yet again, and found myself talking to Phil Urquhart, whose voice sounded strained.

'I've just phoned the lab for the results of Dozen Roses's tests.' He paused. 'I don't think I believe this.'

'What's the matter?' I asked.

'Do you know what a metabolite is?'

'Only vaguely.'

'What then?' he said.

'The result of metabolism, isn't it?'

'It is,' he said. 'It's what's left after some substance or other has broken down in the body.'

'So what?'

'So,' he said reasonably, 'if you find a particular metabolite in the urine, it means a particular substance was earlier present in the body. Is that clear?'

'Like viruses produce special antibodies, so the presence of the antibodies proves the existence of the viruses?'

'Exactly,' he said, apparently relieved I understood. 'Well, the lab found a metabolite in Dozen Roses's urine. A metabolite known as benzyl ecognine.'

'Go on,' I urged, as he paused. 'What is it the metabolite *of*?'

'Cocaine,' he said.

I sat in stunned disbelieving silence.

'Derek?' he said.

'Yes.'

'Racehorses aren't routinely tested for cocaine because it isn't a stimulant. Normally a racehorse could be full of cocaine and no one would know.'

'If it isn't a stimulant,' I said, loosening my tongue, 'why give it to them?'

'If you *believed* it was a stimulant, you might. Knowing it wouldn't be tested for.'

'How could you believe it?'

'It's one of the drugs that potentiates adrenalin. I particularly asked the lab to test for all drugs like that because of what you said about adrenalin yourself. What happens with a normal adrenalin surge is that after a while an enzyme comes along to disperse some of it while much gets stored for future use. Cocaine blocks the storage uptake, so the adrenalin goes roaring round the body for much longer. When the cocaine decays, its chief metabolic product is benzyl ecognine which is what the lab found in its gas chromatograph analyser this afternoon.'

'There were some cases in America . . .' I said vaguely.

'It's still not part of a regulation dope test even there.'

'But my God,' I said blankly, 'Nicholas Loder must have known.'

'Almost certainly, I should think. You'd have to administer the cocaine very soon before the race, because its effect is short lived. One hour, an hour and a half at most. It's difficult to tell, with a horse. There's no data. And although the metabolite would appear in the blood and the urine soon after that, the metabolite itself would be detectable for probably not much longer than forty-eight hours, but with a horse, that's still a guess. We took the sample from Dozen Roses on Monday evening about fifty-two hours after he'd raced. The lab said the metabolite was definitely present, but they could make no estimate of how much cocaine had been assimilated. They told me all this very carefully. They have much more experience with humans. They say in humans the rush from cocaine is fast, lasts about forty minutes and brings little post-exhilaration depression.'

'Nice,' I said.

'In horses,' he went on, 'they think it would probably induce skittishness at once.'

I thought back to Dozen Roses's behaviour both at York and on the TV tapes. He'd certainly woken up dramatically between saddling box and starting gate.

'But,' Phil added, 'they say that at the most it might give more stamina, but not more speed. It wouldn't make the horse go faster, but just make the adrenalin push last longer.'

That might be enough sometimes, I thought. Sometimes you could feel horses 'die' under you near the finish, not from lack of ability, but from lack of perseverance, of fight. Some horses were content to be second. In them, uninhibited adrenalin might perhaps tip the balance.

Caffeine, which had the same potentiating effect, was a prohibited substance in racing.

'Why don't they test for cocaine?' I asked.

'Heaven knows,' Phil said. 'Perhaps because enough to wind up a horse would cost the doper too much to be practicable. I mean . . . more than one could be sure of winning back on a bet. But cocaine's getting cheaper, I'm told. There's more and more of it around.'

'I don't know much about drugs,' I said.

'Where have you been?'

'Not my scene.'

'Do you know what they'd call you in America?'

'What?'

'Straight,' he said.

'I thought that meant heterosexual.'

He laughed. 'That too. You're straight through and through.'

'Phil,' I said, 'what do I do?'

He sobered abruptly. 'God knows. My job ends with passing on the facts. The moral decisions are yours. All I can tell you is that some time before Monday evening Dozen Roses took cocaine into his bloodstream.'

'Via a baster?' I said.

After a short silence he said, 'We can't be sure of that.'

'We can't be sure he didn't.'

'Did I understand right, that Harley Ostermeyer picked up the tube of the baster and gave it to you?'

'That's right,' I said. 'I still have it, but like I told you, it's clean.'

'It might look clean,' he said slowly, 'but if cocaine was blown up it in powder form, there may be particles clinging.'

I thought back to before the race at York.

'When Martha Ostermeyer picked up the blue bulb end and gave it back to Rollway,' I said, 'she was brushing her fingers together afterwards . . . she seemed to be getting rid of dust from her gloves.'

'Oh glory,' Phil said.

I sighed and said, 'If I give the tube to you, can you get it tested without anyone knowing where it came from?'

'Sure. Like the urine, it'll be anonymous. I'll get the lab to do another rush job, if you want. It costs a bit more, though.'

'Get it done, Phil,' I said. 'I can't really decide anything unless I know for sure.'

'Right. Are you coming back here soon?'

'Greville's business takes so much time. I'll be back at the weekend, but I think I'll send the tube to you by carrier, to be quicker. You should get it tomorrow morning.'

'Right,' he said. 'We might get a result late tomorrow. Friday at the latest.'

'Good, and er . . . don't mention it to Milo.'

'No, but why not?'

'He told Nicholas Loder we tested Dozen Roses for tranquillizers and Nicholas Loder was on my phone hitting the roof.'

'Oh God.'

'I don't want him knowing about tests for cocaine. I mean, neither Milo nor Nicholas Loder.'

'You may be sure,' Phil said seriously, 'they won't learn it from me.'

It was the worst dilemma of all, I thought, replacing the receiver.

Was cocaine a stimulant or was it not? The racing authorities didn't think so: didn't test for it. If I believed it didn't effect speed then it was all right to sell Dozen Roses to the Ostermeyers. If I thought he wouldn't have got the race at York without help, then it wasn't all right.

Saxony Franklin needed the Ostermeyers' money.

The worst result would be that, if I banked the money and Dozen Roses never won again and Martha and Harley ever found out I knew the horse had been given cocaine, I could say goodbye to any future Gold Cups or Grand Nationals on Datepalm. They wouldn't forgive the unforgivable.

Dozen Roses had seemed to me to run gamely at York and to battle to the end. I was no longer sure. I wondered now if he'd won all his four races spaced out, as the orthopod would have described it; as high as a kite.

At the best, if I simply kept quiet, banked the money and rode Dozen Roses to a couple of respectable victories, no one would ever know. Or I could inform the Ostermeyers privately, which would upset them.

There would be precious little point in proving to the world that Dozen Roses had been given cocaine (and of course I could do it by calling for a further analysis of the urine sample taken by the officials at York) because if cocaine weren't a specifically banned substance, neither was it a normal nutrient. Nothing that was not a normal nutrient was supposed to be given to thoroughbreds racing in Britain.

If I disclosed the cocaine, would Dozen Roses be disqualified for his win at York? If he were, would Nicholas Loder lose his licence to train?

If I caused so much trouble, I would be finished in racing. Whistleblowers were regularly fired from their jobs.

My advice to myself seemed to be, take the money, keep quiet, hope for the best.

Coward, I thought. Maybe stupid as well.

My thoughts made me sweat.

CHAPTER NINETEEN

June, her hands full of pretty pink beads from the stock-room, said, 'What do we do about more rhodocrosite? We're running out and the suppliers in Hong Kong aren't reliable any more. I was reading in a trade magazine that a man in Germany has some of good quality. What do you think?'

'What would Greville have done?' I asked.

Annette said regretfully, 'He'd have gone to Germany to see. He'd never start buying from a new source without knowing who he was trading with.'

I said to June, 'Make an appointment, say who we are, and book an air ticket.'

They both simultaneously said, 'But . . .' and stopped.

I said mildly, 'You never know whether a horse is going to be a winner until you race it. June's going down to the starting gate.'

June blushed and went away. Annette shook her head doubtfully.

'I wouldn't know rhodocrosite from granite,' I said.

'June does. She knows its price, knows what sells. I'll trust that knowledge until she proves me wrong.'

'She's too young to make decisions,' Annette objected.

'Decisions are easier when you're young.'

Isn't that the truth, I thought wryly, rehearsing my own words. At June's age I'd been full of certainties. At June's age, what would I have done about cocaine-positive urine tests? I didn't know. Impossible to go back.

I said I would be off for the day and would see them all in the morning. Dilemmas could be shelved, I thought. The evening was Clarissa's.

Brad, I saw, down in the yard, had been reading the *Racing Post* which had the same photograph as the *Daily Sensation*. He pointed to the picture when I eased in beside him, and I nodded.

'That's your head,' he said.

'Mm.'

'Bloody hell,' he said.

I smiled. 'It seems a long time ago.'

He drove to Greville's house and came in with me while I went upstairs and put the baster tube into an envelope and then into a jiffy bag brought from the office for the purpose and addressed it to Phil Urquhart.

To Brad, downstairs again, I said, 'The Euro-Securo couriers' main office is in Oxford Street not very far from the Selfridge Hotel. This is the actual address . . .' I gave it to him. 'Do you think you can find it?'

'Yerss.' He was again affronted.

'I phoned them from the office. They're expecting this. You don't need to pay, they're sending the bill. Just get a receipt. OK?'

'Yerss.'

'Then pick up my friend from the Selfridge Hotel and bring her here. She'll phone for you, so leave it switched on.'

'Yerss.'

'Then go home, if you like.'

He gave me a glowering look but all he said was, 'Same time tomorrow?'

'If you're not bored.'

He gave me a totally unexpected grin. Unnerving, almost, to see that gloom-ridden face break up.

'Best time o' my life,' he said, and departed, leaving me literally gasping.

In bemusement, I went along to the little sitting room and tidied up a bit more of the mess. If Brad enjoyed waiting for hours reading improbable magazines it was all right by me, but I no longer felt in imminent danger of assault or death, and I could drive my car myself if I cared to, and Brad's days as bodyguard/chauffeur were numbered. He must realize it, I thought: he'd clung on to the job several times.

By that Wednesday evening there was a rapid improvement also in the ankle. Bones, as I understood it, always grew new soft tissue at the site of a fracture, as if to stick the pieces together with glue. After eight or nine days, the soft tissue began to harden, the bone getting progressively stronger from then on, and it was in that phase that I'd by then arrived. I laid one of the crutches aside in the sitting room and used the other like a walking stick, and put my left toe down to the carpet for balance if not to bear my full weight.

Distalgesic, I decided, was a thing of the past. I'd drink wine for dinner with Clarissa.

The front door bell rang, which surprised me. It was too early to be Clarissa: Brad couldn't have done the errand and got to the Selfridge and back in the time he'd been gone.

I hopped along to the door and looked through the peep-hole and was astounded to see Nicholas Loder on the doorstep. Behind him, on the path, stood his friend Rollo Rollway, looking boredly around at the small garden.

In some dismay I opened the door and Nicholas Loder immediately said, 'Oh, good. You're in. We happened to be dining in London so as we'd time to spare I thought we'd come round on the off-chance to discuss Gemstones, rather than negotiate on the telephone.'

'But I haven't named a price,' I said.

'Never mind. We can discuss that. Can we come in?' I shifted backwards reluctantly.

'Well, yes,' I said, looking at my watch. 'But not for long. I have another appointment pretty soon.'

'So have we,' he assured me. He turned round and

waved a beckoning arm to his friend. 'Come on, Rollo, he has time to see us.'

Rollway, looking as if the enterprise were not to his liking, came up the steps and into the house. I turned to lead the way along the passage, ostentatiously not closing the front door behind them as a big hint to them not to stay long.

'The room's in a mess,' I warned them over my shoulder, 'we had a burglar.'

'We?' Nicholas Loder said.

'Greville and I.'

'Oh.'

He said, 'Oh' again when he saw the chrysanthemum pot wedged in the television, but Rollway blinked around in an uninterested fashion as if he saw houses in chaos every day of the week.

Rollway at close quarters wasn't any more attractive than Rollway at a distance: a dull dark lump of a man, thickset, middle-aged and humourless. One could only explain his friendship with the charismatic Loder, I thought, in terms of trainer-owner relationship.

'This is Thomas Rollway,' Nicholas Loder said to me, making belated introductions. 'One of my owners. He's very interested in buying Gemstones.'

Rollway didn't look very interested in anything.

'I'd offer you a drink,' I said, 'but the burglar broke all the bottles.'

Nicholas Loder looked vaguely at the chunks of glass

on the carpet. There had been no diamonds in the bottles. Waste of booze.

'Perhaps we could sit down,' he said.

'Sure.'

He sat in Greville's armchair and Rollway perched on the arm of the second armchair which effectively left me the one upright hard one. I sat on the edge of it, wanting them to hurry, laying the second crutch aside.

I looked at Loder, big, light-haired with brownish eyes, full of ability and not angry with me as he had been in the recent past. It was almost with guilt that I thought of the cocaine analyses going on behind his back when his manner towards me was more normal than at any time since Greville's death. If he'd been like that from the beginning, I'd have seen no reason to have had the tests done.

'Gemstones,' he said, 'what do you want for him?'

I'd seen in the Saxony Franklin ledgers what Gemstones had cost as a yearling, but that had little bearing on his worth two years later. He'd won one race. He was no bright star. I doubled his cost and asked for that.

Nicholas Loder laughed with irony. 'Come on, Derek. Half.'

'Half is what he cost Greville originally,' I said.

His eyes narrowed momentarily and then opened innocently. 'So we've been doing our homework!' He actually smiled. 'I've promised Rollo a reasonable horse at a reasonable price. We all know Gemstones is no world-beater, but there are more races in him. His cost price is perfectly fair. More than fair.'

I thought it quite likely was indeed fair, but Saxony Franklin needed every possible penny.

'Meet me halfway,' I said, 'and he's yours.'

Nicholas raised his eyebrows at his friend for a decision. 'Rollo?'

Rollo's attention seemed to be focused more on the crutch I'd earlier propped unused against a wall rather than on the matter in hand.

'Gemstones is worth that,' Nicholas Loder said to him judiciously, and I thought in amusement that he would get me as much as he could in order to earn himself a larger commission. Trade with the enemy, I thought: build mutual-benefit bridges.

'I don't want Gemstones at any price,' Rollo said, and they were the first words he'd uttered since arriving. His voice was harsh and curiously flat, without inflection. Without emotion, I thought.

Nicholas Loder protested, 'But that's why you wanted to come here! It was your idea to come here.'

Thomas Rollway, as if absentmindedly, stood and picked up the abandoned crutch, turning it upside down and holding it by the end normally near the floor. Then, as if the thought had at that second occurred to him, he bent his knees and swung the crutch round forcefully in a scything movement a bare four inches above the carpet.

It was so totally unexpected that I wasn't quick

enough to avoid it. The elbow-rest and cuff crashed into my left ankle and Rollway came after it like a bull, kicking, punching, overbalancing me, knocking me down.

I was flabbergasted more than frightened, and then furious. It seemed senseless, without reason, unprovoked, out of any sane proportion. Over Rollway's shoulder I glimpsed Nicholas Loder looking dumbfounded, his mouth and eyes stretched open, uncomprehending.

As I struggled to get up, Thomas Rollway reached inside his jacket and produced a handgun; twelve inches of it at least, with the thickened shape of a silencer on the business end.

'Keep still,' he said to me, pointing the barrel at my chest.

A gun . . . Simms . . . I began dimly to understand and to despair pretty deeply.

Nicholas Loder was shoving himself out of his armchair. 'What are you doing?' His voice was high with alarm, with rising panic.

'Sit down, Nick,' his friend said. 'Don't get up.' And such was the grindingly heavy tone of his unemotional voice that Nicholas Loder subsided, looking overthrown, not believing what was happening.

'But you came to buy his horse,' he said weakly.

'I came to kill him.'

Rollway said it dispassionately, as if it were nothing. But then, he'd tried to before.

Loder's consternation became as deep as my own.

Rollway moved his gun and pointed it at my ankle. I immediately shifted it, trying desperately to get up, and he brought the spitting end back fast into alignment with my heart.

'Keep still,' he said again. His eyes coldly considered me as I half-sat, half-lay on the floor, propped on my elbow and without any weapon within reach, not even the one crutch I'd been using. Then, with as little warning as for his first attack, he stamped hard on my ankle and for good measure ground away with his heel as if putting out a cigarette butt. After that he left his shoe where it was, pressing down on it with his considerable weight.

I swore at him and couldn't move, and thought idiotically, feeling things give way inside there, that it would take me a lot longer now to get fit, and that took my mind momentarily off a bullet that I would feel a lot less, anyway.

'But *why*?' Nicholas Loder asked, wailing. 'Why are you doing this?'

Good question.

Rollway answered it.

'The only successful murders,' he said, 'are those for which there appears to be no motive.'

It sounded like something he'd learned on a course. Something surrealistic. Monstrous.

Nicholas Loder, sitting rigidly to my right in Greville's chair, said with an uneasy attempt at a laugh,

'You're kidding, Rollo, aren't you? This is some sort of joke?'

Rollo was not kidding. Rollo, standing determinedly on my ankle between me and the door, said to me, 'You picked up a piece of my property at York races. When I found it was missing I went back to look for it. An official told me you'd put it in your pocket. I want it back.'

I said nothing.

Damn the official, I thought. So helpful. So deadly. I hadn't even noticed one watching.

Nicholas Loder, bewildered, said, 'What piece of property?'

'The tube part of the nebulizer,' Rollway told him.

'But that woman, Mrs Ostermeyer, gave it back to you.'

'Only the bulb. I didn't notice the tube had dropped as well. Not until after the race. After the Stewards' enquiry.'

'But what does it matter?'

Rollway pointed his gun unwaveringly at where it would do me fatal damage and answered the question without taking his gaze from my face.

'You yourself, Nick,' he informed him, 'told me you were worried about Franklin, he was observant and too bright.'

'But that was because I gelded Dozen Roses.'

'So when I found he had the nebulizer, I asked one or two other people their opinion of Derek Franklin as a person, not a jockey, and they all said the same. Brainy. Intelligent. Bright.' He paused. 'I don't like that.'

I was thinking that through the door, down the passage and in the street there was sanity and Wednesday and rain and rush hour all going on as usual. Saturn was just as accessible.

'I don't believe in waiting for trouble,' Rollway said. 'And dead men can't make accusations.' He stared at me. 'Where's the tube?'

I didn't answer for various reasons. If he took murder so easily in his stride and I told him I'd sent the tube to Phil Urquhart I could be sentencing Phil to death too, and besides, if I opened my mouth for any reason, what might come out wasn't words at all but something between a yell and a groan, a noise I could hear loudly in my head but which wasn't important either, or not as important as getting out of the sickening prospect of the next few minutes.

'But he would never have suspected . . .' Loder feebly said.

'Of course he did. Anyone would. Why do you think he's had that bodyguard glued to him? Why do you think he's been dodging about so I can't find him and not going home? And he had the horse's urine taken in Lambourn for testing, and there's the official sample too at York. I tell you, I'm not waiting for him to make trouble. I'm not going to gaol, I'll tell you.'

'But you wouldn't.'

'Be your age, Nick,' Rollway said caustically, 'I import the stuff. I take the risks. And I get rid of trouble as soon as I see it. If you wait too long, trouble can destroy you.'

Nicholas Loder said in wailing protest, 'I told you it wasn't necessary to give it to horses. It doesn't make them go faster.'

'Rubbish. You can't tell, because it isn't much done. No one can afford it except people like me. I'm swamped with the stuff at the moment, it's coming in bulk from the Medellin cartel in Madrid . . . *Where's the tube?*' he finished, bouncing his weight up and down.

If not telling him would keep me alive a bit longer, I wasn't going to try telling him I'd thrown it away.

'You can't just shoot him,' Nicholas Loder said despairingly. 'Not with me watching.'

'You're no danger to me, Nick,' Rollway said flatly. 'Where would you go for your little habit? One squeak from you would mean your own ruin. I'd see you went down for possession. For conniving with me to drug horses. They'd take your licence away for that. Nicholas Loder, trainer of Classic winners, down in the gutter.' He paused. 'You'll keep quiet, we both know it.'

The threats were none the lighter for being uttered in a measured unexcited monotone. He made my hair bristle. Heaven knew what effect he had on Loder.

He wouldn't wait much longer, I thought, for me to tell him where the tube was: and maybe the tube would in the end indeed be his downfall because Phil knew whose it was, and that the Ostermeyers had been witnesses, and if I were found shot perhaps he would light a long fuse . . . but it wasn't of much comfort at that moment.

With the strength of desperation I rolled my body and with my right foot kicked hard at Rollway's leg. He grunted and took his weight off my ankle and I pulled away from him, shuffling backwards, trying to reach the chair I'd been sitting on to use it as a weapon against him, or at least not to lie there supinely waiting to be slaughtered, and I saw him recover his rocked balance and begin to straighten his arm, aiming and looking along the barrel so as not to miss.

That unmistakable stance was going to be the last thing I would see: and the last emotion I would feel would be the blazing fury of dying for so pointless a cause.

Nicholas Loder, also seeing that it was the moment of irretrievable crisis, sprang with horror from the armchair and shouted urgently, 'No, no, Rollo. No, don't do it!'

It might have been the droning of a gnat for all the notice Rollo paid him.

Nicholas Loder took a few paces forward and grabbed at Rollway and at his aiming arm.

I took the last opportunity to get my hands on something . . . anything . . . got my fingers on a crutch.

'I won't let you,' Nicholas Loder frantically persisted. 'You mustn't!'

Rollo shook him off and swung his gun back to me.

'No.' Loder was terribly disturbed. Shocked. Almost frenzied. 'It's wrong. I won't let you.' He put his body against Rollway's, trying to push him away.

Rollway shrugged him off, all bull-muscle and undeterrable. Then, very fast, he pointed the gun straight at Nicholas Loder's chest and without pausing pulled the trigger. Pulled it twice.

I heard the rapid phut, phut. Saw Nicholas Loder fall, saw the blankness on his face, the absolute astonishment.

There was no time to waste on terror, though I felt it. I gripped the crutch I'd reached and swung the heavier end of it at Rollway's right hand, and landed a blow fierce enough to make him drop the gun.

It fell out of my reach.

I stretched for it and rolled and scrambled but he was upright and much faster, and he bent down and took it into his hand again with a tight look of fury as hot as my own.

He began to lift his arm again in my direction and again I whipped at him with the crutch and again hit him. He didn't drop the gun that time but transferred it to his left hand and shook out the fingers of his right hand as if they hurt, which I hoped to God they did.

I slashed at his legs. Another hit. He retreated a couple of paces and with his left hand began to take aim. I slashed at him. The gun barrel wavered. When he pulled the trigger, the flame spat out and the bullet missed me.

He was still between me and the door.

Ankle or not, I thought, once I was on my feet I'd smash him down and out of the way and run, run . . . run into the street . . .

I had to get up. Got as far as my knees. Stood up on my right foot. Put down the left. It wasn't a matter of pain. I didn't feel it. It just buckled. It needed the crutch's help . . . and I needed the crutch to fight against his gun, to hop and shuffle forward and hack at him, to put off the inevitable moment, to fight until I was dead.

A figure appeared abruptly in the doorway, seen peripherally in my vision.

Clarissa.

I'd forgotten she was coming.

'Run,' I shouted agonizedly. 'Run. Get away.'

It startled Rollway. I'd made so little noise. He seemed to think the instructions were for himself. He sneered. I kept my eyes on his gun and lunged at it, making his aim swing wide again at a crucial second. He pulled the trigger. Flame. Phut. The bullet zipped over my shoulder and hit the wall.

'Run,' I yelled again with fearful urgency. 'Quick. Oh, be quick.'

Why didn't she run? He'd see her if he turned.

He would kill her.

Clarissa didn't run. She brought her hand out of her raincoat pocket holding a thing like a black cigar and she swung her arm in a powerful arc like an avenging fury. Out of the black tube sprang the fearsome telescopic silvery springs with a knob on the end, and the kiyoga smashed against the side of Rollway's skull.

He fell without a sound. Fell forward, cannoning into me, knocking me backwards. I ended on the floor, sitting, his inert form stomach-down over my shins.

Clarissa came down on her knees beside me, trembling violently, very close to passing out. I was breathless, shattered, trembling like her. It seemed ages before either of us was able to speak. When she could, it was a whisper, low and distressed.

'Derek . . .'

'Thanks,' I said jerkily, 'for saving my life.'

'Is he dead?' She was looking with fear at Rollway's head, strain in her eyes, in her neck, in her voice.

'I don't care if he is,' I said truthfully.

'But I . . . I hit him.'

'I'll say I did it. Don't worry. I'll say I hit him with the crutch.'

She said waveringly, 'You can't.'

'Of course I can. I meant to, if I could.'

I glanced over at Nicholas Loder, and Clarissa seemed to see him for the first time. He was on his back, unmoving.

'Dear God,' she said faintly, her face even paler. 'Who's that?'

I introduced her posthumously to Nicholas Loder, racehorse trainer, and then to Thomas Rollway, drug baron. They'd squirted cocaine into Dozen Roses, I said, struggling for lightness. I'd found them out. Rollway wanted me dead rather than giving evidence against him. He'd said so.

Neither of the men contested the charges, though Rollway at least was alive, I thought. I could feel his breathing on my legs. A pity, on the whole. I told Clarissa which made her feel a shade happier.

Clarissa still held the kiyoga. I touched her hand, brushing my fingers over hers, grateful beyond expression for her courage. Greville had given her the kiyoga. He couldn't have known it would keep me alive. I took it gently out of her grasp and let it lie on the carpet.

'Phone my car,' I said. 'If Brad hasn't gone too far, he'll come back.'

'But . . .'

'He'll take you safely back to the Selfridge. Phone quickly.'

'I can't just . . . leave you.'

'How would you explain being here, to the police?'

She looked at me in dismay and obstinacy. 'I can't . . .'

'You must,' I said. 'What do you think Greville would want?'

'Oh . . .' It was a long sigh of grief, both for my brother and, I thought, for the evening together that she and I were not now going to have.

'Do you remember the number?' I said.

'Derek . . .'

'Go and do it, my dear love.'

She got blindly to her feet and went over to the telephone. I told her the number, which she'd forgotten. When the impersonal voice of the radio-phone operator said as usual after six or seven rings that there was no reply, I asked her to dial the number again, and yet again. With luck, Brad would reckon three calls spelled emergency.

'When we got here,' Clarissa said, sounding stronger, 'Brad told me there was a grey Volvo parked not far from your gate. He was worried, I think. He asked me to tell you. Is it important?'

God in heaven . . .

'Will that phone stretch over here?' I said. 'See if it will. Push the table over. Pull the phone over here. If I ring the police from here, and they find me here, they'll take the scene for granted.'

She tipped the table on its side, letting the answering machine fall to the floor, and pulled the phone to the end of its cord. I still couldn't quite reach it, and edged round a little in order to do so, and it hurt, which she saw.

'Derek!'

'Never mind.' I smiled at her, twistedly, making a joke of it. 'It's better than death.'

'I can't leave you.' Her eyes were still strained and she was still visibly trembling, but her composure was on the way back.

'You damned well can,' I said. 'You have to. Go out to the gate. If Brad comes, get him to toot the horn, then I'll know you're away and I'll phone the police. If he doesn't come . . . give him five minutes, then walk . . . walk and get a taxi . . . Promise?'

I picked up the kiyoga and fumbled with it, trying to concertina it shut. She took it out of my hands, twisted it, banged the knob on the carpet and expertly returned it closed to her pocket.

'I'll think of you, and thank you,' I said, 'every day that I live.'

'At four-twenty,' she said as if automatically, and then paused and looked at me searchingly. 'It was the time I met Greville.'

'Four-twenty,' I said, and nodded. 'Every day.'

She knelt down again beside me and kissed me, but it wasn't passion. More like farewell.

'Go on,' I said. 'Time to go.'

She rose reluctantly and went to the doorway, pausing there and looking back. Lady Knightwood, I thought, a valiant deliverer with not a hair out of place.

'Phone me,' I said, 'one day soon?'

'Yes.'

She went quietly down the passage but wasn't gone long. Brad himself came bursting into the room with Clarissa behind him like a shadow.

Brad almost skidded to a halt, the prospect before him enough to shock even the garrulous to silence.

'Strewth,' he said economically.

'As you say,' I replied.

Rollway had dropped his gun when he fell but it still lay not far from his left hand. I asked Brad to move it further away in case the drug man woke up.

'Don't touch it,' I said sharply as he automatically reached out a hand, bending down. 'Your prints would be an embarrassment.'

He made a small grunt of acknowledgement and Clarissa wordlessly held out a tissue with which Brad gingerly took hold of the silencer and slid the gun across the room to the window.

'What if he does wake up?' he said, pointing to Rollway.

'I give him another clout with the crutch.'

He nodded as if that were normal behaviour.

'Thanks for coming back,' I said.

'Didn't go far. You've got a Volvo . . .'

I nodded.

'Is it the one?'

'Sure to be,' I said.

'Strewth.'

'Take my friend back to the Selfridge,' I said. 'Forget she was here. Forget you were here. Go home.'

'Can't leave you,' he said. 'I'll come back.'

'The police will be here.'

As ever, the thought of policemen made him uneasy.

'Go on home,' I said. 'The dangers are over.'

He considered it. Then he said hopefully, 'Same time tomorrow?'

I moved my head in amused assent and said wryly, 'Why not?'

He seemed satisfied in a profound way, and he and Clarissa went over to the doorway, pausing there and looking back, as she had before. I gave them a brief wave, and they waved back before going. They were both, incredibly, smiling.

'Brad!' I yelled after him.

He came back fast, full of instant alarm.

'Everything's fine,' I said. 'Just fine. But don't shut the front door behind you. I don't want to have to get up to let the police in. I don't want them smashing the locks. I want them to walk in here nice and easy.'

CHAPTER TWENTY

It was a long dreary evening, but not without humour.

I sat quietly apart most of the time in Greville's chair, largely ignored while relays of people came and efficiently measured, photographed, took fingerprints and dug bullets out of the walls.

There had been a barrage of preliminary questions in my direction which had ended with Rollway groaning his way back to consciousness. Although the police didn't like advice from a civilian, they did, at my mild suggestion, handcuff him before he was fully awake, which was just as well, as the bullish violence was the first part of his personality to surface. He was on his feet, threshing about, mumbling, before he knew where he was.

While a policeman on each side of him held his arms, he stared at me, his eyes slowly focusing. I was still at that time on the floor, thankful to have his weight off me. He looked as if he couldn't believe what was happening, and in the same flat uninflected voice as before, called me a bastard, among other things not as innocuous.

'I knew you were trouble,' he said. He was still too groggy to keep a rein on his tongue. 'You won't live to give evidence, I'll see to that.'

The police phlegmatically arrested him formally, told him his rights and said he would get medical attention at the police station. I watched him stumble away, thinking of the irony of the decision I'd made earlier not to accuse him of anything at all, much less, as now, of shooting people. I hadn't known he'd shot Simms. I hadn't feared him at all. It didn't seem to have occurred to him that I might not act against him on the matter of cocaine. He'd been ready to kill to prevent it. Yet I hadn't suspected him even of being a large-scale dealer until he'd boasted of it.

While the investigating activity went on around me, I wondered if it were because drug runners cared so little for the lives of others that they came so easily to murder.

Like Vaccaro, I thought, gunning down his renegade pilots from a moving car. Perhaps that was an habitual mode of clean-up among drug kings. Copycat murder, everyone had thought about Simms, and everyone had been right.

People like Rollway and Vaccaro held other people's lives cheap because they aimed anyway at destroying them. They made addiction and corruption their business, wilfully intended to profit from the collapse and unhappiness of countless lives, deliberately enticed young people onto a one-way misery trail. I'd read that people could snort cocaine for two or three years before the physical damage hit. The drug growers, shippers, wholesalers knew that. It gave them time for steady selling. Their greed had filthy feet.

The underlying immorality, the aggressive callousness had themselves to be corrupting; addictive. Rollway had self destructed, like his victims.

I wondered how people grew to be like him. I might condemn them, but I didn't understand them. They weren't happy-go-lucky dishonest, like Pross. They were uncaring and cold. As Eliot Trelawney had said, the logic of criminals tended to be weird. If I ever added to Greville's notebook, I thought, it would be something like 'The ways of the crooked are mysterious to the straight', or even 'What makes the crooked crooked and the straight straight?' One couldn't trust the sociologists' easy answers.

I remembered an old story I'd heard sometime. A scorpion asked a horse for a ride across a raging torrent. Why not? said the horse, and obligingly started to swim with the scorpion on his back. Halfway across, the scorpion stung the horse. The horse, fatally poisoned, said, 'We will both drown now. Why did you do that?' And the scorpion said, 'Because it's my nature.'

Nicholas Loder wasn't going to worry or wonder about anything any more; and his morality, under stress, had risen up unblemished and caused his death. Injustice and irony everywhere, I thought, and felt regret for the man who couldn't acquiesce in my murder.

He had taken cocaine himself, that much was clear. He'd become perhaps dependent on Rollway, had perhaps been more or less blackmailed by him into allowing his horses to be tampered with. He'd been frightened I would find him out: but in the end he hadn't been evil, and Rollway had seen it, had seen he couldn't trust him to keep his mouth shut after all.

Through Loder, Rollway had known where to find me on Sunday afternoon, and through him he'd known where to find me this Wednesday evening. Yet Nicholas Loder hadn't knowingly set me up. He'd been used by his supposed friend; and I hadn't seen any danger in reporting on Sunday morning that I'd be lunching with Milo and the Ostermeyers or saying I would be in Greville's house ready for Gemstones bids.

I hadn't specifically been keeping myself safe from Rollway, whatever he might believe, but from an unidentified enemy, someone *there* and dangerous, but unrecognized.

Irony everywhere . . .

I thought about Martha and Harley and the cocaine in Dozen Roses. I would ask them to keep the horse and race him, and I'd promise that if he never did any good I would give them their money back and send him to auction. What the Jockey Club and the racing press would have to say about the whole mess boggled the mind. We might still lose the York race: would have to, I guessed.

I thought of Clarissa in the Selfridge Hotel struggling to behave normally with a mind filled with visions of violence. I hoped she would ring up her Henry, reach back to solid ground, mourn Greville peacefully, be glad she'd saved his brother. I would leave the Wizard's alarm set to four-twenty pm, and remember them both when I heard it: and one could say it was sentimental, that their whole affair had been packed with sentimental behaviour, but who cared, they'd enjoyed it, and I would endorse it.

At some point in the evening's proceedings, a highly senior plain-clothes policeman arrived whom everyone else deferred to and called sir.

He introduced himself as Superintendent Ingold and invited a detailed statement from me, which a minion wrote down. The superintendent was short, piercing, businesslike, and considered what I said with pauses before his next question, as if internally computing my answers. He was also, usefully, a man who liked racing: who sorrowed over Nicholas Loder and knew of my existence.

I told him pretty plainly most of what had happened, omitting only a few things: the precise way Rollway had asked for his tube, and Clarissa's presence, and the dire desperation of the minutes before she'd arrived. I made that hopeless fight a lot shorter, a lot easier, a rapid knock-out.

'The crutches?' he enquired. 'What are they for?'

'A spot of trouble with an ankle at Cheltenham.'

'When was that?'

'Nearly two weeks ago.'

He merely nodded. The crutch handles were quite heavy enough for clobbering villains, and he sought no other explanation.

It all took a fair while, with the pauses and the writing. I told him about the car crash near Hungerford. I said I thought it possible that it had been Rollway who shot Simms. I said that of course they would compare the bullets the Hungerford police had taken from the Daimler with those just now dug out of Greville's walls, and those no doubt to be retrieved from Nicholas Loder's silent form. I wondered innocently what sort of car Rollway drove. The Hungerford police, I told the superintendent, were looking for a grey Volvo.

After a pause a policeman was despatched to search the street. He came back wide-eyed with his news and was told to put a cordon round the car and keep the public off.

It was by then well past dark. Every time the police or officials came into the house, the mechanical dog started barking and the lights repeatedly blazed on. I thought it amusing which says something for my light-headed state of mind but it wore the police nerves to irritation.

'The switches are beside the front door,' I said to one of them eventually. 'Why don't you flip them all up?'

They did, and got peace.

'Who threw the flower-pot into the television?' the superintendent wanted to know.

'Burglars. Last Saturday. Two of your men came round.'

'Are you ill?' he said abruptly.

'No. Shaken.'

He nodded. Anyone would be, I thought.

One of the policemen mentioned Rollway's threat that I wouldn't live to give evidence. To be taken seriously, perhaps.

Ingold looked at me speculatively. 'Does it worry you?'

'I'll try to be careful.'

He smiled faintly. 'Like on a horse?' The smile disappeared. 'You could do worse than hire someone to mind your back for a while.'

I nodded my thanks. Brad, I thought dryly, would be ecstatic.

They took poor Nicholas Loder away. I would emphasize his bravery, I thought, and save what could be saved of his reputation. He had given me, after all, a chance of life.

Eventually the police wanted to seal the sitting room, although the superintendent said it was a precaution only: the events of the evening seemed crystal clear.

He handed me the crutches and asked where I would be going.

'Upstairs to bed,' I said.

'Here?' He was surprised. 'In this house?'

'This house,' I said, 'is a fortress. Until one lowers the drawbridge, that is.'

They sealed the sitting room, let themselves out, and left me alone in the newly quiet hallway.

I sat on the stairs and felt awful. Cold. Shivery. Old and grey. What I needed was a hot drink to get warm from inside, and there was no way I was going down to the kitchen. Hot water from the bathroom tap upstairs would do fine, I thought.

As happened in many sorts of battle, it wasn't the moment of injury that was worst, but the time a couple of hours later when the body's immediate natural anaesthetic properties subsided and let pain take over: nature's marvellous system for allowing a wild animal to flee to safety before hiding to lick its wounds with healing saliva. The human animal was no different. One needed the time to escape, and one needed the pain afterwards to say something was wrong.

At the moment of maximum adrenalin, fight-or-flight, I'd believed I could run on that ankle. It had been mechanics that had defeated me, not instinct, not willingness. Two hours later, the idea of even standing on it was impossible. Movement alone became breath-taking. I'd sat in Greville's chair for another two long hours after that, concentrating on policemen, blanking out feeling.

With them gone, there was no more pretending. However much I might protest in my mind, however much rage I might feel, I knew the damage to bones and ligaments was about as bad as before. Rollway had cracked them apart again. Back to square one . . . and the Hennessy only four and a half weeks away . . . and I was bloody well going to ride Datepalm in it, and I wasn't going to tell anyone about tonight's little stamping-ground, no one knew except Rollway and he wouldn't boast about that.

If I stayed away from Lambourn for two weeks, Milo wouldn't find out; not that he would himself care all that much. If he didn't know, though, he couldn't mention it to anyone else. No one expected me to be racing again for another four weeks. If I simply stayed in London for two of those and ran Greville's business, no one would comment. Then once I could walk I'd go down to Lambourn and ride every day . . . get physiotherapy, borrow the Electrovet . . . it could be done . . . piece of cake.

Meanwhile there were the stairs.

Up in Greville's bathroom, in a zipped bag with my washing things, I would find the envelope the orthopaedic surgeon had given me, which I'd tucked into a waterproof pocket and travelled around with ever since. In the envelope, three small white tablets not as big as aspirins, more or less with my initials on: DF 1–1–8s. Only as a last resort, the orthopod had said.

Wednesday evening, I reckoned, qualified.

I went up the stairs slowly, backwards, sitting down,

hooking the crutches up with me. If I dropped them, I thought, they would slither down to the bottom again. I wouldn't drop them.

It was pretty fair hell. I reminded myself astringently that people had been known to crawl down mountains with much worse broken bones: they wouldn't have made a fuss over one little flight upwards. Anyway, there had to be an end to everything, and eventually I sat on the top step, with the crutches beside me, and thought that the DF 1–1–8s weren't going to fly along magically to my tongue. I had still got to get them.

I shut my eyes and put both hands round my ankle on top of the bandage. I could feel the heat and it was swelling again already, and there was a pulse hammering somewhere.

Damn it, I thought. God bloody damn it. I was used to this sort of pain, but it never made it any better. I hoped Rollway's head was banging like crazy.

I made it to the bathroom, ran the hot water, opened the door of the capacious medicine cabinet, pulled out and unzipped my bag.

One tablet, no pain, I thought. Two tablets, spaced out. Three tablets, unconscious.

Three tablets had definite attractions but I feared I might wake in the morning needing them again and wishing I'd been wiser. I swallowed one with a glassful of hot water and waited for miracles.

The miracle that actually happened was extraordinary but had nothing to do with the pills.

I stared at my grey face in the looking glass over the basin. Improvement, I thought after a while, was a long time coming. Perhaps the damned things didn't work.

Be patient.

Take another . . .

No. Be patient.

I looked vaguely at the objects in the medicine cupboard. Talc. Deodorant. Shaving cream. Shaving cream. Most of one can of shaving cream had been squirted all over the mirror by Jason. A pale blue and grey can: 'Unscented,' it said.

Greville had an electric razor as well, I thought inconsequentially. It was on the dressing chest. I'd borrowed it that morning. Quicker than a wet shave, though not so long lasting.

The damn pill wasn't working.

I looked at the second one longingly.

Wait a bit.

Think about something else.

I picked up the second can of shaving cream which was scarlet and orange and said: 'Regular Fragrance'. I shook the can and took off the cover and tried to squirt foam onto the mirror.

Nothing happened. I shook it. Tried again. Nothing at all.

Guile and misdirection, I thought. Hollow books and green stone boxes with keyholes but no keys. Safes in concrete, secret drawers in desks . . . Take nothing at face value. Greville's mind was a maze . . . *and he wouldn't have used scented shaving cream.*

I twisted the shaving cream can this way and that and the bottom ring moved and began to turn in my hand. I caught my breath. Didn't really believe it. I went on turning . . . unscrewing.

It would be another empty hiding place, I told myself. Get a grip on hope. I unscrewed the whole bottom off the can, and from a nest of cottonwool a chamois leather pouch fell out into my hand.

Well, all right, I thought, but it wouldn't be diamonds.

With the help of the crutches I took the pouch into the bedroom and sat on Greville's bed, and poured onto the counterpane a little stream of dullish-looking pea-sized lumps of carbon.

I almost stopped breathing. Time stood still. I couldn't believe it. Not after everything . . .

With shaking fingers I counted them, setting them in small clumps of five.

Ten . . . fifteen . . . twenty . . . twenty-five.

Twenty-five meant I'd got fifty per cent. Half of what Greville had bought. With half, Saxony Franklin would be safe. I offered heartbursting thanks to the fates. I came dangerously near to crying.

Then, with a sense of revelation, I knew where the rest were. Where they had to be. Greville really had taken them with him to Ipswich, as he'd told Pross. I guessed he'd taken them thinking he might give them to the Maarten-Pagnier partner to take back to Antwerp for cutting.

I'd searched through the things in his car and had found nothing, and I'd held his diamonds in my hand and not known it.

They were . . . they had to be . . . in that other scarlet and orange can, in the apparent can of shaving cream in his overnight bag, safe as Fort Knox under the stairs of Brad's mum's house in Hungerford. She'd taken all Greville's things in off the street out of my car to keep them safe in a dodgy neighbourhood. In memory, I could hear Brad's pride in her.

'Smart, our Mum . . .'

The DF 1–1–8 was at last taking the edge off the worst.

I rolled the twenty-five precious pebbles around under my fingers with indescribable joy and thought how relieved Greville would have been. Sleep easy, pal, I told him, uncontrollably smiling. I've finally found them.

He'd left me his business, his desk, his gadgets, his enemies, his horses, his mistress. Left me Saxony Franklin, the Wizard, the shaving cream cans, Prospero Jenks and Nicholas Loder, Dozen Roses, Clarissa.

I'd inherited his life and laid him to rest; and at that moment, though I might hurt and I might throb, I didn't think I had ever been happier.

DRIVING FORCE

Dick Francis has written forty-one international bestsellers and is widely acclaimed as one of the world's finest thriller writers. His awards include the Crime Writers' Association's Cartier Diamond Dagger for his outstanding contribution to the crime genre, and an honorary Doctorate of Humane Letters from Tufts University of Boston. In 1996 Dick Francis was made a Mystery Writers of America Grand Master for a lifetime's achievement and in 2000 he received a CBE in the Queen's Birthday Honours list.

Also by Dick Francis in Pan Books

DEAD CERT
NERVE
FOR KICKS
ODDS AGAINST
FLYING FINISH
BLOOD SPORT
FORFEIT
ENQUIRY
RAT RACE
BONECRACK
SMOKESCREEN
SLAY-RIDE
KNOCK DOWN
HIGH STAKES
IN THE FRAME
RISK
TRIAL RUN
WHIP HAND
REFLEX
TWICE SHY
BANKER
THE DANGER
PROOF
BREAK IN
BOLT
HOT MONEY
THE EDGE
STRAIGHT
LONGSHOT
COMEBACK
DECIDER
WILD HORSES
COME TO GRIEF
TO THE HILT
10lb PENALTY
FIELD OF THIRTEEN
SECOND WIND
SHATTERED

THE SPORT OF QUEENS (autobiography)

LESTER: The Official Biography

DICK FRANCIS OMNIBUS ONE:
Long Shot, Straight, High Stakes

DICK FRANCIS OMNIBUS TWO:
Forfeit, Risk, Reflex

DICK FRANCIS OMNIBUS THREE:
Slay-Ride, Banker, Proof

DICK FRANCIS OMNIBUS FOUR:
Enquiry, Rat Race, Smokescreen

SID HALLEY OMNIBUS:
Odds Against, Whip Hand, Come to Grief

KIT FIELDING OMNIBUS:
Break in, Bolt

Dick Francis

DRIVING FORCE

PAN BOOKS

First published in Great Britain 1972 by Michael Joseph Ltd

This edition first published 1974 by Pan Books
an imprint of Pan Macmillan Ltd
Pan Macmillan, 20 New Wharf Road, London N1 9RR
Basingstoke and Oxford
Associated companies throughout the world
www.panmacmillan.com

ISBN 0 330 32951 0

21 23 25 27 29 28 26 24 22

A CIP catalogue record for this book is available from the British Library.

Typeset by Intype, London Limited
Printed and bound in Great Britain by
Mackays of Chatham plc, Chatham, Kent

My thanks to

LAMBOURN RACEHORSE TRANSPORT

and

JOHN HUGHES

ROBERT SCHULMAN

PROFESSOR ELLIE J. C. GOLDSTEIN

PROFESSOR JEREMY H. THOMPSON

and

MERRICK AND FELIX

as always

CHAPTER ONE

I had told the drivers never on any account to pick up a hitchhiker but of course one day they did, and by the time they reached my house he was dead.

The bell by the back door rang as I was heating up leftover beef stew for a fairly boring supper, consequence of living alone, and with barely a sigh and no premonition I switched off the hotplate, put the saucepan to one side and went to see who had come. Friends tended to enter at once while yelling my name, as the door was seldom locked. Employees mostly knocked first and entered next, still with little ceremony. Only strangers rang the bell and waited.

This time it was different. This time when I opened the door the light from inside the house fell yellowly on the stretched scared eyes of two of the men who worked for me, who stood uncomfortably on the doormat shifting from foot to foot, agonisedly and obviously expectant of wrath to come.

My own response to these clear signals of disaster was the familiar adrenaline rush of alarm that no amount of dealing with earlier crises could prevent. The old pump quickened. My voice came out high.

'What's the matter?' I said. 'What happened?'

I glanced over their shoulders. The bulk of one of the two largest in my fleet of horseboxes stood reassuringly in the shadows out on the tarmacked parking area, the house lights raising gleams along its silvery flank. At least they hadn't run it into a ditch: at least they'd brought it home. All else had to be secondary.

'Look, Freddie,' Dave Yates said, a defensive whine developing, 'it's not our fault.'

'What isn't?'

'This four-eyes we picked up . . .'

'You *what*?'

The younger one said, 'I told you we shouldn't, Dave.'

In him the anxiety whine was already full-blown, since wriggling out of blame was his familiar habit. He, Brett Gardner, already on my list for the chop, had been hired for his muscles and his mechanical know-how, the whinging nature at first unsuspected. His three months' trial period was almost up, and I wouldn't be making him permanent.

He was a competent watchful driver. I'd trusted him from the start with my biggest and most expensive wagons but I'd had requests from several good customers not to send him to transport their horses to the races, as he tended to sow his own dissatisfactions like a virus. Stable lads travelling with him went home incubating grouses, to their employers' irritation.

'It wasn't as if we had any horses on board,' Dave Yates was saying, trying to placate. 'Just Brett and me.'

I'd told all the drivers over and over that picking up hitchhikers while there were horses on board invalidated the insurance. I told them I'd sack any of them instantly if they did that. I'd also told them never, ever, to give any lifts at all to anyone, even if the box was empty of horses, and even if they knew the lift-begger personally. No, Freddie, of course not, they'd said seriously; and now I wondered just how often they'd disobeyed me.

'What about the four-eyes?' I said, my annoyance obvious. 'What's actually the matter?'

Dave said desperately, 'He's dead.'

'You . . . *stupid* . . .' Words failed me, drowned in anger. I could have hit him, and no doubt he saw it, backing away instinctively, fright rising. All sorts of scenarios presented themselves in rapid succession, none of them promising anything but trouble and lawsuits. 'What did he do?' I demanded. 'Try to jump off while you were moving? Or did you run him over . . .' And dear Christ, I thought, let it not be that.

Dave's surprised shake of the head put at least those fears to rest.

'He's in the box,' he said. 'Lying on the seat. We tried to wake him when we got to Newbury, to tell him it was time to get off. And we couldn't. I mean . . . he's dead.'

'Are you sure?'

They both reluctantly nodded.

I switched on the outside lights to flood the tarmac with visibility and went over with them for a look-see. They skittered one each side of me, crabbing sideways, making unhappy deprecating flapping movements with their hands, trying to shed their guilt, to justify themselves, to get me to understand it was unfortunate but not, definitely not, as Dave had said, their fault.

Dave, of about my own height (five nine) and age (mid-thirties), was primarily a horseman and secondarily a driver, usually travelling with animals that for some reason weren't being sent with enough attendants of their own. I'd seen him and Brett off that morning to pick up nine two-year-olds locally for a one-way trip to Newmarket, their owner being in the process of transferring his entire string from one perfectly good trainer to another in a typical bad-tempered huff. It wasn't that man's first expensive across-country flounce, and no doubt not his last. I'd shipped his three-year-old colts for him the previous day and was booked for fillies on the morrow. More money than sense, I thought.

I knew the nine two-year-olds had arrived safely in their new home as Brett had made the customary calls to my office both when he reached his destination and at the start of his return journey. All the boxes were equipped with mobile phones: the regular reporting calls were a useful routine, even if the older drivers thought one fussy. Fussy Freddie they might well call me behind my back, but with a fleet of fourteen boxes zig-zagging round England most days carrying multi-million fortunes on the hoof, I couldn't afford ignorance or negligent mistakes.

The front cabs of big horseboxes were always pretty roomy, having to accommodate several attendants besides one or sometimes two drivers. The cabs of my nine-horse rigs could hold eight people at a pinch, not in pullman comfort but at least sitting down. Behind the driver and the two front passenger seats a long padded rear seat usually gave support to four or five narrow bottoms: on this occasion, its entire length was occupied by one man lying on his back, feet towards me, silent and no longer worried about time.

I climbed into the cab and stood looking down at him.

I'd expected, I'd realised, some sort of tramp. Someone with a stubble, smelly jacket, grubby jeans, down on his luck. Not a prosperous-looking middle-aged fat man in suit, tie and gold onyx signet ring, with leather-soled polished shoes pointing mutely to heaven. Not a man who looked as if he could have bought other more suitable transport.

He was certainly dead. I didn't attempt to feel for a pulse, nor close the sagging mouth or the half-open lids behind the thick-lensed glasses. A rolled up horse rug had provided him with a pillow. One arm had fallen by his side, the hand with the ring resting laxly on the floor, near but not touching a black briefcase. I jumped down from the cab, shut its door and looked at the worried faces of my men who would no longer meet my eyes.

'How much did he pay you?' I asked bluntly.

'Freddie!' Dave wriggled in embarrassment, trying to deny it, happy-go-lucky always, likeable, but of variable good sense.

'I'd never . . .' Brett began, fake indignation always ready.

I gave him a disillusioned stare and interrupted, 'Where did you pick him up, why did he want a ride, and how much did he offer?'

'Dave fixed it,' Brett said accusingly.

'But you had your cut.' I took it for granted; not a question.

'Brett asked him for more,' Dave said with fury. 'Demanded it.'

'Yes, well, calm down.' I began to walk back towards the house. 'You'd better sort out what you're going to tell the police. Did he give you a name, for instance?'

'No,' Dave said.

'Or a reason for wanting a lift?'

'His car had broken down,' Dave explained. 'He was at the South Mimms service station, pacing about and sweating round by the diesel pumps, trying to get the driver of an oil tanker to take him to Bristol.'

'So?'

'So, well, he had a fistful of readies but the tanker was going to Southampton.'

'What were you doing by the diesel pumps anyway?' I asked.

They'd had no need to take on more fuel, not just going to Newmarket and back.

'We'd stopped there,' Dave said vaguely.

'Dave had a stomach ache,' Brett enlarged. 'The squits. We had to stop to get him something for it.'

'Imodium,' Dave confirmed, nodding. 'I was just walking past the pumps on my way back, see?'

Bleakly I led the way into the house, going through the back door into the hall and then wheeling left into the big all-purpose room where I customarily spent much of my time. I drew back the curtains, revealing the horsebox out on the tarmac, and stood looking at it while I phoned the police.

The local constable who answered knew me well, as we'd both spent much of our lives in the racing centre of Pixhill, a big village verging on small town sprawling across a fold of downland in Hampshire, south of Newbury.

'Sandy?' I said briefly, when he answered. 'This is Freddie Croft. I've a slight problem . . . One of my boxes picked up a hitchhiker who seems to have died on the journey. Do you mind coming over? He's outside my house, not along at the farm.'

'Dead, do you mean?' he asked cautiously, after a pause.

'I mean dead. As in not breathing.'

He cleared his throat. 'You're not having me on?'

'Sorry, no.'

'Well, all right. Ten minutes.'

Pixhill's token police force consisted of Sandy alone, a Wild West outpost on the frontiers of law and order. Pixhill's police station consisted of an office-room in Sandy's house, where his chief activity was writing up records of his daily patrols. Out of hours, like now, he would be watching television in scruffy clothes, drinking beer and casually cuddling his children's mother, a plump lady perennially in bedroom slippers.

In the ten promised minutes before he sped importantly onto my tarmac in his official car with every available light flashing, I learned not much more about our unwelcome deceased guest.

'How was I to know he'd die on us?' Dave said aggrievedly as I put down the receiver. 'Do someone a favour . . . Yeah, well I know you told us not to. But he was going on something chronic about how he had to get to Bristol for his daughter's wedding or something . . .'

I looked at him in disbelief.

'Yeah, well,' Dave said defensively, 'how was I to know?'

'It was all Dave's idea,' Brett assured me.

'Did you talk to him?' I asked them.

'Not that much,' Dave said. 'He chose that seat behind us, anyway. Didn't seem to want to talk.'

'I told Dave it was all wrong,' Brett complained.

'Shut up,' Dave said angrily. 'You could have refused to drive him. I didn't notice you saying you wouldn't.'

'And neither of you noticed him dying, either?' I suggested with irony.

The idea discomfited them, but no, it appeared, they hadn't.

'Thought he was asleep,' Dave said, and Brett nodded. 'So then,' Dave went on, 'when we couldn't wake him . . . I mean, you saw how he looks . . . well, we'd just pulled off the motorway at the Newbury junction . . . we were going to drop him at the Chieveley service station there so he could get another lift on to Bristol . . . well . . . there he was, dead, and we couldn't roll him out onto the ground, could we?'

They couldn't, I agreed. So they'd brought him to my doorstep, like cats bringing home a dead bird.

'Dave wanted to dump him somewhere,' Brett whined virtuously. 'Dave wanted to. It was me said we couldn't.'

Dave glared at him. 'We *discussed* it,' he said, 'that's all we did.'

'You'd have been in real trouble if you'd dumped him,' I said, 'and not just from me.'

Sandy, still buttoning himself hastily into his dark blue uniform, arrived at that moment to take charge in the slightly pompous manner he'd developed over the years. One look at the corpse set him summoning help over his radio, resulting presently in a doctor and a host of unanswerable questions.

The dead man did, it seemed, at least have a name, discovered via a walletful of addresses and credit cards. Sandy brought the wallet down from the cab and showed it to me, where I waited on the ground outside.

'K.K. Ogden. Kevin Keith Ogden,' he said, picking his way through the contents with stubby fingers. 'Lives in Nottingham. Mean anything to you?'

'No.' I shook my head. 'Never heard of him.'

He hadn't expected anything else.

'What did he die of?' I asked.

'A stroke maybe. Doc won't say before the post-mortem. No sign of foul play, if that's what you mean.'

The archaic words 'foul play' had always seemed faintly ridiculous to me, but in this case I was grateful to hear them.

'I can use the box tomorrow, then?' I asked.

'Don't see why not.' He thought it over judiciously. 'You might want to clean it, like.'

'Yup,' I said. 'Always do.'

He looked at me sideways. 'I thought you had a rule never to give lifts.'

'Dave and Brett are in big trouble.'

With a glimmer of sympathy for the two men, he looked across to where they waited by the house door and said, 'You didn't get your iron-fist reputation for nothing, Freddie.'

'What about the velvet glove bit?'

'Uh huh. That too.'

Sandy at forty had thickened round the waist and softened to puffiness of cheek and jaw, but the resulting air of rustic unintelligence was misleading. His superiors at one time had posted him away from Pixhill, in accordance with their belief that a policeman became too cosy and forgiving if left too long in one small neighbourhood, and had sent cruising cars in from outside to do his rounds. In Sandy's absence, however, the petty crime rate of Pixhill had soared while the detection rate plummeted, and after a while P.C. Sandy Smith had been quietly reinstated, to the overall dismay of the mildly wicked.

Smart young Dr Bruce Farway, a recent Pixhill arrival who had already alienated half his patients by patronising them insufferably, climbed down with agility from the cab and told me brusquely not to disturb the body before he could arrange for its removal.

'I can't imagine why I should want to,' I said mildly.

He eyed me with disfavour. We'd disliked each other on sight a few months ago and he'd not forgiven me for disagreeing with his diagnosis on one of my drivers and paying for a private second opinion that had proved him wrong. No humility and precious little humanity could be diagnosed in Bruce Farway, though he could be nice to sick children, I'd heard.

Leaving him issuing brisk instructions over his car

phone, Sandy and I went across to the house where he took brief statements from Dave and Brett. There was bound to be an inquest, he informed them, but it shouldn't take up much of their time.

Too much, I thought crossly, and they both unerringly read my expression. I told them I'd see them in the morning. They weren't comforted, it seemed.

Not much later, Sandy freed them to walk away down to the pub where they would spread their news item through the local lightning grapevine. Sandy shut his notebook, gave me an insouciant grin and drove back to his house to phone the hitchhiker's home town police force. Only Bruce Farway remained, impatiently waiting out by his car for the arrival of Kevin Keith Ogden's onward transport. I went out to him, for an update.

'They wanted to leave him here until tomorrow,' he exclaimed, affronted. 'Sandy and I insisted they came tonight.'

Grateful for that, I asked if he'd like to wait in the house and, with a hesitant shrug, he accepted. In the big sitting-room, I offered him alcohol, Coke or coffee. Nothing, he said.

He looked with a downturned mouth at the row of framed racing photographs along one wall, mostly pictures of myself in my jockey days sitting on the backs of high-leaping horses. In a village dedicated to thoroughbred racing, where the four-footed aristocrats brought more jobs and more prosperity to the area than all other industries put together, Bruce Farway had been overheard to say that lives lived in racing were wasted. Only selfless service given to others, as for example by doctors and nurses, was praiseworthy. Jockeys' injuries, he considered, were self-inflicted. No one understood why such a man had come to Pixhill.

I thought I might as well ask him, so I did. He gave me a surprised glance and went over to the window to cast his gaze briefly at the cooling immobile horsebox.

'I believe in general practice,' he said. 'I believe in a continuing service to a rural community. I believe in treating the family, not the illness.'

All marvellous, I thought, if he hadn't looked at me superciliously down his nose in a conscious glow of superiority while he spoke.

'What did our body die of?' I asked.

He compressed his already thin lips. 'Obesity and smoking, I dare say.'

In another century, I thought, he would have condemned witches to the stake. For the good of their souls, of course.

Thin, fervent, bigoted, he fidgeted impatiently by the window and finally asked a question of his own.

'Why were you a jockey?'

The answer was too complicated. I said merely, 'I was born to it. My father trained steeplechasers.'

'Does that make it inevitable?'

'No,' I said. 'My brother captains cruise ships and my sister's a physicist.'

He removed his attention wholly from the horsebox with his mouth opening in astonishment. 'Are you serious?'

'Certainly. Why not?'

He couldn't think why not and was saved from fishing for a reply by the telephone's ringing. I answered and found Sandy on the line, slightly out of breath and fluttering notebook pages.

'The Nottingham police,' he said, 'will want to know where South Mimms is, exactly.'

'They've surely got a map!'

'Mm. Well, tell *me*, like, then I can make a better report.'

'You've surely got a map as well.'

'Oh, come on, Freddie.'

I relented, smiling. 'The South Mimms service station is north of London on the M25. And I'll tell you something, Sandy, our friend Kevin Keith was not taking a direct route from Nottingham to Bristol. In fact, from Nottingham to Bristol you'd never go near South Mimms in a million years, so just tell the Nottingham police to go easy on the relatives because whatever our corpse was doing in South Mimms he wasn't going straight from home to any daughter's wedding.'

He digested the information. 'Ta,' he said, 'I'll tell them.'

I put down the receiver and Bruce Farway asked, 'What daughter's wedding?'

I explained how Dave had been persuaded to give the lift, even against express orders.

Frowning, Farway said, 'You don't believe in the daughter, then?'

'Not all that much.'

'I don't suppose it matters why he was in . . . where did you say . . . South Mimms?'

'Not to him, any more,' I agreed, 'but it'll waste my drivers' time. The inquest, and so on.'

'He couldn't help dying!' the doctor protested.

'He's a damn nuisance.'

With plain disapproval Farway went back to watching the horsebox. A boringly long time elapsed during which I drank scotch and water ('Not for me,' Farway said), thought hungrily of my recongealing stew and answered two more phone calls.

The news had travelled at warp speed. The first voice demanding facts was that of the owner whose two-year-olds had gone to Newmarket, the second that of the trainer who was having to see them leave his stable.

Jericho Rich, the owner, never wasted time on polite opening chat, saying without ceremony, 'What's this about a dead man in your box?' His voice, like his personality, was loud, aggressive and impatient. His name, on official documents, was Jerry Colin Rich. Jericho suited him better, if only for the noise.

While I told him what had happened, I pictured him as I'd very often seen him in parade rings at the races, a stocky grey-haired bully given to poking holes in the air with a jabbing finger.

'You listen to me, fella,' he said now, shouting down the line. 'You pick up no hitchhikers while you work for me, understand? That's what you've always said and that's how I like it. When you take my horses, you don't take anyone else's. That's the way we've always done business and I don't want any changes.'

I reflected that once his whole string had gone to Newmarket I wouldn't be doing much more business for him anyway, but alienating the cantankerous old beggar would all the same be unwise. Give him a year or two and I might be ferrying him back.

'What's more,' he was saying, 'when you take my fillies across tomorrow, take them in a different box. Horses can smell death, you know, and I don't want those fillies upset.'

I assured him they would go in a different box, even though, as I didn't bother to tell him, the cab would be reeking of disinfectant, not death, come pick-up time in the morning.

'And don't send the same driver.'

It wasn't worth arguing about. 'All right,' I said.

He began to run out of steam, which is to say, to repeat himself. I offered him always a soft cushion of agreement as being the fastest way to blunt the sword of his anger, especially when his grievances reached the third or fourth recycle. We went through the same conversation twice more. I promised yet again to send a different box and a different driver and finally, though muttering away and still not satisfied, he clicked himself off.

He'd owned five or six hurdlers in the past, which I'd ridden for him regularly. I'd had a lot of practice in absorbing the Jericho tantrums with my own temper intact.

Thanks to the Rich decibels, Farway appeared to have heard the whole repetitious exchange because he gave me his unexpected opinion.

'It wasn't your fault your drivers picked the man up.'

'Maybe.' I paused. 'The captain goes down with the ship, my brother says.'

He stared. 'Do you mean you think it *was* your fault?'

I thought chiefly that it wasn't a good time to discuss ultimate responsibility in the abstract. I wished more simply that Kevin Keith had given up the ghost in someone else's cab. A pity, I thought, that the oil tanker had been going to Southampton.

Michael Watermead, in striking contrast to Jericho Rich, spoke in soft hesitant super-educated tones over the telephone and started by asking if the nine two-year-olds that had left his care that morning had arrived safely in Newmarket.

I was certain he already knew, but I assured him that they had.

Resentment at having had to part with them would have been natural, but Michael seemed to have his feelings well in control. Tall, fair and fiftyish, his habitual air of dither fronted an effective, above middle-rank operation of sixty good stables in three attractive quadrangles, usually healthily full. His horses liked him, always a good character reference. They nuzzled his neck if he were near enough; they came to look out of their boxes at the sound of his step in the yard. I'd never ridden for him, as he trained only Flat horses, but since I'd acquired the transport business and had grown to know him, we'd become, on a business level at least, good friends.

The third son of a baron, he trained for a distantly royal personage thirty-somethingth from the throne, a snob-value combination that had brought him Rich's custom in the first place. The deterioration in the first flush of gratification on both sides – there were no longer many owner-strings as big as Rich's nor as talented in depth – had been complete, both men throwing me asides along the way from euphoria to disillusion.

'The man's impossible!' Michael had exclaimed over some particular transport demand from Jericho. 'Totally unreasonable.'

'My horse lost the race on the journey to Scotland,' Rich complained. 'Why does he send them so far? It costs too much and they arrive tired.' He overlooked entirely Michael's successful forays to France with the same animals.

I remained strictly neutral and non-partisan through all owner-trainer differences out of a strong sense of self-preservation, starting right back in my early racing days over fences when an incautious criticism had got back to its target and very nearly cost me my job. I'd become adept at sympathetic noises with the minimum of actual comment, even to friends.

Getting my own way softly had eased my whole path through life and in business had served me well. I was better at placating than confronting, at persuading than commanding; and I wasn't defeated much.

Michael said slowly, 'Is it true your box brought back . . . a *dead* man?'

''Fraid so.'

'Who?'

I explained yet again about Kevin Keith Ogden, and I told him that Jericho Rich had already demanded a different box and driver for his fillies on the morrow.

'That man,' Michael said bitterly. 'Despite the hole it makes in my yard, I'll be glad to see the last of him. Vile-tempered oaf.'

'Will you fill up the holes?'

'Oh sure, in time. I've got ten boarded out that I can bring in now, for a start. Losing Jericho's a blight, but not a disaster.'

'Great.'

'Lunch on Sunday? Maudie will call you.'

'Fine.'

'Bye.'

A man could drown in Maudie Watermead's blue eyes. Her Sunday lunches were legendary.

Farway, still by the window, was growing impatient, repeatedly consulting his watch as if the constant checking would make time go faster.

'Scotch?' I offered again.

'I don't drink.'

Dislike or addiction, I wondered? Probably plain disapproval, on the whole.

I looked round my spacious familiar room, wondering how he would see it. Grey carpet with a scattering of rugs. Cream walls, racing photographs, my mother's china parrot collection in an alcove. Edwardian mahogany desk, green leather swivelling chair. Sofas with ancient fading chintz, tray of drinks on a side table, padded cream curtains, table lamps everywhere, book-shelves and a pot plant, all leaves, no flowers. A lived-in room, not excessively tidy, not a decorator's triumph.

Home.

An unenthusiastic black van at long last crawled onto the tarmac and parked between the horsebox and my door. It had long black windowless sides and black windowless rear doors, and I realised it was, in fact, a hearse. Sandy in his official car returned in its wake.

Farway, exclaiming, hurried out to meet him and the three men who emerged phlegmatically from the hearse to set about their task. I followed in Farway's wake and watched the unloading of a narrow stretcher which seemed to be covered on the upper surface with a lot of dark canvas and several sinewy straps.

The man who seemed to be in charge of things said he was the coroner's officer and produced paperwork for Farway to deal with.

The other two climbed with the stretcher up into the cab, followed by Sandy, who soon descended again bringing with him a grip and a briefcase. Both bags were of leather, battered but originally good.

'Belongings of the deceased?' the man asked.

Farway thought so.

'They are not my men's,' I agreed.

Sandy put the bags on the tarmac and then went aloft again to return with a plastic bag containing booty collected from the body – a watch, a cigarette lighter, a packet of cigarettes, a pen, a comb, a nail file, a handkerchief, glasses and the onyx and gold ring. He itemised them aloud to the coroner's officer who wrote at his dictation, then attached a label saying 'property of K.K. Ogden' and stowed them in his car.

While Sandy and the coroner's officer climbed back into the cab, I squatted down beside the bags and unzipped the top of the grip.

'I don't think you should do that,' Farway protested.

The grip, half-full, held overnight necessities; shaving kit, pyjamas, clean shirt, nothing very new, nothing out of the ordinary. I closed the zip and snapped open the briefcase, which wasn't locked.

'Hey,' Farway said.

'If a man dies on my property,' I said reasonably, 'I'd like to get to know him.'

'But you've no right . . .'

I looked anyway through the meagre contents, which seemed to me wholly uninformative. A calculator. Writing pad, nothing written on it. A bunch of post-cards in an elastic band, all the same, a view of a country hotel, advertisement hand-outs. A bottle of aspirins, a packet of indigestion tablets, two small air-line size bottles of vodka, both full.

'Look here,' Farway said uncomfortably.

I shut the briefcase and stood up. 'All yours,' I said.

The undertakers took their time, and when they finally brought Kevin Keith out it was through the front passenger door, not via the grooms' door further back through which we had all so far climbed to reach the rear seat. It appeared that, death having done its stiff-ening work, the only way out for the body was to load it forward onto the stretcher laid along the front seats: so it came out that way, feet forward, wrapped amorph-ically in canvas, retaining straps in place.

As bodies went, it appeared that this one was heavy and awkward in shape, the bent right arm being impos-sible to straighten. Certainly respect for the dead as such was markedly absent, the problem seeming to present itself rather as of the order of extricating an obstinate grand piano from a small angular attic. I supposed body-collectors got used to it. One of the men, besides remarks like 'Heave now' and 'That arm's jamming on the door,' was assessing the chances of his football team on the following Saturday. They lifted the stretcher unceremoniously through the open back doors of the black hearse as if engaged in rubbish disposal and I saw them transfer the canvas-wrapped Ogden off the stretcher into an opened metal coffin.

Faraway too, more used to corpses than I, was taking the removal of this one prosaically. He told me he wouldn't be doing the post-mortem himself but it looked to him like straightforward cardiac arrest. Plain unlucky. The inquest should be a brief formality. He would be certifying death. I might not be called.

He said goodnight neutrally, folded himself into his car and followed the hearse as it rolled away off my tarmac. Sandy, taking with him the grip and the brief-case, drove off peacefully in the rear.

All suddenly seemed very quiet. I looked up at the stars, eternal in the face of mortality. I wondered if Kevin Keith Ogden had known he was dying, lying along a leatherette bench seat behind a thundering engine.

I thought quite likely not. There had been times when I'd been knocked out in racing falls, when the last thing I'd seen had been a whirling blurring vision of grass and sky. After the impact, I wouldn't have known if I'd died; and I'd thought sometimes, gratefully waking up, that an unaware death would be a blessing.

I climbed yet again into the cab. The rolled up horse rug still bore the imprint of Ogden's head and there was an unappealing stain halfway along the seat, threat-ening action on the morrow. Damn the man, I thought.

Brett had left the key in the ignition, another taboo

in my book. I stepped over into the front compartment and removed the keyring, checking that at least the brakes were on and all but the cabin lights were off. Finally, switching off those interior lights also I jumped down from the passenger door, locking it behind me.

The front passenger door and the driver's door both locked with the same key that started the engine, a large complicated key supplied by the manufacturers. I locked the driver's door – Brett hadn't – and with the second more ordinary key on the ring locked the grooms' door. A third key locked the small compartment under the dashboard that contained the mobile telephone power switch and various documents, which I'd checked and found secure.

I walked again right round the box, making a last inspection. Everything seemed as it should be. The two ramps for horses were up and bolted. The five doors for humans, two for the front seats, three for the attendants, were similarly immovable. The flap over the intake to the diesel tanks, fastened by the fourth and last key on the keyring, was proof against siphoning thieves.

Feeling all the same uneasy I went back to the house and locked the back door behind me, which I didn't do always. I stretched out a hand to switch off the outside lights and then changed my mind and left them on.

The fleet usually spent the night inside a large brick-walled converted farmyard, the wide strong entrance gates padlocked. The nine-box standing alone on my tarmac seemed unaccustomedly vulnerable, even though trucks of that size were seldom stolen. There were too many identity numbers engraved on too many parts, quite apart from the name CROFT RACEWAYS painted in about six places, the whole thing hardly inconspicuous for anyone trying to avoid notice.

I reheated the old stew, sloshed some red wine into it for excitement and ate the result while leaving the sitting-room curtains open so that I could see the horsebox all the time.

Absolutely nothing happened. My unease slowly abated, and I put down its existence simply to the fact of Ogden's demise.

I made and received a few more telephone calls, checking particularly with my senior driver that all the other boxes were back at the farm. The rest of the day's journeys, it seemed, had for once gone uneventfully to plan: no mix-ups over time, no engine troubles, no equipment or attendants left behind. All the drivers had filled in their log sheets and popped them as requested into the letter-box of the office. The padlocks were on the gates. No keys were anywhere accessible. Despite the dead passenger, the overall message I received was that the boss could relax and go to bed.

The boss, in the end, did just that, though from my bedroom, which was over the sitting-room, I still had a clear view of the horsebox out under the lights. I left the curtains wide open and although I never slept with them fully closed I nevertheless woke several times because of the continuing unusual brightness outside.

At about three in the morning I became suddenly fully alert, disturbed by more than plain light. Disturbed by a moving flash across the ceiling, indistinct, like sheet lightning, seen through my eyelids.

The weather had been mild recently, though it was still early March, but it seemed to me that the temperature had dropped ten degrees in the past few hours. In bare feet and sleeping shorts I stood up and went to the window, shivering.

At first sight nothing seemed changed. Shrugging, I half turned to return to the warm bed and then stopped stock-still in serious alarm.

The grooms' door, through which we'd all climbed, was slightly open, not securely locked, as I'd left it.

Open.

I stared hard, but there was no mistake. There was a black line of shadow where the door no longer fitted flat and snugly into position. The flash of light I'd seen must have been a reflection from its window as the door had been opened.

Without considering clothes, I sprinted headlong downstairs and along to the back door, unlocking it, throwing my feet into gumboots and snatching an old raincoat from a peg. Trying to fit my arms into its sleeves I ran across the tarmac and pulled the door wide.

There was a figure inside there, in black, as surprised to see me as I to see him. At first he had his back towards me, then when he whirled round with a fierce exclamation, more an explosion of escaping breath than an actual word, I saw that his head was covered with a black hood, his eyes alive through holes, the cliché disguise of robbers and terrorists.

'What the hell are you doing?' I yelled at him, trying myself crazily to climb up after him. Stupid thing to do in gumboots: the stepholes weren't designed for their clumsy width.

Black-mask snatched up the rolled horse rug, gave it a fast shake to open its folds and threw it over me while I was still halfway up. I slid off the toe-holds, stepped back unbalanced into a void and landed in a heap on the tarmac. The black figure, dimly seen, jumped over onto the driver's seat, unlatched the door on that side, leaped athletically to the ground and ran for the shadows, lithe and scudding.

Perhaps in trainers I could have made it a contest. In gumboots and an unbelted raincoat still only half on, it was hopeless. I stood up disgustedly, disentangling myself from the horse rug, fastening the raincoat belatedly and listening in vain for any sound of departing footsteps.

None of it made sense, nor did standing around shivering in inappropriate clothes in the middle of the night. There was nothing worth stealing in the horsebox save perhaps the radio or phone, but the black figure hadn't seemed to be attacking either. He hadn't in fact seemed to be doing anything in particular, when I looked back to my first sight of him, but simply standing in the cab with his back to me. There had been dust and streaks of dirt on his clothes. As far as I could remember he hadn't been carrying anything. No tools, not even a torch. If he'd opened the grooms' door with either a key or a lock-pick, he must have put it in a pocket.

The keyhole of the grooms' door was in the handle itself. There was no key in the lock, nor, when I looked, any obvious scratches or signs of force or tampering.

Cold and cross, I threw the horse rug back into the cab, shut the grooms' door and the driver's side door and went back to the house to fetch the keys again to relock them.

Out of respect for my carpets I slid my feet out of the gumboots and padded through the hall and across the sitting-room to the desk, not bothering to switch on any lights in there owing to being able to see perfectly well because of the glow outside. I retrieved the keys from the desk drawer, retraced my steps, resumed the gumboots and clomped back towards the wheels.

Coming close, I saw without belief that there was a black moving shadow again inside the cab. Monstrous, I thought, and what in God's name could he want? He was standing behind the driver's seat, feeling forward into the storage shelf that spread across the whole width of the cab high and above the front seats, projecting out over the windscreen. The spacious shelf, common to all of my fleet, was used by the drivers and attendants to stow their personal belongings, often changes of clothing and occasionally a sleeping-bag and pillow. There was a full-length mattress installed for the use of several of the drivers who slept there habitually on overnight stops, preferring it to cheap lodgings. Brett had told me he expected better. Your own choice, I assured him.

The busy figure in the cab saw me coming and was out and away again before I could reach him. I ran in his wake sluggishly, as if through treacle, my bare feet half-sliding out of the boots at every stride. He headed down the drive and seemed to melt into the shadows of the trees by the exit to the road.

Uselessly, I followed him to the road itself, but he was nowhere to be seen. It was a country road, unfenced, with open gateways to other houses. Trees and bushes by the hundred, hiding places unlimited. It would have taken half an army to find him.

Puzzled and dispirited I retraced my way back to the box. The driver's door stood wide open, as he'd left it. I climbed up clumsily and stood behind the seat, as he had, looking into the storage shelf, switching on the cabin light for a better view.

The shelf was empty except for the mattress and a plastic carrier-bag which proved on inspection to contain remains of Brett-type sustenance; screwed up wrappers from chocolate bars, an empty sandwich-shaped casing bearing a label announcing 'Beef and Tomato', with the price underneath, and two empty Coke cans.

I put the bag back where it had been. It was each driver's business to keep his own box clean and I didn't feel like picking up after Brett. Whatever he and Dave had been doing that day, giving lifts to moribund businessmen seemed just the start of it. Those two would have a lot of explaining to do in the morning.

I carefully locked the doors again, and again walked back to the house, but once inside felt far from reassured. The agile visitor had got into the box the first time without breaking a window or other observable force and presumably could get in again the same way.

Without knowing in the least what he wanted, I still didn't like the idea of his returning a third time. It also occurred to me disturbingly that perhaps he intended to *leave* something, or destroy something, or disable the box altogether. In alarm and doubt I shed the gumboots and raincoat and ran upstairs for substitutes in the shape of two sweaters, jeans, socks, and shoes I could run in. I pulled my own old sleeping-bag from a cupboard and with a last check through the window to see if a third visitation was in progress – no sign of it – I went downstairs for a padded jacket and gloves.

With all these aids to warmth, I crossed yet again to the box and settled myself in the front passenger seats, moderately comfortable in body if not in mind.

Time slid by.

I dozed.

No one came.

CHAPTER TWO

Predictably, I woke stiff and cold as soon as nature's lighting system began creeping into the electric stuff, and I trailed yawning across to the kitchen for warmth and coffee. The newspapers and the post arrived. I sorted through the bills, read the headlines and turned to the racing pages, ate some cornflakes and answered the first phone calls of the new day.

My routine working hours started at six or seven and normally ended at midnight, Sundays included, but it was a way of life, not a hardship. It was the same for trainers, all of whom seemed to believe that if they were up and caring for their horses by or before dawn, everyone who worked for them should be available likewise.

Plans tended to change overnight. The first call on that day, a Friday, was from the trainer of a horse that had got cast in his stable and injured himself by thrashing about on the floor, trying to get himself back onto his feet.

'The bugger's twisted his off-hind. My head lad

found him, hopping lame.' The big healthy voice reverberated into my ear. 'He can't run at Southwell, sod it. Strike him off your list, will you?'

I said I would. 'Thanks for letting me know.'

'I know you run tight schedules,' he boomed. 'The four for Sandown are OK. Don't send that Brett for them, he's a whiner, he upsets my lads.'

I assured him he wouldn't get Brett.

'Right, Freddie. See you at the sports.'

Without wasting time, I buzzed my head driver and asked if the boxes for Southwell had already left.

'Warming up,' he assured me.

'Miss out Larry Dell. Their horse got cast.'

'Got you.'

I put down the kitchen receiver and went through to the sitting-room where most of the desk-top was taken up by the week's comprehensive chart indicating which box was going where with whose horses. I wrote it always in pencil because of the constant changes.

On an adjacent table, easily reached by swivelling the green leather chair, stood a computer, monitor and keyboard. Theoretically, it was easier to call each box to the screen to enter or rearrange its journeys, and actually I did keep the details of the journeys recorded there permanently once they'd been completed, but for an advance overview I still clung to my pencil and rubber.

Along at the farm, in the main office, my two bright secretaries, Isobel and Rose, kept the computer competently accurate and up to the minute, and despaired of my old-fashioned methods. The terminal in my sitting-room was a sort of sub-station upon which appeared all the changes they'd made on the main computer, and that was what I chiefly used it for: checking what had been organised in my absence.

In return, I typed in any changes which came in before or after their office hours and, one way or another, we had not so far left any expectant runner waiting in vain for the coach to take it to the ball.

I checked down the list on what looked like a typical Friday for the first week of March. Two boxes going north to Southwell, where the all-weather track held both flat and jumping races all winter. Four boxes collecting runners for that afternoon's programme of steeplechasing at Sandown, south of London. One nine-horsebox taking broodmares to Ireland. One six-box taking broodmares to Newmarket, one taking broodmares to Gloucestershire, another taking mares to a stud down in Surrey: the thoroughbred breeding season in full flood.

One box was out of action, scheduled for maintenance. One was going to France. One would be taking Jericho Rich's fillies to Newmarket. Brett and his nine-horser, standing outside my window in the strengthening dawn, were due to spend the day shuttling a whole string for a trainer moving to Pixhill from out on Salisbury Plain: not long journeys but multiple and, from my point of view, good profit.

The following week would see the Cheltenham Festival, peak of the steeplechasing year, with the Flat season proper getting into gear the week after, its crowded programme bringing me six months of good business. March was sigh-of-relief time, the fogs and freezes of winter relaxing their paralysing menace: there was no income to be made from a row of boxes standing silent in the snow, but the drivers had to be paid all the same.

My head driver phoned back. Harve by name, short for Harvey.

'Pat's got flu,' he said. 'She's in bed.'

'Shit.'

'It's a bugger, the flu this year. Knocks you out. It's not her fault.'

'No,' I said. 'How's Gerry?'

'Still bad. We could put those broodmares off till Monday.'

'No, they're near to foaling. I promised they'd go to Surrey today. I'll sort something out.'

Pat and Gerry were reliable drivers: if they said they were too ill to work, then they were. Reshuffle required.

'Dave can do the Gloucestershire broodmares, instead of Pat,' I said. Dave was a slow driver, and I didn't send him out behind the wheel unless I had to. 'Those mares have no deadline.'

'Yeah. OK.'

'I want him here first though. When he turns up at the farm, send him along here. Brett too.'

'Will do,' he said. 'Is it about the dead man?'

'It is.'

'Silly sods.'

'And tell Jogger I need him p.d.q. Tell him to bring his slider.'

'He won't be in for half an hour.'

'That will do.'

'Anything else?'

'Sure to be, in five minutes.'

He laughed and went away, leaving me thinking, as I often did, that I was lucky to have him. When I'd been a jockey Harve had been my weighing-room valet, bringing my cleaned saddles and fresh breeches to the races every day. Valets were a bit like theatrical dressers, although one valet would 'do' ten or so jockeys regularly. It was a close personal service: one could keep few physical secrets from one's valet.

When I'd hung up my boots and bought the transport business, he'd appeared to my surprise on my doorstep.

'I'm here to see if you'll give me a job,' he said for openers, coming straight to the point.

'But I don't need a valet any more.'

'Not that. I don't want to keep on with that. My old dad's died and the weighing-room's not the same as when he was there, and I want a change. I'm sick of the wash-tub. How about it if I drive for you? I drive hundreds of miles every week anyway; have for years.'

'But,' I said slowly, 'you'd need a Heavy Goods Vehicle licence.'

'I'll get one.'

'The boxes aren't like cars. You'd have to take a course.'

'If I get the licence, will you give me a job?'

I'd said I would because we'd always got on easily together, and in that casual way I'd acquired the best lieutenant one could imagine.

He was sandy-haired, strong-armed, about my own age, an inch or two taller. Dryly disillusioned, he was quick to denigrate but in a way that made one smile. Brett, he had remarked to me once, shifted the blame before you even realised there was a fault. 'He carries a bagful of alibis around with him, ready to pull one out.'

I went upstairs, showered, shaved, tweaked the duvet straight on my bed and returned in short time to my desk and the uninterrupted view of the horsebox.

Jogger, the company mechanic, swept up the drive in his van and squeaked to a halt nose to nose with the horsebox. Spry, bow-legged, bald and cockney, he eeled out of the van and stood looking at the horsebox while scratching his head. Then he came over to the house in the peculiar gait that had earned him his nickname, a rolling motion like that of speed walkers, almost running but with one foot on the ground all the time, elbows tucked in.

I went to the door to meet him and we walked back

to the box together, he impatiently slowing his scuttling progress to match mine.

'What's the boil, then?' he said.

He spoke his own sort of cockney rhyming slang, and indeed I often thought he made most of it up himself, but I was used to it by that time. For boil, read boil and bubble, trouble.

'Just check it all over, will you?' I answered. 'Take a good look at the engine. Then slide under, make sure we're not leaking or carrying additions.'

'Gor,' he said.

I watched him check the engine, his eyes swift, fingers delicate, head nodding with certainties.

'All hunky-dory,' he said.

'Good. Go over the rest.'

He went along to his truck and brought out the flexible stick, with mirror attached, that could be angled to reveal invisibilities round corners, and also the low platform on castors, on which he lay on his back to slide under the boxes for quick underguts inspections.

'When you're done, I'll be in the house,' I said.

'Am I looking for anything particular?'

'Just for anything you don't understand.'

He peered at me speculatively. 'This box went to Italy earlier, dinnit?'

I agreed that it had. 'Went last Friday, returned by Tuesday evening.' There had been no problems or hold-ups, though; as far as I knew, of course.

'That Brett never cleans it proper. Got no Jekyll.'

Jekyll and Hyde, I thought: pride.

'Brett had Wednesday off,' I said. 'Harve drove a load of colts to Newmarket that day in this box. Brett took it to Newmarket and back yesterday. A couple of odd things have happened, so . . . carry on with the check.'

'You talking about that stiff?'

'Partly.'

'He didn't have no chance to duff the box up, though, did he?'

'I don't know any more than you,' I said. 'And get a move on, Jogger, I've got to get this thing cleaned and out on the road within an hour.'

He lay down philosophically and shoved himself trustingly out of sight, except for his feet, under ten or so tons of steel. Just the prospect of it gave me a sort of claustrophobia, which Jogger knew about but loftily forgave. My failing increased his self-esteem: it did no harm.

I went back to the house and Harve phoned.

'Dave's on his way along to you now,' he said with agitation. 'But he says Brett's packing his bags.'

'He's doing *what*?'

'Dave says Brett's not a complete thicko, he knows his trial three months is nearly up and that you won't keep him on. He's ducking out first. That way he can go around saying he gave you the chuck, not the other way round. He'll be whinging all over the place about how hard he worked here, Dave says, and how you never appreciated him.'

'He can get on with it,' I said. 'The thing is, what about today?'

'The Marigold shuttle,' Harve said. 'Brett was doing that.'

'Exactly. Who else have we got?' I knew the answer as soon as I asked. We had me.

'Well . . .' He hesitated.

'Yes, all right. I'll do it if there's no one else.'

'It's not just the shuttle,' he went on unhappily. 'Vic's wife says he's got a temperature of a hundred and three and no way is he driving to Sandown.'

One of those days.

'They're both here at the farm,' Harve went on, 'Vic and his missus. He says he wants to go, she says she'll divorce him. You can see he's got a fever, though.'

'Send him home, he'll just spread the flu around more.'

'OK. But . . .'

'Give me a minute. Inspiration will strike.'

He laughed. 'Hurry it up,' he said, disconnecting.

I sucked my teeth. If racehorse trainers hadn't been as fussy as they normally were, I could have travelled the two Surrey-bound broodmares in one of the boxes taking 'chasers to Sandown. The box could have dropped off the two racers, taken the mares to their destination and returned to Sandown to bring the 'chasers home. I might have risked it if I hadn't been sure the trainer in question would get to hear of it from his lads: and the trainer in question would never ever let his own horses travel with any horses from any other stables. Sending his runners in company with broodmares would lose me his custom instantly and evermore.

I went out to the nine-horsebox. Jogger was nowhere to be seen but when I yelled his name a pair of boots slid out into view, followed by grease-clogged trousers, filthy army sweater and a dirt-streaked face.

'You're right, we've picked up a stranger,' he reported, and added, grinning with yellow teeth. 'Did you know? You must have known.'

'No, I didn't.' Nor was I pleased. Very put out, in fact.

'Have a decko,' he encouraged me, removing himself from the slider and slyly offering me his place.

'I'll take your word for it,' I said, staying upright. 'What have you found?'

'I'd say it's stuck on with a magnet.' He gave me his opinion judiciously. 'It's a sort of tin box. Like a big cash box, lid downwards.'

'Shiny?' I asked.

'Course not. Want it out?'

'Yes, but wait . . . um . . . we've got three drivers now with flu. Would you do a run yourself, just to help out?'

He rubbed his greasy hands down his trousers and looked dubious. Driving meant cleaning up and there was no doubt he felt happier dirty. I seldom asked him to drive more than his regular test runs on all the boxes, when he listened to their resonances as to a language and heard trouble before it happened.

'Broodmares, not to the races,' I explained.

'Well then . . . when?'

'Lunch time.'

'Bonus?'

'Sure, if you do your regular maintenance work as well.'

He shrugged, lay down again on the slider and disappeared. I went back to my desk, phoned Harve and told him, 'Jogger.'

'He's driving?' He sounded incredulous. 'He agreed?'

'The broodmares to Surrey,' I confirmed. 'It's Phil whose box is in for maintenance, isn't it? Wake him up, twist his arm, sob stuff if you like, tell him his day off's postponed, we need him to take Vic's box to Sandown.'

'OK.'

'That should cover it,' I said.

'Fingers crossed.'

'Come down here yourself, would you, when you have a minute?'

After the briefest of pauses he said, 'Right.'

He would be wondering what I wanted but not to the level of worry. At least, I hoped not.

Dave at that point bicycled in across the tarmac and leaned his rusty conveyance against my wood pile.

Dave did have a car, even rustier than the cycle, but it spent most of the time out of action. One day, he'd been saying for months, he would equip it with retreads and get it back on the road. No one believed him. He spent his money on greyhounds.

He knocked on the outside door on his way in and appeared in the sitting-room doorway with the martyred air of having stepped out of a tumbril.

'You wanted me, Freddie?' He was nervous but trying for bravado: not a success.

'I want you and Brett to clean that box. It's due out again before nine.'

'But, Brett – ' He stopped.

'Go on.'

'Harve told you, didn't he? Brett says he'll be waiting at the office door for his P45 the second Isobel gets there, then he's off.'

'He's due some wages and holiday money,' I said, unruffled. 'You get back on your bike and go and tell him he can have it now, here, in cash, but cleaning that box is yesterday's job, and if he doesn't finish it, his unemployment dates from yesterday morning. No pay for yesterday, understand?'

'You can't do that,' Dave said uncertainly.

'Want to bet? By rights, he should give me a week's notice. And ask him if he thinks he might ever need a reference.'

Dave gave me a hollow look.

'Hurry and fetch him,' I said. 'And come back yourself.'

When he'd gone I switched on the computer and brought Brett and his affairs to the screen. Every journey he'd done for me was listed there, with dates, times, horses' names, expenses and notes. The day before's journey of nine two-year-olds to Newmarket had been entered only as 'proposed': no dead bodies yet cluttered the entry.

His terms of employment were there, along with days worked and holiday entitlement earned: no problem at all to put together his present due. I printed a copy of the income information, ready to give to him.

Through the window, I watched Jogger heel-and-toe his way towards the house, a greyish-brown shape like a big shoe box in his hands. He came into the sitting-room and plonked the object down on my chart, not caring about mundane considerations like dirt. He looked surprised when I asked him to lift the box up again so that I could spread a newspaper under it.

'I had a hell of a job getting it off,' he said. 'Like a limpet mine, it was.'

'Where's the magnet?' I asked.

'Still stuck to the chassis, behind the second fuel tank. Super-glue job, most like. This box came off in the end, though I had to use a tyre lever. No one meant it to move, I'll telling you.'

'How long would you say it's been there?'

The box was thick with grime except for a clean

circular saucer-sized patch on its underside where it had been in contact with the magnet.

Jogger shrugged unhappily. 'It's not in a place I need to inspect all that often.'

'A week? A month? More?'

'Dunno,' he said.

I picked the box up in the newspaper and shook it. It was comparatively light, with no rattle.

'Empty,' Jogger said, nodding.

About fifteen inches by ten by six deep, it was a strong old-fashioned grey metal cash box with rounded corners, a recessed carrying handle and a sturdy lock. No key, naturally. A dent on one edge from the tyre lever. The carrying handle, stuck into its recess, wouldn't lift up.

'Can you open it?' I asked. 'Without breaking it.'

Jogger gave me a sideways look. 'I could pick the lock if I fetch my tools and you squint the other way.'

'Go on, then.'

He decided to take the box out to his van for the job and presently with a yellow grin returned with it open.

Nothing inside, not even dust. I put my nose down to it. It smelled surprisingly clean inside considering the grime on the outside. It smelled even fresh, like talcum powder or soap.

'How difficult was it to search underneath?' I asked.

'Easy, on a slider. Very easy over an inspection pit, if you knew where to look. I nearly missed it, though.

It's the same colour as everything else under there. See, that's it, you wouldn't expect to see it, unless you knew it was there. You'd have to park that bit over the pit, too, which you wouldn't normally do.'

'How long since you had Brett's box over the inspection pit?'

He raised his eyebrows. 'Did an oil change, checked the air brakes, say five weeks ago. Total overhaul must've been before Christmas. Don't remember the day.'

'The computer will have it,' I said.

Jogger looked across at the dark screen without favour. He liked to be able to invent memories, not have them checked.

'Thanks, anyway,' I said warmly. 'I wouldn't have found this cash box myself in a million years.'

The yellow teeth made a brief appearance. 'You want to get under there,' he said.

But no, I didn't.

Dave came back on his bicycle followed by Brett, slowly, in his car, neither of them showing much appetite for the morning. They came into the sitting-room, greeted Jogger unenthusiastically and looked without reaction at the dirty grey cash box lying open on the newspaper.

'Has either of you seen that before?' I asked neutrally.

Uninterestedly, they said they hadn't.

'It's not my fault the horsebox wasn't cleaned,' Brett

said defensively. 'Sandy Smith wouldn't let me near it last night.'

'Clean it now, will you, while I assemble your pay packet?'

'It was Dave's idea to give that man a lift.'

'Yes, so you said.'

'I wouldn't have done it on my own.'

'That's bloody unfair,' Dave protested furiously.

'Both of you shut up,' I said. 'Clean the box.'

Seething, they both went out and through the window I watched the rigidity of their anger as they marched towards the task. Undoubtedly the picking up of the hitchhiker had been Dave's doing, but I found I could forgive his irresponsibility more easily than Brett's self-righteousness. They had both for sure pocketed Kevin Keith Ogden's money, although nothing would get them to say how much.

Jogger said, pointing at the cash box, 'What do you want me to do with that?'

'Oh . . . just leave it here. And thanks.'

'Where's Brett off to in that box today?' he asked, following my gaze through the window.

'Nowhere. He's leaving the firm. I'll be driving it myself.'

'Straight up? Then I'll do you a favour.'

I switched my attention to his grubby, lined, fifty-three-year-old face, the wily exterior of an old soldier who knew every skiving trick of the trade but lived by his own code of strict honesty in some respects, notably for anything that moved on wheels.

'You've got a strong active uncovered magnet under that box,' he informed me. 'If you're not careful, it'll pick up iron bars and such and you could catch them on something or back onto them and maybe pierce a fuel tank or worse.'

I moved my head in appreciation. 'What's best to do?'

'I'll stick something over it, if you like.'

'Thanks, Jogger.'

He heard the real gratitude in my voice and nodded briefly. 'What've we been carrying, eh?' he asked. 'Carpets?'

I was mystified. '*Carpets*?'

'And rugs. Drugs.'

'Oh.' I understood belatedly. 'I hope not.' I pondered briefly. 'Keep it to yourself for now, Jogger, will you? Until I get it sorted out.'

He said he would, a promise easily given that might last into the third pint that evening in the pub, but no further.

At close quarters he smelled of oil and dust, those constant companions, and also of stale smoke and a general earthiness. I found it less objectionable than the overpoweringly sweet aftershave and clashing medicinal mouthwash of one of the other drivers, whose odour pervaded his whole horsebox even overriding the scent of horses.

As far as possible, each driver drove one particular horsebox all the time, making it his own. I'd found they all preferred it like that, and they also looked after the vehicles better that way, kept them cleaner, understood their idiosyncrasies and generally treated them with pride as their personal property. Each driver kept the keys of his own box in his possession and could personalise his own cab if he cared to. Several of them who liked to sleep on board had rigged curtains for the windows. Pat, now sick with flu, carried fresh flowers and an ingenious folding changing room in hers. I could almost infallibly have told which box I was in simply by the cab.

Brett's cab was consistent with how little of himself he'd committed to the job; devoid of anything personal. I would be glad to see the back of him even though it compounded the driver shortage.

Saying he'd fetch something for the magnet and that he'd better get on with things if he was going to Surrey with the broodmares, Jogger joggled his way back to his van, loaded the slider and drove off. Dave hosed down the outside of the horsebox and cleaned the windows with a squeegee. Brett swept internal debris carelessly out through the grooms' doors onto the tarmac.

The inside plan of the 35-foot long horsebox made provision for three sets of three stalls, with spaces between the sets. The horses' heads protruded forwards into these spaces, where often sat an attendant travelling near them.

The width of the box allowed for three stalls only if the horses travelling were of average build. Heavily muscled horses, like older steeplechasers, needed more room and could travel only two side by side. The same for broodmares. When we took mares with foals, the three stalls across converted to one single large one. So nine two-year-olds or three mares with foals could be accommodated.

These versatile arrangements were easily achieved by many cleverly designed swinging partitions, all of them of wood, covered with soft padding, to avoid injuries and bruising. We loaded the horses and bolted the stalls as needed around them.

The floors of the stalls were of thick black rubber to stop the horses sliding about, and sometimes we sprinkled the surface with shavings to catch the droppings, especially on long journeys. At each destination, the attendants or the driver would sweep the stalls clean of the muck: the nine-horsebox had therefore arrived home reasonably clean already, having come back empty from Newmarket.

A narrow cupboard at the rear of each box contained brooms, a shovel, hose, squeegees and mop. We also took a bucket or two, feed sometimes for the horses, and several plastic containers of drinking water. The locker under the attendants' bench seat – where Ogden had died – housed spare tack in the form of head collars, ropes, straps, a horse blanket or two and a first-aid kit. Behind the driver's seat lay an efficient fire-extinguisher; and that was about all we carried except for the attendants' own belongings up on the shelf with the mattress. The lads mostly took with them clean tidy clothes to change into for leading their charges round the parade ring, changing back into working things for the return home.

Day after day, all over the country, fleets of horse-boxes like mine ferried all the runners to the races, most days about a hundred runners to each meeting, on bad days, down to, perhaps, thirty. Most of the runners that were trained in Pixhill travelled, luckily, in my boxes and as at least twenty-five trainers were in business in the district, I was making money, if not a fortune.

For all steeplechase jockeys in their early thirties the urgent question arose, *what next*? One life lay behind, unfilled time lay ahead. I'd been driving horseboxes by the age of eighteen for my father, who had owned his own transport; driving some of his horses to the races, looking after them, riding them in amateur races, driving home. By twenty, turning professional, I'd been retained by a top stable, and for twelve years after that I'd finished each season around second to sixth in the jockeys' list, riding upwards of 400 jump races a year. Few jump jockeys lasted longer than that near the top owing to the physical battering of falls, and at thirty-two time and injuries had caught up with me, as they'd been bound to do in the end.

From jockey to full-time horse transporter had been a jolting change of outlook in some ways, but familiar territory in others. Three years into the new life, it seemed as if it had been inevitable all along.

I made up Brett's pay packet with cash from my safe as promised and typed the information into the computer, so that along in the office Rose could incorporate it into the P45. One way and another she hadn't had much practice at P45s, as the turnover in drivers had proved small.

Brett's envelope in hand, I went out to the horsebox where he and Dave were now standing on the tarmac glaring at each other. Having removed the hose from the outside tap beyond the wood pile, Dave stood with its green flabby plastic loops over his arm, apparently childishly arguing that it was Brett's job to put it away in its cupboard.

Give me strength, I thought, and asked Dave nicely to put it away himself. With bad grace he climbed with it into the box and Brett watched him spitefully.

'That's not the only time Dave's picked up a hitchhiker,' he said.

I listened but didn't reply.

Brett said, 'It's him you ought to sack, not me.'

'I didn't sack you.'

'As good as.'

His sharp young face lacked any sort of humour and

I felt sorry for him that he should go through life making himself disliked. There seemed to be no way of changing him; he would go whining to the grave.

'You'll have to leave a forwarding address with Isobel,' I said conversationally. 'You might be called on for the inquest on yesterday's passenger.'

'It's Dave they'll want.'

'All the same, leave an address.'

He grunted, accepted his pay packet without thanks and drove off, Dave coming to earth again by my side and looking after him balefully.

'What did he say?' he asked.

'That you'd picked up other hitchhikers.'

Dave looked furious. 'He *would*.'

'Don't do it, Dave.'

He listened to the weight I put into the words and, unsuccessfully trying to joke, said, 'Is that some sort of threat?'

'A warning.'

'It don't seem fair to leave people standing by the roadside.'

'It may not seem fair to you,' I said, 'but just grit your teeth and do it.'

'Well . . . OK.' He gave me a half-hearted grin and promised not to give any lifts on his way back from leaving the broodmares in Gloucestershire that afternoon.

'I'm serious, Dave.'

He sighed. 'Yeah. I know it.'

He retrieved his rusty bike from the wood pile and squeaked away down the drive, wobbling aside for Jogger who was returning in his van.

Jogger had brought with him a book-sized piece of wood with a cluster of nails driven into it. The nail-heads would stick to the magnet, he said, but not so firmly that he wouldn't be able to get the whole thing off at the next overhaul. The wood would prevent the magnet from picking up anything else.

I took his word for it, and watched him roll expertly under the chassis without using the slider, taking only seconds to put the insulating wood in place. He was up on his feet giving me a sideways yellow smile in an instant.

'That didn't take long,' I said thoughtfully.

'If you know where to look, it's a piece of cake.'

Harve arrived at that moment, crossing with Jogger's departure. We walked together to the house and I showed him the grime-laden cash box, explaining where Jogger had found it. He looked as puzzled as I felt.

'But what's it *for*?' he said.

'Jogger thinks we've been entertaining drugs unawares.'

'What?'

'Smuggling cocaine, perhaps?'

'No.' Harve was adamant. 'No one could do that without us knowing.'

Ruefully I said, 'Maybe one of us does know.'

Harve didn't agree. Our drivers were saints, he implied.

I told him about the night visitor, who'd come in black disguise and entered the horsebox.

'He had a key to the grooms' door,' I said. 'He must have done. There's no damage to the locks.'

'Yes,' Harve said, thinking, 'but you know those groom-door keys don't open just one box. I mean, I know for a certainty that my own box has the same key as Brett's, here. Quite a lot of them are duplicated.'

I nodded. The ignition keys were individually special and couldn't be copied, but the grooms' door locks came from a different smaller range, and several of the boxes had keys that fitted others.

'What was he doing *inside* the cab?' Harve asked, 'if this thing . . . this hiding place . . . was underneath?'

'I don't know. He had dirt on his clothes. Maybe he'd already looked underneath and found the hiding place empty.'

'What are you going to do about it?' Harve said. 'Tell Sandy Smith?'

'Maybe. Sometime. I don't want to run us into trouble if I don't have to.'

Harve was happy with that. 'We don't want the Customs to hear of it,' he said, nodding. 'They'd hold us up for hours, every crossing. They'd treat it as specific information received, I wouldn't wonder.'

His pleasant face was only lightly anxious; and the

unwelcome discovery, I supposed, didn't merit the instant pushing of panic buttons.

'OK,' I said, 'let's get on. I'll come along to the farm for fuel and start the shuttle.'

I locked the house while Harvey left, then followed along to the farmyard, less than a mile away, nearer to the heart of Pixhill.

Harve, his wife and four tow-headed children lived next door to the farmyard, in what had been the old farmhouse. The old farm barn was now Jogger's domain, a workshop with inspection pit and every aid to mechanical perfection that he could cajole me into buying.

What had once been a cowshed was now a small canteen and a suite of three offices with windows looking into the farmyard, from where one could watch the horseboxes come and go, each to and from its own allocated parking space. A small stable block with room for three horses was sited in the space between the end of the stretch of offices and the high wall of the barn. We sometimes housed our passengers there temporarily if they were due to leave or arrive in the middle of the night.

Several of the day's sorties had already begun. The other nine-box had already left to collect the broodmares bound for Ireland. The two Southwell boxes' spaces were empty also. Jogger was driving Phil's box over to the barn for its overhaul.

I drew to a halt by the diesel pump and topped up the tanks.

Normally we refuelled on return in the evenings to avoid water problems from air condensing overnight in quarter-full tanks, a tip I'd learned from a pilot friend. We also hosed down the boxes at that point and cleaned the insides with disinfectant so they were fresh and ready to go in the mornings.

Brett, I noticed, had removed the remains of his picnic, but his solution to the stain on the bench-seat had been not to clean it off but to fold the horse rug and lay it along the seat to cover it. Typical, I thought.

In the offices, Isobel and Rose were consulting their machines, turning up the heaters and drinking coffee from the canteen next door. Rose said she had already given Brett his P45 and taken his mother's address and was glad to be rid of him.

Rose, plumply middle-aged, kept the financial records, seeing to the pay packets, sending out bills, preparing cheques for my signature, keeping track of the pennies. Isobel, gentle, young, clear-headed, answered the telephone, took the bookings and chatted usefully with many trainers' secretaries, harvesting advance notice of their stables' requirements.

Rose and Isobel had an office each, in which they worked from eight-thirty to four. The third office, less busy-looking, less personal, was technically my own but was used just as much by Harve. The documentation of the boxes was kept in there, and also duplicates of the ignition keys, in a locked drawer.

In spite of the flu, in spite of Brett, in spite of Kevin Keith Ogden, that Friday's work seemed to be going smoothly.

The driver due to transfer Jericho Rich's six fillies to Newmarket had already arrived in the farmyard, as for some unspecified reason Michael Watermead had wanted them to leave his stable earlier in the morning than the load of two-year-olds the day before.

I explained to Nigel, the driver, that Michael wouldn't be sending any of his own lads to care for the fillies ('Jericho can whistle for favours, bloody man') but that a car with a couple of lads would be coming over from the destination trainer in Newmarket.

'They did the same yesterday with Brett and the day before with Harve, so you shouldn't have any trouble,' I said.

Nigel nodded.

'And don't pick up any corpses on the way home.'

He laughed. He was twenty-four, insatiably heterosexual, found life a joke and could call on inexhaustible stamina, his chief virtue in my eyes. Any time we needed long night-driving I sent him, if I could.

Trainers often had a favourite among the drivers, a particular man they knew and trusted. In Michael Watermead's case, there was a driver called Lewis, at that moment warming his hands round a mug of tea and listening to Dave's self-justifying account of the last ride of K.K. Ogden.

'Didn't he say anything?' Lewis asked interestedly. 'Just snuffed it?'

'Makes you think, doesn't it?'

Lewis agreed about that, nodding his close-cropped head. In his twenties, like the majority of the drivers, he was willing, resourceful and strong, with a tattoo of a dragon on one forearm and a reputed past as a biker. The rave-up history had raised my doubts to begin with, but he'd proved thoroughly reliable at the wheel of his glossy super-six box, and Michael, who had exacting standards, had taken to him firmly.

In consequence, Lewis drove prestigious horses to big meetings. The Watermead stable at that moment housed 'Classic' contenders, with representative runners in both the Guineas and Oaks; and all of the drivers had already put their money on the Watermead star three-year-old colt, Irkab Alhawa which, if all went well, Lewis would be driving to Epsom, in June, for the Derby.

He was, that morning, setting off to France to collect two two-year-olds that an owner had bought to be trained in Michael's yard. As he was going alone, without a relief driver – agreed with Michael – he would have to take rest stops on the way and wouldn't be back until Monday evening. He would sleep as usual in his cab, which he preferred.

I checked with him that he had the right documents

and food and water for the two-year-olds, and watched him set off cheerfully on the errand.

Harve having gone through the rest of the day's programme again with me, I set off myself towards chilly gale-swept Salisbury Plain to get to grips with the yo-yo shuttle which could take until evening and give me a headache. The headache would result from the voice and personality of the trainer on the move, a forceful lady in her fifties with the intonation and occasionally the vocabulary of a barrack-room parrot. I wanted nevertheless to please her, aiming for all her future business.

She strode across to the box when I pulled up in her yard and produced the first squawk of the day.

'The boss himself!' she proclaimed ironically, seeing my face. 'Why the honour?'

'Flu,' I said succinctly. 'Morning, Marigold.'

She peered beyond me to the empty passenger seats. 'Didn't you bring a handler? Your secretary said there would be two of you.'

'He's had to drive today. Sorry.'

She clicked her tongue in irritation. 'Half my lads have got the bug. It's a pest.'

I jumped down from the cab and lowered the two ramps while she watched and grumbled, a wiry figure in a padded jacket and woolly hat, her nose blue with cold. She was moving to Pixhill, she'd told the racing press, because it was warmer for the horses.

She'd made lists laying out the order in which her

string was to travel. Her depleted force of lads led the horses up the ramps into the box and I bolted the partitions round them until the first nine were installed.

Marigold – Mrs English, as the lads called her – encouraged the loading with various raucous epithets and an overall air of impatience. I certainly could have done with Dave's knack of imparting confidence to horses while leading them up ramps: Marigold's method tended to frighten them upwards so that I bolted several of them quivering and wild-eyed into their stalls.

She had decided to drive herself in her car to Pixhill to be ready in the new yard when I and the horses arrived. Four of her lads travelled with me in the cab, all of them apparently enthusiastic over the move, the night-life of Pixhill being seen as hotly wicked when compared with the winds of Stonehenge.

Her new yard was an old yard in Pixhill, now modernised and enlarged. Its first nine inhabitants clattered down the ramps and were directed loudly to their new homes by Marigold with a list. I shovelled the droppings onto muck sacks supplied by her lads and put the wagon ship-shape for the second foray.

Pleased, Marigold told me that as I was doing the work myself she wouldn't need to travel backwards and forwards all day to supervise and would entrust the next loading to me entirely. She gave me the list. I thanked her. She looked on me kindly. I thought with satisfaction that I would glue her to me as a permanent customer by nightfall.

With such profitable thoughts I set off back to Salisbury Plain and had my complacence shattered by Jogger on the phone.

'Hi ho Silver,' he said cheerfully, 'we've got another couple of Lone Rangers.'

'Jogger . . . you've lost me.'

'Limpets,' he said helpfully. 'Barnacles. Stuck to the ships' bottoms.'

'Where are you, exactly?' I asked.

'In your office.'

'Is there someone else with you?'

'Nothing wrong with your uptake, is there? Do you want to talk to Constable Smith? He's here now.'

'Wait,' I said, 'do you mean what I think you mean? For Lone Rangers, do I understand strangers?'

'You got it.'

'Like the cash box?'

'Like, but not twins.' Jogger paused, letting me hear a rumble from Sandy Smith's familiar voice. 'Constable Smith,' Jogger said, 'wants to know when you'll be back. He says there was a warrant out for that stiff.'

CHAPTER THREE

I spoke to Sandy.

'What warrant? What for?'

'Fraud. Dud cheques. Skipping hotels without paying. Petty stuff, mostly, it seems. The Nottingham police wanted him.'

'Too bad,' I said.

'Had you ever seen him before, Freddie?'

'Not that I know of.'

'He'd welshed on a bookie or two.'

People who failed to pay bookmakers weren't necessarily my best buddies, as I pointed out.

'No,' Sandy agreed, 'but he must have had something to do with racing if he asked for a lift in a horsebox.'

'Dave said he was propositioning a tanker driver first. Maybe he had something to do with oil.'

'Oh, very funny.'

'Let me know the result of the post-mortem, will you?'

'Well, all right, but I don't expect I'll get it today.'

'Any time,' I said. 'Come in for a drink.'

He liked to do that, because sometimes I would keep him up to date with any local villainy I didn't like the look of. On the other hand, the villainy going on on the undersides of my boxes needed more understanding before, or if ever, I told Sandy about it.

I spoke to Jogger again briefly, asking him to phone me without fail when he returned from Surrey.

'Won't hammer or bucket.'

With a sigh I heard him disconnect and reached Marigold's old yard again before it clicked. Hammer and nail or bucket and pail.

Fail.

Most of the way I thought of the limpets and wondered what to do about them. I thought I might usefully set up an opportunity for advice without committing myself, so I pulled the horsebox into a roadside parking space, fished out my diary for the number and got through to the Security section of the Jockey Club in Portman Square in London, asking for the head man.

Everyone professionally engaged in racing knew Patrick Venables by name and most of them by sight. Transgressors wished they didn't. Such sins as I'd been guilty of having luckily escaped his notice, I could go to him for help when I needed it and probably be believed.

Fortunately I found him in his office. I asked him if he would by any chance be going to Sandown races the next day.

'Yes, but I'm also going this afternoon,' he said. 'If it's urgent, come today.'

I explained about the flu and the driver shortage. 'But I can drive one of my boxes to Sandown tomorrow,' I said.

'Right. Outside the weighing-room.'

'Thanks very much.'

I resumed the journey, loaded the appointed horses, drove them and the two lads to join Marigold. She told me loudly I should have brought more than two lads with nine horses and I explained that her head lad had said two only, he'd had another one go home sick and he wasn't feeling too well himself.

'Blast the man,' she screeched.

'You can't argue with a virus,' I said pacifyingly.

'I've got to get all the horses over here today,' she yelled.

'Yes, well, we will.'

I cleaned out the box, smiled reassuringly, shut up the ramps and made the third leg of the shuttle. Twenty-seven deliveries, I thought, seeing the third load rattle down the ramps into their new home, and supposedly two more trips to make, though the head lad had ominously told me Mrs English hadn't counted right, she'd overlooked her own hack and two unbroken two-year-olds.

The yards were approximately thirty miles apart and each shuttle, with loading and unloading, was taking me two hours. By dusk at seven in the evening all but the oddments were safely settled in and Marigold for once looked tired. Her head lad had given best to the flu and gone home to bed and my own muscles were aching. When I suggested finishing the job early the next morning, the lady resignedly agreed. I tentatively kissed her cheek, an intimacy I would normally not have attempted, and to my utter astonishment her eyes filled with tears, instantly repudiated with a shake of her woolly-hatted head.

I offered, 'It's been a long day.'

'A day I've looked forward to . . . and planned . . . for years.'

'Then I'm glad it went OK.'

She was lonely, I perceived, surprised, the hard outer lady a gallant way of playing the cards life had dealt her. I knew moreover that I had indeed secured her future business, and was happy I'd had to do the shuttle myself.

Leaving her trudging with reviving voice round the new stables, I drove the nine-box along to the farmyard, pulled up by the pumps and wrote up the log books, both the box's and my own. I'd spoken to Isobel on the phone several times during the day, hearing at one point that Jericho Rich had actually turned up in her office checking her records. Cheek, I thought. I'd also learned from Harve that all the planned work had been completed without trouble except that one of Jogger's pair of broodmares had started to foal on the way to Surrey and that Jogger, mechanic, had unwillingly become midwife.

Jogger in his turn had reported the incident to me with shocked indignation because the stud groom at the destination had refused to move the mare from the horsebox until the foaling was complete, delaying Jogger's return to Pixhill by a couple of hours. Jogger, it appeared, had never seen a foal born before: he had found it both eye-opening and disgusting.

'Did you know the mare *eats* all that stuff? Fair turned me up.'

'Don't think about it,' I advised him. 'Tell me which boxes have sprouted little strangers.'

'Eh? Oh . . . Phil's and the one Dave's driving, which is Pat's box usually. But, see, most of the others had gone out by the time I found those. There may be more.'

He sounded cheerful, but then it wasn't his business at stake. By the time I'd completed the log books, filled the tanks and moved the nine-box to the corner where we customarily cleaned the fleet, he had still not returned.

Under the strong outdoor lights, I hosed down the nine-box and squeegeed the windows, not a big job for once as the weather had been dry all day. In the farm-yard, the cleaning water came out like a mist under pressure, driven through a pump with compressed air: more effective and more economical with water than a plain hose.

The interior took me more time, as forty-five horses

and a relay of lads had left their mark despite the intermittent sweepings out, and I was dog-tired myself by the time I'd mopped the floors with disinfectant and fastened all the partitions ready for the morrow.

The front cab itself was a mess, littered with screwed-up sandwich wrappers and awash with the ropes, reins and other paraphernalia used and borrowed from the underseat locker.

I opened the locker and replaced all the gear in it. Even inside the locker, the lads had left their meal-remains. I picked out a small paper carrier and replaced it with a couple of re-folded horse rugs. Shutting the lid, I noticed again the stain on the seat from the previous night and wondered how to get rid of it, short of re-covering the whole thing. Certainly none of the lads that had sat on it that day had complained, but then they hadn't known about Kevin Keith Ogden's last ride.

Smiling a shade ruefully I swept the rubbish into the sack I'd provided but the lads had resolutely ignored, and stood it beside the small carrier which would have gone into the sack also, except that it proved heavier than empty and contained, I found, a thermos flask and a packet of uneaten sandwiches. Yawning, I thought I would get it back to Marigold's lads in the morning, whether or not I did the last shuttle myself.

Finally I drove the box along to its usual parking space, locked everything, threw the rubbish sack into our own skip, carried the thermos flask and bag into the offices and typed my day's records into Isobel's computer. That done, I sat for a while calling to the screen the requirements for the next day, trying to work out if we would have enough drivers and hoping no one else would be ill by the morning.

I phoned Jogger to find out where he was. Ten minutes from the boozer, he said. The boozer, Jogger's natural home, was the pub where he drank with his cronies every night. Ten minutes to the boozer meant maybe twelve to the farm.

'Don't stop on the way,' I said.

While I waited for him I ran through the computer notes for the day; everything, that's to say, that had been entered before Isobel and Rose had left at four o'clock.

The only hiccup, a very minor one, seemed to have been that Michael Watermead's fillies had set off an hour and a half late to Newmarket.

'Nigel reported,' the screen informed me, 'lads from Newmarket didn't show until ten-thirty. Tessa's message yesterday ordered box for nine a.m. Nigel set off with fillies at eleven. Reported arrival Newmarket one-thirty. Reported leaving Newmarket two-thirty.'

Nigel had returned uneventfully, Harve had said, and his box stood clean and shipshape in its accustomed place.

The Tessa in question was Michael's daughter, so no one's head would roll over the mistake; mix ups over time were all too common. If that was the worst that had happened it had been a near-perfect work-day.

Isobel's last snippet of information read, 'Mr Rich

in person called at the office, checking our records on his transfer. I satisfied him on all points.'

Jogger's lights swooped in through the gates and he rolled along to the pumps. I went out to meet him and found him still shaken by the confrontation with the bloody realities of birth. I myself had seen several foals and other animals delivered but never, I idly reflected, an actual human baby. Would I, I wondered, have found it more traumatic? My only child, a daughter, had been born in my absence to a girl who'd persuaded another man he was the father, and married him quickly. I saw them all sometimes, along with their two subsequent children, but I felt few paternal longings and knew I would never seek to prove the truth.

Jogger filled his tanks, moved to the cleaning area and grumbled his way through the mopping out. In the belief that if I interrupted I would be left with an incomplete job, I waited until he'd finished before I asked him the vital question.

'Where exactly are these limpet strangers?'

'You'll never see them in the dark,' he said, sniffing.

'Jogger . . .'

'Yeah, well, you can't hardly see them in broad daylight – ' he wiped his nose on the back of his hand, 'unless you want to get under on the slider with a torch?'

'No.'

'Didn't think so.'

'Just tell me about them.'

He walked along the row with me, pointing.

'Phil's box. I had it over the pit. There's a tube container stuck on top of the rear fuel tank, in that space above the tank but under the box's floor. It's hidden by the side of the horsebox, and you can't see it either from the front or the back of the box if you're looking casually under the chassis. Bloody neat job.'

I frowned. 'What would it hold?'

'Search me. Half a dozen footballs, maybe. It's empty now, though. It must have had a screw-on cap. The screw-thread's there, but the cap is missing.'

Phil's box was a super-six, as were half of the fleet. A super-six carried six horses in comfort, had an extra-spacious cab, a generous general layout, and could accommodate a seventh horse standing crossways at a pinch. I liked driving them better than the longer nine-boxes. Half a dozen footballs in a tube on the underside sounded macabre as well as downright improbable.

'Pat's box,' Jogger said, pointing, 'that's the one Dave drove with broodmares, remember?' He broke off, recalling his own frightful day. 'Don't never ask me to drive no broodmares no more.'

'Er, no, Jogger. What about Pat's box?'

Pat's box, smaller, took four horses. Five of the fleet were that size, handy, less thirsty, the runabouts. In the Flat racing season, Pat's box was retained full time by another Pixhill trainer with a phobia about sharing journeys with other trainers' horses. Pat's box went often to France, though not with her driving.

'Under there,' Jogger said, 'is another tube, the same size. It's empty. It has a screw-on cap, too, and the cap is there, on that one.'

'Been there a while?' I asked. 'Dirty?'

'Natch.'

'I'll maybe take a look in the morning. And Jogger, keep it to yourself, will you? If you spread it around the boozer you'll frighten off whoever stuck the things there, and we'll never have a chance of finding out what's going on.'

He could see the point of that. He said he'd be as silent as the wash (wash and shave: grave) and again I wondered if his reticence would outlast the evening's pints.

On Saturday morning early, I drove one of the four-boxes to Salisbury Plain, collected Marigold's oddment horses and delivered them to her by nine, realising along the way that I'd forgotten to take with me her lads' lunch carrier bag. When I mentioned it to her, she enquired loudly of her employees about ownership but received no claims.

'Throw it away,' she counselled. 'I'm sending horses to Doncaster. You can take them, I hope?'

Doncaster races, twelve days ahead, represented the prestigious opening of the Flat season. I assured her I'd be delighted to take anything she wanted.

'In a box on their own,' she added. 'I don't want

them picking up other stables' germs. My horses never share transport.'

'Fine,' I said.

'Good.' She brought forth a smile, more a matter of eyes than of lips: as good a pledge as shaking hands on a contract.

Home again I drank coffee, ate cornflakes, talked to Harve, talked to Jogger ('Didn't say a dicky bird down the boozer.') and checked the day's list, again juggling the dearth of drivers and pressing Dave and Jogger again into behind-the-wheel service.

Rather against his will, I redrafted Phil into the nine-box and took his super-six myself, picking up jumpers from three different stables and delivering them and their lads to Sandown racecourse for the afternoon's sport.

Over Sandown's fences I'd ridden more winners than I could remember, its testing course so imprinted in my subconscious that I could probably have ridden it blindfold and had certainly navigated its intricacies familiarly in countless dreams. Of all courses, it evoked in me the strongest nostalgia for the close world I'd lost, the intimate body-to-body blending with a non-human powerhouse, the mind-into-mind flowing of courage and intent. One could speak to strangers of race-riding as being a 'job like any other' but the slightest introspection gave that the lie. Racing on horses over jumps at thirty or more miles an hour was, to me at least, a spiritual exaltation never achieved or even envisioned in any other way. To each his religion, I supposed. Big horses over big fences had been mine.

Nowadays at Sandown I felt excommunicated; no doubt a blasphemy, but a deep truth nevertheless.

I met Patrick Venables outside the weighing-room, as he'd promised.

The head of racing's Security Service, a tall thin man with suitably hawk-like eyes, had in his time, one understood, been 'something in counter-espionage', no details ever supplied. Racecourse wits said he'd been sired by a lie-detector out of a leech, in that one couldn't fool him or shake him off.

Like others in his job before him, he ran the comparatively small Security section with brisk efficiency and was largely responsible for the reasonably honest state of racing, sniffing out new scams almost before they were invented.

He greeted me with the usual skin-deep friendliness, never to be mistaken for trust. Looking at his watch he said, 'Five minutes, Freddie. Is that enough?'

Condense it, he meant, and, faced with his deadline and obvious lack of time, I began to retreat from asking his advice.

'Well, it doesn't matter really,' I said lamely.

My hesitancy, instead of releasing him, seemed to switch on his attention. He told me to follow him into the weighing-room and led me through to a small inner office containing a table, two chairs and very little else.

He closed the door. 'Sit down,' he said, 'and fire away.'

I told him about the three containers Jogger had so far found under the boxes. 'I don't know how long they've been there or what they contained. My mechanic says he can't swear he won't find more, as they're pretty well camouflaged.' I paused briefly. 'Has anyone else come across anything like this?'

He shook his head. 'Not that I know of. Have you told the police?'

'No.'

'Why not?'

'Curiosity, I suppose. I want to find out who's been using me, and what for.'

He pondered, studying my face. 'You're using *me* as insurance,' he said eventually, 'in case one of your boxes is caught smuggling.'

I didn't deny it. 'I'd like to catch them myself, though.'

'Mm.' He pursed his mouth. 'I'd have to advise you not to.'

I protested, 'I can't just do nothing.'

'Let me think about it.'

'Thank you,' I said.

'I suppose,' he frowned, 'this hasn't anything to do with the man who died in one of your boxes? I heard about that.'

'I don't really know.' I told him about the masked searcher. 'I don't know what he was looking for. If it was the dead man's belongings, he wouldn't have had any success because the police had them all. But then I wondered if he'd been *leaving* anything. And he had dirt and dust on his clothes, which was why I wondered if he'd been on the ground, and why I asked my mechanic to see if he'd stuck anything on the box underneath.'

'And you think he had?'

'No. The container under there had been in place for some time. It was filthy, with layers of grime.'

I told him that the box I had driven to Sandown that day had a capacious tube stuck above the fuel tank. 'You can't see it at all easily even if you're looking for it, up from underneath,' I explained. 'Horseboxes are all coach-built so that the sides are nearer the ground than the chassis. For aerodynamics and good looks. I expect you know that. Mine are built in Lambourn. They're very good. Anyway, the sides hide and shield the underside mechanisms, same as cars. Bombs can be hidden there.'

'I do understand,' he assured me. 'Are bombs what you fear?'

'I suppose drugs are more likely.'

Patrick Venables looked at his watch and stood up. 'Have to go,' he said. 'Come back to the weighing-room after the last race.'

My nod of agreement was made to his departing back. I wondered what he would make of it; shrug it off or take a look. Sometime during the afternoon he would decide, but in telling him I'd come to my own conclusion, that I really did need and mean to find out what was going on, with or without his help.

I went outside and spent a good deal of the afternoon in conversation, useful sometimes for business but a far cry from the urgency of race-riding, changing colours, weighing out and in, hurrying, racing, changing colours . . . Oh, well. On the good side, I no longer starved to remain artificially thin, no longer broke my bones and hid large bruises, no longer feared losing big races, good owners, my nerve or my job. I was now free in a way I'd never been and reflected that if I still had to please owners and trainers, then to prosper almost everyone had to please *someone*; performers, the paying public, presidents and prime ministers, their population.

On afternoons like that at Sandown I'd found I behaved like all my drivers, that is to say I took especial note of those particular runners that I'd brought to the course. A winner lifted the spirits of every driver; a horse killed, as occasionally happened, sent them home in depression. The undoubted if illogical feelings of proprietorship had a noticeable effect on how cheerfully, fast and thoroughly the boxes got serviced on their return.

As two of the horses I had ferried that day belonged to a trainer I'd ridden for intermittently in the past, it was natural that I'd end up talking to him and his wife.

Benjy Usher and Dot appeared to be quarrelling as

usual when he shot out an arm and grabbed my sleeve as I passed.

'Freddie,' he demanded, 'tell this woman which year Fred Archer shot himself. She says 1890. I say that's rubbish.'

I glanced at Dot's normal mixed expression of resignation and anxiety. Years of living with an irascible man had carved permanent facial lines that even her infrequent smiles could barely override, yet although they'd been figuratively spitting at each other for as long as I'd known them, the pair were still grimly together.

They were both unusually good-looking, which only made it odder. Both were well dressed, in their forties, socially practised and intelligent. Fifteen years earlier I wouldn't have given their union five minutes, which just shows how little an outsider can see of a marriage.

'Well?' Benjy challenged.

'I don't know,' I said diplomatically, though I did know actually that it had been in 1886, when the brilliant champion jockey was twenty-nine, and had won 2,749 races, travelling everywhere by train.

'You're useless,' Benjy said, and Dot looked relieved.

Benjy changed the subject, mercurial always. 'Did my horses get here all right?'

'Yes, they did indeed.'

'My lad tells me you drove them yourself.'

I nodded. 'Three of my drivers have flu.'

Many trainers came out into their stable yards to

see their runners load safely into the transport, but Benjy seldom did. His idea of supervision was to yell out of the window if he saw anything to displease him, which I understood was often. Benjy's turnover of stable-lads was higher than most. Benjy's head travelling lad, who should have accompanied the runners to Sandown, had walked out on the previous day.

Benjy asked if I knew of that awkward fact. Yes, I'd been told, I said.

'Then do me a favour. Saddle my runners and come into the ring with us.'

Most trainers in the circumstances would have saddled their own runners, but not Benjy. He scarcely liked touching them, I'd observed. I guessed the question about Fred Archer had been only a pretext; grabbing me on the wing had been the purpose.

I told him I'd be glad to saddle the horses. Not too far from the truth.

'Good,' he said, satisfied.

Accordingly I did the work while he and Dot chatted to the first runner's owner, and the same for the second runner later in the afternoon. The first ran respectably without earning medals and the second won his race. As always in the winner's unsaddling enclosure on such occasions, Benjy's handsome face reddened and sweated as if with orgasmic pleasure. The owners petted their horse. Dot told me seriously I would have made a good head lad.

I smiled.

'Oh dear.'

'Well, I would,' I said.

There was always something I didn't understand about Dot; some deep reserve in her nature. I knew her no better after fifteen years than I had at the beginning.

Benjy's odd training methods were due, one understood, to his not having to make training pay. Benjy's inherited multi-millions, moreover, had been deployed in acquiring good horses overseas which were trained there by other trainers and which won better events in France and Italy than Benjy's horses in England. Benjy, like many owners, preferred the higher prize-money of mainland Europe, but he chose still to live in Pixhill and to train for other people as a hobby and to use my horseboxes for his transport, a fact guaranteed to earn my approbation.

He and Dot took me for a drink: double gins for them, tonic for me. The one thing I couldn't afford to lose was my driving licence.

Benjy said, 'I've a colt in Italy that's pulled a tendon. I want him back here to heal and rest. Care to fetch him?'

'Very much so.'

'Good. I'll tell you when.' He patted my shoulder. 'You do a good job with those boxes. We can trust you, can't we, Dot?'

Dot nodded.

'Well . . . thanks,' I said.

One way and another the afternoon passed quickly and after the last race I waited for Patrick Venables outside the weighing-room. He came eventually at a half-trot, still pressed for time.

'Freddie,' he said, 'you told me yesterday you were short of drivers. Is that still the case?'

'Three have flu, and one's left for good.'

'Er, um. Then I suggest I send you a replacement; one who can look into your problem.'

I wasn't immediately enthusiastic. 'He'd have to know the job,' I said dubiously.

'It's a she. And you'll find she does. I've arranged for her to go to Pixhill tomorrow morning. Show her your operation and let her take it from there.'

I thanked him unconvincingly. He smiled faintly and told me to give her a try. 'Nothing lost if nothing comes of it.'

I wasn't so sure, but I'd asked his help and could see no way of backing out. He hurried off with a last piece of information. 'I gave her your address.'

He'd gone before I thought to ask her name, but it hardly mattered, I supposed. I hoped she would have the decency to arrive before I went to Maudie Watermead's lunch.

Her name was Nina Young. She swept up the drive onto my tarmac at nine a.m., catching me unshaven and reading newspapers in a towelling robe, coffee and cornflakes to hand.

I went to the door to answer her ring, not realising at once who she was.

She'd been driving a scarlet Mercedes and, although not young, she wore slender skin-tight jeans, a white shirt with romantically large sleeves, an embroidered Afghan waistcoat, heavy gold chains and an expensive scent. Her shining dark hair had an expert cut. Her high cheekbones, long neck and calm eyes reminded me of noble ancestor portraits, bone structure three hundred years old. My idea of a working box-driver, she was not.

'Patrick Venables said to come early,' she said, offering a nail-varnished hand. The voice was Roedean – Benenden – St Mary's, Calne, the social poise learned in the cradle. From my male chauvinist point of view, the only drawback was her age, near mid-forties at a guess.

'Come in,' I invited, standing back and thinking she was good for the scenery if not for the matter in hand.

'Freddie Croft,' she said, as if seeing a cardboard cut-out come to life. 'The man himself.'

'Well, yes,' I agreed. 'Like some coffee?'

'No, thank you. Do I detect a faint air of exasperation?'

'Not in the least.' I led the way into the sitting-room, and indicated any chair she chose to sit on.

She chose a deep armchair, crossing the long legs to show fine ankles above buckled leather shoes. From a shoulder bag of equal pedigree, she produced a small folder which she waved in my general direction.

'Driving licence with Large Goods Vehicle qualification,' she assured me. 'The real McCoy.'

'He wouldn't have sent you without it. How did you get it?'

'Driving my hunters,' she said matter-of-factly. 'Also my show horses and eventers. Any questions?'

The sort of horseboxes she would have been driving had home-from-home large living quarters in front of the stalls, the nomadic luxury motors for eventing at Badminton and Burleigh. She had to be a familiar figure in that world, widely recognisable to too many people for the present purpose.

'Perhaps I ought to know you?' I suggested.

'I shouldn't think so. I don't go racing.'

'Er,' I said mildly, 'here you'd need to be able to find the racecourses.'

'Patrick said you were bound to have a map.'

Patrick, I thought, had taken leave of his senses.

She watched my no doubt obvious misgivings with cool amusement.

'My horseboxes are basic transport,' I said. 'No fridges, no cookers, no bathrooms.'

'They've Mercedes engines, haven't they?'

I nodded, surprised.

'I'm a good driver.'

I believed her. 'All right, then,' I said.

I reflected that whatever she might lack as an investigator, I definitely did need an extra pair of hands for my wheels. What Harve and Jogger would make of her I dreaded to think.

'Good,' she said prosaically and after a brief second's pause asked, 'Do you take *Horse and Hound?*'

I fetched that week's as yet unread copy of the magazine from a side table and handed it to her, watching as she flicked through towards the end, to the many pages of classified advertisements. She came to the horse-transport section where about once a month I advertised Croft Raceways, and tapped the page with a rose-pink fingernail.

'Patrick wants to know if you've seen this?'

I took the magazine from her and read where she'd pointed. In an outlined, single-column-width advertisement were the simple words:

TRANSPORT PROBLEMS?
We can help.
Anything considered.

A fourth line gave a telephone number.

I frowned. 'Yes, I've seen that. It's in the transport ads now and then. Rather pointless, I've thought.'

'Patrick wants me to check it out.'

'No one,' I objected, 'would advertise a smuggling service. It's impossible.'

'Why don't we try?'

I passed her a cordless telephone. 'Go ahead.'

She pressed the numbers, listened, wrinkled her nose and switched the phone off.

'Answering machine,' she reported succinctly. 'Leave name and number and they'll get back.'

'Man or woman?'

'Man.'

We looked at each other. I didn't believe there was anything sinister in the advertisement, but I said, 'Perhaps Patrick Venables could use his muscle on *Horse and Hound* and find out where that ad comes from.'

She nodded. 'He's doing it tomorrow.'

Impressed despite my disbelief I went over to the desk and consulted the chart.

'I've probably got two boxes going to Taunton races tomorrow,' I told her. 'My woman driver Pat's got the flu. You can take her box. It can carry four horses but you're only likely to have three. You can follow my other box to Taunton so that you arrive at the right place at the right time, and for the pick-up this end I'll send a man called Dave with you. He knows the stable the horses are going from. After you've collected the horses, drop him back at our base and follow the other box from then on.'

'All right.'

'It would be better if you didn't report for work in that car out there.'

She gave me a glimmering smile. 'You'll hardly know me in the morning. And what do I call you? Sir?'

'Freddie will do. And you?'

'Nina.'

She stood up, tall and composed, every inch the opposite of what I needed. The trip to Taunton, I thought, would be her first and last, especially when it came to cleaning the box after the return home. She shook my hand – her own was firm and dry – and went unhurriedly out to her car. I followed her to the door and watched the scarlet excitement depart with its expensive distinctive Mercedes purr.

No one, I reflected, had mentioned pay. Rose would want to know what I'd agreed. Not even undercover missions for the Jockey Club could be conducted without ubiquitous paperwork.

Sundays were always comparatively quiet, business-wise, with rarely as many as half the fleet on the road. That particular Sunday, the driver shortage posing no problem, Harve, Jogger and Dave could all take their accustomed day off, along with a bunch of others. Most of the drivers liked Saturday and Sunday work as they were paid more for weekends, but I was lucky in general with all of them as a team, as they hated to see work go to rival firms and would drive on their allotted days off to prevent it. According to the law, their hours and compulsory rest periods were strictly set out; I sometimes had difficulty persuading them that I could be prosecuted if they bent the rules too far.

Like most jobs in racing, driving horseboxes was more a way of life than simply a means of earning a living and, as a result, only people who enjoyed it, did it, Stamina was essential, also good humour and adaptability. Brett had been a mistake.

The news of his leaving had spread already through the racing grapevine, and before eleven that morning two applicants had phoned for his job. I turned them both down: one had worked for too many other firms, the other was over sixty, too old already for the intense physical demands and no good as a long-term prospect.

I phoned Harve and told him I'd engaged a temporary woman driver to take Pat's place until she was well again. She would be doing the Taunton run planned for Pat.

'Good,' Harve said, unsuspecting.

So far, the week ahead looked less busy than the one just completed, not a bad thing in the circumstances. I would be able to go to Cheltenham races in spectator comfort, to watch other lucky slobs win the Gold Cup and smash their collarbones.

Jericho Rich on the telephone bounced me out of unprofitable regrets.

'You got my fillies to Newmarket okay, then,' he shouted.

'Yes, Jericho,' I held the receiver an inch from my ear.

'I expect you know I checked everything in your office. A good job well done, I'll say that for you.'

Good grief, I thought. The heavens would fall.

'I've got a daughter,' he said loudly.

'Er, yes, I've met her at the races.'

'She's bought a showjumper, some damned fancy name. Can't remember it. It's in France. Send a box for it, will you?'

'Pleasure, Jericho. When and where from?'

'She'll tell you. Give her a buzz. I said I'd pay for the transport if it was you who fetched it, so she's doing you the honour.' He laughed, fortissimo but for him almost mellow. 'Don't send that driver, though. That one that picked up the hitchhiker.'

'He's left,' I assured him. 'Didn't my girls tell you?'

'Well, yes they did.' He read out his daughter's phone number. 'Give her a buzz now. No time like the present.'

'Thanks, Jericho.'

I buzzed the daughter as directed and began on the details of the showjumper: age, sex, colour, value, all for the agents who would arrange the paperwork for the horse, and overnight provision for the driver. She sounded straightforward and less fussy than her father, merely asking me to complete the transfer as soon as I could as she needed to practise before the show-jumping season started. She gave me an address and phone number in France and asked if I could arrange for a groom to travel over with the horse.

'I could provide a good man from here,' I suggested. 'One I trust.'

'Yes. Great. Send the bill to my father.'

I said I would and, to do him justice, Jericho Rich

was a prompt payer. Mostly I billed the trainers for the transport of all their runners, the trainers then billing the individual owners, but Jericho always wanted his bills sent direct to himself. Jericho believed trainers would charge him more than they'd paid, all of a piece with his general mistrust of anyone working for him.

On the whole, people accused others of doing what they would do themselves. Dishonesty began at home.

He'd accused me in his time of taking bribes from a bookmaker to lose on one of his hurdlers. I'd told him very politely that I wouldn't ride for him any more, and a week later, as if nothing had happened, he'd offered me an enormous retainer to ride all his jumpers the next season. It had turned out profitably: I put up with his yelling and he gave me lavish presents when I won. A permanent stand-off perhaps described our ongoing relations.

I took a quick look at the time and switched the phone through to Isobel, who took bookings on Sundays when I was busy. Then I got on with such small things as dressing and tidying and going out into the garden to pick flowers. This peaceful activity was the result of strong promptings from my absent sister and brother who considered that flowers should occasionally be put on our parents' grave. As it was I, the youngest, who had inherited the family home, and as it was I who lived near the cemetery, they felt it only right and proper that it was I who picked the flowers and put them in place. The whole point, for them, was that the flowers should come from the right garden. Bought flowers would not be the same.

There was little but daffodils in the first week of March, though I also scavenged some crocuses and an early hyacinth along with evergreen sprigs of cupressus, and drove them to the gates of the orderly cemetery on a hillside where we'd buried the parents within two years of each other some time ago.

Actually, I never minded the errand. The grave was high on the hill but the view was worth the walk up there, and as I had no sense of their being around in any way, I tended to leave the flowers as thanks for my own satisfactory childhood, their gift.

The flowers would die, of course. It was delivering them that mattered.

Maudie Watermead's lunch began in spring sunshine in the garden, with her younger children and guests bouncing on a trampoline and their elders playing tennis. Still too chilly for standing around in, the March air drove faint-hearts back through the garden door to the drawing-room to enjoy the bright log fire and Maudie's idea of champagne cocktails, which began with angostura bitters on sugar lumps and fizzed to the brim with cold pink bubbles.

Benjy and Dot Usher were playing in long trousers on the hard court, arguing about balls being in or out. We engaged in unathletic mixed doubles, Dot and I being out-argued by Benjy and the Watermeads' daughter, Tessa. Benjy and Tessa were enjoying their partnership in a way that had Dot hissing, to my private amusement and our public defeat.

Benjy and Tessa, as victors, took on the Watermeads' son, Ed, and Maudie's sister, Lorna. Dot glowered until I persuaded her into the drawing-room, where the numbers had swelled and the chatter-level risen to the point where individual voices were lost in conglomerate noise.

Maudie handed me a glass and gave me a smile with the friendly blue eyes that as usual set me thinking powerfully adulterous thoughts. Thoroughly aware of my dilemma, she was for ever trying to transfer my feelings to her sister Lorna who, while alike in platinum hair, shapely waist and endless legs, simply lacked for me anything but physical attraction. Maudie was fun, Lorna was troubled. Maudie laughed, Lorna earnestly championed praiseworthy causes. Maudie cooked roast potatoes, Lorna worried about her weight. Maudie thought I would be good for Lorna but I had no intention of becoming her therapist: that way threatened boredom and disaster. I thought Lorna would be perfect for Bruce Farway.

The worthy doctor himself was at that moment standing near the fire with Maudie's husband. The bubbles in the Farway glass were colourless. Mineral water, I surmised.

Maudie followed my gaze and answered my unexpressed surprise.

'Michael thought that as it looks as if he intends to stay in Pixhill, we'd better teach the good doctor that we're not all rogues and fools.'

I smiled. 'He'll have trouble being supercilious with Michael, that's for sure.'

'Don't you believe it.'

My attention moved on towards the woman now talking to Dot, a younger woman, blonde like Maudie, blue-eyed like Maudie, light-hearted, left-handed, a pianist and thirty-eight.

'Do you know her?' Maudie asked, again following my gaze. 'Susan Palmerstone. Her family are all here somewhere.'

I nodded. 'I used to ride her father's horses.'

'Did you? It's easy to forget you were a jockey.'

Like many flat-racing trainers' wives, Maudie seldom went to jump meetings. I'd come to know her only through the transport.

From across the room, Susan Palmerstone looked in my direction and finally walked over.

'Hello,' she said. 'Hugo and the children are here.'

'I saw the children on the trampoline.'

'Yes.'

Maudie, making nothing much of the exchange, wandered over to Dot.

Susan said, 'I didn't realise you'd be here. We don't

know the Watermeads very well. I would have said we couldn't come.'

'Of course not. It doesn't matter.'

'No, but . . . someone told Hugo he couldn't have a brown-eyed child and he's been fussing about it for weeks.'

'Hugo's a green-eyed redhead. He can have anything as a throwback.'

'I thought I'd better warn you. He's halfway to obsessed.'

'OK.'

The tennis players came in from the garden and also Hugo Palmerstone, who'd been watching the children. Through the window I could see my daughter standing on the grass, arms akimbo, disparagingly critical of her straight-haired blond brothers' bouncing. Cinders, my daughter, had brown eyes and dark curly hair like mine and was nine years old.

I would have married Susan. I'd loved her and been devastated when she chose Hugo, but it had been a long time ago. Nothing remained of the emotion. It was difficult, even, to remember how I'd felt. I didn't want the long-buried past casting a shadow over that child's life.

Susan moved from my side the moment Hugo entered the room, but not before he realised we'd been talking together. His expression as he made his way directly to me was not promising.

'Come outside,' he said curtly, stopping a yard away. 'Now.'

I could have refused him but I thought, perhaps wrongly, that if I didn't give him the opportunity to say what he clearly intended to say it could fester in his mind and do harm to his family. Accordingly I quietly parked my glass and followed him out onto the lawn.

'I could kill you,' he said.

It was a remark to which there seemed to be no answer. When I said nothing, he added bitterly, 'My bloody aunt told me to open my eyes. My father-in-law's ex-jockey! Take a look at him, she said. Do some sums. Cinders was born seven months after your marriage. Open your eyes.'

'Your aunt has done you no service.'

He could see, of course, that she hadn't, but his anger was all for me.

'She's *my* daughter,' he insisted.

I glanced over towards Cinders, now somersaulting high with exuberance.

'Of course,' I said.

'I saw her born. She's mine, and I love her.'

I looked regretfully at Hugo's furious green eyes. He and I were almost totally unalike in nature as in looks. A middle-rank City executive, he had an incandescent temper as fiery as his hair, allied to a strong streak of sentimentality. Our lack of affinity with each other had proved, until now, a natural barrier to my getting too close and too fond of my daughter, and I saw clearly, even if he didn't, that allowing myself to be drawn into a fight with him would destroy what should never be touched.

He was clenching and unclenching his fists but with still a degree of control.

I said, 'You won the girl I wanted. You've a daughter and two sons. You're lucky. You'd be a fool to light a bonfire. What good would it do?'

'But you . . . you.' He spluttered with hurt incoherent rage, wanting me dead.

'Hate me if you like,' I said, 'but don't take it out on your family.'

I turned away from him, more than half-expecting him to haul me back and hit me, but to his credit he didn't. I thought uneasily, all the same, that if he came across a less direct and physical way of doing me harm, he might take it.

I walked back through the garden door and Maudie, by the window, said, 'What was that about?'

'Nothing.'

'Susan Palmerstone looks scared.'

'Yes, well, I had a disagreement with Hugo, but forget it. Introduce Lorna to Bruce Farway and don't put me next to her at lunch.'

'*What*?' She laughed, then looked thoughtful. 'If I do, in return you can detach Tessa from Benjy Usher. I don't like her flirting with him, and Dot is livid.'

'Why did you ask them?'

'They live practically next door, dammit. We always have Benjy and Dot.'

I did my best for her, but detaching Tessa from Benjy proved impossible. Tessa was a great whisperer and thought nothing of turning her back to prevent people hearing what she was spilling into Benjy's ear. I got the turned-back treatment a couple of times and left Benjy alone to his foolishness.

Bruce Farway was taking an interest in Lorna, the delectably pretty sister full of good works. Susan stood with her arm through Hugo's, talking brightly to Michael about horses. Intrigue and woven threads, typical of racing villages. Change partners and dance.

We ate Maudie's splendid ribs of beef with the crunching roast potatoes and honey-walnut ice cream after. I sat between Maudie and Dot and behaved with propriety.

The younger children chattered about the rabbit run in the garden where the family pets had doubled themselves in number within the past year. 'They'll go to the butcher one of these days,' Maudie muttered to me darkly. 'They get out and eat my dahlias.'

'One of the bunnies is *missing*,' her younger daughter was insisting.

'How can you possibly tell?' Michael asked. 'There are so many of them.'

'There were fifteen last week and today there are only fourteen. I counted them.'

'Probably the dogs ate one.'

'Daddy!'

Lorna talked to Bruce Farway about pensioned-off steeple-chasers, one of her current charities, and he listened with interest. Unbelievable.

The talk turned to Jericho Rich and his desertion of Michael's stable.

'Ungrateful beast,' Maudie said vehemently. 'After all those winners!'

'I *hate* him,' Tessa said with enough intensity to earn a sharp glance from her father.

'Why especially?' he asked.

She shrugged, tight-mouthed, denying him an answer. Seventeen, full of unspecified resentments, she was one of those children who'd never lacked for anything but couldn't settle for being one of life's favoured mortals. She was a head-tosser besides a whisperer and she didn't like me any more than I liked her.

Ed, her brother, sixteen and pretty stupid, said, 'Jericho Rich wanted sex with Tessa and she wouldn't, and that's why he took his horses away.'

As a conversation stopper it was of Oscar-earning calibre, and in the breath-held aghast silence the front doorbell rang.

Constable Sandy Smith had called. Apologetically he told Michael that he needed Dr Farway and also Freddie Croft.

'What's happened?' Michael asked.

Sandy told Michael, Bruce Farway and myself privately out in the front entrance hall.

'That mechanic of yours, Freddie. That Jogger. He's just been found along at your farmyard. He's in the inspection pit. And he's dead.'

CHAPTER FOUR

Jogger's neck was broken.

We stood looking down at him, the sideways angle of his head to his body impossible in life.

'He must have fallen in,' Farway said as if stating the obvious.

From the other side of the pit Harve met my eyes, clearly thinking, as I was, that for Jogger to have fallen accidentally into an inspection pit he would have to have been reeling drunk, and even then I would have bet on his instincts to save him.

As if catching the thought, or at least the first half of it, Sandy Smith sighed, 'He had a right skinful last night in the pub. Raving on about aliens under the lorries. Lone rangers, stuff like that. I took his car keys off him and drove him home in the end. I'd've had to arrest him for being drunk in charge, otherwise.'

Bruce Farway asked him officiously, 'Have you informed his wife of this?'

'Not married,' Sandy said.

'No next-of-kin at all,' I amplified. 'I have next-of-kin listed for all my employees, and Jogger said he hadn't any.'

Farway shrugged, climbed down the metal ladder bolted to the inspection pit wall and bent clinically over the crooked body, lightly touching the bent neck. Then, standing upright, nodding, he reported to me almost accusingly, 'Yes, this one's dead as well.'

Two corpses found on my property in four days, he seemed to imply, were suspiciously excessive.

Michael Watermead, who had deserted the tail-end of his lunch party to follow me along to the disaster in the farmyard, asked curiously, 'As well as what?'

'The hitchhiker,' I said. 'Thursday.'

'Oh yes. Of course. I was forgetting. On the way back from taking Jericho's two-year-olds.' The thought of Jericho brought a scowl to the naturally patrician features, his son Ed's appallingly casual revelation as yet undigested, unprocessed.

Michael, I guessed, had been prompted to be present now in my barn by a mixture of straightforward morbid interest, supportive friendliness and the typical fuzzy overall sense of responsibility in the community which kept much of rural English life within sane parameters. He brought anyway a weight of authority to the proceedings which Harve, Sandy, Farway and myself might have lacked.

'How long has he been dead?' I asked. 'I mean . . . hours? Last night?'

Bruce Farway said hesitantly, 'He's pretty cold, but I'd say fairly late this morning.'

We understood, all of us, that a closer guess was impossible at that point. The pit itself and the air temperature were cold also. The doctor climbed up the ladder and suggested that he and Sandy should again call for the ultimate in removers.

'How about photographs?' I said. 'I've a camera in the office.'

Everyone solemnly agreed on photographs. I walked through the yard, unlocked the offices, collected my Nikon and returned to the barn. The others were still where I'd left them, standing round the pit looking down at Jogger with unreadable thoughts.

Although there was a certain amount of daylight in the barn from a window looking into the farmyard we always had to top it up with electricity for work. The overhead lights were all on, but even so I used flash for the pictures, taking several shots from round the rim of the pit and several others from its floor, down beside my poor mechanic.

I didn't touch him, though I bent near to photograph his head. He lay in the angle between wall and floor; rough grease-streaked concrete walls, oil-blackened floor. He seemed to be looking at the wall six inches from his nose, his eyes, like those of so many suddenly dead, still open. The yellow teeth showed in two uneven rows within his mouth. He wore the old army jersey, the dirt-clogged trousers, the old cracked boots. He still smelled, extraordinarily, of oil and dust; of earth, not death.

The pit was five feet deep. Standing upright, my direct line of sight was roughly level with the ankles of Sandy, Harve and Michael. Bruce Farway was behind me. For a petrifying second, a primitive instinct warned me against standing up with my neck sticking out of a hole in the ground and I turned quickly but saw Farway harmlessly writing in a small notebook, and felt foolish.

I hauled myself up the ladder out of the pit and asked Harve how he'd happened to find Jogger at that particular time.

Harve shrugged. 'I don't know. I just wandered round the yard, like I often do. The boxes working today had all left. I was here earlier checking them out, see, to make sure. Then to waste time, sort of, while I was waiting for lunch to be ready, I walked round again.'

I nodded. Harve liked to be on his feet always, and on the move.

'So then I noticed the lights were on in the barn,' he said, 'and I thought I might save us a bit of electricity so I walked over here thinking that I hadn't seen anyone come over here earlier. No one needed to. I wasn't worried, see, only I just came over for a look around and, like I said, to switch the lights off.' He paused. 'Don't ask me why I got as far over as the pit. I don't know why. I just did it.'

The pit in fact was well over to the far side of the barn, expressly to stop people stepping over its edge unawares. A large roll-back door at one end of the barn made it possible to drive a horsebox straight in over the pit. The small door nearest the farmyard, which people on foot used, opened into a general workshop area, with tools kept in a large locked store in one corner.

I asked, 'Do you think Jogger was lying here all the time while drivers came in to work and took the boxes out?'

Harve was troubled. 'I don't know. He could have been. Gives you the shudders, doesn't it?'

'The post-mortem will tell us, eh Bruce?' Michael said, and Bruce, preening slightly at the intimacy of the use of his first name, agreed that speculation could be safely left for that event.

Michael caught the satirical glance I gave in his direction and came very close to a wink. The winning over of the doctor was clearly succeeding.

Farway and Sandy between them produced their mobile phones and summoned the necessary cohorts. Michael asked if he could use the phone in my office. Help yourself, I said, it's open. He sauntered off on his errand and when Harve and I followed, feeling upset and insecure, Michael was saying, 'Damned shame for poor old Freddie,' into Isobel's phone, the first one he'd come to, and 'Oh, accidental, undoubtedly. Must go now. See you.'

He rang off, said thanks and goodbye and left smiling with universal benignity, happy in the knowledge that he wouldn't have to feel any personal repercussions from Jogger's death.

'What do you reckon?' Harve asked as we reached our jointly used sanctum and paused for consideration.

'Do you believe he fell in?' I asked.

'Don't want to think of the alternative.'

'No,' I agreed.

'But if he didn't fall . . .'

He left the words hanging, and so did I.

I said, 'Who was in the pub last night with Jogger?'

Harve began answering automatically, 'Sandy, of course. Dave was bound to be . . . I wasn't . . .' He broke off, aghast. 'Do you mean . . . who was in the pub to hear him talking about aliens under the lorries? You can't mean . . . you *can't* . . .'

I shook my head, though how could one help wondering?

'We'll wait for the cause-of-death report,' I said. 'If it's proved he skidded on a patch of oil and fell and hit his neck on the edge of the pit – which is possible – we'll decide then what to do.'

'But that cash box hiding-place was *empty*,' Harve insisted. 'No one would kill Jogger just because he'd found an empty thing like that. They wouldn't. It *can't* be anything like that.'

'No,' I said.

Harve stared worriedly out at the row of horseboxes.

'When I found him,' he said, 'I went back home and phoned your personal line from there, but I got your answering machine saying you'd phone back soon, like it does when you're only going to be away an hour or two. But, well, I didn't think it could wait, so I phoned Sandy. Was that all right?'

'The only thing you could do.'

'We didn't know where you were. In the end we tried Isobel and she said she thought you'd be at the Watermeads', as Nigel had told her you were going to lunch there when he phoned to say the daughter had mixed up the departure time. It seems Tessa told Nigel. So Sandy said he'd go round and fetch you.'

'Mm.' News travelled in Pixhill in dizzying spirals.

Harve began showing troubled signs of indecision, which from our long proximity I identified immediately as doubt over whether or not he should tell me something I might not want to hear.

'Spit it out,' I said resignedly.

'Oh! Well . . . Nigel said Tessa wanted to go to Newmarket with him, with the fillies. She climbed into the box and sat ready in the passenger seat.'

'I hope he didn't take her.'

'No, but he was flummoxed. I mean, he had you on one side threatening the sack to anyone giving lifts, and her on the other side, the trainer's daughter, wanting a ride.' He paused. 'She's a proper little madam, that girl, and Nigel's a sexy hunk, so my wife says, and . . . don't take me wrong . . . I thought you'd better know.'

'I'm grateful,' I said with truth. 'That's a mess we can do without. I don't want to lose Michael Watermead's work just because his daughter fancies one of our drivers. We'd better not send Nigel there again, though it's damned annoying, to say the least.'

Lewis, of course, was Michael's driver of choice, but very often Watermead horses needed more than one box. Not being able to send Nigel cut down my options.

Harve said with humour, 'We could put Pat on the extra Watermead runs, when she's better, and your temporary replacement could do any before that.'

'Good thinking!' I stifled too broad a smile and made a note for Isobel to allocate Nigel chiefly to Marigold English, whose pulses he might race to good effect.

In time, a police car crept carefully through the gates, bringing CID investigators, an official doctor and a photographer. Harve and I went out to the barn, where Sandy was showing Jogger to his plain-clothes colleagues and Bruce Farway was talking importantly to his police counterpart. The official photographer took bright flash official photographs from the same angles as my own.

A statement from Harve about finding the body was taken down and read out to him in the curiously stilted English such proceedings seemed to incur. Harve signed the result even though the words weren't his own, and Farway, Sandy and I confirmed that the body was as we'd found it, and that nothing had been added or subtracted from the scene.

Sandy's colleagues were impersonal, without humour. All fatal accidents had to be thoroughly investigated, they said, and there would be further questions, no doubt, on the morrow.

The same black hearse that had collected Kevin Keith Ogden, or one very like it, arrived in the farmyard, and presently another finished life left my land under canvas and straps in a metal coffin.

The police, unsmiling, followed. Farway, Sandy and I watched them go, I, at least, with relief.

'All very sad,' Farway said with a certain briskness, not caring one way or the other.

'A local character,' Sandy said, nodding.

Not much of an epitaph, I thought. I said, 'Sandy, when you drove Jogger home last night, was it in your car or his?'

'Last night? My car. That old wreck of a van will still be at the pub.'

'That old wreck is actually mine,' I told him. 'I'll collect it later. Do you still have the keys?'

They were in his house, it seemed, for safekeeping. I said I would pick them up shortly and with a sigh of relief he left to salvage the remains of his Sunday off.

Bruce Farway followed, not wasting on me any of the slightly fawning regard he'd lavished on Michael or the police doctor, merely nodding a cool farewell. Harve walked back to his own house for his long-postponed lunch and I wandered round in the barn, staring into the now empty pit and checking that nothing in the tool store was out of place.

The tool store was a spacious twenty feet by ten, windowless. I unlocked the wide door, switched on the light and stood looking at Jogger's domain; at the pair of heavy-duty hydraulic jacks, the vast array of spanners and wrenches, the labelled boxes of spare parts, the rolls of cable, the chains, cans of oil, drums of grease, a set of six new Michelin tyres waiting for installation.

The floor was filthy but the tools were clean, often the way with Jogger. As far as I could see, nothing had disturbed the general tidiness he miraculously maintained in the storeroom. The van in contrast would contain a hopeless-looking jumble from which he would nevertheless pluck just the pliers he needed.

I switched off the light, locked the store and walked out beside the long workbench in the barn, a sturdy shelf which bore nothing at that moment but a small and a large vice, both bolted on. There were no tools anywhere lying about. Nothing a man could trip over, however drunk.

Morosely I left the barn, turning off the lights but as usual not locking the door to the yard. Enough was enough, I'd always thought. We kept the tools locked away and there was the padlock on the outer gate. Security could become an obsession, and anyway I'd been guarding against thieves, not against smugglers.

Not against murder.

I shied painfully away from that word. I couldn't believe it. Didn't want to believe it.

Murder couldn't happen. Not to Jogger. Not because of an empty cash box and two empty tubes. Not because he'd shot his mouth off down at the boozer.

I had a sense of jumping to over-dramatic conclusions. It would be best to wait for the post-mortem findings.

I sat in the office thinking of Jogger: not of the manner of his death, but of the man he had been.

A loner, an old soldier, a driver of army trucks whose only active service war zone had been the Northern Irish border. He almost never spoke of it, though his mates in a truck ahead of him had been blown apart by a bomb.

I'd acquired his services as a fixture or fitting along with the farmyard and the horseboxes, the transaction apparently to his liking, and I'd counted myself lucky to have him and didn't now know where I would find anyone else as expert, undemanding and committed.

I mourned him also simply, without self-interest. Grieved for him as a man. In his own way he'd been a whole person, not needing what others might think he lacked. No one should impose their own perception of fulfilment on anyone else.

A little later, when the afternoon faded to dark, I walked down to Sandy's house and collected the keys of Jogger's van. Sandy gave them to me without question; I merely signed for them, as Sandy knew the van belonged to me. It didn't seem to occur to him that perhaps a couple of keys on the ring were Jogger's own. Continuing on, I walked to the pub that Jogger favoured and duly found the van in the car park there. At first sight there was nothing wrong with it. On second sight, I found that the two rear doors were slightly ajar, and inside, where there should have been the slider and a jumble of tools in a big red plastic crate, there was nothing but rusty dust on the bare metal floor.

I sighed. A whole pub full of people had seen Sandy take Jogger home, leaving a van full of easy pickings behind him. I supposed I should be pleased that the van itself hadn't gone too, and that it still had wheels, tyres, petrol and an engine.

I drove it the short distance to Jogger's quarters, which I so far knew only externally as a rickety-looking garage with an upper storey.

In some distant past, the place had been a chauffeur's lodging, although the house it had served had long gone. Keeping me up to date on developments, for months and months Jogger had conducted a running battle with good souls on the local council who wanted to declare the building unfit for habitation, Jogger maintaining that his home was as it always had been and that it was the council whose ideas had changed. I thought that one could probably defend even a cave on those terms, but Jogger's strong and quasi-logical indignation had to date won him the day.

I laboriously opened one of the old creaking wooden front garage doors, leaving the van outside and letting enough street-lamp in to show me the empty space inside. The way to Jogger's room, he'd said, lay across the garage and up some narrow stairs by the back wall, and up there I came to a flimsy door that opened easily when I tried the handle. No need for keys. I found a light switch and stepped for the first time into Jogger's private world, feeling both that it was a terrible intrusion and also that he would have wanted someone to care enough to go there, to see it for him one last time and make sure there was no desecration.

Jogger's home was as he'd left it, a mess untouched by whoever had stolen the tools. He'd earned good money for years yet had evidently chosen to live as if poverty breathed down his neck, his sagging armchair covered with a grubby old tablecloth, the table covered with newspaper, the floor with linoleum. The army might once have coerced him into spit-and-polish in general, but only in his work had that training prevailed over what I guessed might have been the familiar manner of his childhood. This was the way he felt comfortable, this his old shoes.

There was no kitchen, merely a few mugs and plates on top of a chest of drawers with tea, sugar, dried milk and biscuits in packets alongside. The one drawer I opened revealed a tangle of old clothes. The suit and shirt he wore for driving were draped on a hanger on a hook on the back of the door.

His bed, a matter of jumbled khaki-coloured blankets on a divan, was by conventional standards unmade. Impossible to tell whether or not he'd slept there during the past night.

I realised that the place wasn't as cold as the day outside and came across the first sign of luxury, a small convection heater taking the edge off nature. There was also a colour television, three crates of beer, a shining electric kettle and a telephone. Against one wall leaned a stack of mildly pornographic magazines, representing one copy a week for a couple of years, and in a shoebox on a shelf I came across his birth certificate, his army discharge papers and the passbook of a building society, the total of his savings raising my eyebrows and showing exactly what he'd done with his pay packets.

I left his papers where I'd found them and looked into a sketchy bathroom which was what I by then expected, hardly spotless but not disgusting, basic with throwaway razors and a gap-toothed comb.

Walking back through his room I left everything as it was, including the heater. The whole place still smelled of him, of oil, earth and dust. While his smell remained, so would he. The worthy council would sweep it all away soon enough.

I locked his door, closed the outer garage door and drove the van to the farmyard wondering why Jogger had gone to the barn without his keys or his wheels . . . and when . . . and how . . . and *who with*?

In the office, Jogger's log-book lay on Isobel's desk, ready for her to type the details into the computer. I took the book with me into my own office and sat reading what Jogger had written.

The bare bones of the trip only. No comments. No frills. He'd collected four named steeplechasers from a Pixhill stable and driven them down the M4 to Chepstow races. Time of leaving base, time of pick-up, time of arrival, time of departure from racecourse, time of delivery back at stable, time of return to base. Diesel intake recorded in litres. Odometer readings entered. Cleaning completed. Total number of hours worked. Number of those hours spent behind the wheel.

Nothing about aliens or lone rangers.

Depressed, I replaced the log-book on Isobel's desk and thought I couldn't do any more there that was useful. Four of the fleet were still out, not counting the one in France and the one in Ireland, but Harve would see them return. I would hear soon enough if anything went wrong. I yawned, locked up and went home.

Revived by the product of Scotland I sat in my swivelling armchair and rewound the tape of the answering machine on my private line. I'd transferred the business line to Isobel for receiving and making bookings for the fleet, but personal calls came in on a different number. On that Sunday, I'd switched the private answering machine on when I went upstairs to shower, left it on while I picked flowers and took them to the cemetery, left it on of course for the Watermeads' lunch, and it had been on ever since. The tape wound busily back.

I pressed the play button and nearly fell out of the chair.

The first voice was Jogger's, hoarse, cockney, unhurried, unafraid.

'I hate this bloody machine,' he said. 'Where have you gone, Freddie? Someone's half-inched the van. It's not in the garage here, some tea-leaf's bloody nicked it while I was zizzing. You'd better tell Sandy – No . . . wait . . . hang about . . .' His voice stopped for a while and then in some embarrassment went on, 'Er, um, cancel that, Freddie. I know where it is. It's down the boozer. Forget I said it, OK?'

The line clicked off, but the second call was also from Jogger. 'I remembered, like, about the van. Sandy's got the keys. I'll walk along to the farmyard first for a decko and then I'll get the keys. Anyway, I want to tell you, take a butcher's at them nuns. I found a dead one in the pit last August, and it was crawling and Poland had the same five on a horse last summer and it died. What do you think?'

His voice stopped, leaving me with the problem that I didn't know what he'd been talking about.

Nuns in the pit! Dead, moreover, like himself. Poor old Jogger, poor old exasperating man.

Why couldn't he ever say things straight out? His

rhyming slang hadn't seriously mattered before this, but now it was infuriating. Half-inched meant pinched, a tea-leaf was a thief, a butcher's came from butcher's hook, look. All those were common parlance, part of the general language. But what were nuns and crawling and Poland?

What I needed, I decided, was a rhyming dictionary, and in the morning I would buy one.

I'd switched my private-line answering machine on at about eleven o'clock that morning. Jogger had been alive then. To be 'pretty cold' in the pit by three in the afternoon, he must have died not long after his phone calls. I sat for a while simply looking at the machine as if in some stupid way it could bring my mechanic back to life. If I'd been able to speak to him myself, maybe he *would* have been still alive. I couldn't hear the phone's chirrup when I was in the shower or through the buzz of my electric razor. Perhaps he'd phoned then, but I hadn't noticed the 'message received' light shining. More likely he'd tried when I'd left to pick and take the flowers. I must have missed him by seconds.

With unassuageable regret I ran through a couple of other messages on the tape and I told one or two people about Jogger. The whole village, one way or another, would know of it by bedtime.

By seven-thirty the next morning, after a troubled night's sleep, I was along at the farmyard talking to the two drivers who were taking runners to Southwell. There was an all-weather track up there, just north-east of Nottingham, giving an underfoot surface which had proved popular because it didn't crack, freeze or flood like turf. Its only drawback as far as Pixhill trainers were concerned was its distance of a hundred and fifty miles from home: as far as Croft Raceways was concerned, the distance filled the coffers. It was about the furthest the boxes went out and back in one day, entailing early starts and late returns. Anything much further meant overnight stops or two drivers to work in spells.

On that Monday, we had six boxes going to race-courses, two taking broodmares, two abroad and four standing idle, which in view of the persistent flu situation was just as well.

I was out in the farmyard when a woman drove through the gates in a small Ford runabout that had been a long time out of the showroom. She stopped outside the offices and emerged from behind the wheel stretching to a tall thin height in jeans, padded jacket and dark hair scraped back into an untidy pony tail. No make-up, no nail varnish, no pretence at youth.

She was, as she'd said she'd be, almost unrecog-nisable.

I went across. 'Nina?' I said.

She smiled briskly. 'I'm early, I'm afraid.'

'All the better. I'll introduce you to the other

drivers . . . but first I'd better tell you what's filling their minds.'

She listened to the finding of Jogger with a frown and immediately asked, 'Have you told Patrick Venables about this?'

'Not yet.'

'I'll do it. I'll reach him at home.'

I took her into my office and listened to her make the call. 'It could well be an accident,' she told her boss. 'Freddie hopes so. The local police have it in hand. What do you want me to do?'

She listened for a while and said 'Yes' a few times, and then handed the receiver to me. 'He wants to talk to you.'

'Freddie Croft,' I said.

'Let me get this right. This dead man is the one who found the empty containers stuck to your horseboxes?'

'Yes. My mechanic.'

'And besides you and me, who knew he'd found them?'

'Everyone who heard him saying so in a pub in Pixhill on Saturday night and understands rhyming slang.' He cursed with feeling and I explained about Jogger's linguistic habits. 'The local policeman heard him but it didn't make total sense to him. It *would* have made total sense, though, to anyone who knew the containers were there. Lone rangers and aliens under the lorries, Jogger said. By lone rangers he meant strangers. Clear as daylight.'

'I agree.' Patrick Venables paused. 'Who was in the pub?'

'It's a popular place. I'll ask the landlord. I'll go in at lunchtime and tell him I'll stand a pint to everyone who was there on Saturday night, on Jogger's last visit. In memory, sort of.'

With humour in his voice, he said, 'It can't do any harm. Apart from that, I'll put out feelers towards your local police to see what they're thinking. This Jogger's death may be just an unfortunate coincidence.'

'I hope so, indeed,' I said fervently.

He wanted to speak to Nina again and she said 'Yes' a few more times, and 'Goodbye Patrick' at the end.

'He wants me to phone him later,' she said. 'And on second thoughts, he advises you to be careful in the pub.'

I told her about Jogger's last message on the answering machine.

'I'll write it down for you when I go home,' I said, 'but it's pretty incomprehensible. He used to make up his own rhymes and I've never heard him use these before.'

She gazed at me. 'You've had more practice than most.'

'Mm. I thought of buying a rhyming dictionary, though it's more a matter of guessing. I mean, when he said carpets he meant drugs. Carpets and rugs. You don't have to just find the rhyme, you have to find the word that goes with the rhyme, and that association arose solely in Jogger's own brain.'

'And if he hadn't died,' she said, nodding, 'you could simply have asked him what he meant.'

'Yes. He just liked to play games, to challenge me, I suppose, in a quiet sort of way. But don't get me wrong, he thought naturally in that rhyming fashion. It was no sort of effort. It would come out spontaneously. The trouble is that I don't know if what he said yesterday morning was of desperate importance or only a passing comment. I don't know if desperate importance would come out in rhyme. Passing comments did often.'

Harve came into the office at that moment and I introduced Nina as the new temporary driver. Harve tried not to look dubious, knowing I preferred younger drivers because of their relative tirelessness and seeing the present substitute as halfway to granny-hood.

'We have to give Pat at least two weeks to recover from this sort of flu,' I pointed out, having discovered from past experience that too early a return to such a physical job caused further days off in the end. 'Nina's very experienced with horses and with driving horse-boxes and we'll give her good help with directions.'

He listened to the firmness in my voice and made the best of it. I asked him to show her the canteen and then how to fill out a temporary log and also to explain to her the refuelling and cleaning routines. She followed him meekly out of the office, a shadow of yesterday's woman and not half as interesting.

The day's work began. The two Southwell boxes set off to pick up their loads and the other drivers began arriving, most of them making straight for the tea and toast in the canteen. Dave creaked along on his rusty bicycle. Nigel came running, keeping fit. All of them already knew about Jogger, as did Isobel and Rose, who drove to work in small cars, collecting milk and newspapers on the way.

Out in the yard I had a quick private word with Nina before she set off with Dave to collect her horses for Taunton.

I said, 'The box you're driving is one with an empty container stuck on the bottom. You'd better know, though I can't think it will be used for anything today.'

'Thanks,' she said dryly, 'I'll keep a look out.'

I watched her start up and drive off. She certainly managed the horsebox competently, manoeuvring through the gates easily and turning economically into the road. Harve, watching her departure with his head on one side, could find nothing to criticise. He gave me a shrug and raised eyebrows, judgement deferred.

Half an hour later, when she returned, pausing outside the gate, Dave jumped down from the cab and with a grin reported to Harve and me that, 'The old girl can twiddle a horsebox on a penny and the horses are purring all over her. Where did you find her?'

'She applied for Brett's job,' I said. 'So did four others by phone yesterday. I've two coming for interviews this morning. The word's flown around that we're short of a driver.'

'Isn't this Nina bird staying then?' Dave asked, disappointed.

'We'll see how it goes.'

The second box bound for Taunton rumbled past Nina, hooting, and she set off after it, following in convoy.

'Could do worse,' Harve said generously. 'She seems sensible so far.'

I told Dave that once the paperwork was fixed he would be going to France to collect Jericho Rich's daughter's new showjumper. Phil would drive, and they would stay overnight. Dave looked pleased, as he liked such excursions, but when he'd ambled off Harve queried my choice of Phil.

'Do you mean Phil in his super-six? Just for one showjumper?'

I nodded. 'He's experienced. It's best he goes. It's a valuable horse and I don't want anything going wrong with any other journey to do with Jericho Rich. Phil will come back without hitchhikers, dead or alive.'

Harve winced, smiled and agreed.

Back in the office, I urged Isobel to chase the agents for documentation for that trip. We used the services of specialists for overseas paperwork, as they understood the needs, worked fast and seldom made errors.

'Prompt and perfect,' she said cheerfully. 'Croft Raceways' motto.'

'Er . . . prompt and passable will do.'

I took the day's newspapers along to my own office and flicked through them. There was never much hard racing news on Mondays. Jogger wasn't mentioned. The lead story in one paper was about the equine flu plaguing several racing stables in the north, virtually putting whole yards out of action for months. There was speculation that the virus might spread to Newmarket. Trainers, the writer said, were unwilling to share transport with horses from other stables in case of infection.

Hooray for that. I was all for separate journeys. Just as long, of course, as Pixhill itself stayed free. It was bad enough having *drivers* home sick, but the equine version of flu could hang around much longer, severely depleting the number of runners needing my services.

Equine flu, an infection of the upper respiratory tract, the paper said, had been known in the past as 'the cough'. There was no cure but time. So what else was new?

I turned to another paper. This one, still on the gloom and doom trail, discussed the previous summer's outbreak of debilitating fever and diarrhoea in horses in mainland Europe. No one had satisfactorily identified the cause and trainers feared there might be a recurrence.

Diesel prices might rise again, I read. I hated 'might' stories; non-stories. Like 'Doctors warn', I put 'might' stories bottom of my list. Anxiety raisers, all of them. Doctors should warn against 'Doctors warn'.

It was a 'might' sort of morning. Sunny Drifter might not run in the next day's Champion Hurdle. There might be an increase in betting tax in the Budget. Michael Watermead might run the brilliant Irkab Alhawa in a warm-up race before the 2,000 Guineas.

Marigold English, I read open-eyed, reported that she had successfully completed her move to Pixhill, 'Owing to Freddie Croft's personal services, the transfer went smoothly in all respects.' Bully for the old trout, I thought, and phoned her on the spot to thank her.

'You did a good job,' she said, pleased.

By nine-thirty the phone was ringing almost continuously as it always did on Mondays, the trainers making transport plans for the week ahead.

Isobel answered everything, coming along to my door at one point and saying, 'There's someone enquiring for Brett's job. He sounds all right. What shall I do?'

'Ask him if he can come for an interview this morning.'

She went away and returned to say that he would. Ten minutes later we had another applicant, and then another. We would have a line of them round the farmyard if it went on.

I started the interviews at about ten o'clock. Four men had already arrived and a fifth appeared within an hour. All of them had the necessary licences, all had experience, all said they'd worked in racing before. The fifth one said he was also a mechanic.

Most drivers were mechanics to some extent. This one gave me a reference from a Mercedes garage in London.

His name was Aziz Nader. Age, twenty-eight. He had curly black hair, olive skin, shining black eyes. Confident and outgoing in manner, he was looking for a job but not offering subservience. He spoke with a Canadian accent but didn't look as if he should.

'Where do you come from?' I said neutrally.

'Lebanon.' He paused a second and amplified his answer. 'My parents are Lebanese but they went to Canada when the trouble started. I was raised in Quebec mostly and I'm still a Canadian citizen, but we've been here eight years now. I've a resident's work permit, if that's what's worrying you.'

I looked at him thoughtfully. 'What language do you speak with your parents?'

'Arabic.'

'And . . . um . . . how about French?'

He smiled with white teeth and spoke to me rapidly in that language. The French I knew was racecourse stuff; he was too fast for me.

In the summer I shipped many horses for Arab clients, most of whose employees fumbled along in hopelessly tongue-tied or non-existent English. A driver who could converse with them, and could also feel at home in France, seemed too good to be true.

'How good are you with horses?' I asked.

He seemed uncertain. 'I thought you wanted a driver-mechanic.'

No one after all was perfect. 'Horsebox drivers are better if they can handle horses.'

'I'd . . . er . . . learn.'

It wasn't as easy as he thought, but it didn't rule him out.

'I've told everyone I'll go with them on a test drive before deciding who gets the job,' I said. 'You came last, can you wait?'

'All day,' he said.

The test drives were important because the cargo had to go steadily on its feet. Two of the applicants were jerky with brakes and gears, one was very slow, the fourth I would have engaged if he'd been the only remaining choice.

I found, as I climbed into the super-six cab beside Aziz, that I already intended to give him the job on the strength of his languages and his mechanical experience, just as long as he was half-way proficient at driving. He proved in fact not dazzling but at least smooth and careful, and my mind was made up long before we returned to the farmyard.

'When can you start?' I asked, as he braked to a halt.

'Tomorrow.' He gave me another flashing smile, all eyes and teeth, and said he would work hard.

I thanked the other applicants who were waiting

hopefully and got them to give their names to Isobel, in case. They went away disappointed. Isobel and Rose met Aziz with fascination and a visible increase in femininity, and Nigel, it was plain, had found strong competition.

Three months' trial, subject to his references being OK, I suggested, offering appropriate pay and conditions. Rose said she would put him into her computer, asking for his address. He would rent a room in the village, he said, and let her know later. Rose tentatively told him where Brett had stayed: the room might still be available. Aziz thanked her, listened to her directions, and drove off cheerfully, as he'd come, in a very old, well-tended small-sized Peugeot.

I wondered how much one could really tell of a person by the car they drove. Sunday's Nina matched her Mercedes; Monday's Nina, her old runabout. Aziz seemed too strong a character for his wheels. I, on the other hand, owned a Jaguar XJS, loved and left over from the jockey days. I took it still to race meetings but moved around Pixhill in a workhorse four-wheel-drive Fourtrak. Perhaps everyone, I thought in passing, had a two-car personality, and wondered what Aziz would drive from choice.

To be prudent, I checked his references. The London garage he'd worked for said he knew his job but had left some time ago. The trainer whose private horsebox he had driven proved to have gone out of business recently in financial difficulties. Aziz Nader had been a satisfactory employee but everyone on the payroll had lost their jobs.

While I was on the phone two cars arrived together, not, as it transpired, in tandem but both on fact-finding missions. The first disgorged the press in the shape of a spindly young man with a large nose and a spiral notebook; the second, the area bloodhounds in plain clothes, different men from the day before. I went out without enthusiasm to greet them. There were no smiles, no handshakes, merely minimal introductions, badges flapped in my face. No one seemed intent on overfriendliness or engaging my best help trustingly. Both press and police subsequently asked invasive and borderline-rude questions with visible scepticism at my answers.

Apart from Sandy, my experiences with the larger police world had been few but enough to show me one should never say a word to them that one didn't have to, on the probability of being adjudged guilty of any old thing before conclusively proved innocent, and very likely after. One should also never, ever, on any account, make jokes. Not even to Sandy. The police, to my mind, had only themselves to blame for the public's prevalent mistrust of them, great chaps though no doubt most of them were. Pouncing, however, came as a natural instinct to them all: they wouldn't have been effective without it. No one that I knew of, particularly if innocent, cared to be prey.

The pressman seemed to see his role as being *Wash-*

ington Post-type investigative journalism. The police, to my quiet amusement, saw him as a nuisance who would do no investigating at all if they could help it. I listened to them match verbal swords until the young man retreated discomfited to wait in his motor and the force produced notebooks of their own.

'Now, sir,' they began, an opener full of menace if ever there was one, 'you will hand over the house keys of the man found dead here yesterday, if you please.'

I would have given them Jogger's keys willingly. The brusqueness of their demand reinforced my hovering antagonism and ensured I didn't help them as I might have done, as I should have done, no doubt.

Without a word, though, I went back to the office, finding them following me with sharp suspicious eyes as if I were planning to destroy evidence, given half a chance. Isobel and Rose both watched the procession with open mouths. I didn't bother with introductions.

The two plain-clothes men drew up beside my desk. I opened a drawer, brought out Jogger's keys and removed his house keys from the ring.

They took the keys without comment and asked what Jogger had been doing in the farmyard on a Sunday morning. I replied that all my employees could come and go in the farmyard on any errand they cared to, Sundays included, as it was a workday.

They asked me about Jogger's drinking habits. I said he had never turned up drunk for work. Apart from that, it was his own affair.

If Jogger had been drunk when he fell into the pit, I thought, the post-mortem would show it. Speculation was pointless, really.

The elder of the two policemen next asked if anyone had been present with Jogger when he fell. Not that I knew of, I said. Had I, personally, been there? No. Had I been to the farmyard on Saturday night after ten o'clock or on Sunday morning at any time? No.

I asked why they were asking such questions and was told that all accidents had to be investigated, of course. The coroner would want answers at the inquest. In police experience, he chillingly added, people with information could remain silent so as not to become involved. I refrained from asking whose fault he thought that might be.

The interview proceeded for several more minutes without fruit to either side, as far as I could see. They watched me keenly while telling me they would be making enquiries from my employees. I nodded neutrally, taking it for granted.

They asked for a list of all drivers who had been working on Saturday or Sunday. I took them along to Isobel's office and asked her for a computer print-out of the times everyone had left and returned.

She shook her head disgustedly.

'Look, Freddie,' she said, 'I'm so sorry, but I can't get a thing out of the computer today. When I've sorted it out, I'll do the records straight away.' She picked up a pile of log-books. 'The information is all in here, it's just a matter of typing it.'

'Sure,' I said, easily. 'Can you just write down the names, for a start? Using old-fashioned pencil and paper?'

Obligingly she wrote the names from the log-book covers and handed the list to the policeman who took it stolidly. When they'd gone Isobel made a face after them. 'They might have said thanks, even if I did balls up the computer.'

'Yes, they might.'

The spindly pressman came out of his car like a rabbit from his hole once the police car had driven away and I spent the next ten minutcs assuring him that Jogger had been a great mechanic, his loss would be sorely felt, the police had been investigating the accident, we would have to await the result of their enquiries, and so on and so on, a whole lot of platitudes but the truth as far as it went. He drove away finally in dissatisfaction, but I couldn't help that.

A quick look at my watch showed I'd drifted through much of lunchtime without remembering my intention of organising the Jogger memorial pints in the pub, so I scooted down there at once to talk to the landlord.

He, comfortably fat with a beer belly of his own, presided over a no-frills house geared to the psychological comfort of those made uneasy by too much luxury. He pleased a clientele of both stable workers and austere local intellects, talking easily with both groups.

'Old Jogger was harmless,' he pronounced. 'Got pissed regular on Saturdays. Not the first time Sandy's driven him home. Sandy's a good fellow, I'll say that for him. What can I do for you?'

Make a list, I said, of everyone who had been in the pub with Jogger on his last night and give each of them two or three pints in his memory.

'Very decent of you, Freddie,' he said, and began his list there and then, starting off with Sandy Smith and adding Dave and Nigel and two others of my drivers and proceeding to lads from almost every stable in Pixhill, including a new bunch from Marigold English's yard, individual names unknown. 'They'd asked in the village for the best pub,' he told me complacently, 'and were steered here to me.'

'Quite right,' I said. 'Get their names and we'll make a sort of memorial scroll and frame it and hang it here on your wall for a bit.'

The landlord became enthusiastic. 'We'll do old Jogger proud,' he said. 'He'd be tickled pink.'

'Um,' I said thoughtfully, 'I suppose he didn't leave any famous last words?'

' "Same again!" ' the landlord said, smiling broadly. 'Same again' were his favourite words. 'He'd been rambling on about aliens under your lorries, I ask you, but by the time he left, "same again" was about all he could manage. But always the gentleman, that Jogger, never any trouble when he'd had a skinful, never fighting drunk like that Dave.'

'Dave,' I asked in astonishment. 'Do you mean *my* Dave?'

'Sure. He'll take a swing at anyone, given enough ale on board. He never connects, mind you, he can't see straight by then. I stop serving him then, of course, and tell him to go home. Sandy takes him home too, sometimes, when he's too far gone even to balance on that bike. A good lad, Sandy. Pretty good for a copper.'

'Yes,' I said, and gave him a cash advance for the memorial pints, promising the rest after the list had been drawn up and everyone served.

'How about it if we get their own signatures, then? Make it more personal. Start tonight, shall I?'

'Great idea,' I said, 'but put their full names beside the signatures, so everyone will know who was here.'

'Will do.'

I bought a home-made Cornish pasty from him for a take-away lunch and left him as he began to seek out a sheet of paper worthy of the roll of honour.

During the afternoon I went through the latest print-out of the accounts with Rose and then with Isobel's input drew up my own sort of pencil-and-paper chart for the week. While Isobel was still in my office I inadvertently kicked the carrier left by Marigold English's lads, and, picking it up, I asked Isobel to throw it away.

She took it out of the office but in a few minutes came back, undecided.

'There's quite a good thermos flask in that carrier. I thought it was too good to throw away so I took it into the canteen in case one of the drivers would like it. And . . . well . . . would you come and look?'

She seemed puzzled enough for me to follow her along to the canteen to see what was on her mind. She'd taken out the packet of sandwiches and laid them on the draining-board of the sink there, and she'd unscrewed the flask and removed the top from the vacuum bottle inside. She'd poured most of the contents away into the sink, and found more in the flask than liquid.

I looked where she pointed, though there was no missing what was worrying her. Lying in the sink were four glass containers, each a small tube three and a half inches long, more than a centimetre in diameter, amber in colour with a black stopper fastened on with what looked like waterproof adhesive tape.

'They fell out when I poured,' Isobel said. 'What are they?'

'I've no idea.'

The tubes were covered with the opaque milky liquid that had been in the flask. I picked up the flask and looked into it and, finding some of the liquid still inside, poured it into a canteen mug.

Two more tubes fell into the mug.

The liquid was cold and smelled faintly of milky coffee.

'Don't drink it!' Isobel exclaimed in alarm as I raised the mug to my nose.

'Just smelling it,' I said.

'It's coffee, isn't it?'

'I'd think so.'

I took a paper plate from the stack always ready to hand and put the four tubes from the sink onto it. Then onto a canteen tray I put the plate, the mug, the thermos, its screw-on top and the packet of sandwiches, and with the carrier itself under my arm took the whole lot along to my desk in my office, Isobel following.

'Whatever can they be?' she asked for about the fourth time, and all I could say was that I would find out.

With a paper towel, I cleared the milky residue off one of the tubes. There were a few numbers etched into the glass which at first raised expectations, but all they announced was the container's capacity, 10 cc.

I held the tube up to the light and tipped it up and down. Its contents were liquid and transparent but moved more sluggishly than water.

'Aren't you going to open it?' Isobel asked, agog.

I shook my head. 'Not just now.' I put the tube back on the plate and pushed the tray away as if it weren't important. 'Let's get back to work and I'll decide about this stuff later.'

The tray to one side and with Isobel gradually losing

interest in it, we finished my preliminary pencil-and-paper chart and Isobel went back to her office to bring it up to date in the computer.

She was back in my doorway within five minutes, looking very frustrated, dressed for going home at the end of her shift.

'What's the matter?' I asked.

'The computer is totally on the blink. I can't do a thing with it, nor can Rose. Can you get that man to fix it?'

'OK,' I said, stretching a hand to the phone book. 'Thanks for everything and see you in the morning.'

Before I could find the number, my glance fell on the small glass phials on the tray, and instead of summoning the computer man, I phoned my sister.

CHAPTER FIVE

She was, as usual, hard to find. I left messages for her all over the physics department of Edinburgh University and in the administrative section there and the affiliated research laboratories and in an observatory, and tried the Rector's wife's private line, all numbers left over from former searches. No results.

Waiting until she went home in the evenings was fruitless as she spent all her time in inaccessible meetings and committees, and catching her between waking and departure in the mornings fine-tuned things to a variable five minutes. 'Please ask her to phone Freddie'; after six attempts I gave up and went back to raising the computer people a dozen or so miles up the road.

From that effort I got the number-unobtainable noise and also presently a voice assuring me that the line had been disconnected. Trying again produced the same result. Irritated, I phoned my barber who operated four shops along from the computers, and asked what was going on.

'They vanished overnight one day last week,' he told

me in carefree tones. 'Did a bunk. Just upped and scarpered. Took everything, left the place bare. We're all struggling along here since they put our rents up diabolically and I shouldn't wonder if the shoeshop doesn't go next.'

'Dammit,' I said.

'Sorry, mate.'

I did a bit of yellow-fingers walking and secured a shaky promise from a stranger to 'put me on the list'. 'Can't come tomorrow, sorry, not a chance.'

Sighing, I flicked again over the yellow pages, as I had them in my hand, and tracked down a rhyming dictionary in one of the bookshops. The last one they had, I was warned, but they would keep it for me.

When I put the receiver down this time, the phone rang immediately. I snatched the receiver up again and said 'Lizzie?' hopefully.

'Expecting a lady friend, are you?' Sandy Smith teased heavily. 'Sorry, can't oblige.'

'My sister.'

'Oh, sure.'

'How can I help you?'

'Other way round,' he said. 'I said I'd let you know about your hitchhiker. They did the post-mortem and he died of a heart attack. Myocardial infarction. Ticker stopped working. They've scheduled the inquest for Thursday. A half-hour job, evidence of identity, that sort of thing. Dr Farway's report. That driver of yours might be wanted. That Brett.'

'He's left. Won't Dave do?'

'Oh aye, I dare say.' Not his responsibility, I gathered.

'Thanks, Sandy,' I said sincerely. 'How about Jogger?'

'That's a bit different.' He sounded cautious suddenly. 'There's no report yet on him. As far as I know, they haven't cut him up so far, like. They're always busy on Mondays.'

'Will you let me know when you hear?'

'Can't promise.'

'Well, do your best.'

He said doubtfully that he would, and I wondered if he'd been subverted by my two plain-clothes visitors into casting me as opposition. All the same, he'd kept his word over Kevin Keith Ogden, and maybe our long acquaintanceship would remain a durable bridge.

I sat for a while thinking of everything that had happened over the past five days, until eventually the phone rang again and this time it was indeed my sister.

'Who did you leave unturned?' she demanded. 'I've been deluged by a veritable flood of "Phone Freddie's". So what's up?'

'First of all, where are you and how are you doing?'

'You surely didn't send all those SOSs just for a fireside chat!'

'Er, no. But if we should get cut off, where are you?'

She read out a number, which I added to the list. 'Professor Quipp's lodgings,' she said crisply.

I wondered if everyone except me had known where to find her. She'd had several lovers, nearly all bearded, all academics, not always scientists. Professor Quipp sounded the latest. I didn't make the mistake, however, of uttering aloud an unretractable guess.

'I was wondering,' I said diffidently, 'if you could get something analysed for me. In the chemistry school, perhaps.'

'What sort of thing?'

'Some unknown liquid in a 10 cc tube.'

'Are you serious?' She sounded as if she thought me crazy. 'What is it? Where did you get it?'

'If I knew what it was I wouldn't need to find out.'

'Oh brother . . .' She sounded suddenly more friendly. 'Tell me all.'

I told her about the carrier found in one of my boxes and the six tubes in the thermos.

'Quite a lot of weird things have happened,' I said. 'I want to know what my horsebox was carrying and, apart from you, the only person I could ask would be the local vet or else the Jockey Club. Actually, I'll give the Jockey Club a tube or two to be fair, but I want to know the answer myself, and if I entrust it all to any sort of authority I've lost control of it.'

She understood very well about losing control of research results. It had happened to her once, and she'd never stopped resenting it.

'I thought,' I went on, 'that you'd be sure to know

someone with a gas chromatograph or whatever it's called, and could get the job done for me privately.'

She said slowly, 'Yes, I could do it, but are you sure it's necessary? I don't want to waste a favour I'm owed. What else has happened?'

'Two dead men and some empty containers stuck to the undersides of at least three of my lorries.'

'What dead men?'

'A hitchhiker and my mechanic. He found the containers.'

'What sort of containers?'

'For smuggling, maybe.'

She was silent, evaluating. 'There's a chance,' she said slowly, 'that you could be thought guilty of whatever's gone on.'

'Yeah. A certainty, given the attitude of the two policemen who came here today.'

'And you love the police, of course.'

'I'm sure,' I said, 'that there are any number of civilised intelligent cultured policemen doing brilliantly compassionate jobs all over the place. I just seem to have met those who've had the laugh kicked out of them.'

She remembered, as I did, a time in the past when I'd begged the police (not Sandy, and not in Pixhill) to preserve a young woman from her violent husband. Domestic affairs weren't their business, I'd been told sniffily, and a week later she'd died from a beating. It had been the subsequently shrugged police shoulders which had infuriated me, not any sort of blighted passion, as she'd been barely more than an acquaintance. Official indifference had been literally deadly. Too late that years afterwards a new directive had decreed 'domestics' to be worthy of action: in me, the damage had been done when I'd been idealistic and twenty.

'How are things in general?' Lizzie said.

'The business is busy.'

'And the love life?'

'On hold.'

'And how long since you delivered flowers to the forebears?'

'Yesterday, actually.'

'Really?' She didn't know whether to be impressed or disbelieving. 'I mean . . . truly?'

'Truly. The first time since Christmas, mind you.'

'There goes your fatal honesty again. I tell you, it gets you into more trouble . . .' She broke off, pondering. 'How do you propose to get these mysterious tubes up here to me?'

'Post, I suppose. Courier, better.'

'Hm.' A pause. 'What are you doing tomorrow?'

'Going to Cheltenham. It's Champion Hurdle Day.'

'Is it? Since you stopped hurling your soul over those fences I've lost touch with racing. What if I fly down? I'm due a couple of days off. We could watch the races on TV, you could tell me all and take me out to dinner and I'll fly back on Wednesday morning. Get my old room ready. What do you say?'

'Will you come to the house or the farm?'

'The house,' she said with decision. 'It's easier.'

'Noon?'

'As near as dammit.'

'Lizzie,' I said gratefully, 'thanks.'

Her voice was dry. 'You're one tough cookie, brother dear, so less of the sob-stuff.'

'Wherever did you hear such language?'

'In the cinema.'

Smiling, I said a temporary goodbye and put down the receiver. She would come, as she always had, driven by an inbuilt compulsion to hurry to the aid of her brothers. The eldest of the family by a gap of five years, she had mothered first our brother Roger and then six years later myself, a fierce hen with chicks. Had she had children of her own, those instincts might have died naturally on my account, as they had for Roger, who'd achieved a cosy wife and three boys of his own, but as I, like her, had never married – or not so far – I seemed still to be not only brother but surrogate son.

Shortish and thin, her bobbed dark hair lately peppered with grey, she whisked around her own habitat either in black academic gowns or white laboratory overalls, her darting mind engaged with parsecs, quantum leaps and black and white dwarfs. She published papers, she taught intensely, she'd made a name;

she was, in or out of bed with the latest beard, as far as I could see, fulfilled.

It was a good six months since I'd taken the train to her Scottish door to spend two days with her. Two days compressed six months' conversation into a span she preferred. Her one-night trip to Pixhill was typical; she would never sit still for a week.

Thinking about her, I sat on at the farmyard until Nina came back, her box empty, the runners safely returned to their stable. She parked by the pumps and filled the tanks and came yawning over to the office to put the day's log through the letter-box, as she'd been asked.

I went out to meet her. 'How did it go?' I asked.

'Utterly uneventful in any meaningful way. Fascinating in others. Has anything happened here?'

I shook my head. 'Not really. The police came again about Jogger. I arranged his memorial at the pub, we should get a good list of names tomorrow. The computer's acting up. And after you've cleaned that horsebox I've something to show you.'

She glanced in disfavour at the dusty vehicle. 'Do you really mean I should clean it?'

'Harve will expect it. Inside and out.'

She gave me an old-fashioned sideways look of irony. 'I don't think Patrick Venables intended this at all.'

'Under cover is under cover,' I said mildly. 'If I do it for you and Harve comes back in the middle, my authority in this place is down the drain with the disinfectant.'

To do her justice, she complained no more but drove the box to the cleaning area and attacked it with the pressurised water, squeegeeing until the windows shone.

Harve did in fact return while she was busy and took her industry for granted. While he filled his tanks and waited his turn with the water I returned to my office and slightly rearranged the items on the canteen tray, removing four of the puzzling little tubes from sight and stowing them deep in a desk drawer. With time to spare, I picked up the unopened packet of sandwiches and read the label on it: 'Beef and Tomato'. There was also a price sticker label and a sell-by date, which identified the Friday just past.

Friday was the day I'd done Marigold's shuttle and found the carrier with the thermos. Friday's sandwiches. But I hadn't stopped anywhere for the lads to buy sandwiches or anything else.

I frowned. 'Beef and Tomato.' I'd seen a 'Beef and Tomato' sandwich wrapper, empty, only a day or two ago, but *where* exactly? The answer arrived slowly. In Brett's rubbish in the nine-box, of course.

Nina came into the office and sprawled in the chair across from mine, the desk between us.

'What do I do tomorrow?' she asked. 'I learned a lot about racing today but damn all about smuggling. I think Patrick believed I would instantly spot what's going on, but I could be here a month and see nothing if today's anything to go by.'

'No one,' I reminded her, 'has seen anything going on. Perhaps you're here to see how anything could.'

'Which you could see better than me.'

'No, I don't think so. I'd say nothing much happens when I'm around simply *because* I'm around. I'd like to send you on a trip to France or Italy or Ireland, but there we hit a bit of a snag.'

'What snag? I don't mind going. I'd quite like it, in fact.'

'I have to send two drivers because of the hours.'

'That's OK.'

I smiled. 'Not really. The wives of the married drivers take exception to me sending their husbands abroad with a woman. My usual woman driver, Pat, consequently never goes abroad, to her disgust. I could of course send you with Nigel, who's not married, but Pat herself won't go with him, he'd seduce a nun.'

'Not me, he wouldn't.' She was definite, but I wondered.

'We'll see if a trip comes up,' I said. 'As for tomorrow, we won't be very busy here, we never are in Cheltenham Festival week because there aren't many other meetings held on those three days. We'll be busy again on Friday and it'll be hectic again on Saturday, if we're lucky. Can you work Saturday?'

'It looks as if I'd better.'

'Mm.' I leaned forward, picked up one of the

remaining two tubes lying on the paper plate and asked her if she'd seen anything like it before.

'I don't think so. Why?'

'They were being carried in one of my horseboxes, hidden inside this thermos flask.'

She came to full alertness, all the tired lines shed.

'What are they?'

'I don't know. But it's possible – possible's the strongest I'd put it – that they might be what the masked intruder was looking for in the cab of my nine-box, because that's where they were, in the cab. In a carrier with these uneaten sandwiches, in this thermos full of undrunk coffee.'

She took the tube from me and held it up to the light.

'What's inside?'

'I don't know. I thought Patrick Venables might be able to find out.'

She lowered the tube and looked at me, smothering excitement and saying, 'They're the first concrete piece of evidence that *anything's* going on.'

I picked up the packet of sandwiches and showed her the labels.

'Brett, the driver who took the nine-box to Newmarket last Thursday with the two-year-olds . . .'

'And who has left?'

I nodded. 'Brett – I think probably Brett because Dave had diarrhoea – anyway, one of them bought sandwiches like these on that journey, because there was an empty packet just like this in some rubbish that came back in the cab. They threw the rubbish away on Friday morning when they cleaned out the box. Anyway, suppose Brett's sandwiches came from the shop in the South Mimms service station, and suppose . . . well, why not suppose . . . that these sandwiches here came from the same place . . .?' I paused, but she simply listened, not commenting or disagreeing. I went on, 'Dave picked up our hitchhiker at South Mimms. So . . . well . . . what if these sandwiches and this thermos were travelling with Kevin Keith Ogden?'

Given the supposition, her reasoning followed the same path that mine had and came up with the same observations.

'If the tubes belonged to the dead passenger, they can't be relevant to the containers *under* the lorries. They might well not have anything to do with you at all. The man didn't know he was going to die. He probably meant to take these tubes with him.'

'I was afraid you'd say that.'

'All the same, very interesting. And . . .' She stopped pensively.

'Yes?'

She told me her emerging conclusions, and I nodded. 'Makes you think, doesn't it?'

'You don't need me, really, do you?' she said.

'I need your eyes.'

Harve finished his chores and joined us in the office, asking Nina how she'd fared and whether she had any questions. She thanked him, cutting down, I noticed, on the purity of her blue-blooded vowels, but not to an insulting extent. I wondered how often and how regularly she transformed herself for Patrick Venables.

The phone rang and I answered it, finding Sandy on the line.

'Inquest on Jogger,' he said. 'It's just come through. Wednesday, ten a.m., Winchester Coroner's Court. All they'll do is open the inquest and adjourn it pending results of enquiries. Normal for accident cases. I asked if they'd need you but they said not yet. They'll want Harve, as he found him, and Dr Farway, of course. Also the inquest on Kevin Keith Ogden, they want Dave to attend. I'll brief him about where to go. OK?'

'Yes, thanks, Sandy.'

I put down the receiver and told Harve he'd be needed briefly on Wednesday. Harve made a face of disinclination and shrugged. The phone rang again at once as if in continuation of the same conversation, but in fact there was a strange nasal voice in my ear, full of self-importance and busy-busy.

'John Tigwood here,' he said.

'Oh. Yes?'

'Maudie Watermead told me to get in touch.'

'John Tigwood. Friend of Maudie's sister, Lorna?'

He corrected me briskly. 'Director of Centaur Care.'

'Yes, I know.'

'John Tigwood,' Harve muttered disapprovingly. 'Potty little pipsqueak. Always on the cadge.'

'What can I do for you?' I asked the phone temperately.

'Collect some horses for me,' Tigwood said.

'Certainly,' I agreed with warmth. 'Any time.' Business was business after all. Whatever I thought of John Tigwood personally, I was all for taking his money.

'A retirement farm is closing in Yorkshire,' he told me gravely, making it sound portentous. 'We've agreed to take the horses and find new homes for them. The Watermeads have agreed to put two in their bottom paddock. Benjy Usher's taking two others. I'm on to Marigold English, even though she's new here. How about you, yourself? Can I rope you in?'

'Sorry, no,' I said firmly. 'When do you want them transported?'

'Tomorrow do you?'

'Certainly,' I said.

'Good. Lorna herself wants to go with your box, acting as groom.'

'All right, fine.'

He gave me directions and I told him the fee.

'Oh, look here, I was hoping you'd do it for charity.'

'Sorry, no.' I was friendly and apologetic as far as it went.

'But it's for Lorna!' he insisted.

'I don't expect Maudie said I would do the job for nothing.'

After a pause he said grudgingly, 'She did warn me.'

'Mm. So do you want me to fetch them, or not?'

A shade huffily he said, 'You'll get paid. Though I do think you might be more generous. After all, it's a good cause.'

'You could ask someone else to fetch them,' I suggested. 'You might get someone else to do it for nothing.'

His silence suggested that he'd already tried someone else. Several someones, perhaps. It was a long way from Pixhill to the place in Yorkshire from where he wanted me to collect seven geriatric cases, shaky on their old legs, to deliver them to their new homes.

When Tigwood had gone off the line I handed the directions to Harve. Nina, having listened to my side of the exchange, asked what it had been about.

Harve told her disgustedly, 'There's this wacky home for very old horses. This John Tigwood, he boards them out all over the place. He charges the owners of the old horses for looking after them, but he doesn't pay the people who give the horses homes. It's a racket! And then he has the cheek to ask Freddie for free transport, in the name of charity.'

I smiled. 'It's one of the local good causes. People organise fundraisers. They twist a lot of arms. I daresay I ought to have offered the transport for nothing but to be honest I don't like being pressured or conned, and as I'll bet the owners of the horses will have to pay Tigwood to get their old pensioners brought down here, I don't see why he shouldn't pay *me*.'

'The point is,' Harve said, 'who's doing the job?'

'Whoever goes, takes Lorna Lipton, Mrs Watermead's sister, as groom,' I told him, looking over the chart. 'We'll have to send a nine-box. The new driver, Aziz what's his name, will be driving Brett's nine-box from now on. He may as well start with the geriatrics.'

'What new driver?' Harve said.

'I engaged him this morning, after you'd gone. Best of five who came for interviews.'

I wrote Centaur Care in the chart square for the nine-box, and put 'Aziz' at the head of the column.

Centaur Care, the name of Tigwood's outfit, sounded so like *Centre* Care that for years I'd thought that was how it was spelt. A tiny institution of its kind, the Centaur Care office occupied a small one-storey economically built *hut*, for want of a grander word, on the edge of a two-acre paddock on the outskirts of Pixhill. Adjoining ramshackle wooden stables, capable of holding six pathetic customers with low expectations, just about passed county regulation inspections, the charitable status of the enterprise shielding it from blasts of ill authoritarian will. John Tigwood's public manner elevated this set-up in Pixhill's collective consciousness to major good works: I was sure that many who gave to the noble cause hadn't set eyes on its headquarters.

There were 'Centaur Care' collecting boxes scattered throughout Pixhill, round tins with slots into which one was exhorted to pour 'long life for old friends'. John Tigwood came round regularly to empty the containers and write fulsome receipts. He'd left one tin in our canteen but had fumed to find gifts in it of buttons, biscuits and an out-of-date condom. 'Be glad it hasn't been *used*,' I'd said, which he hadn't seen as funny.

Harve was looking over the whole chart, and shrugging philosophically at the news that the computer wasn't working. Like me, he still preferred a written chart, though he inclined to the blackboard on a wall we'd had until I got rid of it. Too much chalk dust in the air, once we'd installed the computer.

I told Harve that all the tools had been stolen from Jogger's van. He swore briefly but saw no great significance in it. We would need, I said, another slider for inspecting the undersides of the boxes and Harve, nodding, suggested I ask Nigel to make one.

'All he needs is a bit of plasterboard and some casters,' Harve said. 'He's good with his hands, I'll say that for him.'

I smothered a smile. 'He can do it tomorrow, then,' I said. I pondered briefly and came to a decision. 'On Wednesday Nigel can go to France to collect the showjumper for Jericho Rich's daughter. Nina, here, will go with him as a second driver.'

Harve gave her a startled sideways glance and raised his eyebrows to me comically.

'I did warn her,' I said. 'She says she's Nigel-proof.'

'She doesn't know him!'

'She's experienced with horses,' I explained. 'Jericho's

daughter wants us to send an attendant to travel back with the horse. Nina can double that with driving.'

'But you said Dave was to go, with Phil driving his six-box,' Harve protested.

'I've changed my mind. Nina's going with Nigel. They can take the four-box Nina was driving today. It will be better, more economical.' To her I said, 'You'll need overnight things. OK?'

She nodded and, when Harve had gone out to meet the other incoming box, said, 'You'll want one of us to sleep in the box, won't you?'

'It has that tube on its underside,' I said, agreeing.

'Yes. Well, hang out the bait. Let everyone know that that particular box is going to France. Someone might bite.'

'Um,' I said hesitantly. 'No one expects you to do anything dangerous.'

She smiled slightly. 'Don't be too sure. Patrick can be bloody demanding.' She seemed unconcerned. 'And I won't exactly be parachuting into occupied France behind German lines.'

She was, I saw, exactly the type of woman who had done just that in World War II and, as if reading my thoughts, she nodded and said, 'My mother did it, and survived to have me afterwards.'

'That takes a bit of living up to.'

'It's in the blood.'

'Do you have any children?' I asked.

She wiggled long fingers in the dismissive gesture

of unsentimental nanny-assisted mothers. 'Three. All grown out of Pony Club age, all flown the nest. Husband long dead. Life suddenly empty, boring, no further point in showing or eventing. So . . . Patrick to the rescue. Need any more?'

'No.'

I understood her deeply, and she realised it, moved despite herself to an internal wave of emotion and self-knowledge. She shook her head as if to disown the moment and got to her feet, tall and competent, a horsewoman for whom horses ultimately were not enough.

'If you don't need me tomorrow,' she said, 'I'll deliver the tubes to Patrick in London and discuss things with him, and be back on Wednesday. What time?'

'You'll need to set off from here at seven. You'll cross from Dover to Calais and reach your French destination at about six. Returning on Thursday, you'll have to go to Jericho Rich's daughter's place, of course, to deliver the horse. You'll be back here late, perhaps ten o'clock.'

'Right.'

She wrapped the two amber tubes carefully in a handkerchief and stowed them in her handbag. Then with a brief nod of farewell she walked out to her car and inconspicuously departed.

Retrieving the four other tubes from the desk drawer, I wrapped each one in a tissue and put them in my jacket pocket. Then I poured the mug's contents back into the thermos, screwed on the inner stopper and the outer cap and restored it with the sandwiches to the carrier for onward transport to my house.

The work day was ending. There were still boxes out on the road, though I wouldn't wait for their return. The drivers never expected it and might have taken too much close checking as a lack of trust. There had, however, been phone messages during the day both from the nine-box I'd sent to Ireland with broodmares and from the box in France that was bringing the two two-year-olds over to join Michael Watermead's stable, all the calls to the effect that neither box would be arriving back until two or three in the morning.

For us, that was quite normal. For Michael Watermead, it was bound to be an intolerable inconvenience. I had already arranged with the driver to come straight back to home base and to keep the two young horses in the farmyard's stables until morning, but remembered I'd forgotten to tell Michael himself.

Stifling a yawn, I pressed his numbers and found him at home.

'Two in the morning!' he protested. 'You know I don't like it. It disturbs the whole yard, noise and lights when the other horses are asleep. They do need a good sleep, you know.'

'If you like, we could keep your two-year-olds here in the farmyard stables until morning.' I suggested it as if I'd just thought of it. 'They'd come to no harm.

They're travelling well, my driver says. They're calm and eating.'

'You might have organised it better,' Michael grumbled, gently reproving, as usual converting any strong feeling into good-mannered restraint.

'There's been a hold-up with the ferry in Calais,' I explained. 'Your horses won't reach Dover until about ten tonight, they say. I'm very sorry, Michael, but it's out of our hands.'

'Yes, yes, of course, I do see. But blast it, it's bloody irritating. Still, yes, I suppose those two-year-olds won't come to much harm. Bring them over first thing, though. Six-thirty or soon after, when my lads come to work. Eh?'

'First thing,' I confirmed.

'All right then.' He paused for a change of subject. 'Any . . . er . . . more news of your mechanic, poor fellow?'

'The police were asking accident-type questions.'

'Too bad he fell.'

'Rotten.'

'Let me know if I can do anything.'

'Thanks, Michael.'

'Maudie sends her love.'

I put the receiver down with a sigh, wishing Maudie meant it, and after a moment's thought got through to the stud farm that was expecting the delivery from Ireland.

'Your four mares with foals,' I said soothingly, 'are

on the ferry right now but they won't get to Fishguard until eleven tonight and if we bring them straight on to you they'll be with you sometime after three. Is that all right with you?'

'Fine. We'll be up all night anyway, with mares foaling.'

Jobs done, I stood up tiredly, picked up the carrier, locked the outer office door, leaving the canteen open for the drivers, and went out to shift gears in the Four-trak, my workhorse buggy. I sometimes felt, climbing behind that practical wheel, as if the Jaguar XJS persona was leaving me altogether; but somewhere below the businessman the jockey still had a pulse, and I now saw that it was essential to keep him alive, not to let him slip away, to be still *willing* for him to risk his neck daily, even if he no longer did.

I drove home, ate, went to bed.

I would unleash the Jaguar more often, I thought.

Soon after six-thirty in the morning I was up, dressed and breakfasted, and driving along in the strengthening daylight to the farmyard to see what was what.

The box from France with Michael Watermead's two-year-olds stood quietly in its accustomed place, its cargo dozing in the stable, its driver nowhere about. There was a folded note from him, however, tucked under the windscreen wiper. I opened it and read, 'Can someone else take them to Watermead's? I'm bushed,

I'm out of hours, and I think I've got flu. Sorry, Freddie.' It was signed 'Lewis' and dated 2.30 a.m., Tuesday.

Damn the flu, I thought forcefully. Damn all invisible enemies, in fact.

I unlocked the outer office door and went along to my own room to fetch the duplicate keys of Lewis's box, deciding that it was easier to drive it along to Michael's yard myself rather than wait for another driver to be ready. Accordingly, I unlocked the horsebox, loaded the patient untroubled guests from my stable and took them the scant mile to their destination.

Michael was already out in his yard, looking pointedly at his watch, which stood nearer to seven than the appointed six-thirty.

When I climbed down from the cab his displeasure lessened a little but not altogether. He was, for him, in a comprehensively bad mood.

'Freddie! Where's Lewis?' he said.

'Lewis came back with flu,' I said ruefully.

'Dammit!' Michael did some arithmetic. 'What about Doncaster? This flu takes so long.'

'I'll give you a good driver,' I promised.

'It's not the same. Lewis is helpful with saddling and so on. Some of those lazy buggers get to the races and sleep in their cabs until it's time to go home. That Brett was one of those. I couldn't stand him.'

Making sympathetic noises, I lowered the ramp for

access to the two-year-olds and untied the nearest one to lead him out.

'I thought the bloody French were sending a lad with them,' Michael grumbled, his fair head back, his mild voice plaintive.

In anyone else, the displeasure level would have come roaring out in full-blown anger. In Jericho Rich, for example, intemperate man.

'Lewis told us yesterday on the phone that the French lad went back home from Calais,' I explained. 'He apparently thought he would be sea-sick on the crossing. Lewis assured me he could manage on his own, so we decided not to lose even more time in finding a substitute attendant. Where do you want me to put this fellow?'

The two-year-old was skittering around playfully at the end of his rope. Michael's head lad, half running, came to take him into custody and lead him away to his new home.

With the second import safely unloaded, Michael's irritation subsided into his normal bonhomie and he suggested a cup of coffee before I went on my way. We walked together into his house, into the bright warm welcoming kitchen where frequent visitors sat unceremoniously round a long pine table and helped themselves to juices and toast.

Maudie was there in jeans and sweat-shirt, blond hair still tousled from sleep, face bare of make-up. She received my hello kiss absent-mindedly and asked for Lewis.

'Flu,' Michael said succinctly.

'But he helps the children with the rabbits! Bother and damn. I suppose I'll have to do it myself.'

'Do what?' I incautiously asked.

'Clean out the run and the hutches.'

'Be careful,' Michael teased, 'or she'll have *you* mucking out the wretched bunnies. Let the children do it, Maudie. They're quite old enough.'

'They'll be dressed for school,' she objected, and indeed her two younger children, boy and girl in tidy grey, came bouncing in with gleeful appetites and good morning hugs for their father. They were followed, to my severe surprise, by my own daughter, Cinders.

She wore the same grey clothes. I gathered from the chatter that she went to the same school and had stayed with the Watermeads overnight. Hugo, I reflected, couldn't have reckoned on my coming to breakfast.

She said 'Hi' to me nonchalantly as someone she'd met in passing at lunch two days ago, as someone who knew her parents. Her attention reverted at once to the other children with whom she giggled, at ease.

I tried not to watch her, but I was as conscious of her as if I'd grown new antennae. She sat opposite me, dark-haired, neat and vivacious, secure and loved. Not mine. Never mine. I ate toast and wished things were different.

Maudie's daughter said, 'If Lewis has flu, who's doing the rabbits?'

'Why not Ed?' Maudie said, suggesting her elder son.

'Mother! You know he won't. He's a dead loss as a brother. Lewis loves the bunnies. He strokes them, strokes their fur. They hop all over his hands. There's no one as good with them as Lewis. I wish Lewis was my brother.'

Michael raised his eyebrows at Maudie, neither of them relishing the promotion of Lewis to son.

'Who's Lewis?' Cinders asked.

'One of Freddie's drivers,' the children told her, explaining the fleet of boxes, explaining they were mine.

'Oh,' she said, lacking much interest.

Michael said he would get one of the stable-lads to clean the hutches that afternoon and Maudie chivvied the three children like a flock of sparrows to finish their breakfast, bundle up in coats and scramble out to the car for her to drive them miles to reach school by eight-thirty.

The kitchen seemed quiet and empty after they'd gone. I finished my coffee and rose to my feet, thanking Michael for the company.

'Any time,' he said amiably.

My glance fell on one of John Tigwood's ubiquitous round collecting tins standing on the window sill.

'Oh yes,' I said, remembering. 'One of my boxes is

fetching a load of ancient steeplechasers from Yorkshire today. John Tigwood says you're taking two of them in your bottom paddock. What shall I do about them? Do you want the whole lot to come here first? I mean, *which* two do you want?'

Not surprisingly he looked faintly exasperated. 'Lorna talked me into it again. Let her and that wretched little man sort them out at that awful little place. But see if you can bring me two here that aren't on the point of expiring. I told Tigwood to take the last two to the knackers to put them out of their misery. It's a lot of sentimental rubbish, keeping those poor tottering wrecks on their feet, but of course I can't say that in front of the children. They don't understand the need for death.'

He came out into the stable yard to drive up to the Downs to watch his horses complete their morning exercise, and on an impulse asked if I would like to go with him, as Irkab Alhawa would be up there doing fast work.

I accepted at once, intensely pleased at what I knew to be a compliment and a gift. He drove us in his high-wheelbased Shogun and pulled up at a vantage point near the end of his upland all-weather exercise track. From there we had a clear view of horses galloping uphill towards us three abreast, and a closer look as they swept past us, to pull up a hundred yards further on.

I'd spent innumerable mornings most of my life

riding training-gallops. I still did it, given the chance. There wasn't going to be any chance I would exercise Watermead horses, though, as steeplechase jockeys of my size, whether retired or not, tended to be too heavy and too strong for young flat-racers.

'How's Irkab coming along?' I asked tentatively.

'Doing just great.'

Michael's voice was full of satisfaction, the anxiety of training a horse fancied to win the Derby hovering well below sweat-level so early in the year. Come June he'd be insomniac.

We watched three or four trios of his string come past us in a prearranged order, and Michael said, 'Irkab will be in the next three, on this side nearest to us. You'll see the white blaze down his nose.'

'Great.'

The three horses came into sight, moving easily, fast shadows on the brown track. Irkab Alhawa, with his awkward Arab name, had been a late-developing two-year-old, not revealing the extent of his athletic ability until the Middle Park Stakes in October the previous year. Lewis had driven him to Newmarket that autumn day as merely another Watermead runner and had returned with a revelation that had attracted newsmen to Pixhill like a flock of starlings.

The promise of the Middle Park had been confirmed two weeks later by a scintillating six-length victory in the Dewhurst Stakes, the final top two-year-old event of the season, slaughtering the best that Newmarket could muster on its own turf, with the result that during the peaceful inactive winter Irkab Alhawa had become almost a cult, the odd-sounding syllables part of his mystique. The press had translated the words into English as 'Ride the Wind', which had caught the public's imagination, though somewhere I'd heard that that rendering wasn't quite right. Never mind; Irkab Alhawa was good news for Michael, for Pixhill, for Lewis, and not least for Freddie Croft.

The brown sensation with the narrow white blaze, recognisable afar off, swept effortlessly up the track towards us in the smooth coordination of muscle and mass that was nature's gift to the lucky few, horses and humans, in whom grace of movement equalled speed.

I felt, as always in the presence of great horses, an odd sort of envy: not to be on their backs, but to be *them*, riding the wind. In rational terms it was nonsense, but after so many years of closeness with the marvellous creatures they were in a way extensions of myself, always hovering in the back of consciousness.

Not everyone had rejoiced with Michael over the emergence of a prodigy in his stable. Human nature being what it was, a certain portion of the racing world would have been happy to hear that ill had befallen the horse. Michael shrugged it off. 'There will always be spite and envy. Look how some politicians encourage it! It's not my problem if people grudge and bitch, it's theirs.' Michael, easy-going and civilised, couldn't understand the force of unprovoked hate.

Irkab Alhawa galloped past us, majestically strong. Michael turned to me with a glimmering smile and saw he needed to make no comment. For a horse like that, comment was inadequate, banal.

We drove back to the stables. I thanked him. He nodded, and in an odd way, because of that gallop, we'd come closer to a positive friendship, not just friendly business relations.

I took Lewis's super-six back to the farmyard, its daily bustle embracing me, bringing my feet back to earth.

Aziz had reported for work, his vitality and flashing smile having already produced a sort of glaze in Harve's less shiny eyes. Harve greeted my arrival with relief and told me he'd been trying to explain to Aziz, disappointed with his first assignment, that a job was a job was a job.

'There's a whole lot of no glamour in this business,' I assured Aziz. 'Some days you take seven terminal has-beens. One day, maybe, a Derby winner. Getting the cargo alive and well to journey's end is all that matters.'

'OK.'

'And do remember that all horses doze off and dream while you're driving at a constant speed on the motorway, but when you leave the motorway and slow down and come to a roundabout they'll wake up and not know where they are and judder about trying to stay on their feet. All horses are like that but these very old ones will be shaky on their pins to start with, so be extra careful or you'll come back with all seven thrashing about on the floor and, even if they survive, at the very least we will not get paid for our efforts.'

Aziz listened to this homily at first with a disbelieving grin and latterly with thoughtful attention. He should, though, have been nodding throughout.

I said slowly, 'You *have* been driving racehorses, haven't you?'

'Yes,' he replied instantly. 'Of course. But local, round Newmarket. And to Yarmouth races. No motorways, really.'

Harve frowned but didn't pursue it, and question marks rose like a prickly hawthorn hedge in my own mind. It was true there were few if any long motorways in East Anglia, but it passed credibility that a Newmarket stable would never have sent runners further afield.

I might have asked Aziz a few searching questions but at that moment Maudie's sister, Lorna, swept through the gates in her expensive crimson Range Rover, the aristocrat of safari cars, built to withstand raw African veldt and the smooth roads of Pixhill.

Lorna, concerned and intense, hopped down from behind the wheel and strode across to give me a peck on the cheek. Blonde, blue-eyed, long-legged, richly divorced and thirty, lovely Lorna looked me firmly in the eye and told me I was a pig to charge for fetching the pensioners.

'Um,' I said, 'is John Tigwood charging the pensioners' owners?'

'That's entirely different.'

'No, that's getting it both ways, or trying to.'

'Centaur Care needs the money.'

I smiled a usefully bland smile and introduced Aziz as the day's driver. Lorna blinked. Aziz, shaking her hand, gave her a white blinding smile and a flash of dark eyes. Lorna forgot about my meanness and told Aziz animatedly that they were going on a wonderful Errand of Mercy and that it was a Privilege to be involved in Saving Old Friends.

'Yes, I agree,' Aziz said.

He gave me the ghost of a sideways grin as if daring me to denounce his hypocrisy. Aziz was a rogue, I thought, but rogues were good for the spirits, up to a point.

John Tigwood chose that moment to give us the benefit of his company, which I could certainly have done without. The potty little pipsqueak, as Harve had called him, emerged from a coffee-coloured van emblazoned all over with 'Centaur Care for Aged Horses' in titanium white letters, and strode in our direction with thrusting important steps. He wore grey corduroy trousers, an open-necked shirt and a heavy-knit sweater and was carrying an anorak.

'Good morning, Freddie.'

His voice tried hard, but the self-important fruitiness couldn't disguise the lack of substance beneath. Tigwood was essentially an inadequate man inventing a role for himself: not, I supposed, an unusual phenomenon or even one necessarily reprehensible. What else could he do? Slink along, wringing Uriah Heep hands?

I'd always taken the Centaur Care charity to be a long-established facet of the local community. That Tuesday morning I wondered whether Tigwood himself had set it up, and whether he lived off the collecting boxes, and whether, if he did, should Pixhill object? There were always old horses around dozing in sunshine. Such a cause had to be worthy, if compassion meant anything.

'Morning, Lorna,' the charity man said.

'John, dear.' Lorna pecked his thin cheek somewhere above the sparse beard that straggled round his pointed chin. Even the beard, I thought, trying to stifle my impatience, was inadequate. So in a way was his thin neck with the sharp larynx, neither of which he could help.

'What can I do for you, John?' I asked, welcoming him.

'Thought I'd go with Lorna,' he announced. 'Seven horses . . . two pairs of hands will be better than one. Is this our driver?'

Lorna gave a quick glance at Aziz, not sure that she wanted John with her after all, but the potty little pipsqueak had made up his mind, had come dressed for the journey and would stick obstinately to his plan, it was clear.

'How nice,' Lorna said insincerely.

'You've a long way to go,' I told them in general, 'you may as well get started.'

'Yes, yes,' Tigwood said, taking bustling charge. 'Come along, driver.'

'His name is Aziz,' I remarked mildly.

'Oh? Come along then, Aziz.'

I watched them climb aboard, two totally incompatible men with the well-intentioned Cause-embracer between them. Aziz looked grimly out of the window in my direction, all relish for the day, small at best, evaporating. I couldn't blame him. I'd have hated to have taken his place.

Under that nine-box, I reflected, as Aziz turned competently out of the gate, was the magnet Jogger had found. I'd taken it on trust that the nails in the insulating block of wood were still holding fast. I hadn't warned Aziz it was there. I hadn't told him to look out for strangers trying to roll under the fuel tank section of the chassis. I couldn't envisage anyone seeking to transport anything in such awkward secrecy between Yorkshire and Pixhill, when all they'd have to do was drive down in a car.

Harve left in Aziz's wake, setting out five minutes after, in time to pick up two runners for the later races at Cheltenham. Another box had already left for the same destination, two had gone to Bristol airport to collect Irish horses flying over for Gold Cup day and three were out with broodmares. Not bad, considering.

I went into the offices where Isobel and Rose were looking in frustration at blank computer screens and asking what they should do with the day.

'Type letters on the old-fashioned typewriter?' I suggested.

'I suppose we'll have to,' Rose said, disgusted.

'The man promised he'd come tomorrow,' I assured her.

'Not before time.'

Tigwood's collecting box stood on Isobel's desk and I picked it up and shook it. The result was a hollow rattle, three or four coins at most.

'Mr Tigwood came to empty it last week,' Isobel said. 'There wasn't much in there. He thinks we should try harder.'

'Perhaps we should.'

I went out to my jalopy and drove to Newbury to leave my film of Jogger with a one-hour developing outfit and to collect the ordered, reserved and ready rhyming dictionary. I hadn't actually seen one of these before and sat in the car park flicking over the pages to pass the hour's wait, finding that the rhymes were listed not in regular alphabetical fashion but all starting with vowels.

'Amely', I read. 'Gamely, lamely, namely, tamely'.

'Etter – better, debtor, fetter, getter, letter, setter, sweater, wetter . . .'

'Oard – board, floored, ford, gourd, hoard, horde, oared, pored, sword, toward, aboard, afford . . .'

Hundreds and thousands of rhymes, available but useless. I realised I needed to have Jogger's cryptic statements under my eyes, not just in my memory. Maybe if I could simultaneously see what he'd said, some spark might fly out of entries like 'unch – brunch, bunch, crunch, hunch, lunch, munch, punch, scrunch . . .'

Always remembering, I thought in depression, that in Jogger's cockney accent bike became boike and lady, lidey, and ts and ds could be swallowed and not heard.

Closing the book, I collected the sharp sad pictures of his death and drove home to tidy the house and get my sister's room ready, which meant making the bed and opening the windows to let in whatever March cared to deliver.

I picked more daffodils and put them in a vase, and punctually at noon my sister Lizzie arrived.

She flew in literally, from on high, in a helicopter.

CHAPTER SIX

Lizzie owned a quarter share of the tiny Robinson 22, her only extravagance and the way she chose to use her inheritance from our parents. To my mind, the helicopter was her equivalent of Roger's cruise ships and my steeplechasing, the elder sister's statement that if boys could have toys, so could girls. She had shown us each in turn as children how to run a complicated train set. She'd taught us how to bat unafraid at cricket, she'd climbed trees like a cat; in her teens she'd led us into jungle woods and scary caves and defended us and lied for us in our wrong doings. Because of her, we'd grown up understanding many faces of courage.

She cut the engine and, when the rotor had stopped, jumped down from the little glass bubble and walked collectedly to meet me on the tarmac.

'Hi,' she said; small, light, wiry, pleased with life.

I hugged her.

'Have you fixed lunch?' she asked.

'No.'

'Good. I brought a picnic.'

She returned to the helicopter and retrieved a carrier, which we took with us into the house. She never came empty-handed. I never wasted time catering for her except to put champagne on ice. I popped the cork and poured it straight, and she relaxed in a big chair, taking a deep fizzy gulp and looking me over as sisters do.

'How was the flight?' I asked.

'Bumpy over the moors. Some snow still lying about. I dropped down at Carlisle to refuel. Four hours, door to door.'

'Three hundred and fifty miles,' I said.

'Near enough.'

'It's great to see you.'

'Mm.' She stretched, almost purring. 'Tell me all.'

I told her a good deal, explaining who everyone was: Sandy Smith, Bruce Farway, the Watermeads, Jericho Rich, Brett, Dave, Kevin Keith Ogden and Jogger. I told her about Nina Young and her metamorphosis.

She inspected the empty cash box standing in all its grime on the newspaper. I showed her the rhyming dictionary and played her the tape of Jogger's last message, but all the mental agility under the greying dark cap of hair couldn't unlock the old soldier's meaning.

'Silly man,' Lizzie said. 'Did he fall or was he pushed?'

'Pushing someone into a five-feet deep inspection pit is not a sure fire way of killing them.'

'An accidental push, then.'

'No one has owned up to it.'

With some hesitation I offered to show her the photographs of Jogger in the pit.

'I'm not squeamish,' she protested. 'Hand them over.'

She studied them at length. 'There's nothing to tell, one way or another.'

'No,' I agreed, taking the photos back and returning them to their packet.

After a pause she asked, 'What about these tubes in the thermos flask?'

I took two of the tubes from my safe, where I'd kept them overnight, and gave them to her. She unwrapped each from its tissue and held them up to the light.

'Ten ccs,' she said, reading the small numbers. 'In other words, one tablespoonful.'

'Only one?' I was slightly surprised. I'd thought the tubes held more.

'Only one,' Lizzie confirmed. 'A large mouthful.'

'Yuk.'

'Well, yes, it wouldn't be prudent to drink this.' She put the tubes back into the tissues, and into her handbag, just like Nina. 'I suppose you want the results like, say, yesterday?'

'It would be helpful.'

'Day after tomorrow,' she promised prosaically. 'The best that can be done.'

'I'll try for patience.'

'Never your best virtue.'

She sniffed the contents of the thermos and poured a little into a spare glass, putting her nose down close to the surface.

'Coffee,' she said, 'and the milk's off.'

'It's been in the thermos since Thursday at least.'

'Do you want this analysed as well?'

'What do you think?' I asked.

She said, 'I'd think the coffee was just there to cushion the tubes.'

'Leave it, then,' I said.

We drank more champagne and unpacked the picnic, which was the glorious gift of arguably the best restaurant in Scotland, La Potinière at Gullane in East Lothian. 'The Browns send you their love,' Lizzie said, referring to the owners. 'They want to know when you're coming back.'

They would want to know six months in advance and even then one might not get a table. Sometimes Lizzie, their close friend, had been down on her knees. This time, they'd sent chicken breasts stuffed with a mousseline of cream, hazelnuts and Calvados and a watercress salad with its hazelnut oil dressing packed separately, followed by a light lemon cheesecake that melted to ambrosia on the tongue.

I seldom cared much what I ate. Lizzie deplored it and educated me when she could. I'd have been willing to have graduated at La Potinière.

We companionably watched the first of the Cheltenham races on television, and it was no use looking back, it was three years since I'd finished second in the Champion Hurdle, a bitter-sweet loss on the day.

'Be glad you're out of the worry of it,' Lizzie said, watching me watching the jockeys.

'What worry?'

'The worry of someone else being given your rides.'

I smiled. That was, for all jockeys, the worst of worries, and I said, 'You're right. It's a relief. Now I only have to worry about other transport firms pinching my customers.'

'Which I don't suppose they do, much.'

'Not so far, luckily.'

The phone rang with a call from Isobel, reporting progress.

'Everything's OK,' she said. 'That new man, Aziz, has phoned from Yorkshire to say they want him to bring back eight animals, not seven, and the eighth is a half-bald old pony that can hardly walk. What do you want him to do?'

'John Tigwood's there,' I said. 'If he'll be responsible if the pony dies on the way, we'll ship it. Tell Aziz to get Tigwood to write a note absolving us, and sign and date it, including the time.'

'Right.'

'How did Aziz sound?'

'Fed up,' Isobel said cheerfully. 'Can't blame him.'

'What's all that about?' Lizzie asked lazily as I put down the receiver, and I explained about the geriatric expedition and gave her a run-down on John Tigwood, profit-making philanthropist.

'A fanatic?'

'He has to be.'

We watched the rest of the races, all, that is, that were shown. Isobel phoned again in mid-programme at four to report all well; she was going off home. One of the local horses Harve had driven to Cheltenham had won, had I noticed?

'Yes, terrific.'

'Good for custom at the pub,' she observed, bright girl, reminding me, as it happened, that I hadn't checked that day on Jogger's memorial.

I told Lizzie about the memorial, and the reason for it.

'So you don't think it was an accident!' she said.

'I want it to be.'

When the races had finished, we switched off the television and just talked in general, and later Aziz telephoned direct to my house, saying he hoped I didn't mind but the office was shut with my own number on its answering machine.

'No, of course not, I don't mind. Where are you?'

'Chieveley service station; that place north of Newbury. I'm inside, in a phone booth. I wanted to talk to you without them listening.'

'What's the matter?'

'It's my first day with you, and I . . .' He stopped, seeking the words. 'Do you mind,' he said in a rush, 'coming to meet this box wherever it is that I'm taking it?'

'Centaur Care.'

'Yes. These horses aren't fit to travel. I told Mr Tigwood but he insisted we bring them. Mrs Lipton's worried they'll die before we unload them . . .'

'All right,' I said decisively. 'When you get near Pixhill, call me again on the horsebox phone and I'll drive round at once. Don't let the ramps down until I get there. Sit in the cab and write up the log sheet. Do *anything*. Understand?'

'Thanks.' One short word; a dictionary full of meaning.

'See you,' I said.

When I told Lizzie the problem she asked to come with me, and after Aziz had phoned again, round we went.

The scrubby Centaur Care paddock had been over-grazed to the point where the dark earth showed between the straggling tufts of grass. The roughly hard-topped parking area had weeds growing through cracks and the small concrete office was streaked with rusty rain marks. Behind it, the stables looked as if a good breeze would flatten them. Lizzie gazed at this magnificent spread speechlessly as we pulled up beside the elderly green paint of the front door.

We'd been there barely a minute before Aziz turned in slowly from the road and brought the nine-box to an exceedingly gentle halt. I walked across to his window as Tigwood and Lorna disembarked from the passenger seats on the other side.

Aziz opened the window and said, 'They're all still alive, I hope.'

There were sounds of the ramps being unbolted on the far side and I hurried round the front and told both Tigwood and Lorna to stop.

'Don't be silly,' Tigwood said. 'Of course we must unload them.'

'I'd be happier to see them first,' I told him reasonably.

'Whatever for?'

'Old horses might like five minutes rest at this point. There's no mad hurry, is there?'

'It'll soon be dark,' he pointed out.

'All the same, John, I'll just rub their noses.'

I opened the rear grooms' door without waiting for any further objections and heaved myself up to horse level. Three patient old sets of eyes gazed at me, tiredness showing in the angle of the necks and in the lethargically turning ears.

In the space in front of their heads, where often an attendant travelled, stood an untouched bale of hay and the row of plastic water containers, all full.

I jumped down from that compartment and opened the centre grooms' door, climbing up again into the space between the middle three stalls and the front three. In the middle three stalls stood another shaky trio, their heads hanging low with fatigue. I wriggled forward through the empty third of the front stalls and inspected the rest of the load, a horse so feeble that it looked as if the partitions themselves were all that were holding him on his feet, and a pathetic pony with acres of hairless skin and its eyes shut.

I descended to ground level and told Tigwood and Lorna that I wanted the vet round to see them before they were unloaded. I wanted an authoritative opinion, I said, that my firm had delivered them in as good a condition as possible.

'It's none of your business,' Tigwood said furiously. 'And it's an insult to Centaur Care.'

'Look, John,' I said placatingly, 'if the owners of those horses care enough about them to give them good homes in their old age, they'll certainly pay for a vet to make sure they've come to no harm from the journey. They're nice old horses but they're very tired and I should think you should be grateful to have help with their well-being.'

'John,' Lorna said, 'I'm sure Freddie's right. I do think we should. They were a lot feebler than I expected.'

'Did they drink before they set off?' I asked.

Lorna looked at me worriedly. 'Do you think they're thirsty?' she said. 'Aziz was driving so dreadfully slowly.'

'Hm.' Through the open passenger door I asked Aziz to hand me the phone and without more ado got through to the local veterinary surgeon, explaining what I wanted. 'Five minutes look-see, that's probably all. But right now, if you could.'

He promised the right now and was as good as his word, a long-time friend who knew I wouldn't call him out for nothing. He made the same brief inspection as I had and at the end gave me a hollow-eyed look, meaning more than he said.

'Well?' John Tigwood demanded, and listened crossly to the verdict.

'They're mildly dehydrated and probably hungry. Thin, too, though they've been adequately looked after in general. They'll need good hay and water and a lot of rest. I'll stay while you unload, I think.'

During the wait for his arrival, I'd introduced Lizzie to Tigwood and Lorna. They paid her scant attention, having thoughts only for the horses, and Lizzie herself was content just to watch and listen.

I lowered the rear ramp finally and John Tigwood untied the first of the passengers and led him to the ground, the old legs slipping and unsteady, hooves clattering, eyes frightened. He reached firm footing and stood still, quivering.

'Lorna,' I said, 'how old are they?'

She produced a list and handed it to me mutely. The names, ages, and owners of the horses were there, some of them so familiar as to raise my interest sharply.

'But I rode two of them!' I exclaimed. 'Some of these were great horses.'

'Surely you realised that?' Lorna said tartly.

'No, I didn't. Which is which?'

'They have labels on their headcollars.'

I went to the horse Tigwood was holding while the vet looked it over and read the name, Peterman. I fondled the old nose and thought of the races we'd won and lost together twelve and more years earlier, days when the shaky frame had been taut and powerful, a proud head-tossing prince, a star in his time. At twenty-one, his age on the list, he was the equivalent of roughly ninety, in human terms.

'He's fine,' the vet said. 'Just tired.'

Tigwood gave me an 'I told you so' look of triumph and led my old friend off towards the stables.

'He's the youngest,' I remarked, reading the list.

The daylight faded as the unloading progressed and I switched on all the horsebox's lights, inside and out, to give passable illumination. The vet gave a provisional thumbs up to all of the travellers except the last two from the forward-most stalls, both of which had him shaking his head.

The aged pony was worst. The poor creature could hardly stand, let alone walk down the ramp.

'Advanced laminitis,' the vet said. 'Best to put him down.'

'Certainly not,' Tigwood pronounced indignantly. 'He's a much-loved pet. I *promised* a comfortable home, and that's what he'll get. His owner's fifteen. She made me *promise*.'

I thought of Michael Watermead's remark about his

own children: 'they don't understand the need for death'. Tigwood understood it all right, but keeping life going at any cost was where both his income and his fanaticism seemed to lie.

'At least let me dress his alopecia,' the vet suggested, referring to the hair loss, and Tigwood resentfully said, 'Tomorrow, then,' and literally pushed the poor little beast until he had to totter down the ramp or fall down altogether.

'It's disgusting,' Lizzie said under her breath.

Lorna heard and snapped at her, 'It's the people who kill horses just because they're old who are disgusting.' She was busy stifling her own doubts, I saw. 'Old horses have a right to life. Centaur Care is a wonderful institution.'

'Yes,' Lizzie said dryly.

Lorna gave her an unfriendly stare which she then transferred to me.

'You don't appreciate John's work,' she accused. 'And don't give me all that crap about putting animals out of their misery. You can't be sure they're miserable.'

I thought it quite easy to be sure when they were, but I was not going to argue, and besides, I'd known many old horses live healthily and happily into their middle twenties. My father, the trainer, had looked after his favourite horses until they died in the fields, feeding them oats all winter to keep them well-fleshed and warm. They had all looked better than the thin crowd of today.

I said, 'It's nice to see old Peterman again and I'm sure the owners will appreciate your personal attention.'

'And John's!'

'And John's,' I said.

We all three watched Tigwood lead the pony towards the paddock, the sore hooves flinching at every slow step, the head bobbing low with pain. The fifteen-year-old owner, I thought, was full of love but had no mercy, a cruel combination.

Lorna tossed her fair hair, admitting no criticism. The vet shook his head, Lizzie went on looking disgusted, Aziz shrugged. He'd brought them back alive: his involvement ended there.

Tigwood let the pony loose in the paddock and returned to open his office door. We all trooped in behind him, filling a functional space about fifteen feet square, lit by fluorescent strips and lined with filing cabinets. The brown composition flooring was softened by two large patterned rugs, and framed photographs of old horses in sunlit fields crowded the walls. Tigwood crossed to a pair of metal desks standing side by side, one holding a computer and printer, and the other the normal impedimenta of the pre-computer age. A row of collecting tins stood on one of the filing cabinets and a tea-making machine on another. Bookshelves conspicuously displayed publications on the medical problems and care of aged thoroughbreds. There were three comfortable-looking wool-covered armchairs and some decent blue curtains at the two windows. If any of the horses' owners ever turned up on the doorstep, the set-up would give the message that here every penny was devoted to the cause, while at the same time due regard was paid to the luxury level normal to racehorse owners.

Give him his due, I thought, Tigwood had got it right; inside, at any rate.

He demanded, and the vet wrote, a brief statement to the effect that six horses (names attached) had travelled without incident from Yorkshire and had arrived in good condition. One horse (name attached) showed signs of exhaustion and required special care. One pony with laminitis needed veterinary attention. All had been transported by Croft Raceways and entrusted to Centaur Care.

Satisfied, Tigwood made a photocopy and handed it to me with a smirk, saying, 'You've made a lot of fuss about nothing, Freddie. You can pay the vet's bill, I'm not going to.'

I shrugged. I'd called for the help and received it, and I didn't mind paying. The statement, in fact, had insulated me from any accusation of negligence Tigwood might think of making once he received my account. I said I was very glad the horses had been all right, but that it was nice to be sure, wasn't it?

With varying emotions we all left the office again, the vet driving off with a wave and Tigwood and Lorna climbing back into the horsebox for the run to the farmyard, where they'd both left their cars that morning. Lizzie and I followed the box, Lizzie asking whether it hadn't all been a storm in a teacup.

'Didn't your driver over-react?' she said.

'Maybe. But he's new today. And there can't be much wrong with his driving if he got them all here on their feet.'

Lorna and Tigwood left the farmyard separately in individual shades of huff.

Aziz said awkwardly, 'Sorry for all that.' No white teeth. Shiny eyes downcast.

'Don't be sorry,' I reassured him. 'You did right.'

Lizzie and I left him refilling his fuel tanks and went home, deciding to pause there briefly and go out to eat.

There were three call-back messages on the answering machine, two business, and one Sandy Smith.

I called him back first and listened to him tell me that this was out of hours, like, and unofficial.

'Thanks, Sandy.'

'Well, they did the post-mortem on Jogger yesterday in the morgue of Winchester Hospital. Cause of death, broken neck. He hit the back of his head at the bottom of his skull, the top two vertebrae were dislocated, same as in hanging, but he wasn't hanged, no rope marks. Anyway, the inquest opens tomorrow in Winchester. They'll only want identification, which I'm doing myself as there's no next of kin, and Dr Farway's statement, and the police photos. Then the coroner will adjourn the inquest for three weeks or so for enquiries. Routine for all accidents. You won't be needed.'

'Thanks very much indeed, Sandy.'

'The Ogden inquest's first thing on Thursday, same place, that's to say the coroner's court, which is a room in the police station in Winchester. The verdict will be natural causes. They won't adjourn that one. Dr Farway will give his report. Mrs Ogden's identified her husband. Seems Ogden had heart trouble on and off but was bad at taking pills. Dave had better attend, though they might not call him. I'll be there too, of course.'

'Great, Sandy. Thanks again.'

'I drank to Jogger last night in the pub,' he said. 'There was quite a turn out. Loads of people signing his memorial. You'll get an astronomical bill.'

'All in a good cause.'

'Poor old Jogger.'

'Yes,' I said.

Lizzie and I settled for dinner on an old country inn ten miles from Pixhill where the speciality was duck roasted in a honey glaze to a crisp blackened skin with succulence inside. La Potinière it was not, but an old favourite place of Lizzie's, who liked the heavy oak beams, the authentically crooked walls and the low-to-dim lighting.

As Pixhill people often ate there, I was not much

surprised to see Benjy and Dot Usher side by side at a booth table across the room from us. Impervious to their surroundings they were in mid-quarrel as usual, the two faces tight with fury six inches apart.

'Who are they?' Lizzie asked, following my gaze.

'A Pixhill millionaire who plays at training and his inseparable wife.'

'Ask a silly question . . .'

'And you get a dead accurate answer.'

'Really?'

'I reckon if they ever stop fighting that marriage will collapse from boredom.'

I told her about my day with them at Sandown races and about Benjy's odd habit of not touching horses.

'And he's a *trainer*?'

'Of sorts. But he's also a customer, which makes him OK by me.'

She studied my face with elder-sister indulgence. 'I remember you once saying,' she said, 'that if you rode races only for people you liked you'd have missed winning the Gold Cup.'

'Mm. Same theory. I'll hire out my skills to anyone for the prospect of reward.'

'It sounds like prostitution.'

'What isn't?'

'Pure research, for one thing. You're an absolute philistine.'

'Goliath was a Philistine . . . a giant of a man.'

'Brought down by a slingshot.'

'Sneaky.'

Lizzie smiled with pleasure. 'I miss you,' she said.

'Me too. Tell me about Professor Quipp.'

'I *knew* I shouldn't have said that about everyone finding me. You never miss a trick.'

'Well, go on.'

'He's nice.' She sounded fond, not defensive. A good sign, given the characters of some of the past beards. 'He's five years younger than I am and he adores skiing. We went to Val d'Isère for a week.' Lizzie positively purred. 'We raced each other down mountains.'

'Um . . . What colour beard?'

'No beard. You're a beast. No moustache either.'

It sounded serious. 'What subject?' I asked.

'Actually, organic chemistry.'

'Ah.'

'Any more ahs and you won't get your tubes analysed.'

'Not another ah shall pass my lips.'

We ate the crisp black duck and during our coffee Benjy Usher took his attention off Dot long enough to notice me across the room.

'Freddie!' he shouted uninhibitedly, turning every other diner's head his way. 'Come over here, you bugger.'

It seemed easiest to go. I stopped at their table and said hello to Dot.

'Come and join us,' Benjy commanded. 'Bring the bird.'

'She's my sister.'

'Oh sure, pull the other one.'

Benjy had had one drink too many. Dot looked embarrassed. It was for her sake, really, that I went and persuaded Lizzie to cross the carpet.

We accepted coffee from Dot and resisted Benjy's offer of huge glasses of port. When Benjy summoned another for himself, Dot said conversationally, 'He's now at impotence. Paralysis next.'

'Vicious bitch,' Benjy said.

Lizzie's eyes widened.

Dot remarked, 'Followed by vomiting, ending in tears of maudlin self-pity. He calls himself a man.'

'Pre-menstrual tension,' Benjy mocked. 'Chronic case.'

Lizzie looked at their handsome faces and casually good clothes, at the diamonds on Dot's fingers and at Benjy's gold watch. No comment was possible. None was needed. Their pleasure depended not on money but on spite.

'When are you going to Italy for my colt?' Benjy asked me.

'Monday,' I suggested. 'It'll take us three days. He could be here by Wednesday evening.'

'Which driver? Not that one called Brett. Michael says never Brett.'

'He's left. It won't be Brett.'

'Send Lewis. Michael swears by *him*, and he's driven my horses a lot. That colt's valuable, you know. And send someone to look after him on the journey. Send that man of yours, that Dave. He can handle him.'

'Is he difficult to handle?'

'You know colts,' Benjy said expansively. 'You send Dave. He'll be all right.'

Dot said, 'I don't know why you don't stand him at stud in Italy.'

'You keep your tongue off what doesn't concern you,' her husband replied.

To try to stop their argument, I mentioned that we'd that day brought the load of old horses from Yorkshire and I gathered he was giving a home to two of them.

'Those old wrecks!' Dot exclaimed. 'Not *more* of them.'

'Do you have some already?' Lizzie asked.

'They died,' Dot told her. 'I hate it. I don't want any more.'

'Don't look at them,' Benjy said.

'You put them outside the drawing-room window.'

'I'll put them *in* the drawing-room. That should please you.'

'You're utterly childish.'

'You're utterly stupid.'

Lizzie said sweetly, 'It's been terribly nice meeting you,' and stood up to leave, and when we were out in the Jaguar asked, 'Do they always go on like that?'

'I can testify to fifteen years of it.'

'Good grief.' She yawned, well-fed and relaxed, sleepy. 'Beautiful moon tonight. Terrific for flying.'

'But you're not going tonight!'

'No, it's just a habit of mind. I think of the sky in flying terms, you think of the ground as hard or soft for horses.'

'I suppose I do.'

She sighed pleasurably. 'Lovely car, this.'

The Jaguar hummed through the night, powerful, intimate, the best wheels I'd owned. The jockeys lately seemed to have stopped buying speed in favour of middle-rank family saloons, ultra-reliable but rather dull. My bit of flamboyance, alive in my hands, was no longer politically correct with the new serious lot in the changing room.

Bad luck for them, I thought. Looking back, I seemed to have laughed a lot in those years. And cursed and ached and seethed at injustices. And had a sizzling good time.

The last stretch of the road from dinner to bed went past the farmyard. I slowed automatically to glance at the row of transport gleaming in the moonlight. The gates were open, which meant that one or more boxes were still out on the road, and I completed the short distance to the house wondering which one it was.

Lizzie's Robinson 22 shone in the moonlight, standing on the tarmac where the nine-box had stood with Kevin Keith Ogden on board.

'I'll leave about nine in the morning,' she said, 'and get your analysis started in the afternoon.'

'Great.' I must have sounded preoccupied. She turned her head to study me.

'What's the matter?' she asked.

'Nothing really. You go in, go to bed. I'll just nip back to the farmyard to lock the gates. There aren't any boxes still out, or anyway there shouldn't be. I won't be long.'

She yawned. 'See you in the morning, then.'

'Thanks for coming.'

'I've enjoyed it.'

We hugged briefly and she went in smiling. I hoped Professor Quipp would love her for a long time, as I'd never known her so at peace.

I drove the Jaguar back to the farmyard and stopped outside the gates. Someone was walking about in the yard, as Harve often did, taking care of things, and I walked towards the half-seen figure, calling 'Harve?'

No answer. I walked on, reaching the nearest box to Harve's own, and passing into a patch of shadow.

'Harve,' I shouted.

I heard nothing, but something hit me very hard on the back of the head.

I worked out later how long I spent unaware of the world: one hour, forty minutes.

The first sensation of the daze I awoke to was a pain in the head. The second sensation was of being carried.

The third was a matter of hearing, with a voice making a nonsensical remark.

'If this doesn't give him flu, nothing will.'

I was dreaming of course.

Of course.

Soon I would wake up.

I felt I was falling. I hated dreams about falling: they were always about falling off buildings, never off horses.

I fell into water. Breathtakingly cold.

I went down into it without struggling. Wholly immersed. Went down deep.

Terrible dream.

Instinct, perhaps, switched me to reality. This was no dream, this was Freddie Croft, in his clothes, drowning.

The first awful compulsion was to take a deep breath, and it was again subconscious knowledge, not present thought, that stopped me.

I kicked, seeking to go upward, and felt sucked to one side and clutched by currents, a rag doll in limbo.

I kicked again with growing horror, urgency flooding finally into a response from arms and legs, muscles bunching, working hard, chest hurting, head hammering.

Swim up, for God's sake.

Swim . . . up.

I swam up in crazy panic-driven breaststrokes. Swam as if horizontal, arms sweeping, legs kicking, knowing I was also going sideways, being swept without choice.

Probably I spent barely more than a minute under water. I breaststroked through the surface into the night and gulped air into my starved lungs with a whooping roar, and the moment I stopped swimming my heavily saturated clothes and water-filled shoes dragged me down again, down like a see-saw, ultimate terror.

The drowning come up twice, and the third time stay down . . . the bad news wisdom. I swam with ebbing strength to the surface against the weight of my clothes and the drag of the water and its inexorable swirling suction, seeing no light anywhere, only darkness enough for one struggling gasp, and my head went under again, will power urging me up and the salt sea claiming me for its own.

Salt sea . . . I swallowed it, gagging. Pretty well every vestige of athleticism went into lifting my nose above the surface, and kicking to stay there. In a way I knew it was a losing battle, but I couldn't accept it. If I'd been dropped off a boat, if I were alone far from land, an end would come soon, and it was intolerable. I protested furiously, vainly, against being murdered.

I saw a glitter on the water, a flash of light. The current was taking me into it, out of darkness.

Electric light.

A lamp . . . high above the water . . . on a *lamp standard.*

I hadn't realised how far I'd lost hope until the knowledge that electric lamp standards didn't grow in mid-ocean hit my brain like a more friendly blow on the skull. Lamp standards equalled land. Land meant life. Life meant swimming to the lamp standard.

Simple.

Not so simple. It was all I could do to stay up. All the same, the current that had floated me from darkness to light continued its benign work, taking me towards the lamp standard, but slowly, casually, indifferent to its flotsam.

Two lamp standards.

They were above me, on top of a wall. I bumped eventually into the wall, no longer able to see the lights on their tall stalks, but knowing they were there. I was in shadow again by the wall but, looking back, I could see little lights everywhere, bright, unmoving, a whole forest of lamp standards.

The wall was smooth and slimy, without handholds. The water carried me along it slowly, sucking me away and slapping me back against it, while I kicked fearfully and with insidiously growing feebleness to stay up to breathe.

I tried shouting for help. The suck and slap and gurgle of the eddies smothered my voice. When I took a deep breath to shout again, the salt water rushed into my mouth and set me choking.

It seemed ridiculous to drown when I could actually touch land, while the swell lifted me against safety and pulled me away again, while ten feet above me there was a dry place to walk.

I lived by luck. Lived thanks to the designer who'd

built a staircase into his wall. One surge of water lifted me into a sort of hollow in the smooth cliff and the retreating ebb all but floated me out again. Almost too late I thrust my arms and hands against slippery concrete, desperate not to be dragged away, waiting . . . waiting . . . for the water to lift me again into the hollow and knowing it was the last chance, the miracle of deliverance if only I had the strength.

I rolled with the water into the hollow and pressed my body onto a sharp step; felt the tug of the receding swell and rolled against it, using the killing weight of shoes, trousers and jacket as anchor. With the next swell of water I rose to the step above and lay there immobile, head and shoulders out of the water, legs and feet still submerged. The next wave achieved for me one more step up so that I was lying on the slope of stairs, feeling hard land embrace me as if in forgiveness, as if saying, 'All right, then, not yet.'

The stairs were inset, parallel with the wall, the seaward side being always wide open to the water. I crawled up one step more and simply lay there, exhausted, shuddering, frozen and concussed, with almost nil activity going on in the brain-box. My feet, still in the water, lifted and fell with liquid rhythm and it wasn't until one wave slapped over my knees and tried to float me out again that I sluggishly realised that the tide had to be rising and that if I didn't climb upwards I would be back where I'd come from with no strength for another fight.

I slithered up two steps. Three steps. At the top, as I looked up, stood a lamp standard.

When some semblance of strength oozed back I continued crawling, pressing myself against the inner wall, cravenly frightened of dropping off the open edge back into the sea. True nightmares weren't about falling off buildings, I thought, they were about falling off steps built for embarking onto boats.

The endless-seeming climb ended. I slithered onto hard dusty flat dry road-surface, crawled weakly to the lamp standard and lay full length beside it, face down, one arm hooked round it as if to convince myself that this, at least, was no dream.

I had no idea where I was. I'd been too busy trying to survive to worry about such minor details. My head throbbed. When I tried to work out why, memory got lost in a fog.

There were footsteps approaching, grittily scrunching. For a shattering moment I thought the people who'd thrown me in had found me again, but the voice that spoke above me carried a different sort of threat, the heavy resentment of affronted petty authority.

'You can't lie here,' he said. 'Clear off.'

I rolled onto my back and found myself staring straight into the eyes of a large purposeful dog. The dog pulled against a leash held by a burly figure in a navy uniform with a peaked cap and a glinting silver badge. The dog wore a light muzzle which looked inadequate for the job.

'Did you hear what I said? Clear off.'

I tried to speak and achieved only an incoherent croak.

Authority looked displeased. The dog, an unfriendly rottweiler, lowered his head to mine hungrily.

Trying again, I said, 'I fell in.' This time the message reached its target but with moderate results.

'I don't care if you swam the Channel, get up and clear off.'

I made an effort to sit up. Got as far as one elbow. The dog warily retreated a step, leaving his options open.

'Where am I?' I said.

'In the Docks, of course.'

In the docks. Where else?

'Which docks?' I said. 'Which port?'

'*What*?'

'I . . . don't know where I am.'

He was far from reassured by my obvious weakness. With the dog at the ready, he said suspiciously, 'Southampton, of course.'

Southampton Docks. Why Southampton Docks? My bewilderment grew.

'Come on. Get going. No one's allowed on here when the dock's shut. And I can't stand drunks.'

'I hit my head,' I said.

He opened his mouth as if to say he didn't care if I'd been decapitated, but instead said grudgingly, 'Did you fall off a ship?'

'I don't really know.'

'You can't lie here, all the same.'

I wasn't so sure I could get up and walk and he must, I thought, have seen it, as he suddenly thrust down a reaching hand to be grasped. He pulled me vigorously to my feet and I held on to the lamp standard and felt dizzy.

'You want a doctor,' he said accusingly.

'Just give me a minute.'

'You can't stay here. It's against orders.'

Seen at level height, he was a truculent-looking fiftyish individual with a large nose and small eyes and the thin grim mouth of perpetual wariness. He'd been afraid of me, I saw.

I didn't mind his manner. To be a nightwatchman in a dock area was to face dangers from knaves and thieves, and a man lying where he shouldn't had to be treated as a hazard until proved to be harmless.

'Do you have a telephone?' I asked.

'In the guardroom, yes.'

He didn't say I couldn't use it, which was invitation enough. I let go of the lamp standard and tottered a few shaky steps, lurching sideways off a straight line and trying hard to behave with more sense than I felt.

'Here,' he said roughly, grabbing my arm. 'You'll fall in again.'

'Thanks.'

He held my sleeve, not exactly supporting me but certainly a help. With feet that seemed hardly to belong to me I made a slow passage down a long dock and arrived finally at some large buildings.

'This way,' he said, tugging my sleeve.

We went through tall iron gates in a high fence and out onto a pavement. A car-parking area lay ahead, followed by a low wall, with a public roadway beyond that. No traffic. I tried looking at my watch to see the time and hit a slight snag: no watch.

I peered feebly along the road in both directions while the nightwatchman fed a key into a lock, and I found I was looking at a recognisable landmark, somewhere I'd been before, an orientating building telling me exactly *where* I was, if still not why.

'Come in,' the nightwatchman invited. 'The phone's on the wall. You'll have to pay for it, of course.'

'Mm.' I nodded assent, felt for wallet and coins, and found neither. Nothing in any of my pockets. The nightwatchman observed the search judiciously.

'Have you been mugged?'

'It looks like it.'

'Don't you remember?'

'No.' I looked at the telephone. 'I can reverse the charges,' I said.

He made an assenting wave. I took the receiver off the wall and realised that if I phoned my own house what I would get would be my answering machine. It was possible to de-activate it from a distance but not on a reverse charge call. Sighing, I got through to the number, listened to my voice saying I was out and to leave a message, and went through the switch-off routine. The nightwatchman asked crossly what I was doing.

'Getting the operator,' I said, redialling.

The operator tried my number and said there was no answer.

'Please keep trying,' I said anxiously. 'I know someone's there, but she'll be asleep. You need to wake her.'

Lizzie's bedroom was next to mine, where the phone would be ringing. I exhorted her silently to wake up, to tire of the ringing, to get up and answer it. Come on, Lizzie . . . come on for God's sake.

Ages seemed to pass before she finally said, 'Hello?', thick with sleep. The operator, following my instructions, asked if she would take a call from her brother, Mr Croft, in Southampton.

When she spoke to me direct she said, astonished, 'Roger? Is that you? I thought you were in the Caribbean.'

'It's Freddie,' I said.

'But you can't be in *Southampton. Roger's* ship goes to Southampton.'

Explaining was impossible, and besides, the nightwatchman was listening avidly to every word.

'Lizzie,' I said desperately, 'come and collect me. I've been robbed of money . . . everything. I've been in the water and I'm freezing and I hit my head, and to be honest I feel rotten. Come in the Fourtrak, it's outside on the tarmac. The key's on a hook beside the back door. Please do come.'

'Heavens! Come *where?*'

'Go to the main road to Newbury, but turn south. That's the A34. It joins the Winchester bypass. Then follow the signs to Southampton and when you get there take the road to the Docks and the Isle of Wight ferries. There are signs everywhere. I'm . . . I'm down there by the Docks. The Isle of Wight ferry terminal is just along the road. I'll go there . . . and wait for you.'

She said, 'Are you *shivering*?'

I coughed convulsively. 'Bring me some clothes. And some money.'

'Freddie . . .' She sounded shocked and unsure.

'I know,' I said contritely, 'it's the middle of the night. It'll take you three-quarters of an hour, about . . .'

'But what *happened*? I thought you were here in bed, but you didn't answer the phone. How did you get to *Southampton?*'

'I don't know. Look, Lizzie, just come.'

She made up her mind. 'Isle of Wight ferry. Southampton Docks. Forty-five minutes. Five more while I dress. Just hang in there, buddy boy. The cavalry's coming.'

'The cinema has a lot to answer for.'

'At least your sense of humour's still working.'

'It's a close-run thing.'

'I'll be there,' she said, and put down the phone.

I thanked the nightwatchman and told him my sister

would come. He thought I should have telephoned the police.

'I'd rather go home,' I said, and realised I simply hadn't thought of asking for police help. That would involve too many questions and I had not enough answers. And also not enough stamina left for sitting on a hard chair in a police station, or for having my bumps read. The source of my troubles lay not in Southampton but back in Pixhill, and if the transit from one to the other was wholly a blank, I did vaguely remember driving the Jaguar to the farmyard and calling to Harve.

The troubles lay on my doorstep, in my farmyard, under my lorries, in my business. I wanted to go home, to sort them out.

CHAPTER SEVEN

Lizzie, true to form, came to rescue her little brother.

The nightwatchman let me spend most of the wait in his under-heated guardroom, even going so far as to brew me a cup of tea to alleviate my shivers, all under the baleful eyes of his attentive dog. When the hands of the clock on his wall stood at two, he said I'd have to leave as it was time for his rounds, so I thanked him and walked . . . well, shambled . . . along the road to the ferry terminal and sat in shadow on the pavement there at one end of the building, my spine against the wall, my arms hugging my knees. I'd known worse conditions, just.

Not far away, on the other side of an openwork metal fence, light glinted on water. I looked at the scene vaguely, then with speculation. I suppose there were many places like that, where in darkness semi-conscious people could be slid into the briny with nobody noticing. There were miles of available shoreline in Southampton Docks.

The Fourtrak came, slowed, moved hesitantly into

the parking area and stopped. I stood up, pressing against the wall for support, and took a few paces forward into the light. Lizzie saw me and came running from the vehicle, stopping dead a few feet from me, wide-eyed and shocked.

'*Freddie*!'

'I can't look as bad as all that,' I protested.

She didn't tell me how I looked. She came and draped one of my arms over her shoulders and walked with me to the Fourtrak.

'Take off that wet jacket,' she commanded. 'You'll die of exposure.'

Marginally better than drowning, I thought, though I didn't say so.

Once inside the butty little vehicle I struggled out of all the wet things and put on the dry substitutes, including fleece-lined boots and the warmest padded jacket I owned. When Lizzie coped she did nothing by halves.

I got her to drive as near the guardroom as we could manage. The nightwatchman and his dog were at home again and issued forth suspiciously. When I offered him money for the first telephone call and for his trouble and kindness he at first refused it with indignation, raising one's regard for the salt of the British earth.

'Take it,' I urged, 'I owe you. Drink to my health.'

He took the note dubiously, only half concealing his pleasure.

'You'll get pneumonia anyway, shouldn't wonder,' he said.

The way I felt, he might well be right.

Lizzie drove back home the way she'd come, darting glances at me every few seconds. The cold-induced shudders and shakes gradually abated in my body until eventually even my guts felt warmed again, but conversely along with warmth came overwhelming tiredness so that all I wanted was to lie down and sleep.

'But what *happened*?' Lizzie asked.

'I went to the farmyard.'

'You said you were going to close the gates,' she said, nodding.

'Did I? Well . . . someone hit me on the head.'

'Freddie! Who?'

'Don't know. When I woke up I was being dropped into water. Just as well I did wake up, really.'

She was predictably horrified. 'They meant you to drown!'

'I don't know about that.' I'd been puzzled ever since I'd been conscious. 'If they wanted me dead, why not finish the job on my head? Why take me all the way to Southampton Docks? If they wanted particularly to drown me, there's a perfectly good pond in Pixhill.'

'Don't joke about it.'

'May as well,' I said. 'All I remember about them is

someone saying, "If this doesn't give him flu, nothing will." '

'But that's nonsensical!'

'Mm.'

'How many of them?'

'There had to be two at least. If not, why bother to talk?'

'Are you *sure* that's what they said?'

'Pretty sure.'

'What sort of accent? Did you know the voice?'

'No.' I answered the second first. 'Not an Eton accent. Rough, sort of.'

Lizzie said, 'You'll have to tell the police.'

I was silent, and she glanced at me too lengthily, even for light traffic.

'You'll have to,' she said.

'Keep your eyes on the road.'

'You're a shit.'

'Yep.'

She drove, however, with more attention to getting us home safely and I wondered what good it might really do if I bothered to tell the police.

They would take a statement. They might check with the nightwatchman that I had in fact crawled out of Southampton Water. I could tell them that as I hadn't known until five minutes beforehand that I was going along to the farmyard, there hadn't been any sort of premeditated ambush. I'd walked in when I was unexpected and been smartly prevented from finding out who was there and what they were doing.

Taking me to Southampton must equally have been impulsive. Throwing me in alive but apparently unconscious meant they hadn't much cared if I lived or died . . . almost as if they hadn't made up their minds on that point and were leaving it to fate.

Nonsensical, as Lizzie'd said. Anyone, especially the police, would be sceptical. And what would the force do about it? They couldn't and wouldn't guard me day and night against illogical possible attempted murder. If I didn't walk unexpectedly into shadows at night, why should anyone attack me again?

Probably a lot of that creaky reasoning was the result of concussion. More likely it stemmed from the usual aversion to less than friendly questioning, where crime was seen to be the fault of the victim.

I gingerly felt the back of my by then mutedly-throbbing head, wincing at the actual contact. Any blood that had been there had been washed away. My hair had dried. There was a lump and a soreness, but no gaping cut and no dent in my skull. As injuries went, compared with the assaults of steeplechasing, it was of the 'it'll be all right tomorrow' kind. To have been knocked out racing meant to be grounded by the doctors for up to three weeks. I would ground myself for the rest of the night, I thought, and maybe I wouldn't go to Cheltenham until Thursday. That should do it.

The Fourtrak hummed us home, the road direct. Southampton Docks was the nearest deep water to Pixhill, the nearest tidal place where unseen bodies could wash out on the ebb before dawn.

Stop thinking about it, I told myself. I was alive and dry and nightmares could wait.

Lizzie turned into the driveway and curled round the house and we found something absolutely rotten had happened while we'd been away.

My Jaguar XJS, my beautiful car, had been run at full tilt into Lizzie's Robinson 22. The two sweet machines were tangled together, locked in deep metallic embrace, both twisted and crushed, the Jaguar's buckled bonnet rising into the helicopter's cab, whose round bubble front had been smashed into jagged pieces. The landing struts had buckled so that the aircraft's weight sank into the car's roof; the rotor blades were tilted at a crazy angle, one of them snapped off on the ground.

All one could say was that nothing had caught fire or exploded. In every other way, the two fast engines, our pleasure, our soul-mates, were dead.

The house's outside lights were on, raising gleams on the double wreck. It was spectacular, in a macabre sort of way; a shining union.

Lizzie braked the Fourtrak to a jolting halt and sat hand over mouth, disbelievingly stunned. I slowly stepped down from the passenger's seat and walked towards the mess, but there was nothing to be done. It would take a crane and a tow-truck to tear that marriage apart.

I walked back towards Lizzie who was standing on the tarmac saying 'Oh, my God, oh my God . . .' and trying not to weep.

I put my arms round her. She sobbed dryly against my chest.

'Why?' She choked on the word. '*Why*?'

I had no answer, just an ache, for her, for me, for the wanton destruction of efficiency.

In Lizzie the grief turned quickly to rage and to hatred and to hunger for revenge.

'I'll *kill* the bastard. I'll kill him. I'll cut his throat.'

She walked round the helicopter banging it with her fist.

'I love this bloody machine. I love it. I'll kill the bastard . . .'

I felt much the same. I thought mutely that at least we ourselves were alive, even though in my case only just, and that perhaps, that was enough.

I said, 'Lizzie, come away, there's fuel in the tanks.'

'I can't smell any.' She came to my side, however. 'I'm so furious I could *burst*.'

'Come inside and have a drink.'

She walked jerkily with me to the back door.

The door had a pane of glass broken.

'Oh *no*!' Lizzie said.

I tried the handle. Open.

'I locked it,' she said.

'Mm.'

It had to be faced. I went into the big room and tried to switch on a light. The switch had been hacked out of the wall. It was only by moonlight that one could see the devastation.

At a guess, it had been done in a frenzy, with an axe. Things weren't just broken, but sliced open. There was light enough to see the slashes in the furniture, the smashed table lamps, the ruin of the television set, the computer monitor sliced in two, the rips in my leather chair, the raw pieces gouged out of my antique desk.

Everything, it seemed, had been attacked. Books and papers lay ripped on the floor. The daffodils I'd picked for Lizzie had been stamped on, the Waterford vase that had held them crushed to slivers.

The framed photographs of my racing days were off the walls and beyond repair. Our mother's rare collection of china birds was history.

It was the birds that seemed to upset Lizzie most. She sat on the floor with tears running into her mouth, holding the pathetic irreplaceable pieces to her lips as if to comfort them. Grieving for our childhood, for our parents, for life gone by.

I went on a wander round the rest of the house but no other rooms had been invaded; only the heart of things, where I lived.

The telephone on my desk would never ring again. The answering machine had been hacked in two. I went out to the phone in the Fourtrak and woke Sandy Smith.

'Sorry,' I said.

He came in his car with his uniform pulled on over his pyjamas, the navy blue jacket unbuttoned, hairy chest visible. He stood looking in awe at the amalgam of Jaguar and helicopter, and brought a torch with him into the house.

The beam shone on Lizzie, the birds, the tears.

'Done you proper,' Sandy said to me, and I nodded.

'Morning, miss,' he said to Lizzie, the polite greeting bizarre but the intention kind enough.

To me he said, 'Do you know who did it?'

'No.'

'Vandalism,' he said. 'Nasty.'

I felt the most appalling, heart-bumping apprehension and asked him to drive down with me to the farmyard.

He understood my fear and agreed to go at once. Lizzie stood up, still holding a wing and a bird's head and said she would come with us, we couldn't leave her alone in the house.

We went in Sandy's car, its lights flashing but its siren silent. The farmyard gates still stood open, but to my almost sick relief the horseboxes themselves were untouched.

The offices were locked. My keys had long vanished but, seen dimly through windows, the three rooms looked as orderly as usual. The canteen, door open, had been left alone.

I went along to the barn. The tool store was secure. Nothing looked out of place. I went back to Sandy and Lizzie and reported: no damage and no one about.

Sandy stared at me strangely.

'Miss Croft,' he said, 'tells me someone tried to kill you.'

'Lizzie!' I protested.

Lizzie said, 'Constable Smith wanted to know where we were when all that . . . that wicked destruction . . . was going on at the house. I had to tell him. I couldn't avoid it.'

'I don't know that anyone actually meant to kill me,' I said. I told Sandy briefly about waking up in Southampton. 'Maybe the reason for taking me there was to give time for attacking my house.'

Sandy thought things over, buttoned his tunic absent-mindedly and announced that all things considered he had better report to his headquarters.

'Can't it wait till later this morning?' I said. 'I could do with some sleep.'

'You've had two dead men on your premises since last Thursday,' Sandy pointed out. 'And now this. I'll be in trouble, Freddie, if I don't report it at once.'

'The two dead men were accidental.'

'Your house isn't.'

I shrugged and leaned on his car while he telephoned. No, he was saying, no one was dead, no one was injured, the damage was to property. He gave the address of my house and listened to instructions, relaying them to me after. In effect, two plain clothes detectives would come in due course.

'How long is due course?' Lizzie asked.

'There's a major flap on in Winchester,' Sandy said. 'So . . . whenever they can.'

'Why do you say no one was injured?' Lizzie sounded indignant. 'Freddie was injured.'

Sandy eyed me with long knowledge. 'Injured to him means both legs broken and his guts hanging out.'

'Men!' Lizzie said.

Sandy said to me, 'Do you want me to call out Doc Farway?'

'No, I don't.'

He listened to my emphatic reply and smiled at Lizzie. 'See?'

'What time is it?' I asked.

Sandy and Lizzie both looked at their watches. 'Three thirty-two,' Sandy said with precision. 'My message to headquarters was timed at three twenty-six.'

Still leaning on Sandy's car, I couldn't decide which to guard, my business or my home. The damage already done might not be all. With such wanton pointless behaviour as stamping on daffodils, logical prediction could get nowhere. The graffiti mind, the urge to throw stones at windows, looting, destruction for its own sake, they were the natural glee of untamed humanity. It was civilisation and social conscience that were artificial.

The side door of Harve's house opened directly into the farmyard. He came hurrying out in jeans, shrugging his arms into an anorak, anxiety plain.

'Freddie! Sandy!' His relief was partial. 'One of my kids got up for a pee and woke me to say there was a police car by the horseboxes. What's happened?' He looked along the intact row of vehicles and repeated, puzzled, 'What's the matter?'

'Some vandals broke into my house,' I explained. 'We came to see if they'd been here too, but they haven't.'

Harve looked more worried, not less.

'I walked round late,' he said. 'It was all OK.'

'What time?' I asked.

'Oh, I'd say about ten.'

'Um,' I said, 'you weren't out here by any chance an hour or so later? You didn't hear anything?'

He shook his head. 'When I went in I watched a video of a football match for a while, and went to bed.' He still looked anxious. 'Why?'

'I came here at roughly half-eleven. The gates were open and someone was moving about. I thought it was you.'

'No, not that late. I shut the gate at ten. Everyone was back by then, see?'

'Thanks, Harve.'

'Who was here at half-eleven?' he demanded.

'That's rather the point, I don't know. I didn't see anyone close enough to recognise whether I knew them or not.'

'But if they didn't do any damage . . .' Harve frowned, 'what were they here for?'

It was a question worth answering but I was not at that moment going to put forward the one reason I could think of. It was logical, besides: perhaps too logical for the poltergeist-type irrationality of so much that had happened that night.

Sandy and Lizzie between them told Harve about my bit of seaside bathing, Harve looking increasingly horrified.

'You might have drowned!' he said, exclaiming.

'Mm. But there we are, I didn't.' I belatedly asked Harve to keep watch in the farmyard for what was left of the night. 'Doze in your own box,' I suggested, 'and phone me the minute you see anything odd.'

With his promise to do that once he'd told his wife and brought a hot drink and a blanket, I went back to my house with Sandy and Lizzie and left them in the kitchen tut-tutting at life over steaming tea. As for me, I went wearily upstairs, decided to shower, lay down instead on top of the duvet for a minute still in fleecy boots and padded jacket, felt the world whirl briefly and fell instantly and comprehensively asleep.

I didn't wake until Lizzie shook me, her voice urgent.

'Freddie! Freddie, are you all right?'

'Mm.' I struggled from the depths. 'What is it?'

'The police are here.'

'What?'

Realisation and remembrance came back with unwelcome clarity. I groaned. I felt unwell. I inconsequentially thought of Alfred, King of Wessex, who delivered his country from Danish invaders although suffering from half the diseases known to the ninth century. Such fortitude! And he could write and translate Latin as well.

'Freddie, the police want to talk to you.'

King Alfred had had haemorrhoids, I'd read once. With all that on his mind, no wonder he'd let the cakes burn.

'Freddie!'

'Tell them I'll be down in five minutes.'

When she'd gone I took off the night's clothes, showered, shaved, dressed again in fresh things, combed my hair carefully and, at least on the outside, began to look like F. Croft Esquire, master of a few things he would rather not have surveyed.

The sitting-room looked no better in the opal light of dawn, and the soul had gone out of the tangled heap of metal that had been my precious car. I walked from one disaster to the other with the policemen, who weren't the two who had come to Jogger. These were older, wearier, hard-worked and unimpressed by my troubles, which they seemed to suggest I had brought on myself. I answered their questions monosyllabically, partly from malaise, chiefly from ignorance.

No, I didn't know who had done all the damage.

No, I couldn't guess.

No, I knew of no one who held a business grudge against me.

Had I dismissed a worker? No. One had recently left of his own choice.

Had I had any personal enemies? None that I knew of.

I must have some, they said. Everyone had enemies.

Well, I thought privately, reflecting on Hugo Palmerstone, I had no personal enemy who could be sure my house would be empty at two a.m. on the Wednesday morning of Cheltenham races. Not unless, of course, they'd tapped me on the head . . .

Who hated me this much? If I knew, I said, I would certainly tell.

Had anything been stolen?

That question stopped me short. So many things had been smashed that I hadn't thought of theft. My car could have been stolen. My television, my computer, the china birds, the Waterford vase, all had had value. I hadn't, I said lamely, inspected my safe.

They accompanied me indoors again, looking as if they couldn't believe I hadn't checked the safe first.

'There isn't much in there,' I said.

'Money?'

'Yes, money.'

How much was not much? Less than a thousand, I said.

The safe stood in the corner behind my desk, its fireproof metal casing camouflaged inside a polished wooden cabinet. The unharmed cabinet doors opened easily but the combination lock inside had been chopped about with the same heavy cutting edge as everything else. The lock had withstood the assault, but its mechanism proved to be jammed.

'Nothing's been stolen,' I said. 'The safe won't open.'

The fax machine on top of the safe's cabinet would send no more messages. The copier on the table alongside had copied its last. A simple blow to each had ended their lives.

My own anger, not blazing, immediate and tearful like Lizzie's, but a slow inner burn of fury, increased sharply at the spiteful splitting of two machines I – and the insurance – could easily replace. The cruelty got to me. Whoever had done all this, whoever had thrown me into the water, had meant me to suffer, had meant me to feel as I felt. I would give no one the extra pleasure, I resolved, of hearing me scream and moan. I would find out who and why, and even the score.

The police asked about my trip to Southampton but I could tell them very little: I'd been dropped into water, I'd swum, I'd climbed out, I'd phoned my sister to collect me.

No, I hadn't seen who hit me.

No, I hadn't seen a doctor. No need.

In the middle of telling them I didn't remember anything at all of the journey to Southampton, I began to know that at some point or other I had had my eyes open. I'd seen the moonlight. I'd even spoken. I'd said, 'Beautiful night for flying.' Delirious.

'If this doesn't give him flu, nothing will . . .'

They had known, I thought, that I was at least semi-conscious when they tipped me in.

Concussion was unpredictable, as I'd found at other times. Bits of memory could surface long after the impact. One could also appear to be conscious – people would say one had walked and talked – but afterwards one couldn't remember that. Total recall could happen hours, days or weeks after the event, or sometimes remain blank for ever. I could remember the grass hitting my face one time; I could remember the fence I'd fallen at in the second race of the day and I could remember which horse I'd been riding. I still had no memory of driving to the racecourse that morning, or of the first race which, the record books told me, I had won by seven lengths half an hour before the fall.

I had travelled to Southampton in the boot of an ordinary car. The knowledge drifted in. I didn't know how I knew, but I was sure.

The police had brought a photographer who took a few flash shots and departed, and a fingerprinter who stayed longer but gave his opinion in one succinct word, 'Gloves.'

Lizzie mooned round her helicopter, stroking it now and then and muttering 'Bastards' under her breath. She said she would have to fly back to Edinburgh on the shuttle, as she had a lecture to give that afternoon.

She vowed her partners in the helicopter would *strangle* whoever had crunched it.

Find him first, I thought.

The morning seemed disjointed. The police wrote a statement which put what they'd found and what I'd told them into police-force language, and I signed it in the kitchen. Sandy made tea. The other policemen, sipping, said 'Ta.'

'Ta,' I said too. Lightheaded, I thought.

One of the policemen said he believed the damage to my property to be a personal vendetta. He suggested I should think about it. He thought I might know who had attacked me. He cautioned me against taking a personal revenge.

'I don't know who did it,' I said truthfully. 'I would tell you if I did.'

He looked as if he didn't believe me. 'Think it over, sir,' he said.

I stifled a spurt of irritation and thanked him for coming. Lizzie walked into the kitchen saying 'Bastards' quite loudly. I wanted to laugh. She took a mug of tea and walked out.

When his colleagues had gone, Sandy said awkwardly, 'They're good lads, you know.'

'I'm sure.'

'They've seen too much,' he said. 'I've seen too much myself. It's hard to feel sympathy over and over. We end up not feeling it. See what I mean?'

'You're a good lad yourself, Sandy,' I said.

He looked gratified and gave me his own commendation in return.

'You're well-liked in Pixhill,' he said. 'I never heard anyone bad-mouth you. I reckon if you'd had enemies this bad, I'd have heard of it.'

'I'd have thought I'd have heard of it, too.'

'I reckon this was destruction for its own sake. They enjoyed it.'

I sighed. 'Yes.'

'Three times this last week,' he said, 'someone's run a supermarket trolley straight into the side of a car in the car park in Newbury. Smashed the sides of the cars right in, all crumpled and scratched. Not for any reason except just to do damage. People come back to find it and it's their frustration that's the worst. The supermarket employs a guard, but no one's caught the vandal yet. You can't deal with that sort of vandalism. And if he's caught red-handed one day, all he'll get is probation.'

'He's probably a teenager.'

Sandy nodded. 'They're the worst. But arsonists, remember, are usually a bit older. And it wasn't no teenager, I'd reckon, that got into this house.'

'What age, then?'

Sandy pursed his lips. 'Twenties. Thirties, perhaps. Not much older than forty. After that the driving force weakens. You don't get sixty-year-olds doing this sort of thing. It's fraud that sees *them* in court.'

I pondered a few things and said, 'You know Jogger's tools were stolen from his van?'

'Aye. I heard.'

'He had an axe in the van.'

Sandy stared. 'I thought it was mechanic's tools.'

'There was a slider, and in a big open red plastic crate he had a hydraulic jack, spanners, tyre levers, jump leads, pliers, wiring, a grease gun, cleaning rags, all sorts of oddments . . . and an axe, like firemen use, that he'd carried ever since a tree fell across one of the boxes. Before I owned the business, that was.'

Sandy nodded. 'I remember. In one of those hurricane-like winds.'

'You might keep an eye out for Jogger's stuff, in the village.'

'I'll put the word around,' he said earnestly.

'Say there would be a reward. Nothing fancy, but worthwhile for good information.'

'Yeah, right.'

'It'll be Jogger's inquest at any minute,' I said.

Sandy looked at his watch in alarm. 'I'll have to be going. I've not shaved yet, or dressed.'

'I expect you'll phone later.'

He promised he would, and drove away. Lizzie yawned into the kitchen and announced that if I needed her she would be upstairs asleep. I would wake her, please, at eleven, and drive her to Heathrow to catch the shuttle. She had just on my bedroom phone told one of her partners of the demise of the Robinson

22. He was speechless, she said. He would inform the insurers when he got his voice back and probably I would be hearing from them, as they were bound to send an inspector. Did I mind leaving my car where it was until after that? No, I supposed I didn't.

She gave me an absent-minded kiss on the cheek and advised me to go back to bed.

'I'm going to the farmyard,' I said. 'Too much to do.'

'Then lock the door behind you, there's a dear.'

I locked the back door and drove to the farmyard, finding Nina there drinking coffee in the canteen with Nigel. They were discussing the journey to fetch Jericho Rich's daughter's showjumper from France, Nina seeming oblivious of Nigel's dark-lashed eyes and sultry mouth. They had heard from Harve all about the night's alarms and were glad, they said, to find me functioning.

Nina brought her coffee and followed me into the office.

'Are you really all right?' she enquired.

'More or less.'

'I've some news for you,' she said, and paused, 'but . . .'

'Fire away. Is it the little glass tubes?'

'What? No, not those, there hasn't been a report on those yet. No, this is that advertisement in *Horse and Hound*.'

I thought back. So much seemed to have crowded

in since Sunday. 'Oh yes . . . the transport ad. "Anything considered." '

'Yes, that's right. Patrick got the magazine to tell him who had inserted it. And it's rather extraordinary . . .'

'Do go on.'

'It was a Mr K. Ogden of Nottingham.'

'No!' My eyebrows shot up. 'Well, well, that really is extraordinary.'

'I thought you'd think so. The magazine said they checked him out the first time he ran the ad. They wanted to make sure there was nothing criminal in it. Seems they were satisfied Mr Ogden was harmlessly offering his services as an adviser or personal courier, rather on the lines of a universal aunt. The phone number in the advertisement is that of his own house. The magazine checked it. They supposed he must be getting work from the ad, as he's kept on paying for the insertions.'

'Wow,' I said blankly. 'He can't have been doing too well, though. He was wanted for bouncing cheques and other pathetic bits of fraud. He might have seemed bona-fide to *Horse and Hound* – and maybe he was once – but I'd guess he'd stopped worrying about the legality of every transaction, as long as he was being paid.'

'You can't assume that,' she protested primly.

'Stands to reason.' I shrugged. 'But I'll give him the benefit of the doubt. Maybe he didn't know there were six tubes in the thermos. Just maybe. I wouldn't bet on it.'

'Cynic.'

'I'd be cynical about anything after last night.'

'What do the police think about last night?'

'They didn't say much. They said it was a wise man who knew his own enemies, or words to that effect.'

'Oh.' She blinked. 'And do you?'

'I think Sandy Smith's right. Smashing up my things was out-of-control vandalism, done on the pleasure principle. I think I walked into the farmyard when I wasn't expected, and the rest was embroidery. Infantile glee. Sly childish impulse to hurt.'

'Some child, by the sound of things.'

'An immature adult, then.'

'Or a psychotic.'

'A better word for it.'

She finished her coffee. 'I suppose we'd better get on if we're to catch that ferry. Realistically, is anything odd likely to happen on this trip?'

'I don't know. Did I tell you exactly where the container is, under your lorry?'

'Not exactly, no.'

'It's a metal tube fixed fore and aft in a space that runs beneath the floorboards and above the fuel tanks. That space is outside the main longitudinal struts of the chassis, but hidden by the coachwork sides. You can't see the space from the outside or from underneath, but if you know the tube's there, it's easily accessible. You can screw the end of it on and off without trouble, Jogger said.'

'I might go under and take a look.'

Rather her than me. 'Nigel was going to make a new slider for rolling underneath,' I said.

'Yes, he made it. He was showing it to Harve.'

'If you want to look, use the slider. Tell Harve and Nigel I told you there's a diesel inspection sort of glass bowl screwed on underneath, on the fuel line between the tanks and engine. You can check by that that the diesel's clean. If it is, the bowl will look clear. Any dirt in the diesel drops into the bowl and one can unscrew it and clean it out. We had a filthy lot of fuel delivered once. The inspection globe was black with muck. Anyway, tell Harve you want to see it.'

'I had an inspection arrangement in my own box.'

'Sorry, I forgot.'

She smiled. 'I'll take a look.'

She went out and did so. Harve and Nigel thought her fussy, she said, coming back and brushing off dust. 'And you could smuggle anything in that tube,' she added. 'I'll keep an eye on it.' She looked at the telephone. 'A quick word with Patrick, do you mind?'

'Go ahead.'

She phoned him at home because of the early hour and told him Harve's version of the night's events, checking each statement with me with her eyebrows. I nodded a few times. The gist was right; the omissions had been my own.

'Patrick,' she said to me, 'wants to know what it was you walked in on.'

'When I find out, I'll tell him.'

'He says to be careful.'

'Mm.'

Harve rapped on the window, pointing at his watch.

'Got to go,' Nina said. 'Bye Patrick. Bye Freddie. I'm on my way.'

I was sorry to see her depart. Except for Sandy and Lizzie, she was the only person around that I found I trusted. Suspicion was a nasty, unaccustomed companion.

Nigel drove out of the farmyard. From the cab Nina waved back to me as I watched from the window.

Reckoning that all good horse people by that time would be up and about I phoned Jericho Rich's daughter and told her that her transport was rolling and she should have her new horse with her by the next evening, soon after eight o'clock, if that would suit her.

'So soon? What service!' she exclaimed. 'Did you send that groom – Dave, is it? – that my father suggested?'

'Not Dave, but someone as good.'

'Oh, well, great. Thank you.'

'A pleasure,' I said, meaning it. And that's what it was: a pleasure to get a neat job done and more than satisfy customers.

Another more-than-satisfied customer at that

moment drove into the farmyard in a jeep from which every comfort had been stripped by time and hard usage. Marigold English, again in basic clothes and woolly hat, jumped out of her vehicle almost before it had stopped rolling and looked about her for signs of life.

I went out to meet her.

'Morning, Marigold. How are you settling in?'

'Hello, Freddie. Feel as if I've lived here for centuries.' Her smile came and went. Her voice, as always, was geared to the deaf. 'I'm on my way up to the Downs but I thought I'd just call in for a brief word. I phoned your house but some female said you were here.'

'My sister,' I said.

'Oh, yes? Well, look, what do you know about this John Tigwood and some sort of ancient horse retirement scheme? The fellow wants to rope me in. What do I do? Tell me frankly. No one can overhear you. Give!'

I gave it to her as frankly as seemed prudent. 'He's a dedicated sort of man who persuades a lot of people round here to give old horses good homes. Michael Watermead's taking two of the new batch we brought to Pixhill yesterday. So is Benjy Usher, unless Dot puts her considerable foot down. There's no harm in it, if you've got room and grass.'

'Would you say yes to him, then?'

'It's a regular charity in Pixhill.' I thought for a

moment and said, 'Actually, one of this new lot is a horse I used to ride long ago. A great performer. A great buddy. Could you ask John Tigwood to let you have that particular horse? His name's Peterman. If you'd feed him oats regularly to keep him healthy and warm, I'll pay for them.'

'So there's a soft heart inside there!' she teased me.

'Well . . . he won races for me.'

'OK, I'll phone this Tigwood and offer the deal. Peterman, did you say?'

I nodded. 'Don't mention the oats.'

She gave me a slanted glance of friendly amusement. 'One of these days your good deeds will find you out.'

She sped back to the jeep, revved up the engine and tore another millimetre off the tyre treads. Out of where there might once have been a window she yelled as she rolled forward, 'My secretary will contact yours about Doncaster.'

I shouted thanks which she probably didn't hear above the whine of ancient gears. I thought she would be good for Pixhill and hoped she would prosper.

Various drivers came to work and went into the canteen. Harve's account of my nocturnal experiences had them all coming outdoors again, gaping, carrying coffee mugs and inspecting me as if I were somehow unreal.

One of the drivers was the Watermead family's favourite, Lewis, the whizz with the rabbits, supposedly nursing his woes in bed.

'What happened to the flu?' I asked him.

He sniffed and with a hoarse throat said, 'Reckon it's just a cold after all. No temperature, see?' He coughed and sneezed, spraying infections regardless.

'It's better you don't scatter your germs anyway,' I said. 'We've too many sick drivers as it is. Take another day off.'

'Straight up?'

'Come back on Friday, work Saturday too.'

'OK,' he wheezed nonchalantly. 'I'll sit and watch Cheltenham. Thanks.'

Phil, obliging, phlegmatic, unobservant, incurious and unimaginatively reliable, said to me, 'Is it true your house got trashed?'

''Fraid so.'

'And *that* Jag?'

'Yeah.'

'I'd kill the bugger,' he said.

'Just give me the chance.'

The others nodded, understanding the feeling. No one, in their collective ethos, no one messed with their belongings without reprisals.

'I suppose,' I said, 'that none of you came past the farmyard after eleven last night?'

No one had, it seemed.

Lewis said, 'Didn't you see who had a go at you?'

'Didn't even hear anyone. Ask around, will you?'

They said they would, dubious and willing.

Many of the drivers looked superficially alike, I

thought, surveying the group. All under forty, none of them fat. Mostly dark-haired, all with good eyesight, none very short or over six feet: the physique that went best with the job. In character . . . different matter.

Lewis had joined the force two years ago with ringlets. When the other drivers called him 'girlie', he'd grown a slab of moustache and thrown his fists about to silence sarcastic tongues. He'd then produced a blonde bimbo in scarlet stilettos and again thrown his fists about to silence wolf whistles. During the last past summer he'd cut the hair and shaved off the moustache and the bimbo had brought forth a son over which both parents drooled. Lewis couldn't wait, he often said, to play football with his infant. The complete instant father, transformed.

'Don't sneeze on the baby,' I told him, and, alarmed, he said 'No way.'

Dave creaked in through the gates on his rusty bicycle, cheeky and cheery and as irresponsible as ever. His grin and his freckles gave an impression of eternal youth, the Peter Pan syndrome. Dave's wife mothered him along with their two daughters, putting up large-heartedly with his pub-haunting habits and his betting on greyhounds.

Aziz arrived also, dark eyes and white teeth a-flashing. Harve detailed the day's jobs, checking with a list, making sure each driver knew exactly where to go, which horses to collect and when they had to arrive.

I left them all telling Dave and Aziz of my night's

adventures, hearing mistakes creeping into the retelling but not bothering to interrupt and put them right.

'Portsmouth Docks,' Phil was erroneously saying, with Dave understandingly nodding. Although we never used Southampton for horses we did occasionally ship them by ferry from Portsmouth to Le Havre. The drivers all knew Portsmouth Docks, even though I preferred to send horses by the Dover–Calais route, because the sea-crossing was shorter. Many horses suffered from sea-sickness on long crossings, made all the worse through being unable to vomit. A horse had died once of sea-sickness in one of my boxes, which made me especially aware of the danger.

'Portsmouth Docks.' The drivers were all nodding. Portsmouth, just along the coast from Southampton, sounded more familiar. 'Bull-dozed his Jaguar . . .' 'Broke all the glass in the house . . .'

Down the boozer, as Jogger would have said, they'd have me dropped over the side of the Portsmouth–Le Havre ferry by nightfall, with my car through the window in the sitting-room.

Isobel and Rose arrived and complained again about the defunct state of the computer. I thought of the even more defunct state of the terminal in my sitting-room and with an effort remembered that this was the day appointed for the man to fix it. Isobel and Rose took the shrouds off the superseded mechanical typewriters and looked pathetically martyred.

I phoned the central agency that kept my credit card

numbers and asked them to get busy putting a stop on my accounts, and I got through to the insurance company who said they would send a form. Would they be sending a *man*, I asked, or of course a woman, who would verify the write-off of the Jaguar and so much else of my property? They said a copy of a police report would probably be enough.

After that I sat and listened to my head aching while Harve finished getting the day's work organised. Aziz came into the office with his double ration of vitality and asked if there were any personal errands he could run for me. I considered it thoughtful of him, particularly as his manner was casual and, as far as I could see, not self-serving.

'Harve says there isn't a driving job for me today,' he said. 'He said to ask if you wanted me to do maintenance, as you've lost your mechanic. He said two of the boxes need oil changes.'

'It would be helpful.' I picked the tool store keys out of the desk and handed them to him. 'You'll find all you need in there. Get a check list from Isobel and return it to her when you've filled it in and signed it.'

'Right.'

'And Aziz . . .' My aching head came up with a therapeutic idea. 'Would you mind driving my Fourtrak to Heathrow, to take my sister to catch the shuttle to Edinburgh?'

'Be glad to,' he said willingly.

'Eleven o'clock at my house.'

'On the dot,' he agreed.

With Aziz driving Lewis's box along to the barn for its oil change and with the others thinning out as they left on the day's missions, I drove home to say goodbye to Lizzie and beg her forgiveness for sending her with Aziz.

'You're more concussed than you want to say,' she accused me. 'You should be in bed, resting.'

'Oh, sure.'

She shook her head in older-sisterly disapproval and rubbed her hand down my back in the gesture she'd always used to show affection for two little brothers who'd thought kissing was sissy.

'Look after yourself,' she said.

'Mm. You too.'

The phone rang: Isobel's agitated voice. 'The computer man's here,' she said. 'He says someone's killed off our machine with a virus.'

CHAPTER EIGHT

The computer man, perhaps twenty, with long light-brown hair through which he ran his fingers in artistic affectation every few seconds, had given up trying to resuscitate our hardware by the time I got back to the office.

'What virus?' I asked, coming to a halt by Isobel's desk and feeling overly beleaguered. We had flu, we had aliens, we had bodies, we had vandals, we had concussion. A virus in the computer could take the camel to its knees.

'All our *records*,' Isobel mourned.

'And our *accounts*,' chimed Rose.

'It's prudent to make back-ups,' the computer man told them mock-sorrowfully, his young face more honestly full of scorn. 'Always make back-ups, ladies.'

'Which virus?' I asked again.

He shrugged, including me in his stupidity rating. 'Maybe Michelangelo . . . Michelangelo activates on March 6th and there's still a lot of it about.'

'Enlarge,' I said.

'Surely you know?'

'If I knew, I've forgotten.'

He spelled it out as to an illiterate. 'March 6th is Michelangelo's birthday. If you have the virus lying doggo in your computer and you switch on your computer on March 6th, the virus activates.'

'Mm. Well, March 6th was last Sunday. No one switched on this computer on Sunday.'

Isobel's large eyes opened wider. 'That's right.'

'Michelangelo is a boot-section virus,' the expert said, and to our blank-looking expressions long-sufferingly explained. 'Just switching the machine on does the trick. Simply switching it on, waiting a minute or two, and switching off. Switching on is called booting-up. All the records on the hard disk are wiped out at once with Michelangelo and you get the message saying "Fatal disk error". That's what's happened to your machine. The records are gone. There's no putting them back.'

Isobel stared at me, conscience-stricken, appalled and distressed. 'You did tell us to make back-up floppy disks, I know you did. You kept on telling us. I'm ever so sorry. I'm so *sorry*.'

'You should have *insisted*,' Rose told me. 'I mean you should have *made* us.'

'You don't even seem *worried*,' Isobel said.

To the computer man I said, 'Would the virus activate on back-up floppy disks?'

'Pretty likely.'

'But we've got hardly any,' Isobel wailed.

We did, as it happened, have comprehensive back-up disks containing everything the two secretaries had entered up to and including the previous Thursday. I knew they'd found the daily back-up procedure a bit of a bore. I'd seen them leave it for days, sometimes. I'd reminded both of them over and over to make copies and was aware they thought I nagged them unnecessarily. The computer seemed everlastingly reliable. In the end I'd taken to making daily back-ups myself on the terminal in my sitting-room, storing the disks in my safe. If you want a thing done properly, as my mother had been accustomed to say, do it yourself.

At that exact moment, though the copies existed, they couldn't be reached owing to the axed state of the safe's combinations.

I could have reassured them all about our records and normally would have done. Suspicion stopped me. Suspicion about I didn't know what. But it was altogether too much of a coincidence for me that the computer should crash at that particular time.

'You're not alone,' the computer man said. 'Doctors, law firms, all sorts of businesses, have had their records wiped out. One woman lost a whole book she was writing. And it costs *nothing* to make back-ups.'

'Oh dear.' Isobel was near tears.

'What exactly *is* a virus?' Rose enquired miserably.

'It's a programme that tells the computer to jumble up or wipe out everything stored in it.' He warmed to his subject. 'There are at least three thousand viruses floating around. There's Jerusalem II that activates every Friday the thirteenth, that's a specially nasty one. It's caused a lot of trouble, has that one.'

'But what's the *point*?' I asked.

'Vandalism,' he said cheerfully. 'Destruction and wrecking for its own sake.' He ran his fingers through his hair. 'For instance, I could design a sweet little virus that would make all your accounts come out wrong. Nothing spectacular like Michelangelo, not a complete loss of everything, just enough to drive you mad. Just enough to make errors so that you'd be forever checking and adding and nothing would ever come out right.' He loved the idea, one could see. 'Once you've written a programme like that, you have to *spread* it. I mean, one computer can catch the virus from another, that's the beauty of it. All you need is a floppy disk with the virus in it. Feed the disk into any computer and transfer the data on the disk into the computer – which is done all the time – and bingo, the computer then has the virus inside it, lying in wait.'

'How do you stop it?' I asked.

'There are all sorts of expensive programmes nowadays for detecting and neutralising viruses. And a whole lot of people thinking up ways to invent viruses that can't be got rid of. It's a whole industry. Lovely. I mean, *rotten*.'

Viruses, I reflected, meant income, to him.

'How do you find out if you have a virus?' I asked.

'The way to do it is to scan the info in any given computer. The disk I use to do that has more than two hundred of the commoner viruses on it. It will tell you if you've been infected by Michelangelo or Jerusalem II. If you'd called me last week, I could have done it.'

'Last week we saw no need.' I said. 'And . . . um . . . if this Michelangelo thing activates only on March 6th, then obviously we didn't have it on our computer *last* year on March 6th.'

Our expert parted with more information. 'Michelangelo was invented some time after March 6th in 1991 and only works on IBM compatible machines like yours.'

'That's no comfort,' I said.

'Er . . . no. Still, I can clean up these machines for you and give you a virus-free set-up for the future. But you have to be careful what you feed into computers from the outside. Friends can lend you infected disks. And . . . do you have any other terminals?'

'There's one in my house,' I said. 'But someone's vandalised it.'

The expert looked shocked. 'You mean, a different virus?'

'No, I don't. I mean an axe.'

The physical smashing of a computer pained him, one could see. Internal malignant illnesses were his stock in trade. Axes came into malicious damage, he said.

'Computer viruses are malicious damage, it seems to me,' I said.

'Yes, but it's a *game*.'

'Not if you've lost your life's work,' I pointed out.

'If you don't make back-ups, you're a nutter.'

I agreed with him entirely about back-ups, but I didn't think viruses a game. I thought them as wicked as chemical warfare. I'd heard of a computer virus that had wiped out a whole geological survey with the result that wells for water weren't drilled in time and more than a thousand people in a desert region died. The author of that particular virus had been reported to be delighted with its effectiveness. Too bad about the dead.

I said, 'I suppose there's no way of telling whether this virus of ours was introduced into our system on purpose or by accident?'

He stared at me earnestly, hand busy through the hair.

'It would be unfriendly to do it on purpose.'

'Yes.'

'Most viruses are spread by accident, like AIDS.'

'How long can they lie dormant?'

'You could have a virus quite a long time before it was triggered into life.' His eyes held all the sad knowledge of his generation. 'You have to take precautions.'

I told him I wished we'd known him sooner and mentioned the name of the firm we had dealt with in the past.

He laughed. 'Half the computers they sold were

awash with viruses. They used infected diagnostic disks themselves and they used to re-wrap vermin-ridden disks that people had returned to them in anger and sell them again to the great unsuspecting public. They vanished overnight because they knew March 6th would mean an army of furious customers suing their pants off. Even though March 6th was a Sunday, we've dozens of cases like yours to clean up this week. Not our own customers, but *theirs*.'

Isobel looked shocked. 'But they were always so nice and helpful, coming out here whenever we needed them.'

'And feeding in programmes that would *keep* you needing them, I shouldn't wonder,' the expert said with only half-disguised admiration.

'If *you* do that to me,' I said pleasantly, 'your pants will be off for life.'

He regarded me thoughtfully. 'I wouldn't,' he said, and added, as if safeguarding himself from future accusations of which he would be innocent, 'Don't forget the commonest reason for losing all files is pilot error. I mean, you can wipe everything off the hard disk just by typing DEL for Delete, followed by a Directory identification.'

We looked blank.

He said to Isobel, 'Suppose you typed DEL star full stop star, that's all it would take. Just as effective as Michelanglo. You'd lose everything for ever.'

'No!' She was horrified, predictably.

'Yes,' he smiled. 'But people who write viruses see no fun in that.'

'But why?' Isobel asked, unhappily wailing. '*Why* do people want to write viruses to cause such trouble?'

'To show off,' I said.

The expert's eyes widened. He didn't care overmuch for that assessment, I thought. He tended too much to admire the expertise, not despise the self-indulgence.

'Well,' he said slowly, 'it's true a lot of virus-writers sign their names into the programmes. There's one called Eddie, he's invented several.'

'Just put us back in business,' I interrupted, tiring suddenly of the whole subject. 'Keep us clean from now on with regular checks. We'll work out a maintenance agreement.'

'Delighted,' he said, the hand doing double time through the hair. 'You'll be up and running by tomorrow.'

I left him preparing to go while writing a list (expensive) of what we would need, and went along to my own office to telephone the makers of my safe.

'An *axe*?' They exclaimed, shocked. 'Are you sure?'

'I need the safe opened,' I confirmed. 'What can you do and how soon?'

They gave me the phone number of their nearest agent. The nearest agent would no doubt send a lock-smith to look-see. 'Thank you,' I said.

The nearest agent sounded unenthusiastic and doubtfully suggested a visit the following week.

'Tomorrow,' I said.

There was a sharp intake of breath. I could imagine the pursed lips, the judicial shaking of the head. Possibly Friday afternoon, they said. Possibly. As a great favour they might manage it.

I put the phone down reflecting that if I myself let that sort of general back-pedalling unwillingness creep into responses to requests for my services, I'd be twiddling my thumbs in no time. Not only did I myself drive anywhere anytime if I had no other driver available, but often at five minutes' notice I'd hire an extra horsebox from a rival so as not to turn work down. I'd almost never been unable to get wheels out on the road. It was a matter of pride, of course, but the sort of pride that got things done.

Aziz came into the office to collect the keys of the Fourtrak in order to drive Lizzie to Heathrow. I handed them to him and reflexively asked him to drive her carefully.

'Slow down for roundabouts?' he asked, eyes brilliant.

'Oh, God.' I felt like laughing for the first time that morning. 'Yeah. Get her to the shuttle on time.'

When he'd gone, I sat for a while thinking of this and that, and then I phoned the computer expert again. He answered at once, reporting contentedly that he was fixing yet another Michelangelo casualty and assuring me he'd be back with us tomorrow morning.

'Fine,' I said, 'but . . . er . . . could you answer a question?'

'Fire away.'

I said, 'Can you change the date in the computer? Could you change its internal clock so that March 6th in the computer wouldn't turn up at all? Could you change March 6th to March 7th?'

'Sure,' he said readily. 'It's a well-known way of avoiding March 6th. Switch the clock forward to March 7th then switch it back to the right date a couple of days later. Easy, if you know what you're doing.'

'And . . . you could advance or retard March 6th so that it activated on the actual March 5th or on the actual March 7th?'

'Yes.' A pause. 'That would be positive malice. You'd have to know the virus was in there.'

'But it would be possible? Possible to change the hours, too?'

'Yes.'

'How long would it take you to change the clock?'

'Me personally? Say a minute, maximum.'

'And if I did it myself?'

'Well,' he said thoughtfully, 'if someone wrote down for you exactly what to do, step by step, or if you had an instruction book, you'd have to allow maybe five minutes of privacy, because you'd have to concentrate.' He paused again. 'Do you seriously think someone changed your clock? Because it's set to the right date and time now, I'll tell you.'

'I don't know,' I said. 'I just asked.'

'Anytime,' he replied. 'So long. See you tomorrow.'

I was fighting shadows, I thought. Seeing villains behind every bush. The great probability was that my computer, like so many others, had accidentally crashed. And if it hadn't . . . then somewhere in its records there must be information I needed for unlocking surrounding mysteries. Information that some foe or other must know I possessed.

To destroy the records, it was easiest to type DEL star full stop star. Yet to do that one had to be present, and the disk failure would be instantaneous. Changing the computer's clock to activate Michelangelo meant that any future hour could be chosen, like a time bomb going off.

Sandy Smith drove his police car into the farmyard and parked it outside the office window. He came in to join me, taking off his peaked cap and sitting, uninvited but welcome, in the chair across from mine.

'Jogger's inquest,' he said, wiping his forehead.

'How did it go?'

He shrugged. 'Opened and adjourned, like I said. I identified him. Dr Farway gave evidence of death. The coroner looked at the photos and he'd read the post-mortem report. He adjourned pending further enquiries.' Sandy sighed deeply. 'I'd better warn you he wasn't happy. I heard it said that Jogger died from crushing and dislocation of the atlas and that there were particles of rust embedded in his skin at the site of the injury.'

'*Rust!*' I repeated, not liking it.

'There must be rust round the edges of your inspection pit,' Sandy said.

'I hope to God there is.'

We looked at each other blankly, still not wanting to put the obvious surmise into words.

Sandy said, 'The post-mortem put his time of death at about noon.'

'Did it?'

'There will be a lot of enquiries.'

I nodded.

'They'll want to know what you were doing at the time,' Sandy said. 'They're bound to ask.'

Picking flowers, putting them on my parents' grave and driving to Maudie Watermead's lunch. Not brilliant, as alibis went.

'Let's go along to the pub for a drink,' I suggested.

'I can't.' He looked a shade scandalised. 'I'm on duty.'

'We could drink Coke,' I said. 'I have to go and settle up for Jogger's memorial.'

'Oh.' Sandy's face looked relieved. 'All right then.'

'Can we go in your car? My Fourtrak's out on an errand.'

He was reluctant to take me and uncomfortable in his refusal.

'Don't worry, Sandy,' I said, tiredly teasing him. 'I

won't compromise you. I'll drive Jogger's old van. You don't have to come if you don't want to.'

He did want to, however. We drove in convoy to Jogger's boozer and I gave the landlord a heavy cheque. The landlord was well pleased with the trade and had done his best with the signatures, which filled a sheet of paper the size of a tabloid newspaper and were accompanied by encouraging comments. 'Poor old Jogger, jogged his last.' 'Up the apples and pears to the pearlies. Go for it, Jog.'

'Upstairs to the pearly gates,' Sandy interpreted, reading with me.

'Gone to the great oil change in the sky,' the landlord said, pointing. 'That's mine.'

'Most appropriate,' I assured him.

Half of Pixhill seemed to have signed their names but unfortunately all over the place, not in the tidy columns I'd envisaged. Most of my drivers were there, including Lewis, who had been in France collecting Michael's two-year-olds on that Saturday night. I commented on it. The landlord agreed that more people had signed the memorial than had been with Jogger on his last evening. 'They wanted to pay their respects,' he explained.

'And to drink the free beer,' Sandy said.

'Well . . . old Jogger was a good mate.'

'Mm,' I agreed. 'So which of these people were actually here on Saturday? Sandy, you were here. You'll know.'

'I was off duty,' he protested.

'Your eyes were still working.'

Sandy looked at the crowded names and pointed out a few with a stubby finger.

'Of your drivers, Dave definitely, he pretty well lives here. Also Phil and his missus, and Nigel who was chatting her up to Phil's disgust, and Harve looked in. And Brett, the one who drove that dead man, Ogden, he was there definitely, even though he was supposed to have left Pixhill. He was grousing about you having got shot of him.'

His gaze moved over the names.

'Bruce Farway! He's signed it. I didn't see him here.'

'The doctor?' The landlord nodded. 'He often comes in with those book people who sit in that far corner putting the world to rights. He drinks Aqua Libra.' He concentrated on the sheet, reading upside down. 'A whole bunch of Watermead's lads were here and some from half the stables in Pixhill. That new lady, Mrs English, some of her lads came. New faces. Not a bad bunch. And John Tigwood, he's always in and out with those collecting boxes. And Watermead's son and daughter, they were here Saturday, but they haven't been in since so their names aren't down, see?'

I asked, surprised, 'Do you mean Tessa and Ed?'

'Aye.'

'But they're under age,' Sandy said pompously. 'They're not eighteen.'

The landlord took mild offence. 'I'd only serve them

soft drinks. They both like diet Coke.' He glanced at me slyly. 'She likes that Nigel, too. That driver of yours.'

'Does he encourage her?' I asked.

The landlord laughed. 'He encourages anything with tits.'

'You'll be in trouble serving them without an adult,' Sandy said.

'She said Nigel was buying.'

'You'll be in trouble,' Sandy repeated.

'They didn't stay long,' the landlord said defensively. 'They'd probably gone before you got here.' He sniffed. 'I daresay some of those lads aren't eighteen either, if the truth were told.'

'You be careful,' Sandy warned. 'You can lose your licence faster than blink.'

'How early did Jogger get drunk?' I asked.

'I don't serve drunks,' the landlord said virtuously. Sandy snorted.

'How early, then,' I rephrased it, 'did Jogger start talking about aliens, little green men and lone rangers?'

'He was here from six o'clock until Sandy drove him home,' the landlord said.

'What rate of pints per hour?'

'Two at least,' Sandy said. 'Jogger could knock 'em back with the best.'

'He wasn't drunk,' the landlord maintained. 'Maybe not fit to drive his van, but not drunk.'

'Reeling a bit,' Sandy said. 'He was on about the aliens before I got here at eight or thereabouts. And telling the world, he was, about Poland having five on a horse last summer.'

'Why?' the landlord asked me. 'What does it matter?'

'Yes,' Sandy said, 'and what did Jogger mean?'

'Heaven knows.'

'Jogger knows in heaven.' The landlord was delighted with his own wit. 'Hear that? Jogger knows in heaven.'

'Very good,' Sandy said heavily.

'Did anything else happen?' I asked. 'Who stole the tools out of his van?'

The landlord said he hadn't a clue.

'Dave told Jogger to shut up,' Sandy said.

'What?'

'Jogger was getting on his nerves. Jogger just laughed so Dave took a swipe at him.'

The landlord nodded. 'He knocked Jogger's drink over.'

'He *hit* Jogger?' I said, astonished. Jogger, because of his fancy footwork, had been instinctively quick on his feet.

'He missed him,' Sandy said. 'You have to get up early to hit Jogger.'

We all listened in silence to what he'd just said.

'Yes, well . . .' Sandy said, stirring. 'Time I reported back on duty. Are you staying, Freddie?'

'Nope.'

I followed him out, leaving the memorial with the landlord for framing and hanging on the wall.

'That Tessa,' Sandy said, putting on his official hat, 'she's a wild one. Not high-spirited, I don't mean. I mean, well, borderline delinquent. I'd not be surprised if she ends up in court.'

I thought he exaggerated, but I took his estimation seriously. He spent his life with minor offenders: every local bobby did in villages, but he was particularly good at prevention as opposed to retribution. 'I don't suppose you could *warn* Michael Watermead, could you?' he asked.

'Difficult.'

'Try,' he said. 'Save Mrs Watermead's tears.'

I was startled by his imagery. 'OK,' I said.

'Good.'

'Sandy . . .'

He stopped in mid-step. 'Yes?'

'If someone killed Jogger . . . if he didn't just fall . . . well, *catch the bugger*.'

He listened to the commitment in my voice. 'And catch the bugger who took you to Southampton? Catch the bugger who smashed your car and your house and your sister's little wings?'

'If it's possible.'

'But you don't trust my colleagues. You don't help them.'

'If they treated me as an ally, not a suspect, we'd get on better.'

'It's just their way.'

We looked at each other peacefully, long-time friends up to a point. Alone together, we'd have been allies in any investigation. With his colleagues taking charge, the professional fence rose between us like dragons' teeth. No-man's-land would keep him loyally in the opposing trenches, though surreptitiously he might send me semaphore messages. I'd have to settle for that. So would he.

I drove Jogger's old van back to the farmyard and parked it again beside the barn. Its two rear doors were still unlocked and inside there was still nothing but some reddish grey dust. I drove my fingers through the dust and looked at them, not in the least happy with what I saw. The reddish particles among the grey were, to the unmagnified eye, suspiciously like rust.

Brushing the dust off my fingers I went into the barn and stood looking at the floor there, especially at the edges of the pit. There was grease in plenty, and general dirt. There would certainly be rust embedded in it. Steel and damp weather infallibly shed ferric oxide. Rust would be there.

All the same, in memory I surveyed Jogger's lost tools; the old slider, the sharp axe, the jumbled small spanners, the loops of wire . . . all those, and the tyre lever. An old strong tyre iron, as long as one's arm. Ferrous metal, a wide open invitation to rust.

I walked back to my office and wondered how much of my hovering nausea was due to the blow on my own head or the imagined scrunch of a rusty tyre iron into Jogger's.

You'd have to get up early to hit Jogger . . .

He'd died about noon in broad daylight.

It *had* to have been an accident. I didn't want him to have died simply because he'd worked for me. I could deal with attacks on myself. I didn't want to bear the guilt of someone else's death.

Aziz came back from Heathrow, his irrepressible good spirits hovering in a liquid smile even while he commiserated with me over the Jaguar.

'It can't have been easy to get a car to run at that speed into a helicopter. Not on flat land. Not without risking your neck.'

'That's no comfort,' I pointed out.

'I took a quick decko into the wreck,' he said, bright-eyed. 'I'd say the accelerator pedal was wedged down with a brick.'

'A *brick*? I haven't any bricks.'

'What's a brick doing there, then?'

I shook my head.

'You'd have to be nippy,' he said. 'You'd have only seconds to get clear once you'd got up enough speed.'

'It has automatic gears,' I said thoughtfully. 'It sets . . . set . . . off slowly, left to itself.'

He nodded happily. 'Nice little problem.'

'How would you solve it, then?'

He had already been thinking about it, as he answered without hesitation, 'I'd wind down the driver's window, for a start. I'd have a brick lashed to one end of a stick with the other end through the window. I'd slide into the driver's seat, start the engine, put the gear lever in drive, slide out again at slow speed and shut the door, then through the window I'd push the accelerator down hard with the brick and jump away just before impact.' He grinned. 'Mind you, it would take nerve. And you'd have to start a good way back from the helicopter to get up enough speed for that amount of damage. You'd have to be running by the end.'

'There must be a simpler way,' I said. 'No one would risk their life like that.'

'You're not dealing with common sense,' Aziz said. 'Your sister showed me the havoc in your sitting room. You've got a gold-plated wrecker on the loose. Can't you hear him? He's shouting at you, "Look at me, look at what I can do, see how clever I am." That sort of character *likes* taking risks. It's life's blood. It gives him his buzz.'

I said flatly, 'How do you know?'

The shining eyes flickered. 'Observation,' he said.

'Observation of who?'

'Oh, this person and that.' He flapped a hand vaguely. 'No one particular.'

I didn't pursue it. He wasn't going to tell me. I was interested, all the same, in his assessment. It matched pretty faithfully what the expert had said about the pattern of computer virus writers, the look-at-clever-me syndrome. The overpowering self-regard that could express itself only in destruction.

'Does one wrecker,' I asked slowly, 'egg on another?'

His expression was street-smart beyond any other I'd met. 'Ever heard of football yobbos?'

Murderous, I thought.

I thanked Aziz for driving Lizzie.

'Nice lady,' he said. 'Any old time.'

I rubbed a hand over my face, asked Aziz to check with Harve about jobs for the next day and told Isobel and Rose I'd be back in the morning.

On the short way home I noticed that my neighbour had a small pile of bricks beside his gate. The bricks had been there for weeks, I realised. I'd never paid them any attention.

I stopped the jalopy by the wreck of the Jaguar and looked through the space that had once been the driver's side window. There was indeed a brick – or the remains of one – jumbled in the squeezed space. The brick had broken into three pieces. Bricks were brittle. Brick dust was reddish, like rust.

I'm delirious, I thought.

I let myself into the house with the keys Aziz had brought from Lizzie and switched on the television in my bedroom to watch the racing at Cheltenham.

I sat in the armchair and then lay on the bed and then fell inexorably asleep as if brain-dead and stayed that way until long after the last horse had passed the winning post.

Thursday morning, Cheltenham Gold Cup day, once greeted with raised pulse and thudding hope, found me that particular week with a creaking stiffness in my limbs and a craving to curl up and let the world pass by.

Instead, driven by curiosity more than a sense of duty, I put on shirt and tie and drove to Winchester, pausing for five minutes on the way with Isobel and Rose. They could fill in the time before the arrival of the computer-reviver, I suggested, by making a list of everyone they could think of who'd set foot in their offices the previous week.

They looked at me blankly. Dozens of people had crossed their doorstep, it seemed, starting with all the drivers. I would take the drivers for granted, I said. Just list everyone else, and put a star against those that had been in on Friday. They were doubtful if they could remember. Try, I said.

I collected Dave from the canteen and took him with me to Winchester, though he was reluctant to go and spent the whole twenty-minute journey in unaccustomed silence.

The inquest on Kevin Keith Ogden proved, as Sandy had promised, to be a comparatively simple affair. The coroner, quiet and businesslike, had read the paperwork before coming to the proceedings and, though thorough, saw no benefit in wasting time.

He spoke with kindness to a thin, miserable woman in black, who agreed that yes, she was Lynn Melissa Ogden, and yes, she had identified the dead man as her husband, Kevin Keith.

Bruce Farway, consulted, reported that he'd been called to the house of Frederick Croft on the previous Thursday evening and had determined Kevin Keith to be deceased. The coroner, reading aloud from a paper, accepted the post-mortem report that death had resulted from heart failure caused by a string of abstruse medical conditions that probably no one in the room understood except Farway, who was nodding.

The coroner had received a letter from Kevin Keith's own doctor detailing the patient's history and the pills he had been advised to keep taking. He asked the widow if the pills had been faithfully swallowed. Not always, she said.

'Mr . . . er . . . Yates?' asked the coroner, looking around for a response.

'Here, sir,' Dave answered hoarsely.

'You gave a lift to Mr Ogden in one of Mr Croft's horseboxes, is that right? Tell us about it.'

Dave made it as short as he could, sweating and uncomfortable.

'We couldn't wake him, like, at Chieveley . . .'

The coroner asked if Kevin Keith had shown any physical distress before that.

'No, sir. He never said a word. We thought he was asleep, like.'

'Mr Croft?' the coroner said, identifying me easily. 'You called Police Constable Smith when you'd seen Mr Ogden?'

'Yes, sir.'

'And Constable Smith, you called Dr Farway?'

'Yes, sir.'

The coroner shuffled the papers together and looked neutrally at those present. 'The finding of this court is that Mr Kevin Ogden died of natural causes.' After a pause, when no one moved, he said, 'That's all, everyone. Thank you for your attendance. You have each behaved with commendable promptness and common sense in this sad occurrence.'

He gave Mrs Ogden one last sympathetic smile, and that was that. We trooped out onto the pavement and I heard Mrs Ogden enquiring forlornly about taxis.

'Mrs Ogden,' I said, 'can I give you a lift?'

She focused weak-looking grey eyes on my face and indecisively fluttered her hands. 'It's only to the railway . . .'

'I'll take you . . . if you don't mind a Fourtrak?'

She looked as if she'd never heard of a Fourtrak but would have settled for an elephant if all else failed.

I persuaded Sandy to take Dave back to Pixhill and set off with Mrs Ogden who was not exactly crying but in a definite state of shock.

'It didn't take long, did it?' she said defeatedly. 'It

didn't seem much of a thing, did it? I mean, not at the end of someone's life.'

'Not a great thing,' I agreed. 'But you'll have a service of thanksgiving, perhaps.'

She didn't look cheered. She said, 'Are you Freddie Croft?'

'That's right.' I glanced at her, thinking. 'When does your train leave?' I asked.

'Not for ages.'

'How about some coffee, then?'

She said wanly that it would be nice and settled apathetically into an armchair in the empty front lounge of a mock-Tudor hotel. Coffee took its time coming but was fresh in a Cafetière pot, with cream and rosebudded china on a silvery tray.

Mrs Ogden, until then huddled palely into her black shapeless overcoat, began to loosen a little by undoing the buttons. Under the coat, more black. Black shoes, black handbag, black gloves, black scarf. An overstatement.

'A terrible shock for you,' I said.

'Yes.'

'Your daughter must be a comfort.'

'We never had a daughter. He made that up, to get lifts.'

'Did he?'

'He had to make things up.' She gave me a sudden look of panic, the first crack in the ice. 'He lost his job, you see.'

'He was . . . a salesman?' I guessed.

'No. He was *in* sales. Under-manager. The firm got taken over. Most of the management were made redundant.'

'I'm so sorry.'

'He couldn't get another job, you see. Not at fifty-four, with a bad heart.'

'Life's unfair.'

'He's been unemployed for four years. We've spent the redundancy money and our savings . . . the building society's repossessing the house . . . and . . . and . . . it's all too much.'

And he'd bounced cheques, I thought, and failed to pay hotel bills, and tried to live on scraps gleaned from a feeble transport scheme, travelling around free by lifts cadged on the basis of a sob-story about a non-existent daughter's wedding.

Lynn Melissa Ogden looked as hammered into the ground as a tent peg. She had greying straight brown hair tied back in the nape of her neck with a narrow black ribbon. No cosmetics. Pinched lines round her mouth. The cords of age in her neck.

I asked sympathetically, 'Do you yourself have a job?'

'I used to.' The greyness in her skin looked like despair. 'I worked in a greengrocer's but Kev . . . well he's gone now, it can't hurt to say it . . . Kev took some money out of their till, and they were pretty good about it, they didn't get the police but they said I'd have to go.'

'Yes.'

'We were *eating* on that money.' She trembled with futile anger. 'Feeding ourselves on my wages and the things like rotting fruit and veggies that the shop couldn't sell. How *could* he?'

'He could have sold that ring, perhaps,' I suggested. 'I saw it on his finger . . . gold and onyx.'

'That was a fake,' she said dully. 'He sold the real one months ago. He missed it so much . . . He cried, you know. So I bought him that one . . . it was rubbish, but he wore it.'

I refilled her coffee cup. She drank absently, the cup clattering on the saucer when she put it down.

'Why did your husband want to go to the Chieveley service station?' I asked.

'He had to – ' She stopped and considered, then said, 'I don't suppose it matters any more. He can't get into any more trouble . . . I told him I couldn't *bear* any more of it, but I did, of course. We'd been married thirty-three years . . . I loved him once but then . . . for a long time . . . I've been *sorry* for him, you see, and I couldn't kick him out, could I? Because where would he go? And he hadn't been home for weeks because the police had been round . . . I don't know why I'm telling you . . .'

'Because you need to tell *someone*.'

'Oh, yes. And *appearances*, you see? I can't tell our

neighbours and we hardly have any friends left because Kev borrowed money from them . . .'

And never repaid. The words were as stark as if she'd actually said them.

'So why was he going to Chieveley?' I asked again.

'People used to phone the house and ask him to take things for them from one place to another. I said he'd get into trouble doing that. I mean, he could have been carrying bits to make *bombs*, or drugs, or anything. Quite often he took dogs or cats . . . he quite liked that. He put an ad in *Horse and Hound* sometimes. People would pay his train fare to take their animals but he'd cash in the tickets and go thumbing. I mean, he hadn't any *pride* left, you see. Everything had come apart.'

'Wretched,' I said.

'We paid the phone bill,' she said. 'We always paid the phone bill. And I'd take the messages for him and he would phone me whenever he could use someone's phone for nothing. But we couldn't have gone on much longer . . .'

'No.'

'It's a blessing for him, really, that he died.'

'Mrs Ogden . . .'

'Well, it is. He was *ashamed*, you see, my poor old boy.'

I thought of all their awful shared misery and judged that Kevin Keith had been undeservedly lucky to have had Lynn Melissa.

'He wasn't carrying an animal in my horsebox, though,' I said.

'No,' She looked doubtful. 'It was something to do with animals, though. It was an answer to the *Horse and Hound* ad. A woman phoned. She wanted Kev to meet someone at Pontefract service station and go to South Mimms service station and then go in your horsebox to Chieveley.'

'Ah,' I said.

She didn't understand the depth of comprehension in my voice, but looked simply surprised by it.

'Who was he going to meet at Chieveley?' I asked.

'She didn't say. She just said someone would meet him when he got out of the horsebox. Someone would meet him and pay him and take what he was carrying, and that would be the end of it.'

'And you agreed to that?'

'Well, yes, of course I did. We *lived* on it, you see.'

'Who was he meeting at Pontefract?'

'She just said "someone" would meet him and give him a small carrier bag.'

'Did she say what would be in it?'

'Yes, she said a thermos flask but he wasn't to open it.'

'Mm. *Would* he have opened it?'

'Oh, no.' She was definite. 'He'd be afraid of not being paid. And he always said what he didn't know couldn't hurt him.'

A recipe for disaster if ever I heard one.

She looked at her watch, thanked me for the coffee and said she'd better get along to the station, if I didn't mind.

'How about the train fare?' I asked.

'Oh . . . they gave me a voucher. The police or the court or someone. They gave me one to come down last Saturday, too, to identify him.' She sighed heavily. 'Everyone's been kind.'

Poor Mrs Ogden. I drove her to the station and waited with her until her train came, though she said I needn't. I would have liked to give her money to see her through some of her present troubles, but I didn't think she would take it. I would get her address from Sandy, I thought, and send her something in remembrance of Kevin Keith, her poor old boy who seemed to have precipitated me into a maelstrom.

CHAPTER NINE

As I was leaving Winchester the car phone rang. Isobel's voice said, 'Oh, good, I've been trying to reach you. The police are here about Jogger.'

'Which police?'

'Not Sandy Smith. Two others. They want to know when you'll be back.'

'Tell them twenty minutes. Did the computer man come?'

'He's here now. Another half-hour, he says.'

'Fine.'

'Nina Young phoned. She and Nigel have picked up the Jericho Rich showjumper and they're on their way back. No incidents, she said to tell you.'

'OK.'

I completed the journey and kept the police waiting while I checked with the young computer expert in Isobel's office. Yes, he confirmed, he had brought with him a replacement computer for my house, as requested, and he would come straight away to fix it up.

After I'd talked to the police, I said.

He looked at his watch and ran his fingers through his hair. 'I'm due at Michael Watermead's stables. Same job as this. I'll do him first, then come to you.'

'*Michael?*' I asked, surprised.

He smiled. 'Rather apt, I thought, being Michelangelo, but he didn't think it funny.'

'No, he wouldn't.'

Barely digesting the news, let alone the significance, of the failure of the Watermead hard disk, I went along to where the policemen waited in my own office.

They proved to be the two whose manner had so easily raised my antagonism on their Monday visit. I resolved for Sandy's sake to be cooperative, and answered their questions truthfully, politely and briefly. They exuded suspicion and hostility, for which I could see no reason, and they asked most of Monday's questions over again.

They needed, they announced, to take scrapings of the dirt surrounding and inside the inspection pit. Go right ahead, I said. They told me they were in the process of asking my staff what had brought Jogger to the farmyard on the Sunday morning.

Fine.

Had I instructed him to go to the farmyard on that morning?

No, I hadn't.

Did I object to his going there on a Sunday morning?

'No. As I mentioned before, all the staff could go in and out of the farmyard whenever they liked.'

Why was that?

'Company policy,' I said, and didn't feel like explaining that the drivers' pride in their vehicles led them to make them more personal, which they did chiefly on Sundays. Curtains were hung on Sundays. Seat and mattress covers were fitted. Bits of carpet appeared underfoot. Wives helped with the homes-from-homes. Metal and furniture polish accompanied pride. Loyalty and contentment were the products of Sundays.

Did Jogger normally go to the farmyard on Sundays?

I said that the horse transport business was always working on Sundays, though usually not as busily as on all other days. Jogger would certainly consider it normal to go to the farmyard on a Sunday.

They asked, as Sandy had predicted, what I had been doing on that Sunday morning. I told them. They wrote it down dubiously. You say you picked daffodils from your garden and put them on your parents' grave? Yes, I did. Was I in the habit of doing that? I took flowers there from time to time, I said. How often? Five or six times a year.

I gathered, both from their general attitude and the limitations of their questions, that there was still in the collective police mind a basic indecision as to how to view Jogger's death; accident or worse.

Rust, I thought, would decide for them.

I went with them and watched them take scrapings from all round the pit. They fed the patches of dirt into small plastic bags, closing and labelling each with its area of provenance. North end of pit floor . . . east, west, south. North interior wall of pit . . . east, west, south. North rim of pit . . . east, west, south.

They were thorough and fair. One way or another, rust would tell.

They drove away finally, leaving me to my ambivalent feelings and two alarmed secretaries.

Isobel said, scandalised, 'They asked us how you and Jogger got along! Why did they ask that? Jogger *fell* into the pit, didn't he?'

'They have to find out.'

'But . . . but . . .'

'Mm,' I said, 'let's hope he fell.'

'All the drivers say he must have. They've been saying so all week.'

Trying to convince themselves, I thought.

I drove home, where the computer whizz soon joined me. He stood with his legs apart in the centre of my devastated sitting-room, the hand combing through the hair non-stop.

'Yes,' I said to his stunned silence. 'It took a bit of strength and a lot of pleasure.'

'*Pleasure*?' He thought it over. 'I guess so.'

He put the wreck of the old computer onto one of the few free areas of carpet and installed the new version in its place, attaching it to its phone line to the computer in Isobel's room. Although I would still maintain my pencil charts, it was reassuring to see the screen come alive again with the active link to the office.

'I guarantee that this new disk is clean,' the expert said. 'And I'm selling you a disk you can use to check that it stays that way.' He showed me how to 'scan' the disk. 'If you find any virus on there, please phone me at once.'

'I certainly will.' I watched his busy fingers and asked a few questions. 'If someone fed the Michelangelo virus into the office computer, would it also infect the computer here?'

'Yes, it would, as soon as you called the office programmes onto your screen. And the other way round. If someone fed the virus into here, the office would catch it. It would then spread to all the computers on the same network.'

'Like Rose's?'

'Is Rose the other secretary? Yes, sure, into hers in a flash.'

'And . . . um . . . if we make back-up floppy disks, would the virus be in those, too?'

He said earnestly, 'If you *do* have any back-ups, let me check them before you use them.'

'Yes.'

'But your girls said they hadn't made any for ages.'

'I know.' I paused. 'Did Michael Watermead's secretary make back-ups?'

He hesitated. 'Don't know if I should tell you.'

'Professional etiquette?'

'Sort of.'

'She'll tell Isobel, anyway.'

'Then . . . er . . . yes, she did, and the back-up floppy she's been using lately has Michelangelo on it. I'm having to clean up their whole act.'

'Will you save their records?'

'Every chance.'

He finished the installation and gave me a cheerful pitying look. 'You need lessons,' he said. 'You need to know about write-protect and boot-up floppy disks, for a start. I could teach you, if you like, though you're pretty old.'

'How long have you been in computers?' I asked.

'From before I could hold a pen.'

The way I could ride, I thought.

'I'll come for lessons,' I said.

'Really? Great, then. Really great.'

After he'd gone I managed to stay awake to watch all the racing at Cheltenham and had the bitter-sweet satisfaction of seeing a horse I'd schooled and taught his business win the Gold Cup.

I should have been riding him. I might have been . . . Well, it had to be enough to remember the first of his triumphs, a scramble of a two-mile hurdle. Enough to remember his first steeplechase, a high-class novice race that he'd won by outjumping the opposition though nearly giving it away by floundering all over the place in the last hundred yards. I'd ridden him eight times in all into first place past the winning post, and now here he was, nine years old and a star, charging up the Cheltenham hill as straight as a die with all the panache and courage a jockey could hope for.

God dammit . . .

I shook off the sickening self-pitying regrets. I should have got over it by this time, I told myself. A decent period of mourning was reasonable, but three years along the road I should have stopped looking back. I supposed rather uneasily that I wouldn't be free of nostalgia until the last of the horses I'd ridden was heading towards Centaur Care. Not even then, if many like Peterman turned up on my doorstep.

The minute I switched off the set the telephone rang and I listened to Lizzie's voice sounding surprised.

'Hello! I thought I'd get your answering machine. I thought you'd be at Cheltenham.'

'I didn't go.'

'So it seems. Why not? Is your head all right?'

'Nothing to worry about. I keep wanting to go to sleep.'

'Thoroughly natural. Listen to nature.'

'Yes, ma'am.'

'Thanks for lending me Aziz. What a fascinating young man.'

'Is he?'

'Too bright for his job, I'd say.'

'Why do you think so? I need bright drivers.'

'Most drivers can't discuss the periodic table of elements, let alone in French.'

I laughed.

'Just think about it. Anyway,' she said, 'I've a report on your tubes.'

It took me a few seconds to work out which tubes she meant, typical of the sluggish state of my brain.

'Tubes,' I said. 'Oh, great.'

'They each contained 10 ccs of viral transport medium.'

'Of *what*?'

'To be precise about the ingredients, the tubes contained bovine albumin, glutamic acid, sucrose and an antibiotic called Gentamicin, all in sterile water at a balanced pH of 7.3.'

'Er . . .' I said, reaching for a pencil. 'Spell all that slowly.'

She laughed and did so.

'But what's it *for*?' I asked.

'For transporting a virus, as I said.'

'But *what* virus?' My mind thought irrationally of Michelangelo, which was nonsense. Michelangelo needed a different sort of tube.

'Any virus,' Lizzie said. 'Viruses are highly mysterious and barely visible even under an electron microscope. One can usually only see their results. You can also detect the antibodies the invaded organism develops to defend itself.'

'But . . .' I paused to organise a few scattering thoughts, 'was there any virus in the tubes?'

'It's impossible to say. It looks likely, considering that the tubes were carefully sealed and were being carried in the dark in a vacuum flask – and incidentally, the vacuum flask would have been necessary to maintain the tubes in a *chilled* environment, say 4° C, not a hot one – but you've had those tubes for days, haven't you?'

'They were being carried in one of my horseboxes a week ago today.'

'That's what I thought. Well, viruses will only survive outside a living organism for a very short time. Viral transport medium is used for taking virally infected matter from a sufferer to a laboratory for testing, and for infecting another organism for research purposes, but viruses don't live long in the medium or on culture plates.'

'How long?'

'It would depend. The conflicting views here in the university say for as little as five hours or for as many as forty-eight. After that, any virus would be inactive.'

'But Lizzie . . .'

'Yes, what?'

'I mean . . . I don't really understand.'

'You're hardly alone,' she said. 'There are about six hundred known viruses, probably there are at least double that number, and they are all unidentifiable by sight. They're particles of DNA or RNA surrounded by a coating of protein. They are cylindrical or polyhedral in shape, but you can't tell what they do by looking at them. They're not like bacteria, where the organisms are recognisable individually by their appearance. Most viruses look the same. They live by invading living tissue and reproducing in animal cells – for animal, read also human. Flu, colds, polio, smallpox, measles, rabies, AIDS, dozens of things. Everyone knows their effects. No one knows how they evolved. Some, like flu, are constantly changing.'

In silence I thought about what she'd told me until in the end she said, 'Freddie? Are you still there?'

'Yes,' I said. 'Do you mean,' I asked slowly, 'that you could take some flu virus from someone and transport it for miles and infect someone else, without the people even meeting?'

'Sure, you *could*. But why would you?'

'Malice?' I suggested.

'Freddie!'

'You could, couldn't you?'

'As far as I gather, you'd have to have a large inoculum in a small amount of medium, the pathogenicity of the virus would have to be high and the receptor would have to be highly susceptible.'

'Is that straight Professor Quipp?'

She said tartly, 'Since you ask, yes.'

'Lizzie,' I said apologetically, 'it's just that I need it in plain English.'

'Oh. Well, in that case, what it means is that you'd

have to have a very active virus and as much of it as possible in relation to the amount of medium, and the person receiving it would have to be likely to catch the infection. It wouldn't be any good trying to infect someone with the present strain of flu if they'd been inoculated against it. You couldn't give polio to anyone who'd taken the Salk vaccine, or give smallpox or measles to protected people. There's no proven vaccine yet against AIDS, and AIDS is terrifying because it may be that it changes, like flu, though that's not established so far.'

'If it was flu virus in the tubes,' I asked, thinking, 'would you inject it?'

'No, you wouldn't. Flu is spread through respiratory droplets or saliva. You'd have to squirt the medium up someone's nose. That might do it.'

'Or sprinkle it on their cornflakes?'

'Not really reliable. A respiratory virus would have to go into the respiratory tract, not the stomach. From the nose or lungs it could invade the whole system, but it might not have any effect if you injected it into a muscle or straight into the bloodstream.' She paused. 'You do have gruesome thoughts.'

'It's been a gruesome week.'

She agreed with the assessment. 'Is my dear little helicopter still exactly where I left it?'

'Yes. What do you want me to do with it?'

'My partners suggest putting it on a low-loader and bringing it home.'

'Do you think it can be salvaged?' I probably sounded surprised, but there were bits of it, she said, that looked unharmed. The tail rotor, for example, and the main rotor's linkage, the most expensive part of the works. A helicopter could be rebuilt. It would have to stay as it was, though, she said, until after the aircraft crash inspector had been to see it and made a report. Even ground accidents, it seemed, had to go through the mill.

'Talking of viruses,' I said, 'we've had a doozy in the computer.'

'A what?'

'A killer. No vaccine given in time, alas.'

'What exactly are you talking about?'

I told her.

'Inconvenient,' she said. 'Let me know if you need anything else.'

'I will. Incidentally, Aziz said you were a nice lady.'

'So I should hope.'

I laughed with affection and disconnected and from my bedroom window watched a zippy small car drive onto my tarmac and stop with a shocked jolt within first sight of the Jaguar–Robinson embrace.

My visitor, as I was delighted to see as she stood up in the open air to stare at the wreckage, was Maudie Watermead; blonde, slight, forever legs in blue denim.

I opened my window and yelled down to her.

'Hi,' she shouted back. 'Can I come in?'

'I'll be straight down.'

I leapt down the stairs and opened the door for her.

I said, kissing her cheek, 'I don't suppose you've come to hop into bed?'

'Not a chance.'

'Come in for a drink, then.'

She took the less dramatic invitation for granted and followed me into the house. The state of the sitting-room opened her mouth.

'Wow,' she said breathlessly. 'All of Pixhill's *heard* about this, but I never . . . I mean . . .'

'The thoroughness,' I said dryly, 'is impressive.'

'Oh, Freddie!' She sounded truly sympathetic and gave me a hug. Too chaste, however. 'And your super car . . .' She bent down and picked up one of the chopped photographs, sharp pieces of glass falling in a cascade from an old soaring flight over The Chair fence in the Grand National. 'How can you bear it?'

'Without tears,' I said.

She gave me a swift sideways glance. 'You're as tough as ever.'

What was tough, I wondered. Unfeeling? Yet I felt.

'I was talking to the computer boy,' Maudie said. 'He described all this. He said if anyone had done this to *him*, he'd have taken an axe to him himself.'

'Mm. But you have to axe the right person and he didn't sign his name.' Something flickered deep in my brain. Something about signing names. Flickered and vanished. 'What will you drink?' I asked. 'There's champagne in the fridge.'

'If you really feel like it,' she said doubtfully.

'Why not?'

So we went into the kitchen and sat at the table there and drank from my best glasses, all unshattered inside a kitchen cupboard.

'Michael was furious about our computer. That young genius who's fixed it for us told us we hadn't had the virus lurking inside there for more than a month. Betsy started using new floppy disks as back-up disks a month ago. The virus was on those, but it wasn't on the back-up disks she'd used earlier. So the wizard says we didn't have the virus then.'

I thought about it. 'So Betsy hasn't used the old back-up disks recently?'

'No. No need. I mean, you only use back-ups if the computer itself goes haywire, don't you?'

'Yeah.'

'The wizard says there are *hundreds* of these wretched viruses about. Michael's on the point of returning to parchment and quill pens.'

'Can't blame him.'

'Betsy says your Isobel's told her they didn't make back-ups, even, in your office.'

'One lives and learns.'

'But what will you *do*?'

'Oh,' I said, 'start on the parchment and quills, I suppose. I mean, all the records and figures in the computer are still around on paper. Rose kept paper copies of the bills she sent out. We've all the invoices for supplies coming in. The drivers' log books still exist.'

'Yes, but what a mammoth task.'

'Infuriating,' I agreed.

'Why aren't you snarling and gnashing your teeth?'

'Doesn't do any good.'

She sighed. 'You're amazing, Freddie, you really are.'

'But I don't get what I want.'

She knew what I meant. She almost blushed, then said, 'No, you don't,' much too firmly, and drank her champagne. 'I came to see if I could help you in any way,' she went on, and before I could say anything added quickly, 'and not in *that* way, don't be a fool.'

'Pity.'

'Michael said to ask you to lunch on Sunday.'

'Tell Michael yes, thank you.'

Tell Michael, Sandy had said, that his daughter, Tessa, had criminal potential. I looked at Maudie's high cheekbones, at her fair eyebrows, her delicious mouth; looked at her good sense and generous spirit. How could one warn such a mother or such a father to look out for trouble in their daughter? Maybe a critical aunt could have managed it, but I certainly could not.

I had no right to do it and no inclination, and moreover I wouldn't be believed and would lose a welcome friendship. I might privately suspect that Sandy was on target, but that was what the thought would remain; private. I could, on the other hand, alert Maudie to less nebulous dangers.

I said tentatively, 'Have you come across one of my drivers called Nigel?'

The fair eyebrows rose. 'We nearly always have Lewis.'

'Yes. But . . . um . . . Nigel's a sexy hunk, my secretaries say, and . . . um . . .'

'Get on with it,' Maudie urged.

'I just thought . . . you might not want him seeing too much of Tessa.'

'Tessa! Oh God. I thought it was Lewis she was keen on. She's always whispering with Lewis.'

'The pub landlord mentioned to me that Nigel was buying Cokes there for Tessa and Ed one evening. I'm sure there's absolutely nothing to worry about, but perhaps you should know.'

'Stupid kids!' She seemed basically unworried. 'Coca-Cola in a pub!' She laughed. 'In my young days it was "my needle or yours" that had parents hopping.'

I refilled her glass. She frowned, not at the champagne, but at a sudden memory, and thoughtfully said, 'You sent that Nigel to us last week to take Jericho Rich's damned horses off to Newmarket, didn't you?'

'Yes. Friday. But I won't allocate him to your work any more.'

'Betsy told me . . . He came too early, or something, and Tessa climbed into his cab and said she wanted to go with him, but Michael saw her and said she wasn't to go.'

That version of what had happened sounded much

more likely than the one I'd heard from Isobel, that Nigel had virtuously said he wouldn't take her because of my ban on hitchhikers.

Maudie said, 'Michael told me he couldn't imagine why she wanted to go with Jericho's horses when she said she detested the man, but if it was *Nigel* she wanted to go with, it makes more sense. Do you really think we might have a problem there?'

'He's unmarried and has powerful pheromones, I'm told.'

'What a way of putting it.' She was amused. 'I'll keep an eye on things. And thanks.'

'I don't like to tell tales.'

'Tessa can be a bit of a handful, sometimes.' She looked mildly rueful but forgiving. 'Seventeen's a rebellious age, I suppose.'

'Did you rebel?' I asked.

'No, actually. I don't think so. Did you?'

'I was too busy riding.'

'And here you still are, in your father's house.' She mocked me gently. 'You never even left home.'

'Home is wherever I am,' I said.

'Wow. How's that for utter security!'

'You wouldn't care to leave Michael, I suppose?'

'And four children? And an integrated life? And I'm older than you, anyway.'

The thing that made the game most worth playing, I thought, was the certainty that I wouldn't win it. She finished her drink happily, my desire for her as pleasurable an intoxification as the bubbles. Casual consummation would have spoiled the future and she was too nice to allow it. She put down her glass and stood up, smiling.

'If you need anything, let us know.'

'Yes,' I said.

'See you on Sunday, then.'

I walked out to her car with her and got an affectionate, passionless kiss and a carefree wave as she turned her car and departed. Celibacy, I thought, returning to the house, could go on for too long, and too long, at that point, was a year. The older I grew, the more I saw consequences in advance and the more I cared, like Maudie, about not doing damage for the sake of a passing pleasure. I looked back over the years with horror, sometimes. After I'd lost Susan Palmerstone, I'd drifted in and out of several relationships without understanding that I might have awoken much deeper feelings than I felt myself; and I'd dodged a thrown plate or two and *laughed* about it. How dreadfully long it had taken me to stop grazing. All the same . . . I sighed.

I went into the sitting-room to see what I could retrieve from the mess, and stood considering the answering machine, which had been split into two pieces with its guts, in the shape of recording tape, unspooling onto the floor.

On the tape, I thought, was Jogger's voice.

I hadn't in the end written down exactly what he'd

said, and although I could more or less remember, I wasn't certain of being exact. No amount of rhyming dictionary would help if I got the original words wrong. I rummaged in the kitchen for a star screwdriver and other tools and liberated the hacked pieces of cassette from the answering machine, trying not to tear the tape itself but finding that the axe, in going through one of the spools, had severed a lot of it into very short lengths.

Cursing, I sought and found an old cassette with nothing of note on it, and took that apart and removed all the tape from it. Then I carefully unrolled the whole of the longest section of tape from the answering machine's one undamaged spool and wound it from its beginning onto one of the newly freed spools. I attached the severed end to the second freed spool and replaced them into their cassette, screwing it shut again.

Then I searched the house for an old seldom-used pocket-sized cassette player which I knew I had somewhere, but naturally when I finally ran it to earth its batteries were flat.

A short pause ensued while I raided another gadget with the same size batteries in working order, but finally, with a sort of prayer, I pressed the 'play' button and held my breath.

'I hate this bloody machine,' Jogger's voice said. 'Where have you gone, Freddie?'

Loud and clear. Hallelujah.

The whole of his message was there, though slightly distorted by my not having wound the tape evenly enough. When I ran it back and then forward again the distortions had disappeared. I took a sheet of paper and wrote down what he'd said, word for word, indicating his pauses with dots, but I still didn't understand his meaning.

A dead nun in the pit last August.

Most unlikely! Someone would have told me about it even though I'd spent a good deal of August in France (Deauville races) and America (Saratoga, ditto).

What rhymed with nun? Bun, done, fun, run, sun . . .

No. What *paired* with nun?

Nun and monk.

Monk . . . bunk, chunk, dunk, drunk, funk, hunk, junk, punk, sunk, stunk, chipmunk.

A dead chipmunk? A dead funk? A dead hunk? Hunk of what? Dead junk. Dead punk? A dead *drunk*?

I would give the transcript to Nina, I thought, and let the collective brains of the Jockey Club Security Service loose on it. I laid the nonsense aside feeling that even if we cracked the code the message could turn out to be irrelevant. Jogger obviously hadn't known he was going to die. He hadn't been leaving me an intensely significant message, fearing it to be his last.

With a shift of focus I switched on the new computer, hoping there wouldn't be a flash and a fizzle and another total collapse of hard disk. Amazingly, however, the wizard had restored me to smooth computer life, everything working as before. I called up Isobel's office machine to see what, if anything, she and Rose had entered and filed since that morning.

They'd been busy, both of them. They'd been quick, conscientious, generous with their time. I'd told both of them to start with that day's entries and go slowly backwards between their other jobs, if they could, but not to go further back in any case than the beginning of the month.

'Leave it on paper for now,' I said.

'But the spreadsheets . . .' Rose said.

'Leave the spreadsheets.'

'If you say so,' she agreed doubtfully.

'It's our own fault we lost everything,' Isobel said dolefully.

'Never mind.' I still didn't tell them I might produce full back-up copies if, first, the safe cracker didn't somehow destroy them in getting the safe open, and if, second, the Michelangelo virus hadn't already wiped them out. I also didn't want to incur a repeat attack on myself or my belongings if someone heard the disks existed and knew they could reveal high risk information. The bruise on my head might be fading, but my car and my sitting-room continually reminded me that melodrama in Pixhill had come through my gates and might not yet be extinct.

On the screen I read the next day's engagements for the fleet. Not bad for that week: steeplechasers to Wolverhampton and Lingfield Park. Broodmares to three studs. Irish horses to Bristol airport, returning home from Cheltenham.

Advance plans for Saturday looked good.

I called up the directory of files to see what else Isobel and Rose had entered and found an unusual one there: 'Visitors'.

'Visitors' turned out to be the list I'd asked them for of everyone they could remember who'd visited the farmyard office lately.

The dears, I thought, pleased. Helpful beyond duty.

The list read:

All the drivers except Gerry and Pat, who have flu. (They'll both be working again next week or soon after, they say.)
Vic and his wife (they both now have flu).
Tessa Watermead (looking for Nigel or Lewis).
Jericho Rich (about his horses).
Constable Smith (about the dead man).
Dr Farway (about the dead man).
Mr Tigwood (collecting box).
Betsy (Mr Watermead's secretary).
Brett Gardner (when he left).
Mrs Williams (cleaner).
Lorna Lipton (looking for FC, but he was driving the shuttle).
Paul (Isobel's brother, borrowed some money).
Man delivering disinfectant chemicals.

I typed a thank you message onto the list and made a back-up copy of the new work onto a clean unused floppy, though I suspected the office would be ankle-deep in back-ups from now on. I switched off the computer, made some food, drank the rest of the champagne and thought a lot about viruses, both organic and electronic.

Nina telephoned, yawning, at about ten.

'Where are you?' I asked.

'In the cab of the horsebox, in the farmyard. We've refuelled and Nigel's hosing down the outside of the box, thank God. I'm knackered.'

'What happened?'

'Nothing, don't worry. The trip went according to plan. We've delivered the showjumper. The owner's father, Jericho Rich, he was there when we unloaded, shouting orders all over the place. What a bloody awkward man. I nearly snapped his head off but thought I'd better not, for your sake. No, nothing much else happened, it's just that this long-distance driving lark is a job for strong young men, you're right about that.'

'How did you get on with Nigel?'

'My God, he's randy. Had his hand on my knee a couple of times and I'm old enough to be his mother. Actually he's not bad fun. No complaints. We chatted a lot. Can I tell you tomorrow?' She yawned again. 'He's nearly finished the cleaning. He's got inexhaustible stamina.'

'His chief virtue,' I agreed.

'See you in the morning. Bye.'

In the morning I went to the farmyard early, wanting to see some of the drivers before they set off. Harve himself was down for an early start to Wolverhampton, and in such absences of his I very often wandered around in case there were last-minute queries or alterations.

Early starts were normal, as most trainers insisted on their horses arriving at a course at least three hours before they were due to race. In the winter, when racing could start at noon in order to complete the programme in the abbreviated daylight, the drivers could be loading at six or seven in the dark and unloading in the dark twelve hours later, according to the length of the journey. By the vernal equinox, we were loading and unloading at dawn and dusk with the long light summer days beckoning, and in the three years I'd had the business I'd seen a regular pattern of energy enhanced by the sun. The workload might be the same in January and June, but not the fatigue level.

Most of the drivers were in the canteen when I arrived on that Friday. The sky outside was gloriously pink and ginger, high, clear and cold. In the canteen the tea looked the colour of teak with strength to match, and white plastic teaspoons stood upright in the sugar bowl.

'Morning, Freddie . . .'

I answered the chorus. 'Good morning.'

Harve had already set off to Wolverhampton. I checked the other assembled drivers against the list I'd copied from the computer screen and found them all well briefed by Harve and Isobel. I realised I'd left a lot to those two since Tuesday night and had been more affected than I'd acknowledged by the rattling of my brain.

Phil, Dave and Lewis were there, Lewis showing no sign of flu. Nigel, despite his late return the evening before, exuded undiminished animal strength. Aziz smiled, as ever. A bunch of others looked at their watches, drank their tannin, used the washroom and ambled out on a collective mission to pick up most of the Pixhill horses that were running that afternoon at Lingfield Park.

Dave was down to go with Aziz in the nine-box on a broodmare mission to Ireland. Both men had arrived in plenty of time, and I asked Dave to come along to my office as I had something to discuss with him. He came in his usual happy-go-lucky way, carrying his tea mug and wearing an amiable unsuspecting expression.

I gestured to him to sit in the chair in front of the desk and closed the door behind us.

'OK, Dave,' I said, taking the chair behind the desk and feeling irritation with him, rather than outright anger, 'who arranged your diarrhoea?'

'*What?*' He blinked, dismissing the thought crossing his mind. Dismissing the possibility that I knew what he'd done. Dismissing it wrongly, too soon.

'Diarrhoea,' I reminded him, 'needing a stop at South Mimms service station to buy Imodium.'

'Oh . . . yes. That. Mm. That's right.'

'Who arranged that stop?'

'What? Well, no one. I had the squits, like.'

'Let's just face it, Dave,' I said a shade wearily, 'you did not pick up Kevin Keith Ogden by accident.'

'Who?'

'The hitchhiker. And let's stop playing games. You know perfectly well who I mean. You went to his inquest yesterday. You and Brett stopped at South Mimms not because of any mythical squits but to pick up a passenger in order to take him to Chieveley. All of which you did not tell the coroner.'

Dave's mouth opened with automatic denials ready and closed on account of what he saw in my face.

'Who arranged it?' I repeated.

He didn't know what to say. I could almost chart the tumbling thoughts; could clearly see the indecision. I waited while he consulted his tea and searched for answers in the brightening sky beyond the window. The little-boy freckles as always lent his expression a natural air of innocence but the half-sly artful assessing look he finally gave me spoke of a more adult guilt.

'There was nothing wrong in it,' he said wheedlingly.

'How do you know?'

He tried one of the ingratiating grins to which I was by then immune. 'What makes you think it was arranged? Like I said, there was this geezer cadging a lift . . .'

'Stop it, Dave,' I said sharply. 'If you want to keep your job, you'll tell me the truth.'

Shock stopped him. I'd never looked forbidding to him before. 'The truth,' I urged.

'Honestly, Freddie, I didn't mean no harm.' He began to look worried. 'What harm could it do?'

'What was the arrangement?'

'Look, it couldn't do no harm to give a man a lift.'

'Who paid you?'

'I . . . well . . .'

'*Who?*' I insisted. 'Or you get on your bike now and you don't come back.'

'No one,' he said desperately. 'All right. All right. I was supposed to be paid, but I never was.' His disgust looked genuine. 'I mean, you weren't supposed to know about him, but then he died . . .' His voice faded, the realisation of his admission hitting home. 'They said I would find an envelope in the cab of the nine-box first thing Friday, but of course the box was outside your house and there was no envelope in it in the morning, though I looked for it when we were cleaning, like, and I've never heard no more, and it's *not fair*.'

'Serves you right,' I said unsympathetically. 'Who are *they?*'

'What?'

' "They" who said you would find an envelope in the cab?'

'Well . . .'

'Dave!' I said, exasperated. 'Get on with it.'

'Yes, but, see, I don't *know*.'

I said sarcastically, 'You agreed to do something you knew I had over and over again forbidden, and you don't know who you jeopardised your job for?'

'Yes, but . . .'

'No buts,' I said. 'How did "they" get in touch with you, and were "they" a man or a woman?'

'Er . . .'

I would strangle him, I thought.

'All right,' he said, 'all right.' He took an unhappy breath. 'It was a she, and she phoned me at home and my wife answered it and she didn't like it being some strange woman, not Isobel, like, but anyway this woman just said it would be worth my while to give this man a lift, and you don't turn down windfalls like that. I mean . . . well . . . it's all beer money, isn't it?'

'Did you recognise her voice?'

He shook his head miserably.

'What accent did she have?'

He seemed merely puzzled by the question. 'She was English,' he said, 'not foreign.'

'What did she say?'

'Like I said, she said to pick up this man . . .'

'How were you to know him?'

'She said he would be near the diesel pumps and he'd see us pull up and he would speak to me . . . and he did.'

'Who thought up the diarrhoea?'

'Like, she did. See, she said I had to have some way of getting Brett to stop at South Mimms. So I told Brett if he didn't stop, I'd have to drop my trousers in the cab and he would have to clean it up.' He laughed uneasily. 'Brett said he would rub my face in it. But anyway, he stopped.'

'So Brett wasn't in the scheme?'

Dave looked furious. 'Brett's a *shit*.'

'Why, exactly?'

Dave's sense of injustice overcame caution. 'He said he wouldn't take the man unless he paid us. So I asked this Ogden, but he said he hadn't any money. He *must* have had some, but he said that wasn't in the bargain, I would be getting paid later, and I said Brett wouldn't agree to it without being paid first, and this Ogden got sort of purple, he was so upset, and he found some money after all, but not a lot, and Brett said it wasn't enough and so *I* gave Brett some money and I had to tell him I'd be getting it back, so then he said he'd be wanting some of that if I didn't want him to tell you that I'd fixed up a hitchhiker for money. And not only *that*,' Dave's fury increased, 'but Brett came to the pub on Saturday evening and made me pay for his beer and he was effing *gloating*, and I told him the pay envelope hadn't turned up but all he said was, "Too bad, mate, that's your bad luck" and went on drinking.'

'And you took a swipe at Jogger,' I said.

'Well, he wouldn't shut up and I was raging about

Brett, and Jogger was going *on* and *on* about things stuck on the bottom of the horseboxes, on and on about the cash box in your sitting-room, that filthy old cash box, on and on about things being carried under the lorries . . .'

'Did you understand what he was talking about?' I asked, surprised.

'Yes, of course.'

'About lone rangers?'

'Yeah, of course. Strangers.'

'What about nuns and Poland?'

'Eh?'

His face was blank. Nuns and Poland meant nothing.

'Did Jogger,' I asked, 'know about your private enterprise?'

'What? Do you mean that Ogden? Of course Jogger knew he'd died, like. I didn't tell him the ride had been fixed in advance. I'm not loony, see, he'd have been round to you in five minutes telling on me. Always on your side, was Jogger.'

'I thought *you* were, too,' I observed.

'Yeah.' He looked very faintly ashamed. 'Well, like, there's no harm in a bit of beer money on the side.'

'There was, this time.'

'How was I to know he'd *die*?' Dave asked aggrievedly.

'What was he carrying?' I asked.

'Carrying?' His forehead wrinkled. 'A bag. One of them briefcases. And, um, a sort of carrier-bag with sandwiches and a flask. I helped him put them all up in the cab.'

'What did he do with the sandwiches?'

'Ate them, I suppose. I don't know.'

'Did you and Brett buy sandwiches?'

He looked puzzled by the questions but found them easier to answer than earlier ones. 'Brett did,' he said readily, though sourly. 'He went off laughing and bought some with *my* money, the *turd*.'

'Brett said you'd picked up hitchhikers on other occasions.'

'He's a *shit*.'

'Well, did you? And were they arranged in advance?'

'No, they were casual, like. Brett never minded, if he got some of the dosh.'

'What about the other drivers? Have they done the same?'

'I'm not snitching on anyone,' he said virtuously.

'Meaning that they have?'

'No.' He physically squirmed.

I left it. Instead I asked, 'How long before you went to Newmarket was the stop at South Mimms arranged?'

'The night before.'

'Time?'

'After I got back from the Folkestone races.'

'That means late.'

He nodded. 'My wife didn't like it.'

'Had the woman tried to reach you before you got back?'

'My wife would have gone on about it if she had.'

He seemed to be well under his wife's thumb, and it didn't seem to have occurred to him to ask how the woman on the telephone had known he wouldn't be home until late, and had also known he would be going to Newmarket the next day. She had known, moreover, that he could be bribed to pick up a hitchhiker.

She had known a good deal too much.

Who, for God's sake, had told her?

CHAPTER TEN

Dave and Aziz set off for Ireland, Dave looking only moderately chastened, apparently confident that I wouldn't actually sack him. He was probably right, as he didn't appear to have broken any laws except my own and could go off to an industrial tribunal muttering about wrongful dismissal if I gave him grounds and he had a mind to. There was nothing new in his irresponsibility. He was still very good and reliable with horses and an adequate driver. I hoped he would think twice in future about taking money for lifts, but I wouldn't bet he'd never do it. The main change, as far as I could see, was in my own attitude towards him, my indulgent liking having faded towards irritation.

Out in the farmyard Lewis was showing photographs of his baby to Nina who had arrived in her working persona and her working car.

'He's a right little raver,' Lewis said, looking adoringly at his offspring. 'You know what, he likes soccer on the telly, he watches it all the time.'

'How old is he?' Nina asked, dutifully admiring.

'Eight months. Look at this one, in the bath, sucking his yellow duck.'

'He's lovely,' Nina said.

Lewis bcamed and said, 'Nothing's too good for him. We might send him to Eton, why not?' He tucked the photos away in an envelope. 'Better be off to Lingfield, I guess,' he said. 'Two for Benjy Usher. Last time I went to that yard,' he told Nina, 'they led out the wrong horse, and not for the first time, either. I'd loaded up and was driving out of the gate when one of the lads came tearing along yelling and screaming. I ask you! The wrong horse! And there's Mr Usher yelling out of his upstairs window as if it was my fault, not his head lad's, the stupid git.'

Nina listened, fascinated, and asked me, 'Is it easy to pick up the wrong horse?'

'We take the horses they give us,' I said. 'If they're the wrong ones, it's not our fault. As you know, our drivers have worksheets with times, pick-up points, destinations, and the names of the horses, but it's not their job to check identities.'

'We took two of Mr Usher's all the way to the wrong races, last year,' Lewis said, enjoying it.

I enlarged. 'We were taking one from Usher's to Leicester and one to Plumpton, and although Lewis and the other driver each said clearly which box was going to which destination, the Usher head lad mixed them up. They didn't find out until the first one arrived at the wrong place. There was quite a fracas.'

'Frack-ass,' Lewis said, grinning. 'I'll say.'

'Look in a newspaper and check you've got the right names of the Usher runners,' I told Lewis, 'so we have no more mix ups today.'

'OK.'

He walked off to the canteen where he could be seen consulting the racing programmes, then with a wave took himself over to his super-six to set off on his journey.

'When he came here first,' I told Nina, 'Lewis had ringlets. Now he has the baby instead. He's handy with his fists if you ever need defending. There won't be many people messing with his boy.'

'School bullies beware?'

'And their dads.'

'They're all very different from each other when you get to know them,' Nina said.

'The drivers, do you mean? Yes, they are.' She came with me into my office. 'Tell me about Nigel.'

She settled herself comfortably into the second chair while I perched on the edge of the desk.

'He drove nearly all the way, there and back, regardless of hours, but we wrote up the logbooks as if we'd shared it more evenly.'

'Tut.'

She smiled. 'He said I could look after the horse. He's not too fond of horses, did you know? He said some drivers he talks to at race meetings are downright scared of them.'

'So I've heard.'

'Nigel thinks you aren't too bad to work for. A bit fussy, like, he said.'

'Oh, really?'

'He's proud of his body. He gave me a run-down of the state of his muscles, practically each of them separately. He told me how to develop my pectorals.'

I laughed in my throat. 'How useful.'

'I have a message for you from Patrick Venables.'

Abrupt change of subject. 'What is it?' I asked.

'Those tubes you gave me for analysis. He says,' she frowned indecisively, 'he says they held something called viral transport medium.'

I made no immediate comment, so she went on, 'It's a liquid apparently made up of sterile water, sucrose – it sounds odd but that's what he said – and bovine albumin which is what keeps the virus going, and glutamic acid, that's an amino acid or something, and an antibiotic called geranium . . . er, no . . . Gentamicin . . . which kills off invading bacteria, but won't act on a virus. The whole stuff's used for transporting a virus from place to place.'

'Did they find a virus in it?'

'No. They said a virus wouldn't last very long out of a body. They apparently don't use the word "live" with viruses, as viruses can't go on working or reproducing, or whatever it is they do, once they're away from a living host cell. It's all a bit complicated, it seems to me. Anyway, Patrick wants to know where the tubes came from.'

'From Pontefract service station in Yorkshire. Before that, I don't know.'

I told her what I'd learned from Lynn Melissa Ogden, relict of Kevin Keith.

'Poor woman,' I said. 'They led a wretched existence.'

'There are so many awful lives. And you never expect it when you're starting.'

I told her about my confrontation with Dave, earlier that morning.

'So you were right!' she exclaimed. 'You said he had to have arranged that hitchhiker in advance.'

'Mm. But he didn't react when I asked him what Kevin Keith was carrying. I'm sure he didn't know.'

'So it couldn't have been him who came in the black balaclava to search the cab.'

'I'm certain it wasn't. He wouldn't have needed to disguise himself. He could have come back openly. He was hoping for his pay to be left in the cab, but, not surprisingly, it wasn't. The person who came disguised was *searching*, not leaving an envelope.'

'So who was it?'

'Good question.' I thought a bit. 'There are two minds at work here. Two at least,' I said. 'One is logical but destructive. The other's as illogical as a poltergeist.'

'Two at least? You mean, more than two?'

'I think it was two *men* who dropped me into the

Southampton Docks. One was male, certainly. And they carried me easily. But the person who arranged the transport of the virus medium was female.'

'Or falsetto?'

'What would be the point? And not easy to do.' I paused. 'What we *don't* know,' I said, 'is whether Kevin Keith was supposed to take the virus medium with him when he got off at Chieveley, or whether he was supposed to leave it in the cab so that it would arrive in Pixhill. Arrive here at the farmyard, that is. Also we don't know whether there was in fact any virus in the tubes on the way here, or whether someone in this general area had ordered the medium for future use.'

'Oh Jeez.'

I fished in a pocket and gave her a folded piece of paper bearing the transcript of Jogger's phone call.

'Get Patrick Venables' cockney friends to unscramble it,' I suggested.

'What cockney friends?'

'He's bound to know the London brotherhood.'

'Such faith. All right.' She read the words aloud. 'Take a butcher's at them nuns . . . ye Gods.'

'Does it mean anything to you?'

'Poland had the same five on a horse last summer . . . It's all rubbish.' She put the paper in her handbag. 'No one came near us on the French trip,' she said. 'No one anywhere showed the slightest interest in the underside of the horsebox. Nigel said he didn't like driving Phil's super-six because it has heavier steering than his own.

He approves of the one-man one-box arrangement and he likes driving for some trainers more than others. He would like to drive for the Watermeads more often, but Lewis is jealous if he does. Lewis drives for Benjy Usher too, but Nigel doesn't like Benjy Usher's ways. He says Harve told him he'll be driving for a new trainer, a Mrs English, and he's heard she's a dragon.'

'Mm.' I smiled. 'She'll get on well with Nigel, all the same. He'll chat her up. She's demanding, but he's tireless. By the end of the summer she won't want anyone else.'

'You go in for quite a lot of applied psychology,' she observed, 'pairing the drivers to the jobs.'

'Happier drivers work better. It's obvious. Happier trainers don't employ my rivals.'

'So it's all for profit?'

'And . . . um . . . no harm in all-round contentment, is there?'

'I do see,' she said, half mocking, 'why everyone likes you.'

I sighed. 'Not everyone, by a long shot.' I stood up off the desk, pleased to talk to her but with things to get on with. 'You're not on the driving chart today, are you? You could take a day off after the French trip.'

'I don't want to. I'll spend the morning here, looking around in general and available if you get a last-minute driving job.'

'Fine. Good. Well, Isobel's arrived.' We'd both seen her car drive in. 'Come and listen while I try to find out who knew that Dave would be going to Newmarket the day he picked up Kevin Keith.'

Her eyes widened in comprehension. 'Like I said before,' she said, 'you don't need me here.'

'I like you here.'

'As a witness, Patrick said. I'm the insurance you apparently wanted. Your vindicator. He said you were that subtle, and I didn't really believe him.'

'Devious, he probably meant.'

'He approved of the idea, anyway. That's why I'm here.'

I thought her almost too frank and wondered what her boss would have said. We went along to Isobel's office, where I said thank you for the visitors' list, and Isobel brought it onto the screen. She gave me a flashing smile of thanks for my message at the end, but shook her head when I asked her if she could remember which actual day each of the people on the list had been to her office.

'Can you remember,' I asked neutrally, 'which of them were here the day before Brett and Dave picked up the hitchhiker? That would be nine days ago, on the Wednesday.'

She shook her head. 'I could call up the drivers' list for that day.' She turned automatically to the computer and then looked stricken. 'Oh . . . that day's wiped out.'

'It's all right.' I'd pieced together various scraps of the pencil-and-paper chart that had been on the desk in my sitting-room, and had written them down in a list.

'Harve took the first load of Jericho Rich's horses from Michael Watermead to Newmarket,' I said. 'Was anyone from the Watermead yard here in the office that day? Was Jericho Rich here? Was anyone here from Newmarket? Anyone who could have had a sight of the Thursday schedule? You usually have the schedule on the screen a lot of the time. Who could have seen it?'

She looked bewildered. I'd asked the questions too fast. I went back and asked them again slowly.

'Oh, I see. Well, obviously all the drivers could see who was going where. I mean, they always come in for a look.'

'And beside the drivers?'

She shook her head. 'It's so long ago. People are in and out of here all the time.' She considered. 'They didn't need to come here themselves to know who was doing that trip. I told Betsy when she called here that it was down for Brett and she said both Mr Rich and Mr Watermead wouldn't be thrilled about it because Brett was such a whiner, and I said . . . well, I said don't tell them, but I expect she did.'

I read the list on her screen. 'What about Dr Farway?'

'Oh no, he came the day *after*, when that hitchhiker had died. He came on the Friday.'

'And . . . er . . . John Tigwood?'

'He's such a bore with those collecting boxes. Sorry, I shouldn't say that.'

'Why not? He is. Which day did he come?'

'That must have been Friday as well. Yes, Sandy Smith was here too. I remember them all talking about the dead man.'

'OK. What about Tessa Watermead?'

'She must have come before Friday because that was the day she wanted to go with Nigel to Newmarket and he wouldn't take her.' Isobel frowned. 'Tessa's often in and out. I think she gets bored. She wants me to teach her how to do this job . . . do you mind if I show her?'

'Not as long as she's not a nuisance to you, or wastes your time.'

'She does a bit,' Isobel said frankly. 'I asked her why she didn't go to a secretarial college and learn properly and she said she'd think about it.'

'Well,' I said, 'how about Mr Rich?'

'Friday. While you were doing the shuttle.'

'Any other day?'

'Um . . . yes, of course, he came in on the Tuesday, fussing about his transfer. I told you, do you remember?'

'Yes, vaguely.'

'I told him you'd arranged it for three consecutive days. I went through it all with him.'

'Mm. How about Lorna Lipton, Mrs Watermead's sister?'

'She walks her dog past here. Well, you know that.

She . . . er . . . drops in to see *you*, now and then. She came in on that Friday when you were doing the shuttle.'

'What about earlier in the week?'

Isobel said doubtfully, 'I can't remember which days.'

'Um,' I said, 'do you remember if anyone asked for Dave the day before he went to Newmarket?'

'What?'

I repeated the question. 'Did anyone want to speak to him?'

Her forehead wrinkled. 'I don't remember anyone asking, but I couldn't *swear*. I mean . . . oh yes! Mr Rich wanted to know if Dave was going to Newmarket with his first lot of horses but I said no, we were short of drivers because of the flu and he'd have to take some runners to Folkestone. It was Folkestone, wasn't it?' She looked despairingly at the computer, feeling lost without its memory but not doing too badly with her own. 'I expect I did tell him Dave would be going with the nine two-year-olds on the Thursday, though.'

I thanked her with a stroke down her arm and went on out into the yard, Nina following.

'It's a maze,' she said. 'How do you keep it all in your head?'

'I can't. I keep losing bits.' And I still kept wanting to go to sleep, which didn't help.

The fleet was steadily leaving, the farmyard looking empty with most of its herd of monsters out on the trail. Only three boxes remained in separated slots, quiet, clean, gleaming in the sunshine and, in their way, majestic.

'You're proud of them,' Nina exclaimed, watching my face.

'I'd better not be, or something will happen to them. I loved my Jag . . . oh, well, never mind.'

Isobel came to the office door and looked relieved to see me still there. She had Benjy Usher's secretary on the phone, she said: could we please send another box immediately as Mr Usher had forgotten he was running a pair in the second division of the novice hurdle at Lingfield, the last race of the day?

'She says he clean forgot they were declared,' Isobel reported. 'Then just now he let out a yell and said they must be sent off at once. She says the blacksmith's there now, putting racing plates on them and swearing blue murder. What shall I tell her? She's waiting to know. Mr Usher's yelling at her elbow. I can hear him. Lewis has left there with the first two and Mr Usher says there's no time for him to go back. What do you think?'

'Say we'll send another box at once.'

'But . . . will you drive it yourself? Everyone else has gone.'

'I'll do it,' Nina said.

'Oh, yes. Sorry . . . yes, of course.' Isobel hurried inside and presently came out again to confirm the journey, pleasurably saying 'Mr Usher's frantically trying to reach his second jockey.'

'Find a good map for Nina, will you?' I asked her. 'Mark the racecourse.' To Nina I said, 'I'll lead you to Benjy's stable. Can you manage from there?'

'Sure. Which horsebox?'

We looked at the remnants. 'Pat's,' I said, pointing at a four-box, 'the one you drove the first day. There's a lone ranger under it, don't forget, though I can't see that mattering.'

'I'll keep a look out anyway,' she smiled. 'What an incredible trainer, forgetting his runners!'

'Not so incredible, really. Trainers make shattering mistakes, declaring the wrong horse sometimes, even in big races, and forgetting others altogether. Benjy's eccentric, but he's not the only last-minute merchant we deal with. Many trainers change their minds violently, some when the clock's begun striking. Makes life more interesting.'

'As long as you're happy.'

I checked the map with her, marking the road clearly, made sure she had the right paperwork and then drove ahead of her to Benjy's yard, not the easiest of places to find.

He was leaning out of his upstairs window when we arrived, issuing a stream of invective and instructions to his luckless lads and greeting me personally with, 'Don't let your driver go without the jockeys' colours.'

Nina helped the lads load the two young upset hurdlers who were reacting with trembles and rolling eyes to the general scramble. Nina, I saw, had a calming effect as powerful and natural as Dave's, so that in the end the nervous creatures walked docilely up the ramp without needing blindfolds or brute force. Benjy stopped complaining, Nina and the head lad closed the ramp, the jockeys' colours were put on board, a couple of scurrying lads climbed into the passenger seats to accompany their charges and the circus was ready to roll.

Nina gave me a laugh through the window. 'They say there's a new head travelling lad in Lewis's box ahead of us, and he doesn't know these other two horses are coming. He has to declare them, *and* saddle them. What a to-do.'

'Phone Isobel and ask her to tell Lewis,' I said.

'Yes, boss.'

She went on her way in good humour and I found myself regretting her stay would be temporary. Highly competent and good company, Nina Young.

Benjy withdrew and closed his window like one of the characters exiting in *Jeffrey Bernard is Unwell.* I half expected him to reappear on his doorstep but when he didn't I drifted off in the Fourtrak to go home.

A short way along the road I slowed before passing a man leading a horse, hardly an unusual sight in Pixhill. The horse was swinging from side to side with his attendant yanking down again and again on the leading rein in a sharp manner guaranteed to produce more skittering, not less. I passed the pair with caution, stopped ahead, and walked back to meet them.

'Can I help you?' I asked.

'No, you can't.' He was brusque, if not downright rude. Young, belligerent, surly.

I realised with minor shock that the badly behaved horse was my old friend Peterman, his name plain on his headcollar.

'Would you like me to lead him?' I asked. 'I know him.'

'No, I wouldn't. It's none of your effing business.'

I shrugged, went back to the Fourtrak and sat watching the erratic and potentially dangerous progress along the road. When he passed me, the groom raised two fingers in my direction with a jerk.

A fool, I thought him. I watched him turn right a good way ahead, taking the road towards Marigold English's yard. I followed slowly to the turning, stopping on the main road but watching until horse and man turned off the side road and in through Marigold's gates. At least, I thought, old Peterman had reached his new home safely, and I would check with Marigold to make sure he was all right.

Outside my own house, when I reached it, there seemed to have sprouted a well-filled car park. Clustered around the Jaguar and the Robinson 22 were cars in all directions with their drivers in chatting groups. These, on my arrival, attempted to introduce themselves all at once.

'Hey,' I protested, 'who got here first?'

The simple order of precedence identified the crowd

into various insurance assessors, air-accident inspectors, a transport firm surveying the possibility of shipping the helicopter to Scotland, a salesman hoping I would order a new Jaguar and the man to open the safe.

I took the last one pronto into the house, even though he was apparently the latest on the scene. He looked at the hatchet job, scratched his head, asked if there was anything fragile inside (yes, I said, computer disks) and said he thought it a case for a drill.

'Drill away,' I said.

The rest of the men outside had sprouted notebooks and were discussing the mechanics of bricks-on-sticks on accelerators. By no means impossible, they agreed. Very dicey, but possible. The helicopter-shipper asked questions about fuel in the tanks. Not much there, I told him. My sister had said she would have to refuel at Oxford. Full, the tank and auxiliary tank held about 130 litres, she'd said, but she'd flown from Carlisle on that. The shipper began discussing technical ways to disassemble the tri-hinge rotor, and lost me.

The air-accident inspector produced a letter from Lizzie which he asked me to read and confirm. Neither of us had seen the collision, she wrote. I confirmed it.

Insurance assessors, hers and mine, said they'd never seen anything like it, not right outside someone's back door, that was. They'd studied Sandy's report. They asked me to sign various forms. I signed.

The Jaguar salesman told me about the Jaguar

XJ220. Made in Bloxham, near Banbury, he said. Only 350 of them built, costing £480,000 each.

'*Each*?' I repeated. 'Four hundred and eighty thousand pounds each?'

Did I want to order one?

'No,' I said.

'Just as well. They're all sold.'

I wondered if it were I who was surreal and whether my concussion was worse than I suspected.

'Actually,' the salesman said, 'I came to see if your XJS could be salvaged.'

'And can it?'

Shaking his head, he looked with regret at the whole-looking white rear end of my pride and joy. 'I might find you another one like it. That same year. Advertise for one, secondhand. And they're still in production. I could get you a new one.'

I shook my head. 'I'll let you know.'

I wouldn't seek a twin, I thought. Life had changed. I was changing. I would buy a different car.

The flock of notebooks returned to their vehicles and drove away, leaving only the workmanlike van of the safe-cracker beside the wreck on the tarmac. I went in to check on his progress and found my safe door open but minus its lock mechanism, which lay bent on the floor.

We discussed the possibility of mending the safe but he advised me to take the insurance money and buy a newer and better model which he would be happy to sell me. It would not, he assured me, have a lock that could be assaulted by an axe.

He went out to the van for a pamphlet with illustrations and an order form, and I signed my name again. He shook my hand. He asked me to check that the contents of the old safe were untouched and, when I'd done that, to sign his worksheet. I signed.

When he'd gone, I retrieved the packet of money and the back-up floppy disks and went into the kitchen to phone the computer wizard. Sure, he agreed, bring the disks in for a check as soon as I liked; he would be in his workshop all afternoon and would wash Michelangelo out of my hair with his little virus scrubbers. Did all computer wizards talk like that, I wondered?

'Great,' I said.

I made coffee and drank it and thought a bit, and after a while telephoned the local Customs and Excise office.

I explained who I was. They knew of me, they said. I explained that as my horseboxes went fairly regularly across the Channel, I wanted an up-to-date list of what could and could not be carried in them, in view of the ever-changing European regulations. My drivers were confused, I said.

Ah, they said understandingly. They didn't themselves deal with import and export, but mostly with tax. If I wanted the up-to-the-minute gen on international movement of goods I would need to see their Single Market Liaison Officer in the regional office.

'Which regional office?' I asked.

'Southampton,' they said.

I almost laughed. They enlarged. The Southampton regional office was actually in Portsmouth. The Single Market Liaison Officer there would answer all my questions and give me the latest copy of the Single Market report. If I wanted to go there in person, they suggested I should arrive well before four o'clock. It was Friday, they explained.

I thanked them and looked at my watch. Plenty of time. I drove to Newbury, shopped for a week's food and ran the wizard to earth in his workshop, which proved to be a smallish room half lined with large brown cardboard boxes bearing words like 'Fragile' or 'This way up ALWAYS'. A busy desk bore piles of papers – letters, invoices, pamphlets – held down by public house ashtrays used as paperweights. Ceiling-high bookshelves supported instruction manuals and catalogues by the score. Plastic-covered leads snaked everywhere. A table along one wall bore a keyboard, two or three computers, a laser printer and a live colour monitor showing a bright row of miniature playing cards apparently halfway through a game of patience.

'Black jack on red queen,' I said, looking.

'Yeah.' He grinned, ran his hand through his hair, and with a mouse moved the cards around on the screen. 'It's not coming out,' he observed, and switched it all off. 'Did you bring your disks?'

I handed them to him in an envelope. 'There are

four,' I said. 'A new one for each calendar year since I took over the business.'

He nodded. 'I'll start with the latest.' He fed it into a drive slot in one of the computers on the table and called up onto the monitor the directory of the files stored for the current year.

Muttering under his breath he pressed a series of keys on the keyboard and in a while the screen was flickering rapidly with letters and numbers as he scanned my disk for deadly strangers.

Lone rangers, I thought. Aliens everywhere.

'There we are,' he said, when the flickering steadied to a single message. 'Scan complete. No virus found.' He grinned at me. 'No Michelangelo. You're safe.'

'That's . . . er . . . rather more than extremely interesting,' I said.

'How?'

'I used the disk last to back-up the work entered on the main office computer a week ago yesterday,' I said. 'That was March 3rd.'

His eyes savoured the knowledge.

'On March 3rd, then,' he said, 'I'd say there was no Michelangelo in your office. Right?'

'Right.'

'So you caught it on the Friday or Saturday . . .' He pondered. 'Ask your secretaries if they fed anyone else's disks into your machine. Say, for instance, someone lent them a game disk, like the patience game, which no one should do, really, it's an infringement of copyright, but say they *did*, well, Michelangelo could have been lurking in the game disk and it would leap across to your machine instantly.'

'The monitor in the office is black-and-white,' I said.

'Kids would play patience in black-and-white,' he replied. 'Like Nintendo. No problem. Did you have any kids in the office?'

'Isobel's brother, Paul,' I said, remembering his name on the list. 'He's fifteen. Always cadging money from his sister.'

'Ask him, then. I'll bet that's where your trouble lies.'

'Thank you very much.'

'I may as well scan your other disks, just to be safe.' He fed the three others through the scanning process, all with nil results. 'There you are, then. At present they're clean. But, like I said, you have to patrol your defences all the time.'

I thanked him and paid him, took my clean disks out to the car and set off on the drive south to Portsmouth, giving Southampton Docks a wide berth.

Customs and Excise were fortunately helpful, extending the impression that talking to the general public made a change from regular bureaucracy. The near-top man I was finally steered to, who introduced himself briefly as 'Collins', offered me a seat, a cup of tea and a willing expression. An office around us:

desk, green plant, second-generation Scandinavian decor.

'What may your drivers carry and what may they not?' Collins repeated.

'Yes,' I said.

'Yes. As you know, it's all different from the old cut-and-dried days.'

'Mm.'

'We're positively forbidden to make spot checks on anything coming in from the EC.' He paused. 'European Community,' he said.

'Mm.'

'Even drugs.' He spread his hands in what looked like a long-standing frustration. 'We can act – search – only on specific information. The stuff floods in, I've no doubt, but we can't do anything about it. Customs checks on goods are now allowed only at the point of entry into the Community. Once inside, movement is free.'

'I expect it saves a lot of paperwork,' I said.

'Tons of it. Hundreds of tons. Sixty million fewer forms.' The plus side lightened his scowl. 'Saves time too, saves days and months.' He searched briefly for a booklet, found it and slid it towards me across his desk. 'Most of the present regulations are listed in there. There's very little restriction on alcohol, tobacco and personal goods. One day there'll be none. But of course there'll still be duty and restrictions of goods entering from outside the EC.'

I picked up the booklet and thanked him.

'We spend a good deal of our time juggling with VAT,' he said. 'Different rates, you see, in different EC countries.'

'I was wondering,' I murmured, 'what one may still *not* bring into this country from Europe, and . . . er . . . what one may not take out.'

His eyebrows rose. 'Not take *out*?'

'Anything that doesn't have free movement.'

He pursed his lips. 'Some things need *licences*,' he said. 'Are your drivers breaking the law?'

'I came to find out.'

His interest sharpened as if he'd suddenly realised I was there from more than normal curiosity.

'Your horseboxes come and go through Portsmouth, don't they?'

'Sometimes.'

'And they're never searched.'

'No.'

'And you have the necessary permissions, of course, to move live animals across the Channel.'

'All that's done for us by a specialist firm.'

He nodded. He thought. 'I suppose if your boxes carried *other* animals than horses, we'd never know. Your drivers haven't been bringing in cats or dogs, have they?' His voice was censorious and alarmed. 'We maintain the quarantine laws, of course. The threat of rabies is always with us.'

I said calmingly, 'I've never heard of them bringing

in cats or dogs, and if they had it would be common knowledge in my village, where news travels faster than lightning.'

He relaxed slightly; a fortyish man with receding hair and white careful hands.

'As a matter of fact,' he said, 'thanks to vaccines, no one has died of rabies contracted in Europe for the past thirty years, but we still don't want the disease here.'

'Um,' I said, 'what do you need a licence for?'

'Dozens of things. From your point of view, I suppose veterinary medicines would be interesting. You'd need to get a separate licence for each movement, a Therapeutic Substance licence from the Ministry of Agriculture and Fisheries Veterinary Medicines Directorate. But there would be no check on the substance here on entry through Portsmouth. Enforcement of licensing would be a matter for MAFF itself.'

MAFF? Oh, Ministry of Agriculture, Fisheries and Food. Shades of Jogger.

'Well,' I said, 'what else isn't one supposed to bring in and out?'

'Guns,' he said. 'There are still exit checks, of course, for firearms in baggage at airports. No import checks here. You could bring in a horseboxful of guns, and we'd never know. Smuggling in the old sense has vanished within the EC.'

'So it seems.'

'There are intellectual property rights,' he said. 'That's about the infringement of existing patents between member states.'

'I don't think my drivers are into intellectual property rights.'

He smiled briefly, a quick movement of lips. 'I'm afraid I haven't been of much help.'

'Indeed you've been most kind,' I assured him, rising to go. 'Negative results are often as helpful as positive.'

I thought, however, as I drove back to Pixhill with the Single Market booklet on the seat beside me, that I was as far as ever from understanding why anyone should need or want to fix hiding-places under my lorries. If smuggling was out, what were they *for?*

At home I sat in my poor green leather chair with the stuffing coming out of the axe-holes and one by one fed my clean disks and their information into my new computer. Then, feeling rusty and all thumbs and impatient to begin my lessons with the wizard, I looked up my original computer manuals and worked out how to organise all the data now inside the machine into various categories, both chronological and geographic.

I studied in turn each driver's work over the past three years, looking for I knew not what. A pattern? Something worth destroying my records for, if that should happen not to be the work of Isobel's brother. I tended to doubt it was Paul's doing as, first, he was more idle than bright and, second, Isobel would never let him play games in the office.

The patterns I was looking for were definitely there, but told me nothing I didn't know. Each driver went most often to the racecourses favoured by the trainers they mostly drove for. Lewis, for instance, drove most regularly each summer to Newbury, Sandown, Goodwood, Epsom, Salisbury and Newmarket, Michael Watermead's preferred prestigious destinations. At other times he went where Benjy Usher sent his jumpers, Lingfield, Fontwell, Chepstow, Cheltenham, Warwick and Worcester. Most of his overseas journeys had been for Michael, all to Italy, Ireland or France.

Although there was horseracing all over Europe, British trainers rarely sent horses anywhere but Italy, Ireland and France. Often British runners travelled by air (and had to be taken to the airports), but Michael much preferred to go all the way by road; all the better for me.

Nigel had made the most overseas journeys, but that was my doing, owing to his long-distance stamina. Harve had made few, both my choice and his. Dave had made dozens as relief driver and horse-handler, often with broodmares rather than racers.

All in all, the categories were informative but told

me nothing surprising, and after about an hour I switched off, as puzzled as ever.

I phoned Nina, reckoning she would be in her horsebox on the way back from Lingfield, and she answered immediately.

'Phone me when you get to Pixhill,' I said briefly.

'Will do.'

End of conversation.

I phoned Isobel at her home. Nothing unusual had happened during the day's work, she assured me. She'd told Lewis that Nina was following him, and all the Usher horses had run in the right races at Lingfield. Aziz and Dave had arrived in Ireland with their mares. Harve and Phil had each taken a winner to Wolverhampton, great rejoicing. None of the other drivers had hit snags.

'Great,' I said. 'Um . . . your brother Paul . . .'

'I've *told* him not to bother me at work.' She sounded guiltily apologetic.

'Yes, but, um, how is he with computers?'

'*Computers*?'

I explained the wizard's game-virus theory.

'Oh, no,' she said positively, 'I'd never let him near your computer and, to be honest, he wouldn't know *how* to load data in our machine.'

'You're sure?'

'A hundred per cent.'

Another good theory down the drain.

'Did anyone else,' I asked, 'know enough to get near

enough to the computer last Friday to feed any disk into it?'

'I've thought and thought . . .' She stopped. 'Why last Friday?'

'Or Saturday,' I said. 'Our computer wizard thinks we picked up the infection as late as that.'

'Oh golly.'

'Nothing comes to your mind?'

'No.' It was a wail of regret and worry. 'I wish I knew.'

'Did you leave any of those people on your list of visitors alone in your office?'

'But . . . but . . . oh dear. I can't remember. I might have done. I wouldn't have seen anything wrong in it. I mean, there weren't any *strangers* there, not right in my office, and I can't believe . . .'

'It's all right,' I said. 'Don't think about it.'

'I can't help it.'

I put the phone down just as Sandy Smith rolled onto my tarmac. He came towards the back door taking off his peaked cap and combing his flattened hair with his fingers.

'Come in,' I said, meeting him. 'Whisky?'

'I'm on duty,' he said doubtfully.

'Who's to know?'

He squared it with his conscience and took the Scotch with water. We sat in the kitchen, one on each side of the table, and he relaxed as far as unbuttoning his tunic.

'It's about Jogger,' he said. He frowned at his glass, his rounded face troubled. 'About rust.'

His gloom spread to me fast. 'What did they find?' I asked.

'I've heard,' he began, and I reflected that this was Sandy's semaphore at its best. 'I've . . . er . . . *unofficially* heard that they did find rust all round the pit and on the edges. But the rust was everywhere mixed with oil and grease. And there wasn't any oil or grease in the wound on Jogger's head.'

'*Damn*,' I said.

'They're going to treat it as murder. Don't say I told you.'

'No. Thanks, Sandy.'

'They'll be asking you questions.'

'They've asked questions already,' I said.

'They'll want to know who had it in for Jogger.'

'I want to know that too.'

'I knew old Jog for years,' Sandy said. 'He wasn't one to have enemies.'

'I would think,' I said neutrally, 'that he may have done what I did on Tuesday night, which was to walk into the farmyard unexpectedly. Maybe both of us were hit on the head to prevent us seeing . . . whatever . . . but Jogger *died*, and was put into the pit to make it look like an accident.'

Sandy gazed at me thoughtfully.

'What's going on there, in the farmyard?' he asked.

'I don't know. I bloody don't *know*, and it's driving me crazy.'

'Did Jogger know?'

'It's possible he found out. That's perhaps why he died, and I didn't want it to be that. I've been sort of praying for it to be proved an accident.'

'You've thought all along, though, that it was murder.' He scratched his neck absent-mindedly. 'What did Jogger mean about lone rangers under your lorries? My colleagues will want to know.'

'I'll show you,' I said. 'Come into the sitting-room.'

We went into the jumbled wreckage and I led him across to where I'd left the cash box Jogger had prised from under the nine-box a week ago.

I led Sandy to the place, but the cash box wasn't there.

'That's odd,' I said. 'It was right here on this spot on the newspaper . . .'

'What was?'

I described the cash box: grey metal, ordinary, fresh-smelling inside, empty, unlocked by Jogger, the round mark of where it had been held onto a magnet the only bright section on its filthy grime-laden exterior.

I looked round the room for it and so did Sandy, poking about in the general mess.

No cash box.

'When did you last see it?' Sandy asked.

'Tuesday, I suppose. I showed it to my sister.' I

frowned. 'When this room was done over, I didn't think to look for the cash box.'

He supposed, he said, that he could understand that, and asked if anything else was missing.

'I don't think so.'

'Jogger said lone rangers. Plural. There must have been more than one.'

'Two of the other boxes have been trundling about with containers fixed to their undersides: but the containers are empty, same as the cash box was.'

Sandy said doubtfully, 'Everyone in the pub last Saturday heard him talking about it. I mean, he can't have been killed to stop him telling anyone about them because he'd already done it.'

'What's more,' I said, 'Dave, Harve and Brett, besides Jogger, saw the cash box here in this room, just after Jogger levered it off the nine-box. It was on my desk at that point, in plain sight. I put it down on the floor sometime later.'

'You must have an idea what it was for,' Sandy said, a policemanlike suspicion creeping into his voice despite the non-adversarial status between us.

'We thought of drugs, if that's what you mean? Harve, Jogger and I discussed that. But drugs don't just appear out of thin air. Someone had to supply them. Harve and I don't believe that any of our drivers deal in drugs. I mean, there would be *signs*, wouldn't there? And money going around. We would *notice*.'

'Why didn't you tell me about this last Tuesday?'

Still the suspicious tone. 'You should have told me, I reckon.'

'I wanted to find out for myself what's happening. I still do, but I haven't much chance if there's a murder investigation going on. You'll have to admit that once your colleagues get to looking at the containers under the lorries, those containers will never be used again. I wanted to leave them in place, to keep quiet about them and to *wait*. I implored Jogger not to talk about them in the pub, but the beer got the better of him. I'm afraid that he said too much. I'm afraid he blew the whole operation and frightened the fish away. I've been hoping he didn't. But your colleagues will certainly frighten him away for ever and I will never find out . . . and that's why I didn't tell you, because you're a policeman first and a friend second, and your conscience wouldn't have let you keep silent.'

He said slowly, 'You're right about that.'

'It's Friday evening,' I said. 'How long can you sit on what I've told you?'

'*Freddie . . .*' He was unhappy.

'Till Monday?'

'Oh shit. What do you want to do before then?'

'To get some answers.'

'You have to ask the right questions,' he said.

He didn't promise even temporary silence and I didn't try to crowd him with a decision. He would do whatever sat comfortably in his own mind.

He buttoned his tunic round his solid waist. He said

he'd better be going. On his way out he picked up his peaked cap and put it on, reaching his car as a fully uniformed and thorough policeman, looking uncompromising in his vocation.

I poured the remains of his whisky down the kitchen sink and hoped our friendship wasn't sliding away with it down the drain.

CHAPTER ELEVEN

I drove along to the farmyard when Nina phoned to say she was back, and found her filling her tanks, yawning as before.

Lewis had finished cleaning his box and was positioning it in its usual place. Harve and Phil weren't back so far from Wolverhampton but except for Aziz's nine-box, which had gone to Ireland, the broodmare force had returned.

Lewis slid his completed log through the office letter-box, told me briefly that he'd taken his pair safely back to Mr Usher and that he'd had to help the Usher head travelling lad saddle all the runners as their lads were useless and Nina had said she wasn't dressed for it. He thought little of Nina, I gathered, for letting him do so much work. The approval she'd lavished that morning on the photos of his baby had, I thought in amusement, been wasted.

Nina drove along to the cleaning area and set to work with the pressure hose. Looking at her old jeans, the unsmart sweater and the scraped back hair escaping in wisps, one could see why she'd backed away from public gaze, quite apart from the fact that someone in the horse world might have recognised her and asked astonished questions.

Lewis left. I went over to Nina and offered to clean her box for her if she would do a different job for me. She agreed with relief, saying, 'What if Harve comes back?'

'I'll think of something.'

'OK. What do I do?'

'Fetch the new slider from the barn and look at all the fuel tanks to see if there are any containers stuck on them.'

She was surprised. 'I thought Jogger looked and there were only the three.'

'Looking back,' I said, 'he told me of three. I don't know for sure if he'd looked under all the others. I just want to check.'

'All right,' she agreed. 'Don't you want to do it yourself?'

'Not particularly.'

She gave me a curious look but made no comment, just fetched the slider from the barn and started methodically along the row. I finished the cleaning, inside and out, and positioned her box where it belonged, joining her afterwards by the office door.

'Well,' she said, rubbing dirt off her elbows, 'there's one more, and it's under Lewis's box, but it's empty, like the others. Lewis! So we took *two* hidden containers to

Lingfield today, but I stayed with the lorries the whole time, to Lewis's disgust, but he could perfectly well manage to help the head travelling lad saddle up on his own, he didn't need me really, but I'm in his bad books.' The thought hardly upset her. 'No one came near either box, I'd swear it. No one showed the slightest interest in their undersides.'

I thought back. 'Lewis's box was on its way to France when Jogger found the second and third container. Lewis went on Friday, and got back at about two on Tuesday morning.'

'There you are, then. Jogger didn't know about Lewis's box. He was dead before Lewis got back.'

Harve drove into the farmyard, his lights bright in the gathering dusk.

'Do you want me to check Harve's?' Nina asked.

'If you have a chance. And any others we've missed.'

'OK.' She yawned again. 'Am I driving tomorrow?'

'Isobel's got you down again for Lingfield.'

'Oh, well . . . at least I know the way, now.'

I said penitently, 'I don't even know where you live. Do you have a long drive home?'

'Near Stow-on-the-Wold,' she said. 'It takes me an hour.'

'That's a fair commute. Um . . . how about if I give you dinner somewhere on your way home?'

'I'm hardly dressed for going out to dinner.'

'A pub, then?'

'Yes, all right. Thank you.'

I went over to talk to Harve as he filled his tanks and found him happy to have taken a winner to Wolverhampton, as he'd also backed it. The lad with the horse had told him it was a certainty. 'For once, he was right.'

When his tanks were full I asked him to come over to the office to look at the next day's schedule. He came as a matter of course while, looking back, I saw Nina taking the opportunity to slide underneath his box for an inspection.

We went through the list, which was healthily busy. He himself was down for Chepstow, one of his favourite runs. 'Good,' he said. I told him about Benjy Usher overlooking the hurdlers. 'How he ever trains a winner I'll never know,' he said. 'Mind you, he has the luck of the devil. Who else had *three* walkovers last summer? You remember there was that bug going about in Pixhill? All those Classic Trial weight-for-age races, they always cut up to five or six runners every year anyway, and Mr Usher's always keen to win them. He won the Chester Vase last year against only two opponents. I know, because I drove his winner myself, if you remember?'

I nodded. 'He's always tended to enter horses in races that are likely to have very few runners,' I agreed. 'I won several two- and three-horse races for him myself, mostly three-mile chases.'

'He runs the poor buggers on rock-hard going too,' Harve went on disapprovingly. 'Doesn't seem to care if they finish lame.'

'They limp all the way to the bank.'

'You can laugh,' Harve objected, 'but he's still a rotten trainer.'

'We have that colt of his to bring back from Italy next week,' I reminded him. 'Isobel's arranged the paperwork and the ferry for Monday.'

'A broken-down colt,' Harve said, sniffing.

'Er . . . yes.'

'Who's going?'

'Who do you suggest? He asked for Lewis and Dave.'

Harve shrugged. 'We may as well please him.'

'I thought so, yes.'

Across the farmyard Nina emerged from her search and shook her head exaggeratedly.

I said to Harve, 'You remember that cash box container that Jogger found stuck under the nine-box? Has anything occurred to you about what it could be for?'

'I haven't thought about it,' he said frankly. 'Jogger found two more, didn't he, and they were all empty? Whatever was in them is history.' He sounded as unconcerned as ever. 'Poor old Jogger.'

As Sandy had told me off the record that the Jogger enquiry was veering to murder, I didn't mention it to Harve. Everyone would find out only too soon. Harve and I went back towards his box and he eyed the backview of Nina, who was disappearing into the barn.

'This job's too much for her,' he observed, not

unkindly. 'She's a good driver by all accounts, but Nigel says she gets tired easily.'

'She's temporary,' I said. 'One more week, if we get no one else down with flu.'

The other Wolverhampton box returned. I left Harve to supervise the end of the day and followed Nina's car as she waved to Harve and drove through the gates. She stopped after half a mile to walk back and suggest I follow her to a place to eat that she passed every day, and half an hour later we both pulled into the busy car park of a restaurant where good cheap food was important and the bar itself secondary.

She had loosed and combed her hair and applied lipstick, so that the Nina I had dinner with looked younger and halfway back to the original. The place was crowded, the tables small and close together. We ate steak, chips and fried onions with a carafe of house red wine and a chunk of cheddar cheese. 'I get fed *up* with healthy eating,' Nina said, secure in her slender body. 'Did you starve when you were a jockey?'

'Grilled fish and salads,' I said, nodding.

'Have some butter.' With a smile she passed me a small silver-wrapped packet. 'I adore junk food. My daughter despises me.'

'Black forest chocolate cake?' I suggested, handing her the menu.

'I'm not that mad.'

Companionably we drank coffee, neither of us in much hurry to be gone.

I told her the police thought Jogger had been murdered and that perhaps I now only had hours to find solutions before we were swamped by heavy boots.

'You're unfair to the police,' she observed.

'I dare say.'

'The solutions, I do agree, seem as far away as ever.'

'Sandy Smith,' I said, 'says it's a matter of asking the right questions.'

'Which are?'

'Yes, well, there's the rub.'

'Think of one.' She drank her coffee, smiling.

'All right,' I said. 'What do you think of Aziz?'

'What?' She was surprised; almost, I would have said, disconcerted.

'He's odd,' I remarked. 'I don't know how he could have caused any of my troubles, but he turned up in my farmyard the day after Jogger died and I gave him Brett's job because he speaks French and Arabic and had worked in a Mercedes garage. But my sister says he's far too bright for what he's doing and I respect my sister's insight. So why is Aziz working for me?'

She asked how my sister knew Aziz and I explained about the day he fetched the old horses, and that he'd driven Lizzie to Heathrow the next morning.

'That Tuesday night, when I ended up in Southampton Docks, I don't know if Aziz helped to put me there.'

'Oh, no,' she said, shocked. 'I'm sure he didn't.'

'Why are you so sure?'

'It's just . . . he's so cheerful.'

'One can smile and smile and be a villain.'

'Not Aziz,' she said.

To be honest, my gut reaction to Aziz was the same as Nina's: he might be a rogue but not a villain. Yet I did have villains about me, and I badly needed to know them.

'Who killed Jogger?' she asked.

I said, 'Who would you put your money on?'

'Dave,' she said, without hesitation. 'He's got a violent streak that he never shows you.'

'I've heard about it. But not Dave. No, I've known him too long.' I could hear the doubts creeping into my own voice, despite my conviction. 'Dave didn't know about the containers under the floorboards.'

'One can grin a little boy grin and be a villain.'

Against all probability I laughed, my cares unaccountably lifting.

'The police will find Jogger's killer,' Nina said, 'and you will have no more trouble and I will go home and that will be that.'

'I don't want you to go home.'

I said it without thinking, and surprised myself as much as her. She looked at me thoughtfully, unerringly hearing what I hadn't meant to say.

'That's loneliness speaking,' she said slowly.

'I'm happy alone.'

'Yes. Like I am.'

She finished her coffee and patted her mouth on a napkin with an air of finality.

'Time to go,' she said. 'Thanks for the dinner.'

I paid the bill and we went out to the cars, hers and mine, both our workhorse wheels.

'Goodnight,' she said matter-of-factly. 'See you in the morning.' She climbed without pause or tension into her seat, adept at unembarrassing partings. 'Goodnight, Freddie.'

'Night,' I said.

She drove away with a smile, friendly, nothing else. I wasn't sure whether or not to feel relieved.

Sometime during the night I woke suddenly, hearing again in my mind Sandy's insistent voice, 'You have to ask the right questions.'

I'd thought of a question I should have asked, and hadn't. I'd been slow and dim. I would ask the question first thing in the morning.

First thing in the morning, rousing me from depths of renewed slumber, the telephone bell brought Marigold's loud voice into my wincing ear.

'I'm not too happy about your friend Peterman,' she said, coming at once to the point. 'I'd like your advice. Can you call round here? Say, at about nine o'clock?'

'Mm,' I said, surfacing as sluggishly as any half-drowned swimmer. 'Yes, Marigold. Nine o'clock. Fine.'

'Are you drunk?' she demanded.

'No, just asleep.' In bed, supine, eyes shut.

'But it's seven already,' she pointed out severely. 'The day's half over.'

'I'll be there.' I fumbled the receiver towards its bedside cradle.

'Good,' her voice said from a distance. 'Great.'

Sleep was alluring, sleep a temptress, sleep as beckoning as a drug. Only the remembrance of the essential question I hadn't asked got me out of bed and into the bathroom.

Saturday morning. Coffee. Cornflakes.

Still bleary-brained, I padded from the kitchen into the wreck of the sitting-room and switched on the computer. There was no crash of hard disk. I called up Isobel's new entries of details of the drivers and found them still basic and abbreviated: names, addresses, dates of birth, next-of-kin, driving licence numbers, journeys driven that week, hours spent at the wheel.

Invading her privacy, I typed Nina's name, and read her address, care of Lauderhill Abbey, Stow-on-the-Wold, and her age, forty-four.

Nine years older than myself. Eight and a half, to be accurate. I drank my second cup of coffee very hot and wondered how much that age gap mattered.

I answered four telephone calls in quick succession, receiving, altering, agreeing to trips for that day and typing them into the programme for Isobel, who worked in the office most Saturday mornings from eight until noon. At ten to eight she phoned me herself, reporting her arrival, allowing me gratefully to switch the business line to the farmyard.

I drove along there myself to watch the day's journeys begin and to sort out any last-minute hitches, but again Isobel and Harve seemed to have everything running smoothly.

Nina (forty-four) gave me a small hello smile as she arrived to go to Lingfield, her appearance as determinedly unattractive as ever. Harve, Phil and the crowd were in and out of the canteen, stretching, picking up worksheets, flirting mildly with Isobel. Any Saturday morning. Another raceday. Twenty-four hours in a life.

Most of the fleet had gone by eight-thirty. I went into Isobel's office to find her typing the day's adjusted programmes into her computer, working mostly from what I'd typed in at home.

'How's things?' I asked vaguely.

'Always frantic.' She smiled, happy enough.

'I want to ask you to remember something.'

'Fire away.' She went on typing, looking at the screen.

'Um,' I said, 'last August . . .' I paused, waiting for more of her attention.

'What about last August?' she asked vaguely, still typing. 'You go away in August.'

'Yes, I know. When I was away last August, what did Jogger find in the inspection pit?'

She stopped typing and looked at me in puzzlement.

'What did you say?' she asked.

'What did Jogger find in the pit? Something dead. What did he find dead in the pit?'

'But Jogger . . . *he* was dead in the pit, wasn't he?'

'Last Sunday Jogger was dead in the pit, yes. But last August, apparently he found something else dead there . . . a dead *nun*, he said, but it can't have been a dead nun. So can you remember what he found? Did he tell you? Did he tell anyone?'

'Oh.' Her forehead developed lines of thought as she raised her eyebrows. 'I do vaguely remember, but it wasn't anything to worry you about. I mean, it was so silly.'

'What did he find?'

'I think it was a rabbit.'

'A *rabbit*?'

'Yes. A dead rabbit. He said it was crawling with maggots or something and he threw it in the skip. That was all.'

'Are you *sure*?' I asked doubtfully.

She nodded. 'He didn't know what else to do with it, so he threw it in the skip.'

'I mean, are you sure it was a rabbit?'

'I think so. I didn't see it. Jogger said it must have hopped in there somehow and once it had fallen into the pit of course it couldn't get out.'

'No,' I agreed. 'Do you remember what day it was?'

She shook her head decisively. 'If you can't remember it, it must have been when you were away.' She turned automatically to the computer and again the familiar frustration crossed her face. 'It might have been in the records we lost, though I don't really think so. I can't remember bothering to enter anything like that.'

'Did anyone else see Jogger's rabbit?'

'I simply can't remember.' It was clear from her expression that she couldn't see any importance in it either.

'Oh, well. Thanks anyway,' I said.

She smiled without guile and turned back to her work.

Nuns, I thought. Rabbits. Nuns and monks, nuns and sisters . . . nuns and *habits.*

Jogger's words. 'Take a butcher's at them nuns. There was a dead one in the pit last August – and it was crawling.'

The only rabbits that I could think of that he might mean were the rabbits belonging to the Watermead children, but even if one of those rabbits had somehow escaped and got as far as the inspection pit, it would hardly have been crawling with maggots unless, of course, it had been there dead for days when Jogger found it. It didn't seem to be of any importance . . . but to Jogger it had seemed important enough for him to tell me about it – in his own unintelligible way – seven months after the event.

I looked at my watch. Approaching nine o'clock. What was I supposed to be doing at nine o'clock? The sleep-filled assignation with Marigold English swam to the surface.

I told Isobel where I was going and to reach me by mobile phone for a while if she needed me, and drove to Marigold's yard.

She was outside in her woolly hat and came hurrying towards me when I appeared, carrying with her a bowl of horse nuts.

'Don't get out,' she commanded. 'Drive me to look at Peterman.'

Accordingly I followed her directions, which involved bumping down a grassy track to a distant paddock behind her house. The paddock sloped down to a brook and was edged with tall willow trees that would give great shade for old horses when the leaves came out.

Peterman, however, was up near the gate and looked thoroughly miserable. He put his nose down to Marigold's offered horse nuts and then moved his head away as if offended.

'See?' she said. 'He won't eat.'

'What are the nuts?' I asked.

She mentioned a standard brand much-used and well-respected. 'All horses like them, they never fail.'

I looked at Peterman, puzzled. 'What's the matter with him, then?'

Marigold hesitated. 'I phoned my old vet on Salisbury Plain to ask him, but he said just to give the old chap time to settle in. Then I came down here again yesterday evening, and you know what a nice sunny evening it was? The sun was shining low and yellow on the old horse, and you could see them.'

'See what?'

'Ticks.'

I stared at her.

'Tick bites,' she said. 'I think that's what's wrong with him. I phoned John Tigwood not half an hour ago to tell him to do something about it and he said it was rubbish and impossible, and anyway you, Freddie, had got the local vet round on Tuesday when the horses got to Pixhill, and you'd insisted on an examination, and the vet had passed the horses fully fit and had signed a document to that effect which he would show me if I liked, and really, I didn't like his tone much and I nearly told him to fetch the horse back again, but then I'd already asked you to come and look, and knowing that you wanted this old thing well looked after . . . well, I decided to wait until you came and to ask you what you thought.' She stopped, running out of breath. 'What do you think?'

'Um . . . where were the ticks?'

'On his neck.'

I peered at Peterman's neck, but could see only his bay coat, still thick for the winter. Come warmer weather he would shed a lot of it, revealing the short cooler coat of summer.

'What were they like?' I asked Marigold.

'Tiny brown things. The same colour as his coat. I

would never have seen them except for the sun, and because one of them *moved*.'

'How many?'

'I don't know . . . maybe seven or eight. I couldn't see them very clearly.'

'But Marigold . . .'

'You think I'm potty? What about the bees?'

'Er . . .'

She said impatiently, 'Bees, Freddie. Bees. *Varroa jacobonsi*.'

'Start at the beginning,' I begged.

'They are *mites*,' she said. 'They live on bees. They don't kill them, they just suck their blood until the bees can't fly.'

'I didn't know bees *had* blood.'

She gave me a withering look. 'My brother *panics* about varroa,' she said. 'He's a fruit farmer and half his trees don't bear fruit because the bees are too weak to *pollinate*.'

'Oh. Yes, I see.'

'So he smokes a pipe at them.'

'For God's sake . . .'

'Pipe tobacco smoke is about the only thing that knocks out varroa mites. If you blow pipe tobacco smoke into a beehive all the mites fall down dead.'

'Um,' I said. 'It's fascinating, but what has it got to do with Peterman?'

'Don't be so *slow*,' she commanded. 'Ticks carry

illnesses, don't they? I can't risk the ticks on Peterman hopping onto my two-year-olds, now can I?'

'No,' I said slowly, 'you can't.'

'So regardless of what John Tigwood says, I'm not going to keep this old horse here. I'm very sorry, Freddie, but you'll have to find him another home.'

'Yes,' I said. 'I will.'

'When?'

I thought of her star-studded stable and of my own strong desire to transport them for ever to the winners' enclosures.

I said, 'I'll walk him down to my house. There's a patch of garden he can stay in temporarily. Then I'll walk back for my car. Would that do?'

She nodded with approval. 'You're a good lad, Freddie.'

'I'm sorry to have given you this trouble.'

'I just hope you understand.'

I assured her I did. I drove back along the grassy track to her stable yard, where she lent me a leading-rein for Peterman and then led me by the arm to peer over a half-door at her absolute pride and joy, the three-year-old colt that, if all went well, would be contesting the 2,000 Guineas and the Derby against Michael Watermead's sensation, Irkab Alhawa. In her, as in Michael, the fledgling excitement shimmered in the eyes, the wild hope growing.

'You do see,' she reiterated, 'about Peterman.'

'Of course,' I said. I kissed her cheek. She nodded.

I could slaughter John Tigwood, I thought, for putting me in such an awkward position, even though, I thought more fairly, it wasn't actually his fault, as I had myself asked Marigold to take specifically Peterman.

Sighing at my folly I returned to the paddock, put on the leading-rein and led my old friend out of his idyllic pasture and along the road to the very much smaller patch of shaggy lawn in the walled garden behind my house.

'Don't eat the bloody daffodils,' I told him.

He looked at me balefully. As I took off the leading-rein to walk away, I noticed he wasn't even interested in the grass.

I collected my Fourtrak from Marigold's yard and went home again. Peterman stood more or less where I'd left him, looking miserable, the daffodils intact. If it hadn't been for the fallacy of endowing animals with human feelings, I'd have said the old horse was depressed. I gave him a bucket of water, but he didn't drink.

Various thoughts had been popping into my mind, almost as if a couple of sleeping cylinders had resumed firing. I sat down at the computer in my battered room and looked up the instruction manuals again for a renewed expedition through the old information on the healthy disks.

In surveying the drivers' journeys I had not, I'd remembered, pulled out Jogger's own. Even when I did, I learned little, as he'd driven very seldom; barely half a dozen times the previous year and nearly all on Bank Holiday Mondays, the days when with all the holiday race meetings countrywide, we were always scraping the barrel for chauffeurs.

I rubbed my nose, thought a bit more, and began to bring to the screen the horseboxes themselves, one by one, identifying them by registration number.

The columns on the screen came up looking completely different: the same information as before but illuminated from the side, like Marigold's view of otherwise invisible ticks.

Identified by registration number, each box's history now gave me dates, journeys, purpose of journey, drivers, engine hours logged, odometer readings, maintenance schedules, repairs, licensing, roadworthy certificates, unladen weights, fuel capacity, fuel actually used day by day.

After some taxing cerebration, much consultation with the manuals and a few false starts, I came up next with details of all maintenance work performed by Jogger the previous August. This time I'd sorted the work by chronology, and had provided myself more simply with the date, the horsebox registration number and the work done.

Day by summer day I looked back through that one month in Jogger's life, and there I found her, the dead nun.

August 10th. The registration number of the horsebox regularly driven by Phil. Oil change over the inspection pit. Tanks of air for the air brakes drained. Air brake compressor checked. All grease nipples filled. At the end, a note entered on the day by Isobel and forgotten: 'Jogger says a dead rabbit fell out of the horsebox into the pit. Crawling with ticks, he said. Disposed of in skip.'

I sat looking vaguely into space.

After a while I went back to the beginning and called Phil's records to the screen, to find out where he'd been on August 10th or 9th or 8th.

Phil, my faithful aid told me, had not been driving that particular horsebox on any of those days. He'd been driving another box, an older one, which I had, I remembered, subsequently sold.

Back to the drawing board: back to registration numbers, the sideways illumination.

On August 7th the horsebox Phil nowadays drove had gone to France with two runners for Benjy Usher. They had run on the 8th at Cagnes-sur-Mer, down on the Mediterranean, and returned to Pixhill on the 9th.

That horsebox, on that journey, had been driven by Lewis.

Lewis had actually driven that particular box most of the previous year, as I knew perfectly well once I'd thought about it. I'd transferred Lewis to the sparkling new super-six I'd bought in the autumn to replace the old one; transferred him so that the Usher and Watermead horses should go in my best style to their destinies. Lewis had driven one of Michael's horses to

Doncaster in September in the new super-six to win the last Classic race of the year, the St Leger.

At about ten-fifteen I telephoned Edinburgh.

'Quipp here,' a pleasant voice said. English, not a Scot.

'Um . . . excuse me phoning you,' I said, 'but do you happen to know where I could find my sister, Lizzie?'

After the briefest of pauses he said, 'Which are you, Robin or Freddie?'

'Freddie.'

'Hold on.'

I held, and heard his voice yelling, 'Liz, your brother Fred . . .' and then she was, moderately startled, saying, 'Is it your head?'

'What? No. Except it's been slow and stupid. Look, um . . . Lizzie, do you know anyone who knows anything about ticks?'

'*Ticks*?'

'Yeah. Little biters.'

'For God's sake . . .'

She told Professor Quipp what I wanted and he came back on the line.

'What sort of ticks?' he asked.

'That's what I want to find out. The sort that live on horses and . . . er . . . rabbits.'

'Do you have any specimens?'

'I've got a horse in the garden which probably has some.'

After a silence Lizzie came back. 'I've tried to explain to Quipp that you're concussed.'

'Far from it, at last.'

'What horse in the garden?'

'Peterman. One of the geriatrics from last Tuesday. Seriously, Lizzie, ask your professor how I get information about ticks. There are too many multi-million animals in Pixhill for messing about if ticks could make them ill.'

'Ye *Gods.*'

I listened to three full minutes of silence, then Professor Quipp said, 'Are you still there?'

'Yes.'

'I've a friend who's a tick expert. He says can you bring him some specimens?'

'Do you mean . . . put the horse in a horsebox and drive it to Edinburgh?'

'That's one way, I suppose.'

'The horse is terribly old and shaky. Lizzie knows, she saw him. He might not last the journey.'

'I'll phone you back,' he said.

I waited. My Jaguar and Lizzie's helicopter sat uselessly on the tarmac. Lovely fast transport at a standstill.

Quipp came back quite soon.

'Lizzie says if you say this is urgent, it's urgent.'

'It's urgent,' I said.

'Right. In that case, fly up here on the shuttle. We'll

meet you at Edinburgh Airport. Say . . . one o'clock? Soon after?'

'Er . . .' I began.

'Of course you can't bring the *horse* with you,' Quipp said, 'just bring some ticks.'

'But I can't actually *see* them.'

'Quite normal. They're very small. Use soap.'

Surreal.

'Wet a bar of soap until it's sticky,' he said. 'Rub it over the horse. If you find any round brown specks on the soap, you've got ticks.'

'But won't they die?'

'My friend says perhaps not, if you don't waste time on the way here, and anyway, it might not matter. Oh, yes, bring a blood sample from the horse.'

I opened my mouth to say it would take an hour or more to get the vet but Lizzie's voice in my ear forestalled me.

'There's a hypodermic needle and a syringe in my bathroom cupboard,' she said. 'Left over from my wasp allergy days when I lived at home. I saw it the other day. Use that.'

'But Lizzie . . .'

'Get on and do it,' she commanded, and Quipp's voice said, 'See you on the lunchtime shuttle. Phone if you're going to be later.'

'Yes,' I said dazed, and heard the disconnecting click at the other end. A far from absent-minded don, I reflected. A good match for my sister.

What Peterman himself would think about my sticking needles into him I dreaded to think. I went upstairs to the little pink and gold bathroom off Lizzie's bedroom and found the syringe, as she'd said, in the mirror-fronted cabinet there. The syringe, disposable, instructions 'for single use only', was inside an opaque white plastic envelope and looked much too small for anything equine. Still, Lizzie had said to use it, so I took it downstairs along with her cake of soap, moistened to stickiness, and approached the old fellow in the garden.

His apathy seemed complete. I merely held his forelock while I traced the visible vein running along his lower jaw, sticking the fine needle into it gently. His head remained still, as if he'd felt nothing. I found I needed two hands, in my inexperience, to pull back the plunger in order to draw blood into the syringe, and even then he remained unmoving, as if half asleep. The little syringe filled easily with the red stuff. I pulled the needle out again, laid the syringe aside, picked up the bar of soap and wiped it around Peterman's head and down his neck. Despite my doubts and disbelief there were, after three or four passes, a few discernible dark brown pinhead dots on the soft white surface.

Peterman went on paying no attention as I packed my trophies into a nest of scrumpled tissues inside a plastic food container from the kitchen and firmly closed the lid. Automatically I raised a hand to pat the old fellow, to say thanks, and in mid-gesture stopped dead. What if, I thought, in patting him, I transferred his ticks to myself? What if I'd already done it? Would it matter? I hadn't even thought of wearing protective gloves.

Shrugging, I left my old friend unpatted, washed my hands in the kitchen, and within five minutes I was spinning along the road in the direction of Heathrow Airport.

I phoned Isobel on the way.

'You're going *where*?' she said.

'Edinburgh. Be a dear and keep all the phone lines switched to you until I get back. Bonus, of course.'

'OK. How long will you be gone?'

'A day or two. I'll keep phoning you, to stay in touch.'

By luck I had a clear run to the airport, parked in the short-stay car park and caught the last seat on the noon shuttle at nothing faster than a flat-out sprint. My only luggage was the kitchen food container and the envelope of money from the safe. My clothes were the jeans and sweatshirt I'd worn to work. Everyone else on the aircraft seemed to be sporting huge scarlet-and-white scarves and loudly singing bawdy songs. 'Swing Low, Sweet Chariot', with the obscenest of gestures. Life grew steadily weirder. I held the container on my lap and slept away the hour in the air.

Lizzie was waiting at the other end beside a man who looked more like a ski instructor than a professor of organic chemistry, the impact of his dark beardless good looks heightened by a rainbow jacket straight off the slopes.

'Quipp,' he introduced himself, extending a hand. 'I suppose you're Freddie.'

As I'd just kissed Lizzie, this seemed a reasonable assumption.

'I told him you'd get here,' she said. 'He worked out that you couldn't do it in the time. I told him your jockey instincts made you faster across country than a hurricane.'

'Hurricanes are slow across country,' I said, 'actually.'

Quipp laughed. 'So they are. Forward speed, not much more than twenty-five miles an hour. Right?'

'Right,' I said.

'Come on, then.' He eyed the kitchen container. 'You've brought the goods? We're going straight to the lab. No time to waste.'

Quipp drove a Renault with a verve to match his jacket. We pulled up at what looked like a tradesmen's back entrance of a private hospital and entered a light featureless corridor that led round a corner to a pair of swing doors with 'McPherson Foundation' painted in black letters on non-see-through glass.

Quipp pushed familiarly through the doors, Lizzie and I following, and we entered first a vestibule, and then a room windowed solely by skylights.

From pegs in the vestibule, Quipp issued to each of us a white lab overall-coat which buttoned at the neck and needed to be tied round the waist with tapes. Inside the lab itself we met a man similarly dressed who turned from a microscope on our arrival and said to

Quipp, 'This had better be good, you son of a bitch. I'm supposed to be at the International rugby match at Murrayfield.'

Quipp, unabashed, introduced him to me as Guggenheim, the resident nutter.

Guggenheim, who seemed, like Quipp, to prefer to be identified solely by his last name, was audibly American and visibly about as young as the computer wizard.

'Disregard his youth,' Quipp advised. 'Remember that Isaac Newton was twenty-four when he discovered the binomial theorem in 1666.'

'I'll remember,' I said dryly.

'I'm twenty-five,' Guggenheim said. 'Let's see what you've brought.'

He took the plastic container from me and retreated to one of the work benches that lined two of the walls. With time to look around, it seemed to me that except for the microscope there wasn't a single piece of equipment there that I could identify. Guggenheim moved in this mysterious territory with the certainty of a Rubik round his cube.

He was slight in build with light brown crinkly hair and the well-disciplined eyes of habitual concentration. He transferred one of the brown dots from the soap to a slide and took a quick look at it under the microscope.

'Well, well, well, we have a tick. Now what do you suppose he's carrying?'

'Er,' I said, but it appeared that Guggenheim's question was rhetorical.

'If it came from a horse,' he said cheerfully, 'perhaps we should be looking for *Ehrlichia risticii*. What do you think? Does *Ehrlichia risticii* spring to mind?'

'It does not,' I said.

Guggenheim looked up from his microscope in good humour. 'Is the horse ill?' he asked.

'The horse is standing still looking depressed, if that doesn't sound fanciful.'

'Depression is clinical,' he said. 'Anything else? Fever?'

'I didn't take his temperature.' I thought back to Peterman's behaviour that morning. 'He wouldn't eat,' I said.

Guggenheim looked happy. 'Depression, anorexia and fever,' he said, 'classic symptoms.' He looked at Lizzie, Quipp and myself. 'Why don't you three go away for a bit? Give me an hour. I might find you some answers. I'm not promising. We've some powerful microscopes here and we're dealing with organisms on the edge of visibility. Anyway . . . an hour.'

We retreated as instructed, leaving our lab coats in the vestibule. Quipp drove us to his lodgings, which were masculine and bookish but bore unmistakable signs of Lizzie's occupation, though her expression forbade me to comment. She made coffee. Quipp took his cup with the murmured thanks of familiarity.

'How's my little Robinson?' Lizzie asked me. 'Still in the same place?'

'A low-loader's coming on Monday to bring it up here.'

'Tell them to be careful!'

'It'll reach you in cotton wool.'

'They'll have to disassemble the rotor linkage . . .'

We drank the coffee, strong and black.

I telephoned Isobel. All going well, she reported.

'What exactly *is* the McPherson Foundation?' I asked Quipp.

'Scottish philanthropist,' Quipp said succinctly. 'Also a tiny university grant. Small public funding. It has state-of-the-art electron microscopes and at present two resident geniuses, one of whom you met. It pushes out the frontiers of knowledge, and people in obscure places cease dying of obscure illnesses.' He drank some coffee. 'Guggenheim's speciality is the identification of the vectors of *Ehrlichiae*.'

'I don't speak that language,' I said.

'Ah. Then you won't understand that when I asked him about ticks on horses he was, for him, riveted. It's remotely possible that you've solved a mystery for him. Nothing less would have torn him away from Murrayfield.'

'Well . . . what are erlic . . . whatever you said?'

'*Ehrlichiae*? They are,' he said with a touch of mischief, 'pleomorphic organisms symbiotic in and transmitted by arthropod vectors. In general, that is.'

'*Quipp*!' Lizzie protested.

He relented. 'They're parasitic organisms spread by ticks. The best known make dogs and cattle ill. Guggenheim did some work on *Ehrlichiae* in horses back in America. He'll have to tell you about it himself. All I'm sure of is that he's talking about a new disease that arose only in the mid-nineteen eighties.'

'A *new* disease?' I exclaimed.

'Nature's always evolving,' Quipp said. 'Life never stands still. Diseases come and go. AIDS is new. Something even more destructive may be just round the corner.'

'How fearful,' Lizzie protested, frowning.

'Dear Liz, you know it's possible.' He looked at me. 'Guggenheim has a theory that the dinosaurs died not of cataclysmic weather upheavals but of tick-borne rickettsial-like pathogens – and those, before you ask, are parasitic micro organisms that cause fevers like typhus. Guggenheim thinks the ticks and their parasites died with their hosts, leaving no trace.'

I pondered. 'Could you transport these er – pathogens – in viral transport medium? The stuff in those small glass tubes?'

He looked momentarily startled but decisively shook his head. 'No. Not possible. *Ehrlichiae* aren't viruses. As far as I know, they won't live at all in any sort of medium or on a culture dish, which makes the research difficult. No. Whatever was in your virus transport medium, it definitely did not come from ticks.'

'That doesn't,' I said ruefully, 'make anything any clearer.'

'Lizzie is an astro physicist,' he said, 'listening to the cosmic ripple from the beginning of the universe, and Guggenheim looks inward into parasitic elementary bodies detectable only by magnifying them a million times in a beam of electrons instead of light. Outer deeps and inner deeps, with our puny intellects here and now trying to see and understand incredible mysteries.' He smiled self-deprecatingly. 'The humbling truth is that with all our discoveries, we're only on the fringe of knowledge.'

'But from the practical point of view,' I said, 'all we need to know is that arsenic can cure syphilis.'

'You're no scientist!' he accused me. 'You need Guggenheim lookalikes to *find out* that arsenic can cure syphilis.'

The ultimate squelch, I acknowledged. Lizzie patted my shoulder kindly.

'I suppose you didn't know,' Quipp said, 'that it was Ehrlich himself, after whom *Ehrlichiae* are named, who first showed synthetic arsenic to be active against syphilis?'

'No,' I said, astonished. 'I've never heard of Ehrlich.'

'German scientist. Nobel prize winner. A founder of immunology, pioneer of chemotherapy. Died, 1915. You'll never forget him.'

In 1915, I thought, Pommern won the war-time Derby. The quirks of life were endless.

After an hour Quipp drove us back to the McPherson Foundation to find Guggenheim pale and trembling, apparently from excitement.

'Where did these ticks come from?' he demanded, as soon as we appeared in our white gear. 'Did they come from America?'

'I think they came from France.'

'When?'

'Last Monday. On a rabbit.'

He peered at me, assessing things. 'Yes. Yes. They *could* have travelled on a rabbit. They wouldn't live long on soap. But transfer them from a horse to a rabbit by soap . . . there's no reason why they couldn't live on a rabbit . . . The rabbit wouldn't be receptive to the horse *Ehrlichiae* . . . the rabbit could carry the live ticks with impunity.'

'And then one could transfer the ticks to a different horse?' I asked.

'It's *possible.* Yes, yes, I can't see why not.'

'I can't see *why,*' Lizzie said. '*Why* would anyone do that?'

'Research,' Guggenheim said with certainty.

Lizzie looked at me doubtfully but didn't pursue it.

'See,' he said to me, 'equine ehrlichiosis is known in America. I've seen it in Maryland, and Pennsylvania, though it's a very new disease. Not ten years old yet. Rare. When it's caused by *Ehrlichia risticii* it's been called Potomac horse fever. That's because it's been found mostly near big rivers like the Potomac. How did these ticks get to France?'

'France imports racehorses bred in America. So does Britain, come to that.'

'Then why the rabbits?'

'Suppose,' I said, 'that you know where to find the ticks in France but not in England.'

'Yes. Yes.' His excitement, though internalised, was catching. 'You realise that the ticks you've brought me have *no name*? No one has so far identified the vector of *E. risticii*. Do you realise that if . . . *if* these ticks are the vector – a vector is a carrier of a disease – then we're on the verge of a breakthrough in identifying the path of Potomac horse fever?' He stopped, overcome.

'Practically,' I said. 'Could you answer some questions?'

'Fire away.'

'Well, what happens to a horse if it gets Potomac horse fever? Does it die?'

'Not usually. Eighty per cent live. Mind you, if it's a thoroughbred racehorse, which presumably you're most interested in, it will probably never win another race. What I've seen of the disease, it's very debilitating.'

'How, exactly?'

'It's an enteric infection. That's to do with the intestines. Apart from the anorexia and so on, there is usually fierce diarrhoea and colic. The horse is much weakened by the fever.'

'How long does the fever last?'

'Four or five days.'

'So short?'

'The horse develops antibodies so the *Ehrlichiae* don't affect it any more. If the vector is a tick, the tick would go right on living. Ticks, I may say, are themselves not much understood. For instance, only the mature ones are brown. Your soap was crowded with nymphets, young ticks, which are almost transparent.' He paused very briefly. 'Do you mind if I come to see what you've got there, down in Pixhill? Can I see, for example, your rabbit?'

'I'm afraid I deduced the rabbit.'

'Oh.' He looked disappointed.

'But come,' I invited him. 'Stay in my house.'

'Soon? I mean, I don't want to upset you, but you said your horse was *old*, and it's typically old retired horses out at pasture that get this illness, and the older they are, the more likely to die. Sorry. Sorry.'

'Can younger horses be affected?'

'If it's racehorses in a stable that you mean, then yes, they can, but they're *groomed*, aren't they? The grooming might get rid of the tick. Yes, that's a theory. In America it is mostly horses out at pasture that get ill.'

'Um,' I said, 'is there a cure for it?'

'Tetracycline,' he said promptly. 'I'll bring some for your old boy. It may be in time. It depends.'

'And . . . er . . .' I said, 'can humans catch this disease?'

He nodded. 'Yes. They can. It's usually not properly diagnosed as there are so many confusing symptoms. It gets mistaken for Rocky Mountain spotted fever, but it's different. It's rare. And tetracycline does the trick there, too.'

'How could it be diagnosed?'

'Blood test,' he said promptly. 'The amount you brought wasn't really enough.'

CHAPTER TWELVE

I travelled back on the last Edinburgh to Heathrow flight of the day, again surrounded by shoals of red-and-white scarves belting out bawdier-than-ever verses. Bass and baritone voices, tuneful, reverberating. The red and white scarves, it was clear, had won the International at Murrayfield. Beer disappeared at a Jogger-like pace. A naked flame would have exploded the alcohol fumes in the cabin. The flight attendants got their bottoms pinched. The ecstasy level rose, if anything, during the hour in the air.

I sat with my head whirling from different stimuli, hearing in flashbacks the facts that had poured out of Guggenheim.

The man himself was somewhere among the scarves, sitting separately because there hadn't been two seats available together. He had brought with him minimal overnight necessities, a huge amount of hope and a large bag of scientific field instruments. Nothing would have stopped him in his quest for the unnamed vector of *E. risticii*. He quivered with hunger. He reached out with percipient fingertips, like Handel to Hallelujah, like Newton to calculus, like Ehrlich, no doubt, to arsenic for syphilis. Reached out with genius towards recognition.

'It's early in the year for Potomac fever,' he had said. 'It's a warm weather thing, usually . . .'

'The ticks came from down south in France,' I told him. 'From the Rhône Valley.'

'A river! But usually May through October.'

'We had a dead rabbit crawling with ticks in August last year.'

'Yes. Yes. August.'

'We had a bug going round locally in Pixhill last summer that put a small number of horses out of action for the season.'

He groaned. With pleasure, as far as I could see.

'They had the same sort of unspecified feverish illness also in places in France,' I said. 'I read it again in the newspaper only this week.'

'Find the newspaper.'

'Yes, OK.'

'No one would have tested for equine ehrlichiosis . . . it's still almost an unknown infection. Rare. Sporadic. Not an epidemic. Hard to find. This is *wonderful*.'

'Not to the horse owners.'

'But this is *history* . . .'

It was a hopeless disaster, I thought, if I couldn't clear everything up quickly. 'Freddie Croft's horseboxes brought Potomac horse fever to Britain.' I could just see the headlines. 'Freddie Croft's *drivers* brought fever to Britain.' Perhaps it would be safer not to employ Freddie Croft's transport? Sorry and all that, Freddie, but I can't take the risk.

Confidence was fragile. Loyalty was fickle. Rabbits bringing ticks? No, thanks very much.

Freddie Croft Raceways out of business.

I sweated.

One of the Watermead rabbits had been missing, on the previous Sunday. There were only fourteen, not fifteen, the children had said. Maybe Lewis, the trusted rabbit handler, had taken that one rabbit with him to France. Taken it in a hidden compartment, out of sight above the fuel tanks. Last August it had been Lewis who had brought from France the dead rabbit crawling with ticks . . . Jogger's dead nun.

Ticks. Jogger's voice came distinctly through the roaring rugby songs . . . 'Poland had the same five' . . . A childhood rhyme presented itself in synchronising time with the singing. One, two, buckle my shoe: three, four, knock at the door: five, six, pick up sticks . . . 'Poland had the same five, six' . . . six, sticks, ricks, mix, fix . . . Poland had the same . . . *ticks.*

Poland had the same ticks on a horse last summer, and it died.

Who was Poland?

Oh *God*, I thought. Not Poland and Waleska. Not Poland and coal or Poland and Danzig or Poland and corridor or Poland and Solidarity. No . . . Poland and *Russia*.

Russia . . . *Usher*.

Benjy Usher had the same ticks . . .

Dot's voice, 'Those old wrecks. They died. I hate it. They were always outside the drawing-room window . . .'

A well-pinched flight attendant asked if she could fetch me anything, raising her voice above the joyful surrounding din.

'Treble Scotch . . . well, no, just one. Got to drive home.'

Pictures crowded my inner eye. Benjy Usher, training through his upstairs window. Benjy never touching his horses. Benjy getting me to saddle his runners at Sandown.

Benjy couldn't have known, surely, that his old dying lodgers probably carried *Ehrlichiae* . . . Could he? Benjy . . . afraid the microscopic organisms would hop onto himself?

But if he'd feared that, why was he proposing to take two more old horses? Did he know that they, too, might carry ticks?

Lewis drove for him often.

The flight attendant brought my drink.

Benjy entered his horses in small-field races and had had the luck of the devil with walk-overs.

It had to be coincidental. Benjy was rich.

What if what he hankered for were *winners*, not money? Harve's voice, 'Mr Usher's a rotten trainer . . .'

It was nonsense. It had to be.

From somewhere, mingled with the rugby songs, a sentence I'd read once surfaced into consciousness: 'It isn't necessary to speculate about the driving force within us, it leaps out and reveals itself. Under pressure, it can't be hidden.'

What if Benjy Usher's driving force were a hunger for winners, a hunger his own skill wasn't enough to assuage . . .?

No. Impossible. Yet winners gave him orgasmic pleasure.

Lewis often drove for Benjy.

Lewis had cut off his ringlets last summer.

Had Lewis been afraid he would get ticks in his long hair?

He'd transported the tick-infested nun in Jogger's pit.

Jogger.

Benjy hadn't killed Jogger. Benjy had been playing tennis on the Watermeads' court at about the time Jogger had died.

Lewis hadn't killed Jogger. He'd been in France.

Lewis had come back to the farmyard later than intended, at two in the morning on Monday-to-Tuesday night. He'd stabled Michael's two-year-olds in the farmyard and left me a note to say he had flu. I'd driven his super-six on Tuesday morning with the two-year-olds to Michael's yard, and I'd had breakfast and watched Irkab

Alhawa gallop. Then the super-six had gone racing for the day with one of the fleet's other drivers.

What if Lewis had in fact taken the missing rabbit to France to pick up its sick-making cargo? What if it had still been there, now tick-infested, in the hidden container, when I'd driven the super-six to Michael's yard? What if it had still been there until the box returned from the races in the evening? What if Lewis, with only a cold after all, had gone late to the yard to retrieve the rabbit . . . and what if I had walked in there while this retrieval was in progress?

Did it make sense?

As much sense as anything else.

What had *Jogger* walked in on, then?

What had occurred on Sunday morning in the farm-yard that Jogger had seen, and would tell me about, that it wasn't intended that he should see?

What had happened in the farmyard on that Sunday morning?

'Ask the right questions,' Sandy had said.

That Sunday morning had been March 6th, the day the office computer had been switched on in order to activate the Michelangelo virus. Jogger wouldn't have understood the computer. It wasn't *what* he'd seen in the farmyard office that mattered, but *who*.

The rugby songs swelled around me.

I had an acute sense of danger.

*

On the way home from Heathrow I phoned Isobel, apologising for the lateness of the hour.

Think nothing of it, she said. The day had gone well. Harve had taken two winners to Chepstow. Aziz and Dave had returned all right from Ireland but Aziz had said Dave wasn't in good shape. Dave, Isobel thought, might be developing flu.

'Bugger,' I said.

Nina had taken a winner to Lingfield, and so had Nigel. Lewis had driven three of Benjy Usher's jumpers to Chepstow, and had been reminded to bring his overnight things on Monday for going to Italy. Phil had been phlegmatically to Uttoxeter. Michael Watermead and Marigold English had both booked two boxes for Tuesday to take horses to Doncaster sales.

'Great,' I said thankfully. Marigold had disregarded Peterman's problem: so far, at least.

Jericho Rich had reportedly fallen out already with his new trainer, Isobel said. She thought we might be bringing the whole string back to Pixhill any day soon.

'The man's mad,' I remarked.

'I hear you're going to the Watermeads' for lunch again tomorrow,' Isobel said. 'I'll go on doing the bookings, shall I?'

'Yes, please,' I said gratefully. 'And who told you?'

'Tessa Watermead. She came by. I taught her a few things. That's all right, isn't it?'

'Yes, sure.'

'Goodnight, then.'

'Goodnight.'

Guggenheim, sitting beside me in the Fourtrak, repudiated my suggestion that we stop for something to eat. I'd had no lunch and was hungry. Guggenheim's hunger for truth won the day. Besides, he said, rationalising it and silencing me, Peterman needed the tetracycline as soon as possible.

For poor old Peterman, however, it was already too late. When Guggenheim and I went out into the dark garden, my game old partner was lying in the shadows on my lawn barely a yard from where I'd left him, his visible eye already dull, the stillness of death unmistakable.

Guggenheim's grief was for his own career; mine for the long-ago races and the speed of a great horse.

Guggenheim had brought not soap for finding ticks but a very small battery-powered hand-held vacuum cleaner. He tried his best all over Peterman, but an inspection of the collected debris from the horse's skin disappointed him abysmally.

He bent over his microscope in my kitchen uttering soft despairing moans.

'Nothing. Nothing. You must have brought all of them on the soap.' He sounded almost accusing, as if I'd ruined things on purpose. 'But this is typical. The carrier of *E. risticii* is brutally elusive. Ticks feed on blood. They burrow their heads right through the skin of their host. The *Ehrlichiae* that live in the tick pass from the tick into the blood of the host and combine with certain blood cells. I won't bore you with it, it's incredibly complicated . . . but they're only viable in *living* cells, and this horse has been dead for *hours.*'

'Have a drink?' I suggested.

'Alcohol's irrelevant,' he said.

'Mm.'

I poured for myself, however, and after a minute he took the whisky bottle out of my hand and half filled the glass I'd set out for him.

'Anaesthetic for lost hopes,' he said. 'I suppose you're right.'

'When I was your age,' I said, 'I rode the wind. Quite often.'

He looked at me over his glass. 'You're saying there will be other days? You don't understand.'

'I do, you know. I'll try to get you some more of those ticks.'

'How?'

'I'll sleep on it.'

We found a dinner of sorts in the fridge and cupboard, and he slept in Lizzie's room silently all night.

In the morning I telephoned John Tigwood and told him Peterman was dead.

Tigwood's voice, pompous as ever, full of bogus fruitiness, was also defensive and querulous.

'Marigold English complained to me that the horse was ill and she said he had *ticks.* Rubbish. Utter rubbish, I told her so. Horses don't have ticks, dogs and cattle do. I'm not having her or you going round spreading such malicious rumours.'

I saw with clarity that he feared his whole act would fall apart if no one would board his geriatrics. No more collecting tins. No more self-important bustling about. He had as powerful a reason for keeping quiet as I had.

'The horse is at my house,' I said. 'I'll get the knackers to collect him, if you like.'

'Yes,' he agreed.

'How are the other old horses?' I asked.

'Perfectly well,' he said furiously. 'And it's *your* fault Peterman went to Mrs English. She refused point blank to take any of the others.'

I made soothing noises and put down the receiver.

Looking about sixteen, Guggenheim came mournfully downstairs and stared out of the window at Peterman's carcass as if willing him back to tick-infested life.

'I'd better go back to Edinburgh,' he said despondently, 'unless any other horses are ill.'

'I can find out at lunch. All the gossip and news in Pixhill will be available then, at Michael Watermead's house.'

He said if it was all right with me he would stay until after that and then leave: he had on-going work in the laboratory that he shouldn't be neglecting. Fine, I agreed; and he could come back instantly, of course, if anything significant happened.

He gloomily watched the knackers position their van by my garden gate and winch the thin old corpse away. What would become of him? Guggenheim asked. Glue factory, I said. He looked as if he'd just as soon not have known.

He couldn't believe, he said, the state of my sitting-room, still in a mess. He couldn't believe the impact that had destroyed the helicopter and the car. The mind that had done it, I told him, was still wandering around somewhere, still in possession of the axe.

'But aren't you . . . well . . . scared?' he asked.

'Careful,' I said. 'That's why I'm not taking you with me to lunch. I don't want anyone knowing I know a scientist, especially one who's an expert on ticks. I hope you don't mind.'

'Of course not.' He looked at the axe-slashed room and shivered.

I took him to the farmyard, though, and showed him the horseboxes which impressed him by their size. I explained about the containers under three of them and said I thought the ticks had come into England that way on the rabbits.

'There would have to be air holes in the containers,' he said.

'So there would.'

'Haven't you looked?'

'No.'

He was surprised, but I didn't explain. I took him

back to my house and left him there while I went to the Watermeads' lunch.

Maudie greeted me with affection and Michael with warmth. Many of the usual people were there: the Ushers and Bruce Farway included. Tessa indulged in back-turning and whispering into Benjy's ear. The younger children were missing: they'd gone to stay with Susan and Hugo Palmerstone for the weekend. 'They get on so well with Cinders,' Maudie said. 'Such a nice little girl.' I realised that I'd hoped Cinders would again be at the Watermeads'. Don't think about her, I told myself. Couldn't help it.

I asked Michael if he'd accepted any of the old horses yet.

'Two of them,' he said, nodding. 'Skittish old things. Running about in my bottom paddock like two-year-olds.'

I asked Dot the same question and got a different answer.

'Benjy says we can put Tigwood off for a few days. Don't know what's got into the old shit, actually doing what I asked.'

'What did that old horse die of, last year?'

'Old age. Some sort of fever. What does it matter? I hate having them about the place.'

The vet who'd given my geriatric passengers the all clear was there, comparing notes with Bruce Farway.

'How's trade?' I asked them. 'How are the sick of Pixhill? Anything interesting?'

'I hear the knackers were at your house this morning,' the vet observed.

'News zooms round,' I said, resignedly. 'One of the old horses died.'

'You didn't call me in.'

'I didn't know he was that ill, or I would have done.'

He nodded. 'They're old. They die. Can't be helped, it's nature.'

'Is anyone else in trouble? Anyone got last year's bug?'

'No, thank goodness. Just the usual tendons and teeth.'

'What was last year's bug?' Farway asked.

The vet said, 'Some unspecified infection. Horses got feverish. I gave them various antibiotics, and they recovered.' He frowned. 'It was worrying, really, because all those horses lost their speed and form after it. But, thank goodness, it wasn't widespread.'

'Interesting, though,' Farway said.

'You'll be involved in Pixhill's fortunes before you know it,' the vet teased him, and Farway looked disconcerted.

Maudie's sister, Lorna, came proprietorially to Farway's side, taking his arm and eyeing me with the disapproval left over from my not having transported the geriatrics without payment. I found her disapprobation much less alarming than her earlier interest in me. Farway gave her a fond look while sharing her opinions of myself.

I drifted away from them, feeling isolated by how much I had discovered and wondering what else I didn't know.

Ed, Tessa's brother, stood alone, looking surly. I talked to him for a bit, trying to cheer him up.

'You remember your show-stopper last week?' I asked him. 'About Jericho Rich making a play for Tessa?'

'It was true what I said,' he insisted defensively.

'I don't doubt it.'

'He was pawing her. I saw him. She slapped his face.'

'Really?'

'Don't you believe me? No one believes a word I say.' Self-pity swamped him. 'Jericho Rich swore at her and told her he would take his horses away and Tessa said if he did she'd get even. Silly little bitch. How could she get even with a man like that? So, anyway, he did take the horses away and what has Tessa done about it? Bloody nothing, of course. And Dad isn't even angry with her, only with me for telling everyone why Jericho Rich left. It isn't *fair*.'

'No,' I agreed.

'You're not too bad,' he said reluctantly.

I sat next to Maudie at lunch but there was little left of the enjoyment I'd found at that table a week ago. Maudie sensed it, trying to dispel my sadness, but I left after the coffee with no great regrets.

There were no feverish horses in Pixhill, I reported to Guggenheim, and drove him in his own depression back to the airport. On the way home I stopped for petrol and, after a bit of thought, phoned Nina's Stow-on-the-Wold number.

'Um,' I said, 'when you come to work tomorrow, bring a parachute.'

'What?'

'For landing behind the enemy lines in occupied France.'

'Is this the concussion?'

'It is not. You don't have to go if you don't want to.'

'I wish you'd explain.'

'Can I meet you somewhere? Are you busy?'

'I'm alone . . . and bored.'

'Good. I mean, how about the Cotswold Gateway? I could be there before six.'

'All right.'

Accordingly I changed direction and drove west and north to arrive an hour and a half later at a large impersonal old hotel on the A40 main road which ran across the top of the Cotswold town of Burford. I parked outside the great old-fashioned charming pile, a landmark passed endless times in my life on the way to Cheltenham races.

She was already there when I arrived, having had by far the shorter journey, and she was the original compelling Nina, not the scrubbed and workaday version.

She was sitting in a chintz armchair beside a glowing

log fire in the entrance hall, a tea tray primly before her on a low table.

Post-Cheltenham but before the summer tourist season, the place was almost empty. She rose when I came in, and enjoyed my admiration of her appearance. No jeans, this time; the long slender legs were covered instead by black tights. No sloppy old sweater but a black skirt, black waistcoat, white silk shirt with big sleeves, large gold cufflinks and a long neck-chain of enough half-sovereigns to fund a ransom. She smelled, not of horses, but subtly of gardenias. The economical bones of her face were revealed and softened by a dusting of powder. Lips, softly red.

'I hardly like to ask you . . .' I said, kissing her cheek as if from long close habit, 'looking as you do . . .'

'You sounded serious.'

'Mm.'

We sat down near enough to each other to talk, though there was no one to overhear.

'First of all,' I said, 'I found out what's been carried under my lorries, and it is not as simple as drugs.' She waited while I paused, her interest sharpening to acute. 'I went to see a top Customs man in Portsmouth,' I said, 'to ask what *couldn't* move freely in and out of Britain under the EC regulations. I expect you know, the Customs men never search any traffic nowadays unless they have specific information that drugs will be found in a certain vehicle. In practice, it means that anything – guns, cocaine, whatever, coming here from

Europe – has untroubled entry. But he got very excited about cats and dogs, and rabies . . . and it seems the quarantine rules apply, and also one needs a licence for things like veterinary medicines. Anyway, my boxes *have* been carrying extra livestock, though not cats and dogs, I don't think, because they would both make a noise.'

'Make a *noise*?'

'Sure. If you carried a cat in one of those containers, someone would hear it complaining.'

'But why? You've lost me. Why take livestock in those containers?'

'So that the lads with the horses wouldn't know about it. If any horsebox carried anything in public out of the ordinary, half the village would hear about it in the pub.'

'Then who's been carrying secret livestock?'

'One of my drivers.'

'Which one?'

'Lewis.'

'Oh no, Freddie. He has that baby!'

'One can love one's offspring and be a villain.'

'You don't mean it . . .'

'Yeah. And I don't like it.'

'Do you mean . . . you can't mean . . . that Lewis had been deliberately trying to bring rabies into England?'

'No, not rabies, thank God. Just a fever that makes horses temporarily ill, but takes the edge off their speed so drastically that they don't win again.'

I told her that Jogger's dead nun had been a rabbit.

'Nun – rabbit – *habit*.' She sighed. 'How did you find out?'

'I asked Isobel what Jogger found dead in the pit, and she told me.'

'So simple!'

'Then I looked at the computer files for last August, for the time when I was away, and there it was. August 10th. Jogger reported a dead rabbit fell into the pit from a box he was servicing, and it was on the day after Lewis brought that box back from France.'

She frowned, 'But the computer files were lost.'

I told her about the back-ups in my safe.

'You didn't tell anyone! You didn't tell *me*. Don't you trust me?'

'Mostly,' I said.

She wouldn't meet my eyes. I said, 'Jogger told Isobel the rabbit had ticks on it and she put a note about that in the computer. The computer also lists each box's journeys individually, and two of those boxes that have hidden containers, Pat's box, that you drove, and Phil's box, both of those were driven to France by Lewis last year. This year he's driving my newest super-six, and it too, as you found, has a container under it. Last weekend, the Watermead children missed one of their tame rabbits, that Lewis looks after for them, cleaning their runs and so on, and also last weekend Lewis drove the super-six to France, and this weekend a horse has died in Pixhill of a tick-borne fever.'

She listened wide-eyed, her mouth opening. I went over it all again, slowly, telling her about Benjy's training habits, about Lewis's shorn ringlets, about Peterman and finally about Guggenheim.

Once an old horse had come through the fever stage, I said, he could live with ticks on him all summer. A continual source of potential illness for other designated recipients. An *Ehrlichiae* farm, in fact. A quick wipe over an old horse with a wet bar of soap and, within an hour, a wipe of the same soap onto a new host. Tick-transfer completed. Enough of the ticks would survive. The transfer, I said gloomily, might even have been done by Lewis when he drove the unfortunate victims to the races in my boxes.

When the weather grew cold, the ticks would die. A new lot had to be brought in by a temporary host for the new year, and then, without much delay, transferred to their natural host, a horse. Peterman hadn't survived it.

Whatever doubts she had at the beginning, they had gone by the end.

'When we first found the containers,' I said, 'I begged Jogger not to talk about them. But he did, of course, down at the pub on the Saturday night. I reckon he'd been thinking a lot about them. Turning them over in his mind, I'd think he remembered the rabbit, which must have seemed to him at the time to appear from nowhere, and perhaps he'd worked out that it might have fallen out of one of those containers, the one under what is now Phil's box, because that container had lost its screw-on end. I don't know if anyone understood Jogger plainly in the pub. They might have done. Anyway, in the morning he left me the message . . . and he told me, Jogger told me . . . about rabbits and ticks and Benjy Usher's horse that died.'

She was silent for a while and then asked, 'Was it Lewis who wrecked your car and the house?'

'I don't know. I'm sure he was one of the people who dropped me into the water at Southampton. The one who said, "If that doesn't give him flu, nothing will." His voice was hoarse because he had a cold, and in my memory, that voice reverberated a bit, as I was half unconscious, but yes, I'm sure that was him. Whether he hates me enough for the rest . . . I don't know.'

'That's *awful*.'

'Mm.'

'So what next?'

'Tomorrow,' I said, 'Lewis is driving the super-six to Milan, in Italy, to fetch home one of Benjy Usher's colts, that has a dicky leg. It's a three-day trip, mostly through France.'

She grew still. Then she said, 'I'll go. Have parachute, will travel.'

'I don't want you to *do* anything,' I explained. 'I don't want you to alarm him. I want him to have every opportunity to pick up another rabbitful of ticks, because if all of last weekend's cargo were on Peterman and have died with him, and if no other horses are ill, then perhaps this is a chance for them to get some replacements. Those ticks are highly perishable, and also hard to find. I'd think they'd need some more. All I want you to do is to note where you go. The route Lewis will take to Italy is down to the Rhône Valley, which is where he went last weekend also. He should be going through the Mont Blanc tunnel from France to Italy but if he takes another route, don't remark on it. If he wants to stop anywhere at all, let him stop. Don't ask questions. Agree to whatever he suggests. Notice nothing. Don't watch him. Yawn, sleep, act dumb.'

'He won't want me with him, you know.'

'I know he thinks you tire easily. So *tire*. This time, he may be glad of it.'

'And don't, I suppose, look under the box?'

'No, don't. If the place is littered with lettuce leaves and rabbit droppings, ignore it.'

She smiled.

'Be careful,' I begged. 'I'd go myself, except that if I did, nothing would happen. All I want to know is *where* Lewis goes.'

'All right.'

'You don't have to.'

'Nor did my mother.'

'Lewis might be just as dangerous.'

'I promise,' she said emphatically, 'that I'll be as blind as a bat.' She paused. 'There's only one thing.'

'What?'

'I want to tell Patrick Venables where I'm going.'

'Would he stop you?'

'Probably the opposite.'

'Don't let him *do* anything,' I said anxiously. 'Don't let him frighten them off.' My instinct was against the Jockey Club knowing too much, too soon, but perhaps also for this possibly risky mission I might need the insurance of Venables' foreknowledge.

'I don't want to be prosecuted,' she said, half playfully, 'for trying to nobble half Pixhill's best colts.'

'You won't be. I – ' I stopped dead, a revelation presenting itself to me with breath-thieving force. 'Bloody *hell*!'

'What is it?'

'Um. Nothing. When you get back on Wednesday you'll be met. Don't worry about anything except not frightening Lewis.'

We ate dinner in the dining-room, discussing the trip to begin with but passing pretty soon to our lives in general. I enjoyed being with her. I was growing unfaithful to Maudie, I thought ironically. I asked Nina how old her eldest child was.

'Twenty-four.' She smiled down at her pasta. 'Much younger than you.'

'Am I that transparent?'

'You're no toy-boy,' she said.

'Your children might think so.'

'Your sister is older than her professor, isn't she?'

'Yes, she is,' I said, mildly surprised. 'Who told you?'

'Aziz told me.'

'*Aziz?*'

'Your sister told *him*. He told *me*. We drivers hang together, you know.'

'Wipe that demure smile off your face.'

The smile, however, deepened. I thought of all the empty bedrooms upstairs in the hotel. I thought of the year-long celibacy and felt a strong desire to end it. She must have known what was in my mind. She simply waited.

I sighed. 'It's not what I'd prefer,' I said, 'but I'm going home.'

She said passively, 'All right.'

I rubbed my eyes. 'When this is over . . .'

'Yes. We'll see.'

We went out together, as before, to our separate cars. She had come in her Mercedes.

I kissed her mouth, not her cheek. She drew her head away, her eyes gleaming in the car park lights. I saw that I didn't displease her. I could so easily . . . so easily . . .

'Freddie . . .' Her voice was soft, non-committal, leaving it to me.

'I have to . . . I really do have to go,' I said almost desperately. 'I'm not sending you off to France without sensible preparations. Bring your overnight things in the morning and pick up a travel kit from the office. It will hold money and phone numbers and a precaution or two against thieves. Lewis always takes a similar kit.' I stopped. Travel kits were not what I wanted to talk about. I kissed her again and felt resolution draining away.

'Do the kit in the morning,' she suggested.

'Oh, God.'

'Freddie . . .'

'I'll tell you tomorrow why I have to go.'

I kissed her hard, then turned away and went over to the Fourtrak, feeling clumsy and annoyed with myself for going so far and inexplicably retreating. She didn't seem to mind. There were no hurt rejected feelings in the smile she gave me as she shut herself into the red car.

'See you,' she said through the opening window, starting the engine.

'Goodnight.'

With a wave she drove away, as self-possessed as ever. I watched her tail lights into the distance and strove to quieten my pulse. The basic drives of nature were so bloody powerful after all. And I'd thought I had the turmoil licked, which only showed that dormant volcanoes were simply that; fires temporarily asleep.

Eight and a half years. Did they matter? I didn't know, and I understood that she didn't know either. She was attracted to me; I had to believe it. She was also, I thought, in an odd way shy, not wanting me to think she had rushed me. She was making me decide whether what I felt was a passing arousal or a longer commitment.

I belted the Fourtrak back to my house, pushing decisions away for the night, and changed into soft black shoes and the darkest of clothes I could find. Then, with my eyes adjusting to night vision, I walked in the shadows along to the farmyard and unlocked the padlock on the gates to let myself in, locking it again behind me.

It was after midnight. The sky was clear and cold, stars blazing. All those distant suns, I thought; as mysterious and inaccessible as *Ehrlichia risticii*.

All the horseboxes were home in the roost, subduedly shining in the light of the night bulb over the canteen door. A quiet Sunday evening, peace after bustle. I had not, this time, walked into a mortal situation.

Harve, I imagined, had done his last rounds, and was watching video football. I unlocked the offices and, without switching on the interior lights, went along to my own room, enough glow creeping in through the windows for me to locate the torch I kept in the desk there and to check that its batteries were functioning. Then, relocking the office door on my way out, I padded across the farmyard to Jogger's old van from whose front seats I could see all my monsters partially, and one or two of them clearly.

The super-six Lewis would drive to Milan was one

of those. I settled into the dark interior of Jogger's van and tried resolutely to stay awake.

I managed it for an hour.

Dozed.

Woke with a jerk. Two o'clock. Sentries could be court-martialled for sleeping on duty. No one could help going to sleep. When the brain wanted to switch off, it did.

I tried reciting old verses. Nursery rhymes. One two, buckle my shoe.

Went to sleep.

Three o'clock. Four. Half the night passed across my shut eyes. Absolutely no good. Waste of time, sitting there.

When he came, the padlock clicked and rattled on its chain, and I was fully alert instantly.

I held my breath, not moving.

Lewis's unmistakable short haircut passed in silhouette between me and the outside light. Lewis, carrying a shapeless bag, moved unhesitatingly towards his own lorry, where he lay down on the ground and disappeared from my sight.

He remained out of sight for what seemed a long time, until I began to think he must have left without my noticing. But then, there he was, standing up, moving away, returning with his bag to the main gate and fastening the padlock with an almost inaudible click.

Gone.

I sat for another half hour, not entirely from wanting to be sure he wouldn't come back but from reluctance to face the next bit.

Phobias were irrational and stupid. Phobias were paralysing, petrifying and all too real. I slowly emerged from the van, took the torch, tried to think of race-riding . . . anything . . . and lay down on my back beside Lewis's box in the location of the fuel tanks.

The cold stars up there didn't care that my skin sweated and my courage shrank to the size of a nut.

The horsebox would not collapse on me. It obviously would *not.*

For fuck's sake, do it, I told myself. Don't be so fucking *stupid.*

I shifted my shoulders and hips over the ground and wriggled sideways until I was totally under the tons of steel, and of course they did not collapse on me, they hung over me immobile and impassive, a threat unfulfilled. I stopped under the fuel tanks and felt the stupid sweat wet on my face and came near to complete panic when I tried to raise my hand to wipe the sweat away and hit metal instead.

Fuck, I thought. No word was bad enough. I didn't habitually think in that casual expletive universal on the racecourse, but there were times when no other word would do.

I'd *chosen* to lie where I was. Stop bloody trembling, I told myself, and get on with the matter in hand.

Yes, Freddie.

I felt for, and found, the round end of the container above the rear fuel tank. I unscrewed and laid it on the ground beside me. I switched on the torch and raised my head to look into the container.

My hair brushed against the metal. Tons of steel. Shut *up*. My hands were slippery with sweat and I could hardly breathe and my heart pounded, and I'd risked death in racing thousands of times over fourteen years and I hadn't cared . . . it had been nothing like this.

Inside the tubular container there lay what seemed to be a long flat narrow plywood tray stretching away into shadow. Standing on the plywood was an oblong plastic kitchen food-box very like the one I'd taken to Scotland, except that this one had no lid.

Gripping the torch convulsively I stuck my arm with the torch into the tube for a deeper look.

The kitchen food-box held *water*.

Little stars appeared above the tubular container, showing on the underside of the horsebox floor above. The stars were from the torch-light inside the tube. The stars were the result of holes in the tube.

'There would have to be air holes in the container,' Guggenheim had said.

There *were* air holes.

I peered straight into the tube, my head hard against the metal above, arms constricted by metal on both sides, nerves shot to pathetic crumbs.

Deep along in the tube something moved. An eye

shone brightly. In his metal burrow, the rabbit seemed at ease.

I switched off the torch, screwed the end back onto the tube and wriggled out again into the free night air.

I lay on the hard ground, regrouping, heart thudding, ashamed of myself. Nothing, I thought, *nothing* would get me to do anything like that ever again.

In the morning, life in the farmyard looked normal.

Lewis, predictably, was annoyed that I'd allocated Nina to go with him instead of Dave.

'Dave wasn't well on Saturday,' I said. 'I'm not risking him getting flu away in Italy.'

Dave at that moment creaked into view on his bicycle, obligingly flushed and heavy-eyed. Flu wasn't going to stop him, he said.

'Sorry, but it is,' I replied. 'Go home to bed.'

Nina arrived looking the epitome of feminine frailty, yawning artistically and stretching. Lewis regarded her thoughtfully and made no more objections.

He and she both collected their travel kits from Isobel and went over the paperwork requirements with her. When Lewis went into the washroom I had a private moment to murmur in Nina's ear.

'You're taking a nun with you.'

Wide-eyed, she said, 'How do you know?'

'I saw her arrive.'

'When?'

'Five this morning. About then.'

'So that's why . . .'

Lewis reappeared, saying if they were going to catch the ferry they'd better be off.

'Phone home,' I said.

'Sure thing,' he agreed easily.

He drove out of the gate without a worry in the world. I hoped to hell that Nina would come back safely.

From the business point of view it was not an overpoweringly busy day, but the plain clothes police swept in with sharp eyes to take over the place before nine, setting up an interview room in my office. Dispossessed, I showed them whatever they wanted, offered them the run of the canteen and sat for a while on a spare chair in Isobel's office, watching her work.

Sandy drove in in his uniform, still confused in his loyalties.

'Tell them about the containers,' he blurted. 'I haven't.'

'Thanks, Sandy.'

'Did you find your answers?'

'I asked some questions.'

He knew I wasn't being open with him, but he seemed to prefer ignorance. In any case, he joined his colleagues and ran errands for them all day.

The colleagues found out about the containers from the landlord of the pub.

'Lone rangers?' I repeated when they asked me out

in the farmyard. 'Yes, Jogger came across three containers under the lorries. All empty. We don't know how long they've been there.'

The Force wanted to inspect them. Go ahead, I agreed, though Phil wouldn't be back with his own horsebox until evening.

Lewis had reached the ferry in good time, Isobel reported, and was now in France. I metaphorically bit my nails.

The police interviewed everyone they could reach and spent time sliding in and out under the boxes. Rather them than me. When Phil returned they removed the tube from above the fuel tanks (with my permission) and brought it out to where it could be easily inspected. Four feet long, eight inches in diameter, empty except for dust, small holes punched through it, screw cap missing.

They took it away for examination. I wondered if they would find rabbit hairs in it.

I drove home. The little helicopter had gone. My poor crunched car stood alone and forlorn, awaiting a tow-truck on the morrow. I patted it. Silly, really. The end of a big part of my life. Saying goodbye.

I went early to bed and tossed and turned.

In the morning Lewis reported to Isobel that he had cleared the Mont Blanc tunnel and would collect the colt before noon.

The police asked more questions. Half the fleet set off to take merchandise to Doncaster sales, Nigel driving for Marigold. I progressed from metaphorical nail biting to actual.

At noon Lewis reported that Benjy Usher's colt was unmanageable.

I talked to him myself.

'I'm not driving it,' he said. 'It's a wild animal. It'll damage the box. It'll have to stay here.'

'Is Nina around?'

'She's trying to pacify it. No chance.'

'Let me talk to her.'

She came on the line. 'The colt's scared,' she agreed. 'He keeps trying to lie down and thrash about. Give me an hour.'

'If he's really unmanageable, come back without him.'

'OK.'

'Anything else?' I asked.

'No. Nothing.'

I sat watching the clock.

After an hour, Lewis phoned back. 'Nina reckons the colt suffers from claustrophobia,' he said. 'He goes berserk if we try to shut him in a single stall in the horsebox, and also if we try to tie him up. She's got him quiet, like, but he's loose in a big stall, like we arrange it for a mare and foal. You know. Room for three, all to himself. And she's opened all the windows. The colt's standing with his nose out of one of them at the moment. What do you reckon?'

'It's up to you,' I said. 'I'll tell Mr Usher we can't bring his colt out, if you like.'

'No.' He sounded indecisive but finally said, 'OK, I'll give it a try. But if he goes mad again when we start off, I'll scrub it.'

'Right.'

A claustrophobic horse. We did sometimes come across animals that no amount of persuasion or brute force would get them up a ramp into a horsebox. I sympathised with them, especially after the previous night, but I could have done, this time, with a dozy docile passenger giving Lewis no trouble.

I waited. Another hour crawled by.

'They must be on their way.' Isobel said, unconcerned.

'I hope so.'

Another hour. No news.

'I'm going to Michael Watermead's,' I told Isobel. 'Call me on the mobile phone if Lewis reports.'

She nodded, busy with other things, and I trundled down to Michael's trying to work out how best to tell him something he wouldn't want to hear.

He was surprised to see me in the hour of afternoon doldrums before the lads arrived to feed and water the horses and prepare them for the night.

'Hello!' he said. 'What can I do for you? Come along in.'

He took me into a small friendly sitting-room, not the big imposing room of Sunday-lunch champagne cocktails. He'd been reading newspapers, which lay scattered over a low table and nearby armchair and he roughly gathered them together to make a space for me to sit.

'Maudie's out,' he said. 'I'll make some tea in a minute.'

He waved for me to sit down, obviously waiting for me to begin. And *where* to begin . . . that was the problem.

'You remember,' I said, 'the man who died in one of my horseboxes?'

'Died? Oh yes, of course. On the way back from taking Jericho's two-year-olds, wretched man.'

'Mm.' I paused. 'Look,' I said awkwardly, 'I wouldn't bother you with this, but I do want to clear something up.'

'Carry on, then.' He sounded receptive, not impatient, simply interested.

I told him that Dave had picked the man up not casually but by arrangement. Michael frowned. I explained about the carrier-bag with the thermos flask that I'd found in the nine-box the next evening, and I showed him the last two tubes that had been carried in the thermos, that I'd had in my safe.

'What are they?' he asked curiously, holding one up to the light. 'What's in them?'

'Viral transport medium,' I said. 'For transporting a virus.'

'Virus . . .' He was shocked. 'Did you say *virus*?'

Virus, to all trainers, meant 'the virus', the dreaded respiratory infection that made horses cough and run at the nose. The virus could put a stable out of winners for most of a year. The worst news possible, that was 'the virus'.

Michael handed the tubes back as if they'd stung him.

'They came from Pontefract,' I said. 'From Yorkshire.'

He stared. 'They've got the virus up there. Two or three yards have it.' He looked worried. 'You haven't mixed any of my horses in with horses from up north, have you? Because, if so . . .'

'No,' I said positively. 'Your horses always travel alone, unless you give specific permission otherwise. I'd never ever put your horses in danger of infection in my transport.'

He marginally relaxed. 'I didn't think you would.' He was eyeing the tubes as if they were snakes. 'Why are you telling me this?'

'Because I think . . . er . . . if the hitchhiker hadn't died, the virus that was in these tubes might have found its way into the last of Jericho Rich's string – the fillies – on the last day of the transfer to Newmarket.'

He stared some more. He thought it over. 'But *why*?' he asked. 'That's *criminal*.'

'Mm.'

'*Why*?' he said again.

'To get even with Jericho Rich.'

'Oh no,' he said protestingly, standing up sharply, striding away from me, anger rising. 'I would *never, never* do a thing like that.'

'I know you wouldn't.'

He swung round furiously. 'Then *who*?'

'Um . . . I think . . . you might ask Tessa.'

'*Tessa*!' His anger increased; at me, not at her. 'She wouldn't. What's more she *couldn't*. This is utter rubbish, Freddie, and I'm not listening to any more of it.'

I sighed. 'All right.' I stood up to go. 'Sorry, Michael.'

I went out of his house and over to my Fourtrak and he followed me indecisively as far as his door.

'Come back,' he said.

I retraced a few steps in his direction.

'You can't make accusations like that and simply bugger off,' he said. 'Do you or don't you want to go on driving my horses?'

'Very badly,' I admitted.

'Then this is not the way to go about it.'

'I can't let my business be used for carrying viruses from place to place and do nothing to stop it.'

'Huh,' he said on a low breath. 'When you think of it like that . . . but Tessa? It's preposterous. She wouldn't know how to do it, for a start.'

'I'd like to ask her,' I said reasonably. 'Is she at home?'

He looked at his watch. 'She ought to be here at any minute. She only went shopping.'

'I could come back,' I said.

He hesitated, then jerked his head towards the inside of the house, bidding me to follow. 'You might as well wait,' he said.

I followed him through to the sitting-room.

'*Tessa*,' he said, not believing it. 'You've got it all wrong.'

'If I have, I'll grovel.'

He gave me a sharp look. 'You'll need to.'

We waited. Michael tried to read a newspaper and put it down crossly, unable to concentrate.

'Nonsense,' he said, meaning what I'd said about Tessa. 'Total nonsense.'

His daughter returned, looking into the sitting-room as she passed, festooned with boutique bags, on her way upstairs. Brown-haired, light-eyed, perpetually sulky-looking, she glanced at me with disfavour.

'Come in, Tessa,' her father said. 'Shut the door.'

'I want to go upstairs.' She peered into one of the bags. 'I want to try this dress on.'

'Come in,' he said, sharply for him, and frowning, ungraciously, she did so.

'What is it, then?' she asked.

'All right, Freddie,' her father said to me. 'Ask her.'

'Ask me what?' She was displeased, but not frightened.

'Um . . .' I said, 'did you arrange for some tubes containing virus to be brought to Pixhill?'

It took a moment for my deliberately casual tone of

voice to reach her understanding. When she realised what I'd asked her, she stopped fidgeting with her shopping and grew still with shock, her face stiffening, mouth open, eyes wary. Even to Michael it was plain that she knew what I was talking about.

'Tessa,' he said despairingly.

'Well, what of it?' she said defiantly. 'What if I did? It never got here. So what?'

I took the two tubes out of my pocket again and put them on the table. She looked at them vaguely, then worked out what they were. A bad moment for her, I thought.

'There were six tubes,' I said. 'What were you going to do with them? Pour the contents up the noses of six fillies belonging to Jericho Rich?'

'Dad!' She turned to him, imploring, 'Get rid of him.'

'I can't,' Michael said sadly. 'Is that what you intended?'

'I didn't do it.' She sounded triumphant more than abashed.

'You didn't do it,' I agreed, 'because your courier died of heart failure on the journey and failed to deliver the thermos.'

'You don't know *anything*,' she said. 'You're making it up.'

'You wanted to get even with Jericho Rich for taking his horses away because he made a pass at you and you slapped his face. You thought you would make his horses ill so they couldn't win, serve him right. You saw an advertisement in *Horse and Hound* saying more or less "anything transported anywhere", so you phoned the number in the ad and arranged for Kevin Keith Ogden – the man who died – to pick up a thermos at Pontefract service station and bring it down the A1 to the junction with the M25 at South Mimms. You arranged with my driver, Dave, to get Ogden picked up there and to bring him to Chieveley. You phoned Dave late in the evening after he got back from Folkestone, as you knew it was no good trying to reach him earlier because you knew his schedule. You're always in and out of Isobel's office and you could see the day's list. Ogden was supposed to disembark at Chieveley and hand over the thermos, but as he'd died my men brought him all the way to my house. I expect you may have been surprised when Ogden didn't appear at Chieveley, but it was soon all over the village why not, and certainly your father knew about it almost at once.' I paused briefly. Neither father nor daughter tried to speak.

'When you found Ogden was dead,' I went on, 'you knew the thermos had to be still in the horsebox, so you came looking for it, Tessa, disguised in dark clothes with a black balaclava over your head, so that if I saw you I wouldn't know you. I found you in the cab, if you remember, and you ran away.'

It was Michael who said, 'No.'

'You couldn't find the thermos,' I told Tessa. 'You

tried twice. Then I decided to sleep in the cab, which put an end to it.'

Michael said, 'I don't believe it.' But he did.

'I'll make a deal with you,' I said to Tessa. 'I won't tell Jericho Rich what you intended for his fillies if you'll answer a few questions.'

'You can't prove a thing,' she said, narrowing her eyes. 'And that's blackmail.'

'Maybe. In return for my never mentioning this again to anyone, I want a few answers. It's not a bad bargain.'

'How do I know you'll keep it?'

'He will,' Michael said.

'Why do you trust him so much?' his daughter demanded.

'I just do.'

She didn't like it. She tossed her head. She said tightly, 'What do you want to know?'

'Chiefly,' I said, 'where did the virus transport medium come from?'

'What?'

I repeated the question. She went on looking blank.

'The liquid in those tubes,' I said, 'is a mixture used for transporting viruses outside a living body.'

'I don't understand.'

'If you simply collected the nasal discharge of a horse with the virus,' I said, 'the virus would disappear in a very short time. To bring the infection to Pixhill from Yorkshire by road, the way it came, you'd need to combine the nasal discharge with a mixture that would keep the virus active. That's what's in these tubes, that mixture. Even in these, a virus won't survive more than two days. This mixture here is harmless now. But where did it come from?'

She didn't answer. Michael said, 'Where, Tessa?'

'I don't know. I don't know what you're talking about.'

'All you knew,' I suggested, 'was that if you held a horse's head up and poured the mixture down his nostril, he would be infected?'

'Well, probably. *Probably* be infected.'

'Who told you?' I asked. 'Who got the stuff for you?'

Silence.

'Tessa?' Michael said.

'Was it Benjy Usher?' I asked.

'No!' She was truly astonished. 'Of course not.'

'Not Benjy,' Michael agreed, amused. 'But who, Tessa?'

'I'm not saying.'

'That's unfortunate,' I murmured.

A silence lengthened while the head-tosser, the whisperer, thought it over.

'Oh, all *right*,' she burst out. 'It was Lewis.'

Michael was as surprised as I was not. I would have been astounded if she'd said anyone else.

'I don't *know* where he got it from,' she said wildly. 'All he said was he could get a pal up north to collect some snot from a horse with the virus – that's what he said, snot, not all posh like nasal discharge – and this pal would take it to Pontefract service station if I could get someone to collect it. The pal couldn't get away to bring it down here and I'd no chance of going to Yorkshire without making endless excuses, so yes, I'd seen the ad in the magazine and suggested to Lewis that I could use it and he said get Dave to pick the man up; Dave was down for the trip to Newmarket and he would do anything for money, and the man would get to Chieveley, where I could meet him easily, and how was I to know he was going to *die*? I phoned Lewis and told him what had happened and asked him to find the thermos for me but all he would do was give me the key to get into the cab with. And if you want to know, you looked pretty stupid when you caught me searching, when you were trying to run in sleeping shorts and gumboots and a raincoat half off. Pretty silly, you looked.'

'I expect so,' I said equably. 'Did you look *under* the horsebox as well as in it?'

'Mr Know-all, aren't you? Yes, I did.'

'Er, why?'

'Lewis told me one day you could carry anything under the horseboxes if you wanted to.'

'Why did he say that?' I asked.

'Why does anyone say anything? He liked saying things to get you going. He said he'd carried soap in a container under one of your boxes, but he'd given it up, it didn't work.'

'*Soap*,' Michael said, hopelessly lost, 'why ever soap?'

'I don't know. How should *I* know? Lewis just says weird things. Just his way.'

'So . . . er . . .' I said, 'did you find any soap under my horsebox?'

'No, of course I didn't. I was looking for a thermos. There was nothing at all under there. It was all filthy dirty.'

'When you tried to get Nigel to take you to Newmarket with the fillies,' I said, 'were you still hoping to find the virus container and infect the horses on the journey?'

'What if I was?'

'It was a different horsebox,' I said.

'It wasn't . . . well, they all look alike.'

'Many do.'

She looked shattered.

'Did you pay Dave?' I asked mildly.

'No, I didn't. I mean, I never got the stuff, did I?'

'And you didn't pay Ogden, because he was dead. Did you pay Lewis?'

After a pause she said sullenly, 'He wanted it in advance. So, yes.'

Michael said, 'Tessa,' again, almost wailing.

'Well I did it for you, Dad,' she said. 'I *hate* Jericho

Rich. Taking his horses away because I slapped his face! I did it for *you*.'

Michael was overcome, full of too-easy indulgence. I didn't believe her, but perhaps Michael needed to.

CHAPTER THIRTEEN

Isobel was still in the office when I returned to the farmyard although it was by then nearly five. Rose had gone home.

Lewis had phoned, Isobel said. I had just missed him. He and Nina were back through the Mont Blanc tunnel and had stopped for a sandwich and refuelling. Nina had been driving. The colt had had its head out of the window all the way but had not gone berserk. Lewis would be driving north through the night, though he would stop somewhere to fill the jerrycans with French water for the colt.

'Right,' I said.

French water, pure and sweet from springs, was good for horses. Such a stop would be unremarkable.

'Aziz asked for tomorrow off,' Isobel said. 'He doesn't want to drive tomorrow. Something to do with his religion.'

'His *religion*?'

'That's what he said.'

'He's a rogue. Where is he now?'

'On his way back from taking horses to Doncaster sales.'

I sighed. Religions were difficult to argue with, but Aziz was still a rogue, if not something worse.

'Anything else?'

'Mr Usher asked if we'd collected the colt. I told him he'd be in Pixhill by six tomorrow evening, if there were no ferry delays.'

'Thanks.'

'Fingers crossed,' Isobel said.

'Mm.'

'You look awfully worried,' she said.

'It's this Jogger business.'

She nodded in understanding. The police, she said, had been irritated to find so many drivers away out on the road.

'They don't seem to realise we've a business to run,' she said. 'They think we should all down tools. I told them we couldn't.'

'Thanks again.'

'Get some sleep,' she said impulsively, young but no fool.

'Mm.'

I tried to take her advice. Concussion no longer did the trick. I lay awake thinking of Lewis stopping somewhere to fill the cans with French water. I hoped to hell Nina would keep her head down and her eyes – partially – shut.

On Wednesday morning I saw off the lorries going

out again to Doncaster, where the Flat racing season would open the next day. The March meeting of Doncaster sales and races were the start of Croft Raceways' busiest time: we were entering six months of work, work, improvisation and scramble, an atmosphere I usually loved. Juggling the number of boxes, the number of drivers, against the prospects of profitability: normally it excited me, but this week so far I could barely concentrate.

'The whole fleet,' Isobel said, cheeringly, 'will be rolling tomorrow.'

I cared only that Lewis would roll home today.

At nine, when the telephone rang for the nth time, Isobel answered it, frowning.

'Aziz?' she said. 'Just a moment.' She put her hand over the receiver. 'What's "hold on" in French?'

'*Ne quittez pas*,' I said.

Isobel repeated '*Ne quittez pas*' into the instrument and rose to her feet. 'It's a Frenchman, for Aziz.'

'He isn't here today,' I said.

She replied over her shoulder as she went through the door, 'He's in the canteen.'

Aziz came in hurriedly and picked up the receiver from Isobel's desk.

'*Oui . . . Aziz. Oui.*' He listened and spoke rapidly in French, stretching out a hand for a piece of memo paper and a pencil. '*Oui. Oui. Merci. Monsieur. Merci.*' Aziz wrote carefully, thanked his informant profusely, and put the phone back in its cradle.

'A message from France,' he said unnecessarily. He pushed the memo sheet towards me. 'It seems Nina asked the man to phone here. She gave him money for the phone call and an address. This is it.'

I took the paper and read the scant words. 'Ecurie Bonne Chance, près de Belley'.

'Good Luck Stables,' Aziz translated. 'Near Belley.'

He gave me the usual brilliant smile and smartly left the office.

'I thought Aziz had the day off,' I said to Isobel.

She shrugged. 'He said he didn't want to *drive.* He was here already in the canteen when I arrived for work. Reading and drinking tea. He said, "Good morning, darlin' ".'

Isobel faintly blushed.

I looked at the French address and phoned the Jockey Club. Patrick Venables must have been sitting there, waiting.

'Nina sent an address via a Frenchman,' I told him. 'Ecurie Bonne Chance, near Belley. Can you ask your equivalents in France for any information about it?'

'Spell it.'

I spelled it. 'Aziz took the message in French,' I said.

'Good.' He sounded decisive. 'I'll ask my French colleagues and phone you back.'

I sat for a few seconds looking at the telephone after he'd disconnected, and then went and found Aziz in the canteen and invited him into the open air.

'What's your religion?' I asked, out in the farmyard.

'Er . . .' He gave me a sideways look with his bright eyes, the smile untroubled.

'Do you work for the Jockey Club?' I asked flatly.

The smile simply broadened.

I turned away from him. Patrick Venables, I thought bitterly, and Nina also, had trusted me so little that they'd sent another undercover man, one I wouldn't know of, to make sure I wasn't myself the villain I purported to be looking for. Aziz had turned up the day after Jogger died. I suppose I shouldn't have minded, but I did.

'Freddie,' Aziz took a step and grasped my sleeve, 'listen.' The smile had faded. 'Patrick wanted Nina to have back-up. I suppose we should have told you, but . . .'

'Stick around,' I said briefly, and returned to my office.

An hour later, Patrick Venables came on the line.

'First of all, I think I owe you an apology,' he said. 'But I'm curious. How did you suss out Aziz? He phoned to say you'd rumbled him.'

'Little things,' I explained. 'He's too bright for the job. I'll bet he never drove for a racing stable. The phone caller from France asked for him specifically, which meant Nina had arranged for Aziz to be available. And you, yourself, didn't ask who Aziz was when I mentioned him.'

'Dear God.'

'As you say.'

'Ecurie Bonne Chance,' he said, 'is a small stable run by a minor French trainer. The owner of the property is Benjamin Usher.'

'Ah.'

'The property is south of Belley and is situated near the River Rhône where the river runs from east to west, before turning south at Lyons.'

'Very thorough,' I commented.

'The French know nothing against the place. They have had some sick horses there, but none have died.'

'Thank you very much.'

'Nina insisted on going on the journey,' he said, 'and she was adamant we don't intercept your box on its way back.'

'Please don't.'

'I hope you know what you're doing.'

I hoped so too.

I phoned Guggenheim. 'I can't promise,' I said, 'but fly down and come to the farmyard today, in a taxi, and bring something to carry a small animal in.'

'Rabbit?' he asked hopefully.

'Pray,' I said.

The hours crawled.

Lewis phoned Isobel eventually in the afternoon and said they had crossed on the ferry and were leaving Dover.

After another slow hour Isobel and Rose went home and I locked the office and went over to the Fourtrak, starting the engine. The passenger door opened, with Aziz standing there.

'Can I come with you?' he said. Bright eyes. No smile.

I didn't immediately answer.

'You'll be safer if I do. No one, anyway, will hit you on the head when you're not looking.'

I made a non-committal gesture and he swung into the seat beside me.

'You're going to meet Nina, aren't you?' he asked.

'Yes.'

'What do you expect will happen?'

I drove out of the yard, turned out of the village and drove uphill to a place where one could look down on Pixhill below.

'Lewis,' I said, 'should come over the brow of that far hill and drive into Benjy Usher's yard. If he does, I'll drive down there to meet them. If he goes anywhere else we can see that from here too.'

'Where do you think he might go?'

'I don't know how much you know.'

'Nina said the method was complicated but the simple matter is that someone is bringing sickness to Pixhill's horses.'

'Roughly, yes.'

'But why?'

'Partly to make a certain category of races easier to win by methodically infecting all the horses of that category that can be got at in Pixhill.' I paused. 'Halve the runners in the Chester Vase, for instance, and you more or less double your chances of winning. There are seldom more than six or so runners in the Chester Vase, or the Dante Stakes at York. They are nice prestigious races. Winning them puts a trainer in good standing in the profession.'

Azir sat digesting the implications. 'A blanket illness?' he said.

'Occurring here and there,' I nodded. 'It's not like nobbling the favourite for the Derby.'

'Irkab Alhawa,' he said. 'Ride the Air.'

'Ride the Wind.'

'No,' he said, 'in Arabic it means "ride the air". It's the way jockeys ride, standing in the stirrups, sitting on air, not the saddle.'

'Ride the wind's better,' I said.

'But you don't think anyone's going to make *that* horse sick?'

After a pause I said, 'Lewis didn't kill Jogger, he was in France. I don't think Lewis destroyed my car or took an axe to my house. I'm sure Lewis didn't crash the hard disk in my computer. As I said, that Sunday he was in France.'

'He couldn't have done it,' Aziz agreed.

'I thought I was up against two forces,' I said. 'Muscle and money. But there's a third.'

'What is it?'

'Malice.'

'The worst,' Aziz said slowly.

The driving force within you, I thought, leaps out. Under stress, it can't be hidden.

Apply the stress.

'Do you have any *reason* to think anyone would destroy Irkab Alhawa?' Aziz asked, frowning.

'No. I just intend to use the thought as a lever.'

'To do what?'

'Wait and see, and guard my back.'

Aziz leaned sideways against the passenger door and assessed me quizzically, the irrepressible smile reappearing.

'You're not like you look, are you?' he said.

'How do I look?'

'Physical.'

'So do you,' I said.

'But then . . . I am.'

An odd ally, I thought; and unexpectedly, I was glad he was there.

A Croft Raceways horsebox came over the opposite hill. I raised a pair of binoculars and focused, and saw the horse's head sticking out of the window.

'That's them,' I said. 'Lewis and Nina.'

The horsebox turned into the road towards Benjy Usher's stables, almost next door to Michael's. I started the Fourtrak and drove down the hill, reaching Benjy's yard almost before Lewis switched off his engine.

Benjy's head appeared in his upstairs window, poking out rather like his colt's from the horsebox. He issued orders to his lads below with his customary force, and Lewis and Nina lowered the ramp. I got out of my jalopy and watched them.

My presence there was taken for granted by everyone. Nina noticed Aziz still sitting in the Fourtrak and threw him an enquiring glance, to which he responded with a quick thumbs-up.

The colt clattered wild-eyed down the ramp, led by Nina, and limped away in the hands of Benjy's head lad. Benjy shouted an enquiry to Lewis about the journey: Lewis went nearer to the window and shouted up, 'It all went right.' Benjy, relieved, retreated and closed his window.

I said to Nina, 'Did you stop anywhere since Dover?'

'No.'

'Good. Go with Aziz, now, will you?'

I went over to Aziz and spoke to him through the Fourtrak's window.

'Please take Nina with you and go to the farmyard. There may be a young man wandering about there, carrying a small animal transporter. His name's Guggenheim. Collect him and in about a quarter of an hour take him on with you.'

'Where to?'

'To Centaur Care. That place where you took the old horses. I'll drive this horsebox and meet you there.'

'Let me come with you,' he said.

'No. Look after Nina.'

'As if she needed it!'

'Everyone needs their back watched.'

I left him, walked over to the horsebox while Lewis was lifting the ramp back into place, and climbed into the driver's seat.

Lewis was surprised, but when I waved him towards the passenger side he climbed in there without demur. He'd worked for me for two years: he was accustomed to doing what I said.

I started the powerful engine and drove carefully out of Benjy's yard, continuing on down the road towards Michael's place. Opposite Michael's gate, where the road temporarily widened and the space allowed it, I pulled the box over to the side, stepped on the foot-brake, rolled gently to a stop, applied the hand-brake and switched off.

Lewis looked surprised, but not very. The vagaries of bosses, his manner seemed to imply, had to be tolerated.

'How's the rabbit?' I said conversationally.

His expression gave new meaning to the word flabbergasted. He looked for a moment as if his heart had actually stopped beating. His mouth opened and no sound came out.

Lewis, I thought, with his biker past, his tattooed dragon, his expert fists; Lewis with his bimbo and his ambitions for his baby, Lewis might be a dishonest muscle-man out to make money, but he was no actor.

'I'll tell you what you've been doing,' I said. 'Benjy Usher owns a stable in France where he discovered last year by chance that the horses there were falling ill with an unspecified fever. He learned that there was a possibility that the fever was carried by ticks. So he thought it a good wheeze to bring the illness to England and give it to a few horses here so as to clear his path a bit to winners he might not otherwise have. The problem was how to bring the ticks to England; and first of all, you tried to bring them on soap which you carried in a cash box stuck to the bottom of one of my nine-boxes that you were driving at the time.'

Lewis went on looking dumbfounded, a pulse throbbing now in a swelled vein on his forehead.

'The ticks didn't survive that journey. They don't, as you now know, survive long enough on soap. A different way of travel had to be found. An animal. A hamster, maybe. Or a rabbit. How are we doing?'

Silence.

'You looked after the Watermeads' rabbits. Perfect. You thought they wouldn't miss one or two, but they did. Anyway, last year, driving Pat's four-box, you went to France to the Ecurie Bonne Chance, that's Benjy Usher's place outside Belley, down near the River Rhône, and you wiped ticks onto a rabbit. You brought it back here, wiped the ticks from the rabbit on to two old horses that Benjy Usher had in a paddock outside his drawing-room window, and although one of them died, there you both were with flourishing live ticks on the other, ready to be transferred to any horse that Benjy decided on, and that *you* could get close to by driving it to the races.'

I wondered what incipient heart failure looked like.

'The ticks are unpredictable,' I continued, 'and in the end probably just disappeared, so in August you went again to France, but this time taking the box Phil drives now, which you used to drive regularly at that time. But on that occasion, things went wrong. The horsebox was due for maintenance and was driven straight to the barn on your return. The cap had unscrewed itself from the tube, perhaps from vibration. Before you could retrieve the rabbit, it fell into the inspection pit and died, and Jogger threw it away, ticks and all.'

Strangled silence.

'So this year,' I said, 'you went in the new super-six to fetch the two-year-olds for Michael Watermead, and you took a rabbit with you. The ticks came back alive and were transferred to the old horse, Peterman. But Peterman went to Marigold English, not Benjy Usher, and Peterman died. The ticks died soon after him. So now we have the Flat season about to start and all the Chester Vase and Dante Stakes contestants this year are strong and healthy still, so you set off with the rabbit to fetch Benjy Usher's colt from Milan, and on the way back you stopped at the Ecurie Bonne Chance, and what will you bet that in the tube container above the fuel tanks of this horsebox we'll find a rabbit with ticks on?'

Silence.

I asked, 'Why didn't you just wipe ticks straight onto Benjy's colt?'

'He wants it to race again when its leg gets healed.'

The admission slipped painlessly out. Lewis's voice was hoarse. He didn't even try to protest innocence.

'So now,' I said, 'we're going to take the rabbit straight to Centaur Care, where the two old horses destined for Benjy's field are waiting. This time you are not going to have to retrieve the rabbit from the tube at eleven o'clock at night, and hit me on the head when I catch you at it.'

'I never,' he said fiercely. 'I never hit you.'

'You did drop me into the water, though. And you said "If this doesn't give him flu, nothing will." '

Lewis seemed to have gone beyond being astounded and had reached the stage of anxiety to salvage whatever he could.

'I needed the money,' he said, 'for my kid's education.'

One more shock, I thought, and he would really start talking.

I said, 'If it came to a choice, which would you prefer, to drive Irkab Alhawa to the Derby and maybe bring him back as the winner in your own box on the television to this village, or to infect him with ticks to stop him even running?'

'He'd never do that!' he said. His horror, indeed, looked genuine.

'He's violent and spiteful,' I said, 'so why not?'

'No!' He stared at me, belatedly thinking. 'Who are you talking about?'

'John Tigwood, of course.'

Lewis closed his eyes.

'Benjy's reward is winning,' I said. 'Yours is money. Tigwood's is the power to spoil other people's achievements. That's a commoner sin than you may think. Knocking people is a major sport.'

To win by cheating. Ambition for one's child. Malice and secretly enjoyed destructive power, bolstering an inadequate personality. To each his driving force.

And mine? Ah, mine. Whoever understood his own?

Lewis looked sick.

'Does Benjy Usher pay Tigwood?' I asked.

Lewis said without humour, 'He gives him wads of the stuff in one of those collecting tins, right out in public.'

After a pause I said, 'Tell me what happened the night you chucked me in the water.'

He practically moaned, 'I'm no grass.'

'You're a witness,' I said. 'Witnesses get off lighter.'

'I didn't do your car.'

'You didn't kill Jogger,' I pointed out, 'because you were in France. But as for my car, you certainly could have done it.'

'I didn't. I never. *He* did.'

'Well . . . *why*?'

Lewis stared at me, his eyes deep in their sockets.

'See, he was like a wild thing. Going on about you

having everything so easy. Why should you have everything, he said, when he had nothing. There you were, he said, with your house and your money and your looks and your business and being a top jockey all that time and everyone *liking* you, and what did he have, people never looked pleased to see *him*, they turned away from him. Whatever he did, he would never be *you*. He absolutely *hated* you. It turned my stomach, like, but I reckoned he might turn on *me* if I contradicted him so I went along with him . . . and he had the axe with him in his car . . .'

'Did he hit me with the axe?' I asked incredulously.

'No. A rusty old tyre lever. He had a lot of tools in his car, he said. When he hit you we put you in the boot of my car, as there was more room, and he told me to drive to the docks. He was *laughing*, see!'

'Did you think I was dead?'

'I didn't know, like. But you weren't. You were talking, sort of delirious, when we got there. I never meant to kill you. *Honest*.'

'Mm.'

'He said we were in it together. He said how would I like him to get me in trouble. How would I like to lose my job and not drive the best horses any more.'

Lewis stopped talking, looking now at a future which meant all those things.

'Bloody *bugger*,' he said.

'So you came back from Southampton,' I said, taking

it for granted, 'and collected the axe and chopped up my house and my car and my sister's helicopter.'

'*He* did that. He did it. He was shouting and raving and *laughing*. He chopped all the stuff in your room. So bloody *strong*. I'll tell you, he frightened me rigid.'

'You watched him?'

'Well . . . yeah.'

'And enjoyed it?'

'Never.'

But he had, I saw. He might just possibly have been frightened by the vigour of that attack but deep down there had been an awestruck guilty pleasure.

Ruefully, I restarted the engine.

'Like,' Lewis said, 'how did you know about the journeys?'

'They're in the computer.'

'He said he'd wiped out your records on the Sunday with a Michelangelo or something, and not to worry.'

'I had copies,' I said succinctly.

Tigwood had been in the pub the night everyone heard Jogger say he'd found the secret containers. From spite he must have stolen Jogger's tools. Then if Jogger found Tigwood tampering with my computer on the Sunday . . . I could see Tigwood going to his car for Jogger's own tyre lever, walking along to the barn after him and aiming just one lethal blow. Jogger wouldn't have expected it. He knew of no reason to fear.

I released the brakes and started down the road.

'I suppose,' I said, 'that it was Tigwood with all his

medical journals who understood about ticks? And who knew what you needed for bringing the virus from Yorkshire for Tessa Watermead to infect Jericho Rich's horses? You couldn't give the Jericho Rich horses tick fever, because by then you hadn't been over to collect this year's ticks.'

He was again speechless. I glanced at him.

I said, 'You haven't much chance if you're not willing to be a witness. Tessa told me and her father what you did.'

I phoned Sandy Smith's number and, finding him at home, invited him to drive along to Centaur Care. 'Bring your handcuffs,' I said.

It took Lewis a slow painful mile to make up his mind, but as I turned through the gates of the crumbling headquarters of a disgraced charity, he said, mumbling, 'All right. A witness.'

The decrepit place was alive with people.

Lorna Lipton's Range Rover stood in the driveway. Lorna was talking to Tigwood and there were children – *children* – running about. Maudie's two youngest children . . . and Cinders.

Aziz was out of the Fourtrak, also Nina, also Guggenheim. They stood indeterminately, not knowing what to expect.

John Tigwood looked bewildered.

I stopped the horsebox and jumped to the ground. Sandy Smith joined the crowd, lights flashing, uniform buttoned, no siren.

'What's going on?' Tigwood asked.

I wasn't sure how he would react. The trail he'd left with his axe on my property urged any defence I could think of. Keeping the children safe was a first priority.

I said to Maudie's young ones. 'Take Cinders and wriggle under the horsebox and play being in a pirate's cave there, or something.'

They giggled.

'Go on,' I said, urging them. 'Crawl in there.'

They did, all three of them. Lorna, watching, said merely, 'Won't they get dirty?'

'They'll clean.'

Tigwood said, 'Why are you here?'

I answered him. 'We brought back your rabbit.'

'*What?*'

'Lewis and I,' I said, 'have brought back the rabbit – with ticks.'

Tigwood strode to the passenger seat side and yanked open the door.

'*Lewis!*' he yelled. It came out as a screech, all fruitiness gone.

Lewis shrank away from him. 'He knows it all,' he said desperately. 'Freddie knows *everything*.'

Tigwood stretched an arm into the cab and pulled Lewis out. Tigwood's weedy-looking appearance was misleading. Everyone could see the stringy power that tweaked the bigger man out onto the ground with a crash. Lewis's shoulders landed first, then his head, then his legs.

Lewis, rolling in pain, took a rough swing at Tigwood. Tigwood kicked him in the face and turned his attention to me.

'You *bastard*,' he said, white-faced, intent. 'I'll kill you.'

He meant it. He tried. He rushed me, smashing me by sheer speed against the side of the horsebox.

He hadn't an axe, however, or a tyre lever, but only his hands; and they, had we been alone, might have indeed been enough.

Aziz came up behind him and hauled him off. Aziz displayed a timely and useful skill in twisting a man's arm up behind his back until it reached the point of cracking.

Tigwood screamed. Sandy produced his handcuffs portentously and with help from Aziz locked Tigwood's wrists together behind his back.

Sandy said to me out of the side of his mouth, 'What's going on?'

'I think you'll find that John Tigwood axed my house.'

'*Bastard*,' Tigwood said, his voice a snarl.

I asked Sandy, 'I don't suppose you have a search warrant handy?'

He shook his head bemusedly.

'I don't need one,' Aziz said. 'What am I looking for?'

'An axe. A rusty tyre lever. A thing for sliding under lorries. A bunch of tools in a red plastic crate. And perhaps a grey metal cash box with a round bright patch amid the dirt. They might be in his car. If you find them, don't touch them.'

His smile shone out, bright, white and happy. 'Got you,' he said. He left Tigwood to Sandy and bounced away out of sight.

Lorna bleated in bafflement, 'John? I don't understand . . .'

'Shut up,' he said furiously.

'What've you *done*?' Lorna wailed.

No one told her.

Tigwood stared at me with unnerving naked hatred and in a taut white rage called me a bastard again, among other things, repeating what Lewis had told me. I'd never imagined the overpowering strength of his murderous corrosive loathing, not even with his axe's handiwork all around me. I felt shrivelled by it, and weak. Sandy, who had seen so many dreadful things, looked deeply shocked.

Lorna swung round at me with loathing of her own. 'What did you do to him?' she accused me.

'Nothing.'

She didn't believe me, and never would.

Aziz reappeared from the direction of the ramshackle stables.

'Everything's there,' he reported, beaming. 'They're in one of the stalls, under a horse rug.'

Sandy smiled at me briefly, pushing Tigwood hard

against the horsebox. 'Reckon it's time to call my colleagues.'

'Reckon it is,' I agreed. 'They can take it from here on.'

'And the Jockey Club can take on Benjy Usher,' said Aziz.

Another car joined the mêlée. Not the colleagues yet, but Susan and Hugo Palmerstone, with Maudie. Michael had told them that the children were here with Lorna, they said. They'd come to take them home.

Tigwood in handcuffs appalled them. Lorna told them it was all my fault. Hugo believed her easily.

'Where *are* the children?' Susan asked. 'Where's Cinders?'

'They're safe.' I bent down and looked under the horsebox. 'You can come out now,' I said.

Guggenheim touched my arm as I straightened. 'Did you . . . I mean . . .' he said. 'Is the rabbit there?'

'I think so.'

He, at least, looked happy. He was carrying a white plastic small-animal carrier and wearing protective gloves.

Maudie's two children wriggled out on their backs and stood up, brushing off dirt. One of them said to me, in a quiet little voice, 'Cinders doesn't like it under there. She's crying.'

'Is she?' I went down on my knees and looked underneath. She was lying flat on her stomach, her face pressed to the ground, her whole body quivering. 'Come on out,' I said.

She didn't move.

I lay down on the ground on my back and put my head under the side of the horsebox. I shuffled backwards on heels, hips and shoulders, until I reached her. I found there were things I would go under tons of steel for without a second thought.

'Come on,' I said. 'We'll go out together.'

She said, shivering, 'I'm frightened.'

'Mm. But there's nothing to be afraid of.' I looked up at the steel of the chassis not far above my face. 'Turn onto your back,' I said. 'Hold my hand and we'll wriggle out together.'

'It'll fall on me.'

'No . . . it won't.' I swallowed. 'Turn over, Cinders. It's easier on your back.'

'I can't.'

'Your mother and father are here.'

'There's a man shouting . . .'

'He's stopped now,' I said. 'Come on, darling, everything's fine. Hold my hand.'

I touched her hand with mine and she grabbed it tightly.

'Turn over,' I said.

She turned slowly onto her back and looked upwards to the steel struts.

'It's pretty dirty under here,' I said prosaically. 'Keep your head down or you'll make your hair filthy. Now, our toes are pointing to where your parents are, so just shunt along beside me and we'll be out in no time.'

I began to wriggle out, and she wriggled, sobbing, beside me.

It was after all only a few feet. It can't have seemed much to the people outside.

When we were out I knelt beside her, brushing dirt from her clothes and her hair. She clung to me. Her little face, close to mine, was so like the pictures of myself at her age. The tenderness I felt for her was devastating.

Her gaze slid beyond me to where her parents stood. She let go of me and ran to them. Ran to Hugo.

'Daddy!' she said, hugging him.

He put protective arms around her and glared at me with the green eyes.

I said nothing. I stood up: brushed some grit off myself; waited.

Susan put one arm round Hugo's waist and with the other enclosed Cinders; the three of them a family.

Hugo brusquely turned them away with him towards their car, looking fiercely over his shoulder. He shouldn't fear me, I thought. Perhaps in time he wouldn't. I would never upset that child.

I was aware that Guggenheim and Aziz were slithering under the horsebox. Guggenheim scrambled out with visions of immortality in his eyes, cuddling the white plastic carrier as if it contained the Holy Grail.

'The rabbit's here,' he said joyfully, 'and it's got ticks!'

'Great.'

Nina came to stand beside me. I put my arm round her shoulders. It felt right there. Eight and a half years didn't matter.

'Are you OK?' she asked.

'Mm.'

We watched the Palmerstones' car drive away.

'Freddie . . .?' Nina murmured tentatively, 'that little girl . . . when your heads were together, she looked . . . almost . . .'

'Don't say it,' I said.

DICK FRANCIS

Flying Finish

£6.99

'Extremely exciting . . . lots of action'
Sunday Times

Lord Henry Grey was an amateur jockey and pilot. But when he decided to abandon his desk-bound job for an active career in the bloodstock market, he found there was more to couriering valuable horses around the world than he'd ever suspected . . .

Meeting Gabriella in Italy is the first, most pleasurable surprise. But a colleague's disappearance on the next Milan trip gives him a nasty jolt: for two of his predecessors have already gone absent without leave.

Thousands of feet up, in the hands of a sadistic killer, it seems that Grey has discovered the truth too late . . .

'With this book, Dick Francis takes his place at the head of the field as one of the most intelligent thriller writers in the business'
Sunday Express

DICK FRANCIS

For Kicks

£5.99

'Absolutely first class . . . warmly recommended'
Sunday Times

Proprietor of a stud farm in the breathtaking region of Australia's Snowy Mountains? Or muck-raking stable boy in Yorkshire?

The Earl of October persuades young Australian Danny Roke to accept the English alternative. It's the change of scene and the challenge that pushes Danny undercover, on the scent of a suspect racehorse dope scandal.

But the pain involved, dealing with vicious swindlers and the Earl's two attractive daughters, could overturn all his pleasure in the chase . . .

'Very lively, hard-bitten account . . . some jolting action scenes'
Financial Times